The Mysteries of London

Volume 3

George W. M. Reynolds

Alpha Editions

This edition published in 2024

ISBN : 9789361473906

Design and Setting By
Alpha Editions
www.alphaedis.com
Email - info@alphaedis.com

As per information held with us this book is in Public Domain.
This book is a reproduction of an important historical work. Alpha Editions uses the best technology to reproduce historical work in the same manner it was first published to preserve its original nature. Any marks or number seen are left intentionally to preserve its true form.

Contents

- CHAPTER I. THE TRAVELLING-CARRIAGE. - 1 -
- CHAPTER II. TOM RAIN AND OLD DEATH. - 7 -
- CHAPTER III. BOW STREET. - 14 -
- CHAPTER IV. ESTHER DE MEDINA. - 21 -
- CHAPTER V. THE APPEAL OF LOVE. - 31 -
- CHAPTER VI. DR. LASCELLES. - 38 -
- CHAPTER VII. THE BEAUTIFUL PATIENT. - 45 -
- CHAPTER VIII. SEVEN DIALS. - 49 -
- CHAPTER IX. A DEATH-SCENE.—LOCK'S FIELDS. - 58 -
- CHAPTER X. A SCENE AT THE HOUSE OF SIR CHRISTOPHER BLUNT. - 68 -
- CHAPTER XI. THE TWO THOUSAND POUNDS.—TORRENS COTTAGE. - 75 -
- CHAPTER XII. ADELAIS AND ROSAMOND. - 82 -
- CHAPTER XIII. THE ELOPEMENT. - 89 -
- CHAPTER XIV. LADY HATFIELD AND DR. LASCELLES.—ESTHER DE MEDINA. - 97 -
- CHAPTER XV. THE OPIATE. - 104 -
- CHAPTER XVI. THE LOVER AND THE UNCLE. - 107 -
- CHAPTER XVII. THE MYSTERIOUS LETTER.—JACOB. - 111 -
- CHAPTER XVIII. THE LOVERS. - 122 -
- CHAPTER XIX. MR. FRANK CURTIS'S PLEASANT ADVENTURE. - 129 -
- CHAPTER XX. HAPPINESS.—THE DIAMOND-MERCHANT. - 140 -
- CHAPTER XXI. THE OATH. - 148 -
- CHAPTER XXII. THE ALARM.—THE LETTER. - 154 -

- CHAPTER XXIII. OLD DEATH. — 162 —
- CHAPTER XXIV. CASTLE STREET, LONG ACRE. — 169 —
- CHAPTER XXV. MATILDA, THE COUNTRY-GIRL. — 177 —
- CHAPTER XXVI. THE LADY'S-MAID. — 186 —
- CHAPTER XXVII. LONDON ON A RAINY EVENING.—A SCENE IN A POST-CHAISE. — 190 —
- CHAPTER XXVIII. TOM RAIN'S LODGINGS IN LOCK'S FIELDS. — 197 —
- CHAPTER XXIX. THE MYSTERIES OF OLD DEATH'S ESTABLISHMENT. — 210 —
- CHAPTER XXX. THE STORE-ROOMS. — 220 —
- CHAPTER XXXI. ANOTHER DEED OF INFAMY BROUGHT TO LIGHT. — 225 —
- CHAPTER XXXII. RAINFORD IN THE SUBTERRANEAN. — 236 —
- CHAPTER XXXIII. MRS. MARTHA SLINGSBY. — 241 —
- CHAPTER XXXIV. THE PIOUS LADY. — 246 —
- CHAPTER XXXV. MR. SHEEPSHANKS. — 255 —
- CHAPTER XXXVI. THE BARONET AND HIS MISTRESS. — 261 —
- CHAPTER XXXVII. TOM RAIN AND JACOB. — 265 —
- CHAPTER XXXVIII. THE HISTORY OF JACOB SMITH. — 273 —
- CHAPTER XXXIX. CONTINUATION OF THE HISTORY OF JACOB SMITH. — 295 —
- CHAPTER XL. CONCLUSION OF THE HISTORY OF JACOB SMITH. — 304 —
- CHAPTER XLI. FRESH ALARMS. — 317 —
- CHAPTER XLII. THE PARAGRAPH IN THE NEWSPAPER. — 324 —
- CHAPTER XLIII. LORD ELLINGHAM AND TOM RAINFORD. — 331 —

CHAPTER XLIV. MR. FRANK CURTIS AGAIN. .... - 339 -

CHAPTER XLV. MR. DYKES AND HIS MYRMIDONS... - 350 -

CHAPTER XLVI. EXPLANATIONS. .... - 357 -

CHAPTER XLVII. FARTHER EXPLANATIONS. .... - 364 -

CHAPTER XLVIII. LORD ELLINGHAM AND TOM RAIN. .... - 371 -

CHAPTER XLIX. A PAINFUL INTERVIEW. .... - 379 -

CHAPTER L. THE LAWYER'S OFFICE. .... - 389 -

CHAPTER LI. LORD ELLINGHAM IN THE DUNGEON. - 396 -

CHAPTER LII. LORD ELLINGHAM'S EXERTIONS. .... - 406 -

CHAPTER LIII. THE EXECUTION. .... - 412 -

CHAPTER LIV. GALVANISM. .... - 418 -

CHAPTER LV. THE LABORATORY.—ESTHER DE MEDINA. .... - 422 -

CHAPTER LVI. A HISTORY OF THE PAST. .... - 432 -

CHAPTER LVII. A FATHER. .... - 461 -

CHAPTER LVIII. THE RESUSCITATED. .... - 469 -

CHAPTER LIX. THE JEW'S FAMILY. .... - 482 -

CHAPTER LX. SIR CHRISTOPHER BLUNT'S DOMESTIC HEARTH. .... - 487 -

CHAPTER LXI. CAPTAIN O'BLUNDERBUSS. .... - 493 -

CHAPTER LXII. FRANK'S EMBARRASSMENTS. .... - 503 -

CHAPTER LXIII. THE MEETING IN BATTERSEA FIELDS. .... - 508 -

CHAPTER LXIV. OLD DEATH AND HIS FRIEND TIDMARSH. .... - 514 -

CHAPTER LXV. THE EXAMINATION. .... - 520 -

CHAPTER LXVI. MRS. SLINGSBY AND THE BARONET AGAIN. .... - 538 -

CHAPTER LXVII. THE MARRIAGE.—ROSAMOND. ...... - 549 -

CHAPTER LXVIII. DR. WAGTAIL.—ROSAMOND T ORRENS. ....- 557 -
CHAPTER LXIX. MISERY AND VICE. ....- 572 -
CHAPTER LXX. TIM THE SNAMMER. ....- 580 -
CHAPTER LXXI. THE HISTORY OF TIM THE SNAMMER. ....- 585 -
CHAPTER LXXII. MR. AND MRS. CURTIS. ....- 632 -
CHAPTER LXXIII. CAPTAIN O'BLUNDERBUSS AGAIN. ....- 646 -
CHAPTER LXXIV. THREE MONTHS AFTER MARRIAGE. ....- 656 -
CHAPTER LXXV. THE KNIGHT AND THE CAPTAIN. ...- 665 -
CHAPTER LXXVI. TIM THE SNAMMER AND JOSH PEDLER OUT ON BUSINESS. ....- 672 -
CHAPTER LXXVII. THE FATHER AND DAUGHTER. ....- 679 -
CHAPTER LXXVIII. RETRIBUTION. ....- 686 -
CHAPTER LXXIX. THE EARL OF ELLINGHAM AND LADY HATFIELD AGAIN. ....- 695 -
CHAPTER LXXX. MRS. SLINGSBY AND MR. TORRENS. ....- 705 -
CHAPTER LXXXI. ROSAMOND AT HOME. ....- 717 -
CHAPTER LXXXII. THE FORGED CHEQUE. ....- 727 -
CHAPTER LXXXIII. THE REWARD OF CRIME. ....- 736 -
CHAPTER LXXXIV. OLD DEATH'S PARTY. ....- 746 -
CHAPTER LXXXV. THE HISTORY OF A LIVERY-SERVANT. ....- 755 -
CHAPTER LXXXVI. CONCLUSION OF THE HISTORY OF A LIVERY-SERVANT. ....- 776 -
CHAPTER LXXXVII. THE BLACKAMOOR. ....- 796 -
CHAPTER LXXXVIII. SCENES AT THE BLACKAMOOR'S HOUSE. ....- 808 -

CHAPTER LXXXIX. THE SURPRISE.—JEFFREYS AND OLD DEATH. .... - 820 -

CHAPTER XC. THE NEW JUSTICE OF THE PEACE. .... - 827 -

CHAPTER XCI. CAPTAIN O'BLUNDERBUSS AGAIN.—ANOTHER STRANGE VISITOR. .... - 835 -

CHAPTER XCII. THE CONFESSION. .... - 847 -

CHAPTER XCIII. NEWGATE. .... - 854 -

CHAPTER XCIV. "THE STOUT HOUSE." .... - 866 -

CHAPTER XCV. CLARENCE VILLIERS AND HIS AUNT. .... - 877 -

CHAPTER XCVI. SIR CHRISTOPHER BLUNT A HERO. - 885 -

CHAPTER XCVII. CARLTON HOUSE. .... - 892 -

CHAPTER XCVIII. AN ACQUITTAL AND A SENTENCE. .... - 907 -

CHAPTER XCVIX. THE CONDITION OF THE WORKING CLASSES. .... - 912 -

CHAPTER C. THE EARL OF ELLINGHAM AND ESTHER DE MEDINA .... - 920 -

CHAPTER CI. THE BLACKAMOOR'S STRANGE ADVENTURE. .... - 929 -

CHAPTER CII. A STATE OF SIEGE. .... - 943 -

CHAPTER CIII. THE SURPRISE.—A CHANGE OF SCENE. .... - 952 -

CHAPTER CIV. THE VISIT.—THE HABEAS CORPUS. ... - 964 -

CHAPTER CV. THE KING'S BENCH PRISON. .... - 972 -

CHAPTER CVI. A FARTHER INSIGHT INTO THE KING'S BENCH. .... - 983 -

CHAPTER CVII. A TALE OF SORROW. .... - 994 -

CHAPTER CVIII. CONCLUSION OF THE TALE OF SORROW. .... - 1013 -

CHAPTER CIX. THE PRISONERS. .... - 1024 -

CHAPTER I.
THE TRAVELLING-CARRIAGE.

It was about nine o'clock in the evening of the 2nd of November, 1826, that a travelling-carriage stopped, on its way to London, to change horses at the principal hotel in the little town of Staines.

The inmates of the vehicle were two ladies:—an elderly domestic in livery and a female attendant occupied the box.

The night was clear, fine, and frosty: the moon shone brightly; and the carriage lamps threw a strong glare to a considerable distance in front of the vehicle.

The active ostlers speedily unharnessed the four wearied steeds, and substituted as many fresh ones in their place: the two postboys leapt into their saddles; the landlord cried "All right!"—and the carriage rolled rapidly away from the inn, the horses' shoes striking fire against the stones.

"If there be any thing particularly calculated to raise the spirits," said one lady to the other, a few minutes after the chariot had left the peaceful town behind, "it is travelling upon such a beauteous night as this."

"I am delighted to observe that you *are* in good spirits this evening, my dear Lady Hatfield," was the reply. "After passing four long months at Sir Ralph Walsingham's country seat, London will present fresh attractions for your ladyship."

"My dear Miss Mordaunt," returned Lady Hatfield, in a serious tone, "you are aware that I am indifferent to those formal parties and ceremonial assemblies which are reckoned amongst the pleasures of the fashionable world; and I can assure you that had not my uncle purported to return to London in a few days, my own inclinations would have urged me to prolong my stay at Walsingham Manor."

"For my part," said Miss Mordaunt, "I am quite delighted with the idea of hastening back to the great metropolis. A summer in the country is only tolerable because each day brings one nearer to the enjoyments of a winter in town. But really, my dear Lady Hatfield, you are not reasonable. Rich, young, and beautiful as you are—your own mistress—and with the handsomest man in England dying to lay his coronet at your feet——"

"I shall never marry, Julia," hastily interrupted Lady Hatfield. "Pray let us change the conversation. A few minutes ago I was in excellent spirits; and now——"

She paused—and a deep sigh escaped her bosom.

"Did I not say that you were quite unreasonable?" exclaimed her companion. "Here am I—five years older than yourself,—for I do not mind telling you, my dear friend, that I shall never see thirty again;—and yet I have not renounced the idea of changing my condition. I know that I am neither so good-looking nor so wealthy as you;—still I have my little ambition. Sir Christopher Blunt would deem himself honoured were I to smile graciously upon him; but my brother, the lieutenant—who, by the by, expects his captaincy in a few days, thanks to the interest of your kind uncle Sir Ralph—declares that if ever I marry a mere knight, he will never speak to me again."

Lady Hatfield had fallen into a profound reverie, and paid not the slightest regard to the confidential outpourings of her garrulous companion.

Miss Mordaunt, who laboured under the pleasing impression that Lady Hatfield's silence was occasioned by the deep interest which she took in the present topic, continued to rattle away with her tongue as fast as the carriage did with its wheels.

"I am sure it was a very great act of kindness in you to ask me to spend the winter with you in London; for as papa is compelled to reside in Ireland, in consequence of the unsettled state of his tenantry, I should have been under the necessity of returning to the Emerald Isle, after my four months' visit with you to Walsingham Manor, had you not taken that compassion on me. But let us speak of yourself, dear Lady Hatfield. Without a soul in the world to control your actions—with the means of procuring every enjoyment—and with Lord Ellingham going mad on your account——"

"Julia," said Lady Hatfield, with a start,—"again I beseech you to drop this subject. And, as you will be my companion for some months to come, let me now, once for all, enjoin you to abstain from such topics. As you cannot read the secrets of my heart, pray bear in mind the fact that many a light word uttered thoughtlessly and with no malicious intent, may touch a chord that will thrill," she added calmly, but bitterly, "to the inmost recesses of my soul."

"Oh! my dear Lady Hatfield," exclaimed Miss Mordaunt, who, in spite of her loquacity, was a very good-natured person, "I am rejoiced that you have given me this warning. And how foolish of me not to have observed—what indeed I now remember—that the topic of Love never was agreeable to you. To be sure! it was during the sermon upon the felicity of the wedded state, that you fainted and were taken into the vestry!"

Lady Hatfield writhed in mental agony; and bitterly at that moment did she repent the invitation which she had given her thoughtless companion to pass the winter with her in London.

The carriage had now reached the little town of Bedfont, which it traversed without stopping; and continued its rapid way towards Hounslow.

But all of a sudden the course of the chariot was checked—as if by an unexpected impediment in the way; and the horses began to plunge frightfully.

At the same time the lady's-maid on the box uttered a dreadful scream.

Lady Hatfield drew down the window nearest to her: the chaise that moment came to a full stop; and a stern, but evidently disguised voice exclaimed, "Keep your horses quiet, you damned fools—and don't mind me! If you stir till I give you leave, I'll blow out the brains of both of you."

"Robbers!" shrieked Miss Mordaunt in a despairing tone: "Oh! what will become of us?"

Lady Hatfield looked from the window; and at the same instant a man, mounted on horseback, with a black mask over his countenance, and a pistol in each hand, was by the side of the vehicle.

"Villain!" cried the livery-servant on the box. "But you shall swing for this!"

"Perhaps I may," said the highwayman, coolly, though still speaking in a feigned tone, as is the custom with individuals of his profession upon such occasions as the one we are describing: "and if you attempt to move, old fellow, from where you are, an ounce of lead shall tumble you down from your perch. Beg pardon, ma'am," continued the robber, turning towards Lady Hatfield, who had shrunk back into the corner of the carriage the moment the desperado appeared at the window; "sorry to inconvenience you; but—your purse!"

Lady Hatfield handed the highwayman her reticule.

"Good!" said he, perceiving by its weight and a certain jingling sound which it sent forth, that it contained gold. "But you have a companion, ma'am—*her* purse!"

Miss Mordaunt complied with this demand, and implored the "good gentleman" not to murder her.

The highwayman gave no reply; but vouchsafed a most satisfactory proof of his intended forbearance in that respect, by putting spurs to his steed, and darting off like an arrow in the direction of Hounslow.

"Cowardly villains that you are!" ejaculated the livery-servant, hurling this reproach against the postboys.

"And what are you, old fool?" cried the postillion who rode the wheel-horse. "But he'll be nabbed yet."

"Drive on—drive on!" exclaimed Lady Hatfield from the window. "We are all frightened—and not hurt."

"Indeed, my dear," said Miss Mordaunt, as the carriage started off rapidly once more, "I am seriously hurt—grievously wounded!"

"You, Julia!" cried her ladyship, in unfeigned surprise.

"Yes—in pocket," was the answer, implying deep vexation. "All the remainder of my quarter's allowance——"

"Oh! compose yourself on that head," interrupted Lady Hatfield. "You shall not be compelled to acquaint Mr. Mordaunt with your loss."

This assurance, conveying a promise of pecuniary assistance, materially tended to tranquillise the mind of Miss Mordaunt; but the event which had just occurred—apart from the mere robbery of her reticule—awoke the most painful reflections in the mind of Lady Hatfield.

"By the by," said Miss Mordaunt, after a short pause—for she never remained long silent,—"this audacious outrage reminds me of something your uncle Sir Ralph Walsingham was telling me one day, when you interrupted him in the middle. I think he informed me that about six or seven years ago—when you were only eighteen or nineteen—you were staying at your dear lamented father's country-house, where you were quite alone—for of course one does not call the servants anybody; when the mansion was broken into by robbers during the night——"

"Julia!" exclaimed Lady Hatfield, her whole frame fearfully convulsed by the powerful though useless efforts which she made to subdue her agitation: "never, I implore you, again allude to that dreadful event!"

"Well—I never will," said Miss Mordaunt. "And yet, if one must not speak of Love—nor yet of marriage—nor yet of midnight burglaries——"

"Nay—I was wrong to cut you short thus abruptly," remarked Lady Hatfield, now endeavouring to rob her prayer of the importance with which her solemn earnestness of manner had invested it: "only, do choose some more enlivening topic after the fright which we have just experienced."

"The first thing to-morrow morning," said Miss Mordaunt, who had not noticed the full extent of the impression which her allusion to the burglary of some years back had made upon her companion—for Julia was too flippant, superficial, and volatile to pay much attention to the emotions of others,—"the first thing to-morrow morning we must give information to the Bow Street runners concerning this highway robbery: secondly, we must write to the landlord at Staines to tell him what a couple of cowardly fellows he has got in the shape of these postillions;—and thirdly, you must discharge old Mason, who is evidently incapable of protecting his mistress, much less her friends."

"Discharge old Mason!" exclaimed Lady Hatfield: "impossible! How could he have protected us! He is unarmed—whereas the highwayman flourished two large pistols, doubtless loaded. But here we are safe at Hounslow!"

The carriage drew up at the door of the hotel in this town; and the postillions immediately narrated the particulars of the robbery to the landlord and his attendant tribe of hangers-on.

"Well, this is fortunate!" cried the landlord, when the tale was told: "quite a God-send, as one may say."

"As how, please, sir?" exclaimed the elder postboy, astonished at the remark.

"Why—it happens that Dykes, the famous Bow Street officer, is in the hotel at this very instant," said the landlord. "John," he added, turning to a waiter who stood near, "beg Mr. Dykes to step this way."

"And what's Dykes doing down here?" asked the postboy, when the waiter had disappeared to execute the commission he had received.

"He's been investigating a 'cendiary fire," replied an ostler; for the landlord, disdaining to hold any farther converse with a postillion, had stepped up to the window to inquire whether the ladies chose to alight.

Having received a negative answer, accompanied with an intimation that the sooner the carriage was allowed to proceed the more agreeable it would be to Lady Hatfield and Miss Mordaunt, the landlord returned towards the spot where the postillions, the hangers-on of the hotel, and other loungers were grouped together.

Mr. Dykes almost immediately afterwards made his appearance in the form of a tall, stout, heavy, but powerfully built man, shabby-genteel in his attire, and carrying a strong ash-stick in his hand.

The particulars of the highway robbery were described to him in a very few moments.

"How was the fellow dressed?" asked the officer.

"A black coat," said the first postboy.

"No—it wasn't," cried the second.

"Then what was it?" demanded Mr. Dykes.

"I don't know—but I'm sure it wasn't a black 'un," was the highly satisfactory answer.

"Describe his horse," said Dykes impatiently.

"Brown—switch tail—standing about fourteen hands——"

"Nonsense!" ejaculated the second postillion, interrupting his companion who had volunteered the explanation. "It was a light bay—the moon fell full upon it—so did the carriage-lights."

"Come, I see we are only losing time," cried the officer. "Which way did he go?"

"He galloped off in this direction," was the reply, which remained uncontradicted.

"Then he'll be in London to-night, whichever road he took," said Mr. Dykes. "If your ladies will give me a cast as far as town, I'll be after the villain. Perhaps he turned off to the left towards Hatton, and so over by Hanwell and then Shepherd's Bush; or else he made straight for Richmond, and so over into Surrey. But, one way or another, he's sure to be in London by midnight; and ten to one if I don't pounce on him. My business is done down here; and I may just as well toddle back to-night as to-morrow morning."

The substance of these remarks was communicated to Lady Hatfield, who could not well do otherwise than accord a seat on the box to Mr. Dykes, Charlotte, the lady's-maid, removing to the interior of the carriage.

These arrangements having been effected, the vehicle pursued its way; and shortly after eleven o'clock it drew up at the door of a mansion on Piccadilly Hill.

Mr. Dykes, having asked the ladies a few questions, promised to communicate the result of his efforts to capture the highwayman; and then took his departure.

Lady Hatfield and Miss Mordaunt shortly retired to their respective bed-chambers: the latter to dream of the delights of London—the former to moisten her pillow with tears; for the recent adventure had awakened in her mind feelings of the most agonising description.

CHAPTER II.
TOM RAIN AND OLD DEATH.

It was about half-past eight on the following morning, when two individuals entered a public-house in White Hart Street, Drury Lane.

One was a man of about thirty years of age, with florid complexion, light hair, and red whiskers,—yet possessing a countenance which, viewed as a whole, was very far from disagreeable. His eyes were of a deep blue, and indicated not only good-humour but a certain generosity of disposition which was not impaired by an association with many less amiable qualities—such as a wild recklessness of character, an undaunted bravery, a love of perilous adventure, and a sad deficiency of principle on particular points, the nature of which will hereafter transpire. He was evidently proud of a very fine set of teeth, the brilliancy of which compensated for the somewhat coarse thickness of his lips; and the delicate whiteness of his hands showed that he did not earn his livelihood by any arduous labour. In person he was about the middle-height—by no means inclined to corpulency—and yet possessing a well-knit frame, with a muscular power indicative of great physical strength. His dress partook of the half-sporting, half-rakish character—consisting of a high chimney-pot kind of hat, with very narrow brims, a checked blue silk neckerchief, fine linen, a buff waistcoat, cut-away Newmarket-style of green coat, drab-breeches, and top-boots. The proper name of this flash gentleman was Thomas Rainford; but his friends had taken the liberty of docking each word of a syllable; and he was invariably known as Tom Rain.

The other individual was an old man, of at least sixty, with white hair, but eyes of fire glaring from beneath a pair of thick, shaggy grey brows. He was upwards of six feet in height, and but little bowed by the weight of years which he bore. Having lost all his teeth, his mouth had fallen in so as to form a complete angle, the depth of which was rendered the more remarkable by the extreme prominence of his hooked nose and his projecting chin. He was as thin as it was possible to be without having the bones actually protruding through the skin, which hung upon them like a tanned leather casing. He was dressed in a long grey surtout coat, reaching below his knees; a pair of shabby black trousers, very short; and black cloth gaiters fitting loosely over that description of shoes generally denominated high-lows. On his head he wore a greasy cap, with a large front: his linen was by no means of the cleanest; and his appearance altogether was excessively unprepossessing—if not absolutely revolting. What his real name was, very few of even his most intimate acquaintances were aware; for his dreadful emaciation of form had procured for him the frightful pseudonym of *Old Death*.

Tom Rain and his hideous companion entered the public-house in White Hart Street, nodded familiarly to the landlord as they passed by the bar, and ascended the stairs to a private room on the first floor.

Having seated themselves at the table, Tom Rain began the conversation.

"Well, have you considered my proposal?" he asked.

"I have," replied the old man in a deep sepulchral tone; "but I am cautious—very cautious, my good friend."

"So you told me when I saw you three days ago for the first time," observed Rain impatiently. "But Tullock, the landlord of this place, is a pal of yours; and he knows me well too. Hasn't he satisfied you about me?"

"Well—well, I can't say that he hasn't," answered Old Death. "Still a cautious man like me never says *yes* in a hurry. Tullock knew you eight or nine years ago down in the country; and there's no doubt that you was then a right sort of blade."

"And so I am now!" cried Tom Rain, striking the table angrily with his clenched fist.

"Softly-softly, my good friend," said Old Death. "We shall agree better afterwards if we have a good understanding at first. I was going to observe that for some years Tullock loses sight of you; he comes up to town, takes this public, and doesn't even remember that there's such a fellow in existence as yourself until you make your appearance here a few days back."

"When he received me with open arms, and introduced me to you," added Tom Rain. "But go on: what next?"

"Ah! what next?" replied Old Death, with a horrible chuckle that issued from his throat as if it come from the depths of a tomb. "Why—you frankly and candidly told me your intentions and views, I admit;—but you can't do without me—you can't do without me, my dear boy—and you know it!"

Again the hideous old man chuckled in his cavern-like tones.

"I never denied what you say," answered Tom Rain. "On the contrary, I am well aware that no one in my line can think of doing business about London, and making London his head-quarters, without your assistance."

"To be sure not!" said the old man, evidently pleased by this compliment. "I've had the monopoly of it all for this thirty years, and never once got into trouble. But then I do my business with caution—such caution! I've dealings with all that are worth having dealings with; and not one of them knows even where I live!"

"Only let me find a sure and ready-money market for *my* goods," exclaimed Tom Rain, "and I'll do more business with you than all the chaps you speak of put together."

"Well, I suppose we must come to terms," said Old Death after a short pause. "Tullock assures me that you were straight-forward when he knew you in the country, and though time changes men's minds as well as their faces, I'll take it for granted that you're all right. You remember the conditions?"

"Not a word you uttered three days ago has escaped my memory," answered Rain.

"Good. When shall you commence business?"

"I opened my shop last night," replied Tom with a hearty laugh.

"Nonsense!" cried the old man, fixing a glance of delight upon his new friend. "You don't mean to say that——In a word, is *this* yours?"

As he spoke, Old Death drew from his pocket the morning's newspaper, pointed to a particular advertisement, and held the journal towards his companion.

Tom Rain's countenance was overclouded for a moment; but almost immediately afterwards it expanded into an expression of mingled surprise and satisfaction; and snapping his fingers joyfully, he exclaimed, "Is it possible? could it have been *her*? Oh! this business is speedily settled!"

And rising from his seat, he rang the bell violently.

A pot-boy answered the summons.

"Pen, ink, and paper, and a messenger to carry a letter," said Tom Rain, with extraordinary rapidity of utterance.

The boy disappeared; and Old Death, recovering partially from the astonishment into which his companion's ejaculations and manner on reading the advertisement had thrown him, exclaimed, "What the devil are you after now?"

"You shall see in a moment," was the reply; "but I don't promise you any explanation of what you *will* see," he added with another hearty laugh.

The boy returned, bringing writing materials, and intimating that he was willing to be the bearer of the letter.

Tom Rain told him to wait; then, having hastily written a few lines upon a sheet of paper, he tossed the note over to Old Death, who read as follows:—

"Remember the night of the 27th of October, 1819;—and stop the inquiries instituted in respect to the little business referred to by the advertisement in this morning's *Times*."

"This is past all comprehension," exclaimed the old man, still keeping his eyes fixed upon the paper. "The note has not even a signature."

"It does not require one," coolly observed Tom Rain, as he snatched the letter from his companion, and proceeded to fold it up.

"And do you hope to crush the business by means of that scrap of writing?" asked Old Death, evidently perplexed what to think.

"I don't merely hope—I am certain of accomplishing my object," was the reply.

"Now mind you ain't deceiving yourself, Tom," said Old Death. "The man who has taken up the affair is persevering as a beaver and crafty as a fox. You may see that he is in earnest by the expedition he must have made to get the advertisement into this morning's paper. I should have hardly thought it possible to be done. However, done it is—and, though it gives no description of the person, yet it offers a good reward for his apprehension. No one knows what trivial circumstance may afford a trace; and——"

"Enough of this, old friend," cried Tom; and handing the letter, now duly folded, wafered, and directed, to the boy, he said, "Take this to the address written upon it: see if there's any answer; and I shall wait here till you come back. Look alive—and you'll earn a crown by the job."

The boy hastened away to execute the commission which he had received.

"And so that was your business, Master Tom?" observed Old Death, as soon as the messenger had disappeared. "Well—you have made a good beginning: it promises bright things."

"What! do you fancy that I haven't had plenty of experience down in the country?" cried Rainford. "Ah! I could tell you a tale or two—but no matter now."

"And the little business, Tom," inquired the old man,—"did it turn out worth the trouble? The advertisement says——"

"Hark'ee, Master Death," exclaimed Rainford, firmly; "that business does not regard you. Our compact dates from this morning——"

"Oh! very good—very good!" interrupted Old Death in a surly tone. "Be it as you say: but remember—if you *do* get into any trouble on account of this, you mustn't expect me to help you out of it."

"Neither do I," answered Tom. "However, I am a generous chap in my way, and I don't mind yielding to you in this instance; for you must suppose that I can see your drift plain enough. The advertisement says '*A purse containing a Bank-note for fifty pounds and eleven sovereigns, and a reticule containing a purse in which there were three ten-pound notes and sixteen sovereigns.*' This is accurate enough. The reticule I flung away: the two purses I kept—and here they are."

Thus speaking, Tom Rainford threw upon the table the objects last mentioned.

Old Death's eyes glared with a kind of savage joy as they caught a glimpse of the yellow metal and the flimsy paper through the net-work of the purses.

"Pretty things—pretty things!" he muttered between his toothless gums. "I think you'll do well, Tom."

"And I am sure I shall. But turn the money out on the table: you care more about the handling of it than I do."

Old Death "grinned horribly a ghastly smile," and lost no time in obeying the hint conveyed.

"Twenty-seven golden boys, and eighty pounds in Bank-notes," said the hideous man. "The gold is yours—that's part of our conditions: half the value of the Bank-notes is mine, for the risk and trouble in cashing them—that's also part and parcel of our conditions. So if I give you forty sovereigns—forty golden sovereigns, Tom—we shall be square."

"Just so," carelessly observed Rain.

Old Death produced a greasy leather bag from a pocket in the breast of his grey-coat, and counted thence the forty sovereigns on which he had laid such emphasis.

Tom Rain thrust the coin into his breeches' pocket without reckoning it; while his companion first secured the Bank-notes in the greasy bag, and then threw the two purses into the fire.

"You're a good fellow, Tom—a generous-hearted fellow—and I'm much pleased with you," said the old man. "I shall leave you now, as I have some little trifling matters to attend to in another part of the town. When you want me, you know where to leave a message."

"All right," ejaculated Tom Rainford, who did not appear over anxious to detain his new friend.

They accordingly separated—Old Death taking his departure, and the other remaining behind to await the return of his messenger.

It is necessary to state that when Old Death quitted the public-house, he was joined a few paces up the street by a sharp-looking, ill-clad youth of about fifteen, whose pale countenance, bright eyes, and restless glances denoted mental activity struggling against bad health.

Approaching the old man, the youth walked by his side without uttering a syllable.

"Jacob," said Death, after a brief pause, and sinking his voice to a whisper, "you saw that swell-looking chap who went into Tullock's with me just now. Well—I told you to be here this morning at a particular hour, on purpose that you *might* see him. He will be useful to me—very useful. But I must know more of him—and he is not the man to be pumped. Do you wait here, and watch him. Dog him about—find out where he goes—where he lives—whether he has a mistress or a wife, or neither——"

"Or both," added Jacob, with a low chuckle.

"Yes—any thing that concerns him, in fine," continued Old Death. "I am going to Toby Bunce's in the Dials, where I shall be for the next three or four hours if I'm wanted."

"Very good—I understand," said Jacob; and retracing his steps, he hid himself in a court which commanded a view of Tullock's public-house.

Let us now return to Tom Rain, who was waiting for the reappearance of his messenger.

It was shortly before ten when the pot-boy once more stood in his presence.

"Well?" said Rainford, interrogatively.

"I seed the lady herself," was the reply; "and I gived her the note. I thought it was somethink partickler—and so I told the flunkey I'd on'y deliver it into her hands."

"And how did she receive it?" asked Tom.

"I was showed into a parlour and told to wait. In a few minutes the door opened and in come a lady—such a splendid creatur! I never seed such a fine 'ooman in my life before. Our bar-gal's nothink to her! So I gived her the note: she looked at the writing on the outside, but didn't seem to know it. Then she opened the letter—and, my eye! didn't she give a start? I thought she'd have fell slap on her face. For a minute or so she couldn't recover herself: at last she says, '*Tell the writer of this note that it shall be attended to;*'—and she put half-a-crown into my hand. That's all."

"I knew it would be so!" cried Tom Rain in a triumphant tone. "Here's the five shillings I promised you, my boy; and I don't think you've made a bad morning's work of it."

The lad grinned a smile of satisfaction, and withdrew.

Rainford soon after descended to the bar, conversed for a few minutes with his friend Tullock, the landlord, and then took his departure—duly watched by Jacob.

He had reached the corner of Drury Lane, when he felt himself somewhat rudely tapped on the shoulder.

Turning hastily round, he was confronted by a tall stout man, who, without any ceremonial preface, exclaimed, "You're wanted, my good fellow."

"I know I am," replied Tom coolly, as he measured the stranger from head to foot with a calm but searching glance: "and I'm now on my way to the place where my presence is required."

"Just so," said the stout man: "because you are going to favour me with your company, that I may introduce you to a party who wishes to become better acquainted with you."

"Who's the friend you speak of?" asked Tom in an easy, off-hand kind of manner.

"Sir Walter Ferguson," was the reply. "So come along."

With these words, the stout man took Rainford's arm and led him away to the Police Court in Bow Street.

Jacob, who was an unsuspected witness of the whole proceeding, immediately took the shortest way to Seven Dials.

CHAPTER III.
BOW STREET.

The moment Mr. Dykes had lodged his prisoner in one of the cells attached to the court, he hurried off to Piccadilly Hill, and knocked loudly at the door of Lady Hatfield's residence.

Upon explaining the nature of his business to the domestic who answered the summons, he was admitted into an apartment where Lady Hatfield and Miss Mordaunt almost immediately joined him.

Lady Hatfield was the orphan daughter of the Earl and Countess of Mauleverer. She was an only child: the proud title of Mauleverer had become extinct with the demise of her father; but the family property had devolved to her. She was in her twenty-fifth year, and surpassingly beautiful:—the style of her loveliness was fascinating and intellectual—rendered the more interesting, too, by the tinge of melancholy which characterised her countenance. Her eyes were large and of a deep blue: the soul sate enthroned on her pale and lofty forehead;—her smile, though always plaintively mournful, denoted amiability and kindness. In stature she was of the middle height; and, though in the least degree inclining to *embonpoint*, yet the fulness of her form marred not its lightness nor its grace. The bust was rounded in voluptuous luxuriance—and the hips were expanded;—but the waist was naturally small—the limbs tapered gradually downwards—and her step was so elastic, while her gait was easy though dignified, that even the most critical judge of female attractions could not have found it in his heart to cavil at her symmetry.

Miss Mordaunt was a lady who had seen thirty-five summers, although she would have gone into hysterics had any one suggested that such was really the fact. She was short, thin, and not particularly good-looking; for her hair was of so decided a red that it would have been a mockery instead of a compliment to term it auburn: her eyes were grey, and her nose suspiciously inclining to the species called "pug:"—but her complexion was good, her teeth well preserved and white, and her hand very beautifully formed. Thus, when she looked in her glass—which was as often as she passed near it—she mentally summed up the good and the bad points of her personal appearance, invariably striking a balance in favour of the first, and thence arriving at the very logical conclusion that she should yet succeed in escaping from a condition of single blessedness.

It was a little after eleven o'clock when Lady Hatfield and Miss Mordaunt were informed that Mr. Dykes requested an immediate interview with them. Some event of that morning's occurrence had already produced a strange— an almost alarming effect upon Georgiana—such was Lady Hatfield's

Christian name: and in order to regain her spirits—to recover indeed from a sudden shock which she had received—her ladyship had proposed an early airing in the carriage. To this Julia, who had some "shopping to do," readily assented. They had accordingly just completed their toilette for the purpose, and were now waiting in the drawing-room for the arrival of the chariot, when the announcement of Mr. Dykes's name called such an ejaculation of anguish from Lady Hatfield's lips, that Miss Mordaunt was seriously alarmed.

But Georgiana,—the expression of whose countenance indicated for an instant the agony of a heart wounded to its very core,—subdued her emotions by a violent effort; and then, in answer to her friend's solicitous inquiries, attributed the temporary agitation she had experienced to a sudden pain passing through her head.

It was nevertheless with feelings of mingled terror and repugnance that Georgiana accompanied Julia to the room where the Bow Street officer awaited them.

Her very eye-lids quivered with suspense, when she found herself in the presence of the celebrated thief-taker.

"Well, ladies," exclaimed Mr. Dykes, rising from a chair, and making an awkward bow as they entered, "I've good news for you: the highwayman is———"

"Is———" repeated Georgiana, with nervous impatience.

"Is in custody, my lady; and all I now want———"

"Who is in custody?" demanded Georgiana, hope for a moment wildly animating her.

"The man that robbed you last night, my lady," answered the officer; "or else I'm dam———beg pardon—very much mistaken."

"But how do you know he is the same?" exclaimed Lady Hatfield. "Perhaps you may have erred—your suspicions may have misled you———"

"Ah! my lady," interrupted Dykes, totally mistaking the cause of Georgiana's warmth; "you surely ain't going to plead in favour of a chap that stopped you on the King's highway, and did then and there steal from your person and from the person of your friend———"

"Describe the individual whom you have arrested," said Lady Hatfield abruptly.

"To a nicety I will," answered the officer, who was now completely in his element. "About thirty years of age—good complexion—light curly hair—red whiskers—dark blue eyes—splendid teeth—thick lips———But here's your carriage come round to the door, my lady; and nothing could possibly be more convenient. Please not to waste time—as I think we can get him committed to-day."

The moment Dykes had begun his description, Lady Georgiana's eyes expressed the agonising nature of the suspense which she endured; but as he continued, and his portraiture became the more definite, an ashy paleness overspread her countenance.

This agitation on her part was not however perceived by either the Bow Street officer or Miss Mordaunt; for the former had a habit of fixing his eyes on the knob of his ash stick when he was engrossed in a professional topic; and the latter was drinking in with greedy ears the description of the supposed highwayman, whom she was quite astonished to hear represented as so very discrepant from her idea of what a midnight desperado must be.

The arrival of the carriage was, under the circumstances, quite a relief to Georgiana; and, without uttering another objection, she allowed Mr. Dykes to have his own way in the matter.

That experienced officer rang the bell as coolly as if the house was his own, and desired that the man-servant and lady's-maid, who were in attendance on their mistress the preceding night, would prepare to accompany him to Bow Street.

Mason and Charlotte speedily obeyed this request, and the chariot, instead of taking the ladies up Bond Street, conveyed them, the two servants, and Mr. Dykes, to the police-office.

On their arrival, Mr. Dykes conducted his witnesses into a private room, and, after an absence of about five minutes, returned with the intelligence that the night charges were just disposed of, and that the prisoner was about to be placed in the dock.

A shudder passed through Georgiana's frame; but, with a desperate effort to compose herself, she followed Mr. Dykes into the court, Miss Mordaunt and the two servants remaining in the private room until they should be summoned individually to give their testimony.

As Georgiana was a lady of rank and fortune she was not treated as a humble witness would have been, but was accommodated with a chair, Mr. Dykes assuring her, in a confidential whisper, that she need not stand up to give her evidence.

The body of the court was crowded with a motley assembly of spectators, the news that a highwayman was about to be examined having spread like wildfire throughout the neighbourhood.

Scarcely was Georgiana seated, when a sensation on the part of the crowd enabled her to judge that the accused was being brought in; and as Tom Rain leapt nimbly into the dock, she cast a rapid glance towards him—a glance in which terror was combined with indescribable disgust and aversion.

The accused affected not to notice her, but lounged in a very easy and familiar fashion over the front of the dock; surveying, first Sir Walter Ferguson, and then the clerk, with a complacency which would have almost induced an uninitiated stranger to imagine that *they* were the prisoners and *he* was the magistrate.

Mr. Dykes, being called upon by Sir Walter to explain the nature of the charge against the prisoner, declared that, "in consequence of information which he had received," (the invariable phraseology of old police-officers,) "he had arrested the accused on suspicion of having stopped Lady Hatfield's carriage on the preceding evening, and robbed her ladyship and her ladyship's friend of certain monies specified in an advertisement which he had caused to be inserted in that morning's paper." Mr. Dykes further stated that, having searched the prisoner, he had found upon him a considerable sum in gold; but none of the Bank-notes stolen.

Lady Hatfield was then sworn, and she corroborated the officer's statement relative to the robbery.

"Has your ladyship any reason to suppose that the prisoner in the dock is the person by whom your carriage was stopped?" inquired the magistrate.

"I feel well convinced, sir," was the reply, delivered, however, in a tremulous tone, "that the prisoner at the bar is *not* the man by whom I was robbed."

A smile of triumph curled the lips of Tom Rain; but Mr. Dykes surveyed Georgiana with stupid astonishment.

"Not the man, my lady!" he ejaculated, at length: "why, last night, your ladyship could give no description of what the robber was or what he was not!"

"Dykes, hold your tongue!" cried the magistrate: "her ladyship is upon her oath."

"Your worship," said Georgiana, in a firmer voice than before, "I was so bewildered last evening—so overcome with terror——"

"Naturally so, Lady Hatfield," observed the magistrate, with a very courteous smile, which seemed to say that he would rather believe the bare word of a member of the aristocracy—especially a lady—than the oaths of all his officers and runners out together. "In fact," continued Sir Walter blandly, "you were too much flurried, to use a common expression, to reply calmly and deliberately to any questions which Dykes may have put to you last evening."

"Such was indeed the case, your worship," answered Georgiana. "This morning, however, I have been enabled to collect my ideas, and to recall to mind the smallest details of the robbery. The highwayman had a black mask upon his face; but, by a sudden movement of his horse, as he stood by the carriage window, the mask slipped aside, and I caught a glimpse of his countenance by the moonlight."

"And that countenance?" said the magistrate.

"Was quite different from the prisoner's," replied Lady Hatfield firmly.

"Your ladyship did not make that statement when I gave you the description of the prisoner just now," said Dykes, evidently bewildered by the nature of Georgiana's testimony.

"Because you hurried me away, together with my friend and two of my servants, in a manner so precipitate that I had no time to utter a word," returned Lady Hatfield. "Moreover, as you had taken the prisoner into custody, I believed it to be necessary that his case should be brought beneath the cognizance of his worship."

Georgiana spoke in a tone apparently so decided and calm, that the officer knew not how to reply; although in his heart he suspected her sincerity.

The magistrate consulted the clerk; and, after the interchange of a few whispers, Sir Walter said, "I see no reason for detaining the prisoner: there is evidently some mistake on your part, Dykes."

"Your worship," exclaimed the officer, "I know not what to think. Can the prisoner give a good account of himself? He rides into London from Richmond at six o'clock this morning; puts his horse up at an inn in the Borough; goes to a coffee-house in another street to have his breakfast, and leaves a pair of pistols for the waiter to take care of for him; then walks over to a suspicious public not a hundred miles from this court; meets there a man that me and my partners have long had our eyes on; and, when he is searched, has a large sum in gold about his person."

"Do you hear what the officer says, prisoner?" inquired the magistrate.

"I do, your worship," answered Tom Rain, coolly; "and I can explain it all. I come up to London on business, which requires the sum of money found upon me. I put up my horse where I think fit; and I go elsewhere to get my breakfast, because I can have it cheaper than at the inn. I was armed with pistols because I had to travel a lonely road in the dark; and I left them at the coffee-house because I did not choose to drag them about with me all day long."

Mr. Dykes was about to reply, when two decently-dressed men, who had entered the court a few minutes previously, stepped forward.

"Please, your worship," said the first, "I have known Mr. Rainford the last four years; and a more respectable man does not exist. He came up to London to buy a couple of horses of me; and he was to pay ready money. My name's Watkins, your worship; and I've kept livery and bait stables in Great Queen Street, Lincoln's-Inn-Fields, for the last seventeen years."

"And I, your worship," said the other person, in his turn, "can answer for Mr. Rainford. If you doubt my respectability, your worship, send one of your officers round to Compton Street, and see if the name of Bertinshaw isn't painted up in precious large letters over the best jeweller's shop——"

"*And* pawnbroker's," interrupted Mr. Dykes significantly.

"Well—and pawnbroker's, too," added Bertinshaw: "I'm not ashamed of the calling."

"Then you are both prepared to guarantee the prisoner's appearance at any future time?" said the magistrate.

"Certainly, your worship," was the joint reply.

"To answer any charge that may be brought against him?" continued Sir Walter.

The response was again in the affirmative on the part of Watkins and Bertinshaw.

The magistrate stated the amount of the recognizances which were to be entered into, and Tom Rain was desired to stand down from the dock.

This intimation he obeyed with the same air of calm indifference which had characterized him throughout the proceedings, and which had only been for a moment disturbed by the profound astonishment he had experienced when two men, whom he had never before seen nor even heard of in his life, stepped forward to give him so excellent a character and become his bail. But a moment's reflection convinced him that Old Death was the unseen friend who worked the machinery of this manœuvre.

While the clerk was filling up the bail-bond, Lady Georgiana retired from the office, her bosom a prey to feelings of a strangely conflicting nature,—joy at having passed through an ordeal which she had dreaded—grief at having stained her soul with the fell crime of deliberate perjury—and agony at the sad reminiscences which the presence of Rainford had recalled so forcibly to her mind.

Miss Mordaunt and the two servants were astonished to hear the unexpected turn which the proceedings had taken; but their attention was almost immediately absorbed in the condition of Lady Hatfield, who scarcely had time to communicate to them the result of her examination in the court, when a sudden faintness came over her. She had exhausted all her energies in the endeavour to maintain an air of calmness, and to reply in a tone of sincerity when in the presence of the magistrate; and now a reaction took place—her courage gave way—the weight of fearful reminiscences overpowered her—the glow of excitement which had mantled her cheeks changed to a death-like pallor—and she fainted in the arms of her friend.

Fortunately, Miss Mordaunt had a bottle of volatile salts with her; and by these means Georgiana was speedily recovered. She was then led to her carriage; but she did not appear to breathe freely until the vehicle was some distance from the police-court.

CHAPTER IV.
ESTHER DE MEDINA.

Let us now return to the interior of the police-office.

The clerk was drawing up the bail-bond; the two securities were conversing in whispers with Tom Rain, whom they had affected to greet, when he descended from the dock, as an old acquaintance; and Mr. Dykes was leaning gloomily against the partition which separated the magistrate's desk from the body of the court,—when the entrance of two persons produced a new sensation amongst the crowd.

One was an officer of the court: the other was a lady, closely veiled, and enveloped in a cloak of rich material.

Her form was tall; and, even though her entire frame was now convulsed with intense anguish as she passed amidst the gaping throng to the chair which Lady Hatfield had occupied two or three minutes previously, yet that excess of grief and terror did not bow her down, nor impair the graceful dignity of her gait.

The officer motioned her to seat herself, an intimation which she evidently accepted with gratitude.

"What is it, Bingham?" inquired the magistrate of the officer.

"Please, your worship," was the reply, "it's a serious charge; and the prosecutor will be here in a moment."

"Very well," said the magistrate: "I will take it directly."

"Who is she?" whispered Dykes, accosting his brother officer.

"Her name is Esther de Medina, she tells me," returned Bingham.

The question and answer were overheard by Tom Rainford, who was standing close by the officers; and the announcement of the lady's name produced a strange and almost electrical effect upon him.

The devil-me-care recklessness of his manner suddenly disappeared; and a sentiment of profound commiseration and deep interest, in respect to Esther de Medina, seemed to occupy his mind.

He was about to question Mr. Bingham relative to the charge which he had against her, when the clerk called upon him and his securities to sign the bond. This ceremony was speedily performed; and Rain's money was returned to him by Mr. Dykes, who, however, looked at him in a manner which seemed to say—"I know I am not mistaken in you, although you have contrived to get off: but I'll have you another time."

Tom cared nothing for the sinister looks of the Bow Street officer; neither did he pay much attention to the gold which he now poured back into his pocket; for all his thoughts appeared to be absorbed in the presence of the veiled lady.

"Come along with us," whispered Bertinshaw, "and we'll celebrate your escape over a bottle of wine at my place."

"No—not now," replied Tom, hastily: "I mean to stay and hear this case: it interests me."

"Will you join us presently?" asked his new friend, who had just now pretended to be a very old one.

"Yes, yes," answered Tom: "in an hour or so."

Bertinshaw and Watkins then took their departure.

"Now, Bingham," cried the clerk; "what is it?"

At that moment a gentleman of handsome appearance and middle age entered the court.

"Here's the prosecutor who will explain the matter," said the officer.

The prisoner, suddenly remembering the respect due to the bench, raised her veil; and, at the same time, she glanced in an eager, inquiring manner towards the individual who now appeared against her.

But we must pause to describe her.

She was not more than eighteen years of age, and surpassingly lovely. Her complexion was a clear transparent olive, beneath which the delicate tinge of carnation was not entirely chased away from her cheeks by the terror and grief that now oppressed her. Her face was of the aquiline cast—her forehead broad, high, and intelligent; her nose curved, but not too prominent in shape; her mouth small, with thin vermilion lips, revealing teeth of pearly whiteness; her chin sweetly rounded; and her eyes large, black, and brilliant. And never did more splendid orbs of light mirror the whole power of the soul, or flash brighter glances from beneath richly-fringed lids. Then her brows were so delicately pencilled, and so finely arched, that they gave an air of dignity to that lovely—that fascinating countenance. Her hair, too, was of the deepest black—a black so intense, that the raven's wing might not have compared with it. Silken and glossy, the luxuriant mass was parted above the forehead, and, flowing in two shining bands—one on each side of the face, for which they appeared to form an ebony frame,—was gathered behind the ears.

In stature she was tall, sylph-like, and graceful. Her shoulders had that fine slope which the Italian masters so much admired, and with which they were delighted to endow the heroines of their pictures. Her waist was admirably proportioned, and not rendered too thin by the unnatural art of tight-lacing. Her hand was of exceeding beauty; her feet and ankles were in perfect keeping with the exquisite symmetry of her form; and her gestures were full of dignity and grace.

She was a Jewess; and, if the most glorious beauty were honoured with a diadem, then should Esther de Medina have become Queen of the Scattered Race.

The moment she raised her veil, all who could catch a glimpse of her countenance were struck with astonishment at the dazzling loveliness thus revealed; and even the magistrate felt anxious to learn what misadventure could have placed so peerless a being within the grasp of justice. Her crime could scarcely be robbery; for she was well-dressed, and had the appearance of belonging to even a wealthy family. Besides, her face—her eyes seemed to denote a conscious purity of soul, in spite of the painful emotions which her present situation had excited within her bosom.

But the person who was most interested—most astonished by the sudden revelation of that exquisite countenance, was Tom Rain. It was not with lustful desire that he surveyed her; it was not with any unholy passion: on the contrary, it was with a sentiment of deep devotion and profound sympathy. He also manifested extreme curiosity to learn upon what possible charge Esther de Medina could have been brought thither.

On her part, she was evidently altogether unacquainted with the person of Tom Rain; for as she cast a rapid and timid glance around, her eyes lingered not upon him.

The middle-aged, handsome-looking man who had just entered the office, was now desired to state the grounds upon which Esther de Medina was in custody.

This witness deposed that his name was Edward Gordon, and that he was a diamond-merchant, residing in Arundel Street, Strand. On the 31st of October, at about five o'clock in the evening, a female called upon him and requested him to purchase of her a diamond ring, which she produced. He examined it by the light of the lamp burning in the apartment where he received her; and, finding that it was really a jewel of some value, he offered her a price which he considered fair. That sum was thirty guineas. She endeavoured to obtain more; but he did not consider himself justified in acceding to her wish. Finally, she accepted his proposal, received the amount, left the ring, and departed. He went out immediately after, carefully locking the door of the room. Having an engagement to dine with a friend, he returned home late, and did not enter that particular room until the following morning; when he discovered that a set of diamonds, which he remembered to have been lying in an open case upon the table at the time the female called on the preceding evening, was missing. He searched vainly in all parts of the room; and at length came to the fixed conclusion that the female in question had stolen the diamonds. He gave immediate information to Bingham, the officer, together with an accurate description of the suspected person; for she was upwards of twenty minutes with him on the evening of the 31st, and he had therefore seen enough of her to know her again.

"Moreover," added the prosecutor "two clear days only have elapsed since the interview which took place between us; and I appeal to your worship whether the countenance of the prisoner, when once seen, can be readily forgotten; for painful as it is to accuse so young and interesting a person of such a crime, my duty to society compels me to take this step; and I have no hesitation in declaring that the prisoner is the female who sold me the ring."

A profound sigh escaped from the bosom of Esther; but she uttered not a word.

Bingham, the officer, then proved that he called about half an hour previously upon Mr. Gordon to inform him that he had vainly endeavoured to discover a clue to the supposed thief. Mr. Gordon was on the point of going out upon particular business, and the officer, in order not to detain him, walked a part of the way in his company, so that they might converse upon the subject of the robbery as they went along. They were passing through Lincoln's-Inn-Fields, when they met the prisoner at the bar. Mr. Gordon instantly recognised her, and the officer took her into custody. She manifested much indignation, and said that there must be some mistake; but when the nature of the charge was stated to her, she turned deadly pale, and burst into tears.

Rainford had listened to these statements with the deepest—the most intense interest; and his countenance underwent various changes, especially while Mr. Gordon was giving his evidence. At one moment Tom exhibited surprise—then indignation,—and, lastly, the most unfeigned sorrow.

But suddenly an idea seemed to strike him: for a minute did he reflect profoundly; and then joy animated his features.

Hastily quitting the court, he hurried to the coffee-house opposite, called for writing materials, and penned the following letter:—

"*Nov. 3, 1826.*

"MY LORD,—Esther de Medina is at Bow Street, accused of a crime which is alleged to have been committed at about five o'clock in the evening of the

31st of October. It is for you to prove her innocence. Delay not, then, an instant.

"AN UNKNOWN FRIEND TO ESTHER."

Throwing a shilling upon the table, Tom Rain hurried away, took a hackney-coach at the nearest station, and desired to be driven to the mansion of Lord Ellingham, Pall-mall, West.

A half-guinea which he slipped into the coachman's hand as he entered the vehicle, produced the desired effect; for the horses were urged into a pace the rapidity of which seemed to astonish themselves as a proof of what they could do if they chose; and, in a very short time, Rainford leapt out at the door of his lordship's abode.

The nobleman was fortunately at home; and Tom Rain delivered the letter to the servant who answered his summons.

Then, having desired the coachman to wait, as he might have "a fare" back to Bow Street, Rainford hurried away at his utmost speed, retracing his steps to the police-office.

In the meantime, the clerk had taken down the depositions of Mr. Edward Gordon and Bingham; while the most extraordinary sensation prevailed in the court. The youth—the loveliness—the modest, yet dignified appearance of Esther de Medina enlisted all sympathies in her favour; and many a rude heart then present felt a pang at the idea of believing her to be guilty.

She had stood up when the prosecutor was called against her; but when he reached that point in his evidence which mentioned the loss of his diamonds, she clasped her hand convulsively together, and, trembling with agitation, sank into the chair from which she had risen.

When the depositions were taken down, the magistrate said, "Prisoner, you have heard the very serious charge made against you: have you any thing to say in your defence?"

Then she spoke for the first time since she had entered the court; and though her words were delivered with impassioned emphasis, the melodious tones of her voice sounded like a silver bell upon the ears of all present.

"Sir, I am innocent—I am innocent!" she exclaimed. "Oh! God knows that I am innocent!"

The glance she darted from beneath her darkly fringed lids spoke even more eloquently than her words; and every feature of her fine countenance seemed to bear testimony to the truth of her declaration.

"Would you not do well to send for your friends?" asked the magistrate, in a kind tone.

These words seemed to touch her most acutely: they summed up as it were all the painful features of her most distressing position.

"Oh! my father—my dear, dear father!" she exclaimed, her countenance expressing so much bitter—bitter anguish, that there was scarcely an unmoistened eye in the court.

"Your worship, I do not wish to prosecute this case—I am sorry I have gone so far," said the diamond-merchant, wiping away the tears from his cheeks—for he was really a good-natured man.

"It is not in my power to stay the proceedings," replied Sir Walter Ferguson. "The evidence is unfortunately strong against the prisoner. She would do well to send for her friends. Let the case stand over for half an hour."

Esther was accordingly conducted into the magistrate's private room, where she was visited by the female-searcher, who endeavoured to persuade her, with as much gentleness as she could command, to mention the residence of her parents.

"Alas! my mother has long been dead," was the mournful reply; "and my poor father—oh! it would break his heart were he to know——"

She checked herself, and fell into a profound reverie—despair expressed in her countenance. During the remainder of the half hour which intervened ere she was led back to the office, she replied only in vague and unsatisfactory, but not self-inculpating, monosyllables to the questions addressed to her.

At length the female-searcher gave her an indirect intimation, that her punishment on trial would be more lenient if she admitted her guilt and expressed her contrition.

"What!" she exclaimed, with a recovering sob; "do you really deem me culpable of this most heinous charge? My God! have the Christians no mercy—no compassion? Oh! I should not speak thus to you! But I know that our race is looked upon with suspicion: we are prejudged, because we are Jews! And yet," she added, in a different and prouder tone, "there are as noble sentiments—as generous feelings—as estimable qualities amongst the members of the scattered tribe, as in the hearts of those Christians who have persecuted our nation for centuries and centuries!"

The woman, to whom these words were addressed, was astonished at the enthusiastic manner in which the beautiful Jewess spoke; for there was something at that moment sublimely interesting—eloquently commanding about Esther de Medina, as the rich colour glowed more deeply upon her cheeks, the blue veins dilated on her proud forehead, and the whole power of her soul seemed thrown into her magnificent eyes.

It was at this moment that the usher of the court entered to conduct the Jewess back into the office.

Once more she stood in the presence of the magistrate,—now no longer subdued and crushed with terror; but nerved, as it were by conscious innocence, to meet the accusation brought against her.

Tom Rain had returned to the court; and, by mingling with the crowd of spectators, anxiously watched the countenance of Esther de Medina.

"Prisoner," said the magistrate, "have you anything now to offer in your defence? Or have you sent to communicate with your friends relative to the position in which you are placed?"

"Sir," answered Esther, her soft and musical tones falling like a delicious harmony upon the ears, "I have but one word to utter in my defence; and if I did not speak it when I first stood before you, it was simply because this terrible accusation, bursting so abruptly upon the head of an innocent person, stupefied me—deprived me of the power of collecting my ideas. Neither was it until within a moment of my return into the court that the fact which I am about to state flashed to my memory. Sir—I was not in London from two o'clock in the afternoon until half-past ten o'clock at night, on the 31st of October."

A gentle—a very gentle smile played upon her vermilion lips as she uttered these words.

"And it was during the interval which you name that the prosecutor was visited by the female whom he believes to have robbed him of his diamonds?" observed the magistrate.

"I deny having visited the prosecutor at all," answered Esther, in a firm but respectful tone. "I never sold him a ring—I never sold an article of jewellery to a living being. Placed by the honest industry of my father above want," she continued proudly, "I labour not under the necessity of parting with my jewellery to obtain money."

At this moment, a fine, tall, handsome young man, of about six and twenty years of age, entered the court. He was dressed in an elegant but unassuming manner: his bearing was lofty, without being proud; and his fine blue eyes indicated a frank and generous disposition.

Slightly inclining in acknowledgment of the respect with which the crowd made way for him to pass, he advanced towards the magistrate, who instantly recognised him as an acquaintance.

At the same moment, Esther started with surprise, and murmured the name of Lord Ellingham.

To the astonishment of all present—Tom Rain, perhaps, excepted,—the nobleman shook Esther kindly by the hand, saying, "In the name of heaven, Miss de Medina, what unfortunate—or rather ridiculous mistake has brought you hither?"

Sir Walter Ferguson immediately directed the clerk to read over the depositions.

"What!" ejaculated Lord Ellingham, who had scarcely been able to restrain his indignation during the recital of the previous proceedings: "the daughter of a respectable and wealthy gentleman to be placed in such a position as this! But in a moment I will make her innocence apparent. At the very time when this robbery was alleged to have taken place—at the hour when the female, for whom this young lady has evidently been mistaken, called upon the prosecutor—Miss de Medina was not within six miles of Arundel Street."

These words produced in the court a sensation which was the more lively because they seemed to corroborate the prisoner's own defence—a defence which Lord Ellingham had not heard.

Mr. Gordon, the prosecutor, looked astounded—and yet not altogether grieved at the prospect of the prisoner's discharge.

"Mr. de Medina," continued Lord Ellingham, "has only recently arrived in London, having retired from an extensive commercial business which he long carried on at Liverpool. He has become my tenant for a house and small estate situated at a distance of about seven miles from the metropolis; and on the 31st of October I accompanied him and his daughter—the lady now present—on a visit to the property thus leased. We left London in my own carriage at about two o'clock on the day named; and it was between ten and eleven at night when we returned. During that interval of several hours Miss de Medina never quitted her father and myself."

A murmur of satisfaction arose on the part of the spectators; but it was almost immediately interrupted by the entrance of an elderly and venerable-looking man, whose countenance—of that cast which ever characterises the sons of the scattered tribe—had once been strikingly handsome. Though not deficient in an expression of generosity, it nevertheless exhibited great firmness of disposition; and his keen black eyes denoted a resolute, unbending, and determined soul. He was upwards of fifty-five years of age, and was plainly, though neatly, dressed.

Advancing into the body of the court, he cast a rapid glance around.

"My father!" exclaimed Esther; and springing forward, she threw herself into her parent's arms.

He held her tenderly for a few moments: then, gently disengaging himself from her embrace, he murmured in her ear, "Oh! Esther—Esther, I can understand it all! You have brought this upon yourself!"

But these words were heard only by Lord Ellingham, who had advanced to shake hands with the Jew.

That reproach appeared for the moment to be singular and altogether misplaced, as it was impossible that Esther could have perpetrated the crime imputed to her: but the nobleman had not leisure to reflect upon it, for Mr. de Medina now perceived him and accepted the outstretched hand.

"I was accidentally passing by the court," said the Jew; "and hearing my own name mentioned by some loungers outside, paused to listen. Their conversation induced me to make inquiries; and I learnt all the particulars of this charge."

"And some unknown friend of Miss de Medina sent me a hasty note conveying the unpleasant intelligence," answered Lord Ellingham. "But I believe that I have fully convinced his worship of your daughter's innocence."

These last words were uttered in a louder tone than the former part of the observation, and were evidently addressed to the magistrate.

"For my part," said Mr. Gordon, "I am perfectly satisfied that there is a grievous misunderstanding in this matter. Miss de Medina is evidently unconnected with it; and yet," he added, as his eyes dwelt upon her countenance, "never was resemblance so striking! However—I am well pleased to think that Miss de Medina is *not* the person by whom I was plundered; and I most sincerely implore her pardon for the inconvenience—nay, the ignominy to which she has been subjected."

Esther turned an appealing glance towards her father, as if to remind him of some duty which he ought to perform, or to convey some silent prayer which he could well understand: but he affected not to notice that rapid but profoundly significant glance.

The magistrate then declared that the young lady was discharged, without the slightest stain upon her character.

Hastily drawing down her thick black veil, Esther de Medina bowed deferentially to the bench; and passed out of the office, leaning on her father's arm, and accompanied by the Earl of Ellingham.

Tom Rain followed her with his eyes until the door closed behind her.

For a few moments he remained wrapped up in a deep reverie: then, heaving a profound sigh, he also took his departure.

CHAPTER V.
THE APPEAL OF LOVE.

It was about eight o'clock in the evening of the day on which so many strange incidents occurred at Bow Street, that Lady Hatfield was reclining in a melancholy mood upon the sofa in the drawing-room of her splendid mansion.

She was dressed in black satin, which set off the beauty of her complexion to the greatest advantage.

One of her fair hands drooped over the back of the sofa: the other listlessly held a book, to the perusal of which she had vainly endeavoured to settle herself.

There was a mysterious air of mournfulness about her that contrasted strangely with the elegance of the apartment, the cheerful blaze of the fire, the brilliant lustre of the lamps, and the general appearance of wealth and luxury by which she was surrounded.

That sorrowful expression, too, was the more unaccountable, inasmuch as the social position of Georgiana Hatfield seemed to be enviable in the extreme. Beautiful in person, possessing rank and wealth, and free to follow her own inclinations, she might have shone the star of fashion—the centre of that human galaxy whose sphere is the West End of London.

Oh! bright—gloriously bright are the planets which move in that heaven of their own:—and yet how useless is their brilliancy! The planets of God's own sky are made to bestow their light upon the orbs which without them would revolve in darkness; but the planets of the sphere of aristocracy and fashion throw not a single ray upon the millions of inferior stars which are compelled to circle around them!

To Lady Hatfield the pleasures and dissipation of the West End were unwelcome; and she seldom entered into society, save when a refusal would prove an offence. Up to the age of seventeen or eighteen she had been remarkable for a happy, joyous, and gay disposition: but a sudden change came over her at that period of her life; and since then her habits had grown retired—her disposition mournful.

But let us return to her, as she lay reclining on the sofa in the drawing-room.

The robbery of the preceding night and the events of the morning had evidently produced a powerful impression upon her mind. At times an expression of acute anguish distorted her fair countenance for a moment; and once or twice she compressed her lips forcibly, as if to restrain a burst of mental agony.

The time-piece upon the mantel had just proclaimed the hour of eight, when a domestic entered the room and announced the Earl of Ellingham.

Georgiana started up—assumed a placid expression of countenance—and advanced to receive the young nobleman, who, as he took her hand, respectfully pressed it to his lips.

"Your ladyship will, I hope, pardon me for intruding at this hour," he said, as he conducted her back to the sofa, and then took a chair at a short distance; "but I was not aware of your return to town until an hour ago, when I perused in the evening paper an account of the outrage of last night and the investigation at Bow Street this morning. How annoying it must have been to you, my dear Lady Hatfield, to have gone through the ordeal of a visit to a police-court!"

"There is something gloomy and dispiriting in the aspect of these tribunals which the crimes of the human race have rendered necessary," observed Georgiana. "The countenances of those persons whom I beheld at the police-office this morning, had all a certain sinister expression which I cannot define, but which seemed to proclaim that they never contemplated aught save the dark side of society."

"The same idea struck me this day," said Lord Ellingham: "for I also paid a visit to Bow Street—and scarcely an hour, I should conceive, after you must have left the office. But enough of this subject: the words *Bow Street—Police*—and *Tribunal* grate painfully upon the ear even of the innocent,—that is, if they possess hearts capable of sorrowing for the woes and crimes of their fellow-creatures. Lady Hatfield," continued the Earl, drawing his chair a little closer, "it was to converse upon another topic—yes, another and a more tender topic—that I have hastened to your presence this evening."

Georgiana was about to reply;—but the words died upon her quivering lips—and an oppressive feeling kept her silent.

"Yes, my dear Lady Hatfield," continued the Earl, drawing his chair still more nigh,—"I can no longer exist in this state of suspense. During the whole of last winter I was often in your society: you were kind enough to permit my visits—and it was impossible to be much with you, and not learn to love you. You departed suddenly for the country last July: but I dared not follow—for you had not even informed me of your intended retirement from London at so early a period. Pardon me if I say I felt hurt,—yes, *hurt*, Lady Hatfield,—because I loved you! And yet never—during that interval of four months—has your image been absent from my mind: and now I am again attracted towards you by a spell stronger than my powers of resistance. Oh! you must long ago have read my heart, Georgiana:—say, then—*can* you, *do* you love me in return?"

There was something so sincere—so earnest—and yet so manly in the fluent language of the Earl of Ellingham,—his fine countenance was lighted up with so animated an expression of hope and love,—and his eyes bore such complete testimony to the candour of his speech,—that Georgiana must have been ungenerous indeed had she heard that appeal with coldness.

Nor was it so; and the Earl read in the depths of her melting blue orbs a sentiment reciprocal with his own.

"My lord—Arthur," she murmured, "you ask me if I *can* love—if I *do* love you:—and, oh! you know not the pang which that question excites in my heart! Yes," she added hastily, seeing that the Earl was astonished at her words, "I *do* love you, Arthur—for you are all that is good, generous, and handsome! But—my God!—how can I force my lips to utter the sad avowal——"

"Speak, Georgiana—speak, I conjure you!" exclaimed Lord Ellingham: "you alarm me! Oh! keep me not in suspense! You say that you love me——"

"I never loved until I knew you—I shall never love another," answered Georgiana, fixing her deep, silently expressive, and intellectual eyes upon the countenance of the Earl.

"A thousand thanks for that declaration, my heart's sole joy!" he cried in an impassioned tone; and, falling on his knees by the side of the sofa, he threw his arms around her—he clasped her to his breast—his lips pressed hers for the first time.

But that joy lasted only for a moment.

With rebounding heart—and with almost a scream of anguish—Georgiana drew herself back, and abruptly repulsed her ardent lover: then, covering her face with her hands, she burst into a flood of tears.

"My God! what signifies this strange conduct?" ejaculated the Earl, as, with wounded pride, he retreated a few paces from the weeping lady.

"Forgive me—forgive me, Arthur!" she wildly cried, turning her streaming eyes towards him in a beseeching manner. "I am unhappy—very unhappy—and you should pity me!"

"Pity *you*!" exclaimed the Earl, again approaching the sofa, and taking her hand, which she did not attempt to withdraw: "how can *you* be an object of pity? Beautiful—beloved by one whose life shall be devoted to ensure the felicity of yours——"

"Oh! your generous affection, Arthur, gives me more pain than all the rest!" cried Georgiana, in a rapid—half-hysterical tone. "As a weak woman, I have dared to love you—as an imprudent one, I have confessed that love;—but now," she added, in a slower and firmer tone, while her vermilion lips quivered with a bitter smile,—"now, as a strong woman—as a woman restored to a sense of duty—do I make the avowal—and my heart is ready to break as I thus speak———"

"Good heavens! relieve me from this cruel—this agonizing suspense!" passionately exclaimed the Earl.

"I will—I will," returned Lady Hatfield. "Arthur—dearly, fondly, devotedly as I love you,—proud as I should be to call you my husband,—happy, happy as I should feel to link my fate with yours,—alas! it cannot be:—never—never!" she added with a frantic vehemence that caused every chord to thrill in the heart of her admirer.

"Georgiana, is this possible?" he asked, in a faint tone, while a deadly pallor overspread his countenance.

"Would that it were *not*!" she murmured, clasping her hands together in visible anguish of soul.

"And yet it is incomprehensible!" cried the Earl, starting back, and even manifesting somewhat of impatience. "You are not a foolish girl who takes delight in trifling with the sincere attachment of an honest man who adores her:—you are not a heartless coquette, looking upon her admirer as a slave whom she is justified to torture. No—no: you yourself possess a generous soul—you have no sympathy with the frivolous portion of your sex—you are as strong-minded, as sincere as you are beautiful. Tell me, then, Georgiana—what signifies this strange contradiction? You love me—you would be happy and proud to become mine;—and yet—my God!—and yet you the next moment annihilate every hope in my breast!"

"Alas! how unpardonable must my conduct seem—how inexplicable my behaviour!" exclaimed Lady Hatfield, in a tone of despair. "I am not indeed a heartless coquette—nor a weak frivolous girl:—in the sincerity of my heart do I speak, Arthur;—and if you be generous you will forgive me—but I never can be thine!"

"Then you love another!" cried the Earl, impatiently.

"Have I not solemnly assured you that I never loved till I knew you—and shall never, never love again!" she added, with a convulsive sob, as if her heart were breaking.

"But perhaps you were betrothed to another in your youth:—peradventure that *other* has some sacred pledge—some irrevocable bond———"

"No—no: I am my own mistress—none can control me!" interrupted Georgiana, her nervous state of excitement growing each moment more painful.

"And your uncle—your friends—your advisers?" said the Earl,—"it is possible that *they* have become acquainted with my attachment towards you—that *they* have some motive to counsel you against my suit?"

"On the contrary——But, my God! do not question me thus!" almost shrieked the unhappy lady. "I shall go mad—I shall go mad!"

"Oh! there is some dreadful mystery in all this!" cried the Earl; "and I too shall go mad if it be not explained! Merciful heavens! a terrible suspicion flashes across my mind. And yet—no—no, it cannot be,—for you declare that you never loved another! Still—still, what motive, save *that*, can render you thus resolute not to become mine? Georgiana," he said, sinking his voice to a low tone, and speaking with a solemn seriousness which had something even awful in its effect,—"Georgiana, I conjure you to answer me,—*me*, who am your devoted lover and your sincerest friend,—as you would reply to your God! Say—if in your giddy and inexperienced girlhood—ignorant through extreme innocence of the snare spread for you—and in a moment of weakness—you——"

"Just heavens! that you should suppose me criminal—guilty!" shrieked Georgiana, covering her face with her hands.

"Pardon—pardon!" cried the Earl, again falling on his knees at the feet of her whom he adored; and, forcibly possessing himself of one of her hands, he conveyed it to his lips. "Pardon me for the outrageous idea that I dared to express—forgive the insulting suspicion which for a moment occupied my mind! Alas! alas! that I should have provoked the look of indignation which you ere now cast upon me, when I withdrew your hand from before your eyes! But, ah—now you smile—and I am forgiven!"

Georgiana *did* smile—but in a manner so plaintively melancholy, that, although it implied forgiveness for the injurious suspicion, it still conveyed no hope!

There was a long and mournful pause.

The Earl of Ellingham burned to penetrate the deep mystery in which the conduct of Lady Hatfield was shrouded; and yet he knew not what other hypothesis to suggest.

He had no rival in her affections—her friends offered no objection to his suit—she was under no pledge to bestow her hand upon any particular individual—and the evanescent suspicion that she might have once been frail and was too honourable to bring a polluted person to the marriage-bed, had been banished beyond the possibility of return:—what, then, could influence her conduct?

He knew not how to elicit the truth; and yet his happiness was too deeply interested to permit him to depart in uncertainty and suspense.

"Georgiana," he said, at length, and speaking in a tone which showed how profoundly his feelings were excited,—"I appeal to your sense of justice whether you have acted candidly and generously in respect to me? Throughout the whole of last winter you permitted my visits—I will not say encouraged them, because you have too much delicacy to have done that. But you were never denied to me; and you gave me not to understand that my calls were unwelcome, when they began to exceed the usual limits of mere friendly visits. At length my attentions became marked towards you,—and you must have read my feelings in my manner—my language—and my attentions. Alas! why did you permit me to encourage the blossoming of hopes which are now so cruelly blighted by the unaccountable decision that you have uttered to-day?"

"Oh! do not reproach me, Arthur!" exclaimed Georgiana: "and yet I know that I have acted imprudently. But it was so sweet to be beloved by you, that I had not courage to destroy the charming vision! At length I took a decided step—or at least what seemed to me to be so: I departed suddenly to my uncle's country-seat, without previously intimating my resolution to you. And remember—no avowal of affection on your part had then met my ears; and it was impossible that I could have acquainted you with my proposed departure, even if I had wished so to do—because I did not *see* you on the day when I determined to quit London: and had I *written* to you then, would you not have thought that my note conveyed a hint for you to follow me?"

"Fool—idiot that I was not to have declared my passion months and months ago!" ejaculated the Earl. "But say, Georgiana—had I solicited your hand last summer, ere you left London, would those reasons which influence you now——"

"Yes—they were in existence then," was the hasty reply.

"And am I to remain in ignorance of the motives which compel you to refuse my suit?" asked Lord Ellingham bitterly. "Is there no chance of their influence ceasing? Oh! give me but a glimpse of hope, and so powerful is my attachment—so devoted my love——"

"Merciful heavens!" exclaimed Georgiana wildly,—"am I then to lose such a man as this?"

And again she clasped her hands convulsively together.

"Oh! you love me—you *do* love me, my angel," cried the Earl; "and yet you refuse me! What stern fate—what terrible destiny can possibly separate us! This mystery is appalling!"

"And a mystery it must remain," said Georgiana, suddenly assuming that quiet and passive manner which indicated despair.

"Then farewell, Lady Hatfield," exclaimed the Earl; "and be not surprised if I must attribute the disappointment—the anguish—the deep humiliation which I now experience, to some inexplicable caprice of the female mind. But, madam," he added, drawing himself up haughtily, and speaking in a tone of offended pride, "the Earl of Ellingham, whose wealth and rank may enable him to vie with the mightiest peers of England, will not be made the sport of the whims and wavering fancies of even the beautiful Lady Hatfield."

Thus speaking, the nobleman bowed coldly, and advanced towards the door.

"Oh! this is cruel—this is cruel!" cried Georgiana, throwing herself hysterically back upon the sofa.

"No, madam—it is you who are cruel to reject the honourable suit of one like me without deigning to vouchsafe an explanation," said the Earl, persisting in his severity of tone and manner against the promptings of his generous nature, but with the hope of eliciting a satisfactory reply.

"Then go, my lord—depart—leave me!" cried Georgiana; "for I never can be yours!"

The Earl lingered for a moment: convulsive sobs broke from the lips of the unhappy Lady Hatfield—but not a word to invite him to remain!

His pride would not permit him to offer farther entreaty;—and, suffering cruelly at heart, he rushed from the room.

In less than a minute Georgiana heard the street-door close; and then, burying her face in the cushion of the sofa, she gave way unrestrainedly to all the violence of her grief.

CHAPTER VI.
DR. LASCELLES.

The interview between Lady Hatfield and the Earl of Ellingham was as long as it was painful: and ten o'clock struck by the thousand churches of London, as the nobleman quitted the mansion.

There was such a fierce struggle in his breast between wounded pride and fervent affection, that his sorrow for the blighted hope of the latter was rendered less acute by being united with the indignation inspired by the former.

In spite of his generous nature, he could not help thinking that he had been trifled with to some extent; for it naturally seemed preposterous that Georgiana should refuse him without a candid explanation of the motives, and when every earthly circumstance appeared favourable to their union.

Then, again, he pondered upon the wildness of her grief—the delirious anguish which she had shown at several stages of their interview—her solemn avowal of love for him alone—and her voluntary assurance that she should be happy and proud to call him her husband. He moreover reflected upon the steadiness of her character—her aversion to the frivolities of the fashionable world—her apparent candour of disposition—and her total want of any thing approaching to coquetry;—and he endeavoured to persuade himself that he had acted harshly by leaving her in anger.

"Yet what alternative had I?" he asked himself; "and would not any other man have in the same way cut short an interview of so mysterious and unsatisfactory—so perplexing and humiliating a nature?"

Alas! the Earl of Ellingham found himself the very next minute dwelling with an aching and compassionate heart upon the agonised state in which he had left the being whom he so tenderly loved:—he thought of her fascinating beauty—her bewitching manners—her well-cultivated mind—her amiable disposition;—and then he said within himself, "Oh! if I have indeed lost *her*, I have lost an angel!"

He had reached the immediate vicinity of Hatchett's Hotel, when he turned back with the resolution of seeking another interview with Georgiana.

But scarcely had he retraced ten steps of the way, ere he stopped short, and asked himself what advantage could be gained by such a proceeding?

"The decision is given," he reasoned: "she can never—*never* be mine! Wherefore should I renew *her* grief and *my* humiliation—evoke fresh tears from *her* eyes, and add sharpness to the sting of *my* disappointment? No: it may not be! Some terrible mystery shrouds her conduct from my penetration;—but shall I, who am defeated in love, give way to a base sentiment of curiosity? It would be unmanly—ignoble—cowardly to attempt to extort her secret from *her*,—for a profound secret she doubtless cherishes—a secret which has this evening influenced her conduct! And perhaps," he thought, following the natural channel of his meditations, "that secret is of a nature which a modest woman could not reveal to one of the opposite sex?"

This idea, suddenly flashing across his brain, suggested a proceeding which, after a few minutes of profound reflection, he determined to adopt.

Passing rapidly up Dover Street, Lord Ellingham entered Grafton Street, where he knocked at a door on which was a brass-plate engraved with the name of DR. LASCELLES.

The physician was at home; and the nobleman was immediately ushered into a parlour, where he was shortly joined by the individual whom he sought.

Dr. Lascelles was a short, thin, sallow-faced man of about fifty. He had small, restless, sparkling eyes, a prim mouth, and an intelligent though by no means prepossessing countenance. He was devoted to the art which he practised, and was reputed the most scientific man of the whole faculty. His anatomical researches had been prosecuted with an energy and a perseverance which afforded occupation to half the resurrection-men in London, and more than once to the doctor's own personal danger in respect to the law. It was whispered in well-informed circles that he never hesitated to encounter any peril in order to possess himself of the corpse of a person who died of an unusual malady. His devotion to anatomy had materially blunted his feelings and deadened the kinder sympathies of his nature; but his immense talents, added to a reputation acquired by several wonderful cures, rendered him the most fashionable physician of the day.

Such was the medical gentleman whom Lord Ellingham called to consult.

"Excuse this late visit, doctor," said the Earl; "but I knew that I might take the liberty of intruding upon you."

"The words *early* and *late* are not in my vocabulary, so far as they regard myself," was the reply. "My hours are at the disposal of my patrons, amongst whom I have the honour to include your lordship."

"Then, without farther apology, I shall proceed to state the object of my visit," said the nobleman.

"Give me your hand—you look dejected—you are very pale—your pulse——"

"It is not concerning myself altogether that I have to speak," interrupted the Earl, withdrawing the hand which the doctor had seized: "I wish to consult you upon a subject intimately affecting my happiness."

The physician looked surprised, and drew his chair closer to that in which the Earl was seated.

"To tell you the truth," continued Arthur, "I am deeply enamoured of a lady whose social position, beauty, fortune, and intellect render her in every way worthy to become my wife."

"Well—why don't you propose to her?" demanded the physician drily.

"I have—and am rejected," was the answer, accompanied by a profound sigh.

"The devil!" said the physician. "But what can I do for you in the matter? Surely your lordship does not believe in philtres and love-draughts?"

"Ridiculous!" cried the Earl impatiently. "If you will grant me a few moments, I will explain myself."

Dr. Lascelles folded his arms, threw himself back in the chair, and prepared to listen to his young friend's narrative.

"The lady to whom I am attached," continued the Earl, "is, as I ere now informed you, in every way worthy of an alliance with me; and she is moreover deeply attached to me. She has never loved another, and declares that she never can. No apparent circumstances interfere with our union; and she has done me the honour to assure me that she should be alike proud and happy to own me as her husband. She is entirely her own mistress; and, even if she were not, her friends would present no barrier to our marriage. Yet she refuses me—and for some mysterious cause which she will not explain. I have just left her,—left her in a state of anguish such as I never before witnessed—such as I hope never to behold again!"

"Perhaps she has been guilty of some weakness which she is afraid you would discover?" suggested Dr. Lascelles.

"Oh! no—no," exclaimed Arthur, enthusiastically: "in an unguarded moment—carried away by a hasty suspicion of the kind—I hinted at that possibility,—and I soon repented of my rashness! The lady's countenance flushed with a glow of honest indignation; and, instantly veiling her blushes with her hand, she burst into tears. I could pledge my existence, doctor, that she is purity itself."

"But wherefore do you consult me in the matter?" asked Lascelles.

"You must admit, doctor," answered Ellingham, "that my position is a singular one in reference to the lady of whom I speak. What am I to conjecture? Suspense is terrible; and yet, not for worlds would I again attempt to extort her secret from her."

"The motive may be a physical one," said the doctor.

"That was the idea which ere now struck me, and which has brought me hither to consult you!" exclaimed the Earl.

"She may be the prey to some insidious disease which impairs not her exterior aspect at present," continued Doctor Lascelles; "say, for instance, a cancer in the breast. Or again, her motive may be a moral one; inasmuch as she may be aware, from some secret warnings, that she is in danger of suffering an aberration of reason."

"And if the lady were a patient of your own, doctor," asked the Earl, "should you be enabled to judge whether she were menaced by that dreadful mental malady to which you have alluded?"

"Decidedly so," replied the physician.

The Earl rose from his seat, and walked two or three times up and down the apartment.

Dr. Lascelles followed him with his eyes; and as he surveyed the strong, well-knit, but slender and graceful form of the young nobleman, the votary of science could not help thinking what a splendid skeleton he would make.

At length the Earl stopped abruptly opposite the doctor, and said in an impressive tone, "You will never reveal the particulars of this interview?"

"It is scarcely probable," returned Lascelles, with a smile.

"But you promise me—you pledge your word never to breathe a syllable which may betray the motive of my present visit or the topic of our conversation?" persisted the Earl.

"Never," exclaimed the physician.

"Then listen," said the Earl, sinking his voice almost to a whisper;—"the lady of whom I have spoken, is——"

"Lady Hatfield," observed Lascelles.

"What! you have guessed——"

"Simply because every one said last winter that you were dying for her," interrupted the doctor coolly; "and therefore I presume you have availed yourself of her ladyship's return to town to place your coronet at her feet."

"Yes—I do allude to Georgiana, whose professional attendant you are," cried the Earl. "And believe me when I solemnly declare that no sentiment of impertinent curiosity——"

"Never mind the motives," said the doctor: "let us keep to the facts. I have known Lady Hatfield for upwards of five years; and I can positively assure your lordship that there is not the slightest cause, physical or moral, with which I am acquainted, that can influence her conduct towards you."

"Then, what can this mystery be?" exclaimed Arthur, more perplexed than ever. "My God! must I again fall back upon the hypothesis of a woman's idle caprice—the theory of her unaccountable whims? Is she the victim of an idiosyncracy which she cannot control? and must I be made its sport?"

"Throughout the sphere of my extensive practice," observed Dr. Lascelles, "I know not a woman less likely to be swayed by idle caprice or unaccountable whims than Lady Hatfield. Her mind is strong—her intellect bright and uncharacterised by the slightest eccentricity. I have, however, frequently observed that her ladyship is the prey to a secret melancholy—that she has her dark moments, as one may denominate them; but at those times the vigour of her soul is not subdued to a degree that would produce so strange a result as a decision affecting her own happiness. You say she loves you——"

"I have not a doubt of the sincerity of her attachment!" cried the Earl emphatically.

"And yet she will not marry you?" said the doctor. "I cannot comprehend it."

"Nor I," observed Arthur, with exceeding bitterness of tone. "My happiness is at stake. What can I do? Had she explained the motive of her refusal, and were that motive a strong one,—did it reveal some cause which would render our union infelicitous,—I might have borne up against this cruel—cruel disappointment. My love for her would then have been converted, by admiration of her generous candour, into a permanent friendship; and we might henceforth have met as brother and sister. But how can I ever visit her again? how can I meet her? Beautiful and amiable as she is, I adore her;—and yet I dare not in future trust myself in her presence! No:—I must crush this love in my heart—stifle it—subdue it altogether! Oh! fool that I am to talk thus;—as if it were practicable to forget her—as if it were possible to cease to worship her! Ere now, as I walked through the streets, I endeavoured to blunt the keenness of my affection by placing it in contact with the amount of wrong which I deemed myself to have experienced at her hands. But, unjustly perhaps as she has treated me—humiliated as I felt and still feel myself to be—chagrined—disappointed—rejected without explanation,—oh! all these injuries are absorbed in the immensity of the love which I bear her!"

And in a state of extraordinary excitement, Arthur paced the room with agitated steps.

The doctor sate musing upon his chair. He had ever been too much devoted to scientific pursuits to afford leisure for the delights of love; and though he was married, he had entered the connubial state only through motives of self-interest. Well aware that ladies prefer a medical attendant whose propriety of conduct is—or at least appears to be—guaranteed by marriage, he had one day cast his mental eyes around the circle of his acquaintance; and his glances were at length fixed upon a wealthy widow who was one of his patients. Jumping into his cab, he called upon her, and, in order not to waste time, proposed while he felt her pulse: she simpered an assent—and, as she could not name the day, he did it for her while he wrote out a prescription. Then he pocketed her guinea all the same—not through meanness, but from the regularity of professional habit; and had she offered him a fee as an acknowledgment for his loss of time on the morning when they issued from the church, he would also have taken it. This union was sterile; but the doctor found that he had obtained an excellent wife, who kept his house in good order—did the honours of his table to admiration—and never interrupted him when he was engaged in his study.

We have only introduced this little episode in the life of Dr. Lascelles, just to convince our readers that he was not at all the man to comprehend the vehemence of Lord Ellingham's love. Thus, while the nobleman was pacing the apartment in the manner described above, and declaiming in reference to his passion, the physician was meditating profoundly upon the conduct of Lady Hatfield in refusing so excellent a match. His mind, habituated to connect every thing as much as possible with the special sphere of science wherein he moved, soon lost itself in a field of conjecture as to whether there might not be some physical cause, carefully concealed even from himself, which would elucidate the mystery. The result of his meditations was not at all satisfactory to himself; but he resolved that he would not allow the matter to remain just where it was.

This determination he did not, however, communicate to Lord Ellingham, who took his leave more bewildered than ever as to the motive which could have possibly induced Lady Hatfield to assure him of her love and yet refuse him her hand.

CHAPTER VII.
THE BEAUTIFUL PATIENT.

Ten minutes had scarcely elapsed since Lord Ellingham took his departure from the doctor's abode, and the learned gentleman himself was still pondering on the strange communication which had been made to him, when a loud and hasty knock at the front-door echoed through the house.

A servant answered the summons, and in a few moments ushered Tom Rain into the presence of Dr. Lascelles.

"Sir," said the visitor, who was painfully excited, "a female—a young woman in whom I am deeply interested—has taken poison. Come with me this instant, I implore you."

Dr. Lascelles snatched up his hat, and followed Rainford without pausing to ask a single question. A hackney-coach was waiting at the door: the two individuals leapt in; and the vehicle drove rapidly away.

The doctor now thought it expedient to make a few inquiries relative to the case which was about to engage his attention.

"What poison has the young woman taken?" he asked.

"Arsenic," was the reply: "for I found the paper which had contained it."

"And how long ago?"

"Ten minutes before I knocked at your door."

"Has there been any vomiting?"

"I did not delay a single moment in hastening to fetch you, after the unhappy creature took the poison; and therefore I am unable to answer that question."

The physician remained silent; and in a few minutes the coach stopped at a house in South Moulton Street.

The door was opened by a servant-girl; and Rainford led the physician to a bed-room on the second floor, whither the servant-girl followed them.

By the light of a candle placed upon a chest of drawers, Dr. Lascelles beheld a young female of great beauty, and with no other garment on than her night-dress, writhing in excruciating agonies upon the bed. From the reply given by the servant-girl to a question put by the doctor, it appeared that the young lady had been seized with violent vomiting the moment after Tom Rain had left to procure medical aid; and Lascelles accordingly proceeded to adopt the usual treatment which is pursued in such cases.[1]

In the course of half an hour the patient was pronounced to be out of danger; and Tom Rain, who had in the meantime manifested the utmost anxiety and uneasiness, now exhibited a proportionate liveliness of joy.

"Shall I recover, sir! Oh! tell me—shall I recover?" asked the young woman in a strange, thrilling, piteous tone, as she fixed her large dark eyes upon the countenance of the physician.

"You are in a fair way to survive this mad—this wicked attempt upon your life," answered Lascelles, in a compassionately reproachful rather than a severe tone. "But you must be kept quiet—and all sources of mental irritation must be removed or forgotten as much as possible," he added, glancing towards Rainford.

"Oh! sir—do not imagine for a moment that *he* will upbraid or ill-treat me!" exclaimed the young woman, darting a fond look towards Tom Rain: then, drawing a long and heavy respiration, she said in a different and more subdued tone, "In justice to *him*, doctor, I must assure you that no harshness on *his* part urged me to this shocking deed: but——"

"Yes, my dearest girl," interrupted Rain, rushing to the bed, and taking one of her hands which he pressed fondly to his lips, "I *did* upbraid you—I *did* speak severely to you——"

"No—no—not more than I deserved!" cried the young woman: "for I was very wrong—oh! I was very wrong! But say, Tom, can you forgive me?"

"He does forgive you—he has forgiven you," exclaimed the physician. "And now abandon that subject, which is naturally a painful one. To-morrow morning I shall call and see you early."

Dr. Lascelles took up his hat to depart, and Rainford followed him into the passage, where he said in a low but earnest tone, "One word, sir, in private! Please to step into this room."

And he conducted the physician into a front apartment, the door of which he carefully closed.

"In the first place, sir," began Rainford when they were thus alone together, "allow me to thank you for your prompt and effectual aid in this most painful affair;"—and he slipped five guineas into the doctor's hand. "Secondly, let me implore of you to grant the favour which I am about to ask."

"Speak, sir," said Lascelles; "and if your request be not inconsistent with my honour as a physician and as a gentleman——"

"Far from it!" exclaimed Rainford. "It is this:—Promise me, on your solemn word of honour, *as a physician and as a gentleman*, that, when once your professional visits here have ceased, you will forget that you ever beheld that young woman who is lying in the next room. Promise me, I say, in the most binding manner, that should you ever henceforth meet her, alone or in company, you will not even appear to recognise her, much less attempt to speak to her, unless you be formally introduced to her, when you will consider your acquaintance with her to begin only from the moment of such introduction. Promise me all this, sir, I implore you—for you know not what vitally important interests may be compromised by your conduct in this matter."

"I have not the slightest objection to tranquillise your mind by giving the pledge which you demand," returned Dr. Lascelles, without a moment's hesitation.

"A thousand thanks, sir!" cried Rainford joyfully. "You fully understand the precise nature of the reserve and silence which I require?"

"Never to allude in any way to the incident of this night, nor to appear to recognise elsewhere nor henceforth the young lady whom I have just seen," said the doctor. "You may rely upon me: the secret shall never transpire from my lips."

"Again I express my gratitude," cried Rainford, with undisguised satisfaction.

Dr. Lascelles then took his leave; and, as he retraced his way to Grafton Street, he never once ceased to think of the strange promise which he had been required to give in respect to the beautiful creature who had made so resolute an attempt upon her own existence.

On the following morning, shortly after eight o'clock, the physician's cab stopped at the door of the house in South Moulton Street; but, to his surprise, he learnt from the landlady that Mr. and Mrs. Jameson (by which names Rainford and the young woman had been known at their lodgings) had taken their departure at seven o'clock, before it was even light.

"Had they resided long with you?" inquired the doctor.

"Only a week, sir," was the answer. "The lady kept herself very quiet, and seldom went out. When she did, she always had a thick black veil over her face; and, you may think it strange, sir—but it's true for all that—which is, sir, that I never once caught a glimpse of her countenance all the time she was in this house. But the servant-gal says she was very beautiful—very beautiful indeed! *You* must, however, be able to judge whether that report is true or not, sir?"

"I know little, and think less of those matters, my good woman," said the doctor hastily; and, returning to his cab, he drove off to visit another patient.

<u>1</u>. The first great object which we must keep in view, is to promote the speedy evacuation of the stomach: if the poison itself has not produced vomiting, from ten to twenty grains of sulphate of zinc must be given if it can be readily procured; this generally acts as a powerful emetic. If this, however, cannot be obtained, a mustard emetic should be administered, and the vomiting promoted by drinking large quantities of barley water, linseed tea, milk or tepid water: the two first being of a mucilaginous nature are to be preferred; tickling the back of the throat with a feather will often cause the stomach to reject its contents. It frequently happens that this treatment alone is sufficient for relief in accidents of this nature. After the stomach has been cleansed by the emetic, &c., as described above, lime-water, or chalk diffused in water, if it can be procured, may be given in large quantities. Hahnemann has recommended soap to be dissolved in water, in the proportion of a pound to four pints, and a tea-cupful to be given every five or six minutes; this undoubtedly is the best treatment if lime-water is not at hand. Powdered charcoal may also be administered with advantage if the other remedies are not immediately attainable. The above remedies may be used with some degree of confidence, although their good effects are not sufficiently certain to establish them as "antidotes."—*Ready Remedies in Cases of Poisoning, &c. By James Johnson, M.R.C.S.*

CHAPTER VIII.
SEVEN DIALS.

There is not in all London a more extraordinary locality than that which bears the denomination of Seven Dials.

Situate in the midst of one of the lowest and worst neighbourhoods throughout the metropolis, and forming a focus where seven streets, converging towards that point, meet like as many streams flowing into a common reservoir, the open spot of ground called Seven Dials is a lounge for all the idle vagabonds and ill-looking persons, men and women, who occupy the cellars and garrets in the vicinity.

From the centre of the open space alluded to, the eyes may plunge their glances down into the circumjacent thoroughfares—narrow, dark, filthy, and formed by dwellings of an appearance so miserable or so repulsive that they equally pain the heart and shock the sight.

If the wanderer amidst the mazes of this vast city were desired to point out the chosen abode of poverty and crime, taking as his guide the physical aspect of all the worst neighbourhoods, he would probably indicate Seven Dials and its branching streets.

The shops are all of the lowest and dirtiest description; nauseous odours impregnate the atmosphere. In winter the streets are knee-deep in mud, save when hardened by the frost; and in summer they are strewed with the putrefying remnants of vegetables, offal, and filth of every description.

Half-naked children paddle about in the mire or wallow on the heaps of decomposing substances just alluded to,—greedily devouring the parings of turnips and carrots, sucking the marrow out of the rotting bones, and rejoicing when they happen to find a mouldy crust, a morsel of putrid meat, or the maggot-eaten head of a fish. Neglected beings, too, are they—knowing nothing save blows, curses, and hunger at home, and learning naught save every corrupt habit and ruinous vice abroad.

How can we be surprised if such an infancy becomes imbued with those evil principles which gaols and treadmills only tend afterwards to confirm, and which give ample promise of occupation for turnkeys, penal-settlements, and the hangman?

The Established Church is maintained at an annual expense of several millions sterling; the clergy belonging to that Church claim the right of educating and instructing the people;—and yet in no country in the civilised world is there such an appalling amount of juvenile depravity as in England!

For ourselves, we declare—we repeat that our Government, our Legislature, our Clergy, and our Great Landowners are all guilty of the blackest turpitude in permitting hundreds of thousands—aye, millions of children to be neglected in so horrible a manner. If a child be seized with a malignant, infectious, and dangerous disease, what would be said of the father who looked on indifferently—who omitted to call in medical advice—and who beheld, with equal calmness, the furious malady spreading amongst the rest of his offspring! Should we not denounce—should we not execrate such a man as a monster deserving of any penalty which our statutes could inflict?

Yes—a thousand times *yes*!

By a parity of reasoning, then, do we hold up to abhorrence those men who seize upon the reins of power merely to gratify their own selfish ambition; also those men who accept seats in the legislative assemblies, and fritter away the time of a great nation in their own party-squabbles,—those men, too, who put on black gowns, preach sermons as a duty rendered in return for the enjoyment of enormous revenues, and then declaim against the wickedness of those millions whom they do not attempt to reform,—and, lastly, those men who wring the sweat from the poor man's brow to distil pearls for themselves, but who care not for the welfare of that poor man's offspring!

Hundreds of thousands of pounds are annually subscribed to further the objects of foreign missions, the scene of whose labours is in far-off lands scarcely known to us by name, and amongst a race with whom our sympathies cannot exist;—but beneath our very eyes—crossing our paths—constantly displaying their loathsome rags to our view, are small children innumerable, whose only training is for the prison, the hulks, and the gallows!

Talk not to us of christianizing Barbarians in the remote islands of the South Seas, when the children of so many of our own fellow-countrymen and country-women are but barbarous Christians at home!

Let the reader who imagines that we exaggerate the amount of the evil we denounce,—let him take his stand, any evening, in the midst of Seven Dials, and well consider the scenes around him.

It is said that there are Seven Cardinal Sins: at the point where we would wish our sceptical reader to post himself, he may command a view of seven streets, each one presenting to his contemplation some new phase in the common sphere of hideous poverty and terrible demoralisation.

Mark the population of that neighbourhood, consisting of seven principal streets, with all their connecting lanes and alleys—with their dark, filthy courts, and their murderous-looking nooks and passages!

Of what does this population consist?

Men brutalised by drink, or rendered desperate by poverty, and in either state ready to commit a crime,—women of squalid, wasted, and miserable appearance, who, being beaten by their husbands and fathers, revenge themselves upon their children or their little brothers and sisters,—poor shopkeepers who endeavour to make up for the penury of their petty dealings by cheating their famished customers,—wretched boys and girls whose growth is stunted by suffering, whose forms are attenuated through want, and whose minds are poisoned by the scenes of vice, dissipation, and immorality which open upon them at their very birth!

What hope—what promise for the future do such beings as these hold out?

In consternation and sorrow, mingled with the most awful misgivings, do we survey the picture which we are now compelled to draw;—and our feelings are thus painful because we know this picture to be correct!

And yet we call our country "MERRY ENGLAND!"

Merciful Heavens! what a mockery is this name! Can England be merry while the most hideous poverty is the lot of half her population; while her workhouses are crowded with miserable beings who must for ever resign all hope or idea of again enjoying the comforts of "home;" while the streets are filled with loathsome wretches, clad in filthy rags, which barely cover them,—shivering with the cold, or fainting beneath the intolerable heat—and spurned from the doors not only of the rich, but also of the very officers appointed to relieve distress; while the poor mother, maddened with the idea of her own destitution and houseless condition, presses her famishing child to her breast which yields no milk, and then rushes in desperation to consign the innocent being to the waters of the nearest stream; while the wretched father stifles his children that he may hush for ever in their throats the cry of "Bread! bread!"—that vain and useless cry to which he cannot respond; while innocent babes and prattling infants bear upon their countenances and exhibit in their attenuated frames all the traces of the dread and agonising pangs of a constant gnawing—craving—never satisfied hunger; and while hundreds annually *die* around us of starvation and absolute want?

Merry England, indeed! What? is England joyous when the shop of the pawnbroker thrives royally upon the immense interest wrung from the very vitals of the poor; when the gaols, the hospitals, and the workhouses are more numerous than the churches; when the hulks are swarming with convicts pent up in frightful floating dungeons, amidst a fœtid atmosphere; when the streets throng with unfortunate girls who ask to be redeemed from an appalling traffic, but who see no avenue of escape from their loathsome calling; when the voice of starvation, the voice of crime, the voice of discontent, and the voice of barbarian ignorance echo up to Heaven, and form such a chorus as could scarcely be expected to meet the ears beyond the precincts of hell; and when seven-tenths of the entire population are wretched—oppressed—enslaved—trampled on—miserable—degraded—demoralised!

Merry England!!!

But let us continue the thread of our narrative.

Two of the thoroughfares which converge to Seven Dials, bear each the name of Earl Street.

Passing from High Street, St. Giles's, towards St. Martin's Lane, we must request the reader to turn with us to the right into that Earl Street which lies between the Dials and one extremity of Monmouth Street.

Half way up Earl Street stood a house of even a darker and more gloomy appearance than its companions. Its door-way was lower than the level of the street, and was reached by descending three steps. The windows were small; and, as many of the panes were broken, the holes were mended with pieces of dirty paper, or stopped up with old rags. Altogether, there was something so poverty-stricken, and yet so sinister, about the appearance of that tottering, dingy, repulsive-looking dwelling, that no one possessing an article of jewellery about his person, or having gold in his pocket, would have chosen to venture amongst its inmates.

And who were those inmates? The neighbours scarcely knew. Certain it was, however, that over the rickety door of the house were painted the words—TOBIAS BUNCE, TAILOR; but few were the jobs which Mr. Bunce ever obtained from the inhabitants in the vicinity; for his manners were too reserved—too repulsive to gain favour with the class of persons who might have patronised him. And yet there appeared to be no signs of absolute poverty in that dwelling. Mrs. Bunce was one of the adjacent butcher's best customers: a public-house in the Dials was known to be regularly visited by her for the beer at dinner and supper times; and pints of gin were occasionally purchased by the same mysterious customer at the same establishment. She was as averse to gossiping as her husband; and her neighbours declared that they could not make her out at all. She always paid ready money for every thing she had; and therefore the tradespeople were the stanch defenders of the Bunces whenever a word of suspicion was uttered against them.

Who, then, were these Bunces?

Let us step inside their dwelling, and see if we can ascertain.

It was about eight o'clock in the evening, a few days after the incidents related in the preceding chapters, that Toby Bunce, his wife, Old Death, and the lad

Jacob sate down to tea in the ground-floor back room of the house which we have been describing.

Toby Bunce was a short, thin, pale-faced, sneaking-looking man of about forty. He was dressed in a suit of very shabby black; and his linen was not remarkable for cleanliness. His coarse brown hair was suffered to grow to a considerable length; and, as he seldom treated it to an acquaintance with the comb, it hung in matted curls over his shoulders. His nails were equally neglected, and resembled claws terminating with blackened points.

His better-half—as Mrs. Bunce indeed was, not only figuratively, but also literally—was a tall, thin, scraggy, lantern-faced woman, with a sharp green eye, a vixenish pug-nose, and a querulous voice; for although she was excessively reserved when she went out "to do her marketing," she made up for that silence abroad by an extra amount of garrulity at home. Her age exceeded by a year or two that of her husband, and, as she was totally devoid of that sentiment which is so generally ascribed to the sex—we mean vanity—she did not scruple to acknowledge the above fact. Indeed, she often advanced it as an argument to prove that she must know better than he, and as a reason for her assertion and maintenance of petticoat government. But if vanity were not her failing, avarice was her ruling vice; and to gratify her love for gold she never hesitated at a crime.

In this latter respect Mr. Bunce was no better than his spouse—save that his anxiety to obtain money was not always equalled by his readiness to face the danger occasionally involved in procuring it. Any act of turpitude that might be accomplished safely and quietly would find no moral opponent in the person of Toby Bunce; but when some little daring or display of firmness was required, he was forced to supply himself with an artificial energy through the medium of the gin-bottle.

The room to which we have introduced our readers was furnished with bare necessaries, and nothing more. A rickety, greasy deal-table; four or five of the commonest description of rush-bottomed chairs; a long form to accommodate extra company; an old portable cupboard, fitting into one of the angles of the apartment; and a shelf to serve as a larder,—these were the principal articles of the domestic economy. The table was spread with a varied assortment of crockery, none of the cups matching with the saucers, and no two cups or no two saucers alike.

Toby Bunce, having succeeded in inducing the kettle to boil by means of sundry bits of wood sparingly applied, his wife Betsy made the tea, while Jacob cut the bread-and-butter.

"I wonder whether Tom will keep his appointment?" said Old Death, as he sipped his tea. "It's a full hour past the time that I told him to be here."

"And we've been a waiting for him till the fire got so low that it took a power of wood to make it burn up again," observed Toby Bunce.

"S'pose it did?" cried his wife. "You know very well that we don't care about any expense when our best friend Mr. Bones is with us," she added, glancing towards Old Death; for the Bunces were amongst the very few of that individual's acquaintances who knew his real name.

"And yet I should think he would not fail," continued Old Death in a musing strain. "His conduct seemed straight-forward and right enough the very first day we agreed to terms; and he even gave me my regulars in a matter that I'd nothing to do with. But it was well for him that he did so; or else he'd have been laid up in lavender for want of bail."

"Bertinshaw and Watkins did it pretty tidy," said Jacob, who was making prodigious inroads upon the bread-and-butter.

"Keep your observations to yourself," growled Old Death in a surly tone. "Remember, I haven't forgot your negligence in losing sight of Tom Rain the other day, when he left the police-office."

"It wasn't my fault," returned the lad, his dark eyes flashing angrily. "I kept lurking about the court after I had been up here to tell you that Dykes had nabbed Mr. Rainford: I saw him go over to the coffee-house soon after he was discharged—I followed him when he went in a coach to Pall Mall—I dogged him back again to Bow Street—and then——"

"And then when the Jewess's case was over, you saw him come out, and you lost sight of him," interrupted Old Death angrily. "But never mind," he added, softening a little: "I will set you to watch him another day when you've nothing better to do, and we will find out all *I* want to know about him."

"When did you see him last?" inquired Toby Bunce.

"This morning, at Tullock's; and——"

Old Death was interrupted by a knock at the street door, to which summons Jacob hastened to respond.

In a few moments he returned, accompanied by Tom Rain, who sauntered into the room, with a complaisant air and the chimney-pot hat stuck on the right side of his head.

"So you are come at last, Tom," said Bones, *alias* Old Death, his toothless jaws grinning a ghastly satisfaction. "Well, better late than never. But let me introduce you to my very particular friends Mr. and Mrs. Bunce; and as they are good friends of mine, they will be good friends to you. This crib of theirs is convenient in more ways than one," added the old man significantly; "and you will find it so if you ever want to lay up for a time until the storm which must menace one sometimes, blows over."

"The hint may not prove useless at a pinch," said Tom carelessly, as he seated himself on the form. "But there's some one present whose name you've not yet mentioned, old chap?"

And he glanced towards the sickly lad, who was still occupied with the edible portion of the repast.

"Oh! that's my Mercury—my messenger—my confidant—or any thing else you like to call him," said Bones. "His name Is Jacob Smith, for want of a better—and he's a perfect treasure in his way. He can scent an officer two streets off, and would prove the best scout that ever a general commanding an army could possibly employ. Now you know his qualifications; and if you ever want to make use of them, he is at your service."

"Well, my lad," exclaimed Tom Rain, "your master gives a good character of you; and mind you continue to deserve it," he added with an ironical smile. "But what is to be done now, old fellow?"

This question was addressed to Bones, who accordingly prepared himself to answer it.

"There's something to be done to-morrow night, my dear boy," began the old villain, his dark eyes gleaming from beneath their shaggy, overhanging brows; "and there's money—much money—to be got. But the thing is a difficult one, and requires great tact as well as courage."

"You must suppose beforehand that I am the person to manage it properly," said Rain; "or I should think you would not have applied to me."

"Very true, Tom," returned Old Death, with a sepulchral chuckle: "very true! The fact is, you're a dashing, genteel-looking, and well-spoken fellow when you choose; and you can insinuate yourself into the good graces of the best-born gentlemen in the land. I am sure you can do this—don't you think you can, Tom?"

"I should rather fancy I can," replied Rainford, by no means displeased with the compliment just paid him. "But go on—explain yourself—and we shall then see what can be done."

"Listen attentively," said Old Death. "Between Streatham and Norwood there stands a pretty but lonely house, occupied by a gentleman named Torrens. He is a widower, and has two daughters. The eldest of these girls is to be married the day after to-morrow to a certain Mr. Frank Curtis, the nephew of the wealthy Sir Christopher Blunt. It appears that Mr. Torrens has fallen into some difficulty through over-speculation in building houses at

Norwood; and Sir Christopher has consented to advance him five thousand pounds, on condition that this match takes place. For the girl, it seems, is totally opposed to it: she has another lover whom *she* loves—and she hates Mr. Frank Curtis. But the father insists on sacrificing his daughter, to whom Curtis is greatly attached; and Curtis possesses influence enough over his uncle Sir Christopher to persuade him to advance the money."

"All this is clear enough," said Rain; "and nothing would give me greater pleasure than to baulk Sir Christopher, Frank Curtis, and the selfish old father. But I do not see how the business can in any way benefit us."

"I will tell you, my dear boy," replied Old Death, with another chuckle expressive of deep satisfaction. "To-morrow evening Sir Christopher, the nephew, and Sir Christopher's lawyer will set out for Torrens Cottage, as the place is called. They will settle all the preliminary business with the father to-morrow night, so that the marriage may take place the first thing on the ensuing morning."

"Well?" said Tom inquiringly, seeing that Old Death paused.

"And two thousand pounds out of the five will be conveyed from London to Torrens Cottage to-morrow night," continued Bones: "*unless*," he added significantly, "something happens to stop the money on its way."

"But who will have the money about him—Sir Christopher, the nephew, or the lawyer?" demanded Tom.

"Ah! that's the point to ascertain," cried Old Death. "You must exercise your tact in solving this doubt; and your courage will afterwards effect the rest. Did I not say that the business required alike tact and courage?"

"You did indeed," answered Rain; "and I can scarcely see how the deuce the thing is to be managed. Still two thousand pounds would prove very welcome. But how came you to learn all this?"

"The knight's servant, my dear boy, is in my pay," returned Old Death, with a triumphant grin. "Ah! I have many gentlemen's and noblemen's domestics devoted to my interests in the same manner; and by their means I learn a great deal. But to return to our present business. Two thousand pounds are to be paid down as an earnest of the bargain to-morrow night; and those two thousand pounds will be much better appropriated to our uses."

"I perfectly agree with you, old fellow," said Rain. "Could not the knight's servant inform you who is likely to take charge of the money?"

"Impossible!" cried Bones. "He will most probably accompany the party; and——"

"How will they go?" demanded Rain, a thought striking him.

"On horseback," answered Old Death. "Sir Christopher and his nephew have a great opinion of themselves as riders; and the lawyer, Mr. Howard, is a sporting character. It is, therefore, sure that they will all go on horseback."

"Then leave the rest to me," cried Tom Rain, snapping his fingers. "What time do they set out?"

"At six o'clock," was the answer.

"Good again," observed Tom. "It's as dark then as at midnight this time of the year. Say no more upon the subject: the thing is just the same as if it was done—provided your information is correct, and no change takes place in the plan as at present laid down by these gentlemen. One word, however;—describe Sir Christopher's servant to me."

"A short—thin—dapper-made fellow—dark curly hair—face marked with the small-pox," replied Old Death. "Drab livery, turned up with red. His name is John Jeffreys."

"Enough," said Tom. "I shall call at Tullock's to-morrow between two and three in the afternoon; and if you have any thing fresh to communicate, you can either leave a note or meet me there. If I neither see nor hear from you at that time and place, I shall consider that all remains as you have now represented. You have nothing more to say at present?"

"Nothing," returned Bones, after a moment's reflection.

"Won't you take a drop of brandy-and-water, Mr. Rainford—just a *leetle* drop?" inquired Toby Bunce, with a deferential glance towards his better half..

"A leetle drop, stupid!—a good big drop, you mean!" cried the shrew. "Isn't Mr. Rainford a friend of Mr. Bones?—and ain't all Mr. Bones's friends *our* friends? I'm sure if Mr. Rainford would drink a—a quar—a *pint* of brandy," she added, emphatically defining the quantity she felt disposed to place at the service of the new acquaintance, "he is quite welcome."

"No, thank'ee," said Rainford. "I must be off. The business of to-morrow night requires consideration; and——"

He was interrupted by a knock at the street-door; and Toby Bunce hastened to answer the summons.

CHAPTER IX.
A DEATH-SCENE.—LOCK'S FIELDS.

The room-door was left open; and the inmates could therefore hear every thing that took place in the passage.

Toby Bunce opened the street-door cautiously, and said, "Who's there?"

"In the name of heaven, grant me a night's lodging," exclaimed the appealing voice of a female: "if not for myself—at least for this poor dear child!"

"Toby, shut the door!" screamed the querulous tones of Mrs. Bunce from the back-room. "We don't want beggars and poor children here."

"Stay!" cried Tom Rain: "never be hard-hearted!"

And, hastening to the street-door, he saw, by the light of a shop-window opposite, the form of a miserable-looking female crouching upon the steps, and with one arm round the neck of a little boy who was crying bitterly.

"Come in, my good woman," said Rainford. "I will pay any expenses that your presence may entail on the people of the house:—come in, I say."

But the poor creature fell back insensible.

"Toby, take care of the child," cried Tom Rain in an authoritative tone; "while I lift the woman off the steps."

And, suiting the action to the word, he raised the senseless being in his arms, and conveyed her into the passage, Toby following with the little boy, who seemed to be about five or six years old.

"Surely you're mad, Tom," exclaimed Old Death, advancing from the back-room, "to bring strangers into this house."

"I should be a brute to see a dying woman turned away from the door of this or any other house," said Rainford firmly. "Stand back, and let me have my way. My purse shall satisfy the Bunces for any trouble this business may give them."

"Well, well—be it as you will," growled Old Death: then, in a hasty whisper to Betsy Bunce, he added, "You had better let him do as he likes. He is a queer fellow, but very useful—and must not be offended."

Thus advised, and cheered moreover by Rain's liberal promise of payment, Mrs. Bunce suddenly exhibited a vast amount of sympathy on behalf of the poor creature; and, having fetched a candle from the back-room, she lighted Rainford, who carried the still senseless woman in his arms, up stairs to a chamber where there was a sordid kind of bed.

Rainford placed his burden on the miserable pallet, and Betsy Bunce applied such restoratives as the circumscribed economy of her household furnished.

In the meantime Toby had brought the little boy into the chamber; and the child, hastening towards the bed, exclaimed, "Mamma—dear mamma—speak to me—why don't you speak to me?"

The woman opened her eyes languidly; but the moment they encountered the face of the child, they were lighted up with joy; and snatching the boy to her breast, she murmured in a faint tone, "I thought I had lost you, Charles—I dreamt that we were separated! Oh! my head—it seems to split!"

And she pressed her open palm to her forehead with all the appearance of intense suffering.

We must pause a moment to observe that this woman seemed to be about five-and-thirty years of age; that she was dressed in widow's weeds of the coarsest materials; and that her entire aspect denoted dreadful privations and great sufferings, mental as well as physical. The boy was also attired in mourning garments; and though his little cheeks were wan, and his form emaciated, still was he a very interesting child.

"My good woman," said Tom Rain, approaching the bed, "banish all misgivings relative to the present; for you shall be taken care of."

Then, turning towards Mrs. Bunce, he directed her to procure food and to send Jacob for a surgeon.

"No—no, it's useless," cried the poor woman, alluding to the latter order. "I feel that I am dying—my last hour is come!"

The child threw his little arms about her neck, and wept piteously.

"Oh! my God!" cried the wretched stranger, "who will now take care of you, my poor dear—dear little Charles! I who have been to you as a mother——"

"Yes—you are my mamma—my own mamma," exclaimed the child, his heart ready to burst, although he scarcely understood the real nature of the misgivings which oppressed him.

"Sir," said the woman, after a few moments of profound silence, during which the sobbings of the boy and the uneasy palpitations of her own breast were alone heard in the chamber,—"sir," she said, addressing herself abruptly to Rainford, "you spoke to me kindly—you look kindly upon me,—and, if I may judge by your countenance, you possess a kind heart——"

"Speak, poor woman!" cried Rain, softened almost to tears. "If there is any thing I can do for you, confide in me—and I swear——"

"The gratitude of a dying being is all that I can offer you in return for what I am about to ask," interrupted the woman in a faint, yet hurried tone—for she seemed to feel that she had not long to live. "Draw near, sir—there—and now listen attentively. Dreadful privation—exposure to the cold—sleeping in the fields—and painful wanderings have reduced me to this state. But I shall die contented—nay, even happy, if I thought————"

"I understand you," cried Rain. "You are anxious for the welfare of this boy? Compose your mind—banish those painful reflections—I swear to protect him!"

There was something so earnest and sincere in the manner, the voice, and the countenance of Rainford, who was a creature of the most generous impulses, that the dying woman believed him; and her heart bounded with fervent gratitude.

Then, making a sign for Rainford to draw nearer to her still, she collected all her remaining force to utter a few last words; but physical exhaustion almost completely choked her utterance.

"This boy," she murmured in a faint and dying voice, "is not mine. Do not weep, Charles, love—I am not your mamma————although I love you————as if you was my own child. But the moment you were born————in secret————and mystery————the nurse brought you to me————all having been so arranged————and————from that moment I————but, my God! I am dying!————oh! give me strength to declare that————your mother————is————"

"Speak, speak!" cried Tom Rain: "breathe but the name of his mother—I shall catch it—and I declare most solemnly————O God! she is dead!"

And it was so! Vain were her last, last efforts to give utterance to the name which trembled upon her tongue: the death-rattle stifled the words in her throat—her eyes glazed—her countenance settled in inanimation—and she was no more!

The little Charles would not believe that she was really dead; to him she only appeared to sleep;-and this infantine delusion Tom Rain gradually dissipated, making him aware of his sad bereavement in so delicate a manner, that a stranger would have believed him to be a father himself as well as an individual of the most upright and noble principles.

But if Rainford's morality was in some points of the most indifferent nature, he nevertheless possessed kind feelings and a generous heart; and the tears trickled down his cheeks, as he exerted himself to console the little stranger.

Children seem to be endowed with an intuitive power of discrimination between those who would treat them well, and those whose dispositions are severe and harsh; and Charles speedily acquired confidence in the good intentions of Rainford.

At length, when Tom fancied that he had obtained some degree of influence over the boy's mind, he led him away from the chamber where the poor woman had breathed her last.

Old Death had remained in the room below; and Jacob had been sent to fetch a surgeon, who now arrived, but departed again immediately upon learning that his services could no longer be rendered available. Toby and Mrs. Bunce had quitted the chamber of death the moment Rain ejaculated, "O God! she is dead;"—and thus the child had no leisure to take particular notice of any one save the individual who manifested so much kindness towards him.

Fearing that the repulsive appearance of Old Death might alarm the boy, and even fill his mind with misgivings relative to the person who now took charge of him, Rainford stopped in the dark passage down stairs; and calling Mrs. Bunce from the back-room, he placed five guineas in her hand, saying, "The burial of that poor creature who has just breathed her last, must be your care. See that it is performed decently; and if there are any papers about her person—any proofs of who she is—keep them for me. Be faithful in this respect—and what I have now given you may be considered as an earnest of additional recompense."

Rainford then left the house, leading the boy by the hand.

Proceeding to the nearest hackney-coach stand, Tom hired one of the vehicles, and desired to be driven to the Elephant and Castle.

Previously, however, to entering the vehicle, the thoughtful Tom Rain purchased some of the very best cakes which a shop in such a neighbourhood could produce; and, though the little boy kept sobbing as he repeated to himself, "Mamma is dead,"—for he was too young to understand that she had denied this maternity with her dying breath,—yet he ate greedily of the food—for he was famished.

Rainford said but little to him, beyond a few occasional cheering and consolatory words, as they rode along, because the heavy rumbling of the vehicle rendered it difficult to hear what was uttered within.

In about three-quarters of an hour the coach stopped at the Elephant and Castle; and Rainford, conducting the boy tenderly by the hand, plunged into the maze of streets which form a neighbourhood requiring a detailed description.

Any one who is acquainted with that part of London, or who, with the map of the great metropolis before him, takes the trouble to follow us in this portion of our narrative, will understand us when we state that, almost immediately behind the Elephant and Castle tavern, there is a considerable district totally *unexplored* by thousands and thousands of persons dwelling in other parts of the English capital. This district is now bounded on the north by the New Kent Road, on the east by the Kent or Greenwich Road, on the south by Walworth, and on the west by the Walworth Road. Built upon a low, damp, and unhealthy soil, the dwellings of the poor there throng in frightful abundance,—forming narrow streets half choked up with dirt, miserable alleys where the very air is stagnant, and dark courts, to enter which seems like going into the fœtid vault of a church. Many of the streets, that appear to have been huddled together without any architectural plan, but merely upon a studied system of crowding together as many hovels as possible, have their back windows looking upon ditches, the black mire and standing water of which exhale vapours sufficiently noxious to breed a pestilence. When the sun shines upon these noisome ditches, their surface displays a thousand prismatic hues, thrown out by the decomposing offal and putrid vegetables which have been emptied into those open sewers. But sewers they cannot be called—for instead of carrying off the filth of the neighbourhood, those ditches preserve it stagnant.

A considerable portion of the district we are describing is known by the name of Lock's Fields; and the horrible condition of this locality can only be properly understood by a visit. The pen cannot convey an adequate idea of the loathsome squalor of that poverty—the heart-rending proofs of that wretchedness—and the revolting examples of that utter demoralization, which characterise this section of the metropolis. The houses for the most part contain each four rooms; every room serving as the domicile of a separate family. Perhaps one of the members of such a family may be afflicted with some infectious malady: there he must lie upon his flock mattress, or his bundle of rags, or his heap of straw, until he become, through neglect, so offensive as to render one minute with him intolerable; and yet his relatives—four, five, or even six in number—are compelled to sleep in the same apartment with him, inhaling the stench from that mass of putrefaction, hearing his groans, breathing the steam from his corrupted lungs, and swarming with the myriads of loathsome animalcule engendered by the filth of the place. In another room, perhaps, we shall find some old man, living by himself—starving upon the miserable pittance obtained by picking up bones or rags, doing an odd job now and then for a neighbour, and filling up the intervals of such pursuits by begging,—his entire furniture consisting of a cup, a kettle, and a knife—no chair, no table—but with a heap of rubbish in one corner for a bed, on which he sleeps with his clothes on. In a third room there is most likely a family consisting of a man and his wife, who at night occupy one mattress, and their grown-up sons and daughters who all pig together upon another. Shame and decency exist not amongst them—because they could never have known either. They have all been accustomed from their infancy to each other's nakedness; and, as their feelings are brutalised by such a mode of existence, they suffer no scruples to oppose that fearful intercourse which their sensuality suggests. Thus—for we *must* speak plainly, as we speak *the truth*—the very wretchedness of the poor, which compels this family commingling in one room and as it were in one bed, leads to incest—horrible, revolting incest! The fourth room in the house which we take for our example of the dwellings in Lock's Fields, is occupied by the landlord or landlady, or both; and there is perhaps no more morality nor cleanliness in their chamber than in either of the others.

The shops in Lock's Fields are naturally in keeping with the means and habits of their customers. Beer-shops and public-houses abound: the lower and the poorer the locality, the greater the number of such establishments. But who can wonder? Crime requires its stimulants—and poverty its consolation. Men drink to nerve themselves to perpetrate misdeeds which are attended with peril: women drink to supply that artificial flow of spirits necessary to the maintenance of a career of prostitution;—and the honest poor drink to save themselves from the access of maddening despair. Children drink also, because they see their parents drink, and because they have acquired the taste from their earliest infancy;—and thus beer-shops and public-houses thrive most gloriously in the most wretched neighbourhoods.

Lock's Fields abound with small "general shops," where every thing is sold in the minutest detail—a pennyworth of sugar, a penny-farthing-worth of tea, a farthing candle, or a quarter of a pound of bacon for a penny. There are also many eating-houses where leg-of-beef soup can be procured for five farthings the bowl. The knackers do a good business with the owners of those establishments. Tripe-shops are likewise far from rare; and upon their boards in the open windows, may be seen gory slices of black-looking liver, tongues and brains in a dish, sheep's heads, huge cow-heels, chitterlings, piles of horses' flesh and rolls of boiled offal upon sticks—the two last-mentioned species of article being intended for cat's-meat,—but the whole heaped pell-mell together, loathsome to behold, and emitting odours of the most fœtid and nauseating description. Coal-sheds, where potatoes and greens may likewise be purchased, abound in Lock's Fields; as do also pie-shops and that kind of eating-houses where pudding fried in grease, stocking-pudding, and sop-in-the-pan are displayed in the windows, to tempt with their succulent appearance the appetites of hungry men passing to their work, or of half-famished children wearied of playing in the gutter.

It is wretched—heart-rending to linger on a description of this kind: but we must endeavour to make it as complete as possible. The generality of the inhabitants of Lock's Fields are in a state of barbarian ignorance. Nine-tenths of the children, even of ten or twelve years old, are unable to read, and know not who Jesus Christ is, nor that the Saviour of Mankind suffered upon the cross to save *them*, as well as the proudest peers or the most brilliant peeresses that shine in the realms of fashion. Look more closely at the aspect of the population in Lock's Fields. What care is depicted upon the pale cheek of that emaciated woman who is hanging the *one* change of linen upon the elder-bushes skirting the black ditch behind her dwelling! And yet she is better off than many of her neighbours—because her family does possess the *one* change of linen! Behold that man sitting on the threshold of his door, smoking his pipe:—his elbows rest upon his knees—he stares vacantly before him—not even the opiatic influence of tobacco soothes him. He is thinking of what will become of his wife and children when he shall be out of work—because the job on which he has lately been engaged will be finished on the coming Saturday. His wife comes out to speak to him—and he answers her harshly: his children approach him, and endeavour to climb up his knees—but he knocks them away. Yet that man is not brutal by nature: he loves his wife and children—and was even debating within himself whether he should not soon turn thief in order to support them, when they thus accosted him and were repulsed. Let another person insult his wife—let a stranger lay a finger upon that man's children, and the demon will be raised within his breast. But he speaks harshly and treats them all brutally, because he is miserable—because he is dissatisfied with every thing and every body— because he is reduced to despair. The unfeeling aspect of the cold world around him—that world which frowns so sternly upon poverty, and smiles so sweetly upon wealth—has rendered *him* unfeeling. His hard fate drives him to the public-house:—talk of the infamy of which that man is guilty in spending a few pence—the pence which would buy his children more bread—upon beer or gin,—it is ridiculous! That man *must* drink—he *must* drown his care: thought drives him mad—and from thought he must therefore fly. But whither can he fly? The rich and the well-to-do have their theatres and places of amusement: if a penny tea-garden or a penny theatre be opened in Lock's Fields, or in any other poor neighbourhood, the magistrates must put it down;—it is a source of demoralisation—it is a focus of thieves and prostitutes! But the swell-mob and flash women frequent the Haymarket Theatre—and the Lyceum—and the Surrey—and the Victoria— aye, and Covent-Garden and Drury Lane Theatres also. "Oh!" cries the magistrate; "*that* is very different!" Yes—every thing in this country is different when the wealthy or the well-dressed are concerned on one side, and the poor and the ragged on the other. Then, whither can this pauperised despairing man in Lock's Fields go to escape the bitterness of his reflections? To the public-house—or to throw himself into the canal:—those are the only alternatives!

Is it not dreadful to think that we have a sovereign and a royal family on whom the country lavishes money by hundreds of thousands,—whose merest whims cost sums that would feed and clothe from year to year *all* the inhabitants of such a place as Lock's Fields;—that we have also an hereditary aristocracy and innumerable sleek and comfortable dignitaries of the Church, who devour the fruits of the earth and throw the parings and the peelings contemptuously to the poor;—in a word, that we have an oligarchy feasting upon the fatted calf, and flinging the offal to the patient, enduring, toiling, oppressed millions,—is it not dreadful, we ask, to think how much those millions do for Royalty, Aristocracy, Church, and Landed Interest, and how little—how miserably little, Royalty, Aristocracy, Church, and Landed Interest do for *them* in return?

But let us go back to Thomas Rainford and the little boy, whom we left on their way to Lock's Fields—for it was to this district that the excellent-hearted man was leading his young charge.

And, as they went along, many were the kind words that Tom Rain uttered to cheer his artless companion.

"Come, don't cry, my dear little fellow," he would say: "here is another cake—and when we get home you shall have something nice for supper. Are you cold, Charley? Well, you shall soon warm yourself by the side of a good blazing fire. And to-night you shall sleep in a soft bed; and to-morrow morning you shall have some new clothes. I am going to take you where you will find a pretty lady, who will be as kind to you as the mamma you have just lost. Are you tired, Charley? Well, I'll take you up and carry you."

And Tom Rain lifted the poor child in his arms and kissed away the tears which ran down his cheeks. The boy threw his little arms around the neck of his kind protector, and said, "Oh! you are as good to me as my dear papa was."

"And how long has your papa been dead, Charley?" asked Rainford, supposing that the child meant by his father the husband of the woman who had died that evening in Toby Bunce's house.

"Not very long—but I don't know how long," was the reply. "Oh! stay—I think I heard mamma say this morning that he died six months ago."

"And where did you live then, Charley?"

"At a cottage near a great town—Oh! I remember—Winchester."

"Winchester!" cried Rainford. "I know all that part of the country well—or at least I ought to do so," he murmured to himself, with a profound sigh. "But what made you leave your cottage?"

"When papa was buried, mamma had no money," replied the child; "and some naughty people came at last and took away all the things in the cottage, and turned mamma and me out of doors. And then mamma cried so much—oh! so much; and we were very often hungry after that—and we sometimes had no bed to sleep in."

"Poor little fellow!" cried Rainford, hugging the child closer still to his breast. "What was your papa's name?"

"Watts—and my name is Charley Watts," said the boy.

At this moment Rainford stopped at one of the few decent-looking houses in Lock's Fields, and knocked at the door, which was immediately opened by a young and beautiful woman, who appeared overjoyed at his return.

"I have brought you a present in the shape of this poor little boy," said Rainford as he entered the house. "If you wish to please me, you will behave to him as kindly as I shall."

The young woman took Charley in her arms, and kissed him as a proof that Tom's request should be attended to; and Rainford, well pleased at that demonstration, closed the street-door behind him.

CHAPTER X.
A SCENE AT THE HOUSE OF SIR CHRISTOPHER BLUNT.

On the following afternoon, shortly after four o'clock, three gentlemen sate, sipping their wine after an early dinner, in a magnificently furnished room in Jermyn Street.

The one who occupied the head of the table was a red-faced, stout, elderly gentleman, with hair of that blueish-black which denotes the use of an artificial dye, and with large bushy whiskers of a similar tint. He was dressed in a blue coat with brass buttons, white waistcoat, and black kerseymere trousers fitting very tight. A massive gold chain depended from his neck; and on his fingers he wore several rings of great value. In manner he was authoritative, even to rudeness: for, being immensely rich, he firmly believed that money constituted an aristocracy which had a perfect right to command. His pride was the more excessive too, as he had risen from nothing: that is, he had begun life as an errand boy in a linen-draper's shop, and had finished his mercantile career as a warehouseman in Wood Street, where he amassed a considerable fortune. He had filled the office of Sheriff, but had vainly endeavoured to procure an aldermanic gown; and, having failed to persuade the livery-men of Portsoken Ward that he was the very best person they could possibly choose to represent them in the superior City Court, he had ever since affected to rejoice at his rejection, and to look upon all City men and City matters with contempt. In reality, too, he was dreadfully mortified at the fact of his low origin; but, with that clumsy duplicity which vulgar minds often employ in such cases, he pretended to make a boast of his humble beginning, and used the subject as a means of constantly reminding his friends and acquaintances of what he had done for himself. While he held the Shrievalty, it fell to his lot to present an address to the Prince Regent; and on that occasion he received the honour of knighthood. Such was Sir Christopher Blunt.

The gentleman who sate at the bottom of the table was Mr. Frank Curtis, Sir Christopher's nephew. He was a tall, spare, thin, sickly-looking young man, of three-and-twenty; with long, straight, black hair, large staring dark eyes, very bad teeth, and a disagreeable, impudent, pert expression of countenance. He was an orphan, and totally dependent upon his uncle, who had brought him up to no business, inasmuch as he had looked upon the young man as his heir. Sir Christopher, however, having reached his fiftieth year without ever thinking of matrimony, was suddenly smitten with Miss Julia Mordaunt, Lady Hatfield's friend; and as Miss Mordaunt belonged to a very ancient though a greatly impoverished family, Sir Christopher thought that he should gain his darling wish—namely, obtain standing and consideration in the fashionable world—by conducting that lady to the hymeneal altar. This ardent desire he nevertheless kept to himself as much as possible; his first object being to get rid of his nephew in some way or another. For Mr. Frank Curtis had acquired considerable influence over his uncle; and the latter was too much of a moral coward to be able to tell his nephew boldly and frankly that he proposed "to change his condition." The passion which Frank had conceived for Miss Adelais Torrens seemed to furnish the knight with an opportunity to settle the young man, and thus throw off an influence which impeded his own matrimonial designs: hence the readiness of Sir Christopher to lend Mr. Torrens five thousand pounds as an inducement for that gentleman to compel his portionless daughter to accept Mr. Frank Curtis for a husband. We must add, that Frank had passed six months on the continent; and this brief sojourn in France had supplied the staple commodity of his entire conversational powers. Nor must we forget to observe that he was as arrogant a boaster as he was in reality a coward; and that he was so afflicted with the vice of mendaciousness, he could scarcely speak the truth by accident.

The third gentleman present in Sir Christopher's splendid dining-room, was Mr. Howard, the knight's solicitor. We need not say more relative to this individual than that he was about five-and-forty years old, enjoyed an excellent practice, was considered a fine-looking man by the ladies, and was noted for his devotion to the Turf.

The table was spread with a choice dessert and an assortment of the most exquisite wines, to which the three gentlemen appeared to be doing ample justice. Sir Christopher drank copiously, because he felt particularly well pleased at the prospect of getting rid of his nephew, for whom and the intended bride he had taken and furnished a beautiful house at Clapham: Frank had frequent recurrence to the bottle, because he felt nervous and anxious;—and the lawyer stuck fast to the Burgundy, because he liked it.

"Take care, Frank, how you fill your glass too often," said Mr. Howard; "or the young ladies will not find you very agreeable presently."

"Don't mind me, old fellow," exclaimed Curtis: "I can drink you under the table any day. Why, when I was in Paris I used to think nothing of a bottle of brandy with my breakfast. I recollect once betting thirty napoleons with an old Major of grenadiers at Boulogne——"

"A drum-major, I suppose, Frank," said the lawyer with a smile.

"Frank could not so far forget himself as to associate with a *drum*-major," observed Sir Christopher, in a voice like that of a man who goes about with a Punch and Judy show. "Thanks to my honest exertions, I have placed myself—and, in placing myself, have placed *him*—in a position which you will permit me to call brilliant. You know I make no secret of what I *was*. I rose from nothing—and I'm proud of it. And if his gracious Majesty, in acknowledgment of my humble merits, condescended to bestow upon me the honour of knighthood——"

"Oh! blow that old story, uncle!" cried the dutiful nephew. "I was telling you how I laid fifty napoleons with a Colonel of French engineers that I would drink two bottles of champagne to every one of his share——"

"What time will the horses be round at the door?" demanded Howard of the knight; for the lawyer was anxious to escape the menaced tale.

"At six o'clock precise," answered Sir Christopher. "I am always punctual. I learnt punctuality when I was a lad; and I firmly believe it helped to make me what I am. When I look around and see how I am now situated, and think of what I was——"

"Do let me tell you this story," interrupted Frank, re-filling his glass: "it is a capital one, I can assure you. Well, so the French Major-General and me, we sate down at table, and spread out the hundred and fifty napoleons that we had bet. Then we rang the bell, and ordered three bottles of Burgundy to begin with—two for me, and one for him."

"Burgundy was it?" said the lawyer, sipping his wine.

"No—claret, and I told you so," exclaimed Curtis. "But how provoking you are! Well, so the Lieutenant-General and me, we began to drink the champagne just as if it was so much water—both of us eyeing the two hundred napoleons——"

"Half-past four," said Mr. Howard, looking at his watch, and with difficulty suppressing a yawn.

"For I felt sure of winning—and so did he," continued Frank Curtis. "Well, I soon disposed of my *two* bottles of Port, and the General drank his *one* like a Trojan. To work we went again—two more for me, and another for him. Then I proposed cigars, because I knew that I could stand smoking better than him. He agreed; and we puffed away like two factory-chimneys. At last he showed signs of distress——"

"Ah! got quite groggy, like a prize-fighter at the fortieth round," observed Mr. Howard.

"Exactly," said Frank: "and so by the time I had finished my sixth bottle of Sherry, and the Field-Marshal had only got half-way through his third, he was completely sewn up. I pocketed the five hundred napoleons, as a matter of course—rang the bell to desire the waiter to take the Admiral off to bed—and then went and did the amiable at an evening party, where no one could tell that I had ever been drinking at all."

"And so you think that a very pleasant adventure, Master Frank?" said Sir Christopher. "Now, for my part, I leave guzzling and hard-drinking to those vulgar citizens the other side of Temple Bar. Do you know, Howard, that I really believe it was the most fortunate day of my life when I lost the election for Portsoken? If I had become an Alderman———"

"You would have *looked* the Alderman to perfection, Sir Christopher," observed the lawyer.

"Well—well—I might have been dignified on the bench—or I might not," said the knight complacently: "that is a mere matter of opinion—although I *have* been told by a friend who is not accustomed to flatter, that I have more sense—sound sense, I mean—in my little finger, than all the Aldermen and Common Councilmen put together. But it was fortunate for me—very fortunate—that I escaped from the vulgar contact of those citizens."

At this moment a servant entered the room, to announce that a gentleman desired to speak to Sir Christopher Blunt.

"Show him up—show him up," cried the knight. "I have no secrets that my nephew and solicitor may not hear."

The domestic retired; and in a few minutes he re-appeared, ushering in Rainford by the name of Captain Sparks.

Tom was dressed in his usual sporting garb, over which he wore a white top-coat—an article of attire much in vogue in those days amongst gentlemen who were accustomed to ride much on horseback. As he walked, his silver spurs clinked on the heels of his well-polished boots; and in his right hand he carried a whip.

"Beg your pardon, gentlemen, for this intrusion," said Tom, as he entered the room; "but having heard from my very particular friend Mr. Torrens of the little affair that is to take place to-morrow morning———"

"Pray sit down, Captain Sparks," interrupted Sir Christopher. "Any friend of Mr. Torrens is welcome in this house. I do not, however, remember that he has mentioned your name in my hearing."

"Very likely not," said Rainford, drawing a chair close to the table. "The fact is I have been travelling in the north, for my amusement, during the last two years; and I only returned to town this morning. The first thing I did was to run down and see my dear friend Torrens: and you may fancy how surprised and pleased I was to learn what an excellent match his eldest daughter was about to make."

"There is the bridegroom, Captain Sparks," said the knight, pompously waving his hand towards his nephew.

"Very happy to form your acquaintance, Mr. Curtis," exclaimed Tom, with a polite bow.

"Equally delighted to know you, Captain," replied the nephew. "Here's a clean glass—and there's the bottle. Help yourself."

"With much pleasure," said Tom, suiting the action to the word. "But I was about to tell you that Mr. Torrens did me the honour to invite me to the wedding; and as I was obliged to come back to town to have my portmanteau sent down to the Cottage, I have made bold to intrude myself upon you, gentlemen, with the view of joining your party—that is, if you will permit me."

"We shall be quite charmed, Captain Sparks," answered Sir Christopher Blunt. "I need not inquire if you proceed to the Cottage on horseback!"

"Oh! yes—none of your coaches or carriages for me," returned Tom. "I have put up my horse at the stables close by in York Street; for my groom was taken ill a couple of hours ago——"

"Our horses are also there," interrupted Sir Christopher; "and one of *my* grooms," he added ostentatiously, "shall bring round yours when he fetches ours. But I beg pardon for my rudeness, Captain Sparks:—this gentleman is Mr. Howard—*my* solicitor."

Rainford and the lawyer bowed to each other; the wine went round; and Tom chuckled inwardly at the success of his stratagem to obtain access to the knight.

"You see, Captain Sparks," said Sir Christopher in a dictatorial tone, "this projected alliance has met with some little opposition on the part of the young lady herself."

"So Torrens told me this afternoon," observed Tom coolly. "But the qualifications of your nephew, Sir Christopher, are doubtless such——"

"I flatter myself," exclaimed Curtis, pleased with this compliment, "that I have the knack of making myself agreeable to the women when I choose. Why, the day that I left Paris, a French Marchioness took poison, and a Countess went melancholy mad—both without any apparent cause: but *I* knew deuced well what was the reason, though."

"You're a sad fellow, Frank," said the lawyer.

"Now why should you assert that?" cried the young man, affecting to be annoyed by the remark. "Did I tell you that any thing particular occurred between me and those ladies? Suppose the Duchess *did* have a little partiality for me—and suppose the Baroness *was* the least thing jealous—eh? What then?"

"Ah! what then, indeed?" said Tom Rain. "Mr. Curtis is too much a man of honour to betray those fair ones who were weak enough to be beguiled by his soft nonsense."

"Egad! you're right," exclaimed Frank, in whose good opinion the self-styled Captain was rapidly rising. "I would not give a fig for a fellow that boasts of his conquests. But if any one *might* boast on that subject, I think it is your humble servant. What do you say, Howard? Haven't I told you some queer tales at times?"

"You have indeed," answered the lawyer drily.

"Talking of boasting, Captain Sparks," said the knight, who now found means to thrust in a word, "it is *my* opinion that the only legitimate boast is that which a man can make of having risen from nothing. Now I never attempt to conceal my origin: on the contrary, I glory in it. Why, sir, I began life without a sixpence, and without a friend: and now look at me!"

Tom Rain did look at Sir Christopher, as he was requested to do; and it struck our friend that there was nothing very particular to admire in the worthy knight after all.

"You see me, Captain Sparks?" continued Sir Christopher, in an authoritative tone. "Well, sir—such as I am now, I made myself."

"And the more to your credit," said Tom, who could not help thinking that if the knight's words were to be taken literally, it was a great pity that he had not made himself a trifle handsomer while he was about it.

"Come, Howard, pass the bottle, old fellow," cried Frank Curtis, who always got disgustingly familiar when he was in his cups—which was so often that he was seldom out of them: and, as is the case with all persons who boast of the quantity they can drink, it did not require much to upset him. "Remember," he added, "we have rather a lonely road to travel part of the way——"

"Why—you surely cannot be afraid of robbers, Mr. Curtis?" exclaimed Tom, bursting out into a merry laugh.

"I afraid!" ejaculated the young man; "not I! I should think not, indeed! Why, when I was travelling from Abbeville to Paris in the mail, we were stopped by three highwaymen in the middle of the night. The government-courier and myself tackled them in a moment: we were the only persons in the mail, and the postboy was so frightened that he got off his seat and hid himself under one of the horses. Well, the poor courier was soon disabled; but I was not easily done up. Egad! in less than three minutes I forced the whole five scoundrels to sheer off."

"Oh! I have no doubt of it," said Tom very quietly. "A powerful and courageous young gentleman like you must be a match for any five highwaymen in the world."

"Come, come now," exclaimed Frank: "I don't say *that* exactly. But I will assert this much—that I have no more fears of a robber than I should have of a child's stopping me on the highway."

"In that case," observed Mr. Howard, throwing a pocket-book across the table towards Curtis, "you had better take charge of the money that's to be paid over to Mr. Torrens presently."

"Oh! as for *that*——But, never mind," cried Frank, not appearing particularly to relish the office of treasurer thus forced upon him, yet unable to decline the trust after his magniloquent vaunting: "I'll keep the two thousand safe enough, depend upon it."

Sir Christopher looked at his watch; and, finding that the hour for departure was approaching, he rang the bell to order the horses.

Precisely as the clock struck six, the party, attended by John Jeffreys, with whom Rain had found an opportunity to exchange a word or two, quitted Jermyn Street, and rode towards Westminster Bridge.

CHAPTER XI.
THE TWO THOUSAND POUNDS.—TORRENS COTTAGE.

The evening was bright, clear, and frosty; and the stars shone resplendently on the wide arch of heaven.

Well wrapped up in their great coats, the party of horsemen pursued their way; and at about seven o'clock they turned from the main-road near Streatham Common, into a bye-lane leading towards Torrens Cottage, thus leaving Streatham itself on their right hand.

Sir Christopher and the lawyer rode about a hundred yards in advance, Tom Rain and Frank Curtis having stopped at a public-house to procure cigars. Jeffreys, the groom, was about fifty yards in the rear.

"You must come and see us, Captain Sparks, after the honeymoon," said Curtis. "We shall be delighted to make you welcome."

"I shall avail myself of your kind offer," returned Tom.

"And you and me will try who can stand his bottle best," continued the young man. "But what atrocious cigars these are! I remember when I was in Paris, I was very intimate with a certain foreign Prince who was staying there—and I don't mind hinting to you that I was a great favourite with the Princess too. She was a charming woman—a very charming woman. I never saw such eyes in my life! Well, the Prince was a great smoker; and he one day gave me a box of his prime cigars—such cigars! I never smoked such beauties before or since. Poor fellow! he was killed in a duel shortly afterwards."

"Killed in a duel!" exclaimed Tom: "what—by you?"

"Oh! no—I was his second," replied Curtis, who, as usual, invented the story as he went on. "It seems that an officer of French horse-guards had been boasting of the favours which he pretended to have received from the Marchioness; and the Marquis heard of it. He instantly sent for me, and desired me to carry the grenadier-officer a message. I did so; and the hostile encounter took place in Boulogne-wood. The hussar-officer pinked the Count slap through in no time; for it appeared that he was the best swordsman in all France. Well, of course I was desperately savage to see my poor friend the Duke knocked off the hooks in that unceremonious way; and I determined to avenge him. So I challenged the light-infantry officer on the spot; and we fought for six hours without either of us getting a scratch or yielding a foot of ground. Our swords were worn as thin as skewers——"

"I have no doubt of it," said Tom coolly. "It must have been a splendid sight."

"It was indeed," returned Frank. "But at last I obtained a trifling advantage. The artillery-officer had a cold; and I watched him anxiously to catch him off his guard when he sneezed. Egad! that was a glorious idea of mine; and it succeeded too;—for after nine hours' hard fighting, I ran him through just as a cook spits a joint. You cannot imagine what a reputation that affair gave me in Paris. Every one was desirous to see the young Englishman who had killed the best swordsman in France. And, after all, without boasting, it was a feat to be proud of."

"Decidedly so," observed Tom. "But you are too brave a man, Mr. Curtis, to indulge in idle boasts."

"Of course," cried Frank. "Fellows like you and me, Captain, who know what swords and pistols mean, are the last to brag of their exploits."

"Do you carry pistols with you, Mr. Curtis?" asked Tom.

"Generally—generally," was the reply. "But I did not think it necessary to take them with me this evening."

"Well, I did," said Rainford. "And here is one," he added, producing the weapon from the pocket of his white great-coat.

"Pray don't hold it near me, Captain!" cried Frank, reining in his horse with a trepidation most remarkable on the part of a gentleman who had performed such gallant deeds in resisting highwaymen and as a duellist.

"Yes—but I shall not only hold it near you," said Tom: "I shall also fire it—unless you instantly, and without noise, hand me over that pocket-book which you have about you."

"Captain Sparks!" ejaculated the trembling young man: "this passes a joke. Come, now——"

"I never was more serious in my life," interrupted Rainford sharply. "Give me the pocket-book; or——"

And the sharp click of the pistol, as Tom cocked it, sounded like a death-warrant upon the cowardly boaster's ears. In fact, he sate paralysed—motionless—speechless upon his horse, at a loss how to act.

"Come, be quick!" cried Rain, seizing him by the collar of his coat: "I have no time for any of your nonsense."

"You—you—can't—mean——" stammered the young man, "that—you———"

"Yes—I mean that I am a highwayman, if you like to call me so," interrupted Tom impatiently: "and so give me the pocket-book."

Curtis obeyed with trembling hand and sinking heart.

"And now," said Tom, as the sounds of the trampling of a horse announced that the groom was approaching, "one word of caution! You are going to drag a young lady into a match most unwelcome to her. Beware how you accomplish her unhappiness by forcing her to accept as a husband such a contemptible boaster and arrant liar as you are: beware, I say—or you will see more than you like of Captain Sparks."

Having thus spoken, Rainford turned his horse round, and galloped away with lightning-speed.

John Jeffreys, whom he passed in the lane, did not of course attempt to molest him.

But when the groom overtook Frank Curtis, he said, "Any thing the matter, sir? I saw the Captain gallop back again like an arrow."

"Captain!" ejaculated the young man: "he is a robber—a thief—a gallows-bird!"

"What do you mean, sir?" asked Jeffreys, affecting profound astonishment.

"He has plundered me of two thousand pounds, John," cried Frank, in so lamentable a tone that the groom could hardly suppress a violent indication to laugh.

"Robbed you, sir!" exclaimed Jeffreys. "You're joking, sir: no two men in England could rob you."

"We had a desperate tussle for it, John," replied Curtis; "but the villain knocked me off my horse with the butt-end of his pistol. It was a cowardly blow—and I was not prepared for it."

"Most likely not, sir," said the groom drily. "But I thought he must have used some underhand means, because I know what sort of a customer you must be."

"You're right enough there, my man," returned Curtis. "I had got the better of him at one time; and although he has gone off with the two thousand pounds, he has carried away with him such a drubbing that he won't forget in a hurry. But let us ride after my uncle and Mr. Howard—because he might come back," added Frank, casting a terrified glance behind him.

The young gentleman and the servant put spurs to their horses, and in a quarter of an hour overtook the knight and the lawyer, to whom Frank related in his own style the adventure which had just occurred.

"And you mean to say that you surrendered the pocket-book—that you gave up two thousand pounds?" exclaimed Sir Christopher, in a passion.

"What could I do?" said Frank. "The scoundrel took the money from me by main force."

"He was stronger than the five highwaymen in France," observed the lawyer quietly.

"Stronger! I believe you," cried Curtis. "And then he was armed to the very teeth. Why, when he threw open his green cut-away coat, I could see by the starlight a belt stuck round with pistols, daggers, and sharp knives. Or else do you think for a moment that he could have mastered *me*?"

"Well, the mischief is done," said the knight in a doleful tone; "and a pretty figure we shall cut at the Torrens's. I dare swear that the rascal is no more an acquaintance of the family than he is of the King of England."

"It is to be hoped he is not," observed Mr. Howard, who was mightily pleased to think that he had handed over the money into Frank's keeping previously to setting out:—"it is to be hoped not—otherwise your nephew, Sir Christopher, would be marrying into a nice family."

"Really, Mr. Howard, this is no time for jesting," exclaimed the knight. "But why didn't you try and stop the Villain, John?"

"I, sir!" said the groom. "How should I know that he had committed a robbery when he galloped past me? Besides, if he is such a terrible chap as Mr. Frank represents him, it would have been useless for me to try my hand with him."

"Certainly! John is quite right," observed Mr. Curtis. "If I could do nothing with him, I'm sure no one else could. He is as strong as a lion; and, egad! how he did swear! It was quite horrible to hear him. But what shall we do?"

"Do, indeed!" ejaculated Sir Christopher. "We shall look like so many fools when we arrive at the Cottage."

"But Mr. Torrens will take your cheque, Sir Christopher," remarked the lawyer.

"True. We can manage it in that way," said the knight. "Still the cash would have appeared more business-like on such an occasion. But it is growing late: let us push on."

"Yes—let us push on," echoed Frank, casting troubled glances around, and trembling lest the highwayman should take it into his head to return and rob the remainder of the party.

In twenty minutes they reached Torrens Cottage, the inmates of which we must pause to describe.

Mr. Torrens was a widower, and had numbered about five-and-fifty years. He was a tall, thin, dry-looking man, with a very sallow complexion, a cold grey eye, and a stern expression of countenance. After having long held a situation in a Government office, he retired with a pension; and just at the same period a relation died, leaving him a few thousand pounds. With this sum he bought a beautiful little villa, which he denominated Torrens Cottage, and the leasehold of some land at Norwood, where he set busily to work to build a row of houses to be called Torrens Terrace. He had long made architecture an amateur-study during his leisure hours; and the moment he was enabled to retire from his situation in the Ordnance Office, and became possessed of capital, he resolved to put his numerous architectural theories into practice. But, as it frequently happens in such matters, he grew embarrassed; and the works were menaced with stoppage for want of funds, when Mr. Curtis became enamoured of his eldest daughter, whom he met at the house of some of Mr. Torrens's relations in London. The bargain, already described, was soon after struck between Sir Christopher Blunt and Mr. Torrens, who did not hesitate to sacrifice his daughter's happiness to his own pecuniary interests. Unfortunately, too, for the young lady, he did not regard the contemplated union in the light of a sacrifice at all; inasmuch as he naturally looked upon Frank Curtis as Sir Christopher's heir, not dreaming that the worthy knight entertained the remotest idea of perpetrating matrimony. Mr. Torrens therefore considered that his daughter Adelais was about to form a most eligible connexion; and, although he was aware that her affections were engaged in another quarter, he acted upon the belief that parents must know best how to ensure their children's happiness.

His two daughters, Adelais and Rosamond, were both charming girls, of the respective ages of eighteen and sixteen. Their dark clustering locks, their deep hazel eyes lustrous with liquid light, and their symmetrical figures filled all beholders with admiration. Adelais was now pale, melancholy, and drooping; for she loathed the alliance that was in contemplation for her—loathed it, not only because her heart was another's, but also because the manners, conversation, and personal appearance of Frank Curtis were revolting in her estimation. Rosamond possessed a rich complexion, in which glowed all the innate feelings of her soul, animating and imparting to every feature of her beautiful face an additional charm. She was naturally the confidant of her sister, whose hard fate she deeply deplored; and many were the plans which the amiable girls had devised and discussed, with a view to overcome their father's cruel pertinacity in insisting on the sacrifice of Adelais to Frank Curtis. But each and all of those projects had either failed, or involved proceedings repugnant to their pure and artless minds. For instance, they had thought of abandoning the paternal roof, and endeavouring to seek their livelihood by needlework in some safe retirement: then Adelais would not permit Rosamond to dare the misfortunes of the world by flying from a home which she—the younger sister—had at least no personal motive to desert; and Rosamond on her side would not allow Adelais to set out alone. Again, a clandestine marriage between Adelais and her lover was often debated: the young man urged it himself;—but the daughters dreaded the father's eternal anger; and thus this project had been abandoned also. To be brief, the dreaded moment was now at hand; and the seal of misery was about to be set on the roll of the elder maiden's destinies.

And who was the lover of Adelais? A handsome, generous-hearted, honourable young man, occupying a situation in the very Government office where Mr. Torrens had himself served for many years. But, although Clarence Villiers was so far provided for, and had every prospect of rising rapidly on account of his steady habits and assiduous attention to his employment, yet he was at present only a poor clerk with ninety pounds a-year; and he had no capital. Mr. Torrens, as we have seen, required capital; and thus Frank Curtis was preferred to Clarence Villiers.

We cannot quit this description without alluding to the ardent affection which existed between the sisters. Having lost their mother in their childhood, and their father being almost constantly from home throughout the day, they were naturally thrown entirely upon each other for companionship. An illimitable confidence sprang up between them—a confidence more intimate far than even that which usually subsists between sisters; because this confidence on the part of Adelais and Rosamond extended to a mutual outpouring of their most trivial as well as of their most important thoughts, hopes, or aspirations. Thus, the reader will cease to be astonished that, when Adelais, in the anguish of her heart, had contemplated flight from the paternal roof as the only alternative save a hateful marriage, Rosamond insisted upon accompanying her. Much as they loved and revered their father, they were both prepared to sacrifice even filial affection and filial duty for each other's sake. This feeling may be looked upon as one involving a grievous fault on their side: it was not, however, the less firmly rooted in their minds,—for they were all and all to each other!

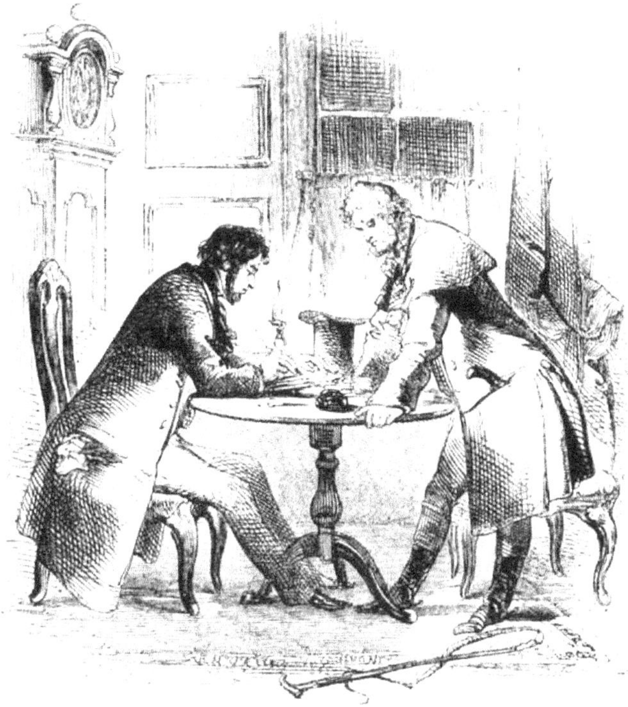

CHAPTER XII.
ADELAIS AND ROSAMOND.

Sir Christopher Blunt, Mr. Howard, and Frank Curtis were soon seated in Mr. Torrens' comfortable parlour, the walls of which were adorned with an infinite variety of architectural plans set in carved oaken frames.

A cheerful fire blazed in the grate; wine was placed upon the table; and the travellers were speedily as much at their ease as they could wish, or as their host could render them.

The young ladies were in another apartment, Mr. Torrens having desired them to remain in the drawing-room while the commercial part of the projected matrimonial arrangement was being settled in the parlour.

When the usual complimentary phrases had been exchanged, and Sir Christopher had observed that the weather was remarkably fine but very cold—a proposition to which Mr. Torrens entirely assented—for somehow or another people never *do* contradict each other when commenting on that subject;—when, also, a glass or two of wine had been imbibed by each, the knight inquired whether Mr. Torrens happened to be acquainted with a Captain Sparks?

The answer was a negative.

Sir Christopher then began to relate the adventure of the evening; and, although he was constantly interrupted by his nephew, who was anxious to interpolate in the narrative certain saving clauses respecting his own valour towards the highwayman, the worthy knight nevertheless succeeded at length in bringing the tale to an end.

"It is clear," said Mr. Torrens, "that you were first duped and then robbed by an infamous scoundrel. But have you any notion how he could have learnt enough of the pending arrangements to be enabled to talk so familiarly with regard to them, when he first introduced himself to you?"

"That puzzles me, my dear sir," returned Sir Christopher.

"And it is likely to continue to puzzle you, uncle," observed Frank; "for the whole business defies conjecture. I remember, when I was in France———"

"The villain evidently knew that you would leave town with a considerable sum of money in your possession," said Torrens; "and his aim was to get it. He did get it too."

"But not without a deuced good thrashing into the bargain," cried Frank; "and that's some consolation."

"I dare say Captain Sparks, as he calls himself, would gladly be thrashed every hour in the day on the same terms," observed the lawyer. "But I think that when our little business is concluded, I should do well to return to London and give information at Bow Street as speedily as possible."

"By no means," exclaimed Sir Christopher. "We must keep the tale to ourselves. If it got into the newspapers, with all the particulars, it would only make us look ridiculous. We might punish the man; but we should never get back the money. No—no: let the matter drop—for all our sakes. Thank heaven," continued the knight, assuming a slower and more pompous tone, "the loss is paltry—very paltry in my estimation. I shall not miss the amount, I can assure you."

"But you have no objection to my giving the scoundrel another good drubbing, uncle, the first time I meet him again?" inquired Frank Curtis, with great apparent earnestness.

"Oh! there can be no objection to that—if the Captain will allow you so to operate on him," said the lawyer drily.

"Allow me, indeed! I should like to know how he could prevent it," exclaimed Frank, affecting deep indignation at the remark. "You should have seen the struggle we had!"

"Very likely: but I noticed your great-coat when we came in just now—and it was not soiled," said Howard.

"Of course not: I had him down all the time."

"Then it was a great pity you did not keep him there."

"Come—come—enough of this fencing," cried Sir Christopher. "Produce the deeds, Mr. Howard: my friend Torrens will take my cheque for the two thousand."

"Oh! certainly," replied the venal father.

"And to-morrow, let us hope that I shall have to give you another for three thousand more," added Sir Christopher. "Thank heaven! my cheque is as good as a Bank-note. But it wasn't twenty years ago, though. Times have altered since then. And yet, as my friend Howard knows, I am proud of my humble origin."

"Yes—yes, uncle," exclaimed Frank: "we all know that perfectly. But let's to business, and then join the young ladies. I shall make them laugh with the story of the highwayman. It's the first time in my life I was ever conquered—ever overcome: and now it hasn't been by fair means. I remember once, when I was at Montreuil, three French peasants had some of their nonsense with me; but I just——"

"Here are the documents, gentlemen," said Mr. Howard. "Frank shall conclude his story presently."

The agreements for the loan of the five thousand pounds were then read over; Mr. Torrens signed them; Sir Christopher Blunt wrote him a cheque for two thousand on account—the remaining three to be advanced only on condition that the proposed marriage took place;—and thus terminated the commercial part of the business.

The four gentlemen then proceeded to the drawing-room, where the two young ladies were seated.

Adelais was excessively pale; and when the odious Mr. Frank Curtis tripped smirkingly up to her, and, taking her fair hand, pressed it to his lips,—his breath, heated with wine and rendered offensive by the fumes of the cigar, steaming upon that delicate skin,—the maiden recoiled as if from something loathsome.

Her father, who observed her narrowly, cast upon her a rapid but ireful glance; and Adelais exerted herself strenuously to recover her composure.

Like a victim about to be sacrificed at the altar of some avenging god, she suffered her admirer to lead her to a seat in a remote part of the room; and placing himself by her side, Frank Curtis darted a triumphant look at Howard and Sir Christopher, as much as to say, "Just see how successfully I am going to play the amiable in this quarter."

Then, turning towards the lovely Adelais, whose large blue eyes were bent timidly down, and whose bosom palpitated with a variety of painful emotions, he observed, in what he considered to be a most endearing whisper, "Come, my sweet gal, cheer up: there's nothing to be frightened at in marriage. I know that I'm not quite a lady's man; but we shall get on better together by and bye. You see, my dear, I've always been used to manly sports or to seeking adventures where some glory was to be gained—such as knocking down watchmen, or fighting with highwaymen, or killing my man in a duel—and things of that kind. But I've no doubt it will be pleasant enough to be tied to your apron-string—if the string itself isn't too tight."

Adelais raised her fine blue eyes, turned them for a moment upon her admirer, and then again fixed them on the carpet, a profound sigh escaping her bosom at the same time:—but that glance, so involuntarily thrown towards her companion, was one of sudden curiosity—as if she were anxious to discover by the expression of his face whether he were indeed serious in the insufferable rhodomontade with which he sought to captivate her.

"There—that's right, my dear gal," said Curtis, mistaking the motive of that rapid look which was directed towards him; "don't stand on any ceremony with me. In a few hours more we shall be husband and wife——"

Adelais shuddered visibly.

"Ah! I like this little modesty—it's all very proper on your part," continued the disgusting young man; "but it will soon wear off—naturally so."

The young lady now started indignantly—her countenance became crimson—and then large tears burst from her eyes. Curtis caught hold of her hand—but she withdraw it,—she literally snatched it away, as if from the jaws of a hideous reptile.

"You needn't think I'm going to eat you, Miss," said Frank in a surly tone. "But I forgot to tell you what an adventure I had just now with a couple of highwaymen," he continued in a milder voice. "You see, as me and my uncle and Howard were coming down the lane, I fell back a little—just to think of you, my dear, at leisure; when all of a sudden three chaps jumped over a bank, and pointed their blunderbusses at me. I didn't care a rap for that; but taking the riding-whip by the thin end, I knocked down three of them—one after the other—with the handle-part, you know, and had just made up my mind to tackle the fourth, when my horse reared and threw me. For a moment I was insensible; and during that time the fifth scoundrel picked my pocket of the two thousand pounds which I may call the purchase-money of your own dear pretty little self."

"Sir!" exclaimed Adelais, aloud: "is it your intention to insult me?"

And, without waiting for a reply, but yielding to the tide of anguish and indignation which now impelled her, she rushed from the room.

Rosamond, who, while engaged in conversation with her father, Sir Christopher, and Mr. Howard at the other end of the room, had never ceased to watch her sister with the most lively interest, now immediately followed the almost heart-broken girl.

The moment the sisters had reached their bed-chamber, Adelais threw herself into Rosamond's arms, exclaiming, "I will never marry him—I will die sooner!"

"Has he offended you?" inquired Rosamond, affectionately embracing her disconsolate sister. "But I need not ask! Your changing countenance—your anxious looks—your convulsive movements—and then your tears, while he sate by you——"

"Oh! my very soul revolts against him!" cried Adelais, emphatically, the conflicts of agonising emotions painfully expressed on her countenance. "At first—when he approached me—it required all the exertions of which my fortitude was capable to subdue the feelings of aversion and disgust—of bitter woe and heart-felt misery—with which I was agitated;—but when his coarse language met my ears——Oh! Rosamond!" exclaimed the distracted maiden, "I must fly—I must avoid this dreadful fate—or my heart will break!"

At this moment Mr. Torrens slowly opened the door, and entered the room.

His countenance wore an expression which gave evidence that anger and compunction were maintaining a fierce struggle in his breast; but the former feeling was rapidly obtaining the ascendancy.

"Rash—disobedient girl," he exclaimed, fixing his stern cold eyes upon Adelais, who still clung to her younger sister, "what signifies this folly?"

"Spare me—spare me, my dearest father!" cried Adelais, suddenly tearing herself from Rosamond's embrace, and falling on her knees before her sire: "I cannot marry that horrible man!"

Mr. Torrens bit his lip almost till the blood came.

"Listen to me, my dear father," continued the despairing girl, joining her hands together, while her cheeks were of marble whiteness, unanimated by a tinge of vital colouring,—"I am your daughter, and must obey you; but if you persist in saying, '*Receive that man as your husband*,' it is the same as if you were to utter the word, '*Die!*' Oh! no—you cannot—you will not sacrifice me in this cruel, cruel manner! What have I done to offend you, that my unhappiness has become your aim? Dearest father—relent—I implore you: on my knees, I beseech you to save me ere it be too late!"

"Adelais," exclaimed Mr. Torrens, arming himself with that fatal sophistry which led him to believe that *he* was the only judge of what was fitting for his daughter's welfare and happiness,—"Adelais, rise—I command you!"

The miserable girl obeyed, but staggered with vacillating and irregular steps towards a chair, in which she sank, the agony of her soul now expelling all power of reflection from its seat.

"I have gone too far to retreat—even if I were so disposed," continued Mr. Torrens. "Your happiness will be ensured by this union."

"Her happiness, father!" said Rosamond, reproachfully. "Oh! no—never, never!"

"Undutiful girl!" cried the venal parent: "do you league with your sister against me? I tell you that Adelais is about to become the wife of a young man who can give her an enviable position in society, and who at his uncle's death, will inherit an immense fortune. It is true that Mr. Curtis is somewhat rough in manner and incautious with his tongue; but perfection exists not in this world. To be brief, this marriage shall take place—it *must*—I dare not retract."

"Father, one word more," exclaimed Adelais, suddenly recovering her power of thought and speech—those powers which anguish had for a few minutes completely subdued: "you are about to *sell* your daughter to that man—he boasted to me that a few thousand pounds were the purchase-money—and hence my abrupt departure from the room."

"The phrase was wrong—ill-chosen—coarse," ejaculated Mr. Torrens, evidently smarting under this announcement: "but we must not judge of words themselves—we must only look to the motives of him who utters them. Mr. Curtis is incapable of insulting you——"

"Oh! you know not how abhorrent is the coarseness of his language!" cried Adelais, bursting into a torrent of tears.

"You provoke me beyond the limits of human patience!" ejaculated Mr. Torrens, stamping his foot with rage. "But no more of this. You know my will—prepare to obey it. I ask you not to return to the drawing-room to-night;—to-morrow morning let me hope that you will show yourself a dutiful daughter towards a father who is anxious only to ensure your prosperity."

Mr. Torrens then imprinted a cold kiss upon the fair foreheads of Adelais and Rosamond, and hastily quitted the apartment.

For some minutes after the door had closed behind them, the sisters sat gazing upon each other in the silence of painful and awful reflection.

Yet beautiful were they in their sorrow; for the unstudied attitudes and abandonment of limb which such a state of mind produces, gave additional grace to the just proportions of their forms, and imparted an expression of the most tender interest to the perfect composition of their features.

"Sister," at length said Rosamond, in a soft and mournful tone, as she approached Adelais, "what will you do?"

This question suddenly aroused the unhappy young lady to a sense of the urgent necessity of adopting some decisive measure.

Winding her arms around Rosamond's neck, she said, "I must fly from my father's house—I must abandon the paternal dwelling. O heaven! wherefore am I reduced to so fearful an alternative?"

"Speak not only of yourself, beloved Adelais," murmured Rosamond chidingly; "for you know that my fate, as well as my heart, is inseparably linked with thine."

"Oh! I doubt not the sincerity of your love for me, dearest sister," exclaimed Miss Torrens; "but I tremble at the idea of making you the companion of my flight. Have we not read in books, dear girl, that London is a dreadful place—abounding in perils of all kinds, and concealing pit-falls beneath its most pleasant places? Oh! Rosamond, you are so young—so very young to quit your father's home and venture in that great city of danger and crime!"

"But with you as my companion, Adelais, I shall have courage to meet all those perils of which you speak," responded Rosamond, the tones of her voice becoming so gentle, so melting, and so persuasive, that never did she seem so dear—so very dear unto her sister as at this moment.

And now all hesitation was banished on the part of Adelais:—it was settled—it was determined—Rosamond should become the companion of her flight!

CHAPTER XIII.
THE ELOPEMENT.

Let us now return to Rainford, whom we left on his way back to London, after having so triumphantly eased the vain-glorious Mr. Frank Curtis of the two thousand pounds.

The highwayman,—for such indeed was the gay, generous-hearted, and brave Tom Rain,—scarcely condescended to bestow even a chuckle of satisfaction upon a victory so easily won—an exploit so readily accomplished.

He would have valued the prize far more, had it been obtained by means of hard blows and as the result of a desperate encounter; for the love of adventure was inherent in his disposition—and he had often courted danger in his life, for the exciting pleasure of freeing himself from its intricacy.

Having galloped his good steed to the beginning of the lane, he checked its celerity, and then proceeded at a moderate pace along the main road to the public-house where Curtis and himself had stopped to purchase their cigars about half an hour previously.

Riding up to the door of the little establishment, the highwayman leapt from his horse, and threw the reins to a dependant of the place who was conversing with the postillion of a chaise and pair that had stopped at the door.

When Rainford sauntered leisurely up to the bar, with his chimney-pot hat set rakishly on one side, his white coat comfortably buttoned up, and his riding-whip in his hand, the landlord instantly recollected him again, and observed, as he drew the liquor which the highwayman ordered, "Back to London, sir, to-night?"

"Yes," replied Tom carelessly: "I just escorted my friend as far as Torrens Cottage, and shall now get home again."

These words produced a visible emotion on the part of a tall, handsome, dark-haired young man, who was also standing at the bar. He was well protected by a great coat against the cold; and Tom therefore very naturally concluded that he was the traveller journeying in the post-chaise outside.

"Torrens Cottage!" cried the landlord. "Why, I do declare that's the very ticket. This gentleman here was just making inquiries whether I had any one that could take a note there in a confidential way."

The landlord blurted forth this announcement without heeding the significant coughs and "hems" of the tall young gentleman, who seemed greatly annoyed that the object of his call at the public-house should thus be published to the very first stranger who entered the place after him.

"You should keep a closer tongue in your head," said Tom Rain. "How do you know what harm might be done by your stupidity in letting out the gentleman's business in this kind of way? Fortunately, I am not the kind of fellow to do mischief; and in this case, it may be, that I can effect some good."

"Indeed!" exclaimed the tall young gentleman, his countenance suddenly exchanging the expression of annoyance which the landlord's garrulity had excited, for one indicative of hope and joy.

"Yes—I think so," said Tom. "But we must have a few words in private."

"Walk into the parlour, gentlemen," cried the landlord. "There's no one in that room at present."

Rainford and the tall stranger followed this suggestion; and when the door was closed behind them, the highwayman said, "If I am not very much mistaken, you must be the gentleman whom that lying braggart Frank Curtis is endeavouring to cut out?"

"My name is Clarence Villiers, sir," was the guarded reply.

"And you are the lover of Mr. Torrens's eldest daughter," continued Rainford. "Now do not waste valuable time by reflecting whether you shall make me your confidant, or not. I am disposed to serve you: tell me how I can do it."

"You will excuse me," said Villiers in a polite but somewhat reserved tone, "if I first request to be informed to whom I have the honour of speaking."

"Captain Sparks," was the immediate reply. "I happen to know old Sir Christopher and his precious nephew; and I rode down with them nearly as far as the cottage. But I did not accept their invitation to go in—for particular reasons of my own. You may, however, suppose that I am well acquainted with all the particulars of this infamous case. Miss Adelais Torrens loves Mr. Clarence Villiers and hates Mr. Frank Curtis; but Mr. Frank Curtis is the successful suitor with the mercenary father, because a certain five thousand pounds——"

"Enough, Captain Sparks!" ejaculated Villiers. "I see that you do indeed know all. And will you serve me in this strait?"

"I will—honour bright!" cried Tom. "There's my hand upon it. Now say what is to be done. It is already past eight o'clock," he added, after a hasty reference to a handsome gold watch which he drew from his fob.

"My object was to obtain an interview with Adelais in some way or another, and urge her to—to———"

"Speak plainly, my friend," cried Rain. "To elope with you. Well?—do you mean every thing that is honourable?"

"As God is my judge," said the young man solemnly. "I have frequently urged the dear girl to consent to a clandestine marriage with me; but the purity of her soul has ever revolted against a course which she considers to be marked with duplicity."

"Where would you convey her during the interval that must necessarily elapse before you can marry her?" asked Rainford. "Because, as she is a minor, I suppose you could not obtain a special licence without her father's consent."

"I have an aunt in London devoted to my interests," answered Clarence; "and she would receive her with even maternal affection until I should acquire a legal right to protect her."

"So far, so good," observed Tom. "And yet a young lady eloping at night with a young man———remember, I am only speaking for the good of both of you."

"I had foreseen that difficulty also," said Villiers hastily. "The fact is, Adelais and her sister Rosamond are so linked together by the tenderest bonds of affection, that the one would not move a step unaccompanied by the other."

"The devil!" cried Rainford: "two ladies to carry off! That increases the embarrassment of the business. Now it is very clear that it is perfectly useless for us to send a messenger down with a note: it would be intercepted by the father. But if you will sit down and write what you choose, I will undertake to have it delivered to the young lady herself."

"You?" exclaimed Clarence joyfully.

"Yes: what I promise, I will perform," said Rainford. "Follow my directions—and all shall go well."

Clarence rang the bell, ordered writing materials, and in a few minutes completed a note to his beloved Adelais, which he read to his companion.

"Seal it," said Tom; "because it may pass through the hands of another person, after it leaves mine, and before it reaches Miss Torrens."

This suggestion was instantaneously complied with; and Rainford secured the letter about his person.

"Now," he continued, after a moment's reflection, "do you proceed with the chaise down the lane, and stop as near the cottage as is consistent with prudence. I shall retrace my way there at once. Fear nothing—but wait patiently at the place where you pull up, until I make my appearance."

Villiers promised to fulfil these instructions; and Rainford, having taken a temporary leave of him, remounted his horse and galloped towards Torrens Cottage.

The highwayman had his plan of proceeding ready digested by the time the white walls of the building, rendered particularly conspicuous in the starlight, met his view.

Alighting from his horse at a distance of about a hundred yards, he tied the animal to a tree, and then repaired towards the dwelling.

Having reconnoitred the premises, he speedily discovered the stable; and, to his infinite joy, a light streamed from one of the windows of that building.

Leaping over the palings which separated the kitchen-garden from the adjacent fields, Tom Rain proceeded to the stable; and there, as he had anticipated, he found John Jeffreys, the groom, busily employed with his master's horses.

John was alone; and his surprise was great, when, upon being tapped on the shoulder, he turned round and beheld the highwayman.

"Silence!" said Tom in a whisper; "we have no time to lose in idle chatter. Here's five guineas for you; and you must get this note conveyed secretly to Miss Torrens—Adelais, the eldest—you know."

"It shall be done, sir," replied Jeffreys. "I am already far in the good graces of the housemaid; the cook is old and deaf; and so there's no fear of my not being able to succeed."

"Good. And you will bring me the answer up the lane, where I shall wait for you."

"And how can you read it, when you get it?" demanded Jeffreys. "The night is not quite clear enough for that."

"The answer will be a verbal one—*yes* or *no*," replied Tom.

Jeffreys promised that no delay should occur on his part; and Rainford retraced his steps to the spot where he had left his horse.

Many novelists would here pause for the honest but somewhat tedious purpose of detailing all the reflections which passed through the mind of Rainford during the mortal half-hour that elapsed ere the sounds of footsteps upon the hard soil announced the approach of some person. But as we do not wish either to spin out our narrative with dry material, or to keep the reader in any unnecessary suspense, we will at once declare that at the expiration of the aforesaid thirty minutes John Jeffreys made his appearance at the appointed spot.

"What news?" demanded Tom impatiently.

"All right——"

"And the answer?"

"Is *yes*."

"That's well!" exclaimed Rainford. "You may now go back, John. All that I require of you is done."

"But I have something to say to *you*, sir," observed the servant. "Just now, Sir Christopher sent for me up into the parlour to give me some orders; and I heard Mr. Frank, who is uncommon far gone with brandy-and-water, making a boast to the lawyer-fellow that he'd walk all round the grounds to see that every thing is safe. It seems that the lawyer has been twitting him about his little business with you just now up the lane, you know; and so Mr. Frank is as bumptious as possible. I only thought I'd better tell you of this—in case you've any business in hand that's likely to keep you about the place."

"I am very much obliged to you, John," said Rainford. "Here's another five guineas for you—and I shall not forget to speak to Old Death in your favour. But you had better get back as soon as you can, for fear you should be missed."

Jeffreys thanked the highwayman for the additional remuneration, and returned to the cottage.

It was now past nine o'clock, and Rainford murmured to himself, "I wonder how much longer they will be?"

His horse, which was a high-spirited animal, began to grow impatient of this long stoppage; and he himself shivered, in spite of the good great coat, with the nipping chill.

Another quarter of an hour elapsed; and, to the infinite joy of Tom Rain, he suddenly beheld two female figures, well muffled in shawls and furs, emerge from the obscurity at a short distance.

"All right, ladies," he said, in as loud a voice as he dared use consistently with prudence.

Adelais and Rosamond hurried towards him, as affrighted lambs to their shepherd; and yet, when they were close to him, they seemed unable to utter a word.

"Fear not, ladies," exclaimed the highwayman. "I am the friend to whom Mr. Villiers alluded in his note."

"Save us, then, sir—save us," said Adelais, in an urgent and imploring tone; "for Mr. Curtis saw us leave the house: he was in the garden———"

At that moment the sounds of voices were heard in the direction of the cottage; and they were evidently approaching.

"Hasten up the lane, young ladies—hasten, for God's sake!" said Tom Rain. "Mr. Villiers is there with the post-chaise—and I will remain here to bar the way."

Adelais and Rosamond could not even give utterance to the thanks which their hearts longed to express: terror froze the words that started to their lips; and, not daring to glance behind them, they hurried up the lane.

Tom Rainford now mounted his horse, and took his station in the middle of the way; for several persons were rapidly approaching from the house.

In a few moments they were near enough to enable Rainford to catch what they said.

"The disobedient—self-willed girls!" exclaimed one, whom Tom was right in supposing to be Mr. Torrens.

"But wasn't it fortunate that I twigged them?" said Curtis. "Egad!———"

"It will be much more fortunate if we overtake them," observed the lawyer.

"Bless me!—I'm out of breath," cried Sir Christopher. "I wish John would come on with the horses. Did you tell him, Frank?"

"To be sure I did. We cannot fail to overtake them. But, poor things! suppose that highwayman should fall in with them—and me not there to defend them!"

"I think it would be all the same———"

Howard was interrupted by a sudden ejaculation on the part of Mr. Torrens, who was a few paces in advance of the others, but who now abruptly came to a full stop.

"What is it?" demanded Curtis, shaking from head to foot, in spite of all the liquor he had imbibed during the day.

"Some ruffian on horseback—there—don't you see?" exclaimed Mr. Torrens. "But I am not afraid of him: his presence here is in some way connected with my daughters."

And the incensed father rushed furiously towards the highwayman.

"Stand back!" cried Tom in his clear, stentorian voice; and this command was followed by the sharp clicking of the two pistols which he cocked.

"The robber!" exclaimed Frank Curtis, clinging to the coat-tails of Mr. Torrens, who had retreated a few paces at the ominous sound of the pistols. "At him, my dear sir—at him! I'm here to help you."

"Villain—give up the two thousand pounds, and we will let you go—on *my* honour as a knight!" ejaculated Sir Christopher, keeping as far remote as he deemed prudent from the sinister form which, wrapped in the white great coat, and seated composedly on the tall horse, seemed, amidst the obscurity of the night, to be a ghost disdaining to touch the earth.

"I am very much obliged to you for your kindness, Sir Christopher," said Tom: "but I am not at all in fear of the necessity of purchasing my liberty at any price whatsoever. I however give you every one due warning, that the first who tries to pass this way——"

"Scoundrel! my daughters—where are they?" vociferated Mr. Torrens.

"That's it—give it him!" cried Frank Curtis. "I'll be at him when you've done."

"Go on at once," cried Howard.

"And why are you standing idle there?"

"Because it is not my business to interfere."

"Well done, lawyer!" exclaimed Tom. "No fees can recompense you for an ounce of lead in the thigh: for if I do fire, I shall only try to lame—not kill."

"Mr. Curtis—Sir Christopher—will you not help me to arrest this villain who beards us to our very faces?" exclaimed Torrens, in a towering passion.

And again he rushed forward, while Frank Curtis beat a precipitate retreat behind his uncle.

"Stand back! or, by God, I'll fire!" thundered Rainford, suddenly spurring his horse in such a manner that the length of the animal was made to block up nearly the entire width of the bye-lane.

"You dare not murder me!" cried Torrens. "My daughters will escape!"—and he attempted to pass in front of the horse.

But by a skilful manœuvre, Rainford baffled him—arrested his progress—and kept him at bay, using all the time the most desperate menaces, which he did not, however, entertain the remotest idea of putting into execution.

"Mr. Curtis, sir—will you help me?" cried the infuriate father. "My daughters are escaping before your very eyes—you are losing your bride——"

"And you the rest of the money that was to have purchased her," said Rainford coolly. "Mercenary old man, you are rightly punished."

With these words, the highwayman suddenly wheeled his horse round, and disappeared in a moment.

He had succeeded in barring the way for upwards of ten minutes against the pursuers of the two fugitive ladies; and he calculated that in less than half that time they must have reached the post-chaise which Clarence Villiers had in readiness to receive them.

Jeffreys had purposely delayed getting the horses out; and even when he did appear with them, several minutes had elapsed since the highwayman had left the path free to those who thought fit to avail themselves of the services of the animals.

These were only two—Mr. Torrens and Jeffreys himself: the latter volunteering his aid for the purpose of misleading and embarrassing the father, rather than of assisting him.

Frank Curtis affected to be suddenly taken very unwell: Sir Christopher was really so; and the lawyer, although by no means a coward, did not see any utility in hazarding his life against such a desperate character as Captain Sparks (for by that denomination only did he know Tom Rain) appeared to be.

Thus, while the knight, his nephew, and the attorney retraced their steps to the cottage, leading back the horses which had been brought out for their use, Mr. Torrens and Jeffreys galloped away towards London.

CHAPTER XIV.
LADY HATFIELD AND DR. LASCELLES.—ESTHER DE MEDINA.

Two days after the incidents which we have just related, Dr. Lascelles received a message, at about noon, requesting him to repair immediately to the dwelling of Lady Hatfield, who was seriously indisposed.

He obeyed this summons with more than usual alacrity; for ever since Lord Ellingham had made him his confidant, the curiosity of the worthy doctor had been strangely piqued by the unaccountable fact that Lady Hatfield should reject the suit of a man whom she not only professed to love, but who was in every way worthy of her.

On his arrival at Lady Hatfield's residence, he was surprised to learn from Miss Mordaunt that his patient was too unwell to quit her couch; and when he was introduced into Georgiana's bed-chamber, he found her labouring under a strong nervous excitement.

In accordance with the sacred privilege of the physician, he was of course left alone with her ladyship; and, seating himself by the side of the bed, he questioned her in the usual manner.

Georgiana explained her sensations; but, although she alluded to nothing beyond those physical details which directly came within the province of the medical man, still Dr. Lascelles had no difficulty in perceiving that the *mind*, rather than the *body*, was affected.

"My dear Lady Hatfield," he said, in as gentle and mild a tone as he could possibly assume, "it is in the power of the physician to administer certain drugs which may produce temporary composure; and an opiate will encourage a good night's rest. But you will forgive me for observing that the condition in which I now find you, is scarcely one to which medical science will apply successfully—*unless* seconded by aid of a more refined and delicate nature."

"I do not comprehend you, doctor," exclaimed Georgiana, casting upon him a glance of mingled surprise and uneasiness.

"I mean, Lady Hatfield," resumed Lascelles, "that you are the prey to some secret grief—some source of vexation and annoyance, which medical skill cannot remove. The aid of a refined and delicate nature to which I refer, is such as can be afforded only by a sincere and confidential friend. Without for an instant seeking to draw you into any explanations, it is my duty to assure you that unless your mind be tranquillised, medicine will not successfully encounter this nervous irritability—this intense anxiety—this oppressive feeling of coming evil, without apparent cause—and this sleeplessness at night,—of all which you complain."

"I thank you most sincerely for this candour and frankness on your part, doctor," said Lady Hatfield, after a long pause, during which she appeared to reflect profoundly. "To deny that I *have* suffered much in mind during the last few days, were to practise a useless deception upon you. But I require no confidant—I need not the solace of friendship. To your medical skill I trust for, at all events, a partial restoration to health; and travelling—change of scene—the excitement of visiting Paris—or some such means of diversion, will effect the rest."

These last words were, however, accompanied with a deep sigh—as if upon the lady's soul were forced the sad conviction that happiness and herself must evermore remain strangers to each other.

"I should scarcely recommend travelling in the winter time, Lady Hatfield," observed Doctor Lascelles. "Surely our own city can afford that constant variety of recreation and those ever-changing scenes of amusement, which may produce a beneficial effect upon your spirits."

"I abhor the pleasures of the fashionable world, doctor," said Georgiana emphatically. "There is something so cold in the ostentation of that sphere— so chilling in its magnificence—so formal in its pursuits—so ceremonial, so thoroughly artificial in all its features and proceedings, that when in the crowded ball-room or the brilliant *soirée*, I even feel more *alone* than when in the solitude of my own chamber."

"And yet, Lady Hatfield, throughout the extensive circle of your acquaintance," said the physician, "there must be at least a few endowed with intellectual qualifications adapted to render them agreeable. The most pleasant parties, composed of these select, might be given: your rank—your wealth—your own well-stored mind—and, pardon me, your beauty,—would ensure to you——"

"Oh! doctor," exclaimed Georgiana, "I can anticipate the arguments you are about to use; but, alas! my mind appears to be in that morbid state which discolours all objects with its own jaundiced thoughts. I speak thus candidly to you, doctor—because I am aware of your friendship for me—I know also that the admission I have now made will be regarded by you as a solemn secret—and perhaps your advice," she added, slowly and hesitatingly, "might prove beneficial to me. But, no—no," she exclaimed, her utterance suddenly assuming great rapidity, "it is useless to say more: advice cannot serve *me*!"

"There is scarcely a possible case of human vexation, grief, or annoyance, which cannot be relieved by the solace, or ameliorated by the counsel, of a friend," observed Doctor Lascelles, dwelling emphatically upon his words.

Georgiana played abstractedly with the long, luxuriant hair which streamed over her shoulders, and spread its shining masses on the white pillow; but at the same time the snowy night-dress rose and sank rapidly with the heavings of her bosom.

"Believe me, Lady Hatfield," continued Doctor Lascelles, after a short pause, during which he vainly awaited a reply to his former observation, "I am deeply grieved to find that one who so little deserves the sting of grief or the presence of misfortune, should suffer from either the sharpness of the first, or the menaces of the latter. But is it not possible, my dear lady,—and now, forgive me if I avail myself of the privilege of a physician to ask this question,—is it not possible, I say, that you have conjured up phantoms which have no substantial existence? Remember that there are certain conditions of the mind, when the imagination becomes a prey to the wildest delusions———"

"Doctor, I am no monomaniac," said Lady Hatfield abruptly. "But justly, indeed—oh! most justly and truly did you ere now assert that I little deserve the sting of grief! If through any crime—any weakness—any frailty on my part, I had merited the sore displeasure of heaven—at that time———"

She checked herself abruptly, and burst into a flood of tears; and for a few moments her countenance appeared to be the sad index of a breaking heart.

"Doctor," she observed at length, "pardon this manifestation of weakness on my part; but my spirits are so depressed—my mind feels so truly wretched, that I cannot control these tears. Think no more of what we have been saying: I wish that we had not said so much! Leave me a prescription, and visit me again in the course of the day."

Lascelles wrote out a prescription, and then took his departure, wondering more than ever what secret cause of grief was nourished in the bosom of Lady Hatfield.

That this secret grief was the motive which had induced or compelled her to refuse the hand of Lord Ellingham, he could not doubt:—that it arose from no *crime*—*weakness*—nor *frailty* on her part, he felt assured; inasmuch as her own words, uttered in a paroxysm of mental anguish and not in a calm moment when deception might be her aim, proved that fact;—and that it was associated with any physical ailment, he could hardly believe. Because, if she were the prey to an insidious disease, no feeling of shame—no false delicacy could possibly force a woman of her good sense and naturally powerful mind to keep such a fact from her physician. What, then, could be that secret and profoundly-rooted cause of grief? Was it monomania of some novel or very rare kind? The curiosity of the man of science was keenly whetted: he already began to suspect that he was destined to discover some new phase in the constitution of the human mind; and he resolved to adopt all the means within his reach to solve the mystery.

This curiosity on his part was by no means of a common, vulgar, or base nature. Considering the profession and researchful disposition of the man, it was a legitimate and entirely venial sentiment. It was not that curiosity which loves to feed itself upon the materials of scandal. It was purely in connexion with the thirst of knowledge and the passion for discovery which ever animated him in that sphere of science to which he was so enthusiastically devoted.

The doctor was proceeding homewards, when he encountered Lord Ellingham. The Earl was walking by the side of an elderly gentleman, on whose arm hung a tall and graceful young lady; but the physician did not immediately catch a glimpse of her countenance, as it was turned towards Lord Ellingham, who was speaking at the moment.

The nobleman shook Lascelles warmly by the hand, and immediately introduced his companions by the names of Mr. and Miss de Medina.

The doctor bowed, and then cast a glance at the countenance of the young lady: but he started as if with a sudden pang,—for in the beautiful Jewess who now stood before him, he beheld—apparently past all possibility of error—the same female who a few days previously had attempted self-destruction in South-Moulton Street.

But, almost simultaneously with this unexpected conviction, the solemn promise which he had made to Tom Rainford (whom he only knew on that occasion by the denomination of Jameson) flashed to the mind of Doctor Lascelles; and, instantly composing himself, he uttered some observation of a general nature.

"I am glad we have thus met, doctor," said Lord Ellingham, who had not noticed his sudden, but evanescent excitement; "for my friend Mr. de Medina is a comparative stranger in London, and it is as well," added the nobleman, with a smile, "that he should become acquainted with the leading physician of the day."

"I believe that no one enjoys health so good as to be enabled to dispense altogether with our assistance," said the physician, bowing in acknowledgment of the compliment thus paid him. "The most perfect piece of mechanism must necessarily need repair sometimes."

"Decidedly so," said Lord Ellingham. "But we will not assert that physicians are necessary evils, doctor—in the same sense as the lawyers are."

"I appeal to Miss de Medina whether his lordship be not, by implication, too hard upon my profession," exclaimed Lascelles, laughing.

"His lordship," replied Esther, "was yesterday riding a very high-spirited horse; and had he been thrown in such a manner as to have incurred injury, I question whether he would have believed that his medical attendant was an evil, however necessary."

"I owe you my profound gratitude for this powerful defence of my profession, Miss de Medina," said the doctor, who had thus succeeded in compelling the young lady to speak.

He then raised his hat and passed on; but he had not proceeded many paces, when he was overtaken by Lord Ellingham, who had parted from his companions to have a few minutes' conversation with the doctor.

"That is a lovely girl to whom your lordship has just introduced me," said Lascelles.

"And as good in heart as she is beautiful in person," exclaimed the nobleman.

"Ah!" cried the physician, with a sly glance: "is Lady Hatfield already forgotten?"

"Far from it!" said Arthur, his tone instantly becoming mournful and his countenance overclouded. "You cannot think me so fickle—so vacillating, doctor. No: the image of Georgiana is never absent from my memory. I had only encountered Mr. de Medina and his daughter a few minutes before we met you; and, not only am I bound to show them every attention in my power, as they are tenants of mine and were strongly recommended to me by mutual friends at Liverpool—but also I am glad to court intellectual society, wherever it can be found in this city, to distract my mind from the *one* topic which so constantly and so painfully engrosses it."

"Are Mr. de Medina and his daughter such very agreeable companions?" inquired Lascelles, apparently in quite a casual manner.

"Mr. de Medina is a well-informed, intelligent, and even erudite man," answered the Earl. "His daughter is highly accomplished, sensible, and amiable. I feel an additional interest in them, because they belong to a race whom it is the fashion to revile and often to despise. It is true that my acquaintance with Mr. de Medina and his daughter scarcely dates from a month back; but I have already seen—and if not, I have *heard* enough of them, to know that he is the pattern of integrity and the young lady the personification of every virtue."

The doctor made no reply. Certain was he that he "could a tale unfold" which would totally undeceive his noble friend relative to the character of Esther. But his lips were sealed by a solemn vow; and, even if they were not, there was no necessity to detail how he had been summoned to attend on the young lady and rescue her from the fate and crime of suicide,—how he had good cause to know that she was either a wife or a mistress, but he suspected the latter,—how he had seen that splendid form stretched half-naked upon the bed, the bosom heaving convulsively with physical and mental agony, and the exquisitely modelled arms flung wildly about with excruciating pain,—how the large black eyes had been fixed imploringly upon him, and the vermillion lips had parted to give utterance to words demanding from himself the fiat of her life or death:—there was no necessity, we say, to narrate all this, even if no vow had bound him to silence, because Lord Ellingham sought not that lovely Jewess as a wife.

That Esther de Medina and the lady of South Moulton Street were one and the same person, the doctor felt convinced. The tones of Esther's voice, flowing upon the ear with such silver melody,—the two rows of brilliant, beautiful teeth,—the face—the hair—the eyes,—the configuration of the form, with its fine but justly proportioned bust and slender waist,—all were identical! But what chiefly amazed—nay, bewildered the physician, was the calm indifference with which Esther had met his rapid, searching glance,—

the admirable composure with which she had encountered him—the firmness, amounting almost to an insolent assurance, with which she had spoken to him,—never once quailing, nor blushing, nor manifesting the slightest embarrassment, but actually treating him as a person whom she saw for the first time, and as if he were totally unacquainted with any thing that militated against her character;—all this was naturally a subject of ineffable astonishment and wonder.

Lord Ellingham accompanied the doctor to Grafton Street; and when they had entered the house, Dr. Lascelles made him acquainted with Lady Hatfield's indisposition.

"She is ill!" ejaculated Arthur, profoundly touched by these tidings: "and I dare not call even to inquire concerning her!"

"And wherefore should you not manifest that courtesy?" asked the doctor.

"I must forget her—I cannot demonstrate any farther interest in her behalf!" exclaimed the nobleman. "If there really exist reasons which render it impossible or imprudent for her to change her condition by marriage, it is useless for us to meet again:—and if she be swayed by caprice, I cannot suffer myself to be made the sport of her whims."

"There are the wanton, wilful whims of a coquette," said the doctor, impressively; "and there are the delusions of the monomaniac—but the latter are not the less conscientiously believed, although they be nothing save delusions."

"Is it possible?" cried Arthur, a sudden ray of hope breaking in upon him. "Can Georgiana be subject to phantasies of that nature? Oh! then she can be cured, doctor—and your skill may yet make us happy!"

"Rest assured, my dear Earl," was the reply, "that all the knowledge which I possess shall be devoted to that purpose."

"My eternal gratitude will be due to you, doctor," said the nobleman. "With your permission I shall return in the evening to learn from you how your charming patient progresses."

The physician signified his assent; and Lord Ellingham took his departure, new hopes animating his soul.

CHAPTER XV.
THE OPIATE.

It was about seven o'clock in the evening when Dr. Lascelles returned to Lady Hatfield's house on Piccadilly Hill.

Miss Mordaunt, whom he encountered in the drawing-room, informed him that Georgiana had become more composed and tranquil since she had taken the medicine which he had prescribed for her, and that she had requested to be left alone, as she experienced an inclination to sleep.

"It is nevertheless necessary that I should see her," said the physician.

Julia accordingly hastened to her friend's apartment, and speedily returned with the information that Lady Hatfield was not yet asleep, and that the doctor might walk up.

Lascelles immediately availed himself of this permission; but he found—as indeed he had fully anticipated—that his patient was rapidly yielding to the invincible drowsiness produced by the opiatic medicine which he had prescribed for her.

He seated himself by the bed-side, asked her a few ordinary questions, and then suffered her to fall undisturbed into slumber.

At length she slept profoundly.

A smile of satisfaction played for a moment upon the lips of the physician; but it yielded to a sombre cloud which almost immediately succeeded it—for a powerful struggle now suddenly arose in the breast of Dr. Lascelles.

In his ardent devotion to the science which he professed, he longed to satisfy himself on certain points at present admitting of doubt and involved in uncertainty: and, on the other hand, he hesitated at the accomplishment of a deed which he could not help regarding as a gross abuse of his privileges as a medical man. By virtue of the most sacred confidence he was admitted to the bed-chamber of his female patient; and he shrank from exercising that right in an illegitimate way.

Then, again, he reasoned to himself that if he were enabled to ascertain beyond all doubt that no physical cause induced Lady Hatfield to shrink from marriage, he must fall back upon the theory that she had become subject to certain monomaniac notions which influenced her mind to her own unhappiness; and he at length persuaded himself that he should be acting for her best interests, were he to put into execution the project which he had already formed.

Such an opinion, operating upon a man who possessed but few of the delicate and refined feelings of our nature, and who was ever ready to sacrifice all considerations to the cause of the medical science, speedily banished hesitation.

Having convinced himself that Georgiana slept so profoundly that there was no chance of awaking her, he locked the door, and again approached the bed.

And now his sacrilegious hands drew aside the snow-white dress which covered the sleeping lady's bosom; and the treasures of that gently-heaving breast were exposed to his view. But not a sensual thought was thereby excited in his mind: cold and passionless, he surveyed the beauteous spectacle only as a sculptor might measure the proportions of a marble Venus or Diana the huntress.

And not a trace of cancer was there: no unseemly mark, nor mole, nor scar, nor wound disfigured the glowing orbs that, rising from a broad and ample chest, swelled laterally over the upper part of the arms.

Yet wherefore did Dr. Lascelles abruptly start? and why did his countenance suddenly assume an expression of surprise—or rather of mingled doubt and astonishment—as his glances wandered over the fair bust thus exposed to his view?

Carefully and cautiously refastening the strings of the night-dress, he now assumed the air of a man who had discovered some clue to a mystery hitherto profoundly veiled; and unhesitatingly did he resolve to clear up all his doubts and all his newly-awakened suspicions.

Five minutes afterwards Dr. Lascelles left the room, Lady Hatfield still remaining buried in a deep slumber.

His countenance expressed surprise mingled with sorrow; and, cold—phlegmatic though his disposition was, he could not help murmuring to himself, "Is it possible?"

Having just looked into the drawing-room, to take leave of Miss Mordaunt, and state that his patient was progressing as favourably as could be expected, Dr. Lascelles returned home.

Lord Ellingham was waiting for him; and this interview the physician now dreaded.

"Are your tidings favourable, doctor?" was the nobleman's hasty and anxious inquiry.

"I regret, my dear Earl," answered Lascelles, "that I should have encouraged hopes——"

"Which are doomed to experience disappointment," added Arthur bitterly. "Oh! I might have anticipated this—unfortunate being that I am! But how have you ascertained that your ideas of this morning are unfounded? How have you convinced yourself that Georgiana is *not* a prey to those mental eccentricities which your skill might reach? Has she revealed to you her motive for refusing—for rejecting me,—*me* whom she professes to love?"

"She has revealed nothing, my lord," replied the doctor solemnly. "But I have satisfied myself that monomania and Lady Hatfield are total strangers to each other."

"Then must I abandon all hope!" exclaimed the Earl; "for it is evident that I am the victim of a ridiculous caprice. And yet," he added, a sudden thought striking him, "I will see her once again. She is ill—she is suffering—perhaps she will be pleased to behold me—and who knows——"

"Not this evening, my lord—not this evening!" cried the doctor, stopping the nobleman who had seized his hat and was darting towards the door. "Lady Hatfield sleeps—and she must not be disturbed."

But Lord Ellingham was too full of his new idea to pay any attention to the physician; and he rushed from the house.

CHAPTER XVI.
THE LOVER AND THE UNCLE.

A few minutes brought Arthur to the residence of Lady Hatfield; and his hand was already upon the knocker, when a sudden idea struck him—and he asked himself, "How can I demand admission to the bed-chamber of Georgiana?"

The madness of his project now being evident to him, he mournfully turned away, when the door suddenly opened, and a tall, stout, fine-looking man, dressed as a country squire, issued from the house.

Lord Ellingham immediately recognised Sir Ralph Walsingham, Georgiana's uncle, with whom he was well acquainted. The baronet also perceived the Earl; and they shook each other cordially by the hand.

"Were you about to call?" inquired Sir Ralph.

"I was," answered Lord Ellingham. "Hearing of Lady Hatfield's illness———"

"She is better—much better," interrupted the baronet. "I have just left her; and she has not long awoke from a profound and refreshing slumber."

"I am delighted to hear these tidings," said the nobleman.

The servant, seeing that Sir Ralph had stopped to converse with the Earl, still kept the door open; and, as Arthur had admitted that he was about to call, there was now no alternative save for him to leave his card.

The baronet then took his arm; and they walked away together.

"Georgiana is a singular being," observed Sir Ralph; "and although she is my niece, yet there are times when I hardly know what to make of her. She is too intellectual—too steady—to be capricious; and still———"

"My dear Sir Ralph," interrupted the Earl, "you have touched upon the very topic concerning which I longed to speak the moment I met you. Will you accompany me to my abode, and favour me for a short period with your attention to what I am so anxious to confide to you?"

"With pleasure," was the reply. "But I have already learnt from Georgiana's lips the principal fact to which your lordship doubtless alludes; and it was indeed for the purpose of introducing the subject that I ere now made the remark relative to the occasional incomprehensibility of her character. Let us not, however, continue the discourse in the public street."

The nobleman and the baronet speedily reached the mansion of the former in Pall-Mall West; and when they were seated in an elegantly furnished apartment, with a bottle of claret before them, they renewed the conversation.

"Georgiana," said the baronet, "has informed me that your lordship has honoured her by the offer of your hand; and I need hardly assure you how rejoiced I should feel to welcome as a relative one whom I already esteem as a friend. But—to my inexpressible surprise—I find that—that———"

"That she has refused me," exclaimed the Earl;—"refused me without assigning any reason."

"I cannot think how it is to be accounted for," continued the baronet; "but Georgiana has invariably manifested a repugnance to the topic of marriage whenever I have urged it upon her. Of course, as her uncle—and double her age, my lord—I can give her advice just as if I were her father; and for some years past I have recommended her to consider well the propriety of obtaining a legal protector, her natural ones being no more. But all my reasoning has proved unavailing; and if your lordship cannot persuade my obstinate niece," he added, with a sly laugh, "then no one must hope to do so."

"I will frankly admit to you," said the Earl, "that my happiness depends on your niece's decision. I am no hero of romance—but I entertain so sincere, so ardent an affection for Lady Hatfield, that my life will be embittered by a perseverance in her refusal to allow me to call her mine."

"She will not persist in this folly—she cannot," exclaimed Sir Ralph emphatically. "It is a mere whim—a caprice; and indeed I have often thought that her disposition has somewhat altered ever since a dreadful fright which she sustained six or seven years ago———"

"Ah!" said the Earl. "What was the nature of the incident to which you allude?"

"I must tell your lordship," returned the baronet,—"unless, indeed, you are already acquainted with the fact,—that Hampshire was for three or four years—between 1818 and 1821 or 22—the scene of the exploits of a celebrated highwayman———"

"You allude to the Black Mask, no doubt?" interrupted Lord Ellingham interrogatively.

"Precisely so," answered the baronet. "The Black Mask—as the villain was called—was one of the most desperate robbers that ever infested the highways. He would stop the stage-coach as readily as he would a single traveller on horseback; and such was his valour as well as his extraordinary skill, that he defied all attempts to capture him."

"I remember reading his exploits at the time," said the Earl. "The most conflicting accounts were reported concerning him. Some declared he was an old man—others that he was quite young; but I believe that all agreed in ascribing to him a more forbearing disposition than usually characterises persons of his class."

"I will even go so far as to assert that there was something chivalrous in his character," exclaimed the baronet. "He invariably assured travellers whom he stopped, that he should be grieved to harm them; but that if they provoked him by resistance, he would not hesitate to punish them severely. If he fell in with a carriage containing ladies, he never attempted to rifle them of their jewellery and trinkets, but contented himself with simply demanding their purses. Those being surrendered, he would gallop away. I never heard of any unnecessary violence—nor of any act of cruelty which he perpetrated. Neither did I ever meet a soul who could give anything like a credible description of his countenance. The invariable black mask which concealed his features, and from the use of which he derived his name, seemed a portion of himself; and although gossips did now and then tell strange tales about his appearance, they were all too contradictory to allow a scintillation of the real truth to transpire."

"But in what manner was the Black Mask connected with the fright which Lady Hatfield experienced some years ago?" asked the Earl impatiently.

"You are perhaps aware that the late Earl and Countess of Mauleverer possessed a country-seat between Winchester and New Alresford—not very far distant from Walsingham Manor, my own rural abode," said Sir Ralph. "It must have been seven years ago that Georgiana, who always preferred Mauleverer Lodge to the town-mansion—even during the London season,—was staying alone there—I mean so far alone, that at the time there were no other persons at the Lodge save the servants. Well, one night the Black Mask broke into the place—the only time he was ever known to commit a burglary—and such was the fright which Georgiana experienced, that for weeks and months afterwards her family frequently trembled lest her reason had received a shock."

"It must indeed have been an alarming situation for a young lady—alone, as it were, in a spacious and secluded country dwelling——"

"And Georgiana was but eighteen, I think, at the time," interrupted Sir Ralph Walsingham. "She certainly experienced a dreadful fright; and although, thank God! her reason is as unimpaired as ever it was, still we cannot say that the sudden shock might not have produced some strange effect which may probably account for the otherwise inexplicable whimsicality—for I can denominate it nothing else——"

"Oh! I thank you, my dear Sir Ralph, for this explanation," cried Lord Ellingham, in the joy of reviving hope. "Yes—I see it all: your niece experienced a shock which has produced a species of idiosyncratic effect upon her; but the constant kindness—the unwearied attention of one who loves her, and whom she loves in return, will restore her mind to its vigorous and healthy condition. To-morrow will I visit her again:—Oh! how unkind—how ungenerous of me to remain away so long!"

There was a pause, during which Arthur gave way to all the bright allurements of the pleasing vision which he now conjured up to his imagination.

At length Sir Ralph Walsingham felt the silence to be irksome and awkward; and he ventured to break it.

"We were talking just now, my lord," he said, "of the famous highwayman known as the Black Mask. He disappeared from Hampshire very suddenly; and the old women declared that his time being out, he was carried off by the Devil, who had protected him against all the devices and snares imagined by the authorities to capture him."

"And perhaps the highwayman who robbed Lady Hatfield the other day," observed Lord Ellingham, "may be the very one who rendered himself so notorious in Hampshire a few years ago?"

"Your lordship judges by the fact that the scoundrel who stopped my niece near Hounslow wore a black mask," said the baronet; "but the generality of robbers on the high roads adopt that mode of disguise. Thank heaven! public depredators of the kind are becoming very scarce in this country!"

In such conversation did the nobleman and the baronet while away the time until eleven o'clock, when the latter took his leave, and Arthur retired to his chamber to dream of the charming but incomprehensible lady who had obtained such empire over his soul.

CHAPTER XVII.
THE MYSTERIOUS LETTER.—JACOB.

On the same evening that the interview between the Earl of Ellingham and Sir Ralph Walsingham took place, as narrated in the preceding chapter, the following scene occurred at the house of Toby Bunce in Earl Street, Seven Dials.

Mrs. Bunce was alone in the dirty, dingy back room, which could not be said to be lighted, but merely redeemed from total darkness, by the solitary candle that stood on the table; and she was busily employed in lighting the fire.

Having succeeded in this object, she placed the kettle on the grate to boil; and then took from a cupboard a bottle half full of gin, two common blue mugs, a broken basin containing a little lump sugar, and a couple of pewter spoons, all of which articles she ranged around the brass candle-stick with a view to make as good a show as possible.

Then she seated herself by the fire, and consulted an old silver-watch which she drew from her pocket, and which was in reality the property of her husband, whom she would not however trust with it under any consideration.

"Eight o'clock," she said aloud in a musing tone. "He can't be very long now; and Toby won't be in till ten. If he is, I'll send him out again—with a flea in his ear," she added, chuckling at the idea of her supremacy in her own domestic sphere. "I wonder who'd be ruled by a feller like Toby? Not me, indeed! I should think not. But I wish old Bones would come," she continued, with a glance of satisfaction at the table. "Every thing does look so comfortable; and I've put 'em in such a manner that the light falls on 'em all at once. Toby never would have thought of that. It's only us women that know what tidiness is."

Tidiness indeed! The windows were dingy with dirt—the walls were begrimed with smoke and dust—the floor was as black as the deck of a collier—and the cob-webs hung like filthy rags in the corners of the room.

Scarcely had Mrs. Bunce completed her survey of the place and its arrangements, when a low knock summoned her to the street-door; and in a few moments she returned, accompanied by Old Death.

The hideous man was very cold; and, seating himself as near the fire as possible without actually burning his knees, he said, "Now, Betsy my dear, brew me a mug of something cheering as soon as possible."

"That I will, Ben," returned Mrs. Bunce, in as pleasant a tone of voice as she could assume; then she bustled about with great alacrity until the steaming liquid was duly compounded, and Old Death had expressed his satisfaction by means of a short grunt after the first sip.

"Is it nice, Ben?" asked Mrs. Bunce endearingly.

"Very. Now make yourself some, Betsy; and sit down quietly, for we must have a talk about you know what. Business has prevented me from attending to it before; but now that I have got an evening to spare—and Toby is out of the way——"

"Oh! you know very well, Ben," interrupted Mrs. Bunce, "that I can always manage *him* as I like. He's such a fool, and so completely under my thumb, that I shouldn't even mind telling him I'd been your mistress for years before I was his wife."

"Keep your tongue quiet, Betsy—keep your tongue quiet," exclaimed Old Death, with a hyena-like growl. "Never provoke irritation unnecessarily. But let's to business. Jacob is out on the watch after Tom Rain; and I told the lad to come up here before ten. And now about this letter," he continued drawing one from his pocket-book: "it proves, you see, that the child is well-born—and if the address had only been written on the outside, we might make a good thing of the matter."

"Just so," observed Mrs. Bunce. "When Mr. Rainford called this afternoon he was so particular in asking me whether I had found any papers about the woman's clothes; but I declared I had not—and he was quite satisfied. He paid me, too, very handsome for the funeral expenses and all my trouble. If he was to know about that letter, Ben?"

"How can he know?" exclaimed Old Death impatiently. "Now what I think," he continued in a milder tone, "is just this:—the woman Watts was reduced to such a desperate state of poverty, that she wrote this letter to the mother of the boy Charles——"

"Why, of course," interrupted Mrs. Bunce. "She says as much *in* the letter."

"Will you listen to me?" growled Old Death angrily: "you don't know what I was going to observe."

"Don't be cross, Ben: I won't stop you again," said the woman in a coaxing tone.

"Mind you don't, then," ejaculated Bones, allowing himself to be pacified. "Well, this Sarah Watts wrote that letter, as I was saying, with the intention of sending it, no doubt, either by post or by an acquaintance to the lady in London. I think that is plain enough. Then, when she had finished writing it, something evidently made her change her mind, and resolve on coming up to London herself. This is also plain; because, if it wasn't so, why did the letter never go—and why did she come to London?"

"How well you do talk, Ben," said Mrs. Bunce.

"I talk to the point, I hope," observed Old Death. "Now how stands the matter? Here is a very important letter, wanting two main things to render it completely valuable to us. The first thing it wants is the name of the place from which it would have been dated, had it ever been sent: and the second thing it wants is the name of the lady to whom it was intended to be sent. In a word, it wants the address of the writer and the address of the lady to whom it was written, and who is the mother of that boy Charles."

"What good would it do you to have the address of the writer, since she is dead and buried?" asked Mrs. Bunce.

"Because I could then visit the place where the woman was when she wrote this letter," replied Old Death. "I could make inquiries concerning the late Sarah Watts; and I know too well how to put two and two together not to arrive at some certainty in the long run."

"To be sure!" ejaculated Mrs. Bunce. "How clever you are, dear Ben."

"I don't know about being clever, Betsy my dear," returned the hideous old man; "but *this* I do think—that I'm rather wide awake."

And then he chuckled so heartily, while his toothless jaws wagged up and down so horribly, that he appeared to be a corpse under a process of galvanism; for if a dead body could be made to utter sounds, they would not be more sepulchral than those which now emanated from the throat of Old Death.

Mrs. Bunce considered it to be her duty to chuckle also; and her querulous tones seemed a humble accompaniment to the guttural sounds which we have attempted to describe.

At length the chuckling ceased on both sides; and Mrs. Bunce replenished the mugs with hot gin-and-water.

"But even as it is," suddenly observed Old Death, after a hasty glance at the letter, which he now slowly folded up and returned to his greasy pocket-book,—"but even as it is, we may still make something of the business. If we could only find a clue to the mother of that boy, it would be a fortune in itself. I tell you what we must do!" he exclaimed emphatically.

"What?" asked his ancient mistress.

"Get that boy into our own keeping," replied Bones, with a sly smile; "and then we can pump him of all he may happen to know concerning the deceased Sarah Watts."

"Excellent!" cried Mrs. Bunce, clapping her hands, "But how will you find out where Mr. Rainford lives?"

"Jacob is after him. For several reasons I want to know as much as I can about that strange fellow. The very day that I made the bargain with him about smashing all the flimsies he might bring me, he wrote an extraordinary note to the very lady whom he had robbed the night before; and he made her go into the witness-box at Bow Street and deliberately perjure herself to serve him. Then he starts off to Pall Mall, when the Jewess prisoner was brought up, and delivers a note at the house of Lord Ellingham; and Lord Ellingham comes straight down to the Police-Court and swears black and blue that the Jewess is innocent."

"And was she?" asked Mrs. Bunce.

"That's more than I can say," answered Old Death; "seeing that I know nothing at all about the affair. Well, these two strange things, showing an extraordinary influence on the part of Rainford over Lady Hatfield on the one side, and Lord Ellingham on the other, have quite puzzled me. He is an enigma that I must solve."

"Does not Tullock know all about him?" demanded Mrs. Bunce.

"Tullock knows only that Tom took to the road some years ago, down in the country; for Tullock then did at Winchester just what I do now in London: only," added Bones, with a knowing glance and a compressed smile of the lips which puckered up his hideous face into one unvaried mass of wrinkles,—"only, my dear Betsy, Tullock never had the connexion which I have. He had no correspondent at Hamburg to whom he could send over the notes that are stolen, and stopped at the Bank: he had no well-contrived places to receive goods—places," continued Old Death, emphatically, "which have baffled the police for thirty years, and will baffle them as long again——if I live."

"And why should you not, dear?" said Mrs. Bunce coaxingly.

"Because I cannot expect it," replied Old Death abruptly. "However—you know what I have done for myself, and in what way I manage my business. You only, Betsy dear, are acquainted with my secrets."

"And you are as safe with me as if I was deaf and dumb and unable to write," rejoined the woman.

"I know that—I know that," said Bones, hastily: then in a slower tone he added significantly, "Because if there was a smash, we should all go together, Betsy."

"Lor! Ben—don't talk in that way—don't!" cried Mrs. Bunce. "Let's see—what were we saying? Oh! you was telling me about Mr. Rainford."

"I was only observing that Tullock lost sight of him for some years, and knows nothing that happened to him till he turned up in London the other day."

"I don't suppose Rainford is his proper name?" observed the woman inquiringly.

"Tullock never told me," answered Bones; "and as he and Tom are thick together, I can't ask him too many questions. The fact is, Rainford will prove the most useful man I ever had in my service, as I may call it; and I must not risk offending him. See how neatly he did that job the other night—how beautifully he came off with the two thousand!"

"And it never got into the papers either," observed Mrs. Bunce.

"Not a bit of it!" cried Old Death, with another chuckle. "Tom calculated all that beforehand—or he never would have been fool enough to go so quietly and introduce himself as Captain Sparks to the very people he meant to rob. Ha! ha! clear-headed fellow, that Tom! He first ascertained the precise character of all the parties concerned; and he knew that he might plunder them with impunity. Sir Christopher and Mr. Torrens were sure not to talk about it, for fear of the whole disgraceful story about the purchase of the daughter coming out. Frank Curtis is a cowardly boaster, who would not like it to be known that a single highwayman had mastered him;—the lawyer was sure to speak or hold his tongue, just as his rich client Sir Christopher ordered him;—and Jeffreys was safe. Tom weighed all this, and boldly introduced himself to them without the least attempt at disguising his person. Oh! It was capitally managed—and Tom is a valuable fellow!"

Mr. Bones seldom spoke so long at a time; but he was carried away by his enthusiastic admiration of Tom Rainford; and he accordingly talked himself so effectually out of breath, that a fit of coughing supervened, and he was nearly choked.

Betsy, however, slapped him on the back; and the old man gradually recovered himself—but not before his fierce-looking eyes were dimmed with the scalding rheum which overflowed them.

"You are afraid to offend Mr. Rainford," said Mrs. Bunce, after a pause, "and yet you think of taking away that boy from him."

"Pshaw!" cried Old Death, whom the coughing-fit had put into a bad humour; "do you think I should steal the child and then tell him of it?"

"Of course not," said Mrs. Bunce. "I am a fool."

"You are indeed, Betsy," rejoined Old Death. "And yet you are the *least* foolish woman I ever knew; or else I never should have made you my confidant as I have done. And now I tell you, Betsy, that I have many great schemes in my head; and I shall require your assistance. In the first place we must get hold of that boy Charley somehow or another—provided we can find out Rainford's abode, which I think is scarcely doubtful. Then we must act upon all the information we can glean from the child, and find out who his mother really is. In the next place I must ascertain all I can concerning this Jewess—this Esther de Medina. If she *did* steal the diamonds, she is the cleverest female thief in all England—for she has managed to get clean off with her prize; and such a woman would be invaluable to me. Besides, if she pursues the same game—supposing that she has really begun it—she will want my assistance to dispose of the property; and she will gladly listen to my overtures. Such a beautiful creature as I understand she is, could insinuate herself anywhere, and rob the best houses in London. Ah! Betsy, I must not sleep over these matters. But, hark! That's Jacob's knock!"

"Poor Jacob!" cried Mrs. Bunce, with a subdued sigh: "If he only knew——"

"Silence, woman!" cried Bones in a furious manner. "Go to the door."

Mrs. Bunce was frightened by the vehemence of Old Death's manner, and hastened to obey his command.

In a few moments she returned, followed by Jacob, who seemed sinking with fatigue.

"Well," said Old Death impatiently, "what news?"

"Give me something to eat first—for I am famished," cried Jacob, throwing himself upon a chair.

"Not a morsel, till you tell me what you have done!" exclaimed Bones angrily, as he rose from his seat.

"I will *not* speak a word on that subject before I have had food," said Jacob, his bright eyes flashing fire, and a hectic glow appearing on his pale cheeks. "You make me wander about all day on your business, without a penny in my pocket to buy a piece of bread——"

"Because he who has to earn his supper works all the better for it," ejaculated Bones, his lips quivering with rage. "Now speak, Jacob—or, by God——"

"You sha'n't bully me in this way," cried the lad, bursting into tears, and yet with all the evidences of intense passion working upon his countenance. "By what right do you treat me like a dog? You fling me a bone when you choose—and you think I will lick your hand like a spaniel. I tell you once for all, I won't put up with it any longer."

"You won't, Jacob—you won't, eh?" said Old Death, in a very low tone; but at the same time he dealt the lad such a sudden and severe box on the ears, that the poor youth was hurled heavily from his chair on the hard floor.

But, springing up in a moment, he flew like a tiger at Old Death, whose small amount of strength was exhausted by the effort which it had required on the part of so aged a man to deal such a blow; and Jacob would have mastered him in another instant, had not Mrs. Bunce interfered.

With a loud scream, she precipitated herself on the lad; and, seizing him in her bony arms, forced him back into his seat, saying—"There, Jacob—for God's sake be quiet; and I'll give you something nice directly."

The lad made no reply, but darted a look of vindictive hate towards Old Death, who had sunk back exhausted on the chair which he had ere now quitted.

Then Mrs. Bunce hastened to the cupboard and produced a loaf and the remains of a cold joint, which she placed before Jacob, who, enraged as he was at the treatment he had just received, could not help wondering within himself how Toby's wife had become so liberal as to place the viands without reserve at his disposal.

The woman seemed to penetrate his thoughts; for she said, "Eat as much as you like, Jacob: don't be afraid. I sha'n't mind if you eat it—*nearly* all."

The lad smothered his resentment so far as not to permit it to interfere with his appetite; and he devoured his supper without once glancing towards Old Death, who on his side appeared unable to recover from the surprise into which Jacob's unusually rebellious conduct had thrown him.

A profound silence reigned in that room for several minutes.

At length Jacob made an end of his meal; and then Old Death spoke.

"And so this is the reward," he said, "which I receive for all my kindness towards you. Without me, what would have become of you? Deserted by your parents—a foundling—a miserable infant, abandoned to the tender mercies of the workhouse authorities——"

"Would that I had died *then*!" interrupted Jacob emphatically. "You make a boast of having taken care of me—of having reared me—such a rearing as it has been!—and yet I wish you had left me to perish on the workhouse steps where, you say, you found me. I have tried to be obedient to you—I have done all I could to please you; but do you ever utter a kind word to me? Even when I succeed in doing your bidding, what reward is mine? Blows—reproaches—sorry meals, few and far between———"

"Well, well, Jacob—I think I have not *quite* done my duty towards you," said Old Death, who in reality could have murdered the boy at that moment, but who was compelled to adopt a conciliatory tone and manner in order to retain so useful an auxiliary in his service: "but let us say no more about it—and things shall be better in future. Instead of having no regular place of abode and sleeping in lodging-houses, you shall have half-a-crown a week, Jacob, to hire a little room for yourself."

"There—Jacob; only think of that!" cried Mrs. Bunce, in a tone expressive of high approval of this munificence on the part of Old Death.

"And you shall have threepence every day for your dinner, Jacob," continued Bones, "in addition to your breakfast and tea which you always get here."

"But will you keep to that arrangement?" asked the lad, considerably softened by this prospect, which was far brighter than any he had as yet beheld.

"I will—I will," replied Old Death. "And if you have brought me any good news to-night, I'll give you ten shillings—ten whole shillings, Jacob—to buy some nice clothes and shoes in Monmouth Street."

"Put down the money!" cried Jacob, now completely won back to the interests of the crafty old villain who knew so well how to curb the evanescent spirit of his miserable slave.

"I will," said Bones; and he laid four half-crowns upon the table.

"That's right!" exclaimed Jacob, his eyes glistening with delight at the prospect of fingering such a treasure: then he glanced rapidly at his ragged apparel, with a smile on his lip that expressed his conviction of shortly being able to procure a more comfortable attire.

"Go on," said Old Death. "What have you done?"

"When Mr. Rainford went away from here this afternoon," returned Jacob, "I followed him at a good distance—but not so far off that I stood a chance of losing sight of him. Well, first he went to Tullock's; and there he stayed some little time. Then he walked into an eating-house in the Strand; and at that place he stopped about a couple of hours—while I walked up and down on the other side of the way. At length he came out, with another gentleman———"

"What was he like?" demanded Old Death.

"A fine—tall—handsome man—with dark hair and eyes," responded Jacob.

"I don't know him," said Bones. "Never mind;—go on with your story, and let it be as short as possible."

"Well," continued the lad, "this gentleman and Mr. Rainford walked together as far as Bridge Street, Blackfriars: and there they parted. The gentleman went into a house in Bridge Street—and Mr. Rainford crossed the bridge. It was now getting dusk; and I was obliged to keep closer to him. But he seldom turned round—and when he did, I took good care he should not see me. So, on he went till he came to the Elephant and Castle; and close by there he suddenly met a lady with a dark veil over her face, and holding a little boy by the hand. They stood and talked for a moment just opposite a shop-window which was lighted up; and I saw well enough that the little boy was the very same that was brought here the other night by the woman who was buried so quietly this morning."

"Then we know that the boy is still in *his* care!" ejaculated Old Death, exchanging significant glances with Mrs. Bunce. "Go on, Jacob. I can see that the ten shillings will be yours."

"Yes—that they will!" cried the lad, apparently having forgotten the blow which he had recently received. "Well, so I knew the boy at once, though he is much changed—nicely dressed, and already quite plump and rosy. Mr. Rainford patted him on the face, and the boy laughed and seemed so happy! Then Mr. Rainford gave the lady his arm; and they walked a little way down the road till they came to a jeweller's shop, where they stopped to look in at the window. Mr. Rainford pointed out some article to the lady; and they went into the shop, the lady still holding the little boy carefully by the hand. The moment they were safe inside, I watched them through the window; and I saw Mr. Rainford looking at a pair of ear-rings. In a few moments he handed them to the lady. She lifted up her veil to examine them; and I knew her again in a moment. But who do you think she was?"

Old Death shook his head.

"No—I don't think you ever could guess," cried Jacob.

"Then who is she?" demanded Bones impatiently.

"The Jewess who was accused of stealing the diamonds at Bow Street the other day," answered Jacob.

"Esther de Medina!" cried Old Death. "The very person we were speaking about just now!" he added, exchanging another glance with Mrs. Bunce. "But go on, Jacob—go on."

"I was rather surprised at that discovery," continued Jacob; "because I thought it so odd that both Mr. Rainford and the Jewess should have been had up on the very same day at Bow Street, on different charges, and that both should have got off."

"It is strange—very strange!" murmured Old Death. "But did you find out Tom Rain's address? That is the chief thing *I* want to know."

"Don't be in a hurry," said Jacob: "let me tell my story in my own way. Well, so the Jewess seemed to like the ear-rings; and she gave Mr. Rainford such a sweet smile—Oh! what a sweet smile—as he pulled out his purse and paid for them. I don't know how it was—but it really went to my heart to think that such a beautiful lady should——"

"Never mind what you felt, Jacob," interrupted Old Death abruptly. "Make an end of your story."

"Well, the ear-rings were put into a nice little box, with some wool to keep them from rubbing; and the lady drew down her veil again, before she left the shop."

"Now, Jacob—tell me the truth," said Old Death: "did either Tom Rain or the Jewess take any little thing—at a moment, you know, when the jeweller's back was turned——"

"No—not a thing!" cried the lad emphatically. "I can swear they did not."

"You are quite sure?" observed Old Death.

"As sure as that I'm here; for I never took my eyes off them from the moment they entered the shop till they came out," responded Jacob. "And when they did come out, I was very near being seen by Mr. Rainford—for I was then in front of them; and I had only just time to slip into the shade of the wall between the windows of the jeweller's shop and the next one. Then I heard Mr. Rainford say to the Jewess, '*Now this little present is in part a recompense for the diamonds which I made you give up.*'—The lady said something in a low tone; but I could not catch it—and they went on, the little boy with them."

"Then she did steal the diamonds!" exclaimed Old Death. "But how could such a man as Lord Ellingham feel any interest in her? and how could he have been induced to perjure himself to save her?"

"Isn't it strange?" said Mrs. Bunce.

"I'm all in the dark at present," returned Bones. "But go on, Jacob."

"They walked on till they came to a street on the left-hand side; and into that street they turned. I never lost sight of them once; but two or three times I thought Mr. Rainford would have twigged me. He did not, though; and I at last traced them to a house in Lock's Fields———"

"Lock's Fields—eh?" cried Old Death. "Can they possibly be living there?"

"They are," returned Jacob; "and I can take you over to the very street and the very house any time you like."

"Well done!" ejaculated Bones, indulging in another long and hearty chuckle, which was echoed by Mrs. Bunce; and then they both rubbed their hands gleefully to think that they had made such important discoveries through the medium of Jacob.

Fresh supplies of grog were brewed; and the lad was not only permitted to consign the four half-crowns to his pocket, but was also regaled with an occasional sip of gin-and-water from Mrs. Bunce's own mug.

The return of Toby at ten o'clock prevented any further conversation on the interesting topics which had previously been discussed; for Mrs. Bunce's husband was not admitted to the entire confidence of his spouse and of Mr. Benjamin Bones, alias Old Death.

CHAPTER XVIII.
THE LOVERS.

It was noon; and Lady Hatfield sate alone in her drawing-room.

She felt herself so much better, and Dr. Lascelles had that morning so earnestly recommended her to quit the bed-chamber and seek the change of scene which even a removal from one apartment to another ever affords—especially to an invalid, that she had not hesitated to follow her own inclination and his advice, both of which were fully of accord.

Her uncle, Sir Ralph Walsingham, was announced shortly after Lady Hatfield had descended to the drawing-room.

"My dear Georgiana," exclaimed the honest and kind-hearted man, as he entered the apartment, "I am delighted to find you here. But why are you alone? Where is Miss Mordaunt?"

"In the parlour below," replied Lady Hatfield. "Julia has a visitor," she added with an arch smile, in spite of the melancholy which still oppressed her mind.

"A visitor!" ejaculated the baronet. "Sir Christopher Blunt, I'll be bound!"

"You have guessed rightly, my dear uncle. But how———"

"How should I know anything about it?" interrupted Sir Ralph. "Surely, Georgiana, you must be too well acquainted with your friend's disposition to suppose that she could have possibly held her tongue relative to the presumed attachment of the worthy knight? Why, all the time she was at the Manor, did she not absolutely hurl Sir Christopher's name at every soul whom she could engage in conversation? Was it not 'Sir Christopher had told her *this* last season,' and 'Sir Christopher had assured her *that?*' and did she not go much farther than merely to hint that Sir Christopher was dying for her? For my part, I was sick of Sir Christopher's name. But now I suppose he has come to lay his title and fortune at her feet, as the newspapers say: or else what could possibly signify a visit at so unseemly an hour as mid-day?"

"It will be an excellent match for Julia," remarked Georgiana, by way of saying something. "She is not one of those who believe that marriage should be only a convention of hearts, and not of worldly interests."

And as Lady Hatfield made this observation, a profound sigh escaped her bosom.

"What means that sigh, niece?" demanded the baronet. "Are you envious of Miss Mordaunt's worldly-mindedness? I am convinced you are not. By the way, I met Lord Ellingham last evening——"

"His lordship left his card," said Lady Hatfield, casting down her eyes, while her bosom again rose and fell with a long and painfully-drawn sigh.

"Georgiana," exclaimed Sir Ralph, seating himself by the side of his niece, and taking her hand in a kind manner, "your conduct towards that young Earl is not just—is not generous—is not rational."

"Oh! my dear uncle," cried Lady Hatfield, starting wildly, "for heaven's sake renew not the discussion of last evening!"

"Pardon me, my dear niece," said Sir Ralph, affectionately but firmly, "if I give you pain by referring to the topic of that discussion. I am your nearest relation—I am a widower, and childless: you know that my property is extensive—and my fond hope has ever been, since the death of your aunt Lady Walsingham, that you would marry, and that your children should inherit those estates and that fortune which I can bequeath to whomsoever I will. But you refuse to accept the hand of a man who is every way worthy of you—you reject an alliance which, in every human probability, would be blessed by a progeny to whom my wealth and yours may alike descend. Nay—interrupt me not, dear Georgiana: I am old enough to be your father—I love you as if you were my daughter—and I have your welfare deeply at heart. To speak frankly, I had a long conversation last evening with Lord Ellingham——"

Georgiana's attention was for an instant broken by a wild start of despair.

"My God! what signifies this grief, Georgiana?" asked her uncle. "I thought to give you pleasure by the assurance I was about to disclose,—an assurance which conveys to you the unalterable fidelity of the Earl's affection—his readiness to bury in oblivion any little whim or caprice which induced you to subject him to the humiliation of a refusal the other day—his determination to study your happiness so entirely that any cloud of melancholy, or unknown and unfounded presentiment—any morbid feeling, in a word—which hangs upon your mind, shall speedily be dissipated. Such are his generous intentions—such are his tender aspirations, Georgiana:—can you reject his suit again?"

This appeal, made to the unhappy lady by an individual who, though only related to her by the fact of having married her mother's sister, had still ever manifested towards her the sincerest affection and friendship,—this appeal, we say, came with such overwhelming force upon the mind of Georgiana, that she knew not how to answer it.

"You consent, Georgiana—you consent!" exclaimed Sir Ralph, entirely mistaking the cause of her profound silence; and, starting up, he rushed from the room before her lips could give utterance to a syllable that might have the effect of stopping him.

"Merciful God! what does he mean to do?" cried Georgiana, clasping her hands together, while a species of spasmodic shuddering came over her entire frame.

Hasty footsteps approached the door.

Wildly did the unhappy lady glance around her—with the terrified and imploring air of one whom the officers of justice were about to fetch to the scaffold.

The door flew open: Georgiana averted her eyes;—but at the next moment her hands were grasped in those of another, and warm lips were pressed upon each fair hand of hers—and for a single instant there streamed through her whole being the electric warmth of ineffable delight, hope, and love!

She sank back upon the sofa whence she had risen: her eyes, which for a moment had seemed to lose the faculty of sight, were involuntarily turned toward the Earl of Ellingham, who was kneeling at her feet;—and simultaneously her uncle's voice, sounding like the knell of destiny upon her ears, exclaimed, "I told you she had consented, Ellingham: be happy—for Georgiana is yours!"

The door of the apartment was then closed hastily; and Lady Hatfield now knew that she was alone with her lover.

"Oh! my dearest Georgiana," murmured Arthur, still pressing the lady's hands in his own, "how happy have you at length made me—and how can I ever express the joy which animates me at this moment! My heart dances wildly with joy and gratitude; and all the anguish which I have lately experienced, is forgotten—as if it never had been. Indeed, my beloved one, it is for me to implore your pardon—for I should not have remained absent from you so long. But now that we are re-united, and your indisposition has passed,——now that your mind has recovered its naturally healthy tone,—there is nothing, my Georgiana, to interrupt the free course of our felicity."

Lady Hatfield was seized with a certain involuntary horror, which completely stupefied her, as these impassioned exclamations fell upon her ears: and vainly—vainly did she endeavour to reply.

Arthur rose, and seating himself by her side on the sofa, passed his arm around her slender waist, and drawing her gently towards him, said in a subdued tone, "From this day forth, beloved Georgiana, you must have no secrets unknown to me. Confide in me as your best and sincerest friend—and the tenderest sympathy shall flow from my heart to solace you in those moments of melancholy which no mortal, however prosperously placed, can hope altogether to avoid. In the society of a husband who will never cease to love you—whose constant care shall be to ensure your felicity—and whose unwearied attention shall be devoted to the promotion of your happiness, your life will be spent in an atmosphere into which a cloud shall seldom intrude. Oh! what pictures of perfect bliss present themselves to my imagination!"

The enamoured nobleman pressed the fair one closer to his breast, as he thus poured forth his soul with all the ardour of his sincere and devoted love; and she—in spite of herself,—bewildered, stupefied, intoxicated as she was by the suddenness with which this scene had been brought about,—she gazed with mingled rapture and surprise upon that handsome countenance which the glow of inward passion and ineffable joy now rendered still more expressive.

She felt as if the hysterical shriek, which for some moments past had threatened to burst from her lips, were subdued—stifled by some unknown power, whose influence was strangely sweet and consoling:—her soul almost sickened in the bliss of that love by which she was surrounded, and to which her woman's heart could not do otherwise than respond.

Then, again, she felt as if she must start from his arms—reject his love—dash down that chalice of honied happiness from which they both were drinking deep draughts—and proclaim to him that it was all a hideous mistake—that she had never consented to receive him as her husband—that her uncle had committed a fearful error—and that they must separate, never, never again to meet!

But at the very moment when she was about to do all this, Arthur drew her nearer to him;—his breath, sweet as that of flowers, fell on her burning cheek—his hand pressed hers—she found herself linked to him in heart by a spell which no mortal courage could at such a moment have broken—then she caught herself looking into his fine eyes, and reading the thrilling language of love that was written there—and in another moment their lips met in one long and delicious kiss.

"Sweet Georgiana, I adore you!" murmured Arthur, his glances speaking more eloquently than his words. "And now there breathes not a happier man on the earth's wide surface than I. Say, Georgiana—say, does not that happiness which I myself experience impart pleasure to you? Could you now do aught to torture my soul again with the agony of suspense—with the despair of baffled hope? Believe me, my dearest angel, that if destiny, in its malignant spite, were now to separate us—if to-morrow I came and found you gone, or here but cold and altered,—in a word, if any impediment were to arise to the accomplishment of our union, I should not survive the blow! As a distracted maniac should I be borne to a mad-cell—or, if my reason were left me, my grave would be stained with a suicide's blood!"

Georgiana was appalled by this terrible announcement; and in the agony of feeling which it excited within her, she cast a glance of profound tenderness upon the Earl, unwittingly pressing his hand at the same time.

"Oh! now I know that you entertain the same sentiments as myself," he cried, mistaking those convulsive movements on her part for the tender evidences of love: "now I know that your heart beats in unison with mine. Oh! thrice happy day—the happiest that I ever yet have known. And happier does it seem, too, because it has dissipated so much previous anxiety—healed so much acutely-felt pain. Yes—dearest Georgiana—I am almost glad that you rejected my suit the other day; for the wretched feelings of the interval have, by contrast, made the present moment indescribably sweet. And shall I tell you, my beloved one, that I am now acquainted with the nature of that secret——"

"That secret!" cried Georgiana, with a cold shudder—which Ellingham did not perceive, for at the moment he pressed her fondly towards him.

"Yes, dearest," he continued: "I know all the power which that secret influence must occasionally have over you: and, believe me when I declare that—instead of being any longer annoyed at the fact of that circumstance having induced you to refuse my hand the other day—I deeply sympathise with you! And if I now allude to that event—that incident which years ago, at your late father's country-residence in Hampshire——"

A short convulsive sob burst from Georgiana's breast.

"Oh! pardon me—pardon me, beloved one!" cried the Earl, again imprinting a kiss upon her lips: "I know that I was wrong to allude to an event which you can never entirely forget. But if I mentioned it ere now—it was for the first and the last time—and merely to convince you that he, whom you will soon receive as your husband, is aware of that secret influence which holds a sway over your mind; and that he implores you to forget it—to abandon yourself only to the thoughts of that happiness which our love and our brilliant social position must ensure us. And now, my dearest Georgiana, no more on that head: never again let the topic enter into our discourse—never let us allude to it, even by a single syllable!"

"Oh! generous—excellent-hearted—noble-minded man," exclaimed Georgiana; "and is your love for me indeed so strong as this?"

"Can you doubt it, dearest?" said the Earl. "If so—tell me how I can prove its sincerity?"

"Have you not given me a proof the most convincing that man can give to woman?" asked Lady Hatfield, concealing her blushing countenance on Arthur's breast. "Are you not content to receive as your wife one who——"

"No more—no more!" exclaimed the Earl, tenderly hushing her words with kisses. "Have we not agreed never again to allude to that topic?"

"But one word, Arthur," said Georgiana: "only one word! Who could have acquainted you——"

"Your uncle, dearest," answered Lord Ellingham;—"that excellent man who has been mainly instrumental in procuring me the happiness which I now enjoy!"

"My uncle!" murmured Lady Hatfield, her soul subdued with astonishment of the most overwhelming nature.

But the Earl's ears caught not the repetition of his answer; neither did he notice the effect which it produced upon Georgiana;—for her head was pillowed upon his breast—his hand clasped hers—her fine form leant against him—and he had no thought save of the pure but intoxicating happiness which he now enjoyed.

Oh, Love! thou art the sweetest charm of life—the dearest solace in this sphere of trial and vicissitude—the sentiment that, shining on us as a star, adds the most refulgent brightness to our lot. Ambition never imparted consolation to the breaking spirit, and places no curb on the wild passions and insatiable vices which too often dominate the human heart. Wealth makes its possessor envied, but also encourages the daring of the robber, or sharpens the knife of the murderer who seeks to grasp it. Honours engender hatred in the breasts of those who once were friends. Pleasure is bought by gold, and must be paid for over and over again by the health. Genius is a consuming fire: like the spur to the gallant steed, it urges its votary on, but draws the life-blood in the act. Glory is the eruption of the volcano—bright, majestic, and resplendent to gaze upon—yet bearing death in its halo. But thou, O Love! art the star which beams brighter as the gloom of this cold and selfish world becomes darker:—thou art the sunshine of the soul—teaching man to emulate the gentleness, the resignation, and the holy devotion of woman—and raising woman but one remove from the nature of angels!

CHAPTER XIX.
MR. FRANK CURTIS'S PLEASANT ADVENTURE.

About half an hour previous to the visit of Lord Ellingham, Mr. Frank Curtis was lounging along Piccadilly with a swell-mob kind of ease and a Bagnigge Wells' independence, when a young female, of good figure and pretty face, attracted his notice.

As he was proceeding in one way, and she in another, they passed each other; and, Mr. Curtis having nothing to do, it struck him that he would endeavour to scrape an acquaintance with the young person alluded to.

He accordingly turned round—hesitated for a moment how to devise an excuse for addressing himself to her—and then, drawing forth his own white cambric pocket-handkerchief, hurried after the object of his interest.

"I beg your pardon, Miss," he said, tapping her gently upon the shoulder; "but I think you dropped this handkerchief."

The young female immediately replied in the negative; but a smile played upon her lips, and her blue eyes assumed an arch expression, implying that she fully saw through the young man's trick, which was indeed transparent enough.

"I really thought it was yours, Miss," exclaimed Curtis, by no means abashed. "But if it isn't—why, I must keep it till I find the owner—that's all."

"I rather think it is with the owner now, sir," answered the young woman.

"Well, my dear," said Frank, "I see you suspect my stratagem. But you are such a sweet pretty creature, that I was resolved to introduce myself to you. Now don't be angry, my love: I mean all I assert—and if you will only tell me where and when I can see you again, I'm sure you won't be sorry to make my acquaintance."

"Upon my word!" cried the young woman, in that dubious manner which might have meant disgust, or which might be taken as encouragement.

Mr. Curtis, strong in his self-conceit, adopted the latter view, and became more pressing in his attentions.

"Now do let me see you again, there's a dear," he exclaimed, continuing to walk by her side. "If you'll only agree to meet me this evening, I'll take you to the play—and I'll buy you a gold chain. Money is no object to me, my love: a man with ten thousand a-year—*and* a peerage in the perspective—may indulge his little fancies, I hope."

These falsehoods, conveyed by implication, were uttered in such a tone of assurance, that the young woman was evidently dazzled by their splendour; and she threw a rapid, but encouraging glance towards the mendacious Frank.

"Come, now—will you meet me again?" he demanded. "I *was* going over to stay a few days with the Prime Minister of France early next month; and I *had* promised to pass my Christmas with his Holiness the Pope at Rome:—but if you was only kind, now—why, there's no saying that I might not send excuses to both of them, and stay in London for the pleasure of seeing you."

"But you men are such gay deceivers," said the young female.

"Well—we may be—sometimes!" ejaculated Frank, rather looking upon the imputation as a compliment than a reproach. "But you're too pretty for a man to find it in his heart to deceive you, my dear. In one word, where shall you be at seven o'clock this evening?"

"I *did* think of calling upon a friend which is lady's-maid in a family living in Conduit Street," replied the young woman.

"And if your friend is a lady's-maid, my dear," said Frank, "what may you be?"

"The same, sir," was the answer.

"The very thing!" cried Curtis. "If there's one class of young ladies that I like more than another, it is the ladies'-maids. Why, my dear, when I left Paris—where I stayed some time with the Archbishop of that city,—for his Grace and I are as thick as two thieves—the ladies'-maids held a meeting, and appointed a committee to draw up an address expressive of regret and all that sort of thing at my going away. They did, upon my honour! But let us come to the point, my dear. Shall you be in Conduit Street this evening at about seven?"

"I think it's very likely, sir," was the answer. "But you must not go with me any farther now—for I live at the house with the bay-windows there."

"But whose service are you in, my dear?" asked Frank.

"In Lady Georgiana Hatfield's," replied the young woman.

"Indeed!" cried Curtis. "I've heard an uncle of mine speak of her ladyship, I think. But this is a great nuisance, though."

"What is?" asked Charlotte, whom our readers may remember to have been mentioned at the opening of this tale.

"Why—that you and me must separate just at the moment that we are getting so friendly together—and without a single kiss, either."

Charlotte giggled—but said nothing.

"You will really be in Conduit Street this evening, my dear?" urged Frank Curtis, after a brief pause.

"I think I shall be able to get out," responded Charlotte. "But her ladyship is an invalid; and Miss Mordaunt—her friend, or companion, or whatever she is—may want me to dress her for some ball or party; and so I cannot promise for sure."

"But you will try?"

"Yes," murmured the young woman; and she hurried on to the front-door of Lady Hatfield's house.

Curtis stopped at a short distance and watched her as she tripped along, her pretty feet and ankles peering from beneath the folds of her dress.

Now it happened that at the very moment when Charlotte was about to ring the bell, the front-door opened, and a livery-servant issued forth, doubtless upon some errand. After exchanging a word or two with Charlotte, he passed on, and the young woman entered the house. But ere she closed the door she turned a sly glance upon Frank Curtis, who, the instant he saw the livery-servant make his appearance, sauntered very leisurely along in the most innocent-looking manner in the world.

The livery-servant was now out of sight—and the pretty face of the lady's-maid lingered at the door which she kept ajar.

Curtis looked hastily around; and, the coast being tolerably clear at the moment, he darted up to the entrance.

Charlotte had merely remained on the threshold to give him a parting glance of intelligence for the purpose of assuring him of the sincerity of her promise that she would endeavour to meet him in the evening,—for the young lady was of an intriguing disposition, and flattered herself that she had captivated some very great, or at all events some very wealthy person:—but, when she saw him thus precipitately rush towards the entrance, she drew back and endeavoured to shut the door.

Frank was, however, too quick for her: and he fairly thrust himself into the hall, closing the street-door behind him.

"For God's sake, go away, sir," said Charlotte imploringly.

"Not till I have had one kiss—just one," cried Frank; and he threw his arms round the lady's-maid's neck.

"Oh! do let me go, sir—the servants will come—and I shall be ruined," she murmured, vainly struggling with the young man, who not only considered the adventure a capital joke, but was also excited by his present contact with a pretty girl.

He glued his lips to hers, and pressed her closely to him, when a loud double-knock suddenly echoed through the hall.

"Good heavens! what shall I do?" exclaimed Charlotte, in a tone of despair: then, in another moment, she recovered her presence of mind, and throwing open a side-door, said in a rapid and earnest tone, "Go in there, sir—and, if any one comes, pray invent some excuse for your being here—but don't compromise me."

Curtis darted into the parlour with which the side-door communicated: the lady's-maid hurried away: and old Mason speedily made his appearance to answer the summons conveyed by the double-knock.

"Is Miss Mordaunt at home?" inquired a voice which Curtis, who was listening anxiously on the inner side of the parlour door, immediately recognised to be that of his worthy uncle.

"Yes, Sir Christopher—Miss Mordaunt is at home," replied Mason. "Please to walk in, sir. This way, sir—Miss Mordaunt is with Lady Hatfield in the drawing-room."

"I wish to see Miss Mordaunt alone, if you please," said Sir Christopher. "Give my compliments, and if Miss Mordaunt will accord me a few minutes—upon some little matter of a private nature——"

"Certainly, Sir Christopher," responded the domestic. "Have the goodness to step into this room, sir."

And Frank Curtis—now as miserable as he was insolent and exulting a few moments previously, when embracing Charlotte in the hall—heard the footsteps of Mason and his uncle approaching the very door at which he was listening.

Not a moment was to be lost. He was too much confused—too much bewildered to think of meeting the embarrassment of his position with a good face and a bold excuse: and concealment instantly suggested itself to his coward-mind.

A cheerful fire was burning in the grate; and near it was drawn a sofa, the cushion of which had rich fringes that hung all round, and drooped nearly to the carpet. To thrust himself beneath this friendly sofa was the work of an instant with Frank Curtis; and so rapidly was the manœuvre executed, that the fringes had even ceased to rustle, when Sir Christopher Blunt stalked pompously into the apartment.

Mason withdrew to deliver the knight's message to Miss Mordaunt; and in the meantime the knight himself paced the room in somewhat an agitated manner.

At length he walked straight up to a handsome mirror, and looking fully at his image as it was reflected in the glass, began to apostrophise himself.

"Sir Christopher Blunt—Sir Christopher Blunt," he exclaimed aloud, in a solemn tone, "what is it that you are about to do? Are you taking a wise, or an imprudent step? Are you, in a word, about to ensure your own happiness, or—or—to make a damned old fool of yourself?"

Frank Curtis was astounded at this language which came from the lips of his uncle. Despite of his fears and the unpleasant predicament in which he found himself, he was on the point of yielding to his natural propensity for mischief and blurting forth an affirmative response to the latter portion of the knight's self-interrogation, when the door opened and a lady entered the room.

Curtis accordingly held his peace, and his breath too as much as he could; for his curiosity was now so intense as to master even his fears.

"Miss Mordaunt," said the knight, suddenly turning away from the glass and advancing as jauntily as his massive frame would permit, to meet the lady, "I have to apologise for this early visit——"

"Oh! no apology, Sir Christopher," exclaimed Julia, in a most affable manner. "Pray be seated."

"Allow me," said the knight; and taking her hand, he led her to the very sofa beneath which his nephew lay concealed. Then, seating himself at a respectful distance from her—but also on the sofa, he continued thus:—"I hope, Miss Mordaunt, that I shall not offend you with what I am going—that is, with what I am about—I mean, with what I am on the point of——"

"Very intelligible, all this!" thought Frank Curtis to himself.

"Sir Christopher Blunt is incapable of offending a lady—especially a young one," observed Miss Julia, blushing in the most approved style on such interesting occasions—for she could anticipate what was coming.

"Sir Christopher Blunt thanks you for that compliment, Miss Mordaunt," said the knight pompously, and encouraged also by the lady's tone and manner. "Yes—I am indeed incapable of giving offence wilfully; although there *are* certain vulgar people east of Temple Bar who pretend that I treat them cavalierly. And, thank heaven! Miss Mordaunt, I was *not* elected Alderman of Portsoken; for I never could have put up with all the filthy guzzling and swilling—excuse the expressions, ma'am—that seem inseparable from City affairs. You know, perhaps, Miss Mordaunt, that my origin was humble—I may say that it was nothing at all. But I glory in that fact: it is my boast—my pride."

"True merit is sure to force its way in the world, Sir Christopher," observed Julia, with a smile which, displaying her white teeth, quite enchanted the amorous knight.

"Again I thank you for the good opinion of me implied by that remark," he said, edging himself a little closer to the lady. "My large fortune—for large it notoriously is, Miss Mordaunt—has all been acquired by my own honest industry; and the title which I have the honour to bear, was bestowed upon me by a gracious Prince in approbation of my conduct as a public officer."

"You occupy an enviable position in society, Sir Christopher," said Julia.

"Do you really think so, Miss?" asked the knight, endeavouring to assume a soft and plaintive tone, but with as little success as if he were a boatswain labouring under a severe cold: "do you really think so?"—and again he edged himself nearer to his companion. "Ah! my dear Miss Mordaunt, how happy should I be to lay my fortune—my title—my all, at the feet of some charming lady, who, like yourself, would not despise the man that has risen by his own honest exertions to I may say affluence and honour."

Miss Mordaunt cast down her eyes and worked herself up into a most interesting state of blushing excitement; while Sir Christopher boldly took her hand and pressed it to his lips.

The knight's foot was thrust some little way under the sofa; and as he wore blucher boots, it was not difficult to stick a pin into the calf of his leg, if any one had felt so disposed. Such an idea certainly struck his dutiful nephew at that instant; for Mr. Frank Curtis now fully comprehended the object of his uncle's visit to Miss Julia Mordaunt; and the matrimonial designs of the said uncle foreboded any thing but essential benefit to himself. Then—although he was not the brightest young man in existence—the selfish motive of Sir Christopher, in agreeing to *purchase* Mr. Torrens's elder daughter as his (Frank's) wife, flashed upon his mind; and in an instant he comprehended the entire policy of Sir Christopher as well as the reader already understands it, with regard to the recent matrimonial speculation, which Tom Rainford had so materially aided to render abortive.

We digressed just at the point where Sir Christopher was venturesome enough to press the hand of Miss Mordaunt to his lips.

"Oh! Sir Christopher," murmured the lady, apparently quite abashed, and forgetting, most probably in the agitation of the moment, to withdraw her fair fingers.

"Julia, my love—for so you must now permit me to call you," exclaimed the enamoured knight, "will my suit be rejected? can you receive it favourably? At this moment you see before you a man whom it is in your power to render happy or miserable for life. And, ah! dear me—what a dreadful dream I had last night! It was that dream which made me come to you so early to-day, to know your decision. For whether it was your image, my beloved Julia—or the cold roast pig that I eat for supper, I'm sure I can't say; but true it is that——Oh!" screamed the knight, in a fit of agony.

"My dear Sir Christopher, what—what *is* the matter?" asked Miss Mordaunt, alarmed by the sudden ejaculation, which was accompanied by an equally sudden start.

"Oh! nothing—nothing," said the knight, endeavouring to compose himself: "a sudden twitch in the leg—just like the pricking of a pin—but it is nothing—a mere sensation! I was going to tell you, my dear Julia, about that horrid dream——"

"Pray, Sir Christopher, don't tell me any thing about horrid dreams," exclaimed Miss Mordaunt: "you will frighten me out of my wits."

"Well, dearest, I will not. But you have not told me yet whether I may consider that this fair hand which I now press to my lips——Oh!"

And again the knight started violently.

"What *is* the matter, Sir Christopher?" asked Julia earnestly.

"Really—I can't make it out—I don't know—but this is the second time that the same sensation has seized me in the left leg," stammered the knight: "just for all the world like the pricking of a pin. And yet of course it cannot be that. But pray, pardon these unpleasant interruptions, Julia; and relieve me from suspense at once. Say—tell me, dearest one—will you, will you consent to be mine?"

"Oh! Sir Christopher, what do you ask?" murmured Miss Mordaunt, as if there were any thing extraordinary or unexpected in the question.

"What do I ask?" repeated the enamoured knight: "I ask you to bestow upon me this fair hand."

"How can I refuse you, Sir Christopher?" sighed the lady. "You are so killing!"

"Am I, dearest!" ejaculated the knight; and, encouraged more than ever by this assurance, he boldly kissed his companion. But almost immediately a cry of agony burst from his lips; and, starting up from the sofa, he exclaimed, "My leg! my leg! the—the devil's in it—and that's the fact!"

The fact was however somewhat different; for Mr. Frank Curtis, having very quietly and deliberately taken his breast-pin from the frill of his shirt, was amusing himself with the very pleasant pastime of thrusting the point into his uncle's leg.

On the third occasion of the application of the aforesaid breast-pin, Sir Christopher started up and danced about the room, while Miss Mordaunt, who was most anxious to bring the delicate topic of discourse to such a point that she might satisfy herself as to the very day on which she was to change her condition, endeavoured to her utmost to console him.

Convinced that the pain he experienced could be nothing more than some sudden but very galling spasmodic attack, neither Sir Christopher nor Julia entertained the least thought of looking beneath the sofa: they therefore re-seated themselves upon it, and continued their tender discourse.

"And when shall it be?" asked Sir Christopher, taking it for granted that it *was* to be.

"Whenever—that is—so soon—I mean—when you choose," murmured Miss Mordaunt. "But you will communicate your intentions to my brother, who obtained his captaincy a few days ago, and whom I *must* consult."

"And why consult him?" asked Sir Christopher, a misgiving entering his mind.

"Oh! he might—I do not say that he will—but he *might* object," answered Miss Mordaunt.

"Then perhaps you wish me to state my views to my nephew also," said the knight somewhat testily: "as *he* might also object."

"But a nephew, Sir Christopher," urged the lady,—"a nephew is not a brother."

"Very true," replied Blunt, as if some grand truth had just been made apparent to him. "And yet it appears, Julia," he added, in a coaxing tone, "that we have each a relation to whom we would rather not mention the matter—until after it was over."

"Oh! you killing man—what would you have me understand by that remark?" cried Miss Mordaunt.

"Simply that we should——"

"Should what, dear Sir Christopher?"

"Should be married privately—or run away to Gretna Green," answered the knight. "And now the truth is out."

"Oh! naughty—naughty man!" exclaimed Julia, casting on her swain one of her most bewitching smiles: but at the same time she imagined to herself all the excitement attending a run-a-way match to Gretna—the rapidity of travelling—the bustle that would be excited at the way-side inns—the sensation that must arise in the fashionable world—the paragraphs in the newspapers—the *éclat* attached to such a proceeding—and the importance with which her reappearance in town, after the union, would be attended:—of all this she thought—and the knight's proposal was therefore most welcome to her; for, while she contemplated the agreeable side of the picture, she never once reflected on the ridicule and absurdity that must attach themselves to such a step on the part of two persons of the respective ages of Sir Christopher Blunt and herself.

"Well, dearest, what are you thinking of?" asked the knight.

"Of what you were saying, dear Sir Christopher," murmured the lady in a languishing tone.

"Then, how shall it be! a private marriage—or Gretna?"

"The arrangements for a private marriage might be suspected," sighed Julia, casting down her eyes and managing a blush, which was respectable enough, seeing that it scarcely came voluntarily to her aid.

"Just my opinion!" ejaculated Sir Christopher. "I would not have that prying nephew of mine, Frank Curtis—the young scapegrace—getting a hint of it beforehand, for any money."

"Nor would I wish my brother to know of it until it is all over, dear Sir Christopher," returned Julia.

"Then be it Gretna!" exclaimed the knight. "And now when shall it take place?"

"I could not say to-day, Sir Christopher—but to-morrow—to-morrow——" murmured the lady in a faint tone, as if quite overpowered by the importance of the step she was about to take, but which she would willingly have taken long before, had the proposal been made to her:—"to-morrow," she added, "I shall be prepared—to——"

"I understand you, my angel," interrupted the knight; and this time he caught the lady fairly in his arms and subjected her to a process of hearty kissing.

Mr. Frank Curtis had in the meantime restored his breast-pin to the frill of his shirt; for, since the conversation had turned upon a regular elopement, the matter had become far too serious for him to trifle with. He suddenly found himself menaced with something bordering on total disinheritance in respect to his uncle's property; for, even if this projected union should yield no issue, still the lady might obtain so much influence over the knight as to induce him to will all his fortune to herself. Frank was therefore in rather an unpleasant state of mind, as well as being in an uneasy predicament under the sofa. He nevertheless saw that cunning must be met with cunning; and he now lay as quiet as a mouse, in order to avoid detection. But he vowed seriously that the moment he should escape from the kind of prison in which he found himself, he would not let the grass grow under his feet ere he adopted measures to defeat the matrimonial scheme of Sir Christopher Blunt and Miss Julia Mordaunt.

At length, to his unspeakable relief, the knight took his leave of Miss Mordaunt, after having settled the hour and place where they were to meet on the following evening.

Sir Christopher being gone, Julia also left the room; and poor Charlotte, who had been on the tenter-hooks of suspense and alarm ever since Frank Curtis had first entered the house, now hurried to the parlour, wondering how he could possibly have managed to avoid an exposure.

But when she entered the room, and perceived no one, she was more astonished still.

Her surprise was not, however, of long duration; for Curtis, having peeped through the fringe and ascertained who the new-comer was, suddenly emerged from his hiding-place.

"Oh! dear me, sir," exclaimed the young woman, "what a fright I have been in, to be sure!"

"And what a pickle I have been in!" cried Frank sulkily.

"You cannot say that it was my fault, sir," observed Charlotte reproachfully.

"Nor more I do, my dear," answered Curtis, warming himself into a better humour by means of a kiss or two on the lady's-maid's red lips. "But, I say, my dear," he continued, after a few moments' dalliance of that sort, "you *must* come to meet me this evening; because, independent of my desire to chat with you and all that sort of thing, you can be of service to me."

"Lor'! sir," cried Charlotte, astonished at this intimation.

"Indeed you can: but I must not stay to explain myself now," returned Curtis. "Here, my dear—take these five guineas as an earnest of what I will do for you; and mind and be punctual in Conduit Street at seven o'clock this evening."

"I shall not fail, sir," replied Charlotte.

"And in the meantime," added Frank, "watch Miss Mordaunt well. Don't ask me any questions now—I will tell you all about it this evening. But mind you watch her; and if possible, get into conversation with her. Should she ask you to do her any service—no matter of what kind—promise her that you will; and leave the rest to me. Do you hear?"

"Yes, sir—and I will do as you tell me," was the answer.

"Well, then—that's right," said Curtis. "And now let me see if I can't slip out without running plump up against one of your liveried flunkeys here."

"Wait an instant," cried Charlotte; and she disappeared from the room, closing the door carefully behind her.

In a few moments she returned, with the welcome tidings that the coast was clear; and Frank Curtis succeeded in quitting Lady Hatfield's house without being perceived by any one save the faithful Charlotte.

CHAPTER XX.
HAPPINESS.—THE DIAMOND-MERCHANT.

When Lord Ellingham took his leave of Lady Hatfield, the latter hurried to her bed-chamber; and, locking the door behind her, sate down in an arm-chair near the fire to ponder unconstrainedly upon the conversation of the previous hour.

And that hour—what changes had it worked in respect to the mind and prospects of this patrician lady!

"Oh! how generous and noble-hearted is my Arthur!" she mused inwardly: "how boundless is his love for me! But is it possible that I am really to become his wife? or am I the sport of a wild and delusive dream? No—it is all true: I am awake—I see the various objects around me—there is no confusion in my brain. Yes—it *is* all true; and he will marry me—he will make me his wife—in spite of——But let me avoid thinking of the past! The future is now bright and glorious before me. My own Arthur—whom I love so fondly, and who alone has ever possessed and will possess my heart,—my own noble, generous Arthur has surmounted all prejudice—flung aside all disgust—and has promised to make me happy! Oh! not in the wildest of my dreams could I have imagined so much bliss. The clouds which have so long hung heavily around the star of my destiny, have been suddenly dispersed by one who views my heart aright—who understands me—who knows my sad history, but recognises my innocence—who, in a word, rises superior to all the prejudices which shackle the world. Oh! dearest—dearest Arthur! how can I ever reward you adequately for this generosity on your part? All the love which I bear you—all the adoration I feel for you—all the devotion I shall manifest towards you, will not repay the immense debt that I owe you! It is true that I possess great wealth—that the services of my father to the State induced his Majesty to create me a Peeress in my own right—and that I have some pretensions to beauty:—all this is true—but it is not sufficient to induce my noble-hearted Arthur to make me the partner of his bed. No: for he himself is rich far beyond his desires—he also owns a proud and ancient name—and England has daughters far lovelier than I. But he loves me for myself—apart from all selfish considerations: and, Oh! what bliss to be thus loved!"

Lady Hatfield sank her head upon her fair hand, and gave way to the new and ineffable bliss which had so suddenly enveloped her in its halo.

At length another idea struck her.

"But my uncle—how could *he* have known my secret?" she exclaimed aloud. "And how did he discover it? Oh! he must have been aware of it from the very first! The good—the kind-hearted man—never to have even appeared to——"

Georgiana's reverie was interrupted by a hasty knock at her door.

She rose, unlocked it, and gave admission to her friend Julia.

"My dear Lady Hatfield," exclaimed Miss Mordaunt, her entire countenance illuminated with joy, "congratulate me. It is all settled!"

"That you are to become Lady Blunt?" asked Georgiana, smiling.

"Yes, my dearest friend—Lady Blunt! How well it sounds! only think of '*Lady Blunt*' upon a card—printed, for instance, in the old English letter—or German text—or whatever it is. And then—'*Lady Blunt's carriage!*'—and all that sort of thing! Really I am so happy—I don't know whether to dance or sing—or both!"

"I am delighted to see you so happy, my dear Julia," said Lady Hatfield; "and most sincerely do I congratulate you. But have you acted prudently to accept Sir Christopher without communicating his proposal to your relations?"

"I think that I am quite old enough to manage my own affairs in this respect at least," answered Julia, laughing: "and yet—after all—I am not so very old—only just thirty. Still it is high time to settle one-self in life. But for the present, my dear Lady Hatfield, I must implore you to keep my engagement a profound secret—for reasons which I will explain in a few days——"

"I shall keep your secret, Julia, without seeking to learn your motives until you may choose to communicate them," replied Georgiana. "And now I am about to surprise you in respect to myself. Lord Ellingham has been here this morning."

"So I heard from old Mason just now," said Miss Mordaunt. "But you knew he would call, my dear friend, after leaving his card last night. And—if you speak candidly—you will confess that you *hoped* he would."

"I *did* hope he would call, Julia," answered Georgiana; "but I could *not* imagine that our interview would have terminated——However," she added, checking herself, and smiling joyously, "you must now congratulate me; for in a few weeks I shall become the Countess of Ellingham."

"I do indeed congratulate you, my dearest Lady Hatfield," replied Miss Mordaunt. "But upon my word, wonders will never cease. Here were you only a few days ago rejecting the Earl in opposition to every thing like common sense—and certainly against the wishes of your very best friends———"

"Let us not talk of the past, Julia," interrupted Georgiana. "The future opens so brightly before me, that I am almost dazzled by its brilliancy. And I am happy—supremely happy—Oh! almost too happy!"

As she uttered these words, Georgiana threw herself into the arm-chair which she had quitted for the purpose of giving admission to Miss Mordaunt; and never did the beauty of her soul-speaking countenance shine to greater advantage than at that moment.

And no wonder that even her friend, whose volatile disposition seldom permitted her mind to settle its attention on subjects concerning another, was struck by the loveliness of Lady Hatfield on this occasion:—no wonder, we say, that Julia gazed with admiration for a long time on that beauteous woman: for happiness seemed to have invested her with new charms.

Her cheeks—lately so pale with mental anxiety and partial indisposition—were now tinged with a warm carnation hue:—joy flashed from her large liquid eyes, usually of so mild though lustrous a languor;—and smiles played upon those rosy lips which were wont to remain apart with serious expression.

The Earl of Ellingham, upon taking leave of Georgiana that morning,—but, be it well understood, with the promise of returning to pass an hour or two in the evening,—experienced that kind of heart-felt happiness which requires a vent by means of imparting the fact of its existence to a friend.

To the abode of Dr. Lascelles was the Earl accordingly hastening, when he was suddenly accosted by a gentleman; who addressed him by name, and whom in another moment he remembered to be Mr. Gordon, the diamond-merchant.

"I beg your lordship's pardon for thus stopping you," said that individual: "but I thought you might be gratified to learn that the jewels which I lost so mysteriously, have been restored to me."

"Indeed!" exclaimed Arthur. "I am rejoiced to hear these tidings. And now, I presume, you are fully convinced that Miss Esther de Medina was entirely innocent of the theft so ridiculously imputed to her."

"On the contrary, my lord," answered the diamond-merchant: "I am more than ever certain that Miss de Medina was the person who took them."

"Mr. Gordon," exclaimed the Earl indignantly, "I should have thought that, after the investigation which took place at the office in Bow Street, you would not have clung to an opinion so dishonourable—so unjust towards an innocent young lady. Moreover, sir, I should have conceived that my testimony to that young lady's character would have dispelled any doubts which had still hung on your mind."

"That your lordship gave such testimony conscientiously, I cannot for an instant question," was the firm but respectful answer. "At the same time that your lordship was and is still deceived in that young lady, I am confident."

"Perhaps, sir," observed the Earl coldly, "you will have no objection to communicate the reasons which have thus induced you to change your opinion; for, if I remember rightly, you yourself declared, in the public office, that you were satisfied there was some grievous mistake, and that Miss de Medina was innocent of the deed imputed to her at first."

"I admit, my lord," replied the diamond-merchant, "that I was staggered by the singularity of the turn given to the proceedings when your lordship appeared to speak in Miss de Medina's defence. But listen, my lord, to the subsequent events which revived all my suspicions. Upon leaving the Police-Court I returned home, but was scarcely able to attend to my business, so bewildered was I by the occurrences of the morning, and so annoyed was I also at the loss which I had so mysteriously experienced. It was probably four o'clock in the afternoon, when a lady was announced; and the moment she raised her veil, I recognised Miss de Medina. You may conceive, my lord, how surprised I was by this visit: but much greater was my astonishment, when she said to me, without a single word of preface, '*Sir, what is the value of the diamonds which you have lost?*'—'*Six hundred pounds*,' was my answer.—Miss de Medina immediately drew forth a small packet from her dress, and counted six Bank-notes, each of a hundred pounds, and which she placed before me on the table,—'*Here is the amount, sir*,' she said; and I offered her a receipt, which she however declined. For a few moments she lingered—as if anxious to say something more: then, suddenly turning away, she abruptly quitted the house."

"Extraordinary!" cried the Earl of Ellingham. "And yet———"

"One instant, my lord," interrupted Mr. Gordon: "the most mysterious part of the whole transaction is yet to be revealed to you. Not ten minutes had elapsed from the moment of Miss de Medina's departure, when a person, whom I remembered to have seen in the court, was announced. I do not know whether your lordship observed at the office a man of florid complexion—light curly hair—red whiskers—and dressed in a sporting suit———"

"I not only observed him," replied the Earl; "but from the description subsequently given by one of my servants, whom I questioned after my return home from the police-office, I have every reason to believe that the individual whom you describe was the bearer of a letter which had induced me to hasten to Bow Street to give my testimony in proof of Miss de Medina's innocence."

"And does your lordship know that man?" inquired the diamond-merchant.

"I never saw him, to my knowledge, until that day, when the attention he appeared to devote to the proceedings attracted my notice—although he was in the midst of the crowd congregated near the door. But please to continue your own narrative."

"This individual, my lord, of whom we have been speaking," returned Mr. Gordon, "was the person introduced to my office a few minutes after the departure of Miss de Medina. He seated himself in a free and easy, off-hand manner, and said, '*I think I can give you some little information concerning the diamonds which you have lost.*'—'*Indeed!*' I exclaimed: and, anxious to hear what he was about to state, I said nothing relative to the visit of Miss de Medina and the payment of the amount at which the lost jewels were valued.—'*Yes*,' he continued: and, with the utmost coolness, he produced a pistol from one pocket and a small parcel, wrapped up in brown paper, from the other.—

'*What is the meaning of this strange conduct?*' I demanded, glancing towards the weapon which the man held in his hand.—'*Oh! it is soon explained,*' he said. '*This pistol is merely to defend myself in case you should take it into your head to give me into the charge of a constable on suspicion of being connected with the person who stole your property: and as for the parcel, open it, and see what it contains.*'—Thus speaking, he tossed the packet across the table to me, crossed his legs, and began to hum a tune. I opened the parcel; and to my surprise perceived the diamonds which I had lost.—'*Is the set complete?*' asked the man.—'*Quite perfect,*' I replied in the most unfeigned astonishment at the singularity of the whole proceedings. '*But how does it happen,*' I continued,'*that you have come to restore them to me, when a quarter of an hour has scarcely elapsed since Miss de Medina herself called and paid me six hundred pounds at which they are valued?*'—It now appeared to be the man's turn to be surprised: but, in another moment, he exclaimed,'*Oh! I understand it all.*'—'*What do you understand?*' said I: '*for I must candidly confess that I understand nothing of the whole transaction, which is one involved in the deepest mystery.*'—'*So let it remain,* he cried abruptly: '*and now mark me,*' he added in a slower and more impressive tone; '*beware how you ever utter a word derogatory to the honour of Esther de Medina.*' And he quitted the apartment, leaving me in possession of my jewels and of the six hundred pounds also."

"This narrative is so singular, Mr. Gordon," said the Earl of Ellingham, "that were you not a respectable merchant, and that you can have no possible interest in amusing me with a fiction, I should not believe the portion which relates to Miss de Medina."

"I declare before my Maker," ejaculated the diamond-merchant solemnly, "that I have not exaggerated one tittle of my history. I have even more to state. The restoration of my property convinced me that I had no right to retain the money which Miss de Medina had paid to me as a recompense for its loss. I therefore determined to give it back to her. But I was unacquainted with her residence. Then I recollected that your lordship had stated that Mr. de Medina had become your tenant for a house and small estate about seven miles from London. I immediately repaired to your lordship's residence in Pall Mall to inquire the address of Mr. de Medina; but you were not at home. Your valet, however, furnished me with the information I required; and on the following morning I proceeded to Finchley. I called at the house to which I had been directed, and learnt that Mr. de Medina and his daughter did not intend to settle there until the Spring; but from the servant in charge of the premises I ascertained where Mr. de Medina resided in town. I accordingly returned to London, and forthwith repaired to Great Ormond Street, where I obtained an interview with Miss de Medina. Her father was out—a circumstance which, on the occasion, appeared to give her pleasure; because she asked the servant who announced me, whether Mr. de Medina were in his study; and on receiving a reply to the effect that he had gone out a few minutes previous to my arrival, she was evidently relieved of some anxiety. I communicated the nature of my business; but when I mentioned the particulars of the visit I had received from the light-haired gentleman, her countenance suddenly assumed so singular an expression that I can scarcely define its meaning. It was not alarm alone—nor surprise—nor shame—nor sorrow, which her looks denoted; but a feeling composed of all those sentiments blended together. Then, when I explained to her that this man had restored my lost diamonds, her countenance suddenly assumed an expression of joy. I handed her the six hundred pounds, which she received; and then—as on the occasion of her visit to me the preceding evening—she seemed anxious to make some remark, to which she could not, however, give utterance. The silence became awkward—and I took my leave. Your lordship now knows all."

"And can you for one moment imagine that Esther de Medina was the person who stole your diamonds?" exclaimed Lord Ellingham: "or that she was in any way connected with that man who restored them to you?"

"My belief is that she parted with them in some way to that man," answered Mr. Gordon; "and that her father most probably gave her the money to recompense me for my loss; but that when she paid it, she was unaware that the man had the intention of restoring the jewels."

Lord Ellingham made no answer: for there suddenly flashed upon his mind a reminiscence which staggered him.

The reader will recollect that when Mr. de Medina encountered his daughter at the police-court, he said to her, "*Oh! Esther—Esther, I can understand it all. You have brought this upon yourself!*" These words were overheard at the time by Lord Ellingham: but they had since escaped his memory—or else failed to make any very deep impression upon him,—his own mind, since that day, having been a prey to much acute anxiety, suspense, and conflicting feelings, on account of Lady Hatfield.

But now, when he recalled those words, and considered them in all their significance,—when he pondered upon the tale which he had just heard from the lips of the diamond-merchant,—when he remembered that the man who had restored those jewels was doubtless the same who had conveyed to Pall Mall the letter which so mysteriously urged him to hasten to the police-court and give his testimony in Esther's defence,—he began to share Mr. Gordon's belief that there must be some connexion between that florid, light-haired man and Miss de Medina.

At the same time, Lord Ellingham was convinced that Esther had *not* stolen the diamonds; or that, if she had, Mr. Gordon had mistaken the hour of the day, if not the day itself, on which such theft was committed. Because Arthur remembered, beyond all possibility of error, that from two o'clock on the afternoon until near eleven o'clock at night, on the day specified by the diamond-merchant, Esther was engaged in visiting the house which her father had hired from him (Lord Ellingham), and which was situate about a mile beyond Finchley. Arthur himself accompanied Mr. de Medina and Esther on that occasion; and Esther was never absent from his sight, save perhaps for a few minutes at a time, during the interval above named.

There was a profound mystery somewhere: and though the Earl was not characterised by any feeling of impertinent curiosity, yet he longed to clear up the doubts and misgivings which had at length arisen in his mind. He entertained the greatest respect for Mr. de Medina, and—until now—the same sentiment towards Esther, whom he had hitherto looked upon as a model of purity, amiability, and innocence. He therefore felt grieved—vexed—disappointed—annoyed, for the honour of the human race, and especially for the credit of the female sex, to think it possible that he had been so grossly deceived in that beautiful Jewess.

He walked slowly along, the diamond-merchant by his side.

"Well, my lord," said the latter, at length breaking the protracted silence, "what is your opinion now?"

"I confess that I am bewildered," was the reply. "But I shall not judge hastily. In the meantime, I pray you so far to suspend your opinion upon the subject as to avoid the utterance of aught prejudicial to Miss de Medina's character; and if I succeed in fathoming this mystery, the fact of that young lady's guilt or innocence shall be duly communicated to you."

The diamond-merchant bowed respectfully, and departed in another direction; while Lord Ellingham continued his way towards Grafton Street.

CHAPTER XXI.
THE OATH.

Dr. Lascelles was at home, and immediately granted an audience to the Earl of Ellingham.

Popular physicians are potentates in their way, and access to them, save on matters of professional business, is frequently difficult.

But the doctor had taken a greater fancy to the young nobleman than he was ever known to entertain for any of his acquaintances; and he therefore received him as one who did not encroach on his very valuable time.

"Well," said the physician, as the Earl made his appearance in the professional reception-room, "something new about Lady Hatfield, I'll be bound?"

"You are right, my dear doctor," answered the lover: "and I am the happiest of men."

"I am charmed to hear it," said Lascelles, casting a glance of curiosity, not unmingled with surprise, towards the Earl.

"Yes, doctor," cried the latter, his handsome countenance irradiated with the lustre of complete felicity, "the beautiful Georgiana has consented to become my wife."

"Your wife!" ejaculated the physician.

"And wherefore not?" asked the Earl, astonished at the tone and manner of his friend. "Do you think that I will allow what must be considered a misfortune to stand in the way of my happiness?"

"Certainly—if you can rise superior to a prejudice which influences the generality of the world," said the physician, thrown off his guard by Lord Ellingham's last observation. "I do not see——"

"Ah! then you also know all?" ejaculated the Earl. "But let us not dwell on this topic. Suffice it that I have heard from Sir Ralph Walsingham enough to convince me that his niece is to be commiserated in a certain respect; and I have had a full explanation with her on the subject. In a few weeks she will be Lady Ellingham; and it shall be my duty—as it will also prove my delight—to make her so completely happy that she shall forget the incident which has had so powerful an effect upon her mind."

"I sincerely wish you all possible felicity, my dear Earl," said the doctor, shaking the young nobleman warmly by the hand.

"A thousand thanks, doctor," exclaimed Arthur, cordially returning the pressure. "But how became you acquainted with that incident in Georgiana's life which has exercised such influence over her? I thought you told me yesterday that she had not entered into any explanations with you?"

"Neither had she—nor has she, my dear lord," observed the physician, who seemed slightly surprised, if not puzzled, by the observations of his young friend. "But—as you yourself ere now said—let us not dwell on that topic;—it is of too delicate a nature."

"It *is* delicate, my dear doctor," responded the Earl. "But as I am my own master, and labour not under the necessity of consulting my relatives as to those proceedings which are connected with my interest or happiness——"

"Oh! certainly," said the doctor. "You love Lady Hatfield—and she loves you in return. It is quite natural. I have known many such cases—more, perhaps, than you could imagine."

"I do not doubt you," replied the Earl. "But I will not longer intrude on your valuable time," he added, smiling; "for I know that you are not in the habit of receiving visits of a merely friendly nature at this period of the day."

"To you only am I accessible on such terms," replied the physician.

The Earl then took his leave, and was about to return home, when he bethought himself of the strange communication he had received from Mr. Gordon, the diamond-merchant; and, as the weather was fine and frosty, he determined to walk as far as the residence of Mr. de Medina in Great Ormond Street.

On his arrival at that gentleman's house, he found the servant standing at the front-door in the act of receiving some articles from a tradesman's boy; and this trivial fact is only recorded, inasmuch as it explains the reason how Lord Ellingham ascended to the drawing-room without being duly announced. He considered himself to be on terms of sufficient intimacy with Mr. de Medina to take such a liberty; and when the domestic made a movement to conduct him up stairs, Arthur desired him in a condescending manner not to take the trouble, as he knew the way.

Accordingly, the Earl proceeded to the drawing-room, where he did not, however, find Mr. de Medina and his daughter, although, from the statement of the servant, he had expected to meet them there.

The floor was spread with a thick, rich Turkey carpet, on which his footsteps fell noiselessly. He was about to seat himself, when voices in the adjoining apartment, which was only separated from the drawing-room by folding-doors, met his ears.

"Esther," said Mr. de Medina, speaking in an earnest and solemn tone, "this is the third anniversary of that dreadful day which——"

"Oh! do not refer more than is necessary to that sad event, dear father!" exclaimed the Jewess, in an imploring voice.

"Heaven knows, my child," responded her sire, "that—if you feel as I do———"

"I do—I do, dearest father!" cried Esther.

"Yes:—but not all the degradation—the infamy—the shame——"

"All—all, father,—even as acutely as yourself!" she said, in a voice denoting the most intense anguish.

"And yet, undutiful girl that you are," exclaimed Mr. de Medina, "you persist in seeing that lost—abandoned——"

The sudden rattling of a carriage in the street drowned the remainder of this sentence.

"Oh! my dearest father, forgive me!" cried Esther in a tone of the most earnest appeal. "You cannot imagine the extent of my love—my boundless love—for that unfortunate——"

"Unfortunate!" repeated Mr. de Medina angrily: "no—no! Say that most wretched—guilty—criminal——"

"My God! use not such harsh terms!" almost shrieked the beautiful Jewess; and the Earl of Ellingham could judge by the sound that she fell upon her knees as she spoke.

"Yes—Esther—on your knees implore my forgiveness for your oft-repeated disobedience!" exclaimed Mr. de Medina. "Consider, undutiful—ungrateful girl—of the position—the scandalous, disgraceful position in which you were placed a few days ago. That ring which was sold to the diamond-merchant——"

"Pardon me, dearest father—oh! pardon me!" cried the young lady, her voice becoming wildly hysterical.

Again a vehicle rolled along the street; and of the Jew's reply all that the Earl could distinguish were the words——"those diamonds, Esther—the theft of those diamonds! Oh! my God—I shall yet go mad with the dreadful thought!"

"Oh! this is cruel—most cruel, after all I have suffered!" cried Esther. "Wherefore revive those terrible reproaches now? Say—speak, father—what do you require of me? wherefore this conversation?"

"Again I must remind you," answered Mr. de Medina solemnly, "that this is the third anniversary of that day——"

"I know it—I know it? Oh! how can I ever forget it?" said Esther in a tone of the most painful emotion.

"And now," continued Mr. de Medina, apparently but little moved by his daughter's grief,—"now must you swear, Esther—upon that book which contains the principles of our creed—that you will never, under any circumstances——"

Mr. de Medina here sank his voice to so low a tone, that the Earl could only catch a few disjointed phrases, such as these—"renew your connexion with——acknowledge that——such infamy and disgrace——honoured name——family——seduced my daughter——robbed her of her purity———although the world may not suspect——degradation on yourself——discard you for ever——Thomas Rainford——"

"I swear!" said Esther, in a tone which led the Earl to imagine that she took the proscribed oath with a dreadful shudder.

"And now rise," exclaimed Mr. de Medina. "It is over."

These words suddenly awoke the Earl to a consciousness of his position: and his face became scarlet as the thought flashed upon his mind that he had been playing the part of an eaves-dropper. He despised himself for having listened to the dialogue between Mr. de Medina and his daughter: but his attention had been so completely rivetted to this strange—mysterious—and exciting conversation, that he had unwittingly remained a hearer. An invisible spell had nailed him as it were to the spot—had forced him to linger and drink in that discourse which, alas! appeared to speak so eloquently to the discredit of her whose character he had so warmly defended two hours before!

And now, suddenly awaking—as we said—to a sense of his position, he perceived that a subterfuge could alone save him from the imputation of being an eaves-dropper: and to that subterfuge was this really noble-minded peer compelled to stoop.

Hastily stepping to the drawing-room door, he opened it and closed it again with unusual violence, so that the sound might fall upon the ears of Mr. de Medina and Esther, and induce them to believe that he had only just entered the room.

The stratagem succeeded; for Mr. de Medina immediately made his appearance from the inner apartment, and welcomed the Earl with his wonted calmness of manner.

In reply to Arthur's polite inquiries relative to Miss de Medina, the father replied that his daughter was somewhat indisposed, and hoped the Earl would excuse her absence.

A quarter of an hour passed in conversation of no particular interest to the reader; and Lord Ellingham then took his leave.

When he found himself once more in the open street, he could scarcely believe that he was not the sport of some wild and delusive dream. Had he heard aright? or had his ears beguiled him? Was it true that all those reproaches had been levelled by an angry father at the head of a daughter who did not attempt to deny her guilt, but who was compelled to implore that outraged parent's forgiveness? Had he not prescribed to her an oath which seemed to imply, in plain terms,—although the Earl had caught but detached portions,—that Esther had been seduced—robbed of her purity,— and that the villain was one Thomas Rainford? Had not that oath been administered for the purpose of binding her to break off her connexion with this Thomas Rainford? And did not Mr. de Medina assure her that, though the world might not suspect it, yet she had not the less brought degradation on herself? In fine—did not the angry father threaten to discard her for ever, unless she swore to obey his injunctions?

In what other way could the blanks in the terms of the oath—as Ellingham had gathered them by means of the few but significant disjointed passages thereof,—in what other way could those blanks be filled up than in the manner above detailed?

"It is too apparent!" thought the Earl within himself: "and Esther is an abandoned—lost—degraded girl! And yet how deceptive is her appearance—how delusive her demeanour! Purity seems to be expressed in every glance:—innocence characterises every word she utters! Merciful heavens! what must I think of the female sex after such a discovery as this? And yet, let me not judge harshly of the whole, because *one* is frail. My own Georgiana is quite different from that artful hypocrite, Esther de Medina. Georgiana conceals not a tainted soul beneath a chaste exterior: she is purity in mind as well as in appearance. And, after all, Esther *did* steal the diamonds: her father upbraided her with the theft! He even alluded to the ring which she sold to Mr. Gordon. Yes—it is indeed too apparent: she is utterly depraved! But that name of *Thomas Rainford*—surely I have heard it before?"

The Earl strove to recollect himself.

"Oh! I remember now!" he thought at the expiration of a few moments: "it was Thomas Rainford who was accused of robbing my Georgiana on the highway! How strange is this coincidence! And yet it was *not* that man who plundered her—for she proved his innocence of at least this imputation. But it was doubtless Rainford who sent me the letter desiring me to appear in the defence of Esther; and it must also have been he who restored the diamonds to the merchant! That Esther stole those diamonds is clear—for her father accused her of it. At least such is the inference that must be drawn from his words. But that Gordon was wrong as to the day, or the hour of the day on which the theft was committed, is also clear; inasmuch as Esther was at Finchley at the time stated! Still Gordon was so positive—and, when he appeared to prosecute the Jewess at the police-office, so short a time had elapsed—only a few hours, indeed—since the act was perpetrated, that it is difficult to believe how he could have mistaken the date! There is a mystery yet attending on this affair;—but that its elucidation would establish Esther's innocence, cannot for a moment be believed!"

Such was the train of thought into which the Earl of Ellingham was naturally led by the dialogue he had overheard between the Jew and his daughter.

He was sincerely grieved to be forced to come to the conviction that Esther de Medina was a lost and ruined girl, instead of the pure and artless being he had previously believed her to be. Although his affections were undividedly Georgiana's, yet he had entertained a sentiment of friendship for the Jewess; and he was pained and shocked to think that he had ever experienced any interest—even the slightest—in a female so utterly unworthy his notice. For the father he still felt respect, which was also now blended with profound commiseration; for he beheld in him an honest and honourable man, who was cursed with a daughter characterised by bad passions and evil propensities.

The Earl was well aware that Mr. de Medina was a very rich man: he could not therefore suppose that necessity had induced Esther either to dispose of the ring or to steal the jewels. What, then, could he conclude? That she required funds to support a worthless, abandoned, and lost man—her paramour! Hence the sale of the ring—hence the theft of the diamonds.

Arthur now remembered his promise to Mr. Gordon to make him acquainted with any particulars which he might discover relative to that business. But how could he fulfil his pledge? He shrank from the contemplation of the circumstance which had made him acquainted with Esther's guilt: he felt annoyed and vexed with himself for having allowed his curiosity so far to dominate his honourable principles as to render him an eaves-dropper. He would not therefore aggravate his offence by imparting its results to another; and, with an endeavour to banish the subject from his memory and turn his attention to more pleasurable topics, he hastily pursued his way homeward.

CHAPTER XXII.
THE ALARM.—THE LETTER.

In the meantime Esther de Medina had retired to her own apartment, immediately after the strange, painful, and exciting scene which had taken place with her father.

Seating herself upon a sofa, she burst into a violent flood of tears.

The delicate tinge of carnation which usually appeared beneath the clear, transparent olive hue of her complexion, was now chased away; and she was pale—very pale.

Her grief was evidently intense: anguish overwhelmed her spirit.

Oh, Esther! if thou art indeed a guilty—frail—fallen being, the eye cannot refuse a tear of pity to thy lost condition!

No:—for never has even the enamoured poet in his dreams conceived a form and face more perfect than nature had bestowed upon her. There appeared, too, such a virgin freshness about that charming creature who was just bursting into womanhood,—such a halo of innocence seemed to surround her,—so much modesty, so much propriety characterised her slightest attitudes and her most unimportant words, that to contemplate her for a few minutes and yet retain the stubborn conviction that she was a wanton, amounted almost to an impossibility.

And now—to behold her plunged in grief—alone with her own wretched thoughts, and weeping,—who could believe that the lips, on which purity appeared to dwell, had ever been pressed by those of the seducer,—that the sylph-like form, whose sweeping, undulating outlines were so gracefully set forth by the mournfulness of her attitude, had ever unveiled its beauties on the bed of illicit love,—that the rude hand of licentiousness had ever disturbed the treasures of the bosom so carefully concealed:—who could believe all this?

Nevertheless, says the reader, appearances are so completely against her—the evidences of her guilt seem so damning—that, alas! there is not a hope of her innocence!

But let us continue the thread of our narrative.

For half an hour did Esther remain absorbed in the most profound affliction—a prey to thoughts and reminiscences of a very painful nature.

At length she rose abruptly, and evidently strove to conquer her grief.

She wiped away the tears from her fine black eyes, and advanced towards the window, from behind the curtains of which she gazed into the street with the view of directing her thoughts into some new channel.

Suddenly an idea struck her; and she hastened to her writing-desk, at which she sate down and began to pen a letter.

While she was thus engaged, the crystal drops ever and anon started from her eyes, and trembled on the jetty fringes, the glossy darkness of which no oriental dye could have enhanced.

In the midst of her occupation—the progress of which was marked by many an ill-subdued sob—a female servant entered the room to acquaint Miss de Medina that her father had just received a letter on some business that required his immediate attention, and that she was not to expect him home to dinner.

The domestic then withdrew; and Esther finished her letter, which she folded and concealed in her bosom.

It was now five o'clock; and she descended to the dining-room;—but she had no appetite—and the ceremony of the repast, to which she was compelled to sit down alone, was by no means calculated to enliven her spirits.

Quitting the table as soon as possible, she returned to her chamber, put on her bonnet and shawl, and hurried into the fresh air, which she hoped would have an exhilarating influence upon her.

Esther drew her veil closely over her face, and proceeded to Southampton Row, where she entered a shop at which the local post-office was stationed.

The woman who stood behind the counter appeared to recognise her, and immediately handed her a letter which was addressed simply to "*A. B. C., Post-Office, Southampton Row. To be left till called for.*"

Miss de Medina purchased a few articles of fancy stationery—evidently with the view to recompense the shopkeeper for the trouble of receiving her letters, and not because she required the things; and while the woman was occupied in making up the parcel, Esther proceeded to read the communication just placed in her hands.

For this purpose she raised her veil, and approached the light which burnt near the window.

The letter was short: but its contents drew tears from the eyes of the beautiful Jewess.

Scarcely had she terminated the perusal, when she was startled by hearing a voice at the door distinctly exclaim, "There she is, by heaven!"

Instinctively glancing in that direction, she beheld a very pale-faced lad of apparently fifteen or sixteen gazing intently upon her from the immediate vicinity of the threshold of the shop; and close behind him—with his eyes also fixed upon her—stood a very tall, thin, old man of most repulsive aspect.

The instant Esther looked towards them, the old man laid his hand on the lad's shoulder and hurried him away; and Esther—somewhat alarmed by the incident—took up the little parcel of stationery, wished the woman a courteous "good evening," and quitted the shop.

When she again found herself in the street, she drew down her veil, and hastened towards the nearest hackney-coach stand.

A vehicle speedily drew alongside of the kerb-stone for her accommodation; and as she was stepping into it, she distinctly beheld, through the folds of her veil, the tall old man and the pale lad entering another vehicle at a little distance.

She could not be mistaken—for the shops sent forth a flood of light which rendered the forms of those two persons plainly visible.

The coachman had to repeat his inquiry whither he was to drive, ere Esther could recover her presence of mind sufficiently to reply.

"To the nearest post-office in Holborn," she at length said.

"Why, Lord bless you, ma'am—there's one close by here—not ten yards off," answered the Jarvey, who was an honest fellow in his way.

"Never mind," said Esther. "I wish to be taken to another."

The man urged no farther objection, but mounted his box and drove away—quietly settling in his own mind that his "fare" was either mad or tipsy, he neither knew nor cared which.

Miss de Medina could not shake off an oppressive suspicion which had forced itself upon her. She fancied that she was watched;—and, for the simple reason that she knew nothing of the old man and the lad, her uneasiness increased into actual alarm.

This feeling was enhanced, too, when her quick ears caught the rumbling sound of another vehicle behind: and she began to blame herself for having ventured abroad at such an hour.

Then she reasoned with herself that no harm could possibly happen to her in the midst of a densely populated city, and while people were walking about in all directions:—but still, in spite of this attempt at self-assurance, the pale countenance of the lad and the sinister looks of the old man haunted her like spirits of evil.

But in a few minutes the hackney-coach entered Holborn; and the blaze of light—the bustle—the throng of vehicles—the crowd of foot-passengers—and the animated appearance of the whole scene, dispelled nearly all her alarms.

The vehicle draw up nearly at the corner of Fetter Lane; and Esther alighted.

Another hackney-coach stopped simultaneously at a short distance; and her eyes were immediately directed towards it.

"Here's the post-office, ma'am," said the driver of the vehicle which she had hired.

Miss de Medina started—recollected herself—and hastened to thrust into the letter-box the epistle which she had written ere she left home.

The address on that epistle was—"*T. R., No. 5, Brandon Street, Lock's Fields.*"

This superscription was caught by the sharp eyes of the pale-faced boy, who had stolen—quick as thought—up to the shop-window, and now stood by Esther's side as she dropped the letter into the box.

When Esther turned hastily to regain the vehicle, she beheld the lad retreating with strange speed from the spot.

"What can this mean?" she thought within herself. "Who is it that is thus watching my movements?"

And, seriously alarmed, she hurried back to the coach, giving orders to be driven direct to Great Ormond Street.

Away went the vehicle again; and the noise of crowded Holborn prevented the Jewess from judging by sounds whether the other hackney-coach was following——for that she was watched, she had no longer any doubt.

Suddenly a suspicion struck her like an icy chill. Could her father have employed spies to dog her—to mark her movements? Circumstances, on the one hand, suggested the probability of such an occurrence; while, on the other, the character of her parent was of a nature repugnant to such a proceeding. He was stern and severe, but strictly honourable; and Esther knew that he was not a man likely to adopt underhand measures.

Then wherefore was she watched? and why had the lad crept close up to her as she put the letter into the box?

The coach had turned up Gray's Inn Lane, which thoroughfare was more quiet than Holborn; and Esther could hear no sounds of a second vehicle.

Our readers are probably aware that the generality of hackney-coaches have, or rather *had* (for they are nearly extinct at the present day) a little window behind, covered with a sort of flap made of the same material as the lining.

Esther turned round and raised the flap to assure herself that there was really no vehicle following the one in which she was. But at the same instant a face disappeared as if it had suddenly sunk into the earth; but not before the Jewess had recognised the pale features and dark eyes of the lad.

A faint cry escaped her lips; and she fell back on the seat, a prey to vague but serious alarm.

In a few moments she recovered her self-possession, and again endeavoured to dispel her fears by arguing that no harm could possibly befall her—that, if any outrage were intended, her screams would speedily bring hundreds to her rescue—and that after all no real cause for apprehension might exist.

She arrived without accident in Great Ormond Street; and when she alighted at her own door, the lad who had terrified her was no longer to be seen.

Her father had not yet returned; and she was therefore again left to the companionship of her own thoughts. But when she was seated by the cheerful fire in the drawing-room, and with the bright lamp burning on the table, she smiled at those alarms which had ere now oppressed her.

The entire adventure now wore quite another aspect in her imagination. The old man and the boy were probably thieves who prowled about to pursue their avocation where they could: she had most likely been mistaken in the idea that they had entered a hackney-coach in Southampton Row simultaneously with herself; but they had followed her vehicle on foot; and when she stepped out to post her letter, the lad had taken that opportunity of creeping close up to her to pick her pocket. Having failed by the suddenness with which she had turned round, he had afterwards got up behind the coach to dog her to the end of her journey, with the hope of still succeeding in his predatory design; but when she had looked through the back-window, he had disappeared.

Such was the explanation which she now arranged in her mind for her own satisfaction. But, then, what could mean the words uttered at the door of the shop in Southampton Row—"There she is, by heaven!"

Fancy again came to her aid to set this point at rest:—she had most probably been watched by the old man and the lad before she was aware of the fact; and they had lost sight of her; but when they passed the shop her presence there had elicited the ejaculation from the youth.

Such was the manner in which Esther tranquillised herself relative to the little occurrence that had so much alarmed her:—whether her conjectures were well-founded, or not, the reader may judge by what we are about to relate.

No sooner had she posted her letter in Holborn, than Jacob, who had managed to get sight of its superscription, darted back to the second hackney-coach which had stopped near the top of Fetter Lane, and leaping in, said to Old Death, who was inside, "The letter is addressed to *'T. R., No. 5, Brandon Street, Lock's Fields.'*"

"And that is Tom Rain's place," ejaculated Bones. "Well—do you follow her—get up behind the coach—and meet me at Bunce's presently."

Away started Jacob; and when he was gone, Old Death alighted from the vehicle which he had hired in Southampton Row to follow Esther, dismissed it, and walked boldly into the shop where that young lady had posted her letter.

A lad was in attendance behind the counter.

"My boy," said Old Death, in as pleasant a tone as he could assume, "I just this minute dropped a letter into the box; and I remember that I have made a mistake in a particular circumstance mentioned in its contents."

"You can't have it back again," replied the boy. "It's against the rules."

"Well, I know it is," said Old Death coaxingly. "But it's of the greatest consequence to me to alter a particular part of it; and, if you'll oblige me, here's half-a-crown for your trouble."

Thus speaking, he displayed the proffered coin.

Now half-a-crown was a great temptation to a lad who only earned eighteen-pence a week in addition to his food: moreover, the master of the shop was absent at the moment, and not very likely to return in a hurry—for the boy knew he was with a party of friends at a neighbouring public-house:—and thus Old Death's silver argument was effectual.

"Well—I s'pose I must," said the youth. "But don't tell any body about it, though. What's the address?"

"*T. R., No. 5, Brandon Street, Lock's Fields.*"

The boy unlocked the letter-box, selected the particular epistle, and handed it to Old Death, who threw the half-crown on the counter, and marched off with the letter.

He could not restrain his curiosity until he reached Seven Dials or any other place which he was in the habit of frequenting, and accordingly turned into a public-house in the neighbourhood. There he ordered some refreshment, seated himself in a corner of the parlour, and carefully opened the letter in such a way that it might be re-sealed without exciting a suspicion of having ever been tampered with.

He then read the contents, which ran as follow:—

"I sit down in anguish of heart to pen a few lines to you—to you whom I love so sincerely, but whom I must never see more. My father has just made me take a terrible oath to that effect; and so determined was his manner—so resolute was he—so stern—so severe—(alas! that I should be compelled to say so!)—that I dared not refuse to obey his command. And yet you know that I am as devotedly attached to you as ever:—all I have suffered—all I have undergone on your account, must convince you of my unchanged, unchangeable affection. Do not, then, think ill of me on account of the oath which my father wrested—tore from me! My God! how my heart palpitates, as I write these lines! Oh! If you knew the state of my mind you would pity me! I am wretched:—heaven send that you are more happy than I! Alas! cannot you take compassion upon me—upon *me*, your own tender Esther—and quit the path which you are pursuing? It is not too late to do so—it is never too late. All might yet be well: my father would forget the past—and we should be re-united. Think of this—ponder well upon it—and remember how much happiness will be wrecked for ever, if you persist in a course which I tremble to reflect upon. To be connected with a highwayman is dreadful! Pardon me—forgive me for speaking thus plainly;—but you know how sincerely I love you—and if I write that terrible word '*highwayman*,' it is merely to fix your thoughts the more seriously on that point. What must be the end of this course of life? Public infamy—or perhaps a scaffold! Again I say, forgive me for writing thus:—I scarcely know what I commit to paper—there are moments when my brain reels as I contemplate the subject of my letter.

"I can write no more. Perhaps I shall find a note from you at the post office in Southampton Row: I hope so—and I also hope that I may discover in it some cause of satisfaction to myself. Adieu—dearest, adieu.

"ESTHER."

The contents of this letter sadly puzzled Old Death. They were quite different from what he had expected to find them; but without waiting to reflect upon their nature, he obtained a piece of sealing-wax from the waiter, and so cleverly closed the letter again that even a clerk in the General Post-Office could not have told it had been opened.

He then retraced his way to the shop in Holborn where it was originally posted, and threw it back into the box.

This being done, he bent his way towards Toby Bunce's house in Earl Street, Seven Dials.

CHAPTER XXIII.
OLD DEATH.

When Bones reached the place whither he had bent his steps, he learnt to his satisfaction that Toby Bunce had been sent out by his wife on some errand which would keep him at least an hour away. He accordingly followed Mrs. Bunce into the back room, and explained to her all that had occurred.

Having stated how he and Jacob had followed Esther in the hackney-coach from Southampton Row to Holborn, he said—"When Jacob first pointed her out to me as she was reading a letter in a shop, I felt sure he must be mistaken; for I could not conceive why she should be up at that part of the town, since from what Jacob discovered last night, I thought she was certainly living with Tom Rain in Lock's Fields. However, I determined to follow her; and when she got down at a shop in Holborn, I told Jacob to jump out and get another good look at her, if possible. But, instead of going into the shop, she merely stopped there to post a letter; and Jacob was quick enough to catch sight of the address. Well, when he came back to me, and told me what that address was, I desired him to follow her directly; for I thought that if she was writing to Tom Rain, it was clear she didn't live with him, and therefore it was as well to find out where she does live."

"To be sure," said Mrs. Bunce approvingly.

"Then it struck me," continued Old Death, "that if I could only get sight of the contents of that letter which she had posted to Tom Rain, it might open some farther clue to the nature of their connexion. And I did get the letter——"

"Oh! you clever fellow!" interrupted Betsy, shaking her head with mock gravity. "But what did the letter say?"

"Why, it was a regular sermon," answered Old Death. "It talked about how much she loved him—all she had done and suffered on his account—and a lot of gammon of that kind. She told him how her father had made her take an oath not to see him any more, and how unhappy she was. Then she begged of him to repent and leave a course of life that is sure to end at Tuck-up Fair."

"Did she use them words?" demanded Mrs. Bunce.

"No, you fool!" cried Old Death. "She writes quite like a lady, and in a beautiful hand too! But, after having said all I have told you, she let him know that she shuddered at the idea of being connected with a highwayman: and she begged his pardon for calling him so."

"A pleasant letter for Tom to receive!" observed Mrs. Bunce.

"Very. And she drops a hint," continued Old Death, "that if he will give up his business, there is a chance of her father forgiving Tom for what is past, and of their being *re-united*—that's the very word."

"Do you think they are married, then?" asked the woman.

"I should say not," replied Bones; "because she talks of being *connected* with a highwayman—and that's not a word a wife uses to her husband. Besides, the whole letter didn't look like one written by a wife—but rather a mistress. And then it ends by saying that she hopes to find a letter from him at the post-office in Southampton Row."

"Find a letter—when?" asked Mrs. Bunce.

"Why, to-day—this evening, I suppose," said Old Death. "She had evidently written *her* letter *before* she went to the post-office in Southampton Row, where she *did* find one from him—because she was reading a note when Jacob first twigged her. And it was singular enough that we were just talking of her at that very identical moment."

"Then the letter you read wasn't an answer to the one she received in Southampton Row?" said Mrs. Bunce.

"Of course not, stupid!" cried Old Death. "We followed her straight down to Holborn, and she never stopped or went in any where to write an answer. The letter I read was already written—written too in the afternoon, most likely just before she came out to go to Southampton Row. And another reason that made me anxious to get hold of her letter to Tom Rain, was that she didn't post it at the office where she received *his*, but took the trouble to go down to Holborn to put it into another box."

"I wonder why she did that?" said Mrs. Bunce.

"Oh! most likely to avoid exciting any suspicion or curiosity at the office in Southampton Row. Then there's another thing that puzzles me:—she was with Tom Rain last night—Jacob saw them together, and followed them home to Lock's Fields; and she is away from him to-day—writes to him this afternoon—and hopes to find a letter from him when she goes to Southampton Row this evening. One would think, by this, that they have been in the habit of corresponding together, and that the place in Southampton Row is where he directs his letters to her. So it's pretty clear that they don't live together for good and all. But what perplexes me most is the sermon that she wrote him. It's plain she stole the diamonds, from what Jacob overheard Tom say to her when he gave her the ear-rings last night; and yet she doesn't reproach herself a bit in the letter to him. She only tries to convert Rainford; and, to read that letter, one would think she was as innocent of a theft or such-like thing as a child unborn."

"Oh! I dare say she wrote the letter for some object or another which we can't see," observed Mrs. Bunce.

"I scarcely think so," returned Bones: "there was so much seriousness about it."

"But she's a precious deep one, depend on it," said Betsy. "Look how she got off about the diamonds. And, after all, perhaps her father had been talking her over; and so, if she wrote to Tom Rain in a serious way, the humour won't last very long."

"Well—we shall see," exclaimed Old Death. "I should like to secure her in my interests."

"What did you do with the letter she wrote to Tom Rain?" asked Mrs. Bunce.

"Put it back into the post," was the reply. "Fancy if Esther and Tom *did* get together again, and, on comparing notes, he found that the letter from her had miscarried, he might suspect a trick somewhere, and fix foul play on me. No—no: it was more prudent to let the note go, since I had gathered its contents."

"Well—perhaps it was," said Mrs. Bunce. "One thing is very clear, Ben——"

"What's that, Betsy?"

"Why—that since Esther isn't any longer with Mr. Rainford in the Fields, it will be much easier to get the little boy away."

"I thought of that just now," said Old Death: then, after a pause, he added, "And I'll tell you what's to be done. The boy most be got into our power to-morrow night."

"To-morrow night!" repeated Mrs. Bunce.

"Yes—to-morrow night," returned Bones emphatically. "I'll trump up something to get Tom out of the way; and me, Toby, and Jacob, will go over and kidnap the child. If we don't do it quick, the Jewess will be getting spooney on Tom again and going back to live with him in spite of her oath to her father; and then we may not find such another chance for some time to come."

Mrs. Bunce smiled an approval of this scheme, and was about to offer a comment, when a knock summoned her to the front-door.

She shortly returned to the back-room, followed by Jacob.

"What news?" demanded Old Death.

"I found out where the Jewess lives," was the lad's answer; and he named the address in Great Ormond Street.

"Good!" exclaimed Bones. "That shows why she has her letters sent to Southampton Row;—it is close by; and as she's known in the neighbourhood, she posts her answers at another place. But give Jacob his supper—and brew me some grog, Betsy."

While Mrs. Bunce was busily employed in executing these orders, another knock at the front-door was heard. Jacob hastened to answer it, and returned with a letter directed to "MR. TOBY BUNCE;" but which, having a peculiar mark placed somewhere amidst the writing, was instantly discovered by Old Death to be intended for himself.

He accordingly opened it, and read as follows:—

"Tim put on the tats yesterday and went out a durry-nakin on the shallows, gadding the hoof. He buzzed a bloak and a shakester of a yack and a skin. His jomen Mutton-Face Sal, with her moll-sack queering a raclan, stalled. A cross-cove, who had his regulars, tipped the office '*Cop Busy!*' and Tim twigged that a pig was marking. So he speeled to the crib, while his jomen shoved her trunk too. To-day Tim sent the yack to church and christen; but the churchman came to it through poll, as Tim's shaler had slummed on him a sprat and an alderman last week. So Tim didn't fight cocum enough, and was grabbed. The skin had three finnips and a foont, which I've got at the padding-ken, T's 23, where I'll cop them to you for edging the gaff. A fly kidden-gonnoff will leave this flim.

"TWENTY-FIVE."

Old Death having read this singular composition to himself, threw it into the fire.

He then sate pondering for a few moments upon the course which he should pursue under the circumstances just made known to him.

And while he is thus engaged in meditation, we will lay before our readers a translation of the slang document:—

"Tim dressed himself in rags yesterday, and went out disguised as a beggar half-naked and without shoes or stockings. He robbed a gentleman and a lady of a watch and a purse. His mistress Mutton-Face Sal, with her reticule, and looking like a respectable female, was on the look-out close at hand. A confederate-thief, who went shares with Tim, suddenly gave the alarm, so that Tim might hand him over the plunder; and Tim saw that a person was watching him. So he hurried off home, while his woman got off safely also. To-day Tim sent the watch to have the works taken out and put in another case and to get the maker's name altered; but the watch-maker informed against him through spite, because Tim's mistress had passed off on him (the watch-maker) a bad sixpence and half-crown last week. So Tim wasn't wary enough, and was taken into custody. The purse had three five-pound notes and a sovereign in it, which I have got at Thompson's lodging-house, No. 23, where I will hand them over to you if you will try and get Tim off. A sharp boy-thief will leave this letter."

The signature "TWENTY-FIVE" indicated the number attached to the writer's name in Old Death's private list of those thieves who were accustomed to do business with him.

"Any thing new?" inquired Mrs. Bunce, handing him a glass of hot gin-and-water.

"Nothing particular," was the reply. "Only Tim the Snammer[2] got himself into a scrape. But I shall go and see about it directly."

"Tim isn't on your list—is he?" demanded Mrs. Bunce.

"No: but Josh Pedler—that's Number Twenty-five—has got Tim's money, and will hand it over to me. So———"

A loud knock at the door interrupted Old Death's observation.

Jacob was sent to answer the summons; and in a few moments Tom Rain walked jauntily into the room.

"Well, my prince of fences," he exclaimed, addressing Old Death, as he cast himself unceremoniously into a chair, and stretched out his legs in a free and independent manner, "any thing new in the wind?"

"Yes—a trifling job—for to-morrow night, Tom," answered Bones. "But you'll be making your fortune at this rate?" he added, with one of his hideous chuckles.

"The sooner, the better," cried the highwayman.

"And then you'd be able to retire from business—marry—and settle yourself comfortably," said Old Death, with apparent indifference of manner, but in reality watching Rainford's countenance attentively as he uttered the word "*marry*."

"Oh! as for settling," exclaimed Tom, laughing, "I am not the chap to bury myself in a cottage in Wales or Devonshire. I don't like that sort of thing. Business and bustle suit me best."

"But what do you say to marriage, Tom? A good-looking fellow like you might do something in that line to great advantage," observed Old Death.

"That's my own affair," returned the highwayman hastily.

"By-the-bye, what have you done with the boy that was thrown on your hands t'other night?" asked Old Death.

"I am taking care of him, to be sure," was the answer. "If I abandon him, he must go to the workhouse. But what is the little job you were talking about?"

"A worthy citizen and his wife will pass over Shooter's Hill to-morrow night, at about eleven o'clock, in a yellow post-chaise," replied Bones, inventing the tale as he went on. "The cit will have enough in his pocket-book to make it worth while to ease him of it; and the postboy will stop when he's ordered to do so. They were to have gone to-night; but something has happened to put off their journey till to-morrow."

"Good," said Tom. "The business shall be done. Any thing else to communicate to-night?"

"Nothing," was the answer.

"Won't you stay and take a drop of something warm, Mr. Rainford?" asked Betsy Bunce, in her most winning way.

"No, thank 'ee," returned Tom. "I must be off. Good night."

And the highwayman took his departure.

When the front-door was closed behind him, Old Death said, with a chuckle, "Well, he'll be out of the way to-morrow night; and we shall get hold of the boy. But I shall now just step up to Castle Street, and see what's going on at twenty-three."

"Shall you come back here to-night?" asked Mrs. Bunce.

"I can't say. It's now nine o'clock; and if I do, it will be by ten. Jacob, my boy, you needn't wait unless you like."

Old Death then left the house.

---

2. Snammer—a thief.

CHAPTER XXIV.
CASTLE STREET, LONG ACRE.

To the north of Long Acre runs Castle Street—for many years notorious as a nest of thieves, prostitutes, and juvenile vagabonds of the most degraded description.

At the period of which we are writing, a person, of the name of Thompson, owned—and probably still possesses—the lodging-houses numbered 23, 24, and 25 in Castle Street. This individual resided in Mint Street, Borough, where he had similar houses, in addition to others in Buckeridge Street, St. Giles's.

The houses in Buckeridge Street would make up one hundred beds; and those in Castle Street sixty.

At lodging-houses of this description the rooms are filled with low truckle-beds, each having a straw mattress, two coarse sheets, a blanket, and a rug. The price of half a bed is threepence; and it need scarcely be observed that men, women, and children sleep together in these filthy receptacles without the slightest regard to decency or modesty. Sometimes, when the lodging-houses are particularly crowded, three persons will share one bed;—or motives of economy frequently compel a poor family thus to herd together. It is by no means an uncommon occurrence for a grown-up girl to sleep with her father and mother, or with her brothers:—a poor married couple will even share their bed with a male friend;—and no shame is known!

Who can define where the shades of doubtful honesty and confirmed roguery meet and blend in these low lodging-houses? The labouring man is in nightly company with the habitual thief—his wife and his as yet uncorrupted daughter are forced to associate with the lowest prostitutes. How long will that wife remain faithful—that daughter taint-less? The very children who breathe that infected atmosphere soon become lost, and triumph in their degradation!

The principal frequenters and patrons of these low lodging-houses are regular customers, and consist of thieves, prostitutes, beggars, coiners, burglars, and hawkers. The casual lodgers are labouring men and their families whom poverty compels to sleep in such horrible places.

The hawkers make a great deal of money. They can buy steel-pens for 9*d.* a gross, pocket-books for 3*d.* each, snuff-boxes for 6*d.* each, and penknives for 4½*d.* each. On every article they can gain one hundred per cent. Many of these hawkers consider nine or ten shillings to be only a reasonable, and by no means a good, day's work.

Some of the women who frequent the lodging-houses in Castle Street and elsewhere, and who have no children of their own, hire infants for 4*d*. or 6*d*. a day, and obtain in the shape of alms at least four or five shillings a day each. Females of this class care not whether their husbands or lovers work or remain idle; for they boast that they can keep them—and keep them well, too. Some of these women knit caps in the streets; and they make more money than those who merely trust to the children accompanying them as the motive of charitable persons' compassion.[3]

In the low lodging-houses of Castle Street, and wherever else they may be found, the most frightful dissipation as well as the most appalling immorality prevails. Drunkenness is the presiding genius of these dens.

And how much has STRONG DRINK to answer for?

It is strong drink that helps to fill the gaols—the hulks—the asylums for the wretched, the diseased, and the insane. It is strong drink that calls forth so many sighs and such bitter tears—shortens existence—perpetuates family disease—and fosters maladies of all species and of all kinds. Strong drink often places the criminal in the condemned cell, and reduces the beautiful girl to barter her charms for bread. Strong drink strews the land with old rags and bleaching bones.

Let Temperance and Moderation be the guides of all:—for what are the results of Intemperance and habitual Drunkenness? Behold them in all the poor and low neighbourhoods of London! And if you ask, reader, by what signs you are to recognise them, we will tell you:—by the leaden eyes—the tottering steps—the shaking limbs—the haggard countenances—the feverish brows—the parched lips—the dry and furred tongue—the hot and pestilential breath—and the tremulous voices, of the confirmed votaries of strong drink. Apoplexy—palsy—delirium tremens—enlarged liver—ossified heart—impaired digestion—yellow jaundice—cancerous stomach—and dropsy,—all these attend upon strong drink. And the hideous catalogue of evils includes, also, broken limbs—fearful accidents and gushing wounds,—as well as many of those hereditary maladies which are handed down from father unto son!

In an earlier chapter we ridiculed the phrase of "Merry England." Oh! is it merry to see so much misery—so much crime—so much oppression—so much sorrow—so much absence of sympathy? If all this be joyous, then, of a surety, is England the merriest country, and London the merriest city, on the face of the earth. If a man can find music in the cries that issue from our crowded prisons and the wails that flow from our barbarous workhouses, then may he dance long and heartily to that melody—for it never ceases. If poverty can excite felicitous sensations within him, heaven knows he need never be sad. If crime can bring smiles to his lips, his countenance need never wear a melancholy aspect. And if he can slake his thirst in the heart-wrung tears of human agony, he need never step out of his way to look for a fountain or a spring!

In this light, England is indeed merry; for the observer of human nature, as he walks through the crowded streets of London, is jostled and hemmed in by all the gaunt and hideous forms that bear the denominations and wear the characteristics of Crime—Poverty—Disease—Sorrow—and Despair!

Old Death knocked at the door of No. 23, Castle Street, and was instantly admitted by a tall, pale, and rather handsome girl, who exclaimed, "Ah! my fine fellow—I thought you would come."

"Is it you, Mutton-Face?" said Bones, with a grim smile.

"Me—and no one else," answered the girl. "But walk in."

Old Death accepted the invitation, and followed Mutton-Face Sal into a room where about two dozen persons, male and female, were crowded round a large fire.

One was a young man, of the name of Quin, and who obtained a handsome income by means of imposture. He was accustomed to appear in the streets as a wretched-looking, deplorable old man, bent double with age and infirmity, supporting himself on a stick, and crawling along in a painful manner at the slowest possible rate. He used to swallow a dose of some strong acid every morning to make himself look ghastly pale; and he succeeded so well in counterfeiting an aspect of the most lamentable nature, that he seldom returned to Castle Street at night with less than ten shillings in his pocket. He had now thrown off his disguise, and was whiling away the time, after a good supper, with a quart of egg-hot.

Next to him sate a young woman, stout, florid, and rather good-looking. She was in her stays and petticoat, having very quietly taken off her gown to mend a rent; and she experienced not the slightest shame at thus exposing all the upper part of her person to the mixed society present. Neither did they appear to think there was any thing at all remarkable in her conduct. How, indeed, could it be otherwise?—since she would presently undress herself entirely in that very room—and before all her companions, who would do the same—male and female—when the hour arrived to repair to the beds ranged along the wall. This girl was known as Jane Cummins, and was the mistress of the impostor Quin.

Farther on was a fellow who was sitting upright enough in his chair then, but who appeared daily in the streets as a bent cripple. He was accustomed to go about imitating a cuckoo, by which avocation he made a good living. He invariably got drunk every night.

Next to this impostor was a little deformity who was tied round the body to his chair. He had no legs, and was dragged about the streets of a day in a kind of cart drawn by two beautiful dogs, and having a banner unfurled behind him. The woman in charge of No. 23 paid him the greatest attention—put him to bed at night—helped him to rise in the morning—carried him out to his vehicle—strapped him in—and saw him safe off on his excursion about the metropolis. He usually returned at four to his dinner, and did not go out afterwards. His "earnings" were on the average ten shillings a-day.

A woman of about thirty, dressed in widow's weeds, and far advanced in the family way, sate next to the little deformity. She had never been married, but was possessed of five children, who were now playing in one corner of the room. She was accustomed to take her stand in some public thoroughfare, with her children drawn up in a row; and this game she had carried on, at the time of which we are writing, for four years—rather a long period of widowhood. She disliked fine weather, because the hearts of the charitable are more easily touched by the spectacle of a "destitute family" standing in the midst of a pouring rain or on the snow; and she reckoned that in bad weather she could earn eight or nine shillings a-day. Every Saturday night she took her station in some poor neighbourhood—such as Church Street (Bethnal Green), Leather Lane, Lambeth Marsh, High Street (St. Giles's), or Clare Market; and on those occasions she often obtained as much as fifteen shillings. But then, as she very justly observed, Sunday was a day of rest; and so it was indeed to her—for she was in the habit of getting so awfully drunk every Saturday night, after her return home to Castle Street, that she was compelled to lie in bed all the next day until three or four o'clock, when she rose to a good dinner. She always kept herself and children remarkably neat and clean—not from any principle, but as a matter of calculation. Charitable people thought she was a good mother, and a deserving though distressed woman; and alms poured in upon her. When questioned by any individual who relieved her, she would reply that "her husband was a bricklayer who had fallen off a ladder and killed himself six weeks ago;" or that "he was an honest, hard-working man whose career was suddenly cut short by his being run over by a gentleman's carriage:" or some such tale.

Next to her sate a young woman who was wont to take her stand in the evening, after dusk, close by the entrance to Somerset House. In the summer she would hold a few flowers in her hand: in the winter, laces and bobbins; and her invariable cry was "Oh! pray, dear sir"——or "dear lady," as the case might be——"pray do assist me: I have only this moment come out of the hospital, and have nowhere to sleep." By these means she realized her five shillings in three or four hours, and hastened back to Castle Street to spend them with a worthless fellow—her paramour.

Another individual whom we must mention, was an elderly man, who in his youth had been apprenticed to a chemist. He obtained his living by displaying a fearfully ulcerated arm, having himself originally produced the sores by means of corrosive acids and by the juices of various plants—such as the ranunculus acris and sceleratus, the sponge-laurel, euphorbium, arum maculatum, &c. He regularly revived and aggravated the ulcers every time they began to heal, and his arm was really shocking to contemplate. He would take his stand before a window, and, raising his shirt-sleeve, display the ulcers, so that the ladies or gentlemen at the casement sent him out a sixpence or a shilling as much for the purpose of getting rid of so loathsome a spectacle as through motives of charity. It was this man's boast that three hours in a fashionable street or square would produce him seven or eight shillings.

Another impostor present on this occasion was a man of about forty, who was a perfect adept in disguising his person, and who feigned a different malady for every change in his attire and outward appearance. At one time he was suffering from ophthalmia, produced by the application of irritants—such as snuff, pepper, tobacco, blue vitriol, salt, alum, &c. At another he would actually produce blindness for a time by the application of belladonna, henbane, or sponge-laurel; and then he was led about by a little boy. Again, he would appear as a miserable creature afflicted with a horrible jaundice—the yellow colour being produced by a dye. He was also perfect in the counterfeit of spasmodic complaints, paralysis, and convulsions. His earnings were usually considerable: but on one occasion, "when things were very bad," he obtained admission into a hospital as an epileptic patient; and so well did he assume the dreadful attacks at particular intervals, that he remained in the institution for several weeks.

Lying on one of the beds, in a filthy state of intoxication, was a miserable object who was accustomed to go about the streets on his hands and knees, holding iron grapnels. His spine was bent upwards—rounded like that of a cat in a passion; and his legs were moreover deformed. His supine position was no counterfeit: he could not walk on his feet like other human beings. Thus far he certainly was an object of compassion: but in his character he was a worthless fellow—abusive, insolent, drunken, and addicted to thieving.

Sitting on another bed, and so far gone in liquor that he could scarcely hold the pipe he was smoking, sate a man about forty years of age, named Barlow. He had been a clergyman and was now a begging-letter impostor. He possessed an excellent address, and was most plausible in his speech as he was fluent with his pen; but the moment he obtained any money, he was never sober until it was spent. He had travelled all over England—knew every nobleman's or gentleman's country seat—and had carried on an excellent business by means of his begging-letters.[4]

A labouring man, his wife, and daughter were amongst this precious company. The girl was about fifteen, and tolerably good-looking. The family had been three days in that lodging-house; and she already laughed at the obscene jest and applauded the licentious song.

Two or three hawkers—a couple of juvenile thieves—and some young girls, confirmed prostitutes, made up the amount of the precious company into whose presence Mutton-Face Sal had conducted Old Death.

Those who were acquainted with him saluted him respectfully; for he was a great man—a very great man—amongst persons of a particular class.

"Who is that horrible old wretch?" asked the labourer's daughter, in a whisper to Jane Cummins.

"The richest fence in London," returned the other in the same low tone of voice.

"And what's a *fence*, Miss?"

"A fence, you fool, is a buyer of stolen goods, as the beaks call it. That old covey is rolling in riches—shabby and mean as you see him. He has been at it, they tell me, upwards of thirty years, and has never got his-self lumbered yet. But the best of it is, no one knows where his stores are: no one even knows where he lives. He has certain houses of call; but the cunningest Bow Street Officer can't find out his abode."

"What do you mean by *lumbered?*" asked the girl, whose name was Matilda.

"Put into quod, to be sure. But how green you are. We must teach you what's what, I see that. Here—help me to put on my gown—it's mended now. Thank'ee. Now come with me to the window, and I'll tell you what a happy kind of life I lead—and how you may do the same if you like."

But even as she uttered these words, Jane Cummins heaved a sigh—although she strove hard to subdue it.

The girl walked aside with her; and they continued their conversation in whispers at the window.

"I'm afraid our Tilda'll get no good here," said the labourer, in a low tone, to his wife, as he glanced uneasily towards his daughter.

"Nonsense, you fool!" returned the woman. "You can't get no work—and we must starve if we don't do something. Our gal can keep us, if she will—and she must too. Sooner or later it will come to *that* with her—and as well now as ever."

The poor labourer sighed: he would have remained honest, and kept his wife and daughter so, if he could; but want and houseless wanderings in the cold street stared him in the face—and he resigned himself to the bitter destiny that was thus forced upon him and his family!

In the mean time Old Death had taken a seat near the fire, and was deep in a whispered conversation with Mutton-Face Sal.

"Where's Josh Pedler?" he asked.

"He'll be in shortly," was the answer. "He's only gone out to fetch something for his supper."

"And so Tim the Snammer is lumbered?" said Old Death.

"Yes: he's in Clerkenwell. But you'll get him off when he goes up again 'afore the beak on Saturday—won't you, old chap?—now, won't you?"

"I don't know—I don't know. He isn't one of my men: he never would give me a turn. His name doesn't appear against a number on my list."

"But he will give you all his business in future, if you'll get him off this time—just this time," said the girl coaxingly.

"We shall see what Josh has to tell me—I never promise in a hurry," returned Old Death. "Besides, it's not the rule to assist a man that goes to others to do his business. Tim gets his notes changed at old Isaacs[5]—or at Milberry's[6]—or at Mrs. Davis's[7]—or at Rayner's[8]—or——"

And as Old Death enumerated his competitors, telling them off on his fingers slowly, one after the other, his jealousy arose to such a pitch that the workings of his countenance became absolutely frightful.

"Now, what's the use of going on like this?" said Sal. "I tell you that Tim shan't have no more to do with them people, if you'll only get him off this time. None of them can do it as sure as you; and if you only tell me it shall be done, why—it's as good as done."

At this moment the door opened, and a tall, rather good-looking, but rakish and shabbily-dressed man, of about five-and-twenty, made his appearance.

"Here's Josh!" cried the girl.

The thief and Old Death exchanged greetings; and the latter proposed to adjourn to a public-house in the neighbourhood to talk over the business. Thither the two men, accompanied by Mutton-Face Sal, accordingly repaired; and Bones suffered himself to be persuaded to receive the three five-pound notes and the sovereign, mentioned in the flash letter, as the price of his endeavours to procure the discharge of Tim the Snammer.

The old man then took his departure, and Josh Pedler returned with Sal to the lodging-house.

3. A police-serjeant, from whom we have obtained much valuable information relative to the poverty, mendicity, immorality, and crime in London, one day informed us that he knew of two sisters, both single women, who were confined at about the same time, and who took it by turns to go out with the children. They passed the babies off as twins, and made upon an average seven shillings a day by this imposture. The money was spent in riotous living and debauchery, in the evening, along with their flash men, who existed in complete idleness, living, however, far better than many a poor tradesman. One evening, the police-serjeant above alluded to had occasion to visit the room which the sisters occupied at one of Thompson's houses in Castle Street (a robbery having been committed in the dwelling), and he found the two young women and their paramours at supper. On the table were a baked shoulder of mutton and potatoes, two quarts of porter, and a bottle of gin. One of the sisters is at the present moment a prostitute in Fleet Street.

4. All the characters just depicted are real ones. Some of them are still about town.

5. A notorious fence living in Liquorpond Street.

6. A flash public-house at the corner of Laurence Lane, St. Giles's.

7. A fence living in Belson Street.

8. A stick-maker, and a noted fence, living in Coach and Horses Yard, Drury Lane.

CHAPTER XXV.
MATILDA, THE COUNTRY-GIRL.

In the meantime Jane Cummins had been using all her eloquence for the purpose of inducing Matilda Briggs, the poor labourer's daughter, to become as bad as herself.

"You don't know what a pleasant life we lead," she repeated, when she had drawn the girl aside to the window. "Quin—my man—earns lots of money—and we know how to spend it. To-night we'd a roast loin of pork and apple-sauce for supper at a slap-up eating-house: then we'd some rum-and-water: and then we came home here. Look how Quin's enjoying himself with that egg-hot. Isn't he a capital fellow to be able to get so much money—and all so easy too? and don't you think I'm happy to have nothing to do but to help him spend it?"

Again the young woman struggled fruitlessly to keep down a sigh; for—in reality—she loathed, she abhorred the life which she was leading.

"And what do you suppose will become of you and your father and mother?" she continued. "Why—if it wasn't for that good-natured fellow Josh Pedler you'd have all been turned out last night into the streets. And when the woman came in just now to collect the three-pences, didn't he take and pay for you and the old people? And didn't he give you all the grub you had to-day?"

"Why do you speak so much about *him*?" asked the country-girl.

"Oh! I don't know—only because he seems to have taken a fancy to you," returned Jane Cummins. "And I tell you what it is—you may become his jomen if you like."

"His what?" said Matilda, blushing—for she half understood the meaning of the word.

"Why—his wife, over the left, if you choose," was the answer. "But what a fool you are! You're not so innocent as you pretend to be. Come—tell me—have you ever had a lover?"

"Never," replied the girl.

"Then it's high time you should. The truth is, Josh told me to sound you," she added in a mysterious manner; "and if you only say the word, we'll have a wedding here to-night. Josh has got plenty of money at this moment. He found a purse the day before yesterday——"

"Where?" inquired the country-girl.

"In a gentleman's pocket, at the theatre," returned Jane coolly; "and he talks of setting up a mint——"

"A mint! what with?" asked Matilda.

"With Queen's metal, to be sure," responded the other; "and I think he's a very thriving young fellow. You'd be as happy as a princess along with him;—and wouldn't he come out strong to-night with the lush, if you was to say *yes*."

"But my father—my mother——" murmured the girl hesitatingly.

"Oh! leave them to me!" said Jane Cummins. "Go and sit down again—I'll manage the old woman—and she can manage the old man herself."

Matilda returned to her seat; and Quin, who could pretty well guess what his mistress had been about, handed the country-girl the quart-pot of egg-flip. She declined to partake of it; but he pressed her hard—and she drank a few drops.

"Oh! that's nothink—a mere taste!" cried Quin. "Take another sip. Come."

And she did as she was desired.

"Lord bless the girl—she's quite afraid of it!" said Quin. "But you must and shall have a good draught."

Resistance was vain: Quin held the pewter-pot to her lips, and forced her to imbibe a considerable quantity.

He then passed the measure to her mother, who did not require any entreaty to drink; and the labourer himself was not one likely to refuse good liquor when it was offered to him.

Quin thus got upon very pleasant terms with the poor family; and, making Briggs sit next to him, he began to chatter away in a familiar style, not forgetting to hand round the quart-pot at short intervals.

Meantime Jane Cummins had drawn Mrs. Briggs aside, and made certain representations to her—the result of which was that Matilda should that very night become the mistress of Josh Pedler. The arrangement was, however, to be kept quiet until Josh should return, for fear that he might have altered his mind since he spoke to Jane on the subject in the morning.

At length Pedler came back, accompanied by Mutton-Face Sal; and, as he entered the room, he exclaimed, "Well, pals, it's all right! Old Death has took it in hand—and so Tim is as good as out. I've ordered round a gallon of gin-punch to make merry in consequence."

This announcement was received with loud cheers.

"Come you here, Josh," cried Jane Cummins: "I want to say a word to you."

"Well—what is it?" demanded the thief.

"Oh! nothing bad," she replied, with a significant look at her paramour Quin, who laughed heartily—as if an excellent piece of fun were in preparation.

Jane then whispered a few words in Josh Pedler's ears: the man did not, however, wait to hear all she had to say; but, bursting away from her, caught Matilda Briggs in his arms, and, giving her three or four hearty smacks with his lips, shouted, "A wedding, pals! a wedding!"

"A wedding!" repeated those who were only now let into the meaning of all the mysterious whispering that had been going on—first between Jane and Matilda—then between Jane and Mrs. Briggs—afterwards between Mrs. Briggs and her husband—and lastly between Jane and Josh Pedler:—"a wedding!" they cried: "hooray!"

"Yes—a wedding, in right good earnest!" exclaimed Josh. "But where's that drunken old file Barlow?"

"He's fallen asleep on his bed," observed Mutton-Face Sal.

"Then rouse him—and be damned to him!" cried Pedler.

Sal approached the bed, and speedily awoke the parson, who was at first mighty wroth at what he considered to be a very great liberty: but when he was informed that his services were required to perform a matrimonial ceremony—that he was to have five shillings for the job—and that a gallon of gin-punch was expected immediately, he uttered a tremendous oath by way of expressing his joy, and leapt up with as much alacrity as the fumes of liquor, which still influenced his brain, would permit him to display.

A circle was then formed, in the midst of which Josh Pedler, Matilda Briggs, and the begging-letter-impostor parson took their station. One of the hawkers produced a common brass ring, which he handed to Barlow, over whose person Quin threw a sheet by way of surplice, while another individual gave him an obscene book.

The greatest excitement now prevailed amongst the rogues and loose women present: and even Matilda herself entered into the spirit of the proceeding—for she was excited with the liquor which Quin had forced upon her. Her poor father alone experienced a qualm of conscience:—but he dared not utter a word calculated to betray his scruples or manifest his regrets—for his wife, of whom he stood in dread, cordially approved of the arrangement.

The drunken parson now commenced the ceremony; and assuming, as well as he could, the seriousness of former days, he recited the following slang chant:—[9]

"I, parish prig and bouncing ben,

Do here, within this padding-ken,

Josh Pedler—if thou wilt agree—

Cop that young shaler unto thee.

To her a fancy bloak be thou:—

Tip mauleys—she's thy jomen now."

Barlow made the bride and bridegroom join hands, and then continued thus:—

"When thou art out upon the cross,

May she be faithful to thy doss.

If things go rough, and traps are nigh,

May she upon the nose be fly."

The company then repeated in chorus the last line; after which display of their vocal powers, the ceremony was continued by the parson in the following words:—

"If you should pinch a lob—or plan

A sneezer, or a randlesman—

Or work the bulls and couters rum—

Or go the jump and speel the drum—

Or turn shop-bouncer at a pinch,—

Should you do this and get the clinch,

May she, while thou art lumbered, be

Still true and faithful, Josh, to thee."

The parson paused for few moments, and concluded with this distich:—

"Be witness, all, to what is said:—

And with this fawney ye are wed!"

Barlow handed Josh the ring, which the thief placed on the girl's finger, and then gave her a hearty kiss.

The spectators immediately set up a shout of acclamation; and at that instant the gin-punch made its appearance.

A scene of debauchery—noise—quarrelling—and ribaldry now followed. The parson was voted into the chair, which was constituted by the foot of one of the beds; and the punch went rapidly round in pewter-pots.

The bowl was soon emptied; whereupon Josh Pedler sent to the public-house and ordered another. The little deformity, without legs, sang a filthy song: even the man with the curved spine, and who went about on grapnels, forgot his wonted ill-humour and insolence, and joined in the mirth.

The woman, who had charge of the house, was summoned; and, for a consideration of seven shillings and sixpence, she agreed to provide a separate room for the accommodation of the "happy couple." This amount was duly paid; and the woman was made drunk into the bargain for her trouble.

At length some one proposed a dance; to which the parson objected, and moved "another bowl of punch" as an amendment. Jane Cummins, however, put an end to the argument by undressing herself, and performing sundry saltatory evolutions in a complete state of nudity—an example which was very speedily followed by Mutton-Face Sal, whose grief for the loss of her paramour, Tim the Snammer, was temporarily drowned in punch. Even the woman in widow's weeds was about to adopt the same course; but she was too tipsy to accomplish her purpose, and, on rising from her chair, fell on one of the beds and into a profound sleep at the same time.

The noise, confusion, and disgusting licentiousness of the scene increased to an extraordinary degree; but Josh Pedler led Matilda away—or rather carried her; for the unfortunate girl was now in a complete state of intoxication.

Revolting as the contemplation of such a scene as that just described must be to the rightly-constituted mind, it was nevertheless requisite to introduce it into such a work as the present.

Its details prove how necessary it is to establish in the great metropolis cheap and well-conducted lodging-houses for the use of poor but honest families.

This cannot be done by private speculators, because an efficient management could only be secured by legislative enactment.

The Government, then, should direct its attention to this very important subject.

A poor man is compelled to quit his native town or village in the provinces, and comes to London to seek for work. He is accompanied by his wife and daughter. Penury compels him to fix upon the cheapest lodging he can find; and a cheap lodging-house cannot be a respectable one. Its landlord and landlady have neither the time nor the means—even if they possess the inclination—to discriminate between the various applicants for admission:—on the contrary, they are well aware that the worst characters are most likely to prove their best customers. Their only consideration is to make their establishment answer; and so long as their lodgers pay for the accommodation they seek, no questions can be asked.

To such a den, therefore, is the poor man forced to take his wife and his daughter. The obscene language which falls upon this young girl's ears—the fact of being compelled to lay aside her garments in the presence of several males, who unconcernedly undress themselves before her—the debauchery of the day—the licentiousness of the night,—to all these elements of ruin is she immediately exposed. A veil drops suddenly, as it were, from before her eyes; and she finds herself hemmed in by moral corruption—surrounded by temptation—excited by new desires—and encouraged to go astray by her companions. How can she leave that sink of impurity, otherwise than impure? how can she quit that abode of infamy, otherwise than infamous? Many a high-born lady has succumbed to the seducer under circumstances less venial,—under influences admitting a far less amount of extenuation!

Were the Government, with the consent of the Legislature, to establish lodging-houses for poor but honest persons, an immense benefit would be conferred upon that class, and the fearful progress of immorality would receive a check at least in one point. The respectability of such institutions might be ensured by placing trustworthy married couples at their head, and applying a system of rules which would enforce regular hours, exclude ardent spirits, and only permit a moderate quantity of beer to be brought in for the use of each individual, and likewise empower magistrates to punish those who might be brought before them charged with breaking the regulations, or otherwise subverting the wholesome discipline enjoined.

Thieves, prostitutes, and bad characters would not attempt to obtain admission to establishments if this description:—no more than a person enjoying a competency would endeavour to become the inmate of a workhouse. Scenes of debauchery and unbounded license alone suit abandoned males and females;—and thus every guarantee would exist for the respectable management of those institutions which would save the honest poor from the low lodging-houses of London.[10]

9. The following is a glossary which will enable the reader to comprehend the flash terms used in the thieves' marriage-service:—

- *Parish prig*, clergyman.
- *Bouncing ben*, learned man.
- *Padding-ken*, lodging-house.
- *Cop*, make over.
- *Shaler*, girl—young lady.
- *Fancy bloak*, paramour—fancy man.
- *Tip mauleys*, shake hands.
- *Jomen*, paramour—fancy girl.
- *On the cross*, out thieving.
- *Doss*, bed.
- *Traps*, constables.
- *Upon the nose*, on the watch.
- *Fly*, alert.
- *Pinch a lob*, rob a till.
- *Plan*, steal.
- *Sneezer*, snuff-box.
- *Randlesman*, a silk pocket handkerchief.
- *Work the bulls*, pass bad 5s. pieces (a favourite specie with coiners in those days).
- *Couters*, sovereigns.
- *Rum*, bad—spurious.
- *Go the jump*, steal into a room through a window.
- *Speel the drum*, run away with stolen property.
- *Shop-bouncer*, shop-lifter.
- *Get the clinch*, be locked up in gaol.
- *Lumbered*, imprisoned.
- *Fawney*, ring.

10. When Mr. Mills was instructed to draw up his "Report on Prison Discipline," he obtained the necessary information and evidence from

a variety of sources. One of the witnesses whom he examined was Inspector Titterton of the Metropolitan Police Force. This intelligent officer deposed as follows:—"St Giles's abounds with low lodging-houses. The most notorious are kept by Grout. He is a rich man, and has elegant private houses at Hampstead, and the lowest sort of lodging-houses in every part of London. He generally visits these dens daily;—keeps his horse and gig. Price of these houses, as all others, threepence or fourpence a night in a room with a score or two of other people. Men and women sleep together anyhow. A man and woman may have a place screened off, which they call a room, for eightpence a night; but they are seldom so delicate. These houses are brothels. Grout is the monopolist of low lodging-houses. The St. Giles's prostitutes commit many robberies upon drunken countrymen whom they entice to those places, and either bully or *hocus* them. The last is to stupify them with opium or laudanum in their drink. Girls club, and keep a man between them. Inspector has known instances of girls robbing men even of their clothes. In one case the victim had been deprived absolutely of his shirt, because it was a good one: this man the inspector carried home in a policeman's great coat. At the census Grout returned that 140 persons slept in one of his houses in Laurence Lane. His ground landlord is Nugee, the great tailor. The lodging-houses in St. Giles's are like rabbit-burrows: not an inch of ground is lost; and there are stairs and passages, innumerable. While Grout is thus the landlord of hundreds and hundreds of thieves, vagrants, and prostitutes, he lets his beautiful Hampstead villas to genteel and fashionable families."

We have already shown that Thompson was (and perhaps is still) a lodging-house proprietor in a considerable way of business. A person named Southgate is also eminent in the same line. He possesses houses which make up altogether 309 beds. These houses are as follow:—Nos. 2, 3, 4, 8, and 9, Charles Street, Long Acre; seven houses on Saffron Hill; five in Mitre Court, St. John Street, Clerkenwell; No. 11, New Court, Cow Cross, Smithfield; and two in Turnmill Street, Clerkenwell. These last are exclusively occupied by Italian boys and their masters. A man named Elliott has also lodging-houses in Charles Street: namely, Nos. 23, 24, and 45. In Shorts' Gardens, a person called "Lucky Dick" has Nos. 8 and 9.

An officer whom Mr. Mills examined, deposed thus:—"To return to lodging-houses, there are cheap ones in all towns; most of them have two sorts of kitchens. The labourers and hawkers live in a better room, and pay fourpence a night for their bed, halfpenny for coals, halfpenny for the use of plates and hot water, and a halfpenny for the cooking apparatus. Regular beggars, the low sort of cadger fellows, live in the other kitchen, and pay a halfpenny for coals, and have nothing found them. The beggars go on very bad at night in the lodging-houses. They can make 5*s*. a day in the country by begging, let alone what they make by thieving. They never think of work, unless they can contrive to carry something in hopes of an opportunity to slip off with it."

And it is in such dens as these that honest poverty must seek shelter and a bed!

CHAPTER XXVI.
THE LADY'S-MAID.

In the meantime Mr. Frank Curtis had met the buxom Charlotte, according to appointment, in Conduit Street.

The youthful lady's-maid, who had not numbered quite nineteen years, but who concealed a warm temperament and a disposition ripe for wanton mischief, beneath a staid and serious demeanour, when in the presence of her mistress or of those in whose eyes it was prudent to be looked upon as "a very prudent and steady young woman,"—the youthful lady's-maid, we say, walked quietly along the street, and pretended not to notice Mr. Curtis, who was leaning against a lamp-post, smoking a cigar.

But the light of the lamp fell upon her pretty countenance; and he, having immediately recognised her, stretched out his hand and caught her by the shawl, saying, "Well, Miss—do you mean to pretend you didn't see me?"

"Lor'! you there now!" exclaimed Charlotte, affecting to be quite surprised at this encounter.

"Just as if you thought I shouldn't come!" cried Frank, laughing. "But take my arm, my dear; and though this very arm has often supported duchesses—and marchionesses—and even on one occasion the young and beautiful queen of the Red-Skin Indians,—yet I don't know that it was ever more agreeably pressed than by your pretty little fingers."

"How fine you do talk!" said Charlotte, by no means displeased with the compliment. "But where are you going?"

"Oh! I'll show you, my dear," returned Frank, as he led her along. "And now tell me—has anything happened in respect to you know what?"

"Yes—a great deal," answered Charlotte. "But here I am walking with a gentleman whose very name I don't even know! Isn't it odd?"

"Very, my dear. I will, however, soon satisfy you on that head. My name is *Mr. Curtis* to the world—but *Frank* to you; and some day or another I hope to be Baron Dumplington. But what was it that you had to tell me?"

"Something about Miss Mordaunt," replied the girl, who firmly believed the Dumplington story and entertained a proportionate amount of respect towards the young gentleman who was heir to so honourable and distinguished a title.

"Come—out with it, my dear," exclaimed Frank. "Business first, and love afterwards—as my dear lamented friend the Prince of Cochin-China used to say when we were intimate together in Paris, before he hung himself for love in his garters."

"Did he, though?" cried the lady's-maid. "How shocking!"

"Shocking enough, my dear. But pray tell me what you have to say about Miss Mordaunt."

"Why, sir," resumed Charlotte, "this evening when I was dressing her for dinner, she began to sound me about how I liked my place in Lady Hatfield's service, and whether I should be glad to better myself. So, keeping in mind what you had told me to do, I seemed to fall in to all she asked me, and gave her to understand that I shouldn't object to better myself. Then she began to simper and smile, and at last let out plump that she was going to run away with a gentleman—but she didn't say who—to-morrow night."

"That gentleman, my dear, is an uncle of mine," said Curtis.

"I'll be bound, then, it's the same Sir Christopher Blunt———"

"The very same, my dear. But go on: you speak almost as well as I did when I was in Parliament—or as my uncle the Earl of Dumplington."

"Do I, though? Well," continued Charlotte, "and so Miss Mordaunt told me how she couldn't think of travelling alone with the gentleman, and that she must have a lady's-maid———"

"And you agreed to go with her?" cried Frank.

"I did," answered Charlotte; "and we settled and arranged every thing quite comfortable."

"Did she tell you where she is to meet my uncle to-morrow night?" inquired Frank.

"No: but she told me to mind and be ready to leave in the evening at about seven o'clock," returned Charlotte.

"Well—fortunately I *do* know where they are to meet—and that's close by the turnpike at Islington Green," said Frank. "She's to go up in a hackney-coach, and be there punctual at eight o'clock; and the old chap is to have the post-chaise and four in readiness. Doesn't he already fancy himself tearing along the great north road, as if the devil was after him! And so nice too did he arrange his plans with his Julia, that there's to be a supper prepared for them at St. Alban's—and off again! Egad! he's settled it pleasant enough: but I'll be even with him!"

"What do you intend to do?" asked Charlotte.

Curtis did not immediately reply; but, after a few moments' consideration, he abruptly exclaimed, "Can you trust any female friend of yours in this business?"

"Well—I don't know—unless it is my own sister Alice, which is a very nice girl, and will do any thing I tell her," was the reply.

"The very thing!" ejaculated Frank. "Is she out at service?"

"No—she's at home with mother," answered Charlotte.

"And will she just consent to take a short ride in a post-chaise and four along with you, if I give her a five-pound note?" demanded Frank.

"To be sure she will," returned Charlotte, who, with the quickness of female perception, began to comprehend Mr. Curtis's design.

"Then I'll tell you how we must contrive it," said Frank. "It's of the greatest consequence to me, my dear, to prevent this marriage: and if I can only expose my stupid old uncle, I shall fairly laugh him out of it. Now, don't you think you could manage to pass yourself off as his Julia, and get your sister to play the part of yourself, as far as St. Alban's? and I would be there with three or four friends of mine—all jolly dogs—ready to receive Sir Christopher and you girls. You might cover your face well with a thick veil; and as he will be sure to hurry you into the post-chaise the moment you get down from the hackney-coach just beyond the turnpike on the Green, you needn't speak a word. Then you can pretend to be so overcome with fear and anxiety——"

"Oh! leave all that to me!" exclaimed Charlotte, who relished the joke amazingly. "But what shall I do about my place at Lady Hatfield's?" "Deuce take your place, my dear!" cried Frank. "I'll secure beautiful lodgings for you in some nice, quiet, retired street at the West End, and you shall be as happy as the day's long. We'll have such fun together—and I'll take you to plays and all kinds of amusements. Lord bless you! I think no more of a cool thousand or two than I should of blowing out a chap's brains if he was to insult you."

"Oh! dear me, don't talk so horrid!" exclaimed Charlotte, laughing. "And you really will do all you say—if I help you in this business?"

"Yes—and much more," returned Frank. "And now the only thing to manage, is to prevent Miss Mordaunt keeping the appointment by herself. Oh! I have it!" he exclaimed, after a minute's reflection. "I can imitate my uncle's handwriting to a *t*. He writes just as if he had a skewer instead of a pen—and so do I, for that matter. So I'll just tip Miss Julia a note to-morrow afternoon about four, as if it came from Sir Christopher; and I'll tell her in it that the elopement must be postponed until the next night. Egad! this is a stroke of policy that beats hollow any thing my cousin the Duke of Dumplington ever did."

"I thought he was your uncle, sir?" remarked Charlotte.

"I meant my uncle, love," replied Frank: "but it's all the same. The Marquis of Dumplington is my relation—and that's enough. And now, my sweet creature, that we have settled all this business—suppose we adjourn to a nice quiet place that I know——"

"But I must see my sister to-night and tell her all that there is to be done," interrupted Charlotte.

The fact is that the pretty lady's-maid had kept the appointment given her by Frank Curtis, with the full intention of abandoning her person to him; for she was alike wanton in her passions and mercenary in her disposition; and the five guineas which he had given her in the morning had stimulated her with the desire of making farther inroads upon his purse. Nay—she had even hoped that he would fulfil the sort of promise he had given her at their previous interview, and, in plain terms, establish her as his mistress in a comfortable manner. But the intrigue just concocted for the purpose of defeating the matrimonial design of Miss Mordaunt and Sir Christopher Blunt, had engendered new ideas in the breast of the lady's-maid; and she resolved that her intimacy with Mr. Curtis should progress no farther for the present.

The young man, who at this moment cared much more for the success of his scheme against his uncle than for the attractions of Miss Charlotte Styles, willingly allowed her to repair at once to the abode of her mother for the purpose of tutoring Alice how to play the part which that younger sister was to enact in the great drama planned by Mr. Curtis.

Charlotte accordingly separated from Frank, with a promise to write to him if any thing should go wrong; but with an understanding, on the other hand, that her silence was to be construed by him into a proof that all was progressing favourably to his views.

CHAPTER XXVII.
LONDON ON A RAINY EVENING.—A SCENE IN A POST-CHAISE.

London has a strange appearance on those evenings—so peculiar to our climate—when a cold, drizzling, mist-like rain is falling. The lustre of the gaslights in the shops is seen dimly, as if through a gauze; and the lamps in the streets have an air as though they struggled to preserve themselves from total extinction. Clogs and pattens create a confused rattling on the pavement; and to a bird's-eye view, such crowded thoroughfares as Cheapside, Fleet Street, the Strand, and Holborn, must appear to have their *trottoirs* arched with umbrellas.

Then aristocracy seems to urge the horses of its carriage more quickly on, as it whisks to the club, the Parliament, or the dinner-party:—the member of the middle class buttons his taglioni or his great-coat over his chest;—the individual of a humbler sphere tries to make his scanty tweed cover as much of his person as it will;—and poverty wraps its rags around its shaking limbs, apparently forgetful that in drawing them over one place they leave another bare.

In the entrances of courts and covered alleys and in deep doorways the "daughters of pleasure" (oh! the frightful misnomer!) collect and huddle together in their flaunting attire, the pattering of the rain rendering their poor thin shoes as pulpy as brown paper, and splashing over their stockings—and thus aiding ardent spirits and nights of dissipation to plant the seeds of consumption more deeply in their constitutions.

The drivers of cabs and omnibuses thrust their heads as far into their hats—or else push their hats as far down on their heads—as possible; and, shrugging up their shoulders, sit with rounded backs and faces bent downward, on their vehicles;—while the conductors or omnibus-cads, in their oil-skin coats, seem to find consolation for the unpleasantness of the weather in the fact that they can speedily fill their vehicles without the usual exercise of the lungs or gymnastic movements of the arm.

And, on a rainy evening such as we are attempting to describe, what business—what bustle prevail in front of the Angel Inn at Islington! Omnibus after omnibus comes up, from every direction, discharging and receiving their animated freight with wonderful rapidity. The red-nosed man at the booking-office seems to have something better to do than merely lounge at the threshold, with his right shoulder leaning against the door-post off which it has worn the paint in one particular spot: for inquiries now multiply thickly upon him. Indeed, we are afraid that that last share of "a quartern and two outs" which he took with the Elephant and Castle six o'clock cad, has somewhat obfuscated his ideas: for he thrusts an elderly lady with a bandbox into a Chelsea, although she particularly requested to be placed in a Bank omnibus; and he has sent that tall lady with her three children and a baby over to Kennington, in spite of her thrice repeated anxiety to repair to Sloane Square.

What a paddling and stamping of feet, and pattering of clogs, and collision of umbrellas there are in every direction,—up the New Road, and down the City Road,—along St. John Street and Goswell Street Road,—and also up towards the Green! The most addle-pated writer may find some food for his pen, if he only take his stand at the Angel door—with a cigar in his mouth, too, if he like—on a rainy evening.

Does he wish to see how a party of pleasure may be spoiled by a change in the weather? Let him study that little procession of a family who have passed the day at Copenhagen House, and are now returning home, wet—cold—uncomfortable—and sulky: the husband dragging the chaise, in which two children are squalling—a lubberly boy of eight or nine pushing behind—and the wife, with a baby on one arm, and holding up her gown with the left hand, paddling miserably through the rain, and venting her ill-humour on her husband by declaring that "it was all his fault—she knew how it would be—she had begged and prayed of him to come home an hour before—but he *would* stay to have that other glass of gin-and-water!"

If our moralist, whom we station at the door of the Angel, be an admirer of pretty feet and ankles, he may now gratify his taste in that respect; for, of a surety, those who have good ones raise their dresses above the swell of the leg. Ah! ladies—it is really too bad of you:—we almost suspect that you care little for the rain, since it enables you to display those attractions!

The policeman, with his oil-skin cape, emerges from the public-house close by, drawing the back of his hand across his lips, just for all the world as if he had been taking "something short" to keep the cold out:—and very likely he has, too—for we are sure that the most rigid disciplinarian of an inspector or serjeant would not quarrel with him for so doing on such an unpleasant evening. The apple-stall woman puts up an umbrella, and maintains her seat on the low basket turned bottom upwards; for she dares not absent herself from her post, for fear of the hungry urchins that are prowling about.

Within the door-way of the Angel a knot of young gentlemen, in pea-coats, and with sticks in their hands, are smoking cigars. They are not waiting for the omnibuses, but are merely collected there because the bustle of the scene amuses them, and they like to "look at the gals." Listen a moment to their conversation:—they are talking about some favourite actress at an adjacent theatre—and, to hear their astute observations, one would think that they must at least be the dramatic-critics of the newspapers assembled there. Or else, perhaps, their discourse turns on politics; and, then, one would be apt to imagine that they were Under-Secretaries of State in disguise, so profound are their remarks! They call the Minister of the day by his surname without any titular adjunct; and one of them, no doubt wiser than the rest, shakes his head solemnly, and very kindly prophesies the said Minister's approaching downfall. Then the conversation flies off at a tangent to some less important subject; and they most probably proceed to comment upon the "excellent lark" they had the other night at such-and-such a place. Presently one of them proposes a "go of whiskey" each; and they accordingly adjourn to the public room of the Angel, where, what with the goes of whiskey and the going of their tongues, they create so much noise that the old gentleman at the next table flings down the last Sunday's paper in despair, before he has read through the third murder.

Well, reader, it was on such a rainy evening as this that two grand events in our history were to take place:—we mean the affair of Sir Christopher Blunt on the one hand, and the project of Old Death to kidnap Charley Watts on the other.

It is our intention, however, to proceed with the former little business in this chapter.

At a quarter to eight o'clock a post-chaise and four passed through the turnpike at Islington, and drew up in the lower road, alongside the enclosure of the Green.

The right-hand window was then lowered; and a head, enveloped in a fur travelling-cap, with lappets over the ears and tying under the chin, was protruded forth.

This head—which belonged to Sir Christopher Blunt—looked anxiously up and down the thoroughfare, and was then withdrawn again.

But the worthy knight's patience was not tested to any great extent; for in a few minutes after his arrival at the appointed spot, and before the clock had struck eight, a hackney-coach rattled up to the place where the chaise was waiting.

Sir Christopher threw open the door of the chaise, kicked down the steps, and leaped out with the agility of a small elephant; and in a few moments he very gallantly handed two females, well muffled up in cloaks, boas, and veils, from the hackney-coach.

"Dearest Julia!" he murmured to the taller of the two, as he assisted her to ascend into the post-chaise.

An expressive squeeze of the hand was the reply to this affectionate apostrophe on the part of the knight.

The shorter female, whom Sir Christopher concluded to be his fair one's attendant,—inasmuch as Miss Mordaunt had informed him by note in the morning that she had secured a faithful maid to accompany her,—was also handed into the post-chaise: the knight followed—and the vehicle hurried away like wildfire.

Sir Christopher and the female whom he believed to be Miss Mordaunt, sate on the back seat, and the other young lady occupied the seat facing them.

For some time there was a dead silence inside the chaise; but at the expiration of about ten minutes, Sir Christopher began to fidget like a gentleman at a public dinner, who, though "unaccustomed to public speaking," nevertheless experiences a nervous anxiety to address the audience.

"My dear Julia—ahem!" began the knight: "I hope you—you don't feel cold, dear?"

The female thus addressed threw her arms round Sir Christopher's neck, and clasped him so fondly that, what with the tightness of the embrace and the contact of the fur in which she was enveloped, he might have been pardoned had he fancied for a moment that he was being hugged by a bear.

"Oh! dearest Julia—how happy I am!" exclaimed Sir Christopher, nearly suffocated by this display of fondness. "And you, Julia—are you happy, my love?"

"Quite—too happy!" murmured his companion.

"And yet—methinks your voice sounds strange, Julia," said the knight. "What—what *is* the matter with you?"

"Only this, Sir Christopher—that I am not Miss Mordaunt——"

"Not Miss Mordaunt!" ejaculated the knight, preparing to throw down the window and order the postillions to stop.

"No—not Miss Mordaunt," was the answer: "but one who loves you as well—or better—and is, I flatter myself, six times as good-looking."

"Then who are you, in the name of heaven?" cried the knight, so completely bewildered that he knew not how to act.

Charlotte—for it was she—threw back her veil, and, by the light of the shops which they were just passing in the outskirts, Sir Christopher recognised Lady Hatfield's dependant, whom he had seen on two or three occasions when he had called on Miss Mordaunt in Piccadilly.

"And who is your companion?" he demanded hastily.

"My sister Alice—at your service," replied Charlotte. "But listen to me for one moment, Sir Christopher!"

"Well—for one moment, then," said the knight, so strangely perplexed and annoyed that he could take no decisive step.

"Miss Mordaunt never loved you, Sir Christopher," continued the wily Charlotte.

"Never loved me! Then why did she tell me so?"

"Only to laugh at you. It was all planned between her and your nephew Mr. Frank Curtis——"

"The devil!" ejaculated the knight. "Go on."

"They determined to make themselves merry at your expense, and yourself ridiculous at the same time."

"By heaven! I will be revenged!" cried the hero of this pleasant adventure, slapping his thigh emphatically with his open palm.

"They accordingly hired me and my sister to personate Miss Mordaunt and a lady's-maid," proceeded Charlotte; "and we were to carry on the deceit till we got to St. Alban's, where Mr. Frank Curtis and a party of his friends are already waiting to receive you."

"The villain!" shouted Sir Christopher, completely deceived by this plausible tale.

"But I always admired you, sir," continued Charlotte; "and I was resolved not to be made a party to carry out the trick to the end. I should have written to you—or called to explain it: but I feared you might not believe me;—and so I thought it best to let matters go as far as they have gone now, just to convince you that what I say is perfectly true."

"Oh! I believe it all:—It is too clear—too apparent!" exclaimed the knight. "That scoundrel Frank—I'll discard him—I'll stop his allowance—I'll never speak to him again! To get a party of friends to meet us at St. Alban's—eh? Just where I'd sent word to have a good supper in readiness!"

"Miss Mordaunt told him all that, sir," observed Charlotte, who had kept one of her arms round the knight's neck, and had gradually approached her countenance so closely to his that her breath now fanned his cheek.

"Yes—I understand it all!" cried Sir Christopher. "I have been grossly deceived—vilely treated—basely served! But I am not the man to put up with it. At the same time, Miss," he added, in a softening tone, "you are a very good girl to have saved me from cutting so ridiculous a figure at St. Alban's!"

"I have only done my duty, sir," murmured Charlotte, with a profound sigh; and—of course by accident—her cheek touched that of the knight.

"A good girl—a very good girl!" repeated Sir Christopher: "as good as you are pretty—for you *are* pretty—and I've often remarked it."

The arm thrown around Sir Christopher's neck pressed him gently.

"And I really do not know how to reward you sufficiently, my dear girl," he added, new ideas entering his mind.

Again the arm pressed him tenderly.

Sir Christopher could resist the exciting contiguity no longer; and he fairly kissed the cheek that was so close to his lips.

Charlotte sighed again, but did not withdraw her face.

"Really this is very ridiculous!" exclaimed the knight. "Here we are, galloping along like lightning—and without any particular object that I know of. Upon my word, I have a great mind—a very great mind to revenge myself on both Miss Mordaunt and Master Frank at one and the same time!"

"In what way, Sir Christopher!" asked Charlotte, in a languidly murmuring tone.

"By marrying *you*, my dear," was the emphatic response.

"Oh! Sir Christopher—is it possible—such happiness!" sighed Charlotte, again embracing him in the most tender manner.

"It is so possible, my dear," answered the knight, "that if you consent to have me, the horses' heads need not be turned back again towards London."

"How can I refuse you, dear Sir Christopher?" exclaimed Charlotte;—"I, who always thought what a fine-looking—handsome—kind—genteel—fashionable man you was from the first time I ever saw you!"

"I'm sure I always heard sister speak in the highest terms of you, sir," said Alice, now taking up her cue.

"Well, then, my dear—what is to hinder us from being happy?" cried Sir Christopher.

With these words, he pulled down the window, ordered the postillions to stop, and gave them directions to change their route in such a manner as to avoid St. Alban's.

The vehicle then whisked along with renewed speed; and while Sir Christopher felt wonderfully elated at the idea of punishing his nephew and avenging himself on Miss Mordaunt by showing her that she was not the only female in the world to whom he was compelled to address himself,— Charlotte, on the other hand, rejoiced at the success of a scheme which had been suggested by the part she was originally engaged to play in this pleasant drama, and which, as the reader will now perceive, was the motive that prevented her from extending her intimacy with Mr. Frank Curtis on the previous evening.

CHAPTER XXVIII.
TOM RAIN'S LODGINGS IN LOCK'S FIELDS.

Nearly opposite to the house where Tom Rain lived, in Brandon Street, Lock's Fields, there was a boozing-ken, well known to Old Death; and shortly after nine o'clock on the same evening which marked the events related in the preceding chapter, that cunning fence, accompanied by Toby Bunce and the lad Jacob, were introduced by the landlord into a front room on the first-floor of the said flash establishment.

Jacob was ordered to station himself at the window and watch for Tom Rain to take his departure on the expedition devised for him by Old Death; while Bones himself and his acolyte Toby seated themselves opposite a cheerful fire, to discuss hot gin-and-water until the hour should arrive for putting into execution the scheme that had brought them thither.

Although the rain was falling with a mist-like density, and no gas-company had been enterprising enough to lay down pipes in such a neighbourhood as Lock's Fields,—so that there were neither stars nor lamps to light the street,—still the eagle-eyes of Jacob could distinguish sufficient of the scene without, to quiet any fear lest the movements of Tom Rain should escape him. Old Death moreover stimulated his energies by means of a sip of hot grog; and the lad remained as motionless at the window and as earnestly intent on his object as a cat watching near the hole into which a mouse has escaped.

"Well," said Old Death, as he sipped his liquor complacently, "I suppose we shall have no difficulty in managing this little job by-and-by? Jacob watched all day long in Great Ormond Street, until we joined him to come over here; and the Jewess never stirred out once—did she, Jacob?"

"No—not once," was the answer.

"But you knew that she was at home?"

"Yes: because I saw her at the window for a moment, every now and then," replied the lad, speaking without averting his eyes from the street.

"Good!" exclaimed Old Death. "It is not at all likely that she has come over to Tom's lodgings this evening, or that she will come—'specially after the long sermon she wrote——"

Bones checked himself; for he was not in the habit of being communicative with Toby Bunce; and Toby, on his side, never sought to pry into the motives or designs of the old fence by whom he was made so complete a tool.

"Who is there in the house besides Mr. Rainford and the boy?" asked Toby, after a pause.

"Only the old widow woman that keeps it," responded Mr. Benjamin Bones.

"There!" cried Jacob, suddenly: "the door opens—and Mr. Rainford comes out! He's gone."

"All right!" said Old Death. "I suppose he's going for his horse, wherever he keeps it."

"I could see by the light in the passage, when the door was opened, that he had his white coat on and his great riding-whip in his hand," remarked Jacob. "It was a woman that held the candle—because I could just catch a glimpse of her shadow, and that's all."

"You don't think it was the Jewess?" asked Bones.

"I couldn't say, because the shadow wasn't plain enough," returned Jacob. "But it's hardly probable that she could have got over here before us, even if she was coming to Mr. Rainford's lodgings to-night."

"Well said, Jacob," observed Old Death. "You're getting a knowing lad—you are; and now you shall have a glass of grog to yourself."

"What! a *whole* glass?" ejaculated Toby Bunce, in astonishment at this unwonted liberality on the part of Old Death.

"Yes—a whole glass—a sixpenny glass," responded Bones; and, having summoned the landlord, he gave the requisite order.

The liquor was brought for Jacob's express behoof; and Old Death drew forth the money to pay for it. But, as he did so, a paper with writing upon it fell upon the floor, unperceived by any one save Jacob.

The lad instantly drew a chair near the fire, and as he seated himself, placed his foot upon the paper, which, being somewhat dingy in hue, he took to be a bank-note.

The landlord withdrew; and the conversation was resumed between Old Death and Toby Bunce.

"I hope Betsy will have something nice for supper when we get back again," remarked the latter.

"She's sure to do that," replied Old Death. "You ought to be very fond of your wife, Toby—for she's very fond of you."

"D'ye think she is, Mr. Bones?" exclaimed Bunce.

"I'm sure of it. Doesn't she take great care of you?"

"Rather too much," was the reply, which came from the bottom of Toby's heart: then, perceiving that he had uttered something which seemed to imply that he had dared to form an opinion for himself, he hastened to add, "Not but what it's very kind of her to keep the money—and my watch too—and every thing else in her own care, because I know I'm an old fool——"

"No—you're not a fool, Toby," interrupted Bones; "but you want looking after. Ah! it was a blessed day for you when I recommended you to marry that virtuous—well-conducted—pattern-woman, as one may say, who is now your wife. I had no interest but your good—and hers——"

"I'm well aware of that, Mr. Bones," cried Toby: "and you've been an excellent friend to us. I'm sure Betsy respects you as if you was her——" Toby was about to say "father," but he remembered that Old Death did not like to be reminded of his age, and so he substituted "brother."

"Well—well," said Bones: "I've no doubt of what you tell me; and so long as you're happy together, that's every thing."

Toby smothered a sigh with a deep draught of gin-and-water;—Old Death poked the fire; and Jacob availed himself of the opportunity to stoop down and pick up the paper, which he dexterously conveyed to his pocket, unperceived by either of his companions. But a sudden disappointment seized upon him—for he could feel that it was too stiff for a bank-note, and was moreover folded like a letter.

The time passed away; and at length Old Death, after consulting his watch, declared it to be close upon eleven o'clock.

There were no lights visible in the house opposite; and it was therefore determined to commence operations without farther delay.

"Before we leave here," said Old Death, "remember what you are to do. Jacob and you, Toby, will put on your masks, rush in, shut the door, and make the old widow secure. Then you, Jacob, will come out and fetch me. It won't do for the woman to see me at all, because I'm so tall that if she described me to Tom Rain when he comes back, he would know who it was directly; but as there's nothing particular about either of you, he can't make you out from description."

"We'll take care, Mr. Bunce, how the thing is managed," said Toby.

The trio then quitted the public-house; and, while Toby and Jacob crossed to the other side of the street, Old Death walked a little way on.

The coast was quite clear, and a profound silence reigned throughout the neighbourhood.

Toby Bunce and the lad stopped at the door of the widow's house, slipped on their black masks, and knocked. In a few moments the door was opened by the widow herself. Quick as lightning, the candle was knocked from her hand, and the scream that half-burst from her lips was arrested by a large plaster which Toby instantaneously clapped upon her mouth. The poor woman fainted through excess of terror, and was borne into the nearest room, where Jacob hastened to strike a light.

Having succeeded thus far, Toby remained in charge of the landlady, while Jacob hastened to fetch Old Death.

In a few moments the lad returned with that individual; and the front-door was again carefully closed.

The widow continued in a swoon; and Toby did not give himself any trouble to recover her.

"Do you remain here," said Old Death, addressing himself to his myrmidon Bunce; "and if the woman revives and attempts to struggle or any nonsense of that kind, give her a knock on the head just to quiet her—but no more."

"All right," returned Toby, rejoiced to find that he had only a female to deal with.

Old Death then took the light, and, followed by Jacob, cautiously ascended the stairs.

They entered the front-room on the first-floor. It was a parlour, very neatly furnished: but no one was there.

"The boy must be in the back chamber," murmured Old Death; and thither they proceeded.

Having opened the door as noiselessly as possible, they advanced slowly into the room; but scarcely had the candle shed its light upon the bed, when they beheld the boy—the object of their enterprise—cradled on the bare and beautifully modelled arm of a female also wrapped in slumber, and whose coal-black hair spread itself over the white pillow, and partially concealed her glowing bust.

"The Jewess!" whispered Jacob, in a rapid, concentrated tone.

Old Death instantly shaded the light with his hand, and retreated from the room, followed by the lad.

But at that moment a loud knock at the front-door was heard; and simultaneously a piercing shriek burst from the apartment below, where Toby Bunce had been left in charge of the landlady.

Old Death muttered a terrible curse, extinguished the light, and hastened down stairs as noiselessly as possible—Jacob following with equal caution.

"The back way," murmured Old Death: "but first go and help Toby, who is in some trouble or another with the landlady."

Jacob darted into the front-room; and as it was quite dark, he stumbled over a chair.

The struggle between Toby and the landlady, who had succeeded in getting off the plaster, was now renewed; and, releasing her throat from the suffocating grasp which her assailant had upon it, she screamed for help a second time.

The knocking at the front-door was redoubled; and in a few moments a light gleamed from the head of the stairs.

"Perdition!" murmured old Death: "it is the Jewess!"

Then, rushing into the front room, he exclaimed, "Come off this moment!" and he was about to beat a retreat by the back way, when the house-door was forced in with a vigorous push.

"What the devil is doing here?" cried the well-known voice of Tom Rain, as he banged the door behind him and drew the bolt. "Who was screaming? What——"

"Oh! Tom—is that you?" exclaimed a melodious, though excited voice on the stairs; "there are thieves—murderers in the house!"

And the half-naked lady, with her coal-black hair floating around her shoulders and over her bosom, suddenly appeared at the turning of the narrow staircase, holding a candle.

The light illumed the small passage below, and showed Tom Rain, standing with his back against the front-door, and with a pistol in each hand.

A third scream burst from the parlour.

Rainford rushed in; and, encountering Toby and Jacob, dragged them—or rather hurled them, as if they were two children in his grasp, into the passage.

There the light revealed to him their countenances—for their masks had been torn away in the struggle with the landlady; and Rainford was for a few moments so astounded at the recognition of Old Death's agents or confederates, that he was unable to utter a word.

"The villains!—the murderers!—the assassins!" cried the landlady, rushing forward, with her hair all in disorder, her garments torn to rags, and the blood streaming from her nose. "Shall I go and fetch a constable, Mr. Rainford?"

"No, I thank'ee," returned Tom: "leave me to manage these scoundrels. Here, my love," he continued, addressing himself to the Jewess, who had remained half-way up the stairs, "give me that light, and do you retire to your room. I must speak to these rascals in private. My good woman," he added, turning once more to the landlady, "have the kindness to go up stairs and keep my wife company; and fear nothing—now that I am here."

The two women hastened to obey these injunctions; and Rainford, provided with the candle, made an imperative sign for Toby Bunce and Jacob to precede him into the room from which he had dragged them a few minutes previously.

"Answer me directly," said Tom, in a stern—resolute manner, as he closed the door behind him, and deliberately drew forth the pistols which he had thrust into the pockets of his white great-coat when he first entered the parlour to rescue the landlady,—"answer me directly—either one of you, I care not which:—what brought you here?"

"Jacob knows best, Mr. Rainford," replied Bunce, eyeing the pistols askance.

"No—I don't," said the lad, in a sulky tone.

"You are game to your employer, I have no doubt, Jacob," ejaculated Rainford. "And now, Toby Bunce, answer for yourself—or, by God! I'll shoot you through the head! In short, what brought you here?"

At this moment there was a low knock at the room-door, against which Tom Rain was leaning.

"Who's there?" demanded the highwayman.

"Me," replied the sepulchral, hollow voice of Old Death.

"Ah! the plot thickens," said Tom; and, opening the door, he gave admittance to Mr. Benjamin Bones.

"It's all a mistake, Tom—it's the wrong house!" exclaimed Old Death. "You don't know how annoyed I am—you don't indeed!"

"Well—I confess I do not," said the highwayman coolly; "and it will take you a long time to persuade me that you are speaking the truth. If it was the wrong house, why didn't these people of yours tell me so when I first questioned them?"

"Because I saw you would not believe me," cried Jacob hastily.

"And I was so flurried by them barkers," added Toby, pointing to the pistols.

"I'm not such a fool as you take me to be," observed Tom Rain. "Without being able to fathom your intentions, I can smell treachery as easy as I could gunpowder. How did you find out that I lived here? You must have had me dogged and watched, Old Death. And perhaps the very job you sent me after to-night, was a mere subterfuge to get me out of the way? Fortunately I did not wait for the yellow chaise, because I picked up something better the moment I reached Blackheath; and I thought I had done quite enough for one evening's work—so I returned without delay. Lucky it was that I did so. But am I to have an explanation of this affair?—or do you mean us to break with each other for good and all?"

"What can I say—what can I do to prove to you that this is all a mistake?" cried Old Death, sadly perplexed between the fear of complete detection and the dread of losing the valuable services of the highwayman.

"I will tell you," answered Tom, after a few moments' consideration. "Let these two followers of yours go their ways—and you and me will have a little discourse in private."

A sudden misgiving—a horrible suspicion flashed to the mind of Old Death. Could Rainford mean to murder him?

"Why do you hesitate?" demanded the highwayman, penetrating his thoughts. "Do you suppose for an instant that I intend you any harm? Why, you miserable old wretch," he added, with a proud contempt which rendered him strikingly handsome for the moment, "I would sooner blow out my own brains than defile my hands by laying them violently on such a piece of withered carrion as you are—unless you give me ample cause."

Old Death's lips quivered with rage; but, subduing his emotions as well as he was able, he made a sign for Toby Bunce and Jacob to depart.

This hint was obeyed; and in a few moments Bones was alone in the room with the highwayman.

"What is it you require of me?" asked the old man, in a tremulous voice—for there was something in Rainford's tone and gesture which alarmed him.

"I will explain myself to you," said Tom. "When we first knew each other, you boasted that all your transactions were conducted with so much caution, that none with whom you had dealings even knew where you lived. Was it not so?"

"Very likely—very likely," returned Old Death. "But what of that?"

"Simply that as it suited you to keep your place of abode secret from me, so did I wish that my residence should remain unknown to you," answered Rainford, "Now, mark me, Mr. Bones—or whatever the devil your name may be:—you shall have no advantage over me. Hitherto our compact has been fairly kept; but at length I find you practising falsely towards me. You need not interrupt me with vows and protestations—because I shall not believe you. But I tell you what you will do—and this night, too."

"What?" groaned Old Death.

"You will place us on even ground—you will give me the same advantage that you have gained over me: in a word, you will take me straight to the place where you live, and you will show me your stores where you keep all the property you receive or purchase from those who are in league with you."

"I—I have no stores," said Old Death; "and, as for my lodging—I—I have no settled place. I sleep sometimes in one crib—sometimes in another——"

"All lies!" ejaculated Tom, in a determined tone. "You have enormous dealings with all the housebreakers and thieves in London; you have said as much to me—and you have boasted that they are ignorant of your residence. Now then, you *have* a residence—and I swear that before I am six hours older, I will know so much about *you*, that you shall never dare to practise any treachery towards *me*."

"What treachery could I practise against you, Tom?" asked Old Death in a conciliatory tone.

"I will tell you," replied Rainford. "You boast that for thirty years you have monopolised the business of fence to all the people worth dealing with in London; and, during that time, you have never got into a scrape. But how could you have enjoyed so wonderful a safety—so uninterrupted a security, unless you now and then sacrificed—yes, *sacrificed*—an accomplice or two?"

"I!" ejaculated Old Death, starting in spite of himself.

"Yes—*you*," rejoined Rainford, fixing his eyes sternly and searchingly on the ancient villain's hideous countenance. "Do you think that I am unacquainted with your real character? do you suppose that I was at a loss to understand you, even the very first moment we ever met? That flippancy of manner—that off-handedness—that reckless indifference, which characterise me, are a species of mask from behind which I can penetrate into the deepest recesses of the hearts of others. I know you as well as you know yourself—or nearly so. At all events, I know enough to render me cautious and wary; and, by the living God! you shall never have an opportunity of selling me to save yourself!"

"Tom—my dear Tom!" exclaimed Old Death, now actually frightened by the other's manner, and astonished at his words; "you cannot think of such a thing seriously!"

"So seriously do I think of it," replied Rainford, "that I will drag you into the pit, if I am destined to fall. So now, without another word, prepare to reveal to me all the mysteries in which you have for thirty years enveloped yourself."

"And if I refuse?" said Old Death, doggedly.

Rainford deliberately cocked his pistol.

"You have inveigled me into a snare—you have sent away those who might protect me—and now you seek an excuse to murder me!" exclaimed Old Death, his voice sounding like ringing metal.

"Did I not say ere now that I would not harm you, unless you gave me just cause?" demanded Rainford. "And think you that your refusal to comply with my present wish does not constitute such just cause? You have discovered my lodging, which it does not suit me to leave on that account:—you may also have found out that I am not *alone* here——"

"I know that a certain Jewess is your mistress," said Old Death, with a savage leer—for all the vindictive passions of his nature were aroused by the conduct of the individual who dared to coerce him—*him*, who had never been coerced before!

"A certain Jewess!" repeated Rainford, surveying Old Death with a singular expression of countenance.

"Yes—Esther de Medina," added Bones.

"Esther de Medina is as pure and innocent as the babe that is unborn!" cried the highwayman, with impassioned emphasis.

"Then she must be your wife," said Old Death.

"Liar!" thundered Tom Rain, rushing forward and seizing the ancient villain by the throat: then, as if ashamed of the sudden transport of rage into which he had suffered himself to be betrayed, he withdrew his hand, and said in a more quiet but still determined manner, "Mention not the name of Esther de Medina with disrespect—or I warn you that my vengeance—yes, *my* vengeance—will be terrible! And now prepare to lead me to your place of abode—for I am wearied of this long parley."

He again drew forth one of his pistols, which he had consigned to his pocket when he rushed on the old man in the way just described.

"You'll repent this, Mr. Rainford," said Old Death, endeavouring to impress the highwayman with vague and undefined alarms.

"You see how evil your nature is, since you can threaten me thus," cried Tom. "But I care little for your menaces. I have but two alternatives to choose between:—one is to blow your brains out at once—the other is to get you as much into my power as you have got me into yours. Either way will answer my purpose. So now make up your mind which it shall be. The people in Lock's Fields wouldn't take much notice if they heard a pistol fired; and there's a pretty deep ditch at the bottom of the yard behind the house."

Old Death shuddered; for there was something awfully determined in the highwayman's manner.

"Well—and if I take you to a certain place," he said, "how do I know that you will not split upon me?"

"Trust to me as I shall *then* trust to you," ejaculated Rainford. "Shall we not continue to be necessary to each other? And on my part, I shall at least experience more confidence, since I shall know that you cannot ruin me without bringing destruction on yourself!"

"Be it as you say," growled Old Death; and, fixing his greasy cap upon his head, he prepared to depart.

"One moment—while I say a word up stairs," said Rainford; and, hastily quitting the room, he locked the door behind him.

Scarcely a minute elapsed ere he returned—to the great relief of the old man, who had begun to entertain serious misgivings at being made a prisoner.

"There are marks of dirty boots upon the carpet in the bed-room above," said Tom, confronting Bones, and fixing upon him a searching look. "What were you doing there?"

"I was not there——" began Old Death, quailing beneath that glance.

"Damnable liar!" cried Rainford. "I have half a mind——But, no," he added, checking himself: "time will show what your purpose was in invading this house; and I shall know how to punish any treachery on your part. And now mark me! You will lead the way—and I shall follow you. Avoid great thoroughfares——"

"Had we not better take a coach?" asked Old Death.

"No—we will walk, be it to the other end of London," replied the highwayman resolutely. "I shall follow close behind you:—beware how you attempt to address yourself to a soul whom you may meet—beware also how you trifle with me. But stay—I will have a guarantee for your good faith. Give me your pocket-book!"

"My pocket-book!" ejaculated Old Death, with something approaching a shudder.

"Yes—your pocket-book," replied Rain. "I know that it contains Bank-notes, and memoranda of value or utility to you; and I will retain it in this house, until we return from the expedition on which we are about to set forth. Come—quick! I have no time for idle delays!"

"My pocket-book!" repeated Old Death, with increasing dismay.

"Do I not speak plain enough?" demanded the highwayman. "If I cannot make myself intelligible by words, I may by deeds: so permit me to help myself to the article I require. It will not be the first time I shall have rifled a pocket," he added, with a merry laugh.

"Do you know that you are treating me in a manner that I never experienced before?" said Old Death, his hideous countenance convulsed with rage.

"I can very well believe what you state," returned Tom Rain coolly. "Hitherto you have had to deal with men whom you got completely into your power—whose lives hung on a thread which you could snap without endangering yourself—who were mere puppets in your hands, and did not dare say their names were their own. Oh! I am well aware how you have played the tyrant—

the griping, avaricious, grinding miser—the cruel, relentless despot! But now,—*now*, Mr. Bones, you have another sort of person to deal with,—a man who will be even with you anywhere and everywhere,—and who will never let you gain an advantage over him without acquiring one in return."

"Who are you," demanded Old Death, in strange bewilderment, "that talk to me thus?"

"Why—Thomas Rainford, to be sure!" cried the highwayman, laughing—yet with a certain chuckling irony that sounded ominously on the old fence's ears. "And I need not tell you," he continued after a few moments' pause, "that I am rather a desperate character, who would as soon shoot you in the open street—aye, or in the midst of a crowd, too—if you attempted any treachery towards me, as I would ease a gentleman of his purse upon the lonely road. But we are wasting time: give me your pocket-book."

Old Death's courage had gradually oozed away during this strange colloquy; and he now mechanically obeyed the command so imperiously addressed to him.

But suddenly recollecting himself, as he was about to hand the pocket-book to the highwayman, he said, "There is one letter here—just one letter—which I should like to keep about my own person."

"Well—take that one letter," returned Tom; "and beware how you endeavour to secrete any thing else."

Old Death's hand trembled as he unfastened the clasp of the greasy old pocket-book; and, when he had opened it, he sighed deeply, as his eyes alighted first on a roll of Bank-notes. Then he turned the papers over—one after another; and clouds gathered thickly and more thickly upon his countenance.

"This is strange—very strange!" he muttered, as he fumbled about with the letters and memoranda.

"What is strange?" demanded Rainford.

"That I cannot find the letter I want," returned Old Death, with increasing agitation. "Surely I cannot have lost it? And yet—I remember now—I was referring to it this afternoon—and——Oh! yes—I recollect—I put it into my pocket——"

But the search in his pockets was vain: the letter was nowhere to be found.

"Come—there's enough of delay and such-like nonsense," exclaimed the highwayman, snatching the pocket-book from his hand.

Again Rainford quitted the room, locking the door behind him; and in a couple of minutes he returned, saying, "Your pocket-book is safe where no one will meddle with it till we come back. It is now past eleven: let us set off. Come—you go first!"

Old Death led the way, and Tom Rain followed, the latter conveying some pleasant intimation, as he closed the front-door behind him, about an ounce of lead in the other's back if he showed the slightest sign of treachery.

CHAPTER XXIX.
THE MYSTERIES OF OLD DEATH'S ESTABLISHMENT.

From the back of the Sessions House on Clerkenwell Green, towards Smithfield Market, runs a thoroughfare the upper portion of which is known by the name of Turnmill Street, and the lower part as Cow-Cross Street.

Numerous rag-shops and marine-stores here meet the eye,—establishments where the thief in a small way may obtain a ready sale for the proceeds of his roguery. It is really curious to stand for a few moments and observe the miscellaneous assortment of articles crammed together in the dingy windows of these places,—as if they were receptacles for all the rags that misery could spare, and all the rubbish which domestic neatness throws into the street.

Some of the old clothes-shops in the thoroughfare which we are describing, are strikingly characteristic of the neighbourhood; for you cannot gaze a minute upon the silk handkerchiefs, the bonnets, the shirts, the gowns, the coats, the trousers, and the waistcoats, and other articles hanging outside the windows, or suspended to nails stuck into the walls, without being able to form a pretty accurate computation of the proportion which has been stolen, and that which has been obtained by legitimate purchase.

The women lounging at the doors in Turnmill and Cow-Cross Streets are of dissipated, dirty, and loathsome appearance: nor have the men any advantage over them in these respects.

Take a duchess from the saloons of fashion,—a duchess in her satin or velvet, with her feathers and her diamonds, her refined manners, her elegant demeanour, her polished discourse, and her civilising influence,—and place her by the side of one of those degraded women in Turnmill Street,—a woman with hoarse voice, revolting manners, incrusted with dirt, clothed in the meanest apparel, if not in absolute rags, and interlarding her conversation with oaths and obscenities,—place those two specimens of the female sex together,—and how astounding is the contrast!

But the duchess has no more claim to praise for the polish—the fascinations—the exquisite refinement which characterise her, than the poor woman of Turnmill Street deserves to be blamed for the degradation and repulsiveness in which she is steeped to the very crown of her head.

Had the two been changed at their birth, she who is now the duchess would have become the dissipated, loathsome, ragged wretch of Turnmill Street; and the babe who has grown to be this ragged wretch, would have sprung up into the splendid lady with the ducal coronet on her brow.

The rich and the high-born do not reflect upon this fact:—they fancy that their very aristocracy is innate as it is hereditary, and that the poor are naturally degraded, vicious, and immoral. Oh! the terrible error—the fearful mistake! For, after all, many a proud peer is in reality the son of his reputed father's groom or footman; and many a dazzling beauty owes her being to her mother's illicit amours with a butler or a page!

The young Prince of Wales, if he live, will doubtless become one of the most polished gentlemen in the universe:—but had he been stolen at his birth, and brought up by poor people, he would even now be running bare-footed in the streets—groping in the gutters for halfpence—gnawing cabbage-stalks and turnip-parings—thieving pudding from cooks'-shops and bacon from cheesemongers' windows—easing old gentlemen of their handkerchiefs—and familiar with all the horrible vocabulary of the slang language!

No credit, then, to the aristocracy—no blame to the poor! Neither can help being what they are. The influences of the sphere of refinement must have a tendency to refine: the miseries of the poor must produce degradation, immorality, and recklessness.

Ah! my Lord Duke—how ineffable is your contempt for yon poor trembling wretch who now stands in the dock at the Old Bailey, before his judge! Your Grace never did a dishonourable action—your Grace has never committed even a crime so genteel as forgery! But has your Grace ever known what starvation is? has your Grace wandered for hours, like a madman, through the streets of a city teeming with all the luxuries of the earth, while a wife and children were weeping for bread in a cheerless garret up some filthy court? No—your Grace has never been placed in such a position; or, believe me, you would probably have purloined a loaf of bread or filched a handkerchief or a purse—even as did that poor trembling wretch in the dock, whose guilt has filled your Grace with so much disgust!

And you, too, my Lady Duchess—how closely your Grace wraps that elegant, warm shawl around your form, lest its mere hem should happen to touch the garments of that poor unfortunate girl who is passing just at the moment when your Grace is stepping from the Opera-door into the splendid equipage which is to whirl your Grace to your palace-home! Oh! I well understand the loathing—the disgust which the menaced contact with that wretched creature excites in the bosom of your Grace. But—ah! does she deserve no pity—no sympathy, as well as such sovereign contempt—such boundless aversion? The entire sex is not outraged by her fall;—and consider, my lady Duchess—had you been a poor man's daughter and so hemmed in by miseries of all kinds from your very birth until the age of womanhood, that emancipation from such incessant privations were a very paradise, even though purchased by a crime,—thinkest thou, my lady, that thy virtue would have been stronger than that of the poor wretch who seems to insult you by even breathing the same air that surrounds your aristocracy?

Merciful heavens! how unjust the upper classes are to the lower! The great lord and the haughty lady blame where they should pity—turn away with loathing where they should commiserate—proclaim as innate wickedness that social aspect which is the inevitable result of poverty and oppression—denounce as inveterately depraved those unhappy beings who never were taught nor had a chance to be good!

The infamy of the upper class towards the lower in this country, is immense. A landowner gives his labourer eight shillings a-week, and says, "Go and live comfortably—be neat and clean—attend divine worship on the Sabbath—educate your children—let them read good books—keep them tidy in their appearance—and avoid debt!" Then when this landowner finds the family naked and starving—the man frequenting the public-house in despair, instead of the church in holy gratitude—the wife a slattern and a gin-drinker—the children incipient prostitutes and thieves,—when he sees all this, he raises his hands, exclaiming, "Oh! the inveterate, innate wickedness of the working classes!"

The aristocracy and the landowners of this country are, as a whole, the most cruel and heartless set of legalised robbers that ever preyed upon the vitals of suffering millions:—they are now what the French aristocrats and landlords were previously to the Revolution of 1796;—and solemnly—solemnly do we declare our belief that the despotic—tyrannical—remorseless oligarchy which usurps the right of domination, is hurrying the United Kingdom to a similar catastrophe!

But to continue our narrative.

The mist-like rain was still falling, and midnight had struck some time, when Old Death, closely followed by Tom Rain, merged from Cow-Cross Street, and stopped at the entrance to a narrow court in Turnmill Street.

Casting a glance around, to assure himself that Rainford was at his heels, Old Death plunged into the court; and Tom, fancying that the ancient fence meant to elude him, sprang after him and caught him by the skirt of his grey coat.

"No noise," whispered Bones. "Here we are."

Thus speaking, he opened a side-door in the court with a key which he took from his pocket, and, hurrying Tom Rain with him, closed the door carefully again behind them.

The place into which the highwayman was introduced, was as dark as pitch; and, not choosing to be led into an ambuscade, Rainford said, "One moment, my worthy friend! If you have no means of obtaining a light, I will very soon get those means from some public-house———"

While he was yet speaking Old Death procured a light from a tinder-box; and a candle, which stood ready on a low shelf near the door, soon diffused sufficient lustre around to enable the highwayman to observe what kind of place he had been introduced into. It was a small, dingy-looking room, without a vestige of furniture in it, and having the entrance to a narrow staircase on one side, and a second door, facing that by which he and Old Death had entered, on the other.

When a thief arrived at this place with any stolen property, he pulled a wire the handle of which hung against the wall in the court: a bell rang within—the outer door opened by unseen means, and the thief closed it behind him on entering the little room. He then tapped at the inner or second door which we have noticed, and which had a hatch in it that immediately drew up: no one appeared—but the thief threw in his bundle or parcel. The hatch then closed. In a few moments—or according to the time required for the inspection of the goods—the hatch was raised again, but merely high enough to admit the passage of a small piece of paper, whereon was marked the highest price that would be given for the articles offered for sale. If the paper were immediately returned by the thief, the money was thrust forth; the door in the court opened again by invisible means, the thief departed, and the door was closed behind him: if, however, he did not return the paper, it was considered that he would not accept the amount proffered, and the bundle was restored to him through the hatch.

"Thus, you perceive," said Old Death, whom Rainford compelled to reveal the mysterious use of the hatch in the inner door, "no one is seen by those who come here to dispose of their property."

"And who manages this business for you?" demanded the highwayman; "for it is clear that you cannot be here—there—and every where at one and the same time."

"I have a faithful and trustworthy man who has been in my service for many—many years," answered Old Death.

"But the people who have dealings at this place must know that it is your establishment?" said Rainford.

"Quite the contrary!" exclaimed Bones, with a grim smile. "This fencing-crib is called *Tidmarsh's*—and none of the flash men in London know that I have the least connexion with it. It takes its name from my managing man. When I have business to do that I must transact in person, I meet my friends at public-houses and patter-cribs—and my very intimate ones, such as you, at Bunce's. But come up stairs."

Old Death led the way to an indifferently furnished room, where a man as well stricken in years and as repulsively ugly as himself, though apparently not near so tall, was in bed.

"It's only me, Tidmarsh," said Old Death.

"Only you!" growled the man, sitting up in bed, and staring suspiciously at Rainford.

"Me and a friend—a very particular friend, Tiddy," added Bones. "Indeed, it's Mr. Rainford."

"Oh! that's different!" said Tidmarsh, in a more conciliatory tone. "Your fame, sir, has reached me even in this crib. Take some rum, sir."

And he pointed to a bottle and glasses standing on a table.

"Well—I don't mind if I do—just to keep out the damp, and drink your health, Mr. Tidmarsh," cried Rainford, in his usual merry, off-hand strain; and, suiting the action to his words, he took a small dram.

Old Death followed his example; and Mr. Tidmarsh suffered himself to be prevailed upon to imbibe a like quantum.

"Now, go to sleep, Tiddy," said Bones, in a patronising manner. "We shan't disturb you any more."

Mr. Tidmarsh gave a species of grunt by way of assent to the recommendation offered, and threw himself back upon his pillow.

Old Death conducted Rainford into the adjoining rooms on the same storey, and then to the upper chambers; but they were all quite empty! Their walls were black with dirt—the ceilings seemed as if they had originally been painted of a sombre hue—the window-panes were so grimed that it was evident they could admit but a feeble light even in the broad day—the floors sent up clouds of dust as the feet trod upon them—and dense masses of cob-webs actually rounded off all the corners. There was, moreover, an earthy, infected smell in those rooms, which would have made a weak stomach heave with nausea.

Tom Rain was quite surprised to find all the chambers empty. He had expected to be introduced into warehouses teeming with the produce of three-parts of all the roguery committed in the great metropolis: but not even so much as an old rag met his eyes. Indeed, the rooms appeared as if they had not been tenanted, or even scarcely entered, for many—many years.

"This may be your reception-house," he said, in a jocular manner; "but it certainly does not contain your stores."

"All the goods are sent away as soon as they are received," replied Old Death.

"And where are they sent to?" demanded Rain.

"To the small dealers—and some to the continent," answered Bones, eyeing him askance.

"Well and good," observed the highwayman coolly. "But you have not a hundred errand-boys to distribute the bundles and parcels about: neither are there vessels sailing for Holland and France every hour in the day."

"What—what do you mean, Tom?" asked Old Death.

"I mean that you are trying to deceive me," exclaimed the highwayman, sternly. "But, look you! we are alone in this house—for I consider your old man down stairs as nobody; and, by God! if you attempt any of your nonsense with me, I'll fell you with the butt-end of this pistol."

"What would you have me do?" said Old Death, trembling at the determined manner in which his companion spoke.

"I would have you show me where you keep your stores," was the resolute answer. "And now—delay not—or it will be the worse for you."

Old Death still hesitated for a moment; but, seeing that Rainford stamped his foot impatiently and raised his pistol in a menacing manner, he disposed himself to do with a good grace what he could not avoid.

Raising the candle high up so as to light the way thoroughly, he retraced his steps down the narrow, precipitous, and broken staircase, Tom Rain following close behind.

Having reached the little room on the ground-floor, and which we have already described as the place where stolen property was purchased, Old Death opened the door containing the hatch, and led Rainford into a small back chamber, having the air of an office. Its furniture consisted of a desk, a high stool, and one of those large, old-fashioned eight-day clocks, which used to be seen in the kitchens of genteel houses, and the wall-nut cases of which were as big as coffins. On the desk were writing materials, and a huge ledger, especially dirty, as if it had been well thumbed by hands not too intimately acquainted with soap.

"This is Tidmarsh's crib, I suppose?" said Rainford inquiringly.

Old Death nodded an affirmative.

The highwayman opened the book, in which the entries of each day's transactions were regularly made. We shall quote a specimen of these accounts, prefacing the extract with the necessary explanation that the numbers prefixed to some of the memoranda were those which tallied with the names of the thieves, burglars, or prostitutes entered in Old Death's books, as was stated on a previous occasion:—

No. 31. Two belchers, a cream-fancy, a randlesman, and a blue billy; three wedge-feeders, a yack, and a dee. £1 15*s.*

A Stranger—*looked like a shallow cove.* Roll of snow, six snooze cases, three narps, and a blood-red fancy. 8*s.*

A Stranger—*looked like a spunk fencer.* Green king's-man, water's-man, yellow-fancy, and yellow-man; pair of kicksters, a fan, and a dummie. 13*s.* 6*d.*

No. 4. A cat, six pair of shakester's crabs, and a cule. 12*s.*

No. 53. Yack and onions. £1 12*s.* 6*d.*

A Stranger—*looked like a snow-dropper.* Twelve mill-togs. 6*s.*

A Stranger—*looked like a peterman.* Busy-sack, redge-yack, six wedge-feeders, and togs in busy-sack. £2 15*s.*

A Stranger—*looked like a mushroom-faker.* Lily benjamin. 3*s.* 6*d.*

A Stranger—*looked like a crocus.* To smash three double finnips. £12 10*s.* 6*d.*

A stranger—*looked like a high-fly.* Redge-fawney. 8*s.* 6*d.*

Lunan. To smash a single finnip. £2 2*s.* 6*d.*[11]

"Quite a secret police-book, this," observed Tom Rain, after he had gained an insight into its contents.

Old Death smiled grimly.

"But do you mean to say," continued Rainford, "that these persons who are noted by means of numbers—for I can understand the meaning of all that—do not know that this is your crib?"

"Not they!" replied Bones. "I tell you that they call it *Tidmarsh's*: and I may add that not one out of one hundred who come here, even know old Tidmarsh by sight."

"And how does he recognise these fellows who are denoted by the numbers?" asked Tom Rain.

Old Death pointed to a small hole, not larger than a pea, in the wood-work which separated the two rooms; and this hole was covered with a little moveable piece of wood on the inner side—that is, in the office where Tidmarsh was accustomed to sit.

"Things begin to grow a little plainer," said Rainford. "And now, my worthy old fence, to the store-rooms and to your own special residence."

This command was significantly backed by the motion of Rainford's right hand towards the pocket where he had deposited the pistol with which he had ere now menaced his companion.

Mr. Benjamin Bones swallowed a profound sigh—for it went to his heart to think that he was compelled to yield to the coercion of one whom he had marked out for a slave, but who had become a master.

But as he took up the candle from the desk whereon he had placed it to enable the highwayman to examine his memorandum-book, a gleam of horrible satisfaction shot athwart his countenance—as if some idea of a consolatory nature had suddenly struck him.

Tom Rain whistled a tune with an air of the most perfect indifference: but that abrupt change in Old Death's features—that scintillation of delight, momentary as its expression was, had not escaped the notice of the highwayman.

The ancient fence now approached the clock, which was ticking in a gloomy, monotonous manner; and, as he laid his hand upon the key which opened the door of the case, he turned sharply towards Rainford, saying, "You persist in going farther to-night?"

"Yes—such is my determination," answered Tom.

Old Death opened the clock, and touched some secret spring inside. This was immediately followed by the noise of wheels, accompanied by a peculiar sound as of a windlass turning rapidly; and in a few moments Rainford perceived that the entire clock itself was moving slowly along the wall, revealing by degrees an aperture in the floor.

In about a minute the working of the machinery ceased—the clock-case was once more stationary—and in the place where it first stood was an opening cut in the boards, large enough to admit the passage of even a moderately stout man.

"Shall I go first?" asked Old Death, with a sardonic smile, which seemed to indicate his opinion that Rainford would not venture to follow him.

But if such were really his idea, he was disappointed; for the highwayman said in the coolest manner possible, "By all means, old chap. And make haste about it—for the night is passing away, and as yet I have seen scarcely anything."

Old Death made no answer, but began to descend an iron ladder, to which the aperture led; and as he gradually went down the steps, he held up the candle in one hand, and with the other supported himself by means of a rope hung for the purpose.

Tom Rain unhesitatingly followed him; and when he reached the bottom of the ladder, he found himself in a long, narrow, vaulted passage, apparently stretching far underground, but to the end of which it was impossible for the eye to penetrate, so feeble and flickering was the light afforded by the candle.

"Wait an instant while I close the entrance," said Old Death: "it is a precaution I never neglect."

"Quite right," observed Tom coolly; and while he affected to be leisurely whistling a tune, he was in reality keeping a most careful watch upon his companion's movements.

Old Death pulled a thick wire which hung down from the top of the vault, and the mechanism of the clock was again set in motion, until the clock-case itself had resumed its usual station over the entrance to the vaulted subterranean.

11. The ensuing glossary will explain these otherwise enigmatical entries:—

- *Belcher*—close striped handkerchief.
- *Cream fancy*—any pattern of handkerchief on a white ground.
- *Randlesman*—green handkerchief, with white spots.
- *Blue billy*—blue ground handkerchief, with white spots.
- *Wedge-feeders*—silver spoons.
- *Yack*—watch.
- *Dee*—pocket-book of small size.
- *Shallow cove*—a fellow dressed in a Guernsey jacket, and looking like a sailor.
- *Roll of snow*—piece of Irish linen.
- *Snooze-cases*—pillow-cases.
- *Narps*—calico shirts.
- *Blood-red fancy*—handkerchief all red.
- *Spunk fencer*—match-seller.
- *Green King's-man*—handkerchief of any pattern on a green ground.
- *Watersman*—sky-coloured handkerchief.

- *Yellow fancy*—yellow handkerchief, with white spots.
- *Yellow-man*—handkerchief all yellow.
- *Kicksters*—trousers.
- *Fan*—waistcoat.
- *Dummie*—pocket-book of large size.
- *Cat*—muff.
- *Shakesters' crabs*—ladies' shoes.
- *Cule*—reticule.
- *Yack and onions*—watch and seals.
- *Snow-dropper*—one who steals linen from hedges or drying grounds.
- *Mill togs*—linen shirts.
- *Peterman*—a robber who cuts trunks from the back of carriages.
- *Busy-sack*—carpet bag.
- *Redge yack*—gold watch.
- *Togs*—clothes.
- *Mushroom faker*—a man who goes about ostensibly to buy old umbrellas, but really to thieve.
- *Lily benjamin*—white upper coat.
- *Crocus*—an itinerant quack doctor.
- *Smash*—change.
- *Double finnips*—ten-pound notes.
- *Highfly*—genteel begging-letter impostor.
- *Redge fawney*—gold ring.
- *Lunan*—common woman.
- *Single finnip*—five-pound note.

CHAPTER XXX.
THE STORE-ROOMS.

The reader has already seen and heard enough to be fully aware that Thomas Rainford was a man of undaunted courage: nor did he now tremble when he found himself immured, as it were, in that subterranean, along with a character so full of cunning and malignity as Old Death.

Although completely ignorant of the dark and gloomy locality to which he had been brought, and well aware that his companion was quite capable of the foulest treachery, the highwayman followed the old fence with so firm a step, and whistled away in a manner indicative of such utter recklessness of danger, that his guide was himself astonished at so much daring.

But Rainford was keenly observant of all the movements of his companion; and, resolutely as he walked, he was nevertheless careful in following as precisely as possible in the steps of Old Death, so that he might not be entrapped by any pitfall in that gloomy place.

On his part, Old Death proceeded at a somewhat rapid pace, shading the light with his hand so as to protect it from the strong current of air which rushed through the passage.

This passage, or long subterranean vault, was about ten feet wide and six high. It was walled and arched with rough stone, and paved with huge flags. The masonry at the sides and overhead was green with the damp; and, even by the fitful light of the candle, Rainford could perceive that this strange place must have been in existence for many—many years.

Here and there he observed little niches in the wall; and in one there was the remnant of an image of the Saviour on the cross. It instantly flashed to the mind of the highwayman that this sinister-looking subterranean had once been connected with some monastic establishment; and his imagination suggested that he was probably treading on the very place where the victims of ancient Popish tyranny had been confined and left to perish through famine.

Old Death and Tom Rain had proceeded about sixty yards, as well as the latter could guess, along the vaulted passage, when the former suddenly stopped, and the highwayman perceived that their farther progress was barred by a huge door, studded with iron knobs.

"You are now about to enter my sanctuary—as I may call it," said Old Death, turning abruptly round on Rainford; "and again I ask you what guarantee I have that you will not betray me?"

"The same security which I have that you will not prove treacherous to me," answered Tom.

Old Death hesitated for a few moments, as if he were about to make another observation: but, yielding to a second thought, which most probably showed him the inutility of farther remonstrance, he proceeded to unbar the massive door.

It opened inwards, and led to a spiral flight of stone steps, up which the two men mounted, Rainford having previously secured the door, which had huge bolts on each side.

Having ascended some forty steps, Old Death, who went first, placed the candle in a niche, and pushed up a trap-door, which immediately admitted a strong current of air: but the precaution observed in respect to the light, prevented it from being extinguished.

"I ought to have brought a lantern with me, by rights," murmured Old Death. "But come along."

"You go on first," said Rainford; "and I'll take care of the candle."

"No—give it to me," replied Bones hastily; and he extended his hand to grasp it.

But Rainford hit him a hard blow on the wrist with the butt-end of his pistol, and then seized the candle.

"What did you do that for?" demanded Old Death savagely.

"Because I suspect you of treachery," returned the highwayman, in a severe tone. "But, remember—I am well armed—and, at the least appearance of evil intent on your part, I fire!"

"You are wrong, Tom—my dear fellow," said Old Death, coaxingly, as he still lingered at the top of the steps.

"Well—I may be; and I shall be glad to find that I am," exclaimed Tom: "and now lead on."

Old Death ascended the few remaining steps; and Rainford followed with his pistol in one hand and the candle in the other.

They were now in a small room furnished as a bed-chamber; and when Old Death had let down the trap-door again, he unrolled and spread a small carpet over it.

"This is your residence?" said Rainford inquiringly.

The old man nodded a grim assent.

"And your store-rooms are in this house?—for I can perfectly well understand that *we have come into another house*—and, by the direction of the subterranean, I should say it must be in Red Lion Street."

"You know London well," said Old Death.

"I do," replied Rainford.

"Although you lived so long in the country," added Bones.

"Right again, old fellow!" exclaimed Tom, "And now for a farther insight into the mysteries of your abode."

With these words the highwayman approached a door on one side of the room; but Old Death, hastily advancing towards another door, said, "This way, Tom—this way: there is nothing in that quarter—worth seeing."

But the ancient fence seemed agitated; and this was not lost upon his companion.

"Well, as you choose," observed the latter, resuming his careless, off-hand manner. "Lead on."

Bones had already opened the door; and he now conducted the highwayman into a spacious apartment, surrounded by shelves, whereon were ranged an assortment of articles of the most miscellaneous description.

Clothes and china-ware—candlesticks, plated and silver, all carefully wrapped up in paper—piles of silk pocket-handkerchiefs, and heaps of linen garments—carpet-bags and portmanteaus—every species of haberdashery—silk dresses and cotton gowns—velvet pelisses and shawls of all gradations of value—muffs, tippets, and boas—ladies' shoes and gentlemen's boots—looking-glasses and candelabra—lamps and pictures—tea-urns and costly vases—meerschaum-pipes and dressing-cases—immense quantities of cutlery—piles of printing paper—saddles and bridles,—in short, an infinite variety of articles, to detail which would occupy whole pages.

"Your magazine is crowded, old fellow," said Rainford, who, even while surveying the curious place in which he found himself, did not the less keep a strict watch upon his companion.

"Are you satisfied now?" demanded Old Death.

"Not quite," answered Rainford. "You must have another room where you keep your jewellery and all those kinds of things?"

"What kind of things?" asked Bones sharply.

"Oh! things that require to be packed away with caution, to be sure," replied Tom Rain.

For an instant the old man cast upon him a glance of searching inquiry, as if to penetrate into the most secret profundities of his soul; but the highwayman affected to be very intent in his contemplation of a picture, and the countenance of the fence grew more composed.

"Well," said Rainford, after a few moments' pause, "there's no use in delaying the matter. I *must* and *will* make myself acquainted with every nook of this place."

Old Death moved towards a door facing the one by which they entered the apartment; and Rainford was conducted into a smaller room, but fitted up with shelves like the first.

On those shelves were several boxes, of various dimensions, and numerous jewel-cases wrapped up in paper.

"Watches and plate, I suppose?" said Rainford, pointing to the boxes.

"Something in that way, Tom," replied Old Death. "Would you like to see any of them?"

"No, thank'ee," was the answer. "I am not particularly curious in that respect."

Then, as he appeared to glance casually round the room, his eyes dwelt for an instant upon an iron safe let into the wall.

"Well—have you seen enough?" asked Old Death. "It's getting very late."

"It must be early, you mean," replied the highwayman, with a smile. "But still there is time for the business that I have in hand," he added, his manner suddenly changing to seriousness.

Old Death glanced towards him uneasily. Indeed, for some time the fence had been suspecting that Rainford had an ulterior object in view, independent of the mere wish to become acquainted with his abode; and vague alarms now filled his mind. What could the highwayman mean? Was he other than he seemed? Did he intend to betray him?

All these ideas rushed rapidly through the imagination of the horrible old man; and, though *he* had formed a plan whereby to avenge himself on *the only individual who had ever yet dared to coerce him*, he trembled lest he should be unable to put it into execution. He knew that Rainford was a man of dauntless bravery, and believed him to be a desperate one; and now he found himself completely in this formidable person's power. Not that Old Death lacked courage himself: and he certainly was not deficient in treachery. But he wanted the strength—the physical strength to maintain a deadly struggle with the highwayman, if it should come to *that!*

Thus was it that for the first time, perhaps, the hardened miscreant trembled for his life.

To throw open the window and call for assistance, in case of danger, was to invite the entrance of persons who would discover all the mysteries of his abode; and death were an alternative scarcely more frightful!

"Yes—there is time enough for the business that I have on hand!" repeated Rainford, his countenance assuming so stern—so determined an expression, that Old Death trembled with a colder shudder than before.

"What do you mean?—what is that—that——" stammered Old Death.

"Sit down—there—on that seat!" thundered the highwayman, pointing imperiously to a chair. "Sit down, I say—or, by heaven! this pistol——"

"Well—I will—I will, Tom," said Bones, perceiving the deadly weapon levelled point-blank at his heart: and he sank into the chair accordingly. "But do tell me—if I have offended you—if——"

"Hold your tongue!" ejaculated Rainford, in so authoritative a manner that the ancient villain's powers of utterance were suddenly paralysed. "And now mark me," continued the highwayman: "I have a certain task to perform, which nothing save a superior physical strength on your part can prevent. But, in the first place it is necessary that I should bind you—that I should render you incapable of molesting me."

Old Death was unable to reply: but he stared with vacant terror on the individual whose proceedings were alike so mysterious and so alarming.

Rainford took a coil of rope from a bale of goods that stood upon the table, and with extraordinary rapidity proceeded to fasten Old Death's arms and legs to the chair, uttering terrible menaces the whole time that this operation lasted; while the appalling state of the aged fence's mind was indicated only by low moans and convulsive movements of uneasiness.

Having made fast the end of the rope to the iron bars of the fire-place, in such a manner that Old Death could not shift the chair beyond the length of the tether thus formed, Rainford leant himself against the table and proceeded to address his prisoner.

CHAPTER XXXI.
ANOTHER DEED OF INFAMY BROUGHT TO LIGHT.

The scene was now a striking one.

In that small chamber—the shutters of which were securely closed,—by the light of a dimly-burning candle, two men of criminal avocations but of entirely discrepant characters, were seated opposite to each other,—one fastened, pinioned to a large arm-chair—the other placed in a determined attitude against the heavy oaken table.

Fear and vague alarms rendered the always repulsive countenance of Old Death now truly hideous; while excitement and a certain air of bold triumph invested the features of the highwayman with an expression which made him appear perfectly, though sternly handsome.

The gleaming eyes of Old Death flickered in sparkles beneath his shaggy, overhanging brows—for fierce, ferocious malignity mingled with the terrors that oppressed him;—while Rainford surveyed him with combined abhorrence and contempt.

"Thirty years and ten months have elapsed," said the highwayman sternly, "since one Benjamin Bones sold his half-sister Octavia to a nobleman who purchased the prize of her virtue for gold!"

For a few moments a dead silence ensued, after these words had fallen from the lips of Rainford: but, when that interval was past, a wild—a savage—a, hyena-like howl, expressive of mingled rage and astonishment, burst from the lips of Old Death.

"Silence, miscreant!" exclaimed the highwayman, in a tone and with a manner of terrible earnestness. "Ah! I have doubtless surprised you by this announcement—this denunciation of a secret that you little deemed to be known to me!"

"My God! who are you?—how came you to learn that secret?" demanded the old fence, writhing in the agony of suspense and wild excitement.

"I will tell you who I am presently," was the answer: "and you will also see wherefore I have compelled you to conduct me hither this night."

"Then you *had* another motive, besides the mere wish to become acquainted with my abode?" said Old Death, perceiving that he had been over-reached in this respect—as indeed he had for the last half-hour suspected.

"Fool!" ejaculated Rainford, contemptuously: "of what use was it to me to know where you lived, or to visit your secret repositories of plunder, unless

I had some essentially important motive? The fact of your having discovered my abode gave me in truth but little uneasiness—for I could have moved elsewhere in a few hours. That fact, however, furnished me with an apparent excuse to force you to conduct me to *your* den; for I knew that were I to acquaint you with my real object in coming here, you would have risked every thing to prevent it!"

"Again I say, who *are* you?" demanded Old Death, a kind of superstitious awe now taking possession of him.

"Listen to me," said Rainford. "Nearly thirty-one years have elapsed since you sold your half-sister Octavia Manners for the gold which laid the foundation of the immense fortune you have amassed. Yes—this atrocious deed was perpetrated; and one of England's proudest peers was the purchaser of that young creature's virtue—for she was but sixteen, old man, when her ruin was effected through your vile agency! She was sold to the embrace of a man old enough to be her father—aye, even her grandfather;—and the affection which she entertained for a deserving youth in her own sphere of life, was blighted—crushed! She died of a broken heart—leaving behind her a male child whom *you* swore to protect!"

Old Death seemed to recoil from this averment as from a hideous spectre suddenly starting up before him; for, in spite of his confirmed wickedness, the present topic had awakened painful reminiscences and compunctious feelings within him.

"Yes," continued Rainford, fixing his eyes reproachfully upon the old fence; "she forgave you on her death-bed—forgave you the wrong that you did her,—forgave you, because you promised to make amends for your conduct towards her by your behaviour to the babe whom she left to your charge."

"And who can say that I did not fulfil my promise?" demanded Old Death, trembling in suspense at what might be the nature of the reply which Rainford would give.

"Who can say that you did not fulfil your promise?" repeated the highwayman, in a slow—deliberate—bitter tone, while his eyes appeared to send daggers to the heart of the old man bound helplessly in the chair. "There is damning evidence against you in that respect!"

"Where?—how?" ejaculated Old Death.

"You shall soon learn," replied Rainford. "The nobleman who had *purchased* your half-sister, provided liberally for the support of her child—*their* child—and gave a large sum to be used for the offspring of that sad connexion. But you——"

"I—I did my duty—towards the child," stammered Old Death, "till—it died——"

"Liar!" thundered Rainford, advancing in an appallingly menacing manner towards the helpless, captive wretch. "You sold the child to a tribe of gipsies——"

"Mercy! mercy!" groaned Old Death. "Do not kill me, Tom—do not hurt me! I am in your power—spare me!"

Rainford had raised his pistol as if to dash the butt-end against the forehead of the old man: but, mastering his passion, he consigned the weapon to his pocket—for he was afraid to trust his hand with it while his excitement was so terrible.

"Mercy, indeed!" exclaimed Rainford in a tone of bitter hatred, not unmingled with contempt: "what mercy did you show towards that hapless child? When Octavia Manners was on her death-bed, that nobleman to whom you sold her virtue, visited her—implored her forgiveness—and placed in your hands a thousand guineas to ensure a provision for the boy."

"My God!" ejaculated Old Death, a terrible suspicion now flashing like lightning to his mind: "how can you know all this?—even if——you, yourself——"

"Yes—*I* am the son of that nobleman and your half-sister Octavia!" cried Rainford, placing himself in front of Old Death, on whom he gazed with eyes flashing fire from beneath sternly contracted brows.

"Spare me—spare me!" murmured the wretched man, hanging down his head—for the glances of his injured nephew seemed to scorch and sear his very heart's core.

"Look up—look up!" thundered the highwayman; "and meet the gaze of him whom, when a child, you sold to gipsies—sold, that you might grasp all the gold which was supplied to you for my benefit! Yes—you sold me to strangers—even making a profit of me by the very way in which you rid yourself of my presence in your dwelling! Had it not been for your treachery—your vile avarice in this respect, I might have grown up to be an honest man. But, no—no," added Rainford bitterly—and a tear trembled on his eye-lash,—"had you kept me with you, I should have been worse—aye, a myriad, myriad times worse than I even now am!"

At the imperious command of the highwayman, Old Death had raised his head; and Rainford then beheld a countenance so fearfully distorted with varied emotions, that he felt he was already partially avenged in having been able to produce such a powerful effect on that aged—that inveterate sinner.

"What do you mean to do to me, Tom?" asked the hideous old fence, now more than ever trembling for his life.

"Not to harm your person," replied the highwayman scornfully: "especially," he added, in a tone of bitter sarcasm, "as you and I can boast of kinship. But I am wearied of the life I am leading—and my aim is to settle in some foreign clime, where the evil reputation of my deeds in this may not follow me. There are times when I abhor myself—happy, reckless, and indifferent as I usually seem;—for my career has been marked with many a deed at which I blush—all robber, plunderer that I am! And this discourse, which has turned upon the foul crime perpetrated against the honour and happiness of my mother—Oh! it has reminded me of *one* act in *my* life that presses sorely—God knows how heavily upon my conscience!"

Rainford walked thrice up and down the room, apparently oblivious of the presence of Old Death, who had never before seen him exhibit so much painful emotion.

"But regrets are useless—save as they prepare our minds for a better course of life," exclaimed Rainford, abruptly starting from his reverie: then, again confronting Old Death, he said, "And now comes the moment of punishment for all your misdeeds towards me!"

The fence groaned audibly.

"Fear not for your life," continued the highwayman: "I am no murderer:—my hands were never stained with blood—neither shall they be now! But, in regaining that which is my own—and with interest—aye, compound interest, too—I shall teach a heartless, grasping wretch a lesson that may render him more cautious in future how he sacrifices every human tie at the shrine of avarice! For even amongst such as you—such as I—such as the veriest wretches whose villany has helped to fill these stores,—the claims of kinship—the bonds of relationship have a recognition and a name. Many and many a man who is noted for his misdeeds—or who has even shed the blood of a fellow-creature—would respect the vow which he pledged to rear his dead sister's child. But you—*you* ruthlessly thrust away the helpless infant,—you cast off the offspring of that connexion which your own fearful thirst for gold had brought about! Now, then, shall I punish you through the medium of that passion which prompted you to sell my mother to the nobleman, and myself to the gipsy!"

With these words Rainford advanced close up to his prisoner, and said in a short, commanding manner, "The key of that safe—where is it?"

"The key?" repeated Old Death, his countenance becoming ghastly white.

"Yes—the key!" cried the highwayman; and he thrust his hands into the pockets of his captive's grey coat.

"No—no: you shall not have my gold!" howled the fence, agitating convulsively on his chair.

"Keep quiet!" thundered Rain; "or I shall do you a mischief yet! Keep quiet, I say.—Ah! here is the key! And now roll about, and rave, and foam as you will—I care not!"

"Villain! what are you doing?" exclaimed Old Death, his eyes glaring with ferocious hate—with infernal spite—with blood-thirsty malignity,—glaring, indeed, like those of a famished tiger caught in the snare of the hunter, and beholding a stately deer at a little distance: "what are you doing? You are going to rob me—to plunder me—after all I have done for you—all the good things I have put in your way! But I will be revenged yet—I will send you to the scaffold—I will wreak a terrific vengeance on your head. Keep off, I say—touch not that safe! Damnation light upon you!—perdition seize you! Oh! Tom—dear Tom—don't rob me—don't! You'll drive me to despair—I shall die of grief—and you will be my murderer Tom—do listen to me! Ah! he opens the safe—the wretch—the villain!"

Thus did Old Death menace and pray—coax and moan by turns; but at last his voice swelled into a howl of fiend-like rage, which rose like the wailing of a damned soul upon the silence of that early morning-hour.

But Rainford seemed indifferent alike to his earnest beseechings and his paroxysms of fury.

That last, ferocious outburst of rage had completely exhausted the old man; and gasping as if under the influence of strangulation, he fell back in the seat to which he was fastened by the strong cords. But his convulsive motions—his hollow, flashing eyes—his parched lips—and the quivering of his hands, denoted how acutely—how keenly he felt the work of depredation that was in progress.

For Rainford had opened the safe, and was now busily engaged in examining the various drawers, and also sundry pocket-books which he found therein. The former contained hoards of gold coins, and the latter were filled with Bank-notes, making an aggregate of immense value.

The highwayman secured about his person a sum of five thousand pounds, murmuring to himself, "This is sufficient to enable me to become an honest man: I will not leave the old villain penniless."

He then searched the safe for any private papers that might be deposited there; and in a drawer which he had well-nigh overlooked, he found a small leather case containing a roll of letters, tied round with a piece of riband so faded that it was impossible to determine what its colour might have originally been. A single glance at these documents awakened such emotions of mingled pleasure and pain within his breast, that he determined to possess himself of them; and replacing them in the leather case, he secured them about his person with even more care than he had bestowed on the Bank-notes.

Having thus rifled the safe of as much as he chose to take away, he closed the iron door, locked it, and placing the key on the table, said to Old Death, "I am now about to take my departure from this house. Is there any one living here besides yourself?"

The fence only stared at him in a fierce and sombre manner; for the brain of the old man had become a chaos of wild and terrible thoughts at the contemplation of the daring robbery which was thus practised on *him*—the patron of robbers!

Indeed, the incidents of this eventful night were sufficient to level the powers of a mind stronger even than that of Old Death,—for those incidents had followed each other in such rapid, whirlwind-like succession, and were all so hostile to his interests, that he felt as if he were the victim of a hideous nightmare composed of all the most frightful images that the terrors of a guilty conscience can possibly conjure up during the long dark nights of winter.

The failure of his expedition to Lock's Fields—the exposure of his treachery to Tom Rain—the discomfiture he had undergone in the presence of Toby Bunce and the lad Jacob—the coercion exercised to force him to discover the secrets of his receiving-house and the mysteries of his store-rooms and dwelling-house—the discovery of his deeply injured nephew in the highwayman, and the revival of the history of his villany in reference to one long since dead,—and, lastly, the robbery of his money and papers,—all these events, occurring with such consecutive rapidity that they appeared to form but one single dreadful blow, were sufficient to paralyse the energies of the old villain.

"Is there any one living in *this* house besides yourself?" repeated Rainford. "It is for your own good that I ask; for I shall leave you bound in this chair—but, if you are really alone here, I will hasten to drop your friend Tidmarsh a hint, that he may come presently and release you, by which arrangement I shall get as long a start of you as I require."

"There is no one here but myself," at length replied Old Death, aroused from his torpor by the words thus addressed to him.

"Then good bye," said Tom; and, taking up the candle, he quitted the room, heedless of the prisoner's intercession to be released from his captivity.

On gaining the bed-chamber situate above the spiral staircase leading to the subterranean passage, the highwayman remembered two circumstances which made him pause ere he raised the trap-door.

In the first place he recalled to mind the anxiety of Old Death to prevent him from securing the candle at the moment when they were about to emerge from the secret avenue; and it struck Rainford that the old man had intended to have extinguished the light as if by accident—but whether for motives of treachery, or merely to avoid the discovery of something that the fence wished to be concealed, Tom was at a loss to conjecture.

Secondly, Rainford remembered that Old Death had manifested considerable uneasiness when he had approached the first of the two doors opening from that bed-chamber; and he now thought it probable that the fence had been desirous of extinguishing the light in order to prevent Rainford from observing that there were two doors in that room.

"At all events," said Tom to himself, "let us see where this other door leads to."

It was unlocked—as he had expected to find it; because, had it been otherwise, Old Death would not have manifested so much anxiety when he had approached it on their entrance into the bed-chamber.

Proceeding with caution—so as not to incur the risk of having his light extinguished, and equally to avoid any sudden surprise in case the house might really have other occupants besides Old Death—Rainford entered a spacious room which seemed to be fitted up as a chemical laboratory. On a large oaken table were galvanic batteries, and an infinite variety of electrical apparatus as well as the articles on which experiments are usually made with the subtle fluid,—such as pieces of glass, amber, sulphur, wax, silk, cotton, loaf sugar, phials containing a variety of oils, metallic oxides, several common stones, metallic ores, the metals and semi-metals, &c. Leyden jars, batteries, electrophori, electrometers, discharging rods, &c., were also crowded together on the table. In a large earthen pan under the table were the flayed carcasses of several rabbits, frogs, and such vermin as rats and mice, all of which appeared to have been only very recently stripped of their skins—for they emitted no putrid smell, and the blood was still oozing from them.

On a shelf were plaster of Paris casts of upwards of fifty heads of men and monkeys. On the base of some of the heads there were inscriptions in black letters, stating the originals from which the casts were made; and, with a rapid glance, the highwayman read the principal ones, which were these:—

ARTHUR THISTLEWOOD.

Executed for High Treason, 1820.

DAVID HOGGART.

Executed for Murder, 1821.

GEORGE BARRINGTON.

The Notorious Pickpocket—died 1811.

HENRY FAUNTLEROY.

Executed for Forgery, Nov., 1824.

JOHN THURTELL.

Executed for Murder, 1824.

WILLIAM PROBERT.

Executed for Horse-stealing, 1825.

There were casts from the heads of several other celebrated criminals; but we need enumerate no more.

Intrepid—dauntless—bold as Tom Rain was, he nevertheless experienced a cold shuddering as he surveyed the objects ranged upon that long shelf; for this thought forced itself upon him—"*I wonder whether a cast of* MY *head will ever be there!*"

In order to chase these gloomy reflections from his mind, Rainford turned away from the contemplation of the shelf and its sinister contents. A cupboard-door stood partially open in one corner of the room; and he hastened to inspect the recess.

But what pen can depict his horror—what language can describe his astonishment, when upon a shelf within that cupboard he beheld four human heads staring out at him with eyes wide open but perfectly motionless, and on the pupils of which the rays of the candle flashed with extraordinary brilliancy!

For an instant the highwayman felt afraid:—in what description of place was he? what meant that ghastly spectacle?

But, conquering his terrors, of which indeed in another moment he was ashamed, he approached nearer: and the idea struck him that he beheld admirable models in wax. Still the flesh was so closely resembling that of the dead—the appearance of the countenances and of the crown of the heads, which were all closely shaven, was so natural, that he extended his hand and touched the cheek of one of those appalling objects.

Great God! it was indeed human flesh,—icy cold, and producing a sensation which the touch of naught beside *can* produce!

In spite of himself, Rainford cast a shuddering glance around him: then, once more ashamed of his weakness, he resumed his inspection of the heads.

They were evidently prepared for preservation; for an odour of strong spices emanated from them, and the eyes, fitted into the sockets, were of glass. Hence the strange brilliancy produced by the reflection of the candle.

The highwayman was still absorbed in the contemplation of these frightful objects, when a door at the farther end of the room slowly opened; and a man, enveloped in a loose dressing-gown, and holding a lamp in his hand, appeared on the threshold.

But the instant he beheld Rainford, he uttered an ejaculation of surprise and alarm—hastily retreated—and barred and bolted the door behind him.

He had, however, been long enough in the room for Rainford to obtain a full view of his countenance; and it was with profound astonishment that the highwayman had recognised Dr. Lascelles!

"What!" he thought: "that respectable physician in league with Old Death?"

And he stood for some moments gazing vacantly at the door by which the doctor had entered and also so abruptly disappeared again.

Then it suddenly struck him that the physician might discover the state of bondage in which Benjamin Bones had been left; and not only would the immediate release of the old fence follow, but an active pursuit be probably instituted by both individuals after himself.

He accordingly determined to beat a retreat as speedily as possible. Not that he was afraid of encountering Old Death and the doctor; but he knew not what principles of danger the establishment possessed, and which might be turned against himself. He had seen quite enough of the house in Turnmill Street and of that where he now was (in Red Lion Street) to be well aware that they were no ordinary places of abode; and he was also sufficiently well acquainted with the character of Old Death to feel conscious that no mercy was to be expected at his hands, should he fall completely into his power.

It is, therefore, no disparagement to the heroism of the highwayman to state that he was now anxious to effect his exit from the strange place wherein he found himself; and it naturally struck him that there must be a more speedy and convenient avenue of egress than the subterranean. He readily comprehended that the underground passage was used as a medium of transferring goods from the house in Turnmill Street to the store-rooms of the establishment in Red Lion Street; and that it might also serve, at a pinch of need, as an avenue of escape for Old Death from his own bed-room.

But that the subterranean was the only means of ingress and egress in respect to the house in Red Lion Street, Tom could not for an instant suppose; as a dwelling without a door, or with a door that was never opened, would soon become an object of suspicion in the neighbourhood.

Judging by the direction of the subterranean passage, the highwayman was enabled to conclude that the room in which he now found himself was at the back of the house, and that the one where he had left Old Death was in the front, as was also that into which Dr. Lascelles had retreated; and he was moreover convinced that these apartments were all on a first or upper storey, but decidedly not on the ground-floor.

Now as the laboratory, Old Death's bed-chamber and the larger store-room formed the suite at the back of the house, and there was no flight of stairs connecting them with the ground-floor, it was clear to Rainford that the means of communication with that ground-floor must be from the front part of the house; and into the rooms looking on the street he did not choose to penetrate, because he might there encounter the doctor and Old Death. He therefore came to the conclusion that he must escape by the back part of the house, or else dare the subterranean.

All these calculations, which have occupied us some time to record, were made and summed up in a few moments by Tom Rain.

Nor did he now hesitate what course to adopt.

Placing the candle upon the table, he hastened to throw up a window; but, to his annoyance, he found it securely barred:—and his hand assured him that the bars could not be removed by mere physical strength.

He had not time nor implements to attempt to force a way through this difficulty; and the only alternative appeared to be the subterranean.

Resuming possession of the candle, he returned into Old Death's bedroom—drew away the carpet—raised the trap-door—and commenced the descent of the spiral staircase, closing the trap after him and bolting it inside.

But scarcely had he proceeded ten steps downwards, when his foot suddenly slipped; and, in the attempt which he made to recover himself, the light went out.

At the same instant he heard heavy steps treading upon the trap-door overhead, and then the hum of voices—but whose he could not distinguish—in the room which he had just left.

"Now, Tom Rain, look alive, old fellow!" he murmured in self-encouraging apostrophe; and, with a resolute step, he hastened rapidly down the spiral staircase, amidst a darkness so intense that it was all but *felt*!

CHAPTER XXXII.
RAINFORD IN THE SUBTERRANEAN.

Tom Rain reached the bottom of the stairs in perfect safety; and, as he had carefully noted the geography of the subterranean when he traversed it an hour previously with Old Death, he experienced but little difficulty in threading his path along it, even amidst the black darkness through which he literally seemed to be pushing his way.

In a few minutes his progress was stopped by a wall, which his extended arms encountered; and he now knew that he had reached the extremity communicating with the house in Turnmill Street.

Having succeeded in grasping the wire which, passing through the top of the vault, was connected with the mechanism of the clock overhead, he pulled it vigorously.

But the machinery moved not!

Then, for the first time during this eventful night, the highwayman became appalled at the dangers on which he had entered.

Again he tugged at the wire; it snapped short close by the roof, and the long piece thus broken off, fell at his feet.

"Damnation!" cried Rainford; and he stamped impatiently on the cold, damp stones.

Suddenly it struck him that there might be one wire to move the clock over the opening at the head of the iron ladder, and another wire to move it away from that opening.

He accordingly began to feel with his hands for this second wire the existence of which was suggested by his imagination; but at the end of a minute he was compelled to admit to himself that it did indeed exist only in imagination.

No such second wire was to be found!

He then hastily ascended the ladder, and endeavoured to hurl the clock from off the opening which it covered: but the huge machine was as solidly fixed there as if it had formed a portion of the vaulted roof itself.

Escape seemed to grow every moment more hopeless; and now came the appalling thought that Old Death and the Doctor would soon have had sufficient time to repair from the house in Red Lion Street to that in Turnmill Street, and thus secure against him the avenue covered by the clock—even if it were not sufficiently secure already!

What was he to do?

Again and again he tried to force away the heavy clock: but there it stood, immoveable—and when he paused to reflect, its steady, monotonous ticking fell ominously upon his ears.

At length it struck him that he would retrace his way to the other extremity—force up the trap-door leading to Old Death's bed-chamber—and, with a pistol in each hand, dare every thing.

But what if that trap-door were secured on the other side?

No:—he remembered to have observed that there was not a bolt nor a bar to break the level of its upper surface as it fitted in flush with the floor.

Encouraged by the scintillation of hope that thus gleamed in upon him, Rainford hurried back to the other end of the subterranean—ascended the spiral staircase—grasped his pistols—and listened attentively.

All was still in the room above:—not the murmur of a voice—nor the creaking of a footstep!

He then slowly and carefully drew back the bolt of the trap-door, and tried to raise it.

But it moved not!

He applied additional force, under the impression that some heavy piece of furniture might have been dragged over the trap: but still it was as motionless as the thick, solid, substantial flooring in which it was set.

Rainford returned the pistols to his pockets, so that nothing might impede the application of all his strength to the task on which his liberty depended: but no—the door moved not!

The highwayman bit his under lip almost till the blood started forth—for he felt that his calmness was abandoning him.

Then how bitterly did he repent the course which he had adopted after his interruption in the laboratory by the appearance of Doctor Lascelles. Instead of trusting himself to that hideous subterranean, he should have essayed an escape by means of the front rooms of the house.

Regrets were, however, useless:—he must act—and not waste time in self-reproach!

Yes: he must act—if he would not die in that dreadful place, where the vindictiveness of Old Death would be sure to leave him!

To act!—oh! how easy to think of acting!—But how *was* he to put his thought into execution?

A stone pavement beneath—stone walls on either side—a stone ceiling overhead—at one end an avenue closed by a huge clock—at the other a trap-door evidently secured on the outside,—these were the obstacles—these were the barriers against which he had to contend.

And what were the implements within his power?

His two hands—a clasp-knife—and a pair of pistols!

Quick as lightning the idea flashed across him that the iron ladder at the other extremity of the subterranean was moveable, and that it would serve him as a battering-ram.

Rejoiced at this thought, he once more retraced his way along the vaulted passage, and eagerly grasped the ladder.

His conjecture was right: it merely hooked on to two iron rings fixed into the masonry just below the aperture covered by the clock; and, heavy though it was, yet Rainford now bore it as easily as if it were of wood—for renewed hope had rendered him strong and bold as a lion.

It was, however, somewhat difficult to drag the iron ladder up the spiral staircase; but in a few minutes this portion of the task was accomplished; and Rainford now prepared to assault the secret entrance to Old Death's dwelling.

Placing himself in such a position that he might deal a vigorous blow upwards with his ponderous engine, and then be able to seize his pistols the instant they might be required, he went to work with a stout arm and a still stouter heart.

Once—twice—thrice—and up swung the ladder:—that single blow was sufficient—and the trap-door burst from its setting.

Quick as thought, Rainford seized his pistols, and thrusting up the trap, ascended the last few steps of the spiral staircase.

Throwing back the carpet which had been replaced over the trap-door, he found, to his infinite surprise, that there was no resistance to his egress from that subterranean where, at one time, it seemed probable that he was destined to find a tomb; and, gazing rapidly around the room, he neither perceived Old Death nor the Doctor—nor indeed a single living soul.

Recovering all his wonted calmness, he proceeded to examine the trap-door, for the purpose of ascertaining how it had been secured against him: and, on a close inspection, he observed a spring-bolt let into the side of the trap-door in such a way that, when the trap was closed, it neither appeared above nor below it. This bolt was either held back within the wood, or made to fly into a hole made to receive it in the beam against which the trap-door closed, by means of two screws that could easily be pressed inwards. But the force of Rainford's battering-ram had unsettled this artfully-contrived piece of mechanism.

It was clear that some one had secured the trap-door; because even if the spring-bolt had flown into its socket by accident, still the carpet could not have spread out of its own accord. Moreover, when Rainford had retreated to the subterranean, he had heard footsteps and voices in Old Death's room. It therefore struck him that those who had so secured the trap-door, had departed to protect the avenue of escape in Turnmill Street, in the confidence that the said trap-door was too strong to be forced.

Nevertheless, it was necessary to guard against the possibility of an ambuscade; and Tom held his pistols in a manner calculated to render them instantaneously available.

He determined to proceed by way of the laboratory; but, on trying the door, he found it locked.

Without an instant's hesitation he forced it open with one vigorously applied blow of his foot: but here again he encountered no resistance.

Passing through the laboratory, he tried the door by which he had seen Dr. Lascelles appear and disappear again so abruptly; and this time he was spared the necessity of violent exertion,—for the door was not locked.

He now entered a passage leading to a flight of stairs; down which he hastened, and reached a kind of hall, from whence the street-door opened.

But he did not immediately issue forth. He experienced an invincible curiosity to ascertain if Old Death had in reality been released from the state of bondage in which he had left him; and, forgetting the terrible dangers whence he had escaped with so much difficulty, he re-ascended the staircase.

The appearance of this part of the house was dirty and neglected. Indeed, it afforded no evidence that the tenement was inhabited at all; but conveyed quite the contrary impression. The fan-light above the front-door was boarded over; and thus the hall itself was nearly dark, the only light it enjoyed being admitted through the ill-closed joints of the boarding just mentioned. The paper was falling away from the walls of the staircase; and dust and dirt had accumulated wherever the hand touched or the eye could penetrate.

On regaining the landing on the first-floor, Tom Rain tried a door opposite to that by which he had issued from the laboratory; but it was locked. He forced it open, and found himself, as he suspected he should, in the very room where he had left Old Death; for that apartment had two doors.

And, to his ineffable surprise, Old Death was still there,—still sitting in the chair to which he had been fastened with a strong cord;—and that cord had not been removed.

The head of the fence was bent forward, and hung—or rather drooped, upon his breast.

The highwayman was alarmed, and hastened towards him.

But the moment he caught a glimpse of his features, he started back horror-stricken,—and stupefied as it were by the hideous spectacle that presented itself to his view.

For the old man's countenance was fearfully distorted, and nearly black—the eyes protruded from their sockets, and seemed staring on vacancy—and the under jaw had fallen.

"Holy God! he is dead!" ejaculated Rainford at length: "and I—I have killed him!"

At that instant the door leading from the inner apartment was slowly and cautiously opened; and the highwayman, yielding to a natural impulse, turned and fled abruptly by the one communicating with the passage, and which he had forced open a few moments previously.

This movement on his part was so sudden and so quickly executed, that he did not perceive the person who was entering the room; but whether that person observed him, or not, he was unaware.

Descending the stairs three or four at a time, the highwayman quitted the house by the front door, and did not breathe freely until he had closed it behind him and found himself at length in the open street.

Dauntless—daring as he was, the idea that he had caused, though unintentionally, the death of the old fence, prostrated for a time the powers of a naturally vigorous mind; and horror threw all his thoughts into chaotic confusion.

He did not even pause a moment to examine, as well as the darkness of the hour would have permitted him, the outward appearance of the house which he had just left; but hurried away as quickly as he could go from the vicinity of a place where he had seen and undergone so much in such an incredibly short space of time.

For it was about one o'clock when he and Old Death had entered the house in Turnmill Street; and Saint Paul's proclaimed the hour of three as Rainford crossed Smithfield Market.

CHAPTER XXXIII.
MRS. MARTHA SLINGSBY.

The reader who is acquainted with the West End of the great metropolis of the British Empire, cannot have failed to notice the air of gloomy grandeur which characterises the aristocratic mansions of Old Burlington Street.

The dingy brick-fronts—the massive doors, all of a sombre colour—the windows, darkened by heavy hangings—and the dead silence which seems to prevail within, produce upon the passer-by a strange and almost melancholy effect.

There is nothing bustling—nothing cheerful in that street: on the brightest day of summer its aspect is cold—mournful—prison-like.

It seems to be the last refuge of the aristocracy of the old school,—that aristocracy which still clings to all its ancient prejudices, its haughty notions, its exclusive pride,—an aristocracy which finds its influence each day narrowing into a smaller compass, in proportion as that of the masses expands around it.

And God grant that every thing in the shape of hereditary aristocracy may shortly expire altogether—crushed by the weight of new interests and modern civilisation!

In one of those gloomy-looking houses of Old Burlington Street dwelt Mrs. Slingsby—a lady of about forty-two, but who, enhancing by art a natural conservation of beauty truly miraculous in a female of her age, seemed at least five or six years younger.

Her hair was very dark; and as she wore the sweetest French caps that Parisian fashion could suggest, she was invested with that air which bewilders the common observer between its admirable coquettishness and its matronly sedateness.

Her complexion was clear and delicate; and a careful but regular use of cosmetics concealed those incipient wrinkles which appeared at the corners of the eye-lids. Her teeth were perfect, white, and even; and her figure, though upon a large scale, was maintained in fine symmetry by the skill of her dress-maker. She had naturally a splendid bust; and as she usually wore very high dresses, she was the better enabled to maintain its appearance of youthful firmness in spite of the prominent expansion it had experienced as the lady herself increased in years.

Mrs. Martha Slingsby was the aunt of Mr. Clarence Villiers, the lover of Adelais Torrens. When very young, she was sacrificed by her parents to a gentleman double her age, and who had acquired a fortune while he lost his health in India. Shortly after this union, circumstances compelled Mr. Slingsby to return to Calcutta; and his youthful wife accompanied him. There they remained about eight years, at the expiration of which period Mr. Slingsby died of a broken heart, his immense wealth having been suddenly and entirely swept away by the failure of a great mercantile and banking establishment in the Anglo-Indian capital. Mrs. Slingsby, however, found a friend in the person of Sir Henry Courtenay—a baronet who had long held a high office in the Council of India, and who was about to return to England, having relinquished the cares of employment in the public service. He was upwards of fifty at that period—a widower—but having a family of young children. The moment that the misfortunes of Mrs. Slingsby were reported to him by a mutual friend, Sir Henry proposed to her that she should enter his family to supply, as far as possible, the attentions of the mother whom the children had lost. This offer was gratefully accepted; and Mrs. Slingsby, who had no offspring of her own, returned to England with the baronet.

For some years after her arrival in London, she remained in the family of Sir Henry Courtenay,—where she appeared to be treated as a near relation, and not as a dependant. But when the boys and girls were old enough to be placed at school, she removed to the house in Old Burlington Street, in which we now find her. Rumour declared that she was enabled to take so handsome an establishment, in consequence of the sudden and unexpected recovery of a portion of that fortune which was supposed to have been irretrievably swallowed up in the failure of the bank at Calcutta, and the loss of which had broken her husband's heart. At all events, she paid her way regularly—and was famed for her numerous charities. Calumny had never assailed her; for she was so regular in her religious duties—so retired in her mode of life—so ready to assist the deserving poor—so constant in her donations to all humane and philanthropic institutions—and so zealous a patroness of Missionary and Bible Societies, that her neighbours looked upon her as a very pattern of Christian virtue.

Between herself and the Courtenay family the most sincere attachment appeared to exist. Whenever the young gentlemen and the young ladies returned home for the holidays, they invariably passed a week with her whom they almost looked upon as a mother; and Sir Henry himself, in speaking of her to his friends, seemed to take a delight in eulogising the manner in which she had performed her duty towards his children. The consequence was that his relations and acquaintances echoed these praises elsewhere; and Mrs. Martha Slingsby was quoted at the West End as the perfect model of a good and excellent woman.

Thus, at the age of forty-two, Mrs. Slingsby had escaped that ordeal through which so many beautiful widows are doomed to pass: we mean, the whisperings of calumny. Not a breath had ever sullied her fame;—not a hint had ever been dropped to her disparagement. Scandal seemed to avoid her threshold as an evil spirit is supposed to recoil from the vicinity of the temple of worship.

We must observe that Sir Henry Courtenay was now close upon sixty-three—thirteen years having elapsed since Mrs. Slingsby had entered his family in India. He was nevertheless a fine man, on whose brow time seemed to sit lightly, considering how great a portion of his mortal career was already run. It is true that he wore false teeth and false hair; but art had rendered those substitutes so natural in appearance, that few suspected they were really false. Elegant in his manners—endowed with a mind which had treasured up the richest stores of intellectual wealth—fascinating in his conversation—and evincing in his attire the taste of a polished gentleman, Sir Henry Courtenay was one of the brightest stars of the fashionable world—a favourite at Court—and welcome in every gay circle.

It was about three o'clock in the afternoon of that day which followed the events related in the few preceding chapters, that Mrs. Martha Slingsby was seated in her elegantly furnished drawing-room, revising the list of her usual Christmas donations to the humane, philanthropic, and religious Societies.

Adelais and Rosamond Torrens were seated one on each side of her, and aiding their kind friend in her pious task.

Rosamond held in her hand a memorandum-book from which she read the names of the various associations alluded to;—Mrs. Slingsby had a cash-box open before her;—and Adelais made entries, according to this lady's dictation, in another memorandum-book.

The two beautiful girls appeared to be the daughters of the elegant and handsome woman who sate between them; and there was so much sweetness in the countenances of all three—so much animation, and so much modesty—that a painter would have been rejoiced to depict the group as Charity dictating to Benevolence and Mercy.

"Proceed, dear Rosamond," said Mrs. Slingsby, when Adelais had finished a note in her memorandum-book.

"*The Orphan Children's Free-School Association*, madam," read the young maiden thus addressed; "and last year you gave ten guineas."

"This Christmas I shall subscribe fifteen, my loves," observed Mrs. Slingsby, in a mild and silvery tone of voice. "There is no duty so sweet—so holy as to contribute to the religious instruction of those poor creatures who are deprived of their natural protectors. Besides, the committee have manifested the most praiseworthy readiness to attend to any suggestions which I may deem it right to offer. For instance, it was the custom until lately to have three multiplication-table lessons to only one Bible-reading; and this, you must admit, my loves, was very indiscreet—I will not use a harsher term. But, in consequence of my recommendation, the dear children have now *three* Bible-readings to *one* multiplication-table lesson. Have you written down *fifteen guineas*, my dear?" she inquired, turning towards Adelais.

A reply was given in the affirmative; and Mrs. Slingsby wrapped the amount up in an elegant sheet of rose-coloured paper, and, having noted in pencil the contents of the little packet, added it to several others which were ranged before her on the table.

Rosamond then read the next item.

"*The Poor Authors' Assistance Fund*; and last year you gave five guineas, madam."

"And this year I shall only send two, my loves," said Mrs. Slingsby. "Authors and journalists are ruining the country, both politically and morally, as fast as they can. They are writing *for* the people, and *against* the aristocracy; and this, my loves, is a crying abomination. Heaven forgive me for speaking in such harsh terms—so inconsistent with pious meekness and Christian forbearance; but it would disturb the patience of a saint to behold the attacks made by these men upon our blessed Constitution—our holy Church, and its most necessary union with the State—the prerogatives of our monarch—the rights of the upper classes—the privileges of wealth—and all those institutions which were perfected by the wisdom of our ancestors. Do you understand me, my loves?"

"Oh! quite, madam," answered Adelais, who already began to look upon liberal-minded authors and journalists as a set of incarnate fiends banded against every thing worth preserving in society.

"Besides, my dear girls," added Mrs. Slingsby, "the *Poor Authors' Assistance Fund* does not publish a Report of its proceedings nor a list of those who subscribe to it; and, under all circumstances, I think that I should be acting more consistently with my duties as a Christian and as an Englishwoman devoted to the blessed institutions of her happy country, to decline any donation whatever to a Society encouraging infidels and republicans. So you may draw a pen through the name, Rosamond, love. There!—now my conscience is at rest. Which is the next item?"

"*The Distressed Milliners' Friends Society*, madam," was the answer.

"That is another Association from which I must withdraw my patronage," observed Mrs. Slingsby, her countenance losing its serene placidity in an air of severity. "You are too young and too pure-minded to understand my motives, dear girls; but when I tell you that most of these distressed milliners are very naughty women, you will perceive the justice of my conduct. And then they endeavour to make their penury an excuse for their turpitude! Oh! how wicked—how sinful is human nature, my loves! Erase that name also, dear Rosamond. And now what is the next?"

"*The South-Sea Island Bible-Circulating Society*, madam; and last year you gave twenty guineas."

"That is indeed a blessed institution!" exclaimed Mrs. Slingsby, turning her eyes piously upward; "and it is to this Society's rooms that we are going in the evening to hear that estimable man, Mr. Joshua Sheepshanks, give an account of the mission from which he has just returned. I shall increase my donation by five guineas in this instance."

Adelais accordingly wrote down thirty-five guineas, which sum was duly wrapped up in rose-coloured paper and added to the other packets.

Rosamond then read the next item in her memorandum-book.

"*The Naked Savages General Clothing Association*; and last year———"

"Pardon me, dearest girl," said Mrs. Slingsby, "I cannot support that Society any longer. There is in its title a word most offensive to the ears of decency; and I do not know how I could have ever been prevailed upon to lend it the countenance of my name and the aid of my purse. Besides, I do not think the object of the institution is useful; for in India one sees the natives of the lower orders in the country districts, going about in a state bordering on nudity, and one gets so accustomed to it that it produces no disagreeable effect whatever. The name of the Association is decidedly indelicate; but there is nothing repulsive in the fact of savages going about in a state of nudity. You may strike out the item, Rosamond love."

"I have done so, madam. The next is, *The*———"

Rosamond was interrupted by a loud knock at the front-door, which resounded through the house.

In a few moments Sir Henry Courtenay was announced.

CHAPTER XXXIV.
THE PIOUS LADY.

The baronet entered the room with a smiling countenance and a graceful salutation.

"Pray be seated, ladies," he exclaimed, addressing himself to Adelais and Rosamond, who had risen from their chairs. "My dear Mrs. Slingsby, I need not inquire concerning your health—for you look quite charming this morning."

"You know, Sir Henry, that I am not pleased by flattery," said the lady in a reproachful tone.

"A thousand pardons, my dear madam," returned the baronet. "But you must remember that we have now been acquainted for some years—that our friendship is not only of yesterday's date—and that if I venture on a little freedom with you, it is as a brother might address himself to a sister for whom he has the highest esteem. Yes, ladies," he added, turning towards Adelais and Rosamond, "this excellent woman—this almost angel, as I may denominate her—was a mother to my children; and *that* is a circumstance which I can never forget."

"You attach more importance than is necessary, Sir Henry, to the mere performance of a duty," observed Mrs. Slingsby, in a calm and modest manner.

Adelais and Rosamond exchanged glances, which seemed to say, "Admirable woman! we already love her as much as if she were our maternal parent!"

"But I am afraid that I am interrupting an occupation of more value than my idle chit-chat can possibly prove to be?" exclaimed Sir Henry, who surveyed Rosamond with an ill-concealed admiration. "Some useful or pious labour was engaging you, young ladies, no doubt;—for, in the society of Mrs. Slingsby, not a moment is likely to be passed without producing a benefit to at least some section of the great human family."

"The anniversary of that holy day on which the Saviour of Mankind suffered on the cross, is approaching, Sir Henry," observed Mrs. Slingsby, in a tone and manner suiting the solemnity of her remark; "and you know that I am in the habit of forwarding my mite at this season of the year to those humane, religious, or philanthropic institutions which deserve support."

"I never forget any of those pious duties which you have taken upon yourself, my dear madam," said the baronet. "And, indeed, the object of my present visit is——But the act of charity of which I am desirous to make you the instrument," he added, glancing towards the young ladies, "involves details of so painful a nature, that——"

"I understand you, Sir Henry," interrupted Mrs. Slingsby; "and this consideration for the feelings of those who are not accustomed to look upon the dark side of the world's picture, is worthy of your generous disposition. Adelais, my love—Rosamond, dearest—pray retire for a short period."

This request was conveyed in a manner so affectionate and with such witching softness, that the maidens to whom it was addressed, could not help embracing their kind friend ere they left the room.

The moment the door had closed behind them, Sir Henry drew his chair close to that of Mrs. Slingsby, and, placing his arm round her waist, imprinted a kiss of burning desire upon her lips.

"Martha, you are really surprisingly beautiful to-day," he whispered in her ear.

"Do you think so, Henry?" she murmured, her eyes lighting up with the excitement of that contiguity. "And yet I have fancied that your behaviour has been somewhat cold towards me of late."

"Do not entertain such a suspicion, my dearest creature!" exclaimed the baronet, plunging his hand into the bosom of this pious lady's dress. "Had either of us a right to complain, I think it would be myself; for——"

"Oh! do not reproach me, Henry!" she murmured, abandoning herself to his lustful toyings. "But ever since the difficulty I experienced in producing that last miscarriage, I have been so frightened lest——"

"Nonsense, Martha! do not alarm yourself without a cause," interrupted the baronet. "Even if it did come to *that*, the matter could be easily arranged. A few weeks' retirement into the country, on some charitable mission—ha! ha!"

"True!" said the frail fair one. "But the chances of detection—oh! I shudder when I think of it! Consider how admirably we have hitherto managed——"

"And how completely the world is deceived in regard to us," added the baronet, laughing. "There is nothing like a religious demeanour to throw dust in people's eyes. Were a syllable of scandal breathed against you, you have the patrons of all those humbugging Societies to defend you. But what are you going to do with yourself this evening? Can you not devote a few hours to me?"

"I wish I could, Henry," returned the lady; "but it is impossible! A dreadful bore named Sheepshanks is going to entertain the devout with his nonsense; and it would seem so odd—so very odd if I were not present."

"It is now upwards of three weeks since we slept together," said the baronet, in a tone of reproach.

"Yes—but you know that I cannot pretend too often to pass the entire night by the sick-bed of some poor woman," returned Mrs. Slingsby. "And now, dearest Henry, I have a favour to ask of you."

"Name it," said the baronet, in a low murmur—for his passions were furiously excited by his voluptuous toyings with his mistress.

"You must write me a check for a thousand pounds," replied the lady, winding her arms round his neck, and then literally glueing her lips to his.

"Oh! you are becoming very extravagant, Martha," said the baronet. "But I suppose I must yield——"

"You are a dear, generous fellow," murmured the lady, as she suffered herself to be led to the sofa.

A quarter of an hour afterwards, Mrs. Slingsby rang the bell; and a sleek, comfortable-looking footman answered the summons.

The lady was then sitting, in her usual quiet, placid manner, in a chair near the table; and the baronet was placed at a respectful distance from her.

"Bring up luncheon, James," said Mrs. Slingsby. "Sir Henry, you will take a glass of champagne? I know you are somewhat partial to it. But a decanter of water for me, James."

"Yes, madam;"—and the domestic withdrew.

In a short time he returned, bearing a tray, which he placed on the table, and then retired again.

Having paid their respects to the cold viands placed before them, the lady and gentleman did honour to the champagne, both drinking out of the same glass, the servant having only brought up one of the description suited to that particular wine.

When the collation was ended, Mrs. Slingsby drank a tumbler of water to take away the smell of the champagne from her mouth; but she did not appear to relish the limpid beverage quite so well as the rich juice of Epernay.

The baronet then wrote the lady a cheque on his banker for a thousand pounds; and, having made a certain little appointment with her for a particular evening in the ensuing week, and at a place of *rendezvous* as convenient as it was safe, he took his departure.

Immediately after Sir Henry had left the abode of Mrs. Slingsby, that lady's housekeeper sought the presence of her mistress, and was forthwith admitted to the private interview which she desired.

"What is it, Magdalen?" inquired Mrs. Slingsby, when the housekeeper stood in her presence.

"I'm sorry, ma'am, to have any thing unpleasant for such ears as yours," was the answer; "but I am convinced that scullion-girl is in the family-way."

"Magdalen!" ejaculated the pious lady, horrified at the mere idea. "Oh! do not utter any thing so uncharitable!"

"I am sure of it, ma'am, I repeat," persisted the housekeeper. "In fact I've had my suspicions about it for a long—long time; and now I'm certain."

"Magdalen," said Mrs. Slingsby, in a tone of profound solemnity, "this is a dreadful occurrence to take place in a house which, I may safely assert, has never yet been tainted with the breath of scandal—at least so long as I have occupied it. Are you sure that your conjecture is right?"

"I would take my salvation oath that it is, ma'am," responded the housekeeper.

"That expression on your part is incorrect, Magdalen," observed Mrs. Slingsby, in a tone of mild reproach. "But I of course believe all you tell me relative to that miserable—degraded girl. Let her be sent from the house this minute, Magdalen—this very minute! Pay her any wages that may be due to her, and inform her that her box shall be sent after her to her parents, with a note acquainting them of the reason for her abrupt discharge."

"She has no parents, ma'am—she is an orphan."

"But she has friends, no doubt?" said Mrs. Slingsby, inquiringly.

"No, ma'am: I took her from the workhouse, on the recommendation of lady—a friend of yours, ma'am—who visits them kind of places on a Sunday, distributing hymn-books."

"Disagreeable as the duty is, it must nevertheless be performed, Magdalen. And that duty, so incumbent upon us, is to turn the lost girl into the street. Pay her the wages——"

"She has nothing to receive, ma'am. I advanced her money to buy herself decent clothes——"

"Then let her go away without any money—since she has none to receive," interrupted Mrs. Slingsby. "To give her a single shilling, were to encourage her in that shameless career of profligacy whereon she has already so far entered."

"Your orders shall be obeyed, ma'am," replied Magdalen; and she withdrew to execute them—for she had a spite against the poor scullery-girl, who had been intriguing with one of this over-particular housekeeper's own lovers.

Shortly after this little occurrence which we have just related, Mr. Clarence Villiers made his appearance in Old Burlington Street.

He found his aunt alone in the drawing-room; and, the moment he had paid his respects to her, he inquired for his much-beloved Adelais and her sister.

"They are safe and well, Clarence," answered Mrs. Slingsby. "But before I summon them, it will be necessary that we should have a little conversation relative to the proper and prudent course now to be adopted. Sit down, Clarence, and grant me your attention."

The young man obeyed, and prepared to listen with all the patience he could call to his aid; for much as he respected and really loved his aunt—whom he looked upon as a pattern of moral excellence and virtue—he nevertheless experienced the anxiety of a lover to find himself in the presence of Adelais.

"I shall not detain you long, Clarence," resumed Mrs. Slingsby: "and it is for your good that I am about to speak. In the first place, I feel it due to myself to explain to you that, in receiving those young ladies into my house the other evening—and at so late an hour—I was influenced solely by that affection which I entertain towards you, and by my conviction of your thorough integrity of purpose."

"The mere fact of my bringing those almost friendless girls to seek an asylum with you, dear aunt," said Clarence, "must prove to you how careful I was of their reputation."

"And it was to assist your upright views that I received them without a moment's hesitation," added Mrs. Slingsby. "You know that if I had the means, you should long ago have been put in possession of a sufficient fortune to have enabled you to compete with Mr. Francis Curtis in bidding with the mercenary Mr. Torrens for his daughter. But—although my income is sufficient for my wants, and, thank heaven! for a few little purposes of charity——"

"My dear aunt!" interrupted Villiers; "wherefore renew an explanation so unnecessary?"

"Because I would not have you suppose, Clarence, that I would for an instant sanction any underhand proceedings in respect to your union with Miss Torrens, had it been possible to have ensured that aim by means of her father's consent. But," continued Mrs. Slingsby, "I conceive that there are so many extenuating features in the case, that I cannot regret having granted an asylum to that dear girl and her sister, and in thus securing them alike from the perils of London, and from the pursuit of their father."

"Your kindness towards them will render their hearts as grateful as mine is," exclaimed the young man warmly.

"During the few days that my house has become their home," continued Mrs. Slingsby, "they have endeared themselves to me by their affectionate dispositions—their tranquil habits—their readiness to please—and a thousand amiable qualities; and therefore—for their own sakes, as well as yours—I am ready to do all in my power to serve them. But should Mr. Torrens happen to discover their abode, conceive the scandal that would be created—the observations that would be excited!"

"My dear aunt, I would not for worlds compromise you in any way!" ejaculated Clarence. "But still——"

"Do not fear that I am anxious to rid myself of their charming company," added Mrs. Slingsby. "I am only desirous that you yourself should adopt due caution, so as to avoid being followed hither by any one who might be employed by Mr. Torrens to watch you."

"No imprudence on my part shall mar the success of my plans," returned Clarence. "The banns have been published at St. George's once already—and next Sunday will be the second time! It is scarcely probable that Mr. Torrens will become aware of this circumstance; and he certainly would not, without any previous hint, conjecture that the preliminaries for our union had been adopted in so fashionable a church as that in Hanover Square," added Clarence, with a smile. "Let two more Sundays pass without the abode of my Adelais being discovered, and she will then become indissolubly mine!"

"Have you seen any more of your kind friend, who so generously took your part the other evening?" inquired Mrs. Slingsby, after a pause.

"Captain Sparks!" exclaimed Clarence. "Not since I met him, as I before informed you, at a tavern in the Strand——"

"Avoid taverns, my dear nephew!" interrupted Mrs. Slingsby, a cloud overspreading her countenance; "for—by all I have ever heard or read concerning them—they are fearful sinks of iniquity."

"Oh! not the respectable taverns, aunt," replied Villiers. "I had purchased a very handsome pair of pistols to present to the Captain as a token of my esteem; and then I recollected that I was totally unacquainted with his address. I flew to the great army-agents at Charing Cross; but there was no such name as Captain Sparks in the List. Well—I thought he might be in the Navy, and off I went to the Admiralty; but no Captain Sparks! I therefore considered it fortunate when I accidentally met him in a tavern which I entered to procure some refreshment. He positively refused to accept the pistols—declaring that he had done nothing more than I should have done for him under similar circumstances. But I thought there was something singular in the merry laugh which burst from his lips, when I proffered the case containing the pistols. However, he is an excellent-hearted fellow—and I shall always hold myself his debtor. We walked together, on that occasion, as far as my own lodgings in Bridge Street, and he entertained me with a perfect fund of anecdote all the time. Indeed, I am as much pleased with him, as I feel myself under an obligation to him."

"Gratitude is a rare virtue in this world," remarked Mrs. Slingsby, who seldom lost an opportunity of letting drop a moral maxim. "And now," she continued, with a smile, "having taxed your patience to such an extent, I must give you the well-merited reward. My kind and generous friend, Sir Henry Courtenay, has advanced me a certain sum of money, one half of which I require for charitable purposes of my own; but the other I place at your disposal, to enable you to hire and furnish a suitable dwelling to receive your bride. Take this cheque, and to-morrow you can bring me my moiety."

"Oh! my dear aunt, have you borrowed of your friends to assist me?" exclaimed Clarence, overwhelmed by so much apparent generosity.

"Not entirely to assist you, my dear nephew," was the calm reply; "but partly, as you perceive, for myself. However,—say no more about the trifle which I present to you; and reward me by making a good use of it."

Clarence embraced his relative: Adelais and Rosamond were then summoned; and the lovers were soon happy in each other's society.

We must now afford the reader some explanation relative to Mrs. Slingsby's behaviour towards her nephew: and, in so doing, we shall throw additional light upon the character of this lady.

She was of a crafty—calculating disposition, and seldom performed any act, however trivial, without a selfish motive. The fact was that she had a very difficult part to play. Devoured with raging desires, she was compelled to adopt a calm, modest, and reserved exterior, and to conceal her debauchery beneath the cloak of religion. Sir Henry Courtenay was necessary to her in more ways than one: necessary as a lover—and necessary as a treasurer, for she was totally dependent upon him in a pecuniary sense. The report relative to the recovery of a portion of her late husband's fortune, was a mere fabrication to account for her comfortable mode of life. Still she considered her position to be so dangerous, that she was compelled to fortify it by all possible means. She really loved her nephew—for it often occurs that women of her description are capable of a strong attachment of this nature:—but even had she entertained no regard for him at all, she would have pretended to do so—because he was necessary to her. He was a means by which she could constantly trumpet forth her "charitable deeds," while she herself appeared unconscious that they ever transpired. Taking good care that he should know all she did in the cause of religion or humanity, she led him to believe in a great many things which she did not do; and the consequence was that Clarence was never wearied of repeating, wherever he went, those praises which he conscientiously considered to be his aunt's due.

Now, when a near *relation* corroborates the statements made by *friends*, those statements receive a weight which places them beyond the pale of disbelief. Thus the world read Mrs. Slingsby's character as Clarence himself read it and reported it; and with such an amount of testimony in her favour, she could defy scandal. Even the most maliciously-inclined dared not venture a shake of the head, nor a shrug of the shoulder; for "surely her own nephew must know whether she were as good as she was represented? Relations seldom praise each other behind their backs; and when a dashing young fellow, like Clarence, was so enthusiastic in praise of his aunt, it was that he was thoroughly convinced of the sterling merit of her character?" Such would have been the arguments opposed to any detractive observations that scandal might dare to let drop concerning Mrs. Slingsby.

The lady, finding her nephew so necessary to her interests, naturally sought not only to maintain the most complete deception relative to herself in his mind, but also to attach him towards her by substantial acts of kindness. Thus she had readily consented to receive Adelais and Rosamond into her house, to oblige Clarence; and she now, with the same interested motive, made him a handsome pecuniary present. She let him know that she had been compelled to borrow the money (in advance of her imaginary income), to enhance the value of the gift, and also that the natural impression should arise in his mind—"Excellent aunt! she embarrasses herself to benefit me!"

The reader now fully understands how complete a mistress of duplicity—hypocrisy—and deceit was the widow of Old Burlington Street. Beneath that calm and placid demeanour—under that veil of sanctity—raged the most ardent lusts, and agitated the most selfish feelings. She was a living—walking—breathing lie. Her existence was one immense falsehood; and yet so well did she maintain the semblance of even the sternest virtue, that her real character was known only to two persons—Sir Henry Courtenay, and another whom it is not at present necessary to name.

CHAPTER XXXV.
MR. SHEEPSHANKS.

In a large room, on a first-floor in St. Martin's Lane, some three or four hundred persons, male and female, were assembled.

At one end of the apartment was a raised platform, in the middle of which stood a capacious arm-chair behind a desk; and on the said platform several sleek, oily, comfortable-looking gentlemen, all dressed in black, and wearing white cravats with no shirt-collars, were grouped together in conversation.

The body of the room was occupied by chairs for the accommodation of those who had "front-seat tickets," and forms for those who possessed "back-seat tickets."

It is a remarkable fact that the votaries of the Established Church invariably create social distinctions in the very places instituted to propagate or maintain their creed. Thus every church belonging to the "Establishment" has its pews for the rich and its pauper-seats; and in the assembly-rooms of the religious associations the same distinction is drawn between aristocracy and democracy. And these lines of demarcation are traced by men practising—or rather pretending to practise—a religion which proclaims that all are equal in the eyes of God!

Oh! the vile hypocrisy of these canting psalm-singers!

The room to which we have introduced our readers, was well lighted with wax-candles, and had two cheerful fires blazing away in the grates.

The atmosphere was warm—there were no unpleasant draughts—and the floor was covered with a thick drugget;—for your religious people are mightily fond of comfort; and comfort was certainly studied at the offices of the *South Sea Islands Bible-Circulating Society*.

In the second row of the "front-seat ticket" department, sate Mrs. Slingsby and the Misses Torrens. The two latter had their veils carefully drawn over their faces; for Mrs. Slingsby had insisted upon their accompanying her to this "pious and soul-refreshing entertainment," as they had not previously stirred out of doors from the moment they had taken up their abode with her.

At a quarter-past six o'clock, two ushers, bearing white wands, passed up the room, preceding a short, stout, brandy-faced gentleman, who tried to look as demure and humble as he could, but who could not, however, subdue that consciousness of importance which seems to say, "Ah! now I am causing a sensation!"

And a sensation, too, he produced, sure enough; for the gentlemen began clapping their hands and stamping on the floor, while the ladies waved their handkerchiefs as if he were some victorious general who had just defeated a French army of a hundred thousand men.

Upon reaching the platform, the brandy-faced gentleman shook hands with the sleek and oily individuals before alluded to; and the "sensation" became more exciting on the part of the spectators, as if it were a very clever thing indeed to shake hands in public.

Then the brandy-faced man stepped a few paces back, and pretended to enter into very earnest conversation with some leading member of the Committee, while another member moved, in a drawling sing-song tone, "that their respected President, Mr. Jonathan Pugwash, do take the chair."

This proposal was received with renewed applause; and the brandy-faced gentleman (for he it was who delighted in the euphonious name of Pugwash) started as if quite astonished that such an honour should have been destined for him. He then proceeded to establish himself in the large arm-chair before mentioned; and in a voice which sounded as if he were talking inside a barrel, called upon "their respected friend, the Reverend Malachi Sawkins, to open the meeting with prayer."

Mr. Sawkins—a very demure-looking man indeed—proceeded to drawl out a long extempore prayer, in the course of which he led his audience to infer that heaven favoured that particular Society more than all others; and when he had concluded, the chairman rose to explain the object of the extraordinary assembly that evening, although the said object was already well known to every individual present—aye, and to every soul who, passing up or down St. Martin's Lane, might choose to stop and peruse the enormous bills placarded at the entrance.

Mr. Jonathan Pugwash commenced by expressing his thanks for the high honour done him by selecting him to preside over that meeting—an honour the more distinguished, inasmuch as it had been perfectly unexpected on his part. [*This was completely false, it having been settled in Committee three days previously that he was to preside on this occasion; but your zealots do not mind a white lie at times.*] He was well aware of his own unworthiness (*Cries of "No! no!"*): yes—he *was* an unworthy vessel—but he hoped the Lord would sustain him in the onerous duty thrust upon him. (*"Amen!" in a hollow, sepulchral tone from the Rev. Malachi Sawkins.*) He thanked the ladies and gentlemen—or he should rather say his Christian sisters and brethren present, for the kind—the handsome—the feeling manner in which they had contradicted his expressed belief of his own unworthiness. (*Cheers, and "Go it, Pugwash!" from a drunken gentleman in a remote corner of the room.*) He need scarcely inform the highly respectable and influential meeting then and there assembled, that the object of such assembly on that occasion was to hear certain accounts of the progress of the good cause, from the lips of a revered brother (*cheers*) who had just returned (*renewed cheers*) from a long (*more cheering*)—arduous (*prolonged cheering*)—and most perilous (*vociferous cheering*)—mission to the islands of the South Seas (*tremendous cheering, mingled with "Bravo!" from the drunken gentleman in the remote corner.*) He need scarcely say that he alluded to their dear—venerated—respected—highly-prized—gifted—talented—persevering friend, Mr. Sheepshanks! (*Cheers.*) With these few observations, he would introduce Mr. Sheepshanks to the meeting. (*Prolonged cheering.*)

The chairman sate down in an awful state of perspiration; but, in another moment he rose again; for a little door at the back of the platform had just been opened by one of the ushers—and behold! Joshua Sheepshanks appeared before the enraptured spectators.

It would be impossible to describe the enthusiasm which now prevailed in the room. The cheering was tremendous—the waving of the ladies' handkerchiefs created a perfect gale of chill air—and the drunken gentleman in the corner shouted so vociferously that one old lady who sate near him would certainly have fainted (as she subsequently observed) if another old lady next to her had not happened, "by the merest accident in the whole world," to have a small flask of cognac in her muff, and most charitably to place the said flask at her disposal.

Mr. Sheepshanks was a tall, thin, sallow-faced man, with black hair combed sleekly over his forehead, and sharp, piercing grey eyes, which seldom settled anywhere—but when they did, it happened (singularly enough!) that they were sure to fix themselves on the prettiest faces in the room.

Order being restored, Mr. Sheepshanks rose to address the audience. Having expressed his gratitude for the truly Christian reception he had received, he entered upon the subject so dear to all who had the good cause at heart. He stated that in the year 1823 the Committee of the Society had determined to send a missionary to some of the South Sea Islands to pave the way for the effectual carrying out of the objects of the Association. A sum of five hundred pounds was voted for the purpose; and he (Mr. Sheepshanks) had offered himself as a willing sacrifice to the good cause, although, as he perfectly well knew, at the risk of being roasted and eaten by the savages amongst whom he was to venture. Understanding that a French ship was to sail for the South Seas, from Cherbourg, on an exploring expedition, he had repaired to that port, and had taken a passage in the vessel alluded to. In due time, and after experiencing tremendous weather, the ship touched at the Cape of Good Hope, and thence proceeded towards the southern islands. "It was on the 14th of March, 1824," continued Mr. Sheepshanks, "that we anchored off the beautiful island of Squizzle-o-Koo; and I fell on my knees on the deck, to return thanks to that Providence which had at length brought me within sight of the scene of my labours. A refreshing influence came over me; and my heart leapt, like a porpoise on the wide waters, at the cheering thought that I was about to render myself useful amongst the benighted savages so near at hand. A boat was lowered; and the captain, the third mate, the purser, and myself were rowed ashore. I was provided with my Bible; the captain and the mate took with them quantities of looking-glasses, buttons, and toys; and the ungodly purser armed himself with a bottle of rum."

An awful groan burst from the Rev. Mr. Sawkins, whereat Mr. Pugwash, who had fallen asleep, woke up.

"Yes—dear Christian friends," exclaimed Mr. Sheepshanks; "a bottle of rum!"

"And no fool he!" cried the drunken gentleman in the corner.

"Order! order!" vociferated Mr. Pugwash, rubbing his eyes.

At this crisis, a gentleman of foreign appearance, well-dressed, and adorned with a pair of very fierce moustachios, advanced from the body of the room towards the platform; but at every three steps he took, he paused for a few moments to examine Mr. Sheepshanks with strict scrutiny by the aid of an eye-glass. At first he seemed uncertain relative to some idea which had entered his head; but the nearer he approached the platform, and the more closely he examined Mr. Sheepshanks, the fainter became his doubts and the stronger his suspicions.

At last—just as the missionary was about to resume the history of his adventures in respect to the island of Squizzle-o-Koo—the foreign stranger leaped upon the platform, confronted the pious gentleman, and said in an ironical tone, "How you do, Monsieur Shipshang? me vare much delight to see you dis vonce again."

Mr. Sheepshanks seemed confounded at the sudden apparition of the foreign gentleman: but, speedily recovering his self-possession, he said, "Really, sir, you have the advantage of me. But if you will step into the private office—behind there—for a short time, I———"

"Oh! yes—you really have de advantage on me, Monsieur Shipshang," interrupted the foreigner; "but you no get it again, do you see? How do Madame Shipshang, and de little Shipshang as was born at my house?"

"This gentleman, sir," said the Reverend Mr. Sawkins, addressing the foreigner in a tone of awful solemnity, and pointing towards Mr. Sheepshanks, "is not married and has no children. His life is devoted to celibacy and good works."

"Good works!" ejaculated the Frenchman: "den vot for he come and swindle me———"

"Oh!" groaned the Reverend Mr. Sawkins, holding up his hands in horror at the supposed baseness of the imputation against the most savoury vessel of the whole Society.

"Oh!" reverberated in a long echoing groan throughout the room; for, as the reader may suppose, this strange scene had excited a powerful sensation amongst all present.

"Ah! it all vare well," exclaimed the Frenchman, indignant at the awful groaning with which his words were received; "but let dis fellow Shipshang look me in de face, and———"

"Call in a constable!" roared Mr. Pugwash, the chairman.

"Give the Frenchman fair play!" cried several voices.

"Dat is all me do ask of de British public," said the Frenchman.

But while he turned to address those words to the audience, Mr. Sheepshanks disappeared with remarkable abruptness by the private door at the back of the platform.

"Where's our reverend brother?" demanded Mr. Pugwash, looking anxiously around.

"I am afraid he must be taken ill," returned Mr. Sawkins. "I will go and see."

And this reverend gentleman followed the pious missionary.

The Frenchman then proceeded to acquaint the audience that he kept an hotel at Cherbourg, where Mr. Sheepshanks arrived at the beginning of the year 1823; that the reverend gentleman continued to reside with him for upwards of ten months, spending money as profusely as if he possessed the purse of Fortunatus; that at the expiration of that period Mr. Sheepshanks departed, but returned at the end of a month, accompanied by a lady whom he represented to be his wife, and who presented him with a pledge of her affection some eleven months afterwards; that Mr. Sheepshanks and the lady, with the child, continued to honour the hotel with their presence until the middle of the year 1826, when they suddenly evaporated, leaving behind them a heavy bill unpaid and a portmanteau full of stones and straw; that business had brought the Frenchman to London, and curiosity had induced him to enter that assembly upon reading the placard, wherein the euphonious name of Sheepshanks prominently figured, at the door.

This narrative produced, as may be supposed, an extraordinary sensation amongst the saints gathered together on this occasion.

And no wonder! Was it, then, all a fabrication relative to Mr. Sheepshanks' visit to the South Sea Islands? Had he never proceeded farther than Cherbourg? were the funds of the Society lavished in riotous living and on a mistress? was it the better to carry out the deception that he had pretended to sail in a French ship, instead of an English one? was he, in a word, an unmitigated impostor? and were all the members of the Society his dupes?

These opinions seemed to be confirmed, when the Reverend Mr. Sawkins came back with the astounding intelligence that Mr. Sheepshanks was nowhere to be found in any part of the Society's offices.

Mrs. Slingsby was overwhelmed with grief, and her two fair companions with astonishment; and as they rode home in a hackney-coach, the pious widow never ceased from dilating on the tremendous injury which the "good cause" would receive from the exposure of the flagrant turpitude of Mr. Sheepshanks.

CHAPTER XXXVI.
THE BARONET AND HIS MISTRESS.

On the following day—at about twelve o'clock, and somewhat to the surprise of Mrs. Slingsby, who did not expect to see him so soon again—Sir Henry Courtenay paid the lady a visit.

She happened to be alone when he was announced; and there was a constraint—amounting almost to an embarrassment—in his manner which she immediately perceived, and which alarmed her.

"Has any thing happened, Henry?" she inquired anxiously, as he took a seat at some distance from her.

"Nothing, Martha—nothing," answered the baronet. "But I wish to have some very particular conversation with you."

"I am all attention," she said, her suspense increasing.

"Now do not be frightened," exclaimed Sir Henry. "Nothing has happened to annoy either you or me; but what I am about to propose to you, is rather of an embarrassing nature—and——"

"Then pray be quick and let me know what brings you hither this morning," said the lady, somewhat impatiently.

"Have patience!" cried the baronet. "The fact is I have taken a fancy in a certain quarter—and, though I have striven hard to wrestle against it, it is every hour growing more powerful than my opposition."

"What *do* you mean? what *can* you mean?" asked the widow, completely bewildered.

"Why do you receive into your house two young ladies of a beauty so ravishing——"

"Henry! is it possible?" exclaimed Mrs. Slingsby, a light suddenly breaking in upon her mind.

"It is very possible that I should feel an unconquerable—an invincible passion for Rosamond Torrens," added the baronet, growing bolder now that the ice was fairly broken.

"And you tell me this to my face!" murmured the widow, in a hollow tone, while her countenance became purple with a rage which she dared not suffer to explode.

"It is expressly to you that I am compelled to make the avowal," was the deliberate reply; "since it is at your hands that I expect assistance."

"At my hands!" almost shrieked the widow.

"Beware how you alarm the house!" said the baronet. "You will do much better to listen to me attentively."

"Proceed," gasped Mrs. Slingsby.

"You are well aware that there are certain natures which cannot master their inclinations, however strenuously they may endeavour to do so," resumed Sir Henry Courtenay, drawing his chair closer to that on which his mistress was seated. "You yourself are of such a disposition—and I am not less so. It would have been impossible for you to remain chaste: your passions are of that ardour which must be gratified—or they would consume you."

"Wherefore this strange expatiation upon my failings?" inquired the widow bitterly.

"Simply to prove an extenuation for myself," was the response. "I have seen Rosamond but three times, and have not spoken a dozen words to her; and yet I am maddened with desire—devoured with cravings which the possession of her can alone assuage. I again assure you that I have essayed to conquer these feelings, for my sake—for hers—but principally for *yours*,—and all in vain! I do not love you the less—I shall not neglect you on her account. And, as a woman of the world," he added, fixing his eyes in a penetrating manner upon her countenance, as if to read the impression his words made on her mind,—"as a woman of the world, I repeat, you cannot imagine that it is possible for me always to remain faithful to you!"

"At least you are candid with me," observed the widow, her tone expressing bitter irony.

"That is the great merit of my present avowal," said the baronet calmly. "But how foolish you are to manifest so much annoyance. You are well aware that I cannot subdue my feelings, nor control my passions more than yourself; and it will be better for you to assist me——"

"Assist you in debauching that young girl—the sister of her whom my nephew is to marry!" ejaculated Mrs. Slingsby.

"Listen, Martha," exclaimed Sir Henry. "I have formed this sudden caprice—or whim—or whatever you may choose to term it; and I will spare no money and no trouble to accomplish my purpose. A man with twenty thousand a-year can afford a trifle to gratify his wishes in this or any other respect."

"But the idea is perfectly insane!" cried the widow. "Even if I were to consent to aid you in your purpose, the result must inevitably involve a fearful exposure."

"Not at all," replied the baronet. "The means are easy, and can be rendered perfectly secure. I gave you a thousand pounds yesterday—the largest sum you have ever yet had from me at one time; and I will present you with a cheque for *two* thousand more the day that Rosamond becomes mine."

"You would not marry her?" exclaimed Mrs. Slingsby, in a tone of unconcealed alarm.

"Yes—rather than not possess her," replied the baronet.

"Oh! this is truly absurd!" said the widow. "What! so powerful an attachment towards a young girl whom you have only seen three times!"

"Strange as it may appear, it is nevertheless a fact!" cried Sir Henry. "But there is a wide difference between the feelings I entertain towards you and her. You are necessary to me, to a certain extent—because you are an agreeable companion as well as a desirable woman. She is a mere child—but a very beautiful one; and, moreover, the sudden fancy I have taken for her is so strong that I cannot resist it. You see that my resolution is fixed. With or without your aid, I prosecute my purpose."

"If you are really so determined——"

"I am," said the baronet.

"Then I must assist you in this dangerous—difficult proceeding," added Mrs. Slingsby, somewhat consoled by the idea of the two thousand pounds that were to find their way into her purse as the price of her services. "But when I reflect on the matter, I behold a thousand perils from which I recoil. Were an exposure to take place, the entire fabric of—of——"

"Hypocrisy," suggested the baronet. "You and I need not mince words together."

"Well—hypocrisy," continued the lady, "would be thrown down—and I should stand revealed to the world in the most dreadful colours. Then, the real nature of *our* connexion would be instantly perceived——"

"But all these terrible evils are to be avoided by prudence," interrupted the baronet. "I am not more anxious for exposure than yourself; nor should I wish to compromise you. Our amour has existed for years—and the world suspects it not, even in the most distant manner:—we will contrive to retain the veil over it until the end."

"Then how do you wish me to proceed?" inquired the widow, with a cold shudder, as she thought of the perils attending the undertaking.

"By operating on the mind—by modelling the imagination of that young girl to suit my purpose," answered Sir Henry. "With a woman of the world like you, this is an easy task. Insinuate certain notions into her bosom—inflame her—excite her———"

"This is more difficult than you imagine," interrupted Mrs. Slingsby: "because she and her sister are constantly together."

"Devise a means to employ Adelais in one room for two or three hours at a time, while you have Rosamond with you in another," said Sir Henry. "If you enter on the task with a good will, you will find it easy enough."

"But in ten days Adelais will become the wife of Clarence; and the sisters, accompanied by him, will repair to Torrens Cottage to throw themselves at the feet of the incensed father. Rosamond will then quit my house altogether."

"Ten days are sufficient to imbue her now innocent mind with such new sensations—such voluptuous thoughts—such eager desires, that her surrender will be easy and certain," persisted the atrocious villain, who thus calmly reasoned on the means of undermining so much virtue.

"I do not think so," observed Mrs. Slingsby. "If I proceed too rapidly, I shall alarm her, instead of inflaming her imagination. Besides, you judge the world by what you yourself are, and by what you know of me. But, frail and guilty as I am, Henry," she added in an impressive tone, "believe me when I declare my conviction that more virtue is to be found in woman than you would be inclined to suspect."

Sir Henry laughed heartily at this observation; then, rising from his seat, he took up his hat, saying, "At all events, dearest Martha, act so that I may present you with the cheque as soon as possible."

He kissed her, and departed from the house, chuckling at the success of his endeavour to make his mistress the instrument of his diabolical design against the pure—the beautiful—the unsuspecting Rosamond.

CHAPTER XXXVII.
TOM RAIN AND JACOB.

It was Saturday evening; and Rainford was proceeding up Gray's Inn Lane, wrapped in his white great coat, and with a woollen "comforter" reaching up almost to his nose, when he suddenly felt some one pull him by the sleeve.

He turned round, and, by the light of a lamp, beheld the lad Jacob.

"Well, you young rascal!" exclaimed Tom—but with an anger more affected than real, for he was not a man to cherish vindictive feelings towards an enemy so utterly unworthy his resentment as that pale, weak, and sickly boy: "I wonder you have the face to accost me, after joining in that abominable scheme to intrude upon the privacy of my dwelling three or four nights ago."

"I hope you will forgive me, Mr. Rainford," said the lad: "for you *must* know," added he emphatically, "it wasn't altogether my fault. I was bound to obey the man who gave me food. But do you know, sir, what has become of *him*? Oh! Mr. Rainford—I am well aware that he *did* deserve punishment at your hands; but—pray forgive me—I hope———"

"You hope that I did not kill him?" said the highwayman in a deep, hollow-toned voice. "Why—do you suppose that I am a likely person to commit murder—intentionally?"

"Oh! no—no," replied the boy. "And yet———"

"And yet what?" asked Rainford.

"And yet it is so strange that he should never have been seen at any of his usual haunts," added Jacob.

"Come along with me," said Rainford abruptly. "We cannot stand talking in the street—and I want to have some conversation with you. But do you know any place close at hand—any public-house, I mean—where we could have a private room for an hour or so?"

"Yes, sir," replied Jacob, after a moment's reflection. "This way."

He turned abruptly down into a narrow, dark, dirty thoroughfare, called Baldwin's Gardens, and conducted the highwayman into a low public-house, where, upon inquiry, they were immediately accommodated, with a private room on the second floor.

Rainford ordered the fire to be lighted and a bottle of wine to be brought up; and when these instructions were complied with, he renewed the conversation with Jacob.

"And so nothing has been heard of Old Death?" he said, in as tranquil a manner as he could assume.

"Nothing," replied Jacob. "A man named Josh Pedler called at Bunce's this morning early, and wanted to see Mr. Bones, on account of a thief, known as Tim the Snammer, who was to go up before the magistrate to-day; and it appears that Mr. Bones had promised to get him off. Pedler was in a dreadful way when he heard that we hadn't seen any thing of the old man for two or three days; and he swore that it was all a hoax, and that Bones wanted to stick to the money that had been paid him, and shirk the job. Then comes a girl about an hour afterwards; and she said she was Tim the Snammer's wife—Mutton-faced Sal they call her;—and a deuce of a rumpus she made also."

"Do you know a person called Tidmarsh?" demanded Rainford, after a few moments' reflection—for he was anxious to learn if the boy were acquainted with the establishments in Turnmill and Red Lion Streets.

"I know him by name very well—and that's all," replied Jacob. "He is a fence, and lives somewhere in Clerkenwell. But pray tell me, Mr. Rainford, if you know what has become of the old man."

"I can tell you nothing about him, my boy," said the highwayman. "Surely he was not so very kind to you———"

"He kind! Oh! no—far from that!" cried Jacob, in a tone of evident sincerity. "But I was so dependant on him, that—unless I turn thief again—as I once was———"

He stopped short, and burst into tears.

"My poor lad," said Tom Rain, affected by this ebullition of grief on the part of the wretched boy, "if you are afraid of wanting bread, you may banish those alarms—at least for the present."

And he threw a handful of sovereigns upon the table.

"Are these for me?" cried Jacob, scarcely able to believe his eyes.

"Yes—every one of them," answered the highwayman. "But on this condition—that you tell me how Old Death discovered my *late* abode in Lock's Fields, and what was his object in entering it along with you and that sneaking fellow, Toby Bunce."

"I will tell you all—everything I know, Mr. Rainford," exclaimed Jacob. "But," he added slowly, "you will find that I do not deserve this kindness at your hands."

"I can scarcely blame you for obeying the person on whom you were dependant," said the highwayman. "Come—gather up the money, and make haste with your information."

As Jacob secured the gold about his person, his dark eyes were lighted up, and his cheeks were flushed with a glow of animation.

"I can tell you much more than you suppose, Mr. Rainford," he resumed in a few moments; "and if I begin at the proper place, what I have to say will go farther back than the affair the other night in Lock's Fields."

"Then begin with the beginning, Jacob," said Tom, lighting a cigar. "There—drink another glass of wine; and now fire away. But mind and tell me nothing save the truth; for I shall soon see if you are deceiving me."

"I won't deceive you, Mr. Rainford," cried the boy; "and will soon convince you that I am in earnest. Besides, it is my interest to make a friend of you—even if it wasn't my inclination. And now to begin. You remember the morning you was had up at Bow Street? Well—Old Death had told me to watch you when you came out of Tullock's—to dog you about—to find out where you lived and any thing else I could glean concerning you."

"What was that for?" demanded Tom.

"He did not tell me *then*," answered Jacob; "but I have ascertained since—and you will be able to guess by and bye. Well, I *did* follow you that morning—I saw you nabbed by Dykes, the runner—and I went up to Bunce's to tell Old Death what had happened. Then he cut off to Watkins and Bertinshaw, who came and bailed you. I was ordered to watch about the police-court, and see where you went to; and I followed you to Pall Mall—then I dogged you back again—and when the Jewess's case was over, I lost sight of you somehow or another."

"And you duly made your report to Old Death?" said Tom inquiringly.

"Of course," replied Jacob. "Two or three days afterwards I was set to watch you again, when you left Bunce's one afternoon; and I followed you down to an eating-house in the Strand. You stayed there about two hours; and at length you came out with a tall, handsome young gentleman———"

"Ah! I recollect!" cried the highwayman: "it was Clarence Villiers. But go on, my boy."

"I only mention all these little things to convince you that I am telling the exact truth," said Jacob. "Well—from the Strand I followed you and the gentleman as far as Bridge Street, Blackfriars, where you parted. I dogged you, Mr. Rainford, over to the Elephant and Castle Tavern, where you met a lady and the little boy———"

"Yes—Charley Watts!" ejaculated the highwayman, gradually becoming more interested in Jacob Smith's narrative, because each successive step thereof afforded fresh evidence of its truth.

"You joined the lady and the little boy," continued Jacob; "and when you all stopped for a short time at the window of a jeweller's shop, the lady lifted up her veil—and I knew her again."

"Ah!" cried Tom, with a sudden start.

"Yes, sir,—I recognised Miss Esther de Medina——But are you angry, sir? have I said anything to offend you?"

"No—no, Jacob," returned the highwayman, the cloud which had gathered upon his countenance suddenly disappearing. "Go on, my boy."

"Then I saw you take the lady and the little boy into the shop, and you bought a pair of ear-rings, which you gave to the lady; and as you came out again, I heard you say to her, '*This present is a kind of recompense for the diamonds which I made you give up,*'—or something to the same meaning."

"Yes—I remember that I did make use of those or similar words!" cried Rainford. "But how the deuce did it happen that I never once caught a glimpse of you?"

"Oh! sir—I acted with so much caution," replied the lad; "and then you did not suspect that you was watched."

"True!" said Tom thoughtfully. "And of course you reported all this to Old Death?"

"I followed you on to Lock's Fields, and then returned to Seven Dials, where I told Mr. Bones and Mrs. Bunce all I had seen and heard."

"And what did they say? Tell me every thing, Jacob," exclaimed the highwayman.

"They seemed very much surprised to think that you and Miss Esther were intimate together——"

Jacob suddenly paused—for again did a dark cloud overspread Tom Rain's countenance.

"Go on, Jacob," he said, observing that the lad was alarmed. "I am subject to a sudden pain——but it is nothing at all. Go on, I say. You were telling me that Old Death and that disgusting woman, Mrs. Bunce, were very much astonished at a certain circumstance. Well—and what did they say?"

"They asked me whether either you, sir, or the lady took any little thing—when the jeweller's back was turned," replied Jacob, timidly; "but I assured them that you did not."

A scornful smile curled the highwayman's lips and then he puffed away violently at his cigar—apparently wrapped in deep reflection.

"Shall I tell you any more, sir?" asked Jacob, when a few minutes of profound silence had elapsed.

"Yes, my boy: go on!" cried Tom, turning towards him again.

"The very next night," resumed Jacob, "Mr. Bones and me were walking down Southampton Row, Russell Square, you know—when I observed Miss Esther de Medina in a shop——"

"Where there was a post-office?" ejaculated the highwayman, hastily.

"Just so, sir. And she was reading a letter," continued Jacob. "Then me and Old Death followed her down to another post-office—it was in Holborn—where she posted a letter which she had with her. I crept close up to her and saw the address on it just before she dropped it into the box."

"And what was that address?" demanded Rainford.

"*T. R., No. 5, Brandon Street, Lock's Fields*," was the answer.

"And you of course told *that* to Old Death?"

"Yes—and he desired me to follow the lady to see where she lived; which I did, and traced her to Great Ormond Street. Then I went back to Bunce's, and acquainted Mr. Bones with this fact also. He was very much pleased; and soon afterwards you came in. He then told you about going to Shooter's Hill to stop a tradesman and his wife; but I afterwards found out that it was only a gag to get you out of the way next night."

"Ah! I thought as much!" cried Rainford. "And now, I suppose, we come to the visit which Mr. Bones, Toby Bunce, and yourself paid to my lodgings?"

"Exactly so," said Jacob. "Early the next morning I was ordered by Old Death to post myself all day long in Great Ormond Street, and see that Miss Esther didn't go out. I kept watch, and saw her several times at the window just for a moment: so I knew she was at home. In the evening Old Death and Mr. Bunce came and fetched me, and we went over to a public-house opposite your lodgings in Brandon Street. On the way I learnt what they meant to do; for it was to carry off the boy——"

"Poor little Charley Watts!" ejaculated Rainford, totally unprepared for this announcement. "But what harm had he done to them? or what could they want with him?"

"I don't exactly know, sir," replied Jacob. "Indeed, I don't think Toby Bunce knew himself. But I can't help thinking that it was somehow or another connected with a certain letter which Old Death let fall, and which I picked up and kept. It bears the signature of *Sarah Watts*——"

"The poor woman who died at Bunce's house!" cried the highwayman. "Where is that letter?"

"Here, sir," answered Jacob; and with these words he produced the document from his pocket, and handed it to Tom Rain.

The highwayman hastened to peruse it with the greatest interest and attention; but he was evidently disappointed when he perceived that it afforded no clue to the person to whom it was originally intended to be sent.

"I shall keep this letter, Jacob," he said, after some minutes of profound reflection.

"Do so, Mr. Rainford," returned the lad. "And now you see that I am acting sincerely with you."

"Quite," remarked the highwayman, in an absent manner; for he suddenly remembered the circumstance of Old Death declaring that he had lost a particular letter on the memorable night which was marked with so many strange occurrences. "Yes, Jacob," he continued, after a long pause, "you are right. It must have been in connexion with this letter that the old man wanted to carry off the boy. Perhaps he had discovered some clue to unravel the mystery of Charley's birth, and meant to turn the secret to his own advantage? But, if so, he must have had some better trace than this letter, which certainly says a great deal, and yet leaves the one grand point—*who Charley's mother really is*—in complete darkness! However," added Tom, who had been musing aloud, rather than addressing his remarks to Jacob, "time will perhaps clear up all."

"You see, sir," continued Jacob, "I was set to watch in Great Ormond Street to find out whether Miss Esther went over to you——"

"To *me*!" ejaculated Rainford, as if taken by surprise. "But—go on, my boy—go on!"

And as I knew that she was at home when Old Death and Toby Bunce came to join me there," pursued the lad, "we of course thought it was all right. You may, therefore, judge how Old Death and me were surprised, when we went up into the bed-room at your lodgings——"

"Enough of that, Jacob!" cried Rainford, starting uneasily. "And now tell me why Old Death seemed so anxious all along to find out every thing he could about me?"

"Lord! sir, can't you guess?" exclaimed the boy. "He knew that you could be useful to him, and he wanted to get you completely into his power. By knowing all that concerned you, he——"

"I understand, Jacob," again interrupted the highwayman; "and it is just as I suspected. You are a good lad for telling me all this—and I will not leave you to want—in case," he added hastily, "your old master should not happen to turn up again. But I do not think I shall stay many days in London, Jacob. However, I will see you again shortly—and we will have a talk together about what is best to be done for you. One word, by the bye—do you know how this letter which you gave me, happened to fall into Old Death's hands?"

"Not all, sir—unless Mrs. Bunce found it about the poor woman who died the other night at her house."

"That is what I suspect," observed Rainford. "Indeed, it must have been so. The deceitful woman!—after my paying her so handsomely, to keep back the document! But it has found its way to my pocket at last, in spite of her and Old Death. And now, Jacob, tell me about yourself. How long have you been in the service of Mr. Benjamin Bones?"

"I wish you had time sir," said the boy, "to listen to my story: it would be a relief to me to tell it—for I already feel towards you as I never felt to any one before. Indeed, I was sorry to be employed against you in any way: but I couldn't help myself. I remember the evening that I watched you over to Lock's Fields:—I was so moved—I hardly can describe how—at seeing that little boy Charley with you; for I thought how good you were towards him, and what an excellent heart you must have,—and when I got back to Bunce's, I couldn't pluck up courage to tell Old Death any thing about you, for fear he might mean you some injury. However," added Jacob, wiping his eyes, "he *did* get it all out of me at last——"

"Never mind, my lad," interrupted Rainford, moved by Jacob's contrition: "all you have told me this evening has fully atoned for the mischief you previously did me. Besides, as I before said, you were forced to obey your master. And now," he added, after referring to his handsome gold repeater, "I don't mind if I sit another hour with you here; and while I smoke my cigar, you shall tell me the history of your life."

"I will, sir," exclaimed the boy, eagerly. "But I warn you beforehand it is a long one—that is, if I tell it as I should like to do."

"Tell it in your own way, my boy," cried Rainford; "and never mind the length."

The highwayman settled himself in a comfortable manner in his chair; and Jacob proceeded to relate the history of his life.

CHAPTER XXXVIII.
THE HISTORY OF JACOB SMITH.

"My earliest recollections are associated with the occupation of playing all day long in the streets, in company with other infants. This was in Upper Whitecross Street, St. Luke's; where I and those other children lived with a woman, who pretended to keep a boarding-school at which she received children to live with her altogether for one shilling and eightpence a-week each: but she used to turn us all out early in the morning with a piece of hard mouldy bread to nibble for our breakfast, and fetch us home again when it grew dusk in the evening. She would then give us each another piece of bread for supper, and we went to bed. But what a bed! A few old sacks thrown over a heap of straw in a little room about six feet long by four and a half in width, served upwards of a dozen children as a sleeping-room. There we used to cry ourselves to rest, famished with insufficiency of food—and awake again in the morning to undergo fresh privations.

"I said there were about twelve of us under the care of this Mother Maggs—as she was called. They chiefly belonged to very poor parents, who were engaged all day long at work, and were therefore glad to get rid of their children, who would otherwise only be an encumbrance to them. Some few were, however, the illegitimate offspring of poor servant-girls in place; but nearly all had parents who came to see them from time to time and perhaps gave them a few pence. I was not, however, so fortunate as the rest; for no one ever came to see me—at least that I was aware of—until I was about nine years old; and I heard that the twenty-pence a-week allowed for my board and lodging, was left regularly for Mother Maggs at the neighbouring chandler's shop every Saturday morning. Mother Maggs seemed to think that I had really no friends—for, though she bullied us all pretty well, she bullied *me* ten thousand times more than the rest.

"The habit of turning a dozen little children, some of whom were only just able to walk, into the street in the way I have described, was not likely to be always unattended with disagreeable consequences. Sometimes a child was run over, and either severely wounded or killed. In the latter case, no Coroner's Inquest ever sate on the body: the exposure of Mother Maggs's neglect towards us, would have drawn the attention of the parochial authorities towards her. But when a death happened in that way, the old woman used to put the body into a sack and carry it some distance into the country, where she would sink it in a pond or ditch. Often, however, the corpse of a dead child has been allowed to remain in our room till it was quite putrid, Mother Maggs not having time or inclination to remove it before. And, on those occasions, we *who were alive in that room* were so frightened to be with the dead body in the dark, that we shrieked and screamed till the noise reached the old woman's ears in the public-house next door; and so savage was she at being disturbed in her gin and her gossip, that she has half murdered us by way of making us hold our tongues!

"Sometimes a child was lost; and if the parents, on being informed of it, expressed regret or anger, Mother Maggs would take some trouble to find it again: if not, she did not put herself out of the way respecting the matter. In addition to her boarding-house for children, she let out lodgings to persons of either sex; and, as she was not particular so long as she got paid, her house was nothing more or less than a common brothel. She was always saying she had no time to do any thing which ought to be done: and if being all day in the public-house was a necessary duty, she certainly had no time for other purposes. Though not often tipsy, she was never actually sober—but in a constant state of muzziness. Liquor did not improve her temper: on the contrary it made her irritable—sometimes ferocious; and I have seen her fight with other women until her face was covered with long seams made by the finger-nails, and pouring with blood.

"You cannot suppose that *all* these things which I have just told you or that I am going to tell you directly, in connexion with Mother Maggs's establishment, were noticed or understood by me when I was quite a child there: but you must remember that I stayed at that den until I was nine, and in the course of those years all I saw made a deep impression on my mind; and what was then dark and unintelligible to me, has since been made clear and plain by experience and by reflection on those scenes and circumstances.

"You will wonder how my wretched companions and myself managed to live, since we only had a piece of bread each, night and morning. We kept body and soul together in a variety of ways, chiefly feeding, like swine, upon all the offal and remnants of vegetables, cooked or raw, that we found in the street. There was a dust-bin in the court where Mother Maggs's house was in Whitecross Street; and every day, just upon one o'clock, we used to crowd round it, waiting till the neighbours came to empty their potato-peelings or the refuse of their meals into that general receptacle. Then we would greedily appropriate to our use the scraps which not even the very poorest of the poor chose to eat. The potato-peelings (most poor families skin their potatoes after they are boiled) were quite a dainty to us: the heads and bones of fish and such-like refuse were also welcome to our empty stomachs. Then we were accustomed to go prowling about the street to snatch a slice of raw bacon or a bit of cheese from the board in front of a butter-shop; or steal a turnip or a carrot from an old woman's stall; or else lay unlawful hands upon the horses' flesh in the cats'-meat shops. This last article of food was much fancied by us. It was comparatively easy to steal; and when we did get such a prize as a large lump of carrion, with a stick thrust through it, we felt as happy for the time being as if we had found a treasure. Then we used to conceal ourselves in some dark court, and take a bite round—each in his turn—until it was all gone. I am afraid I disgust you with these details; but you desired me to tell my story in my own way—and I want you to understand the dreadful mode of life which thousands of poor children lead in the wealthiest city in the world. I am sure, when I have thought of it all since, and when I see little boys and girls paddling in that neglected manner about the streets, my blood runs cold at the idea that while some human beings are riding in their carriages and living in palaces, others are prowling in the low neighbourhoods, happy if they can steal a lump of putrid carrion!

"You may next ask what we did for clothes—it being very clear that Mother Maggs could not supply us with wearing apparel out of twenty-pence a-week. Well—the fact is we scarcely had any clothes on at all. As for a cap or shoes and stockings, I declare solemnly I never wore any one of those articles from the earliest period of my recollection until I was nine years old. A little ragged frock, and that was all: yes, that was all—summer or winter! But where did even the ragged frock come from? I really hardly know: I am at a loss to say exactly how we did get even that one garment each. Sometimes a child would be taken away by its parents, who might, perhaps, bring it some decent clothing: then the cast-off rags in this case would fall to the lot of the most ragged of those who were left behind. Now and then a slop-seller in the neighbourhood would give one of us some old frock which was useless to himself: and occasionally we would steal one, when we could. You may ask me why we did not steal shoes also? So we did, if an opportunity served: but then we could do without shoes, and the eldest of the lot of us was on those occasions commissioned to sell the plunder at a rag-shop, to afford means to buy a little better food than usually fell in our way. These occurrences were, however, rare—so rare, that they constituted perfect holidays in the hideous monotony of our famished lives;—for the shopkeepers in poor neighbourhoods are constantly on the alert to watch the movements of the juvenile prowlers.

"The ages of the children under the care of Mother Maggs averaged from three to ten; and the eldest of course bullied the youngest, while Mrs. Maggs bullied us all. Misery did not make us little ones friendly together. On the contrary, we fought, quarrelled, and ill-treated each other as much as we could. I must relate to you one anecdote—although I now shudder when I think of it, and have often since shed tears of repentance. There was one boy, named Tib Tucker, about eight years old, who used to behave in a more merciless manner towards me than the rest did. He would take away my bread from me whenever he caught me eating it apart and alone; and he laid to me many thefts on Mother Maggs's cupboard which he himself committed. These false reports got me many and many a good beating from the enraged hag; and, in a word, this boy's tyranny became so insufferable, that I was resolved to adopt some desperate measure to put an end to it. I was then but little more than six years old: a fiendish instinct of revenge, however, urged me to act. I secreted a pin about my rags; and one day when Tib Tucker was trying to take away the morsel of mouldy bread which Mother Maggs had just given me, I suddenly thrust the pin into his right eye. He screamed in dreadful agony, and brought down Mother Maggs into the court. I had not run away—terror, or rather horror at what I had done, nailed me to the spot. The bully's tale was soon told. I expected to be half murdered by the dreadful woman: but, to my surprise, she suddenly took my part—declared that I had shown a proper spirit—and consoled Tib Tucker with the assurance that if he would only permit me to operate on the other eye in the same manner, he would prove a perfect fortune to his parents. 'There's nothing like a blind child to draw alms,' she said: 'but one eye's no good—you should be blind of both.'—I remember her words as well as if they had only been uttered yesterday; and, the more so, as they seemed to be prophetic—as I shall explain presently.

"The terrible vengeance which I had taken upon my persecutor, who lost his eye in consequence, not only awed him in future, but made me feared by all the rest; and my existence grew somewhat less wretched—at least in reference to the treatment I experienced from my companions. Mother Maggs also seemed to change towards me—whether through fear, or admiration at what she termed '*my spirit*,' I cannot say. I was less bullied by her—but not a whit better fed.

"About six weeks after the incident which I have related, the parents of Tib Tucker returned to London from the country where they had been harvesting. They passed the evening with Mother Maggs, and great quantities of gin were sent for from the public-house. This I afterwards learnt from my companions; for, as to myself, I kept out of the way through fear of being punished by the boy's parents for the vengeance which I had wreaked upon him. When it was quite dark, I returned to the house, and stole up to the miserable garret where my companions were already huddled together on the straw and old sacks. Tib Tucker was amongst them; for I heard him talking about a promise his parents had made to take him with them into the country, where they were going again in a few days. One of the eldest girls—for, I forgot to say, Mother Maggs's juvenile boarders were of both sexes—asked him what his parents had said about the accident. He replied that they had laughed at it, and had declared that they would turn it to some good account. Scarcely had he thus spoken, when the door opened, and Mother Maggs appeared, with a candle in her hand. Ordering Tib Tucker to get up and follow her, she added that his father and mother had a little treat in store for him, and had meant him all along to sit up to supper. Tib was overjoyed at these news, and made haste to accompany Mother Maggs to a lower room where she had left his parents; and we, in our miserable dark garret, envied the boy who had a good supper in view.

"I remember—Oh! well do I remember, how I cried that night, to think that no friends ever came to see me, and that indeed I was ignorant whether my parents were alive or not. I had often asked Mother Maggs whether she knew my father and mother; but I invariably received a cuff by way of reply—and therefore at length grew tired of putting the question. There were, however, times when my wretched—forlorn—abandoned condition almost broke my heart; for, young as I was, I knew that there were boys and girls in the world much better off than myself!

"While Tib Tucker was absent, the other children began to discourse amongst themselves, saying how lucky he was to come in for a good supper: and then they set to work to guess what the meal was likely to consist of. But all on a sudden a dreadful shriek echoed through the house, and startled us in our miserable garret. There we lay—crouching and huddling nearer to each other, holding our breath, not daring to utter a word, and filled with vague alarms, as if some dreadful danger hung over us. At length sleep came to my relief. When I awoke in the morning and ran down into the court, the first object that met my view was the wretched boy Tib Tucker, being led away by his parents—*for he was now blind of both eyes!*

"I was so frightened, that I ran into the street, where I wandered about all day—forgetting even the pangs of hunger. I had suddenly conceived such a dreadful terror of Mother Maggs, that I had not dared to present myself at her room-door to obtain my usual morsel of bread, along with the rest. It was a very rainy day, and yet I remember that I roved and roved about the whole neighbourhood, at one time crying bitterly—at another stupified, though still moving about like a sleep-walker. When the evening came on, I was so tired and hungry that I was forced to retrace my way to the horrible den, which I only discovered again with the greatest difficulty. Mother Maggs did not take any notice of my absence from the morning distribution of bread, but gave me my evening ration along with the rest; and once more did I return to the straw and filth of the close garret.

"Months and years passed—and I reached the age of nine. The last few months opened my eyes to more wickedness than I had as yet known or dreamt of. I just now told you that Mrs. Maggs's juvenile boarders consisted of boys and girls; and I believe you understood that we all huddled together in the same garret. It was a regular pig-sty, in which we wallowed like swine: and like that of brutes also was the conduct of the eldest boys and girls. If the other rooms in the house were used as a brothel by grown-up persons, no stew could be more atrocious than our garret. The girls were more precocious than the boys, and the latter were corrupted by the former. Mere children of nine and ten practised the vices of their elders. But, my God! let me draw a veil over this dreadful scene. Oh! sir—I have seen much—gone through much; but the mere thought of the horrible licentiousness—the beastliness—the monstrous depravity that took place there, even now makes my blood run cold in my veins!

"And can you wonder that such should be the case? Not one of all us children had ever been taught what virtue was; and all that we knew of crime was that it was something which a constable took you up for. We had not the least notion of the Saviour—none of us had ever heard that the Son of God died for the sins of the world. I had once seen a Bible, because I stole one from a book-stall; and the eldest girl, who went to sell it, gathered from what was said by the person who bought it, that it *was* a Bible. But even if I had previously known that the book was called a Bible, I should not the less have stolen it; because I could not read, and no one had ever told me at that time what the Bible really was. We had all heard of the name of God, and used it pretty often too—for oaths were familiar to us even when we could only lisp them: but we knew not who God was, and had no one to tell us—even if we had wished to learn. You may think it strange that there should be children of even ten years old in London who are completely ignorant of every thing concerning religion; but I can assure you that I have met with youths and girls of fifteen or sixteen who were equally in the dark in that respect.

"I was nine years old when Mother Maggs one day fetched me out of the street where I was playing in the gutter with my companions, and took me into her own room, where I saw Mr. Bones for the first time—I mean the first time as far as my recollection is concerned. He looked at me a long time; and then turning to the old woman, said, 'I don't think you have taken the very best care of him.'—'Yes, I have,' she answered, 'He has had his bellyfull every day of his life: bread-and-butter for breakfast and supper; potatoes for dinner on week days, with may-be a bit of pudding or so now and then; and always a good dinner on a Sunday. Haven't you, Jacob, dear?'—and, as she asked me this question, she gave a terrific frown, unseen by Old Death, and the meaning of which I well understood. So I muttered a 'yes;' and she seemed satisfied.—'But I am going to take him away all the same, Mrs. Maggs,' said Mr. Bones; 'because he is of an age now to be useful to me.'—'I hope you will recommend me where you can,' cried Mother Maggs. 'I do all I can to make the poor little dears happy; and if Jacob is so shabby just the very day you drop down upon us, like, it's only because his new frock is in the suds; and as for shoes and stockings, it makes boys hardy to go without them.'—I do not remember that Old Death made any answer to these observations; because the portion of the dialogue which I have just detailed, produced so deep an impression on my mind—young as I was—that had it been continued, I should most probably have recollected the rest. But *this* I cannot forget—that when Old Death told me to follow him, and Mother Maggs took me in her arms to embrace me at parting, I screamed with affright—for the spectacle of the blind boy instantly recurred to my memory!

"Old Death took me to a shop in Whitecross Street, and bought me a complete suit of clothes—shabby and mean, it is true; but royal robes compared to the rags I now threw off. And how great was my astonishment—how wild was my delight, when I was actually supplied with a pair of stockings and shoes! Never before—never since, have I known such perfect joy as I felt at that minute. Sight restored to the blind could not be more welcome than were those articles. Not that I required them—for my feet were inured to nakedness, and to walk even on the pointed flints:—but I experienced an indescribable sensation of mingled pride and satisfaction which made me supremely happy. My joy was, however, somewhat rudely interrupted by a hard blow on the head which Old Death bestowed upon me, because I dared to laugh in the fulness of my poor heart; and then I burst into tears. He cursed me for a 'snivelling fool,' and ordered me to put on the cap which he had also bought me, and make haste to accompany him. The cap was another article of clothing till then quite strange to me; and once more my tears were succeeded by smiles!

"At length the purchases were complete; and I followed Old Death from the shop. But I walked as if I was tipsy. The cap seemed to be quite a weight on my head; and the shoes threatened every moment to trip me up. I have never worn skates,—but I can fancy how a person must feel when he puts them on for the first time; and I imagine that my awkwardness in stockings and shoes was something of the same kind. Near the point where Upper Whitecross Street joins Old Street Road, I beheld my late companions huddled together at the mouth of a passage belonging to a pawnbroker's shop. They did not know me, till I called some of them by name; and then they could not believe their eyes. I must have seemed a kind of prince to them. They instantly overwhelmed me with questions—but Old Death looked back and called me in a cross tone, and I hurried away. I declare solemnly that the tears started from my eyes as I thus separated from the companions of all my infant misery; and though I knew not whether my own fate was about to be improved, still my heart was smitten with the idea that I was leaving them behind to their wretchedness—their rags—their starvation—and their fœtid den at Mother Maggs's house. Never until that instant had I experienced the least sympathy in their behalf: but then—at that moment—I felt as if I could have remained with them, and loved them!

"Mr. Bones conducted me to some public-house—I can't recollect where it was, but I think it must have been in Brick Lane, St. Luke's,—and there he ordered bread and cheese and ale. What a glorious dinner did I make that day! Never had I tasted any thing so delicious before! The cheese was so nice—the bread so white and new,—and the ale—it was good beyond all description. At least, so the food and drink then appeared to me: and what was better still, was that I was allowed to eat as much as I chose! When we had ended our meal, Old Death began to talk very seriously to me—for we were alone in the room together. He gave me to understand that he had found me, when quite a baby, lying on the steps of a workhouse—that he had taken me to some good, kind woman whom he knew, and who had treated me well—that afterwards he had been obliged to place me, when I was three years old, with Mother Maggs—*and that I therefore owed every thing to him*. I naturally believed at the time that I was under the deepest obligations to him; and then he proceeded to inform me that I might be useful to him in certain ways, and that if I did all he told me and was a good boy, he would never desert me. I of course listened with as much respect as it was in my power or nature to show; and, though I did not quite understand all he said to me, I was nevertheless impressed with the conviction that he had a right to do what he chose with me, and that I was bound to obey him.

"We remained some time at the public-house—indeed, if I remember right, until it was dusk; because Old Death had a great deal to say to me, and as I was so very young and so miserably ignorant, it was not an easy matter for him to make me understand his meaning. But there can be no doubt that he laboured to convince me of the right which certain privileged persons had to prey upon others who were not so privileged;—or, in plainer terms, that whenever I could obtain a handkerchief, a purse, or any thing else worth taking, and in such a manner that there was no chance of my being detected, I was perfectly justified in availing myself of the opportunity. My morals had not been so carefully attended to, as to excite any repulsive feelings at this species of reasoning: on the contrary, having from my infancy practised the art of pilfering pudding from cooks'-shops, bits of bacon from cheesemongers' windows, carrots and turnips from old women's stalls, and lumps of tripe or carrion from the boards of cats'-meat establishments, I was well prepared to go a step farther. There can be no doubt that Old Death was all along aware of the real nature of Mother Maggs's house and of the manner in which she reared the children entrusted to her. A man of his experience could not help knowing all this; and it was not probable that he was deceived by the lying statements she made to him relative to the manner in which I had been treated—although he took, as far as I recollect, no notice of her words. In fact, he had intentionally placed me in a position to learn everything that was bad—to fulfil an apprenticeship of petty vice, that I might enter on a career of crime, whereof the profits were to be his own!

"Taking me now in a somewhat kind manner by the hand, he led me down to St. Paul's Churchyard. Although having hitherto lived within a mile of that place, I had never been there before. It is true that from the garret windows of Mother Maggs's dwelling, I had sometimes seen the huge dark dome surmounted by the cross which shone like gold on a bright, sunny day; but I had never thought of asking what it was—nor had I any notion that it was so near. Often, too, in the silence of the night, when cold and hunger kept me awake in that hideous den, had the deep but glorious sound of the mighty bell, booming through the air, and proclaiming the hour, fallen on my ears: but still I had never thought of inquiring which clock it was that struck so loud and was so tediously long in striking. Thus, when I entered Saint Paul's Churchyard for the first time, in company with Old Death, I was struck with amazement to find myself at the foot, as it were, of that tremendous giant of architecture. Just at that moment, too, the mighty bell began to strike six; and I started—for, young as I was, that well-known sound, though never heard so near before, re-awakened a thousand conflicting thoughts within me. All the misery and wretchedness I had endured at Mother Maggs's house rushed to my mind; and again I shed tears as I reflected on the poor children whom I had left behind me *there*!

"Oh! Mr. Rainford—if any kind and benevolent person had taken me then under his protection and care, and taught me to do good and practise virtue, as Old Death was teaching me to do evil and practise vice, I feel—yes, I feel that I should not have been unworthy such humane attention!

"But let me not interrupt the thread of my narrative more than I can help. Mr. Bones kept me by the hand, and walked slowly—very slowly through the churchyard, pointing out to me the beautiful shops, and telling me that if I was a good boy and only did what he told me, I should soon be rich enough to be able to walk into those shops and treat myself to jewellery, or fine clothes, or anything else I might fancy. This assurance gave me the most heart-felt joy; and I already began to determine in my mind what I should buy when the happy period of such affluence might arrive. All on a sudden my gay reverie was interrupted by Old Death, who, dragging me hastily to the entrance of a passage leading into Paternoster Row, pointed to an elderly gentleman standing at a shop-window at the corner where this passage joined St. Paul's Churchyard. 'Do you see his handkerchief peeping out of his coat-pocket?' demanded Old Death hastily.—'Yes,' I replied.—'Then go and get it, and I will give you sixpence, if you bring it to me, without the old fellow perceiving that you have taken it.'—Sixpence! It was an inexhaustible treasure, such as I had often heard of, seldom seen, and never touched. Without a moment's hesitation I proceeded to execute the task. It was winter-time; and though the evening was dark, yet the shop-windows were brilliantly lighted. This was against me—but on the other hand, the place was crowded with people passing both ways, and this circumstance was in my favour. Old Death stood watching me at the entrance of the passage—no doubt ready to glide away in case of me being detected. But my skill in cribbing victuals and other little articles in Upper Whitecross Street had been so well practised, that it only required to apply the same art to another and rather more difficult branch of thieving, to be completely successful. And this success far exceeded Old Death's expectations; for when I returned to him in the passage, I was enabled to place in his hands not only the old gentleman's pocket-handkerchief, but also his gold snuff-box.

"You may suppose that Mr. Bones was well-pleased with me; and he testified his approval of my conduct by placing a shilling in my hand. I could scarcely believe that I was indeed the possessor of such a sum; and I immediately made up my mind to ease as many old gentlemen as possible of their handkerchiefs and snuff-boxes, as long as a deed so simple was so generously rewarded.

"Old Death now conducted me to Drury Lane, and showing me a public-house, said, 'Jacob, though a young boy, you are a very good and clever boy, and I think I can trust you. If you assure me that you will do just as I tell you, I will give you a treat.'—I gave him the assurance he required.—'Well, then, walk boldly into that public-house; run up stairs, just as if you had been there a hundred times before; and go straight into the large concert-room that you will come to. You will have to pay a penny for going in. Then sit down at a table, call for bread and cheese and a glass of ale—of the nice ale that you like so much, you know; and enjoy yourself. You will find several other young lads there, who will no doubt speak to you; and you may talk to them as much as you like. I shall come into the room presently; but don't come near me; and don't tell any one there that you know me. I have my reasons; and if you do all I tell you, you shall often have a treat to a concert and such like places. When you see me going away, you can follow me at a little distance. Now do you understand?'—I assured him that I did; and I then walked into the public-house as bold as if I had been a grown-up person and a constant customer. I had money in my pocket, and for the first time in my life felt that confidence which the possession of coin produces.

"The concert-room was speedily reached: my shilling was changed to pay the entrance fee; and I entered the place of amusement. It was—or had I not better say, it *is* a very large room; for it was at the *Mogul*, in Drury Lane, to which I had now introduced myself. The place was crowded; and the music and singing were going on. I was quite delighted, and, seating myself at a table near some other boys, all older than I was then, I told the waiter to bring me bread and cheese and a glass of ale. 'Better say a pint, old feller,' observed one of the boys to me: 'and I'll help you to drink it.'—I threw down the eleven-pence, saying, 'Bring bread and cheese and ale for all this.'—I remember that the waiter looked at me for a moment in a strange way, before he gathered up the money; but he said nothing, and hurried off. In a few minutes he returned with a pot of ale, bread and cheese, and several glasses.

I was already on friendly terms with the boys at the same table; and we now got quite intimate over the ale. They soon let me know that they were all *prigs*; and I answered 'Yes' to every question they put to me about my own pursuits. Presently I saw Old Death walk slowly up the room: but I pretended to be looking quite another way.

"The conversation which I had on this occasion with the boys at the penny-concert, completed what was no doubt Old Death's design in sending me there: namely, to render me as familiar as possible with that class of lads at whose hands I was to receive my initiation into the career of roguery to which I was destined. The ale excited me to such a degree that I was even then ready to obey any one who would suggest a deed by which money could be obtained; for I saw that money was the key to all kinds of enjoyment. Presently Old Death walked slowly out of the room; and two or three minutes afterwards I followed him, having told my new companions that I should be sure to meet them again there next night. In the street I joined Old Death, who asked me how I liked all I had seen? You can guess what my answer was. 'Well,' said he, 'it is for you to get a handkerchief and a snuff-box, or any thing of that kind, every day; and then you shall have money to go to concerts, and to buy nice ale, and to enjoy yourself along with those pleasant boys that you met there.'—I was delighted with this prospect; and I thought Old Death the kindest gentleman in the world, in spite of the box on the ears he had given me at the slopseller's shop in the morning. But all this time, remember, I did not know either his real or his nick-name; nor did I trouble myself about such matters.

"He now conducted me to Castle Street, Long Acre, and putting sixpence into my hand, pointed to a particular house. 'Go and knock at that door,' he said, 'and ask for a bed. You will have to pay two-pence for it. The fourpence left is to buy your breakfast in the morning, which the woman of the house will give you for that money. If the people you meet there ask you any questions, say as little as possible, and don't speak a word about me. If you do, I shall be sure to know it, and I will never see you again. Be a good boy; and at nine o'clock to-morrow morning, meet me at the corner of this street.'—I promised to mind all he told me; and he hurried away, while I gained admittance into one of those filthy lodging-houses that swarm in Castle Street.[12]

"At this place, where I procured the half of a bed, my companion being a young girl of thirteen, who had already been a prostitute eighteen months, I received further lessons in the school of vice. In the morning I obtained a cup of coffee and a couple of rounds of thick bread-and-butter for my fourpence: having disposed of which, I hastened to my appointment with Old Death. He was waiting for me at the corner of the street, and asked me a great many questions about the people I had seen at the lodging-house. I satisfied him as far as I could; but, through some lingering feeling of shame, I did not tell him that a prostitute had been my bed-fellow. He desired me to follow him at a considerable distance, but to mind and not lose sight of him. He then led me for a long walk all about the West-end of London,—proceeding slowly, so that I might have an opportunity of looking at the shops and obtaining some knowledge of the position of the different streets: in a word, that I might be able to find my way about by myself another time. At about one o'clock we went into a public-house, where we had something to eat and drink, and rested for two or three hours. Then we set out on our wanderings again, and at about seven o'clock in the evening, we came to a halt in St. Giles's, where Old Death gave me money to enter a penny-theatre. I had not practised my hand at stealing any thing all day long; because he had not instructed me to do so. Neither, from that moment, did he ever put my abilities in that way to the test in his presence: so I suppose that the little affair in St. Paul's Churchyard was merely an experiment made to enable him to judge whether I had any *talent* in the art of *conveyancing*, or not. In fact, he had tried me to ascertain whether I could be made useful; and, finding that I could, his object was now to introduce me to scenes and places where my morals might become confirmed in iniquity, or where there was a sphere for the exercise of my abilities.

"I need not therefore dwell on this part of my story; for in a few days the use which Old Death calculated to make of me was fully explained. I was to thieve where I could and when I could, and every evening I was to meet my employer at some place that he would appoint, and hand him over the articles so stolen; when he was to give me enough money for the following day's expenses. I was, moreover, charged to enlist in the same service as many boys as I could; and now for the first time I learnt that my hitherto unknown protector was named Mr. Benjamin Bones, and my companions soon informed me that he was a famous *fence*, usually bearing the denomination of 'Old Death.' I must not forget to state that my employer counselled me never to allude to him in any manner, unless it was in the way of enlistment, as just now mentioned. He said, 'It will perhaps happen, Jacob, that a constable or a Bow Street runner may catch hold of you sometimes; but do not breathe a word about me, and I will always get you out of the scrape. If, on the other hand, you confess that you are employed by me, or that you are in my service, it will do you no good, and I should cast you off for ever. Indeed, I should leave you to rot in prison; whereas, hold your tongue, whatever may happen, and you will find me your best friend.'

"I promised to obey him; and now, behold me at the tender age of nine, the companion of the worst juvenile pickpockets, and a pickpocket myself! No link had we to bind us to society: the world was our harvest-field, in which we considered that we had a right to glean; and whenever a member of our fraternity got 'into trouble,' we clubbed together to maintain him well in prison. If he was condemned to punishment, he and ourselves looked upon it as a piece of *bad luck*—and that was all. I found that my companions were as reckless and improvident as could be,—ever fulfilling the old adage, '*Light come, light go*.' They used to play at 'pitch and toss,' or skittles, the stakes varying, according to their means at the moment, from a halfpenny to a sovereign. I was not often enabled to join in these sports; because Old Death kept me rather short, and he had obtained such an astonishing influence over me that I dared not attempt to deceive him. Sometimes I thought of appropriating a portion of a '*day's work*' to my own private use; but his image haunted me like a ghost—and I could not do it. He constantly told me that he had the means of ascertaining every robbery that was committed, and who perpetrated it, and that if I attempted to play him any tricks, I should be sure to be found out. I believed him—for he occasionally gave me proofs of the most extraordinary knowledge of all that was passing. He would say, for instance, 'Your friend Such-a-one filched a snuff-box and a pocket-book yesterday in Regent Street: he gave *his* employer the book, and pawned the box on his own account. Now, mark me,' Old Death would add, 'that boy will get into trouble soon, and no one will help him out of it again.'—And this prophecy would come true. I was therefore alarmed at the mere idea of deceiving Old Death—or rather, attempting to deceive him; and, though my companions often jeered me and urged me to '*set up on my own account*,' I lacked the moral courage to break with Mr. Benjamin Bones.

"I was very expert in the art of pickpocketing, and seldom had to disappoint Old Death when I met him in the evening. If I did, he gave me my money all the same: I suppose I was too useful to him to be lost; and perhaps he knew that I always did my best. He allowed me three shillings and sixpence for each day's expenses; and this money was usually laid out in the way I will now explain:—

Breakfast.—Pint of coffee, 2*d.*; loaf of bread, 2*d.*; butter, 1*d.*	0*s.*	5*d.*
Dinner.—Beef, 3*d.*; potatoes, 1*d.*; bread, 1*d.*; beer, 2*d.*	0	7
Tea.—Half-pint tea, 1½*d.*; toast, 3*d.*	0	4½
Supper.—Leg of beef, 3*d.*; bread, 1*d.*; potatoes, 1*d.*; beer, 2*d.*	0	7
Gin and water, 1*s.*; bed, 4*d.*	1	4
	3	3½

—leaving me 2½*d.* a day for any casual expense. This allowance of 3*s.* 6*d.* may perhaps seem rather liberal; but it was seldom that my *earnings* during the day were not of sufficient value to produce Old Death at least fifteen or twenty shillings—and often a great deal more.

"There are various grades, or classes, of juvenile thieves.[13] The most aristocratic amongst them are those who have been admitted into the fraternity of swell-moabites, or who have taken a hand in housebreaking. The next class, on the descending scale, is the pickpocket who dives only for purses, watches, pocket-books, or snuff-boxes, but who would scorn to touch a handkerchief. The third section consists of those who dive for any thing they can get, and whose chief game *does* consist of handkerchiefs. The fourth division comprises shop-sneaks and area-sneaks: the former enter a shop slily, or crawl in on their hands and knees, to rob the tills; the latter get down area-steps and enter kitchens, whence they walk off with any thing they can lay their hands on. This same section also includes the shop-bouncer, who boldly enters a shop, and, while affecting to bargain for goods, purloins some article easily abstracted. The fifth division is made up of thieves who prowl about shop-doors; or who break the glass in shop-windows, to abstract the goods; or who rob mercers by introducing a bent wire through the holes of the shutter-bolts, and draw out lace, silk, or ribands. The sixth, and last division or grade, consists of the very lowest description of thieves—such as pudding-snammers, who loiter about cooks'-shops, and when customers are issuing forth with plates of meat and pudding, or pudding alone (as is often the case), pounce on the eatables and run away with them before the persons robbed have even time to recover from their astonishment. These miserable thieves sell all they cannot eat, to other boys, and thus manage to get a few halfpence to pay for a lodging. I mention all these circumstances to you, sir, because I do not believe that you can have ever found yourself in a position to have seen what I am now relating.[14]

"On one occasion a certain robbery in which I was concerned, made some noise; and the Bow Street runners got a pretty accurate description of me. This I learnt from Old Death, who advised me to go up into the Holy Land—which I need scarcely tell you is St. Giles's—and remain quiet there for a few days until the thing was pretty well blown over. I followed this advice, which was very welcome to me; because Mr. Bones gave me plenty of money to make myself comfortable, and I was not expected to do any '*work*' for at least a week. I happened to take up my quarters at a lodging-house in Lawrence Lane, and found it chiefly used by the very lowest Irish. Never did I see such a set as they were! Filth, misery, and drunkenness were familiar enough to me, heaven knows!—but there I saw such filth, so much misery, and yet such constant and such horrible drunkenness, that I was perfectly shocked—and it required something strong to shock *me*, Mr. Rainford! The house was a brothel; and the daughters of the man who kept it were their own father's best customers. The most dreadful debauchery prevailed there. Old women used to bring young boys, and old men young girls—mere children,—to that beastly stew. I have seen a dozen men and women all dancing together stark naked in the largest room in that house; and some of them brothers and sisters![15] On another occasion I saw an Irish wake in the same place: the corpse, which was that of a prostitute, was laid upon the floor, with candles placed round it: and the friends and relatives of the deceased woman all got so awfully drunk that they commenced a dreadful battle, tumbling about in all directions over the dead body!

"I stayed at this lodging-house in St. Giles's about a week, and never went out except of an evening for about an hour, when I looked in at Milberry's—the flash public-house in Lawrence Lane. Were you ever there, sir? No. Well—it is worth your while just to give a look in any time you are passing. The public room is fitted up with fine tables and high-back partitions. Fronting the door is a large black board, whereon the following inscription may be read:—

My pipe I can't afford to give,

If by my trade I wish to live;

My liquor's proof, my measure's just:

Excuse me, sir, I *cannot* trust.

'To prevent MISTAKES all liquors to be paid for on delivery!'

"As soon as the little affair, which had driven me up into St. Giles's, was blown over, I returned to my old haunts, and fell in again with my old companions. I was now ten years old, and was considered so cunning and clever that Old Death began to employ me in other ways besides thieving. If he required to know any thing concerning a particular party, he would set me to dog and watch him, or to make inquiries about him. Sometimes I was sent to the flash public-houses frequented by gentlemen's servants who were accustomed to arrange with the cracksmen for burglaries in their master's houses—or '*put up cracks*,' as they are called. These public-houses are principally at the West End:—the most famous are in Duke Street (Manchester Square), and Portland Street. There I got into conversation with the servants, or merely acted the part of a listener; and all the information I could glean was of course conveyed to Mr. Bones, who no doubt knew how to turn it to his greatest advantage.

"I was also a visitor to every flash-house in London, at different times, and on various errands for Old Death. The more his business increased, the more necessary did I become to him; and at that period he was not so near and stingy as he since became. Whenever I succeeded in any difficult undertaking, he would reward me with something like liberality; and I don't know whether I actually liked him—but it is certain that he exercised an immense power over my mind. I was, in my turn, much looked up to by my companions: they considered me Old Death's lieutenant; and moreover I was so skilful as a pickpocket, that no one could excel, and few equal me. I had all the qualifications necessary for the art—a light tread, a delicate sense of touch, and firm nerves. For I was then strong and healthy: now I am sickly—wasted—and have within me the seeds of an incurable malady! I used at that time to wear shoes of a very light make—as indeed do nearly all professional pickpockets. It is very easy for one who is any thing of an acute observer, to recognise juvenile pickpockets in the street. Their countenances wear an affected determination of purpose, and they always seem to be walking forward, as if bent on some urgent object of business. They never stop in the street, save to '*work*.' If they wish to confer with their pals, or if they meet a friend, they dive into some low public-house, or court, or alley. A knowing pickpocket never loiters about in the street; because that is the very first thing that draws suspicions glances towards lads. I have read—(and how I came to be able to read, I shall presently tell you)—in the newspapers that many people have a notion that pickpockets use instruments in easing gentlemen or ladies of their purses or other articles of value: but the only instrument I ever knew a pickpocket to use, or used myself, is a good pair of small scissors, which will either rip a pocket up or cut it off in a twinkling.

"I do believe that London thieves[16] are the very worst in the whole world. Their profligacy commences so early; and there is every thing to harden them. Imprisonment raises them into heroes amongst their companions. Only fancy a boy of twelve or thirteen, perhaps,—or even younger,—placed behind huge massive bars which ten elephants could not pull down! He of course thinks that he must be a very clever fellow, or at least a very important one, that the law is compelled to adopt such wonderful precautions to restrain him. He believes that society must entertain a marvellous dread of his abilities. That boy, too, is the superior in the eyes of the whole fraternity of thieves, whose punishment is the heaviest. A lad who has been tried at the Old Bailey, thinks much more of himself than one who has only passed through the ordeal of the sessions. The very pomp of justice,—the idea that all those judges and barristers in their gowns and wigs should be assembled for the sake of a boy,—that the Old Bailey street should be crowded with policemen,—that newspaper reporters should be anxious to take notes,—that spectators should pay shillings to obtain sittings in the court,—in a word, the whole ceremony and circumstance of the criminal tribunals actually tend to imbue juvenile thieves with a feeling of self-importance. Now, might not this very feeling be acted upon to a good and beneficial purpose,—to the advancement of industry and honest emulation? I think so; but society never seems to adopt really useful measures to *reform*—it contents itself with *punishing*. You may be surprised to hear such reflections come from my lips: but who is better able to judge than one who has passed through the entire ordeal?"

Here Jacob paused, and then inquired if he were wearying Tom Rain with his narrative.

"So far from your doing so, my good fellow," replied the highwayman, "that although I have several things to attend to, I mean to stop and hear you to the end. Come, drink a glass of wine. There! now you will be the better able to proceed. I will light another cigar—for I fancy that I can attend more earnestly while smoking."

Rainford once more settled himself in a comfortable posture; and the lad pursued his narrative in the following manner.

> 12. Although our aim is to render the "History of Jacob Smith" a regular and connected narrative of the initiation of a neglected child in the ways of vice and the career of crime, there are necessarily many phases in the history of juvenile iniquity which cannot be introduced into the text, as it would be impossible that the boy who is telling his story could have gone through all the scenes alluded to. We must, therefore, farther illustrate our aim by means of a few notes, derived from authentic sources: and this course we are the more inclined to pursue, inasmuch as we hope that the episode formed by the "History of Jacob Smith" may have the effect of directing public attention more seriously than ever to the awful nature and extent of juvenile depravity in this metropolis. Mr. Miles, in his "Report to the House of Lords on Poverty, Mendicity, and Crime," places on record the following observations:—
>
> "The women and the girls in these districts live with their men as long as they can agree together, or until one or the other be imprisoned or transported. The very children are prostitutes, living with their "fancy lads;" and it is difficult to say which are the most degraded, the men or the women, the girls or the boys. It is thus that I suppose crime is more engendered in low neighbourhoods, where the poorest and the most idle congregate: and I now beg to continue my remarks upon the second head, namely, the neglect of parents. The various pursuits of these parents call them from home during the greater portion of the day, and their children are left to play and idle in the streets, associating with other lads of more experience than themselves, until, seeing and hearing how easy it is to steal, they commence their career of crime, unchecked on the one hand and applauded on the other. There are some parents who turn their children out every morning to provide for themselves, not caring by what means they procure a subsistence, so that the expense of feeding them does not abstract from their means of procuring gin or beer. Other parents require their children to bring home a specified sum every night, to obtain which they must beg or thieve. Others hire out their children to beggars, for 3*d.* a day (a cripple is considered worth 6*d.*); and many women hire children in arms about the same age, to pass them off in the public

thoroughfares as twins. Groups of these young neglected vagabonds herd together, and theft becomes their study; even if a child was well disposed, it is not probable that he could escape the contagion of such bad example. There is a *community of children*, who live and are separated from persons more advanced in years. Moreover, there is so rapid and so certain a communication among them all over the metropolis, that if they discover any of their slang or flash words to be known out of their circle, they will substitute another, which in the course of a day or two will be adopted by the fraternity. There are lodging-houses exclusively for their accommodation, public-houses which are chiefly supported by their custom, and the landlords of both sorts of establishments are ever ready to purchase any plunder they may bring. With this neglect of parents on the one hand, and the faculties to crime on the other hand, can it be expected that these children can resist temptation? The wonder would be if a boy was honest. My conclusion, therefore, is, that the neglect of parents in these low neighbourhoods renders them *nurseries* of crime. The number of boys in London who live by plunder is very—very considerable: and thus society is maintaining them at a great expense, either in the shape of prison expenses, or by the value of the property they steal, especially when it is considered that the receivers never give one quarter the value: and there is not a boy thief who, on the average, does not expend 5*s*. per diem."

13. In the First Series of the "MYSTERIES OF LONDON," Vol. II. ch. CXCII., there is a detailed account of an association denominated "The Forty Thieves." Soon after the Weekly Number containing that chapter appeared, we were inundated with letters, chiefly expressing unqualified disbelief of the astonishing particulars recorded in respect to the Forty Thieves. We answered all those which contained the real names and addresses of the writers, assuring them that the details related were strictly true, and that we actually possessed a printed copy of the regulations by which the Forty Thieves were governed. Still, most of our correspondents were sceptical. It was therefore with a feeling almost bordering on satisfaction that we saw in the *Morning Chronicle*, a few weeks ago, a report of a police-case in which the prisoner who figured before the magistrate was described as "belonging to an association denominated the 'Forty Thieves,' and whose head-quarters were in the Mint, Southwark." We take this opportunity of assuring our readers that of what they find recorded in the "MYSTERIES OF LONDON," far—far more is based on fact than they might at first suspect.

14. Mr. Miles, in his Report (from which we have previously quoted) says, "In considering the subject of juvenile delinquency, it is requisite to take into account the various causes which compel them to be vicious; and though we must condemn, still we must regret that no efficient means have been adopted to prevent this lamentable evil. Young thieves have often confessed to me, that their first attempts at stealing commenced at apple stalls, and that having acquired confidence by a few successful adventures, they have gradually progressed in crime, allured by others, and in their turn alluring. They find companions to cheer them and instruct them, girls to share their booty and applaud them, and every facility to sell their daily booty. There is, moreover, a kind of lottery adventure in each day's life; and as these excitements are attainable at so easy a rate, is it strange that these children are fascinated with and abandon themselves to crime? Imprisonment to a young urchin who steals and has no other means of subsistence is no punishment; for it is indifferent to him where he exists, so long as he has food and raiment. It is in prison that boys form acquaintants, more mischievous than themselves. Many lads have owned to me that they had learned more in a gaol than out of one. I once asked a lad if there was any school where boys were taught to pick pockets? Upon which he significantly observed, 'No occasion for one, sir: the best school for that sort of thing is HERE!' alluding to the prison in which I saw him."

15. We cannot allow the readers to attribute to *our* imagination a fact so disgusting as this. We received the information from a police-officer who was an eye-witness of such a scene, and from whom (as stated in a previous note in this Series) we have gleaned many remarkable facts relative to the lowest orders.

16. Mr. Miles's Report says, "London thieves have no sense of moral degradation; they are corrupt to the core; they are strangers to virtue and character, even by name; for many of them are the children of thieves or of exceedingly dissolute people, consequently they can have no contrition; they are in a state of predatory existence, without any knowledge of social duty; they may lament detection, because it is an inconvenience, but they will not repent their crime; in gaol they will ponder on the past, curse their 'evil stars,' and look forward with anxiety to the moment of their release; but their minds and habits are not constituted for repentance. Mr. Chesterton, of the House of Correction, informed me that he considers reformation among juvenile offenders to be utterly hopeless; he observed, that 'boys brought up in a low neighbourhood have no chance of being honest, because on leaving a gaol they return to their old haunts, and follow

the example of their parents or associates.' Lieutenant Tracy, of the Westminster Bridewell, has pointed out to me lads who live constantly in gaols.

"Captain Kincaid, of the City Bridewell, informed me that one-half of the number under his lock on the day that I inspected the prison (June the 9th) had been more than once committed, many of them several times, especially the boys. Mr. Teague, of the Giltspur-street Compter, is of opinion that young thieves are mostly incorrigible—that nothing will reform them; an opinion which, he says, he has formed from the experience of many years. Mr. Capper, of the Home Office, stated, in his evidence, that out of 300 juvenile convicts, on board the hulk *Euryalus*, the eldest of whom was not 17, 133 had been committed more than once; and an experienced burglar told me that young thieves cannot and will not reform. 'The only thing, sir,' he remarked, 'that may save them is transportation, as it removes them from evil companions.'

"The young thief is a nucleus of mischief. A young pickpocket, named Stuart, aged 13, informed me that his parents daily sent him into the streets to 'look about,' that is, to plunder whatever he could lay his hands upon; that his principal associates were three young thieves with whom he 'worked,' or robbed; that when he was 10 years old he stood at a horse's head while his companion stole a great coat from the gig; that he got sixpence for his share of the plunder; that he had committed many robberies because he was made to do it; and that he lived entirely by plunder. Mr. Chesterton states, in his evidence before the select committee of the House of Commons in answer to query 474, 'Some of the parents lead their children into evil courses. It is no uncommon thing, when we are listening to the conversation between the prisoners and their parents, to hear a conversation that shows at once the boy's situation; but the old thieves are in the habit of bringing in with them young inexperienced lads. Whenever the elder thieves are recommitted, they are frequently recommitted with another.' He also observes (522) that 'the elder thieves are continually corrupting young lads, and bringing them into prison.'

"I am informed that Captain Brenton considers the total number of juvenile offenders within the bills of mortality to be 12,000. Dr. Lushington, I believe, computed the number still higher; and from the evidence above quoted it is evident that each elder offender is daily spreading the mischief far and wide.

"There is a youthful population in the metropolis devoted to crime, trained to it from infancy, adhering to it from education and circumstances, whose connections prevent the possibility of reformation, and whom no punishment can deter; a race '*sui generis*,' different from the rest of society, not only in thoughts, habits, and manners, but even in appearance; possessing, moreover, a language exclusively their own. There are lodging-houses kept by old thieves where juvenile offenders herd together, and their constant intercourse tends to complete corruption. It is in these hotbeds of vice that they revel in the fruits of their plunder; and though extremely young, they live with girls, indulging in every kind of debauchery."

CHAPTER XXXIX.
CONTINUATION OF THE HISTORY OF JACOB SMITH.

"I now come to an important event in my life—in fact, that portion of it which will account for this sickly condition of health in which you see me. Old Death one evening took me with him to supper at a place where he had never introduced me before. This was Bunce's in Earl Street, Seven Dials. Mrs. Bunce immediately seemed to take a great fancy to me—made me sit next to her—and, in spite of her meanness, helped me to the best of every thing on table. It was a very good supper; for Old Death, who provided it, had declared that he meant to launch out for once. But I suppose it was only to put me into such a good humour that I was the more likely to fall into the scheme which he had in view. This was not, however, the reason of Mrs. Bunce's kindness; because since then she has often treated me in a manner that has made me forget many a sorrow. It is true that these likings only take her by fits and starts—and she has not unfrequently used me cruelly enough. I can scarcely make that woman out, as far as I am concerned; and there are moments when I think a great deal of any kind words she has ever uttered to me, or any kind treatment she has ever shown me.

"But I am wandering from the subject which I had entered upon. You remember that I was telling you about the supper at Bunce's house. Well, after the things were cleared away, and the grog was going round pretty fast,—I used to drink then as much as a man, although little more than ten years old;—Old Death began to talk a great deal about the money that might be made by a clever lad like me being able to get admittance into the houses of rich people. He went on to say that I should begin to think of doing business that would leave me more time to amuse myself, and be also less dangerous than going about the streets picking pockets. I assured him that I was heartily sick and tired of the life I was leading, and that I wished I was old enough to be a housebreaker. 'For,' said I, 'a cracksman does have some time which he can call his own. If he does only one job a week, he is satisfied: but I am obliged to gad about all day to get the means of living on the next. Besides,' said I, 'I am of course running a thousand times more risks by doing so many jobs each day, than I should if I only did one or two a week.'[117]— 'Everybody must have his apprenticeship,' returned Old Death, 'and you have now served yours. I agree with you that it is high time for you to be doing something better; and I have a plan ready chalked out for you.'—Mrs. Bunce mixed me another glass of grog: I produced my short pipe, and blew a cloud while Old Death explained his scheme. At first I did not much relish it: but he backed it with so many arguments, that I agreed to try it.

"And, sure enough, at six o'clock one morning—a few days afterwards—a boy, black as a devil, with soot-bag over his shoulder, and brush and scraper in his hand, was making the round of Bloomsbury Square, bawling, '*Sweep!*' as lustily as he could. That boy was myself. Presently a garret-window opened, and a female voice called me to stop. I obeyed. In a few minutes down came the cook to the front door, and I was desired to walk in and operate on the kitchen-chimney. The cook was a fat, middle-aged, good-natured body, and asked me a great many questions about myself,—how long I had been a sweep—how it happened that I became one—whether I had any father or mother—and a host of such queries; to all of which I replied in the most sorrowful manner possible. I assured her that I had been a sweep from infancy—that I had swept a chimney when I was only five years old—that I had no parents—that my master beat me cruelly—and that I had had nothing to eat since the morning before. The good creature shed tears at my narrative; and, when I had swept the chimney—which I did in a manner that scarcely bore out the assertion of my long experience—she gave me a quantity of broken victuals in addition to the money earned. I then took my departure, having very quietly deposited half-a-dozen silver forks and spoons in my soot-bag, while her back was turned.

"This business I carried on successfully enough for some months; till at last Old Death told me that he had seen several paragraphs in the papers, warning people against thefts committed by sweeps. I therefore gave up the employment, and once more took refuge in St. Giles's. But my health was seriously injured by the occupation I had just renounced; and from that time I have always been ailing and sickly. Although I had seldom turned sweep more than twice a week, and an hour after each robbery that I thus committed was as clean again as if I had never been near a chimney in my life,—yet the seeds of disease were planted in me, and I feel the effects here—here—in my chest!

"The life that I led when I gave up the chimney-sweep business, did not certainly tend to improve my health. I hired a room in St. Giles's, and took a girl into keeping—I being then eleven, and she thirteen. Of all profligate creatures, Peggy Wilkins was the worst. The moment she awoke in the morning, she must have her half-quartern of gin; and then she would go on drinking at short intervals all day long. If I attempted to stop the supplies, she would fly into the most dreadful passions, break every thing she could lay her hands on, or else throw the domestic articles at my head. When tipsy, she would loll half naked out of the window, and chaff the people passing in the street. In the evening she went to the penny concerts or penny theatres,[18] and generally came home so gloriously drunk that the entire house, much less our little room, would scarcely hold her. You may wonder why I continued to live with her: but the fact is, I liked her in spite of her outrageous conduct, and as I was sometimes very dull and low, her noisy, rackety disposition positively helped to put me into good spirits. She knew nothing of my connexion with Old Death; but she was aware that I was laying hid in St. Giles's in consequence of having robbed houses disguised as a sweep; and she used to laugh heartily when I told her several amusing anecdotes relative to that portion of my career.

"One night—after having lived about a month in idleness in the Holy Land—I was compelled by the falling short of supplies, to call at Bunce's in Seven Dials, for the purpose of seeing Old Death. After waiting there a short time, he came in; and I immediately noticed that his face was more serious than usual,—a certain sign that he had something new on hand. I did not, however, venture to ask any questions; for I still stood in the greatest awe of him, and knew that his disposition was irritable and easy to be provoked. At length he said to Mrs. Bunce, 'Give that lad a good strong glass of grog: he's shivering with cold.'—I was not, but I took the grog, because I never refused spirits at that time. When Old Death thought I was primed enough to embrace any new plan with eagerness, he said, 'Jacob, I have something for you to do that I am convinced will yield a good harvest.'—I instantly became all attention.—'There's a widow lady,' he continued, 'living at the West End, in a swell street; and, by all I can learn, she is very well off. She is also very charitable, and belongs to a number of what's called Religious Societies; and I am sure you could get into her house as easy as possible. The chimney-sweep business has well-nigh blown over, if not quite; and it's high time to begin a new dodge.'—He then explained his plan; and I agreed to adopt it.

"When I got back to my lodging in St Giles's, I found Peggy sitting in company with a young fellow of about fifteen, drinking raw spirits. She had not expected me home so early, and was for a moment quite taken aback. But soon recovering herself, she put a good face on the matter, and introduced the young chap as her brother; saying that she had not seen him for many years before that evening, when she had met him by accident. I pretended to believe her; but the moment he was gone, I gave her a good beating and overwhelmed her with reproaches. She showed less spirit than I had expected, and did not attempt to return the blows; neither did she treat me with sulkiness or ill-humour.

"On the following evening, at about nine o'clock, I very quietly laid myself down on the door-steps of a house in Old Burlington Street. I was in such rags and tatters as to be almost naked; and having pricked my feet, with a pointed bit of wood, in several places, they were almost covered with blood, as if chapped with the cold and cut by the sharp stones. This was in the depth of winter; and my appearance was most miserable. Presently a carriage drove up to the house, and a fine, tall, elderly gentleman got out. I was crouched up close by the threshold of the door, and I purposely let him tread on one of my naked feet. Then I began to sob as if with pain; and he now observed me for the first time. He muttered an oath; but at that instant the front-door opened, and his manner changed directly. He spoke kindly to me, and put half-a-crown into my hand. A lady was crossing the hall while the door stood open and this gentleman was still speaking to me; and she immediately turned to ascertain what was the matter. 'Here's a poor, wretched creature,' said the gentleman, 'who was so huddled up against the door, that I did not observe him; and I am afraid I trod on his leg somewhat heavily.'—The lady instantly spoke in the most compassionate terms, and desired that I might be brought into the house. The man-servant raised me, for I affected to be unable to walk; and the lady said, 'Poor boy, he is paralysed with the cold!'—When I was moved into the hall, and placed in a chair, the state of my feet was observed; and this increased the compassion I had already excited. She ordered the servant to take me into the kitchen, and give me a good supper, while I warmed myself by the fire.

"All these commands were immediately executed; shoes and stockings were also supplied me; and in the course of an hour the lady herself came down to speak to me. She asked me who I was. I told her a long and piteous tale, already prepared for the occasion,—how I had been apprenticed to a tradesman at Liverpool, and had undergone the most dreadful treatment because I refused to work on the Lord's Day and insisted on my right to go to church; how the cruelty of my master had increased to such an extent, that I was obliged to run away; how I had wandered about the country for the last two months, subsisting on charity, but often half-starved; how I had that morning found my way to London, and had been obliged to sell my shoes for a penny to buy a roll, which was all I had eaten during thirty-six hours: but that I had an aunt who was housekeeper to a certain Bishop, and that I knew she would do all she could for me. The lady seemed to eye me suspiciously until I spoke of the aunt and the Bishop; and then her countenance instantly changed in my favour. 'Well, my poor lad,' she said, 'you shall remain here to-night; and the first thing to-morrow morning, one of my servants shall take a message from you to your aunt.'—I of course expressed my gratitude for this kindness; but the lady assured me that she required no thanks, as heaven rewarded her for what she did towards her suffering fellow-creatures. I really thought that there was something very much like what I and my usual associates were accustomed to call '*gammon*' in all this; and then I actually reproached myself for the idea, and began to repent of imposing on so much virtue and goodness.

"When I was well warmed with the cheerful fire and plentiful supper, the housekeeper of this lady conducted me to a little room on the top storey, and having wished me a 'good night,' retired, locking the door behind her. But this did not give me much uneasiness; for beneath my rags I had concealed the necessary means to counteract such a precaution. Accordingly, about an hour after I had heard the servants withdraw to their bed-rooms, which were on the same floor as the one where I was placed,—and when I thought the house was all quiet,—I took off the lock of the door by means of a little turn-screw, and crept carefully down stairs. Just at that minute the clock struck eleven. My intention was to visit the drawing-room first; but when I reached the door, I perceived there were lights within. I listened, and heard the gentleman and lady talking together. 'Oh! ho,' thought I, 'I shall have time to inspect the lady's bed-room first, and perhaps secure her jewels.'—So, naturally conceiving that this chamber must be the one immediately over the drawing-room, I retraced my way up stairs, and entered the front apartment on the second floor. A rush-light was burning in the room; but no one was there. I lost no time in commencing my search in all the cupboards; but I found nothing except clothes. There was, however, a mahogany press which was fast locked. I drew forth a small skeleton key, and was about to use it, when I was alarmed by footsteps in the passage. In another moment I was safely concealed under the bed.

"Some one almost immediately afterwards entered the room, and only closed the door without shutting it. I dared not move even to peep from beneath the drapery that hung round the bed to the floor: but I could tell by the rustling of silk and the unlacing of stays, that the person in the room was undressing herself—and I felt satisfied it was the lady of the house. I was now seriously alarmed. She was evidently going to bed; and my only chance of escaping from the chamber was when she should be asleep. But might I not disturb her? My situation was very unpleasant—and a prison seemed to open before my eyes.

"In about a quarter of an hour the lady stepped into bed. How I longed to catch the first sound that should convince me she was asleep! But she was not dreaming of closing her eyes yet awhile; for scarcely had she laid herself down, when the door was gently opened—then carefully closed again—and *another person*, evidently without shoes or boots on, came into the room. They said a few words to each other; and to my astonishment I found that the gentleman who had arrived in his carriage (which of course had been sent away) was going to pass an hour in company with the charitable lady. 'Well,' thought I, 'this is the way in which heaven rewards her for all she does towards her suffering fellow-creatures!'

"The gentleman undressed himself, and got into bed. Nearly two hours, instead of an hour, passed away—very pleasantly, it seemed, for the lady and gentleman, and very much to my amusement. I was now no longer under any alarm on account of myself—for I had learnt a secret which placed the lady in my power. Well, the gentleman got up at last and dressed himself; and the lady went down stairs with him to bolt the street-door after him. Their movements were so cautious, that I could plainly perceive the servants must have fancied that the gentleman had gone away long before, and that this care was taken to avoid disturbing them with any noise likely to excite suspicion.

"The moment the lady had left the room with her lover, I thought of beating a retreat. But should I go empty-handed? No: and yet I had not time to force open the mahogany press, which I believed must contain her jewels, before she would come back, as she had gone down in her night-clothes. I therefore resolved to stay where I was, and accomplish my purpose when she was asleep; because if matters did come to the worst and she should awake, she dared not expose me. So I laid quiet; and she came back in a few minutes, shivering with the cold—for I could hear her teeth actually chatter. Half an hour afterwards she was fast asleep—as I could tell by her deep and regular breathing. The rush-light still burnt in the room; and I crept carefully from beneath the bed. Yes—she was sleeping; and, though not a young woman, she appeared very beautiful. But I had not a minute to lose: my skeleton key was again at work—the bolt of the lock flew back—and the door of the press moved on its hinges. Move! yes—and creak, too, most awfully; so that the lady started up in bed, and uttered a faint scream. I instantly rushed up to her, saying in a low but determined tone, 'Madam, not a word—or I betray you and your lover!'—By the feeble light of the candle, I saw that she became as red as crimson.—'Yes, madam,' I continued, 'your tricks are known to me; and I have been all the while concealed under this bed.'—'You!' she exclaimed: 'why, surely you are the poor boy that I received into the house this evening?'—'To be sure I am, ma'am,' was my answer; 'and, being troubled with a habit of sleep-walking, I found my way to this room.'—'But what were you doing at the bureau?'—'Merely examining it in my sleep, ma'am.'—'This is ridiculous,' she said impatiently. 'I understand what you are; but I will treat you well on condition that you do not mention to a soul what you have been a witness of this night.'—'I have no interest in gossiping, ma'am.'—'And were you to do so, I can deny all you may state,' added the lady, who was dreadfully excited and nervous, as you may suppose. 'But if you follow my directions, I will reward you well.'—I readily gave a promise to that effect. She then took a reticule from a chair by the side of the bed, and drawing out her purse, emptied its contents into my hands. At a rapid glance I saw there could not be less than fifteen or sixteen sovereigns, besides a little silver. She then took from her bag a Bank-note for twenty pounds, which she also gave me.

"I secured the money about my person, and she asked me whether I was satisfied? I said, 'Perfectly.'——'Then stand aside for a few moments, and I will show you how to act.'——I stepped behind the curtain, while she rose and put on a dressing-gown; having done which, she took the rush-light in her hand and desired me to follow her as noiseless as possible. We went down into the kitchen, where she told me to take all the cold victuals there were in the larder; and she gave me a napkin to wrap them up in. There happened to be a silver spoon in one of the dishes—left there most probably by accident. This she also desired me to take; and you may be sure I did not refuse. These arrangements being made, she led me to the front door, and having reminded me of my promise not to talk about a certain affair, let me out of the house. I have no doubt that there was a great deal said next morning in Old Burlington Street, about the ungrateful lad who was taken in as an object of charity, and who decamped in the middle of the night with the contents of the larder and a silver spoon into the bargain."

"But you have not mentioned the name of this lady, Jacob?" interrupted Tom Rain.

"I did not think it was worth while, sir—as she used me very well——"

"Still I have a very particular reason for wishing to be informed on that head," said the highwayman.

"Oh! if that's the case, I shall not hesitate," replied Jacob. "The name of that lady was Mrs. Slingsby."

"I thought so from the very first moment you began to speak of her!" cried Tom. "And the name of the gentleman—did you learn *that*?"

"Yes, sir," answered the lad: "I heard the servants talking about him, when I was in the kitchen. His name was—let me see?—Oh! yes—I remember—Sir Henry Courtenay."

"Thank you, Jacob," exclaimed Tom: then, in a low, musing tone, he said, "Poor Clarence! you are woefully deceived in your saint of an aunt!"

"Shall I continue my story, Mr. Rainford?" asked Jacob. "It will not last much longer now."

"By all means go on, my boy. I would sit here till day-light, sooner than miss the end."

Thus encouraged, Jacob continued in the following manner.

17. Every juvenile delinquent is as anxious to rise in his "profession" as the military or naval officer, or the member of any other hierarchy. But with the votaries of crime the apex of promotion is—the gibbet! Mr. Miles says, "I have questioned many boys of shrewd understanding concerning their opinions, and the opinions of their associates, as to their ultimate fate (for all thieves are fatalists). They

look upon their inevitable doom to be either sooner or later transportation or the drop! It is difficult to imagine a state of more gloomy wretchedness and more despairingly horrible than the self-conviction of condign punishment, without one gleam of hope to clear the melancholy perspective. Punishments and whippings are therefore useless, for the mind is prepared to endure more, and every imprisonment is only looked upon as another step in the ladder of their sad destiny. The lad is hopeless, consequently reckless in his conduct,—hardened to the present, and irreclaimable as to the future. It is not by prison discipline that reformation can be effected: the temptations, the facilities, and the love of idleness are too alluring. Crowds of young thieves will wait round a prison-gate, to hail a companion on the morning of his liberation, and to carry him off to treat him and regale him for the day. I have asked boys under sentence of transportation if they thought they *could* reform, if returned again upon society, and the general reply has been, 'No.' Their reasons for that conclusion I give in their own words:—'If we were to be free to-morrow, we must go to our old haunts and our old companions, for where else *can* we go? If we try to be honest we cannot, for our 'pals' (associates) would torment us to return; in short, we should only have to come back here at last, but we are now going to another country, where we hope to be honest men.'

"I have, moreover, questioned many lads as to what method they would adopt to prevent other boys from falling into crime, and their remarks have been, 'Stop playing in the streets, for a pocket is soon picked, and there are many who show others how to do it;—and the next thing is to stop those cursed receivers; for if a receiver knows a boy to have dealt with him, (that is, to have sold him property,) he will make him go out to thieve; he will never let him rest; and even should we get into employment, he will teaze us till he makes us rob the master, or will tell of us to the police.' These remarks prove the boys to be good judges of their own cases; so, like a skilful physician, they know where to apply the remedy; and as I feel convinced that many of these urchins possess every requisite to be good and useful members of society, so am I certain that their reformation, in a majority of cases, is as practicable, under proper means, as their ultimate ruin is now certain, under the present system."

18. Mr. Brandon, in his Preface to Mr. Miles's Report, makes the following observations, which are too important to need any apology for their quotation:—

"If a religious fanatic brings a Bill into the House for the 'better observance of the Sabbath,' whose comforts are to be abridged? Why, the poor man's and those of the middling classes; for it is the stage-coaches and omnibuses that are to be prohibited from making their appearance, while the streets may be thronged with carriages; and though the labourer is not permitted to purchase his necessary food on that sacred day, unable to have accomplished it before from not having received his wages till too late the preceding night, yet the fishmonger may keep the turbot cool that is to grace his lordship's Sunday table, and send it home on the very day, just in time to be prepared for dinner.

"Penny theatres, too, are decried and suppressed, while the larger ones are permitted—the reason assigned being that the company who frequent the former render the step necessary, but the delinquency does not arise from cheap exhibitions—it is from the inefficiency of the law to restrain the audience; for in the plays themselves there is no improper language used. Holland, a notorious thief, in his examination, said he had heard bad language at those places before the curtain drew up, *but never any thing indecent on the stage*. This is a damning proof where the fault lies; if the laws were such as to restrain vice, and those properly administered, it would effectually prevent the improper conduct of the loose individuals, and preclude the necessity of reducing the pleasures of the poor; pockets are picked every night at the royal theatres, and scenes of the worst description carried on in the lobbies; yet it never entered into the cranium of the wiseacres that if the theatres were shut up, these abominations would be effectually eradicated. It is highly gratifying to witness the order and pleasure with which cheap diversions are conducted on the continent, even so close to us as Boulogne and Calais, where may be seen the lowest classes enjoying themselves in dancing and visiting the various public gardens, the entrance to which is a fee equivalent to our penny. Another proof of the difference with which our laws are administered according to the parties affected, is manifest in the proceedings against the various houses for play in the metropolis, the clubs of the aristocracy and the 'little goes,' little hells, &c. of the poor."

CHAPTER XL.
CONCLUSION OF THE HISTORY OF JACOB SMITH.

"On my return to Earl Street, Seven Dials, which was at about three o'clock in the morning, I found Old Death and Mrs. Bunce sitting up for me, Toby having gone to bed. I related the adventures which I had met with, but said not a word about the intrigue of the lady and the baronet; for I could not help thinking that the kind treatment I had in the first instance received from Mrs. Slingsby, deserved the reward of secresy on that head. Old Death *very kindly* permitted me to retain five pounds out of the money which I myself had obtained; and I hurried back to my lodging in St. Giles's. Peggy was in bed and fast asleep; and I lay down by her side without awaking her.

"When I again opened my eyes, the sun was shining in the brightness of a frosty air even through the dingy panes of my window; and I started up. Peggy had already risen; and I supposed she had gone out to get things for breakfast. But something like a suspicion arose in my mind—and I felt uneasy. I searched the pockets of the ragged pair of trousers I had purposely worn on the previous night, and the five sovereigns were gone. Now I was really alarmed: Peggy had certainly decamped. A farther search showed me that she had even carried off the few little articles of decent wearing apparel that I had, leaving me only the miserable rags in which I had appeared at Mrs. Slingsby's house. Yes—Peggy had run away with all I possessed that was worth the taking; and now the question naturally rose in my mind—'*Will she betray me?*' I thought her conduct was so suspicious, that I determined not to give her a chance if I could help it; particularly as I remembered the manner in which she took the beating I gave her, and which now made me think that she had resolved on being revenged. So I dressed myself in my tatters as quick as I could, and got away from the house. But at the end of the street I met a certain Mr. Dykes—the Bow Street runner, whom you happen to know, Mr. Rainford—and though I endeavoured to dive into a narrow court, he pounced upon me in a twinkling.

"In less than an hour I stood in the felons' dock at the police-court, Bow Street, charged with a robbery committed by me in Bloomsbury Square, in the disguise of a sweep. I was remanded for a week, and sent in the meantime to Clerkenwell Prison. There I was placed in No. 12, Reception Yard, where Mrs. Bunce, who pretended to be my aunt in order to get admittance to me, visited me in the afternoon. She told me that Mr. Bones could not possibly come to see me, but that he would do all he could for me if I remained staunch and did not mention his name in any way—not even to my fellow-prisoners. 'We are afraid that you will be committed for trial,' said Mrs.

Bunce; 'but all shall be done that can be done to buy off the witnesses. If that won't succeed, such evidence of former good character shall be given, that your sentence will be a light one; and in the meantime you shall have as much money as you want to live gloriously in prison. Mr. Bones has sent you up a sovereign for the present, and I will bring you a good suit of clothes tomorrow, so that you may go up swell before the beak next time. Be staunch, Jacob; and Mr. Bones will never desert you. But if you only mention his name to a soul in an improper way, he'll leave you to your fate, and you'll be transported.'—Mrs. Bunce impressed all this on my mind; but I assured her it was unnecessary, as I knew that I should not better my own plight in any very considerable degree by nosing against Bones, whereas he might be useful to me if I behaved well in the matter. She went away satisfied; and I spent the rest of the day in jollification with my fellow-prisoners, amongst whom my money raised me to the rank of a hero.[19]

"That night I slept in the Receiving Ward; and next morning I was taken to the bathing-room, a new suit of clothes having been already sent in to me by Mrs. Bunce. But I found that I was to bathe in the same water which had already served to wash the filthy bodies of several trampers who had also been sent to prison the day before on a charge of robbery; and I knew that when they entered they were covered with vermin. I therefore gave the turnkey half-a-crown to allow me to dispense with the bath, put on my new clothes, and was turned into the Felons' Yard. There I found persons, who had committed all degrees of crime, huddled together as if there was no difference in the charges against them. A boy who had stolen a pound of potatoes, value *one penny*—myself, who had stolen plate in a dwelling-house—a *gentleman*, who had wounded another in a duel and could not get bail, but who was a very superior person—a burglar—a coiner—and a man charged with *murder*, were all in one room together! It did not strike me then—but it has often struck me since—how wrong it was to put that boy who had stolen potatoes, along with a burglar, a coiner, and a practised thief as I was,—how unjust it was to put the gentleman with any of us,—and how shocking it was to put a murderer along with prisoners whose hands were not at least stained with blood. And what were the consequences? The boy, who had merely stolen the potatoes because his mother was ill and starving, and who had never done any thing wrong before, was entirely corrupted by the coiner, and made up his mind to turn prig the moment he got out;—the gentleman was worked up to such a pitch of excitement, by being in such society, that he was removed to the infirmary, and died of brain fever, as I afterwards heard;—the burglar helped the murderer to escape, and got safely away with him!

"Our amusements in gaol were chiefly gambling and drinking. Money procured as much liquor as we could consume; and with such I was well supplied. Cards and dice were not allowed, it is true; but we used to play with bits of wood cut and marked like dominoes, or by chalking the table into a draught-board, or by tossing halfpence. Then there was such fighting, quarrelling, and bad language, that nothing could equal the place! In the upper, or sleeping ward, things were much worse: the prisoners robbed each other. The very first night the duellist-gentleman was there, he lost his purse containing several sovereigns; and when he threatened to complain, he was quietly informed by the burglar and the murderer that if he did, he would be hung up to the bars of the window with his own handkerchief the very next night, and his end would be attributed to suicide.[20]

"At the end of the week I was had up to Bow Street once more; and the evidence was so conclusive against me, that I was committed to Newgate for trial. This I had expected, and cared but little for, as Mrs. Bunce at each visit which she paid me at Clerkenwell Prison, assured me that Mr. Bones would do all he could for me. And he kept his word—but more, I suppose, for his own sake than mine. What a dreadful place I found Newgate to be! Hardened as I was—acquainted with all degrees of debauchery—and familiar with vice, I declare solemnly that I shrank from the scenes I there witnessed. Fighting, quarrelling, gambling, thieving, drinking, obscene talking, bullying, and corrupting each other,—all those took place to a great degree in the Clerkenwell Prison; but in Newgate they were carried out to an extent dreadful to think of, and associated with other crimes impossible to mention.[21]

"I now seemed to awake, for the first time, from a long dream of wickedness, and to become aware of the frightful precipice on which I stood. My eyes were suddenly opened—and I shuddered. A man was hanged at the debtors' door, while I was in Newgate: and I saw him pass from the condemned cell to the kitchen, which is just within the debtors' door. I experienced a sudden revulsion of feeling, and took a solemn oath within my own breast that I would never thieve again. But as I knew nothing of religion, and could not read or write, I was not likely to reform very rapidly nor very completely. I still laughed and joked with my fellow-prisoners, and appeared to enter into most of their fun, though I really began to loathe them. But when the chaplain visited us, and the other boys jeered and mocked him, I stood by and dwelt on every word of gentle remonstrance that fell from his lips. Next Sunday I paid great attention to his sermon, while pretending to be asleep: for if I had been caught actually lending a patient ear to his discourse, my fellow-prisoners would have led me no peace afterwards. I understood but little—very little of that sermon: still I gleaned some notion of the existence of a Saviour a belief in whom was the stepping-stone to virtue. I also heard the happiness of heaven explained for the first time: but I must confess that I was greatly puzzled when the chaplain declared that the man who was hanged for a dreadful murder on the preceding Monday, had gone to that place of joy, because he had repented in his last moments—for I thought to myself, 'Well, then, a human being is quite safe in leading as terrible a life as he chooses, as long as he repents at the end.' And, again, I was bewildered when I heard the clergyman say these words, which made so great an impression on me that I have never forgotten them, and never shall:—'*As I stood with that penitent man on the drop, last Monday morning*, I ENVIED HIM HIS FATE, *because I knew that his soul was about to ascend to heaven*!'[22]

"The day of my trial came; and I was placed in the dock before the Common Serjeant of London. The clerk of the Court asked me, '*How will you be tried—by God and your country?*'—I knew not what reply to make, and was actually on the point of saying 'that I would rather not be tried at all this time, since it seemed to be left to my own choice; and that I would faithfully promise never to thieve again,'—when the turnkey who had charge of me, whispered in my ear, 'You damned young fool, why don't you speak? Say '*By God and my country*,' damn you.'—I did as I was directed; and the trial commenced. The charge against me was fully proved; and a verdict of *Guilty* was recorded. The Common-Serjeant asked if I had ever been convicted before. The keeper of Newgate, who was present, said I had not. The counsel who had been retained for me by Old Death, then requested to be allowed to call witnesses to character. This was permitted; and three or four tradesmen, who I well knew were Old Death's friends, got up one after the other, and swore that I had been in their service (each one of course giving different periods of time), and that I was an honest, hard-working, and industrious lad, until I fell into bad company and got into trouble. Dykes, the runner, was then questioned about me; and he said that I was not known as a thief—although he knew the contrary perfectly well. But Old Death had kept his word, and had not spared his gold. My offence was, however, a grave one—robbing in a dwelling-house; and there were two or three other indictments of the same kind against me, though the prosecutors did not come forward. Old Death had made it right with *them* too. I was accordingly condemned to seven years' transportation, with a hint that this sentence would be commuted to two years' imprisonment at the hulks.

"I was but little more than eleven when my career of crime was thus interrupted; and I was glad that it *was* so interrupted—for I resolved that it should not be renewed when I regained my liberty. This was scarcely a resolution produced by moral considerations, but by fear; and it therefore required strengthening. Whether it was, or not, I shall soon inform you.

"A few days after the sessions terminated, I was removed with several other boys to the *Euryalus* Convict-Hulk at Woolwich. This vessel has three decks: the upper is appropriated to lads convicted the first time, the second to the next grade of juvenile criminals, and the third, or lowest, to the worst kind of offenders. I was assigned to the upper deck, where there were about sixty of us. On being received on board we were first sent to the wash-house, where we were bathed and well cleansed; and we then received the suit of dark grey that denotes the felon. Our employment was to make clothes for the entire establishment: that is, shirts, jackets, waistcoats, and trousers. The person who taught us was a convict-boy, who had been a tailor: the cutters-out belonged to the second deck, and visited our department as often as their services were required.

"We were divided into sections, each having at its head a boy selected as the chief on account of his good conduct when in prison. I will describe the routine of the day—taking the period when the summer regulations are in force. At five o'clock in the morning all hands were called, the ports were opened, the hammocks were lowered and lashed up, and we washed ourselves for chapel. At half-past five the signal was given for prayers; and we went to the chapel in sections, or divisions, taking our seats in profound silence. The morning hymn was sung: the schoolmaster read the prayers; and we returned to our wards on the upper deck. There we stood in ranks till six o'clock, when breakfast was served. The steward of the ship superintended the giving out of the provisions, and saw that each boy had his fair allowance of bread and gruel. This being done, the steward ordered each rank, one after the other, to approach the tables, hold up the bread, say grace, and then sit down and eat. At half-past six, we were marshalled on the quarter-deck, in divisions; and the officers of the hulk were then prepared to hear any complaints or receive any reports that might have to be submitted to them. Such complaints were noted down for after investigation. Some of the boys were kept above to wash the quarter-deck, and the remainder were sent down to cleanse their own deck. At eight o'clock we were all set to work at tailoring, a strict silence being preserved. At nine o'clock the report upon the complaints was received from the commander of the hulk, and the punishments awarded were made known:—such as a good thrashing with a cane, stopping the dinner, or solitary confinement on bread and water. At twelve o'clock the dinners were served out, the steward superintending. The quartermasters and guards were also present, to see that one boy's allowance was not taken from him by another. From half-past twelve to half-past one we were allowed to take air and exercise on the quarter-deck, but without making any noise. At half-past one we were marched down again to our work. At two, a section of one-third of us was sent into the chapel, where we were taught reading and writing by the schoolmaster. At five we left off work or schooling, cleaned the wards, and then washed ourselves. This being done, supper was served out; and we went on the quarter-deck again for air and exercise till seven, when we were once more marched to the chapel for evening prayers and the catechism. At eight o'clock we returned to our own deck, where the signal was given for getting out the hammocks and slinging them up. At nine profound silence was ordered; and the whole ship was then as quiet as if there was not a soul on board,—this deep tranquillity being only broken by the striking of the bell and the cry of '*All's well!*' every half-hour.

"Such was the life led on board the *Euryalus* convict-hulk. But I was happier—much happier there than I had ever been before. The schoolmaster was an excellent man, and took a delight in teaching those who were anxious to learn. I was of this number, and my improvement was rapid. I quite won his regard, and he devoted unusual pains to instruct me; so that at the end of a year he obtained leave for me to give up the making of clothes and assist him as an usher. This was an employment that pleased me greatly, and allowed me plenty of time to read the books lent me by the worthy schoolmaster. So fond was I of reading, that I used to take a book with me on the quarter-deck at those times devoted to air and exercise; and sitting apart from the others, I would remain buried in study until it was time to go below again. I examined how books were written and how I was accustomed to speak: that is—I compared the language of those books with my own; and I was shocked to find how wretchedly ignorant I had hitherto been in respect to grammar. This ignorance I strove hard—oh! very hard to surmount; and the good schoolmaster assisted me to the utmost of his power. I read and studied the Bible with avidity; and the more I became acquainted with it, the more fixed grow my determination to avoid a relapse into the ways of crime when I should be released.

"During the two years that I passed at the hulk, Mrs. Bunce came very often to see me, passing herself off as my aunt; but relations were not allowed to speak to us except in the presence of a guard, and so the name of Old Death was never mentioned by either of us. But Mrs. Bunce used to tell me that 'my *uncle* would give me a home when my time was up;' and I supposed by this, that she meant her husband Toby. I knew that Old Death was the person who had directed these assurances to be given me; and often and often did I lay awake of a night, deliberating within myself what I should do when I was set free, to earn an honest livelihood and avoid the hateful necessity of returning to the service of Mr. Benjamin Bones.

"At length the day of liberation came—and I had no plan of proceedings settled. My clothes were given to me, and a shilling was put into my hand by the steward. The old schoolmaster was absent at the time; and I was sorry that I had not an opportunity of thanking him for all his kindness and imploring his advice how to proceed. It struck me that I would appeal to the commander of the hulk. I did so, and solicited him to counsel me how to get an honest livelihood. He burst out laughing in my face, exclaiming, 'I suppose you think I am to be deceived by your humbug, and that I shall put my hand into my pocket and give you half-a-guinea to see your way with. No such thing, my lad! I used to do so when I was first here; but those I assisted in that way were always the first to come back again.'—And he turned on his heel, leaving me quite astounded at the reception my sincerity of behaviour had experienced. But a few moments' reflection showed me that I could scarcely blame him for his conduct; and I quitted the ship in tears.

"The moment I stepped from the boat that landed me in Woolwich, I met Mrs. Bunce. She threw her arms round my neck, and called me her '*dear Jacob*,' in such a loving manner that one would really have believed her to be my aunt, or even my mother if she had chosen to represent herself so. Then, pointing to a public-house at a little distance, she said, 'Your good and kind friend Mr. Bones is there; and he will be so delighted to see you. He has ordered a nice steak and some good ale, and we mean to let you enjoy yourself.'—The idea of having such a glorious repast after being kept on short commons on board the *Euryalus*, made my mouth water; but then I remembered all the influence Old Death had been accustomed to exercise over me—and I knew that if I once again entered within its range, I should never have the moral courage to withdraw from it. So my mind was made up; and suddenly darting down a bye-street, I was beyond Mrs. Bunce's view in a twinkling. I heard her shrill, screaming voice call after me; but I heeded it not—and hurried onward, as if escaping from a wild beast.

"Presently I relaxed my speed, and at length entered a public-house, where I called for a pint of beer. Two or three soldiers and as many young women were sitting at another table, drinking, and indulging at the same time in the most filthy discourse. Suddenly one of the females started up, advanced towards me, and, after considering me for a few moments, exclaimed with a terrible oath, 'Well, I thought it must be my old fancy cove Jacob:'—and she offered to embrace me. I however repulsed her with loathing; for in the miserable, tattered, sickly wretch before me, I had already recognised Peggy Wilkins. She seemed ashamed of herself for a minute; then, recovering her impudence, she said, 'Damn and blast you for a sulky, snivelling hound! Who the devil are you that you can't treat me civilly? Do you think I don't know all that's happened to you? Why, you've only this moment left the hulks—and you can't deny it.'—The soldiers, hearing this, demanded if it was true; and, without waiting for my answer, thrust me out of the place. I had reached the end of the street, when I recollected that I had not received the change for my shilling, which I had tendered in payment of the beer. I therefore went back to ask for it; but the pot-boy who had served me, swore that I never gave him a shilling at all; and the landlord evidently believed that I was a vagabond endeavouring to swindle his servant. So I was kicked out—penniless!

"I was for some time before I could muster up courage to adopt any plan for my support. Indeed, I sate down in a retired nook and cried bitterly. I even regretted having left the hulk, so miserable did I feel. At last hunger compelled me to act; and I entered a shop to inquire if a boy was wanted. The man behind the counter said he did not require the assistance of a lad, but that a neighbour of his would probably hire me. I went to the place pointed out to me, and, having explained my business, was asked for testimonials of good character. I candidly confessed that I had just been discharged from the *Euryalus*, but that I thought the schoolmaster on board would recommend me. The man flew into a dreadful passion, and rushing round from behind the counter, would have kicked me out of the shop, if I had not run away of my own accord.

"I am sure that I tried twenty different shops that day in Woolwich. At some I explained my position—at others I carefully concealed the fact of my late ignominious punishment. But character—character—character! where was it? Even for a starving lad who only asked a fair trial—who promised to work from sunrise to sunset, and to be content with a morsel of bread to eat and a cellar to sleep in, as a recompense for his toils,—even to one who offered so much and required so little in return, *character* was necessary! Night came—I was famishing and in despair. At length a charitable baker gave me a roll; and my hunger was appeased. It struck me that the tradesmen at Woolwich were perhaps more cautious than people elsewhere how they engaged the services of young lads, in consequence of that place being a station for the convict-hulks; and I therefore resolved to try my luck in another quarter. I set out for Greenwich, which I reached at midnight, and slept till morning in a shed near some houses that were being built. Cold, famished, and dispirited did I awake; and with a sinking heart I commenced my rounds. Before noon I had called at a hundred shops, public-houses, or taverns, without success. Few required the service of boys; and those people who did, demanded references. I begged a piece of bread of a baker, and then set off for London.

"So slow did I walk, and so often was I compelled to rest, that it was evening before I reached the Blackfriars Road. There, again, did I endeavour to procure honest employment—but in vain! I remember that when one shopkeeper—an old man—listened to me with more attention than the rest, I burst into tears and implored—besought—prayed him to receive me into his service, if it was only *to save me from becoming a thief*! I did not tell him I had already been one. But he shook his head, saying sorrowfully, 'If you have already thought of turning thief, your morals must be more than half corrupted.'—He gave me a few halfpence, and I went away.

"I balanced for some minutes between the cravings of my stomach and the fatigue of my limbs—that is, whether I should spend those halfpence in food or on a bed. I decided in favour of the food, and having satisfied my hunger, crept into a timber-yard on the bank of the Thames, and slept there till morning. I awoke at sunrise, and crossed Blackfriars Bridge. My limbs shivered with ague, and my clothes were damp with the dews of night. I knew not what to do—which way to turn. Hope had deserted me. There was I, a poor—wretched—houseless—friendless—starving being, anxious to remain honest, yet impelled by circumstances towards a relapse into the career of vice. I prayed as I went along the streets,—yes, I prayed to God to save me from that dreadful—that last resource. But no succour came. All day long did I rove about: night arrived again—and for twenty-four hours I had eaten nothing. I dragged myself back to the timber yard; but there was a great dog prowling about—and I dared not enter. I sought shelter elsewhere, for the rain began to descend in torrents; but I was wet through before I could even find the entrance of a court to screen me. I never slept a wink that night: I was afraid to lie down on the cold stones—they were so chill. Morning came again—and I was now so weak that I could hardly put one foot before another. I was moreover starving—yes, *starving*! I passed a baker's shop and saw the nice hot bread smoking in the windows, and I went in to implore a stale crust. But I was ordered out; and then the idea struck me that in a few minutes I might obtain money to buy a good breakfast—not only bread, but meat and tea! That was by picking a pocket! The idea, however, assumed a horrible aspect a moment afterwards—and I recoiled from it. No: I would sooner plunge into the river and end my woes there—than steal again!

"To the river's brink I hurried—dragging myself slowly no more—but running, yes—absolutely running fast to terminate my wretchedness by suicide. It was near Westminster Bridge that I was on the point of throwing myself into the Thames, when my collar was suddenly grasped from behind, and I was drawn back. I turned—and saw Old Death!

"Then I uttered a scream, and struggled dreadfully to get away, that I might still accomplish my purpose; but he held me tight, saying, 'Silly boy! why do you fly from life, since it may yet have many pleasures for you?'—'No!' I cried: 'I will never become a thief again!'—'And I will never ask you to do so,' he replied. 'But come with me, and let us talk over your prospects.'—'Prospects!' I repeated in a hysterical manner; and then I followed him mechanically to an early breakfast-house close by. He ordered a plentiful meal; and I ate ravenously. The food and hot coffee cheered me; and I began to feel grateful to Bones for having supplied the means to appease the hunger that was devouring me. Moreover, one looks with quite a different eye upon suicide after a good meal; and I could not do otherwise than regard him as the saviour of my life. I was therefore already prepared to listen to him with attention; and when he proposed that we should repair to Bunce's, where we could converse without fear of being overheard, I willingly agreed to accompany him. But during our walk to Seven Dials, I constantly repeated within my own breast the most solemn vows not to yield to any threats or representations—menaces or coaxings—to induce me to become a thief again!

"When we reached the house in Earl Street, Mrs. Bunce received me with more kindness than I had expected to meet at her hands, after the trick I had played her a few days before at Woolwich. But she did not treat me thus without a motive; for when once she and Old Death got me between them, they endeavoured to the utmost of their power to persuade me to resume my old avocations. I was faithful to my vow, and assured them that they might kill me sooner than I would again do any thing to risk imprisonment in that horrible Newgate. It was not the hulk I so much dreaded—nor yet transportation, because I knew nothing of it; but I shrunk from the mere idea of going through the ordeal of Newgate a second time. Old Death saw that I was not to be moved—at least then; and he gave up the point. 'But,' said he, 'you must do something to get a living: you can't starve; and *we* won't maintain you in idleness. If you like, I'll take you into my service to run on errands, look after people that I want to learn any thing about and make yourself useful in that way; and I'll give you a shilling a-day.'—I agreed—for I could not starve.

"Now, of course it is as plain to you as it was even then to me, that Old Death was playing a deep game with me. I was the cleverest thief that ever served him; and he had received ample—ample proofs that he could trust me. He knew that he was safe with me. I was therefore too useful a person to lose; and he thought that by throwing me again amongst my old companions, and keeping me on very short allowance, the disagreeable impressions of gaol would soon wear away, and I should relapse into my old habits. He was quite mistaken. I don't pretend that any particular idea of virtue made a great change in me; but I had been in Newgate—*and there I had seen a man going out to be hanged*; and I thought that if I got into that dreadful gaol *a second time*, I should become hardened, *and that I also should go out some day to be hanged!* So I resisted all temptation—and lived as well as I could on the shilling a day, without increasing my means by theft or villany.

"This mode of life on my part did not suit Old Death. A few weeks passed, and when he found that I was resolved not to return to my former ways, he stopped my allowance altogether. I was now steeped to the very lips in wretchedness and misery: but somehow or another I managed to get a crust here and there just to keep body and soul together—although I oftener slept in the open air than in a bed. Mrs. Bunce showed me a little kindness now and then, but quite unknown to Old Death; and, to my surprise, she did not urge the necessity of my returning to the career of theft. For several weeks I saw nothing of Mr. Bones; but at last he fished me out in some low place, and told me I might return into his service if I liked, and that he should pay me according to the use I proved myself to be to him. To glean information for him—run on errands—dog and watch persons—or even loiter about in police-courts to hear what cases came up before the magistrates,—these were my chief duties; and badly enough they were paid. But I was now permitted to get my breakfast and tea regularly at the Bunces'; and that was something. As for my lodging, if I got together a few pence to enable me to hire a bed, or a part of a bed, in one of those low houses that I have already described to you, I was contented,—for I always had this consolation, that I could walk about the streets without being afraid of meeting a Bow-Street runner."

Jacob paused—for his tale was told.

"Well, my boy," said Tom Rain, "you have gone through much, and seen enough to form a good stock of experience. I commend your resolution never to put yourself within reach of the law again; for that's just my determination also. You have got money in your pocket now; and I will do something more for you before I leave England."

"Ah! Mr. Rainford," exclaimed Jacob, much affected, "how I wish that I had met with such a friend as you earlier in life! And how I wish, too, that I could go with you—wherever you are going—and be your servant—your slave!"

"Well—well, Jacob, we will talk of that another time," said Tom. "Rest assured I will not desert you. Call at Tullock's on Monday evening, and you will either see me there or find a note from me."

Jacob was overjoyed at the species of promise thus held out to him; and, as it was now midnight, Rainford intimated his intention of taking his departure from the public-house where he had passed the evening with the poor lad.

When they had issued from the door, the highwayman bade Jacob "Good night;" and they separated—pursuing different roads.

In fact, Jacob went towards Leather Lane, while Tom Rainford repaired in the direction of the lodgings which he at present occupied in Gray's Inn Lane—he having removed to that locality from his former abode in Lock's Fields.

19. The discipline of criminal prisons was particularly lax at the time of which Jacob Smith is supposed to be speaking.

20. This dreadful state of things continued in the New Prison, Clerkenwell, up to the year 1838.

21. The Report of the Prison Inspectors of the Home District contains these observations upon the state of Newgate:—"The association of prisoners of all ages, and every shade of guilt, in one indiscriminate mass, is a frightful feature in the system which prevails here; the first in magnitude, and the most pernicious in effect. In this prison we find that the young and the old—the inexperienced and the practical offender—the criminal who is smitten with a conviction of his guilt, and the hardened villain whom scarcely any penal discipline can subdue, are congregated together, with an utter disregard to all moral distinctions, the interest of the prisoners, or the welfare of the community. In such a state of things, can it be a matter of wonder that the effects should be such as have been described? Every other evil is aggravated by this; and it would be worse than idle to attempt a remedy for the rest, while this demoralising intermixture of criminals of all ages and degrees of guilt is suffered to frustrate the very ends of Prison discipline, and to give tenfold violence to all their mischievous inclinations, and passions, upon which it is incessantly operating, and which is the design of justice to discourage and repress. Apart from higher considerations, sound policy demands that such a system should be instantly rectified, for so long as it continues, society is nursing a moral pestilence in its bosom, and maintaining an institution in which are forged those weapons that are destined to be wielded with fatal dexterity against the community itself. Every device by which the fences of property may be overcome is here framed, and divulged to ready agents. Every fraudulent artifice, every successful trick, every ingenious mode of over-reaching the cautious, or of

plundering the unguarded, is perfected here, and communicated to those who had not hitherto been initiated in the mysteries of crime.

"But the most distressing circumstance connected with this system, is the cruel indifference with which it regards the condition and necessities of those on whom the extreme penalty of the law is doomed to fall. Prisoners actually awaiting the execution of the awful sentence of death are placed, by the evil influence of companionship, in the most unfavourable circumstances for self-reflection. Religion and humanity combine to point out the imperative necessity of providing men, brought by the sentence of the law to the verge of eternity, with the means of spiritual improvement and consolation; but the system of Prison Discipline in Newgate practically defeats every such merciful design. No human authority has a right thus to trifle with the eternal interests of a dying criminal. Against this serious evil the chaplain has repeatedly and loudly protested; and it is in evidence that the unhappy victims themselves have earnestly implored the officers to deliver them from a situation in which it was impossible for them to devote the few remaining hours that the law allowed them to reflection and prayer. The companions in guilt of these wretched men become further hardened by the influence of this association. The indulgence of thoughtless apathy, unfeeling mirth, or revolting ribaldry, are productive of incalculable mischief to the minds of those who are subjected to their influence. The prisoner who witnesses with levity or indifference the last moments of a culprit in Newgate, comes forth a greater villain than when he went in. In him the evil principle has done its work, and the very exhibition of terror which justice designed for the reclaiming of the survivors, by a perversion of moral influence, irremediably hardens the heart which it was intended to soften and amend. If human ingenuity were tasked to devise means by which the most profligate of men might be rendered abandoned to the last degree of moral infamy, nothing more effectual could be invented than the system now actually in operation within the walls of the first metropolitan prison in England!"

22. Fact.

CHAPTER XLI.
FRESH ALARMS.

Rainford was within twenty yards of the house in which he dwelt, when a woman jostled him somewhat violently as she endeavoured to pass him while pursuing the same direction.

There was no excuse for this rudeness on her part, inasmuch as the pavement was wide in that particular spot, and no other person was on the footway.

"I beg your pardon, sir," said the female; "I'm sure——But, bless me!" she cried, in a shrill, unmistakeable voice,—"if it isn't Mr. Rainford!"

"Ah! Mrs. Bunce," returned the highwayman; "what are you doing in this neighbourhood so late?"

"I'm going to pass the night with a relation of mine that's ill, and which lives at the top of the Lane," answered Mrs. Bunce. "But, Oh! Mr. Rainford, what a shocking thing this is about poor dear Mr. Bones!"

"What?" ejaculated Tom, with a kind of guilty start.

"Why, sir—he's dead, poor man!" sobbed Mrs. Bunce: "dead and buried, sir!"

"Dead—and buried!" repeated the highwayman mechanically. "And how came you to know this?"

"His friend Mr. Tidmarsh came and told me and Toby about it this blessed morning; and in the afternoon we all followed the poor old gentleman to the grave in Clerkenwell churchyard."

"His death was sudden, then?" said Tom, anxious to glean how far the woman might be informed relative to the particulars of the event which she was deploring.

"Mr. Tidmarsh isn't given to gossiping, sir," replied Mrs. Bunce; "and he said very little about it. It was quite enough for us to know that the poor dear old gentleman is gone—and without having made any Will either: so me and Toby are thrown as you may say on the wide world, without a friend to help us."

"But Mr. Bones was rich—very rich—was he not?" demanded Tom, who felt particularly uncomfortable at this confirmation of his worst fears—for he to some extent looked upon himself as the cause of the old fence's sudden death.

"Rich, God bless ye! Ah! as rich as a King!" exclaimed Mrs. Bunce. "But no one knows where he kept his money—unless it is that Tidmarsh."

"And where did he die?" asked Rainford.

"At Tidmarsh's own place in Turnmill Street, Clerkenwell," was the answer. "Poor old man! But you must have seen him only a short time before he went off, Mr. Rainford," she added, as if recollecting the fact: "for it was on that very night when he took Toby and Jacob over with him to a house in Lock's Fields, and which turned out to be where you lived. You know he stayed with you while Jacob and Toby went away. Poor old man! he's a great loss—a very great loss!"

"Were you so dependent on him, then?" asked Rainford.

"Yes, almost entirely, as I may say," was the reply. "And then there's poor Jacob, too: what in the world he'll do, I'm sure I can't say—for me and Toby can't afford to keep him now that our best friend's gone. But good night, Mr. Rainford: I must go on to my cousin's—for it's very late, and *she*, may be, will pop off the hooks before I get to her."

"Good night," returned Tom, slackening his pace so as to allow the woman to proceed as far a-head of him as possible ere he entered his own dwelling, which was now close at hand.

In a few moments the form of Mrs. Bunce was lost in the darkness of the night.

Rainford was now convinced that Old Death was indeed no more—that no prompt assistance had resuscitated him, even if the vital spark were not extinct at the moment when he saw him for the last time, bound to the chair, at the house in Red Lion Street. Yes—it was clear enough—too clear: Benjamin Bones was dead—and Tidmarsh had pounced upon all his property.

"Well—let him enjoy it," thought Rainford within himself. "I have enough for my purposes, and do not wish to dispute the inheritance with him—even if I had the right or the power. And yet—and yet," he mused, with a feeling like a contraction of the heart, "I would give ten years of my own life so that I had not been the instrument of abridging his! But it's too late to repent or regret. Repent, did I say? I have nothing to repent of. I did not do this deed wilfully: it was not murder. And as for any share that I had in the matter at all, *that* does not seem to be suspected. Oh! I can understand Master Tidmarsh's proceedings! It was no doubt he who entered the room just at the moment when I discovered that Old Death was dead. Of course he would say nothing about finding him tied in a chair, or of me having been with him that night: a word on these heads would have excited suspicions— led to inquiries—Coroner's inquest—and all that sort of thing. Then some relation might have turned up, claimed the property, and cut Tidmarsh out. Yes—yes; it is plain enough—and Tidmarsh is a prudent as well as a lucky fellow! But what *could* the laboratory in that house mean? what were those pickled human heads kept in the cupboard for? and why was Dr. Lascelles familiar with that den?"

Even in the midst of his musings, Rainford did not hazard a conjecture to account for the mysteries just enumerated. They indeed appeared unaccountable.

The highwayman walked some distance past the door of his lodgings, to convince himself that he was not watched by Mrs. Bunce; and having assured himself on that head,—at least so far as he could judge in the darkness of the night,—he turned back and entered his dwelling.

The next day was the Sabbath; and Rainford was sitting, after breakfast, reading a Sunday paper in the neat parlour of his lodgings.

On the other side of the fire sate a young—beautiful—and dark-eyed woman—in all the rich flush of Jewish beauty,—the softly sweeping outline and symmetrical undulations of her form being developed, rather than concealed, by the loose morning wrapper which she wore; while the ray of the frosty morning's sun glanced on the glossy surface of her raven hair.

Little Charley Watts, nicely dressed, and with his rosy countenance wearing the smiles of happy innocence, was seated on a footstool near Tom Rain, looking at a picture-book, but every now and then glancing affectionately towards those whom he had already learnt to love as if they were his parents.

"Do the advertisements tell you when the next ship will sail from Liverpool for New York, Tom?" inquired the lady.

"Next Friday, my love," answered Rainford. "We will therefore leave London on Thursday."

"Four more days," remarked his female companion. "Oh! how glad I shall be when we are out of sight of England! And yet," she added, with a profound sigh, "I can scarcely bear the thought of parting—perhaps for ever———"

"You must not give way to those mournful reflections," interrupted Tom, in a kind tone. "Remember that we are going to a country where my personal safety will not be endangered,—where we shall not be obliged to shift our lodgings half-a-dozen times in a fortnight,—and where, too, we need not start at every knock that comes to the door. We shall be as happy as the day is long; and, with the money which I now have at my disposal, I may embark in some honest pursuit and earn myself a good name."

"The money will be at the New York banker's before we reach America, I suppose?" said the lady, inquiringly.

"To be sure," replied Tom; "since I paid it all into the hands of the London agent two days ago. Have you taken care of the receipt, or acknowledgment?"

"I locked it up in the little iron box, together with all your other papers," was the answer.

"And those documents that I brought home with me the other night—or rather morning———"

"All safe, dear Tom. But really when you allude to that dreadful night, you make me shudder. Oh! how long—how long did those weary hours seem, until you returned! When you came up into the bed-room and told me that you were going away with that dreadful man Bones—that the time had at length come—that opportunity had at last served your purposes———"

"Well, my dear girl—I recollect all that took place," interrupted Tom, laughing. "You begged me not to go with him—you said you had your misgivings: but I was resolved—for such an occasion might not have occurred again. Did I not tell you beforehand, when we were down in the country, that if I came up to London and purposely threw myself in the way of Old Death, accident would be sure sooner or later to enable me to wrench from his grasp that gold of which he had plundered me? And have not my words come true? You must not reproach me now, dear girl, at all events—for the danger is over."

"Yes—and the dreadful man is dead!" exclaimed the Jewess, in a tone which expressed a thanksgiving so unequivocally that a cloud for a moment gathered on Rainford's brow.

"He is dead—and can molest us no more," he observed, in a serious tone. "But I could have wished———However," he added, abruptly, "let us avoid that subject: it is not altogether an agreeable one. And now, to return to our intended departure for America, I am somewhat at a loss how to act in respect to that letter, which I obtained last night from Jacob Smith, and which so deeply regards———"

He paused, and glanced significantly towards Charley.

"What can you do in the matter, Tom?" said his beautiful companion. "The letter is too ambiguous———"

"Scarcely ambiguous—but deficient in certain points of information," interrupted Rainford.

"Which is equally mortifying," added the Jewess. "You cannot risk your safety by remaining in England to investigate the affair—even if we had not gone so far in our arrangements for departure———"

"Certainly not," replied Tom: "but I was thinking that I would entrust the letter to my friend Clarence Villiers; and who knows but that some accident may sooner or later throw him into the way of sifting the mystery to the very bottom?"

"Your project is an excellent one," answered the Jewess. "But are you sure that he does not suspect——"

"Suspect what I really am!" ejaculated the highwayman, with that blithe, merry laugh of his which showed his fine white teeth to such advantage. "Not he! He does not know Sir Christopher Blunt—nor the lawyer Howard; and his acquaintance with that consummate fool Frank Curtis was always slight, and not likely to be improved by all that has occurred: for Frank *must* suspect that Clarence had something to do with the elopement of Old Torrens's daughters. So, all things considered, Clarence cannot have heard of the little affair by which Sir Christopher lost his two thousand pounds."

"Then you will entrust Mr. Villiers with the letter?" said the lady, inquiringly.

"Yes: I will call upon him this evening," responded Tom; "for I have a little hint to give him relative to a certain aunt of his——"

At this moment there was a knock at the front-door of the house; and the servant presently made her appearance to inform Rainford that a young man named Jacob Smith wished to speak to him.

Tom's brow darkened—as the thought flashed across him that the lad had dogged him on the preceding night. But instantly recovering his self-possession, he desired the Jewess and Charley to retire to another room, while he received the visitor.

When Jacob entered the parlour, Rainford looked sternly at him, but said nothing.

"I know what *is*—what *must be* passing in your mind, sir," said Jacob hastily; "but you wrong me—that is, if you think I found out your address by any underhand means of my own."

"Sit down, my boy," cried Tom frankly: "I am sorry if I suspected you even for an instant. But what has brought you here this morning? and how——"

"I will explain all in a few moments, Mr. Rainford," said Jacob. "Two hours ago—at about eight o'clock—I went up to Bunce's, just to see if they had heard any thing of Old Death; and, to my surprise, I learnt that he was buried yesterday."

"So I have already heard. But go on."

"You know I told you last night that yesterday morning two or three people called in Earl Street to inquire about Old Death, as he had promised to get a thief off at the police-court? Well—at that time, it seems, neither Mrs. Bunce or Toby knew what had become of Mr. Bones: but just afterwards, as I'm told, and when I had gone away from the house, up goes old Tidmarsh, the fence, with the news that Mr. Bones was dead, and that the funeral was going to take place in a couple of hours. Quick work, wasn't it, sir? So Toby Bunce and his wife went to the funeral; and now it's certain what has really become of Old Death. Tidmarsh told them he died suddenly three or four days ago at *his* house—of apoplexy. I'm sure he didn't look much like an apoplectic man."

"The best part of all this I learnt last night, soon after I left you," said Rainford.

"And I only heard it when I went up to Bunce's this morning," remarked Jacob. "Well, sir—when Mrs. Bunce had told me this, she said, '*Jacob, I want you to do a particular favour for me, and I will give you a sovereign.*'—I asked her what it was. '*I'm pretty sure,*' she says, '*that Mr. Rainford lives somewhere in Gray's Inn Lane, between Liquorpond Street and Calthorpe Street, on the same side of the way as those streets; and you must find out where it is, because I want particularly to know.*'—So I promised her I would; and I of course took good care not to say that I had seen you last night. But I was determined to give you notice of Mrs. Bunce's desire to have you watched; and I have been knocking at every door in the neighbourhood, asking if such a gentleman as yourself lived there. In describing you, however, I did not mention any name."

"That was right, Jacob," said Tom; "because I am not known as Rainford here. But what the devil can that old wretch want with me? Has she inherited Old Death's scheming disposition? or does his vengeance pursue me, even from the tomb?"

These last words were totally unintelligible to Jacob, who knew not that the highwayman had had any share in the death of Mr. Benjamin Bones.

"Of course, sir," remarked the lad, after a pause, "I shall go to Mrs. Bunce this evening and assure her that no such person as yourself lives in this neighbourhood. I hope you are not offended with me for hunting after you?"

"Far from it, Jacob," returned Tom: "for I am sure I can trust *you*. At the same time, you must be cautious how you act, so as not to let Mrs. Bunce imagine that you are playing *her* false. Try and find out what she wants with me, and meet me at Tullock's to-morrow evening, between seven and eight. No—not at Tullock's either—because that woman knows I am in the habit of going there: but come to me at the public-house in Baldwin's Buildings where we were last night. Remember—to-morrow evening, at about half-past seven."

"I shall not fail, sir," responded Jacob: and he then took his departure.

The moment he was gone, Rainford hastened up stairs to the bed-room, whither the Jewess and little Charley had retired; and closing the door, he said, "My dear girl, we must be off directly. That horrid woman Mrs. Bunce, of whom I have spoken to you, is after me—and I am afraid for no good."

"Off!" exclaimed the lady: "what—to Liverpool at once?"

"No: but to another lodging—or to a tavern rather—for it will be difficult to obtain apartments on a Sunday. I must stay in town for a day or two longer—or at least till I have seen Villiers. Come—pack up your things, my love—and let us be gone."

"Are you afraid of that lad who has just been?" demanded the Jewess.

"Not a whit! He is staunch to the backbone—I will swear to it! But *he* might be followed—or he might commit himself somehow or another, and betray me involuntarily. By-the-bye," ejaculated Tom, after an instant's pause, "I tell you what we will do! We will return to Lock's Fields. It is clear that Mrs. Bunce has found out that we are *not* living there now—otherwise she would not have set this Jacob to watch me, which she has done; and she would never suspect that we have gone back to our old quarters. So look alive, my love; and pack up the things, while I settle with our landlady here and send for a coach."

Tom Rain's directions were speedily obeyed; and by mid-day the Jewess, Charley, and himself were once more located in Lock's Fields.

CHAPTER XLII.
THE PARAGRAPH IN THE NEWSPAPER.

Having partaken of a good dinner and imbibed a glass or two of wine, Tom Rain returned to the perusal of the Sunday newspaper, which he had brought with him to his old lodgings; for the highwayman loved a newspaper dearly—especially the police reports and Old Bailey trials.

But as his eye glanced down a column principally devoted to "Fashionable Intelligence," he was struck with mingled horror and astonishment by the ensuing announcement:—

"It is rumoured that the young and wealthy Earl of Ellingham will shortly lead to the hymeneal altar, the beautiful and accomplished Lady Hatfield. Her ladyship is a peeress in her own right, that distinction having been conferred upon her in consequence of the eminent services of her ladyship's deceased father."

Tom Rain was absolutely stupefied by this paragraph:—so stupefied, indeed, that he sate gazing upon it in a species of vacant wonderment,—not starting, nor uttering any ejaculation—so that neither the Jewess nor Charley Watts, who were both in the room, noticed his emotion.

At length he recovered himself, and read and reread the paragraph until he could have repeated it by heart.

The shades of evening were gathering fast over this hemisphere; and he had therefore now a good excuse for going out—for that announcement in the Sunday paper had produced such an effect upon him that he felt he could not rest until he had performed a duty—an imperious but most painful duty!

Having hastily arranged his toilette in the bed-room up stairs, and put on a dark upper coat and a large woollen "comforter," he sallied forth—but not without having previously kissed both the Jewess and little Charley.

At the nearest coach-stand he entered a hack-vehicle, and ordered the driver to take him to the residence of Lady Hatfield, in Piccadilly.

But ere the coach arrived quite opposite the front door of the fair patrician's abode, Rainford alighted, and dismissed the vehicle.

Then he advanced to the house:—but it was with the step of a man who would rather—oh! a thousand times rather—have fled in any other direction.

His hand was on the knocker, and he hesitated,—yes, he hesitated; and that hand trembled.

It must have been some powerful cause that could have made the gallant—dauntless—almost hair-brained Tom Rain manifest so much emotion.

But at length the summons was given; and a livery-servant opened the door.

To Rainford's inquiry whether Lady Hatfield were at home, an affirmative answer was given.

"Say to your mistress," returned the highwayman, "that a person wishes to speak to her upon very particular business—and do me the favour to show me to a room where I can see her ladyship alone."

The servant hesitated a moment—for the excited tone in which the request was made somewhat surprised him. But remembering that it was not his business to question his lady's visitors, he conducted Rainford into a parlour where a fire was burning in the grate; and, having lighted the candles, the domestic retired to deliver to Lady Hatfield the message which he had received.

The few minutes which elapsed ere the door of that room again opened, seemed like an age to Tom Rain. He first sate down: then he rose again and stood before the fire in a state of extraordinary nervousness. In fact, he appeared perfectly unmanned.

We can conceive the feelings of appalling doubt—hope mingled with terrific fear—and agonising suspense, that must be experienced by an individual accused of a capital crime, and awaiting in the dock the return of the jury in whose hands are his life and death.

Such was the state of Tom Rain during the five mortal minutes that elapsed ere the door again opened.

At length it *did* open—and, though he had his back turned towards it, yet the rustling of silk and a light, airy tread convinced him that the lady of the house was now in that room.

He turned: the light streamed full upon his countenance—for he had laid aside his hat and woollen comforter; and Lady Hatfield—for it was she—uttered a faint scream as her eyes met his.

"Pardon this intrusion—fear me not *now*, my lady!" exclaimed Rainford hastily: "but grant me five minutes' attention, I implore you—not for *my* sake—for *yours*!"

Georgiana had started back, and had become pale as death when she recognised the highwayman: but even while he was yet speaking, she recovered herself sufficiently to approach the spot where he was standing.

Then, without sitting down—but leaning her arm upon the mantelpiece, as if for support—she said in a hoarse and hollow tone, "My God! what would you with me?"

"Lady Hatfield," returned Rainford, in a mournful and even solemn tone, "forget the *past*—if you can—for a few minutes——"

"Forget the past!" repealed Georgiana hysterically, her whole frame convulsed with horror. "Oh! terrible man, wherefore have you come hither? have you not injured me enough? what do you now seek?—*my life?*"

And, as she uttered these last words, the syllables seemed to hiss between her set teeth—and her bosom heaved and fell rapidly with spasmodic palpitation.

"Listen to me, madam—I implore you!" exclaimed Rainford, cruelly perplexed and deeply touched by the agonising emotions which his presence occasioned. "I know that the sight of me must be abhorrent—loathsome to you; but it will be your fault if our interview is protracted beyond the few minutes which I ask you to grant me."

"Speak, sir—speak quickly!" cried Georgiana hysterically. "But mark me, sir," she added in a firmer and more resolute tone, while her usually placid glances seemed to glare with deadly hatred against the highwayman,—"mark me," she repeated—"if your intention be to coerce me again to commit a crime for your sake, you will not succeed. But a few days have elapsed since the stain of perjury—rank, abhorrent perjury—was fastened on my soul—and to save *you*! Oh! that I could have been so weak as to yield to your insolent command to swear to that which was false—atrociously, vilely false, at the bar of justice! And now proceed, sir, with the business which has brought you hither!"

"Lady Hatfield—I cannot, I dare not explain myself, while you labour under this dreadful excitement!" said Rainford, himself painfully excited. "Calm yourself, I implore you—for what I have to say most nearly concerns your interests."

"*My* interests!" repeated Georgiana in a sorrowful voice. "But proceed—go on, sir:—I *will* be calm."

"I observed in a newspaper of this day's date," continued Rainford, "that your ladyship is about to become the wife of the Earl of Ellingham."

Lady Hatfield gazed upon the highwayman in that vacant manner which left it doubtful whether she were the prey to feelings of surprise—terror—or despair.

"And if that rumour be true, my lady," added Rainford, after a moment's pause, "I would have you reflect on the propriety of this matrimonial connexion."

"My God! he assumes a right to dictate to me!" almost shrieked Georgiana, as she sank back upon a sofa, clasping her hands together in the excess of her mental anguish.

"No—my lady—not to dictate!" said Rainford. "I have not a shadow of a right to do that: it were the height of madness—the height of presumption—an insolence beyond all parallel on my part—in fact a deed so monstrously inconsistent with even common sense——"

"That you are surprised I should have entertained the idea?" added Georgiana, with an irony and bitterness which seemed lent her by despair.

"My God! I foresaw all the terrors of this interview!" exclaimed Rainford with feverish impatience.

"Then wherefore did you come?" demanded Georgiana. "Is it to expose me—to persecute *me* who have never offended *you*, but who have suffered so deeply—deeply——"

"Madam, I came to perform a painful duty," interrupted the highwayman; "and the sooner I accomplish it the better. Oh! you know not—you will not give me credit for the ineffable pity—the profound commiseration which I feel for you,—as well as the loathing—the abhorrence—the shame—the disgust in which I hold myself:—but I cannot recall the past. Would to God that I could!"

"Then you mean me no harm?" exclaimed Georgiana eagerly.

"Mean you harm, madam!" repeated Rainford enthusiastically: "merciful heavens! if to mitigate one single pang of the many—many with which your breast must throb, poor innocent sufferer that you are—a sufferer through my detestable crime,—if to relieve you of any portion of the load that weighs upon your mind—were that portion no heavier than a hair,—if to do this my life would suffice, I would lay it down, madam, at your feet! Think you that I glory in what I have done? No—no: bad as I am—criminal as I am—robber, plunderer as I am, and as you know me to be,—yet I have feelings—aye, and a conscience too! And, often—often, my lady, when the smile is upon my lip, that conscience is gnawing my heart's core—for I think of *you*! And all this is true as God's own justice is true,—true as that you are an innocent and a noble lady, and that I am a despicable villain!"

And Tom Rain—the gallant, dashing, almost hair-brained Tom Rain—burst into tears.

Georgiana gazed upon him in astonishment—in profound astonishment; and she was softened towards that bold and desperate man who wept on her account!

"But wherefore have you sought me this evening?" she said, in a milder and more gentle tone than she had yet used during this remarkable—this solemnly interesting meeting.

"It is not to demand your pardon, madam," returned Rainford, dashing away the tears from his manly countenance; "because *that* you can never give! It is not to assert any presumed right to dictate to you in respect to your marriage, because *that* were adding the most flagrant cruelty to the most atrocious wrong. But it is to inform your ladyship that if you contract this marriage with the Earl of Ellingham, you wed one who is——"

"Who is what?" gasped Georgiana, almost suffocating.

Rainford paused for a few moments: it required these few moments to enable him to conquer emotions of so terrible a nature that they almost choked his powers of utterance:—then, bending down until his very lips touched Georgiana's ear, and his hair mingled with hers, he whispered a few words in a faint and scarcely audible tone.

But she heard them plainly—oh! far too plainly: and when he withdrew his face from its proximity to her head, and glanced upon her countenance, he saw, with feelings awfully shocked, that she sate mute—motionless—the image of despair.

Alas! she spoke not—she looked neither to the right nor to the left: her eyes seemed to be fixed upon the face of the highwayman;—and yet she saw him not—she was gazing on vacancy.

This dreadful state of stupefaction—the paralysis of despair—lasted for upwards of three minutes,—a perfect age alike to her who endured, and to him who beheld it.

Then suddenly burst from Lady Hatfield's lips a long—loud—piercing scream,—a scream so appalling that the very house appeared to shake with the vibration of the air which was cut by that shriek as by a keen-edged sword.

"Merciful God! the whole place will be alarmed!" ejaculated the highwayman. "Compose yourself, madam——"

But vainly did he thus address himself to the unhappy Georgiana: she had fallen back insensible upon the sofa.

The door opened abruptly; but Tom Rain was rooted to the spot where he stood gazing on the motionless form of that wretched lady,—stood gazing too in horrified amazement at the effect which his whispered words had produced.

The scream to which Lady Hatfield had given vent in the paroxysm of her ineffable anguish, had reached the ears not only of the domestics in the kitchen but also of the company in the drawing-room—for there were guests that evening at Georgiana's residence.

Thus, when the door burst open, a crowd of persons poured in,—Lord Ellingham, Dr. Lascelles, Sir Ralph Walsingham, three or four ladies, and all the servants.

Miss Mordaunt, we should observe, was no longer an inmate of Lady Hatfield's abode—for reasons that will be explained hereafter.

Lord Ellingham was the foremost of the crowd; and the first object that met his eyes, as he rushed into the room, was his Georgiana stretched senseless on the sofa. He saw a man standing near, but did not pause to cast a second glance upon him: the state in which he found his beloved engrossed all his thoughts.

He raised her in his arms—the ladies produced their smelling-bottles—the female servants hastened to fetch water, vinegar, and anything else that struck them as useful under the circumstances—and Dr. Lascelles, who *had* recognised Tom Rain, though without appearing to do so, professionally superintended all the means resorted to for the purpose of restoring suspended animation,—while the highwayman still looked on with a kind of mechanical attention.

At length Georgiana opened her eyes slowly; but the moment they caught a glimpse of Lord Ellingham's countenance, a faint cry escaped her lips—and she covered her face with her hands as if to shut out some terrible object from her view.

"Georgiana, dearest—'tis I," murmured Arthur in her ear.

But a dreadful shudder seemed to convulse her entire frame.

"Some one has terrified her—alarmed her!" exclaimed the Earl, colouring with anger; and as he glanced rapidly around, his eyes met those of the highwayman.

At that moment Dr. Lascelles desired that Lady Hatfield should be supported to her own chamber; and this suggestion was immediately followed by the female friends and servants, the physician accompanying them.

CHAPTER XLIII.
LORD ELLINGHAM AND TOM RAINFORD.

Lord Ellingham and Sir Ralph Walsingham remained behind in the apartment, where Rainford also still was.

"Sir," said the nobleman, advancing towards the highwayman, "you will perhaps be kind enough to explain the cause of her ladyship's emotion?—for the scream which reached our ears, and the condition in which we found her, denote something more serious than sudden indisposition. This gentleman, sir," added the Earl, indicating Sir Ralph Walsingham with a glance, "is Lady Hatfield's uncle: you therefore need not hesitate to address yourself to *him*—even should you decline to vouchsafe an explanation to me, who am a total stranger to you."

"Yes, my lord—for I know you well by sight—we *are* total strangers to each other," replied Rainford in a singularly mournful tone. "And yet——"

But he stopped short, seized his hat, and was about to hasten from the room, when the Earl caught him somewhat rudely by the arm, saying,—"Mr. Rainford—for such I believe to be your name—we cannot part with you thus! A lady—dear, very dear to me, and who indeed will shortly be my wife,—dear also to Sir Ralph Walsingham, who is now present,—that lady has been alarmed—terrified in some manner, by you; and we must insist upon an explanation."

"My lord," returned Tom Rain in a tone of deep emotion, as he gazed with peculiar—almost scrutinising attention upon the Earl's countenance,—"no other man on earth would thus have dared to stop me with impunity. As for explanations," he continued, his voice suddenly assuming a little of its usual reckless indifference, "I have none to give."

And again he moved towards the door.

But Lord Ellingham hastened to place his back against it in a determined manner: while Rainford, as if discouraged and daunted, fell back a few paces.

"Mr. Rainford," exclaimed the Earl, "this matter cannot pass off thus. I insist upon an explanation; or I shall consider it to be my duty to detain you until Lady Hatfield be sufficiently recovered to declare the nature of the treatment she has experienced at your hands. Moreover, sir," added the nobleman, observing that Rainford's lip blanched and quivered nervously, "you are to a certain degree an object of suspicion in my eyes. A variety of circumstances have combined to prove to me that you were implicated, to some degree, in the theft of diamonds which lately caused so much embarrassment at the police-court."

"My lord, that business does not regard you," replied the highwayman. "The diamonds were restored to their lawful owner; and—more than *that*—I even ascertained from Mr. Gordon's own lips that they were paid for, before their restoration, by one who——But let me depart, my lord, I say!" ejaculated Tom, his manner suddenly changing from nervous trepidation to the excitement of impatience.

"You must remain here, sir," said Arthur coldly, "until we ascertain whether it be Lady Hatfield's pleasure that your detention should assume a more serious aspect."

"Allow me to pass, my dear Earl," exclaimed Sir Ralph; "and I will hasten to ascertain how my niece is now, and what her intentions are with respect to this person."

Rainford paced the room in an agitated manner, while Lord Ellingham afforded egress to the baronet, and then resumed his position of sentinel with his back placed against the door.

"My lord," at length said the highwayman, advancing close up to the Earl, and speaking in a low, oppressed tone, "you will find that her ladyship has no complaint to make against me. Permit me to take my departure; and again I tell you that of no other living soul would I solicit as a favour what I would command by force."

"I cannot allow you to leave this room—at least until the return of Sir Ralph Walsingham," answered the Earl. "Lady Hatfield must have been insulted or menaced by you in some way——"

"I take God to witness that I neither insulted nor menaced her!" interrupted Rainford, warmly.

"If your liberty be endangered," said the nobleman, "it is well worth a falsehood to attempt to avert the peril."

"My God! this from *him*!" muttered Rainford bitterly to himself, as he once more turned round to pace the room: then, at the expiration of a minute, he said in a calmer tone, "Well, my lord—I am content to wait until the decision of her ladyship is made known in respect to me. And since it appears that we shall have a few moments more of each other's society, permit me to ask,— your lordship having just now alluded to a certain transaction at a police-court,—permit me to ask, I say, whether you really believe that Miss Esther de Medina was innocent or guilty of the charge imputed to her?"

"This is rather a singular question—coming from *you*, Mr. Rainford!" exclaimed the Earl; "and before I answer it, allow me to ask whether it was not you who left a certain letter at my house, desiring me to repair to the police-office on that occasion?"

"I will not deny the fact, my lord," replied Rainford. "Indeed, I did not particularly study concealment respecting it—else would I not have afforded your lordship's servants an opportunity of describing to you the personal appearance of the individual who left that letter. But if your lordship entertains even the shadow of a suspicion injurious to the character of Miss de Medina, you are wrong—you are in error!—yes—as grievously in error as ever mistaken man could be. Besides, my lord," added Rainford hastily, "you are well aware that the *alibi* which your lordship proved was correct."

"And how knew you that Miss de Medina was with her father and myself at Finchley on the very day, and at the very hour, when the diamonds were alleged to have been taken?" demanded the Earl.

"It would be useless to pretend that accident gave me the information," answered Tom Rain. "But think not that *she* employed *me* as an agent or as a messenger to obtain the intervention of your lordship——"

"Mr. Rainford," said the Earl haughtily, "I dislike the present conversation. I have the highest opinion of Mr. de Medina, and should be sorry to think ill of any one connected with him. But I must candidly confess that there is so much mystery respecting the character of his daughter—a mystery, too, existing on account of yourself, for which reason alone do I condescend to discuss with *you* any affair relating to Mr. de Medina or his family——"

"Lord Ellingham," interrupted Rainford in a hasty and impetuous tone, "Esther de Medina is the very personification of innocence and virtue! As God is my judge, she was ignorant of my interference in her behalf on that day when she was accused of a deed from which her pure soul would recoil with horror:—she knew not even that I was in the court——"

"And yet you were there, Mr. Rainford," exclaimed the Earl: "for I noticed you—although at the time I knew not who you were."

"But Miss de Medina was *not* aware of my presence," rejoined Rainford emphatically; "*for she does not know me by sight*!"

A smile of incredulity curled the nobleman's lip—for the oath which Mr. de Medina had administered to his daughter, and in which her connexion with Rainford was so emphatically mentioned, was uppermost in his mind. But he dared not allude to that circumstance; although he would have been truly rejoiced to receive the conviction that Esther was indeed far different from what he was at present compelled to believe her to be.

"Your lordship said ere now," resumed Tom Rain, "that you noticed me in the court, although at the time you knew not who I was. Those were your words. Does your lordship now know who I am?"

"I cannot boast of a very intimate acquaintance with you or your affairs, Mr. Rainford," returned the nobleman with a hauteur bordering on contempt; "and what I do know of you is so little in your favour that you see I am detaining you here on the suspicion that your visit to Lady Hatfield was for no good purpose. In fact, the first I ever heard of you was in reference to the charge on account of which you yourself figured at Bow Street some short time since,—a charge of which, I am bound to say, you were honourably acquitted, Lady Hatfield having satisfactorily proved that you were not the person who robbed her on the highway."

"Thus far, my lord," said Rainford, "you have no just ground to speak disparagingly of my character."

"Certainly not. But then comes the affair of the diamonds; and I do not hesitate to inform you that Mr. Gordon related to me all the particulars of your interview with him, when you called to restore the jewels, and when he made you aware of the fact that Miss de Medina had already been to pay him the full value thereof."

"Ah! Mr. Gordon was thus communicative?" observed Rainford.

"Yes—and not sparing of his aspersions against the character of Miss de Medina," returned the Earl. "But I defended her, Mr. Rainford—I defended her *then*———"

"And wherefore should you not defend her now, my lord?" demanded the highwayman. "Oh! were I to reveal to you by what wondrous combination of circumstances———But, no! I dare not. And yet, my lord," he added in an earnest, solemn tone, "you are an upright—a generous-hearted man; and I appeal to your good feelings—I implore you not to trust to outward appearances. As there is a God above, Esther de Medina is innocent of every thing—any thing that scandal or misconception may have imputed to her. Again you smile incredulously—and yet mournfully, my lord! Ah! I can assure you, that Esther is innocent—oh! believe her to be innocent!"

At this moment footsteps were heard approaching the door, which Lord Ellingham accordingly opened; and Sir Ralph Walsingham re-appeared.

"How is Georgiana now?" inquired the nobleman hastily.

"My niece is ill—very ill," returned the baronet.

"Ill!" ejaculated Arthur. "Ah! villain—this is your work!" he cried, rushing towards the highwayman.

"Keep off!" thundered Rainford: "you know not whom you would strike!"

"No—touch him not!" cried Sir Ralph, catching the Earl by the arm, and holding him back. "I have seen my niece—Dr. Lascelles is now alone with her: she is more composed—though very far from well;—and she begs that this person may be allowed to depart without the slightest molestation."

"Her ladyship shall be obeyed, Sir Ralph," returned the nobleman. "Mr. Rainford, you have heard the message that has been sent relative to yourself."

Having thus spoken, Arthur turned aside;—for a strange misgiving—a vague suspicion—no, not a suspicion either,—but a feeling of dissatisfaction had stolen into his mind. If Rainford had alarmed or insulted Lady Hatfield, wherefore should she allow him to go unpunished? Was it not more probable that he had brought her some evil tidings? But how could there exist any connexion, however remote or slight, between that man of equivocal character and Georgiana Hatfield? What business could possibly bring them together, and produce so strange—so powerful an impression upon *her*?

All these ideas rushed to the Earl's mind in rapid and bewildering succession; and the reader need not be astonished if we repeat that a sentiment of dissatisfaction—almost amounting to a vague suspicion, but of what he knew not—had suddenly taken a firm hold of his imagination.

Who was this Rainford, after all? Was he other than he seemed? Could he be in any way connected with that narrative of the Black Mask which the Earl supposed to have partially affected his Georgiana's mind, and which he looked upon as the cause of that apparent fickleness or caprice which had first led her to refuse his proffered hand? The more he involved himself in conjecture, the deeper did he plunge into a labyrinth which grew darker and more bewildering at every step.

When he turned round again towards the place where he had left Rainford standing, that individual was gone; and the noblemen was alone with Sir Ralph Walsingham.

"You have seen Georgiana?" said Arthur, advancing towards the baronet and grasping his hand with the convulsive violence of deep emotion.

"I have, my dear Earl; and she appears as if she had received some severe shock," was the reply.

"What, in the name of God! does all this mean?" exclaimed the nobleman, with wildness in his tone.

"I know not—I cannot comprehend it," answered the uncle, as much bewildered as the lover.

"But did you not question your niece? did she offer no explanation? did she not state the cause of her emotion—that piercing scream—that fainting—that movement of horror when she recovered?" demanded the Earl, impatiently.

"I questioned her; but, perceiving that it only augmented her agitation, I did not press a painful interrogatory," replied Sir Ralph. "When I informed her that you had detained that man, whom I heard you address by the name of Rainford, and whom I therefore supposed to have been the person suspected of robbing my niece,—when I informed her that you had detained him, I say, she was greatly excited, and desired me to hasten and request you to allow him to depart immediately, as she had no cause of complaint against him."

"Strange!—most strange!" murmured the Earl.

"Have patience, my dear Arthur," said Sir Ralph. "To-morrow Georgiana will be better; and then she will doubtless explain——"

"To-morrow—to-morrow!" repeated the nobleman impatiently. "Oh! what suspense—what terrible suspense! Ah! Sir Ralph, you know not how wretchedly will pass the weary hours of this night! If I could but see her—only for a moment! Would it be indiscreet? Dear Sir Ralph, have pity upon me, and ask Lascelles to come and speak to me."

The baronet, who was a kind-hearted man, instantly departed to execute this commission; and in a few minutes he returned, accompanied by the physician.

To the latter the Earl repeated the same question which he had already addressed to Sir Ralph Walsingham:—"What, in the name of God! does all this mean?"

And the Doctor gave almost a similar reply:—"I know not—I cannot understand it."

But there was less sincerity in this answer as given by Lascelles than there was in the same response as uttered from the heart by the frank and honest baronet:—for the physician *had* his suspicions relative to the mysterious connexion which now appeared to subsist between Lady Hatfield and the individual whose visit had caused so much painful excitement.

"That villain Rainford! I am sorry even now that I suffered him to escape!" ejaculated the Earl, scarcely knowing how to act or speak.

"Rainford!" cried the physician. "Why, that is the name of the man who was taken up on suspicion of having robbed her ladyship near Hounslow!"

"And that was Thomas Rainford who was here ere now!" returned Arthur, with bitter emphasis, as if he hated the name.

"Rainford!" repeated the physician, in astonishment. "I thought that man's name was Jameson?"

The reader will remember that such was the denomination under which the highwayman passed when residing in South Moulton Street.

"What! do you know him?" demanded the Earl, gazing upon the doctor with unfeigned surprise.

"I once attended a patient at his abode," was the laconic reply: for Lascelles remembered the solemn promise which he had made to Tom Rain on that occasion.

"And where did he live?" inquired Arthur, eagerly. "I may wish to see that man again."

"Where he lived then, he does not live now," returned the physician; "for he moved away the very next day after I was called in; and whither he went to, the people of the house knew not."

"I believe him to be a man of bad character," observed Arthur hastily. "But enough of him—at least for the present. Doctor, can I be permitted to see Lady Hatfield for a few minutes?"

"Impossible for to-night, my dear Earl," replied the physician. "Her ladyship is in a state of nervous agitation—feverish excitement, indeed,—and must not be disturbed. Her maids are now with her, and she is about to retire to rest. To-morrow, my dear Ellingham, you shall see her—that is, provided she is more composed."

"Then must I submit to this weary night of suspense!" exclaimed the young nobleman. "But to-morrow, Doctor, I may see her. You have promised that I shall see her to-morrow! My visit will be somewhat early. Will it be indiscreet if I call at eleven?"

"Call at eleven, then," returned the physician, smiling at his friend's impatience. "But I think I ought to administer a composing draught to you."

The Earl and Sir Ralph Walsingham shook hands with Dr. Lascelles, and took their departure. The other guests had already gone; but the physician remained behind to see his fair patient once more ere he returned home.

When Lascelles found himself alone in the apartment which the young nobleman and the baronet had just left, he fell into a train of reflection which, like the Earl's state of mind, was strangely characterised by perplexity. Were the Doctor's thoughts put into words, they would assume as nearly as possible the ensuing shape:—

"Well, this is an evening of unpleasant adventure! That Jameson, or Rainford, or whatever his name is, has brought confusion and dismay into the house. Perplexities increase rapidly. I remember all that Ellingham said to me the day that he called to inform me that he was the happiest of men, and that her ladyship had accepted him. He declared then that he knew all—that he would never allow what must be considered a misfortune to stand in the way of his happiness—and so on. I also remember complimenting him on his moral courage in rising superior to a common prejudice; and then we dropped the conversation because we agreed that it was a delicate subject. And so it was, too: a devilish delicate subject! And I had found out the grand secret by stealth! Ah! the effects of that opiate were powerful, and she has never suspected that I *did* find out the secret. But Ellingham scarcely seems to have his wits about him; or else he *must* suspect the object of this Rainford's visit. It's as clear as day-light! Rainford is the man—and now he wants to extort money from her ladyship. But Ellingham cannot put two and two together as I can:"—and the physician rubbed his hands complacently, little suspecting that his sapient conjecture relative to the object of the highwayman's visit was totally wrong, as the reader is aware.—"This Rainford is an extraordinary character; and I do believe that he really robbed her ladyship, but that she did not dare say so in the police-court. He has the cut of a dashing fellow who would as soon rifle a pocket as drink a bumper of wine. Curse him, for having intruded on the mysteries of my laboratory! Oh! if Ellingham only knew what I know about the beautiful Esther de Medina—the charming Jewess! What deceivers some women are! To look on Esther, one would think she was purity itself? And yet——"

The physician's reverie was interrupted by the entrance of a female servant, who came to inform him that Lady Hatfield had retired to her bed, and that the Doctor might now visit her again. He accordingly repaired to her chamber, and having prescribed some composing medicine, took his departure, without once alluding to the incidents of the evening; for he was anxious that Georgiana's mind should remain as free from causes of excitement and agitation as possible.

CHAPTER XLIV.
MR. FRANK CURTIS AGAIN.

In the meantime, Thomas Rainford had quitted the abode of Lady Hatfield with a heavy heart: for the duty which he had felt himself called upon to perform, in making a particular statement to Georgiana, had pained—acutely pained his generous soul.

He had not proceeded many yards from that lady's dwelling, when he suddenly encountered Mr. Frank Curtis; and as at that precise moment the glare of a lamp streamed full upon Rainford's countenance, he was immediately recognised by that impertinent young gentleman.

"Ah! Captain Sparks!" ejaculated Frank: "so we meet again, do we? Well, it's very fortunate that I did *not* accept my friend the Duke's invitation to his select dinner-party; or else I should have missed this pleasure. Now what is to prevent me from collaring you, my fine fellow, and raising a hue and cry?"

"*Fear*, Mr. Curtis—*fear* will prevent you," returned Tom Rain, recovering all his wonted presence of mind: and, taking the young man's arm, he said, "Walk a little way with me. I want to have a few minutes' chat with you. Here—put your hand on my great coat pocket: that's right! Now you can feel a pistol inside—eh? Well its companion is in the other pocket; and you must know enough of me already, to be fully aware that any treachery on your part would meet with its reward; for I would shoot you in the open street, if you attempted to place my liberty in danger."

"I'm sure I—I don't want to injure you, Captain Sparks," stammered Frank, trembling from head to foot as he walked along, arm-in-arm with the highwayman. "I always took you for a capital fellow—and I should very much like to drink a bottle of wine with you. What do you say? Shall we go into the *Gloucester*, or *Hatchett's*——"

"Neither one nor the other, Mr. Curtis," interrupted Rainford. "I thank you for your civility all the same."

"Oh! it's nothing, Captain. I learnt politeness in France, where, to be sure, I had excellent—I may say peculiar advantages. The King was very much attached to me—and as for the ladies of the Court—Oh! don't ask me to speak about them, Captain Sparks!"

"Indeed I will not," returned Tom drily. "I want you to let me know how your uncle gets on. Does he still remember that pleasant little adventure—ha! ha!"—and the highwayman's merry laugh denoted that his spirits were reviving once more.

"Sir Christopher! Oh! the old fool—don't talk to me about him!" ejaculated Frank Curtis. "I have done with my uncle—I shall cut him—I can never speak to him again, Captain Sparks. He has disgraced himself—disgraced his family, which was a very ancient one———"

"I always thought Sir Christopher made a boast of having risen from nothing?" said Tom ironically.

"Ah! so he did. But that was only a part of his system of gammoning people," continued Frank. "His family was originally the celebrated Blondevilles of France: about three thousand years ago they settled in Scotland, and their name was corrupted to *Blundevil*;—then a branch came to England about fifteen hundred years ago, and in process of time they spelt their name with a *t*—*Bluntevil*. At last the *e* was left out, and it became *Bluntvil*; and God only knows why, but three hundred and seventy-seven years ago, come next Michaelmas, the *vil* was dropped, and the name settled down into simple *Blunt*. So you see, Captain, that Sir Christopher is of a good family after all."

"Why don't you try and get a situation in the Herald's College?" demanded Rainford. "You would be able to find pedigrees for all the Browns, Jones's, Thompsons, and Smiths in the country."

"Come—come, Captain Sparks," exclaimed Frank: "this observation isn't fair on your part. I may have my faults—I know I have; but I don't shoot with the long bow. I hate that kind of thing!"

"But let us return to the subject of your uncle Sir Christopher," said Tom. "What has he been doing?"

"Run away with a lady's-maid—gone to Gretna with Lady Hatfield's female servant Charlotte!" cried Frank, with great bitterness of tone. "The damned old fool!—but I'll cut him—cut him dead—and that's some consolation."

"Gone to Gretna with Lady Hatfield's maid!" exclaimed Rainford.

"Maid, indeed! I hope he'll find her so!" said Curtis. "The hussey! But I'll be even with her yet!"

"And when did this happen?" inquired Tom.

"Oh! only a few days ago. They are not come back yet. I dare say Sir Christopher already repents his bargain. But I'll cut him!"

"I'm afraid if you cut his acquaintance, he'll cut off your supplies," observed Rainford jocosely.

"And what does that matter?" ejaculated Frank. "Do you think there are no rich women in London that would be glad to have a decent-looking fellow like myself. Egad! I've already got introduced to a widow as wealthy as if her late husband had been a Nabob. It's true that she's blest with five pledges of the said late husband's affection; but then she's got five thousand a-year—and one five is a good set-off against the other, Captain Sparks. Rather so—eh? old fellow?"

"Well, I think it is," returned the highwayman. "But how did all this happen about Sir Christopher and the lady's-maid?"

"I'll tell you," answered Curtis. "You see, Sir Christopher was going to run away with Miss Mordaunt, Lady Hatfield's friend, and I found it out in one of my clever ways. So I resolved to baulk Sir Christopher; and I bribed this lady's-maid Charlotte—in fact, I gave her five hundred pounds and a gold watch, the hussey!—to go to the appointment, get into the carriage, personate Miss Julia Mordaunt, and keep up the farce until they got to St. Alban's, where me and a parcel of my friends were to be at the inn to receive them. That was to be the joke."

"And how did the joke turn so completely against yourself?" asked Tom.

"Why, me and my friends waited—and waited—and waited at the infernal hotel at St. Alban's; and no Sir Christopher—no Charlotte came. We had a glorious supper, and made a regular night of it. All next day we waited—and waited again; but no Sir Christopher—no Charlotte. '*What the devil can this mean?*' thought I to myself. So I came up to London, leaving my friends at the inn at St. Alban's in pawn for the bill—for somehow or another none of us had money enough about us to settle it. Well, when I came back to town, I went home: that is, you know, to my uncle's house in Jermyn Street; and there I found a letter that had just come for me by the post. It was written from some town a good way north, and was from Sir Christopher. I began to think something was wrong; and sure enough there was! For, when I opened the letter, I found that my silly old uncle had written to thank me for throwing in his way a delightful and most amiable woman, who had consented to take his name and share his fortune. The letter went on to say that they were then pretty far on their road to Gretna, and that as they should stop at St. Alban's *as they came back*, I might be there, if I chose, to have the pleasure of handing my *aunt* out of the carriage. That was all said to irritate me, you know, Captain Sparks; and most likely that vixen Charlotte made Sir Christopher write the letter just to annoy me. But I'll cut them both dead; and we shall see what my precious *aunt*—for such she is by this time, I suppose—will say *then!*"

"This is really a very pleasant little adventure," cried Tom Rain. "But I think you carried your joke too far, Mr. Curtis; and so it has recoiled on yourself. Have you seen Mr. Torrens lately?"

"Not I!" exclaimed Curtis. "But don't you confess, Captain, that you carried matters a trifle too far that night? Never mind the two thousand pounds: I'm glad my old hunks of an uncle has lost *that*! But I allude to the affair of helping the gals to run away. I suppose you were in league with Villiers all the time?"

"What makes you think that Villiers had any thing to do with the matter?" inquired Rainford.

"Simply because I don't imagine you carried off the gals for your own sake. However," continued Frank, "I care but little about the matter now. I certainly liked Adelais very much at the time; but there are plenty of others in the world quite as handsome. Besides, I now see through all Sir Christopher's trickery in wanting me to marry Miss Torrens in such a deuce of a hurry, and in giving me a separate establishment. The old bird wanted to commit matrimony himself; and I should have been poked off with a few paltry hundreds a-year."

"And so you will now," said Tom. "Or matters may be even worse, after the trick you endeavoured to play upon your uncle."

"Not a bit of it!" cried Frank. "Had old Blunt's scheme succeeded, I should have been married to a portionless gal, and forced to live on whatever he chose to give me. Now that his project has failed, I am free and unshackled, and can secure myself a position by marriage. I might even look as high as my friend the Duke's niece; but she is horribly ill-tempered, and so I think of making an offer of my heart and hand—I *can* do the thing well if I like, you know, Captain—to Mrs. Goldberry, the widow I spoke of just now."

"The name sounds well, I confess," observed Tom. "But did your uncle never—I mean, did he not instruct his lawyer to adopt any proceedings about that little affair of the two thousand pounds?"

"Not he, Captain!" exclaimed Frank Curtis. "As far as my uncle is concerned, you may rest quite satisfied that he will never take any notice of the business: and Howard wouldn't act without his instructions."

They had now reached Charing Cross; and Tom Rain, having had quite enough of Mr. Curtis's company, signified his desire that they should separate.

"You won't pass an hour with me over a bottle of wine?" said the young man. "I really should like to have a chat with such a gallant, dashing fellow as you are, Captain; for you're quite after my own heart—barring the——"

"The highway business—eh?" cried Tom, laughing. "Why, you cannot for a minute suppose that it is my regular profession, Mr. Curtis? No such a thing! I merely eased you of the two thousand pounds for the joke of it—just as you played off your tricks on Sir Christopher."

"You talk about easing me, Captain," returned Frank; "but I can assure you that you're the first man that ever got the better of me. Don't fancy for a moment that I—I'm a coward, Captain Sparks———"

"Far from it, my dear sir," exclaimed Tom. "I know you to be as brave as you are straight-forward in your conversation. So good night—and pray take care not to follow me; for I've an awkward habit of turning round and knocking on the head any one that I imagine to be watching me."

With these words the highwayman hurried off up the Strand: and Frank Curtis entered a cigar shop, muttering to himself, "Damn the fellow! I almost think he meant that for insolence. Egad! if he *did*, the next time I meet him———"

But the valiant young gentleman did not precisely make up his mind what he should do, in the case supposed: and any resentment which he experienced, speedily evaporated with the soothing influence of a cheroot.

Meantime Tom Rain pursued his way along the Strand and Fleet Street, and repaired to the lodgings of Mr. Clarence Villiers in Bridge Street.

That gentleman was at home, and received his visitor in a very friendly manner.

"You are most welcome, Captain Sparks," he said; "and the more so if you intend to pass an hour or two with me; for my aunt is so very particular that she *would* take the girls to church with her this evening; but of course I did not offer to accompany them, as I could not wear a veil over my face, you know," he added, laughing; "and were I recognised by Mr. Torrens or any of his friends, attention would be immediately directed to any ladies who might happen to be in my company. So I shall not visit Old Burlington Street this evening; and if you will bear me company over a bottle of wine———"

"I cannot possibly remain many minutes," interrupted Rainford. "In fact I am going to leave England very shortly———"

"Leave England!" ejaculated Clarence. "I am truly sorry to hear that announcement—just as we begin to get friendly together."

"Circumstances compel me to take this step," answered Rainford; "and my time for preparation is short. I have called to-night upon business—for, in a word, you can do me a service, perhaps, if you will."

"As if there were any doubt relative to my inclination, provided I have the power," exclaimed Clarence, who was busily employed in decanting a bottle of port-wine: then, having placed upon the table two glasses, which he filled, he said, "You know, Captain Sparks, that I am under the greatest obligation to you. Through your kind—your generous intervention, Adelais will be mine. The banns were published at St. George's, Hanover Square, a second time to-day; and to-morrow week we shall be united. The bridal breakfast will take place at my aunt's: shall we not have the pleasure of your company? Pray, do not refuse me."

"It is impossible—much as I should rejoice at being the witness of that union which no severe or mercenary father will be able to subvert," said Rainford in a feeling tone. "My affairs compel me to leave this country—at least for a time; and for that reason I am anxious to place in your hands a certain document, the mystery of which some accident might probably lead you to clear up."

Rainford then produced the letter which had been found about the person of the deceased Sarah Watts, and which he now requested Villiers to peruse.

"You observe that there is no address to indicate the name of the lady to whom that letter was written," continued the highwayman, when Clarence had read it with attention. "The child to whom it refers is now in my care: accident threw him in my way—and his adopted mother, who was the writer of that letter, is no more."

"Will the child accompany you?" asked Villiers.

"He will. But I will write to you the moment I reach America—to which country I am going—and let you know my address, or at all events through what channel a letter will come direct to me. Then, should you have made any discovery—which is however scarcely to be expected—still, as a wise precaution, I have adopted this step——"

"You are right, Captain," said Villiers; "and I shall not forget the trust you have now confided to me. Should anything transpire respecting this matter, I will not fail to communicate with you. But will you not pass one evening with me in the society of my aunt and the two young ladies, who will all be delighted to receive you? Mrs. Slingsby is a most amiable and excellent woman——"

"A little of a saint—is she not?" exclaimed the highwayman drily.

"She is certainly of a religious turn of mind—indeed, I may say, enthusiastically so," answered Villiers. "But she is extremely charitable—and her benevolence embraces a very wide circle."

"I believe she is a handsome woman, too!" observed Tom Rain.

"She is possessed of personal as well as mental attractions, Captain Sparks," responded Villiers seriously. "But, when in her society, you would think of her only as the pious—benevolent—and compassionate woman, whose heart is ever ready to sympathise with the woes of her fellow creatures."

"To speak candidly, Mr. Villiers," said Rainford, "I am no friend to the *saints*. It may be a prejudice on my part—but I can't help it. Excuse me for my frankness—I beg of you to take it in good part: still I always think that the stillest water runs deepest; and I would not——"

"Remember, Captain Sparks," interrupted Villiers, somewhat warmly, "that you are speaking of my aunt, who is a most worthy and estimable woman. Deeply as I am indebted to you—much as I am inclined to esteem you—yet——"

"I understand you, my dear Mr. Villiers," cried Tom: "you cannot permit me to breathe even a suspicion against Mrs. Slingsby in your presence. Well—I know that it is most ungracious on my part: still, as I was more or less instrumental in inducing those too artless, confiding young ladies to quit their father's home—to abandon the paternal dwelling——"

"Good heavens! what do you mean?" ejaculated Clarence, now seriously alarmed. "I see that there is something at the bottom of all this! Captain Sparks, I implore you to explain yourself. You are evidently well-intentioned—you have shown the greatest friendship for me—I reciprocate the feeling most cordially: fear not, then, to speak."

"My dear Villiers," answered the highwayman, "how can I enter upon particulars the narration of which would be most painful for you to hear? And yet I should not be acting consistently with my duty towards those young ladies—no, nor towards yourself who are about to make one of them your wife——"

"Hesitate not: speak freely!" exclaimed Clarence, seeing that his companion paused. "Should the breath of scandal have wafted to your ear anything prejudicial to the character of my aunt, I cannot blame your motive in confiding the fact to me. And I the more earnestly solicit you to be frank and candid—that is, to act consistently with your nature, which is all frankness and candour,—and reveal to me the cause of this distrust—this want of confidence relative to Mrs. Slingsby,—because I have no doubt of being able to convince you that you have been misled."

"And should I succeed in convincing *you* to the contrary?" asked Rainford.

"Then I should say that you had indeed performed the part of a friend," replied Villiers emphatically. "Although I know beforehand that such a result is impossible—yet, for your complete satisfaction, do I declare that should you prove my aunt to be in any way an unsuitable guardian for that dear girl Adelais, and her sister, I shall conceive it to be my duty immediately to seek for them another home—yes, another home—even for the few days that remain to be passed ere I shall acquire a right to protect Adelais as her husband and Rosamond as her brother."

"You have spoken well and wisely, Villiers," said Rainford; "but I do not recommend any extreme measure, which might only irritate your aunt, and perhaps lead to the forced restoration of the young ladies to their father before you can have obtained the right you speak of. I merely wish you to be on your guard——"

"But the grounds of your suspicion, Captain?" cried Clarence impatiently. "Pardon my interruption—and pity my suspense."

"I do both," returned the highwayman. "And now remember that I am no mischief-maker between relations or friends; and were it not for the peculiar circumstances of this case, in which two innocent young ladies are concerned, I should never have thought it worth while to utter a word of any thing I know injurious to Mrs. Slingsby's character—no, not even to unmask the most disgusting hypocrisy," added Rainford warmly.

"Do you still allude to my aunt?" demanded Clarence, colouring with indignation.

"I do. But start not—I am not seeking a quarrel with you, Villiers—and you promised to listen patiently."

"To no other living being should I have listened so patiently as I have already done to you," said Clarence. "But pray let us hasten to dispose of so disagreeable a topic in one way or the other."

"I am most anxious to do so," continued the highwayman. "Do you know Sir Henry Courtenay?"

"Certainly: he is my aunt's best friend."

"And her lover," added Rainford coolly.

Villiers started from his seat, exclaiming, "Captain Sparks! you presume upon the obligation which I owe you, to calumniate——"

"Then good evening, Mr. Villiers," interrupted the highwayman. "If this is the fair and impartial hearing which you promised to give me,—if this is the manner in which you treat one who has not—cannot have an improper motive in offering you wise counsel——"

"Stay, my dear friend—stay!" exclaimed Clarence, actually thrusting Rainford back into his seat; "and pray forgive my impetuosity. But this accusation—so sudden—so unexpected—so very strange——"

"And yet it is substantially true," added Rainford emphatically: "and it is proper that you should know it. For my part, I am not the man to blame Mrs. Slingsby for having a lover—nor yet the lover for having her as his mistress: it's human nature both ways. But when I know that she has been entrusted by you with the guardianship of two young ladies of tender age and spotless innocence, and one of whom is so very, very dear to you, I consider it necessary for you to be enlightened as to her true character. I've no doubt that you must feel deeply this communication: but it is better for you to learn that your aunt is something that she ought not to be, than to find out when it is too late that your wife or her sister have been corrupted by bad example."

Clarence paced the room in an agitated manner: then, at the expiration of a few minutes, he turned suddenly, exclaiming, "Not for a moment, Captain Sparks, do I suspect you of any sinister object: but you will pardon me for soliciting the proof of this charge which, if substantiated, must so completely and so painfully change my opinion of a relative whom I have until now vaunted as the pattern of virtue and propriety."

"The mode of proving the charge may be left to yourself," replied the highwayman. "Did you ever hear the circumstance of your aunt's house being robbed by a boy to whom she gave a night's lodging, some four or five years ago?"

"Certainly," exclaimed Villiers. "I recollect the incident well. Mrs. Slingsby herself communicated it to me. The ungrateful young villain——"

"I know that boy," interrupted Tom Rain drily; "and I am convinced that he told me the truth when he declared that, during the night—or rather the portion of the night, which he passed in Mrs. Slingsby's house, accident made him a witness to a scene which leaves no doubt as to the fact that Sir Henry Courtenay and Mrs. Slingsby are as intimate as man and wife together."

"And would you receive the testimony of a thief———"

"When well corroborated," added the highwayman.

"But how happened it that you should have any connexion with this lad, Captain Sparks!" demanded Clarence, in a cold and suspicions tone.

"Suppose that the boy has repented of his errors—that he has merited my interest by a service which accident enabled him to render me—that he related to me his entire history, in which this incident is comprised—and that, on questioning him closely, I learnt that the occurrence took place at the residence of your aunt?"

"I am bewildered—amazed—grieved—profoundly grieved!" ejaculated Villiers. "To suppose for an instant that this kind and affectionate relative—who has always been so good to me, and through whose bounty I am enabled to prepare and fit up a suitable dwelling for the reception of my beloved Adelais,—to think that this much-respected and long-revered woman should conceal the greatest profligacy beneath the mask of charity and religion—oh! it is a cruel blow!"

"Again I say that the mode of proving the charge may be left to yourself," observed Rainford. "Seek an opportunity to be alone with Mrs. Slingsby—make some pointed allusion to the incident—and mark how she receives it."

"I will call at my aunt's residence to-morrow morning early—the very first thing," exclaimed Villiers. "The whole affair is most serious; and, now that I can at length contemplate it with something bordering on calmness, I am bound to confess———But let us quit the topic," he added, in a tone of deep vexation, in spite of his asserted self-possession.

"And you bear me no ill-will for the course I have pursued?" said Rainford.

"Far from it. You have acted in a most friendly manner—whatever the result may be!" cried Villiers, grasping the highwayman's hand most cordially.

"I have performed a very painful duty," rejoined Tom: "and now I must take my leave of you—perhaps for a long, long time—if not for ever."

"Farewell," said Clarence; "and may prosperity attend you in another clime."

"Farewell," replied Rainford; "and may you be happy with your Adelais."

The highwayman then hurried from the room, considerably affected by this parting from one for whom he already experienced a most sincere regard.

Nor was Villiers unmoved by this farewell scene; for, on his side, he was particularly attached to the individual who had not only rendered him so essential a service on that memorable night which first made them acquainted with each other, but whose apparent frankness of disposition and manliness of character were well calculated to engage the good opinion of the confiding, warm-hearted, and unsuspecting Clarence.

CHAPTER XLV.
MR. DYKES AND HIS MYRMIDONS.

It was midnight; and profound silence reigned throughout the region of Lock's Fields.

But suddenly that silence was broken by the tread of several persons, who emerged from a bye-alley in the immediate vicinity of Brandon Street.

At the corner of this street they paused to hold a hasty conference.

They were six in number—five men and a woman.

"This is the street," said the woman.

"Oh! this is it, Mrs. Bunce—eh?" returned Mr. Dykes, the Bow Street officer, rubbing his nose with the knob of his stout ash-stick, while his countenance, on which the bright moon-beams played, showed an expression of calm determination.

"Yes: and that's the house—there: the ninth on t'other side of the way," added Mrs. Bunce.

"Well—now we don't want you no more, ma'am," said Dykes; "'cos women is all very well in their place; and darling creatur's they are too. But when a grab is to be made, they're best at home, a-bed and asleep. So good night to you, ma'am."

"Good night, gentlemen all," responded Mrs. Bunce; and she hurried away.

"Now, Bingham and you fellers," said Mr. Dykes, "we must mind what we're up to; for we shan't catch a weasel asleep. You, Bingham, take one of the runners and get round to the back of the house. Me and t'other chaps will make the entry in front. But we shan't stir a peg for one quarter of an hour; and by that time you'll be at your post."

"All right," returned Mr. Bingham; and this individual accordingly moved off, followed by one of the subordinate runners.

In the meantime, Tom Rainford was sleeping, not dreaming of danger, in the arms of the beautiful Jewess.

Charley Watts was cradled in a little bed made up for him in the warmest corner of the room.

A light burnt in the apartment, where naught was heard save the slow, regular breathing of the sleepers.

The clear, transparent olive complexion of the beautiful Jewess contrasted strongly with the florid countenance of the highwayman; and the commingling of the raven hair of the one with the light, almost yellow locks of the other, produced a strange effect, as the marked discrepancy of hues was set off by the snowy whiteness of the pillow. By the feeble light of the candle, it appeared as if ebony and gold were blending on a white ground.

But, hark! what is that sound which breaks on the silence of the chamber?—and wherefore does the highwayman start from his sleep?

He awakes—and listens.

The Jewess also awakes—and also listens,—one of her beautifully modelled arms thrown around the neck of him whom she loved so fondly.

"Some one is trying the back-door," whispered Rainford at length; and he leapt from the bed.

In less than a minute he had thrown on his clothes; and grasping his pistols, he hastened to the window.

But at the same instant the back-door was forced in;—more violently, no doubt, than Bingham and his co-operator had intended; and the sound was too unequivocal to permit Tom Rain to doubt the meaning of the disturbance.

Returning to the bed, he said in a hurried but solemn and deeply impressive tone, "Dearest, I am betrayed. If I escape, you shall soon hear from me: if I am captured, I charge you—by all the love I bear for you—by all the love you bear for me—not to attempt to visit me in prison! Farewell—dearest, dearest girl!"

He embraced her fondly—affectionately,—oh! most lovingly; while she sobbed as if her heart would break.

Then in a moment he tore himself away:—footsteps—many footsteps were already ascending—nay, rushing up—the stairs.

He darted from the room, sprang up a ladder which stood on the landing—pushed up a trap-door—and in another moment was on the roof of the house.

The officers were close upon him. Dykes and his two men had effected an entry by the front-door of the house almost at the same moment that Bingham and his follower had broken in at the back; and the entire *posse* reached the landing just at the moment that the trap-door fell down heavily into its place.

"He has escaped by the roof!" cried Dykes. "Bingham, my boy, take a couple of chaps, and watch the backs of the houses: he can't get away by the front—

it's too high for him to leap into the street. Me and t'other chap will after him to the tilings."

Thus saying, Dykes ascended the ladder as quickly as his unwieldly form would permit. The trap-door was easily raised, as it only fastened inside; and the portly body of the Bow Street officer, who possessed more courage than alacrity, was forced through the small aperture. The operation was slow and difficult; but at last Mr. Dykes stood on a narrow ledge which ran along the whole row of houses, and from which the roof rose obliquely behind. This ledge was only protected by a parapet about two feet high; and the officer felt his position to be any thing but a safe one.

But he was not the man to shrink from danger.

"Come along, you feller," he cried out to his follower, who speedily emerged from the opening. "You cut along that way, and I'll go this."

And they proceeded in different directions on the roof of the house.

The moon shone brightly, but Thomas Rainford was not to be seen.

Suddenly an exclamation of triumph burst from the yard at the back of one of the adjacent houses.

"Holloa?" vociferated Dykes, from the eminence on which he stood.

"We've got him, fast enough," returned Bingham.

A piercing shriek from a window that had been thrown open, denoted the anguish of the Jewess, whose ears had caught these words.

Mr. Dykes and his attendant subordinate now retraced their way to the trap-door, through the aperture of which they once more forced themselves; and when they had regained the landing Dykes said, "Now you go and join my partner Bingham, 'cos this Rainford is a desperate feller, and the more there is to guard him the better."

The man accordingly took his departure, and Mr. Dykes knocked gently at the door of the bed-room.

"Who is there?" asked a voice within,—a voice soft and melodious, but now expressive of the most intense anguish.

"Beg pardon, ma'am," said Dykes; "but I must do my duty; and if so be you'll have the kindness to dress yourself, I should like to examine the boxes and cupboards, and such like—just for form's sake, and that's all."

"Must you thus add to the grief which is already——"

The plaintive voice was interrupted by a violent fit of sobbing, with the mournful sounds of which the crying of the little boy now commingled.

"I don't want to annoy you, ma'am," returned Dykes.

"I should hope not, indeed!" exclaimed the landlady, who, having been alarmed by the disturbance, had got up and dressed herself, and was now ascending the stairs. "But what is it all about? and why do you break into a respectable house in this way? I don't suppose you're thieves—or else——"

"I am an officer, ma'am," exclaimed Dykes, drawing himself up with offended dignity, as the candle which the landlady carried in her hand lighted the landing-place:—"I am an officer, ma'am—and my partners have just taken one Thomas Rainford, a highwayman——"

"A highwayman!" ejaculated the widow, who had never suspected the character of her lodger, and who was a prudent woman that never troubled herself about other people's business so long as her rent was regularly paid.

"Yes—a highwayman," added Dykes. "But I've no time to stand palavering. I b'lieve there's a lady in this room here; and as I must overhaul the place—as the case is a serious one—you'll do well to step in and let me do the job quietly. I don't want to annoy her: the law isn't at loggerheads with her—and so she's nothing to fear. As for me, I'm as gentle as a lamb when a lady's concerned."

The widow urged the afflicted girl within the room to open the door; and as the latter had by this time dressed herself, the request was complied with.

But the Jewess wore a deep black veil over her head, when the officer and the landlady entered the bed-chamber; and, taking Charley in her arms, she seated herself in a chair near the bed, whispering a few words of consolation to the little boy even amidst the terrible violence of her own grief.

As for Charles, he knew that something wrong was occurring; but he was too young to comprehend the real nature of the appearances which terrified him.

Dykes just opened a cupboard, plunged his hands into a trunk, and turned out the contents of a carpet-bag: but he did not prosecute his search any farther; for he was too much experienced in the ways of robbers and rogues to suppose for a moment that he should find on the premises any portion of the money stolen from Sir Christopher Blunt,—this being the charge on which Rainford was arrested.

The search, such as it was, was merely for form's sake; because the magistrate was sure to inquire whether the prisoner's lodgings had been carefully examined; and this superficial glance at the contents of the boxes would enable Mr. Dykes to give an affirmative answer without any very great deviation from the actual truth.

He accordingly quitted the room within a minute after entering it; but he turned on the landing just to beg "the dear young lady not to take on too much," and also to assure the mistress of the house that she should be recompensed for the injury done to her abode by the violent entry effected by himself and his companions.[23]

We must leave the landlady to console—or endeavour to console the unhappy Jewess,—and accompany Mr. Dykes, who passed out of the house by the back way, and stepped over two or three low fences which separated the yards of the respective dwellings, until he reached that one where Tom Rain was in the custody of Bingham and the subordinate runners.

It appeared that the gallant highwayman, finding how hotly he was pursued when he was escaping by means of the trap-door, and dreading lest the whole neighbourhood should be alarmed ere he could possibly get away, had resolved on the dangerous expedient of sliding down from the roof to the back of the buildings, by means of the perpendicular leaden water-pipe. But when he was half-way down in his perilous descent, he missed his hold, and fell upon the stone pavement of the yard beneath. He endeavoured to get up and escape—but could not: his right ankle was sprained, almost to dislocation; and in a few minutes he was discovered and captured by the detachment under the orders of Bingham.

He heard the piercing scream which followed the announcement of his arrest by this officer; and that scream—oh! it went to thy generous heart, Tom Rain!

But he uttered not a word: he offered no resistance, although he had his pistols about him. He not only shrank from the idea of shedding human blood: but he was also well aware that his case was now too desperate to be benefited by even desperate means. For, even if he slew all the officers, he could not drag himself away ere the neighbours would collect and capture him.

And by this time, the whole line of houses was awake with bustle and excitement. Light after light appeared at the different casements: windows were thrown up; and the rumour spread like wildfire, that a famous highwayman had just been arrested.

The reader may well conceive the nature of the sensation which now prevailed all along the back of Brandon Street;—but in one room there was a beauteous woman convulsed with torturing—maddening anguish,—for deep was her love for thee, Tom Rain!

"Now, then," cried Dykes, as he made his appearance in the yard, where the highwayman was sitting on an inverted wash-tub, surrounded by the runners, to whom he had surrendered his pistols;—"now, then lads—let's off with him to quod. How d'ye do, Mr. Rainford! Don't want to crow over a gentleman in trouble—but thought I should have you some day or another." Then, stooping down, he whispered in Tom's ear, "I was obleeged to give a look in at the crib up there just now; but I only stayed a moment, and shan't trouble the poor lady any more. She had a veil over her face—and so I don't know who she is: that is, you see, I *shan't* know, if I'm asked any questions by the beak:—but of course I'm aware it's the handsome Jewess that did the diamond business."

"You are mistaken—you are mistaken," said Rainford, emphatically. "But, if you showed her any civility, I sincerely thank you——"

"Lord bless you! Mr. Rainford—I wouldn't do any thing to annoy you for the world. I can't help admiring a brave man—and you're one. The poor dear lady will be troubled no more by us; and it's nothing to me who she is, or who she is not. The law don't want *her*, at all events."

"One word more," said Tom. "Who has done this business for me?"

"A lawyer named Howard," was the answer. "But I can't say no more——"

"Then what is the charge against me?" asked Tom, a considerable load already removed from his mind.

"Sir Christopher Blunt's little business—that's all," replied Dykes. "But come along: we must be off to Horsemonger."

Mr. Dykes and Mr. Bingham politely offered Rainford their arms; and the procession passed through the house, in the yard belonging to which the capture had been made. The occupants of that dwelling—men, women, and children, all in their night-dresses—crowded on the stairs to catch a glimpse of the "terrible highwayman," whose good looking appearance excited the sympathy of the female portion of the spectators.

Half an hour afterwards Tom Rain was lodged in a cell in the criminal department of Horsemonger Lane Gaol;—but his heart was lighter than the reader might possibly suppose—for he was relieved of the first and most natural fear that had assailed him: namely, that it was on account of Benjamin Bones's death that he was pursued!

"If I must be hanged," he thought within himself, "I would rather it should be for highway robbery than aught else!—But, O Tamar! Tamar! what is to become of *thee*?"

And, as he sate on the humble pallet in the darkness of his solitary cell, he buried his face in his manacled hands.

In another moment a moonbeam penetrated through the barred window; and in that silver ray glistened the tears which trickled between his fingers.

And yet it was not for himself he wept:—thou wast no coward—but thou hadst a generous heart, Tom Rain!

> 23. We should observe that at the time of which we are writing, it was by no means unusual for Bow Street officers to be employed in the pursuit or capture of desperate characters in Surrey, although this county was not strictly within their district.

CHAPTER XLVI.
EXPLANATIONS.

At eleven o'clock on the following day, Lord Ellingham, who had passed a sleepless and wretched night, called at the house of Lady Hatfield, and was immediately conducted to the drawing-room, where Georgiana was alone in readiness to receive him.

She was dressed in a morning garb, and, though very—very pale, looked surpassingly lovely.

"My dear friend," she said, extending her hand, which, as he offered to press it with rapture to his lips, she gently but still resolutely withdrew,—"my dear friend—for such henceforth must I call you——"

"Georgiana!" he exclaimed, starting back: "what means this coolness?"

"Be seated, Arthur—and listen to me attentively," she said in a plaintive and sweetly touching tone. "I am not very well—my nerves are not strong to-day—and you must not manifest any impatience towards me. Indeed, I ought to have postponed this interview: but I considered it to be my duty—a paramount duty owing alike to yourself and to me—to enter into as early an explanation as possible."

"This preface forebodes nothing favourable to my happiness," murmured the Earl, as he sank into a seat to which Georgiana pointed—but which was not by her side!

"Arthur," she continued, with difficulty maintaining sufficient control over her emotions to enable her to speak calmly and collectedly, "you know not how much I love you—how dearly I am devoted to you. For your sake, and to bear the name of your wife, I could consent to become a mendicant—a wanderer on the face of the earth,—renounce fortune—rank—society—all, in fine, that we women are generally deemed to hold so dear,—yes, all this could I do for your sake, so that you were my companion! Then, conceive how hard it is for me—oh! how very hard, my well-beloved Arthur, to be compelled to say that henceforth we must know each other only as friends!"

"Merciful heavens!" ejaculated the Earl, uncertain whether the imagined capriciousness of his Georgiana was about to assert its tantalizing influence again, or whether any thing of a more serious nature, and connected with the incidents of the preceding evening, was about to present an insuperable bar to his happiness.

"Yes—Arthur," continued Georgiana, in an impressive tone, "henceforth we must be but as brother and sister to each other. And as a dear, fond, affectionate sister will I ever be to you; for your generosity would have made me your wife in spite of——But you cannot wish me to refer to *that*! And yet it *is* that one sad episode in my life which now asserts an inexorable influence over the conduct which we must *both* pursue. It is that event, which you—in the noble candour, in the warm liberality of your admirable disposition——"

"You praise me too highly, Georgiana," exclaimed the Earl. "I loved you—I love you dearly; and in spite of all that you now say, hope is not quenched within me. But, my God! when will this painful suspense pass? When shall I behold you no longer a prey to an influence——"

"Alas! that influence must endure for ever!" murmured Lady Hatfield, tears now trembling upon her eye-lashes.

"No—no!" cried the Earl with impassioned energy. "When, but a few days ago, we entered into explanations with each other—when I informed you that I was aware of the nature of that secret influence which tyrannised over you,—did I not assure you that, as a loving husband, I would so completely study your happiness——"

"Oh! yes," interrupted Georgiana; "and did I not declare that you had given me a proof of affection such as man seldom gave unto woman? Believe me—believe me," she added earnestly, "I felt all that there was great—generous—and noble in your conduct: for, knowing that secret—that sad, that fatal secret—you banished all prejudice—discarded even those scruples which the most high-minded of men so often entertain under such circumstances——"

"Dearest Georgiana!" exclaimed the Earl; "you attach far too much importance to the secret of which you speak. What man that truly loves a virtuous—beautiful—accomplished—and amiable woman, would allow himself to be swayed——"

"Ah! every heart is not so generous as yours!" interrupted Georgiana. "You recognise the complete innocence of my soul——"

"I cannot believe that you would be guilty of the wanton cruelty of inflicting these tortures upon me, Georgiana," said the Earl, "were it not for that strange—that almost morbid state of mind which is at times produced by the recollection of a serious fright which you experienced some years ago, and from the effects of which you have not completely recovered. But, after all, wherefore do you praise me so highly—wherefore do you thank me so much for the simple fact of not allowing the knowledge of this occasional access of morbid feeling to weigh with me——"

"Arthur!" almost shrieked Georgiana, losing all control over herself; "then, you know not the secret—the dreadful secret——"

"Yes: have I not proved to you that I know it?" exclaimed the Earl, surprised and grieved at the strange manner of Lady Hatfield. "Your uncle put me in possession of the facts: and what is there in them, after all? It is a mere adventure which one would now tell only as a Christmas tale—or to amuse children,—had it not produced so serious an influence upon your nerves, and——"

"Arthur! Arthur! is this a cruel pleasantry?" demanded Georgiana hysterically; "or have we misunderstood each other all along?"

"You know that I am incapable of turning to ridicule or making a jest of any thing that regards you, Georgiana," returned the Earl. "And as for any misunderstanding between us, there is none. Our explanation the other day was full—complete—satisfactory——"

"No—no," cried Lady Hatfield, painfully excited. "I see that I am mistaken—that you have learnt a bare fact——"

"Yes: and since we are now conversing on the topic," said the Earl, "let us enter fully into it and then abandon it for ever. I see that you attach much importance to this subject—and that, when we are united, there may be no necessity ever to recur——"

"If ever we are united!" repeated Georgiana, clasping her hands in anguish of heart.

"Yes, my well-beloved," continued the Earl. "And now listen to me. About seven years ago you were staying alone at Mauleverer Lodge in Hampshire———"

"Oh! the fatal time—the fatal place!" cried Georgiana hysterically; and though she would have given worlds to cut short the conversation, she had not the power—for her mind was agitated like the ocean in a storm.

"You were staying alone at Mauleverer Lodge," proceeded Arthur, not observing the extent of her emotion; "you were alone, save in respect to the servants: but you had no relation—no friend there at the moment. And one night—a man broke in——"

"A man—with a black mask——" murmured Georgiana, almost wringing her hands.

"And bearing the denomination, too, of the *Black Mask*," continued Lord Ellingham;—"this man broke into the house—and——"

"And—merciful heavens! Spare me the recital of the rest!" shrieked Lady Hatfield, covering her face with her hands.

"Good God! do not thus give way to a reminiscence which, though painful, should no longer exercise any influence over a strong mind!" said the Earl, in a kind and soothing tone, as he approached and seated himself next to Georgiana. "Consider, my dearly beloved—my angel—my intended wife!—reflect, I implore you, upon the childishness of this behavior!"

"Childishness!" repeated Georgiana, with a convulsive shudder.

"Pardon the expression," said the Earl; "but I would reason with you—I would endeavour to persuade you that an occurrence which is past and gone, and which happens frequently in other houses, should not thus paralyse all the naturally fine energies of your soul. What, in the name of heaven! can it matter now, if a robber broke into a dwelling some six or seven years ago? Your uncle told me that for some months fears were entertained for your reason: but——Oh! my Georgiana, I do implore you now—now that we are once again touching on this painful—most painful theme—to exercise more command over yourself. You praise me—you thank me, because I am willing to espouse one whose reason was shocked long years ago;—for that is your secret, after all, Georgiana—dearest Georgiana;—and you perceive that I know it!"

"My God! how have we misunderstood each other!" murmured the unhappy lady:—"my secret—he knows it *not*!"

But the Earl could not catch the sense of the words which she thus whispered to herself; and, with the fond hope of consoling her—for the events of the preceding evening were for the time banished from his memory—he took her hand, pressed it to his lips, and began to utter syllables of tenderness and love.

Then, how terrible was his surprise—how acute the anguish which filled his soul, when Georgiana, suddenly starting from the half-embrace in which he was already enfolding her, exclaimed in a tone indicative of the most exquisite mental agony, "No—Arthur—no: you are not acquainted with my secret—and *now*, never, never will you learn it! We have misunderstood each other—and I consented the other day to become your wife, while labouring under a dreadful—oh! a dreadful error! But heaven has interposed to prevent the consummation of *your* misery—and *mine*! And now," she added, with the calmness of despair, "let us separate, Arthur—and henceforth be unto each other but brother and sister;—for your wife I cannot become!"

"Georgiana, this is cruelty the most refined—the most wanton!" exclaimed the Earl. "Am I again to pass through all the phases of suspense—uncertainty—mystery—and doubt?—and will you in a few days repent of all you have said, and recall this stern decision? But—much as I love you—

deeply as I am attached to you—I cannot—cannot endure a treatment——"

"Pardon me—forgive me!" cried Georgiana; "but you do not comprehend me! My reason is not unhinged,—I am subject to no whims—no caprice, Arthur! A fatal mistake on my part alone induced me the other day to consent to become your wife. That error has now been cleared up—our conversation of this morning has convinced me of the tremendous misunderstanding that had nearly wrecked all *your* happiness! But, even had it not, there was *another* reason which would imperatively command us to think no more of each other in the same light as we so lately did!"

"Ah! you allude, perchance, to the incident of last evening!" exclaimed Lord Ellingham. "Permit me, then, to ask the object of that Rainford's visit? Did he insult you? did he attempt to extort money from you? If so——"

"No—no!" cried Georgiana, in whose bosom the mere mention of the highwayman's name appeared to excite the most agonising feelings. "I sent down a message to that effect last night. He did not insult me—he did not come to injure me——"

"But his presence excited you most painfully, Georgiana!" interrupted the Earl; "and it has also revived in your imagination——Oh! I understand it all!" he cried, suddenly interrupting himself: "this Rainford is the Black Mask—the noted highwayman of Hampshire!"

Lady Hatfield cast upon the young nobleman a look expressive of so much mental suffering, that he was deeply touched—profoundly affected: and yet he knew not how to administer consolation.

"Georgiana," he at length said, in as calm and collected a tone as he could assume, though his heart was in reality rent by the most painful emotions, "there is some terrible mystery in all this! I begin to believe—as you yourself ere now endeavoured to persuade me—that your reason is in no way affected—that you are not subject to mere whims and caprices. No—the cause of your grief—your anguish—your horror at the reminiscence of that event in Hampshire,—an anguish and a horror cruelly revived last night by the presence of that Rainford, who is doubtless identical with the Black Mask,—an anguish and a horror perpetuated, too, until now," continued Arthur, more emphatically,—"the cause of all this is far—far more serious than I had at first imagined. You say that you cannot become my wife—and that you have laboured under a misapprehension: you wish us to look upon each other as brother and sister. And yet you do love me well enough to become my wife—did not some terrible and fearfully mysterious obstacle stand in the way. Oh! if you really love me—then pity me, and tell me this dreadful secret which weighs upon your mind! Unless, indeed——"

And he paused abruptly, as an awful suspicion rushed into his brain.

Georgiana only turned her head aside, and sobbed convulsively.

"Unless, indeed," continued the Earl, after a few moments' silence, "it would bring a blush to your cheek to enlighten me; and I cannot—cannot ask you to humiliate yourself in my presence!"

"Arthur, I *dare* not become your wife!" exclaimed Georgiana, suddenly falling upon her knees before him; "and if you demand the reason—as, after all that has passed between us, you have a right—I will confess——"

"Georgiana, no more!" cried the Earl, hastening to raise her. "Not for worlds would I bring a blush to your cheek." Then, in a different—more serious—and very mournful tone, he added, "Henceforth we will be to each other as sister and brother."

With these words he touched her hand lightly with his lips, and was about to hurry from the room; when, animated by a sudden thought, Georgiana held him back, saying in a hollow, thick tone of voice, "Whatever suspicion you now entertain—you do not believe that I—*was guilty*?" she added, as if the very words were choking her.

"No, much injured woman!" cried the young nobleman warmly. "A light has broken in upon my mind—and I understand it all."

"Yes—for a pure soul dwells in a tainted body," murmured Lady Hatfield; "and if I have said this much—and you can well believe how painful to my feelings the mere necessity of making such an assertion must be,—but in making it, I am influenced only by the hope—the earnest hope of removing from your mind—the mind of one whom I so much respect—so highly esteem——"

"Say no more, my dearest *sister*!" interrupted the Earl emphatically; "for as a sister do I now look upon you—and as a *brother*," he added sternly, "will I avenge you. For *that* was I ere now hurrying away so abruptly!"

"Avenge me!" repeated Georgiana, looking wildly on the young nobleman's countenance, which wore a calm but determined expression.

"Yes, Georgiana," replied the Earl: "wrongs so deep as yours demand a deadly vengeance. And who so fit to become the instrument of that vengeance, than he whom those wrongs which *you* have sustained so cruelly redound upon? But for that incarnate fiend Rainford, would you not already—yes, already have been my loved and loving wife? Am I not, then, also wronged by him? Have I not something to avenge?" he demanded bitterly. "And to consummate this vengeance, Georgiana, I—your *brother* henceforth—will forget my proud title—cast aside the remembrance of my elevated rank;—and, dressed in mean attire, I will visit the noisome dens—the foul courts—the low neighbourhoods of London, until I discover that miscreant Rainford. Then will I—still forgetting the proud title and the elevated rank—dare him to meet me in a duel, from which at least but one shall depart alive, and wherein both may haply fall! I will not yield him up to the hangman, Georgiana," continued the Earl, fearfully excited; "because in his last moments he might confess his crimes, and include amongst them the foul wrong he has inflicted on thee, my sister! But I will descend to make myself his equal—I will place myself on a level with that black-hearted ruffian——"

"Hold! hold!" screamed Georgiana, suddenly recovering the powers of utterance which had been paralyzed by this tremendous explosion of generous indignation on the part of that proudly-born noble who proclaimed himself her champion. "Hold! hold! Arthur—you know not whom you calumniate—whom you would provoke to the duel of death!"

"Yes—too well I know the miscreant!" cried the Earl furiously.

"No—no—you know him not!" screamed Georgiana wildly.

"This is childish—silly!" said the Earl impatiently. "Was it not Rainford who——"

"Yes—yes: but this Rainford——"

"Is a fiend, with a heart so black——"

"Hold! hold! again I say," ejaculated Lady Hatfield, clasping her hands in despair. "That Thomas Rainford whom you would make the victim of your vengeance, is——"

"Is what?" demanded the Earl hastily.

"Is—is——"

"Who? in the name of heaven!"

"YOUR BROTHER!" was the hysterical reply.

CHAPTER XLVII.
FARTHER EXPLANATIONS.

"My brother!" repeated the Earl of Ellingham, with a wild glance and a sudden start, indicative of the most painful surprise. "My brother! Georgiana!—oh! no—impossible! 'Tis true that my father——but no—— that child died——"

"I can give you no particulars—offer you no evidence in this most strange and mysterious matter," said Lady Hatfield, endeavouring to subdue the excitement produced in her much-agitated mind by the preceding scene. "All that I know is—all that *he* told me was that secret which I have now revealed to you! Thus, Arthur, you perceive that—independent of the *other* reason which would prevent *me* from becoming yours, and *you* from receiving me as your wife——"

"But wherefore did you not mention this at first—at the commencement of our conversation this morning?" demanded the nobleman, utterly bewildered by the revelation that had been made to him, and scarcely knowing whether to regard it as a substantial fact or a miserable fiction.

"Because Rainford himself appeared to tell it to me as a profound secret," observed Georgiana. "Not that he desired me to consider it as such: but his manner—and then the nature of the revelation itself, which could not be gratifying to your feelings—oh! I scarcely know what I am saying, Arthur— but I would have spared your feelings, had you not compelled me to make that revelation, to prevent the mad—the insane designs of vengeance which you had formed——"

"I understand you, Georgiana," interrupted the Earl: "and deeply—oh! deeply do I feel your generous consideration on that point. But there is one question that I wish to ask you—a question——"

"Speak, Arthur! This is the day of mutual outpourings of confidence," said Lady Hatfield: "and, remember—we are henceforth to stand in the light of brother and sister to each other!"

"The question I would ask is relative to the robbery that was perpetrated on you and Miss Mordaunt a short time back near Hounslow," continued the Earl. "Was that highwayman——"

"He was—he was!" exclaimed Georgiana, once more painfully excited. "But do not look coldly on me, Arthur—do not despise me for that dreadful crime of perjury which I committed to save him. He wrote me an imperious note, commanding me to stop all proceedings instituted in reference to that matter. What did such a note imply? It was a menace—a dreadful menace,—a threat to expose me, if I did not obey his mandate! Consider, Arthur—oh! consider how I was placed—my reputation at stake—my fame in the hands of one who——But can you wonder that I preferred the dread alternative of perjury to the danger of disgrace and infamy which seemed to impend over my head?"

"Alas! I cannot blame you, poor, suffering woman?" ejaculated the Earl in a tone of deep commiseration. "We never know how we should act until we find ourselves placed in circumstances of difficulty and embarrassment; and then—then even the most rigid integrity often yields! But let us sit down quietly, Georgiana, for a short half-hour—compose ourselves, if we can—collect our scattered thoughts—and converse together as sister and brother. For I will now communicate to you the little I know concerning the birth of Thomas Rainford—if he indeed be the offspring of that amour——"

Arthur ceased, and passed his hand over his brow as if to calm the warfare of thoughts and conjectures which agitated his brain.

Georgiana seated herself on the sofa, and the Earl at length took a chair near her.

He then continued in the following manner:—

"My father, the late Earl, was married twice: his first matrimonial connexion was formed when he was thirty; and this union was unproductive of issue. Lady Ellingham, as I have heard, was a woman devotedly attached to the dissipation of a fashionable life. She seemed to exist only to shine in the gay assemblies of the West End; and, as she had no children, and her husband was immersed in politics, she possessed no ties to bind her to her own fireside. She played deeply—for play was very fashionable then amongst ladies, and is even now to a considerable extent. Her extravagances were great, and she made rapid inroads upon my father's fortune. By the time he was forty he found himself involved in debts; and moreover, rumour began to be so busy with the name of his wife, imputing to her the most shameless infidelity, that he determined to separate from her. I should not allude to this circumstance—I would not for a moment revive statements prejudicial to the memory of a woman who has long ago gone to render an account of her deeds to her Maker—were it not that respect for the name of my lamented father renders me anxious to discover any extenuation which offers itself for his subsequent conduct. Well, a separation was resolved upon: a certain income was settled upon Lady Ellingham; the estate was put 'to nurse,' as the law-phrase has it; and my father, who was a proud man, retired to a small property which he possessed in Ireland, ostensibly for the purpose of giving up the cares of public life, but in reality to conceal the necessity of retrenching his expenditure. Ten years passed away: and when my father was upwards of fifty, he returned to London, his estates having in the meantime been relieved of all their incumbrances. Lady Ellingham was still living: but the smallness of her income and the impaired condition of her health, forced her to dwell in the strictest retirement. She had moreover become a devotee, and manifested no desire to return into the dazzling scenes of fashionable life.

"I am now speaking of about thirty-one years ago; when I was not born. It was at that period that my father encountered a young and very beautiful girl, named Octavia Manners. She was the half-sister of a marine-store dealer, who bore the disagreeable appellation of Benjamin Bones. By all I have heard, Octavia must have been a charming creature; and her manners, acquirements, and conversation were far superior to her humble condition in life. I cannot give you any details respecting the way in which my father became acquainted with her: suffice it to say that he grew deeply attached to her, and his visits were encouraged by her brother. But, alas! from all that I have heard, I have grounds—oh! too strong grounds to believe that those visits were most unwelcome to Octavia; for she was beloved by a young man in her own sphere of life, and whom she loved in return. And it is now that I would palliate—as far as possible—the conduct of my sire, while I am bound to admit that his proceedings in respect to that unhappy girl were most unworthy the noble and the man. My heart aches, too, as I utter these words: but I am telling you a history, the truth of which must not be disguised nor in any way misrepresented. But some allowance—some little excuse may be found for a man who was separated from a wife whom he had not seen for many years, and to whom there were positively no moral ties, although the legal ones still existed, to bind his fidelity. He was devotedly attached to a young and beautiful girl who unfortunately could not return his love, and who did not even seem flattered by his visits, as so many maidens in her sphere would have been. No—she shrank from his addresses, and implored him not to persecute her!

"But he persisted in his visits; and the first sad result was that the young man to whom Octavia's faith was plighted, would not believe that she discouraged the attentions of the nobleman who condescended to appear at that humble dwelling. I cannot of course inform you, although we may both imagine, how the young man reproached Octavia, and how she defended herself: but it is certain that he suddenly quitted the neighbourhood, leaving behind him a note declaring that he should never see the unhappy girl again. Alas! that I should now be compelled to recite the tale of my father's guilt—my father's crime! His love for Octavia knew no bounds—he was determined to risk all—every thing——"

"Spare your feelings, Arthur—dear Arthur!" exclaimed Lady Hatfield; "for I can fully appreciate the grief which this revival of such a subject must cause you!"

"Octavia, then, was purchased—purchased with gold—my father's gold, Georgiana;—and the deed of—dare I call it aught save *infamy*?—was consummated!" said the Earl, in a low and subdued tone, as if he were overcome by the enormity of his sire's guilt—that guilt which, with a venial filial affection, he had vainly endeavoured to palliate. "Yes—'twas done," he continued sadly; "and the vile half-brother sold the honour of that young and already too deeply afflicted girl. Too deeply afflicted, I say, because she had lost him on whom the affections of her youthful heart were set. The very day after her disgrace—her ruin, she fled from her brother's house; and for several months no trace was discovered of her. It was feared she had committed suicide; and my father was almost distracted. At that precise period his wife died, having ended as a devotee that life of which so much of the early portion was passed in dissipation and illicit amours. She had not been laid many weeks in the family vault, when my father, by some means unknown to me—perhaps, by accident—discovered that Octavia was living, and that she was in the way to become a mother. He hastened to the miserable garret which she occupied, and found her in the most abject state of poverty—endeavouring to earn a subsistence with her needle. A girl of the gipsy tribe, and whose name was Miranda, was the friend and companion of poor Octavia. How they grew acquainted—how they came to live together, I am not aware: but Miranda was much attached to poor Octavia, and was nearly her own age. Indeed Octavia was not seventeen even at that time; and this Miranda of whom I speak, was about fifteen. Much mystery envelopes this portion of the sad tale: it is, however, certain that my father visited Octavia for several days—that he passed hours with her—that she even appeared to be reconciled to his presence—and that they went out together, and remained absent for hours, on two or three occasions. Again she disappeared—suddenly—abruptly—without having intimated her intention to my father, and without even having confided her design to her friend Miranda. For Miranda remained behind at the lodging, and when my father called and found Octavia not, he was seized with a paroxysm of the deepest grief.

"Another year passed away; and behold, poverty and distress drove the unfortunate Octavia to seek an asylum at the house of her half-brother. She would not, doubtless, have gone near that fatal dwelling where her ruin was accomplished, had it not been for the child which she held in her arms. That child—a boy—was the fruit of her connexion with my father,—or rather of the dreadful deed which gave her, when under the influence of an opiate, into his arms. But she was dying—yes, she was dying, when she knocked at her brother's door; and on her death-bed she implored that my father might be sent for. He flew to her: he knelt by her side—he took the child in his arms, and embraced both the dying mother and the innocent babe. By a strange—a wondrous coincidence, Miranda entered the house at that moment: she had come to make inquiries concerning Octavia—and found her dying. The poor mother forgave those who had wronged her,—forgave her half-brother—blessed my father—yes, blessed him—and recommended her infant to his care—that infant being also his own! Then my father requested to be left alone with her; but scarcely had the villain Bones and the faithful Miranda quitted the room, when they were recalled by a dreadful cry which burst from my father's lips;—and they hurried back to find that Octavia was no more."

Arthur paused to wipe away the tears which were trickling down his cheeks; nor were Georgiana's eyes unmoistened by the sweet dews of sympathy.

"When my father had sufficiently recovered himself to attend to more worldly matters," continued the young Earl, "he gave directions for the funeral of his victim; and to Miranda did he entrust the child. Then he placed in the hands of Benjamin Bones, in the presence of Miranda, a thousand guineas to be placed out at interest, in order to provide the means of supporting the infant and his nurse. I should also inform you that a small roll of papers, carefully wrapped up in a piece of thick brown paper, was found upon the person of Octavia, shortly after her death; and these were taken possession of by Benjamin Bones, my father having previously quitted the house. Of the nature of those documents I know nothing; but I have been informed that when the half-brother read them, he was greatly excited, and secured them under lock and key.

"A year elapsed, during which my father called several times to see the little boy, who throve well in Miranda's care. But at the expiration of that period his visits ceased altogether;—for he was about to marry again. Twenty-nine years ago the Honourable Miss Stamford became his second wife; and twenty-six years ago I was born. But before the date of *my* birth—and within six months after the marriage of my father appeared in the newspapers—Bones discharged Miranda on some pretence; and she returned to her tribe. Some few months afterwards she fell in with another tribe; and to her profound surprise, she discovered the child Thomas in the possession of a woman named Egyptia. Of the child's identity Miranda had no doubt, because it had a peculiar mark near the shoulder of the right arm. She and her sister-gipsy then compared notes, and Egyptia told her that she had received the child from a man named Benjamin Bones—a marine-store dealer in Greville Street, Hatton Garden; that Bones had given her twenty guineas to take the child; that the money was all gone; and that she already repented of the bargain. Miranda, who was attached to the child, offered to take it; and her proposal was accepted. For seven years did the faithful Miranda rear that boy as if he were her own; but at last she fell dangerously ill—was long delirious—and when she awoke to consciousness again, she learnt from her companions that the boy had died of the same epidemic malady beneath which she herself had nearly succumbed."

Again the Earl paused for a few moments; and when he again broke silence, it was to conclude his narrative.

"My father, as you are aware, Georgiana, died when I was only a year old; and I was brought up by my mother. At the age of nineteen I went to Oxford; and it was in the neighbourhood of that city I one day fell in with a party of gipsies. They offered to tell my fortune; and I consented for the amusement of the farce. The young female who undertook the task commenced by giving me my real name; for I had doubtless been pointed out to her in the city, as the gipsies had been there and in the vicinity for several days.[24] But the moment my name was mentioned, another gipsy-woman, who had probably seen forty summers, uttered an ejaculation of surprise—looked hard at me—and then inquired abruptly whether I was the son of the late Earl of Ellingham. I answered in the affirmative; and she let drop some observations which excited my curiosity. I took her aside, thrust a guinea into her hand, and demanded of her the meaning of her words. She returned me the money, and, after much persuasion, narrated to me the whole history of Octavia Manners—that is to say, as much of it as I have now told to you. You now understand, Georgiana, how it is possible that this Thomas Rainford may be my half-brother: but, if he be, the account of his death, received by Miranda from her companions, must have been false;—for I need hardly tell you that the elderly gipsy who unfolded to me the details of my father's fatal conduct towards poor Octavia, was none other than Miranda herself. Shortly afterwards my mother died; but I never revealed to her the story of her late husband's guilt and Octavia's wrongs."

Scarcely was this strange narrative concluded, when the door of the apartment opened, and Sir Ralph Walsingham entered the room.

"Well," he exclaimed, "Mr. Rainford, who honoured this house with a visit last night, and frightened you, Georgiana, so sadly, has got himself into a pleasant scrape at last——"

"Indeed!" exclaimed Lord Ellingham hastily; "what——"

"He is arrested on a charge of highway robbery—a robbery, in fact, committed on no less a person than our acquaintance Sir Christopher Blunt," returned the baronet.

"Arrested!" ejaculated the Earl, exchanging a rapid glance with Georgiana, as much as to enjoin her not to allow the subject of their previous conversation to transpire in the presence of Sir Ralph Walsingham.

"Yes—arrested last night—lodged in Horsemonger Lane Gaol, as a character too desperate to put into the usual lock-up—and examined before the Magistrates at the office in the Borough this morning," continued Sir Ralph. "I happened to be in the neighbourhood an hour ago, and heard all about it. But he is remanded for a week, at the solicitation of Mr. Howard, the attorney for the prosecution, Sir Christopher not being in London. Well, poor fellow! I am really sorry for him—for he seems to be a dashing, daring, gallant blade, by all accounts. Pardon me, however, my dear Georgiana," he added, seeing that his niece was deadly pale; "I ought not to have spoken a word in favour of a man who terrified you so: but——"

Lord Ellingham interrupted Sir Ralph by taking his leave of him and Georgiana; and as the nobleman took the latter by the hand, he said in a hasty whisper, "I will go and see him at once!"

He then left the house, entered a hackney-coach at the nearest stand, and ordered the driver to take him to Horsemonger Lane Gaol.

---

[24]. For the mode adopted by Gipsies to glean information relative to persons in the various neighbourhoods they visit, see "The History of Skilligalee" in the First Series of "THE MYSTERIES OF LONDON."

CHAPTER XLVIII.
LORD ELLINGHAM AND TOM RAIN.

The interview between Lady Hatfield and the Earl of Ellingham had lasted a considerable time; and it was close upon three o'clock in the afternoon when his lordship reached Horsemonger Lane Gaol.

He communicated to the governor his desire to see Thomas Rainford; and although visitors were usually compelled to speak to prisoners through an iron grating, yet the rank of the nobleman and the fact of his being in the commission of the peace for another county (Middlesex), procured him immediate access to the highwayman's cell.

Rainford was sitting in a pensive attitude at a table on which his dinner remained untouched. We have before said—and we now repeat—that he cared but little for the peril of his own predicament: there were, however, ties which bound him to the existence that was now in jeopardy, and to the freedom that was lost.

He started from his seat with unfeigned surprise, when the Earl of Ellingham entered the cell.

"You are astonished to see *me* here, Mr. Rainford?" said the nobleman, in a mild and mournful tone.

"It is a visit, my lord," was the answer, "that I certainly did not expect."

"And yet—if the statement you made to Lady Hatfield be true—I am but performing a duty——"

"Ah! then she has told you *that*!" exclaimed the prisoner.

"She has told me that you claim a near—a very near relationship to me," rejoined the nobleman, his voice trembling with emotion—for the reader has seen enough of him to be aware that he possessed a generous heart.

"Yes—my lord," replied Rainford: "the same father was the author of our being—although our mothers were different."

"Is this true?—is it really true?" demanded the Earl hastily.

"As true as there is an Almighty God who now beholds the great peer and the prisoned highwayman face to face!" replied Rainford solemnly; and divesting himself of his coat, he bared his right arm and exhibited a particular mark.

"I cannot doubt it—I cannot disbelieve you!" exclaimed the nobleman, tears starting from his eyes.

And then the great peer and the prisoned highwayman were folded in each other's arms.

"But, my God!" exclaimed Arthur, when the excitement of this fraternal recognition had somewhat passed away; "in what a condition do I find you, my poor brother!"

"Grieve not for me, Arthur," said Rainford: "my fate will soon be decided now; and whatever it may be, I shall be prepared to meet it as becomes a brave man."

"Talk not thus, Thomas!" cried the nobleman, pressing his hand warmly. "I have money to buy off your prosecutors—interest to use in your behalf——"

"If I say to you, '*Yes, use both*,' Arthur," replied the highwayman, "it is only because there is *one* who loves me well, and for whose sake I could wish to live."

"I understand you—you allude to Miss Esther de Medina," said the Earl. "But there is *another* for whose sake you must hope to live and enjoy freedom again: and that is the brother who now stands before you, and who, for our father's sake, will never—never desert you!"

"My dear Arthur, your kindness unmans me," said Rainford; "and yet—if you knew all—you would perhaps think that I am not altogether unworthy of your sympathy! But, sit down, and let me show you that, though of lost and ruined reputation, I am not without some feeling!"

The Earl took one of the two chairs that there were in the cell; and Rainford seated himself near his half-brother on the other.

"That you are acquainted with a considerable portion of my history, I know," resumed the highwayman; "for some seven or eight years ago you encountered a gipsy-woman near Oxford, who revealed to you——"

"The faithful Miranda indeed told me all she knew!" interrupted the Earl. "But at that period she believed you to have been long dead."

"Yes—and it was only a short time ago that I met her in Hampshire," answered Rainford; "and accident led us to converse together. A word or two which I dropped without anticipating the result, induced her to make certain inquiries: then she requested me, in a hurried and excited manner, to bare my right arm—and it was only on the occasion of which I am speaking, and which occurred a few months since, that I learnt the real narrative of my birth. It appears that when Miranda had fallen so dangerously ill, and had become delirious, the gipsies considered me to be a burthen to them, as I was not born of their race; and one of them took me to Winchester, in the neighbourhood of which city the tents were pitched at the time; and there he purposely abandoned me. What subsequently became of me I have not time now to relate; my history has been most eventful, and could not be compressed into a short narrative. But should the laws of my country demand that my misdeeds be expiated on the scaffold, I will leave that history, written out in all its remarkable details, for your contemplation."

"Talk not thus, Thomas—oh! talk not thus!" cried Arthur. "I will save you yet—even if I throw myself at the feet of my sovereign, and proclaim that you are my brother!"

"God grant that you may prove successful, for the sake of *one* who loves me well!" said Rainford, solemnly. "But let me pursue the thread of that much of my story which I have now to relate to you. It appears that when Miranda *did* recover from her serious illness, the gipsies did not like to tell her the truth relative to myself; and they therefore invented the tale of my death to account for my disappearance. Thus was it that, until a few months ago, she remained in ignorance of the deceit that had been practised upon her; and the same day which revealed to her the fact that I was still alive, made me acquainted with the history of my birth. Miranda also told me that Benjamin Bones was still in existence and was reputed to be a rich man. She had recently been in London; and curiosity had prompted her to make inquiries concerning him. All that she had gleaned, she communicated to me. It then struck me that I would come to London—that I would throw myself in the way of that man who had plundered me of my inheritance—and that I would watch for some favourable opportunity to wring from him the amount with interest and compound interest, that was fairly mine. I learnt from Miranda that certain papers had been found about the person of my poor mother, after she was dead, and that the perusal of them had excited the interest of this Bones. It therefore struck me that I might recover those documents, as well as the money of which I had been plundered. If the documents should prove in any way interesting or valuable, I thought, so much the better: if not, no harm would be done in obtaining possession of them. I came to London; and accident enabled me, through the intervention of a mutual acquaintance named Tullock, to meet with Benjamin Bones. I offered him my services in a particular way—and he accepted them. To be candid, he was to plan deeds of villany—and I was to execute them. His terms were so ridiculously exorbitant that I should have laughed at them, had I not a particular object to serve in connecting myself with him. And the opportunity which I sought presented itself sooner than I had anticipated. In a word, I had succeeded in all I had undertaken: I was enabled to help myself to as much as I chose of his hoarded treasures—and I discovered the papers that I have alluded to."

"And were they of any interest?" asked the Earl.

"Of such interest and of such value, Arthur," returned Tom Rain, "that perhaps there is no other man in England who would have failed to avail himself of the brilliant prospects that they opened to my view. But I was not to be dazzled by them—not to be led away by the temptation. No: I knew that my character was gone—that my reputation was tarnished—that my misdeeds were numerous and great;—and I felt also for *you*, Arthur—as well as for the haughty name of Ellingham!"

"What do you mean, my dear brother?" cried the noble, struck by the impressive tone in which Rainford uttered these words.

"I mean," answered the debased highwayman to the great peer, "that within the last few days there has been within my reach a jewel which I might have had, and might still have, for the mere trouble of extending my hand to reach it: a jewel such as men toil all their lives to gain! This jewel is a proud title and a princely fortune——"

"Thomas!—my brother!" ejaculated the Earl, a strange and exciting suspicion flashing through his brain.

"Yes—a proud title and a princely fortune, Arthur," repeated Rainford: "but I desire neither! Yet—solemnly and seriously do I declare that, amongst those papers which I discovered in the den of Benjamin Bones, there was one which would make me rich at the expense of another—ennoble me to the prejudice of one whom the proud title better becomes,—and that individual who would thus suffer is *yourself*! For Octavia Manners was the Countess of Ellingham—and I—the debased highwayman, am thine elder brother, legitimately born!"

"Oh! what do I hear?" exclaimed Arthur: "and how much generosity does your conduct display! But think not, dearest brother, that I grieve at the announcement which you have just made! No—far from that! To know that my father did justice to your poor mother—to be able to entertain the conviction that the author of our being was less guilty than I imagined—is a source of satisfaction so pure—so sincere—so heart-felt, that I would gladly purchase it even with the loss of title and of fortune!"

"It is you who are generous, Arthur," said Rainford—for so we shall continue to call him, at all events for the present. "But that coronet which sits so gracefully on your noble brow, and that fortune which enables you to do so much good, shall never be lost to you. No—never, Arthur! Titles I care not for—great wealth I do not crave;—and even if I yearned for the one or aspired to the other, of what avail would be that idle—ineffectual ambition? Here am I in a vile dungeon—accused of a serious offence—my life endangered! And, even if your interest should save me, must I not for ever become an exile from the land of my birth? Yes: for whether you deter the prosecutors from farther proceedings in my case,—or, should they push the matter to the extreme verge, and my life be saved only at your intercession,—can I remain in England? If released from custody, how can I hope to gain an honest name in this clime?—if condemned to death, and then reprieved, will not this leniency on the part of the Crown be conceded on the condition of banishment for the remainder of my days? Thus, Arthur, even did I desire to possess the proud name of Ellingham—did I aspire to that coronet which adorns thy brow—I could not be mad enough to yield to the temptation. But, I repeat—I care not for rank—I need not much wealth; and thus neither my position nor my inclination will for an instant permit me to disturb you in the enjoyment of the family honours and the hereditary estates."

"Alas! how much—how deeply do I regret that we had not met before to embrace as brothers!" exclaimed the Earl. "Though crimes are imputed to you, Thomas,—yet do you possess a heart endowed with the loftiest—the most generous feelings! Ah! well do I now understand wherefore you were agitated last night at Lady Hatfield's house—and why you told me that from no other man in England would you ask as a favour that right of egress from the mansion which you could command by force! And I, who was once on the point of striking you! But wherefore did you not then reveal to me what you have told me now?"

"The secret of my birth you should never have learnt from *my* lips," answered Rainford. "No—I would not have allowed you to know that you possessed a relative for whom you would have to blush. But I was compelled to make that revelation to Lady Hatfield—because——"

"Ah! let us not talk of her, brother!" said Lord Ellingham mournfully. "I would not for worlds reproach you—and yet you know not how profoundly I have loved that woman—how tenderly I love her still! But my hopes there——Let us change the topic, I say!" he added, hastily interrupting himself. "And now tell me if there be any thing I can do in order to soften the grief which must be experienced by that *one* to whom you alluded ere now—any message that I can take to her——"

"Yes: you must see *her*," said Rainford, after a moment's reflection; "and you must tell her that she is to give up to you all those papers which relate to the marriage of our father and my mother and to my birth. She is acquainted with every thing that concerns me and my affairs. It was my original intention to keep those papers—not to serve any purpose—never to use them,—but to gratify one of those unaccountable whims which sometimes influence the most strong-minded amongst us. I thought that, perhaps, when in a foreign land,—for it was my intention to have quitted this country in a few days,—I might sometimes feel a pleasure in contemplating documents so closely connected with my parentage and my birth. Perhaps, too, I might have been swayed by some little sentiment of pride in being able to say to myself, '*A title and a princely fortune are within my grasp; and I will not take them, because I feel myself so utterly unworthy of the first, and because I require not the other.*'—But now, let my fate be whatever it may, it is prudent that those papers should be destroyed. She, who has them in her keeping, loves me—adores me: but she has one foible—one weakness which has already produced serious embarrassment. She is fond of gay apparel—of costly jewels—of those trinkets and that outward show which dazzle the minds of so many women; and this passion on her part is stronger than herself. In a word, then, I would rather that the papers should not remain in her hands—I would sooner that they should be burnt at once than become the source of a temptation which circumstances might perhaps some day render irresistible to *her*. If you really wish to ease my mind of any portion of that weight of anxiety which now hangs upon it, you will at once visit her; and when you tell her all that has passed between you and me ere now, she will give you up those documents, which I enjoin you to commit to the flames, when you have perused them."

"I will do your bidding, Thomas, in all respects save one," returned Lord Ellingham: "and that is with regard to the destruction of the papers. No—if you are generous to a degree, I must at least be just; and I will keep those documents for you—safely, religiously keep them—to be at your disposal at any time, however remote, should altered circumstances induce you to claim them."

"Then you imagine," said Rainford, with something of bitterness in his tone, "that should the future smile upon me, I might be tempted to pluck the coronet from your brow to place it on mine own? You wrong me—yes, you wrong me, Arthur!"

"Heaven knows that I would not willingly—wantonly do so!" cried the nobleman enthusiastically. "But, justice———"

"Well—be it as you say," interrupted Rainford, with a view to terminate the discussion on this topic. "Obtain the papers—they will be safer with you than with her, much as she is devoted to me. And now must I reveal to you another secret—a secret of a strange and romantic nature, connected with *her* whom you are about to visit———"

"With Esther?" said the Earl hastily.

"Ah! ever harping upon that name!" exclaimed Rainford. "Did I not assure you last night that Esther is as pure and innocent as woman can be, and that she does not even know me by sight? See, then, if I have deceived you:—but I will not keep you in suspense———"

At this moment, the turnkey entered with an intimation that it was impossible to allow the interview to be protracted any longer on the present occasion, as the hour for locking up had already passed some time.

"To-morrow, then, you will come again," said Rainford, in a low whisper to his brother. "And now go to No. 5, Brandon Street, Lock's Fields—it is not very far from here—and inquire for Mrs. Rainford."

The Earl pressed his hand in assurance of obeying the directions thus given; and, as the turnkey appeared impatient, the young nobleman hurried away from his brother's cell.

But the mystery relative to Esther de Medina—whatever it might be—was not so soon to be cleared up as the Earl of Ellingham expected.

Upon leaving the prison, he observed an ill-looking fellow lounging about at the gate, and on whose forbidding countenance the light of the lamp streamed fully when the wicket was opened to afford the nobleman egress:— for our readers will remember that all the incidents yet related in this narrative occurred in the winter time, when it is dark at four o'clock.

But it was now nearly six o'clock; and the atmosphere was heavy with mist.

The Earl walked rapidly away from the prison-gate; but when he had proceeded about thirty yards, he inquired of a passer-by the way to Lock's Fields.

The man was a stranger in the neighbourhood, and could not tell him.

"Please, sir, I'll show you the way," exclaimed another individual, stepping officiously forward.

Lord Ellingham immediately recognised, by the light that glimmered from a window in Horsemonger Lane, the ill-looking fellow whom he had noticed at the door of the prison; and for an instant he hesitated to accept his services. But at the next moment he felt ashamed of this vague alarm, and directed the man to lead on.

The fellow turned abruptly round, saying, "You are going out of your way, sir. We must get down to the Fields by the back of the prison."

And he led the way, the Earl following him, down Horsemonger Lane towards Harper Street. But as they passed along the prison-wall, Arthur observed two or three men loitering about at short intervals from each other; and it struck him that his guide coughed in a peculiar fashion as he passed them.

A misgiving, which he vainly endeavoured to resist, was now excited in the Earl's mind; but still he would not turn back nor question his guide.

Suddenly he was seized from behind, and pulled violently backward, while a strong hand fastened itself as it were over his mouth. He struggled desperately: but his guide turned on him, and he was now in the grasp of four powerful men, whose united strength it was impossible to resist.

Still he endeavoured to release himself: and once he managed to get the hand away from his mouth, an advantage of which he instantly availed himself to cry out for help.

But in another instant he was stunned by the blow of a pistol on the head.

When he awoke, he was in total darkness, and lying on a hard bed.

He instinctively stretched out his arms: his right hand encountered a rough and damp stone wall.

He rose and groped cautiously about him;—but it required not many moments to convince him of the terrible though mysterious truth—that he was the inmate of a narrow dungeon!

But where was he thus imprisoned?

Who were the authors of this outrage?

And for what purpose was he made a captive?

These three queries defied all conjecture; and the young nobleman was left to the darkness of his dungeon and the gloom of his meditations.

CHAPTER XLIX.
A PAINFUL INTERVIEW.

We must now go back a few hours—only to the morning of this eventful day—in order to describe the interview which Mr. Clarence Villiers had with his respectable aunt Mrs. Slingsby, at her residence in Old Burlington Street.

He called at her abode as early as nine o'clock,—for he had passed a sleepless night, in consequence of the communication made to him by the individual whom he as yet knew only as Captain Sparks, and of whose arrest on the preceding night he was as yet ignorant.

Mrs. Slingsby, Adelais, and Rosamond were seated at breakfast in a comfortable little parlour, when Clarence was announced.

At first his appearance at so unusual an hour and when he was supposed to be on his way to his office in Somerset House, excited some alarm, lest he had bad news to communicate; and the sisters already trembled for fear their father had discovered their abode. But he speedily reassured them by declaring that he intended to give himself a holiday that morning, and had therefore come to join them at the breakfast-table.

"You are welcome, Clarence," said Mrs. Slingsby, while Adelais appeared so pleased at this unexpected visit that the enhanced carnation tinge of her cheeks and the joy that flashed in her fine eyes rendered her transcendently beautiful.

But Rosamond seemed pensive and even melancholy—although she endeavoured to smile and appear gay.

"I had a visit from Captain Sparks last evening," observed Clarence. "He is going to America, and he called to take leave of me, as well as to entrust me with some little commission, which I of course undertook."

"And we heard a most wholesome and beneficial discourse from the Reverend Mr. Sawkins," observed Mrs. Slingsby.

"Was Mr. Sheepshanks present?" inquired Villiers, without looking at his aunt, and apparently intent only on carving the ham.

"My dear Clarence," said Mrs. Slingsby in a serious, reproachful tone, "your question is light and inconsiderate. You doubtless intended it as a jest, but the object to which it refers is one painfully calculated to wound those who have the good cause at heart. Mr. Sheepshanks has conducted himself in a manner that has produced the most lively grief as well as the greatest astonishment in what may be strictly termed the religious world. Sir Henry Courtenay was shocked when I narrated the incident to him."

"Oh! Sir Henry was shocked, was he?" exclaimed Clarence. "Well, for my part, I should have conceived that a man of fashion would have cared very little for all the Sheepshanks' and Sawkins' in the universe."

"Clarence!" said Mrs. Slingsby, "what *is* the matter with you this morning? There seems to be an unusual flippancy in your observations———"

"Not at all, my dear aunt. Only, I conceive that a man who is fond of gaiety—who goes to parties—mixes with the *élite* of the West End, and so on, can have but little time to devote to the interests of Cannibal-Clothing Associations."

"My dear nephew, you astonish me!" exclaimed Mrs. Slingsby. "Is it to affix a vulgar nick-name to an admirable institution, that you call it a Cannibal-Clothing Association? I once thought you had some degree of respect for the philanthropic and religious establishments which are the boast and ornament of your native land. But———"

"My dear aunt, pardon me if I have offended you," said Clarence—but in a cool and indifferent tone. "I really forgot at the moment the name of the institution to which that arrant hypocrite and scoundrel Sheepshanks belonged."

"Use not such harsh words, Clarence," enjoined Mrs. Slingsby, who knew not what to think of her nephew's unusual manner and discourse. "Mr. Sheepshanks has lost himself in the estimation of all persons of rightly constituted minds; but the Christian spirit of forgiveness commands us to be lenient in our comments on the actions even of the wicked."

"That may be," said Clarence. "But as I read the account in the newspapers, it certainly looked so black against this Sheepshanks, that had he been sent to Newgate, he would have had no more than his due. Now, my opinion is this:—robbery is always a heinous crime; but he who robs his fellow-creatures under the cloak of religion, is an atrocious sinner indeed. Hypocrisy, my dear aunt, is a detestable vice; and you, as a woman of sound sense and discerning judgment, must admit the truth of my observation. But we were talking of Sir Henry Courtenay."

"You must not utter a word against him," said Adelais, in the most artless manner possible; "for Rosamond has conceived so high an opinion of him———"

"Because dear Mrs. Slingsby has represented his virtues—his mental qualifications—his admirable character to me in terms which make me as enthusiastic as herself in extolling so good and amiable a man," exclaimed Rosamond, speaking with an ardour which was the more striking, because the natural purity of her soul prevented her from seeing the necessity of checking it.

Mrs. Slingsby coloured and glanced uneasily towards her nephew, who did not, however, appear to notice that the conversation had taken a turn which was disagreeable to her.

In fact, the suspicions originally excited in his mind by the communications of the preceding evening, were now materially strengthened; and the more he contemplated the character of his aunt, the more transparent became the film that had so long blinded him as to its real nature.

"And so you are a great admirer of Sir Henry Courtenay, Rosamond?" he said, endeavouring to maintain as calm and placid an exterior as possible.

"Rosamond is fully aware that virtue deserves respect, wherever it exists," returned Mrs. Slingsby hastily.

"And Sir Henry Courtenay is the pattern of all virtue, dear madam—is he not?" exclaimed Rosamond.

"He is a very good man, my dear, as I have frequently assured you," said the pious widow. "But let us change a conversation which does not appear agreeable to Clarence?"

"I would not for the world manifest so much selfishness," observed Villiers, coolly, "as to quit a topic which gives so much gratification to Rosamond. At the same time—as the future husband of Adelais, and therefore soon to be your brother-in-law, dear Rosamond—I must warn you against conceiving extravagant notions of the integrity and immaculate virtue of any man who belongs to what is called the Fashionable World."

"But dear Mrs. Slingsby has assured me, Clarence," ejaculated Rosamond, warmly, "that Sir Henry Courtenay is an exception to the general rule—that he is the very pattern of every thing generous and good—and that no one could err in following his advice, whatever it might be. Oh! I can assure you——"

Rosamond stopped short; for Mrs. Slingsby, seeing that her nephew's countenance was becoming purple with indignation as the artless girl thus gave vent to the enthusiasm excited in her soul by the most insidious representations,—Mrs. Slingsby, we say, had touched her with her foot beneath the table—a movement naturally construed by Rosamond into a hint to cut short her observations.

"You can retire, dear girls," said Mrs. Slingsby. "I wish to have a little conversation with Clarence."

"Do not keep us away long, dear madam," exclaimed Adelais, in a playful manner, as she rose to quit the room with her sister.

Clarence and Mrs. Slingsby were now alone together; and the position of each was a most painful one.

The aunt saw that something was wrong; and her guilty conscience excited a thousand vague fears within her bosom; while the nephew felt convinced that the relative, whom he had hitherto loved and respected, was worthy only of his abhorrence and contempt.

There was a long pause in the conversation after the sisters had left the room; but at length the silence, so irksome to both nephew and aunt, was broken by the latter.

"Clarence—something appears to have vexed—to have annoyed you this morning," she observed, in a tremulous tone.

"Do you know," he said, turning abruptly round towards her, and fixing a searching glance upon her countenance, "that you act most unwisely—most indiscreetly—nay, most incorrectly, to expatiate so much upon the virtues of Sir Henry Courtenay? When I first entered the room this morning, I found Rosamond pensive and thoughtful; and she said not a word until that man's name was mentioned, when she became as it were enthusiastic in his defence, although no actual attack was made by me upon his character. What is the meaning of this strange conduct?"

"Clarence—if, in my respect for Sir Henry Courtenay—I have been too warm in my praises of his character,—if——"

"Aunt, there is no supposition in the case," interrupted Villiers, almost sternly. "You *have* been too warm—and heaven only knows with what object! God forbid that I should impute the worst motives to your conduct in this respect: but a dreadful suspicion has been excited in my mind——"

"A suspicion!" murmured Mrs. Slingsby faintly, while the glance which she threw upon her nephew was full of uneasiness.

"Yes—a suspicion!" he repeated; "and most painful—oh! most painful is it to me to be compelled to address you in this manner. But the case is too serious to allow me to remain silent. In one word, have you not made an impression on the mind of that artless girl which may endanger her peace?—have you not been encouraging in her breast an admiration for a man old enough to be her grandfather—an admiration which is not natural, and which is calculated to inspire her with feelings towards a sexagenarian dandy——"

"Clarence!" exclaimed the pious lady, in a hysterical manner; "how dare you address me in this dictatorial tone? Would you seek to invest my conduct in bestowing well-merited praise on a good man, with an aspect so black——"

"Your indignation is well feigned!" cried Villiers, his lips quivering with rage. "But the day of deception has passed—hypocrisy shall no longer impose upon me. If I accuse you unjustly, I will grovel as an abject wretch at your feet to manifest my contrition. Before I thus debase myself, however, you must prove to me that you are indeed the noble-minded—the open-hearted—the immaculate woman I have so long loved and revered! Tell me, then, the real—the true history of that night when a boy was received into this house through charity—a few years ago——"

Mrs. Slingsby became as pale as death, and sate gazing with haggard eyes upon her nephew—unable to avert *her* glance, and yet shrinking from *his*.

"Then you are guilty, madam," he said, after a few moments' pause; "and the excellent—the virtuous—the upright Sir Henry Courtenay is your lover! My God! did the world ever know hypocrisy so abominable—so black as this?"

These words were uttered with extreme bitterness—and Mrs. Slingsby burst into a flood of tears, while she covered her face with her hands.

Clarence possessed a generous heart; and this sight moved him.

"My dear aunt," he said, "I do not wish to mortify you—much less to humiliate you in my presence. In your own estimation you must necessarily be humiliated enough. Neither will I dwell at any length upon the pain—the intense grief which I experience in finding you so different from what I have ever believed you to be—until *now!*" he added, in a mournful tone. "Were you my sister, or did you stand with reference to me in a degree of relationship that would permit me to remonstrate and advise, I should perhaps both reproach and counsel you. But it would ill become a nephew to address his aunt in such a manner."

"Clarence, will you expose me? will you ruin me?" demanded Mrs. Slingsby, in a hysterical tone.

"Not for worlds would I injure you!" ejaculated the young man. "But I must receive no more favours at your hands! Here—take back the money which you gave me a few days ago. Thank God! I have not yet expended any of it— and the arrangements I had made to furnish a house for the reception of my Adelais, can be countermanded. *She* will not object to share a lodging with me—until, by my own honest exertions," he added proudly, "I may be able to give her a suitable home."

And, as he spoke, he cast a roll of Bank-notes upon the table.

"Oh! Clarence—if I have been weak—frail—culpable," cried the widow, "you are at least severe and cruel; for I have ever done all I could to serve your interests."

"Were I to express my real opinion on that head," answered Villiers, "I might grieve you still more than I have already done. A bandage has fallen from my eyes—and I can now understand how necessary an instrument of publicity I have been for your assumed virtues. But, in the name of God! let us argue the point no further; for sincerely—sincerely do I assert my unwillingness to give you additional pain. Pardon me, however, if I declare how impossible it is—how inconsistent it would be—to leave those innocent girls in a dwelling which is visited by such a man as that Sir Henry Courtenay."

"How could you remove them elsewhere, without exposing me, Clarence?" demanded his aunt in an imploring tone. "What explanation can you or I give them, to account in a reasonable manner for the suddenness of such a step?"

Villiers paced the room in an agitated manner.

He knew not how to act.

To leave Adelais and Rosamond in the society of his aunt was repugnant to his high sense of honour and his correct notions of propriety; and whither to remove them he knew not.

He had seen and heard enough at the breakfast-table, to convince him that Mrs. Slingsby had some sinister motive in creating in the mind of Rosamond,—that innocent, artless mind, which was so susceptible of any impressions which a designing woman might choose to make upon it,—a feeling of admiration in favour of the baronet; and although he had to a considerable extent curbed the resentment and the indignation which his aunt's conduct in this respect had aroused within him, still to leave that young maiden any longer within an atmosphere of infection, was impossible! No: he would sooner restore the sisters to their father, and leave to circumstances the realization of his hopes in regard to Adelais!

While he was still deliberating within himself what course to pursue, and while Mrs. Slingsby was anxiously watching him as he paced the room with agitated steps, the servant entered with the morning's newspaper.

Clarence took it from the table in a mechanical manner and glanced his eye over the first page: but his thoughts were too painfully pre-occupied to permit him to entertain, even for an instant, any idea of reading the journal.

No:—it was one of those unwitting actions which we often perform when sorely embarrassed or bewildered,—an action without positive motive and without aim.

But how often do the most trivial deeds exercise a paramount influence over our destinies!

And this simple action of glancing at the newspaper proved to be an instance of the kind.

For at the moment when Clarence was about to throw the journal back again upon the table and resume his agitated walk, his eyes encountered an advertisement which instantaneously arrested his attention.

Then, with beating heart and with an expression of joy rapidly spreading itself over his countenance, he read the following lines:—

"TO A. AND R.—Your distressed and almost heart-broken father implores you to return to him. The past shall be forgotten on his side; and no obstacle shall be opposed to the happiness of A. Your father is lying on a sick bed, and again implores that this prayer may not be made in vain."

"God be thanked!" cried Villiers, no longer able to restrain his joy; and handing the newspaper to his aunt, he directed her attention to the advertisement.

"Here is an apology at once for the removal of the young ladies from this house, Clarence," observed Mrs. Slingsby. "And now that you are saved from the embarrassment in which you were plunged but a few minutes back, will you promise never—never to reveal—and, if possible, to forget——"

"You allude to your conduct towards Rosamond?" said Villiers. "Tell me its motive—and I swear solemnly——"

"In one word, then," interrupted his aunt, "let Rosamond beware of Sir Henry Courtenay! And now answer me a single question—for I see you are impatient to be gone:—How came you to discover——what meant your allusion—to—to the boy who was received into this house——"

"I cannot stay to explain all *that*," cried Villiers. "But rest assured that your character stands no chance of being made the subject of scandalous talk—unless, indeed, your future actions——"

"Enough, Clarence!" exclaimed Mrs. Slingsby. "I know that you must despise me: but spare me any farther humiliation!"

She then rang the bell, and desired the servant to summon Adelais and Rosamond.

We need not pause to describe the joy which those fair beings experienced when Clarence showed them the advertisement inviting them to return home; although tears immediately afterwards started into their eyes, when they read that their father was upon a bed of sickness.

They once more retired to their bed-chamber to prepare their toilette for departure; and, when a hackney-coach drove round to the door, they took leave of Mrs. Slingsby with demonstrations of gratitude which struck to her heart like a remorse.

Clarence accompanied them back to the cottage; and his heart palpitated violently—he scarcely knew wherefore—when he assisted them to alight.

The front door was opened by the female servant, who uttered a cry of joy on beholding the young ladies once more; and with trembling steps Adelais and Rosamond entered the parlour, followed by Clarence.

To their surprise—and, at first, to their great delight—the sisters found themselves, on crossing the threshold of the room, in the presence of their father, who was looking pale, it was true—but with concentrated anger, and not with illness.

Adelais and Rosamond fell on their knees before him, exclaiming, "Forgive us, dear father—forgive us!"

"How am I to receive you, Adelais?" he asked in a cold voice: "as Miss Torrens—or as——"

"As Miss Torrens at present, sir," answered Clarence stepping forward, and speaking in a firm though respectful tone. "But, in accordance with the promise held out in that advertisement which appears in to-day's journal, I hope that your elder daughter will soon be mine—and with your permission and blessing also."

"Where have my daughters been residing during their absence, sir?" inquired Mr. Torrens, without appearing to notice the latter portion of Villiers' observations.

"Under the protection of a female relative of mine, sir," answered Clarence, with increasing misgivings at the cold demeanour of the father of his beloved.

"Thank you for the information, sir," said Mr. Torrens, with a smile of triumph. "At least you have so far disarmed my resentment, that you have brought me back my daughter pure and innocent as when you enticed her away, with the aid of a villanous robber."

"A robber!" ejaculated Clarence indignantly.

"Yes, sir," continued Mr. Torrens, in a sneering tone; "your worthy colleague, Captain Sparks, is a common highwayman—a thief—properly named Thomas Rainford; and at this moment he is a prisoner in Horsemonger Lane Gaol. Scarcely ten minutes have elapsed since I received a note from Mr. Howard, a solicitor, informing me of the fact."

Clarence was so astounded by this announcement, that for a few moments he could make no reply; and the young ladies, who had in the meantime slowly risen from their suppliant posture and were now standing timidly by their father's side, exchanged glances of painful surprise.

"Yes," resumed Mr. Torrens in a stern and severe tone, "that man, who aided you to effect the abduction of these disobedient girls, is a common highwayman—and you could not be ignorant of that fact!"

"As I live, sir," ejaculated Clarence, at length recovering the power of speech. "I *was* ignorant of the fact; and even now——But," he added, correcting himself, "I cannot doubt your word! At the same time, permit me to assure you that I had never seen him until that night——"

"I require no farther explanation, sir," interrupted Mr. Torrens. "My daughters are now once more under the paternal roof—inveigled back again, it is true, by a stratagem on my part——"

"A stratagem!" repeated Clarence, while Adelais uttered a faint shriek, and sank weeping into her sister's arms.

"Yes—a stratagem, sir!" ejaculated Mr. Torrens. "And now learn my decision, Mr. Villiers! Sooner than she shall become your wife," he continued, pointing towards the unhappy girl, "I would give her to the meanest hind who toils for his daily bread. Depart, sir:—this house is at least a place where my authority can alone prevail!"

"Mr. Torrens—I beseech—I implore you——" began the wretched young man, whose hopes were thus suddenly menaced so cruelly.

"Depart, sir!" thundered the angry father; "or I shall use violence—and we will then see whether you will strike in return the parent of her whom you affect to love!"

And he advanced towards Villiers in a menacing manner.

"I will not stay to irritate you, sir," said Clarence, feeling as if his heart were ready to burst. "Adelais—remember one who will never cease to remember you! Rosamond, farewell!"

Mr. Torrens became more and more impatient; and Villiers quitted the house with feelings as different from those which had animated him when he entered it, as the deepest despair is different from the most joyous hope.

But the anguish of his heart was not greater than that which now filled the bosom of her from whom he was so unexpectedly and cruelly separated.

CHAPTER L.
THE LAWYER'S OFFICE.

A few days after the events just related, the following scene took place at Mr. Howard's office in Golden Square.

It was about four in the afternoon, and the lawyer was seated in his private room, at a table covered with papers, when a clerk entered and announced that Sir Christopher Blunt and his lady had just arrived.

"His lady with him—eh!" exclaimed the solicitor. "Well—show them in at once."

And, accordingly, in a few minutes the worthy knight, with Charlotte—or, we beg her pardon, Lady Blunt—hanging upon his arm, entered the office.

The old gentleman was all smiles—but the quick eye of Mr. Howard immediately perceived that they were to some extent forced and feigned; and that beneath his jaunty aspect there was not altogether the inward contentment, much less the lightsome glee, of a happy bridegroom.

As for Lady Blunt—she was attired in the richest manner, and in all the colours of the rainbow,—looking far too gaudy to be either genteel or fashionable.

"My dear Sir Christopher, I am quite charmed to see you" exclaimed Mr. Howard, rising to welcome his client and the bride. "Your ladyship——"

"Yes—this is my loving and beloved Lady Blunt, Howard," said the knight pompously: "a delightful creature, I can assure you—and who has vowed to devote herself to my happiness."

"Come now, you great stupid!" said the lady; "finish your business here, and let us see about the new carriage. Of all places in the world, I hate a lawyer's office—ever since I was once summoned to a Court of Conscience for seventeen shillings and ninepence-halfpenny, and had to call on the thief of an attorney to get him to take it by instalments of sixpence a-week. So, you see, I can't a-bear the lawyers. No offence, sir," she added, turning towards Mr. Howard; "but I always speak my mind; and I think it's best."

"My dear creature—my sweet love!" ejaculated Sir Christopher, astounded at this outbreak of petulance on the part of his loving and beloved wife.

"Pray do not distress yourself, my dear Sir Christopher," said the lawyer. "We are accustomed to receive sharp rebukes from the ladies sometimes," he added, with as courteous a smile as he could possibly manage under the circumstances. "But pray be seated. Will your ladyship take this chair?"—and he indicated the one nearest to the fire.

Lady Blunt quitted her husband's arm, but made an imperious sign for him to bring his chair close to hers; and he obeyed her with a submission which left no doubt in the lawyer's mind as to the empire already asserted by the bride.

"I am very glad you have called to-day, Sir Christopher," said the lawyer; "for——"

"He couldn't very well come before, sir," interrupted Lady Blunt; "because we only came back from the matrimonial trip last night."

Mr. Howard bowed, and was preparing to continue, when the knight exclaimed, "My dear sir, what *is* all this to-do about the highwayman who robbed me of the two thousand pounds? I thought I told you so particularly that I would rather no steps should be taken in the matter; and now—the moment I come back to town——"

"Instead of having all our time to ourselves, to gad about cozie together," again interrupted Lady Blunt, "we are forced to come bothering here at a lawyer's office."

"The ends of justice must be met, Lady Blunt," said Mr. Howard drily. "In consequence of particular information which I received, I caused this Thomas Rainford to be apprehended; and I appeal to Sir Christopher himself—who has served the high office of Sheriff——"

"And once stood as a candidate for the aldermanic gown of Portsoken, until I was obliged to cut those City people," added the knight, drawing himself up.

"And why should you cut the City people?" demanded his wife. "For my part, I'd sooner see the Lord Mayor's show than Punch and Judy any day; and that's saying a great deal—for no one *can* be more fonder of Punch and Judy than me."

"My dear Charlotte," exclaimed the knight, who now seemed to be sitting on thorns, "you——"

"Charlotte at home—Lady Blunt in public, Sir Christopher—if *you* please," interrupted the bride. "But pray let Mr. Howard get to the end of this business."

"Well, my dear," exclaimed Sir Christopher, "if it annoys you, why *would* you come? I assured you how unusual it was for ladies to accompany their husbands to the office of their solicitors——"

"Oh! I dare say, Sir Christopher!" cried Charlotte. "You don't think that I'm going to trust you out of my sight, do you now? I'm not quite such a fool as you take me for. Why, even when we are walking along the street together, I can see your wicked old eye fixed on the gals———"

"Lady Blunt!" exclaimed the knight, becoming literally purple; "you—you—you do me an injustice!"

"So much the better. I hope I am wrong—for both of our sakes," returned her ladyship. "Depend upon it———But, no matter now: let Mr. Howard get on with his story."

"With your permission, madam, I shall be delighted to do so," said the lawyer. "I was observing just now that having received particular information, I caused this scoundrel Thomas Rainford, *alias* Captain Sparks, to be apprehended; and on Monday morning, Sir Christopher, you must attend before the magistrate to give your evidence."

"But who authorised you to proceed in this affair, Mr. Howard?" demanded the knight.

"What a strange question?" exclaimed the lawyer, evidently unwilling to give a direct answer to it. "Only reflect for a moment, my dear Sir Christopher. A robbery is committed—you, your nephew, and myself are outwitted—laughed at—set at defiance,—and when an opportunity comes in my way, I very naturally adopt the best measures to punish the rogue."

"Quite proper too, sir," said Lady Blunt. "The idea of any one daring to laugh at Sir Christopher! I'd scratch the villain's eyes out, if I had him here. To laugh at Sir Christopher, indeed! Does he look like a man who is meant to be laughed at?"

Lady Blunt could not have chosen a more unfortunate opportunity to ask this question; for her husband at that moment presented so ludicrous an appearance, between his attempts to look pleasant and his fears lest he already seemed a henpecked old fool in the eyes of his solicitor, that a man possessing less command over himself than Mr. Howard would have laughed outright.

But with the utmost gravity in the world, the lawyer assured her ladyship that nothing could be more preposterous than to laugh at a gentleman of Sir Christopher Blunt's rank and importance; and he also declared that in arresting Thomas Rainford, he had merely felt a proper anxiety to punish one who had dared to ridicule the knight, after having robbed him.

Lady Blunt was one of those capricious women who will laugh at their husbands either as a matter of pastime or for the purpose of manifesting their own independence and predominant sway, but who cannot bear the idea of any other person taking a similar liberty. She therefore expressed her joy that Mr. Howard had caused Rainford to be apprehended, and declared, of her own accord, that Sir Christopher should attend to give his evidence on the ensuing Monday—"for she would go with him!"

"Well, my dear, since such is your pleasure," observed the knight, "there is no more to be said upon the subject. I *will* go, my love; and I think that when the magistrate hears my evidence, he will feel convinced that I know pretty well how to aid the operation of the laws, and that I have not been a Sheriff for nothing. Although sprung from a humble origin——"

"Oh! pray don't begin that nonsense, Sir Christopher!" exclaimed the lady; "or I shall faint. It is really quite sickening."

At that moment the door opened somewhat violently; and Mr. Frank Curtis entered the room.

"Ah! Sir Christopher, my jolly old cock—how are you?" exclaimed that highly respectable young gentleman, whose face was dreadfully flushed with drinking, and who smelt so strong of cigars and rum-punch that his presence instantly produced the most overpowering effect.

"Mr. Curtis!" began the knight, rising from his chair, and drawing himself up to his full height, "I——"

"Come—it's no use to be grumpy over it, uncle," interrupted Frank. "Matrimony doesn't seem to agree with you very well, since you're so soon put out of humour. Ah! my dear Char——my dear aunt, I mean—beg your pardon—quite a mistake, you know;—but really you look charming this afternoon."

"Get out with you, do!" cried Lady Blunt, who was somewhat undecided how to treat Mr. Curtis.

"What! doesn't matrimony agree with you, either, my dear and much respected aunt?" ejaculated Frank. "Why, I once knew a lady who was in a galloping consumption—given up, in fact, and the undertaker who lived over the way had already begun to make her coffin—for he knew he should have the order for the funeral; when all of a sudden a young chap fell in love with her, married her, and took her to the south of France—where I've been, by the bye—and brought her home in six months quite recovered, and in a fair way to present him with a little one—a pledge of affection, as it's called."

"Mr. Curtis, I am surprised at you," exclaimed Sir Christopher, in a pompous and commanding tone;—"to talk in this way before a lady who has only recently passed through that trying ordeal."

"I'll be bound to say it wasn't so recent as you suppose, old buck," cried Frank, staggering against the lawyer's table.

"Sir, Lady Blunt has only been recently—very recently married, as you are well aware," said the knight sternly. "And now let me tell you, sir, that the detestable devices schemed by Miss Mordaunt and you have recoiled upon yourselves——"

"Miss Mordaunt and me!" exclaimed Frank, now unfeignedly surprised: "why—I never spoke to Miss Mordaunt in my life!"

"The monster!" half screamed Lady Blunt.

"The audacious liar!" vociferated the knight.

"Pretty names—very pretty," said Frank coolly; "but I'm rather tough, thank God! and so they won't kill me this time. But I can assure you, uncle, you've got hold of the wrong end of the stick when you say that me and Miss Mordaunt planned any thing against you. As I once observed to my friend the Count of St. Omers,—'My lord,' says I.—'What?' asks the Marquis.—'My Lord Duke,' I repeated, in a firmer tone——"

"Cease this nonsense, Mr. Curtis," interrupted Sir Christopher Blunt sternly.

"Yes—and let us come along, my dear," said Lady Blunt, rising and taking her husband's arm. "Your nev-vy does smell so horrid of rum and cigars———"

"And very good things too," cried Frank; "ain't they, Howard? Me and a party of young fashionables have been keeping it up a bit to-day at my lodgings—on the strength of my intended marriage with Mrs. Goldberry, the rich widow——"

"Your marriage, Frank!" exclaimed Sir Christopher. "What—how—when———"

"Lord bless you, my dear uncle," said Mr. Curtis, swaying himself to and fro in a very extraordinary manner, "you don't half know what kind of a fellow I am. While you was away honeymooning and nonsense——"

"Nonsense, indeed!" exclaimed Lady Blunt, indignantly. "Come, Sir Christopher—it's no good staying here talking to Mr. Imperance."

"Going to Conduit Street—eh, aunt?" said Frank, with a drunken leer. "But, by-the-bye, you regularly choused me out of five guineas, you know, aunt—and something else, too——"

"Eh?—what?" said Sir Christopher, turning back. "Mr. Curtis, do you dare to accuse Lady Blunt——"

"Of having made a very great fool of me, but a much bigger one of you, old fellow," added Frank; and, snapping his fingers in his uncle's face, he exclaimed, "I don't care a penny for you, Sir Christopher! In a few days I shall marry Mrs. Goldberry—you are very welcome to be as happy as you can with your Abigail there. So remember, we're cuts in future, Sir Christopher—since you want to come the bumptious over me."

The knight was about to reply; but his better-half drew him hastily away from the lawyer's office, saying, "Come along, you great stupid! What's the use of staying to dispute with that feller?"

The door closed behind the "happy couple;" and Mr. Frank Curtis, throwing himself into the chair which Lady Blunt had just quitted, burst out into a tremendous fit of laughter.

"You have gone too far, Frank—a great deal too far," said the lawyer, shaking his head disapprovingly. "Sir Christopher has been a good friend to you; and although he has committed an egregious error in running off with that filly, still——"

"What do I care?" interrupted Frank. "I proposed to Mrs. Goldberry yesterday—and she accepted me, after a good deal of simpering and blushing, and so on. She's got five thousand a year, and lives in splendid style in Baker Street. I made her believe that I wasn't quite a beggar myself: but all's fair in love and war, as my friend the late Prince of St. Omers used to say in his cups. But what about this fellow Rainford? and how the deuce did he come to be arrested?"

"I received information of his residence," answered Howard coolly; "and I gave him into custody accordingly."

"It's very odd," continued Frank, "but I met him last Sunday night; and I don't mind telling you that we went into the middle of Hyde Park and had an hour's wrestling together, to see who was the better man. I threw him nineteen times running, and he threw me seven; then I threw him three times—and he gave in. So we cried 'quits' for old scores, and I gave him my word and honour that nothing would ever be done against him in respect to the little affair of the two thousand pounds. You may therefore suppose that I'm rather vexed——"

"The officers had already received instructions to apprehend him at the time your *alleged* wrestling match came off," said the lawyer; "and your evidence will be required next Monday morning."

"And I suppose the whole affair of the robbery will come out?" observed Curtis interrogatively.

"Decidedly so. You must state the exact *truth*—if you can," added Mr. Howard.

"If I can! Damn it, old fellow, that observation is not quite the thing—coming from you; and if any body else had uttered it, egad! I'd send him a hostile message to-morrow morning—as I did to my most valued friend, the Marquis of Boulogne, when I was in Paris. I'll just tell you how that was——"

"Not now Frank," interrupted the lawyer; "because I'm very busy. It's getting on for post time—and I have not a minute to spare. But mind and be punctual at the Borough police-office on Monday morning at ten."

"Well—if I must, I must," said Curtis. "But, after all, I think it's rather too bad—for this Sparks, or Rainford, or whatever his name is, seems a good kind of fellow, after all."

"The law must take its course, Frank," observed the attorney in an abrupt, dry manner.

Curtis accordingly took his leave, and returned to his lodgings, where by dint of cold water applied outwardly and soda-water taken inwardly, he endeavoured to sober himself sufficiently to pay a visit to Mrs. Goldberry.

For it was literally true that there *was* such a lady—that she lived in splendid style in Baker Street—that Frank had proposed to her—and that he had been accepted;—but we have deemed it necessary to give the reader these corroborative assurances on our part, inasmuch as the whole tale would otherwise have appeared nothing more nor less than one of the innumerable children of Mr. Curtis's fertile imagination.

CHAPTER LI.
LORD ELLINGHAM IN THE DUNGEON.

Four weeks had elapsed since the arrest of Tom Rain and the extraordinary adventure which had snatched the Earl of Ellingham from the great world and plunged him into a narrow—noisome cell.

Yes—four weeks had the nobleman languished in the terrible dungeon,—ignorant of where his prison-house was situated—why his freedom was thus outraged—and who were his persecutors.

Every morning, at about eight o'clock, a small trap in the door of his cell was opened, and food was passed through to him. A lamp had been given him the day after he became an inmate of the place; and oil was regularly supplied for the maintenance of the light. His food was good, and wine accompanied it;—it was therefore evident that no petty spite nor mean malignity had led to his captivity.

Indeed, the man who brought him his food assured him that no harm would befall him,—that his imprisonment was necessary to suit certain weighty and important interests, but that it would not be protracted beyond a few weeks,—and that the only reason for placing him in such a dungeon was because it was requisite to guard against the possibility of an escape.

Often and often had Lord Ellingham endeavoured to render his gaoler more communicative; but the man was not to be coaxed into garrulity. Neither did he ever allow the nobleman to catch a glimpse of his features, when he brought the food to the trap-door. He invariably stood on one side, and spoke in a feigned tone when replying to any question to which he did vouchsafe an answer.

The day after his strange and mysterious arrest, Arthur received from this man the assurances above mentioned; and a considerable weight was thereby removed from his mind. His imprisonment was not to be eternal: a few weeks would see the term of the necessity that had caused it. But still he grieved—nay, felt shocked to think of the state of suspense in which those who cared for him would remain during his long absence. This source of affliction he mentioned to the man who attended upon him; and the reply was to some extent satisfactory.

"I will supply you with writing materials, and you can address letters to your friends, stating that sudden business has called you abroad—to France, for instance; and that you may probably be absent six weeks. Write in this manner—the excuse will at least allay any serious fears that may be entertained concerning you; and those letters shall be sent through the post to the persons to whom they are addressed. But you must deliver them unsealed into my hands, that I may satisfy myself as to the real nature of their contents."

Small as the satisfaction resulting from this proceeding could be to Lord Ellingham, it was still far preferable to the maintenance of a rigid silence in respect to his friends. He accordingly wrote a laconic letter in the sense suggested by his gaoler; and addressed copies to Lady Hatfield, Thomas Rainford, and Mr. de Medina. The next time his gaoler visited him—or rather, came to the door of the dungeon, the prisoner was informed that the three letters had been duly forwarded through the twopenny post.

The reader will scarcely require to be informed of the mental anxiety which the nobleman suffered during his incarceration. This was naturally great—very great. He was also frequently plunged in the most bewildering conjectures relative to the authors, the motives, and the locality of his imprisonment. Nor less did he grieve—Oh! deeply grieve, when he thought of the surprise—the alarm—and the sorrow with which Lady Hatfield on one side and Rainford on the other must view his mysterious absence. He had left the former with the intention of seeing the latter, and she would naturally expect him to return if for no other reason than to give her an account of their interview; and he had quitted Rainford with the promise to perform a certain task, and also having pledged himself to use his influence and his wealth in his behalf.

The idea of the feelings that must be entertained by Rainford relative to his absence, afflicted him more than any other. That generous-hearted man had told him to keep his coronet and his fortune to the prejudice of *him—the elder brother, legitimately born*; and yet that interview in Horsemonger Lane Gaol seemed destined to be the last which they were to have together! What would the poor prisoner think when the Earl returned not, and when a letter containing a cold and wretched excuse was put into his hands? Oh! this was the maddening—maddening thought; and the Earl shrank from it far more appalled than from the stern reality of his dungeon! Because Rainford might be judged, and, alas! the law might take its course—its fatal course—ere *he*, the Earl, could stretch out a hand to save that generous-hearted half-brother.

But amidst all the bitter and bewildering reflections which tormented him during his imprisonment of four weeks in that dungeon of unknown neighbourhood, there was still a predominant idea—a gleam of hope, which, apart from the assurance that his captivity would soon have a term, cheered and animated him often.

For whither will not the rays of Hope penetrate? Even when Hope is really gone, her work is often done by Despair; and the latter feeling, in its extreme, is thus often akin to Hope herself.

The hope, then, that cheered and animated the Earl at times, was—ESCAPE!

Yes: he yearned to quit that dungeon, not so much for his own sake—oh! not nearly so much, as for that of his half-brother, who was involved in such peril, and who needed influence and interest to save him! For the Earl well knew that the law in criminal cases is not so tardy as in civil matters; and that to take away a man's life, all its machinery is set into rapid motion—although to settle his claims to a fortune or to give him justice against his neighbour, it is, heaven knows! heart-breakingly slow and wearisome!

To send a man to the scaffold, takes but a few weeks at the Old Bailey:—to decide the right of this man or that man to a particular estate, or legacy, occupies years and years in the Court of Chancery. Oh! how thirsty do our legislators appear to drink human blood. How rapidly all technicalities and causes of delay are cleared away when the capital offender stands before his judge! A day—perhaps an hour is sufficient to decide the death of a human being; but half a century may elapse ere the conflicting claims to an acre of land or a few thousand pounds can be settled elsewhere.

And, strange—ah! and monstrous, too, is it, that the man who loses a case in which he sues his neighbour for twenty pounds, may appeal to another tribunal—have a new trial granted—and, losing that also, perhaps obtain a *third* investigation of the point at issue, and thus three verdicts in that beggarly business! But the man who is doomed to die—who loses his case against the criminal prosecutor—cannot appeal to another tribunal. No judges sit solemnly *in banco* for him: *one verdict* is sufficient to take away a life. Away with him to the scaffold! In this great commercial country, twenty pounds—consisting of pieces of paper printed upon and stamped with particular figures—are of more consequence than a being of flesh and blood! What though this being of flesh and blood may have others—a wife and children—dependent on him? No matter! Give him not the chance of a new trial: let one judge and one jury suffice to consign him to the hangman! There can be no appeal—no re-investigation for his case, *although it be a case of life and death*: but away with him to the scaffold!

What blood-thirsty and atrocious monsters have our law-givers been: what cruel, inhuman beings are they still, to perpetuate so abominable—so flagrant—so infamous a state of jurisprudence! For how many have been hanged, though innocent,—their guiltlessness transpiring when it is too late! But there is no court of appeal for the man accused of a capital crime: he is a dog who has got a bad name—and public opinion dooms him to be hanged, days and weeks before the jury is sworn or the judge takes his seat to try him!

And wherefore is not this infamous state of the law, which allows appeals to the case of money-claims, but none to the case of capital accusations,—wherefore is not this state of the law altered? Because our legislators are too much occupied with their own party contentions and strifes;—because they are ever engaged in battling for the Ministerial benches—the "loaves and fishes" of power: because it seems to them of more consequence to decide whether Sir Robert Peel or Lord John Russell shall be Prime Minister—whether the Conservatives or the Whigs shall hold the reins of power. Or else, gentle reader, the condition of Greece—or Spain—or Turkey,—or even perhaps of Otaheite,—is a matter of far greater importance than the lives of a few miserable wretches in the condemned cells of criminal gaols!

But, in *our* estimation—and we have the misfortune to differ from the legislators of the country—the *life of one of those wretches* is of far greater consequence than the state of tyrant-ridden Greece—the Spanish marriages—the quarrels of the Sultan and his Pachas—or the miserable squabbles of hypocritical English missionaries and a French governor in Tahiti. Yes—in *our* estimation, the life of *one* man outweighs all such considerations; and we would rather see half a session of Parliament devoted to the discussion of the grand question of the PUNISHMENT OF DEATH, than one single day of that session given to all the foreign affairs that ever agitated in a Minister's brain.

It was the twenty-eighth day of Lord Ellingham's imprisonment; and it was about six o'clock on the evening of this day.

The nobleman was at work upon the masonry of his dungeon,—his efforts being directed to remove the stones from the immediate vicinity of a small square aperture, or sink in the corner of the cell.

His implements were a knife and fork, and one of the screws of the framework of his bed.

But with these he worked arduously.

Nor was this the first day of his labours. No! for twenty-six days had he been toiling—toiling—toiling on, to make an opening into what he believed to be the common sewer,—even at the risk of inundating his dungeon, and thus perishing miserably!

But all those toils, and all that risk, were sustained and encountered for thee, Tom Rain!

Slowly—slowly—slowly had the work progressed; but now—on the twenty-eighth day—Arthur found himself so far advanced that escape from the dungeon was at least open to him.

But escape into what region?

Into those drains and sewers which run beneath the streets of London, and form a maze to which the only clue is a knowledge of the point whence he, who enters the labyrinth, originally starts! And this clue was not possessed by Arthur; for in what part of London his dungeon was situate, he had not the least idea. It could hardly be said that he was confident of this dungeon being in the metropolis at all;—and yet he had many reasons to believe that it was. For, in the first place, his gaoler had mentioned the fact of his letters having been sent by the *twopenny post*; secondly, he had ascertained that his cell was situate in the very vicinity of a common sewer, and sewers were not at that time formed in the villages surrounding the metropolis; and thirdly, he could scarcely believe that those who had arrested him *in* London, would have run the risk of removing him out of its precincts—for he was well aware that atrocious outrages and diabolical crimes may be perpetrated with greater chances of impunity in the metropolis than elsewhere.

But, although he was thus tolerably well convinced that his prison-house was within the boundaries of London, he had not the least notion of the precise locality. And when he had removed sufficient of the massive masonry to form an aperture large enough to permit a full-grown man to pass into the sewer,—and when he heard the muddy, slimy waters gurgling languidly in the depths below, he shuddered, and his blood ran cold—for he thought within himself, "I have heard of men who venture into these places in search of treasures, and who, having wandered for miles and miles beneath the streets of London, have issued safely forth again. But *they* knew whence they started; and thus that starting-post was a clue to guide them in the maze. But *I* know not whether, on entering that slimy shallow, I should turn to the right or to the left,—nor which channels to pursue in that terrible labyrinth!"

Then, ashamed of his fears—reproaching himself for his hesitation, he drank a deep draught of the wine that had been supplied him in the morning; and holding the lamp in one hand, and in the other a stout stick cut from one of the cross-beams that supported the mattress of his bed, he entered the common sewer.

His feet sank down into the thick slime, and the muddy water reached to his knees. There was a nauseous odour in the dreary passage, and the filthy fluid was very thick. These circumstances convinced him that it was low water in the river Thames; and by examining the masonry forming the sides of the sewers, he saw that the tide was running out. He therefore resolved to follow the course of the muddy stream, with the hope that he might at length reach one of the mouths by which the sewers discharge their contents into the river.

Armed with his stick to protect himself against the rats as well as to sound his way so as to escape any hole or abrupt depth that there might chance to be in the bottom of the sewer,—and holding the lamp in his left hand, the great peer of England pursued his appalling path in a channel seven feet wide and beneath a vaulting twelve feet high.

From time to time the sudden rush of a number of vermin along a ledge by the side of the channel, and then the sound of their plunge into the slimy water, startled him to such a degree that he almost dropped his lamp: and then the conviction which flashed to his mind *that if he lost his light, he should be inevitably devoured by those vermin*, caused such a chill to pass through him—as if ice were unexpectedly placed upon his heart—that his courage was oftentimes nearly subdued altogether.

But he thought of his half-brother who had manifested so much generosity towards him,—he thought of her whom he had promised to love as a *sister*,—and he also remembered that were he to retrace his steps, *even if he could find the way back*, he should be returning to a dungeon:—of all this he thought—and he went on—on, in that revolting and perilous maze!

Yes: with lamp held high up, and stick groping in the filthy mud—stirring up nauseating odours,—on—on went the daring, enterprising, chivalrous nobleman—breathing an infected and almost stifling air,—an air formed of such noxious gases, that it might explode at any moment, ignited by the lamp!

But, hark! what is that rumbling sound—like thunder at a vast distance?

Arthur pauses—and listens.

The truth in a few moments flashed to his mind: he was beneath a street in which vehicles were moving. Oh! now he felt convinced—even if he had entertained any doubts before—that he was in London.

Watching the progress of the slimy stream, he turned first to the left, up a channel that branched off from the one which he had originally entered;—then he turned to the right into another—the hollow rumbling sounds overhead gradually increasing in volume and power.

Suddenly he beholds a light glancing upon the putrescent surface of the slimy stream through which he is wading knee-deep. That light is half-a-dozen yards in front of him—flickering playfully.

He advances: sounds of footsteps—human footsteps—come down from overhead. He looks up—and, behold! there is a grating in the street above; and through that grating the light of the lamp streams and the sound of the footsteps comes.

He hears voices, too—as the people pass,—the voices of that world from all communication with which he is for the time cut off!

Shall he cry out for assistance? No: a sense of shame prevents him. He would not like to be dragged forth from those filthy depths, in the presence of a curious—gaping—staring crowd. He prefers the uncertainty and the peril of his subterranean path, in the fond hope that it may speedily lead to some safe issue.

The Earl accordingly passed on—disturbing the water on which the light from the street-lamp played,—disturbing, too, the vermin on either side with the splash of the fetid fluid as he waded through it.

But when he had proceeded a dozen yards, he looked back—as if unwilling to quit the vicinity of that grating which opened into the street.

In another moment, however, he conquered his hesitation, and pursued his way in a straight line, without again turning off either to the right or to the left.

Upwards of an hour had elapsed since he had quitted the dungeon—and as yet he had found no issue from that labyrinth of subterranean passages.

Grim terrors already began to assume palpable forms to his imagination, when suddenly he beheld a dim twinkling light, like a faint star, at a great distance a-head.

That light seemed a beacon of hope; and as he drew nearer and nearer, its power increased. At last he saw another twinkling light, struggling as it were betwixt glimmer and gloom;—and then a third—and then a fourth. The air appeared to grow fresher too; and the Earl at length believed that an opening from the maze must be near.

Yes: he was not mistaken! The lights increased in number and intensity; and he was soon convinced that they shone upon the opposite bank of the Thames.

A few minutes more—and all doubt was past!

The fresh breeze from the river fanned his cheek—and, as he reached the mouth of the sewer, and hurled away his lamp, he saw the mighty flood stretched out before him—a bridge spanning its width at a little distance on his left hand.

He knew that bridge;—he recognised it by the pale lustre of the moon—for the evening was clear and fine.

It was Blackfriars Bridge!

Then, from which direction had he come?

Remembering the turnings he had taken, he could fix upon the district of Clerkenwell as the scene of his late imprisonment. But he did not pause to reflect on a matter now so trivial,—trivial, *because he had escaped, and was once more free*!

It was low water—and a bed of mud received him knee-deep, as he leapt from the mouth of the sewer.

But what cared he for his uncouth and filthy appearance?—*since he had escaped, and was once more free?*

For four weeks his beard had not been shaved, nor his toilette carefully performed; and his hair, too, was long and matted. It was therefore necessary to cleanse himself and change his attire as soon as possible.

Hastening along the muddy margin of the river's bed, he ascended the steps of a wharf, and plunged into the district of Whitefriars. There, selecting the humblest-looking public house he could find, he entered; and, as he had his purse about him (for those who had imprisoned, did not rob him), he was enabled to command the necessaries and attentions which he required. Indeed, the landlord willingly supplied a complete change of linen and a suit of his own clothes to a guest who spared not his gold; and as "mine host" and the Earl happened to be of the same height and equally slender in figure, the garments of the former suited well enough the temporary need of the latter.

A hundred times, while performing his hasty toilette, was the Earl on the point of summoning the landlord, and making inquiries concerning Tom Rain; but the extraordinary appearance which he himself had worn on entering the public-house, must, he felt convinced, have already engendered strange suspicions concerning him; and prudence suggested to him the necessity of avoiding any conversation which might strengthen these suspicions, and thereby lead him into some embarrassment from which the revelation of his name and rank might alone extricate him.

But, oh! how painful—how acutely painful was the suspense which he endured while passing through the details of ablution and change of attire; and, although never were the duties of the toilette more necessary, yet never had the Earl hurried them over with such feverish excitement.

At length, as St. Paul's Cathedral proclaimed the hour of eight, on that eventful evening, Arthur sallied forth from the public-house—leaving the landlord and landlady a prey to the wildest and most unsatisfactory conjectures as to what he was, and how he had happened to be in the condition in which he at first presented himself at their establishment. They, however, both agreed that it was a very good evening's work for them; inasmuch as their strange guest had paid them with a liberality which would have rendered a similar visit every night of their lives a most welcome God-send.

In the meantime the Earl of Ellingham had gained Fleet Street, with the intention of entering some tavern or hotel where a file of newspapers was kept. But he was struck by the deserted appearance of the great thoroughfare—for the shops were all shut, and the vehicles, instead of pouring in two dense streams running different ways, were few and far between.

It then struck him that it was Sunday evening:—for though, in his dungeon, he had been enabled to count the lapse of each day through the date afforded by the morning visits of his gaoler, yet he had not kept so accurate a calculation as to mark each day by its distinctive name.

As he stood in Fleet Street, uncertain how to proceed, it suddenly struck him that he would purchase a newspaper. The office of the *Weekly Dispatch* was facing him: he entered, and bought that day's number.

Such was his intense curiosity—nay more, his acute and agonising suspense,—and so awful were the misgivings which crowded upon his soul,—that he lingered in the office to glance over the newspaper.

And, my God! How he started—how his brain reeled—how crushed and overwhelmed did he feel, when his eyes encountered the dreadful words at the head of a column—

THE CONVICT RAINFORD.

He staggered against the wainscot of the office, and the journal nearly dropped from his hands. He endeavoured to master his emotions, and refer to the fatal column for farther particulars: but his brain swam—his eyes were dim—his glances could not settle themselves upon the point which he vainly endeavoured to make the focus of his attention.

The clerk in the office fancied that he was suddenly attacked with indisposition, and made a polite inquiry to that effect. But the Earl, without giving a direct reply, put hasty and impatient questions to him; and, though his ideas were strangely confused, he nevertheless understood the appalling announcement—*that Rainford had been condemned to death and that the sentence was to be carried into execution on the following morning at Horsemonger Lane Gaol!*

The Earl threw down the paper—and darted from the office,—recovered from his state of stupefaction, but only to become the prey to the most maddening feelings of despair.

An empty hackney-coach was passing at the moment: he stopped it, and leapt in—exclaiming to the driver, "To Horsemonger Lane Gaol."

The coachman saw that his fare was impatient to reach that place; and he whipped his horses into a decent pace. Over Blackfriars Bridge—down the wide road went the vehicle: then it turned to the left at the Obelisk—and, in a short time, it stopped in front of the gaol.

The Earl sprang forth, and was rushing up to the entrance of the governor's house; when an ominous hammering noise fell upon his ears.

He instinctively glanced upwards:—and there—on the top of the gaol—standing out in bold relief against the moon-lit sky, *were the black spars of the gibbet which the carpenters had already erected for the ensuing morning's work*!

CHAPTER LII.
LORD ELLINGHAM'S EXERTIONS.

Not a cry—not a word—not even a moan betrayed the feelings of the Earl of Ellingham, as this frightful spectacle met his eyes.

He was paralysed—stunned—stupified.

Despair was in his heart;—and he could not lower his glances, which were fascinated—rivetted by that awful engine of death on the summit of the gaol.

This state of complete prostration of all the intellectual energies was suddenly interrupted by a gentle pull at his sleeve; and turning abruptly round, he beheld, by the pale light of the moon, a young lad of sickly appearance standing at his elbow.

"Do you know me? what would you with me?" demanded the Earl sharply.

"Yes—my lord, I know you," was the answer, delivered in a mournful—melancholy tone; "and I also know that good—generous, man who——"

The lad burst into an agony of tears, and pointed wildly towards the gibbet.

"Oh! you know Rainford!" exclaimed the Earl eagerly. "Tell me, my boy—speak—have you seen him lately?"

"This day—this evening," replied Jacob Smith—for it was he: "and I have taken leave of him—for ever! He begged me not to visit him—to-morrow——"

"For ever!" echoed the Earl, in a low and hollow voice. "But," he continued, again speaking eagerly and rapidly, "how does he support his doom?"

"With a courage such as the world has seldom seen," replied Jacob: "and he frequently speaks of you, my lord!"

"He speaks of me, my boy——"

"Yes: my lord—he fears that some tidings—some evil reports which you have probably heard, have set you against him—for he received a letter from you a day or two after his arrest——"

"My God! he suspects me of coldness!" exclaimed the Earl, in an impassioned tone. "Oh! I must see him—I must see him this moment——"

And he was rushing towards the governor's door, when Jacob again caught him by the sleeve, saying, "It is useless, my lord! you cannot be admitted to-night."

"The keeper of the prison dare not refuse me," cried the Earl; and he hastened to the door.

"Would it not be better, my lord," asked Jacob, who had followed him, "to use the valuable time now remaining, for the purpose of saving him?"

"True!" exclaimed the Earl, struck by the observation. "An interview with him at this moment would effect no good, and would only unman me altogether. Come with me, my lad: you take an interest in Rainford—and you shall be the first to learn the result of the application which I will now make in the proper quarter."

Thus speaking, Arthur hurried back to the hackney-coach, and as the door closed upon himself and Jacob, he said to the driver in a firm tone, "TO THE HOME-OFFICE!"

During the ride, the Earl put a thousand questions to Jacob Smith relative to the convict.

From the answers he received it appeared that Rainford was well convinced that neither Sir Christopher Blunt nor Mr. Curtis had directed Mr. Howard to prosecute him for the robbery for which he was doomed to suffer: indeed, they had declared as much when giving their evidence at the police-court and at the Old Bailey. Neither did he believe that Howard had instituted the proceedings through any personal motive of spite; but he entertained the conviction that some secret and mysterious springs had been set in motion to destroy him, and that Howard had been made the instrument of the fatal design.

It seemed that Jacob had visited him as often as the prison regulations would permit; and that he had been the bearer of frequent letters between Rainford and the beautiful Jewess, who had removed from Brandon Street a few days after his arrest—this change of residence being effected by the express wishes of Tom Rain, who was afraid lest the malignity of his unknown enemies might extend to herself. Jacob also casually mentioned that the very first time he had been sent to see the Jewess (which appeared to have been the morning after Lord Ellingham's laconic letter was received by Rainford) she enclosed a number of papers in a packet, which she carefully sealed and which Jacob conveyed to the prisoner.

"When I was with him this evening," added the lad, "he gave me that packet, which he re-directed to your lordship, and desired me to leave it at your lordship's residence to-morrow—when all should be over; but since I have thus unexpectedly met you——"

Sobs choked the youth's utterance, as he passed the sealed packet to the Earl, who received it in profound silence—for well did he divine the nature of its contents, and his heart was rent with anguish as he felt all the generosity of that deed on thy part, Tom Rain!

But, in a few moments, the spark of hope that already scintillated within him, was fanned into a bright and glowing flame: for he now possessed proofs to convince the Secretary of State that in allowing the law to take its course, an individual rightly entitled to an Earldom would suffer death; and Arthur was well aware of the influence which such an argument would have in supporting his appeal for a commutation of the sentence.

"Thy generous act in giving up the papers which *thou* mightest have used to save thy life," he thought within himself, apostrophising his doomed half-brother, "shall not be thrown away on me! Ingratitude to thee were impossible!"—Then, turning to Jacob, he said aloud, "I am much mistaken, my boy, if these papers which you have placed in my hands will not effect the great object that we have in view."

"Oh! my lord," exclaimed Jacob, with the most sincere joyfulness of manner, "is there really so much hope? Ah! if not for him—at least for that poor lady who loves him so deeply——"

"Has she seen him?" hastily inquired the Earl.

"Once—once only," answered Jacob: "and that was this afternoon. I was not present at the farewell scene: but I was in the neighbourhood when *she* came out again—and I do not wish ever to witness a beautiful woman's grief again. My lord, I have passed through much—seen much,—and distress and misery in all their worst forms are known to me. But as long as I live will the image of that poor creature, as the wind blew aside her veil for few moments—— Oh! I cannot bear to think of it!"

"He shall be restored to her, my lad!" exclaimed the Earl emphatically. "The more I ponder upon the case, the more firmly do I become convinced that it is one in which the Home Secretary may exercise the prerogative of mercy. It is not as if blood had been shed——"

At this moment the hackney-coach stopped at the door of the Home Office; and the Earl alighted, bidding Jacob await his return.

But what language can describe the violence of that sudden revulsion of feeling which Arthur experienced, when, on inquiry, he learnt that the Home Secretary was neither at his official nor his private residence in London, as he had set out on the preceding evening for his country-seat in the north of England!

With the rapidity of lightning did the Earl calculate the chances of overtaking him by means of fleet horses: but a few moments' reflection showed him the impossibility of accomplishing that undertaking in time to make its result, supposing it were successful, available to the doomed victim. The reprieve might be granted—but it would arrive in London too late!

The Earl was well aware that it was useless to seek the Prime Minister; as that functionary would have no alternative save to reply that he could not possibly interfere in a case so essentially regarding the department of the Home Secretary.

Arthur's mind was accordingly made up in a very few moments:—he would repair at once to the King, who, as he learnt at the Home Office, was, fortunately for his purpose, at Buckingham Palace!

It was now ten o'clock at night: there were but ten hours before him—but in that interval much might be done.

Returning to the coach, he desired to be driven to his own house; and, while proceeding thither, he acquainted Jacob with the cruel disappointment he had sustained by the absence of the Secretary of State, and stated his resolution to repair at once to the dwelling of the King.

Thus the poor, wretched lad became, by his generous sympathy for Tom Rain, the companion and confidant of the great noble!

Great was the joy which prevailed amongst the Earl's household, when he made his appearance once more at his own abode. The servants had indeed heard from Dr. Lascelles as much as the physician himself had learnt through the medium of the vague and laconic letter which the Earl was permitted to write to him from his dungeon: but still the protracted absence of their master had occasioned them the most lively uneasiness; and they were therefore heartily glad to behold his return.

But he was compelled to cut short the congratulations proffered him; and the orders that he issued were given with an unwonted degree of impatience.

"Let the carriage be ordered round directly. Let some one hasten to acquaint Lady Hatfield with my return; and also send up to Grafton Street to request Dr. Lascelles to come hither as soon as possible, and to wait for me—never mind how late. Let this lad be taken care of," he added, indicating Jacob: "and see that he wants for nothing."

Then, hastening up stairs to his own chamber, he locked himself in, having declined the attendance of his valet.

He tore open the packet which Jacob had given him, and beheld a small leathern case. This case contained a roll of letters and other documents, *tied round with a piece of riband so faded that it was impossible to determine what its colour might have originally been.* There was also, accompanying this roll, a brief note addressed to himself.

With trembling hand he opened the note, and, with beating heart and tearful eyes, read the following words:—

"I have sent you the papers, my dear brother—for so I shall make bold to call you still,—to convince you that I did not forge an idle tale when we met last. Whatever your motive for abandoning me in my last hours may be, I entertain no ill feeling towards you: on the contrary, I hope that God may prosper you, and give you long life to enjoy that title and fortune which in so short a time will be beyond the possibility of dispute.

"I had promised to leave behind me a written narrative of my chequered and eventful history for your perusal: but—need I explain wherefore I have not fulfilled this promise?"

"T. R."

The Earl wept—Oh! he wept plenteously, as he read those lines.

"He thinks that I have abandoned him—and he expresses the most generous wishes for my prosperity!" he cried aloud. "Oh! my God—I must save him—I must save him!"

He waited not to examine the roll of papers: his half-brother intimated that the necessary proofs were *there*—and, though no human eye watched the Earl's motions at that instant, still he would not imply a doubt of Rainford's word by examining the documents.

But he hastened to dress himself in attire suitable to his contemplated visit to the King; and his toilette was completed just as the carriage drove round to the door.

A few minutes afterwards he was rolling rapidly along in the vehicle towards Buckingham Palace, the papers carefully secured about his person, and his heart palpitating violently with the cruel suspense of mingled hope and fear.

Alas! he was doomed to another disappointment.

Though it was but little past eleven o'clock, King George the Fourth had already retired to rest,—or rather had been borne away in a senseless state from one of those beastly orgies in which the filthy voluptuary so often indulged.

This much was intimated to the Earl by a nobleman attached to the royal person, and with whom Arthur was well acquainted.

Quitting the palace in disgust combined with despair, Lord Ellingham returned home.

But, no—we were wrong: he did not entirely despair. One hope of saving Rainford's life—one faint hope remained,—a hope so wild—so extravagant—and involving a chance with such fearful odds against it, that it could only have been conceived by one who was determined to leave no means, however difficult, unadopted, in order to attain a particular end.

On crossing the threshold of his door, Arthur's first inquiry was whether Doctor Lascelles had arrived.

The reply was an affirmative; and the Earl hastened to the apartment to which the physician had been shown.

It is not however necessary to relate the particulars of their interview; inasmuch as the nature of the conversation which passed between them will be developed hereafter.

CHAPTER LIII.
THE EXECUTION.

The fatal Monday morning broke, yellow—heavily—and gloomily; and the light stole—or rather struggled by degrees into the convict's cell.

Shortly before seven o'clock Tom Rain awoke; and casting his eyes rapidly around, they successively fell upon the turnkey who had sate up with him—the still flickering lamp upon the common deal table—the damp stone walls—and the massive bars at the windows.

For an instant a cold shudder convulsed his frame, as the conviction—the appalling truth burst upon him, that the horrors of his dreams were not to cease with the slumber that had given them birth.

But, with knitting brow and compressed lip—like a strong-minded man who endeavours to conceal the pain inflicted on him by a surgical operation of a dreadful nature—he struggled with his emotions; and, when the governor and clergyman entered the dungeon, they found him firm and resolute, though not insolent nor reckless.

The chaplain offered to pray with him; and he consented to join in devotion.

There was profound sincerity—but no affectation, no hypocrisy, no passionate exclamation—in the prayer which Tom Rain uttered extemporaneously.

As the clock chimed half-past seven, he arose from his knees, saying, "I am now prepared to die."

But there was yet another half hour before him.

Scarcely had the clock finished chiming, when the door was opened, and the Earl of Ellingham entered the cell.

Heedless of the impression which his conduct might produce upon the prison authorities present, Arthur rushed forward and threw himself into Rainford's arms, exclaiming, "No—I had not willfully abandoned you, Thomas!"

"Just now I said that I was prepared to die," answered the convict, returning the embrace with congenial warmth; "and now I may even add that I shall die contented!"

"The time is too precious to waste in mere details," returned Arthur; "or I would tell you how I have been kept away from you by force—by a vile outrage. But you do not now believe that I was willingly absent—that I wantonly neglected you?"

"No—no," exclaimed Rainford. "I seek not an explanation—I require none. It is enough that you are here now—at the last hour!"

The Earl then related, in a few hurried words, the vain exertions he had made on the preceding evening on behalf of Rainford, who expressed his lively gratitude.

Arthur next requested the governor to permit him to have a few minutes' private conversation with the prisoner: but this favour could not be granted—and the Earl dared not persist in his demand, as the chaplain hinted that the convict had bidden adieu to the affairs of this life, and had but little time left for devotion.

Thus was it that Arthur and Rainford had no opportunity of speaking together in private,—although the former had something important to communicate, and the latter perceived that such was the fact.

"Arthur," said Tom, approaching close to his half-brother, and speaking in a low solemn tone, "is there any hope?"

"None—*on this side of the scaffold*," returned the Earl, with a significant glance as he dwelt on his words: and, as he spoke, he took the prisoner's hand as if to wring it fervently.

But Rainford felt something in the Earl's palm, and instantly comprehended that it was an object which he was to take unnoticed by the gaol authorities. Then, rapid as the lightning flash, he perceived a double meaning in the words—"*on this side of the scaffold*;" because he knew that Arthur would not use those awful words, "*the scaffold*"—but would have said "*the tomb*," had he not had some special, profound motive.

And Rainford *did* comprehend the hint—the hope conveyed; and though he thanked his half-brother with a rapid, expressive glance, yet a sickly smile played upon his lip—indicative of the faintness of that hope so created.

At the same instant heavy footsteps were heard approaching the cell; and the chaplain said in a solemn tone, "The hour is almost come!"

Then Arthur once more threw himself into the prisoner's arms, and whispered rapidly in his ear, "Keep the tube in your throat—and you will be saved!"

Rainford murmured an assent; and the brothers embraced with a fervour which astonished those present, to whom their relationship was totally unknown.

Arthur then tore himself from the cell:—not for worlds could he behold that horrible process termed *the toilette*.

He had also another motive for quitting the dungeon before the last moment:—this was to meet the Sheriff of the County in the passage.

And, behold! in the corridor, he encountered that functionary, the javelin-men, and the under-sheriff, behind whom came the executioner and his assistant.

The Earl accosted the Sheriff, with whom he was acquainted, and who was naturally surprised to meet the nobleman there.

Drawing him aside, Arthur said in a hasty tone, "I have a favour—a great favour to ask of you. The convict is well connected, and his friends demand the body to bury it decently. The earnest prayer that I have to offer you on their behalf, is that you will not prolong the feelings of shame and ignominy which they will experience during the time the corpse remains suspended."

"My lord," replied the Sheriff, "the body shall be cut down at twenty minutes past eight, and delivered over to the unhappy man's friends."

"A thousand thanks!" said the Earl, pressing the Sheriff's hand.

He then hurried away; and the procession moved on to the cell.

Immense was the crowd gathered around the gaol to witness the execution of the celebrated highwayman who had been proved on his trial to be none other than the notorious Black Mask who some years previously had performed the most extraordinary deeds of daring and audacity in the county of Hants.

Yes: immense was the crowd;—and not only did the living ocean inundate all the open spaces about the gaol and all the thoroughfares leading thither,—but it seemed to force its off-shooting streams and channels *up* the very walls of the surrounding dwellings, so densely filled with faces were the open windows—even to the house-tops.

Near the front gate of the gaol stood a black coach and a hearse;—and concealed between the vehicles and the prison wall, were the Earl of Ellingham, Dr. Lascelles, and three of the nobleman's own men-servants, all muffled in black mourning cloaks, and holding white handkerchiefs to their faces so as to hide their features as much as possible.

Lord Ellingham was convulsed with grief. Far—far more than the convict himself did the generous-hearted nobleman suffer on this terrible morning. He was benumbed with cold—his body felt like a dead weight which his legs could scarcely sustain—his tongue clave to the roof of his mouth—a suffocating sensation oppressed him—and he felt as if all the most frightful misfortunes had suddenly combined to fall with crushing burden on his own head!

The clock of St. George's in the Borough began to strike eight—the clock of the prison echoed those iron notes, which sent upon the wing of the air the signal for death.

Suddenly the hum of the multitudes ceased; and an awful silence prevailed.

The Earl and the physician knew by those signs that the convict had just appeared on the roof of the gaol.

But from where they were stationed they could not command a view of the dreadful scene above: and even if they had been differently placed, Lord Ellingham at least would not have raised his eyes towards the fatal tree!

And now, amidst that solemn silence, a voice was heard,—the solemn, deep-toned, monotonous voice of the chaplain, saying, "*I am the resurrection and the life, saith the Lord: he that believeth in me, though he were dead, yet shall he live. And though after my skin worms destroy this body, yet in my flesh shall I see God.*"

The voice ceased: a sudden sensation ran through the crowd like an electric shock;—and the Earl of Ellingham groaned deeply—groaned in the bitterness of his spirit,—*for he knew that the drop had just fallen*!

"Compose yourself, my dear friend," whispered the physician: "for now is the time to arm yourself with all your energies!"

"Thanks, doctor—a thousand thanks for reminding me of my duty," said the Earl. "But this is most trying—most horribly trying! I have lived a hundred years of agony in the last few minutes!"

"Hope for the best, my dear Earl," rejoined the physician. "Do you think that he fully understood you——"

"He did—I am convinced of it!" replied Arthur, anxious to argue himself out of all doubts as well as to convince his companion. "He received the silver tube, and I saw him conceal it in his sleeve. But, alas! we had no opportunity to speak alone—though I had so much to say to him—so many explanations to give—such numerous questions to ask——My God! if after all, *this* plan should fail!"

"If that boy Jacob will only follow my instructions to the very letter," answered Lascelles, "I do not despair of success!"

"Oh! he will—he will!" returned the young nobleman, as he glanced towards the hearse. "He is as intelligent as he is attached to my dear brother!"

The railings in front of the gaol kept the crowd at a considerable distance from the mourning vehicles; and thus the observations which passed between the Earl and the physician were not heard by any save themselves.

And now how languidly—how slowly passed the interval of twenty minutes during which the Sheriff had stated that the body must remain suspended.

To the Earl it seemed as if each minute were a year—as if he were living twenty years in those twenty minutes!

And the crowds had broken the silence which had fallen upon them like a spell;—and ribald jests—obscene remarks—terrible execrations—and vile practical jokes now proclaimed how efficacious is the example of public strangulation!

At last the prison-clock chimed the quarter past eight; and more acute—more agonising grew the suspense of the Earl of Ellingham.

A thousand fears assailed him.

Rainford might not have been able to use the silver tube,—or its imagined effect might have failed,—or the knot of the rope might have broken his neck? Again—the Sheriff might forget his promise, and allow the convict to hang an hour according to the usual custom? And even if all these fears were without foundation, the physician might not be able to fulfil his expectations?

Cruel—cruel was the suspense,—appalling were the apprehensions endured by the young nobleman.

He looked at his watch: it was seventeen minutes and a half past eight.

Two minutes and a half more—if the Sheriff had not forgotten his promise!

But, no: he was even better than his word;—for scarcely had Arthur returned the watch to his pocket, when a sudden sensation again pervaded the multitude—and several voices cried, "*They are going to cut him down!*"

Then came a dead silence.

An intense heat ran, like molten lead, through the Earl's veins; and, at the next moment, he turned death-like cold, as if plunged into an ice-bath.

If he had hitherto lived years in minutes—he now seemed to exist whole centuries in moments!

All the fears which had previously struck him one by one, now rushed in an aggregate crowd to his soul.

The next two minutes were all of fury and horror—fury in his brain, horror in his heart!

But at last the gate of the gaol opened; and a gruff voice exclaimed, "Now then!"

The Earl's three men-servants hastened to range themselves near the door of the hearse, which one of them opened: and when the gaol-officials appeared, bearing the coffin, these servants advanced a few paces to relieve them of their burthen, and thrust it into the hearse, while Dr. Lascelles diverted the attention of the officials by distributing money amongst them.

This proceeding, which had been pre-arranged by the Earl and the physician with the three servants, was absolutely necessary: *because Jacob Smith was concealed within the hearse*!

The affair having proceeded successfully thus far, the hearse moved away; and the five persons who acted as mourners entered the black coach, which also drove off.

For the sake of appearances it was necessary that the vehicles should move slowly along, until the outskirts of the multitude were entirely passed: and then—when Blackman Street was reached—the hearse and the black coach were driven along at a rate which is adopted by funeral processions only when the obsequies are over.

CHAPTER LIV.
GALVANISM.

By the time St. George's Church was passed, the drivers had whipped their horses into a furious gallop;—and on—on went the mourning vehicles like the wind.

The sleek and pampered black horses panted and foamed; but the coachmen cared not—they were well paid for what they were doing.

Down Union Street rolled the chariot and the hearse—into the Blackfriars Road—up the wide thoroughfare to the river—over the bridge—along Farringdon Street—and through Smithfield to Clerkenwell Green.

In an incredibly short space of time, the two vehicles stopped at the door of a house in Red Lion Street.

Dr. Lascelles was the first to leap from the mourning coach, and, taking a key from his pocket, he opened the door of the house, into which, quickly as active men could move or work, the coffin was borne from the hearse.

Jacob Smith was helped out immediately afterwards, and he followed the Earl, the physician, and the three servants into the house, while the mourning coach and the hearse still waited at the door.

A quarter of an hour afterwards, the coffin, *with the lid now screwed down*, was borne back to the hearse;—the three servants returned to the mourning coach, and the funeral procession was set in motion again—but with slow and suitable solemnity.

In another half hour, the coffin, with the name of "THOMAS RAINFORD" upon the plate, was interred in St. Luke's churchyard; and thus ended this ceremony.

But did that coffin really contain the cold corse of the once gallant highwayman?

No: it had been hastily filled with stones and straw at the house in Red Lion Street.

And the body——

The moment the coffin was borne into the house in Red Lion Street, in the manner already described, Jacob Smith closed the door behind him, and exclaimed in a triumphant tone, as he produced the silver tube from his pocket, "It was in his throat! I took it out—and I rubbed his temples with hartshorn and applied it to his nostrils the whole way from the goal to this place! Oh! he will be saved—he will be saved!"

The lid of the coffin, which had not been screwed down, was removed; and in the shell lay the highwayman—with eyes closed—and pale as death!

The Earl of Ellingham shuddered convulsively, and uttered a groan of anguish; but Dr. Lascelles gave his instructions with so much presence of mind and yet such rapidity, that the intensity of the nobleman's grief was soon partially absorbed in the excitement of the scene that now followed.

The body was removed as hastily as possible up stairs, and carried into a spacious laboratory, where it was immediately stretched upon the table.

The three servants then retraced their way down stairs, filled the coffin with stones and straw, screwed the lid tight, and departed with it, as already stated, to St. Luke's churchyard.

In the meantime, the physician, the Earl, and Jacob Smith remained in the laboratory; and now was the profound scientific knowledge of Dr. Lascelles about to be applied to the most wonderful act of human aims—*the resuscitation of a convict who had been hanged*!

The poles of a powerful galvanic pile were applied to the body, from which the animal heat had not altogether departed when it was taken from the coffin; and the force of the electric fluid almost immediately displayed its wondrous influence.

An universal tremor passed over the frame of Rainford; and ejaculations of ineffable joy burst from the lips of Lord Ellingham and Jacob Smith.

Dr. Lascelles continued to let fall upon the body a full quantum of the electric fluid; and in less than a minute the right arm of the highwayman moved,—moved with a kind of spasmodic quivering: then, in a few seconds, it was suddenly raised with eagerness and impatience, and the hand sought the throat.

With convulsive motion that hand kept grasping the throat as if to tear away something that oppressed it—as if the horrible rope still encircled it.

Then Rainford's chest began to swell and work with the violence of returning respiration—as if a mighty current of air were rushing back to the lungs.

"He breathes! he breathes!" cried Ellingham and Jacob Smith, as it were in one voice.

"He will be saved," said the physician calmly, as he again applied the poles of the battery;—"provided congestion of the brain does not take place—for that is to be dreaded!"

But the nobleman and the poor lad heard not this alternative of sinister and dubious import: they had no ears for anything save those blessed words—"He will be saved!"

And they were literally wild with joy.

Lascelles, without desisting from his occupation of applying the electric fluid, and apparently without noticing the excitement—the delirium of happiness and hope which had seized upon his two companions, began leisurely to explain how it was necessary to adopt means to equalise the reviving circulation; and though he called for hartshorn, he was not heard. At length he stamped his foot violently on the floor, exclaiming, "Will neither of you give me the hartshorn? Do you wish him to die through *your* neglect?"

The Earl instantly checked the exuberance of his joyous emotions, and hastened to obey all the instructions which the physician gave him.

The hartshorn was applied to Rainford's nostrils; and in a few moments his lips began to quiver:—then, on a sudden, as Lascelles let fall upon him a stronger current of the electric fluid, a terrific cry burst from the object of all this intensely concentrated interest!

But never was cry of human agony more welcome to mortal ears than now; for it told those who heard it that life was in him who gave vent to it!

The physician felt the highwayman's pulse: it beat feebly—very feebly—but still it beat!

And now his limbs moved with incessant trembling,—and he waved his right hand backwards and forwards, his breast heaving with repeated sighs, and gasps, and painful moans.

The doctor applied a small mirror to Rainford's mouth and nostrils; and it was instantly covered with a cloud.

He now opened his eyes slowly; they were much blood-shot—but the pupils indicated the reviving fires of vitality.

His breathing rapidly grew more regular; and though he retained his eyes open, yet he seemed unconscious of all that was passing around him, and gazed upwards with the most death-like indifference.

Lord Ellingham cast a glance of frightful apprehension towards the physician; but the countenance of Dr. Lascelles wore an expression of calm and complacent satisfaction—and the Earl was reassured.

Twenty minutes had now passed since the galvanic operation had commenced; and at last Dr. Lascelles said emphatically, "*He is saved!*"

The Earl embraced him as if he were a father who had just manifested some extraordinary proof of paternal love, or who had forgiven some deep offence on the part of a son.

"We must put him to bed immediately," said the physician, with difficulty extricating himself from the nobleman's embrace, and fearing lest he should be compelled to undergo a similarly affectionate process at the hands of Jacob Smith, who was equally enthusiastic in his joy:—"we must put him to bed immediately," repeated Dr. Lascelles; "and fortunately for us, there is a bed-chamber in the house."

The three then carefully lifted Tom Rain into a small room furnished as a bed-chamber, and where they undressed him and deposited him in the bed.

"And now," said Jacob Smith, "we should remember that there is one, who will feel as much joy as ourselves——"

"True!" cried the Earl. "But where does she live?"

"I am acquainted with her abode," returned the lad. "If your lordship will allow me——"

"Yes, my good boy," interrupted Arthur. "It is for you to convey these joyous tidings. But perhaps she may have returned home to her father—for, after all that has occurred, and considering Mr. de Medina's affection for his daughter——But all this while we are talking enigmatically in the presence of my excellent friend the doctor, from whom there must be no secrets——"

"Never mind me," said Lascelles laconically, who perfectly well comprehended the nature of their allusions. "I care little for your secrets; and, even if it were otherwise, I am too much occupied with my patient here——"

"Then we will not trouble you with explanations at present," interrupted the Earl. "Jacob, my lad, hasten to the lady of whom we speak—break the happy tidings to her gently—and bring her hither."

"Yes, my lord," answered the lad, delighted at being chosen as the messenger of good tidings in such a case. "Fortunately, Miss de Medina moved from Brandon Street into the heart of the City, by Mr. Rainford's positive directions: and I shall not be long before I come back with her."

The Earl put gold into his hand; but Jacob returned it, declaring that he was not without money; and in another minute the front door of the house closed behind him.

CHAPTER LV.
THE LABORATORY.—ESTHER DE MEDINA.

When Jacob had taken his departure, Dr. Lascelles returned to his laboratory, mixed some liquid ingredients in a glass, and returning to the bed-chamber, poured the medicine down Rainford's throat.

He then felt his pulse, applied his ear to his chest to listen to the pulsation of his heart, and carefully examined his eyes, which were far less blood-shot than when they opened first.

"He is getting on admirably," said the physician, "his pulsation is regular, and neither too quick nor too slow—but just as I could wish it. He seems inclined to sleep—yes—he closes his eyes; and he will awake to perfect consciousness.—But do you know, my dear friend, that in order to oblige you, I have incurred an awful risk?" continued the doctor. "The law would not believe me, were I to declare that it was in the interest of science I made these galvanic experiments, and that having succeeded in recalling the man to life, I was not capable of delivering him up to justice."

"Let us hope that there will be no necessity to make such an excuse at all," said the Earl. "You have rendered me an immense service, doctor——"

"Then I am satisfied," interrupted Lascelles; "for, after all you told me last night, I cannot help liking your half-brother here. He is a generous-hearted fellow; and one would risk much to save such a man from death."

"You had frequently mentioned to me your galvanic experiments," said the Earl: "and last night, when nearly driven to desperation by the absence of the Home Secretary, the reminiscence of all the wonders you had at different times related to me in respect to galvanism, flashed to my mind—and I sent for you as a drowning man clings to a straw."

"In the adjoining room," observed the physician, "I have tried the influence of galvanism upon thousands of animals and on several men. I have paid high prices to obtain the bodies of convicts as soon as they were cut down;—but never until this day did I succeed in restoring the vital spark. Neither would this experiment have been successful, had we not adopted all the precautions I suggested. The tube in the throat to allow respiration—and Jacob Smith in the hearse to remove the suffocating night-cap from Rainford's head, and the tube from his throat, and then to apply the hartshorn to his nostrils and his temples. Step with me again into the laboratory: you have not yet had time to examine its curiosities," added the physician with a smile. "Rainford sleeps," he continued, glancing towards the bed; "and we shall have a little leisure to inspect the laboratory."

They accordingly proceeded into the adjacent room, where Lascelles directed his companion's attention to the various galvanic and electrical apparatus.

"I am also a devoted disciple of Gall and Spurzheim," observed the physician, when he had expatiated upon the discoveries of Galvani.[25] "Behold that row of plaster of Paris casts of heads," he continued, pointing to a shelf whereon upwards of fifty of the objects mentioned were ranged: "they have afforded me much scope for curious speculation and profound study."

"I observe that you have casts of the heads of several celebrated criminals amongst them," said the Earl: "Arthur Thistlewood—Daniel Hoggart—George Barrington—Henry Fauntleroy—John Thurtell—William Probert——"

"And many others, as you perceive, my dear Earl," interrupted Lascelles. "The prejudice is as yet so strong amongst people, in respect to phrenology and craniology, that it is difficult to obtain the casts of living heads: I am therefore forced to make friends with the turnkeys in gaols and with the relations of criminals who are hung or who die in prison, to get casts. Moreover, the heads of men who have led remarkable lives, or who have suffered for their crimes, afford such interesting subjects for study and comparison——"

"Comparison between the head of the man and the monkey!" said the Earl with a smile.

"Decidedly," exclaimed the physician. "But I will not bore you with my theories and speculations on this subject. You may, however, suppose that I am not a little enthusiastic in the matter, since I have taken the trouble to have human heads prepared and articulated to facilitate my studies."

Thus speaking, he opened the door of a cupboard.

The Earl started back—for four human countenances met his astonished and horrified gaze, and four pairs of human eyes seemed to glare ominously upon him. At the same time his nostrils were assailed with a strong odour of spices.

"You need not be afraid of them!" ejaculated the physician, laughing: "they will not speak to you."

"But how—whence did you obtain——"

"I suppose you think I murdered four men for the sake of their heads?" cried Lascelles, laughing more heartily still. "Why, my dear Earl, you would be surprised, perhaps, to learn that I often pass whole nights in this laboratory, making galvanic experiments, or pursuing my phrenological and craniological researches. But these heads were obtained from the hospitals, and I myself embalmed and prepared, as you now see them."

"I was not aware that you possessed this laboratory," observed the Earl, "until you stated the fact last night."

"Nor would you ever have known it, had it not been for the desire which you expressed that science should exert itself to rescue your half-brother from the grasp of death," answered the physician. "The truth is, I have had this laboratory upwards of seventeen or eighteen years. I was always devoted to science, especially that on which my own profession is based; and the spirit of anatomical inquiry made me anxious to obtain as many *subjects*—or in plain terms, dead bodies—as possible. I was therefore thrown into perpetual intercourse with resurrection-men, who, of course, are not the best of characters. But I was afraid of having corpses brought to my own house in Grafton Street; and I was also desirous to fit up for myself a laboratory in some retired neighbourhood, where I could pursue my studies without the least fear of interruption, on such occasions when the humour might seize me. I hinted as much to one of the rascals who sold me *subjects*; and he put me in communication with a man of the name of Tidmarsh. After some haggling and hesitation on the part of Tidmarsh—and when he had consulted, or pretended to consult, his principal—he introduced me to this house, and I hired this room at an enormous rental. I did not, however, care about the high rate demanded of me for the use of the place, because it is not only in a most retired neighbourhood, but there is also a private and subterranean means of egress and ingress from another street, which is useful, you know, for one who has to deal with resurrectionists."

"And are you the only tenant of this house?" inquired the Earl; "for I presume that the bed-chamber in which poor Thomas lies is not your own."

"No: some old man occasionally visits the house, and now and then sleeps in that room," returned the physician. "But I have only seen him once or twice and do not even know his name. I have my own key for the front-door, and I am acquainted with the secret of the subterranean passage; but I never hold any communication with Tidmarsh, beyond paying him the rent when it is due;—and when I happen to meet the old man I have alluded to, we merely exchange a word and pass on. He has his rooms in the house, and I have mine; and as he does not interfere with me, I never trouble myself about him nor his concerns."

"Then, for aught you know, doctor," said the Earl, "you may occupy an apartment in the house of bad characters?"

"What do I care?" exclaimed Lascelles. "I could not well have such a laboratory as this at my own residence—my servants would talk about these human heads, and those plaster casts, and the galvanic experiments, and I should be looked upon as a sorcerer, or at all events with so much suspicion and aversion as to lose all my practice. And, by the bye, my dear Earl, you should be the very last," added the doctor, with a smile, "to hint at the possibility of this house being connected with bad characters; for had I not a laboratory in so quiet a street—a street, too, where no questions are ever asked nor observations made—your poor brother might have waited long enough for the chance of resuscitation by galvanic means."

"True, my dear doctor—I was unjust," said the Earl. "But you will forgive me?"

"Say no more about it, Arthur. Were men of scientific research to be over particular, they might as well abandon their studies at once. The experiments I have made on corpses in this room, could scarcely have been performed at my own residence; and, to tell you very candidly, I believe that the old man who has the other apartments on this floor, is either a miser or a rogue;— but I care nothing about him or his affairs. And now I will mention to you one very extraordinary circumstance. It must have been, as near as I can guess, five weeks ago that I was one night pursuing my galvanic experiments in this room—I had been operating on divers rabbits, frogs, and rats—and, may be, for anything I recollect, a few cats,—when I was compelled to go down stairs for a particular purpose. On my return, as I came back by that door," he continued, pointing to one at the farther end of the room, "and which leads to the staircase, I was startled—nay, positively astounded at seeing a man standing near this cupboard, and gazing fixedly on the human heads. I confess I was alarmed at the moment, because I had heard voices in the house during the half-hour previously; and I remember that I rushed back and instinctively barred and bolted the door. But the man turned round before I had time to close the door—and I caught a glimpse of his face. That man—now who do you think he was?"

"It is impossible to guess, doctor," said the Earl.

"He was your half-brother, who now lies in the adjoining room!" added Lascelles.

"Thomas!—here!" cried Arthur, profoundly surprised.

"I could not possibly make a mistake, because I had seen him before—no matter how or where—and knew him immediately," continued the physician. "Well, I must confess that I was uncertain how to act. I did not wish him to recognise me—although perhaps he had already done so; and I could not very well leave the house and return to Grafton-street at once, because I had on a dressing-gown, and had left my coat in this room. I was half-way down the stairs leading to the hall, when I heard some one opening the front door with a key. Knowing that it must be either the old man I have before mentioned, or Tidmarsh, as they alone besides myself had keys of the front door, I waited till the person came in; and it *was* Tidmarsh. I immediately told him what I had seen.—'*Ah!*' said he, '*I suspected there was something wrong, and that made me get up, dress, and come round.*'—His words astonished me; and I requested an explanation; but he seemed sorry that he had uttered them inadvertently, and gave some evasive reply. He however accompanied me up stairs: we entered the laboratory, and no one was there. We went into the next room—the one where Rainford is now sleeping—and there we found the carpet moved away from the trap-door———"

"The trap-door!" exclaimed the Earl.

"Yes—a trap-door that leads to the subterranean passage which I have mentioned to you," added Lascelles; "but you must remember that all I have told you about this house is in the strictest confidence. Well, we found the carpet moved away from the trap-door, though the trap itself was closed. Old Tidmarsh instantly fastened the trap with a secret spring which there is to it, and spread the carpet over the floor again.—'*But does he know the means of getting out at the other end?*' I inquired, shocked at the thought of Rainford being immured in the subterranean.—'*Do you think he would venture down there if he were not acquainted with the secrets of the place?*' demanded Tidmarsh. This struck me as being consistent with common sense; and moreover I began to fancy that Tidmarsh and Rainford must be connected together—pardon me, my dear Earl, for saying so: and that suspicion was encouraged in my mind by the singular and mysteriously significant observation that Tidmarsh had dropped when I met him on the stairs. So I felt no farther uneasiness; but took my departure for Grafton Street. Tidmarsh quitted the house with me, and left me at the corner of Turnmill Street close by—as he lives there."

"Do you know," said the Earl of Ellingham, who now appeared to be occupied with an idea which had just struck him,—"do you know that all this conversation about subterraneans, and secret passages, and trap-doors, has created a strange suspicion in my mind?"

"Relative to what?" demanded the physician.

"I briefly explained to you last night the cause of my disappearance for four long weeks," continued the Earl; "I also acquainted you with the manner of my escape. Now, I am convinced, by the direction I took, in threading those dreadful sewers, that I was a prisoner somewhere in Clerkenwell; and perhaps—who knows—indeed, it is highly probable, that the very subterranean, of which you have spoken, may contain dungeon——"

"You shall soon satisfy yourself on that head," interrupted the physician. "I confess that I have never been there more than three or four times—and then only to help old Tidmarsh convey to my laboratory a *subject* for my galvanic or anatomical experiments, and which the resurrectionists had deposited at his house in Turnmill Street. So you may believe that I know but little of the precise features of the subterranean. But we will visit it at once; and if there be a dungeon or cell there, such as you describe, we shall discover it."

The physician and the Earl proceeded into the bed-chamber, where Rainford still slept. Lascelles felt his pulse, examined his countenance attentively, and turned with a smile of satisfaction to the young nobleman, to whom he whispered, "He is beyond all danger."

Arthur pressed the doctor's hand with fervent gratitude, while tears of happiness trembled upon his long lashes.

The physician then proceeded to raise the trap-door; and, having procured a lamp from his laboratory, led the way down the spiral staircase of stone.

But the huge door at the bottom was bolted on the other side; and thus further investigation was rendered impossible on that occasion.

They accordingly retraced their steps to the bed-room, closed the trap-door, and spread the carpet over it again.

The Earl nevertheless made up his mind to institute farther search in those mysterious premises at some future day.

"My dear young friend," said the physician suddenly, as they stood by the side of the bed, watching the countenance of the sleeper, "I had almost forgotten that when *he* awakes presently, it will be necessary to administer a little stimulant—either port-wine, or good brandy, if such a thing can be got in this neighbourhood."

"I will hasten and procure both immediately," returned the Earl. "Give me the key of the front-door that I may let myself in without troubling you to descend to open it."

Lascelles handed the key to the nobleman, who immediately sallied forth to purchase the spirits required.

Having procured a pint-bottle of brandy at the most respectable tavern which he perceived in St. John Street, whither he repaired for the purpose, he was retracing his way, when his eyes were suddenly attracted by a lovely female form crossing the street just mentioned, and proceeding in the direction of Northampton Square.

But the lady was not dressed in mourning; and therefore he conceived that he must be mistaken relative to the idea which had struck him.

And yet that symmetry of form, set off rather than concealed by the ample shawl which she wore,—that dignified elegance of gait,—that gracefulness of carriage, were well-known characteristics of Esther de Medina.

The Earl hastened after her, and pronounced that name.

The lady turned—raised her veil—and extended her hand to the nobleman.

Yes—it was Esther;—but how pale—how profoundly mournful her countenance!

"I am rejoiced to meet you," said the Earl in a rapid and excited tone; "for I have news to communicate which will give you joy! But—come with me—I implore you—I know all—look upon me as a friend—and in my presence you need not blush. Delay not—I beseech you—come with me at once!"

And drawing her arm in his, he hurried her away towards Red Lion Street.

"My lord," she said, "I am at a loss to understand——"

"Oh! you know not how nearly that which I have to communicate—to give you evidence of—affects your happiness!" interrupted Arthur. "But I must not tell you all in a breath—it would be too much for you to hear:—and I am glad—Oh! I am rejoiced that I have thus met you—for I had dispatched a messenger to seek you—and he might have broken the happy tidings too abruptly——"

Esther gazed upon his countenance in astonishment mingled with an expression of surprise and even alarm: but the Earl perceived not the strange impression that his words had produced, as he hurried her along at a rate which in a more refined neighbourhood would have attracted disagreeable attention.

The house in Red Lion Street was reached; and the nobleman opened the door with extraordinary impatience.

For an instant Esther hesitated to follow him; but, confident of the honourable intentions of the Earl, and anxious to relieve herself from the state of wonder and suspense into which his words had thrown her, she entered the gloomy-looking tenement.

He led her up the dirty, decayed staircase into the laboratory, where he begged her to wait for a moment. He then softly opened the door communicating with the bed-chamber, in order to acquaint Dr. Lascelles with her presence there, and in a few hurried words explain the motives which had induced him to bring her thither; for he supposed that all those circumstances which had led him to believe that the Jewess was the mistress of his half-brother, were unknown to the doctor.

But the moment he opened the door, he started—and an ejaculation of the wildest surprise burst from his lips.

For there—standing by the bed, with hands clasped and eyes upraised in thankfulness to heaven—was the living counterpart of Esther de Medina!

Arthur turned hastily round to convince himself that Esther had not passed in before him: but Esther was indeed a few paces behind him—alarmed by the exclamation which had burst from his lips.

The truth flashed like lightning to the Earl's brain:—Esther de Medina had a sister—so like herself that, when apart, they might well be taken for each other:—yes—that must be the solution of the enigma which had bewildered him so often!

"Miss de Medina!" he said, hastily taking her hand, "I have been labouring under a strange mistake. But you will perhaps understand how it arose, when——"

He led her into the room:—she started back, exclaiming, "Oh! heavens—my oath!"—but in the next moment the sisters—for such indeed they were—rushed into each other's arms!

---

25. Mr. Peck, B. A., in his interesting papers on Electricity in *Reynolds's Miscellany*, gives the ensuing particulars:—"The discovery of

galvanic electricity was the result of accident. Madame Galvani, the wife of a distinguished Italian philosopher, being recommended by her medical adviser to partake of broth prepared from frogs, several of these little animals were procured, and were placed prior to their being cooked, in the laboratory of her husband. Some of Monsieur Galvani's friends happened to be amusing themselves with an electrical machine, which was standing in the room, and, by chance, one of the frogs was touched with a scalpel. To Madame Galvani's surprise, she observed the limbs of the frogs exhibit a convulsive motion. Upon examining them closely, she perceived that the muscles were affected at the very time when sparks were received from the machine. When her husband returned, she acquainted him with the circumstance. For some time previously M. Galvani had entertained a belief that muscular action was affected by electricity, and had been experimenting for the purpose, if possible, of verifying this hypothesis. Delighted by the discovery, he lost no time in trying a variety of experiments. At first he tested the effect of sparks alone, on dissected frogs, gradually varying the intensity of the spark. In every case, however, even when the electric action was feeble, he noticed that the muscles of the frogs gave evidence of susceptibility to its influence. He next made experiments with atmospheric electricity. The same result ensued as when the electric action had been elicited by artificial means."

In another paper of the same interesting series, the following account is given:—"On the evening of January the 28th, during a somewhat extraordinary display of northern lights, a lady became so highly charged with electricity, as to give out vivid electrical sparks at the end of each finger, to the face of each of the company present. This did not cease with the heavenly phenomenon, but continued for several months, during which time she was constantly charged; and giving off electrical sparks to every conductor she approached; so that she could not touch the stove, nor any metallic utensils, without first giving off an electrical spark, with the consequent twinge. The state most favourable to this phenomenon was an atmosphere of about 80 deg. Fahrenheit, moderate exercise, and social enjoyment. It disappeared in any atmosphere approaching zero, and under the debilitating effects of fear. When seated by the stove, reading, with her feet upon the fender, she gave out sparks, at the rate of three or four each minute; and, under the most favourable circumstances, a spark that could be seen, heard, or felt, passed every second! She could charge others in the same way, when insulated, who could then give sparks to others. To make it satisfactory that her dress did not produce it, it was changed to cotton and woollen, without altering the phenomenon. The lady is about thirty, of sedentary pursuits, and delicate state of health."

We avail ourselves of the digressive facility afforded us by this note to the text, to relate *a true history* of the resuscitation of a man who had been hanged—a history which is perhaps one of the most extraordinary "romances of real life" upon record. It is as follows:— Ambrose Gwinett was hanged at Deal for the murder of a man who merely disappeared, and whose body was not found. Circumstantial evidence certainly pointed strongly to Gwinett as a murderer; but still it was not proved in the first instance that a murder had been really committed. Gwinett and another man, of the name of Collins, arrived together at an inn in Deal. Gwinett borrowed Collins's clasp-knife during supper-time, in the presence of the waiter. On the following morning Collins was missing; and Gwinett had been met on the stairs, in the middle of the night, coming up from the garden. Blood was found in the garden, and in the midst of the blood was the clasp-knife, open. The traces of blood were continued down to the sea-side, and there they ceased. Gwinett was moreover found to have in his pocket Collins's purse, which the waiter had seen over night in Collins's possession. Gwinett's defence was that he had received the purse, after the waiter left the room on the preceding evening, in consequence of an arrangement that he (Gwinett) should be paymaster for them both; that he had gone down stairs in the night, for a certain purpose, to the garden; that his nose had bled dreadfully; that he had used the clasp-knife to raise the latch of the door, and had dropped it in the dark; and that he had walked down to the sea-side close by to wash his face and hands, and stop the bleeding at the nose with the cold salt-water. This tale was not believed; Gwinett was found guilty of *Murder*, and hanged on Sandown Common. But a shepherd, passing by the gibbet a few hours after the execution, and while the victim was hanging in chains, perceived signs of life in him, and cut him down. Gwinett was recovered: and the kind-hearted shepherd sent him abroad. In a distant colony, Gwinett met Mr. Collins, *the very man for whose alleged murder he had been hanged*! An explanation immediately ensued. On the night in question, Collins had also gone down stairs to the garden, and had been carried off by a press-gang who passed along the sea-shore at the time. He was conveyed to a boat, and in that transported to the tender-vessel lying in the Downs: the vessel sailed next morning, and Collins had heard nothing of the dilemma of his friend until they met as just described.

CHAPTER LVI.
A HISTORY OF THE PAST.

Mr. de Medina was the son of a Spanish merchant, who died, leaving a considerable fortune behind him, and of which this son was the sole inheritor. But, by the villainy of his relations and the corrupt decision of a Spanish judge, Mr. de Medina found himself despoiled of the riches which were rightfully his own; and at the age of two-and-twenty he quitted his native land in disgust, to return to England, where indeed he had been educated, and the language of which country he spoke as fluently as his own.

It is hardly necessary to state that Mr. de Medina was of the Jewish persuasion; and on his arrival in London, he naturally applied to the eminent merchants of his own creed for employment. It is the fashion in this country to decry the Jews—to represent them as invariably sordid, mercenary, avaricious, and griping—indeed, to carry the charges laid against them to such a length, as to associate with their names a spirit of usury amounting to the most flagrant and dishonourable extortion. And these charges have been repeated so often, and echoed seriously by so many persons deemed a respectable authority, that the prejudice against the Jews has become interwoven with the Englishman's creed. But the exceptions have been mistaken for the rule; and—strange as the assertion may sound to many ears—we boldly proclaim that there is not a more honest, intelligent, humane, and hospitable class of persons on the face of the earth than the Jews.

The fact is, when an Englishman is broken down in fortune, and can no longer raise funds by mortgage on his estate, nor by the credit of his name, he flies to the money-lender. Now Jews are essentially a financial nation; and money-broking, in all its details, is their special avocation. The class of Israelite money-lenders is, therefore, numerous; and it is ten to one that the broken-down individual, who requires a loan, addresses himself to a Jew—even if he take the money-lender living nearest to him, or to whom he is first recommended. Well—he transacts his business with this Jew; and as he can give no security beyond his bond or his bill, and his spendthrift habits are notorious, he cannot of course obtain the loan he seeks save on terms proportionate to the risk incurred by the lender. Yet he goes away, and curses the Jew as an usurer; and thus another voice is raised to denounce the entire nation as avaricious and griping. But does this person, however, reflect that had he applied to a Christian money-broker, the terms would have been equally high, seeing that he had no real security to offer, and that his name was already tarnished? Talk of the usury of the Jews—look at the usury practised by Christians! Look at the rapacity of Christian attorneys!—look at the greediness of Christian bill-discounters!—look, in a word, at the money-making spirit of the Christian, and then call the Jew the usurer *par excellence*! It is a detestable calumny—a vile prejudice, as dishonourable to the English character an it is unjust towards a generous-hearted race!

We deem it right to state that these observations are recorded as disinterestedly and as impartially—as honestly and as conscientiously, as any other comments upon prejudices or abuses which have ever appeared in "THE MYSTERIES OF LONDON." Not a drop of Jewish blood flows in our veins; but we have the honour to enjoy the friendship of several estimable families of the Jewish persuasion. We have, therefore, had opportunities of judging of the Israelite character; and the reader must be well aware that the writer who wields his pen *against* a popular prejudice is more likely to be instigated by upright motives than he who labours to maintain it. In following the current of general opinion, one is sure to gain friends: in adventurously undertaking to stem it, he is equally certain to create enemies. But, thank God! this work is addressed to an intelligent and enlightened people—to the industrious classes of the United Kingdom—to those who are the true pillars of England's prosperity, glory, and greatness!

When Mr. de Medina arrived, friendless and almost penniless, on the British soil, he addressed himself to the heads of several eminent commercial firms in the City of London,—firms, the constituents of which were of his own persuasion. The Jews always assist each other to the extent of their means:—do the Christians? Answer, ye cavillers against the persecuted race of Israel! Mr. de Medina, accordingly, found occupation; and so admirably did he conduct himself—so well did he promote the interests of his employers, that by the time he reached the age of thirty, he found himself a partner in the concern whose prosperity his talents and his industry had so much enhanced. He then repaired to Liverpool, to establish a branch-house of trade, and of which he became the sole manager. His partners dying soon afterwards, he effected an arrangement with their heirs, by which he abandoned all share in the London business, and retained the Liverpool house as his own.

His success was now extraordinary; and his dealings were proverbially honourable and fair. He went upon the principle of doing a large business with small gains, and paying good wages to those who were in his employment. Thus, though naturally of a stern and severe disposition, his name was respected and his character admired. At the age of thirty-five—twenty years before the opening of our tale—he married a lady of his own nation—beautiful, accomplished, and rich. Within twelve months their union was blessed with a daughter, on whom the name of Tamar was bestowed; and at the expiration of another year, a second girl was born, and who was called Esther. But in giving birth to the latter, Mrs. de Medina lost her life; and for a considerable time the bereaved husband was inconsolable.

The kindness of his friends and a conviction of the necessity of subduing his grief as much as possible, for the sake of the motherless babes who were left to him, aroused Mr. de Medina from the torpor of profound woe; and he became so passionately attached to his children, that he would fondle them as if he himself were a child. As they grew up, a remarkable resemblance was observed between them; and as Esther was somewhat precocious in a physical point of view, she was as tall when ten years old as her sister. Strangers then took them for twins, although there was really twelve months' difference between their ages. But they actually appeared to be counterparts of each other. Their hair was of precisely the same intensely black and glossy shade: their eyes were of the same dark hue and liquid lustre;—their countenances presented each the same blending of the white and rich carnation beneath the transparent tinge of delicate olive or bistre which marked their origin; their very teeth were of the same shape, and shone, too, between pairs of lips which Nature had made in the same mould, and dyed with the same vermilion. Twin-roses did the lovely sisters seem,—roses on the same stalk; and by the time Tamar was sixteen and Esther fifteen, the ripe beauty of the former and the somewhat precocious loveliness of the latter, appeared to have attained the same glorious degree of female perfection.

But their minds were not equally similar. Tamar was vain of her personal attractions, while Esther was reserved and bashful: the former was never so happy as when she was the centre of attraction in a ball-room, while the latter preferred the serene tranquillity of home. In their style of dress they were equally different from each other. Tamar delighted in the richest attire, and loved to deck herself with costly jewels; and, well aware that she possessed a splendid bust, she wore her gowns so low as to leave no room for conjecture relative to the charming fullness of her bosom. Esther, on the contrary, selected good, but not showy materials for her dress, and never appeared with a profusion of jewellery. Though of proportions as rich and symmetrical as her sister, yet she rather sought to conceal their swelling contours than display them. Tamar was of warm and impassioned temperament, and her breast was easily excited by fierce desires; but Esther was the embodiment of chaste and pure notions—her soul the abode of maiden innocence!

Mr. de Medina often remonstrated with Tamar upon her love of splendid attire, and her anxiety to shine in the circles of gaiety. But her ways were so winning, that when she threw her arms around his neck, and besought him not to be angry with her, or to allow her to accompany some female friends to a ball or concert to which she had been invited, he invariably yielded to her soft persuasion.

Tamar was a few weeks past the age of sixteen, and Esther had accomplished her fifteenth year, when an incident occurred which was fated to wield a material influence over the career of the elder sister. One night Mr. de Medina, while returning home on horseback from a neighbouring village where he had dined with a friend, was stopped and plundered of his purse and pocket-book. He was by no means a man who was likely to yield without resistance to the audacious demands of a highwayman; but he was unarmed at the time—and by some accident he was unattended by his groom. The robber, who wore a black crape over his countenance, was armed to the teeth, and seemed resolute as well as desperate: Mr. de Medina, therefore, risked not an useless contest with him, but surrendered his property as above mentioned. On his return home, and while conversing on the incident with his daughters, he suddenly recollected that the pocket-book contained a paper of great value and importance to himself, but of no use to any other person. He accordingly inserted advertisements in the local newspapers, offering a reward for the restoration of that document, and promising impunity to the robber, if he would give it up. But for several days these notifications remained unanswered.

A week elapsed, and one morning an individual, dressed in a semi-sporting style, called at the house and inquired for Mr. de Medina. But Mr. de Medina had just left home for the purpose of conducting Esther to the dwelling of some friends who resided in the neighbourhood of Liverpool, and with whom she was to pass a few days. Tamar was, however, at home; and as the servant informed her that "the gentleman said his business was important," she desired that he might be shown up into the drawing-room. He was evidently struck by the dazzling beauty of the Jewess who had thus accorded him an audience; and there was something so dashing—so rakish—so off-hand, without vulgarity, in his manner,—a something between the frankness of an open-hearted man and the easy politeness of one who knows the world well,—that Tamar did not treat him with that degree of cold courtesy which seems to say, "Have the kindness to explain your business, and then you may depart." But she requested him to be seated; and when he made a few observations which led to a connected discourse on the gaiety and "doings" of the Liverpool folks, she suffered herself to be drawn into the conversation without pausing to ask the motive of his visit. Thus nearly half-an-hour passed away: and while Tamar thought to herself that she had never met a more agreeable gentleman in her life—and certainly never one who possessed such a brilliant set of teeth, or who looked so well in tops and cords,—the stranger came to a conclusion equally favourable concerning herself. Indeed, he was quite charmed with the personal attractions and the conversation of the beautiful Jewess; and when he took his leave, she forgot that he had not communicated his business, nor even his name.

When her father returned home in the afternoon, she mentioned to him the visit of the stranger; but added that he only remained a few moments, and would not explain his business to her. Mr. de Medina immediately expressed his belief that the call had some reference to his advertisement concerning the lost paper. But Tamar enthusiastically repelled the suspicion; declaring that, though he had not stayed a minute, yet his manners, appearance, and address, were of too superior a nature to be associated with a dishonourable avocation. Mr. de Medina asked if he had intimated when he should call again; to which question Tamar, fearful that it would appear strange to give a negative reply, answered—"In a few days." Thus terminated a conversation in which Tamar had been guilty of much duplicity, and which was marked by the first deliberate falsehood which she ever unblushingly told her father.

On the following day the stranger returned; and Mr. de Medina, not having expected him so soon, was not at home to receive him. But Tamar was in the drawing-room, to which he was conducted as on the previous day. It was summer-time, and she was engaged in tying up the drooping heads of some flowers in the large balcony. The stranger begged her not to desist from her occupation; but, on the contrary, offered, in his gay manner of frank politeness, to assist her. She could not refuse his aid—she did not wish to refuse it; and they were soon engaged in a very interesting conversation. He held the stalks of the flowers, too, while she tied the thread; and her beautiful hand passed over that of the stranger's—*not* without touching it; while her breath, sweeter than the perfume of the flowers themselves, fanned his cheek. Once, when he stooped a little lower, under pretence of examining a particular rose-bud more closely, his hair mingled with hers, and he could see that the rich glow of excitement flooded her countenance—her neck—and even extended to the bosom, of which he was enabled, by her stooping posture, to catch more than partial glimpses.

When next their eyes met, there seemed to be already a tacit kind of intelligence established between them,—an intelligence which appeared to say she knew he had allowed his hair to mingle with hers on purpose, and that she had not withdrawn her head because the contact pleased her. The interesting conversation was continued; and an hour had passed before either the stranger showed the slightest sign of an intention to take his leave, or Tamar remembered how long they had been alone together. When he did at length take up his hat and his riding-whip, he also picked up a flower which Tamar had accidentally broken off from its stem in the balcony; and placing it in his buttonhole without making the slightest allusion to the little incident, he bowed and quitted the room.

He had been gone at least ten minutes ere Tamar again recollected that he had not mentioned his business nor told his name. She had been thinking of the incident of the flower;—yes—and also of the commingling of her raven locks with his fine, manly light hair. When her father returned home on this occasion, she did not mention the fact of the stranger's visit at all.

Throughout the remainder of that day she wondered whether he would return on the following one; and she made up her mind, if he did, not to suffer him to depart before she had elicited his business and his name. In the evening she went out to make a few purchases at a shop in a neighbouring street; and she was retracing her way, when two young men, walking arm-in-arm, and smoking cigars,—having withal something most offensively obtrusive in their entire appearance,—stopped short in front of Tamar, literally barred her way, and began to address her in that flippant, coarse style which, without being absolutely obscene, is nevertheless particularly insulting. "Gentlemen—if such you be," said Tamar, in a dignified manner, "I request you to let me pass."—"Well, won't you let us escort you home, wherever it is?" demanded one; "for you're a devilish sweet girl, upon my honour."—Scarcely were these words uttered when the long lash of a riding-whip began to belabour the backs of the two young swells in a fashion that made them almost scream with agony; and Tamar, who instantly stepped aside, recognised in the champion that had thus come to her assistance, the very individual who was uppermost in her thoughts at the moment when she was stopped in the insulting manner described.

The two swells were for an instant so taken by surprise that they dropped each other's arm and their cigars simultaneously, and began to caper about in the most extraordinary manner, the stranger continuing to lash them with so good a will, and yet in such an easy, unexcited manner, that Tamar could scarcely forbear from laughing heartily. But when they perceived that there was only one assailant, they rushed in upon the stranger, and endeavoured to close with him. He did not retreat a single step, but hitting one of them a heavy blow on the wrist with the butt-end of his whip, he sent *him* off roaring, while with his left hand he caught the *other* by the collar of the coat and swinging him round—apparently without any extraordinary effort—laid him on his back in the dust. He then offered his arm to Tamar, and led her away as quietly as if nothing had happened, at the same time commencing a discourse upon some totally different topic, as if he would not even give her an opportunity of thanking him for the manner in which he had chastised the insulting youngsters.

But Tamar *did* thank him—and very warmly too; for this feat was just one of the very nature calculated to improve the hold which the stranger already had upon the heart of the beautiful Jewess. She now looked upon him with admiration; for all women love bravery in a man;—and his bravery was so real—so natural—so totally devoid of impetuous excitement when called into action, and so free from any subsequent desire to elicit flattery,—that she beheld in him a character at once generous and noble. She could have thrown her arms round his neck, and said, "Stranger! whoever you may be, I admire—I love you!" And when he *did* take her hand, as she leant upon his arm, and when he pressed it gently—then let it fall without uttering a word, but fixed his deep blue, laughing, and expressive eyes upon her countenance with a steadiness that meant much though his tongue was silent, a soft—a delicious languor came over her, congenial with the moonlight hour.

He conducted her to within a few doors of her father's house, and then took leave of her, saying, "I shall see you again to-morrow." She entered her dwelling, and retired immediately to her chamber; for her heart was filled with a happiness which she knew that her countenance would betray. When she met her father at supper, she was more composed; and she said not a word to him concerning the occurrence of the evening.

On the following day the stranger called again; and again did he find Tamar alone in the drawing-room. On this occasion she extended to him her hand, which he took and pressed to his lips. The maiden did not withdraw it; and her cheeks—her neck—her bosom were flushed with the thrilling glow of excitement, while her eyes expressed a voluptuous languor. The stranger drew her towards him—their lips met: they embraced tenderly. Then he declared his love for her—and she murmured words in reply which convinced him that he was loved in return. Thus, on the fourth occasion of their meeting, did they pour fourth the secrets of their hearts; and Tamar plighted her affection to one whose name she as yet knew not!

Their happy interview was suddenly disturbed by a loud knock at the street-door; and Tamar exclaimed, "My father!" The stranger implored her to compose herself; and she had succeeded in assuming a collected and tranquil demeanour, when Mr. de Medina entered the room. Her lover was standing at a respectful distance from Tamar, with whom he appeared to be exchanging the mere courteous observations which usually pass between perfect strangers. Mr. de Medina requested him to be seated, and inquired his business. "I have called relative to the advertisements which you inserted in the newspapers," was the reply.—"I thought as much!" ejaculated Mr. de Medina: then, turning towards his daughter, he said, "Tamar, my love, you can leave us."—The maiden dared not disobey the hint thus conveyed; but as she passed behind her father to quit the room, she darted upon her lover a look so full of meaning—so expressive of ardent affection, that it seemed to say, "Be you who and what you may, I shall never cease to adore you!" And he returned that look with a glance more rapid but equally significant of tenderness.

When she had left the room, Mr. de Medina continued by observing, "May I have the pleasure of learning your name?"—"Certainly," was the off-hand answer. "I am called Thomas Rainford."—"And your business with me, sir," added Mr. de Medina, in a cold tone and with suspicious manner, "is relative to the paper of which I was robbed?"—"Precisely so," exclaimed Tom Rain.

"A more suitable person than myself could not possibly have called respecting the affair."—"How so, sir?" demanded Mr. de Medina, his manner growing still more suspicious.—"Simply, because it was I who robbed you," was the cool answer; and Tom Rain's merry laugh rang through the room.—"You!" ejaculated Mr. de Medina, starting from his seat. "Then how dare you show your face here?"—"Oh! very easily," replied Rainford, without moving from his chair. "In the first place your advertisements promise impunity to the robber, on condition that he restores the document; in the second place, if you contemplated any treachery, it would only be the worse for you and would not injure me; and thirdly, it struck me that I had better come in person to give you up the paper, because it might have miscarried through the post, or a messenger might have lost it. However, here it is, Mr. de Medina; and had you not advertised for it, I should have restored it to you. I am no rascally extortioner: I never hold men's private papers as a means of drawing money from them. What I do, I do boldly and in true John Bull fashion. A jolly highwayman, Mr. de Medina, is as different from a sneaking pickpocket or a low swindler, as an attorney in grand practice is different from the paltry pettifogger who hangs about the doors of criminal courts or police-offices. It is not often I boast in this way, Mr. de Medina; but I thought you might as well understand that a principle of honour alone, and neither fear nor hope of reward, has induced me to restore you that document. As for fear, I never knew it; and as for reward, I should not think of taking it, were you to offer any."—Mr. de Medina gazed upon Rainford in astonishment, as much as to say, "You are really a very extraordinary person!" But his lips uttered not what the countenance expressed.

The highwayman rose, bowed with easy politeness to Mr. de Medina, and quitted the room. As he was crossing the landing towards the stairs, the door of an apartment adjoining that where he had just left Mr. de Medina, was cautiously opened, and Tamar thrust a note into his hand. He caught a glimpse of her countenance as he received it; and he saw that she had been weeping. When he reached the street, he tore open the note, and read as follows:—"*I have overheard all! But I do not love thee the less, my brave—my gallant Rainford! This evening, I shall have occasion to call at two or three shops in the same street where you rescued me from insult yesterday.*"—Need we inform our readers that Tom Rain kept the appointment thus given him? Or need we say how the lovers subsequently met as often as Tamar could leave the house without exciting suspicion? Yes—they met frequently; and each interview only tended to strengthen the profound attachment which they had formed for each other.

And no wonder that Tom Rain loved his beautiful Tamar; for beautiful—ravishingly beautiful she indeed was! To behold her countenance, was passion;—to gaze on her admirable shape, was rapture;—to meet the glances of her fine black eyes was fascination! And, oh! how devotedly she loved Rainford in return! To her he was a hero; for, although she knew him to be a highwayman, yet well was she aware that he never stooped to a petty meanness, and that his soul was endowed with many noble—many generous qualities. One daring feat which he performed a few weeks after she first became acquainted with him, converted her admiration into a positive enthusiasm; so that the Empress Josephine could not have more ardently worshipped Napoleon than did Tamar her Tom Rain!

Thus it happened:—One night the Liverpool and Manchester coach was stopped on its way to the former town, by a single highwayman, who wore a crape over his face, was well mounted, and equally well armed. Although the coach was crowded with passengers, most of whom were men, yet so terrible was the robber even in his very coolness—so formidable with his easy air of unconcern, that all were paralysed with fear. No resistance was offered him; and he reaped an excellent harvest from the purses of the passengers. One gentleman, who happened to be the Mayor of Liverpool, was so bewildered by terror, that though only asked for his money, he handed to the highwayman both purse and watch. The latter was returned, the robber declaring that he scorned any thing save the current coin of the realm or good Bank notes. From the female passengers he took nothing; and, perceiving by the moonlight a poor shivering girl of about fifteen seated outside at the back of the coach, he asked her a few questions. The brief and timid replies which she gave were ample enough to render intelligible a tale of suffering and woe; and the highwayman, drawing forth five guineas, said, "Here, my dear, you need not be afraid to accept this trifle. It comes from a pocket into which none of these gentlemen's gold has gone."—And before the poor girl could utter a word in reply, the highwayman put spurs to his horse, and disappeared in a few moments.

But this action on his part did not disarm the male passengers, who had been robbed, of their rage and their rancour. The Mayor was particularly indignant: the entire town of Liverpool had been insulted—grossly insulted in his worshipful person! Such wrath required a vent; and it found an issue by means of advertising the daring robbery. The Mayor announced, in all the local papers and by means of placards, "*that any one who should be instrumental in bringing the highwayman before him, would receive the sum of two hundred pounds as a reward*." But a week elapsed before these proclamations received any answer. At the expiration of that time the following incident occurred. One evening, the Mayor entertained a select party of friends at a splendid banquet. The cloth had been removed some time—the ladies had retired to the drawing-room—and the gentlemen, about a dozen in number, were passing the wine rapidly round, when a servant entered to inform his master that a person wished to speak to him in the hall. The servant's manner was somewhat embarrassed; and, upon being questioned, he said that the stranger seemed to wear a mask, as his face was too hideous to be possibly a human one. The Mayor trembled; and his guests caught the infection of his terror. His worship hazarded an opinion that the visitor was perhaps in some way connected with the highwayman who had robbed the Manchester and Liverpool coach; and he directed the servant to show the stranger into the study and then run and fetch a constable. But scarcely were these commands issued, when the door opened; and in walked the object of interest and fear. The Mayor and his guests uttered simultaneous ejaculations of terror; for never did mortal man possess so frightful a face; and as it was partially shaded by a huge quantity of hair and a large slouched hat, it was impossible to decide whether it were really a mask or a natural physiognomy. The nose was enormous, and studded with carbuncles and warts: the cheeks were fiery red; and the chin was of dimensions proportionate with the nasal promontory. This terrible being was enveloped in a long cloak; but through the holes cut for the purpose appeared his arms, the hands holding each a tremendous horse-pistol as big as a blunderbuss.

Placing his back against the door, the intruder said, in a voice which he rendered as hollow and fierce as possible, "Most worshipful Mayor! you have advertised that any one who is instrumental in bringing a certain highwayman before you, shall receive the sum of two hundred pounds as a reward. *I am* the highwayman alluded to: I have brought myself before you; and I appeal to the wisdom and justice of the intelligent gentlemen seated round your board, whether I have not fairly earned the recompense promised?"—"But," stammered the Mayor, "I meant that any one who would bring the robber a prisoner before me, should be entitled to the reward."—"I don't care what you meant," returned the highwayman: "I only know what your advertisements and placards say. You should get the corporation to vote funds to enable you to attach a grammarian to your establishment. He would be more useful than the sword-bearer, I think," added the audacious robber, with a merry laugh in his natural tone. "But I have no leisure to bandy words with you. Tell out the two hundred pounds; or I shall be under the disagreeable necessity of allowing one of these little instruments to empty its contents in the direction of your head."—And, with these words, he raised a pistol. The Mayor uttered an exclamation of terror, and cast an imploring glance rapidly around. But all his guests were sitting like statues—in blank dismay. The Mayor saw that he must not look to them for assistance; and yet he was very loath to part with two hundred pounds in such an unsatisfactory manner.—"But how do I know that you really are the person who robbed the coach?" he asked, the words evidently costing him a most painful effort to enunciate them.—"Because I can tell you every incident that occurred on the occasion," was the answer.—"That information you may have received from hearsay or gleaned from the papers," returned the Mayor, gathering courage as he found the robber willing to argue the point with him.—"I will give you another proof," said the robber. "There was a bad guinea in the purse I took from you. Are you satisfied now?"—"Not quite," rejoined the Mayor, hoping that by gaining time, some chance might place the daring visitor in his power.—"Then I have one more proof to offer you," said the robber. "In a corner of the purse there was a scrap of paper containing the receipt of an overseer of some parish in Manchester for the quarter's money due for the maintenance of your worship's bastard; and so I suppose you had been to that town to pay it."—The Mayor was aghast as this announcement burst upon him; for, though he had lost the receipt in question, it had never struck him that he had placed it in his purse when he paid the money at Manchester. The guests surveyed their worshipful host in astonishment; and the servant giggled behind his chair.—"*Now* are you satisfied?" demanded the highwayman. "Remember, you brought it on yourself."—The Mayor, partially recovering his presence of mind, affected to laugh off the matter as a capital joke on the part of the robber; but he made no farther objection to pay the two hundred pounds. This he was enabled to do, by borrowing all the money that his guests had about them, and adding it to the contents of his own pocket; for the highwayman would neither take a cheque nor allow him to quit the room to procure the requisite sum from his strong-box. The robber would not even leave his post at the door, but compelled the Mayor to rise from the table and bring the cash and notes to him—a proceeding which his worship liked as little as might be, seeing that it brought him into awful vicinity with the nose, the chin, and the pistols. At length the business was settled; and the highwayman withdrew, locking the door behind him,— but not before he had assured the company that if they attempted to open the windows and raise an alarm in the street after him, he would instantly return and put them all to death.

This incident was in every body's mouth next day, throughout the good town of Liverpool and its environs; and the Mayor was most heartily laughed at. But Tamar alone knew the name of the daring individual who had perpetrated so audacious a feat.

The beautiful Jewess carefully concealed her amour from her sister and her father. Indeed, Esther never saw Tom Rain during the whole time that he remained in Liverpool. But one day Tamar disappeared, leaving a note behind her, addressed to her sister, whom she begged to break to their father her flight and its cause. She stated that her happiness—her life were wrapped up in Thomas Rainford: and that as she was well aware her sire would never consent to her union with him, even if the usages of the Jewish nation sanctioned an alliance with a Christian, she had taken a step which she should regret only on account of the distress it might create in the minds of her father and sister. Esther could scarcely believe her eyes when she read the appalling contents of this note. She fancied that she was in a dream: then, when the full conviction of the truth burst upon her, and she comprehended that her sister had really fled with Rainford, she gave way to all the wildness of her grief—for she was deeply, deeply attached to Tamar!

But how did Mr. de Medina bear this cruel blow? He wept not—he gave vent to no passionate exclamation—he manifested no excitement. But, after remaining wrapt up in profound meditation for upwards of an hour, while Esther sate near, watching him with the deepest—most acutely painful suspense,—a long, long hour of utter silence, broken only by the frequent sobs that told the maiden's anguish,—Mr. de Medina spoke in a calm, deliberate, but stern and relentless tone:—"Henceforth, Esther, I have but one daughter—*thyself!* Let the name of Tamar never more be uttered in my presence. Destroy every thing in the house which may tend to remind me that there once dwelt such a being here—the music whereon her name is written, the drawings which she executed, the very window-hangings which she embroidered. Destroy them all, Esther—keep them not—I command you, as you value my blessing! And henceforth—whatever may occur, never speak of your sister. In the presence of those who are aware that you *had* a sister, cut short any allusion that the thoughtless might make respecting her, by observing emphatically—'*I have no sister now!*'—for should such allusion be made before me, my reproof and my response would be, '*I have but one daughter—and her name is Esther!*' It is my intention to wind up my affairs as speedily as possible and retire from business. Had not *this* occurred, I should have toiled a few years longer to amass an immense fortune to be divided between *two*: now the fortune which I possess will be immense enough for *one*. And that *one*, Esther, is thyself! But two or three years may elapse before I shall be enabled so to condense the vast details of my undertakings into such a narrow compass that I may terminate them all prosperously. During these two or three years we must remain in Liverpool: but our sojourn here shall not last a day—no, nor an hour longer than my affairs render imperatively necessary. We will then repair to London; for it is in the giant metropolis alone that we may hope to conceal from the world this disgrace—this infamy—this blight which has fallen upon a family whose name, I had fondly hoped, would have gone down untainted from generation to generation—even as it had descended to me from a long line of honourable and honoured ancestors! These, Esther, are my resolves: seek not to move me.—I am now inflexible! Nay—implore me not to change my determination, stern though it may appear: it is immutable as those Median and Persian laws whereof mention is made in the Book of Books. *Henceforth I have but one daughter!*"

And having thus announced the inexorable resolves on which his mind had settled itself during that long, long hour of deep and silent meditation, the Jew bent down and kissed the brow of his kneeling daughter with an affection which in its tenderness contrasted strangely with the stern severity of the conduct that he had determined to pursue in respect to the lost—the guilty—the disowned Tamar! He then hurried from the room; and Esther—poor Esther! was left alone to shed torrents of unavailing tears, and give vent to fruitless sobs and sighs.

But, oh! what pen can describe the acuteness of her affliction—the anguish of her gentle heart, when, not daring altogether to disobey the will of her sire, she removed from their frames the charming landscapes which Tamar had painted in water-colours, and placed out of sight the music copies whereon the name of Tamar was penned in her own sweet, fluent handwriting! And blame not Esther, gentle reader—no, blame her not, if, disobedient as to the literal meaning of her father's commands, she retained those paintings and that music,—retained them as memorials of the lost sister whom she so fondly loved! But she secured them in her own chamber; and, alas—poor girl! as she placed the pictures one by one in a drawer, their best tints and their brightest colours were marred by the scalding tears that fell upon them! For, oh! acute as the pain inflicted by the merciless knife which the surgeon wields to amputate a limb, was this task to the sensitive heart of Esther,—a task involving a deed wearing in her eyes the semblance of profanity,—for little short of *that* appeared the removal from their wonted places of those memorials of the disowned and cast-off Tamar. 'Twas like crushing all the reminiscences of a sweet sisterhood,—'twas like cutting away from her heart the brightest thoughts that had hitherto clung around it—tearing rudely off the flowers that encircled Hope's youthful brow, and entombing the choice memories of a happy girlhood!

Then, when the music-books and the pictures were thus removed from the places where she had so long been accustomed to see them, how mournful to her was the sight of the tuneful, but now silent piano on which the former had been piled up—how naked appeared the walls to which the latter had hung! And next she was compelled to take down the very hangings which Tamar had embroidered for the drawing-room windows; and there was fresh cause for tears—fresh motive for the renewal, or rather for the continuation of her grief! But the task was nevertheless completed; and the drapery was also retained by Esther as a memorial of her sister. Not for worlds could she have brought herself to that frame of mind which would have been necessary to enable her to achieve the *destruction* of all those objects,—no—not even were her father to menace her with his direst curse! When Mr. de Medina again appeared in the suite of rooms which had been subject to the changes just detailed, he cast a rapid glance around him, and perceiving that his orders had been obeyed so far as *removal* went, asked not a question relative to the manner in which the various objects had been disposed of: but, settling his looks upon Esther's countenance, after that hasty survey, he said emphatically, "*Thank God! I possess an obedient—a dutiful—an affectionate child!*"

In the meantime Tom Rain and the beautiful Tamar were far away from Liverpool, on their road to London; and when they reached the great metropolis, they hired a neat lodging in a secluded neighbourhood—for they entertained apprehensions that Mr. de Medina might endeavour to trace his fugitive daughter. Tamar did not, in this respect, know her father's disposition well. Judging by his past kindness, she argued accordingly—little imagining that he had strength of mind sufficient to adopt the fearful alternative of casting her off for ever! Rainford had so well stocked himself with coin during his sojourn in Liverpool and its neighbourhood, that there was no immediate necessity of exercising his *professional skill*, or rather *valour*, to supply resources; and several weeks glided away happily—the happiest of his life! He loved Tamar most tenderly and devotedly; and she not only loved him in return—but absolutely adored him. Oh! how she worshipped her gallant highwayman, who was so brave—so generous—and withal so kind to her. Never was there a better temper than that of Tom Rain: it was impossible for him to be put out of humour. He would have scorned the idea of raising a quarrel for the mere sake of making it up again. He saw no amusement in such maudlin proceedings: dissensions, bickerings, and domestic feuds were his abhorrence. He looked upon woman as the weaker vessel, whom man was bound to protect. He thought it beneath him to dispute with a female; because with him it could be a mere warfare of words, to which none but a coward would put an end by means of a blow. Besides, he hated that strife which is waged with the tongue: if a man offended him, he did not wait to argue the point, but quietly knocked him down. That was his first and last reason when irritated: but he could not adopt the same course with a woman, and he therefore most rationally concluded that it was perfectly useless to quarrel with her.

Tamar, like all young and beautiful women—especially being placed as it were in an equivocal position—was jealous. Tom Rain loved to visit all the strange places in which London abounds, that he might make himself acquainted with the "lights and shades" of metropolitan life; and sometimes Tamar complained that he was too long absent. "Now, my dear girl," he would say, "I give you as much of my time as possible; and when I tell you that I shall be home at a certain hour, I never disappoint you. But do not show ill-humour because I take a couple of hours to myself. So now kiss me, and do not teach that pretty face to frown." His good temper invariably proved irresistible; and in the course of time his mistress never thought of manifesting any opposite feeling. Indeed, he was so kind—so good—so attentive towards her, that, had it not been for the frequent intrusion of a painful reminiscence concerning her father and sister, Tamar would have been completely happy.

After remaining for some months in London, Rainford and his beautiful mistress set off for the northern counties, where the highwayman reaped a rich harvest. His midnight expeditions were frequent, because his mode of living was by no means economical: he delighted in good cheer—denied himself nothing that he fancied—and yet was neither a drunkard nor a glutton. He was moreover generous and liberal to an extreme, and, emulative of the character of Robin Hood, gave to the poor no inconsiderable portion of what he took from the rich. Tamar was, moreover, fond of handsome apparel and resplendent jewellery; and Rainford took a delight in gratifying all her whims and fancies. Thus money was lavishly expended by them; but the highway was an inexhaustible treasury to which Rainford never had recourse in vain. The perils he incurred, in these predatory expeditions, were of course numerous and great; but his dauntless valour—his wonderful presence of mind—and the determined resolution with which he as it were met danger face to face, invariably saved him from capture. At first Tamar was dreadfully frightened when Rainford took leave of her to "get a draught on his treasury cashed," as he laughingly termed his nocturnal expeditions; but as he invariably returned home about the hour he had promised, those apprehensions wore off, and she at length became comparatively easy in her mind during his absence.

Thus did time pass away, until nearly three years had elapsed since Tamar first met Rainford at Liverpool. During the whole of this period she had heard nothing of her father and sister; and no allusion was ever made to them by her lover or herself when together. But she did not the less devote frequent thoughts to the author of her being and the much-loved Esther, both of whom she longed—oh! ardently longed to embrace once more.

The reader has already learnt the motives which induced Tom Rain to visit the metropolis towards the close of the year 1826. The important information which, during his travels about England in company with Tamar, he gleaned from the gipsy Miranda, led him to betake himself once more to London. It happened that Mr. de Medina and Esther arrived in the capital almost at the same time; for the merchant had not been able to wind up his affairs until that period. Retiring from business with a large fortune, he had resolved to quit Liverpool—a place which constantly brought back the most painful reminiscences to his mind, in spite of his stern resolve to disown his elder daughter for ever. But Esther—had she forgotten Tamar? Oh! no—the memory of the fond sister was immortal; and she would have given whole years of her life to clasp Tamar in her arms again!

This tender aspiration was speedily destined to be gratified. One afternoon, towards the close of October, 1826, Esther de Medina was returning home to Great Ormond Street, after having been to make a few purchases in Holborn, when she encountered her sister Tamar, who was also alone at the time. Fortunately the street where they thus met was in a quiet neighbourhood and at that moment almost deserted: otherwise, the ejaculations of surprise and delight which the sisters uttered, and the eagerness with which they flew into each other's arms, might have drawn upon them an attention by no means agreeable. As it was, they escaped any particular notice; and hastening to the least frequented side of Queen Square, they entered into long and serious conversation together. Tamar implored Esther to tell her how their father had received the tidings of her flight; and the younger sister was so overcome by her emotions, that she allowed the entire truth to be extracted from her by the questioning and cross-questioning of the impatient Tamar. Thus was it that the latter learnt how she had been disowned—cast off for ever! Terrible were the efforts which it cost her to subdue a violent outburst of grief; and her heart seemed as if it would break, when in a low tone she addressed her sister thus:—"Esther dearest, my father has no cause to apprehend that I shall proclaim myself his daughter. No—let him boldly declare that he has but *one* child—*thyself*! I know not how long I may remain in London; but this I faithfully promise you, that I will appear abroad as little as possible, and then only with my countenance concealed by a dark veil, so long as the interests of him whom I love may compel him to dwell in this city. That we shall be long here, I do not believe. Tell our father, Esther, that we have thus met; and communicate to him those assurances that I have now given thee."—Esther clung to her sister for support: that language was distressing to the young maiden to hear.—"And are you happy, Tamar?" she asked, weeping bitterly.—"As happy as woman can be, whose father has disowned her and who is separated from her sister," replied Tamar, now weeping also. "Yes, dearest Esther, I am happy with *him* whom I love so well, and who is so kind, so fond towards me!"—"This assurance diminishes my grief," murmured Esther. "Oh! how glad I am that we have thus met: this interview has suddenly relieved me of a tremendous weight of cruel uncertainty regarding thee! But, alas! Tamar, why did you desert your happy home? why did you abandon a father and a sister who loved you so tenderly?"—"Esther, hast thou not yet known *that love* which is so different from the affection existing even between parents and their children, or between those who are so closely linked in the bonds of kinship as yourself and I?"—"No!"—"Well, then, Esther, I can scarcely make you comprehend how much more deserving of pity than blame I am! He whom I love so well came to the house—I did not seek him; and my heart soon—oh! full soon became his. Could I help it? It were vain and idle to say that we can control those feelings which constitute the passion of Love! No earthly power could have restrained the current of that attachment which hurried me along to the accomplishment of what became my destiny. And when one loves as I loved and still love, Esther,—and as I am loved in return,—father, sister, home, kindred, friends—all are forgotten! Oh! this is true—so true, that you would not blame me, did you know what it is to love as I love!"—"Blame you, dearest sister!" exclaimed Esther. "Never! never!" And she clasped Tamar fervently in her arms; but it was now dark, and that part of the square to which they had retired for the purpose of unrestrained discourse, echoed to no voices save their own.

When the sisters were a little more composed, Esther informed Tamar of all that had occurred since they had last seen each other,—how their father had renounced the cares and fatigues of business, and had resolved to settle altogether in London; and how he was then negotiating with the Earl of Ellingham for the tenancy of a small but compact estate near Finchley. The sisters then agreed to correspond together; for Esther secretly hoped that her father would not deny her the pleasure of receiving letters from her sister. Tamar was accordingly to address her correspondence to Great Ormond Street; and Esther was to direct her letters to "*T. J., South Moulton Street*," where Rainford and his mistress were then passing under the name of Jameson. The sisters were now about to part, when, Esther, drawing a diamond ring from her finger placed it in Tamar's hand: then taking a small pair of scissors from her reticule, she cut off the end of one of her own ringlets, which, having folded in a piece of paper, she also presented to her sister, saying in her softest, sweetest tones,—"Tamar, the love which subsists between us, no circumstances can destroy—no length of absence impair. We are about to separate: and, though with the hope of meeting again, still that meeting might be deferred by accidents at present unforeseen. I would that you should possess some memorial of your sister——"—"Oh! is it necessary?" exclaimed Tamar, in an impassioned tone of profound sincerity.—"If not necessary, it would be at least soothing to my feelings," said Esther; "for I possess memorials of you, in your drawings and your music. Grant me, then, the favour which I am about to ask you."—"Name it, sister," replied Tamar, now deeply affected in her turn.—"It is, dearest," continued the amiable Esther, "that you dispose of the ring which I have now presented to you, and that with the proceeds you will have made a locket in which my hair may be set, and on the inner side of which my name may be engraved. This I implore you to do, my sister; and I know that you will not refuse me."—"The next time we meet, Esther," said Tamar, in a tone tremulous with emotion, "I will show you the locket."—The sisters then separated with aching hearts.

On her return home, Esther frankly and candidly confessed to her father all that had occurred. For some minutes Mr. de Medina remained silent; and Esther observed that a tear trembled upon his lash. But the hope thereby excited within her, died away, when her father turned abruptly round, and said, "Esther, you have not acted well. That you should speak to her who was once my daughter, is natural. But that you should arrange with her the means of correspondence, was wrong. I desire that the first letter which she may address to this house, shall also be the last."—The Jew then quitted the room, leaving his daughter in tears.

On the very next day Tamar wrote a long and most affectionate letter to her sister; and Esther was compelled to inform her, in the reply, of the harsh command issued by their father. But that very severity on the part of Mr. de Medina to some extent—at least in this particular instance—destroyed that frank and open-hearted confidence which Esther had hitherto manifested towards him, and which was inherent in her nature. She could not make up her mind to break off all correspondence with her sister; and yet she dared not receive any future letters at the house in Great Ormond Street. The idea of having Tamar's letters addressed elsewhere, naturally suggested itself, therefore, to her imagination; and she accordingly made an arrangement at the post-office in Southampton Row, by which the woman who kept the shop consented to receive and keep for Esther any missives that might be thus addressed:—"*A. B. C., Post Office, Southampton Row. To be left till called for.*" That same evening Esther wrote another letter to her sister, acquainting her with this arrangement; and we should observe that Tamar duly communicated all these circumstances to Tom Rain, who was delighted to find that she whom he so fondly loved had experienced so much happiness by thus meeting and corresponding with her sister. The highwayman was not, however, a little astonished when he had learnt from Tamar that Mr. de Medina was about to become the tenant of the Earl of Ellingham; and it was then for the first time that he communicated to his mistress the full particulars of all that the gipsy Miranda had told him, and which had made him acquainted with his parentage,—particulars already so well known to the reader.

The seventh day after these events was the 31st of October—a date rendered memorable, so far as this narrative is concerned, by the affair of the diamonds. It was about five o'clock in the afternoon of the day named, that Tamar called on Mr. Gordon, the diamond-merchant in Arundel Street, to dispose of her ring. Rainford would have transacted the business for her, but he was occupied at the time in effecting his negotiations with Old Death; and, moreover, Tamar considered it to be a matter exclusively regarding herself. We must confess that the idea of possessing the means of procuring a beautiful locket shared in her mind the place that ought to have been entirely occupied by the proofs she had received of her sister's devoted attachment. But Tamar was passionately enamoured of resplendent jewellery; and when, in Mr. Gordon's apartments, she beheld a beautiful set of diamonds lying in an open case upon the table, the temptation became irresistible. It cannot be supposed that she had been very nearly three years the companion of a highwayman without having her notions of *mine* and *thine* considerably shaken; and through her brain instantly flashed the thought—
—"Wherefore should not I make myself the mistress of those charming jewels, as well as Tom render himself the possessor of a purse on the main road?" Scarcely was the idea conceived, when she resolved to execute it; and she haggled with the diamond-merchant relative to the price which he was to pay for the ring, merely to gain an opportunity to self-appropriate the diamonds. That opportunity served; and she departed alike with the produce of the ring and of the theft!

But scarcely had she reached the street, when her sentiments underwent a complete revulsion; and she would have given worlds to be able to recall the last ten minutes. For an instant she paused, hesitating whether she should not return into the presence of Mr. Gordon and restore him the diamonds. Fear, however, prevented her,—a fear lest he might consider her deserving of punishment for having abstracted them at all. She accordingly hurried away towards South Moulton Street. But during her walk thither, she reflected that Rainford might be much annoyed with her for the deed she had committed; and the more she pondered thereon, the more powerful became her conviction that he would be more than annoyed—in fact, deeply incensed. She accordingly made up her mind to conceal the circumstance from him, and seek the earliest possible opportunity of sending back the diamonds, by some safe means, to Mr. Gordon.

On her arrival in South Moulton Street, she found a letter from Esther. It contained assurances of ardent affection, but apologised for its brevity, on the ground that it was then already one o'clock in the day, and that at two Lord Ellingham's carriage was to be at the door to convey his lordship, her father, and herself to view the mansion and estate near Finchley. She added that they were to dine at the mansion, and were not to return until late in the evening. Tom Rain was present in the room when Tamar read this note; and she communicated its contents to him. Two nights afterwards he departed on a little expedition; and on this occasion Lady Hatfield was robbed by the highwayman near Bedfont.

On the ensuing morning Rainford was arrested, and conveyed to Bow Street; but he escaped with impunity, in the manner already described. But how great was his astonishment when he heard the name of Esther de Medina pronounced in the court; and with what interest—with what respectful admiration, did he survey the sister of his Tamar—that sister who loved her whom the father had disowned! When Mr. Gordon was called forward, and stated his name and calling, Rainford began to grow uneasy; for he knew that Tamar had sold him the ring three evenings previously. But as the diamond-merchant gradually explained the details of the robbery of the diamonds, the highwayman's heart sank within him—for he had no difficulty in penetrating the mystery. He was still meditating upon the course that should be adopted to prove Esther's innocence, when it suddenly struck him that she must have been at the estate near Finchley, at the very moment when the theft of the diamonds occurred. The reader knows the rest: Lord Ellingham's attendance at the court was ensured by the intervention of Rainford, and Esther was discharged. Her father, it will be remembered, appeared at the police-office just as the case was about to terminate; and the expression which he made use of to his daughter,—"*Oh! Esther—Esther, I can understand it all! You have brought this upon yourself!*"—is now accounted for. When Esther turned *an appealing glance towards her father, as if to remind him of some duty which he ought to perform, or to convey some silent prayer which he could well understand,*—it was to beseech him to satisfy the diamond-merchant for the loss of his jewels, and thus save Tamar from any unpleasant consequences which might ensue were the theft traced to her. But, as we have seen, *he affected not to notice that rapid but profoundly significant glance.*

During the few minutes that Mr. de Medina remained in the court, Rainford was concealed as it were—or at least shrouded from observation—amongst the crowd; and thus he escaped the notice of the Jew. We should also state that it was on this occasion Rainford first beheld his half-brother, the Earl of

Ellingham, *whose fine blue eyes indicated a frank, and generous disposition*, and in whose favour the highwayman was immediately prepossessed; for it must be remembered that *his eyes were also of a deep blue, and indicated not only good humour, but a certain generosity of disposition*. Indeed, it was only in respect to the eyes and the brilliant teeth, that the Earl and Rainford possessed the slightest family resemblance to each other. Yes:—it was on this occasion that Rainford first saw him whom he knew to be his half-brother; and the Earl noticed him also,—noticed him amongst the crowd of spectators who thronged the court;—but he knew not then how nearly that good-looking man, with the florid complexion and light hair, was related to him!

When Rainford returned home to South Moulton Street, he upbraided Tamar for the deed which she had perpetrated, and which had involved her sister in such a cruel embarrassment. But he did not reproach her in harsh nor brutal terms: of such conduct he was incapable. He spoke severely and coldly—manifesting his displeasure in a way which touched her to the quick, but provoked no recriminations. She was almost wild with grief when she heard the narrative of her sister being dragged to a police-office upon so degrading a charge; and, producing the diamonds, she implored Rainford to hasten and send them back to their owner. He intimated his intention of performing that duty in person; and ere he went away, Tamar implored his forgiveness. "I have no right to assume to myself the power of pardon," he answered; "seeing that my example has done this. But, oh! Tamar—if not for *my* sake—if not for *your* sake—at least for that of your estimable sister who is so devoted to you, abstain from such deeds in future!"—He then embraced her, and issued from the house.

In the meantime Esther de Medina had succeeded in persuading her father to advance the money,—advance to *her* the means wherewith to liquidate the amount of the value at which the jewels were estimated. But in giving the sum required, Mr. de Medina said sternly, "Esther, it is to *you* only that I concede this favour—and not for the sake of her who was once my daughter, and whom the infamy this day brought to light has estranged more remotely than ever from my heart!"—He then retired to another room, as was his wont when he wished to avoid an unpleasant topic: moreover, he thought that his daughter had suffered enough that day to render any further reproach on his part unnecessary—indeed cruel; and he knew that were the subject of conversation persisted in, he should not be able to restrain his ire.

The reader has already seen how Esther de Medina called upon the diamond-merchant, and paid him the sum of six hundred pounds—the amount at which he valued his jewels. He offered her a receipt; but she declined to take it—for she thought that as she was settling the affair from motives purely honourable and through regard towards *another*, it would appear as if she were really interested *personally* in the transaction were she to reduce it to a mere matter of business. Not that she meditated a revelation of the fact that she had a sister so like herself that, when seen apart, they might well be taken for each other, and that this sister was the real culprit:—oh! no—she would not, even if she had dared, admit that her father had *another* daughter! And if she *lingered—as if anxious to say something more*—'twas merely because her feelings of natural pride prompted her to exclaim, "Oh! sir, believe that I am innocent of this dreadful charge!"—but a second thought convinced her that such a declaration would not be credited, unless supported by a feasible explanation; and she *abruptly quitted the house*—bearing the stigma, in Mr. Gordon's eyes, of having committed a deed of which she was utterly guiltless!

Scarcely had Esther quitted the diamond-merchant's dwelling, when Tom Rain called to restore the diamonds; and great was his surprise upon learning *that Miss de Medina herself had called and paid the six hundred pounds at which they were valued*. He, however, left the diamonds, with the certainty that Esther would hear of their restoration either from Mr. Gordon himself or direct from Tamar. Rainford then returned to South Moulton Street, where he found Tamar in a very excited state. The occurrences of the day had made a profound and most painful impression upon her mind: the indignity offered to her sister—the certain indignation of her father—the upbraidings of Rainford, who had never spoken to her so severely before—and the bitter regrets which she experienced when she contemplated her conduct,—all these circumstances had combined to madden her. Thinking that Rainford was absent longer than the business on which he had set out seemed to warrant, she was filled with the most fearful misgivings. At one moment she fancied that, in disgust at her behaviour, he had abandoned her for ever: then she imagined that he must have been arrested as the possessor of the stolen diamonds. Her mind was agitated like the ocean in a storm. She went out in a fit of desperation, and purchased some arsenic at a chemist's shop. She returned;—Rainford had not yet arrived. She sate down, and tried to wrestle with her maddening thoughts: but an invincible idea of suicide dominated them all. She struggled—Oh! she struggled bravely against that terrible sentiment; and at length Rainford came back. He exerted himself to calm her—said all he could to tranquillise her mind. He declared that he forgave her from the bottom of his heart, and lavished every token of tenderness upon her. She endeavoured to triumph over the fearful excitement under which she was labouring; but all she could do was to *appear* calm. Two or three hours passed away, and Rainford hoped she was recovering her equanimity. But a species of delirium suddenly seized upon her: she rushed to the bed-room, and, before Rainford even knew her intention, she swallowed the poison. By the time he had followed her into the room—alarmed at the precipitate speed with which she had hurried thither—the deed was accomplished; and the paper which he picked up, as she threw herself frantically at his feet, explained to him the whole truth.

Not a moment was to be lost. Entrusting Tamar to the care of the servant-girl, Rainford rushed from the house; and, as a hackney-coach was fortunately passing at the moment, he leapt into it, desiring the driver to take him to the nearest physician of eminence. The name of Dr. Lascelles was best known to the honest jarvey, and to Grafton Street did the vehicle accordingly proceed. The physician accompanied Rainford to South Moulton Street, and Tamar was saved. But ere Lascelles took his departure, the highwayman had resolved on adopting some plan to prevent any disagreeable consequences occurring in respect to Esther de Medina on account of this attempted suicide on the part of Tamar. For Rainford naturally reflected, that as the physician was constantly moving in society, and must necessarily have an immense circle of acquaintance, it was more than probable that he might, sooner or later, encounter Esther, whom he would mistake for the sister—his real patient. Hence the solemn promise which Rainford exacted from Lascelles—*that when once his professional visits had ceased in South Moulton Street, he would forget that he had ever beholden Tamar; and that, should he ever meet her, alone or in company, he would not even appear to recognise her*—much less attempt to speak to her—*unless formally introduced, when he would consider his acquaintance with her to be commenced only from the moment of such introduction.* On the ensuing morning, at seven o'clock, Rainford and Tamar took their departure from South Moulton Street, and repaired to Lock's Fields, where the highwayman had already engaged lodgings previously to the affair of the diamonds, as he was anxious, for many obvious reasons, to dwell in a spot as secluded and retired as possible. Tamar then wrote a long and pathetic letter to her sister, imploring her forgiveness for the indignity which she had undergone on account of one so worthless as herself; and requesting her to address all future letters to her (until further notice) in this manner:—"*T. R., No. 5, Brandon Street, Lock's Fields.*"

On the same day that Rainford and Tamar thus removed to the vicinity of the Elephant and Castle Tavern, Mr. Gordon called upon Esther de Medina in Great Ormond Street. Esther was much embarrassed when the diamond-merchant was announced; for she feared that if her father were at home, he would naturally hasten to the drawing-room to learn the object of this call, and a renewal of many painful reflections, as well as of much unpleasant observation, would follow. It was therefore with a feeling of pleasure that Esther found, upon inquiry of the servants, that Mr. de Medina had gone out a few minutes previous to Mr. Gordon's arrival. When the diamond-merchant mentioned *the particulars of the visit which he had received from the light-haired gentleman*, Esther instantly comprehended that the individual alluded to must be Rainford; for though she had never seen him to her knowledge, yet she had heard a few details relative to his personal appearance, three years previously, at Liverpool. Mr. Gordon acquainted her with the restoration of the diamonds, and *her countenance suddenly assumed an expression of joy*, because she could not help recognising a certain evidence of good principle, and of kind feeling towards herself, in the fact of such restoration.

Two days afterwards Tamar and Esther again met; and the younger sister breathed the most tender expressions of forgiveness in the ear of her whom, though so guilty, she loved so tenderly. On the following evening they met for the third time; and then Esther used all her powers of persuasion to induce Tamar to accompany her home—to throw herself at the feet of their father, and implore his forgiveness. But Tamar answered in a firm tone, while tears nevertheless streamed down her countenance,—"It is impossible, Esther! Rainford loves me so devotedly, that I should esteem myself the veriest wretch upon the face of the earth to desert him; and on this condition alone could I hope to obtain my father's pardon. No: my destiny is fixed; to him I am linked until death shall separate us! Think not, dearest Esther, that I love thee the less because I cannot, dare not, take a step that would probably unite us again at the blessed domestic hearth, and beneath the sacred roof of our father's dwelling. Oh! God knows how sincerely, how earnestly, I wish that such happiness was in store for me! But it is impossible, Esther,—impossible!" And the sisters parted again, each weeping bitterly. Mr. de Medina had noticed that Esther was absent from home a long time on those two occasions; and he taxed her with having seen Tamar again. She did not deny the charge; but falling at her father's feet, she implored him to leave her that source of consolation. Her grief was so excessive, that Mr. de Medina, who in his heart admired these evidences of sisterly affection, gave no reply on that occasion: a negative trembled upon his tongue—but he dared not utter it. He recognised all that was generous and noble in the disposition of Esther; and he felt proud of her as his daughter—the *only* daughter whom he considered himself to possess. But, when in the solitude of his study, he reflected maturely upon these interviews which were taking place between the sisters, and which, if not at once checked, would naturally become more frequent, his mind was impressed with an idea that Tamar was utterly and irredeemably profligate—abandoned in character beyond all hope: and he feared lest Esther should be corrupted by her conversation. He therefore resolved, painful as the duty was, to put an end to those meetings, and yet mitigate the severity of this blow by winking, as it were, at the continuation of their epistolary correspondence—but still with the firm intention of crushing that indulgence also at a very early period. He knew that oral communication is far more dangerous than written interchange of thought; the former therefore was to be suspended first. He accordingly chose the anniversary of the day on which Tamar fled with Rainford to administer to Esther a solemn oath, binding her never to see her sister again. And to this vow was the unhappy girl compelled to pledge herself. It was the conversation which passed between the father and daughter on this occasion, that Lord Ellingham overheard—or rather, detached portions of which met his ears, producing such strange misgivings in his mind relative to the purity of Esther de Medina.

When the weeping Esther retired to her chamber, after having taken that oath, it struck her that her father had not prohibited her from *writing* to Tamar: and Esther was too glad to avail herself of this circumstance, to unburthen her grief to her sister through the medium of that epistle which Old Death intercepted and perused, but which he afterwards returned to the letter-box in Holborn. And if the reader will refer to that letter, he will perceive that it was specially addressed to Tamar, although when first glanced at, and while the impression remained unfavourable to Esther's character, it might have seemed to appeal to Rainford himself.

We have now cleared up all the mysteries relating to the family of Mr. de Medina; and we doubt not our readers will be pleased to find that Esther is indeed a model of purity—innocence—and sisterly affection. Oh! despise not, then, the Jewess—for Christians might be proud to emulate her virtues! And Rainford was a man who readily recognised and appreciated all the excellence of her disposition—all the glorious traits of her character, though he knew her not. But he admired—enthusiastically admired the soul that could cling so devotedly to its love for a sister; and from the first moment that the sisters met in London, he vowed that Esther should never again be compromised by any act or deed on the part of Tamar, if he were able to prevent it. Thus was it that, on the night when Mr. Dykes and his myrmidons invaded the house in Lock's Fields, Tom Rain gave such positive injunctions to Tamar not to visit him in prison, should he be captured; for he feared lest any one acquainted with Esther might meet Tamar under such circumstances, the inevitable result being that the one would be mistaken for the other. But on the day previous to his execution, he yielded to the imploring—beseeching letters which Tamar sent to him by means of Jacob Smith; and consented that she should take a last farewell of him, on condition that she concealed her face as much as possible with a veil.

When Esther read in the newspapers of Rainford's arrest, she felt deeply—deeply for her poor sister, whom she knew to be so devotedly attached to the highwayman. And, oh! Esther herself had begun to comprehend the feeling of love; for she had not beheld with indifference the handsome—the elegant—and the generous hearted Earl of Ellingham;—and all that Tamar had said relative to the wondrous influence of that passion, would at times recur strangely to her memory. Yes—Esther loved the good young nobleman; but her soul was too pure—her manners to deeply fraught with maidenly reserve, to betray the slightest evidence of her attachment. Nor had she yet so far admitted, even in the secret depths of her own mind, the existence of this inclination towards him, as to ponder upon it seriously, or to invest it with the aspect of reality. She knew that he was attached, and believed him engaged to be married to Lady Hatfield and she sighed involuntarily—scarcely comprehending wherefore—when she thought thereon. Still she loved him—while she believed, in the innocence of her own heart, that she merely felt interested in him as a friend. Nor did her imagination define the true distinction between the feeling which she actually experienced, and that which she only conceived to animate her,—no, not even when the glowing description of love which her sister had drawn on one occasion of their meeting, presented itself to her mind. But she could yet the more easily understand how it was possible for Tamar to love Rainford so devotedly as she did. Hence the acute anguish that Esther experienced, on account of her sister, when she read the arrest of the highwayman. Mr. de Medina did not of course remain ignorant of the occurrence; but he made not the slightest allusion to it in the presence of Esther. Nor did he put into force his previously contemplated plan of forbidding any future epistolary correspondence between the sisters. He felt deeply for Tamar, in spite of his stern silence respecting her; and he would not deprive her, under the weight of such dire afflictions, of the consolation which he naturally conceived the letters of Esther must prove to her. He even gave Esther, though unasked, a considerable sum of money, casually observing "that she might wish to purchase herself a new piano, or any thing else she might fancy;"—and the young maiden pressed her father's hand, for it struck her that he meant her to be the medium of conveying assistance, in case it should be needed, to Tamar. But Tamar, in reply to the letter which Esther wrote proffering pecuniary aid, gave her the assurance that, though bowed down by the weight of affliction, poverty was not amongst the sources of her deep sorrow.

Day after day did Esther fondly hope that her father would speak to her relative to the now unfriended position of her sister; but Mr. de Medina preserved a profound silence. There were, however, moments when Esther fancied that his countenance looked anxious and care-worn, as if a struggle were taking place in his mind. Still time wore on, and he said nothing respecting Tamar:—he mentioned not her name! But one night, when Esther could not sleep, she thought that she heard a moaning sound in her father's room, which was on the opposite side of the passage communicating with her own; and, alarmed lest he might have been seized with sudden indisposition, she stole silently from her chamber and listened at his door. He was pacing the room with agitated steps, and speaking aloud in a manner indicative of acute mental anguish. "O Tamar! Tamar—my daughter Tamar! wherefore didst thou ever abandon me? God of my fathers! that such misery—such disgrace—such infamy should have fallen upon my race! And yet—though I have disowned thee—though I have cast thee off for ever—though, obedient to a stern duty, I have interdicted thy meetings with Esther, the darling of my heart,—nevertheless, my heart yearns towards thee, my Tamar! Oh! to reclaim thee—to bring thee back to the paths of virtue—to see thee happy and gay as thou once wast,—Oh! to do all this, I would consent to become the veriest beggar who crawls upon the face of the earth!" There was a long pause; and Mr. de Medina continued to pace his room with steps still more agitated than hitherto—while Esther stood in breathless suspense at the door, not daring to make her father aware that she had overheard him, and yet unable to retrace her steps to her own chamber. "But it may not be!" suddenly exclaimed the Jew, in an impassioned—rending tone; for the triumph which he had achieved over his softer feelings, cost him pangs as acute as if his heart-strings were being torn asunder. "No—it may not be! I have pronounced the fatal words, Tamar—I have disowned thee; and I may not recall the *fiat*! But if that man——who led thee astray——should be cut off by the hand of justice——" and the Jew's voice grew tremulous as in broken sentences he uttered these words——"then thou will be alone in the world——friendless——perhaps in want——starving—— Oh! my God! my God!"

And Esther knew that her father was overcome with the bitterness of grief. For a moment her hand was raised to knock at the door; but in the next the thought struck her that she would be doing wrong to wound, and even humiliate him, by suffering him to know that she had become aware of the sorrow which he devoured in secret! And it also flashed to her mind that beneath the cold, stern, and severe demeanour which he had maintained ever since the flight of Tamar from the paternal roof,—beneath, also, that unbroken—profound silence which he had maintained towards her in respect to the misfortune that had fallen upon Tamar by the arrest of Rainford,—beneath all this, there agitated within his breast feelings and emotions keenly sensitive, but which were seldom if ever allowed to reflect themselves in the mirror of the countenance. Deeming, therefore, her father's grief too sacred for intrusion—too solemn to be broken in upon, Miss de Medina stole back to her chamber, and moistened a sleepless pillow with her tears. Nevertheless, a gleam of light penetrated the dark clouds of grief which hung upon her mind; for she had ascertained, beyond all possibility of doubt, that Tamar was not entirely unloved by her father—that his heart was not a tomb in which her memory was interred!

For, oh! that heart yearned towards thee, Tamar—lost, fallen though thou wast! and this conviction was an anodyne to the lacerated feelings of thy sister Esther! Time passed on—and still Mr. de Medina remained silent respecting the matter to which the charming maiden daily and hourly hoped to hear him allude. At length the trial took place—and the gallant highwayman was condemned to death. Oh! had it not been for that terrible oath—an oath from which her sire only could release her—Esther would have flown to console her sister at that season of her bitter grief. But, alas! all she could do was to impart solace by means of letters; and how cold is even the most fervent language of the pen when compared with that which the heart feels it should utter through the medium of the tongue! Tamar replied to those letters; and Esther was astonished to perceive that the afflicted woman wrote with a certain degree of calmness:—but she feared that it was indeed the calmness of despair! A second time did Mr. de Medina place in Esther's hands a considerable sum of money, telling her to use it as she thought fit; and the beauteous maiden, while her heart fluttered with hope and anxious expectation, exclaimed in an appealing tone, "Oh! my dear father—God grant that I do not misunderstand thy motives! Thou knowest that I have no need for all this gold; and *she* requireth a sire's pardon, but not the aid of his purse."—"I do not—I dare not understand you, Esther," returned Mr. de Medina, with difficulty assuming a cold tone, but with tears starting into his eyes:—and then he hastily quitted the room. Esther saw how deeply he was moved: and hope increased—not diminished—within her gentle breast. Then, when she pondered on all her father had uttered aloud, on that night when she had listened at his chamber door,—and when she reflected on all his proceedings since the day of Rainford's arrest,—she fancied that she could fathom his motives and intentions. "Should my dear—dear sister," she thought within herself, "be left friendless and alone in the world, by the hand of justice striking at the existence of him whom she loves—*then*, and only *then*, will the door of the paternal dwelling be opened, and a father's arms be extended, to receive the exile once more."

At length the fatal morning came—the morning on which Rainford was to suffer, and to which date we have now brought up our history. On the preceding Saturday Tamar had written to Esther to say that the hours of her bitterest—most crushing trials were now at hand; and that if she survived the soul-harrowing anguish then in store for her, it would be only with the hope of yet finding herself restored, sooner or later, to the sweet companionship of her sister, and also for the sake of the little boy whom Rainford's kindness had adopted, and who was so completely dependent upon her. "The moment all shall be over on Monday morning," added Tamar in her letter, "my preparations to leave London will commence. It is my intention—my firm intention to proceed to America, and there remain—burying my woes in a strange land, and devoting myself to the care of this boy—until it may please God to move my father's heart to recall me home! Let me receive a letter from thee, then, my beloved sister, on Monday morning—a letter that may console me by the assurances of thy continued love—if consolation there be for me in this life! Let your much-coveted communication reach me, sweetest Esther, at about ten o'clock on Monday. May God bless you, dearest—dearest Esther!"

Accordingly, on Monday morning, at about half-past nine, Esther despatched a letter, by a messenger, to Tamar's lodgings in the City. Need we say that this epistle contained all the tender assurances of love and unvarying affection which the affectionate disposition of the Jewish maiden could suggest, or which were calculated to console where consolation was so difficult? When the messenger, whom she had gone out to hire, had departed with the letter, Esther de Medina felt too restless—too nervous—too unsettled, to return home again immediately. The idea that one whom her sister loved had suffered an ignominious death that morning, and that Tamar was at that very moment crushed down to the earth by the weight of her afflictions,—this idea was more than Esther could contend against. She wandered listlessly about—unmindful whither she was going; and it was in this frame of mind that she suddenly heard her name pronounced. She knew the voice, which somewhat recalled her to herself; for it was the voice of Lord Ellingham, whose absence from home had been made known to her by means of the laconic letter which he had addressed to her father from his dungeon.

The reader knows the rest:—with strange rapidity was she hurried away by the Earl towards Red Lion Street; and in the house to which she was conducted, she found her sister, who had arrived there only a few minutes previously, guided by Jacob Smith.

CHAPTER LVII.
A FATHER.

While the scenes related in the fifty-fifth chapter were taking place at the house in Red Lion Street, Mr. de Medina was pacing in an agitated manner his private apartment at his own residence.

Esther had rightly divined his thoughts and intentions: he had indeed been debating in his own mind, for some time past, whether his duty, as a father and as a man, did not command him to forgive a daughter whom the hand of the Lord had so severely stricken.

The Jew thought of his wife long dead, and murmured to himself—"Were she alive still, she would be kneeling at my feet, imploring me to pardon the erring Tamar! And does she not now look down upon me from those empyrean heights where her sainted spirit is numbered with the blest? Nay, more; do I not see her image now kneeling before me? Oh! can this be imagination? Yes—it is,—it is,—and yet how like the reality!"

Mr. de Medina was so painfully excited that his fancy for a moment conjured up the semblance of his deceased wife, as she had appeared in the pride of her loveliness, long years before.

But when the evanescent illusion had passed away, he again paced the room, a prey to the most painful indecision and doubt.

He longed to recall Tamar to his favour; and yet he feared to compromise his character for firmness and decision;—so strange and yet so sure it is, that, even in those moments when our best feelings are agitating within us to the purest and holiest ends, a miserable sentiment of worldly vanity intervenes, and if it do not altogether mar good deeds, at least impairs the merit of their excellence, by engendering hesitation, wavering, and delay.

Mr. de Medina's conflicting—battling meditations were suddenly interrupted by a loud knock at the street-door; and a servant shortly after announced to his master that the Earl of Ellingham was waiting in the drawing-room.

The Jew remained in his chamber a few minutes to compose his countenance, and collect his scattered ideas, ere he descended to meet the nobleman.

When he entered the drawing-room, he immediately saw by Arthur's face that it was no visit of mere ceremonious courtesy which was now paid to that house.

"My dear Earl," said Mr. de Medina, "you have been lost to the world for some weeks; and I must confess that when I received the letter which you did me the honour to address to me nearly a month ago, I entertained fears lest business of an unpleasant nature called you thus abruptly away from England."

"That letter, my dear sir," answered the Earl, "was not precisely such an one as I should have written to you had I been free from restraint."

The nobleman then related, in as few words as possible, the outrage that had been perpetrated upon him—the imprisonment he had endured for four mortal weeks—and the manner in which he had escaped.

Mr. de Medina expressed his indignation and surprise at the treatment which the young nobleman had undergone, and inquired if the motive could be accounted for.

"I am totally at a loss to conjecture who were my enemies, and the cause of their abominable proceedings," answered the Earl. "But let us waive that subject for the present, my dear sir," he continued; "as it is my duty to engage your attention with other and more important matters."

Mr. de Medina pointed to a seat near the fire, and then drew a chair for himself to within a short distance of that taken by the Earl.

"I am about to mention a name to you, my dear Mr. de Medina," continued the nobleman, "which may perhaps—nay, will certainly sound unpleasantly upon your ears; but you know me too well to imagine for an instant that I should thoughtlessly or wantonly give you pain. I allude to Thomas Rainford."

The Jew started, and his countenance fell.

"This Thomas Rainford, Mr. de Medina," resumed Arthur, "has wronged you—wronged you deeply; and not for a moment do I attempt to defend his conduct."

"But how know you, my lord, that the wretched man, who is now no more, and against whose memory common humanity orders me not to nourish animosity——"

"Mr. de Medina," interrupted the Earl in a low and solemn tone, as he bent towards the Jew, "Thomas Rainford lives!"

"Lives!" ejaculated Mr. de Medina, in a voice loud with excitement and surprise.

"Hush! speak low—in a whisper—the walls have ears!" said Arthur impatiently. "In the name of heaven! compose yourself—calm your mind, Mr. de Medina—for I have much to communicate to you—and that much of the first importance."

"Proceed, my lord," said the Jew coldly: "I am all attention."

"It is, then, true that Rainford lives——"

"And yet scarce an hour has passed since men were crying the account of his execution for sale in the street—beneath this very window," observed Mr. de Medina, in an incredulous tone.

"It is as true that he is now alive as that he underwent the ordeal of the terrible rope, even as the pamphlet-venders proclaimed beneath your window," continued the Earl. "In a word, he has been resuscitated by the wondrous agency of galvanism."

"Good God! my lord—is this possible?" cried Mr. de Medina: "or do my ears deceive me?"

"Again I implore you to master your feelings," said the Earl; "for I have another circumstance, almost equally strange, to reveal to you. Thomas Rainford is nearly related to me——"

"To you—to your lordship!" exclaimed Mr. de Medina.

"Yes: the same father was the author of our being—though different mothers bore us. He is my half-brother—and all the proofs thereof are in my possession. Nay, more—and *this* I reveal to you to prove the confidence I place in *you*—he is my elder brother, legitimately born, and is the rightful Earl of Ellingham!"

Mr. de Medina gazed on the young nobleman in speechless astonishment,—with an amazement, indeed, so profound, that it seemed as if he were suddenly paralysed by the announcement which had just met his ears.

The Earl then rapidly sketched the outline of Rainford's birth; and, without in any way alluding to Lady Hatfield, stated that accident had brought them together, and had led to the revelation of all those wondrous circumstances. Arthur did not however forget to mention the generous conduct of Rainford in refusing to avail himself of papers which would have placed a coronet on his brow and vast estates at his disposal, and also in consigning those papers to the possession of Arthur himself.

Mr. de Medina was perfectly astounded at all he heard; and he listened in silent wonderment—no longer interrupting the narrator with comment or question.

The Earl proceeded to inform him how the whole scheme for the resuscitation of the doomed man had been arranged between himself and Dr. Lascelles, and how it had perfectly succeeded.

"Indeed," added Arthur, "I left my half-brother just awakened from a profound sleep, and, though much enfeebled, still beyond the reach of danger. But spare me the necessity of describing to you the first moments of horror—boundless, appalling horror—which he experienced, when, slowly opening his eyes, he awoke to the recollection of all he had this morning gone through, and to the wildest doubts as to where he was and what had actually become of him! Oh! Mr. de Medina, it was a scene which the memories of those who beheld it, never—never could fail to retain—even though madness were to destroy the discriminating powers of the intellect! But all that is passed—gone by; and my brother lives—conscious, too, of resuscitated existence!"

"My dear Earl," said Mr. de Medina, at length breaking the long silence which had been maintained on his part, "I have read and heard many wildly wonderful narratives in my time,—truths also far stranger than fictions,—genuine occurrences which outvie all the marvels of romance. But never—never, do I firmly believe, has mortal tongue related, nor mortal ear listened to, a history more amazing—more solemnly interesting, than this. Should these facts ever transpire to the world, and be seized upon by the novelist as the basis of a tale, those who may read, having been previously unacquainted with those facts, would exclaim, *'Tis impossible!* Oh! what a work might be written, under the title of THE MYSTERIES OF LONDON! But pardon me for wasting your valuable time with these comments:—I say, pardon me—because I perceive that you have more yet to relate."

"I have indeed," said the Earl, trembling for the success of the mission which had taken him to Mr. de Medina's house; "and I am now compelled to touch upon a subject which cannot be otherwise than painful to you——"

"I understand you, my lord," interrupted the Jew: "proceed—for I know that you would not refer to that topic without a well-intentioned motive."

"Such is indeed the case," said the Earl. "But not to use more words than are necessary—as time is precious—I shall at once inform you that I am acquainted with the sad episode in my half-brother's life, which relates to—to—your elder daughter."

"Go on, my lord," said the Jew, mastering his emotions.

"But not until this morning—till within an hour ago," continued the Earl, "was I aware that you possessed *two* daughters. The moment that Rainford was pronounced to be out of danger, I despatched a faithful messenger to break the tidings to her who loves him, and whom he loves so well; but while this messenger was absent, I had occasion to leave, for a short time, the house where Thomas Rainford now lies; and accident led me to encounter Miss Esther. Pardon me, when I state that a variety of circumstances, which I will some day explain, had for several weeks past induced me to believe that she—whom I now know to be an angel of purity and goodness—was the being so dear to my brother; and, anxious to relieve her mind, as I thought, from the agony of grief into which the supposed fate of Rainford must have plunged her,—anxious also that her presence should greet *his* eyes upon awaking from the deep sleep that followed the galvanic resuscitation,—I led her—dragged her, with me to the house I ere now spoke of—saying heaven only knows what incoherent things to her as we sped along, and to which, I remember now, she listened and replied with an amazement since explained. But, in the meantime, Jacob Smith—the messenger whom I had sent to your elder daughter—had arrived with *her*; and thus—you perceive how innocently on my part,—the sisters were brought together by the bed-side of my brother!"

"Esther and Tamar together!" ejaculated Mr. de Medina, starting from his seat, in mingled anger and surprise: then, suddenly changing to an aspect of profound sorrow, he murmured, "Oh! Esther! thine oath—thine oath!"

"She did not violate it, Mr. de Medina," said the Earl emphatically. "As well might it be asserted that, had you sworn never to enter my house, and were you carried thither by force, your vow would be wilfully—wickedly broken. No:—Miss de Medina knew not whither she was going—knew not whom she was to see—knew not that her sister would be there! If any one has erred in all this, 'tis I; and yet I, Mr. de Medina," added the Earl proudly, "am incapable of doing a bad deed. There lives not the man who, with truth, could impute to me aught that I should be ashamed to have published before all the world. And it is not to boast of untarnished rectitude—of a bright fame—of an unsullied reputation, that I now speak;—but it is to convince you—you, Mr. de Medina, a man of the world—yourself upright beyond all doubt—honourable beyond all possibility of impeachment,—it is to convince you, that if I have incurred your displeasure, I did not the act wantonly—and that I deserve forgiveness."

"Excellent young man!" exclaimed the Jew, grasping the Earl's hand, and wringing it with even paternal warmth: "who shall dare to impute sinister motives to one like you? No,—Oh! no:—were all the scions of the aristocracy as noble-hearted as yourself—endowed with such feelings as you possess, they would be a blessing instead of a curse and a shame to this country. I was unjust," added Mr. de Medina, more slowly,—"unjust towards my beloved and amiable Esther—and unjust also in respect to you. But, oh! my lord," continued the Jew, while tears rolled down his cheeks, "it is hard—it is hard to have the honour of one's name tarnished by a disobedient daughter:—and such is the lost—the unhappy Tamar!"

"The best of us in this world are but poor, erring, sinful mortals in the eyes of Him who is all-perfect but who is likewise all-merciful," said the Earl in a solemn and impressive tone. "Alas! but a few minutes have passed since I proclaimed my rectitude, vain boaster that I was—and lauded your integrity, miserable flatterer that I was! But I then spoke as men speak—as we mortals are accustomed to estimate our characters for honour and probity. Nevertheless, in the sight of heaven, we are sinners—wretched sinners; and our only hopes are in God's illimitable mercy! Then, Mr. de Medina,—as you hope for salvation in another world,—as you expect forgiveness at the hands of the Almighty for those failings wherewith the very best of us are characterised,—I implore—I beseech you, to pardon your daughter Tamar!"

Glorious—almost god-like, was the enthusiasm with which the fine young nobleman urged his strong appeal—the stronger for all the sincerity of the argument which prefaced it.

Mr. de Medina gazed upon him with mingled wonder and admiration: but when the Earl had done speaking, the Jew turned aside and paced the room in a manner betraying the most painful agitation.

"Think not," resumed Arthur, also rising from his seat, "that I am one of those wretched hypocrites, who, in their sickly cant, make use of the holiest names and the most sacred arguments to win a cause in which they are interested only through selfish and worldly motives. No!—I should scorn to reduce myself to such a level—I should hate myself were I capable of such contemptible duplicity. It is not he who prays longest and loudest, that is the most sincere. But I appeal to you by all things sacred—I, the Christian, appeal to you, the Jew—by those doctrines which form the basis of the creed in which we both put faith,—doctrines which teach us the goodness of the Almighty, as manifested towards the Israelites,—by all HE did for your forefathers—thereby do I appeal to you to receive an erring daughter back to your arms, and assure her of your pardon!"

Still Mr. de Medina replied not—but continued to pace the room.

"Were your daughter Esther—the amiable, the excellent Esther here," continued Lord Ellingham, "she would not perhaps intercede so vainly as I. During the rapid explanations which were ere now vouchsafed to me by the repentant Tamar herself,—explanations which have shown me how ineffably beyond all human praise is the conduct of the younger towards her elder sister,—I learnt more of the heart of woman than ever I knew before. My ideas—my sentiments, concerning woman and her mission here, have always been of the loftiest kind: but now I am led to recognise something angelic—something heavenly in her disposition. Oh! Mr. de Medina, had I such a sister as Esther, never—never, would I permit a tear to dim the brightness of her eye, if it were in my power to wipe it away!—never—never, would I allow a pang to steal into her gentle breast, if deed or word of mine could avert it. For I declare your younger daughter to be a very angel of excellence and moral worth; and your entire nation should be proud of the name of Esther de Medina!"

"My lord—my dear Earl," faltered the father, approaching the young nobleman, and taking his hand, "if the Jews should be proud of Esther, the Christians may with good cause glory in their Arthur of Ellingham! But if this *must* be—if Tamar should once more receive from me the name of DAUGHTER—how——"

"I understand you, my dear friend," interrupted the nobleman: "you would ask—you would know what course is to be pursued in respect to my half-brother."

The Jew made a hasty sign for his companion to proceed.

"I must confess that this difficulty struck me forcibly ere I came hither just now," continued Arthur. "My half-brother is devotedly attached to your daughter; and Tamar is equally wrapped up in him. To separate them, in my opinion, would be the height of cruelty: for you to forgive your daughter and consent to allow her to dwell in concubinage with Rainford, are things I know to be incompatible. But is there no course open to them? Listen to the plan which I suggested before I left those who are no doubt so anxiously waiting my return. It is this: To-morrow night, if Dr. Lascelles accord his permission, I shall accompany my half-brother to France, whence he will proceed as soon as possible to the United States of America. For in the hasty explanations which ere now took place between us all, I learnt that he had already expedited thither a considerable sum of money, his intention having been to proceed with Tamar to the New World when his project was suddenly marred by his arrest. While he is away, and in safety, I shall exert myself to obtain his full pardon; for I shall privately represent to the Minister all the circumstances of this most extraordinary case. To-morrow night, then, we proceed to Dover, whence we shall embark for France. 'Tis for you and your daughters to follow us to Paris; and there the hands of Tamar and Thomas Rainford may be united in the chapel of the British Embassy. I am well aware that it will be a Protestant marriage only;—that in your eyes it may be insufficient, so far as it regards the creed of your daughter;—but it is the least of two evils. For, believe me, Tamar and my brother are so devoted to each other that they would never consent to separate:—no—Tamar would not quit him even to receive her father's pardon! Thus they would continue to live in that state which is repugnant to the feelings of society—a state unhallowed by the rites of the Church. But where two hearts are thus closely connected and are wedded to all intents and purposes, by the mere fact of their binding affections,—tell me—tell me, does it matter much at which of

God's altars the blessing of heaven shall be invoked? You will pardon your daughter—you will receive her back into your arms,—you will give her to one who loves her most tenderly and who has ever treated her as if she were his wife—and, after the ceremony shall have been performed, albeit a Protestant one, you may say proudly and unblushingly to those who learn that you have another daughter, and who inquire concerning her,—you may say fearlessly, 'She is married!'"

Mr. de Medina walked towards the window for a few moments to conceal his tears.

But he could not conceal them; and with the holy dew trickling down his cheeks, he turned again to the nobleman, saying in a tremulous and broken voice,—"My friend—my dearest friend, I yield!—you have subdued me! It shall all be as you have designed it!"

The Earl pressed Mr. de Medina's hand with fervent warmth—with the ardour of gratitude.

"Come with me at once—delay not a moment!" exclaimed Arthur, his own eyes also dimmed with tears.

And he hurried Mr. de Medina to the hackney-coach, which was waiting at the door.

CHAPTER LVIII.
THE RESUSCITATED.

Touching was the scene in the bed-chamber at the house in Red Lion Street,—that scene which the return of the Earl of Ellingham, accompanied by Mr. de Medina, was to render more touching still.

But previously to their arrival, the group was interesting and must be specially noticed.

Rainford was seated in the bed, propped up with the pillows; for he still felt very weak, though all danger had completely passed.

Standing by his side, with one hand locked in his, was Tamar, clad in deep mourning—a mourning now no longer necessary, and which covered a heart beating with ineffable joy.

Dr. Lascelles and Esther de Medina were also standing close by the bed; and Jacob Smith was leaning over the foot-board, surveying Rainford with eyes dimmed by tears, and in a kind of wonderment as if he were scarcely able to convince himself of the miracle the *living evidence* of which was before him.

The hearts of all were too full for connected discourse; for even the doctor himself was more moved by the incidents in which he had that day performed so prominent a part, than ever he had felt before.

At length Tamar turned towards her sister, and said in a low, tremulous tune, "Do you think, dear Esther, that Lord Ellingham will succeed—can you hope it?"

"I have every hope," replied Esther, firmly. "His lordship suggested a plan by which all our father's scruples may be overcome."

"And by which we shall not be separated, save for a few days, Tamar," observed Rainford.

"I would not quit you even for an hour," answered the elder sister, emphatically; "were it not that I was previously assured of being speedily re-united to you."

Rainford pressed her hand tenderly.

"If my friend Arthur does not succeed with Mr. de Medina," said Dr. Lascelles, "I must go myself, and see what I can do. But I confess that I should despair of producing any effect, were Arthur's eloquence to fail."

"Hark!" cried Jacob Smith: "the front door opens!"

The physician hastened to assure himself that no unwelcome step was approaching; and the sisters exchanged looks indicative of the most acute suspense.

"Bravo!" cried the good doctor, returning in a few moments, and clapping his hands together.

But before he had time to give any explanation as to the cause of a joy so unusual in one of his calm and unexcitable disposition, footsteps approached the room.

The eyes of Rainford, the sisters, and Jacob Smith were anxiously cast towards the door.

Lord Ellingham entered first—his countenance radiant with joy. Another moment—and Tamar bounded forward to meet her sire, in whose arms she was immediately received.

"Oh! my dear—dear father!" exclaimed Tamar; "is it possible that you can forgive me—that this happiness is not a dream?"

"Let the past be forgotten, my child!" said Mr. de Medina, pressing her again and again to his breast: for now that she *was* forgiven, all the long-smothered generosity and tenderness of his heart in respect to her revived with fresh vigour. "And you, Esther, my well-beloved," he added, "come also and share your father's joy that the day of pardon has at length arrived!"

Most affecting was the scene. The physician pretended to be busily occupied in wiping his eye-glass; but the tears fell fast upon it:—Rainford and Lord Ellingham both wept aloud; and Jacob Smith whimpered like a little child.

At last the party grew somewhat composed; and Mr. de Medina advanced towards the bed.

"Mr. Rainford," he said, extending his hand, which the resuscitated highwayman grasped with grateful warmth, "to you also do I say, '*Let the past be forgotten.*' From the very bottom of my heart do I forgive you; and this forgiveness I the more readily accord, because I learn that your conduct has been uniformly kind and tender towards my daughter,—because you are prepared to make her your wife according to the ritual of your creed,—and also because I have heard from your noble relative—far more noble in nature even than in name—that you have manifested so many proofs of an excellent heart and a generous disposition towards *him*, that it is impossible not to admire your behaviour in this respect. I have now said all that I intend to utter upon these subjects; for if I be stern and severe in my displeasure, I am equally sincere and profound in my forgiveness."

"My dear Earl," whispered Dr. Lascelles, in the most solemn manner possible, and in a tone audible only to himself and the young nobleman, "I did not think of asking you for any reward for all I have this day done to serve you and yours. But I am so charmed with this Jew, who positively shows more good feeling than many Christians whom I know, that I would give any thing to possess a cast of his head. Do you think———"

"Depend upon it, my dear Doctor, I will not forget your wish," said the Earl, smiling: "but you must admit that this is not precisely the time to ask a favour of so delicate a nature."

"True!" observed Lascelles. "And yet the interests of science———"

"Hush!" said Lord Ellingham: "you will be overheard."

As soon as the party were sufficiently composed to deliberate upon the course now to be adopted, considering the position of Rainford, a solemn conclave was held.

The results of the council may be thus summed up:—Dr. Lascelles, feeling convinced that Rainford was totally out of danger, proposed to return without delay to the West End, to visit his patients who would be otherwise astonished and vexed at his absence. Mr. de Medina was to repair home with his two daughters: and while the young ladies made all the necessary arrangements for the trip to France, their father undertook to proceed to Dover, and secure a sailing-vessel to be in readiness by the time that Lord Ellingham and Rainford should reach that port. Mr. de Medina would then return to London to fetch his daughters; and the family would follow the half-brothers as speedily as possible to Paris. On his side, Lord Ellingham expressed his intention of remaining with Rainford until the moment for their departure together should arrive. Jacob Smith was to stay also in the house in Red Lion Street, and to accompany Tom Rain not only to France, but also to America; for the poor lad was devotedly attached to him, and Rainford felt it almost a duty to remove the youth from the scene of his former temptations and miseries.

Dr. Lascelles accordingly quitted the house, first having promised to see Rainford again next day. Mr. de Medina and his daughters next took their departure, Tamar having taken a tender farewell of him whom she loved, and whom, according to present arrangements, she was not to meet again until they arrived in Paris. As for Esther, ere she turned to quit the room, she gave her hand to Rainford, who respectfully touched it with his lips.

At length the Earl and Jacob were left together with the resuscitated highwayman, who now lost no time in narrating to them the particulars of his visit to that very house a few weeks previously. For when, on awaking from his deep sleep, he was sufficiently recovered to collect his scattered ideas,—and when the first emotions attendant upon his meeting with Tamar had passed,—he had recognised the chamber in which he was lying. But finding himself under the care and protection of Dr. Lascelles, whom he had seen, it will be remembered, in the house on the night of his memorable adventures beneath that roof, he had so far mastered his surprise and momentary alarm, as to maintain a profound silence relative to his recognition of the place.

But now that there was leisure to converse on matters of secondary importance, and that she in whose breast he was fearful of exciting fears for his safety was no longer present, he detailed at full length all the particulars with which the reader is acquainted, not even omitting the impression existing in his mind that Old Death was no more. Then Lord Ellingham learnt how Rainford had happened to visit the laboratory when he was disturbed by the entrance of Lascelles; and he also heard for the first time how his half-brother had recovered his money, with compound interest, and had obtained all the private papers proving the history of his birth and the marriage of the late Earl of Ellingham with Octavia Manners. Jacob, likewise for the first time, learnt that the very house in which he then was, contained the store-rooms of Old Death; and he now also ascertained the cause of that individual's sudden and mysterious disappearance.

Arthur, in his turn, related the entire particulars of the outrage perpetrated upon him—his imprisonment in a dungeon for four long weeks—the reason of his writing the laconic letter which Rainford had received in prison—his escape by means of the sewers—and his suspicion, in consequence of all he had heard that morning from Dr. Lascelles, that the scene of his late incarceration was not altogether unconnected with the mysterious subterranean of that very house.

But conjecture was useless in respect to all these circumstances; and the only point to which any positive decision could be arrived at, was the absolute necessity that existed for defending the house from all intruders so long as Rainford should remain in it.

Jacob Smith went out to purchase refreshments; and Rainford felt himself so well that he was enabled to make a hearty meal.

Hour after hour passed; and at length evening came.

"Arthur," said Tom Rain, breaking a silence during which he had partially dozed, and now aroused by a sudden idea that had struck him,—"Arthur, I have a strange fancy—a whim, which I much desire you would gratify——"

"Name it, Thomas," returned the nobleman.

"I should like to see the evening paper," continued Tom Rain. "I need scarcely tell you that never again will the highways of this nor any other country be rendered dangerous by me—never shall this right hand of mine perpetrate a crime. My career as a desperate plunderer terminated this morning—on the roof of the gaol: from the instant of my resuscitation I date a new term of existence—new in a moral as well as in a physical sense. But I *should* like to see what is said of me *in my last moments*."

For an instant the Earl hesitated—but only for an instant; and Jacob Smith was sent to purchase the evening newspaper.

In due time he returned; and Rainford sate up in bed *to read the account of his own execution*!

"I am glad of that!" he exclaimed, as his eyes ran down the column headed with the awful words—EXECUTION OF THOMAS RAINFORD; and his countenance became flushed with excitement, as he read aloud, in a tone that trembled not in the least degree, a few of the sentences which seemed to give him pleasure:—"*He underwent the dreadful process of pinioning with extraordinary courage*"—"*his footsteps were as firm as if anything save a scaffold were his destination*"—"*he ascended the stairs leading to the roof of the prison with steps that faltered not*"—"*the same dauntless courage sustained him as he mounted the fatal ladder which conducted him to the drop*"—"*nor did he once exhibit signs of fear; no, not even when the executioner descended beneath the platform to draw the bolt that was to launch him into eternity.*"—"*Thus died a man who possessed a courage that would have rendered him distinguished had his destinies cast him in the profession of arms.*"

"For heaven's sake, no more of this, my dear brother," exclaimed the Earl, painfully excited.

"Burn the paper, Arthur," said Tom Rain, handing it to the nobleman, and then throwing himself back on his pillow. "I have seen enough—and never wish to read that narrative again. But pardon me for having given you pain; and think not it was any frivolous sentiment of vanity that made me desirous to peruse the account, or that excited me as I read it. I merely wished to convince myself that no injustice was done me, Arthur," he added, very seriously; "for, of all things, I abominate a coward; and I confess—it may be a weakness on my part—that I should not like *my last moments* to have been misrepresented. But let us talk no more on this topic—since it gives you pain. And now, by way of changing the conversation, I will tell you some of the plans I have shadowed out in my mind. Perhaps they may never be realized:—I hope they may."

Arthur had set fire to the newspaper by means of a lamp which was burning upon the table; and, having crushed out the expiring flames with his foot, he drew his chair towards the bed, to listen with attention to his half-brother.

Jacob Smith leant over the foot-board, anxious to drink in the words which Rainford was about to utter.

"I have been thinking," resumed this individual, "that my past life requires a great atonement through the medium of my new existence. I am not, however, one of those men who turn saints, and who hope to win the good opinion of the world and the favour of heaven by means of incessant prayer. No—my ideas are quite at variance with such proceedings. I believe that one good *deed* is worth ten thousand *psalms*. It certainly is more beneficial to our fellow-creatures, and must therefore be more acceptable to the Almighty. I have been thinking, then, how pleasant it would be for one who possesses an independence, to employ his leisure time in seeking out those poor, unhappy beings whom adverse circumstances, or even their own faults, have plunged into misery. If they be cast down through misfortunes unconnected with errors, it would be delightful to aid them: but doubly pleasing must it be to reclaim those who have erred, and to afford even the felon a chance of quitting his evil ways and acquiring an honest livelihood."

"Oh! it would—it would, indeed!" ejaculated Jacob Smith, all the adventures and incidents of his own chequered life rushing to his memory.

"I have been reflecting, moreover—not merely within the last few moments," continued Rainford, "but ever since I heard the narrative of one who became an ill-doer in spite of himself,"—looking significantly for an instant towards the lad,—"but who struggled successfully at last against temptation, cruel attempts at coercion, and almost unheard-of wretchedness,—I have been reflecting, I say, that society is wrong in refraining from the adoption of strenuous means to reform those whom it considers to be the most abandoned. The reformist does not enter the criminal gaol: he considers it to be useless. But whither should he go, if not *there*? He should reason with himself that it is impossible for men willingly to cling to the unnatural—the feverish excitement of a life of incessant crime, if they had any chance of adopting pursuits unattended with constant peril. Setting aside the morality of the case, nine-tenths of those very persons who sing the loudest, swear the hardest, and appear the most depraved, would gladly quit a course that makes their conscience see a constable in every shadow. I think I can give you a parallel case, which will fully illustrate my meaning. It is the custom to vilify the Irish—to declare that they cling with a species of natural tenacity to their rags, their dirt, and their penury—to assert that they themselves are the foes to any civilizing principles which may be applied to them. But look at Irish labourers in England—look at the Irishman when in *this* country, supplied with plenty of work, earning adequate wages, and removed from scenes of political excitement. Does he not work hard? is he indolent? does he adhere lovingly to rags and misery? No such thing! Well, then, it is equally absurd to suppose that criminals cling with affection to crime, prisons, and an existence harassed by constant apprehensions. Remove the thief or the housebreaker from the sphere into which circumstances have cast him, and from which he cannot extricate himself,—give him a chance of earning an honest livelihood, and of redeeming his character,—and in nine cases out of ten, he may be reclaimed. There are, of course, exceptions to all rules; but I am convinced, from all I have seen and heard, that I am now speaking of a rule, and not of the exceptions. Well, then, these considerations lead me back to the starting point which I chose; and I repeat my former words,—that were some man to devote himself to the visitation not only of the dwellings of the honest poor, but also the haunts of crime, and the abodes of vice, the deep sinks of impurity, and even the felons' gaols themselves, he would be able to effect an immense amount of good. You may be surprised to hear such sentiments come from my lips——"

"I am delighted—ineffably delighted!" exclaimed Lord Ellingham, speaking with the enthusiasm of unfeigned joy; "and I agree with every opinion you have put forth. I see that our laws are miserably deficient, while they seek only to punish and not to reform—that our legislators are short-sighted if not actually wicked, in neglecting to adopt means to prevent crime by reforming the criminal, rather than encourage turpitude by rendering the criminal a desperate outcast."

"Oh! my dear brother," cried Tom Rain joyfully, "how happy I am to hear you thus express your adhesion to those theories which I have so rapidly glanced at. And are not you a legislator of England—an hereditary legislator? and do you owe nothing to your country? Believe me, when I declare that were you to apply your intellect—your talents—your energies, to this great question, you would render your name so illustrious that the latest posterity would mention it with veneration and gratitude!"

"Rest well assured, Thomas, that these words of your's shall not be thrown away upon me," returned Arthur solemnly.

"And, on my side—humble individual that I am, *and that I intend ever to remain*," added Rainford, with a significant glance towards the Earl, "my resolution is fixed to make some atonement in another part of the world for all the bad deeds I have committed in this. Should I reach America in safety, it will be my task to reduce to practice some of these theories which I have just now broached; and I believe that the results will fulfil all my expectations."[26]

"There is no doubt of it—oh! there is no doubt!" exclaimed Jacob Smith, catching the enthusiasm which now animated him who was *once*—and so lately—a lawless highwayman, but whom circumstances, and the never altogether crushed sentiments of a rightly constituted mind, had suddenly imbued with the hope of atoning for the past by means of the good which he meditated towards his fellow-creatures.

"Poverty is a fertile source of crime," observed Lord Ellingham; "but then it is declared that many are poor only through their own idleness. How are such persons to be reformed? I am prepared to answer the question. Education will teach them the value of industry, and the necessity of rendering themselves independent of parochial relief and eleemosynary assistance. If a child offend, we say, '*He knows no better.*' The uneducated individual is as ignorant of the real principles of right and wrong as the lisping child; and therefore must instruction—not merely religious, but an enlightened species of education—be provided for the millions."[27]

"It is for you to urge those great and glorious points in the proper place—in the Parliament of England!" said Rainford: "and, I repeat, posterity will honour your name!"

"I am not such a hypocrite as to deny the existence of those charms which a laudable ambition possesses," returned Arthur; "no selfish considerations will, however, influence me in the public course which I am now determined to adopt. But I am forgetting, dear Thomas, that this prolonged discourse on an exciting topic may be prejudicial to you, weak and enfeebled as you are. Let us not, therefore, pursue the theme at present: it is now growing late—and you stand in need of repose. Jacob and myself will watch by your bed-side."

Rainford pressed his brother's hand, and composed himself to woo the advance of slumber.

In about ten minutes he was fast asleep!

The Earl of Ellingham was seated close by the head of the bed: Jacob drew a stool near the foot, and the two observed a profound silence.

The Earl looked at his watch: it was half-past ten o'clock.

The lamp burnt upon the table.

Suddenly, slow and heavy steps were heard *beneath*—as if some one were ascending the flight of stairs under the floor.

Lord Ellingham placed his finger upon his lips to enjoin Jacob to maintain the strictest silence, and then instantly extinguished the light.

In another moment some one was heard preparing to raise the trap-door—a proceeding which Arthur did not attempt to thwart. He knew that if the person or persons now approaching were debarred the ingress which was sought, the front door would be the alternative next essayed; and he therefore resolved that, come what might, he would endeavour to capture and secure any intruders whose presence threatened in any way to interfere with his plans.

These calculations were all weighed in a single moment by the energetic and brave young nobleman.

The trap-door was raised slowly—the carpet was thrust aside from the aperture by the arm of him who was ascending; and a light suddenly gleamed from beneath.

The intruder carried a lamp in his hand.

Arthur and Jacob Smith maintained the most death-like silence—the former nerved for the trying scene, the latter ready to sink with apprehension on account of Rainford, who still slept soundly.

Having removed the carpet from the aperture,—a task which occupied nearly a minute, as the intruder held the lamp in his left hand and was compelled to support the trap-door in a half-open position with his head or back, while he worked with the right hand,—the individual—for Lord Ellingham was by this time pretty well satisfied that only one person was approaching—prepared to ascend into the room.

But the moment he had removed the carpet, and advanced another step or two upwards, the lamp was dashed from his hand, and he was violently seized by the collar, in the powerful grasp of Lord Ellingham, who exclaimed at the same instant, "Be silent—or you are a dead man!"

The individual thus captured, uttered a low growl, but said nothing.

Then, quick as thought, and with a degree of strength which astonished even him who exercised it, the Earl dragged the man up the steps into the room, but fortunately without awaking the soundly-sleeping Rainford.

All this took place amidst the most profound darkness, be it remembered; but, acting with wonderful energy and presence of mind, Arthur dragged the man along the floor of the bed-chamber into the laboratory; and then, without relaxing his hold, he exclaimed, "Jacob, light the lamp and bring it hither!"

"Jacob!" muttered the prostrate intruder, "Jacob!"

"Silence!" cried the Earl. "You are in the grasp of a desperate man," he added in a menacing tone; "but if you mean no harm, you will receive no injury."

Scarcely were these words uttered, when Jacob Smith, having hastily relighted the lamp, entered the laboratory, closing the door behind him—for he fully comprehended the Earl's motive in dragging the man, whoever he might be, away in the dark from the chamber where Rainford was lying.

But hardly had the light of the lamp fallen upon the countenance of the individual who was now half-lying—half-sitting on the floor, restrained by the vigorous grasp of Lord Ellingham, who bent over him,—when Jacob uttered a cry of mingled horror and alarm, exclaiming, as he staggered back, "*'Tis Old Death!*"

The lamp fell from his hand, and was instantly extinguished.

> 26. Mr. Brandon, in his admirable preface to Mr. Miles's work on *Poverty, Mendicity, and Crime*, places on record the ensuing observations:—
>
> "It is a generally-admitted axiom that among the uneducated, the human mind is more prone to evil than virtue; how greatly, then, must vice be disseminated, and the evil propensities encouraged, by persons of all descriptions, from the hardened murderer to the truant-playing apprentice, mingling and without one admonitory antidote to check them, all unemployed, all uneducated in the proper school of morality. The idlers, tyros in crime, or petty misdemeanants, be they boys or adults, will listen with eager curiosity to the gossiping of the old and

hardened offenders, while relating to each other the exploits they had achieved, or when giving instruction how to escape detection in certain situations, which from their own experience they have been led to conceive the best, and to hear them plot fresh depredations to be committed as soon as they shall have finished the term of their captivity, or be set at large upon a verdict of 'not guilty;' what but evil can arise from such a state of congregating? the mind cannot fail to become contaminated in some degree, even in the best disposed among them; whilst others, incited by the picture of pleasure they have described in the event of a successful enterprise, and from the encouragement given to the growing desires by the hardened wretches, enter recklessly into the path of vice as soon as they have turned their backs on the prison door; future accomplices and companions of the 'gaol bird,' who had been their tutor; commencing their career perhaps by a robbery planned whilst in prison. Minds, not over strong nor sufficiently guarded by moral education, are easily led astray, and the very punishment they are enduring as a requital for faults committed, will be used as the rudder by which they are steered to crime, in persuading them that they are aggrieved victims instead of criminals paying the penalty due to offended justice. This is the certain effect of the present system, and to expect any thing like repentance or thorough reform in a criminal, would be ridiculous.

"In a work published some time since, which is generally considered authentic, 'The Autobiography of James Hardy Vaux,' a notorious thief, is the following anecdote, which, as it corroborates and is illustrative of the facts above stated, namely, that vice is taught in prison, is here inserted:—

"He (Vaux) had in a most systematic manner robbed jewellers' shops, and, as he conceived, every one of note had fallen under his lash. He was at length taken up for stealing a gold snuff-box, and committed to Newgate, where he made acquaintance with two brothers, both of the same profession as his own, and committed for a similar offence; they were very communicative to each other, and Vaux discovered that there were some of his favourite shops which had escaped his notice. 'They pointed out,' says the text, 'about half a dozen shops which it appeared I had omitted to visit, arising either from their making no display of their goods, or from their being situated in private streets where I had no idea of finding such trades. Although I had little hopes of acquittal, it was agreed that in the event of my being so fortunate that I should visit these tradesmen I had overlooked, and I promised, in case I was successful, to make them a pecuniary acknowledgment in return for their information.' He was further instructed in what manner to proceed, and what sort of goods to order, and a Mr. Belger, a first-rate jeweller in Piccadilly, was particularly recommended to his notice as a *good fiat*. He succeeded in getting acquitted, and in robbing the shops pointed out to his notice, when, like a 'man of honour,' he did not fail to perform his promise to the two brothers—his associates in Newgate. The *good fiat* he robbed more than once, and once too often, for Vaux was discovered by him at last, and through his instrumentality convicted."

27. Mr. Brandon has these remarks in his Preface, just quoted from:—"Poverty is one of the great causes, and proceeds from both public and private abuse. It is the originator of minor crime, when it arises from want of employment commensurate to earn sufficient to maintain a large and growing family so often to be found in the hovels of the poor; of the greater offences, when it is owing to idleness, and a total dislike to labour, of which there are but too many instances, the individuals never attempting to work more days than will procure food, and of that a scant portion for the family, while for their particular self they make up the deficiency by a quantity of those pernicious spirits so destructive to health, and become besotted the rest of their time, until they are compelled to labour for a supply of provision; at length work fails altogether, either from a slackness in trade, or the party having become too enfeebled or besotted to use proper care and exertion. Then, with poverty staring him in the face, his favourite liquor refused, and he turned out of the same house in which he had squandered so much, when flushed with cash, he becomes half mad, the inflamed state of his mind from drink adding to it, and the wretches he had associated with in his boozing hours, being of the worst description, giving bad advice, he is tempted and fails.—But there are others who struggle in vain, and can only get a partial employ at most; who find, strive to their utmost, they cannot gain sufficient to drive 'the gaunt wolf, famine' from the door, and are doomed to behold the wife and children of their love, dearer to them than life, in a state of starvation—what wonder that they should be induced to steal food to soften the cravings of hunger, and alleviate the bitter cries of the young and helpless infants? Parental affection is strong, and what for himself a man would scorn to do, for the sake of his poor and suffering child he rushes to, and rather than behold his family dying in the agony of starvation, he begins by robbing victuals; for this he is placed in prison with a set of reckless vagabonds, by whom he is taught to become as degraded as themselves, and crime following crime, he stops not till he rises to the acme of his profession. Whereas, if this description of prisoners had been kept apart, he would have returned to society nothing the worse for his

incarceration.—Early marriages are one of the great causes of poverty, a folly to which the labouring classes are greatly addicted, getting large families before they are enabled by their strength or abilities to maintain them. Dr. Granville made a very curious table, showing the ages at which they marry, and as his calculation is made upon his Lying-in Hospital Practice, which is confined to the lower classes, none else taking the benefit of such institutions, it is confirmatory of the fact, and of the extent of this evil."

CHAPTER LIX.
THE JEW'S FAMILY.

In the meantime Mr. de Medina had passed a happy afternoon in company with his two daughters and little Charley Watts.

Tamar acquainted her father and sister with the generous conduct of Rainford towards the boy, who was accordingly fetched by a servant from the lodging which he and his adopted mother had recently occupied in the City.

Tom Rain's kindness in respect to Charley made a deep impression upon Mr. de Medina, who had already heard and seen enough to convince him that the seducer of his daughter possessed many good qualities; especially a generosity of disposition which might have made the envy of a monarch.

Charley had been fortunately retained in complete ignorance of the real cause of the protracted absence of him whom he called by the endearing name of "father." He was too young to entertain suspicions or misgivings on the subject; and the excuses which Tamar had constantly made to account for that absence, had so far satisfied his mind, that he entirely believed them, although he pined for the return of Rainford. When he beheld Tamar weep, which was often—very often—he exerted himself to console her, throwing his little arms round her neck, and yet weeping also! Even when Tamar, with the bitterest anguish, arrayed herself in deep black on the awful morning the results of which she could not have possibly anticipated, she had not the heart to exchange Charley's coloured garments for the mourning ones which had been prepared for him. No—she threw them aside: she had not strength sufficient to place before her own eyes an evidence of the dreadful loss which she deemed herself that hour to sustain!

The dinner-table at Mr. de Medina's house that day, was gayer—oh! far more gay than usual; for a forgiven daughter sate at the board—and Charley Watts was so happy to see his "dear mamma" smile once more, and to receive the positive assurance that he would meet his "papa" in a few days, that it was delightful to behold his sweet countenance animated with such heart-felt, innocent joy.

The attendance of the servants was dispensed with, in order that the conversation might flow unreservedly; and Mr. de Medina felt the full amount of that pleasure which consists in pardoning, as Tamar experienced the ineffable happiness of being by a father pardoned.

And, Esther—beauteous, amiable, generous-hearted Esther,—oh! she was as gay and smiling as she was ever wont to be in her girlhood, ere Tamar's disgrace had carried sorrow into the heart of the family!

In the evening Mr. de Medina bade adieu to his daughters and little Charley, and departed in a post-chaise for Dover, according to the arrangements already made.

That night, when the sisters retired to rest, a touching scene occurred in Esther's chamber; for this amiable girl led Tamar to her drawers, in which she showed her all the music-books and the pictures that had been so religiously preserved.

Then Tamar threw herself, weeping with gratitude and joy, into Esther's arms; and delicious was the embrace of purest affection in which the sisters clasped each other.

"Oh! how can I ever repay thee for so much love, dearest Esther?" murmured Tamar in a tone expressive of her unfeigned sincerity.

"By thinking of me frequently when you are far away," replied Esther, the tears streaming from her eyes as she reflected that they were no sooner re-united than they were about to separate again—for a long, long period—perhaps for ever!

"I shall never cease to think of thee, my Esther," answered the elder sister, as she now began to set at liberty the shining masses of her rich black hair, preparatory to retiring to rest; for she was to share Esther's bed, little Charley being already asleep in an adjoining chamber, the door of communication being left open in case he might awake:—"no, never shall I cease, to think of thee, Esther!" repeated Tamar; "for thou hast always manifested so much devoted affection towards me—and then, too," she added, casting down her blushing countenance, "thou hast endured so much for my sake!"

"Oh! have we not agreed that the past is to be forgotten?" hastily exclaimed Esther, for a moment desisting from the occupation of laying aside her garments. "The deeds that are gone should only engage our thoughts when no hope survives for the future. And how much hope is there yet for *you*!" she added, with an emphasis upon the pronoun.

Tamar started, and gazed steadfastly upon her sister's countenance; for, apart from that emphasis which was not unnoticed, there seemed something mournful in the sweet, liquid tones of Esther's voice.

"Hope for me!" exclaimed Tamar. "Yes—there *is* hope of happiness for me and for him whom I love so tenderly! But you spoke, my beloved sister, as if there were hope for me *alone*—and that there was none for you. Ah! Esther, have no secret from me—for I will never henceforth refuse you my fullest confidence, in the letters which I shall address to you so often—so very often! Esther, my sweet sister—you love!"

The maiden buried her countenance in Tamar's bosom.

"I am not deceived!" continued the latter. "Yes—you love, Esther; and perhaps you are not loved in return? But tell me all, and I may counsel you."

Esther murmured a name; and, as she thus whisperingly pronounced it, her face was burning in its contact with Tamar's bosom—so deeply did she blush in the confusion and shame of that confession of virgin love.

"The Earl of Ellingham!" cried Tamar, echoing the name which her sister had breathed.

"Alas!—yes," answered Esther, raising her beauteous countenance, still suffused with the rich carnation hues of modesty; "I can conceal the truth from my own heart no longer! But he loves another———"

"Whom he can never marry," added Tamar; "and therefore, my beloved sister, there is hope for thee!"

"Can never marry Lady Hatfield!" exclaimed Esther, in a tone of profound surprise.

"Rainford assured me that such is the case," continued Tamar. "I am not aware of the reason, because he did not volunteer an explanation; and it never has been my habit to question him respecting affairs on which he has not spoken freely of his own accord. But this much I can assure you—that Lady Hatfield and the Earl of Ellingham will never be united, and that they no longer entertain even the idea of such union. Do not, therefore, perplex yourself relative to the cause of their severance, my darling Esther; but nourish hope—for, oh! it is delicious to feed love upon the manna of hope! And, believe me, the Earl of Ellingham already surveys you with so much admiration—already entertains so exalted an opinion of your character—already looks upon you with such respect, that he cannot fail to experience feelings more tender still!"

"O Tamar! talk not thus—I may not listen to thee!" exclaimed Esther, with fluttering heart and swelling bosom; for, model of purity and innocence as she was, the words of her sister excited pleasurable sensations within her breast.

And thus ever is it with the most chaste, most virtuous, and most unsophisticated maiden, who loves for the first time!

"Nay—do not compel me to keep silence on a topic which *is*—which *must be* dear to your soul, my Esther," said Tamar. "Were human beings to feel shame at loving, there would not be an unblushing cheek in the whole world, save amongst children. Sooner or later, dear sister, every one must feel the influence of that passion, which spares no one. Oh! cold and cheerless, indeed, would this world be, were not the hearts of those who have grown up, and who have cast aside the frivolities of childhood, warmed and irradiated by the beams of Love! Feel not ashamed, then, dearest Esther, on account of this passion which has so imperceptibly stolen upon thee."

"But, after all you have said, Tamar," returned the coy and bashful maiden, "I shall not be able to meet the Earl again without blushing! And then—were I mad enough to indulge in such a hope as you would have me nourish—remember the difference of our creeds!"

"Was it not the Earl himself who suggested the means by which matrimonial rites could be celebrated between his own half-brother and myself?" demanded Tamar eagerly.

"Yes," replied Esther, every feature of her fine aquiline countenance deriving additional charms from the crimson hues which mantled on that splendid face, and spread themselves over her arching neck, her gracefully sloping shoulders, and the rich contours of her virgin bust, which, in the presence of her sister, no invidious drapery now concealed:—"yes, Tamar," she replied; "but there are other—oh! and far more important considerations. Consider how exalted is the rank of that great nobleman—and consider, also," she added, in a mournful tone, "how much our race is still despised even in this land, which boasts of an almost consummate civilisation!"

"The Earl of Ellingham, I feel convinced, despises such absurd—such pitiful prejudices," said Tamar, labouring only to render her sister happy by means of joyous hope. "As an enlightened man, he must recognise how deeply his country is indebted, in respect to its wondrous prosperity, to the commercial enterprise and the financial skill of our nation. Moreover, do we not believe in the same God? For the Almighty whom the Christians worship, is the same who brought our forefathers out of Egypt, and gave them the promised land. In a word, my beloved Esther, Arthur of Ellingham is too noble-minded a being to despise you because you cling to the creed in which you were brought up; and something tells me that my sister is destined to become the Countess of Ellingham."

Esther sighed, but made no response.

Tamar continued to discourse in the same inconsiderate strain for several minutes. She was actuated by the most generous motives towards her sister; but, in the enthusiasm of her affection and gratitude, she forgot that she might only be exciting hopes destined never to receive a fulfilment, and encouraging a passion which, after all, was perhaps doomed to experience the bitterness of disappointment.

At length Esther turned towards her, and exclaimed hastily, "Tamar—if you love me, speak on this topic no more. It may be false shame on my part,—but it seems to me that it is unmaidenly thus to discourse on a subject in which one, who is separated from me by so wide a gulf, is concerned. Alas!

deeply do I regret that, in a moment of weakness, I admitted aloud that which my heart had not hitherto dared to whisper even to itself! I should have exercised more command over myself. Oh! I have been foolish—very foolish to permit such a thought even to assume the faintest shape in my imagination. But we will abandon the topic;—and again I say, Tamar—if you love me, renew it not!"

There was a minute's pause, at the expiration of which Esther began to converse gaily and rapidly on Tamar's future prospects in the clime to which it was contemplated that herself and Rainford were to proceed; and the amiable girl communicated to her sister all that she had read concerning the United States of North America.

This little manœuvre on the part of Esther was to change the topic of discourse: and Tamar did not attempt to renew a subject which offended the maiden pride of her sister.

Oh! happy was Tamar to sleep beneath her father's roof that night—to know, to feel that she was in the parental dwelling again! When she awoke once, while it was yet dark, she fancied that she had been dreaming—so strange did all the incidents of the preceding day appear to be—so truly incredible! But, as she stretched out her arms, they encountered the form of her sister; and then—in the silence and obscurity of the night—Tamar joined her hands and prayed fervently,—far, far more fervently than she had prayed for some years past!

And, Christian! darest thou believe that the prayers of the despised Jewess were not wafted with thine own to the throne of the Eternal?

CHAPTER LX.
SIR CHRISTOPHER BLUNT'S DOMESTIC HEARTH.

It was the morning following the incidents just related; and the scene changes to the house of Sir Christopher Blunt, in Jermyn Street.

The worthy knight and his lady were seated at breakfast.

The table literally groaned beneath the weight of the cold viands placed upon it; for the ex-lady's-maid was particularly addicted to good things, and she moreover thought that it was "quite the rage" to see cold fowls, ham, tongue, Perigord pie, and all kinds of marmalades spread for the morning repast.

Lady Blunt was in her glory of premeditated negligence and studied *deshabillée*. She was arrayed in a pea-green silk wrapper, trimmed all down the front with scarlet bows; and the cape was braided with the same glaring hue, so much affected by a certain Lady of Babylon. Her cap was decorated with ribands likewise of scarlet, and she wore red slippers. Her appearance was indeed most flaming, as she lolled, in delightful lassitude, in a capacious easy chair, with her foot upon an ottoman.

A stranger would have thought that so fine a lady could not possibly touch any thing more substantial than a thin slice of toast or half a muffin for her breakfast; but she had in reality paid her respects—and with a good will also—to every dish upon the table.

Sir Christopher was seated opposite to her, looking like a fish out of water; for, in order to please his dear wife—or rather, to have a little peace and quiet in the house—he had consented to adorn his person with a light blue dressing-gown, fastened by a gold cord and huge tassels at the waist, and a pair of bright red trowsers, large and loose like a Dutchman's. Moreover, a scarlet silk cap, with a long gold tassel, was perched airily over his left ear; so that altogether he seemed as if he were dressed out to enact the part of a Turk at a masquerade.

"Shall I cut you a *leetle* slice more ham, my love?" enquired Sir Christopher, in a mincing tone, as if he were afraid of receiving a box on the ears for not speaking civilly enough.

"No, Sir Christopher," answered the lady sharply: "you shan't send me a *leetle* ham, as you call it. I don't like the ham—and that's flat."

"And yet, my love—that is, my dear—" remonstrated the knight gently.

"And yet what?" demanded his wife.

"I *think* I had the pleasure of helping you three times, my love," added Sir Christopher, astonished at his own boldness in uttering the words, the moment they had escaped his lips.

"Three times!" ejaculated the lady, turning as red as her ribands or as her husband's trowsers. "And if I like to be helped six times—or nine times, Sir Christopher—what should you say *then*?"

"Well, my love—I should say——"

"What should you say?" again asked the lady, assuming a menacing attitude.

"Why, my love—that you had a very good appetite," responded the knight, looking as miserable as if he expected eight finger nails to fasten on his cheeks the very next moment.

"I have no appetite, Sir Christopher!" cried the lady in a petulant tone, as she sank back again into her lounging attitude: "three miserable bits of ham, and a trifle of cold pie, with may be a taste of the chicken, and just one cut out of the tongue——"

"And two eggs, my love," suggested Sir Christopher meekly.

"Well—and two tiny eggs," continued the lady;—"I am sure all that doesn't say much for one's appetite. Why, when I was at Lady Hatfield's, I used to eat three great rounds of bread-and-butter, crustinesses and all."

"But you are no longer at Lady Hatfield's, my angel," said Sir Christopher, simpering; "you are with one who adores you—who has given you his name—a name, I flatter myself, that carries weight with it, in certain quarters; although, when I did so far forget myself as to put up for Portsoken——"

"Now, Sir Christopher, pray let us have none of that nonsense, if *you* please!" interrupted Lady Blunt, in a tone and with a manner which showed that she knew full well she should be obeyed. "I can't a-bear to hear even the word *Alderman* mentioned, ever since a lady I lived with once in the City talked something about the Guildhall police-court when she missed the silver spoons——"

"My dear, my dear," said Sir Christopher; "you forget that you are now Lady Blunt! Pray let us change the topic."

"Well, so we will," she cried sharply; "and I'll tell you what we'll talk about."

"What, my best love?" asked the knight.

"Your best love!" almost shrieked the lady. "Then you must have other loves, if I'm your best! Oh! Sir Christopher, was it to hear this that I gave up every thing—all my prospects in life—to become yours?"

"My dear girl," said the knight meekly, "I most humbly submit to you that I do not think you had so very much to give up when I asked you to become Lady Blunt."

"What! do you call a good place and being my own mistress, nothing to give up?" cried Charlotte. "Twenty-four guineas a-year, and the chance of marrying a Duke or a Prince!"

"Well—well, my love, we will not dispute," said the knight, who in his heart wished to God that she never *had* given up the prospects she spoke of; or that she *had* married some Duke or Prince—in which latter case Sir Christopher would not have envied either his Grace or his Royal Highness, after the trifling experience he had already enjoyed relative to the fair one's temper.

"No—I should think *you* would *not* dispute, either, Sir Christopher!" cried the vixen, tossing her head. "But I was going to tell you what we would talk about, when you interrupted me so rudely. I was going to say that I do not approve of that ham—or yet the chicken—or yet the tongue; and I do not mean to have my breakfast spoilt in this way. Ring the bell, Sir Christopher."

"My dearest Charlotte——"

"Ring the bell, Sir Christopher!" repeated the lady in a still more authoritative tone, as she looked daggers—nay, regular bayonets—at her miserable husband.

The knight rang the bell accordingly, gulping down a sigh—a very profound sigh—at the same time.

A footman answered the summons.

"John!" said the mistress of the house.

"Yes, my lady," was the reply.

"Tell Mrs. Bodkin to step up—*immediately*," added the wife of Sir Christopher's rash choice.

"Yes, my lady;"—and the footman disappeared, thanking his stars that *he* was not "in for it,"—the bad humour of his mistress being very evident indeed.

In due time Mrs. Bodkin made her appearance, in the shape of a stout, matronly-looking female, "of a certain age," as a housekeeper ought to be;—for Mrs. Bodkin was neither more nor less than that high female functionary in the establishment.

"Mrs. Bodkin!" said Lady Blunt, endeavouring to distort her really pretty face into as stern an expression as possible.

"Yes, my lady," returned the housekeeper.

"That ham is detestable, Mrs. Bodkin."

"Indeed, my lady."

"The cold fowl's abominable!"

"Sure now, my lady!"

"And the tongue frightful!"

"Lawk-a-daisy!—your ladyship don't say so!"

"I *do* say so, though, Mrs. Bodkin!" cried Sir Christopher's better half; "and I just tell you what it is—I don't mean to have my breakfast spoilt in this way; and if you can't find tradesmen who'll supply good things——"

"Why, please your ladyship," interrupted the housekeeper, quite astounded at these accusations against comestibles which she knew to be excellent: "Mr. Smuggs, who sent in the ham and tongue, is purveyor to His Majesty; and——"

"Then if His Majesty chooses to put up with Mr. Smuggs's rubbish, Lady Blunt will *not*!" exclaimed the mistress of the house, glancing indignantly, first at the petrified Mrs. Bodkin and then at the dumb-founded Sir Christopher.

There was, as romancists say, an awful pause.

Mrs. Bodkin knew not whether she were standing on her head or her heels: Sir Christopher was in an equally strange state of bewilderment as to whether he had heard aright or was labouring under a delusion; and Lady Blunt was triumphant in the impression she had evidently made upon her audience.

"But, my dear angel—my love," at length stammered the knight, "surely you will not—that is, you cannot—I appeal to you, my sweet, as a woman of sound judgment——"

"Sound fiddlestick, Sir Christopher!" interrupted her ladyship contemptuously. "I know what I am saying, and I mean what I say. Mrs. Bodkin, I order you once for all not to deal no more at Smuggs's; and if you can't choose good things, you'd better pack up your things and go about your business."

Now it happened that Mrs. Bodkin had managed, during long years of servitude and by rigid economy, to scrape together a very comfortable independence; and, feeling that she *was* independent, she did not choose, as she afterwards observed to a friend, "to put up with any of missus's nonsense."

"Go about my business, eh!" she accordingly exclaimed. "Well, ma'am—the sooner I do that the better, I think: for since I can't give saytisfaction here, I'd much rayther resign at once."

"Resign!" echoed Lady Blunt, again turning red as her ribands.

"Yes, ma'am," continued the housekeeper; "*resign* I said; and *you* ought to know that's the right word—for I b'lieve you wasn't always used to sit in the parlour."

"Oh! you wretch!" exclaimed Lady Blunt, now manifesting a violent inclination to go off into hysterics. "Sir Christopher! can you sit there and hear me insulted by that owdacious woman? Turn her out of the house, Sir Christopher—let her bundle, neck and crop, this minute!"

"I rayther think there's no need for bundling in the matter," said the indignant Mrs. Bodkin. "Sir Christopher is too much of a gentleman to ill-treat me, after being eleven years in his service come next Aperil. But I don't require no favours at *your* hands, ma'am—leastways, I wouldn't except them if they was offered."

And in a most stately manner Mrs. Bodkin walked out of the room, leaving the door wide open behind her.

"Sir Christopher!" exclaimed Lady Blunt, bursting into tears—but tears of rage, and not shame.

"Yes, my love," said the knight, who was rendered so nervous by this scene that he appeared to be labouring under incipient *delirium tremens*.

"You're a brute, Sir Christopher!" cried the angel in the pea-green wrapper and the red bows.

"My dear!—my love!" stammered the knight. "It was not my fault—you brought it on yourself—I really think——"

"Oh! I did, did I?" screeched Charlotte; and, unable to control the fury of her passion, she darted upon Sir Christopher, adown whose cheeks the marks of her nails were in another moment rendered most disagreeably visible.

"Lady Blunt!" vociferated the miserable man, struggling to extricate himself from the power of the fury.

"There! now I've taught you not to nag me on another time," said Charlotte, throwing herself back into her chair, already sorry and ashamed for what she had done, but too deeply imbued with vulgar and mean-spirited pride to manifest the least proof of such compunction.

Sir Christopher wiped his bleeding face with his cambric pocket-handkerchief: but his heart was too full to speak. He felt all the indignity which he had just sustained—and yet he had not courage enough to resent it.

The embarrassment of the newly-married pair was relieved, or rather interrupted, by a loud and unusually long double knock, which at that moment awoke every echo, not only in the house itself, but also half-way up Jermyn Street.

A few minutes elapsed, and then the footman entered the breakfast-parlour to announce to Sir Christopher that a gentleman, who had been shown into the drawing-room, wished to speak to him immediately upon most urgent business.

At the same time the servant placed upon the table a card, bearing the name of CAPTAIN O'BLUNDERBUSS.

"Tell the gentleman I'll be with him in a moment, John," said Sir Christopher.

The servant bowed and retired.

"Do you know who he is?" asked Lady Blunt.

"No, I do not," responded the knight, more sulkily than he had ever yet dared to speak to his wife.

"Come, now, Sir Christopher," exclaimed her ladyship; "don't have any of your ill-humours with me, because I can't a-bear them. Say you're sorry for what you've done, and I'll not only forgive you, but also patch your face for you with diakkulum plaster. Come, now—do what I tell you."

And as her ladyship seemed to examine her finger nails, as she spoke, in a manner which portended her readiness to make another onslaught, the miserable husband muttered a few words of abject apology for an offence which he had not committed, and the amiable Charlotte vouchsafed a pardon which she should rather have besought than bestowed.

Then there was a little fond—or rather foolish kissing and hugging; and this farce being concluded, the lady hastened to fulfil her promise relative to the diachylon plaster.

When this operation was likewise ended, Sir Christopher cast a rueful glance into the looking-glass over the mantel; and never did a more miserable wight see reflected a more woefully patched countenance. The wretchedness depicted on that face, apart from the long slips of plaster stuck upon the cheeks, contrasted in a most ludicrous fashion with the absurd splendour of the knight's morning attire; and, to use a common phrase, he wished himself at the devil, as he wended his mournful way to the drawing-room.

CHAPTER LXI.
CAPTAIN O'BLUNDERBUSS.

Captain O'Blunderbuss was a gentleman of Irish extraction, and, according to his own account, possessed of vast estates in the Emerald Island; but it was evident to all his friends that the rents were very irregularly paid, inasmuch as their gallant proprietor was frequently under the necessity of soliciting the loan of a guinea, and when he could not obtain that sum, his demand would suddenly drop to half-a-crown or even eighteen-pence.

But whenever the Captain talked of his estates, no one ventured to suggest a doubt relative to their existence; for the gallant officer was a notorious duellist, having been engaged as principal in thirty-seven of those pleasant little contests, and as second in ninety-two more.

He was about forty-five years of age, and of exceedingly fierce appearance. His crown was entirely bald; but huge bushes of red hair stuck out between his temples and his ears—enormous whiskers of the same meteoric hue and portent covered half his face—and a formidable pair of moustaches, red also, curled ominously over his upper lip, the ends being twisted and greased so as to look like two small tails.

In person he was tall, thin, but not ill-made. He held himself particularly upright; and as he wore a military undress coat, all frogged and braided in the Polish fashion, and grey trousers with red stripes down the legs, he really looked like what he called himself and was called by others—namely, a CAPTAIN.

But he was not wont to be more explicit relative to his military services than he was definite concerning the locality of his estates. No one knew, and assuredly no one ever ventured to ask him, to what regiment he had belonged. He stated himself to be *unattached*; and that was sufficient.

We should, as faithful chroniclers, observe that it *had* been whispered—but then, scandal is so rife in this wicked world!—that Captain O'Blunderbuss was never in the army at all, and that his formidable name was merely an assumed one; and the newsmongers who propagated these reports behind the gallant gentleman's back, not only ridiculed the idea of his estates, but actually carried their malignant spite so far as to insinuate that he was once the driver of a jaunting-car in Dublin, and at that period bore the name of Teddy O'Flaherty.

Be all this as it may, it is nevertheless very certain that Captain O'Blunderbuss was a great man about town—that he was nodded to by loungers in the Park—shaken hands with by dandies in Bond Street—and invariably chosen as a second in every duel that took place on Wormwood Scrubs, Wimbledon Common, or Battersea Fields.

Such was the terrible individual who was standing on the rug, in a most ferocious attitude, when Sir Christopher Blunt entered the drawing-room.

The Captain desisted from twirling his moustaches, and indulged in a good long stare at the knight, whose half-ludicrous, half-doleful appearance was certainly remarkable enough to attract an unusual degree of attention.

"You resayved my car-r-d, Sir Christopher Blunt?" said the Captain, speaking in a strong Irish accent, and rattling the r in a truly menacing manner.

"Yes, sir—I received the card of Captain O'Blunderbuss," replied Sir Christopher, not knowing what to think or make of his strange visitor.

"And, sure, I'm Capthain O'Blunther-r-buss!" exclaimed the military gentleman, twirling his moustache; "and I've come on the par-rt of my friend Capthain Morthaunt—an honour-r-able man, Sir-r Christopher Blunt!" added the gentleman emphatically, looking awfully fierce at the same time, just as if the unfortunate knight entertained the idea of questioning the honour of Captain Mordaunt.

"I—I've no doubt of it, sir," stammered the intimidated Blunt, looking more wretched in proportion as the tone of his visitor became more excited.

"By the power-rs, I'm glad ye don't doubt it!" cried the Captain; "or you'd find yerself desayved in yer man. Well, Sir-r Christopher, the shor-t and the long of the affair is just this:—My friend Capthain Mordaunt feels himself aggraved on behalf of his sisther-r, and he's put the little business into my hands to manage for-r him."

"I'm convinced that Captain Mordaunt could not have chosen a better friend, Captain O'Blunderbuss," said the knight, scarcely able to utter a word, so sorely was he oppressed by vague alarms. "But I hope—that is, I mean, I— in a word——"

"What do ye mane?" demanded the Captain, advancing a pace or two towards the knight.

"Oh! nothing—only——" stammered Sir Christopher, dodging round the table, for fear that the formidable O'Blunderbuss intended an attack upon him.

"Only what, man?" vociferated the Captain. "Sure, now, ye don't think I'm afther ayting ye up!"

"No—oh! no! I'm not afraid of any gentleman eating me, exactly," observed Sir Christopher. "But if you would state the object of your visit——"

"Be Jasus! and that's soon done!" exclaimed Captain O'Blunderbuss. "The shor-rt facts is these:—Capthain Morthaunt is mightily attached to his sisther-r, Miss Julia, who's a most amiable lady—for I've jist been breakfasting with her-r and her-r brother at their lodgings in Half Moon Street. Miss Morthaunt, as per-rhaps you are aware, returned home to her father's mansion—a sweet place, by the bye, in Connamar-r-ra—when you desayved her in the most gross—the most infamous manner, by running away with a lady's-maid instead of her dear self——"

"Captain O'Blunderbuss," said Sir Christopher, "she of whom you speak is now Lady Blunt."

"And much good may she do ye, Sir Christopher!" exclaimed the Captain. "But, as I was saying, Miss Morthaunt comes back to London again, smar-rting under the influence of her wrongs, which her brother has resolved to avenge. And, therefore, Sir Christopher, you'll be so good as jist to say whether it shall be on Wor-rmwood Scr-rubs or Wimbledon Common; and we'll be there punctual to-morrow morning at eight o'clock."

The worthy knight looked perfectly aghast. He began to understand the real drift of Captain O'Blunderbuss's visit; and he entertained the most unmitigated abhorrence of the mere idea of a duel.

"Well, Sir Christopher, say the wor-rd!" resumed the gallant gentleman with as much unconcern as if he were making arrangements for a party of pleasure. "But per-rhaps ye'd like to consult a frind—or refer-r me to him. That's the best way! Leave it to your frind and me; and we'll settle everything so comfortable that you'll not have the least throuble in the wor-rld. You can get your breakfast a thrifle earlier than usual——"

"Breakfast!" echoed Sir Christopher, in a deep sepulchral tone; "breakfast—when one is going out to be shot at!"

"Be the power-rs! and why not?" demanded the warlike Captain. "But here we are, wasting our precious time, while we ought to be settling the little business and thrying the pisthols at the Gallery."

"The pistols!" groaned Sir Christopher, his visage lengthening most awfully, and his under-jaw completely dropping through intense alarm.

"Be Jasus! and what would ye fight with, if it isn't pisthols?" cried the Captain.

"But pistols—pistols are so apt to—to—kill people," observed the knight, shaking from head to foot.

"Is it afraid ye are?" demanded Captain O'Blunderbuss, twirling his moustache, as he surveyed Sir Christopher with cool contempt.

"I do not admit such an imputation," answered the knight; "but I will not fight with this mad-cap Mordaunt. The law shall be my protection. I am my own master—I married whom I chose—and I will not be bullied by any man living."

The astonishment depicted on the countenance of Captain O'Blunderbuss, as these words met his ears, was mistaken by the knight for a feeling of apprehension; and thus he had grown bold, or at least energetic in his language, as he had proceeded.

"Yes, sir," he added emphatically, "the law shall protect me."

"Is it shir-rking that ye mane?" asked the Captain. "Because, if it is, I shall feel myself bound to administer a dacent drubbing to ye, Sir Christopher. Why, sir—it's a rale insult to *me* to refuse to fight with my frind!"

And, as he uttered these words, the Captain advanced in a menacing fashion towards the knight.

"Keep off, sir! don't attempt violence against me!" exclaimed Sir Christopher Blunt, rushing towards the fire-place to seize the poker. "I'll not stand it, Captain O'Blunderbuss—I have been a Sheriff in my time—I once put up for Portsoken—and I'll not submit to any insult."

"Then name your frind, sir!" thundered the gallant officer; "or-r I'll not lave a whole bone in your skin."

"Well—I will, I will!" ejaculated Sir Christopher, anxious to get rid of his fire-eating visitor on any terms. "Go to my nephew, Mr. Frank Curtis: he has killed his man often enough—according to his own account——"

"Be the power-rs! that jist suits me to a tay!" exclaimed the Captain; "for may be he and me could jist amuse ourselves with an exchange of shots afther you and my frind Morthaunt have settled your own small thrifle. 'T would be a perfect God-send to me; and I've no doubt your nev-vy will be of the same mind. Where does he hang out?"

Sir Christopher hastily mentioned the address of Mr. Frank Curtis; and Captain O'Blunderbuss stalked away, hugely delighted at the idea of being about to form the acquaintance of a gentleman every way so worthy of his friendship as the knight's nephew appeared to be.

Fierce indeed was the aspect of Captain O'Blunderbuss as he marched through the streets to the address indicated by the knight; and to the great joy of the military gentleman, he found, on his arrival, that Mr. Frank Curtis was at home.

"But he's not up yet, sir," said the spruce-looking tiger who opened the front door at which the Captain had given one of his tremendous double knocks.

"Never mind, my boy," exclaimed the visitor in an awe-inspiring tone. "Your masther will be glad to see me, or I'm mightily desayved."

"What name shall I say, sir?" inquired the tiger.

"Faith! and I'll just take my name up along with me, my lad," returned the Captain. "Which floor may it be now?"

"First floor, sir,—and the bed-room's at the back."

"By Jasus! you're a smar-rt lad, and a credit to your masther!" exclaimed the Captain. "The next time I come, I'll make ye a present of sixpence."

And with these words Captain O'Blunderbuss marched up stairs.

On reaching the landing, he knocked at the back-room door with his fist, as if he were practising how to fell an ox; and to this peremptory summons an invitation to "come in" was returned.

The Captain accordingly stalked into the chamber, where Mr. Frank Curtis was breakfasting in bed, a table well spread being drawn up close by the side of his couch.

"Be Jasus! I knew you was a boy afther my own heart!" ejaculated the Captain, as he caught sight of a bottle of whiskey which stood near the tea-pot: then, closing the door, he advanced up to the bed, and, pulling off his buckskin glove, said, "Misther Curtis, here's my hand. Tip us your's, my boy—and let's know each other without any more pother."

Mr. Frank Curtis accepted the proffered hand with delight; for the amiable deportment of the visitor now relieved his mind from the vague fears that had been excited in it by the unceremonious entry and ferocious appearance of the Captain.

"And how are ye, Misther Curtis?" continued this gentleman, drawing a chair close to the bed, and depositing his gloves in his hat, and his hat on the table.

"Quite blooming, old fellow, thank'ee!" returned Frank, to whom all this familiarity was by no means displeasing. "But what will you take? shall I ring for another cup and plate? or will you take a dram of the whiskey?"

"The potheen, my boy—the potheen for me!" exclaimed the Captain, grasping the bottle.

"You'll find it rather good, I fancy," said Curtis. "My friend the Russian Ambassador sent it round last night, with his best respects——"

"And my respects to him and to you both!" cried the Captain: then, having drained his glass, he drew a long breath, and said, "Be Jasus! that's some of the right sor-rt!"

"Help yourself then, old fellow!" said Frank, in as free and easy a manner as if he had known his visitor all his life. "I can get plenty more where that came from. Old Brandyokouski, the Polish Ambassador's butler, has had orders to give me the entire run of his master's cellar; for me and his Excellency are as thick as two thieves. He is pestering me from morning to night to dine with him——"

"No wonther, Misther Curtis!" interrupted the Captain; "for you're the most agreeable jintleman I've the honour to be acquainted with."

"And what's your name, old boy?" asked Frank, as he proceeded with his breakfast.

"Captain O'Blunderbuss, at your service, my dear frind," was the answer, while the individual who gave it helped himself to another glass of the whiskey, which was certainly the best that the *Stilton Cheese* round the corner could supply.

"Delighted to form your acquaintance, Captain!" exclaimed Curtis, suddenly becoming a trifle less familiar,—for the name was well known to him, in connexion too with the notoriety of a duellist. "And might I inquire what business——"

"Oh! we'll talk about that presently," interrupted the Captain. "Your uncle, Sir-r Christopher Blunt, recommended you to me in the strongest ter-rms—the most flatter-ring ter-rms, I may say——"

"Indeed!" ejaculated Mr. Curtis, with unfeigned surprise—for he had not seen, nor spoken to the knight for some weeks.

"Be the power-rs! he gave you a splindid char-r-acter, Misther Curtis!" cried Captain O'Blunderbuss; "and it was quite longing to know ye, I was. But we'll talk on business presently. I'm in no hurry—and we'll have a cozie chat first. May be my name is not altogether strange to ye?"

"By no means," answered Curtis, now thoroughly convinced that the object of his new friend's visit was altogether of an amicable character. "I have heard of your renown, and must say that I have envied it. But I've done a little in the same line myself—chiefly in France, though. I'll be bound the name of the Marquis of Soupe-Maigre is not unknown to you."

"Yes—I've heard spake of it," returned the Captain, helping himself to another glass of whiskey.

"Well—the Duke and me fought with small swords for three hours one morning," continued Frank; "and at length I managed to scratch the little finger of his left hand. In France, you know, a duel always ends when the first blood is drawn; and so the Count flung away his sword, acknowledged that I'd beat him, and we've been bosom friends ever since."

"Give me your hand, my broth of a boy!" exclaimed the Captain: "I was not desayved in you! You're as fine spirited as your potheen. Why! be the power-rs, you're a confir-rmed duellist."

"To be sure! and I have killed my man, too," responded Frank, delighted to perceive that he had made a deep impression on his companion. "There was the famous Spaniard, you know—what was his name again? Oh! ah! Don Juan Stiletto del Guerilla! He was a dreadful fellow—the terror of all Paris, where he was staying when I was also there. Well, one evening—it was at the King's fancy-ball—this Portuguese fellow gave himself such airs that there was no bearing him. He insulted all the gentlemen, and smirked at all the ladies. At length the Archbishop of Paris, who was in full canonicals, appealed to me to put down the insolent Italian; I undertook the task—and picked a quarrel with him in no time. The ladies all looked upon me as one devoted to death: and though I say it who shouldn't, a great deal of tender sympathy was shown towards me. Well, next morning me and the German met on the very top of Montmartre; and in a quarter of an hour my gentleman was weltering in his blood. That affair won for me the love of the beautiful Countess of Dunkirk:—but she is gone down to the tomb—and I am left behind to mourn her loss!"

And Mr. Frank Curtis took a large bite of a muffin, doubtless to subdue the sigh which rose to his lips at this sad reminiscence.

"Be the holy poker-r! it's a touching business," cried the Captain, who had by this time fully seen through the mendacious braggadocio of Mr. Frank Curtis, and had come to the conclusion that he was as great a coward in reality as his uncle.

But the gallant Captain O'Blunderbuss did not choose to suffer the young gentleman to perceive that he understood him, as the whiskey was too much to his taste to allow him to lose the chance of emptying the bottle by a too precipitate rupture.

Frank, firmly believing that all his fine stories were taken as gospel by his visitor, rattled away in his usual style—heaping lie upon lie at such a rate, that, had his falsehoods been mountains, the piling thereof would have outdone the feats of Titan with Ossa and Pelion.

At length the Captain began to thrust in a few words edgeways, as the contents of the bottle got lower and lower.

"Your uncle, Misther Curtis, seems a nice old jintleman. His face was rarely plasthered this mornin', as if he'd been in the war-r-rs a thrifle or so."

"Perhaps his wife had been giving him a taste of her claws?" said Frank, with a coarse giggle.

"Be Saint Path-rick! and that's just what struck me!" exclaimed the Captain.

"She's a very devil, I know," continued Frank. "But, I say, old fellow—what little business was it that took you to old Sir Christopher's, and made him refer you to me?"

"Is it the little business?" cried the Captain. "Och? and be Jasus! then, it's jist that affair of my friend Morthaunt, who manes to shoot Sir Christopher-r to-mor-r-row mor-r-r-ning before breakfast."

"Shoot Sir Christopher!" ejaculated Frank, apparently more surprised than annoyed.

"Or else jist get shot himself, be the power-rs!" added Captain O'Blunderbuss. "And it's becase it's myself that's Morthaunt's frind, Sir Christopher has referred me to you as his frind."

"Then it's a regular duel?" said Frank, opening his eyes wider and wider.

"The purtiest little affair I ever had a finger in, Misther Curtis," responded the Captain, now looking tremendously fierce; for although he had imbibed at least a pint of pure spirit without experiencing the least inconvenience in respect to his brain, the effects were nevertheless apparent in an awful rubicundity of countenance: "the purtiest little affair, certainly," he continued; "and it now only remains for you and me jist to settle the place—time being of cour-rse in the mornin at eight."

"And do you mean to say that my old uncle has agreed to fight this duel with Captain Mordaunt?" inquired Frank.

"Be Jasus! it's for you to bring him to the scratch, Misther Curtis; or else——"

"Or else what?" demanded the young gentleman, oppressed by a vague presentiment of evil.

"Or else, be the holy poker-r! you must fight *me*!" returned Captain O'Blunderbuss, twirling his moustache in the coolest and calmest manner possible.

"Fight *you*?" ejaculated Frank, turning ashy pale.

"As a matther of cour-rse!" answered the Captain. "A famous duellist like Misther Curtis, can't be at a loss on a point of honour."

"But why the devil should I fight *you*?" demanded the young gentleman, his heart palpitating audibly.

"Why the devil shouldn't ye?" vociferated Captain O'Blunderbuss. "Answer me that, my frind?"

"My dear sir—it's really—I mean, you—that is to say, I think, with all due deference——" stammered Frank, growing every moment more and more alarmed.

"Be Jasus! I've said nothing I don't mane to stick to!" exclaimed the martial gentleman, now assuming an expression of countenance so fierce that Frank Curtis began to have serious misgivings that his visitor intended to assault him then and there.

"But, my dear Captain——this proceeding——" said Frank, assuming a tone of excruciating politeness.

"Is going on beautifully, Misther Curtis. And so, as you seem to have a little delicacy in putting yourself too for-rward in the matther," continued the Captain, "we'll jist say Battersea Fields, to-morrow mornin', at eight o'clock. Good bye, Misther Curtis."

With these words the Captain took up his hat, and stalked majestically out of the room, banging the door violently after him.

Frank Curtis fell back in his bed, and gave vent to his feelings in a deep groan.

The door opened again with a crash; and the Captain thrust in his inflamed visage, exclaiming, "Ye'll remember, Misther Curtis, that I hould ye responsible in this matther; and that if ye can't bring the uncle to the scratch, ye must come yourself; or, be Jasus! I'll be afther ye to the inds of the ear-rth!"

The head was withdrawn again, and the door once more slammed violently.

Frank Curtis gave a hollow moan, thrust himself down in the bed, and drew the clothes over his face, as if to shut out some dreadful spectre from his sight.

CHAPTER LXII.
FRANK'S EMBARRASSMENTS.

Thus remained Mr. Frank Curtis for some minutes—each moment expecting that the bed-room door would again open, and that the voice of the terrible Irishman would once more convey some hideous menace to his ears.

But Captain O'Blunderbuss had fairly departed this time; and at length the miserable young man slowly pushed down the clothes, and glanced timidly round the room.

It was no dream—as for an instant he had endeavoured to make himself believe that it was; for there was the chair in the very place where the Captain had sate—there also was the bottle which the Captain had condescended to empty.

"A duel!" groaned Frank, in a sepulchral voice—he who had fought so many in imagination!

Then he remembered that there existed a means of averting all danger from himself; and, elated by the sudden thought, he leapt nimbly from his bed, with the affectionate intention of proceeding forthwith to his uncle, and compelling the old gentleman to go forth and be shot at, whether by Captain Mordaunt or Captain O'Blunderbuss, Frank did not care a fig.

Having hastily dressed himself, the young gentleman hurried off to Jermyn Street: and, on his arrival, he was surprised to find the knight's travelling-carriage at the door, while the servants were busily employed in piling up portmanteaus, and hat-boxes, and bandboxes, and carpet-bags.

"Halloa!" cried Frank to Jeffreys, the groom, who was in the act of hoisting one of the aforesaid articles of luggage to another servant who stood upon the roof of the vehicle: "what does all this mean?"

"Means travelling, Mr. Frank," responded the domestic. "The order was given in a violent hurry—and so I haven't a moment to spare. But here's master and her ladyship."

And, sure enough, Sir Christopher and Lady Blunt made their appearance at that instant, the former enveloped in his great coat and with a silk handkerchief tied round all the lower part of his face,—and Charlotte muffled in a splendid cloak.

"I say, Sir Christopher!" cried Frank: "this won't do at any price, you know."

"What won't do, sir?" demanded the knight in a stern tone. "Now, then, Jeffreys—down with the steps."

"Yes, sir:"—and the steps were lowered accordingly.

Frank stood aghast, as he saw the knight hand his better half into the carriage: and the said better half pouted up her really pretty mouth in a disdainful manner as she passed the forlorn youth.

Sir Christopher was about to follow her into the vehicle, when Frank suddenly seized him by the skirts of his great coat, exclaiming, "You shan't sneak off in this manner: you shall stay to—to——"

"To what?" growled Sir Christopher from the depths of the silk handkerchief which came up to his nose.

"To be shot at!" returned Frank, almost driven to desperation.

The lady inside uttered a scream—Sir Christopher gave a desperate groan, and, breaking away from his nephew, rushed into the carriage—Jeffreys put up the steps and banged the door—and the vehicle rolled away, leaving Curtis standing alone on the pavement, the very picture of the most ludicrous despair.

What was to be done now? The formidable Captain O'Blunderbuss held him—yes, *him*—Frank Curtis—answerable for the appearance of Sir Christopher Blunt on the field of battle; otherwise——but the alternative was too dreadful to think of!

What, then, *was* to be done? Frank saw the impossibility of nerving himself so as to encounter the desperate fire-eater; and yet he knew that the Captain would find him out, even if he removed his abode from the West-End to West Smithfield.

Yet something *must* be done—and that speedily; for it was now two o'clock in the afternoon—and next morning at eight the Captain would expect him at the place of appointment.

An idea struck Frank:—he would go and consult Mr. Howard, the attorney.

To that gentleman's offices he accordingly repaired, composing himself by the way as well as he could, so as not to express by his countenance the alarms which agitated within his breast.

Mr. Howard was disengaged, and gave him an immediate audience.

"Well, I hope you're satisfied, now that you hanged that poor fellow yesterday morning," said Frank, as he took the chair to which the solicitor pointed.

"It was a duty which I owed to society," returned Howard, laconically, as if the subject were not altogether a pleasant one.

"What an idea!" ejaculated Frank. "But, however, it is done, and can't be undone. After all, he was a brave fellow—a man just such as I could have admired, barring the highway part of his calling. And now, you who are such a stickler about duties to society, and so on—suppose you heard, for instance, that a duel was going to take place between some friends of yours and another party—of course you'd do all you could to stop it—you'd go to Bow Street, and you'd give private information concerning the *where* and the *when*;—or perhaps you'd speak openly, and get the persons bound over to keep the peace—eh?"

"I should not do anything of the kind," answered Howard, who already began to suspect that Mr. Frank Curtis had some special reason of his own for speaking with so much earnestness—indeed, with such an air of appeal, as he now displayed.

"You wouldn't—eh?" exclaimed Frank, grievously disappointed at the ill-success of his little manœuvre. "And why not?"

"Because I should only lose my time for nothing," responded Mr. Howard.

"The devil! Then, did you get Tom Rain hanged because the prosecution put money into your pocket?" demanded Frank.

"Did you merely come to chatter with me, or on business?" asked the lawyer evasively. "If the former, I am busy—if the latter, make haste and explain yourself."

"Well—the fact is," continued Frank, now feeling certain that the entire affair of Tom Rain's prosecution was a very sore subject with the lawyer,—"the fact is, I wanted to speak to you about a little matter—in which my precious old uncle has placed me in a complete fix———not that I care about a duel, you know—I'd see a duel damned first, before I'd care for it—still———"

"Still you would rather not fight it?" observed Mr. Howard, with a slight curl of the lip.

"You see, my dear fellow," proceeded Curtis, "that I have so many affairs of my own to attend to, I really cannot undertake to conduct those of other people. There's my marriage with Mrs. Goldberry coming off in a few days——and now, bother to it! up starts this duel-business———"

"Do explain yourself, Frank!" exclaimed Howard impatiently.

"Well, I will—and in a few words, too. It seems that Captain Mordaunt has taken a tiff at my uncle's conduct towards his sister; and so he sends Captain O'Blunderbuss———"

"Captain O'Blunderbuss, eh!" ejaculated the attorney, now becoming suddenly interested in the narrative of Mr Curtis.

"Yes: a terrible-looking, wild Irishman," returned this young gentleman: "but he didn't frighten me, though——*I* should think not! Do you know him?"

"Only by name," answered Mr. Howard coolly, as he glanced at a suspicious-looking slip of parchment that lay upon his desk. "But go on."

"Well, this O'Blunderbuss, it appears, goes to my uncle, who refers him to me—naturally enough, seeing that I am pretty well experienced in all matters of duelling," pursued Frank. "So the Captain calls on me a couple of hours ago; and we discuss the business in a very friendly way. Every thing is settled pleasantly enough; but before the Captain takes his leave, I catch hold of him by the button, and let him know that if he fails to produce his principal on the ground to-morrow morning, after all the trouble entailed on me, I shall hold *him* answerable accordingly. The Captain looks rather glum at that, because I did tumble down upon him a little unexpectedly with my threat. However, he agrees; and we separate. But, lo and behold! I go to Sir Christopher to tell him how comfortably I have settled the whole business for him—and he is gone—fled—bolted—mizzled—cut his stick—baggage and all, including his wife!"

"And, therefore," observed Howard coolly, "you will have to fight Captain O'Blunderbuss, because *you* will not be able to produce *your* principal."

"It's just this that bothers me," exclaimed Frank. "If the man had offended me, I shouldn't of course mind: in that case, one of us should never quit the ground alive—for I'm a desperate fellow, when once I am in earnest. But here's a poor devil who has never done me any injury, but who seems to me to be a capital hand at the whiskey-bottle,—and my fire-eating temper places us both in that position which compels *him* almost, poor creature! to insist on our exchanging shots. I really feel for the Captain——"

"And not at all for yourself, Frank?" said the lawyer, in his usual quiet manner.

"Oh! not an atom!" ejaculated Mr. Curtis. "But don't you admit that something ought to be done to prevent Captain O'Blunderbuss from becoming the victim of a display of temper so unjust and uncalled for on my part? I wish to heaven my friend the Duke of the Tower Hamlets was in town—he would pretty soon put matters on a proper footing, and save me from the chance of killing a man that has never injured me. But as his lordship the Marquis is *not* in town, why—I must throw myself on your friendship."

"Well—I will undertake to prevent the duel, in this case," said Howard, speaking as quietly as if he believed every word of Mr. Frank Curtis's version of the affair.

"Will you, though?" cried the young man, unable to conceal his joy.

"I will indeed," returned Howard: "so make your mind perfectly easy on that head. Where is the duel—or rather, where ought it to take place?"

"In Battersea Fields, to-morrow morning, at eight precisely," answered Frank.

"Very good," said the lawyer. "Now, you must be with me at a quarter before seven—here, at my office; and I will have a chaise ready to take us there."

"But need we go at all?" asked Frank, his countenance suddenly assuming a woeful expression again.

"We *must* go to the field," replied the solicitor; "but trust to me to settle the matter when we *do* get there. Again I tell you not to make yourself uneasy: I will guarantee the complete settlement of the affair—and in a most peremptory manner too."

"Thank'ee kindly," returned Frank, again reassured. "You have taken a load from my breast: not that I care about fighting, you know—but it must be in a good cause. That was just what I said when my best friend, the Prince of Scandinavia——"

"There's enough of it for the present, Frank," interrupted the lawyer. "Leave the affair to me—and I shall manage it to your complete satisfaction. Be here at a quarter to seven—not a minute later—to-morrow morning,—and now you must permit me to attend to my own engagements."

Frank Curtis took the hint and his leave accordingly, wondering how the lawyer would so manage matters as to subdue the terrible fire-eating propensities of the redoubtable Captain O'Blunderbuss. Nevertheless, the young man placed implicit reliance upon Mr. Howard's promise; and it was with a comparatively light heart that he sped towards use dwelling of Mrs. Goldberry, in Baker Street.

CHAPTER LXIII.
THE MEETING IN BATTERSEA FIELDS.

According to instructions given to his landlady, Mr. Frank Curtis was called at a quarter to six on the morning following the incidents just related; and leaping from his warm bed, he proceeded, with quivering limbs and chattering teeth, to strike a light.

Having, after a great deal of trouble, persuaded the short wick of his candle to catch the flame of the match which he held to it, he drew aside the window-curtains and looked forth to ascertain the nature of the weather.

The result of this survey was by no means reassuring; for a mizzling rain was falling, and a cheerless mist appeared to hang against the window.

Frank closed the curtains again, and looked wistfully at the bed, as if he were more than half inclined to return to it, and leave Captain O'Blunderbuss to do his worst;—but, on second thoughts, he knew that this was a hazardous venture—and, accordingly, he began to huddle on a portion of his garments.

Then commenced the process of shaving—always an unpleasant one, but doubly so by candle-light, and when the hand is so nervous that the chances are equal whether you mow off the hirsute stubble or the tip of your nose.

"Bother to this razor!" cried Frank: "it won't cut at all this morning!"

The fault was not, however, in the razor, but with him who wielded it.

At length, by dint of reiterated scraping, and steadying the right wrist with the left hand, Mr. Frank Curtis managed to achieve this portion of his toilette.

When occupied with his ablutions, he thought that the water had never appeared so icy cold before; and his teeth chattered like a box of dominoes rattling.

The fact was, that the nearer the eventful moment approached, the more alarmed became this heroic young gentleman, lest the lawyer should disappoint him, or deceive himself, in the task of taming the formidable Captain O'Blunderbuss.

It was half-past six before Mr. Curtis quitted his bed-room; and he had just time to take a cup of coffee in his sitting apartment while the girl of the house ran to fetch a cab. She speedily returned with, or rather *in* the vehicle; but when Mr. Curtis had taken her place, he perceived to his dismay that the horse had such an unpleasant knack of suddenly bolting round each corner he came to, and the driver was already so drunk, even at that early hour in the morning, that the chances were decidedly in favour of an upset.

He, however, reached the lawyer's office in safety, though not before the clocks at the West-End were striking seven.

A hackney-coach was already waiting at the door; and the moment Frank rang the office-bell, Mr. Howard appeared.

"Come, jump in—we have not a minute to lose," said the latter.

Frank accordingly entered the coach, in which, to his surprise, he found two ill-looking, shabbily-dressed fellows ensconced. Mr. Howard followed him—the door was closed hastily—and away rolled the vehicle in a westerly direction.

Mr. Curtis was now enabled to examine at his ease—or rather at his leisure, for easy he was not—the two individuals just mentioned.

One was a man of about forty, dressed in seedy black, and with a beard of at least three days' growth, and a shirt that seemed as if it had been worn and slept in too for a fortnight. His face was pale and cadaverous, and its expression sinister in the extreme. His companion was worse-looking and dirtier still; but *his* countenance was red and bloated with intemperance. He carried a stout stick in his hand, and smelt awfully of rum.

"Got your pistols, Frank?" inquired Mr. Howard, when the coach had moved off the pavement.

"Pistols!" repeated the young gentleman, turning dreadfully pale. "I thought you—you—you——"

And his teeth chattered violently.

"I know what I promised; and what I promised I will perform," responded the attorney. "But I thought you might like to make a show of an intention to fight, before I interfered."

"Oh! you know I never bully," exclaimed Frank. "If I made a show of fighting, as you call it, I *would* fight—and not pretend merely."

"Well—just as you like," observed Howard. "We will settle the business the instant we get down there."

"But is the gen'leman sartain the Cap'ain'll be there?" asked the man with the stout stick and the red face.

"Hold your tongue, Proggs!" growled his companion in the shabby black. "These gen'lemen know what they're up to."

Silence then prevailed in the vehicle; and Frank Curtis sate wondering who the strange-looking twain could be. At last he came to the conclusion that they must be constables whom Mr. Howard had called into requisition for the laudable purpose of putting a stop to the duel. Still, such seedy constables were seldom seen: but then, reasoned Frank within himself, they might perhaps be in a state of insolvency—a suspicion certainly warranted by their outward appearance.

The mist-like rain continued; and, though the morning grew a trifle brighter, it was in a very sickly manner. Frank had seldom felt more dispirited in his life, the weather leaguing itself with his own vague apprehensions to render him utterly miserable.

At length the coach reached the vicinity of Battersea Fields; and Mr. Howard pulled the check-string as a signal for the driver to stop.

He then descended; Frank Curtis followed; and the two queer-looking gentlemen alighted also.

"You will keep at a decent distance, Mr. Mac Grab," said Howard, addressing himself to the individual in seedy black.

"Wery good, sir. Proggs," continued Mr. Mac Grab, turning to his companion, "you make a circumbendibus like, so as to cut off the Captain's retreat down yonder. I'll skirt the river a short way, and then drop down on him.".

"All right," growled Mr. Proggs; and off he set in the direction indicated by his master, Mr. Mac Grab.

Howard then took Frank's arm; and they walked on together, the young gentleman shivering and trembling violently.

"What *is* the matter with you?" demanded the lawyer. "You shake just like an aspen."

"Oh! nothing—nothing!" returned Frank, in a faltering tone. "Only it's very cold this morning—and this cursed mist——But there's the Captain already!" he suddenly ejaculated, making a full stop.

Howard glanced in the same direction towards which Frank's eyes were turned, and beheld two individuals at a short distance. One, who was wrapped in a cloak, was standing still; the other was pacing rapidly up and down in the immediate vicinity of his companion, and tossing his arms about as if in a perfect fury of indignation.

"Come on," said the lawyer, dragging forward the terrified Frank Curtis. "There! the person who is walking up and down like a maniac, has caught sight of us——"

"That's the Captain!" almost whimpered the young man. "Oh! my stars! how fierce he does look!"

"Now, then, ye shir-rkers! is it keeping us waiting ye mane?" vociferated the terrible Captain, sending his voice half-way across a field in a tone of awful indignation. "Be Jasus! it's a rale insult to me and my frind, to be seven minutes and a half behind time in this way!"

"We are coming, sir, as fast as we can!" exclaimed Howard: "and may be a little faster than you will find to be agreeable."

"My God! don't irritate him!" implored Frank. "He's capable of——of—— shooting us both—as we walk along."

"Don't be such a fool, Frank. You will see a rare bit of fun in a few minutes. Come along!"—and the lawyer dragged his shrinking companion forward.

"Be the holy poker-r!" vociferated the Captain, as Howard and Curtis now drew near enough for him plainly to recognise their countenances: "be the holy poker!" he repeated, his eyes glaring furiously, "Sir Christopher is not here! Morthaunt, my dear frind, ye are swindled—robbed—plunthered— chated of the pleasure of a duel this cold mornin'. But I'll avenge ye, my boy—for I tould that Misther Curtis there that I'd hould him responsible— —"

"Come, come, Captain!" exclaimed Howard, as he and Frank now stopped at the distance of a few paces from the warlike officer and his friend Mordaunt: "don't bluster and sputter in this fine fashion——"

"Is it blusther and sputter to me ye mane!" cried Captain O'Blunderbuss. "Be Jasus; sir-r—ye shall ate the wor-rds afore we're done. But I'll shoot Mr. Curtis first; and 'tis yourself I'll send headlong afther him. Morthaunt, my frind, instead of being principal now, 'tis second ye must be. So give us the pisthol-case from under your cloak, man."

"With all my heart, Captain!" said Mordaunt, who was a tall, awkward gentleman, about thirty-five years of age, and as like Miss Julia as brother could be to sister.

"Howard—my dear friend—my good fellow," gasped Frank Curtis in the ear of his companion; "is it possible that—that—you've——"

"Be Jasus! we're watched!" suddenly exclaimed the Captain, whose quick eye now caught sight of a man approaching from the next field.

"It's only my servant, sir, who is bringing my case of pistols," remarked Howard. "Not knowing whether you would be here, we kept them in the coach at a short distance."

"Not be here!" repeated the Captain. "Do ye take us for as great cowards as ould Sir Christopher Blunt? Be Jasus——But that man don't look like a servant anyhow!" ejaculated the warlike gentleman, interrupting himself, and fixing a ferocious look upon Mr. Mac Grab, who now came running up to the spot, completely out of breath.

Howard glanced rapidly to the left, and beheld Proggs approaching from that direction.

"Here's another fellow!" exclaimed Mordaunt, who had marked and followed the lawyer's scrutinizing look. "Gentlemen, what *does* this mean?"

"Yes—and be Jasus!" vociferated Captain O'Blunderbuss: "what does this mane? Have ye had recourse to the dirthy expadient of getting constables to come for-ar-rd to spile the purtiest little affair that was ever to come off on a misty mornin'?"

"It don't mean nothink of the kind, Captain," said Mr. Mac Grab gruffly: then, as with a side glance he convinced himself that his follower Proggs was now only a few paces distant in the rear of the warlike Irishman, he continued thus:—"The fact is, I'm a hofficer—and you're my prisoner."

"An officer-r-r!" vociferated Captain O'Blunderbuss, his countenance becoming actually purple with rage, while Frank Curtis, suddenly assured that all prospects of a duel were at an end, began to enjoy the scene amazingly.

"Yes, sir—this person is an officer," said Mr. Howard, in the calmest manner possible; "and I am the attorney for the plaintiff—Mr. Spriggins—at whose suit you are now captured for three hundred and forty-seven pounds, including costs."

"Blood and thunther-r!" roared Captain O'Blunderbuss, swelling so tremendously with passion that he seemed as if about to burst through his military frock-coat with its frogs and braidings: "this is a rale insult not ounly to me, but also to ould Ireland. Mor-r-thaunt, my boy——"

"It's a very awkward business, Captain," said the gentleman thus appealed to. "But I do not see why it should prevent the business on which we met. Pistols first—prison afterwards."

"That won't do," said Mr. Mac Grab.

"Not a bit," growled Proggs, who was now stationed close behind the Captain.

"Bastes of the ear-rth!" roared O'Blunderbuss: "do——"

"Come now—enough of this gammon," interrupted Mac Grab. "If you won't walk quiet off with us, we must see what force will do."

"It is no use to resist, my boy," whispered Mordaunt to his friend, who was literally foaming at the mouth. "But we will find another occasion to punish these cowardly fellows," he added aloud, casting fiery glances upon the lawyer and Frank Curtis.

"Be Jasus! and I'll have some of it out of 'em now!" ejaculated Captain O'Blunderbuss; and springing upon the unfortunate Frank, he administered to this young gentleman three or four hearty cuffs, before a hand could be stretched out to withhold him.

Curtis roared and wriggled about with the pain; but he was speedily released from the effects of this onslaught, Mac Grab, Proggs, and the lawyer, hastening to his assistance.

The warlike Captain was then borne away to the hackney-coach, in which he was safely deposited, Mordaunt obtaining leave from Mr. Howard to accompany his friend in the same vehicle as far as the prison to which he was to be consigned.

Frank Curtis declined forming one of the party; and while the coach proceeded in as direct a line as possible for Horsemonger Lane gaol, the young gentleman sped merrily along alone and on foot, delighted, in spite of the drubbing which he had received, to think that the redoubtable Captain O'Blunderbuss was on his way to a place where his warlike propensities stood every chance of being "cribb'd, cabin'd, and confin'd," at least for a season.

You may conceive, gentle reader, that Captain O'Blunderbuss was in a dreadful rage at being interrupted in the midst of his favourite pursuit—especially as the interruption was of so unpleasant a nature as that described. But his vapouring and blustering produced little effect upon Messrs. Mac Grab and Proggs, who never spoke a word during the journey from Battersea Fields to Horsemonger Lane, save to answer in an affirmative when Mr. Howard proposed that they should stop at a public-house for a few moments to partake of some refreshment; and then they each responded—"Yes—rum, please."

The Captain himself was accommodated with a glass of whiskey: Mordaunt and the lawyer took nothing.

The vehicle then proceeded, without stopping, to the prison, where the gallant Captain—oh! most ignominious fate!—was handed over to the care of the turnkeys in the debtors' department of the establishment.

CHAPTER LXIV.
OLD DEATH AND HIS FRIEND TIDMARSH.

The incident which occupied the preceding chapter occurred, as will probably be recollected, on the morning of the Wednesday after the Monday on which Thomas Rainford was hanged and resuscitated.

It was on the evening of the same Wednesday, and at about eight o'clock, that we must again introduce the reader to the laboratory in Red Lion Street.

A cheerful fire burnt in the grate; and before it sate Dr. Lascelles and the Earl of Ellingham, engaged in conversation and also in the discussion of a very excellent bottle of claret conveyed thither from the Earl's own cellar in Pall Mall.

"I wish Jacob Smith would return," said the young nobleman, looking anxiously and nervously at his watch.

"In the same manner have you renewed the conversation after every pause that has occurred during the last two hours," observed the physician. "My dear Arthur, there is nothing like patience in this world. You may depend upon it, all goes on well—or you would too soon have received the tidings of any evil that might have occurred. Bad news fly uncommonly fast."

"I wish that I possessed a small amount of your calm and unexcitable temperament, doctor," returned the Earl. "But I am so fearful lest any untoward accident should mar the success—the complete success of all our plans."

"Do not meet evils half way," said the doctor. "Every thing has gone on well as yet. Mr. de Medina acted with the dispatch of a regular man of business. No one could possibly have managed better. He left on Monday evening for Dover, where he remained but just long enough yesterday morning to hire a cutter and arrange with the captain to have her in readiness to leave at a moment's warning. He was back in London again last night by seven; and fortunately your half-brother was so far recovered as to be able to depart in company with Jacob. The disguise you procured for him was impenetrable to even the eyes of the most experienced Bow Street runner. He and his young companion reached Dover early this morning; and I dare swear that long before this hour gallant Tom is safe in Calais, where Mr. de Medina and his daughters will also be some time to-morrow. Then off they all go to Paris, where you are to rejoin them."

"Yes: all has been well arranged by Mr. de Medina," said the Earl; "and I have no doubt that the results will be as you anticipate. But I charged Jacob to return post-haste to London—I begged him not to spare the gold with which

I furnished him, so that he might be back here as soon as possible to assure us of my brother's safe embarkation for France. And yet the lad is not with us yet! You must admit, doctor, that I am not to be blamed for my apprehensions: for misadventures and obstacles, altogether unforeseen—never dreamt of, indeed—do start up so suddenly, that I confess I shall enjoy no peace of mind until I receive from Jacob's own lips the assurance that the object of my anxiety is beyond the reach of all danger."

"How can it be otherwise than that he is already safe?" demanded the physician somewhat impatiently.

"Who can tell what may happen?" asked the Earl. "On Monday night, while Thomas was sleeping and profound tranquillity as well as perfect security seemed to prevail in the house, was not the grand secret suddenly menaced by the appearance of one whom only a few hours previously I had been led to consider numbered with the dead? Yet doubtless you thought at the moment, while at your house in Grafton Street, that all was calm and unendangered in Red Lion Street."

"The sudden turning up of that old scoundrel whom Thomas Rainford supposed to be dead, and of whom you have since told me so much, was certainly very remarkable," observed the physician. "But you certainly managed the matter most cleverly—the more so, too, inasmuch as my patient knew nothing of the transaction until it was all over."

"Fortunately he slept, as I have already told you," said the Earl. "That excellent lad Jacob was for a few minutes completely overcome—stunned—stupified, indeed, when he recognized the countenance of Benjamin Bones; and I myself was strangely excited when those terrible words, *'Tis Old Death!* fell upon my ears—for I knew to whom they applied. Moreover, Jacob let the lamp fall; and I dared not move to obtain another light—for Bones began to struggle furiously. I was sadly alarmed lest my half-brother should awake: but fortunately his slumber was profound."

"And then, I believe, Jacob Smith recovered himself and procured another light?" said the physician interrogatively.

"You see, doctor," returned the Earl, with a smile, "that you did not listen very attentively to my narrative of the transaction, when you came back to the house yesterday morning."

"Because, I remember, you would persist in telling me the story at a time when I was thinking of the best restoratives for my patient," answered Lascelles, also with a good-natured laugh. "But pray give me all the details now—and the occupation will while away the time until Jacob makes his appearance."

"God grant that he may soon come!" exclaimed the Earl. "But let me resume at the point where we interrupted ourselves."

"I asked you if Jacob did not procure another light the moment he had recovered his presence of mind," said the physician: "but I remember now that you availed yourself of the opportunity afforded by the darkness, to drag the old man back to the staircase leading into the subterranean, and that the terrible menaces you whispered in his ears reduced him to the passiveness of a lamb. He is a hideous-looking man—for, after all you learnt from your brother concerning him, it is clear that he is the same whom I had seen in this house on one or two occasions, but whose name I did not then know."

"He is clearly the same person," said the Earl.

"Well—and so you got him down the break-neck stairs," added the doctor; "and *then* it was you called to Jacob to procure another light, Rainford continuing asleep the whole time. But, after all that had taken place in the morning, his slumber would necessarily be heavy."

"I can assure you that a more dangerous task I had seldom undertaken than that of dragging the old villain down those stairs," said the Earl; "and how it was that we both escaped broken necks, I am at a loss to divine. However, I did get him safely down to the bottom; and the great door being then bolted only on the same side as the stairs, I had no difficulty in opening it. Jacob came down with the light; and I compelled the old man to rise, and enter the subterranean with me."

"I will be bound his hideous countenance was convulsed with rage and alarm?" exclaimed the doctor. "But I must get a cast of his head when he dies—which I dare say will be upon the scaffold."

"Yes: he was positively horrible with mingled wrath and fear," continued the Earl. "But I had no pity for him—as I have none now. I made him walk a few paces in front of me, Jacob accompanying us with the light. Once he turned round, and fixed on the lad a look so full of infernal spite—of demon-like malignity, that I was horrified to think that such hateful emotions could find an abode in the breast of any human being. Jacob Smith recoiled in affright—as if from the glare of a serpent's eyes; but I whispered a word to reassure him—and almost at the same moment I beheld, by the light of the lamp, a door in the side of the subterranean. You know the suspicions which had already filled my mind: they then returned with renewed vigour to my memory—and I felt convinced that I touched on the threshold of a discovery. I commanded the old man to stop—suffering him to believe that I had pistols about me, and should not hesitate to use them in case of need. The door was speedily opened——"

"And it led into the very dungeon where you were confined for four weeks," said Dr. Lascelles. "The villains—the scoundrels, who perpetrated such an outrage!"

"Yes—it was the very same dungeon," continued the Earl; "and my blood ran cold as I glanced within. Jacob Smith understood the discovery that I had made, and uttered an ejaculation of horror. '*I now know at least one of the authors of* my *imprisonment!*' I said, turning to Old Death, whose eyes were again glaring fiercely upon the lad. '*But*,' I added, '*this is no time for question and answer on that head.*'—Then, taking the lamp, I held it in such a manner as to be able to throw its light upon that part of the cell where I had opened to myself the means of escape; and I perceived that the masonry had not been replaced. I accordingly resolved not to imprison the old man there: and yet, what could I do with him? Turning round to examine more minutely the nature of the place, I beheld another door, on the opposite side of the subterranean. Old Death marked the fact of my eyes lingering thereon; and he gave vent to something between a menace and a prayer.—'*I seek not to harm you,*' was my reply; '*but as it once suited* your *purposes that I should become a captive here for a few weeks, it is now expedient according to* my *views that you should become a prisoner for a few days. In with you, old man!* I added, having in the meantime opened the door of this second cell!"

"And there the old reprobate is now cooped up, along with his friend Tidmarsh," exclaimed the physician, laughing at the idea of the two cronies being caught in one of their own snares;—for that they *were* companions in iniquity he had now but little doubt.

"You must admit that the case was a desperate and an urgent one," continued the Earl. "From all you had told me concerning this Tidmarsh, I felt well persuaded that he was likely to visit the subterranean; and I knew that, were such a casualty to ensue, Old Death had merely to raise his voice in order to obtain his release."

"And so you quit the subterranean and run round to Turnmill Street to tell old Tidmarsh that Dr. Lascelles wishes to see him immediately in his laboratory?" exclaimed the doctor, again laughing heartily—for the entire affair seemed to have touched a long slumbering chord of merry humour in his breast.

"Precisely so," returned the young nobleman. "Tidmarsh, however, eyed me very suspiciously, and muttered something to himself about the doctor being very indiscreet;—but I affected not to notice his peculiarity of manner. He came round to the house—and you know the rest."

"Yes: you took him down to join his friend Old Death, as it seems the rascal is called," observed the doctor.

"And there they must remain until Jacob Smith shall have returned with the tidings of my brother's safe embarkation," continued the Earl. "It is true that they are both utterly ignorant of his escape from death—his extraordinary resuscitation, thanks to your profound knowledge and generous aid, doctor;—but, as we have every reason to believe at least one of them to be Thomas's enemy, they shall neither obtain a chance of discovering the secret of his *new existence*, as I may indeed term it—at all events not until he shall be beyond the reach of danger. And, do you know, it strikes me most forcibly that Tidmarsh was the gaoler who attended upon me during my incarceration in the dungeon below? Although the person who *was* my gaoler, invariably spoke in a feigned tone, and as laconically as possible, yet I am almost certain that it was the voice of Tidmarsh. Moreover, he seemed for a moment so astounded—so struck, when I presented myself at the door of his dwelling in Turnmill Street, to deliver the forged message which induced him to accompany me round to this house, that I am convinced he knew me. For, though he never permitted me to catch a glimpse of his countenance, when he used to visit me at the trap in the dungeon-door—still he might have seen my face. However, when I presented myself at his abode in the way which I have described, my manner appeared so off-hand and sincere, that had any suspicions of treachery entered his mind, they were dispelled almost immediately. But, doctor, I abominate the necessity of having to use duplicity even towards villains of that stamp!"

"Your compunction is carried too far, my dear Arthur," returned Lascelles. "It was necessary to get that scoundrel Tidmarsh into such a snare, as to place him beyond the possibility of doing mischief; and, though the narrative which you have now given me more in detail than you did yesterday morning, when you hastily sketched these incidents to your brother and myself,—though, I say, it makes me laugh—a habit not frequent with me—I really commend your foresight in averting danger, as well as your bravery in carrying into effect the requisite precautions."

"I deserve and require no praise, doctor," answered the Earl. "What would I not have done to ensure the safety of him who has behaved so generously to me? During the whole of Monday night, I sate by his bed-side, anxiously awaiting the moment when slumber should leave his heavy eye-lids; for I knew that I had welcome—most welcome tidings for his ears. But he slept on until you came: and then, doctor, you were a witness of the joy which he experienced on learning that he had not been the cause of the death of Benjamin Bones—miscreant though the man be!"

Scarcely were these words uttered, when a low but hasty knock at the front door caused Lord Ellingham to spring from his seat—seize the lamp—and hasten to answer the summons.

Dr. Lascelles could hear the Earl ejaculate the words—"Jacob Smith!"—then a hurried whisper took place in the hall;—and, in another moment, the joyous exclamation—"Thank God! thank God!" bursting from the young nobleman's lips, met the physician's ears.

And Dr. Lascelles thereby knew that Rainford had succeeded in quitting the shores of England in safety!

CHAPTER LXV.
THE EXAMINATION.

The reader will remember that, according to the arrangements originally chalked out, Lord Ellingham and Jacob Smith were to have accompanied Tom Rain to France. But this project was disturbed by the appearance of Old Death in the house in Red Lion Street, and the incidents to which it gave rise, as narrated in the last chapter.

For, the Earl—having succeeded in making Old Death and Tidmarsh his prisoners—resolved to remain in the house, not only that he might, by means of frequent visits to the subterranean, guard against their escape, but also to supply them with food and to liberate them when circumstances should render their farther confinement unnecessary.

Thus was it that Tom Rain and Jacob had proceeded without the Earl to Dover, and that the lad had returned thence to London the moment he had seen Rainford safe on board the cutter which Mr. de Medina had hired especially to convey him to France. Nay—Jacob was not content with merely witnessing the embarkation of the individual to whom he had become so deeply attached; but, in spite of the instructions he had received alike from the Earl and Tom Rain himself to return with the least possible delay to the metropolis, he had lingered on the pier at Dover until the white sails of the cutter were no longer in sight.

He therefore arrived somewhat later in London than had been expected, although he travelled post and spared not the gold placed at his disposal to urge the postillions on: but when he frankly admitted to Lord Ellingham and the doctor the reason of his retarded appearance in Red Lion Street, they could not find it in their hearts to utter a word of reproach or blame.

No:—for Lord Ellingham's joy was now as exuberant as his apprehensions had a short time previously been strong and oppressive; and he wrung the hand of the humble Jacob as if that lad had been his own brother!

"We will presently liberate our prisoners," said the Earl, when Jacob had related the particulars of his journey with Rainford to Dover, and of the latter's safe embarkation. "But, before I suffer them to go at large, it behoves me not only to adopt the means requisite to elicit certain explanations interesting to myself, but also to take those steps that will effectually prevent the mysterious subterraneans and dungeons of this establishment—or rather, of the *two* houses—from being accessible or available to the miscreants whom we are about to set free. Conceiving that Jacob would be sure to come back this evening, and intending that his return should be followed by the examination and liberation of those two men, I have ordered the three faithful domestics who assisted us so materially on Monday morning, and on whose fidelity I can rely with so much confidence, to be here at half-past nine o'clock."

"For what purpose?" demanded the physician, in astonishment.

"To increase our number so as to overawe the wretches who are to appear before us," replied the Earl. "It is not that I fear to give them an inch of vantage-ground; but were they to find themselves in the presence of only two men and this lad, they might attempt resistance, and use a violence that would alarm the neighbourhood;—and I need hardly say, doctor, how necessary it is for all our sakes that we should not be placed in a position which would compel us to give to a magistrate any explanation of the modes in which we severally became acquainted with this establishment or those two vile men."

"Your precautions are most admirably forecast, my dear Earl," responded Dr. Lascelles. "Hark! there is a single knock at the front door!"

"Run, Jacob, my boy," said the Earl: "my servants have arrived."

The lad left the room without taking a light, but the young nobleman almost immediately rose and followed him—a second thought suggesting the prudence of assuring himself against the coming of any unwelcome intruder instead of his servants.

By the time the Earl reached the middle of the stairs leading down into the hall, Jacob had opened the street-door.

"Mrs. Bunce!" exclaimed the lad, starting back half in affright, as he recognised her wizen countenance by the feeble light that streamed from an adjacent window.

"What! Jacob—you here!" cried the woman. "Why—how come you in this house? and what have you been doing with yourself lately? I began to think you was playing us false: but now that I find you here, I suppose you know all about the trick of Mr. Bones's pretended death, and have made every thing right with him. But is he here?"

"Yes," answered Jacob boldly—for he had by this time recovered his presence of mind. "Walk in:—he wants very much to see you."

"And so do I want to see him," added Mrs. Bunce as she entered the hall, while Jacob barred the door carefully. "I haven't seen him ever since Monday night; and he was to be sure and come up to the Dials last evening. So I got alarmed, and come down to see, I went to Turnmill Street—but I could make no one hear there—for I suppose you know by this time all about Tidmarsh and the other crib——"

"Yes—and the subterranean too," added Jacob: "all the secrets, so long kept from me, are now revealed. But walk up, Mrs. Bunce—walk up."

The woman, suspecting nothing wrong, and not altogether displeased to find (as she believed) that Jacob had risen so high in favour with Old Death as to become one of his confidants,—the woman, we say, walked up the staircase, which was well known to her; but, scarcely had she reached the first turn, when she was suddenly grasped by a vigorous hand, and a voice exclaimed, "Make no noise, Mrs. Bunce—or it will be the worse for you."

"Thank God, you are there, my lord!" cried Jacob now hastily running up the stairs. "This woman is one of the gang which it has fallen to your lordship's lot to disperse."

"Oh! Jacob," ejaculated Mrs. Bunce, "you don't know what you are doing! But who is this lord—and what have I done to injure him?"

"I am the Earl of Ellingham, woman," said Arthur; "and perhaps you are not ignorant of the long imprisonment which I endured in this place. But proceed—I will follow you: and remember that you are in the power of those who will not suffer you to escape."

At that instant there was another knock at the door.

"Remain here," said the nobleman to Mrs. Bunce. "Jacob, let me answer that summons."

Arthur accordingly proceeded to the door, and gave admittance to his three men-servants.

They then all repaired to the laboratory together, where the Earl made Dr. Lascelles acquainted, in a hasty whisper, with the cause of Mrs. Bunce's appearance on the stage of their present proceedings.

The moment the woman emerged from the darkness of the landing outside to the light of the laboratory, she cast a hasty and inquiring glance around on those present; but her eyes settled on Jacob Smith, and she was evidently much astonished to see him dressed in a plain but most respectable manner, and looking neat, clean, and even interesting in his appearance. For the lad possessed good features—very bright eyes—and a set of white, even teeth; and though his countenance was still somewhat indicative of a sickly constitution, it nevertheless showed a state of health considerably improved by the excitement of travelling and by the happiness imparted to his soul by the successful escape of Thomas Rainford.

Jacob saw that Mrs. Bunce surveyed him with interest; and at the moment he felt pity for the woman who had on many occasions shown him some kindness, and towards whom he had also experienced at times unaccountable heart-yearnings;—but he could not blame himself for having just now entrapped her into the power of Lord Ellingham, because he knew how important it was to assemble in the presence of that nobleman as many of Old Death's accomplices as possible. Besides, he was well aware that no harm was intended her; and this assurance he conveyed to her in a hasty whisper—though not in such a way as to induce her to believe that he was any longer an accomplice also.

"You will now accompany me *below*," said the Earl, addressing himself to his three servants.

Jacob hastened to light another lamp (of which there were several in the laboratory); and the Earl, attended by his domestics, proceeded into the adjoining bed-room, whence they passed down into the subterranean.

Dr. Lascelles, Mrs. Bunce, and Jacob were left together in the laboratory.

"What does all this mean?" demanded the woman, accosting the lad in an imploring manner—for she was afraid, in spite of the whispered assurance she had received from him.

"I cannot give you any explanation," answered Jacob aloud. "But I may go so far as to promise you—and this good gentleman," he added, turning towards the doctor, "will confirm my words—that no harm is intended to you, provided you give faithful replies to the questions that will be put to you presently."

"The lad speaks quite properly, woman," said the physician; "and you had better hold your tongue until *the prisoners* make their appearance."

"The prisoners!" muttered Mrs. Bunce; and it struck her that allusion must be made to Old Death and Tidmarsh.

Nor was she mistaken; for, in a few minutes, the Earl and his domestics re-appeared, escorting into the laboratory those two individuals, whose hands were fastened by strong cords.

Benjamin Bones looked more hideous than ever. A white bristling beard, of three or four days' growth gave an additional death-like aspect to his countenance; and his eyes glared, from beneath their shaggy brows, with mingled rage and alarm.

Tidmarsh manifested less emotion; but, on entering the laboratory, he cast a rapid and scrutinizing glance around, as if to ascertain who were present.

Old Death did the same; and when his eyes caught sight of Jacob Smith, his forehead contracted into a thousand wrinkles with the intense ferocity of his malignant hate: then he exchanged a rapid glance with Mrs. Bunce, who gave him to understand, by a peculiarly significant look, that she was not there as a witness against him, but as a prisoner herself.

Dr. Lascelles stood with his back to the fire, contemplating the various persons assembled, in a manner which showed that he was far from being an uninterested spectator of the proceedings: indeed, he not only prepared to listen with attention to all that was about to be said, on account of the friendly feelings which he experienced towards the Earl of Ellingham,—but he likewise occupied himself in studying the physiognomies of Old Death, Tidmarsh, and Mrs. Bunce—a survey which led him to the comfortable conclusion that if they did not all three perish on the scaffold sooner or later, it would not be their own fault.

Lord Ellingham ordered the three prisoners to be accommodated with chairs; and, when they were seated, he addressed them in the following manner:—

"You are now in the presence of one who has the power to punish you for your numerous misdeeds, and who, should you refuse to answer the questions to be put to you, will not hesitate to hand you all three over into the grasp of justice. The individual who possesses that power, and who is now about to question you, is myself. All your secrets are known or suspected—and, even should you refuse to answer my queries, or if you reply to them falsely, I have the means of arriving at the truth. To you, Benjamin Bones, do I address myself first:—answer me, then—and say wherefore your agents or accomplices waylaid me, and bore me off to that dungeon opening from the subterranean. Speak, villain—and see that you speak truly!"

"One word, my lord," said the arch-miscreant, his sepulchral tones quivering and tremulous with mingled rage and alarm: "let me say one word to you in private!"

"Not a syllable! Speak openly—and cause not idle delay," exclaimed the young nobleman.

"Do you know," asked Old Death, "that it is in my power to publish a secret which would not redound to your honour?"

"I can well divine to what you would allude," returned Arthur; "and I despise your menace. Go and say, if thou wilt, that the Earl of Ellingham is the half-brother of him——"

"Who was hanged on Monday morning!" growled Old Death; and then he chuckled horribly in the depth of his malignity. "Ha! ha! ha! the proud and wealthy Earl of Ellingham the brother of a highwayman who was hanged,—and that brother, too, the elder one, and born in lawful wedlock! Ah! this would be a pretty tale to circulate at the West End!"

"Scoundrel! you cannot provoke me to anger," said the Earl, calmly; "but you may move me to invoke the aid of justice to punish you for daring to imprison me during four long weeks in a noisome dungeon—a crime for which the penalty would be transportation for the remainder of your miserable life. Moreover, that same justice would require of you full and ample explanations respecting those rooms filled with property of immense value, and of such a miscellaneous nature that the various articles could not have been honestly obtained! Ah! you shrink—you recoil from that menace! Think you that any ridiculous punctilio has prevented me from forcing the locks of those rooms and examining their contents? No: the day after *you* became *my* prisoner here, and when I ascertained beyond all doubt that *you* were the tenant of those rooms, I hesitated not to visit them, to glean evidence against you. Now, old man, you see that you are in my power; and you will do well not to push my patience beyond the sphere of indulgence."

"And what if I tell you all you want to know?" said Benjamin Bones, appalled by the unveiling of the fearful precipice on which he stood.

"Give me the fullest and completest explanation of many circumstances in the unravelling of which I feel a special interest—spare me the trouble of adopting other means to obtain the solution of those mysteries to which I possess a clue," exclaimed the Earl; "and I shall forthwith liberate you and your companions, having previously taken measures to prevent you from holding any farther interest in this house or the tenement in Turnmill Street, with which the subterranean passage communicates."

"And—and my property?" gasped Old Death.

"To allow you to retain it, were a sin," answered the Earl emphatically: "to give it up to the magisterial authorities, or to dispose of it for the benefit of the poor, would be to court an inquiry which must inevitably lead to the mention of your name and the consequent apprehension of your person—a result which would be an indirect forfeiture of the promise I have given and now repeat: namely, to permit yourself and companions to depart with impunity on condition that you make a full and complete confession in regard to all the points wherein I am interested. What, then, can be done with that property?" exclaimed the nobleman: "there is but one course to pursue—and that is, *to destroy it*!"

"Destroy it!—destroy it!" groaned Old Death, writhing with mental anguish on his chair: "what? destroy all that hard-earned wealth—those treasures——"

"Every article!" interrupted the nobleman emphatically; "and consider yourself fortunate in quitting this house to breathe the air of liberty, rather than to be consigned to a gaol."

"Oh! my God! my God!" cried Old Death, reduced to despair by the lamentable prospect now placed before him.

"Blaspheme not, villain!—invoke not the sacred name of the Almighty!" ejaculated Arthur. "Rather implore pardon for your manifold iniquities!"

"It would take a long life of repentance to purge *his* soul of all the atrocity that harbours in it," observed the physician, who had intently watched all the variations of the old man's countenance during this colloquy.

"My dear doctor," said the Earl, "there is hope for even those who are most deeply stained with sin—yes, even for this miserable man, who would sooner cling to his ill-got wealth than adopt the only means now open to him of avoiding the grasp of justice. But it is useless to prolong this discussion. Benjamin Bones! once for all, do you consent to make a full confession, as the first atonement for a life of crime, and to surrender all your treasures as the second?—or shall I send forthwith to summon hither the officers of justice?"

"But, if you take mine all, you send me forth into the world a beggar!" cried Old Death, in a tone which seemed to indicate that he was about to weep for very rage.

"On that night," said the Earl solemnly, and almost sternly, "when Thomas Rainford took from thy treasury the money which he conceived to be his due, did he not leave ample sums behind? and wilt thou tell me that thou hast not since disposed of those sums in other places of security? Thou seest, villain, that I can read all thy secrets: so prate no more about being reduced to beggary."

Old Death's eyes fell beneath the fixed gaze of the Earl of Ellingham, who thereby perceived that the conjecture which he had just hazarded was indeed the right one.

"And you will let us go free if I answer all your questions?" said the arch-miscreant, after a brief pause, during which he consulted his companions in iniquity by means of a rapid interchange of glances.

"I will," replied the nobleman emphatically.

"But what if I should tell you more than you already seem to suspect—through ignorance of the precise extent of your real knowledge," said Old Death,—"and thus make you acquainted with things likely to render you vindictive——"

"I scorn a mean and petty vengeance!" exclaimed the young nobleman. "My word is pledged to a certain condition; and that promise shall be redeemed, whatever the nature of your revelations may be."

"Then I consent!" exclaimed Old Death. "Bear witness, Dr. Lascelles—for you are an honourable man——"

"The Earl of Ellingham is too lenient," interrupted the physician. "But, as it is, I guarantee my word of honour that his lordship will faithfully fulfil his promise."

"In spite of any thing that may transpire, and for which he may not be prepared?" added Old Death, determined to drive as sure a bargain as possible: "because," he continued, "it is quite impossible for me to foresee the nature of the questions you are going to put to me, my lord—and, in answering them, I may only commit myself. I am in your power; but pray use that power mercifully."

"Mercifully!" cried the Earl, in a tone of mingled scorn and disgust. "I have no sympathy with you of any kind, old man—you are loathsome to me! I merely make a compact with you—and that bargain shall be adhered to on my part, if it be fulfilled on yours. I however warn you, that should I detect you in aught at variance with the truth, our compact ceases—my promise is annulled—and you remain at my disposal as completely as if no pledge relative to your safety had ever issued from my lips. Weigh well, then, the position in which you stand," continued the young nobleman sternly: "for I am not to be trifled with!"

"I will tell you all you require to know—all—all," responded Old Death, gasping convulsively: "only let this scene end as soon as possible—for it does me harm."

"We will proceed at once to business," said the Earl: then seating himself in front of the prisoners, he addressed his questions to Old Death, saying, "In the first place, why was I imprisoned in the subterranean dungeon?"

"To prevent you from using your wealth to bribe the gaol-authorities to let Rainford escape, or your interest to save him if he was condemned," answered Old Death, in a slow and measured tone.

"Then, villain that you are," cried the Earl, scarcely able to subdue his resentment, "you had an interest in hurrying the son of your own half-sister Octavia to the scaffold!—Oh! I understand it all! Thomas felt assured that some profound, secret, and malign influence was at work against him; for those who were put forward as the prosecutors—the knight and his nephew—went as unwilling witnesses! Then it was you," continued the nobleman, in a tone of fearful excitement,—"it was *you* whose gold doubtless bribed the attorney Howard to institute those fatal proceedings!"

"It was—it was!" ejaculated Old Death, trembling from head to foot. "But Rainford deserved it;—he outraged me—I was good and kind to him—I threw excellent things in his way—but he made me bring him to this house—he learnt all my secrets—he robbed me of my treasures—he carried off my private papers——"

"Silence!" exclaimed the Earl, in a tone which made the arch-villain and his fellow-prisoners all three start convulsively: "give not a false colouring to that transaction! Rainford learnt, when in the country, who you were and how nearly you were allied to his late mother;—he knew also how you had plundered him of his inheritance—and he was justified in the conduct he pursued towards you. The money which he took was legitimately his own, allowing for the accumulation of interest and compound interest; and the papers were not *yours*—but rightfully his property!"

"Then why did he not tell me who he was?—why did he entrap me, and compel me at the muzzle of the levelled pistol to conduct him to my secret places?" demanded Old Death impatiently.

"Your villany and your craft could only be met by stratagem and counterplot," returned the Earl emphatically; "and in that way did Rainford meet you. And yet—for the truth of my assertion you cannot deny—you have sent your own nephew to the scaffold!"

"It was his own fault!" persisted Old Death doggedly. "He should not have crossed my path—he should not have proclaimed warfare against me. I would have been his friend——"

"His friend!" exclaimed the Earl, in a tone of bitter scorn.

"Yes—his friend, after his own fashion—in the way he wanted a friend!" continued Old Death, becoming garrulous with nervous excitement. "But he outraged me in a way I could not forgive nor forget—he penetrated into all my secrets—he might have returned and helped himself again and again from my stores—*he knew too much* for me to be safe—and moreover he bound me to a chair in such a way that I fell into a fit, and should have died had it not been for this man here," added the miscreant, indicating Tidmarsh. "All those things combined to render Rainford's death necessary—and he has paid the penalty of his conduct towards me."

Lord Ellingham recoiled in horror from the fiend-like man who could thus seek to palliate the foul deed of having sent his own relative to the scaffold, through no moral motives, but merely to gratify his vengeance and remove one who seemed to be dangerous in his path.

"Let us know more of the sham-death business on your part, Mr. Bones—or whatever your name is," said Dr. Lascelles.

"You remember that night I came round to the house here and met you, sir?" hastily exclaimed Tidmarsh, thinking that he should serve himself by exhibiting a readiness to volunteer any explanation that was required. "Well—you recollect that it was the night you saw Rainford in your laboratory, and we knew that he had gone down into the subterranean. Then, if you please to remember, we went away together—and I took leave of you at the corner of Turnmill Street. But I suspected there was something wrong—although I did not dare offer to go into Mr. Bones's rooms while you were with me. As soon as you had left me, however, I returned to the house—not by the subterranean, be it well understood,—and passing through your laboratory——"

"Then you possess counterpart keys, rascal!" exclaimed the physician angrily. "But go on."

"Well, sir—I passed through your laboratory into the bed-room there, locking the door of communication after me. Then I entered the first store-room; but I had scarcely put foot therein when I heard a violent noise as if some one was trying to break through the trap-door in the bed-chamber. I confess that I was frightened—because I knew it must be Rainford, and I suspected him to be a desperate man who meant no good in that house. I remained quite still—heard him break open the trap and come forth. I also heard him, dash open the door of your laboratory, through which he passed;

but as I had neglected to lock the other door there—leading to the landing—he was not compelled to force that also. Well—I waited a few minutes, till I thought he had left the house; and then, having great misgivings on account of Mr. Bones, I went into the next store-room. But there I caught a glimpse of Rainford, standing over Mr. Bones, who was tied in his chair. I was about to retreat, I must confess—but Rainford bolted away like a ghost; and I ran up to my friend, who I thought was dead. I however saw enough, at a second glance, to convince me that he was only in a kind of trance-like fit; and in a short time I recovered him. That's my part of the story, sir; and, I hope——"

"Enough!" exclaimed Lord Ellingham abruptly. "*I* have now a question to ask *you*, Mr. Tidmarsh:—Were you not my gaoler when I was a prisoner in the subterranean?"

"Well, my lord—it's no use denying it," answered the man; "but——"

"Spare your comments. I cannot complain of the way in which you executed a task doubtless imposed on you by your master here. Moreover, you even showed me some indulgence, by permitting me to write those letters to my friends——"

"Give my friend Bones his due, my lord," interrupted Tidmarsh; "for I showed 'em to him first before I posted them."

"And as they could do no harm, I let them go," hastily exclaimed Old Death; "for I did not want to punish *you* more than I could help. Besides, I was glad you wrote them;—in the first place because they prevented any noise amongst your friends on account of your disappearance—and, secondly, because the one you wrote to Rainford was enough to convince him he had nothing more to hope from you."

"Even while you seek to conciliate me, you cannot prevent the manifestation of your fiendish hate against him who was the son of your sister Octavia!" said the Earl, gazing upon Old Death in profound surprise,—surprise that his heart could be so irredeemably black. "But now answer me another question," he continued after a few moments' pause: "how came you to know that I was likely to use my interest or my gold on behalf of Thomas Rainford?"

"My spies were stationed about Horsemonger Lane gaol," answered Old Death; "and I had a lodging in the immediate neighbourhood. They came and told me that you had just gone into the prison to see Rainford; and I concluded that you must already be aware of the relationship which existed between you. To resolve and to act with me are the same thing; and I sent back my men to seize you and convey you to the subterranean."

"And why had you stationed spies about the gaol?" demanded the Earl.

"Because I suspected that Rainford would send for you, or that you would go to him of your own accord," replied Old Death; "for he had taken from me the papers which *proved* who he was—and I supposed that his first act on possessing them, must have been to communicate with you; and in that I cannot have been far wrong."

By dint of questioning and cross-questioning, the following additional facts were elicited;—

When Tidmarsh recovered Old Death from the species of trance or fit into which he had fallen when bound to the chair, the latter determined to encompass at least the transportation, if not the execution, of Tom Rain. For two or three days he remained quiet at Tidmarsh's abode in Turnmill Street, brooding over his scheme of vengeance, and communicating with none of his friends elsewhere—not even with the Bunces. In planning the punishment of Tom Rain, Old Death knew that he had a most delicate and difficult game to play; for the highwayman was to be sacrificed to his hatred and his interests—and yet in such a manner that the victim should not know by whom the blow was struck nor the source whence his ruin came. The deed must be effected with so much dark mystery that Rainford should not even have any ground for supposing that Bones was the real prime mover of the prosecution; and in this case the arch-villain felt convinced that Rainford would not even mention his name nor allude to his establishments in Clerkenwell, when placed before the magistrate or on his trial. The affair of Sir Christopher Blunt's three thousand pounds seemed the best point on which to set the whole of this complicated machinery in motion; and Old Death knew sufficient of Mr. Howard's cold, calculating, and money-making disposition to be well aware that his aid in the business could be readily secured. He communicated all his plans to Tidmarsh; and this latter individual suggested that Rainford should be led to believe that Old Death was no more. "For," said Tidmarsh, "when I entered your store-room and saw Rainford gazing at you in your fit, I concluded you were really dead, and I am certain that such was the impression of the highwayman. Besides, he fled in horror; and Rainford is not the person thus to act save under extraordinary circumstances." This hint was adopted; and it was resolved that Rainford should be induced to suppose that Benjamin Bones was positively defunct—a belief that would of course preclude the possibility of any suspicion that the said Bones was the individual who set in motion the springs of that conspiracy which was to carry the victim to the scaffold. These projects being all settled between Old Death and his man Tidmarsh, the latter was despatched to Mrs. Bunce to whom the entire scheme was communicated. She was instructed to set spies to watch Tom Rain, and to convey to him, if possible, the information that Benjamin Bones was dead.

It was also determined not to trust Jacob Smith with the plan of vengeance to be carried out, but, as a precaution on the right side, to let even him also believe that Old Death was no more. At the same time the lad was to be used as a spy on Rainford, his devotion to whom was not of course suspected. When Mrs. Bunce met, or rather overtook Rainford in Gray's-Inn-Lane on the Saturday night previous to his arrest, it was really by accident; and she availed herself of that opportunity to inform him that Old Death had gone to his last account, according to the instructions communicated to her in the morning of that very day. She endeavoured to watch whither Rainford went, after she parted from him; but he disappeared, and she concluded that he had entered some house in that vicinity. That he had quitted Lock's Fields was known to her; and she therefore imagined that his new domicile must be in the Lane. Jacob was accordingly set to watch that neighbourhood; but he misled her purposely, as will be remembered, by stating that he had knocked at every house in the street, and had ascertained that no such person as Rainford lived there. Tom was, however, seen by one of the spies, in Piccadilly, on the ensuing (Sunday) evening, as he was returning from Lady Hatfield's house; and he was dogged over to his old abode in Lock's Fields. In the meantime, Tidmarsh had been to Mr. Howard, whom he bribed heavily with gold supplied by Old Death for the purpose; and the lawyer was induced to instruct Dykes, the Bow Street runner to arrest Rainford on the charge of robbing Sir Christopher Blunt. This arrangement with the solicitor was effected on the Saturday afternoon: it was on the Sunday evening that Rainford was dogged to his own abode; and that very night, as soon as the spy could communicate with Mrs. Bunce and Dykes, the arrest of the victim was accomplished in the manner described in a previous chapter. Throughout all these and the subsequent proceedings, Jacob Smith's friendly disposition towards Rainford was not suspected; nor were his visits to Horsemonger Lane Gaol known to the conspirators—inasmuch as the spies, who had been placed in that neighbourhood to watch for Lord Ellingham, had no farther business there when once the Earl was captured and secured.

Such was the substance of the confession, partly elicited fairly and partly extorted from the three worthies—Old Death, Mrs. Bunce, and Mr. Tidmarsh—who were now so completely in the power of the Earl of Ellingham.

"Thus," said Arthur, who, as well as the physician and Jacob Smith, was appalled at the dreadful discoveries now brought to light,—"thus was this tremendous conspiracy to take away the existence of a human being, minutely—I may almost say, scientifically planned in all its details, and carried on with a secrecy and a success that manifested the most infernal talent for wicked combinations! Monsters that ye are!" he cried, unable to retain his feelings any longer; "what vengeance do ye not merit at my hands? But, no—

vengeance is for cowards and grovelling miscreants like yourselves! Were I inclined—did I stoop to retaliate and repay ye in your own coin for this enormous misdeed—for you, old man," he added, turning his indignant glances upon Benjamin Bones, who shrank back in dismay,—"you ere now alluded to that cause which makes me interested in all that regards—or rather regarded," he said, correcting himself, "your unfortunate victim Thomas Rainford! But, as I was observing—did I choose to wreak revenge on ye three, how easy were it done! I might imprison ye for the remainder of your lives in your own dungeons: I might gag and bind ye in such a way that no cry could escape your lips, and no avenue of escape be possible, and then either leave ye to starve—yes, to starve to death in this room; or I might set fire to the house and consign ye to the torture of flames!"

Mrs. Bunce uttered a faint shriek, and Old Death gave vent to a low moan, as these awful words fell upon their ears: but Tidmarsh remained passive and silent.

Jacob Smith and the domestics gazed upon the Earl in anxious suspense, not unmixed with awe; for, as he spoke, he seemed as if he were armed with an iron eloquence to reproach, and a vicarious power to punish fearfully.

The physician surveyed the three prisoners with ineffable disgust.

"But, no!" resumed the Earl: "I would not condescend—I would not degrade myself so low as to snatch from your hands the weapons with which you work, and then use them against you! I have yet another point on which I require information: and when your answers, old man," he continued, again addressing himself to Bones, "shall have been given, all that will remain for me to perform is the destruction of your ill-got property, and the adoption of a measure to deprive you of any future interest in these houses with their dark subterranean passage and their horrible dungeons. Benjamin Bones," exclaimed Arthur, after a few moments' pause, "wherefore did you seek to possess yourself of that little boy whom Thomas Rainford had so kindly—so generously—so charitably adopted?"

Old Death explained that as he hoped to be enabled to discover the maternal parent of the lad, and as he conceived that Charley might afford him information calculated to assist him in that pursuit, he had endeavoured to get the child into his power.

"The letter which was found on the person of the deceased Sarah Watts," said the Earl, "doubtless furnished you with ideas of enacting a scheme of extortion against the boy's mother, should you be enabled to find her out, and believing as you do that she is high-born and perhaps wealthy. That letter fell into the hands of Rainford—no matter how; and, though I have not seen it, yet the nature of its contents have been communicated to me. Now, answer me—and answer me truly, if thou canst,—have you any farther clue beyond that which your acquaintance with the nature of that letter furnishes?"

"I have not—I have not," replied the old villain hastily: "if I had, I should not have wanted to get the boy into my power, that I might glean from him as much as he could impart to me."

"I now, then, warn you to think no more of that child, old man," said the Earl; "for he is already beyond the reach of your vile aims—and, even were he not, *I* would protect him. You see that all your atrocity—all your intriguing—all your black wickedness does not invariably conduct you to the goal of success. But moral lessons are thrown away on such as you. We will therefore terminate this scene as speedily as possible." Then, turning to his domestics, he added, "You will repair into the store-rooms of this house, and you will so destroy and ruin all the rich garments and the larger articles which are there piled up, that they will become comparatively valueless. The jewellery you will convey into the subterranean; and all those trinkets you will throw into the sewer, to which there is an opening from one of the dungeons. Jacob, you will guide my servants in this task."

"No, Jacob—Jacob!" exclaimed Mrs. Bunce hysterically: "have nothing to do with a business which——"

"Silence—silence, I command you!" growled Old Death, turning a savage glance upon the woman, and then fixing a look of demoniac hatred upon the lad, who was already leading the servants into the adjoining rooms.

Mrs. Bunce remained quiet, in obedience to the order she received from Old Death.

"And now relative to these houses—this, and the one in Turnmill Street?" said the nobleman. "Whose property are they?"

"They are my own freehold," responded Bones,—"bought with my money, long, long ago. But you will not——"

"I will not rob you," interrupted the Earl emphatically. "Where are the papers proving your title to the possession of this freehold?"

"In the iron-safe, in one of the store-rooms."

The nobleman quitted the laboratory, but presently returned, saying in a tone of authority, "The key of that safe!"

"It is here—here, in my pocket," muttered the arch-villain. "But my hands are bound——"

The Earl took the key from the pocket of Old Death and again left the laboratory. In a few minutes he re-appeared, holding a bundle of papers in his hand.

"I see by the endorsement that these are the deeds which I require," he said. "Now set a value upon your property, and I will pay you the amount. But stay—I will release you, so that you may execute a document which my solicitor has already prepared, and which simply requires the necessary filling up to render it available."

The nobleman drew a parchment deed from his pocket; and, aided by the papers which he had brought from the store-room, inserted the requisite particulars in the blanks left for the purpose.

He then removed the cords which confined Old Death, who named a large sum as the purchase-money of the freehold, and for which the Earl wrote a cheque on his banker without hesitation.

Then the deed of sale and transfer was duly signed by Old Death, and witnessed by Dr. Lascelles.

"This proceeding on my part," said the Earl, when the business was concluded, "may appear arbitrary and even vindictive; but it is necessary, and is not instigated by the spirit of revenge. I have paid you more than double the value of the property; and, therefore, you cannot complain. If you feel aggrieved, remember that it is in my power to transport you for life, on account of the outrage you perpetrated upon me by making me your prisoner in the subterranean which shall never be rendered available to you again. I have now performed the whole of the task which I had imposed upon myself; and you may all three depart!"

Thus speaking, the Earl unbound Tidmarsh; and, having compelled this individual, as well as Old Death, to surrender their pass-keys to the two houses, he followed those two villains and the equally vile Mrs. Bunce to the front-door.

The three passed out into the street; but before they sped away, Old Death raised his hand, and shaking it ominously, exclaimed, "Lord Ellingham, I will yet be avenged!"

The young nobleman did not condescend to offer a reply, but closed the door, and retraced his way to the laboratory.

"Well, my dear Arthur," said the physician, "I think you have had to deal with as pretty a sample of miscreants as ever underwent examination. None of those," he added, pointing towards the shelf on which the casts of the felons' heads were ranged, "could possibly have competed with them."

"Do you approve, doctor, of all the steps which I have taken?" demanded the young nobleman.

"You have acted admirably," replied Lascelles. "Indeed, you have behaved too well to the chief of those fiends, by paying him double the value of his houses."

"I would not allow even so vile a wretch as he to think that I had wronged him," returned the nobleman. "You can now remain in uninterrupted possession of your laboratory, doctor," he added with a smile. "But let us see how progresses the work of destruction in the other rooms."

Thither the doctor and the Earl proceeded accordingly.

It would have broken Old Death's heart outright to contemplate the rapid work which the nobleman's servants and Jacob Smith were making of the task allotted to them. In the room adjoining the bed-chamber, two of the domestics were employed in breaking the china, tearing the clothes, burning the silk handkerchiefs and the parcels of rich lace, ripping to pieces the muffs and boas, smashing the looking-glasses and pictures, and committing a havoc such as only the peculiar circumstances of the case could have justified. In the other store-room, the third servant and Jacob Smith were unpacking boxes and cases of jewels, and crushing the various valuables with billets of wood.

The fires were lighted in both rooms, and as much property was destroyed as it was safe to consume by those means: the jewellery was all conveyed to the subterranean, and thrown into the common sewer through that aperture which the hands of the nobleman had so lately hollowed in the wall of the dungeon.

The day dawned ere the work of destruction was completed: and then the store-rooms exhibited an appearance forming a strange contrast with their late wealthy aspect.

The physician returned to his house in Grafton Street; and Lord Ellingham hastened home to Pall Mall, leaving his servants and Jacob Smith to follow at their leisure.

In the course of the day he called upon Lady Hatfield, to whom he had already written two or three notes, acquainting her with the outlines of the numerous incidents which had so rapidly occurred since the moment of his escape from the dungeon: and he now gave her a detailed and oral account of all those exciting occurrences.

Their demeanour towards each other was that of an affectionate brother and a fond sister; and when the Earl bade her adieu, they embraced with feelings far different from those which once had filled their hearts.

In the evening, Arthur, accompanied by Jacob Smith, and attended by only a single valet, departed in his travelling-carriage for Dover, whence on the ensuing morning he embarked for France.

CHAPTER LXVI.
MRS. SLINGSBY AND THE BARONET AGAIN.

A few days had elapsed since the events related in the preceding chapter.

We must now again introduce our readers to the abode of Mrs. Slingsby, in Old Burlington Street.

It was about ten o'clock in the morning; the breakfast things had just been cleared away; and the pious lady was sitting in an abstracted—nay, positively mournful mood, holding in her hand the *Morning Herald*, on which, however, her looks were not fixed.

There was something on her mind. She was the prey alike to a source of disquietude and to the embarrassment caused by a projected scheme, beset with difficulties which seemed insuperable.

At length a double knock at the door interrupted her painful reverie; and in a few minutes Sir Henry Courtenay, whom she had been expecting, was announced.

The baronet's countenance was lighted up with an expression of joy and triumph; and, as soon as the servant had retired, he embraced his mistress with more than his wonted ardour. Still that ardour seemed not to exist on account of her, but rather to arise from feelings which required a vent: it was an embrace that appeared to say, "Congratulate me, for I have succeeded!"

"You are unusually gay this morning, my dear Henry," observed the lady, somewhat piqued at his manner; for her perception was quite keen enough to comprehend the real nature of the baronet's emotions, as we have just described them.

"Martha, my love," responded Sir Henry, "I have just brought a well-laid plot to a successful issue—at least, so far successful, that there can be no doubt as to the result."

"I dare say the project has but little interest for me," exclaimed the lady. "You have become a general *intriguant* I am convinced, Sir Henry; and your conduct is not fair or proper towards me."

"My dear Martha, I have before told you that it is impossible for me to remain completely faithful to you," answered the baronet. "I would not bind myself to any one woman, for all the world. If there be a woman to whom I could so bind myself, it is decidedly yourself."

"Thank you, Sir Henry, for the compliment," said Mrs. Slingsby, a little softened.

"But it is impossible, I repeat. Moreover," continued the baronet, "you must not complain of me—for I do all I can to render you happy. My banker's book is at your service——"

"Well, well," interrupted Mrs. Slingsby, "we will not dispute. Indeed, I have matters of too great an importance upon my mind to permit me to devote attention to petty jealousies and idle frivolities; and I perceive that you have also much to occupy your thoughts. But the revelation shall commence with you. Come, Henry, tell me all you have to say; and when we have discoursed on your affairs, you shall listen to mine."

"Be it so, Martha," said the baronet; then drawing his chair close to that of his mistress, he continued thus: "You are well aware how vexed and annoyed I was when you allowed the two girls to depart in so sudden a manner from the house."

"And you are also aware how cruelly I was discovered and reproached by my nephew Clarence," added Mrs. Slingsby.

"I have not forgotten all you told me on that head, Martha," returned the baronet; "and perhaps what I am going to tell you may set your mind at ease relative to that same nephew of yours."

"Poor Clarence!" exclaimed the lady, really touched as she thought of him. "He has been dreadfully ill ever since that shabby trick which Mr. Torrens played him. For three weeks he was confined to his bed, and was delirious———"

"I know all that, Martha," interrupted the baronet somewhat impatiently. "But do listen to me, as I am going to tell you things which I have hitherto kept altogether to myself. Well, you must know, then, that I was determined not to be discomfited by the abrupt return of Rosamond to her father's house; and I was well aware that, after all which had occurred between Villiers and yourself, you could not possibly give me any further assistance. So I acted for myself. I ascertained every requisite particular relative to this Mr. Torrens; I discovered that he is overwhelmed with difficulties—trembling on the verge of insolvency—and anxious to do any thing that may save him from so ignominious a fate. I also learnt that he is a man who will sacrifice his best feelings and principles for money. He has a mania for building speculations; and he conceives that if he be only assisted with adequate funds, he shall make a rapid and princely fortune. Love for his daughters he has not: he merely regards them as beautiful objects, to be sold to the highest bidder—and on what terms he scarcely cares, so that they become the means of producing him money. Such is the person on whom I have had to work—and I have not worked ineffectually."

"Then you have formed an acquaintance with him?" exclaimed Mrs. Slingsby.

"An acquaintance!" cried the baronet, chuckling; "I have formed an intimate friendship."

"What! in four or five weeks!" said Mrs. Slingsby.

"Exactly so. I obtained an introduction to him through his surveyor, who also happens to be mine; and under pretence of bargaining with him for the purchase of some of his houses, I wormed myself into his confidence. He at length informed me that there were heavy mortgages on all his buildings, and that he was anxious to sell some in order to be able to proceed with others. When I encountered the young ladies, I affected to be greatly surprised that they should prove to be the daughters of the very Mr. Torrens to whom my surveyor had recommended me."

"You have worked systematically indeed!" exclaimed Mrs. Slingsby, with pouting lips. "But pray proceed."

"Sometimes I was enabled, when I called," continued the baronet, "to obtain a few minutes' conversation with Rosamond alone; for Adelais, the elder sister, usually remains in her own chamber, a prey to the deepest melancholy. But Rosamond never appeared to comprehend any of the significant though well wrapt up hints which I dropped relative to my feelings concerning her. It is evident that you proved either a bad tutoress, Martha, or she a dull pupil."

"I presume you are coming to a crisis, Henry," said Mrs. Slingsby; "for your narrative is somewhat of the most tedious."

"I will endeavour to render it a little more interesting," observed the baronet complacently. "A few days ago I called at Torrens Cottage, and found the house in the greatest confusion. An execution had been levied in the morning, and the broker was there, putting a value upon the property. Mr. Torrens was in a state of dark and sombre despair; the young ladies were in their own apartment. I had a long private conversation with the father. He made me acquainted with the entire position of his affairs; and I discovered that five thousand pounds would be required to redeem him from utter ruin. It was then that I gradually unveiled my purposes—it was then that I dropped mysterious hints of my objects and views. At first he was astounded when the light began to dawn upon him, and he caught a glimpse of my meaning; but as I carelessly displayed a roll of notes before him, he grew attentive, and appeared to reflect profoundly."

"*The man who deliberates, is lost*," said Mrs. Slingsby, quoting the hackneyed proverb, and shuddering—bad, criminal, worthless as she was—at the tremendous amount of guilt which she now more than half suspected to be already perpetrated, or at all events to be approaching its consummation.

"While we were yet far from coming to an open explanation," continued the baronet, as calmly as if he were narrating a history of but little moment, "an event occurred which hastened the affair to the catastrophe that I contemplated. A sheriff's officer entered and arrested Mr. Torrens for a considerable amount—seven hundred pounds. The execution levied on the property in the house was for three hundred and forty; and thus he required an immediate advance of upwards of a thousand pounds to save himself from a prison, and his furniture from a public sale in due course. I requested the officer to withdraw from the room for a few minutes, stating who I was, and pledging myself that Mr. Torrens should not attempt to escape. I will not tell you all that then took place between me and the father of those girls: let it suffice for you to learn, that at the expiration of nearly an hour's discourse—varied on his part by appeals, threats, prayers, and imprecations—*he agreed to sell his daughter Rosamond!*"

"As your wife?" exclaimed Mrs. Slingsby, in a hoarse, hollow tone.

"No: as my mistress—as any thing I choose," returned Sir Henry Courtenay, emphatically.

Mrs. Slingsby shuddered from head to foot.

"How silly of you to affect horror at such an event!" exclaimed the baronet.

"Yes—it *is* silly on my part!" cried Mrs. Slingsby, bitterly; "silly, because I ought to have played a different part when first you touched upon the subject a few weeks ago. But, my God! Henry—you cannot mean—you will not, surely—surely——"

"Martha, this passes all endurance," said the baronet sternly. "If you do not choose to listen to me, I can retire: if you will not assist me, there is an end to every thing between you and me—and then, how will you live?"

"What assistance do you require?" asked the widow, in a low and tremulous tone—for she was shocked at all she had heard, and she was terrified by the menace which the baronet had just uttered.

"You shall learn," answered the latter. "I advanced the sums necessary to save Mr. Torrens from a prison and his furniture from the effects of the levy, taking his note of hand, payable on demand, for the amount—so that should he wish to retract from his bargain, he is completely in my power. I have agreed to give him five thousand pounds in all—*as the price of his daughter.* But he represented to me that the project can never be carried into execution, until Adelais and Rosamond shall have been separated. I was not unprepared for such an objection; and I accordingly proposed that he should permit Clarence Villiers to marry Adelais without delay—her drooping health serving as the plea for this relenting disposition on his part. I moreover promised my special protection on behalf of Clarence, for whom I can speedily obtain a government situation of far greater emolument than the paltry clerkship which he now holds. Then, when the wedding is over, and the young couple have quitted London, to pass the honeymoon somewhere in the country, *you will request Rosamond to spend a few days at your house.*"

And the baronet fixed a significant look upon his mistress as he uttered these words, so pregnant with terrible meaning.

"Impossible!" exclaimed Mrs. Slingsby: "if the deed were done here—beneath this roof—it would ruin me!"

"Ridiculous!" cried the baronet; and he proceeded to argue his hellish project in a manner which showed how fully he had considered it in all its details, and how artfully he had devised the means to render an exposure improbable.

But we cannot place on record all that was urged by him, or objected to by his mistress, on this particular point; suffice it to say that, influenced by the menaces more than by the reasoning which came from his lips, the pious lady at last consented to become the pander to his damnable machinations.

"Mr. Torrens shall this day write a letter to your nephew and invite him to the Cottage," said the baronet, when the whole plan was fully agreed upon. "Clarence will not of course be suffered to know that any interference on my part has brought about a reconciliation between him and the father of his beloved. The marriage will be hurried on as much as possible, and then Rosamond will become mine! But is Clarence sufficiently recovered from his illness to leave his dwelling?"

"He is much better than he was a few days ago," returned Mrs. Slingsby; "but when he first awoke to consciousness, after a month's duration of alarming illness and almost constant delirium, he received a severe shock, which produced a partial relapse. In a word, he inquired concerning the highwayman Thomas Rainford; and, on hearing that he had suffered the penalty of death, he exhibited the most painful and heart-rending emotions."

"But can he leave his room? Is he well enough to move out again?" demanded the baronet impatiently.

"Yes: he was here yesterday," answered Mrs. Slingsby. "Moreover, a letter conveying to him such joyful news as those which Mrs. Torrens will have to impart, cannot fail to restore him speedily to health and good spirits."

"Thus far all goes well," said Sir Henry Courtenay. "And now, Martha, my love, it is your turn to speak."

"I have consented to serve you, Henry, in a most difficult and dangerous scheme," observed the lady, after a few moments' reflection; "may I hope for aid and support from you in a plan which *I* have formed?"

"Certainly. Proceed—my curiosity is already excited."

"Henry," said Mrs. Slingsby, sinking her voice to a low and serious tone; "I am again——"

The baronet started.

"Yes—again with child," added the widow; "and on this occasion I intend to turn to a good account what would otherwise be deemed a terrible misfortune."

"I cannot for the life of me understand you," exclaimed Sir Henry Courtenay.

"I will explain myself," resumed Mrs. Slingsby. "You are well aware of the readiness which even well-informed persons in this country manifest to put faith in anything monstrous or preposterous that may be proclaimed or established under the cloak of religion. The greater the falsehood, the more greedily it is swallowed. There is that scoundrel and hypocrite Sheepshanks, for instance, who was so completely exposed a few weeks ago: he has taken a chapel somewhere in the Tottenham Court Road, and preached for the first time last Sunday. He has now become a dissenter; and in his initial sermon he dwelt boldly and long on the errors of which he had been guilty. He declared that he had been sorely beset by Satan, to whom he had for a time succumbed: hence his disgraceful fall. But he proceeded to aver that he and Satan had since then had a long and desperate struggle together, throughout an entire night, in his bed-chamber; and that he eventually succeeded in sending the Evil One howling away just as the day broke. He therefore proclaimed that he had now emancipated himself from the thraldom of hell, and was a chosen vessel of heaven once again. This discourse produced such an effect, that when he descended from the pulpit, many of the congregation pressed forward to shake him by the hand; and he is now in a more fragrant odour of sanctity than ever."

"To what is all this to lead, Martha?" inquired Sir Henry, completely bewildered by the long tirade relative to Mr. Sheepshanks.

"I merely mentioned the circumstances which I have related, for the purpose of convincing you how easily the world is duped by persons professing extreme sanctity," continued Mrs. Slingsby.

"To be sure!" ejaculated Sir Henry: "there are always plenty of fools to assemble at the beck and word of a knave."

"And it is with these impressions," added the widow, "that I intend to convert my present misfortune into an honour and a source of immense profit."

"May I be hanged if I understand one word of all you are saying!" cried the baronet, completely bewildered. "You are in the family way again, it appears; and yet you glory in the circumstance!"

"Doubtless you have heard the story of Johanna Southcott?"[28] said the widow, with a glance full of meaning.

"And you would imitate that imposture!" exclaimed Sir Henry: "'tis madness—sheer madness! Your nephew, who knows how intimate you and I are together, would expose the miserable trick."

"That is the principal difficulty which I should have to encounter," said Mrs. Slingsby, in a calm tone: "and even that is not insurmountable. I require your aid, indeed, on that very point. The change which, to suit *your* views, has taken place—or will speedily take place—relative to the position of Clarence and Adelais, already smoothes down much of the difficulty alluded to. Clarence will receive the benefit of your interest: exert that interest, then, to procure him a situation in some distant colony—or the East Indies, if you will—and his absence will alike render *you* more secure in the enjoyment of your Rosamond's person, and will remove to a distance the only individual who could possibly interfere with *my* project."

"Martha, this scheme of yours is utter madness, I repeat," exclaimed the baronet. "I will have nothing to do with it. If you attempt to palm so ridiculous a deceit on the world, all sorts of prying inquiries will be made, and the real nature of our intimacy must in that case be inevitably discovered. No—it shall not be done! I will give you money to go abroad, if you choose, when your situation may render necessary a temporary disappearance from London; but to consent to this insane project——"

"Well, well, Henry," interrupted the lady, terrified by the vehemence of the baronet's manner, "you shall have your own way."

"Now you are reasonable," said Sir Henry, drawing his chair closer to that in which she was seated, and beginning to toy with her.

But we need not prolong our description of this interview. Suffice it to say, that Mrs. Slingsby consented to abandon her atrocious scheme of representing herself as a second Johanna Southcott, and on the other hand promised to lend her aid to the no less infamous conspiracy formed against the honour of the unsuspecting Rosamond Torrens—for which concessions the pious and excellent lady received a cheque for a considerable sum on Sir Henry Courtenay's bankers.

The plan which Mrs. Slingsby had conceived, would never for one moment have obtained any degree of consistency in her imagination, had she not been well aware that there were thousands and tens of thousands of credulous gulls—superstitious dolts and idiots—miserable and contemptible fanatics, who would have greedily swallowed the impious, blasphemous, and atrocious lie.

In earnest belief of the Christian religion, and for profound veneration of all the sublime truths and doctrines taught by the Bible, we yield to no living being:—but it is not with common patience that we contemplate that disgusting readiness which so many of our fellow-countrymen exhibit to put faith in the false prophets and hypocrites who start up on all sides, each with some saving system of his own.

Not many years have elapsed since the Reverend Mr. Irving electrified all England with his "unknown tongues;" and there were impostors and fanatics, or fools and knaves, prompt to give an impulse to that memorable delusion by lending themselves to the cheat.

In this civilized country, too—in the nineteenth century—in a land whose sons proclaim themselves to be farther advanced in knowledge and enlightening principles than any other race on the surface of the earth—in one of the counties, moreover, where the refinement of intellect is supposed to prevail to a degree of brilliancy certainly not excelled in other parts of the kingdom,—there—in the neighbourhood of the cathedral city of Canterbury—did a madman, at no very remote date, assemble a host of enthusiastic believers in his horrible assumption of the name and attributes of the SAVIOUR OF THE WORLD! Yes—in the vicinity of a town presumed to possess all the benefit which the knowledge and learning of innumerable clergymen can possibly impart, did Mad Tom successfully personate the Messiah for several days!

But, oh! how sad—how mournful is it to contemplate the course which the Government of England is taking at the instant while we are penning these lines! A General Fast, to propitiate the Almighty, and to induce Him to avert his wrath from Ireland! Holy God! do thy thunders sleep when men thus blaspheme thy sacred name—thus actually reproach Thee with the effects of their misdeeds?

When misgovernment has brought Ireland to the verge of desperation,—when landlords have drained the country of its resources to be expended in the British metropolis,—when the agents and middlemen have exercised the full amount of petty tyranny and goading oppression upon the unhappy tenants,—when the Irish pride has been insulted by the symbols of subjection until endurance is no longer possible,—when the ambition of many gifted minds has been chafed and irritated at being excluded from a career of honour they would otherwise have pursued,—when all the humanizing effects of civilization have been restricted by a perpetual collision between the triumphant Protestant religion on the one hand domineering with insolence, and the defeated Catholic religion on the other looking for the chance of regaining a lost ascendancy,—when, too, an unprincipled system of agitation has fanned the flame of the worst feelings and extorted the few pence from the pockets of the half-starving peasantry,—when all these influences, forming an aggregate powerful enough to crush the most flourishing country upon the face of the earth, have been brought to bear upon unhappy Ireland, and have reduced her population to a misery which with such fertile causes was inevitable,—there are to be found men who are bold enough, in their deplorable ignorance or their abominable impiety, to accuse the Almighty of having purposely afflicted Ireland!

People of the British Isles! be not deceived by this blasphemous proceeding—a proceeding that would shift an awful responsibility from the shoulders of incompetent statesmen, and lay it to the account of heaven! Our blood runs cold as we write these lines—we shudder as we contemplate the wickedness of this impious subterfuge!

A General Fast to propitiate the Almighty—when the misgovernment and the misdeeds of men have worked all the horrible results complained of! Carlile, Hone, Richard Taylor, Tom Paine, and the whole host of avowed infidels were never prosecuted by the Attorney-general for blasphemy worse than that which attributes to the Almighty the effects of the errors, ignorance, despotism, and short-sightedness of human beings!

God has given us a fair and beauteous world to dwell in,—he has endowed us with intelligence to make the most of the produce of the soil,—and his revealed laws and doctrines have supplied us with precepts competent to maintain order and regularity in society. HE manifests no caprice—no change: the seasons come in due course, each bringing its peculiar bounties;—and it depends on ourselves to render our abiding-places here scenes of comfort, happiness, and contentment. But if by our own ignorance, wickedness, or tyrannical behaviour, we succeed in rendering any one spot of this fair and beauteous world a prey to famine and its invariable attendant—pestilence,—if we undertake to govern a country which we have conquered, and instead of applying beneficial and suitable measures, heap insult, wrong, error, and oppression upon its people,—how can we be surprised that the worst results should ensue? and how can we be so wickedly blind, or so vilely hypocritical, as to attempt to cast upon the dispensations of Providence those lamentable evils which we ourselves have engendered?

Again we say that a more abominable insult to the Majesty of Heaven was never perpetrated, than that conveyed by the motives set forth as a reason for a General Fast! The Ministers who have advised Queen Victoria to assent to such a hideous mockery, are unworthy the confidence of the nation. England will become the laughing-stock—the scorn—the derision of the whole world. Oh! we feel ashamed of belonging to a country in which such monstrous proceedings are set in motion under the solemn sanction of the Sovereign and her Ministers!

28. Partington's "Dictionary of Universal Biography" contains the following brief but faithful account of that impious and abominable impostress, Johanna Southcott:

"She was a singular fanatic, whose extravagant pretensions attracted a numerous band of converts in London and its vicinity, said to have, at one period, amounted to upwards of 100,000. She was born in the west of England, about the year 1750, of parents in very humble life, and, being carried away by a heated imagination, gave herself out as the woman spoken of in the book of Revelation. In this capacity she for awhile carried on a lucrative trade in the sale of seals, which were, under certain conditions, to secure the salvation of the purchasers. A disorder subsequently giving her the outward appearance of pregnancy, after she had passed her grand climacteric, she announced herself as the mother of the promised Shiloh, whose speedy advent she predicted. The faith of her followers, among whom were several clergymen of the established church, rose to enthusiasm. A cradle of the most expensive materials, and highly decorated, was prepared by her expectant votaries at a fashionable upholsterer's, and every preparation made for the reception of the miraculous babe that superstition and credulity could induce. About the close of the year 1814, however, the prophetess began to have her misgivings during some comparatively lucid intervals, in which she declared that, 'if she was deceived, she had, at all events, been the sport of some spirit, either good or evil;' and the 27th December in that year, death put an end to both her hopes and fears. With her followers, however, it was otherwise; and though for a time confounded by her decease, which they could scarcely believe to be real, her speedy resurrection was confidently anticipated. In this persuasion many lived and died, nor is her sect yet extinct: but, within a short period, several families of her disciples were living together in the neighbourhood of Chatham, in Kent, remarkable for the length of their beards and the general singularity of their appearance. The body of Johanna underwent an anatomical investigation after her death, when the extraordinary appearance of her shape was accounted for upon medical principles; and her remains were conveyed for interment, under a fictitious name, to the burying-ground attached to the chapel in St. John's Wood."

CHAPTER LXVII.
THE MARRIAGE.—ROSAMOND.

A fortnight had passed since the interview between Mrs. Slingsby and Sir Henry Courtenay; and the machinations of the latter had so successfully prevailed in accelerating the matters in which he was interested, that on the morning, when we must request our readers to accompany us to Torrens Cottage, the marriage of Adelais and Clarence Villiers was to take place.

The young man was still pale from the effects of recent and severe indisposition; but the happiness which he had experienced during the last fourteen days had worked a greater physical improvement in him than six months' sojourn in the south of France could possibly have done.

Firmly believing that the declining health and drooping spirits of Adelais had alone induced Mr. Torrens to revoke a decree which was to have separated them for ever,—and not over anxious to revive past topics in connexion with the subject,—Clarence gave himself completely up to the happiness which now awaited him; and his Adelais was equally ready to bury in oblivion any disagreeable reflections relative to the late conduct of her father.

Mr. Torrens was cold, moody, and distant: but this was his manner—and, as the young people knew not what fierce fires raged beneath that aspect of ice, they did not bestow any unusual attention on the subject.

The only source of grief which the sisters knew was their approaching separation; for Mr. Torrens had arranged for the young couple to proceed into Devonshire and pass the honeymoon with some distant relations of his own, who were anxious to see their beautiful cousin Adelais. Rosamond was to remain with her father, Mrs. Slingsby not having as yet sent her an invitation to Old Burlington Street, for fear that Clarence might throw some obstacle in the way of its being accepted.

Thus stood matters on the bridal morning,—when Adelais appeared pre-eminently beautiful in her garb of virgin white—emblematical of the innocence of her own heart,—and when Clarence Villiers could scarcely persuade himself that he was actually touching on the threshold of complete felicity. Rosamond—poor Rosamond smiled amidst the tears that flowed fast down her pale cheeks; for she felt as if she were losing her best—her only friend in the approaching departure of Adelais.

There was a young lady—a friend—who acted as joint bridesmaid with Rosamond; and there were two or three other acquaintances of the family;—and of the persons thus enumerated consisted the bridal party. The sisters had naturally invited Mrs. Slingsby; but that lady, aware that her presence would not be agreeable to her nephew, had sent to plead indisposition as the excuse for her absence.

And Mr. Torrens—what was the nature of his feelings now? Forced by his necessities—or rather by that indomitable pride which urged him to make every sacrifice rather than boldly meet his embarrassments in the Bankruptcy Court—he had assented to bestow his elder daughter on a young man whom he disliked, and to sell his younger child to an atrocious villain, who had not even manifested the delicacy of hinting at marriage!

Reader! think not that when we record the dreadful fact of *a father consenting to sell his own daughter for gold*, we are fabricating for a romance an incident which never occurred in real life! Such things have been done often—are done often—and will be done often, so long as the human species shall exist. The immense wealth of that corrupt and detestable monster, the late Marquis of Hertford,[29] enabled him to purchase the favours not only of Lady S⸻, but also induced that profligate woman to sell to him every one of her daughters! And those daughters have since married titled men, and live splendidly upon the riches bequeathed to them by the horrible voluptuary. Again, but a few years have elapsed since a certain Lady H⸻sold her beautiful daughter Priscilla to a most ignoble lord; and the atrocious deed became the topic of numerous articles in the English and continental newspapers, the tribunals of France having taken cognizance of the scandal!

We could make mention of innumerable instances of this kind, the greater portion of which are, however, confined to the aristocratic circles. For it must necessarily occur that the "upper classes," as they insolently denominate themselves, are the most profligate, unprincipled, and licentious of all the sections into which society is divided. Wealth and idleness, associated, must, as a general rule, give a fearful impulse to immorality: rich viands and generous wines must heat the blood; and nights of dissipation—balls, routs, *soirées*, and card-parties—inflame the imagination. The voluptuous dances which prevail in those fashionable assemblies—the indecent manner in which the ladies of the "upper class" display so much of the bosom that but little scope is left for the exercise of fancy—the positive encouragement that is given in high life to men whose reputation as vile seducers is notorious,—all these circumstances foster licentiousness, and provide a constant aliment to sustain immorality.

Again, the morals of the fashionable world have not recovered from the effects of that dangerous poison which was instilled into them by the evil examples of the family of George the Third, and the flagrant conduct of the beastly voluptuary, George the Fourth. The licentiousness of the Princesses of that family became the public scandal of the day; and from the ladies of the Court emanated the fashion of wearing hoops to their dresses, for a purpose which need not be particularly described. But fashion subsists by the artifice of constant change; and when hoops had enjoyed their day, those ladies who had found them so convenient, actually devised the scheme of giving vogue to a padding in front *to make the wearers appear in the family way*! This is no fiction; and young, unmarried girls, as well as married ladies, actually submitted to this disgraceful and immoral fashion through servile obedience to the example of the Princesses. This was positively holding out a premium to licentiousness—because the fear of a false step indicating itself by its consequences, was annihilated.

Everyone knows that many titled ladies gloried in the reputation of being (as they really were) the mistresses of George the Fourth. With all these frightful examples in view, how could the entire sphere of the fashionable world fail to become dreadfully demoralised? and how was it possible to prevent the contaminating influence from spreading to the inferior grades? Therefore is it that the fashionable world especially—being the first to experience that influence and the most likely to perpetuate it—has not yet recovered from the effects of the evil example of the Court. True is it, thank God! that Queen Victoria has not followed the same course which so many of her near relatives adopted: but still even her bright example can only gradually mitigate, and not in a moment destroy, the effects of the moral poison instilled into fashionable society by her royal predecessors.

Previously to the first revolution in France, the aristocracy were steeped in licentiousness and profligacy. But a glorious nation rose in its might—hurled down a throne encrusted with the miseries of the people—annihilated the bloated and infamous nobility—and even gave the proud and arrogant clergy such a lesson as they have never since forgotten. The aristocracy of France have never recovered that blow—and, thank heaven! never will. The hereditary peerage exists no longer in France; and titles of nobility are valueless. Thus, by virtually destroying the aristocracy of rank and birth, France has suppressed a sewer of filth and corruption which distilled its abominations through every grade and phase of society. The aristocracy of talent has been substituted; and the mechanic may now rise to be a minister—the ploughman has his fair chance of becoming a politician—the delver of the soil can aspire to the post of deputy. France is regenerated: England can become so only by the destruction of its hereditary aristocracy.

From this long digression, we return to the bridal party assembled at Torrens Cottage, and now about to repair to the adjacent church, where the nuptial bond was to be indissolubly tied.

And to that church did the party proceed,—the father, who looked upon his daughters as the means of filling his purse,—the daughters, who knew not the utter selfishness of their sire,—the young man, who was so indescribably happy in at length accompanying to the altar her whom he loved so well,—and the guests, who thought as much of the excellent breakfast which followed as of the solemn ceremony itself.

The banquet passed—and the time came for the departure of the newly married couple. A post chaise drove up to the door—the trunks were hastily conveyed to the vehicle—and Adelais was torn away from the arms of her young sister Rosamond, who clung frantically to her.

An hour afterwards, the guests were gone—and Rosamond remained alone with her father.

"God grant that my dearest sister may be happy!" said the maiden, her voice almost completely lost in sobs.

"If she is not, it will be her own fault," observed Mr. Torrens harshly, as he paced the room. "She would have the young man—she set her heart upon him—and I have yielded. I suppose you are now sorry that she is gone; and yet I dare swear you thought me a brutal tyrant for separating the love-sick pair a few weeks ago."

"My dearest, dearest father!" exclaimed Rosamond, profoundly afflicted and even annoyed at the manner in which she was addressed,—"wherefore speak to me thus! Have I ever given you any reason to suppose that I was so undutiful as——"

"As to run away from the house with your sister—eh?" interrupted Mr. Torrens in a biting, satirical tone. "A young lady who could take such a step, would not be very particular in her observations on her father's conduct."

"Heavens! how have I deserved these reproaches—at least to-day?" asked Rosamond, bursting into an agony of tears. "Shall not the past be forgotten? will you ever continue, my dear father, to recall those events which are naturally so painful——"

"Well, well—let us say no more about it, Rosamond," cried Mr. Torrens, ashamed of having vented his ill-humour upon his daughter.

And he paced the room in a manner denoting a strange and indomitable agitation.

The fact was that the miserable father recoiled in horror from the atrocity he had agreed to perpetrate; and, with an idiosyncracy so common amongst men who tremble upon the verge of committing a fearful crime, he turned on the intended victim as if she were the wilful and conscious cause of those black feelings that raged within his breast. He had not moral courage sufficient to retreat while it was yet time:—he dared not make the comparatively small sacrifice of himself to avoid the immeasurably greater one which involved the immolation of his daughter.

Rosamond was already deeply afflicted at parting with her sister—that sister from whom she had never been separated until now:—but she was doomed to experience additional sources of grief in the harsh manner and alarming agitation of her father.

At length, unable any longer to endure the state of suspense and uncertainty in which she was suddenly plunged concerning him, she rose from her seat—advanced timidly towards him—and, throwing one of her snowy arms over his shoulder, murmured in a plaintive tone, "Father—dearest father, what dreadful cause of sorrow oppresses you now? Are you fearful that Adelais will not be happy—that Clarence will not always be good and kind to her? Oh! yes, dearest father—I am sure he will——"

"I am not thinking of the daughter who is gone," exclaimed Mr. Torrens, suddenly interrupting the maiden, and speaking in a tone no longer harsh, but positively wild with despair: "my thoughts are intent on the daughter who is left behind!"

"Am I a source of affliction to you, father?" asked Rosamond, contemplating her sire in so plaintive, melancholy, and yet tender a manner that his vile heart was for a moment touched, and he felt ready to throw himself at her feet and implore her pardon for the ill he meditated towards her. "Tell me, my beloved parent," she said, "have I given you offence in any way—by word or deed? Oh! if I have, bitter will be the tears that I shall shed; and sincerely—most sincerely shall I beseech your forgiveness."

"No, Rosamond," said Mr. Torrens, crushing the better feelings of his soul as he thought of the ruin that would envelop him were he to retract his engagements with the baronet: "you have not offended me—and I believe I spoke harshly to you just now without a cause. But let us talk no more on that subject. Compose yourself—wipe away those tears. I shall now retire to my study—for I have letters of importance to write."

But at that moment the well-known knock of the postman resounded through the house; and almost immediately afterwards a servant entered the room, handed a letter to Rosamond, and then withdrew.

"A note for *me*!" exclaimed the young lady, in surprise, while Mr. Torrens' blood ran cold and his brain whirled. "Oh! it is from dear Mrs. Slingsby—I recognise the handwriting."

And hastily opening it, she glanced over the contents.

Mr. Torrens was about to leave the room, as if the arrival of the letter were a matter of perfect indifference to him.

"One moment, dear father," said Rosamond, detaining him by the arm: "you must read this beautiful letter which Mrs. Slingsby has written to me; and though I cannot think of accepting the kind invitation which it conveys——"

"What does Mrs. Slingsby say in her letter, then?" demanded Mr. Torrens, all his ill-humour returning as this further step in the hideous plot re-awakened his most poignant reflections; "what does she say, that you speak in such enthusiastic terms of a mere letter?"

Rosamond placed the note in his hand; and Mr. Torrens, turning aside towards the window, read the contents, as follow:—

"It has greatly distressed me, my beloved young friend, to have been unable to attend at the solemnization of the holy and yet deeply affecting ceremony, which, by the time this reaches you, will have united my excellent nephew and your sweet sister. But it has pleased the Almighty, in his inscrutable wisdom, to afflict me with a severe rheumatism at this time, as I assured you in a previous note; and although I sincerely hope that, by the blessing of that all-wise Being and the aid of the lotion which Dr. Wagtail has sent me, I shall be well in a few days, yet I am compelled for the present to remain within the house. It is my most sincere and heart-felt hope that your dear sister and my beloved nephew may experience all that happiness which the Omnipotent may deign to bestow upon his elect. One circumstance must essentially tend to smooth down those mundane asperities which, alas! they will have to encounter in the rough path of life; and that is the religious faith with which they are both imbued. For myself, I can safely declare that if it were not for the consolations which the Holy Bible imparts to all who study its divine doctrines, and for the solace afforded me by a few kind friends (amongst whom I must include that most choice vessel of the Lord, Sir Henry Courtenay), I know not how I should bear up against the grievous pains wherewith it has pleased the Most High to afflict me, and which have just passed from the right foot into the left. Doubtless it is for my eternal welfare, in a better world, that I am thus chastened in this; although Dr. Wagtail, with a levity unbecoming a professional man of his age and standing, declares that if I keep my feet well swathed in flannel and take mustard baths on going to bed, I shall triumph over the ailment. But, oh! my dearest young friend, what is flannel without the blessing of heaven? what is mustard without the aid of the Most High? I am very lonely, sweet Rosamond; and I am fearful that you must miss your dear sister much. I know that Mr. Torrens' occupations take him much from home; and thus you cannot always enjoy the presence and the consolations of your excellent father, whom, I regret to say, I only as yet know by good report, but whose hand I hope to press some day in friendship. Will you, my love, come and pass a week or two with me? It will be a perfect charity on your part; and I am convinced also that change of scene will cheer your spirits. Come to me, my dearest Rosamond, early tomorrow morning (God willing)—if your good kind father can spare you.

"Ever your sincere and attached friend,

"MARTHA SLINGSBY."

The vile hypocrisy which characterised this letter enhanced, if possible, the blackness of that crime towards the consummation of which it was so material a step; and Mr. Torrens stood gazing upon the document until all its characters seemed to move and agitate on the surface of the paper like a legion of hideous reptiles swarming together.

But at length mastering his horribly painful emotions, he turned towards his daughter, saying, "And wherefore, Rosamond, should you not accept an invitation as kind as it is considerate?"

"Oh! my dear father," exclaimed the maiden, "I could not think of leaving you at a time when you have just lost the society of one of your children. Moreover, I perceive that you are not entirely happy—I fear that those recent embarrassments——"

"Speak not of them, Rosamond," interrupted Mr. Torrens sternly; for so great was his pride, that he could not endure the idea of his own daughters being acquainted with his late pecuniary difficulties. "To return to the subject of that letter," he added, after a few moments' pause, "I think you cannot do better than accept the invitation:—indeed, it would appear unkind were you to refuse it. Mrs. Slingsby is suffering from indisposition—and she is evidently anxious to have a companion. Therefore, Rosamond, I must beg you to commence your preparations for the visit."

The young lady urged various remonstrances against this resolution; but her father over-ruled them all—and it was accordingly determined at length that she should repair to Old Burlington Street on the following morning.

But when the morning came, and the vehicle which was to convey her to London drove up to the door, how appalling were the feelings which agitated,—nay, absolutely raged in the breast of Mr. Torrens!

Acute—intensely acute was the pain which he endured in endeavouring to subdue those emotions,—or rather in composing his features in such a way that his countenance might not indicate the awful warring that disturbed his soul.

With streaming eyes did Rosamond take leave of her father; and as she stepped into the chaise, a presentiment of evil flashed across her imagination.

But she was young—naturally inclined to look upon the bright side of things—and too inexperienced to know much of the dreadful pit-falls which the artifice of man has hollowed in the pathways of the moral world. Her misgiving was therefore forgotten almost as soon as it was entertained; and she was in comparatively good spirits—though still affected by her recent separation from her sister—when she alighted at the door of Mrs. Slingsby's residence in Old Burlington Street.

> 29. Represented as the Marquis of Holmesford in the First Series of "THE MYSTERIES OF LONDON."

CHAPTER LXVIII.
DR. WAGTAIL.—ROSAMOND TORRENS.

Rosamond Torrens found the pious lady reclining on a sofa, and so profoundly absorbed—at all events, apparently so—in the perusal of a chapter in the New Testament, that she did not immediately look up when the drawing-room door opened to give the young maiden admission.

"Ah! my dearest girl—is it indeed you?" at length said Mrs. Slingsby in a dolorous tone of voice, as she laid aside the sacred volume. "Come and embrace me, sweet Rosamond."

"I hope you are better to-day, my dear madam," was the sincere observation made by the intended victim of a damnable plot, as she pressed her pure lips to Mrs. Slingsby's polluted brow.

"Heaven blessed me with a good night's rest, my love," returned the pious lady; "and Dr. Wagtail would insist upon my taking a little warm brandy-and-water—although, as you well know, I loathe alcoholic liquor, which I do not consider to be a '*good creature of God*,' nor '*fitted for our use*.' But, as a medicine, Rosamond—and when accompanied by urgent prayer—it is beneficial. And now tell me, sweet girl, how passed off the bridal ceremony? Was the conduct of my nephew becoming and proper? I could scarcely suppose otherwise—seeing that for years he has been benefited by the advice and example which it has been my happy lot to afford him. And Adelais—was she much affected, my love?"

Rosamond described the particulars of the wedding; and Mrs. Slingsby was in the midst of some very comforting remarks thereon, when the door opened and Dr. Wagtail made his appearance.

This gentleman was a short, fat, important-looking personage—with a powdered head and a pig-tail—delighting, too, in small-clothes and black gaiters, and carrying a thick bamboo cane, the gold head of which he invariably applied to his nose when he wanted to appear more than usually solemn. He enjoyed a large practice, and was yet miserably ignorant of the medical art. What, then, was the secret of his success? We will explain the mystery.

His father was a very wealthy man, and paid a premium of £800 to apprentice the subject of this sketch to the house-surgeon of one of the great metropolitan hospitals. But young Wagtail, though cunning and crafty enough, was a wretched dolt, and only succeeded in passing his examination by dint of the most extraordinary cramming. By these means, however, he became a Member of the Royal College of Surgeons, and set up in business for himself. The house-surgeon of the hospital soon after hinted to him that he intended to resign; and Mr. Wagtail senior, on hearing this private communication made to his son, immediately sent the house-surgeon a five-hundred pound note in a gold snuff-box, "as a token of esteem for his high character and of admiration for his splendid talents." This was intelligible enough. The house-surgeon immediately began to canvass his friends on behalf of young Wagtail as his successor; and when the resignation of the said house-surgeon was publicly announced, the majority of the persons who had a right to vote were already enlisted in the cause of Mr. Wagtail. Several of the most eminent surgeons became candidates for the vacancy; but their abilities stood no chance when weighed against Mr. Wagtail's interest—and Mr. Wagtail was accordingly elected. He thus jumped into renown and handsome emolument almost as soon as he entered the profession; and things went on smoothly enough for three or four years, until he one morning took it into his head to cut off a man's leg, when amputation was positively unnecessary. A disturbance ensued—the thing got into the newspapers—and Mr. Wagtail employed three poor authors constantly, for six months, at half-a-crown a day each, to get up the pamphlets which he issued in his defence. He so inundated the British public with his printed statements that he literally bullied or persuaded the majority into a belief that he was right after all; and then, with becoming indignation, he threw up his berth at the hospital—took a magnificent house at the West End—got his doctor's diploma at the same time—and announced through the medium of the *Morning Post, Morning Herald*, and *St. James's Chronicle*, that "Dr. Wagtail might be consulted daily, at his residence, from 2 till 7." His father died soon afterwards, leaving him a handsome fortune; and as the doctor, when the time of mourning (which he cut as short as possible) had expired, began to give splendid entertainments, his dinners procured him friends, and his friends procured him patients. In fact, he eventually rose so high in public estimation at the West End, that he was quoted as the rival of the celebrated Dr. Lascelles;—but wise men shook their heads, as much as to intimate that Dr. Lascelles had more medical knowledge in his little finger than Dr. Wagtail possessed in his entire form. But then Dr. Wagtail was so important-looking, and had such a knowing and mysterious way with him;—and he never insulted his patients, as Dr. Lascelles sometimes did, by telling them that they had nothing the matter with them, but were mere hypochondriacs. On the contrary, he would gratify their fancies by prescribing pills and draughts till he made them ill in reality; and then he had some little trouble in curing them again. But as he administered plenty of medicine—shook his head a great many times even when ordering a foot-bath or a bread poultice—and dropped mysterious hints about its being very fortunate that he was called in just at that precise moment, or else there would have been no answering for the consequences,—as he did all this, and was particularly liberal to nurses, valets, and ladies-maids, he had worked his way up to a degree of eminence which real talent, legitimately exercised, struggled fruitlessly in ninety-nine cases out of a hundred to arrive at.

Such was the physician who now entered the drawing-room where Mrs. Slingsby was reclining on the sofa with Rosamond seated near her.

Bowing with important condescension to Miss Torrens, the doctor quietly took the chair which she vacated, because it was close to his patient.

Rosamond was about to quit the room, when Mrs. Slingsby desired her to remain, adding, "Dr. Wagtail does not require your absence, my love: there is nothing so very important in my case—is there, doctor?"

"Important, my dear madam, is not precisely the word," returned the physician, with his gold-headed cane to his nose; "inasmuch as your ailment *is* important—as all ailments are, when, though trivial in themselves, they *may* lead to dangerous consequences. But how are we to-day, my dear madam? how is the pain in our legs? did we suffer much last night? or did we feel a *leetle* easier?"

"Yes, doctor—thank you," replied the sufferer, who had nothing at all the matter with her, but who had merely simulated indisposition as an excuse for absenting herself from the bridal: "I passed a better night—by the blessing of heaven!"

"Well—come—and so we are getting on nicely, eh?" observed the doctor. "And what did we take for supper last evening?"

"A little gruel, doctor—as you ordered," answered Mrs. Slingsby, in a lachrymose tone—which was really natural enough, seeing that she could have eaten a roast fowl instead of the farinaceous slop.

"And did we take a very *leetle* brandy-and-water hot?" asked Dr. Wagtail, in a most insinuating voice, as much as to say that he knew very well how revolting such a beverage must have been to Mrs. Slingsby; although, in his heart, he had recommended it simply because experience had taught him that ladies of a certain age did *not* object to a small dose of cognac:—"did we take a *leetle* brandy-and-water?"

"I did so far follow your advice, doctor," replied Mrs. Slingsby; "but I hope I am not to continue it?"

"Indeed but we must though, my dear madam," exclaimed the physician, shaking his head most solemnly and with all the air of a man enforcing the necessity of swallowing a nauseous draught:—"indeed but we must though,—and a trifle stronger, too—a mere trifle;—but stronger it must be, or I really cannot answer for the consequences."

And here he looked at Miss Torrens, as much as to imply that Mrs. Slingsby's life would perhaps be endangered if his advice were not punctually and accurately followed.

"Well, doctor," said the suffering lady, in a more doleful tone than ever, "if it must be stronger, it shall be: but pray make a cure of me (God willing) as soon as possible, so that I may renounce that vile alcoholic beverage."

"We must have patience, my dear madam—great patience," said Dr. Wagtail with increasing solemnity, as he rubbed his nose against the gold-headed cane. "Indeed, so long as this nasty rheumatism hangs about us, we must keep to the brandy-and-water."

The physician knew very well that his words would cause the rheumatism to hang about the excellent lady for a considerable time,—indeed that she would be in no hurry to get rid of it, so long as he proscribed "the vile alcoholic beverage";—and he foresaw a goodly number of fees resulting from the judicious mode which he thus adopted of treating an ailment that did not exist.

"And now, my dear madam," he continued, "how is our tongue! Ah—not quite right yet! And how are our pulse?"

Then, as the case was pronounced to be important, the doctor lugged out an enormous gold stop-watch, and bent over it with a mysterious and even ominous expression of countenance as he felt the patient's pulse.

"Well, doctor—what do you think?" asked Mrs. Slingsby, looking as anxious and miserable as if she had been in the dock at the Old Bailey, about to hear the verdict of the jury.

"We must take care of ourselves, my dear madam—we must take care of ourselves," said the physician, shaking his head: "our pulse is not quite as it ought to be. How is our appetite? do we think we could manage a little slice of boiled fowl to-day? But we *must* try, my dear madam—we *must* try; and we must take a glass or two of wine—Port wine, of a good body. We must not reduce ourselves too low. And this evening, for supper, we must take gruel again—and the brandy-and-water as an indispensable medicine, afterwards."

"I will endeavour to follow your advice, my dear sir," said Mrs. Slingsby; "though heaven knows that the idea of the old Port wine at dinner——"

"Well, my dear madam—I know it is repugnant to you—very repugnant," interrupted the physician in a calmly remonstrative tone: "but the world cannot afford to lose so excellent a member of society as yourself. Consider your friends, my dear madam—exert yourself on their account. Triumph over these little aversions to wine and brandy—and take them as medicines, in which sense do I offer them. And now, my dear madam, I will write you out a *leetle* prescription. You had better get it made up as usual at Timmins and Jakes, in Bond Street. I have no interest in recommending them, you know—not the slightest;—but I am sure their drugs *are* good, my dear madam."

Which was as much as to imply that the drugs of other chemists were *not* good; and we may here observe that the disinterested physician merely received a thousand a-year from Messrs. Timmins and Jakes for recommending all his patients to send prescriptions to their shop.

The doctor wrote some professional hieroglyphics upon a slip of paper, and scrawled at the bottom something which would have represented the name of Snooks, or Brown, or Thompson, quite as well as it did Wagtail.

He then rose, received from Mrs. Slingsby his fee neatly wrapped up in a piece of tissue paper, and took his departure, holding his stick to his nose all the way down stairs.

The afternoon passed away somewhat tediously for Rosamond; and when dinner was placed on the table, Mrs. Slingsby contrived to do honour to the boiled fowls; and though she held forth at considerable length upon her abhorrence for Port wine, she managed to swallow four glasses of the generous juice in a manner which Rosamond considered highly creditable to her moral courage, seeing how much she detested it.

Shortly after dinner, which was served in the drawing-room, Sir Henry Courtenay made his appearance.

The baronet's eyes sparkled with delight when he beheld his intended victim at the pious lady's abode, and looking more sweetly beautiful—more divinely interesting than she had ever yet appeared to him. The blood boiled in his veins, as his glances rapidly swept her slight but symmetrical form, and as he thought within the recesses of his own iniquitous heart, "This night thou shall become mine!"

It will be remembered that, during the last few days of her previous sojourn at Mrs. Slingsby's abode, Rosamond had been taught to form a very high opinion of the baronet; but the pious lady had not gone so far as to instil any voluptuous sentiment into the mind of the young maiden. Thus, when the baronet, on the occasion of his visits to Torrens Cottage, had addressed her in a somewhat equivocal manner, she did not comprehend him; and hence Sir Henry's reproach against Mrs. Slingsby, "that she was but an indifferent tutoress."

Still Rosamond was predisposed to admire the baronet's character, as it had been represented to her by Mrs. Slingsby; and she was by no means sorry that he had arrived to vary the monotony of the evening.

He exerted all his conversational powers to please her; and she could not conceal from herself the delight which she experienced in listening to those outpourings of a well-informed mind and a richly cultivated intellect.

The supper-hour arrived while she thought the evening was still young—so rapidly had the time passed away. Mrs. Slingsby partook of her gruel with as good a grace as she could possibly assume; but she ever and anon cast a longing glance towards the more substantial and succulent viands spread upon the board. The brandy-and-water was, however, a consolation; and this the baronet, who mixed for her, made as strong as she could wish, and much stronger than Dr. Wagtail, were he really sincere in his advice, could have possibly intended her to take it.

Shortly before eleven the baronet rose and took his departure, Mrs. Slingsby ringing the drawing-room bell for the servant, to open the front door for him, with a ceremony the object of which was to let every one in the house know that he had departed, and the hour at which he went—*in case of any exposure following the dread plot now in progress*!

Mrs. Slingsby and Rosamond then remained in conversation for a few minutes, the topic being the excellent qualities of Sir Henry Courtenay.

"Rosamond, my love," at length said Mrs. Slingsby, "before you retire to your own chamber, have the kindness to lock the side-board in the drawing-room and bring me the keys. For really servants are so neglectful——"

The beautiful girl departed with the alacrity of an obliging disposition to execute this little commission:—but the moment she had quitted the drawing-room, Mrs. Slingsby emptied the dark contents of a very small phial into the only half-finished glass of Port wine which Rosamond had left.

The infamous woman then resumed her recumbent position upon the sofa; and—oh! the abominable mockery!—appeared to be occupied with her Bible, when the artless, innocent, and unsuspecting maiden returned to the room.

"Here are the keys, my dear madam," said Rosamond; "and every thing is safe down stairs. I shall now wish you a good night's rest."

"Finish your wine, my love, before you retire," observed Mrs. Slingsby, in a softly persuasive tone: "I am not mean, but you know that I am averse to waste in any shape."

Rosamond blushed at having merited the species of reproach thus conveyed, and drank the contents of her wine-glass: then, as it struck her that the flavour of the *wine* was somewhat less pleasant than it should be—but without attaching the least importance to the idea, and forgetting it altogether a moment afterwards—she ate a small piece of bread to take away the disagreeable taste.

"Good night, my dear madam," said the maiden, bending over the pious lady and kissing her cheek.

"Good night, Rosamond my love," returned Mrs. Slingsby. "I shall remain here for a quarter of an hour to perform my usual devotional exercises; and then I shall retire to my own chamber."

Rosamond withdrew, and sped to the room prepared for her.

She felt wearied, and made haste to lay aside her garments and arrange her hair. But in the midst of her occupation a sensation of deep drowsiness came over her; and she was glad to step into bed as speedily as possible—omitting, for perhaps the first time since her childhood, to kneel down first in prayer.

A minute afterwards—and she was sound asleep.

Three persons at that precise period had their minds filled with the image of Rosamond!

In the solitude of his chamber, at his lonely cottage, Mr. Torrens endured the torments of the damned,—mental torments, indescribably more severe than the most agonising of physical pain could possibly be.

Mercenary—selfish—cold—callous as he was, he could not stifle the still small voice of conscience, which told him he had done a flagrant—a vile—an awful deed, which would fill his cup with a bitterness, that no earthly pleasure, no mundane reward, could possibly counteract or change.

He felt that he was a monster in human shape: he was afraid to catch a glimpse of his own countenance in the glass—for when he once surveyed it rapidly, its workings were horrible to behold!

To sell his daughter for the filthy lucre which had tempted him!—It was horrible—atrocious!

And then,—then, at that very moment while he was pacing his chamber, the fell deed might be in consummation!

He walked to the window:—how black was the night—how menacing were those clouds that seemed laden with storm!

He started back with a look of horrified amazement: was there not some dreadful shape in the air?—assumed not those clouds the form of a tremendous being, with a countenance of lowering vengeance and awful threatenings?

No: it was fancy—and yet the temporary creation of that fancy was dreadful to behold,—as cloud piled on cloud, for an instant wore the semblance of a supernal, moving phantom, black and menacing with impending storm!

The guilty, wretched father clenched his fists—gnashed his teeth—knit his brows—and compressed his lips together to prevent his voice from suddenly shrieking forth in accents of heart-felt agony.

Having remained for about twenty minutes in the drawing-room, Mrs. Slingsby summoned her maid, by whose assistance she gained her own chamber—although she in reality no more required such aid than did the servant who afforded it.

The maid helped her mistress to divest herself of her clothing, and then retired.

And now Mrs. Slingsby, instead of seeking her couch—that couch which had been the scene of guilty pleasure, when Jacob Smith had lain concealed beneath it—seated herself in a large arm-chair, to wait until the house was quiet.

"I could wish that any thing rather than *this* was to take place!" she murmured two or three times. "Heaven only knows what will be the end of it! But Henry appears so confident of being able to appease her—so certain of reducing her even to the position of one who beseeches instead of menacing—that I am inclined to suppose he has well weighed all the difficulties of his task. At all events he has promised to spare me—to make me appear innocent! But will Rosamond be so deceived? No—no: she will view me with suspicion—her eyes will gradually open——And yet," thought Mrs. Slingsby, suddenly interrupting the current of her reflections, "she will be so completely in my power—at my mercy,—her honour will be in my hands—her reputation will depend on my secresy——Oh! how I wish this night was past!" she cried passionately: "for the deed which is to mark it, is horrible to contemplate!"

And the third person whose mind was so full of the image of Rosamond Torrens, at the time when she lay down—beauteous and chaste virgin as she was—to rest beneath the roof of one whom, in her ingenuous confidence, she believed to be a pattern of female excellence and virtue,—that third person was Sir Henry Courtenay.

The baronet, on quitting Mrs. Slingsby's house, had returned home in his carriage, which was at the door ready to convey him thither; and, on entering his abode, he had immediately repaired to his own chamber.

Dispensing with the services of his valet, he sate down to pass away in voluptuous reflections the hour that must elapse before he could set forth again, to return to the dwelling of his mistress in Old Burlington Street.

He was of that age when the physical powers somewhat require the stimulus of an ardent and excited imagination; and he now began to gloat in anticipation of the joys which he promised himself to experience in the ruin of the hapless Rosamond.

Remorse and compunction touched him not:—if he thought of the grief that was to ensue, it was merely because he re-arranged in his head all the details of the eloquent representations he must make to soothe that woe! Besides, his licentious imagination represented to him the beauteous Rosamond, more beauteous in her tears; and he had worked himself up to a pitch of such maddening desire, by the time it was necessary for him to sally forth, that he would not have resigned his expected prize—no, not if the ruin and disgrace of ten thousand families were to ensue.

Leaving his house stealthily, by a means of egress at the back, Sir Henry Courtenay hastened back to Old Burlington Street.

A few moments after he had reached the immediate vicinity of Mrs. Slingsby's residence, the clocks of the West-end churches proclaimed the hour of one.

That was the appointed time for his admission into the house.

Nor had he long to wait—for the front-door was soon opened noiselessly and cautiously, and by a person bearing no light: but the voice which whispered, "Is it you, Henry?" was that of Mrs. Slingsby.

And noiselessly and cautiously, too, she led the way up stairs, he having previously put off his shoes, which he carried in his hand.

At the door of her own bed-room, Mrs. Slingsby made the baronet pause for an instant while she procured a taper; and as she handed it to him, and the light revealed their countenances to each other, they shrank from each other's gaze,—for human nature at that instant asserted its rightful empire, and while the woman recoiled with horror from the man who was about to commit an awful outrage on a member of her own sex, the man felt a momentary loathing for the woman who was aiding and abetting in the work of this foul night.

Mrs. Slingsby hurriedly pointed towards a door at the bottom of the passage, in the most retired part of the house; and she then retreated into her own room, a prey to feelings which a convict in Newgate need not have envied.

Meantime Sir Henry Courtenay had passed on to the extremity of the passage: and now his hand is upon the door.

He opens that door—he enters—he closes and fastens it behind him.

Advancing towards the bed, he holds the taper so that its light falls upon the pillow; and the soft, mellow lustre of the wax-candle reveals a charming countenance, with flushed cheeks and with rosy lips apart.

For Rosamond's slumber is uneasy, though profound,—doubtless the effect of laudanum upon the nerves of one so entirely unaccustomed to its use, and who has imbibed so large a dose!

And one of those flushed cheeks reposed on a round, full, and naked arm, like a red rose-leaf upon Parian marble;—and the other arm was thrown over the bed-clothes, which had been somewhat disturbed by the uneasiness of the maiden's sleep, and left exposed the polished shoulders of dazzling whiteness and the bosom of virgin rotundity and plumpness.

Oh! what a charming picture was thus revealed to the eyes of the lustful miscreant, whose desires were increased to almost raging madness by the spectacle!

He placed the taper on the mantel, and hastened to lay aside—nay, almost to tear off his garments; and in less than three minutes he was lying by the side of the young virgin.

But scarcely had his rude hand invaded the treasures of her bosom, when she awoke with a faint scream and a sudden start—the result of some disagreeable dream; and then the baronet clasped her with all the fury of licentiousness in his arms.

A few moments elapsed ere she was aroused sufficiently to comprehend the dreadful—the horrible truth; but when the torpor produced by the laudanum had somewhat subsided, she became a prey to the most frightful alarms, produced by the conviction that some one had invaded the sanctity of her couch—and a glance showed her the features of Sir Henry Courtenay.

She would have given vent to her anguish and her horror in appalling screams; but he placed his hand over her mouth—he muttered fearful menaces in her ears—he called God to witness his resolution to possess her; and, though she became bewildered and dismayed—though her brain whirled, and her reason seemed to be deserting her—yet she battled with the ravisher—she maintained a desperate, an awful struggle,—and so unrelenting was the violence which he used to restrain and overpower her, that murder would have perhaps been done, had not the poor victim become insensible in his arms!

And then her ruin was accomplished.

Oh! ye clouds, laden with storm, why gave ye not forth your forked lightnings—why sent ye not abroad your thunders—to smite the hero of that foul night?

For, oh! while the father was still pacing his chamber in his own dwelling, the hell that raged in his breast defying all hope of slumber,—while, too, the no less infamous woman who had pandered to this work of ruin, was trembling rather for what might be the consequences than for the deed itself,—there, in that room to which Rosamond had retired in the pride of innocence and chastity—there was she despoiled—there became she the victim of the miscreant ravisher!

"Release me—let me depart—let me fly!" implored the wretched Rosamond, in a tone so subdued with anguish and with weakness, that there was no fear of its alarming the house.

"Rosamond, hear me—I beseech you!" exclaimed the baronet, as he held her by the arms in such a manner that she could not escape from the bed. "Hear reason, if you can! What would you do? Whither can you fly? The past cannot be recalled; but there is much to think of for the future. The occurrence of this night is a secret known only to yourself and to me: your dishonour need never transpire to the world?"

"Oh! my God! my God!" murmured Rosamond, in a tone of ineffable anguish: "my dishonour!—my dishonour!"

And she repeated the word—the terrible word, in so thrilling, penetrating, and yet subdued a voice, that even the remorseless baronet was for a moment touched.

"O Rosamond!" he said, in a hurried and excited manner; "do not repine so bitterly for what cannot be recalled! Think how I love you, dearest one—remember that my passion for thee amounted to a frenzy,—and it was in frenzy that I acted thus. Instead of loathing me——"

"No—no, I do not loathe you!—my God—no!" said Rosamond, becoming the least degree calmer. "I now perceive how dependant I am upon you—how necessary it is that your love should console me! But my dear father—should he learn his daughter's disgrace—Oh! heaven, have mercy upon me!"

And she once more burst into an agony of weeping.

"Rosamond—Rosamond, compose yourself!" said Sir Henry Courtenay, with that tenderness of tone which he so well knew how to assume, and on which he had so much relied as an emollient means to be applied to soothe the grief of the victim of his desires. "Shall I repeat how deeply I love thee—how ardently I adore thee? Oh! my best beloved, do not thus abandon yourself to the wildness of a vain and useless despair!"

"But have I not been made the victim of a dreadful conspiracy?" said Rosamond; "was I not inveigled hither to be ruined? Oh! I will fly—I will fly—I will hasten home to my father—I will throw myself at his feet and tell him all—and he will pardon and avenge me!"

Again she endeavoured to spring from the bed; but Sir Henry Courtenay held her back—and, through sheer exhaustion, she fell weeping on his breast.

Then the task of consoling her—or rather of somewhat moderating the excess of her anguish, became more easy; and the baronet reasoned and vowed—argued and protested—and pleaded for pardon so touchingly and with so much apparent contrition, that Rosamond began to believe there was indeed some extenuation for one who loved her so passionately, and who had been led away by the frenzy of those feelings of which she was the object.

"Oh! why, my adored girl, are you so beautiful?" murmured the baronet: "rather attribute my crime to the influence—the irresistible influence of thine own charms, than to any deeply-seated wickedness on my part! I should have become raving mad for love of thee, had not the fury of my passion hurried me on to that point, when, reckless of all consequences, I had recourse to this stratagem. I know that my conduct is horrible—that it is vile and base in the extreme;—but I sue to thee for pardon,—I, so proud and haughty—yes, I implore thee, my darling Rosamond, to forgive me! And, oh! if all the remainder of my life, devoted to thine happiness, can atone for my turpitude of this night,—if the most unwearied affection—the most tender love can impart consolation to thee, my angel—then wilt thou yet smile upon me, and the past shall be forgotten."

"Then you will make me your wife?" murmured Rosamond.

"Yes, sweet girl—thou shall become mine—mine in the sight of heaven!" said the baronet, who would have made any pledge at that moment, in order to solace and reassure his victim.

"But wherefore not have told me that you loved me—why not have demanded my hand of my father, and have married me as Clarence did my sister?" asked Rosamond, a doubt striking to her heart's core.

"I said many things to make you understand how dear you were to me," answered the baronet; "and you did not comprehend my meaning. Remember you not that, one day when I called at your father's house, I met you alone in the parlour; and as you offered me your hand, I said, '*Happy will the man be on whom this fair hand shall be bestowed!*' And on another occasion, when you and I were again alone together, the conversation happened to turn upon death, and I remarked that '*it was dreadful to contemplate the idea of dying, but that I could lay down my life to serve you!*'"

"Oh! yes—I remember now!" murmured Rosamond. "And I even thought of those observations after you were gone; and they seemed to afford me pleasure to ponder upon them."

"Do you not now understand, then, dearest angel, how disappointment at finding that I was not at once comprehended, drove me to despair?" said the wily baronet. "Can you not pardon me, if—thus driven to desperation—I vowed to possess you—to make you mine—so that you would be compelled to accept my hand, as you already reigned undisputed mistress over my heart?"

"If you will fulfil your solemn promise to make me your wife, I shall yet be happy—and this dreadful night may be forgotten. No—not forgotten," continued Rosamond, hastily; "because the memory is immortal for such hours of anguish as these! But you will, at least, make all the atonement that lies in your power—and I may yet look the world in the face!"

"Rosamond—my sweet Rosamond, within a month from this time thou shalt be my wife!" said the baronet.

"With that assurance I must console myself," returned the still weeping girl. "And now, I adjure you—by the solemnity of the pledge which you have made me, and which I believe—I implore, you, by that love which you declare you entertain for me,—to leave me this moment!"

The baronet was fearful of reviving the storm of grief which his perfidious language had succeeded in quelling; and he accordingly rose and resumed his apparel.

Not a word was spoken during the two or three minutes which thus passed; and when Sir Henry was once more dressed, he approached the ruined girl, saying, "One embrace, Rosamond, and I leave thee till the morrow."

"One word ere we part," she said, in a hurried and almost hollow tone: "does Mrs. Slingsby know——But surely, surely, she could not have lent herself——And yet," added the bewildered Rosamond, a second time interrupting herself abruptly, "how could you have gained admittance into the house, and in the middle of the night? Oh! heavens, the most fearful suspicions——"

"Calm yourself—compose your feelings, dearest," said the baronet. "Mrs. Slingsby knows that I adore you—is aware that I love you: because the long acquaintance—indeed the sincere friendship which exists between us—prevents me from having any secrets unrevealed to her. But wrong not that amiable, that excellent, that pure-minded woman, by unjust suspicions! I entered her house like a thief—by means of a window accidentally left unfastened; and in the same manner must I escape now. Not for worlds would I have her suspect the occurrences of this night! Therefore, my angel, compose yourself, so that your appearance may not engender any suspicion in her mind when you meet at the breakfast table in the morning:—for, remember, my Rosamond, you will shortly become my wife,—and then, as you yourself observed, you will be enabled to look the world in the face!"

"And until that moment comes," said Rosamond, with a deep sob, "I shall blush and be compelled to cast down my eyes in the presence of every one who knows me. Oh! my God—what cruel fears—what dread thoughts oppress me! And my sister is doubtless so happy! Heaven grant that she may never know the anguish which wrings my heart at this moment!"

"By every thing sacred, I conjure you to compose yourself, Rosamond," exclaimed Sir Henry Courtenay, now afraid to leave her, lest in the dread excitement which was reanimating her, she might lay violent hands upon herself:—for, by the light of the taper, he could perceive that her countenance was ashy pale, and that while she was uttering those last words relative to her sister, her features were suddenly distorted by an expression of intense mental agony.

"Compose myself! Oh! how can I compose myself?" she exclaimed; and then she burst into a torrent of tears.

The baronet knew the female heart too well not to allow her to give full vent to the pearly tide of anguish; and three or four minutes elapsed,—he standing by the bed, contemplating with but little emotion, unless, indeed, it were of lust, the beauteous being whom he had so ruthlessly ruined,—and she burying her face in her hands, the tears trickling between her fingers, and her agonising sobs alone breaking the solemn stillness of the night.

Sir Henry Courtenay waited until the violence of this renewed outburst of ineffable woe had somewhat abated; and then he again endeavoured to console the unhappy victim of his foul desires—the ruined sufferer by his hellish turpitude!

And Rosamond had so much need of solace, and was so dependent on hope for the future to enable her to sustain the almost crushing misery of the present, that she threw herself upon his honour—his mercy—his deceitful promises; and she even smiled—but faintly—oh! very faintly—when he again employed his infernal sophistry to prove the deed of that dread night to be the surest testimony to his ardent love.

At length she was sufficiently composed to induce him to take his departure; and, like a vile snake as he was in heart, he crept away from the chamber of the deflowered—the ravished girl.

As he stole thus stealthily along the passage, he observed a light streaming from Mrs. Slingsby's room, the door of which had been purposely left ajar.

He entered, and found his accomplice still up; nor had the abandoned woman felt the least inclination to retire to rest.

For her mind had been a prey to the most terrible alarms, from the moment when the baronet had first set foot in Rosamond's chamber.

"I have succeeded—and she will not proclaim the outrage to the world," said Sir Henry Courtenay, in a low tone. "I have, moreover, kept my word with you, and have made her believe that you are innocent of any share in the proceeding."

Mrs. Slingsby gave no answer, but bit her under lip forcibly—for vile as she herself was, she could hardly prevent herself from exclaiming to her companion, "You are a black-hearted monster!"

Sir Henry did not, however, notice that she was influenced by any emotion hostile to him; or if he did, he cared not to show that he perceived it;—but, wishing his mistress "good night," he quitted the room, and stole out of the house.

CHAPTER LXIX.
MISERY AND VICE.

A week had elapsed since the perpetration of the atrocity described in the preceding chapter.

The scene changes to a miserable garret in one of the foul courts leading out of King Street, St. Giles's.

It was about eight o'clock in the evening; and the rain pattered on the roof and against the little window of the wretched room, which, small as it was, was scarcely lighted by the candle that flickered with the draught gushing in from beneath the door.

On a mean and sordid mattress stretched upon the floor, and with but a thin and torn blanket to cover him, lay a man who was not in reality above five-and-twenty, but who seemed nearly double that age—so ghastly was his countenance, and so attenuated was his form with sickness and want.

Near him a young female—almost a mere girl—was seated on a broken chair. Her apparel was mean, and so scanty that she shivered with the cold; and though the traces of famine and care were plainly visible upon her features, yet they had not carried their ravages so far as to efface the prettiness which naturally characterised the composition of that countenance.

Beautiful she was not, nor ever had been; but good-looking she decidedly was;—and though attired almost in rags, and with an expression of profound misery upon her face, there was something interesting in the appearance of that poor creature.

The reader will remember that, in the earlier chapters of this tale, we introduced him to one of those dens of iniquity called low lodging-houses, in Castle Street, Long Acre; and he will also recollect that a mock marriage took place in that "padding-ken," between a thief, called Josh Pedler, and a poor labourer's daughter, named Matilda Briggs.

The man lying on the mattress in the garret, was Josh Pedler; and the girl sitting near him, was Matilda Briggs.

"Well, now," suddenly exclaimed Pedler, as he raised himself with difficulty to a sitting posture, "what do you say in answer to my last question? are we to die of starvation? or are we to have bread by some means or another?"

Matilda burst into tears, and wrung her hands bitterly.

"Don't sit whimpering there, damn your eyes!" cried the ruffian. "Blubbering won't do no good—and you know that as well as me. Here have I been on my beam-ends, as one may say, for the last three weeks, and unable to go about to pick up a single farthing—the landlord swears he will have some money to-morrow morning—all the things is pawned—and here am I only wanting a little proper nourishment to set me on my legs again; but that I can't get."

"God knows I have starved myself to give you all I could, Josh," said Matilda, her voice broken with frequent and agonising sobs. "When you have asked me if I had kept enough meat or bread for myself, I always answered yes; and I turned my back towards you that you mightn't see how much—or rather how *little* I had kept back. But what can I do? My father and mother are gone back into the country to throw themselves on their parish—I have no friends to apply to—and your's seem unable to assist you at present."

"Something must be done, Tilda," said the man. "We can't starve—we must do any thing rather than that. I am as hungry as the very devil now—and I know that if I had a good steak and some porter, it would put me all right again."

"But, my God! we have not even the means to buy a penny roll!" almost shrieked the young woman. "There isn't a thing left to pawn. I have nothing but this old gown on my back—every thing else has gone—gone!" she added hysterically, as she threw a wild glance around the naked and dismantled garret. "How cold it is, too! What can we do? what can we do?"

And she rocked herself to and fro in a manner denoting an utter despair.

"You keep asking what can be done," said Josh Pedler, brutally, "and yet you know all the time that there's only one thing to be done, and that it must come to *that* at last."

Matilda started, and turned a glance of horrified amazement upon her companion.

"Well—so I suppose you understand what I mean," continued the ruffian; "and, therefore, there's no use in gammoning about it no longer. We're starving, and there's the rent to pay: that's one side of the question. You're a good-looking young o'oman, and can do as other vimen do: that's t'other side of the question."

"Oh! Josh—and would you have me become a prostitute?" shrieked Matilda, in a tone of mingled horror and reproach.

"Come—none of your nonsense, my lady," said Josh Pedler; "or I shall precious soon know how to settle your hash. Either go and earn some tin, or cut your lucky altogether. If I starve, I'll starve by myself——"

"My God! I will not abandon you!" murmured the unhappy young creature, terrified by this menace of separation from one to whom she had grown greatly attached. "No—I cannot—I will not leave you, Josh: and yet——"

"Let's have no more of this humbug, Tilda!" exclaimed the man, brutally. "Leave off whimpering—or, ill as I am, I'll give you something worth crying for. Come, put on your bonnet and tramp; or, by hell——"

"Oh! you could not—you would not do me a mischief!" she cried, clasping her hands together. "And if I obey you now, in what you have ordered me to do, shall you not hate and detest me ever afterwards?"

"Not a bit of it," returned Josh Pedler, softening a little as he perceived that his point was already well nigh gained: for the poor young woman found powerful incentives to yield to the commands of the ruffian—she herself being almost famished. "Not a bit of it!" he repeated. "You ought to have turned out when I was first taken ill; and then if I'd had common necessaries I should have got well by this time. So be a good girl, and see if you can't bring back something good to eat and drink, and a trifle to pay the landlord."

With a bursting heart, Matilda rose from her seat, and put on her bonnet and her scanty shawl—a poor rag which the pawnbroker had refused to advance a single penny upon.

"Give us a kiss afore you go, old gal," said Josh Pedler, by way of affording her some encouragement to begin the frightful course of prostitution to which he strove to urge her.

She bent down, and pressed her lips upon his forehead, murmuring, "Are you sure that you will not loathe me *afterwards*?"

"Don't have any more of that gammon, Tilda," he cried; "but cut along—or else I shall be tempted to bite a piece out of your face, I'm so thundering hungry."

Matilda shuddered from head to foot, and rushed from the room.

As she was about to quit the house, a door in the passage opened, and a stout ill-looking fellow, without a coat, and smoking a short pipe, came forth, exclaiming, "Ah! I know'd it was you by your sneaking step. Now I tell you what it is, Mrs. Pedler—if so be I don't have my rent, or a good part on't to-night, you and your man must tramp before I shuts up. I've got people as will be glad to have a airy and comfortable room like your'n and as will pay; leastways I'll get rid of *you*."

Matilda stayed to hear no more, but rushed wildly from the house, the threat of the landlord ringing like the knell of hope in her ears.

She observed not which direction she was pursuing;—she saw not the passengers who jostled her on either side:—her eyes were open—and yet the surrounding and the passing objects formed only one vast void—one tremendous blank to her.

Her pace was hurried, like that of a person intent on some important mission, and having some defined and positive end in view:—and yet she had even forgotten the motive that had sent her forth into the streets that evening, to dare the cold wind and face the pattering rain,—she who had but so scanty a clothing to protect her!

There was a humming noise in her ears: but she could not discriminate the sounds of voices from the roll of carriages;—and even when she crossed a street, it was through no caution exercised on her part that she was not ran over.

At last her ideas began to assume a more settled shape; and her thoughts, rescuing themselves as it were from utter confusion, settled gradually down into their proper cells in the brain—the racking brain which held them!

She walked slower, and with more apparent uncertainty of aim; objects assumed a defined shape to her eyes; and her ears recognised the various sounds which raised the echoes of the streets.

At length she stood still in the midst of Holborn, and tears burst from her eyes; for she now remembered that she was there—there, in the wide and open thoroughfare—to commence the dread avocation of a prostitute!

She shuddered from head to foot—but with no ordinary tremor: it was a convulsion which began at the very heart, and vibrated with electric rapidity and spasmodic violence throughout the entire form.

"Now then, young voman—out o' the vay!" cried a porter carrying a huge load upon his head.

And, like a startled deer, Matilda hurried along.

She glanced to the left and to the right, and beheld magnificent shops teeming with merchandise, and crowded with purchasers:—she lingered in front of the pastry-cooks' establishments;—and she stopped to devour with her eyes the smoking joints, the piles of vegetables, and the large tins full of pudding, in the windows of the eating-houses!

But she knew it was useless to implore a meal;—and moreover it was something beyond food that she required,—for money to pay her heartless landlord she must have!

She resumed her mournful, melancholy walk, now slow in pace and drooping in gait.

Time was wearing on—nine o'clock would soon strike—and if she were ever to take the first step in a loathsome trade, now was the moment!

Think not, reader, that because this young woman had become the mistress of a thief, and had passed through all the training of a low lodging-house and several weeks of misery and want,—think not that she was prepared to rush at once and in a moment on a career of public prostitution! No: she was attached to her lover, in the first place;—and secondly, she was no brazen-faced slut, whose mind had derived coarseness from intemperance, or callousness from ill-treatment.

She shrank from the path which alone seemed open to her: she recoiled from the ways into which a stern necessity commanded her to enter.

While she was endeavouring to subdue the bitterness of the reflections which crowded upon her soul, a young woman, scarcely a year older than herself, accosted her, and said, "My dear, are you come on this beat to be one of us?"

Matilda saw by a glance that the female was one of the lowest class of prostitutes; and she burst into tears.

"Oh! then, you *are* come out for that purpose!" exclaimed the other. "Well, you must pay your footing at all events;"—and making a signal to several of her friends who stood at a short distance, she cried, "Here's a precious lark! a gal which wants to be one of us, and is blubbering at it!"

Matilda was now surrounded by loose women, who vowed that she should treat them, or they would tear her eyes out.

Vainly did she protest that she had no money: tears and remonstrances were of no avail; and the prostitutes were growing more clamorous,—for, it must be remembered, there were no New Police in those days,—when an old man, decently dressed, but horribly ugly, stopped near the group and asked what was the matter.

"Here's a young gal which wants to go upon the town, and can't pay her footing," explained one of the loose women; "and so she shan't come on our beat."

"Come, come," said the old man; "don't tease the poor thing! Which is she? Oh! rather good-looking. Well, my dears—here's half-a-crown for you to get something to drink—and I'll get the young woman to take a little walk along with me."

Thus speaking, the old man handed the coin to the girl who had given him the above recorded explanation; and she and her friends were too much rejoiced at the receipt of this unexpected donation, to trouble themselves further concerning Matilda Briggs.

When the loose women had disappeared, the old man turned towards Matilda, and said, "Take my arm, my dear; and I'll conduct you to a nice place where we can have a chat together for half an hour or so; and I'll make you a present of half-a-guinea before we part."

The unfortunate girl obeyed in silence; but not quite mechanically:—gratitude for the seasonable assistance she had received from the old man, and the idea of obtaining enough money not only to buy food but also liquidate the greater portion of the arrears of rent due to the merciless landlord, were powerful motives to stifle compunctious feelings in her breast.

The old man was one of those sexagenarian voluptuaries who dishonour gray hairs—one of those hoary sinners who prowl about the streets after dusk, to pick up girls of tender age, and who seldom choose females of ripe years. Under ordinary circumstances this old man would not have bestowed the slightest notice upon Matilda; because she was between fifteen and sixteen, and he affected children of eleven and twelve. But the incident which had brought them together had given him a sudden zest for novelty; and thus the gray-headed reprobate, who was old enough to be Matilda's great grandfather, tucked her under his arm and led her off to the nearest brothel with which he was acquainted.

It was eleven o'clock when the door of the garret in which Josh Pedler was lying, opened abruptly and Matilda made her appearance.

"Well, what news?" demanded the man anxiously "You've left me long enough——"

"I could not return sooner," answered the young woman, in a hoarse and strangely altered tone. "But sit up and eat your fill, Josh—for here is a good plate of meat——"

"And the landlord?" interrupted the thief joyfully.

"Is paid every farthing. I have earned a sovereign by yielding to the hideous embraces of an old man," she added in a tone expressive of deep and concentrated emotion,—"an old man whose touch was horrible as the pawings of an imp or some filthy monster. But he gave me double what he first promised; and now you may eat—if you can," she exclaimed, with a hysterical laugh.

"And you will sit down and eat with me, Tilda," said the thief in a coaxing tone—for he now saw that his mistress might become serviceable to him, and he was anxious to conciliate her.

"No—not a morsel," she replied impatiently. "I am not hungry—*now*: besides, even if I was, it would seem to me that I was eating my own flesh and blood. But I have got some spirits in a bottle, Josh—and I can drink a drop with you."

"I thought you didn't like spirits, Tilda?" observed the man, contemplating with some degree of alarm her pale countenance on which there appeared an expression of settled despair.

"Oh! I dare say I shall like spirits well enough now!" she said. "At all events I feel an inclination for them to-night. But, come—sit up and eat."

Thus speaking, she spread open a large brown-paper parcel before the thief, whose eyes sparkled when he beheld a quantity of slices of recently cooked meat, a loaf of bread, and some cheese.

Forgetting how the viands were procured, Josh Pedler began to devour them with the voracity of one who had fasted a long time; and Matilda hastened to fetch him some beer.

When she returned, she sate down, and drank two glasses of raw gin, with but a few moments' interval between the drams; and then, bursting out into a hysterical laugh, she said, "Blue ruin is capital stuff! I feel myself fit for any thing now!"

"That's right, old gal—cheer up!" exclaimed Josh Pedler. "Take another glass—and then you'll be able to eat a bit of this meat."

"Well—perhaps I may," cried Matilda. "I was tipsy when you and me were married by the old parson in the padding-ken; and I'll be tipsy to night, as it's the first of a new period of my life."

"Damn it! you are coming out strong, Tilda!" ejaculated Josh Pedler. "*Blue ruin*—*padding-ken*—why, I never heard you patter flash before."

"Oh! you don't know what you may see me do yet," said the young woman, in a voice indicative of unnatural excitement. "And what does it matter? Perhaps you'll hear me cursing and swearing to-morrow! Any thing—any thing," she added, her voice changing to a tone of deep, intense feeling,— "any thing, so long as one can only grow hardened!"

And having tossed off a third glass of liquor, she accepted and ate the portion of food that Josh Pedler handed to her—although but a few minutes before she recoiled from it, as if it were her own flesh and blood!

"Now you are acting like a sensible woman," said Josh; "and you make me feel more comfortable. But when you first come in, I couldn't make out what the devil possessed you: you looked all queer like—just as if you was going to commit suicide."

"Suicide!—ha! ha!" laughed Matilda strangely. "Well—I did think of it as I was coming home; but I remembered that you was here—hungry—starving—and too ill to get up and shift for yourself. So I came back, Josh. But won't you have some gin? You don't know what good it does one. If I had only taken some before I went out just now—that is, if I had had the money to buy it—I shouldn't have gone whimpering along the street as I did. No wonder all the poor girls who walk the pavement drink so much gin. I am already quite another person. I do declare that I could sing. But here comes some one up the stairs: it can't be for us."

"Yes, it is though," said Josh Pedler, as the heavy steps of a man halted at the door, to which a fist was applied by no means lightly. "Come in!"

The visitor obeyed this invitation without farther ceremony; and the moment Josh caught sight of his countenance, he cried joyfully, "Tim the Snammer!"

CHAPTER LXX.
TIM THE SNAMMER.

The individual who rejoiced in the name of *Tim the Snammer*, was a tall, athletic, well-built man of about thirty-two, and tolerably good-looking. His attire consisted of a shabby bottle-green surtout, a dark waistcoat, and drab trousers; and he wore his hat very far down on his head—probably because it was too large for him, his hair being particularly short, all his superfluous curls having fallen beneath the unsparing scissors of a gaol-barber.

"Holloa! Josh, my boy!" cried Tim, as he closed the door behind him. "Why, you are taking it cozie there in bed."

"I have been desperate bad, Tim," was the answer; "or I shouldn't lie quiet in such a damned empty garret as this here, you may take your davy. But when did you get out?"

"My time was up to-day at eleven o'clock," returned Tim. "I called at the old crib in Castle Street—Thompson's, twenty-three, and stayed with Mutton-Face till now. She told me you'd been ill, and also where I should find you. So I've come round to see you, old feller—and, may be, arrange a little job that I've got in my head. But since you're unable to get up——"

"Tim, my boy," interrupted Josh, "I've just had a deuced good supper, and I'm sure of a breakfast and a dinner too, and may be a supper also, to-morrow; and if I ain't well with all that in two days' time, my name isn't Pedler. So, if you've got any thing that'll keep so long, do let me be in it. Matilda, my dear, this is my friend Mr. Timothy Splint, generally knowed as Tim the Snammer: and Tim, this young o'oman is my jomen. We was regularly spliced at the padding-ken by old Barlow; and she's staunch to the backbone. So now you're acquainted with each other; and you needn't be afraid, Tim, of talking secrets. But how goes the gin, Tilda?"

"There's plenty left—and I borrowed two glasses of the landlord as I came up," answered the young woman: "so here's one for Mr. Splint."

"Call me Tim, my dear," said that individual "We have no *misters* and *missuses* among us. Here's your health, Tilda, then—since that's your name: here's to ye, Josh."

"Thank'ee. But what plan is it that you've got in your head?" asked Pedler.

"I'll tell you in a brace of shakes," returned Splint, smacking his lips in approval of the dram which he had just imbibed. "You may very well suppose that I've no great reason to be pleased with the conduct of that scoundrel Old Death."

"The damned thief!" cried Josh. "He sacked the sixteen pounds, and then never made a move to help you when you was had up again afore the beak."

"No thanks to him that I wasn't transported," said Tim Splint, with a fierce expression of countenance. "The prigging wasn't proved very clearly, and so I got off with two months at the mill as a rogue and vagabond. But, by hell! I'll have my revenge on the bilking old scoundrel that humbugged you and Mutton-Face Sal. And what's more, I know how to go to work, too."

"What do you mean, Tim?" demanded Josh Pedler.

"Why, I mean this—that Mutton-Face knows where Old Death is hanging-out," responded the Snammer. "She saw him last night in the Borough; and she dogged him into some crib. This was about eight o'clock. Well, she was determined to see whether he lived there, or not—and she was afraid of raising suspicion and alarming him by making any inquiries: so she watched near the place for a matter of three hours, and he didn't come out. So it's pretty clear he does live there. But to make all sure, Mutton-Face has gone over there again to-night; and she'll watch to see when he comes in, if he does at all—and then she'll stay to see whether he comes out again. If it's all right, you and me will just pay a visit to Old Death; and I'll be bound we shall find something worth the trouble of going for."

"Old Death always has money about him," observed Josh; "and I should think that there's no one wants blunt more than you and me, Tim, at this moment."

"I haven't a blessed mag," returned Splint. "If it wasn't for Mutton-Face Sal, I shouldn't have had a dinner to eat, when I got out of quod this morning, till I'd prigged the money to pay for one. And after all I've spent in Thompson's padding-kens, I couldn't get a lodging there for love, I know. But Sal has managed to keep herself while I've been lumbered; and now I must begin to keep her again. She's got just enough to carry us on till either this business of Old Death or some thing else turns up: and that's all I care about."

"Well," said Josh Pedler, "I hope I shall be able to get up in two or three days; and then I'm your man for any thing you like. But, I say, Tim, what a life this is of our'n, to be sure!"

"You don't mean to say you're a-tired on it—do you?" cried Splint, with a species of anxiety and almost convulsive shudder, proving that a truth of an unwelcome nature, and to which he never liked to be awakened, was suddenly recalled to his contemplation.

"By God! I wish I could turn honest man, Tim!" exclaimed Pedler, with unmistakeable sincerity. "It's all very well while the excitement of drinking or *business* goes on; but it's when one is lumbered in bed, as I've been for some weeks, that one feels queer and qualmish, Tim. That's why I always hate to have the least thing the matter with me. I can't a-bear to have time to brew and mope over things. I wish there wasn't no such thing as *thought*, Tim."

"Blest if I didn't often say so to myself when I was cooped up in that cursed prison, Josh!" exclaimed the Snammer. "I tell you what it is. People say we're reglarly depraved—that's the word, Josh—and so they invent treadmills and all them kind of things. But it's quite enow for chaps like us to be left alone with our own thoughts—and there's no denying it. Now my idear is jist this:—Put a man like us into gaol, if you will and don't torture him with hard labour: but let him have time to *think*. Then, when he comes out, say to him, 'Here's work for you, and a chance to get an honest living.' My opinion is that nine out of ten would await themselves of the offer. But suppose only one or two did it—why, it must be a blessin' to society to reduce the number of them as preys upon it. What do you think, Josh?"

"I can't a-bear to think about it, Tim," returned the invalid thief. "Now, then, Tilda—what the hell are you piping your eyes for? I s'pose you think my friend Splint is a Methodist parson? But he ain't though—and don't mean to be. Damnation! Tilda, leave off blubbering like that—and hand round the gin. There—that's a good girl. Blue ruin is the mortal enemy of unpleasant thinking—and that's why we all takes to it as nat'ral as one does to opium when he's accustomed to it."

"I've often thought, Josh," said Tim Splint, after draining the glass which Matilda handed him, "that I should like to go over to America, and bury myself in the backwoods that you hear talked of or read about. I wish I had a chance! And, raly, if we do get a good haul from Old Death, I think I shall try the game. For, arter all—and you and me may say it between ourselves in this here room, 'cause Matilda, being a o'oman, goes for no one,—but, arter all, there's few on us that wouldn't give up prigging if we could. I wonder why they don't establish societies to reclaim and provide for men-thieves, as they do for unfortunit vimen. Blowed if I wouldn't go into such a place in a minute!"

"And do you mean to say," exclaimed Matilda, wiping her eyes, and speaking with strange energy, "that if you choose to leave off this kind of life, you can't? Why, you'd be happier, Josh, as a labourer with only twelve or fifteen shillings a week, than you are now;—for I never heard so much from your lips as I have to-night."

"Who the devil will employ people without characters?" demanded Josh Pedler. "Do you think that if you tried to get a place even as a scullion in a gentleman's family, you could obtain it? No such a thing. Lord bless your dear heart! them as talks most about the depravity of the lower classes, is always the last to give us a chance."

"Yes:—and yet we wasn't all nat'rally wicked," said Tim the Snammer. "Some on us was made so by circumstances; and that was the case with me."

"How came that about?" asked Josh Pedler, who, being in no humour to sleep, was well disposed for conversation.

"Yes:—how came that about?" inquired Matilda, feeling interested in the present topic.

"You don't mean to say you would like to hear me tell my story, do you?" exclaimed Tim.

"I should, by all means," answered Josh Pedler.

"And I too——Oh! above all things!" cried Matilda: "particularly, if you can show——what you said," she added hesitatingly.

"You mean to say, if I can prove that I didn't become what I am through my own fault?" observed the Snammer. "Well—I think I *can* prove it. But you shall judge for yourselves. So, here goes."

And, with this free-and-easy kind of preface, the thief commenced his narrative, which we have expurgated of those grammatical solecisms and characteristic redundancies which, if preserved, would only mar the interest and obscure the sense. At the same time, we have kept as nearly to the original mode of delivery as possible.

CHAPTER LXXI.
THE HISTORY OF TIM THE SNAMMER.

"My father was a small farmer in Hampshire. He had about thirty-six acres of his own, all well cultivated and well stocked, and free of all mortgage and encumbrance of that kind. The farm was small enough, God knows; but it yielded a decent living,—for my father was as industrious as a bee,—always out by sunrise,—and my mother was as saving, thrifty, and prudent a housewife as any in the county. They were not, however, mean: no—very far from that. The beggar was never turned away unassisted from their door; and if a neighbour got a little behind-hand with his rent, and deserved aid, it was ten to one if the china tea-pot in my mother's cupboard did not contain a few pounds, which were speedily placed at his disposal. Farmer Splint, as my father was called, was always regular in his attendance at the village church on Sunday; and the only person who looked upon him as a mean-spirited fellow, was the landlord of the ale-house—because my father so seldom entered the *George and Dragon* even to take a glass of beer at the bar,—and never stopped there to pass an evening.

"My mother was a very handsome woman, and had been the village-belle before her marriage with Farmer Splint. This marriage was one of affection on both sides; for though my mother's parents were very poor and unable to give their daughter any thing, yet Farmer Splint preferred her to the wealthier young women of the neighbourhood. On her side, though my father was nearly ten years older than herself, she refused the offer of a rich young farmer, and became the spouse of a man whom she could respect and esteem as well as love. The fruits of this marriage were two children,—a daughter, named Marion, and myself. Our mother found time, even amongst the numerous duties and cares of the household, to teach us to read and write. The village schoolmaster then taught us a little arithmetic, history, and geography; and we were as well instructed as the children of poor parents were likely to be, and much better than those of even many richer people living in our neighbourhood.

"Now, from all I have just told you, you will see plain enough that our mother and father were good, honest, moral, and well-intentioned people. Their only care was to toil with all possible diligence, to make both ends meet,—put by a little savings, when the harvest was very plentiful,—and bring up their children in a respectable and decent manner. My father was particularly anxious to prevent his boy from resembling the young black-guards of the village: he would never let me play about in the high road at marbles,—nor yet go bird's-nesting, which he said encouraged cruelty, and was also the first step to poaching. But he did all he could to render me hardy, and promoted innocent sports of an athletic nature. Altogether, farmer Splint's family was considered to be the best-behaved and the happiest in all the county.

"It was in the year 1807, that my history now dates from. I was then thirteen years old: my sister, Marion, was eighteen, and a sweet beautiful girl she was, with fine blue eyes, flaxen hair, and a figure that couldn't have been made more graceful if clothed in silk or satin. She was at that time engaged to be married to the only son of a farmer in the neighbourhood, and who was well to do in the world. A finer fellow than young George Dalton you would never wish to see; and when he and Marion walked to church arm-in-arm, on a Sunday, every one noticed them, as much as to express a conviction of the fitness of the intended union of such a handsome, manly youth, and such a modest pretty girl. Well, it was the summer of 1807, and the marriage was to take place in October, when all the harvest was got in, and the good ale was brewed for the ensuing year. Every thing appeared gay and smiling for the young people; for George's father had promised to give up his farm to his son, but to continue to live in the house, as soon as Marion should have become his daughter-in-law.

"About three miles from our farm stood the beautiful seat of Squire Bulkeley. This gentleman had been left an orphan when young; and his estates were managed by his guardians, until he came of age, he living with one of them in London. But when he attained his majority, he soon showed himself to be tired of a London life; and he came down to take possession of Bulkeley Hall, and settle there. This was in the beginning of 1807; but for two or three months the Squire kept himself pretty quiet. All of a sudden, however, he became as gay as he was before tranquil and retired; and this change, we learnt, arose in consequence of his guardians leaving him, they having accompanied him to the Hall and remained there until all the papers and deeds connected with his accession to his property were signed. The moment they were gone, a number of fashionable gentlemen from London arrived as guests at the old mansion; and the long silent rooms echoed to the sounds of their late revellings. Then there were steeple-chases, and horse-racing, and cock-fighting, and badger-baiting, and all kinds of sports of that nature; and sometimes the young squire was more than half tipsy when he lounged into church in the middle of the Sunday evening service. His residence at the Hall did no good to the village tradespeople, because he had every thing sent down from London;—and thus no one was rejoiced at his settling in that neighbourhood. My parents, particularly, had no good opinion of Squire Bulkeley; but, as the farm was their own, they had no positive fear of him, although our land joined his estates. This was not so, however, with the Daltons, who were only tenant-farmers, and rented their fifty or sixty acres of the Squire. The farm had been in old Dalton's family for many, many years, and was one of the best tilled and best stocked in the county; and as Mr.

Dalton was always regular with his rent, it did not seem probable that the lease, which was shortly to expire, would be refused renewal.

"One morning,—it was in the month of June, I remember, Marion and myself happened to be alone together in the house, when the Squire, attended by his groom, rode up to the door. Marion sent me out to learn the cause of his visit. 'This is Farmer Splint's, my boy, I believe?' said the Squire, who, I should observe, was a handsome young man in spite of his dissipated appearance. I replied in the affirmative, adding, that my father was not at home. 'Who is at home, then?' asked the Squire; 'for I caught a glimpse of a face so pretty just now at the window, that I should not mind beholding it again.'—'That was my sister, Marion, sir,' I answered, not seeing any thing insolent in his remark; but, perhaps, rather pleased by it, as it flattered a sister of whom I was very fond.—'Well, my boy,' said the Squire, leaping from his horse, 'here is a crown for you; and now be off and try and find your father, as I want to speak to him. In the mean time I will walk in and rest myself.' Catching the coin which he threw me, I hurried away, delighted with the handsome present, and naturally thinking that the visit of so liberal a gentleman must be with a motive beneficial to my father. But after hunting every where for him about the farm, I remembered that he and my mother had gone to the village to make some purchases. The village was a mile and a half distant from our house; and as I knew that they would be back to dinner at one, I returned straight home, expecting to find them already arrived. The groom was walking the horses up and down at a little distance; and, therefore, I was convinced that the Squire was still waiting within. My hand was just upon the latch of the door, when a scream burst upon my ears; and immediately afterwards I heard Marion's voice reproaching the Squire bitterly for some insult which he had offered her. I hastened into the house, and my presence appeared to disconcert Mr. Bulkeley completely. He was standing in the middle of the room, as if uncertain what course to adopt in a case of embarrassment; and he turned as red as scarlet when he saw me. Marion was at the further end of the apartment, near a door opening into the kitchen; and she was arranging her hair, which had been disordered; while her cheeks were also crimsoned, but, as I thought, with the glow of indignation; whereas the face of the Squire was flushed with shame.

"I advanced towards Marion, asking, 'What is the matter? why did you scream out? and what has he been doing to you?'—'Nothing, Tim,' she replied, but with a profound sob. 'Have you met father?'—'No; I forgot that he'd gone to the village; but he will be home in a minute or two, as it's close on one.'—'I shall call another day, then, Miss,' said the Squire; and he hurried abruptly away. For some minutes neither Marion or myself spoke a word. I suppose she was endeavouring to compose herself, and also deliberating what course she should pursue; while, on my side, I did not like to question her. At length she approached me, and said, 'Tim, you are a good boy, and always do what sister tells you. Now, mind and don't mention a word about that gentleman having been rude to me. I have reasons of my own for it. And don't say either, that you were so long away when he was here.' I promised to follow Marion's injunctions; for I was very fond of her, as I have before said. Accordingly, when my father and mother had come back, and we were all seated at dinner, Marion remarked in an indifferent manner that the Squire had called to see our father, and that he had given me a five-shilling piece. 'I wonder what he can want with me?' said my father: 'it was certainly very kind of him to make Tim such a handsome present; but after all I have heard of him, I would rather that he should honour us with his visits as rarely as possible. However, he can do us no harm—nor any good, that I know of; for he has no land to let at present, and I am not disposed to hire any even if he had.' There the subject was dismissed, at least so far as remarks thereon were concerned; but I saw that Marion was thoughtful and even melancholy during the remainder of the day.

"About a week had elapsed, and my father and I were one afternoon proceeding along the borders of our land, just where it was separated by a quick-set hedge from the Squire's estate, when Mr. Bulkeley himself, alone and on foot, suddenly appeared at a stile. My father and I touched our hats with the usual respect shown by country people to great folks; and the Squire, who had for a moment shrunk back on seeing us, exclaimed, 'Farmer Splint, you are the very man I wanted to fall in with; and that very field in which you are standing is the object of my business with you.'—'How so, sir?' asked my father.—'Why,' returned the Squire, 'you see it cuts awkwardly into my estate, and breaks in on the very best preserves I have in this quarter.—'Begging pardon, sir,' said my father, 'I could wish it broke a little more on your preserves: for your hares and pheasants do a world of harm to my fields when the corn is just springing up. I lost more than an acre by them last year, sir.'—'So much the greater folly on your part, Farmer Splint,' exclaimed the Squire, 'to persist in remaining a landowner. You never can get a good living out of so small a farm as your's.'—'I get enough for all our wants sir, and am able to assist a friend now and then,' said my father.—'Well, but if you sell your land and become a tenant-farmer, you will be much better off,' observed the Squire. 'Suppose, for instance, I bought the land? why, you would have received compensation for the injury done to your crop by the game in my preserves.'—'But I should lose my independence, sir,' said my father, in a firm though perfectly respectful manner.—'Your independence!' ejaculated Mr. Bulkeley, with a sneer. 'Then, I am to imagine that you consider yourself a regular landowner, one of the lords of the soil. May be you will dub yourself *Squire* next! Squire Splint, eh?'—'I am plain Farmer Splint, sir, and so I hope to remain,' was the answer.—'Then you will not sell me that field?'—'I had rather not, sir.'—'But you may have an equivalent portion of my seven-acre field over by the mill yonder; and your property will be much more compact.'—'But the land is not equally serviceable, sir,' answered my father, 'and therefore I must decline the bargain. Besides, it may be fancy on my part; but it is true notwithstanding, that I am rather superstitious in making boundary changes in a farm that has been so long in my family; unless it was to extend it by a purchase of land, and *that* I can't afford. So good day, sir;' and my father, touching his hat, walked on. I saw the Squire's lips quivering with rage as he stood looking after us; and, young as I was, yet I thought my father had made an enemy of him—for the conversation which I have just detailed, produced a deep impression upon me.

"Six or seven weeks had passed away since this little incident, when I one day met the Squire as I was going on an errand for my mother to the village. He was on horseback, and his groom was in attendance. I was thinking whether I ought to touch my hat to him or not, after his insolence to my father, when he pulled up, exclaiming, 'Holloa! youngster—your name is Splint, I believe?'—'Yes, sir.'—'Ah! I remember. You are a very good lad, and I should wish to become a friend to you. I think I gave you a crown once: well, here's another. And now answer me a question or two. Did your sister ever say a word to her father or mother about that visit of mine some weeks past, you know?'—I was so bewildered by the apparent liberality of the Squire, and, boy-like, was so rejoiced at the possession of the coin which I was rolling over and over in my hand, that I suffered myself to be sifted by him at will; and I acquainted him with the injunctions that my sister Marion had given me on the occasion to which he had alluded. He seemed much pleased, but not particularly astonished. In fact, it is of course easy to understand what was passing in his mind, although I could not *then* fathom his thoughts. The respect which my father had shown him when they met in the fields, evidently induced him to believe that Marion had *not* acquainted her parents with his rudeness to her; and now he was pleased to receive from my lips a confirmation of his conjecture on that point. It was also natural for him to imagine that Marion was not in reality so much offended with him as she had appeared to be; and it was doubtless with this impression upon his mind that he proceeded to address me in the following manner:—'To tell you the truth, my boy, I behaved rather rudely to your charming sister; and I have repented of it ever since. I do not like to call and offer an apology, because your father or mother, or both, might be present. But if you will deliver a note to her privately, I will write one; for I shall not feel happy till I have convinced her that I am sorry for the past.'—'I am sure, sir,' I replied, 'I shall be most happy to deliver such a letter to my sister, and she will be most pleased to receive it; because she has often told me that we always ought to forgive those who show repentance for their errors.'—'An excellent maxim, my boy!' cried the Squire. He then desired me to wait for him in a particular shop, which he named, in the village; and, turning back, he rode thitherward, followed by his groom. I walked on, thinking that the Squire was a much better man than he had at first seemed,—wondering, too, how he could have been so harsh and unjust in his observations towards my father, and yet so ready to acknowledge the impropriety of his conduct towards my sister.

"Arrived in the village, I performed the commission entrusted to me by my mother, and then repaired to the shop of Mr. Snowdon, chemist and druggist, as directed by the young Squire. This gentleman was leaning on the counter, writing on the sheet of paper with which the obsequious Mr. Snowdon had provided him; and when it was terminated, the Squire folded it, sealed it, and addressed it to *Miss Marion Splint*. Mr. Snowdon caught a glimpse of the superscription, although he pretended to be looking quite another way. The letter was then handed to me by the Squire, accompanied by a whispered injunction to be sure and give it privately to Marion; while another crown-piece anointed my hand at the same time. I promised compliance with the instructions given, and hurried back home. George Dalton was there, and he stayed to dinner; but he departed soon afterwards, taking an affectionate leave of Marion as usual. My father also went out to his work; my mother repaired to the dairy; and I was now alone with my sister. 'Marion, dear,' said I, 'I have got a surprise for you.'—'A surprise for me, Tim!' she exclaimed.— 'Yes; a letter from Squire Bulkeley.'—'Tim!' she cried, 'you surely———.'— 'Pray read it, Marion dear,' I interrupted her. 'Its contents are a most respectful apology for his conduct some weeks ago. In fact, he spoke quite like a gentleman about it, and said how sorry he was.' Marion no longer hesitated to open the letter; but I saw that her countenance suddenly became crimson, and she hastened up to her own chamber, without uttering another word.

"An hour passed away, and she came down again. Having assured herself that our mother was still occupied in the dairy, she said to me, 'Tim dear, you must do me a kindness this very evening.'—'That I will, Marion,' I answered. 'What is it?'—'Here is a letter for Squire Bulkeley,' she said; and it struck me that there was something singular, and not altogether natural in her voice and manner. 'If you meet father on the way, say that you are going to inquire after neighbour Jones's little daughter; and never tell any one, Tim, that you did this for me. You are not old enough yet to understand my motives; but when you are, you shall know them.'—I was never accustomed to question my sister, nor even to deliberate on any thing she did; and away I sped to Bulkeley Hall. The Squire was not at home; and so I left the letter. On my return to the farm-house, I told Marion what I had done: she said I was a good boy, and repeated her injunctions of the strictest secrecy.

"About a week after this incident, George Dalton took me out for a ramble with him. I never saw him so happy and in such excellent spirits. He spoke of the prospects of a good harvest; and observed that every thing seemed to hold out a promise of happiness for Marion and himself. Then he told me how glad he would always be to see me at his farm when my sister should have become his wife. In this way he was talking, and I was listening very attentively, when, as we were crossing a field on Squire Bulkeley's estate, that gentleman suddenly appeared on the other side of the hedge. 'Holloa! you fellows,' he cried; 'don't you know you're trespassing?'—'I wasn't aware of it, Sir,' replied George, touching his hat: 'the field has always been used as a short cut by the people of the village; and there have been a foot-path and a stile at each end, ever since I can remember.'—'And if my guardians chose to permit the village people to use this short cut, it is no reason why I should,' exclaimed the Squire, purple with rage. 'And so I order you off at once, both of you.'—'Well, sir,' said George, still respectfully but firmly, 'we shall never trespass again, now that we know it is trespassing.'—'Go back, then!' cried Mr. Bulkeley.—'As we are nearer the other end of the field, we may as well continue our walk in that direction, sir,' returned George. 'It can't possibly make any difference to you.'—'Yes, but it does though,' shouted the Squire. 'I order you off; and you shan't advance another step.' Thus speaking, he sprang through the hedge, and came towards us in a menacing manner.— 'Look you, Squire Bulkeley,' said George Dalton, without retreating a single pace: 'you warn me off your grounds, and I am prepared to obey. But you shall not bully me, for all that.'—'Bully you!' cried the great man, now turning perfectly white: 'do you think a gentleman like me knows what it is to bully?'—'I think it seems very much as if you did, sir,' answered George coolly.—'Low-bred scoundrel, insolent clod-hopper!' exclaimed the Squire: 'you are not fit to stand in the presence of a gentleman. Go back to your Marion, and console yourself with my leavings in that quarter!'—'Villain! what do you mean?' cried George, rushing forward to grasp the Squire by the throat.—'Wait one moment!' exclaimed the latter, raising his arm and stepping back a few paces. 'I tell you that Marion knows how to prefer a gentleman to a swineherd; and that boy there can prove it,' he added, pointing to me.

"George Dalton turned a hasty and angry glance upon me; and I saw him become deadly pale and tremble violently—I suppose because he saw that my manner was embarrassed and confused. 'Tim,' he said, in a hoarse and thick voice, 'do you know what this person means?' and he pointed disdainfully towards the Squire, who seemed to feel a diabolical delight at the evident pain which he was inflicting upon my sister's lover.—'If that boy tells the truth,' said Mr. Bulkeley, 'he will admit——.'—'The children of Farmer Splint were never known to tell a falsehood,' interrupted George Dalton; 'and though you, sir, have made most cowardly and insulting allusions to Marion, you are well aware that there breathes not a purer being than she is, nor a greater scoundrel and liar than you are. And if I restrain my hands from touching you, it is only because you are too contemptible for serious notice.

Come, Tim: let us move on.'—'One word, George Dalton!' cried the Squire, his lips quivering with rage. 'Ask that boy whether he knows of any thing that has ever taken place between me and Marion. Remember, I am your landlord; and your father's lease expires next Christmas.'—'We don't care for the threats of a man like you, who endeavours to cause a breach between me and a young lass that never did you any harm.'—'Oh! not at all; but a great deal of good, on the contrary,' said the Squire, with a chuckle of triumph. 'Why, it is but a week ago since that boy was the bearer of the last notes which passed between us.'—'Liar!' thundered George Dalton; and he was again on the point of rushing on the Squire, when he checked himself, and turning to me said, 'Now, Tim, you are no story-teller; and, indeed, I ought scarcely to insult Marion so far as to ask such a question. But can you not tell this man to his face that he is what I just now called him; namely, a liar?'—'Not if he tells the truth,' observed Mr. Bulkeley coolly.—I hung down my head, and wished at the moment that the earth would open and swallow me up.—'Tim,' said George Dalton, again speaking in a hoarse tone, as dark suspicions were revived in his mind, 'does this person who calls himself a gentleman utter facts? did you ever convey letters between him and your sister? Come, answer me, my boy: I cannot be angry with *you*.'—I faltered out a faint 'Yes.'—'Then God have mercy upon me!' exclaimed George Dalton, in a voice of piercing anguish, as he clasped his hands convulsively together.

"The Squire stood gazing upon him with fiend-like malignity. I cannot describe the dreadful picture of despair which George at that moment seemed to be. At length he turned again towards me, and, grasping my shoulder so tight that I nearly screamed out with pain, he said, 'Tim, tell me all, or I shall do you a mischief. Does Marion receive letters from Mr. Bulkeley?'—'She did one,' I stammered in reply, 'because I took it to her. The Squire wrote it at Mr. Snowdon's.'—'And did Marion answer it?' he demanded.—'She did,' I answered: 'but——'.—'Have you ever seen the Squire and Marion together?' he asked in a hurried and now dreadfully excited tone.—'Yes, once,' I said: 'but——.' And again I was about to give certain explanations relative to what the Squire himself had represented to me to be the nature and object of his letter to my sister—namely, to apologise to her for some insult which he had offered her: but George Dalton had not patience to hear me. Rushing upon the Squire, he struck him to the ground, exclaiming, 'Vile seducer! you glory in the ruin you have accomplished!' and then he darted away, clearing the hedge with a bound, and was almost immediately out of sight.

"The Squire rose slowly and with pain from the ground, muttering the most dreadful threats of vengeance; and I, afraid that he might do me a mischief, hurried off as quick as possible. I was old enough to comprehend that George Dalton believed my sister to have been faithless to him; and the same impression rapidly forced itself on my own mind. Still I was sorry that George had not waited to hear all the additional circumstances which I was about to relate; and it somehow or another struck me that he would call on Mr. Snowdon, the chemist. I cannot now account for this idea which I entertained: but I suppose it must have been because that person's name was mentioned in the conversation, and because I must have thought it probable that George would seek the fullest confirmation of his cause of unhappiness. It is, however, very certain that I hastened off to the village as quick as my legs would carry me. But just as I entered Mr. Snowdon's shop, I caught sight of George Dalton, standing at the counter talking to that individual. He had his back towards me; and the chemist was so occupied with the subject of conversation, that he also did not notice my entrance. I knew not whether to advance or retreat; and while I stood hesitating, I overheard Dalton say, 'And you are sure that the letter was addressed to Marion?'—'I happened to catch a glimpse of the direction,' answered the chemist, 'and I saw the Squire give the lad Timothy some money.'—'Then am I indeed a wretched, miserable being!' exclaimed George Dalton; and he rushed wildly from the shop, not noticing me as he hurried by. I was so alarmed by his haggard looks and excited manner, that I was nailed as it were to the spot; and it was not until Mr. Snowdon had asked me two or three times what I wanted, that I recollected where I was. Then, without giving any reply, I quitted the shop, and repaired homewards.

"I was afraid to enter the house; for I felt convinced that poor Marion's happiness was menaced, and that even if she was not already aware of the presence of the storm, not many hours would elapse ere it would burst upon her head. And when I did reach the farm, my worst fears were confirmed. The place was in confusion; Marion was in a state bordering on distraction; and my father and mother were vainly endeavouring to comfort her. An open letter lay upon the table:—without reading its contents I could too well divine their nature and whence the missive came. For some minutes my entrance was unperceived; but when at last the intensity of Marion's grief was somewhat subdued, and her eyes fell on me, she exclaimed, 'Oh! Tim, what have you done? what have you been telling George, that he has written to say he will abandon me forever, and that *you* can explain the cause?'—'Reveal the whole truth, boy,' said my father sternly, 'as some atonement for the misery which you have been instrumental in producing.'—I then related all that had occurred with the Squire and at the apothecary's shop.—My father and mother showed, by their lowering countenances and searching glances towards my sister, that they were a prey to harrowing suspicions; but they did not interrupt the current of my story. Then, when I had concluded, Marion, without waiting to be asked for an explanation, gave it in the following manner:—

"'You cannot, my dear parents, think for a moment that I have acted unworthily. Imprudent I may have been—but guilty, Oh! no—no! One day the Squire called here, as you are well aware; and he sent Tim to search after you, father. This was most probably a mere vile subterfuge on his part; for when Tim had departed, the bad man began to speak to me in a disparaging way of George; and when I begged him to desist, as he was wronging an excellent being, his language took a bolder turn. He paid me some compliments, which I affected not to hear; and at last his language grew so insulting, that I was about to quit the room, when he caught me round the waist. Oh! how can I tell you his insulting language?—but he proposed to me—to me, your daughter, and beloved by George Dalton as I then was,—the detestable man implored me to fly with him to his mansion—to become his mistress!'—Here my father and mother made a movement indicative of deep indignation; and Marion then continued thus:—'I started away from him—I was rushing towards that inner room, when Tim returned. I was now no longer alarmed, though still boiling with anger: nevertheless I had presence of mind sufficient to command my emotion so far as not to utter a word of reproach or complaint in the presence of my brother. For, in a moment, did I perceive how necessary it was to retain in my own breast the secret of the gross insult which I had received. I reasoned to myself that the Squire was the landlord of the Daltons—that their lease would expire at the end of the year—that it would break the old man's heart to be compelled to quit a farm which had been in his family for so many years—and that George possessed a fiery spirit, which would render him blind to the consequences of avenging on the Squire the insults offered to me. Of all this I thought: those ideas flashed rapidly through my brain;—and I therefore not only resolved to remain silent in respect to the insolence of Mr. Bulkeley, but also tutored Tim to be so reserved, that you, my dear father and mother, should not notice any thing unusual having occurred. When Tim brought me the Squire's note, a week ago, I scarcely hesitated to read it, thinking that it might indeed contain an apology. But, oh! you may conceive my feelings, when I discovered that it repeated the insulting proposals made to me on the first occasion. I knew not how to act; and prudence struggled with wounded pride. But I reflected that Mr. Bulkeley was wealthy and powerful enough to crush us all—for we *have* seen instances, my dear parents, of the rich landowners ruining the small farmers, who to all appearance were independent of them: and again I resolved to adopt a cautious line of conduct. I accordingly answered the Squire's note. I implored him, as he was a gentleman and a Christian, not to molest me more with importunities from which my very heart revolted; I besought him not to ruin for ever the happy prospects of two families by any means of vengeance with which circumstances or accident might supply him; and I conjured him to believe that, in keeping secret all that had hitherto passed between us, I was actuated only by the best of motives. That letter was the one which Tim conveyed to the Squire; and now, my dear parents, you know all.'

"I remember perfectly well that my father and mother were greatly affected by the narrative which my pure-minded sister thus related to them, and which was frequently interrupted by bursts of bitter anguish on her part. She moreover added that she possessed the Squire's letter to her and a copy of the one which she had written to him.—'Give me those papers, my dear child,' said my father: 'and I will at once proceed to neighbour Dalton's house. If I find George at home, I will undertake to bring him back with me to pass the remainder of the day, and to implore your forgiveness for his unjust suspicions; and if he is not there, I am sure to see my old friend, to whom I will give all the necessary explanations.'—Marion was somewhat soothed by the hopes thus held out; and our father departed to the Daltons' farm, which was about a mile off. Two hours elapsed before he came back; and when at last we perceived him returning through the fields, he was alone. Marion burst into tears: a presentiment of evil struck a chill to her heart; and as our father approached, the serious expression of his countenance filled us all with alarm. He entered and seated himself without uttering a word. Marion threw herself into his arms, saying in a broken voice, 'Father, tell me the worst: I can bear every thing save suspense.'—'My dearest child,' answered the old man, tears trickling down his cheeks, 'it has pleased heaven to afflict thee, and all of us likewise through thee. George has quitted his home, and——.'—'And what?' demanded Marion hastily.—'And his father knows not whither he has gone,' continued he: 'but when the first fever of excitement is over, there can be no doubt that he will return. Old Mr. Dalton is perfectly satisfied——.'

"But Marion heard not the words last addressed to her: she had fainted in her father's arms;—and, when she was restored to consciousness, she was so unwell that she was immediately removed to her own chamber. For three weeks her life was despaired of; and she was constantly raving of George Dalton. But at last, youth, a good constitution, and the care taken of her, triumphed over the rage of fever; and she was pronounced out of danger. Alas! what replies could be given to her anxious, earnest questions concerning George? Old Dalton had not heard of him since the fatal day when he disappeared. Was he no more? had he in a moment of frenzy laid violent hands upon himself? There was too much reason to suppose that such was the case: otherwise, would he not have written, or returned? As gently as possible was the fatal truth, that no tidings had been received of him, broken to Marion; and a partial relapse was the consequence. But in another week she rallied again; and then the first time she spoke of him, she said in as excited a tone at her feebleness would allow, 'Had he ceased to love me—had he loved another, I could have borne it! But that he should think me lost—faithless—degraded,—oh! that is worse than even the bitterness of death!'

"Slowly—slowly did Marion recover sufficiently to rise from her bed: but how altered was she! The gay, cheerful, ruddy girl, blooming with health and rustic beauty, was changed into a pale, moping, mournful creature, whose very presence seemed to render joy a crime and smiles a sacrilege. The autumn came—the corn was cut—the harvest, as plentiful as had been expected, was gathered in. Had George been there then, that was the period settled for the wedding. And, strange as it may seem, it was precisely on the day originally resolved upon as the one to render the young couple happy,—that old Dalton *did* receive tidings of his son. George was alive, and had enlisted in a regiment then stationed at Chatham, but shortly to embark for India. The young man wrote a letter communicating these facts, and referring to a former letter which he had written to his father a few days after he had quitted home, but the miscarriage of which had produced so much uncertainty and painful suspense. The colour came back to Marion's cheeks when she heard that her lover was alive; and she said, 'Even though I may never see him more, I can yet be happy; for he will now learn that I am still as I have ever been, his faithful and devoted Marion!' Meantime, old Dalton and my father were deliberating together what course to pursue; and it was determined that the discharge of George should be immediately purchased. The proper steps were taken, under the advice of an attorney in the nearest market-town; and in the mean time his father wrote to him a full account of the Squire's treachery and Marion's complete innocence. The return of post brought the tenderest and most pathetic letter to Marion, imploring her forgiveness, and assuring her that his extreme love had driven him to such a state of desperation as to render his native district hateful to him, and had induced him to enlist. I need scarcely say, that Marion now enjoyed hopes of happiness again: her cheeks recovered their lost bloom—her step grew light as formerly, and her musical voice once more awoke the echoes of the homestead. In six weeks time we heard that George was free, and on his way home. He came:—it is impossible to describe the unbounded joy of the meeting!

"And now there was no longer any obstacle to the union of the lovers, nor any wish in any quarter to delay it. The marriage was accordingly celebrated and a happier pair never issued from the village-church; nor did ever the bells appear to ring so merrily before. There were grand doings at our farm-house, for my mother was determined to give a treat to all her neighbours;—and the feast was such a one as I never can forget. Long after George had borne away his bride to his father's house, which, as already long before arranged, was to be the young couple's home, the dancing was kept up on the green in front of our dwelling, though the cold weather had already begun to show itself.

But all hearts were gay and happy, and warm with good feelings; and the old ale and the punch flowed bountifully; for it was one of those days in people's lives which are a reward for whole ages of care. Ah! when I look back at those times, and think of what I was—and now reflect for a moment on what I am——But, no; I must not reflect at all. Let me continue this history without pausing for meditation!

"The happiness of both families was now complete; for even old Dalton declared that he had so much reason for joy in the turn which circumstances had lately taken, that he could even make up his mind to receive a refusal when he should apply for the renewal of his lease. But just at this time fortune seemed determined to be propitious; for Squire Bulkeley, who was in London when the return of George and the marriage took place, sent down a legal gentleman to make arrangements with his steward for the sale of a part of his estate in Hampshire, as he wanted to make up the money to purchase a small property in Kent. He was a wild and reckless fellow, and full of whims and fancies; and he cared not which portion of his land was sold, so long as his preserves and park were left. Well, it happened that old Dalton, hearing of this, went straight to the lawyer, and proposed to purchase the farm which had been rented by his family for so many years. The offer was accepted: by the aid of my father the money was made up and paid. Dalton was now a landowner; but he did not remain so long—for he made over all his newly acquired property to his son George, who laboured hard to improve it.

"Shortly after this transaction, it was rumoured in the neighbourhood that the Squire had flown into a tremendous passion when he received the news that the Daltons had purchased the farm. He had no doubt intended to turn them out at Christmas; but he had omitted to except their farm from the part of the estate to be sold. The Daltons cared nothing for his anger; and George even said that he now considered himself sufficiently avenged upon the perfidious gentleman. Shortly after Christmas the Squire came down to Bulkeley Hall with a party of friends; and the mansion once again rang with the din of revellers. And now I come to a very important incident in my narrative.

"One day George Dalton had occasion to visit the neighbouring market-town to buy a horse; and he stayed to dine in company with the other farmers at the principal inn. The landlord of the inn dined at the same table with his guests; and, during the meal, he informed the company that a poor discharged gamekeeper had died at the house on the preceding evening, leaving behind him his only possession—the only thing that he had been able to retain from the wreck of his former prosperity,—namely, a beautiful greyhound. The farmers were interested in the tale, and instantly made a subscription to defray the expenses of the poor man's funeral, and remunerate the good landlord for the care and attention which he had bestowed on the deceased during his last illness. The hound was brought in, and every one admired it greatly. The landlord observed that his wife had such an aversion to dogs, he did not dare keep it on the premises; and he proposed that the farmers should raffle amongst them to decide to whom the hound should belong. This was assented to; and the lot fell on George Dalton. He accordingly took the dog home with him, and related all that had occurred to his father and his wife, both of whom were much pleased by the acquisition of such a fine animal, and under such interesting circumstances. The poor gamekeeper's dog accordingly became an immediate favourite.

"About a week or ten days afterwards, and in the month of February, George went out early, accompanied by the hound. The morning was fine and frosty, but excessively cold; and George whistled cheerily as he went along, Ponto trotting close at his heels. Suddenly a hare started from her form; and away dashed the greyhound after her. George knew that he had no right to pursue game even on his own land; and he ran after the dog as hard as he could, calling him back. But he might as well have whistled against the thunder: Ponto was too eager in the chase to mind the invocations of his master. Well, after a short but exciting run, the hound caught and killed the hare in the very last field belonging to George's farm, the adjoining land being the Squire's. And, sure enough, at that very instant Mr. Bulkeley appeared, accompanied by two gamekeepers, on the other side of the boundary palings. 'George Dalton, by God!' cried the Squire, with a malignant sneer on his countenance.—But George took no notice of his enemy; for he had promised Marion in the most solemn manner to avoid all possibility of quarrelling with so dangerous an individual.—'I did not know that you took out a certificate, Mr. Dalton,' observed the Squire, after a pause.—'Neither do I, sir,' replied George in a cold but respectful manner; 'and I have done nothing that I am ashamed of; for, if you have been here many minutes, you must have heard me trying to call the dog off.'—'We know what we heard, Mr. Dalton,' said the Squire, with a significant grin at his gamekeepers;—and away the gentleman and keepers went, chuckling audibly. The very next day an information was laid by the Squire against George Dalton, who accordingly attended before the magistrates. Squire Bulkeley was himself a justice of the peace; and he sate on the bench along with his brother magistrates, acting as both judge and prosecutor. The two gamekeepers swore that they saw George encourage the dog to pursue the hare; and it was in vain that the defendant represented the whole circumstances of the case. He was condemned in the full penalty and costs, and abused shamefully into the bargain. Smarting under the iron scourge of oppression, and acting by the advice of an attorney whom he had employed in the case, George Dalton gave notice of appeal to the Quarter Sessions. His wife, my father, and old Mr. Dalton implored him to settle the matter at once and have done with it: but he declared that he should be unworthy of the name of an Englishman if he suffered himself to be thus trampled under the feet of the despotic magistracy. The attorney, who was hungry after a job, nagged him on, too; and thus every preparation was made to carry the affair before the Sessions.

"The event made a great stir in that part of the country, and the liberal papers took George's part. They said how utterly worthless, as an engine of justice, was the entire system of the unpaid magistracy; and they denounced that system as a monstrous oppression, instituted against the people.[30] Well, the case came on before the assembled magistrates; but on the bench sate not only the justice who had condemned George Dalton, but likewise Squire Bulkeley, the prosecutor himself! Judgment was given against my brother-in-law; and he suddenly found himself called upon to pay about sixty pounds—the amount of all the aggregate expenses which the original case and the appeal occasioned. The money was made up with great difficulty, and not without my father's aid; and though George Dalton was thus relieved from any fears of the consequences, yet he became an altered man. He went to work with a heavy heart, because he could not prevent himself from brooding over his wrongs. He also found frequent excuses for visiting the village; and on those occasions he never failed to step into the ale-house for a few minutes. There he found sympathizers; and his generous nature prompted him to treat those who took his part. One pot led to another; and every time he entered the ale-house, his stay was prolonged. Care now entered both the farm-houses. In one, old Dalton and Marion deplored the change which had taken place in George; and in the other, my parents could not close their ears to the rumours which reached them, nor shut their eyes against the altered manner of their son-in-law. The great proof of dogged obstinacy which George gave, was in his conduct respecting the hound. Those who wished him well, implored him to dispose of it; but he declared that he considered himself bound, by reason of the manner in which he had acquired the dog, to maintain and treat the animal kindly. He, however, kept Ponto chained up in the farmyard.

"Time wore on; the summer arrived and passed; and the autumn yielded so good a harvest that the produce was a complete set off against the heavy expenses entailed on the two families by the unlucky appeal. This circumstance somewhat cheered George's spirits; and the birth of a fine boy restored him almost completely to his former gaiety. In the evening, instead of finding some pretence to repair to the village, he sate with his beloved Marion; and happiness once more entered the homestead. But misfortune was again impending over the head of George Dalton. It was one morning in the month of November, that he was repairing to his work, with a spade and a hoe over his shoulder, whistling as he was wont to do ere oppression had wronged him; and wondering, also, how he could ever have been so foolish as to pay such frequent visits to the public-house in the village. His mind was occupied, too, with the image of his Marion, whom he had left nourishing her babe; and perhaps his heart was never lighter than at that moment. But suddenly, he heard a slight noise behind him; and, turning round, he beheld Ponto, who, having succeeded in slipping his collar, had scampered after his master. George's first impulse was to secure the dog; but, as the devil would have it, at that very instant a hare jumped from her form close by. Ponto escaped from George's grasp, and the chase ensued. My brother-in-law was bewildered—he knew not how to act; but at last he pursued the hound, taking care, however, not to call him. Away went Ponto—the hare doubled and turned—George managing to keep them in sight. At length, to his horror, the hare swept towards a hedge, which in that point separated the Daltons' property from the Squire's preserves:—the hedge was passed by the pursued and the pursuing animals, and the chase was now maintained on Mr. Bulkeley's estate. But the run soon terminated by the death of the hare; and George, after casting a rapid glance around to assure himself that the coast was clear, sprang through the hedge to secure Ponto. He was, however, doomed to misfortune on this, as on the former occasion. The gamekeepers were up before he could retrace his steps into his own property; and he was immediately seized as a poacher and a trespasser. In dogged silence he accompanied the keepers to the house of the same magistrate who had before convicted him; but that 'worthy gentleman' was absent in London, and the prisoner was accordingly taken before the rector of the parish, who was also in the commission of the peace. The Squire was sent for, and the case was entered into under all the unfavourable circumstances of a previous conviction—a fruitless appeal—the exaggerated or positively false representations of the gamekeepers—the malignity of the Squire, and the readiness of his Reverence to believe every thing that was set forth to the prejudice of the prisoner. The parson-justice determined to send the case to the Sessions; and George was ordered to find bail. This was easily done, and he was accordingly liberated.

"This second misfortune, of the same kind, plunged the two families into the deepest affliction, and made Marion very ill. George said but little on the subject: he refused this time to employ any legal advice in getting up his defence, both on account of the expense, and because it was notorious that the unpaid magistrates always dealt more harshly with those persons who *dared* to show fight with the weapons of the law. Again there was a great sensation in the neighbourhood; and every one waited anxiously for the day of trial. That day came; and George left his Marion on a bed of sickness, to repair to the market-town. The Squire, the parson-justice, and the magistrate who had convicted the defendant on the previous occasion, and who had by this time returned from London, were all on the bench. The two gamekeepers swore that George Dalton had coursed with the same hound which had led him into trouble before—that he had persisted in keeping the dog in spite of the remonstrances of his friends—that in the case then under the cognisance of the court, he had encouraged the dog to chase the hare— that he had followed into the Squire's land—and that he was in the act of concealing the hare about his person when he was stopped by the keepers. George told the entire truth in defence, and implored the magistrates not to allow him to be crushed and ruined by the malignity of Squire Bulkeley. He was then about to enter into explanations to show wherefore the Squire persecuted him; but the chairman stopped him abruptly, saying, that he had no right to impute improper motives to any member of the court. The Squire, moreover, indignantly—or, at least, with seeming indignation—denied any such selfish purposes as those sought to be imputed to him; and it was very evident, that even if the magistrates were not already prejudiced against Dalton, this attempt at explanation on his part fully succeeded in rendering them so. George was sentenced to three months' imprisonment in the County House of Correction; and he was forthwith removed thither without being allowed to go home first and embrace his sick wife.

"You may suppose that Marion was distracted when she received this intelligence, although my mother went and broke it to her as gently as possible. Old Dalton was so overwhelmed with grief that he became dreadfully ill, took to his bed, and died three weeks after his beloved son's condemnation. My mother went to stay altogether with Marion until George's return, which took place at the expiration of his sentence. But how he was altered!—altered in mind as well as in personal appearance. He was gaol-tainted: his honourable feelings were impaired—his generous sympathies were ruined. He was still kind and tender to Marion and his child; but his visits to the ale-house soon re-commenced, and he neglected his work more and more. One night, about six weeks after his release from prison, a tremendous conflagration was seen in the immediate neighbourhood of the Squire's mansion: all the out-houses and farms were on fire; and, despite of the assistance rendered by Mr. Bulkeley's people, those premises were reduced to ashes. That it was the work of an incendiary was clearly ascertained; and suspicion instantly pointed to George Dalton. He was taken before a magistrate and examined; but nothing could be proved against him. The magistrate, however, observed, that he felt convinced of George's guilt, and deeply regretted the necessity there was to discharge him. I well remember that my father and mother evinced by their manner their fears that George was indeed the incendiary.

"From that moment a dreadful change came over my sister Marion. She grew profoundly melancholy; but not a murmur nor a complaint escaped her lips. There can be no doubt that *she* was aware who the incendiary was; and that knowledge was the death-blow to her happiness. The child, deprived of its proper nutriment—for Marion wasted to a mere shadow—drooped and died; and the poor mother declared hysterically that its loss was the greatest blessing which could have happened to her. This was the only allusion she was ever heard to make, direct or indirect, to the unhappy state of her mind and of her home. George continued kind to her; but kind rather in the shape of forbearance than in tokens of affection: that is to say, he never said a harsh word to her—nor beat her—nor slighted her; but he gave her little of his society, and was usually silent and thoughtful when in her presence.

"One day the parson-justice, whom I have before mentioned, called on the Daltons, and remonstrated with George on his conduct in absenting himself from church.—'I shall never go again, sir,' was the dogged answer.—'And why not?' demanded the clergyman.—'Because I got no good by it,' replied Dalton. 'The more I strove to be respectable, the more I was persecuted. The hound I liked, almost as if it was a human being, and which got me into two dreadful scrapes, was obliged to be given away; my father was killed by grief for my wrongs; and my wife's sorrow has led to the death of my child. My character is gone; and I know that sooner or later, I must be ruined, as I have no heart for work. Every thing that one prays for, and that I have so often prayed for, has been swept away: I mean an honest reputation; the bread of industry; a cheerful disposition, and the health and long life of those who are near and dear to us.'—'Then you refuse to go to church any more?' said the parson-justice.—'I do,' was the answer; 'and the law can't compel me.'—'We shall see,' observed the Rector; and away he went. A few days afterwards the Squire issued a summons for George Dalton to attend before him. George went, and found that the Rector had laid an information against him, under an obsolete Act of Parliament,[31] for having absented himself from divine service during a period of six months. George was astounded at the charge, but could not deny its truth. The Squire accordingly sentenced him to a month's imprisonment in the House of Correction; and George was taken back to his old quarters—to the farther contamination of a gaol!

"This was another dreadful blow for Marion; and it produced such an effect upon our father, that, like old Dalton, he fell ill, and soon died. When George was liberated once more, he was compelled to part with his farm at a great loss; for his misfortunes and his absence on two occasions had left it but indifferently cultivated; and, moreover, as my father was now gone, it was thought better that we should all live together. Dalton's farm was accordingly put up for sale; and the Squire became the possessor of the land once more. George was now almost constantly at the ale-house. Instead of expending the money realised by the sale of the farm, after paying the debts due, in increasing the stock and improving the tillage of our land, he squandered it away on worthless companions. His wife never remonstrated when he came home late; but would sit up for him patiently and resignedly: and if ever my mother said any thing, she would observe, 'Poor George feels his wrongs too acutely to be able to bear up against them: there are great allowances to be made for him.' Thus did about two years pass away; and, though I and the two labourers whom we kept worked hard on the farm, yet it wanted the master-hand to superintend; and we found that its produce now scarcely yielded a bare maintenance when every thing was paid. Marion gradually got worse; but her endurance was inexhaustible. It often gave me pain to look at that poor, pale, wasted young woman, and think of her blooming charms when she first loved George Dalton. Her heart was breaking slowly—slowly—slowly! Had she been passionate, or liable to the influence of strong emotions, she would have gone rapidly down to the tomb; but she was so meek—so amiable—so resigned—so patient—so enduring, that her very weakness was her strength.

"Upwards of two years had passed since George's second liberation from confinement, when it was found necessary to raise money to increase the stock of the farm, and buy seed for sowing. George applied to the same attorney who had got up his defence on the occasion of his appeal; and this man offered to induce one of his clients to lend a certain sum on George's and my mother's joint bill of exchange, which he said would save all the expense of a mortgage. My mother objected strongly; but George promised so faithfully to amend his conduct if she would consent, that she did agree. The money was raised; but a considerable portion found its way to the public-house before any purchases were made. Even then, George forgot his pledges, and became, if possible, more idle and dissipated than before. The bill became due, and there were no assets to meet it. The lawyer, however, undertook to manage the affair; and he induced George and my mother to sign some parchment deed, which he previously read over in a hasty mumbling way, and in which blanks were left for the names of another person who appeared to be interested in it; and also blanks for certain dates, fixing the particular conditions as to time. My mother inquired why the name of the other party was not filled in; and the lawyer replied, with a chuckle, 'Oh! that is for the name of my client; and as he has only lent the money to serve you, and not as a mere lender, motives of delicacy induce this suppression for the time being.'—My mother did not like it; but George urged her to sign, and she did so.

"Three months after that an execution was levied upon the farm, at the suite of Squire Bulkeley, the lawyer's accommodating client, who had hitherto kept his name secret! George Dalton was at first a prey to the most terrific rage; but he mastered his feelings at the intercession of Marion and our mother. We were compelled to quit the farm, which now became the property of the Squire, by virtue of the roguish deed which had been drawn up by the unprincipled attorney; and we retired to a humble lodging in the village. Need I say how we all felt this sad reverse—this dreadful degradation? My mother and Marion strove hard to subdue their anguish, in order not to irritate the already much excited George; but there were moments when his outbursts of rage were furious in the extreme. He invoked curses upon the head of the Squire, whom he denounced as the murderer of his father and of mine, and also of his child; and he vowed to wreak a deadly vengeance upon him. At the ale-house, it seems, these threats were repeated, accompanied with the bitterest imprecations. On the following day George was arrested, and conveyed before the parson-justice, on a charge of threatening the life of Squire Bulkeley. He was ordered to find good bail for keeping the peace; but security was impossible in respect to one so fallen, lost, and characterless as he. To prison, then, again he was sent; and for three months he languished there, doubtless brooding over the awful wrongs which the Squire had heaped upon him. And all this time the Squire held up his head high; and no one in his own sphere of life seemed to think that he had acted at all unjustly or tyrannically. On the contrary, the gentry and the influential farmers in the neighbourhood, looked on George Dalton as an irreclaimable scamp, who had only got what he well deserved. Even those persons of the poorer class, who were formerly our friends, looked coldly on us, and shook their heads when the name of George Dalton was mentioned. So sure is it that if you give a dog a bad name, you may hang him.

"We lived as sparingly as possible on the wreck of our little property, during the three months that George's third imprisonment lasted; but I found it very difficult to get work, as the farmers said '*that I was as bad as my brother-in-law.*' And yet there was not a steadier lad in the whole county than myself; and, though invited, I never set foot in the ale-house. I was moreover regular in attendance at church, along with my mother and sister. But I got a bad name without deserving it; and even when I could procure a little employment, I was subjected to a thousand annoyances. Unpleasant hints would be dropped about the burning down of the Squire's out-houses, and the name of George Dalton was darkly alluded to in connexion with that business; or, if I refused, on a Saturday night, to accompany my fellow-labourers to the ale-house, I was taunted with knowing something that I was afraid of confessing in my cups. At that time I often thought of running away, and seeking my fortune elsewhere; but when I looked at my poor mother, now deprived of almost necessaries, and my sister pining away, I had not the heart to do it. Besides, I was greatly attached to George Dalton, and was anxious to see in what state of mind he would come out of prison. Three times during his incarceration was Marion allowed to visit him; and on each occasion she returned home to our humble lodging weeping bitterly. Neither my mother nor myself ever questioned her much; for we knew her extreme devotion to George, and that she would not only always endeavour to conceal his failings as much as possible, but that she likewise strove to hold out hopes of his complete reformation. But when he was emancipated once more, he had become sullen, dogged, and morose—*forbearing* only in respect to Marion, to whom he could no longer be said to be positively *kind*. He did not mention the name of the Squire, nor in any way allude to him; neither did he visit the ale-house—and thus my mother and I began to hope that Marion's fond hopes were likely to be fulfilled.

"Having recruited his strength by a few days' rest, after his half-famished sojourn in the gaol, George one morning said to me, 'Now, Tim, you and me will go out and look for work.' We accordingly set off, but applied fruitlessly at all the farm-houses in the neighbourhood. Some did not want hands:

others positively refused to have any thing to do with George Dalton or any one connected with him. We were returning homeward, mournful enough, when we passed a large lime-kiln, the owner of which had been very intimate with George's father and mine. He happened to be coming up from the pit at the moment when we were passing; and stopping us, he entered into conversation. Finding that we were in search of work, he offered to employ us in the chalk-pit; and we readily accepted the proposal. Next day we went to work; and when the Saturday night came round, we were paid liberally. Thus several weeks elapsed; and we earned enough to keep the home comfortably. Our master was good and kind to us; and the spirits of my brother-in-law appeared to revive. But he never mentioned the Squire, nor alluded to the past oftener than he could help.

"We had been employed in this manner for about three months, when one evening George and I stayed later than the other labourers in the chalk-pit, to finish a job which we knew the owner wanted to be completed as soon as possible. It was ten o'clock before we made an end of our toil; and we were just on the point of retiring, when we saw two persons walking slowly along the brink of the chalk-pit. The moon was bright—the night was beautifully clear; and we obtained a full view of the two figures: but as we were at the bottom of the precipice, they could not have seen us, even if they had looked attentively downward. 'Tim,' said George, in a low, hoarse whisper, 'one of those men is the Squire. I recognised his infernal countenance just now when the moonlight fell full upon it.'—We remained perfectly quiet at the foot of the chalky side of the pit; although I do not believe that George had any bad intention in view, and I only stayed because he did.

"The Squire and his companion began to talk together; and by the name in which Mr. Bulkeley addressed the other, George and I immediately knew that he was one of the very gamekeepers who had twice perjured themselves in mis-stating the circumstances connected with the exploits of Ponto.—'And so you say that the scoundrel Dalton works in this pit now, eh?' observed the Squire.—'Yes, sir,' replied the other: 'he's come down to that at last.'—'By God! I never shall be contented till I send him to Botany Bay, or to the scaffold!' exclaimed the Squire. 'But sooner or later, you see, I obtain vengeance on those who offend me. Old Splint refused to sell me his field, and spoke insolently to me: he died of grief through all that has happened, and the entire farm is now mine. Old Dalton contrived to buy his land, through my cursed neglect in forgetting to tell my agent to except his property from any part that might be sold; but he also died of grief, and the land has come back to me. Ah! ah! I bought that in again too, no doubt to the vexation of young Dalton. Then, next we have the insolent jade Marion: she refused my overtures, and persisted in marrying Dalton; and what has she gained? Nothing but misery. As for George Dalton himself, he insulted and struck me, besides carrying off Marion as it were before my very eyes and making her his wife, when she was much more fitted to become my mistress;—and what has *he* got for his pains? I have crushed and ruined him, and I will never stop till I have shown him what it is to dare to offend an English landowner. But you say that this is the pit where he works?'—'Yes, sir,' answered the gamekeeper.—'Well, I shall see his master to-morrow,' continued the Squire; 'and I'll be bound to say George Dalton will not do another week's work in this place. You may now go and join your men in the preserves; and I shall return to the Hall, by the short cut through the fields. The night is uncommonly fine, however, and is really tempting enough to make one stay out an hour or two.'—'It is very fine, sir,' answered the gamekeeper. 'Good night, sir;'—and the man walked rapidly away, the Squire remaining on the edge of the pit, about thirty feet above the spot where George and I were crouched up.

"'Tim,' said George at last,—and his voice was deep and hollow, although he spoke in a low whisper,—'do you remain here quite quiet: I must have a word or two with that man.'—'For God's sake, George,' I said, 'do not seek a quarrel.'—'No, I won't seek a quarrel exactly,' returned my brother-in-law; 'but I cannot resist the opportunity to tell my mind to this miscreant who is now seeking to deprive us of our bread.'—And before I had time to utter another word, George was gliding rapidly but almost noiselessly up the craggy side of the chalk-pit, holding by the furze that grew in thick strong bunches. I confess that a strong presentiment of evil struck terror to my soul; and I remained breathless and trembling, where he had left me, but gazing upwards with intense anxiety. 'Holloa!' suddenly exclaimed the Squire, who had remained for nearly three minutes on the top of the precipice after his gamekeeper had quitted him—most likely brooding over the new scheme of vengeance which his hateful mind had planned: 'holloa!' he said; 'who is there?'—'I, George Dalton!' cried my brother-in-law, suddenly leaping to within a few paces of where the Squire was standing, and confronting the bad man like a ghost rising from a grave in the presence of the murderer.—'And what the devil do you want here, scoundrel?' exclaimed the Squire.—'Rather what do *you* want, plotting against me still?' demanded George. 'I overheard every word that passed between you and your vile agent; and if there was any doubt before as to your detestable malignity, there is none now.'—'Listeners never hear any good of themselves,' retorted the Squire; 'and if I called you a rascal, as perhaps I might have done, I meant what I said, and you heard yourself mentioned by your proper name.'—'Villain! miscreant!' cried George, now quite furious; 'you shall no longer triumph over me!'—And in another moment they were locked in a firm embrace, but not of love; and in the next moment after that, they rolled over the edge of the precipice, down to within a few paces where I was standing.

"A scream of terror escaped me; for I thought that they must be killed. The Squire lay senseless; but George leapt upon his feet—and almost at the same instant a low moan denoted that his enemy was not dead.—'Thank God, murder has not been done!' I exclaimed.—'But murder *will* be done, Tim, this night,' said George, in a voice not loud, but so terrible in its tone that it made my blood run cold in my veins. 'Yes,' he continued, 'my mortal enemy is now in my power. For a long time have I brooded over the vengeance that I had resolved to take upon him when no one should be near to tell the tale; for *you* will not betray me, Tim—you will not give me up to the hangman on account of what I may do?'—'George, I implore you not to talk thus,' I said, falling on my knees at his feet.—'As there is a living God, Tim, above us,' said George, solemnly, 'if you attempt to thwart me, I will make away with you also!' And having thus spoken, he raised the Squire in his arms, while I still remained on my knees, horrified and speechless. Never, never shall I forget the feelings which then possessed me! The Squire recovered his senses, and exclaimed, 'Where am I? Who are you?'—'George Dalton, your mortal enemy,' was the terrific reply.—'Oh! I recollect now,' cried the Squire, wildly. 'But do not murder me!'—'Your last hour is come! and your death shall be as terrible as human revenge can render it!' said George, in a voice which I should not have recognised without a foreknowledge that it was actually he who was speaking.—'Mercy!' cried the Squire, as George dragged him away towards the middle of the pit.

"Oh! then I divined the dread intent of my brother-in-law; but I could not move a hand to help, nor raise my voice to shout for assistance in behalf of the victim. There I remained on my knees—speechless, stupified, deprived of motion,—able only to exercise the faculty of sight; and that showed me a horrible spectacle! For, having half stunned the Squire with a fearful blow, inflicted with a lump of chalk, George dragged him towards the kiln in which the lime was still burning, diffusing a pale red glow immediately above. 'Mercy!' once more cried the Squire, recovering his senses a second time.—'Mercy! miscreant,' exclaimed George; 'what mercy have you ever shown to me?' and, as he uttered these words, he hurled his victim, or rather his oppressor, into the burning pit! There was a shriek of agony—but it was almost immediately stifled; and the lurid glow became brighter, and the form of my brother-in-law seemed to expand and grow vast to my affrighted view; so that he appeared some dreadful fiend bending over the fiery receptacle for damned souls!

"Still was I a motionless, speechless, stupified spectator of that horrible tragedy, at a distance of about twenty yards. But no words can describe the dreadful feelings that seized upon me, when I suddenly beheld an object reach the top of the burning kiln, and cling there for an instant, until George Dalton with his foot thrust him back—for that object was indeed the

Squire—into the fiery tomb! Then a film came rapidly over my eyes—my head seemed to swim round—and I fell back senseless. I was aroused by a sensation of violent shaking; and, on opening my eyes, I saw George Dalton bending over me. I shuddered fearfully—for all the particulars of the dreadful deed so recently performed, rushed to my mind with overwhelming force; and I remember that I clasped my hands together in an agonising manner, exclaiming, 'My God! George, how could you do it?'—'Tim,' he replied, 'I do not repent what I have done. Human endurance could not stand more. If I had to live the last hour over again, I would act in the same manner. *Your* father—*my* father—and my child, were all as good as murdered by that man: and he has deserved death. Death he has met at last; and the sweetest moments I ever tasted were when I saw him crawling painfully up from the smouldering bottom of the pit, with his flesh all scorched, his clothes singed to tinder, and his face awfully disfigured,—clinging, too, with his burnt hands to the burning lime, and too wretched—yes, too full of horror, even to utter a moan. Then I kicked him back, and I watched his writhings till all was over. He died with difficulty, Tim; and my only regret is that he was not ten hours in the tortures of that death, instead of as many minutes. But, come, get off your knees, and let us be going. I do not ask you whether you mean to tell of me, because that would not prevent you if you have the intention.'—'George, do you think it possible!' I exclaimed, scarcely able to recover from the horrified sensations which were excited by the cold, implacable manner in which he had described the dying efforts and agonies of his enemy.—'Well, Tim,' he said, 'I don't ask you for any promises: you can do as you like. One thing is very certain, I could never harm you; and so, if you do take it into your head to turn round upon me, you would be treating me as I never should treat you. Let us say no more about it; and if you *can* keep a composed countenance before the women, do.'

"We left the pit; and when we reached the top, George said, 'You go one way, and I will go another. If you are met out late by any one, you would not be suspected; but I should—and I would not involve you in any danger by your being seen with me; for, remember Tim,' he added, as we were about to separate, 'if I should happen to be caught out, I shall never say that you were present. And now get home as soon as you can; and say that you left work an hour ago, but that you took a walk, or something of that kind, before you went home. You can also seem surprised that I have not yet come back: that is, if I don't get home before you.' We parted, and I took the nearest road to the village, which I reached a little after eleven. Marion and my mother were rather uneasy at our absence; and I was quite unable to master my feelings so far as to appear composed and comfortable. Indeed, they were already overwhelming me with questions, when George made his appearance. I was astonished to see how happy he appeared: there was, positively, a glow of animation in his countenance, as if he had done some admirable deed.

Somehow or another, his good spirits were catching; and I began to think that an admirable deed had really been accomplished, in ridding the earth of a monster whose delight was to crush and oppress the poor. George said that he had been to deliver some message to the owner of the kiln, after he had separated from me; and that made him so late. I had already stated that I had taken a good long walk, and our tales were believed. But, when the two women retired to rest, and George and I were left alone for a few minutes, his manner suddenly changed, as he said in a hoarse, low whisper, 'Tim, there is danger menacing *me*. A few minutes after you and I parted, I met the Squire's gamekeepers near the pit, as they were going their rounds on account of the poachers; and they recognised me. My only chance of safety is in the probability that the lime will consume the body entirely. At all events I shall be the first at the pit in the morning.' I was horror-struck at what he told me, and conjured him to seek safety by flight; but he declared his resolution to await the issue of events, and trust to fortune. He said that he felt perfectly happy in having wreaked his vengeance upon the Squire, and should not experience other feelings, were he on the scaffold. He then rose and went to join Marion, while I prepared to spread my bed as usual on the floor of our little parlour.

"It was not yet day-light when I was awakened by hearing a noise in the room; and on inquiry, I found that it was George, about to sally forth, as he had intimated to me on the preceding night. I offered to get up and accompany him; but he said, 'Not for the world, Tim. Should any thing happen to *me, you* must be at least safe, for those poor creatures of women cannot be left without a friend and protector.' He then left the room, and in a few moments I heard the street-door closing gently. I lay down again and tried to sleep, but could not. An indescribable feeling of uneasiness was upon me, and I found myself, even against my will, balancing and calculating the chances for or against the detection of the murder. At length my mind was worked up to such a pitch of excitement that I could remain in bed no longer; and I rose and dressed myself. Having opened the shutters, I found that the day was just breaking. I cleared away the bedding, and laid the breakfast-table, as was my custom. Presently my mother and Marion made their appearance; and we sate down to the morning meal. But I could eat nothing; and my uneasiness was soon perceived. 'Tim,' said Marion, 'there is something upon your mind: I know there is. You cannot conceal it; and if you deny it, you will not be speaking the truth. In the name of heaven, tell me what grieves you! And why has George gone out so unusually early and without his breakfast this morning?'—I assured both my sister and mother that there was nothing the matter with me, and that George had merely gone out early to do a good day's work, as he hoped to get an increase of wages. Marion was not satisfied; but she saw that it was useless to question me, at least before our mother: accordingly, when the latter left the room after breakfast, my sister again urged me to make her acquainted with the cause of the secret anxiety which she knew was preying upon me. I renewed my protestations that she was mistaken. 'Well, Tim,' she said in her quiet, plaintive manner, while her blue eyes filled with tears, 'if any thing should happen, the blow will be certain to kill me, because I shall be unprepared for it.'—For a few moments I hesitated whether I would confide to her the terrific secret of the murder; but I had not the courage, and hurried away to join my brother-in-law at the kiln.

"As I passed through the village, with my pickaxe on my back, I met a person whom I knew. 'Splint,' said he, 'have you heard any thing?'—I know that I turned deadly pale, as I stammered out, 'No, nothing particular.'—He did not notice my change of countenance, but added, 'The Squire is missing, and foul play is suspected. That is all I have heard. But where is George?'—'Why should you instantly ask that question, after mentioning the report about Squire Bulkeley?' I asked; and it was with the utmost difficulty that I could restrain my feelings so as to speak in a manner at all composed.—'Oh! only because if any thing should be wrong, you know, I am afraid that George Dalton would be suspected first; as every one is aware that he is no friend to the Squire;'—and the man passed on his way, not having intended to say any thing cruel or cutting, for he was a good kind of a fellow. My alarms increased; and I felt so terribly uneasy, that I knew not whether to throw down my pickaxe and run away altogether, or whether I should proceed to the chalk-pit. But while I was still weighing in my mind all the chances for and against detection, I came within sight of the fatal spot where the dreadful murder had been perpetrated. There was the height from which my brother-in-law and the Squire had rolled down, so firmly locked in each other's hostile embrace: there was the chimney of the kiln, in the burning-pit of which the wretched man had endured such fearful agonies before death released him!

"I know not how it was—but, though I really wished to fly from the fatal spot, some strange influence urged me on, or rather attracted me thither. When I reached a point from which I could command a view of the depths of the chalk-pit, an icy chill struck to my heart. George was in the grasp of the Squire's two principal gamekeepers; and the labourers of the pit were gathered round the mouth of the kiln, in a manner which convinced me that they had made some discovery. At that instant the words which George had addressed to me that morning, flashed back to mind:—'*Should any thing happen to me, you must be at least safe; for these poor creatures of women cannot be left without a friend and protector.*'—My soul recovered all its power, and I felt that the truth of those words was strong indeed. Yes—what would become of my poor mother and the unhappy Marion, if both of their protectors were snatched away from them? Never was presence of mind more necessary. With a firm step I descended the sloping path leading into the pit, and affected extreme surprise when I beheld George in the custody of the gamekeepers. A rapid but significant glance on his part encouraged me to maintain the part I was playing; and fortunately no one suspected that a mere lad of fifteen or sixteen like me had any hand in the dreadful deed of which there was now evidence to prove the perpetration. It was however with no affected horror that I gathered from the hurried words of the labourers the particulars of the discovery. It appeared that the absence of the Squire from home all night had created an alarm; and this was augmented when it was ascertained that the Squire had been with one of his gamekeepers at the chalk-pit, and that half an hour afterwards this same keeper and another had encountered George Dalton in the same vicinity. The gamekeepers, finding that the Squire had not returned home all night, repaired direct to the chalk-works, where they found George Dalton had just arrived; and the dawn of day showed them enough at the bottom of the lime-pit to convince them that murder had been perpetrated. To the questions put to him by those who arrested him, George replied that he had parted from me at about a quarter to ten o'clock on the previous evening—that I had returned home—and that he had remained behind to finish his work;—but he denied having seen the Squire at all.

"I may as well state now, although I was not aware of the fact till some hours later on that terrible day, that the Squire's bailiff had been sent for the moment George was arrested and the murder was discovered; and that, having heard George's answers to the questions put to him, he set off for the village by a short cut over the Bulkeley estate; whereas I took the main road to the pit, and therefore had not met him. It appears that on his arrival at the village, the bailiff went straight to our lodgings, and began to question Marion and her mother as to whether George had been home at all during the night; and if so, at what hour he had returned. Marion named the hour at which he had returned; adding, that he was so late because he had been, on leaving off work, to deliver a message to the owner of the chalk-pit. The bailiff then brutally revealed the whole terrible truth to the two females; and though I was not there to witness the same, yet it is easy to believe that it was terrible and heart-rending indeed. But, heedless of the misery which his abrupt discourse had produced, the bailiff hastened off to the owner of the chalk-pit, and learnt from him that George had *not* been near him on the preceding evening. Back to the pit went the bailiff, now accompanied by its owner; and the next step was to convey the prisoner before the nearest magistrate, who happened to be the rector of the parish. I was desired to go with the party; but no suspicion was attached to me. It was proved that the calcined remains of a human body were found in the hole where the lime was burnt; and that the metal buttons picked up were those which belonged to the coat the Squire had on the previous evening. I need not detail the nature of the evidence which appeared to tell against George Dalton; because you can well understand it from all the circumstances I have already related. He conducted himself with wonderful calmness and presence of mind throughout the long examination, which lasted for several hours; and when the magistrate asked him if he had any thing to say in his defence, or to show why he should not be committed for trial, he answered in a firm tone, 'I am innocent, and have nothing more to say.' He was accordingly committed for trial—handcuffs were put upon him; and he was removed to an out-house, guarded by constables, until a cart could be got in readiness to convey him to the County Gaol.

"But in the yard of the rector's abode a heart-rending scene took place. Marion was there, waiting to see her husband, of whose guilt *she*, poor thing! could entertain no doubt. She had left our mother, who had fallen down in a fit when the disclosure was so rudely made by the bailiff, to the care of the landlady of the house in which we lived; and, crushed with deep affliction—weak—sickly—almost heart-broken as she was, she had dragged herself to the place where she heard the examination was going on. 'Oh! George, George!' she exclaimed, as she rushed forward to embrace her husband, whose manacles rattled, as, forgetting that he wore them, he endeavoured to extend his arms to receive her. How poor Marion wept!—what convulsive sobs escaped her bosom! George wept also; but he said every thing fond and endearing to console her. The parson-justice appeared at the door of his house; and, perceiving the sad spectacle, said, 'Take that woman away: I will not have such scenes under my windows. She is no doubt as bad as he.'—Never shall I forget the look of imploring anguish which Marion turned towards that *minister of the Gospel*, who spoke so sternly and so unjustly; then, in the next moment, she fell senseless upon the ground. The constables rushed upon George to drag him off to the out-house: but he hurled them away, manacled as he was, crying in a voice that struck terror to my soul, 'I will not move an inch till I see this poor innocent creature properly cared for. Keep off—or I shall do *another murder*!'—'Another murder!' exclaimed the rector: 'then he confesses that of the Squire!'—But George heard not the observation; nor did he seem to notice the tremendous oversight which he had committed in the bewildering anguish of the moment. Bending over Marion, he raised her with his chained hands, while one of the rector's servants, more humane than his master, brought out water to sprinkle upon her countenance. At length she slowly opened her eyes; and George, beckoning to me, said, 'Now, Tim, take her away: I cannot bear this scene any more!'—I approached, and lent my support to poor Marion, while George, of his own accord, hurried to the out-house, not once casting a look behind him.

"I know not how I got my wretched sister home;—and I was nearly as wretched as herself. But at length we reached our humble lodging, where the landlady, who appeared to be the only friend left to us in the world, did all she could to console the miserable young wife. Had it not been for that kind-hearted woman, we must all have perished through sheer want; for I received notice from the owner of the chalk-pit that my services would be dispensed with in future, and no one else would give me work. A week after George's committal, my mother died; and she, who was once the wife of a farmer well-to-do in the world, was now buried at the expense of the parish! When the funeral was over, and Marion grew somewhat more composed, she insisted upon removing to Winchester, so as to be near the gaol wherein her husband lay. 'If we go,' said I, 'we must beg our way.'—'Then we will beg our way, Tim,' answered Marion; 'for, whether innocent or guilty, George is my husband, and I can never cease to love him.'—I offered no farther remonstrance; so, bidding our kind landlady farewell, we set out, with only half-a-crown in our pockets; and for that sum we were indebted to that same good landlady.

"On our arrival at Winchester, we took a small lodging near the gaol; and Marion went to see her husband. She insisted upon going alone; and I did not thwart her in any of her wishes. When she returned to me, she seemed a little more tranquil than she had yet been since the dreadful disclosure of George's arrest on an accusation of murder. She was consoled by having seen her husband, although she could not do otherwise than believe him guilty. But of that she never spoke to me; and I was very careful not to touch upon the point. I now tried to obtain work; but, at some places where I applied, *character* was inquired about, and at others no assistance was wanted. At last I was actually compelled to go into the streets and beg, for Marion was attacked with severe indisposition. One evening, as I was returning home without having succeeded in obtaining a single halfpenny all day long, and in a state bordering on despair, I was warned by a beadle that if I was seen begging in the streets again, I should be taken up as a rogue and vagabond. Frightened by his threats, I hurried away, and was already in sight of the house in which we lived, and where I had left my poor sister in the morning, when, by the light streaming from a shop-window, I saw an old gentleman drop something on the ground as he drew out his pocket-handkerchief. He went on without noticing the occurrence; and I picked up the object, which proved to be his purse. Gold glittered through the net-work at one end—silver was in the other. I ran after the gentleman as hard as I could, hoping to receive a reward for my trouble; but I could not find him. Thinking he had entered some house in the street, I waited for nearly an hour—but still he appeared not. It came on to rain hard: I was soon wet through to the skin, for my clothes were old and tattered; and the pangs of hunger were now dreadful. The idea of using a small portion of the money in the purse, by degrees grew stronger and stronger in my mind. I thought of poor Marion, who was famished as well as myself;—the temptation was too strong—and I yielded. Rushing to a baker's shop, I procured bread: thence I proceeded to a general-dealer's, and purchased a little tea, sugar, butter, and other necessaries. I then returned home, and told Marion that a charitable gentleman had given me half-a-crown, and that I was also promised work. 'Alas! my poor brother,' she said, 'you are compelled to think of supporting me as well as yourself: but it will not be for long, Tim,' she added: 'I feel it *there* now,'—and she touched her forehead,—'as well as *here*,'—and she placed her hand on her heart.—I burst into tears, and implored her not to talk in that mournful way. She shook her head, sighing piteously—but said nothing.

"Next day I went out and remained absent until night. When I came home again I said that I had obtained work, at the rate of two shillings a day and was to be paid every evening. So I laid two shillings on the table. I forgot to observe that the purse contained about eleven pounds in gold and silver; and I was determined to dole it out in such a way that Marion should not suspect me of deceiving her. As often as the gaol regulations would permit, she visited her husband; for the little comforts which I was now able to provide for her, restored her strength in a trifling degree—at all events, sufficiently so to enable her to drag her drooping form along to the dungeon which held all she deemed most dear. Once only did I see George before the day of his trial; for Marion preferred to visit him alone. He was greatly affected at beholding us together, and thanked me for my kindness towards my sister.

"At last, after the lapse of about three months, the Assizes commenced; and on the second day the trial came on. George had counsel to defend him: for I supplied the means from the purse, having invented some tale to account for the possession of the requisite sum to fee the barrister, so that Marion was satisfied. It was with the greatest difficulty that I could persuade her to remain at home during the proceedings, at which I was compelled to be present as a witness. I need not detail all the particulars of the evidence given against my unhappy brother-in-law: circumstances all told in his disfavour, and the observation which he had let slip, '*I shall do another murder*,' was made the most of by the counsel for the prosecution. I was examined, and I swore that I had quitted the prisoner at the lime-kiln at a quarter to ten on the night in question. It was proved that it was not until *past* ten that the gamekeeper accompanied the Squire to the neighbourhood of the fatal place; and therefore no questions were put likely to embarrass me. The counsel for the defence argued most ingeniously in George's favour; but the Judge summed up against him.[32] The Jury did not deliberate ten minutes; and the verdict was *Guilty*! George was standing in the dock all the time that the Jury were whispering together and when the foreman pronounced his doom; and a slight muscular twitching of the lips was the only sign of emotion. The Judge put on the black cap,[33] and sentenced him to death in the usual horrible terms. I must confess that, though I had but little room in my soul for reflection of any kind—so much was it occupied with the *one* dreadful fact of the day—I shuddered and looked with loathing upon the Judge,—to hear that old man, himself having one foot in the grave, uttering such a disgusting, cruel, and inhuman sentence as this:—'*You shall be taken back to the place whence you came, and thence to a place of execution, where you shall be hanged by the neck until you are dead!*' Then, when man has done his worst, and will not forgive nor attempt to reform the criminal, the awful atrocity concludes with the damnable mockery—'*And may the Lord have mercy upon your soul!*' I call it a mockery, because it is insulting to heaven to invoke that pity and compassion which human beings so positively refuse. But then the old Judge was a mere mouthpiece through which the blood-thirsty law spoke; and he was compelled to do a duty for which he was so well paid. Still I loathed that old man who could *sell* his feelings for money, and who could be allured by the temptation of a large income to undertake an office which constrained him to doom his fellow-creatures to die the deaths of mere dogs. I wondered whether he could sleep comfortably in his bed afterwards; and I thought at the time that I would sooner be the veriest beggar crawling on the face of the earth, than a Judge with all his money—all the respect shown to him—and all his titles of Lordship!

"But I have wandered away from my subject. Poor George was removed from the dock:—I mean, he accompanied the turnkeys back to the gaol; for he walked as firmly as I could do at this moment. I now had a most dreadful duty to perform—to convey the result to Marion. But I hastened back to her, fearful lest she should learn that result from lips which might not break the horrible tidings slowly to her. When I entered the garret where I had left her, I found her on her knees praying aloud and fervently. The sight was too much for me; and I burst into tears. She rose slowly, took me by the hand, and said, 'Tim—dear Tim, you need not attempt *to break it gently to me*, as I know you have come to do. I feel—something tells me, indeed—that it is all over: and I have been long prepared for this awful moment! I have never allowed myself to indulge in vain hopes. The world, I was convinced, would persecute my poor husband until it drove him to——but I cannot, cannot say where! That he was guilty of the deed, Tim, I have known all along; and, dreadful as that deed was, I could not reproach him for it. He was goaded to desperation by wrong heaped upon wrong; and, instead of being treated as a criminal, he should be looked upon as a victim himself.'—Marion had spoken with an unnatural calmness, which made me tremble lest her reason was deserting her; but when she had concluded her address to me, she threw herself into my arms, and burst into a violent flood of weeping. I endeavoured to console her: she grew frantic. The command which she had maintained over herself throughout that dreadful day, and in the solitude of that garret, had tried her powers of endurance too severely; and now that her long pent-up anguish burst forth, it was awful in the extreme. 'Oh! my God!' I exclaimed; 'what have we done that we should be thus tortured on earth, as if we were in hell?'—and then I thought of the crime I had committed in appropriating the contents of the purse to my own use—and I felt ashamed. But in a few moments other feelings came over me: it struck me that there was no use in being good. Old Dalton—my father—my mother—poor Marion—and, until the date of that one deed, myself,—none of us had ever been wicked—and yet, how awfully had we suffered. The three first had positively been *killed* by misfortune. And George too,—there was not a more upright, honourable, generous-hearted man in existence than he, until oppression and cruel wrong wrought a change in his nature. Such were my thoughts; and again I asked myself, what was the use of being good? From that moment I determined to do as I saw the world doing around me.

"The execution was fixed for the second Thursday after the trial, which took place on a Tuesday; and during the interval Marion saw her husband three times. I accompanied her on each occasion; for I was afraid to allow her to venture out alone. George maintained his courage in an astonishing manner; but never alluded to the crime in our presence. He showed the greatest affection towards his wife, and the warmest attachment for me; and implored her not to give way more than she could help to grief on his account. The third interview was on the evening previous to the fatal day; and that was heart-rending indeed. Marion, no longer resigned and enduring, was absolutely frantic; and she was borne away, raving wildly, from the condemned cell. I managed to get her home; and some female lodgers in the same house put her to bed. A surgeon was sent for, and he pronounced her to be in the greatest danger. I sate up with her all that night, throughout which she slept at intervals, awaking to rave after her '*dear murdered husband*!' Had she not been my sister, I never could have supported the horrors of that awful night. Towards morning she seemed quite exhausted, and fell into a deep slumber. The execution was to take place at twelve precisely; and I hoped, sincerely hoped, that she might sleep until all should be over. Hour after hour passed—eleven o'clock struck, and still she slept. Every now and then she started convulsively, and murmured the name of her husband. Oh! how anxiously did I then wait for the chimes that proclaimed the quarters! and how slowly went the time! 'Poor George! what are your feelings now?' I kept repeating to myself. A quarter past—half-past eleven,—a quarter to twelve,—these had all struck, and still she slept. As I sate by her bed-side, I could hear the rushing crowds in the street below; and I also heard all the lodgers hastening down the stairs to witness the execution! But still Marion slept; and, in the bitterness of my own grief, this circumstance was a slight consolation.

"At length the chimes announced the hour—the fatal hour! Scarcely had they done playing, when Marion awoke with a sudden start, and raised herself to a sitting posture in the bed. Wildly she glanced around—and again she started fearfully as, the chimes being over, the clock began to strike the hour. '*One—two—three*,' she began in a tone of piercing anguish; and on she went counting the strokes till her tongue had numbered *twelve*! 'My God! 'tis the hour!' she exclaimed, with a dreadful shriek; then extending her arms wildly, she cried, 'I come, George—I come!' and fell back heavily in the bed, as if shot through the heart. She was no more!

"It appeared that the drop fell about half a minute after the last stroke of twelve; and, therefore, by a strange chance, poor George must have breathed his last almost at the very instant when Marion uttered those words so wildly—'*I come! I come!*'—Thus died my persecuted brother-in-law and my poor sister; and I was now left alone—friendless—unprotected in the wide world.

"A strange whim now suddenly entered my head: I would bury the remains of the ill-fated couple in the same grave! Such was my idea; and so determined was I to carry it into execution that I set out deliberately and calmly for the purpose of robbing some one to obtain the means for the purpose. When I got into the street I found the crowds dispersing after having witnessed the execution of my brother-in-law. How I loathed the inhuman creatures, who had shown such eager curiosity to view the last struggles of a man hung up like a dog by the blood-thirsty mandates of the law! Some were laughing and joking together as they walked along; and such observations as these caught my ears:—'How game he died, didn't he?'—'That Jack Ketch is a devilish clever fellow at his business!'—'It was the best turnoff I have seen for a long time.'—'I propose that we don't go to work to-day. Let's make a holiday of it? For my part, I never fail to attend all executions that take place in the county, and I always look upon it as a holiday; just like Easter Monday or Whit Monday for instance.'—'What fun it was to see that old chap whom I bonneted in the crowd! How he did curse and swear just as the parson was reading the last prayer on the scaffold!'—'I never had such a jolly good lark in my life. I had my arm round Tom Tiffin's wife's waist all the time.'—'What a precious sight of pickpockets there was in the crowd!'—These, and a hundred other observations of the same kind, met my ears as I walked along the streets through which the people were returning from the execution. At length I passed the door of a public news-room; and there several gentlemen were standing, in conversation about the hideous spectacle, which one of them had witnessed, and which this individual was describing with wonderful minuteness to his companions. I pretended to be looking at some pictures in the shop-window, but was in reality surveying the group, thinking that one of them might become paymaster (though against his will) for the funeral of my sister and brother-in-law.—'You don't mean to say that the woman really did it?' cried one of the gentlemen.—'I mean to say,' answered the person who had witnessed the execution, 'that immediately after the criminal was dead, or rather as soon as he had ceased to struggle, the woman went up on the scaffold and the executioner put the murderer's hand upon her face to cure the King's evil; and when she had gone down again, a countryman ascended to the platform, and was touched in the same way for a wen which he had got upon his head. I saw it all myself.'—'Well, I could scarcely believe it,' said the other gentleman who had spoken.—'I will lay you ten guineas,' exclaimed the one who had witnessed the execution, 'that if you ask any other person who was present, he will tell you the same thing: and, thus speaking, the gentleman drew out his purse. His friend, however, declined the wager; and the purse was re-consigned to the pocket, but not before I had seen enough of it to convince me that its contents were worth having. I felt the less remorse in robbing that man, because he had described, with such methodical cold-bloodedness, all the minute details of the execution; and, availing myself of on opportunity when the group had got deep into a loud and excited discourse on the incidents of touching for the King's evil and the wen, I managed to extract the purse in even a far more skilful manner than I had expected. The robbery was not immediately perceived; and I got clear away.

"On returning to my miserable garret, and by the side of the bed whereon lay the remains of my once beautiful and amiable sister, I counted the contents of the purse. 'Eleven guineas!' I murmured to myself; and, as I glanced tremblingly at the corpse, it actually seemed to me at the moment as if an expression of deep gloom and sorrow suddenly passed over its countenance. 'Oh! my sister—my dear sister!' I cried; 'I have done it for your sake:'—and then, unable to remain any longer near one who seemed to reproach me even in death, I hurried away to the prison to claim the body of my brother-in-law. This request was granted without difficulty; and in the course of the day the husband and wife lay together upon the same bed—side by side—motionless, white, and cold,—the former murdered by the law, the latter by cruel wrong and diabolical oppression. The undertaker had received my instructions, and the preparations for the funeral were in progress. But two nights did I pass in the same room with those dead bodies; for, although I was afraid, yet something seemed to whisper to me within, that it would be heartless and cruel to abandon even those inanimate remains until the grave should close over them! And as I sate by their side, while a candle burnt dimly on the table, I thought to myself, 'All this tremendous amount of sorrow, calamity, and woe has been caused by a wealthy and unprincipled landlord! Had it not been for Squire Bulkeley, those two would still have been alive, and would have been happy, prosperous, and useful to society. But the tenant or the small landowner has no chance against the proprietor of great estates, if the latter chooses to be a tyrant. The herring has as much right as the whale to swim in the waters which God has made; and yet the whale swallows up the herring! So is it with the great and the small landholder!'

"Well, the funeral took place—and there were four mourners, one real and three sham. The real one was myself—the three sham were the undertaker and two of his dependants. Nevertheless, my aim was accomplished: George and his wife slept in the same grave; and the money of a man who had greedily devoured the hideous spectacle of public strangulation had served to bury them! In spite of my grief I chuckled at this idea; it seemed something like retributive justice. I had now no object in staying at Winchester; and, with eleven shillings in my pocket, I set out to walk to London. During my journey I passed the chalk-pit where the dreadful deed had taken place—I passed it purposely, because I now wanted to harden my mind as much as possible, for I saw it was no use for a poor friendless orphan like me to think of being honest. In the most civilised country (as it is called) in the world, I had seen such abominable acts of oppression perpetrated, under colour of law, that I envied those naked savages in islands a great way off of whom I had read in books; *for I thought that it was better to be barbarians without the pretence of civilisation, than to be barbarians with that pretence.* I had heard a great deal said by my father, by old Mr. Dalton, and also by the clergyman from the pulpit, about the paternal nature of the English Government; but I now began to perceive that it had been mere delusion on the part of my well-meaning parent and Mr. Dalton, and rank hypocrisy and wanton deception on the part of the parson. All I could now think of the paternal Government was, that it favoured institutions by means of which poor men might be driven to desperation, and then they were coolly and quietly hanged for the deeds to the perpetration of which they had been so goaded. I began to look upon the English people as the most chicken-hearted and contemptible nation in the world for allowing the aristocracy to ride rough-shod over them; whereas the great and high-minded French people, as I had read in books, had risen up like one man and overthrown *their* aristocracy altogether.[34] But let me continue my history. Having passed by the chalk-pit—the fatal chalk-pit—I visited the immediate neighbourhood of the farm-house where a happy family had once dwelt—my own! Now it was tenanted by strangers. I went on, and came to the house to which George Dalton had borne my sister Marion a blooming bride: that tenement was now deserted—and it struck horror to my heart to observe—or rather to *feel*—that death-like silence which pervaded a place where the joyous laugh of George Dalton and the musical voice of my dear sister had once been heard. O God! that so much misery should have fallen upon *two* families who strove so hard to live honestly and in peace with all mankind!

"The tears streamed down my face as I turned back into the high road and pursued my way towards London. I now thought, as I went along, that if I could, *possibly* obtain honest employment in the great city, honest I would endeavour to remain,—I say *remain*, because although I had committed two thefts, yet I was far from being utterly depraved. The tears which painful remembrances had called forth, had softened my heart; and the image of my lamented sister appeared to urge me to virtue. Armed with this resolution, I proceeded towards the metropolis. It was evening when, after two days' fatiguing journey, I entered London, and put up at a miserable lodging-house in the window of which I saw a bill stating that single men might have a bed for fourpence a night. Eight hours' good rest gave me strength and spirits to begin my search after employment. I went into the City and inquired at several warehouses if a light porter was wanted. Having met with many refusals, and being wearied with walking about, I went into a public-house to get some refreshment; and happening to mention my situation to the landlord, he very kindly recommended me to apply at a certain warehouse which he named and where he knew that a porter was wanted. I did so, and was fortunate enough to succeed in obtaining the place, with a salary of twelve shillings a week.

"I commenced my new avocation on the following morning, and exerted myself to the utmost to obtain the good opinion of my master. I was regular in the hours of attendance, and frequently remained behind at the office, when the clerks had departed, to finish the labours which had been assigned to me in the morning. I was economical and prudent in my expenditure; and the pittance which I received was ample to keep myself. At the expiration of four months from the time when I first entered this establishment, I had entirely gained the confidence of my employer. My salary was increased; and I began to think that fortune was once more inclined to smile upon me; when a circumstance occurred which convinced me that the long lane of life had not yet taken a turn. My employer one morning desired me to proceed to a particular address, at the West End of the Town, and insist upon the payment of a bill, which, in the course of business, had fallen into his hands, and which had been protested. I instantly set out for the place intimated; and, having inquired for the gentleman, whose name was familiar enough to me, though I could not suspect the identity which proved to be the case. I was shown into an elegant apartment, where a gentleman was sitting with his face to the fire and his back to the door, smoking a cigar. 'Who the devil's that?' demanded the occupant of the room, without turning his head, but in a voice which was not unknown to me. 'If you're a dun, I ain't at home.'——'I have called for payment——,' I began.—'Holloa! who have we here?' ejaculated the gentleman; and, rising from his chair, he disclosed the features of the magistrate who had first committed George Dalton for poaching. 'What! Tim Splint!' he cried: 'is this you?'—'It is I, the brother-in-law of the man whom you helped to persecute,' I returned, equally surprised at this unexpected encounter.—'No impudence, my good fellow,' said the magistrate, very coolly; 'or else I shall be compelled to kick you out of the room. But what vulgar thing have you got in your hand there?'—'A bill, with your name to it, and the payment of which I am come to require,' was my immediate answer.—'Oh! that's it—is it?' ejaculated the magistrate, casting his eyes over the document which I displayed to his view. 'Well, let me see, how shall I pay this? In Bank notes, or by kicking you out of the house, or by recommending the holder to read his bill again this day six months? Oh, I have it;'—and, sitting down to an elegant writing-table, he penned a hasty note, sealed it, and desired me to give it to the person who had sent me. I then withdrew, anxious to avoid a dispute which would be perfectly useless, and which would probably prejudice the interests of my employer. I returned to the office in the City, and delivered the note. The merchant opened it, and his countenance changed as he perused its contents. For some moments he remained absorbed in thought; and then, apparently acting in obedience to a sudden impulse, passed the note to me, who had been anxiously watching the strange demeanour of my master. The letter contained the following words:—'Mr.——*would be much obliged to the holder of his acceptance, for a hundred and sixty-eight pounds, if he would forbear from sending the brother of a man who has been hanged, to demand the amount, as such persons are by no means welcome at the abode of Mr.——, however well they may suit the holder of his bill. The meaning of this request would be ascertained, were the porter Timothy Splint, questioned as to his connexion with the murderer George Dalton.*'—I folded up the letter, returned it to my employer, and said, 'I cannot deny the truth of its contents; but I am innocent, although my poor brother-in law died on the scaffold.'—'You should have been candid at the commencement,' interrupted my employer, firmly but mildly. 'Whether you are innocent or not, matters not now. Had you told me your real position when you first came to me, I should have admired your frankness, and given you a fair trial. As it is, we must part at once.'—I attempted to justify my silence respecting the ignominious end of my relative; but the merchant was inexorable in his determination not to hear any thing in the shape of an explanation. He paid me the wages due to me, with a sovereign over, and dismissed me.

"I forthwith began to look after a new situation; and I remembered the parting words of the merchant whom I had left, resolving to be candid in the first instance, when soliciting a new place. My duties at my recent situation had compelled me to visit other mercantile firms on many occasions; and I had formed the acquaintance of several of the persons employed in those establishments. To some of them I repaired to ascertain where vacancies were to be filled up; and, having obtained a considerable list, I set out upon a round of applications. The first house I inquired at was that of a general merchant and warehouseman, who required a porter and collector of monies.—'Have you ever served in that capacity before?' was the first demand.—'I was in the employ of a highly respectable merchant,' I returned, mentioning his name, 'whose service I only left a few days ago.'—'I remember that you were engaged there; I thought your face was familiar to me,' said the merchant. 'And I also recollect that I heard you spoken of in the highest possible terms,' he continued; 'indeed, you were represented to me as being invaluable in your particular department. But, of course, you did not leave your late employer for any misconduct on your part?'—'Not at all, sir,' was my answer. 'I must, however, explain a certain circumstance———.'— 'Well, I will just send round, merely for the form's sake, you know, and ascertain that it is all right; and if you will call to-morrow morning, I have no doubt I shall be enabled to give you a favourable answer.'—'I must really, sir,' said I, 'speak to you very seriously for a moment before you take any trouble on my behalf. If you will have the kindness to listen to me, I shall explain my real position. The truth is, though perfectly innocent of any crime myself, I have the misfortune to be related to a persecuted man, who was driven by despair to commit a deed for which he suffered on the scaffold.'— 'The scaffold!' ejaculated the merchant in dismay.—'Yes, sir,' I continued, hastily endeavouring to give a full explanation; 'and if you will but permit me to tell you in a few words the melancholy history, you will see no reason to be displeased with my candour. On the contrary, you will, I am sure, pity me, sir.'—'I thank you for such candour,' interrupted the merchant, buttoning up his breeches-pockets, and locking his desk; 'but I regret that, under circumstances, I cannot think of taking you into my service.'—'But do pray listen to me, sir,' I exclaimed: 'you are doubtless a man of sense, of justice, and of impartiality; and I appeal to you———.'—'My good young man, it is no use to take up my time,' interrupted the merchant impatiently; 'I am certainly not going to receive you into my service, under existing circumstances.'

"I was compelled to take my departure. I left the house, ashamed and abashed—fearful that my evil doom was sealed—afraid to look those whom I met in the face—and fancying that every one seemed to know who and what I was. But a few moments' reflection taught me to believe that I had no reason to anticipate failure every where, because I had met with a repulse in one place. I accordingly proceeded to another establishment where a light porter was also required. The head of this firm was a venerable old man, with long grey hair falling over his coat-collar, a bald head, and a huge pair of silver spectacles on his nose. There was altogether something so kind, so unassuming, and so philanthropic in the appearance of this individual, that I was immediately inspired with confidence. I began my narrative, and related the main incidents, without interruption from my hearer, who listened to me with the greatest attention and apparent interest.—'My good young man,' said the merchant, taking off his spectacles, and wiping them, 'I feel deeply for you. Every word which you have told me, I firmly believe; your manner and your language inspire me with confidence. Merciful God! into what a state would society be plunged if innocence that had been wronged, could not obtain the credence of those to whom it offered its justification! I repeat, I am interested in you; I feel deeply for you. You have had your share of misfortune, poor young man! Most sincerely do I hope that your future prospects will not be equally embittered. I have a son of just your age;—he has gone to the East Indies in a free-trader in which I have a share; and, if it were only for his sake, I should feel interested in you, for you resemble him in person. Heaven! what a world this is! Why, man is a cannibal in a moral sense, for he is constantly devouring his fellow-man! Upon my word, I could weep, I could shed tears, when I think of the misfortunes which you have endured.'—'I am overcome by your kind sympathy,' said I, now certain that this time I had encountered the man who would not allow my misfortunes to stand in the way of my appointment to the vacant situation. 'How much did you receive per week at your last place?' asked the old gentleman.—I named the sum.—'And what hours did you keep?'—This question I also answered.—'Was your master kind and considerate?' proceeded the venerable merchant, in a compassionate tone of voice.—'He was very kind in his manners; but at parting he behaved harshly and ungenerously, when he discovered all I have just told you; and I think I had reason to complain.'— 'Ah! it was cruel, it was ungenerous,' said the venerable old gentleman, musing. 'But don't you see,' he added, 'that as society is at present constituted, and I admit that its constitution is vitiated in the extreme, it is impossible for a man who depends upon the world for his subsistence, to act contrary to the received notions and usual habits of that world. Now, for my part, I should be glad, I should be delighted to take you in a moment; but I dare not. I am very sorry, but I really *would* strain a point to serve you, if I possibly could.'—You may suppose that I was astonished at this announcement. I had made sure of the situation from the first moment that the old merchant had addressed me; and I now saw my hopes cruelly and fatally defeated. With a heavy heart I went away; and the tears ran down my cheeks, as I reflected upon all I had just heard. Never did my situation in the world appear more lonely—never more truly desperate!

"My position was too hopeless to allow me to apply at another mercantile establishment for upwards of an hour. It required that interval to soothe and soften down my feelings; and I then ventured into the warehouse of an export merchant upon a very extensive scale, whose name was down upon my list. I was introduced into the presence of a young man, who wore a large blue figured satin stock with an enormous gold pin, and a chain hanging over an elegant silk waistcoat. This gentleman sate on one side of a desk; and his partner, who was dressed as well as he was, occupied the other. I immediately attracted their attention; and the elder partner, laying down his pen, exclaimed, 'Why, you're a devilish smart looking fellow. Here, sit down and take a glass of porter; you seem tired. By the bye, we haven't had our cigars yet, Dick,' he added, addressing his partner; 'let's smoke and talk over this business at the same time. Sit down, my man: we have no humbug about us, I can tell you.'—And so indeed it appeared; for the two gentlemen produced cigars and bottled porter, and I was very soon engaged in a most comfortable chat with them. At length they began to speak about the business which had taken me there, and when I told them my story in a straight-forward manner, they declared, with an oath, that 'they would take me on my word, and that they didn't want any damned reference, or any thing of that kind.' The terms were agreed upon, and I was to commence my duties on the following morning. When I took my leave the two partners shook hands with me, expressing their conviction that 'I was a damned good fellow and understood what was what,' and also that 'I was just the kind of bird they had some time been looking for.' I accordingly entered on this new place; but I had not been there long, before I began to notice, though I was regularly paid, that a great many persons called for money, and never could obtain a settlement of their accounts. On some occasions the partners were denied, although they were in the counting-house, drinking and smoking; and then the applicants were very much disposed to be insolent, making use of such terms as 'swindlers,' 'rogues,' &c. Some would express their conviction 'that it was all a regular *do*,' while others felt equally certain 'that it was nothing but a *plant*.' There was also another circumstance which astonished me; and that was the singular mode in which the business of the firm was conducted. No sooner did the bales of goods arrive by the front door, than they were carried out at the back, and sent away in vans. Altogether it was a most extraordinary firm; and one morning I discovered that the doors were closed, the partners had bolted, and the City-officer was inquiring after them, in consequence of a warrant which he had with him for their apprehension. Thus I lost a place where the duties were easy, but where the respectability attached to it was not very likely to increase my own.

"I was thus thrown once more upon the world; and again was I compelled to look out for a situation. I applied at numerous warehouses and offices; but when I stated my real condition,—when I revealed the secret that I was related to a man who had been hanged,—I was thrust from the doors of some, reproached for my impertinence in calling by others, and treated with coolness or contempt by a third set of men. No one seemed to believe that I could possibly be honest. Day after day saw the renewal of disappointment, and that sickening at the heart which leads to despair;—night after night did I return to my lodging, to meet a landlady who wanted the money I owed her. At last she would have no further patience; and one night when I went back late, she poked her head out of a window, desiring me to begone and loading me with abuse. I slunk away, almost-heartbroken at the treatment I had just received, and at the deplorable situation to which I was reduced. Accident, or rather necessity, conducted me back to the low lodging-house at which I had put up on my first arrival in London; and there I fell in with some persons who were very willing to assist me in a certain way. In fact they proposed that I should join them in a robbery which they were arranging; and after vainly struggling with my better feelings, I consented. It is no use to tell you how I got on from bad to worse:—you can both very well guess how it is that when once a man gets regularly into this line, he seldom or ever gets out of it again till his career is cut short by transportation or the scaffold."

Thus terminated Tim the Snammer's History, which, as we stated at the conclusion of the preceding chapter, we have greatly modified in style and changed in language, without however omitting, altering, or exaggerating any one incident, nor any one sentiment.

It was now late; and the Snammer took his leave of Josh Pedler and Matilda Briggs, having promised to call again next day, and arrange with the former the contemplated robbery of Old Death.

> 30. Taken as a body, there is not a more infamous and tyrannical set of authorities on the face of the earth than the unpaid magistracy of England. How the high spirited people of this country can endure such an atrocious system, is to us surprising. Almost entirely irresponsible—chosen on account of their wealth and influence in their respective counties, but without the least reference to their

abilities—and, by the very circumstances of their position, opposed to the interests of the masses, the justices of the peace are so many diabolical tyrants vested with a power which completely coerces the industrious and labouring classes. If it be necessary to have *paid barristers* as magistrates in the cities and great towns, why should not the same rule apply to smaller towns and to rural districts? To invest an irresponsible, narrow-minded, and prejudiced body of men with such immense powers as those wielded by magistrates, is a foul blot upon our civilisation. Prison-chains, fines, and treadmills are at the disposal of these justices; and the use they make of their power proves that the entire system on which their attributes and jurisdiction are based, deserve universal execration. Thousands and thousands of honest, well-meaning, hard-working families have been ruined by this hierarchy of terrestrial fiends. Talk of the freedom of the British subject, and boast of the trial by jury! Why, any magistrate, by his own *single* decision, can award heavy fines or months of imprisonment! The unpaid magistracy exists as a protection and also as an agency for the infernal Game Laws. Their local powers and influence give them immense weight in general elections, for poor people are afraid to offend them. But the worst kind of unpaid magistrates are the clergymen who are in the commission of the peace. These men usually act more like off-shoots of the Czar of Russia than as magistrates in a civilised country and as ministers of the charitable and generous doctrines of the Christian faith.

31. This act is not only still unrepealed, but was put in force about eighteen months or two years ago, by certain county magistrates against two or three poor labourers.

32. It is generally understood that the Judge should be merely an expounder of the law affecting the cases brought under the cognizance of the court, and also a means of refreshing the memories of the jurymen by reading over his notes, or the salient points in them. At least, to our thinking, a Judge should never allow his own opinion on the point at issue to transpire. If he do, he is almost sure to bias the jury. But, unfortunately, nearly all the Judges in this country act in a dictational manner with regard to juries. They *direct* the verdicts returned. This assumption on the part of the Judges of the privileges and attributes of juries, renders the latter perfectly unnecessary. For ourselves, we believe that trial by jury is in these islands a mere farce—an idle mockery—a contemptible delusion: the Judges are the real juries after all. And yet we boast of the institution! That institution would indeed be a glorious one, were the Judges to discharge their duties properly: *but, in nine cases out of ten, they do not.*

33. There is something uncommonly barbarous in many of our institutions and customs. Were it not associated with such solemn occasions, we should laugh at the mountebank piece of solemn humbug of the black cap—as if the Judge himself could not assume a demeanour serious and dignified enough for the awful and atrocious duty which the law imposes upon him in pronouncing death sentences. The custom of Judges and barristers disfiguring themselves in huge wigs is a mere relic of barbarism, and unworthy of a civilized age. If the law cannot maintain its solemn majesty without such wretched aids, heaven knows there must be something radically wrong either in the constitution of the tribunals themselves or in the conduct of the functionaries of justice. Away with all such mockeries and fools'-play as wigs and black caps, and let men distribute the justice *of* men *as* men, and not muffled up and disguised like old women. The maintenance of all customs which our barbarian ancestors handed down to us shows an aversion to *progress* on the part of the Government and the Legislature. The wisdom of those ancestors existed, we imagine, only in the *wig*: let the wisdom of the present day show itself by the fact of discarding all useless pomp and vain ostentation.

34. "The Aristocracy of England, a History for the People," by John Hampden, Junior (the pseudonym of a very clever writer, whatever his real name and whoever he may be) is a work which should be read by all classes—by the aristocratic sections of society, because it may warn them of the impending storm; and by the middle and poorer grades, because it will shew them their oppressors in their true characters. This and William Howitt's "History of Priestcraft" (both published by Messrs. Chapman, Newgate Street) are glorious signs of the times in which we live. From the first-mentioned book we quote the ensuing passage:—

"Look at France. Every one is familiar with the dreadful condition to which its proud and imbecile aristocracy reduced it. Every one knows in what a storm of blood and terror the oppressed people rose and took an eternal vengeance on their oppressors. If we read the accounts of France, just previous to the Revolution, we cannot avoid being struck with a terrible similarity of circumstances and features with those of our own country now. Nay, the following description by their own historian, Thiers, seems to be that of England at present:—'The condition of the country, both political and economical, was intolerable. There was nothing but privilege—privilege vested in individuals, in classes, in towns, in provinces, and even in trades and professions. Every thing contributed to check industry and the natural genius of man. All the dignities of the state, civil, ecclesiastical, and military, were exclusively reserved to certain individuals. No man could take up a profession without certain titles, and the compliance with certain pecuniary conditions. Even the favours of the crown were converted into family property, so that the king could scarcely exercise his own judgment, or give any preference. Almost the only liberty left to the sovereign was that of making pecuniary gifts, and he had been reduced to the necessity of disputing with the Duke of Coigny for the abolition of a useless place. Every thing, then, was made immoveable property in the hands of a few, and every where these few resisted the many who had been despoiled. The burdens of the state weighed on one class only. The noblesse and the clergy possessed about two-thirds of the landed property; the other third, possessed by the people, paid taxes to the king, a long list of feudal *droits* to the noblesse, tithes to the clergy, and had, moreover, to support the devastations committed by noble sportsmen and their game. The taxes upon consumption pressed upon the great multitude, and consequently on the people. The collection of these imposts was managed in an unfair and irritating manner; the lords of the soil left long arrears with impunity, but the people, upon any delay in payment, were harshly treated, arrested and condemned to pay in their persons, in default of money to produce. The people, therefore, nourished with their labour, and defended with their blood, the higher classes of society, without being able to procure a comfortable subsistence for themselves. The towns-people, a body of citizens, industrious, educated, less miserable than the people, could nevertheless obtain none of the advantages to which they had a right to aspire, seeing that it was their industry that nourished and their talents that adorned the kingdom.'—Is not that a wonderful fac-simile of our own present condition? But these circumstances produced revolution in France; what will they produce here! If they are allowed to continue they will produce the very same thing. The French historians assert, that had the cries of the people been listened to before they grew maddened with their miseries, there would have been reform instead of revolution, and their nation would have been spared the years of unexampled horror and self-laceration through which it had to wade. Now is the same saving crisis with us! The people, the most industrious of them in town and country, starve by tens of thousands, or lead a sort of half life in incessant labour, rags, and hunger. All parts of our social system call out for relief. The manufacturer, the farmer, equally complain; the agricultural labourers are reduced to a condition worse than serfdom—to a condition of unparalleled destitution; and in some districts gangs of them are driven to the field, as we learn from parliamentary reports, under gang-masters, and are lodged promiscuously like cattle—men, women, and children, in temporary booths, fitter for beasts than human beings. In many parts of this once happy country the agricultural labourers are getting but five and six shillings per week; while they are asked 8*l.* an acre for bits of land to set a few potatoes on."

The author of "THE MYSTERIES OF LONDON" would not have his readers imagine him to be in favour of "physical force." No—we abhor war even with foreign powers; but no words are strong enough to express our loathing and abhorrence of the bare idea of that infernal scourge—a civil war. Another quotation from the work of John Hampden, Junior, will serve to express also our opinions on the point:—

"The neglect of the public interest it extends to the whole frightful mass of *delegated taxation*, under which the nation groans, even more heavily than under the direct national imposts. The reviewer justly remarks that the maxim of legislators is 'Every one for himself, and the public for us all!' But could this state of things possibly exist if Englishmen did their duty, if they resolved to do their own *public* business, as they do their private—to do it themselves, and not foolishly intrust to men who have shown themselves at once so incapable and so unworthy of trust in every respect? Is there any reason why the people of England, who conduct their commerce, their manufactures, their domestic trade and affairs so admirably, should not conduct the affairs of their government just as well if they were to set about it? Is there any reason that a man who guides a ship round the world, clear of rocks and breakers, should not as well help to steer the vessel of state? Why should not he who governs a steam-engine just as well govern or assist in governing a country? The great Oxenstiern, Chancellor of Sweden, said to his son, 'Mark, my son, with what a small stock of talent a nation may be governed.' But our aristocracy have for ages demonstrated that they do not even possess this 'small stock of talent,' or of as much honesty; and the remedy for the evils they have covered us with is as clear as the day-light:—*The power must be wrested from them!* But how? By arms? No: Englishmen know too well the dangers of revolution: they have too much to lose; and they have too much humanity. The soil of England will not willingly drink in the blood of its children, as in the barbarous ages; the remedy is alike simple and conspicuous. It lies in one joint rising and stern demand of all and every class in the country. All—manufacturer and farmer, gentleman and ploughman, merchant and shop-man, artizan and labourer—all must combine, and with one dread voice, like another Cromwell, command the aristocrats to quit the people's house, and 'give place to better men.' This is the simple and sole remedy. A thousand evils are complained of. 'The whole head is sick and the whole heart is sore;' but 'THE GREAT ROOT OF ALL' is the usurpation of the Commons House of Parliament by the aristocracy. One party proclaims that the whole people is corrupted by the bribery of these patrician senators, and demand the *universal franchise*, and in that they demand the true and only remedy. But because some are for this, and some for that, and do not all join in the *hearty rending shout* for the FRANCHISE—*that magic word in which lies the constitution*—that cure for all bribery (for who can bribe thirty millions of people)—that guarantee for the steady maintenance of the constitution—for, once in the hands of the totality, the totality will never relinquish it again—they cry, but they cry in vain. Till we obtain the *franchise* we obtain *nothing*; when we obtain *that* we obtain *every thing*. Every petition, every demand, however stern or resolved, that asks for any thing short of the UNIVERSAL FRANCHISE, is the preparation of an absurdity, and the greatest of all absurdities. He is just as wise who asks short of this, as if he prayed the Pope to abolish the Catholic religion, or a Jew to give you all he is worth. The aristocracy have usurped the House of Commons—for what? Just for this very purpose—of resisting the proper demands of the people—of maintaining and perpetuating all the evils for whose removal you pray. It is true the people, combining on some great emergency—driven, as it were into this combination by some desperate pressure—may alarm the aristocracy into some individual concession, as in the case of the Reform Bill. But this is a stupendous exertion, a violent and convulsive sort of action in the political system, which wrests only, at the point of famine or national ruin, its own rights from the usurping party. Public opinion is said, in this country, to be the actual ruling power; but it is a fitful and irregular power. Like the Indian, or the boa-constrictor, it is aroused to action only by hunger or imminent impending danger; at the smallest return of ease it pauses; it becomes drowsy again, and the mischief goes on for another period. If public opinion really rules, it should lift itself to the necessary height of command, and do its work effectually. That would save us all much trouble. There is but one perfect permanent remedy—but one means of absolute cure for our perpetually recurring evils: *We must have these usurpers out of the people's house, and rule in it ourselves!* and this is to be done only by insisting on *the franchise, the whole franchise, and nothing but the franchise.*"

CHAPTER LXXII.
MR. AND MRS. CURTIS.

It was about two o'clock on the following afternoon that a travelling-carriage with four posters thundered along Baker Street, to the great admiration of that semi-fashionable neighbourhood, and at length stopped at a house the door of which was immediately opened by a footman wearing a livery of such varied colours that the rainbow was nothing to it.

Divers countenances appeared at the windows of the neighbouring dwellings; for it would seem that the travelling-carriage—or rather the persons whom it contained, were an object of curiosity and interest to the elderly ladies in turbans in the drawing-rooms and the servant-maids in the garrets, the latter of whom completely flattened their noses against the panes in their anxiety to obtain a view of the fashionably dressed gentlemen who handed the magnificently attired lady from the vehicle, while the footman in the transcendent livery assisted the lady's-maid to alight from the high seat behind.

And since all the neighbourhood of Baker Street appears to know right well who the arrivals are, we shall not affect any mystery with our readers; but plainly, distinctly, and at once declare that the fashionably dressed gentleman was Mr. Frank Curtis, and the magnificently attired lady was Mrs. Curtis, late Mrs. Goldberry.

This excellent couple had just returned home, after passing their honeymoon in the country, as all rich and fashionable people are bound to do; and five little Goldberrys were crowding at the front door to welcome their mamma and their "new papa." These specimens of the Goldberry race formed, in respect to their ages, an ascending scale commencing with Number 5 and terminating with Number 13, and exhibiting as much pleasing variety as could possibly exist in the pug-nose species and the chubby-face genus.

These delightful children set up a perfect yell of joy, which was heard at least ten houses off, when their "new papa" assisted their old mamma to alight from the carriage; for Mrs. Goldberry could not be said to be *young*, she being on the shady side of forty, though blessed with such a juvenile family.

"Happy is the *man*," says the psalmist, meaning also *woman*, "who hath his quiver full of them:" but Mrs. Goldberry fancied that it rather spoilt the effect of a bride's return, to behold a hall full of them. Nevertheless, she gave them each a maternal hug; and the youngest set up a shout because she did not give him a box of toys into the bargain.

Let us suppose half an hour to have elapsed since the return of the "happy pair." At the expiration of that period we shall find them seated in the drawing-room, enjoying a pleasant *tête-à-tête* chat until the early dinner which had been ordered should be duly announced by the rainbow-excelling footman.

Mrs. Goldberry was, as above stated, a trifle past forty; although she never acknowledged to more than thirty-one. She was somewhat stout, had coarse masculine features, a tolerably good set of teeth, certainly fine eyes, and was as yet independent of the adventitious aids of the wig-maker and rouge manufacturer. Little of her history was known by Mr. Curtis until the period (a few weeks previously to the marriage) when he became acquainted with her through the simple process of picking up her youngest boy who happened to fall into some mud one day when the lady and her children were taking a walk in the vicinity of Baker Street. This little act of politeness on the part of Frank had naturally led to the exchange of a few observations; the exchange of a few observations brought Mrs. Goldberry to her own door; her own door admitted her into the house, whither Frank was politely invited to follow her; the following her in was followed by the serving up of luncheon; the luncheon led to increased communicativeness; and the communicativeness made Frank aware that his new acquaintance was the widow of the late Mr. Goldberry, gentleman, and the undisputed possessor of a clear income of five thousand a year. Glorious news this for Frank, who suffered the lady to understand that he enjoyed a similar income; and then they laughed a great deal at the funny coincidence. When Frank took his leave, he requested permission to call again; and this favour could not be refused to a gentleman who had picked the child out of the mud and who had five thousand a year. Thus frequent visits led to tender proposals; the tender proposals ended in marriage; and the marriage ended in——

But we were going on much too fast; and therefore we must pause at the point indicated ere we commenced this brief digression—namely, at the *tête-à-tête* discourse while awaiting the announcement of dinner.

"Well, my love," said Frank, "here we are once more in London. Upon my word, there's nothing like London after all—as my friend the Earl of Blackwall says."

"And yet I think we were very comfortable in the country, Frank?" observed Mrs. Curtis, late Mrs. Goldberry, with a simper as fascinating as she could possible render a grimace formed by a large mouth.

"Oh! but you and I can be happy any where, dear," said Frank. "We mustn't remain in Baker Street, though: I shall take a slap-up house in Grosvenor Square, if I can get one there: at all events, somewhere more in the fashionable quarter. Now, I'll tell you what I've been thinking of—and I'm sure that you'll approve of my plan. You see, there's all those dear children of your's—I'm sure I love them as well as if I was their real father, the darlings——"

"You're quite a duck, Frank," exclaimed Mrs. Curtis, tapping him slightly on the face.

"Well—I don't think I'm a bad fellow at all," continued the young gentleman, smoothing down his hair very complacently; "And the plan I'm going to propose to you will prove it. Indeed, it's just what my very particular friend the Marquis of Woolwich did, when he married under similar circumstances—I mean a lady with a young family."

"And what did his lordship do?" inquired Mrs. Curtis.

"He made this arrangement with his wife," explained Frank:—"All his own property was to be left in the funds to accumulate for the benefit of the children—never to be touched—to be locked up like a rat in a trap, as one may say; and the lady's property was to serve for the household and all other expenses. Now, this is just what I propose we shall do. My hundred and forty thousand pounds shall be so locked up; and your income, my love, will do for us to live upon. In fact, I'll make a will to-morrow, settling all my fortune on you in case you survive me, or on the children at your death."

It is astonishing how blank Mrs. Curtis's countenance became as her beloved husband proposed this arrangement: but she managed to hide her confusion from him by means of her handkerchief, while he flattered himself that his generous consideration of her children had drawn tears from her eyes.

"This little arrangement will decidedly be the best," continued Frank; "and I shall have the satisfaction of knowing that your dear children are well provided for. In fact, it was but the day before the happy one which united us, that I met my friend the Duke of Gravesend, and he was advising me how to act in the matter, saying what he had done, as I told you just now. And his Grace's authority is no mean one, I can assure you, my dear. But you don't answer me: what are you thinking about?"

Mrs. Curtis was thinking of a great deal;—a horrible idea had struck her. Was it possible that Frank's vaunted property was all moonshine, and that he was now inventing a means of concealing this fact from her. She had been vain enough to suppose all along that he was enamoured of her person far more than of her alleged five thousand a year; and he had given her so many assurances of the disinterestedness of his affection, that she had congratulated herself on hooking him most completely. She knew that he was the nephew of the rich Sir Christopher Blunt, and had readily believed, therefore, that he himself was rich also; and, experienced though she were in the ways of the world, she had not instituted any inquiries to ascertain the truth of his assertions relative to his property. In a word, she fancied she had caught a green, foolish, but wealthy young fellow; whereas she was now seized with the frightful apprehension that she had laboured under a complete delusion. And this alarm was the more terrible, as the reader may conceive when we inform him that she herself was a mere adventuress—without a farthing of annual income derivable from any certain source—and overwhelmed with debts, her creditors having only been kept quiet for the last few weeks by her representations that she was about to marry a young gentleman of fortune. In a word, she had only taken the house in Baker Street on the hopeful speculation of catching some amorous old gentleman of property: and she had deemed herself particularly fortunate when she received the proposals of an amourous *young* gentleman who, in the course of conversation, happened to intimate that he possessed five thousand a year.

Mrs. Curtis's confusion and terror,—nay, absolute horror, may therefore be well conceived, when the dreadful suspicion that she herself was as much taken in as her husband, flashed to her mind.

"You don't answer," repeated Frank: "what the deuce *are* you thinking of?"

"I was thinking, my love," replied the lady, subduing her feelings as well as she could, and still clinging to the faint hope that all might not be so bad as she apprehended,—"I was thinking, my love, that your arrangement is not feasible, for this simple reason—that *my* fortune is so locked up and settled on my children, I can only touch the dividends: and I shall have nothing to receive till July. Moreover, I run very short at my banker's now—indeed, I believe I have overdrawn them—and so, all things considered, it will be impossible, and unnecessary even if possible, to carry your generous proposal into effect."

"I didn't know your money was so locked up!" exclaimed Frank, looking mightily stupid, in spite of his strenuous endeavours to appear perfectly happy and contented. "I thought your fortune was at your own disposal?"

"Certainly—the interest," responded Mrs. Curtis, now finding by her husband's manner that her worst fears were considerably strengthened.

"The devil!" murmured Frank petulantly.

"What did you say, dearest?" asked the lady.

"Oh! nothing, love—only that it doesn't signify at all, so long as we have the interest of the money settled on your children—and that's five thousand a year."

"Which, with your five thousand a year, makes us ten, love," added the lady, eyeing him askance.

"To be sure!" said Frank: and, walking to the window, he hummed a tune to conceal his desperate vexation.

This worthy pair had, however, each a consolation left—one real, the other imaginary.

The real consolation was on the side of the lady, who had saved herself from the danger of a debtor's prison by marrying Mr. Curtis. The imaginary consolation was the idea which this gentleman nourished that his amiable spouse enjoyed at all events the annual income of five thousand pounds. Moreover, as he glanced round the elegantly furnished drawing-room, and in imagination at all the other apartments in the dwelling, he thought to himself, "Well, hang it! with five thousand a year and this splendid house, I think I can manage to make myself pretty comfortable. Of course every thing's paid for—and that's a blessing!"

Scarcely had Mr. Curtis disposed of this solacing reflection, when the livery servant entered to announce that "dinner was served up."

Frank offered his arm to his lady in the most jaunty manner possible—for, as the reader may suppose, he had many reasons to induce him to be uncommonly attentive to one who (as he thought) held the purse; and the lady, on her side, accepted in a most charming manner the homage thus paid her—because she was not as yet quite certain that her husband's property was really aerial, and even if it should prove so, he must become the scapegoat between herself and her ravenous creditors.

Indeed the little tokens of endearment which the "happy couple" thought it fit to lavish upon each other as they descended the stairs, created such huge delight on the part of the livery servant following them, that this individual, totally forgetting the dignity which should have accompanied such a gorgeous livery, actually and positively diverted himself by means of that wonderful arrangement of the hands commonly called "taking a sight."

The dinner passed off in the usual way; and when the cloth was removed and the domestic was about to retire, Frank exclaimed in an authoritative manner, "John, bring up a bottle of claret."

"Yes, sir—claret, sir?" said the servant, fidgeting about near the door, and glancing uneasily towards his mistress, who did not however happen to observe him.

"I specified claret as plain as I could speak, John," cried Mr. Curtis angrily; "and so make haste about it."

"Yes, sir,—only—" again hesitated the domestic.

"Only what?" vociferated Frank.

"Only there ain't none, sir," was the answer.

"No claret, John?" cried Mrs. Curtis, now taking part in the discussion.

"No ma'am. There was but two bottles of wine left when you went away, ma'am—with master—and them's the Port and Sherry on the table now ma'am."

"John, you must be mistaken!" exclaimed Frank. "Your mistress assured me that the cellar was well stocked——"

"Yes, my dear," interrupted Mrs. Curtis: "and I was so far right in telling you what I did, because on the very morning—the happy morning, dear, you know—when we went away, I wrote to Mr. Beeswing, my wine-merchant—or rather *our* wine-merchant, I should say—to order in a good stock of Port, Sherry, Champagne, and Claret."

"And what the devil, then, does Mr. Beeswing mean by this cursed neglect?" cried Frank. "There's Log, Wood, and Juice, my friend Lord Paddington's wine-merchants, who would be delighted to serve us. Did you know of this order, John, that your mistress gave?"

"Ye-e-s, sir—I did," was the stammering reply, delivered with much diffidence and many twirlings of the white napkin.

"Well, my dear—it is no use to make ourselves uncomfortable about the business," said Mrs. Curtis, evidently anxious to quash the subject at once. "You can put up with what there is to-day; and to-morrow you can give an order to your noble friend's wine-merchants. That will do, John—you can retire."

"No—by God! that will not do!" vociferated Frank. "This fellow Beeswing has behaved most shamefully. It's a regular insult—as the Prince of Gibraltar would call it! But I dare say he forgot it: and since you knew of the order, John, why the devil didn't you see that it was executed while we were away?"

"My dear——" began Mrs. Curtis, in a tone of remonstrance.

"Answer me, you fellow!" cried Frank, turning in a threatening way towards the domestic, and unable to resist the opportunity of indulging his bullying propensities. "Why the devil didn't you attend to the order given by your mistress?"

"Well, sir—and so I did," responded the servant, now irritated by the imperious manner of his master. "I went a dozen times to Beeswing's while you and missus was away."

"Frank, dear—do leave this to me," urged the lady.

"No, my dear—this concerns me, as the master of the house," exclaimed Frank, looking very pompous and very fierce. "Well, John—and what the deuce did Beeswing say when you did see him?"

"Please, sir, he said he'd rayther not," was the astounding answer.

Mr. Frank Curtis looked aghast.

"I always knew he was the most insulting fellow in the world—that Beeswing!" cried the lady, colouring deeply and affecting violent indignation. "But we will never deal with him again, I vow and declare! John, tell him to send in his bill——at once, mind——"

"He has, ma'am," interrupted the servant "In fact, there's a many letters waiting for master."

"Then why the devil didn't you give them to me before?" exclaimed Frank, not knowing precisely what to think of Mr. Beeswing's conduct, but in a very bad humour on account of the disappointment relative to the claret.

John, the servant, made no reply to the question last put to him, but advancing towards the table, produced from his pocket about thirty letters and other documents, all of which he laid before his master, his countenance the while wearing a most curious and very sinister expression, as much as to say, "You're a very bumptious kind of a young man; but these papers will, perhaps, bring you down a peg or two."

"You may retire," said Frank, savagely; and this intimation was forthwith obeyed. "Very curious conduct, that of Beeswing, my dear?" continued Mr. Curtis, as soon as the door had closed behind the servant.

"Very, dear—I can't make it out," responded Mrs. Curtis. "But pray don't bother yourself with those letters and papers now. They can't be very particular; and you will have more time to-morrow, dear."

"Oh! I can look over them, and we can go on talking all the same," said Frank: "because I can't think how the deuce so many letters should be addressed to me *here*—instead of at my own place;—I mean, I shouldn't have thought that such a lot of my friends would have already heard of our union, love," he added, with a tender glance towards the lady, who was sitting very much in the style figuratively represented in common parlance as being "on thorns."

And Mr. Curtis's visual rays, having thus benignly bent themselves on his companion, were once more fixed on the pile of letters and documents lying before him.

The lady tossed off a bumper of Port, and filled her glass again, in an evident fit of painful nervousness; while her husband opened the first letter, the contents of which ran as follow:—

Oxford Street.

"SIR,

"We beg to enclose our account for furniture supplied to Mrs. Curtis, late Mrs. Goldberry, and respectfully solicit an early settlement, as the bill has been running for a considerable time.

"Your obedient Servants,

"TUFFLE and TUNKS."

"The devil!" ejaculated Frank, as he cast his eyes over the inclosure: "'*Bill delivered*, £876 6*s*. 6*d*.' God bless my soul! that's a stinger! Why, I thought all the furniture must have been paid for, my dear?"

"Not exactly, love—you perceive," returned the lady. "One never pays an upholsterer's bill for so long a time, you know: indeed—it quite slipped my memory, it's such a trifle!"

"Well, so it is, dear," observed Frank, reassured by the calm and indifferent way in which his wife disposed of *the trifle*: and he proceeded to open another letter, which announced a second trifle in the ensuing manner:—

Furnival's Inn.

"SIR,

"We are desired by Messieurs Ore and Dross, jewellers, to apply to you for the payment of 377*l*. 10*s*. being the amount of debt contracted by your present wife, late Mrs. Goldberry, with our clients; and unless the same be paid, together with 6*s*. 8*d*. for cost of this application, within three days from the date hereof, we shall be compelled to have recourse to ulterior measures without farther notice.

"Your obedient Servants,

"DAWKINS and SMASHER."

"What a thundering lot of jewellery you must have, to be sure, dear!" exclaimed Frank, as he handed this letter to his wife. "But, 'pon my soul! I think you've been rather extravagant, love—haven't you?"

"Oh! my dear—ladies *must* have jewellery, you know," returned Mrs. Curtis; "and, after all I have paid Ore and Dross, I really am surprised at their importunity. But we will pay them, and have done with them, dear."

"So we will, love," responded Frank; "and I'll ask my friend the Duke of Hampstead to recommend *his* jeweller to us. But here's a precious letter! Why—what the deuce? There's a dozen pawnbroker's tickets in it, I declare!"

Mrs. Curtis fell back almost senseless in her chair, while her husband perused the ensuing letter:—

"i rite maddam 2 inform u that I can't sel the dewplikets wich u Placed in mi ands as seckeuraty for mi Bil and has u've married a gent wich as propperti i ope u'll now settel my Bil wich as bin a runnin for 18 munce and i ope u'll settel it soon leastways as soon has u cum ome becaus i ham in rale want of it being a loan widder wich as lorst mi Usban 2 yere cum missummer an having 5 young childern an another cumming bi axident but i shan't do so no more an shal be verry appy to go on washin for u wen u've pade this Bil wich is thirty fore pouns thrippense dere maddam pray do this 2 oblege me the instunt u cum ome u can send it upp by mr jon yure futman or els mi Littel gal shal wate on u at anny our u no i've never prest u an i tuk the dewplikits 2 oblege u but coodn't dew nuththink with them an now they've run out and its no falt of mine becaus i'd no munny to pay the interesk and u was gorn out of town with ure new usban wich i ear is a very fine young man wich I'm glad to ear for ure sak dere maddam eggskews this long letter becaus the doctor should say i shal be konfined this weak an its hard lines to ave no munney at such a time i arn't sent ome the last batch of linning becaus i ware obleged to mak a way with it butt I send the dewplikit of that has wel has the dewplikit of the wotch and chane an other trinklets wich i ope u'll reseave saf an now as u'r all rite and r a ritch wumman u'll not be angree with me for puttin ure linning upp the spont att such a crittikal moment dere maddam pray eggskews this riting wich i no is verry bad butt mi pen is verry bad an ime in grate pane wile i rite ure obejent umbal servant kummarn susan

spriggs.

mary lee bone

"Mrs. Kirtis lane wigmore strete

baker cavenditch

strete squair."

"Madam, it's all a cursed plant!" vociferated Frank Curtis, starting from his seat, and throwing down the letter, during the perusal of which he had been scarcely able to control his impatience. "I see it all—it's a cursed imposition—an infernal plant—and I'm a—a—damned fool!"

Thus speaking, the young gentleman shook his better half violently by the shoulders; and she, having nothing to urge in explanation of the extraordinary letter of her washerwoman, screamed just loud enough to appear hysterical without alarming the servants and went off into a fit, as a matter of course.

"Fooled—duped—done brown, by God!" exclaimed Curtis, as he began to pace the room with no affected agitation. "Saddled with a wife and five children—overwhelmed with her debts and my own—and, what's a deuced sight worse, made an ass of! I've regularly sold myself, as my friend the Duke——no, damn the Duke! I'm in no humour for Dukes and that kind of nonsense now—I don't know a Duke, and never did—and never shall—and so it's no use telling a parcel of lies any more! Plague take this old cat with her half-dozen brats—or near upon that number——"

"And plague take you, then!" screeched the newly-married lady, recovering with most surprising abruptness from her fit, and starting up like a fury. "Why, you swindling scoundrel, how dare you call me names? I'll tear your eyes out, I will, if you say over again what you've just said."

"I say you're a regular adventuress!" cried Frank.

"And you are an impostor—a cheat!" yelled the lady.

"Your fortune is all a gammon!" exclaimed Curtis.

"And your's all moonshine!" retorted his wife.

"You've taken me in shameful!"

"And you've done the same to me!"

"You're——" cried Frank, nearly suffocated with rage.

"And so are you, whatever you're going to call me!" vociferated the late Mrs. Goldberry.

Curtis was unable to give forth any rejoinder; and Mrs. Curtis, resuming her seat, had recourse to the truly feminine alternative of bursting into tears.

A long pause ensued, constituting a truce to recriminations and vituperations for several minutes, and affording the pair leisure for reflection.

We will describe the ideas that gradually expanded in their minds, as such explanation will the more easily prepare the reader for the result of the quarrel.

Frank Curtis, on his side, recognized the grand truth, that what was done could not be undone; and then he came to the philosophical conviction, that it would be prudent to make the best of a bad job. He reflected on the folly of an exposure, which would be attended with immediate ruin;—bringing about his ears a host of creditors, who would only become the more clamorous when they were brought in contact with each other, and were placed in a condition to ascertain their number and compare the amounts of their claims. He fancied that by allowing himself to be represented as a man of property his wife might silence the creditors for a time, during which the war could be carried on; and though an explosion must sooner or later take place, yet it was some consolation to the young gentleman to think that the evil day might be postponed by keen manœuvring and skilful generalship. He feared being laughed at much more than the idea of a debtor's prison; and delay was every thing to a man in his desperate circumstances. "There was no telling what might turn up;" and he thought that if he could only dazzle the eyes of his uncle Sir Christopher with fine stories relative to the brilliancy of the match which he had formed with the late Mrs. Goldberry, he might contrive to wheedle a large sum of money out of the old gentleman on some such pretext as a desire to discharge divers debts, and a disinclination to confess to his wife that he had contracted them.

On the other hand, Mrs. Curtis fell into a similar train of thought. It would, she fancied, be easy for her to visit the numerous creditors, assure them that she had as yet intercepted all the letters they had written to her husband, and implore them not to ruin her in his good opinion by exposing her liabilities to him. She even arranged in her head the very words which she would use when calling on them:—"My husband is about to sell an estate in Ireland, and the moment the purchase money is paid, I am sure to be enabled to obtain from him a sum sufficient to liquidate all my debts. Have a little forbearance, therefore, and all will be well." Thus *she* also recognised the utter inutility and monstrous folly of exposing themselves by means of quarrels; and as their minds were, by these parallel systems of reasoning, prepared for reconciliation—or at least the show of it—the making up of their dispute was no very difficult matter.

Frank was the one to break the ice with the first overture.

"Well, I think we're two pretty fools," he said, approaching the chair in which she was rocking herself to and fro: "don't you?"

"To alarm all the house, and let our servants know every thing," added the lady.

"No—no: it isn't so bad as *that* yet," returned Frank. "But I vote that we have no more quarrels."

"I am sure I agree to the proposition, Frank," was the answer.

"It's carried then, without a dissentient voice," exclaimed Curtis; "as my friend the Duke——"

"Let us have no more falsehoods," interrupted his wife. "You said just now that you knew no Duke—never had known one—and never should——"

"But I thought you was in a fit at that moment, my dear?" said Frank.

"Maybe I was—but still I could hear all that passed, as you very well know. However, let us be good friends, and hold a consultation how we are to proceed."

"Good!" cried Frank. "And we will begin with a glass of wine each. There—let us drink each other's health. Here's to you, my dear. And now to business. I suppose all these letters and bills are about unpaid debts of yours?"

"Precisely so, love," answered Mrs. Curtis.

"How much do you think they amount to?"

"About eighteen hundred pounds, I should say?"

"And how much money have you got towards paying them, dear?" inquired Frank.

"Eighteen-pence, love," responded the lady, extracting that sum from her pocket.

There was a pause, during which Frank Curtis refilled the glasses; and then the "happy pair" looked inquiringly at each other, as much as to ask, "Well, what shall we do?"

"This is devilish awkward!" observed Frank. "But I'll tell you what I've been thinking of."

"I am all attention, dear," said his better half.

Mr. Curtis then conveyed in words the substance of those reflections which we have recorded above, and which had bent his mind towards a reconciliation.

"I entirely approve of all you say," remarked Mrs. Curtis; "and I will now tell you what I have been thinking of."

"Fire away, love," was her husband's encouraging observation.

The lady detailed, in her turn, the reflections which had occupied her mind a few minutes previously.

"Then we both hold the same opinions?" exclaimed Frank.

"Exactly. And if we play our cards well, there is no immediate danger of any thing," remarked the lady.

"But all the threatened writs—the probability of a sudden arrest—and the clamours of such small tradesmen or other persons as your delectable washerwoman, who is about to add to her family two years after the death of her husband?" exclaimed Frank interrogatively.

"I have trinkets, plate, and such like things which will realise a hundred pounds," said Mrs. Curtis; "and with that sum we can settle the little claimants, who are always more noisy and clamourous than the large ones."

The colloquy had just reached this highly satisfactory point, when a tremendous double knock threatened to beat in the front door, and the bell was instantaneously afterwards set ringing in frantic accompaniment.

"Some one's ill," cried Frank, "and they take this house for a Doctor's."

"At all events it is no dun," observed Mrs. Curtis.

Here the thundering knock and insane ring were repeated.

"I just tell you what, my dear," resumed the young gentleman, rising from his chair, and looking as fierce as possible: "I've a deuced great mind to go out and ask who the devil it is that dares knock and ring twice in half a minute at our door in that fashion. I'm certain it's no friend of your's—and it's none of mine. So—as sure as my name is Francis Curtis, Esquire, of Baker Street—I'll—"

But at this instant the dining-room door was thrown open by the domestic in gorgeous livery; and the countenance of the warlike Francis Curtis, Esquire, of Baker Street, grew white as a sheet, when the servant announced—"CAPTAIN O'BLUNDERBUSS!"

CHAPTER LXXIII.
CAPTAIN O'BLUNDERBUSS AGAIN.

"Be Jasus! and it is my dear friend, Misther Frank Cur-r-tis!" exclaimed the redoubtable officer, as he stalked into the room: then, perceiving the lady, he untied his head in a most graceful manner—or, in plain terms, removed his foraging cap with a certain rounding sweep of his right arm, saying, "Your servint, Mim. I presume that I have the honour-r to pay my rispicts to Mrs. Curtis?"

"Ye-es—that is Mrs. Curtis, Captain," said Frank, while the lady gave a somewhat cold inclination of the head.

"And a sweet and iligant wife ye've got, ye dog!" cried the Captain, bestowing a friendly poke in the ribs of the newly married gentleman. "Come, shake hands, Misther Cur-r-tis: men like you and me mustn't harbour animosity against each other. Let the past *be* past, as the saying is: and an excellent saying it is too, ma'am," he added, in a tone of bland appeal to the lady, as he nearly wrung her husband's fingers off in the enthusiasm of his anxiety to convince him that *this time* at least he came for no hostile purpose.

"Sit down, Captain," said Frank, now feeling more at his ease than he had done since the unexpected appearance of the famous duellist. "Will you take a glass of wine? There's Port and Sherry on the table; and there's Champagne, Claret, Hock, and Burgundy in the cellar—as well as capital whiskey."

"Be the holy poker-r!" exclaimed Captain O'Blunderbuss, "and I'll jist throuble ye for the potheen. The thrue Irish potheen, ma'am," he continued, turning once more towards Mrs. Curtis, "is the most iligant beverage unther the sun. On my estates in ould Ireland I allow no water at all; and my pisanthry is the finest to be seen in the whole country."

"Indeed, Sir," observed Mrs. Curtis, beginning to grow amused with the strange character who had thus intruded himself upon the momentous discussion which she and her husband were carrying on at the time.

"Be Jasus! Mim, and it's as thrue as you're sitting there!" exclaimed the Captain. "In my own counthry, Mim, I'm a Justice of the Pace, and I never allow my pisanthry to be interfered with by the gaugers. I let them keep as many illicit stills as they like; and the consequence is they adore me."

"I should think that to be very likely," said Frank. "But here's the whiskey—and there's hot water. Now, John, put the sugar on the table: that's right!"

The servant having retired, Captain O'Blunderbuss proceeded to compound his favourite beverage by mixing equal parts of spirit and water, and adding thereto three lumps of sugar.

"I always brew the first glass sthrong Mim," he observed, "in honour to ould Ireland. Your health, Mim."

"But I'm not Irish, sir," responded the lady, laughing.

"Then I'm sure ye ought to be, Mim," cried the Captain; "and, be Jasus! if ye was, ye'd be an honour to the counthry!"

Mrs. Curtis simpered, and bowed in acknowledgment of the compliment.

"Come, old fellow," said Frank, "you needn't mind my wife being present—she's a woman of the world, as my friend the Archbishop of Paris used to say of his niece;—and so you may as well tell us how you managed to get out of a certain place and what made you think of honouring us with this visit."

"Och! and be Jasus, I'll answer the last question fir-rst, Mr. Cur-rtis," responded the Captain. "Well, thin, ye must know that I've taken a great affection for ye, because, be the power-rs! I've heard spake of your bravery in a many quar-rters; and it isn't me that would cherish animosity against a gallant fellow."

The Captain might have added that, being in want of grog, supper, and lodging, he had racked his brain all day to think of some soft, easy individual amongst his acquaintance, on whom he could quarter himself for a week or so; and having at length remembered to have seen the marriage of Mr. Curtis and Mrs. Goldberry duly announced, at the time, in the fashionable newspapers (the said announcements having been duly paid for, as a matter of course), it had struck him, that he might make himself very comfortable in Baker Street for a short period.

"Well, I feel highly flattered by your good opinion of me," said Frank. "It's quite true that I've killed a man or two in my time, and winged half a dozen others;—but really those are trifles which one scarcely thinks of any value. At the same time, Captain, we duellists, you know, are devilish chary of our reputation; and so it's just as well that the world should talk in a respectful way about us—eh?"

"Be the holy poker-r! and ye're right, my boy!" exclaimed the Captain, mixing the second glass of grog; then, turning towards Mrs. Curtis, he said, "I always make my second jorum, Mim, a little stronger than the first, for the honour of ould England; because that's always my second toast! So here's for ould England! And now," continued Captain O'Blunderbuss, after having taken a long draught of the potent liquor, "I'll answer your first question, Misther Cur-r-tis. And sure it's how I got out of limbo that ye was asking about. Well, I'll tell ye; and, be Jasus! ye'll say that such a rum start never was seen. The cowardly bastes locked me up in Horsemonger Lane, ye know, at the suit of one Spriggins, for three hundred and forty-seven pounds, including costs.

For three whole days I was jest for all the world like a rampagious lion. There's an infer-r-nal iron grating all round the yar-rd where the prisoner-rs have to walk about; and, be Jasus! I chafed and foamed inside those bar-rs, till the other prisoner-rs got so frightened they sent a petition to the governor to get me locked up in the sthrong room. So the governor sends for me, and says he, '*Capthain O'Bluntherbuss, ye're a terror to the other people in the debtors' department of the prison, and ye'd betther be after thinking of making some arrangement with your creditor, or I shall be forced to put you by yourself in the sthrong room.*'—'*Be Jasus!* says I, '*and I'll skin any man who shall dar-r to lay even the tip of a finger on me for such a purpose.*'—'*Well,*' says the governor, '*but if you've ever so little in the shape of ready money to offer your creditor, I'll see him myself and thry what I can do for ye.*'— So I pulled out my purse; and behold ye! I'd jest two pound three shillings, and sixpence, to pay three hundred and forty-seven pounds with.—'*Is it three-halfpence in the pound ye'll be afther offering?*' asks the governor.—'*Jest that same,*' says I; '*and if ever Misther Spriggins gets another farthing out of me, then I'll skin myself!*'—So away goes the governor to the creditor; and heaven only knows what blarney he pitches him;—but in the course of a day or two, down comes a discharge on condition that I pay the three-halfpence in the pound.—'*Now,*' says I, '*that's trating an Irish jintleman as he deserves*;' and so I got clean out of that infer-r-nal place. Here's your health, Mim."

And the Captain emptied his glass.

"You managed that business capital," exclaimed Frank Curtis, who began to think that it would be no bad speculation to maintain the martial gentleman altogether in Baker Street to frighten away the creditors,—or, at all events, to employ him to go round to them, in case they should prove inclined to act in a hostile manner towards him.

At that moment his eyes met those of his wife; and the glance of intelligence which was exchanged between them, showed that the same thought had struck them both, and at the same time.

"Help yourself, Captain," said Frank. "That whiskey was sent me as a present by the Crown Prince of Denmark, for having been second to his illustrious wife's uncle's stepmother's first cousin's nephew, in a duel three years ago."

"Blood and thunther-r!" ejaculated Captain O'Blunderbuss, "what a disthant relation! But the potheen is beautiful. I always mix my third glass sthronger than the two first, because in this same thir-rd I dhrink to the ladies—the sweet-hearts—and God bless 'em!"

Mrs. Curtis again acknowledged the compliment with a simper and an inclination of the head; and by the time the Captain had disposed of his third glass, the domestic in transcendent livery announced that coffee was served in the drawing-room.

Thither the party accordingly proceeded; Captain O'Blunderbuss escorting Mrs. Curtis, with a politeness which would have been perfectly enchanting had he not smelt so awfully of poteen.

And now, in a few minutes, behold the trio seated so cozily and comfortably at the table in the drawing-room, sipping the nectar of Mocha; while a friendly little contest took place between Frank and the Captain, to decide who could tell the greatest number of lies in the shortest space of time.

"Be Jasus!" cried O'Blunderbuss; "this coffee is an iligant beverage! But, saving your prisence, Mim, it don't come up to the coffee which I grew on my own estate in ould Ireland. The thruth was, I had such a vast extent of bog-land that I was at a loss what use to tur-rn it to—so I sent my steward off to Arabia,—yes, be the holy poker-r, direct off to Arabia,—to buy up as much coffee as he could get for money. Och! and with a power-r of coffeeberries did he come back, in the next West Indiaman, up the Meditherranean; and wasn't it a sowing of them same berries that we had in the bog! Ye should have seen the land eight months afterwards, with the coffee-plants grown up bigger than gooseberry bushes, and making the whole counthry smell of coffee for eight miles round. I rayalized seven hunthred pounds by that spec the first year; and I have gone on with the culthure of coffee ever since."

"Oh!" said Frank, "it is astonishing what improvements might be introduced in that way, if one only had the sense to do it. When I was staying in Paris, I was very intimate with the Governor of the Bank of France, and he had a beautiful conservatory on the top of the Bank. He took me up one day to see it: 'twas in the middle of winter, and cold as the devil in the open air—but warm as a toast inside the conservatory. Well, there I saw melons as large as a bumb-shell growing in flower-pots no bigger than that slop-bason—pine-apples hanging over the sides of tea-cups—and a kind of fruit the name of which I've forgotten; but I know that it was as large as a horse's head, and of the same shape. So I said to my friend the Governor of the Mint, says I——"

Mr. Curtis stopped; for the radiant footman entered the room, saying, "Please, sir, two men wish to speak to you immediately."

"Two men!" exclaimed Frank, casting an uneasy glance towards his wife, who, it was evident, shared her husband's very natural apprehensions.

"Yes, sir——But here they are," added the footman: then turning round towards the intruders, he said, "Why didn't you wait quiet down in the hall till I'd informed master that you wanted to speak to him?"

"'Cos we doesn't do business in that ere way, old feller," responded a voice which was not altogether unknown to either Mr. Curtis or the Captain.

"Proggs, the officer-r—by God!" vociferated the latter, starting from his seat.

"Yes—it's me and my master, Mr. Mac Grab, at your service, gen'lemen," said Proggs, pushing his way past the footman, and entering the room with his hat on his head and his stout stick in his hand. "Please, Mr. Curtis, sir—you're wanted."

And as these words were uttered by the subordinate, the principal himself—namely, Mr. Mac Grab—made *his* appearance (and a very dirty one it was too) in the door-way; while the footman stood aghast, and Mrs. Curtis went off into hysterics.

"Wanted!" cried Frank, casting an appealing glance towards the Captain: "who the devil wants me?"

"Whose suit is it at, sir?" asked Proggs, turning towards his superior.

"Beeswing, wine-merchant—debt, two hundred pounds, owing by the lady," answered Mr. Mac Grab.

"Is it arresting my friend Misther Curtis, ye mane?" demanded Captain O'Blunderbuss, advancing towards the officers with tremendous fierceness, now that he found his own personal security unendangered.

"And why not?" growled Mac Grab, shrouding himself behind his man Proggs.

"Is it why not, ye're afther asking?" shouted Captain O'Blunderbuss. "Now, be Jasus! and if ye don't both make yourselves as scarce as ye was before ye was bor-rn, it's myself that'll tayche ye a lesson of purliteness in the twinkling of a bed-post."

"Oh! that's all gammon," muttered Proggs. "Mr. Curtis must either pay the money or come along with us."

"He won't do neither the one nor the t'other, ye bastes of the ear-rth!" exclaimed the Captain.

"I say now——" began Mac Grab: but, before he had time to utter another word, the redoubtable Captain wrenched the short stick from the hands of Mr. Proggs, and throwing it to a distance, boldly attacked the officers with his long sinewy arms in such an effectual manner, that they disappeared from the drawing-room in as short a space of time as their assailant had represented by that beautiful figure of rhetoric—"the twinkling of a bed-post."

Mrs. Curtis had deemed it most prudent to go off into a fit—Frank was nailed to the floor by the terror of being captured and dragged off to a debtor's prison—the footman considered it wise to remain a mere spectator of the fight;—and thus the Captain was unassisted in his gallant onslaught upon the sheriffs' officer and his man.

The Captain, however, had an advantage on his side: namely, that when he had once succeeded in driving the enemy back as far as the staircase, it was comparatively an easy matter to fling them headlong down—a feat which he performed without the least ceremony or hesitation, to the infinite alarm of the female-servants in the kitchen, who came rushing up into the hall from that lower region, screaming as heartily as they could under the conviction that the house was tumbling about their ears.

"Hold your pace! my dears," exclaimed Captain O'Blunderbuss, rushing down the stairs after the vanquished enemy,—his countenance purple with whiskey and excitement—every vein in his forehead swollen almost to bursting—and his fists clenched for a renewal of the onslaught.

"We'll make you smart for this, my man!" growled Mac Grab, as he rose painfully from the hall-floor.

"I'm jiggered if we don't too!" added Proggs, picking himself up as it were from the last step, and feeling his legs and arms to see if any of his bones were broken.

"Out of the house, ugly bastes that ye are!" thundered the Captain.

The officers had received sufficient evidence of the redoubtable gentleman's warlike propensities, to induce them to beat a rapid retreat,—and the moment they had evaporated by the front-door, the Captain banged it violently after them, securing it with bolts and chain.

"That's the way we serve out the riptiles in ould Ireland, my dears," he exclaimed, turning towards the female servants, who, having at length comprehended the nature of the amusement going on, had ceased to scream and were enjoying the animated scene as much as if it had been a play.

Frank Curtis had heard the front door close violently; and the drawing of the bolts afterwards convinced him that the house was cleared of its invaders. He accordingly descended the stairs, laughing heartily now that the immediate peril had been averted by the prowess of the Captain. The resplendent footman was following close behind his master—very anxious to solicit his wages and his discharge there and then, and only prevented from acting thus abruptly by the formidable presence of Captain O'Blunderbuss.

"Now, my frinds," exclaimed this gallant gentleman, who was quite in his element under existing circumstances, "the house is in a complate state of siege! Ye must look to me as the commander of the garrison. So let the area and the ground-floor windows be all properly fastened: take care of the back door, wherever it leads to—and, be Jasus! we'll keep the rascals out! I know 'em well! They'll be thrying all manner of dodges to get in: but they'll find themselves as mistaken as the old lady was when she scratched the bed-post and thought she was scratching her head."

Then, with wonderful alacrity, Captain O'Blunderbuss hastened to superintend the arrangements and the precautions which he had briefly suggested. He examined the windows in the drawing room—he descended to the kitchen—went out into the area—poked his nose into the coal-cellar—inspected the yard at the back—issued his orders—saw that they were executed—and then drank off half a tumbler of whiskey neat, both as a slight refreshment after the exertions of the evening, and as a token of his satisfaction at the various measures which he had adopted with a view to convert the house into an impregnable fortress.

By this time Mrs. Curtis had made up her mind to recover from her fit; but she was so dreadfully shocked at the exposure which had taken place before the servants, that she retired to her bed-chamber forthwith.

The Captain and Frank then sat down to hold, as the former gentleman expressed it, "a council of war-r-r;" and as one bottle of whiskey had been emptied, and there was not another in the house, the martial gentleman was kind and condescending enough to put up with gin, of which exhilirating fluid he found, to his great satisfaction, there was a large supply in the cellar.

"What the devil would you have me do in this cursed embarrassment?" asked Frank.

"Be Jasus! and I'll jest tell ye now," answered the Captain. "Let me see?—this is Thuesday. Well, we must maintain the siege until Sunday; and then you must give the traps leg bail into another county. Whose furnitur-r is it in the house?"

"Why—it's ours, and it isn't," responded Frank.

"Och! and be asy now—I understand ye, my boy!" cried the Captain. "It isn't paid fur, ye mane—but possission is nine points of the law; and, be the holy poker-r! we'll make it the whole twilve. Jest allow me to carry ye through this little affair. Next Sunday night, me lad, ye must be off into Surrey with the lady and little ones; and lave me to manage here. On Monday, at the top of the mornin', I'll have in a broker and sell off every stick; and I'll bring ye over the proceeds like a man of honour-r as I am."

"So far, so good," said Frank. "But how are we to get things to eat between this and Sunday, if no one is to stir out of the place?"

"Is it ayting ye mane, when there's three gallons of gin in the house?" demanded Captain O' Blunderbuss, with something like indignation in his tone and manner.

"Well, but the wife and the children can't live upon gin, Captain," observed Frank; "even though the servants should have no objection."

"Not live upon gin, me boy!" vociferated Captain O'Blunderbuss, in a state of astonishment as complete and unfeigned as if some one had just shown him his own name in the Army List, or presented him with the title-deeds of his often vaunted Irish estates: "not live upon gin, Misther Curtis!" he repeated, surveying Frank as if this young gentleman were actually taking leave of his senses. "Show me the discontended mortal, my frind, that says he *won't* live upon gin, and I'll jest———"

"Just what?" asked Frank, somewhat dismayed at this irascibility on the part of his companion.

"I'll skin him—by the holy poker-r!" cried Captain O'Blunderbuss, rapping his clenched fist violently upon the table.

There was a long pause, during which the two gentlemen emptied and refilled their glasses.

"Be the way, me boy," suddenly exclaimed the Captain, as if an idea had just struck him, "is that old uncle of yours in town at present?"

"Yes: he came back some days ago, I understand," replied Frank.

"D'ye think he'd bleed?" asked the Captain: "for 'tis supplies to carry on the war-r in an iligant style for a long time to come, that we want; since now that we're once on a frindly footing together, Curtis, I'm not the boy to desert ye in your throubles."

He might have added that he would stick to Mr. and Mrs. Curtis so long as they had a bottle of spirits to give, or a shilling to lend him.

"I really think that it's very likely you might be able to draw the old bird," said Frank: "and to tell you the truth, I had already entertained the idea. Besides, he won't *dare* refuse *you*, Captain."

"Be Jasus! I should take it as an insult if he did," exclaimed the man of war, caressing his moustache. "But let us strike the ir-r-ron while it is hot. Dthraw up a letter to Sir-r Christopher-r in your best style; and I'll be off with it at once. Trust me for getting out of the garrison safe and coming back again in the same way; but mind and keep a sharp watch while I'm gone."

Frank promised compliance with this injunction, and hastened to pen a letter to his uncle, the Captain kindly undertaking to dictate the sense in which it was to be written.

The precious document ran as follows:—

"My dear Uncle,

"I hope this will find you blooming, as it leaves me; and as you and me have both made ourselves happy by marriage, don't let us have any more animosity between us. In fact, I will show you at once that I mean to forget the past, and treat you as an uncle ought to be treated by his dutiful nephew.

"Well, then, to come to the point. My friend, Captain O'Blunderbuss, whom you have the pleasure of knowing, and who improves vastly on acquaintance, has kindly lent me five hundred pounds, just to settle a few pressing debts which I had contracted during the time that I was so unfortunate as to be on bad terms with you; and as the Captain wants his money again, and I don't like to tell my wife so soon after marriage that I owe this sum, you will greatly oblige me by giving the Captain a cheque for the amount—or else Bank notes at once—he isn't very particular which, I dare say;—and I will repay you the moment I get my quarter's allowance, as the beloved and angelic creature, whom I shall have so much pleasure in introducing to you and to my dear aunt Charlotte, has promised me seven hundred pounds every three months to spend as I like and no questions asked.

"So no more at present, my dear uncle, from your dutiful, attached, obliged, and grateful nephew,

"Francis Curtis."

"What do you think of *that*?" demanded Frank triumphantly, when he had read the letter aloud for the opinion of his friend.

"Is it what I think?" exclaimed the Captain. "Be the power-rs! and it's as well as I could have done it myself, if I'd studied it for a week."

"Thanks to your suggestions," added Frank. "And now I'll just seal and direct it, while you finish your glass."

Captain O'Blunderbuss *did* drain the contents of his tumbler, as Frank foresaw that he would do; for it was one of that gallant gentleman's maxims never to waste good liquor;—and, being thus fortified with upwards of a pint of whiskey and ditto of gin—the effects of which were evident only in the fiery hue of his complexion, but by no means in his gait nor speech—he prepared to set out on his expedition to the dwelling of Sir Christopher Blunt.

"Frank," said he, putting on his foraging cap and conveying the letter to his pocket, "take the poker-r."

"The poker!" repealed the young man, with mingled surprise and dismay.

"And what else would ye take to dash out the brains of any man who should thry to spring in at the door while I go out!" exclaimed O'Blunderbuss. "That's right, me boy," he added, as Curtis shouldered the fire-implement. "Not that it's likely for any of them bastes of the ear-rth to be lur-rking about so soon afther the little affair of jest now: but it's as well to be on our guar-rd."

Accordingly, Frank Curtis stood behind the front door, poker in hand, as the redoubtable officer issued forth; but the coast was clear so far as the retainers of the Sheriff were concerned; and the peace of the garrison remained unmolested.

Frank closed, chained, and bolted the door again; and Captain O'Blunderbuss wended his way with an awful swagger down the street, frightening by his fierce looks all the small children whom he happened to encounter.

CHAPTER LXXIV.
THREE MONTHS AFTER MARRIAGE.

Sir Christopher Blunt was pacing his drawing-room in a very agitated manner; and the expression of his countenance was so ludicrous, in its reflection of the thoughts that were stirring within his breast, that it was impossible to say whether he was influenced by commingled hope and suspense on the one hand, or by fear and shame on the other.

It was pretty evident that he had not been out all day; for he was unshaven—and he wore the light blue dressing-gown, the bright red trousers, and the scarlet silk cap, which his dear wife had devised as a most becoming morning costume, but which gave him the appearance of a Mussulman quack-doctor, as the golden lustre of the handsome lamp brought forth all the flaunting effects of the garb.

Advancing towards the time-piece, Sir Christopher compared his watch with that dial.

"A quarter to nine!" he murmured to himself, as he restored the huge gold repeater to his fob; "and the doctors have been an hour with her already! Well—I never heard of such a thing before—three months after marriage—it's impossible—quite impossible! Dr. Wagtail is a very clever man, no doubt—but he's wrong for once in his life. If it was six or seven months, now—one might suppose that a premature birth—but three months——"

And the worthy knight paced the apartment in a manner which showed that "he didn't know wha the deuce to make of it."

"Well," he continued, again speaking in a murmuring tone, after a short pause, "it may be so, after all! For really science does discover such wonderful things now-a-days, and the world seems to undergo so many strange changes, that upon my word I should not be at all surprised if, on going out some morning, I was to see the people walking on their heads along Jermyn Street. Ah! things weren't like this when I was a boy! But then I must recollect that I live in the fashionable quarter of the town *now*, and ladies at the West End ain't like those vulgar citizens' wives. Thank God that I didn't get in for Portsoken! It was quite enough to have filled the high and responsible office of Sheriff, and to have received the distinguished honour of knighthood——But, three months!" exclaimed Sir Christopher, interrupting himself, and flying back with ludicrous abruptness to the idea that was uppermost in his mind; "three months! And, after all, who knows but that it's the fashion at the West End; and I'm sure that if it is, I shall be very glad that it has happened so. And yet the most extraordinary part of the business is that—

when I suspected something of the kind, and just hinted at it to Lady Blunt—she—she scratched my face to pieces for me. Very extraordinary, indeed!"

Sir Christopher now became lost in a maze of conjecture, vague suspicion, and bewilderment, through which he certainly could not find his way; and heaven only knows how long he might have remained in the labyrinth, had not Dr. Wagtail appeared to his rescue.

"Well, doctor?" exclaimed the knight, hastening to meet the physician.

"My dear Sir Christopher, I congratulate you!" said Dr. Wagtail, considering it decent and becoming to assume a joyous and smirking expression of countenance for the occasion, while he wrung the knight's hand with most affectionate warmth: "for it is my duty," he continued, now suddenly adopting the pompous and important style of the fashionable physician to a rich family,—"for it is my duty, Sir Christopher, to announce to you that you are the happy father of a charming boy, with whom her ladyship has been kind enough to present you."

"A boy—eh, doctor?" faltered the knight. "But of course it isn't—I mean—it can't be—a—a—full grown child?"

"Well, my dear Sir Christopher," responded Dr. Wagtail, who perfectly understood where the shoe pinched, "from what Mr. Snipekin, the talented and much-sought-after accoucheur whom I deemed it prudent to call in just now,—from what Mr. Snipekin says, Sir Christopher, I do believe that the dear little creature has come a leetle before his time. But pray don't make yourself uneasy on that account, my dear Sir Christopher; for the sweet babe is in no danger, and is an uncommonly fine child, to be sure!"

"Then it is a little before its time, doctor—eh!" said Sir Christopher. "But—doctor—you and me are old friends, and you can speak candidly, you know——and—the truth is——you must remember that—that—our marriage only took place—three months ago—and it seems to me rather unusual—not that I suspect dear Lady Blunt's virtue for a moment—on the contrary—I know her to be a perfect paragon of morality: at the same time—three months, doctor—and a fine boy——"

"My dear Sir Christopher," responded Dr. Wagtail, foreseeing that the amount of his fee would depend vastly upon the state of mind in which the Knight might be when he should give it, and acting moreover upon his favourite principle of humouring the whims and wishes of all persons with whom he had any professional connexion,—"my dear Sir Christopher," he said, looking very solemn indeed, "your avocations in the world have not allowed you time to dive into the mysteries of science and investigate the arcana of learning—much less to pursue with sesquipedalian regularity the routine of that course of study which, in the abstract, and also considered in a purely professional point of view—and having due regard to the wonders of physiological science,—in fact—ahem!—you understand me, Sir Christopher?"

"Ye-e-s, doctor," drawled forth the bewildered knight. "But I think you were going to satisfy me—you know—about the three months—and a fine boy—doctor——"

"I was coming to that point, my dear Sir Christopher," said Dr. Wagtail. "In fact, I was about to observe that *physiology*, properly considered in its etymological signification, comprehends the entire science of Nature; but I must impress upon your mind, Sir Christopher, that the ratiocinative propensities of modern physicians have induced them, doubtless after much profound cogitation, to restrict the term to that department of physical knowledge relating, referring, and belonging exclusively to organic existence. And thus, Sir Christopher——ahem!—you follow me?"

"Oh! quite easy—indeed!" returned the knight, wondering in his own mind whether it were dog Latin that stunned his ears, and also how any one individual could possibly pick up and retain such an immense amount of knowledge. "But—the point was, doctor——"

"Precisely, my dear Sir Christopher!" exclaimed the physician, looking as wise as all the seven sages of Greece put together: "it was to that very point which I was coming;—but I thought that a detailed and full explanation would prove most satisfactory to you."

"Oh! decidedly, doctor:—and I am sure I am very much obliged to you for taking the trouble to—to———"

"Well, then, my dear Sir Christopher," interrupted the fashionable physician; "all my premises being granted, and the arguments which I have adduced being fully admitted, I think that the demonstration is easy enough. Consequently, Sir Christopher, it is quite apparent that a child *may* be born three months after marriage; at the same time, I think I can assure you, that in future your excellent and amiable lady will not be quite so premature in her accouchements."

"It is not unusual, then, doctor, amongst your female patients?" said Sir Christopher, who was not entirely satisfied yet.

"It is by no means unusual that a *first* child should be born a few months after marriage, my dear Sir Christopher," answered the physician.

"And perhaps—perhaps, it's rather fashionable than otherwise?" asked the knight, in a hesitating manner.

"Well—I don't know but what it is, Sir Christopher," replied Dr. Wagtail, taking a pinch of snuff. "And now that your mind is completely set at rest on this point—as indeed it must and ought to be, after the full and professional explanation which I have given you,—I will return to the chamber of your amiable and excellent lady, and see whether you can be permitted to visit her for a few moments."

"Do, my dear doctor. And, doctor," cried the Knight, as a sudden idea struck him; "pray don't—I mean, it is not necessary to let Lady Blunt know that—that—in a word—that I asked you any questions———"

"Oh! certainly not, my dear Sir Christopher," exclaimed the physician; and he then quitted the room.

"Well," thought the knight to himself, as soon as he was again alone; "and so I am the father—the happy father,"—and he made a slight grimace,—"of a fine boy. A fine boy—eh! 'Pon my honour, I'm very glad—very glad, indeed! A son and heir—a little Christopher! How very kind of my dear wife: it is a tie which will bind us together—perhaps soften her temper a leetle—and make her more sparing in the use of her finger nails. Well—if it's only for that, the coming of this child will be a great blessing—a very great blessing. But I really do wish the dear babe had made its appearance about six months later. Not that it matters much—seeing that I must be its father, and that the thing is rather fashionable than otherwise. Besides—Doctor Wagtail is such a clever man—such a very clever man—and his explanation was so completely satisfactory—so very lucid and clear—a fool might understand it. Well, I really ought to be a very happy fellow!"

But all the knight's attempts at self-persuasion and self-consolation were futile: there was a weight upon his spirits that he could not throw off—and in the depths of his secret soul there was an awful misgiving, to the existence of which he vainly endeavoured to blind his mental vision. He strove to be gay—he tried to establish the conviction that he was perfectly happy and contented—he did all he could to make himself admit *to* himself that the doctor's reasoning was conclusive:—still he could not shut out from his heart the ever recurring thought that the physician's argument might be very conclusive indeed, but that he was totally unable to understand a word of it.

Then came the fear of ridicule;—and this was the most galling sentiment of all. But, on the other hand, there was an apprehension which was not without its weight: namely, the anger of his wife, in case she should discover that he had dared to doubt her virtue.

Thus, by the time the doctor came back, the silly old gentleman had determined to take matters just as he found them: and, though half suspecting that there was something wrong in the business, he resolved to maintain as contented an air as possible, as the only means of combatting ridicule should he experience it, or of quieting his wife should she hear of any thing to excite her irritability.

"We are getting on so well, my dear Sir Christopher," said the physician, "that we can see you for a few minutes; but we cannot bear any loud speaking as yet, and we establish it as a condition that you do not attempt to kiss our child more than once, for fear you should set it crying and make our head ache."

Sir Christopher attempted a pleasant smile, and followed Dr. Wagtail to the chamber of the indisposed lady.

The moment the door was opened, the shrill but nevertheless apparently half-stifled cry of a newborn child saluted the knight's ears; and, hastening up to the bed, he bent over and kissed his wife.

"See what heaven has sent us, Sir Christopher!" said the lady, in a low and weak voice, well suited to the solemnity of her observation; and, slightly uncovering the bed-clothes, she exhibited a tiny object, looking amazingly red, but which she assured him was "the sweetest little face in the world."

"That it is—the pretty creatur!" observed a hoarse voice, which appeared to emanate from the chimney, but which in reality came from no further off than the fire-place, and belonged to an elderly woman of tremendous corpulency, who was arranging some baby-linen on a clothes-horse. "I've nussed a many ladies," continued the stout proprietress of the hoarse voice, "but never such a patient dear as your'n, Sir Christopher: and I never see such a angel at its birth as that babby. Why," continued the woman, advancing towards the knight and giving him a good long stare, while, potent odours of gin assailed his nostrils all the while, "I do declare that the babby is as like his father as he can be."

Sir Christopher "grinned horribly a ghastly smile," and slipped half-a-guinea into the nurse's hand, at which proof of his generosity she dropped him a curtsey that shook the house so profoundly as nearly to drop her through the floor.

"Yes—the babby's as like you, Sir, as two peas is like each other," continued the nurse, while Dr. Wagtail and the accoucheur exchanged rapid but intelligent glances at the excellence of the idea, and Sir Christopher grunted like a learned pig which has just put its snout upon the right card in a show. "I'm sure, Sir, you ought to be wery much obleeged to missus for presenting you with such a cherub. Poor dear! she had a sad time of it—but she bore it like a saint, as she is. Won't you let master have just one kiss at the little dear, my lady?"

The saint was just at that moment wondering whether the child, as it grew up, would bear any resemblance to a certain tall footman in a certain family at the West End: but why such an idea should enter her head, we must leave to the readers to divine.

The nurse repeated her question, adding, "Do let the little dear's pa just kiss it once; and then we must turn him out, you know, ma'am, for the present."

"Yes, Sir Christopher—you may kiss the little cherub, if you like," said Lady Blunt, in a tone which was meant to impress on her husband's mind a full sense of the favour conferred upon him: "but pray don't make the sweet child squeal out—for you're so rough."

The knight accordingly touched the babe with his lips, which he smacked to make believe that the kiss was a hearty one in spite of his wife's injunction; and, this ceremony being completed, he was turned out of the room by the nurse, whose power on such occasions amounts, as all fathers know, to an absolute despotism.

"The nurse" is a species exhibiting but little variety. Stout and in good spirits she must always be; and bottled stout and ardent spirits she highly esteems. She moreover has an excellent appetite, and is fond of many meals in the course of the day. She awakes at five or six in the morning, and makes herself strong hot coffee and a couple of rounds of toast, putting a great deal of sugar to the former, and a vast quantity of butter to the latter. At nine she is ready for her *breakfast*—the first meal not being so denominated and in fact considered as nothing at all. If her mistress be awake, the nurse will amuse her with innumerable stories relative to her former places; and she will not fail to make herself out the very best nurse in the world. She will describe how one lady was inconsolable because she could not have her at the desired time; how another lady would eat nothing unless prepared by the said nurse's own hands; how a third would have died if it had not been for her care and attention; and how she never slept a wink nor put her clothes off once for a whole month while in attendance upon another lady. Then she is sure to be well connected and to have seen better days: and if asked for her address, she is certain to reply, "Lord bless you, my dear: all you have to do is to send and inquire for me in such-and-such a street, and any body will tell you where I live." In fact she is as well known in her quarter of the town as the Queen is at Pimlico. But—to continue the category of meals—at eleven o'clock she is quite prepared for a mutton-chop and half a pint of stout; and she forces a basin of gruel down her mistress's throat, accompanied with many a "Poor dear, I'm sure you must want it!" At two o'clock she has a good appetite for her dinner; and then she manages to get on pretty comfortably till tea-time. The nurse is very fond of her tea, and likes it strong. After tea, as her mistress most likely sleeps, she gets hold of an odd volume of a romance, or a newspaper not more than a week old; and it is ten to one that she believes every word she reads in both. If her mistress happen to be awake, the nurse will comment upon what she reads. The newspaper, especially, is sure to set her talking on the "hardness of the times," and arouse all her reminiscences of "when she was a gal." She will often express her mysterious wonder at "what the world is coming to," and invariably speaks as if every thing had undergone a great change for the worst. She is sure to know a poor family whom she is mainly instrumental in saving from starvation; and she is equally certain to descant upon the necessity of sobriety and frugality amongst the working classes. Then she remembers that it is time "for missus to take her medicine;" but when she goes to the shelf or the cupboard, she stays a little longer there than is quite necessary to pour out the medicine aforesaid; and, as she approaches the bed to administer the same, she wipes her mouth with the back of her hand, and her eyes are observed to water. The invalid lady may now thank her stars if she be not assailed with an odour of ardent spirit while she receives her medicine from the hand of the nurse. Well, the time passes away somehow or another until the supper hour; and it is a remarkable fact, that the nurse never seems wearied of the monotony of her avocation. But, then, in the evening she manages to get half-an-hour's chat with the servants down stairs; and the chat is rendered the more pleasant by a little drop of something short out of a black bottle which the cook mysteriously produces from the cupboard. On these occasions the nurse exhibits all her importance. She assures the listening domestics that it was very fortunate *she* happened to be sent for to attend upon "missus," as if any other nurse had been called in the results would have been most unpleasantly different. She then expresses her opinion of the medical attendant; and her estimation of this gentleman is invariably regulated by the amount of his liberality towards her. If he gave her the odd shillings which accompanied the sovereigns in the little piece of paper containing the fee, then he is sure to be a very clever man indeed; but if he forgot this important duty, then in the nurse's estimation he is certain to be a most unfit doctor to call in; and "it was quite a wonder that he didn't kill poor dear missus." Having thus delivered her opinion, which is received as gospel by the servants, she hastens up stairs again, and relates to her mistress her own version of the conversation which has taken place down below. After supper she no longer partakes of ardent spirit on the sly, and unblushingly brews herself a potent glass. But then she is sure to have an excuse—such a dreadful pain in the stomach, or a bad cold; and her mistress, whose peace of mind depends on keeping her attendant in a good humour, says in a mild, languid voice, "Do make yourself comfortable, nurse!" And the nurse obeys the hint to the very letter. The liquor induces her to descant upon spirits in general; and she is sure to inform her mistress that the *Duke of Wellington* doesn't sell near such good things as the *Duck and Drake*; but that "the beautifullest gin is at the public round the corner." Sometimes—and this is one of the worst features in her character—the nurse will take it into her head to relate gloomy stories to her mistress; and when once she gets on this subject, the devil himself could not stop her. She tells how she knew a lady who went on very well for ten days, and then popped off all on a sudden; or else she was once in a house which caught on fire in the middle of the night, and the poor lady and child were burnt to death. If the husband should happen to be out late, the nurse, when she is in this gloomy vein, talks mysteriously of the danger of the streets; and says how she knew a gentleman who was run over by an omnibus during the fog. But, in justice to the nurse, we must observe, that these horrible subjects are not very frequently touched on by her—and only when she gets somewhat maudlin with too much ardent spirit or bottled stout. For the first week she is in her place, no one comes to see her; but in the course of the second, she is visited by her married daughter and her married daughter's eldest girl. During the third week, the nurse is constantly wanted by people who come to see her, or inquire for her; and at the beginning of the fourth the front door bell is rung frantically, and the nurse hears, with a countenance so innocent that it is almost impossible to think she has pre-arranged the whole matter, that Mrs. So-and-so, whom she has pledged herself to attend upon, is just taken in labour, and she (the nurse) must go to her directly. Her mistress is by this time well enough to do without her; and the nurse receives her full month's wages for three week's attendance.

But let us return to Sir Christopher Blunt, whom we left at that pleasant point when, having undergone the ceremony of embracing the babe which, according to his lady's account, heaven had sent him, he wended his way back to the drawing-room.

At that precise moment Sir Christopher would have given just one half of his fortune to be enabled to undo all he had done three months previously. He had married in haste, and he now repented at leisure. But it was too late to retract; and he found, to his infinite mortification, that he must "grin and bear it."

The accoucheur shortly entered the room to report that "all was going on as well as could be expected;" and, having received his fee, he took his departure.

Soon afterwards the pompous and self-sufficient Dr. Wagtail made *his* appearance, and received *his* fee, which, out of sheer ostentation, the knight rendered as liberal as the physician had anticipated.

These little matters being disposed of, Sir Christopher rang the bell, ordered up a bottle of claret and was about to console himself with the solitary enjoyment of the same, when an astounding double knock and tremendous ring at the front-door startled him so fearfully that he spilt the wine over his red trousers and nearly upset the table on which his elbow was leaning.

"Who can this be?" he exclaimed aloud.

"Captain O'Blunderbuss!" cried the footman, throwing open the door as wide as possible to afford ingress to the swaggering officer.

CHAPTER LXXV.
THE KNIGHT AND THE CAPTAIN.

"Captain O'Blunderbuss!" murmured Sir Christopher, in a faint tone, as he sank back dismayed into his seat.

"Be the power-rs! and how are ye, my hearty old cock?" was the polite salutation of the gallant gentleman, as, advancing close up to the knight, he grasped his hand and shook it with as much energy as if he were a policeman carrying off a starving mendicant to the station-house for the *heinous crime* of begging.

"Thank you, Captain—I—I'm pretty well," responded Sir Christopher.

"Well, that's a blessing, be Jasus!" cried the Captain, coolly taking a seat. "Is it claret that you're after dhrinking, Sir-r Christopher?" he demanded, taking up the bottle and holding it between his eyes and the lamp. "Iligant stuff in its way—but not my lush. Have ye no potheen in the house, Sir Christopher-r?"

"Potheen?" repeated the knight, not understanding the name nor half liking the intrusion.

"Is it you, Sir-r Christopher, that don't know what rale Irish potheen is?" cried the Captain. "Why, there's niver a child in ould Ir-reland that can't spell potheen. Whiskey, Sir Christopher—whiskey! But I'll save ye the throuble of ringing for it yourself:"—and, with these words, Captain O'Blunderbuss applied his hand most vigorously to the bell-pull.

The footman answered the summons.

"Your masther says, sirrah," exclaimed the Captain, "that ye're to bring up a bottle of the best Irish whiskey—rale potheen—with a tumbler, a spoon, a lemon, hot water, and sugar and look shar-rp about it, too!"

The domestic retired, and Sir Christopher stared in amazement at the Captain; for the worthy knight was so astounded by the free and easy manners of his visitor, that he was not quite certain whether he, Sir Christopher Blunt, was actually in his own house at the moment, or whether he was in some public coffee-room where every one had a right to order the waiter about as he chose.

"I hope you're not offinded with me, Sir Christopher-r, by making myself at home?" said the Captain: "but it isn't me that's the boy to stand on any ceremony."

The knight thought that his visitor could never have said a truer thing in his life.

"Not I, be Jasus!" continued Captain O'Blunderbuss. "But thin I'm the man to let others do the same with me; and if you should ever find yourself in the wilds of Conamar-r-ra, Sir Christopher, jist ask the first naked urchin ye meet with to show the way to Bluntherbuss Park, and see if I won't trate ye as ye deserve to be trated. Blood and murther! it's me that keeps open house save whin the sheriff's-officers are prowling about the neighbourhood, which is generally from the 1st of January to the 31st of December in every year."

The servant now made his appearance with the whiskey and the *et ceteras* which the gallant gentleman had ordered; and the said gallant gentleman straightway began to brew himself some toddy, with the air of an individual who had had nothing stronger than mild ale to drink all day long.

"May I request to be informed——" began Sir Christopher, his courage reviving now that the Captain's visit appeared to be one altogether of an amicable nature.

"Faith! and is it to be informed ye'd be?" ejaculated O'Blunderbuss, as he stirred his whiskey-and-water up with the spoon. "But don't alarm yourself, Sir Christopher-r: my call this evening was merely jist to ask ye how ye do and present ye with a little note from that rale broth of a boy, Misther Frank Curtis."

"Frank—my nephew!" exclaimed Sir Christopher: "what can he want with me? Surely 'tis not to congratulate——But, no—he can't have heard of *that* yet."

Be the power-rs! and is there any thing to congratulate ye upon, Sir Christopher?" cried the Captain. "Have ye been made a baronet—or elected an alderman?"

"I would have you know, Captain O'Blunderbuss," said the knight, in a solemn tone, "that I was once so unadvised as to put up for Portsoken——"

Be Jasus! have nothing to do with Port—it lies heavy on the stomach, my frind!" interrupted the gallant officer. "Dhrink potheen—and you'll niver grow old nor yet gray. But we were spaking of congratulations. Is it possible that your dear wife has tumbled down stairs and broken her neck? or has she presented ye with a pledge of her affiction?"

"Since you must know, Captain O'Blunderbuss," responded the Knight, "it is——the latter."

"I give ye joy, old brick!" vociferated the gallant officer and seizing Sir Christopher's hand, he subjected it to such a process of violent shaking, that the victim almost yelled out with agony. "But from what Frank tould me," continued the Captain, at length relinquishing the hand which he had so unmercifully squeezed, "I thought you hadn't been married long enough for such a happy evint to take place. However—I wish ye joy, my frind; and now to business. Read this little bit of a note, and ye'll be charmed with the kind way in which Frank Curtis spakes of ye."

The knight received the letter which the Captain handed to him; but ere he had time to break the seal, the door opened and the nurse made her appearance.

"Well, nurse—what is it?" demanded Sir Christopher.

"Please, sir," was the reply, "missus wants to know who it was as come with such a chemendous knock and ring that it has set her poor head a-aching ready to split, and the blessed babby a-crying as if he was in fits."

"Tell your misthress, nurse," exclaimed the visitor, in an imperious tone, "that it's Captain O'Bluntherbuss, of Bluntherbuss Park, Ir-r-reland," with an awful rattling of the r's; "and prisint my best rispicts to your lady and the babby."

"Thank'ee, sir," replied the nurse; "but missus says, Sir Christopher, please, that she hopes you won't make no noise in the house."

"Very well—very well, my good woman!" exclaimed the knight hastily. "Tell your mistress I shall not be engaged long, and will come up and see her presently."

"Wery good, sir;"—and the nurse withdrew.

Sir Christopher then proceeded to open the letter; but it was with trembling hands,—for the visit of the nurse had thrown him into a most unpleasant state of nervousness—he being well aware that he should receive a blowing up on account of the Captain's call,—although no one could possibly wish more devoutly than himself that such a call had not taken place.

"Ye thrimble, Sir Christopher!" cried the Captain; "but there's no need to be alar-r-med—for your nev-vy hasn't sent ye a challenge. So let your mind be at pace—and read the little note at your leisure. I'm in no hurry for an hour or two."

And indeed the Captain appeared to be quite comfortable; for he brewed himself a second glass of whiskey and water—threw some coals upon the fire—and trimmed the lamp in such a way that the flame rose above the globe.

Meantime Sir Christopher perused the letter with great attention, and did not altogether seem to relish its contents.

"I really cannot oblige my nephew in this respect," he said, fidgetting the paper about in his hands. "The truth is—he has not behaved altogether well to me—nor to Lady Blunt;—and if I was to do this for him, Lady Blunt would be so angry. He must fight his own way in the world, Captain O'Blunderbuss, as I did; for I have no hesitation to admit that I rose from nothing—indeed, I glory in the fact: and having filled the high and responsible office of Sheriff, with credit to myself and advantage to my fellow-citizens——"

"Damn the high office of Shiriff!" exclaimed the gallant gentleman, striking his fist upon the table. "I want my money—and it isn't Captain O'Bluntherbuss that ye'll be afther putting off in this snaking fashion."

"But, my dear sir," said the knight, in a tone of gentle remonstrance, "*I* don't owe you the money."

"Be Jasus! but your nev-vy does—and therefore it's all in the family!" cried the Captain.

"That is a proposition I cannot agree to, my dear sir," returned the knight.

"D' ye mane to differ from me?" demanded the Captain, looking desperately ferocious.

"Why—as for that—I—I——"

"D' ye mane to differ from me, I repate?" vociferated Captain O'Blunderbuss, again striking the table with his fist, but so violently this time that the bottles and glasses danced a hornpipe: "answer me that, Sir-r Christopher-r!"

"I don't wish to offend you, Captain—I couldn't wish to do that; but," added the knight, "I must beg leave most respectfully to dissent from the proposition that I am in any way answerable for the debts of Mr. Curtis. And since he has married a lady of fortune, let him be candid with her at once; and——"

"Is it candid that he's to be, when the wife would kick up hell and blazes?" cried O'Blunderbuss. "But I tell you purty frankly, my frind, that if ye don't shell out the seven hunthred pounds——"

"Seven hundred!" ejaculated Sir Christopher. "It says only five hundred in the letter."

"I don't care two r-raps for the letther," answered the Captain: "all I know is that Misther Frank Curtis, your nev-vy, had seven hunthred of me—and, be Jasus! I'll have seven hunthred of you."

"It can't be done," said Sir Christopher doggedly.

"Then, be the holy poker-r! I'll shoot ye to-morrow mornin'!" vociferated the gallant officer: "so name your frind; and I'll take care that ye shan't be afther shir-r-king this time as ye did when ye had to mate my frind Morthaunt."

"Really, Captain O'Blunderbuss, this strange conduct on your part—is—is—" stammered the knight, scarcely knowing what to say or do; while his countenance became elongated to an awful extent.

"Sthrange!—sthrange! do ye say?" exclaimed the Captain. "Why, ye're adding insult to injury, man. But don't desayve yourself—ye won't come the counterfeit-crank over me, be Jasus! I'm not the boy to be bullied afther this fashion, Sir Christopher-r. So shell out the eight hunthred—or be the Lor-r-d Harry!——"

"Eight hundred!" murmured the miserable knight, now cruelly alarmed at the ferocious manner and the progressive attempt at extortion on the part of his visitor.

"Eight hunthred is what I lent, and eight hunthred is what I'll have back," said the Captain, in a determined tone: "and if ye're afther denying your debts of honour-r, Sir Christopher, I'll make such an example of ye as shall let all the wor-rld know what ye are—as soon as I've shot ye dead, which I'll do in the mornin'."

"You surely wouldn't commit such a crime—without—without just provocation?" urged the knight, in a coaxing manner.

"I'll not hear another word of palthry excuse, sirrah," replied the Captain, starting from his seat; "and if the money isn't forthcoming in the twinkling of a bed-post, I'll flay ye first and shoot ye afterwards."

"Oh! dear—Oh! dear," said the wretched Sir Christopher: "what shall I do?—I wouldn't mind the five hundred that my nephew asks for—since he promises so faithfully to pay me again· but eight hundred——"

"Nine!" thundered the Captain. "D'ye mane to tell me as good as that I'm a liar-r, and that I can't recollect amounts?—Be Jasus! I niver was so insulted in my life—and nothing but blood can wash it away!"

"Blood!" murmured Sir Christopher: "my blood! and I the father of a family, as I may say."

"So much the more dishonour-r-able for ye to dispute a just debt, and thry to shir-rk off in this bastely fashion!" cried the Captain, twirling his moustache, and eyeing Sir Christopher in a way which made the latter tremble in every limb. "I always thought that ye was a man famous for your straight-for'ard dalings; but I'm desayved—grossly desayved;—and I'll sind my frind to ye to-morrow mornin', before you've had time to break the shell of your first egg at breakfast."

"Well, Captain—to oblige *you*," said Sir Christopher, "I don't mind if I write a cheque for five hundred pounds; but I positively will give no more—I won't indeed—I can't."

"Put down the palthry five hunthred, then, on the dhraft," exclaimed the Captain; "and I'll make Misther Curtis fork me out the rest at his convaynience."

The miserable Sir Christopher, though feeling that he had been completely bullied into the settlement of the demand made upon him, nevertheless stood in such awful dismay of the warlike Irishman, that he wrote a cheque for the five hundred pounds, which said cheque the Captain secured about his person, exclaiming, "And now, my frind, I'll look over all the insulting words ye have applied to me this evening. But, be the power-r-s! if I hadn't a great respict for ye, I'd make a mummy of ye before ye was twelve hours oulder."

Having thus spoken, the Captain tossed off the remainder of his whiskey-and-water, shook the knight violently by the hand once more, and took his departure, just as the nurse was coming down to desire that Sir Christopher would get rid of his guest and send up the keys of the wine-cellar to her ladyship.

Now, strange as it may appear to the reader,—considering all that they know relative to the character of Captain O'Blunderbuss,—it is nevertheless a fact that he never once thought of appropriating to his own use the amount just extorted from the knight. He was a man who would not hesitate to get into debt, without the least intention of ever paying the same,—he moreover thought that he had accomplished a highly meritorious deed in extorting the five hundred pounds from Sir Christopher: but he was honourable after his own fashion—that is to say, he would scorn to perpetrate an actual robbery, or to betray the trust reposed in him by an accomplice. He was, in fact, one of those curious, but not uncommon beings, who might be trusted with a thousand pounds to convey to the bank for a friend, but who would borrow eighteen-pence without the remotest intention of ever repaying it, and who thought that the most brilliant act a gentleman could achieve was to chouse a creditor.

Accordingly, the clock had scarcely struck eleven, and Frank Curtis was already beginning to get uneasy, when the Captain's thundering knock at the front door in Baker Street, proclaimed his return; and in a few moments the young gentleman was made acquainted with the success experienced by his friend.

"And now, be the holy poker-r! we'll make a night of it," said the Captain, when, the front-door having been duly secured, the two worthies were once more seated in the dining-room: "and it's myself that'll tell ye stories and sing ye rale Irish songs to keep ye awake, my boy."

And a night they did make of it, heaven knows!—and tremendous inroads were effected upon the supply of gin then in the "garrison," as the Captain now termed the house. Such lies, too, as the Captain and Frank Curtis told each other! until the latter gentleman began to entertain the pleasing idea that the room was spinning round, and that there were four candles on the table instead of two. The gallant officer, on the other hand, carried his liquor like a man who was inaccessible to its inebriating fumes; and when Curtis fell dead drunk upon the carpet, the Captain considerately picked him up, tossed him over his shoulder as if he was a sack of potatoes, and thus transported him to the door of his wife's bed-room, at which he deposited the senseless gentleman, having intimated in stentorian tones that Mrs. Curtis would do well to rise and look to her husband.

The Captain then went down stairs again, finished the bottle last opened, and, throwing himself on a sofa, fell into a sound sleep.

CHAPTER LXXVI.
TIM THE SNAMMER AND JOSH PEDLER OUT ON BUSINESS.

He who delights in wandering amongst the mazes of this mighty city of London,—this wilderness of brick and mortar,—and who can view, with the eye of a philosopher or a moralizer, the various phases in which the metropolis is to be considered, may find ample food for reflection, and much changing interest of scene, if he post himself at that point in the Borough of Southwark, called Newington Butts.

From this point diverge Blackman Street, the Newington Road, the Borough Road, and Horsemonger Lane.

Blackman Street and the Newington Road constitute the great thoroughfare between London Bridge and the *Elephant and Castle* tavern; and incalculable are the multitudes—innumerable are the vehicles, which pass along the busy way,—oh! so busy, because the love of money and the love of pleasure cause all those comings and goings,—those hurryings hither and thither,—those departures, and those returns!

What a tremendous conflict of interests,—what a wondrous striving to accomplish objects in view,—what an energy—what an activity—what an unwearied industry, are denoted by a great thoroughfare like this! Nor less does that bustle speak of recreation and enjoyment—parties of pleasure to end in dissipation—amusement, diversion, and holiday, too often to be dearly paid for thereafter!

Close by Newington Butts you behold a portion of the wall of the Bench Prison, with its *chevaux de frise*, denoting rather the criminal prison than a place of confinement for unfortunate persons. What a horrible cruelty it is to incarcerate men who are unable to liquidate their liabilities—as if such immurement would place within their reach the philosopher's stone. Where one dishonest debtor finds his way thither, a dozen human beings who are enclosed within that gloomy wall, would gladly—willingly, acquit themselves of their responsibilities if they had the means. And shall the law be so framed that, in order to punish one, it must cruelly oppress twelve individuals? Is such a principle consistent with common sense, justice, or civilisation? Many and many a heart has been broken within those walls: many and many a fine spirit has been crushed down to the very dust; and the man who went into that prison with honourable feelings and generous sympathies, has gone forth prepared to play the part of a sneaking swindler. For a creditor to lock his debtor up in prison, is the same as if a master took away the tools from a mechanic and said, "Now do your work as usual." The Legislature does not understand this. It allows an expensive process to take place, so that the debtor who cannot originally pay 50*l.*, for instance, has his liabilities immediately increased to 60*l.*: then, when responding negatively to the demand for this larger sum, he is taken away from the avocations by pursuing which he might obtain the means to settle with his creditor, and is thrown into prison. The routine is precisely this:—If a person cannot pay a debt, you increase it for him: and, having increased it, you tie his hands so that he shall have no chance of paying it at all! Merciful heavens! is this common sense?[35]

The system of imprisonment for debt falls trebly hard upon the poor. The gentleman, though reduced himself, has friends who can assist him; but the poor are too poor to aid each other. Then money can purchase bail when a schedule has been filed in the Insolvents' Court; but the poor man must languish in prison until his hearing. Oh! the advantages of wealth or wealthy connexions in this mercenary land!—oh! the benefits of being by birth *a gentleman*!

It was about ten o'clock in the evening, when Tim the Snammer and Josh Pedler encountered each other, by appointment, at Newington Butts; and, as it was yet too early for the business which they had in hand, they repaired to a public-house hard by, where they drank porter, smoked pipes, and conversed, until the clock in the tap-room denoted the hour of eleven.

They then rose, paid their score, and took their departure,—bending their way into Horsemonger Lane.

Tim the Snammer now fell a few paces behind his comrade, Josh Pedler, who hurried a short distance up the lane, and stopped at the door of a house of mean, sordid, and sombre appearance.

He knocked at the door, which was opened by an old and hideous-looking woman, holding in her hand a candle, by the light of which she surveyed the visitor in a very suspicions manner.

"I want to speak to a genelman of the name of Bones which lives here," said Josh, placing his foot, with apparent carelessness, in such a way over the threshold that the door might not be shut against his inclination.

"No sich a person don't live here," returned the woman gruffly; and she was about to close the door, when Josh again addressed her.

"Well," said he, "if he don't pass by that there name, he does by another—and it's all the same. We ain't partickler, ma'am, as to names; but my business is partickler, though—and I've got an appintment with Mr. Benjamin Bones—or Old Death—or whatever else he calls his-self or is called by others."

"It ain't of no use a standing bothering here, my good man," said the woman, "'cause vy—no sich a person lives here, I tell you—and I don't know sich a person by sich a name at all."

"Humbug!" cried Josh and, giving a low, short whistle, he pushed into the house.

A moment had not elapsed ere Tim the Snammer was at his heels—the door was forcibly closed—the candle was wrested from the old woman's hand—and she was threatened with throttling if she attempted to raise an alarm.

The two men bound her with a cord, and carried her into the room opening from the passage. They then left her, vowing with terrible oaths to return and "do for her," if she dared make the slightest disturbance.

"There isn't a room on t'other side of the passage, is there, Tim?" demanded Josh of his companion, who carried the light.

"No. And now let's creep up stairs as gentle as if we was mice," said the Snammer.

"You've got your barkers, Tim?" asked Pedler.

"Yes—and a damned good clasp knife too," replied the ruffian, with a significant leer at his accomplice, and speaking in a low whisper. "I don't think we shall find any one else in the house besides that old woman and Ben Bones his-self, 'cause Mutton-Face Sal is a devilish keen one—and she would have found it out if there was any lodgers."

"Well, cut up stairs, Tim," said Josh Pedler, "and don't let us be a-standing here palavering—or the old scamp may overhear us and get out by the back windows, or some such a dodge. I'll go fust, if you like."

"No—I'll go fust, Josh," answered the Snammer; "for it's me that has got the most spite agin the ancient willain."

With these words, Tim Splint crept cautiously up the narrow and dirty staircase, Josh Pedler following close behind him.

The robbers stopped at the door on the first landing, and knocked; but, no answer being returned, they broke it open in a few moments by means of a small stout chisel such as housebreakers are in the habit of using.

"Who's there?" cried the deep, sepulchral voice of Old Death, as he started from the arm-chair in which he had been taking a nap.

"It's only two of your friends," returned Tim the Snammer; "and *as* friends you had better treat us, too—or it'll be the wuss for you."

"I don't know that I ever treated you in any way but as friends," said old Death, glancing somewhat uneasily from the one to the other. "As for you, Tim—I can guess why you're angry with me; but I wasn't at liberty—I wasn't my own master, I can assure you—on that Saturday when I promised to get you out of the Jug; or I should have kept my word. But it's too long a story to tell you now—even if I was disposed to do so; and so the shortest way to make us all right, is for me to give you back the money that was placed in my hands by Josh Pedler."

"And what'll pay me for the two months of quod that I had all through you, you cheating old fence?" demanded Tim Splint, placing his back against the door in a determined manner.

"I couldn't help it, Tim—I couldn't help it," returned Old Death with a hideous grin. "And may be—may be," he added, with the hesitation habitual to him, "I can put something in your way, that will make up for the past."

"Well—that looks like business, at all events," observed Tim, exchanging a rapid glance with his companion; for it struck the two robbers at the same moment, that they should perhaps act prudently to join Old Death in any enterprise which he might have in hand, and then plunder him afterwards—provided that the affair he had to propose, gave promise of a better booty than that which they stood the immediate chance of obtaining from him.

Old Death looked leisurely round the small, mean, and ill-furnished room, as much as to say, "What can you hope to get out of me?"—for the meaning of the glances which he had observed to pass between the two robbers, was perfectly well understood by him.

"Is the business you hinted at for to-night?" demanded Josh Pedler, after a brief pause.

"For to-night," replied Benjamin Bones. "But sit down, my good friends, and may be I can find a dram of brandy in the bottle for you."

"Thank'ee, we'll stand, old chap," said the Snammer; "but we shan't refuse the bingo, for all that."

Old Death regaled his two visitors each with a wine glass full of brandy, and then took a similar quantity himself.

"Yes," he said, continuing the discourse: "it is for to-night—and a good thing may be made of it, if you're staunch and resolute. In fact, I wanted to meet with a couple of such active fellows as you are, for I have been sadly used lately—in more ways than one."

"Well, what is it?" demanded Tim the Snammer. "You know that we're the lads to do any thing it ought to be done; and I don't see the use of wasting time, if the business is really for to-night."

"I have had positive information," continued Old Death, his dark eyes gleaming snake-like beneath the shaggy brows that overhung them, "that a gentleman, who lives in a lonely house not many miles off, this morning received a considerable sum of money at a banker's, on a cheque which he get cashed there; and in a few days he will pay it all away to his creditors—for he has been building a great number of houses at Norwood; and so I think," added Bones, with a horrible chuckle, "that it would be just as well to anticipate him."

"And can you rely on this information?" asked Tim the Snammer. "Come—let us know all the particklers."

"Two or three days ago he took into his service a man named John Jeffreys—a groom who was lately in the household of a certain Sir Christopher Blunt," said Old Death; "and this person sells his secrets to those who pay him best."

"In plain terms he's in your pay," exclaimed Josh Pedler. "Well—that's all right. What next?"

"Nothing more than that if you like to crack that crib, you can do it to-night; and I'll smash the notes, which will be of no use to you till they're melted into gold," answered Old Death; thereby intimating to them, first that he should take no active part in the business, and secondly that it would not be worth their while to cheat him of his share of the plunder, inasmuch as they were totally dependent on him for rendering the hoped-for booty at all available.

Tim the Snammer and Josh Pedler consulted together for a few moments in low whispers.

"But how do we know," said the former, suddenly turning round upon Old Death, "that this isn't all a cursed plant to get us out of the house here—or may be to inveigle us into some infernal trap—eh? Answer us that."

"Read John Jeffreys' note," said Old Death coolly, as he produced the letter from the pocket of his capacious old grey surtout coat.

Tim the Snammer, and Josh Pedler, accordingly read the contents of the paper, which ran as follow:—

"This cums to tel you, sir, that Master resceved a chek for about twelve undred pouns yesterday from Sir enry courtenee, a barrow-night, and that master got it keshed this mornin at the benk, wich I no becos I had to go with him in the gigg to the benk, and I see him cum out of the benk a-countin the notes, and I no he will pay it all away in 2 or 3 days to his bilders and arkitecks and carpinters at norwood. anny thing you leeve for mee in a broun paper parsel at the ushoul crib will reech mee. Yure fatheful servant,

"J. J."

"Satisfactory enow," exclaimed Tim the Snammer, with an appealing glance to his comrade, who nodded his head approvingly. "Well," continued the thief, "give us the necessary description of the place; and we'll be off at once. It's fortnit that we've got our tools about us."

"Which you have used against my miserable lodging," observed Old Death, with a grim smile. "However, I would rather you'd have introduced yourselves in that way, than not come at all; for I should have let this matter," he added, pointing to Jeffreys' note, which now lay on the table, "go by without attending to it. So it's lucky for us all that you did make your appearance; and if you serve me well in this case, you shall not want employment of my finding."

"Good again, old tulip," said Tim the Snammer; "and now tell us where this Mr. Torrings lives—or whatever his name is—and we will lose no time."

Old Death gave the necessary explanation; and the two men took their departure, having first acquainted their employer with the condition in which they had left the old woman down stairs—a piece of information which made him hasten to her rescue.

---

35. The records of the Insolvent Debtors' Court prove that the average dividend paid upon the estates of persons who take the benefit of the Act is *one farthing* in the pound!

CHAPTER LXXVII.
THE FATHER AND DAUGHTER.

Proceed we now to Torrens Cottage, on the road to which place we have just left Tim the Snammer and Josh Pedler.

It was past eleven o'clock, and Mr. Torrens was seated alone in his parlour, examining a pile of papers which lay before him. A decanter more than half emptied of its ruby contents, and a wine-glass also stood upon the table; and the flushed countenance of the unprincipled man showed that he had sought to drown the remorseful feelings of a restless conscience by means of the juice of the grape.

But he could not;—and though ten days had now elapsed since the sacrifice of the beautiful Rosamond had taken place, there were moments when the father felt even more acutely than on the fatal night when, in the solitude of his chamber, he endured the torments of the damned,—*mental torments, indescribably more severe than the most agonising of physical pain could possibly be*!

He had received the price of *his* infamy and *her* dishonour: the last portion of the "price of blood" he had drawn from the bankers in the morning—and he was now arranging and casting up his accounts to satisfy himself that he had actually obtained sufficient to settle all his liabilities.

But his occupation was every moment interrupted by a gush of terrible thoughts to his maddening brain;—and if he laid down the pen, it was to grasp the bottle.

What would the world say if his black turpitude were to transpire?—how should he ever be able to meet Clarence Villiers and Adelais again, if they were to become acquainted with Rosamond's dishonour? He knew that the baronet had hitherto managed somewhat to tranquillise the ruined girl by promises of marriage and eternal affection;—he was also aware that Rosamond had endeavoured to subdue her anguish as much as possible in order to avoid the chance of arousing any suspicion on the part of Mrs. Slingsby! But a term must at length arrive to those specious representations and mendacious assurances adopted by Sir Henry Courtenay to lull the agonising feelings of the unhappy girl;—and then—oh! it was then, that the danger would be terrible indeed! Of all this Mr. Torrens thought; and he suffered more acutely from his fears than from his consciousness of infernal iniquity.

The time-piece upon the mantle had struck the hour of eleven some time, and Mr. Torrens was in the midst of his terrible meditations, when a loud, long, and impatient knock at the front-door caused him to start from his seat.

He had already desired the servants not to sit up on his account, as it was probable that he should be occupied with his papers until a late hour in the night; and he was therefore now compelled to answer the summons himself.

A cold chill struck to his heart—for he entertained a presentiment of what was about to occur: indeed, such an anticipation was natural on his part when we reflect that his soul was a prey to conscious guilt, and that the knock at the door was hasty and imperative.

For a moment he staggered as if about to fall: then, calling all his firmness to his aid, he proceeded to open the front-door, the knocking at which was repeated with increased vehemence.

His presentiment was correct;—for, scarcely had he drawn back the bolt, when the door was pushed open—and Rosamond rushed into the house.

"My dearest father!" she exclaimed, and fell insensible into his arms.

He conveyed her to a sofa in the parlour, tore off her bonnet and shawl, and sprinkled water upon her pale—her very pale countenance.

Merciful heavens! how acute—how agonising was the pang which shot to his heart, as he contemplated that lovely brow on which innocence had so lately sate enthroned, until the spoiler had pressed the heated lips of lust thereon! Then for a few moment all the father's feelings were uppermost in his soul; and he gnashed his teeth with rage at the thought that he himself was dishonoured in that dishonoured daughter!

Oh! to have given her back her purity and her self-respect,—to have known that she could raise her head proudly in maiden pride,—to have been able to embrace her as the chaste and spotless being she was ere hell suggested its accursed machinations to achieve her destruction!

But it was too late!—Here lay the ruined child—and there were piled the notes and gold which had purchased her virtue!

Three or four minutes elapsed, and still Rosamond gave no signs of returning animation. Suddenly the father desisted from his endeavours to restore her; for an infernal thought flashed to his mind.

He would suffer her to die!

No sooner did the atrocious idea enter his soul, than he longed to see it fulfilled. He dared not meet her eyes—even should she be unsuspicious relative to his unnatural treachery. No—it were better that she should die!

But the infernal hopes of the wicked man were not to be realized;—and, monster that he was, he could not slay her with his own hands!

Slowly, at length, her bosom began to heave—a profound sigh escaped her—she opened her eyes, and gazed vacantly around.

"Rosamond," said her father, now mastering his feelings of bitter disappointment so far as to be able to speak in a kind tone: "Rosamond, dearest—what ails you? Fear not—you are at home! But why do you look at me so wildly!"

"Oh! my God—what have I done, that I should have deserved so much misery!" exclaimed the young girl, in a voice of the most piercing anguish, as she covered her face with her hands and burst into a flood of tears:—then, raising herself to a sitting posture on the sofa, she seized her father's hands, saying in a different and more profoundly melancholy tone, "My parent—my only friend! I am unworthy to look you in the face!"

"Do not speak thus, Rosamond," said Mr. Torrens, seating himself by his daughter's side, and maintaining a demeanour which bespoke the deepest interest in her behalf. "Something has cruelly afflicted you?" he added interrogatively—as if *he* had yet the fatal truth to learn!

"Oh! heavens—your kindness kills me, dearest father!" shrieked Rosamond. "Yes—never did you appear so kind to me before—and I—I——But, merciful Saviour! my brain is on fire!"

"My sweet child," returned Mr. Torrens, whose soul was a perfect hell as he listened to the words which came from his daughter's lips,—"you can surely have no secrets from me? Has any one caused you chagrin? has any one dared to insult you? And what means this sudden arrival at home—at so late an hour—and when I fancied that you were staying with that excellent woman, Mrs. Slingsby?"

"Mrs. Slingsby!" repeated Rosamond, with a shudder which denoted the loathing and abhorrence she entertained for that woman. "Oh! my dear father, that Mrs. Slingsby is a fiend in human shape—a vile and detestable hypocrite, who conceals the blackest heart beneath the garb of religion!"

"Rosamond—Rosamond—you know not what you are saying!" exclaimed Mr. Torrens, affecting to be profoundly surprised and even hurt at these emphatic accusations.

"Alas! I know too well—oh! far too well, the truth of all I am saying!" said Rosamond, a hectic glow of excitement appearing upon her cheeks, hitherto so ashy pale. "Yes, father—that woman is a disgrace to her sex! This evening—but two hours ago—I accidentally heard a few words pass between her and Sir Henry Courtenay——"

"Sir Henry Courtenay is at least an honourable man," said Mr. Torrens.

"Sir Henry Courtenay is a monster!" cried Rosamond emphatically: then, bursting into tears again, she threw herself at her father's feet, exclaiming, "Oh! that I had a mother to whom I could unburthen all the woes that fill my heart:—but to you—to you—my dearest parent—how can your daughter confess that she has been ruined—dishonoured—undone?"

"Unhappy girl!" cried the hypocrite, affecting a tone and manner denoting mingled indignation and astonishment: "what dreadful things are these that you have come home to tell me?"

"The truth, my dear father—the horrible, the fatal truth!" continued Rosamond, in a fearfully excited tone.

"Speak lower—lower, my child," said Mr. Torrens: "the servants will be alarmed—they will overhear you. And now resume your seat near me—rise from that humiliating posture—and——"

"Humiliating indeed," interrupted Rosamond, sinking her voice to a comparative whisper, but with an utterance that was almost suffocated by the dreadful emotions raging within her bosom:—"because I myself am so signally humiliated!" she added. "And yet I am innocent, dear father—it was not my fault—not for worlds would I have strayed from the path of virtue! But a hideous plot—a diabolical scheme of treachery—devised between that bad woman and that still more dreadful man——"

"No more—no more, Rosamond!" exclaimed Mr. Torrens, still maintaining a well-affected semblance of indignation and astonishment. "I understand you but too well—and you shall be avenged!"

"Alas! vengeance will not make me what I once was—a happy and spotless girl!" said Rosamond: "and now that I am dishonoured, it would require but the contumely with which the world would treat me, to drive me to utter desperation—to madness, or to suicide!"

Mr. Torrens said all he could to console his unhappy child; and he very readily promised her to abandon all ideas of vengeance on those who had been the authors of her shame.

"Until this evening," said Rosamond, her head reclining upon her father's shoulder, "I had hoped that Sir Henry Courtenay would repair the wrong he had done me by means of marriage,—for, alas! my dear father, I loved him! But—two hours ago—I overheard a few words pass between him and Mrs. Slingsby,—a few words which rivetted me to the spot where I was at first only an involuntary listener. Then I became a willing and attentive eavesdropper,—for, oh! the little which had already met my ears, intimately—too intimately regarded myself! And, dear father, you can conceive with what horror and dismay I learnt enough to convince me, that she whom I had loved and esteemed as a dear friend and a model of perfection, was a vile—an abandoned—an infamous woman,—the mistress of Sir Henry Courtenay, and in the way to become a mother also! I could not believe my ears—I fancied that I was dreaming. But, alas! it was indeed a frightful reality;—and then I heard that I had been sold,—yes, *sold*—I, your daughter, *sold* to Sir Henry Courtenay,—and, I suppose, by that dreadful woman! Yes—yes—father," she continued wildly, "I was sold to his arms,—and he never intended to marry me! I screamed not,—I uttered not a word: I was crushed too low—I had too great a load of misery upon my soul to be able to give vent to my feelings; but I dragged myself away from the spot where I had overheard that terrible discourse,—a veil had fallen from before my eyes, and I saw all the extent of my hopeless position in its true light. How I managed to reach my bed-room I know not: my brain began to whirl, and I thought that I should go mad! Of what followed I have but a dim recollection; but methinks that, having put on my bonnet and shawl, I was flying from the house, when Sir Henry Courtenay pursued me down the stairs—and how I escaped from him I cannot say! There was a chaos in my bewildered brain; and when I was enabled to collect my scattered thoughts—when consciousness, as I may term it, came back, I found myself hurrying along the streets. I looked round, fearful of being pursued; but there was no cause for alarm. Nevertheless, I hastened on,—and all that long distance have I accomplished on foot, dear father; for, oh! I felt that home was the place where my deep sorrows would receive sympathy, and where only I could hope to enjoy security. And now, my beloved parent," added Rosamond, throwing her arms around his neck, "you will not spurn your unhappy daughter,—you will not thrust her from you! My God! why did I ever reveal to you all this? Oh! it was because my heart was so full of woe, that if I had not unburthened it to you in the hope of receiving consolation, it would have broken—it would have broken!"

"Rosamond," said Mr. Torrens, "you did well to reveal all these dreadful things to me; because I alone am the proper person to counsel and console you. A fearful crime," he continued, shuddering at his own monstrous duplicity, "has been perpetrated; but, alas! the criminals must go unpunished. Yes,—Rosamond, you were right when you declared that vengeance would lead only to exposure; and that exposure would kill you. My poor child, not even your sister must be made acquainted with this awful calamity."

"No—no!" exclaimed Rosamond: "it is sufficient that *you* are aware of the ignominious treatment which I have received! Not for worlds would I have the bridal happiness of my dearest sister poisoned by the revelation of my wrongs! And Clarence, too—Clarence—oh! from him, of all men, must this secret be kept; or he would, perhaps, be urged to wreak on his aunt, and on that vile baronet, a vengeance which would lead to exposure, and render Adelais miserable for ever!"

"It charms me, Rosamond," said Mr. Torrens, "to perceive that the wrongs heaped upon you have not impaired your prudence. Between you and me shall this secret now remain,—for, depend upon it, the authors of this cruel outrage will not themselves be anxious to publish their own infamy. You are now beneath the paternal roof—and here you are certain to enjoy security; and from this night forth, Rosamond, let us place a seal on our lips so far as the *one* dread topic is concerned."

"And you, my father," asked the ruined girl,—"shall you not love me the less? Shall you not look with loathing and abhorrence upon your daughter? Oh! if there be a change in your sentiments towards me, I shall have no alternative save to die!"

The miserable and criminal father embraced his dishonoured child, and said every thing he could to console her.

Rosamond then retired to her chamber,—that chamber which she had left ten days previously a pure and spotless virgin, and to which she now returned a deflowered and ruined girl!

Mr. Torrens remained in the parlour.

Amidst all the horrible thoughts that forced themselves upon his mind, he saw one glimmering of consolation: and this was that Rosamond suspected not his complicity in the nefarious plot which had destroyed her. It was evident that in the conversation which she had overheard between Mrs. Slingsby and the baronet, *his* connivance had only been hinted at,—too darkly and mysteriously for Rosamond to comprehend the meaning of those words which alluded to the fact of her having been *sold*!

But what pen can describe the tortures which the guilty man experienced, as he pondered on the scene that had just occurred? In spite of that gleam of solace he was the prey to ineffable anguish,—for he could not help feeling as a *father*: nature asserted her empire,—and he was in despair as he contemplated the awful crime which had led to the dishonour of his own child!

Never had she appeared to him so beautiful as when, ashy pale, she had awakened from the deep trance into which she fell on crossing the parental threshold;—never did he feel more inclined to love her, or to be proud of her charms, than when he afterwards saw her kneeling at his feet, the light of the lamp falling with Rembrandt effect upon her upraised countenance! Alas! through him was she ruined—by his machinations was she destroyed! And of what avail was that beauty now, since honour was lost?

He fixed his eyes upon the gold, and endeavoured to console himself with the contemplation of the glittering metal.

It seemed dross—vile dross in his eyes; and could he have recalled the deeds of the last ten days, he would gladly have fallen back into the inextricable labyrinth of his pecuniary difficulties, and have dared even the disgrace and punishment of a debtors' prison, so that he might not have had to reproach himself with *the sale of his daughter's virtue*!

CHAPTER LXXVIII.
RETRIBUTION.

It was long past midnight—and Mr. Torrens was still pacing the parlour with uneven steps, when a low double knock at the front-door aroused him from his painful meditations.

Wondering who could visit the cottage at that late hour, he hastened to reply to the summons; and, to his surprise, the lustre of the parlour-lamp which he carried in his hand, streamed full upon the pale and agitated countenance of Sir Henry Courtenay.

Making a sign to the baronet not to speak, Mr. Torrens led the way into the parlour; and the visitor, in the excitement of the feelings which had brought him to the cottage, neglected to shut the front-door close as he entered, but merely pushed it back in such a way that the bolt of the lock did not catch.

This little incident was unperceived by the two gentlemen.

When they were both in the parlour, Mr. Torrens shut the room-door, and said in a low whisper, "She has come home!"

"Thank God! she is safe then!" observed the baronet, also in a subdued voice. "The fact is, Mrs. Slingsby and myself were so dreadfully frightened that she might either make away with herself, or else adopt some measure that would lead to a certain exposure, that we have both been hunting for her through all the streets at the West End; and at last I determined, late as it was, to come over and acquaint you with her flight. But it never struck me that I should hear of her return home."

"She is unaware of my sad complicity in the dreadful business," replied Mr. Torrens sternly. "But pray repeat to me the whole conversation which took place between Mrs. Slingsby and yourself, and which she unfortunately overheard. I shall then be enabled to judge whether reflection on that discourse may lead her to imagine that her own father was indeed a party to her ruin; for I must confess that I have terrible fears lest she should indeed imbibe such a suspicion."

"Give me a tumbler of wine, Torrens," said the baronet, throwing himself upon the sofa which had so lately been pressed by his victim when in a state of insensibility: "I am regularly exhausted, for I have walked all the way hither;—and, when I have a little recovered myself, I will detail all the conversation which took place between me and Mrs. Slingsby, as nearly as I shall be able to recollect it."

Mr. Torrens produced a bottle of wine from the side-board, he having already emptied the decanter upon the table.

"Help yourself, Sir Henry," he said: "and in the meantime I will steal cautiously up stairs and see if Rosamond be yet retired to rest—for I would not for worlds have her come down and find you here."

"A wise precaution," observed the baronet.

Mr. Torrens accordingly quitted the parlour, and hastened up stairs. He stopped at the door of his daughter's chamber, and listened. Profound sobs and impassioned ejaculations, indicative of terrible grief, met his ears; and he grew alarmed lest she should feel herself so thoroughly wretched and lonely as to be unable to sleep, and perhaps return to the parlour.

He accordingly knocked gently at the door, and Rosamond speedily opened it.

She had not as yet divested herself of a particle of her clothing, nor made any preparation to retire to rest; and her countenance was so truly woebegone—so thoroughly the picture of a deeply-seated grief, that even her iron-hearted father was affected to tears. She threw her arms around his neck, and thanked him for his kind solicitude. He remained with her nearly half-an-hour, exerting all his power of language to console her; and the anxiety which he experienced to induce her to seek her couch, so that he might return to the parlour and get rid of Sir Henry Courtenay as soon as possible, rendered him so eloquent and so effective in the (to him) novel art of administering solace, that he succeeded fully.

"Now I am convinced that you do not loathe, despise, and hate your daughter," said Rosamond at length; "and this impression has removed an immense weight from my mind. Though true happiness may never more be mine, yet shall I find a substitute in Christian resignation to my fate; and henceforth, dear father, I will not make *you* unhappy by compelling you to act the part of a comforter. And now, good night, my only friend—my beloved parent; and fear not that I shall give way again to that violent outpouring of grief in which you so kindly interrupted me."

Mr. Torrens embraced his daughter, and a pang shot to his heart as he thought of his infernal conduct towards that good and affectionate girl!

As he descended the stairs he heard her lock her chamber-door; and he was just congratulating himself upon the success of his attempt to console her, when the murmuring sounds of voices, apparently coming from the front parlour, caused him to redouble his pace thither—for the idea flashed to his mind that Mrs. Slingsby might also have visited the cottage in her alarm concerning Rosamond, and that the baronet had probably afforded her admission while he was up stairs with his daughter.

Tim the Snammer and Josh Pedler, bent on their predatory intent, and hoping to reap a good harvest at the house of Mr. Torrens, approached that dwelling nearly half an hour after Sir Henry Courtenay had entered it.

Perceiving a light gleaming from the divisions in the parlour-shutters, they crept cautiously up to the window, and through those crevices beheld the glittering gold piled upon the table, and a person lying upon the sofa, apparently in a profound sleep.

The fact was that the baronet was completely exhausted with his long walk from Old Burlington Street to the Cottage; and, having tossed off a tumbler of wine, he lay down on the sofa to await Mr. Torrens' return.

But we have seen that the father had found his daughter in such a state of profound affliction as to be totally unable to leave her for nearly half an hour; and during that interval an irresistible drowsiness stole over Sir Henry Courtenay,—speedily wrapping him in a deep slumber.

Tim the Snammer and Josh Pedler were determined to risk "the crack," in spite of the sleeper whom they descried upon the sofa, and whom they believed to be Mr. Torrens; for neither was this gentleman nor the baronet known to them by sight.

With their housebreaking implements they were on the point of making an attempt on the front-door; when it yielded to their touch, and swung noiselessly open. At this they were not at all surprised; for it immediately struck them that John Jeffreys had expected the visit that night, and had left the door ajar on purpose.

They stole into the house, and succeeded in entering the parlour without arousing the baronet.

Tim the Snammer instantly drew forth his clasp-knife, and, bending over Sir Henry Courtenay, held the murderous weapon close to his throat, while Josh Pedler hastily secured the notes and gold about his person.

"We may as well have the plate, if there is any," whispered this individual to his companion. "In fact, we'll have a regular ransack of the place; and if he awakes——"

"I'll cut his infernal throat in a jiffey," added Tim the Snammer.

Josh grinned an approval of this summary mode of proceeding, and opened one of the side-board drawers. But the noise which a sugar-basin or some such article made inside the drawer, by falling over with the sudden jerk, aroused the sleeper.

Sir Henry Courtenay started—opened his eyes—beheld a strange countenance hanging over him—and was about to utter a cry of alarm, when the terrible clasp-knife was drawn rapidly and violently across his throat.

There was a dull, gurgling noise—a convulsive quivering of the entire frame,—but not a groan—much less an exclamation of terror,—and Sir Henry Courtenay was no more!

"Come along, Tim," said Josh Pedler, whose face was ghastly pale. "We've done enough for to-night."

"Yes—let us be off," returned the murderer, now shuddering at the dreadful deed which he had just perpetrated.

And they were issuing from the room, when the noise of footsteps on the stairs made them redouble their speed to gain the front-door.

It was Mr. Torrens who had thus alarmed them; but they escaped without molestation—for when that gentleman reached the hall, and beheld two men rushing towards the front-door, he was himself seized with such profound terror—painfully strung as his feelings had been that night—that he was for a few moments stupified, and rivetted to the spot.

But when he saw the front-door close behind the strangers, he took courage—hastily secured it within—and then hurried to the parlour, in agony of fear lest his gold and notes should have become the prey of plunderers!

One glance at the table was sufficient:—the money was gone!

Mr. Torrens dashed his open palm against his forehead with frantic violence, and was about to utter a cry of rage and despair, when the remembrance of his unhappy daughter sealed his lips.

At the same instant he looked towards the sofa:—but, holy God! what a spectacle met his view!

For there lay the baronet with his head nearly severed from his body,—murdered—barbarously murdered upon the very sofa where his victim had so lately reposed in trance-like insensibility. On that sofa slept he his last sleep; and, even in that appalling moment when Mr. Torrens recoiled, shuddering and shocked, from the dreadful sight, it struck him that there was something of retributive justice not only in the loss of his own treasure but also in the death of Sir Henry Courtenay!

The frightened man uttered not a murmur as that spectacle encountered his eyes. His amazement was of so stupifying a nature that it sealed his lips—paralysed his powers of utterance. With staring orbs he gazed on the grisly corpse from which he recoiled staggeringly; and several minutes elapsed ere he could so far command his presence of mind, as even to become aware of his own dreadful predicament.

But as the truth dawned upon him, he was seized with indescribable alarms—with horrible apprehensions.

The double crime of robbery and murder, had been perpetrated so speedily and so noiselessly, that not a soul in the house was alarmed by any unusual sound—and Mr. Torrens felt the sickening conviction that it would be a difficult thing to persuade a jury that *he himself* was innocent! Suspicion must inevitably attach itself to him:—circumstantial evidence would be strong against him! In a word, the appalling truth broke in upon him, that *he* would be accused of the assassination of Sir Henry Courtenay!

Mr. Torrens sate down, and, burying his face in his hands, fell into a profound but most painful meditation.

Should he raise an alarm—arouse Jeffreys and the female-servant, as well as his daughter—and proclaim all he knew about the horrible transaction! No:—something whispered in his ear that he would not be believed. Rosamond, not knowing that he was the baronet's accomplice in achieving her dishonour, would naturally conceive that the murder was the result of paternal vengeance. It was, then, impossible to suffer the occurrence to transpire. But what was he to do with the body?—how dispose of it? Terrible dilemma!

All the atrocity of his crime towards his daughter now returned with a tremendously augmenting intensity to his mind. His punishment on earth had already begun:—he was doomed—accursed. Wretched man! gold was thy destroyer! Ah! gold—but thou hast lost thy gold,—and in a few days the creditors who yet remain unpaid, will be upon thee! But——

What!—does such an idea actually strike him?—urging him to plunder the murdered victim of any coin which there may be about the corpse! Yes:—and now behold the father, who sold the honour of his child, about to examine the pockets of that child's assassinated ravisher?

The purse contains some fifteen or sixteen sovereigns; and these Mr. Torrens self-appropriates. The pocket-book of the deceased is next scrutinized. But there are no Bank-notes—nothing save papers and memoranda, totally valueless.

Mr. Torrens stamps his foot with rage:—his predicament is truly awful. Ruin still menaces him on one side in respect to his affairs—for, having reckoned on the money to be produced *by the sale of his daughter's virtue*, he had contracted fresh liabilities within the last ten days: and on the other side is the terrible danger in which the presence of that corpse may involve him! Add to these sources of agonising feelings, the conviction that the sacrifice of Rosamond will, after all, have proved ineffectual in respect to the complete settlement of his affairs, even should he succeed in burying the more serious event—namely the murder—in impenetrable mystery,—and the wretched state of mind in which Mr. Torrens was now plunged, may be conceived.

He rose from the chair, on which he had a second time flung himself, after plundering the corpse, and approached the time-piece.

It was half-past one o'clock.

But as Mr. Torrens glanced at the dial, which thus told him how short an interval remained for him to take some decisive step, if he really intended to dispose of the corpse before the servants should be stirring, he caught a glimpse of his countenance in the mirror over the mantel.

He recoiled—he shrank back with horror.

Was it indeed *his own* countenance that he saw?

Or was it that of some unquiet ghost, wandering near the spot where its mortal tenement had been cruelly murdered?

He turned round suddenly, to avoid farther contemplation of that ghastly visage;—and again he recoiled from an object of terror—staggered—and would have fallen, had he not caught the back of a chair for support.

For in the half open door way he beheld a human face, which was withdrawn the moment his eyes encountered it.

Driven to desperation, and reckless now of what might happen to him, the maddened man rushed into the hall, in time to observe a figure turn the angle of the staircase.

In another moment he had caught that figure by the arm; and, dragging the person forcibly down, beheld his new man-servant John Jeffreys, by the light of the lamp streaming from the open parlour-door.

Totally forgetful at the instant of the presence of the corpse in the room,—so terribly excited and bewildered was he,—Mr. Torrens dragged Jeffreys into the parlour to demand the reason why he was up and *dressed* at that hour of the night—or rather morning:—and it was not until he saw the man himself turn ghastly pale as his eyes encountered the hideous spectacle on the sofa, that Mr. Torrens remembered the frightful oversight which he had committed.

Then, hastening to close the room-door, which he locked also, Mr. Torrens said, "Why are you up? and wherefore were you prying about the house?"

The fact was that Jeffreys had expected a visit from some of Old Death's gang that night, and had never retired to bed at all. He heard the two double-knocks at the door—the first being that given by Rosamond, and the other by the baronet;—and when the robbers had quitted the house, closing the front-door after them, Jeffreys thought it must be the last visitor (whoever he might be) going away. After that the house had remained quiet for some little time; and Jeffreys fancied that Mr. Torrens had retired to bed. He had accordingly stolen down from his bed-room to unfasten a window shutter, and thus render the ingress of the expected robbers an easy matter: but perceiving a light in the parlour, he began to suspect that they must be already there. Accordingly he crept cautiously up to the door, and was for a moment stupified when he obtained a glimpse of the reflection of his master's ghastly countenance in the mirror, a view of which he could command from the hall.

"Why are you up? and wherefore were you prying about the house?" demanded Mr. Torrens.

"The truth is, sir, I heard a noise, just now, and I was afeard that thieves was breaking in," was the ready reply: "so I got up and dressed; but, sir—"

And he glanced significantly towards the dead body.

"Jeffreys," said Mr. Torrens, in a hurried and excited tone, "a dreadful event has occurred to-night. This gentleman came to call upon me late—on very particular business—I left him here, while I went up stairs to speak to my daughter, who has returned home—and, on coming down stairs again, I saw two men escaping from the house. When I entered the parlour, a considerable sum of money, which I had left on the table, was gone—and my poor friend was as you now see him!"

The man-servant believed the tale; but he affected not to do so—for he was villain enough to rejoice at such an opportunity of getting his master completely in his power.

"You smile incredulously, John," said Mr. Torrens; "and yet I take heaven to witness——"

"It's orkard, sir—very orkard," observed Jeffreys; "and may be it'll lead to scragging, if the stiff'un isn't put away."

Mr. Torrens shuddered from head to foot.

"What *do* you mean to do, sir?" asked Jeffreys. "I am quite ready to assist you; but it's getting on for two o'clock——"

"Yes, I know it," interrupted Mr. Torrens. "I am mad—I am driven to desperation! What would you advise? But will you be faithful? Will you keep the secret? I can reward you——"

"We'll talk of that another time, sir," said Jeffreys; "for the present let's think of making away with the stiff'un. We must bury it. Stay here a moment, sir, while I go and get the stable lanthorn and a sack."

"Or rather," observed Mr. Torrens, "I will fetch some water to wash the carpet; fortunately, the blood has not trickled upon the sofa."

Noiselessly the two crept away from the parlour—one to the stables, the other to the kitchen.

In a few minutes they met again by the side of the corpse, which they thrust into the sack; and between them the load was conveyed to the stable.

"You go and clean the carpet, sir," said John Jeffreys, whose superior presence of mind served to invest him with authority to direct the proceedings; "while I dig a hole in the garden."

Mr. Torrens hastened to obey the suggestion of his servant, and returned to the parlour, where he cleansed the carpet, as well as he could. He then took a bottle of Port-wine from the side-board, and broke it over the very spot where the blood had dripped down, leaving the fractured glass strewed about, and drawing the table near the sofa, so as to produce the appearance of the bottle having been accidentally knocked off it.

Nearly half an hour was consumed in this occupation; and Mr. Torrens, whose mind was already much relieved, hastened back to the garden, where Jeffreys was busily engaged in digging a grave for the murdered baronet. When the servant was tired, his master took a turn with the spade; and, as the soil was not particularly hard, an hour saw the completion of the labour.

The corpse was thrown into the hole, and the earth was shovelled over it— each layer being well stamped down by the feet.

When the task was accomplished, Mr. Torrens and Jeffreys re-entered the house; and, ere they separated to retire to their respective rooms, the former said, in a low whisper, "Once more I conjure you to maintain this secret inviolable, and I will find means to reward you well. For the present take this!"

And he slipped ten sovereigns—a portion of the murdered baronet's money—into the hands of Jeffreys.

"Don't be afeard that I'm leaky, sir," responded the man, clutching the gold, and consigning it to his pocket, where he had already stowed away the baronet's handsome repeater and gold rings—to which valuables he had helped himself, while his master was busily engaged in cleansing the carpet in the parlour;—for Mr. Torrens had merely plundered the corpse of the contents of the purse, and had not touched the jewellery, through fear that it might lead to the detection of the murder, if seen in his possession.

Master and man now separated—the former to seek a sleepless couch, and the latter to dream of the good fortune which that night's adventure had brought him.

And in his unconsecrated grave—a victim to the assassin's knife—slept the once gay, dissipated, and unprincipled Sir Henry Courtenay!

CHAPTER LXXIX.
THE EARL OF ELLINGHAM AND LADY HATFIELD AGAIN.

It was about two o'clock, on the day following the incidents just related, that we shall find the Earl of Ellingham seated with Lady Georgiana Hatfield, in the drawing-room at the residence of the latter.

Arthur had returned on the preceding evening from France, accompanied by Mr. de Medina and Esther, after having seen Tom Rain, Tamar, and Jacob Smith embark at Havre-de-Grace for the United States.

Rainford and Tamar were united in the bonds of matrimony in Paris; and Mr. de Medina had insisted upon placing in the hands of his son-in-law a sum of ten thousand pounds, as a proof of his perfectly cordial feeling towards him, and of his determination, also, fully to recognise Tamar as his daughter again.

The Earl communicated all these incidents to Lady Hatfield, who listened to them with the greatest interest.

"I propose to introduce the Medinas to you shortly, Georgiana," said the young nobleman. "You will find the father a person of very gentlemanly manners, well read, and particularly agreeable in conversation; while his daughter, Miss Esther, is as amiable and accomplished as the child of such a man should be."

"Arthur," replied Lady Hatfield—for they now addressed each other in the same friendly, or rather familiar manner, when alone together, as if they were brother and sister—"I would rather not form the acquaintance of your friends for the present."

The Earl appeared surprised and vexed.

"Georgiana," he exclaimed, in a tone of gentle remonstrance, "is it possible that you entertain any of those ridiculous prejudices[36] which only very ignorant or very narrow-minded persons can possibly entertain towards a most estimable race?"

"Oh! no—no," cried Lady Hatfield emphatically. "I have read much concerning the Jews, and I feel convinced that they are most unjustly treated by Christians. Heaven knows, Arthur, that I have no bad prejudices of that nature; and were I imbued with them, I would never rest till I had stifled such evidences of an illiberal and narrowed mind."

"I am delighted to hear you thus express yourself," said the Earl. "During my sojourn in France with the Medina family, I have obtained a great insight into the Jewish character; and I am convinced that it is fully as benevolent, as generous, and as liberal as that of the Christian. But we were speaking of my proposed presentation of Mr. de Medina and his daughter Esther to you. From all that I have said to them concerning you, they are most anxious to form your acquaintance; and you have yet to explain to me the meaning of your observation that you would rather postpone the introduction."

"To justify myself," returned Georgiana, blushing, "against your suspicion that I entertain illiberal prejudices, Arthur, I will frankly state my motives for expressing that wish. Indeed, I know not why any consideration should induce me to retain those motives a secret—especially as the explanation of them will afford me an opportunity to give you my advice. For have we not agreed to be unto each other as brother and sister?—and in what can a sister more conscientiously advise her brother than in matters regarding his happiness?"

"My happiness!" exclaimed the Earl, starting slightly, and evincing some degree of astonishment at Lady Hatfield's remark.

"Yes, Arthur—your happiness!" repeated Georgiana, with difficulty suppressing a sigh. "Now, listen to me attentively. I have heard that Miss Esther de Medina is eminently beautiful—excessively accomplished—very amiable—and endowed with every qualification to render her worthy of becoming even a monarch's bride."

"Georgiana!" cried the Earl of Ellingham, his heart fluttering with mingled suspense, surprise, and joy.

"Yes," observed Lady Hatfield; "and since you have learnt," she added more slowly, and in a softly plaintive tone—though she endeavoured to subdue the emotion which so modulated her voice,—"since you have learnt that *our* union is impossible, Arthur,—since you have ceased to look upon me otherwise than as a sister,—it is probable—nay, it is both natural and certain that you cannot have beheld Esther de Medina with indifference."

"Georgiana," exclaimed Arthur, in a solemn tone, "I never can forget that my first love was devoted to you; and—although circumstances have, alas! prevented our union—yet I should be unwilling to promise to another that heart which I so freely—so gladly gave to you!"

"It is alike unjust and ridiculous for me to suppose that, as I cannot become your wife, Arthur, you may never marry. No," continued Lady Hatfield; "I should despise myself, were I to entertain such abhorrent selfishness. My ardent desire is to know that you are happy; and Esther de Medina is well qualified to ensure your felicity. Nay—interrupt me not: remember, it is now a sister who counsels a brother! Granting even that you could never love another as you have loved me—and this is a supposition which I have not vanity enough to entertain for a moment—but, even granting it, for argument's sake, you may yet treat a beautiful and affectionate wife with that tenderness—those delicate attentions—and that cherishing kindness which will make *her* happy. Oh! believe me, such a state of bliss would soon beget love in your heart,—a love for Esther as ardent and sincere as that with which you honoured me; for it is the mere idle theory of romance-writers, that the same heart cannot love twice. Nature herself proclaims the falsehood of the doctrine; and the experience of all wise legislators, whether secular or ecclesiastic, declares the same, by the mere fact of allowing second marriages. Believe me, Arthur, I am speaking solely in regard to your happiness; and the day shall come when your lips breathe the words, '*Georgiana, I thank thee for the counsel thou gavest me.*'"

The Earl surveyed with respectful admiration that noble-hearted woman who thus stifled her own feelings through generous solicitude for his felicity.

"And now," she resumed, after a moment's pause, "you can divine the reasons which induced me to express a wish that my introduction to the Medinas should be postponed for the present. I am but a weak woman;—and though I can proudly say that no petty feeling of jealousy would ever enter my heart—yet I would rather not awaken in my mind painful recollections of *what might have been,* by beholding you in the society of one to whom you would be engaged. Moreover, as Miss de Medina has doubtless heard that *our* union was once resolved upon," added Lady Hatfield, now unable to suppress a profound sigh, "it would not be agreeable for her to visit me, if she accept you as her husband, until after your marriage. Those are my motives, Arthur: and now you will admit that, so far from entertaining any illiberal prejudices against the Jews, I have proved the very contrary, by earnestly recommending you to espouse an amiable and beautiful lady belonging to that nation."

"Dearest sister—for such indeed you are to me," said the Earl of Ellingham, "I appreciate all the excellence of your intentions in thus advising me; and I will frankly admit to you, that did I now think of uniting my fate with any woman, Esther de Medina would be the object of my choice, since my alliance with yourself has been rendered impossible. But I am not quite prepared to take that step—nor do I even know whether Miss de Medina would accept my suit, were I to proffer it."

"If her affections were not engaged before she saw you—before she knew so much of you," exclaimed Georgiana, "she loves you now. Oh! of this I am convinced," she continued enthusiastically. "Consider how much you have done to render her grateful to you; and gratitude in woman is the parent of affection! You have saved her beloved sister Tamar from the depths of despair by adopting those wondrous schemes, by which he who is now her husband, was snatched from the jaws of death;—you reconciled a father to a long discarded daughter;—and you have at length seen that daughter made a wife—the wife of the man she adores! Oh! Arthur, think you not that Esther ponders on all this? Yes—and, in the gratitude of her generous soul, she already sees a god-like being in the Earl of Ellingham."

"You will render me quite vain, Georgiana," said the young nobleman; "for you are magnifying into glorious achievements a few very common-place acts on my part."

"I am giving you your due for all that is great and noble in your disposition—all that is excellent and estimable in your character," replied Lady Hatfield, in a tone of fervent sincerity. "And that you are every thing I describe is so much the more to your credit, inasmuch as you belong to a class not famous for good qualities. The aristocratic sphere is characterised by intense selfishness—by a love of illegitimate power—by an abhorrence of the inferior grades,—and by a hollowness of heart which brings shame and reproach upon their hierarchy. When, then, we find this corrupted and vicious sphere possessing a glorious exception such as yourself, the world should be the more ready to recognise your merits. But I will say no more on this head, my dear Arthur," added Georgiana, with a smile, "for fear that you should think I wish to coax you into following that counsel which I, ere now, so seriously and so conscientiously gave you."

"And on that advice will I reflect deliberately," replied the Earl, who could not conceal from himself that he was rejoiced it had been given. "And now, Georgiana, I must take my leave of you for the present," he added, rising from his seat: "for I have a commission of a somewhat important nature to execute for my half-brother. Indeed, the mention thereof reminds me that I have never made you acquainted with one of the best traits in his character. But does it annoy you,—does it vex you to hear me speak of him?"

"No—no," answered Georgiana, somewhat hurriedly. "Since I have known that he is your brother, I have been pleased to hear you say as much good of him as possible."

"And this incident to which I allude," continued the Earl, "is not the least praiseworthy of the many fine deeds which must be placed to his account on the bright side. It appears that about three months ago he adopted a little boy under very peculiar circumstances. A poor woman died suddenly, through want and exposure to the inclemency of the weather, at an obscure house in Seven Dials. Rainford happened to be there at the time, and he took compassion on the little boy whom this poor woman had in charge. The boy was not the woman's child—as a certain letter found upon the person of the female proved. This letter was at first detained by those miserable wretches who so persecuted my poor brother: but it subsequently fell into his hands; and he entrusted it to a Mr. Clarence Villiers, in order that this gentleman might institute inquiries relative to its contents. I am now about to seek Mr. Villiers, and obtain the letter from him; because, it appears from all I have heard, that it is indubitably addressed to some lady of title, although no name be mentioned in it. In fact, the poor woman—whose name was Sarah Watts——"

"Sarah Watts!" repeated Lady Hatfield, with an hysterical scream, a deadly pallor overspreading her beautiful countenance.

"That is the name——But, my God! you are ill!"—and the Earl rushed forward to catch Georgiana in his arms, as she was falling from her chair.

He conveyed her to the sofa; but for some moments she seemed insensible. He was about to summon her female attendants, when she opened her eyes, glanced wildly around her, and then said in an excited tone, "Do not ring for any one,—I shall be better in a minute—remain with me, Arthur,—I have now much to tell you!"

Surprised and grieved at the effect which his words had produced on Lady Hatfield—yet unable to comprehend wherefore the mere mention of a name should have so seriously touched her feelings,—the Earl gazed upon her with interest and curiosity.

At length a faint tinge of red appeared upon her cheeks; and, with reviving strength, she sate up on the sofa, motioning the young nobleman to take a chair near her.

"Arthur," she said, "I ought not to have kept that *one* secret from you—for are we not now brother and sister? But, alas! you—with your generous heart and fine feelings—can well understand how painful it is for me to speak of my own dishonour,—and the more so, since that degradation—that deep disgrace was caused by *him* who is nearly allied to you."

"What! can it be possible?" exclaimed the Earl, a sudden light breaking in upon him: "that child—that boy, whom Rainford has adopted as his own———"

"Is mine!" said Georgiana, in a voice of despair;—and, covering her face with her hands, she burst into an agony of tears.

The Earl of Ellingham started from his seat, and began to pace the room in a manner denoting the most painful excitement.

He was, indeed, deeply afflicted.

How wronged—how profoundly wronged had Georgiana been!—and by *him* who, as she herself had said, was so nearly allied to him!

Oh! Tom Rain—Tom Rain! that was the darkest episode in thy life!

Thus thought the Earl likewise;—and bitter was his sorrow at the revival of such appalling reminiscences as those which now rent Lady Hatfield's heart with anguish, and called forth the floods of grief from her eyes.

"Arthur," at length she said, exercising a violent effort to subdue her sorrow, "give not way to bitter reflection on my account. For *your* sake, all has been forgiven—though it may never be forgotten; for memory is immortal! But that child—that boy of whom you speak—he is indeed with his own father; and Providence doubtless willed that it should be so!"

She paused, and stifled the sobs which rent her bosom.

"You may think me a cruel and heartless mother, Arthur," she resumed at length, now speaking in a mournful, plaintive tone, "thus to have abandoned my offspring: but reflect ere you blame me! I was as it were alone in a house situated in a retired part of the country—a man entered at night—he found his way to my chamber—he took advantage of my loneliness——O God! how have I survived that disgrace—that infamy? Desperate was my resistance—but vain: and the ravisher, as you already know, was Rainford! Alas! pardon me if I then mentioned his name with bitterness; but human patience could not speak it calmly when such a cloud of crushing reminiscences come back to the soul."

Again she paused: the Earl remained silent. What could he say? He loathed—he abhorred the conduct of his half-brother, whom he would not attempt to justify;—and his good sense told him that it were worse than mockery to aim at consoling the victim of that foul night of maddened lust and atrocious rape.

"Some weeks afterwards," continued Lady Hatfield, in a voice scarcely audible and deeply plaintive, "I found that I was in a way to become a mother. You may conceive——But no: it is impossible to imagine the state of mind into which this appalling conviction threw me. And yet I was compelled to veil my grief as much as possible;—for at that time a suspicion of my condition on the part of the world, would have driven me to suicide. I need not—I could not enter into the details of the plan which I had adopted to conceal my dishonour. Suffice it to say, that I succeeded in so doing—and, in a small retired village, and under a feigned name, did I give birth to a son. To Sarah Watts was the babe confided;—and, for a sum of money paid down at once, she agreed to adopt it as her own. By an accident she discovered who I was—my name was on an article of jewellery which I had with me. But she promised the strictest secrecy, and I put faith in her words. Oh! do not blame me, if I acted as I have now described—if I abandoned that child whose presence near me would only have been a proof of my dishonour, and a constant memorial of the dread outrage which no levity—no encouragement—no fault on my part had provoked!"

"Blame you, Georgiana!" exclaimed the Earl, approaching and taking her hand kindly;—"how could I blame you? You acted as prudence dictated—and, indeed, as circumstances inevitably compelled you. But—now that the parentage of this child is at length discovered—how do you wish me to act? Remember, Georgiana, every thing in this respect shall be managed solely with regard to your wishes—solely according to your directions. Shall I communicate in a letter to my half-brother the secret which has thus strangely transpired this day?—or shall I leave him in ignorance of the fact that he has adopted his own son?"

"He knew not that the outrage he perpetrated led to that consequence," said Lady Hatfield, now cruelly bewildered and uncertain how to decide. "No—he could not even suspect it—for I never met him again until that night on the Hounslow road—and even then I recognised him not—and it was only at the police-office in Bow Street that I again beheld him who had been my ruin!"

"I am convinced," observed the Earl, "that Rainford has not the least suspicion that you indeed became a mother. And, oh! when I touched upon the subject of his atrocious behaviour towards you—while we were in Paris—had you seen the tears of contrition—heart-felt contrition which he shed——But, no," added the Earl, suddenly interrupting himself,—"it were impossible that you could forgive him!"

"I forgive him for *your* sake, Arthur," said Georgiana, in a mild but firm tone. "And now, relative to that child—yes—he shall know that he is with his father; and your brother must be informed that he has adopted his own son! Providence indeed seems to have so willed it; for we cannot believe that accident alone threw the child thus wondrously into the way of the author of its being. Arthur," she added, taking the young nobleman's hand,—"you will write to Rainford—and you will tell him all. It is not necessary to enjoin him to treat the child with kindness—for you say that his disposition is naturally generous. Nevertheless—I should wish," continued the lady, looking down as she uttered these words, and sinking her voice almost to a whisper—for *maternal feelings* were stirring within her bosom,—"nevertheless, I should wish that you impress upon the mind of your half-brother the necessity of bringing that child up in the paths of virtue and honour."

"Your wishes shall be complied with," answered the Earl. "But fear not that Rainford would inculcate evil principles into the mind of his son. No—he is thoroughly changed, and will become a good, and, I hope, a happy and prosperous man."

The young nobleman then took leave of Lady Hatfield, whom he left a prey to emotions of a very painful nature.

For deeply and tenderly did she love Arthur; and great violence did she to her feelings when she so generously and conscientiously counselled him to take the beautiful Jewess as his wife!

And as the Earl returned home to his mansion in Pall Mall, to pen a letter to Rainford, who was then on his voyage, under an assumed name, and accompanied by Tamar, Jacob Smith, and little Charley, to the United States,—he reviewed all the details of that long and interesting conversation which had that afternoon passed between Lady Hatfield and himself;—and he found that the tendency thereof was to make him ponder more seriously and more intently upon the image of the charming Esther than he ever yet had done.

36. We have been much gratified by observing that our attempt to vindicate the Jews against most of the unjust charges which it seems to be a traditionary fashion to level against them, has not passed unnoticed. All the Jewish papers have quoted the exculpatory passage at page 172 of this Series of "THE MYSTERIES OF LONDON:" many provincial journals have also transferred it to their columns; and in No. 173 of *Chambers's Edinburgh Journal* (New Series) it was printed, with the following record of approval on the part of the Editors of that well-conducted periodical:—"*We cordially agree in this manly defence of a cruelly misrepresented people.*"

In this enlightened age it is really horrible to think that the most abominable prejudices should prevail amongst Christians against the Jews. England boasts her high state of civilisation; and yet the Jews labour under innumerable disabilities, which have been abolished in France. After all, the French understand what civilisation really is much better than the English. The idea of a Jew sitting in the House of Commons would send all the Church party raving mad: but in France there are many Jews in the Chamber of Deputies. The learned Selden said very justly, "Talk what you will of the Jews, that they are cursed, they thrive where'er they come; they are able to oblige the prince of their country (and others too) by lending him money; none of them beg: they keep together; and for their being hated, my life for your's, Christians hate one another as much."

The worst feature in the malignant persecution and misrepresentation of the Jews, is that the evil prejudice against them has been, and still is, fostered by Christian Divines and Theological writers. A Spanish theologian has placed on record the following infamous specimen of malignity:—

"The tribe of Judah treacherously delivered up our Lord, and thirty of them die by treason every year.

"The tribe of Reuben seized our Lord in the garden, and therefore the curse of barrenness is on all they sow or plant, and no green thing can flourish over their graves.

"The tribe of Gad put on the crown of thorns, and on every 25th of March their bodies are covered with blood from deep and painful wounds.

"Those of Asher buffeted Jesus, and their right hand is always nearly a palm shorter than the left.

"Those of Napthali jested with Christ about a herd of swine, since when they are all born with tusks like wild boars.

"The tribe of Manasseh cried out, 'His blood be on us and on our children,' and at every new moon they are tormented by bloody sores.

"The tribe of Simeon nailed our Lord to the cross, and on the 25th of March, four deep and dreadful wounds are inflicted on their hands and feet.

"Those of Levi spat on the Saviour, and the wind always blows back their saliva in their faces, so that they are habitually covered with filth.

"The tribe of Issachar scourged Christ, and on the 25th of March blood streams forth from their shoulders.

"The tribe of Zebulon cast lots for the garments, and on the same day the roof of their mouth is tortured by deep wounds.

"The tribe of Joseph made the nails for crucifying Jesus, and blunted them to increase his sufferings; and therefore their hands and feet are covered with gashes and blood.

"Those of Benjamin gave vinegar to Jesus; they all squint and are palsied, and have their mouths filled with little nauseous worms, which, in truth (adds our author), is the case with all Jewish women after the age of 25, because it was a woman who entreated the tribe of Joseph not to sharpen the nails used for the crucifixion of our Lord."

That wretchedly prejudiced and unprincipled writer, Justin Martyr, wrote as follows, while apostrophising the Jews:—

"God promised that you should be *as the sand on the sea shore*; and so you are indeed, in more senses than one. You are as numerous, and you are as barren, and incapable of producing any thing good."

CHAPTER LXXX.
MRS. SLINGSBY AND MR. TORRENS.

While the scene, related in the preceding chapter, was taking place at the residence of Lady Hatfield, in Piccadilly, incidents requiring mention occurred elsewhere.

Mrs. Slingsby was seated in her drawing-room, a prey to the most frightful alarms.

Sir Henry Courtenay had left her the evening before to acquaint Mr. Torrens with Rosamond's flight, and consult with him relative to the necessary steps to be taken to prevent the exposure which himself and Mrs. Slingsby so much dreaded. On thus parting with her, the baronet had faithfully promised to call early in the morning and inform her of the particulars of his interview with Mr. Torrens;—but it was now past one o'clock in the afternoon, and he had not made his appearance.

What could his absence mean?—had any thing disagreeable occurred?—was it possible that Rosamond could have made away with herself, and that Sir Henry had taken to flight through dread of an exposure and its consequences?

The suspense which Mrs. Slingsby endured, was horrible—horrible!

Guilty consciences invariably magnify into giants even the most dwarf-like causes of apprehension; and there was no exception to this rule on the present occasion.

A hundred times had she glanced at the elegant or-molu clock on the mantel—and as hour after hour passed, and he came not, her restlessness increased to such a degree that it at length reached a state of nervous excitement no longer endurable.

She accordingly hurried to her chamber, dressed herself in her walking-attire, and having left word with her servants that in case Sir Henry Courtenay should call, he was to be requested to wait until her return, sped to the nearest hackney-coach stand, where, stepping into a vehicle, she ordered the driver to take her over to Torrens Cottage.

Yes—thither she was determined to proceed without delay, even at the risk of encountering Rosamond; though she could scarcely believe that the wronged girl had returned home. For, not precisely remembering all the details of the conversation which took place between herself and the baronet, and which Rosamond had overheard, the guilty woman imagined that something more than mere allusions might have been made to the connivance of Mr. Torrens in the ruin of his daughter; and hence Mrs.

Slingsby's very natural supposition that the victim of the infernal plot had not returned to the parental dwelling.

The coach did not proceed with particular celerity, and the distance from the West End to Torrens Cottage was great:—Mrs. Slingsby had therefore ample leisure to continue her harrowing meditations upon the real or supposed dangers which menaced her.

In sooth, her position was by no means an enviable one—unless indeed a convict under sentence of death might have preferred her state to that of imminent and ignominious death. For circumstances appeared suddenly to combine against her. She was in the family-way—and this was alone sufficient to cause her the most serious chagrin, especially as her impious scheme of proclaiming herself a second Johanna Southcott had been so completely frustrated by the determined opposition of her paramour. Then there was the affair of Rosamond Torrens, one word from whose lips would have the effect of tearing away the mask of hypocrisy which Mrs. Slingsby had so long worn, and exposing her to the world in all the hideous nudity of her criminal character. Lastly, the unaccountable absence of the baronet filled her mind with the most serious misgivings; for she knew that if he had indeed absconded, and if he should cease to maintain her in a pecuniary sense, her position would become lamentable in the extreme.

All these maddening reflections raised a storm of agitation in her guilty mind; and she could scarcely subdue her excitement so that it should escape the notice of the coachman, as he opened the door of the vehicle when it stopped opposite Torrens Cottage.

Mr. Torrens was at home; and Mrs. Slingsby was immediately conducted by Jeffreys to the parlour—the very parlour where her paramour had been murdered on the preceding evening!

Rosamond, from her bed-room window, had observed the arrival of the hateful woman, and was lost in surprise at her conduct in daring to visit her father's abode.

Mr. Torrens received Mrs. Slingsby in the apartment where, as we have just stated, the awful tragedy of the previous night had been enacted; and this was the first time the criminal pair had ever met.

Bad as Mr. Torrens himself was, he could not help feeling a sentiment of extreme loathing and disgust for the woman who concealed so black a heart beneath the garb of religious hypocrisy;—and, though he endeavoured to speak politely to her as he desired her to be seated, his manner was cold, reserved, and indicative of the influence which her presence produced upon him.

"We know each other by name, Mr. Torrens," began Mrs. Slingsby; "but it is only now that we have met. You can doubtless conjecture the object of my visit——"

"Yes, madam," exclaimed Rosamond, suddenly bursting into the room, evidently in a state of fearful excitement: then, hastily closing the door, she added, "My father can too well divine the purport of this insolent intrusion. You doubtless seek to recover possession of *me*—to take me back to your infamous abode—to surrender me up to your own vile paramour! Oh! my dear father, surely—surely you will not allow this polluted creature to remain beneath your roof a minute longer!"

"Rosamond—Rosamond," said Mrs. Slingsby, becoming the colour of scarlet, "you will regret those harsh words. I came for the purpose of giving certain explanations to your respected parent——"

"Explanations, madam!" cried the young girl, with a bitter smile of contempt. "What explanations can *you* offer which *I* have not already given?"

"I have every reason to believe that you overheard a conversation between Sir Henry Courtenay and myself," said Mrs. Slingsby, growing bolder as she perceived that the atrocious complicity of Mr. Torrens was not suspected by his daughter; "and that conversation seems to have alarmed you—for your flight from the house was wild and precipitate."

"Had I not already tarried there too long?" demanded Rosamond emphatically. "Oh! think not to be able to delude me any more with your specious misrepresentations—your disgusting sophistry! A veil has fallen from my eyes—and I now behold *you*, madam, and that baronet whom you so much vaunted, in your proper colours."

"You are wrong thus to suspect us so cruelly," said Mrs. Slingsby. "The conversation which you overheard was but the repetition of another conversation which Sir Henry Courtenay had himself overheard between two persons whom you know not, and which he was relating to me. But I appeal to your father whether *he* believes me——"

"Enough, madam!" exclaimed Rosamond, in a tone which convinced the base woman that she was indeed no longer to be imposed upon. "My father knows you to be a degraded hypocrite—and your insolence is extreme in thus daring to violate the sanctity of the paternal dwelling to which I have been forced to return for shelter and refuge. And were it not," she added bitterly, "that I should be proclaiming my own dishonour, not a moment's hesitation would I manifest in tearing away the mask from your face, and exposing you to the world. Oh! when I think of all the insidious wiles which you have practised—all the abhorrent tutoring which you have brought to play upon my mind, I deplore—yes, deeply do I deplore that necessity which compels me to place a seal upon my lips!"

Mrs. Slingsby had heard enough to satisfy her that no exposure would take place at the hands of Rosamond; and she was not very solicitous to prolong her visit. The cause of the baronet's absence she had yet to learn; but she concluded that it was not at Torrens Cottage she must seek to have her curiosity in that respect gratified.

She accordingly rose—bowed to Mr. Torrens, who had remained a mute but most alarmed spectator of the whole scene—and hastily withdrew, just in time to avoid coming in collision with John Jeffreys; for that worthy, judging by the excited manner in which he, himself unobserved, had seen Rosamond rush into the parlour, that something extraordinary was connected with the arrival of Mrs. Slingsby, had very coolly and quietly listened at the parlour-door to every word that was uttered within.

Mrs. Slingsby returned home, somewhat consoled by the conviction that her character was safe from any vindictiveness on the part of Rosamond: but she was still alarmed in respect to the baronet;—and this fear increased greatly, when, on her arrival in Old Burlington Street, at about four o'clock, she learnt that he had not called.

She immediately despatched a note to his residence; but the domestic returned with the answer that Sir Henry Courtenay had not been home since the preceding day—a circumstance which caused no small degree of alarm in the baronet's household, inasmuch as though he often slept away from his abode, his servants were invariably kept ignorant of those proofs of irregularities on his part. In a word, he was accustomed so to arrange matters, that his nocturnal outgoings were never suspected at his own residence—and thus his absence on this occasion had naturally inspired some degree of apprehension.

Mrs. Slingsby was astounded at the message which her servant had brought back. She could not even hazard a conjecture relative to the cause of Sir Henry Courtenay's disappearance; and she was at a loss where to search for him.

She therefore resolved to remain at home in the hope that he would presently call upon her; but time passed—and still he came not.

At length there was a loud double knock at the door; and she fancied it was the announcement of Sir Henry's arrival. But, instead of the object of her anxiety, Mr. Torrens was ushered into the drawing-room.

"I fancied, madam," he said, "that you had some particular reason in calling upon me just now, and which the presence of the unfortunate Rosamond prevented you from explaining. I therefore lost no time in waiting upon you."

"My alarm was somewhat appeased by the words which fell from your daughter's lips," answered Mrs. Slingsby, motioning to her visitor to be seated; "inasmuch as she expressed her intention of remaining silent on a subject which neither I nor you would wish to become a matter of public gossip. But I am astonished and grieved at the behaviour of Sir Henry Courtenay, who left me last night with the intention of proceeding direct to your house, and whom I have not since seen."

"He came not to me, madam," answered Mr. Torrens, with an unblushing countenance.

"This is most extraordinary—most alarming!" cried Mrs. Slingsby; "for he has not been home all night—nor yet to-day—and I begin to have vague suspicions that something wrong must have occurred."

"Sir Henry Courtenay is a gallant man——"

"Yes," interrupted Mrs. Slingsby hastily, as if the subject were not a very agreeable one: "but he also *maintains* a character for propriety and good conduct—and his dependants are never suffered to know that he stays away from home at night. You see that I am compelled to be candid with you—for the affair is most serious. Now, only reflect for a moment, Mr. Torrens, upon what my state of mind would be, were I questioned relative to Sir Henry's disappearance. Suppose, I say, that he did not soon come back—that he continued to be missing,——it would transpire that he was with me until late last evening—that we went out together,—for we *did* go out, to search for Rosamond,—and that I came back alone."

"No one could suspect *you*, madam, of having made away with him," observed Mr. Torrens.

"No—but I should be overwhelmed with the most embarrassing questions," exclaimed Mrs. Slingsby hastily. "And, do you know, that remark of your's has inspired me with horror and alarm? No one would suspect *me* of having made away with him! Of course not:—how could a weak woman assassinate a man in the streets of London, and not leave a trace of the dreadful deed behind? But might not inquiries be made—might it not be discovered that Sir Henry and myself were frequent visitors—I must speak candidly to you—to a house of ill-fame? And then—oh then! what a dreadful exposure would take place!"

"You are torturing yourself with vain apprehensions, Mrs. Slingsby," said Mr. Torrens, experiencing the greatest difficulty to conceal his own agitation.

"I should have thought that *you*, Mr. Torrens, would have assisted me with your advice—considering how we have been involved in the same transaction—rather than treat my fears with levity," said Mrs. Slingsby, in an excited manner. "And, if I tell you the candid truth," she added, fixing her eyes upon his countenance in a way which seemed intended to read the inmost secrets of his soul, "I must declare my conviction that *you* know more of the cause of the baronet's disappearance than you choose to admit."

"I—madam!" exclaimed Mr. Torrens, shrinking from the accusation in spite of himself.

"Yes—*you*," returned the lady, growing more and more excited: "and that suspicion which I hazarded, I scarcely know why, is now confirmed by your manner. I again say, yes—you know more of the cause of Sir Henry Courtenay's disappearance than you are willing to admit. I am convinced that he *did* visit you last night—and if he never came back, what account will you give?—what explanation will you render? Your anxiety in coming after me just now,—the singularity of your remark that no one would suspect *me* of foul play towards the baronet,—and your trepidation when I named the suspicion which had flashed to my mind concerning you,—all these circumstances convince me that you are no stranger to the cause of Sir Henry Courtenay's disappearance."

"Madam—this outrageous charge—implying a crime of which I am utterly incapable———" began Mr. Torrens, scarcely knowing how to meet the accusation, and seriously inclined to divulge the whole truth.

"I do not say that you have *murdered* Sir Henry Courtenay," interrupted Mrs Slingsby, speaking in a low tone, and giving a strong, hollow emphasis to that dreadful word which few can breathe without a shudder: "but that some quarrel may have taken place between you—that you were compelled to appear violent and vindictive in respect to him, your daughter perhaps being present—and that all this led to a fatal issue, are things which now seem to form a complete and connected train of horrible impressions in my mind. At all events, Mr. Torrens," she added, sinking her voice to a low whisper, "be candid with me—tell me the whole truth—and we will consult together, circumstances having already rendered us colleagues in *one* transaction."

"I have nothing to tell you, Mrs. Slingsby, in respect to this business," said Mr. Torrens; "and I am as astonished at Sir Henry Courtenay's disappearance as yourself."

"Then, if I were questioned," observed the lady, "you would have no objection to my saying that I parted last night from Sir Henry Courtenay near St. James's Church, Piccadilly, his last words being to the effect that he was about to call at Torrens Cottage on particular business?"

As she thus spoke, Mrs. Slingsby fixed her eyes in a searching—nay, a piercing manner upon the countenance of her companion, who for a moment quailed and betrayed evident signs of the desperate efforts he was making to conceal his agitation.

"Yes—you may safely say *that*, if you perceive any utility in so doing," returned Mr. Torrens at length: then, his features suddenly assuming a ferocious expression, he added, "But why proclaim war against me! Do we not know too much of each other to render such a warfare safe or useful to either? Were you not the paramour of Sir Henry Courtenay?—did you yourself not admit ere now that you visited a house of ill-fame with him?—and are you not at this moment with child by him? Woman—woman," muttered Torrens between his teeth, "provoke me not,—or it shall be war indeed—war to the knife!"

"Be reasonable, sir," said Mrs. Slingsby, now assuming a cold and resolute air; "and let us talk as two accomplices ought to converse—and not with menaces and threats."

"Agreed, madam—but be you reasonable also," returned Mr. Torrens.

"Then wherefore keep anything secret from me?" demanded Mrs. Slingsby. "I have read the truth—I have divined it—and your language has just confirmed my impression. But think not that I care for Sir Henry Courtenay, as a loving mistress or wife might care for him. No," she added contemptuously: "any affection which I may ever have experienced towards him, has long since vanished."

"And of what avail would it be to you to know that Sir Henry Courtenay was no more, even for a moment granting that he indeed exists no longer?" asked Torrens.

"I will tell you," replied Mrs. Slingsby in a low and hoarse whisper, while she looked intently and in a manner full of dark meaning into her companion's eyes, as she bent her countenance towards him. "If I were assured that Sir Henry Courtenay was indeed no more, I would become possessed of two thousand pounds by ten o'clock to-morrow morning."

"Ah!" ejaculated Mr. Torrens, his mind instantly conceiving the idea of sharing the produce of whatever plan the lady might adopt to accomplish her purpose—for we have already said that his necessities were still great, and that, unless he shortly obtained funds, he would be as badly off as he was ere he sold the virtue of his daughter.

"Yes," resumed Mrs. Slingsby; "and to show you that I have more confidence in you than you have in me, I will give you a full and complete explanation.

Sir Henry Courtenay promised me two thousand pounds as a reward for my connivance in the plan respecting Rosamond."

"Go on—go on," said Mr. Torrens hastily.

"That reward I have not received, because the payments which Sir Henry had to make to you, and other claims upon him, had caused him to overdraw his bankers. But yesterday morning he paid in eight thousand pounds; and he intimated to one of the partners that he should give me a cheque for two thousand in the course of the afternoon. The fact is," continued Mrs. Slingsby, "those bankers believe that I have property in India, which Sir Henry Courtenay's agent there manages for me, and that the proceeds therefore pass through Sir Henry's hands. This tale was invented to account for the numerous and large cheques which I have received from the baronet on that bank:—it was the saving clause for my reputation. Now, those two thousand pounds which were promised me I can have for little trouble and a small risk."

"Indeed!" said Mr. Torrens, becoming more and more interested in this explanation.

"Yes," continued Mrs. Slingsby, "and I will tell you how almost immediately. But I must first observe that I should have received the cheque last evening had not the sudden flight of Rosamond interrupted the discourse which I was having with the baronet, and thrown us into confusion. But,"—and again she lowered her voice to an almost inaudible whisper—"I can imitate the handwriting of Sir Henry Courtenay to such a nicety that it would defy detection. Now, do you understand me?"

"I do—I do," answered Mr. Torrens.

"And you perceive that I have full confidence in *you*," added the widow.

Mr. Torrens rose and paced the room for a few minutes. He was deliberating within himself whether he should repose an equal trust in Mrs. Slingsby; and he decided upon doing so. She saw what was passing in his mind, and remained silent, confident as to the result.

"My dear madam," he said, resuming his seat, "I will at once admit to you that Sir Henry Courtenay is indeed no more."

The lady heard him with breathless attention; for though she was fully prepared for the avowal, yet when it came it sounded so awfully—so ominously, that she received it with emotions of terror and dismay.

"It is indeed too true," continued Torrens: "but think not for a moment that I am a murderer! No—no; bad as I may be—as I know myself to be, in fine—I could not perpetrate such a deed as that. A strange and wonderful combination of circumstances led to the shocking catastrophe. Listen—and I will tell you all."

Mr. Torrens then related every incident of the preceding evening, suppressing only that portion of the tale which involved the fact of his servant John Jeffreys being acquainted with the occurrence, and having lent his aid in disposing of the body. This circumstance he concealed through that inherent aversion which man ever has to confess that he is in the power of any one; and he made it appear, by his own story, that, unassisted, he had buried the corpse.

At first Mrs. Slingsby was incredulous relative to the version of the murder which she heard. She thought that Torrens was himself the perpetrator of the act; but when he declared how cruelly the robbery of his money had embarrassed him, and when she reflected that there really could have been no reason urgent or strong enough to induce him to make away with the baronet, she ended by fully believing his narrative.

"Then he is indeed no more!" she exclaimed. "But, my God! what will be thought of his disappearance?—and will not those enquiries, which I so much dread, be made?"

"As no suspicion can possibly fall upon either yourself or me," responded Mr. Torrens, "it is far from likely that any such enquiries will be instituted. No—you need not be alarmed on that head, my dear madam. I should rather be inclined to entertain apprehensions for the success of your own scheme of——the forgery," he added, after a moment's pause.

"No danger can possibly attend that undertaking," said Mrs. Slingsby. "The baronet stated at the bankers' that he should give me the cheque yesterday; and it will be paid in a moment, even if they have already heard of his disappearance, which is scarcely probable, because the fears excited by that fact have not as yet become so strong as to lead to the suspicion that he has indeed met with foul play."

"You are, then, confident of being enabled to counterfeit his handwriting successfully?" asked Mr. Torrens.

"Beyond all possibility of doubt," replied the widow.

"And shall you want my assistance?" inquired Torrens, thinking how he could start a pretext for claiming a portion of the expected proceeds of the nefarious plan.

"Listen to me," said Mrs. Slingsby, after a few moments' deliberation, and now speaking as if she had finally come to a settled resolution on a particular point, which she had been revolving in her mind almost ever since Mr. Torrens entered the room: "I have something to propose to you which regards us both, and which may suit yourself as well as it would suit me. You are involved in embarrassments?"

"I am indeed," replied Mr. Torrens, now awaiting breathless suspense the coming explanation, which, by the leading question just put, appeared to relate to some scheme for relieving him of his difficulties.

"And these embarrassments are very serious?" continued the widow.

"So serious that they are insurmountable, as far as I can see at present," was the response.

"Then you fear executions—arrest—prison—and all the usual ordeal of an insolvent debtor?" asked the lady.

"Just so: and sooner than enter on that ordeal, I would commit suicide," rejoined Mr. Torrens.

"The alternative I have to propose to you is not quite so serious nor alarming as that," resumed Mrs. Slingsby. "I have shown you that I can put myself in possession of two thousand pounds to-morrow morning: will that sum relieve you completely from your difficulties?"

"And enable me to carry out those speculations which must produce a large fortune," answered Torrens.

"Then those two thousand pounds are at your disposal, on one condition," said Mrs. Slingsby.

"And that condition?" gasped Mr. Torrens, in mingled joy and suspense.

"Is that you marry me," returned Mrs. Slingsby, as calmly as if she were making a bargain of a very ordinary nature.

"Marry you!" exclaimed her companion, quite unprepared for this proposal.

"Yes—marry me," repeated the widow. "You want money to save you from ruin—I want a husband to screen me from disgrace. You are involved in pecuniary troubles—I am in a way to become a mother. I can save your person from a gaol—you can save my character from dishonour."

"The arrangement is indeed an equitable one," said Mr. Torrens, not without the least scintillation of satire in his remark: "but I see one fatal objection."

"And that is your daughter Rosamond," observed Mrs. Slingsby. "Surely the whim—the aversion—or the phantasy of a girl will not induce you to reject a proposal which will save you from ruin and imprisonment?"

"And yet, what could I say to her? how could I explain my conduct? what would she think, after all she knows of you?" demanded Mr. Torrens.

"She has not the power to prevent the match; and that is the principal point in the matter," returned Mrs. Slingsby coolly. "You may as well urge as an objection that Clarence Villiers, my nephew, is your son-in-law; but I am not so foolish as to be alarmed at such scruples, and you must have seen too much of the world to allow yourself to be irretrievably ruined for the sake of a few idle punctilios. Give me your decision at once—aye or nay. If it be the former, the marriage may be celebrated by special license to-morrow evening; if it be the latter, there is at once an end of the business, and we need not be the less good friends."

"You regard the whole proposition, then, entirely as a matter of *business*," said Mr. Torrens. "Well—that is indeed the way to look at it. Of course, if we strike a bargain and unite our fortunes, we shall require only one establishment. Will you break up this in Old Burlington Street, and be contented to dwell at my Cottage?"

"Certainly," was the reply. "The sale of my furniture will pay my debts, and perhaps leave a surplus; at all events we shall have the two thousand pounds clear."

"And that sum you will place in my hands to-morrow morning?" said Mr. Torrens interrogatively.

"No—to-morrow evening, *after* the ceremony," responded the widow.

"Then we cannot trust each other?" continued Mr. Torrens.

"I think we should act prudently to adopt as many mutual precautions as possible," observed Mrs. Slingsby coolly.

"Granted!" exclaimed Mr. Torrens. "And what guarantee have I that, when once the indissoluble knot shall have been tied, you will hand me over the promised sum?"

"Simply the fact that I do not wish to marry a man who will be the next morning conveyed away to a prison."

"That is a mere assertion, and no security," remonstrated Mr. Torrens; "we are talking the matter over in a purely business-like sense. Now, as far as I can see, the advantages will be all on your side. If you happen to be in debt, you will have a husband on whose person your creditors will pounce instead of on your own; and, at all events, as you are with child, you will have a person whom you can represent as the legitimate father of the expected offspring."

"I will tell you how the business can be managed," said Mrs. Slingsby, after a pause. "A thought has struck me! I will lodge the money in the hands of a very respectable solicitor whom I know, and you can accompany me to his office for the purpose. In his keeping shall it remain, with the understanding that it is to be paid to you on your becoming my husband."

"Good!" observed Mr. Torrens. "Who is the solicitor?"

"Mr. Howard," was the answer.

"I know him, and have no objection to him as the agent in the business. I think we have now got over all obstacles in that respect. A difficult task will it however prove to me to prepare my daughter this evening for the step which I am to take to-morrow."

"Oh! I have no doubt you will succeed," said Mrs. Slingsby: "it would be indeed hard if a father could not overcome, with his reasoning, the objections of his own child."

"I must do my best," observed Torrens, rising. "At what hour to-morrow shall I call to accompany you to the lawyer's?"

"At about twelve. I shall go to the bank between ten and eleven; and you can in the meantime obtain the marriage-license."

"It shall be done," returned Mr. Torrens. "The ceremony will be performed here?" he added interrogatively.

"Yes—at seven o'clock in the evening. I will make arrangements with two ladies whom I know, to be bridesmaids, and Dr. Wagtail will give me away. After the ceremony we will repair to Torrens Cottage."

Thus, calmly and deliberately, was settled the solemn covenant between the man who had sold his daughter's virtue and the licentious woman who was now prepared to commit a forgery!

And the worthy pair separated, Mr. Torrens having embraced his intended wife, because he considered a kiss to be as it were the seal of the bargain just concluded, and also because Mrs. Slingsby by her manner appeared to invite the salutation.

CHAPTER LXXXI.
ROSAMOND AT HOME.

We shall follow Mr. Torrens homeward, and see how he acquitted himself of the disagreeable and difficult task of breaking his matrimonial intentions to his daughter, the fair but ruined Rosamond.

It was past nine o'clock in the evening when he reached the cottage; and Rosamond, with a charming filial solicitude to render her parent's home as comfortable as possible, had superintended the preparations for supper. Exercising a command, too, over the sad feelings which filled her bosom, and invoking resignation with Christian fortitude to her aid, she even manifested a species of cheerfulness as she opened the front-door at the sound of his well-known knock. But, alas! it was not the innocent—artless cheerfulness of other days:—it was merely the struggle of the moonbeam to pierce the mass of dark and menacing clouds!

And now behold the father and daughter seated at the supper-table—that repast which the care of Rosamond had endeavoured to render as agreeable as possible, but which was disposed of hastily and without appetite on either side.

At length, when the things were cleared away and Mr. Torrens had fortified his courage with sundry glasses of wine, he prepared to enter on the grave and important subject which occupied his mind.

"Rosamond, my love," he said, speaking in as kind a tone as it was possible for his nature to assume, "I have something to communicate to you, and shall be glad if you will hear me calmly and without excitement. I have this evening seen Mrs. Slingsby."

"That woman!" exclaimed the daughter, starting. "Oh! I had hoped that her name would no more be mentioned in this house."

"I begged of you not to give way to excitement—I warned you to be reasonable," said Mr. Torrens severely. "Surely you can accord me your attention when I am anxious to discourse with you on matters of importance?"

"Pardon me, dearest father—and, oh! do not blame nor reproach me if I manifest a very natural irritability—a loathing—an abhorrence——"

She could say no more, but burst into a flood of tears.

Mr. Torrens suffered her to give full vent to her emotions; for he knew that the reaction would produce comparative calmness.

"Rosamond," he at length said, "you *can* be reasonable when you choose—and I do hope that you have sufficient confidence in your father to accord him your attention and to believe what he may state to you. Listen then—and rest assured that I should never take the part of any one against my own daughter. I have seen Mrs. Slingsby."

Rosamond gave a convulsive start; but her father, appearing not to observe it, proceeded.

"It struck me," he continued, "that she would never have had the presumption and impudence to call here this morning, if she were really as guilty as you supposed her to be. I therefore deemed it an act of justice to ascertain the nature of those explanations which she proffered in this room, and which your presence cut short. With that object in view, I proceeded to her abode; and she assured me that she was entirely innocent of any connivance in the atrocity perpetrated by Sir Henry Courtenay——"

"Innocent!" almost shrieked Rosamond. "Oh! my dear father, you know not how specious—how plausible that woman can be when she chooses; and it has suited her purpose to be so with you. But be not deceived——"

"Do you imagine that I am not old enough and sufficiently experienced to discriminate between sincerity and duplicity?" demanded Mr. Torrens. "I tell you, Rosamond, that you wrong Mrs. Slingsby—that your suspicions are most injurious! Reflect—consider before you thus condemn! You overheard a few words which immediately threw you into a state of such excitement that your imagination tortured all the subsequent discourse into an evidence of guilt on the part of a lady who is deeply attached to you—who loves you as if she were your own mother—and who will die of grief if you continue thus to misjudge her. Yes, Rosamond—Mrs. Slingsby has declared that she will put a period to her existence if you persist in your present belief! She accuses you of ingratitude towards her, after all her affectionate kindness in your behalf; and, should she carry her dreadful threat into execution—which I much fear, for she seems literally distracted—her blood will be upon your head!"

"Merciful heavens!" exclaimed Rosamond, appalled by this terrible announcement. "But if I cannot command my own convictions?" she added hastily.

"You must cherish a Christian spirit—you must be less prompt in forming opinions—less ready to arrive at those convictions which you represent to be uncontrollable," said Mr. Torrens, endeavouring to bewilder his daughter, and thereby render her spirit ductile and her mind pliant, so that he might manage both as he pleased. "So far from nourishing malignity against Mrs. Slingsby, you should seek consolation with her; for your own mother is not here to console you!"

"God be thanked that my mother is not here to witness my disgrace!" ejaculated Rosamond, clasping her hands fervently.

"For the sake of my daughters I was wrong—yes, I was wrong not to have married again," said Mr. Torrens, as if musing to himself. "I should have given a protectress to my children—a lady who would have been a second mother to them; and then all this would not have occurred! But it is not yet too late to ensure your future welfare, Rosamond, by those means," he added, turning towards his daughter, who had listened with surprise to her father's previous observations; "and in accomplishing that aim, I may at the same time afford a convincing proof to a deserving, wrongly-suspected, and misjudged woman of my own esteem, and inferentially of your regret at the calumniatory sentiments you have cherished concerning her."

"My dear father—I do not understand you!" cried Rosamond, a dreadful suspicion weighing on her mind; and which, nevertheless, seemed so wild and ridiculous—so utterly impossible to be well-founded, that she fancied she had not rightly comprehended the sentiments of her parent.

"I am thinking how I can best ensure your welfare and happiness, Rosamond," he said, "by giving you a substitute for that maternal protectress whom you have lost—one who will be a companion and a friend to you——"

"Father!" exclaimed Rosamond, horrified at the idea of having a step-mother, and trembling with indescribable alarms lest she had indeed too well read her sire's intentions respecting the *one* whom he proposed to invest with that authority.

"Will you hear me with calmness?—will you subdue this excitement, which amounts to an undutiful aversion to all I am projecting for your sake?" demanded Mr. Torrens, again assuming a severe tone: then, perceiving that his daughter was dismayed by his manner, he hastily added, as if determined at once to put an end to a painful scene, "If I have consulted you, Rosamond, on the step that I propose to take, it was because I deemed you sensible and reasonable enough to merit that proof of confidence on my part, and obedient enough to submit becomingly to the dictates of my superior wisdom and experience. Know, then, that it is my intention to marry again—*for your sake*—and that my inclinations, as well as my interests, induce me to fix my choice upon Mrs. Slingsby."

Rosamond uttered not a word, but fell back senseless in her chair.

"Obstinate fool!" muttered Torrens between his teeth, as he hastened forward to save her from slipping off on the fender. "But I will neither argue nor consult any more—I will command, where I wish to be obeyed."

He applied a scent-bottle to her nostrils; and she soon gave signs of returning animation. Opening her eyes, she glanced wildly at her father, as if to interrogate him whether that were really true which appeared to have been haunting her like a horrid dream.

"Father—father," she murmured, grasping his hands; "you will not—no, you will not do what you have said! Oh! I implore you—I conjure—sacrifice not your own happiness and mine at the same instant! I was not mistaken in one syllable that I overheard between that woman and that man—and their discourse filled me with horror. She is his paramour, father—she is in a way to become a mother——"

"Silence, daughter!" cried Mr. Torrens, sternly. "And now listen to me, while I make you acquainted with my *commands*! Not only is it my intention to marry Mrs. Slingsby, but I desire that you will treat her with respect—if not with affection. And as you value my love and the continuance of my kindness, you will observe these instructions. If any thing more be wanting to induce you to comply with my desire, that additional argument will, perhaps, be found in the fact that if I do not marry Mrs. Slingsby, I shall be ruined—utterly undone—my property wrested from me—my person conveyed to a prison—and *you* thrust out, houseless and penniless, into the wide world, without a soul to protect or befriend you. Now I have told you all—and it is for you to decide whether your prejudices shall prevail against my most substantial interests."

Rosamond was astounded at the words which met her ears; and she knew not how to reply.

For a few moments she stood gazing vacantly upon her father's countenance, as if to read thereon a confirmation of words, the import of which seemed too terrible to be true: then, probably experiencing the necessity of seeking the solitude of her own chamber for the purpose of giving vent to the overflowing fulness of her heart's emotions, she hurried from the room.

Poor friendless girl! dreadful was the position in which she found herself placed! Oh! why were not Clarence and Adelais near to console her—to receive her beneath their protecting influence? Alas! she would not have dared to face them, even were they in the metropolis at the time; for she could not have revealed to them her dishonour—Oh! no, she would sooner have died!

Throwing herself on a seat in the privacy of her bed-chamber, she burst into tears, and gave vent to her anguish in heart-rending sobs.

An hour passed—and still she thought not of retiring to rest;—she was in a state of utter despair!

She heard her father ascend to his chamber: but this circumstance reminded her not that the usual hour when she herself sought her couch had gone by.

Suddenly she was aroused from the deep reverie of woe that had succeeded the violent outburst of her anguish, by the movement of the handle of the door, as if some one were about to enter her room.

She started and listened, the bed being between the place where she was and the door, so that she could not see the latter.

Yes—some one was indeed entering the chamber.

With a faint scream she darted forward, and beheld a man in the act of closing the door behind him.

The intruder was Jeffreys, the recently-hired servant.

"What has brought you hither, John?" enquired Rosamond, in hasty and anxious tone—for she feared lest something had happened to her father.

"Nothink but your own beautiful self, Miss," answered the ruffian, advancing towards her as well as he was able—for he was much intoxicated.

"Begone!" cried Rosamond, her whole countenance becoming suddenly crimson with indignation. "Begone, I say—and to-morrow my father will know how to punish this insolence."

"Your father, Miss, won't do no such a thing," returned Jeffreys; "and it'll be all the worse for you if you holler. I know a many things that wouldn't render it safe for master to quarrel with me. So give me a kiss——"

"Villain!" exclaimed Rosamond, bursting into tears: "how dare you thus insult me? Leave the room—or I alarm the house at any risk!"—and she rushed towards the bell-pull.

"None of that nonsense, Miss—*or I'll hang your father, as sure as you're alive!*" said Jeffreys, placing his back to the door, folding his arms, and surveying Rosamond with the insolence of a licentious, drunken bully.

"Hang my father!" repeated the unhappy girl, staggering back and sinking into a chair—for so many dreadful things had recently occurred, that her mind was more attuned to give immediate credence to evil than to receive good tidings.

"Yes, by jingo!" said Jeffreys: "I can hang him any day I like. But what's more, I know pretty well all that's happened to you. I didn't listen for nothink at the parlour door this morning when that Mrs. Bingsby or Stingsby, or whatever her name is, was here."

"My God! my God!" murmured Rosamond, pressing her hands to her brow with all her might—for she felt as if she were going mad.

"Now don't take on so, Miss," said Jeffreys: "I'm sure I didn't mean to vex you like that. But the fact is I've took a great fancy to you: and if so be I let out that your father did draw a knife across the throat of that baronet which come here last night, and which I s'pose was the same you spoke of this morning to Mrs. Bingsby——"

"Monster!" shrieked Rosamond, in a shrill, penetrating tone—for she was unable any longer to subdue the horrible emotions which racked and tortured her, goading her almost to madness.

In another instant Mr. Torrens was heard to rush from his chamber—a moment more, and he forced his way into his daughter's room, hurling the villain Jeffreys forward with the violence exerted in dashing open the door.

"Father—dear father!" exclaimed Rosamond, springing into his arms; "save me—save me from that monster, who has told me such dreadful—dreadful things!"

"Be calm, Rosamond," said Mr. Torrens in a low and hoarse tone; "or you will alarm the other servant. Jeffreys," he added, turning towards the fellow who was swaying himself backwards and forwards, in the middle of the room, in that vain attempt to appear sober so often made by drunken men, "how dare you to intrude here? But follow me—I must speak to you alone."

"Father—one word," said Rosamond, in a voice indicative of deep feeling. "This man uttered a frightful accusation against you—Oh! an accusation so terrible that my blood curdles——"

"Nonsense, Rosamond!" interrupted Mr. Torrens, cruelly agitated: "you see that he has taken a drop too much—he is a good well meaning fellow—and will be very sorry in the morning——"

"Sorry! why the devil should I be sorry?" cried Jeffreys, with the dogged insolence of inebriation. "I don't know what I've got to be sorry for——"

"Come, come," said Mr. Torrens, gently pushing his daughter aside, and approaching the man-servant in a coaxing, conciliatory way; "this is carrying the thing too far, John——"

"Well—well, we can talk it over in the morning, Miss—and I dare say we shall make matters right enough together," stammered the drunken hind, as he allowed himself to be led away from the chamber by Mr. Torrens. "You're a pretty gal—and if I said anythink amiss——"

The almost maddened father hurried him over the threshold, and Rosamond hastened to secure the door behind them both.

Then flinging herself into a chair, she exclaimed, "My God! what horrors have met my ears this night! Misfortunes—crimes—woes—fears—outrages have entered the house, like an army carrying desolation along with it! But my father—a murderer—Oh! heavens—no—no—it cannot be! And yet that dread accusation—so cool—so systematic——my God! my God!"

And she wept as if her heart would break.

From this painful—or rather most agonising condition of mind, she was aroused by a low knock at her door; and, in answer to her question who was there, the voice of her father replied.

She hastened to admit him;—but, as he entered, she started back, appalled by the ghastliness of his countenance, every lineament of which denoted horror and fearful emotions.

"Father, tell me all—keep me not in suspense—let me know the worst!" exclaimed Rosamond, clasping her hands in an imploring manner. "Dreadful things have happened, I am sure—and my brain is reeling, maddening!"

"Daughter," said Mr. Torrens, taking her hand, "you *must* and you *shall know* the worst now—for I find that the miscreant Jeffreys has indeed told you too much for me to attempt to conceal the truth——"

"Just heavens! my father—stained with blood—the blood of vengeance on account of his dishonoured daughter;" said Rosamond, speaking in broken sentences and with hysterical excitement, while her eyes were fixed intently and with a fearfully wild expression upon the haggard countenance of her sire.

"No—not so, Rosamond," answered Mr. Torrens emphatically. "Sit down—there—and try and compose yourself for a few moments, while I give you an explanation which circumstances have rendered imperative."

The wretched girl suffered herself to be placed on a seat: her father then drew another chair close to the one which she occupied—and, leaning with folded arms over the back of it, he continued in these terms:——

"Last night—after you had retired to your room—Sir Henry Courtenay called. Yes—he dared to visit the house into which such dishonour and so much misery had been brought by his means. But he came to offer every possible atonement which it was in his power to make; and then I ascended to your room—here—to make you aware of his presence in the parlour below and of the proposals which I had received. But I found you in a state of mind too profoundly excited to bear the announcement—I remained with you to console and tranquillise you—and, when I saw that you were growing more calm, I retraced my way down stairs. Merciful heavens! what a spectacle then met my eyes!"

And Mr. Torrens, having introduced his fearful history by this deceptive and well coloured preface, proceeded to narrate the facts of the murder precisely as they had really occurred,—not forgetting to mention the robbery of a sum of money which he had left on the table. He then explained the part which John Jeffreys had subsequently performed in the occurrences of the preceding night; and he wound up in the following manner:——

"Thus you perceive, dear Rosamond, how a fearful combination of circumstances would fix dark and dreadful suspicions on me, were this tragedy to be brought to light. And now, too, you can understand how that miscreant Jeffreys dared to presume upon his knowledge of the shocking event—how, believing me to be completely in his power, he fancied that I dared not defend my own daughter from his licentious ruffianism. And, more than all this, Rosamond—Mrs. Slingsby holds me also beneath the rod of terrorism! For she knew that the baronet came hither last night—she knew also that he did not return—and I was compelled to reveal to her the whole truth, even as circumstances have now forced me to reveal it to you. And this is the secret of my intended marriage with her—a marriage that will take place to-morrow, and into which she has coerced me! Thus, Rosamond, if you ever loved and if you still love your unhappy father—pity him, pity him—but do not reproach him—nor aggravate his grief and his mental anguish by thought or deed on your part!"

So ingeniously had Mr. Torrens blended truth and fiction in his narrative, to work upon the feelings of his daughter,—so artfully had he combined and explained the various incidents in order to represent himself as the victim of cruel circumstances—that the generous-minded Rosamond felt the deepest commiseration and sympathy on behalf of her father rapidly taking possession of her soul.

"My dearest parent," she said, "I crave your pardon—I implore your forgiveness, for having wronged you by the most unjust—the most horrible suspicions! But the conduct of that man Jeffreys—his awful accusation—the reluctance you appeared to exhibit in dealing summarily with him, when you entered the room the first time this night,—all these things operated powerfully upon my mind, which has been attenuated by so many dreadful shocks within the last ten or twelve days! Alas! what sorrows have overtaken us—what perils environ us! Let us fly from this neighbourhood, dear father—let us leave England——"

"It is impossible, Rosamond!" interrupted Mr. Torrens hastily. "I had myself thought of that means of ensuring personal safety: but I abandoned the idea almost as soon as formed—for it was better to stay here, surrounded by danger, yet having bread to eat, than seek a foreign clime to starve!"

"We can work, dear father—we can toil for our livelihood! But, no—never should you be reduced to such a painful necessity, so long as your daughter has health and strength to labour for our mutual support!" exclaimed the excellent-hearted girl. "Oh! let us fly—let us quit this country—let us repair to France! I have some few accomplishments—drawing—music—a knowledge of all the branches of needlework; and it will be hard indeed if I cannot earn enough to procure us bread."

"No—no, Rosamond—it cannot be!" said Mr. Torrens, tears now trickling down his cheeks—for the better he became acquainted with the admirable traits of his daughter's character—traits which adversity, misfortune, and danger now developed—the more bitterly did his heart smite him for the awful treachery he had perpetrated with regard to her.

"And wherefore is it impossible?" she asked. "Consider, my dear father, by what circumstances you are now surrounded. On one side is Jeffreys whom you dare not offend—whom you cannot discharge—and from whose ruffianism your daughter is not safe. On the other side, is this marriage with Mrs. Slingsby—a marriage which I now perceive to be forced upon you—a marriage that will bring into this house a person whom neither of us can ever love or respect!"

"Enough! enough! Rosamond," exclaimed Mr. Torrens: "all these sad things—these dangers and these sacrifices—have become interwoven with the destiny which it is mine to fulfil; and I must pursue my painful course—follow on my sad career, in the best manner that I may. I cannot risk starvation in a foreign land—I could not support an existence maintained by the toils of my daughter. Besides, I am confident of being able to realise a fortune by my speculations in this neighbourhood. Here, then, must I remain. And now, Rosamond, it remains for you to decide whether you will receive the mother-in-law whom imperious circumstances force upon you—or whether you will abandon your father!"

"Never, never will I leave you!" cried the affectionate girl, throwing her arms around her parent's neck, and embracing him tenderly.

The interview—the painful interview between the father and his child then terminated. The former retired to his own apartment, a prey to feelings of the most harrowing nature; and the latter sought her couch, to which slumber was brought through sheer exhaustion.

But the horrors of the early portion of the night were perpetuated in her dreams!

CHAPTER LXXXII.
THE FORGED CHEQUE.

Oh! what a strange, and, at the same time, what a wondrous world is this in which we live;—and how marvellous is human progress! The utmost attainments effected by the wisdom of our ancestors were but ignorance and short-sightedness compared with the knowledge of the present day. Antiquity had its grand intellects and its sublime geniuses; but it furnished not the same abundance of materials to act upon as is afforded by the discoveries and likewise by the spirit of this age!

But are we proportionately happier, on this account, than were our forefathers? Is the working-man, for instance, more prosperous, more comfortable, more enviable as to his condition, than the aboriginal Briton who lived in a cave or the hollow of a tree, and who painted his body to protect it against the cold?

With all our prosperity—with all the grandeur, the glitter, and the refinement of our civilisation—with all our moralising institutions and our love of social order and mental improvement, we yet find the national heart devoured, tortured, and preyed upon by that undying serpent—PAUPERISM!

Yes: the millions are not so happy, so prosperous, or so comfortable as they ought to be;—for they are compelled to gnaw the tares of civilisation's field, while the proud and heartless oligarchy self-appropriate the corn!

Proud and heartless, indeed, are the rulers and the mighty ones of this land; and if the millions remain passive and patient, that pride and that heartlessness will grow, the one more despotic and the other more selfish.

It was but a few days ago that we marked two distinct articles in the morning newspapers, which formed a contrast fearfully significant in its evidence of the pride and the heartlessness which we abominate on the one hand, and of the distress and suffering which we so deeply deplore on the other.

One of these articles consisted but of *four lines*: the other occupied nearly *two columns*.

The first stated as laconically as possible that bread had risen to thirteen-pence the quartern loaf, and recorded a rapidly-disposed of regret that provisions should be so dear, on account of the poor. The second gave a laboured, fulsome, and tediously wire-drawn narrative of "Her Majesty's State Ball."

Thus the misery endured by millions in consequence of dearness and scarcity, is a trivial matter deserving only of *four lines*; whereas the trumpery nonsense and childish tom-foolery of a royal dance are deemed of sufficient importance to merit nearly *two columns*!

Oh! instead of giving balls and splendid entertainments at such a time, if the Sovereign of this land were to say to the people, "Ye are starving, and it makes my heart bleed to think that from your very vitals are wrung the hundreds of thousands of pounds which are wasted by myself and the other members of the Royal Family on our frivolities, our whims, our caprices, and our wanton extravagances: therefore will I give ye back one half of the enormous income which I have hitherto enjoyed, in the full confidence that my example will be imitated by many others who prey upon you;"—did the Sovereign thus speak to the nation, the nation would be justly proud of its Sovereign; and yet this Sovereign would only be performing a duty dictated by humanity and common justice.

What would be thought of the father of a family who feasted on turtle and venison, accompanied by generous wines, every day, while his children were thrust into the cold, humid cellar, to devour a mouldy crust and drink water?

Yet the Sovereign delights in the attribute of a general and comprehensive paternal solicitude in the welfare of the people: but it is an attribute which exists only in the imaginations of grovelling courtiers or lick-spittle historians.

Royalty and Aristocracy are intensely—necessarily—and thoroughly selfish: and as for any anxiety on behalf of the toiling and suffering millions, the idea is absurd—the notion is a mere delusion—the assertion that such a feeling exists, is a lie—a monstrous, wicked, atrocious lie!

There is more of the milk of human kindness in a single cottage than in all the palaces of Europe taken together.

There is more true philanthropy in one poor man's hovel, than in a thousand mansions of the great and wealthy in the fashionable quarters of London.

Oh! if the father or the mother can dance and be glad while the children are famishing, the sooner all ties are severed between such worthless parents and such an oppressed and outraged offspring, the better!

Nero danced and sang on the summit of a tower at the spectacle presented to his eyes by burning Rome;—and festivity and rejoicing reign in our English palaces, at a moment when scarcity menaces the land with famine and its invariable attendant—pestilence!

People of England! ye now understand how much sympathy ye may expect on the part of those who derive all their wealth from the sweat of your brow!

People of Ireland! ye now comprehend how much pity your starving condition excites on the part of your rulers!

People of Scotland! ye now perceive how worthy the great ones of the realm are of your adulation!

But it is sickening, as it is sorrowful, to dwell on this subject. Some of our readers may perhaps ask us wherefore we broach it at all? We will reply by means of a few questions. Is not every individual member of a society interested in the welfare of that society? or ought he not at least to be so? Is he not justified in denouncing the errors or the downright turpitude of the magistrates whom that society has chosen to govern it, and who derive their power only from its good will and pleasure? or is it not indeed his duty to proclaim those errors and that turpitude? Should not this duty be performed, even if it be unpleasant? and can we ever hope to ameliorate our condition, unless we expose the abuses which oppress, degrade, and demoralise us?

Oh! let no one rashly and in a random manner say that he cares nothing about politics! Such an assertion denotes a wilful disregard not only of his neighbour's interests, but also of his own. Were all men to entertain such an indifference, the people would be the veriest slaves that an unrestrained despotism and an unwatched tyranny could render them. It is as necessary for the industrious classes to protect their rights and privileges by zealously guarding them, as to adopt precautions to save their houses from fire.

One word more. It is a common saying, and as absurd as it is common—"Oh! women have no right to meddle in politics." Women, on the contrary, have as much right as "the lords of the creation" to exhibit an interest in the systems and institutions by which they are governed. For the sake of their children, as well as for their own, they should assert and exercise that right. It is a lamentable delusion to suppose that the intellect of woman is not powerful nor comprehensive enough to embrace such considerations. The intellect of woman is naturally as strong as that of man; but it has less chances and less opportunities of developing its capacity. The masculine study of politics would aid the intellect of woman in putting forth its strength; and we hope that the day is gone by when the female sex are to be limited to the occupations of the drawing-room, the nursery, or the kitchen. We do not wish to see women become soldiers or sailors, nor to work at severe employment: but we are anxious to behold them *thinkers* as well as *readers*—utilitarians as well as domestic economists. And we know of no greater benefit that could be conferred on society in general, than that which might be derived from the influence of the well developed intellect of woman. Her mind is naturally better poised than that of man: far-seeing and quick-sighted is she;—a readiness at devising and combining plans to meet emergencies, is intuitive with her. Her judgment is correct—her taste good;—and she profits by experience far more usefully than does man. Is it not absurd, then—is it not unjust—and is it not unwise to deny to woman the right of exercising her proper influence in that society of which she is the ornament and the delight?

Alas! that there should be such exceptions to the general rule of female excellence, as Martha Slingsby,—a woman whose principles were thoroughly corrupt, whose licentious passions were of the most devouring, insatiable kind, and whose talent for wicked combinations and evil plottings was unfortunately so great!

Let us return to this hypocritical and abandoned creature, and follow her in the vile scheme which now occupies all her attention.

Having breakfasted at an early hour, she seated herself at her desk, whence she drew forth a packet of letters received by her at various times from Sir Henry Courtenay, and the signatures of which now became the objects of her special study. The art of counterfeiting the late baronet's autograph was practised by her for nearly half an hour; for though she was already tolerably confident of her ability to forge his signature most successfully,—as she had assured Mr. Torrens,—she nevertheless deemed it prudent to render the imitation as perfect as possible.

At last the atrocious deed was accomplished to her complete satisfaction; and a cheque for two thousand pounds lay, drawn in a thoroughly business-like manner, upon her desk!

She was bold and courageous in the execution of plots and the carrying out of deep schemes;—but this dark and dangerous crime which she had just perpetrated, caused her to shudder from head to foot! Hitherto all her wickedness had been of a nature calculated only, if detected, to involve her in disgrace, and not in peril—to ruin her character, but not place her life in jeopardy! Now she had taken a step—a bold and desperate step—which at once set her on the high road that conducts all those who are found treading its pathway, to the foot of the scaffold!

Yes—she shrank back and she trembled violently as she rose from the desk whereon the forged cheque now lay; and for a moment she was inclined to seize it—to rend it into a thousand pieces—and thus to dispel at once and in an instant the tremendous black cloud of stormy danger which she had drawn over her own head.

But, no—she had courage enough to be wicked and rash; but she had not strength of mind sufficient to render her prudent. She therefore decided on daring all—risking everything, by the presentation of the forged cheque!

Having dressed herself in a style of unusual elegance, she proceeded in a hackney-coach to Lombard Street, and alighted at the door of the banking-house on which the cheque was drawn.

Saying to herself,—"Now for the aid of all my courage!"—she entered the spacious establishment, and advanced towards the counter.

One of the numerous clerks in attendance instantly received the cheque which she handed across to him;—and, as it left her hand, a chill struck to her heart—and she would at that moment have given worlds to recall it.

Her composure was now only the effect of utter desperation: but so unruffled was her countenance, that not a lineament was so changed as to be calculated to engender suspicion.

The clerk took the cheque to the nearest desk upon the counter; and after reading it with more than usual attention, as Mrs. Slingsby thought, he said, "This is dated the day before yesterday, madam. Have you seen Sir Henry Courtenay since then?"

"I have not," answered Mrs. Slingsby, wondering how she was able to speak in a tone so cold and collected. "I believe," she added, "that he is gone out of town."

"Pardon the question, madam," observed the clerk; "but one of his servants was here last evening, just before closing time, to enquire if we had seen Sir Henry:"—then, after a few moments' pause, he said, "How will you have this?"

Immense was the relief suddenly experienced by the guilty woman! She seemed as if drawn abruptly forth from the depths of an ocean in which she had been suffocating—drowning. The revulsion of feeling was so great, that, whereas she had been enabled to stand without support throughout the few minutes of frightful ordeal just passed, she was now compelled to cling to the counter, though the clerk observed not her emotion.

Having specified the manner in which she desired the amount of the cheque to be paid her, Mrs. Slingsby received the produce of her crime, and quitted the bank.

She was now so astounded at the complete success of her scheme,—although, when able to reflect calmly upon it, she had never once doubted the issue,—that she could scarcely believe in its realization. Her brain whirled—her heart palpitated violently, as she ascended the steps of the hackney-coach;—and its motion, as it rolled away from the door of the bank, increased the excitement under which she was now labouring.

On her return to Old Burlington Street, she found Mr. Torrens waiting for her, it being nearly twelve o'clock—the hour appointed for their visit to the solicitor.

The moment she entered the drawing-room, Mr. Torrens rose from his seat, and advanced towards her, his eyes fixed intently upon her countenance.

In fact Mr. Torrens was deeply anxious to learn the result of the bold venture which Mrs. Slingsby was that morning to make. With him it was now a matter of pecuniary ruin or salvation; and he had overcome so many difficulties already,—stifling his own scruples at taking an immodest woman for his wife, and reducing his daughter to a belief in the necessity of his submitting to this matrimonial arrangement,—that he trembled lest some unforeseen accident should thwart him just at the moment when he appeared to be touching on the goal of success. Moreover, he had that morning, ere quitting home, so contrived matters with John Jeffreys as to induce this man to leave his service without delay; and he had enjoyed the supreme satisfaction of seeing that dangerous person leave his house ere he himself had set out to keep his appointment with Mrs. Slingsby. Thus every thing had progressed in accordance with Mr. Torrens' views and wishes, so far as the preliminaries to his change of condition were involved.

"Well, my dear madam, what tidings?" he eagerly demanded, as he approached to meet Mrs. Slingsby.

"I have succeeded," she said, throwing herself into a chair. "But I would not for worlds undergo again the same dreadful alternations between acute suspense and thrilling joy—cold tremor and feverish excitement."

"And yet the transaction has given a charming glow of animation to your countenance," observed Mr. Torrens, now for the first time inflamed by desire in respect to the amorous widow whom he was shortly to make his wife. "I have procured the license; and——"

"And Rosamond—what of her?" demanded Mrs. Slingsby hastily.

"She will receive you with a respectful welcome at Torrens Cottage," was the answer. "By dint of reasoning with her, I overcame all her scruples, and rendered her pliant and ductile to our purposes."

"All progresses well, then," said Mrs. Slingsby. "Let us now away to Mr. Howard."

And to that gentleman's office did the pair proceed. Their business was soon explained to the attorney, who manifested no surprise nor any particular emotion at the singularity of the transaction; for Mr. Howard was a perfect man of business, ready to receive instructions without expressing any feelings at all calculated to annoy his clients, and never indicating a curiosity to learn more than those clients might choose to confide to him.

"I am to keep this sum of two thousand pounds until such time as Mr. Torrens may claim it in the capacity of your husband?" he said, as coolly and quietly as if he were receiving a deposit on the purchase of an estate.

"Exactly so," answered Mrs. Slingsby.

"And to-morrow morning, my dear sir," added Mr. Torrens, with a smile, "I shall come to claim it."

"Good," exclaimed Mr. Howard, locking up the bank-notes and gold in his iron safe. "I give you joy, Mr. Torrens: Mrs. Slingsby, I wish you all possible happiness."

Thus speaking, the attorney bowed his clients out of the office.

Mr. Torrens escorted Mrs. Slingsby back to Old Burlington Street, and then repaired as fast as his horse and gig would take him to his own dwelling, to sit down to an early dinner, and afterwards dress himself for the interesting ceremony of the evening.

But on his arrival at the Cottage, he learnt from the female servant who opened the door, that his daughter Rosamond had left home an hour previously.

"Left home!" ejaculated Mr. Torrens. "But she will return?" he continued interrogatively. "Did she not say that she would return?"

"She desired me to give you this note, sir," answered the domestic.

Mr. Torrens tore open the letter placed in his hands, and read the following impressive lines:—

"Pardon me, dearest father, for the step which I am now taking; but I cannot—cannot support the idea of dwelling beneath the same roof with that lady who is soon to be my mother-in-law. I know that I promised not to desert the paternal home: that promise was given in sincerity—though maddening reflections now render me incapable of keeping it. You are well aware how dreadfully my feelings have been wounded—how cruelly my heart has been lacerated, during the last few hours; and I have struggled against the violence of my grief—I have endeavoured to subdue my anguish;—but the occurrences of last night—the outrage attempted by that villain Jeffreys—the revelation of the terrible secret relative to Sir Henry Courtenay——Oh! my dear father, a mind ten thousand times stronger than that of your unhappy daughter could not endure the weight of all this aggregate of misery! Therefore, sooner that my presence should render my father's house unhappy, I depart thence, hoping to be followed by your blessing! Grieve not for me, dear father—heaven will protect me! From time to time I shall write to you; and should happier days arrive——but of that, alas! I dare entertain no hope at present. To you must I leave the painful task of accounting to my dearest, dearest sister and her esteemed husband for my absence when you see them again. Farewell—farewell, my beloved father! I scarcely know what I have written—my brain is on fire—my heart is ready to burst—my eyes are dimmed with tears."

The servant watched the countenance of her master with evident interest and curiosity as he perused this note.

"Did Miss Rosamond appear much excited?" he asked, in a tremulous tone, and without raising his eyes from the letter which he held in his hand.

"She was crying very much, sir," responded the servant; "and it made me quite sad to see her. I attempted to comfort her; but she only shook her head impatiently, and then sobbed as if her heart would break. I knew that she was going to leave, because she had a small package in her hand; and she did cry so dreadful when she told me to give you this note."

Mr. Torrens turned aside, and hastened to his chamber, where he remained until half-past five o'clock. He then descended to the parlour, dressed for the nuptial ceremony. To the servant's enquiry relative to the serving up of the dinner, he replied that he had no appetite, and immediately gave orders for the horse and gig to be got ready by a stable-boy, who had been hastily hired in the morning to take the place of Jeffreys until a more efficient substitute could be found.

This command was soon obeyed, and shortly before seven o'clock Mr. Torrens arrived in Old Burlington Street.

The flight of his daughter from home had proved a more severe shock to him than the reader might imagine, considering the cold and heartless disposition of this man. It was not that he felt he should miss her society;— no—he did not love her enough to harbour a regret of that nature;—but her departure from the paternal dwelling had made him writhe beneath the maddening—the galling conviction that his independence was in a measure gone, and that a stern necessity had compelled him to assent to link his fate with that of a woman so vile and abandoned, that his own child fled at the idea of her approach.

Influenced by such feelings as these, it was no easy task for Mr. Torrens to assume a complacent demeanour suitable to the occasion of his nuptials. He, nevertheless, managed to conceal the emotions which wrung him so acutely, and played his part with tolerable satisfaction to Mrs. Slingsby as she introduced him to Dr. Wagtail and the other guests, including a clergyman, who were already assembled at her house.

The ceremony was performed by the reverend gentleman just alluded to, Dr. Wagtail giving the bride away. A splendid banquet was then served up; and shortly after ten o'clock Mr. and Mrs. Torrens departed together for the Cottage.

CHAPTER LXXXIII.
THE REWARD OF CRIME.

At half-past eleven on the following morning, Mr. Torrens entered the office of Mr. Howard, the solicitor.

His countenance wore a smile of satisfaction, in spite of the various events which had lately occurred to harass him; for he was about to receive a large sum of money—and his fingers itched to grasp the bank-notes and the gold which he had seen stowed away in the safe on the preceding day.

He already beheld his debts paid—his mind freed from pecuniary anxieties—and his speculations prospering in a manner giving assurance of the realization of a splendid fortune; and these pleasing visions, with which his imagination had cheered itself during the drive from the Cottage to the attorney's office, naturally tended to bestow on his countenance the expansiveness of good humour.

And, after all, it is a pleasant thing to enter a place where one is about to receive a good round sum of money, even though the amount will not remain long in pocket, but must be paid away almost as soon as fingered.

Mr. Torrens had never felt more independent than he did on this occasion; and the look which he bestowed upon a poor beggar-woman with a child in her arms, as he ascended the steps leading to the front-door of Mr. Howard's abode, was one of supreme contempt—as if a pauper were indeed a despicable object!

Well—Mr. Torrens entered the office with a smiling countenance:—but he was immediately struck by the strange aspect of things which there presented itself.

The place was in confusion. The clerks were gathered together in a group near the window, looking particularly gloomy, and conversing in whispers;—several gentlemen were busily employed in examining the japanned boxes which bore their names and contained their title-deeds;—and two or three females were weeping in a corner, and exchanging such dimly significant observations as—"Oh! the rascal!"—"The villain!"—"To rob us poor creatures!"

Mr. Torrens recoiled, aghast and speechless, from the contemplation of this alarming scene. A chill struck to his heart: and, in common parlance, any one might have knocked him down with a straw.

"Good heavens! gentlemen," he exclaimed, at length recovering the use of his tongue: "what is the meaning of this?"

"Ask those youngsters there, sir," said one of the individuals engaged in examining the tin-boxes: and the speaker pointed towards the clerks in a manner which seemed to imply that the news were too shocking for *him* to unfold, and that it was moreover the duty of the lawyer's subordinates to give the required information.

"Well, gentlemen, what *is* the matter?" demanded Mr. Torrens, turning to the clerks. "Has any thing sudden happened to Mr. Howard?"

"Oh! very sudden indeed, sir," was the answer vouchsafed by one of the persons thus appealed to, and accompanied by a sinister grin.

"Is he dead?" enquired Mr. Torrens, his excitement now becoming absolutely intolerable.

"No, sir—he isn't dead exactly—but——"

"But what?" cried Torrens, trembling from head to foot.

"He's bolted, sir!" was the astounding answer.

"Absconded!" murmured Mr. Torrens faintly;—and, reeling like a drunken man, he would have fallen had he not come in contact with the wall.

Yes—it was indeed too true: Mr. Howard—the cold, phlegmatic, matter-of-fact, business-like lawyer—had decamped no one knew whither, though numbers had to mourn or curse his flight!

"Are you ill, sir?" enquired one of the clerks, at the expiration of a few moments; for Mr. Torrens was leaning against the side of the room, his countenance pale as death, his eyes rolling wildly in their sockets, and his limbs trembling convulsively.

"No—no—I shall be better in a minute," groaned the unhappy man. "But this blow—is cruel—indeed!" he gasped in a choking voice. "Two thousand pounds—ruin—ruin!"

"Ah! there's many who'll be ruined by this smash, sir," said the clerk: "you're not the only one—and that's a consolation."

A consolation indeed!

It was none for Mr. Torrens, who saw himself ruined beyond all hope of redemption,—ruined in spite of the immense sacrifices he had made to avert the impending storm—the sacrifice of his daughter's innocence to Sir Henry Courtenay, and the sacrifice of himself to an abandoned and profligate woman!

Miserable—miserable man! what hast thou earned by all thine intriguings—thy schemings—thy black turpitude—and thy deplorable self-degradation?

Oh! better—better far is it to become the grovelling, whining beggar in the streets, than to risk happiness—character—name—honour—all, on such chances as those on which thou didst reckon!

And now, behold him issue forth from that office into which he had entered with head erect, self-sufficient air, and smiling countenance:—behold him issue forth—bent down—crushed—overcome—ten years more aged than he was a few minutes previously,—and an object of pity even for that poor beggar-woman whom ere now he had treated with such sovereign contempt!

Miserable—miserable man! has not thy punishment commenced in this world?—is there not a hell upon earth?—and is not thy heart already a prey to devouring flames, and thy tongue parched with the insatiate thirst of burning fever, and thy soul tortured by the undying worm? Oh! how canst thou return to thy house in the vicinity of which lies interred a corpse the discovery of which may at any time involve thee in serious peril?—how canst thou go back to that dwelling whence thine injured daughter has fled, and over the threshold of which thou hast conducted a vile strumpet as thy bride?

When we consider how fearfully we are made,—how manifold are the chances that extreme grief—sudden ruin—and overwhelming anguish may cause a vessel in the surcharged heart to burst, or the racked brain to become a prey to the thunder-clap of apoplexy,—it is surprising—it is truly wondrous that man can support such an enormous weight of care without being stricken dead when it falls upon him!

And yet to what a degree of tension may the fibres of the heart be wrung, ere they will snap asunder!—and what myriads of weighty and maddening thoughts may agitate in the brain, ere reason will rock on its throne, or a vein burst with the gush of blood!

In the meantime occurrences of importance were taking place at Torrens Cottage.

Mrs. Torrens—late Mrs. Slingsby—was whiling away an hour in unpacking her boxes and disposing of her effects in the wardrobe and cupboards of her bed-chamber; congratulating herself all the time on the success which her various schemes had experienced. She had obtained a husband to save her from disgrace; and that husband had set out to receive, as she fancied, a considerable sum of money, which would relieve him of his difficulties, and enable him to pursue his undertakings in such a manner as to yield ample revenues for the future! She was moreover rejoiced that Rosamond had quitted the house;—for, shameless as this vile woman was, she could not have failed to be embarrassed and constrained in her new dwelling, had that injured girl met her there!

While Mrs. Torrens was thus engaged with her domestic avocations and her self-gratulatory thoughts in her bed-chamber, the stable-boy, who had been hired on the preceding day, was occupying himself in the garden.

"Well, what do you think of your new missus?" he said to the maid-servant, who had just been filling a stone-pitcher at the pump in the yard.

"She seems a decent body enow," was the reply. "But I haven't seen much of her yet. What are you doing there, Harry?"

"Why, you must know that I'm rather a good hand at gardening," answered the lad, desisting from his occupation of digging a hole in the ground, and resting on his spade: "and I'm going to move that young tree to this spot here—because it's all in the shade where it stands now, and will never come to no good."

"Ah! that's one of the young trees that Jeffreys planted—him who went away so suddenly yesterday morning, and which made me come and fetch you to help us here," observed the maid. "But, come—go on with your work," she added, laughing; "and let me see whether you really know how to handle a spade."

"Well—you shall see," returned the boy; and he fell to work again with the more alacrity because a pretty girl was watching his progress. "But I'll tell you fairly," he said, after a few minutes' pause in the conversation, "this digging here is no proof of what I can do; because the ground is quite soft—and the more I dig, the surer I am that the earth has been turned up here very lately."

"That I am certain it has not," exclaimed the maid-servant.

"But I say that it has, though," persisted Harry. "Look here—how easy it is to dig out! Do you think I don't know?"

"You fancy yourself very clever, my boy," said the female-domestic, laughing: "but you're wrong for once. We had no man-servant here before Jeffreys come—and he never dug there, I declare."

"Now, I just tell you what I'll do for the fun of the thing," cried the lad. "I'll dig out all the earth as far down as it has been dug out before—because I can now see that a hole *has been dug* here," he added emphatically.

"You're an obstinate fellow to stand out so," said the maid. "But I'll come back in five minutes and see how you get on."

The good-natured servant hastened into the kitchen with the pitcher of water in her hand; and the lad continued his delving occupation in such thorough earnest that the perspiration poured down his forehead.

By the time the maid-servant returned to the spot where he was digging, he had thrown out a great quantity of earth, and had already made a hole at least three feet deep.

"Still hard at work?" she said. "Why, you have made a place deep enough to bury that little sapling in! And what a curious shape the hole is, to be sure! Just for all the world like as if it was dug to put a dead body in! I wish you wouldn't go on digging in that way, Harry—I shall dream of nothing but graves——"

A cry of horror, bursting from the lips of the boy, interrupted the maid-servant's good-natured loquacity.

"What is it, Harry?" she demanded, peeping timidly into the hole, from which the boy hastily scrambled out.

"You talk of dead bodies," he cried, shuddering from head to foot, and with a countenance ashy pale;—"but look there—a human hand——"

The maid shrieked, and darted back into the kitchen, uttering ejaculations of horror.

Mrs. Torrens heard those sounds of alarm, and hastily descended the stairs.

"Oh! missus," cried the boy, whom she encountered in the passage leading from the hall to the back door of the house; "such a horrible sight—Oh, missus! what shall we do?—what will become of us?"

"Speak—explain yourself!" said Mrs. Torrens, amazed and frightened at the strange agitation and convulsed appearance of the boy.

"Oh! missus," he repeated, his eyes rolling wildly, and his countenance denoting indescribable terror; "in that hole there—a dead body—a man's hand——"

"Merciful heavens!" shrieked Mrs. Torrens, now becoming dreadfully agitated in her turn—for, rapid as lightning-flash, did the thought strike her that the corpse of Sir Henry Courtenay was discovered.

"Yes, missus—'tis a man's hand, peeping out of the earth," continued the lad; "and I'm afraid I hacked it with the shovel—but I'm sure I didn't mean to do no such a thing!"

The newly-married lady staggered, as these frightful words fell upon her ears—and a film spread over her eyes.

But a sudden and peremptory knock at the front-door recalled her to herself; and she ordered the trembling maid, who was now standing at the kitchen entrance, to hasten and answer the summons.

The moment the front-door was opened, two stout men, shabby-genteel in appearance, and smelling uncommonly of gin-and-peppermint, walked unceremoniously into the hall.

"Is Mrs. Torrens at home, my dear?" said one, who carried an ash-stick in his hand: "'cos if she is, you'll please to tell her that two genelmen is a waiting to say a word to her."

"What name?" demanded the servant-maid, by no means well pleased at the familiar tone in which she was addressed.

"Oh! what name?" repeated the self-styled gentleman with the ash-stick: "well—you may say Mr. Brown and Mr. Thompson, my dear."

"*I* am Mrs. Torrens, gentlemen," said that lady, who having overheard the preceding dialogue, now came forward; "and I suppose that you are the persons sent by the auctioneer about the sale of my furniture in Old Burlington Street."

"Well—not exactly that neither, ma'am," returned the individual with the ash-stick. "The fact is we're officers——"

"Officers!" shrieked the miserable woman, an appalling change coming over her.

"Yes—and we've got a warrant agin you for forgery, ma'am," added the Bow Street runner, who was no other than the reader's old acquaintance Mr. Dykes.

Mrs. Torrens uttered a dreadful scream, and fell senseless on the floor.

"Come, young o'oman, bustle about, and get your missus some water, and vinegar, and so on," exclaimed Dykes. "Here, Bingham, my boy, lend a helping hand, and we'll take the poor creatur into the parlour."

The two officers accordingly raised the insensible woman and carried her into the adjacent room, where they deposited her on the sofa—that sofa which had proved the death-bed of her paramour! In the meantime the servant-maid, though almost bewildered by the dreadful occurrences of the morning, hastened to procure the necessary articles to aid in the recovery of her mistress; and in a few minutes Mrs. Torrens opened her eyes.

Gazing wildly around her, she exclaimed, "Where am I?"—then, encountering the sinister looks of the two runners, she again uttered a piercing scream, and clasping her hands together, murmured, "My God! my God!"

For a full sense of all the tremendous horror of her situation burst upon her; and there was a world of mental anguish in those ejaculations.

"She's a fine o'oman," whispered Dykes to his friend, while the good-natured servant endeavoured to console her mistress.

"Yes, she be," replied Bingham; "what a pity 'tis that she's sure to be scragged!"

"So it is," added Mr. Dykes. "And now, you stay here, old chap—while I just make a search about the place to see if I can find any of the blunt raised by the forgery."

Thus speaking, the officer quitted the room.

"Oh! ma'am, pray don't take on so," said the good-natured servant-maid, endeavouring to console her mistress. "It must be some mistake—I know it is,—you never could have done what they say! I wish master would come home—he'd soon put 'em out of the place."

"My God! my God! what will become of me?" murmured Mrs. Torrens, pressing her hand to her forehead. "Oh! what shall I do? what will the world say? Just heavens! this is terrible—terrible!"

At that moment the parlour door was opened violently, and Mr. Dykes made his appearance, dragging in the lad Harry, who was struggling to get away, and blubbering as if his heart were ready to break.

"Hold your tongue, you damned young fool!" cried Dykes, giving him a good shake, which only made him bawl out the more lustily: "no one ain't a going to do you no harm—but we must keep you as a witness. Bless the boy—I don't suppose you had any hand in the murder."

These last words brought back to the mind of Mrs. Torrens the dread discovery which had ere now been made in the garden, and the remembrance of which had been chased away by the appalling peril that had suddenly overtaken her: but at the observation of the Bow Street runner to the boy, she uttered a faint hysterical scream, and fell back in a state of semi-stupefaction.

"Murder did you say, old fellow?" demanded Bingham.

"Yes—summut in that way," returned Dykes. "At all events there's a man with his throat cut from ear to ear lying at the bottom of a hole in the garden——"

"You don't mean to say he was left all uncovered like that?" exclaimed Bingham.

"No—no," answered Dykes. "Them as did for him, buried him safe enough; and it seems that this boy has been a-digging there, and comes to a hand sticking out of the ground. So he's too much afeared to go down any farther; but I deuced soon shovelled out the earth—and, behold ye! there lies the dread-fullest spectacle you ever see, Bingham, in all your life. But it wont do to waste time in talking here. You cut over to Streatham and get a couple of constables—'cos there's plenty of work for us all in this house, it seems."

Bingham departed to execute the commission thus confided to him; and Dykes remained behind in charge of the premises.

It would be impossible to describe the wretchedness of the scene which was now taking place in the parlour. The lad Harry was crying in one corner, despite the assurances which Dykes had given him;—the maid-servant, horrified and alarmed at all the incidents which had occurred within the last quarter of an hour, was anxious to depart from a house which circumstances now rendered terrible; but she could not make up her mind to leave Mrs. Torrens, who was in a most deplorable condition;—for the unhappy woman lay, gasping for breath and moaning piteously, on the sofa—her countenance distorted with the dreadful workings of her agitated soul, and her eyes fixed and glassy beneath their half-closed lids!

Dykes accosted the boy, and, was beginning to put some questions to him with a view to ascertain when it was likely that Mr. Torrens would return, when that gentleman suddenly drove up to the door in his gig.

"Now, my lad," said Dykes, "go and open the door, and mind and don't utter a word about what has taken place here this morning."

The boy hastened to admit Mr. Torrens, who passed him by without even appearing to notice his presence, and proceeded straight to the parlour in a mechanical kind of manner, which showed how deeply his thoughts were occupied with some all-absorbing subject.

But the moment the ruined, wretched man opened the door, he shrank back from the scene which offered itself to his view; for the condition of his wife, and the presence of so suspicions-looking a person as Mr. Dykes told the entire tale at once—the forgery had been discovered!

"Oh! master," exclaimed the servant-maid, "I am so glad you're come back;— for your poor dear lady——"

"Yes, master—and that dreadful sight in the garden," interrupted the boy, whimpering again,—"the murdered man in the hole——"

Mr. Torrens staggered—reeled—and would have fallen, had not Dykes caught him by the arm, saying, "Sit down, sir—and compose yourself. I'm very sorry that I should have been the cause of unsettling your good lady so, sir: but I'm obleeged to do my dooty. And as for t'other business in the garden—I s'pose——"

"I presume you are an officer?" cried Mr. Torrens, suddenly recovering his presence of mind, as if he had called some desperate resolution to his aid.

"That's just what I am, sir," answered Dykes.

"And you have come here to—to——"

"To arrest Mrs. Slingsby that was—Mrs. Torrings that is—for forgery, was my business in the first instance," continued Dykes; "and now its grown more serious, 'cos of a orkard discovery made in the garden——"

"What?" demanded Torrens, with strange abruptness: but he was a prey to the most frightful suspense, and was anxious to learn at once whether any suspicion attached itself to him relative to that discovery, the nature of which he could full well understand.

"The dead body—the murdered gentleman, master!" exclaimed the lad Harry, throwing terrified glances around him.

"I do not understand you!" said Mr. Torrens, in a hoarse-hollow tone: "what do you mean? All this is quite strange—and therefore the more alarming to me."

But the ghastly pallor and dreadful workings of his countenance instantly confirmed in the mind of Dykes the suspicion he had already entertained—namely, that Mr. Torrens was not ignorant of the shocking deed now brought to light: and the officer accordingly had but one course to pursue.

"Mr. Torrens, sir," he said, "the less you talk on this here business, perhaps the better; 'cos every word that's uttered here must be repeated again elsewhere; and it will be my dooty to take you afore a magistrate——"

"Take me!" ejaculated the wretched man: and his eyes were fixed in horrified amazement on the officer.

"I'm sorry to say I must do so," answered Dykes.

"Martha—Martha!" ejaculated Torrens, starting from the seat in which the officer had just now deposited him, and speaking in such wild, unearthly tones that those who heard him thought he had suddenly gone raving mad: "why do you lie moaning there? Get up—and face the danger bravely—bravely! Ah! ah! here is a fine ending to all our glorious schemes!"—and he laughed frantically. "Howard has run away—absconded—gone, I tell you! Yes—gone, with the two thousand pounds! But I did not murder Sir Henry Courtenay!" he continued, abruptly reverting to the most horrible of all the frightful subjects which racked his brain. "No—it was not I who murdered him—you know it was not, Martha!"

And he sank back, exhausted and fainting, in the seat from which he had risen.

"Sir Henry Courtenay!" cried Dykes. "Well—this *is* strange; for it's on account of forging his name that the lady is arrested—and notice of his disappearance was given at our office this morning."

Late that evening the entire metropolis was thrown into amazement by the report "that a gentleman, named Torrens, who had hitherto borne an excellent character, and was much respected by all his friends and acquaintances, had been committed to Newgate on a charge of murder, the victim being Sir Henry Courtenay, Baronet." And this rumour was coupled with the intelligence "that the prisoner's wife, to whom he had only been married on the previous day, and who was so well known in the religions and philanthropic circles by the name of Slingsby, had been consigned to the same gaol on a charge of forgery."

CHAPTER LXXXIV.
OLD DEATH'S PARTY.

While these rumours were circulating throughout the metropolis, Old Death was preparing for the reception of visitors at his abode in Horsemonger Lane.

The aged miscreant, assisted by the old woman who acted as his housekeeper, arranged bottles, glasses, pipes, and tobacco on the table—made up a good fire so that the kettle might boil by the time the guests should arrive—and carefully secured the shutters of the window in order to prevent the sounds of joviality from penetrating beyond that room.

When these preparations were completed, the old woman was despatched to the nearest cook's-shop to procure a quantity of cold meat for the supper; and shortly after her return with the provender, the visitors made their appearance—arriving singly, at short intervals.

The housekeeper was dismissed to her own room: and the four men, having seated themselves at the table, began to mix their grog according to their taste.

"I s'pose you've heard the news, Mr. Bones?" said Jeffreys.

"About your late master and his wife—eh?" asked Old Death.

"Just so. They're in a pretty pickle—ain't they?" exclaimed Jeffreys, with a chuckle. "We little thought last night, when we was a talking over the whole business and dividing the swag, that the corpse would so soon turn up again. But, I say," he added, now breaking out into a horrible laugh, and turning towards Tim the Snammer and Josh Pedler, "it was rather curious, though, that I should have had a hand in burying that there feller which you made away with."

"And still more curious," replied Tim, "that we should have done for a stranger, while the master of the house his-self escaped altogether. But 'tis no use talking of that there now. I wish it hadn't happened. It was however done in a hurry——"

"Never mind the little windpipe-slitting affair," said Josh Pedler impatiently. "We got the swag—Old Death here smashed the screens[37]—and that's all we ought to think of. Twelve hundred between us wasn't such a bad night's work—although it did lead us to do a thing we never did afore."

"And now my late master is certain sure to be scragged for it," exclaimed Jeffreys; "for no one could believe such a tale as he must tell in his defence.

Well—I'm not sorry for him: he is a harsh, reserved, sullen kind of a chap. But there's one thing I'm precious sorry for——"

"What's that?" demanded Old Death.

"Why—he promised me fifty pounds, to be paid this evening at seven o'clock," answered Jeffreys; "on condition that I'd leave his service at an instant's notice: and the blunt isn't of course forthcoming."

"Never mind that—don't make yourself uneasy, my boy," said Old Death, with a significant chuckle. "You've got plenty of money for the present: and the business which we've met to talk about, will put ever so much more into your pocket."

"Well—let's to business, then," exclaimed Jeffreys. "The fact is, I shan't go out to service no more; for, since I'm reglarly in with you fellers now, I shall stick to you."

"And I can always find you employment, lads," observed Old Death. "Come—help yourselves: we shall get on so much more comfortable when we're a little warmed with good liquor."

"The cunning old file!" exclaimed Tim the Snammer, laughing and winking at his comrade, Josh Pedler; "he wants to make us half lushy so as to get us to undertake anythink, no matter how desperate, on his own terms."

"'Pon my word, Tim," said Old Death, affecting a pleasant chuckle, which however sounded like the echo of a deep-toned voice in a cavern, "you are too hard upon me. I don't mean any such thing. I'll treat you liberally whatever you do for me."

"And so you ought, old boy," returned Tim Splint: "for you know how I suffered by you—and how cursed shabby you behaved towards me."

"We agreed yesterday to let bygones be bygones," said Benjamin Bones, somewhat sternly. "Do you mean to keep to that arrangement? or am I to consider that you still bear me a grudge?"

"No—no," cried Tim. "What I said was only in fun. So tip us your hand, old boy. There! Now we'll each brew another glass—and you shall explain your business, while we blow a cloud."

The fresh supplies of grog were duly mixed: Jeffreys, Josh Pedler, and Tim Splint lighted their pipes;—and Old Death addressed them in the following manner:—

"There is a man in London who has done me a most serious injury—an injury so great that I can never cease to feel its consequences as long as I live. In a word," continued Old Death, his features becoming absolutely hideous with the workings of evil passions, "he discovered my secret stores—he destroyed all the treasures, the valuables, and the possessions which I had been years and years in accumulating."

"Destroyed them!" cried Tim Splint. "Stole them, you mean?"

"No—destroyed them—wantonly destroyed them—destroyed them all—all!" yelled forth Old Death, his usually sepulchral voice becoming thrilling and penetrating with hyena-like rage. "The miscreant!—the fiend! All—all was destroyed! Thousands and thousands of pounds' worth of valuables wantonly—wilfully—methodically destroyed! I did not see the work of ruin: but I know that it must have taken place—because the man of whom I speak is what the world calls honourable! Perdition take such honour!"

"But of what use was all that property to you, since you didn't convert it into money?" demanded Josh Pedler.

"Of what use?" cried Old Death, again speaking in that yelling tone which manifested violent emotions. "Is there no use in keeping precious things to look at—to gloat upon—to calculate their value? To be sure—to be sure there is," he continued, with a horrible chuckle. "But of that no matter. It is sufficient for you to know that I was deprived in one hour—in one minute, as you may say—of that property which had been accumulating for years. And the house, too, which was mine so long—which I had purchased on account of its conveniences,—even those premises this man of whom I speak, made me sell him. But I swore to have vengeance on him—I told him so when we parted—and I will keep my word!"

"Who is this person that you speak of?" asked Tim the Snammer.

"The Earl of Ellingham," was the reply.

"He is a great and a powerful nobleman, I suppose," observed Tim. "It will be difficult and dangerous to do him any harm."

"What's a nobleman more than another?" cried John Jeffreys. "I for one will undertake any thing that our friend Mr. Bones may propose."

"And so will I—if we're well paid," added Josh Pedler. "But there's one thing I must mention while I think on it. Don't none of you ever speak about that affair down at Torrings's, you know—the cut-throat business, I mean—before my blowen, Matilda. I like to have a little comfort at home; and a woman's tongue is the devil, when it's set a wagging in the blowing-up way."

"We'll mind our p's and q's before 'Tilda," said Tim the Snammer. "It isn't likely that any of us would be such fools as to talk of that business to women, or to others besides ourselves. But let Mr. Bones continue his explanations."

"I have told you enough," resumed Old Death, "to convince you that this Earl of Ellingham deserves no mercy at my hands: and if I say that I will give each of you a hundred pounds—yes, a hundred pounds each—to do my bidding in all things calculated to accomplish my vengeance on that man,—if I make you this promise, I suppose you will not refuse to enlist yourselves in my employ. But, mark you!" he added hastily, and with a sinister knitting of the brows; "before you give me your answer, bear in mind that my vengeance is to be terrible—terrible in the extreme!"

"You mean to have the Earl murdered, I suppose?" said John Jeffreys.

"Murdered—killed!—no—no," exclaimed Old Death; "that would be a vengeance little calculated to appease me! *He must live to know—to feel that I am avenged*," added the malignant old villain. "He must experience such outrages—such insults—such ignominy,—that he may writhe and smart under them like a worm under the teeth of the harrow. He must be made aware whence the blow comes—by whose order it is dealt—and wherefore it is levelled against him. Will you, then, for one week devote yourselves to my service? If you agree, I will at once give you an earnest of the sums promised as your recompense: if you refuse, there is an end of the matter—and I must look out elsewhere."

"But you haven't told us what we are to do to earn our reward," said Josh Pedler.

"There is no murder in the case," observed Old Death, emphatically.

"Then I for one consent without another minute's hesitation," exclaimed Josh Pedler.

"And me too," said Tim the Snammer.

"And I'm sure I'm not going to hang back," cried John Jeffreys.

"Good!" continued Benjamin Bones. "Though you've all got plenty of money in your pockets, there's no harm in having more. I will give you each thirty pounds on account of the business I have now in hand," he added, taking his greasy pocket-book from the bosom of his old grey coat.

The specified amount was handed over to each of the three villains, who received the bank-notes with immense satisfaction.

"Three or four more things like Torrings's and this," observed Tim the Snammer, "and we shall be able to set up in business as genelmen for the rest of our lives."

"Now listen to me," resumed Old Death, his countenance expressing an infernal triumph, as if his vengeance were already more than half consummated. "In the first place I must tell you that I'm going to move to-morrow morning up to Bunce's house, in Earl Street, Seven Dials; and to-morrow night must you perform the first duty I require of you."

"And what's that?" demanded Josh Pedler.

"You know that a few weeks ago a certain person, named Thomas Rainford, was hanged at Horsemonger Lane Gaol," proceeded Old Death, glancing rapidly around from beneath his shaggy, overhanging brows.

"The very prince of highwaymen—a glorious fellow,—a man that I could have loved!" exclaimed Josh Pedler, in a tone the enthusiasm of which denoted his heart's sincerity.

"Well—well," said Old Death, impatiently: "but he's put out of the way—dead—and gone—and it's no use regretting him. I suppose," he added, "that if you saw Tom Rain's body here, you wouldn't mind spitting in the face of the corpse, or treating it with any other kind of indignity, if you was well rewarded for your pains!"

"Why—my respect for the man while he was living wouldn't make me such a fool to my own interests as to refuse to do what you say now that he's dead," answered Josh Pedler. "Besides, a dead body's a lump of clay, or earth—or whatever else you may choose to call it: at all events it can't feel any thing that's done to it. But what in the world has made you touch on such a queer subject?"

"Because it is with Tom Rain's body that you will have to come in contact to-morrow night!" responded Old Death, in a low, sepulchral voice, and now fixing his eyes as it were on all the three at the same time.

And those three men started with astonishment at this extraordinary and incomprehensible announcement.

"Yes," proceeded Benjamin Bones: "it is just as I tell you—for the late Thomas Rainford was the elder brother of the Earl of Ellingham, and was legitimately born!"

This declaration excited fresh surprise on the part of the three men to whom it was addressed.

"And therefore," continued the aged miscreant, his countenance contracting with savage wrinkles, "it must be by the desecration of the corpse of Tom Rain, that the Earl will be alike exposed to the whole world and goaded to desperation by the insult offered to the remains of his brother. Now do you begin to understand me? No! Well, then I will explain myself more fully. It is known that the Earl demanded of the Sheriff the corpse of the highwayman—that his request was complied with—and that the body was interred privately in consecrated ground. I set people to make enquiries; and it was only this morning—this very morning—I learnt that a coffin, with the name of THOMAS RAINFORD on the plate, was buried in Saint Luke's churchyard. This intelligence my friend Tidmarsh gleaned from the sexton of that church. To-morrow night," added Old Death, "it is for you three to have up that coffin and convey it to the Bunces' house in Earl Street, Seven Dials."

"Do you want us to turn resurrectionists?" demanded Josh Pedler, in unfeigned surprise.

"I wish you to do what I direct, and what I am going to pay you well for," answered Benjamin Bones. "If you refuse, give me back my money, and I'll find others who will be less particular."

"Oh! I don't want to fly from the bargain," said Josh; "only you'll allow me the right of being astonished if I choose—or rather if I can't help it. As for the resurrection part of the business, I'd have up all the coffins in Saint Luke's churchyard on the same terms."

"I thought you were not the man to retreat from a bargain," observed Old Death. "Well—when you have brought the coffin to Earl Street, we'll take out the body, put a rope round its neck, and a placard on its breast: and that placard shall tell all the world that *it is the corpse of Thomas Rainford, the famous highwayman who was executed at Horsemonger Lane Gaol, and who was the rightful Earl of Ellingham*! This being done, it will be for you to convey the body to Pall Mall, just before daybreak, and place it on the steps of the hated nobleman's mansion."

"There will be danger and difficulty in performing that part of the task," said Tim the Snammer.

"Not at all," exclaimed Old Death. "A light spring cart will speedily convey the burthen to Pall Mall; and it will be but the work of a few moments to achieve the rest. Besides, at that hour in the morning there is no one abroad."

"All this can be managed easy enough," observed Jeffreys. "I don't flinch, for one. Is that every thing we shall have to do?"

"No—no," replied Ben Bones, with a grim smile: "I can't quite give three hundred pounds for one night's work. But since we are on the subject, I may as well explain to you what else I require in order to render my vengeance complete."

The three men replenished their glasses and their pipes; and Old Death then proceeded to address them in the following manner:—

"From certain information which I have received, I am confident that the Earl of Ellingham experiences a great friendship towards Esther de Medina, who was, I am pretty certain, Rainford's mistress."

It must be remembered that Benjamin Bones knew nothing of those incidents which have revealed to the reader the existence of Tamar—her beautiful sister's counterpart.

"This Esther de Medina is now in London, having been absent for a short time with her father. Another important point is that the newspapers some weeks ago announced the intended marriage of the Earl of Ellingham and Lady Hatfield. We are therefore aware of these two facts—that the Earl is attached to Esther de Medina as a friend, and to Lady Hatfield as her future husband."

It may also be proper to remind the reader that as Old Death knew nothing more of the position in which the nobleman and Georgiana stood with regard to each other, than what he had gleaned from the fashionable intelligence in the public prints,—so he was completely ignorant of all the circumstances which had tended to break off the alliance thus announced.

"Now," resumed the malignant old fiend, his eyes glistening with demoniac spite, as he glanced rapidly from Josh Pedler to Tim the Snammer, and from Tim the Snammer to John Jeffreys,—"now, it is my intention to wound the heart of that hated Earl—that detested nobleman, through the medium of his best affections! Yes—by torturing those ladies, I shall torture him: by subjecting them to frightful inflictions I shall punish him with awful severity. For to-morrow night, my good friends, your occupation is chalked out: for the night after, the task will be to inveigle Esther de Medina to the house in Earl Street; and on the night after that, Lady Hatfield must also be enticed thither. How these points are to be accomplished, I will tell you when the time for action comes."

"And what do you mean to do with the two ladies when you get them there?" demanded Tim the Snammer.

"What will I do to them?" repeated Old Death, his features animated with a malignity so horrible—so reptile-like, that he was at the moment a spectacle hideous to contemplate: "what will I do to them? I will tell them all I have endured—all I have suffered at the hands of the hated—the abhorred Earl of Ellingham;—and you three will be at hand to hold them tight—to bind them—to gag them,—so that I, with a wire heated red, may——"

"What?" demanded Jeffreys impatiently.

"Blind them!" returned Old Death, sinking his voice to a whisper, which sounded hollow and sepulchral.

The three villains—villains as they were—started at the frightful intention thus announced to them.

"Yes—I will put out their beautiful eyes," said Benjamin Bones, clenching his fists with feverish excitement: "then I will leave them bound hand and foot in the house, and will send a letter to the Earl to tell him where he may seek for them! Will not such vengeance as this be sweet? Did you ever hear of a vengeance more complete? The Earl I leave unhurt, save *in mind*—and *there* he will be cruelly lacerated! But *he* must have *his eyes* to see that those whom he loves are blind—he must be spared *his* powers of vision, that he may read in the newspapers the account of those indignities which will have been shown to the corpse of his elder brother!"

And, as he feasted his imagination with these projects of diabolical vengeance, the horrible old man chuckled in his usual style,—as if it were a corpse that so chuckled!

The three miscreants, whom he had taken into his service, expressed their readiness to assist him in all his nefarious plans; for the reward he had promised them was great, and the earnest they had received was most exhilirating to their evil spirits.

The infernal project having been fully discussed, and it having been agreed that Tidmarsh should proceed with one of the three villains in the morning to Saint Luke's churchyard, to point out the precise spot where the coffin bearing the name of Thomas Rainford had been interred,—all preliminaries, in a word, having been thus settled, the old housekeeper was summoned to place the supper upon the table.

The meal was done hearty justice to; and when the things were cleared away, Old Death, who was anxious to conciliate his friends as much as possible by a show of liberality, commissioned John Jeffreys to compound a mighty jorum of punch, the ingredients for which were bountifully supplied from the cupboard, the wash-hand basin serving as a bowl.

And now the four villains—four villains as hardened and as ready for mischief as any to be found in all London—dismissed from their minds every matter of "business," and set to work to do justice to the punch.

"Come—who'll sing us a song?" exclaimed Tim the Snammer.

"Don't let us have any singing, my dear friend," said Old Death: "we shall alarm the neighbours—and it's better to be as quiet as possible."

"Well, we must do something to amuse ourselves," insisted Timothy Splint. "If we get talking, it will only be on things of which we all have quite enough in our minds; and so I vote that some one tells us a story: I'm very fond of stories—particklerly when they're true."

"I'll tell you a true story, if you like," said Jeffreys: "for I don't mind about smoking any more. In fact, I'll give you my own history—and a precious curious one it is, too."

"Do," said Josh Pedler. "But mind and don't introduce no lies into it—that's all."

"Every word is as true as gospel," observed Jeffreys.

The glasses were replenished—Old Death snuffed the candles with his withered, trembling hand—and Jeffreys then commenced his narrative, which, as in former instances, we have modelled into a readable shape.

37. Changed the notes.

CHAPTER LXXXV.
THE HISTORY OF A LIVERY-SERVANT.

"My parents were very poor, but very honest; and I was their only child. My father was a light porter in a warehouse, earning fifteen shillings a week; and my mother took in washing to obtain a few shillings more. We lived in a court leading out of High Holborn, and occupied one room, which was very decently furnished for people in my parents' condition of life, the things moreover being all their own. My father had a good suit of clothes, and my mother a nice gown, bonnet, and shawl, for Sundays and holidays; and they also took care to keep me neat and decent in my dress. Neither of them ever went to the public-house except just to fetch the beer for dinner and supper; and they were always regular in their attendance at church. In addition to all these proofs of good conduct and respectability, they put by two or three shillings a-week as a provision against a rainy day; and you may be sure that to be able to do this, they lived very economically indeed. In fact a more industrious couple did not exist than my father and mother; and you will admit that they deserved to succeed in the world. This much I have heard from people who knew them; for they died when I was too young to be able to understand their ways or judge of their merits.

"It seems that my mother was a very pretty young woman. She had been a servant in the family of the merchant in whose warehouse my father was; and, an attachment, springing up between them, they married. The merchant, whose name was Shawe, had a son—a dissipated young man, addicted to gaming and bad company, and consequently a source of great uneasiness to his parents, who were highly respectable people. During the time that my mother was in service at the merchant's, Frederick Shawe was on the Continent, his father having sent him to a commercial establishment at Rotterdam, in the hope that he would amend his ways when under the care of comparative strangers. But this hope, it appears, was completely disappointed; and the young man was after all sent back to his father's house as irreclaimable. At this time my parents had been married three years, and I was two years old. My mother was in the habit of taking my father's dinner to him at the warehouse, whenever his duties prevented him from running home to get it; and on one of these occasions, Frederick Shawe saw her as she was going out of the establishment. He followed her, made insulting proposals, and behaved most grossly. She had me with her; and this circumstance rendered his conduct the more abominable, if any thing was wanting to aggravate it. Indeed, his persecution was carried to such an excess, that she was obliged to take refuge in a shop, where she went into hysterics through fright and indignation. Shawe sneaked away the moment he found that the master of the shop was disposed to take my mother's part against him; and when she was a little recovered, she was sent home in a hackney-coach. On the return of my father in the evening, she told him all that had occurred; and it seems that she had scarcely made an end of her narrative, when Frederick Shawe entered the room. He declared that he had come to express his sincere penitence for what he had done, and to implore that his father might not be made acquainted with his behaviour. He seemed so earnest, and so excessively sorry for his infamous conduct, that my parents consented to look over it. He thanked them over and over again, and took his departure. My father, however, desired his wife never to come to the warehouse to him any more, as he was unwilling to expose her to even the chance of a repetition of the insult.

"A few weeks after this occurrence Frederick Shawe one evening, when under the influence of liquor, called at our lodgings, my father being absent, and renewed his outrageous conduct towards my mother. An alarm was created in the dwelling—a constable was sent for—and the young gentleman was taken off to the watch-house. Of course the matter was now too serious to be hushed up; and the elder Mr. Shawe necessarily learnt all the particulars. His son was fined and held to bail to keep the peace towards Mrs. Jeffreys; and my father obtained another situation—for though the old merchant knew that his son was alone to blame, yet my father thought that he could not prudently remain in a place where he must daily meet a person who, he felt convinced, was now his sworn enemy. And such indeed did Frederick Shawe prove to be; for by misrepresentations and heaven only knows what other underhand means, he so successfully avenged himself that my poor father soon lost his new situation, and was totally unable to find another. The most infamous reports were circulated concerning him; and he took the cruel treatment he had received so much to heart, that his spirit was completely broken—he fell ill, and died in a few weeks.

"Poverty and despair thus seized upon my mother at the same moment. She saw all her happiness suddenly blasted by the agency of a reckless villain; and, to add to her afflictions, the only friend who showed any compassion for her or who came forward to assist her in the midst of her wretchedness—namely, the old merchant—was suddenly snatched away by the hand of death, ten days after the earth had closed over my father's remains. The poor woman was unable to bear up against her sorrows: she languished for a few months, and then departed this life, leaving me a friendless and unprotected orphan at the tender age of three years! You may guess what then became of me: I was taken to the workhouse!

"I have sketched these circumstances just to show you how unfortunate I was in my earliest infancy. My parents would have lived to thrive and prosper had it not been for the miscreant Frederick Shawe; and under their protection I should have been happy. However, it was destined that my father and mother should be cut off thus early; and their cruel fate threw me as a pauper-child upon the parish. At the workhouse I remained until I was thirteen; and it was from an elderly couple whom distress brought to the same place, and who had known my parents well, that I learnt all the particulars which I have related to you. Well, at the age of thirteen I was transferred to the care of a surgeon and accoucheur, who took me into his house to clean the boots and shoes, run on errands, and beat up drugs in the mortar. Finding me active and, as he said, a good-looking lad—for I was not then seared with the small-pox as I am now—he put me into the regular livery of a doctor's boy after I had been with him a few months; and I was then entrusted with the delivery of the medicine. My master was an old man; and his wife was a bustling, active, elderly lady, in whom implicit confidence might be placed as long as she was well paid for her services and her secresy. You will understand what I mean very shortly. In fact one day I noticed a great deal of whispering between the doctor, his wife, and the housekeeper; and their looks were mysterious and important. Certain preparations, too, commenced, which showed me that a visitor was expected; for I was a shrewd and observing boy for my age. I was ordered to clean the windows in the spare bed-room and the well-furnished little parlour communicating with it; and while I was thus occupied, the housekeeper put the two apartments into the nicest possible order. I asked her if any one was coming to stay at the house, and was desired to mind my own business. I accordingly held my tongue; but my curiosity was only the more excited in consequence of the answer I received and the mystery in which the motive of the preparations in progress was involved. At an earlier hour than usual I was ordered to retire to my own room; but as it commanded a view of the street—it was Brook Street, Holborn—I sate up, watching at my window—for I felt sure that I had not been dismissed to my attic without some good reason. Nor was I mistaken. At about half-past ten a hackney-coach drove up to the door: two trunks were carried into the house, and a lady, muffled in a cloak, was assisted to descend from the vehicle by the doctor and his wife, who seemed to treat her with the greatest respect. I was able to notice all that passed, because the moon was bright and I was looking out of the open window. The lady accompanied the doctor and his wife in-doors; and the coach drove away.

"Next morning I saw the housekeeper take up a breakfast-tray to those rooms which I had now no doubt were occupied by the lady who had arrived the night before; but I was cautious not to appear even to notice that any thing unusual was going on, much less to ask questions,—for I remembered the rebuff I had already received in this latter respect. The cook and housemaid were as mysteriously reserved as the housekeeper herself; and I could not for the life of me make out what it all meant. To be brief, a month passed away; and though I never saw the tenant of the spare-rooms all the while, yet I knew that a tenant those rooms had; for the meals were regularly taken up—the doctor looked in there two or three times a day—and his wife passed hours together there. At length the housemaid, who was a pretty, wicked-looking girl of about nineteen, undertook to initiate me into the secret which so much puzzled me; and, taking advantage of a Sunday evening when she and I were alone together, the other servants having gone out, she explained how some young lady, who was not married, was about to become a mother—and how the spare-rooms were always kept for lodgers of that kind.—'Have you seen her?' I asked.—'No,' she replied; 'nor am I likely to see her. I have been four years in this house, and during that time there have been eight or ten ladies here in the same way; but I never caught a glimpse of the face of any one of them. They pay, or their friends pay for them, a good round sum to master for the accommodation; and that is the manner in which he has made so much money; for you can see that his regular practice is not very great. But you must not tell any body that I have been talking to you in this style, John; or else I shall lose my place.'—I promised her not to betray her.—'How old are you, John?' she asked.—'Going on for fourteen,' I said.—'You are a pretty boy,' she continued. 'Would you like to give me a kiss?'—'You would think me very rude,' I answered.—'No, I shouldn't: try.'—'But I should feel so ashamed,' I said.—'Then you are a fool, John,' exclaimed the pretty housemaid; and she got into a pet, which lasted all the rest of the evening.

"I lay awake a long time that night thinking of what I had heard concerning the lady in the private apartments; and, I can't say how it was—but I felt an extraordinary longing to catch a glimpse of her. The more I reflected on this wish, the stronger it grew: and at last I determined to gratify it somehow or another. Having come to this resolution I fell asleep. Next morning the twopenny postman at eight o'clock brought a letter directed to my master; but in the corner were two or three initials which I could not quite make out. I took it into the parlour, where the doctor was seated alone at the time; and, when he had glanced at the address, he said, 'Oh! it is to go up stairs: give it to the housekeeper:'—and he went on reading his newspaper. Here was an opportunity which presented itself almost as soon as my desire to see the tenant of the spare-rooms had been formed; and, without any hesitation, I hurried upstairs. I knocked at the door of the parlour communicating with the bed-chamber; and a sweet voice said, 'Come in.' I accordingly entered the room and beheld a beautiful creature of about seventeen or eighteen, dressed in a morning wrapper, all open at the bosom, and reclining in an arm-chair. She uttered an exclamation of surprise when she saw me, and drew the wrapper completely over her breast. It was evident that she had expected to see either the housekeeper or my mistress. I handed her the note, stammered out something about 'Master having told me to bring it up,' and then retired, awkward and embarrassed enough. A few minutes afterwards the bell of the spare-rooms was rung rather violently; and the housekeeper went up. She shortly came down again, and went into the parlour, to which I was presently summoned. The doctor and his wife were seated at the breakfast-table, looking as gloomy and solemn as possible, and the housekeeper was standing in the middle of the room. I suspected that a storm was brewing. 'John,' said the doctor, 'what induced you to take such a liberty as to enter the apartments of a lady who is lodging in my house?'—'Please, sir,' I answered, as boldly as possible, 'you told me to take up the letter; and I did so.'—The doctor, his wife, and the housekeeper looked at each other by turns; and then they all three looked very hard at me. 'Well,' said the doctor, 'I suppose it *was* a misunderstanding on the boy's part;'—for I did not blush nor seem at all confused while they were all staring at me.—'But you must not tell any one that you saw the lady up stairs, John,' exclaimed my mistress.—'I don't know a soul who would care about knowing such a simple thing, ma'am,' I replied, pretending to be very innocent indeed. I was then told to withdraw; and thus passed off this little affair.

"Throughout that day I saw the pretty housemaid showing great anxiety to speak to me alone; but circumstances so occurred, that we had not an opportunity of exchanging a word in private together. At half-past nine I went to bed as usual, an hour before the other servants; and I soon fell asleep. But I was awoke by some one shaking me gently; and I was also startled by seeing a light in the room. In another moment my fears subsided; for my visitor was the pretty servant-girl in her night-gear. She sate down on the edge of the bed, and asked me what I was called into the parlour for in the morning. I told her all that had occurred. 'You are a dear boy,' she said 'not to have confessed that I had put you up to any thing; for that was what I was afraid of:'—and she gave me two or three hearty kisses. Then she asked me a great number of questions about the lady I had seen—what she was like—how old—the colour of her hair and eyes—and all sorts of queries of that kind. I replied as well as I could; and she seemed vastly to enjoy the idea of my cool impudence in taking up the letter just for the sake of getting a peep at the lady. In fact she was so much pleased with me, that she kept on kissing me; and all this ended just as you might suppose—for the pretty housemaid shared my bed during the remainder of the night. This occurrence was most unfortunate to us both; for we over-slept ourselves,—and the housekeeper, doubtless having vainly searched for us down stairs, came up to look after us. We were discovered fast asleep in each other's arms; and a terrible scene ensued. The housekeeper alarmed the doctor and his wife with her cries—for I suppose the old lady was quite scandalised, though she herself had often chucked me under the chin in a tender manner. The result was that the pretty housemaid was packed off without delay; and I was stripped of my livery, compelled to put on my workhouse clothes again, and sent back to the parish officers.

"At the very moment when I was conveyed into the presence of the overseers by the doctor, a middle-aged lady, magnificently dressed, was returning to her carriage which waited at the door. She immediately recognised the doctor as an acquaintance, and he addressed her by the name of Mrs. Beaumont. The exchange of a few remarks led the lady to observe that she had applied to the parish officers for a well-conducted, genteel-looking lad to take the place of a page in her household; and, as she spoke, she eyed me very attentively. The doctor informed her that I had been in his service and was a good boy in all respects save one:—and he explained to her the indiscretion which had compelled him to part with me; adding, 'The lad was no doubt won over by the young woman herself; but as my professional success depends on the reputation of my house, I could not overlook this occurrence.'—The lady declared that she entertained great compassion for me, and said what a pity it was that such a nice boy should be thrown back on the parish. In a word, the business ended by her agreeing to take me on trial; and, before the doctor left me, he whispered in my ear, 'You see, John, that I have not ruined your character as I might have done; and therefore you must be a good lad, and never mention to any one that you saw the lady who is now lodging at my house.'—He then took his departure; and Mrs. Beaumont, having arranged with the overseers relative to receiving me into her service, desired that I might be sent to her abode in the evening. The instructions were obeyed; and I entered my new place, the first appearances of which pleased me much.

"Mrs. Beaumont was a widow-lady of about six-and-forty, and was still a very handsome woman considering her age. Her house was in Russell Square; and she lived in an elgant style—keeping a butler, a footman, and three female domestics. She had a Miss Stacey residing with her as a companion; and this lady was about five or six-and-twenty—somewhat stout—and rather good-looking. The moment I entered my new place, I was supplied with a page's livery, and was informed that I was to consider myself at the orders of the butler. I soon found that I had got into very comfortable quarters; for the best of provisions were consumed in the kitchen as well as in the parlour, and the butler, who was fond of a glass of good liquor himself, often treated me to some likewise. Mrs. Beaumont saw a great deal of company; and there were dinner-parties or evening-parties at least three or four times every week. I had not been many days in this place, before I began to notice that both Mrs. Beaumont and Miss Stacey treated me with much the same kind of innocent familiarity which the housekeeper at the doctor's had shown towards me. They would pat me on the cheek, or chuck me under the chin, and tell me I was nice boy: but this they never did before each other—only when I happened to be alone with either one of them. Indeed, when they *were* together, and I entered the room to answer the bell or for any other purpose connected with my duties, they would both appear as indifferent towards me as if they had never shown any other feeling in my behalf. Of the two I liked Miss Stacey much the best, because she was younger; and I felt a strange excitement come over me whenever she began to toy about with me in the way I have described. One day, when I entered the drawing room, where I found her alone at the time, she said to me, 'John, you are a very nice boy; and here is half-a-guinea for you to buy what you like. Only don't let any one know that I gave you the money.'—'Certainly not, Miss,' I replied.—'And now, John,' she continued, 'I want you to answer me a question which I am going to put to you. Will you tell me the truth?'—I of course declared that I would.—'Then tell me,' she said, patting my face, and looking full at me with her large blue eyes, 'does Mrs. Beaumont ever play about with you as I do?'—'Oh! never, Miss,' I answered immediately, and without undergoing the least change of countenance.—'You are a good boy, John,' she said; and pulling me towards her, covered me with kisses. A double-knock at the front-door interrupted her amusement, which, as you may suppose, I took in very good part; and she hurried me out of the room, enjoining me not to tell any one that she played about with me.

"The next day Mrs. Beaumont was rather indisposed, and kept her own chamber until the evening, when she descended to the drawing-room. Miss Stacey had gone out to a party at a married sister's; and, the footman being absent likewise, it devolved upon me to take up the tea-tray. 'Well, John,' said my mistress, 'are you comfortable in your present place?'—'Quite, thank you, ma'am,' I replied.—'You like it better than the doctor's?' she continued, smoothing down my hair, and then passing her hand over my face.—'Oh! a great deal ma'am.'—'But do you not miss the pretty servant-girl, John?' she asked, with a sly look and a half smile. 'Why, what a naughty boy you must be, and at such an age too!'—'It was all the young woman's fault, ma'am,' I said; 'and I hope you do not think any the worse of me for it.'—'If I had I should not have taken you into my service, John,' she answered. 'And to show you that I am really attached to you and consider you to be a very good boy, here's a sovereign for you. It is not on account of your wages, mind; but a little gift. You must not however tell any body that I gave it to you, or else you will make the other servants jealous.'—'I'll be sure not to tell, ma'am,' I said: 'and I thank you very much.'—'And now, John,' continued Mrs. Beaumont, 'I have one question to put to you, and you must tell me the truth. Does Miss Stacey ever speak kindly to you? I mean, does she ever do any thing to show you that she likes you better than the other servants?'—'No, ma'am,' I replied. 'On the contrary, I fancy she sometimes speaks sharp to me.'—'Oh! indeed,' said Mrs. Beaumont; and she then subjected me to the same kissing process that I had undergone on the part of Miss Stacey—only I did not like it quite so well. The old lady hugged me very tight, and seemed as if she wanted to say something, but did not exactly like to do so. At last she spoke out plainly enough, though in a whispering tone. 'John,' she said, 'I just now gave you a sovereign, because you are a good boy; and I will give you another if you will do what I ask you and not tell any one about it. Should you like to have another sovereign?'—'Very much indeed, ma'am,' I answered.—'Well, then,' continued Mrs. Beaumont, 'you must come to my room to-night, when the house is all quiet; because I want to speak to you very particularly indeed.'—'But I promised the servants, ma'am, to sit up to let Miss Stacey in,' I answered.—'So much the better,' observed Mrs. Beaumont. 'Miss Stacey has promised to be back by twelve at latest; and as soon as you have let her in, you can go up to your own room, and then a few minutes afterwards come down to mine.'—I promised to do exactly as I was desired; and, having received a few more kisses and pawings about, was suffered to return to the kitchen.

"The footman came back at eleven; and as Mrs. Beaumont had already retired to her chamber, all the servants except myself went off to theirs. I then remained alone in the kitchen, thinking of what had occurred between my mistress and myself, and not half liking the idea of sleeping with her—for I knew very well what her object was in asking me to go to her room. I wished it had been Miss Stacey who had made such an appointment with me; for, young as I was, I was greatly smitten with that lady; and I thought she had never looked so well as when I saw her that evening dressed for the party to which she had gone. She had on a very low gown, and her neck was so beautifully white, and her naked arms seemed so plump, that I was really quite in love with her. It gave me great pleasure to think that I had been chosen to sit up for her, and I longed for her return. The clock struck twelve; and a few minutes afterwards a vehicle stopped at the door. I knew it must be Miss Stacey who had come back; and I did not wait for the knock and ring, but hurried to the hall to admit her. She seemed pleased when she saw who it was that opened the door for her; and I observed that her countenance was rather flushed, as if she had been drinking an extra glass of champagne, of which I knew she was very fond. The moment I had closed and bolted the door, she asked me in a low whisper, whether any of the other servants were up. I answered in the negative.—'Does your mistress know that you are sitting up for me?' she next inquired.—'No, Miss,' I unhesitatingly said.—She began to caress me, and I found that she smelt rather strong of wine; but she looked so nice that I did not care about that; and I was so excited that I kissed her in return.—'Light me up stairs, John,' she at length said; 'and let us go as gently as possible, so as not to make any noise, on account of Mrs. Beaumont, who is unwell.'—I led the way up stairs, my heart beating violently; for I more than half suspected that I should not keep my appointment with my mistress that night. Nor was I mistaken: for, on reaching the door of Miss Stacey's chamber, she took my hand, drew me towards her, and said in a low, hurried whisper, 'Come down to my room in about a quarter of an hour: I wish to speak to you very particularly indeed.'—I promised to do so, and hurried up to my own chamber, Miss Stacey having previously lighted her candle and said, 'Good night, John,' in a tolerably loud voice, but making a sign to convince me that it was only a precaution on her part. When I reached my room, I sate down on the bed to think how I should act. My inclination prompted me to keep the appointment with Miss Stacey: my fears urged me to keep the one given me by Mrs. Beaumont. I cared nothing about the sovereign promised me by my mistress, now that I had received such an invitation from her pretty companion; and I thought that it would be very easy to excuse myself to Mrs. Beaumont, should she question me next day, by saying that I fancied her to be only joking, or perhaps trying me. So, at last, I resolved to follow my inclinations, and disregard my fears; and I acted in pursuance of this determination. I accordingly repaired to Miss Stacey's room, and was completely happy.

"We had been an hour together, when a knock at the door alarmed us. Who could it be? what could it mean? We remained silent as the dead. The knock was repeated, and was immediately followed by Mrs. Beaumont's voice, saying, 'Miss Stacey, dear! Miss Stacey!'—'Good God! what can she want?'

whispered Miss Stacey to me; 'she is perhaps unwell, and will come into the room to speak to me. John, my dear boy, you must get under the bed, and keep as quiet as a mouse.'—This was done in a moment, and Miss Stacey bundled my clothes under the bed after me. She then opened the door, and, sure enough, my mistress entered the room, saying, 'I am sorry to disturb you, my dear; but I am so unwell I cannot sleep. I have got such nervous feelings that I am really afraid to be alone.'—'Had I not better call up one of the servants and send for the doctor, my dear madam?' asked Miss Stacey, her voice trembling; I could well conjecture why.—'No, thank you, dear,' answered the lady; 'if you have no objection, I will pass the remainder of the night with you.'—'Oh! with pleasure, ma'am,' exclaimed Miss Stacey. 'I will accompany you to your room directly.'—'We may as well remain here,' replied Mrs. Beaumont; and it struck me that there was something strange in the way that she spoke. Miss Stacey urged that it was very injurious for persons in delicate health to change their beds; but Mrs. Beaumont declared it to be a mere prejudice. Miss Stacey invented some other frivolous excuse, and I suppose that this confirmed Mrs. Beaumont's suspicions; for she immediately exclaimed, 'Really, one would suppose that you wished to get rid of me, Miss Stacey!'—'To speak candidly, my dear madam,' was the reply, 'I can't bear sleeping with another person.'—'Indeed!' said Mrs. Beaumont. 'Hey day! what shoes have we here? Why, surely these cannot be your's, my dear?'—I have noticed that the more spiteful ladies are together, the more they '*dear*' each other.—'It must be some oversight on the part of one of the servants,' said Miss Stacey, in a faint tone.—'It's very strange!' cried Mrs. Beaumont; and I heard her stoop down and take up the unfortunate shoes. Oh! how I did shiver and tremble! and how sincerely I wished both the amorous ladies at the devil at that moment! But matters grew speedily much worse; for, in stooping down to pick up the shoes, Mrs. Beaumont had spied my trowsers; and these she fished up in another moment. Miss Stacey shrieked; Mrs. Beaumont raised the drapery hanging round the bed to the floor—and, behold! by the light of the candle which had been left burning in the room, she discovered unfortunate me!

"I cannot tell you what a scene ensued. Mrs. Beaumont raved like a madwoman, and Miss Stacey protested her innocence. The house was alarmed—the other servants came down to the door—and Mrs. Beaumont's reproaches and upbraidings, levelled against Miss Stacey and myself, made every thing known to them. I scarcely know how I had pluck enough to play the part which I did play; but it is, notwithstanding, a fact that I was resolved to screen Miss Stacey, and throw all the scandal on Mrs. Beaumont. I accordingly begged to be allowed to explain; and when I could obtain a hearing, I swore that Mrs. Beaumont had given me a sovereign, and promised me another to sleep with her—that I had mistaken the room—and that the moment I had seen Miss Stacey enter and perceived my error, I had managed to creep under the bed, unnoticed by her. Mrs. Beaumont went into strong hysterics at this accusation, and was conveyed away to her own apartment by the female servants, while I hurried off to my own room. You may suppose that I scarcely slept a wink all the remainder of the night. I knew that I had lost both my place and my character—but I felt satisfied in having done all I could to screen poor Miss Stacey, though it did not strike me at the time that my version of the business could not possibly be taken as a very probable story. Next morning the butler came up to me very early, and in a long, humbugging speech, assured me that, out of good feeling towards me, Mrs. Beaumont had consented to keep me in her service, and look over the affair, if I would confess the truth. I however persisted in my original statement, and displayed the sovereign that Mrs. Beaumont had given me. The butler went away, telling me not to leave my room until he came back. Half an hour passed before he returned, and again he tried to argue me into his views; but I was obstinate, and the interview ended by his desiring me to pack up my things and leave the house directly. This I very willingly agreed to, and in a few minutes my preparations were complete. 'Where are you going to, youngster?' asked the butler, when he had paid me the amount of wages due.—'I don't know,' was my reply.—'Well,' he said, 'I should advise you to take a room at the family washerwoman's. She has got one to let, I know; and if you hold your tongue about what has occurred in this house, I will try and get you another place.' I readily gave the required promise, and also followed the advice relative to the lodging, in which I was installed in another half hour.

"In the evening the butler came to me, and gave me the addresses of several families in whose service pages were wanted. 'You will have to apply to the butlers at those houses,' he said, 'and therefore you can refer them to me. I will endeavour to make it all right for you, as I should be sorry to see a promising young lad ruined for want of a character.' I thanked him very much, pretending to see nothing but pure friendship in his conduct, although I was quite enough experienced in the ways of the world to understand that Mrs. Beaumont herself had instigated this lenient treatment as a means of sealing my lips. I ventured to ask him about Miss Stacey, and he at once told me that she had left the house at a very early hour in the morning. I longed to enquire if he knew where she was gone, but dared not. On the following day I called at the various addresses which the butler had given me, and was not considered suitable at any. At one I was thought too young—at another too old: here I was too short—there I was too tall. In fact, the objections were trivial, but fatal. I was returning to my lodging along Great Russell Street, Bloomsbury, when I saw in a shop window a notice that a livery boy was wanted, and that applications were to be made within. I entered the shop, and received the address of a house in the same street. There I went, and was shown into a small parlour, where I was kept waiting for nearly a quarter of an hour. At last a gentleman and lady—an elderly couple—entered the room, and I was immediately subjected to no end of questions, all of which I answered in the most satisfactory manner, because I did not hesitate to say 'Yes' when an affirmation was required, and 'No' when a negative was necessary. At last the gentleman said to the lady, 'Well, my love, what do *you* think?'—'What do *you* think, my dear?' asked the lady.—'I think, my dear——' began the gentleman.—'So do I, Mr. Turner,' exclaimed the lady, without waiting to hear what her husband *did* think. It however appeared that they perfectly well understood each other; for the lady, turning towards me, said, 'We will give you a trial if the butler at your last place speaks as well of you as you assure us he will. But you will have to be very active here, for I must tell you that this is a boarding-house——'.—'A boarding-house of the highest respectability,' interrupted the gentleman, looking very solemn indeed, as if he was afraid that I was going to say I didn't believe him.—'And there are many ladies and gentlemen to wait upon,' continued Mrs. Turner: 'but we shall see.' I then withdrew. Mr. Turner went about my character in the evening, and found every thing satisfactory; and next day I entered my new place, wondering what adventures would befal me here.

"This boarding-house proved to be the hardest place I ever was in. I had to get up at five in the morning to clean six pairs of boots and ten pairs of ladies' shoes. If they did not shine well, I was blown up on all sides; and if I did make them shine well, Mrs. Turner blew me up for wasting the blacking. Then I had to bees-wax heaven knows how many chairs and tables, and to clean the windows from top to bottom at least twice a-week. In the middle of my work I was constantly interrupted by knocks at the door, or errands to run upon. Then at meal-times something was always wanting—something had always been forgotten. The cleaning of knives and plated forks and spoons would have alone been a good four hours' work for a strong man. If I did them properly and devoted time to them, I was scolded for being slow and lazy: and if I knocked them off in a hurry, they were sure to be found fault with. Sometimes the bells of half a dozen rooms would ring in the morning, when the boarders were getting up, all at the same instant; and if I was long in taking up any particular gentleman's hot water to shave, or any lady's shoes, I was certain to hear of it when Mrs. Turner came down into the kitchen. In fact, it was a hard life, and an unthankful office; for when I did my best, I could not give satisfaction; and yet the cook and housemaid—the only servants kept besides myself—were candid enough to declare that I was the best lad that had ever been in the house during their time.

"There was one elderly lady—a Miss Marigold—who seemed to have taken a particular hatred for me; and only because when, one day, she began to caress me in the same way that Mrs. Beaumont and Miss Stacey had done, I laughed in her face and told her to keep her wrinkled old hands to herself.

From that minute she grew desperately malignant against me, and was always finding fault. I determined to have my revenge, and waited patiently for the opportunity. That occasion came at last. One evening Miss Marigold retired earlier to bed than usual; and Mrs. Turner rang for me in the parlour. I went up and found my mistress alone. 'John,' she said, 'go directly with this box,'—pointing to a round paste-board one on the table—'to the hair-dresser's, and tell him that you will call for it at eight precisely to-morrow morning. Then, in the morning, when you come back with it, send it up by the housemaid to Miss Marigold's room.'—I took the box, which was tied round with string, and was particularly light. It immediately struck me that it must be Miss Marigold's wig: for I was convinced she wore one. Accordingly, as I went along the street, I stepped up an alley; and by the light coming from the window of a house, unfastened the strings to peep inside. Sure enough, it was Miss Marigold's wig. It immediately struck me that her going to bed earlier than usual was only an excuse to be able to send her wig in time for the hair-dresser to do it up that night; and this circumstance, joined to the fact that she wanted it the very next morning, convinced me that Miss Marigold had but one wig belonging to her. I therefore resolved that some accident should occur to the wig before it went back to her; but in the meantime I took it to the hair-dresser. He seemed to understand what it was; for without opening the box, the strings of which I had carefully re-fastened, he promised me that I should have *the article* when I came back in the morning, shortly before eight.

"I must now inform you that there was an elderly gentleman at the boarding-house, whose name was Prosser. Captain Prosser he was called; and a jovial kind of old bird he was too. He was amazingly fond of breaking out now and then, staying away all night, and coming home between six and seven in the morning, so precious drunk that he could not see a hole through a ladder. But he was always sensible enough to know that he must not make a noise; and when I let him in on these occasions, he would put his fore-finger by the side of his nose in such a comical fashion, as much as to say, 'Don't let any body know it!' that I could scarcely keep from laughing. Well, on this very night, when the affair of the wig occurred, the Captain went out for a spree; and it happened that he came home rather later than usual the next morning. I had just returned with the wig-box, and had it still in my hand, when the Captain's low sneaking knock at the door summoned me to open it. He came in worse than I had ever seen him before: he could scarcely keep upon his legs, and his head rolled about on his shoulders just as if he had no bones in his neck at all. His hat, too, was smashed completely in; and his coat was slit completely up the back to the very collar. Such a comical figure I never saw in my life. He staggered into the hall, seeming quite to forget where he was, or what he wanted there. A thought struck me, and I resolved to put it into execution. He was so uncommonly drunk, and yet so quiet and tractable, that

I saw I could do with him just as I liked: so I led him into the parlour where the long table was laid for breakfast; but no one had come down yet. I seated him on the sofa in such a way that he could not fall off, and in a few moment he was in a sound sleep. I removed his hat, took the wig from the box and fixed it all awry upon his head, purposely tumbling all the curls, so as to make it appear as if he had thus adorned himself with his own hand. I then stole away from the room; and, having suffered about ten minutes to elapse, so as to bring the time nearer to breakfast before the exposure should take place, I went into the kitchen to tell the housemaid that there was a box in the parlour which she must presently take up to Miss Marigold. But she, not knowing what the box might contain, waited a few minutes more to finish something that she was about; and I did not choose to hurry her. At last Miss Marigold's bell rang; and I laughed in my sleeve to think that the poor lady would vainly wait for her wig. The housemaid hastened to answer the summons, and I followed her as far as the parlour, under pretence of taking up some plates for the breakfast-table. But just before we reached that room, seven or eight of the boarders, ladies and gentlemen alike, came pouring down stairs to breakfast; and the moment they entered the parlour, such screams of amazement burst from the women, and such roars of laughter from the men. The housemaid hurried into the room, and I behind her; and almost immediately afterwards in came Mr. and Mrs. Turner, and all the rest of the boarders, except poor Miss Marigold!

"And what a sight burst upon their view! The screams and the roars of laughter had awoke Captain Prosser; and he was sitting, propping himself up, in the corner of the sofa, and looking stupidly about him, as if quite unconscious of where he was, and certainly ignorant of the reason which drew all eyes upon him. Such a comical spectacle as he was, with the wig perched all crooked upon his head! At length the ladies began to give vent to their indignant feelings. 'Shameful!' said one.—'Well, I never!' cried another.—'And *this* in a respectable boarding-house!' exclaimed a third.—'It all comes of having such a monster as the Captain in the place!' observed a fourth.—'But whose wig is it?' cried one of the gentlemen, a humorous fellow in his way; and, approaching the leather box, he took it up. 'MISS MARIGOLD!' at length he exclaimed, his eyes catching some writing in the inside.—Mrs. Turner, who had suspected the ownership of the wig, declared that she should go into hysterics; but her husband begged her not to do any thing of the kind; and so she followed his advice. Of course no suspicion fell upon me. When questioned, I said that I had brought home the box without knowing its contents; that I had put it on the sofa; and that before I had gone down stairs to tell the housemaid to take it up to Miss Marigold, I had opened the front door to let in the Captain. The thing was therefore clear:—the Captain had come in, in a state for which he ought to be ashamed of himself; and nothing would please him but he must decorate himself with poor Miss

Marigold's wig! Such was the explanation agreed upon by all present; and while two or three of the gentlemen conveyed the Captain up to his own room, the wig having been previously removed from his head, Mrs. Turner went up to break the fatal news to Miss Marigold. To make an end of this part of my story, I need only say, that Miss Marigold left the house on the sly the moment her wig was done up again by the hair-dresser; and Mrs. Turner easily persuaded the ladies to forgive the Captain, on condition that he would stand a dozen of wine—which he did.

"Several months passed away after this incident without any adventure worth relating. It was a most unpleasant place; but there was amusement in it; and moreover there was a certain love-affair in progress, in which I felt interested, and the end of which I was determined to wait and see. Not that I was an actor in it at all; but only a go-between. The fact was, that amongst the boarders there was a widow-lady, of about seven or eight and twenty—a very pretty woman, whose name was Percy. There was also a young gentleman of very effeminate appearance, but possessing a handsome—or rather a beautiful countenance, and a very slight figure. He was also short—a complete doll of a man; for he was within four years as old as the widow. His name was Hulse. This couple fell in love with each other: or rather, I think, the love was all on the side of the young gentleman, who possessed some little property and better prospects, whereas the widow was notorious as a husband-hunter ever since she had been in the boarding-house, and was moreover very poor. She was however sweetly pretty; and she had such wicked eyes that it gave me strange sensations to meet her looks. It was in this way that I came to know of the love-matter existing between Mr. Hulse and Mrs. Percy. About the time when the adventure of the wig took place, Mr. Hulse one evening asked me to give a letter privately to the widow-lady; and he slipped half-a-crown into my hands. You may have already seen that I possessed no small degree of curiosity, and I longed to know what that letter could possibly contain. I took it up into my own room with me, and tried to catch a glimpse at the writing inside; but it was so carefully folded that I could not. At last, to my joy, I perceived that the wax was stamped with a seal which was invariably left lying in the ink-stand drawer in the parlour, for the general use of the boarders. I therefore hesitated no longer to open the letter, breaking the wax as carefully as possible. The letter was a declaration of love, the writer stating that he had not courage to make the avowal in words; and he implored a written answer, observing that the lad John was to be trusted, as he seemed a quiet steady youth. I was much amused by the letter, and early next morning I re-sealed it by means of the stamp in the ink-stand drawer: then, watching the opportunity when Mrs. Percy descended to breakfast, I gave it to her as she was coming down stairs. In the evening she put into my hands an answer, accompanied by a shilling for myself; and as she smiled significantly, and showed her pretty white teeth,

I felt that I could do any thing to obtain a kiss from that sweet mouth. Fortunately this letter was also fastened with the house-seal, and I was therefore able to read its contents. It thanked Mr. Hulse for the favourable opinion he had entertained of her, and stated that she felt she could love him, but that she required a more explicit avowal of his intentions. This letter I re-sealed and gave to the young gentleman. A reply was ready in the evening; and another half-crown was slipped into my hand. This letter I likewise read, and found that Mr. Hulse professed the most honourable intentions, but begged that their engagement (should the correspondence have that result) might be kept a secret, as he had an uncle (from whom he had considerable expectations) to consult, but who was at present abroad and would not be in England again for several months. The lady's answer, which also passed through my hands, was quite satisfactory; and in the course of a few days I saw that the tender pair exchanged significant looks when they thought themselves unperceived, and that Mr. Hulse was gradually losing much of his bashfulness. Nevertheless frequent notes passed between them, and several presents were made to the lady by the young gentleman, all of which went through my hands and were duly inspected by me. It may seem strange that two people living in the same house should require the aid of a go-between; but such was the fact—for I believe Mr. Hulse to have been one of the very sentimental and romantic class of lovers who are fond of mystery and of tender correspondence.

"This absurd courtship went on for several months; and the lovers little suspected that I was as well acquainted with its progress as themselves. At length I perceived by one of Mr. Hulse's letters that his uncle was expected home in a few days, and he spoke of the necessity which would compel him to go on a visit to the old gentleman, but also expressed his hopes that the result would be according to the wishes of the lady and himself. And in less than a week he did depart on the proposed visit, having previously exchanged most tender and affectionate letters with the widow. The very next morning a new boarder arrived—a gentleman who in every respect was quite different from Mr. Hulse. He was tall, largely-made, and wore a great deal of hair about his face. Without being handsome, he was a very fine man; and he talked away at a rapid rate, getting on good terms with all the other boarders by the time breakfast was over, and very intimate indeed before the cloth was removed after dinner. He sate next to the widow, to whom he paid great attention; and she appeared very well satisfied with his civilities. In fact, in one single day he made more progress in thrusting himself into the good graces of Mrs. Percy than Mr. Hulse had done in a week. The name which the gentleman bore at the house was Jameson; but I did not believe it to be his right one, because his hat had the initials of F. S. in it; the same letters were marked, as I heard from the housemaid, on all his linen; and they were also described by means of brass nails on the lid of his trunk. However, a few days passed; and I saw that Mr. Jameson and Mrs. Percy were becoming more and more intimate. They sate together at meals—they lounged together on the sofa in the drawing-room—and, as I watched them narrowly, I saw that they exchanged glances which convinced me that Mr. Hulse had been forgotten by the faithless lady. Somehow or another I took an immediate hatred to Mr. Jameson, the moment he set foot in the house; and this feeling was increased by his harsh and commanding ways towards me. I was moreover sorry for Mr. Hulse, who had been kind and generous in his behaviour to me; and I longed to do Jameson some evil turn. The opportunity arrived sooner than I expected; for one morning—about a fortnight after he had arrived at the establishment—I was accosted in the street, when going on an errand, by an ill-looking fellow who was loitering about, and who said he wanted to speak to me particularly. I asked him his business; but he would not exactly explain it. He however said he was very anxious to learn some tidings of a certain gentleman, and that he had received a hint of the person alluded to being at a boarding-house in Great Russell Street, under a feigned name. It instantly struck me that the gentleman thus enquired about was Jameson; and I was moreover convinced, by the appearance of the enquirer, that he had no good intentions towards the individual whom he was seeking. I therefore readily gave such information as convinced the man that Mr. Jameson was the person he was looking for; and I then learnt, to my astonishment, that this Mr. Jameson's real name was Frederick Shawe! I now showed myself so much interested in the affair, and expressed myself in so hostile a way relative to Mr. Frederick Shawe, that the man at last admitted to me that he was a sheriffs'-officer's follower, and had a writ against the man who, I was convinced by all I now heard, was the same that had treated my deceased parents in so scandalous a manner. We did not part before we came to an understanding together; and I returned to the boarding-house, overjoyed to think that the moment of vengeance was not very far distant.

"The dinner-hour was five o'clock; and on the day of which I am speaking, there was company present besides the boarders. Mr. Jameson, as usual, sate next to Mrs. Percy; and his attentions were of the most amiable description. Had Mr. Hulse returned at the moment, he would not have been very well pleased at the way in which she received them. But a storm was brewing over the head of the successful rival; and I was longing for it to burst. Towards the close of the meal Jameson asked me for a glass of porter. I pretended not to hear him, and waited on some one else. He called me again; and when I at length drew near his chair to serve him, he said in a harsh voice, 'You're very neglectful, John; and I wonder how Mrs. Turner can keep such a stupid boy in the house.'—'Then why don't you ask her to discharge me, *Mr. Shawe*?' I said.—You should have seen how he turned—first as white as a sheet, and then as red as scarlet.—'*Mr. Jameson* you mean, John,' exclaimed Mr. Turner.

'Call gentlemen by their proper names, and don't be rude, sir, or you shall leave the house directly.'—'I did call *this gentleman* by his proper name, sir,' I answered: 'and that name is *Shawe*.'—'The poor boy is labouring under a mistake,' said Shawe, dreadfully confused and stammering as he spoke; 'but don't be harsh with him: he did not intend any harm.'—'I do not want *you* to speak in favour of me, sir,' I exclaimed; 'and perhaps you'll guess why, when you know that my name is *Jeffreys*.'—The villain's countenance now showed the most awful dismay; and the scene produced great excitement amongst all present. But at that moment, a knock at the front-door was heard; and I ran to answer it, well knowing who were there. How my heart beat with joy when I admitted the officer and his follower (the man I had seen in the morning) into the house; and, without caring how my master and mistress might take it on my part, I threw open the dining-room door, led the officers in, and, pointing to the person they wanted, said, '*This* is Mr Frederick Shawe!' The officers instantly arrested him; and a scene of extraordinary confusion followed. Mrs. Turner fainted in right earnest, and while several of the ladies flocked round her, others began tittering and whispering, and Mr. Turner requested Mr. Shawe to pay his bill before he went to prison. But the conduct of Mrs. Percy was the most extraordinary part of the whole performance. It is, however, most probable that she acted in the way she did to conceal her vexation and annoyance. For, bursting out into a loud laugh, and casting a look of contempt at the man with whom she was on such good terms a few minutes before, she expressed her surprise that '*fellows of his stamp* should dare to force their way into *genteel society*!'—To be brief, Mr. Turner could not get the amount of his claim on Shawe, whose trunks he accordingly detained; and the scoundrel was conveyed away by the officers. I followed the party to the street-door, and took good care to let Shawe know that it was I who had betrayed him. The exposure of this person caused such a sensation in the house, that my share in it created a feeling of curiosity; and, when questioned by Mr. Turner before all the company, I explained how he had treated my parents, so that I was rather praised than blamed for what I had done. But Mrs. Percy applauded me the most, and spoke warmly in my favour—at which I was very much pleased.

"Two or three days after this occurrence, Mr. Hulse returned—but only for a few hours; and during that time he was alone with Mrs. Percy in the parlour. The nature of their interview was soon known throughout the house; for it appeared that the news he had brought from his uncle were favourable, and their engagement was now no longer kept secret. It was fortunate for the widow that he did not remain in the boarding-house until their marriage; for, if he had, some kind friend would have been sure to tell him of the flirtation that had gone on between herself and the scoundrel Shawe. As it was, every thing turned out well: Mr. Hulse took and furnished a nice house in Bloomsbury-square, and in a few weeks he and Mrs. Percy were married. My former services were not forgotten by either; but, on the contrary, were rewarded on the wedding-day by a guinea from the gentleman and half that sum from the lady. I had thus seen the end of this very extraordinary courtship, and being thoroughly tired of my place, began to look out for another. I accordingly made the usual enquiries, and heard of several vacancies. My very first application was successful, and I was engaged by the Honourable Mr. Ilverton, Mr. Turner giving me a good character and expressing no dissatisfaction at my desire '*to better myself.*'

"The Honourable Mr. Ilverton resided in St. James's Square. He was a gentleman of about forty years of age, and was on the point of marriage with a lady much younger than himself, and who was one of the numerous daughters of the Marquis of Mountcharlton. But as Mr. Ilverton was very rich, and the Marquis was but a poor peer, the match was considered a very desirable one by the friends of Lady Hortensia Stanhope. I heard my fellow-servants in my new place say that she was a very beautiful creature; and I longed to see her; but six weeks were yet to elapse before the celebration of the marriage. The place was a very nice one; and the establishment was on a large scale. There were six female servants, and four men, besides the butler and coachman. Two of the footmen were constantly on duty in the hall, that is, they had nothing to do for the four hours that their turn lasted, but to look out of the hall-windows, and attend the front-door. When their four hours expired, the other two took their place for a like interval. There was a great deal of aristocratic feeling amongst these servants. The butler had *his* room, and the housekeeper had *her* room; and they took their meals apart from the rest. The other servants were obliged to say '*Sir*' to the butler, and '*Ma'am*' to the housekeeper. The cook and the two housemaids were likewise above the kitchen-maids, who said '*Miss*' when addressing either one of them. The footmen also considered themselves above the coachman; but they allowed the latter to take his meals at their table. As for myself, I was looked upon as a mere child by the men; and probably by the women too—for they were very much addicted to fondling me when I happened to be alone with either one of them.

"Well, the six weeks passed away; and the day came on which Mr. Ilverton was to be married. The ceremony was performed at St. George's, Hanover Square; and the 'happy couple,' as the newspapers always call new-married people, started off for Mr. Ilverton's country-seat. A fortnight elapsed; and then came the day when the town-mansion was to receive its new mistress, whom I had not yet seen. I remember the profound curiosity which I felt on that occasion, my fellow-servants, who had frequently beheld her, having spoken so high of her beauty. It was about six o'clock in the evening when they were expected to arrive, dinner having been provided for seven. I stationed myself in the hall to obtain as early a view as possible of Lady

Hortensia Ilverton; and shortly after six the carriage drove up to the door. From the hall-window I saw her ladyship alight; but she had a veil over her face. I was, however, enabled to admire the beauty of her figure, which was very finely proportioned; and I thought, as she stepped from the vehicle, that I had never before seen such a charming foot and ankle. The loveliness of her form rendered me the more anxious to behold her face; and this curiosity on my part was soon gratified. For, on entering the hall, the lady threw back her veil;—but no words can explain the full extent of my astonishment, when I beheld the very same charming creature of whom I had once before caught a hasty glimpse at the doctor's house in Brook Street! A faint exclamation of surprise escaped my lips; no one however heard it—and I instantly mastered my feelings. Lady Hortensia passed through the hall, leaning on her husband's arm, without looking either to the right or to the left;—and as she did not therefore observe me, I had no opportunity of knowing whether she would remember me or not.

"It was a part of my duty to help to wait at table; and I longed for the dinner-hour to arrive, to clear up that point. At length my doubts were set at rest;—dinner was served up—the lady saw me; and I felt convinced that she had completely forgotten my face. I was not however quite a year older than when I saw her at the doctor's, and therefore not much changed: nevertheless, she evidently did *not* know me again. I really felt relieved on her account; for she was such a beautiful creature, and seemed so amiable, that I should have been sorry for her to have experienced any annoyance or vexation on my account. During the whole of dinner, I took my station near her chair, and watched her attentively; and though she conversed pleasantly enough with her husband when he started a subject, or addressed himself to her, yet it struck me that she was not altogether happy—for she seldom commenced a topic of her own accord, but seemed rather to love silence; and I now and then fancied that she sighed in a subdued manner. I don't know when I ever felt a deeper interest in any one than I did in this lady; and it seemed to me as if I could do any thing to serve her. But I am afraid that I am tiring you with this long story;"—and Jeffreys abruptly broke off.

"Not at all, old fellow," exclaimed Tim the Snammer. "It's only just struck twelve by St. George's; and we don't mean to separate yet awhile."

"No—not quite yet, I should hope," observed Josh Pedler. "Besides I'm getting deucedly interested in that Lady Hortensia of your's. I all along expected that the beautiful young creature at the doctor's would turn up again somehow or another."

"To be sure," said Old Death: "it wouldn't be a regular romance if she didn't."

"It's all as true as gospel!" cried Jeffreys. "Do you think I could invent such a pack of curious adventures? If you don't believe what I've told you already,

I'm sure you won't believe what there is to come; and so I'd better hold my tongue."

"Now don't be angry, my dear boy," said Old Death: "I was but joking. I like your story amazingly: so pray finish it. We're in no hurry, and there's plenty of drink."

Jeffreys accordingly complied with the solicitations of his comrades, and proceeded uninterruptedly to the end of his narrative.

CHAPTER LXXXVI.
CONCLUSION OF THE HISTORY OF A LIVERY-SERVANT.

"I am now going to take a leap of about six months in my story; because, during that time, nothing of any importance occurred in the establishment of the Honourable Mr. Ilverton. I may, however, observe that my suspicion relative to the unhappiness of his wife was confirmed the more I saw of her; for she was often dull and melancholy—and once or twice I saw that she had been shedding tears. Her husband was very kind and attentive to her; but he was a great deal from home, as he had large estates in the country which he was frequently obliged to visit, and he was also canvassing a borough for the approaching elections. Her ladyship preferred remaining in town, because she could then enjoy the society of her mother and sisters, who were almost constantly with her. Well, as I just now said, six months had passed away without any adventure of importance, and I was already wearied of the sameness of the life I was leading, when something occurred which tended to excite my curiosity and interest. It was about four o'clock, one summer afternoon that the little incident took place; and this was it. A letter came, addressed to her ladyship; and the hall-porter gave it to me to take up into the drawing-room. I went up stairs, and my hand was on the drawing-room door, when sounds of sobbing and low whispering, coming from inside, met my ears. I stopped and listened. 'My God! you know that I love you, Herbert,' said the voice of Lady Hortensia, who no longer spoke in a whisper.—Then another voice made some reply which I could not catch; and several minutes passed in a whispered conversation, not one single word of which did I overhear. At last I could judge that the visitor was about to take his leave; and I entered the room, first making as much noise as I could with the handle of the door so as to warn those inside that some one was coming in. But a single glance was enough to show me that Lady Hortensia was in great confusion, while a tall, handsome, young gentleman who was with her turned aside and walked towards the window. They were both standing when I went in; but her ladyship seated herself the moment after I entered and passed her handkerchief rapidly over her charming face. I endeavoured to appear as if I saw nothing to excite my curiosity, handed my mistress the letter, and retired. I waited in the hall to catch another glimpse of the gentleman when he went out; and in a few minutes he took his departure. I asked the hall-porter who he was. 'I never saw him before,' was the answer; 'but I heard him desire the footman to announce him by the name of Mr. Herbert Remington.'—'Well,' thought I to myself, 'Mr. Herbert Remington is a very fortunate man to be loved by such a beautiful lady.' But I did not breathe to a soul what I had overheard, nor any thing that I knew concerning my mistress.

"Mr. Ilverton was in the country at this time; and I now observed that Mr. Remington called regularly every day at about four o'clock. The other servants did not appear to notice it as at all extraordinary; but I had my own reasons for thinking a good deal on the subject. Several times, on the occasion of these visits, did I creep to the drawing-room door, and listen; and much of their conversation did I thus overhear. From that I gleaned that Mr. Remington and Lady Hortensia had been attached to each other for a long time; but that their marriage had been rendered impossible by his poverty. I also learnt enough to convince me that he was the father of a child of which she had been delivered at the doctor's house, but which had died a few hours after its birth. I felt no small degree of importance in knowing myself to be acquainted with all their secrets; and I considered myself not only bound to keep those secrets to myself, but also to assist them in any way I could, if an opportunity served to render my humble aid available. And the time to put me to that test soon came. Mr. Ilverton returned home from the country much sooner than was expected; and the servants, when talking together in the kitchen, said that he had come back in a very queer humour. He was, however, more amiable than ever with her ladyship at dinner on the day of his return; and I saw nothing to prove the truth of what I had heard down stairs. Lady Hortensia retired early that evening, saying she was unwell; and her maid observed on returning to the servants' hall, after attending on her mistress in her bed-chamber, that her ladyship appeared very unhappy. Then for the first time did the servants speak of the constant visits of Mr. Remington; and as they talked on the subject, suspicions seemed to spring up in their minds. But the entrance of the housekeeper put an end to the gossip; and soon afterwards the drawing-room bell rang. I hastened up to answer the summons, and found Mr. Ilverton walking up and down the apartment in so excited a manner that he did not even notice my entrance. At length he perceived me; and, throwing himself in a chair, beckoned me towards him. 'John,' said he, laying his hand on my shoulder, and speaking in a strange tone of voice, 'I think you will tell me the truth, if I ask you a few questions,'—I said that I would.—'And will you keep to yourself whatever I am going to say to you?' he asked.—'I will, sir, certainly,' was my answer.—'I thought you were a good and discreet lad,' he continued, putting a couple of sovereigns into my hand: 'act as you ought towards me, and you shall never want a friend. Now, tell me, my boy, whether a gentleman named Remington has called here every day during my absence this last time?'—'Not every day, sir, I should think,' was my reply; for I saw that a storm was brewing, and felt determined to screen my mistress as much as possible.—'Yes, but he has though,' returned Mr. Ilverton sharply; 'you may not, however, have observed it,' he added immediately afterwards, in a milder tone: 'now answer me truly my next question; and don't be afraid that I shall be angry, or shall say any thing about it if you reply in the affirmative. Do the servants talk amongst themselves of Mr. Remington's visits?'—'I have never heard a word said on the subject, sir,' was my answer.—'Then I am not laughed at in that quarter!' he muttered to himself; but I heard his words plain enough, although he seemed to forget that he had spoken them a minute after they had left his lips. 'John,' he continued, his fingers actually griping my shoulder, 'you can do me a great service if you will; and I will reward you handsomely.'—'It is my duty to do all I can for you, sir,' I replied.—'Yes,' he said; 'but what I now require is something out of the way of your ordinary duties, and is rather the part of a friend, than a servant towards a master.'—'I will do any thing I can, sir, to oblige you,' I exclaimed.—'And you will swear solemnly not to breathe to a soul a word of all that now takes place between us, or that you may have to do for me, unless I call upon you to proclaim any thing in a court of justice.'—'I will obey you in all things, sir,' I replied.—'You are a good lad,' he said; 'and I am not mistaken in you. To tell you the truth,' he continued, 'I have received an anonymous letter, creating the most painful suspicions in my mind. This letter assures me that a gentleman whom I do not know, and whose name is Remington, is a too frequent visitor at this house. But before I act, I must be satisfied that his visits are injurious to my honour. Do you understand me, my boy? You see, I am obliged to be open and candid with you, as I require an important service at your hands.'—'I understand you perfectly, sir.'—'What, then, do I mean?'—'Why, sir, that my lady should not receive that gentleman's visits so often, and while you are away,' I answered, pretending first to reflect for a few moments.—'Exactly so!' he cried. 'And now I will explain what I require of you. To-morrow at about half-past three o'clock,' he continued, 'I will give you a letter addressed to some friend of mine at a little distance; and you must tell the butler you are going to take it, and that you shall be upwards of an hour away. By these means you will not be missed by the servants. But, instead of leaving the house, you must steal up to the drawing-room, and conceal yourself under the sofa. There must you lie as quiet as possible, and listen to all that may take place between Lady Hortensia and Mr. Remington, who, not knowing of my return, will be sure to call at his wonted hour.'—'But suppose, sir,' I said, 'that I should be discovered?'—'Then leave it to me to extricate you from the difficulty, which is not likely to arise,' answered Mr. Ilverton.—'But,' I again argued, 'if her ladyship should happen to come down earlier to the drawing-room than usual, how shall I be able to conceal myself beneath the sofa?'—'Should this occur, I will devise some means to induce Lady Hortensia to quit the room for at least a few minutes, at about half-past three. Be you on the watch.'—'I will sir,' was my answer.—'And if you serve me faithfully, John,' he added, 'you will find a friend in me; but if you disobey me in one single point, I will find means to punish you somehow or another.'—I, of course, made all the necessary promises; and he dismissed me, apparently well satisfied with my assurances of fidelity.

"I slept but little all that night. I saw that a dreadful storm hung over the head of my mistress; and I lay awake, planning a thousand schemes to avert it. It was very easy for me to hide myself under the sofa; and, whatever I might overhear, afterwards assure my master that not a word had been said which he could possibly be angry at. But I was experienced and cunning enough to fear that Mr. Ilverton wanted a witness; and that though I might be listening under the sofa, he would also be listening at the door, and would burst into the room in case his suspicions respecting his wife should receive confirmation. Even if he should not adopt this plan, but merely use me as a means of ascertaining whether his wife was faithful or not, and take my word respecting the particulars of the anticipated interview between herself and Mr. Remington,—nevertheless, I saw the necessity of warning my mistress that such suspicions did exist concerning her, and put her fully upon her guard. This I resolved to do; and at last I made up my mind to speak frankly to her next day. But when that day came, I saw no chance of having an opportunity of carrying my intention into effect;—for her ladyship did not come down stairs to breakfast nor to luncheon, she being still indisposed, as I heard from her own maid. I loitered upon the landing near the drawing-room as much as I dared; and once or twice, when my master went up or down stairs, he nodded approvingly of my conduct, thinking that I was there only to serve his interests. At last, just as the clock had struck three, to my joy I saw Lady Hortensia descend from her own chamber, and enter the drawing-room. Not a moment was to be lost. I rushed in after her, closed the door, and said, 'My lady, listen to me for one instant, I implore of you.' She looked at me with mingled surprise and anger; for my manner must have appeared not only strange, but also boisterously rude. I am sure I do not recollect now—for I did not remember ten minutes after this scene occurred—what words I used, or how I introduced the subject; but it is very certain that I told her how I was the very lad who had seen her at the doctor's; how her husband had bribed me to watch her; how I was determined to warn her of the plot in progress against her; and how I would do any thing in the world I could to serve her. She seemed perfectly astounded at all I told her: she sank on the sofa, turned red and white a dozen times in a minute, and then burst into tears. I dared not say a word: the idea of a poor servant like me venturing to console a great lady like her was ridiculous. But I was in a dreadful state of alarm lest Mr. Ilverton should come in.—'John,' she said at last, wiping away her tears, 'if all you have told me is true, you are one of the best lads that ever lived. But how am I to know that this is as you represent it?'—I understood what she meant: she feared lest it was only a trap to ensnare her into something amounting to a confession.—'My lady,' I answered, 'if I wished to injure you, could I not have at once revealed to Mr. Ilverton all that took place at the doctor's house in Brook Street?'—'True!' she said, blushing scarlet. 'Yes—you are faithful!' and she put her purse into my hand. I returned it to her, declining to take any reward; but she forced it upon me, and I was compelled to accept it. 'Now retire,' she said hastily; 'and follow your master's bidding in respect to concealing yourself. I shall afford you an opportunity,' she added: then, turning away, she again burst into tears.

"I hastened from the room, well pleased with the success of my interview with her ladyship, and feeling myself so important a person that I scarcely knew whether I stood on my head or my heels. The secrets of the family were in my keeping,—in the keeping of a boy not sixteen years old; and it was enough to make me proud. Besides, I felt so satisfied with my conduct in respect to her ladyship, that it seemed to me as if I had done a great and a glorious deed. Well, on quitting the drawing-room, I went up to my own chamber, to compose my feelings; for I was really so much elated as to be quite unfit to meet my master for a few minutes. But at the expiration of that time I hastened down stairs, received the letter which he had in readiness for me, and, after looking in at the servants' hall for a moment, just to say I was going out on an errand, stole up to the drawing-room, where I found no one. I therefore thrust myself under the sofa, and awaited anxiously the termination of the adventure. Just as the time-piece on the mantel struck four, her ladyship returned to the room; and almost immediately afterwards

Mr. Remington was announced. Hasty whispers were exchanged between them in a language—most likely French—which I did not understand; and then they seated themselves on chairs at some distance from each other, Lady Hortensia having previously rung the bell. I was surprised at this proceeding: what could she possibly mean? But I was more astonished still, when, on the entrance of one of the footmen, she said, 'Ask your master if he will have the kindness to favour me with his company for a few minutes.' The servant retired to execute this command; and I was now frightened lest her ladyship intended to accuse her husband of his stratagem, and thereby expose my want of faith towards him. But second thoughts convinced me that this was not the case; because her ladyship must remember that it was in my power to ruin her effectually if she meditated any treachery towards me. A few minutes elapsed, during which Mr. Remington and my mistress conversed on the most common-place subjects—such as the weather, the new opera, and so on; and at length Mr. Ilverton entered the room. 'I am sorry to disturb you, my dear,' said Lady Hortensia, speaking in her most amiable manner, 'since I know that you are so fully engaged with election matters and other important business; but I have a favour to ask of you. This gentleman is Mr. Remington. Mr. Remington,' she added, 'Mr. Ilverton:' thus calmly and quietly introducing them.—I do not know how my master looked, but I could fancy that he felt very queer: at all events, he said nothing.—'Mr. Remington, my dear,' continued Lady Hortensia, speaking with a tranquil affability that quite astonished me, 'is a gentleman to whom our family are under the greatest obligations; for it was he who saved my brother Edward's life at Oxford a few years ago.'—'I remember to have heard that your brother Edward had a narrow escape from being drowned in the river on a boating excursion,' said Mr. Ilverton; 'but I was not until now acquainted with even the name of the gentleman who so generously risked his life to save him.'— 'It was a deed which scarcely deserves such warm praise, sir,' observed Mr. Remington.—'On the contrary, Mr. Remington,' exclaimed Lady Hortensia, 'Mr. Ilverton must, as my husband, experience the same gratitude which I feel towards you, and ever shall, for your noble conduct.'—'Certainly, most decidedly,' exclaimed my master, who, I could very well suppose, was now feeling particularly sheepish.—'And I am convinced, my dear,' continued her ladyship, addressing herself altogether to her husband now, 'that you will approve of certain steps which I have taken in order to convince Mr. Remington of the gratitude of the near relatives of him whom he saved from a premature death. Mr. Remington has a sister who has been left a widow, and who is anxious to turn her accomplishments to a good account. She is desirous of entering some family as a governess; and I have supplied Mr. Remington with letters of introduction on behalf of his sister to several of our friends and acquaintances. He has this day called to inform me of his sister's success in obtaining the situation she requires, by means of one of those letters.'—Mr. Ilverton expressed his entire approval of this proceeding on the part of her ladyship; and Mr. Remington rose, and took his leave in that formal manner which seemed to show that he did not even pretend to be considered in any other light than a mere acquaintance.

"When he was gone, Lady Hortensia said, 'I am really glad that I have been able to serve that young man's sister, for they are both very poor, it seems and the service which he rendered our family in saving the life of my brother was not one that should have gone unrewarded.'—'Oh! decidedly not, my love,' said Mr. Ilverton. 'But will you accompany me to the library now, and see the new picture that I bought some weeks ago, and which has been sent home this morning? It was kept to be framed.'—'Certainly,' answered Lady Hortensia; and she quitted the room with her husband. I of course understood that he had purposely enticed her away to allow me an opportunity of leaving my hiding-place; and I was very glad to get from under the sofa, where I was most terribly cramped, not having dared to move, and scarcely able to breathe free through fear of being heard. I was highly delighted at the clever manner in which Lady Hortensia had got herself out of the serious scrape that for a time seemed to threaten her with total ruin; and I was heartily glad to think that her husband must be thoroughly ashamed of having exposed himself so completely to me. At dinner-time Lady Hortensia gave me a glance which seemed to thank me again for the part I had acted towards her; whereas Mr. Ilverton never once looked me in the face—not even when I was close by his side and he ordered me to serve him with any thing. Shortly after dinner her ladyship retired to the drawing-room; and the moment I was alone with my master, he beckoned me to approach him, and said in a low tone, 'John, what took place between your mistress and that gentleman before I came in?'—'Mr. Remington said he came to thank her ladyship for her kindness towards his sister,' I answered, taking my cue from what I had heard before; 'and then her ladyship said that you was at home, sir, and she would introduce Mr. Remington to you.'— 'Then I have been altogether misled, John,' he observed: 'and mind that you never breathe a syllable of what has passed to a living soul.'—'Certainly not, sir,' I replied. He put a couple of sovereigns into my hand, telling me I was a good boy, and repeating his injunction of strict secresy.

"I was now a very great favourite with both my master and mistress, though, in each other's presence, they neither showed any particular kindness towards me. Mr. Remington came no more to the house; but her ladyship now and then gave me letters to put privately into the post for her, and which were addressed to him. Thus three months more passed away; and the general election came on. Mr. Ilverton went out of town; and he had not left the house an hour, before Lady Hortensia gave me a note to convey by hand to Mr. Remington's lodgings in Sackville Street, with directions to wait for an answer. Mr. Remington seemed greatly delighted at the contents of the note, and gave me the reply, which, in his hurry and joy, he omitted to seal, although he had lighted a taper on purpose. I hastened away, and went into a public-house to read the letter. To my surprise I found, by its contents, that an appointment had been made for the lover to pass the night with Lady Hortensia, she having already admitted her maid into her confidence, thereby arranging for his admission into the house at twelve o'clock. I was now dreadfully annoyed at being no longer treated as a confidant, I who had done so much to protect them from exposure! My interest in behalf of my mistress suddenly turned to hate; and I thought seriously of revenging what I considered to be a slight. I however ran back to Mr. Remington's lodgings, and said to him, 'Sir, you have not sealed this letter; and I would rather not take it like this to her ladyship, for fear she should think I had read it, which I would not do for all the world.'—He looked very hard at me, and seemed dreadfully confused at his oversight; but, perceiving that I did not change colour, and that I met his gaze steadily, he was more satisfied. Having sealed the letter, he returned it to me, putting half-a-guinea into my hand; and I then hastened away with it to my mistress, from whom I received double that sum. But a wonderful change had come over my mind. I saw that I was made a mere tool of; whereas so long as I thought myself important as a confidant, I was happy. I had moreover hoarded near twenty pounds, by means of the presents I had received; and I thought how foolish I was not to turn my knowledge of certain secrets to account, and extort a good round sum from her ladyship. In a moment I grew avaricious and spiteful. I know how it was: while my vanity was flattered, I was contented; but the instant I saw that I was a tool, and not a confidant, I was mortified, and therefore changed. It did not strike me then that delicacy would of course prevent Lady Hortensia from making use of me to give admittance to her lover; and I looked on myself as a person badly used. I did nothing that day; but I lay awake during the best part of the night settling in my mind how I should proceed. Thus, while the lovers were in each other's arms—as I had no doubt they were—a storm was brewing against them in a quarter from which they little expected it.

"The very next day I went into the drawing-room when I knew that her ladyship was there alone, and, shutting the door, advanced in a resolute manner towards her. She seemed astonished, and asked me what I wanted. 'A hundred pounds,' I answered in a dogged style.—'Do you mean to request that sum as a favour, or to demand it as the price of the secrets you have promised to keep faithfully?' she said in a mild and reproachful way, which made me more than half repent of my conduct; but I had gone too far to retreat.—'Whichever your ladyship likes,' I replied.—'I will give you *two* hundred if you will leave the house this minute, and let me make what excuse I choose for sending you away,' she said.—The offer was too tempting to be rejected; and I immediately accepted it. Two hundred pounds! it was a fortune, and I fancied that I should never be able to spend it.—'Pack up your boxes, and prepare to depart,' said Lady Hortensia, 'If the servants ask you any questions, steadily refuse to answer them, beyond merely stating that I have ordered you to leave immediately; and if you will call on Mr. Remington this evening at eight o'clock, he will give you two hundred pounds in gold.'— I was overjoyed at this arrangement, and gladly took my departure on such terms, caring little what reason her ladyship might allege for the abruptness with which I left. Two hundred pounds to be received in a few hours! Oh! how happy I was!—and what castles did I build in the air! I removed my trunk to a public-house in St. Martin's Lane; and having had a pint of wine to celebrate the occasion, strolled out to purchase new clothes—for I had of course left my livery at Mr. Ilverton's house, and was not overwell dressed. Having bought all I required, thereby making a considerable hole into the twenty-five pounds which, with my hoardings and wages, I had in my pocket when I came away, I returned to the public-house, and put on my new things. I then went out again to while away an hour till eight o'clock, it being now seven. As I was going along Piccadilly, I saw an elegantly dressed lady step out of a carriage at a shop-door; and to my joy I recognised Miss Stacey. She immediately knew me; and, seeing me so well attired, did not hesitate to stop and speak to me. We conversed together for a few minutes, during which I told her that I was no longer under the necessity of working for my living, as fortune had been kind to me. She expressed her pleasure, gave me her address, and asked me to call upon her; telling me, however, that I must be sure to come between two and seven, and at no other time. I promised to visit her; for she looked sweetly pretty and very amorous;—and we parted.

"Precisely as the clock struck eight, I knocked at Mr. Remington's door,—none of your sneaking single knocks; but a good loud double one—for I felt all the importance of a man who has two hundred pounds to receive. Mr. Remington was at home, and I was shown up into his room. He desired me to be seated; but in a very cold tone and with a haughty manner. I did not however care one fig for that: the idea of the two hundred pounds rendered me as independent as possible. When I sate down, Mr. Remington rose from his chair; and, advancing close up to me, he said in a low, savage tone, 'You are a contemptible villian!'—'I did not come here to be abused,' I exclaimed insolently: 'give me my money, and let me be off.'—'Your money, indeed!' he cried: 'not one farthing will you receive of me, or of Lady Hortensia Ilverton. Now, listen, young man, and be cautions how you act. Had you conducted yourself fairly, you would always have found friends in me and her ladyship; but you have shown yourself a villain, and we are determined to crush you at once. You think you have us in your power; but you are mistaken. Her ladyship has already stated to her entire household that you were discharged suddenly for an atrocious attempt to extort money from her:

and say but one word of scandal, utter one syllable against her, and you will be handed over to justice. Begone, sir; and take care how you conduct yourself. One word, by the way, before you leave me—and that is a word of friendly warning. The hall-porter in St. James's Square has instructions to give you over to the care of a constable, if you present yourself again at that mansion.'—'You cannot bully me,' I exclaimed; 'I know too much! Every thing shall now be made known to Mr. Ilverton.'—'And he will not believe a word you utter,' answered Remington. 'This night's post bears to him a letter in which Lady Hortensia declares that you threatened to expose both him and her if she did not give you a sum of money; and that you dared to assert that her husband had bribed you to conceal yourself under a sofa. *She* of course pretends to think her husband incapable of such mean and cowardly conduct; and he will be sure to deny it; at the same time he will never forgive nor believe you.'—'But there is the affair at the doctor's house in Brook Street,' I cried.—'The doctor will deny that such a lady was ever there,' returned Mr. Remington, with a triumphant smile.—'And the maid who knows that you passed an entire night with her mistress?' I said, my courage sinking rapidly.—'You had better ask her what she knows of the business! Now, mark me, young man; every precaution is taken to put you to confusion. You are forestalled in every possible way. Say what you will, positive contradictions and denials will meet your assertions; and the result will be to you transportation for life, for attempting to extort money! Now, then, reflect well before you plunge yourself headlong into difficulties.'—'But I am thoroughly ruined!' I exclaimed, tears starting into my eyes, as I saw the truth of all he said. 'I have lost my place and my character!'—'It is your own fault,' replied Mr. Remington. 'At the same time,' he added, after a few moments consideration, 'I do not wish you to be crushed completely down to the very mire. I will give you one chance. Sign a paper, stating that all your accusations are so many falsehoods, and that you make this acknowledgment to save yourself from being handed over to justice; and I will then present you with fifty guineas.'—Thus speaking, he took out a handful of notes and gold, to tempt me to conclude the bargain.—'But every thing I can state is true!' I exclaimed.—'Never mind *that*,' he answered: '*we* can prove it to be all false. So, haste and decide: my time is precious.'—What could I do? I wanted money, and I saw that he was determined to resist all attempts at positive extortion. I therefore expressed my readiness to sign the paper, which was already drawn up; and, having done so, I received the fifty guineas promised.—'Now,' said he triumphantly, as he folded up the document and placed it in his pocket-book, 'you know the consequence of a single slanderous whisper!'—I took my departure, terribly nettled, but still somewhat consoled by the possession of the fifty guineas; for I thought that one third of the sum at first expected, was better than none at all.

"I longed to be revenged on Lady Hortensia and Mr. Remington; but I knew not how. I smarted dreadfully under the treatment I had received;—I uttered bitter words against my folly in consenting to leave the house before I had the money paid down; and I pondered on a thousand different ways of venting my spite on my enemies. For several days I rambled about by myself, racking my brain with devices. At last I resolved to abandon the idea, at least for the present; and then I set to work to enjoy myself—or rather to see how soon I could make away with my money. A few weeks beheld the bottom of my purse—and I was astonished to think that so many guineas should have disappeared in so short a time. I was now seriously troubled what to do for a living; because I had no character. Suddenly I bethought myself of Miss Stacey's invitation, and hastened to call on her, it being then about three o'clock in the day. I found her living in elegant lodgings in Maddox Street: and she received me most kindly. I told her, word for word, all that had occurred to me since I last saw her; and she was equally candid with me. In fact, she was then in keeping by one of the Cabinet Ministers, who allowed her ten guineas a week, paid her rent, her milliner's and her wine-merchant's bills, and also the hire of her carriage. We soon came to an understanding together; she wanted a page, or tiger, just at that moment, and I accepted the post. The very next day I entered my new place—the most comfortable I had ever yet been in, because I shared my mistress's bed nearly every night. But I soon discovered that the Cabinet Minister and myself were not the only persons who enjoyed the favours of Miss Stacey. Several gentlemen called during those hours when she knew there was no chance of her 'friend' making his appearance: in fact, the lady had become a regular wanton. It was not however for me to make any observations on her conduct: I was well satisfied with my place—and that was enough. I learnt from her that Mrs. Beaumont had died a few months previously, having just before married her butler, who came into possession of all her fortune and had set up as a gentleman, driving his cab and finding plenty of people to honour his champagne parties with their presence. Miss Stacey also gave me a little sketch of herself. She had been seduced, when only fifteen, by the husband of a lady with whom she was placed as companion; and she unhesitatingly admitted that in all the families where she had lived, she had maintained an intrigue with some one, either master, man-servant, or page. Since she had left Mrs. Beaumont she had been in keeping with the Cabinet Minister;—'but,' she added with a smile, 'you see that I am not particular where I take a fancy.' She was indeed a licentious woman, but very good-natured, and possessing a temper that nothing could ruffle.

"I had been with her about three months, when I saw in the newspaper an account of the sudden death of the Honourable Mr. Ilverton, M.P., who was found a corpse in his bed one night by the side of his wife. There was a Coroner's Inquest; and the verdict was 'Died of apoplexy.' I however had my suspicions that some foul play had been practised. In a little less than a year afterwards, I learnt, by the same channel of intelligence, that Lady Hortensia Ilverton had become the wife of Herbert Remington, Esq. About the same time I met Mrs. Hulse—the pretty lady, you remember, who played such pranks with her two lovers at the boarding-house. She stopped and spoke to me. I inquired after Mr. Hulse; and she said that he was quite well, and that they lived very happy together. I then asked her slyly if she had seen Mr. Frederick Shawe lately.—'What!' she exclaimed, 'do you not know all that happened to him?'—I assured her I did not.—'He committed a forgery some months ago,' she replied, 'and was hanged for it. It was down in the country; but I forget where. The whole account was, however, in the papers at the time.'—I was delighted to hear that the enemy of my parents had come to such a miserable end. Mrs. Hulse gave me half-a-sovereign, and bade me good bye.

"A short time after these little incidents, and when I had been in Miss Stacey's service nearly eighteen months, the Cabinet Minister suddenly withdrew his protection from her—I never heard why. It is however more than probable that her numerous intrigues reached his ears. The immediate result of the stoppage of funds in that quarter was a bolt from the lodgings, my mistress being over head and ears in debt. She removed to Norfolk Street, Strand: and I accompanied her. It was at this time that I was attacked by the small-pox, and obliged to leave. I went to the hospital, where I remained dangerously ill for several weeks; and, when I did recover, I was marked as you now see me. I may therefore say without vanity, that before this unfortunate occurrence I was a very good-looking lad; and it was no wonder that the women used to take a fancy to me. Well, I left the hospital with only a few shillings in my pocket, which I had about me when I went in; and my first step was to enquire after my late mistress in Norfolk Street. But there I learnt a sad tale. She had been greatly reduced in circumstances, and had made away with the things in her ready-furnished lodgings. The landlady gave her into custody; she was committed for trial, and sentenced at the Old Bailey to transportation for seven years. But this sentence was commuted to imprisonment for two years, by an order from the Home Office, although the judge who presided at the trial declared it to be a most aggravated offence. I thought I could understand the secret of this leniency; nor was I mistaken; for, on calling upon my poor mistress in Newgate, where she was imprisoned, she told me that she had written to her late 'friend,' the Cabinet Minister, who had procured the alteration in her sentence. She was very happy, and made me promise to call and see her again. But I never had the opportunity; for some Member took up the case in the House of Commons, and asked the Home Secretary the reason why the original sentence was not carried out, seeing that the jury had given no recommendation to mercy, and that the judge had pronounced a strong opinion on the matter. The affair made such a noise, and the *Weekly Dispatch* took it up in such strong terms, that the Government was obliged to order the sentence of transportation to be put into immediate effect.[38] The consequence was that the poor lady was sent out of the country as soon as possible; and I never saw her any more. I felt for her deeply: she had been kind to me—and, with all her faults, there were many excellent points in her character. But, somehow or another, I never did meet a woman who, let her be ever so bad, had not some redeeming qualities. I have met hundreds of men so thoroughly bad, that they had not a single thing to recommend them: but it has not been so in my experience with the other sex. I don't believe that any woman can become so utterly depraved, as not to retain a little amount of good feeling about her. I wish I could say as much for men.

"But let me make haste and bring this story to an end. I was now a miserable, friendless wretch in the world, and knew not what to do for a living. I had no character, and could not get a place. At last, when driven to desperation, I resolved to call on the person whom Mrs. Beaumont married, and who was for many years her butler. I accordingly went up to Russell Square, and knocked at the well-known door. A servant in splendid livery answered the summons; and I was shown into the hall, where I was kept waiting for nearly two hours. At last I was shown up into the drawing-room, where the ex-butler lay lounging on the sofa, reading the *Morning Post*. 'Just sit down, young man, for a moment,' said he, with an affected drawl, although he was an old fellow of sixty, 'while I finish the *Fashionable Intelligence*; because, you see, I'm interested in it.'—So I took a seat, and was kept waiting for another half-hour. At last the *gentleman* laid aside the paper, and enquired my business. I told him who I was, and how distressed was my position. He stared at me for a long time, as if to make sure that I was really the John Jeffreys whom he had once known—for I was cruelly disfigured; and when he was convinced that I was no impostor, he gave me half-a-guinea, saying that he had been a looser by the late Derby, and had lent his friend Lord Mushroom so much money lately, that he could do no more. I thanked him very sincerely and went away. I walked on to Great Russell Street, being in the neighbourhood, and called at the Turners' boarding-house. But I learnt from the servant that Mr. Turner was dead, and Mrs. Turner had *declined* business in consequence, and would see nobody. I went away with a heavy heart; for I knew that the half-guinea would not last for ever. At length I was so tired with walking about, that I entered a public-house to get some refreshment. Two men were sitting in the parlour, drinking ale; and their conversation, singularly enough, happened to turn on a friend of theirs who, as I heard them say, had just got a situation as footman in a good family.—'But how the devil did he manage, though?' asked one; 'since he only came out of quod for stealing that plate, you know, ten days ago.'—'Why, he got a character of that chap who lives at the house with the balcony, up in Castle Street,

Portland Place, to be sure,' was the answer.—'You don't mean old Griffiths, do you?' said the other.—'Of course I do,' replied his friend: 'he's been in that line now for the last six months, and makes an excellent thing by it. I've recommended several poor devils of men-servants to him.'—'The deuce you have!' I exclaimed: 'I wish to God you would recommend me!'—'Are you out of place and got no character?' demanded the man.—'Just so,' I answered; 'and if I don't get a situation soon, I shall starve.'—'Have you got any tin about you?' asked the man.—'Ten shillings, when I've paid for what I've had,' I replied.—'That'll just do the trick!' cried the man: 'you must stand a pot to me and my friend here; and you'll have to pay seven-and-sixpence entrance fee to old Griffiths. Then you'll have a trifle left to take you on till to-morrow.' I readily paid for a pot of the best ale; and when we had disposed of it, I received a note of recommendation to the Mr. Griffiths spoken of. He was an old, respectable-looking man, with a bold crown, and grey hair at the back and sides of his head; and he was sitting in a neat office, with a large book before him. He read the note, which explained my business, and then demanded the entrance fee. This I paid; and he put down my name in the book. 'I will give you the addresses of several families who require a young livery-servant,' he said; 'and you may refer them to Captain Elphinstone, No.—, Mortimer Street, Cavendish Square. You may say that you lived with that gentleman for three years, and only left him on account of ill health. And now I must tell you the nature of the bargain which exists between you and me. You are sure to obtain a situation; and when your first quarter's wages are paid, you must bring me a sovereign; and a sovereign from second quarter. You will then always have me as your friend, and need never be afraid of remaining long out of place. But if you do not keep faith with me, I shall find means to make you repent it.'—I assured the old gentleman I would do the thing that was right; and took my leave of him, rejoiced at the prospect of obtaining a situation.

"Next morning I made myself as tidy as I could, and called at the places pointed out by Mr. Griffiths. I was soon successful, and gave Captain Elphinstone as my reference. The gentleman of the house said he would call on the captain in the course of the day, and I was to return in the evening for the answer. This I did, and found that an unexceptionable character had been given of me. I was therefore admitted into the gentleman's service at once. It was a quiet place, and a small establishment, only consisting of myself and two female servants—a cook and housemaid; for Mr. Farmer, our master, was an elderly bachelor. There I stayed for several years, and was very happy and comfortable indeed. But one day Mr. Farmer took it into his head to marry the cook; and as she could not bear to have in her house the same people who had known her as a fellow-servant, the housemaid and myself both got our discharge. We, however, had good characters, but we did not avail ourselves of them—for, having each scraped up a little money, we agreed to club our savings, and open a shop in the chandlery line. We had long been intimate enough to render the parson's services quite unnecessary in enabling us to live together; and so we commenced business, passing ourselves off as man and wife. The thing did not, however, succeed; and care drove me to the public-house. It was then that I met you, Mr. Bones; and you suggested how much good might be done if I would go back into service, and give you notice of any little things worth your knowing. This I resolved to do; and, leaving my female companion to do what she liked with the shop, I took leave of her. We parted very good friends; and by the aid of old Griffiths I very soon obtained a place. I need not say any more,—unless it is that since then I've been in situations at many houses, and have generally managed to do a pretty decent amount of business with Mr. Bones."

Jeffreys ceased speaking; and his three companions expressed the amusement they had derived from his narrative.

A few more glasses of grog were drunk, as well as a few more pipes smoked; and it was not until past three in the morning that Old Death's visitors left him.

We cannot close this chapter without a few observations relative to that large and important class—domestic servants.

And first of female servants. It is said that great numbers of them are immodest, and that from their ranks the class of unfortunate women, or prostitutes, is largely recruited. We believe that the immorality of female servants is considerably exaggerated by these representations, and that the cases of frailty are the exceptions and not the rule. There are thousands and thousands of females amongst this class as respectable and well conducted as women ought to be, and who take a pride not only in maintaining a spotless character, but in so behaving themselves that there shall be no chance of its becoming tainted. And this is the more creditable to them—the more to their honour, inasmuch as the temptations to which they are exposed are very great. Sent out on errands at all hours—compelled to go to the public-houses to fetch the beer and spirits for the use of the family—constantly placed in contact with the serving-men belonging to the family's tradesmen—exposed to the chance of sustaining insulting liberties at the hands of the visitors to the house—and often persecuted by the lustful addresses of some male inmate of the establishment, such as a brother or son of the master, and perhaps the master himself,—what strength of mind—what moral courage must the servant-maid possess to resist these temptations and escape from so many perils! We mean to say, then, that if she do fall, there is far more scope for pity and a far greater amount of extenuation on her behalf, than on that of the lady who surrenders herself, unmarried, to the embraces of her lover!

And in many—too many instances—what a life of slavery is that of the female servant!—and how little enviable is the lot of the poor maid-of-all-work! Talk of the hard fate of the negress—think of the hard fate of the maid-of-all-work! Excellent saint of Exeter Hall! you need not send your sympathies travelling some thousands of miles across the sea: there is plenty of scope for their exercise at home, if you be really sincere—which we know you are *not*! Look to the maid-of-all-work—up at five in the winter, and heaven only knows when in the summer,—compelled to keep an entire house neat and decent—to black all the boots and shoes—to run on all the errands—to put herself in awful peril by standing or sitting outside the windows which she is compelled to clean—and very frequently half-starved by those whom she serves so assiduously and so faithfully,—what a life is hers![39]

Female servants are treated with much greater kindness in France than in England. In the former country they are considered rather in the light of humble friends of the family than as mere slaves, which is the estimation in which they are usually held, we are sorry to say, in the British Islands. Let them be treated with kindness and forbearance: they have much to try their patience and sour their tempers by the very nature of their condition and the miscellaneous character of their avocations. A man or a woman who is unkind to a servant, is a wretch deserving obloquy and execration. But a master or a mistress who, through petty spite or sheer malignity, refuses to give to a discharged servant the good character which such servant may in reality deserve, is a very fiend, unfit to remain in civilised society.

Before we take leave of this subject, we cannot resist the opportunity of expressing our opinion relative to a practice adopted at Court: we mean the fact of the Queen being waited upon in her private apartments by ladies of high rank and good family, instead of by female servants. Who is Queen Victoria, that a Duchess must select her gown, and a Marchioness hook it? Is she a goddess that a Countess must help her to put on her shoes, and a Baroness tie them? Must not royalty be touched by the hands of a female servant? Alas! we strongly suspect that Queen Victoria is a woman made of the same flesh and blood as the most ordinary mortals: and we feel confident that the practice of attaching ladies of rank and title to her august person is as pernicious to her, as it is degrading to the ladies themselves, and as flagrantly insulting to the entire class of well-conducted ladies'-maids. But royalty in this country must be idolized—deified: no means must be left untried to convince the credulous public that royalty is something very different from commonalty. This delusion shall, however, be dispelled;—the people must be taught to look on Victoria as nothing more than the chief magistrate of the country, deriving her power from the nation at large, and holding it only so long as the majority of the inhabitants of these realms may consider her worthy to retain it. The contemptible farce of firing cannon to announce her movements—of illuminating dwelling-houses on her birthday—of cheering her whenever she appears in public, just as if she cared two figs for the bawling idlers who gaze on Majesty with awe and astonishment,—all this miserable humbug should be abolished. *The more a Sovereign is deified, the more the people are abased.* Instead of the nation being obliged to Queen Victoria for ruling over it, Queen Victoria ought to be very much obliged to the nation for allowing her to occupy her high post. For the only real *sovereign power* is that of the people; and the individual who looks on royalty as something infallible—divine—supernally grand and awe-inspiring, is a drivelling, narrow-minded idiot, unworthy of the enjoyment of political freedom, and fit only to take his place amidst the herds of Russian serfdom.

38. This incident is founded on fact. Many of our readers will doubtless recollect the case of J——N——and her mother, who were convicted of robbing ready-furnished lodgings about ten years ago. Miss J——N——had been the mistress of a noble lord who was a Cabinet Minister at the time of the condemnation of her mother and herself, *and who is a Cabinet Minister at the present moment.* The affair created a great sensation at the time; but the *Dispatch* and other independent newspapers took it up; not in order to persecute the unhappy women, but on public grounds. The result was that the original sentence passed upon them, and which Ministerial favouritism sought to commute to a much milder penalty, was carried into force. The entire business, so far as the noble lord was concerned, was vile and scandalous in the extreme.

39. We avail ourselves of the opportunity afforded us by the glance which we are taking at this subject, to recommend to perusal an admirable little work, written by our esteemed and talented friend, Mr. John Taylor Sinnett, and entitled "The Servant Girl in London." It is published by Hastings, Carey Street, Lincoln's Inn Fields; and is a little book which should be found in all families, as it contains sentiments and precepts useful alike to the employer and the employed.

In a work from which we have frequently quoted in the Notes belonging to the present Series of "THE MYSTERIES OF LONDON,"—we allude to "Poverty, Mendicity, and Crime,"—we find an important passage bearing strongly upon the subject of the text. It runs as follows:—"We must now direct attention to the class of female servants, and they form no insignificant number: from these the higher ranks of our prostitutes are recruited. Thirst for dress and finery, which has crept on to such a degree that it is not a very rare sight to behold them waiting on their mistress in the morning, bedecked in silks and ornaments equal to the young ladies themselves, even where the ladies are of the highest class of the community. Great censure is due to ladies, especially those who are mothers, for not restraining their servants from squandering away the whole of their money, loss of place ought to be the consequence of not laying by a small portion of wages to sustain themselves in the event of illness or other unforeseen calamity; the dress of a female servant ought to be good, but perfectly void of ridiculous ornament and frippery. The ladies' maids of our aristocracy are a race the most highly culpable of their sex, aping all the pride and airs of their lady, and desiring to appear abroad with equal *éclat*, to effect which, the wardrobe of the mistress is not unfrequently resorted to, and the purse not always held sacred, or she becomes a prostitute whilst under the roof of her employer, till descending from one false step to another she at length links her fate to some favourite of the swell mob, to whom she at first listened as a suitor, and ends in her being accessary to robbing the family which had fostered her. It is ascertained, beyond doubt, that most of the houses that are robbed, arises from the connexion and intimacy which the servant has contracted with some of the petty workmen who have been employed about the premises, many of whom are thieves themselves, or connected with some gang of villains who resort to that expedient to learn what property is kept on the premises, and how it is disposed of at night. 'A great deal of crime,' says Mr. Nairn, in his evidence, 'is generated in consequence of the tradesmen who employ journeymen to work for them, in gentlemen's houses, not taking care to inquire into their character: by getting acquainted with servants, they get a knowledge of those parts of the house where anything valuable is kept. A number of men that were in the prison were painters, plasterers, and bricklayers, they were in the practice of communicating with thieves, and it is in that secret manner that they get information where property is kept.'—*Vide J. H. Nairn, p. 370, 2nd Report, Lords, on State of Gaols, 1835.*

"There is a most infamous conspiracy existing between the purveyors or housekeepers of the aristocracy and their tradespeople, the latter paying the former a large per centage on the bills for the sake of 'gaining their custom.' Twenty per cent. is often given, and it has been known to rise as high as fifty; unfortunately, the nobleman considers it as derogatory to his high rank to look into his pecuniary domestic affairs; but taking it in a moral point of view, it is his duty to do so for the sake of preventing this species of peculation, which is an absolute theft and one of the stepping-stones to crime generally, as the money so attained is mostly as lightly spent, and the servants out of place for a length of time, the difficulty to procure the wherewithal to keep alive their former extravagance makes them not hesitate to become *regular thieves*, the fine sense of honesty having been destroyed by the transaction with the tradesman, who had not failed, in his turn, to make out a bill more than sufficiently long to cover merely his generosity in bestowing Christmas boxes upon the domestics of his patron. These tradesmen are a rank disgrace to their more honest fellow shopkeeper; they are worse than fences, and it is greatly to be regretted that a complete *expose* cannot take place, and all such tradesmen dealt with according to their merit.

"Another evil in society that is pregnant with mischief is giving a false character to servants, which ladies are constantly in the practice of doing, to avoid being plagued, or 'perhaps,' as they say, 'insulted by the discarded servant,' whose character, if correctly stated, would not be such as easily to procure a new situation; thus a pilferer having once had the luck to start off in a private family with a good name, is from this shameful habit let loose upon the public to commit his depredations at leisure and convenience, with the chance of blame falling upon an honest individual, through the crafty machination of the wicked. By making servants conscious that they would only procure such a character as they really deserve, great good would accrue to the public generally, and the servants themselves would be taught to curb their temper and other bad propensities, by which they would become infinitely more contented and happy beings, and valuable members of society.

"It is too often the case that servants are looked upon as little better than slaves, and so to treat them. To say the least of such conduct it is unwise, for in proportion to the kindness with which they are treated, so will they study in return to make us enjoy numberless little comforts so delightful to experience, and which it is in their power to give life to or destroy. Humanity ought to suggest that the situation in which these persons are placed, witnessing nightly those scenes of pleasure, without being permitted to join in them, is sufficiently grating, for they all have their feelings, in common with the best of us, and it ought to be one of the first cares of the heads of families to lighten, as far as consistent with the rules and shades of society, the state and labours of their dependants. In France the servants are in an enviable condition compared with those of England, and if the plan were followed in this country, giving them their little pleasures, many a one, whose propensities were wavering, would be confirmed in virtue, and become a useful member, instead of a disgrace to society."

CHAPTER LXXXVII.
THE BLACKAMOOR.

Upon quitting Old Death's abode, Tim the Snammer and Josh Pedler proceeded together in the direction of Blackfriar's Bridge; while John Jeffreys, having wished those worthies "good night," pursued his way up Horsemonger Lane, and plunged into the maze of narrow, obscure streets lying at the back of the prison.

Although he had said "*good night*" to his companions, it was in reality *morning*; for the clock of the gaol chimed a quarter-past three as Jeffreys passed by that dismal-looking establishment.

Having reached the door of the house in which he lodged, and which was in one of the streets above alluded to, he drew a pass-key from his pocket, and was about to apply it to the lock, when the sounds of footsteps close by fell upon his ears, and almost at the same moment a heavy hand was laid upon his shoulder.

The conscience of Mr. John Jeffreys was not quite so free from sources of alarm as to prevent him from being painfully startled by this occurrence; and turning suddenly round towards the individual who had thus accosted him, he found himself face to face with a blackamoor.

"Fear not—no harm is intended you," said the negro, in a deep, solemn, and sonorous voice, but without the least peculiarity of accent; "that is," he added, "if you follow my directions."

"And who are you?" demanded Jeffreys, reassured by the certainty that he was addressing no myrmidon of the law.

"It is not for you to question, but to answer," said the Black in a cool and authoritative manner which seemed to indicate the consciousness of possessing the power to enforce his will, even against any resistance that might be offered. "But I have no time to waste in unnecessary discourse. You must accompany me whither I shall lead you."

"And if I refuse?" asked Jeffreys, trembling he scarcely knew why.

"Then I shall summon to my aid those who are ready at hand, and who will carry you off by force," calmly replied the Black.

"But if I raise an alarm," said Jeffreys, gradually yielding to a sensation of awe in the presence of the mysterious stranger who spoke with the confidence of power and authority, "the neighbours will come to my rescue, and——"

"A truce to this argument," interrupted the Black, sternly. "If you accompany me of your own free will, it will be to your advantage, and no harm shall befall you: but if you venture to resist me, I shall unhesitatingly make you my prisoner by force; and we shall then see what account John Jeffreys can give of his long and intimate connexion with Old Death."

"I will go with you—I will do any thing you command," said the villain, trembling from head to foot. "Only——"

"Again I tell you that you have nothing to fear and much to gain," observed the Black; and taking Jeffreys' arm, he led him hastily back towards Horsemonger Lane, neither of them uttering a word as they thus hurried along.

The night—or rather morning, was dark and sombre, and there were no lamps in the streets which they were threading. Thus, although arm-in-arm together, Jeffreys could obtain but a very imperfect view of his companion's features: nevertheless, it struck him that though the stranger's countenance was black as that of an African negro, the facial outline was not characterised by the protuberant thickness of lips and hideous flatness of nose which usually belong to that race. But Jeffreys was too much alarmed—too much bewildered by the sudden and mysterious adventures which had befallen him, to be able to make any very steady reflections; and whenever he threw a furtive glance towards his companion's countenance, he was instantly met by eyes the pupils of which seemed to glare upon him from their brilliant whites like those of a basilisk.

It was, indeed, an awe-inspiring and most uncomfortable situation in which Jeffreys found himself placed. Having numerous misdeeds upon his conscience, he shuddered at the idea of coming in contact with the law; and if he offered any resistance to his strange companion, such contact was the alternative with which he was menaced. But who was this strange companion? who was this Black that spoke with a tone of authority, and acted in a manner denoting a consciousness of power? For what purpose was he now hurrying Jeffreys along through the darkness of the silent night? and whither were they going? Even had the man been armed with conscious innocence, his position was one calculated to engender acute suspense, painful doubt, and wild apprehension;—but, knowing that he had been guilty of many deeds any one of which would be sufficient to involve him in serious trouble with regard to the law, the miserable wretch had every thing to fear, and scarcely any thing to hope.

It was true he had received assurances that no harm should befall him; and that the incident would, on the other hand, prove advantageous to him. But the influence of those assurances was completely absorbed in the vague and terrible alarms which the dread mystery of the adventure was so well calculated to excite. Conscious guilt made him a complete coward; and his ideas became so confused—his nervousness so great—his excitement so wild, that he began to fancy he was in the power of some unearthly being of evil nature and design. As this impression grew stronger in his attenuated mind, he cast in his terror more frequent glances at his companion;—and now it seemed as if the black countenance were rapidly changing—becoming hideous to behold, and lighted up with eyes that burnt in their sockets like red hot coals!

John Jeffreys felt his legs failing beneath him—his brain whirling—his reason going;—and he was on the point of falling to the ground, overcome by the terror that oppressed him, when his companion's voice suddenly broke upon his ear, dispelling all the superstitious portion of his alarms, and recalling him to his senses.

"Step in!" said the Black;—and Jeffreys found himself by the side of a hackney-coach which was waiting beneath the wall of Horsemonger Lane gaol.

He obeyed the command issued in that authoritative tone which he dared not resist; and the Black followed him into the vehicle, which immediately drove away.

"I must now blindfold you," observed the mysterious stranger; "and I warn you not to attempt to discover the road which we are about to pursue. Even in the darkness which prevails in this coach, I shall be able to distinguish all your movements."

"Where are we going?—what are you about to do with me?" asked Jeffreys, in an imploring voice.

"If you are such a coward as you now seem to be, you will prove of little service to me, I am afraid," said the Black, as he fastened a handkerchief over his prisoner's eyes. "Cheer up, man," he added, in a tone not altogether free from contemptuous disgust: "if I meant to deliver you into the hands of justice, for your numerous misdeeds, I should not take this round about manner of accomplishing the task. Once more I tell you that the result of this adventure depends wholly and solely on yourself. It may prove a fortunate occurrence for you, if your conduct be such as to beget confidence and merit forbearance and protection."

"Then you wish me to do something for you?" said Jeffreys, considerably reassured by the words just addressed to him.

"A great deal," was the laconic answer. "But we will not continue the discourse at present, if you please."

This intimation was followed by profound silence; and the vehicle rolled along at a rapid rate. Jeffreys was now so far relieved of the oppressive fears which had recently paralysed his intellectual energies, that he could even smile at the superstitious alarm which had seized upon him; and he endeavoured to follow in imagination the route pursued by the coach. But he soon became aware that it was taking such a circuitous and tortuous way as fully to destroy all possibility on his part of instituting any clue to its course; and he at last threw himself back in the vehicle, to give way to reflections on another subject—thus abandoning the idea of studying the direction in which he was being hurried along.

For an hour did the coach proceed, making numerous turnings into fresh streets, and often appearing to retrace the way it had previously pursued. At length it stopped; and, one of the doors being immediately opened, the Black took Jeffreys' hand and assisted him to alight. The mysterious guide then hurried his prisoner into a house, up a flight of stairs and into a room, where he conducted him to a seat.

"Remove the bandage from your eyes," said the Black.

This command was instantly and cheerfully obeyed; and Jeffreys, casting a rapid glance around, found himself to be in a well-furnished apartment, of which he and his mysterious guide were the only occupants. The curtains were drawn completely over the windows; and Jeffreys had not the least idea of the locality to which he had been brought.

Opposite to him, but in such a manner that the light of the candles did not fall upon his countenance, sate the Black, whose person Jeffreys was now enabled to examine more narrowly than when they were walking arm-in-arm in the neighbourhood of Horsemonger Lane Gaol; and that survey showed him a man of middle height, well-built, and dressed in good but plain attire. His features were too delicate to be of the negro cast: he had no whiskers, and his hair was of the glossiest jet and seemed to curl naturally. On the table near him lay a pair of pistols; and over the mantelpiece two swords hung cross-wise, beneath a formidable blunderbuss.

The Black allowed Jeffreys leisure to examine the apartment, probably with the view of convincing him, by the appearance of the weapons distributed about, that he was in a place where treachery could be punished in a moment, and that it would be prudent for him to resolve beforehand to accept any conditions that might be proposed to him.

After a short pause, the Black assumed an attitude significant of his intention to open the business of the morning's adventure.

"John Jeffreys," he said, in his calm but imposing manner, "I am well acquainted with all that concerns you; and I know your readiness to serve those who pay you well. Now, however well Old Death may have already paid, or may promise to pay you, for any thing you may have done or may have to do for him, I will pay you better. Do you choose to enter my service—my service exclusively, remember; because, in serving me, you can really serve none other?"

"You seem to know me well, indeed, master," said Jeffreys, assuming a familiar tone, now that he began to fancy the Black to be no better than he should be.

"Dispense with jocularity, sir," exclaimed the other sternly; and Jeffreys shrank from the severe look fixed upon him and the haughty manner which accompanied the words just uttered. "Look you," continued the Black,—"I may as well inform you at once that the companionship which you may expect to enjoy with me, will not be of the kind to which you are accustomed with such men as those from whom you parted an hour ago. If you serve me, you must become my slave: you must execute my bidding without even pausing to reflect on the motives which may instigate the commands I shall give you. You must consent to become a mere automaton in my hands—a machine that is to move only as I choose to direct. There will be no familiarity between us—no friendship. All will be enveloped in the strictest mystery; and you will often have to act without comprehending what you are doing, or the objects you are destined to accomplish. You will moreover be watched by invisible spies—at least by persons whose supervision you will not suspect; so that the least attempt at treachery on your part will be sure to meet with instantaneous punishment—and that punishment is *death*."

"I see nothing to object to, sir, in all that," said Jeffreys, now speaking in a respectful tone, "providing the advantages are as great as they ought to be."

"The advantages to you will be immense," resumed the Black; "and I will explain them. In the first place, there is nothing criminal in my service—nothing that can make you tremble when a stranger taps you on the shoulder. On the contrary, I will protect you even from the effects of the crimes which you have already committed, should they transpire by accident or by the treachery of any of your former accomplices. Your salary shall be liberal and regularly paid; and thus you will be freed from those vicissitudes which make such men as you rich to-day and poor to-morrow. When the time shall come—which it must—that I no longer need your services, I will settle on you an income for the remainder of your days. These are the advantages which I offer you."

"If you only fulfil one tenth part, sir———" began Jeffreys, delighted at the prospects opening before him.

"I am not in the habit of promising more than I can perform," interrupted the Black haughtily. "If my service suits you, you enter it from this moment."

"I accept the terms with joy and gratitude," said Jeffreys.

"Good!" exclaimed the Black; and tossing a well-filled purse towards his new servant, he said, "There are a hundred pounds to confirm the bargain. One piece of advice I must give you:—indeed, it involves a condition on which I must insist; and this is, that you do not, through idle vanity, display your gold to those persons who may be likely to suspect that you have not come honestly by it. For you will not be able to give any satisfactory explanation; and I do not choose you to get into any difficulty just that I may have the trouble of getting you out of it again. Why I say that you will be able to give no satisfactory explanation relative to the source of your prosperity, is because you will not know who your master is—nor where he lives—nor any thing concerning him. You will have no one to refer to, in case you fall into difficulty: at the same time, I should hear of it, and would hasten to assist you, if you be worthy of my regard—if you deserve that I should care for your welfare."

"But how am I to receive your orders, sir, if I do not know where you live nor who you are?" inquired Jeffreys, his astonishment and awe increasing with every word that came from the lips of his new master.

"Shall not I know where *you* live?" said the Black, smiling for the first time since they had met: "and can I not come to you when I require your services? Will not the post convey my letters? and have I not messengers to dispatch to you? Leave all those matters to me; trouble not yourself relative to the means of communication between us: and ask no questions which do not bear upon the mechanical and even blind service which you are to devote to me. You will find me a good and liberal master, if you prove faithful, diligent, and sincere; but should you attempt to practise perfidy against me—should you deceive me in any one single thing, however trifling, I shall become a terrible and implacable enemy."

"I can have no interest in deceiving you, sir, considering all the advantages your service holds out," said Jeffreys: "and yet I should like to know a little more of the nature of what you will require at my hands—what I shall have to do, indeed."

"No—I will explain nothing," returned the Black. "I have already assured you that my service is safe, so far as the laws of the country are concerned, and that you will never be called upon to do a deed of which you need be ashamed—supposing that you have any shame in you. I say this, because I know that you have hitherto pursued evil courses—that you have maintained a desperate connexion with Benjamin Bones—and that many robberies have taken place through your instrumentality, if not actually perpetrated by your hands. But if you remain in my service, I hope to render you a better man— I hope to see the day come when you will know what proper shame is, and will blush at many of the actions of your earlier years. Of this enough, however, for the present. I did not bring you hither to listen to moral lectures or sermons from my lips. Neither do I believe that precepts are of much benefit to a man who has pursued a long career of vice and error. Example does much more—but experience most of all. When you shall have learnt the value of good conduct and the advantage of fidelity to him whom you serve, you will see how far preferable it is to dwell without the fear of incurring the resentment of outraged laws than to lead an existence of harassing excitement produced by the perpetual dread of falling into the grasp of justice. But, again I say, of this enough. Do you still adhere to your desire to enter my service?"

"I do, sir," was the answer, delivered in a firm tone.

"I must then warn you," resumed the Black, "that though I exact the most complete fidelity from you—and though I should punish, in a terrible manner, the least perfidy on your part,—yet, in respect to others, you will often be compelled to exercise stratagem and practise plots which at first sight may appear treacherous. You will have to wage war, perhaps, against some of your old companions—to defeat their projects—even to betray their schemes. Are you prepared to agree to all this?"

"I am prepared to obey your orders in all things," was the reply.

"Without even questioning my motives?"

"That was a condition already imposed by you, and agreed to by me."

"And you will undertake never to breathe to a single soul a word relative to the secret service in which you are engaged? Remember," added the Black, hastily, "I merely mention this as a warning; because I should immediately detect any treachery on your part, and should not hesitate to punish it terribly."

"I wish you would at once put me to the test in some way or another, sir," said Jeffreys. "You seem to know all about me—but in what way you got your information, is of course a mystery to me. However, you *do* know me well—and, having that knowledge of me, I can perfectly understand that you do not feel disposed to trust to my bare word in any thing. Now give me something to do—put me on trial in some way or another—and then judge whether I am the man to serve a good paymaster, or not."

"You speak to the point—and I will at once put you to the test you solicit," returned the Black; "and mind how you reply to my questions—because, even were you to amuse me with deceptive answers now, in a few hours I should discover the real truth, and my vengeance would overtake you—aye, even in the midst of those companions whom I am about to ask you to betray. In a word, then, what was the nature of the business which took you and two other men to Old Death's lodgings last evening, and detained you there a great portion of the night?"

"One word, sir, before I answer the question!" exclaimed Jeffreys. "If I reveal to you every thing which took place between myself, those two men and Old Death last night, will you not think that in the same manner I shall betray to them what is now taking place between you and me?"

"I have already told you that the greatest proof of faithful service towards *me* is to betray *others*," returned the Black; "and I have given you ample assurance that if you attempt to betray *me* to *others*, certain vengeance will overtake you."

"Then if you consider my treachery towards others as a proof of fidelity to you, sir," continued Jeffreys, "I am content to be put to such a test. You ask me what took place between Old Death, Tim the Snammer, Josh Pedler, and myself last night; and I will tell you word for word. A few weeks ago one Thomas Rainford was hanged at Horsemonger Lane gaol, and was buried in St. Luke's churchyard. To-night Old Death means to have the coffin dug up, and conveyed to the house of certain people named Bunce, in Earl Street, Seven Dials; to which house he himself will move to-day. It seems that this Rainford was the eldest brother of the Earl of Ellingham, against whom Old Death has a dreadful spite; and so he intends to have the body of Tom Rain taken out of the coffin, a rope put round its neck, and a placard on its breast, stating that the famous highwayman was the Earl's brother. The body is then to be conveyed to Pall Mall, and placed on the steps of the nobleman's house. This is one part of the scheme concocted last night, and which me and the two other men were engaged to execute."

"Go on," said the Black, in a low tone.

"The part that's to come is worse than what I've already told you, sir," observed Jeffreys; "and I am afraid that if you know I consented to serve in the matter——"

"Go on—go on," exclaimed the Black, impatiently.

"Well, sir—since I must, I will tell you all," continued Jeffreys. "Old Death has found out that a lady, named Esther—Esther—I forget——"

"Never mind! Go on, I say," cried the Black, more impatiently than before.

"I was saying that Old Death had found out that this lady was the mistress of Tom Rain, the famous highwayman, and that the Earl has a great esteem for her. He has also heard that the Earl *is* going—or *was* going—to marry another lady, named Hatfield; and he has made up his mind to have these two ladies carried off and conveyed to Bunce's house in Seven Dials. When he has got them there, sir, he intends——But I really——"

"Go on, man!" exclaimed the Black. "What does he mean to do?"

"To put their eyes out," replied Jeffreys, in a low tone, and speaking with considerable hesitation.

"The fiend!—the monster!" ejaculated the Black, starting from his chair; but instantly composing himself, he resumed his seat, saying, "Was that the full extent of the atrocity planned and agreed upon last night?"

"That was the whole scheme, sir," answered Jeffreys. "Benjamin Bones agreed to give us each a hundred pounds for serving him in those matters, and he paid us each thirty on account."

"Show me your share," said the Black, abruptly.

Jeffreys hesitated, and turned pale.

"Beware how you deceive me—take care how you trifle with me!" exclaimed his master. "If you received those thirty pounds from Old Death, you must have them about you now; for *I know*," he added emphatically and significantly, "that between the time you left his lodgings and stopped at your own door, whither I followed you expressly to ascertain where you lived, you entered no place at which you could have deposited the money."

Jeffreys no longer dared to hesitate; but taking a large roll of Bank-notes and a quantity of gold from his pocket, he spread them upon the table, saying, "The thirty pounds I received from Old Death last night are amongst this lot."

"And whence did you obtain such a large sum?" demanded the Black, hastily glancing over the amount, "there are several hundreds of pounds here!"

"Well, sir," said Jeffreys, completely over-awed by the tone and manner of his new master, as well as by the mystery which surrounded him; "I will tell you all about it—and then you will be convinced that I am ready and anxious to secure your good opinion. I was until very lately in the service of a Mr. Torrens——"

"Ah!" exclaimed the Black, starting as if with sudden surprise at the information he had just received: then, again composing himself, he said in his usual calm, but authoritative manner, "Proceed."

"This Mr. Torrens was paid a sum of money a few days ago—about fifteen hundred pounds," continued Jeffreys; "and I put Old Death up to it."

"Benjamin Bones again—Benjamin Bones at the bottom of every villainy!" cried the Black, in an excited manner.

"Well, sir—and so Old Death sent two men—the very same men who was with me at his lodgings last night—to rob Mr. Torrens of the money. They succeeded, and Old Death changed the large notes into small ones and gold; because large notes are useless to such men as Tim the Snammer and Josh Pedler. If they attempted to change a fifty pound note, they would get taken up in a moment; whereas they can manage to smash small notes at the public-houses where they deal. So Old Death had his share of the plunder; and mine is part of that heap. I have now told you every thing, sir———"

"No—not every thing!" said the Black, in a more serious and solemn tone than he had yet adopted during his interview with Jeffreys. "Mr. Torrens is in Newgate—charged with a fearful crime," he continued; "and his daughter Rosamond is in a state bordering on despair at the house of kind and generous people with whom I am acquainted."

"Good God! who are you?" exclaimed Jeffreys, surveying his master in terror and amazement. "You know every thing—every body! The least word that is uttered leads to a subject with which you are sure to be acquainted! Oh! sir—if you have had me brought here to do me a mischief—to get me into trouble—to make me confess things—"

"Fear not, Jeffreys!" interrupted the Black, in a reassuring tone. "I am acquainted with Mr. Torrens' version of the history of that murder—and I know that suspicion rests not upon you. But I now perceive clearly that the tale which Mr. Torrens has told to his daughter, and which his daughter has repeated to those friends of mine who have granted her an asylum,—I perceive that this tale is, alas! too true, strange and incredible as it at first appeared. Yes: Mr. Torrens did not deceive his daughter! The house was entered by two men and robbed, as he described the occurrence—and those two men were the real murderers of Sir Henry Courtenay! Jeffreys," continued the Black, in a lower and more measured tone, "you are now completely in my power. Nay—start not—fear not: it is far from my intention to harm you. But it is as well for you to know that you are now bound to me in two ways: first, because I pay you for your services—secondly, because I will denounce you as an accomplice and an accessory before the fact, in respect to that murder, if you hesitate to fulfil my orders! On the other hand, if you remain faithful—if you serve me with that blind obedience and implicit zeal which I exact from you, you have nothing to fear, but every thing to hope."

"Before I was in your power I had made up my mind to serve you in the manner you state," said Jeffreys; "and now of course I am compelled to do so. Give me your orders—what is there for me to undertake? Shall I inform against Josh Pedler and Tim Splint? or shall I go and set the constables upon Old Death, who was an accomplice in the robbery, since he sent those two men to commit it."

"Silence, Jeffreys!" exclaimed the Black imperiously: "it is not for you to suggest any thing—but to perform what is suggested by myself! And remember—I will not allow you to take a single step in these matters, unauthorised by me. Stir not of your own accord—or you will only involve yourself in ruin. See the position in which you are placed! If the two men who murdered Sir Henry Courtenay, be surrendered up to justice, they may confess all—and their confession would implicate you and Benjamin Bones. Nevertheless, an innocent victim shall not be sacrificed to the blood-thirsty law which authorises the punishment of death: Mr. Torrens must be saved! This is an affair which demands the greatest caution; and if you utter a word more than I direct you to speak, or take a single step unknown to me, you will be undone! But time has passed rapidly—more rapidly than I had expected, while we have been thus conversing together," added the Black, looking at his watch. "It is now day-light—and you cannot depart hence until the evening."

He knew by the hour that morning had dawned some time; but the window-shutters were closed, and the curtains were thick and ample, so that not a gleam of sunshine penetrated into that apartment, where the candles were still burning.

"Yes—you must remain here until the evening," repeated the Black. "At what time was it arranged that you should meet the other agents of Old Death in order to visit St. Luke's churchyard?"

"To-night at eleven," answered Jeffreys; "and the place of appointment is at the back of the burial-ground. But do you intend, sir, that I should fulfil my agreement with Benjamin Bones?"

"Ask me no questions!" cried his master, evidently much excited—if not absolutely perplexed by the various ideas that were agitating in his brain. "I have not yet resolved how to act: I must be alone for some hours to meditate! In the meantime you no doubt stand in need of rest? Follow me."

With these words the Black took up a candle and led the way into an adjoining room, which was fitted up as a bed-chamber. There also the shutters were closed, and the curtains drawn over the windows.

"This will be your apartment until the evening," said the Black: "but as I am accustomed to adopt all proper precautions to ensure the complete carrying out of my views, I shall be compelled to place some one with you, and I most moreover request that those shutters remain closed throughout the day."

Jeffreys' new master rang a bell; and in a few minutes a tall, thin, genteel-looking lad, but of a complexion as dark as his own, answered the summons.

"Cæsar," said the elder Black, addressing the lad, "you will stay in this room until I give you permission to leave it; and you will see that Jeffreys, whom I have taken into my service," he added significantly, "is supplied with every thing which he requires in the shape of refreshments."

"Yes, sir," replied the youth, in a respectful manner.

The Black then quitted the room; and Jeffreys remained with the lad who had been addressed by the name of Cæsar.

CHAPTER LXXXVIII.
SCENES AT THE BLACKAMOOR'S HOUSE.

When the Black returned to the parlour where he had received from the lips of Jeffreys revelations which had produced a strange effect upon his mind, he threw himself upon the sofa, and gave way to his reflections.

Although he had been up all night, yet he experienced no sensation of weariness: he possessed a soul of such indomitable energy that by a natural kind of sympathy between mind and matter, it sustained even the physical powers to a wondrous degree.

We must follow him in the train of meditations into which he was plunged; for the affairs in which he suddenly found himself interested, through the confessions of John Jeffreys, were of so complicated and so difficult a nature,—involving, too, so many delicate points,—that to a mind endowed with one whit less of courage, or with one gleam less of clearness, those affairs would have appeared to be entangled beyond all possibility of a safe and prudent unravelling.

Let the reader bear in mind that there were two distinct affairs in question; although they might at a first glance be confounded, because certain persons who were connected with one were also involved in the other.

The first of these affairs was the scheme of Old Death to avenge himself on the Earl of Ellingham,—a scheme involving many frightful details, such as the exhumation of a coffin, the capture of Esther de Medina and Lady Hatfield, and the atrocity of blinding those fair and interesting creatures.

The other affair was the accusation of Mr. Torrens of a crime which he had not committed, and the necessity of proving his innocence.

"If those miscreants Tim the Snammer and Josh Pedler be informed against," reasoned the Black within himself, "they will be certain that either Benjamin Bones or John Jeffreys has betrayed them, and they will accordingly give a full and complete explanation, the result of which would be that the whole four would swing together. But I am bound to save Jeffreys from that terrible fate; and God forbid that that I should be the means, direct or indirect, of sending Benjamin Bones to the scaffold! And yet, on the other hand, knowing all that I have elicited from Jeffreys, and acting in the true spirit of that mission which I have voluntarily undertaken, I dare not allow this innocent man Torrens to be condemned by a frightful combination of circumstantial evidence, when the utterance of a single word will prove him guiltless and fix the crime on those who really perpetrated it. How stands the matter, then? Torrens must be saved on the one hand; but the real murderers must be allowed to escape on the other! Oh! this is a fatal necessity—a dreadful alternative; and yet it is imperious!"

The Black rose and paced the room with slow and measured steps. He reflected profoundly. He separated all the details of the two complicated matters which occupied his thoughts, and examined them one by one.

"In respect to the vengeance of Benjamin Bones,"—it was thus that his musings were continued after a time,—"*that scheme* must be completely strangled at once—annihilated at its very commencement. Not for worlds must aught scandalous or degrading occur to Arthur, Earl of Ellingham!—not for worlds must the relationship subsisting between him and Thomas Rainford be published and proclaimed! Yes—Benjamin Bones must be rendered powerless for the future;—and yet how can this be accomplished without permitting a legal tribunal to seize upon him?"

The Black continued to pace the room, his sable countenance denoting by its workings the searching keenness with which his mind seized upon and examined each successive project that suggested itself as a means to accomplish all his objects and carry out all his aims in a manner certain to produce the results which he was anxious and resolved to bring about.

At length one particular scheme flashed to his mind; and the smile which appeared on his countenance, as his imagination seized on that project, was an augury of its subsequent adoption. He weighed it well in all its details—he calculated its consequences—he minutely examined all its certain results,—and he arrived at the conviction that, though a large and even a dangerous measure, it was the only one whereby all his designs could be effected.

Having resolved to carry it into execution, the Black felt his mind relieved of a considerable load;—and, seating himself at the table, he wrote the following letter:—

"The account which Rosamond Torrens received from her father relative to the assassination of Sir Henry Courtenay, and which that unfortunate girl recited to you, is strictly and substantially correct. Accident has enabled me to discover the real perpetrators of the crime; *and Mr. Torrens shall be saved!* You will know in what terms to convey this assurance to that poor, suffering creature whom you have taken under your protection."

The Black sealed this note, and addressed it to "*Miss Esther de Medina, Manor House, Finchley.*" He then repaired to the room where he had left Jeffreys and Cæsar together, and found that the former, having partaken of some refreshments, had thrown himself on the bed and fallen into a profound sleep.

"Cæsar," said the Black, "you must hasten to Finchley with this letter. Take your horse and delay not. On your return, come back by way of Grafton Street, and tell Dr. Lascelles that I desire to see him as soon as he can possibly visit me."

Cæsar immediately departed to execute these commissions; and the Black seated himself by the side of the bed on which Jeffreys was sleeping.

Nearly an hour passed, and the man did not awake. The Black rang the bell, and a domestic in plain clothes answered the summons.

"Wilton," said his master, "remain here, and keep watch upon this person,"—pointing to the sleeper. "When he awakes, ring the bell."

The servant bowed obedience to these instructions; and the Black left the room.

Several hours had passed away, and it was three o'clock in the afternoon.

Cæsar had returned with letters for his master, who had scarcely made an end of their perusal when Dr. Lascelles was announced.

"Well, my dear friend," said the physician, "what new scheme have you now in view? in what new project do you require my assistance?"

"Sit down, Doctor, and listen to me attentively," observed the Black; "for many and strange incidents have occurred since I saw you last. But perhaps you have been to Finchley; and in that case, one of those circumstances to which I allude will have been made known to you."

"No, my dear friend," replied Dr. Lascelles, depositing his hat and gloves on one chair and himself in another: "I have not had time to call upon the Medinas since they removed to their country residence. I have been experimentalising on a most splendid brain which the surgeon of St. Bartholomew's Hospital was kind enough to send me as a present. But of what nature is the circumstance of which I should have heard at Finchley, had I called? Nothing disagreeable, I hope?"

"I will explain it to you in as few words as possible," answered the Black, seating himself opposite to the physician. "The day before yesterday—at about five o'clock in the evening—Mr. de Medina and Esther were walking along the high road in the immediate vicinity of the Manor, to which they had removed, as you are well aware, in the morning, when they saw a beautiful young creature sitting on the step of a stile, and evidently a prey to the most heart-rending anguish. They accosted her—spoke kindly to her—and at length induced her to tell just so much of her sorrowful tale as to enlist their warmest sympathies in her behalf. They took her to the Manor; but on their arrival, the poor girl was so overcome by illness, fatigue, and distress of mind, that Esther insisted on her retiring to rest. Yesterday morning she was so far recovered as to render it unnecessary to send for you in your medical capacity; and Esther assured her that she might not only look upon the Manor as her home, but that she should be treated with all the kindness, attention, and respect, due to her misfortunes. It then appears that the poor creature made a confidant of Esther, and revealed her entire story, which shows how deeply she is to be pitied, and how cruel were the circumstances that had driven her from her home, and made her resolve to fly from London as from a city of pestilence. The entire details of that story I will give you presently. Yesterday afternoon I repaired to the Manor, and the particulars connected with the young lady were confidentially narrated to me by Mr. de Medina. Last night the metropolis rang with the rumours of a dreadful murder having been discovered——"

"The assassination of Sir Henry Courtenay," remarked the physician; "and the murderer, a gentleman named Torrens, is in Newgate."

"The *alleged* murderer, you mean, doctor," said the Black, emphatically. "And now prepare yourself to hear an amazing revelation—for the young creature who found an asylum at Finchley Manor, is the daughter of that *alleged murderer*, and her name is Rosamond."

"But surely she could not have been in any way implicated——"

"Patience, doctor—patience," said the Black. "On hearing last night of the arrest of Mr. Torrens, I immediately dispatched Cæsar to Finchley with a note to Mr. de Medina, containing the sad intelligence; and I find by letters which I have just received," he added, glancing towards the documents which lay open on the table, "that the news were broken as delicately as possible to the unhappy girl: nevertheless, she is, as you may suppose, a prey to the most lively grief; and it has been with the greatest difficulty that Mr. de Medina and Esther have restrained her from flying to Newgate to console her father. Let me now relate her history to you."

The Black then detailed those incidents in connexion with Rosamond, which are already known to the reader—save and except the dreadful fact that Mr. Torrens had sold his daughter's virtue to Sir Henry Courtenay; for though the unhappy girl had confessed the outrage which had been perpetrated on her, she knew not—as the reader will remember—that her own father had been an accomplice in the fearful deed.

"I have now some further explanations to give you, doctor," continued the Black; "and then I shall have completed my long, long preface to the business which induced me to request your presence here now. In pursuance of that grand and difficult project, the nature of which is so well known to you, I resolved to enlist one of Old Death's confederates, or rather instruments, in my own service. Accordingly, last night, as soon as I had dispatched Cæsar to Finchley with the note containing the intelligence of Mr. Torrens' arrest, I went into the Borough, and watched in the neighbourhood of Old Death's lodgings: for I informed you a few days ago, if you recollect, that Cæsar had succeeded in discovering the abode of that terrible man. Well, I kept not my watch uselessly; for I soon beheld three men enter the house in Horsemonger Lane, individually and at short intervals. Two of them were unknown to me—although I have since found that their names were by no means unfamiliar; but the third was a fellow of whom I knew something. This was John Jeffreys—once a servant in the employ of Sir Christopher Blunt. Now it immediately struck me that this was the very man who would suit my purposes; for he is crafty—intelligent—and always ready to serve the best paymaster. I accordingly resolved to enlist him in my employ; and to this determination I was the more readily brought, because I felt convinced that mischief was brewing under the auspices of Old Death. The fact of the three men arriving so mysteriously—singly and at short intervals, on the same evening, evidently by appointment—and the length of time they remained in the place, were sufficient arguments to prove to a far less experienced person than myself, that a council of desperate men was being held for no good purposes. It was not until past three this morning, that the villains separated. I had already made up my mind how to act, and a hackney-coach was ordered by me to wait beneath the wall of Horsemonger Lane. I fancied that Old Death's visitors would depart singly as they had arrived; and my expectations were so far realised that Jeffreys went off by himself. I resolved to follow him home first—for I suspected that he lived at no great distance; because, I thought that if I could not succeed in inducing him to accompany me, I should at least know where to find him on another occasion. At his own door I accosted him; and, by working on his fears by means of my mysterious behaviour, as well as by holding out to him vague threats that I was prepared to carry him off by force, if he should resist me, I succeeded in bringing him blindfold to this house."

"Well done!" exclaimed the physician. "And so I presume you have regularly enlisted the respectable Mr. Jeffreys into your service—thereby securing the aid of a spy in the enemy's camp."

"The very object aimed at—the very point gained!," cried the Black, "Jeffreys, under the joint influence of bribery and menaces, is completely mine: and he gave me proofs of his fidelity by revealing to me many interesting matters. Indeed, it was providentially fortunate that I got him into my power and service just at this particular time; as you shall judge for yourself."

He then related the details of the damnable conspiracy planned by Old Death, and to be executed by his myrmidons, against the peace of the Earl of Ellingham and the happiness of Lady Hatfield and Esther de Medina.

"This man is a perfect monster!" ejaculated Dr. Lascelles indignantly. "How is it possible that you can have any forbearance, my dear friend? Set your retainers to watch for him—have him captured—and lock him up for life in one of the dungeons which he himself doubtless rendered serviceable to his own purposes on more than one occasion."

"Patience, doctor," said the Black: "nothing must be done rashly nor without due consideration. Besides, you are well aware that my object is to endeavour to reform that bad man———"

"Reform the devil!" cried the physician impatiently. "You know very well that I ridiculed the idea when you first started it."

"And I intend to try the experiment, doctor," observed the Black, calmly but firmly. "In the meantime, pray listen to me. In the course of the conversation which I had with Jeffreys this morning, he mentioned the name of Torrens; and to my surprise I found that he had lately been in that gentleman's service. When Rosamond told her story to Esther, the poor girl alluded several times to her father's man-servant, as I stated to you just now; but as she did not happen to mention his name—or if she did, it was not mentioned to me—I was unaware of the identity of that domestic and Jeffreys till the latter himself suffered the fact to transpire. Then was it that I also received a corroboration of the truth of the version which Mr. Torrens had given his daughter of those circumstances that led to the death of Sir Henry Courtenay; for Jeffreys instigated the robbery at Torrens Cottage—Benjamin Bones appointed two men to execute it—and those men assassinated the baronet."

"You have thus become the depositor of a very agreeable secret, my dear friend," said the doctor, somewhat ironically. "How do you intend to act? For my part, I consider the position to be embarrassing; for if those two men are arrested, they will perhaps inform against Jeffreys and Old Death,—and, in this case, you lose not only your new dependant, but also the opportunity of trying your great moral theory—which I call great moral nonsense—upon the respectable Mr. Benjamin Bones."

"Doctor—doctor," exclaimed the Black, in a reproachful tone: "is this your friendship for me? is this the way in which you fulfil your promise of assistance?"

"Pardon me, my dear fellow," cried the good-hearted physician, wringing his companion's hand violently. "If I talk to you in that fashion, it is simply because I am deeply anxious for your welfare, and that—in consequence of certain circumstances which we need not specify—I look upon you just as if you were my own son. You know that I am ready to serve you by day and by night—that you may command me at all times, and my purse to its fullest extent——"

"A thousand thanks, doctor, for these proofs of generous friendship," interrupted the Black. "Your assistance I indeed require: on your purse, thanks to the liberality of Mr. de Medina and the Earl of Ellingham, I shall not be compelled to make any inroad."

"Then in what way can I assist you?" demanded the physician.

"I will explain myself," continued the Black. "But first I must tell you that the very two men who murdered Sir Henry Courtenay, are of the gang employed by Old Death to persecute the Earl and the two ladies in whom we all feel an interest—I mean Georgiana Hatfield and Esther de Medina."

"This makes the business more complicated," said the doctor: "because if those two men are arrested on the charge of murder, they may perhaps confess not only that Old Death urged them to the robbery and that Jeffreys was an accomplice in it; but they may also state the services which Benjamin Bones hired them to perform respecting the Earl and the two ladies,—thereby at once publishing to the world that Thomas Rainford was indeed the elder brother of the Earl, and propagating the infamous scandal relative to Esther de Medina having been the said Thomas Rainford's mistress."

"You embrace the whole difficulty—or rather the greater portion of it at once, my dear doctor," exclaimed the Black, delighted to find that his friend entered so minutely and with such keen perception into the affair. "The business presses in every way. In the first place, it is necessary that an innocent man should be relieved as speedily as possible from the dreadful charge hanging over his head; and secondly, the exhumation of the coffin in Saint Luke's churchyard must be prevented this night."

"Certainly it must;" observed Dr. Lascelles. "For if once Old Death knew that the coffin contained not the remains of Thomas Rainford, the discovery might engender certain suspicions in the mind of such an astute old scoundrel as he."

"In a word, doctor, Torrens must be saved; and yet the two men, who rejoice in the names of Joshua Pedler and Timothy Splint, must not be handed over to justice," observed the Black.

"Such ought to be the policy adopted," said the physician: "and, remember, that though these two men are not to be rendered up to justice, they must be taken such care of for the future as to commit no more murders and accept no more employ in the service of such miscreants as Old Death."

"Of that I shall indeed take good care," said the Black.

"But how will it be possible to save Torrens without handing Splint and Pedler over to justice in his place?" demanded the physician. "You will be a clever fellow if you accomplish that difficulty."

"I am prepared to encounter it, doctor," returned the Black; "and you must aid me in the business. Are you so intimately acquainted with any magistrate or justice of the peace, that you could invite him to dinner?"

"What an extraordinary question!" cried Dr. Lascelles, laughing. "How will my asking a magistrate to dinner serve your purposes?"

"Only thus far," responded the Black: "that you would have the kindness to walk a little way with him on his return home in the evening, and that I should have you both very quietly kidnapped, blindfolded, and carried off to some place where you would both have to receive and witness the statements made by two men named Joshua Pedler and Timothy Splint, whom I shall have safe in my own custody within a few hours."

"I understand," said the physician, laughing heartily. "Capital! capital! But, by the bye,—when I think of it—your old friend Sir Christopher Blunt was gazetted two days ago to be one of his Majesty's Justices of the Peace for the County of Middlesex. Would he not serve your purpose? or do you think——"

The physician paused and looked the Black steadfastly and significantly in the face.

"He will answer admirably!" exclaimed the latter, after a few moments' reflection. "Yes—better than any other, all things considered! I will undertake to get him into my power without giving you the trouble to ask him to dinner. But I must request, doctor, that to-morrow night at eleven o'clock you will take a lonely walk in some very retired spot, and at a good distance off too, so that you may lose all trace of the path pursued by your kidnappers."

"You do not require two persons, surely?" said Lascelles.

"Yes—it will be better," responded the Black; "a Justice of the Peace, and a competent and credible witness. Do you happen to have any patient in the neighbourhood of Bethlem, for instance?"

"Let me see," said the doctor, in a musing manner. "Yes," he cried: "an old lady whom I have not visited for some time."

"Very good," observed the Black. "Then you can call on her to-morrow evening; and between ten and eleven, as you are returning on foot—on foot, remember—you will be set upon by half a dozen ruffians," he continued, laughing, "who will blindfold you, shove you into a chaise, and carry you off—you never will be able to say whither."

"I understand you, my dear friend," said the physician, laughing heartily also. "Your scheme is admirable and certain of success."

"Thus far, then, the business is settled," observed the Black.

At that moment Cæsar entered the room, and informed his master that the man Jeffreys had just awoke, having slept uninterruptedly for many hours.

"But you have not left him alone, Cæsar?" exclaimed the Black.

"No, sir—Wilton is with him," was the answer given by the youth.

"Good!" observed his master: then, turning towards the doctor, he added, "If that fellow were to open the shutters and look out into the street, he might recognise the locality; and I intend to allow him no opportunity of playing me false."

"You act wisely," said the physician, who then took his departure, while the Black repaired to the chamber where Jeffreys was remaining.

The man rose and bowed respectfully on the entrance of his master, who, having dismissed Wilton, seated himself and proceeded to address his new dependant in the following manner:—

"I have resolved how to act in the emergencies which have arisen, and to which I have devoted my best consideration. You will not only be saved from the consequences of your connivance with the robbery which took place at Torrens Cottage, and which ended in so tragic a manner; but you will likewise be rendered secure from the possibility of being in any way implicated hereafter. My promises will be faithfully kept, if you prove faithful. But if, on the other hand, you deceive me, I will find you out wheresoever you may hide yourself; and you shall assuredly perish on the scaffold! For you cannot conceive the extent of my power to reward, nor of my ability to punish."

"I have seen enough, sir, to be convinced that you are some great person," said Jeffreys, "and I assure you that you will find me faithful and devoted."

"Act according to your words, and you will bless the day when you first encountered me," observed the Black. "And now listen to my instructions. Soon after it is dark you will be conveyed away from this house; and, at the proper hour, you will keep your appointment to-night with Pedler and Splint. You say that you are to meet them behind St. Luke's church. Do you mean in the road which separates the two burying-grounds from each other?"

"That is the place of meeting, sir," was the answer.

"Very well," continued the Black. "Is there any chance of Old Death forming one of the party?"

"Not the slightest, sir. He loves to plan and plot; but he usually pays agents to execute."

"I could have wished it had been otherwise. However, you will meet your two friends according to agreement; and you will endeavour to keep them in conversation for a few minutes in the road between the two burial-grounds. This will give my people time to surround them, as it were: for it is my intention to arrest those two men this very night."

Jeffreys looked alarmed and said, "They will be sure to think that I have betrayed them, sir."

"Leave all that to me," returned the Black. "I will take care that they shall never have the opportunity of injuring you. Wilton—the servant who has just left this chamber—will conduct the expedition to night; and he will allow you to escape. You will then proceed as quickly as possible to Seven Dials, where Old Death, according to what you told me this morning, must have already taken up his abode;—and you will tell him that when it came to the last moment, Tim the Snammer and Josh Pedler were afraid to undertake the business of digging up the coffin, and resolved to have nothing more to do with him or his affairs. But you will assure him that you remain faithful to him, and that you can recommend two friends of your own who will be delighted to do all he requires for a quarter of the sum he agreed to pay Pedler and Splint. If he accepts the service of your pretended friends, you will make an appointment to meet him in some, low neighbourhood the day after tomorrow, in the evening. Let the time named be a late hour; and should he wish you and your friends to call on him in Earl Street, raise objections, as it does not suit my purpose that the appointment should be there. It must be a place of meeting *from which he has to walk home afterwards*."

"I understand all your commands, sir," said Jeffreys; "and you may depend upon them being faithfully executed."

"I rely upon you," observed the Black; and, after a few moments' consideration, he added, "To-morrow evening at nine o'clock, punctually, you must be in Wilderness Row, beneath the wall of the Charter House gardens; and I shall send some one to receive an account of your proceedings with Old Death, and give you further instructions. But once more I say, be faithful—be prudent—and avoid any vain or foolish display of your money."

"I wish you would have more confidence in me, sir," exclaimed Jeffreys: then, after a brief pause, he said, as an idea struck him, "I have a great deal of money about me, sir—and I wish you would take care of it for me."

"Now I am convinced of your honest intentions, my good fellow," said his master, in a kinder tone than he had yet adopted towards the man. "If you propose to leave your money with me as a guarantee of your good faith, I do not now require any such security: but if your object be to place it in safety, I will accept the trust."

"Well, sir—let it be in the way you have just mentioned," returned Jeffreys.

"Here is a drawer—lock up any thing you choose therein, and take the key with you," said the Black.

Jeffreys did as he was desired: Wilton was again summoned—an excellent dinner was supplied the new dependant and the servant who was appointed to remain with him;—and the Black retired to his own apartment.

Soon after it was dark, Jeffreys was blindfolded and conducted to a private carriage, which was waiting. Wilton accompanied him in the vehicle, which, after driving about for nearly an hour, stopped at last; and Jeffreys, on removing the bandage from his eyes, and alighting, found himself in an obscure street in the immediate vicinity of Shoreditch Church.

CHAPTER LXXXIX.
THE SURPRISE.—JEFFREYS AND OLD DEATH.

The deep tones of St. Luke's bell, proclaiming the hour of eleven, oscillated though the gusty air, as Tim the Snammer entered the narrow road dividing the two burial-grounds belonging to the church. John Jeffreys was already at the place of appointment; and not many moments had elapsed after those two met, ere Josh Pedler joined them, bringing with him the necessary implements for the work of resurrectionists, and which he instantly threw over the wall.

"What a windy night it is," said Tim the Snammer; "and how precious dark."

"All the better for our business," observed Josh Pedler. "I should have been here a little earlier; but I had such a cursed deal of trouble to get rid of that bothering wench 'Tilda. She wouldn't let me come out at first; and swore that if I did, she'd foller me."

"And did she follow you?" demanded Jeffreys.

"Deuce a bit," answered Josh. "I was obliged to give her a good drubbing because she whimpered, and then another to make her hold her tongue; and afterwards we kissed and made it up—and so she went quietly to bed. What strange things women are, to be sure! If you beat 'em, they're sure to love you all the more."

"Well, are we going to stand here talking all night?" cried Tim the Snammer. "Who knows but what there's a watchman about here?"

"I know there isn't," said Jeffreys: "because I made the enquiry in a careless kind of way at a public-house close by, where I bought some brandy in a pint bottle."

"That's capital!" cried Tim. "Give us a dram, old feller."

"I got it on purpose to keep the cold out and our spirits up," said Jeffreys, playing his part admirably so as to gain time, in obedience to the orders he had received from his master. "Who was it that came with Tidmarsh this morning to see the place where Tom Rain is buried?"

"I did," answered Tim the Snammer, smacking his lips in approval of the brandy, and handing the bottle to Josh Pedler.

"Ah! Tom Rain was a fine fellow!" said Jeffreys. "I knew him well. In fact, I was with old Sir Christopher and Frank Curtis the night he robbed them. What a bold, dashing, and yet cool-headed chap Rainford was!"

"The finest highwayman that England ever had," observed Josh Pedler, returning the bottle to Jeffreys.

"Beat your Dick Turpins and your Jack Sheppards all to nothink!" added Tim the Snammer. "I say, Josh, let you and me take to the road when we've done Old Death's business for him, and sacked the blunt he's still got to pay us."

"Well—well, we'll see about it, Tim," answered Pedler. "But—hush! here's some one coming. Let's pretend to be walking on: we haven't time to jump over after the tools."

The three accordingly put themselves in motion; but Jeffreys knew pretty well that the critical moment was now at hand. Tim the Snammer affected to whistle a tune in a careless way; and Josh Pedler began talking loud on some indifferent subject.

Meantime, the footsteps advanced; and it was evident that more than one person was approaching. In fact, there seemed to be three or four; but Josh Pedler and Tim Splint had not the least suspicion of impending danger: they thought that a party of jovial fellows were returning from the public-house—an idea that was excited by the merry song which one of the persons now approaching was singing.

A few minutes brought the two parties within ten paces of each other; when a sudden and suspicious noise was heard, as of a rustling of clothes against the walls which bounded the road. Both Tim the Snammer and Josh Pedler stopped short, alarmed and irresolute: the next instant they, as well as Jeffreys, were seized by two persons who leaped upon them from the walls, and by those who had advanced along the road.

Jeffreys was liberated the moment he mentioned his name; and he hurried away as quickly as possible from the scene of the surprise and capture;—but not before he had witnessed enough, even in the obscurity of the night, to convince him that Josh Pedler and Tim the Snammer were gagged and rendered powerless in the grasp of the agents of the mysterious Blackamoor.

And such was indeed the fact. Before they were able to offer the slightest resistance, or even utter a cry, they were reduced to the condition just described. Their captors immediately divided into two parties, each bearing off a prisoner, so that the villains had not even the consolation of remaining together.

So well were all the arrangements made to ensure the complete success of the affair, that a vehicle was waiting in the vicinity of each end of the road separating the burial-grounds; and the moment the prisoners were thrust inside, bandages were tied over their eyes.

Tim the Snammer was the first who arrived at the place of the villains' destination. At the expiration of an hour from the time of his capture, the vehicle, which had purposely driven about in a circuitous manner, stopped at a house, into which the prisoner was hurried. Up a flight of stairs he was then led—through several rooms—and at length down a long spiral descent of stone steps, a trap shutting with a crashing sound above, and a huge door opening and closing with the din of massiveness below,—then along a place in which the rapid tread of the numerous feet echoed with a gloomy and hollow sound, as if in a paved and vaulted passage,—and lastly into a dungeon, where the wretched man was deposited, unbound, and left to himself, the huge door closing upon him,—such was the hurried progress and ultimate destination of Tim the Snammer in the strange and unknown place to which his captors had borne him!

The treatment experienced by Josh Pedler was precisely the same, save that he did not enter his prison-house until a good half hour after the arrival of his companion in iniquity.

In the meantime, John Jeffreys proceeded to Seven Dials, and found Old Death seated with Mrs. Bunce, Toby having been dismissed—as was usual when Mr. Bones had business to transact in Earl Street—to the public-house to amuse himself with his pipe and his pint.

Old Death was surprised and alarmed when he beheld Jeffreys make his appearance so early, and unaccompanied by Tim Splint and Josh Pedler.

"Is any thing the matter?" enquired the ancient miscreant, as Mrs. Bunce carefully closed the room door.

"No great harm—only something to delay your business," replied Jeffreys.

"Well—if it's no worse, there isn't much harm done," said Old Death. "But where are the others?"

"It's just on account of them that nothing has been done to-night," answered Jeffreys. "In two words, they funked over the affair and have given it up."

"What!" cried Old Death, his countenance becoming grim and ghastly with rage and disappointment: "those scoundrels have received my money—my good money—thirty pounds each, in advance—and have given up the business! You are joking, Jeffreys,—you are bantering me! Why, Tim the Snammer would go through fire and water for such a sum of money as I promised him; and Josh Pedler would sell his skin for half the amount."

"All I can say is this, Mr. Bones," continued Jeffreys, "that I was punctual at the place of meeting at five minutes to eleven; and when Tim Splint and Josh

Pedler made their appearance, they said they had changed their minds and should not proceed farther in the business, and that I might come and tell you so if I liked."

"The villains!—the rascals!" growled Old Death, clenching his fists, and working his toothless jaws about horribly as he spoke.

"I asked them what had made them come to such a resolution," proceeded Jeffreys; "and they said that on account of Torrens's affair they had plenty of money, and it was useless to risk transportation by turning resurrectionists, at least before it was all spent. I argued with them—but it was all in vain: they went away to some public-house; and as I couldn't do the job myself, I started off here to tell you what had occurred."

"Those men don't know me, or they would not attempt to play their tricks in this fashion," murmured Old Death: then, turning towards Jeffreys, he said in a louder tone, and in a conciliating manner, "But you are a good fellow—you are faithful and true, as I always found you; and I am pleased with you. The day will come when Tim the Snammer and Josh Pedler shall bitterly repent of their conduct! But in the meantime I am not to be disappointed in my vengeance—I will not be foiled: I have set my mind on a particular course—and I will follow it."

"There are other men in the world who can do all you require, Mr. Bones, besides Tim the Snammer and Josh Pedler," said Jeffreys. "I wish you had spoken to me first of all———"

"Why so?" demanded Old Death, hastily.

"Because I could have got a couple of chaps to help me to do all the business, and who would have been contented with a quarter of the money you promised those sneaking scoundrels Splint and Pedler," answered Jeffreys.

"Indeed!" cried Old Death eagerly. "You are a good fellow, Jeffreys—an excellent fellow; and you may always calculate upon having me as your friend. But where are these people that you speak of?—who are they?"

"You don't know any thing of them, I fancy," was the reply. "They are like myself—servants out of place; but they are a precious sight worse off than me in respect to money-matters, and would be glad to do any odd job for a ten-pound note or so."

"And when can you see them?" demanded Old Death.

"When can I see them?" repeated Jeffreys in a musing tone, as if he were giving the matter his most serious consideration: "why—I might hunt them up to-morrow night—in fact, I'm sure I could———"

"And you can make an appointment for me to see them the night after?" said Old-Death, with fiendish eagerness to consummate the atrocious vengeance which he had planned.

"I will undertake to do that, Mr. Bones," returned Jeffreys. "Shall I explain to them the nature of the business before they see you, or not?"

"No—let me see them first!" said Old Death. "Or stay—you may sound 'em about the resurrection business—but mention no names at all. Don't tell them who has employed you to treat with them——"

"Mr. Bones is a good judge of people's faces," observed Mrs. Bunce; "and knows by their looks whether they're to be trusted or not."

"Generally speaking, I do—generally speaking," said Old Death. "Now, for instance," he added, staring from beneath his shaggy, overhanging brows, full upon the countenance of Jeffreys, "I know that you're faithful—and I can trust you."

The man to whom these words were addressed, met the searching look fixed upon him with an unchanging cheek and eyes that quailed not; although for a moment he feared lest Old Death had suddenly entertained some suspicion concerning him. But it seemed that the ancient miscreant, with all his boasted skill in reading the human physiognomy, was on this occasion completely at fault.

"To tell you the truth, Jeffreys," he continued, "I never liked the looks of the Snammer: but I thought that good pay would make him faithful. However, he will yet repent his conduct towards me—and so shall Josh Pedler. If it wasn't for their infernal treachery, my vengeance would be by this time in a fair way towards prompt and speedy gratification. For if that Earl was allowed to go scot-free—if I didn't punish him—aye, and fearfully too—for all the injuries he has done to me, I should go mad! My property all destroyed—my riches taken from me—the very house that was so useful to me——"

"Don't take on so, Mr. Bones!" interrupted Mrs. Bunce, in a coaxing manner. "Come—shall I put a leetle brandy on the table?"

"No—gin!" ejaculated Old Death savagely: then, turning towards Jeffreys, he said, "You won't bring those friends of yours here, mind, the night after to-morrow: it will be quite time to let them know where I live and where business will afterwards lead them to meet me, when I have satisfied myself that they are of the right sort."

"You don't think I would ask you to employ any one that I wasn't sure of?" exclaimed Jeffreys, affecting an angry tone.

"No—no, my good fellow," hastily responded Old Death: "but experience—experience teaches us much; and my experience is greater than yours. Come—take a glass of gin-and-water, and don't be annoyed. I didn't mean to vex you."

"Say no more about it, then," observed Jeffreys. "Where shall we meet the night after to-morrow?"

"Let me see," mused Benjamin Bones aloud: "I have an appointment for that evening in the actual neighbourhood of St. Luke's Church; and there's a flash ken in Helmet Row, called the *Stout House*. We will meet there between ten and eleven."

"Agreed," said Jeffreys. "Have you any farther instructions?"

"None—none, my good fellow," answered Old Death: "only don't promise your two friends too much for the services required of them. You see how I have lost already by those scoundrels Pedler and Splint: but I will be even with them—I will!"

"The two persons I shall introduce to you will do your work well and cheap, Mr. Bones," replied Jeffreys; "and I am sure you will be satisfied. I shall now be off—because I may perhaps find them to-night. At all events we meet at the *Stout House*, Helmet Row, the night after next."

"Exactly," said Old Death. "By the way, if you run against Tim the Snammer or Josh Pedler, just try and find out where they are to be met with, and let me know."

"I'll bear it in mind," answered Jeffreys.

He then took his departure, well pleased at the success which had hitherto attended his proceedings in working out the designs and fulfilling the instructions of his master.

But who was that master?—and where dwelt the mysterious personage? Ah! these were points which defied all conjecture.

On the following evening, shortly before nine o'clock, Jeffreys was pacing Wilderness Row, in obedience to the appointment arranged by his employer.

He was not kept waiting many minutes, ere the youth Cæsar accosted him.

"Our master," said the lad, "has sent me to inquire of you the result of your interview with Old Death; and he desires me to assure you that he is well satisfied with your conduct of last night, inasmuch as you effectually amused your companions until their captors came up. But what of Old Death?"

"He has completely fallen into the snare laid for him," answered Jeffreys; "and will meet me and *my two friends*," he added significantly, "at the *Stout House*, Helmet Row, to-morrow night between ten and eleven."

"Good!" observed Cæsar. "Wilton and another of our master's retainers, both dressed in a suitable manner, will meet you at that place to-morrow night shortly before ten, so that you may have time to arrange the plan of proceeding together, before Old Death makes his appearance."

"I shall not fail to be there at a quarter to ten," answered Jeffreys. "Have you any further orders for me?"

"Yes," replied Cæsar: "listen! To-morrow you must endeavour to find out the abode of one Tidmarsh, a friend of Old Death's."

"That will be easily accomplished to-morrow night when I meet Benjamin Bones," said Jeffreys. "You are aware that the object of my appointment with him, is to introduce to him two friends of mine who will undertake to dig up the remains of Tom Rainford, the famous highwayman."

"Yes—yes," said Cæsar hastily.

"Well," continued Jeffreys, "I am supposed to be the leader of the party by whom that task is to be performed; and I shall tell Old Death that he must send Tidmarsh with me in the morning to point out the place where Rainford is buried. He will then let me know where Tidmarsh lives; or else will at once make him write a note to that person to arrange an appointment."

"I understand," said Cæsar. "But suppose that Old Death will do neither, alleging that he will call himself on Tidmarsh and send him to meet you on the following morning at some place named? In this case all will be wrong, because Old Death is to be captured to-morrow night on his way home. Had you not better call in Seven Dials to-morrow morning, tell Old Death that you have found your friends and made the appointment with them for the evening, and then ask him to let Tidmarsh at once afford you the clue you will require to—to—the grave of Rainford?" asked the lad, his voice trembling and hesitating slightly as he uttered the concluding words of his question.

"I understand you perfectly, Cæsar," replied Jeffreys. "Leave it to me to manage as our master desires: I will undertake to be able to give Wilton good news of Tidmarsh to-morrow night."

"Our master will rely upon you," said the youth. "Meantime farewell;"—and he hurried rapidly away, Jeffreys not offering to follow him.

CHAPTER XC.
THE NEW JUSTICE OF THE PEACE.

Sir Christopher Blunt was seated in his library, on the same evening which saw the interview between Cæsar and Jeffreys; and his countenance was animated with a glow of indescribable delight as he glanced his eyes over several letters which he opened one after another.

He was dressed in a very elegant manner; though he had somewhat punished his corns by persisting to wear tight boots in order to make his feet look small, and he might have felt a trifle or so easier at the waist if he had not tied his waistcoat strings so tight. But if Sir Christopher Blunt chose to enhance the fascinations of his appearance by converting himself into a voluntary victim of that all-powerful Inquisition called "Fashion,"—if Sir Christopher Blunt, like a great many other silly, old gentlemen of this age, smiled at his self-martyrdom with the equanimity of a saint broiling on a gridiron,—it is no business of any body save the Sir Christopher Blunt aforesaid.

In spite of the pinching boots end the excruciating tightness of the figured silk waistcoat, the worthy knight was in a most glorious humour. It was not because fortune had favoured him with great wealth: he was so accustomed to riches by this time that a little poverty might have proved an agreeable variation, if only for the excitement of the thing. Neither was it the pleasing fact that his dear spouse had been in such a hurry to present him with a son and heir, that she could not wait longer than three months after their marriage;—for Sir Christopher was already accustomed to the cries of the child, and somehow or another was growing less and less proud of his paternal honours every day, the reasoning of Dr. Wagtail relative to the premature birth appearing more and more illogical each time he sate himself down to reflect upon it. "Then, what *was* the cause of the worthy knight's joyousness and good humour on the evening in question?" demands the impatient reader: to which query we hasten to reply—"Sir Christopher Blunt had just been placed in the commission of the peace, and congratulatory letters from his friends were pouring in on all sides!"

"Well, upon my word, this is very pleasant," said Sir Christopher to himself: "I should not have thought that I was so beloved! Not a man in England has such a host of dear, disinterested friends as I seem to possess. Scarcely does my name appear in the *Gazette*, when—whisk! in come the letters, by twopenny post and general—by hand and by conveyance! And some too are from people that really had no particular cause to be so devoted to me—people that I never spoke to six times in my life! But let's see—what have we here? A sheet of foolscap completely covered—and crossed in some parts.

God bless me! what a letter. Why, it must have taken the man an hour to write it; and I am sure it will take me two to read it. But who does it come from? *Henry Atkins!* Henry Atkins—who the deuce is he? Oh! I remember—the gentleman who allowed me a seat in his pew at Hackney, when I went to lodge there four years ago for the benefit of my health. Well, it's very kind of him to write me this long letter of congratulation—for I never exchanged ten words with him in my life. But let's see what he says. '*My dear Blunt.*' Very friendly indeed! '*It was with indescribable delight and supreme satisfaction that I heard of your appointment to a position which no man in Europe can fill with more suitable dignity than yourself.*' Well, come—that's a good beginning. '*Your business habits, your high standing in society, your great name, your unblemished character, your brilliant talents, and your immense benevolence, render you most eligible to fill that office, and most competent to discharge its functions.*' Upon my honour, it's very prettily worded—quite sonorous! It reads admirably. And this sincere and heart-felt congratulation is from a man whom I scarcely know. But he seems to know me well enough, however. '*In these times of agricultural distress and commercial embarrassment—in this age when England's heaven is overcast with lowering clouds, and the storms of anarchy and discontent menace us imminently—it is delightful to reflect that authority is so judiciously entrusted as in your case.*' That's the best rounded period I ever met with in my life. What a clever, far-seeing, shrewd man this Atkins must be: and what an idiot I have been not to cultivate the acquaintance of such a sincere friend! '*But it is chiefly your benevolence—it is principally your boundless charity, which is the theme of all praise, which is chanted by all tongues, and which is hymned beneath every roof throughout the length and breadth of the land.*' Well, I could not have believed that I was so famous—particularly on that score. However, it must be so, since Atkins says it is. '*Yes, my dear Blunt,*'—very friendly indeed!—'*it is your boundless charity, your anxiety to do good to deserving persons, that will hand your name down to posterity, and send it floating like an eternal bark, over the waves of Time.*' Egad! that's splendid. Milton never wrote any thing finer. I have never read Milton, it is true; but I am sure Atkins can beat him. Let us see how it goes on. '*It is under these impressions, and acting in obedience to these convictions, that I have ventured to address you.*' And I am very glad he has: I'll write to him presently and tell him I shall always be delighted to hear from him. Let's see—where was I? Oh!—'*ventured to address you for the purpose of soliciting your aid under very peculiar circumstances.*' Hem! I don't like that sentence so much as the others. '*I am a man possessing a large family and very limited means; and business having been lately indifferent, I have fallen into sad arrears with my landlord.*' The style gets worse—that's clear! '*At this present moment I have an execution in my house for forty pounds; and when I look around me, I behold a distracted wife on one side, and a grim bailiff in possession on the other.*' This is the least interesting part of his letter: that period was not at all well turned. Milton beats him hollow there.—'*If, then, my dear Blunt,*'——damned familiar, though, with his '*dear Blunt,*' upon my honour!——'*If, then, my dear Blunt, you would favour me with the loan of fifty pounds for three months,*'——Confound his impudence!" ejaculated the knight, throwing the letter into the waste-paper basket. "A man I know nothing of—who knows nothing of me—who never saw me ten times in his life—to ask me for fifty pounds! It is absurd—preposterous!"

And the knight's countenance underwent a complete change, which lasted for several minutes, until its joyous expression was gradually recalled by the perusal of letters which contained congratulations only, without soliciting favours.

Presently a servant entered the room, and stated that a gentleman named Lykspittal requested an interview with Sir Christopher Blunt.

"Show him up—show him up immediately!" exclaimed the knight. "I have been expecting the gentleman this last half-hour," he added, looking at his watch. "It is now nine—and he was to have been here soon after eight."

The domestic withdrew, and speedily returned, ushering in a thin, pale, elderly, sneaking-looking man, dressed in a suit of black which would not bear too close an inspection in the day-time, but passed off well enough by candle-light.

"Sit down, Mr. Lykspittal—pray sit down," said the knight, looking, in contrast with the visitor, just like a wax figure recently added to Madame Tussaud's exhibition, so bright was the red of his animated cheeks, so glossy his coat and trowsers, and so stiff and starch his attitude. "You have been well recommended to me, Mr. Lykspittal, by a friend to whom your literary labours have given complete satisfaction, and who speaks highly of you as a man in whom implicit confidence may be placed."

"I am very much obliged to you, Sir Christopher, for the kind opinion you have formed of me," answered the visitor in a tone of the deepest veneration and respect, and appearing by his manner as if he did not dare to say that his soul was his own. "Allow me to congratulate you, Sir Christopher, on your appointment as one of his Majesty's Justices of the Peace. I am convinced a worthier selection could not have been made."

"Well, you're very kind, Mr. Lykspittal," returned the knight. "All my friends seem to agree that the Lord Chancellor acted in a wise and prudent manner in placing my name before his most gracious Majesty for the purpose: and it will be my endeavour, Mr. Lykspittal," added Sir Christopher, pompously, "to discharge the duties of my office with credit to myself and benefit to my country."

"It is not every one who possesses your advantages, Sir Christopher," observed his visitor, in a cringing tone and with a sycophantic manner which would have disgusted any person endowed with good sense and proper feeling; but which were particularly pleasing to the shallow-pated, self-sufficient old beau.

"At the same time," said Sir Christopher, "whatever advantages I may possess—whatever be those merits which have placed me in this—this——"

"Enviable and responsible," suggested Mr. Lykspittal, meekly.

"Enviable and responsible position," continued the knight, adopting the epithets as coolly and quietly as if they were prompted by his own imagination;—"at the same time," he said, "it will not be amiss if certain measures be adopted to—to——"

"Enhance the popularity of your name," observed Mr. Lykspittal, in the same low, cringing, and meek tone as before.

"Just so," exclaimed the knight. "In fact, I mean to take a high stand in the county—to put myself more forward than I have hitherto done—to attend public meetings and——"

"Public dinners," suggested Mr. Lykspittal.

"Exactly," said Sir Christopher: "in a word, I want to—to——"

"Become a public man," added the ready-witted gentleman, whose business it was to furnish ideas to those who furnished him with cash in return.

"You understand me as well as I understand myself, Mr. Lykspittal," observed the knight.

"It's my business, sir," was the answer. "Besides, you are so enlightened and enlightening a man, Sir Christopher, that you may be regarded as a lamp constantly diffusing its lustre even upon the darkest and most chaotic ideas. Pardon me, Sir Christopher, for being so bold as to express my opinion: but it is the truth—and I never flatter."

"I am convinced you speak with sincerity, my dear sir," said the new Justice of the Peace, playing with his eye-glass. "Well, then, Mr. Lykspittal—to go back to our original subject—the subject of this interview—I think you fully comprehend me: indeed, I know that you do. It is my object and my determination to take a high position in the county—so that I may in a short time reckon upon the honour of being one of its representatives in Parliament."

"Very easily managed, Sir Christopher," said Mr. Lykspittal. "The electors would be proud of such a man as yourself:—pardon me for making the observation—but I never flatter. In the first instance, however, it is necessary that they should know you well."

"Now we are coming to the point, my dear sir," exclaimed the knight.

"Will you permit me to offer my suggestions?" asked Mr. Lykspittal, in a tone of insinuating meekness.

"Certainly—by all means. Proceed."

"Well, Sir Christopher, in the first place I should propose that a pamphlet be written on some taking subject, and addressed to your worship," continued Mr. Lykspittal. "Suppose we say the *Corn Laws*—or *Prison Discipline*—or *Catholic Emancipation*—or *Church Extension*—or *Parliamentary Reform*—or *Labour in Factories*——"

"All good subjects, Mr. Lykspittal—all good subjects," observed the knight. "But I do not mind telling you in private, that I know nothing about any one of them."

"Of course not, Sir Christopher," exclaimed Mr. Lykspittal. "It is not to be expected that a man of your standing will trouble himself about the details of such trivial matters. But which side will you take—the Liberal or the Tory?"

"Oh! the Tory, by all means!" cried Sir Christopher.

"Very good, my dear sir," said Mr. Lykspittal. "It is all the same to me—I can write on one side as well as on the other. Suppose, then, we take up the subject of *Catholic Emancipation*, which begins to make a great noise.[40] A pamphlet must be got up, supposed to be written by '*A Friend to the Established Church*,' and it must be in the shape of a letter addressed to yourself. I should begin by saying,—'SIR,—*The interest which you are known to take in this great and important question—the perseverance you have manifested in making yourself acquainted with all the bearings of the case, its certain results and its inevitable influences—the stanch and long-tried ardour which you have evinced in maintaining and upholding the institutions of the Established Church—the numerous proofs which you have given of your attachment to the Protestant Faith—and the fact that the eyes of the whole country are upon you as a man resolved, at any personal sacrifice, and at all individual risks, to oppose all dangerous innovations and resist all perilous changes,—these motives, sir, have induced me to address the following pages to you.*'"

"Nothing can be better, Mr. Lykspittal!" exclaimed the knight. "I should, however, be glad if you will, in the course of the pamphlet, allude especially—and more than once, too—to the fact that I have been the artificer of my own fortune—that I raised myself from nothing—and that the greatest mistake the livery-men of Portsoken ever made was to reject me as a candidate for the aldermanic gown of that ward."

"I shall not forget, Sir Christopher," observed Mr. Lykspittal.

"And you may add, my dear sir," continued the knight, pompously, "that you are well aware that circumstances have since occurred to make me rejoice at that rejection."

"I will declare it to be a well known fact amongst all your friends," said the accommodating literary gentleman.

"And you may touch upon the zeal—the ability—and the efficiency with which I performed the duties of the shrievalty—the very arduous duties of that office," observed the new Justice of the Peace.

"I shall certainly do so, Sir Christopher," replied Mr. Lykspittal; "and it will only be telling the exact truth."

"You may likewise touch upon the reward which it graciously pleased the illustrious Prince to confer upon me," continued the magistrate: "I mean—the honour of knighthood."

"As a matter of course, my dear sir; and never was that title bestowed upon a gentleman better calculated to wear it worthily."

"I thank you, Mr. Lykspittal," returned Sir Christopher, "for your very flattering opinion of me. When can the pamphlet be got ready?"

"I shall set about it immediately, sir," was the answer. "The moment it is published, you must seize upon some point, which I shall purposely leave open for discussion, and write a letter to a morning newspaper, declaring that you agree with the general tenour of the work, but that you totally dissent from that particular doctrine."

"Decidedly," said Sir Christopher. "You will then write a reply, through the same channel, and signed '*A Friend of the Established Church*.'"

"That is my intention. We shall thus excite an interest relative to the pamphlet, and your name, Sir Christopher, will be kept before the public. The discussion may lead to a second pamphlet——"

"Stay!" exclaimed the knight, smiling with the brightness of the idea which had just struck him: "we will manage better than all that! You shall write a pamphlet which you must address to me in the terms just now specified by you; but the work must contain throughout opinions totally opposed to mine, and the object of the pamphlet must seem to be my conversion to your particular way of thinking. Then I must write another pamphlet in answer—or rather, you must write it for me; and you must cut up, hip and thigh, and completely refute all the doctrines set forth in the first pamphlet. In fact, you must start a theory in that first pamphlet, and knock it down altogether in the second, which must be supposed to come from me."

"A very ingenious idea, my dear sir," said Mr. Lykspittal, "and just such an one as I should have expected from a man of your enlightened mind. I admire the plan amazingly; and will set to work at once."

"Very good," exclaimed Sir Christopher. "I will write you a cheque for thirty guineas on account. You will of course make all the necessary arrangements with the printer and stationer, and you may apply to me for money as you require it. I shall do the thing handsomely, and spend fifty pounds at least in advertising each pamphlet."

Mr. Lykspittal coincided altogether in the propriety of these intentions—indeed, he never was known to differ from a patron in the whole course of his life; and, having received the cheque, he took his leave, walking backwards to the door in homage to the great man who had just been placed in the commission of the peace.

Almost immediately after the departure of Mr. Lykspitttal, a servant entered, announcing Captain O'Blunderbuss.

---

40. The reader will observe that this was said in the year 1827, *before* the emancipation of the Catholics took place.

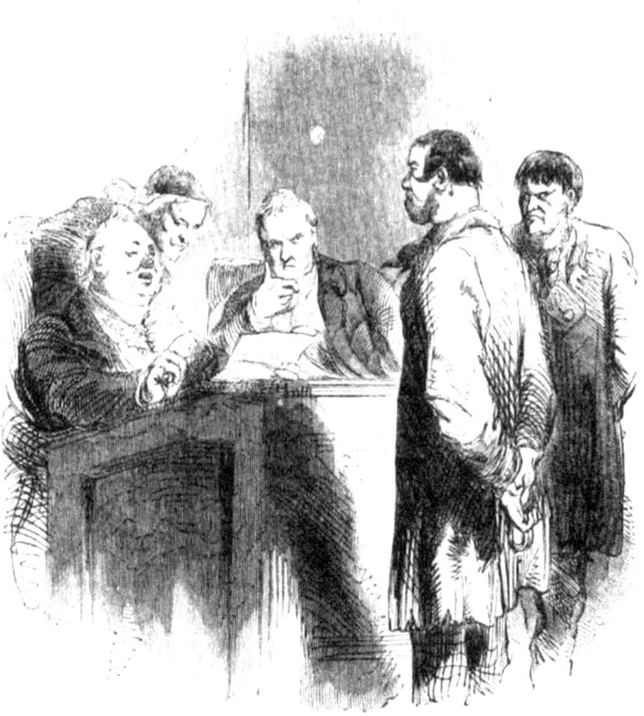

CHAPTER XCI.
CAPTAIN O'BLUNDERBUSS AGAIN.—ANOTHER STRANGE VISITOR.

Sir Christopher Blunt was a man having many antipathies. Since his rejection for Portsoken he had disliked all aldermen, individually and collectively; and since his union with the present Lady Blunt, he had conceived a violent aversion for all lady's-maids. He abominated Italian organ-players, and hated mendicants. Many other dislikes had Sir Christopher Blunt;—but of the whole batch, none was more settled, more genuine, and more sincere than his antipathy for Irishmen generally, and Captain O'Blunderbuss in particular.

His interview with Mr. Lykspittal had left complacent smiles upon his countenance;—but these suddenly yielded to clouds of the darkest description when the domestic announced the name of that dreadful and dreaded man.

"Be the powers, and how is your wor-r-r-ship?" roared Captain O'Blunderbuss, at the top of his stentorian voice, rattling the r most awfully, as he strode towards the knight with outstretched hand: "tip us your fin, my hearty—and allow me to congratulate ye on your appintment to the Commission of the Pace!"

Thus speaking, the captain shook with such exceeding violence the member which he metaphorically designated as a fin, that the wretched Sir Christopher groaned aloud, while tears started into his eyes.

"Be Jasus! and it's proud I am to own ye as my frind, Sir Christopher!" continued the gallant officer, not observing the pain which his proof of extreme cordiality inflicted upon the worthy knight: then, throwing himself into a chair, he exclaimed, "That rascal of a lacquey of your's told me you was out; but I wasn't to be desayved in such a gross fashion any how. So I just tould him my mind—"

"And what was that, captain?" asked the knight, in a half terrified—half sulky tone.

"That he was an insolent blackguard, Sir Christopher," returned O'Blunderbuss emphatically; "and be Jasus! I was just on the point of taching him how to behave towards his superiors, when I saw the gentleman who was last with ye coming out, and he tould me that your wor-r-r-ship was at home."

"But I—I am very particularly engaged, captain," said the knight; "and if you would excuse me now—another time I shall be happy—when you are passing this way——"

"Be the holy poker! and there's no time like the prisint!" interrupted the captain; "and as I want just to have a little cozie chat with you, my dear frind, may be ye'll orther up the whiskey at once, and so save us the throuble of talking dry-lipped."

"Really, Captain O'Blunderbuss," stammered the knight, "as a gentleman—as a—ahem—a person being in the Commission of the Peace—I—must protest against—this—this intrusion——"

"Inthrusion do ye call it?" vociferated the captain: then, after a few moments' pause, during which he surveyed Sir Christopher in a most ferocious manner, he suddenly assumed a milder demeanour, and, coolly ringing the bell, said, "Be Jasus! I'll save ye the throuble of giving any orthers at all, my frind."

"Captain O'Blunderbuss," cried Sir Christopher, plucking up a spirit, "I will not be treated in this manner! One would think that I am not master in my own house. I have already told you that I am very particularly occupied with business—in consequence of my recent appointment to——"

"To the Commission of the Pace!" added the captain. "Well, my frind—and we are going to dhrink success to the Commission and the Pace and all the rist of it. My good fellow," he continued, addressing himself to the footman who now entered the room, "bring up the whiskey and hot wather; with the sugar and a lemon—d'ye hear?"

"Don't do any such thing," exclaimed Sir Christopher, now in a furious passion. "Who are you, sir, that thus dares to give orders in the house of—of an ex-sheriff and an actual magistrate?" demanded the knight, in a stern and pompous tone, for the presence of the servant seemed to be a kind of protection beneath the shield of which the old gentleman grew every moment more valourous.

"Be the powers! and that same is soon answered," said the captain, rising from his chair and drawing himself up to his full height. "Is it myself that ye are afther enquiring about, Sir Christopher? Be Jasus, then—it's Capthain O'Bluntherbuss, I am—of Bluntherbuss Park, Connemara; and it's a pair of pisthols I've got for any man who dares to insult that same Capthain O'Bluntherbuss. So, if you're for war-r-r, Sir Christopher-r-r," roared the gallant gentleman, "it shall be war-r-r; and if ye're for pace, let it be pace—and potheen!"

The captain looked so very terrible—grew so awfully red in the face—seemed to swell out so tremendously at the chest—and raised his voice to such a thundering tone, as he enunciated his name and that of his imaginary estate, that Sir Christopher's valour, like the courage of Bob Acres, oozed rapidly away, and the servant drew back as near the door as possible so as to be able to beat a retreat, in case of need, without any assistance from the warlike Irishman's foot.

"Is it war-r-r, or pace?" demanded the captain, seeing that the enemy was discomfited.

"Peace—peace, captain,—by all means," returned the knight, in a tremulous voice. "You'll alarm Lady Blunt—and—and make the dear baby cry—"

"It's pace—and potheen, sirrah," said the military gentleman, addressing himself in a tone of stern determination to the domestic, who instantly disappeared. "Now, my dear frind, ye're too impatient be half," continued the captain, resuming his chair and again speaking to the knight: "you don't give me time to explain to ye the nature of my business and the rayson of me calling; for sure and it was to tell ye how plazed your nev-vy Misther Frank Curtis is to think that ye're put in the Commission of the Pace—and how sorry he is to think that ye should have lost any thing by that scounthrel Howard—and how plazed he is to learn that your son and heir is flourishing just like a green bay-leaf—and how sorry he is to think that your frind Torrens should have got himself into such a tirrible pother—and how plazed he is to be able to send ye back the thrifling amount of five hunthred pounds which ye was kind enough to advance him t'other day—"

"Oh! he has done *that*, has he?" said Sir Christopher, rubbing his hands, and evidently getting into a better humour. "Well, I am glad he has fulfilled the little engagement, at all events; and I shall not hesitate to receive it, because—because I am sure he would not have sent it, if he couldn't have spared it."

"Your nev-vy, my dear sir, is a man of honour-r—like myself!" cried the captain, striking his breast very hard, so that it gave forth a hollow, rumbling sound, as if he had a small drum buttoned inside his frock-coat. "But, be the powers! here's the potheen; and it's over the glass that we'll settle the little business of the five hunthred pounds."

The servant placed the tray upon the table, and withdrew. Sir Christopher then, with the politeness of a man who is about to receive the payment of money which he had never expected, did the honours in a most affable manner, and only seemed contented when the captain, having poured half a tumbler of scalding hot toddy down his throat, declared that it was excellent!

"And now for the little business," resumed the gallant gentleman; and he forthwith began to fumble in his pockets, producing various pieces of paper, and discarding them one after the other as soon as he consecutively glanced at their contents. "That's not it, be the powers!" he said, laying down a piece of a play-bill;—"and that's not it, be the holy poker!" he added, throwing aside an old account of his washerwoman's: "nor yet that, be Jasus!" he continued, similarly disposing of a tailor's bill. "Why—what the blazes could I have done with the note?"

"Dear me, captain," observed Sir Christopher, in a tone of gentle remonstrance, "it is very imprudent of you to carry notes about loose in that way."

"So it is, my dear frind," returned the gallant gentleman; "but it's a fashion I have, d'ye see—and it's hard to break one-self of habits of the kind. Be the powers! and here it is at last!"

"All right—all right," said Sir Christopher, rubbing his hands.

"Ye can give me change out of a thousand pounds, can't ye, my dear frind?" demanded the captain, crunching a bit of paper in his hand as he spoke.

"Oh! I can write a cheque for the difference, you know," returned the knight. "I presume it's a note for a thousand pounds?"

"Just so," responded the captain; "and as good as a Bank of England note, be the powers— although 'tisn't quite payable at sight."

"Not payable at sight!" exclaimed Sir Christopher, in astonishment. "Why—I never heard of the Bank of England issuing notes that weren't payable on demand."

"Egad, nor I!" said Captain O'Blunderbuss. "But sure it isn't a Bank of England note at all, at all: it's just my own acceptance——"

"Your acceptance!" groaned the knight, his countenance becoming suddenly blank.

"Yes—be Jasus! and here it is, my dear frind," returned O'Blunderbuss, thrusting the rumpled slip of paper into Sir Christopher's hand. "It's as dacent a note for a promissory one as ever you'd wish to see, and as good as any of the palthry flimsy stuff that the Bank of England ever issued—or the Bank of Ould Ireland either: and that's not even saying enough for it."

Sir Christopher—looking indeed like a knight of the rueful countenance—turned the document over and over in his hands, having glanced impatiently at its contents, which were drawn out in the usual style of a bill of exchange, Captain O'Blunderbuss having accepted it in favour of Frank Curtis, for the amount of One Thousand Pounds, and at three months after date.

"Well, Sir Christopher, and what d'ye say to that, my old buck?" cried the captain, apparently surprised that the knight had not already expressed his admiration at the whole proceeding.

"What—what would you have me do with this?" asked Sir Christopher, in a hesitating manner; for the fact is, he could not think well of it, and he dared not speak ill of it.

"Is it what you should do with it?" vociferated the captain. "Arrah! and be Jasus, man, pay yourself out of it and write me a cheque for the balance."

"But, captain—I—I am no discounter," remonstrated the knight. "This little slip of paper is no use to me."

"Why! sirrah, and just now you was prepared to pay me the difference if it had been a Bank-note!" cried O'Blunderbuss. "D'ye suspict the thing, my frind? For if you mane to infer that it isn't as good as a Bank-note, it's a direct insult to myself; and, be the Lord Harry! it's me that'll resint it."

With these words, the captain assumed a most menacing attitude; and Sir Christopher was already in a dreadful fright lest he should be compelled to submit to this new demand on the part of the extortioner, when the footman entered to announce that a gentleman was waiting in the parlour down stairs to speak to him upon very particular and urgent business.

"You must excuse me for a few minutes, Captain O'Blunderbuss," said the knight, rising to quit the apartment.

"By all manes," cried that gentleman. "We can finish the little matther prisintly; and during your absence I'll pay my respicts to the potheen."

Sir Christopher accordingly repaired to the ground-floor parlour, where he beheld a venerable old man who rose from the sofa whereon he was seated, to greet him.

The stranger's aspect was indeed most imposing and respectable. From beneath a black silk skullcap flowed hair as white as silver; and his form seemed bowed by the weight of years. He was dressed in a complete suit of black, having knee-breeches, silk stockings, and shoes with large silver buckles. He supported himself by means of a stick, and appeared to walk with considerable difficulty.

"Pray be seated, sir," exclaimed the knight, already prepossessed in favour of his venerable-looking visitor, who resumed his place on the sofa in such a manner that the light of the lamp should not fall upon his countenance, which however appeared to be very pale and drawn up about the mouth with the wrinkles of age.

"Sir Christopher Blunt," said the old gentleman, in a tremulous voice, "I have ventured to intrude myself upon you, for the purpose of soliciting a very great favour. It is not of the ordinary nature of boons—it involves nothing of a pecuniary kind; for, thank heaven! I am placed far above the necessity of requiring such succour. Indeed, I may say that I enjoy affluence."

"Be assured, my dear sir," returned the knight, whose respect for his visitor was amazingly enhanced by this announcement,—"be assured that if I can serve you in any way—compatible with my honour as a man, and with my position as an individual in the Commission of the Peace——"

"It is just because you are a magistrate, Sir Christopher," interrupted the old gentleman, his tone becoming slightly less tremulous as he continued, "that I have now visited you. Not that any other magistrate would have failed to answer my purpose; but I have heard so much in your favour—the admirable manner in which you filled the office of Sheriff—the becoming way in which you presented the address to his present Majesty, when Prince Regent, and which was so very properly rewarded by the honour of Knighthood—the dignified manner in which you left the ungrateful livery-men of Portsoken to ruminate over their folly in bestowing their votes on your unworthy rival in that grand contest,—in a word, Sir Christopher, the whole tenour of your life, from the period when you were poor and friendless until now that you are a rich, esteemed, and influential member of society——"

"My dear sir—my dear sir," cried Sir Christopher, absolutely whimpering for joy at hearing his praises thus chanted by a gentleman of so venerable and saint-like an appearance; "I really must know you better—I—I—am quite at a loss to express my thanks—my——"

"No thanks are required by one who proclaims the truth," said the stranger, shaking his respectable old head in a solemn and imposing manner. "You will yet be a great—a very great man, Sir Christopher; or my experience, which is of four-score winters, is miserably—miserably deceived."

"Do you really think so, my dear sir?" exclaimed Sir Christopher. "Well, I suppose you know—or perhaps you may not—that I am a very stanch and sincere friend to the Established Church—that I am entirely opposed to Catholic Emancipation—that I have made the subject a profound study, and have devoted——I wish to God Lykspittal was here to prompt me," he muttered in an under-tone to himself.

"I was not exactly aware of all that, my good—my worthy Sir Christopher Blunt," responded the old gentleman; "but I respect you all the more now that I am acquainted with those facts. Indeed, I am proud and delighted to have the honour of your acquaintance—an honour for which I have long craved urgently. But let me return to the subject of my visit? I was saying that you could render me a great—a very great favour, and at the same time convince the world how zealous, how active, and how worthy a magistrate you are."

"My dear sir, I shall be quite delighted to serve you," cried Sir Christopher, catching also at the idea of serving himself by performing some duty which would put him in such a comfortable and desirable light before the world.

"The fact is, most estimable man," continued the stranger, his voice again becoming very tremulous, as if with deep emotion, so that Sir Christopher was positively affected in no ordinary degree, "two men, stained with a dreadful crime, and now in a position which precludes the possibility of their appearing before a magistrate, are anxious to confess their enormity to some competent authority; and I have selected you for the reasons which I mentioned just now."

"You have done me infinite honour, my dear sir," cried the knight. "I presume that this confession will be published to the world——"

"Decidedly so," interrupted the venerable stranger; "and your name will go forth as that of the zealous, trustworthy, and highly respectable magistrate who was selected under such peculiar circumstances to receive the confession."

"Really this is no favour which you ask of me, my venerable friend," exclaimed Sir Christopher, rejoiced at the lucky chance which thus gave promise of publishing his name in so remarkable a manner. "I shall be delighted to serve you in that or any other way. When do you require me to visit these unhappy men?"

"Immediately—at once," answered the old gentleman. "My own carriage is at the door; and we can proceed to the place of destination with a privacy which the nature of the circumstances renders imperative."

Sir Christopher rose and signified his readiness to accompany his venerable visitor, the joy which he experienced entirely obliterating in his mind all remembrance of the fact that he had left Captain O'Blunderbuss in his library.

Giving his arm to his new friend, who walked with considerable difficulty, Sir Christopher led him into the hall, where the knight only stopped for a moment to take down his hat from a peg. They then issued forth together, and Sir Christopher assisted the old gentleman to ascend the steps of the vehicle which was waiting. He then leapt in himself; and the footman belonging to the carriage had just closed the door, when Captain O'Blunderbuss rushed from the house, exclaiming, "Be the powers, and this is the greatest insult 'twas ever my misfortune to mate with in all my life!"

"Oh! the dreadful man!" murmured the knight, throwing himself back in the carriage in a state of despair.

"Sir Christopher-r-r!" cried the captain, thrusting his head in at the carriage window: "Sir Christopher-r-r!" he repeated, with a terrible rattling of the r: "is this the way ye mane for to trate a gintleman? Now, be the holy poker! if ye don't come forth and finish the little business——"

At this moment the captain was abruptly stopped short in a most unexpected manner; for the old gentleman, growing impatient of the delay, and perceiving that Sir Christopher was cruelly annoyed by the presence of the Irishman, suddenly dealt so well applied and vigorous a blow at the gallant officer, that his countenance disappeared in an instant from the window, and he rolled back upon the pavement, exclaiming, "Blood and thunther!" in a tone of mingled rage and astonishment.

At the same moment the coachman whipped his horses, and the vehicle rolled away with extraordinary rapidity; while a merry laugh burst from the lips of the venerable old gentleman who had so successfully discomfited the warlike captain.

As soon as Sir Christopher Blunt had recovered from the alarm and excitement which the conduct of Captain O'Blunderbuss had caused him, he was seized with a strange surprise, not altogether unaccompanied by vague fear, at the sudden demonstration of vigour and strength made by his companion. This feeling was enhanced by the youthful tones of the merry laugh, which lasted long after the performance of the pleasant feat; and the knight began to tremble with apprehension, when that same mysterious companion hastily drew up the windows and the wooden blinds of the carriage, the interior thus being thrown into a state of utter darkness.

"My dear Sir Christopher Blunt," said a voice, now tremulous no more, but still evidently disguised, "you will pardon me for having practised upon you a slight deception, which would indeed have been sustained until the end of the present adventure, had not the chastisement which I was tempted to administer to that bullying fellow convinced you that I cannot be an old gentleman of four-score. In all other respects no duplicity was practised upon you; for I am a great admirer of your character—the object I have in view is precisely the one I named to you—and I selected you to receive the confessions of the two men, because I knew no magistrate better qualified to answer the purpose in every way."

A faint degree of irony marked the manner in which these last words were uttered; but Sir Christopher Blunt observed it not—for he was now a prey to oppressive fears and vague apprehensions.

"Do not alarm yourself, my dear sir," resumed the stranger: "I pledge you my most solemn word of honour that no harm shall befall you. Circumstances which I cannot disclose render it necessary to observe all possible mystery in respect to the present transaction. To you the results will be just as I ere now promised. You will receive and attest the confession of two criminals; and in forty-eight hours the contents of that confession, coupled with an account of how you became possessed of it, will appear in every London newspaper. Thence the whole transaction will be transferred to the provincial press; and in less than a week, the name of Sir Christopher Blunt, Knight, and Justice of the Peace, will be published and proclaimed throughout these islands."

"And you really mean me no harm?" said Sir Christopher, considerably reassured as well as consoled by this intelligence.

"Give me your hand, my dear sir," exclaimed his companion. "There! And now I swear that as there is a God above us, you hold the hand of friendship in your's; and may that hand wither if I forfeit my word, or do you harm."

"I believe you, sir—I believe you," said the knight, pressing the hand which he held, with convulsive ardour. "But who are you that act thus mysteriously? what is your name? where do you live? and whither are we going?"

"Not one of those questions can I answer," was the reply; "and it is expressly to prevent you from ascertaining the route which we are pursuing that I have drawn up the wooden blinds. I must also inform you that ere we alight at the place where you will have to receive the confession of the two men, I must bind a handkerchief over your eyes, so that you may obtain no clue to the point of our present destination. Recollect, the event of this evening will give you an immense popularity: you will become the hero of one of the most romantic—one of the most extraordinary—one of the most unheard-of adventures that have ever occurred, or will again occur in this metropolis. You will be courted by all the rank, beauty, and fashion of the West End, to learn the narrative from your own lips; and if you write a novel founded upon the occurrence," added the stranger, again in a slight tone of unperceived irony, "you will instantaneously become the most popular author of the day."

"Upon my honour—my dear sir," said Sir Christopher, rubbing his hands, "I am not altogether sorry that—that—ahem!—that you should have pitched upon me to become the hero of this adventure: at the same time you must confess that never was a hero placed in a position so well calculated to alarm him."

"The character of a hero is not to be bought cheaply in the world," observed the knight's companion. "To become such a character, one must necessarily pass through extraordinary circumstances; and extraordinary circumstances are never without their degree of excitement."

"Very true, my dear sir—very true," said Sir Christopher. "But I don't care how extraordinary the circumstances may be, so long as I run no risk. It's the risk—the danger I care about; and I shall be very happy indeed, if I can become a hero—as you are pleased to call it—without undergoing any such peril."

"You shall become a hero, Sir Christopher, without having undergone the slightest danger," returned his companion; "and that's even more than can be said by people who go up in balloons or by men who put their heads into lions' mouths in menageries."

"Upon my honour, your observations are most true—most just," exclaimed the knight, now finding himself almost completely at his ease. "I suppose that if I do get my friend Lykspittal to write me———I mean, if I do write a novel founded on the occurrences of this night, you will have no objection to my putting in all our present conversation?"

"Oh! not the least!" cried the stranger. "It is however a great pity that the night is calm, serene, and beautiful."

"Why so?" enquired Sir Christopher, in a tone of profound astonishment.

"Simply because it would be such scope for a splendid opening, if there were a fearful storm, with all the usual accessories of thunder and lightning," observed the stranger, in a cool, quiet, but dry way. "Only fancy, now, something like this:—'*It was on a dark and tempestuous night—the wind blew in fitful gusts—the artillery of heaven roared awfully—the gleaming shafts of electric fluid shot in eccentric motion across the sky;*'———and so on."

"Upon my honour, that commencement would be truly grand!" cried the knight, altogether enraptured by the turn which his companion had given to the discourse. "And, after all, as it would be a novel, I might easily begin with the storm. Let me see—I must recollect that sentence which you composed so glibly. How did it run? Oh! I recollect:—'*It was on a dark and tempestiferous night—the wind roared—the artillery blew in fitting gusts—the streaming shafts of electricity shot across the eccentric sky.*' Eh? that will do, I think," exclaimed Sir Christopher, rubbing his hands joyously. "You see I have not got such a very bad memory, my dear sir."

"Not at all," answered the stranger; "and I should certainly advise you, Sir Christopher, not to lose sight of the novel. If you publish it by subscription, you may put down my name for half a dozen copies."

"But I don't know your name," cried the knight. "And yet," he added, after a moment's pause, "I suppose you must have one."

"I believe that I have," responded the stranger, in a tone suddenly becoming solemn—even mournful; and it struck Sir Christopher that his ear caught the sound of a half-stifled sigh.

But he had not many instants to reflect upon this occurrence—nor even to continue the discourse upon the topic which had so much interested him; for the carriage suddenly stopped, and his companion immediately said, "Now Sir Christopher, you must permit me to blindfold you."

The operation was speedily completed; and the stranger led the knight from the vehicle, into a house, the door of which immediately closed behind them. Up a flight of stairs they then proceeded, and entered a room, where the stranger desired Sir Christopher to remove the bandage.

As soon as this was done, and the knight had recovered his powers of vision, he found himself in a well-furnished room, with the shutters closed, the curtains drawn, and a lamp standing in the middle of a table spread with wine and refreshments of a luxurious description.

His companion still retained the garb and disguise, but no longer affected the decrepitude of old age; and, seating himself with his back to the light, he invited Sir Christopher to take wine with him.

They then sate chatting for upwards of half an hour, when the sound of several footsteps ascending the stairs fell upon their ears: the door opened—and two men entered, leading between them a gentleman with a bandage over his eyes.

The two men retired,—and the stranger desired the gentleman to remove the bandage, adding, "Dr. Lascelles, you will pardon this apparent outrage, the motives of which have doubtless been explained to you by my dependants."

"I am led to believe that my presence is required to witness the confession of two criminals," said the physician, affecting complete ignorance alike of the mysterious master of the house and his affairs; "and if no treachery be intended towards me, I do not feel inclined to complain much of the treatment I have already received."

"I am delighted to hear you express yourself in these moderate terms," observed the prime mover of those widely ramified schemes which are now occupying the reader's attention. "Allow me to introduce you to a gentleman whose name is doubtless familiar to you—Sir Christopher Blunt:" then, turning towards the knight, he added, "Sir Christopher, this is Dr. Lascelles, the eminent physician."

"I think I have had the honour to meet Sir Christopher Blunt on a former occasion—at Lady Hatfield's," said the doctor, offering the knight his hand.

"It is therefore a strange coincidence which has thus brought you together again under such circumstances as the present," observed the stranger. "But you are both no doubt anxious to depart hence as speedily as possible, and I will not detain you longer than is absolutely necessary."

He then rang a bell; and in a few minutes four of his dependants entered the room, leading in Tim the Snammer and Josh Pedler, both strongly bound with cords, and having handkerchiefs over their eyes. These bandages were removed—the two villains cast rapid and searching glances around them—the stranger ordered them to be seated and his dependants to retire—and the business of that memorable night commenced.

CHAPTER XCII.
THE CONFESSION.

"Sir Christopher Blunt," said the stranger, "in your capacity of one of his Majesty's Justices of the Peace, you will have the kindness to receive the confession of the two men now before you; and you, Dr. Lascelles, as a gentleman of the highest respectability, will witness the present proceedings."

Thus speaking, he drew a writing-table close up to the place where Sir Christopher Blunt was sitting; and the knight, inflated with the pride of his official station, and conscious of the importance of the part which he was now enacting, assumed as dignified and solemn a deportment as possible. A Bible was produced; and he directed the two prisoners to be sworn, the stranger administering the oath.

"Now, my men," said the Justice of the Peace, "it is my duty to hear and receive any confession which you may have to make to me. But I give you due warning that it is to be published, and, from what I have already been told, will be used elsewhere. Remember, also, that you are now upon your oaths; and you must consider yourselves in just the same position as if you were in a regular police-court, under usual circumstances."

Having thus delivered himself of what he believed to be an admirable prelude to the proceedings, Sir Christopher glanced complacently towards Dr. Lascelles, as much as to say, "That was rather good, I flatter myself;" and the physician responded with a sign of approval. The knight then fixed his eyes in a searching manner upon the two prisoners, who, however, appeared to be much less in awe of the magisterial dignity than of the presence of the mysterious stranger, at whom they from time to time cast furtive looks of terror and supplication.

"Sir Christopher Blunt," said that individual, who throughout the proceedings spoke in a feigned tone, and sate in such a manner that the light never once fell fully upon his countenance, "it is now necessary to remind you that a gentleman with whom you are well acquainted, and whose name is Torrens, is now in a criminal gaol, charged with the murder of Sir Henry Courtenay."

"I heard the news with grief, and indeed with incredulity as to the truth of the accusation," observed the knight.

"Ask those men, sir," said the stranger, in a low and impressive voice, "what they know of that foul assassination."

"God bless me!" exclaimed Sir Christopher, much agitated: "surely these men now before me are not the—the——"

"The real murderers of Sir Henry Courtenay!" added the stranger solemnly.

"Is this possible?" cried the Justice of the Peace, surveying the prisoners with apprehension and horror.

"That's the confession we have to make, your worship," said Tim the Snammer, in a dogged tone.

"Dreadful! dreadful!" murmured the knight: then, somewhat mastering his emotions, he asked, "What is your name?"

"Timothy Splint, your worship," was the reply.

"And your's?" demanded Sir Christopher, making notes as he proceeded.

"Joshua Pedler, your worship."

"Where do you live?—and what are you?" were the next questions.

"Where we *did* live, your worship means," said Tim the Snammer; "but it doesn't much signify answering that query—since we don't live now where we used to do; and as for what we are, your worship can pretty well guess, now that we've confessed having murdered Sir Henry Courtenay—which was all through a mistake."

"A mistake!" repeated Sir Christopher.

"Yes, sir," continued the Snammer; "and I'll tell you all about it."

"Speak slow—very slow," said the knight; "because I shall commit to paper every word you utter, remember."

"Well, sir," resumed Timothy Splint; "it happened in this way. Me and my companion here, Joshua Pedler, took it into our heads to break into Torrens Cottage, for no good purpose, as you may suppose."

"To rob the house—eh?" said Sir Christopher.

"Just so, your worship. Well, we reached the Cottage between twelve and one o'clock at night—or nearer one, I should think—and looking through the chinks of the shutters, for there was a light in the parlour, we saw a pile of gold and a heap of notes on the table, and a gentleman asleep on the sofa."

"You follow this man, Dr. Lascelles?" said Sir Christopher, turning towards the physician.

"Word for word," was the reply.

"Go on, then," exclaimed the knight.

"We opened the front-door in a jiffey, your worship, and without making any noise," continued Splint; "and we went into the parlour. Josh Pedler secured the notes and gold; and I held my clasp-knife close to the throat of the gentleman sleeping on the sofa."

"Did you know who he was?" demanded the knight.

"Not a bit of it, your worship. We took him for Mr. Torrens, as a matter of course," continued the Snammer. "Josh Pedler went to ransack the sideboard, and upset a sugar-basin, or some such thing in the drawer. The gentleman awoke, and was just on the point of crying out, when I drew the clasp-knife across his throat."

"Merciful goodness!" exclaimed Sir Christopher, shuddering from head to foot, and glancing uneasily around him.

"Shocking! shocking!" said the doctor, with unfeigned emotion.

"The very knife that I did it with was in my pocket," observed Tim the Snammer, "when we was made prisoners and brought here."

The stranger, who had remained silent for some time, now rose from his seat, and took from the mantel the fatal weapon, which he laid upon the table before Sir Christopher, saying, "This is collateral evidence of the truth of the deposition now made."

"Well, upon my honour," observed the knight, recoiling from the ominous-looking instrument, "I have commenced my magisterial functions in an extraordinary—I may say, unheard-of manner. But let the prisoner proceed with his confession."

"I've very little more to say, your worship," answered the Snammer. "As soon as the deed was done, I could have wished it to be undone; and I know that my companion in trouble here, wished the same. We didn't go with the intention of doing it: it come upon us by itself, like—and I hope mercy will be showed us," he added, with a significant glance of appeal towards the mysterious individual of whom he seemed to be so much in awe.

"You and your comrade then left the house immediately, I suppose?" said Sir Christopher, interrogatively.

"Exactly so, your worship," replied Timothy Splint.

"And do you," continued the knight, addressing himself to Joshua Pedler, "admit the truth of all that your companion now states?"

"Every word of it, your worship," answered the man.

"We must therefore suppose," observed Dr. Lascelles, "that Mr. Torrens, upon discovering the dreadful deed, feared lest suspicion should fall upon himself, and buried the corpse in the garden where it was found."

"True!" said Sir Christopher. "And now, Joshua Pedler, you will inform me what you did with the money which you took away with you."

"I divided it, sir; and the big notes was changed into small ones," was the answer. "When me and my companion here was made prisoners, we had ever so much of the money about us; and it was took from us."

The stranger produced from his pocket a small parcel which he handed to Sir Christopher, saying, "There is the amount taken from the two prisoners."

"Very good," said Sir Christopher: then, after a few moments' profound reflection, he turned towards Dr. Lascelles, in whose ear he whispered these words, "To me it is very clear that those men have confessed the truth, and that they are the dreadful villains they represent themselves to be. But, as this statement is to be published, in connexion with our names, we must render the evidence *against* those fellows as complete and satisfactory as possible."

"I am perfectly of your way of thinking, Sir Christopher," returned the doctor, also speaking in a low whisper. "Since we are here on such an unpleasant business, we must do our duty effectually."

"Then those men should be examined separately in respect to the very minutest details of their self-accusing evidence," said the knight, still addressing himself in an under-tone to the physician; "or else the world will immediately declare that the whole thing was a mere farce, contrived by some of Torrens' friends to save him, and of which you and I were the dupes and the instruments."

"A very just fear on your part, Sir Christopher," observed the doctor, who, from the little he knew of the knight, would not have given him credit for so much penetration and forethought.

"But—but," said Sir Christopher, "I hardly like to propose it to the gentleman who had us brought here——"

"Oh! I will take that duty upon myself," interrupted Dr. Lascelles; and, immediately turning towards the stranger—who was however no stranger to him—he said in a loud and firm tone, "We wish to examine these men separately."

"Certainly," was the reply; and the mysterious master of the house forthwith rang the bell.

Wilton answered the summons, and was ordered to conduct Joshua Pedler into an adjoining room.

When this command was obeyed, and the domestic had led the prisoner away, Sir Christopher proceeded to question Timothy Splint again.

"You said just now that when you looked through the window, you saw a gentleman sleeping on the sofa? Now, did your companion also peep through the crevices in the shutters?"

"He did, your worship," was the answer.

"And which way was the gentleman lying?"

"With his feet towards the window, and his head on that end of the sofa which was nearest to the door."

"And when you both went into the house, who entered first?"

"Myself, your worship."

"And when you went away again, who departed first?"

"I think Josh Pedler was in advance—in fact, I'm sure he was, because I remember shutting the front-door behind me."

"Which side of the table were the pile of gold and the heap of notes on?" inquired Sir Christopher, racking his brain for as many minute questions as possible.

"The money was all lying on a large book at that end of the table next to the window, your worship," responded Tim the Snammer.

The knight put several other queries of the same trivial, but really important nature; and Splint was then removed from the room, Joshua Pedler being led back again to his place.

Precisely the same questions which had been asked of the Snammer, were now put to the other villain; and the answers corresponded in the minutest particulars.

"There is no possibility of doubt as to the genuine character of the present scene," whispered the knight to Dr. Lascelles.

"I have been all along of that way of thinking," replied the physician. "At the same time I admire the precautions you have adopted, Sir Christopher, and the skilful manner in which you have examined and cross-examined these self-inculpatory scoundrels."

"You really are of opinion that I have done the thing well—eh, doctor?" said the Justice of the Peace, with a complacent smile. "Well—I am rejoiced to perceive that I have given you satisfaction. Our unknown friend there may now have the other villain brought back again; so that the two partners in crime may sign these depositions."

Dr. Lascelles intimated the knight's desire to the stranger, who forthwith caused Tim the Snammer to be reconducted to his place in the room where this extraordinary scene was enacted.

Sir Christopher then read over, in a slow and measured tone, the whole of his notes—containing the voluntary confession of the miscreants, and the subsequent examination.

"You, Timothy Splint, and you, Joshua Pedler," he said, when that task was accomplished, "will now sign, or otherwise attest, this document."

The unknown rang the bell twice, and the four dependants who had conducted the two prisoners into the room in the first instance, immediately re-appeared; and, on a signal from their master, they loosened the cords which confined the hands of the villains, in such a way that the latter were enabled to affix their signatures to the depositions, Dr. Lascelles acting as the witness.

"You may now remove those men altogether," said the unknown.

The four dependants immediately blindfolded them, and led them away from the apartment, carefully closing the door behind them.

"I presume that Sir Christopher Blunt and myself are now at liberty to depart?" said the doctor.

"Not before you have each given me a solemn pledge that you will not publish nor even hint at the occurrences of this night until twenty-four hours shall have elapsed," returned the stranger.

"For my part I don't at all object to give the promise required," exclaimed the knight hastily; for the mystery of the whole proceeding had imbued him with the utmost awe in respect to the unknown.

"And I will as readily pledge my solemn word of honour to maintain that condition," observed the doctor.

"In that case, gentlemen," said the stranger, "you shall be conveyed hence without delay. I need hardly enjoin you to use that confession, which you will take away with you, in the manner alone calculated to save the life of Mr. Torrens and relieve him from the dreadful charge hanging over his head."

"Rest assured that all shall be done which the emergency of the case requires, and which we have now the means to effect," said Sir Christopher. "And now, with your permission, I shall take a draught of wine and water—for I feel somewhat exhausted with these proceedings."

While Sir Christopher was helping himself at the table, Dr. Lascelles stepped up to the individual whom circumstances compel us to denominate "the stranger" or "the unknown," and said in a low and hasty whisper, "What is the reason of this delay of twenty-four hours in respect to the proclamation of Torrens' innocence?"

"Because Old Death and others must be in my power, ere the occurrences of this might be published," was the answer, likewise spoken in a hurried whisper; "or else *they* will suspect *where* these scenes have been enacted."

"But are you sure of capturing them?" demanded Lascelles.

"Confident," was the brief but emphatic reply.

The unknown then rang the bell, and significantly intimated to Wilton, who answered the summons, that his guests were ready to depart. The domestic bowed and withdrew: but in a few minutes he returned, accompanied by another dependant; and the two domestics proceeded to blindfold both the doctor and the knight, the unknown apologising for the necessity of renewing this process. He himself then conducted them to the carriage which Wilton had ordered round to the door, and into which the stranger followed them.

It then drove away at a rapid rate; and, after taking sundry windings, stopped, at the expiration of an hour, opposite St. James's church, Piccadilly, just as the clock struck two in the morning.

The knight and the doctor descended, having already bade farewell to the mysterious individual whom they left inside; and the carriage instantaneously drove off.

CHAPTER XCIII.
NEWGATE.

Yes—'twas two o'clock in the morning; and the hour was proclaimed by the iron tongues of Time, from the thousand steeples of the mighty metropolis.

How solemnly does the sound of those deep, sonorous, metallic notes break upon the dead silence of that period when darkness spreads its sable wing over an entire hemisphere!

And though 'tis the time for rest, yet repose and slumber are not the companions of every couch.

Crime, sickness, and sorrow close not their lids in balmy sleep, weighed down with weariness though they be: too much happiness has likewise an excitement hostile to the serenity of the pillow.

For sleep is a fickle goddess, who succumbs not to every one's wooing at the hour when her yielding is most desired: now coy and coquettish, she hovers around, yet approaches not quite close:—now sternly and inexorably obstinate, she keeps herself at a great distance, in sullen mood.

And when the iron tongues of Time proclaimed the hour of two, were the eyes of the wretched Torrens or his miserable, guilty wife closed in slumber?

No—no: beneath the same roof, though in compartments far asunder, they writhed and tossed upon their hard pallets, in feverish excitement—craving, longing for sleep to visit them,—and sleep would not!

In those hours of wakefulness, and amidst the solemn stillness and utter darkness of the night, how terrible are the trains of thought which pass in rapid procession through the guilty mind,—as if imagination itself were being hurried along an endless avenue of horrors—grim spectres, hideous phantoms, and appalling sights on the one hand and on the other!

Then with what tremendous speed does memory travel back through the vista of a mis-pent life, all the foul deeds of which become personified in frightful shapes, and muster themselves in terrible array on either side!

In his narrow stone-cell, the wretched Torrens felt as if he were in a coffin, suffocated, hemmed in around;—and yet his imagination possessed boundless space wherein to raise up the awful shapes that haunted his pillow.

Was it possible that he was there—in Newgate? Did he dream—was he the sport of a hideous phantasy? Could it be true that he was dragged away from his comfortable home—snatched as it were suddenly from the world itself—and flung into a felon's dungeon?

No—no: it was impossible—absurd. Ha! ha! the folly of the idea was enough to make one laugh!

But—oh! merciful heavens!—he extended his arms, and his hands touched the cold—rugged—uneven wall: thence they wandered to the iron of the bed-stead—and came in contact with the coarse horse-cloth which covered his burning, feverish limbs!

Then a dreadful groan burst from him,—a groan which, even were he ten thousand, thousand times more guilty than he really was, would have been lamentable, heart-rending to hear,—a groan of such ineffable anguish that Satan himself might have said, "This man hath suffered enough!"

Suffered!—holy God, how deeply—deeply has he suffered since the massive door of that mighty stone sepulchre first closed upon him,—appearing to shut out the pure air of heaven, the golden light of day, and to mark a point where even human sympathies could follow no farther!

Suffered!—the wretched felon whose foot is upon the first step of the scaffold, never suffered more than the crushed, ruined, accused Torrens;—for all his guilt had arisen from the lack of moral courage to meet misfortune face to face; and now that misfortune had thrust itself upon him, and compelled him to gaze on its pale and death-like countenance, he was completely weighed down.

His infamy in respect to Rosamond, lay as heavily upon his conscience as would have lain the crime of murder, had he really perpetrated it; and he suffered more on account of the deed which he had committed, but for which the law *had not* touched him, than on account of the charge of which he was innocent, but for which the law *had* seized upon him.

Miserable—miserable man! Darkness—silence—and sleeplessness were indeed terrible to him,—so terrible that, as he lay tossing upon his feverish pallet, he wished that he was dead:—yet, had he possessed the means of inflicting self-destruction, he would have been afraid to die!

He was not placed in a ward along with other prisoners; because the charge against him was so black and terrible—the charge of murder—that he was lodged in a dungeon by himself—a cell that had seen many, many previous occupants, most of whom had gone forth to the scaffold!

For in Newgate the possession of a room to oneself—if a room such a coffin of masonry can be called—is the horrible privilege of him who is accused of *murder*; and those whose alleged offences are of a less deep dye, herd together in common wards, where a fetid atmosphere is the medium of communicating the foulest ideas that words can convey or ears receive.

Oh! what a plague-spot is that horrible gaol—that pandemonium of Newgate—upon the civilisation of the metropolis of these realms!

Shame—shame, that it should be allowed to exist under the management of an incapable, ignorant, and monstrously corrupt body—the Aldermen of London:—shame, shame that it should be permitted to remain as a frightful abuse of local jurisdiction, just because no statesman has yet been found bold enough to wrest a barbarian charter from an overgrown, bloated, and despicable corporation!

The wife—the newly married wife of Mr. Torrens,—that woman so well known to our readers by the name of Martha Slingsby,—was not lodged by herself:—being accused of a crime one degree less heinous than that of murder, she was placed in a ward with several other females.

And she also heard the iron tongue of Time proclaim the hour of two in the morning;—and she also tossed upon a hard, sleepless, and feverish pallet.

For she had not even the solace of conscious innocence as an anodyne for her lacerated heart and wounded spirit: she knew that she was guilty of the crime imputed to her—and that knowledge lay upon her soul like a weight of lead.

And—O horror! she was well aware that the black deed of forgery would be indubitably fixed upon her: and the penalty of that deed was—*death*!

Yes:—death by the hand of the common executioner—an ignominious death upon the scaffold!

She knew that almost her very minutes were now numbered—that, as the clock struck eight on some Monday morning, not very far distant, she must be led forth to die—that after her trial, which was sure to end in her condemnation, she should be consigned to the condemned cell—that from this cell she must proceed through several dark and dismal passages to that door upon whose very threshold would appear the gibbet, black and sinister—that she would have to ascend, or perhaps be carried up, the steps to the platform of the horrible machine—that she should see myriads and myriads of human beings crowding around to behold her dying agonies—that she would be placed upon a drop soon to glide away from beneath her feet and leave her suspended in the air—that the few minutes during which she must stand upon that drop, while the chaplain said the parting prayer, would comprise whole years, aye, centuries of the bitterest, bitterest anguish—that her attentive ear would catch even the sound caused by the finger of the executioner, when he touched the bolt of the drop an instant before he pulled it back—and that her soul would be yielded up in the agonies of strangulation!

Thus—thus, in spite of herself, did the wretched woman's imagination picture in frightful detail the whole of the dreadful ceremony of a violent death: thus—thus did she shadow forth, in imagination, every feature—every minute particular of the appalling ordeal;—and, in imagination also, did she now pass through it all, as vainly she craved for sleep in the silence and the darkness of the prison-ward!

The dread routine of the whole ceremony assumed an historical exactitude, a palpable shape, and a frightful reality in her mind.

Terrible—terrible was it for her to think upon what she now was, and upon what she might have been.

Not a hope was left to her in this world: she must be cut off in the meridian of her years;—she must bid adieu for ever to all the pleasures, the enjoyments, the delights of society and of life!

Oh! for the power—oh! for the means to avert her maddening, harrowing thoughts from the prophetic contemplation of that fatal morning when she must walk forth to the scaffold—when the close air of that prison would suddenly change to the fresh breeze of heaven, as she stepped forth from the low dark door which the passer-by outside ever beholds with a shudder,—and when she should raise her eyes to that black and ominous frame-work, with the chain hanging from the cross-beam, and her own coffin beneath the drop! All this was horrible—horrible,—sufficient to deprive the strongest mind of its reasoning faculties, and to paralyse the boldest with excess of terror!

For, oh! the reward of crime is dispensed in two ways upon earth,—by the law, and by the criminal's own thoughts;—and far—far more dreadful is the punishment inflicted by the guilty conscience than by the vengeance of outraged justice. Even the horrors of the scaffold, immense—tremendous though they must be in the reality, are magnified a hundred-fold by the terror-stricken imagination!

From the examples of the wretched man and the guilty woman of whom we have been speaking, and on whose heads afflictions and miseries fell with such frightful rapidity and crushing weight,—from their examples let the reader judge of the *folly*—setting aside the *wickedness*—of crime.

Gold—deceitful gold—was the will-o'-the-wisp which led them on through the devious ways of iniquity, until they suddenly found themselves in Newgate!

For the woman forged for gold—and the man sold his daughter's virtue for gold; and from the moment when Torrens consented to that vile deed, every thing went worse with him—nothing was bettered—and the circumstances resulting from that one act, combined to overwhelm him with afflictions, and even to fix upon him a horrible charge of which he was really innocent!

To err, then, is to be foolish, as well as wicked;—and this grand truth has doubtless been felt and acknowledged, when too late, by many and many a wretched being within those very walls and that sombre enclosure of Newgate!

Newgate!—what numberless ties have been severed on its threshold;—and what countless thousands of individuals, on entering that dread portal one by one, have gnashed their teeth with rage at the folly, even though they have felt no compunction for the guilt, of the career which they pursued and which had its natural ending there!

It was ten o'clock in the morning, when a hackney-coach stopped at the door of the governor's house, which stands in the centre of the front part of Newgate; and a fine, tall, handsome young man, having leapt forth, assisted a closely veiled lady to alight from the vehicle.

They were almost immediately admitted into the office of the governor, the young lady clinging to her companion's arm for support, for she was labouring under the most dreadful mental anguish.

These persons were Clarence Villiers and his beauteous bride, Adelais.

Returning from Devonshire, whither they had been to pass the honeymoon, they heard on the road, ere they reached the metropolis, the astounding intelligence that the aunt of the one had been committed to Newgate on a charge of forgery, and that the father of the other was consigned to the same place under an accusation of the murder of Sir Henry Courtenay. They also learnt at the same moment and for the first time, that the wretched pair had only just been united in matrimonial bonds when this fearful fate overtook them; but they were too much shocked by the more grave and serious portion of the tidings which thus burst upon them, to give themselves even leisure to express their surprise at the less important incident of the marriage of Mr. Torrens and Mrs. Slingsby.

They had arrived in London on the preceding evening, and had repaired direct to Torrens Cottage, hoping—and, indeed, expecting as a matter of course—to find Rosamond there.

But they were disappointed—cruelly disappointed that anticipation!

The female servant and the lad were, however, still at the Cottage; and from the former they learnt tidings which enhanced, if possible, the grief that already rent the heart of Adelais, and which excited vague but terrible suspicions in the mind of Clarence.

For the servant informed them that Miss Rosamond went to stay with Mrs. Slingsby almost immediately after the wedding—that she remained there almost ten days, and came home the very night when the murder was committed, and seemed dreadfully unhappy during the short time that she did remain at the Cottage—and that she departed no one knew whither, the second day after her return, leaving a note for her father.

While Adelais sate weeping at these tidings, to her so completely inexplicable, a torrent of suspicions and terrible ideas rolled through the mind of her husband Clarence. For he knew—as the reader will remember—that Sir Henry Courtenay was not only the paramour of his aunt, but that he had likewise cast lustful looks upon Rosamond; and he was equally aware that the young girl's imagination had been excited and inflamed by the false representations his aunt had made in respect to the character of the baronet. Then that second visit of Rosamond to Old Burlington Street—her unhappiness on returning home—the assassination of Sir Henry Courtenay at Torrens Cottage—the sudden marriage of two persons who were almost entire strangers to each other—and the contemporaneous flight of Rosamond from her home,—all these incidents seemed of so suspicious and terribly mysterious a nature as to strike Clarence with dismay.

The version which Mr. Torrens had given Rosamond of the particulars of the murder—and which, as the reader is aware, was the true one so far as the actual perpetration of the deed itself was concerned—was unknown to Clarence, inasmuch as it had not been published in the newspapers;—for, when arrested by Dykes and Bingham, Mr. Torrens had immediately sent for able counsel, to whom he told his story previously to the examination before the magistrate, and by the advice of his legal assistant, the prisoner had contented himself by simply declaring his innocence, stating that he should reserve for his defence the explanations whereon that assertion was founded.

Thus Clarence Villiers could not help believing that Torrens was really guilty of the murder; and he shuddered at the idea which forced itself upon him, that his aunt was an accomplice in the crime. In fact, it naturally appeared as if that woman and that man had suddenly blended their congenial spirits for the purpose of working out deeds of the blackest dye; and he dreaded lest the honour of Rosamond had been wrecked in the frightful convulsion produced by that association.

But none of his awful misgivings did he impart to Adelais. On the contrary, he strove to console her by assurances of his hope that her father must be the victim of a terrible junction of adverse circumstances, and that his innocence would yet transpire. Such ideas he was in reality very far from entertaining;—but it cut him to the quick to behold the anguish of his young wife—and he uttered every thing of a consolatory nature which his imagination was likely in such a case to suggest as a means of imparting hope and affording comfort.

They remained at the Cottage that night; and on the ensuing morning repaired to Newgate, as we have already stated.

The governor, upon learning the degree of relationship in which Mrs. Villiers stood towards Mr. Torrens, expressed himself in terms of the kindest sympathy, and offered to proceed in the first instance to the prisoner's cell to prepare him for the meeting with his daughter and son-in-law. This proposal was thankfully accepted; and the governor, after remaining absent for about ten minutes, returned to conduct the young couple into the presence of the prisoner, with whom he left them.

Adelais threw herself into her father's arms, embraced him with a fondness that was almost wild and frantic, and sobbed bitterly upon his breast,—while Clarence Villiers stood a deeply affected spectator of the sad—the touching scene.

"My child—my dear child," exclaimed the father, more moved by paternal tenderness than he ever yet had been,—"I am innocent—I am innocent!"

"Almighty God be thanked for that assurance!" murmured Adelais, as she fell upon her knees, and bent her burning face over her father's emaciated hands:—for Mr. Torrens had become frightfully thin—altered—and careworn,—and his entire appearance denoted how acute his mental sufferings had been.

"Clarence," he cried, after a few moments' pause during which he raised his daughter, and placed her upon a seat,—"Clarence, did you hear my declaration? I am innocent!"

"I heard it—and I rejoice unfeignedly—oh! most unfeignedly," returned the young man, not knowing what to think, but speaking thus to console his heart-wrung wife.

"But whether I can prove my innocence—whether I can triumph over the awful weight of circumstantial evidence which has accumulated against me," continued Mr. Torrens, "is a point which God alone can determine."

An ejaculation of despair burst from the lips of Adelais.

"For heaven's sake, compose yourself, dearest!" said Villiers. "You have heard your father declare his innocence———"

"Yes—yes," she cried: "but if the world will not believe him? It is not sufficient that *we* should be convinced of that innocence! Oh! my God—wherefore has this terrible affliction fallen upon us?"—then, suddenly struck by another idea, she exclaimed, "And Rosamond, dear father—what has become of my sister Rosamond?"

Mr. Torrens turned away, and burst into tears—for that question revived a thousand agonising reminiscences in his mind.

"My father *here*—my sister *gone*," mused Adelais, her manner suddenly becoming strangely subdued, and the wild intensity of her earnest eyes changing in a moment to an expression of idiotic vacancy;—"and Clarence—where is he? Methought he was with me just now———"

"Merciful God! her senses are leaving her!" exclaimed Villiers, in a frantic tone: then, throwing his arms around her, he said, "Adelais—my beloved Adelais—Clarence is here—by your side! Oh! look not at me so strangely, Adelais—do you not know me?—speak—speak!—I am Clarence—your husband—he who loves, who adores you! My God! she does not recognise me!"

And the young man started back, dashing his right hand with the violence of despair against his forehead; while Adelais remained motionless in the chair, gazing on him with a kind of vacant wonderment,—and the miserable father staggered against the wall for support, murmuring in a tone of ineffable emotion, "Great God! where will all this end?"

But at that moment the heavy bolts were drawn back—the door opened—Adelais uttered a scream of mingled amazement and delight—and in an instant Rosamond was clasped in her arms.

Long and fervent was that embrace on the part of the sisters: nor were Torrens and Clarence Villiers alone the witnesses thereof—for the heavy door of the stone cell had, ere it closed again, given admittance to Esther de Medina.

Fortunate for Adelais was it that Rosamond appeared at such a moment,—a moment when the reason of the young bride was rocking on its throne, and the weight of an idea no heavier than a hair would decide whether it were to be re-established on its seat or overturned for ever!

Faint and overcome by the sudden revulsion of feeling produced by this sudden meeting with her sister, Adelais slowly disengaged herself from Rosamond's arms, and falling back in the chair, beckoned Clarence towards her, saying, "My dearest husband—keep near me—stay with me—for I know not what dreadful ideas have been passing in my mind;—and it seemed to me for a time that I was in utter darkness—or that I was buried in a profound sleep."

"But you are better now, dearest?" exclaimed Clarence, overjoyed at this sudden return of her senses.

"Yes—I am better now," said Adelais; and, falling upon her husband's neck, she burst into a flood of tears.

Meantime Rosamond was weeping also in her father's arms; and the eyes of the generous-hearted—the amiable Esther de Medina were overflowing at the contemplation of this mournful and touching scene.

"Father—father," murmured Rosamond, her voice almost suffocated with the sobs which agitated her bosom,—"there is hope—every hope——"

"Hope!" ejaculated Mr. Torrens, catching at the word as if the halter were already round his neck and the cry of "a reprieve!" had fallen on his ears.

"Hope, did you say?" exclaimed Adelais, now so completely relieved by the issue her pent-up anguish and shocked feelings had found in copious weeping, that all the clearness of her intellect had returned.

"Hush—Rosamond!" said Miss de Medina, advancing towards the group: "hush—my dear madam," she added, turning hastily towards Adelais; "that word must not be breathed here aloud *yet*! Nevertheless, it is true that there *is* hope—and every hope—nay, even certainty——"

"Great God! I thank thee!" cried Adelais, clasping her hands together in fervent gratitude, while Mr. Torrens was so overcome by emotions of joy and amazement that he sank upon that prison-pallet whereon he had passed a night of such horrible watchfulness.

"I implore you to restrain your feelings as much as possible," said Esther, speaking in a low and mysterious tone, which made Torrens, Clarence, and Adelais suddenly become all attention and breathless suspense; "the proofs of your innocence, sir," she added, looking at the prisoner, "have been obtained! Nay—give utterance to no ejaculation—but hear me in silence! Within twenty-four hours from this time your guiltlessness will be proclaimed to the world. Already are the proofs in the hands of a magistrate but circumstances, with which I am not myself altogether acquainted, render that delay imperiously necessary. It would, however, have been cruel to have left you in ignorance of this important circumstance; and——"

"And this admirable young lady, at whose father's house I found a home," hastily added Rosamond, "would not refuse me the joy—the indescribable joy of being the bearer of these tidings. Nay—more: she offered to accompany me——"

"God will reward you for all your kindness to my sister, dear lady," said Adelais, embracing Esther with heart-felt gratitude and affection.

"You are doubtless anxious to learn how the proofs of Mr. Torrens' innocence have been obtained," resumed Esther, after a pause: "but my explanation must be very brief. Suffice it to say that in this mighty metropolis, which contains so much evil, there is a man bent only on doing good. Accident revealed to him certain particulars which convinced him of your innocence, sir," continued the beautiful Jewess, addressing herself now especially to Mr. Torrens: "upon the information which he thus received, he acted—and he has succeeded in obtaining and placing in the hands of a Justice of the Peace the confession of the real perpetrators of the awful deed——"

"Then the murderers are in custody, doubtless?" exclaimed Clarence, astonished and delighted at all he heard.

"They are not in the grasp of justice," answered Esther. "But on this head you must ask me no questions. Rest satisfied with the assurance that the innocence of Mr. Torrens will completely and unquestionably transpire—that he will soon be restored to you all—and that his secret friend watches over him even from a distance. Who that individual is, you cannot know—and perhaps never may. All the recompense he demands at your hands is the subduing in your minds of every sentiment of curiosity that may prompt you to pierce the mystery which shrouds his actions; and remember also that every syllable I have now uttered, is to remain a secret profoundly locked up in your own breasts until the proclamation of innocence shall be made from that quarter to which the solemn duty of publishing it has been entrusted."

"We should be wanting in common gratitude, indeed, to him who has thus interested himself in behalf of the innocent, were we to act in opposition to those injunctions," said Clarence Villiers. "But through you, lady, do we each and all convey our heart-felt thanks for that generous intervention which is to produce so vitally important a result."

"Yes—and to you also, dearest Miss de Medina, is our eternal gratitude due!" exclaimed Rosamond—an assurance that was immediately and sincerely echoed by Adelais, Clarence, and Mr. Torrens.

Hope had now returned to that prison-cell,—hope in all her radiance and her glory,—with her smiling countenance and her cheering influence!

The name of Mrs. Torrens—late Mrs. Slingsby—was not mentioned by a soul during this meeting: her husband uttered it not—Clarence, through motives of delicacy, remained silent likewise in that respect—and the sisters had too much to occupy their thoughts relative to their father's position and the hope of his speedy release, to devote a moment's attention to that woman.

For the interview was necessarily short, in consequence of the severity of the prison regulations; but when Mr. Torrens was again alone in his cell, he could scarcely believe that so sudden a change had taken place in his prospects.

On leaving the gaol, after having taken a tender and affectionate leave of their father, the sisters looked inquiringly at each other, as if to ask whither each was going.

"We have taken up our abode at the Cottage," said Adelais, breaking silence; "where we shall remain, doubtless," she added, glancing towards her husband, "until our father shall be restored to us."

Clarence signified his assent.

"I should be grieved to separate you from your sister immediately after your unexpected meeting to-day," said Esther, addressing herself to Adelais; "but if Rosamond will continue to make our house her home——"

"Yes—yes, my dear friend," exclaimed Rosamond, hastily: "I will intrude a little longer upon your hospitality—for I feel that my nerves have been too much shaken by recent occurrences to allow me to return to the Cottage, at least for the present."

The reader need scarcely be informed that the young lady desired to avoid the painful prospect of being alone with her sister and Clarence: for what explanation could she give of her flight from home?—an explanation which she knew would naturally be required of her.

Adelais, indeed, felt somewhat hurt at the decision which her sister had made in respect to remaining with Miss de Medina: but she concealed her vexation, and they parted with an affectionate embrace.

Thus, Clarence and Adelais proceeded to Torrens Cottage, while Esther and Rosamond returned in Mr. de Medina's carriage to Finchley Manor.

During their ride home in the hackney-coach, Villiers and his wife discussed all the incidents which had just occurred; but during a pause in the conversation, Adelais bethought herself for the first time that day of her mother-in-law.

"Clarence," she said, laying her hand upon her husband's arm, "we have been sadly culpable——"

"I know to what you would allude, dearest," interrupted Villiers. "To-morrow I shall call upon my wretched aunt; but it is by no means necessary for you to accompany me. Your father did not once mention her name during the interview: we will not seek to penetrate his motives for that silence—but we will endeavour to imitate him in that respect as much as possible."

"I do not clearly understand you, Clarence," said Adelais, gazing at him enquiringly.

"I mean that the less we speak concerning my aunt, the more prudent it will be, my love," responded Villiers; "for I fear that *she* will not prove to be innocent of the crime imputed to her—and, under all circumstances, you can owe her no sympathy nor respect, either as my relative or your mother-in-law."

Adelais made no answer; and Clarence immediately changed the conversation.

CHAPTER XCIV.
"THE STOUT HOUSE."

London is a wondrous city for the success with which the most flagrant quackery is accomplished. Things not only improbable, but absolutely impossible, are puffed off with matchless impudence; and, what is more extraordinary still, they obtain an infinite number of believers. Thus we have snuffs which will cure blindness when the most skilful oculists are at fault,—oils and pomatums that will make the hair grow in spite of nature's denial,—cosmetics that will render every skin, though tawny as a gipsey's, white as a Circassian's,—pills so happily compounded as to be an universal panacea, annihilating diseases of even the most opposite characters, and effecting for thirteen-pence halfpenny what all the College of Physicians could not accomplish for millions,—lozenges by which a voice cracked like a tin-trumpet, may become melodious as a silver bell,—ointments that will cure in a week ulcers and sores which have baffled all the experience of famous hospital-surgeons for a quarter of a century,—decoctions prepared on purpose to prolong life, although the *elixir vitæ* of the alchemists has long been regarded as an absurd fable,—boluses competent to restore to all their pristine vigour constitutions shattered by years and years of dissipation and dissolute habits,—pulmonic wafers efficient to wrestle against the very last stage of consumption, and restore lungs entirely eaten away,—tonics so wonderful that they will even give new coats to the stomach, though the old ones have been destroyed by ardent spirits,—and heaven only knows how many more blessings of the same kind!

Seriously speaking, it is deplorable to perceive how tremendously the millions are gulled by all these details of an impudent and most dishonest quackery. The coiner who passes off a base shilling, representing it to be a good one, is punished as a felon and stigmatised as a villain. But the quack who sells articles which he announces to be capable of performing physical impossibilities, is not tangible by the law, nor does he become branded in the opinion of the world. Such are the conventional differences existing in civilised society!

Of all the demoralising species of quackery practised now-a-days, certain medical works are decidedly the worst. We allude to those beastly things which are constantly announced in the advertisement-department of newspapers, but which, with a scintillation of good taste on the side of the printers, are invariably huddled together in the most obscure nook. It is evident that newspaper-proprietors are ashamed of the filthy advertisements, although they cannot very well refuse to insert them. But we warn all our readers against suffering themselves to put the least confidence in the representations set forth in the announcements alluded to. The works thus puffed off are contemptible as regards medical information, demoralising in their very nature, and delusive in all their promises.

An amusing species of quackery exists with repect to many public-houses. Passing along a thoroughfare, or visiting some fresh neighbourhood springing up in the outskirts of the metropolis, you will probably see a new building, destined for the "public" line, and with the words—"NOTED STOUT HOUSE"—painted on a board, or cut in the masonry. The cool impudence of proclaiming an establishment to be famous for a particular article, before it is even finished, is too ludicrous to provoke serious vituperation. The merit of the place is agreed upon beforehand between the architect and the proprietor. Never mind how worthless the beer to be retailed there may eventually prove, it is a Noted Stout House all the same! But so accustomed are the inhabitants of London to behold such things, that the springing up of such a structure causes no sensation in its neighbourhood: good, easy people that we are now-a-days—we take every thing for granted and as a matter of course!

The *Noted Stout House* in Helmet Row, St. Luke's—called by its patrons, for abbreviation's sake, the *Stout House*—was one of those flash boozing-kens which are to be found in low neighbourhoods. And noted it indeed was—not on account of its beer, unless the fame thereof consisted in its execrable nature—but by reason of the characters frequenting it. The parlour was large, low, and dark; and in the evening it was invariably filled with a miscellaneous company of both sexes. Prostitutes and thieves—old procuresses and housebreakers—dissolute married women, and notorious coiners,—these were the principal supporters of the *Stout House*.

Had Machiavelli once passed an evening there, he would not have declared as a rule that "language was given to man for the purpose of disguising his thoughts;" inasmuch as no attempt at any such disguise at all was made in that place. Every one spoke his mind in the most free and open manner possible,—calling things by their right names—and expressing the filthiest ideas in the plainest phraseology. If foul words were capable of impregnating the air, the atmosphere of the *Stout House* parlour would have engendered a pestilence.

At about half-past nine in the evening, John Jeffreys sauntered into the establishment, took a seat at the table, and gave his orders to the waiter for the beverage which he fancied at the moment.

Whenever a new-comer appears in a public room of this kind, the company invariably leave off talking for a minute or so, to enjoy a good stare at him; and they measure him from head to foot—turn him inside out, as it were—and form their rapid and silent conjectures regarding him, just as a broker "takes stock" in his mind, with a hasty survey around, on putting an execution for taxes or rates into a defaulter's house.

We cannot exactly say what opinion the company present on this occasion at the *Stout House* formed of John Jeffreys; but we are able to assure our readers that, much as he had seen of London, and well as he was acquainted with its vile dens and low places of resort, he thought to himself, as he glanced about him, that he had never before set eyes on such a dissipated-looking set of women or such a repulsive assemblage of men.

"Well, and so Mother Oliver's place is broke up at last," observed one of the females, addressing herself to another woman, and evidently taking up the thread of a conversation which the entrance of Jeffreys had for a few moments interrupted.

"Yes—and the poor old creature has been sent to quod by the beaks at Hicks's Hall, till she finds sureties for her good behaviour in future," was the reply.

"What—is that the Mother Oliver you mean, as kept the brothel in Little Sutton Street, t'other side of the Goswell Road there?" demanded a man, desisting from his occupation of smoking, for a few moments, while he asked the question.

"To be sure it is," returned the female, who had previously spoken; "and a bad thing it is for me, I can tell you. I was servant there—and a good living it were. But I'll tell you how it all come about. It was a matter of six or seven weeks ago that a young feller came to the house, quite on his own accord, as you may suppose; and he stayed there three whole days, for he was quite struck, as one may say, with a fair-haired gal which had been lodging with us for some time. Well, he orders every thing of the best, promising to pay all in a lump; and so Mother Oliver gives him tick, like a fool as she was. But at last she wanted to see the colour of his money; and then he bullied, and swore, and kicked up a row, and went away without paying a mag. Well, the debt was given up as a bad job, and we thought no more about it, till we heard a few days afterwards that the house was to be indicted. So off Mother Oliver goes to the Clerk of the Peace: but, lo and behold ye! the young gentleman was a clerk in his office; and not content with reglarly robbing the poor old o'oman, he must try and ruin her into the bargain. Mother Oliver got to see the Clerk of the Peace, and began to tell him all about the trick his young man had played her; but he said he knowed every thing already, that she had enticed the young feller into her house, and that was the reason she was to be indicted. So the thing come on yesterday before the Middlesex magistrates at Hicks's Hall, and Mother Oliver was sent to gaol."

"There's been a reglar rooting out of them kind of cribs all over the parish," observed one of the company; "and it's the same in a many other parishes."

"Yes: but I'll tell you what it is," exclaimed the woman who had related the above particulars; "it's only against the poor sort of houses that these prosecutions is ever got up. Lord bless you! before I went to Mother Oliver's, I was servant in a flash brothel at the West-End—a reglar slap-up place—beautifully furnished, and frequented by all the first folks. It was kept—and still is kept—by a Frenchwoman. I was there as under-housemaid for a matter of seven year; and should have been there till now, only I was too fond of taking a drop the first thing in the morning, to keep the dust out in summer and the cold out in winter."

"Ah—I des say you was always a lushing jade, Sally," observed an individual in his shirt-sleeves, and who seemed to know the woman well.

"Well, old feller—and what then?" cried she, for a moment manifesting a strong inclination to draw her finger-nails down the cheeks of her acquaintance: but, calming her anger, she said, "It don't matter what comes from your lips—so I shan't be perwoked by you. Howsomever, as I was telling you, I was servant in the flash house at the West-End for upward of seven years; and such scenes as I saw! The old Frenchwoman used to entice the most respectable gals there by means of advertisements for governesses, ladies-maids, and so on; and they was kept prisoners till they either agreed to what she proposed, or was forced into it by the noblemen and gentlemen frequenting the place. And all this occurred, I can assure you, in one of the fashion-ablest streets in London. But there was never no notice taken by the parish-authorities; and as for the Society—what's its name again?—that prosecutes bad houses, it didn't seem to know there was such a brothel in existence. And I'll tell you how *that* was, too. The Frenchwoman gave such general satisfaction to her customers, and was always treating them to such novelties in the shape of gals, that she was protected by all the gay noblemen and gentlemen at the West-End. Lord bless you! some of her best customers was the Middlesex magistrates themselves; and two or three of the noblemen and gentlemen that I spoke of, was members of the Committee of that very Society which prosecutes brothels. So it wasn't likely that the house would ever be interfered with. I recollect the old Frenchwoman used to laugh and joke with the great Lords and the Members of the Commons that patronised her, about the way they talked in the Parliament Houses, and the bother they made about the better observance of the Sabbath, and so on. It used to be rare fun to hear the old lady, in her broken English, repeating to them some of their fine speeches, which she'd read in the newspapers; and how the gals used to laugh with them, to be sure!"

"You don't mean to say that them Lords and Members, which is always a-going on about the Sabbath, used to frequent the brothel you speak of?" exclaimed a man.

"Don't I, though?" cried the woman, in a tone of indignation at the bare suspicion against her veracity implied by the question: "I do indeed, my man; and I should think you ought to know the world better than to be astonished at it. It was through having the patronage of all them great people, that the old Frenchwoman never got into trouble. But none of the fine brothels at the West-End are ever prosecuted: no one would think of such a thing! It's only the low ones in the poor neighbourhoods."

"Well, I always heard say that poverty is the greatest possible crime in this country," observed the man who had recently spoken; "and now I'm convinced on it."

"I never had any doubt about it," said another. "A rich man or a rich woman may do anythink; but the poor—deuce a bit! That's quite another thing. Why, look at all these Bishops, and great Lords, and Members of the Commons, which are constantly raving about Sunday travelling: don't they go about in their carriages? and ain't Hyde Park always more filled with splendid vehicles on a Sunday than on any other day? The very Bishops which would put down coaches on a Sabbath, goes in their carriages to the Cathedrals where they preach."

"By all I can hear or learn," observed another individual present, "there's a precious sight more religious gammon in the Parliament Houses than anywheres else."

"I should think there is too," exclaimed the woman who had told the tale relative to the brothel-keepers. "Some of them noblemen and gentlemen that I spoke of was the most terrible fellows after the young women that I ever see in all my life; and they was always a bothering the Frenchwoman to send over to France, or down into the country, to entice more gals to the house. The Frenchwoman used to send out agents to entrap innocent creatures wherever she could—farmers' and clergymen's daughters, and such like. I remember what a spree we had with one of the religious Members of the Commons one night. He had been bringing in a bill, or whatever you call it, to protect young females from seduction, and had drawed such a frightful picture of the whole business, that he made all the other Members shed tears. Well, as soon as he'd done, he came straight off to our place, and asked the old Frenchwoman if she had got any thing new in the house. That very day a sweet young gal—a poor marine officer's daughter, who wanted to be a governess—had been enticed to the brothel, and the Member that I'm speaking of gave the old Frenchwoman fifty guineas for the purchase of that poor creatur'."

The woman was entering into farther details, when Wilton and another of the retainers of Jeffreys' mysterious master entered the parlour of the *Stout House*, both disguised as servants out of place. The place was too much crowded to enable them to converse at their ease: they accordingly all three repaired to a private room, Jeffreys having left at the bar a suitable message to be delivered to Old Death who was well known at that establishment.

Wilton ordered up glasses of spirits-and-water; and when the waiter had retired, after supplying the liquor, Jeffreys proceeded to acquaint his colleagues with the promised tidings relative to Tidmarsh.

"I called at the Bunces' house in Earl Street, Seven Dials, this morning," he said, "and saw Old Death, who was quite delighted when I assured him that I had already found the two friends of whom I had spoken to him, and that that they would be here punctual this evening at half-past ten. I then told him that as the resurrection affair in St. Luke's churchyard would most likely come off to-morrow night, and as I should be engaged the best part of to-morrow on my own business, he had better let Tidmarsh go with me at once and show me the exact spot where Tom Rain was buried. The old man bit directly, and said, '*Well, Jeffreys, you're a faithful and good fellow, and can be trusted. Tidmarsh lives here now, and is up stairs at this moment.*'—So Tidmarsh was sent for; and away him and me went together to St. Luke's. In the course of conversation I found out that Tidmarsh, Bunce, and Mrs. Bunce were to go out with Old Death on some business this evening; and that while Old Death came here to meet me, the other three were to wait for him at another flash house in Mitchell Street close by."

"This is admirable!" said Wilton. "We have now the whole gang completely in our power. Fortunately, I have several of our master's people in the neighbourhood; and I will go at once and give them the necessary instructions. Wait here, Jeffreys, with Harding," he added, indicating his colleague with a look; "until I return. My absence will not be long."

Wilton left the room, Jeffreys and Harding remaining alone together.

In a quarter of an hour the Black's trusty dependant returned.

"All my arrangements are now complete," he said, resuming his seat; "and the entire gang must inevitably fall into our hands."

Jeffreys then acquainted Wilton and Harding with the exact nature of the proposal which would be made to them by Old Death; and scarcely were these preliminaries accomplished when the ancient miscreant made his appearance.

"This is business-like indeed—very business-like, my good fellow," said Old Death, taking a chair, and addressing himself to Jeffreys while he spoke. "And these, I suppose," he continued, fixing a scrutinizing glance upon the others, "are the friends you spoke of."

"Just so," replied Jeffreys. "This is Bill Jones," he added, laying his hands on Wilton's shoulder; "and there's no mistake about him. T'other is named Ned Thompson, and knows a thing or two, I rather suspect."

"All right—all right!" chuckled Old Death, rubbing his hands joyfully together. "I'm glad to make your acquaintance, Mr. Jones—and your's too, Mr. Thompson."

"And we're not sorry to form yours, Mr. Bones," said Wilton, affecting a manner and tone suitable to the part he was playing. "Our pal Jeffreys here has told us quite enough to make us anxious to know more of you."

"And so you shall, my dear friends," exclaimed Old Death. "I can always find business for faithful agents—and I can pay them well likewise."

"Jeffreys has told us *that*," observed Wilton.

"And I've also explained to them what you want done to-morrow night, Mr. Bones," said Jeffreys.

"Good!" ejaculated Old Death. "Well—is it to be done?"

"There's no manner of difficulty that I can see," said Harding; "and as for any risk—why if the reward's at all decent——"

"The reward shall be liberal—very liberal," interrupted Old Death hastily. "What—what should you say to a ten-pound note a-piece?"

"Deuce take it!" cried Wilton, thinking it would look better to haggle at the bargain: "remember, there's the chance of transportation—and my friend and I are not so desperate hard up——"

"No—no—I understand," observed Old Death, fearful that his meanness had disgusted his new acquaintances and that he should lose their services unless he immediately manifested a more liberal disposition: "I meant ten pounds each on account, and ten pounds more for each when the job is done. Besides," he added, "there's other business to follow on: this is only the first scene in the play that I'm going to get up, and in which you must be prominent characters."

And the aged miscreant chuckled at his attempt at humour.

"What you have now said," observed Wilton, "quite alters the case. Twenty pounds each, and the chance of more work, is a proposal that we can accept. What say you, Thompson?"

"I say what you say, Jones," replied Harding.

"Now then we understand each other, my friends," continued Old Death; "and I will at once give you the earnest-money."

Thus speaking, he drew forth a greasy purse, and presented the two men each with ten sovereigns, which they appeared to snatch up with much avidity.

"I have now nothing more to say to you," resumed Benjamin Bones, his fierce eyes sparkling beneath his overhanging brows with the hope of speedy vengeance on the Earl of Ellingham. "You must place yourselves at the disposal of your friend Jeffreys here, who will inform you how to act and show you precisely in what way my wishes are to be executed. I must now leave you: but to-morrow evening," he added, in a tone of savage meaning, "I shall see you in Earl Street with the coffin!"

"You may rely upon us, Mr. Bones," replied Wilton.

"But won't you stay and take a glass with us?" demanded Jeffreys.

"Not to night—not to night," was the answer. "I took something short at the bar as I passed by; but to-morrow night, my friends—to-morrow night," he exclaimed emphatically, "you shall find a good supper ready for you in Earl Street when you come, and a drop of the right sort."

"So much the better," said Jeffreys: "I like a good supper. But what's your hurry at present, Mr. Bones?"

"To tell you the truth, my dear boy," answered the old man, "I have got three friends waiting for me at a ken in Mitchell Street; and I promised not to keep them longer than I could help. So you must excuse me on this occasion; and, therefore, good bye."

Old Death shook hands with the three men, and took his departure—chuckling to himself at the idea of having secured the services of Jeffreys' friends at so cheap a rate, inasmuch as he would cheerfully have given them, griping and avaricious as he was, three or four times the sum stipulated in order to secure their services in the scheme of carrying out his atrocious plans of vengeance.

But for once, Old Death! the laugh was against yourself—as you speedily discovered to your cost!

We must not however anticipate.

The moment the old man had left the room, Wilton, Harding, and Jeffreys exchanged glances of satisfaction and triumph.

"Bunce, Tidmarsh, and Bunce's wife are all three at the flash house in Mitchell Street—that is quite clear," said Jeffreys.

"Yes," observed Wilton: "and the moment for action is now at hand. Let us depart."

The three men accordingly left the tavern, and hastened in the direction which they knew Old Death must pursue in order to reach Mitchell Street.

As they passed by another public-house in Helmet Row, Wilton bade them pause for a moment, while he went in to give the necessary instructions to the persons who were associated with him in the expedition of this night, and whom he had ordered to remain there until his return. He speedily rejoined Jeffreys and Harding; and all three were once more on the track of Old Death.

At the same time, half-a-dozen men, dressed as labourers, issued from the public-house at which Wilton had called; and, dispersing themselves, hurried singly by different ways towards the road separating the two burial-grounds.

Precisely at the corner where Mitchell Street joins Helmet Row, and just as he was in the act of turning into the former thoroughfare, Old Death was suddenly seized by three men, and gagged before he had time to utter a single exclamation. The moon shone brightly; and his eyes flashed the fires of savage rage and wild amazement, as their glances fell upon the countenances of Wilton, Harding, and Jeffreys. He stamped his feet in a paroxysm of fury, and then struggled desperately to release himself: but his efforts were altogether unavailing—though he exerted a strength which could scarcely have been expected on the part of so old and feeble a man. He was borne off to the Black's carriage, which was waiting close by; and, being thrust in, was immediately bound and blindfolded by two persons who were already seated inside the vehicle, which drove away at a rapid rate.

This important feat being accomplished, Wilton desired Jeffreys to proceed to the flash-house in Mitchell Street, and induce Tidmarsh and the Bunces to accompany him into the ambush prepared for them.

Jeffreys accordingly repaired to the boozing-ken alluded to, where he found the objects of his search seated at a table, and occupied in the discussion of bread and cheese and porter.

"Sorry to interrupt you, my friends," said Jeffreys; "but you must come away with me directly. Mr. Bones has sent me to fetch you——"

"Is anything the matter?" asked Mrs. Bunce, in a low but agitated voice, as she glanced towards the strangers present in the room.

"I can't say what's the matter," replied Jeffreys, "because I don't know. But Mr. Bones seems much excited—and he's walking up and down the road between the burying-grounds. He told me to desire you to come to him directly."

"Is he alone there?" inquired Toby Bunce, looking particularly frightened.

"Yes—quite alone. There's no danger of any thing, if that's what you mean: but I think Mr. Bones has met with some annoyance. Come on!"

Tidmarsh and the Bunces accordingly rose, paid for what they had ordered, but which they had not time to finish, and repaired with Jeffreys to the place mentioned by him.

"Where *is* Mr. Bones?" demanded Mrs. Bunce, in her querulous voice.

But ere Jeffreys had time to give any answer, his three companions were set upon and made prisoners by the Black's retainers.

It is only necessary to state, in a few words, that they were gagged, blindfolded, thrust into a second vehicle which was in attendance, and conveyed to the same place whither Tim the Snammer, Josh Pedler, and Old Death had preceded them.

Wilton, having superintended this last transaction, remained behind along with Jeffreys, to whom he addressed himself in the following manner, as soon as the carriage had departed:—

"I am commissioned by my master, who is also your's, to state to you his entire approval of your conduct. Measures have been taken to save Mr. Torrens, in a manner which cannot implicate you. Keep your own counsel: be prudent and steady—and you may not only atone for past errors, but become a respected and worthy member of society. For a few days it will be necessary for you to remain as quiet as possible at your own lodgings; and whatever extraordinary reports you may hear concerning the affairs of Mr. Torrens—however wonderful the means adopted to proclaim his innocence of the crime of murder may be—keep a still tongue in your head! So much depends upon your implicit secrecy, that you would not be now left at large, did not our master entertain a high opinion of your fidelity. But beware how you act! You have had ample proofs not only of his power, but likewise of his matchless boldness and unflinching determination in working out his aims."

"For my own sake, Mr. Wilton," said Jeffreys, "I shall follow all your advice."

"And you will live to bless the hour when you first encountered our master," was the answer. "It is not probable that your services will be required again for some days: but should it be otherwise, a letter or a messenger will be dispatched to your abode. Our master retains in his hands the money that you left with him; and the next time he has occasion to see you, he will advise you in what manner to lay it out to your best advantage. In the meantime he has sent you a moderate sum—not from your own funds, but from his purse—for your present wants; and so long as you remain in his service, your wages will be liberal, but paid in comparatively small and frequent sums, so that the possession of a large amount may not lead you into follies. By this course he will train your mind to recognise the true value of money honourably obtained, and fit you for the position in which the funds he holds of your's may shortly place you."

Jeffreys and Wilton then separated, the former more astonished than ever at the bold and yet skilfully executed proceedings set on foot by his mysterious master.

CHAPTER XCV.
CLARENCE VILLIERS AND HIS AUNT.

The church of Saint Sepulchre on Snow Hill, was proclaiming the hour of nine on the following morning, when Clarence Villiers again entered the office of the governor of Newgate, and solicited permission to see Mrs. Torrens, representing the degree of relationship in which he stood with regard to that unhappy woman.

We have before stated that Mrs. Torrens had been placed in a ward where there were several other prisoners of her own sex; and the governor, animated by a proper feeling of delicacy, and supposing that the interview of relatives under such circumstances was likely to be of a nature which it would be cruel to submit to the gaze of curious strangers, immediately conducted Clarence into his own parlour, whither the guilty aunt was speedily conducted.

When they were alone together, Clarence endeavoured to find utterance for a few kind words; but his tongue clave to the roof of his mouth—and he burst into tears.

Mrs. Torrens threw herself into a chair, covered her face with her hands, and expressed the anguish of her soul in deep and convulsing moans.

"Oh! my dear aunt," exclaimed Clarence at length; "in what a frightful position do I find you! What terrible changes have a few short days effected!"

"Do not reproach me, Clarence—Oh! do not reproach me," said the wretched woman, extending her arms in an imploring manner towards him: "I am miserable enough as it is!"

"My God! I can well believe you," cried Villiers, speaking in a tone of profound commiseration, and forgetting for a moment the iniquity of which his aunt had been guilty: for she was frightfully altered—her plumpness was gone—her cheeks were thin and pale—and she even stooped, as if with premature old age.

"Oh! yes—I am indeed very, very miserable," she repeated, in a tone of intense bitterness, and clasping her hands together in the excess of her mental agony. "Such nights as I have passed since I first set foot in this dreadful place! No human tongue can tell the amount of wretchedness which I endure. In the day-time 'tis too horrible—oh! far too horrible to think of: but at night—when all is dark and silent, and when my very thoughts—my very ideas seem to spring into life and assume ghastly shapes——"

"Oh! my dear aunt, do not allow your imagination thus to obtain dominion over you!" interrupted Clarence. "Endeavour to compose yourself a little—

if only a little—for it does me harm to see you thus! Besides, I have so much to say to you—so many questions to ask you—so much advice to give you———"

"Alas! the only counsel you can give me, Clarence," said the wretched woman, shaking with a cold shudder, though the perspiration stood in big drops upon her brow,—"the only counsel you can give me, Clarence, is to bid me prepare for another world."

"Is it possible?" cried Villiers, shocked by the appalling significance of these words: "have you no hope—no chance———"

"Would you believe me were I to assure you that I am not guilty of the crime imputed to me—the forgery of a draft upon the bankers of the late Sir Henry Courtenay?" demanded Mrs. Torrens, fixing her sunken, lustreless eyes upon her nephew. "No—no: you are convinced that I *am* guilty—and a jury will pronounce me to be so! Think not that I blind myself against all the horrors of my position! I know my fate—I know that I must die eventually by the hand of the executioner———"

"God have mercy upon you!" exclaimed Villiers, pressing his hand to his brow as if to calm the dreadful thoughts which his aunt's language excited in his brain.

"Yes, Clarence—that must be my fate," she continued: "unless I obtain a short respite—of a few months—by confessing———"

"Confessing what?" cried Clarence impatiently.

"Oh! no—not to you can I make that avowal!" she exclaimed, in a shrieking tone.

"But I understand you! Yes—a light breaks in upon me—and———"

"Do not spurn me altogether, Clarence!" said the wretched woman, throwing herself upon her knees before him and grasping one of his hands with convulsive tightness in both her own. "Oh! I know what you would reproach me with! If not for my own sake—yet for that of the unborn child which I bear in my bosom, I should have avoided this awful risk—recoiled from that fatal crime! But I was so confident of success—so certain of avoiding exposure,—and my affairs, too, were so desperate—without resources—Sir Henry Courtenay having disappeared in such a mysterious manner———"

"Aunt," interrupted Clarence, in a firm and solemn tone, as he raised her from her suppliant posture, and placed her in a chair,—"answer me as if you were questioned by your God! Are your hands unstained with the blood———"

"Holy heavens! would you believe me capable of murder?" cried Mrs. Torrens, in a penetrating, thrilling tone of deep anguish. "Listen, Clarence," she continued, her voice suddenly becoming low and hollow, as she rose also from her seat and laid her emaciated hand upon his arm,—"listen, Clarence, for a few moments. I have been of all hypocrites the most vile—I have led a dissolute life, the profligacy of which has been concealed beneath the mask of religion—I have subsisted upon the wages paid to me by a paramour for the use of my person—I have forged—I have become the accomplice of the ravisher of innocence,—but a murderess—no—never—never!"

"God be thanked for that assurance, which I now sincerely believe!" exclaimed Clarence. "But you speak of being the accomplice of the ravisher of innocence? Is it possible—answer me quickly—that Rosamond—my sister-in-law——"

"Oh! kill me—kill me, Clarence!" cried the miserable woman, again throwing herself at his feet in the anguish of her soul: "kill me, I say—for that was the blackest crime which one woman ever perpetrated towards another!"

"Then all my worst fears are confirmed!" groaned Clarence; and, turning abruptly away from her in sudden loathing and horror, he broke forth into violent ejaculations of rage.

But in less than a minute the sounds of grief, more bitter than his fury was terrible, forced themselves on his ears; and glancing round, he beheld his aunt lying prostrate on the floor, her face buried in the carpet, and her whole frame convulsed with an anguish which in a moment renewed all the feelings of commiseration in his really generous heart.

Springing towards the spot where she had fallen when he burst so rudely away from her, he raised the wretched creature in his arms, conveyed her once more to a seat, and endeavoured to address her in terms of consolation and kindness. He even implored her pardon for what he termed his brutality towards her.

"Oh! you have no forgiveness to ask of me, Clarence," she murmured, in a faint and half-suffocating tone. "Your indignation is most natural—and I am the vilest being in female shape that ever cursed the earth with a baleful presence, or brought dishonour on a glorious sex! My God! when I look back and survey all my crimes—all my misdeeds, I despair of pardon in another world!"

"And now you add another wickedness to those of which you spoke," exclaimed Clarence: "for the mercy of God is infinite! It must be so—it would be an awful sin, a monstrous impiety to believe otherwise! A great and good Being, possessing omnipotent power and a will which there is none to question, can have no pleasure in casting your soul—poor, frail, crushed-down woman!—into a lake of eternal fires! Oh! believe me—there is hope even for greater criminals than yourself! But every atonement which it is possible for you to make upon earth, *must* be made; and, whatever be your fate amongst beings who forgive nothing, you will experience the blessings of salvation at the hands of a Being who forgives every thing!"

"I am penitent—oh! believe me, Clarence, I am very penitent!" exclaimed his aunt. "Would to God that I could live the last twenty years of my life over again! Not an error—no, not even a frailty should stain my soul! But these thoughts come upon us when it is too late to take them as the guides of our conduct."

"Alas! such is indeed the case!" said Clarence, mournfully. "And now, aunt, I am about to ask you to perform a duty which will perhaps lacerate your bosom—revive a thousand bitter reflections—"

"I understand you, Clarence," interrupted Mrs. Torrens, subduing her emotions as much as possible, and speaking in a comparatively tranquil tone: "you require from my lips a true and faithful narrative of all that has occurred since you left London with your beautiful bride? Well—that narrative shall be given. Sit down by me—and listen: but, in so listening, you will only receive fresh proofs of my black turpitude! For systematically and coolly—not in the excitement of moments when evil passions were more powerful than reason—have I perpetrated those crimes which now weigh so heavily upon my soul!"

Clarence took a chair by his aunt's side, and prepared to hear her story with an earnest but mournful attention.

His aunt then related to him the particulars of the dreadful conspiracy which had been devised by herself, the late Sir Henry Courtenay, and Mr. Torrens against the honour of Rosamond; and Clarence now learnt for the first time that Mr. Torrens had only consented to his marriage with Adelais in order to get them both out of the way, so that the younger sister might be completely in the power of those who had thus leagued against her happiness and her virtue.

"Although I deplore that such motives should have been the favouring circumstances which led to my union with Adelais," said Clarence, "yet I rejoice that my charming and adored wife is safely removed by the fact of that marriage from the power of such a monster of a parent."

Mrs. Torrens sighed profoundly, and then entered upon those details which explained to her nephew how she became acquainted with Mr. Torrens—the whole particulars of the murder of Sir Henry Courtenay, as she herself had heard them from the lips of Mr. Torrens—the forgery of the cheque, to which crime that individual was privy—the way in which she had compelled him to marry her—and the flight of Howard, the attorney, with the produce of the crime for which she was now in a felon's gaol.

"And you believe that Mr. Torrens is really innocent of the black deed imputed to him?" said Clarence, inquiringly—for he was now anxious to ascertain whether the tale which he had just heard in explanation of that mysterious event, would correspond with the proclamation of Mr. Torrens' innocence which was to be that day made to the world, according to the assurances given on the preceding morning by Esther de Medina.

"I am confident that the account given by Mr. Torrens, and which I have now related to you, is correct," answered Mrs. Torrens: "for," she added, after a few moments' hesitation, "when once we understood each other—when once our hands were united—there was no necessity to maintain any secrets from each other. We plunged headlong into crime, hand-in-hand—and felt no shame in each other's presence. Besides, he had no motive to perpetrate such a deed: on the contrary, he deprived himself of a friend whose purse was most useful to him."

"True!" observed Clarence, struck by the truth of this reasoning.

"In respect to myself," resumed the unhappy woman, "I have made up my mind how to act. I shall not aggravate my enormity by denial: I shall plead guilty to the charge of forgery—and without implicating that wretched man on whom the charge of murder now presses with such a fearful weight of circumstantial evidence. No—I shall not mention him in connexion with that deed of mine; so that if he escape from the cruel difficulty in which he is now placed, no other accusations, beyond those of his own conscience, may injure his peace."

"You have determined to adopt the course which I should have counselled," said Clarence. "It would be useless to attempt the defence of that which is so clearly apparent. The forged signature had not the baronet's private mark attached to it; but the clerk who cashed it for you, did not think of scrutinising it so closely at the moment, as you were well known to him. A subsequent examination of it proved the forgery. Stands not the case so? At least, it was thus reported in the newspapers."

"The statement is correct," answered Mrs. Torrens, mournfully; "and I feel convinced that I shall possess a greater chance of obtaining the royal mercy, by pleading guilty at once and confessing my error. Oh! to escape death—a premature death—a horrible death!" she cried, suddenly becoming nervously excited again.

"Compose yourself, aunt—compose yourself!" exclaimed Clarence; "for you have an act of justice to do towards an innocent man. In a word, I wish you to sign the account of the murder of Sir Henry Courtenay, as you received it from the lips of Mr. Torrens, and as you have now related it to me. I will draw it up briefly; and no one can tell of what benefit the existence of such a document may prove to your unhappy husband."

Clarence hastened to procure writing materials from the governor's office; and, on his return to the parlour, he drew up the statement, combining it with a confession of the forgery, though not mentioning the name of Mr. Torrens in connexion with that latter crime. The penitent woman then signed the paper in a firm handwriting; and it immediately appeared as if a load were taken from her mind.

Villiers now informed her that Rosamond had found an asylum with some kind friends of the Jewish persuasion; but, faithful to his promise to Esther de Medina, he did not drop even so much as a hint of the hopes which that admirable young lady had held out with regard to the expected proclamation and existing proofs of Mr. Torrens' innocence. It struck him, however, that the paper which he had that moment received from his aunt might assist the steps that were in such mysterious progress elsewhere to remove from the head of his father-in-law the dreadful charge which rested upon it.

"I must now leave you, aunt," said the young man, rising from his seat.

"Shall you visit Mr. Torrens?" she inquired, in a hesitating manner.

"Not to-day," was the answer. "The prison regulations do not permit visitors to call on the same inmate of this gaol two days consecutively. In fact—for I abhor every thing savouring of duplicity—I will candidly inform you that Adelais, myself, Rosamond, and the young lady with whom that poor girl is staying, saw Mr. Torrens yesterday."

"You visited him first!" murmured the wretched woman. "But I do not blame you—I cannot reproach you, Clarence," she added hastily. "It was natural that your wife should wish to see her father—and equally natural that you should accompany her. Besides, I know that it must have cost you a painful effort, to enter the presence of one so stained with crime—so polluted—so infamous as I!"

"Your contrition has obliterated from my mind all feelings save those of regret and commiseration," returned Clarence warmly. "Would that justice could so easily forget the past as I!"

"Oh! I thank you for those generous assurances," exclaimed Mrs. Torrens, bursting into tears; "for sympathy in such a place as this is dearer to the soul than all the enjoyments which the great world outside could possibly bestow! The kind word—aye, and what is more, the word of forgiveness—is the holy dew of heaven. For years and years, Clarence, was I a vile hypocrite, and such sentences as those flowed glibly from my tongue—because they were the means whereby I deceived the world. But now—oh! now, I feel all I say; and whatever may be my doom, I shall at last appreciate the sublime truths of that religion which I so long used as a mask. Clarence," she added, in a more measured tone, "always suspect the individual who makes a display of his religion. Be assured that true religious feelings do not obtrude themselves in all unseasonable moments upon society. The man or the woman who enacts the part of a *saint*, is nothing more nor less than a despicable hypocrite; and I believe that more profligacy is concealed beneath such a mask as I so long wore, than can possibly exist amongst those who make no outward display of religion. But I will not detain you longer: I know that Adelais must be cruelly shocked by all that has lately happened. One word, however, before we part:—you will not—you can not acquaint *her* with—with——"

"With the ruin of Rosamond!" cried Clarence, seeing that his aunt hesitated. "Oh! no—no: it would kill my poor wife! Not for worlds would I allow her to learn that dreadful secret! And now I understand full well wherefore Rosamond preferred to remain with her new friends, rather than accompany her sister and myself."

Mrs. Torrens and Clarence embraced and separated; the former returning to her ward in company with the matron, who had waited in an adjacent room during this interview;—and the latter repairing to the office of the governor, to whom he handed the document which his aunt had signed.

The young man then proceeded to the house of some friends dwelling in the City, and with whom he had left Adelais during his visit to Newgate.

We should observe that he was fully enabled thus to dispose of his time according to his own will, he having obtained six weeks' leave of absence from the Government Office to which he belonged.

In the course of the morning, he called at the lodgings which he had occupied in Bridge Street, Blackfriars, previously to his marriage with Adelais, to see if there were any letters lying there for him. There was only one; and the contents of that ran as follow:—

"*Pall Mall West*.

"The Earl of Ellingham presents his compliments to Mr. Villiers, and requests that Mr. Villiers will, on his return to town, favour the Earl with an interview relative to private business of some importance."

"There must assuredly be some mistake in this," observed Clarence, as he showed the letter to Adelais, "for I am totally unacquainted with this nobleman, and cannot understand what private business he can possibly have to transact with me. However, I will call to-morrow or next day and ascertain the point, when the excitement connected with your father's situation shall have somewhat subsided by the declaration of his innocence."

We need hardly say that Clarence had communicated to his beloved wife the fact that his aunt had narrated to him the particulars of the manner in which Sir Henry Courtenay came by his death, and that he had drawn up the narrative, which, upon being signed by her, had been deposited in the hands of the governor of Newgate.

CHAPTER XCVI.
SIR CHRISTOPHER BLUNT A HERO.

It was about mid-day when an extraordinary rumour began to spread like wildfire throughout the metropolis.

The report was, that between ten and eleven o'clock that morning, Sir Christopher Blunt and Dr. Lascelles had presented themselves to the sitting magistrate at Bow Street, and had not only communicated to that functionary a surprising account of certain adventures which had happened to themselves, but had likewise placed in his hands a document which proclaimed the innocence of Mr. Torrens, who was lying in Newgate under an accusation of murder.

The adventures alluded to were of such an amazing character, that, had they been related by persons of a less honourable reputation than Sir Christopher Blunt and Dr. Lascelles, they would have been treated as a pure invention on the part either of maniacs or unprincipled friends of the accused.

But the known integrity of those two gentlemen gave no scope for even the slightest breath of suspicion; and their tale, though wonderful, was so consistent in all its parts, that it was received as one of those truths which are "stranger than fiction."

The entire metropolis was in amazement!

Two respectable gentlemen—an eminent physician and a wealthy Justice of the Peace—had been conducted, blindfolded, to a house where they had received the depositions of two men who confessed themselves to be the murderers of the late Sir Henry Courtenay. There was no appearance of fraud in that confession. The men had been cross-examined apart, and had agreed in the minutest details. Every one therefore believed that Mr. Torrens was indeed innocent; and the sitting magistrate at Bow Street expressed the same opinion.

But who was the individual that had caused Sir Christopher Blunt and Dr. Lascelles to be thus made the recipients of the confession of the murderers? Where was the house to which those gentlemen had been taken? What motive was there for screening the assassins? Why was so much mystery observed in the entire transaction? And wherefore had Sir Christopher and the physician been enjoined to withhold the publication of the matter for twenty-four hours after its occurrence?

These questions were in every body's mouth; but no one could suggest any thing resembling even the shadow of a satisfactory solution.

The weapon with which the crime had been perpetrated, and a portion of the proceeds of the robbery effected at Torrens Cottage at the same time, accompanied the depositions placed by Sir Christopher Blunt in the hands of the magistrate; and a surgeon, on examining the corpse which had been removed to the deceased's house previous to receiving the rites of Christian burial, declared that the throat must have been cut by such an instrument as the one thus produced.

But this was not all. The moment the rumour of what had occurred at Bow Street reached the prison of Newgate, the governor hastened to the police-office, and submitted to the magistrate the confession made that morning by Mrs. Torrens.

This confession not only admitted her guilt in respect to the forgery—but gave such a version of the murder, as completely tallied with the depositions made by Timothy Splint and Joshua Pedler.

Looking at the entire case, as it thus stood, there was no doubt of the innocence of Mr. Torrens; and all that gentleman's friends—who, by the bye, had hitherto kept aloof from him—crowded to Newgate to congratulate him on the facts which had transpired.

The sensation created by the affair, throughout the capital, was tremendous; and when the evening papers were published, the copies were greedily caught up in all directions. It was a fine harvest for those journals; and their sale that day was prodigious.

An individual often spoken of, but never yet seen—namely, "the oldest inhabitant in the metropolis"—was duly mentioned on the occasion.

"Never," said each of the evening papers—as if the reporters had all been suddenly struck by the same idea,—"never, within the memory of the oldest inhabitant of the metropolis, has so extraordinary a case transpired."

And certainly no event for many years had produced such a powerful excitement, animating even the most callous and indifferent dispositions with a desire to know more, and setting a-thinking many who had quite enough in their own affairs to occupy all their thoughts.

The taverns, public-houses, and coffee-shops became the scenes of loud and interesting discussions, but even the knowing-ones found no opportunity of displaying their sagacity, for the mystery of the whole affair positively defied conjecture.

"But who can the man be that is at the bottom of all this? and where can his residence be situated?" were the questions which every tongue uttered, and to which no one could reply.

That such an extraordinary incident could occur in the metropolis, without leaving the faintest trace or the smallest clue to the elucidation of the enigma, appeared almost incredible.

As for Sir Christopher Blunt—he certainly did not appear to know whether he stood upon his head or his heels. The Home Secretary sent for him in the course of the afternoon, and received from his lips a full and complete statement of the whole occurrence; for the Government was naturally indignant that any individual should unwarrantably usurp the functions of the proper authorities by holding murderers in his own custody and adopting his own course to prove the innocence of a man in the grasp of justice. Sir Christopher was, however, unable to afford the slightest information which was likely to lead to the discovery of that individual, or of his place of abode.

On his return to his own house in Jermyn Street, Sir Christopher found several noblemen and influential gentlemen, including three or four Members of Parliament, waiting to see him; and he instantly became the lion of the company.

No pen can describe the immense pomposity with which he repeated his narrative of the mysterious transaction: no words can convey an idea of the immeasurable conceit and self-sufficiency with which he described the cross-examination of the murderers.

In fact, the knight made himself so busy in the matter—was so accessible to all visitors who were anxious to gratify their curiosity by asking a thousand questions—and was so ready to afford the newspaper-reporters all the information which he had to impart respecting the incident, that no one thought of applying to Dr. Lascelles in a similar manner. This circumstance was the more agreeable to the physician, inasmuch as he not only disliked wasting his time in gossip, but was well pleased at escaping the necessity of giving vague answers or positive denials in an affair the details of which were in reality no mystery to him.

To all his visitors Sir Christopher Blunt took care to speak in the following terms:—"You see, the individual who is the prime mover in this most extraordinary proceeding, required the assistance of no ordinary magistrate. He wanted a man of keen penetration—the most perfect business-habits—and of the highest character,—a man, in a word, who would probe the very souls of the two miscreants to be placed before him, and on whose report the world could implicitly rely. *That* was the reason wherefore I was pitched upon as the Justice of the Peace best qualified to undertake so difficult a business."

Sir Christopher became a perfect hero, as the mysterious stranger had predicted; and during the remainder of that memorable day on which the innocence of Mr. Torrens was proclaimed, Jermyn Street was literally lined with carriages, the common destination being the knight's abode;—so that a stranger in the metropolis would have supposed that such a scene of animation and excitement could only be occasioned by the arrival of some great foreign prince, or that the Prime Minister lived in that house and was holding a levée.

When all Sir Christopher's visitors had retired, and he found himself alone in his drawing-room at about half-past ten that evening, he threw himself on a sofa, exclaiming aloud, "Egad! that old fellow, who knocked down the Irish Captain and afterwards turned out to be a young man, was quite right. I am a hero—a regular hero! This popularity is truly delightful. I really do not envy the Duke of Wellington his having won the battle of Waterloo. No, indeed—not I! Sir Christopher Blunt is a greater man than his Grace, although only a knight."

Scarcely had the worthy gentleman arrived at this very satisfactory conclusion, when Mr. Lykspittal entered the room, holding his portfolio in his hand, and bowing so low at every third step which he took in advancing towards the knight, that it really seemed as if he were anxious to ascertain how close to the floor he could put his nose without rolling completely over like the clown at Astley's.

"My revered patron," began Mr. Lykspittal, "I have taken the liberty of bringing the first half dozen pages of the manuscript of the pamphlet——"

"The deuce take the pamphlet, Mr. Lykspittal!" shouted Sir Christopher, leaping from the sofa, and, in the exuberance of his joy, kicking the portfolio from the literary gentleman's hands up to the ceiling, so that the papers all showered down upon the head of their author, who stood amazed and aghast at this singular reception.

But in the next moment it struck the discomfited Mr. Lykspittal that Sir Christopher Blunt had suddenly taken leave of his senses—or, in other words, had gone raving mad; and he rushed to the door.

"Stop—stop!" cried Sir Christopher, darting after him. "What the deuce is the matter with the man?"

"No—don't—don't injure me!" roared Mr. Lykspittal, falling upon his knees, as the knight caught him by the arm.

"Injure you, my good fellow!" exclaimed Sir Christopher, surveying him with the utmost amazement. "What could possibly put such a thing into your head? I am not angry with you: I'm only mad——"

"I know you are!" cried Mr. Lykspittal in a tone of horror, while his countenance expressed the most ludicrous alarm.

"Yes—mad—literally mad—insane—my dear fellow!" vociferated Sir Christopher, quitting his hold upon the literary gentleman and absolutely dancing round him.

"O Lord! O Lord!" groaned Mr. Lykspittal, still upon his knees and nailed by terror to the spot.

"Insane—mad with joy!" cried the knight. "But get up—and don't be frightened. I am not angry with you. But I suppose that the idea of entering the presence of a man like me is too much for you, my poor fellow," added Sir Christopher, stopping short in the midst of his capering antics, and surveying the literary gentleman with immense commiseration.

"Oh! only mad—with joy?" murmured Mr. Lykspittal, considerably relieved by the assurance, and starting to his feet: then, dexterously catching at the suspicion which Sir Christopher, in his boundless self-conceit, had expressed, the literary gentleman suddenly resumed his usual cringing manner, and said in a tone of deep veneration, "Pardon me, my excellent patron, if—for a moment overcome by your presence—the presence of a man whose name is upon every tongue——"

"Say no more about it, my good fellow!" cried the knight, with all the bland condescension of a patron. "To tell you the truth, I am quite beside myself with joy; but I should not expose myself thus to any one save yourself. You are, however, a privileged person—behind the scenes, as it were; and you know how necessary popularity is to me. Egad! Mr. Lykspittal, I little thought when I began life as a poor boy, that I should one day become a great——"

"A *very* great," meekly suggested the sycophant.

"A very great man," added Sir Christopher, emphatically, as he surveyed himself in a neighbouring mirror. "I tell you what, Mr. Lykspittal—those vulgar citizens of Portsoken must now be ready to cut their throats——"

"A person *did* expire in that ward very suddenly to-day, Sir Christopher," observed the literary gentleman, drawing upon his imagination for this little incident, which he knew would prove most welcome to the knight's vanity; "and there's every reason to suppose that his death was caused by vexation."

"No doubt of it!" exclaimed the Justice of the Peace, playing with his shirt-frill. "Don't you see that there will be now no necessity for the pamphlets?"

Here Mr. Lykspittal's countenance fell.

"But you shall write instead," continued the knight, "a complete narrative of my most romantic and extraordinary adventures."

Here Mr. Lykspittal's countenance brightened up again.

"No—you shan't, though," cried his patron, an idea striking him.

Again the sycophant's brow became overcast.

"You shall write the history of my life!" added Sir Christopher.

And again the literary gentleman's brow expanded.

"Yes—*The Life*——"

"And *Times*," suggested Mr. Lykspittal.

"*The Life and Times of Sir Christopher Blunt*," exclaimed the knight triumphantly.

"In three volumes, large octavo, with portraits," added the sycophant.

"Egad! that's a capital suggestion of your's—the portraits, I mean," said Sir Christopher. "But you must show that, although I began the world with nothing, yet I am of an ancient and highly respectable family——"

"Certainly, my dear sir. There was no doubt a Blunt at Crecy or Agincourt," observed Mr. Lykspittal. "At all events it is easy to say there was, and in a note put '*See M.S.S., British Museum.*' That is the way we always manage in such cases, my dear Sir Christopher. The British Museum is a most convenient place——"

"What—to write in?" asked the Justice of the Peace.

"No, sir—to furnish pedigrees for those who haven't got any."

"Ah! I understand!" cried Sir Christopher, chuckling. "Capital! capital! Well, my good fellow, set about the *Life and Times* directly. But, by the bye, I wish the work to begin something in this way—'*It was on a dark and tempestiferous night—the wind roared—the artillery flew in fitting gusts—the streaming shafts of electricity shot across the eccentric sky,*'—and so on. That's a pretty sentence, you perceive; and being entirely my own composition—striking me, in fact, at the moment—and not suggested by any other person——"

"It does you infinite credit, Sir Christopher," interrupted Mr. Lykspittal, with an obsequious bow; "and with a *leetle* correction——"

"Oh! of course you will use your discretion. Well, now we understand each other, Mr. Lykspittal; and you will begin the work immediately. Of course you must introduce a great quantity of correspondence between myself and the leading men of this age, but who are now all dead."

"Have you any such letters by you, sir?" enquired the literary gentleman.

"Not I!" ejaculated Sir Christopher Blunt, speaking bluntly indeed.

"Oh! that's no matter—I can easily invent some," observed Mr. Lykspittal. "I thank you most sincerely for your kind—your generous patronage, my dear Sir Christopher. In fact, I can never forget it—I—I——"

And Mr. Lykspittal, by way of working his sycophancy up to the highest possible pitch—or, shall we not say, down to the lowest degree of self-abasement—affected to burst into tears and rushed from the room.

"Poor fellow! he's quite overcome by his feelings," murmured Sir Christopher to himself. "That's what I call real gratitude, now!"

And, having mused upon this and divers other matters for some few minutes, the worthy knight went up stairs to see his affectionate spouse and the baby, ere he retired to his own apartment.

CHAPTER XCVII.
CARLTON HOUSE.

We are now about to relate an incident which, at present, may appear to have little to do with the thread of our narrative, but which, we can assure our readers, will hereafter prove of immense importance in the development of the tale.

On the evening of that day when the innocence of Mr. Torrens was proclaimed, as related in the preceding chapter, King George IV. gave a grand entertainment at Carlton House.

This splendid mansion was that monarch's favourite residence—not only when he was Prince of Wales and Regent, but likewise while he wore on his unworthy brow the British diadem.

Execrable as the character of this unprincipled voluptuary and disgusting debauchee notoriously was, he unquestionably possessed good taste in choosing the decorations of a drawing-room, selecting a paper of a suitable pattern to match particular furniture, and superintending the fittings of a banquetting-hall. Carlton House was accordingly rendered a perfect gem of a palace under his auspices; and there the King loved to dwell, passing his evenings in elegant orgies and his nights in lascivious enjoyment.

The interior of Carlton House was indeed most sumptuous in all its arrangements. The state-apartments were fitted up with a grandeur properly chastened by elegance; and convenience and comfort were studied as much as magnificence. The entrance-hall was paved with veined marble, the roof being supported by Ionic columns from the quarries of Sienna. The west ante-room contained many fine portraits by Sir Joshua Reynolds. But the most splendid of all the apartments was the Crimson Drawing-room, which was decorated in the richest and yet most tasteful manner. The rich draperies, the architectural embellishments, the immense pier-glasses, the chandeliers of cut glass, and the massive furniture all richly gilt, evinced the state of perfection which the arts and manufactures have attained in this country.

Adjoining the Crimson Drawing-room was the Rotunda, the architecture of which was of the Ionic order, every part having been selected from the finest specimens of ancient Greece. The ceiling was painted to represent the sky, and was in the shape of a hemisphere. Another beautiful apartment was the Rose Satin Drawing-room, fitted up after the Chinese fashion, and in the middle of which stood a circular table of Sevres porcelain, the gift of Louis XVIII. to the King. Many pictures by the old masters likewise embellished that room.

We must also mention the Blue Velvet Room, remarkable for the refined taste displayed in its decorations,—and the Library, Golden Drawing-room, Gothic Dining-room, Bow Room, Conservatory, Armoury, Vestibule, and Throne Room, the last of which was fitted up with crimson velvet, and produced, when illuminated, a superb effect.

This rapid glance at the interior of Carlton House may serve to afford the reader a general idea of the splendour of that palace,—a splendour almost dazzling to contemplate, if we consider it for a few moments in juxta-position with the deplorable misery of thousands and thousands of cottages, huts, and hovels in which so large a number of the working population are forced to dwell!

But kings and queens care nothing for the condition of their people. So long as their selfish desires can be gratified and all their childish whims or extravagant caprices can be fulfilled, the industrious millions may rot in their miserable hovels, crushed by the weight of that taxation which is so largely augmented by the wants of Royalty!

It is absurd to venerate and adore Royalty; for Royalty is either despicably frivolous, or vilely arbitrary:—and he who admires or adores it, is an enemy to his own interests.

Let us, however, return to the subject of this chapter.

It was ten at night; and carriage after carriage, in rapid succession, set down the noble and beauteous guests at the entrance of Carlton House.

The palace itself was a blaze of light; and the brilliant lustre, shed throughout the spacious rooms by the magnificent chandeliers, was reflected on the numerous pier-glasses and enhanced by the splendour of the diamonds worn by the ladies.

Upwards of four hundred guests—constituting the *élite* of the fashionable world—were there assembled; and amongst them moved the King himself—undoubtedly a polished gentleman, although the few—the very few qualifications which he did possess have been greatly exaggerated by writers of the Lykspittal school.

It was a *re-union* of beauty, rank, and fashion, of the most brilliant description, though on a limited scale. A full band was in attendance; and dancing commenced in the drawing-rooms shortly after ten o'clock.

Amongst the guests was the Earl of Ellingham,—conspicuous by his fine form and handsome countenance, and more deserving of respect on account of his noble nature than by reason of his noble name: for a title is a thing which any monarch can bestow—but God alone can create the generous heart and the glorious intellect!

Lady Hatfield was likewise there; for, averse as she was to the assemblies of fashion, yet having received a card of invitation to this *re-union*, she could not refuse to obey the "royal commands."

And beautiful she appeared, too—with diamonds sparkling on her hair, and in a dress which enhanced the loveliness of her complexion and set off her graceful figure and rounded bust to their utmost advantage.

She had accompanied the ladies of a noble family with whom she was intimately acquainted; and when the party was presented to the King, he contemplated Lady Hatfield with an admiration which he did not attempt to conceal. Indeed, he addressed himself particularly to her during the few minutes that he remained in conversation with the party to which she belonged. But other guests speedily demanded his attention, and he moved away, not however without bestowing another long and even amorous look upon Georgiana, who felt relieved when the monarch was no longer near.

The Earl was speedily by Lady Hatfield's side, as soon as she was seated; and, after a few cursory observations upon the entertainment, she said to him, "Have you lately visited Mr. de Medina?"

"Not for the last two or three days," he replied. "I have been kept much at home by the necessity of preparing materials for the speech which I shall have to make on Monday evening next, on moving, according to the notice which I have already given in the House of Lords, for certain papers calculated to throw some light on the state of the industrious classes."

"You at last intend to shine as a great statesman, Arthur?" said Lady Hatfield, with a smile.

"I intend to apply myself to the grand subject of proposing those measures which may ameliorate the condition of millions of human beings," answered the Earl. "Do you not remember, Georgiana, that I told you how one whose name I need not mention, adjured me to do my duty as a British legislator? and have you forgotten that I explained to you the deep impression which his language on that occasion made upon me?"

"I have forgotten nothing that you ever told me," answered Lady Hatfield; "and I am rejoiced to hear that you are now seriously resolved to apply your great talents to so useful a purpose. You must give the necessary orders to enable me to obtain admittance to the House of Lords on Monday evening next; for I would not for worlds be disappointed in hearing your sentiments upon so grand and important a question."

"If we were not in the light of sister and brother to each other, Georgiana, I should say that I am flattered by your words," remarked the Earl: "but, as it is, I can only assure you that I receive the expression of your desire to be present in the House of Lords next Monday, as a mark of that sincere attachment—that profound friendship which you bear towards me, and which is so entirely reciprocated."

"And have you reflected upon the conversation which occurred between us the other day relative to Miss Esther de Medina?" enquired Georgiana.

"I have," was the answer; "but as yet I have arrived at no decision."

"The next time you call upon me, then," said Lady Hatfield, smiling, and yet subduing a sigh at the same moment, "I shall repeat to you all the arguments in that respect which I used on the former occasion. Now give me your arm, and we will walk into the next room through the open folding-doors of which I catch a glimpse of some fine paintings."

To the adjacent apartment they accordingly proceeded, and inspected several fine pictures, some by the old masters, and others by the most celebrated professors in modern art.

While they were thus engaged, the King approached them, greeted the Earl with urbane cordiality, and proceeded to point out to Lady Hatfield the best compositions amongst the works which she was admiring. The monarch then proposed that she should visit the Armoury; and as, when he had first approached, she had, through deference to Royalty,[41] relinquished the arm of the Earl of Ellingham, she was now compelled to accept that of the King. His Majesty, however, implied by his manner that Arthur was to accompany them; and the young nobleman accordingly followed the monarch and Georgiana to the Armoury.

As they passed through the rooms leading thither, many an envious glance was bent upon Lady Hatfield by the wives and daughters of aristocracy, each of whom would have given ten years of her life to obtain so much favour in the eyes of Royalty; although the King was, at this period, upwards of sixty-four years of age.

There was, nevertheless, nothing in Lady Hatfield's manner which indicated a consciousness of triumph: her deportment was modest, yet dignified—and manifesting that ease and self-possession which constitute such important proofs of good breeding.

"This is the first time that I have seen your ladyship at Carlton House," remarked the King, as they passed slowly on towards the Armoury.

"I have never had the honour of visiting your Majesty's palace until the present occasion," was the reply.

"You must not be forgotten in future," said the King: then slightly sinking his voice, he added, "A palace is the fitting region to be adorned by beauty such as your's."

Lady Hatfield affected not to hear the observation; and the Earl of Ellingham actually did not.

"I am an enthusiastic admirer of female loveliness," continued the King; "and I envy those who possess the talent of pourtraying upon canvas the features which are most dear to them. By the way," added his Majesty, as if a sudden idea had just struck him, "I intend to have a Diana painted for my Library. Beautiful Lady Hatfield, you must be the original of my Diana! Grant me that favour—I shall esteem it highly; and to-morrow Sir Thomas Lawrence shall call upon your ladyship to receive your commands relative to the first sitting."

"Your Majesty will deign to excuse me," said Georgiana, in a cold but profoundly respectful tone.

"Indeed, I shall receive no apology," observed the King, laughing. "But here we are in the Armoury; and it will give me infinite pleasure to direct your attention to those curiosities which are the worthiest of notice."

George the Fourth then pointed out to Lady Hatfield and the Earl of Ellingham, the swords which had belonged respectively to the Chevalier Bayard, the great Duke of Marlborough, Louis XIV., that glorious patriot Hampden (would that we had such a man at the present time!), General Moreau, Marshal Luckner, and other heroes. There was also a hunting knife which had belonged to Charles XII. of Sweden; and in addition to these curiosities, there were many military antiquities, especially in costume, all of which the King explained to the lady and the Earl.

From time to time it struck Lady Hatfield that her royal companion pressed her arm gently in his own, and not in an accidental way, as he addressed himself to her; and he also looked at her more than once in a very peculiar manner. Had he been of a less exalted rank, she would have instantaneously quitted him; but she reflected that it would be an evidence of insane vanity and conceit on her part were she to interpret in a particular way attentions which after all might have nothing more than a common significancy. She however remained cold, but respectful; and if the King really meant any thing more than the usual courtesy which a gentleman naturally pays to a lady, he received not the slightest encouragement.

"Ellingham," he said, turning abruptly towards the Earl, "do you carry a snuff-box?"

"I do not, sire," was the answer.

"That is provoking! I left mine on the porcelain table in the Chinese Drawing Room."

The young nobleman understood the hint, bowed, and departed to fetch the box—not however for a moment suspecting that the King had any sinister motive in sending him away from the Armoury, where his Majesty and Georgiana now remained alone together; for that museum had not been thrown open for the inspection of the guests generally.

"Beautiful Lady Hatfield," said George the Fourth, the moment the folding-doors had closed of their own accord behind the Earl, "you will consent to allow Lawrence to copy your sweet countenance for my Diana?"

"Your Majesty will deign to excuse me," was the cold and now reserved answer; for Georgiana's suspicions, previously excited in a faint degree, had gathered strength from the fact of her royal companion having got rid of the Earl in the manner already described.

"No—I will not excuse you, beautiful lady," exclaimed the King, enthusiastically—or with affected enthusiasm. "Your's is a countenance which, being seen once, leaves behind a desire to behold it again; and as I shall have no chance of often viewing the original, I must content myself with the contemplation of the picture."

"Your Majesty is pleased to compliment me thus," said Georgiana, more coldly than before: "and your Majesty is of course privileged. But such words, coming from a less exalted quarter, would be deemed offensive."

"I am unfortunate in not being able to render myself agreeable to Lady Hatfield," observed George the Fourth, drawing himself proudly up to his full height—for he was really piqued by the lady's manner—he who never sued in vain for a beauteous woman's smiles! But, probably reflecting that his haughtiness was little suited either to his previous conduct towards Georgiana or to his aims with regard to her, he immediately unbent again, saying in his blandest and most amiable tones, "Not for worlds would I offend you, charming lady: on the contrary, I would give worlds, did I possess them, to be able to win a single smile from those sweet lips."

Georgiana withdrew her hand from the King's arm, and became red with indignation.

"Forgive me—pardon me," said the monarch hastily: "I perceive that you are vexed with me—and I am very unfortunate in having offended you."

Thus speaking he again proffered his arm, which Lady Hatfield took, saying, "Would your Majesty deign to conduct me back to the company?"

At this moment the Earl of Ellingham returned to the Armoury, and handed the King his snuff-box. The party then retraced their way to the splendid saloons, the monarch conversing the while in a manner which seemed to indicate that Lady Hatfield had no ground to fear his recurrence to subjects that were disagreeable to her. At length he resigned her to the care of Lord Ellingham; but ere he turned away, he gave her a rapid and significant look, as much as to say, "I throw myself upon your generosity not to mention my conduct towards you."

The King now withdrew from the apartments thrown open for the reception of the company, and remained absent for nearly an hour. When he returned, his countenance was much flushed; and it was evident that he had been enjoying a glass or two of his favourite curaçoa-punch, in company with a few boon-companions, who had been summoned to attend him in a private room remote from the state-saloons.

One of the boon-companions just alluded to, was a certain Sir Phillip Warren—an old courtier who was supposed to enjoy the confidence of the King, and who, it was rumoured, had been the means of extricating his royal master, when Prince of Wales, from many a difficulty in financial matters as well as from the danger of exposure in divers amatory intrigues. Without any defined official position about the person of the King, Sir Phillip was nevertheless a very important individual in the royal household—one of those useful, but mysterious agents who, while enjoying the reputation of men of honour, are in reality the means by which the dirty-work of palaces is accomplished. In appearance, Sir Phillip Warren was a stout, red-faced, good-humoured-looking man; and not the least of those qualifications which rendered him so especial a favourite with the King, was the aristocratic faculty that he possessed of taking his three bottles after dinner without seeming to have imbibed any thing stronger than water.

Such was the courtier who, accosting the Earl of Ellingham, shortly after the King's return to the drawing-rooms, drew that nobleman aside with an intimation that he wished to say a few words to him in private.

Taking the Earl's arm, Sir Phillip Warren led him away from the brilliantly lighted saloons, and introduced the nobleman into the Blue Velvet Closet— a small but elegantly decorated room, where a single lamp was burning upon the table.

"His Majesty has been speaking to me concerning your lordship," said Sir Phillip Warren, when Arthur and himself were seated alone together in the Closet; "indeed, our royal master has been graciously pleased to intimate that he is much prepossessed in your favour."

The Earl bowed a cold recognition of the compliment,—for he was far too enlightened a man not to feel disgust at the sycophantic language in which that compliment was conveyed—and he was likewise convinced that there was some ulterior object in view.

"A young nobleman such as your lordship, may rise to the highest offices in the State by means of the royal favour," continued Sir Phillip. "Your talents are known to be great—and your influence in the House of Lords is consequently extensive. But his Majesty regrets to learn that your lordship seems inclined to proclaim opinions so far in advance of the spirit of the age as to be dangerous to the institutions of the country—those institutions which the wisdom of our ancestors devised, and which the experience of ages has consecrated."

"Really, Sir Phillip Warren," said the Earl, unfeignedly surprised at this address, "I am at a loss to conceive wherefore you should seek to lead me into a political discussion on such an occasion as the present."

"I will explain myself," returned the courtier. "His Majesty retired just now, with a few of his faithful servants, amongst whom I have the honour to be included, to partake of a little refreshment; and while we were thus engaged, his Majesty made an observation highly in favour of yourself. A nobleman present thereupon informed his Majesty that your lordship had placed a certain notice upon the books of the House of which your lordship is so distinguished an ornament. The nature of that notice is displeasing to his Majesty, who is graciously pleased to think that the common people already consider themselves of far greater importance than they really are."

"If, sir, by the contemptuous phrase '*the common people*,' you mean that enlightened and respectable body—*the working classes*," exclaimed the Earl indignantly, "I must beg to declare that I differ totally from the opinion which his Majesty has expressed concerning them."

"Well—well, my dear Earl," said Sir Phillip, in a conciliatory tone: "every one has a right to his own opinion—we are aware of *that fact*. But permit me to represent to you that you will gain no personal advantage, by espousing the cause of the masses."

"I seek no personal advantage," cried Arthur, with an impatient gesture, indicative of his desire to terminate the interview at once. "I am not putting myself forward as a factious demagogue—I seek not the honours of a democratic championship: but *this* I intend and contemplate, Sir Phillip Warren—to exert all my energies, use all the little influence I may possess, and devote any amount of talent which God has given me, for the purpose of directing the attention of the Legislature to the neglected, oppressed and impoverished condition of that fine English people which constitutes the pillar of the State."

"By adopting such a course, my lord," remonstrated Sir Phillip, "you will offend his Majesty, who is now so well disposed towards you, that were you inclined to enter his service in the sphere of diplomacy, your wishes might be complied with at once. Indeed, the post of Envoy Plenipotentiary to the important Grand Duchy of Castelcicala is at this moment vacant; and if your lordship——"

"In one word, Sir Phillip Warren," interrupted the Earl of Ellingham, rising from his seat, "you are desirous to tempt me into a compromise. Wherefore do you not frankly explain yourself at once, and say, '*Withdraw your notice from the books of the House of Lords, and depart as Ambassador to the Court of Angelo, Grand Duke of Castelcicala*:' to which I should immediately reply, '*No possible reward which an earthly monarch can give, should induce me to abandon that task which a sense of duty has imposed upon me.*'"

Sir Phillip Warren was astonished at the firmness and boldness with which the Earl spoke; for such manly independence was quite unusual in the atmosphere of a corrupt Court and venal political world. The fact was that Sir Phillip had undertaken the task of effecting the desired compromise with the Earl: the King had specially entrusted the matter to him;—and the courtier trembled at the idea of being compelled to report the total failure of the negotiation to his royal master. He was therefore cruelly embarrassed, and knew not what course to adopt.

But suddenly an idea struck him;—for he perceived that the Earl was not a man to be tempted by reward; but he thought that the nobleman might perhaps be overcome by the powers of eloquent reasoning.

"My dear Earl," he accordingly said, "you are too honourable and too highly-principled a statesman not to yield to conviction. Grant me, in common justice, one favour: I ask it in the name of his Majesty."

"Speak," exclaimed Arthur, resuming his chair to show that he was prepared to listen with courteous attention.

"The Prime Minister is present at the *re-union* this evening," said Sir Phillip: "will you hear any argument which he may address to you upon the subject of your notice for next Monday night, and consider whatever may pass between you to be strictly confidential?"

"I should be unreasonable to refuse to listen to any observations which so high a functionary as the Prime Minister may address to me," answered the Earl; "and I shall consider our interview to be private and confidential, on condition that no insult be offered to me in the shape of temptation or promise of reward. If it can be shown by fair argument that I am wrong in pursuing the course which I have adopted, I will yield to conviction; but I shall spurn with contempt and indignation any other means that may be adopted to induce me to withdraw my notice from the books of the House."

"The Interview shall take place upon the condition your lordship has stipulated. Be kind enough to await my return with the Prime Minister."

Sir Phillip Warren then withdrew, closing the door behind him.

But scarcely had he left the Blue Velvet Closet, when the lamp upon the table suddenly grew dim; and in a few moments the light expired altogether, doubtless through lack of oil—leaving the room in total darkness.

The Earl was uncertain how to act; and while he was still deliberating with himself whether to leave the Closet in search of a servant to procure another light, or await the return of Sir Phillip Warren, the door opened.

"This room is in darkness, sire," immediately said a female voice, which the Earl of Ellingham recognised to be that of Lady Hatfield.

"I pledge you my royal word that I was ignorant of the fact when I conducted you hither," returned the King. "But, pray enter, beauteous lady: we may at all events converse at our ease for a few minutes."

And to the amazement of the Earl, Georgiana complied with the King's request, accompanying his Majesty into that dark room, the door of which was immediately closed. Indeed, so astounded—so shocked was Arthur by this incident, that he sate motionless and speechless in his chair at the further extremity of the apartment.

"My dearest Lady Hatfield," said the King, "I thank you most sincerely for having thrown aside that chilling—freezing manner which you maintained in the early part of the evening, when I sought to make you understand the profound admiration with which your beauty has inspired me. How unfortunate are princes! They cannot obey the dictates of their hearts—they dare not bestow their hand where their affections are engaged. But society is justly lenient in their behalf; and thus the lady who becomes a monarch's favourite, is regarded with envy and respect, and not with contumely or reproach."

"But no lady who entertains the slightest feeling of self-respect," observed Lady Hatfield, in a low and tremulous tone, "will abandon herself in a moment even to a monarch. There must be proofs of real attachment on his side——"

"Granted, beauteous Georgiana," interrupted the King impatiently. "Show me how I can demonstrate my affection towards yourself—ask me any boon which I have the power to grant, and which I dare accord——"

"Oh! if your Majesty would only fulfil this pledge!" exclaimed Lady Hatfield joyfully.

"Do you doubt me?" demanded George the Fourth. "Put me to the test, I say—and you shall be convinced of my readiness, my anxiety to prove how deeply I am attached to you, although the impression made on my heart be so sudden."

"Sire," resumed Lady Hatfield, "I shall be so bold as to take your Majesty at your word. To-morrow your Majesty will receive a certain paper; and I warn your Majesty beforehand that its contents will be most singular."

"I shall ask no farther explanations than you may choose to give, beauteous Georgiana," observed the King. "But when I receive the paper, what next do you require?"

"That your Majesty shall affix to it your royal signature, and likewise direct your Majesty's Secretary of State for the Home Department to countersign it," responded Lady Hatfield. "This being done, the document must be returned to me."

"All that you have stipulated, shall be carried into effect," said the King: then, sinking his voice and assuming a tender tone, he added, "But will there be room for me to hope, sweet lady——"

"Your Majesty must remember the observation I made ere now," interrupted Georgiana. "Before a woman, whose affection is really worthy of being possessed, can consent to surrender herself entirely even to one so highly placed as you, sire, her heart must be won by kindnesses shown—by proofs of attachment given——"

"I accept the condition implied, charming Georgiana," exclaimed the King. "You imagine that I am now influenced by a sudden caprice—that the love which I bear for you is the phantasy of a moment. Well—I will convince you to the contrary; and when I shall have proved to you that my passion survives the passing hour—then—then, sweet lady, you will not suffer me to hope in vain! Come—let us return to the drawing-room; and believe me when I declare that you have made me supremely happy. But, ere we again seek that society where a cold ceremony must keep us under a rigid restraint, allow me to seal upon your lips that pledge for which I have already given my royal word."

"No, sire—not now—not yet!" cried Lady Hatfield, in a tone which showed that she felt herself to be in a position to dictate to her regal admirer.

"Cruel charmer!" said the King: "but I suppose you must be permitted to have your own way. Send me the paper to-morrow—let it be addressed to me under cover to Sir Phillip Warren;—and you shall see by the haste with which it will be returned to you, that I shall count every minute an hour, and reckon every day to be a year, until that happy moment comes when you will be wholly and solely mine."

George the Fourth then opened the door, and led Georgiana away from the room in which this singular scene had taken place.

But what of the Earl of Ellingham?

So completely stunned and stupified was he by all that had occurred, that he never moved a muscle and retained his very breath suspended while his ears drank in every word that passed between the King and Lady Hatfield. Thus did he become an unwilling and unintentional listener to a discourse which created the most painful emotions in his breast.

Was it possible that the Lady Hatfield whom he looked upon as the very personification of virtue, in spite of the terrible misfortune which had deprived her of her chastity,—was it possible that she, whose soul he had imagined to be so pure, though dwelling in a body polluted by the ravisher,—was it possible that she had already suffered herself to be dazzled by the delusive overtures of royalty? and was she seriously about to resign herself to the King's arms—to become the mistress of that regal debauchee of sixty-four?

"My God!" thought the Earl: "I, who had such an exalted opinion of female virtue!"

Then he remembered that portion of the conversation which had turned upon the document Lady Hatfield was to send to the King for his royal signature, and which she had prepared him to find of a most singular character. Of what nature could that document be? Conjecture was vain and useless.

The first impulse of the Earl was to inform Lady Hatfield that he had overheard her conversation with the King, and conjure her to reflect seriously ere she committed a fatal step of which she would assuredly have to repent for the remainder of her life. But second thoughts convinced him that he must retain profoundly secret the fact of his acquaintance with the understanding existing between Georgiana and the monarch; for in confessing himself to have been an eaves-dropper, he should have to blush in the presence of one whom he was to take to task. He saw it would be difficult to make the lady believe that he himself was so stupified by her conduct, as to be totally unable to declare his presence in a room where a private conversation was in progress; and she would naturally upbraid him, he thought, for what might be looked upon as a proof of mean and contemptible curiosity on his part—although, as the reader is aware, he was indeed animated by no such vile sentiment.

Moreover, in resigning all claim to her hand—or rather, in recognising the impossibility of contracting an alliance with a woman whom his brother had ravished—the Earl had ceased to enjoy any right to advise or control her in respect to her moral conduct;—and it now struck him that, painfully situated as she was—unable to become the wife of any honourable and confiding man—she had accepted overtures which would render her a monarch's mistress. In a word, he conceived that he should best consult her happiness, as matters stood, by affecting a complete ignorance of the understanding so suddenly established between herself and George the Fourth.

Having come to this determination, he quitted the Blue Velvet Closet, and was retracing his way to the scene of brilliant gaiety, when he encountered Sir Phillip Warren in the corridor.

"I searched every where for the Minister, and was unable to find him," said the courtier. "At last, upon making enquiries, I learnt that he had taken his departure."

"I am not sorry that it is so," returned the Earl of Ellingham; "for I feel convinced that no argument, although I should have listened to it as a matter of courtesy, could deter me from advocating the cause of the working classes."

With these words the nobleman bowed coldly to Sir Phillip Warren, and passed on to the state-apartments, in one of which he found Lady Hatfield seated with the friends in whose company she had arrived at the entertainment.

Her manner was calm and collected; and if there were any change, it was in the slight—the very slight smile of triumph which played upon her lip:—at least, it struck the Earl that such an expression her rosy mouth wore, as he approached her. But it disappeared as she began to converse with him; and he so subdued his own feelings, that she did not observe any thing to lead her to suppose that he was aware of her understanding with the King.

Precisely at midnight the supper-rooms were thrown open; and a magnificent banquet was served up. We need scarcely say that the most costly wines, the most expensive luxuries, and every delicacy that gold could procure, appeared upon the board, which absolutely groaned beneath the weight of massive plate, superb porcelain, and brilliant crystal.

The festivity was kept up until a late hour: indeed it was past two in the morning before the company began to separate.

But when the Earl of Ellingham was once more at home, and had retired to his chamber, sleep would not visit his eyes, fatigued though he were:—the scene which had occurred in the Blue Velvet Closet was so impressed upon his mind, that he could not divert his thoughts into another channel. It was not that he was jealous of Lady Hatfield:—no—circumstances had changed his love for her into a sincere and deeply-rooted friendship. But he felt disappointed—he felt deceived in the estimate he had formed of her character: he had believed her to be possessed of a mind too strong to be dazzled by the splendours of Royalty, and to yield herself up to a man whom it was impossible for her to love, merely for the sake of becoming a King's mistress.

Had George the Fourth been estimable on account of character, amiable in disposition, and worthy of admiration as a sovereign, the Earl thought that there would in this case have been a shadow—but even then, only a shadow—of an excuse for the conduct of Georgiana. The reverse, was, however, the precise fact;—for the King was notoriously a hardened profligate—a confirmed debauchee—a disgusting voluptuary—and an unprincipled monarch,—in a word, such a man as a refined and strong-minded woman would look upon with abhorrence.

So thought Lord Ellingham;—and when he recalled to memory the frightful behaviour of George the Fourth towards the unhappy Caroline, against whom his vile agents trumped up the most unfounded accusations, and who was hunted to death by the blood-thirsty instruments of a hellish system of persecution,—when the Earl reflected upon all this, his amazement at the conduct of Lady Hatfield increased almost to horror.

At length his thoughts wandered to Esther de Medina—or rather, the beautiful Jewess became mixed up with them; for it was impossible that the scene in the Blue Velvet Closet could be entirely banished from his mind;—and, as he pondered upon *her* innocence—*her* artlessness—*her* amiable qualities, his confidence in woman revived, and he exclaimed aloud, as he lay in his sumptuous couch, "Oh! wherefore do I delay securing to myself the possession of such a treasure? Yes, Esther—dearest Esther—thou shalt be mine!"

> 41. It is contrary to Court etiquette for a lady and gentleman to remain arm-in-arm when conversing with a Royal personage.

CHAPTER XCVIII.
AN ACQUITTAL AND A SENTENCE.

The Blackamoor, in his mysterious abode, beheld the successful progress of his grand schemes; and while all London was busy with conjectures relative to the daring unknown who seemed to have constituted himself the instrument of justice and the champion of innocence wrongly accused, the object of this general interest and curiosity remained in impervious concealment.

The Secretary of State offered a reward of two hundred pounds to any one that should give such information as to lead to the discovery of the person who had enticed Sir Christopher Blunt to his unknown abode, and who had caused Dr. Lascelles to be conveyed thither by force; and the most astute Bow Street agents were employed in instituting enquiries in every part of the metropolis with a view to find out the dwelling of the individual in question.

The newspapers teemed with the most absurd and contradictory reports on the subject; and a thousand wild rumours were constantly circulating throughout the metropolis. The result of all this was that those who were employed in the enquiries above alluded to, were so mystified and bewildered, that they worked like drunken men in the dark,—taking up and following any ridiculous information which they obtained either from wags or from persons who wished to appear more knowing than their neighbours,—and pursuing what at first might seem to be a clue, but which invariably led to nothing satisfactory at last.

The Blackamoor's own retainers, who were all faithful to their master, augmented this confusion of rumours and ideas, by mingling amongst the gossips in places of public resort, and gravely propagating reports which were sure to direct the attention of the Bow Street runners from the very point where its object lay; and all that Dr. Lascelles had been known to hazard in the shape of conjecture in the matter, was a hint that, to the best of his belief, the carriage in which he had been borne away on the memorable night of the confession, had eventually stopped in one of the most easterly suburbs of the metropolis. The consequence of this suggestion was, that Wapping, Whitechapel, Bethnal Green, and Globe Town were regularly explored by the Bow Street officials—but entirely without success.

Although the innocence of Mr. Torrens was universally believed, yet, as he had been committed for trial, it was necessary that he should undergo the ordeal. This ceremony took place a few days after the publication of the confession of the real murderers—indeed, on the very Monday following the grand entertainment at Carlton House.

The prisoner was arraigned on the charge of having assassinated Sir Henry Courtenay; and the Recorder of London presided on the bench. The counsel for the prosecution merely stated the particulars of the discovery of the corpse of the deceased baronet, and the circumstances which had led to the prisoner's committal; but he did not for a moment insist that those circumstances were conclusive against him. Sir Christopher Blunt then detailed in evidence all that he had given in narrative at Bow Street; and Dr. Lascelles corroborated his statement. The confession signed by Joshua Pedler and Timothy Splint, and likewise the one in which Martha Torrens had attested to certain facts in favour of the prisoner, were read by the clerk of arraigns; and the counsel for the defence was about to address the Court, when the jury declared that their minds were already made up.

The *acquittal* of the prisoner immediately followed; and the first person who shook hands with him as he was released from the dock, was Sir Christopher Blunt.

Mr. Torrens accepted a seat in the knight's carriage, and repaired to a friend's house in the neighbourhood, where Clarence Villiers, Adelais, Rosamond, and Esther de Medina were assembled to welcome his acquittal, relative to which none of them had felt at all uneasy.

But it was evident that, although thus relieved from the dreadful charge and appalling danger which had recently hung over him, Mr. Torrens was an altered man. He had received a blow which had shaken his constitution to its very basis:—his mental energies were impaired;—and instead of a hale man of between fifty-five and fifty-six, which was his actual age, he seemed to be a feeble, tottering octogenarian.

When the excitement produced by the meeting with his family after his release had somewhat subsided, Mr. Torrens said with nervous impatience, "Rosamond, my dear child, I shall leave England this very day. Will you accompany your father?"

"Leave us the moment you are restored to us!" exclaimed Adelais, bursting into tears.

"Yes—yes," returned the unhappy man: "I cannot—dare not remain in England. Though released from a criminal gaol, yet I am in danger of being plunged into a debtors' prison; for I am ruined, as you all know—totally, irredeemably ruined. Besides—never, never again could I dwell in that house where so many frightful things have occurred. Yes," he repeated, "I must leave England at once; and you, my poor Rosamond," he added, with tears trickling down his sunken cheeks, "will have to support your father, by means of your accomplishments, in a foreign land."

"No—that must not be," said Esther de Medina, passing a handkerchief rapidly over her eyes: "Rosamond has friends to whom, although they have known her but for so short a period, her welfare is dear. Foreseeing some such decision as that to which you have now come, relative to leaving England, my father has desired me to place a thousand pounds at your daughter's disposal," continued the beautiful Jewess, addressing herself to the wondering Torrens, and at the same time placing a sealed packet in Rosamond's hands.

"Oh! my generous—my excellent-hearted friend," exclaimed Rosamond, embracing the Jewess tenderly: "how is it possible that I could have merited this kindness—this extraordinary bounty at your hands?"

"We are fellow-creatures, though of a different creed," said Esther modestly;—but she was compelled to receive the thanks of the astonished Torrens and of the admiring Clarence and Adelais.

Villiers now drew his father-in-law aside, and spoke to him concerning Mrs. Torrens.

"I cannot see her, Clarence—I cannot meet her again," he replied. "Besides, an interview would be useless. Our marriage was not one of affection, as you are well aware: and, moreover——But," he added, suddenly interrupting himself, and looking tremblingly in the young man's face, while his voice sank to a low, hollow whisper,—"she has doubtless told you *all?*"—and then he glanced toward Rosamond, who was conversing with Esther de Medina and Adelais at the farther end of the room.

"Yes—I know *all*," returned Villiers; and the words seemed to convulse his wretched listener with horror. "But it is too late to amend the past—and it is not for me to reproach you *now*. Your own conscience, Mr. Torrens, will prove a sufficient punishment for the frightful wrong you have done to that poor girl. And fear not that I shall impart the sickening truth to my wife, who is already too deeply affected by all that has lately occurred."

"Thank you, Clarence—thank you, at least for that assurance," said the old man, his voice almost suffocated with terrible emotions. "You perceive how impossible it is that I should remain in England—with so many dreadful reminiscences to make me ashamed to look those who know me in the face. This very instant will Rosamond and myself set out on our way to a foreign land: you will be kind enough to send my trunks after me to Dover."

"I do not attempt to dissuade you from this step," observed Villiers; "because I can see no more agreeable alternative."

Mr. Torrens' decision was then communicated to the three ladies: and the farewell scene between the sisters was affecting in the extreme. Nor less did

Adelais deplore the necessity which compelled her to separate from her father; but she at least had a consolation in the midst of her grief—a solace in the possession of a husband who loved her devotedly, and whom she adored.

A post-chaise was speedily in attendance: and Mr. Torrens took his departure from the English capital, in company with his younger daughter.

Esther de Medina did not take leave of Clarence and Adelais before she had made them promise to pay her an early visit at Finchley Manor; and the young couple returned to Torrens Cottage more than ever prepossessed in favour of the beautiful Jewess, who seemed to delight only in doing good.

On the ensuing day Martha Torrens was placed in the dock, before the Recorder of London, charged with the crime of forgery.

The court of the Old Bailey was crowded with persons belonging to those religious associations of which the prisoner had lately been so conspicuous a member. There was Mr. Jonathan Pugwash, President of the *South Sea islands Bible-Circulating Society*, not only with a face indicative of its owner's attachment to brandy, but also with a breath smelling very strongly of that special liquor: there also was the Reverend Malachi Sawkins, looking so awfully miserable at the scandal brought by the prisoner's conduct on the religious world, that a stranger would have supposed him to be at least her brother, if not her husband;—and there likewise was the Reverend Mr. Sheepshanks, who, having made his peace with the members of the above-mentioned Society, had latterly come out much stronger than ever in the shape of a saint. Many other sleek and oily, or thin and pale, religious gentlemen were present on this occasion; and in the gallery were numerous old ladies, all belonging to the ultra-evangelical school, and who appeared to divide their attention between the task of wiping their eyes with white cambric handkerchiefs and strengthening their nerves by means of frequent applications to little flasks or bottles which they took from their pockets or muffs.

Mrs. Torrens was supported into the dock by two turnkeys of Newgate; for she was overcome with shame and grief at the position in which her crime had placed her. She was indeed a pitiable object; and it was evident that, whatever penalty the Bench might award, her punishment in this world had already begun.

The indictment being read, she pleaded *Guilty* in a faint voice; and the prosecutors strongly recommended her to mercy.

The Recorder[42] put on the black cap, and proceeded to address the prisoner in a most feeling manner. His lordship said that the law left him no alternative but to pronounce sentence of death. He however observed that, considering the contrition manifested by the plea of *Guilty* and the intercession of the bankers who had been defrauded of their money by the forgery, he should recommend the prisoner to the mercy of the Crown. His lordship concluded by an intimation that she must make up her mind to pass the remainder of her days as an exile in the penal settlements, but that her life would be spared.

She was conveyed in a fainting state away from the dock; and the religious gentlemen present gave so awful and simultaneous a groan, that the judge was quite startled upon the bench, and the jury were horrified in their box.

> 42. At the period of which we are writing, this high civic functionary tried cases involving capital penalties as well as those of a less serious nature. Since the establishment of the Central Criminal Court, the great judges of the kingdom preside at the Old Bailey to try prisoners charged with grave offences.

CHAPTER XCVIX.
THE CONDITION OF THE WORKING CLASSES.

In the afternoon of that same Monday on which Mr. Torrens was acquitted and his wife condemned, vast crowds collected in the vicinity of the Houses of Parliament.

The multitude consisted chiefly of members of the industrious classes, many individuals being accompanied by their wives and children. They were attired in the best raiment that they possessed; and their conduct was most orderly and creditable.

At about a quarter to five o'clock, the carriages began to arrive and set down at the respective entrances the Members of the two Houses of Parliament: some, however, proceeded thither on horseback; and others on foot. The crowds neither cheered the popular, nor hissed the unpopular legislators who thus passed through the mass which had divided to make way for them; until at last one long, hearty, and glorious outburst welcomed the appearance of the Earl of Ellingham, as he proceeded on horseback, attended by his groom, to St. Stephen's.

The young nobleman acknowledged this outpouring of a people's gratitude—not with a patronising condescension, but with an affability which seemed to say, "I am one of yourselves—we're all equal—and I am proud of being considered your *friend*!"

Long after he had entered the portals of the House of Lords, and was lost to the public view, did the cheering continue outside; for the multitudes appreciated all that was great and generous in the task which a member of a proud aristocracy had undertaken to perform that day in their behalf.

There was a full attendance of Peers, Temporal and Spiritual; and the strangers' galleries, overlooking the throne and the woolsack, were crowded with fashionable gentlemen and elegantly dressed ladies. Amongst the audience there assembled, were Lady Hatfield, Mr. de Medina, and Esther. Georgiana was not however seated near the Jew and his daughter, she being unacquainted with them otherwise than by name, as the reader is already aware.

Soon after five o'clock the Earl of Ellingham rose from his seat, advanced towards the table, and proceeded to address the House on the motion of which he had given notice.

He began by expressing a regret that so important a subject as that which he proposed for discussion—namely, the condition of the industrious population—should not have been taken up by some noble lord more competent than himself to do it adequate justice; and he declared most solemnly that no selfish idea of obtaining popularity had influenced him in the course which he was pursuing. He then proceeded to expatiate upon the state of the working classes, and to urge upon the House the necessity of adopting measures to ameliorate their lamentable condition. It was too frequently alleged, he observed, that those classes were thoughtless, improvident, ungrateful, and intellectually dull; but this assertion he emphatically denied. Despair, produced by their unhappy condition, naturally led to dissipation in many instances; but were the working-man placed in a position so that his livelihood should be rendered less precarious than it now was—were his labour adequately remunerated—were he more fairly paid by the representatives of property—were a scale of wages established, having a fixed *minimum*, but no fixed *maximum*, the increased comfort thus ensured to him would naturally remove from his mind those cares which drove him to the public-house. His lordship would have no fixed *maximum* of wages, because wages ought always to be increased in proportion to the value of productive labour to employers: but he would have a *minimum* established, to obviate the cruel and disastrous effects of those periods when labour exceeded the demand in the market. This could not be considered unfair towards employers, because when the markets were brisk and trade was flourishing, they (the employers) reaped the greatest benefit from that activity, and enriched themselves in a very short time: therefore, when markets were dull and trade was stagnant, they should still be compelled to pay such wages as would enable their employed to live comfortably. The profits gained during prosperous seasons not only enabled employers to enjoy handsome incomes, but also to accumulate considerable savings; and as the best wages scarcely enabled the employed to make any thing like an adequate provision for periods of distress, it was not fair that the representatives of property should use the labour of the working classes just when it suited them, and discard it or only use it on a miserable recompense when it did not so well suit them. For the labour of the employed not only made annual incomes for the employers, but also permanent fortunes; and the value of that labour should not be calculated as lasting only just as long as it was available for the purpose of producing large profits. Labour was the working man's *capital*, and should have constant interest, as well as money placed in the funds—that interest of course increasing in proportion to the briskness of markets; but never depreciating below a standard value—much less being discarded as valueless altogether, in times of depression. A thousand pounds would always obtain three per cent. interest, under any circumstances; and, at particular periods, might be worth six or seven per cent. Labour should be considered in the same light. Stagnant markets diminished the profits of employers, but did not ruin them: if they did not obtain profit enough to live upon, they had the accumulations of good seasons to fall back upon. But how different was the case with the employed! To them stagnation of business was ruin—starvation—death;—the breaking up of their little homes—the sudden check of their children's education—the cause of demoralisation and degradation—and the terrible necessity of applying to the parish! The supply and demand of labour were necessarily unequal at many times, and in many districts; and the Government should therefore adopt measures to prevent those frightful fluctuations in wages which carried desolation into the homes of thousands of hard-working, industrious, and deserving families. In fact, a law should be passed to ensure the working-man against the casualty of being employed at a price below remuneration. In England the poor were not allowed to have a stake in the country—there were no small properties—the land was in the possession of a few individuals comparatively; and thus the landed interest constituted a tremendous monopoly, most unjust and oppressive to the industrious classes. The only way to remove this evil influence, and ameliorate the condition of the working population—the only way to countervail the disastrous effect of that monopoly, short of a Revolution which would treble or quadruple the number of landed proprietors,—was to compel property to maintain labour as long as labour sought for employment and occupation. The noble Earl then proceeded to state that if the working-classes were thus treated, they would not be driven by their cares and troubles to the excessive use of alcoholic liquors: they would not become demoralised by being compelled to migrate from place to place in search of employment—going upon the tramp, sleeping in hideous dens of vice, where numbers were forced to herd together without reference to age or sex: they would not be unsettled in all their little arrangements to bring up their children creditably and with due reference to instruction;—they would not be made discontented, anxious for any change no matter what, vindictive towards that society which thus rendered them outcasts, and sullen or reckless in their general conduct. But as things now were, the industrious man never felt settled: he knew that the hut which he called his home, was held on the most precarious tenure;— he felt the sickening conviction that if he had bread and meat to-day, he might have only bread to-morrow, and no food at all the day after. It was positively frightful to contemplate the condition of mental uncertainty, anxiety, and apprehension in which millions of persons were thus existing; and those who reproached them with recklessness or sullenness, should blame themselves as the causes of all that they vituperated. Lord Ellingham next proceeded to show that although there had been a vast increase of wealth and comfort amongst the middle and upper classes, yet the condition of the industrious millions was not only unimproved, but had positively deteriorated. The population was increasing at the rate of 1000 souls a day— and pauperism was keeping pace with that increase. Unrepresented in Parliament—without any means of making their voice heard—positively incapacitated from having a stake in the country, the industrious millions were the mere slaves and tools of the wealthy classes. Thus an immense mass of persons was kept in bondage—in absolute serfdom by an oligarchy. Was such a state of things just? was it rational? was it even humane? The millions were ground down by indirect taxes, in which shape they actually contributed more to the revenue, in proportion to their means, than the rich. The only luxuries which the poor enjoyed, and which had become as it were necessaries,—namely, tea, sugar, tobacco, beer, and spirits,—were the most productive sources of revenue. If noble lords reproached the poor for dirty habits, as he well knew that it was their custom to do, he would ask them why soap was made an article subject to so heavy a tax? It was a contemptible fallacy to suppose that because the poor contributed little or nothing in the shape of direct taxation to the revenue, they were positively untaxed. He would again declare that the poor paid more in indirect taxes than the rich did in both direct and indirect ways, when the relative means of the two parties were taken into consideration. From these subjects the Earl passed to the consideration of the inequality of the laws, and the incongruity, severity, and injustice of their administration towards the poor. Every advantage was given to the rich in the way of procuring bail in those cases where security for personal appearance was required; but no poor man could possibly give such security. He must go to prison, and there herd with felons of the blackest dye. Perhaps on trial his innocence would transpire; and then what recompense had he for his long incarceration—his home broken up during his absence—and his ruined family? It was possible—nay, it often happened that a man would lie thus in prison for four or five months previously to trial; and during that period it would be strange indeed if he escaped gaol contamination. Then, again, there were offences of a comparatively venial kind, and for which penalties might be inflicted in the shape of fines, the alternative being imprisonment. These fines were insignificant trifles in the estimation of a rich man; but the smallest of them was quite a fortune in the eyes of the poor. Even a person with a hundred a-year would pay a fine of five pounds rather than go to prison for a month or six weeks: but a labouring man, earning ten or twelve shillings a week, could no more satisfy the demand thus made upon him than he could influence the motion of the earth,—unless, indeed, he pawned and pledged every little article belonging to him; and the infliction thereby became a blow which he never afterwards recovered. Did a poor man offend a clergyman, he was forthwith put into the Spiritual Court, as the common saying was; and the expensive proceedings, which he could not stay, involved him in utter ruin. When a poor man was oppressed by a rich one, it was vain and ludicrous to assert that the Courts of Law were open to him: law was a luxury in which only those who possessed ample means could indulge. In a case where some grievous injury was sustained by a poor man—the seduction of his wife or daughter, for instance—redress or recompense was impossible, unless some attorney took up the case on speculation; and this was a practice most demoralising and pernicious. But if left entirely unassisted in that respect, the poor man could no more go to Westminster Hall than he could afford to dine at Long's Hotel. With regard to the subject of education, the noble Earl declared that it was positively shocking to think that such care should be taken to convert negroes to Christianity thousands of miles off, while the most deplorable ignorance prevailed at home. The Church enjoyed revenues the amount of which actually brought the ministers of the gospel into discredit, as evidencing their avaricious and grasping disposition;—while the people remained as uneducated as if not a single shilling were devoted to spiritual pastors or lay instructors. He boldly accused both Houses of Parliament and the upper classes generally of being anxious to keep the masses in a state of ignorance. Where instruction was imparted gratuitously, it was entirely of a sectarian nature; just as if men required to study grammar, history, arithmetic, or astronomy on Church of England principles. The whole land was over-run by clergymen, who lived upon the fat of it—Universities and public schools had been richly endowed for the purpose of propagating knowledge and encouraging learning,—and yet the people were lamentably ignorant. It was a wicked and impudent falsehood to declare that they were intellectually dull or averse to mental improvement. Common sense—that best of sense—was the special characteristic of the working classes; and those who could read, were absolutely greedy in their anxiety to procure books, newspapers, and cheap publications for perusal. The fact was, that the mind of the industrious population was a rich soil wherein all good seed would speedily take root, shoot up, and bring forth fruit to perfection: but the apprehensions or narrow prejudices of the upper classes—the oligarchy—would not permit the seed to be sown. Now, as the soil must naturally produce something, even of its own accord, it too often gave birth to rank weeds; and this was made a matter of scorn, reviling, and reproach. But the real objects of that scorn—that reviling—and that reproach, were those who obstinately and wickedly neglected to put the good soil to the full test of fertilization. Lastly, the Earl of Ellingham directed attention to the state of the criminal laws. These were only calculated to produce widely spread demoralization—to propagate vice—to render crime terribly prolific. A man—no matter what his offence might have been—should be deemed innocent and untainted again, when he had paid the penalty of his misdeed; because to brand a human being eternally, was to fly in the face of the Almighty and assert that there should be no such thing as forgiveness, and was no such thing as repentance. But the nature of punishments in this country was so to brand the individual, and so to dare the Majesty of Heaven. For the gaols were perfect nests of infamy—sinks of iniquity, imprisonment in which necessarily fastened an indelible stigma upon the individual. He either came forth tainted; or else it was supposed that he must be so. Under these circumstances, he vainly endeavoured to obtain employment; and, utterly failing in his attempt to earn an honest livelihood, he was compelled perforce to relapse into habits of crime and lawlessness. This fact accounted for an immense amount of the demoralization which the Bishops so much deplored, but the true causes of which they obstinately refused to acknowledge. The criminal gaols were moral pest-houses, in which no cures were effected, but where the contagious malady became more virulent. Society should not immure offenders solely for the sake of punishment—but with a view to reformation of character. The noble Earl then summed up his arguments by stating that he was anxious to see measures adopted for a *minimum* rate of wages, to prevent the sudden fluctuation of wages, and to compel property to give constant employment to labour:—he was desirous that indirect taxes upon the necessaries of life should be abolished;—he wished the laws and their administration to be more equitably proportioned to the relative conditions of the rich and the poor;—he insisted upon the want of a general system of national education, to be intrusted to laymen, and to be totally distinct from religious instruction and sectarian tenets;—he desired a complete reformation in the system of prison discipline, and explained the paramount necessity of founding establishments for the purpose of affording work to persons upon leaving criminal gaols, as a means of their obtaining an honest livelihood and retrieving their characters prior to seeking employment for themselves;—and he hoped that the franchise would be so extended as to give every man who earned his own bread by the sweat of his brow, a stake and interest in the country's welfare. The noble Earl wound up with an eloquent peroration in which he vindicated the industrious millions from the aspersions, misrepresentations, and calumnies which it seemed to be the fashion for the upper classes to indulge in against them; and he concluded by moving a number of resolutions in accordance with the heads of his oration.

The Earl's speech was received with very partial cheering by the assembled Lords, to whom its tenor was most unpalatable: but such was its effect upon the auditors in the strangers' galleries, that, contrary to the established etiquette, it was loudly applauded by them. The Lord Chancellor immediately called to order; and in a few minutes a dead silence reigned throughout the House.

The leading Minister present then rose to answer the Earl's oration; which he did in the usual style adopted by official men under such circumstances. Entirely blinking all the main arguments, he declaimed loudly in favour of the prosperity of the country—dwelt upon the happiness of English cottagers—lauded the "wisdom of our ancestors"—uttered the invariable cant about our "glorious institutions"—spoke of Church and State as if they were Siamese twins whom it would be death to sever—and, after calling upon the House to resist the Earl of Ellingham's motion, sate down.

Several noble Lords and Right Reverend Fathers in God took part in the discussion; and at length the House divided, when the Earl's motion was of course lost by an overwhelming majority against it. Arthur was by no means disappointed: he had foreseen this result—but he had made up his mind to renew the subject as often as he could, in the full hope that a steady perseverance would ultimately be crowned with success.

The House adjourned—the strangers' galleries were speedily cleared—and the Lords, Spiritual and Temporal, rolled home in their carriages, the multitudes, who still remained assembled in the vicinity of St. Stephen's, preserving a profound silence, until the Earl of Ellingham was observed to issue forth by those persons who were nearest to the Lords' entrance. Then arose a shout more loud—more hearty even than that which had greeted his arrival a few hours previously: it was the voice of a generous and grateful people, expressing the sincerest thanks for the efforts which the noble patriot had exerted in their cause.

CHAPTER C.
THE EARL OF ELLINGHAM AND ESTHER DE MEDINA.

It was about two o'clock in the afternoon of the day following the scene just described, that the Earl of Ellingham and Esther de Medina were walking in the gardens attached to Finchley Manor.

The beautiful Jewess leant upon the arm of that fine young nobleman who had suddenly appeared before the world in the light of the champion of the industrious classes.

Never had Esther seemed so ravishingly lovely as on this occasion:—a rich carnation hue tinged her cheeks, beneath the clear, transparent olive of her complexion; and her fine large black eyes mirrored the enthusiasm of her soul, as she listened to her companion, who was expatiating upon the wrongs and sufferings endured by the sons and daughters of toil.

Her generous heart beat in entire sympathy with his own in this respect. Until the previous evening she had known little more of the condition of the people than is generally gleaned by young ladies of good education from the works which they peruse. But the Earl's lucid and convincing exposure had shed a marvellous light upon her soul: she comprehended how much the industrious millions were neglected by the Government—how sorely they were oppressed by a selfish, grasping, greedy oligarchy—how noble a task it was which the Earl had imposed upon himself.

His brilliant eloquence—his logical reasoning—the tone of deep conviction in which he had spoken—the conscientious earnestness of his manner—and the honest fervour that animated him when, having disposed of the more argumentative portion of his speech, he burst forth in his impassioned peroration,—all this had made a profound impression upon Esther de Medina. For hitherto her gentle heart had loved him for all those qualities of person and of mind which usually engender tender feelings in the maiden's bosom: but now she felt that she could adore him—that she could worship him as a hero who had stood forth in honest championship of a cause which it was so glorious to undertake.

Therefore was it that her cheeks were tinged with the carnation glow of youthful enthusiasm: therefore was it that her fine dark eyes flashed with the fires of so generous a fervour, as she now dwelt upon every word that the nobleman was uttering in reiteration of those sentiments which he had so boldly enunciated the night before.

But by degrees the conversation took a different and more tender turn; and as they entered an avenue of trees verdant with the foliage of an early Spring, the nobleman found himself speaking in obedience to those feelings of admiration which he experienced towards the beautiful Jewess.

"It was not to treat you with a political disquisition, Miss de Medina," said the Earl, "that I came hither to-day. I had another and very different object in view; for I am about to ask you to bestow upon me a boon which, if accorded, shall ever—ever be most highly prized. Esther—dearest Esther," added the nobleman, sinking his voice to a tender whisper, and gazing upon her affectionately, "it is this fair hand which I solicit!"

"Oh! my lord," murmured Esther, casting down her swimming eyes, while she felt that her cheeks were burning with blushes, "you have not well considered the step which you are now taking."

"I have reflected deeply upon the course which I am adopting," answered the nobleman, "and I am convinced that my happiness depends upon your reply. Tell me, Esther dearest—can you love me? Will you accept me as your husband?'

"Did I consult only my own heart, my lord," replied the beautiful Jewess, her countenance still suffused in virgin blushes, and her voice tremulously melodious, "I should not hesitate how to reply—oh! how could I? But I cannot forget, my lord, that I am the daughter of a despised—a persecuted—a much maligned race,—that the prejudices of your country and your creed are hostile to such an alliance as this, the proposal of which has done me so much honour."

"You are well aware, my beloved Esther," said the Earl, "that I have none of those absurd prejudices. The proudest Christian who wears a crown might glory in being the son-in-law of such a man as Mr. de Medina; and, even were he otherwise than what he is, it were a worthy aim of ambition to become the husband of his daughter Esther."

"I am well aware, my lord," resumed Esther, "that your heart harbours every noble and ennobling sentiment—that you are all that is great, and liberal, and good. Proud and happy, then, must that woman esteem herself who shall be destined to bear your name. But not for me, my lord—not for the despised Jewess must that supreme honour be reserved. No," she continued, her voice faltering, and her bosom heaving convulsively,—"no, my lord,—it may not be!"

"Esther," exclaimed the Earl of Ellingham, in an impassioned tone, "tell me—I conjure you—is this the only motive which induces you to hesitate? Is it simply on account of those absurd prejudices which my illiberal fellow-countrymen entertain in reference to your race? is it solely on this account that you deny me the boon I demand?"

"That reason—and another," murmured the lovely Jewess, in a low—hesitating—and tremulous tone.

"Ah! that *other*—I can divine it!" cried the young nobleman. "You know that I was engaged to Lady Hatfield;—but that engagement exists no longer—has ceased to exist for some time! I will not attempt to persuade you, dearest Esther, that I did not love Georgiana;—but I now feel that my passion in respect to her was very different from the affection which I entertain for you. Georgiana was the idol of my imagination—you are the mistress of my soul. My attachment to her was wild and passionate—to you it is tender and profound. Dazzled by her splendid beauty, I was bewildered—captivated—held in thraldom: but such a love as that contained not those elements which might render it durable. Your modest and retiring charms, sweet Esther—your amiability—your gentleness—your goodness, all combine to render my love permanent and impossible to undergo diminution or change. Moreover, circumstances which I need not—cannot explain to you, suddenly transpired to alter my sentiments in respect to Lady Hatfield—to make me look upon her as a sister, and never more in any other light. But if you will give me your love, my Esther, you shall experience all the happiness which can arise from an alliance with one who will make your welfare the study of his life. Indeed, if you still hesitate on the score of those prejudices to which we just now alluded,—then—sooner than resign my hope of possessing this fair hand of your's, I will renounce the society in which I have been accustomed to move—I will dwell with you, when heaven's blessing shall have united us, in some charming seclusion, where we shall be all in all to each other—I will devote myself entirely to you and to that task which I have taken upon myself in respect to the industrious classes—that fine English people, in whom my sympathies are so deeply interested—"

"Oh! my lord," murmured Esther, in a joyous though subdued tone, "how have I merited all the proofs of attachment which you now lavish upon me?—how can the obscure Jewess flatter herself that she is worthy of becoming the bride of one of England's mightiest nobles?"

"Then you *do* consent to become mine, Esther?" cried the handsome young peer; and, reading her answer in her eloquent eyes, he caught her in his arms—he pressed her to his heart—and on her virgin lips he imprinted the first kiss which Esther had ever received from mortal man save her own father.

A few minutes elapsed in profound silence,—a few minutes, during which the happy pair exchanged glances of sincere, and pure, and hallowed love.

Suddenly the sound of footsteps drawing near fell upon their ears: they turned, and beheld Mr. de Medina approaching down the avenue of trees.

Then the Earl of Ellingham, taking Esther's hand, advanced towards the Jew and said in a firm and manly tone, "Mr. de Medina, I am glad that you have come hither at this moment, for I have a great boon to beg of you—a precious gift to solicit!"—and he glanced tenderly towards the blushing maiden who stood by his side.

"I understand you, my dear Arthur," returned Mr. de Medina, smiling. "But I presume that the whole business is already settled and arranged between you," he added, looking slily and benignantly at his daughter.

"Miss de Medina has consented to bestow her hand upon me, my dear sir," answered the nobleman; "and I scarcely dread a refusal on your part."

"A refusal!" ejaculated Mr. de Medina, the tears of joy and gratitude starting to his eyes: "there is indeed no danger of that! On whom would I consent to bestow my jewel, my pride, if not upon you—*you*, my dear Arthur, who are all that an Englishman ought to be? Yes—I give you my daughter; and may God ensure your happiness!"

The venerable Jew embraced the Earl and Esther; and the happiness of those three deserving and admirable persons was complete.

The Earl of Ellingham passed the remainder of that day at Finchley Manor; and it was past eleven o'clock in the evening when he alighted from his carriage at the door of his own abode.

On the ensuing morning Clarence Villiers called upon the nobleman, by whom he was most courteously received; and the Earl proceeded to explain to him the nature of the business which had induced him to request the favour of that interview.

"Mr. Villiers," said Arthur, "it will be sufficient for me to inform you that I had reasons for experiencing a more than common interest in behalf of Thomas Rainford, with whom you were somewhat intimately acquainted. What those precise reasons were, you, as a gentleman, will not enquire: but I believe that you have in your possession a particular letter, which Thomas Rainford entrusted to you; and circumstances now render it necessary that this document should pass from your hands into mine."

"The high character of your lordship commands immediate compliance on my part," said Villiers, producing the letter from his pocket-book and tendering it to the Earl.

"I thank you for this proof of confidence, Mr. Villiers," observed the nobleman: "but to set your mind completely at rest, I can show you a written authorization, signed by Thomas Rainford, to enable me to receive the paper from you."

"It is not at all necessary, my lord," answered Clarence, rising to take his departure.

"One moment," said the Earl, much struck by the frank, candid, and gentlemanly demeanour of Villiers: "any one who felt an interest in Thomas Rainford—especially one in whom he reposed sufficient confidence to entrust with that letter—has a claim on my friendship. I should therefore be delighted to serve you, Mr. Villiers; and let this assurance tend to convince you that I am animated by no idle curiosity in enquiring relative to your position in life. I believe you hold a situation in Somerset House?"

Villiers answered in an affirmative.

"And the salary you at present receive is only ninety or a hundred pounds a-year?" continued the Earl. "You see that Thomas Rainford made me acquainted with your circumstances, and that I have not forgotten them. Indeed, he requested me to exert myself in your behalf; and I am anxious to fulfil his desire. I called at your lodgings in Bridge Street, and learnt that you had been very recently married. Now, ninety or a hundred pounds a-year," continued the Earl, with a smile, "are little enough to enable you to support your changed condition in comfort; and the state of political parties forbids me to ask any favours of the men in power. I will make you a proposal, which you may take time to reflect upon. I require a private secretary: and that post I offer to you. The emoluments are four hundred a-year, and a house rent-free. The dwelling is a beautiful cottage belonging to me, and situate at Brompton. Moreover, I will give you three hundred guineas for your outfit and furniture."

Clarence Villiers was astonished—nay, perfectly astounded by the liberality of this offer; and, unable to utter a word, he gazed upon the Earl with eyes expressive of the most sincere gratitude, mingled with admiration at his generous behaviour.

"I know," resumed the Earl, "that a government situation is a certainty, and that you have every chance of rising in your present sphere: think not, therefore, that I now offer you a precarious employment. No—whether I continue in that activity of political existence on which I have just entered—or whether I be compelled by circumstances to renounce it,—you shall be duly cared for."

"My lord, I accept your generous proposal," exclaimed Clarence, at length recovering the power of speech; "and I shall exert myself unweariedly to deserve your lordship's good opinion of me."

"The bargain is therefore concluded," said the nobleman. "I will give you a note to my solicitor, who will immediately put you in possession of the lease of the house at Brompton."

The Earl seated himself at a writing-table, and penned the letter to his professional agent: he also wrote a cheque on his bankers for three hundred guineas; and the two documents he handed to Clarence Villiers, who took his leave of the kind-hearted nobleman, his soul overflowing with emotions of gratitude and admiration.

How joyous—oh! how joyous a thing it is to carry glad tidings to the beloved of one's bosom,—to hasten home to a fond, confiding, adoring wife, and be able to exclaim to her, "The smiles with which thou greetest me, dearest, will not be chased away from thy sweet lips by the news which I have in store for thee! For God is good to us, my angel—and happiness, prosperity, and buoyant hopes are ours! From comparative poverty we are suddenly elevated to the possession of affluence; and we enjoy the protection of one who will never desert us, so long as we pursue the paths of rectitude and honour!"

Oh! to be enabled to say this to a loved and loving creature, is happiness ineffable; and that felicity was now experienced by Clarence Villiers, and shared by his charming wife.

Wealth in the hands of such a man as the Earl of Ellingham was like anodynes in the professional knowledge of the physician who attends the poor gratuitously:—the power to do good is the choicest of the unbought luxuries of life, and far more delicious than all the blandishments that gold can procure.

From the midst of a selfish and bloated aristocracy, how resplendently did the Earl of Ellingham stand forth as a glorious example of generosity, manliness, and moral worth! He was the true type of a sterling English gentleman—an Englishman of education, enlightened soul, and liberal sentiments;—not one of those narrow-minded beings, who believe that birth and wealth are the only aristocracy, and whose ideas are limited as the confines of the land to which they belong. Your prejudiced Englishman is a most contemptible character:—borrowing so much as he does from foreign nations—even to the very fashion of his coat and hat, or his wife's gown— he boasts in his absurd and pompous pride, that England is all and every thing in itself. Britain is indeed a wonderful country; but Britain is not the whole world, after all. In all that is useful as far as the solid comforts of life are concerned, she stands at the head of civilisation; but she cannot compete with France in the refinements and elegancies of existence, nor in the progress of purely democratic principles. If Great Britain be a wonderful country, the French are a wonderful—aye, and a mighty and noble nation, likewise; and in France at least the principles of equality are well understood, and the battering ram of two Revolutions has knocked down hereditary peerage—class distinctions—religious intolerance—and that vile *prestige* which makes narrow-minded Englishmen quote the "wisdom of their ancestors" as a reason for perpetuating the most monstrous abuses!

But let us return to the Earl of Ellingham, who, having terminated his interview with Clarence Villiers, repaired to the dwelling of Lady Hatfield.

Georgiana was at home, and Arthur was immediately admitted to the drawing-room where she was seated.

He had not now the same feelings of pleasure which had lately animated him, when entering the presence of one whom he had sought to love as a sister: the scene at Carlton House haunted him like an evil dream;—and as he contemplated the calm and tranquil demeanour of Georgiana, he felt grieved at the idea that beneath this composure must necessarily reign the excitement experienced by a woman who had resolved on becoming the King's mistress.

Nevertheless, in pursuance of the resolutions already established in his mind, he conquered—or rather, concealed his sentiments; and, though a bad hand at any thing resembling duplicity of conduct, he managed to greet her without exhibiting any thing peculiar in his manner.

"I have two important communications to make to you, Georgiana," he said, as he seated himself opposite to her. "The first relates to a delicate subject, which we will dispose of as soon as possible. In a word, I have this morning seen Mr. Villiers; and he has given me this paper."

Lady Hatfield eagerly received the document from the hands of the nobleman, and ran her eyes rapidly over it. Her countenance grew deadly pale, and tears trickled down her cheeks, as she murmured in a tone of subdued anguish, "My God! they were in want—they were starving—that woman and my child—and I——"

Then, stopping suddenly short, she threw herself back upon the sofa, covered her face with her hands, and no longer sought to repress the outpourings of her grief.

The Earl interrupted her not: he understood the nature of those emotions which constituted a subject of self-reproach on the part of the unhappy lady, who was so deeply to be commiserated; and he thought within himself, "She possesses a kind—a feeling heart!"

At length Georgiana broke the long silence which prevailed.

"Yes—there can be no doubt?" she exclaimed: "that boy is my child—and he is now with his father! May heaven bless him!"

"Rest assured that he is with one who will treat him kindly, although some weeks must elapse ere *he* can learn who the boy really is," observed the Earl of Ellingham. "And now for the second communication which I have to make to you, Georgiana," continued the nobleman, desirous to change the topic as speedily as possible. "I have taken your advice—I have followed your counsel——"

"And Esther de Medina is to become the Countess of Ellingham?" said Lady Hatfield, in a low and mournful tone of voice.

"Esther has consented to be mine," added the Earl; "and her father has expressed his joy and delight at the contemplated alliance."

For a few moments Georgiana turned aside her head, and appeared to struggle violently and painfully with the emotions which filled her bosom.

"Arthur," she said at last, evidently scarcely able to stem the flood of her agitated feelings, "I am happy to learn these tidings. You will be blessed in the possession of one who has been represented to me in such an amiable—such an estimable light. I congratulate you—and *her* likewise. You deserve all the felicity which this world can give; and she who is destined to be—your bride," added Georgiana tremulously, "must feel proud of you. Yes, Arthur—your high character—your talents—your generous disposition—your noble nature——"

She could say no more: in summing up all his good qualities, she seemed to be reminded how much she had lost—and she burst into tears.

Arthur was painfully affected: he had not expected such a scene as this!

Was it possible that a woman who, either yielding to the cravings of a voluptuous disposition or dazzled by an ignoble and false ambition, had consented to become the mistress of a King,—was it possible that such a woman could manifest so much true and profound feeling on learning that he whom she had once loved was about to wed another, she herself having counselled the alliance? Was it possible that he was still so dear to her, and that her own generous nature had suggested that union through a conscientious belief that it would result in his happiness, though she herself sacrificed all her tenderest feelings in urging him to adopt a course which must necessarily interfere even with the friendship which had conventionally succeeded their love? He had indeed, in the first instance, fancied that the advice which Georgiana had given him arose from the best and kindest motives; but the scene at Carlton House had made him mistrustful of her. Now, then, all his good opinion of her revived in its pristine strength;—and yet he was bewildered when he thought that one, who was susceptible of such noble conduct, could have become so suddenly depraved as to consent in a single hour to resign all the purity of her soul in homage to the advances of a royal voluptuary.

But Georgiana understood not what was passing in his mind; and she supposed, by his embarrassed manner and air of profound thought, that he felt only for her in regard to the position in which they had been formerly placed.

"Let no thought for me mar your happiness, Arthur—dear Arthur," she said, in a voice of solemn mournfulness. "Believe me, I have your welfare sincerely—deeply at heart—far more than perhaps you imagine," she added, with strange yet unaccountable emphasis. "At the same time, I am but a poor weak woman, and cannot altogether restrain my feelings. I rejoice that you are about to form an alliance with an amiable and beautiful young lady, who is so well deserving of your love: at the same time, my memory—oh! too faithful memory—carries me back to those days—indeed, to only a few months ago, when *my* hopes were exalted and *my* prospects of happiness bright indeed. However," she added hastily, "let me not dwell upon that topic—and pardon my momentary weakness, Arthur. May God bless you!"

With these words, Lady Hatfield hurried from the room; and the Earl of Ellingham took his departure, grieved and bewildered by all that had just occurred.

"If Georgiana be really serious in resigning herself to King George the Fourth," thought Arthur, as he returned in his carriage to Pall Mall, "she sacrifices the purity of the most generous—the tenderest—the noblest heart with which woman ever was endowed,—save and excepting my own well-beloved Esther!"

CHAPTER CI.
THE BLACKAMOOR'S STRANGE ADVENTURE.

It was about nine o'clock in the evening of the same day on which the above-recorded interview took place between the Earl of Ellingham and Lady Hatfield, that the Blackamoor, clad in a very plain—almost a mean attire, sauntered along Pall Mall West, and stopped for a few moments in front of the nobleman's house.

He gazed wistfully at the windows—murmured something to himself—uttered a sigh—and passed on.

His appearance attracted the notice of two gentlemen who were walking arm-in-arm in the same direction; and, as they examined him more closely by the light of an adjacent lamp, one said to the other, "Since his Majesty has taken it into his head to have a black servant, I really think that the very man to suit the purpose is now before us. He is a well-made, good-looking fellow."

"My dear Warren," said the gentleman thus addressed, "you are positively absurd with your notions that you have only to *ask* in a King's name in order to *have*. How do you know that this man wants a situation?"

"He looks as if he did, Harral," replied Sir Phillip Warren. "See—he lounges along as if he had no fixed object in view—his clothes do not appear to be any of the best—and his whole demeanour gives me the idea of a lacquey out of place."

"My dear friend," whispered Sir Randolph Harral—who, like his companion, was one of the King's courtiers, "you are really wrong. That man is something far superior to what you conceive him to be: there is even an air of subdued gentility about him——"

"Pooh! pooh! Harral," interrupted Sir Phillip Warren: "you do not understand these matters so well as I do. At all events there is no harm in questioning that fellow—for I should rejoice to be able to fulfil to-night a whim which our royal master only expressed this afternoon when he saw the French Ambassador's splendid black *chasseur*."

"Well, as you please, Warren," observed Sir Randolph Harral: "but as I do not wish to get myself knocked down for insulting a person of a superior class to what you imagine, I shall leave you to pursue the adventure alone."

This conversation had been carried on so close to the Blackamoor, that, although the two courtiers had spoken in a very low voice, and had not of course intended that their remarks should be overheard, yet scarcely a word had escaped his ears. Affecting, however, all the time to continue his lounging, listless walk, he took no apparent notice of the gentlemen behind him, and even pretended to start with surprise when Sir Phillip Warren—Sir Randolph Harral having re-entered Carlton House—tapped him on the shoulder.

"My good man," said the courtier, in a patronising fashion, "I wish to have a few moments' conversation with you."

"Certainly, sir," exclaimed the Blackamoor, touching his hat just like a lacquey, and assuming the tone and manner of one.

"I thought so—I knew I was right?" exclaimed Sir Phillip, rubbing his hands in proof of his satisfaction; then, attentively scanning the Black from head to foot, by the aid of the lamp at the door of a neighbouring mansion, he said in a less excited tone, "I suspect you, my good fellow, to be a person in search of employment——"

"Yes—sir," interrupted the Blackamoor, now enjoying the farce that he was playing; "I should very much like to obtain a good situation, and can obtain a first-rate character from my late master."

"The very thing!" cried Sir Phillip Warren, hugely delighted at the opportunity of crowing over his friend Sir Randolph Harral: then, once more addressing himself to the Black, he said, "Now what should you think if I proposed to you to enter the household of his most gracious Majesty?"

"I should be afraid that the offer was too good to be realized, sir," was the answer, delivered in a tone of deep respect; although the Blackamoor was laughing in his sleeve the whole time.

"It all depends upon me, my good fellow," said Sir Phillip: "and if *I* am satisfied with you, the matter is settled immediately. But we cannot continue to talk in the open street: so follow me to my own apartments in the palace."

Thus speaking, the courtier led the way to Carlton House, the Blackamoor following at a respectful distance, and saying to himself, "What object I propose to myself in embracing this adventure, I know not. It, however, tickles my fancy, and I will go on with it. Besides, having an hour to spare, I may as well divert myself in this way as any other."

Accordingly, he followed Sir Phillip Warren into the royal dwelling; and in strict silence did they proceed, until they reached an ante-room leading to a suite of apartments which were occupied by the old courtier. In that ante-room they stopped; for Sir Phillip was immediately accosted by his valet, who, starting from a seat in which he had been dozing, said, "If you please, sir, his Majesty has sent twice, during the last half-hour, to desire your presence."

"Very good, Gregory," exclaimed Sir Phillip: "I will attend to the royal command this moment; and do you take the present of hot-house fruit at once to my sister, Lady Maltoun. Her ladyship requires it for her grand supper to-night. Tell her that I am enabled to send it through the goodness of my royal master."

"Yes, sir," answered the valet, and instantly took his departure.

"My good fellow," said Sir Phillip Warren, turning towards the Blackamoor, "you perceive that it is impossible for me to speak to you at present. You must sit down and wait patiently until my return. I shall not be very long away; but, in any case, wait!"

Sir Phillip Warren, having issued these injunctions, hastened into the inner apartments to amend his toilette after his evening's stroll; and in a short time he came forth again, with knee-breeches and silk stockings, all ready to attend upon the king. In passing through the ante-chamber he repeated his command that the Black should await his return; and the latter promised to obey.

When left alone, this individual seated himself, and gave way to his reflections, forgetting for a time where he was. At length he started up, looked at his watch, and found that upwards of half-an-hour had elapsed since the old courtier had left him. He was already wearied of waiting; but a natural love of adventure and of the excitement of novelty induced him to remain a little longer to see the issue of the affair which had led him thither. He accordingly whiled away another half hour with a newspaper which lay on the table; and, that interval having passed, he began to think of taking his departure without farther delay.

Issuing from the ante-room, he proceeded along a well-lighted corridor, from the extremity of which branched off two smaller passages, one to the right, and the other to the left. The Blackamoor was now at a loss which path to pursue; for he could not, for the life of him, remember by which passage the old courtier had led him on his arrival an hour previously.

He was not, however, a man at all capable of hesitating to explore even a royal palace, in order to find a mode of egress, when it did not suit him to wait for the return of his guide: and taking the passage to the right, he hastened on until he reached a pair of colossal folding doors. Perfectly recollecting to have passed through those doors on his arrival—or at all events through folding-doors exactly like them—he pushed them open, and entered a large ante-room, well lighted, and containing four marble statues as large as life.

"Now," thought the Blackamoor, "I am mistaken; for I do not remember to have seen those statues as I followed the old gentleman into the palace just now. And yet I might have passed through this room without noticing them. At all events, I well recollect those large and splendid folding-doors; and so I must be right."

It happened, however, that he was altogether wrong in the path which he had pursued in order to find an egress from the palace; and he was deceived by the fact that at each end of the long passage, from the middle of which the corridor branched off, there were folding-doors of an uniform shape, size, and appearance. But, conceiving himself to be in the right road, he crossed the ante-room, and, pushing open a door at the farther extremity, found himself in a magnificent apartment, the furniture of which was of the French fashion of King Louis the Fifteenth's time. The hangings and drapery were of crimson velvet, of which material the cushions of the chairs and the sofas were also made. Several fine pictures, by old masters, and vast mirrors with elaborately decorated frames, graced the walls; and the whole was displayed by a rich, subdued, golden lustre, diffused throughout the room by lamps, the globes of which were of very thick ground glass. It was a mellow light, sufficient, yet without glare—misty, without being positively dim—and calculated to produce a lulling sensation of voluptuous indolence, rather than to dazzle the eyes with a wakeful brilliancy. In fact, there was altogether something ineffably luxurious in the general appearance of this apartment, which was magnificent without being spacious, and the perfumed atmosphere of which stole like a delicious languor on the senses.

The Blackamoor forgot for a few moments that he was an intruder—or, if he remembered the fact, he was indifferent to it: and, though the instant he entered this apartment he saw that he had indeed taken a wrong path, yet he could not help advancing farther into it to admire its sumptuous elegance and fine pictures. He was thus gratifying his curiosity, when he heard voices in the ante-room through which he had just passed; and, obeying a natural impulse, he slipped behind the rich velvet curtains drawn over the immense window, near which he happened to be standing at the moment.

The door opened, and two persons entered the apartment.

"I will await her here, Warren," said one, in a commanding and triumphant tone: "and see that during our interview, we are secured against interruption of any kind."

"Your Majesty shall be obeyed," answered Sir Phillip. "Have you any farther orders, sire?"

"None, my faithful friend," returned the King. "Stay—have I the document?"

"I gave it to your Majesty ere now, after having myself fetched it from the Home Office," said the courtier.

"True! I have it safe," said George the Fourth. "And now hasten to receive the fair one, Warren: it is past ten o'clock, and I am impatient to behold her charming countenance again."

Sir Phillip departed; and the King, throwing himself upon one of the voluptuous ottomans, exclaimed aloud, "Now for a new pleasure! I know not how it was, but I never before took so sudden and ardent a fancy for any woman, as for this Georgiana Hatfield. There is something truly bewitching—ineffably captivating in her sweet countenance; and the calm repose which characterises the general expression of that face, has for me an influence profoundly voluptuous. Then her bust—oh! her bust—*that* is charming indeed,—so full—so richly proportioned—and yet evidently so firm! She has never been married, and Warren says that her reputation is untarnished. It will be a luxury of paradise to revel in her virgin charms. And yet, somehow or other, the joys of love are not generally unknown to ladies in the fashionable world who have reached the age of four or five and twenty. No matter! be she virgin or not, she is an adorable woman; and I am madly impatient for her coming."

The King rose from the ottoman, and walked slowly across the apartment, stopping opposite a mirror in which he surveyed himself. His admirably fashioned wig was entirely to his taste: there was not a curl nor a wave which he could have wished otherwise than it was. His false teeth were white, fixed firmly in his mouth, and had a perfectly natural appearance. The tie of his cravat—borrowed from the fashion set by his once all-powerful favourite, Beau Brummell—was unexceptionable. The white waistcoat had not a crease, so perfectly did it fit the portly form of the royal voluptuary. The above-mentioned Beau Brummell could not, even in his ire against the King, have found the shadow of an excuse for a cavil against the black dress-coat, so artistically was it made. No tailor in the famous city of Paris could have achieved a greater triumph in respect to the pantaloons: and as for the polished dress-boots——O immortal Hoby!

Well satisfied with the result of his survey, George the Fourth returned to the ottoman, and relapsed into a train of voluptuous imagings with respect to Lady Hatfield. This current of thought, whereby, in his emasculated old age, he endeavoured to invigorate his physical powers through the medium of an excited and heated imagination, led him to reflect upon all the beauteous women—and their name was Legion—who had ever surrendered themselves to his embraces; and his ideas naturally wandered to the enjoyments, luxuries, and pleasures which his exalted rank and immense resources enabled him to procure. Then he chuckled with triumphant delight at the egregious folly of the great and powerful English people tolerating a King at all. But he likewise knew that his own conduct and example had done more harm to the cause of Monarchy than all the republic pamphlets or democratic disquisitions ever published. He was well aware that, without intending to be so, he was the most effectual means of opening the eyes of the civilised world to the insanity and madness of maintaining monarchical institutions: and, though he foresaw that the industrious millions of this realm must inevitably, sooner or later, overthrow Monarchy and establish a pure Democracy, yet he consoled himself, in his revolting selfishness, with the conviction that "the throne would last during his time, at all events."

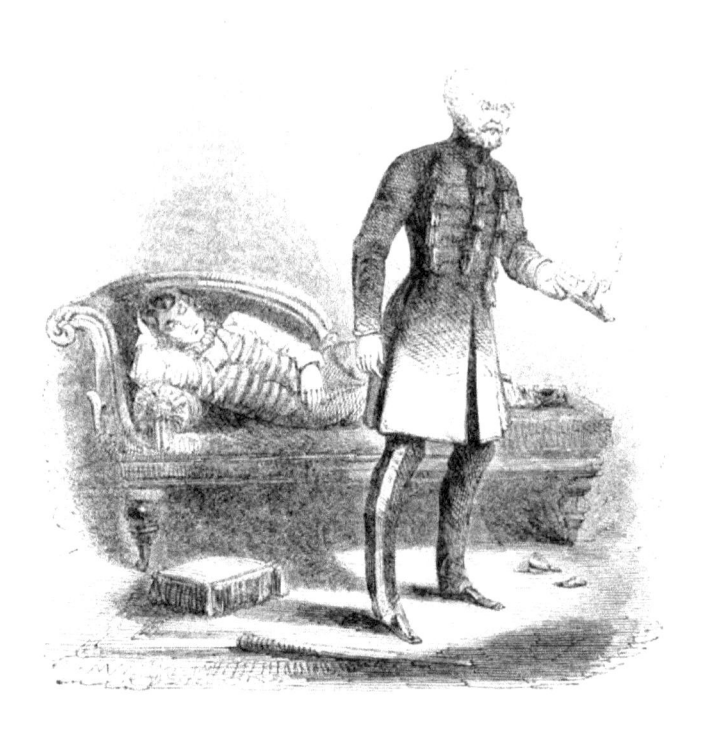

It was about half-past ten, when the door opened; and the Blackamoor, peeping from behind the curtains, beheld a lady, closely veiled, enter the room, the door immediately closing behind her.

"Adorable Georgiana!" exclaimed the King, hastening forward to receive her, and then conducting her to a seat: "I am rejoiced that you have thus yielded to my wishes—that you have come to me this evening."

"But wherefore, sire, did you insist upon this visit?" asked Lady Hatfield, in a low and tremulous tone. "Our compact stipulated that I was first to receive a certain document, as a proof of your Majesty's sincerity———"

"Dearest Georgiana, raise that odious veil—lay aside that invidious bonnet, which conceals your charming countenance!" exclaimed the monarch, in an impassioned voice.

"Oh! sire, I have taken a step at which I tremble," said Lady Hatfield, raising her veil, but retaining her bonnet. "On my way through the corridors, guided by Sir Phillip Warren, I met two or three of your Majesty's retainers; and if they recognised me—in spite of the thick veil——"

"Fear not on that account," interrupted the King. "I admit our compact was as you just now stated it to be, and that the paper should have been forwarded to you. But I was so anxious to see you soon again, that I could not resist the temptation of that idea which suggested to me how much better it would be to solicit you to come hither this evening and receive from my hands the document which you so much desire. Here it is, beloved Georgiana—signed by myself, and countersigned by the Secretary of State."

The King presented the paper to Lady Hatfield, who received it with joy flashing from her eyes: and she immediately secured it about her person.

"My curiosity prompts me to ask an explanation of the extraordinary contents of that document," said the monarch; "but, on the other hand, delicacy forbids."

"And I thank you for this delicacy, sire," exclaimed Lady Hatfield, with earnest sincerity. "It were a long tale to tell—and an useless one——"

"Yes—useless, indeed, when we have a far more interesting topic for our discourse," interrupted George the Fourth, throwing one of his arms round the lady's neck.

"Sire!" cried Georgiana in a reproachful tone, as she hastily withdrew herself from that half-embrace, and retreated to the further end of the ottoman.

"Oh! wherefore play the coy and the cruel?" exclaimed the King. "Have I not given you a signal proof of my attachment, by affixing my signature to a paper the contents of which I scarcely understand, and by ordering the Minister to legalize it with his name? And think you, sweet lady, that it was an easy task to induce that responsible functionary to obey me in this respect? But I menaced and coaxed by turns; and all this for your sake! Do I not, therefore, deserve the reward of your smiles—the recompense of your caresses?"

"I recognise all that is generous in the conduct of your Majesty towards me in respect to this document," said Lady Hatfield: "but were I to succumb to you now, sire, I should loathe myself—I should become degraded in my own estimation—I should feel that I had been purchased by a bribe! No—sire: I cannot renounce every consideration of purity—every sentiment of propriety, in a single moment."

"What further proof do you require of my attachment?" demanded the King, in a tone of vexation which he could not altogether subdue.

"No other proof, save your forbearance on this occasion," answered Georgiana. "Remember, sire, what I told you the other night: I am not a woman of impure imagination—no—nor of depraved character; and I cannot consent to become your mistress, without a mental effort on my part—without wooing on your's. In yielding myself to your Majesty, it will be as a wife who is forced to dispense with the ceremony which alone can make her one in reality; and if your Majesty deem me worth the winning, let me be won by means of those delicate attentions which would be shown in honourable courtship."

"Perdition!" ejaculated the King, who was as much unaccustomed to hear such language as he was to sue at the feet of beauty: "how long will you keep me in this suspense, fair lady?—how long must I endure the tortures of deferred hope? Consider—I love you madly: you are so beautiful—so sweetly beautiful! Oh! to press you in my arms——"

"Pardon me, sire, for daring to interrupt you," said Georgiana; "but if there be nothing save the impulse of the senses in this *liaison* of ours, your Majesty will soon become wearied of me—and I shrink in horror from the idea of becoming the cast-off mistress of even Royalty itself. Let me seek to engage your affections, as you must endeavour to enchain mine; so that our connexion may be based upon the sentiments and feelings of the heart."

"But I already love you sincerely—devotedly, cruel Georgiana!" cried the King, his eyes greedily running over the outlines of the exquisitely proportioned form of the lady, and the rapid survey exciting his desire almost beyond endurance.

"Not with a love calculated to be permanent," said Georgiana quietly; "and unless I become the object of such an affection, never—never shall I so far forget myself——"

"This is cruel—this is maddening!" exclaimed the King; and he extended his arms towards Lady Hatfield.

"Sire, do not treat me with outrage," she said, rising from the ottoman, and speaking in a dignified manner. "If your Majesty supposed that your sovereign rank would so far dazzle my imagination as to make me throw myself into your arms at the very first words of encouragement which fell from your lips, your Majesty has sadly misunderstood the character of Georgiana Hatfield."

"Be not angry with me, adorable creature!" exclaimed the King: "I love you too much to risk the chance of losing you by any misconduct on my part. Name, therefore, your own terms. Or rather, let me ask whether you will consent to visit me every evening for an hour, and allow us an opportunity to become better acquainted with each other?"

"Now your Majesty speaks in a manner calculated to win my esteem," observed Lady Hatfield, avoiding a direct reply to the question put to her; "and when the esteem of a woman is once secured———"

"I understand you," interrupted George the Fourth, hastily: "her love speedily follows. Be it as you say, sweet lady," he continued, in a slower tone; "and let us secure each other's affections. You shall find me docile and obedient to your will—and this is much for *me* to promise. But let me hope that the period of probation will not be long—that the hour of recompense is not far distant———"

"Hush, sire!" exclaimed Georgiana, in a reproachful voice: "this is the language of sense—whereas you must secure my affections by the language of sentiment. If you treat me as a woman who is to be purchased as your mistress, let our connexion cease this moment: but if you will woo me as a wife should be won—although I am well aware that your Majesty's wife I can never be———"

"Would that I could marry you this moment!" cried the King, fixing his eyes upon her beauteous countenance; "for you are ravishingly lovely! I would give a year of my life to obtain all I crave this night. Oh! Georgiana, be not so coy and cruel with me—for you madden me—my veins seem to run with molten lead. Be mine at once—and render my happiness complete. Behold that small low door in yonder corner: it opens into a room which may serve as our nuptial chamber. Come, then, dearest Georgiana—let me lead you thither—not cold, hesitating, and resisting—but warm, and impassioned, and prepared to revel in the delights of love! Our privacy will be complete: no intruder need we fear;—and the world will never know that you have become mine."

"Sire, this language on your part—in spite of all the arguments and remonstrances which I have used," exclaimed Lady Hatfield, "is unworthy of a great King and a polished gentleman."

"The madness of love knows nothing of regal rank nor the shackles of etiquette," said the monarch, speaking in a tone of great excitement; "and, in spite of the promises which I just now so rashly made, I cannot endure delay. No—sweetest lady—you must be mine at once!"—and he wound his arms around Georgiana's form, the fury of his desires animating him with a strength against which she could not long have resisted.

But at that moment succour was at hand!

Forth from his place of concealment sprang the Blackamoor; and an ejaculation of surprise and rage burst from the lips of the King, while a cry of joy emanated from those of Lady Hatfield.

"Who are you? and what signifies this intrusion?" demanded George the Fourth, instantly releasing his intended victim at this sudden apparition.

But, without answering the monarch, the Blackamoor hastily led the half-fainting Lady Hatfield to the door—opened it to allow her to pass out of the room—and, closing it behind her, placed his back against it,—the whole being effected with such speed, that Georgiana had disappeared before the King could recover from the astonishment into which the very first step of the bold proceeding had thrown him.

"Villainous negro!" cried the disappointed monarch, at length recovering the power of speech: "do you know who I am, that you have thus dared to outrage me?"

"I know full well who you are, sire—and I am grieved to the very soul at the idea of being compelled to acknowledge you as my King," returned the Black, in a calm—collected—and somewhat mournful tone.

"This insolence to me!" ejaculated George the Fourth, becoming purple with rage. "Make way, sirrah, for me to pass hence!"

"Not until I have allowed Lady Hatfield sufficient time to escape from this house which the country has given as a palace for your Majesty, but which seems to be used for purposes too vile to contemplate without horror," was the firm reply.

The King fell back a few paces in speechless astonishment. Never before had he been thus bearded:—but in that momentary interval of silence, a crowd of recollections rushed to his mind, warning him that the individual who thus seemed to defy his rank and power, had been present during the whole of the interview with Lady Hatfield,—and that this individual had learnt how the Royal and Ministerial signatures had been given as a means of propitiating a coy beauty, without any reference to the interests of the State:—when the King remembered all this, he was alarmed at the serious manner in which he suddenly found himself compromised. For that Blackamoor could make revelations of a nature to arouse against him the indignation of the whole kingdom; and, reckless as George the Fourth was of public opinion, he trembled at the idea of exciting public resentment.

Thus did a few moments of reflection show him the precipice on which he stood, and carry to his mind a conviction of the necessity of making terms with the sable stranger who had obtained such a dangerous power over him.

But the mere thought of such a compromise was sorely repugnant to the haughty spirit of George the Fourth: and yet there was no alternative! He accordingly addressed himself with the best grace he could assume, to the task of conciliation.

"My good sir," he said, approaching the Black, "I seek not to deal harshly with you: and yet you owe me an explanation of the motives which induced you to penetrate into the palace, and the means by which you gained access to my private apartments."

"I feel bound to answer your Majesty with candour and frankness, in order to clear myself from any injurious suspicion which my concealment in this room might naturally engender," was the reply. "The explanation, sire, is briefly given:—I was accosted by an elderly gentleman in Pall Mall, and asked if I required a situation. In truth I do not; but it being intimated to me that the proffered place was in the royal household, curiosity prompted me to follow the gentleman into the palace. He left me alone in his ante-room for upwards of an hour; and, growing weary of waiting, I sought a means of egress. But, losing my way, I found myself at length in this room; and almost immediately afterwards your Majesty entered with the very gentleman I am speaking of, and whose name I learnt to be Warren. I concealed myself behind the curtains—with no bad intention; and indeed I was about to come forth and explain the reasons of my presence to your Majesty, when certain words which fell from your Majesty's lips made me acquainted with the fact that Lady Hatfield was expected here every moment. That name nailed me to the spot—and I was prompted by an uncontrollable curiosity to wait and satisfy myself whether Lady Hatfield could have become so depraved as to surrender herself to your arms."

"You are acquainted with her, then!" exclaimed the King. "And yet," he added, a moment afterwards, "she did not appear to recognise you."

"No, sire—she did not recognise me," returned the Black.

"But you must know her well, since the mere mention of her name rendered you thus anxious to see the issue of our interview?" said the King, impatiently.

"I know her well, sire," was the guarded response: "and yet she knew not me."

"Who *are* you, then?" demanded George the Fourth, fixing a searching look upon the stranger. "You certainly are not what Sir Phillip Warren took you for——"

"I must firmly, though respectfully, decline to give any account of myself," said the Blackamoor. "Your Majesty will now permit me to withdraw."

"One moment," cried the King. "How stand we in respect to each other? Do you constitute yourself the enemy of your sovereign?—will you publish your knowledge of all that has transpired here this evening?—or can I offer you some earnest that I myself am not offended by the manner in which you ere now thought fit to address me?"

"I have no interest in making known to the public those secrets which have so accidentally been revealed to me," answered the Blackamoor. "It is never a pleasing task to an honest man to publish the frailties or failings of a fellow-creature—much less when that fellow-creature is placed at the head of the nation. As for any reward—or rather *bribe*, to induce me to remain silent, none is necessary. At the same time," he added, hastily correcting himself as a second thought struck him, "it may be as well that I should avail myself of your Majesty's offer; for it might so fall out that the privilege of claiming a boon at your royal hands———"

"May prove serviceable to you some day or another—eh?" added the King, impatiently. "Well—be it so; and, stranger though you be to me, I rely in confidence upon your solemn pledge to place a seal on your lips relative to the incidents of this night."

Thus speaking, the monarch seated himself at the nearest table, and opening a drawer, took forth writing materials: then, with a haste which showed his desire to put an end to a painful interview, he penned the following lines on a slip of paper:—

"We acknowledge a sense of deep obligation to the bearer of this memorandum, the said bearer having rendered us especial service; and we hold ourselves bound to grant him any boon which he may demand at our hands, so that it be not inconsistent with our royal honour, nor prejudicial to the interests of the State.

"Given this 3rd of March, in the year 1827.

"GEORGE REX." (L.S.)

The King lighted a taper, and affixed his royal seal to this document, which he then handed to the Blackamoor, saying, "You perceive what confidence I place in you: see that the good name of Lady Hatfield on the one side, and your Sovereign's honour on the other, be not compromised by any indiscreet revelations on your part."

"Your Majesty may rest assured that I shall maintain the incidents of this evening a profound secret, and that I shall not abuse the privilege conferred upon me by this paper which bears your royal signature."

The Blackamoor bowed, and retired from the presence of King George the Fourth, whom he left in no very pleasant humour at the turn which his meditated attack upon the virtue of Lady Hatfield had taken.

On this occasion, the Black had no difficulty in finding the way to the private staircase up which Sir Phillip Warren had originally introduced him; and he was about to issue forth from Carlton House, when he suddenly encountered that old courtier and Sir Randolph Harral in the hall.

These gentlemen were disputing in a loud tone; but the moment the Blackamoor appeared, Sir Phillip Warren sprang towards him, exclaiming, "Why, where have you possibly been? But no matter," he added, in a triumphant tone, "since you are here at length to settle the question between me and my friend."

"The fact is, my good sir," said Sir Randolph, "I have laid Sir Phillip Warren twenty guineas———"

"Yes—twenty guineas," interrupted Sir Phillip hastily, "that you are———"

"That you are *not*———" cried Sir Randolph.

"I say that you are!" exclaimed Sir Phillip.

"And I say that you are *not*!" vociferated Sir Randolph.

"Gentlemen, pray explain yourselves," said the Blackamoor.

"Well—I say that you are a lacquey out of place," observed Sir Phillip Warren.

"And I say that you are *not*," cried Sir Randolph Harral, in his turn; "whereupon we have bet twenty guineas."

"And you must decide who has won," added Sir Phillip.

"Then, gentlemen," said the Blackamoor, in a merry tone, "I can soon set the matter at rest. So far from being a lacquey out of place, I have upwards of a dozen dependants of my own. I wish you a very good night."

"Why—I am robbed as if it were on the highway!" exclaimed Sir Phillip Warren, his countenance suddenly becoming as awful and blank as such a Port-wine visage could possibly be.

"Ha! ha!" chuckled Sir Randolph: "robbed or not—please to hand me over twenty good guineas."

And the cachinnation of the winning courtier was echoed by the merry laugh of the Blackamoor, as this individual issued forth from Carlton House.

Again, as he passed along Pall Mall, did the Black pause for a few moments opposite the splendid mansion of the Earl of Ellingham, and gaze at it with the attention of no common observer. He was about to continue his way, when two men, belonging to the working class, stopped likewise for an instant in front of the house; and one said to the other, "That is where the Earl lives. God bless him!"

"Yes—God bless him!" repeated his companion, with the emphasis of unfeigned sincerity: "for he is the people's friend."

The two men then passed on.

"Who dares to say that the industrious millions have no gratitude?" murmured the Blackamoor to himself, as he also pursued his way. "O Arthur! you are now indeed worthy of the proud name which you bear: and I likewise exclaim from the very bottom of my heart, '*May God bless you!*'"

CHAPTER CII.
A STATE OF SIEGE.

Return we now to Frank Curtis, his excellent wife, and Captain O'Blunderbuss, who were living in a complete state of siege at the house in Baker Street.

The captain was the commandant of the garrison, and superintended all the manœuvres and the devices which it was necessary to adopt to keep out the enemy. The front-door was constantly chained inside; and every time there was a knock or a ring, John the footman reconnoitred from the area. Whenever any one was compelled to go out to order in provisions, the captain stood at the door, armed with the kitchen poker, and looking so grim and terrible that the officers who were prowling about in different disguises, dared not hazard an encounter with the warlike gentleman.

The grocer, the butcher, and the baker lowered their respective commodities down the area by means of a rope and basket provided for the purpose; but they all took very good care to receive the cash first. The milkman and pot-boy were enabled to supply their articles through the opening afforded by the door with the chain up inside; and they likewise strenuously advocated the ready-money principle.

This condition of siege was a source of great delight to Captain O'Blunderbuss. He was completely in his element. Little cared he for the opinion of neighbours: *his* feelings were by no means concerned. The house, from the first moment he set foot in it, was in a state of perpetual excitement. He was constantly ordering the servants to do something or another: a dozen times a-day did he perform what he called "going his rounds," armed with the poker in case a bailiff should have crept into the place through some unguarded avenue;—and it was indeed with the greatest difficulty that Mrs. Curtis could divert him from a plan which he had conceived and which he declared to be necessary—namely, the drilling of all the inmates of the house, male and female, including the five children, for an hour daily in the yard. As it was, he compelled John, the footman, to mount sentry in the yard aforesaid, every morning while the housemaid was dusting her carpets and so forth—indeed during the whole time that the domestic duties rendered it necessary to have the back-door open. If John remonstrated, the captain would threaten, with terrible oaths, to try him by a court-martial; and once, when the poor fellow respectfully solicited his wages and his discharge, the formidable officer would certainly have inflicted on him the cat-o'-nine-tails, if the cook had not begged him off—she being the footman's sweetheart.

Mrs. Curtis took a great fancy to the captain, and allowed him to do pretty well as he chose. She considered him to be the politest, genteelest, bravest, and most amusing gentleman she had ever known; and it soon struck her that his various qualifications threw her husband considerably into the shade. Whenever she felt low-spirited, he had a ready remedy for her. If it were in the forenoon, he would exclaim, "Arrah and be Jasus, Mim, it's no wonther ye're dull, with the inimy besaging us in this way: and it's a nice mutton chop and a glass of Port-wine that'll be afther sitting ye to rights, Mim." Then forthwith he would ring the bell, and order three chops, so that himself and Frank might keep the dear lady company. If it were in the evening that Mrs. Curtis was attacked by those unwelcome visitors termed "blue devils," the captain would recommend "a leetle dhrop of the potheen, brewed afther the fashion in ould Ireland;" and while he exhausted all his powers of eloquence in assurances that it should be "as wake as wather, and not too swate," he would mix the respectable lady such a stinger, that her eyes would fill with tears every time she put the glass near her lips. Sometimes he would undertake to amuse the children up in the nursery, by going on all fours and allowing them to play at horse-soldiers by riding on his back; and then, what with his shouting and bawling, and their laughing and screaming, it was enough to alarm the whole neighbourhood—and very frequently did.

All these little attentions on the part of the captain either to herself or her children, gave Mrs. Curtis an admirable opinion of him; and he rose rapidly in her favour. His success in obtaining the five hundred pounds from Sir Christopher Blunt was considered by her as sublime a stroke of mingled policy and daring as ever was accomplished; and his tactics in opposing a successful foil to all the stratagems devised by the sheriff's-officers to obtain admission into the dwelling, made her declare more than once that had *he* commanded the Allied Army at Waterloo, it would have been all up with the French in half-an-hour.

The female servants in the house did not altogether admire the position in which they were placed; but, they were so dreadfully frightened at the captain, that they never uttered a murmur in his hearing. They moreover had their little consolations; for Sir Christopher's five hundred pounds enabled the besieged to live, as the captain declared, "like fighting-cocks,"—so that the kitchen was as luxuriously supplied with provender as the parlour; and no account was taken of the quantity of wine and spirits consumed in the establishment.

We have before hinted that the house was a perfect nuisance in Baker Street. And no wonder, indeed, that it should have been so considered; for it seemed to be the main source whence emanated all the frightful noises that could possibly alarm nervous old ladies or irritate gouty old gentlemen. No sooner did the day dawn, than Captain O'Blunderbuss would fling up the window of his bed-room, which was at the back of the house, with a crashing violence that made people think he was mad; and, thrusting forth his head with a white night-cap upon it, he would roar out—"John! John! to arms!" as lustily as he could bawl. This was not only to save himself the trouble of repairing to the footman's chamber to summon him, but also for the purpose of letting the sheriff's-officers, if any were in the neighbourhood, know that he was on the alert. Then John would poke his head out of another window, and answer the captain's call; and a few minutes afterwards the back-door would open and shut with a terrific bang, and John would be seen to sally forth to mount sentry in the yard, with shouldered poker. Then an hour's interval of comparative silence would prevail, while the captain turned in again to take another nap; but, at length, up would go the window again—out would come the head—and, "John! hot wather!" would roll in awful reverberation throughout the entire neighbourhood.

The confusion and dismay produced by these alarms were terrific; and the neighbours all threatened their landlords to give warning on the next quarter. For it was not only in the morning that the noise prevailed, but throughout the entire day—aye, and the best part of the night also. Sometimes the captain would take it into his head to discharge his pistols in the yard: or else he would have a fencing-match with Frank Curtis, the weapons being pokers, which made a hideous clang. Then there were the rows in the nursery, which were truly awful; and, by way of a variety, Captain O'Blunderbuss would occasionally show himself at the drawing-room windows and vociferate the most appalling abuse at any suspicious characters whom he might happen to behold prowling about. These exhibitions frequently collected crowds in front of the house; and the captain would harangue them with as much earnestness as if he were a candidate at a general election. On one of these occasions the parish-beadle made his appearance, and from the pavement remonstrated with the gallant officer, who kept him in parlance until Frank Curtis had time to empty a pitcher of water over the enraged functionary from the front bed-room window.

But the worst part of the whole business consisted in the goings-on at nighttime. Just when sedate and quiet people were getting cozily into their first sleep at about eleven o'clock, Mr. Frank Curtis was getting uncommonly drunk; and, though the captain seemed proof against the effects of alcohol, no matter in what quantity imbibed, he nevertheless grew trebly and quadruply uproarious when under the influence of poteen. Thus, from eleven to twelve the shouts of laughter—the yells of delight—the cries of mirth—and the vociferations of boisterous hilarity, which came from the front parlour, made night perfectly hideous: but no amount of human patience ever possessed by good and forgiving neighbours, could possibly tolerate the din and disturbance which prevailed during the "small hours." Then would the captain and his friend Curtis rush like mad-men into the yard, shouting—roaring—and bawling like demons, so that the residents in the adjacent houses leapt from their beds and threw up their windows in horror and alarm, expecting to find the whole street in a blaze. These performances on the part of Frank and O'Blunderbuss were intended to show the officers that they were upon the alert; and they not only had the desired effect, but accomplished far more—inasmuch as they produced an absolute panic throughout an entire neighbourhood.

Thus it was that Mr. Curtis's abode—lately so serene and quiet in the time of Mrs. Goldberry—became a perfect nuisance and a scandal; and had Bedlam in its very worst days been located there, the noise and alarm could not have been greater.

It will be remembered that the captain's plan, when first he took up his residence in Baker Street, was to get Mr. and Mrs. Curtis and the children away on a Sunday night, and sell off all the furniture on the Monday morning. But this scheme was postponed at first for one week—then for another, because the officers kept such a constant look-out, that the captain saw the necessity of standing the siege until the creditors should be completely wearied of paying those disagreeable spies to watch the premises. This determination was the more readily come to, inasmuch as the five hundred pounds obtained from Sir Christopher Blunt, supplied sinews to carry on the war in grand style.

When the captain paid the second financial visit to the worthy knight with a view to the effecting of a further loan on the assignat which himself and Frank Curtis had resolved to issue, it was not because money was scarce in Baker Street; but simply because the captain admired "the fun of the thing," and also considered it prudent to raise as ample a supply of bullion as possible. The rage which he experienced at his discomfiture on this occasion, can be better conceived than described; and, firmly believing that it was Sir Christopher himself who had dealt him from the carriage window the tremendous blow which sent him sprawling on the pavement in a most ignominious manner, he vowed the most deadly vengeance against the new Justice of the Peace. Picking himself up as well as he could—for the gallant gentleman was sorely bruised—he repaired to the nearest public-house, to "cool himself," as he said in his own mind, with a tumbler of the invariable poteen; and, having reflected upon the insult which he had received, he thought it best not to communicate his dishonour and discomfiture on his return to Baker Street. Accordingly, having returned to "the garrison," into which he effected an easy entry—for no one dared approach the door when it opened to give *him* egress or ingress—he assured Mr. and Mrs. Curtis that the knight was out of town, and would not be back for a week. However, in a couple of days, the wonderful adventures of Sir Christopher Blunt and Dr. Lascelles burst upon the metropolis like a tempest; and, as the morning newspapers were duly dropped down the area of the besieged dwelling in

Baker Street, the entire report was read aloud by Frank Curtis at the breakfast table. It therefore being evident that Sir Christopher was not only in town at that moment, but was likewise in London when the captain had called upon him, the gallant gentleman affected to fly into a violent rage, swearing that the knight was denied to him on purpose, and vowing to make him "repint of his un-gintlemanly conduct." O'Blunderbuss did not, however, in his heart mean to do any such thing as call again in Jermyn Street; for he had despaired of inducing the knight, either by threatenings or coaxings, to advance a further supply; and, now that the worthy gentleman was a Justice of the Peace, the captain thought that it would be somewhat imprudent to visit him for the mere sake of committing an assault and battery. He accordingly invented divers excuses, day after day, for remaining in "the garrison;" and as funds were abundant, no one urged him to undertake another financial mission to Sir Christopher Blunt.

The reader must remember that Messrs. Mac Grab and Proggs were very roughly handled by captain O'Blunderbuss, when they visited the house in Baker Street for the purpose of arresting Mr. Frank Curtis; and, the honour of a sheriff's-officer being particularly dear to its possessor, those worthies considered their's to be at stake, unless they fully vindicated it by capturing the aforesaid Mr. Curtis in the long run. They therefore had recourse to all kinds of devices to obtain an entry into the house, being armed not only with a writ against that gentleman's person on behalf of Mr. Beeswing, but also with an execution against the furniture at the instigation of another of Mrs. Curtis's creditors.

The tricks practised by these worthies to obtain an entry into the besieged domicile, were as varied as they were ludicrous. On one occasion, Mr. Proggs, dressed for the nonce as a butcher, and carrying a leg of mutton in a tray on his shoulder, hurried up to the door, gave the loud, sharp, single knock peculiar to the trade, and shouted "T-cher!" in the most approved style. But the parlour window was thrown up, and out popped the head of the ferocious O'Blunderbuss, the countenance as red as a turkey-cock, and the mouth vomiting forth a torrent of abuse; so that the discomfited Mr. Proggs was compelled to retreat with all the ignominy of a baffled strategist. On another occasion, Mr. Mac Grab, attired as a general postman, rushed along the street, stopped at the door of the besieged house, gave the two clear, rapid strokes with the knocker, and immediately began to look over a bundle of letters with all the feverish haste of the functionary whose semblance he had assumed. But John came forth from the area; and again was the sheriff's-officer's object completely frustrated. Next day, however, two sweeps appeared in the street, as black as if they had never known soap-and-water, and were accustomed to lodge, eat, and sleep in chimneys as well as cleanse them; but upon arriving opposite the parlour-windows, they beheld the captain and Frank Curtis "taking sights" at them, the two gentlemen having "twigged the traps" without much difficulty. Thus, defeated in all their endeavours to accomplish their aims by cunning, Messrs. Mac Grab and Proggs worked themselves up to the desperate resolution of using force; and they accordingly took their post at the front-door of Curtis's house, with the apparent determination to rush in the first time it should be opened. But, when it *was* opened as far as the chain inside would permit, and they beheld, to their horror and dismay, the terrible captain wielding the poker, they exhibited that better part of valour which is denominated *discretion*. At last, however, they could no longer endure the jeerings of their friends exercising the same agreeable and lucrative profession; and moreover, the attorneys who employed them in the Baker Street affair spoke out pretty plainly about gentlemen bribing bailiffs not to execute writs, and so forth. All these circumstances induced Mr. Mac Grab and his man Proggs to hold a council of war over two four-penn'orths of rum-and-water; and the result was a determination, that as the various devices and stratagems they had practised to enter the dwelling had failed, and as they feared to carry it by storm, the stronghold must be reduced by a *surprise*.

It was on the very evening when the Blackamoor experienced so strange an adventure at Carlton House, that the following scene took place in Baker Street.

The clock had struck ten; and, supper being disposed of, the whiskey, hot water, glasses, and *et ceteras* were placed upon the table, at which Frank Curtis, his amiable wife, and Captain O'Blunderbuss were seated—as comfortable a trio as you could wish or expect to see, especially under such adverse circumstances.

"John!" vociferated the captain, as the domestic was about to leave the room; "stop a moment, you rogue, and answer me this. Is the area all safe?"

"Yes, sir," was the ready response.

"And the kitchen-windows—and the back-door—and the yar-rd gate—all right, eh—John?"

"All right, captain: I've just been the rounds."

"And all the provisions in the garrison, John?—plenty of potheen?" demanded O'Blunderbuss.

"Plenty, sir. There'll be no more going out again to-night."

"That's a blissing!" exclaimed the gallant captain. "John!"

"Yes—sir."

"Take a glass of whiskey, mate—and slape with the kitchen poker-r under your pillow, my frind," enjoined the officer. "We must be ar-rmed at all pints, be Jasus!"

"I shan't forget, sir," said John: and having tossed off the spirit, he quitted the room.

"Now then to make ourselves cozie," observed the captain, drawing his chair a little closer to Mrs. Curtis. "Pray, Mim, how d'ye feel your dear self this evening?—is it in good spirits ye are, Mim?"

"Thank you, captain," returned Mrs. Curtis, "I am quite well—but the least, least thing nervous. This strange kind of life we're leading———"

"Strange, Mim!" ejaculated the captain: "it's glor-r-ious!"

"Glorious, indeed!" cried Frank. "I only wish the Marquis of Shoreditch was here along with us—how he would enjoy himself!"

"You will permit me, Mim!" said the captain, grasping the bottle of whiskey, and addressing the lady in an insinuating manner.

"Now, really, captain—if I must take a very *leetle* drop———" began Mrs. Curtis, with a simper.

"Well, my dear madam, it shall be the leetlest dhrop in the wor-rld, and so wake that a baby of a month old might dhrink it and niver so much as thrip up as it walked across the room," exclaimed O'Blunderbuss, whose knowledge of the physical capacities of infants was evidently somewhat vague and limited. "There, Mim!" he added, placing before the lady a large tumbler, the contents of which were equal portions of spirit and water: "you may tell me I'm a Dutchman and unwor-rthy of ould Ireland, if that isn't the purtiest dhrink iver brewed for one of the fair six."

"You're very kind, captain," said Mrs. Curtis, in a mincing—simpering manner.

"It's you that's kind to say so, Mim," remarked the captain, placing his foot close to that of the lady, and ascertaining by the readiness with which she returned the pedal pressure, that the tender intimation he wished thereby to convey was by no means unwelcome.

Frank did not of course notice what was going on under the table, and the conversation progressed in the usual manner—the captain and Frank vieing with each other in telling the most monstrous lies, and the silent interchange of love's tokens continuing with increasing warmth between the gallant gentleman and the stout lady. Mrs. Curtis's spirits, however, seemed to require a more than ordinary amount of stimulant on this occasion: she declared herself to be "very low," although she contrived to laugh a great deal at the captain's lively sallies and marvellous stories;—but as the clock struck midnight and she rose to retire to her chamber, she found that the *three* glasses of toddy which she had been persuaded to imbibe, had somewhat unsettled the gravity of her equilibrium. The captain sprang from his seat to open the parlour-door for her; and as he bade her "good night," she pressed his hand with a degree of tenderness which, as novel-writers say, spoke volumes.

"Curthis, my frind," said the captain, as he returned to his seat, "be the holy poker-r! you possess a rale jewel of a wife. She's the most amiable lady I ever knew and takes her potheen without any nonsense. Be Jove! she's an ornamint in a jintleman's household; and we'll dhrink her health in a bumper!"

"With all my heart," exclaimed Frank, already more than half-seas over. "But, I say, captain—do you know that I'm getting very tired of the life we're leading? I wish we could put an end to it somehow or another."

"Be the power-rs! and that's the very thing I was going to recommend to ye, Frank!" cried the captain, who was more affected by liquor on this particular night than ever he had been before since the first moment he had taken up his abode in Baker Street.

"But—how can it be done?" hiccoughed Curtis.

"Is it how the thing's to be done!" cried O'Blunderbuss. "Can't ye, now, bolt off to France to-morrow night, and lave me in charge of the house? I'll manage to sell every stick to a broker; and then it's myself that'll bring over the wife, the children, and the money to ye as safe as if they were all my own!"

"I don't like the idea of going away alone, captain," observed Frank, as he refilled his tumbler. "But suppose we talk the matter over to-morrow—when we've slept off the effects of the toddy!"

"Be Jasus! the toddy has no effects upon me!" exclaimed O'Blunderbuss, who nevertheless sate very unsteadily in his chair, his body swaying to and fro in spite of all his efforts to the contrary.

The conversation now languished; but the drinking was maintained, until Frank Curtis suddenly fell from his seat in a vain attempt which he made to reach the whiskey-bottle. The captain burst out into a roar of laughter, and while endeavouring to pick up his companion, rolled completely over him. He however managed, by means of many desperate efforts, to place the young gentleman upon the sofa, where he left him to repose in peace; and, taking up a candle, he staggered out of the room, muttering to himself, "Be the power-rs! if I didn't know—hic—that it was impos—sossible—hic—I should say that I—hic—was—dhrunk!"

This was a conclusion which the captain was by no means willing to admit; and, in order to convince himself that he was perfectly sober and knew what he was about, he proceeded to examine the front-door according to his invariable custom ere retiring to rest.

"Well, be the power-rs!" he murmured, as he stood contemplating the door with all the vacancy of inebriation; "it's John that's a clever fellow—hic—afther all—hic! Be Jasus! and it's two chains he's put up—and two bolts at the top—hic—and two bolts at the bottom—hic—and, be the holy poker-r!" exclaimed the captain aloud, his face expanding with an expresion of stupid joy; "the house is safe enough—hic—for there's two doors!"

Supremely happy at having made this discovery, and moreover fancying himself to be lighted by two candles—in a word, seeing double in every respect,—the gallant officer staggered along the passage, and commenced the ascent of the staircase, which appeared to have become wondrously steep, rickety, and uneven. Stumbling at every step, and muttering awful imprecations against the "thunthering fool of a carpenter that had built such a divil of a lath-er," Captain O'Blunderbuss contrived to reach the first landing in safety; but, his foot tripping over the carpet, he fell flat down, extinguishing the light of the candle, though at the same time giving his head such a knock against the balustrades, that a million meteoric sparks flashed across his visual organs.

"Blood and hounds!" growled the gallant gentleman; "there must either be an airthquake—hic—or else, be the power-rs! I'm—hic—raly—hic—dhrunk!"

Picking himself up, the captain groped about for the staircase; and, finding it with some little trouble, he continued his ascent in a pleasing state of uncertainty as to whether he were walking on his head or on his feet, but with the deeply settled conviction that he was spinning round at a most terrific rate.

"Capthain O'Bluntherbuss," he said, apostrophising himself, as he staggered along, "is this raly you or another person? If it's yourself it is—hic—I—I'm ashamed of ye, be the holy poker-r; and I've a precious good mind—hic—to give ye a dacent dhrubbing, captain—hic—O'—hic—Bluntherbuss."

Thus soliloquising, the martial gentleman reached the second landing; but here he paused for a few minutes in a state of awful doubt as to which way he should turn in order to reach his own room. He knew that his door must be somewhere close at hand; though whether to the right or to the left, he could not for the life of him remember. At length he began to grope about at a venture; and, having encountered the handle of a door, he hesitated no longer, but entered the chamber with which the said door communicated.

CHAPTER CIII.
THE SURPRISE.—A CHANGE OF SCENE.

It was about half-past three o'clock in the morning, and profound silence reigned in Baker Street, when four men, bearing a ladder upon their shoulders, passed like phantoms through the obscurity of the thoroughfare, and halted in front of Mr. Curtis's house; where their operations, so far from being at all ghost-like, assumed very much the appearance of those proceedings which are carried on by creatures of flesh and blood.

Thieves, however, they were not: but sheriff's-officers they were,—being our old friends Mac Grab and Proggs, assisted by two other queer-looking fellows of the species which chiefly abounds in the tap-rooms and parlours of public-houses in Chancery Lane.

Mr. Mac Grab having satisfied himself by a close scrutiny of the number on the front-door, that they had pitched upon the right house, the ladder was forthwith placed against the little iron railings forming the balcony at the drawing-room window; and Mr. Proggs was ordered to mount first. But Mr. Proggs, having perhaps recently studied some book upon etiquette, would not think of preceding his master; and Mr. Mac Grab was doubtless too meek a man to take upon himself the post of honour. As for the two underlings, they very bluntly assured Mr. Mac Grab that they would see him unpleasantly condemned before they would venture first; and thus the entire project was threatened with discomfiture, when Proggs, overcoming his fears, consented to lead the way.

Up the ladder did this hero accordingly drag himself; and had he lost his life in the desperate deed, the epic muse would have been compelled to deplore the death of the last of the famous house of Proggs. But fortune beamed upon Proggs, though the moon did not; and he reached the balcony in safety. Mac Grab ascended next—and the two subordinates followed,—by which time the intrepid Proggs had obtained admission into the house by the simple process of cutting out a pane with a glazier's diamond, and thrusting in his hand to undo the fastening of the window.

And now, behold the four men safe in the drawing-room—in actual possession of the place,—four heroes who had just carried a strongly fortified castle—by surprise!

A lanthorn, which Mr. Proggs took from his pocket, was lighted; and a flask of rum, which Mr. Mac Grab took from *his* pocket, was drunk. The heroes then stole gently from the apartment—descended the stairs—opened the front-door—and laid down the ladder along the area railings, so that the watchman, on going his rounds, might not raise an alarm of "thieves." This being accomplished, they re-entered the house, and fastened the street-door, the key of which Mr. Mac Grab secured about his own person.

The officers next entered the parlour on the ground floor, where they found Frank Curtis lying asleep upon the sofa.

"That's our chap," said Mac Grab, in a tone of deep satisfaction, as he threw the light of his lanthorn full upon the young gentleman's countenance. "I shall take him off at once, with one of the men; and you, Proggs, will remain in possession along with t'other."

"Two on us isn't enow to keep possession agin that devil of an Irisher," exclaimed Proggs, bluntly; and the loudness with which he spoke disturbed Mr. Curtis.

Starting up, Frank rubbed his eyes—then stared around him with the stupid vacancy of one who had only half slept off the fumes of whiskey—and at last, as the truth gradually glimmered upon him, he said in a hoarse, thick tone, "Well—who the devil are all you fellows?"

"You'll know soon enow who we be," growled Mac Grab. "Come—get up, young genelman; and don't sit there a-staring at us, as if you was a stuck pig and we was ghostesses."

"So you've got in at last—have you, old fellow?" said Frank, with an awful yawn. "But I feel precious seedy, though. Can't you let me sleep a little longer."

"You won't sleep no more till you gets to Chancery Lane," returned Mac Grab; "and then you can have a turn-in if you like."

"What o'clock is it?" demanded Frank, his teeth chattering and his whole frame shivering alike with the cold and the unpleasant petition to which he had been awakened.

"It's getting on for a quarter to four, or thereabouts," said Mac Grab, consulting a huge silver watch of the turnip species.

"Then I must have been asleep here for some time," mused Frank aloud; and, glancing at the table, he added, "Oh! I remember—I was precious drunk last night——"

"Well, I'm blest if I didn't think you was," said Proggs, expressing his opinion with more bluntness than politeness. "You'll find a many lushing coven over in Spike Island."

"Spike Island?" ejaculated Frank: then, as a light broke in upon him through the mist and fumes of whiskey, he added, "Oh! I understand—the Bench, eh? Well—never say die, my boys; as my friend the Crown Prince of Holland used to observe. If it must be the Bench, it must: but you'll let me tell my wife what's happened."

"We won't let you rouse that Irisher, young gentleman," said Mac Grab. "Let us get you safe off, and then he may wake up, and be damned to him."

"I pledge you my word I will not attempt to rouse the Captain," exclaimed Curtis: "but I must speak to my wife."

"Well, that's only fair and reasonable," said Mac Grab; "although you don't deserve no good treatment at our hands, seeing how we was served by that owdacious Irish friend of yourn. Howsomever, you shall speak to your good lady; but mind, I ain't going to lose sight on you."

"You can come with me as far as the bed-chamber door," observed Frank; "and I shan't keep you many minutes."

"Proggs, you'll come along with me," said Mac Grab. "And now, mind, Mr. Curtis, what you're up to. We've got pistols with us; and blowed if we don't use 'em in self-defence if that Irish friend of your's happens to wake up and tries it on again with any of his nonsense."

"It wasn't my fault that he acted as he did the last time you was here," returned Frank. "But come along, you two—if you must go with me."

Curtis lighted a candle, and led the way gently up stairs, Mac Grab and Proggs following close at his heels. They reached the second landing, where Frank stopped at a door, which he was about to open, when the first-mentioned officer said in a low tone, "Now, mind—no nonsense!—we won't be done a second time, remember."

"I assure you this is my wife's room," returned Curtis, also speaking in a whisper; and he entered the chamber, the two bailiffs remaining at the door, which was left ajar.

Frank, carrying the light in his hand, approached the bed, and was just on the point of saying, "My dear—my dear!"—when he stopped short—aghast—stupefied—his mouth wide open—and every faculty which he possessed, save that of sight, entirely suspended.

For there—by the side of his wife—lay Captain O'Blunderbuss!

Both were fast asleep; and the countenance of the gallant officer seemed absolutely on fire, so red was it in contrast with the white pillow.

"By Jove—this is too bad!" exclaimed Curtis, at length recovering the powers of speech and movement; and, influenced only by the sudden rage which took possession of him, and which rendered him bold and courageous for the instant, he seized a water-jug from the washing-stand and dashed the contents completely over Captain O'Blunderbuss.

"Blood and thunther!" roared the man of war starting up in a towering passion;—and, springing from the bed, he was about to inflict summary chastisement on his friend, when a shriek issued from the couch—and the captain, stopping short and looking around him, ascertained where he was. The cause of Frank's conduct towards him was instantly apparent; and, subduing his anger, he exclaimed, "Be Jasus! and it was all a mistake, me boy! I dhrank too much of the potheen——"

"The Irishman, by goles!" growled a hoarse voice in the landing outside.

"Well—never mind, Proggs!" cried another voice: "if he touches us, we'll fire. Holloa! you fellows down there—come up!—come up!" roared Mac Grab.

And now the whole house was in confusion.

Mrs. Curtis lay screaming and shrieking in bed—the captain rushed upon the landing, with nothing on save his shirt, and looking as if he had just sprung out of a water-butt—Curtis followed, sulky and not half satisfied with the apology he had received relative to the presence of the officer in his wife's chamber—the two men who had been left down stairs were running up as hard as they could—and the servants were calling from the garrets to know what was the matter, but rather suspecting something very much like the real truth in respect to the invasion of the bailiffs.

"Down—down with ye, wild bastes that ye are!" vociferated the captain, as the light which Curtis still carried showed the gallant officer the well known faces of Mac Grab and Proggs.

But the two men, who had worked their courage up to the sticking point, produced each a heavy horse-pistol; at the appearance of which formidable weapons the captain hung back, and Curtis shouted out in alarm, "No violence! I'll keep my word and go off with you quiet enough."

"Be Jasus! and you shan't though, my dear frind!" cried O'Blunderbuss, looking rapidly round in search of some object which he might use as an offensive weapon against the invaders; but the two men from down stairs now made their appearance, and Curtis put an end to all further hostilities by surrendering himself to them without any more ado.

"Frank! Frank!" shrieked his wife from the bed-room.

"Curthis, my frind—don't be a fool!" roared the captain: "we'll bate 'em yet!"

The young gentleman, however, took no notice either of his wife's appeal or his friend's adjuration, and rapidly descended the stairs, followed by the sheriff's-officers. He was not only afraid of the pistols; but he was likewise too much annoyed at the bed-chamber scene to care about remaining in the house any longer. Not having courage enough to resent the wrong which he conceived to have been done him, he was nevertheless unable to endure it passively; and here signed himself, moodily and sulkily, to the lot which circumstances had shaped for him.

Mac Grab and one of the subordinates accordingly departed with their prisoner to the spunging-house in Chancery Lane; while Proggs and the other man remained in possession of the dwelling in Baker Street.

It was about half-past four o'clock on that dark and chilly morning, when Frank Curtis entered the lock-up establishment owned by Mr. Mac Grab, the sheriff's-officer. A racking head-ache, the result of the preceding night's debauch—a cold nervousness, amounting almost to a continuous shiver,—and thoughts of by no means a pleasant nature, all combined to depress the young man's spirits to a very painful degree; and, as the door of the spunging-house closed behind him, he murmured to himself, "Oh! what a fool I have been!" Fortunately, he had plenty of ready money in his pocket; and, putting a guinea into Mac Grab's hand, he said, "Let me have a private room; and have a fire lighted directly."

"Please to sit down for a few minutes in the office here," observed the bailiff, pocketing the coin, "while I call up the servant."

In the meantime the subordinate had lighted a lamp in the little, dirty, cold-looking place, dignified by the name of "the office;" and while Mac Grab went to summon the domestic, Curtis, who was a prey to that fidgety sensation which seems the forerunner of something dreadful, endeavoured to divert his thoughts from gloomy topics by scrutinizing the objects around him.

A sorry desk, much hacked about with a pen-knife and stained all over with ink—a small shelf containing a few old law books—a law-almanack with thick black lines in the calender denoting Term-times—a list of the sheriffs and undersheriffs of England and Wales—printed papers showing the arrangements of the Courts for the sittings in and after Term—two or three crazy chairs—and a Dutch clock, which ticked with a monotony calculated to drive a nervous person out of his senses,—these were the objects which met his view. Every thing appeared musty and worm-eaten;—the office looked as if it never were swept out;—and there was an earthly smell of a peculiarly unpleasant nature.

In this miserable place—so cold and cheerless—Frank Curtis was kept waiting for nearly half-an-hour; while the man who remained with him sate dozing in a chair, and every now and then awaking with a sudden dive down and bob up of the head which painfully augmented the nervousness of the prisoner. At last Mr. Mac Grab returned, smelling very strong of rum, and followed by a dirty-looking old woman, who seemed to have huddled on her clothes anyhow, and to be in a particularly ill-humour at being disturbed so early in the morning.

"Now then," she said, in a short, sulky tone, addressing herself to Curtis, without however looking at him: "this way."

Frank followed her into a short passage, and then up a narrow staircase, the miserable candle which she held in one hand and shaded with the other on account of the draught, affording only just sufficient light to render apparent the cheerless aspect of the premises. It was not that there was any thing mean or poor in the interior of the dwelling, the office excepted: but there was an air of deep gloom, and also of dirt and neglect, which struck even so superficial an observer as Mr. Frank Curtis.

The old woman led the way into a moderate-sized front room on the second floor, where she lighted two candles, and then set to work to persuade a few damp sticks smothered with small coal to burn up in the grate. The apartment was fitted up as a sitting-room, but had a bed in it. The walls were hung with numerous pictures the frames of which were an inch thick in dust and cobwebs; and there was a side-board covered with old-fashioned cut glass. The carpet was worn out in many places, and was also much soiled with grease and beer: the table-cover was likewise stained with liquor and spotted with ink. The curtains, which were of good material, were completely disguised in dust; and the windows were so dirty that at mid-day they formed a pleasantly subdued medium for the sun-light. Altogether, there was an air of expense mingled with the most cheerless discomfort—an appearance of liberal outlay altogether neutralized by neglect and habits of wanton slovenliness.

The fire burnt feebly—the old woman slunk sulkily away—and Frank Curtis threw himself upon the bed. He was thoroughly wretched, and would have given all the money he had left in his pocket for a few hours' tranquil repose. But sleep would not visit his eyes; and, after tossing about for some time in painful restlessness, he got up as the clock struck eight.

His burning, feverish countenance craved the contact of cold water; and the idea of a refreshing toilette rendered him almost cheerful. But the jug was empty; and there were no towels. He rang the bell: five minutes elapsed—and no one came. He rang again; and at last, another five minutes having gone tediously by, the old woman made her appearance. His wishes were expressed; and the harridan took away the jug. A third interval of five minutes passed, ere she returned. Then she had forgotten the towels; and now a quarter of an hour dragged its slow length along before she came back, bringing with her a miserably thin rag of about a foot square. She was about to leave the room again, when Curtis discovered that there was no soap; and ten minutes more were required for the provoking old wretch to produce a small sample of that very necessary article. Yet for all this *discomfort*, the prisoner had paid a guinea in advance!

"Pray let me have some breakfast us soon as you can, my good woman," said Frank, humiliated and miserable.

"As soon as the kittle biles down stairs," answered the servant, in a surly tone, as she turned to leave the room.

"And how long will that be?" demanded Curtis.

"Don't know: the kitchen fire ain't alight yet:"—and she hobbled away.

In a fit of desperation the prisoner addressed himself to his toilette: but the feeling of utter discomfort still clung to him. The water seemed thick and clammy, instead of cool and refreshing; and the towel was so small that it became saturated in a few moments, and he was compelled to dry his face with a corner of one of the sheets. Having no nail brush, he could not cleanse his hands properly; and the want of a comb left his hair matted and disordered. In fact, he positively felt more uncomfortable and dirty after his ablutions than he did before he began them; and that disagreeable sensation kept him dispirited and wretched.

He walked about the room, examining all the pictures one after the other, until he became as thoroughly acquainted with their subjects as if he had lived for years in that room. He then posted himself at one of the windows, and watched the people passing up and down the street. It was now nine o'clock, and the law-clerks were proceeding to their respective offices. Seedy-looking men were hurrying along with mysterious slips of paper in their hands; and now and then a better-attired person, in a suit of black, would be seen wending his way towards the Chancery Court, carrying the blue bag of his master, a barrister. Small parties of threes or fours would likewise pass up the lane, affording to the initiated the irresistible idea—which was also the true one—of tipstaves conducting insolvents to the court in Portugal Street.

At the public house, opposite the barred window from which Curtis was gazing, a small knot of very shabby men had collected; and it required but little knowledge of the specimens of animated nature in Chancery Lane, to recognise their especial calling. In fact they were individuals who belonged to the outworks of the strong entrenchments of the law,—process-servers, sheriff's-officers' assistants, and men who hired themselves out to be left in possession at dwellings where executions were levied. When not actively engaged, they regularly haunted the public-houses, of which they seemed the very door-posts; and if they stepped inside to take something, which was very often indeed, they appeared on intimate terms with the landlord, said "Miss" to the bar-girl, and called the waiter by his Christian name. They had a dirty, seedy, mean, and cringing look about them; and yet, if not adequately recompensed by the unfortunate victims of the law with whom they had to deal, they would become doggedly insolent and grossly abusive.

Half-an-hour passed away; and Chancery Lane grew more attractive. A few barristers, in all the imposing dignity of the black gown and the awful wisdom of the wig, were seen moving along to the Rolls' Court: well-dressed attorneys alighted from their gigs, cabs, or phaetons at the doors of their offices;—and articled clerks, having thrown away their cigars when within view of the windows of their places of business, made up for lost time by cutting briskly over the pavement, flourishing short sticks, and complacently surveying their polished boots, tight-fitting trousers, and flash waistcoats.

Frank Curtis sighed as he beheld so many, many persons in the enjoyment of freedom;—but his mournful reverie was at length broken by the entrance of the old woman with the breakfast-tray. His throat was parched, and he had been unable to drink the water: he now, therefore, eagerly applied himself to the tea. But it was wretched stuff; and even extreme thirst could not render it palatable. He tried to eat a piece of toast; but the butter was so rank that his heart heaved against it. He broke open an egg: it however tasted of straw, and nearly made him sick.

Having forced himself to swallow a couple of cups of tea, Frank rang the bell and ordered the woman to bring him a sheet of paper. This command was complied with, after a long delay; and, by the aid of a worn down stump of a pen and ink which flowed like soot and water, Frank managed to pen a brief note to a lawyer whom he knew, and who dwelt in Carey Street hard by. After a great deal of trouble, a messenger was found, who, for the moderate reward of eighteen pence, undertook to convey the note to its place of destination—just fifty yards distant; and in the course of half an hour, Mr. Pepperton, the legal limb alluded to, made his appearance in the shape of a short, thin, sallow-faced man, with small piercing eyes, and very compressed lips.

"Well, Mr. Curtis," said the lawyer, as he entered the room; "got into a mess—eh?"

"Rather so," replied the young man. "But I don't care so much about that, as on account of being locked up in this cursed place. The fact is I must go over to the Bench; and I dare say Sir Christopher won't let me lie very long there."

"You require a *habeas*, you know," observed the lawyer. "But are you sure that you're sued in the Court of Queen's Bench? because, if it is in the Common Pleas or Exchequer, you will have to go to the Fleet."

"The devil!" ejaculated Frank. "But here's a paper which Mac Grab gave me——"

"Ah! that's right," said Mr. Pepperton, examining the document placed in his hands. "Yes—it's in the Bench, safe enough. Holloa!" he exclaimed suddenly, after a few moments' silence: "here's an error in the description. Your name is Francis, and not Frank."

"Just so!" cried the prisoner, his heart fluttering with the vague hope which his legal adviser's words and manner had encouraged.

"Well—I think—mind, I *think* that it is highly probable we may set the caption aside," continued Pepperton. "At all events it would be worth the trying. But I must apply to the Judge in Chambers this afternoon; and if we *do* happen to fail—mind, I say *if* we *do*—why, then you can pass over to the Bench to-morrow."

Somehow or another, persons locked up in spunging-houses always feel confident of getting out on the slightest legal quibble that their ingenious attorneys may suggest. They do not apprehend the chance of failure, and of disbursing two or three guineas, which they can so ill afford, for nothing: the process of applying to a Judge in Chambers seems so certain of a triumphant issue, and there is such a spell in the bare idea, that the door of freedom appears already opening to the touch.

Frank Curtis was not an exception to the general rule which we have mentioned; and he forthwith desired Mr. Pepperton to adopt the necessary steps, although this gentleman assured him that nothing could be done until the after part of the day.

Poor, deluded captive! Little did he think Mr. Pepperton was well aware beforehand that there was not the shadow of the ghost of a chance of success; but that his only motive in suggesting these proceedings was to make as much out of his client as possible.

When Pepperton had left the room, Frank Curtis began to pace it as if he were a Wandering Jew confined to a very miniature world; and he examined the pictures over and over again, until they seemed the most familiar friends of the kind he had ever known. Then he returned to the window, and beheld Mr. Mac Grab and one of his men just starting in a queer-looking gig upon a suburban expedition; and having watched the equipage until it was no longer visible, he bethought himself of asking for a newspaper. He accordingly rang the bell, and intimated his wishes to the old woman, who, after keeping him in suspense as usual for ten minutes or a quarter of an hour, returned with a *Weekly Dispatch* a fortnight old and a *Times* of ten days back. Curtis could scarcely control his indignation; and, tossing a shilling to the harridan, he desired her to send out and buy him a morning paper. She departed accordingly, and in half-an-hour returned with that day's *Times*, whereby Mr. Frank Curtis was enabled to divert himself until two o'clock, when he partook of an execrable chop nearly raw, a potato that seemed as if it were iced, and a pint of wine which appeared to have been warmed.

Then how heavily, heavily did the weary hours pass away; and Curtis more than half regretted that his friend O'Blunderbuss did not call upon him. He felt that, for the pleasure of his society, he would overlook and forget the treatment he had received at his hands. But the gallant officer came not; and, what with another examination of the pictures, a complete spell of the advertisements (the news being already disposed of) in the *Times*, and a cigar or two, Frank managed to dispose of the time, though miserably enough, until five o'clock.

Mr. Pepperton then came back; and Frank awaited the report in excruciating suspense.

"Well, my dear fellow," said the lawyer, flinging himself in a chair as if regularly worn out by hard work, "we have lost the point; but we have this consolation——"

"What?" demanded Curtis, in the anxious hope of seeing another loophole promising emancipation.

"Why—that we as nearly gained it as possible," returned Pepperton. "It was old Justice Foozlehem that was at Chambers to-day; and, when I argued the point, he rubbed his nose with the feather-end of the pen—he always does that when the thing is very ticklish——"

"Damn Judge Foozlehem!" emphatically cried Mr. Frank Curtis. "A miss is as good as a mile; and that was what the Prince of Malabar said when my bullet whistled close by his ear at that duel which him and me fought at Boulogne three years ago. But, to speak seriously of business—I suppose that there's nothing left for me to do——"

"Save to pay the debt or go to the Bench," added the lawyer, putting the alternatives in as nut-shell a compass as possible.

"Well—the Bench it must be, then!" ejaculated Frank.

"I will take out the *habeas* to-morrow," observed Mr. Pepperton; "and at about five o'clock in the afternoon the tipstaff will be at Serjeant's Inn waiting for you—or may be, you'll have to go over to him at the public-house opposite."

Curtis invited the lawyer to pass the evening with him: but Mr. Pepperton was engaged elsewhere; and the prisoner was therefore compelled to drink and smoke in solitude, occasionally varying the occupation by another spell at the *Times*—another long gaze of envy from the window—and another scrutiny of the pictures.

At last, when ten o'clock struck, Mr. Curtis was thoroughly worn out by feverish excitement, suspense, and annoyances of all kinds; and he retired to rest with the fervent hope of enjoying an uninterrupted slumber till morning. But scarcely had he begun to get drowsy, when a tickling sensation commenced in a thousand parts of his body and limbs; and, to his dismay, he found himself assailed by a perfect legion of those abominable little torturers termed bugs.

Now, Mr. Curtis was most peculiarly sensitive in this respect; and if there were ever a flea or a bug in a bed, it was certain to find him out—aye, and feast upon him too. But never, in the whole course of his life, had he experienced such an attack as on the present occasion: never till now had he known bugs so numerous, nor bites so pungent.

At length he jumped up in rage and agony, and lighted a candle. But vain was all search: not a bug could he find. The legion *appeared* to have suddenly *disappeared*. Like Destiny, they were always to be felt, but never seen. He could not sleep with a light in the room; so, having extinguished it, he laid himself down once more.

For a few minutes he was suffered to remain quiet enough; but at last, back came his tormentors by slow degrees; and scarcely had he torn the skin off one part of his body, than he was compelled to flay another. In this manner hour after hour passed; and, when he did at length fall asleep between one and two in the morning, he was pursued by a legion of bugs and sheriff's-officers in his dreams.

CHAPTER CIV.
THE VISIT.—THE HABEAS CORPUS.

Frank awoke at seven o'clock, depressed in spirits and unrefreshed in body. His head still ached; and he was sore all over through having nearly torn himself to pieces on account of the bugs. His face betrayed marks of the ravages committed upon him by his little tormentors; and his eyes were swollen from the same cause. He had not even the comfort of copious ablutions; for the process of the toilette was not more satisfactory on this occasion than it had been on the previous day. Thus all circumstances conspired to make him wretched.

Before he sate down to breakfast, he despatched a messenger to Baker Street for a few necessaries which he required; and, as he did not choose to write to his wife, and knew not whether O'Blunderbuss might still be there, he sent a verbal intimation of his wishes.

The breakfast of this morning was no improvement on its predecessor: indeed, it struck Curtis that he had got from bad to worse by trying the desperate experiment of ordering coffee instead of tea. He, however, knew that it was useless to grumble; and so, having disposed of the meal as best he could, he sent for the morning paper, with which he whiled away an hour and a half until the return of his messenger, who came laden with a portmanteau.

"Well, who did you see in Baker Street?" demanded Frank.

"Please, sir, I see Mr. Proggs and t'other man which is in possession," was the answer.

"And who else?" enquired Curtis.

"Please, sir, I see a stout lady as give me a glass of gin, and a tall genelman as give me a rap over the head," returned the man.

"And what did he do that for?" cried Frank, laughing in spite of himself.

"'Cos he said, sir, that I didn't speak in a speckful way to him. But here's a note as the genelman give me to give to you, sir."

Curtis tore open a curiously folded letter which the messenger handed to him, and the contents of which ran as follow:—

"Be Jasus, my frind, and it's myself that has a right to complain of unfrindly tratement. Here have I been waiting to resave a bit of a note from ye, and divil a line or a word at all, at all. Your poor wife's distracted and has lost her appetite, and all because of your injurious suspicions; but I do all I can to consoul her. If you come to reflict upon the matther, Frank, ye must admit that though appayrances was against me, yet it isn't Capthain O'Blunderbuss that would wrong ye. For, be the powers! and it's mistaken in the bed I was—what with botheration and potheen and the candle's going out; and divil a hayp'orth did I drame where I was, till ye powred the wather all over me. So shake hands, me boy, and let us be frinds again; and sure it's myself that will bring Mrs. Curtis down to dine with ye at two o'clock this afthernoon, and we'll send in the dinner and the potheen first. Proggs and his man are in possission; and I feel like a defated ginral: but they're on their best behaviour, and so I have not been forced to give either of them a taste of the shillaylee. I'm sadly afraid that the chap you have sent up is a fool; so if he should forget to give you this letter, mind you ask him for it. Your wife sends you a million kisses through me; and believe me, my frind, to remain

"Ever yours,

"GORMAN O'BLUNDERBUSS."

"Very good," said Frank Curtis, as he brought the perusal of this curious epistle to an end: and having paid and dismissed the messenger, he sate himself down to reflect upon the manner in which he ought to receive his wife and the gallant gentleman.

On the one hand was the sense of the injury he had received, or fancied he had received; for he could not well embrace the double conviction that Mrs. Curtis was *not* faithless, and that the captain was *not* treacherous. On the other hand were numerous motives persuasive of an amicable course,—the want of society, the shame of declaring himself to be a cuckold—and last, though not least, the infinite terror in which he stood of Gorman O'Blunderbuss. These reasons were weighty and powerful; and they grew stronger and stronger as the dinner-hour advanced,—until they became completely triumphant when a hamper was sent up, containing cold fowls, ham, wine, dessert, whiskey, and cigars.

No longer hesitating what course to pursue, Frank superintended the laying of the cloth and the arrangement of the provisions upon the table: he decanted the wine—tasted it—and found it excellent;—and, those little proceedings having put him into a thorough good humour, he received his wife and the captain, when they made their appearance, as if nothing had occurred to ruffle his mind with regard to them.

Mrs. Curtis thought it necessary to go into hysterics at the sight of her beloved husband in a spunging-house; but she speedily recovered upon the said beloved husband's kindly recommending her not to make a fool of herself;—and the trio sate down to dinner, at which they made themselves very comfortable indeed. The captain proposed that as the wine-glasses were particularly small, they should drink their Sherry from tumblers; and the motion was adopted after a feeble opposition on the part of the lady.

"Well, Cu-r-r-tis, me boy," exclaimed the gallant gentleman, when they had made an end of eating, having done immense justice to the viands provided, "what are ye afther now? It isn't staying here all your life that you can be thinking of——"

"Nor do I intend to stop in this cursed hole many hours longer," interrupted Frank. "I expect to go over to the Bench, at five o'clock."

"The Binch!" cried the captain, overjoyed at the plan chalked out: "be Jasus! and it's the wisest thing ye can be afther, my frind! The Binch is a glor-rious place—and ye'll be as comfortable there as at home. The porther is the best in all London; and it's worth while to be in the Binch for the pleasure of dhrinking it. Not that I'm a great admirer of malt, Mim," he added, turning politely towards Mrs. Curtis; "but the porther of the Binch is second best to rale potheen. Then the amusements of the Binch, Mim, are delightful! There's the parade to walk upon—and there's the racquet ground when ye're tired of the parade—and there's the dolphin-pump—and the coffee-house, a riglar tavern——In fact," exclaimed the gallant gentleman, quite lost in admiration of all the beautiful views and scenes he was so enthusiastically depicting, "the Binch is a perfect palace of a prison, and I only wish I was there myself."

"I'm sure I should be most happy to change places with you, captain," observed Frank Curtis drily.

"I wouldn't deprive ye of the pleasure, me boy, for all the wor-r-ld!" cried O'Blunderbuss, in a tone of the utmost sincerity. "But what's to be done next? Those bastes of the earth are in possession of the garrison, and every stick will be sould up by them—the ragamuffin scamps that they are!"

"The wife and children must take a lodging over the water, close by the Bench," said Curtis; "and if Sir Christopher won't come forward to assist me, I must either get the Rules or go through the Insolvent's Court—I don't care much which. My friend, the Earl of Billingsgate, did both——"

"Be the holy poker-r! and it's myself that will call on Sir Christopher-r in such a strait as this," vociferated the captain; "and although he did knock me down from the carriage window, the last time——"

"What!" ejaculated Frank, as much amused as astonished at the information which the gallant officer had so inadvertently let slip; "Sir Christopher knocked you down!"

"Blood and thunther!" roared the captain, becoming as red as scarlet; "and was it afther making a fool of myself that I was? For sure and it was Sir

Christopher that was knocked down—and I didn't like to tell ye about it before, seeing that he's your own nat'ral uncle. But it's myself that will call upon him and offer the most abject apology; and I'll skin him alive if he don't come for'ard as he ought to do, and pay all your debts, my dear boy. So you persave that there's some use in having such a frind as Gorman O'Bluntherbuss, of Bluntherbuss Park, Connemar-r-ra, Ir-r-reland!" added the martial gentleman, with an awful rattling of the r's.

"The sooner I move over to the neighbourhood of the Bench, the better," said Mrs. Curtis; "for I am sick and tired of living in Baker Street. Just now, when I came out, it seemed to me that all the people I met laughed in my face, as if they knew our circumstances."

"I wish I had seen them dar-r to laugh!" cried Captain O'Blunderbuss, lifting up an empty bottle, and flourishing it over his head: "I'd have sent them slap into the middle of next week, so that they should miss resayving their money next Saturday night."

In such pleasant chat as this, did the trio while away the time until about a quarter to five, when Mr. Pepperton made his appearance to announce that the office had been searched, that three detainers had been found, and that the *habeas corpus* was all in apple-pie order.

Frank Curtis accordingly rang the bell, and ordered his bill. In about a quarter of an hour it was brought;—and thus it ran:—

Mr. Curtis's Account.

	s.	d.
Room	10	6
Breakfast	3	0
Eggs	0	6
Messenger to Carey Street	2	6
Reading Newspapers	1	0
Dinner	5	0
Porter	0	6
Gin and Cigars	5	6
Bread and Cheese for Supper	2	0

Porter		0	6
Room		10	6
Breakfast		3	0
Eggs		0	6
Messenger to Baker Street		3	0
Use of table-cloth, knives, and forks, &c., gentleman providing his own dinner		2	6
Extras		5	0
	£2	15	6

"Why, my good woman," exclaimed Frank Curtis, amazed as such a terrific attempt at imposition, "this account is absurd. Besides, there are two things in it that I paid for myself—I mean the messenger yesterday and to-day."

"Master says it's all right, sir," observed the harridan.

"And then you charge a shilling for reading two newspapers a fortnight old," cried Frank, more and more bewildered as he studied the items of the bill: "and five shillings for *extras*! Why—what the devil are the *extras*, since it seems to me that you have taken precious good care to omit nothing?"

"The extras is soap, and candles, and so on," said the woman, growing impatient.

"Then, be Jasus! and just let me soap over Mr. Mac Grab with a shillaleh!" ejaculated Captain O'Blunderbuss, starting from his seat. "It's after robbing my frind, ye are—ye bastes of the earth!"

Mr. Pepperton however interfered, and represented to the two gentlemen that there was no possibility of obtaining redress—that sheriff's-officers might charge exactly what they liked—and that it would be much better to pay the bill without any haggling. The amount was accordingly liquidated, and the old woman received half-a-crown as a gratuity, which she took in a manner most unequivocally denoting that she had expected at least four times as much.

"Well," exclaimed Frank Curtis, as soon as she had left the room, "of all infernal impositions this is the greatest! Supposing I was a poor devil———"

"Then you would have been bundled straight off to Whitecross Street at once," observed Pepperton. "Lord bless you, my dear sir—there's an aristocracy amongst debtors as well as in every thing else in this country."

"I always thought the law was the same for rich or poor," said Curtis.

"You never were under a greater mistake in your life," returned the solicitor. "Money is all-powerful in England, and makes the gentleman; and gentlemen are treated quite differently from common people. Such establishments as the Bench and the Fleet[43] are for those who can afford to pay for a *habeas*: while those who cannot, must go to the County Gaol. These spunging-houses, too, are places of accommodation, for the use of which people must pay liberally."

"Or rather be robbed vilely," said Frank. "But never mind—it can't be helped. When shall I have to go over to the Bench?"

"The tipstaff is no doubt already waiting at the public-house opposite," replied the lawyer.

"Then I'll be off at once," exclaimed Curtis, rising from his chair.

"Be the power-rs! but we'll see ye safe over to the Binch," cried Captain O'Blunderbuss; "for it may be that I shall have to thrash the Marshal or skin a tur-rnkey to renther the people dacently civil in that iligant istablishment."

"Yes—you come with me, captain," said Frank, who had been thinking of some means to separate his amiable wife and his devoted friend. "You can put Mrs. C. into a hackney-coach; and to-morrow morning, my dear," he added, turning towards his spouse, "you can look out for a lodging somewhere in the neighbourhood of the prison."

"But you don't mean me to remain all alone to-night in Baker Street, with those odious officers in the house?" exclaimed Mrs. Curtis, not admiring the proposed arrangement.

"It would not be proper for the captain to stay in the house now that I am away," said Frank, hastily, and without daring to look at his gallant friend: indeed, scarcely were the words out of his mouth, when he was surprised at his courage in having dared to utter them.

Fortunately the captain took the observation in good part, and even expressed his approval of it; for it struck the martial gentleman that he should stand a much better chance of amusing himself with Frank Curtis in the Bench, with the interior arrangements of which he was pretty well acquainted from old experience, than in the society of Mrs. Curtis in Baker Street. The lady could not, therefore, offer any farther opposition to the arrangement proposed; but she darted an angry look upon the captain, who responded by one of earnest appeal to her mercy.

She now took leave of her husband, and was escorted by Captain O'Blunderbuss to the nearest coach-stand; and as some time elapsed ere he returned to the spunging-house, it is presumable that he had a little difficulty in making his peace with her.

At length, however, he did re-appear; and, the messenger having conveyed the portmanteau over to the public-house opposite, for which he only charged a shilling, the prisoner proceeded thither in company with Mr. MacGrab and Captain O'Blunderbuss, Pepperton bidding them farewell at the door.

In a little front parlour on the first floor of the public-house alluded to, sate half-a-dozen seedy-looking men, who were delectably occupied in smoking cigars and drinking hot gin-and-water. Their conversation was doubtless very amusing to themselves; but it would have been very boring to strangers;—for the topic seemed entirely limited to what had taken place that day at the Insolvent Debtors' Court, or at the Judges' Chambers. There, in that same room, were those men accustomed to meet every afternoon (Sunday excepted), at about the same hour; and their discourse was invariably on the same subjects. They were tipstaffs—or, more properly speaking, perhaps, tipstaves: they lived in the atmosphere of debtors' prisons and law-courts;—and all their information was circumscribed to the transactions thereof. When they were not hovering about the lobbies of the Fleet or the Bench, they were "down at Westminster," or "up at Portugal Street;" and if not in any of those places—why, then they were at the public-house.

It was to one of these worthies that MacGrab introduced Mr. Francis Curtis; and as the tipstaff thus particularised had not finished his cigar nor his gin-and-water, Mr. Frank Curtis and Captain O'Blunderbuss sate down to keep him company till he had. Half an hour afterwards a hackney-coach was sent for; and the prisoner, his gallant friend, and the officer were speedily on their road to the King's Bench prison.

Curtis spoke but little during the transit: he felt nervous at the idea of going to his new home. But the captain rattled away as if he were determined to speak for himself and his friend both; and the tipstaff was still in a state of uncertainty as to whether he should set the gallant gentleman down as a very extraordinary personage, or as a most wondrous liar, when the vehicle stopped at a little low door in a gloomy brick wall.

"Be Jasus! and here's the Binch already," exclaimed Captain O'Blunderbuss, thrusting his head out of the coach-window. "That house there, with the trees before it, Frank, is the Marshal's—and a very dacent berth he's got of it: I shouldn't mind standing in his shoes at all, at all. But come along, me dear frind."

Thus speaking, the captain leapt from the vehicle, followed by Frank Curtis and the tipstaff; and, having traversed an enclosure formed by the gloomy-looking wall above alluded to and the high spike-topped boundary of the prison itself, the trio ascended a few steps which led them into the upper lobby of the King's Bench.

> 43. Within the last few years the Fleet has been suppressed, and the Bench, under the general name of the Queen's Prison, has become the receptacle for all metropolitan debtors who are enabled to purchase the luxury of a *habeas corpus*.

CHAPTER CV.
THE KING'S BENCH PRISON.

The upper lobby was a small, dirty, and sombre-looking outwork of the vast establishment. A huge clock hung against one of the walls—a roasting fire burnt in the grate—and a stout, elderly turnkey, who spoke with a provincial accent, was seated on a high stool near the inner door, watching the persons who came *out* of the prison, and on whose countenance the glare of a powerful light was thrown by a tin reflector. Grouped near him were several char-women and messengers, engaged in the double occupation of discussing a pot of the best ale and the scandal of the Bench; while another turnkey—a short, active, bustling little fellow, who rejoiced in the nick-name of "Buffer"—was seated inside a small enclosure formed by wood-work breast-high, examining a greasy and well-thumbed book containing sundry hieroglyphics which were supposed to be entries of the prisoners' names.

To Mr. Buffer was Mr. Frank Curtis duly introduced by the tipstaff; and the young gentleman's appellations were forthwith inscribed in the greasy book. He was then desired to pay his gate-fees, which he accordingly did; and, these little matters being settled, Mr. Buffer politely informed him that he might "go inside." The head turnkey—who was the stout, elderly man above alluded to—thereupon opened the door at which he was seated; and Captain O'Blunderbuss led the way, first across a small yard, next through the lower lobby—and thence into the grand enclosure of the King's Bench itself.

Captain O'Blunderbuss turned sharp round to the left, and stopped in admiration before a low building with a roof slanting down from the high wall against which it stood.

"There!" cried the gallant officer, in an ecstacy of enthusiasm: "what place should you be afther taking *that* to be?"

"Why—I should say it was the scullery or the coal-cellars," replied Frank.

"Be Jasus! me dear frind—and you're insulting the finest fature in this fine prison," exclaimed the captain: "it's the coffee-house."

Mr. Curtis did not like to say how deeply he was disappointed at the unpromising exterior of an establishment which his companion seemed so especially to admire; and he therefore silently followed his guide into the coffee-room, which was just large enough to contain four very little tables and yield accommodation to about a dozen people at a time.

There was nearly that number present when Captain O'Blunderbuss and Frank Curtis entered the place; and as there were not two seats disengaged, the gallant officer put his arms akimbo, fixed his eyes sternly on a stout, inoffensive-looking old gentleman, and, without positively addressing his words to him, exclaimed, "Be the holy poker-r! and I should advise some one to be afther making room on a binch for my frind and myself—or I'll know the rayson why!"

The inoffensive-looking gentleman shrank dismayed into a corner, and, two or three others pressing closer together, sufficient space was obtained to afford Captain O'Blunderbuss and Mr. Frank Curtis seats; and the former, as he took his place at a table, cast a particularly ferocious glance around on the assembled company, as much as to say, "Be the power-rs! and ye'd better not be afther having any of your nonsense with me!" But as no one at the moment seemed at all inclined to make even an attempt to interfere with the gallant gentleman, his countenance gradually lost its menacing aspect; and he ordered the waiter—a slip-shod, dirty boy—to bring a bottle of wine, spirits not being allowed.

The company presented to the view of Mr. Frank Curtis rather a motley aspect. There was a sample of nearly all kinds of social distinctions,—a sprig of the aristocracy— a broken-down sporting gentleman—a decayed tradesman—a bankrupt merchant—an insolvent parson—a ruined gamester—a prize-fighter—a horse-chaunter—an attorney, who had over-reached himself—a poor author—and one or two others who bore the vague and much misappropriated denomination of "gentleman." All these were herding together in a glorious state of democratic equality; for a debtors' prison goes far to level distinctions, the lordling being very often glad to obtain a draught of ale from the pewter-pot of a butcher.

The entrance of Captain O'Blunderbuss and Frank Curtis, both of whom were taken for new prisoners and stared at accordingly, seemed to have interrupted a conversation that was previously going on;—and for a few minutes a dead silence prevailed. But at last, when the wine which the captain had ordered was brought in, and that gallant gentleman and Curtis gave evident proofs of an inclination to enjoy themselves by enquiring likewise for cigars, the company recovered the feeling of hilarity on which the awful appearance of O'Blunderbuss had seemed for a few minutes to throw a complete damper.

"Well, how did Jackson get on to-day at Portugal Street?" enquired a rakish, dissipated looking young gentleman, who was smoking a cigar and drinking a pint of Port-wine.

"He got sent back for six months," answered the person to whom the question was put, and who was a stout, big man, in very seedy attire. "It seems that his schedule was made up of accommodation bills, and the opposition was desperate."

"You talk of accommodation bills, Muggles," observed the young gentleman; "why, all my debts are in paper of that kind. There's seventeen thousand pounds against me at the gate; and I'd take my affidavit that I never had more than three thousand in actual value. So I suppose I shall get it from the old Commissioner?"

"No, you won't, Pettifer, my boy," cried a short, elderly, dapper-looking man, putting down a quart pot in which his countenance had been buried for upwards of a minute before he began to speak; "your father's a lord—and that's enough," he added, looking mysteriously around.

"Well, so he is," said the Honourable Mr. Pettifer, lolling back in a very aristocratic manner, and speaking for the behoof of Captain O'Blunderbuss and Frank Curtis; "it's true that my father is Lord Cobbleton, and that I'm his second son. But, after all—what's a nobleman's second son?"

"Be Jasus! and what indeed?" cried the captain. "Why, my grandfather was Archbishop of Dublin—and my father was his son—and I'm my father's son—and yet, be the power-rs! I'm only a capthain now! But if I hadn't half a million, or some thrifle of the kind locked up in Chancery, I should be afther rowlling in my carriage—although I do keep a buggy and a dog-cart, as it is—and my frind Curthis here, jintlemen, wouldn't be in the Binch for two hunthred thousand pounds, as he is and bad luck to it!"

"Well—but you know, captain," said Frank, who was determined not to be behind his gallant companion in the art of lying, and who therefore very readily took up the cue prepared for him,—"you know, captain, that the moment my god-father the Duke comes home, I shall be all right."

"Right!—right as a thrivet, me boy!" vociferated O'Blunderbuss; "and then we'll carry on the war-r-r with a vengeance."

These remarks on the part of the captain and Frank Curtis produced a deep impression upon the greater portion of the company present; but two or three of the oldest prisoners tipped each other the wink slyly, as much as to say, "Ain't they coming it strong?"—although they did not dare provoke the ire of the ferocious Hibernian by any overt display of their scepticism.

"Speaking of Chancery," said an old, miserable-looking man, in a wretchedly thread-bare suit of black, and whose care-worn countenance showed an intimate acquaintance with sorrow,—"speaking of Chancery," he repeated, leaning forward from the corner in which he had hitherto remained silent and almost unobserved,—"you can't know Chancery, sir—begging your pardon—better or more bitterly than I do."

"Ah! tell the gentlemen your story, Prout," exclaimed one of the company. "'Pon my soul 'tis a hard case, and a stain upon a civilised country.

"A stain!" ejaculated the old man, whose name appeared to be Prout;—"a stain!" he cried, in a tone of painful irony:—"it is a horror—an abomination—an atrocity that demands vengeance on those legislators who know that such abuses exist and who will not remedy them! Chancellors—Vice-Chancellors—Judges—Law-Lords—Members of Parliament—Attorney-Generals—Solicitor-Generals—all, all for the last two-and-twenty years, so help me God! have been familiar with my case—and yet the Court of Chancery remains as it is, the most tremendous abuse—the most damnable Inquisition—the most grinding, soul-crushing, heart-breaking engine of torture that the ingenuity of man ever yet invented! Yes—all that—and more—more, if I could find stronger language to express myself in—is that earthly reflection of hell—the Court of Chancery!"

The old man had spoken with a volubility which had increased in quickness and in emphasis until it positively grew painful to hear;—and his countenance became flushed with a hectic, unhealthy red—and his eyes, usually leaden and dull, were fired with an unnatural lustre—and his chest heaved convulsively—and his lips quivered with the dreadful excitement produced in his attenuated and worn-out frame by the remembrance of his wrongs.

Remembrance!—as if he ever forgot them! No—the Chancery Court was the subject of his thoughts by day and his dreams by night: every thing he heard, or saw, or read, was so tortured by his morbid imagination as to bear some analogy, remote or near, to the proceedings of the Chancery Court;—when he had a meal, he wondered that the Chancery Court had left it to him—and when he had none, he said that the Chancery Court made him starve;—if he felt in tolerably good health, it was because he heard of some case in Chancery even more flagrant than his own—and that was a consolation to his diseased mind; and if he felt ill which was nearly always the case, he declared that the Chancery Court made him so:—in fact, he was truly a victim, in every sense and way, of that tremendous tribunal which has instruments of torture far more terrible for the feelings than those which the Inquisition of Spain ever invented for the body!

"Yes," exclaimed Prout, after a few moments' pause, "and all that diabolical tyranny is carried on under the semblance and with the solemn forms of justice. You go into a fine court, where you see a man of splendid intellect, fine education, and profound knowledge, seated in a chair, with the wig and gown; and before him are rows of barristers almost as learned as himself. Well—would you not think that you were in a tribunal worthy of the civilisation of this country! Yet—better were it if savages from the South Sea Islands became your judges; better to die upon the threshold of that court, than enter its walls. It is a damnable and a cursed tyranny, I repeat; and the English are a weak—a pusillanimous—a spaniel-like race, that they do not rise in rebellion against that monstrous tribunal!"

Again he paused, overpowered by excitement:—but there was something terribly real and awfully sincere—aye, and sternly true—in that man's denunciations!

"Yes—I say," he resumed, after having refreshed himself from a pewter-pot near him—though there had been a time when he was accustomed to drink wine,—"the English people are a nation of paltry cowards for allowing this hideous Chancery Court to uprear its head amongst them. Did not the French destroy their Bastille?—and was the Bastille ever half so bad, in one way, as this Chancery Court is in another? It is all useless for two or three people to declaim, or two or three authors to write, against such a flagrant abuse. 'Tis a public grievance, and must be put down by the public hand! The whole body of lawyers are against law-reform—and the profession of the law has vast influence upon both Houses of Parliament. From the Houses of Parliament, then, we have no hope: the strong hand of the people must do it. You might as well ask the Lords to abolish hereditary aristocracy, or the

King to dethrone himself, as expect the Houses of Parliament to sweep away the Chancery Court."

"But could we do without it?" enquired an attentive listener.

"Do without it!" exclaimed Prout, indignantly—almost contemptuously, at the nature of the question: "certainly we can! France does without it—Holland does without it—Prussia does without it—Switzerland does without it—and the United States do without it;—and where is the law of property better administered than in those countries? There the transfer of land, or the bequeathing of other property, is as simple as that of merchandize or stock; but here—here, in England, which vaunts its freedom and its civilization, the process is encumbered with forms and deeds which leave the whole arrangement liable to flaws, difficulties, and endless embarrassments. Talk of Equity indeed! 'tis the most shameless mockery of justice ever known even amongst barbarians. But let me tell you an anecdote? In 1763, a suit was commenced in Chancery relative to some lawful property on which there was a windmill. The cause was not referred to the Master till 1796—thirty-three years having elapsed, and the lawyers, who had grown old during the proceedings, not having been idle. In the Master's office did the case remain till 1815—though the new lawyers who had succeeded the old batch that had died off in the meantime, were as active as the matter would allow them to be. Well—in 1815 the Master began to look into the business; but, behold! the windmill had disappeared—it had tumbled down—it had wasted away into dust—not a trace of it remained!" actually shrieked out the old man, in the excitement of his story.[44]

"Thus the affair was fifty-two years in Chancery, and was knocked on the head after all?" observed one of the company present.

"While Law slept, Time was awake and busy, you see," said Prout, with a bitter irony which actually chilled the hearts of his auditors. "But I can give you plenty of examples of the infernal—heart-breaking delays of Chancery—and my own amongst the rest presently," he continued. "There is the case of *Bute* versus *Stuart*: it began in 1793—and in 1813 *a step* was made in the cause![45] Then, again, you have the case of the *Attorney-General* versus *Trevelyan*: it commenced in 1685, and is an affair involving an endowment for a Grammar-School at Morpeth. This cause never will be finished![46] But how much property do you suppose there is locked up in Chancery—eh? Ah! now I am going to tell you something astounding indeed—and yet as true as the Gospel! *Thirty-eight millions sterling* are locked up in that dreadful tribunal. A tribunal!—no—it is a sepulchre—a tomb—a grave in which all justice and all hopes are interred! But you will say that this enormous fund is only as it were in temporary trust, to be in due time portioned out to its rightful owners. Pshaw!—nonsense! More than *one-third* concerns persons who are dead and have left no heirs, or else whose representatives are ignorant of their rights. The Suitors' Fund is a bank of plunder—of shameful, diabolical plunder effected under the *forms of the law*!"

"But what about your own case, old fellow?" enquired the Honourable Mr. Pettifer.

"I'll tell you in a moment, gentlemen," cried Prout, rejoiced to observe the interest created by his strictures on the most hellish tribunal that ever disgraced a civilised country. "Twenty-five years ago," he said, "I was a prosperous man, having a good business in the City; and I had managed to save four thousand pounds by dint of strict economy and the closest attention to my affairs. A lawyer—a friend of mine—told me of a favourable opportunity to place the sum out at good interest and on the best possible security. A gentleman, in fact, wanted to borrow just that amount on mortgage, he having a capital estate. The matter was fully investigated, and the security was considered unexceptionable. So I lent the money; and for three years the interest was regularly paid, and all went on well. The gentleman suddenly died; and his nephew, who inherited the estate, hunted out an old entail, effected a hundred and fifty years previously, and of the existence of such an entail no mention had been made in subsequent deeds. So the nephew would not acknowledge the validity of the mortgage, and refused to pay me a fraction of my four thousand pounds. He would not even settle the interest. I was therefore forced into Chancery; and seven years afterwards I got a decree in my favour, but I was sent into the Master's Office on account of certain details which I will not stop to explain to you. This was fifteen years ago—and I am still in Chancery! I have spent three thousand pounds in costs—and am totally ruined. The excitement and worry of law made me neglect my business: my affairs fell into confusion—my creditors took all my stock in trade—and here have I been eleven years for the balance of my liabilities. Twenty-two years have I been engaged in *law*—and have not yet got *justice*! And yet I am told that I live in a civilised country, where the laws are based on consummate wisdom, and where the meanest as well as the highest individual is sure to obtain justice. Justice indeed!—such justice as one finds in the Chancery Court! My original claim was for four thousand pounds—and I have spent three thousand in costs, and owe my lawyer five hundred pounds more. But what do you think of this? Eight years ago a *written question* was put by the Master to the respondent in the suit; and it is still a matter of dispute whether he is to answer it or not! Here's law for you—here's justice! Why—it is enough to make a man curse himself for belonging to a country in which such things take place: it is enough to make me ashamed of being an Englishman! Suppose a savage from the South Sea Islands came to England—beheld all the glitter and glory of our outward appearance of civilisation—studied our language, and was then told of such cases as these? What would he think. He would say, '*After all, you are in reality a very barbarous people; and I shall be glad when I get back to my own far-off island!*'"[47]

"As far as all this goes, you are right enough," observed an attorney, who was one of the company present: "but had you gone much farther, you would have been equally correct. You may denounce nearly all our laws and statutes to be radically bad and a disgrace to civilisation. But it is useless to hope that an efficient reform will be ever effected by the Parliament; because the Parliament is loth to interfere with existing usages, and is afraid to meddle with existing rights. Nothing short of a Revolution can possibly accomplish a proper change."

"Why—this is treason!" exclaimed the Honourable Mr. Pettifer, his aristocratic feelings deeply wounded by the lawyer's bold and manly declaration.

"It may be treason—but it is nevertheless the truth," said the attorney, with the cool firmness of a man entertaining an honest conviction of the justice of his observations. "I declare most of our laws to be a disgrace and a shame. In France all the laws are contained in one book, accessible to every person: here, in this country, they are totally inaccessible to the community in general. Do you think France would ever have had her Code without a Revolution?[48] Do you know how silly, absurd, and contradictory are some of our statutes—those statutes which are approved of by the Law-Officers of the Crown, and enacted by wise senators? There is a statute, for example's sake,[49] which decrees that one half of the penalty inflicted in a particular case is to go to the informer, and the other half to the King. And yet under this statute Judges sentence men to transportation—say, fourteen years' transportation, to be halved by the informer and the King! Then there are statutes still upon the book, and which, though unrepealed, could scarcely be put into execution without inflicting an odious tyranny. A statute of Edward VI. forbids agricultural labourers to hire themselves out, or be hired, by the day, and not for less than a year. By a statute of William and Mary, no peasant may sell goods in a town, except at a fair; and a statute of Henry VII. decrees, under severe penalties, that no cattle shall be killed in a walled town, nor in Cambridge. There is also a statute, I forget of which reign, enacting that no shoemaker may be a tanner, nor a tanner a shoemaker. The laws relating to Marriage are in many respects absurd, and in others obscure. A marriage contracted by persons under age, by means of license, without the consent of their parents, is unlawful; but such persons may contract a lawful marriage by banns, although without the consent of their parents. Thousands and thousands of persons have been led to believe that it is lawful for a man to marry his deceased wife's sister; whereas it is *not lawful*, and the issue of such a marriage is illegitimate."

At this moment the learned gentleman was interrupted by the clanging of a loud bell, carried by a person who was proceeding round the main building of the prison, and who every now and then stopped ringing for the purpose of vociferating as loud as he could—"Strangers, women, and children, all out!"

"Shall you have to leave?" demanded Frank Curtis, in a whisper to his friend the captain.

"Divil a hap'orth of it, me boy!" exclaimed O'Blunderbuss. "The person who keeps the Coffee-house will be glad to give me a bed as well as yourself; for money, frind Cur-r-tis, procures everything in this blissed Spike-Island."

Another half-hour was passed in discourse on various topics, the inmates of the Coffee-house parlour having become wearied of commenting upon the laws of their country; and, at the expiration of that interval renewed shouts, now emanating from the immediate vicinity of the lower lobby, warned all strangers to quit the prison. At the same time the parlour was rapidly cleared, O'Blunderbuss and Frank Curtis alone remaining there:—for it seemed to be a rule on the part of the prisoners to rush to the gate, for the purpose of seeing the "strangers" take their departure.

The captain now gave a furious pull at the bell; and, when the slip-shod waiter appeared, he demanded a conference with the keeper of the Coffee-house. This request was speedily complied with; and satisfactory arrangements were entered into for beds. Another bottle of wine was ordered, the captain persuading Curtis that it would be better for him to take his first survey of all the grand features of the Bench in the morning, and to pass the evening in conviviality. This they accordingly did until eleven o'clock, when the lights in the parlour were put out, and the two gentlemen were shown to their respective bed-chambers—the said chambers being each about twice as big as a coffin, and quite as inconveniently angular.

44. The anecdote is a positive fact!

45. It is not terminated yet!

46. Mr. Prout's prophecy seems likely to be fulfilled; for the case pends yet, having now lasted *one hundred and sixty-two years*!!! In 1710 Lord Chancellor Harcourt made a decree commanding the boundaries of the litigated land to be ascertained; and the commissioner appointed to carry this decree into effect, reported that no boundaries could be traced! Proceedings continued; and on the 25th of January, 1846, the case was re-argued before Vice-chancellor Shadwell, eight counsel being engaged for relator, lessee, trustees,

corporation, and the various other parties interested. The Vice-Chancellor of England referred the matter to the Master's Office, where it is not likely to be disinterred for the next half century! Really, we English are a highly civilised people: a law-suit may be perpetuated through a dozen generations, without any delay or fault on the side of the parties interested—*the whole and sole blame resting upon the Chancery Court.*

47. Mr. Commissioner Fane, of the London Bankruptcy Court, was brought up as a Chancery lawyer; and in a recent "Letter to Lord Cottenham" he thus explains the causes of that shameful dilatoriness which characterises Chancery proceedings:—

"In Chancery the suitor applies first to the judge: every thing is done in writing. The judge, after great expense has been incurred and after a long delay, makes a decree: that decree tells the Master, in endless detail, what he is to do (just as if he required to be taught the simplest matters): the decree is drawn up, not by the judge, who might be thought wiser than the Master, but by the registrar, who, in teaching the Master, frequently omits some material direction; the parties then adjourn to the Master's office; there the matter lingers, month after month and year after year; at last the Master makes his report, tells the Court what he has found, and sometimes what he would have found if the registrar had authorised him to do so, and at last the Court either acts or sends the matter back to the Master with new directions. Meanwhile, as Lord Bacon said about two hundred years ago, 'Though the Chancery pace be slow, the suitor's pulse beat quick.' I know of nothing to which to compare this process except the game of battledore and shuttlecock, in which the poor suitor plays the part of shuttlecock, and is tossed from the judge to the Master, and from the Master to the judge, over and over, till the scene is closed only too often by despair, insolvency, or death."

48. "The *Code Napoleon* is sometimes declared to be a failure; but it has been no failure. In place of the previously differing laws of the provinces of the ancient kingdom it has substituted a consistent uniform code for the entire of France. But it is urged, that it has been buried under a load of commentaries. Of course there has risen a pile of judicial constructions, as must be the case with the text of every code. But these constructions have a platform to rest upon, framed in the light of modern science. Ours are wholly different; they have no such foundation to settle upon: they rest upon a mingled heap of rubbish and masonry, of obsolete laws and laws in force. Even the basement storey has not been firmly laid, as in France. This, however, it is that the nation requires to have done; it requires an entirely new

legal edifice to be erected. All that is good in the past it would have preserved under a new and better arrangement; and then the mass of statutes, reports, and text-books from which the analysis had been made, and which had long embarrassed both the learned and unlearned—declared by parliamentary authority to be no better than waste paper—null and void, and no more citable for any purpose of legal argument, illustration, or decision."—*Black Book of England*.

49. 53rd, George III.

CHAPTER CVI.
A FARTHER INSIGHT INTO THE KING'S BENCH.

At half-past seven o'clock on the following morning, the slip-shod waiter knocked at Mr. Curtis's door, exclaiming, "Please, sir, you must get up, and go down to the lobby by eight, 'cos you're wanted."

"Who want's me there?" demanded Frank, leaping from his bed, and suddenly animated by the hope that Sir Christopher had accidentally heard of his predicament and had come to pay his debts.

But the boy had hurried down stairs again; and Curtis was accordingly compelled to hurry over his toilette in a state of profound suspense. By the time his ablutions were performed and he was dressed, it was close upon eight o'clock; and he repaired to the gate, having bestowed *en passant* a thundering knock with his clenched fist on the door of the captain's crib.

The gate of the lower lobby was not as yet opened; but in its immediate vicinity several of the prisoners were collected—some in dressing-gowns, others in their shirt-sleeves, and all having a certain air of seediness not observable elsewhere. At length, when the massive portal *did* expand, in rushed a motley assortment of messengers, char-women, and such itinerant venders as milk-men, water-cress boys, and the fustian-clad individual who sold red herrings and shrimps.

When this influx of varied specimens of animated nature had passed, Frank Curtis entered the lobby and demanded of a one-armed turnkey standing before the fire, "who it was that required his presence?".

"Me and my partners, sir," was the reply.

"And what for?" enquired Frank.

"Just to take your likeness, sir," was the farther explanation given.

"My likeness!" cried the young gentleman, glancing rapidly around in the expectation of beholding an artist with pallet and brushes all ready; but, not perceiving any such individual, he began to look very ferocious indeed, under the impression that the turnkey had a mind to banter him.

"We call it taking the likeness of a new prisoner, sir," observed the one-armed functionary, who was really a very civil fellow, "when we have him here by day-light just to take a look at him—so that we may know him again," he added significantly. "You see, sir, there's between three and four hundred prisoners in the college—we call it a college, sir, sometimes—and it isn't a very easy thing to remember every new-comer, unless we have a good look at him."

"Oh! now I understand you," exclaimed Frank, laughing heartily at the idea of having his likeness taken in such a style.

While he was yet indulging in this expression of his mirth, the other turnkeys made their appearance, and, each individually wishing him a "good morning," they scanned him from head to foot—apparently committing to memory every one of his features *seriatim*. Frank tried to look as unconcerned as possible; but he nevertheless felt very uncomfortable, and was heartily glad when the operation, which lasted about five minutes, was over. The other turnkeys then withdrew; and Curtis remained alone with the one-armed official.

"Nice place this, sir, for a prison—ain't it?" asked the latter, taking his seat on a stool near the door, which stood open, and whence the eye commanded a view of the spacious racquet-ground and a small portion of the main building.

"Well—it might be a great deal worse," replied Frank. "You must have some strange characters here?" he added, enquiringly.

"I b'lieve ye!" exclaimed the turnkey, fixing his looks mysteriously upon the young gentleman in a species of dim intimation that it was indeed a very remarkable place. "You see that old feller in the rugged blue coat, a-rolling the fust racquet-ground there? Well—he come here to this prison twenty year ago in his carriage, and had his livery servants to wait upon him; and now he's glad to drag that roller every morning for a few pence."

"And can't he manage to get out?" asked Frank, with an ominous shudder.

"Lord bless you, sir," cried the turnkey, "he's his own prisoner!"

"His own prisoner!" repeated Curtis. "What—do you mean to say that he keeps himself in the Bench?"

"I do, sir—and a many does the same," continued the turnkey, in a low, mysterious tone. "These poor creaturs, sir, stay in prison so long that all their relations and friends dies off; and if they went out, they wouldn't have a soul to speak to, or a place to go to. So, if their creditors dies too and their discharge is sent 'em, they keep it in their pockets and never lodge it at the gate—'cos they prefer staying inside, where they have companions and can get a bit of something to eat in one way or another."

"This is the most extraordinary thing I ever heard in my life," said Frank.

"There's many things more stranger still *here*," returned his informant, who was pleased with the mysterious importance which his position as narrator of these marvels gave him. "What should you think of men putting themselves into prison, and making up their minds to stay here all their lives perhaps?"

"I should think you were joking if you said so," answered Curtis.

"Joking! Lord bless you, sir, I wouldn't joke about no such a thing," exclaimed the turnkey, with a spice of indignation in his manner. "But I'll tell you how it is. There—you see that stout man in the shooting-jacket a-bargaining for them bloaters with the chap that's sitting on the bench outside the Tap? Well—he committed a forgery, or summut of that kind; and, knowing there was a warrant against him, and not choosing to run away from London for fear of being took in the country, he got a friend to arrest him for debt. So he immediately passed over to the Bench by *habeas*; and the warrant for felony was lodged at the gate against him. But his debts must be paid before the warrant can be executed; and as you see he's in a manner his own detaining creditor—leastways, his friend outside is—he isn't likely to have his discharge till the felony business can be settled somehow or other."

"The Bench is then a most convenient place for people who ought to be in Newgate?" said Curtis. "But live and learn; and the more one sees of the world——"

"The more curiouser it is—ain't it?" cried the turnkey. "Well—now you see that tall, stout gentleman there, walking up and down in front of the State House with the stick in his hand? He's been here some years, and is wery likely to stay a many years longer. His creditors allows him three guineas a week for his kindness in remaining a prisoner in the Bench."

"What!" ejaculated Curtis, now more astonished than ever. "His *creditors* pay him for staying *here*!"

"It's as true as you're alive, sir," was the reply; "and it's easy enough to explain, too. That gentleman has got a good landed estate, which is in the hands of his two or three principal creditors, who manage it and receive all the rents for the purpose of paying themselves their claims upon him. Well, now—if he went through the Insolvents' Court, *all* the creditors would come in for their share of the proceeds of the estate; and so the two or three principals ones allow him three guineas a week to keep him here and prevent him going through the Court. It's a deuced good thing for him, I can tell you; and he's as happy as a King. He has his wife—leastways, his lady with him,—we call 'em all *wives* here;—and he's got a batch of the loveliest and nicest children you ever see. There they are, sir—the little innocents—a-playing there in the mud, just as if there wasn't no such place as prison at all; and yet they was all born up in that room there in the State House, with the green safe at the window and the flower-pots."

"And who is that lame, elderly man, running about with newspapers in his hand?" enquired Frank.

"He's the newsman of the Bench—and a prisoner like the rest on 'em," was the answer. "Ah! some years ago he was a rich man, and in a flourishing way of business. But he got into Chancery, and that's the same as getting into the Bench; 'cos one always leads to t'other—for even to be a vinner in Chancery, one must pass at least a dozen years or so here fust. That seems to be the rule, as far as I can understand it. Well, sir—now that lame man is obliged to turn newsman; so you see there's a many rewerses in this world, sir. Ah! the world's a queer place, ain't it?—almost as queer as the Bench itself!"

What the turnkey's notions of the world might be, it is not easy to conceive: but they were evidently somewhat dim and misty—inasmuch as he seemed impressed with the belief that the Bench and the world were two distinct places:—but, then, the Bench was *his* world, though not a prisoner there himself; and perhaps he established a distinction as existing between the "world within" and the "world without." Alas! many—many who *were* prisoners did the same!

"Who are those two ladies that have just come down to walk on the gravel there, by the side of the racquet-ground?" enquired Frank Curtis, much amused by the turnkey's gossip.

"We call that gravel-walk *the parade*," observed the official. "Those ladies are mother and daughter; and it's the daughter that's a prisoner. She's a devilish fine gal; and the old woman stays with her to take care of her. But she and the Honourable Mr. Pettifer are deuced thick together; and the mother winks at it. Such things will happen in the best regilated families—partcklerly in the Bench, where no one ain't over and above partickler. This isn't the shop for morals. Mr. Curtis: all the young single women that comes here, is sure to get corrupted. But that's no look-out of mine;"—and with this solacing conclusion, the turnkey hit the lock of the door a tremendous blow with his key.

"Be the power-rs! and is it afther staling a march upon me that ye are?" vociferated a well-known voice at this moment; and the captain stalked up to the gate, looking quite fresh and blooming after a good night's rest and copious ablutions.

"They had me down to take my likeness," cried Frank; "or else I dare say I should have slept on till now."

"Well—we'll just make the round of the Binch, me boy," exclaimed the captain; "and by that time the breakfast will be ready. I've orthered it—hot rolls and coffee, with kidneys, eggs, cresses, and such like thriftes; and a walk will give us an appetite."

Curtis accordingly took his friend's arm; and they set out on their limited ramble.

"That building on your right, Frank," said the captain, "is the State House, where Government prisoners and such like spalpeens are kept—or ought to be; but the prisoners for debt get hould of the rooms there, and the divil himself can't turn 'em out. But here's the Tap: and this is the first lion of the Binch."

They entered a low and dirty-looking place, in which there were several common tables of the roughest description, and the surfaces of which were completely carved out into names, initial letters, men hanging, and a variety of devices—these ingenious and very elaborate specimens of wood-engraving having been effected by penknives. A tremendous fire burnt in the grate, round which were assembled several of the poorer class of prisoners and the messengers, eating their breakfast;—and, at one of the tables just alluded to, the newsman was sorting his papers.

As the captain and Curtis were retracing their way from an inspection of the interior of the tap-room, the former stopped at the bar, exclaiming to the man in attendance, "Two half pints, Misther Vernon—and good mornin' to ye."

"You would not drink malt liquor so early, will you?" asked Frank, with a look of astonishment at his companion.

"Be Jasus! and it's for you to taste the porther, me boy!" exclaimed the captain. "Don't you remember all I said yesterday in its praise? Come—dhrink!"

And Mr. Curtis was accordingly compelled to swallow half a pint of porter, though malt liquor before breakfast was somewhat repugnant to his taste. The beer was veritably of first-rate quality; and the captain was as proud to hear the young gentleman's eulogy on its merits, as if he had brewed it himself.

"Now let us continue our ramble," said he;—and away they went, arm-in-arm, the two or three poor prisoners who were lounging at the door of the Tap respectfully making room for them to pass.

Entering upon the parade, Frank now for the first time obtained a full view of the front of the main building—a long, gloomy, barrack-like structure, with half a dozen entrance-ways leading to the various staircases. Fixed to the ledges of many of the windows, were safes in which the prisoners kept their provisions; and in several instances these safes were covered with flower-pots containing sickly plants. Precisely in the centre of the building was the chapel; and over the chapel was the infirmary. Most of the rooms on the ground-floor were fitted up as little shops, the occupants being prisoners, and the business carried on being entirely in the "general line." The lumps of butter—wedges of cheese—red herrings—slices of bacon—matches—balls of twine—candles—racquet balls—sweet-stuff—loaves of bread—rolls—soap—eggs—and other articles of the nature usually sold in such magnificent marts of commerce, were arranged so as to make the best possible show, and carry out the spirit of competition which raged as fiercely in that little community as in the world without. A peep through the window of one of those miniature shops, showed the canisters of tea and the jars of tobacco and snuff standing orderly upon the shelves of three feet in length; and behind a counter, along which Tom Thumb could have walked in two strides, stood the stout proprietor of the concern, examining with rueful looks the wonderful increase of chalk-marks which the morning's sales had compelled him to make upon a slate against the honoured names of his customers.

"Now look this way, me frind," cried the captain, as he forced Frank to turn round towards the racquet-courts. "D'ye see nothing particular?"

"Nothing but the high wall, with the spikes on the top, and the netting to prevent the balls from going over," answered Curtis.

"There—there, me boy!" vociferated O'Blunderbuss, impatiently pointing in a particular direction. "Now d'ye see any thing worth looking at?"

"Well—I see the pump there," said Frank, vainly searching after a more interesting object.

"Be Jasus! and that's jist what I wanted ye to see," exclaimed the captain. "It's the Dolphin-pump, me boy—the finest pump in Eur-r-rope—the pride of the Binch——But, be the power-rs! ye shall taste the wather and judge for yourself!"

Curtis protested that he would rather not;—the captain was however resolute; and a tumbler was borrowed from a prisoner who was smoking an early pipe at one of the ground-floor windows. Then the captain began to pump away like a madman; and Frank was compelled to imbibe a deep draught of the ice-cold water, which would have been pronounced delicious by any one who did not admire alcoholic beverages much better than Adam's ale.

"Don't you mean to take a glass, captain?" enquired Frank.

"Be Jasus! and I know it of ould," returned that gallant gentleman: "so there's no need for me to pass an opinion upon it. Besides it's not to astonish my stomach with any unusual dhrink that I'd be afther, Frank: but you're a young man, and can stand wather better than me."

Curtis did not consider the reasoning altogether conclusive: he however refrained from farther argument;—and the two gentlemen resumed their walk.

Between the eastern extremity of the main-building and that part of the wall which looked directly upon the Borough, was the market-place,—an assemblage of miserable sheds, where a butcher, a fishmonger, a greengrocer, and a vender of coals carried on each his peculiar traffic—the said spirited traders being prisoners as well as the shopkeepers above alluded to.

At a stall in the centre of the market, and at which vegetables, fruit, and fish were sold, stood a tall, thin, weather-beaten old woman, resembling a gipsey in dress as well as in complexion, and having an ancient bonnet perched most airily upon the top of her head. This respectable female was denominated "Old Nanny," and was in such wise greeted by Captain O'Blunderbuss, who informed Frank in a whisper that she was not a prisoner, and, in spite of competition, had pretty well the monopoly of the market.

"The fact is, me boy," he said, "she has the advantage of money. Those fellows in the sheds there, set up in business with a floating capital of eighteen-pence each, and can't afford to give credit: and a tradesman in the Binch who can't give credit, stands no more chance, be Jasus! of getting custom than if he began with an empty shop."

The captain now proceeded to show his friend the public kitchen, which was in the immediate vicinity of the market; and thence they passed up the back of the main building, O'Blunderbuss especially directing Frank's attention to that quarter which was denominated "the Poor-Side."

The Poor-Side!—Yes in every public establishment in England, is the line of demarcation drawn between the rich and the poor,—in the debtors' prison as well as in the church of God! Oh! what a disgraceful thing is poverty made in this country! Why—the contamination of Newgate, if borne by a man possessing a well-filled purse, will be overlooked in society; while the rags that an unsullied character wears, are a ban—a stigma—a reproach! "He has been in the workhouse," or "She has been on the parish," are taunts as bitter in meaning and as keen in spirit, as the phrase "He has been in Newgate," or "She has just come from the treadmill." Aye—and even amongst the lowest classes themselves, it is a deeper stain to associate a name with the workhouse, than to connect it with the felons' gaol! Such is the dreadful—demoralizing consequence of that example set by the upper classes, whose ideas of men's excellence and worth are guided chiefly by the standard of the purse.

The Poor-Side!—And for whom is the Poor-Side of debtors' prisons instituted? For those who go penniless to gaol,—the best proof that they have profited nothing by the losses of their creditors,—the best evidence that their liabilities were legitimately contracted! But the fashionable swindler—your man-about-town—your *roué*—your rake, who gets into debt wherever he can, and without the slightest intention of ever paying a single farthing,—*he* drives down in his cab to the prison—treats the bailiff to wine upon the way—and takes with him into confinement all that remains to him of the plunder of duped tradesmen, there to spend it in riotous living and in the best room which the best quarter of the gaol can afford! If a debtors' prison have a *Poor-Side*, it ought also to have a *Swindlers'-Side*.

No word in the English language is used so frequently and so contemptuously as the monosyllable *Poor*. "Oh! he is a poor devil!" is a far worse character to give of any one, than to say at once, "He is dishonest." From the latter sentence there is a hopeful appeal in the question—"But *can* he pay?" "Yes—he can, if he chooses." "Oh! then, if he *can*, we will trust him and risk it." But from the former sentence there is no appeal; it is a judgment without qualification—a decision too positive and weighty to admit of a doubt. The objection—"Well, he may be poor; but he may also be honest," is never heard. The idea of poverty being honest! Why—in the estimation of an Englishman, *poverty* is a word expressing all that is bad. To say that a man is *poor*, is at once to sum up his character as every thing unprincipled and roguish. Such magic is there in the word, that rich men, and men well-to-do in the world, instantly button up their breeches' pockets when they hear it applied to a person. They seem to consider that a poor wretch can have no other possible object in view than to get the better of them. Poverty, in their eyes, is something that goes about preying upon the rich—something to be loathed and shunned—something that ought not to intrude itself into respectable places. A man may just as well be leprous, as be poor!

So undeniable are these truths—so universally recognised are these facts, that designing individuals always endeavour to seem well off, even if they be insolvent. They dress well, because they know the sovereign influence of a good coat. They talk largely—because they see how necessary it is "to keep up appearances." They toss about their last few guineas, as the only means of baiting a hook to catch fresh dupes. It is impossible that a man, with fine clothes, well-polished boots, elegant guard-chain, and lemon coloured gloves,—it is impossible that such a man can be poor! Oh! no—trust him with anything! Why—what poor man would be perfumed as he is?—the aristocratic odour of wealth surrounds him as with an atmosphere peculiar to the rich. Trust him by all means!—But that poor-looking devil, who sneaks along the shady side of the way—who has a wife and half-a-dozen children at home—and who is struggling from morning to night to earn an honourable crust,—don't trust him—have nothing to do with him—don't assist him with the loan of a single sixpence—on the contrary, give him a thrust farther down into the mud, if you can;—because he is undisguisedly *poor*!

Such appear to be the rules of conduct in this enlightened and glorious country. God help the poor!—for poverty is a terrible crime in "merry England!"

The Poor-Side of the King's Bench struck Frank Curtis as being particularly miserable:—it quite gave him the horrors! And no wonder;—for the architect—a knowing fellow was he!—had so arranged the building, that the windows of the Poor-Side should look upon the dust-bins and the conveniences. Yes—a knowing fellow was that architect! *He* understood what the poor are worth in this free and civilised land,—*he* saw in a moment where they ought to be put;—and therefore he arranged for their use a number of dens where the atmosphere was certain to be one incessant pestilential odour; and where he would have been sorry,—very sorry to have placed the kennel of his favourite hound!

Yes:—well might Frank Curtis feel the horrors—callous and indifferent as the young man naturally was—on beholding the Poor-Side. The ground-floor rooms were even at mid-day in a state of twilight, the colossal wall being only a few feet distant:—the windows were blackened with dirt; and from the upper ones hung a few rags—the miserable duds of the miserable, miserable inmates. Half-starved, pale, and emaciated women—the wives or daughters of those poor prisoners—were loitering at the doorways,—some with children in their arms—children, Oh! so wan and wasted—so sickly and so death-like—that it must have made their parents' hearts bleed to feel how light they were, and how famine-struck they seemed! And yet those little, starving children had their innocent winning ways, as well as the offspring of the rich; and they threw their skeleton arms around their mother's necks—and their lips sent forth those infantile sounds so sweet to mothers' ears;—but still the little beings seemed to be pining rapidly away through actual want and in the prison atmosphere! "God help the poor," we said ere now: but, Oh! with tearful eyes and beating heart do we exclaim—"God help the children of the poor!"

Frank Curtis and the captain, having now completed their walk round the prison, entered the parlour of the Coffee-house, where an excellent breakfast awaited them, and to which they did ample justice.

The repast being disposed of, Captain O'Blunderbuss took a temporary leave of Frank Curtis, it being arranged that the gallant officer should proceed to Baker Street in order to induce the men in possession, either by means of bribes or menaces, to allow Mrs. Curtis to remove as many valuables from the house as possible; and, this notable aim being achieved, the captain was to pay his respects to Sir Christopher Blunt.

Frank Curtis, being now temporarily thrown upon his own resources for amusement, strolled out upon the parade, and was gazing at the racquet-players, when Mr. Prout accosted him.

"Good morning, sir. Have you taken a survey of the Bench yet?" said the Chancery prisoner.

"I have been round the building, and seen all that's worth seeing, I believe," replied Curtis. "But the Poor-Side appears to be a wretched place."

"Wretched!" cried Prout, in a bitter tone: "ah! you may well make that observation, sir! But if my affairs do not end in a speedy settlement, I shall have to move to that quarter myself."

"How is that?" enquired Frank.

"Do you not know—have you not yet learned that you must pay even to have a room in this prison—a place to which you do not come of your own accord?" said Prout. "A shilling a week is the room-rent; and he who cannot pay it, must go over to the Poor-Side. This is English justice, Mr. Curtis! You must pay to live in a prison!"

"It seems to me monstrously unfair———"

"Unfair! 'tis vile—rascally!" cried the Chancery prisoner. "But, talking of the Poor-Side puts me in mind of a strange story connected with that quarter of the Bench; and if you have nothing better to do for an hour or so, and will step up to my room———"

"I shall have great pleasure," interrupted Curtis; "for, to tell you the truth, the time does hang rather heavy on my hands;—and till my friends the Marquis of Aldersgate and the Prince of Paris, who is staying in London, come over to see me, I may just as well amuse myself with your story."

Prout accordingly led the way to his room, which was in the front of the building and commanded a view of the parade and racquet-grounds. It was very plainly furnished, but neat and clean; and its owner informed Curtis that he had a married daughter who visited him every day, was very kind to him, and superintended his little domestic concerns.

"But I will not detain you longer than I can help, sir," observed Prout; "and I can promise you that you are about to hear a true tale of deep interest. I have thought of it so often, and have so frequently repeated its details to myself, in the solitude of this chamber, that I am enabled to give you the whole story in a connected form; although it was not in the same continuous manner that the vicissitudes I am about to relate, became known to me. Alas! 'tis a sad—sad tale, sir; but I am afraid that, bad as it is, it still is not the worst that might be told of human nature."

Frank Curtis seated himself opposite to the old man, who, after a short pause, commenced his narrative in the following words.

CHAPTER CVII.
A TALE OF SORROW.

"It was about thirty years ago that a poor but respectable and kind-hearted tradesman, of the name of Craddock, came up from Plymouth to London to receive a hundred pounds which had fallen to him through the death of a relative of whom he had not heard for years until he received the lawyer's letter announcing his decease and the legacy. Craddock was a linen-draper in a very small way at Plymouth: and though industrious, temperate, and obliging, he never had succeeded in doing any thing better than earning a mere living. He was about forty-five years of age at the time of which I am speaking, and had long been married to a woman as generous-souled as himself. They were childless; and, in spite of their poverty, they often regretted that they had no offspring to become the object of their affection, and to comfort them when old age should overtake them. Indeed, it appears that they had seriously thought of adopting some poor person's child: but circumstances of various kinds had opposed this plan; and they at last ceased to converse upon it—endeavouring to render themselves as happy as they could in each other's society. And happy, for that matter, they were too; for the mutual attachment which linked their hearts together, was firmly established; and, as they advanced in years, they seemed to become so necessary to each other, that when Craddock received the lawyer's letter summoning him to London, it was with the greatest difficulty his wife would allow him to set out alone. He however succeeded in making her understand that a hundred pounds did not constitute an independent fortune,—that it was absolutely necessary to carry on the shop,—and that therefore she must remain at home to manage it. Accordingly, the worthy dame tarried at Plymouth, and her husband came up to London by the stage—at that period a journey of no inconsiderable importance.

"It was the first time Mr. Craddock had ever been in the metropolis: but he did not stay a moment longer than his business absolutely compelled him, which was four or five days. The lawyer with whom he had to transact his little affair, was a kind and conscientious man—for there *are* many good lawyers as well as bad ones;—and he hastened the business as much as possible. Accordingly, Mr. Craddock received his money in less than a week; and he instantly went to the Belle Sauvage on Ludgate Hill to take his place home again by the coach. There was only one inside-seat vacant by the stage that was to start in the evening; and Craddock secured it. He then returned to the little lodging where he had slept during his sojourn in London, and which was somewhere in the neighbourhood of Doctors' Commons. Having packed up his portmanteau, he shouldered it, and was wending his way to the Belle Sauvage, when his attention was drawn to a little boy who was sitting on a door-step in one of the narrow, secluded streets in that district. The child, who was very neatly dressed and about two years old, was crying bitterly. Craddock stopped and spoke kindly to him; and though the boy was too young to give any explanation of the cause of his grief, it was easy to divine that he had strayed from home, or been lost by a negligent servant. Two or three other persons stopped likewise; and some of the neighbours came out of their houses: but the boy was unknown to them. Craddock tried to console him; but the little fellow wept as if his heart would break. By accident the parish-beadle passed that way, and, on learning what was the matter, said, 'Oh! the best thing I can do, is to take the poor child to the workhouse.'—Now, the mere name of a workhouse was terrible to the ears of the kind-hearted Craddock; and, obeying the impulse of the moment, he exclaimed, 'No, no: not while I have a crust to give him, poor child!'—'Why don't you take him home with you, then?' demanded the beadle: 'the parish will be very glad to be quit of such a bargain as a lost child promises to be.'— 'But I live at Plymouth,' returned honest John Craddock.—'Never mind if you live at the devil, so as you agree to take the child,' persisted the parochial authority.—'Well, I have not the least objection: on the contrary, I shall be delighted to do so,' said Craddock, his eyes filling with tears as the poor boy's grief became more heart-rending. 'I will give you my address; and if you hear any enquiries made by the parents of the child, you can let me know.'—'Very good,' exclaimed the beadle, as he received the card on which John Craddock's name, calling, and abode were printed in bold type. The worthy linen-draper then took up the boy in his arms, the beadle consenting to carry the portmanteau; and in this manner they proceeded to the Belle Sauvage, the kind looks, soothing tone, and fond caresses of Craddock having the effect of somewhat diminishing the little fellow's grief.

"The coach was just ready to start; and Craddock took his place, with the child upon his knees. The beadle renewed his promise to write in case he should hear any thing relative to the boy's parents; and the stage rolled out of the old inn yard. It was evening—the shops glared with light; and the scene, as well as the ride in the coach, amused the boy, so that his violent weeping ceased—but frequent sobs agitated his little chest, until at last he fell asleep in worthy John Craddock's arms. It was now for the first time that the linen-draper had leisure to reflect upon the step which he had taken; and it struck him that he had acted imprudently. He was taking away the child from the city to which he most probably belonged, and where he was alone likely to be found by his parents,—taking him away to a far distant town. But, on the other hand, he remembered the beadle's declaration that the lost child must be conveyed to the workhouse; and he likewise felt certain that should the little creature's parents make proper enquiries concerning their child, the parochial authority would know what explanation to give. Craddock therefore came to the conclusion that he had performed a Christian deed and an Englishman's duty; and, having thus set all scruples at rest, he began to reflect upon the pleasure which his wife would experience in receiving the foundling. For the child was a most interesting one—with curly flaxen hair, sparkling blue eyes, and a sweet complexion; and as he lay sleeping in Craddock's arms, and the lights of the shops in the outskirts of London, which the coach was then traversing, beamed through the window upon the boy's countenance, the worthy linen-draper thought that he had never seen a face so truly cherub-like. But tears came afresh into the worthy man's eyes—for he reflected that an afflicted father and a distracted mother might at that moment be calling upon heaven to restore them their lost child; and, as he bent down and kissed its cool and firm cheeks, on which the traces of weeping still remained, he murmured to himself, 'If thy parents never succeed in recovering thee, my boy, I will be as a father, and I know that my wife will be as a mother to thee!'—The other inside passengers admired the child greatly; but when honest John Craddock told them the story connected with his possession of the boy, they merely hem'd and coughed drily as if they thought him a very great fool for so burthening himself. Craddock understood what was passing in their minds; and he only hugged the child closer to his bosom.

"During the night, the little fellow frequently awoke, and cried for his papa and mamma; and the good linen-draper was indefatigable in his exertions to console and comfort him—uttering all possible kind things, and purchasing nice cakes for him at the way-side inns. Throughout the following day, too, Craddock was compelled to persevere in this affectionate and conciliatory treatment, which he, however, maintained with a good heart; and as the long, tedious journey of two hundred and sixteen miles drew towards a close, and evening was again drawing on, he had the satisfaction of observing that his little charge seemed to appreciate—or at least to understand his attentions. At last the coach entered the famous sea-port; and in a very short time Craddock was set down at his own door, the stage passing through the street in which he lived. You may suppose that his wife was greatly astonished when she perceived the present that the worthy linen-draper had brought her: but she was not many moments before she took the child in her arms, and covered it with kisses. Then how the kind-hearted dame wept when Craddock explained to her the manner in which he had become possessed of the boy; and as he spoke she pressed the little being all the closer and all the more fondly to her bosom. The social tea-table was spread, and the servant-girl was sent out to procure some cakes and other nice things for the boy; and then how he was petted and made much of—and how happy the good couple seemed when their attentions and caresses were rewarded with smiles!

"Several days passed, during which Craddock received no intelligence from the beadle who had promised to write to him in case of enquiries being instituted respecting the lost child:—weeks elapsed—and still no tidings! The idea—I had almost said the fear—which the worthy couple entertained that they might be compelled to part with the child just as they were getting fond of it, grew gradually fainter and fainter; and at length, when six months had passed and little Alexander (for so they called the boy) had grown not only reconciled to his condition, but appeared to have forgotten that it had ever been otherwise,—by the time six months had passed, I say, Mr. and Mrs. Craddock ceased to contemplate even the chance of being called upon to surrender their charge. Not but that those excellent people would have rejoiced, in one sense, to restore little Alexander to the arms of his parents; but in another sense they could not quench in their secret souls the fond hope that he might be left undisturbedly in their care. Thus time passed on: Craddock's business, which had only required a little capital to give it an impetus, exhibited every sign of improvement since the investment therein of the hundred pounds received in London; and Alexander throve apace.

"I shall now take a leap of twenty years, which brings us up to a date of only ten years ago; and at that time great alterations—but all for the better—had taken place in the circumstances of the Craddocks. Indeed, they had retired from business, having made a considerable fortune; and were settled in a handsome dwelling at a short distance from Plymouth—their native town. Craddock and his wife had, however, descended tolerably far into the vale of life, sixty-five winters having passed over their heads; but in Alexander—now a fine, tall, handsome young man of twenty-two—they had a source of real comfort and happiness. Though acquainted with the circumstance which had led to his adoption by Mr. and Mrs. Craddock, and, therefore, knowing well that they were not his real parents, his attachment to them was so great—his affection so sincere—and his gratitude so boundless, that he never once manifested any desire to quit them for the purpose of instituting enquiries relative to his birth. His constant and unwearied endeavour was to show himself deserving of all they had done for him,—the tender care they had taken of him in his infancy—the excellent education they had given him in his boyhood—and the affectionate consideration with which they treated him now that he was grown to man's estate; for in all respects did they regard him as their son, and in this light was he looked upon by their friends and dependants. In fact, nothing was wanting to complete the happiness of Alexander Craddock. He had become enamoured of a beautiful girl, the orphan daughter of an officer in the Navy, and who resided at Plymouth with an old aunt. Lucy Middleton had no fortune; but she possessed the invaluable treasures of amiability of disposition—a sweet temper—a kind heart—and those sterling qualities which fitted her for domesticity, and gave promise that she would prove an admirable housewife. Alexander loved her, and was loved in return; and his adopted parents gave their consent to the match. Accordingly, one fine Spring morning, when the heavens appeared as auspicious as the prospects of the youthful pair, the hands of Alexander

Craddock and Lucy Middleton were united; and, after a six weeks' tour in Wales, they returned to Plymouth to take possession of a commodious and handsome dwelling, which the adopted father of the young man had furnished during their absence for their reception. A year passed away, at the expiration of which Lucy presented her husband with a lovely boy; but almost at the same time the family experienced a severe loss in the death of old Mr. Craddock, who was carried off in a moment by the lightning-stroke of apoplexy. Alexander was dreadfully grieved at this shocking occurrence— a feeling in which his excellent young wife largely shared; but they were compelled to restrain their sorrow as much as possible, in order to console the bereaved widow. Mrs. Craddock was, however, unable to bear up against this heavy affliction: the suddenness of its arrival and the awful manner in which her husband fell down dead at her feet, when as it were in the midst of a state of perfect health, gave her a shock which she never recovered. She was spirit-broken, and could not rally, in spite of the tender devotion and unwearied attentions shown her by Alexander and Lucy, as well as by the aunt of the latter. Thus was it that in less than six weeks from the sudden demise of Mr. Craddock, his affectionate relict was consigned to the same tomb which held his remains.

"When Alexander had so far recovered himself, after experiencing these cruel inroads upon his happiness, as to investigate the affairs of his late adopted parents, he found that he was left sole heir to the handsome fortune acquired by their honest industry: but, though the will and other papers were strictly correct and accurate in all points, he found that certain circumstances connected with his inheritance would compel him to repair to London, and probably retain him in the capital for some weeks. He was not sorry at the idea of quitting Plymouth for a time, his spirits having been deeply affected by the deaths of his adopted parents; and he found Lucy and her aunt, who now lived altogether with them, perfectly agreeable to shift their place of abode. It was accordingly about eight years ago that this family arrived in London, and took a house in a genteel but quiet neighbourhood. Alexander found his income, chiefly derived from funded property, to be seven hundred a-year; and on this he knew that he could live well, but not extravagantly. A natural curiosity—which was the more lively now that he had lost his adopted parents—prompted him to make certain enquiries in the district of Doctors' Commons, with the hope of solving the mystery of his birth. The only intelligence he gleaned, was, that the beadle who figured in the opening of the tale, had been dead just twenty-two years; and as Alexander was now twenty-four, he could calculate pretty accurately that the parochial authority alluded to must have been carried off by the hand of the destroyer within a few weeks, if not within even a very few days, from the date when he himself, as a young child, had fallen into the charge of Craddock. Beyond this fact Alexander could ascertain nothing at all calculated to assist in rolling away the veil of mystery which covered his parentage: none of the inhabitants in the street where Craddock had found him sitting on the door-step, remembered any thing of the loss of a child at the period named;—no tradition of the fact remained. Alexander felt somewhat disappointed with these unsuccessful results of his enquiries; but he possessed too many elements of happiness—too many substantial accessories to comfort and mental tranquillity—to remain long affected or dispirited by the apparent permanence of that mystery which enveloped his birth.

"Alexander was naturally of an active disposition, and abhorred a life of idleness. He had been married two years, and was the father of two children; and contemplating the probability of having a numerous offspring, he felt anxious to augment his worldly possessions. 'My adopted father,' he would reason with himself, 'carried on business until a late period of his life, and was happy in the occupation which it afforded him. Why should not I embark in some eligible and safe undertaking which will give me a few hours' employment every day and yield a profit at the same time?' The subject of his musings was communicated to his amiable wife and her aunt; and those ladies joyfully encouraged a spirit so praiseworthy and so indicative of steadiness and prudence. The matter had been under discussion one morning at the breakfast-table, when the daily newspaper was brought in; and an announcement, worded somewhat in this way, met Alexander's eyes:— 'ELIGIBLE INVESTMENT.—Any gentleman having a few thousand pounds at his immediate disposal, and desirous to occupy a few leisure hours each day in a highly respectable and advantageous manner, is requested to apply to Edward Walkden, Solicitor, Bush Lane, Cannon Street.'—Alexander read this advertisement aloud; and the ladies agreed with him that the nature of it was tempting enough to prompt farther enquiry. Accordingly, the young man proceeded in the course of the morning to the address indicated, and found Mr. Walkden's establishment to be large and having every appearance of respectability as well as solidity. Half-a-dozen clerks were busily employed in the front office; and the shelves were covered with japanned tin cases, containing the papers of the most substantial clients. Upon being introduced into the lawyer's private office, Alexander found himself in the presence of a tall man, whose years were upwards of sixty, and whose countenance, once handsome, wore an expression of mingled mournfulness and severity. He was attired in a plain suit of black: his manners were cold and reserved; but there was a business-like air about him and his office, which augmented the good opinion already entertained by Alexander in respect to the lawyer and his establishment.

"Walkden was evidently a man of very few words; and therefore, when Alexander had explained the object of his visit, the information he sought was speedily given. 'I have a client,' said the lawyer, 'who has taken out a patent for a particular purpose; and he requires five or six thousand pounds to work it effectually. The person advancing the amount, will become an equal partner with the patentee, and will find a few hours of pleasant and agreeable occupation daily in superintending the commercial branch of the concern, while the patentee directs the manufacture of the article. There are the papers, sir: take them with you, and read them at your leisure.' Walkden handed the young man a bundle of documents tied round with red tape, and then bowed him out of the office. On his return home, Alexander examined the papers, and was highly delighted with the prospect which they opened to him. He felt convinced that an immense fortune was to be made: the thing was as clear as day-light! The patentee possessed the secret of effecting vast improvements in the manufacture of broad-cloths, which he undertook to produce not only of a superior quality, but likewise at a very reduced price. The calculations showed that large returns were certain to follow a comparatively small outlay, and that the business might be extended to a wonderful degree in proportion to the capital advanced to work upon. In a word, the whole affair was of the most roseate hue: Alexander, his wife, and her aunt were in raptures at the brilliant prospect thus fortunately opened to their contemplation; and it was resolved that he should lose no time in securing a share in so excellent an undertaking. Accordingly, on the following morning, he returned to Mr. Walkden, who received him with cold politeness, and requested his speedy decision in the matter—'as so promising a business had already attracted the notice of several capitalists, who were eager and willing to embark their funds.'—'And you will guarantee the respectability of your client, sir?' enquired Alexander.—'I have been established in this profession for upwards of thirty years, young man,' said the lawyer, almost sternly; 'and never have I allowed my office to be made the means of carrying out an illegitimate transaction. My client, Mr. Scudimore, is a man of integrity and honour; and whatever he promises, *that* will he perform!'—'In this case, Mr. Walkden,' observed Alexander Craddock, 'the sooner I have an interview with Mr. Scudimore, the better.'— The lawyer made no farther observation, but furnished his visitor with the address of the patentee; and Alexander accordingly repaired to Mr. Scudimore's dwelling, which was situated somewhere near Finsbury Square.

"Mr. Scudimore was an elderly person—very well dressed—plausible in his discourse, and over-polite in his manners. In fact, he seemed to be the very reverse of his solicitor in respect to disposition; for he received Alexander as if he had known him all his life; and the young man found himself sitting at lunch, and on the best possible terms with his new friend, almost before he had time to look round him. Then, if the affair which thus brought them together, had looked well upon paper, it assumed so glorious an aspect, when described in the glowing language of Mr. Scudimore, that Alexander Craddock, generous, frank, and confiding as he naturally was, came to a complete understanding with the patentee ere he took his departure. On the following day Scudimore dined at his house; and the ladies were quite charmed with their new acquaintance. Matters progressed rapidly through the business-like attention which Walkden devoted to the affair; and in less than a fortnight the deeds of partnership between Alexander Craddock and James Scudimore were duly signed at the lawyer's office, in Bush Lane, Cannon Street. Immediately afterwards, Alexander sold out six thousand pounds, which he paid into a bank to the joint account of Craddock and Scudimore; and in the course of a few days the latter gentleman took his departure for a manufacturing town, where he was to hire premises and establish a factory without delay, Alexander remaining in London to prepare a warehouse to receive the goods. For some months all appeared to go on to the complete satisfaction of both parties: Scudimore wrote up the most pleasing accounts from the country; and at last he informed his young partner that the factory was in perfect readiness to commence operations. It however appeared that more money was required; and Alexander, after an interview with Walkden, threw a farther sum of four thousand pounds into the business, all the funds being completely at the disposal of Scudimore. But almost immediately after the advance of this second sum, the letters from the provincial town ceased. Several weeks passed away: no communications were received from Scudimore;—and Mr. Walkden appeared to be as astonished as Alexander himself. A visit to the banker created a vague suspicion in the mind of the young man that all was not right;—for though Scudimore had drawn out the first amount by means of a number of successive cheques, he had received the whole of the second advance on one draught, and almost immediately after it had been paid in. A little farther enquiry convinced Alexander that Walkden had presented all the cheques for payment at the bank. Without, however losing a moment by calling on the lawyer for an explanation, Alexander proceeded post-haste to the provincial town where he expected to find Scudimore; and there all his fears were speedily confirmed. No premises had been hired by any such person—no factory established in such a name: but Mr. Scudimore had resided at an hotel in the place for several months, and had taken his departure, no one knew whither, at a date which, on calculation, Alexander found to be precisely four days after he had paid the second sum into the banker's hands. No doubt now remained in his mind that he was the dupe of a designing villain; and he was convinced that Walkden was an accomplice. To London he returned without delay; and, on his arrival, he repaired direct to the lawyer's office. That professional gentleman received him with his usual cold and reserved politeness, affecting not even to notice the excitement under which the young man was labouring.

"'Your friend Mr. Scudimore, sir, is a villain!' exclaimed Alexander.—'Such language is intolerable in my office, sir,' said Walkden, in his chilling, phlegmatic manner.—'Intolerable or not, it is the only language I can use under such circumstances,' cried the young man. 'Scudimore has absconded with the whole sum of ten thousand pounds which I advanced in this swindling concern; and it was through you and your representations, sir, that I have been thus cruelly deceived and basely plundered.'—'Softly, Mr. Craddock, if you please,' observed the lawyer; 'because your language conveys an imputation which I repel with scorn and contempt. My character is too well established to be injured by the calumny of an obscure stranger. You requested me to give you Mr. Scudimore's address in the first instance: I did so; and it was with *him* that you made all your arrangements. You then both came to me, informed me that every thing was settled between you, and employed me professionally to draw up certain deeds.'—'But you gave me the highest character of your friend Scudimore!' ejaculated Alexander.—'I spoke of him as I had always found him up to that hour when you questioned me,' said Walkden: 'but I never pretended to possess the power of prophesying that he would continue honest up to the day of his death!'—'Contemptible, vile sophistry!' exclaimed Alexander, his cheeks glowing with indignation. 'It is a base conspiracy to plunder me; and I will unmask you!'—'And supposing that I have incurred a chance of losing as much as yourself through this Mr. Scudimore?' said the lawyer, without losing his temper, but with a smile of malignant triumph on his lips.—'*You* lose by him!' cried Alexander, in a tone of bitter irony: 'you knew him too well to trust him.'—'At all events I may have somewhat calculated upon *your* joint responsibility,' observed Walkden, fixing his cold, grey eyes upon the young man whom these ominous words startled.—'What do you mean?' he demanded, his heart sinking within him.—'I mean,' answered Walkden, 'that I have discounted your acceptances to the amount of eight thousand pounds; that I have passed away those bills of exchange in the course of business; that when they fall due shortly, I shall be unable to take them up; and that the holder will therefore look to you for the payment of them?'—Alexander sank, speechless and powerless, into a seat as the whole scheme of villainy was thus fully developed to his horrified contemplation.—'As you were in partnership, and all the deeds establishing that partnership were drawn up in the regular way and strictly binding, Scudimore had not only a right to sign bills in your joint name,' proceeded the lawyer, 'but you cannot for an instant dispute your liability in respect to them.'—'Is it possible,' gasped Alexander, 'that I can have been so foolish and you so wicked? Oh! my poor wife—my beloved children, what will become of you, now that I am ruined by my own madness and this awful combination of villainies!'—'Mr. Craddock,' said Walkden, drawing himself up to his full height, while his iron features remained implacable and rigid, 'you must not allow your tongue a license in respect to me. Again I tell you that my character is too well established, and my reputation too substantially good, to be injured by false calumnies. Indeed, I am not at all clear that I have not some grounds to complain of conspiracy and villainy: for it certainly looks suspicious—most suspicious that your partner should obtain from me advances to the amount of eight thousand pounds, and then abscond. You would not come out of court with very clean hands, Mr. Craddock, I can tell you.'—'Wretch!' ejaculated the unhappy young man, now goaded to desperation: 'how dare you hint at any connivance on my part with the scoundrelism of your own friend—*you* who presented at the bank all the drafts for the money which I was insane enough to lodge there!'—'I certainly received several sums on behalf of Mr. Scudimore, to whom I duly remitted them,' said the lawyer, still in that cold, reserved tone which so much aggravated the rage of the ruined Craddock. 'But we will now put an end to this interview, sir,' he added; 'as my time is precious.'—'Yes, I will leave you, treacherous miscreant that you are!' exclaimed Alexander; and rushing into the clerks' office, he vociferated with mad excitement, 'Gentlemen, if you wish to behold the greatest villain on the face of the earth, go and look at your master!'—He then hurried away, the victim of a mingled rage and grief which it would be impossible to describe.

"But how could he face his dear wife—her affectionate aunt—his much-loved children? '*Ruined—totally ruined*!' how awfully do these words sound upon the ears! A man, when alone in the world and with none dependent on him or his exertions, may murmur those words to himself with comparative calmness: but the individual who has a wife and children looking to him for every necessary of existence—ah! *he* indeed feels his heart seared as with red-hot iron when his lips, expressing the conviction which circumstances force on his startled mind, frame the frightful words, '*Ruined—totally ruined!*' Miss Middleton (the aunt) and Lucy were already acquainted with the unpleasant nature of the suspicions which Scudimore's protracted silence had created in the mind of Alexander; and they were likewise aware of the object of his journey into the country. But they had yet to learn the fatal result of the enquiries which he had instituted; and it was still left for him to break to them the particulars of his interview with Walkden. On his return home, his anxiety and mental suffering were betrayed by his countenance,—for he was unskilled in the schools of duplicity, and knew not how to conceal a lacerated heart beneath a tranquil exterior. The ladies pressed him with questions: they saw that something dreadful had occurred—and they implored him not to keep them in suspense. He told them all,—told them how Scudimore had plundered him of ten thousand pounds—how he remained liable to Walkden for eight thousand more—and how the payment of this imminent liability would sweep away the whole of his fortune, leaving him a ruined man! Then, in that hour of bitter trial, he found how dear is woman as a 'ministering angel;'[50] and, having been comparatively soothed and tranquillised by the consolatory language of his Lucy and Miss Middleton, he proceeded to the office of his own solicitor, whom he resolved to consult relative to the posture of his affairs.

"The moment he had left the house, Lucy and Miss Middleton held a hasty council together. 'Do you think it would be imprudent or improper, my dear aunt,' asked the young wife, 'if I were to call upon this Mr. Walkden, and implore him not to press the payment of a debt which will deprive Alexander of all the resources that he might render available for the purpose of retrieving himself?'—'On the contrary, I approve of the step,' was the reply. 'Alexander says that Mr. Walkden was stern and severe; but then Alexander himself may have been hasty and indignant. After all, this Mr. Walkden has perhaps been duped, as well as your husband, by Scudimore.'—'I fear that this is not the case,' said Lucy: 'I am impressed with the conviction that the lawyer and Scudimore were in league together. Nevertheless, as we are entirely at Walkden's mercy, it would be unwise to irritate, but prudent to conciliate him.'—'Go, my dear child,' exclaimed the aunt; 'and may you succeed in softening the heart of this man who holds your dear husband in his iron grasp.'—Lucy accordingly attired herself in a simple and modest manner, and proceeded to the office of Mr. Walkden, who, happening to be disengaged at the time, immediately received her.

"'I have called, sir,' began Lucy, whose courage almost failed her when she found herself in the presence of a man of such stern, cold, and indeed forbidding aspect—for this was the first time she had ever seen him,—'I have called, sir,' she repeated, 'on behalf of my husband, whose ruin is certain unless you show him some degree of mercy.'—'Mr. Craddock behaved in a manner the most insulting, and dared to utter suspicions the must derogatory to my character, even in the presence of my clerks,' observed Walkden, in a tone so chilling that it seemed as if the breath which wafted those words to the young wife's ears, passed over the ice of the poles.—'But surely, sir,' urged Lucy, the tears trickling down her cheeks, 'you will make some allowances for the excited feelings of a young man just entering the world as it were, and so cruelly struck on its very threshold by the hand of misfortune? At least, sir, if not for his sake, I implore you for that of his innocent children to be lenient and merciful.'—'Law forms and ceremonies are not influenced by such considerations, madam,' said Mr. Walkden. 'At the same time, I have no objection to search the Commentaries; and if I there find leniency recommended in filing a declaration, or mercy enjoined in signing judgment, I have not the slightest objection to instruct my common-law clerk accordingly.'—Lucy stared at the attorney in wild bewilderment and uncertainty as he thus delivered himself in a measured tone of such frigidity that it seemed as if an automaton of ice were speaking; but at length she murmured, 'May I then hope, sir, that you will not press for the payment of this heavy debt when the bills become due?'—Walkden fixed his eyes upon the lovely and tearful countenance which was upturned so imploringly towards him; and at the instant he thought within himself that he had never before seen a female face of such surpassing beauty. Then his glance slowly and deliberately wandered from the faultless features to the contours of the well-formed bust, developed even by the plaits of the thick shawl which Lucy wore; and thence his survey was continued until his contemplation had embraced the wasp-like waist, and the flowing outlines of a symmetrical form, terminating in feet and ankles ravishingly modelled.—'You are doubtless much attached to your husband, madam?' he said, his tone becoming the least thing more tender—or rather losing one small degree of its cold severity.—'Attached to him, sir!' exclaimed Lucy, perfectly astonished at the question: 'I love—I worship him! He is the best of husbands and the best of fathers!'—'Then you would make *any* sacrifice to restore him to peace of mind?' said Walkden, his voice becoming more tender still, and his demeanour gradually unbending from its stiff formality.—'Oh! yes,' cried the artless Lucy; '*any* sacrifice would I make to see my Alexander happy as he was wont to be!'—'*Any* sacrifice,' repeated the lawyer, now positively allowing his features to relax into a faint and significant smile, while his voice was lowered and changed into a tone of soft familiarity; 'consider what you say—*any sacrifice*! Well, then on that condition'—and he took her hand.—A light broke instantaneously upon the mind of Lucy; and, snatching back her hand as if from the maw of a wild beast, she started from her seat, uttered a cry of indignation and abhorrence, and disappeared from the office before the baffled and disconcerted lawyer had time to make an effort to detain her.

"Lucy's heart was still swelling with mingled resentment and anguish, when she reached her home; and Alexander who returned at the same time, saw in an instant that she was a prey to no ordinary emotions. Throwing herself into her husband's arms, Lucy burst into tears—her pent-up feelings no longer obeying the control of that restraint which she sought to impose upon them. Then, by dint of questioning, Alexander gleaned enough to convince him that his beloved wife had been flagrantly insulted by the villain who had already heaped such grievous wrongs upon his head. Maddened by this fresh injury, Alexander was about to rush from the house and inflict some dreadful chastisement upon the cold-blooded monster Walkden, when his wife and her aunt threw themselves at his feet, and implored him, with tears and impassioned entreaties, not to aggravate the perils and embarrassments of his position by involving himself in a quarrel with their enemy. Alexander was moved by the prayers of those whom he loved; and he faithfully promised them not to suffer his indignant feelings to master his prudence. When calmness and composure were somewhat restored, he proceeded to explain the result of the visit which he had just paid to his own solicitor. That gentleman had said to him, 'It is as clear as day-light that you are robbed by Walkden and Scudimore conjointly; but I really do not think that you could *prove* a conspiracy in a criminal court. I should, however, decidedly advise you to resist the payment of the bills; and, as Walkden is tolerably sure to push the matter on to trial, the verdict of a jury in the civil case will enable us to judge how far we may hope to punish the scoundrel attorney in another manner.' Alexander had accordingly placed himself entirely in his solicitor's hands; and there rested the business for the present.

"But a serious change took place in the disposition and habits of Alexander Craddock. Smarting under the wrongs which he had received, he grew restless and unsettled—experienced less delight than he was wont to feel in the society of his wife and children—showed signs of irritability, and an impatience of the slightest contradiction, however trivial—and remained longer over his wine after dinner. Lucy beheld all this, and wept in secret: but when with Alexander, she redoubled her attentions, and sought every possible opportunity of proving her devotion. She implored him to give up the house they then occupied, and adopt a more economical mode of life; but his answers were at first evasive—then impatient—and at last so sharp and angry, that she was compelled, though with reluctance, to abandon the topic, at least for the present. To add to Lucy's grief, her aunt, who had so long fulfilled towards her the duties of a mother, was attacked with sudden indisposition, which increased with alarming rapidity, and carried her off in the course of a few days. Alexander manifested far less sorrow than Lucy had expected him to have shown; and this proof of an augmenting callousness on his part, pierced the heart of the amiable young lady to the very quick. But scarcely had the remains of Miss Middleton been consigned to the tomb, when a fresh misfortune occurred to increase the irritability of Alexander. The bills for eight thousand pounds fell due, and were dishonoured by him, in accordance with the advice of his solicitor. He was immediately after arrested: and, as he had resolved to defend the action, he paid into court the whole sum in dispute, a proceeding whereby he could alone save himself from remaining in prison until the trial. He had, however, gone through the ordeal of a spunging-house, and he considered himself disgraced; the irritability of his temper increased—he daily grew more attached to the bottle—and his affections towards his wife and children were evidently blunted. Oh! how ramified and vast are the evil effects of the villainy of one man towards another,—striking not only the individual victim, but rebounding and reacting on his wife, his children, and his friends!

"Lucy again revived the expression of her wish that a cheaper dwelling should be taken and a more economical style of living adopted. But Alexander would not listen to the proposal. He declared his certainty of gaining the suit and of recovering his money from the court—a result, he said, which would enable him to employ his funds in some legitimate commercial enterprise. On this subject he spoke so confidently, that Lucy entertained the most sanguine hopes of beholding happiness restored beneath a roof where naught save happiness had once prevailed; and it was but with little apprehension that she marked the arrival of the day fixed for the trial. The most able counsel had been retained on both sides; and the cause excited immense interest. Walkden had been established for years, and bore an excellent character: indeed, none of his friends or clients could for a moment believe that he was an accomplice of the villain Scudimore. The whole question, as presented to the cognizance of the tribunal, was whether Mr. Walkden had given value for the bills, and was a *bona fide* holder of securities which he had legitimately and honourably discounted in the course of business. The evidence he adduced to establish these points was certainly of a nature likely to prove most convincing to a jury, though Alexander knew full well that Walkden had suborned the grossest perjury on the part of his clerks and the other persons whom he put forward as witnesses. Nevertheless, the verdict was in Walkden's favour; and Alexander returned home a prey to the liveliest grief and the most bitter resentment. Lucy did all that woman's goodness and ingenuity could suggest to console him; but the excitement of his feelings gained upon him with such overwhelming violence and rapidity, that he grew delirious, and a brain-fever supervened. The best medical advice was procured for him by the almost heart-broken Lucy; but weeks and weeks passed away without enabling the physicians to pronounce him beyond the reach of danger. During that period he had many lucid intervals, on which occasions he recognised his wife and children—embraced them tenderly—wept over them—implored heaven to bless them—and then, in the bitterness of overwhelming reminiscences, desired them to look upon him as one who was dead,—his excitement relapsing into delirium again. Poor Lucy! seldom was it that she reposed her aching head upon a pillow, throughout the period of her beloved husband's illness—and never until completely crushed with the fatigue of long vigils and the burthen of a grief beneath which she herself was sinking. At length—just as her pecuniary resources began to fail, and the want of funds excited alarms which augmented her afflictions—Alexander's malady took a sudden turn which filled her mind with the most joyous hope; and when the delirium had altogether passed away, his manner was so kind and gentle—his language so endearing and affectionate—and his temper so entirely devoid of irritability, that Lucy's heart became elate with the most cheering aspirations and delightful visions. Alexander spoke of his misfortunes with calmness and resignation; and said, 'Our property is all swept away, dearest; but I am young, and shall soon be strong and active again; and then I will work to obtain a livelihood for us all. And who knows, my beloved Lucy, but that the bread of honest though perhaps severe toil, may not prove the sweetest we shall have ever eaten?'—Then, when his wife heard him discourse in this manner, she would throw herself into his arms, and thank him—yes, thank him fervently for becoming a consoler in his turn.

"The fond pair had been conversing in this style one afternoon—the first day on which Alexander was enabled to walk down stairs to the parlour without assistance,—and their children were playing in a corner of the apartment, when the door was suddenly and violently opened, and two or three coarse-looking fellows unceremoniously made their appearance. Their mission was soon explained. The money paid into court had only just covered the amount of the bills of exchange which had formed the ground of action; and Alexander was now arrested by Walkden for the costs, which had been taxed at a hundred and odd pounds. The unfortunate young couple had not the money; and Lucy had already made away with their plate, jewellery, and other valuables in order to provide her husband with every comfort and luxury in his illness. The furniture was worth more than the amount of the costs: but arrears of rent were due to the landlord. Lucy implored the bailiffs, with tears in her eyes, not to remove Alexander for a few days, when he might have recovered the shock of this new and unforeseen blow; but they were inexorable, intimating pretty plainly that they were instructed to show no leniency of any kind. She, however, by dint of entreaties—actually going down upon her knees to the officers—succeeded in inducing them to wait while she repaired to his own solicitor. But this gentleman was unable to assist her to the amount she required: he nevertheless manifested the kindest and most respectful sympathy towards her, giving her a few guineas for immediate necessities, and promising to incur the expense of the measures necessary to enable her husband to remove next day from a lock-up house to the King's Bench. It was some consolation to the almost heart-broken young lady, to find that Alexander possessed at least one friend in the world; but even this faint and poor gleam of solace vanished, and gave way to the keenest apprehensions, when on her return she found her husband a prey to all that fearful excitement which had proved the forerunner of his late dangerous malady.

"What was to be done? There seemed but one alternative; and this she was determined, in her affectionate solicitude and zeal, to adopt without the knowledge of Alexander. Indeed, he scarcely appeared to be aware of what was going on; but raved, talked wildly, and menaced and wept by turns in the presence of the officers who surrounded him. Away sped Lucy to Bush Lane; and a second time did she enter the establishment of that individual who had brought such rapid—such signal—such unredeemable ruin on the heads of a once happy family. Walkden received her in his private office, and coldly desired her to be seated, a smile of infernal triumph relaxing his stern and usually rigid features; while his eyes scanned the wasted, but still touchingly beautiful and deeply interesting countenance of that afflicted young lady.

Lucy was for some minutes so overcome by the intensity of her feelings, that she was unable to utter a word; and when she did speak, it was a mere gasping forth of disjointed sentences, broken by frequent sobs of convulsing agony. The lawyer bent over her, like Satan whispering to a desperate creature the terms on which wealth and power might be purchased,—bent over that crushed, much-enduring, and amiable young wife, and murmured in her ears *his* terms of mercy towards her husband. She rose and looked at him in amazement and horror. Was he a human being, or a veritable fiend? His cold, grey eyes sank not beneath the reproachful and indignant glance of that outraged lady; and a smile of demoniac triumph again played upon his lip. Doubtless he thought that her anger was only momentary, and that the sternness of necessity would force her to a compliance with his will. But he knew not the mind of Lucy. 'Villain! monster!' she exclaimed: 'has your infamy no bounds?' and she fled from the presence of the cold-blooded scoundrel as if the atmosphere which he breathed were fraught with the plague.

"With what a heavy heart did she return home—that home from which her husband must now be dragged immediately and before her eyes,—a home which, perhaps, would not long remain so for herself and children. But suddenly, and as if by divine inspiration, she remembered that all her courage was now required to enable her to bear up against her afflictions for the sake of Alexander—for the sake of her offspring;—and it is astonishing how, in the midst of the deepest sorrows, woman can ofttimes display an energy of which the stronger sex is altogether incapable. And so it now was with Lucy Craddock. She even succeeded in comforting her husband and soothing his excitement, by reminding him that the more he appeared to be crushed, the greater would be the delight of his savage and unrelenting enemy. This species of remonstrance, so kindly—so gently administered, had the desired effect; and Alexander, animated with a spirit of endurance, and fortified by the example of his admirable wife, rose if possible superior to his misfortunes, and proceeded with a feeling of proud resignation to the lock-up-house. Thence on the ensuing day he was removed to the King's Bench: and it was here that I first formed his acquaintance, when he entered the prison six years ago.

"Immediately after his arrival, his spirits gave way rapidly; and it was necessary for his wife to take up her abode with him altogether. She accordingly disposed of the furniture in their house, paid the landlord and the few other small creditors, and brought her children over to the small cheerless chamber in which her husband was lying on a bed of sickness. Thus was this once happy family—like so many, many others, reduced from a state of comfort, and even affluence, to poverty and a prison-room. Heaven only knows what misery—what privations they had undergone, when it was first whispered to me by a char-woman that the Craddocks seemed to be in great distress. I was then a little better off than I am now; and I immediately repaired to their room, inventing some excuse for my intrusion. Oh! what a scene of destitution—what a heart-rending spectacle met my eyes! The furniture which the Craddocks had hired, had been all removed away in consequence of their inability to pay for its use: Alexander, pale and emaciated, was sitting upon a trunk; the two children, thin and wasted, were crying for food; and the poor, heart-rent Lucy was looking over a few things in a hatbox, evidently with a view to select the most likely articles to be received by the pawnbroker—while her scalding tears fell fast upon her hands as she turned over the only relics left of a wardrobe once extensive and elegant. It went to my very soul to contemplate that scene! I shall not pause to explain all the particulars which rendered me intimate with the Craddocks: suffice it to say, that they accepted my assistance, and that in a few hours their chamber once again wore an aspect of such comfort as the restitution of the furniture and a well supplied table could possibly afford in a prison. I did not learn their history immediately—nor all its details at once: portions of it were communicated by degrees—some of the particulars oozed out incidentally—and the feelings and sentiments experienced by the sufferers in the various phases of their eventful tale, transpired from time to time,—until at length I gleaned all those facts which I have now related to you. But by far the most terrible portion of the history of the Craddocks is yet to come."

Prout paused for a few moments, and then enquired of Frank Curtis if he were wearied of the narrative. The young gentleman assured him that, so far from being tired of the story, he was deeply interested in its progress; whereupon the Chancery prisoner proceeded in the following manner.

50.

O woman in our hours of ease,

Uncertain, coy, and hard to please,

And variable as the shade

By the light quivering aspen made;—

When pain and anguish wring the brow,

A ministering angel thou!

WALTER SCOTT.

And such is woman's love—the secret power
That turns the darkest to the brightest hour;
That smothes the wrinkles care has learned to plough,
And wipes the trace of anguish from the brow!
And Oh! if spite of war and wasting pain,
Feelings so noble—so divine remain,
Where were the brighter star to cheer our gloom,
Make heaven of earth, and triumph o'er the tomb!

UNIVERSITY PRIZE POEM.

CHAPTER CVIII.
CONCLUSION OF THE TALE OF SORROW.

"Although I was enabled to administer temporary assistance to this unfortunate and persecuted family, and, under the delicate guise of a *loan* of money, *gave* them the wherewith to make themselves comparatively comfortable, it was nevertheless necessary for Alexander to resolve upon some decisive step. To remain in prison was to bury his talents in a manner so as to render them completely unavailable,—to think of liquidating the enormous burthen of debt which lay upon his shoulders, was ridiculous,—and to move the stony heart of Walkden was a hopeless idea. The only alternative was the Insolvents' Court. Good food, medical attendance, and the altered appearance of his wife and children, who had all improved greatly, restored Alexander to some degree of health and spirits; and he soon began to discuss with me and Lucy his present position and plans for the future. The lawyer who had enabled him to pass over to the Bench, returned to town at this precise period, after some weeks' absence; and he not only agreed to provide the funds to take Alexander through the Insolvents' Court, but also promised to give him employment as a clerk on his release. Thus was it that this good man infused hope into the bosoms of the Craddocks; and the necessary steps were adopted to effect the emancipation of the prisoner. But scarcely were the initiatory proceedings set on foot, when intelligence was received to the effect that Walkden was resolved to oppose Alexander's discharge by all the means that were within his power. This intimation, which reached the prison through a private channel, aroused Alexander's fury against the man who so unrelentingly persecuted him; and it required all the attentions of his amiable wife and all the manifestations of friendship which I was enabled to offer, to restore him to comparative tranquillity.

"Well, the day fixed for his examination at the Insolvents' Court arrived; and Alexander proceeded thither in the usual charge of a tipstaff. His case was called on at an early stage of the day's business; and he found a formidable array of counsel employed against him. I shall not pause to dwell upon all the details of the proceeding: suffice it to say that Walkden was placed in the witness-box, and, being examined by the barristers whom he had feed, made the entire case look so fearfully black against Alexander Craddock, that he was remanded to gaol for twelve months, his discharge to take place at the expiration of that period. Fearful was the state of excitement in which he returned to the Bench; and in the course of a few hours he was delirious. It was frightful to hear his ravings, in which the name of Walkden was uppermost, and associated with the bitterest imprecations and menaces. Poor Lucy! I thought her heart would break, as she sate watching by her husband's bed; but she was rewarded to some extent for her vigils and her sorrow, when, on the return of his senses, he recognised her before he even knew his own children, much less me—his humble friend,—and manifested his purest love for her in the most impassioned language and with the tenderest embraces. But though the delirium left him and returned no more, he soon fell into a deep and brooding melancholy, from which it was scarcely possible to arouse him. He fancied himself dishonoured—permanently dishonoured by the sentence passed upon him by the Insolvents' Court; and though the friendly lawyer and myself, as well as Lucy, endeavoured to reason with him against the belief,—pointing out every circumstance calculated to prove that he was a victim, and not a culprit,—he took the matter so to heart that it was evident his spirit was broken!

"My own resources began to fall off at this period, and I was unable to assist the Craddocks as much as I could wish. Moreover, Alexander and Lucy both felt averse to remain dependant upon me; and the friendly lawyer had proved so generous that they were naturally delicate in applying to him. Lucy accordingly made up her mind how to act. She proposed that they should remove over to the Poor-Side, and receive the County money. They would thus obtain a room rent free, and a few shillings a-week to purchase bread. Alexander's pride struggled against this project; but he yielded at last to the entreaties and representations of his excellent wife, who assured him that she felt no shame in showing that she was poor, and that the only real disgrace lay in dishonesty. 'Wherefore, then, should we contract any debts which we cannot pay?' she enquired; 'and if we continue to live in this part of the prison we must keep up certain appearances, which we have not the means to do.'—Alexander succumbed, I say, to this reasoning; and to the Poor-Side they accordingly removed. I never shall forget the day when this change took place. Lucy had made the new chamber look as neat at possible; and she endeavoured to maintain a smiling exterior as she arranged the little furniture and the few things of their own which were left to them. But every now and then she glanced anxiously towards her husband, who sat in a musing—or rather an apathetic manner—watching her proceedings; and I observed that a tear frequently started to her eye, and that every now and then she caught up her children and pressed them passionately to her bosom. I insisted upon providing dinner on that day; and I did all I could not only to make this poor family as comfortable as possible, but also to raise Alexander's spirits. But if he smiled it was so faintly, or sickly, that my heart sank within me as if he had been my own son.

"A few weeks passed away, and I observed that Lucy managed to keep the family pretty comfortably. They had no lack of plain and humble food—and the children were always neat and clean. Whenever I called at their room, I found Lucy busy in some way or another—either washing or mending the clothes, or ironing out her husband's linen, or else plying the needle at work which, though I know little of such matters, did not seem to me to have any reference to the family wardrobe at all. One night I could not sleep, and got up to take a walk round the prison. It was between twelve and one; and, as I passed round by the Poor-Side, I chanced to look up at the window of the Craddocks' room. To my surprise, I observed a light burning; and the truth flashed upon me. Poor Lucy was sitting up to work—to waste her youth, her health, and her spirits over the needle, that she might obtain the means to purchase comforts for her husband and children! The conviction went to my very heart like a pang; and I thought how bitter is often the mission of a good and virtuous woman in this world! I remember that I had no inclination to retire to rest again that night; and I kept walking—walking round the prison, impelled by some invincible influence thus to wander about the gloomy place, as if to watch how long the feeble light would be burning in that one room! It was nearly four o'clock when that light was extinguished; and I heaved a sigh as I murmured to myself the name of poor Lucy Craddock! When day came, and I was enabled to call upon Alexander after breakfast. I examined the young wife and mother with more attention than usual; and it then struck me that she was visibly wasting away. Her health was evidently declining; and her spirits were entirely forced. She was gay and lively as ever; but that gaiety and liveliness were assumed, not real—artificial, not natural,— the veil which an excellent and amiable woman—a most affectionate wife and the best of mothers—put on to cover the secret of her breaking heart!

"Three mouths of the year for which Alexander had been remanded, passed away; and Lucy beheld her children drooping and pining through want of proper air and exercise. This discovery was a new affliction. She would not permit the little things to play about along with the ragged, dirty offspring of the other prisoners on the Poor-Side; and she was unable to spare the time to take them out herself. I understood the struggle that was passing in her mind. If she devoted an hour or two each day to them, she must give up some of the work which, as I found out, she had obtained from a warehouse in the Borough; and by so doing their comforts and those of her husband would be abridged. On the other hand, she could not see those poor innocents confined to a close room and pining for fresh air. She accordingly resolved to take them out for a certain period each day, and to steal another hour or two from her repose. I knew that she did this, because when I either walked about until very late, or else rose early to take my ramble about the prison, I saw the light in the chamber even at five o'clock in the morning! My God! It is as true as I am here, that this poor, devoted woman at length limited herself to only three hours' rest; and though her children improved in health, her own was suffering the most frightful ravages. It was evident that Alexander did not suspect the labour and toil which his wife endured: he had sunk into a species of apathy which blinded him to a fact that I discovered so easily, and which gave me the acutest pain. You may be sure that I did all I could for the family, and in as delicate a way as possible,— always proposing to join my dinner to their's when I knew that I had a better one than they; but my own resources were becoming daily more cramped; and my accursed Chancery business not only lingered on, but absorbed all the funds I could raise or my friends could muster in my behalf. Thus six months passed away—Lucy in the meantime being worn down to a skeleton, and seeming only the shadow of her former self. Still she grew not, slovenly: dirt—that too frequent companion of poverty—was not the characteristic of her little chamber; and her husband always had his clean shirt for the Sabbath, and even decent apparel, considering that he lived on the Poor-Side of the King's Bench Prison!

"It was Term Time; and my business compelled me to take a day-rule. That is to say, I obtained permission to go out for a day to attend to my affairs, my friends giving security to the Marshal of the Bench for my safe return. I resolved to avail myself of this opportunity to call on Walkden, and represent to him the cruelty and absurdity of keeping Alexander in confinement, when by withdrawing the detainer he might restore him to freedom. I was prepared to find Walkden a severe and hard man; but the reception I experienced was calculated to make me set him down as a fiend in mortal shape. The moment I mentioned my business, he stopped me short,—rising from his seat, and saying in a cold, icy manner, 'The name of Craddock is abhorrent to me, sir. I was grossly insulted by his injurious suspicions; and he shall rot in prison before I permit him to escape my vengeance. He thinks that he will be freed in six months' time; but he is mistaken.'—'No, sir,' I exclaimed indignantly, 'it is you who are mistaken. The fiat of the Insolvents' Court is stronger than your vindictive will.'—'We shall see,' observed Walkden, in an implacable tone; and I was compelled to withdraw, not only grieved at the ill-success of my visit, but filled with vague apprehensions that fresh persecutions were in waiting for my unhappy friend. But I did not breathe a word to either Alexander or Lucy relative to the step which I had taken nor the fears thus excited within me; although I could not banish the lawyer's dark menace from my thoughts. Months passed away—Lucy still managing to keep the wolf from the door, as the vulgar phrase goes; while her health was sinking rapidly.

"At length the period drew nigh when Alexander expected to obtain his deliverance; and now his spirits began to rise. He gradually shook off the apathy which had so long clouded his intellect and impaired his energies; and he spoke highly of the prospect of release. But Walkden watched him from a distance, and seemed to gloat over the new scheme of vengeance which he had in store for this hapless family. Indeed, the blow came on a day when Alexander had declared to me that he had not felt his heart so light for a long, long time. A detainer was lodged against him at the gate—a detainer for a thousand pounds! The fact was that a mistake had been committed in Alexander's schedule, and an item to that extent omitted. The judgment of the Court was therefore void and null in respect to a debt not inserted in the schedule; for such is the atrocious law, made on purpose to persecute those unfortunate debtors who do not come within the meaning of the Acts which enable traders to apply to the Bankruptcy Court. The way that I heard first of the detainer being lodged at Walkden's suit was in this wise:—A charwoman came to my room, saying that Mrs. Craddock, who appeared to be in great distress of mind, wished to see me immediately. I hurried to the

Poor-Side, a misgiving preparing my mind to receive intelligence of farther persecution on the part of the fiend Walkden. On entering the Craddock's chamber, I found Alexander lying almost senseless on the bed, deep and prolonged gaspings alone denoting that he was alive. Lucy was on her knees, imploring him not to give way to despair; and the children were crying piteously, although they were too young to understand the nature of the misfortune which had fallen on their parents' heads. I strove to awaken my unhappy friend to the necessity of enduring this new affliction with courage; and in a short time my representations, joined to Lucy's prayers and entreaties, succeeded to some little extent. 'You must petition the Insolvents' Court again,' I said; 'and you are sure of having no farther remand. In six weeks you will be free.'—'But the means—the means to pass this ordeal a second time!' he exclaimed almost frantically.—'The Marshal has some charitable funds at his disposal,' I observed; 'and I will instantly wait upon him, and present the whole circumstances of the case.'—Alexander was in that feverish state of excitement which cannot endure suspense when any gleam of hope is afforded in the midst of despair; and he urged me to lose no time in seeing the Marshal. As I quitted the room, Lucy pressed my hand in a manner expressive of deep emotion, as she murmured in a low tone, 'You are our only friend!'

"Within ten minutes I was seated in the Marshal's private office, explaining the nature of my business. I unreservedly and frankly revealed to him Alexander Craddock's whole history; and you may be sure that I did not forget to dwell upon the admirable conduct of Lucy. The Marshal is a humane man, although nothing more than a superior kind of gaoler; and he listened to me with great interest. When I had concluded my narrative, which was rather long, he said, 'Mr. Prout, I will lose no time in calling myself upon Mr. Walkden, whom I know well by name, and whose character has certainly appeared to me this day in a new light. I am well aware that he is harsh and severe; but I do not think him capable of keeping this man in prison under all the circumstances which you have detailed to me. I will see him, and endeavour to excite his compassion by unfolding to him all the particulars of Craddock's history, as you have now related them to me. If he should persist in retaining him in gaol, I will then from my own pocket advance the necessary funds to enable your poor friend to petition the Court again. In the meantime give Craddock this guinea.'—I returned my warmest thanks to the Marshal for his goodness, and was hurrying back to the Craddocks with the money and the hopeful intelligence I had in store for them, when, as I passed through the upper lobby, my attention was directed to a new prisoner who had just arrived; for on the turnkey asking him his name, he replied—SCUDIMORE! A moment's scrutiny of the man convinced me that he was the same who had plundered Craddock, a description of his personal appearance having been frequently given to me by Alexander. I was sorry to find that he had become an inmate of the same place as the individual whom he had so deeply injured, and whose excited feelings I feared might lead him to some act of violence towards the villain. Well aware that Alexander could not be long before he must inevitably learn the fact of Scudimore's arrest, I resolved to mention it to him without delay, so as to prepare him to meet his enemy within the precincts of the Bench. I, however, communicated my good news first; and Lucy was overjoyed when she learnt that the Marshal had resolved to interest himself in her husband's behalf. But Alexander's manner suddenly became so strange—so unaccountably sombre and gloomy—and so menacingly mysterious, when I revealed to him the circumstance of Scudimore's presence in the prison, that both Lucy and myself grew terribly alarmed. We implored him not to notice Scudimore even when they should meet; but he gave no reply. I, however, whispered to Lucy my hopes that the Marshal would succeed in inducing Walkden to liberate her husband at once; and thereby remove her husband from the vicinity of the scoundrel who had ruined him. I also resolved to be as much with Alexander as possible; and I was delighted to find that he showed no inclination to leave his room for the purpose of taking his usual walk up and down the back of the prison-building.

"In the course of a couple of hours the Marshal sent me in word that he had not succeeded in finding Mr. Walkden at his office, but had made an appointment with the head-clerk to call again in the evening, when the result of his interview with the lawyer should be immediately communicated to me, even if the gates were closed. I therefore saw that the Marshal was in earnest in carrying out the business he had taken in hand; and Lucy was inspired with the same strong hopes that I entertained. But Alexander received the Marshal's message with an apathetic coldness which filled me with alarm; and it was evident that his mind brooded over other affairs, which I could not help thinking were connected with the arrival of Scudimore at the Bench. I was, however, glad to observe that Lucy did not participate in my fears to the same extent as she did in my hopes: poor creature! the thought of seeing her husband soon free was the absorbing sentiment in her mind! I remained with the Craddocks on that eventful day up to almost nine o'clock, when a letter which I received by the last post compelled me to go to my room for a few minutes to look out a few papers connected with my own case, and which my attorney required the first thing in the morning. I assured Lucy that I would return as soon as possible, the promised intelligence from the Marshal being now every moment expected by us.

"And now I come to a frightful portion of my sad tale. I had been about five minutes in my room, and had just sealed up the packet which was to be given to a messenger that night to deliver early next day to my solicitor, when Lucy rushed in without knocking. She fell exhausted upon the floor; and it was some moments before she could articulate a word. I was cruelly alarmed; and my hand trembled so as I poured her out some water that I could scarcely hold the glass. At length I learnt that Alexander had suddenly started from his chair, a minute after I left him, and seizing a knife, had rushed from the room. Before Lucy could reach the bottom of the stairs, he had disappeared; and, in a state bordering on distraction, she had naturally flown to me. While she was gasping forth the few words which thus made me acquainted with the cause of her visit, cries of horror suddenly burst from the parade-ground and struck upon our ears. I cannot at this moment remember what we thought, or what we said—no, nor how we got down the stairs: the next incident that I *do* recollect, after hearing those appalling cries, was finding myself elbowing my way through a group of prisoners assembled on the parade; and then, by the moonlight, what a spectacle met my eyes! A man was lying on the ground, weltering in his blood; and another was passive and motionless in the grasp of three or four prisoners. The former was Scudimore: the latter was Alexander Craddock. Then female shrieks of anguish rent the air; and Lucy threw herself wildly into her husband's arms, exclaiming in a tone so piercing that it still rings in my ears—'You did not do it, Alexander! Oh! no—you could not—you would not! Tell me—I conjure you,—tell me that you did not do it!'

"Almost at the same moment a cry was raised of—'The Marshall'—and immediately afterwards that gentleman came up to the spot, accompanied by *another individual,* whom, as the moonlight fell upon his countenance, I instantly recognised to be Walkden. And that countenance—how was it changed! No longer cold and implacable, every feature bore the imprint of ineffable anguish and black despair. Then, when in a few hurried words, the assassination of Scudimore was communicated by the bye-standers to the Marshal and Walkden, and Alexander Craddock was mentioned as the murderer, a scene of the most wildly exciting interest ensued. For Walkden sprang towards the guilty—unhappy young man, and throwing his arms frantically around him,—poor Lucy shrinking back at his appearance,— exclaimed, 'My son!—my dear, and long-lost son! Pardon me—pardon me— I am the cause of all this—Oh! my God! how frightfully am I punished!'— and the wretched Walkden fell heavily upon the ground, overpowered— stunned—crushed by emotions too awful to be even conceived!

"I must here pause for a few moments to give a word or two of necessary explanation. The Marshal had found Mr. Walkden at his office in the evening, and had begged him to grant Alexander's release. But the miscreant was inexorable, alleging that he had received at the prisoner's hands insults of a nature which rendered mercy impossible. The Marshal, hoping to touch the man's heart by a recital of all the interesting circumstances of Alexander's life, began to tell his story; but scarcely had he explained how Alexander had been found by the late Mr. Craddock in the neighbourhood of Doctors' Commons, when Walkden's whole manner suddenly underwent an appalling change: he turned ghastly pale—trembled like an aspen-leaf—and then, in another minute, covered his face with his hands, exclaiming in a tone of the deepest anguish, '*Merciful God! it is my own son whom I have plundered and persecuted thus vilely! Oh! wretch that I am—miscreant, demon that I have been!*'—The Marshal was naturally overwhelmed with astonishment at these terrific self-accusations, which nevertheless appeared to be too well founded; for it was indeed the only child of the miserable lawyer who had been lost by a neglectful servant years ago in the neighbourhood of Doctors' Commons; and the sudden death of the beadle happening the very next day, had destroyed the only clue to the infant. Mrs. Walkden died of a broken heart; and it was most probably these misfortunes which, acting upon a morbid mind, rendered the attorney the harsh, severe, merciless man which he had so effectually proved himself to be.

"And what miseries had he piled up, to fall on his own head! He had ruined his son—rendered him a murderer—and also endeavoured to seduce that son's wife. Oh! it was a fearful scene, which took place on the parade-ground on that eventful evening. Scudimore lay a corpse at the feet of the man whom he had injured; and senseless by the side of the corpse, fell Walkden who had made Scudimore his instrument and accomplice in the iniquitous transaction which paved the way for this accumulation of horrors. Alexander understood nothing that took place. He saw it all—but comprehended it not. His reason had fled; and it is most probable that he was already a maniac when he rushed from his room armed with the fatal knife—and perhaps even when I observed the strange change come over him on his learning from my lips that Scudimore was an inmate of the Bench. As for Lucy—poor, crushed, heart-broken Lucy—she had fainted when Walkden proclaimed himself her husband's *father*! But I must hasten and bring my story to a conclusion. The Marshal speedily gave the orders necessary under the circumstances which had occurred; and, on Lucy being recovered from her swoon, she found that she had not been the prey of a hideous dream, as she at first supposed—but that her husband had been taken from her, and lodged in the strong-room—a maniac and a murderer! Oh! what a heart-rending duty it was for me to implore her to take courage for her children's sake! Walkden, who had in the meantime been restored to his senses, begged her to make his house her home in future, and look on him as a father;—but she shrieked forth a negative in so wild a tone and accompanied by such a shudder, that the wretched man could not be otherwise than deeply convinced how ineffable was the abhorrence that she entertained for him. The Marshal kindly took charge of the stricken woman and her young children; and the corpse of Scudimore was conveyed to a room there to await the attendance of the Coroner on the following day.

"But little more remains to be told. During the night that followed the deplorable events which I have just related, Alexander Craddock grew furious with excitement, and became raving mad. A brain-fever supervened; and in less than twelve hours from the moment when his hand avenged his wrongs on the villain Scudimore, he himself was no longer a denizen of this world! Ten days afterwards the Marshal received a letter from Walkden, which he subsequently showed to me, and the contents of which ran thus as nearly as I can recollect them:—'*I am about to quit England, and shall never be again heard of by one who has to much reason to shudder at the mere mention of my name. I allude to my deeply-injured daughter-in-law. My share of the ten thousand pounds, of which Scudimore plundered her husband, was precisely one half. This amount, with compound interest, I have placed in the funds in her name; and I implore her to forgive a man who is crushed and heart-broken, and who loathes himself!*'—Lucy, who had only for her children's sake been able to sustain anything like the adequate amount of courage necessary to support her afflictions, was somewhat solaced—if solace there could be in the midst of such bitter, bitter woe—by the certainty that those children were now secure against want. She accordingly removed with them into a small but comfortable dwelling near Norwood—but not before she had called on me, to express all her gratitude for the kindnesses which I had been enabled to show the family. She moreover endeavoured to compel me to receive a sum of money, as she said in repayment for the amounts I had at various times lent them; but that sum was a hundred times greater than any I had ever been able to assist them with. I would not receive a fraction; and I wept on parting with her, as if she had been my own daughter. During the year which she survived the loss of her husband—for she only *did* survive it a year—she came frequently to visit me, always accompanied by her children; and on every occasion she brought me some touching and delicate memorial of her esteem. But her health had been undermined by the long vigils—the deep anxieties—the corroding cares—the serious toils—and the frightful shocks, which had characterised her existence in this accursed prison; and she died in the arms of an affectionate female friend, who dwelt in her neighbourhood, and whose bosom her misfortunes had deeply touched. This friend promised to be a second mother to the poor children; and she has fulfilled her word. Two respectable gentlemen accepted the guardianship of the orphans, so far as their pecuniary interests are concerned; and those orphans will be rich when they become of age,—for Walkden died a short time ago, leaving them all his fortune. Poor Lucy sleeps in the same grave with her husband; and thus ends my TALE OF SORROW."

The old man wiped away the tears from his eyes: and Frank Curtis was not only deeply interested in the narrative which he had just heard, but even affected by its lamentable details, on which he was about to make some remark, when, happening to glance from the window, he espied the captain on the parade staring about him in all possible directions. Curtis therefore took leave of Mr. Prout, after thanking him for the recital of the melancholy tale, and hastened to join his friend.

Captain O'Blunderbuss had no good news to relate. The officers in possession in Baker Street had positively refused to allow Mrs. Curtis to take any thing, beyond wearing apparel, away with her; and the excellent lady had accordingly moved, with her two trunks and her five children, to a lodging in Belvidere Place.

The captain had likewise been unsuccessful in his visit to Sir Christopher Blunt. He had seen the knight, it is true; but neither menaces nor coaxings had proved potent enough to induce that gentleman to draw forth his purse or sign his autograph to a cheque.

"What the devil, then, must I do?" demanded Frank Curtis, shuddering as he thought of the Poor-Side.

"Be Jasus! and go dacently and genteelly through the Insolvents' Court," exclaimed the captain; "and I'll skin the Commissioners alive if they dar-r to turn you back, my frind!"

"I really think there is no other alternative left but to petition the Court," observed Frank Curtis; "and therefore I'll make up my mind at once to do so."

CHAPTER CIX.
THE PRISONERS.

We must leave Mr. Frank Curtis to adopt the necessary measures in order to effect his emancipation from the Bench *viâ* the Insolvents' Court, and suppose that a month has passed since the period when the Blackamoor consigned to his dungeons Tim the Snammer, Josh Pedler, Old Death, Mrs. Bunce, her husband, and Tidmarsh.

It was about nine o'clock in the evening, when the Blackamoor, attended by Cæsar, who bore a light, entered the subterranean passage containing the doors of the cells in which the prisoners were separately retained. Wilton followed, bearing a large basket; and two more of the Black's retainers brought up the rear, one carrying a naked cutlass and the other a pair of loaded pistols in their hands.

Opening the door of the first cell, the Blackamoor took the light from Cæsar's hand, and stopping on the threshold, said, "Timothy Splint, another sun has set, and the close of another day has come. Had you been surrendered up to the justice of the criminal tribunals of your country, you would ere this have ceased to exist: your guilt would have been expiated on the scaffold."

"Oh! I would rather it had been *that*," exclaimed the man, in a tone which carried to the hearts of his listeners a conviction of his sincerity,—"I would rather it had been *that*, than this frightful lingering in utter darkness! The light, sir, is as welcome to me as food would be if I was starving," he added with profound emphasis.

"Are you afraid to be alone and in the dark?" enquired the Blackamoor.

"It is hell upon earth, sir!" cried Tim the Snammer. "What! can you ask me whether I'm afraid, when the place is haunted with dreadful spectres?"

"The spectres are created by your own guilty conscience," answered the Black, mildly but solemnly: then, advancing farther into the dungeon, so that the light fell upon the haggard countenance of the prisoner, he said, "You see that there are no horrible apparitions now; and why should they not remain here when you can enjoy the use of your eyes as well as when you are involved in darkness?"

"That is what I say to myself—that is what I am always asking myself," exclaimed Timothy Splint. "And yet I can't help thinking that *he* is there—the murdered man, you know—with his throat so horribly cut——Oh! yes—when I am alone and in the dark, I am sure he is there—just where you are standing now. He never moves—he stands as still as death—and his eyes glare upon me in the dark. It is dreadful—dreadful!"—and the wretched criminal hid his face in his hands.

"Are you sorry, then, that you killed Sir Henry Courtenay?" asked the Black.

"Sorry!" repeated Splint, in a thrilling—agonising tone. "I wish that I could only live the last few months over again! I'd sooner beg—go to the workhouse—break stones in the road—or even starve, than rob or do any thing wrong again! Oh! I would indeed! For I see now that though a man may only mean for to rob, he stands the chance of taking away life; and it's a horrid—horrid thing to say to one's self, '*I am a murderer!*' But it's more horrid still to see the dreadful spectre always standing by one—quite plain, though in the dark—and never taking his cold eyes off his assassin."

"If you had a light, Timothy Splint, you would no longer think of your crimes," said the Blackamoor; "and then you would be ready to fall back into your old courses, if you had your liberty given to you once more."

"Heaven forbid!" exclaimed the man, his frame convulsed with a horrible shudder. "I wish I had never known such courses at all: I wish I could live over again during the whole period that I've been so wicked. I am sure I should be a good man then—if so be I had all my experience to teach me to be so. I never thought it was such a shocking thing to be wicked till I came to be left alone in darkness—yes, all alone with my frightful thoughts! I would sooner be put to death at once: but—but—" he added, in a hesitating manner—"I haven't the courage to brain myself against the wall, because the spectre of the murdered baronet seems to stand by to prevent me."

"And have you, then, ever thought of suicide, since you first became a prisoner here?" enquired the Blackamoor.

"Often and often, sir—very often," exclaimed Splint, emphatically.

"You never told me this before; and yet I have visited you regularly every evening to bring you food and talk to you for a short time," said the Blackamoor.

"But you never spoke to me so kindly as you do now, sir," cried the criminal, earnestly; "and when a man has been upwards of thirty days—yes, I have counted your visits, and this is the thirty-first,—when a man, I say, has been thirty-one days all alone and in darkness, except for a few minutes every evening, he begins to feel the want of hearing a human voice—and when that voice speaks in a kind manner——"

Timothy Splint's tone had gradually become tremulous; and now he burst into tears. Yes—the villain—the robber—the murderer wept; and those were tears such as he had not shed for a long, long time!

When the river is ice-bound by the cold hand of winter it seems unconscious of the presence of the flower thrown on its impenetrable surface; but when thawed by the warm sun, and flowing naturally again, the stream opens its bosom to receive the rose-bud which it caresses with its sparkling ripples, and wafts gently along as if rejoiced at the companionship. So was it with the heart of this man; and the slightest word spoken in a kind manner was now borne on by the current of feelings thawed from a state of dull and long-enduring obduracy.

"Your crimes are manifold and great," said the Blackamoor; "but there is hope for even the vilest," he added, unable altogether to subdue a profound sigh; "and contrition is all that remains for sinful mortals, who cannot recall the past."

"I *am* penitent, sir—I *am* very penitent, I can assure you," exclaimed the man, in a tone of deep emotion. "A few weeks ago I should have been ashamed to utter such a thing; and now it does me good to say so.—And I'll tell you something more, sir," he continued, after a moment's hesitation; "though I suppose you will not believe me——"

"Speak frankly," said the Blackamoor.

"Well, sir—I have tried to recollect a prayer; and last night when I repeated it, I thought that the spectre gradually grew less and less plain to the view, and at all events seemed less horrible. I was praying again when you came just now—and I shall pray presently—for I know that there is some consolation in it."

"You do well to pray, Timothy," observed the Blackamoor. "Would you not like to be able to read some book?"

"If I only had a candle and a Bible, sir," exclaimed the man, speaking under the influence of feelings deeply excited but unquestionably sincere, "I think I should even yet be happy in this dreadful dungeon."

"What makes you fancy that the Bible would render you happy?" enquired the Black.

"Because I used to read it when I was a lad, and I remember that it contains many good sayings," answered Splint. "Besides, it declares somewhere that there is hope for sinners who repent; and I should like to keep my eyes fixed at times upon God's own promise. I am sure that my mind would be easier; for though I know that the promise *is* given, yet I feel a desire to repeat it over and over again to myself—and also to learn whether God ever forgave any one who was so bad as I am."

"You shall have a light and a book," said the Blackamoor.

"Oh! you are jesting—you are deceiving me!" cried Splint. "But that would be so cruel, sir, on your part——"

"I am not jesting—the subject is too serious to be treated lightly," was the answer: then, making a sign to Wilton to step forward, he took from the basket which that dependant carried, a lamp already trimmed and a couple of books. "There is a volume of Tales—and there is the Bible," he continued: "take whichever you prefer."

"The Bible, if you please, sir," cried Splint, eagerly, while his countenance denoted the most unfeigned joy. "I know not how to thank you enough for this kindness!"—and tears again started from his eyes.

"Had you chosen the Tales, you should not have had either book or light," said the Black.

Wilton now gave the prisoner a plate containing bread and cold meat, and a bottle of water, while Cæsar lighted his lamp; and the door was then again closed upon him.

"That man is already a true penitent," whispered the Blackamoor to Wilton. "Let us now visit his late companion in iniquity."

The party proceeded to the next cell, in which Joshua Pedler was confined, the two armed dependants stationing themselves in such a manner as to be visible to the inmate of the dungeon when the door was opened.

"Thank God! you are come again," he cried, starting up from his bed the moment the light flashed in upon him. "But why do you come with swords and pistols in that fashion?" he demanded, savagely.

"In case you should offer any resistance," answered the Blackamoor. "I do not choose to put chains upon you; and therefore I am compelled to adopt every necessary precaution when I visit you in this manner."

"I really would not harm you, sir—I would not for the world," said Pedler, in a milder tone. "You are not cruel—though severe; and I feel very grateful to you for not giving me up to justice. I hope you are not offended with me for speaking as I did: I try to be patient—I endeavour to be mild and all that——"

"What is it, then, that irritates your temper?" enquired the Blackamoor.

"My own thoughts, sir," answered Josh Pedler, bitterly. "Just before I heard the key grating in the lock, I was a thinking what a fool I have been for so many years, and how happy I might be, perhaps, if I was a labouring-man."

"You are sorry that you have been wicked?" observed the Black, interrogatively.

"And so would any one be when he comes to be locked up here in the dark," returned the man. "It is all very well when one is at liberty, and has friends to talk to, and plenty of drink; because company and gin *can* prevent a body from thinking. But here—here—oh! it is quite different; and my opinion is that a dark dungeon is a much worse punishment than transportation—leastways, judging by all I've heard from men which has been transported and has come home again when their time was up."

"Would you rather be transported at once, then—or remain here?" enquired the Blackamoor.

"I would sooner remain here, for several reasons," said Pedler. "In the first place, I don't want to get into bad company again; because I'm afraid I should go all wrong once more;—and, in the second place, I know that the thoughts which I have are good for me, though they're not pleasant."

"But if you could this minute join some of your old friends to drink and smoke with them, would you not gladly do so?" asked the Black.

"I scarcely know how to answer you, sir," replied Pedler, musing. "I am afraid I might—and yet I am very certain that I should be a fool for my pains. I would sooner earn an honest living somehow or another: I should like to have good thoughts——But that is impossible—impossible!" he added, shaking his head gloomily.

"Why is it impossible?" demanded the Black.

"Because a man to have good thoughts, must do something that is good," was the prompt rejoinder; "and I have been a wicked fellow for so many years. I wish I had been good; but it is too late now!"

"It is never too late to repent," said the Blackamoor.

"I know that the Bible promises that," observed Pedler; "but then people would never believe that a rascal like me could become good for any thing. Besides, after all that has happened, I don't hope for any opportunity of showing that I feel how stupid I have been to lead such a life as I have done. Who would trust me with any work? what honest person would associate with me? It's no use questioning me, sir: you see that even you yourself don't feel comfortable in visiting this place, since you come with armed people."

"If you could obtain your liberty by killing me, would you not do it?" asked the Black.

"As true as you are there, I would not harm a hair of your head!" cried Josh Pedler, emphatically. "I shudder when I think of that dreadful business down at the Cottage yonder—in fact, I can't bear to think of it. I don't say that I am actually afraid at being in the dark; but darkness causes terrible thoughts.

It seems as if the mind had eyes, and couldn't shut them against particular things;—and now that I have found out this much, I should be a long time before I did a wrong deed again, even if I was turned out into the midst of London this very minute without a penny in my pocket."

"What would you do if you were set free this moment?" demanded the Blackamoor. "At the same time, do not suppose that you are about to have your liberty."

"I am not mad enough to fancy it possible," replied Josh Pedler. "But if such a thing did happen, I would go to Matilda—the gal that I spoke to you about, sir——"

"And who is now in a comfortable position," added the Black.

"Yes—thanks to your kindness," said the man; "and I should like you as long as I lived, if it was only on account of what you have done for her. But, as I was going to tell you—supposing I was set free, I would take 'Tilda with me into the country—as far away from London as possible; and then I'd change my name, and try to get work. Ah! I should be happy," he continued, with a profound sigh, "if I could only earn enough to keep us in a little hut. But don't make me talk in this way any longer: I feel just—just as if I—I was going to cry."

The man's voice became faltering and tremulous as he uttered these last words; and his lashes were moistened with tears.

"Should you feel pleasure in writing a letter to Matilda?" asked the Blackamoor, in a kind tone.

"Yes—above all things!" eagerly cried the criminal. "I am no great penman; but she could make out my scribbling, I dare say;—and it would do me good to give her some proper advice—I mean, just to let her know what my thoughts is at times. Besides, now that I'm separated from her, I find that I liked her more—yes—a good deal more than I used to fancy I did; and I should be glad to beg her forgiveness for what I made her do when I was sick and in want."

"You shall have a light and writing-materials," observed the Black.

"You are a good man—I feel that you are, sir!" exclaimed Josh Pedler, the tears now trickling down his cheeks. "If I had only fallen in with such a person as yourself, when I was young, I shouldn't have turned out as I did. But though people may never know that it is possible for a fellow like me to alter, yet altered my mind *is*—and I don't look on things as I used to do."

Wilton gave Josh Pedler a supply of food, a lamp, and writing-materials, the dungeon already containing a table in addition to the other necessary but plain and homely articles of furniture. The criminal was overjoyed at the indulgence shown him on the occasion of this visit: and he saw the door close upon him with feelings which seemed to have experienced a great relief.

END OF VOL. I. OF THE SECOND SERIES.

Milton Keynes UK
Ingram Content Group UK Ltd.
UKHW011122050624
443649UK00006B/487

IMPEI
LUPI

DAYFLY

ADAM BROWNE

Copyright © Adam Browne 2017

Published by Dayfly Publications 2017

Adam Browne asserts the moral right to be identified as the author of this work.

This novel is entirely a work of fiction. The names, characters and incidents portrayed in it are the work of the author's imagination. Any resemblance to actual persons, living or dead, events or localities is entirely coincidental.

All rights reserved. No part of this publication may be reproduced or distributed in any form without the prior permission of the author.

Cover illustration by Mike Nash.
www.mike-nash.com

Interior illustrations by Adam Browne.

Imperium Lupi

For Mum, Dad and the long-suffering Scott

Special thanks to Michael

Giacomo Valerio M-12 *"Springtail"*

Adam Browne

Author's Note

Dear reader. This edition of Imperium Lupi contains a lexicon for your convenience. You may turn to it at your leisure, as every effort has been made to omit any plot particulars that might spoil your enjoyment of the narrative.

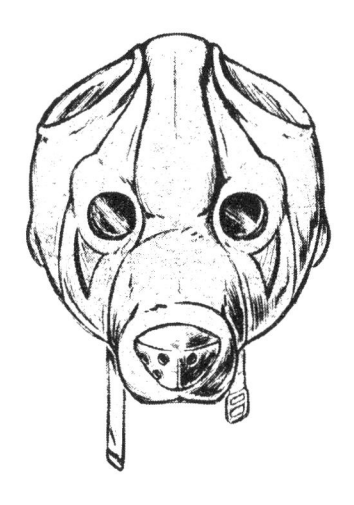

Adam Browne

Live your time as the dayfly that dared, not the nymph who hid in the pond forever.

Giacomo Valerio

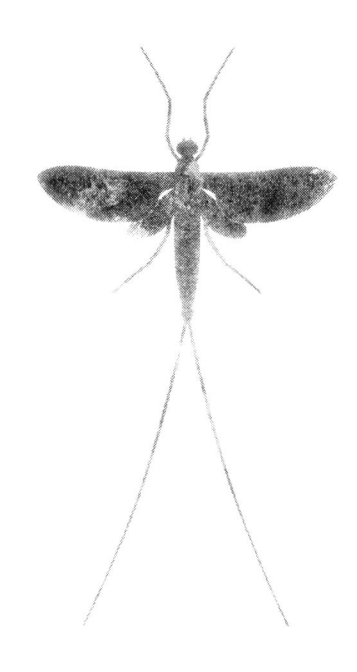

Adam Browne

IMPERIUM LUPI

Contents

Maps	11
Prologue	21
Part I: INDUCTION	23
Part II: EISENWOLF	171
Part III: GELB	311
Part IV: LUPICIDE	445
Part V: BLACK RAIN	569
Epilogue	708
Lexicon	713
Contact Us	723
About the Author	724

Adam Browne

Adam Browne

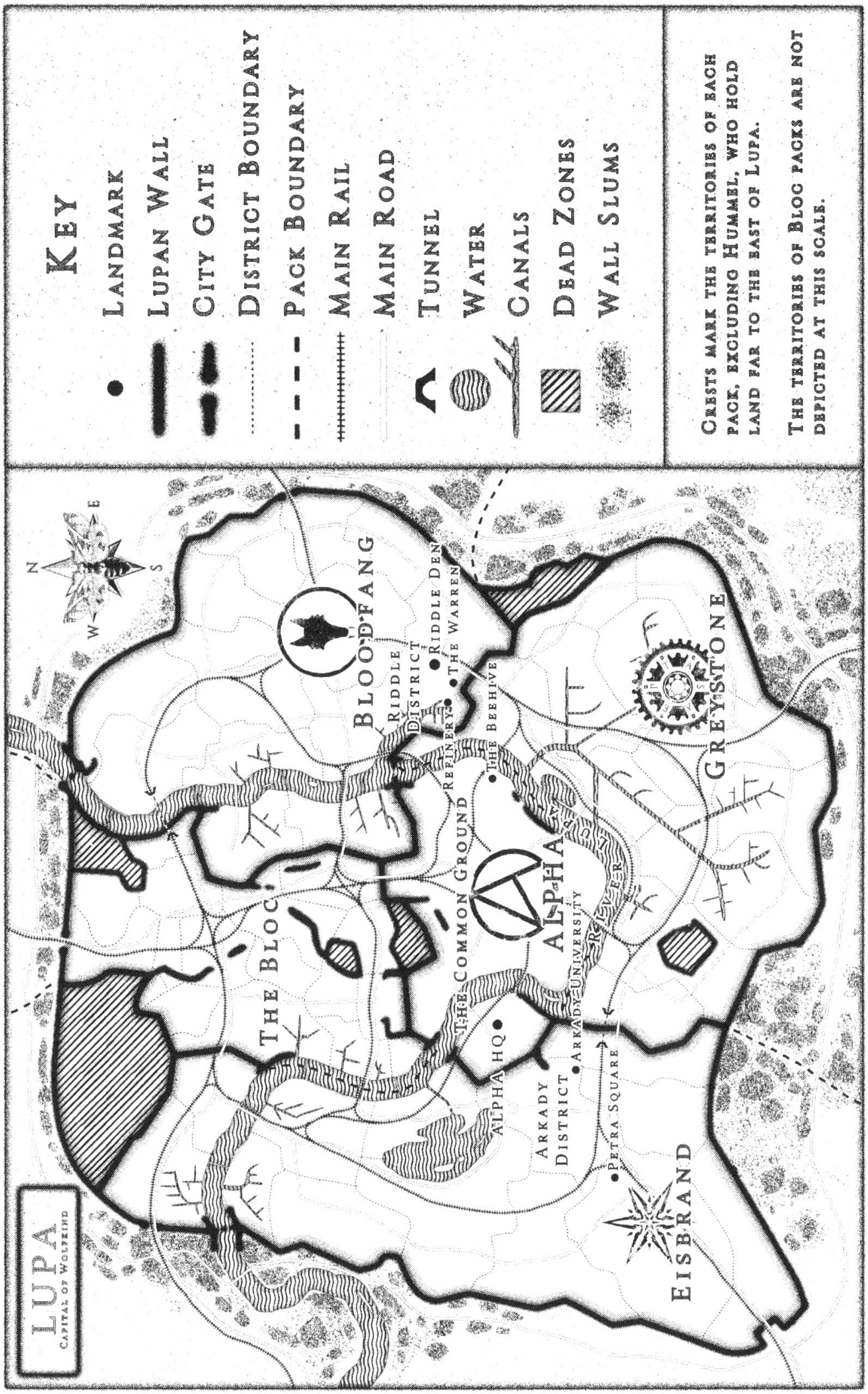

Adam Browne

The Lupine Continent

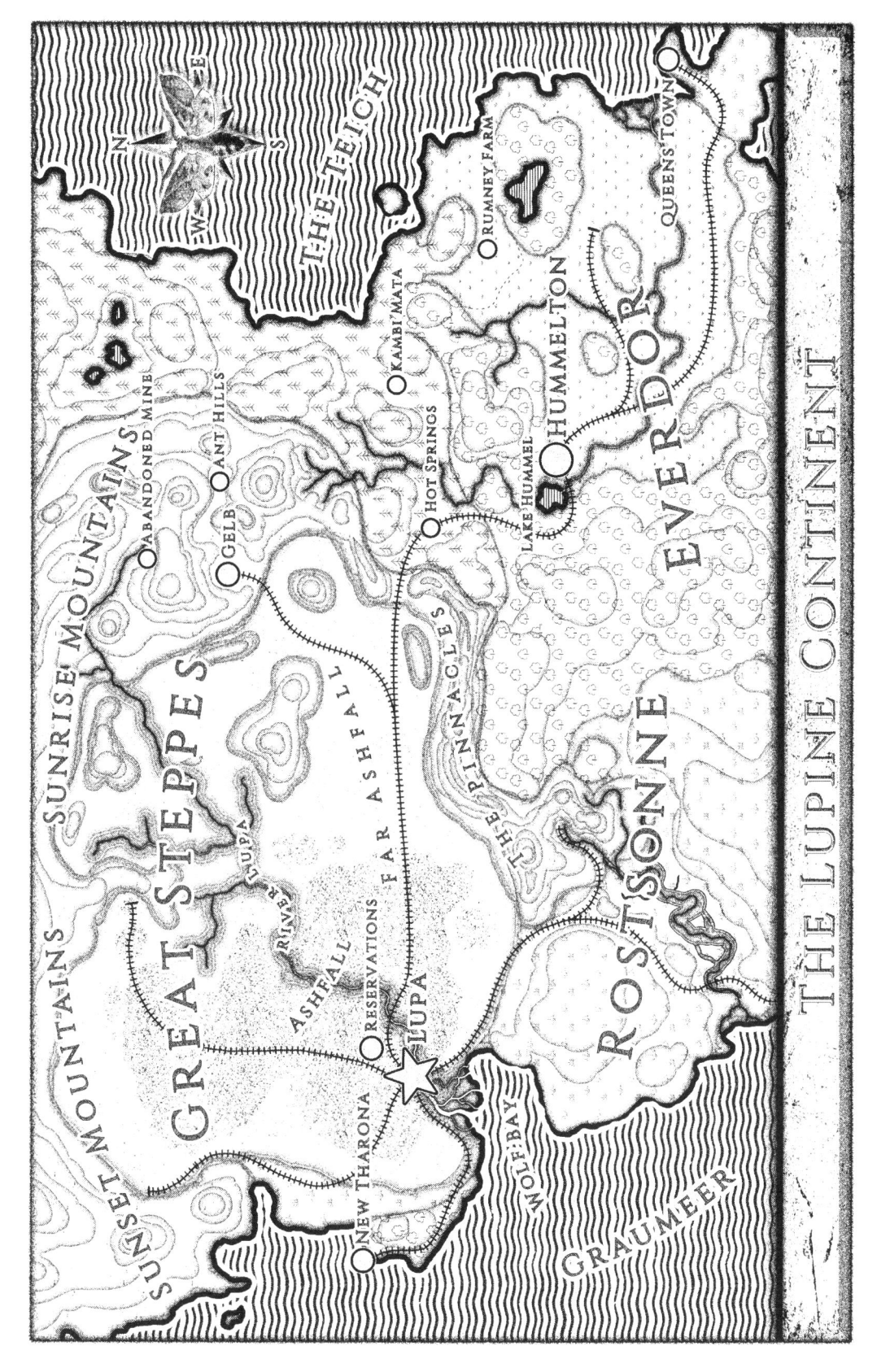

Adam Browne

Imperium Lupi

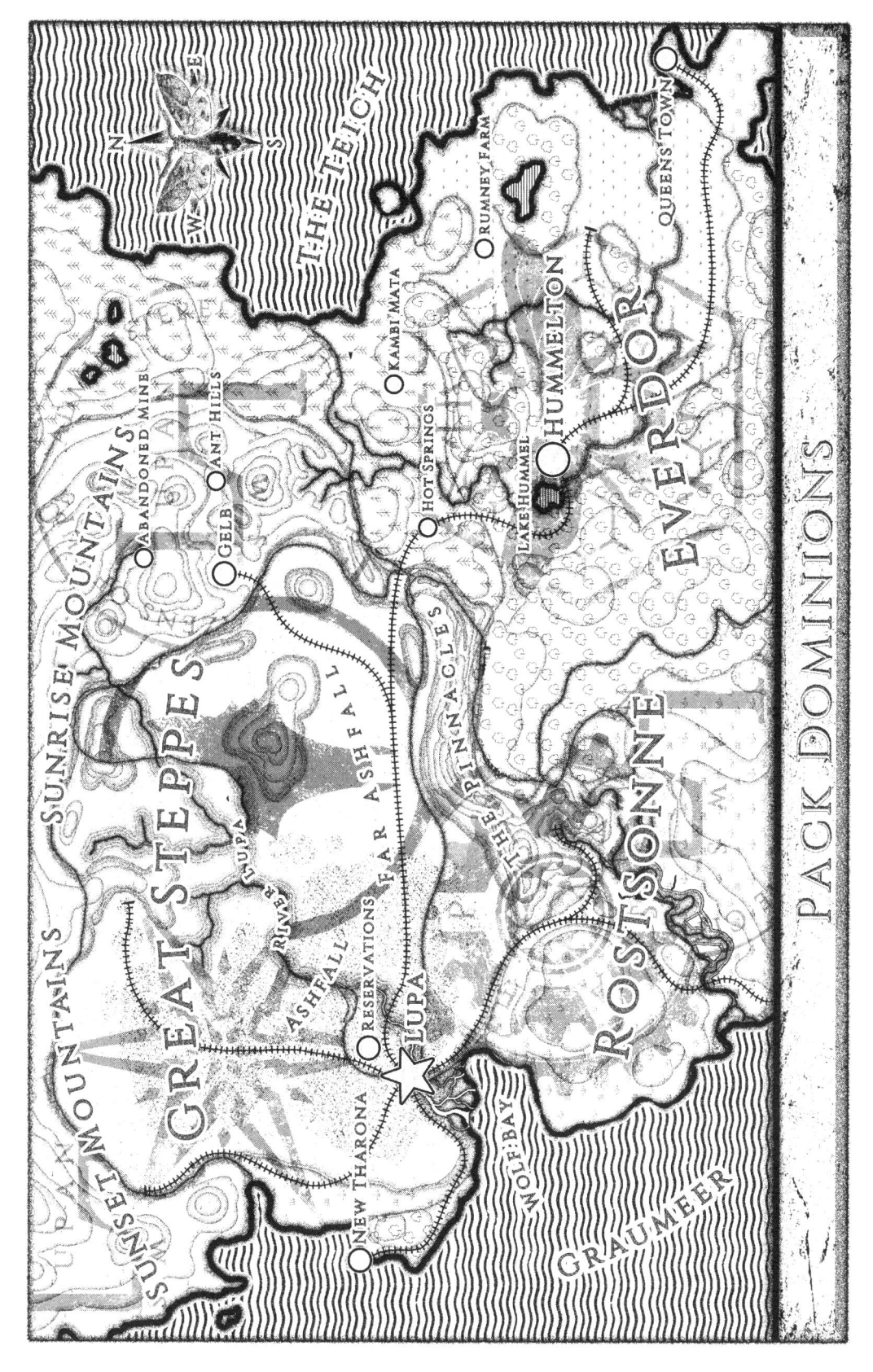

Adam Browne

ELDER CHAMBER NOW IN SESSION

Adam Browne

Prologue: Twelve years Ago

Rain lashed the cobbles and tumbled off the twisted, smouldering ruins of a devastated street, washing ash and paper into Lupa's clogged drains. Another shell roared overhead, slamming into a row of abandoned terraced houses and rending them to dust.

"Schmutz!" a big hog snorted, enveloped in mid-stride by the rolling pall of pulverised brick and mortar. "Casimir!" he coughed, blinded and confused. "Casimir, where you at? Cas!"

"Here, Werner!"

A young white rabbit emerged from the cloud, grabbed the hog's huge, muscled arm and guided him through the choking chaos to the clear.

"You all right?" Casimir asked, setting his helmet straight.

"Yeah," Werner replied, wiping his beady eyes. "You?"

"Aye, fine. I reckon that was the last volley. Come on; the Howlers are gonna be all over the district any minute now they've softened us up."

"Don't need to tell me twice."

Armour and weapons clattering about their frames, hog and rabbit trotted and bounded through the heaps of what was once a happy Lupan street. Bricks, wood, steel and glass, lately ordered into shops, houses and pubs, now lay crushed and jumbled beyond recognition. Occasionally a rotting body broke through the monotonous grey mountains like a strange weed, a rat's tail here, a gaping, eyeless hog face there – Werner tried not to look.

He and Casimir clambered up a mound of unremarkable ruins; whatever it was, it was no more. Upon descending the other side, Werner noticed Casimir's sudden absence. He looked back, sodden chin straps slapping on his jowls, and spied Casimir standing atop the devastation, his face all-a-frown.

"What is it?"

"I can feel something."

Werner cowered, pistol drawn. "Howler?" he seethed.

"Not sure… I…."

Wordlessly, Casimir removed his helmet, sliding it over his long white ears. Taking a sharp breath, the athletic rabbit turned and hopped down the ruins with definite purpose, disappearing from Werner's view.

"Cas!" the hog called. "Cas, what're you doin'?"

"It's down here!"

"What?"

"Just help me!"

Against his better instincts, Werner scrambled over the horrific results of war's recipe book and slid down to where Casimir worked, furiously throwing bricks aside.

"Come on!" the rabbit panted. "He's under here."

Werner eventually joined in, the mighty hog excavating huge chunks of mortar with ease. "He?"

"He, she, I dunno, but its got a corona."

Werner stopped dead. "Then it's gotta be a Howler."

"No. It's too weak, mate, too weak by half."

"We ain't got time, Cas. We gotta go-"

"Keep digging!" the rabbit snapped, rain dripping off his chin.

At length, the grumbling Werner cast aside a broad chunk of plaster, revealing a small hole. Casimir called in, "Hello? Anybody in there? Say something if you can hear me!"

He listened with his sensitive ears.

"Well?" Werner urged.

"Shh shhh!" Casimir hushed.

At considerable length, the rabbit stripped off his backpack and scrabbled head-first into the hole.

"Stay here."

Werner gnarled his thick fingers in frustration. "Casimir, get out of there, it could come down on yer!" He worriedly scanned the ruins. "If I see a Howler I'm leaving you here, I swear. Stupid, thumping, son of a maggot, thinks he's all that with his-"

"Werner!"

"Cas? Cas, where are yer?"

Casimir's white face appeared at the hole. "Here, take him," he said, before shuffling back somewhat and speaking to someone else in a kind, encouraging tone, "Climb out the hole, lad. Go on. Uncle Werner won't hurt yer."

"Uncle?" big Werner snorted, scratching his snout.

A small, quivering, dishevelled beast crawled blinking to the precipice of Lupa's cloudy, wet firmament. His fur and clothes were matted with blood and caked with dust, but his blinking eyes shone even in the overcast daylight like twin embers – a wolf cub and no mistake, perhaps three or four.

"Go on, lad," Casimir urged, hissing at his comrade, "Werner, help him up!"

"Cas… if you can feel him, then-"

"Just take him!"

Rolling his shoulders, Werner reached down and plucked the silent cub from the wreckage, before setting him to once side and standing back, as if he were a ticking bomb.

Casimir extricated himself from the hole, popping forth like a cork from a keg. A moment later and the ground rumbled to a distant explosion. The ruins collapsed further, dust and mortar issuing fourth in jets, choking everyone.

Once the air had cleared, Casimir knelt down and spoke to the cub, "What's yer name, lad?"

The parched cub croaked politely, "Bruno, sir."

"Bruno? I'm Casimir, that's Werner." Casimir doused a hanky with a flask of water and mopped Bruno's face, revealing him to be a rich, chocolaty brown. Smiling for a moment, the rabbit offered the stoical cub his flask. "Where's yer parents, Bruno?"

Wetting his little throat, the cub slowly pointed at the heaps and said simply, "Mummy's not moving anymore."

Casimir dipped his chin, "Aye." Standing up, he took Bruno's tiny paw. "Come on, lad."

Werner's big nostrils flared, "Oi, what're you doing? Just leave him here; the Howlers'll find him."

"Aye, and make him into another one of our oppressors someday!" Casimir scoffed. He spread a paw, "Come on, Werner. He must be from an impartialist family to be living here. We'll take him to HQ and see what can be done."

"But he's afflicted, and bad if you can feel him already!"

"So what're you gonna do, shoot him?"

Silence. Werner looked down at the tiny wolf. "'Course not," he exhaled at last, defeated by those blameless eyes.

"Then we take him," Casimir declared, hefting his backpack and leading Bruno across the grey wastes. "Come on, lad. Don't be scared. Uncle Werner and I will see you right."

Part I
INDUCTION

Adam Browne

Chapter 1

Lupa was a bleak, garbled lattice of bricks and squalor even on the best of days, and positively rancid on such a miserably overcast morning. Streets of decaying houses and towering, ash-belching smokestacks rippled by the drizzle-licked windows as the train trundled through a particularly rough district. The radiant red and white banners marking the border of Bloodfang territory barely stirred Rufus's wolfen heart as they swung into view, for his mind was elsewhere.

Oh for the wilds, the fresh air and open spaces, to study the plants and bugs beyond the confines of Lupa and further wolfkind's knowledge.

One day Rufus, the red-furred wolf convinced himself, as he nursed the file resting on his armoured legs.

"Ticket please."

Hardly hearing for his daydreams, Rufus slowly turned and looked up at the conductor – and kept on looking up, for he was a huge, tusked pig in a blue uniform, complete with cloak and hat. The portly beast was armed with an absurdly small ticket-punch and a truncheon.

"Pardon me, citizen?" Rufus chirped pleasantly.

"I said *ticket*, wolf," the train hog snorted – he was armed with an absurd attitude too.

Maintaining his smile, Rufus pulled the shoulder of his own black cloak round, presenting his brooch – a circular black brooch with a luminous vermillion-red triangle set within, so bright that it injected the conductor's suddenly pale cheeks with some much-needed colour.

"Sorry, Howler!" he excused. "I-I-I didn't think that-"

"You were merely doing your duty, citizen," Howler Rufus assured him. "Though, one could endeavour to go about it with a modicum of cheer, even on such a gloomy day."

"Oh, yes sir. I shall endeavour to do so, sir!"

The hog nervously tipped his hat and vacated the carriage without so much as punching another ticket.

As the swaying train rocked him side to side, Rufus felt a tingle rise up his armoured legs.

Not again. Not now.

The Howler subtly grasped the folds of his waist-length cloak, bracing himself.

Sure enough it came, the pain, rolling through his bones like an icy wave thrashing the rotten scaffold of a pier. Every muscle and sinew in Rufus's powerful arms pressed against his ruddy hide as he suffered in silence.

It passed quickly, with only a dull ache lingering deep down in the marrow of his femurs – they said the legs were the first to go.

The pain subsiding, Rufus leant back into his seat, chest heaving beneath his cloak. He glanced around the dilapidated carriage; his fellow passengers diverted their curious gaze or hid behind newspapers. Little beasts mostly, mice, rats, rabbits, all the lesser races, who wouldn't dare speak to Rufus without being spoken to.

The train slowed and the station panned into view, its fine marbled columns standing proud, each tarnished by the faintly spangled lustre of imperium ash. Rufus reached over and grabbed his helmet from the adjoining threadbare seat. He placed it over his brow; the padded metal hugging his sleek wolfen skull. It was black, save for the cheeks, which were white. Luminous red triangles were set beneath each eye-hole, like that found on Rufus's brooch. Made of the wonder mineral imperium, they glowed even in the muted daylight, and against the helm's white cheeks they resembled two bloodied fangs lying atop freshly fallen snow. The helm's nose was covered by a grille punctured by a dozen round holes that enabled Rufus to breathe. Only his inquisitive green eyes and perky red ears remained visible, endowing him with menacing anonymity.

File in paw, Rufus vacated his seat and made for the nearest exit, leg armour rattling as he walked. He stopped a moment to fasten a stray button on one of the white, knee-high gaiters covering his boots. Satisfied, he opened the carriage door before the train had stopped. The reward for such impatience was a face full of eye-watering ash as the monstrous engine up ahead vented waste imperium. Luckily the helmet's special grille filtered out most of the ash before it got up Rufus's nostrils, not that it would much affect a Howler like him. The induction process had hardened him against such feeble levels of poison long ago.

Pulling the hood of his cloak over his helmet, the Howler braved the rain and strode across the platform towards the station with his usual confident gait. Seeing the trappings of a Howler – cloak, helm, armour – beasts of every sort averted their varied faces even whilst secretly watching, terrified, yet curious.

Rufus remembered the feeling. From the gutters of Lupa he had once observed the mighty Howlers of yesteryear going about their business, taking what they wanted, whenever they wanted, never poor, cold or hungry. How Rufus had envied them, hated them, and yet wished to be one, ignorant cub that he was back then.

Those Howlers were likely all gone now, their bodies decayed from the inside out whilst still living.

Such was the curse of the rot.

Sensing a second twinge brewing in his own contaminated bones, Rufus considered ducking behind the nearest pillar to save himself the indignity of becoming a spectacle. Many citizens secretly desired to see their diseased, parasitic overlords laid low by the very thing that gave them such power.

Any passing sadists were denied their schadenfreude this morning, for the pangs grew into a warm, almost pleasant tingle, not unlike pins and needles – another Howler was near.

Friend or foe? Even in these peaceful times, Rufus took stock. His free paw straying to the rapier slung at his hip, he allowed the ebb and flow of the imperium throbbing in his veins and crackling in his bones to guide him to one of the station's enormous ash-streaked columns.

"It's no good hiding!" he said, apparently challenging an inanimate marble pillar. "Out you come!"

Perhaps reckoning the rot had rendered yet another Howler insane, a passing family of mice gave Rufus an even wider berth than was customary. Had they stayed a moment, they might have been relieved to see a wolf slip out from behind the pillar dressed exactly like Rufus; black mantle, armour, rapier at hip. He was somewhat taller, sporting white ears and piercing blue eyes that shone brightly even in the shadows of his helmet.

"Ivan!" Rufus tutted. "I could've chopped your head off."

"And were I an assassin I could've shot you," Ivan replied, in his rumbling, haughty tenor. He looked to the right, following the departing train with his eyes, then panned back to Rufus again. "You've a perfectly good monobike at your disposal, yet still you ride the rails with the dregs of Lupa," he scolded. "It wouldn't take much for someone to lie in wait for you."

Rufus leant forward slightly, paws and file cupped behind his back. "Next time you're trying to make a point," he said, "try dampening your imperium corona like a real assassin would so I don't feel you halfway across Lupa-"

"I wasn't trying to do anything. Except keep dry."

"Really? Well, I hope you didn't have to wait too long in this rancid drizzle."

"Is a minute long?" Ivan snorted brusquely. "You hop on the same train whenever you stay over at Professor Heath's place. You're excruciatingly predictable."

Rufus raised a finger, "Punctual."

"Just take precautions. Change your route. Take a taxi."

"Oh, but who'd want to do me in?"

"There's always someone when you're a Howler, and you're not just any Howler. You're a little beast-loving impartialist who's banged up more hard criminals than I've had hot meals. You infuriate authority and delinquent alike."

Chuckling throughout Ivan's tirade, Rufus reached up and adjusted the taller wolf's brooch and cloak as if nought but a cub were hiding under that imposing Howler getup.

"Ivan, if I've taught you anything, I hope it's that there's more to life than constantly eluding death," Rufus said, his warm, crackly voice effortlessly overcoming the rain and hubbub. "Live as the dayfly that dared," he instructed, "not the nymph who lurked in the pond forever."

The snowy Ivan brushed away Rufus's ruddy paws. "And what of the carefree grasshopper who fiddled all summer long whilst the prudent ants stored grain for winter. What became of him?"

Rufus beamed, "The ants took pity on him and invited him inside their nest, whereupon he regaled them all winter long."

"That's not the version I'm familiar with."

Slapping Ivan on the shoulder with his rather damp, limp-looking file, Rufus tutted, "That's because beneath that hot Bloodfang exterior you're still a cold-hearted Eisbrand. Come on, a cup of tea'll warm you through."

"Tea?"

"Yes. I dunno about you, but I'm gasping."

Rufus marched purposefully towards the grand station foyer, file in paw.

Ivan stayed put. "What about your hearing with the Elders?" he pointed out, barely turning his masked face as Rufus passed him by. "They're convening at half-seven."

"Oh they can wait five minutes to reject my proposals for another year," Rufus sighed, flapping his folder about. "Which they will."

Ivan caught up with his partner. "They will if you're late." he said, walking beside him.

"They will have decided long before I arrive."

"Still, it can't hurt your chances for next time if you're punctual this time."

Rufus took a golden pocket watch from inside his cloak, "I'll be punctual; I'll be precisely five minutes late."

"Just to irritate them?" Ivan scoffed.

"Humble them. There's a difference."

"You'll be the one humbled by the time Amael gets through with you. Embarrassing him in front of Den Father Vito... again."

Rufus shrugged. "Anyway," he said anew, slapping Ivan on the shoulder with his papers, "I can't very well put forth our proposals on an empty stomach. The very idea!"

"Food as well? I hope you're paying."

"Stinginess; another Eisbrand trait I thought I'd beaten out of you by now."

"Wait," Ivan realised, "did you say 'our' proposals?"

"Professor Heath and I," Rufus clarified, giving him a sideways look and smile. "Not you, Blade-dancer."

"Good! I don't want my name attached to your mad schemes."

"You've a mighty high opinion of yourself this morning, haven't you?" Rufus rebuked, slapping Ivan with his file yet again, on the head this time, betwixt his white ears.

"Will you stop hitting me with that thing?"

"When you stop being a bore."

The pair breezed through the splendid marbled station, past ticket gates and train hogs, before stepping out onto the broad street beyond with the impunity and freedom afforded Howlers. The rain had died down, but the great industrial machine that was Lupa forever chugged along indifferent to all weathers. Pedestrians of every race, though little beasts in the main, walked to work or to the shops, whilst colourful motor cars big and small ambled along the road on their tremulous wheels belching imperious ash in their wake.

Standing atop of the splaying stairway spilling from the station, Rufus announced, "Since we're about breakfast we'll go to that new place I've been meaning to show you."

Starting down the stairs, Ivan snorted, "New place?"

Rufus followed, "Yes, you know, that licensed café I was telling you about the other day. Remember?"

"No."

"Must've been Uther," Rufus tutted. "Charming little joint; popped up right on HQ's doorstep. Run by a rabbit and his son. Remarkable chap, the son; grills the finest waffles this side of Lupa."

Ivan huffed, "I don't much care for waffles."

"Nor I, actually," Rufus mumbled.

"What?"

"Nothing. Come on."

At the bottom of the sprawling stairs, Ivan peeled away from Rufus, keys jangling in paw, and found his monobike parked by the road – and a fine machine it was too, its large, singular wheel housed seamlessly under a chunky, polished black chassis marked on the flank with a small white spider motif.

Brushing globules of rainwater from the seat, Ivan threw an armoured leg over his marvellous bike, inserted the keys, and started it up with a kick of the pedal. Amidst a loud bang and several ear-thumping pops, imperium ash exploded forth from the exhaust in grey, yet slightly glittery clouds. The inside rim of the bike's lone, broad wheel nestled between Ivan's legs lit up in a bright ring of white as the imperium-laced gyroscope came to life. The bike rose up a little and righted itself, like a metallic beetle awakening from hibernation.

Easing himself into the thigh-hugging seat, Ivan looked behind for Rufus – the red wolf stood aloof, arms folded.

"Come on then," Ivan said, patting the back of the seat; a big monobike like his could accommodate two.

"You're driving are you?" Rufus hummed.

"It's my bike," Ivan contended.

"Yes, but I know the way. Don't worry, I'll be gentle with her."

With a grunt, Ivan shuffled backwards and Rufus all too eagerly plonked himself in front. The bike slumped appreciably under their combined weight.

Rufus passed his file over his shoulder to Ivan. "Keep it dry will you?"

Grumbling, Ivan tucked the soggy papers inside his cloak and hugged Rufus around the waist, though not before contemptuously brushing aside his grey-tipped red tail.

Rufus grasped the steering bars, kicked away the stand with his gaitered boot, and twisted the accelerator. The black chassis trembled violently, its singular wheel burning rubber for an instant, before gripping the wet cobbles. With a snap of plasma, monobike and wolfen riders were thrust out onto the road.

The whole ensemble, beasts and bike, reared dangerously backwards, before the gyroscope compensated and righted everything.

"Careful!" Ivan shouted over the thundering engine and wind.

"Hahahaha!"

The amused Rufus should have stayed on the main road to get to what he had earlier called 'HQ', that black pile of towers and walkways looming over the whole district, red and white wolf skull banners drooping in the drizzle. Good to his word, however, he forwent home and leant hard to the left, swaying monobike and riders into an adjoining street.

Houses, shops and beasts cowering beneath umbrellas whizzed by on either side as Rufus and Ivan careened down Lupa's snaking backstreets, black mantles fluttering about their powerful wolfen bodies. With each twist the road ahead grew narrower, the walls closing in on either side like a ghastly booby trap. The skilful Rufus had little difficulty navigating even right-angle turns, for a monobike could swivel on a penny if going slow enough – most advantageous in a city like Lupa. But slow wasn't Rufus's style, who instead leant at crazy angles, applying shocking g-forces to Ivan and his precious mono.

All this, yet the bike's solitary wheel had no mechanical steering whatever. The steering bars were just a conduit between machine and rider. No normal beast could control a mono, only a Howler, or an equivalent imperium-wielder trained to bend the mineral to his or her will. None but they could make the imperium gyroscope within twist and lean appropriately, and so balance and guide the machine to any useful purpose.

Doing so with aplomb, Rufus slowed to a controlled halt in an unremarkable street.

"Here we are," he announced, kicking out the stand and shutting the quivering mono down. The white ring running around the wheel faded and the whole machine settled to sleep. "She feels a little out of tune; you might want to tweak her gyro."

Ivan couldn't leap off quickly enough to check the bodywork for scratches. "More likely *you're* the one out of tune."

"Nonsense," Rufus woofed. "These bikes were invented by my ancestor; if anyone's going to ride them properly it's a Valerio." He held out a paw, "File?"

Not even looking up from his bike, Ivan held the crinkled papers aloft with an annoyed snort.

Leaving Ivan with his baby, Rufus marched straight down the cobbled street and into a dodgy-looking passage with all the pluck of beast who knew nobody with any sense would mess with him.

Satisfied his bike was in one piece, Ivan hurried after Rufus whilst maintaining all dignity, fastidiously avoiding the polluted puddles of water that his partner traipsed carelessly through, thus keeping his pristine white gaiters just so.

Ivan looked this way and that, checking the shadows; Rufus strolled along without a care, as if mocking Ivan's paranoia.

"What's so remarkable about him then?" Ivan asked, catching up to his partner as they traversed the brickwork labyrinth of Lupa.

"Who?"

"The cook."

"Well, it's not his waffles," Rufus admitted, suddenly veering off to the left and pushing open a door, causing a bell to ring. "Try not to stare."

"Stare?" Ivan scoffed in disbelief, "At a rabbit?"

Rufus laughed and disappeared inside, whilst Ivan stepped back to take in the establishment's façade, with its crooked bay window and brand-new sign stencilled in fresh red and white paint.

THE WARREN.

Chapter 2

Ivan entered *The Warren* under the ring of the customer bell and the curious gaze of some questionable patrons. The pokey eatery was dark, the gnarled, yet shiny tables illuminated by overhead imperium lamps burning a warm white. There came a rare flicker of colour from said lamps, red, blue, even green, as imperium gas in various states of decay worked its way through Lupa's ancient piping. The café's creamy walls were cracked and the wooden beams overhead worryingly, or to an estate agent 'charmingly', crooked.

"Looks a dive," Ivan pronounced.

"Oh shush," Rufus tutted, pulling back his rain-flecked hood and removing his helmet.

A white rabbit in a black apron emerged from the dingy corners – what passed for the waiter in this dump, Ivan could only assume. At least the fellow made an effort, with a frilly shirt and red bow-tie.

"Good morning, Rufus," the rabbit chirped, giving the still masked and hooded Ivan a nervous glance.

Rufus adopted a chipper smile. "Casimir," he said. "How're you this fine Lupan morning?"

"Fine indeed!" the rabbit laughed gruffly. He glanced at the ornate clock on the wall and dared, "This is early for you. Don't tell me you're actually working for a living?"

"I have been known," Rufus joked back. "I'm on my way to an important meeting at HQ, actually." He gave Ivan a glance, then said, "Thought we'd have a bite to eat first, if that's not too much trouble."

"By all means. Usual table?"

"Please."

Casimir led the Howlers over to the bay window and quickly wiped down a table. As they walked, Rufus searched the café for someone.

"Bruno round back?"

Casimir shook his head, his long white ears flapping. "He's in bed, I'm afraid."

"Bed? He's up with the bees, usually."

"He's got a bad chest," Casimir murmured, tapping his own. "Yesterday's smog 'en all."

Rufus winced from disappointment. "Oh dear, what a pity," he seethed. "I was going to introduce Ivan here to Bruno's famous three-season waffles, wasn't I Ivan?"

No reply from Ivan.

Casimir waved a paw, "I can whip 'em up for you."

"Sorry, Casimir, but it's just not the same," Rufus sighed, fussing with his cloak. He slapped Ivan on the chest with his file. "Looks like we'll just have to come back another time, Ivan. I know you were so looking forward to it."

This time Ivan rolled his eyes, at least.

Faced with a loss of earnings, Casimir changed tune, "Hang on, hang on, how about I go tell Bruno you're here? It's been a few hours, he might be feeling better-"

"Could you?" Rufus said, all too fast.

"No promises, though."

"Whatever's best for Bruno, Casimir. We can come back tomorrow."

Nodding, the rabbit hurried up the creaky stairs, bob-tail flashing, whilst the wolves took their seats.

Rufus set his helmet on the tabletop, the red fang decoration beneath each eye slowly fading as the imperium left a Howler's influence, or corona. Ivan followed suit, revealing that handsome white-furred face; well Rufus thought it handsome. Wolves were usually two or three colours, Rufus himself was grey on his chest and muzzle and red elsewhere, but Ivan was a uniform white; rare even for the notoriously beautiful Eisbrands.

Like most Eisbrands, Ivan's family, the Donskoys, had originated on the Great Steppes, that vast northern tundra where summer was unbearably hot and winter fatally cold. Even before the

Ashfall it had been a hard country. Ivan himself had been raised in Lupa and orphaned during the war. Upon contracting the rot he had gone to the Eisbrand Pack with only his respected Donskoy name, determined to complete their rigorous Howlership and earn his keep. After induction and graduation, he had been anointed Ivan 'Eisbrand' Donskoy, adopting the name and traditions of the pack, and beginning his career, roaming the streets, maintaining order, and quickly earning a reputation as an exceptional Howler.

Ivan had shown his gratitude to his Eisbrand benefactors by switching allegiance to the Bloodfangs for reasons wolves still guessed at; adventure, pay, companionship, to this day even Rufus wasn't quite sure, but was glad to have him.

Still admiring Ivan, Rufus chucked his crumpled file on the table and delved into the neck of his black cloak, reaching for the inside breast pocket. Taking out a small silver case he flipped it open. Inside were a dozen colourful sticks arranged in a neat rainbow, from red to green to indigo, like so many crayons.

Rufus offered them to Ivan, "Ember?"

The white wolf glowered disapprovingly back, those icy blue eyes unmoved by the warm glow of the nearby imperium lamp.

"Oh yes," Rufus tutted, withdrawing the embers, "you've quit smouldering." He took the red ember, broke the end off and popped it between his lips. It immediately began to glow of its own accord, releasing heady vapours – strawberry.

Whiffing the noxious cocktail of ash, flavourings and even painkillers, Ivan said, "So should you."

"It's a noble effort on your part," Rufus said, red clouds erupting from his mouth, "but I'm past help."

"Don't be absurd."

"D'you know I was aching on the train just now. You complain I don't ride. Well there it is, monos wear me out. You're right, I am out of tune... and out of time."

"You've got decades yet."

Rufus hiked his eyebrows, licked a finger and began to leaf through his crumpled folder. "My dear Ivan, I should be on twice the venom I am to maintain my vague usefulness," he said, the glowing ember wobbling between his lips. "I was all right before they cut our ration again."

"This shortage will pass. They'll find a new white-imperium mine, they always do. You should quit Lupa for a bit. Take the air on the Graumeer, or down Everdor. You're due heaps of leave."

Rufus smiled from ear to ruddy, grey-flecked ear.

"What?" Ivan grunted, shuffling.

"I'm touched, that's all," Rufus chirped back. "First assassins and now health advice. It's almost like you want me sticking around."

"I do."

"Really?"

"Yes! When you snuff it they'll lump me with another partner, some wet-eared cub who actually turns up for work. I'll lose my independence. Think of that before you smoulder yourself into an early grave, Valerio."

Rufus broke into hoarse laughter, clouds of red breath steaming from every viable orifice. Some burly customers of many races sitting at the next table, road workers judging by their attire, quickly paid their bill and left in a hurry without finishing their breakfast, whilst a massive muscular hog walked in, spied the unsmiling Ivan, and performed a none-too-subtle about-face.

"You're bad for business, Donskoy," Rufus tutted, as the hog trotted past the bay window in search of somewhere that didn't harbour Howlers. "Start smiling, or you'll bankrupt Casimir's fine establishment before you even sink your fangs into one of his son's waffles."

Ivan adjusted his cloak and leant forward, "Yes. Only he's not his 'son', is he?"

Rufus played dumb, "Hmm?"

"Bruno, is it?" Ivan pressed, the name sticking to his tongue out of jealously, Rufus felt certain. "He's no rabbit; he's a wolf, and a handsome one I don't doubt."

Grinning, Rufus took a draught of vapour and blew it over his head.

"Afflicted too?" Ivan growled.

Before Rufus could admit to anything, if he even had the intention, Casimir ambled down the stairwell with a noticeable limp, Ivan observed.

"Bruno'll be right with you," the white rabbit informed the wolves. "The rain has cleared the air for him. This drizzle has its upside, I suppose."

"Marvellous, you're a star, Casimir," Rufus declared.

Casimir wasn't so enthused. "My son is," he grunted soberly. He stared at Rufus, particularly the smouldering ember between his fingers, before saying, "Now, what can I get you two gentlebeasts to drink?"

Rufus winked, "Hummel tea, please."

The rabbit turned to Ivan, "And yourself, sir?"

"The same, citizen."

Nodding, Casimir took his leave and disappeared into the kitchen to see about the tea.

There was a quiet moment. Rufus studied his file, no doubt mentally rehearsing his pitch to the Bloodfang Elders, whilst Ivan studied Rufus, sitting there, unassumingly puffing on his ember.

It was perhaps some twenty-five years ago now that a starving, orphaned Rufus Valerio had been discovered picking through bins for edible gleanings by a Bloodfang talent scout; Ivan hadn't even been born at the time. After undergoing a painful induction and enrolling in the Bloodfang Academy, young Valerio had set out like any other Howler. Unlike almost every other Howler, he had exercised both mind and body, finding time to read imperiology and philosophy at the famous Arkady University. Socialising amongst the academics of Lupa, many of them daring, liberal types, Rufus had developed some fanciful ideas, harbouring not only sympathy for the little beasts, but advocating true universal equality – what was known as Impartialism. Worse, Rufus was widely mocked as a 'hyena-lover' for his compassionate stance towards the lately conquered hyena tribes.

It was not a good look for a Howler, all in.

Ivan's thoughts were dashed by a loud creak on the stairs; a big, dark wolf was descending from the above floor, stooping to fit through a gap meant for lesser beasts. He was wearing an off-white tunic and baggy black breeches with knee-high white silk gaiters.

"I knew it," Ivan said.

"Behave yourself," Rufus hushed.

Casimir's giant wolfen 'son' picked his way through *The Warren* and approached Rufus and Ivan without trepidation. He stood with his paws behind his back, his warm face full of smiles. His thick chest and smooth, chocolaty-furred arms bulged with muscles, and he was possessed of extraordinary fiery-orange eyes, like two smouldering charcoals.

"Good morning, Howler Rufus," he greeted cheerily, in a profound yet young and airy tone.

"Good morning, Bruno," Howler Rufus crackled, exhaling strawberry vapour and looking knowingly across to Ivan.

The white wolf was staring.

Kicking Ivan's gaitered shins under the table, Rufus did the honours, "Bruno, this is my partner and dear friend, Ivan Donskoy."

Bruno extended a big, dark brown paw, "Pleasure, Howler."

Ivan, eventually, cleared his throat, crossed his legs and nodded but once, "Citizen."

He conspicuously did not extend a paw.

Rufus growled, "Please excuse Ivan's rudeness. He's a terrible bore sometimes."

Bruno slowly withdrew his paw and shrugged his muscled shoulders. "Well, I know my size can be intimidating," he suggested cheekily, adding, "Maybe a three-season waffle will break the ice, yeah?"

Laughing at Bruno's gall, Rufus wagged his smouldering ember at him. "My thoughts exactly!" he agreed, venting imperium like the very mono that had ferried him here.

With red clouds swirling around his face, Bruno turned away and sneezed loudly into his cupped paws.

"A-aaaa-achoo!"

"Oh, Bruno!" Rufus gasped. He stood up, opened a window and flicked his ember out onto the street, where it proceeded to fizzle in a puddle. "I'm so sorry, I completely forgot!"

He patted Bruno on his vast back.

The youth rubbed his watery eyes. "It's all right, sir," he coughed. "No 'arm done."

"No, it was utterly thoughtless of me, especially since you've been ill. Forgive me."

"Really. Forget it."

Ivan noticed Casimir wiping down tables in a pretence of business, whilst listening to the goings-on with those great white rabbit ears.

Bruno hiked a thumb over his shoulder. "I'm fine, sir," he said, sounding suddenly bunged-up. "I'll, uh… go whib up a couble of waffles, yeah?"

"That'd be splendid," Rufus declared, looking at Ivan and saying with intent, "Wouldn't it Ivan?"

"Oh, splendid," Ivan agreed, with a tinge of sarcasm.

Coughing a little, Bruno headed into the kitchen, donning an apron as he went. Ivan watched Casimir predictably finish up wiping a table and follow his son into the kitchens, whereupon they exchanged heated whispers. Ivan couldn't make out what they were saying.

Rufus initiated his own whispers. "Well?" he urged, leaning across the table, his face alight with excitement.

"Well what?" Ivan said, as if he didn't know.

"Stunning, eh?"

Ivan turned his icy gaze, "Have you no shame?"

Rufus spread his paws. "You saw him!" he woofed, before lowering his tone. "No, you *felt* him. Don't tell me you didn't sense his corona. Your face was a picture."

Ivan shifted in his seat, but said nothing.

"Apparently, he dabbles in boxing," Rufus added.

"A rabbit pastime," Ivan derided.

"Indeed. Still, a body like that's not natural in a wolf his age."

"Dodger then?"

Rufus shook his head, "Doesn't seem the sort. Besides, he's still allergic to ash. If he was a dodger he'd be smouldering embers between stings; he'd be accustomed to them."

Ivan begrudgingly admitted, "But his corona's strong."

"He may have been exposed to imperium somehow without his knowledge; accidents happen. Or he's just exceptionally prone to natural uptake. Either way he's not just another Howler, he's exceptional… perhaps the most exceptional."

"You're not suggesting he's a pure-blood?"

A raised brow, a spread paw.

"Oh Rufus, they're rarer than worms teeth!" Ivan scoffed.

"Nowadays, but Bruno's fifteen or sixteen; he doesn't quite know himself. Still, that'd put his birth in the middle of the war, and some years before the Lupan Laws were amended to exclude Howler marriages. He could be among the last wave of cubs legally and openly born to two Howlers."

"Then how's he gone this long without being noticed?"

"Being a war orphan he's off the records, my dear Ivan. His parents are long-forgotten, even to him. The good Citizen Casimir gave him his own surname; Claybourne."

Ivan had to concede a grumbling, "Mm."

"In any case, Bruno needs to be inducted... and soon. As you say, his condition is a death sentence."

"You're going to bring him in?" Ivan huffed.

"Naturally," Rufus replied. "What do you suggest, let him prowl the streets looking for black-market stings?"

"No, I 'suggest' you urge him to move to Everdor. Out from under the Ashfall he'll get no worse and live a fairly long life."

Rufus dismissed the notion, "He's too far gone. He'll last longer as a Howler than not."

"Even on our meagre sting rations? He'll rot like all the rest of the old, unwanted pure-bloods! You only just about cope yourself."

No reply.

Defeated, Ivan closed the matter down. "Fine, you're the imperiologist, Rufus, not I!" He leant back in his chair, "But be it on your head when Josef has to put him down."

"I was right about Uther, wasn't I?" Rufus chirped. "Wolves said he was too hungry, now look at him. Magnificent."

"No, Den Father Vito was right about him," Ivan corrected acerbically, "you just 'intervened', and look how grateful he's been ever since."

"I didn't do it for gratitude."

"Did you not?"

Rufus scowled, ears low, but before he could speak Casimir emerged from the kitchens, tray in paws, bearing a pot of tea, two rough stoneware teacups and a tiny pot of honey. Whilst the rabbit set them down on the table Rufus chatted away like an old friend, as friendly with him as he had been towards Bruno. From this cordiality, Ivan deduced Rufus must have been coming here for a while, scoping out the talent. Now all he need do was get Bruno to sign away his freedom before another Howler nabbed him.

Ivan knew that nothing he said or did would alter the situation. Bruno was doomed.

"Isn't that right, Ivan?"

Ivan looked up from pouring his tea. "What?"

"See? Miles away," Rufus told Casimir, grabbing the pot and pouring himself a cup. "Away with the butterflies. I can't take him anywhere these days."

"It's a mutual affliction," Ivan countered.

Casimir laughed a little, but no doubt not wishing to upset either Howler, mediated, "I'm sure he was thinking of some lovely girl, Rufus."

Rufus almost choked on his tea.

Fortunately, a timely interruption arrived in chef form. "Here's your three-season waffles," Bruno declared proudly, swooping into the room with two dishes in one vast paw and condiments dwarfed the other.

Rufus checked the old clock behind the bar, "That was quick."

"You're my first customers," Bruno explained, deftly setting down the meals as the Howlers cleared their helmets from the table. He added modestly, "Anyway, it's just pouring batter on a waffle iron; nothing complicated."

Picking up a fork, Ivan prodded his fancy-looking waffle as if inspecting a squashed beetle. It was topped with roasted nuts, fresh fruit and with some kind of sticky gloop Ivan couldn't for the life of him identify.

"What's this?" he asked bleakly, swiping his finger through the red sauce like blood at a crime scene

"Secret sauce, Howler," Bruno claimed proudly, thumbs tucked into his apron straps.

"Patent pending, "Casimir joked.

Someone called from the dark corners of the café, "*Oi, can we get some service over here, please!*"

Casimir excused himself to wait on his few remaining customers, which he had neglected in favour of the illustrious Howlers – no sensible proprietor could do otherwise.

Bruno turned to watch his father go, but stayed put. The young cook was alone with the Howlers.

Rufus pounced. "Tell me, Bruno," he began, without even looking up from his waffles, "have you ever considered working for the Bloodfangs?"

"Bloodfangs?" the youngster laughed. "Doing what?"

"Well, you'd make a fine Politzi Constable, what with all those muscles."

Bruno scratched the back of his neck. "Me, a Politzi?" he guffawed. "Nah, I'm too easy-going, sir."

"Nonsense," Rufus crackled warmly.

Ivan picked silently at his food, watching and listening as Rufus spun his silken trap.

"This is awfully good," the red wolf praised, pointing at Bruno's speciality dish with his fork. "You should come along one day and have a look around Riddle Den. I'll give you a guided tour."

Bruno scratched his head, "I'd love to, sir, but... uh...."

"But what?"

"Well... uhm...."

"Look, you don't have to be afraid," Rufus interrupted in his gravely voice, glancing over at Casimir to check he was still occupied. "I'm here to help you."

Ivan emitted a scoff – it had begun.

"Help me?" Bruno said, anxiously wringing his apron with both big, brown paws. "Whatcha mean?"

Rufus's voice lowered, "Come now, do you think I don't know? That I can't tell? My dear Bruno, I can feel you from across the street." He continued to eat, "Getting pains in your legs yet?"

Surprised, Bruno timidly admitted, "Yeah, sometimes."

"I bet. Excruciating business. I get it all the time, often at a most inopportune moment. Classic symptom of the rot."

"Rot?"

"I'm afraid so, yes."

Seeing at last what Rufus was implying, Bruno woofed, "Aww, no, I've not got rot, sir." He thumbed his mighty chest, "I'm allergic to imperium ash, is all."

Ivan and Rufus exchanged incredulous looks.

"The doctor said so," Bruno claimed, reading their disbelief. "I got a certificate of health; you know, to stop Howler talent scouts pestering me. Not that you are, sir, but-"

Rufus interrupted Bruno's nervous rambling, "What doctor is this?"

"I dunno, sir."

"Well was he a qualified imperiologist?"

"Pff! I dunno, it was ages ago," Bruno said with a nonchalant guffaw. "I was just a cub. I remember he was a cat in a white coat. I can ask dad-"

"Well, I *am* an imperiologist," Rufus said pompously, putting down his knife and fork, "and what's more a Howler, and you're sick, Bruno. Very sick. You need imperium."

Silence.

Bruno's confidence gave way to creeping fear, "But... but I've never worked with imperium. I stay away from it on account of my bad chest."

"Very wise," Rufus said. "Even so, you've been ingesting it by accident ever since you were born. We all do, every day. It's everywhere; in the air, the water; even your fine waffle batter."

Bruno looked hard at the half-eaten waffles, as if he might glimpse the glittering trace of imperium.

Rufus caught sight of Casimir. It appeared the white rabbit was coming back, but he instead gave Rufus a friendly nod in passing to the kitchen. Smiling disarmingly back, Rufus waited for Casimir to disappear before quietly lecturing with his son in imperious science.

"You probably know that exposure to small amounts of imperium does nothing to most beasts," he said, pointing at Bruno. "But you're different. You're one of us."

"You mean-"

"Afflicted, yes, a Howler, if you will."

Bruno let out a sharp breath, "But I-I can't be."

Rufus didn't argue, only stated, "Our muscles are able to metabolise imperium, which makes them stronger and faster than those of healthy folk." The Howler looked Bruno over, raising an eyebrow and flattering, "You're the size of a house, I suspect you've noticed."

That made Bruno smile again, just a little; Ivan on the other paw rolled his eyes as Rufus continued browbeating his ignorant victim with science.

"The imperium in our bodies is what gives us Howlers power," the imperiologist went on, enjoying his role as the wellspring of knowledge, "but there's a price. Whenever it's burnt, whether it be in a car, a train, or our muscles, imperium of all colours decays into imperium ash. It's bad enough when it clogs Lupa's air, but when it fouls our bodies up it causes great pain… as well you know."

Bruno gulped audibly.

"The liver and kidneys deal with most of it within a few hours and we get better," Rufus added cheerfully, before immediately fading again. "However, a tiny fraction of the ash is fully-decayed imperium."

"Black-imperium?" Bruno all but mouthed.

Rufus nodded. "The body doesn't have the plumbing to excrete black-imperium," he said, arms folding on the waxy, pitted tabletop. "It remains within us and starts attacking our flesh, causing localised necrosis – eyes, heart, brain, bits of us start to die."

Ivan silently ate his breakfast throughout Rufus's lecture, as if the weighty subject were of no consequence to him.

Valerio continued, "The body is clever though, and it locks the black-imperium away in our bones, which are made of minerals that do not rot, at least not very quickly." A sigh, "But slowly the poison builds up, more and more, like a terrible secret we should've told someone long ago. Eventually the strain overwhelms our valiant biological countermeasures and we… succumb."

Bruno stammered, "B-but the stings you take, the white venom-"

"White-imperium staves off the rot, Bruno, but even that can't neutralise all the black-imperium," Rufus said. "And besides, white-imperium goes bad itself, once used. The law of nature is an endless spiral into decay. Nothing lasts forever, not you, not mountains, not even this planet."

Bruno kneaded his apron with trembling paws; Rufus recalled his own dry-mouthed terror when told the same bad news by the Howler who had discovered him some twenty years ago.

"You've two choices, Bruno," Howler Rufus told his own discovery. "Either steal venom, for which you might be arrested and perhaps sent to some awful jail, or receive a sting legitimately for a day's work."

"As a Howler?"

Rufus raised his teacup, "You'd look very dashing."

Bruno guffawed sceptically. Rubbing the back of his neck he looked all around, searching for his father, for reassurance, a denial, anything. He looked back to Rufus and tried to speak but words didn't come. "But this can't be … I…." he faltered, leaning on the tabletop for support.

Rufus touched Bruno's paw. "I know, dear boy, it was the same for me," he comforted. "I'm sure your induction will be smoother than mine."

Bruno's eyes darted a little, "Induction?"

"Your marriage, boy," Ivan said drily, toasting with his teacup, "to the spiteful bitch that is white-imperium."

"Oh do shut up, Donskoy," Rufus seethed.

Casimir emerged from the kitchen, carrying a tray of tea for the table he was attending, "Be right with yer, Howlers."

Nodding, Rufus wrapped up. "Don't fret, Bruno. I'll come back later, right after my meeting with the Elders, and we'll chat some more." He tapped his nose, "Don't worry your dad though, eh? Keep this between us."

Gulping hard, Bruno nodded dumbly.

Casimir returned to the table, "Everything all right?" he gruffed, paws clapping together.

"Yeah!" Bruno barked, straightening up with a start.

"You look off, lad. How's the chest?"

"I'm fine."

"Taken your cough syrup?"

"Yeah, yeah." Looking around, Bruno changed subject, "What did they want over there?"

Casimir passed Bruno the latest order, but held onto the notepad long enough to say, "If you feel bad, go to bed. I can manage."

Bruno whined through his teeth, "Dad, don't fuss me in front of everyone!" and departed for the kitchen, giving the Howlers one last glance.

"He's a terrible teenager sometimes," Casimir excused on his son's behalf.

Rufus raised a paw, "Not at all. You've raised a true gentlebeast, Casimir."

"Ah, well, I try my best."

Ivan, to general surprise, spoke to the lowly rabbit. "How is it you have a wolf for a son, citizen?" he asked, his voice dripping with inquisitorial suspicion, rather than curious warmth. "Where are his real parents?"

"Dead, I suppose."

"You 'suppose'?"

"It's like I told Rufus," Casimir explained, arms folding – he had usually strong arms for a rabbit, Ivan thought. "I found Bruno during the closing days of the war, buried under rubble. He was only three or four at most. He said his mother was dead and I just assumed the worst for the rest; the house was a pancake. Once peace broke out I told the Politzi, but they didn't care. They said I could take Bruno to an orphanage or keep him myself. Call me soft, but by then I'd grown attached to the scamp. Aye. We've been rubbing along together ever since. Been over twelve years now."

"The war was that long ago?" Rufus sighed. "Time flies."

"Aye, that it does, Howler."

Ivan nodded a little, "Must be useful having a wolf for a son, especially one of Bruno's... unusual stature."

"Ahahaaa-aye, he's a big 'un!" Casimir laughed, suddenly tugging his collar. "I-I taught him to box from a young age, so he could look after himself, you know? Lad's down the gym all the time these days, really taken it to heart. He's been looking for a new haunt since we moved; do you know any round here, Howlers?"

Casmir's decidedly nervous rant died just as someone passed by the bay window, someone large, another 'big 'un' as the rabbit might say. They lingered for a moment, perhaps looking inside. Ivan ignored them, until he felt a tingle up his spine – a corona? Was it the beast outside the window that set the Howler's bones throbbing, or was it still Bruno? Ivan could not deny the youth coiled with imperious energy, but this felt different, almost... familiar.

By the time Ivan looked up from his meal, the figure at the window had moved on.

"Who was that?" Ivan asked in general.

Casimir scratched his brow, "Looked like a hyena."

Rufus got up from his meal. "Hyena?" he said, peering out the window.

Ivan dispelled the notion, "Don't be ridiculous. Hyenas are restricted to the Reservations; they would not get far traipsing around Lupa in broad daylight."

Casimir agreed, "Well aye, of course. I only caught a glimpse, Howler. Big fella though. Bear maybe? Definitely weren't no hog, he was furry."

Rufus sat back down and chuckled, "No doubt another burly customer you've scared off, Ivan." Reaching into his cloak, he produced his wallet and a fair few colourful Lupan bank notes, known as lupas. "I shall have to recompense Casimir triple-fold for the inconvenience you've caused him today."

"Oh, noooo," the rabbit said, even whilst hungrily eyeing up the cash. "I can't accept all that, Howler."

"I insist," Rufus said, taking Casimir's smaller paw and pressing the money into it. "What with me dragging poor Bruno out of bed just to make me breakfast and Ivan's sour mug frightening off your clients, it's the least I can do."

"Really, I can't-"

"Casimir!" Rufus snapped, adding gently, "Don't be tiresome."

The white rabbit assumed his faux reluctance no further, save to helplessly spread his paws at such generosity.

What a charade, Ivan thought, hurrying to finish his admittedly delicious waffle – the Elders would be expecting Rufus in ten minutes.

Suddenly a tingle, the same as before.

Ivan looked up from his waffle, jaw slightly agape, just in time to catch that cloaked figure passing the window again, only in the opposite direction. He was big all right, massive, with mountainous shoulders and a helmet that covered his face.

A Howler? But what wolf was built like that? Something felt horribly wrong.

"Rufus," Ivan said, getting no further.

Crash!

The mysterious beast effortlessly put a mighty, spot-flecked elbow into one of the window panes, smashing it to pieces and showering the table with shards of glass. In the midst of flinching, Ivan heard and felt something hard and hefty bounce across the table. When he opened his eyes he saw a glowing, spiked ball of yellow-imperium crystal, fizzling and spinning away in the middle of the polished, pitted old wood like a demented puffer fish.

Bruno leapt from the kitchen, greasy spatula in paw. "What in Ulf's name was that?"

Swiftly wrapping his arm in his cloak, Ivan swept the bristling orb from the tabletop, catapulting it clean past Bruno's baffled nose and across the café, spewing a trail of yellow vapour like a sulphurous comet.

"Get down!" Ivan snarled, grabbing Casimir and pulling him under the table.

Coughing and spluttering from the vapours, Bruno didn't have the wherewithal to move.

In the same instant as he hit the deck, Ivan saw Rufus leap up from his chair and shove Bruno into the kitchen. A flash of light overtook them both and a clap of thunder rippled through the café. Bottles exploded, windows blew out and countless brilliant shards of smouldering yellow-imperium fizzled through the air, lodging in the walls, chairs and tables like burning darts.

Silence prevailed.

Ivan opened his eyes and looked around. He pushed himself off the floor and knelt upright, glass fragments tumbling off his cloaked body. He felt no grievances, save for a ringing in his ears.

He checked on Casimir; the little beast was all right, if obviously shaken – rabbits were notoriously panicky.

"Rufus?" Ivan called, looking around.

No sign of him.

Still half-deaf, Ivan plodded to the kitchen and stood in the doorway, his paws resting on the frame.

Rufus lay on top of Bruno, his black cloak shredded by a dozen smouldering holes.

"Rufus!"

Ivan rolled his comrade aside of the cook, revealing his bloodied face and raw, bobbing throat.

"Go!" Rufus snarled at once, chest heaving fitfully beneath his cloak.

"Rufus-"

"Do your... duty, Howler!" he barked angrily, grabbing Ivan's arm. "Get him f-fff-for me!"

With but a moment's hesitation, and many a nod, Ivan ran back into the café, grabbed his helmet from the windowsill and dashed out into the rain-lashed street. He looked left, then right, settling on right.

Ivan's boots faded into the distance, leaving Rufus to grunt and growl in lonesome agony.

Until a big, brown wolf in an apron loomed over him. "Howler Rufus, sir!" he yelped.

"Bruno," Rufus seethed, "You... all right?"

The young wolf nodded, his face filling Rufus's ever more blurred vision. Those eyes, so bright, so beautiful, like fierce imperium embers; that corona, so warm, so strong, like the Rostsonne sun. Pity I'll never get to know him, Rufus thought.

"Bruno!" Casimir shouted discordantly, running in.

"I'm all right, I'm all right!" the cook replied, before crouching over Rufus again. "Dad he's hurt bad; what do we do?"

"Just leave him!" Casimir said, grasping Bruno's mighty shoulder and trying to pull him away. "Come on."

"What?"

"He's done fer, lad. We have to get out of here!"

Bruno threw his father's paws aside. "Dad, what's wrong with you?"

Casimir fumed, "Are you thick, boy? Can't you see it's a hit? There'll be swarms of Howlers here in no time and I don't want us to be swept up in an investigation!"

Bruno thought for a moment. "Bring the truck round; we'll drive him to his Howler Den. It's the one just up the road, 'en it?"

"Bruno!"

"Dad, stop it!" Bruno barked. "I'm not leaving him to bleed to death and neither are you. Now snap out of it and get the truck or I'll do it myself!"

Shaking his head, Casimir conversely gave in. "All right, all right, but you're making a big mistake!" he grumbled, bounding away and grabbing a ring of keys from behind the bar. "Keep him warm, I'll be as quick as I can!"

✦

After a roundabout route, Ivan exploded onto the very street where Rufus had parked his monobike. He cast his eyes up and down the rows of shops and houses, sure from the assassin's aura that he had fled this direction.

I'm losing him, Ivan thought, as the strangely familiar presence faded away.

Little beasts of every sort were gathered at the windows of their properties. Some stood in the doors, curious by the bang they had heard, but afraid to go out.

Ivan turned to a tiny pinafore-clad mouse wife and her two even tinier children she was hurriedly ushering inside and demanded of her, "Which way did he go?"

The terrified mouse wife shook her head and yet conversely opened her lips to say something.

"Tell me, citizen!" Ivan implored. "Please, I won't hurt you!"

One of the children pointed to the right. With a gasp the mother grabbed her offspring and bundled them inside, slamming the door behind her.

Before Ivan could act on the information, he heard the popping of a fierce imperium engine in the distance – a monobike. The engine revved up and then grew louder, closer; it was coming this way!

Sure enough a mono pulled out of a side street, a large, plain grey vehicle topped with an equally large, mantle-cloaked, helmet-clad beast, his legs encased in well-crafted black and white armour, his sandy-brown, muscle-bound arms as thick as Ivan's thighs.

With a snort of fury, Ivan reached round his back, just right of his handsome white tail, and pulled his secondary weapon from his belt – an imperium pistol. It was, in essence, but a fancy-looking metal tube with a grip and trigger. There was an explosive charge of yellow-imperium powder and a hefty imperium pellet stuffed down the barrel, in that order.

"Stop in the name of the Republic!" Ivan demanded, levelling the pistol at the stranger. "Stop, or I'll shoot!"

The beast on the monobike simply turned and accelerated in the opposite direction. He knew what the Howler knew; that there was little chance of a pistol hitting from such a distance.

"Cowaaard!" Ivan snarled.

Dashing to his black monobike, he threw himself over the seat and started her up with one mighty kick of the pedal, before riding his deafening machine down the road in pursuit, its single wheel glowing fiercely, its exhaust spewing a thick pall of ash.

✦

Tentatively wrapping Rufus in his thick, black mantle, Bruno scooped him up in both arms and whisked the wounded wolf outside, the pounding rain beating down on them both.

"The file!" Rufus growled.

Bruno stopped dead, unsure of his own ears after that deafening explosion. "What?"

"Don't… leave it," the Howler grunted. "It's very important the Elders… read it."

"I'll go back in a minute-"

"Now!" Rufus snarled painfully, adding, "Please."

Nodding dumbly, Bruno carried Rufus back inside and searched the shattered café with his fiery eyes. He found the precious file lying in the corner, its cover smouldering from a tiny shard of imperium embedded in the paper.

Bruno gently put Rufus down and patted the folder with a paw until it stopped burning.

"I got it!" he woofed, wafting it in front of Rufus's nose.

Rufus gulped and nodded gratefully, before turning his face to the wall and letting out a long growl of agony. His cloaked body shivered and his bloodied fingers trembled as shock and adrenaline took hold. Howlers were no ordinary wolves; Bruno knew that, everyone in Lupa and beyond knew that, but Rufus doubtless had a dozen needles of poisonous yellow-imperium lodged in his flesh. How could he bare it so quietly?

"Helmet," Rufus spluttered.

"Helmet?"

"If I'm to die, give me… my dignity… Bruno."

The Howler's helmet was lying upside-down amongst the debris like an upturned beetle. Retrieving it, Bruno gently lifted Rufus's head from the wooden floor and slipped the mask over his agonised face, turning him anonymous and fierce, even now. The decorative fangs began to shimmer hot and red amidst the coils of Rufus's corona.

With great care, Bruno ferried his pitiful bundle out onto the street again and waited in the rain.

Shortly, Casimir pulled the family truck round. The rickety vehicle was possessed of a little wooden cabin and a steering wheel on a ridiculously long shaft that vibrated alarmingly. The throbbing engine tucked beneath the rusty grey bonnet spluttered noxious clouds of spent imperium.

Bruno climbed in the rear, between crates and barrels. "Dad, you drive. I got him."

Casimir crunched the gear stick and drove through the gathering onlookers of every race and creed, out onto the main road, towards the towering pile that was the local Howler Den looming large and ominous over Riddle District.

"I got a bad feeling about this lad!" he shouted.

Bruno said nothing. He laid Rufus down and made him comfortable, covering him with some sackcloth and sheltering his head from the rain by leaning over him.

"Hold on, mate."

"Mate?" Rufus replied with amusement. "How droll."

Rocking to and fro as Dad drove the truck through Lupa's cobbled streets, Bruno found Rufus's nearest ruddy paw and held it in his own big brown fingers. The Howler squeezed back, a good, strong squeeze.

Strange.

Bruno looked at his paw. Pins and needles played over his flesh and up his arm, down to his very bone! It was a warm, crackling, numbing sensation, as if he had placed his paw on a vibrating surface for too long. With a panicked snort, Bruno let Rufus go and wiped his throbbing paw on his breeches until the sensation faded. He stared at his forearm, held it with his other paw and opened and closed his fingers.

Nothing seemed amiss.

"Now we're fully… acquainted," Rufus chuckled, his head flopping to one side.

With a pang of dread turning his veins to ice, Bruno pressed his ear to Rufus's chest.

He was still breathing, thank Ulf.

Slowly, reluctantly, Bruno took the Howler's paw again. There was no tingle this time, no warmth, save that of a hot-blooded, living being. Bruno felt somehow disappointed. He looked up from the trundling truck, fiery eyes blinking in the rain, and saw the distant towers of the Riddle Den growing closer, hoping with every breath he was doing the right thing, if not the most sensible thing.

CHAPTER 3

The rain battered Ivan's body, the wind ripped at his cloak, but still he twisted the accelerator another inch, adding another few notches to the monobike's quivering dials. Not that he paid any heed; he felt his machine's beating heart through his legs, his body, his bones, whilst his eyes remained fixed upon the bike in front bearing the beast who had bombed the café.

After a long straight, the road twisted and turned like a marble run, bins were overturned, papers scattered, little beasts sent diving for cover as the assassin tore through Lupa's backstreets at breakneck speed, leaning hard, skidding round corners, sometimes putting a leg down to kick off the cobbles and even a far wall to stop himself from going over, before accelerating away again.

He was good, but Ivan was better.

Foot by foot the Howler closed the distance, shaving off mere fractions of time with every corner, until, at last, another long, straight alley presented itself and with it Ivan's opportunity.

The Howler reached round his back and drew his silver pistol. He hoped it had stayed dry tucked under his cloak, for if the rain had dampened the imperium charge it wouldn't fire so much as fizzle.

Black mantle flapping about his shoulders, Ivan took aim at the rider, but decided in the last second to aim down.

Crack!

A flash of light and puff of ash burst from the pistol's end. A fraction later and a colourful spark dashed off the leading monobike's one wheel. The tyre exploded and tore itself apart in an instant.

The assassin's monobike shuddered and twisted violently to one side, before catapulting itself seat over wheel and flinging the rider in front. He sailed through the air and disappeared amidst the carnage as his machine slid along the cobbles, shedding a shower of sparks and pieces of chrome bodywork all the way, before smashing into a heap of rubbish piled against the end of the alleyway.

Ivan came to a controlled stop. Throwing those long, gaitered legs off the bike, which remained upright of its own volition thanks to the still-spinning gyroscope, the Howler holstered his pistol and drew his cold, bluish rapier.

Sword held loosely, Ivan approached the crash scene, his armoured paws crunching on the dirty, wet ground, his brooch gently illuminating the glistening brickwork and cobbles of the alleyway. The assassin's monobike smoked and crackled as the engine cooled down. Drops of rainwater boiled away on the overheated engine.

Where is he?

The alley was a dead-end with garbage piled high. There was nowhere to go.

Something stirred beneath the refuse and a tin can tumbled down. Using his sword to prise aside an old sheet, Ivan found a roach half as big as him hiding there. Long antenna waving furiously, the giant bug burst forth and scuttled down the alley as fast as any monobike.

Not quite the manner of vermin Ivan was after.

Then a distinct grunt from somewhere ahead – insects didn't grunt. Following the noise, Ivan spied the beginnings of a narrow passage half-buried by the rubbish.

Clambering over the rotting piles, Ivan made it to the alley just in time to catch sight of his quarry vaulting up onto a ten-foot-high brick wall. Despite what Ivan judged to be relatively short limbs for someone otherwise so big, the stranger was evidently very athletic and able, for he hauled himself up with ease.

"Halt, in the name of the Republic!" Ivan demanded, pointing with his sword.

The Howler-like stranger glanced behind with two bright purple eyes gleaming out from under his helmet; one side of the helmet was white the other black. Wordlessly, he swung his alternately black and white armoured legs over the wall and fell down the other side with another pained grunt – no doubt he was bruised from the crash.

Sheathing his sword, Ivan sped down the alley and attacked the wall with rather more aplomb than his hefty foe, reaching the top in a heartbeat, whereupon he glimpsed the assassin fleeing round the next corner and heard his heavy pawsteps.

Jumping down into a puddle, Ivan saved his breath for the chase and pursued in silence.

✦

"Ah, very nice, very nice," the Howler said, tossing the shiny apple into the air a few times before taking another enormous bite. He whirled away from the stall, the hood of his otherwise tight-fitting red mantle swaying outwards, and deigned to bid farewell to the little beast grocers by raising a dark, blue-grey paw.

His fellow Howler, a blonde-furred wolf in the same kind of short red cloak, looked between the impoverished rats and the noble wolf, and raised a finger. "Uh, Uther," he said, rather gently for one so well-built.

"What's up, mate?" Uther replied, stopping a moment, dark ears pricked.

The golden wolf approached, "Well, aren't you g-g-going to pay for that?"

"Pay?" Uther scoffed, his robust brow knitting in bafflement. "P-p-pay!" he mocked further, whizzing round to face his compatriot wolf. "Ahahahahaha!" Slinging a dark, muscular arm around the shorter, stockier wolf he squeezed him close and growled in his coarse, sandpapery tone, "You're funny, Linus. I like you."

Releasing Linus, Uther continued his patrol through the hustle and bustle of the covered marketplace, the iron roof arching overhead keeping out most of the drizzle, save for the odd rusty pellet-hole from the last Howler War, or perhaps even the one before.

Linus surreptitiously returned to the stall. "Here," he said, sliding a Lupan penny to the rat-folk, who were but half his size if that – and he was a height-challenged wolf himself, albeit sturdy. "Good day to you, citizens."

One of the rats, a young female by the looks, bowed graciously. "Thank you, Howler," she said.

Linus hurried back to Uther's side, hoping his charity had gone unnoticed.

Nothing escaped Uther's sharp yellow eyes. "What's wrong with yer?" he snorted.

"W-www-what?" Linus stammered innocently.

"They're under our protection, dummy! Riddle Market is smack bang in Bloodfang territory."

"I know."

"Oh, you know but you shelled out? What fer this time?"

Linus spread a paw, "I... felt sorry for them."

Uther sighed and patted him on the back, "Mate, that's cute 'en all, but you can't help everyone. It's a citizen's duty to provide for us and ours to protect 'em from the scoundrels of this world. We can't run Lupa on good will alone, you know."

"I know, but they pay taxes too."

"Yeah, and we bleed and rot! They don't. Now stop it, you're embarrassing me."

Linus shrugged his burly frame, but said nothing as he and the taller, more athletic Uther continued to patrol the market, keeping one eye and one ear open for trouble. If trouble there be, Uther had twin short swords at the ready, one strapped tightly to each grey armoured thigh, and Linus his sword and shield, the latter slung over his back, turtle-like. The shield was round and white, save for the décor of black wolf skull and glowing red fangs. Their helmets, grey with white cheeks and red fang imperium markings, were hung over their sword hilts by their chin-straps, ready when needed.

Uther bit his apple and further berated his partner through a mouthful of pureed fruit, "That's exactly the sort of thing Rufus does. The fastest way to wind up dead in an alley is to let beasts think you're a pushover like him. Puh! Wolves like that are bad for our hard-won reputation."

As he strolled along, Linus looked down at his armoured feet with his baby-blue eyes. "Forgive me, Uther," he said, "but if he's such a pushover how come he's feared across Lupa?"

"Know him do yer?" Uther asked.

"Well, no, not personally. I've read all his work, though."

"Puh!"

"Captain Rufus puts as much stay in knowledge as strength. I can but strive to emulate such a-a-a great Howler."

Uther grunted, "Even his hyena-loving? Give over!"

There was a break in the conversation, but Riddle Market continued to swirl around the Howlers. Beasts of every kind, colour and creed proffered goods from across the Lupan Republic and beyond; fruit, honey, fish, delicious choice cuts of fried bugs. There were also living bugs; pet crickets on leads, antennae waving all about; massive beetles carrying crates on their armoured backs; and two ants of different colours wrestling in a huge iron cage as bets were placed on their fate by a raucous crowd. Trinkets glittered on stalls by the hundred and racks of clothing wafted in the gentle breeze; compared to a Howler's imperium-laced mantle and brooch, the cloth and jewellery offered here was worthless.

As he patrolled the market with the streetwise Uther, Linus tugged the front of his handsome red cloak. "Is it hyena-loving to w-www-want wolves and hyenas to get along?" he stammered. "All Rufus wants is a better solution than the Reservations. Surely we all do."

"You can bet the hyenas do!" Uther said. "It's their own fault, mind."

"Do you know they call him 'Red-mist'?" Linus said. "He once saved a hyena prince from getting eaten by a sewer centipede and they honoured him with the name-"

"Yeah, yeah, I know, mate. Look, the hyenas only lick his toes 'cause he stands up for 'em."

"I wonder what it m-mmm-means, exactly. Red-mist."

Uther scoffed. "Dunno, mate, but they call me 'Wild-heart'."

Linus piped in surprise, "Wild-heart?"

"Yeah, Uther W. The W is for Wild-heart."

"Oh, so… you've been honoured by the hyena tribes too?"

"Yup."

"When? How?"

"Puh! Long story, mate. Captain Ivan's got one too. Blade-dancer they call him."

"Well yes, everyone knows *that*, Uther."

"Do they now? Well, it's nothing special, mate; them hyenas paw out their silly names like otters do fish 'n' chips."

Linus blinked, "Really? I've been labouring under the impression it's a r-rrr-rare accolade, especially for a wolf."

Uther cocked his head side to side. "Look, whatever, I don't care one fig about them troublemaking hyenas and nor should you, not if you want a quiet life," he sniffed, his pale-furred face squirming a little under Linus's scrutiny. 'Wild-heart' moved on, eager to take control of the discussion again, "Here, piece of advice, mate."

Linus waited patiently for this 'advice'.

"Should ol' Rufus ever take a shine to yer," Uther said, tapping Linus on the shoulder, "remember who you are."

A confused blink.

Uther looked the stocky Linus up and down, "Just remember you finished top of your year, that's why you've started as a Trooper First Class. You're an alpha wolf."

Linus looked down at his toes again.

"You *are* an alpha, aren't you, mate?" Uther scoffed.

The blonde wolf cleared his throat and rubbed the back of his neck. "One likes to think so, but it's n-nnn-not our choice."

"Course it is!" Uther asserted, slapping Linus on his barrel-like chest with the back of a paw. "You're built like a wall, mate! You're an alpha male, make no mistake, not some wimpy beta. So don't let Rufus, or anyone, make you their beta, because if you do everyone is gonna know and you'll never be respected. Ivan made that mistake and he ain't lived it down yet."

"You mean our Ivan, the Blade-dancer himself?"

"Yep. Rufe's finest conquest." Uther winked, "Of course, everyone knows *that*."

"I-I-I thought it was just a rumour."

"Puh! Nah!" Uther woofed. "Ivan used to groom Rufus and everything. Worshipped him, he did. Only Rufe's got a right short attention span, 'en he? Soon as he clapped eyes on Ivan's cousin he dropped Blade-dancer like a stone. And that only lasted five minutes before he tried to work his magic on me!"

"You?"

"Aye! I told him to stick it. Uther Wild-heart ain't nobody's beta. Nobody's!"

Linus looked altogether baffled and concerned.

Uther pinched his partner's cheek like a doting auntie. "Just watch yourself, mate," he cackled drily.

As the Howlers passed by an alley, someone in a hooded cloak stepped out and boldly intercepted them. Startled, Linus almost reached for his sword, but the stranger was just a thin young wolfess, very dark, with bags under her bright green eyes.

"Looking for fun?" she said to Uther, pulling back her hood to reveal her gaunt face and bony shoulders.

Uther declined gruffly, "Sorry, Sweetheart."

The wolfess moved to Linus and placed a paw on his chest to halt him, "Please. I am cheap. Only twenty lupas."

Linus could scarce believe her nerve. "Don't you know who we are?" he growled pompously, removing her paw from his person and contemptuously pushing it away.

The wolfess defensively pulled her cloak up and shook her head a little. "I'm… from far away," she said, in a foreign and now fearful tone. "Forgive me. Who are you?"

"We're Howlers," Linus said.

"Yes, I know this. That is why I come to you. You want fun."

"C-ccc-come to us?" Linus squeaked in amazement. "You come to us when you're clearly a venom addict? Do you want to be arrested?"

She looked down at her feet, "I… I do not know. I just need money, food. Please, anything!"

Uther leant over and whispered in Linus's ear, "Mate, she's a gazer."

"What?"

"Gazer."

Linus drew a blank gaze himself.

Uther took his partner to one side and seethed, "Can't you see she's on illegal stings?"

"Of course I can. You mean she's a dodger… right?"

"Nooo!" Uther woofed. "Ulf almighty, what log did you crawl out from under, woodlouse? A dodger is a wolf who's qualified to be a Howler and knows it, but avoids being drafted and takes imperium to survive, 'en they?"

Linus was all at sea, "So what's a gazer, then?"

Uther nodded to the dewy-eyed wolfess and whispered. "That's a gazer. Whatever she was, she's so far gone she can't think right for rot. Look at her, poor lass is all fur n' bones. Probably been taking krappy street stings to keep alive. Ulf knows what's in 'em. If she keeps on she'll be dead in a month."

Concerned, Linus returned to the wolfess, "Look, miss, whatever lies the sting dealers told you, you can't stop the rot by taking anything except white-imperium. Besides which it's illegal. If you're sick you should report to the local Den for tests and maybe you too can become a Howler-"

"No, no, no!" Uther growled, pushing Linus in the shoulder. "She's too far gone for that, she's a thumping gazer."

Linus defended, "I-I-I was just trying to help."

"Well, don't."

"But-"

"Just shut up a minute! I got this."

Glancing left and right, Uther reached into his cloak and took a fair sum of colourful Lupan notes from the inside pocket. He offered the money to the unfortunate wolfess.

"Here, love, get yourself something to eat."

The gazer stared longingly at the colourful lupas.

"Go on," Uther urged softly. "Where'd you come from originally, the Steppes, yeah?"

A nod, "I-I-I think so. I live in Wall Slums for some time, until I pay Watcher to get inside city. He said he would get me papers, but I never see him again."

Uther huffed, "Aye, I bet. Judging by your accent, you're a Steppes wolf, though. Here, take my advice and get on the next train to Everdor instead. Ever-dor. Right? There's always work on the Hummel plantations; they ain't fussy. It's clean there, see, no ash. In the fresh air n' sunshine you'll bounce back, as long as you stay clean. No stings, not even embers, not even when it really hurts. Do that and you might make it ten, twenny years even. Understand?"

With a whimper of fright, the wolfess snatched the money and hurried into the alley without looking back, lest these Howlers changed their minds.

Linus watched her go. "She didn't even thank you."

"Puh!" Uther snorted. "Well, what did I just say about being soft? Doesn't get you anywhere."

"Then why'd you do that?"

"Dunno, maybe I felt sorry for her," the petulant Uther said sarcastically, tugging at the gathered neck of his cloak and walking on without further ado, leaving his comrade to scratch his head and glance down the alley.

Someone distant was running towards Linus – was the gazer returning to thank Uther? No, it was someone else, someone bigger, much bigger, and growing by the second as they approached at speed, a heap of a beast in a cloak and helmet, armoured legs rattling down the alley, puddles of water splashing underfoot, muscled, spotted arms swaying.

As Linus watched a Howler emerged from a passage behind – he was obviously giving chase.

"Uther!" Linus called, not looking away. He raised a paw to the stranger as they neared the end of the alley. "Halt! In the name of the Repub-oof!"

Ears pricked, Uther turned around the moment a huge cloaked beast burst out the alley and barged into Linus. Much like a stray car being struck by a train, Linus was the loser. He slammed onto his back and rolled tail over head, like a giant pea bug, his shield taking the worst of the impact as it scraped over the cobbled street.

With barely a stumble, the aggressive stranger dashed into the market, scattering traders and shoppers alike.

"Oi, whatcha playing at?" Uther yapped. He ran to Linus and helped him up. "You all right?"

Nodding, Linus rubbed the back of his throbbing skull. "Agh! He... he didn't stop."

"I noticed. Howler was he?"

"I don't know. He looked like a Howler, but...."

"Which pack, mate?"

"I-I-I didn't see any markings, just black and white."

Some echoed footsteps later and a second, unquestionable Howler emerged from the alley, this time clad all in black, save for the white cheeks of his helmet. He was tall, with snow-white fur, from what little could be seen.

"Ivan?" Uther snorted in recognition, half-heartedly reaching out with a paw to stop him. "Oi, Captain!"

"Don't just stand there, Trooper!" Ivan snarled, stopping for no one. "Help me!"

With but a moment's thought, Uther donned his helmet and gestured furiously to Linus. "Come on, Woodlouse, something's going down! Come on, come on!"

"Woodlouse?" the dazed Linus seethed, securing his helmet straps about his chin as he ran.

The athletic Uther flew ahead and was soon level-pegging with the higher-ranking Ivan as they chased the stranger, whilst Linus languished behind. Beasts of every sort kept well clear of the felon and the law as both sides sped through the covered market and into the claustrophobic maze of twisted streets beyond.

"Where d'you want me, sir?" Uther asked Ivan, not in the least breathless as they entered the next alley in pursuit.

"Just... do your... stuff!" Ivan panted back. "Quickly; he tried to kill Rufus!"

"What?"

"Just go! Use any means, go on!"

"Aye aye, sir!" Uther snarled. "I'll get the bastard!"

The still-fresh Uther peeled off from his tiring comrade and started to pull away, slowly at first, but with growing speed. He tore down the alley, ears flat, paws cutting through the air. Puddles splattered and papers swirled in his wake as Uther's body tapped into the power of the imperium woven into his muscles, bones and blood. The lagging Linus had heard rumours about him, but by Ulf was Uther fast! He made the end of the dingy alley and disappeared into the light. Ivan followed, not too far behind.

Embarrassed at his tardiness, Linus tapped into some extra reserve of energy and hurried to remain in the race. He wasn't built for this nonsense, he was no sprinter, a good honest fight was what he and his shield liked.

Bursting out onto the wide-open main street, Linus looked in all directions. Riddle Den loomed to the left and the nearest train station to the right; the Howlers and therefore the chase was heading to the station.

"Halt! In the name... of the Republic!" Linus shouted, woefully maintaining pursuit.

Far ahead, Uther laboured under his helmet, the rain lashing his body, plastering his red cloak to his muscled torso. It was hard to see. Either the rain had grown heavier, or Uther was running into it so fast as to make it feel so. He spotted his cloaked prey ascending the stained station steps; the stranger shoved an unfortunate pig porter out the way, sending trunks and suitcases spilling down the stairway.

He's fast for a big fella, Uther thought, but I'm faster; the fastest thing in Lupa!

Getting his feet in the right position, Uther, with a skip and a jump, sailed up the station stairs in one great bound, the air rippling in his wake as his contorting corona reached out. Landing neatly at the top he continued as before. The rot would make him pay for this later, he knew, but pain was the price of glory.

Into the grand station foyer, through the hustle and bustle, beasts big and small, high and low, gasping and screaming as the huge law-breaker pushed them aside and jumped the barriers. With the path already cleared Uther fared better.

I'm gaining. So close!

There was a train; the carriages were moving. Imperium ash swirled across the platform as the locomotive belched into action. The fugitive vanished into the clouds, but Uther spied his faint silhouette open a carriage door and climb inside. Redoubling his efforts, the Howler veered off to the left, chasing the train. Pulling a door open on the very next carriage he swung himself inside and slammed it shut.

Silence, but for the wheels clacking on the tracks and Uther's panting.

Dripping with water, the Howler looked back and glimpsed Ivan arriving on the platform, only to vanish again as a pall of grey ash passed by the carriage windows.

Surely Ivan's missed the train; I'm on my own.

Wait.

Uther whirled around with a start and glared at the little beasts cowering in the carriage. He sensed it, felt it in his bones, the fuzzy crackle of a fellow imperious presence, a corona. Someone was near, someone powerful. Was it the beast he was chasing?

"Go to the back of the train," Uther told his lesser passengers.

Nobody moved.

"Go on!" the Howler snarled, grabbing the nearest terrified mouse by the scruff of his jumper and ejecting him down the carriage so hard his cap fell off. Uther obligingly picked up the floppy cap and threw it after him, saying to him and everyone else, "Stay outta the way! We could have a rogue Howler on board!"

The passengers filed down the carriage, past Uther, keeping their eyes averted. Once they had gone, Uther slowly started his way up the trundling train.

✦

Linus made the platform just as the last carriage departed the station. As the ash clouds dissipated, Uther was nowhere to be seen, nor was Ivan, even less their quarry. They must all be on the train, Linus realised.

The Howler dashed back to a ticket office, cut to the front of the queue and flashed his brooch at the enormous hog behind the glass.

"Stop that train, citizen!"

The hog squinted hard at Linus's brooch with his beady eyes, his porcine girth all but filling the window as he leant forth with painful lethargy. "I can't," he snorted at last.

"Can't?"

"Not until the next stop. I'll have to telephone ahead. Is that satisfactory, Howler?"

"Yes!" Linus panted. "Just hurry!"

The rotund hog slowly squeaked away on his seat and rummaged around somewhere. He glided back, still seated, and hung a sign up in the window that read, 'No Service', before fetching a stick with a hook on the end and pulling down the booth's metal shutters – procedures, and all that.

Linus assumed the hog was on the telephone. The Howler felt useless waiting here. He agitatedly slapped his fingers on the booth's desk a few times before it dawned on him what next to do. Speeding through the station foyer and down the steps, he went back to the main street. Arms waving, he flagged down the first vehicle he came across; in the event it was a rather fancy motor car, red and black with a soft top and big chrome wheel-guards. There was a handsome ginger cat at the steering wheel wearing a magnificent white coat, a scarf and goggles, and next to him a pure grey catess in a frilly white dress and bonnet.

"Stop in the name of the Republic!" Linus shouted.

"Golly, it's one of them 'Owler chaps," the ginger cat said to his fellow feline, before leaning on the open window and loudly addressing Linus over the churning of the car's imperium engine. "What's the matter, sir, are you lost?"

"Citizen… in the name of the Republic… I need to requisition your vehicle!" the panting, dripping-wet Linus replied, flashing his glowing red brooch.

"Requisition, you say?"

Linus almost opened the front door, but upon seeing the long steering wheel jutting forth from a cornucopia of buttons, levers and dials, remembered he couldn't drive.

"Please drive, citizen," he said, opening the back door instead and sliding across the smooth back seat until he was in the middle. He pointed between the two cats, at the billowing locomotive chugging ahead. "Follow that train!"

"I say, how exciting, it's like being in the pictures!" the cat laughed at the catess, crunching gears and tugging knobs. The car shuddered and coughed, disgorging clouds of spent imperium. "Hold on. Just a tick. Nearly there. Haha!"

For a horrible moment Linus thought he had requisitioned the one vehicle in Lupa that wasn't going anywhere. Finally the red car took off with a mighty jolt, throwing the Howler back into his seat.

Vrrrrrooom!

"Clear a path here!" the goggled cat hollered, honking his horn at pedestrians and waving a paw out the window. "In the name of the Republic, clear off!" Glancing back at his wolfen passenger he cackled gleefully, "Did I say that right?"

"Uh… y-yes, citizen," Linus gulped, hoping he didn't end up going through a wall with this fellow at the controls.

"Citizen indeed!" the cat piped in amusement, driving merrily along the road and giving the train the odd sideways glance as he casually raced to catch up with it. "Penny and I are from Queens Town, actually, down on the Teich. We are but visitors to your fine metropolis, aren't we Sweetpea?"

"Yes, dear," the grey-furred catess said, calm as you like despite everything.

"Welcome to Lupa," Linus said absently.

"Thank you, sir," the ginger cat nodded. "We only arrived here via Hummelton yesterday. Staying at the *Crab and Kettle*, just down the way. Pokey little place, run by a couple of salty otter folk. They swear like sailors, but they've good hearts 'en all. We wanted the authentic multicultural Lupan experience, didn't we Sweetpea? Nothing too posh."

"Oh, absolutely."

"Montague Buttle, by the way," the ginger cat declared, swerving round a bus and honking his horn. "Monty for short. That's me wife, Penelope." He winked at Linus via his mirror, "Ain't she a beaut?"

Distracted by the train, and Monty's driving, Linus eventually nodded, "I'm sure, citizen."

"Well, perhaps not to a wolfen sort like you, eh?" Monty chortled. "What's your label, sir, if I may be so bold?"

"Label?"

"Name, sir."

"Uh, Linus… Linus Bloodfang Mills, Trooper First Class."

"Pleasure, sir!"

Linus Mills shuffled across the back seat to see out the right window as the train slew round to that side.

"So, you're one of them 'Owlers?" the chatty Montague asked Linus, with a little uncertainty in his voice.

"Yes, sir."

"I thought so," Monty said, adding tactlessly, "Got the rot, eh?"

"Monty!" Penny hissed.

"Well he has, you know, they all do, just like our Valours."

"Yes, but mind your manners."

Linus glanced between the bickering cats and finally answered, "I am afflicted, sir. It's n-nnn-nothing you need be polite about."

Monty spread a paw at Penny, "There, you see?"

Penny glanced piteously back at Linus, "Such a terrible disease, Mr. Linus. You bear it with great fortitude. I would never know to look at you."

"Look at him? You can't see his bally face!" Monty pointed out. "Surprised he can breathe with that ruddy great helmet on. Haha!"

"Monty!"

"Only joking, Sweetpea," Monty guffawed. "All in good fun, eh Howler Linus?"

"Indeed, sir."

"See? We understand each other."

Linus tapped his paw on the door as the train started to pull away, "Sorry, but can we not go any faster?"

"Faster? But of course, my good wolf! This beauty packs a six-hundred ant-power reciprocating red-imperium engine under the hood." Montague shifted gears and tapped his wife's paw, "Hold on, Penny, we're going for a spin. All in the name of the law, mind."

"Do be careful, Monty, we can't afford another prang."

"Absolutely, Sweetpea."

Hardly flush with confidence, Linus gripped the edge of his seat with both paws as Monty took him on a white-knuckle ride down the main street, dashing kerb-side puddles over unfortunate pedestrians and gassing them with noxious clouds of imperium ash. The grim towers and walkways of the local Howler Den passed slowly by on the left, far behind the rows of shops and houses whizzing past the window, whilst the train edged painfully back into view on the right, carriage by carriage.

"Oh Monty, look!" Penny gasped, pointing ahead.

"I say, how extraordinary!" Monty laughed. "Linus, there's someone on top of the train!"

Linus shuffled back to the middle and leant between the front seats, "What?"

"There, look!" Monty said, pointing as well.

Sure enough there was a black figure crouched on top of a carriage. He was slowly creeping along the train, his cloak flapping and billowing wildly.

"Is that the rogue you're after, Linus?"

The wolf squinted, "I-I-I don't know. Just do your best to stay with the train."

Montague saluted, "Will do!"

Chapter 4

Uther opened the door leading to the next trembling carriage and stepped across the small gap between them, the grey cityscape of Lupa passing either side of him, rails screaming beneath. The wind and rain buffeted Wild-heart as he checked through the window of the next carriage, irises glowing like fireflies beneath the glazed eyes of his helmet. The passengers were seated in rows. All seemed to be in order, save for a flickering imperium lamp swaying overhead.

Entering the shelter of the carriage, Uther advanced with caution, armoured, gaiter-clad legs rattling. The feeling in his bones was strengthening.

"Did he come through here?" Uther asked the passengers, "A big beast, in a mantle? His armour were black and white."

Little beasts of every kind averted their eyes.

"Well?"

Some nodding

"Anybody hurt?" Uther asked further.

Some head-shaking.

They were just pathetic wee beasts, Uther remembered, small and helpless. Even common wolves were frightening to them, let alone a Howler with the power of imperium at their fingertips. Some abused their right, but Uther liked to think he was one of the good ones.

"All right, everyone go back to the next a carriage," he said. "Go on! I don't want you getting under me feet."

The Howler drew one of his short swords. Holding it loosely by his side he advanced up the carriage.

The next door. Uther passed between the carriages, the deafening noise and lashing rain attacking him once again. He peeked through the window.

The next carriage was strangely empty, save for one large, cloaked beast sitting halfway along the right row. He was facing in the direction of travel – away from Uther – with one leg crossed over the other and one arm slung across the back of the seat in apparent nonchalance.

That's him all right.

Whipping open the door, Uther entered the carriage. He expected the felon to leap up in surprise, or at least look, but he didn't even glance over his cloaked shoulder.

'Arrogant son of a maggot', Uther thought.

He approached, paw over armoured paw. The stranger was no wolf; his ears were erect, but broader and rounded-off. His shoulders and arms were massive, like a bear, but no bear had light-brown arms with dark-brown spots.

"Come to kill me, Howler?" it said.

Uther's heart leapt in the face of that hair-tingling baritone voice, if only for a moment.

"Up to you, citizen," he replied, in his own sandy tenor, albeit slightly muffled by his helmet.

"Citizen?" the stranger scoffed, turning his helmet-clad head a little, so that Uther glimpsed a bright and, he could swear, purple eye. "Since when are hyenas citizens in your glorious republic?" the stranger went on. "Are we not but a plague of savages and vagrants to be rounded up and squashed like locusts?"

Uther grunted, "Don't be cute. Just drop your weapons and put those paws where I can see 'em."

"Who said I have a weapon, Trooper?"

"Call it intuition."

The hyena, or so he claimed to be, laughed rather hysterically, as his kind were wont to do.

"Hahaaahahahhahaaha!"

When he'd finished, he sniffed, "I have no grievance with a wet-eared pup like you." Giving Uther the once-over glance, he added, "You've twenty years before you rot, maybe more. Do not throw your life away on me, little wolf. Turn around and pretend you didn't see me. Who will ever know of your cowardice?"

Uther snorted simply, "Me."

The hyena's eyes narrowed and one could sense him smiling dangerously beneath the anonymity of his helmet. "Answered like a true warrior," he said.

In the next breath, he jumped to his feet and whirled around with something in his right paw.

Crack!

The bright flash came the exact same moment Uther dived onto the nearest seat. The corner of the well-worn upholstery exploded as a pellet of imperium tore through it and ricocheted around the carriage. The hyena had a weapon all right; an imperium pistol!

Two could play at that game.

As he lay in the seat, Uther reached round his back and plucked his own pistol from its holster, nestled just right of his tail. Knowing his foe couldn't have reloaded his pistol so quickly, but accepting he might have two on him, Uther prayed to Ulf, rolled forward and pulled the trigger.

Crack!

A flash and a puff of ash exploded from the end of Uther's pistol. In the same moment, a colourful spark flared off the top of the hyena's helmet and blood took fly.

A hit!

The cloaked hyena staggered down the carriage, but didn't fall over. He gripped the chairs either side of him as blood trickled liberally over his helmet. The pellet had bounced off his forehead and gone through his ear, leaving a nasty dent in his helm and a tear in his ear.

"Hahahahaaaaa!" he laughed, pulling himself upright and shaking his head to dispel the dizziness. "Invigorating!"

Uther got up, said nothing.

The stranger removed his uncomfortably dented helmet and tossed it on the nearest seat, revealing the hyena he claimed to be. He had a broad, dark muzzle, glistening wide nose and a lick of a mane sticking up between his rounded ears. Those eyes, purple without a doubt and crowned with dark, thickset brows.

"Now we have dispensed with the formalities," the hyena said, throwing his pistol on the nearest seat beside his helmet, "let us conduct ourselves as warriors."

Not in the habit of discarding expensive Howler property for the benefit of some nutter's games, Uther simply holstered his pistol. "How's about you let me 'conduct' you to our Den for questioning, before I have to kill yer."

The hyena flashed a mighty, toothy smile, "Do I look like the sort to just roll over, Howler?"

"Attacked Rufus, did yer?" Uther growled.

"Blew him up, yes."

"What?"

"Friend of yours is he? Friend of mine too. It was just business."

Slowly, the hyena reached round his back and under his cloak. Uther tensed up, ready to move in case of a second pistol, but he quickly saw his foe was reaching for a black stick, two feet long if that. The hyena pressed a button with his thumb and the pole extended many times its length, becoming a third as tall again as its wielder. A blade popped out one end, one made of shimmering imperium-strengthened metal.

A spear!

With a knowing look in his glimmering purple eyes, the hyena casually lowered said spear. As its tip touched the floor a bolt of imperious plasma arced forth and lit up the carriage, casting harsh shadows in all directions. The hyena gently tapped his weapon on the floor a few times, producing flashes of light and showers of sparks – the floor became blackened and blasted, with tiny craters blown in the smouldering metal.

"What's the matter, Howler?" the stranger mocked. "Never seen a Chakaa before?"

Uther cocked his head to one side, "What are yer, some kind of wannabe Howler?"

"Takes one to know one."

"Puh!"

After a chuckle, the hyena claimed, "I am of the Chakaa; what you wolves call Howlers we hyenas call Chakaa, we are cousins if somewhat... different." He beckoned with his fingers, which were dark brown, as if he had dipped them in chocolate. "Now for the practical instruction."

Uther drew both swords, one then the other. He tapped one on the nearest seat, sending a curtain of sparks across the cabin, just to prove he too had the strength and wherewithal to release the energy stored in his flesh and bones at will. With a sharp breath, Wild-heart advanced, twirling a sword round for show. There wasn't much room to swing a blade in the narrow carriage, but there was even less room for that spear.

This'll be a piece of honey cake.

Uther launched himself into battle. The Chakaa raised his spear to greet him, but Uther saw that coming a mile away; he was counting on it. Smashing the spear aside with one sword he thrust forward with the other, to run this joker through. Alas, the hyena twisted his massive body to the side, leaving Uther's shimmering blade stabbing vainly at thin air. With a snarl, the Howler slashed sideways, but his adversary's spear shaft was already in the way. Sparks of imperium took fly as weapons and warriors met.

In that moment, that passing flicker of contact, Uther felt the warm crackle of another imperious corona penetrate him right down to the bone. What power!

Ducking and rolling backwards, Uther retreated and took stock of the situation. The hyena hadn't budged an inch during the brief exchange, a veritable wall of muscle.

"Not bad, little Trooper," he cackled, slapping a big paw against his cavernous chest. "I felt you. Right here!"

Uther didn't admit to the same, but betrayed a gulp which he hoped his helmet disguised.

Suddenly, Wild-heart swore he felt a second imperious presence overhead. He glanced up at the carriage ceiling moment, but hadn't time to contemplate for the Chakaa progressed between the seats, imperium spear held level.

"My turn," he said, flashing another bold smile.

With that he thrust at Uther; the wolf weaved aside and slashed the spear shaft with a sword, hoping to cut it; but it was made of sterner stuff than that. Another jab followed, another dodge too, high, low, the slightly flexible spear bending and quivering as the hyena tried to stick Uther like a fish.

Then, with a snarl, the Chakaa whipped his spear up and away in a great arc. Barely clearing the rain-lashed windows as it went, the now hot, glowing tip swept round the cabin, over the tops of the chairs and down again, slapping the floor where Uther had been but a moment ago. Molten metal exploded in all directions, leaving a blackened crater in the carriage big enough to glimpse the sleepers whizzing by beneath!

Ears ringing from the blast, Uther glanced behind – he hadn't much room left. He considered beating a humiliating retreat to the next carriage.

The Chakaa hyena advanced, spear tip low. The deafening wind whistling through the hole he had blown in the floor fluttered the looser folds of his cloak.

Passing said hole, the hyena sensed the wind blowing through a little harder, as if the air had suddenly found an outlet elsewhere in the carriage, like someone opening a window.

Or a door?

"Halt!" someone barked. "Or I'll shoot!"

The hyena froze, save for his rounded ears that pricked and swivelled behind.

Uther looked past him. "Ivan!" he piped in a marriage of surprise and relief. "How'd you get over there?"

"I took the high road," Ivan replied cryptically.

The white wolf looked rather windswept, his mantle soaked through and dripping. In his right paw he held his handsome silver pistol, aimed and doubtless ready to shoot.

"You all right, Wild-heart?" he asked Uther, those icy eyes piercing out from under his helmet.

"Yeah. All under control, sir, all under control. I was just about to finish this uh… Chakaa."

With a surprised scoff, Ivan turned his voice, and his fury, on the hyena. "He is no honourable Chakaa, Uther, but a spineless assassin!"

The 'spineless assassin' turned his head and body slightly.

"Go on!" Ivan urged, stepping forward and growling, "Give me the excuse I need to execute you here and now."

Inviting death, the hyena stood up straight and slowly turned around. "Better to die by your noble paw, Blade-dancer, than be thrown to the ants," he reasoned. "That's still the sentence for a treacherous Howler amongst the Bloodfangs, is it not?"

Ivan's icy eyes softened. "Noss?" he gasped in what could only be recognition.

Uther stared, listened.

This 'Noss' raised his hefty chin. "Not a scratch, I see," he said to Ivan, grinning toothily. "You ought to have more holes in you than a rotten log, yet here you stand."

Ivan just stared in dumb disbelief.

"And Red-mist?" Noss enquired simply.

That snapped Ivan from his stupor. "Why'd you do it, Noss?" he snarled. "Don't say it was money. You'd not do that for money; there must be a better reason!"

The big hyena shrugged his mighty shoulders, "A beast's got to eat, Blade-dancer."

Eyes narrowing, Ivan nodded but once. "I see," he said, his voice quivering with rage. "Remember that when you're staked out for the ants, won't you? Remember as they carve your worthless carcass up and carry it away that 'a beast's got to eat'. I certainly will. I'll stake you out myself if Rufus dies!"

Unable to suppress a gulp at the grim thought, Noss readied his spear. "You'd better kill me, Ivan; pray you've kept your pistol dry, because I shan't hold back."

The Howler lowered his pistol a little. "Death's too good for you," he seethed.

Crack!

From Uther's point of view, Noss dropped his spear and bent double, falling in-between some seats with barely a grunt of pain escaping his lips.

He squirmed, alive still.

The train began slowing down underfoot; ash billowing past the windows in thick clouds as the driver commanded the engine to vent waste imperium before reaching the station.

Ivan let his pistol flop to his side. "Wire that wretch for me, Uther. I can't stand to look at him let alone touch him. His stinking corona sickens me!"

"Yes, sir," Uther said at length – orders were orders.

Striding down the carriage to where Noss lay, Uther peered between the seats, sword drawn just in case there was any fight left in him. "All right you 'Chakaa' you, don't try anything funny."

Noss rolled onto his back. "Too late," he laughed, revealing a grey, metallic sphere about the size of a racquetball. He twisted the sphere's two distinct, mechanically-linked halves in relation to one another. It began to click and whir, before Noss stopped it, holding the halves tight. "Hahaaaahaha!"

"Schmutz!" Uther yelped, stumbling back against a seat. "Ivan! He's got a bomb!"

"Bomb?"

"Aye, sir! It's thumpin' live!"

Ivan zipped down the carriage and looked fearlessly down upon Noss and the bloodied grey sphere in his paws.

"I suggest… you stand clear," Noss grunted from down between the seats, one paw grasping at his heaving, bleeding ribs, the other holding the bomb. "This will not be pretty."

"Noss, don't do this."

"Better this than torture and the ants! It's a black-imperium bomb, Ivan, so do not linger."

"Black-imperium?"

"I will hold the timer awhile. Not too long mind. And if you kill me. Pow! Hahahaaahaha!"

"I don't believe you!" Ivan seethed.

"Then stay and find out, Blade-dancer. We can r-reminisce before we rot together."

Feeling the train braking underfoot, Ivan looked out the windows and saw the station rolling into view, the platform, the innocent citizens of Lupa, waiting to board.

"Noss, you insane fool!" he growled, as the train screeched to a halt. "There's hundreds of citizens out there!"

"Then… you had best not let them in here," Noss replied drily. "Go, do your duty, Howlers!"

"Leave him!" Ivan told Uther, reaching for the nearest door. "Come on, we have to evacuate the station!"

"A-aye, sir."

With a glance back at Noss, Uther gladly followed Ivan off the train and onto the platform, making quite sure to close the door behind him. The nearest citizens were surprised to see a couple of Howlers, even more surprised when one of them started to address them.

"Back!" Ivan shouted. "Everybody stand back!" He grabbed a passing rat that was trying to board regardless and yanked him away from the door. "Citizen, don't board the train. There's been a chemical spill." He raised his paws at a group of curious onlookers, "There's no need to panic citizens, calmly leave the platform and go inside the station. There's been an accident and we need you all to evacuate the area-"

"It's black-imperium!" Uther shouted, waving his paws wildly. "Don't get on the train!"

Ivan whirled on him, "Shut up, you fool!"

"Black-imperium, you say?" a well-to-do cat gasped.

"What?" snorted a hog. "Black-imperium!"

"It's black-imperium!" a rabbit cried, running in circles. "There's been a black-imperium spill! It'll rot us all. Run for your lives!"

Word spread like a conflagration in a silk shop and within moments beasts of every kind and class were fleeing the platform and stampeding the station doors, pushing and shoving, leaving hats and umbrellas in their wake.

"Well done, Uther," Ivan said, sarcastic at best.

"Worked didn't it?" Wild-heart snapped defensively.

There was no time to quarrel, and Ivan didn't. "I'll go this way; you clear the carriages down that way. I'll get the driver to move the train into a siding. If you see a black cloud, climb to higher ground. Black-imperium hugs the floor, understand?"

"Higher ground. Right."

The Howlers parted company. Uther ran alongside the carriages, banging on windows and checking inside, Ivan the same, until he reached the locomotive at the head of the train.

The huge engine was a mass of pipes, funnels and fireboxes, twisting and turning over one another, with a dozen wheels running down each side. Every inch was coated with the shimmering, iridescent sheen of imperious ash, the same ash which polluted a Howler's blood. And just the same, it contained traces of black-imperium. Luckily only minuscule quantities, for were it abundant, everyone here would be dead, every beast, every bug, every plant and bacterium, rotted, for black-imperium devoured everything that lived. It lingered for years, invisible, undetectable, which is what made Noss's little surprise back there so deadly. That tiny bomb contained a marble-sized ball of black-imperium, enough to kill hundreds if applied correctly. The bomb would explode, dashing black-imperium everywhere, then this whole train would have to be pitched into a hole and the platform decontaminated. Noss himself would decay in a matter of seconds, his flesh melting away. What a way to go.

"Driver!" Ivan called.

A badger appeared at the cabin, his spectacles and coveralls impregnated with a glorious sheen of ash. "Yes, Howler?" he replied, wiping his paws on a rag. "I got signalled to stop the train. What's the bother, sir?"

"I need you to…."

Ivan froze, his paws grasping the rails of the cabin's entrance as if to pull him up. He looked along the train and saw grey smoke tumbling rapidly across the platform, pouring from a carriage door.

Noss's bomb!

Ivan staggered backwards in fear as the cloud advanced on him, a rolling wall of black death.

No, wait, the smoke was grey and light, not black and dense.

Steeling himself, Ivan started back down the train, slowly at first, but soon flying as his confidence grew. With a glance around the deserted platform, and a prayer to Ulf, Blade-dancer plunged into the billowing grey smog, climbed inside the carriage and ran to where Noss should be.

Ivan found only the hyena's 'black-imperium' bomb discarded on a seat. A hole in the top was spewing a steady jet of grey smoke – it was just an ash bomb. If it was what Noss had claimed, Ivan wouldn't have made it ten steps, as it was his helmet grille filtered out the mild pollution.

Exiting the carriage, he searched the thick, synthetic fog, turning up Uther taking shelter in a ticket booth of all places.

Ivan opened the door. "As if this would've saved you!" he woofed contemptuously, ash rolling in over his shoulders.

Uther fell backwards in a flailing panic, but soon realised he wasn't dying, even less was Ivan. "Sir?"

"It's just ash. It's blocking Noss's corona, but he can't have gone far. Come on!"

"That lying, cackling hyena!" Uther snarled, extricating himself from the booth. "I'll string him up!"

✢

Opposite the station, Monty and Penny watched from within the trembling cabin of their sporty red motor car as Linus hurried across the broad rain-swept paths of Lupa to the foyer, shield at his back, boots splashing in puddles.

"Well," Monty mewed, nursing the quivering wheel in one ginger paw, "now there's a story to tell everyone when we get home. Haha!"

"Yes, dear," Penny replied.

Monty marvelled, "That one on top of the train! Golly, would I like to shake that fellow's paw. Never seen the like, not even during me military days."

"Remarkable. What a brave beast."

"I'd heard these 'Owlers were all rogues, but Linus seemed a reasonable chap to me."

Penny chided her husband, wagging a moon-grey finger under his pink nose, "You mustn't believe Felician gossip, Monty."

The cat nodded, "I suppose you're right." He licked his lips, "Do you think we can go now?"

"I don't see why not. I'm sure Howler Linus and his friends have everything under control."

"Right ho."

Monty crunched the gears and worked the pedals, spewing ash in all directions, until he noticed strange goings-on out the corner of his goggled eyes. Hoards of beasts of every sort were hurrying down the station steps in apparent panic, whilst billowing grey clouds issued forth behind them.

"I say, what's all that?"

"I don't know," Penny replied, leaning forward to see. "Is it a fire?"

"Looks like ash to me, Sweetpea."

As the cats looked on, a cloaked figure in a helmet emerged from the crowd and hurried towards the road. He was leaning forward somewhat, his pace hampered by a serious limp, and he kept glancing over his shoulder.

"Look, Penny, another 'Owler," Monty pointed.

"He looks hurt," Penny observed with a sympathetic gasp.

Monty cranked up the parking-brake, "Yes. Stay here. Won't be a tick."

"Monty, do be careful. He doesn't look quite right to me."

In one choreographed movement, Monty opened the door and popped up a white umbrella to guard against the rain. He intercepted the ragged-looking Howler just as he passed in front of his motorised carriage.

"I say, old chap, are you all right?"

The huge fellow turned to Monty in a start, then eyed up the fancy red motor car. "Yours is she?" he grunted, standing up straight, but nursing his stomach.

"What? Oh yes," Monty replied. "Look, hate to be a pest, but you're, uh… you're bleeding, sir."

"Am I?" was the reply. "So I am! Silly me." The Howler cackled, spreading a bloodied paw and wiggling his thick, gory fingers at Monty, "Give me the keys, cat."

Monty blinked, "Pardon me?"

The Howler, if Howler he be, produced a pistol from under his cloak and pressed it into Monty's pink nose. Forcing the cat backwards over the bonnet, he repeated himself, albeit with further elaboration, "I said, give me the keys, else I'll repaint your lovely car in shades of brain."

"I say! Steady on. There's no need for-"

"Keys, you pompous fop!"

"Well... uhm, actually, she's already running, old chap."

"So it is!" the Howler laughed. "Sorry, mind's going."

"Now look here, me wife-"

The Howler back-pawed Monty across the face, sending him down into a puddle and splashing his fine white coat with sooty water.

Penny opened her door. "Monty!" she screamed.

As she tried to escape the carriage, the Howler got in the other side, grabbed Penny's dress and pulled her back onto the seat. "Oh no you don't!" he growled.

"Let me go, you brute of a wolf! Let me go, I say!"

"Wolf? You insult me madam!" the 'Howler' said, holding Penny with ease as she slapped his massive arm with both paws. "Brute I can live with, but I am no despicable wolf."

He removed his dented helmet and threw it on the back seat, proving he spoke truly – he was a hyena.

"How do I work one of these infernal contraptions?" he demanded of his feline hostage, looking over the maze of controls and dials. "I'm a little rusty."

"Monty! Monnnnty!"

"By the Wind, madam, cease your whining!" the hyena snarled, clutching at his painful wound a moment. "Aaagh!"

Penny watched as, bloodied paws trembling, her hyena captor produced a red and white cylindrical paper cartridge from his dripping-wet mantle. He bit off the white half, taking it into his mighty mouth, and poured glittering powder from the red half into the pistol's breach chamber. He then spat the round pellet contained in the half of the cartridge he had bitten off down the barrel and pushed it home with the little attached ram-rod.

The pistol was now loaded.

"Don't think... I won't blow your pretty head clean off to shut you up," its owner warned, wiggling it under Penny's delicate nose.

"Oh!"

"Now, swap places. You drive!"

Penny haughtily turned away, "I most certainly will not! Don't you know who I am? I am the Duchess of Felicia, cousin of the Queen herself!"

"Are you now?" he replied, pressing a paw to his vast cloaked chest. "Well I am Prince Noss of the Jua-mata Tribe, son of the Four Winds. Pleased to make your acquaintance."

Penny squeaked in disbelief, "Prince?"

"I prefer it to 'your highness', your highness," Noss cackled gruffly. "Never mind then, I will drive. How hard can it be? Hahahaaaahaha!"

Pushing the pedals and crunching the gears, Noss enticed the car to spew clouds of ash. Good! Confident of success, the Chakaa pressed the pedal right down – alas, the carriage jolted violently backwards, mounting the kerb, hitting a lamp post and throwing the passengers all about the cabin.

"Gfffgh!" Noss growled, falling over the unyielding wheel.

Nursing his throbbing wound he pushed himself upright again, only to discover he was surrounded by on all sides by Howlers, pistols pointing at him through the rain-flecked windows, Ivan, Uther and even that short blonde one that Noss vaguely remembered shoving aside.

"Stop! In the name of the Republic!" he demanded.

In reply, Prince Noss levelled his pistol at the Duchess of Felicia. "Back off, Howlers!" he growled.

"Sweetpea!" the muddied Monty mewed, looking on helplessly.

"We'll shoot!" Uther warned. "Don't think we won't!"

"Your pistols are soaked through!" Noss dismissed. "Do you think I'm stupid as well as mad!"

Knowing Noss was right, and knowing Noss knew he was right too, Ivan lowered his weapon. "Give up, Noss!" he shouted over the rain. "You can't escape!"

"I will blow this pretty cat's block off, Ivan!"

"No… you won't!" Ivan replied, water dripping off his helmet and jaw. "If you were unwilling to poison hundreds of innocents with black-imperium, you'll not kill one innocent either! I know you!"

"I've changed, old friend!"

"You're a noble hyena warrior, not a lowly murderer!"

"Oh really?" Noss laughed. "Tell that to everyone picking imperium out of their bodies in *The Warren*!"

"Which you knew was empty?" Ivan countered. "You waited until almost everyone had gone! I saw you make a pass of the window, checking one last time before you committed. Even then, how it must've pained you, a prince amongst hyenas, to stoop *so* low!"

With a growl, Noss dipped his chin a little.

"What made you do it?" Ivan asked, more reasonably. "It wasn't money, was it? Someone's got you over a barrel, haven't they? Tell me who it is! Let us help!"

"It was money, you fool!" Noss snarled. "Just money! You understand me? Money and nothing more!"

There was a pause.

Ivan nodded, "Fine then. As you say. But you can still die with honour. Let her go and face me. I'll spare you the indignity of capture!"

"Truly?" Noss replied, his robust features softening. "You would… you would do that for me… my old friend?"

A nod.

Slowly, but surely, Noss lowered the pistol away from Penny, only to press it against his own head.

"No, I'll spare you the indignity of... of spilling my worthless, polluted blood… Ivan," he said, laughing, or crying, it was hard to tell. "Arjana, my love, f-fff-forgive me!"

Penny screamed and covered her eyes.

Click! Fssssss-s-sss…

A puff of ash fizzled out of the pistol, but nothing more dangerous. With a baffled look on his face, Noss tapped the pistol with a bloodied, shaking paw, braced himself and tried again.

Click! Click! Click!

A misfire!

"Hahahahahahaaaa!" Noss laughed, falling forwards over the wheel and dropping the pistol, his shoulders rolling in hysterics. "Aaaahahehehehehohooo!"

The Howlers exchanged unbelieving glances.

"He's insane," Linus observed.

"Nutter, mate," Uther growled.

Ivan seized the moment, opening the passenger door and extracting Penny, who ran to her husband.

Uther, meanwhile, quivered with rage. Unable to stand this cackling hyena any longer he opened the driver door.

"Come here, you son of a roach!" he roared, pulling a hysterical Noss from the cabin by his cloaked shoulders and throwing him down in a filthy puddle. He kicked him in the side and generally administered a beating, before forcing his paws behind him and binding them with a length of Howler-proof wire. "You're under arrest in the name of the Republic!"

"Hahahahaaaahaha!"

Linus joined the fray, but Ivan didn't bother. He knew Noss was a broken beast, beyond resistance, beyond caring. To try and shoot himself, to end his life by his own paw, the ultimate sin for his people, he must be utterly spent.

Why, Noss? Why?

No doubt Elder Amael would have someone extract the truth, and no doubt he would get it.

✤

Riddle District's Howler Den loomed large behind its reinforced gates, great buttresses spread wide like roots, dark, ash-licked spires piercing the leaden sky. At the front, above the main doors, was a huge crest, round and white like the moon, with a black wolf's head stamped within, its vermillion-red fangs standing proud. Red banners emblazoned with the same white circle and wolf's head were draped either side, proclaiming that this Den, this whole district, belonged to the Bloodfangs; just one of the many packs that made up the oligarchic cartel that ran Lupa, but to Casimir's mind one of the most terrifying.

Oh why did we move here?

The nervous rabbit stopped his trembling, three-wheeled truck some distance from the gates; leaving its engine ticking over he hopped out the cabin and hurried round back.

The two red-cloaked Howlers at the Den's gate watched him through the stream of passing citizens. Casimir knew they wouldn't hesitate to draw their pistols and blow him away if they thought anything amiss; a truck-bomb perhaps, driven at the gates by some mad rabbit; or one full of terrorists, even rival Howlers, who were about to leap out and attack the Den. Such things happened, not so much since the war had ended, but still.

"Bruno," Casimir said, looking in the back of the truck.

Bruno was holding Rufus's paw; his clothes were stained in the Howler's blood. It looked bad.

"He still alive?" Casimir asked.

"Yeah," Bruno replied.

"All right, give him here."

"What?"

Casimir explained, "I daren't drive any closer, lad, they might get funny. I'll take him on foot."

Bruno scoffed in disbelief, "You can't lift a wolf!"

"I can drag him," the rabbit sniffed.

"Don't be stupid. I'll do it."

"I don't want you being seen to be involved. It could be dangerous."

Knowing reason was useless on Dad, especially panicked Dad; Bruno rolled his eyes, scooped the bloodied Rufus up and stepped off the back of the truck.

"Bruno-"

"Dad!" the big wolf snapped, adding softly, "Calm down, yeah. We're doing 'em a good turn. It'll be all right."

With that, Bruno strode round the truck and across the street towards the gates, Dad following nervously behind. They passed amongst the pedestrians, some of whom noticed the big brown wolf was holding, of all things, a Howler. They gasped and made themselves scarce, whispered, watched, as Bruno and Casimir stepped onto the unmarked patch of no-beasts-land that surrounded Riddle Den's gates.

Once they crossed some invisible line and were deemed too close for comfort, one of the Howlers stepped forward and held up a paw.

"Halt!" he barked.

The other reached for his pistol, ready to back up his partner.

Casimir grabbed Bruno's shirt, pulling the bold youth to a firm stop.

From a distance, the Howler visually inspected the bundle of rags cradled in Bruno's arms and soon recognised it as a fellow Howler, armoured legs and red tail dangling limply.

"What's the meaning of this, citizen?" the guard growled at Bruno.

The wolf licked his lips, "Well... uhm...."

"My premises was attacked, Howler," Casimir explained, stepping in front of Bruno.

"Attacked, by who?"

"Don't rightly know, sir. Someone threw an imperium bomb in the window, right on one of our tables. This Howler was injured in the blast. We brought him straight here. He's badly hurt, I think."

The Howler strode over and checked for himself, lifting Rufus's black and white helmet just enough to see his face.

"Captain Rufus!" he gasped, shouting, "Open the gates!"

Wrenching Rufus from Bruno's arms, the Howler whisked him through the opening gates, leaving Casimir and Bruno standing bewildered in the rain.

"Let's go, lad," Casimir urged. "Quick, before they come back!"

With Dad tugging furiously on his arm, Bruno peeled his fiery eyes from the Howlers rushing Rufus into the Den and hurried back to the truck. Slamming the door, Dad whirled the steering wheel hard over and performed a near-suicidal U-turn. If the truck could skid and screech it would have, but all she managed was a trundle.

Bruno watched the Den's grand entrance recede into the misty distance, until Dad turned onto the busy main street that paralleled the railway, whereupon the wall of another building obscured the Den from view.

With a sigh, Bruno turned round and settled into his seat.

"You all right, lad?" Casimir breathed, possibly for the first time since stopping the truck. "Lad?" he urged impatiently.

"Yeah, yeah," Bruno replied.

Casimir eyed the blood staining Bruno's shirt and gaiters, "You hurt?"

"No."

"Sure?"

"Yeah. It ain't my blood."

Relieved though he was, Casimir conversely shook his head, long white ears flopping about, "That was a right stupid thing to do, my boy. They could've had us!"

Bruno's triangular ears pricked, "Had us? Whatcha mean?"

"Arrested us, lad! Whatcha think I mean?"

"What for?"

"What for?" Casimir repeated in high-pitched disbelief. "Since when do Howlers need a 'what for'?"

He checked the mirror and, half-expecting Howlers on monobikes to come speeding noisily after them, turned into a side-street so as to lose them in advance.

"Where're we going?" Bruno asked, as unfamiliar shops and houses swung by. "This ain't the right way."

"Just taking precautions, lad."

"Aww, Dad come on! I dunno what you're so worried about; Rufus'll tell 'em we helped him."

"If he survives!" Casimir pointed out. "Even if he does, there's no telling what'll go through their minds in the meantime. I don't wanna be locked up and beaten senseless, do you? After everything I ever told you about the Howlers, you pull a stunt like that. It's in one ear and out the other with you."

Bruno's lower lip quivered a moment, "I had to help. I couldn't just leave him. I couldn't."

The brooding Casimir silently nursed the wheel.

With a wolfen grunt, his son looked out the window at the passing streets of Lupa, opening and closing his right paw.

It still tingled, just a little.

Chapter 5

The three Howlers were arranged in size order, the tall Ivan and stocky Linus acting as bookends to the athletic Uther. Helmets tucked under arms they waited smartly in front of their superior's desk, or as smartly as they could after this morning's chase. Fur unkempt, cloaks damp and gaiters stained with ash, they stood in dire need of polish and grooming oil.

The big, black and white wolf behind the desk wrote notes on the paper in front of him with a golden pen. His magnificent white cloak was pinned with a silver Bloodfang brooch and his silver Howler helmet rested upon the desk, its vacant eyelets looking somewhat sad. An imperium lamp flickered warmly overhead, whilst the rain tumbled down the arched window, distorting the cityscape of Lupa far below.

"So, let me get this straight, Donskoy," the big wolf said, leaning forward and twiddling his pen between the white fingers and dark pads of both paws. "Waffles?"

"Yes, sir," Ivan Donskoy confirmed.

"Rufus dallied about town, knowing full-well the Elders were convened and waiting to discuss his proposals, because he fancied a… 'three-season' waffle?"

"In fairness he hadn't had breakfast, sir."

"Breakfast?"

"Yes, sir."

"I see. And this negligent behaviour didn't move you to protest at all, Captain?"

Ivan shrugged a little, "I protested, Grand Howler Vladimir, but Rufus is my partner, not my subordinate. I can't tell him what to do. We're captains both."

Grand Howler Vladimir Bloodfang Oromov, to give him his full title, looked down at his pen and took a sharp breath, "A rank Rufus would have left behind years ago were it not for such indiscretions. He should be in my cloak, or higher … as should you, Donskoy."

Ivan's stony expression remained so.

Vladimir moved on. "Why Rufus? Why would Noss of all beasts attack him when he is famously a hyena-sympathiser?"

"Whatever the reason, I don't believe Noss's heart was in it, sir," Ivan said.

"Oh?"

"If he'd wanted Rufus dead he'd have done it properly. I think he meant to miss."

"Miss? By Ulf's fangs, the wolf's in a coma!"

Ivan nodded once, "Yes sir, but ordinarily a yellow-imperium bomb isn't too much trouble. We had time to get clear; perhaps ten seconds. It was only because Rufus was protecting some… some foolish boy that he was wounded at all. Noss couldn't foresee that."

Vladimir sighed, "What're you saying, Donskoy?"

"I'm not sure, sir. Only that Noss held back. Perhaps it was meant to be a warning?"

"Humph! A warning aimed at who? Rufus? Does Noss want him to stop speaking up for the hyenas?"

"Why would he?"

"I don't know, Donskoy, but when this gets out it'll be a public relations disaster for the hyenas. They'll look like the worst kind of traitors. Noss must be insane!"

"But a great Howler," Ivan interjected. "I served with him for years, he's not some oaf. He's educated, and clearly as fit and strong as ever. He could have killed Uther too, if he'd tried, but he held back even then."

Uther shot Ivan a dirty sideways glare.

"Eyes front, Wild-heart!" Vladimir snapped.

"Sir!"

With Uther admonished, Vladimir said, "Rest assured, Ivan, I'll get to the bottom of this, by rack if need be."

"Sir, I beg clemency," Ivan blurted.

"Clemency?"

"For Noss. Not on my behalf, but it's what Rufus would want were he able."

Vladimir sat up straight, "But he is not able, nor would it make a blind bit of difference if he were. Noss will be tried and dealt with according to the laws of the Bloodfangs and Lupa. Is that clear?"

Ivan nodded but once, "Yes, Grand Howler."

With that, Grand Howler Vladimir leant back and pondered matters in relaxation whilst his lesser Howlers remained standing in relative hardship. Uther was suffering especially, though he endeavoured to hide it. Vladimir could read it on his face; the ache of the rot. The eager youth had worked hard, apparently, running like the wind to catch Noss. Now his body was dealing with the consequences. It would take some time for the ash to work its way out of his blood and muscles. A trace of the ash was black-imperium, and that would never leave him, but go deep into his bones. One day, when there was no more room, it would overwhelm him, rot him, as with every Howler, even Grand Howlers.

There was a rap at the hefty wooden door.

"Come in!" Vladimir barked, nursing the well-worn arms of his ornate chair.

An athletic, red-furred wolfess in a white cloak and tight white breeches entered the office. She had a rapier by her hip and a sparkle in her green eyes. With a quick glance at the Howlers, she addressed Vladimir. "I've found something," she said simply, flapping a folder.

"Already?" Vladimir replied.

The newcomer went to speak, but then flicked her file at the Howlers. "Out," she said.

Vladimir slowly looked to Ivan and his lower-ranking comrades. "Dismissed," he confirmed.

The Howlers saluted by thumping their fists to their chests and then holding them forward.

"Oh, and Mills," Vladimir added firmly.

The blonde Linus Bloodfang Mills faced front again. "Yes, Grand Howler Vladimir?"

His superior gave him a withering look, "Next time you requisition a car, make sure you're not putting Felician dignitaries in mortal danger. Montague and Penelope Buttle are members of the Felician Royal Family."

Linus gulped, "Yes, Grand Howler Vladimir, I realise that now."

"You will apologise to them at once. Is that clear?"

"Y-yyy-yes, sir."

"Off you go."

Despite being dismissed, Linus lingered awkwardly.

"What's wrong, Mills?" Vladimir sighed.

"Where c-ccc-can I find them, sir?" Linus stuttered.

"I don't know, Howler, but you had better find out!"

"Yes, sir."

Linus and the others made good their escape – almost.

"Wild-heart, wait outside," the wolfess said, adding, "I need to see to you."

Uther cringed, shoulders hunched, grumbling something.

"Pardon?" the wolfess barked.

"Yes, Grand Howler Janoah."

"That's more like it."

Once Uther had closed the door a little too loudly, Janoah pulled up an ornate chair and fell into it; she didn't need to ask Vladimir's permission, she was his equal, a Grand Howler, one of only two in Riddle District.

"You've business with Uther?" Vladimir asked her.

Janoah dodged the question, "He looks tired."

"He's the one who ran Noss down. He might've gotten away if Uther hadn't stayed on him."

"Commendable. He's coming along that one. Rufus's eye for talent hasn't failed yet."

"Indeed."

"Who's the dumpling?"

"Mills? He's new," Vladimir said, moving on, "What've you found?"

The red-furred Janoah threw her file on Vladimir's desk with both expert precision and a wry smile. "Dirt, on the long-ears."

"Who?"

"The owner of the café," Janoah clarified.

"Ah yes. We're grateful to Citizen… Claybourne, of course. We'll make sure he's recompensed for his loyalty and common sense."

Janoah checked her claws, "We'll see."

Curious at her circumspect words, Vladimir opened the file. There was an old mug-shot of a young white rabbit looking rather beaten up, along with sundry reports.

"What's all this?"

"The good citizen's extensive criminal record," Janoah said, still checking her claws.

"What of it?"

"He fought in the war; on the wrong side."

Vladimir let out a tiny grunt of annoyance, "So did a lot of beasts, little and noble. We had the amnesty; what's passed is passed. What's the use in aggravating old wounds?"

Janoah let her paws flop down, "Leverage?"

Similarly, Vladimir let the file flop down, "All right. What've you really found?"

"Well, Rufus found him actually."

"You've lost me."

Janoah rolled her green eyes around Vladimir's pokey office of books and trinkets. "Oh come on, Vladimir," she huffed. "You don't think he was frequenting some third-rate café for the fabulous menu? Rufus never just does anything."

"Yes, I gather he was out to embarrass Amael in front of Den Father Vito by turning up fashionably late."

"Well, that may have been half his reasoning," Janoah conceded. "The other half is in that file."

"The rabbit?"

"No, his 'son'."

Janoah said 'son' in such a loaded manner that Vladimir was compelled to pick up the file again and flick through until something stood out.

Some grainy, grey photos of big, dark and very muscular wolf, wearing an apron and breeches; he was unloading barrels from a truck. The pictures were evidently covertly taken, doubtless by one of Janoah's discreet little beast agents. There were more photos of Rufus entering a café and sitting in the bay window, chatting with the big wolf.

Vladimir shook his head. "Spying on your husband, Janoah?" he tutted. "Shame on you."

Janoah ignored the jibe. "Those were taken weeks ago. They weren't brought to my attention until today. I'm going to bring that cub in, as someone should've weeks ago."

"Janoah, you can't arrest wolfen citizens just to prevent Rufus going about his 'business', embarrassing though his antics may be to you-"

"Don't be tiresome, Vladimir!" Janoah cut in sharply. "Those barrels are being delivered, they're full of beer. They must weigh a two-hundred pounds, yet that cub is throwing them around like pillows! Do you think that's natural in a wolf? Look at him!"

Vladimir took another gander at the pictures. The extremely burly young wolf plucked a barrel up in the first, swung it up onto his shoulder in the other, before strolling off in the third without a care in Lupa. Janoah had a point.

"The long-ears adopted him," Janoah said, leaning back in her chair and crossing her long legs. "They've only been on the premises a few months. He's the cook. Rufus probably went in for a cuppa and felt a tingle in his bones."

"Dodger?" Vladimir assumed.

"Well you don't get arms like that just by beating batter," Janoah chuckled. "Werner knows them a little, he says the cub does a little boxing, but still. I've sent him to bring them in; we'll soon find out if he's just a pretty face. If he resists induction I can use his father's past to… change his mind."

Vladimir closed the file with a flick of the fingers. "So where do I come in?"

"Come in, Oromov?"

"You have no reason to tell me any of this, and if you have no reason to tell me something, you don't. I'm a very busy wolf Janoah so spit it out; I've a mad hyena to interrogate before lunch."

Janoah took a sharp breath, then explained, "Rufus... isn't doing so well."

"Oh?"

"Doctor Josef says he needs more venom, but he's already well over his ration."

"These are lean times," Vladimir stated, unmoved.

"Get some for him," Janoah demanded.

"Impossible."

"I know you have contacts in the supply chain. Pull some strings and I'll let you have the boy."

Vladimir sucked his cheek and twiddled his golden pen.

Janoah shuffled in her chair, pawing its arms, "You can present him to Elder Amael and take all the credit."

Vladimir played down the deal, "Even if he's suitable Howler material, Rufus found him first-"

"Rufus is in no position to contest it," Janoah dismissed. "When he's on his feet again, I'll tell him we brought the boy in for questioning and you sensed his corona during the interview."

Vladimir nodded, "You've thought this all through, haven't you?"

"I like to keep you boys quiet."

"All right, but what if the cub turns out to be useless? You've no hard evidence yet just... barrels."

"Then I'll compensate you another way."

"I don't want your money, Janoah, short of paying the paws I'll need to grease."

"Who said anything about money?" Janoah piped indignantly. She yawned a little, "We're so rare, we Howlers of the fair sex, so much more exhilarating than those Common Ground harlots. Can't beat a real wolfess of the blood, eh Vladimir?"

"Humph! Rufus copes without you."

"Unhappily, you're not so inclined," Janoah swiped back.

Pulling back in his chair, Vladimir sniffed officiously, "The Lupan Law states-"

"Oh, spare me! Are you a fusty old cobweb already, or are you a real alpha wolf?"

His honour and strength challenged, Vladimir thoughtfully popped the lid his golden pen on and off with a thumb. He cleared his throat and looked to his office window, watched the rain tumble down. There was no way out.

"One sting for the boy," he stipulated at last.

"Or me," Janoah beamed, "a bargain both ways."

✢

Uther sat on a bench in the dingy hallway watching the imperium lamps flicker overhead. Ivan and Linus had long departed for the washrooms to render themselves presentable for duty again. It was only midday and there was the rest of the shift to get through.

Wriggling his toes, Uther ran a paw down inside an armoured thigh and rubbed his sore muscles. Sprinting at imperious speeds had taken its toll. He needed a hot bath, a massage, a grooming, maybe the company of a fair wolfess later tonight; that would take his mind off the rot.

A red wolfess in a white cloak and silver armour stepped in front of Uther – Janoah.

Wild-heart hopped smartly to his feet, "Grand Howler!"

"At ease," she said.

Uther stood thus; feet apart, paws behind back. To his surprise, Janoah slapped a ruddy paw to his dark, bluish-grey arm and squeezed firmly.

"I want to thank you for bringing my husband's assassin down," she said sincerely, looking Wild-heart in his conversely pale-furred, mask-like face. "You did well, Trooper. Rufus was right to recommend you promoted to First Class."

Uther's bright eyes flitted left and right a little as he fathomed what best to say. "It were my duty, Grand Howler. I couldn't have done it without Blade-dancer 'n' Woodlouse."

"Wood what?"

"Mills, Linus Mills, marm, my new partner. He kinda reminds me of a... well a... a

Woodlouse, like."

"I'm sure."

Uther shrugged and hiked a thumb round back, "It's the shield. Don't see many about."

"No, it's not a popular choice these days," Janoah acknowledged, frowning, "He any good this Mills?"

"They reckon so, marm."

"I'm asking you, Wild-heart."

"Could stand to lose a few pounds, maybe," Uther suggested through a grimace.

"Yes," Janoah hummed, cupping her paws behind her back. "You know, at first I dismissed you as one of my husband's little indulgences… but it seems I was mistaken. You're more than a pretty face, aren't you?"

Gulping, Uther deftly changed subject, "How's Cap'n Rufus doing, if I may?"

Janoah paused, perhaps to weigh up whether or not Uther really cared. "He's in a bad way," she admitted, with a flick of her ears. "It took Josef three hours to pick all the imperium shards out of him. Fifteen in all."

"Thump me," Uther whistled.

"Quite," Janoah agreed. "Still, nothing a little sting can't fix, eh?"

There was a distinctly awkward pause.

The Grand Howler rolled a paw, "I… don't suppose you have any lying around your quarters, Trooper?"

So that's what this is about, Uther realised. Janoah's fishing for venom. Rufus must really be up the proverbial schmutz canal without a paddle.

"No, marm," said Wild-heart, cringing with embarrassment, "I don't even have any for meself, not until the next batch comes in."

"Ah."

"I'm sorry."

"No, I'm being unfair," Janoah sighed. "You've already risked your neck twice for Rufus. You'll get in trouble."

Uther spread his paws, "I'd do it, if I could. I owe him that much for getting me out of…. I mean, for convincing the Bloodfangs to take me on, marm."

A careful nod.

"It's not fair. Imperium ought to be shared out equally, marm. The higher ranks get too much and us foot soldiers too little; we're the ones working the streets, not them-"

"I'll pretend I didn't hear that dissenter talk, Uther!" Janoah hissed. "Imperium is earned, not given. If stings were distributed regardless of rank there would be no incentive to achieve; the pack would be full of rotting gazers staring at walls! Just imagine if every beast received the same wages too, nobody would try harder than the next and nothing would get done."

"But-"

"Rufus is an exception," Janoah interjected, heading off any accusation of hypocrisy. "His academic work has held him back; Ulf knows he should be an Elder by now! As it is I have to beg and borrow to see him through the hard times." The Grand Howler chuckled falsely, "Sometimes I wonder why I bother, I really do."

Silence, but for the humming of imperium lamps.

Janoah made to leave, but lingered long enough to add, "Take the rest of day off, Wild-heart, you and Ivan. I can't offer you stings, but I can offer you rest and recuperation."

"What about Linus?"

"Linus? Oh, yes, your little Woodlouse too. I'll have Boris clear you all for a bonus; Riddle District may be poor, but treat our Howlers right in this Den."

Uther saluted extra smartly, "Thank you, Grand Howler!"

Authority and loyalty expertly sewed, Janoah merely grunted in recognition and took her leave.

Chapter 6

Bruno climbed on the table he was using as an impromptu ladder with a board of wood in his strong paws. He put it against a section of the shattered bay window and hammered it in place. Between hammer strikes, he heard a pained grunt from behind the bar.

"Dad, leave it to me," he tutted at the pair of white ears poking up. "You'll do your knee in."

Casimir got up and emptied his dustpan into a bin. "I'm fine," he said. "There's ash everywhere. I don't want you breathing it in."

With a wince the white rabbit knelt down and continued sweeping up broken bottles. Intermingled with the colourful glass was the occasional smoky-grey shard of opaque, glittery crystal – the shrapnel from that yellow-imperium grenade. Long-since decayed into relatively harmless ash, the shards crumbled under the merest touch from Casimir's brush.

"When you've done the windows I want you to clear off outside whilst I sweep up proper," he said. "It's gonna get right nasty in here."

"Dad, don't fuss."

"You're one to talk! Knee this, knee that! Anyway, we can't open like this, so you're no use to me here. The air's nice and clear after that rain; a walk'll do you good."

Bruno couldn't argue with that. With a sigh, he pushed another board to the window frame.

"Go see your girlfriend-"

"Dad!" Bruno barked.

Casimir ducked behind the bar, as if dodging his son's reproach. Bruno could see his long ears wobbling to and fro as he shook his head and chuckled.

Between boarding up windows, Bruno blurted, "Do you reckon he'll be all right?"

"Eh?"

Bruno said the name quietly, "Rufus."

"Oh," Casimir said, with an awkward sniff, "I dunno, lad. It's no concern of ours. We did our bit."

Bruno hammered another nail in and, given a moment's thought, posed another question. "Why would someone want to kill him, do you think?"

Casimir reluctantly humoured him. "Howler business, lad. Rival pack probably has it in for him over some old grudge. The war's never quite left us."

"Yeah, but he's so nice."

"That's the trouble, 'en it? It's his impartialist streak. He didn't have to give us a penny for his food, not on his territory, but he shelled out. The old guard don't like his sort. They fear another uprising. If it wasn't for the fact Rufus is a war hero they'd have done him in years ago."

"He's right. Every beast should be equal-"

"Don't start lad."

"I'm not, I'm just saying."

"Well *don't* say! Don't even think. Just keep your head down and walk on by."

Bruno huffed and puffed, but kept silent. Boarding up the last strip of shattered windows in brooding silence, the young wolf downed tools and stood back.

"Here, how's that?"

Casimir joined Bruno, inspecting his work like a forebeast. "Beautiful," he declared, patting that vast, wolfen back. "You got a knack with your paws, lad, and I don't just mean in the ring, you got practical skills."

With a wry smile, Casimir suddenly jabbed Bruno in the ribs, reeling off a couple of deft punches before the wolf twisted round and blocked the rest, forearms up and defensive.

"Oi!" he barked.

"Hahahaha!" Casimir laughed. "Getting quicker, lad! Getting quicker, but not quick enough."

"You're such a cheater!" Bruno tutted fondly.

"Beasts don't always fight fair. You got to be prepared."

"Yeah, yeah, I know, I know."

Casimir sniffed, "Hmm. Maybe if I can get this place cleaned up in time we can open for the evening crowd."

Bruno leapt on the premise, tail wagging, "I'll help."

"No, lad."

"I'll cover my nose with a hanky-"

"I said no!" Casimir snapped, adding gently, "I appreciate it, you're a good lad, but if you get sick on my account I'll not forgive myself. I can manage, all right?"

Bruno nodded and forced a smile; even as fear's icy claws pierced his hot wolfen heart. Despite trying to block it from his mind his conversation with Rufus haunted him. The Howler had advised Bruno keep it to himself, but that was before the bomb. Would Rufus ever come back? What if he didn't, could I die?

"Dad, I-"

"I'm proud of you, Bruno," Casimir said, at the same time.

Surprised, Bruno gave way. "Eh?" he laughed, rubbing the back of his neck. "What for?"

"Because of what you did," his father explained. "I'm ashamed of myself for being such a coward. You were right to help Rufus, of course you were. He's a good 'un and everyone knows it."

Bruno said nothing.

Casimir wandered across his deserted café. "I-I got scared, "he admitted, throwing his paws up, "I still am; for you, not me."

Bruno wrung the front of his cream-coloured tunic with both dark brown paws, "I couldn't leave him there-"

"Of course not," Casimir agreed, "but… but I think we should move, lad."

"Move?"

"Aye."

"But we only just got here!" Bruno scoffed.

Casimir tugged his ears, "I know, I know! It's all my fault, lad, I knew coming to Riddle District was a bad idea. It's right rough around here and I swear the Ashfall's gotten worse. Werner said he'd look after us; he certainly got this premises on the cheap 'en all, but I can see why. It's just not safe."

"We can't move!" Bruno piped, paws spread. "I… I'll never make any friends if I keep moving every six months."

"You got Sara haven't you?"

Bruno raised a finger. "One friend, Dad. One! It's bad enough that other wolves always ripped the fur out of me in school for being raised by a rabbit, let alone always being the new cub!"

Casimir folded his arms.

"That came out wrong," Bruno groaned, cupping his paws to his head a moment. "But you know what I mean. For Ulf's sake, I was just making friends with someone, a wolf like me."

It took Casimir some time figure out whom Bruno was referring to. "Who? Rufus?" he gasped.

"Yeah."

"Don't be stupid, lad!" Casimir snorted. "He's a Howler!"

"So?"

"So he's scum!" Casimir blustered, gnarling his fingers at Bruno's stupidity "What're you gonna do, lad, hang out together at bars? What'll beasts think of you? You wanna be shunned by everybody in Lupa for kissing a Howler's arse?"

"But you're friends with him," Bruno whined.

"That's business, lad, it's different! I don't go to the pub with no Howlers, nor even Politzi, not even Werner."

Bruno averted his eyes.

"Look, I know he's a good 'un, but he's still a Howler, and a Bloodfang at that," Casimir explained, calmer now. "Besides, everyone knows Rufus is on the way out. He's too strong for his own good, too hungry for venom. He's like a fancy car lad, he needs a lot of fuel." The rabbit pawed his son's shoulder and grimaced, "With this shortage he'll be dead soon, so don't go getting attached. Stick to Sara and other Freiwolves like yerself-"

Suddenly Bruno whirled away and stomped upstairs, ducking under the low ceiling. Casimir imagined his lonely son was going to throw a tantrum, locking himself in his bedroom as he used to not so long ago, but he instead returned in his dark green greatcoat, buttoning the long garment about his mighty wolfen frame.

Casimir followed him to the door, "Where're you going?"

"For a walk, like you said," Bruno huffed, as the door bell jingled overhead.

"It's still raining; take the umbrella."

"I don't need a stupid umbrella!"

"You'll get soaked. Think of your bad chest, you could get pneumonia-"

"For Ulf's sake, Dad, stop mollycoddling me! I'm not your little cub anymore. You 'n' Werner taught me to fight so I could look after myself, right? Be prepared you always say, but all you ever do is wrap me in fluff. It's embarrassing!"

Slamming the door hard enough that the boarded-up windows rattled, Bruno stormed down the shiny, puddle-strewn street with his paws rammed in his pockets and rain-flecked shoulders hunched.

"Ah, lad," Casimir sighed, watching him go.

The enormous hog secluded in the shadows across the road watched as well.

"Follow him," he snorted at his uniformed compatriots of various races and sizes, before biting the head off a fried locust on a stick. He chewed with relish, before wagging the decapitated insect in Bruno's general direction like a gruesome pointer. "Janoah wants to know where he goes and who he talks to before we bring him in," he said, adding, "I'll deal with my old pal Casimir."

✣

The glazed green tiles of the washroom shimmered by the light of imperium lamps as Linus trimmed his whiskers in the mirror. Older wolves often let theirs grow out, but Linus was young and his facial blossom was patchy and untidy, not at all like Montague Buttle's magnificent feline splays.

The washroom door burst open and Uther moseyed in, humming a little ditty as he went.

"Hello, Woodlouse!" he chirped in his gruff tenor, slapping Linus on his broad blonde back. "Sprucing yourself up for a day out are we?"

"Hardly," Linus replied, adjusting the short towel tied neatly about his hips. "Seven hours until we get off."

"Is it now?"

Uther danced over to his locker and turned the dial on the combination lock, all the while flicking his tail and jigging his legs like some cabaret star. He removed his helmet like a hat, twirling it deftly over one paw and into the darkness of the locker, whereupon the red-imperium fangs slowly lost their lustre. Uther's whole helmet was fortified with imperium not just the fang decoration, his leg armour too. The metal comprising Howler armour was known as eisenglanz, an alloy of steel and, of all things, imperium ash. Eisenglanz was not only physically tough, but the ash melded within the steel acted as an insulator and helped diminish the burning plasmatic attacks Howlers could inflict on one another. The ash gave naked eisenglanz a distinctive grey sheen, like pencil-lead.

Uther unbuckled his twin swords and threw them in with the helmet. They, and indeed all Howler weapons, were made of eisenglanz's cousin, kristahl. Kristahl was steel impregnated with active imperium, blue and red being the most useful and economically viable options, though white-imperium swords were known. The imperium within kristahl performed the opposite task to eisenglanz, it channelled and even enhanced a Howler's plasmatic attacks, like lightning rods.

"Someone's in a good mood," Linus laughed, watching Uther dance. "Have you just been promoted?"

"Hah! It's not that easy, mate."

Uther unpinned his brooch and peeled off his waist-length, hooded cloak, or mantle to give it its proper name, revealing his smart, dark red Bloodfang tunic with its many shiny buttons running exclusively down the left side.

Howler mantles and tunics were made of imperium-weave, woven from the thread of giant silkworms fed upon imperium-laced mulberry bushes. Like eisenglanz, imperium-weave was a kind of armour. The conductive fabric helped spread and dissipate the energy-based attacks of an enemy, but was less disruptive to a Howler's own corona than eisenglanz. Eisenglanz breastplates, gauntlets, greaves and so forth protected a Howler from another but also dampened the wearer's corona, and were cumbersome to boot. The Bloodfangs extolled the speed and strength of their Howlers above defence or mechanical contrivance, so they did not wear breastplates, nor even gauntlets; only their legs which played little role in projecting their imperious fury were well-protected.

Tossing his glowing brooch carelessly in the locker, Uther hung his cloak over a radiator to dry and swiftly unbuttoned his tunic to do the same, exposing his dark, blue-grey back to Linus. His chest and belly were white; a marked contrast. Uther was one of those strikingly dichotomously-coated wolves who looked like they had fallen face-down in a puddle of paint.

More striking still, Uther's fur rippled with muscle and sinew like no other wolf Linus had seen. Broad-chested and wasp-waisted, he looked a matchless athlete even amongst Howlers.

The stocky Linus felt quite inadequate.

"Mate... something's happened," Uther sighed gravely, shaking his head.

His woes forgotten, Linus pushed himself off the sink and approached his partner. "Not Captain Rufus?"

Uther whirled around, paws spread. "I'm afraid we've got the day off!" he whooped.

"What?" Linus gasped in relief, stammering, "S-sss-says who?

"Janoah! She said we deserved it, me and Ivan. I convinced her to let you off too, Woodlouse."

Silence.

Uther gruffed at length, "Well, whatcha say?"

"Thank you," Linus replied. "Sorry I-I was miles away."

Sitting on a bench, Uther unbuttoned his ash-stained white gaiters, removed his boots and made grand plans. "We'll go to the Common, get a little merry, maybe pick up some company, eh?" He looked to Linus, "Anything you wanna do?"

"Do?"

"Yeah, as in fun."

There was a distinct pause.

"You do *do* fun, doncha, Woodlouse?"

"Yes of course," Linus replied, grimacing, "Sorry, what is this 'Woodlouse' thing?"

Uther cackled, glad Linus had finally noticed, "That's yer name."

"It's Mills, Linus Mills-"

"Yeah, yeah, but you remind me of a woodlouse, mate, or a pea bug if you prefer."

"Pea bug?" Linus whined – he did not prefer it.

"Yeah!" Uther went on. "What with yer shield on yer back and short little legs, you look like you're gonna roll up just like a pea bug. Hahahaha!"

"Yes, well, I-I-I can't help my shape," Linus defended.

"No, but you didn't even know what a gazer was. You been living under a log, Woodlouse? Haaaah! You're too funny, mate."

Ears low, Linus looked down and away.

"Aww, come on, Linus," Uther cooed. "It's a term of endearment! Really, I mean it. I give all my partners a name, just like them hyenas do. It's an honorific title, like Blade-dancer and Red-mist. You're Wood-louse. Hahahahaha!"

Succumbing to Uther's contagious laughter, Linus fought a smile for the longest time. Once all merriment had faded, he asked, "So what happened to your last partner?"

"First one, Smiles, he was promoted away," Uther said, continuing on a heavier note, "Second one, Dusty, got topped by a sting dealer. We were raiding an illegal imperium refinery and... bang, some bastard shot him. Dead in a flash."

"I'm s-sss-so sorry," Linus seethed.

"Yeah. Just how it goes, you know."

Another, most protracted silence.

"We could go to the pictures," Linus suggested out of the blue, though it sounded more like a question.

"Pictures?" Uther repeated, breaking from a trance. "Yeah, good idea. We'll take 'em to the pictures. I recommend a horror flick, so we can comfort 'em, if you know what I mean. Eh, eh?"

"Them?"

"The girls!" Uther tutted, slapping Linus in the stomach with the back of a paw. "You in?"

Linus rubbed the back of his neck, "Well… uh…."

Uther threw a paw up, "What? I'll pay. My treat, mate."

With a tiny grunt, Linus caved in, "All right."

"That's better! Oi, where's Ivan; we should invite him too."

"He said he was going to the infirmary wing," Linus said.

"What for, to see Rufus?" Uther scoffed. "There's nothing we can do to help him. Best to take our minds off it. We got the roach who attacked him and that's all we can do."

Linus made his way to the mirrors again. "We shot the messenger, at least," he said.

Uther kicked off the last trappings of Howler armour and donned a towel. He looked perplexed whilst he tied it off, but soon figured out what Linus meant. "Oh, Vladimir'll get it out of him," he growled. "If that cackling hyena knows who hired him, he'll talk. They all talk on the rack."

"Rack?" Linus squeaked. "Do they still use that here?"

"Puh! Everyone does mate, don't you doubt it."

"But… but the Lupan Laws forbid it!"

"Hahaha! Lupan Laws, he says. Oh, Woodlouse, you're killing me. Hahahaha!"

"It's n-nnn-not funny! The Lupan Laws are important-"

"Aye! But he's a hyena, mate! They don't rack us wolves no more, at least not officially, but hyenas are another matter."

Linus looked nonplussed.

"Oi, did you see his eyes, mate?" Uther went on. "Purple! That's the purple-imperium them hyenas take. That stuff is the worst, goes straight to the brain. Makes 'em nuts."

"Yes. He must be very strong to retain his wits."

"Puh! Has he though?"

Without comment, Linus popped the cap off his little white bottle of *Glimmer*, the most trusted brand of wolfen grooming oil in Lupa, and sprayed it over his body. After rubbing in the scented oil he combed his fur through, removing loose hair and flicking it into a special sink reserved for the task of grooming. Linus combed every exposed inch, under his arms and chin, down each leg, but not his back, for he couldn't reach – that's what grooming parlours were for, or failing that, a friend. Some considered it demeaning to groom another wolf, something subservient betas did for dominant alphas.

Uther is unlikely to comb my back, Linus thought, remembering this morning's conversation in Riddle Market. Uther 'ain't nobody's beta' and all that.

"Grrrffaaagh!"

Hearing a growl of pain, Linus looked for Uther in the mirror – he'd disappeared!

"Uther?"

Abandoning all grooming, Linus hurried round the bench, where he found Uther doubled up on the floor.

"Uther!" Linus gasped, crouching down in all fours. "Uther, what's w-www-wrong?" he stammered.

"Aaaah…ffff… it'll pass," Uther seethed, chest heaving fitfully as he grasped one leg, "I'm all right, mate."

"Rot?"

"Yeah. I knew it were comin' on! Gagh!"

Linus looked on helplessly as Uther writhed on the tiled floor. "Is there anything I can do?" he asked.

"Don't… let anyone… see me," Uther begged.

With a moment's hesitation as he figured out what Uther meant, Linus went to the washroom door. He couldn't lock it, but stood guard lest someone came in. Linus was still thinking of what excuse he could feed a fellow Howler who wanted to bathe when Uther suddenly recovered and clambered up onto the bench. He sat there, massaging his right leg, breathing and grunting and swearing.

Linus returned to his side. "Is it going away?"

"Yeah," Uther said, with a mortified chuckle.

"Must've been bad to have you on the floor."

"Yeah."

"I'll get you a sting," Linus suggested.

"No, I used mine weeks ago, mate," Uther admitted. "I'll be all right in a minute. It's only 'cause of all that running. That'll teach me. Puh!"

Glancing around, Linus whispered, "I… I still have a sting."

Uther's dark ears pricked with interest.

"You can have it."

Nodding, Uther conversely declined the offer, "Nah. I'm fine, mate. Best you keep it."

"I-I don't need it as badly as you."

Uther frowned, "You might yet."

Linus spread a paw. "I haven't had any pains for months," he beamed.

"Well la di dah, good fer you!" Uther snarled over his shoulder, ears flat to his skull

Linus backed off.

"I don't need your charity," Uther claimed. "I'm fine."

"Yes, of course. S-sss-sorry, I…."

Giving the proud Uther one last glance, Linus slowly returned to the sink. He opened his white tin of '*Imperator*', the most trusted brand of toothpaste in Lupa, and scraped out the recommended pea-sized amount with the end of his toothbrush. The advice films on dental health promoted brushing for a minute, no more, no less. Linus checked the second-hand on the clock and timed his brushing accordingly. If he went to the pictures with Uther as planned, there was a fair chance Linus would see the same old information reel whilst waiting for the film. There was a fair chance also that Linus's bored mind would wander then, as now.

'Uther doesn't want your pity, it narrated, like one of those info reels. 'One day that'll be you. You're only a couple of years younger. You're healthy now, but you'll feel the insidious rot again soon enough. And one day, just like your parents, you'll be bedridden long before your natural time, your sight failing, your lovely golden fur falling out in clumps, your once-firm muscles withering-'

Minute up!

Linus rinsed his mouth out and splashed cold water on his face to banish mortal thoughts. When he looked up, water dripping off his chin, he saw Uther standing behind him, dark, muscled arms folded across his white chest, his fierce yellow eyes staring right into Linus's soft blue peepers via the mirror.

"Listen," he grunted, clearing his throat, not that it made any discernable difference, "if you wanna give yer sting to someone, give it to Rufus."

"Rufus?" Linus woofed

"Yeah. He needs it more than anyone."

"B-b-but, surely he's being looked after? They must have stings put by for emergencies."

"I dunno so much, Woodlouse."

Linus turned to face his taller partner, eyes darting to and fro as he tried to get his head around Uther's words.

With a check of the door, Wild-heart took the naïve newcomer aside. "Janoah wanted to see me because she was fishing for extra venom," he whispered. "There's none left for Rufus and by the look on her face he's not gonna make it without some."

"B-b-but he's one of the finest Howlers alive!" Linus spluttered in disbelief. "Surely our Elders r-rrr-recognise that."

"Puh! The Elders are out of touch, mate," Uther dismissed, with the certainty of one who knew, at least in his own mind. "They don't walk the streets like we do, not even Elder Amael. They don't see how it is. They've forgotten, 'en they? That's what happens when they stop being Howlers and start being Elders. Too busy jostling and dealing with each other over money and territory to care about us Troopers. Rufus'd be in a Howler Hospice already if Janoah didn't stand up for him all the time. She's always having to scrounge stings off me and Ivan for him, but… we've given all we can. I got nothing left for me."

"I see," Linus said tentatively, wondering how much of Uther's gossip and opinions were true. He believed the last claim at least. "Well, he can have mine, of course."

Uther felt he had to add a caveat. "If someone catches you you'll be in big trouble. Giving stings away is as bad as selling 'em on the black market; at best they'll flog you, and at worst, well… they'll send you down."

"I'm hardly going to sit on a sting whilst another Howler dies."

"Hah! You're no stick-in-the-mud, Woodlouse, I give yer that," Uther tutted fondly, pinching Linus on the cheek like an adorable cub. "All right, we'll go see Janoah about it now."

Linus nursed his cheek, "We?"

"Yeah; me 'n' you." Uther chirped. "What, think Janoah will see you without me to back you up? You're nothing to her mate; ash on her shoe."

"Thanks."

"Ah, but you'll be something now," Uther assured Linus, heading for the baths. "She's tough, by Ulf is she, but Janoah *never* forgets a good turn. She's a good friend to make, not like that slimy git Vladimir."

✢

Grand Howler Vladimir Oromov entered the room in his full uniform; silver helmet, red tunic, white mantle and all. Kicking the door shut he tossed a hefty file onto the table and turned up the desk lamp. As the rate of imperium gas coming in through the lamp's rubber hose changed, the fire within the glass coughed and sparkled with a mini display of beautiful colours, before settling down to a warm, steady light.

Satisfied, Vladimir slowly pulled the simple wooden chair from under the table, its legs scraping painfully over the rough tiled floor, and sat. Tugging at the chest of his white mantle so it hung more comfortably about his robust Howler frame, he busied himself by flicking through his file and making notes with his golden pen, apparently uninterested in the hyena slouched opposite him in the middle of the depressingly stark, off-white room.

This continued for some minutes, before Vladimir said without even looking up, "The Hyena Organisation for Recognition of Nationhood," adding in a mocking tone, "THORN."

No reply.

"Is that what you've become, Prince Noss, a lowly terrorist? Hmm?"

Still nothing.

"Why target Rufus and Ivan?" Vladimir probed. "You're all old friends. Rufus especially is an ally of your people. He's always stood up for you, sung your hyena virtues, still does. He even saved your life. Yet of all the wolves in Lupa you blow him up. Why?"

Faced with Noss's silence, Vladimir nodded at the Howler Troopers standing in the corners of the room. Like the vast majority of Bloodfang rank and file they were both clad in standard red cloaks, which is where the widely recognised nickname for a Bloodfang, a 'Redcloak', originated. Some had black trims on their mantles, some white, some none, depending on the rank, but most of the lower ranks were red.

One of the Redcloaks stepped into the light, grasped the bound Noss by the scruff of the neck and pulled him upright, revealing his bloodied snout and ripped ear.

"Well?" Vladimir urged impassively from under the fierce anonymity of his silver-plated eisenglanz helmet.

Nothing.

With a nod from the Grand Howler, the Redcloak thumped Noss in the ribs, right where Ivan had wounded him.

"Gaaaagh!"

Ivan's shot had only scraped the hyena's muscled ribs, but the wound was doubtless excruciating.

"Such a disgrace," Vladimir tutted, shaking his head and twiddling his pen.

Prince Noss writhed and seethed.

Vladimir sniffed, "Still, I know what you're made of. I know that even the rack may not break you, though that is what Doctor Josef is going to prepare for you once he has finished setting Rufus right."

"So Red-mist lives!" Noss woofed through a toothy grin, twisting his wire-bound wrists – mere rope wouldn't hold a beast who could channel imperium, only Howler-wire made from insulating eisenglanz would suffice. "I never doubted it!"

"You sound pleased," Vladimir said. "Why is that?"

Noss snorted, "I didn't want to kill Rufus. It was just… business."

"What business?"

Silence.

Vladimir nodded at his accomplice again. The obedient Redcloak smacked Noss across his thick snout with the back of a paw, setting off his nosebleed again. Blood dribbled off the hyena's dark chin and onto his mighty chest, the pale fur there being already clotted and darkened with streaks of gore.

"You'll talk, in the end," Vladimir assured. "You should have thrown yourself under that train, not boarded it."

"Hah! During… the morning rush?" Noss replied, licking his nose of blood. "Hahaaaa! Oh, yes. Just think of the disruption caused to Lupa's busy schedule if… if the train-hogs had been forced to scrape my carcass off the rails. Think of the money lost! I could have set Lupa back millions. Now that would've been a terrorist atrocity for the ages. Hahahahahaaaa!"

Vladimir hummed, "I wager the train-hogs would have left your corpse for the ants to pick over sooner than stop the trains."

"Ants he says! What ants?" Noss laughed. "I see none in this nightmare of our creation! No trees, or bees, or wholesome life at all within a thousand miles of Lupa. Only the roaches and the flies that tolerate the ash and feed on our waste, and if it goes on like this the Erde entire will be like the Far Ashfall one day, a rotting, festering sore!"

The same red-cloaked Howler went to hit Noss, but Vladimir stayed him with a wave of the paw.

Noss ranted on, "Rivers of death, withering crops and famine… walking ribcages." The hyena slumped forward and cried, "If you could but see what my people suffer. If it were your kind looking to you and crying out for help, you would not stand by and let their oppressors go unpunished. You would not, Vladimir!"

"Walking ribcages?" Vladimir snorted. "You expect me to believe THORN's slander?"

"It is the truth! Go to the Reservations and see!"

Vladimir slapped the tabletop; the imperium lamp burning beside him flared up along with the Grand Howler's mighty voice, "The truth, Chakaa Noss, is that your arrogant people will not join our republic despite countless military defeats and generous concessions and thus you must now be treated like naughty cubs!" Adjusting his mantle he continued in his usual, measured tone, "You are fed, you are watered, we spend millions of lupas building new towns for the cooperative tribes to live in. We educate your cubs and provide medicine for your sick; real medicine like you never had before, not useless witchdoctor magic! All this and how do you repay our kindness? With bombings and murder." Vladimir flicked his golden pen at Noss, "Just last week a train was de-railed by THORN activists. You probably know, they bombed the tracks and it went into the river. Hundreds drowned, mostly little beasts, innocent in your eyes. And now you try to assassinate the one wolf in all Lupa, who even THORN admits cares about the fate of the tribes, who stifles his own career to exalt your stubborn, arrogant people?" Shaking his head, Vladimir tapped his pen on the tabletop and said to his captive, "I bring you back to my question, sir! Why did THORN try and kill Howler Rufus?"

Noss rocked back and forth a little and sniggered quietly, yet maniacally, "It was not... not THORN. It was my doing alone. I... did it for the money. I am, no longer a member of THORN. I am weary of the struggle."

"I don't believe you."

"A hyena's got to eat!" Noss snarled, tears rolling down his cheeks. "Nothing to eat out there, Howler, not in the barren wastes you've caged my people in, not even for an anointed prince!" Chuckling, he fell back over his chair, his gaze tipped to the ceiling, chest rising and falling. "Rufus's speeches and articles do not put bread on my table," he sniffed, calmer now, "a few thousand lupas does. It was a trade I was willing to make, to... survive." He licked his broad nose, "Do you think I wanted to do it? Do you think I enjoyed it? I... I love that wolf, as a brother, a father; he taught me how to wield imperium like no other. Look at what you've reduced me to. I'm but a worm writhing in a rotten mantle!"

Vladimir frowned, not in anger, but thought; his helmet hid all emotion, such was its simple power.

The Redcloak went to pull Noss forward and make him face Vladimir and probably give him a slap or two, but again Vladimir mercifully waved a paw to stop him.

Outside, Janoah watched through the tiny cell door window, contemplating.

Noss of the Jua-mata was not your average hyena. Not only was he a Chakaa, a hyena able to wield imperium, but a prince too. He had been trained in the Bloodfang Academy a decade ago as part of an early hyena integration programme, a project Rufus himself had championed. It was hoped if Noss of the Jua-mata became a Howler, other Chaka would follow and his tribe would meld peacefully into wolfen society like everyone else. That integration programme had failed when, after some years serving with Rufus and Ivan, Noss had suddenly hung up his mantle and returned to the tribes in protest at the treatment of his people. Even Rufus had not heard from Noss in the last few years.

Now here he was, back in Lupa and trying to murder the wolf who'd been his friend. Who had paid him, or had someone made him? He would go to his grave with such knowledge unless Vladimir upped the stakes. But of course, Grand Howler Oromov hadn't got to where he was by being just another Redcloak.

As Janoah expected, Vladimir opened his file, aimed the all-seeing, all-knowing bureaucracy of the Howlers at his helpless prisoner, and fired.

"Such a lovely little family you have, Prince Noss," he said.

"Family?" Noss sniffed, facing Vladimir. "I have none left, as well you know."

The Howler took out a piece of paper. "Not old family, but new. It seems a hyena princess and her two cubs, a boy and a girl, were arrested trying to pass out of the Jua-mata Reservation the other week." Vladimir looked up from the paper, "The Jua-mata are your tribe, are they not?"

"What of it?"

"Only... they found this on the hyeness. She goes by the name of Arjana, Princess Arjana, next in line to the Jua-mata throne. She's quite the precocious madam I'm told."

Vladimir held up what Janoah assumed was a crumpled photo, judging by the thick, shiny texture of the sizeable paper.

"What a touching portrait," Vladimir said, turning the photo around and looking for himself. "Most traditional. Very noble."

Noss remained unmoved.

Janoah caught a glimpse of the photo, of a bright-eyed female hyena sitting on a ceremonial throne with countless pillows about her. She was wearing traditional hyeness clothing; boldly-striped robes and necklaces made of bug carapaces. Two cubs sat at her feet, a male and female, twins perhaps; they looked the same tender age. A big male hyena knelt beside them all, somewhat apart, as was tradition in hyena society where males, even princes, were subservient to their spouse. He was wearing traditional male hyena clothing, just a sarong marked with bold black and white dazzle patterns, whilst his muscled body was painted in a similar fashion.

"Two cubs, you sly dog," Vladimir chuckled, turning the photo around again and asking,

"Twins?"

Noss stared at the photo for an age, then his eyes flitted to Vladimir. "Who knows?"

"You, I'd hope."

"They're nothing to do with me."

"So that's not you kneeling down?"

"I'm much handsomer," Noss cackled.

"I see," his interrogator huffed, closing the file. "Then you won't mind that they executed Princess Arjana."

"Executed?" Noss mouthed, his lips quivering.

Vladimir spread a paw, "I was unable to stop it. I'm told they took her away and shot her. The cubs are-"

"Bastaaaards!" Noss cried, lunging from his chair and onto the desk. "I'll kill you all! Graaaaaagh!"

Vladimir shot to his feet. "Back to your chair, you treacherous ingrate!" he bellowed, fists clenched by his sides. His white cloak billowed outwards and the imperium lamp on the desk flared up in a bright flash.

Outside, Janoah ducked just in time as an air-warping pulse of imperious energy tore through the cell, punching out the window she was looking through. Inside, the desk shot forward a few feet, catapulting Noss back into his chair so hard he rolled over backwards. The two Howlers were also knocked off their feet by the near-invisible blast, whilst Vladimir's file fluttered across the room shedding papers all the way.

The Grand Howler was the only one left standing, chest heaving audibly in the silent aftermath. He brushed down his cloak and adjusted his brooch.

"Apologies, Howlers," he told his subordinates, calm as you like. He pulled the now bare table back into position and set the lamp back upon it, before sitting down. "Restrain him properly, will you?"

Noss was dragged away from the wrinkled photo lying on the floor amidst the scattered papers, the one Vladimir had shown him, and set back on his chair, to which he was ruthlessly and painfully wired, paw and foot.

The prince felt nothing of it; he just dipped his chin to his vast chest and wept.

Vladimir put him out of his misery, "I lied."

Noss's rounded-off ears pricked and he looked up, mouth agape, his rough hyena fur wetted with tears and matted with blood.

"Arjana still lives," Vladimir admitted coolly, whilst skilfully, if mindlessly, twirling his golden pen with the fingers of one paw so that it climbed along his digits and back again. "I apologise for my cheap tactics," he said, slipping the pen in his cloak pocket. "It was dishonourable of me, but… it was the only way to catch a beast like you out."

Noss squirmed in his bonds and ground his teeth at his own stupidity. If he had only kept his composure Vladimir would have had nothing to work with.

Now he had everything.

Vladimir set out his stall, paws knitted on the desk, "Help me, Noss, and I'll protect her."

"Protect her?"

"Yes. Tell me what you know. Tell me who paid you to kill Rufus and why."

"You… you w-www-would not believe me," the tormented prisoner spluttered.

"Try me."

"They will kill Arjana now anyway after what I did!"

"I'll see her safe."

"You don't have the power, Vladimir."

"It's not about power, Noss. It's about favours and bribes and trust, you know how Lupa works. I've contacts in the Watchers; it will be no trouble to arrange a… clerical error."

Noss took a moment to compose himself, to lick his bloodied lips. "On your honour?"

"With Ulf as my witness. I will see to it Arjana and her cubs are at least treated well. I have no bone to pick with some hyeness. You know me; I'm a reasonable wolf."

The longest time passed.

Noss stared at Vladimir, scrutinising his eyes, the only part he could see. Satisfied, the hyena dipped his gaze.

"They c-ccc-came to me," he said, staring at the floor, "all the way out to the Reservations. They put me in a limo and drove me back in style. Hahaha! I was flattered to be honest."

Vladimir took a sharp breath, "Who?"

Noss didn't answer, but kept talking, "I told them, one does not simply kill the wolf our people call Red-mist. He is too strong, even for me." He chuckled a little, "They said it wouldn't be a problem and furnished me with a... black-imperium bomb, like the one I tricked Ivan with, only this one was no trick, Vladimir, it was real. Not even microbes would've gotten out of *The Warren* alive if I had used that like I was instructed to."

"Then why didn't you?" Vladimir said.

"I'm not so far gone as to use a black-imperium bomb!" Noss spat, adding, "Me, a Chakaa, yet sane compared to them! Hahahaaaaaahahahaaa!"

Vladimir waited patiently – hyenas were such a chore, especially the Chakaa.

Composing himself, Noss continued, "Without telling them I disposed of the vile thing in a pit and procured myself a yellow-imperium bomb. I wasn't proud of that method either, but... this is Rufus, and Ivan. One does not fight such wolves face to face and win. You must use cunning. They offered me a hundred-thousand lupas to do it. It was a mere nothing to those... creatures before me. They pulled it from their cloaks like pocket-change. My people die from hunger, and *they* have a hundred thousand lupas in their cloak pockets? Is this the Republic you fight for, Howler?"

Vladimir wasn't here to discuss politics. "They?" he asked, his patience thinning. "Names, Prince Noss."

Noss smiled briefly and simply continued his story, "I demanded half the money up front, you see, so even if I failed I would come away with something. I secretly made arrangements for Arjana and the cubs to get out of the Reservation, that's what the money was for, to grease the appropriate paws. You're right; I do know how it works." The hyena prince looked down, "But I've been betrayed, evidently. I'm but a naïve fool when it comes to trust. Arjana has always told me so. She loves me for it; I... I know not why."

Vladimir asked again, "Who paid you? I need names."

"Ah, now we come to the part you won't like, Oromov," Noss cackled in his hair-tingling tenor. "You'll call me a liar... and rack me... and I'll be long-since devoured by the ants before you believe me. But one day, when it's too late to act, you shall remember me."

"Noss," Vladimir growled tiresomely, "if you don't start making sense I'm going to rack you personally."

"Come closer, Howler, I cannot speak it out loud."

"You will say it loud and clear!"

"It is for your ears alone," Noss sniffed, his eyes straying to the cell door, "It's... safer for you that way."

Janoah withdrew from the window a little; but remained within earshot.

Giving the cell door a passing glance, Vladimir stood up and walked over to Noss, his fine silver armour rattling. He stooped behind the prisoner, close enough for Noss to whisper in his ear, but not to bite it off if the mood struck; Vladimir was no fool.

The bound Noss leant his head back and whispered in the Grand Howler's ear. Try as she might, Janoah could not hear what was said. The whispering went on for nigh on a minute, perhaps more, with Noss cackling halfway through, as he was wont to do. Vladimir's face was hidden by his helmet and Janoah could not gauge his reaction.

Until he exploded.

"Enough!" he barked, smacking Noss across the face, sending blood spattering across the tiled floor. "You dung beetle!" the Grand Howler snarled, pacing around the cell. "I extend my paw and this is how you repay me, with ridiculous slander? Is this a sick hyena joke?"

"In our culture... dung beetles are noble creatures," Noss replied, through a crooked, bloody grin. "They help clean up the mess others make. Now you have a mess on your paws, perhaps you can clean it up and earn... nobility."

"Do you want your family to die?" Vladimir seethed.

Noss cringed at the thought, but tipped his head back and said philosophically, "Killing those I love won't change the truth. What do you want from me, Howler, a lie that is easier on your ears than the truth? Ah, but you're used to that. You and all your kind. You see and hear only what is convenient, remaining deaf and blind to difficulties. That is how you wolves live with yourselves, how you pollute, rape and enslave. Self-deception. Hahahahaha!"

Noss laughed, his muscled, spotty shoulders trembling, and turned his face away.

Vladimir raised a paw to strike the arrogant hyena, but stayed it. "You must think yourself an intellectual," he said, producing a kerchief from his cloak pocket. He wiped his paw clean of Noss's blood and contemptuously threw it at the prince's face. "You forget who provided you your education, ungrateful savage that you are."

"Must be the rot," Noss cackled. "It'll get round to you too… one day."

As Vladimir turned and strode for the cell door, Janoah stole away.

With one paw resting on the door lever, Vladimir looked back at his subordinates. "Rack him," he ordered, before stepping out and slamming the door in his furious wake.

✦

The rain had ceased and the clouds were breaking, allowing hazy sunshine to play across the buildings and streets far below Janoah's office. Ships chugged along the sparkling river, whilst motor carriages ambled across bridges.

Brrrring!

Janoah snatched the phone from her desk.

"Yes?" she snapped, holding the mouthpiece and stand in one paw and the earpiece in the other. "Who?" she scoffed further, glancing out the window. "I'm busy. Send him away."

Janoah waited and listened.

"Wild-heart as well?" she said, more patiently. "I see. All right let them in."

She put the phone aside and sat in her swivelling chair. Spying her library, she grabbed a random book and opened it up on her cross-legged lap. To add to the air of nonchalance she whipped out a silver case from her cloak pocket and popped an ember between her lips, not even noting the flavour until an orange-flavoured cloud erupted from her nostrils.

Upon hearing the expected knock at her door Janoah said loftily, "Come in."

Not looking up from her book, she glimpsed two wolves out the corner of her eyes, one blonde and stocky – some nobody, Linus Mills or something – the other a duotone black and white bit of athletic young talent – Uther Wild-heart.

Janoah slowly lowered her book and swivelled round to face them. They were out of Howler uniform and into breeches and shirts, Linus a smart, blue, collared top, Uther a sleeveless red tunic. Both had coats slung over an arm. Uniform or not they stood to attention and saluted; fists to chests then out.

"Howlers," Janoah said, removing her smouldering ember and blowing orange mist, "where *are* your uniforms?"

"You… gave us the day off, Grand Howler," Uther gently reminded her.

"I suppose I did. I trust you'll pamper yourselves down the Common?"

"Yes, Grand Howler."

Janoah spread a paws, ember smouldering between fingers, "Then what more do you boys want from me?"

The blonde Linus glanced nervously at Uther, who nodded a little. Linus reached into his pocket and produced a small cardboard tube no bigger than a packet of mints. It had been dipped in beeswax to seal it and was banded with a white stripe at one end, along with some bold warning labels.

Janoah stared awhile, apparently unmoved. Slowly her green eyes strayed to the uneasy Howler Linus.

"What's the meaning of this?"

Linus gulped, "Well… uh… it's for, uhm… I…."

"Spit it out, Howler!"

"Captain Rufus, marm! F-fff-for him, marm. I mean, Grand Howler Janoah. Please give it to him, on my behalf."

More staring, then a crackly-toned inquiry, "Vladimir sent you?"

Uther took that one. "No," he scoffed, sounding insulted.

"Pardon?"

"No, Grand Howler."

On that disclosure, Janoah came over far more intrigued. She snapped her book shut and leant forward across the table to pick up the sting. "Do you have the foggiest idea what you're doing, Howler… Mills, is it?"

Linus nodded, and nodded again. "Linus Mills, marm."

"Possible flogging or banishment to the Gelb mines not off-putting at all, young Mills?"

Linus shook his head, though he had to think about it.

Janoah puffed on her ember, before speaking in a dangerous tone. "Good. Because if I thought you were doing this for material gain, or to procure my favour, I might have to report you. You can't buy me, Linus. Not trying to buy me, are you Trooper?"

"N-nnn-no, Grand Howler."

"You're sure?"

Linus closed his eyes and licked his lips, summoning his courage. "C-c-captain Rufus… he's my hero and I-"

"Hero!" Janoah spluttered, shooting orange vapour in all directions like a boiling pan. "Howler Rufus is your hero?" she finished, with a wry chuckle.

"I-I admire him greatly, Grand Howler."

"Then I had better accept on his behalf, hadn't I?"

Linus nodded, "Please, marm."

Janoah reached for the tube, but paused, asking, "How did you even know he needed it?"

"Uther said that you-"

Uther kicked Linus in the shin, silencing him.

"He said what?" Janoah cooed, looking at Uther. "That my husband is going to croak without your help? What an offensive supposition. Bedridden he may be, but Rufus could still blow the both of you out the window behind me without getting up, such is his power." Janoah hummed, "That's why they did this to him. They fear him. Not the hyenas, no, it's someone else."

Linus and Uther remained silent.

"Very well," Janoah said, snatching the sting and swivelling round to the window amidst a swirling cloud of orange vapour. "This meeting never occurred. If either of you breathe a word of this to anyone, or in any way try and force my paw, you'll be ant food long before me."

Another, prickly silence.

"Dismissed."

The Howlers saluted and filed towards the door.

"And Mills," Janoah called after them.

"Yes, Grand Howler?" Linus barked back, standing smartly to attention again.

"I'll remember this."

Linus said nothing, though his eyes darted about.

Janoah waited an eternity before she deigned to release him, "Off you go."

No sooner had Linus took his leave and shut the door than the phone rang again.

Brrring!

Janoah answered it with the same celerity as before, her paw slightly checked by first slipping Linus's precious donation into her cloak pocket.

"Yes?" she said, facing the window. "Speak up, it's a bad line." Pressing the phone to her ear she repeated, "He's got off the train in the Arkady District, did you say? He's probably headed to the university; Werner says he goes there a lot. He's not a student, but his girlfriend is. Yes, she'll make good leverage if he proves difficult. Stay on him, but *wait* until he's left Eisbrand territory before you move in and arrest him, we can't overstep our jurisdiction. Right. Carry on."

Janoah put the phone down. Stubbing out her ember, she headed for the door, fondling the cardboard tube in her cloak pocket all the way, unbelieving of her luck.

✧

Uther wordlessly led the way through Den's twisting, lamp-lit innards to the ground floor. With his mind dwelling on what had transpired, Linus didn't even think about where Uther was taking him until he got there. The pungent odour of imperium fuel and machine oil woke him from his worries as he stepped into Riddle Den's vast garage, with its rows of cars, trucks and monos, most of them black and red and marked on their bonnets or flanks with the smart Bloodfang crest.

Slipping on his long, dark red coat, Uther marched down the rows, keys jangling, and picked out one of the few monobikes that wasn't painted in Bloodfang livery, or in any way marked for the pack. It was a robust, green-bodied machine with a dragonfly motif stencilled on the side.

Linus hurried over. "You've got your own mono?" he gasped at Uther.

"Yeah."

"It's beautiful. Giacomo Valerio Model 20?"

"Aye, an original GVM-20 *Dragonfly*," Uther chuckled, patting the dark green bodywork and pointing to the dragonfly logo. "Not as fancy as Ivan's *Spider*," he said, glancing across at the intimidating black mono parked nearby, its right flank decorated with a white spider, "but still a rung up from the little *Springtail* all the cubs ride. Hah!"

Linus could but smile and nod.

"Nothing wrong with the *Springtail*, of course," Uther tactfully rowed back. As a fresh face, Linus was likely the proud caretaker of a standard issue Giacomo Valerio Model 12 *Springtail*. "Where's your wheel, mate?"

"I-I-I don't have a wheel."

Uther frowned, "Haven't they sorted you out with one yet?"

After a moment's hesitation and neck-scratching, Linus guffawed, "Not yet."

"Typical! Here, hop on."

Donning his blue coat, Linus sat behind Uther. The seat was firm, but comfortable; the antithesis of his admission.

"Actually, Uther… I-I-I can't really, uhm… ride."

"Can't ride?"

"No. I meant to take lessons at the academy, but I was trying to keep up with my imperiology studies at the same time. Everything went so quickly and well… uh… there it is."

'Woodlouse' braced himself for a tide of mockery.

Opening a compartment in the bike's contoured bodywork, Uther took out some goggles and strapped them about his eyes. He passed a pair back to Linus, sniffing, "It's not unusual, mate; lots of Howlers ain't ready for a mono until they're a bit older. You'll get there."

Linus was surprised to be let off so magnanimously.

Uther gripping the conductive kristahl steering bars and glanced behind at his goggled partner. "Ready?"

A hearty thumbs-up.

"Hold on then."

Linus gripped the edges of the seat with both paws.

"Mate, hold onto *me*," Uther clarified with a laugh. "Thump me! You'll come off tail over tit otherwise."

"Right."

"Never even been on a mono before, have yer, Woodlouse?"

Laughing, Linus said, "Not since my father took me for a ride and he always put me in front."

Hugging Uther around the waist, Linus knitted his paws tight. Even with a big, heavy coat on Wild-heart was enviably trim around the middle. Linus wished he half as fit. Running after that hyena had shown him up.

"Where to?" Uther sniffed.

"Uhm… the pictures, wasn't it?" Linus replied.

"Pub first, yeah?"

"Right," Linus said. "Actually, s-sss-speaking of pubs, do you know the *Crab and Kettle*?"

"Yeah, it's a tavern down on the canals. Run by otters. I wouldn't recommend it. I know better joints."

"Maybe, but I need to see the Buttles."

"Y'what? Buttles?"

"Montague and Penny," Linus clarified, adding, "The cats from this morning."

"Oh, the two lah-di-dahs you hijacked!" Uther hooted humorously.

"Yes. Vladimir wants me to apologise to them."

"Puh! He can thump off. We're not wasting our well-earned rest sucking up to no cats!"

"It's an order, Uther," Linus said worriedly. "What if he finds out? I'll be in for it."

Gauging his partner's unease, Uther caved in. "Fine. Just don't take too long."

"I-I-I won't."

With a kick of the pedal, Uther's *Dragonfly* coughed and spluttered into quivering life, its single wheel lighting up in a fiery ring of red-imperium. Linus felt the gyroscope whirring inside; as a Howler he could sense it and might yet command such a device himself one day, but for now he held on tight as Uther steered his awesome monobike through the garage and out into daylight.

The clouds were dispersing, giving way to muted sunshine and a surprisingly lovely afternoon.

Chapter 7

"The queen produces chemical smells, 'pheromones', which both tell the hive what to do and stops its members maturing into adults. The worker bees, which are the queen's own eternal children, exist solely to serve her, never once having a thought of their own, controlled as they are by these chemical… edicts."

The hoary old bear ceased lecturing and peered over his puny glasses at the small, black-furred wolfess whose paw had shot into the air.

"Yes, Sara?" he urged.

"What about Toggle, sir?" Sara asked, slowly lowering her paw, and only half way.

"What about her?"

"Will she nae think for herself, now that she's nae under control from her queen?"

The bear nodded, "Possibly. There is limited evidence that bees separated from their hive mature into queens, though nobody has observed the entire process satisfactorily."

Clearing his throat, the teacher slipped one huge paw into the pocket of his waistcoat and returned his attention to the black board, using his pointer to pick out the rear end of a honeybee on his lovingly paw-drawn diagram. "Now then, the pheromones are released from the abdomen-"

"How long will she live for, Professor Heath?" came the brown-furred wolfess sitting beside Sara. She glanced at Sara, then back to Professor Heath, "Toggle, that is."

Heath looked to the elegant student. "I can't rightly say, Olivia. We think queen bees last decades, though even records from the Hummel apiary are inconclusive. The rest of the hive may manage a year or two, except the poor males, of course; they reach senescence soon after pupating whether they mate or not."

"Senescence, sir?"

"Natural death," Heath clarified. He wagged his pointer at the class, "So, you boys best be thankful Arkady University's not a hive, for not only would we 'drones' live merely a day, but queens Sara and Olivia here would be in charge for the duration!"

The class, mostly wolfen and male, laughed boisterously. One whistled at Olivia. Sara rolled her eyes.

"Now bee-have!" Heath chided, to a chorus of groans. Looking far too pleased with his terrible pun, the Professor returned to the board and the finer points of bee anatomy. "So then, the sting is located in the…."

Sara switched off and daydreamed; she knew bee anatomy like the back of her paw. Resting her little chin on one palm she cast her golden eyes to her right, beyond the sinks, taps and imperium-burners of science class, beyond the ceiling-high windows, to the university grounds; one of the precious green spaces in Lupa, with its grand cedar tree and well-kept lawn. Sara checked Arkady's ornate clock tower; it was nearly lunch break and some classes, thanks to generous lecturers, were emptying out before the bell. Students hurried back and forth under the cloisters that enclosed the green, mostly wolves, but the odd cat and hog too, even a lumbering bear.

"Saraaa," the present lumbering bear cooed, tapping his pointer on the board. "Are you still with us?"

The little wolfess looked at the board, at where Heath's pointer was on the diagram, and guessed, "Thorax?"

The Professor stared at her with his beady brown eyes, but had to concede, "That's right, yes."

"Nice dodge," Olivia whispered to her friend.

Before Heath could move on, the bell rang and his pupils started piling their books into their bags. "I want your talks ready by tomorrow, please," the Professor shouted over the hubbub of chatter and activity. "Any bug you choose, ant, butterfly, slug, whatever, but please confer and avoid covering the same species, or it'll be a rather dreary exercise for all."

Sara packed her bag and threw her knee-length green coat over her matching tunic and cream breeches. Before she could desert her desk and catch up with Olivia, the enormous Professor

Heath beckoned the diminutive wolfess over.

"Aye, Professor?"

"Sara, I know as a Hummel you're streaks ahead on this subject but do try and look like you're paying attention, for my sake."

"Sorry, Professor, I just…."

"What?"

"Ah keep thinking about Toggle, sir," Sara admitted.

"Ohohooo, I see," Professor Heath woofed, his countenance lifting at once. "Yes, it's rather strange, isn't it? We haven't had a bee come this way for years and just as we're starting on social insects one turns up! It's a gift from Gaia."

"Aye," Sara agreed, picking her claws and looking out the nearest window. "It's so sad she'll nae get tae fly home, though. Do you suppose she came from Hummelton's hive? Ah could take her back there myself if she did."

"It seems too far for a worker bee to wander, even if she were lost," Heath said gently. "And if she's put into a foreign hive they would tear her apart, as you know."

Sara grimaced, "Aye."

A thought crossed her teacher's mind, "If you're not too busy maybe you would you like to help me feed her again?"

Sara squeaked excitedly, "Oh yes, Professor! When?"

Heath checked his pocket watch, even though there was a perfectly good giant clock looming outside. "After lunch, say half one? You can skip your gym class on my authority. What do you say?"

"That'd be grand, sir."

"I'll meet you on the green then," Heath beamed, thumbs tucked in his waistcoat, proud of his munificence. Looking out the window he added, "Let's hope the blasted rain holds off. It's looking quite pleasant out there now."

✦

The blasted rain did hold off as Sara partook of lunch in the shelter of the cloisters. The muted sunlight – about as good as it got under Lupa's eternal shroud of polluted haze – warmed Sara's dark face as she watched passing ash clouds from the university's central heating boiler cast playful shadows across the clock tower, before floating off into the sky to contribute to said haze.

"What're you going to do?" asked Olivia, lying on the floor armed with a pencil and paper

"Eh?" Sara replied, biting into her honey sandwich. "Did you say something?"

"Your presentation. What bug?"

"Oh! Bee."

"Ask a silly question," Olivia snorted, sketching the beginnings of an anatomical drawing on her paper.

Sara recognised Olivia's efforts as a spider. "Well ye always do everything on spiders."

Olivia had to concede, "True. But they're fascinating."

"So are bees!"

"Yes but… spiders are just so…."

"Creepy?" Sara provoked. "Evil?"

"Elegant," Olivia corrected flatly, and also, "Patient." She glanced up at Sara with her wonderful, almost unnaturally violet eyes, "You don't *really* think they're evil, do you?"

"Och! Ah was only pulling your leg. Bugs cannae be evil, they are what they are."

Relieved, Olivia returned to her sketch.

Like many a student at the Arkady University, Olivia Blake hailed from a wealthy Freiwolf family with a prestigious history. The adopted daughter of industrialist from the Greystone Pack's territory, she had never wanted for anything, not even beauty, for she was very lovely-looking in Sara's opinion. Deep brown and elegantly short-furred, sporting a pink blazer and spotless white breeches, she turned heads amongst the male faculty with ease; her stature and poise made Sara feel an inadequate dumpling.

"Any word from Bruno?" Olivia hummed, swinging her long legs and flicking her lovely tail as she sketched away with enviable ease.

"No," Sara replied at length,

"Did you check his gym?"

"Nobody's seen him there either."

Olivia put down her pencil and sighed. "It's been weeks. Maybe he's gone for good this time?"

Sara shrugged, "He'll get back tae me when he's settled in. It's the same old Bruno routine."

"It's not him, it's that daft rabbit, always running from his own shadow, like anyone cares what he did in the war. I feel sorry for Bruno, I really do; can't be easy having a little beast for a dad. If only a nice Freiwolf family had adopted him like mine did me. Makes me feel very lucky, you know."

Sara wasn't listening, for she had noticed something strange out the corner of her eye. A silver, lozenge-shaped object was slowly emerging from behind the university clock tower, as if a giant invisible magician was pulling a penny from behind its ear.

"Och!" Sara gasped. "Olivia, it's an airship!"

Sandwich fluttering in paw, Sara leapt over the cloister wall and ran into the garden to get a better look; the saturated grass squelching underfoot.

Olivia followed leisurely; the airship, being very far away, appeared to stand still whilst the clock tower obligingly shuffled over, at least from her point of view.

The girls watched, necks craned skyward, paws sheltering eyes from the muted sun.

"Isn't it beautiful?" Sara marvelled.

"Is it Professor Heath's cat friends?"

"Maybe."

Suddenly, an enormous dark beast in a long coat appeared beside the girls.

"What's up?" he quipped.

"Bruno!" Sara piped with further joy, looking the big brown wolf up and down. "Och! We were just talking about you!"

"Oh yeah?" he woofed. "All good things, I hope."

"Aye, of course, ye great lump!" Sara giggled, slapping his arm. "Where've ye been? We've been worried sick."

"Sorry, been busy," Bruno said simply, shrugging his shoulders.

Olivia raised a paw and said gently, "Hi, Bruno."

"Olivia. You all right, yeah?"

"Yes, thank you. How are you?"

"Not bad, not bad."

Olivia smiled warmly and swivelled side to side a little, paws behind her back as she looked Bruno over.

He pointed at the balloon. "I was watching it on the train the whole way here."

"Aye. Where'd it take off from?" Sara asked.

"I dunno. It just popped up out of nowhere. It's been circling for ages. I think it's over the Common."

"Must be for a show," Olivia supposed.

"Yeah," Bruno agreed, adding excitedly, "Oi, wanna go see what's happening?"

Sara laughed, "We can't, silly, we've got lessons yet."

"Oh, right. Yeah."

"You go."

Bruno shrugged that off, "Nah. They'll probably be packing up by the time I get there."

Olivia had an idea. "I know," she said, "let's go to the pictures tonight. It might be mentioned on the news reels."

Bruno was eager, "Yeah, all right. What time?"

"Olivia!" Sara growled out the side of her mouth, "We've got our presentations tae prepare fer."

"Prepare what?" Olivia replied airily. "All we have to do is a drawing, the rest is easy. You know bees and I know spiders. We could talk the legs off a millipede."

Sara said nothing, but smiled at Bruno.

"Seven o' clock then?" Olivia asked, looking hopefully across to Bruno.

"Sure. I'll meet you there," he said. "Usual place, yeah?"

Olivia nodded.

Bruno cast his fiery gaze down at Sara. "You coming?" he urged, smiling toothily at her – the rogue.

Sara couldn't help but give in, "Aye. All right."

Once all arrangements had been made, and the silver balloon had circled out of sight, the girls invited Bruno to join them under the cloisters. Sara offered him half her honey sandwich.

"No thanks, I snuck a waffle earlier," Bruno declined, removing his coat and laying it over the low cloister wall.

"Oh aye, the famous three-season waffle," Sara said, sitting on the cloister wall. "You should go one better and make a four-season waffle."

Bruno sat beside her, a giant. "That's a season too far, Sara, it'd spoil it," he said.

"Aye, well, you know me and mah cooking."

"Could burn a salad, you."

As Sara went to hit him in rebuke, a sniggering Bruno deflected her paw deftly aside – Dad had taught him well.

"Too slow."

"Where've you been, Bruno?" Olivia asked, her chin cupped in her paws, her drawing quite forgotten in favour of Bruno's rippling muscles. "Moved again?"

"Yeah, and Dad wants to move *again*."

Sara nearly choked on her dwindling sandwich, "Again? Didn't you just move into that new place last month?"

"Yup."

"What's wrong this time? Is the spot nae good fer business?"

"No, it's great for business, but Dad says it's too dangerous, like he always does," Bruno explained, in a huffy voice. He hiked his shoulders as he filled the girls in on the morning's happenings, "See, there's this one Howler who keeps coming in and he's gotten really friendly. He's really nice, shells out massive tips. Dad was well-pleased."

"So what's the problem?" Olivia chirped.

Bruno spread his big paws. "Well, we got a big bay window in this new place and this Howler likes to sit there every time he comes in. Someone obviously knew his routine, 'cause they lobbed a bomb right on his lap nearly! It blew up and took out half the café. Almost killed me, it did!"

Sara's puny paws clapped to her petite muzzle.

Seeing the look on her little face, Bruno hurriedly toned things down, "Oh, it's not that bad. Just a few windows knocked out, really."

Slowly, Sara lowered her paws, "Is your dad all right?"

"Oh yeah."

"And you?"

Bruno jokingly checked his body for holes, "Yeah."

Olivia and Sara exchanged looks, "Well, thank Ulf for that," said the former.

Bruno rubbed the back of his neck, "The Howler's in a bad way though. We took him to his Den. I dunno if he's even still alive. I don't suppose we'll be told anything."

"What Den?" Olivia asked, trying, failing, to sketch some more.

"Riddle."

"Riddle? But that's Bloodfang territory."

"Yeah, so?" Bruno queried.

Olivia tutted at him, "Brutal bunch they are. You should move into Greystone territory. It's much safer there. My family is close to the Greystones, they'd look after you if I asked."

"Their turf's too ashy for my lungs; too many furnaces and factories."

Sara threw her paws up, "Ah dunno why you don't just leave Lupa altogether instead of going from one district tae the next. They're all the same. Doesn't matter which crooked pack runs them."

"What about yours, Sara Hummel?" Olivia chirped cheekily.

"Mah pack's nae perfect either, but at least over in Everdor there's fresh air and sunshine," Sara Hummel defended. "And life, Bruno, trees and bugs and crops and… and hardly any ash that does your lungs nae good at all!"

"We can't run a business out in the sticks, Sara."

"For the hundredth time, you can set up in Hummelton; plenty of tourists there. Or better yet work on a farm, caring for the land, keeping livestock. Och, you'd love it!"

Bruno guffawed and shook his head.

"What's wrong?" Sara mocked. "Farmer's life too tough fer a soft city wolf?"

"It's not that. Hummelton just sounds…." Bruno hesitated.

"What?"

"Boring."

Bruno was right to hesitate.

"Boring!" Sara piped, glancing at Olivia, who was laughing at them both. "Well it may not be as exciting as having your house blown up, but if it was nae fer Hummelton you'd all starve in Lupa. Nothing edible grows within a hundred miles o' this dump!"

Bruno raised his paws to calm her, "I know, I just… look, I dunno, Sara, I'm not like you. You've always known what you wanted to do. I've never known. I want to be useful. Do something with my life. You know?"

Boooonnnng!

The clock tower chimed for half past one and Olivia leapt to her feet, as if stung by a bee.

"My next lesson!" she yelped, stuffing her satchel with her paper and lunchbox. "Oh by Ulf, I've got an imperiology exam! I should've been revising!"

"Och! Olivia, you're terrible!" Sara laughed.

"I know, I know."

Bruno raised his chin at Olivia, "See you later, yeah?"

"I'll be there!" Olivia replied, hurrying down the cloister.

Sara sighed fondly, "She's such a scatter brain."

"Yeah," Bruno agreed, looking all around. Once Olivia had gone, he began anew, "Oi, Sara, you're an expert on imperium and stuff aren't you?"

"Ah would nae go that far," Sara chuckled modestly.

Bruno remained dead serious, and strangely subdued, "It's part of your course though, 'en it?"

"Nae as much as Olivia's. Why?"

"Well, I… it's just that… I've been told that…." Bruno trailed off and leant his paws on his thighs.

"What?"

"Saraaaa!"

An old bear in a waistcoat ambled across the lawn, puffing clouds of imperium from a pipe like a train and looking a little bit lost as he searched the garden with his beady eyes.

"Here, Professor!" Sara called, waving at him whilst simultaneously gesturing for Bruno to stand up.

Upon arrival under the cloister, the Professor passed the slightly scruffy Bruno a look of near-disdain and addressed only his star pupil. "Had your lunch, Sara?"

"Aye."

"Good, good."

The bear finally looked at Bruno, chin high, chest out, puffing on his pipe. "You are *not* a pupil, sir," he said, with a suspicious and protective air.

"No, sir," Bruno admitted.

"I've seen you lingering about before, who are you?"

"I'm-"

"Cousin Bruno," Sara hastily interjected, locking arms with Bruno and pulling him close. "He's down from Hummelton visiting Lupa… again. Ah said we could meet during lunch today. Ah forgot all about it on account of Toggle."

"You've got bees on the brain!" the Professor chuckled.

Laughing, Sara made introductions, "Bruno Hummel this is mah biology teacher, Professor Heath."

"Oh aye, the famous Professor Heath!" Bruno 'Hummel' flattered, effortlessly adopting Sara's distinct Hummel accent. "Ah'm Bruno Hummel. Pleasure tae meet you, sir. Och, aye!"

"Oh, uh… and you, young Bruno."

They shook paws. Heath, whilst small for his race, still dwarfed the giant Bruno. Still, the discrepancy between bears and wolves was never slimmer, by Sara's estimation.

Unable to excuse himself from Bruno's company so soon without appearing quite rude, Professor Heath was impelled to ask, "Would you like to see our bee, young wolf?"

"Bee?"

Sara leapt on the premise, "Oh yes! Bruno you have tae come see her, she's so beautiful. She crashed in the university the other day, didn't she Professor?"

"Yes. Got lost in the especially bad smog, we think."

"Me and Professor Heath managed tae catch her. We were running around all day with a big net. She's got a broken wing you see, so we had tae save her."

Worried, Bruno accidentally reverted to his rough Lupan twang, "Yeah, but aren't bees dangerous?"

Sara laughed, "Och, Bruno!"

"What?"

Heath explained. "They're only dangerous if you threaten the colony, my boy," he dismissed airily, waving his pipe around. "On their own they're relatively harmless. They only sting as a last resort since it often results in their death, of course."

Bruno held his breath as noxious fumes from the Professor's ember pipe wafted his way; but in the end he still wound up coughing.

"Professor, Bruno's allergic tae ash!" Sara tutted, as if Heath ought to know.

"Oh! I do apologise."

"It's nae problem," Bruno spluttered, remembering to pick up the accent again. "You weren't tae know."

Heath cleared his throat, "In any case, I'd better go empty this out. Shameful habit really."

"You'll catch the rot, Professor," Sara chided.

"Oh, at my age bits of me are falling off regardless."

Bruno felt his heart ice-over upon hearing that dreaded word, rot, but it was too awkward to bring it up now.

Maybe later, after the pictures. There's no rush.

"I'll meet you in the glass house," Heath said, adding, "I'm going to give my associate a call whilst I'm about this pipe. I've been expecting him to ring all morning about his meeting. Something's obviously kept him – Howlers for you. Don't do anything with the bee until I get there, all right?"

"Aye, Professor," Sara replied, tugging Bruno's paw. "Come along, cousin."

"Oh aye, cousin."

Sara sniggered at some joke that Professor Heath wasn't privy to. The bear watched her and Bruno depart, unable to cast that wolf's fiery eyes from his mind.

✢

Sara opened the hefty wrought-iron and glass door amidst a delightfully rusty squeak.

"Age before beauty," she said.

"I'm younger than you," Bruno tutted, "I think."

Warm, humid air billowed into him like the breath of an imperium train, only without the subsequent watery eyes and sneezing. The young wolf found himself amidst a veritable jungle of plants and small trees, flowers and fruits, all enclosed by a delicate-looking web of glass and black-painted iron. It was like a cathedral of crystal made by a parish of plants to please the sky god.

"Phew!" Bruno puffed, writing his name in the nearest pane of steamed-up glass. "Warm 'en it?"

"It's a glass house," Sara tutted, shutting the door. "It's supposed tae be."

"I'm not moaning. It's lovely!"

Shedding her green coat, Sara rolled it up and stuffed it inside her satchel; Bruno had slung his over one shoulder in a rather dapper fashion.

"And I thought you said nothing grows around Lupa," he said, flicking a big, waxy leaf.

"The ash doesn't get in here."

"What about the tree on the green, though, and the grass. How comes they don't die?"

Sara couldn't tell if Bruno was being daft to wind her up or genuinely ignorant. He had lived his whole life in Lupa and dropped out of school by twelve to work for a living and sometimes his lack of formal education showed.

"It's a cedar," Sara explained, "it's as tough as old boots, as is the grass. Some plants can tolerate ash, others even use imperium, just like the Howlers do. Anyway, the Eisbrand territory's cleaner than most. You should move here really."

Bruno shot that idea down in flames. "It's too expensive, we can't afford Eisbrand rent."

"Aye," Sara sighed, "Ah can just about afford mah tiny flat."

"Can't yer mum help you out?"

"Ah don't want her to."

A grimace, a nod.

Ducking and weaving to see through the knotted leaves and stems, Bruno chirped afresh, "Where's the bee then?"

"This way, silly," Sara said, grasping Bruno's arm – her little black paw barely encompassed half his enormous bicep. "Would ye look at those muscles!" she tutted. "You get bigger by the week, ye great lump."

"Maybe you're just getting smaller."

Sara pinched Bruno's arm, "Ah'm serious. Must be all the waffle batter you mix."

"Yeah, or maaaybe it's the gym, Sara."

"Is there one near the new place?"

"Dunno, I haven't had a chance to look yet. Won't bother now."

Navigating the miniature jungle, Sara and Bruno emerged into a clear space, whereupon the massive Bruno stopped dead, tugging puny Sara to a halt.

Before him sat a large iron cage, as big as Dad's truck, and behind its rusty bars lay a quivering bundle of striped black and yellow hair with six splayed legs and shiny, tear-shaped compound eyes. Two transparent, yet iridescent wings protruded from its back, criss-crossed by a network of dark veins, like a leaf – a bee all right, about the size of Sara!

"Come on, she can't get out," the wolfess laughed. "She's called Toggle."

"Toggle?" Bruno said, with a gulp.

With a shake of the head at Bruno's predictable trepidation, Sara dragged him closer. 'Typical city beast, afraid of a wee bumblebee,' she thought.

Leaving Bruno standing, Sara knelt down beside the cage and reached through the bars.

"Oi, careful!" Bruno yelped.

"It's all right, silly," Sara scoffed, patting the bee on its shiny brow. Apart from the way the creature was continuously trembling, like a motor car left ticking over by the side of the road, it didn't move.

"Why's it shaking?" Bruno asked. "Is it scared?"

"No, they're always like that," Sara replied with a shrug. "It's just the way they are."

"Oh."

"Want tae stroke her?"

Bruno waved a paw, "I'm all right, thanks."

"Och, come on," Sara tutted, beckoning him down.

"Your teacher said not to do anything."

"He was talking about feeding her. Now come on, don't be such a wimp. You're a boxer, ye cannae be scared of a fluffy great bumblebee."

Unable to back out after that slight, Bruno put his coat aside and crouched beside Sara.

"Just pat her head," she told him, shuffling to one side.

Against his better judgement, Bruno reached through the bars, his paw reflecting in the bee's shiny eyes. He made contact. The insect's skin, if one could call it that, was rock-hard and dimpled, like an orange made of marble.

Bruno let out a tiny guffaw of surprise.

"See?" Sara said, with that 'I told you so' look in her big yellow eyes, or rather 'Och! Ah told yer so'.

Bruno shuffled a little closer, "All right, Toggle?"

Bvvvvvvvvvvv!

Wings fluttering like a propeller, Toggle suddenly took off amidst a blast of wind and slammed into the roof of her cage, before falling flat on her back.

Bruno also fell on his back, tripping over his own feet in his haste to get away.

"Woaagh!"

Sara knelt, her sides splitting at her friend's expense. "Hahahaaaa! Och, Bruno, ye so daft!"

Toggle lay on her back awhile, six segmented legs kicking, before she fluttered her wings again and flipped upright. Her furry abdomen was pumping in and out like a bellows after that brief flurry of effort, as was Bruno's for that matter.

"She gave me a heart attack!" he said, grasping at his thumping chest. "Ulf almighty."

Stifling her giggles, Sara replied, "She keeps trying tae fly away, but one of her wings is broken, so she just flips over."

Gathering up what scraps of dignity he could, Bruno crawled over for a closer look. Sure enough a fair section of iridescent film was missing from Toggle's right wing.

"It'll grow back, won't it?" Bruno said expectantly.

Sara grimaced, "Their wings don't grow back."

"Ahw, no."

"Aye, isn't it terrible? So sad."

Bruno leant forward, paws on knees, "What'll happen to her then? You can't keep her locked up forever."

Before Sara could summon a reply, Professor Heath pushed his way through the glass house jungle like an explorer, his mighty bulk rustling more than enough leaves to advertise his presence to the young wolves well in advance.

"Sorry, you two, I got waylaid," the bear excused. "Some Bloodfang oaf was loitering around campus."

"Bloodfang?" Bruno said.

"Some rat; a plain-clothes Politzi agent. He denied it of course, but I recognised him. I've a memory for faces."

"But this is Eisbrand territory. What's a Bloodfang Politzi doing all the way over here?"

"That's what I said! The rascal claimed he was tailing a suspect. He couldn't produce an Eisbrand warrant so I escorted him off campus."

Sara was more interested in Toggle. "She tried to fly again, Professor!" she squeaked, hopping to her feet.

"Hmm? Oh, yes yes, she will for a long time," Heath maintained, cleaning his little spectacles. "I don't suppose she's really aware of what's wrong with her."

Bruno looked to Toggle's frayed wing. "What?" he said, before remembering to adopt the correct Hummel dialect. "Och! She must be able tae feel it."

Professor Heath gave Bruno a sideways look. "On the contrary, uh… Bruno, her wings are made of dead material. It's like our fur, or claws, it's not living tissue; you can clip your claws and not feel a thing. It's the same for her wings. In fact a bug's whole exoskeleton is like that; an armoured shell. Some say they don't feel pain."

Sara scoffed, "Och, but they must do."

"Well, maybe," her teacher chuckled. "They certainly feel hunger!"

On that note, Heath ambled over to a nearby chest and unlocked the padlock. The creaky chest housed various pots and gardening equipment, which Heath passed over in favour of a big stoneware jar and a stained old ladle. He brought them over and set them by the cage, before removing the jar's cork lid. It was full of a golden, translucent liquid.

"Honey!" Bruno stated, sticking his finger in and snatching a taste of the sticky goodness. "Yum!"

Heath plunged the ladle into the viscous honey. "Where's her plate, Sara?"

"Here," the wolfess chirped, retrieving an old clay dish from beside the cage.

"Put it inside," Heath instructed.

Sara did so; she had to turn the dish through ninety degrees to fit it though the bars. Heath carefully passed the dripping ladle to his pupil and she poured the honey into the dish. Bruno realised that if Sara had filled the dish prior to putting it inside the cage, she would have tipped the honey out when trying to fit it through the bars.

"Toggle! Din dins!" Sara cooed, tapping the edge of the dish with the ladle.

"Din dins?" Bruno laughed.

"What?" Sara shot back, her brow knitted.

Bruno dodged her disapproval by posing a pertinent question, "Does she even understand you?"

"Aye, she can hear… sort of," Sara explained. "She doesn't have ears like us but, she can hear something, isn't that right Professor."

"Uh, yes yes. She can sense vibrations with her hairs."

Sara waved the ladle at Bruno, "Ah'm going tae teach her tae come for her dinner, you wait and see." She tapped the dish again, "Toggle! Din dins! Come on!"

For a while Toggle remained shivering in the middle of the cage, apparently indifferent to dinner, or 'din dins'. But then her antennae wiggled excitedly, doubtless catching a whiff of sweet honey, and she clambered across the floor to the dish with haste. Out came a long, black blade-like tongue, at least Bruno assumed it was a tongue, stabbing at the honey, lapping it up with great relish.

Beaming with joy, Sara scooped out more honey and served it up for her pet bee.

"There ye go," she soothed, patting its shiny brow.

Smiling broadly, Bruno watched Sara Hummel drip honey everywhere in her race to keep up with the ravenous insect behind the bars. Nothing made her happier than mucking about with bugs. It was her calling.

Bruno decided not to spoil things for her; his trifling troubles could wait.

✢

Janoah breezed down the stark infirmary corridors, shafts of muted sunlight dancing on her white Grand Howler's cloak; a lowly Redcloak passed her by, he saluted, she nodded.

Don't look back, Janoah told herself, just keep going. Nobody knows, nobody even cares, and even if they did suspect you they're too scared of you anyway.

She rounded the corridor and entered the wards where the sick and the dying were kept; Janoah could hear the moans already. With white-imperium thin on the ground, Riddle Den alone had lost several Howlers of late to the dreaded rot, some of them not even particularly 'old', just unlucky. Even the healthy were suffering hardship and putting up with pain, like Uther. If things continued like this the tenuous peace would break and there would be a pack war, Bloodfangs, Eisbrands, Greystones and the rest, openly killing one another for access to venom stocks. Lupa would burn and the little beasts might even rise up in revolt as once they had.

Janoah burst into the last room, maintaining all appearance of confidence.

"You!" she yapped, stopping dead in the doorway, her paw still grasping the lever.

Bathed in sunlight, Ivan stood up from beside the wrought-iron bed and saluted half-heartedly. He said nothing.

Rufus lay on the bed, crisp white sheets tucked up to his waist, bandages and dressings all down his right side, which had apparently taken the brunt of the blast. A drip line went into his arm and a respirator was strapped to his muzzle, itself piped to a churning bellows.

Letting the door close, Janoah walked over to the foot of the bed and grasped the cold rails with both paws.

"Get out," she whispered, not once looking at Ivan.

Blade-dancer collected his helmet from the chair. As he brushed Janoah by she snapped at him, "Wait!"

Ivan stood silent and inert.

"Thank you for sitting with him," Janoah said, her throat bobbing.

A nod.

She produced Linus's donation from her cloak pocket and whispered quizzically, "Stand guard for me, Howler?"

Those icy eyes focussing on the white-striped cardboard tube a moment, Ivan donned his helmet. "Be quick," he grunted, stepping out.

Walking round Rufus's bed, Janoah tore open the tube. Inside was a sting; a glass phial with a plunger at one end and a needle coated with wax the other. The glass portion contained a milky fluid that, even by daylight, noticeably shone. White-imperium, venom, the good stuff; it had many names.

After breaking off the hygienic wax seal and flicking the needle to banish any air bubbles, Janoah parted the ruddy fur of Rufus's forearm, eased the needle into a vein and slowly depressed the plunger.

Within seconds Rufus began to tremble, his fingers twitching by his sides, at first slightly, then with growing violence. His grey chest heaved in and out, his nostrils flared, each hot breath steaming up the glass respirator as the purest of all imperium coursed through his powerful body. Snorting and grunting, the wolf arched his back and squirmed, enveloped in the womb of a nightmare.

"Mum… Dad," he cried. "Leave them alone! Get off me! Get away! No no nohohooo!"

Janoah, in a moment's folly, tried to hold him. "Rufus! Rufus, I'm here," she soothed, looking to the door. "Be quiet, my darling, it's just a bad dream-gagh!"

A white-hot spark of imperious plasma erupted from Rufus's arms and shot up Janoah's, ejecting her across the room whereupon she fell in a heap against the wall.

The wolfess watched, her whole body throbbing, as the chair beside the bed catapulted away from Rufus. A moment later and the drip pouch hanging over him exploded, showering the ward with water. Curtains billowed outwards and window panes rattled, as if in the grip of a gale. It was a storm all right, Rufus's incredible corona, coiling and twisting invisibly as the venom revitalised the Howler, releasing copious energy in the process.

At last, Rufus collapsed and all was silent.

In the serene aftermath, Janoah heard Ivan's boots pat across the ward. He offered her a paw and pulled her groggily to her feet. After a brief stumble and a rub of her numbed forearms, Janoah pushed Ivan away like a drunk and staggered over to Rufus. He was still, save for deep, steady breaths, his muscled, grey-furred torso heaving in and out. The sheets were twisted into a mountain range and the bed itself had come away from the wall, moving a good foot.

Gathering herself, Janoah tidied up. Whilst she brushed beads of water from the sheets and inched the hefty bed back against the wall, Ivan righted the chair and removed the shredded drip pouch from its stand, tossing it out the window.

Kissing Rufus on the forehead, Janoah looked to Ivan. "I've work to do, Blade-dancer."

"I'll stay with him," he offered.

Janoah nodded gratefully and made her getaway.

Chapter 8

Bruno presented his pass to the train hog at the gates. The portly pig squinted at the big brown wolf with extra care before letting him onto the platform with a disgruntled snort and wave of his pen.

"Ta, mate," said Bruno.

As a Freiwolf in a useful trade the trains were free for him, but the surly hogs didn't like anyone getting special treatment, except them, or so Dad always said.

Bruno joined Lupans of every kind and creed gathering on the platform in mutual expectation of the next train, mostly little beasts; the long-tailed rats, the meek mice, the long-eared rabbits and one Howler.

Odd, Howlers rarely took the train.

Bruno kept his distance, but spied on the fellow. He was very impressive; tall, yet thick-bodied, his mighty frame clad head to toe in polished, silvery eisenglanz metal. His helmet was marked on the brow with a blue-imperium snowflake, its subtle glow, whilst drowned in the muted sunlight, still proclaimed its wearer's allegiance to the local Eisbrand Pack, holders of Arkady District and the whole east of Lupa. The Eisbrands didn't wear mantles, preferring instead a knight's surcoat of old, albeit ones made of modern imperium-weave with hoods sewn on to guard against the rain and ash. The front and back of this fellow's handsome blue surcoat were emblazoned with a white Eisbrand snowflake.

Very nice, but above all Bruno envied the big sword slung at the Howler's back. Half as tall as him it must've required both paws to wield. Oh to have a swing of that!

Ah, but I couldn't use it right, Bruno thought, I couldn't channel plasma down it like them Howlers. I'm just allergic. Dad knows about these things, he had me checked out. Why would he lie to me? Makes no sense.

The next train chugged into view, spewing noxious clouds. Beasts shuffled forward in preparation to board, save Bruno, who shuffled backwards whilst holding his breath and squinting his eyes in anticipation of the ash.

He could do without getting ill again.

The train squealed to a halt amidst a swirl of ash and beasts of every sort filed out the carriages. Once the flow of furry bodies had died down, Bruno slipped aboard and found a seat. Any open doors were slammed shut by the train hogs and with a few whistles and a howl of waste imperium the train continued on its way.

The station eased aside, replaced by rows of shops and houses and chugging motor cars. The marble-clad Arkady University and its ornate clock tower passed by in the distance, poking up from the sea of blue tiled roofs like an iceberg. Sara was over there somewhere, still playing with her pet bee, no doubt.

Girlfriend, Dad always ribbed; nothing of the sort, Bruno would ever scoff. Sara had simply walked into one of Dad's previous 'Warrens' and gotten chatty with the young wolfen chef. In two years nothing had ever passed between them, not a kiss, not a hug, just Bruno's hastily scrawled addresses and phone numbers. He had kept in touch with her despite Dad's constant disappearing acts because Sara wasn't like other wolves; she'd not so much as raised an eyebrow upon learning Casimir was his adoptive father, even less said anything derogatory.

Dad said Sara was different because she was a member of Hummel, the only serious pack that still lived outside Lupa's walls. They owned Everdor, the untainted land beyond the Far Ashfall stretching east to the shores of the Teich. Little beasts were well-treated in Everdor and Dad had considered moving there many times, but always pulled back, citing that it was hard to run a business, save farming, about which he knew nothing. Even Hummelton, Everdor's capital district, was subject to strict anti-imperium laws that curtailed industrial processes, managed ash disposal, and even dictated how much imperium one could use to heat one's home; wood coppiced from the extensive forests being preferred. These laws had protected Everdor from succumbing to

Lupa's fate and choking under the umbrella of pollution known as the Ashfall.

Most Everdors steered clear of smoggy Lupa for life; Sara herself had only come to attend the prestigious Arkady University, or 'Ark'. She wished to study the wild world, describe strange bugs and catalogue new plants, and to that ambition she braved the poisonous Ashfall for the time being. Conventional wisdom held that she ran a risk of catching the rot like everyone else, especially being the cub of a Howler, which made a wolf more susceptible. However, Sara was a wolfess and girls were less prone to catch rot. Bruno didn't really understand why. It was something about X's and Y's and girls having extra genes thanks to having two X's whereas boys had an X and a Y chromo-something or other.

Sara had tried, but Bruno couldn't get his head around it.

The city outside was seemingly plunged into utter blackness as the train screamed into a tunnel. With nothing to see out the window, the young wolf cast his eyes around the dimly-lit carriage, watched the imperium lamps sway overhead.

Suddenly pain.

Bruno closed his eyes and grunted as his legs throbbed to every heartbeat. Such a dull, creeping, insidious ache, as if one's bones were being squeezed in a vice.

"Hurts doesn't it?" someone said.

Bruno opened his eyes. Sitting opposite him was the Howler he had seen on the platform!

The fellow adjusted his marvellous imperium-weave surcoat and crossed his eisenglanz-clad legs, cupping his big white paws on his lap in a rather well-to-do manner.

"It'll only get worse, my friend," the Howler said, his big kind eyes, one green and one blue, peering at Bruno from the anonymity of the Howler helmet. "Maybe I can help."

Bruno sat dumbstruck.

The train burst from the tunnel and into the next territory amidst a slightly glittery pall of imperium vapour. Smoke stacks reached for the sky and molten metal glimmered inside huge forges. The land was blasted and rendered grey by imperium ash, more so than anywhere. Every house, every building, roof and façade, was stained with streaks of spent imperium. Even the populace looked grubby.

"Bleak isn't it?" the Eisbrand sighed. "The Greystone Pack lives in filth, but you can't deny they've a brusque charm. They at least have embraced imperium and accept the Ashfall as the consequence of progress, instead of feeling guilty. What my pack wouldn't give for their secret of stabilising yellow-imperium, though!"

Bruno found his courage. "What do you want?"

"To warn you, Citizen Bruno," the Eisbrand replied.

Citizen Bruno didn't ask how the fellow knew his name. "Warn me?" he asked instead.

"Yes. Don't look now but you're being tailed."

Bruno peered over his shoulder. The little beasts in the carriage pretended not to see him, but nobody stood out.

"I said don't look," the Howler sighed.

"Who is it?" Bruno whispered.

"Politzi, naturally. There's a rat in plain clothing who thinks I've not noticed him. He answers to Janoah of the Bloodfangs. You ever heard of her?"

Bruno shook his head, just a little. "No."

"Well, no doubt she's heard about you after what happened at your father's café this morning," the Howler mused. "I bet she's already put together a whopping great file."

"How'd you know about that?"

"Spies, of course."

Bruno emitted a tiny snort at this wolf's candour. Everyone knew the Howlers had eyes everywhere, but still, to just come out and say it was odd.

The forthright Howler went on, "Rufus is Janoah's husband. He's well-known for sniffing out talent."

"Talent?"

"Yes. Why do you think he kept popping by? Not to impugn your cooking, my friend, but it's hardly to sample your menu. Rufus Valerio was grooming you."

"Watcha mean 'grooming' me?"

The Howler spread a paw, "Pretending to be your friend, so he could persuade you to join his pack."

"He's not like that."

"Really? He's never mentioned anything about you joining the Howlers? Induction?"

Bruno dipped his chin.

"There you go-"

"He's still my friend!" Bruno maintained at once. "He wouldn't 'pretend' like that."

The Howler shrugged, "Well let's not fall out over it. Regardless of his motives, Rufus was right to approach you. I can feel you from here, the crackle of imperium in your bones is... deafening. You've quite the corona and you've not even been inducted yet. You could be very powerful one day, with the right care and training."

Bruno remained silent.

"Are you frightened, or angry? I can't tell."

Now Bruno looked out the window, his right leg jiggling nervously.

"The latter," the Howler decided. "Look, you need help," he said matter-of-factly, spreading a paw. "Don't dodge or you'll wind up like the gazers we all bump into on street corners. Join us, let us induct you, train you; you'll make a great Eisbrand."

Bruno's bottom jaw quivered a little. "Look, I dunno what you're on about. I don't have a corona, I'm not a...." He stopped short of saying something in favour of, "I'm just a cook. All right?"

The Eisbrand laughed a little.

Bruno glared at him. "What's so funny?"

"We were all just something or other. I had my dreams too, but the rot changed all that. You're strong all right, but you're starting to get ill. Your bones ache, your eyes water, sometimes you can't even breathe. It's the black-imperium in you, rotting you alive."

Bruno explained it away, "I'm allergic to imperium ash, is all. It was the smog yesterday it affects me bad!"

"Is that what your 'father' tells you?"

"You calling my dad a liar?"

"I'm sure Citizen Claybourne meant well."

Bruno felt such rages, but kept his tongue in check, for he was talking to a Howler who could doubtless kill him and make up an excuse for doing so.

The Howler twiddled his thumbs. "I know you want to believe the excuses," he exhaled. "I did when the rot came for me. You put it down to a cold, or too much drink. But you can't fight it; believe me, I tried. How I tried. At least if you come to our pack you'll have the finest things in life to ease your suffering. Despite what propaganda you may have heard on your travels between territories, we Eisbrands look after our Howlers and we're good to our little beasts too. On a Howler's pay you can set your father up in a good district, perhaps even Arkady. You can see him every day on patrol, I promise, and… Sara too."

Bruno's heart leapt into his mouth. "Sara?" he said with forced ignorance. "Who's Sara?"

The Howler smiled; his helmet hid any emotion, but Bruno could just feel it. "You're a noble wolf to try and keep her out of this, but not everyone is as scrupulous as me. Some would use her against you, and your father's past."

The big brown Bruno shot up, all of him, every massive muscle and mighty bone of his powerful frame looming over the seated Howler, and with courage or stupidity he never knew he had, brandished both fang and fist.

"Leave her alone! Leave me alone and leave my dad alone, or I'll lamp yer. You got that, 'Howler'?"

The little beasts all stared, open-mouthed.

For a moment, Bruno supposed he was a dead wolf, but the Howler merely cocked his helmeted head to one side and said with impeccable calm, "I'm not about to force the issue; we Eisbrands prefer honey to vinegar, but I can't protect you once we reach Bloodfang territory and they already know what you are. They'll make you sign on the dotted line."

"I ain't interested!"

"I said make. Look, what do you think your father's been doing moving you about these past ten years? He's been protecting you from the likes of Rufus. Most Bloodfang talent scouts don't take no for an answer. Understand?"

Bruno's blood ran cold.

Feeling the train slow, the Howler rose from his seat, proving he was almost a match for Bruno in stature. "For what it's worth, pleasure talking to you, Bruno Claybourne. And yes I know your name. I also I appreciate that you stood up for Sara just now; I had doubts, but… she's right to call you a friend."

He held out a knightly paw.

Bruno frowned, "How'd you know Sara?"

"Oh, we're long-acquainted. I'm what she calls a good 'un. She's often spoken to me about you."

Bruno didn't know whether to believe this fellow or not, but decided to part on good terms regardless and shook paws. "Thanks for the warning," he muttered.

A nod. "Listen, get off at the next stop and make a break for it. I'll divert your little admirer."

"Why're you helping me escape?"

"Because if you must be a Howler I'd sooner a wolf like you were on my side than not," the Eisbrand admitted, looking Bruno up and down. "If you reconsider, get out of Bloodfang territory, tonight, and swing by an Eisbrand Den; ask for me, Tristan Donskoy."

"Donskoy?"

"Right. Oh, and bring Casimir. I'll see him safe; Sara wouldn't have it any other way."

As the train entered the next station, Howler Tristan stepped into the midst of the carriage.

"This is an inspection!" he declared. "Have your citizen passes ready, please!"

The little beasts all looked up as one, then delved through their belongings, bags, coats, wallets and purses, pulling out their paper passes of various colours. Tristan's blue and green eyes ignored them all, focused as they were on the suspicious character hunched at the far end of the carriage.

As the train came to a stop, the rat in a coat and hat stood up and slinked for the nearest door.

"Where are you going, citizen rat?" Tristan said loudly, even as he checked someone else's papers.

The rat looked at him, "This is my stop, Howler."

"Well, you'll just have to get off at the next one! There's been too much terrorist activity of late and nobody is leaving this carriage until I have seen their documents."

"But this is Greystone turf. You're not-"

"Sit *down*, citizen, before I make you!" Tristan barked.

The rat looked longingly out the window, but unable or unwilling to blow his cover, gave up and sat down.

Tristan glanced sideways out the carriage and caught a glimpse of Bruno hurrying across the platform, disappearing into the hubbub as best a wolf of such dimensions could.

⁂

The Warren was taking delivery of several beer kegs, which ordinarily the muscular Bruno would lug down the cellar without much ado. However, with his son absent, Casimir helped his fellow rabbits from the brewers roll the kegs across the road and into the boarded-up establishment.

Conversation centred on the bombing, it was the talk of the district and no doubt there would be a mention in the papers tomorrow morning. Any article would be bent to Bloodfang propaganda requirements, accusing whatever group they desired to slander this week of masterminding the dastardly deed. Perhaps they'd finger THORN; that'd keep public opinion firmly against the hyenas. Perhaps rightly for once, for Casimir could swear he had seen a hyena, and had told everyone so. He felt bad maligning a whole race he had sympathy for, but he knew better than to stand up and be counted. Lay low, remain obscure, live a long and quiet life; Casimir had tried the alternative on for size and all it had gotten him was a stint in prison and a busted leg.

"See you next week?" the brewer assumed.

"Uh, I'll bell you about that," Casimir said to his fellow rabbit, making a telephone gesture with one paw.

The surprised youth looked up from his clipboard, which he had been filling in prematurely, "Oh?"

"Not sure when we'll be back on our feet," Casimir excused, thinking how he and Bruno might not be here come tomorrow morning let alone next week, but not wanting to let on the fact to anyone. "I can't sell beer if I'm not open, lad."

"Fair enough, sir," the brewer said, tipping his hat and climbing into his truck with the others. "Good day."

Casimir waved them off and limped inside his deserted café. He stood in the midst of the main room, arms folded, taking things in. The tables were polished, the imperium lamps flickered, glasses stood ready, every speck of ash was gone. Ignoring the boarded-up windows one would suspect nothing untoward. But as a rabbit Casimir saw the taint, smelt the danger; his long-oppressed people were masters of self-preservation.

It was time to go.

Reluctantly shuffling behind the bar, Casimir grabbed the telephone and placed the stand between the beer pumps. He found the secret bit of paper with the usual number on, a number he should know by now but never remembered. Time to forge new passes and new identities for a new territory, but which pack this time? Casimir and Bruno had lived in every major quarter of Lupa, sometimes twice over. The Eisbrand districts were too expensive, the Greystone's too polluted and the Bloodfang's too dangerous. The Bloc was out of question; too violent *and* polluted, whilst the Common Ground was all of the above and a seedy cesspit.

Perhaps it's best to leave Lupa?

Don't kid yourself, Casimir. Even if you smuggle him through the Lupan Wall how will we survive? All your dodger contacts are here. I should've told him. I should've had this out years ago instead of letting it fester. He'll never forgive me when he finds out. Never.

With a shaky sigh, Casimir dialled in the number and slumped on a bar stool whilst call went through. He didn't notice *The Warren's* door open, until the bell rang.

"We're closed!" he said irritably, not even looking over the beer pumps. "Can't you read?"

The patron snorted back, "I thought you'd make an exception for your old comrade in arms, Casimir."

Ears pricked, the rabbit stood up and slammed the phone down in one movement. He found a huge hog dominating the little café with his mighty girth, his ill-fitting red Politzi uniform straining at the buttons, his shiny belt partially smothered by rolls of fat, like a muffin overhanging its paper case.

"Werner!" Casimir chirped, forcing a smile. "What're you doing here?"

Werner dodged the question with his own. "Who were you on the phone to?"

Casimir thought fast. "The glaziers," he said, furtively screwing up the piece of paper. "Gotta get them windows fixed. That's an expense I don't need, let me tell you."

Casting his beady eyes over the boarded up bay window, Werner grunted, "I'll see to it the Bloodfangs recompense you for the damage."

"Oh yeah? How? I thought they were poor?"

"Nooo, they just have different priorities to the Eisbrands. Instead of spending money on pretty headquarters and nice gear, it all goes straight into their Howlers' pockets. That's how they get the best of the best. We Politzi get a fair share too; shifting over to BF territory was the best move I ever made."

"Aye, well, it's not been so rosy for us as you can see."

"Give it a chance, Casimir, you only just got here," Werner said. He smacked his lips, "Where's Bruno at?"

"Out," Casimir said, "I dunno where."

"Not in bed?"

"No no, he's in good nick."

Werner smiled until his little eyes almost disappeared under his flabby cheeks, "Glad to hear it."

Casimir cleared his throat and scratched an ear, "So what can I do fer you, Werner?" he asked, grabbing a pint glass and filling it with golden, bubbling beer.

Werner trotted over and lowered himself onto a bar stool, it creaked alarmingly under the load. The hog knocked back his beer, chugging it down.

"Aaaaah," he gasped. "Very nice, that."

Werner nudged his empty glass towards Casimir, who refilled it. Downing his second beer at a more leisurely pace, though not much more, Werner licked his lips and wiped his snout of foam.

"Listen, Cas," he sniffed at last, "you need to come in for questioning."

Casimir let out a guffaw, "What?"

"Just routine. It's nought to worry about."

"Look," Casimir scoffed, raising his paws, "I didn't have anything to do with what went down."

"I know that!" Werner snorted.

"Then what do you need to question me about? Question me here. I saw a hyena throw a bomb in the window and that's all there is to it. I've told everyone that."

"This comes from high up. My trotters are tied. Janoah herself wants to see you. Probably wants to thank you."

"Thank a rabbit? You're having a laugh!"

"Well… Bruno then."

Upon hearing Bruno's name, Casimir ran a paw over his mouth. Almost without pause he opened the till and took out a wad of cash. He started counting it out in front of Werner, one lupa at a time.

"Casimir, don't bother," the pig dismissed.

"Hundred lupas?" the rabbit interrupted, winking. "Pretend we were gone, yeah? Just like last time. You came in here and the place was deserted. We're going tonight anyway; you can have all the beer. I won't be able to take it with me."

Werner shook his head, "I just can't do it, Cas; I can't keep doing this. It's starting to look suspicious for me-"

"Two-hundred."

"It's not about the money, it's about self-preservation!"

Casimir spread his paws. "Come on Werner. All those years in the resistance, me n' you, like brothers we was. Don't tell me you've forgotten how I saved your hide."

Werner let out a grunt.

"Just look the other way," Casimir urged.

The pig didn't so much look the other way, as down a little. "They want Bruno," Werner whispered, clearing his throat and glancing behind. "I can let you go, but not him, not this time. It's too near."

A strained, confused chuckle escaped Casimir's lips, "Whatcha mean?"

Werner's snout twitched. "The game's up, Casimir," he sighed, shuffling on the stool. "Janoah's figured it all out. You can't fight her, don't even try."

There was a long silence.

"I see," Casimir said, withdrawing his money. "Did you tell her?"

"It's not so bad," Werner replied, neither denying nor confirming. "At least you won't have to spike Bruno's 'cough syrup' no more."

Casimir grimaced.

"Aye, now there's a weight off yer conscience."

"My conscience? That was your idea! It's Uncle Werner's Cough Syrup, not Casimir's."

"Well you wanted to keep him in the first place, not me!"

Silence.

"You don't understand what it's like," Casimir seethed. "He's my boy, Werner. He's part of me."

"I understand better than you and I'm not even rotten," Werner maintained. "Pretty soon

Bruno's corona is gonna bubble over and he'll throw a left hook down the gym so hearty it'll put a hole in a punch bag, if not someone's face! Is that what you want?"

Casimir dipped his chin, "No."

"It's time to stop dodging. Let him go to his fate. Think of it, Cas, your own son, a Howler and a Bloodfang at that!" Werner laughed and snorted, "Nobody will ever mess with us again-"

"They can't have him!" Casimir bellowed. "They don't deserve him, not after blowing up his family!" He leant across the bar, "I've spent the last ten years moving him around, paying neighbours, Politzi and even Howlers to turn the other cheek. I'm not giving in now because you're too cowardly to go on!"

Werner grunted, "You should've told him, not hid him. You should've let him make up his own mind. You're the coward here."

"Don't you dare, you bastard! You would've left him to die under the rubble."

A longer, most prickly silence.

Werner snorted angrily, but said nothing.

"Just let us go one last time," Casimir begged afresh. "We'll disappear for good, I swear. You won't see us ever again. Please!"

"It's not worth my life," Werner sniffed, standing up and turning away. "I'm sorry, Cas, but it's over. Bruno's gonna be picked up and inducted as soon as he's back on BF land-"

"I've got the goods on you!" Casimir warned.

Werner froze.

"Aye, all those payments, all those favours, all that imperium you've embezzled. I bought stings off you enough times, didn't I? If they ask questions I can sing like a cricket and you know it-"

Werner whipped his truncheon round, smashing his beer glass across the café. "Say a word and you're dead!" he snarled, even before the shower of glass shards had settled.

Casimir refrained from gulping, just about.

Once all was quiet again, Werner snorted, "Lot of good it'd do you anyway. If it weren't me they'd only send someone else to bring you in, someone less reasonable. Now shut up and get your coat."

Slowly, Casimir dug out his keys. "Let me lock up at least," he said. "If I ever come out of that Den alive I don't want to find my place cleaned out by thieves."

The hog snorted, "I'll be outside. You got five minutes before I send in my boys. Five minutes, Cas, got that?"

"Aye. Got it."

Werner winked and took his leave.

Once Werner had squeezed his great girth through the café door, Casimir hurried upstairs into the living area of *The Warren*. It was still bare, lacking any personal touches. Moving often and secretly had left Casimir and his son devoid of belongings, sometimes just the clothes on their backs and the old steel box of life savings. The premises was always a rental, their identity papers forged; a new life in a new district never far off. Werner was just one of the many corrupt officials Casimir had dealt with, from train hog to Howler. The deception was such that, even now, Bruno thought Casimir was running from his own chequered past when the fuss was about the cub and always had been.

Werner's right, Casimir decided, I've got to tell him. The lad's old enough to understand and make his own mind up, to carry on dodging or don the mantle.

Just please forgive me, lad. I did it all for you.

Hurrying into his bedroom, a tearful Casimir pulled up a floorboard and grabbed the old metal box. He opened it and took a pistol out from amongst colourful wads of lupas; it was so old the charge had probably decayed, but he could wave it at anyone who tried to stop him at least.

To the wardrobe, dark coat, rounded hat, long ears slotting neatly through the holes.

One last look around, a sigh.

Casimir hurried to the window and checked the back streets below. It was clear; not a Politzi in sight. Either Werner wasn't trying very hard on purpose, or he was just stupid enough not to cover the whole building. Casimir liked to think his old friend was turning his cheek one last time.

Lifting the sash window, Casimir tossed the box onto an adjoining flat-topped roof, one floor below, then eased himself out and hung onto the windowsill to soften his fall. He landed well, his strong rabbit legs taking the force with aplomb, though his old wound played him up somewhat.

No time to linger; he had to find Bruno. The lad would take the usual route home and get off at the nearest station. All Casimir need do is wait for him.

Grabbing his savings, the desperate rabbit hopped silently down onto the street below, abandoning this short-lived incarnation of *The Warren* forever.

✧

Linus peered through the glass desk at the glowing orbs resting on royal blue cushions within.

"Uther look, imperium pearls," he gasped in awe.

"Yeah, yeah, I see 'em," Uther replied, leaning on the counter and impatiently tapping the service bell with his paw.

Ding! Ding! Ding!

"You sure this is where they're staying?" he sniffed, casting his wary eyes over the nautical-themed inn, with nets and harpoons festooning the walls. "Bit flaky for Felician royalty."

Linus peeled his blue eyes from the wonderful pearls, "Monty said they wanted the full Lupan experience."

"Monty?" Uther guffawed, nudging Linus, as he was wont to do. "Listen to you, 'rather old chap'. Hahahahaha!"

"I hardly know the cat; I'm just going to apologise."

"Puh! You're wasting our time, mate. I should be having a massage by now. Not like Vladimir's gonna check."

Ding! Ding! Ding!

Uther slapped the bell and shouted, "Oi, anyone alive back there or what?"

The door behind the reception desk opened and a sleek, brown, muscular beast with a rounded snout and a big tail moseyed in – an otter to be sure, or Lutran as some said. The youth eyed the wolves up as he approached, as if gauging whether they were Howlers or not. Uther and Linus had adopted plain clothes precisely for that reason; to be able to enjoy a night out without ordinary beasts giving them a wide berth, though seasoned eyes could usually spot Howlers.

"What can I do far you gentlebeasts?" the otter said, in laid-back Lutran patois, thumbs finding his short breeches.

Uther went to speak, but instead gestured at Linus, giving him the floor. "Go on, mate."

"Excuse me, citizen otter," Linus said, "but do you have a couple of cats staying here?"

"Cats?" the otter said, looking up at the bigger wolves. "There be no cats here, sirs."

"Fellow going by the name of Montague Buttle?" Linus clarified hopefully.

The otter's rounded head pivoted to and fro atop his long thick neck.

"Oh," Linus said, disappointed.

Uther glanced at his flaxen-furred friend, before taking over. He reached into his pocket and whipped out his Howler brooch. "You absolutely sure there's no cats staying here?" he asked, waving it in front of the young otter. "Maybe your memory is a little hazy, eh?"

"Uther, there's no need for that," Linus said. "Never mind. Let's just go."

Wild-heart wouldn't be deterred. "Well?" he urged the otter.

"I'm not after no Howler brooch," the fellow said, waving a webbed paw. "They be too dangerous to get rid of, yah know what I mean?" He leant on the counter and twiddled his fingers, "I accept lupas though."

With an incredulous glance at Linus, Uther also leant on the counter, "I ain't bribing you, I'm a thumping Howler! My mate here wants to talk to Monty Buttle, so where's he at?"

"Yah be an 'Owler, eh?" the bold otter laughed, equally incredulous. "Where's da fancy cloak n' all dat, den?"

"In da wash!" Uther mocked.

He slapped his paw on the glass desk and the pearls within the cabinet leapt from their cushions and clattered to the top. Gathering beneath Uther's paw, they remained aloft like a bunch of glowing crystal grapes.

The young otter looked on in amazement, his face lit up by the multicoloured imperious glow.

"Uther!" Linus piped.

Wild-heart lifted his paw; the pearls clattered back down like so many marbles. "Well?" he said. "Where's the cats? Or do I confiscate those lovely pearls in the name of the Republic?"

The otter found his tongue. "Room fourteen," he said, adding nervously, "Sorry, 'Owler. They be staying here to avoid da press. They told us not to let anyone know, yah."

Uther pocketed his brooch, "Yeah, yeah." He turned to Linus and sniffed, "Come on Woodlouse, let's get this over with."

Linus looked at the pearls, then at Uther, then back again.

"Come on!" Uther tutted, climbing the rickety stairs.

Watched by the otter, Linus hurried after his partner. Upon alighting the cramped first floor corridor, he said, "You didn't have to do that."

"What?" Uther piped. "Can't let them rudder-tails walk all over yer Linus, 'cause they will. Otters are right cheeky."

Knowing Uther was impatient to be out and about, Linus got back to the task at paw and followed the doors round the twisted, thread-bare carpeted corridor, 11, 12, 13.

"Here," he said.

Uther leant against the wall, arms folded, "Go on then," he said, tipping his head. "Knock."

Linus raised a golden paw, "Yes, right... uh.... W-what should I say?"

"Don't ask me!"

"No. S-sss-sorry."

Uther shook his head in disbelief as Linus rapped on the rough old door.

"Who is it?" a delicate feminine voice replied from beyond.

Linus cleared his throat, "Howler Linus, marm."

"Whom did you say?" the occupant replied, confused.

"Linus Mills, marm, the Howler from this morning," Linus said in a rising tone, hurt that he'd been so quickly forgotten. He consoled himself with the supposition that royalty must meet so many beasts that remembering names was impossible. "Am I addressing Penelope Buttle, Duchess of Felicia?"

A distended silence.

The blonde Linus was thinking about what next to say when the door unlocked and eked open a little, revealing a slither of a pale, grey feline face – Penny Buttle alright.

"Oh!" she gasped. "Howler Linus, of course!"

Linus beamed broadly, "Marm."

"Forgive me, I'm all over the shop, as Monty would say."

"Not at all."

Penny swung the door wide, revealing a similar frilly white dress to this morning's, less the bonnet. She gestured inside her simple room, which had a huge red trunk full of clothes beside the double bed and a half-decent view of late afternoon Lupa from the bay window.

"Do come in, Howler Linus," the catess said.

Linus raised a paw, "No time, marm," he refused. "I uh... I merely swung by to apologise for this morning."

Penny frowned in bafflement, "Apologise?"

"Yes marm, for r-rrr-requisitioning your vehicle and p-p-putting you and your husband in danger."

"Well isn't it normal procedure to requisition cars to aid in a pursuit, Howler? The Valours back home certainly do so."

"Well, yes marm, but-"

"Then think nothing of it!" Penny piped benignly. "We're glad to have been of service in helping you and your brave comrades bring that brutish hyena to justice. I dare say Monty found the whole event thoroughly exciting; he hasn't stopped talking about it all day!"

Linus glanced at Uther, who wound a finger beside his head, mocking the cat's sanity. Ignoring his rudeness, Linus asked Penny, "How is your husband?"

"Very well," she replied. "I'm afraid he's not here at the moment. It takes rather more than a box on the nose and a muddy coat to keep my Monty from his work."

Linus smiled, "Glad of it."

There was a pause.

Something occurred to Linus, "Work? Didn't you say you were here on holiday, marm?"

Penny tipped her head to one side. "More of a… promotional venture," she said with difficulty. "We're combining our holiday *with* Monty's work. Well, our work, really, we're both at it. He's the tinkerer and I'm the PR manager, though I have been dipping my toes in the engineering side lately. I'm sure you know all about it now you know who we are. Monty's so famous these days."

"Oh, y-yyy-yes, of course," Linus claimed, looking to Uther for a clue.

Wild-heart shrugged and pulled a 'I don't know' face.

"I expect he'll be back shortly," Penny said. "I'm just getting ready to go out to dinner. It's all part of wooing our patrons; bit of a bore. Perhaps you'd like to join us, Linus? I'm sure Monty would enjoy your company as much as I would."

Uther frantically waved his paws and mouthed silently, 'No! No!'

"We… wouldn't want to intrude on your, uh… promotional venture," Linus excused, accidentally betraying Uther with both 'we' and another sideways glance.

Leaning forward, Penny discovered the loiterer. "Oh, and who's this strapping gentlebeast?" she beamed, stepping into the corridor a little. "I recognise you from this morning, sir wolf, but, forgive me, I didn't catch your name."

Standing nobly with his paws behind his back, Uther cleared his throat and said gruffly, "Howler Uther, marm."

"Ah yes, of course you are. Thank you for saving me from that hyena brute, Howler Uther, most noble."

"Oh well, weren't nothing, marm. All in a day's work, like."

"I'm sure it is to such marvellous beasts," Penny praised effortlessly. "We have your sort in Felicia too. Valours they call themselves. Oh, but I'm sure you know."

"Yes, marm," Uther said. "Taught us all that in the Academy, marm. Know your enemy."

"Enemy?"

"In case of another war with Felicia marm. Uh, not that we're gonna or anything."

"Indeed, that was long *long* ago," Penny sighed. "I pray we've learnt something from our ancestors' mistakes." Leaning to one side she peered round Uther, "Is… the other chap here as well?"

"Who?" Linus asked her.

"The tall white wolf."

"Ivan?" Uther woofed. "Puh! No, no."

"What a pity, Monty so wanted to shake his paw," Penny tutted, adding, "Still, you'll join us for dinner, won't you, Howlers? It would cap Monty's day."

Uther began to make an excuse, "Well, uh, you see-"

"I insist on paying, of course," Penny interrupted. "It'll be on Monty and I."

"On you?" Uther said, ears pricked.

"Absolutely! Well, we couldn't possibly do otherwise after you saved my life. The very idea!"

Linus rocked on his feet, "That's very kind, but I think we have other plans-"

"Don't be so rude, Linus!" Uther chided. "We're honoured to dine with our Felician neighbours!"

Linus blinked and stammered, "W-www-we are?"

"Of course we are!" Performing an overblown bow, fist pressed to substantial chest, Uther said, "You just let us know where and when and we'll be right there, Mrs Buttle, on my honour as a Howler."

Laughing gently, Penny admitted, "Well, as it happens, Monty and I are rather clueless as to where to wine and dine. We're not Lupans, you see. Perchance you two gentlebeasts have a suggestion? The young otter downstairs is a dear, but his notion of a nice restaurant is a fish and chip shop and that just won't cut it when wooing our investors."

"I know just the place," Uther claimed, raising a finger.

⁕

The otter at the reception desk looked up from tidying his lovely pearl display, nervously watching through the glass worktop as the Howlers descend the creaky stairs.

The stocky blonde one unexpectedly jogged over. "How much for a pearl, citizen?" he asked amiably.

The otter gulped. "Ey?"

"The pearls," Linus clarified, "I'd like to buy one."

Silence.

"Are they for sale?"

After a distended quiet, the young otter beamed, "Yah, they be fer sale!"

Uther moseyed over, paws in pockets. "What're you doing now, Woodlouse?" he scoffed at Linus.

"Buying a pearl."

"What for?"

A shrug, but then an answer, "I collect pearls," Linus professed simply.

With a scratch of the head and wave of the paw, Uther left Linus to it. "Look, I'll be outside, mate. Just hurry up, yeah?"

Uther pushed the door open and stepped out onto the noisy main street, awash with pedestrians, cars, trucks and a blue-green evening light. The Howler immediately took an ember from his case and popped it between his lips, puffing away whilst he watched a mouse with a long stick turn on the imperium gas street lamps one by one.

Uther's ember had nearly fizzled away by the time Linus finally emerged from the *Crab and Kettle*. Reading Uther's stormy, white-furred face, Linus immediately excused, "Sorry, but you have to haggle with otters."

"Yeah and I bet he ripped you off still," Uther growled, flicking his spent ember away. "Puh! Cheeky maggots they are. Dunno their place half of 'em."

Linus just guffawed noncommittally. Otters didn't have a place, he felt; they were one of those midway races that didn't fit tidily into Lupan conventions, being neither cowed by wolves, nor a threat to them. They ran the waterways of Lupa and knew their own worth, and unlike the displaced hogs and hyenas and many other races, whose lands had been swallowed up by Lupa and Felicia and so forth, the aquatic otters still held their own archipelago to the tropical south. They had cities, an intact history and a sense of belonging, which is perhaps what endowed them with such confidence.

"Come on, Woodlouse," Uther said, hopping on his green monobike.

"Where to?" Linus replied, getting on the back.

"To *The Beehive* of course," his partner tutted, adding, "Finally!"

"*The Beehive?* Isn't that where you told Penny and Monty to meet us later?"

"It is, mate. Yeah."

"But they won't be there for hours."

"Aye," Uther confirmed, snapping on his goggles and passing Linus's pair over the shoulder, "but we can get started and have proper fun before they turn up."

Linus took his goggles, "We'd better be careful, Uther."

"Whatcha mean?"

"Well, we'll have to watch ourselves in front of them. I mean, they're Felician royalty and Vladimir-"

"We'll be good as gold!" Uther woofed, revving his *Dragonfly* into life and tearing down the road with Linus clinging on, the distant, hazy glow of Lupa's dazzling Common Ground beckoning.

⁕

The ashen streets of Greystone territory never came clean, not even with rain. Lathes and steam hammers powered by imperium and guided by skilled paws constantly turned and beat metal by the ton, fashioning train and car, rail and wheel, pot, pan, knife and fork, anything and everything, spewing ash by day and by night.

All of Lupa polluted, every engine, mono and lamp contributed to the Ashfall, even Bruno played his small part whenever he cooked a meal for a customer, but the industrious Greystones stood right in the thick of it. Being located to the south, between the Bloodfangs and Eisbrands, the prevailing wind usually blew northeast, carrying the Ashfall over the Common Ground, towards the Bloodfangs and beyond to the Great Steppes. But just occasionally the wind would whip round and carry Lupa's grey firmament southwest across the Eisbrand quarter and subject their citizens to a taste of Greystone life, this twisted landscape of brick and metal choked by the ash of a thousand furnaces, where piles of industrial junk clotted the alleyways and children of every race played amongst poisonous effluent. Bruno remembered it well; this is where Dad had found him, where he had played amidst ash drifts with long-gone friends. Since moving out he had never returned, not even passing through for fear of setting off his bad chest.

Feeling his airways contracting, Bruno picked up the pace. He rounded a corner and came upon his escape route – a familiar stretch of the mighty Lupan Wall.

A huge, ash-streaked, brick and concrete barricade crowned with grim crenulations and brutal-looking towers, the Lupan Wall cut discordantly through the otherwise ordinary streets like a great millipede, twisting and turning into the grey distance as far as the buildings and roofs would allow Bruno to see.

The true Lupan Wall, when beasts generally referred to it, was that which circled Lupa entire. However, sections ran within the city itself, dividing pack holdings. The stretch ahead of Bruno was the Greystone-Bloodfang wall, and on the other side of it lay Riddle District, *The Warren* and Dad. Bruno hoped his memory served anyway, he'd not been this way for years.

Jogging to the end of the next street, he spied a tunnel cut into the thick wall; just one of many that allowed beasts and trade to flow from one pack's land to the next. Red banners fluttered on either side of the tunnel's arching, brick-lined throat, each marked with a white circle encompassing a black wolfen skull and two red fangs – the Bloodfang crest. Greystone banners doubtless flew on the far side, advertising the way into their quarter just the same.

With pack relations running smoothly at the moment the gates were open. There was not even an arm barrier, just two Howlers on duty. The wolf on the Greystone side of the arch wore a dark yellow cloak, the wolf on the Bloodfang side red. Occasionally the Greystone stopped a passer-by and checked his or her papers and inside their coat, before waving them through. The Bloodfang seemed altogether uninterested in the living traffic.

Bruno mingled with the crowds and waited until the Greystone was busy searching someone's luggage before slipping under the dark, dank archway.

The arch felt a mile long, every paw step a labour. Nearly there, Bruno, nearly there.

"Oi, you!"

Bruno cringed, but continued walking, head down, hoping it wasn't him.

"You, wolf in the coat! Halt in the name of the Republic!"

Bruno stopped, turned around and pointed at himself, innocently conveying, 'Me?"

"Yeah, you!" the Greystone Howler snorted, beckoning him with a wave of the paw. "Come here!"

The Bloodfang Howler, meanwhile, turned to look at what his rival was doing.

Bruno slinked over to the Greystone; an athletic brown wolf armed to the teeth, his glowing brooch marked with the crest of his pack – a giant mechanical gear. Or was it a waterwheel? Bruno never could tell. Either way, the brooch was lovingly centred with a stone of bright yellow-imperium, which, whilst usually poisonous and unstable, had been tamed by way of some secret process privy only to the highest Greystone artisans.

Bruno couldn't help noticing the two pistols strapped around the Howler's thighs, not to mention the enormous imperium rifle slung at his back. Oh to have a pop of that!

"Yes, Howler?" Bruno sniffed, friendly as he could muster.

"Open yer coat then," was the slightly snappy reply, as if Bruno ought to know to do so.

Bruno did as bidden and the Howler felt inside the pockets and checked the lining, frisking

Bruno's breeches too, no doubt searching for contraband. During his examination the Howler turned up Bruno's pass and checked it.

"Bruno 'Claybourne'?" he said curiously, looking inquisitively up at the giant Bruno.

"Yes, Howler."

There was a long, tense quiet. The Howler checked the pass, then took a second, longer gander at Bruno.

"Not Casimir's son?"

Bruno's already jumpy heart performed a somersault, "Uh, which Casimir is that, sir?"

"The white rabbit. Used to run *The Warren* down my way. Got a limp."

"I wouldn't know-"

"Yeah, you're his adopted son!" the Howler woofed, slapping Bruno on his mighty chest. "Mate! We used to play down the road every day, us and me big brother, 'til you suddenly moved away without a bye nor leave." He winked, "Changed your surname, I see. Used to be Cranbourne, when we were cubs. Still, that's to be expected from a dodger, eh?"

Bruno said nothing. He just stared; scared.

The Howler laughed, "It's all right, mate, I won't rat!"

He removed his helmet, revealing a friendly wolfen face, brown-furred like Bruno, but a shade lighter. His eyes were pale yellow, almost translucent, like slices of glistening lemon set on the side of a glass.

Bruno frowned. "Gunnar?" he hazarded.

"Yeah, now you're getting it!" Gunnar laughed. "Six, seven years is it? Mate, my dad used to pop in for breakfast every day on his rounds. Remember that?"

"Yeah! Hah!"

"Ah, small town is Lupa," Gunnar cackled, even though Lupa was a megapolis that sprawled for tens of miles in all directions.

Hoping to keep things friendly, if only so he could get through this territorial checkpoint, Bruno made small talk with this long-forgotten friend, "How's your brother?"

"Going up in the world," Gunnar claimed, "Captain Bodvar now."

"Howler then?"

"Yeah, rot got both of us, well, all three of us including you eh?"

Bruno didn't know what to say.

Gunnar stood back and marvelled, "Mate, I could feel you from across the street. I thought you were some idiot smuggling a load of stingers in that coat, but it's just you under there, 'en it? By Ulf, that wily rabbit must've greased paws left right and centre to keep you out of the Howlers this long!"

Bruno dipped his chin. His mind raced. All these years he had ridden the trains and walked the streets and nobody, not one Howler, had stopped him or said anything remotely like this. Now three of them had accosted him in one day, speaking of crackling bones and coronas, and all the strange talk they came out with, which Bruno for the life of him had never once felt. Why now? What's changed? Is it because I've been ill? Is that how the rot starts?

Dad, is Tristan right? Have you been hiding it from me? Do you know? Did you always?

"What're you on?" Gunnar said.

"Eh?" Bruno replied, in something of a daze.

"Venom. What're you taking to, you know, keep yourself going? White I hope."

Bruno scoffed, "I… I don't take anything. I'm allergic to imperium; doctor said so."

Gunnar stared awhile, then snorted and tapped his nose. "Aye, aye, nudge nudge, wink wink." He glanced around the arch and then took Bruno aside, "Seriously mate, if you need a fix you can drop by any time. I skim a bit of scum off the top of my broth, if you know what I'm saying."

Bruno didn't really, but nodded anyway.

Gunnar spoke under his breath, "White-imperium, mate, pure venom, properly packed and sealed. It'll make you feel like a new wolf, not like the watered-down krap they peddle on the streets. For you, I can do a very reasonable price. Favour, for an old mate."

Heart pounding, Bruno decided to nod, and nod some more, judging it to be the fastest way to get out of here. "Sounds good, Gunnar," he said, smiling.

"All right then," Gunnar replied, slapping Bruno on the arm.

"Yeah. Look, I'd better go."

"Sure, sure. Don't be a stranger; I'm on duty here most days."

With a forced friendly wave, Bruno took his leave and passed through the arch, thankfully unmolested by the Redcloak, into Bloodfang territory.

He didn't feel any healthier for it, nor safer.

✤

Brrrri-!

Janoah snatched the phone.

"Yes?" she demanded, rocking to and fro in her office chair, before sitting up straight. "What do you mean you've lost him? He's the size of a house, how could you lose him?"

She waited through the fumbled explanation.

"I see, Tristan's meddling again. That wolf is fast becoming a bore with all his spies. Riddle District must be swarming with Eisbrand informants. If he wasn't Ivan's cousin and Den Father Thorvald's darling I'd do something about him, as it is he's untouchable."

Janoah paused for a thought and an ember.

"Put out a notice to all the border guards to arrest our cook," she puffed. "I'll check the café. Werner should be there to pick him up, but I fancy a boxing wolf with a nascent corona might be beyond Politzi expertise. At least I rather hope he is."

Hanging up, Janoah grabbed her silver Howler helmet from her armour stand and a matching silver pistol from her drawer and left her office.

"All right, boy, let's see what you've got."

CHAPTER 9

"Drink up, Linuuus!" Uther woofed.

Linus humoured his partner with a gulp of his beer.

Satisfied, for now, Uther leant back into the plush green bench and took a huge draught of his beer and then another of his ember. Puffing blueberry vapours from his nostrils, he said knowingly, "You don't get out much, do yer Woodlouse?"

The stocky Linus shrugged his shoulders. "Not as often as I'd like," he admitted.

Uther's white face cracked a wry smile.

Linus cast an umpteenth eye around the interior of *The Beehive Saloon*, at the beasts of every sort laughing and chatting, drinking and smouldering. The air was thick with multicoloured vapours and lounge music; the walls hung with fashionable, imprecise 'new art'; the chairs and tables of good quality, yet a minimalist design. The huge bear bouncers at the doors kept any real hard nuts at bay, Howlers notwithstanding. This was a safe, classy establishment; it didn't feel like somewhere a tough street-wise wolf like Uther would go for raucous fun. Linus supposed he had Penny and Monty in mind, or even his new partner.

"I'm sorry," Linus sighed, shaking his head.

"Eh?" Uther urged over the hubbub.

"I'm not m-mmm-much fun I'm afraid."

Before Uther could mount a reply, an attractive golden-furred wolfess in a frilly red and white dress and matching hat sat down beside him without invitation.

"Why if it ain't Uther Bloodfang," she said, in a lazy drawl. She stroked Uther's chin with a finger and teased, "Whatcha doin', yah no-good Howler scum?"

"Getting merry, Lorna," replied he.

"Is that a fact?"

"Aye, but not too much; I got special guests tonight."

Lorna plucked Uther's ember from his lips and had a puff for herself. "Special guests, huh?" she chirped, blowing vapours over his ears. "Does that mean I ain't wanted, Sugar?"

Uther cast his eye over Lorna, "Depends if you behave."

With a dry chuckle, the wolfess looked across the table at Linus, who immediately buried his nose in his beer to avoid eye-contact with her.

"Who's yer friend?" Lorna asked Uther, giving Linus the once-over with those lovely blue eyes.

"That's my mate Linus."

"Cute."

"'En he!" Uther agreed, with a rough cackle.

Lorna raised her chin, "You a Rostsonner, sonny?"

Upon realising Uther's lady friend was addressing him, Linus looked up from his beer, "Who m-mmm-me?"

"Uh huh. You look like a fellow southerner."

"I-I-I was born there, marm, beyond the canyons, but I hardly remember it now. I-I-I've lived in Lupa since I was a cub."

"So I can hear. You ain't got no hint of our fine frontier accent, have you?"

"I lost it I'm afraid; provided I ever had it. I don't recall."

Lorna purred, "Trust me, the new you's just fine. Nothing more attractive than an educated-sounding wolf, Linus."

The educated-sounding Linus felt his heart flutter, which wasn't so bad, except as he gulped his beer it sloshed down the wrong hole and he spent the next half a minute coughing his guts out, much to the general amusement of Uther.

Mercifully, someone patted Linus on the back and offered him a hanky, which he took and coughed into. Linus looked up to thank whoever it was who had done him such a courtesy, but was struck dumb.

Another wolfess, light brown, in a similar getup as Lorna, but green and black. She was shorter, with a rounded muzzle, button features and grey eyes.

"You awright?" she said, in a harsh and squeaky rendition of a Greystone accent.

With some difficulty Linus articulated a response, "Yes. Thank you, miss."

For a while nothing was said.

"That's Linus," Uther told the newcomer; breaking the end off another ember, strawberry this time. "Linus, meet Rosalina."

Linus nodded, "Pleasure, miss."

Rosalina curtsied, "Pleasure's all mine, Mr. Linus."

"Scoot over then!" Uther tutted at 'Mr. Linus'.

"Oh. Yes, of course."

Linus did as he was told and shuffled along the bench, allowing Rosalina to sit beside him, just as Lorna had sat beside Uther, making two pairs on opposite sides of the waxy table.

"He your new partner?" Lorna asked Uther quietly, though Linus could still hear.

"Yup," Uther replied under his fruity breath.

"But he's too… plump-lookin' to be a Howler," Lorna almost whispered.

'Plump?' Linus thought despairingly.

"Aww, he's just a cub, fresh out of the academy," was Uther's nigh on inaudible response. "You two be gentle with him, yeah? I'll make it worth your while." He leant over and whispered in Lorna's ear; this time Linus couldn't hear.

"Uther Wild-heart, I do declare," Lorna said, playing with her pearl necklace of many colours. "Why, you're just a regular softy under all that muscle n' gristle, ain't yah?"

She ran a paw over Uther's chest, her fingers slipping between the brass buttons and inside his shirt. She pecked him sweetly on the neck and he returned her affections with gusto.

Linus reached for his beer and took a substantial swig to calm his nerves. This was escalating quickly.

"So," Rosalina blurted, "you a Howler too then?"

Linus nearly choked a second time, but luckily avoided the indignity. "Yes," he said, nodding.

"You don't much look it, if I may say."

"Thanks," Linus beamed, "I think."

"It's a compliment," Rosalina insisted. "You dun half get some clapped-out droolers in my line of work."

The next Linus knew, Rosalina had placed a delicate paw on his thigh. The only barrier remaining between her and Linus was the fabric of his breeches.

"Me father was a Howler," she said.

"Really?" Linus all but squeaked. "How nice."

"No, it weren't," Rosalina sighed. "It were horrible. His fur fell out and everythin'. He were so young too."

"No, of course, I… uhm… I'm so sorry."

"Yeah, well. That's how it goes. I'm lucky he never passed on the rot to me. Me mother was healthy, so fingers crossed I'll be all right. Us girls usually get away with it, but you never know."

Nodding, Linus supped some beer.

Suddenly he felt Rosalina's muzzle on his neck, her moist little nose nuzzling into his fur and down to his skin. Spitting beer, Linus pushed a paw up between him and Rosalina and levered the wolfess aside.

"What's the matter?" she squeaked, looking him up and down. "Don't you like me?"

Linus looked across at Uther and Lorna, who disengaged to check what the problem was.

"Uhm… w-www-would you ladies like to go to the p-ppp-p-p-pictures?" Linus stuttered in desperation.

"What?" Lorna sounded across the table. "The pictures?"

"Yes. We're going there, r-rrr-right Uther?"

"Well… we *were*," he replied with intent.

Rosalina contemplated the proposition. "You mean, go there first, before getting down to business?"

Linus leapt on the premise, "Yes! A-a-and maybe join us for dinner too?" he stammered further.

Rosalina looked to Lorna, "Ooh, he's posh, 'en he?"

And Lorna looked to Uther, observing, "Yeah, your friend's a regular gentlebeast. How comes you've never offered to take us to the pictures, Uther, or dinner?"

"'Cause I ain't a gentlebeast?" he suggested, with a puff of vapour.

Lorna slapped him on the shoulder.

"What? You actually wanna go?" Uther cackled.

The girls nodded eagerly – Linus too.

"All right, you're on. We got plenny of time to kill."

Reaching into his breeches, Uther produced some money from his wallet. Lorna tried to snatch it, but Uther was too quick by half. He did, however, count out what Linus estimated to be a few hundred lupas and give them up to Lorna, who stuffed the cash inside the neck of her bodice.

"Half now, half later," Uther stipulated. "Now, let me pay my tab before I'm barred," he grumbled, extracting himself from under the table.

Warning sirens screaming between his ears, Linus was quick to excuse himself from Lorna and Rosalina and follow his partner across the saloon to the bar.

"Uther!" he seethed through his teeth.

"Leaving two vulnerable ladies alone, Woodlouse?" Uther tutted, hailing the black cat bartender in a smart red waistcoat. "Oi, Leroy!" Then finishing, "Not the done thing for a gentlebeast."

"They're hardly ladies," Linus scoffed, "let alone vulnerable-"

"Well listen to you!" Uther growled. "Lah di dah!"

Leroy arrived, his feline eyes alight, "What can I get you, Wild-heart?"

"The bill, mate."

"It's a hundred and sixteen lupas, forty-five pence."

"What the! You sure?"

"Positive."

Uther made grumbling noises as he counted out a wad of lupas.

Linus began afresh, "Uther I-"

"What?" Uther snapped. "Look, I'm paying for everything, don't worry. My treat."

Linus wasn't sure if Uther was referring to the tab or the company. "I-I don't want to appear… ungrateful-"

"Then don't!"

Uther slammed the money down and returned to the table. Grabbing his coat, he offered Lorna his arm and escorted her through the busy saloon towards the door.

Rosalina waited patiently for Linus.

"You Uther's new partner?" Leroy asked, his glittering eyes taking Linus all in.

"Yes."

The cat laughed heartily and bid adieu with a shake of the head and the words, "Good luck."

✦

As late afternoon bowed to twilight, Bruno emerged from a tiny passage into the street he had called home for only a few weeks. He had taken the back alleys to avoid attention, but still found himself glancing nervously over his shoulder for the umpteenth occasion.

Never before had big, confident Bruno been afraid to walk Lupa's streets.

As he approached *The Warren*, Bruno could see warm light playing on the glistening cobbles outside and hear drunken laughter reverberating within. Dad must have opened for the evening crowd after all!

Spurred on by thoughts of Dad and safety, Bruno hurried to the café door and burst inside.

"Dad!" he called.

It wasn't Casimir behind the bar, but a recognisably enormous hog in a Bloodfang-red Politzi getup. Three more Politzi lounged around the place, two rats and another more modestly-built hog. They all stopped laughing and drinking and stared at Bruno as one entity, jaws slightly agape.

Bruno stared back in kind. "Werner?" he guffawed; he knew Dad's crooked old friend anywhere.

"Bruno," Werner replied, wiping his snout and putting his beer down. "Good to see you, lad."

Bruno looked around, "Where's Dad?"

"He's gone to see about the windows," Werner replied without pause, pronouncing 'winders'.

"Oh, right," Bruno nodded – that made sense.

Werner trotted out from behind the bar, pulling up his baggy breeches as he went. "I came by to take Casimir's statement regarding this morning. I said I'd watch the place for him whilst he was gone." He slapped Bruno on the back; Werner was one of the few beasts big and hefty enough to jolt the immovable Bruno. "Don't mind if the lads have a few beers whilst we wait, do yer?"

Dry-mouthed and dying for a pint of beer himself, Bruno cast his fiery eyes over the others. Had he been cleverer, he might've wondered why four Politzi were required to take a statement. As it was he replied, "'Course not, mate."

"That's the spirit," Werner said, patting Bruno's shoulder. "We'll take your statement too. Just need to ask you a few questions. Nothing serious. Formalities, really."

"Fire away, Werner."

"Not here. We'll do it over at Riddle Den."

Bruno glanced at the bay window; ordinarily he might've seen the spires of the local Bloodfang Den in the distance, but of course the broken glass was boarded up.

"Why there?" he asked, a little worried.

"It's just easier to fill out all the paperwork," Werner sniffed logically. He looked Bruno over, "You all right, though? I mean, not hurt or anything are yer?"

"Nah," Bruno dismissed, taking a moment to add, "Howler Rufus saved my life."

"Did he now?"

"Yeah, I think so. He pushed me into the kitchen when the bomb went off. If he hadn't I'd have been shredded." Bruno scratched an ear, "You know about the bomb, yeah?"

"I do; yellow-imperium, nasty stuff," Werner snorted, shaking his head. "You know, most beasts would've just cowered whilst a Howler bled-out, or at best ran for help. It was a noble thing you did, Bruno Claybourne, very noble indeed."

The youth shrugged.

Werner beamed amiably, "I reckon you'll be handsomely rewarded."

For the first time all day, Bruno felt a pang of relief, "Rewarded?"

"Of course! You're a regular hero over at the Den."

"I am?"

"Aye! I reckon they'll strike you a medal and everything."

Bruno woofed with delight, "Cor! Really?"

"Aye!" Werner threw an arm around the wolf and guided him to a bar stool. "Now come and have a beer with Uncle Werner. You've always been like a nephew to me, as Casimir is like my brother. You know that, don't you?"

With all concerns receding rapidly into the distance, Bruno nodded, "Yeah. Dad always says so."

"Good, good-"

Brrrriiing!

Bruno deftly extracted himself from Werner's bulky embrace and went behind the bar to fetch the telephone, saying on the way, "I'd better get that."

"That's the third time it's rung," one of the Politzi rats snorted through his foamy beer.

"Third time?" Werner said, looking at his subordinate.

"Yeah, you were outside last time, boss. Wasn't anybody there though, they just hung up again. Weird."

"Is that right, Denny. Is that right."

Bruno set the phone's fancy base on the bar a moment and put the earpiece to his ear, before grabbing the base again and speaking into it. "Hello, this is *The Warren*, Riddle District, how can I help?"

A familiar voice crackled hurriedly in his ear, *"Bruno, don't say anything! Don't speak, lad! Just listen!"*

Bruno nearly piped 'Dad', but refrained.

"Just keep nodding and saying yeah," Dad whispered down the line. *"Pretend I'm a client, got it?"*

"Yes, sir," the young wolf nodded.

"All right, listen. Is Werner there?"

His heart thumping and mind frazzled by an already strange day, Bruno accidentally made eye-contact with the hog in question. "Yeah," he said, adding, "Yeah, we're open for business, sir. The windows will be fixed by tomorrow."

"Good, lad, that's really clever," Dad praised. *"Listen, whatever Werner's said to you is a lie. Don't go with him. Just get out of there. Hear me? Make an excuse and hop out a window, but don't make it obvious, Werner's no fool."*

"Yeah… yeah, tell me about it," Bruno said, with a convincing chuckle.

"He let me go, I think," Dad explained, *"but I couldn't twist his arm for you."* He drew a deep breath, *"The Howlers are after you lad; the Bloodfangs that is. Whatever Werner tells you, if you go into their Den, you'll not come out the same wolf as you went in, if ever."*

Bruno gulped. "Yeah? Why's that then?"

Casimir sighed, *"I'll explain everything later, but I swear to you, lad, I did what I did to give you a good life. It'll be different from now on. I'll find a way to fix everything, we'll go somewhere. Just get outta there, Bruno. Please!"*

After what felt an eternity, Bruno found his wits.

"All right, so the usual seat then?" he said, grabbing a pen and writing in the reservation book.

"Aye, the usual place," Dad replied fondly. *"You know the emergency drill, lad."*

"Yeah. I got it."

"I love you, lad. Be strong. I'm gonna hang up now."

"See you then."

Bruno slowly set the earpiece on the hook.

"Who was that?" Werner demanded, snout flaring a little.

"Oh… just a regular booking," Bruno sniffed.

"Regular? You've only been here a few weeks."

"Ah, word of my legendary waffles spreads pretty fast, Werner," Bruno joked, paws spread on the bar.

Mind and heart whirring, Bruno removed his suddenly stifling coat and threw it over the bar; hoping at the same time to throw Werner off guard, since someone who planned to flee would surely keep their coat on.

Acting natural, he hoped, Bruno grabbed two glasses and drew the hog and himself a beer.

"Cheers!" Werner said.

Bruno slaked his thirst. He noticed his paws were trembling, so he put the glass down in a hurry lest Werner saw. Luckily the pig had his thick snout in his glass at the time.

Bruno made small talk. "So, how are you anyway?"

"Very well, thanks."

"Good."

Werner nodded, "You're looking well yourself, Bruno."

"Yeah, I'm all right."

"Still boxing and lifting weights?"

"Yeah."

"You get bigger every time I see you."

Bruno scoffed, "So do you, mate."

There was a brief silence; the other Politzi looked at one another. Finally, Werner burst out laughing and slapped his knee. "Ahaahahaaa! Aye, I do, but in the wrong places," the huge pig admitted. "Not like you, lad. Oh, to be young and fit again. I had a body of rock, back in the day, just like yourself. Undefeated in the ring, I were. Werner Iron-snout they called me. Hah! Never boxed yer dad, mind, different weight class see, but... maybe me and you could've gone a few rounds."

Bruno just smiled amiably.

'Time to go,' he told himself, whilst telling Werner, "I'm gonna spend a penny, all right?" and hiking his thumb at the stairs.

Werner chuckled, "It's your house, lad, you don't have to ask my permission."

Bruno forced a convincing laugh.

Wiping his fingers on his shirt, the big wolf climbed the stairs and ducked under the ceiling as usual, leaving Werner and the others below.

Once Bruno was out of sight, Werner set his beer down, reached across the bar and grabbed the reservation book. He flicked through to the last entry.

Not a reservation, but a meaningless scribble.

With a last gulp of beer and a shake of the head, Werner turned to his constables and flicked a trotter at the door. Setting aside their drinks, the Politzi grabbed their hats and truncheons and filed out in silence, save for the door bell, which jingled overhead.

Grunting and sniffing, Werner climbed for the stairs. They creaked under his bulk. Once he had squeezed through the gap between the stairs and ceiling and alighted on the first floor, the layout of which he was already familiar with after superficially searching for the eloping Casimir, Werner clopped to the bathroom and tried the door knob.

It opened. Inside was a tin bath, grooming sink and all the rest, but no Bruno. The window was shut and locked.

Werner picked up the pace, trotting to the nearest bedroom, the one Casimir had leapt out of.

Locked.

Werner rapped on the door. "Bruno, come out," he said. "I know that was your dad on the phone."

Nothing, save for some scuffling.

"Don't be daft, lad!" Werner warned. "Don't try and run, you'll only get hurt!"

No response.

Werner stood back and rammed the door with his shoulder. With his great size and strength, not to mention weight, it buckled in a single blow. Werner stumbled into the room just in time to see Bruno's dark paws release the windowsill.

"Bruno!" Werner shouted, hurrying to the window.

Landing awkwardly on the roof, Bruno fell on his rump. He looked up and saw Werner poke his pink head out the bedroom window.

"Bruno, listen to me!" he called. "Casimir lied to you! He's been lying to you for years!"

Bruno's said nothing, but his face conveyed 'what?'

Glancing around for his fellow Politzi, Werner hissed as loudly as he dared, "He meant well; I know 'cause I was part of it. We did it for your own good, lad. But the truth is you're dying. You're rotten and always have been, ever since you were little. Casimir's kept you going as long as he can, but he can't afford the amount of venom you need now. If you don't go to the Howlers and get some proper juice you'll die, I'm telling yer!"

Bruno sat frowning, ears erect.

Werner held out a trotter. "I won't let no harm come to yer, I swear. You're like my own blood, you know that. Come with me and I'll make it easy for yer."

Without a word, Bruno scrabbled to his feet and hopped off the roof.

"Bruno!" Werner shouted, seething, "Aww schmutz!"

The moment his paws hit the street a great weight slammed into Bruno from the side, knocking him to the smooth yet painfully immovable cobbles.

Bruno made to rise, but his world exploded in a baffling cacophony of trotters and paws, breeches and tails, as Werner's uniformed Politzi thugs descended upon him, hitting him about the back and head with their truncheons and holding him down with their combined weight. They shouted and snarled at one another and at him, but Bruno couldn't make head nor tail of it all. He rolled into a ball and tried to protect his head with his arms, to weather the storm.

It'll be over soon.

No. I'll be taken to a cell, questioned and beaten. Remember Dad's stories, what he suffered at the paws of the Politzi and the Howlers, how so many of his friends just disappeared? Is that what you want to happen?

Get up! Bruno told his trembling, throbbing body. Fight back. Do something, anything!

"Gaaagh!"

Bruno pushed himself off the floor, sending the scuffling bodies tumbling off his back. They hit him, but he felt nothing as the red mist descended. The urge to survive seized the helm and steered Bruno's fist expertly into the nearest Politzi face, all those sparring sessions making it second-nature.

With a fleshy thud the unfortunate rat dropped like a stone, his red hat flopping in a filthy puddle.

Next the pig; Bruno was on him, his whole weight pushing him to the ground, his fists laying into him, left, right, left, blood and teeth took fly and he was out of it.

Crack!

Something slammed into Bruno's back, no mere truncheon, but an explosion of pain.

The wolf fell forward over the unconscious pig and snarling in agony crawled along the cobbles a few yards, trying to get away from the pain, as if he could outrun it. But there was no escaping. His whole left side throbbed like he'd never known, had his arm fallen off at the shoulder? No, it was there, but the pain by Ulf!

I've been shot!

Holding his arm stiff, for that eased it a little, Bruno levered himself upright and turned on the last Politzi rat. The constable had a pistol in his paws, a pistol that he was hurriedly trying to reload. He fumbled with the cartridge right up until the moment Bruno grabbed the pig's stray truncheon from the ground and brought it round into the Politzi's rat's skull.

There was a flash of light, a thunderous clap.

Pfzaack!

"Agaghpff!"

Spiralling through the air, the rat slumped into a concrete gutter, silenced.

Bruno stood, chest heaving, body trembling, hot blood swilling in his throbbing mouth.

The rat didn't move.

Dropping the truncheon like a hot poker and wiping his tingling paw for good measure, Bruno, despite everything, reached down and grabbed the downed rat by the back of his shirt, turning him over, lest he drowned in the putrid ashen water.

There was no danger of that; his skull was caved in on one side, revealing a dark, bloody hole and what Bruno swore was a hint of pale brain.

With a distinctly wolfen yelp, Bruno dropped the rat and fell on his rump. He scrabbled across the slick cobbles on three out of four limbs, kicking with his feet to distance himself from the rat's staring, accusing eyes. The only thing that checked Bruno's panicked crab-like scuttle was the pain. He collapsed to nurse his left arm, to grasp it tight and roll in the street.

Once the agony had subsided a little, Bruno felt a new sensation deep in his gut. It rose up his chest and into his mouth and forced its way through his lips.

He vomited.

It wasn't much, just the beer from a few minutes ago. The acid and alcohol stung his nose and bleeding mouth.

Lips quivering, dripping, he looked at his offending right paw, opening and closing his bloodied, tingling fingers. Beyond them, coming into sharp focus, lay the other rat and the hog, both unnervingly still in the midst of the road.

With a whimper of fright, Bruno got up and staggered down the street, into an alley, overturning a bin in his haste.

Silence prevailed.

Once it was safe to come out, Werner crept round the side of *The Warren* and took in the devastation. He tentatively approached and kicked his comrade hog in the side. Getting no response he slowly crouched to check for a pulse.

He was alive, just.

When the enormous Werner rose again, someone was standing beside him.

"Yahaaagh!" he cried, very nearly falling over.

It wasn't Bruno, but rather a slender, shapelier wolf in a white cloak and silver helm – almost worse.

"Calm yourself, Werner," it said, paw on rapier hilt.

Once he had recovered from his fright, Werner saluted nervously, slapping a fist to his flabby chest. "Grand Howler Janoah, I-"

"Save it!" she interjected firmly. "I observed your incompetence from afar."

Werner's eyes darted about and his jaw shook a little as he found the words, "Then why didn't-"

"I do anything?" Janoah guessed. "Silly pig," she tutted, "I wanted to see what the boy could do. Though... I suspect you've long-known of his condition, haven't you?"

Werner glanced at the rat whose head Bruno had mercilessly bashed in and used it to change subject. "The bastard murdered Denny," he snorted, with a gulp. "Caved his head in with his own stick, I saw it!"

"Denny shot him."

"Yeah, but-"

Janoah growled, silencing Werner, "You Politzi aren't meant to carry pistols without strict Howler authorisation, Werner, for you cannot be trusted! The packs got a taste of Politzi 'loyalty' during the war; we shan't make that mistake again." She added softly, "I'll say nothing to Elder Amael of it, or the fact you knew about this boy and said nothing to us, if you don't mention his ability to anyone. Plead ignorance. Tell anyone who asks, Amael included, that this Bruno is a dullard and a weakling, do you understand me?"

"But why?"

"Do you understand me, or do you want to go to the Gelb mines?" Janoah barked.

Werner nodded once.

Wordlessly, Janoah took her leave of him, dashing gracefully down the street and into the alleyway Bruno had taken.

⁕

Ducking into a passage, Bruno fell against the nearest moonlit wall and heaved again, but like a well-wrung sponge there was nothing left in him.

The pains shooting down his left arm overwhelmed any other; the savage beating administered by the Politzi pale compared to being shot. The young wolf wondered if he might bleed to death here in this alley, far from Dad, far from Sara, far from anyone who cared, which wasn't many.

The war memorial, in the Common Ground, that's the emergency meeting place.

Got to get there. Keep going.

Bruno could hear Dad now, encouraging him whilst sparring in the street, back when he was just a tiny cub smaller than a rabbit.

'You can do it, lad. Pick your feet up! Move! Duck! Weave! That's it!'

With a gulp, Bruno limped along the alley, his bloodied arm held stiff by his side.

His fevered mind wandered, the sickening image of that rat's caved-in face bubbling to the fore like a rotten vegetable in a foul broth. *By Ulf, it wasn't possible. How could I do that? I just hit him with his stick. That's all. I hit him back, is all. The Politzi hit beasts all the time with those things. Werner's big and strong, but he doesn't smash heads in with his truncheon, not like that!*

You're a freak, Bruno. You're one of them, just like Rufus said. You're gonna rot.

"No!" Bruno yelped aloud. "Dahaaad!"

His voice echoed off the walls of the houses. Someone opened their window high above and shook a fist at him, *"Shut up, you thumping drunk!"*

"Please!" Bruno called up at them, "Please, help me... I've been shot! Please!"

At once the window slammed shut and light within the house was extinguished; doubtless this someone didn't want to get involved in any trouble lest they incurred the wrath of the Politzi, or worse, the Howlers. Bruno couldn't blame them, not now he knew what it was to do so. *I'm an idiot. I should've left Howler Rufus to die and disappeared like dad wanted. Should've lain low.*

"Please!" Bruno called pathetically. "Somebody!"

No response; at least, not from up there.

"Perhaps I can be of assistance?"

With a startled gasp, Bruno looked ahead. A cloaked figure stood in the claustrophobic passage, silhouetted by an imperium lamp in the street ahead. They took a few steps forward, Bruno could hear the metallic clink of armour and belt buckles. The stranger had a thin sword at their hip and a helmet on their brow.

A Howler and no mistake!

"Poor boy," she tutted, for she was indeed a she under that uniform, judging by her manner and voice. "You must be frightened and in a great deal of pain."

"Please, Howler… I didn't do anything," Bruno sniffed, clutching his arm. "I'm innocent!"

"I know, I know," she soothed.

Bruno's fiery, yet watery eyes flitted about, "You do?"

"Yes," she replied, raising her chin. "Werner's thugs can be such bullies, can't they? It was merely self defence, wasn't it?" She turned away a little and sighed, "Still, you did kill a beast back there. Murdering a Politzi *is* a capital offence."

Bruno's lower lip quivered, "I didn't mean to!"

"Shh. I know… I know."

"I just… I…."

"Hit back?" the Howler guessed, with a slight titter. "With all your might?"

Bruno nodded dumbly, unwilling to embarrass himself by trying to speak through a flush of tears.

"My dear boy, but you don't know your own strength," the Howler told him, taking a few steps forward. "I do, I can feel your corona half a street away, that's how I found you." She cocked her head, "You… really haven't been inducted, have you?"

Bruno dipped his chin and shook his head; he'd heard this part before. He wanted to laugh.

As if sensing this, the wolfess chuckled, "What is it?"

"Please, Howler. I'm just a cook. I'm nobody."

"Nonsense!" she tutted. "You should embrace what you are, all the better for you. Starting to get the pains, are we? The old legs giving you jip, eh?"

Bruno looked away a little.

The Howler nodded, "They're often the first to go. Werner's many things, but he wasn't lying. You'll rot, and soon, unless you let us help you."

"I'm just allergic!" Bruno growled.

"Allergic? To imperium?" the Howler laughed. "Hahahahaha! By Ulf, your poor boy. What lies have you been told by that long-ears?"

"He's my dad! And he's no liar!"

Her laughter fading, the Howler stepped a little closer, until Bruno could see her helmet and the imperious red fangs glowing on her cheeks. "You really believe it don't you?"

Bruno just pouted.

"Do you believe us to be monsters then?" she mocked. "Are *you* a monster?"

Bruno didn't know what to say.

"No," the Howler answered for him, "You're just… Bruno Claybourne. So why would you become a monster the instant you donned the mantle and helmet? Why would any of us? On the contrary, as a Howler you could protect those you love. Make a difference in this cruel world. Leave a mark."

There was a long pause.

"Until I rot… right?" Bruno said plainly.

The wolfess tipped her head back in understanding. "Is that what you're scared of? Well, we're all going that way, even the healthy die. Better to live as the dayfly than the nymph, Bruno."

Frowning in bafflement, Bruno looked down. "But I'll be hated," he snuffled, with fresh grief. "Sara… I'd lose her. She hates the Howlers; everything about 'em; even her own family!"

"Then she's unworthy of you!" the Howler huffed, as if she knew who Sara was. Then again, perhaps she did. "Only small-minded, petty beasts hate that which they do not understand. That you didn't spurn Rufus despite him being a Howler and your father a little beast who's doubtless filled your head with vitriol and hate shows how worthy a wolf you are. You saved my husband's life and for that I'll help you all I can."

Bruno's ears pricked. "You're… J-Janoah, aren't you?"

"My name precedes me; no doubt Tristan's doing," Janoah hummed, unsurprised. "Look, I won't lie to you, Bruno, being a Howler's no picnic. You have to get up really early, you get told what to do all the time and you have to train constantly. It's rather like… boxing, actually."

Bruno's ears pricked and Janoah smiled.

The apparently all-knowing wolfess went on, "But without us Lupa would fall into ruin and with it the Erde entire. We alone stand against the tide of war and disorder. Anyone can shoot an imperium pistol and kill a beast these days, but only we can turn raw imperium to our will and control the fabric of nature itself. Such power makes us invincible to all but our own kind, and by own kind I mean not only Howlers, but Valours, Chakaa, Kodas, even Seawanders – you know what they are, Bruno?"

Bruno shook his head.

"Well it's not just wolfkind with this power, you know, many races have it, and they'd all take our place if we let them. It's your duty to use your Ulf-given gifts to protect our race's rights. Don't join the ranks of dodgers living in Lupa's underbelly, scavenging rancid imperium to live and gazing vacantly at walls, make something of yourself!"

Silence.

"The sting of imperium's not so bad," Janoah soothed, walking close and cupping a paw to Bruno's cheek. "Once your induction's out the way you'll see there's nothing to be afraid of."

Bruno looked down at his feet and nursed his arm. Every inch of him ached. He smelt of blood and fear. It would be easy to give in.

So very easy.

"All right," he exhaled, nodding and forcing a crooked smile. "All right, Howler. You win."

Janoah gasped a little; relief tinged with surprise. She placed a ruddy paw on Bruno's broad back. "Come along then, let's get your wounds seen to. I'll have to introduce you to our other imperiologist Doctor Josef. He'll fix you up and, when you're better, perform the induction; he's the best in the business."

Bruno limped along, hardly listening.

"Can you walk back to our Den?" Janoah asked him, taking stock of his wounds. "I can call a car."

Bruno seethed, "I'm fine, Howler."

"What a brave chap you are," Janoah praised, ushering Bruno down the alley. "I can see we're going to get along handsomely, you and I. We understand each other."

"Yeah."

"I'm good to my wolves," Janoah said, "You'll see."

"Yeah."

Howler or no, Bruno dwarfed this wolfess, as he did most beasts, and that's what he was counting on.

"Oof!"

A good shoulder-barge from Bruno's muscled bulk sent Janoah stumbling clean across the narrow alley and into a pile of garbage. It was Bruno's wounded arm that did the shoving, but no matter. Suffering through the excruciating pain he sprinted headlong down the alley.

He made the end alive and sped down another, then another, the walls, windows and doors of houses whizzing by either side, dirty puddles exploding underfoot. He stuck to the back streets, out of sight, knowing all he need do was escape from Bloodfang territory. Greystone, Eisbrand, it didn't matter where he wound up, his crime wouldn't carry over, he would be free.

It wasn't far now, just a few blocks. *I'll barge that Bloodfang at the territorial gates out the way. Maybe Gunnar is still on duty. He'll help me. Yeah.*

Bruno rounded the next corner and leant on the wall to rest a moment. He peered back, checking if he was being followed. There was no one. Commanding his battered body to move, he turned to trudge down the next alley.

"Ragh!"

As if by sorcery, Janoah dropped from above and was on Bruno in a split-second, one paw pressed to his chest. She stayed her actions, her bright green eyes narrowing slowly, challenging Bruno, daring him to try that again.

With a boxer's speed and strength of paw, Bruno whipped his good arm up to bat Janoah's touch away.

Too slow.

Pffzaack!

The Howler's white cloak billowed outwards as a bolt of imperious plasma instantly shot up her arm and into Bruno, punching him across the alley and against the far wall with all the force of an invisible wrecking ball. With a yelp the big wolf bounced off the rough bricks at a crazy angle and flopped to the unforgiving cobbles, coming to rest in a puddle enriched by a swirling rainbow film of imperious ash.

Time passed; Bruno's world span.

Spitting blood and rank water he tried to rise, to stagger away, but as he found his feet a smart gaitered boot thumped him right in the side, and with it another explosion of imperious energy. Bruno was sent against the wall a second time, before falling on his back. Plasma licked over his trembling body and played between his teeth. His whole skeleton throbbed in pulsing waves, as if he were being run through a giant mangle again and again.

At last the pain subsided.

Smouldering chest heaving fitfully, the dazed Bruno lifted his bleeding head, tried to focus.

"Stupid boy," a blurry Janoah tutted at him, the ash-laden moon hanging behind her like an apparition. "Still, I expected nothing less from such a splendid candidate."

Bruno fell back, let go.

"Dad," he growled, staring into nowhere, into blackness and beyond, "Sara."

CHAPTER 10

Uther led the way to the bright facade of the cinema and queued at the ticket office, which was occupied by a particularly bored-looking pig squished into the tiny booth.

"Whatcha wanna see?" Wild-heart asked his colourful little posse, glancing at the posters.

"Somethin' romantic," the golden Lorna swooned, hanging on his arm with her elegant gloved paws.

"Puh!"

Linus stepped back and read the well-lit marquee curving overhead. The diminutive Rosalina waddled over to him. "I like a bit of 'orror meself," she said. "What about you, Mr. Linus?"

Linus remembered what Uther had said back in Riddle Den's washrooms about watching a scary film. He pointed at the black letters stuck on the white marquee, "*Night of the Spider Queen* sounds like its 'orror, I mean horror."

"Ooh, yes!" Rosalina giggled shrilly. "And it's on again in ten minutes, look."

"Oi, hurry up!" Uther called, as he and Lorna reached the booth.

Linus hurried over with Rosalina in tow. *"Night of the Spider Queen?"* he said, giving her a glance; she nodded.

Uther looked at his fellow Howler, eyes wide. "Nah, nah," he dismissed, waving a paw. "That sounds krap, mate. How about something… romantic, yeah?"

Leaning on Uther's shoulder, Lorna scoffed, "Romantic? You puh'd me for suggesting that a second ago."

"No I didn't."

"You did!"

"Look, we'll see what you wanna see, Lorna. I don't really care."

"Is that right? Then I wanna see *Night of the Spider Queen*," Lorna cackled, with a mischievous air. "Sounds a real hoot, hey Rosalina?"

"Ooh yeah!"

The hog crammed inside the booth cleared his throat to hurry the wolves along. Uther cast his eyes over everyone, Linus, Lorna, Rosalina. "Fine, whatever," he said, rolling his muscled shoulders and tugging at the chest of his shirt. He addressed the hog, "You heard the lady. Four fer… *Spider Queen,* or whatever it's called."

The hog ripped off some pink paper tickets and went to take Uther's money, but Linus pushed his comrade's arm down and paid for everyone instead.

"M-mmm-my treat this time," he stammered.

Beaming, Uther snatched the tickets, "Much obliged, mate," and shepherded Lorna to the cinema entrance.

"He's cute when he stammers," she laughed in Uther's ear.

"Daft more like."

Arriving in the foyer and wondering where his daft partner had got to, Uther looked behind and saw Linus had set Rosalina down on a bench and was tying one of her shiny green boots, which had, onc could only assume, come undone. Rosalina was chatting away and scrunching up her nose, whilst Linus, down on one knee, nodded a lot.

Lorna sighed, "What're you doing, Uther, mixing a nice boy like that with the like of us Lupanar girls? You're gonna ruin him."

"Puh! Lupa's no place for a 'nice boy'. He's gotta male-up."

"But he might find himself a nice Freiwolf girl one day."

"Yeah, but he's gotta live long enough first, Lorna."

Whilst waiting for Linus and Rosalina, Uther broke out another ember to ease the rot; raspberry flavour. Inhaling its heady vapours, Wild-heart felt a tingle shoot down his spine. Was it the ember vapours doing their work?

Looking behind him, Uther spied a beautiful young brown wolfess in a pink coat, pink beret and white breeches. She was the only beast standing out in the open. She turned away, pretending she hadn't been staring at Uther and was quickly joined by a little black wolfess in a green coat and similar breeches, but no hat. Chatting away, the pair took a seat on a bench together, the taller brown wolfess glancing Uther's direction again as she did so.

"Come on, Uther."

Wild-heart looked up from his musings; Lorna was beckoning him after Linus and Rosalina, who were already heading inside.

At length, Uther rejoined the group.

"Penny for yer thoughts?" Lorna said, looking at the girls and hanging on Uther's arm.

"Nothing," he replied.

As was the natural order of things, the confident Uther overtook Linus and led the way through the vaulted gold and red foyer to the appropriate theatre door. A rat in stripy red clothes tore their tickets and let them through with a tip of his cap. Inside, the screen was still draped in fancy red curtains and beasts of every sort were chatting away, though most fell silent as the intimidating Uther passed by.

He picked out an empty row of medium-sized seats, appropriate for wolves and similar-sized races, and everyone filed in after him. It was right and proper that he and Linus should bookend the girls, and, consciously or not, they did so, thus were Lorna and Rosalina sandwiched between the boys.

No sooner had they settled than the curtain raised and the lamps dimmed, as if the show had been on hold for them alone.

Rosalina shuffled over and slipped a paw round Linus's arm. "If I get frightened you'll hold me, won't yer, Linus?" she said.

"I'm sure it'll be all right," he replied, pointing at the screen. "Anyway, the news reel comes first."

"Oh yeah!" Rosalina giggled, her hysterics punctuated by a snort. "Sorry. Been ages since a wolf took me to the pictures."

Linus asked, "Where do you usually go?"

Rosalina gave him an incredulous look. "Well, upstairs to a room," she said, tugging at her dress.

Linus gulped and nodded. "I-I-I see."

Rosalina brushed a paw on his shoulder. "Oh, you are funny," she marvelled.

Mortified at his own stupidity, Linus looked down at his knees. "Sorry. I've never... uhm... I mean-"

"Don't apologise," Rosalina hushed. She glanced across at the others and tactfully changed subject, "So how long have you known our Uther then?"

Linus was grateful for the question, "Oh, just a few days."

"That all?"

"I was only just assigned to Riddle."

"Well, Uther's a good fella," Rosalina said, scrunching up her little nose. "He's very kind to us." She cocked her head to one side and added with a shrug, "Not many are."

Linus thought back to that unfortunate wolfess on the street that Uther had given money to, and how abominably he himself had spoken to her.

The projector started up, throwing a jittery off-white rectangle onto the screen. Scratches and dust grains flitted by at twenty-four frames a second, followed by an animated countdown, starting at five. Some of the audience counted with the film, including Rosalina.

At zero, they cheered.

The screen turned black, then opened in a vignette. An inky-black cartoon grasshopper in a bow tie popped up and leant on the interior edge of the vignette. He removed his monocle and winked cheekily at the audience.

Linus had forgotten that in any self-respecting cinema the cartoon short preceded the news.

"Charlie Cricket!" Rosalina 'whispered' excitedly, squeezing Linus's arm. "Ooh, he's my favourite."

"He's a grasshopper, actually," Linus blurted.

"What?"

"Oh, uh… well, everyone *says* cricket, but he's clearly a grasshopper."

"Whatcha mean? It said cricket up on the screen."

Linus forwent modesty for a moment's confidence, "I know my bugs, miss." He pointed at the screen, as Charlie 'cricket' waltzed through a greyscale meadow on two legs, his other four tucked behind him, as if he were a civilised beast rather than a mere mindless insect. "Charlie has a long face, look, and a narrow abdomen, and long legs. Crickets are much more… stout."

"Like me?" Rosalina said.

"Well, and me," Linus admitted, "Uther says I remind him of a woodlouse."

"Woodlouse? Why's that?"

Once Linus had explained why, Rosalina laughed aloud.

Lorna elbowed Uther and whispered, "They're getting on like a fire in a silk barn."

"Good," Uther sniffed. "Cub needs loosening up."

Wild-heart raised his paw to hail the passing snack vendor; a peachy-furred young wolfess in a racy red and white-striped skirt.

"Pot of honey-roast crickets please, love," Uther whispered gruffly, winking at her like Charlie Cricket.

"Anything else, Howler?" she asked in a chipper voice – she obviously recognised a Howler's physique when she saw one despite the civilian clothes.

Smiling, Uther looked to Lorna, "You want anything?"

"I'll pass, thanks."

The beaming Uther was given a stripy pot of crickets and paid up, telling the vendor to keep the change. He immediately took a very-dead, very tasty-looking, honey-glazed cricket and popped it in his mouth, crunching noisily away.

Back on screen, the well-to-do Charlie Cricket was accosted in some spooky-looking woods by a mysterious stranger in a cloak and broad-rimmed hat – a fortune teller, according to the rickety old sign. They chatted in musical intonations for a while, until the stranger invited Charlie into his wagon where a crystal ball waited. Charlie sat on a stool, long, spiky legs crossed, and turned his pockets out onto the table at the stranger's insistence. Amongst the paperclips, bottle caps and far more ridiculous paraphernalia, yo-yos and springs amongst them, was a glowing imperium pearl which, reluctantly, Charlie gave up as payment.

Pocketing the pearl, the cloaked stranger waved his baggy sleeves about until the crystal ball exhibited a future Charlie rolling in piles of riches beyond his wildest dreams and throwing corn over his head. The grasshopper leant close to the ball; eyes so wide in joy that his monocle fell out on the floor, forcing him to bend down and retrieve it.

Suddenly the stranger threw off his cloak – he was a hideous spider with eight eyes, eight legs and huge dripping fangs. He was covered in spots and sported a mane that clearly resembled a hyena's. He had a hyena's dentition too, Linus thought, and spiders didn't even have teeth.

Back in the real world, Uther fumbled his tub of crickets, scattering a few of the sticky bugs over the carpet. Lorna glanced at him, but thought no more of his unusual clumsiness.

Meanwhile Charlie was clonked over the head by the spider and the screen faded to black.

The animated hero awoke in a spider's web and looked about. The spider was chopping vegetables nearby and adding them to a broiling pot over an open fire. The chef's cap did nothing to alleviate the spider's menacing appearance, or Charlie's worries, evidently.

With a 'pssst' the well-to-do grasshopper beckoned the savage spider over and whispered in his ear. After enthused nodding on the spider's part, Charlie was plucked off the web by his captor and stood upright, though he was still mostly bound in silk. Nonetheless he stood on one foot and started playing his legs like a violin. The spider enjoyed it immensely and clapped along with six out of eight arms until, against his will, judging by his baffled expression at least, he took to dancing around the campfire. Charlie's music was simply too catchy to resist.

Trying to free himself by burning his silk bonds on the campfire, Charlie couldn't simultaneously play music with his legs. Released of the hero's charms the spider ran after

Charlie, but he hurriedly played on just in time, making the spider dance away across the screen. Charlie had to stop again to further burn his bonds away. The spider, at large, went after him a second time, only to be stopped yet again by the hypnotising music. The charade continued in ever-faster portions with the audience laughing all the way until, at last, Charlie burst out of his silken bonds, held a claw up to the spider's eight-eyed face and indicated the confused fellow to turn round. He did so. Satisfied, Charlie kicked the spider up his bulbous behind to the sound of a loud drum beat, sending him head-first into the pot and rolling down the nearest hill. The shining imperium pearl rolled out of the villain's pocket – spiders had pockets apparently – and Charlie picked it up, polished it off and hopped off into the grey sunset, though not before leaning on the encroaching vignette and proffering a cheeky wink to the audience.

Many clapped and cheered, Rosalina amongst them.

The next feature followed swiftly, the title of which jumped onto the screen with a bit of an incongruous jitter.

'OUR HYENA FRIENDS'

"Puh!" Uther scoffed, turning a few heads.

The screen faded into a sunny scrubland, which panned across to a camp, with tents, a smouldering campfire and carts lashed to mighty horned beetles.

After the establishing shot, the camera moved in and cut to a tribe of traditionally-dressed hyenas; the males standing about in knee-length sarongs of dazzling designs, spears in paw, bodies painted. Then to a mother in a shawl, with a braided mane and cubs about her. Then to old one stooped, over a fire.

"Hyenas, beasts of the wilds, hunters, vagabonds," said the narrator, in perfect Lupan; one imagined a dapper wolf or cat at the microphone though it could as easily be a puny mouse endowed with a profound voice. *"Noble some call them, savages say others,"* the narrator went on. *"Either way our hyena friends remain tragically outside the circle of Lupan citizenship. The Matriarchs, the mothers of the tribes who command the respect of all hyenas, continue to hold back their own people in suffering and squalor."* The narrator chuckled patronisingly, *"They say we are destroying the world! That we Lupans anger the gods; the Sun and the Wind and especially Mother Erde, by digging up her riches and plundering the wilds. Such outmoded superstitions stifle the hyenas, dooming their race to destitution and misery."*

Shots of downtrodden hyena cubs and old folk followed, many clothed in mere shreds of tattered fabric, huddled around campfires and tents.

The camera cut away to a row of shiny wooden buildings; a town so young the trees were mere saplings, with houses, a saloon, a park and even a motor car, all brand-new. New, yet Linus couldn't help but notice the car looked old-fashioned, perhaps ten years old, what with its crank-shaft down front. Nobody made those anymore.

"However, by the power of education and good old-fashioned charity," the narrator said, *"we Lupans persevere in bringing our naïve hyena brothers into the fold of civility, to give them a better life, a life of convenience and cleanliness powered by nature's great gift – imperium."*

To a perfect classroom, with rows of young hyenas at their desks, clean and tidy, diligently doing their sums.

The narrator exalted the gifts of education bestowed upon them by wolfen charity as the teacher, not a hyena but a prim-looking wolfess in spectacles, pointed out the times table. The film was scratched and it jittered alarmingly, as if it had seen better days. Moreover the teacher's clothing looked dated. Who wore blazers with lapels that size anymore, or glasses that large? Perhaps she was just frumpy.

The camera cut to a particularly cute trio of hyena cubs sitting together at a table.

"These little 'warriors' can all spell their names and count to ten already, thanks to Lupan charity," the narrator patronised.

A large and again rather dated microphone was held before the most self-assured and handsome-looking cub of the hyena trio. *"Now then, little Nurka, can you count to ten for the beasts watching back in Lupa?"*

Nurka, who looked no older than six or seven, obliged quickly in his rough little hyena voice,

"One, two, three, four, five, six, seven, eight, nine, ten."

"Very good, Nurka! And what about your friend, Madou?"

To the next hyena, smaller, shier but steady, *"One... two... three... four... five... six... seven... eight... nine... and ten, sir."*

"Good, Madou. And now you Themba, show the nice audience what you've learned."

The largest cub blew a raspberry, arms folding defiant.

"He's got spirit, that one," the narrator chuckled, as did many in the audience.

The trio all beamed perfect smiles, showing off their impressive hyena dentition.

Down below, Lorna melted at the sight. "Aww, ain't they adorable?" she said to Uther.

"Give 'em ten years and they'll be killers," he growled.

"You heard the film; they're being 'civilised'."

"Civilised?" Uther snarled. "So was the one that blew Rufus up this morning! One of us, he was, a hyena prince 'en all, 'civilised' in a Howler Academy. Rufus was his friend, thumping trained him, even saved him from a sewer centipede, Ivan says. So what does the filthy, rotten, son of a maggot do? Turns round and throws a bomb in Rufe's lap. That's gratitude for yer!"

Lorna raised a gloved paw to urge Uther to keep his voice down. Beasts looked at them and whispered, but soon settled again.

Linus had watched the spectacle with little surprise; not many wolves had time for hyenas. Still, the re-education and integration programmes would do their work as with many a people before. By the next generation, the hyenas would be just another facet of the Lupan Republic and indistinguishable from the next civilised beast.

With the propaganda out the way, news from the past week was up next. Linus read the papers and was up to date with events. Sure enough the news wasn't news to him; there was a mention of a new imperium mine opening, with shots of lifts and veins of imperium; then an art museum exhibition being unveiled by some big-shot pig in a suit; and finally, and most interestingly, a bank robbery over in the Eisbrand territory that had escalated into a hostage situation. The Politzi had called in a Howler who had dealt out summary justice; discounting the robbers there were no casualties.

"We spoke to the wolf of the hour as he left the scene of the crime," said the speedy narrator.

On-screen, a big Howler in a light grey surcoat – probably blue but there was no telling when everything was a shade of grey – was accosted by a reporter as he left a marbled building and strode to a parked monobike.

"Beg your pardon, Howler, but what's your name?" asked a bold rabbit correspondent, pushing a metallic microphone at the Howler's grille-clad snout.

"My name?" the Howler growled, the hilt of a big imperium sword shining at his back. *"What for?"*

"You're a hero, sir," the rabbit insisted. *"Say something to the good folks of Lupa, won't you?"*

With a glance left and right, the Howler looked right into the camera with his striking eyes that were clearly of two different shades and said, *"Be good, citizens."*

Jumping on his monobike, he sped away, cloak fluttering.

"Tristan," Uther cackled, "you smooth-talking fleabag."

"You know him?" a surprised Lorna asked.

"Yeah. He's Ivan's cousin. He's all right."

Lorna hiked her blonde brow. "Fleabag passes as a compliment between Howlers these days, huh?"

"It's a term of endearment, Lorna."

Up next was a mention of a diplomatic visit to Felicia by representatives of the Den Fathers – every pack had their own Den Father, but they would never deign to travel across the Teich to Felicia themselves, of course, only their ambassadors were sent to shake paws and smile for the cameras.

A last piece of news was tacked on the end; Linus could see where it had been hurriedly inserted into the reel, for the film jittered for a split-second and some tape whizzed by.

The piece began with beasts in a park, mothers pushing prams and young ones of many races playing on the swings.

"A wonder of the imperium age has come to Lupa," said a different, much livelier narrator, *"To see it all you have to do is... look up!"*

The beasts in the park did indeed 'look up' and the camera cut to a great silvery lozenge with four fins and whirring propellers hovering over Lupa, like a giant fish.

A dirigible!

After shots of the airship from below came amazing views of Lupa from above, from the balloon's gondola no doubt. The chaotic tangle of streets and buildings that were Lupa passed by far below. Chimney stacks belched smoke and vapour, carriages and buses navigated the roads like toys, and mighty imperium trains were reduced to scale models of the sort found in a grandfather's cellar. Gardens were but the size of postage stamps and even a sprawling Howler Den, with its towers and walkways, appeared no more than an elaborate chocolate cake.

"Oh, it's making me all dizzy," Rosalina giggled, covering her eyes. "Tell me when it's over, Mr. Linus."

Mr. Linus was silent, transfixed by the sight of the airship hovering low over a crowd of on-lookers. Twenty beasts or so grabbed the dangling lines and pulled the ethereal behemoth to a stop.

There followed a close-up of a cat in a long white coat and goggles standing on a stage, waving to the crowds.

"What?" Linus woofed, pointing, "Uther, that's Monty!"

"Eh?"

"The pilot, look! That's Montague Buttle!"

"Hah! So it is!"

Lorna looked between them and elbowed Uther, "What's he hollering about?"

"Long story," Uther replied, putting aside his spent pot of crickets and licking his sticky fingers clean. "I'll tell you over dinner."

The newsreel cut to Montague Buttle waving silently into the camera, backed by bombastic orchestration. He kept pointing at the sky, perhaps conveying, 'Look up! Haha!'

As the orchestra reached a crescendo, the stylised logo of an airship with six feline whiskers on its nose cone faded in. The title *Buttle Skyways* was stamped into the surround.

So, that's what Penny had meant by 'promotional venture'.

At long last, the film that everyone had paid to see started to roll. The credits came first, displayed on a painted background of sinister naked tree branches festooned with web, backed by thunder and lighting and all things 'orror.

Suddenly an orchestra strike, and a huge, hairy spider darted across the screen, momentarily filling the theatre with eight-legged terror! It was recorded to film, but real enough, unlike Charlie Cricket's acetate-based cartoon nemesis. Some of the audience jumped, even screamed – Rosalina loudest of all. The same spider scuttled in from the other side of the projected image to much the same reaction as before.

"It got me again!" Lorna woofed, paw to chest and giggling. She looked to an unresponsive Uther and found he had his paws cupped over his eyes. "Uther, whatcha doing?"

Wild-heart snorted and rubbed his eyes. "Eh, what? Oh, just tired, is all. Gonna sneak a nap, I think."

"Nap? What about the film?"

"Puh! Whatever. Wake me when it's over."

"Well *you're* no fun."

Settling down under Lorna's frowning glare, Uther peeked through his squinting eyelids just as a third spider slowly crept onto the celluloid from above, thin, hairy legs waving with calculated creepiness this time.

Sod that.

Uther opened an ember, shut his eyes and prayed to Ulf this wasn't a three-hour epic.

✢

Someone rapped on Janoah's door.

"Come in," she said, swivelling her seat away from the night time lights of Lupa.

Vladimir, cloaked but without helmet, his inquisitorial black and white face plain to see. The big wolf strode into Janoah's warm, fire-lit office and set a cardboard sting tube down on her polished desk without any of Linus's hesitation.

"There," he said. "It wasn't easy, but I got some."

Janoah eyed the wax-coated tube, puffed on her ember, then bluntly informed Vladimir that, "The boy's dead."

"What? How?"

"He tried to run," Janoah explained. "Stepped out into the road and was crushed by a lorry. Just as well, really, he'd only have been sent down."

"Sent down?" Vladimir spluttered.

"For murder. He bashed a Politzi's head in, apparently. One of Werner's; Denny or something. I dunno."

Once the news had sunk in, Vladimir cocked his head to one side and rumbled, "So what you're telling me is, you've reneged on your end of the bargain."

"It was never guaranteed."

"You said-"

"I said," Janoah interjected firmly, "that if the boy turned out to be useless, I'd find some other way to recompense you." She dipped her chin and tempered her tone, "He's dead, my dear Vladimir, and therefore couldn't *be* more useless. Though, if you want his corpse, by all means pop down to the morgue and take it. Compost him, for all I care; I know how you love your horticulture."

Vladimir turned his head to one side.

Janoah went on, "No need to sulk. He wasn't anything special anyway, just a pretty face."

"Says who?"

"Werner."

"And since when was that corrupt hog any judge of a Howler's potential?"

"He knew this Bruno for ten years," Janoah maintained. "He never saw any evidence of dodging or anything else. If he had he'd have reported it."

"Is that a fact?" Vladimir grunted.

Shrugging, Janoah looked down at the file she had open on her desk. She took out the photo of Rufus sitting in the café's bay window chatting to the strapping wolfen cook. "It was just a… silly infatuation," she said, screwing the picture up and tossing it in the fire. "Anyway, if he had a corona it hardly matters now. We can't induct the dead, Oromov."

Vladimir watched the photo shrivel and burn, along with any credit that may have come from adding such a splendid-looking wolf to Bloodfang's ranks. There was no point crying about it.

"I… hear Rufus is much improved," he said, with a sniff.

"Yes," Janoah chirped. "I rather jumped the gun. He didn't need any venom."

"Is that so?"

"There's life in those rotten bones yet."

Vladimir had to concede, "He's an alpha male, despite all his indiscretions… if not because of them."

Janoah snorted, "Careful Vladimir, you're dangerously close to complimenting him."

Vladimir tapped a finger on top of the sting, "Do you still want this or not?"

Janoah looked down at it, then up at Vladimir. He was being strangely magnanimous, so Janoah played nice. "I suppose I can take it off your paws. Rufus may need it before long."

Vladimir smacked his lips. "Actually… I may have a use for it after all. No, I'll keep it."

His sudden change of mind felt like teasing to Janoah, so she swiped back, "For yourself? You do look terrible."

Ignoring Janoah's cheap jab, Vladimir tucked the sting away in his cloak pocket. "I will cover the cost of the venom, since it is mine now," he assured her, stepping forth a little and leaning on the desk with one black and white paw, "However, I expect compensation after I stuck my neck out for you."

"Never fear," Janoah replied at length, "I've a strong stomach."

Oromov weathered the blow. "Humph! You don't fool me with your front, Janoah. You *crave* a Howler's touch. You, one of the few still married to a fellow Howler, denied still…. How delectably ironic." Slapping the desk with a paw, Vladimir turned to leave, stipulating, "Come to my quarters, midnight tomorrow. You'll enjoy yourself, I promise."

He walked to the door, silvery greaves rattling.

"What about Noss?" Janoah asked after Vladimir, staying his paw on the door knob.

"What of him?" he replied.

"What's Josef got out of him so far?"

Vladimir took a deep breath, then said with a glance over his shoulder, "I'm surprised at you Janoah. Didn't you hear?"

"What?"

"He died."

Janoah let out a tiny, incredulous gasp, "Noss?"

"On the rack; he just… gave up."

On that disclosure Vladimir took his leave, abandoning Janoah to her thoughts.

✧

The audience piled out the theatre doors into the night air, laughing and chatting, save Uther, who immediately peeled off to the right and broke out an ember. He took a nerve-calming puff as soon as possible, blowing orange-flavoured vapours to the wind.

"Slow down, Uther!" Lorna laughed, exiting the theatre and joining him under the marquee. She glanced behind to check all was clear, then whispered, "Why didn't you just say you're scared of spiders?"

Uther nearly fell over, "What? Who told you that? I'll lamp 'em the liars!"

"Wild-heart, you had your peepers shut the whole time."

"I was sleeping!"

Lorna dipped her chin and queried the proud Howler from under the brim of her fancy hat. "All through Rosa's screamin'?"

"All right, all right, so I hate 'em!" Uther admitted. "Horrible, disgusting… ugh!"

"You know they were just little 'un's made to look big-"

"Little un's are even worse than big un's!"

Lorna masked a snigger. "Well, if it's any consolation, I was jumping all the way through that flick too."

"Yeah?" Uther said, relieved to hear it.

"Who wasn't? Linus aside; that cub's not as soft as he looks. Must be his tough old Rostsonne blood, huh?"

"Puh!"

Lorna looked suddenly wistful. "You know, back home on the ranch, Mama always told me never to go into the woods nearby on account of the net-casting spiders there."

Uther foolishly probed, "Net-casting spiders?"

"Uh huh. One fine summer's evening, Mama was playing with friends in those woods when a giant creature swept down from the trees and snatched one of the them away." Lorna spread her fists apart to illustrate, "Mama said it was a spider that held a web between its front legs, like a net. It scooped her friend up into the treetops. The whole town went a-hunting, but all they ever found was a dried husk of bone and fur-"

"Ulf fangs, wolfess!" Uther yelped, wheeling away in disgust. "What're you trying to do to me?"

"To make you feel better!" Lorna shrugged. "It's perfectly natural to fear bugs that can eat you."

"Is it, Lorna? Is it really? No schmutz!"

"Well, what about sewer centipedes? You afraid of them too?"

"Don't be daft, it's just spiders," Uther assured. "It's the way they move. And their web makes my fur crawl. Yeeuch!"

Linus and Rosalina sedately emerged from the doorway, chatting merrily away like old friends.

"Well actually a spider's bite only paralyses you," Linus was saying. "You can't move, but you're still alive; that way it can store you in its web and keep you fresh. It's only when it comes to eat you that it injects you with an enzyme that liquefies your flesh and-"

"Linus!" Uther squeaked, paws cupped over his ears

Mills stopped dead, blinking his big blue eyes. "Yes?"

"Just… just shut up, all right? Stop showing off! Rosalina's had her fill of bugs and all that science guff. First a lecture on Charlie thumping Cricket, now this."

Rosalina waved a paw, "Oh no, it's right interesting."

"Yeah well, *I've* heard enough!" Uther insisted, storming to the roadside. "You're such a know-it-all, Woodlouse!"

Lorna raised a paw at Linus and Rosalina, "Don't ask."

Smouldering alone by the kerb, Uther was wondering how best to row back from his regrettable outburst when he felt that weird tingle again. Looking left, he spied two wolfesses sitting on a bench, the same pink and green-clad pair from before the film. Had they been waiting outside this whole time?

Unable to stand by, Uther wandered over, ember glowing between his dark fingers. "You two all right there?" he enquired, his conversely white face pulling as friendly an expression as he could muster.

The tall brown wolfess looked the athletic Uther up and down, and smiled warmly at him; her little black friend pulled her pea-green coat tightly around her, suspicious of Uther's intentions perhaps.

"We're fine, thank ye," the latter huffed coldly.

Uther beamed at the friendlier brown wolfess "Waiting for someone?"

"Aye," the black one answered in her stead.

"For two hours?" the Howler said to them both. "You've been stood up."

Glancing at her brown friend, the black wolfess gave Uther a narrow-eyed glare. "Look, we're nae interested, all right?"

Uther reached into his pocket and held up his Howler brooch; the red-imperium Bloodfang crest glowed brightly at his behest, proving he was a true Howler with a corona. "I'm not a creep, love; I'm just doing me duty."

"See? I told you, Sara," the brown wolfess whispered to the black. "I can tell a mile away."

The black wolfess remained unimpressed. "You've nae duty in the Common Ground, Howler. This place is run by ALPHA, nae the Bloodfangs," she said officiously. "So if we want tae sit here fer two hours, we will. All right?"

Bold little lass, Uther thought.

The Howler pocketed his brooch. "Whatever you say," he chuckled, pointing at the marquee above, "but there ain't no more flicks showing."

The black wolfess twisted round, read the sign, then stood up, paws in pockets. "No, Ah suppose not," she sighed worriedly, talking more to herself than any other. "It's nae like Bruno not tae show up. Something's happened. Och, if only Ah had his new number!"

"Boyfriend, eh?" Uther guessed.

The brown wolfess stood up. "Yes," she blurted.

"Olivia!" came the black.

Uther laughed, "Can't decide between yer?"

"It's a double-date," the brown wolfess explained.

Uther just smiled and took a long, thoughtful drag on his dying ember. "Where'd you girls live?"

They exchanged looks. The brown went to speak, but the black elbowed her into silence.

Uther nodded slowly. "Look, just be careful. Stick to the main streets as far as you can-"

"We can manage, thank ye!" the black wolfess declared haughtily, brushing Uther by. The brown wolfess mumbled her thanks and together the girls trotted briskly into the busy nightlife of the Common Ground. Uther watched and waited until the brown lass gave him the satisfaction of one last glance over her shoulder.

"Still got it, Wild-heart," Uther cackled.

Linus approached, looked in the direction Uther was, then said, "Who're they?"

"I dunno," Uther said, adding, "Cute though."

Clearing his throat, Linus waited a moment. "Want to talk about something?" he asked, "Get it off your chest?"

"Don't be thumping stupid, Linus."

"No. Sorry."

An awkward pause.

"We'd best get back to *The Beehive*," Linus suggested, hiking a thumb. "Monty and Penny will be waiting."

Uther clapped and rubbed his paws, "Oh yeah, our free meal!"

"Well I-I'm not sure we can expect them to pay for Lorna and Rosalina too."

Uther grunted, as if expecting otherwise. With a glance over at the girls, waiting under the theatre marquee, Uther slapped his partner on the chest with back of his paw and asked, "Well, whatcha think of Rosalina then?"

Linus rubbed his neck, "Oh. Well, she's… uhm-"

"Hot stuff, eh?"

"Oh yes, absolutely. Of course!"

Chuckling, Uther flicked his spent ember away and slung a heavy, sinew-streaked arm around Linus, saying, "Steady, mate. We're gentlebeasts, remember?" He shouted and beckoned to Lorna and Rosalina, "Oi, come on you two! Grubs up!"

Linus could but roll his eyes at Uther the 'gentlebeast'.

Lorna and Rosalina glided and waddled respectively over to the boys.

"Now then girls, we're off to meet with royalty," Uther let it be known, wagging a stern finger. "If you want to tag along you'd best behave yourselves.

"Eh?" Rosalina squeaked, holding onto her hat. "Whatcha mean royalty?"

"Royalty! Like what they have in all them backward lands that wolfkind don't run. You know, kings 'n' queens 'n' that. Right Linus?"

"Well, perhaps not quite that royal," Linus guffawed.

"Well how royal we talking?" Uther snorted impatiently.

"Penelope Buttle is the Queen's cousin, a Duchess. I'm not sure if Monty's strictly royal at all, Vladimir didn't say."

Whilst the Howlers discussed their cat cousins, the girls fussed with their hats and dresses.

"Ulf's fangs, Lorna! If I'd only known I'd have worn me best outfit, not this tatty old rag."

"Rosa, have I got anything stuck round back, honey? Those cinema seats are filthy."

"No, you're all right, luv. Here, what about me?"

"You've got a dead cricket stuck to your behind. Hold on."

With much patting, brushing and bother, Lorna and Rosalina rendered themselves presentable again, not that Uther or Linus perceived any change. It was fair to say the boys themselves were hardly dressed for the occasion, but then a Howler's idea of formal dress was mantle, tunic, brooch and gaiters, often with armour and sometimes weapons. Parades, memorials, funerals, even weddings; the ignominy of the Howler getup in Lupa's wider society was lost on the wolf packs themselves, where it was a thing to be respected and worn with pride.

"How do we look, lads?" Rosa queried.

"Beautiful," Uther sniffed, leading the way. "Come on."

Braving the Common Ground, dodging cars and trams, Linus and Uther explained to the curious girls how they came to be meeting with Felician royals. And not just royals but, according to the newsreels, pilots too! Nor merely pilots of some old boat, but newfangled airship pilots! Flight had been but a fantasy up until a decade ago, and in common public parlance the word pilot still meant first and foremost a ship's guide into port rather than someone who took to the air.

"Oi, maybe they'll fly here!" Uther cackled, puffing clouds of ember vapour as he sauntered confidently along and made engine sounds. "Brrrrrrrrrbbbbbbp!"

"And take us for a ride!" Lorna swooned, hanging on his arm. "Oh, that'd really be somethin', wouldn't it?"

"Puh! Yeah."

"Oh, no!" Rosa squawked, paws to face. "I couldn't even look at them pictures let alone do the real thing."

Whilst the others chatted, Linus cast an eye to the stars and pondered the possibilities.

Rounding an alleyway into a main street, Uther's little posse arrived back at *The Beehive Saloon*. The building was shaped vaguely like the eponymous structure, with each floor stepping inwards somewhat from the one below, and pocked with golden hexagonal lead-lattice windows, like so many honeycombs. Patrons filed in and out the similarly hexagon-panelled doors, passing the formidable bear bouncers, or not if they didn't look respectable.

"Can't see 'em," Uther grumbled, eyes casting about.

"Maybe they're inside already?" Linus theorised, heading for the doors.

Before they made *The Beehive*, a familiar sporty red car rolled up on the opposite side of the street and birthed a couple of beautifully dressed cats, a ginger fellow in an elegant white coat and goggles, and grey catess in a frilly pink dress and wide brimmed floral hat – Monty and Penny and no mistake.

"Hahaaah!" laughed Monty. "There they are, Sweetpea!"

Penny waved daintily over the car roof and cooed, "Linuuus!"

Linus bashfully raised a paw to the cats as they crossed the road to the saloon side of the street, Penny's right arm looped through Monty's left. When only halfway, Monty extended a paw and homed in on Linus like a mosquito.

"I say, good to see you again, Linus!" he said, shaking the Howler's blonde paw with gusto. "Or should I say, good to see you for the first time? Haha! You look jolly handsome without that helmet, sir."

"Oh, well, uhm… thank you."

"And you, sir, Uther is it?" Monty recalled, turning to the athletic wolf.

"'Tis, mate, yeah."

Upon that confirmation Monty pitched Uther's paw all over the place, "Mate, he says. I like it! You look fit as a fiddle, my good wolf. Remarkable shape you've got there; must be a lot of jolly hard work, jolly hard."

"Heh, well, I suppose it is."

Monty went on, "I know it is, sir. Used to do a bit of running meself in me soldiering days. Four minute mile would you believe? Not a scratch on you Howler chaps though, of course." He patted his stomach, "It's all gone south now alas. Hahaaah!"

"Keep your voice down, Monty," Penny hissed gently, brushing her raucous husband with a paw.

"Sorry, Sweetpea," he excused, moving on, "So, who're these fine wolfen ladies, your girlfriends?"

"Monty!" Penny seethed further.

"What?"

Linus cleared his throat, "Uhm, well-"

"This is me lovely Lorna," Uther interrupted, throwing a muscled arm around Lorna and kissing her on the cheek, "and Rosalina there is Linus's sweetheart," he added mischievously, pushing Linus stumbling into Rosalina.

"There, you see!" Monty mewed. "Pleasure to meet you, ladies. You've got a couple of top-notch chaps there. Hold onto 'em."

Lorna tweaked Uther's nose and winked at him.

Whilst Linus tugged anxiously at his collar, Rosalina curtsied to Monty, "Honour to meetcha, your highness."

"I'm afraid, your aim's a little off, my dear!" Montague chuckled, hiking a thumb at Penny. "She's the one you're after; the Duchess Penelope. I'm just the ignoble cad who made off with the Queen's cousin. Not a drop of ink in me!"

"Oh! Forgive me, your majesty."

Penny reached out and raised Rosalina up before she could bow again. "Never mind all that, my dear; you're a Lupan citizen, not a Felician." She looked to Uther and especially Linus, "Besides, it's I who should be curtsying to these brave souls after they likely saved my life."

Stepping forward, Linus had to speak up, "I-I-I should never have put you in harm's way, marm."

"Nonsense, sir," Penny dismissed. "As I've said, we're glad to have helped."

"That dashed hyena, clobbering me out of left field, it's just not on!" Monty said, shaking a fiery ginger fist. "Pity about the other chap, Ivan is it? Penny said he wouldn't be here. No show, just like our investors."

"Yes, marm, didn't you say there'd be beasts with you?" Linus queried Penny.

"They backed out, I'm afraid," she grimaced.

"Something spooked 'em," Monty scoffed, feline eyes wide a moment.

"Spooked, sir?"

"Not all plain sailing this dirigible lark, Linus, there's risk involved and beasts won't back a loser."

Penny flapped a paw, "Forget them, we're here to honour Linus and Uther for their good works." The Duchess led the way, passing between the bear bouncers, both of whom gave the overdressed cats a second glance. "Come along everyone!"

Chapter 11

Grand Howler Vladimir Oromov entered the murky, windowless room and shut the hefty metal door behind him. The warm light from the imperium lamps overhead played on his polished eisenglanz helmet as he walked over to the metallic, bed-like machine in the midst of the room and looked down upon the hyena strapped to it, arms and legs outstretched.

"How are you, Noss?" Vladimir asked him.

Noss gulped and breathed deep. His nose was encrusted with blood and mucous, and his eyes were weepy.

"Been better, Oromov," he cackled.

Vladimir suddenly pulled down an overhead lamp and shone it right in Noss's face. The hyena turned his dark muzzle away and shut his purple eyes tight.

"Grraagh!"

"Aversion to light," Vladimir diagnosed. "The rot is bad with you today, my 'Prince'."

The bound Noss spat, "After... a racking? Who would have thought?"

Vladimir watched the hyena's mighty spotty arms twist and tense in a vain attempt to break the metallic clasps and, no doubt, strike his tormentor down. Even were he not restrained, Noss would be unable to do any such thing – Vladimir knew from personal experience that a beast didn't just get up and walk away after a stint on the imperium rack; they hobbled.

"You know, I was racked once," the Howler said, almost wistfully. "It was a long time ago now; I was only a cub really, fresh out of the academy. I was accused of misappropriating venom and found guilty. The Elders were lenient and gave me the rack instead of death." Vladimir took a sharp breath. "One never forgets the feeling of burning from the inside out as too much plasma flows through your body," he sighed, adding, "So you see, Noss, I never ask my Howlers to do something I couldn't do, not even treacherous ones like yourself. I've been there."

No reply.

With a 'humph' Vladimir pushed away the lamp.

The Grand Howler turned to the smoky-grey cat in a laboratory coat standing by a complex panel of dials, buttons and levers wired up to the rack.

"Get him up, Josef."

The grey cat adjusted his tinted spectacles and nodded once. He pressed a button and pulled a lever, keeping one gloved paw in his coat pocket the whole time.

The rack shuddered and slowly rotated, with Noss remaining firmly strapped to it. When it was almost vertical, with the crucified hyena all but hanging by his arms, Josef released the lever and the rack stopped with a jolt.

Vladimir wafted some papers in front of Noss's snout. "Your death certificate; heart failure from imperium shock, signed and dated by our coroner Doctor Josef Grau there. You're dead and nobody is going to know anything different, except us."

"You're... to kill me then?" Noss gruffed. "Thank the Wind! Hahahahaaa!"

"On the contrary I'm preserving your life," Vladimir revealed soberly. "I'm sending you somewhere safe, Noss, to a special penal colony for errant Howlers and other imperium-abusers on the far reaches of civilisation. Perhaps you know of it?"

"Gelb?" Noss guessed, big nostrils flaring.

A nod. "Plenty of hyenas there; you'll blend in nicely. You'll crawl on your belly through Mother Erde, as you call her, digging up imperium ore until such time as I call upon you."

"Hahahahaaaaheheheee!" Noss laughed, "What... w-www-what makes you think... I'll agree to performing such desecration?"

Vladimir said simply, "Arjana."

Noss's defiant laughter died.

"Provided you behave, Arjana and the cubs will be kept safe in one of those re-education towns. I've never been to one personally, but they look charming enough. Perhaps you've seen them on the newsreels? Your cubs will be moulded into perfect citizens, counting to ten in Lupan and everything-"

"Arjana will never accept it!" Noss snarled. "Never!"

"She must. They take cubs away from unruly mothers, I hear. You too must behave in Gelb, and be silent. Understand?"

Noss grimaced. His mighty chest and shoulders started to shake and a tear streaked down his gory cheek.

Vladimir snorted in disgust, "Crying, Noss? Did you shed a tear for Rufus when you agreed to blow him up for a fist full of lupas? You truly are despicable. Almost as despicable as those who put you up to it."

With a gulp, Noss managed to croak, "Throw the s-switch and kill me Vladimir. End my shame... my madness... I beg you."

"I wish I could oblige," the Howler professed. "You should've kept your big hyena mouth shut."

"I'll write it all down. I'll s-sss-sign anything. Please!"

"Not good enough!" Vladimir rejected. "I need you alive, if plausibly punished. Should Elder Amael discover your whereabouts I'll have my explanation for sparing you. You're a prince. I thought we may need you in future negotiations with your people, but for your protection, and to stop your tribe rallying around your name, I engineered your 'death'. He'll understand my deception... then promptly kill you."

"You believe me, then?" Noss said, raising his chin.

"Take consolation in that," Vladimir said, "and in the knowledge that, one day, if all goes well and you do as I ask, I'll set you and your family free. I swear it, on my honour."

"And if all goes wrong?"

"Then I'll see you in Gelb, if not the ant hills."

"I look forward to it! Hahahahaaaaa!" Noss cackled deliriously, his head flopping down. "Hehehee-hahahaa!"

Leaving Noss to his madness, Vladimir offered a sting of white-imperium to the tidy-looking Josef. "When they come for him give him this," he whispered.

"Venom?" Josef hissed. "Why?"

"Because I want him to survive. He needs the best possible start to get through Gelb. Don't worry, by the time he recovers he'll be collared and on the train."

At length, Josef pocketed the sting, "Fine."

"Not a word to anyone, Doctor. Not even Janoah, not until I sound her out."

With that, Vladimir headed to the door, but paused a moment. "Listen out for me, Noss," he said without even looking. "I'll set things in motion when I'm good and ready. Play your part and you'll see daylight yet."

Stepping out, Oromov closed the door.

Once Vladimir had departed, Josef Grau stepped round in front of Noss, paws buried in lab coat pockets. The grey cat filled the hyena's tear-blurred vision, his dark, round glasses catching the lights overhead.

"Typical," he said, "I wait ages for a decent test subject then two come along at once and I get to keep neither for myself."

Noss spat at the cat with what little bloodied saliva he could muster. "Rot!"

Josef simply purred, "You want more?"

Noss tipped his head back. "Come on, worm. Hit me! Hahaaa!"

"Hoping I'll actually kill you by accident like Vladimir's daft cover story?" Josef tutted. "Such a schoolboy error is beneath my expertise. If I had my way I'd dissect you right now to find out what makes you magnificent Chakaa tick, but Vladimir has his silly plans for you and I must humour him. He and Janoah between them keep me so busy with their plotting, and so well remunerated."

Josef walked to the control panel and pulled a lever. The rack jolted and eased flat again. The Doctor then turned an innocuous-looking dial.

"It's a living," he sighed.

Noss braced himself, closing his eyes, breathing deep, clenching every muscle in his powerful frame – it made no difference.

"Gaaaaghaaagh!"

In an instant, white plasma racked Noss's twisting body from paw to foot, the arcs of energy dancing randomly over his fur and flesh like a thunderstorm. Tiny streams of energy flowed between the top and bottom rows of Noss's mighty teeth as he arched his back and twisted in agony, unable to escape, unable to think, his whole world collapsing into a chaotic singularity of bone-burning pain.

Knock! Knock! Knock!

Josef shut his monstrous contraption down and Noss fell back, mighty chest heaving, spotty limbs trembling, the distinctive smell of singed hair rising over his battered body.

Someone was rapping on the door.

Pushing his spectacles up his nose, Josef hissed. "Whoever you are, go away!"

The door knob slowly twisted. Josef had forgotten to lock it! He hurried over and grabbed the knob. "Who is it?" he demanded huffily.

"Janoah," they replied, equally indignant.

Josef let out a slight growl of exasperation. Thinking fast, he opened the door, but only wide enough for him to slip out into the hallway where Janoah waited for him.

"What've you got in there, Josef?" she asked. "Or should I say who?"

"Just testing the new equipment," Josef lied, firmly closing the door.

"I see," Janoah said. "I hear Noss got cooked by your over-zealous application of the rack. Is that right?"

Josef glanced at the door, then frowned, "The hyena died suddenly, but-"

"But?"

"It wasn't my fault; there was a power surge."

"Power surge?"

"Yes. That's why I'm testing the equipment. It won't happen again."

Janoah looked down at her feet, stepped forward, and met the cat's bespectacled eyes. "I don't care myself, good riddance to that deranged hyena, but I can tell you when Rufus hears of this I'll be hard pressed to stop him administering his own 'power surge' to you. He loved Noss. He'll want to look him in the eye to ask him why he did what he did. You've denied him that satisfaction and, as you know, my husband is not a wolf to be denied his... satisfactions."

Josef acknowledged nervously, "It won't happen again."

Satisfied with her little exercise of intimidation, Janoah changed tone. "Glad to hear it. Now, my good doctor, let's pop to Riddle Hospice and find ourselves a dying wolf to lend us his noble name."

"Now?" Josef blurted.

"Yes, right now," Janoah chirped, glancing around the deserted corridor. "Our little secret had to be out of here and on his way before Rufus is well enough to stop me."

"Give me half hour, I just need to tidy up here."

Janoah gave the cat and the door a suspicious look, before parting company with both. "I'll be in the ambulance."

✦

Uther knocked back his beer and puffed on his ember, "So then I sez to Ivan, I sez, 'It's black-imperium, mate, we'd better get everyone clear of the train.' He was panicking of course, as is natural, I mean, the black stuff'll put the fear of Ulf into any one, even Blade-dancer."

"Even you?" Rosalina asked from across the table.

"Even me," Uther insisted. "I was scared, but I kept me head somehow. So we hops off the train and I start telling everyone to back off, calm-like, I didn't want to start a panic. But then Ivan, bless him, he starts waving his paws and shouting, 'It's black-imperium! Run!' and that was that, beasts couldn't get off the platform fast enough. Like a stampede it was. Still it worked out pretty well."

Lorna laughed between chews of her meal and wiped her mouth with a napkin. "Then what?" she urged.

"We started to check the train for stragglers, but then this dark cloud starts pouring out the carriage!"

Monty nearly choked on his food. "I say! You actually saw black-imperium, Uther?"

"Nah, it weren't black-imperium, Monty, just a mock-up."

"Mock up?" Penny queried delicately.

"Ash bomb, marm, that's the smoke you and Monty saw at the station. Pretty harmless, of course, though it will make a beast choke without protection. Just a sneaky hyena trick is all it was. He'd scarpered. Oh, and I found Ivan trying to take shelter in a ticket booth! Puh! As if that'll save yer from real black-imperium, I sez to him." Cackling, Uther took a draught of ember vapours and winked at the cats, "Of course, you two know what happens next."

"That hyena scoundrel decked me!" Monty said to all. "Caught me off guard, mind! If I'd been ready I'd have shown him the what for. Fought for Felicia once or twice in me time; nothing like you chaps I doubt, but I'm tricky with a rifle and bayonet I dare say." The cat whispered, "Incidentally that's how I met Penny here. Got bally wounded didn't I? She'd volunteered as a nurse at the time and the moment I clapped eyes on her that was that, she afflicted me heart for life. Terminal case."

"Oh Monty, away with you!" Penny dismissed.

Linus sat in silence, nursing his drink with both paws and nibbling the remnants of dinner, proffering smiles and laughter whenever appropriate. As the multicoloured haze and lounge-music of the saloon swirled around his ears, he watched Uther effortlessly entertain Lorna, Rosalina, the Buttles and several on-lookers, who secretly listened in to Uther's mesmerising gruff tenor.

That's an alpha wolf, Linus, fit, handsome and best of all charismatic; you'll never be like him, even less a true legend like Rufus or Ivan. Stick to your books and your bugs, that's what you know. You can't even talk properly half the time. Stammering in front of Janoah, what must she have thought?

Linus suddenly stood up. Uther stopped chatting and everyone looked to him.

"You awright?" Rosalina asked, grabbing Linus's paw.

"I'm…uh… I need some fresh air," he excused, brushing her paw off. "I'll be right back."

Leaving his coat behind, Linus headed off, only to stumble on a chair leg.

"Steady, old chap!" Monty said.

"Thump me," Uther cackled, "I do believe he's pissed!"

Mortified, not least by Uther's language in front of the Buttles, Linus pushed open the saloon's inner doors, entering the lobby, then on through the outer doors to the lamp-lit street. Feeling slightly light-headed, he strolled over to Uther's handsome green monobike and felt the smooth, shiny seat with a paw. With a glance at the saloon doors, as if worried Uther might burst out and tell him to get away from his precious machine, Linus sat on it and placed his paws on the cold kristahl steering bars.

Not every Howler could cope with such a powerful beast as the Giacomo Valerio *Dragonfly*, let alone Ivan's legendary GVM-8 *Spider*, only those strong enough to tame the wild imperium gyroscopes within could hope to even go in a straight line.

You can't even ride yet, Linus chided himself, you'd still fall off a little *Springtail*. Better hurry up. It's not so far away, the long sleep. Ten years, twenty, even thirty; it'll fly by. Then you'll rot. Most do by then and you're not special. First in class? Big deal!

Reaching into his coat, Linus took out a silken pouch with a draw string. He tipped it over his paw and the pearl he had bought from the *Crab and Kettle* tumbled into his palm, a perfect, iridescent green orb the size of one's fingertip.

Green was the commonest useful sort of imperium, burnt in hearths and engines up and down Lupa, so the pearl hadn't been very expensive, but it was absolutely pure and so far more potent than the rough green ore mined from the erde and shovelled into fireboxes.

"Linus?" someone said.

It was Rosalina, trotting towards Linus in her similarly imperium-green dress.

"You awright?" she asked again, tipping her hat.

"Yes," Linus insisted, with much nodding. "Just tired."

"I was worried you might be feeling sick or something. I know how it is with you lot."

"You lot?"

"Howlers," Rosalina whispered. "The pains, n' all that."

"Oh. I-I-I don't get that much," he replied. "Not yet anyway."

Rosalina scrunched up her brown nose and scooted round the prickly subject. "Lovely mono," she said, rubbing the bodywork with her gloved paw. "Looks like Uther's."

Linus spread his paws, "It *is* Uther's."

Rosalina tutted at her own perceived silliness, "Oh yeah, so it is." She sat on the back of the mono with both legs one side of the wheel, as if it were a stool. "Whatcha got there?"

"Huh?"

"In yer paw."

"Nothing, just a pearl," Linus said, opening his golden fingers to reveal the perfect green orb. "I-I bought it from an otter earlier."

"Really?" Rosalina said. "What for?"

"No particular reason. I just like to collect them."

"Collect 'em?"

"Yes. I have a drawer full of them. Should be in a cabinet really, but I don't have the room. That'll have to wait until I'm a Howler Captain, if I get that far."

Rosalina was perplexed, "What do you do with 'em all?"

Linus shrugged a little, "Not a lot. I… I practise with them sometimes."

"Practise?"

Linus gave Rosalina a sideways look, then closed a paw over the pearl. His fist quivered a little and he emitted a tiny grunt of effort. When he opened his paw, the pearl was shining and shimmering with a ghostly green light.

Rosalina marvelled, "Oh! Whatcha do to it?"

"I freed some of the imperium's energy," Linus explained, shielding the pearl with his other paw so as to not draw too much attention to himself. "It's what we Howlers do, after all."

"Yeah," Rosalina said, suddenly wistful. "I… I remember me dad doing somethin' like this. He used to make things float about to keep me quiet. I was just a baby."

Spurred on by Rosalina's faded memory, Linus cupped his other paw above the pearl and, as if by magic, but in reality by the imperionic laws, the pearl rose up and stuck to his other palm!

"Like that?"

Rosalina gasped and giggled, "Oh! That's it! That's it!"

Linus laughed, "My dad did it too. I used to pester him to."

The pearl dipped down, then rose up, oscillating to and fro until finally hovering level between Linus's paws, spinning round like a tiny planet with pearlescent seas and continents. Rosalina could plainly read the concentration written on the Howler's face as he performed the delicate balancing act.

"That's real clever."

"It's nothing, really," Linus shrugged. "A Den Father could do this with their sword."

Rosalina shrugged, "Well, I'm still impressed."

Linus let the pearl drop down and popped it back in its silken home. The show was over.

"I reckon you'll be a Den Father one day, Mr. Linus."

Mr. Linus literally winced. "Rosalina you don't have to flatter me," he said, absently playing with one of the bike's chrome switches. "I mean, I know it's your job to pretend that you find me interesting and… and all that, but this is all Uther's idea and… well… what I mean is… uh…."

The wolfess dipped her chin and shook her head, "Oh no. You're easy."

Linus faced her. "Easy?" he squeaked.

"I don't have to pretend, like. You're fun, like Uther. I've not smiled like this for ages."

"R-rrr-really?"

"Really," Rosalina cooed. "Anyway, you don't have to do something you don't wanna do just to impress Uther. He won't think any less of yer. He was probably just trying to help you come out of yer shell, 'Woodlouse'." Giggling, the Lupanar wolfess patted Linus's knee and stood up, "Let's go back inside."

"Thank you," Linus gulped, rising with her, "f-fff-for being so kind to me."

Rosalina took Linus's paw and scrunched her nose. She looked about to say something when a sizeable beast came barrelling out of left field like a rugby player!

"Oh!"

Before Linus knew what was what, both he and Rosalina had been barged to the ground. After a brief kerfuffle, the stranger took off, dashing down the main street. It sounded like a pig to Linus; trotters on cobblestones were always a dead giveaway.

"Oi, watch it!" Linus barked, his well-crafted, gentlebeast's facade giving way to a moment of street-side brusqueness. He pulled Rosalina to her feet, "You all right?"

"Me purse!" Rosalina yelped at once, searching her belt. "He nicked me purse!"

"What?"

"All me money's in there!" Rosalina wailed, paws clapping to her cheeks. "Everything!"

After a moment's hesitation, Linus remembered who he was and what he was and took off in pursuit. "Thief! Stop, in the name of the Republic!"

"Linus, don't it could be dangerous!" Rosalina squeaked, before hurrying into the saloon to summon help. "Uther! Utheeer!"

Linus tore down the path, paws thumping in puddles, his golden fur intermittently illuminated every few seconds as he passed through the warm glow of street lamps. The hefty pig obligingly cleared a path for the wolf, barging pedestrians aside, so that all Linus need do on occasion was leap over shocked citizens still scrabbling around on the floor.

"Howler, coming through!"

The thief had a good fifty feet on the law, but even on a full stomach Linus was not going to be outrun by a pig; lagging behind a Chakaa hyena was excusable, but not a mere hog!

The thief veered into a dark alley, no doubt in an attempt to lose the Howler.

Linus stayed on him, weaving between dustbins and detritus, left turn, right turn, left, left, right, down the grim alleys, deeper into the dangerous Lupan labyrinth that connected the safe main streets of the Common ground.

The pig burst through a gate and slammed it shut. Linus rammed into it seconds later, but rebounded – locked!

The Howler instantly attacked the wall, climbing up and over with aplomb – he wasn't one for jumping, but with an upper body like his any wall Linus could reach the top of was no obstacle.

The strong little wolf landed in a puddle and found himself in a junkyard, with scrap and ash piled high on all sides. There was no sign of the hog, but Linus heard trotters clopping away into the darkness. He hurried after them, following one of many clear paths snaking between the mounds of rusting metal and decaying imperium.

"Stop… in the name of the Republic!" Linus shouted, for the umpteenth time today.

After many twists and turns, he found himself in a clearing overlooking the broad River Lupa. The fire-belching furnaces of the industrial Greystone territory reflected in the quivering waters, whilst a mighty iron railway bridge spanned the gulf.

The Howler looked around, took stock; he was a long way from the warmth and comfort of the saloon.

"What am I doing?" he panted.

Unwilling to give in just yet, Linus ventured a little further into the mysterious junkyard, until he came to the railway bridge and what appeared to be a dead-end. The bridge arced high overhead, its brick struts creating a cave of sorts. It dripped and glistened by the light of a single imperium lamppost jutting out of the seas of garbage like a lonely lighthouse. A train screamed swiftly by, the light from its carriages playing invitingly over Linus's face.

Howler Mills suddenly felt he was being watched and turned around. Scanning Lupa's waste, he picked out an unusual quantity of threadbare furniture; chairs, sofas, desks, all set upright atop the junk as if in use. What looked like crude dwellings were pitched amidst the jumble, their sides constructed from corrugated iron and canvas, sometimes incorporating the inside of a car or bus. Beasts of every sort peered out at the intruder from these makeshift tents and shacks, little beasts in the main, but some bigger sorts.

This was some kind of illegal slum, by the looks; Lupa was rife with them, inside and out.

"I'm a Howler," Linus puffed, chest heaving, turning on the spot and showing the citizens his glowing brooch. "I'm looking for a hog. Where did he go?"

Nothing.

"I know he came this way. There's nowhere to go, so he must be here."

Still nothing.

"He's a thief; he stole a purse," Linus explained, "It's your duty as citizens to help me uphold the law."

"Go away!" someone spat.

"Howler scum!" said another.

Shocked, Linus shouted back, "I'll have this fleapit cleared away if you don't cooperate!"

"I've got your purse right here, Howler!" someone declared from under the bridge. *"There's no need for threats."*

Lowering his brooch, Linus walked tentatively towards the bridge, looking for the owner of that profound voice. The beasts in their dwellings made themselves scarce, closing their tent flaps and doors if they had them, or putting up a sheet of iron or drawing a curtain if they hadn't.

There was something not quite right about this place; Linus felt it in his bones. Is that a corona, or just my imagination?

A lamp coughed into life, illuminating the underside of the bridge and revealing a fantastical grotto of tapestries, paintings, carpets and furnishings, all of it somewhat tired and worn, but still remarkable finds in this otherwise ant-heap world. Nestled amongst the sullied splendour was a fancy-looking high-backed wooden chair draped in purple, imperium-weave cloth and protected by a moth-eaten canopy.

Seated upon this throne, his trotters crossed, was a huge, powerful, tusked hog. His massive body dripped with jewellery and fine clothes; rings, bracelets, chains, ribbons and more. It looked like he had blundered through Riddle Market, arms spread, randomly sweeping up all manner of spoils. Upon his head was a crown of sorts, a jumble of weird circles of metal soldered together. Linus couldn't quite make it out.

"You're trespassing on my kingdom, Howler," grunted the muscled hog, spreading his fingers at his junkyard domain, before settling back, resplendent in what seemed to be an imperium-weave cloak. "I am Gustav, King of Great Bridge. Who might you be?"

Linus had but one lucid thought – what in Ulf's name have I walked into?

Well, here goes.

"Howler Linus Bloodfang Mills," he said, clearing his throat. "Trooper, First Class."

"Welcome to my court, Howler Linus," said King Gustav, gesturing about his so-called court. "You look tired. Please, refresh yourself."

A mouse poured something into a bent golden cup and offered it to the Howler on a dented pewter tray.

"N-nnn-no, thank you," Linus stammered.

Gustav nodded, the fine chains dangling from his tusks rattling, and drank from another, much finer cup. "I must apologise, Howler, for any inconvenience my subject caused you," he said. "He knows it's not the done thing to take from Howlers; he thought you were a mere Freiwolf."

Linus growled, "It is not the done thing to take from anyone, sir, Howler or citizen. That is theft."

"Oh? Yet Howlers take what they want, do they not?"

"A Howler's privilege, as written in the Lupan Laws-"

"I see. Legal theft, then? Hahahaaa! You wolves like to have it all your own way."

Linus paused a moment, perturbed by the hog's manner. "It is taxation, sir," the Howler said, steeling himself. "Now, give up the purse you stole."

Gustav scoffed, "You make demands of me in mine own kingdom?"

"This is Lupa, citizen," Linus pointed out. "It is no one's kingdom, it is a Republic-"

"Insolent wolf, I am no citizen, but king of the Great Bridge!" roared Gustav, standing up and gesturing at the underside of the railway bridge. "This is my world, so be mindful of your insolent tongue!"

Linus could hear Uther now, 'Nutter, mate.'

Gustav sniffed and sat regally, "Still, you were not to know, ignorant soft-footed beast that you are. I shall overlook your transgression. You may go in peace." Snapping his fingers, he said, "The purse!"

The shifty-looking hog Linus had been chasing stepped forth from the shadows, head bowed, and passed his insane leader Rosalina's green purse. Gustav snatched it and tossed it on the ground, making his bejewelled body rattle like a crystal chandelier. The purse landed just short Linus's 'soft' feet.

"Take it," the king snorted, "and get you gone from my sight, little Howler."

Linus ignored the purse, saying, "I'm afraid you don't get off that easy."

Gustav snorted, "Oh?"

"I'm not leaving here without booking the beast who stole the bag."

The pig in question looked up a little.

Gustav laughed, "I'll not forsake a servant over a mere purse!" He leant forward, "Leave my domain and forget you were ever here, or else suffer the consequences of your wanton arrogance."

Unaccustomed to being spoken down to by mere citizens, let alone one of such brazen cheek, Linus boiled over, "Or else what, you mad-beast? I've only to speak to my superiors and the authorities will sweep your 'kingdom' of pickpockets into the river!" Linus looked around, at the countless eyes peering out from the junkyard dwellings pitched roundabout him, and told them, "You'll all find yourselves on the rough edge of Lupan justice if I'm not satisfied!" He then addressed the so-called 'king', "Out of pity I'd rather leave these beasts in peace; I don't want to see their lives destroyed over a purse any more than you. I'll forget I ever saw this place, provided you give up the thief and swear to disband your illegal activities."

Gustav's huge nostrils flared with rage. "I tire of your insolent yapping," said the hog, casting his fat fingers at Linus. "Guards! Seize the intruder."

Four well-built hogs stepped out of the shadows armed with metal poles, surrounding Linus.

"A-a-are you insane?" he spluttered, whirling on the spot, paws raised defensively. "I'm a Howler! Don't you even know what I'm capable of?"

"The imperious rage in your blood? What of it?" Gustav dismissed airily. "You'll quickly break yourself on my legions and become exhausted. Then you will go the same way as all the others."

"Others?"

The king touched his warped crown and it glowed momentarily with a rainbow of colours. It was clear to Linus then that it was made of Howler brooches of every rank and pack, crudely welded together. Gustav's cloak too was a patchwork of Howler mantles, and his guards were wreathed in the same.

"Where did you get all those?" Linus gasped.

"I bade them to leave," Gustav explained sorrowfully, as his guards circled Linus. "I am most gracious towards each Howler who rudely invades my domain looking for trouble, but being such an arrogant sort, few take up my generosity. Most that came investigating have had to… disappear."

"You killed them!" Linus realised. "You're a Howler-killer!"

"I but defend my people."

Ears flat to skull, Linus brandished a quivering fist at the hog. "Murderous scum!" he snarled, as sparks of imperious fire played over his paw. "I'll bring you to justice! I will!"

"Humph! Take him."

At Gustav's command, the cloaked hogs lunged at Linus as one porcine ring; likewise Linus lunged at them, barging into the nearest and slapping his paw into his midriff. There was a loud spark of blinding plasma and the hog was blown clean across the junkyard kingdom, sliding and rolling through the slippery mud.

Shaking his throbbing right paw, Linus whipped around and used his left to deal another shocking coronal explosion to the next hog, sending him down too.

Bzzzt! Crack!

The third hog swung his weapon at Linus. The Howler heard the hollow metal pole whistle an inch from his face as he ducked and weaved, fought as he had been trained in the Bloodfang Howler Academy, fought for his life.

Recovering from the dodge, Linus swept in and slapped both his paws on the guard's distended belly. He summoned the imperium energy locked within his bones and blood, releasing it in a spectacular white spark that blew the surprised hog clean off his trotters.

"Oooaagh!"

He slid across the mud on his back and crashed into a rubbish heap, sending a cascade of cans tumbling over his shoulders and little beasts running for cover.

Meanwhile, Linus stumbled away, his shaking paws throbbing and burning, yet numb and stiff. Without a kristahl sword, or at least something metal to channel the energy away from his flesh, it was wounding him too. He couldn't keep this up for long.

The last hog, wary from witnessing his comrades downed by this tough little wolf, hesitated. At last, seeing the Howler was in serious trouble, he went for him, swinging his rod. The stocky little Linus weaved aside and grabbed the iron rod with both paws in one tidy movement.

Finally, something to channel the imperious fire!

Plasma erupted from Linus's arms and rippled up the rod in a flash, straight into the hog who gripped on tight, unable to let go as the enraged Linus filled him with energy.

"Gaaaahaaaagh!"

Finally, Linus released the rod and the hog collapsed backwards into a puddle, stiff as a drawbridge. Traces of plasma crawled over his trembling body and dissipated into the water. Then he went limp.

He was dead. No normal beast could suffer an imperium shock like that, and Linus knew it. Chest and shoulders heaving, the panting Howler stared at the four downed pigs, horrified at what he had done. He looked at his quivering paws, their pads blackened and raw.

'By Ulf, I'm a killer!'

The sound of thumping trotters and jangling metal quickly brought Linus to his senses. He dived to one side as Gustav himself deigned to descend from his rotten throne and charge him, head down, festooned tusks brandished.

Linus rolled in the mud and back to his feet as the cloaked mountain of a pig stood upright and looked down upon the puny wolf.

"Humph!" he snorted, tramping towards Linus on his mighty legs. "You shall suffer many days of humiliating torture for this, Howler. You will beg me to end your miserable existence. And when I grow weary of your pitiful moaning I'll have you buried alive in the heaps of Lupa's waste. Nobody will hear your screams as you twist and turn, the roaches and mud-worms nibbling your flesh." Gustav raised an eyebrow, "And when your body is picked clean, your bones will go into the stinking mud of the Lupa, and it will be as if you never were... just like all the rest."

"You're insane!" Linus growled, backing away as quickly as Gustav advanced.

"It is *you* who is insane, *your* race who cuts down the forests and chokes the world, who uprooted my noble hoggish ancestors and forced them to live in your vile city as your Politzi scum and servile train hogs!" Gustav's beady eyes widened with a terrible glee. "There will be a reckoning for wolfkind someday, but for you, little Howler, it comes this day!"

With a stomp of trotter, the snorting hog charged Linus, sweeping his head and tusks at the wolf, gold décor rattling melodiously, bracelets falling in the mud.

Linus weaved clear and seeing an opening scrabbled past Gustav's mighty bulk landed an imperious punch on his massive body.

"Ragh!"

Linus expected the hog to be knocked off his trotters like his minions before him, fight over, but the plasma merely dissipated over his imperium-weave cloak and served only enrage him! By Ulf, what kind of monster is this?

The snorting, squealing, red-eyed Gustav swept Linus away with an arm. The wolf rolled in the mud to escape a stomping great trotter and tried to rise, to get away, but then it hit him, a trainload of pain bursting through his body!

"Gaaaagh!"

Up Linus went, levered foot by agonising foot slowly into the air, all the while clutching instinctively at something hard and bony protruding from his stomach. He was brought level, his world reduced to black night, twinkling stars and an infinity of pain. The squirming wolf lifted his head to look down at himself, to try and fathom what was happening, and discovered he was impaled on Gustav's tusks like a maggot on a thorn bush! One had gone straight through him; the one he was clutching uselessly at with both bloodied paws.

"Ulf above!" he cried. "Ulf help me! Gaagh!"

If Linus's moans moved King Gustav, it was only to let the pitiful wolf down with a contemptuous flick of his gory, twitching snout. The Howler tumbled to Erde, landing heavily in the mud. Winded and wounded, he could but cough and splutter as Gustav stood impassively astride him.

The 'king' cast at the dwellings all around, "I give him to you, my subjects! Take your revenge on your oppressors. Drag this one to the shore and bury him up to his neck. Let the mud worms hollow out his eyes!"

As Gustav returned to his throne, the wretched beasts in the ramshackle dwellings set aside their makeshift doors and tent flaps and emerged in filthy rags. Mice, rats, hogs and rabbits, male and female, young and old, descended from the hills of waste and closed in on the helpless Linus like ants on a wounded caterpillar, their dirty paws grasping at his clothes and pulling him through the mud.

"Aaaagh!"

They beat him and kicked him, hit him with sticks, some spat on him and cursed him.

"Howler scum!"

"Your kind murdered my son!"

"Rot!"

And then, amidst the baffling melee, a coarse voice snarled clear over them all.

"Get off him, you gazing vermin! Get back or I'll thumping blow your heads off! Go on, get!"

The mob scattered, dropping Linus on his back, his paws clutching his stomach. Standing over him, pistol in paws, was a black and white wolf in a red tunic.

"Uther!" Linus coughed.

"Mate, get up!" Uther urged, pointing his pistol at some of the bolder 'gazing vermin'. "Come on, come on!"

"I… c-c-can't."

"Aye, you can!" Uther insisted. He glanced down at Linus and saw he had a hole or two in him. "All right… maybe you can't," he agreed.

The gory Gustav stood up, beautified, bloodied tusks dripping. "Another one?" he huffed. "Where one Howler goes, another is bound to follow, like ants to a sugar bowl."

"Stay right there," Uther warned, "or I'll shoot!"

"Humph! You can't shoot us all, Howler. You only have one puny pellet."

"Aye, but I can shoot *you*, freak!"

"Hahaaa! Go ahead; see if you can kill me!" Gustav said, parting his cloak and revealing a weird, malformed breastplate, its surface a beaten patchwork of welded metals. "My body is protected by your very own eisenglanz, fool!"

Uther let out a snort and murmured at Linus. "Woodlouse what have you got us into?"

Linus gulped, "He's… a murderer… a Howler-killer." He grimaced and looked down at himself, at his heaving, bleeding stomach, and he wished he hadn't. "He's insane, Uther."

"No kidding. He looks like a walking Wintertide tree."

"He's afflicted. I f-felt it when I… agh!"

"Hold on Woodlouse, be strong," Uther puffed, aiming left and right, keeping the ragged mob at bay; nobody wanted to be the first to attack and get shot.

"Get help," Linus suggested.

"Shut up! I'm not leaving you to 'em!"

"They'll kill us both if you stay… and then nobody will know. You have to s-sss-stop them, Uther."

"I will too! Just gimme a minute to think here."

As he lie there, Linus's fevered mind wandered. He thought back over the strange day, this morning's chase, Monty and Penny, the *Crab and Kettle*, the pictures, Rosalina, the pearl.

By Ulf, that's it!

Linus slapped a paw to his chest pocket, feeling the hard round sphere tucked away near his heart. "Uther… Uther, the pearl."

"What? What pearl?"

Linus took out the pouch, "The pearl I bought. Use it."

Uther glanced down a few times, "Whatcha mean? You mean bargain with 'em?"

"No… I mean…."

Lying in the mud, Linus tipped the pearl into a cupped palm and closed both paws around it. Snarling for the pain of his burnt pads, the Howler summoned all his imperious might one more time. Plasma trickled down his arms and danced over his shaking paws, exciting the imperium, turning it critical, priming it for use.

With a yelp of pain, Linus opened his smoking paws, revealing the shining orb of pure, green-imperium, smouldering and fizzling away. The mob gasped as one, their sickly faces made even sicklier by the eerie green light.

"Mate, are you serious?" Uther growled.

"Leave me with the pistol!" Linus begged. "I'll do it."

Uther scoffed, "Not on your life!" and quickly snatched the blazing pearl. Breaking open the pistol's breach and removing the normal pellet, he instead dropped the pearl down the muzzle; the usually pitch-black black bore shimmered bright green as the orb slid neatly down – a good fit.

"Now we're cooking with gas," Uther cackled, raising the pistol by his ear and slowly lowering it, levelling it at the filthy mob. "All right you low-life gazer scum, I've loaded this baby with a live imperium pearl. You know what that means do yer? Eh? Aye I can see you do!"

The junkyard mob backed off somewhat.

"Now, I'm gonna count from ten, then I'm gonna blow whoever's in my sights to ash!" Uther declared, stepping slowly forth. "Ten… nine… eight…."

Screaming and shouting, the mob scrabbled for the twisted hills of rubbish, stampeding past their king in their haste to flee the impending catastrophe.

"He can't kill you all!" Gustav told them. "You will protect your king, you cowards! I'll kill you myself if you don't!"

Uther slowly aimed at the 'king', "Seven… six… five."

"You fool it could backfire and kill you!" Gustav told Uther.

"Hahaha, aye! Four... three."

"Howler, wait!" Gustav said, clambering towards his throne. "Let us parley! I will let you both go free!"

"Two."

"Wait! I beg you!"

"One!"

"No!"

Crack!

A stream of green, glittering light shot straight and true from Uther's pistol, passing through Gustav and terminating in the back of his throne, where it stayed, glimmering and fizzling bright.

There was but a moment's grace, a second to think about the end, before the throne vanished, swallowed and incinerated by a sphere of plasma, and Gustav too.

"Eyyyyaaaaagh!"

The resulting explosion ripped across the junkyard, punching a half-blind, half-deaf Uther onto his back and sweeping away any stragglers. Shortly, the wind reversed, sucking everything towards the epicentre, before dying to a calm.

Silence.

Bits of metal rained down, and probably bits of Gustav, or what dust remained. Shaking his head, Uther scooped Linus into his arms and draped him over his back.

"I got yer!" he said, stealing away into the night, "Hold on, Trooper, don't die on me!"

✤

It was a modest drive permeated by silence – preferable for both parties. No gates or checkpoints barred Josef's ambulance as it crunched into the courtyard, imperium-fuelled headlights fading slowly upon the engine's termination. Janoah climbed out and cast her masked face over Riddle District Hospice; a modest affair with six columns and a clock centred on the pediment. It was late, past visiting hours, but a Grand Howler on official business was exempt from all that, especially with Riddle Den's coroner by her side.

Flashing brooch and pass respectively and claiming to be here on an investigation, Janoah and Josef made swift progress through the chequered halls, the distant sounds of coughing and moaning, even downright mad shouting, pricking in their ears.

Nobody challenged them, unwilling as they were to incur the wrath of a Grand Howler.

With Josef Grau her guide, Janoah entered a ward, with its vaulted ceiling and high windows. It was dark and reeked of disinfectant, though not enough to mask the odour of rotting, dying beasts. Beds lined the long walls, many of them occupied by patients, wolves all, thin and tired-looking, many covered in sores and bald-patches with drip lines of water and painkillers going into them from all angles.

These were the Howlers for whom time had run out, whose sting rations had been officially withdrawn, who had no choice now but to die here with honour, or flee and become an old dodger in disgrace.

Janoah entered; she need not steel herself, for she had witnessed many a friend and teacher die thusly. It was the way of things. When stings no longer did the trick, when black-imperium leaked out of the bones and started to kill you, it was better, the Bloodfangs believed, to just let the rot progress and save the pack the expense and indignity of keeping you alive. She too would come here one day, if she lived so long. Rufus too. Perhaps not so long, Janoah thought, if this shortage continues unabated.

With a glance and nod at the night nurse, who Doctor Josef rapidly dismissed, Janoah approached the first bed she happened across and placed a paw on the cold iron bed rails. The patient was a steel-grey wolf, no doubt once a strapping, handsome young Howler, reduced now to a sickly shadow of himself long before the natural order of things. Out of curiosity Janoah checked his records. He was forty, not that much older than herself. Unfortunate, but in general males didn't last as long as females.

The wolf opened his eyes. "Sir?" he croaked.

The masked Janoah put down the clipboard and smiled, "Rest easy, Howler."

He smiled back, and said, "Did we win?"

Janoah nodded, "Yes, we won."

Senility, or insanity; the fellow was probably re-living the glorious past in his feverish brain.

"Rest easy, Howler."

Janoah moved on, scanning the sick and the dying for a wolf who at least vaguely fit the profile; big, brown, young. Some deviation could be tolerated, overlooked, money exchanged for the turning of a blind eye, but only so much. The bureaucracy of the Bloodfangs was pervasive, its all-seeing eye difficult to evade, what with officials crossing the T's and dotting the I's on every Howler's rank, pay and sting rations, from induction to death.

If anyone could pull a fast one, it was Janoah Valerio. At her instruction, Werner had already put it about that the boy was dead, run down by a truck. Editors had been rung, presses stopped, new stories printed just in time. It would all be in the papers tomorrow and a body would be waiting in the morgue for formal identification. All Doctor Josef need do is to provide that body.

Aha!

Janoah swooped on a bed at the far end of the ward, her paws latching onto the iron rail – a big mottled wolf lay before her with drip tubes going into him and a respirator over his muzzle, chest heaving slowly.

Yes, yes he might just do.

Janoah checked his records. Low rank and no next of kin. He would not be missed. Perfect! In her excitement she inadvertently read the patient's name aloud.

"Stenton, Rafe."

The wolf's ears pricked. He slowly heaved his weary eyes open – they were black, as if dilated beyond all reason. It was in fact the decaying imperium that coloured them so. The eyes of healthy Howlers shone with imperious minerals, sometimes taking on a different colour than they were born with, but those days were over for Rafe, whose irises were stained and polluted with ash.

"How are you feeling, Stenton?" Janoah asked, proffering a warm smile.

No reply.

"Is it terrible?" she asked.

This time Rafe Stenton nodded and gulped.

A day, a week, a month, it didn't really matter, there was no way back for this one.

Janoah checked Rafe's records further. He was just a boy really, hardly older than the like of Uther and Linus, but the rot had claimed him all the same. Perhaps this youth had been too zealous in the pursuit of justice, exerting himself beyond the limits of endurance. There were those that burnt bright but quickly, whilst others flickered as mere embers for decades. Some defied the odds, others fell foul. In prosperous times with white-imperium enough for all Rafe might have lived another twenty years regardless, but with supplies thin on the ground there wasn't enough to sustain those with a greater need.

"Rest easy, Stenton," Janoah soothed. "You'll make a difference yet, I promise you. Your name will live on."

Rafe stared at Janoah, black eyes unblinking, unable to see her clearly if at all. Likely he didn't understand what was going on, Janoah supposed, though she could not bring herself to tell even a dying wolf her burgeoning plans.

The grey Josef approached in his lab coat. "There's a definite resemblance," he purred in delight, looking the patient over. "In the dark, at least. I'll have to dye his fur brown to fool any next of kin."

Janoah huffed, "Bruno has none, save his 'father', and he's done a runner."

"Someone will have to positively identify him, preferably a wolf," Josef stipulated. "I can't get round that."

"I'm sure his girlfriend will come."

"That could be problematic. She'll know him intimately."

"I'm sure you'll persuade her, Doctor," Janoah hissed, borderline threatened. She walked around the bed and held one of the dying Howler's paws with both of hers. "Doctor Josef has something for you, Stenton," she said.

"Taubfene?" Rafe croaked through his respirator.

"Yes... all the taubfene you want," Janoah promised him. "Enough to take the pain away forever. You won't have to suffer another minute." She leant near, "Is that what you want, my Howler? I won't do this unless you want it. I'll find another who does."

Rafe let out a piteous whine, then took a deep breath and nodded.

Did he fully understand? Perhaps.

Satisfied this was not murder, Janoah nodded at Josef. "The taubfene, Doctor."

Checking the door, the cat produced a large syringe of yellow liquid from his inside pocket and flicked the air bubbles from the needle, more out of habit than necessity in this case. He disconnected the drip tube from its bag and unceremoniously stabbed the syringe into the line, injecting the contents, all of it, right up to the plunger. The yellow fluid rushed down the tube and into Rafe's bandaged wrist, into his blood.

The effect was immediate. Rafe breathed deep a few times and whined in delirium, "Mum…. Mum, it's sunny out…. Can I go play in the street? Mum."

Janoah felt that grip fade, watched those black eyes glaze over. The last fires went out in him, his imperious corona extinguished in an instant by enough taubfene to execute a bear. It was painless, a blessed release, Janoah told herself, waiting a respectful minute for Rafe Stenton to leave this world.

"You flew well, dayfly."

With that, Janoah gently placed Rafe's paw on his chest and closing those tired, ashen eyes.

Doctor Josef stood impassively by the bed, tinted glasses betraying nothing.

Grabbing the clipboard from the foot of the bed, Janoah stood up and gave it to the doctor, pressing it firmly into his midriff. "Start the ball rolling, we've little time."

Codex: Bloodfang

Eldest of the packs, the Bloodfangs, or Redcloaks, are among the few able to point to a record predating the Founders, Lupa and the rot, back when little beasts wallowed in mud huts, noble beasts cowered in castles, and imperium was but a curiosity, its true power mostly forgotten and untapped.

Some sneer that the Bloodfangs still wallow in filth, their poor, heavily-polluted territory being little more than a collection of slums and markets not unlike those found clinging desperately to the outside of the Lupan Wall. However, the Bloodfangs are not as wretched as all that. The pack jealously holds the Far Ashfall, which, whilst worthless in itself, remains the only gateway to the Everdor plantations and Gelb mines. They therefore control most food and white-imperium currently entering Lupa and tax it accordingly; nominally to pay for the expense of guarding the Far Ashfall's rails and roads from thieves and terrorists, but mostly to line its Howler's pockets. This monopoly is a source of great tension between the packs, since at any time the Bloodfangs could raise taxes, or even cut supplies altogether. To do so would doubtless spark a Howler War with all other packs allied against Bloodfang, but it would not be the first time the pack has stood its ground alone and survived to make a favourable deal, for they are formidable.

Shunning the gadgets and heavy armour of their main rivals, the Greystones and Eisbrands respectively, the nimble Bloodfangs rely on superior coronal manipulation to win out. Only the strongest wolves from across and beyond Lupa are accepted, or if resistant pressed, into service. The pack welcomes drifters, orphans, rivals, and even ex-criminals into its ranks, provided a wolf shows enough promise. Redcloaks therefore have no solid roots, no typical colouration, accent, manner or bloodline to point to, only the ancient name of Bloodfang itself to bind them.

Be they voluntary or coerced, every Bloodfang beneath Elder rank must uphold a high level of fitness, both coronal and physical. There is no room, no provision of stings made, for wall-gazing scroungers. When the rot sets in such that a Howler can no longer perform their duties, the Bloodfangs regard it a kindness to permit a rapid decline instead of a lingering death, and sting rations are completely withdrawn. Some, stripped of their lifeline but desperate to limp on, move to other, less exacting packs; others turn to crime and buy venom on the black market; the honourable retire to their bed and wait for Ulf to collect them.

It is because of this policy of pruning old wood, considered unreasonable by most, that Bloodfangs die statistically younger than their Eisbrand and Greystone counterparts. However, with no imperium pensioners draining limited sting supplies and the tax on two essential imports filling their coffers, active Redcloaks enjoy generous food rations and absurd pay, fuelling in their ranks a culture of hedonistic pleasure-seeking on the Common Ground, which is tolerated as long as it does not impede a Howler's duties. This alone attracts many talented young candidates to sign on Bloodfang's dotted line; the other great attraction being the sheer prestige of donning the red mantle and becoming a member of the toughest pack of wolves on the Lupan Continent, until, that is, the local hospice calls them home.

Chapter 12

Morning nuzzled its way into Sara's third-floor flat and stirred her. She rose in her green nightgown and drew the bedroom curtains, revealing the clear, crisp air of a sunny Lupan dawn; the clearest she had seen for a while. The city was awakening; chimneys coughed into life, pedestrians headed to work, trams and motor carriages trundled by in the street below. Just another day.

To the kitchen; a humble affair. Imperium gas burner on, kettle filled, nice pot of Hummel tea on the way, just the ticket. Sara couldn't wait to get to the campus and see Toggle.

Toast in paw, the little black wolfess hurried downstairs to the mailbox and retrieved the morning paper, *The Lupa*. It was the Common Ground paper which, although heavily biased against 'lesser races' and constricted by its neutrality towards the packs of Lupa, was at least full of actual news, births, deaths, discoveries and more, rather than columns of opinionated propaganda designed to make the local plebs believe their pack was the best one in Lupa. *The Harbinger* was the local Eisbrand Pack's authorised rag useful only for firelighter and lining the bottom of insect cages.

The Lupa open in her paws, Sara headed for the stairs. She hadn't got far when the building's main door opened. Sara expected it to be one of her neighbours returning from an early morning shop, but was instead met with a white rabbit in a coat and hat. He had a steel box in one paw.

"Sara," he panted.

"Casimir!" she replied, with a gasp. "Och! You've caught me in mah nightie," she laughed, performing a mock curtsey.

No smile graced Casimir's lips. "Is Bruno here?" he asked directly, taking a step forward. "I… I thought he might have stayed the night with you."

Sara took a moment to comprehend Casimir's extraordinary proposition. "No," she said. "He was supposed tae meet me at the pictures last night. Ah thought he was sick."

Casimir's face sunk and he fell against the wall, sliding down to the floor.

He wept.

Dropping her half-eaten toast on the stairs, Sara dashed over to him. "Och! Casimir, what's wrong?"

"They've got him!" he cried, curling up into a ball. "They got my boy!"

"Who's got him?"

"Oh, lad. It's all my fault!"

"Casimir, what's happened? Tell me for Ulf's sake!"

Getting no sense out of the rabbit, and not wanting the neighbours to see, the wolfess pulled him to his feet and helped him limp upstairs to her flat.

Ushering him inside before anyone saw, Sara sat Casimir by her pokey kitchen table and hurriedly made him a cup of tea before attempting to tease forth the facts. She knew it concerned Bruno, and knew it was no good, but Casimir was a rabbit and rabbits were known for overreacting and seeing the worst in a situation.

"There now," Sara said, physically grasping Casimir's paws and folding them around the cup of tea. "Have a sip o' that and tell me what's going on. It cannae be the end of the world."

With shaking paws, Casimir supped his steaming tea, then looked at Sara with his tear-streaked eyes.

"The Bloodfangs, they found out," he said.

"Found what out?" Sara asked, guessing, "That you were in the resistance?"

"No. Well, yeah they probably know that, but…."

"What then?"

"Bruno's… sick," Casimir said carefully, his face contorting as he squeezed out the truth, "He's got the rot, lass."

Silence.

"I never told him, but I knew. I've always known, ever since he was a cub."

Sara gasped, "But Ah thought he was just allergic tae ash."

"Aye, he is that; Howlers often start that way, but he's got full-blown rot, always has," Casimir said, forcing a laugh. "He's been getting worse just lately. I just couldn't keep up with his needs, you see. I couldn't afford it."

"Afford what?"

"The good stuff. He needs too much to stay healthy and the prices on the street keep going up on account of the shortage."

Sara was all at sea. "Ah don't understand. You mean he's a proper dodger?"

"Not… exactly."

Silence.

Casimir picked his claws, "I've… been… sneaking him venom without him knowing. I've been doing it for years-"

"Casimir!" Sara gasped.

"I had to!" the rabbit yelped, covering his face with both paws. "I had to. I couldn't tell him, Sara. When he was just a cute little cub I couldn't bring myself to stick him with a sting, so I spiked his cough syrup instead."

"With white-imperium?"

"Aye, it was bitter medicine," Casimir seethed, "so we added lots of honey and lemon. Uncle Werner's Cough Syrup, we labelled it. It was Werner's idea, see. Lad still takes it now, swears by it! It only works whenever I make a batch of course, not when he makes it. Bruno doesn't know the secret ingredient."

"Och, Casimir."

"He's never sussed it out neither. I hoped he would. I hoped he'd force me to come clean. But Bruno's not the brightest ember in the pack, you know."

Sara looked away. She didn't know what to say.

"Now you know why we kept moving, to avoid him being picked up and drafted," Casimir sighed. "I was gonna give him the choice this time, I swear. Go to the Howlers, or carry on dodging. Now he's got no choice. They'll fix my boy good. They'll sting him with all imperium he needs. 'Induction' they call it, aye, and then they'll train him to use it, to be one of our oppressors. And when he starts rotting far sooner than is natural for a beast they'll dump him in bed to die like all the rest." He looked down into his tea, at his trembling reflection within, "I kidded myself this would turn out different, but I think I always knew they'd take him away."

Sara shook her head, "Who took him, exactly?"

Casimir explained. "Werner, I think. I got away, but Bruno wasn't home. I waited by the station for him to come home by the usual train, but when he didn't show I rang home. The Politzi kept picking up. They were sitting around in *my* café just waiting for him. I couldn't go back, so I… I kept on ringing until Bruno picked up the phone. Werner was right there with him, telling him a pack of lies no doubt, trying to bring him in nice and easy-like, 'cause my boy… my boy he's so strong he'd have put up a fight let me tell yer!" After a brief chuckle, Casimir continued soberly, "I told him to get outta there and meet me in the usual place. I waited all night but he never made it. He's always made it before. Always. Werner must've got him. I just hope Bruno punched his fat face in first!"

Sara stayed positive, "He's probably just hiding out somewhere."

Casimir wasn't listening. For the longest time he sat in silence, his lower lip quivering, until suddenly he dashed his mug of tea against the far wall, "That bastard Werner. I'll kill him! I will!"

Then he broke down all over again, falling on his knees beside the table.

Sara comforted him a moment and sat him down, then grabbed her mop and tidied up, sweeping the broken mug into a dust pan.

"I'm sorry, lass," Casimir excused.

"It's all right," Sara replied, perchance slightly sarcastically. "Ah've still got two mugs left, Ah think."

Once she had cleaned up the mess, the wolfess tried to put a positive spin on things. "Casimir, let's just say for the moment you're right and Bruno's been taken in. Let's just assume all that is true. Even if it is, which I doubt, at least he's going to get what he needs."

"Eh?" Casimir snuffled.

"They'll give him imperium," Sara chirped, sitting beside him and grabbing his nearest paw. "There are worse things in this world than being a Howler. Ah know beasts hate them, I do, but it's the system nae the beasts. There's as many good Howlers as not. Ah met a good one just last night, outside the pictures. He wanted tae walk me home. Ah'm ashamed I was so rude tae him now, when Ah think of it. He was a good 'un. Bruno's a good 'un too. He'd nae be like the rest o' them thugs. He'd use his power for good, Ah know it."

Casimir nodded and forced a smile, "Aye. Aye, he would wouldn't he?"

Sara cocked her head to one side, "But Ah'm sure he's all right, you daft rabbit. In fact he's probably worried sick about you. We'll go find him together."

Another nod.

"Just let me get sorted, all right? Chin up."

"Aye."

Leaving Casimir cheered, the wolfess hurried into her bedroom. Upon closing the door she sat on the bed. Tears came swiftly, but silently, dripping onto her knees.

No, crying is no good! What if Casimir comes in? You have to be strong for him. You're a wolf, a Hummel; he's just a wee beast.

Wiping her eyes, Sara composed herself. She brushed her fangs over her tiny bedroom sink and slipped into something decent. A proper grooming would have to wait, Bruno could be out there somewhere, alone and afraid. Sara had no idea how to find him in the sprawling megapolis of Lupa, save to go to the local places they always met. Maybe he's at the university waiting for me? Maybe Professor Heath took him in? It's possible.

Suddenly a wail of anguish erupted from the kitchen. Sara dropped her brush in the sink and burst in on Casimir, finding him sprawled over the table, newspaper open wide.

"Oh lad!" he wailed. "My poor boy.... Ohohohohoooow!"

Even in her ignorance, Sara felt tears welling up inside her just from witnessing Casimir's unbridled grief. "Casimir, what is it?" she begged of him, his sorrow catching in her throat. "Come now, stop this. It's doing nae good at all."

With a seething, frustrated gasp of grief, the rabbit grasped the newspaper with both paws, scrunching it up somewhat, before pushing it away from him in disgust.

Sara snatched it and scanned the crumpled columns.

There was a picture of Bruno, looking handsome and chipper. He was carrying crates into the café. Casimir was also there, albeit an old picture, young and looking beaten-up. The picture must have been nearly twenty years old.

Heart beating faster, Sara latched onto the article's headline.

"Sting peddlers rumbled, one killed, one at large," she said, reading on in silence.

Politzi swooped on a known sting dealer posing as a café owner in the heart of the famously rough Riddle District yesterday. The authorities had been aware of Mr. Casimir Claybourne, rabbit, 35, for some time, but thus far he had evaded the Politzi by moving location. Using forged papers the criminal mastermind slipped between territories, setting up new premises from where to peddle his illegal goods to unfortunate souls, leaving his old lair deserted. His adopted son, a one Bruno Claybourne, wolf, 16, was known as a boxing thug that nobody would cross. It is thought Mr. Claybourne, if that is his real name, used his 'son' as protection during his illegal dealings, and that Bruno was a dodger with the strength of a Howler but the morals of a hyena. Interviewees say Mr. Claybourne had injected his son with venom from a young age and beat him regularly, turning him into a savage killer, yet one who was terrified of a mere rabbit not half his size. Others say Bruno was mentally incapable from years of imperium abuse and easily manipulated.

When the Politzi tried to take the Claybournes peacefully, the cowardly Casimir leapt out an upstairs window and fled with a suitcase of money, leaving his son to face justice alone. The mad

Bruno attacked the Politzi, leaving the heroic Constable Denny Demar, rat, 24, dead at the scene. Bruno fled and was pursued on foot, only to be run down by a truck in the backstreets. Constable Werner Schwartz, hog, 38, said he died instantly and that it was a merciful release for a tortured soul. Casimir Claybourne is still at large and....

There was more, but Sara screwed the worthless article up and let it drop at her feet. She found the strength to contain her grief only by leaning upon her anger.

"Don't you believe it, Casimir," she said, crushing the paper underfoot. "Bruno's nae dead. The whole article is a lie from start tae finish!"

"They killed him!" Casimir wept. "Something went wrong and they killed my boy. They're covering it up."

"It's all nonsense!"

"But I did give him imperium! I did that to him, Sara! I turned Bruno into what he is!"

Sara comforted Casimir as best he could. Tears didn't come to her anymore, because she didn't believe a word of what she had read. It gave her new hope.

Telling Casimir to stay here and not do anything silly, Sara put on her green coat and hurried out the flat. Closing the main door she strode down the gravel path and opened the wrought-iron gate with a mind to go to the university and search there. If nothing else, Olivia would help look.

"It's not wise to harbour a fugitive, Sara."

Sara nearly leapt from her black-furred hide as she whirled around, paws still grasping the gate.

A large Howler of Eisbrand allegiance strolled up the gravel path, his glorious silver armour shining in the muted sunlight, his body wreathed in a blue surcoat marked with a snowflake. He had been hiding in the garden, Sara imagined, waiting for her.

"Tristan?" she said, adding derisively, "Spying on me again?"

The Howler removed his helmet, revealing a robust, young, two-tone wolf of grey and white. His eyes were especially queer, one was green, the other blue, and Sara never knew which one to focus on.

"Forgive my concern," he said, glancing up at the window. "How's Citizen Casimir?"

"Who?" Sara said, feigning ignorance.

Tristan wasn't fooled, "He's a wanted beast, Sara."

"I don't care."

"Nor do I, but you're putting yourself in danger. Hummel you may be, but you're a long way from home."

Sara stood up straight, "Look, what do you want?"

Tristan waited a moment. "I came about your friend," he said, holding up a rolled newspaper.

Sara looked at the paper, "Don't tell me you actually believe that krap? And you a Howler!"

"I don't have to rely on the rags, I have my spies."

"Oh, Ah bet. And what did they tell ye?"

"They told me Bruno was going to be pressed into Bloodfang service at the first opportunity. If he resisted they were going to use his father's unfortunate past as leverage, and possibly yourself."

"Me?"

"Yes. They know all about you, believe me."

Sara could but scoff. "Then they know they can't touch me. Do you think mah mother would stand fer it? Ah'm not some nobody they can just bang up!"

Tristan took a sharp breath and spread his paws in helplessness, "Sara… Bruno… he tried to run away and was shot and killed by a Politzi."

Sara's paws clapped to her muzzle, almost stifling her intake of breath. "No!" she yelped.

"I'm sorry," Tristan said at once. "The paper's a lie, except that Bruno's gone."

Sara turned around and looked out across the city. She remained standing, silent for a time, but eventually the damn broke and she wept into her paws.

Tristan waited for a minute or two before saying, "He cared for you very much."

Sara exploded back, "You didn't even know him!"

"No, but we met on the train yesterday."

"Train? What?"

Tristan explained, "I tried to help him get away. He was very protective of you, when I mentioned you. I thought he was going to knock me out! Bruno was quite a wolf. Sitting opposite him for the first time I felt his strength and... I see what you saw in him-"

"Please, just leave me alone!" Sara seethed, crying afresh.

Tristan cleared his throat, "I would if I could, but I have to escort you to Riddle District's Den."

Sara's ears pricked, "What?" she sniffed. "What fer?"

"Bruno's there," Tristan said, spreading a paw. "Their coroner rang ours looking for you. It's required by the Lupan Laws that a wolfen family member or close wolfen friend identify a fellow wolf, and as Bruno had no such family there's nobody else on file. Casimir doesn't count."

"File? What file?"

"On his pass. You're down as next of wolfen kin."

"Och!" Sara cried afresh. "Bruno, Ah had no idea!"

Tristan grimaced. "They won't release his body unless someone identifies it and I'm not letting you step paw in that nest of scorpions they call Bloodfang Territory alone."

"W-www-what about Casimir?" Sara snuffled.

"Like I said, he's a rabbit; his word isn't good enough to confirm a wolfen death. Besides, he's a wanted beast. Whether the allegations are true or not is immaterial."

"Sorry, Ah'm nae thinking straight."

"It's all right," Tristan insisted. He walked closer, "Can you manage this now, or shall we wait? There's no rush."

"Let's get it over with," Sara croaked.

"It won't be pleasant. You must be prepared for what you may see."

Sara spread a paw over her chest and held back her grief with a gulp, "I have tae do it, so... let's do it."

Tristan donned his helmet and led Sara to his pale blue mono. "All right, but let me do the talking."

✦

Uther Wild-heart Bloodfang sat cross-legged on the cold concrete floor of Riddle Den's garage, elbows resting on knees, chin resting on paws. Despite being on-duty he remained dressed in his casual clothes from last night's revelries, not to mention exploits.

"By Ulf, it could've backfired in the barrel and you'd both have been vaporised!" Ivan hissed, furiously polishing his mono; he was already resplendent in Howler uniform, cloak and all. "Charging an untested pearl to criticality is strictly forbidden by the Howler Codex for a reason; even a good one is above your rank to deploy! I shan't be surprised if Amael gives you both a good flogging for this, not to mention for carrying a pistol in the Common!"

"I left out the pistol, sir," Uther admitted.

"What? So you omitted the pistol, but not the pearl?" Ivan asked, leaning on his black Giacomo *Spider*. "How's that going to look when Amael reads your testimony?"

"I left the pearl out too, actually."

"Right. Did you leave anything in, Wild-heart, or is your report just a series of blank pages?"

"No, no! I said the hog had both the pistol and the pearl. He went to shoot us and it exploded in his face, end of story."

Uther beamed innocently.

"So you lied," Ivan snorted.

"I bent the truth a little, for Linus's sake. The pearl was his idea. You can keep a secret, can't yer, cap'n?"

"Don't bank on it."

Ivan continued polishing.

"You know," he said, stopping again, "I've come to expect this kind of schmutz from you and Rufus, but I'm surprised at this 'Linus'. He looks too... plump."

Uther gruffed, "He was just upholding the law, sir."

"Leave it to the ALPHA Prefects, Wild-heart, the Common Ground's their slice of Lupa. We have no business there."

"Puh! Lot of good ALPHA are!" Uther barked. "That Howler-killer had obviously been there ages and you're telling me none of their Prefects ever happened by? Ten, twenny Howlers must've been murdered by that hog bastard!"

Ivan spread a paw, "Those that noticed disappeared, Uther. Prefects too, no doubt."

Wild-heart grumbled on, "That thief lured Linus in by nicking Rosa's purse. It was all a dirty trap, I reckon."

"Sprung for the last time."

"Aye. Job well done, I say."

Ivan huffed, "You'd best hope Amael sees it that way."

Grand Howler Vladimir stood surreptitiously listening behind the garage's inner door, which had been left slightly ajar. After digesting Uther's story with interest (wildly different to his official account) he entered the garage, folder in paw.

"Ah," he said, "just the wolves for the job!"

Uther jumped to his feet and saluted, whilst Ivan just saluted. Vladimir stayed by the hefty door, paw on lever, and looked down upon the Howlers from the slight vantage point provided by the concrete stairs, like a king on a dais.

"I'm told we've got a special guest," he said, gesturing at the half-open garage doors with his file. "They're sending him round back to park his mono. Take care of him will you?"

"Guest, sir?" Ivan queried.

"A fellow Donskoy, Ivan," Vladimir clarified.

"Not Tristan."

"Yes, Tristan. He's brought a wolfess along to formally identify that cub Werner's bungling oafs killed last night. He's 'escorting her'. We suspect he just wants to snoop around, of course, so watch him, but show him every courtesy all the same. We have to keep relations amicable during these trying times."

Ivan stood perplexed. "Forgive me, Grand Howler, but what cub was killed last night?"

"Rufus's 'chef', was it?" Vladimir sniffed, with much forced uncertainty and nonchalance. "The boy from the café you two were attacked in yesterday."

Ivan wasn't fooled by Vladimir's acting, though he was shocked at the news. "Bruno?"

"Yes, Bruno. Dead apparently. Squashed by a lorry."

Ivan dipped his chin.

"Such a senseless waste," Vladimir tutted. He suddenly looked at Uther as if he had noticed him for the first time in his life. "Why aren't you in uniform, Wild-heart?"

"Sorry, sir. Been up all night making statements and worrying about Linus, sir. I wasn't thinking straight."

Vladimir let it slide, "Yes, well, sort yourself out Howler."

"Yes, Grand Howler."

With an unreadable grunt Vladimir took his leave, shutting the door behind him.

Moments later the popping of a hefty monobike engine stirred Uther and Ivan's ears. Outside, a Howler in a surcoat glided into view on a *Dragonfly* mono, like Uther's, but made-up in Eisbrand livery. It had been sprayed pale blue and the insect motif replaced by the pack snowflake. Seated behind the rider was a little black wolfess in a dark green coat. As the pair pulled into the Bloodfang garage the two native Howlers received them, Ivan taking the lead, being the senior.

"Tristan," he greeted, approximating enthusiasm.

Swinging his armoured legs off the mono, the hefty, knight-like Tristan spread his equally armoured arms wide. He embraced the thinner, lightly-armoured Ivan, and though Ivan didn't return the gesture, he was at least cracking a smile.

"Cousin," Tristan said, standing back. "You look well."

"And you."

"How can you tell? I've not even removed my helmet."

"I can feel your corona," Ivan assured. "It's getting stronger."

Tristan's duotone eyes squinted and one could imagine him smiling under his helmet, which he duly removed and hung over the hilt of the great sword at his back. His attention switched to Uther.

"Ah, the Wild-heart," he said, taking him all in, "Day off?"

Uther was struck by the wolfess on the bike, but answered after a time. "No, just running late, mate. Bit of a busy day."

"Ah."

"Oi, I saw you on the news," Uther added.

"Oh?"

"The bank heist! 'Be good, citizens'. You're a slick bastard, Tristan Donskoy."

They both laughed and shook paws. Then Tristan said gravely to both the Bloodfangs, "I heard about Rufus, of course. All of Lupa knows. I hope he's out of danger."

"He'll live," Ivan said simply.

"Glad to hear it," Tristan replied. "I… know he still means a lot to you, cousin."

Ivan said nothing, but nodded graciously.

There was a silence, then Tristan moved on, "Let's get this over with shall we? I assume you've been briefed."

Another, quicker nod.

Tristan looked behind, "Citizen Sara here is a friend of the deceased. Since she lives on Eisbrand turf I'm obliged to escort her. Not that I don't trust you two of course."

To general surprise, Uther approached Tristan's monobike and the wolfess upon it. Sara's dark cheeks and squat muzzle were wet with tears. "I'm sorry for your loss, Sweetheart," Uther said to her, offering his paw.

Hearing Uther's coarse voice Sara looked up from her grief and chirped, "You."

Uther winked, "Come on, lass. Chin up."

Sara got off the mono. "I don't need your help," she sniffed, standing aloof.

Surprised at the rebuff, Uther backed off.

Tristan looked at him, then cleared his throat and shepherded Sara away from Uther and to his own side. He nodded at Ivan, "Lead on, cousin."

Ivan did so. Uther, scratching his head, followed behind.

Passing rows of cars and monos they climbed the few stairs into the corridor beyond, Sara's watery eyes darting to and fro all the way, as if she had only just now realised where she was being taken. This was a Howler Den, into which few outsiders were privileged to enter short of arrest.

Sara had ventured inside Arkady District's Den with Tristan once or twice. Moreover, and most unusually, she had actually grown up in a Den under the care of her parents, albeit a Den very different to this dark, foreboding place. As they ventured deeper into the twisting innards of Riddle's HQ in grim silence, Sara saw none of the grand interiors she was expecting, none of the carpeted halls and vast marbled offices. Tristan always disparagingly asserted that Bloodfang holdings were filthy dives compared to his opulent Eisbrand surroundings, and their territory was nothing but a seedy slum, worse even than the Common Ground. Olivia said similar things. Sara was beginning to believe them.

Through some double doors, down some stairs. The décor became stark, the air cold, the concrete walls running with damp patches and cracks.

Sara instinctively kept close to Tristan.

The group stopped outside a rust-flecked iron door with a push-bar latch, so that trolleys pushed against the doors would open them. Sara imagined Bruno's lifeless form had come barrelling through here on a trolley. She closed her eyes, trying to dispel the awful involuntary image.

Howler Ivan went to open the door, until a grey cat in a doctor's coat spotted the wolves from further up the corridor and approached, chin high, clipboard in paws. His tinted glasses gave him a somewhat menacing, officious air, in Sara's opinion.

"What's the problem here?" he asked directly.

Captain Ivan released the door and said, "This citizen needs to confirm a wolfen death, Doctor Josef."

"Death? What death?"

"The wolf from the café."

"Ah yes, of course, the young cook," Josef said, before looking down on Sara with his brilliant feline eyes, made smoky by his spectacles. "You must be Sara Hummel?"

"Aye," Sara confirmed.

"Daughter of Den Mother Cora?"

"Aye."

Josef's spectacled eyes explored Sara. "So many healthy cubs delivered by a Howler mother, it defies probability. You know… it'd help my research greatly if I could have a blood sample-"

"Do you mind?" Tristan growled. "This is hardly the appropriate time!"

Doctor Josef shifted his attention to the Eisbrand. "And what brings you here, Howler Tristan?"

"Citizen Sara is from my district. I'm escorting her."

"How noble," Josef mocked. "She's quite safe, all I wanted was a little prick to further imperium science and save lives, but I see progress must wait for you lumbering Howlers to catch up as per usual." He sighed, "Very well, let's get this over with."

Glancing at Tristan, Sara allowed Josef to guide her in.

"Have you ever seen a dead body?" the cat asked, as if making polite conversation.

"No. Well… aye, Ah've dissected bugs."

"Ah! You're a disciple of the sciences?"

Surprised to be asked, Sara nodded, "Aye."

Josef mewed, "I congratulate you," and pushed the door open, revealing a dark room with cabinets set in the walls. He turned a knob on the wall and after a few seconds some imperium lamps set in the ceiling coughed into a colourful rainbow of light, before settling down and burning steady. The room was bone-white, the tiles grey, with black grouting.

"Please," Josef urged, placing a paw behind Sara.

With some trepidation the wolfess shuffled inside. The Howlers made to follow, but Doctor Josef barred their entry with an arm across the door.

"Stay here, please."

Howler Tristan simply thrust Josef's arm away, "I'm not to leave her side," and strode in.

Ivan and Uther made to follow as well, but Josef hissed under his breath, "If you two go in you'll answer to Janoah!"

"Why?" Uther scoffed.

Josef smirked menacingly, "Howler Uther, you're far too lowly to question a Grand Howler's orders." He clicked his fingers before the Howler's nose, "Back off, plodder, or else."

"Oh yeah?" Uther laughed pugnaciously, paws spread. "Is that a threat is it yer-aaow! Ivan!"

Stomping on Uther's foot, Ivan over-talked him, "We couldn't care less about some cook," and ushered him away.

"Ivan-"

"Leave it, Wild-heart. It's nothing to do with us."

Tugging his coat lapels, Josef shut the door. Inside, Sara cast her eyes over all the metal cabinets. There must be bodies behind some of these; Bruno's body. The air was cold and dry, not fresh like a winter's morning, but rather like being at a bug-meat market, with that strange, organic smell of slightly questionable produce.

The smart Josef brushed by, going straight to a cabinet. Putting his clipboard aside, he slipped on some felt-lined black rubber gloves and opened the door. He pulled out a robust metal drawer, like a bed, complete with a sheet. The sheet was slightly bloodied and distinctly wolfen-shaped.

Whoever was under there he was big, Bruno-sized. Oh no.

Sara let out a tiny whimper. Tristan placed an armoured paw on her shoulder. It was cold comfort, literally. Together they approached the sheet-wreathed body and stood over it. Sara's eyes roved across the white folds, already searching for any sign that this was Bruno, or better yet, wasn't.

Josef looked at her. "Ready?" he asked.

Sara nodded.

The doctor rolled the edge of the sheet over and slowly pulled it back. For some reason, Sara had expected the cat might theatrically whip the sheet away, but he didn't, and the reveal was slow, even reverential. Ears first, sporting that rich chocolaty brown hide. The eyes were shut, so their colour was no indication. Then came a broad nose. The mouth was shut, but the front teeth and fangs showed slightly. Then finally that massive neck and strong shoulders.

Bruno? Could it be? No… no, it wasn't!

Sara looked to Josef and gasped with palpable relief, "That's nae him."

The grey cat squinted at her. "Take your time. The mask of death can be quite… changing. He was run down by a motor carriage, he may not look quite right for the swelling and-"

"Ah thought he was shot," Sara blurted.

"Shot?" Josef snorted. "Whoever told you that?"

Without thinking Sara glanced back at Tristan, who remained a picture of calm indifference. He'd claimed Bruno had been shot, the papers claimed he'd been run down. What was the truth? Who had lied and why?

"It was in the papers," Sara lied herself, covering for Tristan.

Josef's whiskers turned up. "You can't believe everything you read."

Sara looked closer. With a gulp she reached forth and placed a paw on Bruno's brow. It was stone cold. With a whine of sorrow and fright, Sara peeled one of his eyelids up, looking for those fiery eyes.

The iris was black!

Sara withdrew in fright and wiped her paw on herself as if she might catch the rot. "That's nae him," she gasped. "His eyes were a… a sort of yellow-orange."

Josef scoffed patronisingly. "My dear wolfess, as a scientist you ought to know his eyes are corrupted by ash. When a Howler dies their cells undergo autolysis; ash and black-imperium leak out and the rot advances rapidly. You can't judge anything by eye-colour now, except he was a dodger."

"Bruno was nae a dodger!" Sara maintained, despite what Casimir had told her. "Everything in the papers is a lie!"

"I'm afraid whatever he appeared to you, he was abusing imperium."

"But… but…."

Ushering Sara aside, the big Howler Tristan had a gander for himself, pulling up the eyelids. He looked at Josef and held the cat in his duotone stare for some time, before saying simply, "That's him."

Sara looked at the Howler in horror, as if he had betrayed her to this cat. "But it can't be!" she growled, before adding with uncertainty, "Can it?"

"I saw him up close on the train," Tristan explained, turning to Sara and presenting his back to Josef, his surcoat's hood draping down over the hilt of his beautiful kristahl sword. He took the distraught wolfess aside with both great paws on her tiny shoulders and said, "I've seen death many times. It changes a beast's look in strange and subtle ways. I'm sorry, but that's definitely Bruno." He stared hard Sara and cocked his head slightly to one side. "I know it's hard to accept, Citizen Sara, but it's true."

Sara's eyes darted over Tristan's face, trying to read him, to fathom his secret message. Her heart filled with hope and dread all at once. What did it all mean?

Tristan squeezed her shoulders firmly. "Trust me."

Sara slowly dipped her chin, "Aye… Ah suppose it has tae be him."

Satisfied, Josef covered the corpse and tucked it away with unseemly haste – so much for his earlier reverence. He grabbed his clipboard and slammed the door, before offering Sara the appropriate papers to fill out.

"Sign here," he said, taking a nice fountain pen from his top pocket and passing it over.

Sara did as bidden.

"And here," Josef directed further.

Again, Sara squiggled her signature as best she could. Her paw was shaking, her heart breaking. She felt she was betraying Bruno somehow, signing him out of existence. That wasn't him on that table, it just couldn't be.

Play their game, Sara told herself, for now.

Josef inspected her autograph. "You have a doctor's paw, Miss Hummel," he remarked with a smile, escorting the wolves from the morgue. "Most untidy. You'll make a great scientist one day."

✦

The gates opened and Tristan whisked his ward clear of the Riddle Den on his powerful blue monobike. They hadn't gotten a mile down the main road that paralleled the railway before Sara started tapping Tristan on the shoulder.

"Stop!" she shouted. "I want tae talk!"

"Not yet," he replied. "Let's get you home first."

"I said stop, Tristan!" Sara bellowed.

Giving in to Sara's wishes, Tristan slowed down and pulled into an alley, parked up, checked over his shoulder and all around, before letting the engine sputter to a halt.

Sara immediately hopped off the seat and said in a tone not unlike that of a mother demanding an explanation from a naughty cub, "Well?"

Tristan's weird eyes looked out at her from under the secrecy of his helmet. "I… I don't know what to make of it all," he admitted.

"You don't know?"

"Are you sure that wasn't Bruno?"

"Weren't you?" Sara squeaked in disbelief. "You seemed pretty sure back there!"

Tristan shrugged, "He's your boyfriend."

"He's not… was not…." Sara faltered to a stop and composed herself. "Where *is* he?" she begged. "You have tae tell me something, Tristan. Ah don't care what, just say something! What did Ah just see? What did Ah just do?"

Tristan dipped his chin and looked at his Eisbrand-blue *Dragonfly*, both paws on the steering bars. "I don't know. But take consolation from the fact that you believe that's not him back there and move on with your life."

"Move on?"

"I'm sorry, Sara."

"No! We have tae do something!"

"Like what?" Tristan snapped.

"Ah'll… Ah'll tell mah mother. Ah will!"

Tristan scoffed, "And what's she going to do? Swoop down from Hummelton and fix everything? She can't accuse anyone without proof. They've got him Sara, dead or alive. Bruno's been disappeared and nobody is going to be able to prove otherwise, not with a body and a signature."

Sara gasped, "Then why'd you let me sign it, for Ulf's sake?"

"To protect you!"

"Me?"

"Cora's daughter you may be, but even Den Fathers are assassinated from time to time. Nobody in Lupa is indispensable, Sara, nobody."

Sara grimaced. The wolfess looked all around, at all the indifferent beasts going about their business. She searched Tristan's inscrutable Howler helmet for clues, for hope, but nothing was forthcoming.

"So, Ah'll never see him again?" she whined.

Tristan shrugged, "Who knows? Perhaps he's been squirrelled away in Howler Academy. That's the best outcome. If he survives his induction he may even come find you. If he remembers you."

"Remembers me?"

"As I've oft told you, induction is cruel and imperium a jealous bitch."

Sara whirled away to hide her grief. Tristan watched her weep, regretting his insensitive choice of words. How he wanted to get off his bike and hold her, this gentle, beautiful wolfess who cared for beast and bug alike, but he was sure she would just throw him off in disgust after what he had made her do.

He looked away, then down at his bike. "Let me take you home," he said, clearing his throat.

"Ah betrayed him!" Sara snuffled. "Ah want tae die!"

"Don't be so stupid!" Tristan scolded. "As if Bruno would want such a thing! You need to be stronger than that. I know you are. It took a lot of guts to leave cosy little Hummelton and come all the way to Lupa to study-"

Sara screamed and punched the air with her fists, "Ah don't care about that! Ah hate Lupa! Ah hate it! Ah wish Ah'd never come here!"

There was a pause as Sara wept.

"You do care," Tristan assured her. "I know nothing in the world matters just now, but it'll pass."

"What do you know?"

"A lot," the Howler asserted. "Almost everyone I ever cared about is dead, long-rotten or missing, or out of my reach one way or another… except you."

Sara whirled round, her yellow eyes darting about, but she said nothing.

Tristan held out an armoured paw, "Now please, let me take you home. We can still help Casimir get away."

Something passed, a thought, a feeling, and Sara wordlessly slipped on the back of the mono. She held Tristan around his middle and rested her head on his back, just left of his sword.

"Ready?" he said.

Sara nodded, "Aye."

Tristan started the monobike and away they went, leaving Riddle Den in the rear-view mirror.

Chapter 13

"What did you put in your report, Janoah?"

"It's a little late to compare notes, Vladimir."

"I just thought we should be on the same page if Amael's going to blow his lid."

"I'll back you up, Oromov, never fear."

The two Grand Howlers sat cosseted in opulence; tall windows, lush blood-red curtains, polished black and white marbled columns and a floor so heartily waxed you could see yourself in it. In fact a mouse was mopping the floor right now, albeit at a respectful distance from the Howlers. This was the inner sanctum of Riddle Den, where only the Elder of this district, or the Bloodfang Den Father himself, could venture uninvited.

Janoah leant back in her red chair and broke out an ember. When offered refreshments by the secretary, Vladimir settled for a cup of tea. It arrived on a tray held in the paws of a nervous-looking brown rabbit in red Politzi uniform. He set the pot down and the teacup, but fumbled with the extra hot water, knocking it over and then catching it again, which only made matters worse as steaming water was catapulted clean across the table.

"Idiot!" Vladimir yelped, jumping to his feet to avoid getting seriously splashed.

"Sorry, Grand Howler!"

Sorry or not, Vladimir clouted the rabbit round the back of the head, sending his Politzi hat spiralling across the room, which was quite a feat where rabbits were concerned, since they had such long ears that hats tended to cling on.

"Just what I need before meeting Elder Amael," Vladimir said sarcastically. "What's your name?"

"Claybourne, sir. Borce Claybou-"

"You're useless, Claybourne, like all your jittering kind!"

"Pity about the boy," Janoah said, with a chuckle, "he'd have made a fine tea boy if nothing else."

"Boy?"

"Rufus's late fancy."

"Humph," Vladimir grunted, sitting back down.

Whilst Claybourne mopped up the mess with a kerchief, the doors leading into the waiting room opened and a big hog clopped in – Werner. The pig's usually ill-fitting uniform looked well-ironed and tidy for once.

"You too?" Janoah said to him, ember smouldering between her ruddy fingers.

However, Werner was distracted by the goings-on at the table. "What happened here?"

"This incompetent rabbit nearly scalded me to death," Vladimir replied. "There's been one assassination attempt already this week, am I THORN's next target?"

"My apologies, Grand Howler," Werner said. He shepherded the rabbit away and admonished him, but didn't hit him. Directing the mouse with the mop to clean up with just a wave of a finger, Werner returned to the table. "Shan't happen again, Grand Howler."

Vladimir grumbled, "What've I told you about hiring rabbits, Werner? They're too nervous for this line of work."

"Making tea, you mean?" Janoah guffawed.

"A decent Politzi, I mean."

"I'll put young Borce to duties elsewhere, sir," Werner assured, adding, "but I must say, rabbits are good at rapport with the citizens, Grand Howler, they don't come across as threatening as some."

Werner was just about to ease himself into a spare seat when the doors on the other side of the room opened and a rough, stocky, mottled brown and white Howler in captain's black stepped in.

"Elder Amael will see you now, Grand Howlers," he announced plainly.

"Thank you, Boris," Vladimir acknowledged, forgoing his tea with a parting sip, whilst Janoah hurriedly stubbed out her ember. Werner nervously toyed with his hat, rolling it over in his pink fingers. All three stepped through the high doors and walked down a long, straight corridor as opulent as the room that preceded it. Glimmering imperium crystal chandeliers passed overhead, their soft light reflecting in the floor below. The walls were beautified with red and gold and the stained-glass windows were draped with curtains. Portraits of long-dead Howlers – Elders and Den Fathers mostly, but sometimes great Howlers of lesser rank – graced the spaces between the windows, their fine cloaks and intricately embossed armour trumpeting their rank, whatever the period. Fashions and technology had changed, but the underlying message of power and wisdom captured in their finery and faces was ageless. Unlike some, Pack Bloodfang had been around a long time, predating the discovery of imperium, the advent of the rot, even the founding Lupa itself, so there were plenty of portraits, enough to line the walls right up to the double doors at the end of the corridor, where two ancient Bloodfang banners were hung just-so. The banners, like the mantles of the Howlers, were imperium-weave, and thus looked as good as the day they were woven despite being a few centuries old.

Two fully-dressed Howlers stood guard at the doors. Their mantles were the usual Bloodfang red, only very long, terminating past the knee. This indicated that they were members of the Den Guard; elite Howlers assigned to protect Elders and the Den Father. Saluting they opened the doors, one each, and stood by as Vladimir and company entered the fabulous Elder Chamber, whereupon they shut the doors and stood smart once more.

The Den's Elder Chamber was as fine as the preceding rooms; circular in plan, with gold and red walls, much drapery and paintings, and an enormous chandelier hanging from the domed ceiling, its crystals playing in the light from the embedded imperium lamps. A huge Bloodfang crest dominated much of the circular floor space; this is where the guests were expected to stand, and did so, Vladimir in the middle. In front of them was the Elder table, an arc of ancient polished wood that spanned a third of the room, with thirteen high-backed chairs, the middle being the grandest, the rest identical. Silver pens and thick papers were set neatly at each space, enough for everyone to make notes in their files during an inquiry, a meeting, or even a trial.

Vladimir, Janoah and Werner stood firmly to attention, eyes front.

"What in Ulf's name has been going on in my district, Howlers?" someone said, from the far right of the room.

Using just his eyes, Vladimir spied a wolf peering out the windows at the cityscape of Lupa below. He was wearing a red cloak with a white stripe running around the edges. His fur was a handsome, uniformly steel grey, his armour golden. Tail flicking thoughtfully, he lifted one muscular, scar-flecked arm and smouldered, blowing the vapour at the window, before turning around. Vladimir's eyes faced front again just in time.

"Well?" the wolf snapped, walking round behind the long, bow-shaped table.

"We're not sure, Elder Amael," Vladimir replied. "We're still ascertaining the facts."

"The facts?" Elder Amael repeated.

"Yes, Elder."

"The facts, Oromov, are this: that someone has tried to blow one of my Howlers to the moon! That the one beast who might know something about it is dead, i.e. that treacherous wretch Noss, racked to death by our incompetent doctor. The facts are you three can't even bring a cub and a rabbit in for questioning and Uther can't go five minutes in the Common Ground without causing chaos!"

Amael picked up a file and slammed it on the desk with contempt.

"That is what your reports amount to," he said. "Do you want to hear *my* report?"

Silence.

"I'll tell you! It's this: that you have embarrassed me in front of my fellow Elders, even Den Father Vito himself, on the very day they came to visit. Not only does Rufus not turn up, but utter chaos reigns in Riddle and beyond. I look like a fool! You could not have planned my downfall better."

Janoah could hold her tongue no longer. "With respect, Elder Amael, you exaggerate."

"Exaggerate, Valerio?" Elder Amael growled dangerously. "I 'exaggerate'?" he said again, louder.

"I believe that you do yourself, and your loyal Howlers an injustice," Janoah said calmly, but firmly. "A notorious traitor was brought to justice in the morning and a Howler-killer in the evening; our district is the envy of Lupa thanks to wolves like Uther and Ivan… and my husband."

"Your 'husband' did nothing, except get blown up!"

"Hardly his fault," Janoah fearlessly pointed out. "He still salvaged his proposals; I sent them along via Boris."

"Yes. They were considered."

"What was the Elders' decision, if I may?"

Amael leant on the table with both paws, ember wobbling between his lips as he spoke. "Rejected," he scoffed. "Tell Rufus from me that we do not have the time or resources to mount a pointless expedition to the Dead Cities. With this shortage we do not even have resources enough to sit around *discussing* a pointless expedition to the Dead Cities! If he didn't have the ear of the renowned Professor Heath and Den Father Thorvald nobody would take a blind bit of notice, as it is great wolves must be seen to humour him. The rot is an incurable condition, we can but manage it; everyone knows that, except loons like Rufus."

Janoah let the matter lie with a nod and the words, "I'll pass on your message, Elder, though I don't suppose my husband will take much heed-"

"Because he is a disrespectful hyena!" Amael barked, slapping the long table with a paw and upsetting the pens. "He should be flogged to within an inch of his life for continuing in this folly and bringing shame on Riddle!"

"He believes it's not folly," Janoah explained. "He feels his time drawing nearer and wishes only to save future lives; he hasn't a care for himself anymore."

"Or you!" Amael blurted.

Janoah remained outwardly composed, but for a dip of the chin.

Elder Amael looked down a moment too. Knocking on the tabletop with his knuckles a few times, he walked around it and stood before Janoah, not a tall wolf by any means, but very strong and imposing all the same. His hide was scarred from many a wound, his eyes were like fire, and his blood was loaded with imperium; Janoah could feel his muscular corona crackling in her bones like static.

Amael looked Janoah up and down, but moved on to the taller Vladimir.

"Noss said nothing?" he grunted.

"He said that he was paid, but gave no names," Vladimir replied simply

"Nothing? You're sure?"

"He was too strong. Josef did his best, Elder-"

"Not good enough! That queer cat is here for one thing and one thing only, to do imperious science for our cause and if he can't even rack a deranged hyena without cooking him he obviously doesn't know his stuff, does he?"

"Chakaa are difficult to rack, Elder, their superior pain-tolerance and purple-imperium psychosis makes them strong, and Noss was the strongest Chakaa I knew."

Taking his ember from his mouth, Amael lectured the lofty Grand Howler, "Justice needs to be seen to be done, Vladimir, out in the open, not in a dark corner. Those days are over, this is a new era with ALPHA snapping at our heels, or so they keep telling us. To keep the peace between the packs is to present a united front to our enemies and the little beasts. If Noss had been a wolf from a rival pack, and not a degenerate hyena from some tribe, his death could have sparked a Howler War."

Vladimir couldn't help but point out, "If Noss were a wolf he would not have been racked, sir. Racking of wolves is prohibited by the Lupan Laws, of course."

"Indeed, Oromov! Indeed."

Vladimir said nothing more.

"And you, Schwartz!" Amael snarled, turning on Werner. "What do we pay the Politzi for? You can't even apprehend a mere rabbit and a wolf cub!"

"Casimir ain't no ordinary rabbit, Elder."

"Ain't no ordinary rabbit?" Amael mocked. "Ain't?"

"He was a big deal during the war," Werner Schwartz explained, hoping his grammatical error would be forgotten. "He's ex-Politzi too. Real tough customer."

"So I read in your ill-written report," the scary Amael sniffed. "Friends are you?"

"Mildly acquainted, Elder."

"I see. Knew his 'son' did you?"

"A little."

"Exactly what manner of wolf was he, this… Bruno?"

Janoah glanced across at the pig; Werner could sense her green-eyed glare without looking. "Just an ordinary lad, sir," he said, "Kind boy, but not too bright. It's his father's fault, what happened I mean. He told Bruno to never trust the Politzi. I tried to bring him in quietly, like, but it just went south for us on account of Casimir's ways. It's a tragedy."

"Indeed. Still, no great loss. He was but an ordinary wolf after all, not the next Den Father in the making. Rufus just fancied a bit of rough, I wager, eh?"

Amael looked to Janoah – she remained composed.

"Very well, get out of my sight all of you," the Elder grunted, turning away. "Dismissed."

The Howlers and the Politzi officer saluted and headed for the doors.

"Oh, one moment Valerio," Amael said, beckoning with a finger, "I, uh… need a word."

Everyone waited.

"Just you," Amael clarified firmly.

Vladimir and Werner carried on their way, opening just the one door and stepping out. Werner, to his surprise, was allowed to take the lead, whilst Vladimir politely stayed behind to close the door. He did so with painful slowness, lingering as long as possible, trying glean what it was Amael wanted to discuss with Janoah. All he caught through the crack of the door, as he finally and inevitably pulled it shut, was a glimpse of Amael offering Janoah a drink.

"To the Republic," he said, pouring Janoah some brandy from a crystal decanter.

Janoah took the glass and chinked it against Amael's, "To the Republic."

She downed her brandy in one go, which brought a smile to Amael's grizzled muzzle. Still with half a glass, he walked around the table and picked up a telephone.

"I'll receive no one for an hour, Boris," he said, talking to his adjutant, that stocky, mottled wolf. "No, I'll be in the Elder Chamber, but do not disturb me. I've work to do."

Putting the phone down he gulped the rest of his drink and said to Janoah, "You shouldn't talk to me like that in front of others. Especially Vladimir, he'll get suspicious."

"I'd have spoken my mind even if Den Father Vito himself were here. Anything less would be out of character and therefore suspicious."

With a disapproving grunt, Amael tapped the file on the table with a finger, "Do you really believe the Greystones are behind the attack on Rufus?"

"They made the bomb, at least. Only they know how."

"Yet it was delivered by Noss of all creatures. Rufus's friend… once."

Janoah shrugged, "Hence we're flummoxed, and Noss has gone to his grave with his secrets."

"How convenient," Amael huffed.

"For someone."

Amael grunted and moved on, "Such a remarkable recovery Rufus has undergone, I hear, and all without a single sting."

"Yes," Janoah agreed blandly.

"You should've come to me first."

"For what?"

"You know what."

The wolfess sniffed, "I'm sure I do not-"

"I would've arranged it," Amael said, over-talking her, "for your sake, not his."

"As I said, I don't know what you mean, Elder-"

"Amael!" the Elder snapped irritably, adding, "We're alone, Janoah; I'm not testing you! For Ulf's sake, do you hold me in such contempt?"

Janoah dipped her chin, "One never knows who might be hiding behind the curtains."

Elder Amael stubbed out his spent ember in a fancy ashtray and strode around the table to stand with Janoah. He reached down and took one of her red paws in his steel grey fingers.

"Come to me for a sting next time, not that fool Vladimir," he chided gently.

Janoah said nothing.

"What?" Amael snorted. "I know you've started dealing with him to get venom for Rufus. As Riddle's only wolfess, you can offer something even the crusty Vladimir can't turn down."

"And who says I have?" Janoah spat.

"That's neither here nor there. What matters, is that I am not minded to share you with that pompous, weakling of a pen-pusher! I will not have it, do you hear me?"

Silence.

Amael tempered his tone, "Besides you could come away with a cub. Then where would you be?"

"I'm barren," Janoah stated, matter-of-factly.

"With Rufus, yes; Vladimir is of a different makeup."

"As are you. Every Howler coupling is different. What if we should come away with a cub?"

Amael rose on his toes a moment, chin high. "As an Elder I have the power and money to hide you for the duration and any cubs you may bear, unlike Vladimir. And if you miscarried... or worse the rot being as it is, I'd have Josef Grau take care of matters discreetly. There'd be no charges brought, no shame."

Janoah was sarcastic at best, "Much obliged, I'm sure."

"In any case, your foolish dealings with Vladimir could bring ALPHA down on us!" Amael blustered. "This shortage has made them zealous in their pursuit of imperium abuse. If you need a sting just ask me. I have the means." Cupping a paw over his handsome silver brooch, the Elder whispered, "You know how much I respect you. You're the rarest of Howlers, Janoah."

"A female one, yes. I'm quite used to it-"

"Yes, female, but a clever one too, a beautiful one! And Rufus does not appreciate you, nor deserve you."

"He can't help his Ulf-given inclinations, Amael."

"Then he's as bad as old Vito!"

Faced with that outburst, Janoah withdrew from Amael. "Do not compare a brilliant alpha male like Rufus to that drooling degenerate we still mistakenly hail Den Father!"

Amael grabbed her arm, "I'm sorry. Forgive me. I'm tired."

"May I be excused?"

"Stay, please!" Amael almost whined. The steel-grey wolf looked around the room, as if checking for those spies hiding in the curtains, then took both Janoah's paws in his and kissed them together. "I love you, you know that," he said. "You alone truly know where my ambitions lie, that I will be Den Father, the only Den Father."

Janoah clucked tiresomely, "So you've said for nigh on a year. I see no movement in that direction."

Amael woofed, "Good, then nobody else will have!" Then he chuckled, "See, that's what I like about you; you doubt me, challenge me. I'll need a wife like you, a Howler, strong, intelligent, someone who understands my pain, not some simpering nothing."

"Again with this 'wife' talk? The nuptial arm of the Lupan Laws states two Howlers cannot marry; you won't get special dispensation."

"Forget dispensation, I will change the Lupan Laws! If they were changed before they can be changed again."

"When you rule?"

"When we rule, Janoah."

"And how long will that take?"

"Not as long as all that," Amael claimed. "Lupa cannot limit her potency much longer. The other races will soon overtake us. Do you think the cats will wait for us? Their Valours are free to breed and make strong offspring still. What if they start a war? They'll have the edge. I know you agree with me."

Janoah stared into space and blinked once. "Amael," she said, quavering a little, "I do agree… and I do love you… but Rufus-"

"Cares more about crystals and bugs than his duty to me or his wife," Amael snorted. "Don't let him waste your talents as he wastes his own. For Ulf's sake, I beg you to proceed with a divorce and leave him to his toys."

"What difference will divorce make when I cannot marry you?"

"It will mean you don't belong to him!"

"We belong to each other!" Janoah snapped, adding calmer. "We married before the Lupan Laws were enacted and that is not something to throw away lightly."

"He threw it away years ago."

Janoah grimaced. "Amael, if you hate him so much why do you say you'll help me keep him alive? Why not just cut off his rations and let him die? I know you could arrange it."

Amael paused a moment. "Because you love him, wolfess that you are," he said a length, stroking Janoah's sweet cheek. "And wolfess that you are, I know you'd never forgive me."

"Yet you ask me to abandon him?"

"That would be your choice. I can only keep asking."

Janoah looked down and away, suddenly so demure and reticent, but Amael knew very well the fire that burnt in her bones. She could simply cup a paw to his chest and blow him across the room right now if she had cause. What a wolfess.

"I will divorce him if and when you change the law," she said. "I see no point before then, do you?"

Amael grunted, "Hedging your bets Janoah?"

"One of us has to."

A nod.

"Lay with me tonight?" Amael asked. "Let me treat you as a wolfess should be treated."

"I can't. Beasts will talk."

The Elder wheeled away, poured another drink. "Can you not console me? I deserve it. Entertaining the Elders yesterday was pure torture." He waved his tumbler side to side, "We processed from restaurant to bar to Lupanar, Vito becoming more drunk and disgusting at every stop. Yet everyone continued to hang on his every word in sycophantic admiration, myself included, even though we all know what he is now. What he always was. We're all such cowards it sickens me! I sat hoping a hyena would toss a bomb through *our* window."

Janoah tutted, "That's treasonous talk."

Amael turned to her, "Treason's all I talk around you. I don't know why I trust you… but somehow I do."

A smile.

"Will you not reconsider my request?"

Janoah dipped her chin, then raised it, "Which one, Elder? You've pitched so many tonight."

Amael cringed, "You know I hate you using that ridiculous title in private. I'm not old! I am very far from the rot. The first thing I'll do when I rule Lupa is abolish the feeble terms 'Elder' and 'Den Father' forever. The Wolf Kings shall return! We'll be like our cat cousins; they know how to rule, how to foster respect and keep the little beasts in their place. The citizens will bow in the streets as we pass when I am king."

"Why merely king?" Janoah tempted. "Why not… emperor? Emperor Amael Balbus of the Pan-Lupan Pack Bloodfang."

"Ambitious," Amael Balbus growled in amazement. "See? You truly are a wolfess after my own heart. That's why I trust you. I know you'll always put Lupa first. She must survive, and the best way is through strength, unity, not these warring factions."

Slowly, gently, Janoah cupped her paws over Amael's mighty cloaked chest; she could feel his crackling aura, and no doubt he could hers. "I have things to do, as always," she said, tapping him on the nose, "I'll call on you later my 'Emperor'."

✦

It took Janoah five minutes to cross the Den, from the opulent Elder wing where Amael Balbus entertained guests, through the relatively understated, even run-down barracks where the Howlers resided, to the stark, clean hospital wing where Janoah threw open the doors to the appropriate ward.

Rufus lay in bed. Beside him; in a second bed and much the same predicament was Howler Linus.

Janoah made her way to Rufus's bedside and stood over her bandaged husband. She stared for an age, wondering whether to wake him and tell him the bad news.

"Well?" he croaked, not opening his eyes – so much for Janoah's little dilemma.

"Rejected," she replied at length, wringing out a flannel and wetting her mate's puckered brow.

"Naturally."

"Your absence didn't help matters."

"My dear Jan," Rufus woofed, "if I thought for a moment I could talk them round… do you think I'd let myself get blown up?"

"Yes, if it garnered your pride."

Rufus smiled, as did Janoah.

"How are you feeling anyway?" she asked afresh.

"I… haven't felt this wretched since I was inducted," Rufus complained.

"That bad?"

Rufus had suffered a famously painful and protracted induction; the sheer volume of white-imperium his body had required to get over the threshold from sputtering, sickly cub to fully-functioning, corona-wielding Howler had been almost too much to bear. He had been bedridden for weeks whilst his pain-wracked muscles and bones adjusted. Some Howlers did not survive their induction, slipping into comas and dying of imperium poisoning; others woke up robbed of long-held memories, or even their sanity. Janoah herself barely remembered her induction, though beasts told her afterwards it had been painless. She could believe it, female Howlers tended to cope with imperium better than their more common male counterparts.

Thinking such thoughts whilst tenderly dabbing her husband's brow and neck, Janoah suddenly said afresh, "For what it's worth, I'm sorry about Noss."

"No… you're not," Rufus chuckled falsely, turning his cheek. "You're not sorry about the boy either."

"Boy?"

"Don't insult my intelligence, wife, I know that you've looked into him. Besides, Ivan's told me everything. Did you send Werner's thugs in to arrest Bruno, or did Vladimir?"

"It was a routine questioning," Janoah claimed.

"For what? He was just a cub!"

"Who bludgeoned a rat to death and hospitalised two others to escape? Some cub, husband."

Seething in pain, Rufus said, "It's... all my fault."

"How?"

"I told him he was dying, that he had to be inducted. I only wanted to help him, stop the pain, all that. Poor boy must've been scared witless all day. He obviously panicked."

"You did what you thought was right. It's not your fault he ran away and got hit by a truck."

Rufus flinched at the mental image. "Ulf's fangs."

Janoah wiped his muzzle. "You should stop talking and rest," she chided. "Amael will get suspicious if you recover too fast."

"Yes," the patient snorted. "I hope you didn't lay with him to get your paws on some venom. Not that you haven't to get favours before, but don't debase yourself further on my account."

With a glance at Linus, who she judged to be a mere insect in the great scheme of things and therefore no threat even if he was awake and listening, Janoah spat haughtily, "At least Amael's a wolf worth lying with!"

"My dear Jan, if he were that I'd be happy for you."

"You've no right to judge me!" Janoah hissed, leaning close, "None! You betray me for… for-"

"For senseless passion," Rufus cut in, turning to Janoah at last and looking at her with one green eye. "You betray me for cold, calculated ambition." Smiling knowingly, he cupped a paw to his wife's cheek, "If you love Amael, really love him, then leave me and go to him. But power alone won't sate your hunger, Janoah Valerio."

"How would you know? You've never had any power!"

"I see it in Amael's eyes. He's always hungry that wolf, hungry and frightened."

Janoah drew back. "Well, as it happens," she revealed haughtily and more than a tad triumphant, "I didn't have to go to Amael or anyone else to save your sorry tail this time. You can blame young Woodlouse over there for your stay on the mortal coil; he gave you one of his stings. So there."

Frowning, Rufus looked to his right, at the unconscious blonde wolf. "Woodlouse? You mean Linus?"

Janoah huffed, "You've spoken? I thought he was out of his head on stings and taubfene."

"Ivan told me," Rufus explained, adding, "Fresh out of the academy, isn't he?"

"Yes. He's Uther's new partner; hence the new title. I think it's going to stick."

"That's the least of his worries. Does he even appreciate the risk he took giving me a sting?"

"I spelt it out," Janoah maintained. "Still, he wouldn't be deterred."

"Jan, if you twisted his arm-"

"If you don't believe me ask Uther. He was there."

Rufus looked the wounded Linus over whilst Janoah wetted the flannel.

"He's very bright," the latter wolf said afresh. "Finished top of his year, bumped straight up to Trooper First Class. Even found time to study imperiology *and* biology. Though not how to ride a mono."

Rufus cast a suspicious eye over his wife, "You've been looking into him."

Janoah meticulously wiped-down her mate's arms. "I thought he might be after something by helping you, thought he might come with some baggage. He seems harmless enough."

"Oh, you're as bad as Ivan. You two see plots everywhere!"

Janoah paused a moment, but said nothing. Eventually she continued in the same vein as before, "Uther says Linus worships you. He's read all your work. Big fan, apparently."

Rufus tried to disguise his delight. "Well," he grunted, "you can't believe what that lying rogue Uther 'Wild-heart' says. He's not even paid me a visit yet. After everything I've done for him. That's gratitude for you! He will be proud, that one."

Janoah checked the nearest clock. "Fun as is it playing nursemaid to my decrepit husband again, I have to go."

"So soon?"

"Don't pretend you'll miss me."

"Have I ever?"

Without even a kiss on the cheek, Janoah left Rufus for the corridor, failing to notice the starkly two-toned wolf lingering in the shadows until he leapt forth.

"How is he, marm?" Uther gruffed after her.

Whirling on him, Janoah assumed, "Linus?"

Uther nodded, "Aye, a-a-and Rufus, marm."

Janoah cast a paw to the doors. "Why don't you go in and see for yourself? I'm sure my husband would enjoy your company. He was just talking about you."

"He was?" Uther said, betraying a smile.

A nod.

"No, I... I'd better let him rest," Wild-heart excused. "He's got enough good stuff now though, yeah?"

A second, deeper nod.

"Aye. Good."

One paw finding her hips, Janoah looked the athletic Uther up and down. "He's never intentionally hurt me, you know," she said, presumably of Rufus. "We were even happy for a time, back when we were young. We stay together because we're friends, you see; it's not like two Howlers have much hope of cubs, especially when one of you is... well, you boys know the score by now."

Uther's white face grimaced.

"What I mean is," Janoah said, with a tiny gasp, "if it's me you're scared of offending, Wild-heart, don't be. I'm not the covetous sort. He might even make you happy... for a time."

She took her leave of Wild-heart before he could even grasp her words, let alone dare to reply.

✦

The young beast twisted his arms. They were bound to his sides. Every part of him was strapped down to a hard, cold surface. He couldn't fathom why, or where, or even when. The room around was dark, yet the light overhead painfully bright. Machines pumped and hissed. Beasts talked. Visions of a stern white rabbit in an apron and a smiling black wolfess kept surfacing and fading away.

Who are they? Who am I?

"Hello?" the beast said, breathing deep as the tendrils of panic started to creep into the sides of his fuzzy mind like a cold, dense morning fog. "Is anybody there?"

A cat in a white coat leant in, he had grey fur and tinted spectacles. His mouth and nose were obscured by a medical mask. "He's awake already," he said, adding, "Remarkable."

"Where am I?"

"You are in a... medical facility," the cat replied vaguely, writing on a clipboard. "My name is Doctor Josef Grau, but you may call me Doctor Josef."

"Oh. All right, but… who am I?"

"Who are you?"

"Yeah, sorry but…" the beast growled, letting out a slight laugh at his own perceived foolishness, "but… I can't remember."

"You're Rafe."

"Rafe?"

"Yes. Howler Rafe Stenton."

Rafe Stenton let out a scoff of amazement, "What? Howler? Me?"

"Well, in a manner of speaking," Josef assured, flipping a sheet up. "You're a very special kind of Howler. I'm saving your life, believe me, but there are certain side-effects to induction. Loss of memory is not uncommon with this much imperium in the blood."

"I'm…. I'm a-a wolf, then?"

"Oh yes."

"Where? I can't see."

"Nurse," the cat said. Someone passed him a small mirror and he held it overhead, blocking out the bright light. "Here, take a look at yourself."

There in the mirror was a dark, handsome brown wolf. He had robust features and big fiery eyes that shone with unnatural brilliance.

"Huh," he said, smiling a little. "That's me?"

"Who else would it be?" Josef scoffed, passing back the mirror. "Now shut up and lay still."

Rafe had no choice but to.

Doctor Josef looked across to his wolfen nurse. "Better sedate him before the pain hits, Nurse Meryl," he said. "Taubfene, one hundred minims."

"A hundred?" Nurse Meryl questioned.

"Plus gas – he's a big lad, he'll cope," Josef assured. Still Meryl hesitated, so the doctor huffed further, "I know he's restrained, but if his corona coils violently now he'll turn the place upside down, perhaps even kill us! He must remain asleep for as long as possible. Besides, we need to take his tail off yet. Might as well get that unpleasantness over with."

"Yes, Doctor," Meryl said guardedly.

A door opened, a hefty metal door by the sound, though Rafe couldn't see. Doctor Josef turned to address whoever had entered the room.

"He's not ready yet-"

"How is he?" the intruder snapped, a female. Rafe strained to look, but the light overhead reduced everything beyond to blurry silhouettes.

He felt something prick him in the arm and his whole body jolted in surprise, though he could not move for his bonds. He saw that wolfen nurse beaming down on him, her smile somehow apparent even behind her mask. She was pretty, with smooth grey fur and tall, elegant ears. Her shirt had a high, black collar and cravat; very smart and modest.

"Shh," she soothed, stroking Rafe's brow. "It'll be over soon. Doctor Josef's going to make you better."

"You're Meryl, yeah?"

"Meryl Stroud. Pleased to meet you, Rafe Stenton."

Rafe smiled as Meryl Stroud placed a cold glass respirator over his muzzle. The hiss of gas escaping a canister echoed down the pipe. For a moment Rafe was alarmed, but as a strange sweet smell overcame him he relaxed, his aches and pains melting away.

"Well?" the intruder demanded of the doctor. "Is the induction taking?"

"Taking? He's off the charts!" Josef mewed with excitement. "His imperium density is staggering. He must have a dozen stings in him and he's still stable."

"I knew it. I knew it! Rufus you've done it again."

As his eyelids grew strangely leaden, a red wolfess in a white cloak walked into the light and peered down upon the prostrate Rafe, inspecting him closely. She cupped a paw to his massive neck. Rafe's body twitched from ear to toe as a tingling, warm sensation crawled down his spine. It was strange, but not unpleasant.

"Ah, can you feel me, dear boy?" the wolfess cooed, stroking Rafe. "I'm Janoah Valerio. We're going to be working together, you and I."

Rafe frowned, but was too weak to speak.

Turning away, Janoah growled at Josef, "Don't lose him!"

"Oh, I won't," the doctor assured. "Where are you going?"

"Back to Riddle Den; I've another obligation to attend to," Janoah replied, closing the door behind her.

Nurse Meryl looked down upon Rafe. That gentle, placid visage nestled atop that high collar was the last thing he saw before the weight of drug-induced sleep banished all thoughts and fears.

✤

Vladimir crossed his sumptuous Grand Howler quarters and pushed aside an antique tapestry to reveal his wall safe. He unlocked it with a deft twiddle of the dial. Inside was a rainbow of test tubes filled with imperium, red, green, blue and more. Vladimir took the green tube and went to his window, which was festooned with potted plants of every kind, some hanging, others climbing, but most content to stay within the confines of their pot.

Adding a few drops of green-imperium to an elegant silver watering can, Vladimir swirled the water within and sprinkled it over his miniature garden with great care.

There was a knock at the door. Vladimir glanced at his ornate clock – midnight.

"Come in," he said, amidst his horticultural duties.

The door opened and Janoah stepped in, devoid of armour and uniform in favour of white breeches and a matching silk tunic with silver thread woven into the seams.

She walked over to inspect Vladimir's window-bound jungle. "Tending to your first love, I see," she cooed. "I had better come back some other time."

"Pour yourself a drink," Vladimir replied absently, "I want to talk to you."

"Talk? I didn't come here to 'talk'."

"How's Rufus?"

"As if you care, Vladimir."

"A great deal," he insisted, putting the watering can aside and facing his rude guest. "If I were able, I would vote for him go on his expedition. In fact I'd go along. I'm sure there are many plant species in and around the Dead Cities that I could describe for the first time. One of them might hold a cure."

Janoah said nothing – science wasn't her field.

She went to Vladimir's cabinet to see about that drink he had offered her.

"What Rufus doesn't appreciate," Janoah complained at last, pouring herself a crystal tumbler of Hummel brandy, "is that, if he'd had the heart to try, he'd be our Den Father by now, what with his strength and guile. Then he could arrange this silly expedition himself instead of canvassing idiots for approval."

"He's a little young to be Den Father."

"No younger than Ulf was," Janoah pointed out. Knocking back her drink she looked into the empty glass. "It's the cruellest of his jokes – Ulf that is – endowing that husband of mine such strength and wit, yet zero ambition. If I'd only known what he was before I married him, or if he'd known himself for that matter. What fools we were. Nothing's ever come of us. Nothing ever will."

The tall Vladimir came up behind Janoah and placed a big black and white paw on her left shoulder. "I've ambition," he said, stroking Janoah's sweet, red neck.

"But no power," she huffed.

"Information *is* power. And my information says that Noss was bundled into a dark room and bribed to kill your husband by certain powerful wolves, not hyenas."

Janoah threw Vladimir's paw from her shoulder, "I could've told you that this wasn't THORN's idea."

Raising a finger to beg Janoah's patience, Vladimir poured himself a stiff drink. "You know, it is thought, by the conservatives amongst the packs," he began, pointing at Janoah with same paw he held his tumbler with, "that if a cure for rot were affected tomorrow, by Rufus or anyone else, it would upset the natural order and bring about Lupa's ruin."

Janoah let slip an incredulous scoff, "Ruin?"

"White-imperium keeps us Howlers in check," Vladimir said, rolling a paw. "We all learnt during the war that a wolf's allegiance to their pack only lasts as long as the sting supply."

"Depends on the wolf."

"But for simplicity's sake, imagine if a few Elders controlled the flow of all venom," Vladimir posited. "They would be able to control the Howlers, enough of us at any rate to take Lupa. Those who wished to live would join the well-supplied uprising, any who didn't would die on the streets within a month or two. If the Den Fathers were then eliminated and the structure of packs destroyed, all papers burnt, district boundaries redrawn, there would be no going back. When the white-imperium tap was turned on again it would be too late, Lupa would be a republic no longer, but an empire."

"A dictatorship," Janoah corrected.

"Semantics, Howler. Either way, a cure precludes such a grand plan, because if we don't need imperium, we cannot be controlled by the packs or anyone else."

"So someone tried to kill Rufus because of a cure?"

"No. That's just their cover story."

Janoah folded her arms. "But you just said-"

"Rufus is not alone," Vladimir dismissed. "Professor Heath searches for a cure, Josef too; hundreds of beasts must. I myself dabble and nobody's tried to kill me."

"Pity," Janoah chuckled.

The jibe pinged off Vladimir's thick hide. "Noss didn't believe in a cure," he said, "but those who paid him *claimed* that their plans to take over Lupa would be in jeopardy if Rufus succeeded in his endeavours. Noss bought their lies, thinking he was dealing with utter fools. All he had to do was bomb Rufus, get paid, disappear, and never look back – there would be no repercussions."

"Except killing Rufus."

"Not even that. Ivan feels Noss's heart wasn't in it, and I agree. His legitimate reservations about using black-imperium should not have got in his way; he could have tossed his yellow-imperium bomb through the window and then shot Rufus and Ivan during the confusion. He didn't, thus sparing them, he hoped, whilst still making a convincing attempt, or enough of one to persuade his contractors that he had followed through whilst he eloped with the cash. He had already sent his family ahead to be smuggled out of the Reservation, though somebody betrayed him. They clearly had no intention of letting Noss or his family get away with all that money thank you very much."

"Noss said all that, did he?" Janoah mocked.

"I surmise somewhat. Either way, Noss was not dealing with fools, Janoah, and nor are we."

"I dunno, I might be looking at one."

Vladimir's temper finally buckled. "These conspirators are hard, ruthless beasts, wolfess! They do not believe in a cure and they certainly did not send Noss after Rufus for so spurious a reason. They only wanted him to think so in the event of his capture. It is ash and mirrors, an artful deception!"

Vladimir took a calming breath, and continued.

"Noss didn't see the big picture. He represents not only his tribe but all hyenas. Look at those barbarians, Lupans will now say. Even their prince has turned on the very wolf who loved him most, who once saved him from a sewer centipede! Can you imagine the papers tomorrow? It'll be utter bile."

Janoah sucked her cheek, "More surmising?"

"I… calculate. It's what we do in this business, Janoah, as well you know."

"Fine, but what's the point, Vladimir?" Janoah sighed, with one paw gnarled. "How does turning opinion against the hyenas, who are banged up on Reservations I might add, help anyone rule Lupa? Tell me that, if you're so clever."

Vladimir attempted to do so. "Difficult times make strange bedfellows, Janoah. Even moderate hyenas may turn to violence under a harsher yoke. If the hyenas are sanctioned for this, and they will be, THORN will only grow stronger. Should they step-up their sabotaging of our railways and refineries, the venom shortage will only get worse, causing further disaffection amongst the wolf packs and helping the conspirators recruit venom-starved Howlers for an uprising. With one act of greed, Noss may have triggered the Republic's fall."

Janoah took a moment to consider Vladimir's hyperbole. "All right, I'm listening," she said, calm as you like. "Who are these so-called 'conspirators'?"

"You know one. Intimately."

Janoah stood, baffled and expectant, the faces of a dozen wolves whirring through her mind like a carousel. At length, a smiling Vladimir stepped close and put her out of her misery.

"Amael Balbus," he whispered to her.

Janoah recoiled. "Vladimir!" she spat, marching to the window in an exhibition of revulsion.

"Shocking isn't it?" Vladimir goaded, chasing after her, his muzzle close to her head. "Much like your acting! You need to work on that if we're to survive."

"Amael's no traitor!" Janoah snarled.

Vladimir pulled back and swirled his drink, "Humph! You mean our glorious leader has never once whispered his ambitions to you during those long, cold nights in your arms? I find that very hard to believe."

"Amael has ambitions like any wolf," Janoah hissed. "We all want to climb the slippery pole, everyone except my gallivanting husband, but there are acceptable ways these things are done. What you are accusing Amael of is high treason against the Republic!"

"Noss is his accuser, not I."

"Oh, a beast will say anything on the rack!"

Vladimir sniffed, "He wasn't on the rack. He whispered it in my ear, the life of his wife and cubs forfeit should he lie. I know you were watching me."

Silence, but for a ticking carriage clock.

"So why'd you hit him?" Janoah scoffed. "If you believed him then who was that for, me?"

"You're not the only actor on Lupa's sordid stage. Even the two Howlers in the room had to think I didn't believe a word Noss had told me; they could be Amael's spies for all I know."

Silence reigned for a long and prickly tenure, broken only by Vladimir supping his drink.

"If nothing else," he said at last, "had Noss killed Rufus, Amael would now have you all to himself at last. Oh, he can't marry you yet, but the marriage laws are unpopular and could be reversed someday." Vladimir raised his glass, "What more reason would he need? What more reason would you?"

"No!" Janoah spat. She looked down and around the room, at all Vladimir's nice things, but seeing none of them for her thoughts. She stared out the window again, but saw nothing of the world beyond either. "This can't be right. Amael knows Rufus is dear to me, despite everything. He would never…."

She stumbled to a silence, defeated.

"I didn't know!" Janoah growled anew. "I only laid with Amael in the first place to protect Rufus and get him his stupid expedition. One thing led to another and now he confides in me. It's true, he does talk treason, king this and emperor that, but I swear to Ulf, Vladimir, I am not part of any plot. I just humour him to get what I want. I… I had him down as an idle dreamer! All he does is bleat and moan about Vito. I've never seen him do anything concrete. Do you think I'd let him kill my Rufus? I love that wolf!"

Vladimir raised a paw to Janoah's panicked rant. "I believe you," he assured her. "Would you offer to lay with me to get Rufus a sting if you planned to kill him? You're good, but you're not that thorough, Valerio."

Valerio let out a sigh of relief and laughed a little, "The things I do for my fool of a husband."

"Indeed," Vladimir seconded. "Now, I suggest you start taking Amael's bleating seriously. He means to act. How and when I don't know, but something's afoot."

"I'm done with him."

"No. You must continue as you are and gather evidence against him. We both must."

Janoah whirled on Vladimir, "Are you mad? Let's go straight to ALPHA and expose his plot."

"What plot? We do not have any proof."

"They'll get a warrant to raid his offices. They'll turn up something."

"And if they don't we're finished!"

Janoah huffed, "Den Father Vito then. I know he's a mad old drooler, but he can still strip Amael of his position for any reason he sees fit."

"And how do you propose we get an audience with Vito without Amael or one of his spies hearing about it first? Noss saw dozens of wolves at the table, most of whom he didn't recognise. This conspiracy is already enormous. Besides, Amael's a hero, with an excellent record running Riddle, everyone respects him. Without hard evidence he would be believed over two ambitious nobodies and a mad hyena."

"A dead, mad hyena," Janoah added.

"Quite. If we break cover now and fail to make the charges stick, we will be snatched off the street one dark night and sent to the bottom of the Lupa."

Janoah ran a paw over her ruddy muzzle, "Then what do we do? Stand by and let them take over?"

Vladimir strolled around his room, equally flummoxed. "I don't know yet. I don't know who we can trust." He glanced sideways at his guest, "I don't even know if I can trust you."

"For Ulf's sake."

"You could crawl into Amael's arms and turn me in."

"What do you want me to say, Oromov?"

"Not say," Vladimir breathed, suggesting, "but perhaps you could let me in?"

"In? Into what?"

Oromov smirked, "You almost had me fooled, Janoah. Bruno must be something special for you to engineer his disappearance. Pure-blood is he? Yes, thought so. What're you and Josef planning? Are you two going to sell him to the highest bidder, or does the good doctor just want to experiment on him?"

Silence.

"Well?"

At last, Janoah raised her chin and said with a distinct smirk on her deceptively delicate muzzle, "I'll tell you… if you tell me what you're planning to do with old Nossypoos."

Vladimir actually laughed. "It appears, Janoah, that we're conjoined at the hip by our mutual need. Perhaps we should make the best of a bad situation?"

Slowly, Janoah turned and moseyed up to her fellow Grand Howler, cupping her paws over his cloaked chest. "Ever the pragmatist, aren't you Vladimir?"

"Humph!"

Peeling Vladimir's tumbler from his fingers, Janoah downed the remaining brandy in one impressive gulp and tossed it over her shoulder onto the sofa. Vladimir emitted a slight wolfen whine of alarm as his antique crystal glassware bounced precariously on the red pillows. Janoah unpinned Oromov's brooch and tossed that onto the sofa too, his imperium-weave mantle slipping away from his powerful, scarred shoulders that had seen many a battle and hardship. She kissed those old wounds, worked her way up his neck, up under his muzzle.

Finally, something snapped in the reserved Vladimir and he embraced Janoah by the dim glow of imperium light.

CHAPTER 14

Amael Balbus poured himself a stiff drink and stood before his plush office window. It was a snowy, early spring morning and Lupa's streets and spires were blanketed in white, looking cleaner and healthier for it. Just an illusion of course, beneath the pristine mask Lupa was still rotten, the streets piled high with garbage and ash. Just like the packs themselves – noble Howlers led by degenerates and fools who were outwardly respectable, but who embezzled money and laid with lowlifes. The well-being of the wolfen race was the last thing on most of their petty, disgusting minds.

One day I'll wash them all into the river, along with the rubbish. Lupa will be cleansed.

Brrrring! Brrrring!

Putting aside his drink and dreams, Amael grabbed the phone with a steel-grey paw. "Yes?" he grunted, before clearing his throat and saying more clearly, "What is it, Boris?"

"Grand Prefect Nikita's here to see you, sir," said his loyal adjutant,

Amael's scoffed, "Nikita?"

"From ALPHA, sir."

"Yes, yes, yes, but what does he want?" Amael snapped, then spoke quietly, "Is it about you know what-"

"No, sir," Boris interjected firmly. *"No, he's here with…. I'm sorry, what's your name, sir?"*

"Silvermane," someone crackled in the background.

Boris came back with, *"Grand Prefect Silvermane, sir."*

Amael's veins ran as cold as the frost painted on the windowpanes. Those thoughts trampled through his mind again, the ones that robbed him of sleep most nights.

The game's up. They're going to drag me out of here and throw me before the Den Fathers. Then I'll be executed in the manner reserved for treasonous Howlers; staked out alive in the wastes for the great ants to feast upon. Better to shoot yourself now, Amael, and take that intolerable ALPHA bastard with you whilst you're at it, the double-crossing son of a-

No! Calm down, it could be about anything. Right?

"Shall I send them through, sir?" Boris asked at length, like Amael had any choice in the matter, as if ALPHA's Grand Prefects hadn't the run of almost every Den in Lupa.

Amael recovered the power of speech, "Yes, yes of course. I'll meet them in the Elder Chamber."

"They're already on their way," Boris confirmed, as Nikita and Silvermane's boot steps squeaked into the distance. *"One more thing, sir. They want me to send for Valerio."*

Amael frowned, "Rufus?"

"Janoah, sir."

More thoughts. Has she betrayed me? Is she coming to denounce me? That bitch!

"What do you want me to do, sir?"

"Just… do whatever they want," Amael said with a gulp.

Boris sensed Amael's anxiety down the line. *"I'm sure it's nothing to do with… all that, sir,"* he whispered. *"There are no Prefects with them to make any arrests."*

Amael grunted, "There's time for some to arrive yet, Boris. Keep an eye out the window. If any ALPHA bikes pull up, let my phone ring twice and get out. Understood?"

"But if Nikita's here-"

"He'd betray us to save his own skin! Now go."

"Sir."

Setting down the phone with shaking paws, the Elder finished his drink in one gulp and grabbed his glorious silvery helmet from his armour stand. Looking in his ornate full-length mirror he adjusted his cloak and brooch and placed his helmet over his head. If he was going to fall, he was going to look noble one last time.

With a deep breath, Amael opened his desk drawer and took out a silver pistol – for himself.

Holstering it by his tail, he vacated his office and headed through Riddle Den. He had started a Howler and worked his way up to Elder in this miserable place, but was this as high as he was destined to climb? He had played the game, they all played the game, but few with stakes as high as Amael.

Through the waiting room he strode, exchanging worried looks with Boris keeping watch at the window, then down the long, grand corridor to the Elder Chamber, the silent paintings on the walls staring at him, their imperious eyes judging him down through the ages.

The long-cloaked Den Guards opened the chamber doors without provocation; the thought crossed Amael's mind that these same guards that had sworn to protect him might be tying his paws in a minute. It wouldn't be their fault, Amael told himself, they would just be doing their duty as you would.

Inside the chamber, sitting on the finest chair reserved for Den Father Vito's rare visits to Amael's district, with his legs up on the table just to add to the insult, was a huge wolf dressed entirely in black. Cloak, armour and helm, even the brooch, all of it was as black as black-imperium itself. Only the symbol etched into the brooch dared break rank; it was a stylised 'A' glowing white with that purest, most valuable form of imperium. What could be seen of the wolf's fur coat was mottled brown and white and heavily muscled, his two-toned arms home to enormous biceps.

"Grand Prefect Nikita," Amael said, saluting, fist to chest then out, albeit rather lacklustre.

"Elder Amael," Nikita replied, with but a wave. There was a distinct pause before he added, "This is Grand Prefect Silvermane."

Amael turned to the silver-furred fellow standing behind Nikita; he looked every bit the wolf in his prime as well – an imperium fuelled wolf, that is.

"Pleasure, Elder Amael," Silvermane said silkily.

After a nod, Amael dared ask, "What brings you to my district, Prefects?"

"I do not like to repeat myself, Amael," Nikita said, his thick, Great Steppes accent as warm and smooth as melted chocolate.

Wolves who had grown up on the Steppes and only later learnt Lupan tended to talk clearly, even deliberately, but often dropped connective words when speaking the official language of the Lupine Continent – Nikita was such a wolf.

"We wait for Grand Howler Janoah," he said. "Your adjutant, Boris, has gone to fetch her. I am sure they will be only minute or two. Then we talk."

A minute or two that felt an eternity to Amael, who wandered over to the nearest window, paws behind back, and looked out over ice-bound Lupa.

"Rather nippy out there isn't it?" Silvermane observed brightly, as if this were but a cordial visit.

"Yes," Amael replied flatly.

It was rather nippy in here too, but Amael had no intention of breaking the ice by offering the likes of ALPHA a drink.

"No bombings of late?" Silvermane went on. "No Howler-killers brought to justice?"

"No. Been quiet for months."

"Indeed. You've an excellent record for keeping order in your district, Elder Amael. The Alpha himself commends you."

Amael almost snarled, 'The Alpha himself commends me? Who does he think he is, Ulf?' but somehow contained his fury at being patronised. "I've some of the finest wolves in Lupa under me," he said. "Commend them."

"Indeed," Silvermane agreed. "Though, unhappily we're here to steal one of your number away."

Both relieved and alarmed by the comment, Amael turned to face Silvermane. Before he could ask who the unlucky Howler was, the Elder Chamber doors opened and a ruddy-furred wolfess entered, saluting everyone.

Of course, Janoah! ALPHA's come for her because of Rufus, because she's been skimming imperium off the top for that degenerate. I warned her, the foolish wolfess!

Silvermane reached into his black cloak and produced a small brown envelope. This was it, the warrant. Amael looked at Janoah, but she just stared impassively ahead. There was nothing even an Elder like Amael could do for her now, ALPHA was immune to interference, only the Den Fathers themselves were above their scrutiny, only they could quash their accusations regardless of evidence.

"By the power vested in my mantle by the Republic of Lupa," the fine-voiced Silvermane declared, passing across the letter, "I hereby accept you into ALPHA, the Agency for Lupan Peace and Howler Accountability." Stepping back and raising a paw to his chest, as if waving, he added, "Congratulations, Prefect Captain Janoah."

Janoah saluted, fist to chest then out. "Thank you, Grand Prefect Silvermane," she said, and to Nikita, "Grand Prefect Nikita."

Nikita merely raised a paw. "Use the ALPHA salute from now on, Prefect."

Janoah did so, raising her paw smartly.

Amael stood dumbfounded at the display of treachery for some seconds before he squawked at Janoah, "Prefect?"

She corrected him, "Prefect Captain, sir."

Grand Prefect Silvermane walked around the arc-shaped Elder table, "Valerio has proven herself a Howler of rare wit and guile, Amael, and it's been decided that she can best serve the whole of Lupa working for ALPHA. It'll be a blow to the Bloodfangs to lose so dedicated a Howler, but as a Prefect she will now strive to root out the decay that gnaws at the heart of every pack and so serve us all."

The insolent Nikita at last removed his black-armoured legs from the table and joined Silvermane. He patted Amael on the shoulder with a big mottled paw, "It is your choice how you fill her position, though Red-mist comes to mind as Grand Howler material, no?"

The confused Amael scoffed angrily, "Rufus?"

"Is long-overdue," Nikita said in his broken dialect. "Of course, this is your district, it is none of my business." With a mere raise of the paw, he moseyed casually on, heading for the door, paws behind his back. "Silver."

Nodding, Silvermane beckoned Janoah, "This way, Prefect."

"May I have a moment, sir?" Janoah asked her new boss, adding, "To… say goodbye to my comrades."

"Take all the time you need," Silvermane assured, paw rising one more time. "We'll be in the car."

Janoah 'saluted' back.

Once the old Prefects had gone, Amael almost leapt on the new one. "What is this?" he snarled in disbelief, though still keeping is voice in check lest Nikita or Silvermane were listening through the door. "You've betrayed us. You've betrayed *me*."

A suddenly bold Janoah waved a paw, "My dear Amael, I'm helping you."

"Helping me?"

"Yes! If I'd betrayed you, you'd be in Howler-wire by now, silly wolf," Janoah chirped patronisingly, as if Amael ought to understand at a stroke. She wandered over to the Elder table and ran her finger along it, "With my new powers as a Prefect Captain I'll be able to cross districts and dominions with impunity. Just think of all the information I will glean working for ALPHA, think of the obstacles I can remove."

Amael let out a snort of amazement; he never knew Janoah had it in her!

Janoah looked around the Elder Chamber. "I'll miss Riddle Den," she hummed, her green eyes settling on Amael, "Give Rufus my old position. He deserves it."

"You're joking!" Amael blustered without delay.

"Do that for him," Janoah insisted, walking over to Amael knotting her arms about his neck, "No, do it for me, and I'll do everything I can for you from within ALPHA."

Silence prevailed.

"But I thought… I thought that you… we…." Amael trailed off and looked down.

"I *do* love you," Janoah professed. "It's because I love you and share your vision that I must do this. If you want to save Lupa you need beasts everywhere working for you. You have to be a spider in a web; a web we'll build together, so that when the time comes we can snare all the flies."

"But you'll not be nearby," the Elder said, walking to and fro. "We'll not be able to lay together and talk of our plans like we do. Who will I turn to?"

Janoah took one of his paws, "A small sacrifice now for glory later, my dear."

Amael could but grumble wolfen sounds.

"I'll visit you," Janoah assured him. "I'll have to see Rufus after all; in fact he's the perfect premise for me to come here without arousing suspicion. He's my husband, nobody can stop my coming and going, and if they do get suspicious they will look into Rufus and find he knows nothing he shouldn't know, for I'll not tell him." The new Prefect chuckled and tickled Amael's chin, "But you? I'll bring you a wealth of intelligence. You'll have all the dirt you need. Which Elder embezzled money, which Elder skimmed imperium, which Elder laid with whom. With such a treasure trove of filth you can force them over a barrel and attain their vote when the time comes to elect the next Den Father of the Bloodfangs. Vito's old and mad; he'll not last much longer. And if he lingers too long, well, we'll just have to give him a push, that's all."

Nodding continuously throughout Janoah's words, Amael let this new reality sink in, drop by drop. He closed his eyes and let out a slightly giddy laugh. "Janoaaaah," he growled happily, clasping her hips. "By Ulf, you're ingenious! I didn't realise you were so committed."

"Lately I've come to believe in you. In us, even. Let's make a go of it, you and I."

Amael marvelled, "But how'd you do it?"

"Do what?"

"Get to be a Prefect Captain. What did you do to secure such a high post?" Amael's jaw dropped, "You didn't… you didn't give yourself to that arrogant dog Nikita."

"Hah!" Janoah laughed. "From what I hear I don't think he'd be that interested in me."

"Well what then?"

Thinking, Janoah walked her fingers up Amael's chest and slipped it under his helmet to feel his cheek. "Let's just say I sent something along to ALPHA a few months ago, something more valuable than myself."

"Something you don't want to tell me?" Amael growled.

"It's a trifle complicated, and I have to go," Janoah assured, changing subject. "May I suggest one more thing before I love and leave you, Amael?"

"If you must go," he said sadly.

"Look after my boys."

"Boys?"

"You know who I mean. Treat them with respect and they'll never let you down, whatever path you take."

✦

Silvermane barely looked up from his files as the smartly-dressed hog driver climbed out the sleek, black motor carriage and opened the back door. The newly-minted Prefect Janoah slipped onto the plush seat opposite her boss, along with a swirl of icy winter's breath and a snowflake or two.

"Grand Prefect," she said with a shiver; she was either cold, or a little nervous in Silvermane's presence.

"All done?" he said cordially, trying to dispel any fears.

"Yes, sir."

Not even looking up from his papers, Silvermane waved his pen at the looming Den, "Don't worry about your belongings. We'll send someone to clear out your office and quarters and have it moved to ALPHA HQ."

Janoah nodded; in the excitement of the moment she had utterly overlooked that prosaic detail. "Much obliged," she said, not letting on.

She watched Silvermane flick through documents and sign his name at speed; search warrants, arrest warrants, recommendations, anything and everything that passed the desk of a Grand

Prefect.

"Where's Grand Prefect Nikita?" Janoah asked.

"Spending a penny," Silvermane replied. "How'd Rufus take the news?" he asked.

Surprised at the personal enquiry, Janoah kneaded her paws and admitted, "I don't know, sir. I left Elder Amael to inform my comrades."

This provoked a reaction, enough for Silvermane to look up from his work, his eyes shining from under his jet-black helmet. "Even Rufus?"

A nod.

"But… he's your husband."

"It's merely a professional relationship," Janoah claimed, looking up at the snow-flecked Den. "He does his thing, and I do mine. It's been that way for years." After a brief pause she added, "With his latest fixation he will hardly notice my absence."

Silvermane sniffed, "I see."

Janoah shuffled in the seat and crossed her legs, "Forgive me, Grand Prefect, I forget myself. Though no doubt you're aware of his leanings."

Silvermane nodded. "In all things," he said, with a sharp intake of breath. "Even so, you should cherish one another whilst you can. You're one of the lucky Howler couples who married before the law, that's not something to throw away lightly."

"Rufus threw it away long ago, sir," Janoah said, flashing a quick, false smile.

"Mm."

Suddenly the car door opened and Grand Prefect Nikita slipped into the front. "Is cold, no?" he woofed affably at Janoah and Silvermane, before addressing the hog at the wheel beside him, "Let's go, comrade hog."

The trembling ALPHA limo pulled away and the Den that Janoah had called home for most of her Howler life slipped from sight.

Part II
EISENWOLF

Adam Browne

Diary Excerpt 1

Apparently it's Uther's birthday! Well, what he decided was his birthday. Being orphaned so young, he doesn't know the actual date. He faintly remembers opening a present one frosty morning around Wintertide. It was a scarf, in which case it could just as well be a Wintertide gift as a birthday present. We may never know.

I do know his 'hyena name' is also a fiction; that's nine months he had me going. Nine months! Captain Ivan finally took pity and set me straight. He says the aforementioned scarf had Uther W. sewn onto it, that's all the information the orphanage had when they took him in, and all the Bloodfang Academy knew later. Ivan says Uther invented Wild-heart to impress Lorna and Rosalina one evening and that it's certainly nothing to do with hyenas. The late Prince Noss bestowed 'Blade-dancer' on Ivan and 'Red-mist' on Rufus during their time together, as only a hyena prince can. If Lorna and Rosa know the truth they haven't let on. I think Uther assumes I know by now. If I bring it up he'll say I was a fool for believing him in the first place. After nine months working together I'm beginning to know how he'd spin it.

Still, everyone calls him Wild-heart, even Vladimir when growling after him down Riddle Den's corridors. I guess it's stuck, rather like my moniker. I get Woodlouse, Uther gets Wild-heart, and his last two partners were dubbed Dusty and Smiles; all I can say is it's a good thing he's not a hyena prince.

Rufus has invited me to the Arkady Symposium next week; all the most eminent scientists and intellectuals are going to be there, including the great Heath himself. Rufus keeps meaning to introduce us. My stomach is already a flutter at the prospect of going; I'm just not good at social gatherings! The only public places where I'm truly at ease are patrolling Riddle's streets with Uther and the Den gymnasium. I've nearly reached 175lbs! Uther's impressed. I'll never be a sprinter like him, but I can get stronger. I must.

Didn't need a sting last week, but feeling weary. Awful weather out. Hoping for a quiet shift.

Howler Linus Bloodfang Mills

Chapter 15

"In the name of the Republic, throw down your weapons and come out with your paws up!"

Linus waited by the wide open doorway, shoulder to the wall, shield at his back, pistol held low in both paws. The relentless Lupan drizzle patted on his helmet and dripped off its grille.

No response was forthcoming.

The blonde wolf looked across to the duotone Uther, who stood on the opposite side of the doorway with his back to the rough redbrick wall, ember smouldering between lips. He wasn't wearing his helmet, but he was sporting that crooked smile, the one he always wore whenever he was in the midst of a mission.

Linus nervously shuffled his feet then shouted through the doorway, "Citizens, if you release the hostages and come out you'll not be harmed! I'm sure nobody here wishes there to be any unnecessary-"

Crack! Crack! Crack!

Several bright sparks exploded around the doorframe as the beasts inside took pot-shots at the Howlers. Linus flinched and hunched his shoulders, whilst Uther hardly batted an eyelid and returned fire.

Crack!

Nervously resetting his helmet, Linus sniffed, "I don't think they're minded to cooperate."

"Puh! Hyenas dunno the meaning of the word," Uther snorted, flicking away his half-spent ember and ripping open a paper pistol cartridge with his teeth. He poured the glittering powder charge into his pistol chamber.

"Keep your powder dry," Linus advised, looking up at the grey, impenetrable firmament hanging low over Lupa.

The soaked Uther spat his pellet down the barrel and rammed it home with a, "Hah! Will do Woodlouse."

Werner Schwartz strode round the corner of the heavily ash-stained, industrial building, looking like a blimp under a tarpaulin with his tent-like rain cloak.

"My boys have got the place covered," the Politzi Chief reported confidently, whilst strolling carelessly around, head craning to look up at the refinery's towering smoke stacks. "Nobody's getting out of there ali-"

Suddenly, Uther grabbed the neck of Werner's uniform and yanked him clear of the door.

Crack!

A tiny, colourful explosion took a chunk out of the already blasted ground, leaving a smouldering crater right where Werner had been standing.

"Mind the door, mate," Uther chided, patting the pig on his flabby pink cheek

The flustered Werner cleared his throat and straightened his hat. "Hyena bastards," he grunted, loosening the collar of his suddenly stifling uniform. "My boys are ready and waiting," he growled. "Just give the word and we'll wipe 'em out!"

"Lead the charge will yer?" Uther laughed.

"Aye, I will!"

Linus raised a paw. "Steady on, Constable Schwartz," he cautioned. "Let's not escalate the situation."

Werner composed himself, "Right you are, Howler."

"We need the terrorists alive to interrogate them. This is the third refinery to be targeted by THORN in a month. We must find out what they're up to."

Werner sniffed officiously, "Aye, of course, but it's better to shoot 'em than let 'em escape; them's Elder Amael's standing orders-"

"Until we're relieved by a superior, Uther and I are in charge here," Linus explained patiently, if firmly, "and we want no unnecessary casualties. Better to let a few escape and catch some alive than none at all. Right Uther?"

Uther just nodded and sniffed.

"Besides, they have hostages," Linus tacked on. "We must be cautious."

"Aye, Howler Mills," Werner said, "but the last few times someone cornered these fanatics they all committed suicide anyway."

"Yes, I know," Linus said.

"They all swallowed black-imperium capsules," Werner went on. "Worst case of the rot you'll ever see. Couldn't go near 'em for contamination, not that you'd want to! Like burnt corpses they were; all black and twisted."

Linus gulped, "Indeed."

Uther pushed off the wall and holstered his pistol. "We can't wait any longer," he said, donning his helmet and strapping it in place, "You two to keep the bastards busy. Start negotiating or somethin'."

Linus and Werner exchanged glances before turning their combined gaze on the third party.

"What're you gonna do, sir?" Werner asked for both.

"Have a pog inside," Uther replied.

Linus seethed, "You can't go in there alone!"

"I'm just gonna snoop around," Uther tutted innocently, looking up at the roof for some reason. He rolled his muscled shoulders and kicked his armoured legs, loosening his limbs for the task. "You just said we gotta find out what they're up to, didn't you, Woodlouse?"

"Yes, but-"

"Well then, let me go put my ear to the ground before things get messy."

"Uther-"

Too late. With a grunt and a growl, Uther leapt at the wall and sprinted up its face! Werner's hat was punched clean off his head as a wobbling blast of invisible imperious energy chased Wildheart up the building, aiding his impossible ascent and carving a void in the falling rain. Grasping the lip of the roof, Riddle District's most athletic Howler vaulted up and over, disappearing from sight without so much as a wave to his comrades.

"How does he do that?" Linus snorted, looking enviously up the three or four story high building. "I-I can barely manage a fence."

Werner retrieved his hat from a colourful, imperium-laced puddle and flicked it off. "Maybe, Howler Linus, sir, but we're the heavy-duty sort, me and you," the massive hog claimed, slapping his gut. "We're built for a fair fight."

The barrel-chested Linus felt he was a far-cry from the barrel-bellied Werner, but, ever-polite, he changed subject sooner than point out the obvious differences in their physiques. "Have you telephoned HQ?"

"Yes, Howler. Vladimir's on his way with reinforcements."

"And Rufus?"

Werner shrugged, "I didn't ask. He's probably away."

"All right," Linus breathed, looking back at the many nervous Politzi officers of various races taking cover behind boxes and barrels, imperium pistols loaded and authorised for use. Linus hoped things didn't come to that, because the war-like hyenas would take a fair few Politzi with them. "Well, we had better negotiate then," Linus declared. "Do we have an expert negotiator?"

Politzi Constable Werner Schwartz smiled and proudly tipped his hat back, "You're looking at one, Howler."

"You?"

"I used to be something of a public speaker, yer know. Just give me a soapbox and a trumpet."

✦

Passing between the ash stacks that were still belching imperium waste of some kind or another into the smoggy Lupan sky, Uther opened a metal trapdoor and slowly poked his head inside the refinery roof.

He saw a ladder leading down onto a metal walkway, and beyond that a great twisting maze of pipes and churning machinery. It sounded noisy down there, which meant the hyenas wouldn't hear Uther sneaking about; the ambient imperium would also mask his corona.

With a last visual check for the enemy, Wild-heart slid down the ladder and ducked into the shadows. He crept along the walkway, using pipes and vats and Ulf knows what for cover, until he spied something of interest down below.

Standing in a clearing amongst the colourful tangle of tubes and trembling dials was an unusually muscular hyena addressing a little band of skinnier comrades. His massive, sandy-furred, spotty shoulders were turned to Uther, paws cupped neatly behind him. He wore nothing from the waist up, but his legs were encased in armour of a striking black and white zigzag design; geometric, abstract squiggles were typical of hyena art. Uther judged from his impressive build that he was a Chakaa, like that prince had been. No hyena grew that big just by eating all his greens, or bugs, or whatever they ate; he was on stings.

The lesser hyenas hanging on the Chakaa's every word were incongruously dressed in a mix of civilised clothes and traditional hyena ornament. Breeches and open waistcoats jostled with bandanas and necklaces strung with claws, horns and iridescent bits of carapace taken from various beetles and other bugs, whilst their stocky bodies and grim faces were painted white, like a hyena skull. They all held spears, some stood proud, others leant on them, as if bored. The spears were tipped with sharp and poisonous yellow-imperium. Strange. It must be stabilised, or else it would be fizzling away, Uther supposed. He also supposed they had stolen it from the Greystones, since only they knew how to fix yellow-imperium. Some hyenas nursed pistols too, though not many. Uther calculated most of the terrorists armed with pistols were posted at the entrances to hold the Politzi at bay.

As the Howler looked on, a second outsized hyena approached the gathering. He was taller than the apparent leader and generally bigger. His legs were housed in the same black and white armour, but of a labyrinthine design of right-angled twisting lines instead of lightning-like zigzags.

Two imperium-guzzling hyenas in one place? This is getting interesting.

The taller Chakaa donned a black helmet embossed with a white skull design – something of a step-up from the skull face-paint employed by the others. The shorter leader faced the taller newcomer and Uther caught a glimpse of his typically thickset hyena face just before he too donned his own skull-themed helmet.

He had striking purple eyes!

There was only one way a beast's eyes turned purple and that was by taking purple-imperium. It was potent stuff, which went to most beasts' heads, sending them insane.

Deciding he had to get closer, Uther crept along the walkway and down some metallic steps, until he was on the ground floor. He relied on his eyes to spot danger, his ears being inhibited by the churning machinery and his coronal senses the polluted atmosphere.

Pipes hummed and vats bubbled in front of Uther as hot, liquid imperium was separated into its constituent grades by a noisy centrifuge spinning overhead, one of several dotted throughout the place. As far as Wild-heart understood from basic imperiology classes foisted on him and every Howler back in academy, each grade of imperium had a different density. Thus, in a spinning centrifuge, light white rose to the top, heavy black sank to the bottom and the rest gathered in layers somewhere in-between to be skimmed off into an appropriately-coloured vat, white first. The dreaded black-imperium remained inside the centrifuge until last, whereupon it was flushed out into special canisters and put aside for disposal in a pit somewhere.

Therein lay a mystery; according to recent briefs by Vladimir, THORN had only been stealing black-imperium canisters, not the valuable white. What for? Were they going to make a dirty bomb? Poison Lupa's water supply? When? How?

Whilst Uther watched and contemplated, the taller of the Chakaa hyenas walked over to a drain cover and lifted it off. He was so strong he set it aside like a dustbin lid.

For a second he looked in Uther's direction, his purple-tinged eyes seemingly piercing through the bubbling vats of imperium into the wolf hiding in the shadows.

Uther didn't move a muscle.

The big Chakaa carried on with his business. He climbed into the hole and a couple of other hyenas, ordinary beasts not nearly as strong, used a rope to pass down a spherical, metal canister stencilled with a black X and multiple warnings.

Black-imperium and no mistake.

Wild-heart watched the lethal black-imperium being gently lowered, canister after spherical canister. Most buildings didn't have a sewer system big enough to crawl down, but here, well, all that pipe-clogging ash from the furnaces had to go somewhere, straight down the tubes and into the River Lupa

The biggest hyena climbed back out of the drain; his coarse spotty fur and admittedly beautiful labyrinthine armour streaked with ash – filthy business, crime. To Uther's surprise, a *third* Chakaa climbed out of the drain. He was shorter than either of the other two afflicted hyenas, but built like a wall – rather like Linus, Uther thought, if Linus was a dirty hyena. The third fellow's armour was decorated with a swirling, wind-like design of black and white lines. These Chakaa had access to some nifty kit.

The three leaders chatted merrily away. What were they planning? Uther couldn't hear.

Suddenly the Chakaa stood alert, rounded ears pricked. It took a moment to tune in, but Uther heard it too – someone was shouting outside the refinery.

It was Werner, his voice magnified by a trumpet!

"Now now, let's not be silly, lads," he crackled, in his friendly, pat-about-the-shoulders manner. *"I know things ain't so dandy between you n' the wolves, but I'm a hog! I understand your pain, your pride. My people, we don't have no country of our own neither, but we rub along, we do. You have to learn to compromise in this life, you know? Lupa is built on sacrifice and cooperation. You don't have to be left out, if you don't want. You can join in our family. Me and you, let's talk this over, my fellow rootless friends. Send a representative out and let's come to an agreement. We'll give you asylum in our fair city. What do you say?"*

Nice speech, Uther thought, for a pig copper.

The three Chakaa in skull helmets shared a brief discussion, then the taller one and the shorter one beckoned some of their hyena comrades to join them. They strode swiftly out of sight, leaving what Uther assumed was the leader and the majority behind to continue their work. Perhaps the other two were going to negotiate with Werner? Or else chuck an imperium-tipped spear in his gob. Either scenario suited Uther provided there were fewer sets of eyes to dodge whilst he located the hostages.

With that in mind, Uther stole away from the pipes and turned to climb the stairs he had descended.

"Oof!"

Bumping snout-first into a hard, furry torso, a wall of rippling muscle and sinew, Uther caught a glimpse of a skull and purple eyes before a massive fist came in from the side and clouted him round the side of the head.

Uther's world exploded as a blast of plasma flashed over his helmet. The eisenglanz dulled the imperious energy, but the punch still knocked him for six.

"Gagh!"

Two powerful paws picked Uther up by his cloaked shoulders and hurled him against the corroded pipes. He slammed into them with a loud clang, his back and shoulders absorbing the worst of the blow. One of the pipes burst and hot, red-imperium vapour spurted in all directions, enveloping Uther in a hot, bloody cloud.

Overcoming the pain and confusion, Wild-heart instinctively brought his pistol to bear on his hazy attacker.

Crack!

His pistol was slapped aside and he received a second plasmatic punch, this time to the ribs. Then those big paws grabbed him again and ejected him headlong from the choking imperium vapours. Uther stumbled and slid across the smooth concrete floor, winded, ribs throbbing.

Coughing and spluttering, a bruised Uther reached for his kristahl swords and made to rise, to fight, or escape, but half a dozen glowing, yellow-imperium-tipped spears descended upon him from all directions, each one held by a ferocious, skeletal-faced hyena. They stopped short of running Uther through, but one or two pressed uncomfortably close, pinning Wild-heart to the cold floor, chest heaving, body aching, yellow-imperium reflecting on his chin.

Some of the hyenas parted, allowing a much larger fellow into the circle of spears. It was the tallest of the three Chakaa that Uther had been spying on, the one with the labyrinthine armour. The impressive beast looked down on him with his purple eyes, his face masked by a skull helmet, one rounded-off ear glinting with decorative studs – his mighty body was home many such piercings.

"I thought I saw a roach hiding here," he spat.

That shorter, burly Chakaa joined the circle, "What now, Themba?"

"My hammer, Madou."

The biggest Chakaa held out a paw and his shorter comrade passed him said hammer. Not some little tool for knocking nails in, but a war hammer as nearly tall as he. The simple, cylindrical head was the size of a brick and had the telltale cold, oily sheen of high quality kristahl.

The powerful hyena hefted his hammer in both paws and casually positioned its head over Uther's, taking aim, before swinging it high above him like a railroad worker preparing to knock in a peg.

"For murdering our prince," he declared, "and suppressing my people, I sentence you to death, Howler!"

"Wait a minute!" Uther yelped.

No use, the Chakaa followed through with his mighty swing.

"Themba!" someone cracked, coarse and sharp, their voice tearing the air like a thunderclap.

A fraction later and the deafening knell of kristahl striking concrete exploded just left of Uther's head, its metallic, corona-bending pulse reverberating in his chest and jolting every fibre of his being with involuntary terror. Breathing hard, Wild-heart opened his eyes. The hammer's head lay nestled beside him, plasma still playing over its glittering kristahl surface, the pale concrete floor shattered in a spider-web pattern around it.

"Schmutz," Uther mouthed.

The big Chakaa slowly withdrew his hammer, scraping its smouldering head along the floor, and looked across at whom had addressed him.

Gulping, the reprieved Uther followed suit.

It was THORN's probable leader. He walked over to the group, paws tucked behind back, zigzag-patterned, eisenglanz-clad legs rattling. "Calm yourself, Themba," he chided in that bristly voice.

"But Nurka-"

"I'm not a barbarian! Are you?"

Themba let out an annoyed grunt and replied in his velvety, yet cavernous tenor, "It would have been a quick death. Better than they gave our prince."

"Justice will be done," this Nurka assured simply. "Their time will come."

Big Themba bowed his head a little, "Chief."

Nurka looked down at Uther with just his purple eyes, his face unreadable behind his skull helmet. "Are there any other Redcoats scuttling around here, Howler?" he asked. "I know you Howlers work in pairs."

"You're surrounded, mate," Uther managed to growl. "If you give up now, we'll go easy on yer."

"Is that right?" Nurka said.

"You bet your spotty arse it is, skull-face."

Unable to abide such an insult to his leader, the shorter Chakaa wearing the swirling leg-armour kicked Uther in the side. "Wolfen scum! You're addressing a chieftain!"

"Madou!" Nurka snapped at him, purple eyes wide. "You disgrace yourself!"

The stocky Madou backed off, ears low with shame.

Satisfied, Nurka looked across at Themba, then down at Uther, "Do this… comedian no serious harm, but send the Howlers a message, one that will convince them to think twice before sending another fool in here."

"Yes, chief," Themba acknowledged.

Nurka looked to Madou, "Search the building. If you find anyone bring them to me."

Madou nodded, "Chief."

Once Nurka and Madou had departed, the latter taking half the hyenas with him to search the refinery, big Themba growled at his remaining compatriots, "Get him up."

The lesser hyenas descended on Uther, a scrum of paws, arms and elbows, pulling him to his feet. The odd punch to the ribs and kidneys was surreptitiously snuck in, but Uther didn't give them the satisfaction of a response.

Held firm, the wolf was relieved of his swords and his paws forced behind his back. Someone bound them with wire, wrapping it around Uther's wrists and twisting it off. Howler-wire? It appeared this lot knew what calibre of beast they were dealing with, they knew Howlers could scorch mere ropes away in a second.

Themba stepped up to Uther, proving he was more than a head taller. Grabbing the back of the wolf's helmet with a big paw he ripped it off without unfastening the chin strap, which scraped painfully along Uther's jaw, pulling out some white fur as it went.

Uther emitted a snarl of pain, and the hyenas laughed at his expense – save Themba that is.

The big hyena took a step back, armour and decorative piercings tinkling. Dropping Uther's helmet on the ground like a tin can he smashed it in with his mighty hammer. Sparks of plasma played over the metal and the fang-shaped red-imperium décor beneath the eyelets flashed one last time, before fading for good.

Uther's nostrils flared with rage; his precious eisenglanz helmet, with which he had suffered through so much pain and toil, was no more. It's just an object, he tried to tell himself, don't let it get to you. That's what he wants.

Themba drew a short, kristahl sword from a scabbard nestled inside his right thigh plate and ran it up inside the prisoner's mantle. Uther tipped his head back to avoid the deadly blade as it popped out the neck of his red cloak, which made the lesser hyenas laugh and snort again.

Themba tugged his blade violently upwards, cutting through the tough imperium-weave and causing Uther's brooch to ping off like one of Werner's brass buttons during the annual Wintertide Riddle Den dinner. The brooch rolled away into the darkness and lost its sparkle, whilst Uther's cloak hung limply around his shoulders in tatters, before Themba ripped it away altogether, leaving only Wild-heart's many-buttoned red tunic.

Staring always at Uther with those purple eyes, Themba threw the torn mantle on the floor and wiped his ash-stained feet on the very symbol of the Bloodfangs.

Uther lunged forward, "You son of a maggot, I'll-!"

Themba instantly punched him on the snout, not a plasmatic punch, just an ordinary one. Even so it was like being cuffed by a bear and Uther would've fallen on his tail but for the other hyenas holding him aloft.

Spitting blood from a split lip and throbbing nose, Uther righted himself. "I'll have you," he spat, chin high.

Satisfied he had teased a rise from the stoic wolf, Themba gathered up Uther's ruined cloak and helmet, "Take him; I'll deliver our message."

✦

Werner stood atop a box at the gates to the refinery's grounds, brass speaking-trumpet held to snout. Fellow Politzi were stationed either side of him and at every exit. Several painted hyenas peered curiously back over boxes and barrels from inside the complex. No pistol could shoot this far, at least not with anything approximating accuracy, so both THORN and Politzi were quite safe, though only the terrorists were warm and dry in their makeshift fortress.

"Do you have any demands?" Werner shouted, rain dripping off his cap and trumpet. "Money? I can do money. Transport? I can arrange it. I'm the Politzi Chief of this whole district, it's no problem. Just come on out and we'll talk over a nice, cold beer."

Silence.

"You hyenas like beer, doncha?"

The hooded Linus looked up at the hog, "I don't think you're getting through to them, Werner."

"No, sir," he freely admitted. "They're fanatics."

"They may not understand much Lupan."

"Reason is lost on 'em, sir," the portly Werner assured, before speaking amiably into the trumpet again. "Do you have a leader? Can we speak to him?"

"Or perhaps her?" Linus suggested.

Werner gave the stout Howler a double-glance, "Her?"

A nod, a stammer, "Hyenas are m-mmm-matriarchal. The females are in charge; males are subservient."

"Really? Huh! I never knew that."

"It still depends somewhat on rank. The matriarchs have consistently denounced THORN, though without a queen amongst them it seems nobody is paying them any mind."

"Queen, sir?"

Linus spread a paw, "The hyenas have queens, but no kings; just princes of the blood that are allowed to sire a queen's cubs. But there are no royal hyenas left amongst the tribes. Their last queen died lately and her only serious heir, Princess Arjana Jua-mata, is still missing, along with the cubs that the late Prince Noss fathered."

Werner snorted, "Arjana Jua-whata?"

"Jua-mata. It's a tribe."

"Huh! You're a wellspring of knowledge, sir."

"It springs from Rufus, originally," Linus admitted. "Anyway, keep talking. As long as they're looking at us they won't be looking for Uther. He's sure taking his time."

Even as he spoke, Linus's attention was drawn behind by the popping engines of several monobikes and an imposing motorised carriage, all marked up in Bloodfang livery. After waiting for the Politzi to let them through, they headed for the refinery gates and parked up nearby.

"That'll be Grand Howler Vladimir," Linus said, with a slightly nervous sigh. "Keep trying," he told Werner, hurrying over to the motorcade.

"Will do," the pig saluted.

The car door opened and Grand Howler Vladimir emerged in his white cloak and silver armour. Pocketing his golden pen and throwing a file on the back seat, he nodded at the saluting Linus and asked, "What's the situation, Mills?"

Linus explained, "Hyenas thought to be from THORN have taken over the refinery, sir. They've a few dozen hostages-"

"Yes, I'm aware of that. What've you done about it?"

"Werner has the refinery surrounded, Grand Howler."

"By Politzi?"

"Yes, sir."

One of the Howlers accompanying Vladimir passed him his silver helmet and he carefully, even reverently, slipped it over his black and white face. "No other Howlers at your disposal, Linus?"

"No, sir," he replied, looking at the reinforcements. "Uther and I were the only ones here, until now."

"And where *is* Uther, dare I ask?"

Linus hesitated a moment, "He went inside, sir."

"Inside?"

"Scouting, sir. I'm sure he'll be back any minute."

Vladimir grunted disapprovingly, "Humph."

Linus thought he should explain, "As you know, Grand Howler, these THORN militants have a record of killing themselves to avoid capture. So Uther and I thought maybe we could find something out before the… uh…."

"The inevitable insane climax?"

"I suppose so, sir."

Vladimir squinted across at Werner, "What in Ulf's name is that cretin doing up there?"

Linus glanced over, "N-nnn-negotiating, sir."

Vladimir actually guffawed, "Negotiating! Don't be ridiculous. Get him down at once."

"Y-y-yes, sir."

Whilst Linus hurried off to coax Werner down from his soapbox, Vladimir was joined by a member of his motorcade, a tall white wolf in black Howler uniform.

"Permission to go in, sir," he said hopefully.

"Denied, Donskoy."

"But Uther-"

"Is big and ugly enough to look after himself," Vladimir interjected, before soothing Ivan's ego, "I don't want both Riddle's best wolves traipsing around in there when I may need you out here at any moment."

Ivan parleyed, "Well, at least let me scout the perimeter and get a feel for the situation, sir."

This Vladimir allowed – he had to let Ivan do something, if only to shut him up.

Despite being soaked to the bone from riding his beautiful black Giacomo Valerio *Spider* all the way from Riddle Den, Captain Ivan still pulled his hood up to guard against the rain, or perhaps just to look even more menacing. Vladimir watched the black-clad white wolf join Linus and Werner just inside the refinery grounds. After a brief exchange, Ivan moved on, disappearing amongst ore silos and outbuildings controlled by the Politzi.

Ivan hadn't long gone when a brown-furred Politzi rabbit bounded across the road towards Vladimir with something in his paws.

"Grand Howler Vladimir!" he gasped, nearly tripping over in his haste.

"Yes, Claybourne, what is it?"

"Sir!" the rabbit said, respectfully holding forth a bundle of red cloth, as if it were an orphaned baby.

Vladimir barely looked at it, "What've you got there?"

"The terrorists… threw it off the roof at us, sir," the Politzi explained, amidst an ill-timed gulp. "It's a Howler's Helmet and mantle, sir; all banged up it is."

Now he had Vladimir's attention. The Grand Howler took the bundle and opened it up. Inside was a mangled grey Helmet with white cheeks. It looked like it had been run over by a car.

"We think it's Trooper Uther's, sir," the rabbit said.

Nodding, Vladimir looked across at the smoking refinery. "Was there a message?" he asked.

"No, sir."

"Nothing?"

"No, sir. No sign of Howler Uther either, sir."

"I see."

"What do we do, sir?"

"Not much we can do, constable. Let's just hope they killed him quickly."

Linus hurried over; Vladimir presented the sad bundle to him. Even with his face obscured by his helmet, one could sense a change come over Howler Mills as he recognised the equipment. After an eternity of staring, he took the red cloak and helm in his trembling golden fingers.

"It's Uther's," Vladimir explained.

Shaking his head a little, Linus looked around, searching for the wolf himself. "I don't understand, sir."

"The hyenas threw that off the roof, I'm told," Vladimir explained. "We don't yet know what's become of Uther. Do we Constable Claybourne?"

Surprised to be consulted, the Politzi rabbit took a while to respond, "Uh, no sir."

"But we can guess," Vladimir sighed, cupping a paw to Linus's shoulder and saying again, "I'm sorry."

Squirming free of Vladimir's conciliatory paw, Linus growled, "Don't say that!"

Under the strenuous circumstances, Vladimir allowed his subordinate's terse response to go unchecked.

In desperation, Linus searched inside the folds of Uther's cloak. Putting the smashed helmet down, he opened the torn, muddied cloak.

"What're you doing, Mills?" Vladimir asked sharply.

"Well, wasn't there a-a-a note or a demand or something?" he stammered. "There's no blood, look!" he added hopefully. "He must be all right. I'll try and talk to them-"

"You'll do no such thing!" Vladimir barked at once.

"What?"

The Grand Howler patiently explained. "Linus, we cannot negotiate for Uther's sake. To negotiate with THORN is to invite further attacks. I will not set such a precedent."

"But… but they might kill him, sir."

Vladimir spread a paw, "He knew the risks."

Linus scoffed in disbelief, blue eyes darting to and fro beneath his hood and helm. "B-b-but you can't do that!" he snarled, "You can't just w-www-write him off-"

Vladimir stepped forward and clouted Linus around the head, sending the stocky wolf staggering sideways more out of surprise than force.

"Remember whom you address!" Vladimir snarled. "I'll have you flogged to within an inch of your life if you speak out of turn again, you disgraceful whelp!"

There was a pause as Linus gathered his wits.

"I'm s-sss-sorry, Grand Howler," he growled, ears flattened against his hooded skull, "but… I-I-I really must insist we negotiate. If Grand Howler Rufus were here he would open dialogue with the hyenas."

Vladimir towered over him. "By Ulf, are you mad?" he said, his tone dangerously low. "Do you want to live out the rest of your natural life shovelling imperium down Gelb?"

"N-nnn-no sir, but-"

"Then back down, you foolish, arrogant pup!"

"But, sir-"

"Linus!"

Slowly, with Uther's frayed cloak still grasped in his trembling fingers, Linus cupped his paws behind his back and stood to attention, eyes forward.

"Sir," he acknowledged shakily.

At once relieved and disgusted, Vladimir turned his cheek to him. "Uther would be ashamed of you, disgracing yourself in this manner," he growled, firm but measured. "I have known him longer than you and I assure you he would not countenance our begging for his life. He's better than that, as are you. Do you understand?"

Linus nodded, a little at first, but then vigorously. "Yes, sir. I-I-I understand, sir," he seethed, secretly gripping Uther's cloak tightly in his paws to vent his frustration. Despite his fury, Linus took a shaky breath and sealed his submission, "I'm sorry, Grand Howler. I don't know what came over me. Please forgive my transgression."

Mollified, Vladimir felt a pang of sympathy. "Very well, I'll forget this lapse of judgement," he said, adding, "Take five minutes, Howler."

"I'm all right, sir."

"That's an order! Have an ember."

"I don't s-sss-smoulder, sir."

"Well, sit down or something," Vladimir insisted, opening his smart motor carriage door and shepherding Linus onto the plush seat. He beckoned the Politzi rabbit, "Constable, look after Howler Mills. Make sure he doesn't do anything stupid whilst I'm gone."

"Sir?"

"You heard me. I've a phone call to make. If there's any developments come find me at once. Understood?"

"Uh, yes Grand Howler. Right away, sir."

Vladimir strode off to requisition the nearest telephone, leaving Linus to pick up Uther's mangled helm and sit with it on his lap.

"It's m-mmm-my fault," the young Howler said, rolling Uther's battered eisenglanz helmet over in his paws, "I should've gone in with him, or stopped him."

Constable Claybourne wasn't sure if he was being addressed by the Howler, but Linus had a growing reputation for being approachable.

"It's not your fault, sir," the rabbit hazarded. "Howler Uther's a daring wolf. You can't tell him what to do."

"No."

"We've all got to take risks, sir, for the sake of Lupa. Why, my uncle Casimir never wanted me to join the Politzi, but I told him life's for living, not hiding in no warren!"

"Yes, of course," Linus sniffed; mortified he was being given a pep-talk by a little beast.

Someone loomed over the odd pair, armoured feet crunching on the ashen ground, someone tall and full of imperious fire – Linus could feel his corona buzzing in the air like a swarm of mosquitoes.

He looked up and through his distorted, salty tears the elegant form of Howler Ivan.

"What's happened?"

"Sir. It's Uther sir, they got him."

A pause. Ivan turned to the refinery, cast his icy eyes up the towering chimneys. "If Vladimir asks," he said, "you haven't seen me."

Chapter 16

Professor Heath grasped either side of the lectern in his great hoary bear paws as he finished addressing the small crowd seated in the hall.

"And so it is with great pleasure," he declared, "that I bestow my colleague and friend of many years now with the Quin Medal for his outstanding contribution to the field of imperiology."

The big bear turned to his smaller wolfen colleague and shook paws, "Congratulations, Rufus."

Rufus nodded and bowed graciously; he wasn't used to wearing a suit and the collar and cravat were stifling, but nothing could wipe the smile off his face today. Heath hung the shining silver Quin Medal around his neck. They posed for the photographer amidst a chorus of applause.

Rarely had a Howler been so honoured, and rarely would Rufus have another opportunity to address so influential a crowd and be noticed. Time to make a splash.

"I'd like to thank Professor Heath and the faculty of the Ark for putting up with me all these years," Rufus joked, upon taking the stand, "as well as countless others who have been there for me over the years, both in the lab and, of course, in the line of duty… for I am a Howler, when all is said. You wouldn't believe the time I had trying to find a suit that fit me as snugly as my dirty old mantle."

Much laughter.

Rufus glanced down at his medal, admiring the geometric, mathematical shapes embossed into its face, then cocked his head to one side. "Appreciated as this is, dear friends, and though my work has helped to extend the lifetimes of the afflicted, a true cure eludes me. I always thought it would be for that I would win the Quin Medal, though I'm not averse to a second."

Some laugher.

"Of course, with a true cure may come true change," Rufus continued. "The power I and my Howler brethren wield would diminish if a method to forever block or flush imperium from our bodies were to be found. The imperious fire, as we colloquially call it from ages past, so long at our fingertips that Lupan civilisation cannot easily recall life before it, would, if we choose to free ourselves of its taint, be ours to command directly no more. Indeed, perhaps the cure *is* to cease abusing imperium itself. When burnt in our furnaces and fashioned unnaturally by us, ash and black-imperium is the result, raining down from the sky, ruining land, crops and lives. Hundreds of thousands of beasts die from its effects every year, not least the hyenas forced unjustly to live in unbearable conditions on the Reservations."

Silence, coughs, shuffles.

"Surely a cleaner, less destructive way of living in comfort can be found; an imperium-free future. That idea frightens some of my Howler kind, as does a cure, but after some twenty-five years now of knowing great power with greater pain, I can tell you I would rather live longer, love longer, and watch my friends and I grow old, than have beasts tremble and cross the street when they see my terrible eyes."

Rufus looked at a paw, cocked his head.

"One's corona is a marvellous tool… yet cold comfort for those in want of love, and the strength it bestows no substitute for the power of the mind. For you see, every day machines advance, every day power trickles down from the chosen few into the paws of the many, like sand through our fingers. An imperium rifle fires as accurately in a mouse's paw as a Howler's, and a dirigible flies under any captain, however meek. The age of the Howlers and their peers elsewhere in the world, the Valours, the Koda, the Chakaa and so on, will come to an end someday as the weak gain their own powers through science and technology; technology waiting to be found in the Dead Cities. You laugh, but the achievements of our ancestors are there. Their ghosts wait for us to come and pick up the pieces, read their messages, and perhaps heed their warning before Lupa, and all of us, join them in everlasting, black silence."

Rufus shrugged and scratched a ruddy, grey-tipped ear.

"That'll do. If I bang on much longer I risk us all being hauled off and 're-educated'."

Professor Health laughed, which allowed others to join in, and soon everyone was clapping. Strength in numbers protected them, made them brave; the powers that be couldn't disappear everyone.

After the inevitable book signings and paw-shakings, Rufus managed to slip out the hall and through the university to his office, whereupon he immediately removed his cravat and unbuttoned his collar. The trappings of academia didn't fit the well-sculpted body of a Howler, just bending one's arms was difficult.

Rufus had just broken an ember out and poured a stiff drink when the office door opened to a very-well sculpted Howler dressed entirely in black. For an instant, Rufus thought he really was about to be re-educated, but the intruder removed her helmet, revealing a familiar red-furred beauty.

"Jan!" Rufus chirped pleasantly. "You gave me a fright."

"I'm not surprised after that speech," she replied grimly, stepping inside and closing the door. "They won't print a word of it."

"Naturally."

"Then why even say it?"

Rufus shrugged and raised his glass. "Because I have a conscience?" he guessed cheerily, knocking it back.

Janoah narrowed her eyes, "Conscience? To agitate the little beasts and perhaps spark an uprising that would lead to death and destruction is... conscionable? Your lack of moral judgement astounds me, husband."

"It's good we can still surprise one another after fifteen years of marriage."

"Fourteen."

"Is it? Seems longer somehow."

Janoah sat on the desk and huffed, "Your brain is atrophying from the rot."

"I'd best effect a cure then," Rufus replied, "then we'll have another fifteen years to surprise each other yet."

"Fourteen!"

"Forty?" Rufus suggested cheekily. "Anyway, I thought your glorious leader, 'the Alpha' was a reformist like me."

"The Alpha seeks reform, not anarchy," Janoah clarified. "What you spout is dissident talk, and if it wasn't for fools like me persuading certain wolves that your scientific acumen outweighs your political ineptitude, you would've been dragged before the courts and sorted out with a stint down Gelb by now."

"ALPHA's got nothing on me," Rufus growled. "Now, dear wife, what can I do for you?"

Janoah spread a paw on her chest, "Me? I merely came to congratulate my husband on his intellectual accolade."

"Really?" Rufus beamed.

"Hahaha! Nooo."

Hopping off the desk, Janoah threw a file before Rufus; she was always brimming with files before becoming a Prefect, but it had gotten worse of late.

Like Janoah's brooch, the folder was stamped with the crest of ALPHA; a black ink circle cut by a stylised capital A whose crossbar rose from left foot to centre-right flank. The stamp meant it was an offence against ALPHA for Rufus to so much as peek inside, as it would be any other pack's secret files. Nonetheless he wordlessly opened it up and several grainy photos spilled out.

"Clumsy," Janoah tutted.

Rufus gathered them up. Three hyenas, he saw, big chaps wearing fine-looking leg armour of a striking dazzle-pattern tribal design with matching cloaks. They and their less well-dressed comrades were going about their business inside what appeared to be a warehouse.

"Who're these handsome chaps?" Rufus asked his wife.

"I was hoping you could tell me."

"Me? Haven't the foggiest, dear. Bit hard to tell with those marvellous skull helmets." Rufus peered at the pictures through a magnifying glass. "Hmm. Definitely Jua-mata."

Janoah frowned, "Noss's tribe?"

"Yes. Their crest is a painted hyena face, like a skull. Their warriors paint their faces the same. Quite terrifying."

"That takes sense."

It was Rufus's turn to frown, "Makes sense, Jan?"

Jan explained, "According to witnesses, these three mention Noss at every opportunity. They say they're avenging their prince; that the Howlers murdered him."

"They're right," Rufus growled, "we did murder him!"

"It was an accident. Anyway, he tried to murder you first, or have you forgotten Noss's attempted lupicide?"

"He should never have been racked, not in *my* name!"

Janoah slapped her chest, "Well it was nothing to do with me!"

"I know, I know. Let's… not go over it again," Rufus sighed, one paw held up. "It's passed now."

Janoah waited, then spread a paw at her husband. "So who are these three? Did you ever meet them back when you used to visit Noss and the tribes?"

"I don't recall. They're clearly Chakaa, though."

Janoah let slip a few more details, "Well they're in THORN; they might even be its leaders. We don't know their names, but they've been involved in thefts all across Lupa; refineries, warehouses, even a train robbery. Strangely they only steal black-imperium; they leave the rest, even white, though they take purple sometimes."

Rufus nodded, "Yes, I know. They're probably after making a black-imperium bomb."

"You 'know'?"

"We've had raids down Riddle way. All the hyenas poisoned themselves, but they weren't Chakaa, or at least they didn't have eisenglanz armour like these three." After a pause, Rufus added acidly, "Of course, such kristahl weapons and eisenglanz armour are rare in the tribes, especially since we've stripped them of all their heritage and left them naked on the Reservations-"

"Save your bleating for those in charge," Janoah interrupted.

"You're in ALPHA, aren't you?"

"It's the packs who manage the tribes; it's nothing to do with us. We stick to interior matters."

"What was the point of joining ALPHA then? I thought you wanted to make a difference?"

"I want to protect Lupa!"

"You did that well enough before."

"Rufus, must we go through this every time we meet?"

Silence.

"My point is," Rufus continued from before, "perhaps these chaps have inside help."

"Inside? You mean a Howler?"

"Someone who can get hold of eisenglanz and kristahl, yes, or perhaps locate the ancestral Chakaa armour that Lupa confiscated. Either way they would have to be high up to move that kind of material around; Grand Howler at least, possibly even an Elder."

Janoah pursed her lips and looked down, taking it all in Rufus supposed, then she looked up again and moved on, "Witnesses say they've got purple eyes, though they also report they seem fairly lucid, so they must be young."

"Not necessarily," Rufus countered, tapping the photos with a finger. "The Chakaa cope with purple-imperium better than we do."

"Not that much better."

"Some have very a high tolerance for it. Noss did. They prefer it to white-imperium, it's not such an affront to the gods to use it – less sacred than white, which is the tears of the Sky, of course."

"Of course it is."

"Anyone would think you've never read my work on hyena culture, Jan," Rufus sighed.

"I'd brush up on it, but it's best not to be seen indulging in anything you've put your paw to, dear," his wife claimed drily. "Not if one wants a long and productive career-"

Brrrring! Brrrring! Brrrring! Brrrring!

Janoah glared at the telephone on Rufus's desk, then at the wolf himself. "Aren't you going to get that?"

"Mm?" Rufus said, preoccupied with his thoughts. "Oh, it won't be for me."

Brrrring! Brrrring!

Janoah cast a paw about, "Isn't this your office?"

Brrrring! Brrrring!

"Yes," Rufus all but shouted, "but I'm never here. It'll be a wrong number."

Brrrring! Brrrr-

"Ugh!" Janoah lifted the phone and immediately slammed it down again. "There! Now I can hear myself think." Peace restored, she returned to the question of the hyenas, "In any case, it's only a matter of time before the usual Chakaa madness catches up with them. They must be pretty far gone to be contemplating a black-imperium bomb; even the mad Noss drew a line there-"

Brrrring! Brrrring!

"Ulf's fangs!" Janoah cursed, snatching the earpiece and adopting her best telephone voice. "Rufus Bloodfang Valerio's office, Grand Howler, winner of the Quin Medal and all round good egg. How may I help you?"

Rufus laughed a little and shook his head, "Flatterer."

Janoah looked to her husband. "Grand Howler… 'Vladimir', you say?" she said with mock bafflement. "No, never heard of you. No, and I'm pretty up on my Howlers. Really? Well, I sincerely hope this isn't a prank call, young wolf, or you'll be in a great deal of trouble with your mother! Get me in trouble will you? Most unlikely."

Rufus gestured with his fingers.

Janoah duly gave the phone up, saying, "It's for you."

"You're terrible," Rufus tutted, pressing the mouthpiece to his chest to muffle his words, before speaking lucidly into it. "Yes Vladimir? Yes, apparently I have a secretary now…. No, I can't fire her…. No."

Janoah chuckled as she listened in.

"What's the problem?" Rufus asked, listening. "You're joking!" he spluttered in surprise, looking at Janoah. "We were just talking about them."

Janoah's ears stood erect. There was a long pause as Vladimir spoke; the Prefect could hear his dulcet mumbles, but no clear words.

"What?" Rufus gasped, recoiling from the earpiece. "By Ulf, how'd he manage that?"

Janoah whispered impatiently, "What is it?"

Unable to concentrate on two things at once, Rufus held up a paw to his wife and spoke to Vladimir, "Yes I know what he's like, but…. Yes, I see. Yes, well that makes sense, but these aren't normal hyenas we're dealing with, there's some Chakaa about." He held up one of Janoah's photos, looking at the extraordinary hyenas. "Trust me, I know. Don't ask me how, Vladimir, I don't ask you for your sources."

Janoah folded her sinewy arms, "He'll guess."

Rufus winked at her. "Hah! No, I haven't seen Jan for nearly a month," he lied, nodding and scratching an eyebrow. "Yes, I'll be right over. Yes, of course I'm up to it, I'm not that far gone. I'll be twenty minutes. Right. Just be careful."

He hung up.

"Well?" Janoah urged.

Rufus leant on the desk with both paws. "THORN is raiding an imperium refinery as we speak."

Those arms unfolded, "You're joking! Where?"

"The one opposite Riddle Market, just across the river. Vladimir's got them trapped."

"Hah! Excellent!"

"Not really," Rufus corrected, turning round and unlocking a wardrobe. He took out his Grand Howler gear, white mantle, silver armour, helmet and rapier, saying, "Uther went in to spy on them and didn't come out. They just threw his gear out the window apparently. Stupid boy's got himself in deep trouble."

"Is he alive?"

"I pray," Rufus sighed, unbuttoning his waistcoat. "He's a bigoted, foul-mouthed fibber sometimes, but I couldn't be doing without him."

Janoah calmly gathered her papers. "You can't protect your boys forever," she said, philosophically. "You're a Grand Howler now. You have to learn to accept casualties."

"And I thought you were fond of him?"

"He's a capable wolf," Janoah admitted, "I've other concerns these days."

Rufus threw his waistcoat over the chair and said, "You've changed, you know that?"

Janoah pondered the comment. "Yes, I have," she admitted, donning her perfectly black Prefect's helmet, "but at least I can." She turned around and opened the door, parting with, "You've yet to leave the comfort of your pond, nymph."

✥

Dialling ALPHA HQ, Janoah waited in the ornate, wrought iron telephone kiosk for a response. The rain lashed the windows, reducing the university campus beyond to a wobbling, distorted artwork of shifting colours.

"Grand Prefect Silvermane's office," a receptionist said, *"how may I-"*

"Put me through to Silvermane at once. Tell him it's Janoah and it's an emergency."

"Please hold, Prefect."

Janoah waited, fingers rapping on the window.

"Silvermane, here," came a soothing tone.

"Sorry to disturb you, Grand Prefect," Janoah apologised, "but I've located a THORN cell in action. There's a raid on-going as we speak."

"Whereabouts?"

"Bloodfang territory; the refinery near Riddle Market."

"Your old district?"

"Yes. I have reason to believe the THORN Chakaa are there."

"How comes?"

Janoah explained, "A Howler's disappeared inside, a very capable Howler that I know personally. He may have blundered, but I think he's been outmatched by something unexpected."

"I see," Silvermane hummed. *"Then ALPHA must rise to the occasion. Do you think he's ready for this?"*

"This could be our best chance to catch THORN's leaders, sir."

"Yes. I'll inform Josef then. I know this may sound ridiculous, but try and keep a low profile. The longer we remain a rumour, the longer we can operate unimpeded."

Peering out the window Janoah spied what had to be Rufus dashing across the university grounds. She made no promises. "I'd better go, sir"

"Good hunting, Janoah. For the Republic Lupi."

"For the Republic."

Slamming the phone down, Janoah burst from the kiosk into the driving rain, pulling her hood up as she went. She hurried across to the university building, with its grand clock tower looming over all. Because of the award ceremonies taking place inside, not just for Rufus but for many an academic, there were a number of motor cars of all shapes and sizes parked up, some with drivers sheltering inside, smouldering amidst a cloud of vapours.

Janoah could have requisitioned any one of them, but settled on familiarity.

"Jan!" Rufus yelped, as his wife jumped onto the back of his *Springtail*. "What're you doing?"

"I need a lift," she replied, adding, "We're going the same way, as in all the way."

Rufus took a moment to figure that out. "I'll be glad to have you, of course, but Amael won't appreciate ALPHA interference."

"Since when do you care what Amael thinks? Anyway, it's only me and one or two others."

With a worried grunt, Rufus started his *Springtail*.

Janoah slipped her paws around his waist. "My you've put on weight," she mused, playfully pinching his stomach. "Watch that waistline, Valerio."

"Do you want to walk?" Rufus growled.

"Hahahaha!"

With that, the wolfen couple pulled away onto the main road, black and white cloaks flapping about them.

They were followed at a respectful distance by another Howler on a blue monobike; a big fellow in Eisbrand livery and with a mighty sword at his back.

Chapter 17

Uther twisted his paws for the umpteenth time, to no avail; the stiff Howler-wire binding his wrists would cut into his flesh sooner than give an inch.

Defeated, the Howler leant his back against the warm, vibrating pipe to which he was tied and watched the hyenas clean out the refinery, lowering hefty black-imperium canisters into the sewers one by one. Uther figured there must be a bucket brigade of terrorists down there ferrying the poisonous imperium away as fast as it was coming; the hyenas above ground were but a fraction of the number.

Whilst the last of the spoils were spirited down the sewers by Themba and Madou, Nurka, most definitely their leader in Uther's opinion, approached the wolfen prisoner, paws behind back, face hidden by his skull-adorned helmet. The hyena was the same height as Uther, but far heftier; even without imperium flowing through their veins hyenas tended to have the upper paw in strength, though not agility, what with their shorter, stouter limbs.

"Uther, the fastest wolf in Lupa, isn't it?" Nurka rasped in his coarse voice, as if admitting to the fact.

Uther snorted in surprise, but nothing more.

Nurka sighed, "Not fast enough, it seems," whilst looking Uther up and down. "Perhaps you're losing your touch, Uther of the Bloodfangs. Perhaps the rot is setting in. This white-imperium shortage must be taking its toll, even on strong young Howlers like you. You must all be weak."

"Is that THORN's big plan?" Uther sneered. "Starve us of imperium? Pretty krappy idea if you ask me."

"I did not," Nurka said, with a shrug. "Nor am I about to discuss my strategy."

"You will on the rack, mate."

"You've to catch me first."

"Oh, we will. Don't worry."

Nurka nodded, "In the event, my wolfen friend, I like to think I would hold out unto death on your vile torture machines, as our noble prince did."

Uther laughed, "Prince? What prince is that then?"

In a flash, Nurka whipped a big paw round and slapped Uther across the face. "Prince Noss of the Jua-mata!" he barked. "Son of the Four Winds, husband to Princess Arjana and father of her sacred offspring!" Grabbing the scruff of Uther's neck he pressed his metal helmeted snout against Uther's soft wet nose and snarled, "You would do well to remember those you have murdered!"

He released Uther with contemptuous flick of the paw.

The Howler shook his head rapidly to correct his ruffled fur. "I ain't murdered anyone!" he protested.

"You are a Howler, and by that token you have indirectly killed thousands of my brother and sister hyenas!" Nurka countered. He snorted beneath his helmet, eyes narrowing, "Once, you used to round us up and put us in the re-education camps. I was sent to one as a cub, put on display for the citizens of Lupa, filmed for your 'propaganda'. Perhaps you've seen me before? We're famous, you know, Themba, Madou and I. How we counted for the cameras. One, two, three, four, five! Hahahahaaa!"

Uther frowned as Nurka laughed.

"It was a long time ago," the hyena sniffed, sobering up. "They… do not bother with trying to change us now. Now wolfkind just wants us gone, so the last camps have been knocked down and we're starved and shot; re-educated in death."

Wild-heart scoffed at the notion.

"You doubt my word?" Nurka said. "Of course; you do not want to believe your kind are so despicable as to commit… genocide."

The mighty-looking Themba emerged from the sewers and walked over to Nurka and his prisoner.

"Time to go, chief."

"How's your wound?" Nurka replied without looking.

Themba's purple eyes widened within his skull-like helmet, then narrowed again, "It's nothing."

Uther looked Themba over and saw his left arm was caked with blood – evidently the Howler's pistol had left a mark, scraped his flesh perhaps. The athletic wolf met eyes with the big hyena and the two engaged in a pugnacious staring match.

"If you're done with him," Themba said, stepping a little closer, "I'll kill him, now."

"No," Nurka replied.

Themba glared at Nurka.

"No, Themba," the chief reiterated firmly, looking at his taller companion. "We're better than that."

"But-"

"He wounded you. He's a great warrior, a Chakaa worthy of our respect. Take that as solace."

Themba snarled, "You promised us revenge!"

Nurka grabbed him by his wounded arm and marched out of earshot.

Uther was surprised at the smaller Nurka's clout with Themba, but was glad of it. He watched as Themba twisted his arm free of Nurka's grip like an unruly teenager and the two exchanged heated words. Uther couldn't hear them over the churning machinery behind his head, and the hyenas' helmets precluded any lip-reading.

"Comfy, Wild-heart?" someone else said.

Uther's fur stood on end and he twisted in his bonds to look behind. "Ivan!" he gasped.

The black-cloaked Howler Captain was nestled behind the contorting pipes. He held a finger to helmet grille, and said, "I was waiting for them to kill you, but it appears they've other ideas, or Nurka does at any rate."

"Untie me," Uther whispered, twisting his paws.

"No."

"What? Whatcha mean 'no'?"

Ivan explained in his most dulcet, honey-glazed tone reserved only for the highest in sarcasm, "Let's not blow your cover, Wild-heart. Ingenious strategy, I must say."

"Strategy, sir?"

"Yes, allowing yourself to get captured to learn of the terrorist plot from their own lips, naturally. I couldn't have done better myself."

"Uh, yeah. Now untie me."

"You've got their names and their grievances, that's a start. Now try and get the location of the hostages out of them."

"Cap'n!"

"I'll be nearby."

"Ivan!" Uther seethed, "Wait!"

But Ivan had already slipped away into the shadows, leaving Uther to his captors.

Meanwhile, the argument between the hyenas had died down and Nurka affectionately patted Themba on the side of his massive neck. The two of them bumped their helmeted snouts together in a show of soldierly accord.

Themba returned to his duties, shepherding fellow hyenas into the sewers, whilst Nurka returned to Uther.

"I apologise for Themba's manners," he rasped. "He's easily provoked."

Uther said nothing.

"His family was murdered, you see," Nurka went on regardless. "His was one of many rounded up and shot by the wolves you call Watchers. Themba only escaped the massacre because he and I were out… hunting. We returned to find his village burnt, his mother and father, brothers and sisters, all gone. They had been led away and shot, their bodies piled in a mass-grave and burnt."

"You hyenas are full of schmutz mate," Uther sniffed nonchalantly. "Look, why don't you just give up and tell me where the hostages are, eh?"

Nurka's reply was swift; he stepped forth and thumped Uther in the gut. The Howler bent double and coughed violently, before Nurka grabbed the scruff of his neck and forced him back over the bend in the pipe. Drawing his short sword, the hyena tickled the wolf's bobbing throat with its sharp, blue-tinged kristahl tip.

Uther wondered where Ivan was right about now.

"For Themba's sake I should kill you, Howler scum, as you've killed so many of my people!" Nurka growled, purple eyes burning. "But I want you to tell your Den Fathers of us. Tell them the Chakaa shall dispense justice to them all. Tell them, if the rape of my people continues, our vengeance shall be a thousand-fold greater than any wrong done to us. They will all rot where they stand!"

Nurka suddenly drew back, one paw clapped to his helmeted skull. He breathed deep, vast chest heaving, then shook his head and blinked rapidly, as if waking from a nightmare.

"Goodbye... Howler Uther," he rasped.

Sheathing his sword, Nurka joined Themba by the entrance to the sewer, leaving the winded and indignant Howler Uther spluttering for breath.

"Ivan!" Uther seethed between coughs, twisting round to see into the maze of pipes. "Cap'n! Come on, they're gonna get away! Ivan?"

Nothing.

"Iv-"

"Aaaaagh!"

Uther whirled round, ears pricked by a blood-curdling scream echoing up from the sewers.

Themba and Nurka looked on in alarm as their fellow hyenas started to clamber back up the ladder and into the refinery, their faces scrawled with terror.

Themba grabbed one of them by the arms and shook an explanation from him. "Howlers?"

Uther heard the hyena yelp, "S-sss-sewer centipede!"

Then the stocky Chakaa Madou popped up through the hole. When only half way clear he slipped and grabbed onto the ladder with both paws.

"Gaaagh!" he screamed. "My foot! It's got my foot!"

Throwing himself on his belly, Nurka grasped his comrade's wrists just in the nick of time. "Hold on, Madou!"

"Chief! Help me! Please!"

Big Themba reached down, took the relatively small Madou by the thickly-furred scruff of his massive neck and together he and Nurka pulled their snarling, squirming comrade up. With a sudden jolt Madou was extricated from the sewers and the three Chakaa hyenas fell about the floor in a heap of spotty fur and black and white armour.

They scrambled clear of the drain just as two enormous, segmented, fiery-orange feelers twitched fitfully up through the hole and whipped around its rim, causing the lesser hyenas to scatter fearfully in all directions.

Whilst Nurka helped Madou limp to safety, Themba grabbed his long, kristahl-headed hammer from where it stood leaning against some pipes and cautiously approached the antennae licking around the drain.

"Themba!" Nurka seethed, in a sort of loud whisper.

"That's the only way out," Themba replied in kind, hefting his hammer in both paws. "Better to die fighting a noble hundred-legs than those Politzi scum, Nurka."

Nurka, given a moment's hesitation, set Madou down and rallied the troops.

"My kristahl bow!" he said.

A hyena passed Nurka his bow and quiver. The bow was indeed made of kristahl, whilst the arrows were fletched with various coloured flights made from the wings of moths and flies. Nurka picked an arrow fletched with iridescent, transparent wings and notched it to his bow; it had a shining kristahl tip. He took aim at the centipede's feelers, waiting for its head to appear.

Despite his wound, Madou limped ahead of Nurka, a long kristahl axe in his paws.

"Out the way, Madou!" Nurka spat.

"Stay back, Chief, it's too dangerous," Madou replied, hefting his axe in both paws. "You could get bitten."

Several lesser hyenas fearfully approached the drain in a circle, spears held protectively forth.

Themba, at the head of them all, spied a piece of metal on the floor – a big rusty bolt. With an armoured foot he chipped it neatly towards those quivering antennae.

In an instant the bug revealed itself, shooting up through the hole – a great orange centipede, perhaps as long as a bus! Its many, shiny legs clacked over the smooth concrete floor and its antennae groped around the bolt, searching for the source of the vibration, for prey.

Themba took his chance. Without a word, the powerful hyena brought his hammer down on the beast's armoured, wedge-shaped head.

Crack!

The giant centipede's segmented body writhed under Themba's kristahl hammer before slipping limply back into the hole, leaving a smear of white blood in its wake. There was a prolonged splash as its doubtless twenty-foot, two ton body flopped into the shallow waters below.

The hyenas stood around in silent astonishment.

"Hahaaah!" Themba woofed, triumphantly raising his hammer over his head. "Jua-mataaaaa!"

Everyone cheered and patted him around his mighty shoulders.

Then, as if to dampen spirits, the gas lights slowly went out, casting the refinery into the grey gloom of an overcast Lupan day. The deafening centrifuges wound down, the bubbling vats silenced, and within a few seconds the only sound was the rain patting on the iron roof high above.

"The Politzi must have cut the gas," Nurka said to his spooked brethren, looking all around. "They're preparing to storm us." He looked to his two Chakaa comrades, "Is the black-imperium all gone?"

"Yes, chief," Madou seethed, standing on one foot.

"Then let's not overstay our welcome."

"Hurry, into the sewers," Themba instructed, looking to Nurka specifically. "You first, chief. You help Madou. I'll bring up the rear this time."

At length, Nurka accepted the plan with a simple nod.

Madou, however, shook his head. "I can't make it with this foot," he said nobly. "I'll stay behind and help hold them off."

"No, Madou," Nurka said flatly.

"Chief, please. Let me do this for you."

"Do what? Die and leave me? I need you by my side!"

Once Madou had accepted his lot, Nurka peered down into the blackness of the sewer. Satisfied all was well, he slung his bow and quiver over his shoulders. One of Nurka's comrades passed him an imperium lantern and he clambered onto the ladder.

Uther watched and listened, silently impressed at how these hyenas had dealt with that centipede.

Suddenly the Howler felt something, a strong imperious presence, strong enough to disturb the overwhelming ambient imperium. Was it Ivan, back to rescue him? He looked behind but saw nobody.

Uther felt something more, something vibrating through the pipe to which he was tied, through the very floor, the clickety-clack of a hundred armoured, bone-like feet moving in rhythmic, chattering waves. The sensation passed rapidly underneath Uther, like an underground train screaming by.

The penny dropped.

"Oh schmutz," Uther mouthed.

Not halfway down the ladder, amidst the slimy, brick-lined stink of the pitch-black sewer, Nurka heard a rapid clicking echoing down the tunnel. It emerged from the gloom, a glistening river of colours, charging down the tunnel, sluicing round and round its cylindrical walls in a writhing spiral that defied gravity and logic. In the last second before impact Nurka's mind made sense of it all – every limb, every segment, every sound, added up to an enormous sewer centipede at least twice the size of the last.

The many-legged beast struck, smashing head-first into the ladder in its haste to snatch the tasty morsel that was Nurka. The corroded ladder protected the hyena, but broke away from its rusted moorings and fell backwards into the water, taking Nurka and his lamp with it.

"Nurkaaa!" Themba cried.

Perhaps sensing better prey, the mighty centipede whirled round in an instant and burst through the hole in pursuit of Themba and the others. Its sinuous, blue body licked around the refinery in a circle like a giant plate armour tongue, knocking barrels and hyenas aside with equal ease as it struggled to pull the remainder of its body through the hole.

Some of the hyenas fired their pistols, but the pellets bounced hopelessly off the creature's thick, iridescent armour and served only to enrage it further. Others threw their yellow-imperium spears, the crystalline tips breaking on impact, then fizzling and exploding. In this enclosed space, however, the resulting fumes and irritation caused the hyenas more discomfort than the centipede.

In the chaos, Themba found himself separated from Madou and the other hyenas. He wound up near Uther. He gave the wolf a few sideways glances, before suddenly turning to him, hefting his hammer, and swinging it at the wolf's head.

Uther cringed, every muscle and sinew, tooth and claw.

Wham!

Themba's kristahl hammer crashed through the pipe to which Uther was tied, splitting it at a join and sending imperium ash venting forth in a noxious cloud. The next Uther knew, Themba grabbed him by the scruff of the neck and bodily lifted him off the broken, ash-spewing pipe, before throwing him down into the shadows behind the machinery.

Coughing and spluttering, Uther rolled to a stop on the cold, hard ground. He looked up at Themba, panting for breath and utterly baffled.

"Go on then!" Themba spat, kicking him, "It is what Nurka would want. Go!"

The hyena turned to leave, to rejoin the fight and help his comrades, but the cold silver pistol that was thrust into his chin stayed him.

"Halt," Ivan said, slowly emerging from the hissing ash cloud; the Howler just said it, as if saying 'hello'. "Drop it," he instructed, tapping Themba's robust hammer with his delicate imperium rapier, adding, "Quietly."

Given a moment's thought, Themba lowered his hammer, letting the hefty, imperium-laden head hit the ground relatively softly, then the rest. With Ivan's pistol and sword digging in his throat and ribs respectively, Themba was pushed deep into the murky maze of pipes and machinery. Amongst the chaos and obscuring clouds of ash, nobody noticed Themba's disappearance, even less Ivan's appearance.

"You all right?" the Howler asked Uther.

"Yeah," he grunted.

With great effort, and some snarls, the gymnastic Uther tucked his feet in and managed to loop his bound paws round in front of him, whereupon he was able to kneel down and tease out the cruel, Howler-wire with his teeth and so begin to free himself.

"I could have killed him," Themba told Ivan.

"You wanted to," he replied coolly.

"Please," the big hyena said, hearing the shouts of his comrades fighting the centipede. "Let me go to them; let me die by their sides-"

"Or escape to terrorise and murder hundreds of innocent citizens? I think not."

"As you murder my kin, wolf!"

"Save it for your interrogators, Chakaa."

Surprised Ivan even knew the term, Chakaa Themba took a moment to growl, "All I need do is shout for help and-"

"And I'll kill you, then all of them," Ivan countered instantly. "Your followers are not Chakaa. They're nothing. Uther and I will squash them. Is that what you want?"

"They are ready to die."

"But they don't have to; my superiors only want the ringleaders," Ivan explained. "Tell your followers to stand down, all of them, and the Howlers will take care of the centipede. You, Nurka and Madou will be executed in the end no doubt, but not the others. I'll see to it."

Themba huffed, "I am not their chief, Howler."

"Become their chief. Take charge. Save their lives."

"I cannot. I will not."

"Shout then," Ivan goaded. "Disgrace yourself and cry for help like a wet-eared pup."

Themba's eyes twitched beneath his skull helmet. After an age, the hyena swallowed hard and said, "If I give myself to you… will you let them go, Howler?"

Ivan met him halfway, "I'll not interfere. If they die, let it be by the centipede. That's an honourable end for a hyena warrior. They'll pass across the Eternal Plains and sit beside the Ancestors. How's that?"

Themba was surprised, "You… you know us well, wolf."

"I had a good teacher, hyena."

After listening to the sounds of battle awhile, Themba closed his eyes and nodded just once – his word was given. Hyenas were many things, in Ivan's experience, but they kept their word more often than wolves.

"Where are the hostages?" Blade-dancer dared ask. "The refinery workers, we know you have them."

With a tinkle of ear-piercings, Themba just raised his chin haughtily.

Meanwhile, Uther slipped his sore wrists free of the wire and joined Ivan. He relieved Themba of his short sword and tucked it down his own armoured leg.

Ivan glanced at the battered Uther. "Tie him up," he instructed insipidly.

Uther paused a moment, but if he harboured any misgivings in the light of Themba's moment of mercy back there, the feeling instantly evaporated when he remembered just how zealously this fanatic had wanted him dead before that.

If anyone had been merciful, it was that Nurka, not his oversized henchbeast.

With that in mind, Uther grabbed Themba's big paws and, using the very same wire that had bound him, got his sweet revenge. "Told you I'd have yer," he said in Themba's ear, twisting the wire especially tight.

"My people will win in the end," Themba snorted.

"Yeah? We'll just see about that."

✦

Rufus weaved through the barriers and parked his standard-issue Bloodfang monobike next to Vladimir's standard-issue Bloodfang car.

The soaked Janoah looked longingly at the car, "Why don't you use your car? I didn't have Amael leave you my rank and privileges for nothing, you know."

"Not my style, Jan," Rufus said, shutting down his mono. "Train or mono for me, you know that."

"I miss my old car."

"Don't you have one in ALPHA?"

"Only Grand Prefects get those," Janoah huffed.

"Oh dear. Hard times."

Standing at the grim refinery gates, Vladimir spied the married couple approach. Rufus took the lead, striding boldly forth as usual, whilst the snoopy Janoah cast her eyes around even more than was normal, as if looking for something, or someone.

Linus saluted Rufus, "Grand Howler!"

Rufus waved the youngster's salute away. "Don't worry, Linus," he said positively, "we'll get Uther out."

"And Ivan," Vladimir added.

"Ivan?" Rufus queried.

"He's simply… vanished," his fellow Grand Howler huffed, looking sideways at Linus, then at the three other Redcloaks who had made up the motorcade, as well as Constable Claybourne. "Nobody's seen him apparently."

The guilty party remained silent.

Vladimir turned to Janoah, "Very amusing, by the way. What were you doing at the Ark, noting down the names of dissident speakers, perhaps?"

Janoah hummed innocently, "Mm?"

Vladimir went on. "You've no business here, Prefect," he stated. "Your remit is to police the Howlers. Since none of us has committed any crimes you will have nothing to do."

"THORN is as much ALPHA's problem as yours," Janoah said. "You'll be glad of my reinforcements."

"We don't need any more zealous Prefects, thank you."

"Who said anything about Prefects?"

Vladimir frowned and looked at Janoah, who cocked her head just a little.

Grunting, Vladimir then filled Rufus in on the situation, though short of Ivan's disappearance nothing much had changed since their phone conversation. Werner and the Politzi had the building surrounded and the power cut off, THORN were pointing pistols right back at them, and Uther was inside, presumably captured or worse.

"What do you suggest?" Rufus said.

"That's what I was going to ask you," Vladimir replied.

"Negotiate?"

"With THORN? The Elders will go insane."

"But if we assault the place they'll kill themselves, if their previous record is anything to go by."

"Short of letting them walk out of there, I don't see a way around that," Vladimir grumbled. "We will just have to storm them and try and catch one before he swigs black-imperium."

Rufus shook his head, "It'll be a bloodbath."

"Doubtless."

"Killing a few more members won't stop the movement. We have to find out what they're up to."

Vladimir mumbled sarcastically, "Why don't we ask your wife?"

Rufus glanced back at Janoah. "She doesn't know any more than us," he whispered.

"Do you think I'm stupid?" Vladimir growled. "I know she shares secret ALPHA files with you. Yes. She was in your office doing exactly that, wasn't she? She was plying you for your extensive hyena expertise, no doubt. What's she got on them?"

"Look," Rufus snapped, "all I want is to get as many beasts out of this mess alive as possible!"

"Your hyena friends too?"

"Terrorists are no friends of mine!"

The sound of a vehicle approaching drew everyone's attention. It was a prison truck, but painted pure black instead of the local Bloodfang livery. Werner's officers stopped it at the Politzi cordon, but after a brief exchange with the cat driver they waved it through.

The truck parked up, revealing a white A symbol stencilled tidily on its side.

ALPHA.

Rufus looked to Janoah for an explanation, but she was already halfway to the truck. She met the driver, a familiar grey cat in a black coat and tinted spectacles, and together they disappeared round the back of the chugging vehicle.

"So that's where Josef Grau went," Rufus said.

"Didn't Janoah tell you?" Vladimir derided. "He gets to rack a lot more beasts now he's in ALPHA. He's free to experiment, more or less."

Quite unaware he was being spoken ill of, not that he would care, Doctor Josef swung the truck doors wide and climbed inside the back. Janoah stayed outside, arms folded.

"What're they up to?" Rufus asked.

"Nothing good, I'm sire," Vladimir replied drily.

Burning with curiosity though they were, Rufus and Vladimir waited, unmoving, unwilling to look concerned or in any way put-out by the appearance of ALPHA.

Unencumbered by such pride, Linus strolled over to get a look. As he approached the truck, he heard Janoah and Doctor Josef talking, their voices just about penetrating the patting rain and chugging engine.

"Is he up to it?" Janoah asked, stroking her neck.

"Why don't you ask him?" Josef replied from within.

"You're the doctor, Doctor."

"His blood-ash levels have been good, lately. As long as he doesn't overdo it he'll be fine."

Then another voice, strong and yet tinny, like someone was entombed in a metal barrel.

"I'M FINE! LET'S JUST GO."

Keeping a respectful distance so as to not appear unduly nosy, Linus circled round the ALPHA truck. Respectful distance or not, he felt an imperious presence growing in his bones; the static crackle of an unfamiliar corona butting up against his own.

Peering inside the truck Linus saw giant of a wolf sitting on a bench, or at least he assumed it was a wolf. The beast was clad from head to toe in hefty-looking, eisenglanz armour, with a black mantle pinned about his mighty body. The armour was scratched and worn, tired-looking, like something from a museum cabinet rather than a modern Howler armoury. Not an inch of the beast beneath could be seen, not a lick of fur, not a single whisker; even his paws were housed in hefty gauntlets. His helmet covered his face, as with any Howler, but more extensively, enclosing him wholly under the jaw and even down the neck with flexible-looking rubber. A tube, perhaps carrying air, ran up into the helmet's snout from a backpack tucked beneath the beast's cloak. Tinted yellow glass covered his eyes, obscuring them utterly and rendering them as vacant orbs. Even the fellow's ears were encased in triangular projections of metal, each perforated like a telephone's mouthpiece to allow for hearing, one assumed. To Linus's further astonishment the ears swivelled and moved, as if alive!

What fine engineering is this?

In his blind quest to get a better look, Linus tripped over an especially wicked cobblestone and stumbled into a puddle beside Janoah.

She looked down at him, "Linus?"

Flicking dirty water from his paws, the mortified Linus got up and saluted, fist to chest, then forward. "Forgive my intrusion, marm."

Janoah saluted back, albeit ALPHA-style. "Not at all, I like such curiosity in a wolf. How've you been these last months?"

"Uh, very well. Thank you."

"You've grown," Janoah observed. "Not up mind you, but that's beyond help."

"Y-y-yes, marm."

"I hear Uther's got himself in trouble."

"It… seems so," Linus said, suddenly subdued.

"Don't worry," Janoah chuckled, patting his arm. "We'll sort this mess out."

Eased by Janoah's kindly manner, Linus blurted with cub-like tactlessness, "Who's that?"

"That? Oh, that's just Stenton, Rafe Stenton."

"Prefect?"

"Of a sort."

A pause, "He's n-nnn-not what I think he is, is he?"

Janoah crackled dangerously, "And what if he is, Woodlouse?"

Woodlouse rubbed his neck, "Well, uh… only that… uhm…."

The armoured bulk in the truck, this Rafe Stenton, suddenly looked out at Linus. His eyes, though obscured by reflective, yellow-tinted glass, somehow conveyed no malice.

Linus nodded at him and raised a friendly paw. "Hello."

The metal wolf raised a gauntlet-clad paw. "ALL RIGHT, MATE?" he rumbled, deep and hollow, like an organ pipe.

"Uh, y-yyy-yes, thank you."

Janoah leant inside and huffed, "Come along Doctor! They could be getting away!"

Josef made some final adjustments, twisting some valves on Rafe's backpack, then pulling the mantle down over it again. "He's ready."

"All right," Janoah beckoned. "Come on, Stenton, let's show these filthy terrorists who's boss."

"AYE," Rafe said simply.

It was only when he stepped down onto the road that Rafe's true stature became apparent to Linus. He was a steel giant, tall and broad, his massive chest jutting out over his stomach like an overhang on an old pub. Yet he was not inelegant, still long-limbed and nipped in at the waist as a wolf should be. His suit looked truly sealed from every angle, the armour plates sliding effortlessly over one another, with some kind of ribbed rubber bridging any gaps between the most flexible joints.

Linus remained transfixed as Rafe clomped past the little Howler as if he didn't exist, the coils of his corona burning him down to the bone.

By Ulf, what a beast!

Composing himself, Linus followed Janoah and her strange, towering champion at a distance, staring always at Rafe's back, watching him thump confidently along, belts jingling, arms swaying, cloak hugging his shoulders and heaping over his backpack. He must weigh a few hundred pounds, Linus supposed, yet he carried his bulk with such apparent ease. He hadn't a tail, only a thick black ribbon where it ought to be. It was common for a wolf who had lost his or her tail to mark its absence with a ribbon. Was his really gone or tucked in his suit?

So many questions – and not all in Linus's head.

"What in Ulf's name is going on here?" Vladimir demanded, taking a step forward as Janoah and her goliath approached. "Explain yourself, Prefect!"

"Calm yourself, Oromov," Janoah replied. "Prefect Stenton's only here to help."

"Prefect my foot! This is highly illegal!"

Illegal, Linus thought. Then is it? Could it be?

"For the packs, yes," Janoah said, "but ALPHA is not strictly a pack and therefore not a signatory of the non-promulgation treaty. We did not even exist at the time to sign it."

Vladimir could but huff, "A legal loophole, then. How ironic."

Janoah fondly brushed her steel companion on the arm with a paw. "Don't worry, Stenton's a kitten."

Rafe looked down at Janoah, head cocked, metal ears rotating. "JAAAN," he hissed, embarrassed.

She chuckled.

For his part, Rufus stared at Rafe, silent, unmoving. Rafe turned to him, stared back. Gasping, Rufus turned away and latched onto the wet iron rails of the fence.

"Rufus?" Janoah chirped in concern, then realised. "Oh! You get used to it after a while. It's the suit. It generates such a searing corona. It made me ill too, at first, made Rafe ill in fact, didn't it Stenton?"

"YEAH," he admitted. "EXCUSE ME, HOWLERS, BUT I'M HERE TO HELP, IF I CAN."

"Indeed," Vladimir sniffed. "That's what they all said… before going mad."

A Politzi rabbit hurried over to Vladimir, "Sir!"

"Yes, Claybourne?"

Claybourne looked twice at Rafe, then said, "Sh-shooting sir, inside the refinery. Something's going on."

"Must be Ivan's doing" Oromov decided. "The fool."

Rufus looked alarmed. "Schmutz!" he cursed. "We can't wait any longer, have to go in!"

"If we storm the gate we'll have multiple casualties!"

Janoah slapped Rafe's cloaked backpack, "You're up, Stenton."

With a nod, and no authority from anyone but Janoah, the iron giant passed gates and Politzi lines with impunity, heading straight for the refinery as if strolling to work. Werner and his constables watched him pass as one baffled entity.

"Who's that?" Werner said, grabbing his speaking horn and shouting at the stranger. *"Oi, you! What're you doing?"*

"DON'T WORRY, MATE! STAY BACK, YEAH?"

Slowly, Werner lowered the trumpet. "It can't be," he scoffed. "Can it?"

Linus expected Rafe to peel off and take a side route into the building, as Uther and Ivan had, but he just kept marching towards the main entrance, bold as brass.

"They'll sh-sh-shoot him!" Linus stammered.

"Don't p-p-panic, Mills," Janoah mocked.

The refinery's gaping entrance was piled high with boxes and barrels. As Rafe approached, the hyenas taking cover within their crude fortress grew agitated.

One jumped up, imperium rifle in paws, shouting, "Get back, Howler scum!"

He fired.

After the flash of the imperium charge came the puff of ash and the 'crack' echoing across the refinery. Linus expected Rafe to fall down wounded, but he kept on going, striding forth unchecked. Had the hyena missed him?

Another took aim and fired – a colourful spark flashed off Rafe's shoulder, tearing his cloak, but he hardly noticed. By now the first hyena had reloaded his rifle. He leant on a box and took more careful aim. He fired. Rafe's armoured head jolted back as the pellet doubtless hit him right between the eyes and he stumbled backwards.

The hyenas whooped.

Their celebrations proved premature. Rafe righted himself, shook his head and continued his stoic advance. Slowly he raised a paw.

"IN THE NAME OF THE REPUBLIC!" he woofed, his voice carrying further than was natural, "LAY DOWN YOUR WEAPONS AND SURRENDER! YOU WON'T BE HARMED!"

Imperious plasma played up his forearm and snapped between his metal-clad fingers in a show of strength that would've burnt any normal wolf's flesh to the bone.

Linus couldn't believe it, "By Ulf's fangs!"

Doctor Josef strolled up behind the Howlers, snug under an umbrella – cats despised the rain. "Their puny weapons won't put him to the test, Janoah," he observed, raising a pair of fancy binoculars to his spectacled eyes.

Janoah snatched them, "Give me those!" and peered through for herself.

Meanwhile, panic set in on the hyena side. Several of them stood up and fired an incongruent volley over the tops of barrels and boxes. The deadly pellets pinged uselessly off Rafe's armour like so many dried peas.

"I DON'T WANNA HURT YOU!" he said.

A desperate hyena produced a metal bauble and twisted it open to reveal a bristling yellow-imperium crystal. Instantly fuming as it made contact with the air, the hyena threw the sizzling bomb at Rafe and dived for cover.

"Get down!" Werner shouted, hitting the deck.

Unafraid, Rafe calmly stepped forward and crushed the crystal with a mighty boot – it exploded. Deflected by the suit's thick, eisenglanz sole, the shards shot away from the Politzi and right back at the hyenas! The burning imperium embedded in the crates and boxes, setting them instantly aflame and clogging the entrance with choking smoke and poisonous fumes.

Then, with seemingly impossible acceleration for a wolf of his dimensions, Rafe hunched down and leapt gracefully into the clouds, vanishing from sight!

Linus held his breath. His ears twitched and eyes darted, listening, searching.

"Gaagh!"

"Get back you-aaarrrgh!"

"Eyaaagh!"

The rolling, yellow-tinged smoke lit up from within, flashing like an angry thundercloud. Amidst the sparks and screams, a hyena was ejected from the chaos. He rolled tail over head and came to a rest on his front, his body trembling and smouldering in the rain as residual arcs of plasma licked over him.

The wind changed, the smoke and ash cleared, and Rafe stood alone, armoured shoulders heaving, the black ribbon that marked his absent tail dripping with water. The bodies of hyenas lay strewn about him like the tragic victims of a Rostsonne whirlwind.

"Are… are they all d-d-dead?" Linus stuttered.

"Toast," Josef said. "Even a Howler cannot take much of a shock from Rafe, let alone nobodies." He turned to Janoah, "Silvermane said there'd be Chakaa here."

"Patience, Doctor."

Observing the devastation, Vladimir remarked, "So much for prisoners."

Suddenly, and to Linus's astonishment, a thick jet of sparkling imperium ash hissed from Rafe's back!

Fsssssh!

The ash came from a short, stout exhaust poking up near Rafe's left shoulder, like the funnel of an imperium train. There was even a neat, well-stitched hole worked into his black mantle to allow for its egress. Linus could see that, just like the flexible tube going to Rafe's helmet, the funnel originated from the same backpack lurking under the folds of his mantle.

Baffled beyond words, Linus looked to the others, Rufus, Vladimir, Janoah – they were in no way surprised. They know what he is, Linus realised. They've seen it all before because they were in the war. Rafe must be one of *them*. But then, how could ALPHA get away with this? Legal loophole, Vladimir had said.

Once the vented ash had billowed away, the long-legged Rafe looked back at his allies, raised a paw, and leapt clean over the boxes into the refinery with Uther-like athleticism.

Shortly thereafter more screams and flashes ensued.

"Come on!" Janoah barked, drawing her rapier. "Let's back him up, Howlers!"

Vladimir growled at the Prefect, "You've no authority here, Janoah!"

"Then stay," she spat, "and let the glory be ALPHA's!"

The red wolfess strode through the gates, rapier held before her nose, left paw on her hip, as bold as Rafe had been before her and yet she hadn't his armoured bulk. One well-placed pellet would go straight through her cloak and tunic.

"Jan, don't!" Rufus shouted, running to the gate and reaching for her. "It's too dangerous! *He's too dangerous!*"

With a glance at his superiors, Linus unbuckled his shield from his back and dashed past Rufus into the refinery grounds after Janoah.

"Mills, what're you doing?" Vladimir snarled. "Mills! You'll be flogged for this!"

Linus Mills pretended not to hear as he slipped in front of Janoah, shielding her advance with his Bloodfang-emblazoned kristahl shield.

"Much obliged, Mills," Janoah said to him.

"Marm," he replied nervously.

With a glance at one another, Rufus and Vladimir drew their rapiers and advanced with the three other Howlers at their backs, ordering Werner and the Politzi to follow their lead.

Soon a ring of Howlers and Politzi officers was closing in on all sides.

The final assault was on.

Chapter 18

The water lapping at Nurka's helmet-clad face brought him to his senses with a start. He was on his front and something was pressing down on him.

Panic set in.

Kicking, splashing and choking, he scrabbled aside of the mysterious bulk and fell against the circular, brick-lined sewer wall, spitting gritty, ash-laden water from his mouth. Chest heaving fearfully he removed his helmet and wiped his stinging eyes, looking all around for the giant centipede, expecting it to snatch him at any moment.

It was gone.

The weight on him had been the ladder, Nurka realised. It had fallen with him and landed on him. That's all.

Satisfied for the minute that he wasn't being eaten, Nurka looked up at the bright, circular drain hole – he saw nobody and heard nothing of the world above.

"Themba!" he rasped, as loudly as he dared. "Madou?"

Cursing the gods, donning his helmet and shouldering his kristahl bow, Nurka searched the shallow water for the ladder. Hefting it onto his bruised shoulders, he discovered it was bent and mangled beyond use; it would not reach the drain. He lowered it gently back down into the water and looked up.

Plan B then.

Nurka prepared himself; taking deep breaths, bending his knees, crouching low.

"Ragh!"

The Chakaa leapt straight up with all his imperious might, his corona pushing out behind him, blasting the water away in a bubble of invisible energy. As the water splashed back into the void below him, Nurka latched onto the lip of the circular hole.

Slowly, carefully, he pulled himself up enough so his skull-covered face could tentatively peer into the ghostly refinery, rounded ears swivelling, purple eyes darting. He could see nothing. The whole place was awash with a dense, grey smog, of the sort Lupa suffered when the Graumeer wind failed to clear the air.

Shapes loomed silently; pipes and machinery silhouetted against the ambient light. Then Nurka looked low and saw the bodies of fellow hyenas strewn about.

Heart pounding, the Chakaa levered himself up and rolled from the sewer mouth. He stole across to the nearest of his followers. The downed hyena lay in a pool of blood, his body ripped open. There was no need to check for life, he was with the ancestors now. The work of the hundred-legs.

Nurka looked up and around but couldn't see it. *Has it retreated back down the sewers?*

"Chief," someone said.

Nurka whirled round and found Madou flat on his back, one paw holding his heaving body. The chief crouched beside his follower and cradled his blood-flecked, helmet-clad head.

"Chief," Madou said, trembling, "I'm... I'm bitten."

Nodding, Nurka looked around again; the centipede could be anywhere in this ashen fog. "Where's Themba?" he asked.

"I don't know," Madou growled painfully. "I lost him in the f-fff-fog. It all happened so fast."

Nurka looked to where Howler Uther should be. The pipe was broken and the Howler was missing. *Had the centipede taken him? Had it killed everyone?*

"It's m-mmm-mad, chief," Madou stammered, as if reading Nurka's mind. "It's... mad from... imperium poisoning. It kills for the sake of killing. It was horrible."

There came distant shouting, screams and the clashing of swords from elsewhere in the refinery.

"The Politzi!" Madou spluttered. "Chief, you must go!"

Nurka hushed him, "Rest easy, Chakaa. I have to find Themba-"

"But, Chief!"

"Don't, Madou! And don't you dare swallow your black-imperium capsule. I'll not forgive you if you abandon me, do you hear? Swear to me you won't!"

Madou, eventually, nodded, "I swear."

Nurka patted his neck, "Hold on. I'll be back."

Notching an arrow to his bow, Nurka explored the choking atmosphere of the refinery like a hunter in a forest. He checked the bodies of his fallen comrades, searching for a hyena bigger than the rest. Themba stood out in a crowd to say the least, a mere glance was all Nurka needed – he was not amongst the dead, not here.

"Themba!" Nurka growled, as loud as he dared. He waited for a response, either from Themba or, if the Wind willed it, the centipede lurking somewhere. "Themba, where are you? It's me, Nurka."

A metallic footstep crunched on the gritty ground.

With a snort of alarm Nurka whipped round, bow taught. His purple eyes met the hazy figure of a Howler, no doubt about it. Nurka waited, heart pounding, tail flicking, expecting the attack, but none came.

The wolf stepped a little closer, emerging from the unnatural fog, rapier held loosely by his side. He was pure white, but dressed in black. "Your ally is in our custody," he declared insipidly.

Nurka gasped back, "Themba?"

A nod.

"Where is he?" Nurka demanded, bowstring creaking.

"Safe," the white wolf replied. "He surrendered to put a stop to this madness, as should you."

"You lie!"

"Tell your comrades to stand down and we'll deal with the sewer centipede. The survivors will receive medical care, you've my word-"

"And be tortured afterwards?" Nurka spat. "Sent to the mines? Executed? Hah!"

"That's beyond my control, but deals can be made," the Howler reasoned calmly. "You can strike an agreement with my superiors, I'm sure. Give yourself up for the sake of your followers. I'll put in a good word."

"Your words are as hollow and rotten as Lupa, Howler. If it's the last thing I do, I'll kill you and as many of your corrupt kind as I can!"

"Then shoot."

Nurka waited.

The Howler huffed, "How old are you, sixteen, seventeen?"

Nurka's purple eyes narrowed. "Old enough," he claimed.

"Old enough for the purple venom you're taking to drive you round the bend yet? How clearly do you think Chakaa? How well do you sleep?"

"I'm ready to end it all, believe me-"

"By choking on your black-imperium capsule? Or will you rot with the black-imperium bomb you plan to set off somewhere?"

"You know nothing of THORN's plans."

"I know they're despicable."

Nurka flared up, "Do not speak to me of what's despicable, you who oppress my whole race!"

There was a silence, but for distant battle.

"Every second we talk hyenas are dying," the Howler went on. "You sound educated. You must realise that even a black-imperium bomb will hardly dent Lupa. You'll perhaps pollute a district, make it uninhabitable. Big deal, the city will hardly notice. All you will do is blacken your people beyond redemption. You want change? So do I. Prove yourselves trustworthy and able, as Prince Noss tried to do before-"

"Don't speak of him! You've not the right!"

"I've every right!" the wolf growled, adding, "We served together for years. I'm Ivan Donskoy. Perchance Noss mentioned me?"

Nurka's eyes widened a little, "The Blade-dancer?"

"A daft epithet," Ivan excused.

"But, you're… a… a great warrior."

"I'm just another Chakaa, brother, albeit in a different body to yours. I know your pain. Surrender, and I'll do what I can for your followers; on my honour."

Time passed. Slowly, imperceptibly, Nurka's tense bow arm lowered somewhat.

"Drop it, Spotty," someone growled from behind, as something cold and sharp tickled Nurka's shoulder blades.

It was Uther, armed with Themba's sword.

Ivan grumbled at him, "Uther, don't."

"I got him, sir," Uther maintained, tapping Nurka's back with the sword. "Drop the bow, scum. Nice n' easy like."

"Treacherous wolves," Nurka spat, glaring at Ivan and keeping a firm hold of his bow. "You've not a shred of honour between you."

Uther snarled more firmly, "Drop iiiit!"

Crack!

Amidst a bright flash and spurt of vapour from somewhere down low, Uther bent double. Without so much as a yelp the Howler fell on his side and rolled into a ball.

"Uther!" Ivan barked.

Down on the concrete ground, awash in his own blood, Madou let an imperium pistol fall from a trembling paw. With a final laugh he collapsed on his front.

Chakaa Nurka charged his arrow with a blast of plasma from his fingers and let it fly at Ivan – a bolt of shimmering blue. In the instant he had, Blade-dancer both jerked to one side and raised a paw. Nurka's shining, plasmatic arrow veered unnaturally off into the fog, deflected by Ivan's corona.

Quietly amazed, Nurka lowered his bow, letting it clatter to the floor along with his quiver. Pulling a short sword from a scabbard built into his thigh plate, he lunged to the attack, thrusting and swinging at Ivan. The Howler dodged nimbly aside and nicked Nurka on the arm with his delicate imperium rapier.

They parted, circled one another.

Stopping still and spacing his armoured legs, Nurka readied himself for another attempt.

"Grrraagh!"

Swinging high, then low, he tried to break Ivan's defences with sheer force, but the wolf was too swift, his seemingly fragile rapier deflecting the hefty blows whilst his lithe, cloaked body weaved aside. His feet shuffled swiftly, lightly repositioning his weight with the skill of gymnast, a dancer.

Again they parted.

"You're aptly named!" Nurka rasped, with a mad, wide-eyed cackle.

Ivan said nothing.

Another lunge, and, as his weapon met Ivan's, Nurka summoned all his strength, every thought, every fibre of his being, as he had been taught. The imperious fire leapt down his arm and up his sword, exploding in a flash of light. Ivan was punched back by the force and tumbled head over tail. He rolled aside as Nurka followed and tried to stab him where he lay. Still on the ground, Ivan raised a paw at Nurka. The air bent and warped as his corona reached out and pushed Nurka stumbling against a tangle of pipes.

Ivan righted himself, as did Nurka, both breathing hard in the foggy silence.

No, not silent.

There came a clicking noise, echoing overhead.

Ivan moved in the nick of time, jumping back as a many-legged, segmented column of iridescent blue swooped down from the foggy ceiling like the bejewelled whip of some gaudy sky giant.

The centipede!

It was so long that its great body disappeared into the foggy ether above, but its rear-end was no doubt clinging to the refinery roof. It twisted and arced towards Ivan, its orange antennae flailing at him as he backed off.

Slowly the centipede lowered to the floor and started to trundle across the refinery. Once enough of its front legs were on terra firma, it released its hold on the ceiling and the rest of its mammoth body arced neatly down, legs clacking on the concrete like spears, almost stabbing Nurka, who had to scrabble away to one side.

With his bluish kristahl rapier held forth, Ivan reversed, paw over armoured paw, silent, waiting. The centipede crept after him as quickly as he backed away, its body undulating, poison barbs twitching either side of its head.

It lunged at Ivan, barbs agape! In the same breath, Blade-dancer thrust his sword forth, stabbing the centipede in the mandibles, right up to the hilt. The beast arced and twisted, flinging Ivan's sword away, before sweeping down and around, barging him aside.

Ivan slammed into a wall of vertical pipes. Thinking fast, he slipped between them as the maddened centipede bore down on him. Its head smashed into the pipes, bending them like cardboard tubes and bumping Ivan forward. Stumbling into the wall opposite, Blade-dancer looked around; a machine to the right, a vat to the left and a sewer centipede behind.

He was trapped!

The silent centipede's weighty feelers tore around Ivan's cramped industrial cell, painfully whipping his cloaked body and clinking against his armour. The Howler backed into a corner to protect himself.

Drawing his pistol he fired. The pellet pinged off the centipede's armoured brow and served only to madden it further. It pushed against the pipes, buckling them inwards, legs scraping over the metal.

Turning his helmeted head to one side to avoid being slapped by the whipping feelers, Ivan calmly tore open another cartridge to reload.

Outside in the refinery, Nurka left the centipede to its devices; bad luck for Ivan, good for him. Sheathing his sword he hurried over to Madou and rolled the hyena onto his back. Had he gone? He was lying motionless, dead if not heading that way. His lips had turned blue, poisoned by the centipede's fangs no doubt.

"Madou," Nurka seethed. "Madou!"

Nothing.

With a snarl of rage, Nurka found Uther amidst the carnage and dived on the wolf.

"Grrrrffffgh!" the Howler groaned.

He was shot and bleeding, a paw holding his raw ribs, but he was still alive.

The massive Nurka sat astride the lighter wolf, pinning his dark arms with his armoured knees, and grabbed his throat with one paw. Uther squirmed, unable to do anything, save choke.

"Gaaagh!"

"Where's Themba?" Nurka demanded, shaking him.

Uther just ground his teeth.

With a mad-eyed snarl, Nurka used his free paw to thump the wolf's wound. "Where is he? Speak!"

"Gaaaahhaaaagh!!" Uther snarled, spluttering, "Go… thump… yourself!"

Another punch, but Uther held out. He was strong. Time was short; there was no time for a lengthy interrogation. Nurka contemplated what to do, how to break him – a mad idea took hold. Taking a pouch from his belt the hyena produced a small tin. Inside the padded tin was a tiny glass capsule, like a crystal bean, with a miniscule glob of black fluid inside.

Nurka held the capsule over Uther's pale face. "Black-imperium, Howler," he almost whispered.

Uther's yellow eyes locked onto the capsule and his whole body jolted in fear, Nurka felt him trembling beneath him already.

Better.

"Speak," Nurka said, his purple eyes as wide and mad as Uther had ever seen them, "or I break this between your teeth and you rot. Have you ever seen a beast die from the rot in ten seconds flat? It is not a handsome death, but you leave a spectacular corpse."

"You… you w-www-wouldn't dare!" Uther stammered.

Grabbing Uther's snout in one vast paw, Nurka forced his dark fingers between the wolf's clenched lips and slipped the capsule down beside his teeth. As the cold glass touched his gums Uther let out a muffled scream.

"Mmmmmphgh!"

Whilst Uther squirmed, Nurka made a fist and drew it back with overblown drama, threatening to punch the wolf's jaw and break the capsule.

Uther shook his head, "Mmm, mmmph!"

Of course, Nurka waited. "Last chance," he said, cocking his head to one side and lessening his grip on Uther's muzzle, just enough for him to talk.

"Take it out!" Uther begged, through his teeth. "Please!"

"Speak first!"

"He's over there! He's over there!"

"Where? Tell me!"

Uther gently flicked his muzzle to the left, worried too violent a motion would break the deadly capsule. "In with all the pipes!"

Nurka released him and stood up. Uther rolled over and spat the capsule into a shaking paw, putting it gently on the ground. No sooner had he than Nurka administered him a final, brutal, plasmatic stomp to the back, sending the Howler down for the count.

"Unffgh!"

Rolling his shoulders and composing himself after that uncomfortable deed, Nurka hurried into the foggy, industrial maze of pipes and machines. He felt a familiar presence growing, even amidst the ambient imperium.

"Themba!"

Nurka's comrade sat crossed-legged by a pipe, bound and gagged. Nurka fell upon him and pulled the dirty cloth from around his thick, black hyena snout.

"Chief!" Themba grunted at once. "Did you kill the Howlers?"

"No, but the centipede might," Nurka replied, setting about unravelling the wire that bound Themba's paws to the piping behind him. "It's killed Madou."

Themba winced in shame and pain.

Suddenly he banged the back of his helmeted head on the pipe and laughed, "By the Wind, I'm a disgrace. Hahahaaaaahaha!"

"Themba!" Nurka barked.

Chakaa Themba banged his head on the pipe a second time, harder than before. "They all died with honour, whilst I surrendered like a coward! Hahahahaaha! How is it… how is it everyone around me dies, yet I continue to suffer? Hahahaaahahaa!"

As he went to bang his head for a third time in self-punishment, Nurka cupped a paw to Themba's thick neck and shook him. "Stop it!" he snarled, then quietly, "Stop it."

Swallowing his grief, Themba asked hopefully, "Did he die well?"

Nurka said simply, "Yes."

Retrieving Themba's hammer and Nurka's bow, the two Chakaa stole across the refinery towards the sewer, sneaking by the centipede's long, undulating rear and passing the bodies of their fallen comrades on the way. There was no point trying to avenge their deaths; there could be no retribution against a centipede, it was an arm of Mother Nature, above morality and justice. It simply was what it was and did what it did; every hyena knew that.

With a last, pensive look at Madou, Themba lowered himself into the sewer. Nurka followed, hanging on and letting go to lessen the fall. Upon landing he fetched his imperium lamp bubbling steadily beneath the ashen water.

The Chakaa splashed along the gloomy tunnel, not getting far before a group of fellow THORN members came the other way, one with a lamp.

"Chief!" the one with the lamp barked in relief. "We were getting worried."

Nurka growled, "You were told not to come back."

"Sorry chief, but… we're lost without you," was the reply.

"We have all the imperium we need. If we die now you must carry on without us."

"Yes, chief. W-w-where is everyone?"

Nurka grunted poetically, "Striding the Eternal Plains. They died well."

The hyenas dipped their heads respectfully.

"Grieve later," Nurka said, sloshing through them. "Our brothers are fighting to the last so we can escape. Honour their brave sacrifice."

Back on the surface, the giant centipede squeezed through the pipes, invading Ivan's hiding space. Slipping its head inside, followed by the first segment of its body and the accompanying legs, the whole writhing, armoured ensemble rattled and scraped against the metal walls, its jaws coming within a few feet of Ivan's face. The feelers snaked all over him, ruffling his fur, tasting him.

Blade-dancer could taste the centipede too. His nostrils flared and throat burnt as the bitter, acidic reek of ammonia penetrated even his helmet's purifying filter. He knew centipedes extruded ammonia through their skin, adding to their already deadly arsenal of speed, strength and venomous fangs.

Desperate, Ivan raised his pistol, aiming at the beast's mouth.

Crack!

The pellet pinged off a rock-hard mandible and ricocheted around the enclosed space, sparking off the walls and pipes and inches from Ivan's head.

Useless.

The centipede suddenly pulled back, writhing and twisting between the pipes. Ivan looked down at his silver pistol in amazement; had it done the trick after all?

No, the Howler saw the beast's back end was flailing about outside like a gargantuan, unattended fire hose as arcs of blue imperious plasma licked along its segmented body, illuminating the foggy factory in harsh light. Eventually, the beast could stand no more punishment and pulled its head from between the pipes altogether.

It began trundling up the walls, retreating to the smoggy ceiling from whence it had come, like a god ascending to the heavens.

Ivan stood astonished. What Howler was powerful enough to imperiously torment a giant centipede into retreat?

"Rufus?" Ivan realised happily, laughing a little and calling louder, "Rufus! In here!"

Once the centipede's thirty-foot body had passed, someone looked in through the mangled pipes, a big, grey-looking beast in a black cloak. He was very heavily built and stood taller than Ivan by the looks.

Definitely not Rufus.

"ALL RIGHT, MATE?" the fellow enquired.

Ivan's ears pricked at the tinny voice that was clearly augmented by a speaker. The stranger was indeed heavily built, but the look was accentuated by the fact he was armoured from head to toe in a hefty suit of plain-looking iron.

"Yes," Ivan said at length – it wasn't often someone asked the great Blade-dancer if he was 'all right'.

"I THINK WE SCARED IT OFF BETWEEN US," the newcomer said magnanimously.

With that he clanked away, taking his potent imperious presence with him; Ivan hadn't even noticed the fellow's overpowering corona until its crackling warmth had moved out of range, leaving Ivan feeling cold.

"Wait!" he barked, slipping through the pipes and into the foggy refinery after the stranger. He found him visually checking the bodies of the fallen THORN members.

Before Ivan could ask who he was, the metal-clad wolf turned to him and said, "WHERE'S THE LEADERS?"

Between casting his eyes over that helmet, with its big filter and metallic ears, and that mighty armoured body, Ivan found his tongue. "The sewers," he said, pointing, "I think."

A look, an incongruous and metallic, "TA." Then the stranger clomped over to the sewer.

Ivan followed, demanding, "Who are you?"

"RAFE," the iron wolf replied, "I'M WITH ALPHA."

"A Prefect?"

"SORT OF, YEAH."

On that cryptic note, this Rafe lowered his legs into the pitch black hole and swung down, clinging onto the lip with his paws long enough to add, "STAY HERE, MATE."

He let go.

Rafe fell quickly at first, but then defied the laws of nature by slowing in mid air. He landed gently, yet with an almighty splash, blasting a perfectly spherical cascade of water against the cylindrical brick walls – he had used the power of his imperious corona to soften his landing. Glancing around, he waved a paw over his brooch. The white-imperium 'A' motif began to shine, lighting up the sewer with a cold, pure light.

Satisfied, the 'sort of' Prefect sprinted down the passage at unnatural speed, his spherical corona pushing aside a torrent of water like a motorboat.

Ivan looked on, astonished.

Torn between curiosity and sympathy, he hurried over to Uther, who lay on his front amidst the smog. With trepidation Blade-dancer rolled him over.

"Urrgh!"

"Still alive?" Ivan said, with a hint of relief.

"Kinda... wish... I wasn't," was Uther's seething reply.

Reinforcements were approaching; Ivan could hear Vladimir shouting orders. The Bloodfangs would soon have the refinery under control.

"Help's on the way," Ivan assured Uther.

"Go get the bastards, sir," Uther growled, laughing through his bloodied teeth, "Some birthday... eh?"

"You'll have many more yet. Tell Vladimir I'm on their tail."

"Aye, sir."

Without time to search for his sword, Ivan grabbed the one Uther had taken from Themba and lowered his legs into the dark, dank sewer. It was a long way down. Clinging onto the lip, Ivan hung for a moment, then dropped.

He landed, stumbled on the mangled ladder hidden in the water and fell on his rump. Rancid water sloshed inside his leg armour and soaked his breeches.

Nice.

Blade-dancer could've spectacularly softened his landing like Rafe, but the cost didn't outweigh damp breeches.

Standing up and waving his paw over his red brooch, Ivan dispelled the gloom like Rafe had, albeit less effectively. Red-imperium was the very worst for lighting, but it was at least subtle, and the Bloodfangs were all about subtle.

Ivan could see well-enough and sloshed down the sewer in pursuit of both THORN and this 'Rafe', whoever, or whatever he was.

✦

Nurka stepped into the curtain of rain; night was falling, hastened by the thickening fog. Before him the polluted River Lupa lapped at the city's flood defences; behind him the gaping maw of the industrial sewer and storm drain, not to mention his comrades, all of them smeared with the ash and filth of Lupa's secret bowels.

One of the downtrodden hyenas slipped in the growing torrent of sewer water. With a yelp of alarm he was nearly washed clean into the river, but Nurka grabbed his paw and set him back on his feet.

"I've lost enough brothers today," Nurka replied, tossing his imperium lamp in the brown water. It bobbed about in the growing waves, before sinking into oblivion.

Under the cover of encroaching darkness, Nurka led his defeated band across to a slimy wooden jetty where a rusty barge piled high with imperium ash waited.

Several slick-looking figures were already aboard – otters, their dark, muscular outlines barely discernable against the grey piles of poisonous ash. Masters of the waterways, otters could be relied upon to smuggle anything in or out of Lupa, provided the price was right.

Arriving at the barge, Nurka nodded at the oldest of the sailors, a tough, salty sea dog with a patch and several scars flecking his greying fur.

"Yah be late, Nurka," the otter said in his people's laid-back patois.

Nurka replied, in his own rasping tone. "We faced some difficulties."

"'Owlers, yah?"

"Amongst other things."

"We is taking a big risk fer you, Chakaa! If dem 'Owlers discover who we are, our lives be over."

Nurka knew where this was going. "You'll be compensated double-pay, otter," he assured. "Just get us clear of Lupa."

Satisfied, the otter nodded at some of his better-built, rougher-looking crew. They climbed on the ash pile and dug out some ropes hidden amongst the spent imperium. They heaved on the ropes and the ash bulged aside as a trapdoor broke the surface, revealing a secret hiding space built beneath the poisonous piles. Some ash tumbled down inside the hole, but not much – the rain was making it cake together with the consistency of fine, damp sand.

Someone popped up through the hole, a rabbit in a gas-mask, his long white ears discoloured by ash. He beckoned Nurka with a grubby white paw, doubtless he was eager to be away – rabbits will be rabbits.

The otters, meanwhile, set down a box of grim-looking gas masks cut for hyena dimensions and the members of THORN each took one in passing, Nurka climbed on the ash and passed his extraordinary bow and quiver to the rabbit in the hole; the little beast passed it along the line to some hyenas already hiding within the barge. Nurka tossed the rabbit his skull helmet too, which he caught and passed along as well.

"What happened?" the rabbit asked, his voice heavily muffled by his gas mask. He took a disappointing head-count of the hyenas, "Where is everyone?"

"Sewer centipede," Nurka replied. "Madou and the others didn't stand a chance."

The white rabbit let out a strained grunt, but no words of any meaning.

Nurka looked on the positive side, "They died well. Besides, it'll take some Howlers with it."

"Aye. All the same, I'm sorry, Nurka."

"We are all ready to die, Casimir."

The hyena chief donned his suffocating gas mask, but didn't climb in with Casimir just yet. He stayed outside, ushering his comrades into the trapdoor one by one.

Themba was last up. He exchanged a sad, violet-tinged glance with Nurka from beneath his own gas mask. They tapped their grille-clad snouts together in camaraderie, in memory of Madou and the others.

The chug of an imperium engine vibrated through the barge's iron hull as the otters hurriedly cast off, putting water between them and the jetty.

The fog rolled in and the shore disappeared but for the tip of the jetty, lolling like a great tongue.

"Get below, Nurka," the otter captain said.

Nurka nodded and ushered Themba down the hole, passing him his kristahl hammer as he did so.

"HALT IN THE NAME OF THE REPUBLIC!"

All ears, eyes and noses, otter, rabbit and hyena, pricked, searched and sniffed for the source of that iron-clad voice. It came from a white light on the foggy jetty. It bobbed about like a firefly a moment, before revealing itself to be a brooch pinned to the cloaked chest of a giant, grey, armoured wolf!

The beast thundered down the jetty and leapt towards the barge with obvious imperious strength. Sailing cleanly across the dark, oily gap, the iron wolf landed heavily on the barge amidst a shockwave of coronal energy that blew ash away in a bubble of choking clouds.

Whilst the otters coughed and spluttered, blinded by bitter ash, Nurka remained unaffected beneath his gas mask, yet stunned all the same. He was met with an all-metal monster, as tall as

Themba and doubtless as strong. It had a Howler mantle draped about its mighty shoulders, secured by that shining white brooch. At its back, Nurka saw an exhaust puffing noxious clouds of ash, like a machine!

A machine shaped like a beast? What blasphemous wolfen contraption is this?

That was the last lucid thought Nurka enjoyed before the wolf raised a paw and blasted him in the chest with a blinding bolt of imperious plasma.

"Oof!"

The thunderous blow hit Nurka like a runaway train, pressing him backwards into the piles ash, which tumbled down over his spotty shoulders.

Unable to breathe and blinking stars from his eyes, Nurka saw one of the otters come up behind the approaching monstrous wolf and hit him over the back with a wrench. There was aloud clang and slight stumble. The wolf turned and simply shoved otter aside, knocking him harmlessly overboard.

"TELL YOUR CREW TO SURRENDER" the wolfen machine said to the nearby otter captain. "I DON'T WANT TO HURT ANY LITTLE BEASTS."

"Little beasts?" the captain spluttered, brandishing a huge imperium pistol. "There be no little beasts here, 'Owler! We otters be a proud warrior race. Take this, yah arrogant Lupan!"

Ka-crack!

The otter's pistol round pinged off the wolf's chest, leaving but a tiny scratch.

The otter's beady eyes gawked in amazement.

With a grunt and a single paw, the wolf shoved the otter captain overboard and advanced on Nurka.

"SURRENDER, THORN SCUM."

Before Nurka could get up, Themba leapt out of the ship's hold where he had been waiting for the right moment and swung his hammer down, hard and fast at the wolf's head. The metal Howler turned to meet the blow with one armoured paw held high. Amidst a blinding, deafening spark of plasma, paw and hammerhead met. The hammer rebounded, as if Themba had struck a trampoline! The weighty weapon tugged him off-balance and dragged him tumbling down the ashen piles.

The metal wolf shook his paw a few times, perhaps injured by the incredible force Themba's hammer had applied, but still standing.

He turned to Nurka with those sad, yellow eyelets. "GIVE UP. YOU CAN'T BEAT ME."

His breath laden with fear and adrenaline, Nurka scrambled to his feet and lunged at the enemy, trying to stick him with his sword. In defiance of his dimensions, the huge wolf weaved aside with a boxer's reflexes, slapped Nurka's sword down, and jabbed the disarmed hyena in the ribs, the resulting plasmatic blast throwing him hard against the secret entrance to the hold.

"Gaagh!"

"HAD ENOUGH, MATE?"

Coughing beneath his stifling gas mask, Nurka looked up and asked, "What… w-www-what are you?"

"Eisenwolf!" someone shouted from below.

The metal wolf looked past Nurka, to the hold. A white rabbit in a gas mask slowly, tentatively emerged from the piles of poisonous ash, paws behind his head.

"All right, mate," he said. "You win."

"Casimir!" Nurka spat.

"He's an Eisenwolf, Nurka," the rabbit said. "We can't beat the likes of him. Trust me, I know from the war."

"Eisenwolf?"

The 'Eisenwolf' stared at Casimir with his unblinking glazed eyes, metallic ears twitching, following the rabbit's every move as he stepped nervously sideways across the barge, out into the open.

"HALT!" the Eisenwolf warned.

"Easy, lad," Casimir replied, nursing the imperium pistol tucked behind his head, the barrel glowing with an eerie green light. "We'll come quietly."

The Eisenwolf cocked his head to one side and stared for an age. "TAKE YOUR MASK OFF," he demanded.

"What?"

"YOUR MASK; TAKE IT OFF. DO IT!"

Baffled, but nodding in compliance, Casimir slowly unbuckled his mask and pulled it over his long ears, away from his white face.

Suddenly, he threw the mask at his feet and raised his pistol at the Eisenwolf.

"Everyone, get down!"

Even before Nurka, Themba and the watching otters threw themselves down in the ash, Casimir pulled the trigger.

"Try an imperium pearl on for size, you monster!"

Crack!

A gleaming, ethereal arrow of green light sped from the pistol barrel and into the Eisenwolf's massive chest. The metal wolf looked down at himself, paws raised to where the pearl had struck, then up at Casimir, his inert helmet somehow betraying such melancholy.

"DAD?"

The pearl exploded and a blinding blast of imperious energy ripped across the deck, bowling Casimir head over tail and sending ash swirling from the polluted barge in great clouds.

Time passed. All was silent, save for waves slapping against the hull of the boat as it rocked to and fro in the aftermath. Coughing and spluttering, Casimir and the others looked all around them.

The Eisenwolf had gone.

Casimir scrabbled across the deck on all fours and grasping the rails peered overboard, into the inky, fog-bound blackness of the River Lupa. There was no sign of life, no sign of anything, not even a shred of cloak floating on the waters.

A big, weighty paw clapped on the rabbit's shoulder, startling him. Half-expecting to be met with the terrifying Eisenwolf, he was instead greeted by Themba, only slightly less terrifying in that gas mask.

"Nice work, long-ears," he acknowledged, his profound voice muffled.

"Thanks, spotty-bum," Casimir replied.

Themba frowned, then cackled, as hyenas ever did.

The otters that had been thrown overboard swam neatly back to the boat. "What was dat explosion?" the captain demanded. "Looked like a pearl."

Nurka tramped over, clutching his ribs. "How did you do that, Casimir?" he marvelled. "You're just a little beast."

Indignant, Casimir hopped to his feet and his full diminutive height, his long ears barely reaching Nurka's masked nose, or, in Themba's case, his chest. "Oi! Little beasts can shoot straight too, you know. I was in the war when you were still on milk, boy!"

"I only meant, Casimir, that you little beasts cannot wield imperium or charge pearls," Nurka explained gingerly.

"Oh yeah?" the 'little beast' scoffed. "Says who?"

His hyena comrade blinked a few times, "Then, you're a rabbit Chakaa?"

"Sort of."

"How can that be?"

Casimir dipped his chin, "During the war I was... I was captured and... experimented on." He whirled away, "These mad doctors and imperiologists. They exposed little beast prisoners to imperium, injected us with stings, racked us, just to see if we could be made into... Howlers, or whatever you call a rabbit like me. Most of us died, but I came through it. I used my power to escape 'em. Been looking over my shoulder ever since, even before I found Bruno." Casimir chuckled fondly, "That's how I found him, how I knew what he was. I was one too. He never knew. Never knew anything."

After a brief, almost respectful silence, Themba said, "Where's your corona?"

"It's weak," Casimir dismissed. "And I've learnt to repress it, that and so many things. No more, though. Now I'm standing up and being counted, for Bruno."

"Well said, Chakaa Casimir," Nurka praised.

"Heh! Chakaa. Yeah, right."

With a last glance at the waters, Themba said, "We should get below, Chief."

Once everyone had regained their wherewithal and otters had sounded the ship, Nurka's party went below. The chief stepped back from the trapdoor, which slammed shut over him, plunging him into blackness. He could hear the otters shovelling ash over the door, burying him and his comrades alive. It was unnerving, even for the stoic Nurka.

Nurka's eyes adjusted to the light of a single swaying lantern and his comrades slowly came into focus, hyenas one and all, except Casimir. They stood and sat nervously amidst the dozen spherical canisters of black-imperium. The tiniest leak would kill everyone in minutes, even Nurka and Themba, though as powerful Chakaa they would agonise the longest. The air was already laden with poisonous fumes from the heaps of decaying imperium all around and without masks everyone would choke regardless. That was the beauty of hiding under a deadly heap of ash; nobody was going to look too hard.

Hanging onto an overhead beam as the boat swayed, Nurka cast his eyes over his dejected brethren, especially Themba, who slumped in a corner, arms crossed over his armoured knees, a mighty warrior, laid low by his own perceived failure and the loss of Madou. The three of them had suffered together for so long. It seemed impossible he was gone.

"We will make their sacrifices count," Nurka said quietly, as if he hadn't meant to say it aloud, before shouting, "By the Wind, we'll make them all count!"

Everyone looked to him, so he continued.

"The time to strike is nearly upon us. You will have your revenge, Themba, for your slain family; and you Casimir, for your son, Bruno – a wolf no less! How low they scrape, these Howlers, they kill even their own kind in their greedy pursuit of power! Not for much longer. We will tear down their oppressive banners and free all the races!"

Breathing heavily under his stifling mask, Nurka suddenly clutched at his right arm and fell sideways against the flaking hull. Everyone jumped to help, none quicker than Themba, who shot to his feet and hurried over to support his chief.

"Nurka!"

"It's nothing," Nurka seethed, nursing his sword-arm.

"Did the iron wolf wound you?"

"No, it's just the ash in my blood. I... I had to use the imperious fire to fend off... Blade-dancer."

"Blade-dancer?" Themba repeated, holding the weakened Nurka up. "What do you mean?"

"The white wolf," Nurka explained.

"He was *the* Blade-dancer? Our Prince's old friend?"

"So he claimed; I believe him."

Casimir's ears pricked, but nothing more.

Themba blinked a few times, "You killed him?"

"Hahahahaaaa!" the reserved Nurka laughed, giving a personally rare display of his people's hysterics, "No, the hundred-legs interrupted our... meeting."

Now it was Themba's turn to pat Nurka on the neck. "Rest, chief," he said fondly. "Save your speeches for those that need to hear them, not us."

Nurka looked up at him.

"We're with you," Themba swore, raising Nurka's paw to the ceiling like a boxing champion, "Jua-mataaaaaa!"

✦

Ivan Donskoy stepped from rank sewers to fresh air; or as fresh as air came in Lupa. He checked the immediate area and found nobody. He hurried down the jetty and looked out across the dark, foggy river, his brooch still shining red, illuminating the mist and passing raindrops, turning them to blood. There was no sign of the hyenas, or Rafe.

Suddenly, bubbles.

Ivan followed the bubbles with his eyes and ears as they broke the surface of the black water, heading past him and with a definite purpose for shore. The Howler swore he could see a white light wobbling deep beneath the waves.

Was it some kind of angler fish?

The bubbles converged by a rusty iron ladder set into the river wall and up popped a massive metallic wolf in a sodden black mantle.

Rafe!

Hardly believing his eyes, Ivan watched Rafe pull himself from the river and back onto dry land without much ado, water cascading from every crevice.

"I TOLD YOU TO STAY BACK THERE," Rafe said, brushing a little red crab from his shoulder.

Ivan found his tongue amidst his astonishment. "I… I don't take orders from ALPHA," he maintained, rolling his neck and tugging at his cloak. "Where'd THORN go?"

"SAILING," Rafe hummed, feeling his massive metal chest, specifically a large, fresh, silvery crater surrounded by soot which wasn't there before. "I'D SWIM AFTER THEM IF I COULD, BUT… I CAN'T."

"Not in that getup," Ivan observed, adding, "Were you *walking* on the riverbed just now?"

"YEAH!" Rafe chirped, tipping water from his sieve-like ears. "PRETTY NEAT, EH?"

"How'd you breathe?"

"BACKPACK HAS AN AIR SUPPLY. IT'S GOOD FOR FIFTEEN MINUTES, DOCTOR JOSEF SAYS."

Ivan cocked his head, "Josef? Not Josef Grau?"

"YEAH," Rafe confirmed. Then he cupped a paw to his head and laughed like a hyena hiding in a barrel. "HAHAAAAHAHAAA! HO BOY IS JANOAH GONNA BE MAD. I'VE SCREWED UP AGAIN."

Josef *and* Janoah.

Ivan frowned beneath his Bloodfang helmet as he slotted the pieces together; the size, the power, the voice – it was all adding up in his mind.

"They didn't," he mouthed.

Rafe's metal ears squeaked round to Ivan, then his head and torso followed, as if delayed by their sheer heft. "SORRY, WHATCHA SAY?"

Ivan swallowed and gathered himself beneath that blank, yellow-eyed gaze. "You're an Eisenwolf, aren't you?"

Rafe wrung out his ribbon for a tail. "NO SCHMUTZ."

Nodding, Blade-dancer looked at Rafe's symbolic, silken prosthetic. "What happened to your tail, Eisenwolf?" he asked, in an obviously calculating manner.

Ivan's insincerity was lost on Rafe. "JOSEF HAD TO CUT IT OFF. CAN'T HAVE ANY HOLES IN AN EISENPELZ, HAS TO BE HERM… HERMETICALLY SEALED. YEAH, THAT'S IT. HAVING A TAIL STICKING OUT IN A BAG OR SOMETHIN' IS A WEAKNESS."

"He's a butcher, that cat," Ivan tutted.

"NAH, HE'S ALL RIGHT. I DON'T MISS IT, YOU KNOW, MY TAIL THAT IS. PART OF THE JOB."

"Pinned up in a frame is it?"

"HA! NAAAAH, IT WENT IN THE BIN, MATE."

Huffing, Ivan suddenly growled, "You do realise, of course, that as an Eisenwolf you're a dangerous and illegal abomination?"

Rafe's ears swivelled, "OH YEAH?"

"I didn't write the law, but as a Howler I must uphold it."

"RIGHT, RIGHT. SO WHAT'RE YOU GONNA DO ABOUT IT, ARREST ME?"

"I should; that or kill you."

Rafe instantly raised a snapping, popping, plasma-charged metal fist. "COME ON THEN, HAVE A GO!"

Blinking slowly, Ivan turned his nose in disgust and looked out across the water, "It won't last, Eisenwolf."

Rafe's paw dropped a little.

"You'll rot faster than a corpse left in the sun the rate you're going," Ivan explained. "Believe me, I know of what I speak-"

"YOU DUNNO NOTHING ABOUT ME!"

With a grunt, Rafe turned to leave, arms held off his body with a slight, unnatural stiffness.

"Thank you," Ivan blurted, almost in pain.

Rafe stopped, head and ears turning just slightly.

It was difficult, but for honour to be upheld Ivan persevered. "You got that centipede off me. I'd be dead if you hadn't. For that I'm letting you go, but if we ever meet again, I won't be able to."

The Eisenwolf laughed, "CHARMING, 'EN YER?"

"Rafe!"

Prefect Janoah dashed from the sewers, sword drawn, and with a couple of obliging Bloodfang Howlers at her back. Giving Ivan a passing glance, she came to a stop by Rafe and looked all around.

"Well?"

Rafe shook his head, "SORRY, JAN. THEY GOT ON A BOAT. I TRIED TO STOP 'EM."

Janoah tramped down the jetty a way, "Where?"

Ivan dismissed, "Forget it, Janoah. We won't find them in this fog. They'll be smuggled from the district before we can even get word about."

"Schmutz!"

"SORRY," Rafe said again. "I SCREWED UP."

"No, you did your best," Janoah said, returning to slap Rafe's arm. In doing so she noticed the crater on his chest and placed her paw there. "What happened?" she gasped.

Rafe looked, "EH? OH! IT WAS A PEARL, I THINK."

"Pearl? You took an imperium pearl to the face? You're joking!"

"WELL I DUNNO, JAN. I'M ONLY GOING BY WHAT YOU TOLD ME ABOUT 'EM. SOME RABBIT POPPED UP 'N' SHOT ME WITH IT. KNOCKED ME OVERBOARD INTO THE RIVER. I THOUGHT I WAS A GONER, BUT THE SUIT NEVER EVEN SPRUNG A LEAK."

"Rabbit, you say?"

"YEAH."

Nodding, then laughing, Janoah looked to Ivan, then patted Rafe's cavernous chest. "Rabbits can't fire pearls, Stenton," and started back down the jetty. "Come on, they need us back there."

"WHAT FOR?"

Janoah was already away, climbing some slimy steps to take the overland route back to the refinery. She stopped long enough to reply, "We're going on a bug hunt."

✦

Removing the wrench that barred the rusty door, Rufus pulled it open and shone his brooch down the steps, beating back the darkness with a blood-red light and revealing dozens of little beasts dressed in coveralls; rabbits, rats, moles and the like, all squinted back at him.

The hostages.

"I've found them!" Rufus shouted to the left, before saying to the trembling beasts, "It's all right everyone. You're safe now. Is anybody hurt?"

Werner joined Rufus at the doorway, his pink face enclosed by a gas-mask since the air in the refinery was thick with pollution. "Well done, sir," he praised, his voice muffled by his mask. "How'd you find 'em? This place is like a labyrinth!"

Rufus glanced sideways at the hog, surprised the word labyrinth was amidst his lexicon. "Doors aren't generally secured with wrenches, Werner," the Howler explained, throwing the hefty tool aside. "Get these beasts clear of the building; with a centipede on the loose it's too dangerous for them to linger."

"Leave it to me, sir."

Rufus did so, hurrying down smoky corridors, passing red-shirted Politzi of every race made somewhat anonymous by their similar gas-masks. Happening across a hyena slumped against a wall, Rufus knelt down and checked for life.

He was disappointed.

Linus came barrelling down the same corridor. "Sir!" the youth said, skidding to a halt. "Vladimir wants you, sir!"

"Tell him I've found the hostages," Rufus huffed, standing up and asking, "Any sign of that centipede yet?"

"No, sir, but-"

"How's Uther holding up?"

"They're putting him on a stretcher, sir."

Patting Linus's sturdy shoulder Rufus made to leave, "Stay with him. I'm going to find Jan. I shouldn't worry about her these days, but I do-"

"But we've got a hyena cornered upstairs!" Linus blurted, adding, "Sir."

Rufus whirled on him, but said nothing.

"He's alive, sir," Linus explained, "but, well… unhinged, you might say. Vladimir was wondering if you wouldn't try talking him down, what with you being uh… well…."

"A hyena-lover?" Rufus guessed.

"Versed in hyena ways," Linus tactfully corrected.

Managing a chuckle despite everything, Rufus looked this way and that, before nodding, "Lead on, Mills."

Linus beckoned his superior through the innards of the refinery, past more bodies, some hyenas, some Politzi, but mostly the former. They hurried up some metallic stairs, boots thumping, and through a door into a relatively fog-free series of nicely furnished offices – this is where the administrators worked, evidently.

Linus slowed to a walk, his boots softened by a red carpet. With Rufus in tow, he picked his way through an office, past several Politzi, to Vladimir's side.

The lofty Grand Howler was stationed by a door, pistol in paw. He turned to his fellow Howlers, Rufus in particular.

"He's in there," he whispered, trusting Linus had filled Rufus in on the situation. "He's got a capsule in his mouth but not the guts to crunch it."

"Yet," Rufus said.

Vladimir nodded, "He's armed too, so watch yourself. We've got one of the Chakaa in custody already, so don't take any unnecessary risks."

Rufus was surprised, "Is that one going to live? I thought he was bitten."

Vladimir tapped his armoured nose, "I brought a sting, just in case of an emergency. He'll live now."

Surprised, Rufus nodded.

It took Linus a moment to work out what Vladimir had just said. "White-imperium?" he gasped, appalled. "You gave venom to a… a THORN terrorist, sir?"

"We need him alive if we're to interrogate him," Vladimir explained. "Now keep your voice down."

"But we're dying from the rot left right and centre; we can't justify wasting venom on criminals. What'll Elder Amael say when he finds out?"

Sighing, Vladimir played his card, "Keep it to yourself, Mills, and I will let your disgusting display of insubordination earlier go unpunished. Or would you prefer being tied to a pole and flogged with an imperium whip?"

Linus dipped his chin, "I-I-I was just concerned, sir."

Smacking his lips, Vladimir turned to Rufus. "He's got a lot to learn, this one," he said of Linus.

Rolling his eyes, Rufus brushed Vladimir by, and peered round the open door, catching sight of a youthful hyena sitting in the corner of a plush office.

"Stay back!" the hyena snarled at Rufus, waving a pistol in his general direction "I'll shoot!"

Rufus drew away. He looked at Vladimir and Linus, then, to their combined tiny gasps, boldly stepped into the open, paws raised.

"Get out, Howler scum!" the hyena howled at once.

"I'm not going anywhere, dear boy. I just want to have a word with you-"

"Get oooouut! Get out, get out, get ouuuuhouhout!"

Rufus waited, paws raised, heart pounding, whilst the hyena's hysterics passed. He was only a cub, sandy cheeks wet with tears, broad nose running, big paws trembling. There was no danger of him shooting straight in his condition, of that Rufus was convinced, taking a surreptitious step closer.

"I'm… going to remove my helmet, so we can talk face to face," Rufus told the hyena, adding with a disarming Rufus-brand chuckle, "These silly old helmets of ours are rather intimidating, I know."

Slowly, Rufus unbuckled his helmet and slipped it off.

The hyena stared at him, mouth slightly agape – Rufus spied the glimmering glass imperium capsule resting on the youth's tongue. By Ulf, how could he bear it? The mere thought of a black-imperium capsule resting on his own tongue made Rufus queasy.

"Perhaps you recognise me?" he said with a gulp. "I'm Rufus Bloodfang."

The hyena nodded a little. "You… you're the one… the one who… who helps us."

"I speak up for your people when I can, yes," Rufus clarified, spreading a paw. "If that small gesture helps at all then I'm glad. I wish I could do more."

The hyena said nothing.

"What's your name?" Rufus asked him.

"My name?"

"Yes."

"Who cares?"

"I do," Rufus insisted, but moved on. "It's wrong how the tribes are treated. If I had my way things would change tomorrow. But I tell you now, my young friend, that this is not the way to go about changing anything. Killing and bombing isn't going to-"

"I've not killed anyone!" the hyena protested. "I never killed anyone! Please, you must believe me!"

"I didn't say you had," Rufus soothed. "But there are beasts lying dead in the corridors below me, beasts on both sides, and they wouldn't be but for THORN. It's a tragedy for us all, it really is."

The hyena wept afresh, "Ohohohoooow."

Rufus took the opportunity to shuffle a little closer, to get within range, he hoped. "I can see you're just a young lad," he reasoned. "It's not your fault. You got sucked into this mess before you even knew what was what. It all looked very romantic from the outside, didn't it? I bet your leaders told you how glorious it is to die for their cause. Now you've seen what death is like you know better."

"It was a monster!" the hyena wailed, cupping his paws over his head and rocking back and forth. "It killed them all. It killed everyone!"

Rufus frowned in thought, "The centipede?"

The hyena looked up, baffled, "Centipede?"

"The hundred-legs," Rufus clarified, using hyena terminology. He changed tack, thinking to give the cub a reason to help, to talk, even to live, "We're trying to find it, you see, before it kills anyone else. If it gets out into the city it might kill hundreds of innocent citizens and I know you don't want that. Did you see where it went, perhaps? Did it go back down the sewers? Can you tell us?"

The hyena shook his head, his features screwing up with fresh grief. "It was… was one of you, wasn't it? How could you do that to one of your own?"

"What?"

"Your monster wolf. I s-sss-saw it. I did! It killed everyone at the doors!"

Rufus realised the cub hadn't seen a centipede, but an Eisenwolf. Best to skirt round that, he thought.

"Just put the pistol down and for Ulf's sake spit out that dreadful capsule," he implored. "Don't do this to yourself. I can help you. I want to help you."

"How can you?" the hyena wept.

"I'm a Grand Howler. I can take charge of you. I won't let anyone hurt you-"

"They'll torture me on the rack!"

"I won't let them."

"You lie! I know it's true! They k-k-killed our Prince on the rack. I won't let you humiliate *me* that way! I won't! Do you hear?"

Before Rufus could think of another avenue of attack, he heard a dreadful, dull crunch from the hyena's mouth.

"Gagh!" he choked. "Grrrgh!"

Rufus grimaced, "Foolish pup," and drew his pistol.

Outside, in the corridor, Linus and Vladimir heard the bang of an imperium round going off.

Crack!

"Rufus!" barked Linus, fearing the worst.

He hurried into the room with Vladimir whereupon they found Rufus still standing – thank Ulf – looking down on the hyena. The terrorist was slumped in the corner of the room, the wall splattered with blood, the carpet beneath his shattered head turning a darker shade of red. His mouth and lips were blackened, as if burnt.

Odd, Linus thought.

Rufus covered his nose and backed off. Linus wondered why. Surely Grand Howler Rufus, a war veteran, had seen death up close before?

And then it happened, the hyena's mouth started to smoulder, to wither and blacken. The gums curled away from the mighty canine teeth as the flesh shrivelled and 'smoked', the face altogether peeling away from the red-raw bone like a ghoulish mask.

"Oh by Ulf!" Linus gasped, nearly falling over backwards.

"Out!" Vladimir barked, grabbing the stocky Howler by the scruff of his neck and yanking him back through the door. "Everybody out!"

Donning his helmet, Rufus calmly shut the door behind him, whilst Vladimir ushered Linus and the gathered Politzi down the corridor and stairs, back into the smoggy refinery proper – smoggy, but not deadly like the office they had hastily evacuated.

Linus removed his helmet and leant against the stark refinery wall. He heaved, but nothing much came up – he and Uther hadn't been able to stop for lunch, thankfully.

Howler Mills felt a paw on his back; Rufus.

"Oh, sir, how c-ccc-could he?" Linus howled at him.

"It's all right, dear boy," Rufus hushed, patting the young Howler's shoulders. He winked at Vladimir, "The poor chap shot himself before the capsule took any real effect. He didn't suffer. Not for a second."

"It's monstrous."

"Yes. I know."

Allowing Linus a moment's grace, Vladimir urged everyone back to work, "Come on. There's a centipede on the loose and I want it found!"

Chapter 19

The rain beat down on Linus as he helped load Uther into the back of the chugging field ambulance, lifting the stretcher onto his shoulders and sliding him in. With a glance back at the refinery, Linus climbed inside the ambulance and stood over his partner as the Howler medic strapped a respirator to his muzzle.

The battered Uther had lost a lot of blood and breathed in a toxic cocktail of imperium from several broken pipes, some of it yellow-imperium. He was coughing and spluttering something awful.

"Don't die," Linus told him.

To which Uther gruffed, "Don't be daft, Woodlouse."

"No, s-sss-sorry." Looking around, Linus whispered, "Did you see him?"

"Eh?"

Before Linus could explain, two Politzi hogs hurriedly bore another stretcher from the refinery to the ambulance; Vladimir Oromov followed closely behind. To Linus's shock he saw the wounded beast was a hyena. It must be the Chakaa that Vladimir had spoken of.

Linus felt a steaming wave of fury wash over him. These THORN fanatics had beaten and shot Uther, and now one was being put into the very same ambulance as him? It was an outrage!

"Sir, what's going on?" Linus demanded, barring the ambulance with his stocky frame. "Uther's in here."

Vladimir took a moment to grasp the problem. "Oh do calm down, Mills, there's room enough for two. We need the Chakaa alive to interrogate him. Even if he was in a position to fight he's well-restrained."

Linus noted the reams of Howler-wire binding the feverish-looking hyena paw and foot.

"You're on thin ice, Howler," Vladimir warned. "One more peep out of you today and I'll send you to Amael for correction, is that understood?"

A nod. "Yes, sir… I-I was just-"

"Shut up, Mills!"

A gulp. "Sir."

"We'll take it from here, Grand Howler," the Howler medic said, breaking Linus from his thoughts. He was ushered from the ambulance and the unconscious hyena slipped in beside Uther like a loaf of bread. Without further ado the doors were slammed shut and the horns atop the ambulance blared out an ear-piercing siren. It charged through the cordon and down the road, headlights beaming.

Momentarily caught in the ambulance's passing lights was a big Howler sitting atop a blue monobike – an Eisbrand? He was parked by the side of the road, watching the goings-on at the refinery.

"Linus, see who that is," Vladimir said. "I'll be inside."

"Sir!" Linus acknowledged extra-smartly, trying to claw back some semblance of obedience.

The Eisbrand saw the Bloodfang approach and Linus half-expected him to ride away, but he stayed put, one armoured foot on the wet, gritty ground, the other on his bike. He was an Eisbrand all right, the blue-imperium snowflake emblem gently illuminating his armoured brow made that plain.

"State your business, Howler," Linus demanded, noting the intimidating sword at the Eisbrand's back.

"Curiosity," he replied.

"This is Bloodfang territory."

"Lupa's a free city. I can loiter where I please."

To which Linus nodded, rainwater dripping off his metallic muzzle. "Yes, but for your own safety I suggest you keep away from here. It could be dangerous."

"Is that a threat?" the stranger growled.

"N-nnn-n!" Linus chirped. "I-I didn't mean it like that!" he guffawed. Shaking his head, he held out paw to mollify his fellow Howler, "Where're my manners? I'm Linus Mills Bloodfang, Trooper First Class."

The Eisbrand cautiously looked Linus up and down, but accepted his paw, "Captain Tristan Donskoy... Eisbrand, of course."

Linus gasped a little, "Ivan's cousin?"

Tristan nodded.

"Honoured, Howler," Linus said, nodding back.

"Honour's mine," Tristan sniffed. "I hear you're quite the Howler, Mills."

"Me?"

"Took down a nest of Howler-killers, didn't you?"

Linus came over all flustered. "That was Uther really. I-I-I got in way over my head."

"Modest too," Tristan observed. He looked past Linus, to the now quiet refinery. "It seems you have everything under control, Howler Mills, you *and* ALPHA."

"I wish. It's a terrible shambles I'm afraid."

"Oh?"

Linus wasn't sure if he should be telling a member of rival pack such things but, "By the looks of it all the terrorists are dead or fled, save one. It's a right sorry sight in there."

Tristan nodded, "I hear they commit suicide by swallowing black-imperium these THORN fanatics."

"Yes. It's awful. They put capsules in their mouths when they know we're coming and crunch them when there's no chance of escape." Linus closed his eyes and shook his head at some awful vision. "Grand Howler Rufus was trying to talk one round just now," he continued. "We had him cornered in an office. He was just a cub."

"No luck?"

"His flesh just... just fell away like wax. I'll never forget it. Never."

"It's a shame they feel driven to such ends."

"It's insane!" Linus seethed. "I don't understand these THORN types. Hyenas don't believe in suicide; it's a sin that bars them from crossing the Eternal Plains. Dying in battle is one thing, but to just kill yourself? It goes against everything a young warrior is taught."

"You know your hyenas," Tristan observed, surprised.

Linus shrugged that off with, "I know Rufus Valerio."

Nodding, Tristan asked, "You said you've a survivor?"

"Yes."

"What's his name?"

Linus was surprised to be asked, "No idea."

"You'll torture him to find out though?"

"Interrogate," Linus corrected.

"That what you Bloodfangs call racking these days?" Tristan chuckled.

Linus wasn't sure how to respond and moved swiftly on to keep things civil. "In any case, friend, it's not over yet. We've a giant sewer centipede on the loose in there, so you should keep your distance."

"Sewer centipede?" Tristan scoffed in amusement. "That's no problem for the mighty Bloodfangs, surely!"

"It's a big one."

"How big?"

"I haven't seen it. The air's so thick in there we can't find it. Uther says it's the biggest he's ever seen."

"Judging by Uther's knack for exaggeration it'll be about two inches long, then," Tristan huffed.

Linus actually laughed, "You know, I hope so-"

Suddenly the peal of breaking glass cut across the refinery grounds. Through the rain and fog, Linus and Tristan saw flashes of light illuminate the windows and heard the subsequent pops and cracks of imperium pistols.

"Excuse me," Linus said, hurrying back.

Tristan stayed put on his mono, but started it up, the wheel's gyroscope bursting into a ring of frosty blue-imperium.

As Linus tore towards the refinery, Werner trotted from the main door with a dozen armed Politzi at his back. They scuttled round the side of the towering building and lined up like a firing squad.

The Politzi aimed upwards as Werner ran his torch beam up the nearest smouldering smoke stack.

They waited.

"Werner, what is it?" Linus panted.

"It's coming up the chimney, sir," the pig replied.

"What is?"

"The centipede."

Sure enough an enormous, many-legged centipede erupted the refinery's chimney, squeezing its way to freedom like vivid blue paint from a tube.

"By Ulf's fangs, look at it!" Linus woofed.

"Aye, it's a whopper," snorted Werner.

The giant bug flopped forward and started trickling down the side of the chimney, its orange legs clacking rhythmically. The beast was so long that its rear end remained inside the great funnel even whilst its front end reached the roof and started to spill over towards the ground.

"Steady!" Werner said. "Hold your fire!"

The Politzi, rabbits, rats, hogs and more, quivered in fear.

"Steady, I say!"

Linus watched, waited.

"Fire!"

Werner's beasts opened a mighty volley, lighting up the refinery for a moment, before they were instantly enveloped in clouds of ash. The resulting pellets pinged harmlessly off the centipede's armour and served only to alert it to the rough whereabouts of its tormentors towards whom it now raced.

"Retreat!" Werner yelped. "Split up! Split up! It can't follow all of us!"

The pig and his Politzi scattered in all directions as the centipede clacked swiftly towards them, antennae slicing the rainy air where they had been but seconds ago. It picked out an unfortunate rabbit from the group and ran him down, cornering him inside an outlying building.

It was Constable Claybourne!

"Aaagh!" he screamed, ducking into a ball. "Help meeheheee! Please!"

Whipping out his short sword, Linus sprinted over to the centipede's back end. As it bore down on Claybourne, he slashed at one of its legs with a bright, plasmatic sword-strike and a gruff, Uther-like, "Oi!"

The centipede arced round, almost indignant, and undulated rapidly towards Linus, claw over giant orange claw, antennae tasting the rainy air.

Realising what he'd done, Linus unbuckled his kristahl shield and brought it to bear. He could see the centipede was wounded, its mouth dripping white blood. Every Howler worth his sting knew that the mouth was the place to strike.

"Get outta there, sir!" Werner squealed from the safety of some crates. "Run, lad!"

Too late.

The colossal centipede lunged at Linus, bloodied maw agape, and he instinctively raised his shield.

Impact!

Trooper Linus was knocked flat on his back and crushed to the hard, rough ground, the air pressed from his lungs. He felt the mandibles of the centipede's mouth scraping over his shield's smooth surface as it tried to get a purchase and bite through to the tasty wolfen morsel beneath. The bitter, acrid stench of centipede ammonia burnt Linus's nose and throat.

Summoning all his strength, the young Howler channelled the imperium down his arm and into the centre of his Bloodfang shield. The kristahl metal pulsed with white-hot plasma, blasting the centipede right in the face! It whipped away in pain and alarm, plasma playing over its mandibles. Linus seized the opportunity to roll to his feet, shield up, sword ready, tail flicking. He knew from the Howler Codex not to flee; this monster could run as fast a car and would just chase him down.

Stand and fight, it was the only way.

The centipede recovered and followed Linus across the refinery grounds, feelers slapping his shield as he retreated backwards, foot over smartly white-gaitered, ash-streaked foot.

Suddenly a light appeared, bright and white; the ear-piercing popping of an imperium engine too. Linus dared look just as a monobike whizzed across the refinery grounds towards him. It thrummed loudly between him and the centipede. There was a flash of steel and spark of plasma as a huge sword slashed the centipede in the head! Writhing about in pain, it reared up and away.

The bike and its rider skidded round and powered back, parking neatly by the awestruck Linus.

"Get on!" Tristan barked.

Linus jumped on the monobike. Burning rubber, Eisbrand whisked Bloodfang away a few tens of feet before slowing to a stop at the refinery's main entrance.

They both looked on as the baffled centipede searched for them in vain, before continuing its rampage elsewhere

"All right," admitted Tristan, "that's pretty big."

Vladimir and Rufus emerged from the refinery amidst utter chaos. Politzi of every race fled before the oncoming tide of living armour as it flowed towards the refinery's perimeter, washing over barrels and boxes and even crushing a Politzi car, spearing its arch-shaped bonnet with its dagger-like legs as if it were paper.

"We can't let it get out into the city!" Rufus said, swishing his sword.

"I'm open to suggestions," Vladimir replied.

Werner guffawed falsely, "Shooting it won't work, that's for sure!"

The Howlers watched the centipede trundle through the gates and onto the road, scattering the law and kicking over monobikes as it went on its merry way. Luckily, Ivan's Giacomo Valerio *Spider* was spared destruction, but Vladimir's pack-issued car was quickly crushed as the centipede trampled it under every single one of its legs, as if taking some perverse pleasure.

Vladimir winced at the sight. "Amael's not going to be happy," he grumbled.

"If it scratches Ivan's *Spider* it's as good as dead," Rufus chuckled.

With that he took the lead, striding across the refinery grounds, and out onto the road, tracing the centipede's wake of destruction and bristly ammonia scent.

Even whilst its back end still crumpled Vladimir's car underfoot, the centipede's head end was starting to scale a warehouse wall. Its segmented body shimmered with ghostly waves of imperium, illuminating the glistening buildings all around and the awestruck faces of the Politzi observing helplessly below.

Vladimir and Rufus stared along with everyone else, as unsure as to how to proceed against such a monster as anyone.

"Magnificent sight, isn't it?" said Doctor Josef, coming up behind them with his umbrella – the cat had a nasty habit of sneaking up on beasts.

"Magnificent?" Vladimir spluttered. "It's a menace!"

Chuckling, Josef ignored him in favour of Rufus, "By the way, may I offer my congratulations, Rufus."

The preoccupied wolf turned to him a moment, "Pardon?"

"On your recent accolade."

Rufus said nothing.

Josef twirled his umbrella. "Such a great mind as yours is wasted here," he said, pushing his dark spectacles up his neat feline nose. "You'd do well to talk to Grand Prefect Silvermane. He did wonders for me. I've my own laboratory, and I've suffered very little interference in my work since I jumped ship."

This time Rufus let out an incredulous snort.

Vladimir too, "Excuse me, Doctor Josef, but this is hardly the time to go head-hunting. We've a deranged centipede on the loose."

Josef dismissed haughtily, "Rafe will take care of it, once he's taken care of the hyenas."

"What is he, the incarnation of Ulf?" Vladimir mocked.

"You doubt the power of my creation?" Josef chuckled. "A common mistake."

Rufus whirled on the grey cat, "So you did it? *You* made that boy into an Eisenwolf?"

Josef bowed a little, "Rafe is what he is; I merely helped him achieve his full potential-"

Grabbing Josef's coat lapels, Rufus heaved the cat off his feet and slammed him into the black ALPHA truck that had brought him and his 'creation' here.

"Bastard cat!" Rufus snarled, his cannonball biceps straining against his ruddy fur. "What gave you the right? Did you even ask him? Did you even go through the motions, or did you just abduct him? Answer me!"

"Rafe was a willing subject in-"

"Rafe? 'Rafe'!" Rufus spluttered, shaking Josef until his spectacles nearly fell off his face. "By Ulf, do you think I don't know, that I can't tell, I who found him first? You stole his future you miserable schmutz-sucking maggot!"

"He… was… dying… Rufus!" Josef said between shakes.

"And he'll die a lot faster now, though not as fast as you when I'm through with you-"

"Rufus that's enough!" Vladimir bellowed, grabbing his shoulder and pulling him away. "Control yourself, for Ulf's sake!"

Rufus let Josef go, but glared at him and pointed like a common brawler. "You'll pay for this!"

"Your wife found him for me," Josef claimed, dusting himself down and resetting his spectacles. "No, in fact, *you* found him. For once your keen coronal senses have served the Republic, instead sating your own lecherous cravings-"

Rufus lunged at Josef a second time, but the bigger Vladimir tugged the furious wolf aside and threw him against the van. "Leave it, Rufus!" he snarled, his helmet grille and profound voice tickling the shorter wolf's ear. "You can't pick a fight with ALPHA. You hit him and they'll throw the book at you! Don't give them any excuse when you're already of interest."

"Josef I expect it from," Rufus laughed falsely, shaking his head. "But my own wife? My dear Jan, sinking so low? I'd never have believed it. Never!"

Vladimir huffed, "She must have good reason."

"Don't defend her!"

"For someone so clever there's much you don't see, Valerio."

Rufus glared at Vladimir.

The noise of Tristan's approaching monobike put paid to any further upset. It rumbled to a stop and Linus hopped off the back.

"Sir!"

"Fraternising with Eisbrands, Mills?" Vladimir joked, releasing Rufus. "Your list of misdemeanours lengthens still."

"Howler Tristan helped me get away, sir."

"Did he indeed? Then we're indebted to him, aren't we Rufus?"

Tidying his mantle, Rufus looked Tristan over and snorted with what Linus sensed was barely-veiled malice, "Grateful, I'm sure."

Vladimir spread a paw, "I don't know what you're doing here, Donskoy, but if you want to help us-"

"We're all prey here, Vladimir, a sewer centipede makes no distinction according to one's brooch," the Eisbrand cut in. He glanced at the centipede twisting its way along the buildings, before asking, "Where's my cousin?"

Vladimir sighed, "Gallivanting through the sewers after THORN, last we heard."

"Dirty old sewers? Ivan Donskoy? Are you sure?"

"Uther said so."

Tristan winked at Linus with the latter of his green and blue eyes. "Ah, well then it must be true."

Linus smiled beneath his helm.

"It's going!" Werner shouted. "It's off, sirs, look!"

Sure enough the centipede's head disappeared round the side of a building and slipped into a narrow alley. Its orange legs picked up the pace, double-time, triple-time, drumming the roof of Vladimir's mangled car and threading its never-ending body into the alleyway.

"We can't lose it," Rufus said.

"Lose it?" Linus scoffed. "How could we even begin to?"

"It'll look for somewhere warm and dark, like the sewers again. Then it could pop out anywhere, kill anyone. We must stop it."

"But how?"

Tristan swung his legs off his monobike and drew his mighty sword from his back, hefting it in both armoured paws he touched it to his metallic nose. "The old-fashioned way," he said. "Lead on, Grand Howlers, age before beauty."

"Watch it, boy, or I'll have you thrown off our land and your bike impounded!" Rufus growled, barging the bigger Tristan with his shoulder in passing. "Come on, Vladimir; let's show this wet-eared pup how it's done."

Vladimir rolled his eyes.

Linus couldn't believe it. What had come over Rufus?

Doctor Josef sighed, "You're all being quite foolish. Rafe will take care of everything. Leave it to him."

Ignoring the cat for fear of throttling him, Rufus strode across the road with growing speed, dashing into the alley. The others followed him, the youngsters first, Vladimir last, and then one or two braver Politzi eager to see the battle – no doubt this was going to be a rare spectacle.

Werner, less brave, or more intelligent, squeezed behind the wheel of a Politzi car along with young Constable Claybourne and drove straight past the alleyway, for it was too small, taking instead the main road. Following his pink porcine nose through the ever-thickening riverside fog, Werner drove round the deserted industrial block and down the next road to where he assumed the alleyway must lead. Judging he was approaching the spot where it ought to emerge, he slowed down and searched for a rent in the otherwise uniform brick walls. The street lamps passed lazily overhead, their warm light dancing on the rain-flecked bonnet, whilst the window wiper squeaked back and forth over the vertical windscreen.

"Sir!" young Claybourne said, pointing at a rift between buildings. It was dark and foggy, like a mysterious chasm leading to another world.

"I see it, lad," Werner snorted.

He stopped the car. They waited. The engine ticked over and the rain patted noisily on the roof. Nothing.

Had they taken a wrong turn? Had the centipede gone elsewhere? It could climb anything, go anywhere, there was no law that demanded it take the alley, except that bugs tended to follow the easiest path they were presented with, as Werner explained to young Claybourne.

"How'd you know that, sir?" the rabbit asked.

"Bugs are like us, Borce," Werner maintained. "On your way home tonight what'll you do, take the roads, or climb over all the houses?"

"The roads, sir, but I'm not a centipede the size of a thumping train."

"Even so, and mind yer language."

Borce looked down the alley, so still and silent, "Maybe… maybe it's killed 'em, sir?"

"Who?"

"The Howlers, sir."

"You sound just like your uncle. What a pessimist! Give 'em a chance, it's only been two minutes-whoooaaagh!"

Werner crunched the gears and slammed a trotter on the accelerator, reversing the car so hard that Borce had to hold his paws forth to keep from head-butting the window. The car whined backwards just in time as a veritable freight train of blue and orange centipede steamed out the alleyway and charged across the road. It curled away from the opposite side of the street and started stampeding down the road after the Politzi car, its bejewelled blue face illuminated by the headlights, antennae whipping the bonnet.

"Faster, chief!" Borce yelped. "Faster!"

Werner shouted back, "I can't go any faster!"

"It's gaining!"

"Shoot it, lad! Quickly!"

"W-w-what?"

"Pop one in its head. Quick, before I run out of road!"

"A pistol won't do schmutz!"

"Just have a crack at it, lad! Go on!"

Borce fumbled with his pistol, spilling glittery imperium powder all over his lap as he tried to reload it. The whining, squealing car swivelled side to side as Werner battled to keep it from skidding round, not wanting to stop, not wanting to find out what might happen if he did.

Werner checked the mirror for obstacles, but couldn't see anything for the fog. "Hurry up, lad!"

Constable Claybourne opened the passenger window and with a shaking paw fired in the general direction of the centipede.

A hit!

The beast reeled away into the rolling fog in an instant, almost the exact instant the car mounted the kerb and hit a lamppost. The engine conked-out and the headlights with it, casting Werner and Borce into the misty, orange gloom emanating from of the bent imperium gas lamppost flickering overhead.

Once they had stopped rattling around in their seats, the Politzi pair took stock. Wiping condensation from the cracked windscreen, they watched flashes of light explode in the mist ahead like giant fireflies. The faint silhouettes of four Howlers danced all over the road, leaping and rolling and letting off bright sparks of imperious energy against the great, swooping, skeletal shadow of the centipede, trying to find a chink in its armour. It was like a giant shadow-puppet show.

"Go on, lads, get it!" Werner laughed, punching the air. "Ohohoooo! Look at 'em go!"

Borce Claybourne sat in silence, straining his eyes. He had never seen the like before. The true power of the Howlers was a thing rarely glimpsed; pistols, threats, merely the presence of an imposing cloaked wolf usually sufficed to maintain order, but a centipede had no respect for Lupa's laws, no concept, it understood only nature's law – kill or be killed.

Four Howlers was too much even for the centipede. The many legged beast twisted round and started fleeing up the road – in the direction of the Politzi car!

"Get down, lad!" Werner shouted.

No sooner had they ducked than the centipede mounted the bonnet, crushing it in. The terrible din of legs clacking and scraping over metal assaulted Borce's ears and he cupped his head in his paws. The car rocked violently to and fro, as if being shaken about by a riotous mob. The windscreen smashed and the roof caved in, inch by inch, step by step, as the centipede's many legs thundered heavily overhead.

Then, as quickly as it came, it was gone.

The passenger door opened, only to fall off its hinges, and Constable Claybourne felt a set of strong paws pull him tail-first from the wreckage – and it was a wreck. The Politzi car had been reduced to a mangled, steaming heap of twisted metal, the Bloodfang crest barely discernable in the crumpled chaos.

Young Borce looked around and saw, of all beasts, that Vladimir had pulled him from the car.

"You hurt, constable?" he asked.

"N-nnn-no, sir," he stammered.

Meanwhile, Linus was having trouble extracting the plump Werner from the wreckage.

"Breathe out!" Linus instructed, tugging on his breeches.

"I am, sir!"

"Suck your gut in!"

"I have, sir!"

Finally, Werner's pink and red bulk popped out the deformed door like a cork and he fell on top of Linus, causing the Howler to 'breathe out', as it were.

"Gaaagh! Gerroff me!"

"Sorry, sir. Getting off, sir."

Werner helped Linus up and adjusted his sodden cloak.

Howlers Tristan and Rufus were nowhere to be seen, nor was the centipede, it had run over the car and up the side of the building into the pea-souper of a fog, vanishing.

For a moment Borce assumed that was it, that Linus and Vladimir had lost the scent and were out of the fight.

"Awooooooo!"

A bright wolfen howl echoed over the misty rooftops, stirring Borce's heart – of course, the Howlers could find each other, even in the foggiest Lupan night, or deepest monotonous forest, they simply sang their ancient song.

"That's Rufus," Vladimir said. "This way, Trooper."

Linus followed the Grand Howler down the nearest alley, leaving Werner and Borce behind.

"Awooooooo!"

Navigating the fog-bound, puddle-strewn alleyways, the Howlers emerged onto an open street whereupon they found Rufus in the midst of a Howl, helmet off, head tipped back.

"Where is it?" Vladimir panted.

"Around," Rufus replied, sniffing the air, "I can smell it."

Tristan appeared from the fog. "Smell it?" he puffed.

Rufus sighed, "Take your helmet off, boy; use your nose."

"I'd rather not in Riddle District, thank you."

Linus explained, "Centipedes excrete ammonia, Tristan. It burns your nose and throat, but it gives them away."

Rufus beamed at Linus, "Looks like Mills knows his stuff… unlike some."

Embarrassed, Linus could but clear his throat.

Tristan grunted a little.

"All right, let's split up," Vladimir declared, removing his helmet and sniffing about. "If you find it, leave it be and howl for backup."

✢

Gunnar rubbed his brown paws together and tightened his sandy-yellow cloak about his shoulders. It was a cold, wet night for guard duty, but his wolfen heart was warmed by the sight of his red-cloaked Bloodfang compatriot materialising from the fog and crossing the Bloodfang-Greystone border, passing beneath the dripping arch with two steaming mugs in his paws.

The hooded Bloodfang cheerily offered a tin mug to the Greystone, "Hot chocolate, mate?"

"For me? Ta very much."

Gunnar pulled back his hood and removed his helmet, slinging it over the imperium rifle at his back. He carefully sipped at the hot chocolate.

"Good eh?" said the Bloodfang, doing the same.

"Yeah," the Greystone agreed. "Mind you, hot water would do in this weather."

"Hah! Yeah, yeah, too right."

"You here all night?"

"Aye."

"Me too. Gonna be a long night."

Fraternising with wolves from other packs was frowned upon, but everyone did it. Gunnar didn't even know this wolf's name, but if he was good enough to share his hot chocolate, he was all right, even if he was a scummy Bloodfang.

"You ain't like the usual fella," Gunnar observed.

"No?"

"Nah. Weird he is. I tell yer, he's only said two words to me in as many years."

"Two words?"

"Yeah," Gunnar said, "'Thump' and 'off'."

"Hahaha!"

"It's true, I swear. All he does is give me funny looks."

"Well," the Bloodfang sniffed, "he probably doesn't want to get in trouble. They're pretty strict regards mingling on our side of the wall."

"I bet," Gunnar whistled.

"Speaking of which, I'd better get back."

"Already?"

"Yeah, can't be seen slacking, we're on high alert. Got to keep me eyes peeled for terrorist scum, 'en I? THORN's been at it again, not far from here. Got half the district's Politzi surrounding some factory or something. Right palaver."

"Daft hyenas," Gunnar said. "All they're doing is making it worse for themselves."

"Yeah, tell me about it."

The wolves tutted as one and shook their heads, before sipping their hot chocolate.

"Funny smell around," the Bloodfang said, sniffing.

"Smell?" Gunnar replied, doing the same.

"Aye. Not so bad here. It was stronger back there."

"Well it ain't me."

"Hahaha! I'll catch you later to collect me mug," said the Bloodfang.

"Nah, nah, I'll drop it off your side," Gunnar insisted, raising his comforting beverage. "Ta again. Much appreciated."

"No problem, mate."

Gunnar watched the Bloodfang mosey through the ghostly arch and vaporise into the fog like a spirit.

What a nice wolf.

He had almost disappeared from Gunnar's sight when a long, black, spiny tentacle swooped down from the ceiling and snatched him up.

"Gaaagh!"

Spitting a shower of hot chocolate, Gunnar dropped the mug, drew a pistol and sprinted under the arch. The sight that met his eyes stopped him in his tracks. Dangling from the top of the arch was a gigantic blue centipede, orange legs splayed, vicious jaws clasping the Howler around the waist, drawing the squirming wolf up and away.

"Help meee!" he cried, punching the centipede's armoured brow to no useful end. "Aaaagh!"

Gunnar found his wits and took aim, "Hang on, mate!"

Crack!

The centipede's shimmering body twisted in pain, but it kept hold of its prize. Gunnar drew his second pistol and had another go, but the effect was the same.

With his heart pounding so hard that his ears throbbed to every beat, Gunnar released the buckle that held his Greystone rifle to his back and skilfully swung the weapon under his arm, round to his front – his helmet fell off the butt and rolled away, no time for that. He unravelled the oil-soaked rag from around the breech and trigger, which had kept the powder dry this dreary night, and raised the rifle's elegant, three-foot-long barrel. Peering down the sight he took aim at the centipede's head as it chewed on the unfortunate Bloodfang.

Too close; can't risk it. Cursing through his teeth, Gunnar aimed a little further along the centipede's body and pulled the trigger.

Ka-crack!

The rifle's muzzle exploded with a thunderous pall, illuminating the monstrous beast, revealing for an instant its full, twisting, coiling body, just before one of its countless legs was blown clean off and sent spiralling away into the fog.

That got a reaction. Dropping its prey the centipede withdrew back to the ceiling. It clicked and clacked swiftly overhead, dripping white blood from its wound as it snaked across the glistening brickwork and down to the ground. Round and round it went, over the walls and across the ground, until Gunnar found himself surrounded, trapped in the tunnel by an undulating noose of armour and legs.

Standing astride his spluttering Bloodfang comrade the Greystone hurriedly reloaded his rifle, tearing the cartridge, pouring the powder, spitting the ball, aiming at the centipede's head as it coiled round.

Ka-crack!

Off came an antenna – Yes!

Gunnar's triumph was brief. The furious centipede swooped towards him in an instant, grasping him in its poisonous pincers and piercing his sides.

"Grrraaaagh!"

Gunnar's world collapsed into a jumbled mess as the beast savagely shook him to and fro, before hurling him against the tunnel wall. He bounced off the bricks and fell in a heap.

It was all over, just like that.

Through dazed eyes, the aching, throbbing Howler Gunnar watched the stampeding centipede approach, jaws agape, eager to feed on its well-earned dinner. But no, the centipede veered off and snatched the Bloodfang lying in the middle of the tunnel instead, dragging him away to the roof.

Within a pitiful scream and bloodied gurgle, the Howler was ripped open and finished off, rendering Gunnar's efforts to save him pointless.

"Ulf's fangs," Gunnar whined.

Trying to close his ears to the sickening crunches of his fellow wolf being devoured, the wounded Greystone rolled over and crawled away. It felt like every bone in his body was broken, that his sides were on fire. He wondered if he should call out for help, howl, anything, or would that simply attract the centipede's attention? Maybe it'll eat its fill and leave me alone. Maybe I can crawl through its legs.

Trembling and panting, Gunnar dragged himself across the cruel, cold cobbles, aiming to creep under the centipede's body and out into the open where someone might find him.

Suddenly, between the centipede's many legs, Gunnar spied a wolfen shape appear in the misty streets beyond the arch. It ran forward and leapt into the air!

Thunk!

With a coronal blast it landed beside Gunnar, a wolf made of iron, his mighty shoulders draped in a jet-black cloak. He looked down at the stricken Gunnar with blank yellow eyes of glass, his face obscured by an all-encompassing helmet. Without pause, he reached down and scooped Gunnar up. The young wolf yelped in fear and pain.

"HANG ON, MATE," the iron wolf soothed.

He bent his legs and leapt, in a single coronal bound, over the centipede and out of the arch, into the open. Sailing through the air, the wind and rain whipping at his face, Gunnar could scarce fathom what was occurring. The next he knew, he was lying on the cold, wet ground and several Howlers were looking down on him, a black-cloaked Bloodfang Captain, two Redcloaks, and an all-black ALPHA Prefect.

"LOOK AFTER HIM," said the iron wolf.

The Prefect, a striking red-furred wolfess, raised a paw and grabbed the iron wolf's arm, "Rafe!"

The iron wolf Rafe waited, metal ears swivelling.

The red wolfess let him go, saying gently, "Be careful. Don't overdo it. All right?"

With a nod, Rafe clomped towards the arch, the damp flags marking the passage to Greystone territory hanging limply either side, the centipede coiled within, snug and happy in its new nest, unaware that this wasn't the wilds, but Lupa, and it could not be allowed to hunt here.

"Shouldn't we help?" said the Bloodfang Captain.

"We'll just get in his way, Ivan," the Prefect replied. "Rafe works best alone."

This Ivan grunted, "So do I."

Several metallic paw steps approached and four more Howlers emerged from the fog, three Bloodfangs and an Eisbrand, all of them panting.

"Jan!" said one, small and ruddy-furred.

"Ah, Rufus," the wolfess replied, affecting a suddenly haughty air. "Where've you lot been?"

"We lost it in the fog," Rufus excused, looking at the centipede. "We heard shooting."

"Yes, same here," Jan admitted. She looked down on Gunnar and sighed, "I think it got one of ours, and this chap's in a right old state."

Rufus crouched beside Gunnar – the closer he got, the stronger the comforting, crackling, imperious fire Gunnar felt emanating from him. Whoever he was, he was very powerful, this 'Rufus'. The name rang a bell. He was some Bloodfang big shot, a scientist, a hyena sympathiser. Gunnar wasn't sure, didn't care, he was more worried about his chest – it was growing tight, heavy, hard to breathe. What's going on?

"I'm dying!" he whined.

"No no, dear boy," Rufus soothed, casting his eyes over the wounded wolf. "You'll be all right. Just keep calm."

Seething in pain, Gunnar burst out laughing. Tears streaked from his lemon-yellow eyes. "Hahaaah! I g-g-got it good," he guffawed, recalling his performance, "I did.... I got it good, sergeant... right good. Pow!"

The Eisbrand snorted, "Sergeant who? He's delirious."

Rufus huffed at him, "It's the centipede's venom, you fool; can't you see he's been bitten?"

Ivan also turned on the Eisbrand, "Tristan, what're you doing here?"

"Helping, cousin-"

"We don't need your help. Patrol your own land!"

Janoah claimed haughtily, "Spying as usual, eh Tristan?"

"I was just passing."

"You're always just passing."

Staying out of the squabble, Rufus stood up and addressed a stocky-looking blond Howler. "Linus, find a telephone and call HQ. This chap needs an ambulance fast or he's not going to make it."

"Yes, sir," Linus acknowledged.

"Insist they bring a sting and some taubfene. All right? The white-imperium will counteract the poison."

"But, he's a Greystone, sir."

"And?"

"Well, n-nnn-not that I mind, but they'll never allow us to squander stings on a rival with this shortage-"

"They'll never know who it's for," Rufus interjected. "Cite my name if you have any trouble; I'm a Grand Howler now and I'm going to use this cloak. There's a pub down the road, the *Silverfish*. They've a phone."

Linus nodded, "Right. Where exactly, sir?"

Another Grand Howler stepped in, tall and imposing. "I'll go; I know where it is," he said. "I'll take the hit for the stings, Rufus; I've more credit with Amael than you."

Surprised, Rufus nodded, "Much obliged, Vladimir."

Whilst Vladimir went to see about that telephone, the remaining Howlers and Janoah looked on.

Rafe reached round his back with a metal paw and twisted a red valve on his backpack. Within seconds the thick funnel protruding from his heaped, cloaked back popped open and expelled a jet of ash, then another and another! Like some imperium-fuelled mechanical contrivance, the Eisenwolf clomped steadily forth, chugging wisps of noxious ash in his wake.

Fearlessly approaching the centipede, he grabbed one of its innumerable orange legs in both mighty paws and simply twisted it off amidst a blast of plasma. The response was immediate, the centipede dropped its prey and whipped down from the arch, its fangs and jaws stained with wolfen blood. The mad invertebrate charged Rafe.

Tossing its leg aside, the Eisenwolf stood his ground and simply let the centipede take him. Pincers clamping around his waist, it swept him away, slamming him against the tunnel wall, sending dust and mortar tumbling over his cloaked shoulders.

At once and together, Linus and Tristan drew their wildly different-sized swords.

"Don't!" Janoah barked at them, raising a paw.

Tristan snarled, "It'll kill him!"

"Rafe has to do this by himself, he must prove he's worth the investment or they'll cut off his imperium rations!" Janoah explained, imploring, "Please... let him be."

Reluctantly, the Howlers stayed put. Rufus looked on, arms folded.

Rafe and the centipede remained locked together, pincers and arms wrestling for control. Try as it might, the centipede was unable slice through Rafe's armoured waist. Realising it had bitten off more than it could chew, it released him and tried to withdraw, but Rafe clung on like a limpet, his long, powerful arms wrapping tight around its neck. Trapped in an iron head-lock, the panicked bug scrabbled about the cobbles, shaking side to side, coiling and squirming, rolling around the tunnel with Rafe, trying to twist him off, but the wolf's grip was indomitable, and his armoured bulk immovable. The centipede couldn't brush him aside as it had so many others. Rafe was a millstone around its neck and the mad beast quickly exhausted itself trying to remove him.

"SORRY, BIG FELLA."

With a sudden, violent jerk and air-wobbling coil of corona, Rafe twisted the centipede's head segment through ninety degrees. There was an audible, stomach-churning crack, akin to splitting a tree. Then, silence.

Rafe let the giant bug flop down like a fire hose. Some of the legs twitched a little and white blood spilled rapidly between the cobbles. It was dead.

"By the Founders of Lupa," Linus mouthed shakily.

"Incredible," Tristan seconded.

Chest heaving, Rafe stepped back from his brutal deed, as if ashamed. With a quick flick of his metallic ears, as if dismissing a mosquito, he hurriedly reached under his cloak and twisted that red valve again, only the opposite way. The funnel projecting from his back ceased puffing ash.

Nursing his head, the Eisenwolf attempted to walk back to the others, but teetered sideways – imperceptibly so to all but Janoah.

"Rafe?" she said, stepping forward. "You all right?"

"YEAH."

The assurance had no sooner left Rafe's iron muzzle than he tripped and staggered across the cobbles, collapsing and rolling to cacophony of scraping metal and jangling belt buckles.

"Rafe!" Janoah yelped. She dashed over and strained to roll the hefty Rafe onto his back, whereupon she clasped his armoured head in both paws. "Rafe, what is it? Speak to me! Come on, don't do this to me, Stenton, not now, not when you've done so well!"

The others gathered round.

Linus asked, "Is he wounded?"

"It's the eisenpelz," Rufus said impassively. "It's too much even for him, isn't it Janoah?"

Janoah ignored her husband. "Find Josef Grau, tell him to bring venom," she said. Hearing no immediate response from the Howlers, she turned and shrieked at them all, "Quickly! He'll die!"

Whilst Linus ran off to do Janoah's bidding, Rufus and Tristan remained, watching Janoah nuzzle into Rafe's mighty body and stroke his metallic brow.

"JAN... JAN... I CAN'T SEE."

"Hold on, Rafe," she soothed. "It'll be all right. I'm here. I'm here."

~BLICK~

"Gaaaaagh-aaagh!"

"I'm here, Rafe! Rafe, look at me; look at me and hold my paw!"

Rafe's bleary eyes focused on the grey-furred wolfess looming over him. She took his paw in hers and he squeezed. He tried not to squeeze too hard for fear of hurting her.

"That's it," she woofed. *"I'm right here. Squeeze as hard as you like, I won't mind a bit."*

"It... hurts!" Rafe panted at her. *"Am I... am I dying?"*

"No. I know it's terrible, I know, but it's normal for a Howler. They all go through this. Your body is adjusting to the imperium. You won't die, I promise."

"Unnnggfffgh!"

As the sweating, heaving Rafe writhed on the bed, his wolfen nurse looked across to the cat in the coat. *"Can't I give him more taubfene, Doctor Josef?"* she implored.

"No," he said, wrestling with a long paper readout, one of many trailing from the machines roundabout. The spikes and troughs traced a wild zigzag, which might alarm an untrained eye, but not Josef's. *"Magnificent,"* he marvelled, deciphering the code.

His assistant seemingly cared nothing for the readouts. *"But I can't stand to see him like this."*

"We've numbed the pain as long as possible," Josef hissed impatiently. *"He can't have any more. I'll not make him a taubfene addict on top of an imperium addict. He's going to have enough difficulties adjusting as it is."* The cat looked to Rafe's beseeching nurse and cocked his head, *"For pity's sake, girl, just hold his paw and mop his brow."*

The nurse did just that. Wetting a cloth she dampened Rafe's forehead and spoke soothingly. *"It'll pass soon, I promise. You'll fall asleep and you won't remember any of this."*

"R-rrr-remember?" Rafe gasped at her.

She nodded. *"Howlers forget their induction all the time,"* she explained, trying to keep Rafe talking, to concentrate his feverish mind on anything but the pain. *"You won't even remember me. It's for the best, I think."*

The panting Rafe flashed a quick smile, *"Meryl Stroud, yeah?"*

"Yes," she said, a little surprised.

"I'll remember you... I will."

"Don't worry on my account," she replied softly.

"Bet you a penny I do!" Rafe laughed, before tipping his head back and enduring another tsunami of bone-melting torture. *"Grrrrrffffaaaagh!"*

✦

"Hold out your paw and concentrate. Tense the muscles in your arm, squeeze out the power within them."

Sitting up in bed with a tube up his nose and a drip in the wrist, Rafe watched Janoah's fingers gnarl, observing the plasma snap and pop between them.

"See? Now try again," she instructed, shaking her paw. *"You can do it. You have the power."*

For the umpteenth time, Rafe opened a big paw on his lap. He stared at it in silence, muscled arm tensing, tendons and veins popping.

"It's... it's not working-"

"It'll come, boy. That and so much more. Give it time-"

Pfffzack!

With a flash of light the bed sheets around Rafe's paw went up in smoke!

"Oh schmutz!" he yelped patting his burning lap.

Thinking fast, Janoah grabbed a glass of water and doused the smouldering sheets with a hiss, then opened a window to let the smoke out. Satisfied, she returned and checked Rafe's shaking paw, turning it over for damage.

Rafe seethed a little, and Janoah squinted knowingly.

"You'll find it numb at first, then it tingles and finally you feel the burn," she explained, letting Rafe go, lest he accidentally set her aflame next. *"That's part of the deal, I'm afraid. With great*

power comes great pain... in all walks of life."

Rafe held his wrist and opened and closed his paw. "I did it."

"Yes, but don't do any more," Janoah said. "Not until you're up and about or Josef's little nurse will have a fit."

"Who?"

"Nobody. I'll get a change of sheets."

"Janoah," Rafe called, staying her at the door.

"What?"

After the longest period of brow-twisting and word-searching, the Eisenwolf said, "Can you tell me who I am? I mean... I'm Rafe Stenton, but... where was I born? Who're my parents."

Janoah sighed, "I don't know, Stenton."

"But-"

"You were orphaned in the war and raised by a rabbit. That's all anyone knows." She smiled briefly, "It's not who you were but who you are that counts. Remember that above all."

Janoah stepped out, leaving Rafe to spread his fingers and make plasma play gently between them.

⚜

"Welcome to ALPHA, I'm Grand Prefect Silvermane," said the young grey wolf in black, his voice as smooth and golden as silk in sunshine. He extended a paw across the desk, "I'm the wolf in charge of this project. If there's anything you need, come to me-"

"Pleasure, mate," replied the giant brown wolf opposite, vigorously shaking paws, his own voice light, but booming, as if coming from the back of the throat. "I'm Rafe... Rafe, uh... Stenton. Aye, that's it."

Silvermane's steely brow rose.

Janoah stepped in and physically pushed Rafe's mighty arm down. "Please excuse him, Grand Prefect," she said, with a disarming chuckle. "Rafe's still confused from his induction."

Silvermane opened and closed his paw, as if a lingering tingle of plasmatic energy were dancing between his fingers. "Of course, but wasn't that weeks ago?"

Before Janoah could excuse Rafe further, Josef purred from the back of the office, "Rafe's induction wasn't like that of any normal Howler, Grand Prefect. It took half a dozen stings to get him up to speed, a number that would've killed you or anyone else. Rafe will never be as... settled as a 'healthy' Howler, not with his elevated imperium levels."

Rafe glanced back at Josef; Janoah elbowed him, making him face Silvermane again.

"There are no 'Howlers' here, Doctor Josef," the Grand Prefect reminded everyone, taking his seat again and tugging on his black mantle. "Whatever institutions you were a part of, you are now loyal only to ALPHA and must put aside all previous connections and sympathies. Prefects, Agents... even Eisenwolves," he said, looking at Janoah, Josef and Rafe respectively, "we exist solely to protect Lupa from those who would abuse her. Whilst the Howlers remain an essential arm of the law, corrupt individuals and their greed for personal gain fermented the conditions that led to the last war, we must see to it this never happens again."

"My greatest fear, Grand Prefect," Janoah said, "having lived through the last war when so many friends didn't."

"Indeed," Silvermane seconded.

A brief, solemn silence took hold amongst the wolves; Josef checked his watch, eager to be off.

"My parents were killed in the war," Rafe blurted, grasping his head and frowning, "I... I think."

Janoah pulled his paw down. "Yes," she said, gently, "and then you were adopted by a rabbit."

"R-rrr-right. He... he...."

"He was a criminal who fed you imperium. Remember?"

"Yeah."

"Until you went mad and attacked a Politzi. You should be in trouble for that, but you've been given a second chance by the good wolves of ALPHA. We've been through all this."

Rafe dipped his chin. Janoah released his paw and urged him to face Silvermane.

Silvermane had watched and listened interest, but tactfully did not press his curiosity. "You will find your quarters stark and our HQ's amenities basic, Rafe," *he continued afresh, spreading his paws at his simple office, devoid of beautification, save for a wall of literature and a potted orchid.* "But we have all you need; a canteen, a gym, a library, you are free to use them as you wish. Your wage will be meagre, our organisation is stretched thin, but be assured we are all paid the same here. Even the Alpha himself takes no more from our coffers than the lowliest recruit."

Rafe slowly raised a huge brown paw, just a little, as if unsure he'd be scolded.

Silvermane nodded, "Yes, Stenton?"

"Who's 'the Alpha', sir?" *Rafe asked, his hefty brows twisting like a cub's.*

"Rafe!" *Janoah hissed.*

Grand Prefect Silvermane was not offended, "A very great wolf, Rafe, the greatest I have ever met."

Chapter 20

Janoah sat in the waiting room nursing an ember and staring at the single basic imperium lamp flickering overhead, her posterior mortified by the uncomfortably thin seat cushion.

ALPHA wasn't one for creature comforts. Unlike the packs of Lupa, the newfangled ALPHA did not squander their budget on chandeliers and plush sofas, paintings and banners. Simple, modern furniture made of 'new materials' sufficed. Beds, chairs and desks were constructed of cheap steel and the latest injection-moulded imperium compounds, not expensive wood, marble or chitin. To spend even a penny on beautifying ALPHA HQ beyond basic functionality would leave the fledgling organisation open to condemnation. Set up after the war to guard against the very extravagance and corruption that had sparked the conflagration in the first place, they could not be seen to be hypocrites.

Still, Janoah thought, would it kill them to hire a tea-boy?

The intercom buzzed, *"Send her in."*

"Yes, my Alpha," the wolfess receptionist acknowledged, pressing the intercom. She was just a Freiwolf, not eligible to wear the mantle of a Howler, or in ALPHA's case Prefect. She was instead dressed in a jet-black ALPHA uniform, like that of the Politzi, only smarter, the blazer's many pockets fastened with bright silver buttons. "They'll see you now, Prefect," she let it be known, with a slightly haughty air.

Janoah snuffed out her ember. Blowing flavoursome vapours at the nobody wolfess in passing, she moseyed through the plain double-doors into the hall beyond.

There was no Den Guard ahead, no paintings or parquet floor, just a plain white hallway with basic windows leading to another set of simple double doors – a layout lifted, consciously or not, from the awe-inducing, glittering majesty of the traditional Elder Chamber and its adjoining hall. Yet if anything this lime washed ghost of Lupan splendour was scarier. The stark unsentimental plainness conveyed no warmth, no sense of history or permanence, as if the glorious past was shameful, an embarrassment to be expunged. Indeed, Alpha Prefects were required to forget their adoptive pack and its ways, to sever all ties and remain neutral – easier said than done.

Janoah rapped on the doors. She was beckoned with a sharp but not angry, *"Enter!"*

Into an Elder Chamber – of a sort. The magnificent, carved wooden table of yore was reduced to some plain new materials composite, grey in colour, whilst the humming chandelier was cast of basic steel, no gold or crystal in sight, and gone were the plush, ancient thrones of a real Elder Chamber, banished by the same uncomfortable, ill-moulded affairs Janoah's behind had been subjected to for an hour already in the preceding waiting room. There were no decanters of finest Rostsonne wine to be had either, just a jug of water and simple tumblers – the Alpha didn't drink. None of the four wolves seated at the table were even smouldering – the Alpha didn't like it.

Janoah stood upon the only nod to decadence, the black and white ALPHA emblem inlaid into the floor. She saluted her superiors by simply raising a paw to chest-height, as if waving hello. None of that outmoded 'fist to chest and out' business was tolerated here. Indeed, Janoah's comrades saluted her back, equally, all four of them, however lacklustre.

Janoah's green eyes flitted to the furthest right of the wolves, Grand Prefect Silvermane. The grey wolf looked fidgety, but not unduly worried. He could and would throw Janoah under the bus to save his own career, of that she was sure.

"Please take a seat, Valerio," he said.

"I'll stand, if it's all the same to you, sir," she replied. "I've been sitting an hour already and my tail is numb."

Silvermane looked to the brown and white wolf seated in the middle of the five places and waited for him respond to Janoah's cheeky remark.

The Alpha set the tone.

"Our apologies, Prefect," he said amiably, flicking through what Janoah recognised as her report. He smiled up at her with his noble-white face and lighting-blue eyes, "We've had a busy day. Please be seated, we'll not detain you long."

"Yes, my Alpha," Janoah said, pulling up one of those awful chairs.

'The Alpha', as the head of ALPHA had come to be known, was a small, albeit very well-built wolf, his thick neck and muscled arms betraying the innate strength common to Howlers in their prime. His fur coat resembled Uther's, another of those pale-faced fellows who looked like they were wearing a white mask over their otherwise coloured fur. Only instead of white on grey, the Alpha was white on brown. His smart black mantle was pinned with a white-imperium brooch bearing the stylised ALPHA 'A'. The black helmet resting on the desk beside Janoah's open report was marked up in the same manner. White-imperium décor was a little extravagant, but symbolised the pure intentions of ALPHA.

A single medal graced the Alpha's impressive chest. It was a smooth, heart-shaped, red-imperium crystal, quite dull, but with facets glinting deep within. A bead of red-imperium hung freely beneath the heart, like a drop of blood. The heart and droplet were both suspended beneath the word 'EXALT', which was embossed into a banner held aloft by twirling, ornate plant stems, all cast in bronze. A tiny, white-imperium pearl was nestled amidst the vines above the heart – easily the most intrinsically valuable detail. The whole ensemble, heart, drop, pearl and suspension, hung on a handsome red and white imperium-weave ribbon.

This rarest accolade was known as the Imperium Heart. Properly speaking it was not a medal, but a decoration; a thing earned for an act of distinguished bravery rather than taking part in a specific campaign. Only the Den Fathers could bestow a Howler with this particular honour and even then *only* when they all met at the annual Pack Summit and unanimously voted to do so – a thing almost unknown.

Some Howlers drooled at the mere thought of holding an Imperium Heart, let alone winning one. Janoah had inspected one up-close many times; it held no mystery for her. Except that, every time she sat down in front of the Alpha she would wonder how he had earned it, then forget to ask Silvermane or anyone else later, and asking the Alpha outright just felt tacky somehow.

Janoah had another question in mind. "Where's Grand Prefect Nikita, if I may?" she asked, looking at the empty seat to the Alpha's right, the one usually occupied by Alpha's unofficial second.

"Checking on your Eisenwolf, I believe," the Alpha replied airily. "He read your report with much interest, Prefect, as did we all. You say the Bloodfangs have a hyena in custody. Is that still the case?"

Janoah nodded, "Yes, my Alpha. He's called Madou of the Jua-mata. Last I heard he's recovered enough from his wounds to be plied over at Riddle Den. I've no doubt my old partner Vladimir Oromov will extract answers."

"It's fortunate for us that he didn't have the gall to swig black-imperium like the rest," the Alpha observed.

"It appears, my Alpha, that this Madou passed out from the centipede's venom before he could kill himself. To even survive a bite he must be a Chakaa and therefore of some importance to THORN, perhaps one of their leaders."

"Chakaa?" scoffed the Prefect to the Alpha's left, a rotund white-furred fellow weighed down not only by his girth, but by dozens of medals jostling for space on his cloak. "Chakaa, Prefect?"

Janoah explained gently, "That's what hyenas call their Howlers, Grand Prefect Horst."

"Yes! *They* do, *we* don't." Grand Prefect Horst chided. "We mustn't add credence to rival hyena institutions."

Janoah skilfully batted Horst's criticism away, "Actually, Chakaa is rather a disparaging term in hyena dialect, sir; it means they're rotten."

"Rotten?"

"Yes, sir. To call them anything else would be complimentary."

"Well… in any case," Horst bristled, trying to regain control, "it should've been ALPHA who came away with such a key suspect not our valued Bloodfang friends,".

Janoah mounted a further rebuff, "Chakaa Madou only fell into Bloodfang paws because he appeared to be dead; Rafe and I were after a live suspect."

The Alpha checked Janoah's report. "Nurka?"

"Yes, my Alpha-"

"These hyena names; they're so... primitive!" Horst chortled like a hog, medals tinkling as he looked left and right at the Alpha and the two other present Grand Prefects. "Nur-ka, Mad-oo and... Tem-ba is it? Ridiculous!"

Nobody else so much as cracked a smile, least of all the Alpha.

ALPHA's leader moved swiftly on, "Are they using their real names, or are they aliases?"

"Who can say?" Janoah replied. "But as Chakaa any family will have disowned them. They'll be pariahs."

"Pariahs?" Horst queried, flabby chin raised. "Why's that?"

Janoah made to speak, but the Alpha took over, "Because hyenas do not believe in using imperium, Horst, especially not white, which they consider to be the tears of the sacred Sky." He continued, perchance showing off in front of the knowledgeable Janoah, "If a Chakaa happens across imperium above ground then it is accepted as a gift from Mother Erde and can be used as they see fit, fashioned into armour or used to sate the rot, but digging it up is *always* theft and white-imperium *always* forbidden."

Grand Prefect Horst thought for a moment. "Then what if these three so-called Chakaa have only using imperium deemed acceptable? Would they still be outcast?"

"Always the awkward question, Horst."

"I like to keep you on your toes, my Alpha."

"So that's why I keep you around," the Alpha joked. Patiently he explained that, "Even if Chakaa follow the rules and only use surface deposits of imperium, they must still consume purple-imperium in lieu of sacred white. They do not inject it via stings as we do, they brew it up into a drink called 'chunta', rather like our own ancestors used to do before we found purer means. Naturally the purple-imperium in chunta settles on the brain and makes Chakaa insane, albeit much slower than it would a Howler. Even so, in the strict and nuanced world of hyena nobility, a Chakaa's crude behaviour is unacceptable. Only the late Prince Noss was exempt; being a sacred Prince he could do no wrong."

ALPHA's premier finished by looking to Janoah, "At least as far as I understand matters."

She nodded a little, like a prim schoolteacher to a star pupil.

"Then they really are primitive," was Horst's assessment. "No imperium mining and a mad monarchy running the show. No wonder they lost."

Grunting, the Alpha flicked through Janoah's report. "I see a lot of this consists of Uther Bloodfang's testimony. He's a reliable fellow, this 'Wild-heart'?"

Janoah nodded, "An exceptional Howler, my Alpha. He infiltrated the refinery and courageously allowed himself to be captured by THORN to gain information that has so far eluded even us."

"Allowed himself to be captured!" Horst heckled, his jowls wobbling in time to the ridiculous array of medals dancing beneath. "You expect us to believe such rubbish?"

"I didn't myself, at first, but his testimony matches with that of Ivan Donskoy, who, as I'm sure you're aware, is a wolf of unquestioned courage and impeccable credentials," Janoah said airily.

Silence, for a moment at least.

"Not quite impeccable," Horst said, knitting his fingers together on the table and leaning forward. "I feel for you, Prefect."

"Sir?" Janoah replied.

Horst delighted in letting it be known that, "It must be very upsetting to know that pretty Eisbrand pair, Ivan and Tristan, turn your husband's eye more readily than you do."

Janoah smiled disarmingly, "Forgive me, but I fear your gossip is a little outdated, Grand Prefect. My husband moved on from those two years ago."

"Did he indeed?" Horst woofed, looking down the table at the Alpha and the others. "Are we to believe now that Howler Rufus has reformed his ways?"

Janoah patronised Horst with aplomb, "You misunderstand me, Grand Prefect. Not reformed, just... found someone else to occupy his feverish mind. Outside of his work, Rufus has the attention span of a cub. Betas come and go, conquered one after the other. Though he seems quite taken with his latest follower-"

"And you remain wedded to this degenerate?" Horst snarled, thumping the tabletop once. "Have you no shame? You two should've divorced a decade ago, as the amended Lupan Laws decreed, instead of carrying on with-"

"Horst!" the Alpha snapped, blinking rapidly and raising a paw. "I do not want a headache at this hour."

Horst was silenced.

The Alpha continued calmly, "Prefect Janoah has nothing to be ashamed of; she and Rufus were wed before the nuptial amendment like many Howlers and that's that. We are not about to retroactively apply law, that way madness lies. Besides, we are not concerned by who's combing Rufus's back from month to month, our only concern is that he receives no more imperium or pay than he is allocated, as with any other wolf. That is ALPHA's remit."

"But his speeches are clearly inflammatory," Horst claimed. "Do you realise he thinks hyenas are our equals?"

"Yes… and he's right."

"My Alpha!"

Glaring meaningfully at Horst, the Alpha pulled a photo of the now identified hyenas from Janoah's file. "Hyenas are not, as is generally put about, stupid, uncultured buffoons. They are clever, resourceful and in THORN's case deceitful. Those terrorists must have enough black-imperium put away by now to murder half of Lupa, and I dare say they've had inside help."

"Inside help?"

"Yes! To have avoided capture, and to have such kristahl arms and eisenglanz armour as they do, there must be a vast network of filth running beneath Lupan society… and I do not mean the sewers. Howlers, Elders, even a Den Father could be involved."

In the ensuing silence, one of the other wolves felt able to speak, a handsome, athletic fellow whose jet-black fur melded almost seamlessly with his mantle. "This Prince Noss the Alpha mentioned," he began, in a faded Hummel accent, "did you nae work with him when you were a Bloodfang, Janoah?"

"Yes, Grand Prefect Duncan," she confirmed.

"He was a Howler, am Ah right?"

"A Watcher, sir."

"Oh aye?" Duncan woofed.

"He had some knowledge of the wilds, so we made him a Watcher. He was part of the Bloodfang's drive to civilise the hyenas by gainfully employing them."

"And what a success that was!" Horst mocked loudly. "He turned round and blew Rufus up! Another of Rufus's ludicrous ideas ends in utter disaster."

"An idea sanctioned by the Den Fathers," Janoah pointed out, "And, I believe, the Alpha too."

The Alpha smiled; Horst tugged his suddenly stifling mantle.

"Well, perhaps it was a mistake," the Alpha conceded.

Silvermane quietly marvelled at the goings-on; Janoah was as hard to pin down as a greased worm.

"He's dead, this Noss?" the black-furred Duncan asked, his golden eyes narrowing.

Janoah nodded confidently, "Yes, sir."

Horst leant over and cackled, "Josef Grau cooked him to death on the rack, I heard."

"Mistakenly," Janoah said, "though he would have been executed regardless for his crime."

Duncan sighed, "Pity. Mayhaps he'd have made for useful leverage, or at least a negotiator. Terrorist or no, a hyena prince must have some clout if he's 'above fault'."

The Alpha impatiently dismissed him, "Since Noss is dead this is an academic debate, Duncan."

Janoah looked down a little.

Duncan went on, "Och, but there must be other hyena princes, my Alpha."

"Not of unquestionable bloodline; Noss was the last with a decent claim. Besides, you overstate a prince's clout. There are no kings amongst hyenas, only queens. If we were hyenas, even princes, we males would have to bow to lady Janoah's every whim on pain of death. Isn't that right, Valerio?"

"I believe so, my Alpha."

"Happily we wolves are a race of equal opportunities."

Janoah smiled, "Yes, although there are times when the hyena way of doing things is tempting."

Baffled silence.

Unfazed, Janoah continued, "What I wouldn't give to have my wayward husband at my beck and call on pain of death, just for once."

The Alpha laughed, "Indeed!"

Everyone else joined in, save Horst.

The Alpha moved on, "Now, Prefect Janoah, we must discuss graver matters, I fear," he said. "About your young 'Eisenwolf', we are concerned at his lack of progress and the mounting costs."

"Rafe's made great strides of late, my Alpha."

Horst made his thoughts known again, "Great strides? We've sunk thousands of lupas into Josef's monstrosity and what've we to show for it? Not a single canister of black-imperium recovered, not a hyena taken into custody, at least not by us, though the Bloodfangs managed perfectly well *without* an illegal Eisenwolf. All your abomination managed last week was a little pest control. How do you account for his failure, Prefect? Explain yourself!"

Before Janoah could mount her defence, Silvermane interjected.

"There have been teething troubles, we'll not deny," he said, looking past Horst to the Alpha. "But Rafe will come good, my Alpha. His raw power is… phenomenal. The wolf broke an imperial centipede in half with his bare paws."

Silvermane's claim was hyperbolic, but his voice remained so measured and convincing that wolves were inclined to believe him.

"I've seen the specimen he killed," he went on, "it's a monster. Had Rafe not intervened there's no telling how many good Howlers would have lost their lives trying to stop it. That aside, he also killed dozens of THORN fanatics; a success by any measure."

"And yet I heard your mighty Eisenwolf fainted on the job, Silvermane," Horst mocked, leaning back in his creaking new-materials chair. "Laid up yet again."

"Too much ash in the blood," Silvermane clarified, with a disarming chuckle. "Who amongst us hasn't overdone it from time to time? The cocktail of poisons in Rafe's body would kill any of us stone dead… even you my Alpha."

The Alpha remained inscrutable.

"Rafe is a remarkable fellow," Silvermane went on, "and genial company, once you get to know him. He is no monster, just a young wolf weighed with a great burden."

Silence prevailed.

The Alpha rubbed his handsome white muzzle with a brown paw, "I'm sure, Silvermane, but our pockets are not inexhaustible. When I go before the Den Fathers and they review our budget I must justify the cash and white-imperium I have diverted. If I have nothing to show for it when good Howlers are dying for want of venom, they will demand an explanation and I will have to come clean about your project. The Pack Summit is not far off. If Rafe cannot prove his worth come springtime, the Den Fathers will close the loophole in the Lupan Laws that has allowed your Eisenwolf to be brought to fruition under ALPHA and then there will be nothing anyone can do for him, not even me."

"You'll have results, my Alpha, and soon," Silvermane insisted. "If not," he said, looking to Janoah, "I'll terminate the Eisenwolf project myself."

✦

"Terminate the project yourself will you?"

"I didn't mean it-"

"Throwing me under the bus are you?"

"Janoah, I am a Grand Prefect; you will speak to me appropriately, or I'll divest myself of you sincerely."

The ALPHA Chamber fell silent. Horst and Duncan and the Alpha had long gone, leaving Janoah to have it out with her patron, Silvermane.

"If you get rid of me, you lose Rafe," she claimed. "He only trusts me."

Silvermane countered silkily, "Not *only* you."

After a moment's thought, Janoah huffed, "If you think that prim little nurse he fancies will help you control him you're mistaken. All Meryl can manage is a hot chocolate and a bedtime story, that's as far as she goes. She won't make Rafe fight for ALPHA."

Silvermane turned his glass of water in his paw, watching the shafts of refracted light sweep across the tabletop. He poured another and passed it to Janoah, like a pathetic peace offering.

"This petty arguing is not helping either of us," he said. "We need to think of something."

Janoah took the water and dipped her chin, looking at her wobbling reflection. "I already have."

"What?"

"I've been thinking about Uther's antics all week."

"You mean his getting captured?"

A nod, an explanation, "He infiltrated THORN back at the refinery. He did so clumsily, but briefly there we had a window. We must manufacture one again, only properly."

"Inserting an agent?" Silvermane scoffed, sipping his water. "It's been tried, even with bought hyenas. They've all learnt nothing or disappeared and time is running out, Janoah."

"I know. But I've a beast the hyenas will *want* to trust. Provided we make his fall believable."

"Fall?"

"From grace," Janoah clarified. "It'll be rough and he's not getting any younger. We'll need to make him an offer even he can't refuse; an offer only the Alpha can make."

Curious, Silvermane knitted his fingers, "Who exactly do you have in mind?"

Janoah raised her glass, "My dear husband."

✦

Linus lay back on the bench and grasped the barbell with both chalked paws. After a few shuffles, adjustments and preparatory breaths, he eased the weight from its cradle and lowered it slowly until the bar nearly touched his chest, then up again, and down again, counting each press on the up-stroke.

"One… two… three… four… five…."

The sounds of other Howlers huffing and puffing, and the clink of changing weights, was momentarily drowned out by sheer concentration.

"Seven… eight… nine…."

Linus stared at the imperium lamp burning overhead, at the cracked ceiling beyond it, to nowhere. His whole focus momentarily collapsed down to the simple yet all-consuming task of lifting an axle-shaped hunk of metal – silly yet necessary.

"Linuuuus!" someone roared.

Linus lost all concentration and down came the barbell, pinning him to the bench.

"Gagh!"

"Oi, oi, careful!" a wolf tutted, silhouetted against the lamp above. Reaching down and grabbing the bar, the stranger helped Linus heft the weights back onto the brackets.

Freed, Linus sat up with one paw clasped to his bruised chest and looked behind.

"Uther!" he piped in surprise.

"Thump me, you trying to kill yourself?" Uther chided, leaning on the cradled barbell. "You're supposed to have someone standing here in case you get stuck. Good job I turned up when I did or you'd be flatter than a flatworm. Puh!"

Linus dusted his chalky paws off on his sensible white training breeches. He decided not to point out it was Uther who had made him jump, he was just glad to see his partner on his feet again.

"How are you?" he asked, looking Uther over; Wild-heart seemed fine, cloaked, armoured and ready for duty, as if nothing had occurred last week. "Have you been discharged?"

"I discharged myself!" Uther claimed in an indignantly high-pitched tone. He slapped his cloaked chest, then winced and rubbed his ribs, "But… don't expect me to lift another barbell off your neck for a few weeks, Woodlouse, I don't wanna bust my stitches."

Linus laughed, "I'll be careful."

"Wanna go down *The Beehive* later for a belated birthday bash? You can tell Lorna and Rosa how you nearly got eaten by a centipede. It'll be a howl."

"You heard about that?" a humbled Linus said.

"Puh! Mate, *everyone* knows. What went down last week is the talk of the district, if not Lupa."

"Goodness."

Uther glanced around the Den's gymnasium. Other Riddle District Howlers were about their business, lifting weights or wrestling on mats, keeping in obligatory shape.

Rufus was fencing across the way, dancing to and fro in friendly combat with a brave opponent. Uther didn't know who Rufus was up against since both their faces were masked by generic grey fencing helmets; similar to the real thing, but lighter. Rufus's red and grey fur and countless small scars gave him away even from afar, that and his skill.

In a few flicks and thrusts Red-mist landed a hit. A weak imperious bolt snapped down his blunt and poorly conductive training rapier, shocking his opponent in the ribs and causing the wolf a moment's discomfort – enough to make him jump and twist away in defeat.

Rufus slipped his helmet off and shook paws with the vanquished Howler, before immediately replacing said helm to face the next foolish youngster.

"Puh!" Uther scoffed. "Rufe's having fun, I see."

Linus marvelled. "He's been on the floor since I got here. I don't think anyone's touched him."

"Yeah? Well, I'd go over there and sort him out if I weren't laid up."

"You any good with a rapier?"

"Who said anything about rapiers? I'd get him on the wrestling mat."

Linus laughed.

Once all mirth had faded, and Rufus had dispatched yet another foe, Linus dipped his chin. "Uther," he said, in the tone of an inquisitive cub to his parent, "that ALPHA wolf last week, was he really an Eisenwolf?"

"You mean you dunno?" Uther snorted. "Woodlouse, I thought you knew everything!"

"I've been asking around Den all week, but nobody wants to talk about it, not even Werner. Vladimir told me to forget it and even Rufus fobbed me off. He just said that Rafe's an unfortunate mad wolf and told me ALPHA won't get away with it."

"I see."

"I know you won't lie to me. You're my best friend."

Uther shrugged, "Well, Rufus ain't lying. Eisenwolves *are* mad. Imperium poisoning 'en it. Goes to their head." He tapped the side of his skull, "Ivan spoke to him. Fruitcake, apparently."

"But… his eisenpelz, and… and the ash it kept venting. It was like a living machine!"

"Kinda is, mate. 'Course, how it's done is a mystery, even to the know-it-all Greystones. Comes from one of the Dead Cities, dun it, before Lupa was founded. We can't make armour like that no more. Not even close."

"Of course, but I-I-I thought the packs agreed never to field eisenpelz again because they're so dangerous. That's why the Lupan Laws were changed, why Howlers can't marry, to stop wolves capable of using them from even being born."

"Yeah, but ALPHA ain't no pack, are they? They get away with all sorts of schmutz because of it. Must've found some cub with Howler parents and conned him. Puh! All well-dodgy of course, but ALPHA is well-dodgy, in case you hadn't noticed." Uther leant close, "Oi, you know what they did whilst I was laid up?"

"No. What?"

"They 'questioned' me."

Baffled, Linus waited for Uther to elaborate – and Uther being Uther, he did.

"A couple of Prefects snuck into the ward and locked the door," he said. "Wedged a chair to it, they did, which is always a bad sign. They pulled me out of bed and whilst one pinned me arms behind me the other thumped me in the gut. I must've told 'em the same story fifty times before a nurse fetched Elder Amael. He sent 'em packing sharpish. They did the same thing to Ivan too, caught him in the washroom. He sent 'em packing himself, needless to say."

Linus blustered, "B-b-but that's outrageous!"

"Aye."

"This is Bloodfang territory! This is our Den!"

"Aye, so?"

"So they can't do that!" Linus squawked, before adding with meek uncertainty, "Can they?"

Uther pinched his partner's cheek, "Woodlouse, ALPHA can do what they please when they please to plebs like us. You gotta be a Grand Howler at least before they have second thoughts about bothering yer."

Linus sat in brooding silence, arms folded.

"Come on," Uther said, "let's go out and have some fun."

"I'm in the middle of gym."

Uther looked the barrel-chested Linus over, "Mate, take it from someone who lives in here himself, you can stand to skip a session. What you need is a little rest and recuperation, a nice bath, an hour in the sauna, maybe a massage. Wind down and forget your worries. It's good fer the rot."

Sighing, Linus unfolded his arms, "Sounds great, but I'm going to the Arkady Symposium at eight."

"Yer what?"

"Symposium."

Uther's vacant expression was priceless.

It was Linus's turn to elaborate, "It's like a… well a… a meeting of minds, I suppose. It's a party – for bookish types."

"Oh that! I know the thing."

"Rufus invited me."

"Ohoo!" Uther woofed further. "I see."

"Sorry. It was arranged weeks ago. I should go."

"No no, it's fine, mate. You uh, you do what you gotta do with ol' Red-mist himself."

Linus had a notion, "Why don't you come? I'm sure he won't mind. All his friends will be there."

"Puh! They'll bore my ears off. Bunch of know it alls they are. I mean, what do I care about ancient elk pottery or otter driftwood carvings? We have museums for that guff anyway."

"Sounds like you've met Rufus's crowd before."

"Yeah. I pity you, mate. I really do."

Linus could but shrug and smile.

"Oh thump me," Uther groaned, subtly turning away. "Look out, here he comes now."

Rufus the conquering hero crossed the gym in his white training breeches, mopping himself with a towel all the way.

"What're you doing out of bed Uther?" he gruffed on arrival.

Uther stood to attention with Linus. "Discharged, sir, and ready for duty," the former explained.

"Discharged my left foot," Rufus snorted, throwing his towel about his shoulders. "You breathed in more imperium than a den of gazers down a mine and took a pellet to the ribs; you need a couple of weeks off."

"I'm fine, sir-"

"Grand Howler's orders, I'm afraid. You'll be on half pay for the duration of your sick-leave whether you clock in or not, so you may as well not. Is that abundantly clear?"

At length Uther capitulated, "Yes, sir."

"There's a good chap," Rufus beamed, looking between his rigid subordinates. "At ease, at ease; this isn't the Parade Grounds."

Released, Linus nodded across to the fencing court where fellow Howlers continued to fight. "You must've beaten half the district, sir. I-I-I lost count."

"Oh, they're just cubs really; barely out of their stripy training mantles. I needed one of you ruffians to come over and show them how it's done."

"Not me, sir," Linus scoffed. "I'm all thumbs with a rapier."

"So's Uther! But he'd at least put up a fight."

"Puh!" Uther denied. "Ivan's the one you want, sir."

"Ivan would've ended my reign in a heartbeat, as well you know. No, I needed a proper run-around to get the blood flowing again – getting podgy apparently."

Linus was baffled. "Podgy, sir?"

Holding his towel with both paws, Rufus shrugged and spread his fingers, "So the wife says."

It was easy to forget Rufus even had a wife these days, they were so seldom seen together. What did Rufus make of Janoah and her Eisenwolf? Was he still angry? Why was he angry? Was it just the legality of the matter? Linus burnt with curiosity.

Uther didn't, "If you'll excuse me, sir."

"Get some proper rest, Wild-heart," Rufus warned.

Saluting, barely, Uther took his leave. "Have fun at yer 'sympodium', or whatever," he murmured at Linus. "Cop you later, Woodlouse."

Once Uther had departed, Rufus said of him, "Too proud that one. I always thought Ivan was the worst." Shaking his head he moved on, "Still on for tonight, Linus, or have you made plans with Uther?"

"No, sir. I-I-I mean yes, sir. We're s-sss-still on for tonight, you and me that is."

Rufus laughed and slapped Linus on the arm. "You'll grow out of that one day," he winked, leaving Linus at once embarrassed and encouraged.

✧

The Alpha rose from his office chair to survey the glittering cesspit that was the Common Ground, with its countless clubs, saloons and Lupanars all mingling like rancid mucous in a spittoon.

It was a joke that the austere ALPHA HQ had been erected in Lupa's putrid heart, this lawless patch over which no true pack ruled and which ALPHA itself could not properly police. They had neither adequate staff nor resources, not even a Politzi force to deal with petty crime, and the citizens took full advantage of it.

The Den Fathers had tied ALPHA's paws from the outset by gifting them the rich Common Ground, yet denying them the revenue it generated. It was not official policy; ALPHA was free to tax goods passing in and out of its boxed-in territory just as any other pack, but taxing imports that had already been taxed elsewhere merely raised prices in local shops to ridiculous sums, driving business away. And exports? There were none! The Common Ground was a place of wanton consumption, not noble production. The only things leaving the Common were staggering, drunken Howlers. The impoverished ALPHA Prefects couldn't even prop up their salaries by demanding tribute from their citizens like the Howlers – the old guard demanded at least *some* privileges be kept out of ALPHA's paws. Fine, let the Howlers take the odd free apple from a stall; the Prefects looked better for not engaging in the practice.

One day, the Alpha presaged to himself, we'll set the moral standard across Lupa, if not the world entire.

"All right," he said aloud, talking to Janoah and Silvermane. "But this does not leave this room. If you fail, I'll deny all knowledge. You accept?"

"Yes, my Alpha," Silvermane replied.

"Completely, my Alpha," said Janoah.

The Alpha turned and saluted smartly yet simply with his self-styled paw-gesture, "For the Republic Lupi."

✧

After a post-gym grooming, Linus returned to his quarters and dressed in his best civilian getup, white shirt, black breeches and knee-high silk gaiters covering his boots. Smart.

Buttoning his cuffs and looking in his mirror he breathed a few deep breaths.

"How do you do?" he said to himself. "I'm Linus Mills. Howler Linus Mills, Howler Trooper First Class, that is."

Idiot.

Uther had the right idea. Stay within your class, Linus. Go down the pub. Go out with Lorna and Rosa. Don't try and climb Rufus's ivory tower with all his educated, academic, arty friends because you won't fit in.

No, you *are* educated. Yes, you had to drop out because of the rot, but you continued to study at the Howler Academy, just like Rufus.

Yes, but unlike him you can't even talk properly. You just panic and start stuttering and mumbling.

Fool.

Trying to ignore his rude brain, Linus grabbed his trusty blue coat from his bed and slipped it on. He was in the midst of tugging out the collar and searching the pockets for his room keys when it struck like lightning.

"Haagh!"

The pain shot up his body, from shin to shoulder, and before Linus knew what was what he was on the hard wooden floor, grasping one of his legs with both paws, trying to stem the pulsing, pumping surge of bone-burning pain. Linus's pokey little room span like a fairground amusement, the desk, the imperium lamp, the frost-flecked window. He closed his eyes to save himself from being sick.

The rot. It's here. Already.

Linus thought he heard a knocking at the door, thought he caught a familiar gravely voice. He thought, in his feverish state, that he told them to go away. Thought he had saved himself the indignity of being seen to succumb.

No, the door opened and a pair of strong, sinewy limbs scooped Linus up and plonked him on his bed.

"Where's your sting?" the stranger asked.

Linus couldn't reply.

"Linus, your venom ration!" they barked.

"Top drawer… bedside cabinet," the youngster growled, writhing in pain. "In the… the music box."

The drawer was opened. The music box played, chiming a lullaby. Time passed. The pain! Ulf, please make it stop!

Something pricked Linus's arm, hot and tingly. That was the needle going in, the white-imperium coursing through his veins, his muscles, his bones. Linus arched his back a moment then collapsed, chest heaving fitfully. Within seconds the mind-numbing throb of a thousand hot pokers cooled and faded. The fog dissipated. Slowly, Linus opened his bleary eyes and looked around the room.

"Grand Howler Rufus!" he gasped, sitting up.

Rufus pushed Linus back on his pillow. "Stay there a minute, young Mills," he said. "Let it pass."

Nodding, Linus gladly did as bidden.

Satisfied, Rufus plopped himself in the one creaky chair gracing Linus's modest quarters and looked all about, at the shelves crammed with well-worn books, fossils, pressed plants and other curiosities, as if he had never been in here before.

Linus realised Rufus hadn't.

With a curious and high-pitched 'Hmm' the Grand Howler stopped his visual tour and broke out an ember. He was dressed in his white cloak and all the rest of his Howler gear, save his helmet.

'Is he going to attend the symposium in that?' Linus thought. 'Should I?'

"Been a while, has it?" Rufus said, blowing a cloud of green vapour overhead and taking another draught.

"Pardon, sir?"

"Your attack. First one for a while?"

"Oh, yes. I've not had one that bad, not since…" Linus closed his eyes and opened them again, "since I found out what was wrong with me."

"I see. Well, you've been stung. It's all right now."

Linus glanced at the bedside table, at the music box and the empty sting. He turned away and covered his face with a forearm. "By Ulf's fangs, I knew it," he seethed.

"Knew what?" Rufus chirped, sitting forward.

"I'm a weakling… I'm going to rot before I'm twenty, aren't I?" Linus growled. He looked to Rufus, a trained imperiologist. "Tell me the truth, sir, I can bear it."

Rufus laughed, ejecting vapour like a saucepan boiling over. "My dear Linus, don't be so melodramatic. Weak indeed, you're nothing of the sort! What kind of weakling takes on a band of Howler-killer thugs with his bare paws? No, no, no. At your age you're expected to have the odd attack, it's quite normal."

Red-mist inspected Linus's music box. The wood was inlaid with a waterside scene; dragonflies clinging to reeds, great diving beetles swimming about below, and a pair of dayflies fluttering towards the languid sun in their first and final nuptial flight.

"Lovely thing," Rufus remarked. "Heirloom?"

"My mother's, sir," Linus replied, adding, "It plays the Dance of Dayflies."

"I heard when I opened it up. Bit out of tune, mind."

"It's very old, sir. Predates the railways, Dad said."

"Now that *is* old," Rufus marvelled. He took out his pocket watch to check the time and stood up, "Speaking of the passage of epochs, we're going to be late."

"Late?"

"For the symposium! You can manage can't you?"

With a little trepidation, Linus sat up and threw his legs off the bed. There was nothing to worry about, the white-imperium had done its work and staved off the dreaded rot, for another month at least.

"Of course, I-I-I wouldn't miss it for the world," Linus stammered, with a slightly giddy laugh – perhaps the sting high was kicking in already.

"Good lad," Rufus beamed, pocketing his watch. He looked Linus over and wiggled his smouldering ember at him, "Handsome as you look, get changed will you?"

Surprised, Linus plucked at his coat, "Changed, sir?"

"Wear your mantle, Howler. Everyone knows what we are, there's no point denying it."

"I thought it would be… uhm."

"What?"

"Well, uh… disrespectful, sir, to go to a… well a meeting of minds dressed in our-"

"I'm sure the Eisbrand Den Father will be wearing his Howler kit," Rufus interjected, opening the door.

Linus squeaked, "Their Den Father will be attending?"

Rufus waited in the door long enough to say, "Yes, old Thorvald Strom. Didn't I tell you? Good friend of mine."

"No, sir."

"Oh. Well, Strom's as harmless as a caterpillar," Rufus assured, stepping out. "I'll be in the garage. We're taking my mono, so don't forget your helmet."

✦

Grand Prefect Nikita stood at the window, his paws cupped behind his back, watching Josef Grau fuss over his creation in the stark interrogation room beyond. The huge, dark brown wolf strapped to the rack breathed slowly and deeply, his muscle-packed torso heaving in and out.

The Eisenwolf was ill. Decaying imperium had built up in his bones and organs, his very blood ran as foul with ash as the River Lupa, enough to kill any normal Howler.

In time Rafe would heal, his tormented organs would expel the ash and all would be well, but it would take weeks at this rate. The only speedy remedy was to manually re-energise the imperium ash in his blood, to enrich it back to higher grades. But, with white venom thin on the ground and ALPHA's shoestring budget fraying, the only way to effect a recovery was to 'rack' the fellow.

Shock imperium therapy, Josef called it; monstrous torture his critics scoffed.

Either way, the young Eisenwolf had agreed to go through with the pioneering treatment. He was not afraid to suffer. He may be insane, but Nikita could respect his courage.

The tidy-looking nurse, Meryl Stroud, placed an inhaler over the patient's muzzle. He nodded at her. She smiled and stroked his big ears. Josef impatiently beckoned his assistant away to the control panel. Once Meryl was clear of danger, Josef worked the dials of the repurposed torture machine, slowly increasing the imperium flow.

Rafe breathed harder and faster, steaming up the inhaler. The specialised rack beneath him shone with a lattice of priceless white-imperium. Suddenly arcs of plasma shot forth, rippling down Rafe's mighty body. He arched his back and cried out.

"Aaaaaaaaaaghgaaahgh!"

Nurse Meryl cupped her paws to her muzzle mask, whilst Doctor Josef looked on with cold indifference, the white plasma reflecting in his tinted spectacles.

"Gaaaaagh!"

After half a minute, Meryl turned to Josef and said something; Nikita couldn't hear her over the snapping bolts of plasma, but whatever it was Josef ignored her.

Not half a minute later, Meryl ran over to a pipe and turned a valve, shutting down the machine by cutting off its imperium gas supply.

The patient collapsed back, his body shaking, fur steaming, teeth grinding.

"What're you doing?" Josef hissed.

"That's enough!" Meryl shouted back.

"You could've damaged the equipment!"

"I don't care!"

Once all was quiet, Meryl hurried over to Rafe and cradled his head in her arms.

"That's enough, Rafe," she said, her voice muffled by the glass. "That's enough for today."

"I... can go again," he rasped. "I need to get better... for Jan. For Lupa."

"She can wait. They can all wait. What good are you to anyone if you die?"

"I can't die.... Not with you to look after me."

Meryl pulled down her mask and kissed Rafe's brow.

Outside, Nikita tutted sympathetically, "Foolish girl, allowing herself to grow attached to your Eisenwolf." He looked in the reflection of the glass, at the wolfess approaching from the shadows behind, "You agree, Prefect?"

"Yes, sir," Janoah replied at length, joining Nikita at the large observation window – he had sensed her corona approaching, Janoah made no effort to hide it. "I'm sure Rafe will be back on his feet soon," she added.

"He's brave wolf," Nikita praised imperfectly in his thick and cosy-sounding Steppes accent. "You did well when you find him for ALPHA, Comrade Valerio. Silvermane had been waiting long for such wolf as this."

"Thank you, sir."

Janoah knew little of Nikita; the wolf remained an enigma to her even after nine months at ALPHA. Common knowledge held that, along with Horst, Nikita was one of the Alpha's oldest friends. They had served in the war as little more than cubs and joined ALPHA upon its inception, clawing their way to the top and running the show ever since. Some said they were rather more than friends, that Nikita was the Alpha's wolf even behind closed doors. It sounded a little too convenient to Janoah, an obvious slander put about by Howlers eager disparage the organisation they despised.

Still, as they say, no ash without embers.

"How went your debriefing?" Nikita hummed, rocking on his boots, tail flicking. "Was Adal in good mood?" he added, using the Alpha's true name, Adal Weiss, a thing rarely dared even by his inner circle.

Janoah dipped her chin, "Fair mood, sir."

"He expect results; as do I."

"As do we all, Grand Prefect. We must crack this plot open by the time the Summit comes around."

Nikita hiked his mottled brown and white brow and said simply, "Why then?"

Janoah replied, "Because there won't be a glorious Republic to protect, otherwise."

"You exaggerate, comrade! The imperium those hyenas have stolen could make one or two districts uninhabitable at worst. It would not be first time Lupa has lost land to a black-imperium spill; there are many Dead Zones, especially in Bloc."

"Yes, sir, but if the Pack Summit is bombed with black-imperium? Surely it's occurred to you."

Nikita scoffed at once, "It occurred to Adal and I years ago! Such plot has been tried many times by many dissidents; always it end in failure. Black-imperium is most difficult to use as weapon. The vapour; it is heavy, it sink down, not rise like yellow. There is no way to deliver it effectively except to stand up high and drop it on beasts. How will hyenas do that and not be stopped?"

"I don't know, but this year it's Hummel's turn to host. I'm not saying Hummelton's security is lax, sir, but it's just not Lupa."

"Indeed. Well, if we only knew for sure."

"The Bloodfangs may yet prise something from the Chakaa they captured in Riddle," Janoah said.

Nikita just grunted and dipped his chin. In the silence that ensued, Janoah watched Josef fiddle with his machine whilst Meryl comforted the trembling Rafe. Janoah burnt with the desire to race in there and hold his paw, but that would be unseemly in front of Nikita. Rafe had Meryl; the pretty young wolfess would comfort him tonight.

Nikita said at length, "I will leave you with your Eisenwolf, Janoah-"

"Actually, Grand Prefect, I came to see you."

"Me?"

"Yes," Janoah said, explaining, "the Alpha has tasked me with executing a special arrest. He suggested I call on you to assist me."

"Oh?"

"The suspect is attending the Arkady Symposium tonight. The Alpha wants as many beasts as possible to witness his arrest, so as to set an example. However, I may have trouble maintaining order. Even Silvermane and the others may find themselves out of their depth. The Alpha trusts you'll have no trouble, you being such an… imposing figure."

There was a long, thoughtful silence.

"If it is Adal's wish, of course," the flattered Nikita sniffed, lifting his chin and cupping his paws in front of him. "Who is this suspect he wants example made of?"

Janoah took a sharp breath, "Rufus Valerio."

"Your husband?"

"Yes, sir."

"Why? Rufus is harmless fool."

"He's a radical impartialist."

"So am I!" Nikita growled. "Is no secret the views I hold. Duncan is not so different. Will we be next?"

Janoah mediated, "You seek reform, sir, as do many here, even the Alpha himself. But of course you do not incite violent unrest. Rufus's speech in Arkady University last week was tantamount to treason; he could make another tonight! Besides, I know he's been misappropriating imperium for years and I can prove it."

Nikita nodded slowly, "You would arrest your own husband?"

"I must."

"For the sake of the Alpha, or your career?"

Janoah's green eyes flitted a little, "Neither, sir, but for the Republic Lupi."

Codex: Eisbrand

The Eisbrand families, by and large, originate from the Great Steppes, a land that was harsh long before the Ashfall rendered it almost uninhabitable. The naturally severe conditions bred not only big, tough wolves, but seeded endless wars and rebellions. These internal conflicts gave rise to a culture of relative equality and toleration, as meagre resources had to be shared more fairly in order to quell the ranks of disgruntled noble wolves and little beast peasants alike. Therefore, it is the Eisbrands and not Hummel who can best lay claim to have given birth to the notion of 'Impartialism', where no beast is born superior to the next. Though the Eisbrands still maintain ultimate control, they go further than any Bloodfang or Greystone to keep the little beasts content, even allowing them some say in how a district is run. Uniquely they have District Councils comprised of citizens voted for by citizens, though the local Elder still has the final say on most matters.

The current Den Father, Thorvald Strom, is especially liberal. Under him there has been a surge of learning and philosophical debate, culminating in the annual Wintertide Arkady Symposium, where all the brightest minds of Lupa gather to share their liberal ideas. There is also the Petra Square Science Exhibition, where the latest inventions are shown off to both the masses and possible investors.

Liberal though they are, the Eisbrands run a tight ship regards their Howlers. They must be as strong as any Greystone or Bloodfang to maintain their borders, and to that end they equip themselves with the very best armour and weapons lupas can buy. Eisbrands revel in their heavy eisenglanz plate and enormous great kristahl swords, all paid for by the taxes on luxury goods the pack imports from across the Graumeer with the help of sea-faring otters. Fine silk, porcelain, spices; all things exotic come to Lupa via the Eisbrands and their otter partners.

Unlike the vast, barren Steppes to the north, Eisbrand holdings both within Lupa and along the west coast remain somewhat uncontaminated, since the prevailing wind blows the Ashfall to the north east. Thus the Eisbrands are able to keep clean streets and gardens of hardy plants within their handsome quarter of the city. Many an Eisbrand, Howler or healthy, maintains a holiday home on the clean Graumeer coast, particularly in and around the otter colony of New Tharona.

For all this, and for their renowned physical beauty, the Eisbrands are looked upon jealously by their wolfen neighbours, particularly the long-suffering Greystones.

Chapter 21

Tristan Donskoy stole round the side of the Arkady University, the golden light from the windows cascading over his freshly polished armour and Howler helmet like liquid gold. Just on the other side of that wall was warmth, light and a fabulous spread. Tristan could hear the belly-laughs of dignitaries and clinking of glasses. He longed to be inside, to be sharing a drink with Sara, beautiful Sara.

Tristan approached the majestic main entrance, with its great marbled pillars. Two heavily armoured Eisbrands were checking the invites of guests and allowing them to pass inside, or not in the case of any uninvited press, spies and other undesirable gatecrashers – there had been a few attempts made already.

Security was especially tight since the Den Father of the Eisbrands was putting in a rare appearance; Old Thorvald liked to be seen to sponsor learning and debate. The annual Arkady University Wintertide Symposium, to give it its full title, was the ideal venue to let it be known how progressive the Eisbrand Pack was compared to the 'other lot', the other lot being whatever pack you fancied, it was a blanket disparagement.

Tristan climbed the steps. "Any more troublemakers?" he asked his wolves.

They saluted, fists to chests and out. "A couple, sir," the one on the right said. "Just some dissident wolves; students by the looks. They were giving out leaflets at the gate."

"What kind of leaflets?"

The Howler pulled a crumpled piece of paper from his cloak pocket and passed it to Tristan.

Tristan opened it. Inside was a grainy, barely discernable photo of a burnt settlement with dead hyenas of every sex and age lying about.

"Fake dissident propaganda, sir," said the Howler.

"Yes," Tristan said at length, clearing his throat.

"What shall we do with them, sir?" asked the gruff Howler on the left.

"Who?"

"The dissidents, sir."

Tristan slipped the leaflet in his own cloak pocket. "Keep them in a cell overnight. Let them go with a warning."

"That all, sir?"

"Do you have a problem with my order, Howler?"

"No, sir."

"Good."

Headlights beaming, a fancy red motor car zoomed down the drive, wheels crunching through the gravel and snow, and pulled up by the entrance. A smartly dressed wolfen valet – or rather a volunteer student acting as a valet – burst from the university foyer and hurried down the steps to open the car door. Before he managed, a dapper ginger cat in a long white coat and scarf popped out.

"I say, you lot, where do you want us to park?" he asked.

Tristan descended the steps, "Leave it to the valet, sir."

"Valet?" the cat scoffed, casting his goggled eyes down the skinny young wolf Tristan was gesturing to. "Do you know what you're doing behind a wheel, young wolf?"

"Yes, sir!" the youth replied confidently.

"You'd better. There's a six-hundred ant-power, turbo-charged, red-imperium engine under that bonnet, and don't you forget it!"

"Six-hundred!" the wolf whistled. "Wow!"

"Put her into a wall, me laddo, and you'll be for it."

"Perish the thought, sir."

An elegant grey catess in a similar white coat emerged from the other side of the carriage. "Monty leave him alone," she chided, walking round, "I'm sure this young gentlebeast is perfectly capable of parking our car."

After a twist of his whiskers, Monty coughed up the tip and gave the young wolf a few lupas.

"Keys are in the ignition," he said.

"Yes, sir. The cloakroom is just inside on your left. The girls will take your coats."

The valet eagerly hopped inside Monty's car and slammed the door. Nursing the gorgeous wheel with his gloved paws he crunched the gears a few times and, after a few false starts and innocent smiles, got things moving.

Monty watched the car crackle its away across the university grounds towards the clock tower, until his wife turned his gaze with a paw. "Manners, Monty," she hissed.

"I'm only thinking of the money we'll get for selling it in good nick, Sweetpea."

"It shan't come to that."

"No? Better pray for some investors tonight, then."

The imposing Tristan greeted the cats, a big wolf, even for an Eisbrand. "Montague and Penelope Buttle?"

"That's right, 'Owler," Monty replied, chipper again. "Call us Monty n' Penny if you will."

Tristan nodded.

With an 'Oh!' Monty hurriedly produced the invitations from inside his coat, but Tristan waved the envelopes away.

"I've seen you on the newsreels," he insipidly assured the famous feline couple. "Please, allow me to escort you to the hall personally."

"Much obliged, sir, much obliged. What's your grip, if I may be so bold?"

"Donskoy, Tristan Donskoy."

"Pleasure, Tristan. Lead on, sir."

The Buttles followed Tristan up the stairs, between the saluting Howlers, and into the ancient magnificence of Arkady University. The main foyer arced high overhead, but was strangely cosy and warm-looking, with its lattice-like structure of struts criss-crossing a hundred times, creating countless geometric nooks and crannies.

"Oh, it's beautiful, Monty," Penny whispered, casting her eyes around.

"Yes, quite. Must be a nightmare to dust, eh?"

Tristan couldn't help himself. "I'm sure it's nothing compared to what you're used to as Felician royalty."

"Hahaa!" Monty laughed, "Did you hear that, Penny? Chap thinks we're rolling in it."

Penny smiled.

"We live on a bally farm, sir," Monty explained

Tristan actually turned to the cats in mid-stride, "Farm? Don't you live in Queen's Town?"

"Absolutely not. No room in Queens Town for me dirigibles, even less Felicia. Open air is what you need. Besides, I'm not part of the club am I, Sweetpea?"

"That's enough Monty."

Deciding not to probe, Tristan wordlessly led the cats to the cloakroom set into the wall. Behind the desk was a little black wolfess in a green blazer and white breeches, her simple beauty unmarred by a disapproving frown, in Tristan's opinion.

"What do you want?" she scoffed at him, busying herself by shuffling hats on the shelf behind. "You're supposed tae be on duty, Howler Donskoy."

"Can't stay away," Tristan whispered, saying aloud to the guests, "Sara Hummel will take your coats-"

"Saraaa!" Penny cooed, fluttering a gloved paw.

Sara whirled around, her countenance altering in a flash, as if someone had hooked fine fishing lines to the corners of her mouth and pulled. "Duchess!" she squealed, just about managing to hug Penny over the desk. "Och! What're you doing here?"

Monty took that one, "Invited, doncha know."

"When? You did nae tell me!"

"We wanted to surprise you," Penny explained. "Monty's giving a talk on his dirigibles, aren't you dear?"

"Indeed. Forgot me notes, but I'll improvise."

Sara laughed, "Ah can't wait."

Monty peered over Sara to the rows of coats and cloaks arranged behind, "You are going to be at the dinner, then?"

She waved a paw, "Of course! Ah'm just helping out here until everyone arrives."

"Ah. That's our little trooper, eh Penny?"

"We should've known you'd be about something," Penny tutted fondly. "Sara's such a dear," she told Tristan. "She helped us last summer, back when we were just getting settled in at Rumney Farm. Feeding the silkworms and milking the aphids, oh she was in her element."

Tristan looked sideways at Sara, "I thought you were visiting your family in Hummelton."

"I did… fer a week," Sara explained. "It was during summer break; six weeks stuck with Mum was a wee bit much."

"For her or you?"

Sara surreptitiously poked her tongue out at Tristan, then said to the cats, "Well, let me take your coats and everything."

The Buttles shed their outermost garments as if they were pupae skins, emerging transformed, like butterflies; Monty in a green suit complete with cravat and gold lace, and Penny in a wonderful white gown with a silver lily brooch.

Once Sara had told Penny how lovely she looked, she directed her and Monty across the foyer to the open double doors guarded by two more Howlers. Beyond was the Great Hall, with a grand table festooned with silver cutlery, winter foliage and ice sculptures, all lit by marvellous imperium chandeliers glowing steady overhead like weird spaceships. The air was thick with vapours and chitchat as beasts mingled before the main event.

Sara spied Professor Heath talking with several of his academic friends, but as the Buttles entered the hall, the big bear excused himself and greeted them, shaking paws and making introductions. He glanced across at Sara and waved.

"You do get around, don't you?" Tristan hummed.

Sara glanced at him. "You still here?" she clucked, labelling the Buttles' coats and hanging them up

"Where's Olivia? I thought she was helping."

"She had tae stay home."

"I see. How is she?"

Sara shrugged and continued her task.

After a long silence, Tristan sighed, "Heath can't keep this up forever. Someone's going to notice the white-imperium missing from the Ark's inventory and when they do-"

"Not now, Tristan."

Tristan emitted a gruff sigh.

At length, Sara heard the crumple of paper, which drew her curiosity back to Tristan, then down at a strange leaflet he had spread over the desk.

"What's that?" Sara asked him.

"Take a look."

Wearing a curious frown, Sara came over and inspected the paper. Tristan kept watch, glancing all about.

"Ulf's fangs!" Sara gasped, paw to mouth, as if she were there amidst the ash and death of the burning village.

"Couple of dissidents were giving them out at the gates," Tristan explained, seemingly unaffected. "Evidence from the Reservations."

"Och, that's terrible. Is it real?"

The Howler dipped his chin, "It could be an old photo from the war. I hope so, but… my sources point to serious abuses in the Reservations."

"Abuses? Tristan, there's dead cubs and everything!"

"I know, I know. Look, don't show that to anybody, I wouldn't want them to think you were giving them out-"

"Donskoy!" someone barked.

Sara hid the leaflet under the desk whilst Tristan whipped round to face a passing superior, an Eisbrand Grand Howler in a suitably grand white surcoat, her armour marked with runes and snowflakes.

"Marm?" Tristan replied.

"Stop flirting with the faculty and get outside," was the order. "Thorvald's due any second. Help him in, wolf, he's doubtless expecting you."

"Yes, marm!"

With a helpless shrug at Sara, Tristan hurried to the main doors. Not knowing what else to do, Sara tucked the leaflet in her blazer and joined the crowds of beasts pouring out the hall to catch a glimpse of the arriving host. She was curious herself, having never before seen the Eisbrand's Den Father in the flesh.

Sara weaved her way through the throngs of 'respectable' beasts; cats, hogs, bears and fellow wolves of course, even a rabbit or two – their kind had always straddled the divide between big and little, strong and meek. The Eisbrands were notoriously liberal and tolerated the odd little beast climbing above their station, especially under old Thorvald Strom. According to Tristan, Thorvald had been a Watcher, a Howler of the Lupan Wall and the Ashfall beyond. He had travelled far in his time, seen many things, lost many friends, and learnt the Lupan way was not the only way.

Emerging onto the university steps and the bitter cold of a winter's night, Sara and the others spread out, making an informal funnel of beasts ready to greet Den Father Thorvald, patron of the prestigious Ark. He was the wolf to whom many, Sara included, owed their education. Others owed him their jobs, like old Professor Heath, who came alongside Sara, a giant in comparison, pipe smouldering in jaw as ever.

The Arkady University gates swung open and the churning of imperium engines filled the bitter evening air. A motorcade of eight monobikes and two impressive, gleaming white motor carriages lit up the courtyard with their blinding headlamps. Stopping at the stairs, the Howlers disembarked their monos and smartly formed up around the leading car, ready to protect it from any would-be assassin or terrorist.

Leaving his comrades at the entrance, Tristan calmly descended the stairs and opened the lead car's passenger door, which was marked with the Eisbrand snowflake. He got down on one knee and dipped his head respectfully.

"Den Father Thorvald," he said.

An armoured leg extended from the car, gold, with silver runes written into the seams. Snowflakes dotted every available space like stars in the firmament. An arm extended from the cabin, equally exquisite, the grey paw at the end grasping Tristan's sturdy shoulder

"Help me rise, Howler," rasped Thorvald Strom, Eisbrand Den Father. "The rot is bad with me today."

"Sir."

Keeping his chin dipped, Tristan slowly stood up. With some difficulty, Thorvald used the virile young Howler to lever himself out and stand, resplendent in his magnificent golden armour and ice-blue mantle.

Eisbrands were a heavily armoured lot, but Thorvald's marvellous gear must weigh more than most, Sara reckoned, watching from the steps. The Den Father's face and age were masked by his bejewelled helmet, but Sara knew Strom was an ancient wolf, especially so for a beast who'd had the rot all his life. He'd once been a tower of muscles, but even if his physical strength was finally deteriorating, he was, Tristan always claimed, an incredible imperium-wielder.

Satisfied the Den Father was steady, Tristan backed away a few steps, head still dipped. Thorvald raised a paw at all the Howlers, Freiwolves, citizens and others gathered before him in recognition of their attendance. They clapped and cheered. Despite the disturbing leaflet in her pocket, Sara found herself politely clapping too.

Thorvald approached Tristan and cupped a paw to his shoulder, "Help an old wolf up the stairs will you, Captain?"

"It'd be my honour, Den Father."

Thorvald raised Tristan's gaze to meet his own with a finger to his chin, "Head up, Donskoy, look smart."

"Sir."

Thorvald hung on Tristan's arm and together they slowly climbed the marble steps of the Arkady. The university faculty lined up at the top to shake paws, Heath included, whilst the Den Guard made a wall around Thorvald, blocking anyone from approaching without the Den Father's invitation.

Thorvald worked his way along the line; paws were shaken, polite enquiries made, Tristan occasionally reminding his master who the beasts were. The zoologist and imperiologist Professor Heath, the pilots Montague and Penny Buttle, and many other academics besides.

Before Sara knew what was what, the Den Father was in front of her!

"And who is this enchanting wolfess?" he asked in a pleasantly crackly old voice, like an evening campfire.

Sara curtsied, "Pleased tae meet you, Den Father, sir."

Tristan formally introduced her, "This is Sara Hummel, sir; Professor Heath's graduate-"

"Ah yes, of course it is!" Thorvald woofed. "I've heard all about your progress from young Tristan here."

"Oh aye?" Sara said, glancing at Tristan, who looked down and cleared his throat.

Thorvald went on, "Forgive me, I forget; you're Den Mother Cora's eldest?"

"Aye, eldest of eight daughters, sir," Sara confirmed chirpily.

"Hahaha! Eight now?" Thorvald chuckled. He leant forward a little and said with a twinkle in his eyes, "There must be something in Everdor's water."

"It's just the ash, sir, or lack of it," Sara replied.

"Ash?"

"Aye. When Ah first came tae Lupa, mah eyes watered for weeks and weeks, and Ah'm nae even allergic! Mah mother has the rot like any Howler, of course, but she's at least had clean air and food when pregnant; that's why she's carried so many cubs through. It's nae mystery tae me."

Tristan subtly made a throat-cutting motion with his paw to ward Sara off the touchy subject.

However, Thorvald was amenable. "Yes. What damage we and our ancestors have done to our poor, wounded country, young Sara," he sighed wistfully. "Perhaps one day we'll wean ourselves off the two-faced mineral that has given us civilisation at the price of our freedom and our health. Alas, I will be long gone." He looked to Tristan and back, "The future is in your paws, you youngsters. It is for you, sick Howler and healthy citizen alike, to plot the next course and find a solution."

Sara and Tristan exchanged glances, then looked down and away from one another.

Tristan and his master moved on, heading inside the warmth and light of the university, followed by Professor Heath, Sara, and the crowd of guests, all swilling in the wake of Thorvald and his fierce-looking bodyguards.

"Where's Rufus?" Thorvald discreetly asked his escort.

"I don't know, Den Father," Tristan snorted. "Running fashionably late, I imagine. He'll stop at nothing to remain the centre of attention."

"Mind your tongue, Howler," Thorvald chided. "He's a better wolf than you and I."

They passed into the glorious dining hall with its chandeliers and sculptures, Thorvald waving at his guests even whilst secretly talking to Tristan.

"It's unfortunate Red-mist lured your cousin away to the Bloodfangs," he said, walking to the grand chair at head of the table, "but Ivan could do worse. Rufus shares so many Eisbrand sympathies that he'd be one by now were it not for his loyalty. The Bloodfangs took him in, gave him a chance, when all other packs refused… including ours. He would have died of rot as a cub without a Bloodfang Howlership. Rufus, as a wolf of honour, will never forget that."

Tristan replied steadily, "Yes, Den Father," like a young wolf listening to his granddad.

He pulled out the marvellous wooden chair at the end of the fabulous spread. Thorvald sat and his long-cloaked Den Guard spread out around the room, some closer than others, but all ready to pounce on any intruder.

Thorvald changed subject. "You still love that girl?" he whispered afresh.

Tristan's duotone eyes widened alarmingly.

"Who wouldn't?" Thorvald chuckled at once. "Ah, Sara's a worthy cause. Ulf knows, you've watched over her since her arrival in Lupa with little thanks."

"It's reward enough that she's safe, sir," Tristan humbly insisted.

"Nonetheless, since we tasked you with this burden, albeit on her noble mother's behalf, I feel I should have a word with her and explain your honourable intentions-"

"No!" Tristan yelped, adding in a measured tone, "No, thank you, Den Father. I… I wouldn't want Sara to feel put upon. Whatever she decides must come naturally, not because such a great wolf as you said so."

Thorvald nodded solemnly. "I was lucky enough to know love. Nothing gave me greater joy than my wife, though nearly all our cubs were stillborn, no doubt because of the poisons in my bones and all around us… as young Sara says. I pray she's sees past the rot and accepts you in her own time, as a wolf first, not a Howler, just as my wife did me."

Tristan watched Sara enter the hall with Professor Heath and take her seat for dinner; the places were all labelled. She glanced Tristan's way, before the raucous Monty Buttle snatched her charming gaze away.

Tristan bowed and excused himself. "Forgive me, Den Father, I must return to my duties."

"Stay awhile, Donskoy; warm yourself."

"I wish I could."

Thorvald nodded and waved him away. Released, Tristan strode from the hall, armour and sword rattling.

Sara watched him pass, before surreptitiously checking his leaflet under the table. As Sara stared at the terrible picture, made somehow more horrific by its grainy texture, the hubbub of dinner faded, the clinking of glass and Monty's laughter ebbing away like the blood of the hyenas lying slain in the rolling Ashfall mud.

Could it be?

✦

Rufus whizzed down the gravel drive on his mono and skidded to a halt by the stairs, kicking up a shower of stones. Linus hopped off the back as quickly as possible, eager to feel terra firma beneath his toes after that hair-raising ride.

Rumour held Rufus was a notorious tearaway on a mono, now Linus could confirm it.

"Here we are," Red-mist declared, shutting his standard-issue, Bloodfang-emblazoned GVM-12 *Springtail* down. "You all right?" he asked Linus.

"What? Oh, yes."

"You look a bit unsteady."

"Must be the rot, sir," Linus excused, clearing his throat.

He cast his baby-blue eyes over the magnificent façade of the Arkady University, its cold, indifferent exterior punctured by elegant glazed cavities through which passers by could glimpse the promise of warmth and good company.

Linus's heart was still racing, and not from the ride. He realised he was excited to be here, albeit nervous.

'I'm going to muck things up,' he thought. 'I'll do or say something stupid.'

"Come on," Rufus chirped, leading the way.

"Sir."

As the Bloodfangs climbed the stairs, the Eisbrands either side of the doors were augmented by another big wolf with a big sword. Linus recognised him as that Tristan character from the refinery, and without even realising it his tail wagged with pleasure at the thought of a friendly face.

"You're late, Howler Valerio," Tristan snorted.

"Traffic was murder, Howler Donskoy," Rufus replied airily, brushing by.

Tristan grabbed Rufus's upper arm, stopping him. "You can't leave your little *Springtail* there."

Rufus slowly looked to him. "That's why I left the keys in the ignition, so *you* could move it." He twisted his arm free and, with his helmet grill an inch from Tristan, added dangerously, "Touch me again and you'll be on your tail. Is that clear, Donskoy?"

Tristan said nothing. He just looked straight ahead.

Rufus moved on, "Come along, Linus."

Baffled by the altercation, Linus hesitated on the stairs whilst Rufus strode fearlessly inside.

"Hello, Tristan," Linus said, with a slightly nervous chuckle. He raised a paw in a quick 'hi' gesture. "Good to see you again, Howler."

"Your master is waiting," Tristan scoffed, cupping his paws before him. "Run along now."

Linus's heart leapt. He let out a slight gasp, but nothing more came, no words. He climbed the steps, giving Tristan a sideways glance, before slipping past the other two Howlers without looking.

Once he was inside, Linus heard muffled laughter behind him. It was the two Howlers with Tristan.

Why?

"Linus," Rufus beckoned from hall.

'By Ulf,' Linus realised, 'they think I'm his beta.'

The young wolf followed his 'master', the grand interior of the Ark passing by without notice. Linus's mind had zoned in on that one thought; the thought that others reckoned him a lesser wolf, a follower, the sort to groom your back and be grateful.

Did Uther think it too?

Linus remembered his friend's reaction in the gym. 'Oh,' he'd said, 'I see.'

Oh dear Ulf, he *did* think it!

"Are you sure you're all right, Linus?" Rufus tutted, dashing Linus's mental meanderings as the youth caught up with him. "You're walking around like a gazer."

Linus nodded a little too enthusiastically, "I'm f-fff-fine, sir. Really."

Rufus waited a moment, then said, "Ignore them."

"Pardon?"

"You heard me," the Grand Howler sniffed. "They're jealous, that's all. You know why?"

Linus couldn't find his tongue to speak.

"Because they think even though you're a rotten Howler you get what they all crave; contact with a fellow Howler, against which all other love pales by comparison, especially the counterfeit sort Uther pays for at the local Lupanar!" Rufus snorted. "They hate me all the more because I married me a genuine 'Howleress' back before it was forbidden. It's all jealousy."

Linus spluttered, "But I'm not-"

"Does it matter?" Rufus interrupted. "To deny it would only make them believe it more. Stay silent and let them stew in their own petty bitterness. What do we care?"

Linus looked at his feet.

Taking a deep breath, Rufus removed his helmet and ran a paw over his ears to tidy his fur. "Well, take your helmet off before we go in!" he chided gently. "There's a Den Father in there. It's bad enough we're late, let's not compound our disrespect."

"Of course, sir."

Linus removed his helmet; Rufus winked at him, "Very dashing."

'Good Ulf, is he trying to make me uncomfortable on purpose?' Linus thought.

They walked on, coming to the doors and the Howlers standing guard, who opened the way.

A cacophony of chitchat and laughter, cutlery and crystal flooded into the silent hallway. Rufus led the charge, battling the noisy current. Linus tagged nervously along, eyes wide, ears pricked, taking in the magnificent spread and the rows of smartly-dressed guests. Beasts of every sort, though wolves in the main, looked up from their dainty starters and delicate wine glasses. Upon recognising the Howlers they immediately started whispering to one another. Were they saying good things or bad things? After what had just occurred at the front door, Linus's gut leant towards the latter.

"Rufus!" said a relatively small old bear who was dressed like a teacher. He stood up from the table and intercepted the famous Howler with a paw-shake and a warm smile. "There you are, I was getting worried."

"Heath, old friend," Rufus said simply, adding, "Thorvald first, all right?"

"Oh yes, protocol. Carry on, carry on."

Linus noticed a little black wolfess who had stood up with the bear. She beamed broadly at Rufus. He returned the gesture with a nod and paw-shake, before marching towards the head of the table.

The wolfess looked at Linus, her eyes exploring him.

She smiled politely.

Linus forced a quick smile that in his own mind came out more like a ridiculous gurn. Eyes down and throat cleared, he hurried after Rufus.

"Who's that?" he heard the wolfess say behind him.

"Not sure," replied the bear, adding, "Tristan said Rufus had found someone new."

"New?"

"Well a... a companion. You know what he's like."

Oblivious, or indifferent, Rufus made the head of the table and immediately prostrated himself on one knee beside the magnificently-dressed wolf seated there.

"Den Father Thorvald," he said.

"Rufus!" laughed the old wolf, his grizzled grey features lighting up. "You're late, you rogue."

"Apologies, sir. Something cropped up."

Linus arrived and also knelt, head down. Whatever pack they belonged to, whatever one thought of them or their policies, every Howler beneath a Den Father was required to display reverence. Anything less would get you in trouble with one's own pack for 'upsetting the peace'.

"Stand up, stand up," Thorvald insisted, waving a paw, "I'll not have a wolf who won the Imperium Heart stay on his knees."

Rufus rose.

Linus stayed kneeling, until Rufus tapped him with his foot, then he got up.

"Not *wearing* the heart, I see," Thorvald noted, looking at Rufus's cloaked chest, it was devoid of decoration beyond the usual brooch. "This is a special occasion, Howler; you're supposed to flaunt your accolades with pride."

"In the rush to be at your side I forgot," Rufus dismissed.

"Oh really?" the Den Father said, not fooled for a moment of course. "And what is it that 'cropped up'?"

"Touch of the rot, sir."

"Ah."

"I was in a bad way," Rufus maintained, turning to Linus and winking at him. "Luckily young Linus here found me in the middle of the attack. He sorted me out, but we lost half an hour whilst I gathered myself. Rather embarrassing."

"But-" Linus began.

Rufus kicked his gaitered shin.

"Linus Mills," Thorvald mused, tipping his head back in a knowing sort of way. "Yes, I hear great things about you. Brave fellow."

Linus nodded, "I'm honoured Den Father, but-"

"But we should take our seats," Rufus finished. "No doubt there's many beasts waiting to speak tonight."

"Yes yes, quite right," Thorvald agreed, adding, "Have you something for our ears, Rufus?"

"I've always something to say. You know that."

"Hah! Indeed."

"Den Father."

With a reverent bow for Thorvald, Rufus led Linus back down the table, past numerous guests, to the two empty spaces beside Heath and the little black wolfess in a green blazer.

"Room for two more?" he said.

Professor Heath, at least Linus assumed he was the great Professor Heath, stood up again, "Yes

yes, take your seats. I'll have them bring your starters."

"No, don't worry. We'll go straight for the main course."

"You sure, Rufus?"

"Absolutely."

Heath peered over his little spectacles at the stocky blonde wolf accompanying Rufus, "So, who's this fellow?"

"This is Linus."

"Linus? Oh! The clever one?"

Rufus ruffled Linus's ears like a cub, "Yes. He's very bright. Right up your alley; knows all about bugs."

"Does he indeed?" Heath said appreciatively.

Linus extended a paw, "Honour to meet you, sir. I-I-I've read all your work."

"You have?"

"Yes, sir, yours and Rufus's."

Heath hiked his hoary brow in surprise. "Well, at least someone has, eh Rufus?" he joked.

He and Rufus laughed aloud.

Linus and Sara shared covert looks and smiles before Heath remembered his manners. "Ah, yes, uh Linus, this is my dear friend and star pupil, Sara Hummel," he said, placing his big paws on her tiny shoulders. "She's into bugs too," he whispered, as if it were something illicit, "Especially bees."

"Aye, we're all mad here," Sara chirped, raising a glass.

Linus smiled at her, barely managing a, "Miss," then clearing his throat.

Sara nodded graciously, but spoke to Rufus, "You look well, Howler."

"Do I?" Rufus replied. "Must be the thought of an evening in your radiant presence, my dear, sweet girl."

"Och, you flatterer! Away with ye."

"Hahaha! How's your mother?"

Sara nodded, "As well as can be."

Rufus gruffed, "Good, good. Been too long."

With introductions and greetings made, Rufus set about making trouble. "I'm sure Sara doesn't want to be sandwiched between two old fogeys all night when there's a strapping young gentlebeast to be had," he said. "Heath, you move over here next to me and let Linus sit in your place. That way we can talk business and leave these two youngsters to get acquainted."

"Oh, very well," Heath replied.

"Ah don't mind being stuck between you," Sara said, as Rufus moved Heath's half-eaten food past her nose to the furthest empty space. "Really."

"Nonsense!" Rufus woofed, deftly swapping the cutlery and the wine glasses too.

By the time the Howler had finished and sat down, the arrangement went Heath, himself, Sara and Linus.

Linus could not politely object, and thus sat. He felt sidelined, dumped on the end as far away from the great Professor Heath as possible. Rufus obviously wanted to be surrounded by his fellow trained scientists tonight, Linus thought, not some enthusiast.

It's enough you're here at all, his conscience reminded him, be grateful.

Then again, maybe I should've gone with Uther.

The waiter poured his wine. He drank some, settled down, watched, listened. Sara and Professor Heath hung on Rufus's every word as he described what had happened last week, mostly regarding the giant centipede. When Rufus got round to mentioning THORN, Miss Sara tugged on his mantle and whispered something.

Reaching into her green blazer she produced a bit of crumpled paper and passed it to Rufus.

The Grand Howler stared for an age.

Linus couldn't see what it was, and Rufus soon tucked it away. He supposed it was something to do with the university and none of his business.

So, this is Rufus's other life, Linus thought, the one Elder Amael and many others frowned upon. The Eisbrands and the intellectuals they protected, these beasts with strange ideas about the rot and where intelligent creatures had originated, were not to be fraternised with beyond what was necessary for cordiality – yet Rufus had a chair here, even lectured on occasion. Were he any less of a wolf he would've been sent down years ago for dissident behaviour, or so Linus had been told by anyone with an opinion. Linus wondered if he too would be frowned upon for attending such an event. He wondered if he wanted to be. It sounded a strangely alluring badge of honour.

"Howler Linus?" someone exclaimed opposite.

Linus looked up from his drink and musings. "Monty Buttle?" he said, almost spitting his wine all over an ice sculpture of a butterfly on a flower.

"Hahaaaa! It *is* you!" Montague Buttle laughed, slapping a paw on the table, making the fine spread wobble. He shook his wife's shoulder, drawing her attention away from a conversation with rotund hog in a suit.

"What is it, Monty?" the catess hissed irritably.

"Sweetpea, it's Howler Linus, look! Remember him?"

Penny cupped a paw to her frilly, laced chest. "Oh! Howler Linus, but of course I remember."

"What're you doing here, sir?" Monty demanded.

Linus explained, "I uh… I'm with Rufus, sir."

"Rufus? What's a Rufus?"

"Sara's Howler friend, dear," Penny tutted quietly, pointing discreetly at Rufus, who remained oblivious to the Buttles as he chatted away with Sara and Professor Heath. "You know, the famous imperiologist? Professor Heath's colleague? We met during one of our demonstrations."

"Oh yes!" Monty recalled. "Capital fella."

Penny rolled her eyes, "You've a memory like a sieve these days. Honestly."

"I remembered young Linus, didn't I?"

Linus nodded, "You did, sir. To my honour."

"To his honour, he says! Did you hear that, Pen? I love the way this chap talks. Like someone from the Dark Age."

Penny laughed, perhaps only to smooth over any offence caused, not that Linus felt any.

"Oh, but we meet so many beasts now Sweetpea," Monty sighed, flapping a ginger paw dismissively. "I can't keep track of them all. That's your job. You're our ambassador."

"Next you'll be asking me to make your speeches," Penny complained.

"Never! I've got it all squirrelled away up here." Monty tapped his skull. "I know me dirigibles like my own paw. Even when I'm reduced to a gibbering wreck, infirm from old age, and you're pushing me about the farm in a wheelchair, my dear, I'll still know how to slap an imperium gas balloon together and fly. Isn't that right, Linus?"

"Oh, uh, ah… absolutely," he replied with a nod. "Do you ever take passengers up, Mr. Buttle?"

"Passengers?" Mr. Buttle bellowed. "Passengers! But of course, my good wolf. That's the whole point. Quick connection from country to country, crossing seas and impassable forests, shrinking the world." The cat made a flying motion with a fork as he talked, "*Buttle Skyways*; from here to there by air! It's the future of travel. Right Sweetpea?"

Penny sipped her wine and addressed Linus, "Once we have enough investors to open the factory again we can start producing a fleet. Then the ticket prices will come down and before you know it dirigibles will be the norm."

"That's why we came, really," Monty chuckled, leaning across the table and attempting to whisper, even though he was incapable of any such thing, "to find beasts *bold* enough to invest in our little enterprise. Yes. Our coffers are rather empty at the moment, I'm afraid."

"But I saw you on the news reels," Linus said, spreading his blonde paws. "You were flying over Lupa."

"Ah yes, well, that was all promotional stuff, you know, we had to pay the wolves in charge of your fair city for the privilege," Monty explained, adding, "Can't do it back home in Felicia at all. No. There's been a lot of resistance from the establishment, you see, they've banned our balloons from the city. If beasts were meant to fly they'd have wings and all that nonsense. We cats can be such sticks, sometimes."

"Banned?" Linus woofed in horror. "But why?"

"We lost a balloon over Felicia once," Penny added, passing Monty a quick glance and nod.

"Lost?" Linus said.

"There was an accident," Monty clarified sadly. "There was a fire and… well, it all went up. Beasts were injured, good friends. It was splashed all over the news back home, of course. The Queen herself turned on us and our backers pulled out overnight. Can't even set up in Queens Town, nobody wants to know. We've had to lay off nearly all our staff this last year. It's really slowed down the construction of our next big project, but it's coming along now. Nearly there."

Penny held Monty's paw, "We'll come through it in the end, dear. We always do."

"Absolutely, Sweetpea. If we were that easy to put off we'd never have tied the knot. Haha!"

Penny laughed, but there was a distinctly awkward pause.

"I'll help," Linus's tongue blurted, before his mind had cleared it for utterance.

"Help?" Monty squeaked.

"I'll invest. I mean, if that's all right."

"All right? But of course it is, Linus. Good show, sir!"

Beaming broadly, Linus reached into his red cloak and pulled out his wallet. "How much is a share?"

"How much you got, sir?"

"Monty!" Penny chided.

"You heard the wolf, he wants to invest!"

Linus didn't notice, but Sara's dark ears twisted round. Her head followed suit, just a little. She discreetly looked at Linus, specifically his wallet and the wad of colourful lupas he was flicking through like mere playing cards.

"How much do beasts usually pay?" the Howler asked, oblivious to Sara's scrutiny.

"A few thousand, sir," Monty sniffed assertively.

Linus stopped counting his money, "Uhm… well, I… I don't have a few thousand."

"Oh. Well what do you have?"

Linus continued to count. "About two-fifty," he admitted, through a mortified cough, checking his wallet again and adding lamely, "And a bit."

"Two-fifty and a bit?" Monty declared. "Sold!"

"It is?"

"One percent stake, sir, how's that for you?"

"One? Uh well, I suppose-"

"Two, sir! Two it is."

"Two?" Linus scoffed.

"More? You drive a hard bargain, Linus, so you do. Three percent, sir, that's me final offer-"

"Monty, stop!" Penny yelped. Excusing herself from Linus, she pulled her husband close and said sarcastically, "Give the whole farm away for beans, why don't you?"

Whilst the cats bickered amongst themselves, no doubt discussing the deal, Linus idly shuffled his money. Time passed, he looked around the table, at all the guests eating and talking. Nobody was paying him any mind.

Good.

The Howler rolled his money up, wrapped it in his napkin, and discreetly whistled at the cats.

Montague reacted just in time to catch Linus's flying napkin. "I say!" he mewed, opening the cloth in his paws to find a wad of hard cash. "Golly, how flash. Three percent share then, eh?"

"No no," Linus dismissed, waving his paws.

"Four?"

"Monty!" Penny hissed.

"No, I-I-I don't want a stake in your business," the Howler explained, thrumming his fingers on the table.

"What?" Penny said, wanting of manners herself for once.

"It's a gift. Please."

"Two-hundred-and-fifty lupas?" Monty spluttered.

Linus shrugged his stout shoulders, "It's nothing, really. I'd only waste it on entertaining myself. We all do. Better it goes to a worthy cause."

"We can't just take your money for nought, young wolf."

"It's not for nothing. I believe in you. Really, I do."

"But-"

"Just… give me a ride one day," Linus suggested ad-hoc, adding with some uncertainty, "Does two-fifty buy a ticket?"

Monty and Penny exchanged incredulous looks. "It buys a lifetime *Buttle Skyways* pass for you, Linus!" Monty confirmed, flapping the cash and raising his glass to the wolf. "It would be an honour to take you up into the big blue, sir."

Linus nodded, "Then I look forward to it."

In the aftermath, Sara made her move – she had seen and heard enough to pass judgement. "So, what's your favourite bug, Howler?" she posed out of the blue.

Surprised, Linus turned to this little wolfess – no shorter than he, but half his weight if that – and blurted, "Termite."

"Termite? Why's that?"

"Because… well, th-they build great castles of mud, even though they're blind and deaf and probably not all that bright they match Lupan civilisation, in their own way."

"Perhaps even better it?"

Linus could but guffaw. "Maybe."

"Have ye ever seen a termite nest?" the wolfess asked.

"I vaguely remember poking one as a cub. They're all over Rostsonne. Only s-sss-small ones, mind."

"Och! Rostsonner are ye?"

"Originally."

"Ah thought so from the fur, but you've nae accent."

"No, but you do."

"Aye! Everdorian guilty as charged. Sara Hummel by the way."

"Yes, Professor Heath said," Linus pointed out. "S-sss-still, whilst we're about it, I-I-I'm Linus, Linus Mills, Howler Trooper First Class. Uhm, Bloodfang… etcetera."

Sara laughed gently.

Linus too, rubbing the back of his neck.

"That was very nice of ye," Sara said afresh, "giving Monty and Penny some help there. They're pretty hard-up."

"Oh, it was nothing."

"Two-fifty is a lot for a Trooper, even a 'first-class'."

"Like I said, I've come to realise lately that I may as well throw it in the bin," Linus explained. He looked at his fingers, picked at his claws and swallowed hard. "We Howlers have no future, after all," he said with a slight, false chuckle. "Nothing to save for, or to try for." Almost immediately, Linus shook his head a little and closed his eyes, "I'm, sorry… I don't know where that came from."

Sara raised her wine. "The drink?" she laughed.

Linus smiled at this bubbly wolfess, before admitting, "Had an attack, you see. Haven't had a-a-a bad one in years. My bones are still throbbing. The rot must be setting in."

"But you look young-"

"Exactly," the Howler said at once, his golden paws trembling a little, "I'm not even eighteen yet. But that's how it goes. Can't complain, eh?"

He took a huge swig of his wine to calm his nerves.

"Bee," Sara said, changing subject.

"What?"

"My favourite bug; it's a bee. Great bees, mind, nae little ones."

"Oh!" Linus woofed. "Yes, Professor Heath said that too. You must see a lot of great bees in

Everdor."

"Aye, but mum never let me work in the Den's apiary, too dangerous and all," Sara complained. "Ah've a pet bee, though!" she hastened to add, as if covering a slip of the tongue.

"A what? A *pet* bee?"

"Aye."

Linus blinked rapidly. "Is that normal over Everdor way?"

Sara laughed, "Och, no! She flew into the university clock tower last year. Did her wing in; she cannae fly. So, Ah look after her now, well, Heath and me."

Linus didn't know what to say, so he just forced a laugh and nursed his wine.

"Have you really read all his work?" Sara enquired sceptically, "Professor Heath, Ah mean."

"Of course," Linus maintained. "Haven't you?"

"No, Ah cannae get into it," Sara whispered, giving Heath a glance. "He's a great teacher, but his writing is so...."

"Dense, I know."

"Do you read it for fun, then?"

Linus nodded vigorously, adding, "I wanted to be a scientist, but… things didn't work out."

"The rot, aye," Sara sighed, as if she could relate.

Could she be afflicted? Linus could feel no corona and female Howlers were vanishingly rare, except Sara was a Hummel and that altered the equation.

"You're… n-nnn-not a Howler, are you?" Linus hazarded.

Sara scoffed, "Me? Nooo!"

Linus raised a paw, "I-I-I didn't think you were, but… if you're Sara *Hummel* then-"

"Ah'm a member by birth," Sara explained, "nae by rot. She knocked on the table, "Ah'm still healthy. Touch wood."

"Shouldn't you have reverted back to Freiwolf status when you became an adult?"

"That's… nae how it works over my way, nae when you're a Den Mother's daughter anyway."

A pause.

"You're the daughter of D-D-Den Mother Cora?" Linus piped.

Sara grimaced. "Aye, that's me." She swirled her drink, "Ah'd be the next Den Mother in training, but without the affliction that's nae happening. Ah'd renounce mah Hummel name tomorrow and become a proper Freiwolf, lose the baggage, but that'd upset mah dad and, well, Ah'm a daddy's girl."

Linus nodded. Before he could enquire further, someone tapped a glass.

Ding! Ding! Ding!

Beasts fell silent and looked to the head of the table, to Den Father Thorvald, who stood up. A Howler rushed to help him, but he brushed him off.

"Esteemed guests," he announced. "Whilst we wait for the second course, we shall hear from the next speaker tonight. He is a very special wolf, a Howler and a philosopher, winner of the Imperium Heart and lately of the Quin Medal. I speak of course of Rufus Bloodfang, who has made a special effort to be here tonight, though I shan't go into all that. Please give him your ears."

Rufus stood up to general applause, which he calmed by raising his paws and nodding a lot.

"Now, I know what you're all thinking," he began, as silence descended. "Even you, Den Father," he added with a slight bow. "You're thinking he's going to bang on about his ruddy expedition again, or the rot, or something controversial that's going to make me squirm like a maggot. Well, not tonight dear friends. I'm a little tired. Tonight I'm giving that drum a rest."

Several 'aaws' filled the air.

"No no, I've something even better. I'm going to recite the fable of the Nymph and the Dayfly." Rufus cocked his head to one side, "Yes, I know. It's an oldie, but a goody. Many of you have probably heard it before, in your beds, read to you by your mother or your father, just like me. But… I think, even as grow-ups, we need reminding of these things from time to time, when the night closes in and the way ahead seems frightening. And besides I do have an exceptionally melodious voice."

"Hahahahaaa!" Thorvald laughed. "More melodious than mine, Howler?" he joked.

"You're a distant second, Den Father."

Laughing, Thorvald slapped the arm of his chair and knocked back some wine, like an ancient Wolf King.

Once all were silent, Rufus began….

Two eggs fell from the sky. They splashed into a pond and drifted slowly down to the silt below. From where they came the bugs in the pond did not know, for none of them had seen such a sight, only the fish had, for he lived longer than most.

Days passed and the eggs hatched, and from them two nymphs emerged, pale little creatures with six legs and no wings.

'What am I?' said the first.

'I know not,' said the second.

'Are you like me?'

'I think we are the same, yes.'

'We should be friends,' the first suggested, to which the second replied. 'That we should.'

'We will need names, friend. Call me… Gold, you can be Silver.'

'No, I'll be Gold,' the second insisted, 'you be Silver.'

'As you will,' said Gold, who was now Silver.

Together they fed, grazing on the plants and algae, growing day by day, shedding their skin each time.

'What do you think is beyond the sky?' asked Silver, looking up at the shimmering blue surface.

'I don't know,' Gold replied, nibbling a leaf, 'but I feel I want to go there.'

'And I.'

'No, you don't want to go up there,' said the big fish, swimming lazily over to the nymphs.

'Why not?' asked Gold.

'You'll die,' Fish replied. 'There's nothing to see anyway. Stay here. It's safe down here.'

'But that's where we came from,' Silver pointed out, 'the others told us so. Our mother must have dropped us from beyond the sky. She must be up there, waiting.'

Fish chuckled, 'No, she is dead.'

'How do you know?'

'Because you're a dayfly. Once you spread your wings and fly away, you will die in but a day. However, if you stay down here you may live forever.'

"But I want to see. I want to fly."

Days passed, weeks, months. The nymphs ate and grew. They swam here, they swam there, they swam everywhere, to every corner of their pond, saw every inch, every twig, cave and pebble.

Then one morning, a year since hatching, Silver felt the urge to climb a reed. So Silver climbed and climbed, determined to break through the shimmering sky.

'What are you doing?' asked Gold.

'If I am to see,' Silver replied, "then I must fly."

'But you'll die.'

'I don't believe the fish.'

'I do. I'm going to stay here and live forever.'

'As you will,' said Silver.

'You'll come back and tell me what it's like?' Gold hoped.

'I'll try."

Silver broke through the sky and disappeared, whilst Gold returned to the bottom to nibble a leaf.

The next day, Silver called to Gold from the edge of the pond. Gold knew Silver's voice, but the bug looked so different, with great iridescent wings and a beautiful three-pronged tail.

'Silver, is that you?' Gold asked.

'It is,' Silver replied weakly.

'What did you see?'

'Everything... yet nothing,' said Silver, 'I have rode the wind, seen forests far below, met great beasts and small. I have kissed the sun, felt its warmth on my wings. I have known love with my mate and shared joy at their smile. And yet there is so much more beyond the horizon, so much yet to see and do! This pond is but a puddle in a great ocean of green. Alas, I cannot go on. My time is done.'

'You're dying?'

'Yes.'

'I knew it!' Gold scoffed. 'The fish was right.'

'No, everything dies,' Silver replied, as the last breath left that weary body, 'but I at least have lived.'

✧

Tristan was distracted from his comforting cup of hot chocolate by a motorcade of cars and monobikes thrumming into the university courtyard. He was not expecting another Den Father to visit.

"ALPHA?" he said, recognising the black livery and white A motif.

Not just any ALPHA, but a big shot, one of the four that sat either side of the Alpha himself, surely.

Passing his hot chocolate back to his subordinates and slamming his helmet back over his brow, Tristan stood firm at the top of the stairs. His mind raced, his heart thumped, his skin iced. What are they here for? The dissidents who were giving out leaflets?

Me?

The motorcade crackled to a halt on the gravel and the doors immediately opened, spitting out black-cloaked Prefects. With their helmets disguising them Tristan didn't recognise anyone in particular straight away, it was only as the Prefects speedily climbed the steps that the leaders became apparent.

The wolf at the front was none other than Nikita himself, with mottled brown and white arms and a white-imperium 'A' gracing his helmet and brooch. At his back was Janoah, ruddy-furred and slender, green eyes lurking under that black helm.

"Grand Prefect Nikita," Tristan said, barely containing his shock.

Nikita calmly raised a paw, ALPHA-style. "Captain Donskoy," he replied, in his thick, warm, Steppes accent. "I'm sorry to intrude on your Den Father's, how you say... 'symposium'?"

"Not at all, sir. You're most welcome."

Cupping his paws before him, Nikita glanced at the inviting windows of the Great Hall, "It is cold night to be left out on porch when others enjoy themselves."

"It is my duty, sir, and I am glad to do it."

"Yes. I know you have great respect for old Thorvald."

"He's my Den Father, sir," Tristan maintained, adding, "He's always been good to my family."

A nod.

"What brings you here, sir?" Tristan asked afresh, glancing at Janoah, but talking to Nikita.

"Grand Howler Rufus," he replied.

"Rufus?" Tristan quizzed, glancing at Janoah again. Her demeanour gave nothing away.

Nikita nodded but once, "He's charged with inciting unrest and misappropriating imperium."

"That's ridiculous!"

"Ridiculous?" Nikita growled. "Misappropriating imperium is ridiculous to you, Donskoy?"

"The charges against Rufus, sir," Tristan explained. "The world knows I'm no admirer," the Eisbrand maintained, "but Valerio's no black-market peddler."

"Then he will be released when found innocent, I assure you," sniffed Nikita. "Please, let us pass. Let us not make scene in front of your Den Father Thorvald."

"He's not here," Tristan said.

"Thorvald?"

"No, Rufus. He... never turned up, sir."

Janoah stepped up and scrutinised Tristan for a few seconds. "He's lying!" she spat, glancing at Nikita. "I don't know why, but he's lying."

"You're arresting your own husband?" Tristan growled under his breath,"

"It is *my* duty," she replied, "and *I* am glad to do it."

She made to pass, but Tristan grabbed her arm, "Wait, there must be some-"

Immediately, Janoah twisted free and thumped Tristan's shoulder with a palm. There was a burst of light, a loud crack and Tristan was ejected from the stairs, landing in a bush.

"Prefect!" barked Nikita.

The two other Eisbrands standing at the doors instinctively reached for their pistols.

"No!" Tristan yelped, as he rolled out of the foliage and staggered forth. "Let her pass," he said, nursing his armoured shoulder with a paw. "We… cannot obstruct ALPHA."

Janoah glared at the Eisbrands. Reluctantly, they put their pistols away.

"Wise move," she told them, brushing by. She lingered in the grand entrance long enough to tell Tristan without deigning to look at him, "If you ever touch me again, I'll see to it you go to the mines. Ivan will not stop me."

On she walked, shaking the paw she had dealt Tristan an imperious blow with – no doubt it hurt her too.

"Careful, Howler Tristan," Nikita advised in his sultry tone, giving the youth a narrow-eyed glare, "I warn you, as friend, you're on the thin ice already."

Tristan dipped his chin, "I was merely objecting to your timing, Nikita. To arrest Rufus in front of our Den Father at such a time-"

"Unfortunate, but necessary," Nikita dismissed. "Justice cannot wait. Den Father Thorvald would not want to stand in the way of the law, would he?"

"Of course not, sir."

"Rufus is here, yes?"

Tristan, eventually, nodded, "Yes."

Nikita huffed, "I pretend it slip your mind." Gesturing to his Prefects with the merest flick of the paw, Nikita climbed the marbled stairs. "Put some ointment on that shoulder, Donskoy," he advised.

✤

"Me dirigibles are held together by a durametal skeleton, which is light but jolly strong!" Montague said to all, pumping a ginger fist. "We wrap the frame in polygreen, which is waterproof, but not gas proof, and then inside that there's the gas bags, usually about twelve, which are also polygreen, but they're lined with beeswax to keep the imperium gas in you see. Hah hah!"

"Isn't imperium gas explosive?" asked the well-dressed hog with a monocle sitting beside Penny. "Isn't that why your dirigible blew up over Felicia, Mr. Buttle?"

"Ah, yes, well, we uh…."

"We use a new compound now, sir," Penny assured him, standing up beside her floundering husband. "It is a mix of certain imperium gases and other additives that are completely inert, but lighter than air. Not as light as standard imperium gas, perhaps, but it provides nine tenths of the lift without the danger of a fire."

"Yes, that's right!" Monty seconded.

"New compound you say?" the hog snorted. "What's it called?"

"Uhm," Monty said, whispering, "Sweetpea?"

"It's called felitium," Penny declared, chin high, "in honour of my home city."

"Is it? Oh, yes, it is!"

The hog squinted at the Buttles, "Invented by a cat was it?"

"Yes, sir, by myself," Penny asserted.

"You, madam?"

The elegant catess bowed slightly, "I'm a imperiologist, sir."

"Imperiologist!"

"Yes, sir. Self-taught."

"Hah! I've never heard such nonsense! New compound indeed, where's the proof? Where is your paper? Frauds, I say. Frauds."

"I say, sir, steady on now!" Monty mewed. "Say what you like about me, but leave Penny out of it. Me wife's a imperiologist, and a very fine one too! I may slap 'em together, but if it weren't for Penny here, me dirigibles would be as flaccid as… as your waistline sir!"

"Monty!" Penny hissed, as the hog's monocle fell out and plopped into his glass.

"Hahahahahaaaa!"

All ears and eyes homed in on the smouldering red wolf across the table – Rufus – whose hysterics resembled those of a hyena.

"Is there something amusing, sir?" snorted the hog, fishing his eyepiece from his glass and shaking it off.

"Not at all, my good hog," the Howler excused, swirling his own drink. "Save that, we all know your own company is exploring dirigibles too, like many others, and would give anything to see such fine competition discredited."

A chorus of gasps and whispers rippled down the table, reaching even Den Father Thorvald.

"It's true!" Rufus said, baffled as to the overblown reaction. "My ancestor was Giacomo Valerio, whose fine monos still whiz around this city like ants, so I know something about pioneering inventors and the troubles they face." Rufus Bloodfang Valerio raised his glass to the Buttles, "Guard your intellectual property, Penny my dear, that's all I can say-"

"Howler Rufus, you are under arrest!" someone barked.

Ears pricked, Rufus slowly swivelled around in his chair, resting one elbow on the back. He was met with Janoah, standing in the midst of the double doors with several black-cloaked Prefects behind her.

Rufus stared for an age, then looked at Linus, Heath, Sara and the rest.

"Hahahahahaaa!" he laughed, raising his glass. "That's very funny, Jan."

It occurred many that Rufus was a little drunk.

"No joke, Howler," Janoah assured coldly, as if she had never met the wolf in her life.

Before Linus or Heath could protest, Den Father Thorvald stood, thank goodness, and did so. "What is this, Prefect?" he bellowed. "Explain yourself, before I have you thrown out of this hall in disgrace and lodge a complaint to your so-called Alpha!"

Janoah calmly bowed to the Den Father, "Apologies, Den Father, but I am merely carrying out my orders."

"Orders?" Thorvald blustered, slapping the tabletop. "Who gave such orders?"

Nikita strode into the hall, "I did, Den Father," he said, adding, "The Alpha himself sends apologies for intrusion, but we were afraid Howler Rufus might… slip away."

Now, without a thought entering his head, Linus stood up. "Slip away?" he woofed, incredulous at best. "What are the charges?"

"And who're you, little wolf?" Nikita hummed.

"I'm-"

"Stay out of this, boy!" Rufus barked. "This is no concern of yours."

Thorvald himself looked momentarily unnerved by Nikita's appearance, but demanded, "The boy is right. What are the charges, Grand Prefect? I will be satisfied before you act. This is Eisbrand territory; I will not have you traipse over it arresting wolves without just cause!"

Nikita looked to Janoah.

"Misappropriation of white-imperium, Den Father," she said flatly, looking down on her mate. "Howler Rufus has not only been taking more than his fair share, but selling excess on the black market."

"Have I, by Ulf?" Rufus laughed. "And what of your enormous 'misappropriation', wife?"

"You will accompany us to ALPHA HQ," Janoah said, hissing quietly, "Get your things husband. Let's not make a scene."

"Ulf forbid."

Rufus stood up and assertively tugged at the shoulders of his cloak. He donned his helmet, the cheeks glowed.

"Linus," he said loudly.

"Sir?"

"Tell Elder Amael I'll be detained for the night."
"Uh… yes sir."
With that, Rufus walked in amongst the Prefects, who led him away.

~Blick II~

"Uff, uff, unff!"

The hefty punch bag swung and spun wildly on its creaking tether. Upon its return journey it met again with the mighty fists that had first set it upon its pendulous trajectory.

"Uff, uff, unff!"

This time arcs of plasma played over the blackened, smouldering bag as its imperium-weave sacking absorbed the boxer's incredible blows; blows that would surely break the body of any mere wolf and send them tumbling across the floor.

Prefects looked on in awe from the corners of the ALPHA gymnasium, some in admiration of that matchless strength, others aghast it was even possible in a wolf. Rumour held the newcomer had been specially brought in by Silvermane and that new wolfess, Janoah, to be an Eisenwolf. Some said he had already been suited up a few times and training was underway, albeit in secret. Certainly his tail had already been cut off, replaced with a black ribbon tucked in his breeches, as if in mourning for it.

Whatever they thought, whatever the facts, none dared approach the intimidating wolf.

Well, save one.

"Ungh, ungh, unfghff!"

As the bag swung away, a grey wolfess in a prim black nurse's uniform appeared out of left field. "Hello!" she piped quickly.

The boxer's gaze settled on her, "Oi... I know you-oof!"

The punch bag slammed into him, sweeping him off his feet and flat on his back, ribbon trailing.

"Oh!" the nurse chirped. "Are you all right?"

The gymnasium broke into raucous laughter at the clumsy boxer's expense. The little nurse shot eye-daggers at the lot of them, but, shaking his head, the boxer got up and dusted down his breeches. He turned to the mocking Prefects roundabout and beamed amiably, shrugging his massive shoulders and spreading his bandaged paws, dispelling at a stroke any air of spite they had projected against him. He had been a fool and knew it.

The laughter faded.

"You're Meryl Stroud, yeah?" the boxer said to the nurse, steadying the still-swinging bag. "I'm Rafe," he added, with a roguish smile. "Rafe Stenton."

"Yes, I know," she replied, surprised. "You... you do remember me, then?"

"Yeah. You looked after me when I was ill."

Meryl dipped her tiny chin over that well-starched high collar of hers, almost touching the white cravat. "I suppose you could say that," she said guardedly. "How are you today?"

A shrug, a sniff, "Fine, fine. You?"

"Me?"

"Yeah. You all right?"

"I'm very well, thank you," Meryl replied at length, as if shocked to be asked.

Rafe nodded, smiled, and hung on the punch bag a moment before giving it a light jab – it still swung appreciably.

Meryl asked, "Did your father teach you to box?"

"Father?"

"He was a rabbit, wasn't he? They're often fond of boxing."

Rafe's brow twisted this way and that. He steadied the bag again and stared down at his feet for the longest time. He clapped a paw to his aching head, "Uhm."

"Never mind," Meryl said quickly. "Rafe, I need you to come along to the infirmary."

Those big brown ears pricked, "What for? I feel fine."

"For a blood test. Quite routine I assure you. Josef says we need to keep an eye on your ash levels."

"Oh. Sure. One second, I'd better unwrap."

"All right."

Rafe hurried over to a bench, silk ribbon flapping in his wake, where he unbound his paws. Spying blood on the discarded bandages, Meryl clomped over in her practical, hard-wearing boots.

"Your paws are red-raw!" she tutted, grasping them and checking the blistered pads.

Rafe shrugged his mighty frame, his enormous muscles rippling beneath his rich brown fur. "That's what happens, 'en it?"

"Happens?"

"To Howlers. I-I mean Prefects. When we use our corona. It burns, dun it?"

"No, not whilst training it shouldn't!" Meryl scolded, amazed Rafe appeared to feel nothing.

"Oh."

"Didn't Silvermane and Jano..." Meryl cut off, looked around, and continued quieter, "Prefect Janoah should have told you that you only use imperium when you absolutely must. If you go on damaging your body like this you won't last five minutes, even if you are an..." Meryl finished in a hushed voice, "an Eisenwolf."

Rafe mischievously leant down and whispered in kind, "I didn't know. Sorry."

Meryl shook her head. Leading Rafe from the gymnasium, she said, "You must learn to control your corona properly. No more training for you, not until someone's taught you a thing or two about self-restraint, young wolf. I'm going to have a word with Janoah and Silvermane at once-"

"Can't you teach me?" Rafe interjected.

"Me?" Meryl said with surprise, stopping in the gym's adjoining hall. "Not really. I'm not even afflicted."

"Aren't you?"

"No. Why, do I look ill?" Meryl rubbed a grey cheek, worried at Rafe's baffled expression. "I know I'm gaunt sometimes. Lack of sleep-"

"No no, I just wondered," Rafe professed, adding, "And no, actually, you ain't 'gaunt'."

Meryl glanced up at the wolfen giant, surprised at his somehow frank, naive gentleness, like that of a cub who meant well but had not the life experience to put his thoughts across. Of course he was no older than sixteen or so; nobody knew for sure, least of all Rafe himself after his frightful induction.

"Come along," Meryl said, clearing her throat, "let's set you right, Rafe."

"Oi, Meryl," he said.

"Yes?"

"You owe me a penny."

Chapter 22

Elder Amael Bloodfang Balbus stood out front Riddle Den's inspiring facade, the huge crest depicting the pack's emblem illuminated from below, the accompanying red banners lit from above. Grand Howler Vladimir stood loftily at Amael's left, his stocky adjutant Captain Boris at his right, whilst the elegant Captain Ivan lingered behind with some more Redcloaks. Everyone was dressed in their best, helmets and all.

It was midnight, and as agreed via a week of ludicrous negotiations – Ivan thought them ludicrous at any rate – the gates opened and several Howlers on industrial-looking monobikes were allowed to chug onto Riddle Den's grounds. Stopping a respectable distance away the Howlers dismounted. Despite the relative gloom one could tell their mantles were a dark yellow, except for the leader, whose cloak was ashen grey. The symbol of a gear was apparent on their brooches from several yards distant, centred as it was with a fluorescent crystal of yellow-imperium. If that didn't give their identity away, their ugly monos did. Not for these wolves the beautiful Giacomo Valerio bikes, but hefty, own-brand models replete with twisting, exposed pipes and valves.

The proud and arrogant Greystones and no mistake, Ivan sighed inwardly.

Their leader, a very tall and powerfully built brown wolf, separated from his followers and strode towards the shorter, pure grey Amael, who did the same. They met halfway and embraced.

"Amael," said the guest.

"Flaid," said the host.

After much arm-patting and pleasantries they separated and got down to business.

Flaid raised a paw. One of his yellow cloaks came forward and placed a metal trunk on the ground.

Amael raised his paw. One of his Redcloaks came forth and took it, checked its weight with his paw. The Howler put it down again and opened the case, revealing shining, translucent ingots of stabilised yellow-imperium crystal.

"What're you doing?" Amael barked at his subordinate.

"Checking it, sir," replied the baffled youth.

"You insult our honoured guest. I would trust Elder Flaid with my life. Shut it immediately!"

"Yes, Elder."

The Bloodfang closed the case and backed off.

At the rear of proceedings, Ivan rolled his eyes at Amael's painfully transparent acting. He had doubtless specifically instructed that Howler to check the case, which is why the poor chap was confused at being pulled up on it.

One of the Greystones, a short burly fellow, stepped forward and snarled, "All right, now where's me brother?"

"Bodvar!" Flaid snapped.

"If you've hurt a hair on his head-"

"Bodvar, enough!" Flaid bellowed. "Do not disgrace us further, or I will disgrace you!"

The wolf called Bodvar backed off, chin dipped.

Despite the insult to his honour, Amael remained outwardly unmoved. "Boris," he instructed simply.

"Sir."

Boris turned and gestured at the Den's grand entrance. The doors opened and two Bloodfang Howlers escorted a young brown wolf on crutches down the stairs, his tattered yellow cloak hanging limply around his shoulders and bandaged midriff showing. It was the border guard who had valiantly fought the giant centipede in the tunnel.

"Gunnar!" Howler Bodvar yelped, waving.

"Bodvar!" Howler Gunnar replied, hurrying along as best a broken leg allowed.

As he passed Vladimir, the bruised Gunnar stopped and nodded, "Thanks for being so kind to me, Grand Howler, you n' Rufus both."

Vladimir nodded graciously back, "Take care of yourself, Howler. Mind those sewer centipedes in future."

Smiling, Gunnar limped on, rejoining his pack whereupon Howler Bodvar hugged his brother close.

"Stupid idiot," he growled, "I thought we'd lost yer."

"Don't fuss!" Gunnar whined.

"Did they hurt yer?" his brother growled.

"No. They were really good to me. Saved me life. It was that Rufus, he's a right good 'un."

Whilst his lesser Howlers let the mask of dignity slip, the mighty Flaid remained utterly composed. "I apologise that you had to squander precious venom on one of ours, Amael," he sniffed. "I hope this meagre offering of yellow-imperium will cover the cost."

Amael cocked his head to one side, "Admirably, Flaid. If any of mine are ever wounded in your district, you'll pay them the same courtesy, I'm sure."

Flaid nodded, "Of course."

"I think we're done here, agreed?"

"Agreed."

They shook paws and patted each other's backs as if they were the best of friends. They were not enemies, it was true, but the Greystones and Bloodfangs had fought before and would fight again if this shortage continued, of that Ivan was sure, as he watched in silence.

"Give my regards to Grand Howler Rufus," Flaid said, not seeing him amongst the gathering. "Wherever he is."

Amael managed a strained chuckle only.

With that, Flaid and the Greystones parted company with their Bloodfang rivals and mounted their still-churning monobikes. No sooner had Gunnar sat on the back of his brother's chunky mono than he was whisked away, out the gates and into the night, destined for the safety of Greystone territory.

"That worthless Rufus," Amael complained, turning and passing through his Howlers, heading up the stairs, "He's embarrassed us yet again. He should've been back from wherever in Ulf's name he is."

"The Arkady Symposium, sir?" Boris reminded his leader, following him.

"Whatever! He said he would be here in time for this exchange, but as usual I am made to look a fool. He's probably lying drunk in a ditch somewhere, the disrespectful dog. I'll have him flogged this time, I swear it."

"Shall I send someone to find him, sir?"

"What's the point?"

As the group entered the Den's reception, with its Bloodfang emblem and polished marbled foyer, Vladimir came up on Elder Amael's left. "One does not excuse oneself from the presence of a Den Father lightly, sir," he said. "Perhaps Thorvald has kept Rufus longer than expected?"

Amael gave Vladimir a questioning sideways look, but in the end just grunted noncommittally at him. Perhaps he thought it odd that Vladimir should stick up for Rufus, Ivan certainly did, as he lingered at the back. Twice in as many weeks now Vladimir had been Rufus's pal. Perhaps he was just repaying a favour, or perhaps he was accruing credit with Rufus to ask a favour later?

"Vladimir, that hyena you have in custody," Amael growled, taking Vladimir to one side, though Ivan listened in.

"Madou, sir?"

"Whatever he's called."

"He's proving most stubborn on the rack, but-"

"Get rid of him," Amael interrupted.

Vladimir was baffled, "Elder?"

"You heard," Amael snorted impatiently, "I want him tried and out of my fur."

"But he may yet reveal THORN's plans-"

"He knows nothing! Just like Noss before him, he's a pathetic pawn. Stop driving up our gas bill frying him on the rack and have him sent down. Is that clear?"

At length, said, "Yes, sir."

Though his interest was piqued by the exchange, Ivan quickly forgot it when a Howler hurried across the foyer and intercepted him.

"Cap'n!" the youngster panted, saluting.

"Yes, Howler?" Ivan acknowledged.

"It's Grand Howler Rufus, sir."

Visions of bombings and lupicide flashed through Ivan's mind as he imagined Rufus had been assassinated. "What's happened?" he said, dreading the answer.

"He's been… been arrested by ALPHA, sir," the Howler said, betwixt a gulp.

Vladimir overheard and approached, "Arrested?"

The Howler saluted him, "Yes Grand Howler. Trooper Linus just got off the phone to us sir. He says they came storming in and arrested Rufus in the middle of a… a party, or something."

"Symposium?" Vladimir suggested.

"That's it, sir. Line was pretty bad."

Vladimir nodded and turned away, "I see. Very good, Howler, carry on."

Ivan also went about his business, apparently relieved.

The puzzled young Howler followed them, "But… but what about Rufus, sir?"

"He'll be back by morning," Ivan assured the youth.

Vladimir explained, "Not a year goes by without Rufus being arrested for something; probably got denounced to ALPHA by a jilted beta. At least this gets him off the hook with Amael."

✦

Rufus sat in the stark, off-white interrogation room, ember smouldering betwixt his lips, ash tumbling onto the table he was leaning on. He reached inside his cloak – as he did so one of the two ALPHA Prefects standing in the corners of the room went for their sword.

"Checking the time, dear boy," Rufus explained, tentatively producing his pocket watch.

The Prefect gulped and cleared his throat, before standing normally again. He glanced nervously at his compatriot across the room, but said nothing to him.

"It's nearly one," Rufus snorted, stowing it away. "Are you chaps planning on keeping me here all night?"

No reply.

"Any chance of a cup of tea? Maybe a biscuit, if it's not too much trouble?"

Nothing, not a peep.

"You know you're very rude," Rufus tutted, blowing a cloud of strawberry ember vapours.

Some minutes passed. Rufus was just wondering how Linus was faring getting home without a ride, what with the last trains long since gone, when the door opened. The Prefects stood to attention and waved the quick ALPHA salute as two more entered the room, one tall, silvery grey and in all-black gear, the other… well….

"Ah, the wife!" Rufus greeted, Janoah's obscuring Howler helmet proving no impediment to recognition. He looked to the wolf accompanying her and had no trouble there either. "And you've brought 'Silvermange' to see me. How lovely. Do have a seat, you two. Kettle's on."

Grand Prefect Silvermane looked to Janoah and growled under his breath, "You said he was sober."

She just shrugged.

Silvermane cleared his throat and approached the table with a file in his paws.

"Grand Howler Rufus," he said, pleasantly enough.

Barely had he than Rufus asked, "Whatcha got there?" in a patronising tone, like a father to a cub, raising his chin at the file nestled in the Grand Prefect's silver paws. "Evidence?"

Silvermane nodded at the two Prefects, "Leave us."

"So soon?" Rufus whined. "I was just getting to know the charming fellows."

The Prefects waved again and shuffled hastily out the room, eager to be relieved, either because Rufus frightened them, or because he annoyed them. Either way, Janoah closed the door in their wake and stood aloof.

Satisfied, Silvermane tossed the file in his paws onto the desk. Rufus looked at it, then at him.

"Go ahead," Silvermane urged, paws cupped before him.

Rufus opened the file. He hadn't read two sentences when he stopped and looked up at his captor, "This is my proposal to go to the Dead Cities."

"Your annually rejected proposal," Silvermane corrected gently, albeit dripping with intent.

Rufus closed the file. "Try, try again," he said, dipping his chin and pushing the offending file away.

Janoah watched in silence. Silvermane glanced at her, then said to Rufus, "You want it to happen?"

"Pardon me?"

"You heard," the Silver sniffed, spreading a paw. "I can make it happen. ALPHA will fund it, give you wolves and supplies, no cabal of ignorant, indolent Elders will stop you."

Rufus looked up at him, "I don't understand."

"Your arrest was just a ruse," Silvermane admitted.

"Ruse?"

"Yes. To make THORN believe you when you say you've defected and wish to help bring down the Republic. We have to make this convincing if we're to succeed."

Rufus's green eyes darted to and fro. "Sorry, but… did I miss a page or something?"

Maintaining outward calm, Silvermane pulled up a chair and sat opposite the cheeky red wolf, "Grand Howler, there is a plot afoot to destroy the Republic-"

"I'm not surprised!" Rufus woofed.

"You condone it?" Silvermane said at once.

"Don't put words in my mouth, Silver, you're not nearly clever enough."

"That's Grand Prefect Silvermane, if you please."

"I don't. So, how's your glorious leader? Does he let you boys smoulder, or is he still an utter bore?"

Silvermane snorted and looked to Janoah, "Am I wasting my time here, Prefect?"

Thus invited, Janoah entered the conversation, "Rufus, THORN are going to murder hundreds, possibly thousands-"

"As we do them?" Rufus replied instantly.

"What?"

Reaching into his cloak, Rufus slammed a dishevelled piece of paper on the desk. It was Sara's leaflet; the one Tristan had given her, with all its horrific imagery.

The Prefects exchanged looks.

"Where did you get this?" Silvermane demanded, taking the leaflet.

"That's hardly the issue."

"Is this what passes for intellectual discussion at the Wintertide Symposium?" Silvermane scoffed, flicking the paper with his fingers. "Are the great thinkers of Lupa stupid enough to fall for such blatant propaganda?"

"Hyenas do not make propaganda, sir!" Rufus countered sternly. "When was the last time you saw a hyena photographing or printing anything? How can they when they are denied basic amenities!"

"Naive do-gooders help spread THORN's rot, do-gooders like you."

"Is it 'do-gooding' to sympathise with starving cubs?"

"Starving? Ridiculous."

Janoah leant in, "Rufus, this isn't even about the hyena tribes, or THORN, not really."

"But you just said-"

"They are being used!" Janoah cut in, before Rufus could go off on one. "They are fools, these… cubs, this Themba and Nurka, and all their followers too! Brainwashed fanatics who are dooming their own people." She grabbed the leaflet and waved it in Rufus's blinking face, "I've no doubt this nightmare *will* come true for them if Lupa falls into civil war because of THORN. The Howlers will have no choice but to wipe the hyenas out to quell the outrage of the citizens, little and noble alike!"

Rufus gulped, "Go on."

Janoah threw the leaflet away and stood up straight, arms folded. "That's the plan, you see. The hyenas will be blamed for causing the next Howler War, whilst their treacherous wolfen puppeteers will reap the reward and rule Lupa as kings, professing to be our saviour in Lupa's time of need... or something equally tacky."

Janoah could see her husband's astute brain working behind his eyes, piecing things together. It was fun watching him struggle on so little information.

"Puppeteers, Jan?" he said, fishing for clues.

"Ah! Now he's intrigued," his wife cackled at Silvermane.

Silvermane reasoned. "Rufus, I know the Republic isn't perfect," he said, in his soothing tone, "but it's all we've got, and it's preferable to a dictatorship which is what we will get if we do not smash this plot before it breaks around our ears."

"All right, all right," Rufus sighed, "I get it." He shrugged his ruddy shoulders, "Look, I love Lupa, for all its ills and injustices, and all our... mistakes. Change will come to our fair city, I've no doubt; but not by dictatorship. That way madness lies."

Silvermane sat back and exhaled a little, perhaps relieved to hear such words.

"Who is it?" Rufus asked in general. "Hit me."

Janoah snorted simply, "Amael Balbus."

"Balbus!"

"Amongst others," Silvermane added quickly.

"I don't believe it!" Rufus blustered.

"Believe it!" Janoah chirped airily. "He does nothing but talk about how he's going to rule Lupa... with me."

Silence.

"With *you*, Jan?"

"Yes, dear. I lay with him."

Rufus nearly went cross-eyed, "What do you mean, you-"

"It's strictly for the sake of the Republic!" Janoah interceded, raising a paw. "I did it for you, once, now I do it for Lupa – a worthier cause, I'm sure you'll agree."

Rufus took a sharp puff on his ember as he digested the news. "I do," he said.

"He loves me, or so he professes," Janoah huffed.

To which Silvermane added, "Not enough to reveal who he's conspiring with, or exactly how it's going to come about, despite your best efforts, Janoah."

"He says he's keeping me at arm's length to protect me, in case he falls," Janoah excused, with a tiny shrug. "I appreciate his concern, but hopefully as the time draws nearer he'll confide in me. Until then I must continue to help him and not push too hard or he may suspect me."

Rufus had to ask, "How're you helping him, Jan?"

"I feed him snippets of ALPHA files, give him dirt on his fellow Bloodfang Elders. Illegal dealings, imperium embezzlement, embarrassing liaisons and so forth – you know the kind of thing you're always brought in for."

"How charming. Why?"

Janoah explained, "So he can blackmail them into voting him Den Father. Amael believes he must be at least that high to strike. Nobody is going to follow a mere nobody Elder, but Den Father of the illustrious Bloodfangs... well maybe."

Rufus pointed out, "Perhaps you should remind Amael that we 'illustrious Bloodfangs' already have a Den Father."

"For now," Janoah said, "but he might fall down the stairs tomorrow. He's very old and doddery, isn't he?"

"Are you saying Amael's going to do him in?"

"It's the logical step."

"Then Vito must be told."

"No."

"No?" Rufus woofed. "What do you mean no? Are you just going to let it happen?"

Silvermane interjected, "If we tell the Den Fathers what's afoot they will initiate their own clumsy investigations all over the shop and Amael's fellow conspirators will go to ground and destroy all evidence. Even racking Amael for their names will not be enough to incriminate conspiring Elders from other packs; no Den Father would stand for it. They mistrust ALPHA as it is and will defend their own from feeble prosecutions. You Howlers seem to think we're all-powerful and can bring anyone down on a whim; the truth is very different. We must have evidence."

"Clearly," Rufus huffed, looking at his dwindling ember. "That's why I'm not down the mines already."

Silvermane grunted, "You must admit, Rufus, that you invite scrutiny at every turn. Your actions have not been above reproach."

"I have never committed a crime against the Republic, unless voicing my concerns is a crime?"

"Concerns?" Silvermane woofed. "You have incited unrest on multiple occasions. You incite it now by even entertaining that vile propaganda leaflet!"

"Can you prove it untrue? Have you ever been to the Reservations and checked what goes on there?"

"Wolves do not do such things! We are not barbarians!"

Rufus burst out laughing, head tipped back.

Silvermane saw red. "Do you mock me, sir?" he bellowed.

"I envy you, young Silvermane," the Howler replied. "I wish I was still so… cute."

Silence, pricklier than a cactus.

"So, other wolves are involved?" Rufus sniffed, as if nothing had transpired.

Flustered by comparison, the 'cute' Silvermane took a moment to compose himself, to clear his throat and adjust his cloak. "The rot runs deep," he said gravely. "We suspect there are dozens of traitors in every pack. One or two in ALPHA itself, we think."

Rufus tutted like a disapproving matron.

"Nobody is more disappointed than me," Silvermane assured him. "Even the pure intentions of ALPHA have been sullied by this… festering decay!" the Prefect snarled, before measuring his tone. "However, fester it must, for now. The game must be allowed to run until Amael plays his cards and reveals his allies, only then can we round them up."

Nodding, Rufus sucked his cheek, then said, "Where do I fit into your scheme?"

"You'll help us?" Silvermane asked expectantly.

"I haven't decided yet. Besides, my price might be too high for you impoverished ALPHA lot."

"Your expedition will be funded and-"

"I'll set my provisos, not you!" Rufus interrupted, looking between the Prefects. "Just tell me what you want me to do and I'll let you know if I can even do it." Stubbing out his ember and breaking open another he said, "And for Ulf's sake, someone make me a cup of tea."

✧

"I shouldn't worry," Heath said, anxiously puffing on his pipe in the deserted university hall. "Someone's denounced him because they don't like what he says. It's intimidation that's all. ALPHA needs hard evidence not hearsay and Rufus is no imperium peddler."

"Aye," Sara agreed, casting her eyes over the sad remnants of the symposium; the dripping ice-sculptures and discarded napkins.

Rufus's arrest had spoilt the evening. Den Father Thorvald had excused himself, professing he was going to make a complaint on Rufus's behalf and taking his Howlers with him, and once they had gone the great and good of Lupa had dispersed also, perhaps afraid they too might be whisked away by ALPHA. One or two stoic individuals had stayed behind awhile, like Penny and Monty, but now only the university faculty remained.

"We should put this outside, Professor," Sara suggested, reaching for the ice relief-sculpture of a butterfly resting on a flower. "It's so beautiful; it'd be a shame tae let it melt straight away. It could last all winter in the grounds."

"What? Oh, yes yes! Quite."

Sara began sliding the sculpture across the tabletop on its decorative tray. "Och!" she puffed,

"It weighs a ton!"

"I'm not surprised!" Heath laughed. "Here, I'll take this end, you take that end."

Together, the bear and wolf eased the butterfly sculpture off the table. It was a struggle for both parties, since Heath was too tall and Sara too short to comfortably hold the beautified block of ice level between them. Nonetheless they made it out the door and down the empty entrance hall, Heath shuffling backwards all the way.

"Professor, Ah can't hold it much longer," Sara complained, as icy water slopped over the tray and sapped her paws of strength. "Mah fingers are going numb!"

"Nearly there," Heath replied, bumping the door open with his behind and letting in some falling snow.

They started down the stairs.

"Ah'm gonna drop it!" Sara cried.

The warning had no sooner left her lips than some blonde wolf in a red cloak swept in out of left field and grabbed Sara's end of the sculpture from her.

"I've got it," Howler Linus assured.

Surprised, but grateful, Sara removed her painfully frozen paws and dried her fingers on her breeches.

"Thanks," she said, breathing life back into her paws.

Linus nodded – his helmet disguised any smile.

Apparently without effort, the powerfully-built Howler helped Heath guide the sculpture down the marbled stairs and set it in the fresh snow by the bushes.

"There we are," Heath said, flicking his paws. "I thought you'd gone home, Howler Mills."

"Yes," he replied, "I started to walk, but… well…."

"Walk back to Riddle HQ? In this weather? Hah!"

"Precisely."

"What about the mono?" Heath said, flapping a paw at Rufus's lonely monobike, the last vehicle remaining on the campus, which now sported a hefty white mantle of freshly fallen snow. "Don't you have the key?"

"I do, sir, I got it off the valet."

"Well then, Rufus won't mind you borrowing it to get home. It's just a pack-owned *Springtail*, isn't it?"

"I… can't ride," Linus admitted awkwardly.

"Oh, I see."

Linus moved on, "Might I use your phone again to call a friend to come pick me up? I'd stay at a hotel, naturally, anywhere really, but I don't have any money on me."

Listening in, Sara snorted in a confused tone, "But you're a Howler, you don't have tae pay."

The Howler explained patiently, "This is Eisbrand territory, Miss, not Bloodfang. I can't abuse my rights."

"Some would."

"Maybe."

There was a brief silence.

Linus looked to Heath, "May I use your phone, sir?"

"Uhm… well, yes yes, of course," the bear replied, momentarily bowled over by this Howler's reserve. "Come in and warm yourself up while you wait, uh… Linus."

"Thank you, sir."

"Been a funny old night, hasn't it?"

"Yes."

Smelling the youth's anxiety a mile away, Heath tried to set him at ease. "Rufus will be all right, you know. He's used to being mucked about by ALPHA, even if we're not. Not a year passes without them breathing down his neck over something he's said or done. It's all nonsense; a mere game."

Linus nodded, but said nothing.

As the trio walked up the snow-bound stairs, Sara cupped her paws behind her back and asked knowingly, "What happened tae all your money, Howler?"

"I blew it all on a *Buttle Skyways* ticket."

✦

In the vaporous atmosphere of the ALPHA interrogation room, Rufus sipped his Hummel tea and puffed on his third ember, blueberry this time, not his favourite, but he hardly noticed for the thoughts jostling for position in his head.

"Who else knows?" he asked, clearing his throat.

Silvermane took a sharp breath and shuffled on his parsimonious new-materials seat, "Just us three, and the Alpha, of course."

"Not Nikita and Horst then?"

"Nor Duncan; any one of them may be a traitor. I doubt it's Horst, though he could be hiding his ambitions behind conservatism. But Duncan is a little-beast-loving ex-Hummel and Nikita is a rabidly impartialist ex-Eisbrand; it could be change is not happening fast enough for them."

Rufus tutted, "I like them already. Perhaps it's you who's the traitor, Silver? Have you checked your own file?"

Silvermane huffed, "If it were me, Janoah wouldn't be alive. Amael would've taken care of her by now, because I would have told him about her double-crossing."

Rufus couldn't deny it.

In the silence, Janoah sighed, "Vladimir needs to know what we're going to do."

"Vladimir?" Rufus guffawed.

His wife grimaced, as if the truth pained her. "He's the one who sussed Amael out in the first place."

"The wily Oromov. How?"

"That doesn't matter, husband, what matters is that he's still my partner in Riddle." Janoah spread a ruddy paw. "How do you think I know half of what I know? Amael didn't tell me THORN's plans, it was Vladimir getting it out of Chakaa Madou. Horst complained earlier that I let the Bloodfangs get away with a key suspect, but I knew Vladimir would set to work and tell me anyway."

"Yes," Rufus gruffed, "Vlad's set to work all right, with rack and iron all week I dare say-"

"You haven't obstructed him have you?" Janoah hissed, leaning on the tabletop.

Rufus removed his blue ember. "Do calm down, Jan. Madou is Vladimir's catch; I've no right to interfere. Besides, hyenas are not covered by the Lupan Laws… are they?"

"That's the most sensible thing you've said all day," Janoah huffed. She stood up again, "Well, in any case, Vladimir needs to be brought aboard. If I betray his trust by holding back information he'll do the same to me and that could be dangerous."

"It could be dangerous if he's told too much," Silvermane observed. "How do you know he's truly on our side? He could be feeding you lies as Amael's double-agent for all you know."

"No, sir," Janoah dismissed. "I know Vladimir's secret, and Amael would kill him if I let it be known, as would I be if Vladimir told Amael about me. We have the goods on each other, Vlad and I."

Silvermane enquired, "And what is this 'secret'?"

"It's of no matter to ALPHA, sir."

"Nonetheless-"

"I *will not* betray Oromov, sir, not even to you," Janoah said firmly. "All will out in good time."

Rufus swirled his tea, watching the brown leafy liqueur spin, "Jan, you never cease to amaze me. I bet you're having fun giving Amael the old run-around, aren't you?"

Janoah chuckled, "Amael's quite the wolf; strong, handsome, ambitious."

"Mad?"

"Clever! It's a pity he's abusing his Ulf-given talents. Rather like someone else I know."

Silvermane watched the couple bounce off one another, apparently enjoying themselves, forgetting, perhaps, that they were in the presence of a Grand Prefect.

Silvermane glanced at Janoah, then asked the pertinent question, "Will you help us, Rufus?"

"Aren't you forgetting something?"

"What?"

"My price."

With an exasperated sigh, Silvermane said, "What more do you want?"

Leaning on the table Janoah hissed at Rufus, "Take the offer. An expedition is your life's ambition, for Ulf's sake! This is your big chance."

Rufus slowly turned to her. "By Ulf, Jan, do you honesty think I want ALPHA breathing down my neck whilst I am trying to catalogue the discoveries of a lifetime? Besides, you can't even stretch to decent chairs for you own Den, let alone the cash required for an expedition."

Silvermane insisted, "The Alpha will back you. He has given us his direct consent to make this deal."

"Hah!"

"You doubt the word of the Alpha?"

"He's your Alpha, not mine."

Janoah stood up straight, arms folded, "All right. What do you want?"

Rufus inhaled a huge draught from his ember and blew it overhead, "That which you took from me."

✦

After tapping the hook a few times, Linus put the phone down as quickly as he'd picked it up.

"Line's dead," he explained.

"It's the snow," Heath complained. "I've told the district council a hundred times they need to clean the ash off the lines more often come winter. The snow sticks to it something awful and the lines break under the weight! Same every year."

"What now?" Sara asked.

Linus looked around Heath's university office, with its many papers, trinkets and fascinating specimen jars with preserved bugs floating inside like pale embryos. "You two can go home," he said, adding, "Just leave me here."

"Leave you here?" Heath snorted, looking to Sara.

"Don't worry, I-I-I can sleep in the foyer," Linus explained, "I mean, if that's all right?"

"No! No it isn't!" the bear woofed. "No associate of my dear friend Rufus is sleeping rough, sir. The very idea! No, you shall come home with me."

"But-"

"I won't hear of it! Rufus would never forgive me. You can sleep on my sofa, how's that?"

Linus, eventually, nodded, "That's v-vvv-very kind of you, Professor Heath. I'm honoured."

"Honoured, he says," the bear chuckled. "It's the least I can do for someone who's read all my books! That's a harder labour than my writing them, I fear."

Linus laughed awkwardly and scratched his neck.

"We'd better lock up, Sara," Heath told his young associate, fishing some keys from his waistcoat. "I'll do the offices, you do the main hall."

"Aye."

Linus was surprised, "Don't you have caretakers here?"

"They've gone home to bed, Howler," was Heath's amused response. "Sara and I were only staying on in the hope ALPHA would bring Rufus back once Thorvald got onto them, but it seems he's been put away for the night."

"Awful bullies they are," Sara growled huffily, "They're worse than the Howlers."

Linus looked at her.

Glancing back at him, Sara wordlessly left the office with Heath's keys jangling in her little paws.

Once she had gone, Heath made excuses, "She's a spirited girl. She doesn't really mean anything by that."

"Forget it," Linus said.

Unbeknownst to them, Sara lingered long enough to hear what was said, before sneaking down the hallway to the main entrance, where the Great Hall was to be found. Checking inside one last time, lest a guest had somehow escaped all notice and was sleeping in a corner, Sara pulled the mighty doors to, so she could grab them both at the same time, and shut with all her might.

The sound of ancient wood and metal slamming together reverberated down the ornate foyer.

"Sara."

"Oh!"

Turning around with a paw to her chest, Sara was greeted by a tall knightly-looking Howler, his armoured shoulders flecked with half-melted snow.

"Tristan!" she barked, hitting him on the shoulder. "You scared me!"

"Sorry."

Composing herself, Sara locked the doors. "Any news?" she asked.

"No," Tristan replied, nursing his shoulder. "The phones are down all over the place. Thorvald will take it up in the morning."

"They'll let him go, right?"

"Grand Howler Rufus has powerful friends. It'll be fine."

"Aye."

Tristan looked around, "Do you still have that flyer?"

"What? Oh, no."

"You destroyed it? Good."

"No, Rufus took it," Sara said innocently.

Tristan snorted in alarm, "What?"

"Ah showed it tae him over dinner and he took it. He said Ah shouldn't be seen with such things."

"Sara!"

"What?"

"How's it going to look to ALPHA when they find that on him? By Ulf's fangs, wolfess, if they didn't have a reason to throw the book at him they do now!"

"But... he just took it off me! Ah didn't know he was going tae be arrested."

Tristan turned away and removed his helmet to run a paw over his aching head.

Deflecting her blunder, Sara snorted after him, "Ah dunno why ye pretend tae care, anyway; everyone knows ye don't even like him." Giving the doors a tug to check they were locked she mumbled, "Ah bet you'd love tae see him go down the mines and never come up again."

With a scoff of disgust, Tristan took his leave, storming down the hall.

Cursing her terse tongue, Sara called after him, "Tristan, come back! Tristan!"

Hurrying after the Howler, Sara grabbed his arm and tugged him to a stop.

"Gagh!"

Sara immediately let go as Tristan whirled round in apparent pain, dropping his helmet in favour of clapping a paw to his shoulder.

"What's wrong?" Sara gasped.

"Nothing, you just... pulled too hard," the Howler excused.

"Don't be daft."

Tristan suffered through obvious discomfort, before admitting begrudgingly, "It was that... that bitch Janoah."

Sara's eyes darted about, "Rufus's wife?"

The Howler nodded quickly, "I tried to stop her going in, or at least ask her why in Ulf's name she was arresting her own husband. She blew me off the stairs."

"Blew you off the stairs?"

"She packs quite the punch," Tristan seethed, with a false laugh. "You'd never believe it to look at her."

Digesting all that, Sara said, "Let me see."

"No-"

"Tristan."

"You can't do anything!"

"Of course I can!" Sara huffed, paws on hips. "Ah know how tae treat plasma burns."

Linus strode into the hall, or as much as such a short stocky wolf could stride. "Everything all right here?" he enquired, ears pricked from the sound of raised voices. "Miss Sara?"

Tristan protectively pushed his way in front of Sara and snorted, "What're you doing here at this time of night, Bloodfang?"

"I could ask you the same thing, Eisbrand."

"This is *my* territory!"

With a gulp, Linus quickly tagged on, "I meant last week, sir, when you were spying on us."

"Spying? Is that the thanks I get for saving your hide?"

"I had everything under control."

"Hah! Right."

In the same manner he had her, Sara pushed in front of Tristan, even if she was a dot by comparison. "Stop it!" she yelped, looking between the Howlers. "Grow up, the both of ye!" She eventually settled on Tristan, whispering, "Don't be so rude. He's Rufus's friend and a good 'un."

"You can't trust that pack of-"

"Yes, Tristan, ah can, and it's nae your business!"

"Have you forgotten Bruno already?" he growled, "What *they* did to him?"

Sara reached up and slapped Tristan across the muzzle, hard enough to turn his head.

There was a brief silence.

"Go home, Tristan," Sara said, looking down and away.

With a last glare at Linus, Tristan retrieved his helmet from the polished floor and strode from the university, slamming the front door behind him.

In the aftermath Linus said, "Sorry. That was my fault. He's right, I shouldn't be here."

Sara shook her head, "Tristan's just… overprotective."

"Of you?"

"Aye. He's such an idiot sometimes."

Professor Heath ambled into the hall, "Ready, you two?" he said chirpily.

"Aye," Sara replied.

"It's just a short walk to my flat," Heath told Linus.

Linus was confused, but said nothing as Professor Heath led him from Arkady University. Locking the main doors behind them they headed out into the night, paws crunching in the deepening snow.

Sara tagged along – and that was the confusing bit. Was she coming to Heath's flat? Was she staying there too, or just coming along for the ride?

"Och! Ah hate this time of year," the little wolfess complained to Linus, amidst an overblown shiver.

"Too cold?" he guessed, with a sniff.

"Well, that and there's nae bugs," Sara replied. "They all die or hibernate, of course. We've had tae keep Toggle cooped up inside for days; she's getting very frustrated."

Linus gave Sara a sideways glance, "Uhm, Toggle?"

"Oh. Sorry. That's mah bee's name."

"Ah."

"You'll see her in a minute," Sara explained. "She's in the Professor's flat. We brought her over so we could show her off tae everyone, but it was too cold tae take her out. Olivia stayed in tae look after her."

"Olivia?"

"Mah best friend."

Heath glanced behind, "She's, uh… got the flu, so don't get too close, Howler."

Linus joked nervously, "I-I-I just hope this flat is big enough for all of us."

✦

"He can't have him!"

"We've no choice."

"He's mine! I found him!"

"He's ALPHA's!" Silvermane snapped. "Or have you forgotten how I got you this position?"

Janoah dipped her chin and looked away in frustration.

Safe in the gloom of the corridor, Silvermane glanced through the one-way mirror, into the brightly-lit interrogation room. Rufus casually puffed on an ember, staring exactly where Silvermane was, meeting his very eyes, as if he could see him and Janoah through the reflective glass. Perhaps he could sense their coronas, even through the ash-infused, aura-dampening glass and walls, what with his extraordinary perceptive powers, which reminded Silvermane.

"Besides," he said, looking to Janoah, "Rufus found him, not you."

"And would've wasted him, sir," Janoah growled back, "as he wastes all the talent that comes his way, even his own! Set him free? He'll send Rafe to a… a home for the afflicted or something, to sit around turning clay pots and painting watercolours, wasting his life when he should be out protecting the Republic!"

"Then he really is fond of the boy?"

"As he was Ivan, Uther and all the rest he's taken under his wing. They're but passing interests."

"In the end," Silvermane reasoned, "it's Rafe's choice. If he wishes to stay with ALPHA, to remain an Eisenwolf and do his duty, Rufus cannot force him otherwise. All we're promising is an imperium pension in the event he does wish to leave, we're not promising to convince him to take it. Are we?"

Janoah nodded, "That's true."

Silvermane cupped his paws before him, "Then we're agreed?"

His subordinate eventually sighed, "Yes, sir."

Back in they went, Silvermane quick and eager, Janoah slow and reluctant. She nibbled a claw and stood behind Silvermane whilst he nodded at the expectant-looking Rufus.

"All right," he said, "you've got a deal."

"Pension for life?"

"If Rafe chooses, yes."

"That's all I ask," Rufus agreed, stubbing out his ember. "Let me see him."

✦

At the top of the stairwell, Heath unlocked the door and shepherded his wolfen guests inside.

"My humble abode," said the bear, his little eyes squinting at Linus from behind a warm smile.

Ever-polite, the Howler removed his helmet as he walked in, blue eyes taking stock. He found himself in Heath's living room, amidst antique sofas and chairs, a smart coffee table and a ticking grandfather clock.

Linus was immediately drawn to the walls. Framed photos plastered every available surface as thickly as wallpaper. In most, a decidedly youthful Heath was standing in the great outdoors, with deserts, forests and even great snowy mountains looming over his sloped bear shoulders. In many of the pictures other beasts stood around him, fellow scientists and naturalists of every race, all dressed in distinctively Lupan clothing, which made them stand out like sore thumbs when posing beside native beasts in traditional garbs – hyenas on the plains, otters at a sunny beach, even a group of noble-looking elk in a deep dark forest. Sometimes the group were standing over a slain bug, a scorpion in one, a centipede in another. In one faded photo, Heath was measuring a presumably dead crab's gigantic claw, and in another he was posing by a huge spider's web stretched between two trees.

There were other things to see, old shields painted with dazzling hyena patterns, crossing spears with sprays of red ribbon, and weird idols representing some kind of squat beetle god; even the carpet beneath Linus's gaitered boots was a thing to behold, the red and gold fibres festooned with stylised insects frolicking amidst a scene of leaves and flowers. The seemingly endless pattern drew Linus in, sucking him into another world, the wild world beyond Lupa.

"Make yourself at home, Howler," Heath said, breaking the youth from his mental meanderings. "I'll make us all a cup of hot chocolate before bed."

"Oh, uh… thank you, sir."

"Call me Heath," the bear said, opening the kitchen door.

Sara had already passed through to one of the adjoining rooms, where she turned up a lamp.

"Olivia?" she called gently. "You awake?"

"Sara?" someone out of view replied groggily – Olivia, Linus could only presume, wondering what manner of beast she might be. "Oh dear, I must've fallen asleep!" she laughed gently. "What time is it?"

"Very late," Sara whispered. "How's the flu?"

"Better," Olivia chirped at length, adding curiously, "Is someone here?"

"Aye, one of Rufus's friends," Sara explained, adding quickly, "Where's Toggle?"

No sooner had Sara enquired after her pet bee than Professor Heath turned up the kitchen lamp and wailed in a chiding tone, "Oh no. Tooooggle!"

Sara sped through the lounge, giving Linus but a glance on her way to the kitchen.

"Och!" she gasped at the door, paws clapping to cheeks.

"Where's Olivia?" Heath asked.

"She was asleep."

"Asleep? How'd she sleep through *this*, it's a disaster!"

Linus quietly wandered over to see what the trouble was, as if, him being a Howler and all, he might be able to mend any problem these normal beasts might come across.

He discovered a very reasonable kitchen – stove, breakfast table, airy windows and terracotta tiles – all of it smeared with what looked like jam. Various jars of all shapes and contents were strewn haphazardly across the floor, some of them broken, others intact. All the broken jars containing sweet preserves and honey looked clean, as if they had been licked out, whilst those containing vinegar-soaked pickles and tart chutney remained where they lay, unadulterated beyond breakage. Is this the work of a deranged, sweet-toothed burglar? Linus thought.

Leaning in a little more he discovered the culprit; a trembling, black and orange ball of fluff with its head stuck in an especially big jar.

"A bee!" Linus woofed.

Sara looked back at him – the Howler was smiling like an excited cub.

Heath wasn't. "Oh dear, oh dear, what a confounded mess," he tutted. "I said to keep this door shut, didn't I? You know what she's like."

Sara went to pick her way through the carnage, "Toggle!"

"Mind the glass!" Heath advised, stopping her.

"Ah think she's stuck, Professor."

Putting his helmet aside Linus said, "Here, let me."

Watched by Heath and Sara, the Howler crunched through the minefield of glass shards, his gaitered boots impervious to damage, approaching Toggle without trepidation.

As Linus advanced, the bee backed into a corner and made aggressive buzzing noises.

Bvv! Bvvvt! Bvvv!

Her abdomen began pumping in and out from the effort.

Hushing the frightened bee, Linus slowly crouched beside her and stroked those shiny, iridescent wings with a paw. They were smooth, yet bumpy with veins. They were also dripping with honey, much like the rest of the bee.

Once all was calm, Linus grabbed the broken jar in both paws and gently twisted it off Toggle's head, leaving the bee's front end coated in a golden film of sticky honey.

Triumphant, Linus stood up, jar in paws, "There we-"

Bvvvvvvvv!

Amidst blasts of air and blurring wings, Toggle flicked honey all over the walls, all over the curtains, and all over Howler Linus.

"Toggle, stop!" Sara gasped, paws to muzzle. "Toggle!"

Toggle stopped, but all too late. She trundled across the kitchen, her naturally armoured legs kicking aside the razor-sharp glass with impunity, leaving Linus behind to look down at himself, his fine Howler cloak and armour dripping with flecks of shiny, delicious, and horrendously sticky honey.

"Oh dear," he said, licking some from his nose – it really was delicious.

"Ah'm so sorry!" the mortified Sara said. "Bad Toggle! Look what you've done. Bad, bad, bee!"

Bvvvt!

Someone else hurriedly pushed their way into the crowded kitchen, an elegant, light brown wolfess in a fluffy pink dressing gown. She took in the devastation with her violet eyes, took in the honey-flecked Howler Linus.

"I see you've met our pet bee," she chuckled.

Linus plucked uselessly at his sticky cloak, "It seems so, Miss… uh…."

"Olivia," she sniffed, "Olivia Blake."

✧

The door opened, but Meryl Stroud ignored it and continued to read.

"I have rode the wind," she said, "seen forests far below, met great beasts and small. I have kissed the sun, felt its warmth on my wings. I have known love with my mate and shared joy at their smile. And yet there is so much more beyond the horizon, so much yet to see and do! This pond is but a puddle in a great ocean of green. Alas, I cannot go on. My time is done.'

Slowly, the nurse closed the book and stood up from her stool. She hailed Janoah and Silvermane with the simple ALPHA paw-gesture.

"Prefects," she said, with little enthusiasm.

"Miss Stroud," Silvermane replied, stepping inside ahead of Janoah, as rank dictated. "Sorry to disturb your work, but Rafe has a guest."

"He knows," Meryl replied.

Rufus entered the room after Silvermane and Janoah. It was quite dark, the only light source being a stark imperium lamp mounted on the wall. As his eyes adjusted, Rufus saw a big comfy chair and a bed. Slumped in the chair, mighty, muscled shoulders wrapped in a blanket, was a huge, dark brown wolf, his eyes covered by a tidy blindfold. The young wolfen nurse standing by him wore a modest black dress and white apron, her neck cosseted in a tall collar and cravat. She had a kind, pure-grey face, etched with worry.

Silvermane turned his gaze on the wolf in the chair and enquired, "How are you, Rafe?"

Rafe cocked his head slightly, "Much better, sir."

"You seem perkier, to be sure. Doctor Josef's therapy must be paying off."

"I think so, sir. Meryl's been helping too."

"Indeed, Miss Stroud is most assiduous in her care," Silvermane agreed. "The Alpha himself sends his regards."

Nodding, Rafe turned his head a little, "Jan?"

Janoah grinned with delight and approached. As the Prefect passed her, Nurse Meryl could hardly disguise the look of disgust – Rufus saw it, if nobody else.

Whether she noticed it or not, Janoah sat on the arm of Rafe's chair and ran a paw round the back of his big head, stroking his muscled neck. "There's a special Howler here to see you, Stenton," she whispered.

"I know," Rafe said, without eyes to see, "I felt him coming a mile away. Meryl didn't believe me."

Janoah tutted, "She doesn't understand your power."

Meryl dipped her chin to her cravat, and likely bit her tongue.

Rafe looked thoughtful. "It's that… that red-furred wolf from the other day, 'en it?"

"Yes."

"He's really strong, Jan."

Janoah expected to see Rufus smile as he usually did when flattered, but he remained stony-faced. "Don't take anything he says to you too seriously, will you?" she told Rafe.

With a sniff, Rufus stepped into the room, but instead of going straight to Rafe, as everyone expected, he veered towards Nurse Meryl.

"You care for this wolf, Miss Stroud?" he asked her.

"Yes, Howler,' Meryl replied, with a tiny curtsy.

Rufus nodded, "How long has he been averse to light?"

Surprised to be asked, Meryl said, "Ever since his induction," adding dejectedly, "It's gotten much worse since last week's... overreaching. It comes and goes, but it's never been this bad before."

"The rot is an uphill struggle," Rufus explained, "though it has its sunny vales on the way. I'm sure you're one of those vales, Miss Stroud."

Meryl smiled bashfully. "Are you..." she began, faltered a moment, then continued, "Grand Howler Rufus Valerio?"

A nod.

Meryl let out a tiny gasp of amazement and fought to hold back a giddy smile. "Oh! It's an honour to meet you, sir. I-I-I've read all your works on the rot."

Rufus winked. "As Janoah here says, you shouldn't take anything I say too seriously."

The youthful Meryl could but say, "You're the reason I became a nurse, sir."

"Then I'm the honoured one," Rufus assured her.

He turned to Rafe, a giant of a wolf, even whilst seated, hunched like an old beast over a fire. He was wearing some breeches with silk coverings up to the knee, but nothing else besides that blanket and blindfold. His rippling hide was in poor condition, his paws bandaged from burns, a far cry from the handsome, well-groomed youth Rufus remembered from *The Warren*.

Rufus's eyes strayed to Janoah, hovering over her creation, stroking his neck and smiling at her husband as if by snatching this prize she had won some great victory over him.

Without a word, Rufus turned away made for the exit. Janoah shot to her feet. "Is that it?" she spat.

"I've seen him, or what's left of him," Rufus huffed, leaning on the doorframe long enough to add, "When this is over, I... I never want to see you again," Rufus told her, slipping into the corridor.

Glancing at the dumbstruck Janoah, Silvermane stormed after Rufus. "Where are you going?" he demanded, shouting down the stark, white corridor. "Howler!"

"Shame on you!" Rufus spat, turning and looking Silvermane up and down. "Both of you. You've destroyed that poor boy and for what? To further your own careers in this miserable pile the Den Fathers misnamed 'ALPHA'?"

Silvermane visibly winced. "You're upset, so I'll pretend I didn't hear that," he growled. "You need to understand what Rafe is-"

"Bruno!" Rufus barked, looking down. "He's... he *was* called Bruno," he said, fists trembling by his sides. "Such a nice young wolf, Silvermane; so kind and funny."

Silvermane nodded sagely, "He remains so."

Rufus snorted in disbelief.

"He bears his burden with grace," Silver continued. "He's a true pure-blood, an exceptional one. He must have come from two powerful Howlers. The chances of him even surviving to birth were a thousand to one, let alone without madness or deformity-"

"Remember who you're talking to, Silver."

"I'm well aware, sir! Likewise, don't insult my intelligence by throwing a pique of moral outrage, as if you were after Rafe yourself for any other reason-"

"I would have inducted him gently!" Rufus protested. "Extended his life, not pushed him until he burnt out or went mad. Ulf have mercy on you if he ever does, you will be as ash in a gale before his might." Stepping back, Red-mist shook his head, "Where were you during the war, eh? How ironic that it's ALPHA who's learnt nothing. When the Den Fathers realise what you're doing they'll stop you, if not disband you for good."

Like a thundercloud skirting the horizon, Silvermane rumbled back, "If one Eisenwolf frightens them so much they can close the loophole during the Summit. They can shut down ALPHA too if they want. Until then, we will continue to fight for the Republic and give the packs the privilege of choice – Amael won't. Janoah says he's going to lift the Lupan Laws, bring back Howler marriage and all that goes with it, no doubt Eisenwolves included."

The Grand Howler and the Grand Prefect stood in brooding silence.

Janoah entered the corridor. Closing Rafe's door she walked halfway over and said to Rufus, "Finished, dearest?"

Red-mist composed himself, wiping his eyes, "Let's just get this circus on the road shall we?"

Silvermane glanced between them. "You're going to help us?" he asked Rufus.

"Though it turns my stomach to line up with ALPHA, I see no other choice."

With a sigh of relief, Silvermane said, "This has to be convincing, Rufus."

"I know."

"Once we begin I can give nothing away, not even to save you."

"Yes, yes, yes."

"Remember, the fable is the code. Wait for-"

"Oh get on with it, wolf, before I change my mind!"

Clearing his throat and taking a nervous breath, Silvermane rolled his neck and shoulders. "Well, you'd better hit me, then. Just don't kill me, Rufus."

"It's more likely your Eisenwolf'll kill me, Silvermane."

"You know him. You know he's not that kind of wolf."

"I *knew* him," Rufus corrected pointedly.

Not wishing to be drawn into a second argument, Silvermane merely nodded. He spread his paws and grimaced, bearing himself to harm. "For Ulf's sake, do it!" he snarled.

"Gladly."

Pff-zzzt!!

With a whining snap of white-hot plasma, Rufus thumped Silvermane in the chest. The sizeable wolf left the floor behind and hit the wall, before flopping to the ground, his black cloak smoking from the blow.

He was out cold!

Rufus huffed, "My, that was satisfying." Shaking his throbbing paw he looked down the corridor, at Janoah.

He nodded. She nodded.

"Help!" Janoah cried, drawing her rapier and striding down the corridor towards Rufus. "Stenton!"

Rafe shouted through the door, *"Jan?"*

Husband and wife met halfway, Janoah half-heartedly thrusting her imperium-laced rapier at Rufus, fully expecting him to avoid it. To her gasp of shock, he merely allowed the needle-like blade to skewer his left shoulder. He snarled in pain, but stood firm.

Janoah narrowed her green eyes. "Fool," she chided.

"Just… making it convincing, Jan," he laughed. Grasping her flexible kristahl sword-blade in his right paw, the wincing Rufus seethed, "Brace yourself, wife."

"Stop showing off and do it."

Rufus obliged. A spark of imperious plasma erupted from his paw and raced down Janoah's conductive sword, blowing her down the hall and sending her weapon spiralling away. She slid to a halt at the feet of a huge brown wolf – Rafe.

"Jan!" he yelped, kneeling down and cradling her limp body. "Jan? You all right?"

No reply, save a groan.

With a whine and a growl, Rafe looked up with his blindfolded eyes, right where Rufus was standing, as if he could see him clear as day through the cloth.

Putting Janoah down and raising a fist, Rafe strode towards Rufus, a big, dark tower of muscle and sinew, overflowing with imperium and rage. With every step Rufus could feel the youth's crackling corona growing, its coils penetrating his flesh down to the bone, such warmth, such strength.

Meryl stepped out into the corridor, "No Rafe!"

Undeterred, Rafe cast his paw at Rufus. The windows and imperium lamps between them exploded, the walls cracked and buckled, even the very air warped and twisted. Reaching Rufus in an instant, the twisting coronal tidal wave blew him off his feet and swept him down the corridor. Bouncing, rolling, whining and yelping, Rufus didn't stop until he slammed into the door at the far end and fell on his side.

Silence.

The furious Rafe loomed over the dizzy Howler, his mighty body silhouetted by a flickering lamp, his right paw licked by imperious plasma. As he raised his right arm to finish the job and send Rufus out of the world, Meryl ran in and hugged him tight.

"Rafe stop it!" she wept, nuzzling into his stomach. "Please don't kill him! Please!"

"Meryl?"

"Please! This isn't you. You're a good wolf. Don't let the rot win."

The plasma left Rafe's paws and he held Meryl close.

That was the last Rufus saw.

Chapter 23

Rejoining the world of wakefulness, Linus watched dawn nuzzle into Professor Heath's flat, its sunny rays splaying out above the thick velvety curtains like sheets of ephemeral gold. He listened to Lupa rising, to motor cars trundling by and newspaper sellers shouting headlines – it was impossible to make out what they were saying, muffled as they were by the window and doubtless thick, fresh snow.

Linus thought about last night; Heath, Sara, Toggle, getting splattered with honey. Heath had offered to wash the Howler's cloak whilst Linus and the girls partook of a nightcap of hot chocolate. Not much was said, outside of humorous remarks about Toggle's mischief and expressing worry over Rufus, for it was very late and everyone had elected to turn in, even Toggle. Plump with stolen honey, the great bee had put herself to bed in Sara and Olivia's room, clinging to the wall of all places. Linus had settled for the sofa in the living room. The plush antique proved perfectly adequate, especially since Linus, being somewhat short for a wolf, fitted easily between the arms.

Yawning and stretching, Linus set aside his blanket and swung his legs off the sofa. He hastily dressed, legs into greaves, feet into boots, smart white gaiters clipped over both. Donning his many-buttoned tunic, he crept over to the living room's hearth where his red mantle was drying by its warm glow. After checking the thick imperium-weave was dry, Linus went to fetch his Bloodfang brooch from the coffee table.

It was missing.

Glancing around his immediate space, Linus got down on all fours and peered underneath the table.

"It's here," someone volunteered.

Linus jumped up to find Olivia standing in the kitchen door, snug in a pink dressing gown and turning Linus's brooch over in her brown paws.

"I was just looking at it," she excused.

Clearing his throat, Linus hurriedly threw his hooded Howler mantle over his shoulders. He temporarily secured the final fold at his left shoulder with his fingers, pinching the fabric.

Smiling, Olivia walked over to him, proving taller by a head. The stocky Linus held out his left paw to receive his brooch, but this elegant wolfess boldly brushed aside both his paws and pinned his mantle for him.

"There," she chirped, brushing a paw on Linus's smartly-buttoned torso.

For a second the Howler could swear the red-imperium fang on his brooch had glowed rather brighter than normal. He quickly checked it. A trick of the light, perhaps?

"Did I pin it right?" Olivia asked, uncertain of Linus's reaction.

"Yes," he replied, twisting a little. "Thank you."

"I hear they're tricky, these mantles."

"It's fine, really."

Raising her chin proudly, Olivia turned around and strolled into Professor Heath's kitchen, as if she owned the place.

"Would you like some breakfast?" she asked, disappearing round the door. "I'm going to attempt waffles."

Linus stayed where he was, "I-I-I should really be going. My Den will wonder where I am."

"Surely you'll have a cup of tea?" Olivia insisted.

"Well… I-I-I suppose so. Yes. Please."

Walking over to one of Heath's interesting photo-festooned walls, Linus glimpsed Olivia through the perspective-skewed doorway, taking big, bear-sized cups down from the cupboards. Most would think her very lovely, he supposed, tall, elegant and all that; Uther would be all over her like a wasp on jam.

"Rostsonne or Hummel?" Olivia blurted from the kitchen, interrupting Linus's thoughts.

"Pardon?"

Olivia held up some tins, "What kind of tea? Rostsonne or Hummel?"

"E-either. I don't mind."

"Professor Heath has some Felician teas too, but they're rather weak I think. Taste like dishwater-"

"Rostsonne's fine," Linus interjected, eager to be away.

With a sharp exhale at her own perceived lack of social dexterity, Olivia opened one of many tins and proceeded to make the tea, pouring in the hot water and all the rest. "You look like a Rostsonne wolf," she observed, steam rising around her, "but you don't have the horrible accent."

'Horrible?' Linus thought, saying, "I-I-I was born there, but I've lived in Lupa since I was three or four."

"I see," Olivia hummed, adding, "Where'd you get those scars?"

"Scars?"

"On your back. Sorry, I couldn't help but notice them. Very impressive."

"Oh! That."

"Am I being terribly nosy?"

"No, no, not at all," Linus lied. "A hog did it."

"Hog?"

"N-nnn-not a 'normal' hog. He was some… insane, imperium-fuelled, gang-leader, down on the Common. He gored me with his tusks."

Olivia seethed in sympathy, "You poor beast!"

For once in his life Linus sailed dangerously close to boasting waters. "One tusk went right through me," he claimed. "Josef said it was nothing short of a miracle that it missed all my vitals."

At length, Olivia emerged from the kitchen with two hefty cups and saucers balanced in her paws. "Josef?" she said curiously, offering one to her Howler guest. "Not Josef Grau, the grey cat with the little black glasses?"

Linus took his tea, "The very beast. He used to be Riddle District's pathologist, amongst… other duties. He works for ALPHA now."

Olivia gasped, "Gosh, so that's where he went."

"Went?"

"He used to lecture at the Arkady. He was one of my imperiology teachers. One day he just disappeared." At length, Olivia cocked her head, "He's a bit strange, isn't he?"

Linus sipped his tea, "I couldn't say."

"I could, but I'm not as polite as you," Olivia hummed mischievously. "Grau's a genius, obviously, but… not entirely with it. Still, goes with the territory I suppose. Rufus Valerio's a bit strange too, don't you think?"

Linus guffawed ambiguously and blew on his tea.

"Well, anyway," Olivia said, "I'm glad that hog's tusks missed your vitals and all."

Howler Mills raised his cup to that, "Me too."

There was an awkward break in the conversation as both wolves sipped their tea.

"I should see about those waffles," Olivia said. "I want to surprise Sara and the Professor when they get up. Sure you don't want any?"

Linus set aside his half-finished tea, "No, thank you. I really have to go." Adjusting his cloak, because Olivia had indeed pinned it somewhat wrong, he added, "Please express my gratitude to Professor Heath and Miss Sara. It was nice to meet you all, despite the circumstances."

Olivia smiled broadly, "You know, you're far too polite for a Howler, especially a Bloodfang."

Linus snorted humorously.

"You must have good breeding," Olivia judged, sipping her tea.

"I'm not one for judging wolves by their breeding," Linus insisted, lightly, if sincerely. Clearing his throat for the umpteenth time, he headed for the door. "I really must go."

"Your helmet, Howler?" his host suggested.

"Oh!"

Linus whirled round and fetched his sad-looking helmet from the coffee table.

"I'd forget my tail if it wasn't screwed on," he laughed, donning his armour.

Olivia chuckled back.

Linus lingered at Professor Heath's door long enough to say, "Goodbye."

"Goodbye."

Linus gently closed the door, blocking out Olivia's intense violet eyes. As he walked along the corridor and down the stairwell, he felt a sudden emptiness, the absence of a presence to which he had grown accustomed.

Linus glanced at Heath's door one last time before heading on down, through the building's main doors, and out onto the pristine snow-bound street. The icy breath of winter rolled over him, but Linus was a wolf, and a Howler, hardened in the Bloodfang Howler Academy – the cold had little effect. His eyes watered not from the bitter air, but from the sheer glare of the snow that coated every level surface.

Crossing the street between ash-belching motorised carriages, Linus happened upon a newsstand run by a mottled wolf cub in a dark blue coat and hat – he looked about ten. No doubt he was the very same youth Linus had heard hollering from up in Heath's flat.

Linus thought no more of it, or the biased Eisbrand rags the cub was peddling, until the boy said, "Rufus Bloodfang is charged with imperium embezzlement and attempted lupicide! Read all about it!"

Heart somersaulting, Linus whirled back to the stand and snatched up a paper. The front page of *The Harbinger* was plastered with an unflattering mug-shot of Rufus accompanied by a worse headline.

'THE FALL OF 'RED MIST'.'

"But, he was only arrested last night," Linus said.

"Hot off the press, sir," replied the cub, little paw outstretched. "That'll be tuppence, please."

✥

Uther rolled out of bed, wincing less from his week-old wounds than a fresh hangover. After cradling his pounding head a moment, the Howler sat on the edge of the bed and nursed his bandaged ribs and upper left arm.

"Schmmmmutz," he seethed.

Locating his mantle amidst the chaotic mix of clothing strewn about the threadbare carpet, he dug out his wallet and counted a few hundred lupas. Leaving the colourful wad of cash under the imperium lamp on the bedside table, he stood up and drew the curtains back, allowing the snow-enhanced sunlight to flood into the pokey hotel room, momentarily blinding him.

A set of slender golden arms snaked around Uther's sinewy black and white waist. "Mornin', Wild-heart," said their owner.

"Good morning, Lorna," Uther sniffed, as the lovely wolfess kissed his thick neck. "Money's on the side."

"Oh no it ain't."

Uther glanced at the bedside table; the cash had magically vanished.

"Puh!" he laughed. "You're quick."

"Well, you can't leave that kind of money lying just around, partner," Lorna defended, tucking the lupas further down into the neck of her bodice, until they disappeared entirely from view. She purposely felt and squeezed Uther's muscled arms, and therefore his wound, making him wince. "My poor, brave soldier," Lorna purred in his left ear. "You should let me and Rosa nurse you back to health for the rest of the week."

"Think I'm made of money?" the Howler scoffed. "I only get half-pay on sick leave as it is!"

"All the more reason to get better quick then," Lorna swiftly pointed out. "We'll do it for half rate, birthday boy."

Uther laughed the offer off, as if it were a joke, but Lorna looked dead-serious.

The door burst open without so much as a knock and the squat Rosalina waddled in.

"Uther-" she said, but got no further.

In stepped Ivan, armoured and cloaked, with a rolled newspaper in his paw. Looking Uther and Lorna over, he threw the rag at his fellow Howler.

Uther fumbled to catch it.

"They've no right!" Ivan snapped. "The lying bastards haven't the right!"

Baffled beyond words, Uther turned the paper over until the front page flopped open.

Lorna leant in. "They've arrested Rufus?" she gasped.

"ALPHA took him last night," Ivan said. "I assumed someone was just trying to scare him and his literati friends into behaving, like always."

Uther looked up from the paper, "They probably are."

"It's going to trial, you fool. They want rid of him!" Ivan paced, growled. "ALPHA moved too fast; from arrest to charges to newspaper story. Someone had this all planned out."

There was a brief quiet, marked only by the sound of Uther folding the paper up and tossing it on the bed. "Well what am I supposed to do about it?" he snorted at Ivan.

"You could at least feign concern!"

"I *am* concerned."

"You don't look it!"

Uther squirmed defensively, "Yeah well, maybe it's because I ain't surprised. With the way Rufus carries on this was gonna happen one day and we all knew it."

Ivan huffed, "You've always been eager to forget what he did for you, 'Wild-heart'. He got Den Father Vito to let you go when anyone else would've walked away. Yet I've never once seen you speak up for him."

"Just because I never combed his back like you! I respect him, and I'm grateful for what he did, but I ain't no beta, never again, not to no wolf. Not even him."

There was a frosty silence.

"Sir," Uther tacked on, sarcastic at best. He turned away and hastily rifled through his cloak for an ember. Taking a deep puff he leant on the wall and peered out the window at the snowy streets of Lupa.

"Just get dressed," Ivan commanded. "You're wanted back at the Den."

"But I'm on sick-leave!" Uther protested indignantly.

"You seem well-enough to exert yourself!" his superior growled, glaring at Lorna and Rosa. "This comes from Amael, so unless you want a flogging, be back by midday. There's to be a meeting in the Elder Chamber about Rufus and you're to attend, though Ulf knows why."

With that, the stormy Ivan took his leave.

Glancing at Rosalina, Lorna picked up the paper and read the headlines once more. Creeping up behind Uther and placing a paw on his shoulder, she said, "I'm sure it'll all come to nothin'."

"Yeah," Uther sniffed at length.

✤

Elder Amael Balbus stubbed out his ember and picked up the ringing telephone. "They're here?"

"Yes, sir," Boris replied. *"Uther just arrived."*

"Send them both in," Amael said, "and yourself," before setting the phone down and pouring himself a tumbler of Hummel brandy, knocking it back for courage. "You're sure this is wise?" he asked aloud.

Not getting an immediate reply, Amael looked at Janoah, standing silhouetted by one of the bright, snow-flecked windows that circled the Elder Chamber, arms folded, ember smouldering.

"They have to join you sooner or later," she said at last, blowing vapour at the frosty window. It condensed into a colourful patch of imperium, before evaporating. "Uther and Ivan are two of the finest Howlers in Lupa. You need them."

"Either one could betray me."

Janoah huffed, "Uther's a gossiping proletarian, a street fighter from the gutter. He despises most Elders and their lack of morals, especially our very own Vito. I assume you're aware of Uther's history with him?"

Amael nodded, "What about Ivan?"

"He'll do anything to save Rufus," Janoah claimed, blowing a perfect vapour-ring, adding, "As will I."

Amael felt his pistol hidden beneath the Elder Table. Not even Blade-dancer could dodge a pellet. He attacked me; I shot him, who could say otherwise? Uther would go the same way if need be.

The Elder Chamber doors eased open, allowing two fully-uniformed Howlers to enter, Uther and Ivan in red and black respectively, followed by a third wolf in black and without a helmet – the mottled brown and white Captain Boris. Uther and Ivan stood on the Bloodfang emblem, removed their helms and saluted. Boris, being Amael's adjutant, stood slightly to one side and saluted only half-heartedly – years of being in Elder Amael's presence all day every day bred familiarity, as well as a sense of privilege, perhaps. Either way, Amael didn't pull him up on it.

"Send the Den Guard away," Amael said to Boris, flicking his grizzled snout at the doors.

"Sir," the mottled wolf acknowledged.

Watched discreetly by Ivan, Boris went to the doors, opened one, and told the two Den Guards to take a break. Supposedly sworn to secrecy though they were, and thick though the Chamber doors may be, the snatching, interrogation and torture of Den Guards for information had been the fall of many an ambitious Elder.

Once the guards had departed, Boris returned to the middle of the chamber and cupped his paws behind his back. He nodded at Amael, who nodded back.

Ivan took note of it all.

Why had Amael taken such a precaution, and why was Janoah here.

"How are you, Uther?" Elder Amael began with unusual cordiality. "On the mend, I trust?"

"Aye, sir," Uther replied, hesitant.

"Well enough to service his regulars over in the Common Ground," Janoah said, with a sardonic chuckle. "Don't overdo it, Wild-heart; you'll bust your stitches."

Uther said nothing, but cleared his throat a little.

Ivan growled without looking, "Are you aware your husband has been arrested, Prefect Valerio?"

"Who isn't, Captain Donskoy?"

"Strange. You don't appear upset. But then I hear you're the one who seized him."

Janoah huffed, "Who told you that; your dear cousin?"

"Is it true? Answer me!"

Amael slapped the table and barked, "Ivan!"

"It's all right," Janoah said, stepping forward. "I'm not his superior any more, just a Prefect."

Ivan waited, nostrils flaring a little.

"I had no choice," Janoah told the lofty white wolf, dipping her chin a little. "ALPHA was testing me. They've grown suspicious of my regular visits to Riddle District. If I had refused to take Rufus in, or warned him, I would've been sent down as well for acting against the peace." Janoah chuckled a little, then sighed, "Besides… if it had to be done, at least I would do it gently."

Ivan erupted, "Gently? In front of the whole world?"

Janoah had her answer immediately to paw, "Better everyone knows about it," she claimed. "Better that ALPHA is seen to arrest Rufus and go to trial than for him to disappear and wolves wonder whom to blame. The citizens know who to blame – ALPHA."

Ivan digested that, then looking between Janoah and Amael said, "Then I take it ALPHA's right to be suspicious of your visits to Riddle. What are you playing at, Janoah?"

She, Amael and Boris exchanged stolen glances, each unsure how to proceed, each looking to the other to set the ball rolling, as if they feared Ivan, the Blade-dancer, could strike them all down in a flash if they said the wrong thing.

"You probably think I'm happy to see Rufus go down the mines," Amael said.

"Well aren't you?" Ivan blurted daringly. "Isn't he an embarrassment to you? That's all you ever say!"

Amael frowned, but instead of calling Ivan out on his cheek, kept his cool. "If anyone was going to send him down the mines it was going to be me, not those jumped-up bastards at ALPHA! Ulf knows Rufus has given me enough cause, but I did more than spare him, I protected him."

Ivan spluttered, "Protected him?"

"Yes! And you, and you!" Amael barked, glaring at Ivan and Uther respectively. "I've looked the other way when you've donated your imperium to him – do not deny it, I know everything that goes on in Riddle!"

Ivan and Uther remained silent.

Amael continued, rumbling away like a distant landslide, "I let you get away with it when I should have referred you to our own Provosts for investigation, let alone ALPHA, because you are good Howlers, my finest, as would Rufus be if he concentrated on his duty as oppose to his idle dreams and desires. As it is, he wastes his talent and brings shame on our whole pack. And now he is finally paying the price." The Elder knitted his paws on the desk, "I can't help him. Only a Den Father can possibly intercede on his behalf, and ours is in no fit state to do anything."

Ivan frowned, "Is Den Father Vito unwell?"

"Unwell? He's mad!"

"Mad, sir?"

"You didn't see him when he came to Riddle last, Ivan, on account of Rufus being blown up by Noss, but don't worry, you didn't miss out," Amael derided. "It's pathetic to see what an embarrassing shambles of a wolf Vito has become. He's always had his… vices, as well you know, but he's led Bloodfang effectively until now and so I've been forced to tolerate his failings for lack of support. Now the rot's spread to his brain; he can't be trusted to remember what happened yesterday let alone make decisions that affect every one of us. All he thinks of is where his next meal is coming from and what street cub next to bed with. It's disgusting!"

Uther's muzzle twitched, and Ivan noticed.

"His adjutants and Den Guard are as guilty as him," Amael claimed, "procuring his every whim and protecting him when they should know better!"

Boris spoke, "Sir, the Den Guard are sworn-"

"If I was an abusive old drooler, I'd expect you to do something about it, Boris, whatever you'd sworn!"

Silence.

Amael growled afresh, "Howlers, our pack is paralysed by lack of sound governance. Every district is plotting their rise, every Elder jostling for votes – myself included. I shan't deny it; I want to be the next Den Father as much as any wolf and I have been laying the foundations. I have great plans, let me tell you. I'll lead Pack Bloodfang into a glorious future, and sweep this city clean. I will cut out the festering rot, starting with ALPHA. Setting them bullies up was the biggest mistake the Den Fathers ever made!"

"Odd you say that when there's a member of ALPHA standing in this very room, Elder," Ivan observed, not a tad sarcastically.

"Janoah works for me," Amael snorted, adding, "But you already knew that, Ivan."

"I work for the Bloodfangs," Janoah corrected Amael.

"For Lupa," Boris corrected them both. "We *all* work for Lupa, not our own ambitions, Howlers."

Amael raised his glass to his adjutant. "Quite right, loyal Boris, quite right," he said, downing his drink. "I can always rely on you to bring me down to Erde."

Nodding, Boris tugged at the neck of his cloak. He looked at Ivan a moment, then down and away.

"Drop of Hummel brandy, Howlers?" Amael said, breaking the awkward moment by pouring some fresh tumblers of the golden liquid.

"No, thank you, sir," Boris said at length.

Ivan shook his head.

Uther glanced at them and, perhaps only then realising that Amael was including the lowly Trooper in the offer, said a little too eagerly, "Yes please, sir!"

Amael laughed and slid one of the modestly-filled tumblers across the polished table. "That's more like it. Finest Hummel brandy lupas can buy, Howler. Get your lips around that."

Uther snapped it up and knocked it back. "Cor!" he woofed, thumping his chest.

"Good eh, Trooper?"

"Aye, sir! Hits the spot."

Chuckling warmly, Amael poured him another.

Ivan glared at Uther – the usually street-wise wolf seemed completely ignorant as to what was transpiring here, or else he was just taking full advantage of the situation to get a free drink; one couldn't put it past him.

Either way, Ivan turned to Amael and said, "If you've got something to say to us, Elder Balbus, then please don't mince your words. Whatever it is, I swear it won't leave this chamber, even if we agree to disagree."

Amael Balbus leant back in his ornate chair. "I appreciate your candidness," he said sagely, fondling the imperium pistol nestled in his lap. "I'll be candid also; you deserve nothing less for your years of exceptional service, 'Blade-dancer'."

Ivan waited.

"I know you… revere Rufus," Amael told him, the penultimate word sticking to his tongue. "And believe me, I don't wish him harm, much as his antics shame our Den."

Ivan moist nostrils flared just a little.

"Help me become Den Father," Amael continued, breaking out an ember and smouldering away, "and I'll get him off the hook. More than that, Boris here will become Riddle District's Elder and you two his Grand Howlers."

"Me?" Uther squeaked. "Grand Howler, sir?"

Amael nodded, "That's right, Uther. I intend to pull my best wolves up with me as I climb Lupa's slippery pole, and you two are the best Howlers in Riddle District, if not Lupa. Between us we'll run the Bloodfang Territory as it should be run, and help make Lupa a fairer, cleaner, safer place. Doesn't that sound worthy of you?"

"Well uh…." Uther hesitated, glancing at Ivan for guidance.

But Ivan had ceased listening long ago, the further delights dangled before him pale before the prospect of keeping Rufus out of the mines and alive.

"How can *you* help Rufus?" Blade-dancer demanded of his superior. "ALPHA must have enough evidence to convict him or they wouldn't dare bring him to trial. Even a Den Father's word can't save him now."

"But it can," Amael began afresh. "If four Den Fathers demand a citizen's pardon during the summit then that citizen is granted it regardless of ALPHA's evidence. It is a Lupan Law, the Den Father Prerogative, a safety net kept in place to curb ALPHA's power and keep them in check, one of the few truly overriding powers that remain. Now, Thorvald is one voice, as you know he's fond of Rufus and furious over the insult ALPHA dealt him. He's already in our camp. Hummel's Cora is another one who admires him, she'll help. I can get Flaid on board."

"He's just an Elder."

"He's sure to become Den Father of the Greystones within weeks; theirs is dying, and he and I have an understanding. That's three."

"I see. And the fourth?" Ivan said.

Amael blew a cloud of vapour overhead, "That's where you boys come in."

Ivan took a sharp breath and nodded.

"If you need time to think I can wait," Amael said, swirling his tumbler, "but Rufus can't. He might last a year in the mines, even two years… or a month, who knows? It's rather unpleasant down there in Gelb. They make you wear imperium collars, but even they're not enough to stop mad beasts stabbing one another-"

"I'll do it," Ivan said.

Amael looked at Boris, then back at Ivan again. Nodding, he turned to Uther.

"Alone!" Ivan stipulated, before Amael could speak. "I work best alone, sir. Leave Uther out of this, he's not the right wolf for the job."

"Oi!" Uther yapped indignantly. "Whatcha think you're doing, Blade-dancer?"

Ivan sneered, "You don't even know what's being asked of you, cloth-ears. Now get out before you hear too much!"

"I know *exactly* what's being asked," Uther growled, nodding at Amael, "and I'm in, sir."

Amael nodded.

"Fool," Ivan spat. "What do you even care?"

Uther turned to Ivan, "I gave him as much venom as you ever did when it could've got me done! Don't tell me I don't care, not when I spent nights burning up from the rot so he didn't have to!" He returned to Amael, "Tell me what to do, Elder, I'm your wolf, sir."

✤

Vladimir answered the knock at his office door without looking up from writing. "Come in."

Linus entered, removed his helmet and saluted with his free paw, before standing smartly to attention. He was breathing heavily, as if he had been in a hurry, and looked somewhat bedraggled.

"Ah, Mills," Vladimir woofed, "so nice of you to turn up for duty."

"Yes, sir. Sorry, sir. The trains were-"

"Delayed, I know. If it's not snow on the lines it's ash. You need to learn to ride a mono."

"Sir."

"And where did you sleep last night," Vladimir asked, giving the youth a disdainful look, "under a bridge?"

"No, sir. I… I stayed at Professor Heath's flat."

"Professor Heath!"

"Yes, sir. He insisted."

"My my, you are moving in high circles," Vladimir huffed in an acidic tone, even for him. "Or should I say were? I shouldn't let it go to your head, Howler, you served Rufus like every wolf that's gone before you – a pretty ornament draped over his arm to show what a potent alpha he is."

Linus cringed, "Sir, I-I-I protest!"

"Protest?"

"I have never… I'm not Rufus's-"

"Beta?" Vladimir guessed. "Yes, then perhaps you've had a lucky escape." Grabbing a newspaper from his desk he showed Linus the headline, "No doubt you've seen all this?"

Linus glared at the offensive front page, at the picture of Rufus photographed like a common criminal, and the claims, written large in bold print, that he had misappropriated white-imperium, embezzled thousands of lupas, laid with all and sundry and tried to murder two ALPHA agents, one of them his own wife, in his bid to escape justice. The papers all across Lupa were unanimous in their condemnation of this treacherous, hyena-loving, debauched wolf – Linus had checked every newsstand he had happened across on his journey home, desperate for a contradiction, a ray of hope, but finding none, not even here in Riddle.

"Yes, sir," Linus croaked, dipping his chin.

"Humph! I told him this was going to happen someday, it was inevitable the way he carried on," Vladimir said, tossing the paper in his crackling fire. "He upsets conservatives with his inflammatory speeches; he upsets reformists by keeping a string of betas like a corrupt old Den Father, and he upsets ALPHA just by being a powerful free agent. He has few friends left."

Linus looked up, "Sir, we have to do something-"

"There's nothing we can do, you foolish little pup."

"But surely if we ask Elder Amael-"

"Linus, do not dare!" Vladimir bellowed, cowing the 'little pup' at a stroke. "Unless you wish to join him, and believe me that's the last thing Rufus wants, you must forsake him," he advised, gentler now. "If ALPHA knocks on your door, and they will, disown him. If they ask about donating venom, it never happened. You only went anywhere with Rufus because he's a Grand Howler and you felt you had no choice to save your career. You didn't even like him. Don't give them a reason to take you to task as well, because they will, by Ulf."

"B-b-but why?" Linus stammered incredulously. "What've I done?"

"It's not what you've done, but what you are. Rufus doesn't pick up just anyone off street corners. Your blood… it crackles with imperium."

Linus let out a tiny scoff of surprise.

Clearing his throat, Vladimir averted his eyes from Linus to the desk. "ALPHA will use any opportunity to clip our wings," he said twiddling his golden pen between his fingers. "Removing talented wolves like you and Rufus from play is one way of going about it. Despite their protestations of 'purity' and 'justice', ALPHA is fast becoming a pack like any other, only with sweeping powers foolishly granted them in haste after the war. There will be a reckoning someday, but for now you need to learn to blend in. Bend and sway, hide your strength, your intelligence. Do that and you may survive. Then, perhaps, if you climb to the top of this termite nest we call Lupa, *then* you can make a difference."

Linus dipped his chin. He said nothing.

At great length, Vladimir got back to his papers, "If anyone asks, I never said any such thing. Dismissed."

"Sir, I-"

"I said dismissed! Go groom yourself, Mills; you're unfit for duty."

Once Linus had departed, Vladimir sighed to himself, "I hope you know what you're doing, Janoah."

✤

Linus burst into the washrooms, threw his cloak down and slammed his palms on the washbasin surround to vent his fury. The mirror in front of him warped and cracked, splitting Linus's shocked reflection in two.

The young wolf checked his tingling paws. He opened and closed them.

"Linus?" someone said.

The Howler in question quickly spied Uther's reflection via the next mirror along. Ivan joined him, stepping out of the shady shower rooms further down. This wasn't so odd, except that both wolves were fully dressed in their Howler gear and could hardly have been grooming. Whispering in the shadows, perhaps?

"You all right, mate?" Uther asked Linus.

"Yes," Linus said, pushing himself off the sink and gnarling his fingers. "No. Sorry I just… I-I-I'll pay for the damage."

"Puh! We never saw nothin', mate," Uther dismissed, clapping a dark paw on Linus's sturdy shoulder. "Right, Ivan?"

Ivan nodded once.

Linus's blue eyes darted between them, then down into the sink. "Have you heard about Rufus?" he asked.

"Who hasn't?" Uther scoffed angrily.

"There are such…." Linus began, faltering and gulping back his grief, before starting again, "Such liars and criminals in Lupa; beasts guilty of things a thousand times worse than anything Rufus has done, yet they're not carted off are they? I-I-I fight so hard to make Lupa a better place, and now… I don't know what to think anymore. It's not fair!"

Uther nodded sagely. He sniffed and glanced at Ivan's inscrutable porcelain face, then said to Linus, "It'll be all right mate, you'll see."

"How can it be?" Linus spat.

"Trust me-"

"Uther!" Ivan growled, walking by. "Come on, Boris is waiting."

"Yeah yeah, comin'."

Ivan stayed in the doorway a little while, giving Uther and Linus a look, before stepping out.

Uther waited until Ivan was quite gone, before licking his lips and saying to Linus, "Listen. I'm not supposed to say anything, but you're gonna notice sooner or later. Me n' Ivan, we're, uh… gonna be away for a little while. All right?"

Linus turned around, "Away?"

"On a special mission, mate. All hush hush. Nothing you need worry about; just keep your nose clean whilst we're gone."

Linus stared at Uther with cub-like bafflement.

Uther laughed and gently knuckled Linus on the chin. "Oi, it'll be your job to hold our patch together whilst I'm gone. Now I know I can rely on you, Woodlouse."

His mind whirring, Linus scrambled about for his power of speech. "H-how long w-www-will you be gone?"

"I dunno. Month, maybe two."

"Two months!"

"Aye. Gonna be going out beyond the Far Ashfall. See a bit of the world. That's all I can tell yer."

Linus gasped in surprise and smiled, "Oh, well, that sounds wonderful! I-I-I'm jealous."

"Yeah?"

"Of course. By Ulf, I've longed to leave Lupa for years."

Uther leapt on the premise, "Right! When I get back we're taking a holiday, mate, just me and you, down on the old Graumeer Coast. We must have some proper leave brewin'."

"Why Graumeer?"

"Rostsonne then. Whatever! Oi, you can show me your homeland."

Linus nodded, laughed.

Slowly, Uther's own smile melted away and he looked around the washrooms. "Well, be seeing yer, Linus," he sniffed bluntly, slapping his friend's arm. "Take care of yourself, all right?"

"I-I-I will," Linus replied, concerned by Uther's melancholic tone. "You too," he added hastily, as Uther made the door.

Linus raised a paw, but Uther didn't look back, he just stepped out and shut the door. Linus heard him and Ivan talking, their muffled voices fading away as they strode down the hall and to Ulf knows where.

✦

"The Alpha will see you now," the overweight Grand Prefect Horst said haughtily, stepping out and breezing by Janoah, his medals jangling about his distended cloak like a jester's bells.

Without a word, and a dirty look, Janoah went inside. She wasn't sure what to expect – the Alpha was in ALPHA HQ's gymnasium of all places, hardly the most discreet of venues for a meeting, but the Alpha was a busy wolf and had to slot supplicants in somewhere, Janoah supposed.

She moved quickly amongst the exercise machines and dumbbell racks, searching for the Alpha. Much of the equipment was the standard fare used for working the muscles and building enviable bodies, but some items were elaborate imperium-laced monstrosities that could only be powered by imperium-wielders, however strong or skinny. Possessed of cogs, discs and spheres made from glittering imperium alloys, they were to be turned, lifted or rolled by manipulating one's imperious field alone.

"My Alpha," Janoah saluted, finding him and Nikita on a gym mat in the middle of the huge space.

The Alpha stood with his brown back to Janoah, paws cupped behind him. Nikita was opposite. Both were wearing white training breeches, nothing more.

The Alpha raised his paw in acknowledgement of Janoah, but didn't turn around. "One moment, Prefect," he excused.

Janoah nodded, waited, watched.

The Alpha and Nikita, both slightly out of breath and a little bedraggled, bowed gracefully at one another, one paw tucked to their chests as if doffing a hat.

Then they continued.

With a growl Nikita lunged at the Alpha, trying to thump him with the palm of a paw, but the Alpha twisted aside and struck the bigger wolf in the ribs with his own deft paw. Amidst a flash of plasma and a little smoke, Nikita was sent staggering sideways, nearly stepping off the mat and out of the bout. He regained his balance, however, and skirted around the smaller Alpha. Nikita bobbed about, rolling his mighty shoulders like a boxer, whilst the Alpha maintained a rather nonchalant stance, one paw held before him as if checking his perfect, moon-white face in a compact mirror, the other tucked neatly behind his brown back.

Nikita attacked again, the Alpha dodged and weaved, but as he made to get away Nikita thumped him in the back, blasting him with a loud snap of imperious energy. The Alpha staggered forward, his back arched in pain, before recovering his stance with a snarl and face-saving chuckle.

Janoah wondered why she was stood here watching the Alpha toy with his second wolf. *Is he really slipping me into his busy schedule, or is this intentional? Am I supposed to be impressed at his masculine virility? Oh dear, boys will be boys, even the Alpha.*

His composure regained, the Alpha goaded Nikita with his fingers and the words, said through a smirk, "Let's not keep the Prefect waiting, Nikita."

Nikita snorted angrily and bowled into the Alpha, who apparently just let him. Grasping him around the midriff Nikita knocked his superior to the ground where they wrestled, Nikita's paws pushing against the Alpha's. Janoah could sense their coronas mingling, twisting. The air hummed with energy, growing stronger and stronger until.

"Grrrrragh!"

With a blast of air-warping, imperious power, enough to punch Janoah back a step, Nikita was blasted clean off the Alpha. Sailing through the air he landed flat on his back with a loud, bony, distinctly organic thump. The mat broke his fall, but it was hardly a soft landing.

The Alpha kicked himself to his feet with a gymnastic grace that was enviable even amongst Howlers and brushed himself down, before offering his downed opponent a friendly paw. Nikita, eventually, took it, and was pulled to his feet whilst nursing his spine.

The Alpha slapped him on the arm. "Invigorating match, Nikita," he said.

"Adal," Nikita replied simply.

Grabbing a towel from a nearby rack and wiping himself down, the Alpha turned to Janoah, his pale face and bright blue eyes arresting her.

"Apologies for boring you, Prefect," he said affably. "I'm sure we looked like cubs play-fighting on a sitting room rug to you, at least compared to your famous Riddle comrades Ivan and Uther."

Janoah deftly batted aside the Alpha's none-too-subtle compliment-fishing. "I've never had the pleasure of seeing them matched, my Alpha."

"Ah."

"But for the record, my husband could take them both at the same time, I'm sure."

After a distended pause, the Alpha looked back at Nikita, who hiked his eyebrows at the incredible notion. Wiping around his robust neck, the Alpha said to Janoah, "Then your husband must be well-guarded. We can't have him embarrass ALPHA again by escaping before his trial."

"I understand Grand Prefect Silvermane is taking personal charge of the matter," Janoah said simply.

A nod. "Rafe's quick actions have been noted, Prefect, as has your loyalty to ALPHA in the face of… personal difficulties."

Janoah nodded, "It was merely happy circumstance Rafe was nearby when Rufus," she paused a moment, then finished, "when he attacked me."

"It must be very shocking."

"Yes."

"How is our young Eisenwolf?"

Janoah smiled, "Improving, my Alpha. Josef's treatment seems to be effective."

"Good, good," the Alpha said, adding, "You will divorce Rufus, of course."

"If he's found guilty, my Alpha, but I mustn't be seen to presume guilt, even though he… he…." Janoah looked into the far distance, then dipped her chin and wiped her eyes. "I'm sorry," she sniffed, turning away.

The Alpha stepped up behind Janoah and gently gasped her shoulder. "Rufus casts no shadow over you," he said. "I know you put Lupa above anything, even him. I'm sorry things turned out this way. Truly."

Janoah slowly turned to the Alpha, taking his paw from her shoulder and rubbing his palm with a thumb, "Thank you, my Alpha."

He nodded and smiled amiably.

With that, Janoah was sent on her way with the Alpha's blessings and the understated salute of his own invention. The brief meeting was over.

Nikita, watching and listening from afar, was left somewhat baffled as he wiped himself down.

"What was all that about?" he scoffed at the Alpha, coming up behind the shorter wolf as Janoah picked her way through the gym and out the door.

"I wanted to let her know her loyalty has been noted," the Alpha explained. "It can't be easy for her, having to finally let Rufus go."

Nikita's brow knitted, "You like her, don't you, Adal?"

"What?"

"You show off in front of her, like big cub!"

"Nikita, what in the world-"

"I do not trust her! Horst; he agrees with me. She goes back and forth to Riddle. Is she Amael's, or is she ours? And that monster she keeps. He could destroy us all. She need only ask him to kill us and he would do it."

Chuckling, the Alpha turned to Nikita, looked the powerful wolf up and down, "By Ulf's fangs, Nikita, are you jealous of that tiny little wolfess?"

"Adal, I am merely-"

The Alpha tossed his towel at Nikita's mottled face. "What do you take me for?"

Nikita ripped the towel from his face and replied, "She is a Howleress, a rare jewel, and many say she is very beautiful."

"Since when did I care for that?"

No reply.

Adal clapped a paw to Nikita's thick, mottled neck and pulled him close. "Nikitaaa... Janoah's clever and resourceful," he said, "and that is why Rufus, despite his every natural inclination, married her; to gain an ally in this insane hive we call Lupa. Ulf knows they stopped laying together years ago. Besides, even were I so inclined where Rufus is not, it's not like I could marry her once they divorce, it's forbidden."

Adal released Nikita and pulled back, "No, with Rufus out of the picture, Janoah will be free and committed to ALPHA, which needs such wolves as her if it is to flourish."

Nikita raised his chin a little, "Is *that* why you get rid of Rufus?"

Winking, Adal turned his back, "Now grab the glimmer and comb, I've work to do."

"Yes... my Alpha."

✦

Vladimir entered the dingy chamber, with its cracked, off-white walls and grim, tiled floor, and gently closed the rusty, metallic door behind him. He cast his eyes over the stocky, muscle-bound hyena standing in the midst of the room, paws wired above his head, black-furred toes just about touching the blood-smeared floor.

"Seems your stay is over, Chakaa Madou," Vladimir said to him. "I regret to inform you you're off to the mines."

The battered Madou twisted in his cruel Howler-wire bonds as he tried to relieve the weight on his arms by standing on his toes. The Redcloaks had strung him up at precisely the right height to make it just possible for him to touch the floor if he tried, but with almost as much agony as merely hanging.

"Kill me... Howler," Madou panted, tipping his head back and seething through his teeth.

"I think not," Vladimir sighed.

"Please! As one... one warrior... to another-"

"You are no warrior, but terrorist scum!" Vladimir snarled in disgust, continuing in a measured tone, "Elder Amael has it in his head to do you in, but I will not let him dispose of a liability that easily. No. You'll rot in the mines, hyena, as many before you. Think on your actions whilst you're down there. If perchance anything comes to mind regards THORN's plans for us all, or perhaps Amael's, let the guards know and perhaps I'll come humour your ravings."

"I've t-t-told you... everything."

"Not how Nurka plans to strike!"

"The black... imperium... at the Summit. He'll k-kill all the Den Fathers-gaaaagh gagh!"

Just by giving Madou a hearty push on the chest, Vladimir was able to set him swaying and inflict unbearable pain.

"Yes, but how, Madou? What day? What time? Under what chair will the bomb be planted? The summit goes on for days, I must have details!"

"I… d-d-don't… know!" a quivering Madou rasped, coming to rest. "Nurka's… told n-nnn-nobody the exact plan. He's k-kept it secret even from Themba and me just in case… in case of this!" He laughed, "Gaaaaghahahaaaa!"

"Then he's clever this Nurka," Vladimir admitted, "for a chunta-swigging madbeast."

Leaving Madou to groan, Oromov stepped outside. Two Redcloaks were waiting.

"Cut him down and give him this," he instructed them, giving one a sting. "Then send him to the Watchers. They know what to do. Tell anybody of what transpired here and I'll string you two up next; by the throat mind you."

~Blick III~

They all felt ridiculous, clunking along the dark, decaying halls in layers of eisenglanz, Janoah most of all. A nimble Bloodfang inducted and trained she had no love for hefty armour, but even the Eisbrands would be ashamed to wear so much plate as to barely be able to move.

Still, better safe than sorry. The building Silvermane had picked for this real world exercise was a rotting derelict and Janoah didn't trust the ceiling not to come down of its own accord, let alone under duress.

"Don't hold back," she told her two comrades, lifting her thick, sight-limiting visor a moment, green eyes peeping out. "For this to mean anything we have to make it a fair test-"

"Gaagh!"

"Oofagh!"

Janoah whipped round, rapier rising instinctively at the sound of not-so-distant wolves being taken out. Flashes of light reflected off the adjoining corridor walls.

"He's coming! Don't let him through!"

She had refused a shield, but her fellow Prefects raised theirs and stepped forward, blocking the way.

"Gas grenade, captain?" one suggested, producing a metallic bauble.

"It shouldn't affect him, but try it. Behave as you would under normal circumstances."

"Aye!"

With a twist of the grenade's opposing hemispheres, the Prefect rolled it neatly down the hall. It spewed a tear-inducing, white smog from one end, slowly filling the corridor with a choking atmosphere which even a Howler's helmet would struggle to filter out. Janoah and her companions retreated backwards as the cloud rolled towards them.

Suddenly a towering, black, wolfen figure clomped audibly into the smog from the next corridor. He turned to face the Prefects with glinting, circular eyes of yellowed glass, fixing them with his blank stare just as he vanished in the rising smog.

The next anyone knew, the fog heaved like a billowing sail, ejecting the enormous, yet graceful wolf into battle, the very air wobbling and warping around him, ribbon flapping behind. First one Prefect then the other were punched aside with imperious fists, slamming into the walls either side and sending plaster crumbling. They were out. Another Prefect ambushed from behind, swinging a great sword. The metal wolf bobbed and weaved like a boxer, the blade clipping his armoured shoulder sending sparks and mantle fabric flying. He staggered aside, then retaliated, raising a quivering metal paw. The air warped and twisted, the coils of his corona reaching out. The walls cracked and bowed around him and, without even touching the Prefect, the metal wolf blasted him yelping down the corridor, the great sword sticking in the ceiling up to its hilt.

Gulping, Janoah stood firm as this mighty Lupine creation turned on her, metallic ears swivelling, listening, vacant glazed eyes staring, sad yet terrifying. The filthy exhaust at his back vented a pall of black ash, like an unfeeling machine.

Perhaps this had been a mistake? Was it still him in there, or had he turned?

"Well?" urged Janoah, dust falling all about her.

The all-metal wolf looked up a little, ears twitching more.

At length Janoah snarled, "Oh come along, Stenton!" rapier swishing. "What are you, scared of a little wolfess? You're an Eisenwolf! Show me what you're capable of-"

"JAN!"

In one great bound, Stenton leapt at Janoah and pushed her, no plasma, no sparks, no unnatural force, just a good hard playground shove, which from Stenton was as good as being hit by an imperium train. Janoah rolled across the hall, her armour clacking like so much pewter dropped by a clumsy maid. No sooner had she gathered her wits about her than she saw Stenton disappear under a heap of dust and rubble as the ceiling caved in.

"Stenton!" Janoah shrieked, bounding over and pulling at the disjointed lumps of concrete.

"Rafe? Rafe, where are you? Help! Someone help us! Wolf down, wolf down!"

The rubble stirred a little, then a lot, as Eisenwolf Rafe Stenton clawed his way out of the piles and stood tall, his cloak torn to shreds, his exhaust bent, his entire suit bleached a dusty, powdery grey.

"YOU ALL RIGHT?" he asked.

"Y-yes," Janoah managed.

Rafe nodded. "WE'D BETTER GET EVERYONE OUT OF HERE," he said, looking up, then around.

A nod.

With two Prefects slung over Rafe's shoulders, and another around Janoah's, the crumbling building was quickly evacuated. Dust, gas and tens of overly-armoured Prefects poured from the entrance where Silvermane and Josef were waiting, along with many a smart-looking ALPHA staff member with cameras and notebooks. The derelict building folded and two of the four walls caved inwards, enveloping everyone in a cloud of mortar and turning every black cloak and uniform grey.

"Is everyone accounted for?" Janoah bellowed, searching the Prefects, counting their heads. When she arrived at fifteen Prefects she counted a second time, only then did her panic subside. "That's the lot," she assured a spluttering ALPHA official.

As the dust cleared, Silvermane checked his pocket watch and crunched over to where Janoah stood with Rafe. "Well that was certainly spectacular... whatever it was."

Janoah removed her helmet and ALPHA-saluted.

Rafe followed suit, twisting the thick neck ring and pulling off his great helmet with a hiss. "Looks like we brought the house down, sir," he quipped.

"Indeed, Stenton," Silvermane said.

Josef demanded of Janoah, "Well? How did it go?"

"I think he's ready for the real thing," she replied, looking proudly to her Eisenwolf. "Nobody stood a chance in there."

"Not even you?" Josef enjoyed needling Janoah.

"Unfortunately, Doctor, the roof came in before I had a chance to whip our Eisenwolf into shape," she said, slapping Rafe on his cloak-draped backpack. "Hahahahaaa!"

Chapter 24

It had been quite the performance, Rufus thought, as he sat in the carriage rocked by the soothing motion of the train, thinking back over the past few days. Then again, he hadn't really been acting, nor had most of those who had sat in judgement of him.

With paws wired, Rufus had been sent before a panel of thirteen high-ranking wolves convened especially for the task of judging his fate. Representatives from each of the packs were there; two Eisbrands, two Greystones, two Bloodfangs and two Hummels, the latter being stationed in Lupa to push their pack's interests. That made eight. The many small packs that dominated the so-called Bloc sent three more judges between them, bringing the number up to eleven. ALPHA, who had brought the case, made up the shortfall with Silvermane and Horst.

Silvermane had proved a consummate actor, whilst Horst had unsuspectingly fulfilled the role required of him by being his natural abrasive self – a cartoon of a wolf, with his flabby jowls and copious war medals, half of which were gongs invented just to keep him placated, Rufus was convinced

Like Horst, Rufus had spoken from the heart, whether Silvermane knew it or not.

"There isn't a wolf among you, I think, who hasn't procured a little extra imperium to stay alive," Rufus had claimed, staring at the Elders dressed in various hues, blue Eisbrands, yellow Greystones, red Bloodfangs and more, all spread in a splendid arcing rainbow of judgement before little Rufus. "We've all done it; begged and borrowed from wolves younger or stronger than us to stave off the pain. They were my friends, who gave it up freely. I did not steal it!"

"You dare accuse *us* of misappropriation?" Horst had growled. "Have you no shame?"

"It doesn't have to be this way!" Rufus had interrupted. "If a cure could be found the cycle of pain would end. Being a Howler could at least become a choice! If you could just… just let me go on my expedition, I would give my life to search. I would not return without answers-"

"By Ulf's fangs, *still* you persist with this nonsense when your life hangs by a thread!" Horst had exploded, standing up and thumping the tabletop. "You stand accused of misappropriation, of embezzlement and of inciting hatred and discord! Your 'expedition' is as far from our consideration as the moon, sir!"

"Horst!" Silvermane had barked, adding quietly. "We're the representatives of ALPHA at this table. Control yourself before our peers."

And so forth.

Some of the fabricated charges were unbearable, that Rufus had skimmed off white-imperium and sold it on the black market, and worse, that he had procured it from malleable, naive young Howlers by flattery and blackmail, that Linus, Ivan and Uther were just the latest victims in a string of exploitation going back a decade. Like the most convincing lies it was half-true, as well Silvermane knew. The gossip and hearsay swirling around Rufus and his betas was public knowledge, almost fact, thus the charges would slip down the throats of the average little beast, Howler, and, perhaps most importantly for the ruse to work, hyena alike. Lupa's contentious champion of equality, of the rights of the hyenas, of the literati, had fallen because of his own desires and vanity, because of his weaknesses.

It was unpalatable, but believable.

The train slowed, brakes whining, straining to bring the great hulk under control. Bright light invaded the carriage through the bars above. They had reached the Lupan Wall.

The sound of activity was quick to follow, of the Watchers barking orders and carriage doors sliding open. The train was being inspected, its cargo turned over and convicts examined, lest the smuggling of imperium or some other commodity was afoot.

With light streaming into the carriage, Rufus could see his fellow inmates for the first time, at least with his eyes rather than their soul. A motley mix of beasts who had fallen foul of the law, a rat, a rabbit, an otter, their auras almost imperceptible, even to Rufus.

Then there was the one beast who had been bothering Rufus this last hour, the overbearing corona that had been jostling with his in this claustrophobic space – a hyena, a stocky, spotty hyena, replete with muscle.

A Chakaa and no mistake. Was it the one from the refinery? The one bitten by the centipede?

Before Rufus could ask, the carriage door rumbled open and light rolled in from the expensive white-imperium crystal flood lamps high overhead. Two cloaked wolfen silhouettes appeared, not ALPHA Prefects this time, nor Howlers, but Watchers – the wolves that not only policed the Lupan Wall and the adjoining Wall Slums, but the Ashfall beyond.

Unlike the great pile of Lupa itself, where the boundaries between packs could be a confounding jigsaw, the hinterlands beyond were sliced like a pie, with each pack's holdings extending outwards from their section of the Lupan Wall, their influence waning with every mile, until only the Lupan Laws remained remotely enforceable, if any laws at all.

However, Rufus had no idea what pack's territory the train was passing through on its way out of the city, nor how rough this stop might be, therefore.

"Up, up!" one of the Watchers shouted whilst climbing aboard. "Get up you miserable maggots! Come on!"

The prisoners stood, Rufus included, clad in nothing but the now tatty breeches he had been wearing under his armour the day he had been arrested. He hoped Janoah had put his Howler gear in a safe place until his return, otherwise they might melt it down and extract the imperium for profit.

A second Watcher climbed aboard with a sizeable red ant on a leash. The eager insect scuttled amongst the prisoners, frantically, yet gently, brushing them with its sensitive antennae. The rat cringed and whined in alarm as the insect frisked him – it was big enough to snip him in half with its jagged maws if it so chose.

But this was a sniffer-ant, raised from a stolen egg and trained to find smuggled goods, especially venom. It was unlikely that anything would be smuggled out of Lupa on a carriage of filthy prisoners headed for Gelb, but there was nothing new under the sun.

Satisfied the rat was hiding nothing, the ant climbed up the carriage wall and across the ceiling, antennae waving wildly, coming down beside to Rufus and checking him out in turn.

The Howler chuckled as the ant tickled him with its baton-like antennae, doubtless finding his fiery, imperium-laden blood especially fascinating.

"Hello there, girl," said Rufus, fearlessly stroking the insect's smooth, rock-hard brow. The ant's frenzied appendages explored his forearm, feeling his ruddy fur, gaining all sorts of secret information.

"Hey!" barked the Watcher holding the ant's leash. "What you doing?" he asked in a soft, Great Steppes accent.

Rufus looked at the wolf, past his obscuring helmet, into his imperious aquamarine eyes that shone almost as brightly as his brooch. "Just saying hello, dear boy," he said to the obvious youth, taking note of the red-imperium fangs on his helmet's cheeks – so this was Bloodfang territory. Good. "That's a lovely great ant you've got there," he added. "What's her name?"

The Watcher stared a while. "He is Scuttle," he said, in a vain attempt at correct Lupan.

"Scuttle?" Rufus woofed in amusement. He scratched an eyebrow and sniffed, "Well, I suppose that's passably genderless."

The Watcher came over worried, "What you mean, genderless?"

"Nearly all ants are girls, my good Watcher, including uh… 'Scuttle' here."

The youngster emitted a little dry laugh, "You joke, yes?"

"No, it's quite true, I assure you. I'm… something of an expert on these matters."

The Watcher tipped his head back a little, "Oh."

The other Watcher approached, evidently older, evidently stronger, and not interested in the gender of Scuttle, or any other ant for that matter. Brushing his callow compatriot aside he thumped Rufus in the gut with a truncheon and shoved him to the floor.

"Shut up, filth! No talking!"

Rufus resisted the urge to spring up and blow this fellow across the carriage for his lack of decorum only by telling himself that getting executed for striking a Watcher wasn't part of

ALPHA's plan. He had to get to Gelb alive.

"What's wrong with you, Tomek?" the older Watcher growled at the younger. "Just get on with it!"

"Yes, Captain. Sorry."

Scuttle and her master, Watcher Tomek, resumed their inspection, giving every beast in the carriage the once-over, whilst Rufus lay recovering.

The unfriendly Watcher Captain threw the downed Howler a funny look, perhaps sensing his imperious fire, or even recognising him as that famous troublemaker Rufus – at least Rufus flattered himself by imagining either was the cause, or both. Regardless, the Watcher didn't linger and vacated the carriage. One prisoner was much like another, Rufus supposed, as he sat against the carriage wall; even fallen Grand Howlers must roll through here on their way to the mines with disturbing regularity.

Tomek and Scuttle scrutinised the stocky hyena last; the Chakaa smiled menacingly.

"Come on, Usenko, they're clean," the Watcher Captain growled, beckoning to Tomek.

"Sir," Tomek Usenko acknowledged.

Pulling Scuttle after him, the young Watcher gave Rufus a sideways glance in passing, before averting his eyes to the floor, perhaps frightened that he might incur his superior's wrath a second time.

The wrath came from elsewhere.

In a split second, faster than Rufus could fathom, the Chakaa hyena at the back of the carriage dashed forth and locked a mighty arm around Tomek's throat.

"Gaaagh!" the Watcher howled.

Wordlessly, brutally, the hyena slammed his second paw into the Watcher's cloaked back. With a loud and blinding explosion of imperious fire the wolf was blasted forth and ejected tail over head from the carriage, landing heavily on the pebbly ground outside, a crumpled, smoking heap of mantle and armour.

Shaking his smouldering paw, the hyena laughed as hyenas were wont to do. He glared triumphantly at Rufus, his unnaturally bright violet eyes alight with fire.

"Want some, Howler?" he woofed, brandishing a fist.

Rufus remained silent and seated.

"Usenko?" the older Watcher yelped. "Tomek, lad!"

Scuttle rushed past on her six segmented legs to be at her fallen master's side. The red ant felt Tomek with her antennae like a mother frantic over his condition, as if she could feel concern, this mere bug.

Blowing a whistle and leaping into the carriage, the grizzled Watcher Captain whipped out his sword and snarled at the grinning hyena, "Bastard! They'll stake you out in the wastes for that, I'll see to it myself! You're ant-food!"

"Come on, wolf," the hyena beckoned cockily, big paws spread wide, his mere life of no concern to him. Like any hyena warrior he wanted to die in battle, Rufus knew, not rot down a mine. That's what this was about. It was this fellow's last chance to die with a modicum of hyena dignity.

Whilst the other frightened prisoners ducked into corners of the carriage, the Watcher Captain slashed at the hyena. For all his obvious strength, the stocky Chakaa was nimble enough to whip his body back, dodging the initial slash and the follow-up thrust. Grabbing the wolf's sword arm he pulled him round, punched him in the side of his helmeted head and swung him deeper into the carriage, relieving him of his sword in the process.

The hyena twirled the dazed Watcher's imperium sword and beckoned him a second time.

Not bad, Rufus thought.

The growling Watcher drew his imperium pistol, took aim at the prisoner and pulled the trigger. The fearless hyena bared his mighty chest, ready to receive the pellet and death.

Fssss!

A dud charge!

"Grrrfgh!" the hyena huffed, disappointed that he wasn't walking amongst the ancestors by now, and that this fellow wasn't skilful enough to send him on his way. He could send the wolf on *his* way, though, and stepped forth with a mind to do just that.

Crack!

The hyena, indeed everyone, flinched as a pellet ricocheted around the carriage, leaving a colourful trail of sparks. The shot came from behind, from the door and Watcher Tomek.

"Cease and desist… in name of Republic Lupi!" he wheezed, stepping aboard, sword drawn, pistol in paw. Had he missed by accident, or fired a warning shot?

Either way, the hyena whirled on the next wolfen challenger with abandon. Whipping his arm through the air and clashing his stolen sword with Tomek's, he all but knocked the breathless youth off his feet. The hyena was going to kill him.

No, Rufus decided, that won't do at all.

In a flash, the Howler leapt to his feet and slapped a ruddy paw against the hyena's immense spotty back, just as the hyena had done to Tomek

Pfzaack!

"Oaaagh!"

And in much the same fashion, he too was ejected from the carriage amidst an even more spectacular plasmatic explosion, flying past Tomek and rolling in the dust and pebbles.

Rufus slowly lowered his throbbing, steaming right paw.

"You all right?" he asked Tomek.

"Yes," Tomek gasped at length. "Thank you."

Within seconds reinforcements arrived from all over the facility and half a dozen Watchers piled on the smouldering hyena as he tried to rise. They quickly restrained the snarling beast, tying his paws with wire and giving him a good kicking, until he was subdued.

Rufus was next. Three of the helmet-clad, cloaked Watchers clambered aboard the carriage and singled him out from the other cowering prisoners, grabbing his arms and forcing him against the wall.

"Wait! He help me!" Tomek explained. He turned to his superior for support, "Captain, this prisoner, he help me."

At length the older Watcher sniffed, "Carry on, lads."

"But, sir-"

"He's a troublemaker, Tomek! I can see it in his eyes. Best to finish him off quick, not send him to Gelb. It's a kindness, believe me."

"You not do that. Is not right!"

"We'll shoot him, lad. Firing squad. He'll have a soldier's death. Not like the hyena. It's for the best."

'Schmutz,' Rufus thought, as his paws were tied, 'I've gone and done it now.'

One of the bigger Watchers grabbed him by the scruff of the neck and roughly marched him from the carriage, down onto the pebbled ground outside. The white-imperium crystal floodlights were blinding and Rufus could make out nothing of the compound around him save the looming shadow of the Lupan Wall, gateway to the Ashfall and the wider world beyond Lupa – a world Rufus was never to see again, by the looks.

'No, I've got to say something,' he thought, 'I can't go out like this.'

"Tomek!" he shouted, twisting free of his escort and running over to the surprised youth. "Tomek, get on the phone and call ALPHA," he growled. "Ask for Prefect Janoah, or Silvermane, tell them what's happening. Tell them it's Rufus."

"What?"

"Just do it, please! I'm a Bloodfang like you. Help me. You owe me that much!"

Before Tomek could so much as nod, the Watchers fell upon Rufus and dragged him away.

"Please hurry!" he cried.

✦

Brrrrriiing! Brrrrriiing! Brrrrriiing!

With a growl of annoyance, Amael Balbus finally rolled over in bed and snatched the phone. "Yes?" he grunted. "By Ulf's fang's, Boris, it's three in the morning!" he complained, blinking at his ornate alarm clock, its glowing imperium-infused arms and numerals lighting up his grizzled, grey-furred face. "Rufus?" he growled. "What do you mean? Just put her through."

There was a click as Boris switched over.

"Jan?"

"Amael, they're going to kill him!" the phone crackled.

"What're you talking about?" Amael growled. "Who's going to kill who?"

"The Watchers. I don't know the details; it was something about a fight. They pulled Rufus and a hyena out of a carriage when they stopped at the Lupan Wall." A moment's pause, before Janoah shrieked, *"Are you listening to what I'm saying? You have to stop them!"*

Amael woofed back, "Are you insane? I can't!"

"Of course you can!"

"For Ulf's sake, wolfess, be reasonable!"

"Reasonable? Reasonable!"

"Think!" Amael explained. "How would it look if I interfered on Rufus's behalf? I can't sully my reputation defending a condemned beast, let alone poke my nose into the affairs of the Elder Watcher. It'd be an insult. I need the Elder Watcher's vote as much as anyone's."

"I see," Janoah said, in her calmest and yet most venomous tone. *"And do you think Ivan and Uther will still help you after this? It's Rufus they're fighting for, not you."*

"They'll not know he's dead until it's too late," Amael said, matter-of-factly.

"Yes, but they'll find out you let Rufus die eventually. Then no force on Erde will stop Ivan killing you in your sleep, you can be sure of that."

Amael gulped.

Janoah offered a solution, *"Send Vladimir."*

"What?"

"Send him down there to stop the Watchers," Janoah explained, the answer formulating in her mind even as she spoke it. *"The death warrant has to be signed, that won't happen until the Elder Watcher gets up. You can deny you had any involvement and say that Vladimir acted out of his own regard for Rufus – he's known as being sympathetic on account of their shared beliefs, it'll stick. You can grovel to the Elder Watcher later."* With a sharp breath Janoah added, *"Does that satisfy you?"*

Amael thought it over, scrutinising that voice for some sign of malignancy, some trick.

The malignancy was there sure enough.

"If you allow this to happen I will wash my paws of you, Amael Balbus-"

"All right!" the Elder snapped. "All right, if he matters *so* much. By Ulf you'd think he was the perfect husband the way you carry on. Ridiculous wolfess."

Switching away from his lover and councillor, Amael returned to Boris's line. "Boris!" he grunted. "Put me through to Vladimir. Yes, I know he's in bed, go wake him yourself if you have to!"

⁕

As dawn's light turned the polluted sky gold, Rufus, his paws still bound behind him, was taken from a cell and led into a grim, bricked courtyard by the very Watcher who had kindly decided he might as well die quickly by imperium pellets than worked to death – he had a point, honestly.

It can only have been an hour or so since the ruckus in the carriage, just long enough for the warrant to be prepared and signed by the Elder Watcher. Not for the hyena, mind, no warrant was needed for lesser races, but for a wolf, even a condemned one, there were protocols to follow, however perfunctory. The Elder Watcher had probably signed Rufus out of existence over a fine cooked breakfast without a second thought, him and many others besides.

Rufus was pushed against a wooden stake and tied up. He was surprised to be joined by the hyena, who was dragged past and set up against the next stake along, his fur matted with blood. It appeared the Watchers had settled for giving him a sound beating and then shooting him. Rufus liked to think someone around here had been merciful, but staking a hyena out in the Ashfall for imperium-fuelled bugs to find and devour was probably too much effort.

The executioners filed in, ten Watchers armed with imperium rifles – one of them was Tomek.

The lad had probably shot quite a few prisoners, Rufus supposed.

"Blindfold?" gruffed the Watcher Captain, offering it to Rufus.

Rufus gulped, "I'd rather not."

"As you will."

"Could you perhaps spare an ember?"

The Watcher waited a moment, mulling over the request. In the end he couldn't deny the last wish of a fellow wolf and produced a silver case from his cloak.

"Red, please," Rufus said.

"I ain't got any reds left. I got orange."

"Oh bother. Couldn't go find a red one, could you? Strawberry's my favourite."

The Watcher simply broke out the orange ember and twiddled it in front of Rufus. "Take it or leave it, Howler."

Rufus nodded a little.

The Watcher snapped the ember and popped it between the condemned wolf's lips. Leaving him to puff nervously away, he walked over to the raw-looking hyena. For a moment, the watching Rufus foolishly thought the Watcher was actually going to offer the hyena a blindfold, an ember even.

"If only I could line up every scum-sucking hyena against this wall and shoot 'em," the Watcher growled instead.

The bound hyena's bloody nostrils flared, but he said nothing, choosing only to stare at the Watcher until the wolf blinked and looked away with a huffy snort.

A noble riposte, Rufus thought.

The Watcher walked across the courtyard towards his wolves. "Let's get this over with," he said, raising a paw. "Fire on my mark."

As the Watchers raised their rifles, Tomek included, so Rufus raised his ruddy face to the sky. He breathed deep, trying to prepare himself. The hyena stared ahead, fearless as ever, confident as to where he was headed after this final trial, across the Eternal Plains to meet the Ancestors.

"Hold it," the Watcher Captain said, stepping forward. "Lower your rifles! Lower 'em!'"

Baffled, Rufus looked about. The Watchers were all saluting smartly, including their captain.

Out of left field marched two impressive wolves, one clearly the Elder Watcher of the Bloodfang share of the Ashfall, looking as resplendent in his cloak as any other Elder from the inner city districts, but with subtle additions to his uniform to set him apart, most notably some black beetle carapaces serving very nicely as shoulder pads. The suburban Watchers were a little closer to nature and its bounty than the city-dwelling Howlers and used, or abused, the wilds accordingly, even if those wilds were ravaged by ashen rain from the city.

Accompanying the Elder Watcher was a recognisably large and lofty Grand Howler.

"Vladimir?" Rufus gasped, his ember mercifully clinging to his lower lip by way of a little dried saliva despite his jaw dropping.

The Elder Watcher walked over to his subordinate. "Captain, return these prisoners to the train," he said simply, as Vladimir lingered behind.

"But sir, they assaulted us!" the Watcher Captain protested.

"I'm aware of that. However, Grand Howler Vladimir here informs me that this wolf is Rufus Valerio, a notorious scoundrel and traitor who has brought unbearable shame on our pack. He's not getting off so lightly. The hyena is a member of THORN and is also deserving of a proper fate. They will work off their debt in Gelb as they were sentenced to, is that clear?"

"Yes, sir."

Vladimir headed over to the bound Rufus, armour rattling, and cupping his paws before him said airily, "An admirable attempt, Rufus. However, you will be punished accordingly and serve your sentence in full. I came down here especially to make sure you get to Gelb alive, you and this THORN terrorist."

"Much obliged," Rufus grunted, trying to piece things together – had Jan done this, had she sent Vladimir?

Well done Tomek!

"Doubtless you were in league with each other," Vladimir proclaimed haughtily, looking between Rufus and the hyena as if they were naughty cubs. "What was your plan? Did one of you set out to cause a diversion so the other could escape, hmm? Or did you both agree to try and end it all quickly?" He walked over to the hyena, "We meet again Madou. Tell me THORN's plans. This is your last chance, Chakaa; save yourself from a lingering death down the mines."

Madou turned his face.

Whilst Vladimir sighed and shook his head, the Elder Watcher moved things along.

"Put these wretches on the next train to Gelb," he instructed. "Keep them away from the other prisoners and collar them so they can't channel the imperium; the hyena's a Chakaa."

The Watcher Captain saluted, "Yes, sir, we know. He blasted young Usenko right in the back, sir."

"Did he, by Ulf?" the Elder Watcher said, looking at Tomek. "How predictably dishonourable."

"Luckily our Tomek's a tough nut, sir."

"Glad to hear it, Captain."

On that note the Elder Watcher extended an arm from under his cloak, beckoning Vladimir away. "My wolves will take it from here, Grand Howler. Now, will you join me for some refreshments? I've a bottle of decade-aged Felician brandy waiting for such a distinguished guest."

Not even winking at Rufus, Vladimir took his leave. "I would be honoured, Elder Watcher," he said, walking with his host. "Though, I am far from distinguished."

"Nonsense! I'm a great admirer of your work, Oromov."

"Work, Elder?"

"Your botanical papers."

"Ah. Then I *am* honoured."

⁂

Back to the tracks, bundled into a carriage, the other prisoners removed to make way for the Howler and the THORN activist alone.

"Collar 'em!" barked the Watcher Captain.

Rufus was forced to kneel, his head pulled back. Unlike the nearby Madou he didn't spit or struggle, that would only make things worse.

In came a Watcher armed with what looked like a giant pair of mechanically-powered pliers with pipes trailing out the back of them.

"Hold still," the Watcher advised gruffly.

Slipping the monstrous pliers around Rufus's neck, the Watcher pressed a button with his thumb. Amidst a hiss of gas and pistons, the jaws snapped violently round the Howler's bobbing throat, making him yelp in alarm despite knowing what was about to happen. His world was instantly enveloped by a cloud of noxious ash as the perverse machine pressed home, venting waste imperium in all directions, choking Rufus like a mechanical murderer.

As quickly as it started, it was over. The vicious clamping mechanism was withdrawn, ripping out a carelessly-snared tuft of Rufus's neck-fur in the process. The pain of some fur being torn from his hide dampened the immediate sensation of being strangled. It was only afterwards Rufus perceived a tightness lingering around his neck.

He couldn't see it, nor reach up to feel it with his paws bound behind him, but he knew it was there – a wretched imperium-weave collar.

The Watcher with the clamp reloaded his dreadful contraption with a simple, broad metallic ribbon, threading it through the mechanism with disturbing deftness. The ribbon was dark grey, yet a subtle swirling rainbow of imperium played on its surface, like a film of oil on a polluted Lupan puddle.

Placing the clamp around the hyena's neck, the Watcher did his work. The clamp closed, somehow stopping short of choking the hyena to death despite him possessing a thicker neck than Rufus. Doubtless the clamp boasted some ingenious automatic breadth-measuring mechanism, designed by someone, sometime, somewhere, who likely never envisaged it being abused for such a cruel purpose. Amidst a pall of ash, the imperium-weave collar was instantly moulded and sealed into place. There was no buckle, no lock, not even a seam of weakness to exploit or pick at, just a perfect, faintly-coloured band pulled snug around the hyena's neck, like some beautiful adornment.

Gulping under his own newfangled collar for the umpteenth time already, Rufus noticed Tomek and his pet ant standing outside, at the fringes of the goings-on.

The Watchers released the prisoners and exited the carriage, save the Captain. "In case you scumbags don't know, those collars ain't just pretty necklaces," he said. "They're negative imperium coils. Any release of imperious energy will make them, well… I'll show you."

The Watcher Captain stepped over to the kneeling Rufus and raised a paw at him, fingers gnarled.

"There's really no need to demonstrate," Rufus insisted.

In response, perhaps, the Watcher spread his paw at the hyena instead. The big, spotty beast immediately gagged and fell about the floor, his back arched and legs kicking.

"Gaaaagh!"

"Stop it!" Rufus barked. "Have you no shame?"

The Watcher lowered his paw and allowed the hyena to collapse panting on the floor, only to whirl round and smack Rufus across the muzzle, knocking him on his side.

"Filthy hyena-lover!" the Watcher Captain spat. Stepping from the carriage he said to Tomek, "Lock 'em up, lad. We're done here."

"Yes, Captain."

Once his captain had departed, Tomek climbed aboard and went straight to Rufus.

"You all right?" he asked, crouching before him.

Rufus spat some blood from his mouth, "Never better, young wolf."

"I'm sorry."

"Sorry? You saved my life back there."

Tomek shook his helmeted head, "No. I call ALPHA on phone. I ask for Janoah. She said it none of her business that some criminal being executed, whoever it is. She tell me not to waste her time again, or else."

Rufus chuckled, "I knew I could depend on her."

"But-"

"You'd best get out of here. Go on, now."

Tomek hesitated a moment, then crouched behind Rufus and began untwisting his wire bonds.

"What're you doing?" Rufus seethed.

"Is long way to Gelb," Tomek explained, unwinding the cruel wire. "I cannot help with collar, but at least you can scratch itchy nose now."

Once he was free, Rufus instinctively reached for the broad collar clutching his throat. "Foolish chap… you could get in big trouble," he chided, sliding a finger under the smooth metal in a vain attempt to loosen it. "But… thank you, Tomek."

Standing up and throwing the wire away, Tomek shrugged it off, "Is all right."

Sitting with his back to the wall, Rufus looked Tomek over and said, "Could I ask one last favour before you go?"

The Watcher evaded committal with another shrug.

Rufus dared regardless, "Take your helmet off for me."

"My helmet? Why?"

"I like to remember the faces of my friends. Besides, it's just good manners, isn't it?"

"Is true," Tomek eventually admitted.

Checking over his shoulder, the Watcher unbuckled his helmet and deftly slipped it off, revealing a grey and white wolfen face capped by hefty, black brows that were knitted over what Rufus swore were a brilliant set of aquamarine eyes – quite a jumble, but somehow it worked.

Tomek spread his paws subtly, as if to say, 'Well?'

"I'll remember you, Tomek Usenko," Rufus assured.

With a retiring guffaw, Tomek donned his helmet and took his leave. Stepping out of the carriage he slowly ground the hefty metallic door shut, peering in at Rufus all the way, until the last crack of daylight was extinguished.

Rufus immediately collapsed on his back, paws to his face, and thanked Ulf he was still alive. That had been too close.

✦

Rocked to and fro by the swaying carriage, Madou drifted on the precipice of sleep despite the cold, hard floor and countless other discomforts. He was brought back from the brink of dreams by the pain of someone tugging at the wire bonds about his sore wrists.

The red wolf, Rufus?

Madou thought better than to question him. *Let the fool untie me if he wishes.*

As the wire fell away, Madou rolled over and scrabbled clear of his fellow prisoner with a defensive snarl.

Rufus remained kneeling, paws on thighs, like a sage.

"Sorry, you looked uncomfortable," he said, in a sandpapery tone acquired from years of smouldering. "It's a long way to Gelb."

Rubbing his bloodied wrists, Madou scoffed, "Why do you care, wolf?"

"You heard the Watchers; I'm a filthy 'hyena-lover'."

Madou said nothing as he crouched in the corner.

"It's not true, of course," Rufus defended, red paw to dark grey chest. "There's as many crooked hyenas as wolves or any other. I've just learnt to reserve judgement."

Again, Madou had nothing to say.

"I'm Rufus," his wolfen inmate said. "You're Madou, the hyena who got bitten by the centipede in the refinery a few weeks ago, right?"

Now Madou scowled, "What if I am?"

"Just curious."

"Well, I *am* Madou. You'd better remember it."

Rufus nodded. "I have rode the wind, seen forests far below, met great beasts and small," he said.

"What?" Madou snorted.

"I have rode the wind, seen forests far below, met great beasts and small," Rufus repeated, rolling a paw.

At length, the baffled Madou narrowed one violet, imperium-laden eye. "What's wrong with you?"

Letting his paw flop down, Rufus dipped his chin and actually chuckled, "Never mind."

"Are you mad?"

"It's nothing. Really."

It didn't sound like nothing to Madou, but he decided not to pursue the matter for fear of being mocked, favouring the plumping up of his injured pride instead. "You know, I should kill you for blasting me in the back," he spat, rubbing the metal band around his throat; it felt suddenly tighter. "I should snap your neck like a twig."

Rufus hummed, "How charming."

"I would be dead if not for you! I would be walking with my ancestors, with my family. Instead, you've doomed me to the mines!"

"Yes, well, sorry about all that, but I wasn't going to let you kill that cub."

Madou snorted, "What cub?"

"Tomek," Rufus replied. "He can only have been sixteen."

"That's no cub!"

"To my sensibilities it is. Now if I were you I'd watch that nasty temper or things will get uncomfortable."

"You're threatening me?" Madou laughed, flashing his mighty teeth in the darkness, "I could… could throttle you to death with one paw…. puny wolf!"

Madou was barely able to squeeze his words through his bobbing throat. *This collar feels tighter than ever! What's happening to me?*

"Grrrfgh!" he growled, grasping uselessly at the invisibly, yet perceptibly contracting band, his fingers unable to find a purchase beneath the metal pressed flush against his coarse hide.

"Gaaagh!"

Rufus watched Madou gag. "Your collar will be the only thing doing any throttling, I suspect," he huffed.

"Stop it!" Madou rasped back. "Please!"

"It's not me, it's you, you daft beast!" Rufus explained sternly, yet maintaining impeccable calm, paws on knees. "The collar is sensitive to your imperious field. Don't panic. Just stay still and keep your fires dampened and it'll loosen its grip. Trust me, I know from experience."

Slowly, and whether he dampened his fires or not, Madou felt the collar widen a fraction. "Wolfen... barbarity," he gasped, sitting back, chest heaving.

"You're half right," Rufus observed. "Collars are used beyond the Republic, there's nothing wolfen about it, though it is a barbaric practice, I'll give you that."

Madou cleared his throat, but nothing more.

Disturbed only by the carriage wheels thumping over joins in the rails with clockwork regularity, Rufus and Madou stared at one another, took each other all in. The hyena had thirty pounds on the wolf, but there was no denying Rufus's strength, least of all on the inside.

"You hit hard... for a wolf," Madou admitted, allowing a smirk. "I've heard you're a very powerful Howler. They call you Red-mist."

"Yes. My apologies if I hurt you."

"It's good. It let's me know I'm still alive."

"Oh? And I thought you wanted to die."

"In battle," Madou clarified, looking down. "Not here... or down some hole," he added, with a gulp. "Are the mines as bad as they say?"

"I wouldn't know," Rufus said simply.

Madou nodded, then began afresh, "You knew Prince Noss of the Four Winds, didn't you? He was your friend."

"Who told you that?"

"Nur...." Madou began, before cutting himself short.

"Nurka?" Rufus guessed.

Madou dipped his chin. "By the Wind," he groaned, cupping his face in his paws. "That bastard Vladimir. He and the Bloodfangs... they... they spent *days* torturing me, trying to make me talk. I... I didn't even acknowledge Nurka's name for days, yet you've teased it out of me already."

"Honey attracts more bees than vinegar," Rufus said, "I'm much sweeter than wily old Vladimir; handsomer too."

Madou laughed falsely, "I suppose it doesn't really matter now, not where I'm going."

Rufus moved on. "Since you asked, Prince Noss was sent to me to be trained as a Howler. He was a good friend," he sighed. "That is, before he tried to murder me."

"That's not true!" Madou snapped.

"Pardon?"

"Prince Noss didn't try and murder you, Howler."

"I've the scars to prove it."

Madou squirmed, "What I meant is he was *forced* to do it, tricked by your own kind!"

"If by forced you mean bribed, then yes-"

"You don't understand!" Madou spluttered, shaking a fist at Rufus. "The Howlers, they held my Prince's tribe in the palm of their paws. If he didn't comply, they'd have killed us all. It was all a filthy wolfen trick, an attempt to blacken our race and turn... turn sympathisers like you... against us!"

Madou clenched his teeth and grasped at his collar as it tightened mercilessly.

"Grrrrfgh!"

"Calm down," Rufus advised. "There's no need to shout. I believe you."

The hyena nodded and gasped.

Whilst Madou rasped for air, Rufus hummed calmly, "It hardly matters. Noss's attempt on my life didn't change my views in the slightest."

"Then you still support our cause?"

"In as much as I believe hyenas, and all other races, should be made wolfkind's equals, yes," Rufus clarified guardedly.

"All races?" Madou said.

"Yes. That is the impartialist stance."

"Even... even the little beasts?"

"And why not?"

Madou snorted in obvious derision, but didn't, or couldn't, mount an argument.

Rufus moved on. "In any case, one can't change Lupa by planting a few bombs and causing mischief," he dismissed. "THORN is just making the situation worse, for the hyenas *and* the little beasts."

"We've tried peaceful means!" Madou protested. "We are ignored!"

"I'm not talking peace."

"But you just said-"

"THORN thinks too small," Rufus explained. "The only way to bring about real change would be to overturn the current government and set up a new regime headed by progressive beasts."

"Beasts like you?" Madou said, strangely expectant.

"I'm flattered," the Howler hummed, amused at the thought. "Ah... but it'll never happen."

Madou looked sideways, then back again, "Why not?"

"You'd have to eliminate every single Den Father in one sitting for a start."

A pause.

Madou threw it out there. "What if someone were to plant a black-imperium bomb?"

"You mean like THORN plans to?" Rufus replied wryly. "That probably won't work, you know."

"Why not?" Madou growled indignantly.

The imperiologist emerged, "Because black-imperium is very dense; it's the densest substance known to beast."

"So?"

"So, any vapour cloud from such a bomb would sink to the ground, not billow across the whole city."

"What about the Ashfall? That's spread miles!"

"The Ashfall? It's taken centuries for that to get as bad as it has. Ash is fluffy and carries much further alright, but there's not much black-imperium in it; if there was we'd all be dead! More than poison plants, the Ashfall physically smothers them. And when they die there's no roots to hold the soil together, so you get soil erosion, making farming impossible. That's the real trouble."

Madou sat forward, "But... but in an enclosed space, like the Pack Summit, the black-imperium would be trapped and-"

"My dear hyena," Rufus woofed, "the Hummel Den where the Summit's being held this year is enormous! Enclosed indeed, it has halls loftier than opera houses. You'll get some I dare say, but the Den Guard will have ample time to whisk the Den Fathers to safety the moment any funny cloud rolls in. Anyway, the fact THORN is stealing black-imperium makes it obvious what you're up to and the Howlers will be ready for it. You won't sneak anything past them, and a front-on attack will never get near the Den Fathers. It's quite foolish."

Rufus was perhaps only reassuring himself.

After a pugnacious staring match, Madou suddenly looked away and clumsily changed subject by rubbing his huge, spotty arms and complaining, "It's cold."

"I didn't mean to burst your bubble-"

"Nurka will find a way!" Madou snapped. "He'll find a way to change things. You'll see, wolf! You'll see."

Silence.

"Well we needn't fall out over it," Rufus said, settling down for the night. "Where we're going none of this is going to matter."

✦

"Well?" a female barked – Janoah perhaps, Werner couldn't be sure.

"He's all right," replied a dulcet male voice – Vladimir of course, it was the phone line to his office that had been tapped after all. "Though by the time I got there," he went on, "Rufus was tied to a stake. A minute later he'd have been shot."

"By Ulf's fangs! I've been worried sick all night. Why didn't you call me sooner?"

Yes, definitely Janoah.

Pressing the earpiece closer to his head to overcome the hiss of white noise, Werner stopped chewing on a sandwich long enough to listen carefully.

"Sorry," Vladimir excused, "I was invited for a drink, which escalated to dinner. I couldn't get away. The Elder Watcher gets desperately lonely out there on the fringes of society. Pathetic really."

The chink of glass and bubbling liquid indicated Janoah was pouring herself a stiff drink. "Rufus only has to hold out a few months until Amael makes his move," she said, "but I know Gelb is no picnic and he's not getting any younger-"

"Don't worry. The Warden will want to keep him alive. Good miners help Gelb turn a profit."

"Since when can Rufus mine?"

"Trust me, with his corona he'll be a natural. Noss is still alive, last time I checked. Why'd you think I hid the treacherous scum there? I knew he'd thrive. We may yet need him to mould Amael to our ends after the dust settles. If we have Noss, we have the hyenas, and the tribes will do anything for him, even go to war with Amael. We can threaten him."

"Clever Vladimir," Janoah purred.

"Look, we shouldn't talk over the phone," Vladimir suddenly grumbled, shuffling in his seat, perhaps leaning closer to the phone or looking over his cloaked shoulder, it was hard to say. "It could be dangerous."

Werner chuckled.

At length, Janoah said, "I'll be in touch."

Click!

Scribbling a few notes, Werner set down the earpiece and turned off the lamp. The cramped, closet-sized space was cast into utter darkness, except for a tiny pinprick of light beaming from a hole in the wall. With a peek through said hole to check his office was deserted, Werner quickly slid the wall aside and squeezed his substantial pink girth through, before sliding the bookcase on the other side into place with a firm click.

His secret room remaining thus, the Politzi Chief grabbed his telephone and dialled a memorised number. He let it ring three times, then hung up.

Seconds later, Werner's phone rang.

"What?" someone urged immediately.

"I got news for our friends," Werner whispered.

"What news?"

"Meet me in the usual place, usual cash."

"I thought you were with us now?" they snarled. "That's what they said."

"I am, I am!"

"And still you want payment, you greedy, fat hog-"

"On my salary? You bet I do! You can afford it, Tristan, you Eisbrands are rolling in-"

"Shut up! Don't use my name, you idiot."

Werner went silent, but for a smack of the lips.

"Fine, fine," came his contact, with a growl, "but this had better be worth it."

Underlining 'Noss' on his notes, Werner said, "Oh it is, mate."

Hanging up the phone, the big hog grabbed his red Politzi hat and headed out. "Popping to the Common Ground, Borce," he told the rabbit, as they passed in the Den's corridors. "Hold the fort for me."

"Will do, sir," Borce confirmed. "What're you going there for, sir?" he asked, adding as Werner whirled on him, "In case Vladimir asks."

Werner beamed, "Just following a lead, lad."

Adam Browne

Part III
GELB

Adam Browne

DIARY EXCERPT 2

It's been a while, but I should write. The trouble is not much is happening around here. Uther and Ivan have been away for nearly two months now, and Rufus remains in Gelb despite several formal protests by Thorvald. I still can't believe he's gone.

Riddle's horribly quiet without them, especially Uther, at least for me. I've been keeping myself to myself, mostly frequenting the gym and going to see Sara over in Arkady during my spare time. I've kept an eye on Lorna and Rosa too; Uther would want that. My actual rounds have been dull and uneventful. I think my run-in with that giant centipede has spoilt me! Still, I shouldn't complain.

Vladimir hasn't forced me to take on a temporary partner yet, for which I'm grateful. I do not want to get involved with another wolf when Uther is due back any day. I feel I'm not taking liberties, since Ivan has remained a lone wolf for months since Rufus's promotion to Grand Howler and now imprisonment. So indeed has Vladimir remained alone, Rufus being his fellow Grand Howler. He has been running Riddle by himself; nominally Boris has been acting as a temporary Grand Howler, but he's rarely seen, Elder Amael even less.

Riddle feels strangely depleted of authority, but Elder Amael rightly refuses to move anyone up to fill the vacancies because all the missing wolves are expected to return; Ivan, Uther, even Rufus, if the charges against him can be quashed at the Summit. There will shortly be an influx of newcomers when the next class of Cubs graduate into Howlers, and Ivan will be assigned a new partner on his return whether he likes it or not, or so I'm told. I myself will be expected to 'show the youngsters the ropes', Vladimir says.

Strange. I've only been a Howler myself a year. Seems longer somehow.

Got another monobike lesson this morning, then I'm off to see Sara again. We're going to the Science Exhibition to have a look at the latest in imperium technology. Sara says Monty and Penny Buttle will be flying there today. Exciting!

Howler Linus Bloodfang Mills

Chapter 25

"All right, now twist the accelerator. Gently, gently! That's it. Good, very good."

The *Springtail's* engine thrummed between Linus's armoured legs as he weaved between the bollards. The glowing imperium gyroscope nestled within the wheel shifted to and fro, right, left, right, its hefty presence butting against Linus's corona as he battled to control it in ways unknowable to those untouched by the wonder mineral.

"Keep your speed up!" his instructor growled over his shoulder, as Linus reached the last bollard. "Not too slow, or you'll just turn on the spot!"

"Yes, sir!"

"Steady, steady. That's it, Mills. Nice!"

Striding across the sunny, if chilly grounds of Riddle Den, Vladimir watched Linus guide his standard-issue grey and black Bloodfang-livery monobike gently round the final bollard and back the way he'd come, weaving through the course with aplomb.

Immediately he finished, Linus panicked and slammed a gaitered boot down, mistrusting the machine to stay upright of its own volition even at rest, though it should and did, as Linus's instructor pointed out.

"Trust your machine, lad. Giacomo Valerio make the best monos in the world, even the little *Springtail;* reliable as the rising sun she is. As long as her gyroscope is spinning she'll stay up until Wintertide, it's only bad riders that make 'em topple."

Linus nodded his helmeted head, "I-I-I know. I do. I just couldn't help fighting it."

"It'll come to yer. You're doing really well."

Patting his pupils shoulder, Linus's instructor climbed off the bike, whereupon he noticed Vladimir's approach and saluted, fist to red-cloaked chest. "Grand Howler."

Shutting his mono down and kicking out the stand, Linus threw his stout legs off the seat and did the same.

"Grand Howler Vladimir."

"At ease gentlebeasts," Vladimir said, turning immediately to Linus, paws cupped before him. "Impressive riding for a learner, Howler Mills."

"Thank you, sir."

"Mills is a natural, Grand Howler," said the instructor.

"Is he indeed?"

"Haven't had a pupil tame a bike this fast since Uther."

Vladimir emitted one of those high-pitched hums that indicated how impressed he was, or at least how impressed he wanted others to think he was, whatever his private thoughts.

"I hate to interrupt your lesson, Linus, but I need to borrow you a minute," he said.

"By all means, sir," Linus's instructor answered in his stead. "We're done for today anyway. Not much more I can teach the lad at present, he's just got to practise. You know how it is."

The lofty Vladimir ushered the stocky Linus away, walking him slowly towards the Den's gaping garage, with all its bikes and cars lined up.

Checking over his shoulder, Linus cleared his throat and asked, "If I may, sir, have you heard anything about Uther and Ivan?"

"No."

"But it's been two months. Uther told me he'd be back by now."

Vladimir shrugged, "He had to tell you something, I suppose." He glanced up at the towering Den, "I myself will be going away shortly; Amael requires me to accompany him to the Pack Summit. He's leaving Boris in charge of Riddle."

"To your honour, sir," Linus said.

"Yes," Vladimir huffed, looking down at young Mills. "You do realise it's Hummel's turn to host this year?"

"I do, sir."

"Humph. Getting to Hummelton is going to be a logistical nightmare. Every Den Father is going, of course, each taking their own train packed with a retinue of Elders, Den Guards and Howlers, not to mention dignitaries, the press and Ulf knows who else. The security arrangements alone are going to be ridiculous! Worse, Lupa will be left depleted of authority at this most dangerous time. Can you imagine the opportunity this presents to enemies of the Republic, to THORN?"

"I can, sir."

"Much as I relish leaving Lupa for a while it's a daunting proposition. I'll need a good Howler to act as my second, someone who shan't embarrass me in front of wolves from other packs, or Amael for that matter."

"Yes, sir."

Vladimir stopped walking, "What do you say, Linus?"

"Me?" the youth squeaked at length, stopping too.

"Well yes. Why do you think we're having this conversation?"

Linus couldn't articulate a reply, "But… but…."

"You refuse?" Vladimir assumed.

"N-nnn-no, sir, how could I?" Linus stammered. "But surely there must be others more suited to-"

"Ordinarily I would take Ivan," Vladimir explained, cutting Linus's predictable sentence short. "However, since he's away, you'll have to do. You're quiet and passably intelligent; I wouldn't drag the like of Uther around."

"Sir."

"You accept then?"

"Yes, sir. A-a-absolutely! I'm honoured. I've longed to travel beyond the Ashfall again."

"Again?" Vladimir said with intrigue. "When did you last go?"

"Oh, n-nnn-not since I was a cub. I'm a Rostsonner, sir, south of the canyon, originally."

"Yes, I know. You must've been very young when you came to Lupa, you've no accent left at all."

Since Vladimir cared to know, Linus enlightened him. "I was about three or four, sir. My father contracted the rot and had to become a Howler, so I had to go to the city with him."

"And your mother?"

Linus's blue eyes squinted into the far distance, looking through Vladimir and time, "She died of the rot before my father even contracted it himself, sir. I hardly remember her, save for the day she died in her bed back in Rostsonne."

Vladimir nodded sagely, asking, "How is it your family was blighted by the rot when you lived down there? I thought Rostsonne was a clean, if naturally unforgiving country."

"My home town was mysteriously blighted, sir. It wasn't just us. I can remember many beasts dying, and the crops too. Everything."

"Strange. An imperium plume, perhaps?"

Linus spread his paws, "Father had his theories, but one of the reasons I wanted to study imperiology and the natural world was to try and find out what happened to my town." He dipped his chin, the enthusiasm dampened, "Of course… that's been put on hold somewhat."

Vladimir grunted, "I know the feeling."

Linus wondered what the Grand Howler's story was; everyone had one, even stuffy old Vladimir.

"I'm sure you'll make a fine adjutant," Vladimir declared, cheering the mood. He parted company with Linus, informing him that, "Make your arrangements. We leave in a week."

✦

Chiirrrrruup!
Chiirrrrruup!
Chiirrrrruup!

"What the thump's that?" Uther whispered, ears and eyes swivelling, searching the darkness beyond the campfire.

"Sand cricket," Ivan said simply, stirring the simmering broth hanging over the crackling campfire. "They're mostly harmless."

Uther turned to him, "Mostly? Whatcha mean mostly?"

"If you don't bother it, it won't bother you," Ivan explained. "It's just calling for a mate. If you come at it from behind it can deal a nasty kick with its back legs. Keep that in mind if you have to hunt one to eat one day."

Pulling his cloak a little tighter around himself this chilly night, Uther said, "Sure, whatever."

Chiirrrrruup!

Chiirrrrruup!

Chiirrrrruup!

The Howler covered his ears, "Oh, how are we gonna sleep with that thing sounding off?"

"You get used to it," Ivan said.

"Puh! Oh yeah?"

Chiirrrrruup!

"Shut up!" Uther barked at the anonymous night, his gruff voice echoing across the desert.

Silence.

"Aye, that's more like it-"

Chiirrrrruup!

Cupping his white face in his dark paws, Uther grumbled, "It's been so quiet up 'til now."

Ivan sipped the steaming broth, "It's spring. Life is returning to the land, even the Ashfall. You wait until we get to Everdor; you won't know where to lay your head at night for bugs."

"Can't wait, mate."

Ivan allowed a rare chuckle. It would be easy to make fun of his comrade, but Blade-dancer was bigger than that. It wasn't the 'Wild-heart's' fault that, despite his bogus epithet, he was a Lupan born and bred. He couldn't tell a cricket from a grasshopper. The sword cut both ways; bright-eyed, healthy folk coming to Lupa from Everdor, Rostsonne, or even the tough Steppes to study or work were all too often eaten alive by the rapacious city, falling into a spiral of imperium-fuelled crime and poverty, often ending in the rot or Gelb.

"Do you reckon Rufus is all right?"

Ivan's pure white ears pricked at Uther's question, more out of surprise that Wild-heart should be seen to care than anything. Ivan nearly expressed just that sentiment, but refrained from stirring up ill-feelings.

"He's stronger than either of us," he replied tactfully.

Uther nodded a little and cleared his throat, perhaps embarrassed he had let slip any feelings for the wolf who had pulled him from the gutter.

Staying his tongue on the matter, Ivan ladled some broth into a wooden bowl and passed it across to Uther.

"Oh, ta," Wild-heart said, rubbing his thighs in great expectation and not caring to ask what Ivan's stew consisted of; after walking all day he was too famished to care.

Ivan watched Uther blow on his spoon before supping the broth. That white, mask-like face of his screwed up as he assessed the flavour.

At length he admitted, "It's good."

"Mushroom and potato," Ivan told him, without pride.

Nodding, Uther stirred the thick mixture and let some dribble off his spoon, "It's got real body to it."

"That's the potato. We wolves might be able to walk forever and a day, but even we can't march twelve-hundred miles on gruel."

"Yeah, nah!"

The Howlers would have liked to ride straight east to Everdor on their monobikes in a day or two, but that was too conspicuous. They would have been necessitated to stop for fuel, and at least take the beaten paths if not the roads. Beasts would have seen them pass, Watchers stopped them at checkpoints, asked questions as to why two city Howlers were out here. They could have donned disguises, made excuses, but what was the rush? The Elder Trains were not due for another week. Better to go north, across the sparsely-populated ashen desert of the Great Steppes and along the foot of the Sunrise Mountains, before dropping down into the lush, unpolluted forests and fields of Everdor, unseen and unsuspected.

This was Ivan's country, Uther knew, where the Donskoys and most other Eisbrand families originally came from. With the ever-spreading Ashfall making farming impossible, few remained now. Ivan's immediate family had been amongst the last clinging on here and he still spoke a little Steppes through them – enough to trade with a passing bear merchant a few days ago. The brazen bear had thrown open his beetle-drawn cart to the wolves, and whilst Uther had naively inspected useless trinkets, Ivan had traded wads of lupas for mere bread and water. Money wasn't worth much out here, Blade-dancer had explained later.

The bread had since gone stale, but Uther didn't complain; naive city-dweller he may be, he still knew he was lucky for anything at all out here. Without Ivan's guidance he would probably get lost and expire, not that he would admit it.

Halfway through his meal, Ivan noticed Uther staring at him across the campfire.

"What?" he snorted pugnaciously.

"Nothing," Uther said, looking down and away.

There was a pause as Ivan doubtless tried to fathom what Uther had been staring at, but he let it pass for fear of looking stupid, or seeming to care, or both.

Blade-dancer curled up under his black captain's cloak, which served very well as a blanket. "You take first watch," he said, pulling his hood up, "the crickets will stop singing in a few hours and then you'll be able to sleep better."

"Don't you want your soup?" Uther said hopefully.

"I'd prefer to have it for breakfast."

"It'll get cold."

"I'll survive, city-boy," Ivan teased, rolling onto his side and presenting his back to Uther. Hearing the ladle clink on the pot as Uther snuck a refill, Ivan growled, "If there's not enough soup there to fill my belly in the morning you'll be eating sand crickets from here on out, Howler."

Chiirrrrruup!

"Puh, suits me!" Uther claimed, speaking loudly into the night. "Did you hear that? I'll be forced to eat yer!"

✦

Sara sat kneading her black paws on her white breeches, watching the simple new-materials glowing clock tick by on the wall opposite.

The clinical-smelling, somewhat stark waiting room was populated by the usual suspects, beasts old and young, little and large, some coughing their guts out, some on crutches, some with bald patches of scabrous skin, and some, like Sara, harboured no outward symptoms at all, though she suspected if she sat here being coughed on much longer she was bound to come away with a souvenir cold.

The surgery door opened and Sara hopped to her feet. She was premature, for a rotund male hog nurse trotted out and crossed to the reception desk.

Sara sat back down again, before immediately getting up and walking to the desk. She butted into the flirty conversation the hog nurse was having with the presumably attractive hogess receptionist nestled behind the desk.

"Excuse me. Sorry, but how long will this take?"

"The doctor'll be right with you miss," the distracted hog nurse said to Sara. "Just take a seat."

"It's not for me. I brought my friend in. The-"

"Yeah, I know, the tall brown wolfess. Miss Blake's still undergoing tests. All right?"

"Still?"

"Doctor Maher will be another fifteen minutes, I reckon."

Sara expressed her thanks to the hog and sat back down, if only for a few seconds before taking the nearest exit and a little fresh air, or as fresh as air got around here.

The clinic's cloister-like gardens weren't really gardens, just raked gravel and some trees that were tough enough to put up with the ashen rain. The muted Lupan sun played through their leaves and danced over Sara's blazer as she sat on a curvy iron bench beneath one of the tree trunks and buried her face in her paws.

"Sara?"

The little wolfess looked up to see her big, surcoat-clad, armoured shadow.

"Tristan," she chirped at him. "What do you want?"

"How is she?" he replied, nodding at the clinic.

"Ah don't know yet."

"You can't hide her much longer."

"I'll hide her as long as she wants."

"If you *love* her," Tristan said, stepping closer, "you'll let me help her before someone else finds out."

"Help her?" Sara spat. "You mean become one of you?"

"Not if I can help it."

Sara grimaced, "Ulf almighty, life's just nae fair, Tristan. Olivia's got so much tae give the world. She's so clever and… and beautiful. And here's little, daft dumpling me, healthy as can be even though mah mother's as rotten as a dustbin. Why was I spared?"

Tristan contemplated sitting beside Sara and comforting her, but thought better of it. "It's not too late," he soothed, spreading a paw. "With fresh air and clean living Olivia might live a relatively normal life for a reasonable time, with minimal stings."

"Reasonable?" Sara sniffed, looking up at the Howler, "Like what?"

"Years to come," he replied vaguely. "Look, can't Penny and Monty put her up on their farm?"

"Aye, gladly, but how will I get her out of Lupa now? The Watchers will sense her when she passes the Lupan Wall's checkpoints, won't they? They'll find her out."

Tristan had obviously been thinking about it for a long time, for he had a plan to paw. "I can get you past them. I'm going to Everdor next week, for the Pack Summit – it's being held at Hummelton this year."

"Aye, Ah know. So what?"

"Well, I can tuck you and Olivia away in my cabin on the Elder Train."

"The Elder Train, are ye mad?" Sara squeaked.

"Where better? There'll be so many Howlers aboard nobody will be able to pick Olivia's corona out. I can get passes, disguises; everything."

Sara thought it through, "You think that'd work?"

Tristan nodded, then looked to the clinic, "Who's she seeing in there anyway?"

"Her usual doctor… Doctor Maher."

"Maher?"

"Aye."

Tristan cocked his head, "I take it he's being paid to keep his mouth shut?"

Sara looked around, "Aye," she confirmed, guiltily.

Tristan sniffed, "I'd better check him out nonetheless."

"Och, he's fine. Olivia's been seeing him years. He's one of Heath's ex students."

A grunt.

Standing up, Tristan took his leave, boots crunching on the gravel. "I'll be in touch."

After tugging on her fingers for an age, Sara finally called after him, "Tristan!" she began, exhaling a second later, "Thank ye."

Tristan saluted with a finger and walked on.

✦

Finally Sara was called into the surgery by the pig nurse, who opened the door for her and ushered her inside. She found Olivia sitting beside the doctor's desk with her bag on her lap and her pink coat tucked close. She looked ready and eager to leave after suffering through a carnival of needles, breathing exercises and questionnaires.

"Sorry," she apologised, as Sara pulled up a seat beside her, "you must've been bored out of your mind."

"Don't be daft," Sara dismissed. She waited a moment whilst Olivia blew her nose in a hanky, then she reached over and clasped Olivia's nearest paw. "Well?" she urged with a gulp. "How bad is it?"

"Hmm? Oh! The blood tests won't be in for a week," Olivia replied chirpily, waving her free paw. "But he says it's nothing to worry about."

"What? But Ah thought it was getting really bad?"

"It's not full-blown rot yet; I've just had a bad reaction."

"Reaction?"

"He reckons I've become allergic to ash now, that's all. You know, like Bruno was? Just the next stage."

Sara looked down a little.

Olivia went on. "I told you it was nothing to worry about. I've got this all under control. A little sting here and there is all I'll ever need. I've been doing it a long time, now."

Another door opened and a steel-grey wolf in a long white coat and black breeches, emerged.

"Yes, yes, strong with honey," he said, "but not so strong the spoon stands up in it, thank you!" Slamming the door he faced the girls and rolled his spectacled eyes, "Sorry, new assistant's never seen a teabag in her life, it seems."

Olivia laughed, whilst Sara made good a polite smile.

"I'm Doctor Maher," said the dashing grey wolf, removing his specs from his blue eyes and holding out a paw. "You must be Sara."

"Uh, aye."

"Olivia here says you're into bugs," the doctor said, as paws were shaken.

Sara nodded vigorously, "Oh, aye. It's mah degree."

"A noble subject, Miss," Maher praised, beaming effortlessly at Sara whilst reclining in a cantilever office chair made of shiny new-materials. "Oh! What a life Professor Heath has led. I took his biology class myself, though in the end I went the imperiology route. No doubt you'll follow the great bear's pawsteps and see the big wide wild world?"

Sara was still processing Olivia's good news and what it might mean for Tristan's plans, but managed to make small-talk, "Aye, that's the idea."

Maher moved on. Donning those circular, wire frame spectacles again he pulled a folded piece of paper from his coat pocket. "Now then, Olivia, I'm going to prescribe some antihistamines to get that swelling under control," he said, scribbling away. "Plus the uh… additional extras."

Olivia duly produced a brown envelope from her bag and passed it to Maher.

The doctor stared at it, then at Sara.

"Oh, Sara knows," Olivia reassured Maher, shrugging her shoulders. "She was the first to know. I used to get my venom from Professor Heath, you see."

"Heath, eh?" Maher said, pocketing the money at once.

"Olivia, what's going on?" Sara gasped. "Where'd ye get all that money?"

"My parents," Olivia said, with a slight, false chuckle. "It was their parting gift. They... never want to see me again. I think they mean it this time." She raised her chin, flicked an ear, "It's all right, though. I'm going to pay my own way from now on. Well, soon I will. What I mean is, I don't want you or Heath getting in trouble on my account. I'll move out of his flat soon."

"But, where will ye go?"

"I'll figure something out."

Sara closed her eyes as thoughts of Olivia becoming a wolfess in a Lupanar flitted through her mind. "Olivia-"

"My mind's made up," Olivia insisted. "I can do this by myself now."

"But-"

"Olivia was telling me about your friend," Maher interrupted, in that clumsy, subject-changing tone of voice.

"Friend?" Sara blinked in surprise.

"Yes, the one who disappeared. Bruno was it? I used to help him as well, but his father kept moving him on and eventually I stopped hearing from them. Pity what happened. The Howlers can be such bullies, can't they?"

"Aye," Sara said, clearing her throat.

"Don't worry," Maher assured, "I'll take extra special care of Olivia."

With pleasantries exchanged and the deal done, the doctor showed his patient and her escort the door, telling the pig receptionist to hold all other patients for five minutes.

"I've an important call to make," he growled.

Locking the door, Maher simultaneously eased into his cantilever chair and dialled the telephone. Whilst waiting, he pulled a folded sheet of graph paper from his coat pocket and set it out on the table. The long sheet was traced by a black line that spiked wildly up and down, like a seismometer.

"Doctor Josef's office," a nasally female said.

"Yes, this is Doctor Maher," replied Maher, following the wild, jagged line with his spectacled eyes. "Put me through to Josef will you? It's urgent."

"The doctor's out of the office. Can I take a message?"

"Why yes, you can!" Maher woofed, his voice dripping with incredulity. "Tell my dear old teacher that I've a possible pure-blood for sale, female, and I'm going straight to the next bidder if he's not in, all right?"

Silence.

Within five seconds there was a click and a recognisable hiss down the line, *"What's this, Maher?"*

"Sorry to bother you, Josef, but I've just had the most charming dodger drop by, very pretty-"

"And?"

"And she's off the charts!" Maher marvelled. "She *must* be a pure-blood. She's finally reached maturity, but I fobbed her off by telling her she's just allergic to ash. She is, but she's going to need rather more than antihistamines soon."

"Name? Address?"

"Ah ah ah… you know my price."

Josef growled, *"You realise I could have ALPHA take you in for helping dodgers whenever I wanted!"*

"Sir!" Maher squeaked, removing his glasses. "Really, is that any way to talk to a star pupil? You know I'm worth every penny."

"We're on a tight budget since we started work on Rafe. I can't afford it."

"Well then I'd better find someone who can. Ta ta-"

"Wait!" Josef mewed. By the sound of things, he sat down in a squeaky new materials chair. *"All right, perhaps we can come to some other arrangement."*

"A position at ALPHA, like you promised?"

"She had better be good, or else."

"Oh she's good," Maher insisted, admiring the wildly spiked imperium graph. "She might even be better than your last Eisenwolf."

~Blick IV~

The atmosphere in the warehouse was thick with ember vapour. Several smouldering hogs nervously counted money whilst a bespectacled white rabbit checked the quality of stings with an eyeglass. Rats, stoats and a single hyena stood guard at the table, doors and windows, with pistols and rifles aplenty lest any Howlers dared show their snouts. They shouldn't, not in a designated Dead Zone, all had agreed.

"C-ccc-can we hurry, please?" a smartly-dressed hog dealer asked; the boss of the others. "This Dead Zone air must be killing us all," he complained, kerchief pressed to snout as a rudimentary guard against any ambient black-imperium.

An enormous brown bear in a suit was overseeing proceedings from the other side of the table, his black lips nursing an equally enormous ember smouldering away. He had murderous purple eyes with which he glared at the hog dealer across the way.

"The puny Howlers exaggerate the danger," he claimed. "It does not hurt to come and go from a Dead Zone."

"As you say, Mister B," the white rabbit agreed.

Mister B, or Mad Bront as they called him, had so much purple-imperium swilling around his veins it didn't take much to upset him and everyone knew it in Lupa's criminal underworld, especially the hog sting dealer, nervously mopping his brow.

Still, all was going well.

"This one's fake," the rabbit suddenly spat, setting a sting aside. He picked out another few and inspected them. Two passed his test, but the third did not. "Looks like they've been filled out with flour, or chalk, Mister B. Not all of 'em, but more than a few have been adulterated."

Mister B's ember rolled in his lips, his eyes flared open.

"What are you on about?" the hog dealer spluttered. "This is good stuff. I checked it myself."

"Aye I bet you did!" the rabbit accused, removing his spectacles and pointing with them. "What're you trying to pull? Our clients are first rate. They're rich Freiwolves helping relatives dodge. If someone's beloved son or daughter dies because we supplied fake stings they won't come to Mister B again!"

The hog looked to the wall that was Mister B. "Mister Bront, sir, I assure you-"

"How many are fake, hog?" Mister B interjected, removing his ember and blowing a veritable cloud of vapours.

"N-nnn-none, it's all-"

"Are you calling my imperiologist a liar?"

"N-nnn-no, he's just mistaken-"

"Incompetent then? I hire only incompetent beasts!"

"Of course not, I am merely saying that-"

"That I'm trying to screw you out of imperium? Because if it's not you it must be me. But the thing is, I know for a fact it isn't me, because, well, I'm me. Do you follow?"

The hog boss mopped his brow – for the last time.

In two or three great strides, a snarling, roaring Mister B climbed across the table, kicking aside wads of money and sending piles of stings spinning. Closing the gap between himself and the hog he clapped both great paws down upon the latter's pink head.

Pfffzaack!

"Eyaaagh-blurp-gggh!"

The dealer hog's skull was crushed and fried both at once, his body quivering wildly under Mister B's plasmatic blast, before going limp. Released like a squashed insect, he flopped on the tabletop and slumped to the floor.

Dead.

"Now look what you made me do," Mad Bront sighed. He looked to the hog's followers, who stood back, aghast. "Well, aren't you going to protect your boss?"

They all shook their heads.

"Little late now, I suppose," Bront huffed. "We will be taking our money back and also the stings as compensation. Do you gentlebeasts have a problem with that?"

More head shaking.

"Excellent. Now be off with you, before I seek further... damages."

The hog contingent of the shady dealings took their leave, hurrying for the exit lest Mad Bront snuffed out their lives as he had their boss. But no sooner had they disappeared than screams and flashes of light erupted from the depths of the warehouse! One hog came running back, stumbling over cardboard boxes in his haste and rolling into Bront.

"It's him! It's him!" he squealed.

Mad Bront grabbed the passing hog, lifting him by the back of his shirt, "Him?"

"The Eisenwolf! They do got one! It's real!"

The clomp of boots announced the approach of an impossibly huge wolf with blank yellow eyes, striding through the warehouse and stopping before reaching the light where Mad Bront's deal was being cut. A cloud of ash erupted from the wolf's left shoulder and swirled overhead. Bront's beasts readied their pistols and rifles, but the wolf was unafraid.

"So... it's true," said Bront, dropping the hog, who crawled rapidly away. "The Eisenwolves walk again."

"LAY DOWN YOUR WEAPONS AND SURRENDER," said the Eisenwolf. "PLEASE."

"Please? Hahahahaha! I don't think so, freak."

A Prefect with ruddy fur joined the Eisenwolf. She looked at Bront, then at the hog slumped under the table. "Looks like murder this time, Bront," she hummed. "Crooked dealer or not, murder is murder, and I bet those hogs back there will testify against you when faced with a hefty Gelb sentence."

Bront huffed, "Howler Janoah Bloodfang, we meet again."

"Prefect, please," she corrected primly.

"I see. Well, whatever filth you work for now, forget you saw us and I'll let you and your abomination there walk... or do I send you both to the bottom of the Lupa in eisenglanz chains?"

Silence.

"Kill em!" Bront snarled at his beasts.

As pellets took fly, Janoah leapt into the shadows and drew her rapier, "Book 'em, Stenton!"

Rafe ducked down, missiles pinging off his shoulders. Hardly moving a muscle he accelerated in amongst Bront's followers by riding a wave of imperious energy that rippled and warped the air around him. The coronal tsunami upturned crates and crashed into the table, catapulting it and all the money and stings across the warehouse. The white rabbit dashed for cover amidst the fluttering cash and imperium rain.

Bront himself stood back whilst the rest of his beasts descended upon Rafe from all sides and angles. Their weapons having been fired and long in the reloading, they tried to club him and stab him instead. Rafe boxed and slapped the feeble rats and stoats aside with barley even noticeable snaps of plasma. The more powerful hyena he wrestled for a time, before sending a bolt of plasmatic blue into his paws and up his arms, shocking him to his knees.

"Gaaagh-aaag!"

As the hyena was being subdued, Mad Bront dived on Rafe from behind, his mighty bears arms clapping clean around even the Eisenwolf's broad frame.

"UNGH!" Rafe barked in surprise; his arms were pinned!

"Let me show you... the ancient greeting we Koda bears used to give Howlers... up on the... Steppes!"

The bulk that was Bront both crushed Rafe and summoned a surge plasma so mighty the sleeves of his own fine suit smouldered and went up in flames. His fur sizzled and smoked, but Mad Bront felt nothing of it as he tried to cook Rafe alive inside his Eisenwolf suit.

"Aaaahahahaahaaaa!"

"Rafe, get out of there!" Janoah yelped. She scurried in from left field and stabbed Bront in the arm with her rapier. The moment she touched him the Koda's immense power channelled down *the sword blade, blasting Janoah back across the room.*

"GAAAGH! JAN!" Rafe snarled, kicking and squirming. "GRRRAAAAGH! GERROFFOFME!"

"W-www-what the-blaaagh!"

The air twisted, bent and altogether exploded in a wave of near-invisible energy. Mad Bront was ejected across the warehouse, slamming against a support girder, so fast, so hard, his body deformed back-first around it like a wet pillow and fell in a heap at the base, whereupon life took its leave. Windows shattered and corrugated walls bowed outwards as Rafe's coronal shockwave continued, upturning the whole building.

Rafe collapsed on all fours, iron chest heaving, his mantle torn to shreds, backpack puffing away.

"JAN?" *he panted metallically in the gloom.* "JAN!"

"I'm here, Stenton. I'm all right. You?"

"YEAH. I THINK GOT HIM. HAH!"

"You did. Just… do yourself a favour and don't look behind you."

Chapter 26

Rufus wriggled through the stony crevice, his belly slithering slug-like on a film of water, his back scraping against the jagged, chalky ceiling.

The red wolf paused for a rest and to tug at his stifling imperium collar. He looked ahead, at the faint creamy light emanating from within the pale rock face. It rekindled a memory in him; that of Janoah smuggling a lamp under the sheets to read past lights out – the faint glow was similar.

It's been a long time since we met at the Academy, Rufus chuckled in his head, dipping his chin a moment to rest his aching neck muscles.

"Anything?" someone urged outside.

"Hold on!" Rufus called back.

He scrabbled behind with a wet paw and pulled his imperium lamp after him, past his stripy convict's breeches and into the cramped space. The lamp's metal housing lodged between the lips of the crevice and Rufus had to wrench it side to side to force it through, gouging crumbs of soft rock from the ceiling. He was appalled he could fit through so narrow a gap himself and supposed he was losing weight; not mere fat, but muscle too.

How much longer? Where's my contact? When do we get out? Perhaps it's all gone horribly wrong. Has Jan abandoned me? I deserve it, the way I've treated her. I do.

Concentrate, Rufus.

The Howler groped blindly behind for his pickaxe. Someone back there realised what his leader needed, grabbed his wrist, and placed the pickaxe grip firmly in his grasp.

Rufus easily recognised that big, rough paw. "Thanks, Madou," he acknowledged.

"Be careful," the hyena rumbled guiltily, crouching on all fours outside – he was no taller than Rufus, but was simply too burly to crawl into so small a crevice.

Grunting and growling, Rufus shuffled within reach of the shimmering vein of imperium. It was white. Rufus could feel it in his bones and, more uncomfortably, at his throat as his cruel imperium collar tightened.

Rolling on his side and bringing his pickaxe to bear with both sore, bandaged paws, Rufus began chipping away at the rock. Flecks of chalky, wet, warm stone spattered in all directions, bouncing off the walls and the would-be miner's muzzle. He squinted to defend his metallic-green eyes from the gritty missiles, rendering himself almost blind to anything but the imperium vein, which shone brighter and sharper with every blow as the translucent rock thinned.

Suddenly a spurt of water, then a stream, then a torrent, tumbling through the hole in the rock and washing over Rufus's shoulders. The wolf gasped and spluttered, turning his face away from the tepid flow.

"Chief?" Madou called, doubtless getting wet paws as water spilled across the cave. *"What's happening?"*

"Just a tick!" Rufus shouted over the surge.

The Howler could see the imperium crystal shimmering brightly through the greenish water. Afraid he would lose it to the violent rapids he grasped it with a paw – at the very same moment his collar tightened unbearably.

"Gaaagh!"

Then the entire, weakened rock face collapsed in a flood of gritty, chalky stone, instantly entombing Rufus in dark, warm, burbling mass!

With every fibre of his being the panicked wolf pushed and kicked, struggling to squirm backwards out of the suffocating pile, but Mother Erde had this thief in her grasp and would not let go so easily. Within seconds Rufus's lungs began to pang for air, to burn and throb.

By Ulf, it's all over!

Someone grabbed Rufus's breeches, then his waist, those big tough hyena paws again. Please get me out of here, Madou. By Ulf don't let it end like this!

Rufus could hear Madou's muffled shouting as the hyena tugged on him with all his might.

"Hold on chief!"

With a gurgling, sucking sound, Rufus was dragged from the crevice and reborn into the world of the living. Blinded by dirt and half-deaf, he could feel Madou looming over him, feel his corona coiling with his.

"Rufus!" the hyena barked, rolling the spluttering wolf over and trying to clear his airways with his thick fingers before someone obligingly tipped a bucket of relatively cold water over his face.

Splosh!

"Gagh! Pleh! Pppst! Ugh!"

Spitting grit and sand all over, Rufus wiped his stinging eyes and sat upright. Slowly the mines came into focus, the slick, humid, dew-laden walls punctuated by wooden struts and flickering imperium lanterns.

"You all right?" Madou asked, his big, dark, rounded-off muzzle filling Rufus's sharpening vision.

"Yes… thank you," the wolf assured him, a picture of calm without, even whilst his body trembled within. "Thought I'd bought it then," he admitted jokily, tugging at his unyielding collar with a muddied paw.

Madou grunted, "Mother Erde doesn't appreciate us stealing her riches, chief. Better luck next time."

Amidst a wry smile, Rufus presented Madou with a clod of dirt, like a cub offering a mud-pie to a parent. The hyena was baffled, until the wolf flicked the mud from his fist, revealing the unmistakable pure shimmer of a white-imperium crystal the size of a pebble, its rough facets quite beautiful.

"Hahaaaa!" Madou woofed, grasping Rufus by the upper arms and giving him a fond shake. "Well done, chief!"

The rest of the team leant in, a motley crew of beasts; a big hog, a second and much skinnier hyena, and a fellow wolf who was as robust and as he was athletic. Everyone wore the same obligatory uniform of Gelb inmates – stripy yellow and black shirts, matching breeches and cloth caps. Rufus could scarce conceive a more tasteless look. Any fugitive would of course stand out a mile away in such a bold getup, even if the colours were faded and obscured by time and filth.

"Look at the size o' that nugget!" whistled the peach-skinned, tusked hog, himself the size of a house. The black and yellow stripes of his threadbare convict's shirt bulged and warped to the contours of every rippling muscle and, it had to be said, his distended belly. "Well done, Rufe!"

The skinny hyena merely nodded and grunted. He was a sorry-looking beast compared to the mighty Madou, with grey fur and black spots instead of the typical browns and tans. He did however sport an impressive upright mane running down his long neck, something Madou lacked.

Rufus's fellow wolf, meanwhile, glanced nervously about the deserted throat of the mine before settling his aquamarine eyes on the imperium crystal.

"Rufus," he said, "Here, I hide it this time."

Standing with Madou's help, Rufus brushed his fellow wolf's offer aside with far greater ease than the dirt clinging to his fur, "No no, I'll do it."

"I want to help," the wolf insisted.

"My corona is stronger. It'll disguise the crystal."

"But you *always* smuggler. Is not fair on you-"

"Tomek!" Rufus snapped, then pinched the youth's cheek and tutted, "Behave. There's a good chap. It wouldn't do to get you in more trouble. I owe you my life already, let's not compound my debt."

"There is no debt, we're equal," Tomek replied, twisting free and rubbing his cheek.

He looked to Madou, who ignored him.

Clearing his throat to distil the tension, Rufus reached up and set Tomek's stripy cap straight so that both his perky grey ears projected through the holes.

"Wear your cap properly," he advised, "don't give the guards an excuse to hit you."

Tomek nodded in consent to Rufus's good sense.

Bzzzzzzzzt!

All ears pricked to the dreaded electronic address system echoing down the damp silence of the mines.

"*All gangs return to base camp,*" the austere announcer warned. "*All gangs return to base camp. You have ten minutes. Loiterers and idlers will be punished. That is all.*"

Hurriedly stowing the imperium crystal into a pouch sewn into the inside of his soggy breeches, Rufus grasped his gang's rickety old mine cart and made to push it along the rails. Before he could get it moving, the massive hog brushed him aside and took over.

"Rest, mate, you've earned it after that," he said through his mighty tusks.

Rufus gladly accepted. "Much obliged, Helmut," he said, allowing the hog to push the cart, which was piled high with glittering imperium ore.

It was safe to say there was no danger of 'Scarab Gang' falling below their quota today.

"We'd all be dead without yer," Helmut snorted, recognising the very fact as he trotted along, the cart apparently weightless to him, "I dunno how you do it, Rufe. How'd you feel a decent imperium vein amongst all the ambience? You've a gift, even for your kind. You'd make a great imperium douser. You could be a rich beast!"

"In kinder circumstances," Rufus admitted, taking his stripy shirt from the back of the mine cart and slipping it over his soiled shoulders, "maybe."

Aided by the powerful Madou, Helmut pushed the cart along the winding, deserted tunnel for some five minutes – this was an old shaft, mined out, or so they had been warned by the kinder guards as they passed. Rufus's nose, his inner Howler nose at least, had proven them false. No doubt some of the other teams would hear of Scarab Gang's success today and swarm this way tomorrow to try and repeat their good fortune, but they hadn't Scarab's 'secret weapon', as Helmut had lately dubbed Rufus, and would fail.

Scarab's 'secret weapon' just hoped nobody around here suffered unduly because of his meddling. Well, nobody more at any rate. It was too late for young Tomek Usenko, who had been sent down thanks to Rufus.

Apparently, so far as Rufus could discern matters through the fog of Tomek's broken dialect, the Bloodfang Elder Watcher had been humiliated by Vladimir's sudden intervention regarding Rufus's summary execution, despite his facade of cordiality at the time. As the Elder Watcher saw it, his authority had been challenged by Amael and Vladimir, two know-it-all, inner-city Howlers who thought they were better than the gate-guarding Watchers. The investigation into who was to blame for such an affront to the Elder Watcher's prestige had quickly percolated right down to Tomek and that phone call he had made to ALPHA.

Tomek's act had been construed as abetting a prisoner, and his punishment, enacted by a Bloodfang court marital, was a stint down Gelb. Rufus knew in reality it was because Tomek had gone to ALPHA like a tattletale that he was being punished.

'I sent down only for one year,' Tomek had insisted, the day he had bumped into Rufus in the Gelb. 'Is not so bad.'

He was optimistic, to be sure.

Rufus felt terrible, especially since he at least was here on a mission for ALPHA and had a way out. He could say nothing to Tomek or the others about it, only his fellow agent.

And where in Ulf's name is this agent? Rufus thought. Two months and no sign, not even a note thrust into my paw. Something's up. Whoever he was, he's died down here, or betrayed us to the conspirators, or been extracted because everything's gone to pot and I've been left to rot to cover ALPHA's tracks and maintain deniability, just like Silvermane warned me.

No, Jan, dear Jan, you wouldn't just leave me down here. Would you?

"Halt!" snapped one of the guards standing at the shaft's crooked exit, thankfully plucking Rufus from his swirling riptide of depressing thoughts.

"Stand away from the cart!" said the other.

Hogs they were, dressed in a revolting vomit-yellow Politzi-like uniform. The guards were not particularly big or muscular individuals, rather flabby if anything. They packed no imperious abilities, no pistol, just a truncheon and a strange black box that hung around their necks on ribbons.

One might think that the Scarab Gang, with two Howlers, a Chakaa hyena and an enormous hog like Helmut to their name, could easily overpower an army of such poorly-equipped sentinels and thus make a bid for freedom.

But this was Gelb and they had methods.

"Eyes down, Usenko!" the first hog snorted at Tomek, who made the simple mistake of meeting eyes with him. The youth looked down at his toes, but too slowly and with too much hatred in his imperious eyes to get away with it.

It was no mistake on Tomek's part, Rufus knew, but an act of defiance as usual.

"I said eyes down, you maggot!" the hog bellowed.

Out came the truncheon, straight to the stomach, knocking the wind from Tomek and sending him down on all fours. Then another blow to the back, knocking him flat to the wet, gritty erde. The tough youth didn't yelp or scream, just grunted and coughed.

Rufus looked on, fists clenching and unclenching.

Don't you fool, he told himself, his collar tightening somewhat as his rage boiled, you can't afford to get in trouble again. Lupa can't afford you to. Keep out of it.

Whilst hog one kicked Tomek in the side, hog two took the black box dangling around his neck and, eying up the other convicts, placed his fingers on the dial. Rufus and the others braced themselves.

Nothing, hog two was merciful… this time.

Leaving Tomek coughing on the ground, hog one inspected the cart. "Quite a haul, Scarab," he sniffed, pushing the glittering imperium ore around with his truncheon, "You're doing well. The Warden *will* be pleased."

He ran his beady eyes over the condemned, at the muscled Madou, his fellow skinny hyena, the giant Helmut, before settling on the relatively little Rufus. He trotted slowly over to the red wolf.

"You look even filthier than usual, Valerio," he said, lifting the prisoner's chin with his truncheon. "You find any good stuff, down there, eh? Any white schmutz?"

Rufus said nothing and kept his green eyes averted.

"Well, scum?"

"No," Rufus said. "No good stuff, sir."

"Not with your famous 'nose'?" the hog mocked.

"Not this time, sir, this mine's exhausted… for now. But I'll be sure to let you know when I *do* find some."

"I'm sure you will," the hog chuckled maliciously. He suddenly jerked forward and sniffed Rufus all over, so hard his nostrils vacuumed up his fur, before withdrawing. "Cor, you stink!" he derided, waving his truncheon at him and the rest of the gang. "You all stink! Get outta here before I catch the rot off you pathetic imperium-junkies. Go on!"

Pulling Tomek to his feet by the back of his shirt, Rufus wordlessly led his team past the bullies and onward.

Leaving their claustrophobic shaft behind, the Scarabs pushed their trundling cart into an open, airy cave with stalactites dangling from the roof like grotesque fangs. One of the giant stalactites had, at some point in its ancient life, met the equally vast stalagmite growing beneath it and together formed a natural, rippling pillar of smooth stone around which imperium lamps and speakers were strung in equal number like some demented Wintertide ornament.

Bzzzzzzzzt!

"All teams return to base camp. You have five minutes. That is all."

The cave's pale, glittering walls were pocked with dark, circular openings, some high, some low, like the gasping mouths of suffocating fish piled one on top of the other. Rails spilled from these ghoulish shafts like iron tongues, lolling across the floor of the huge cave and converging at an elaborate checkpoint operated by yet more vomit-clad hogs. Wretched beasts dressed in stripes and throttled by imperium collars pushed carts along the rails, heading for the checkpoint. Gelb's inmates were wolves mostly, ex-Howlers in the main, sent down for some misdemeanour or other, but there was many a hyena and hog in the mix, even a few cats and a bear or two. However, there were no little beasts; sending their like to Gelb was considered a waste of labour, for they would quickly expire from the workload and bullying. Desperate noble beasts would as likely steal a little beast's rations as look at them – it was bad enough for wee beasts in the real world, let alone this pit of inequity.

The rattle of dozens of mine carts and patting paws congregating at the checkpoint combined to make an awful racket, but it at least allowed the prisoners to talk without being noticed and punished by the guards.

"You all right?" Rufus surreptitiously asked Tomek.

"Of course!" the youngster snorted, nursing his stomach through his shirt. "They nothing. Pathetic."

"You mustn't provoke them."

"I didn't."

"Tomek… I know it's hard for a Howler to suffer such bullies in silence," Rufus sniffed. "How do you think I feel, or Madou, a proud hyena warrior?"

Tomek flashed a brilliant smile and tutted, "Watcher."

"Pardon?"

"I'm Watcher, not Howler. Only one in thirteen chosen to become Watcher. I is special wolf."

On that note Tomek laughed – such boasting was a Steppes wolf's idea of humour, perhaps. Regardless, Rufus allowed Tomek's infectious laughter to catch on. He couldn't remain mad at him, the rogue. Between his handsome grey and white coat and marvellous aquamarine eyes he cut a dapper figure even in filthy prison rags.

Whilst Rufus continued to smile, Tomek's faded. He peered over his shoulder at Madou pushing the cart. The hyena wasn't laughing and merely returned Tomek's look with those unflinching purple-tinged eyes. Snorting, Tomek faced forward and twisted his cap sideways, covering one ear completely whilst leaving the other free.

"Foolish pup," Madou grunted quietly to Helmut.

"Whatever happened between you two," big Helmut advised, "bury it, mate, that is if you want to live."

"It's not me, it's him."

"Yeah, well, I'm sure Tomek'd say the same thing."

The gang members lined up beside their carts in front of the wooden checkpoints, arms by their sides.

Bzzzzzzzzt!
Bzzzzzzzzt!
Bzzzzzzzzt!

That's it, time's up. Rufus glanced around and behind, checking if any of the teams hadn't made it back. He couldn't really tell; there were too many carts to count, too many faces to remember, a sea of filthy, anonymously stripy beasts, like a swarm of wasps. He could see, however, that some of the carts fell short of full, and the teams responsible for them stood with hunched backs and ears low.

Poor fools are scared out of their wits.

More Gelb hogs appeared and took their positions at the checkpoints. Without fanfare they beckoned the first row of carts forward. The mining teams pushed their rickety loads up to the barrier whereupon the hogs inspected the glittering ore within, pushing it around with their truncheons and snorting in a pretence of criticism even when the quota was fulfilled. Some inmates were lazily frisked for contraband, but with hundreds of prisoners there was no time to check everyone, the system relied on chance to deter thieves.

Rufus was counting on such sloppiness to get his white-imperium crystal through. Tomek kept giving his fellow wolf a sideways glance.

The thought occurred to Rufus, as it did every miserable, back-breaking day, to just fill the cart with a useless pile of rocks and then spread a thin layer of pretty ore on top. However, it was made clear to the inmates on arrival in Gelb that the hogs sitting inside the wooden kiosks weren't just there to raise the barrier, but were in fact watching over machines sensitive to ambient imperium levels. If a passing cart was lacking in real ore the sensor's needle wouldn't budge, and then there'd be trouble. Rufus, however, was convinced it was a ruse; if his own strong imperious senses struggled to cope in the invisible imperium fog of the mines any mechanical contrivance would be utterly useless. Certainly Tomek had never heard of reliable mechanised imperium dousing, that's why he and the Watchers used sniffer-ants like Scuttle.

The barriers were raised in their own time and the first row of carts wheeled through. Circular tokens were metered out to the gang members as they passed the wooden kiosks; white for a 'good', grey for 'acceptable', the white tokens being worth twice the rations of the grey.

There was no token for 'unacceptable'.

The gang ahead of Scarab pushed their day's labour forth for inspection. The cart wasn't as full as they might like, and the Gelb hogs looked unimpressed. The convicts were lucky to get away without a beating, let alone without tokens. No tokens meant they would be entitled to no more than a bowl of soup this evening. They would have to do better in future if they wanted to eat properly, let alone buy an imperium fix to stave off the rot in the case of the afflicted and/or addicted, which most inmates were.

No work, no imperium – that at least was the same everywhere.

Just as the flimsy barrier arm wobbled down and the Scarabs' turn came, a black wolf in a green cloak and white Howler armour appeared in the wooden watchtower overlooking the checkpoints. He stood clasping the railing with both paws, his imperious eyes looking down upon the stripy masses below.

"The Warden," Helmut whispered, as he and Madou slowly pushed the cart forward.

"He's looking right at you, chief," Madou said, head down.

"Don't panic," Rufus calmly assured.

"Can he sense it?" Helmut wondered, referring to the crystal in Rufus's secret pocket.

"Give me crystal," Tomek begged Rufus.

"Shut up, boy," he seethed back.

"You're needed more than me. I can take risk-"

"Shush!"

It was too late regardless. Some Gelb hogs approached and hurried Helmut and Madou along.

"Come on, you lazy sacks of maggot slime!" one said, slapping the back of Madou's legs with his truncheon. "Move it! Move it!"

The guard stopped short of hitting Helmut, either because he sympathised with a fellow hog, or because Helmut was frighteningly enormous; it was impossible to know. Either way, hyena and hog pushed the cart to the barrier and stood by along with the others.

Rufus stood furthest forward, chin down, whilst the hogs rifled through the surface of the ore with their dusty truncheons, carelessly spilling some of the smaller lumps over the rusty lip of the cart. Contraband, such a pickaxe that would make for a good weapon, could only be hidden in the surface layers of the ore, any deeper and it would take too long, and be too obvious, to dig something out of the cart during the short and well-guarded walk from checkpoint to emptying.

Whilst the hogs searched, Rufus's shoulders burned. He could feel the Warden's eyes on his back, feel his mighty corona despite the imperious fog – he was quite the Howler.

The hogs frisked everyone, Tomek, Helmut, Madou and his silent hyena friend, each beast coming over more worried than the last for surely Rufus would now be discovered.

No, the hogs backed off, the barrier rose – Rufus went unsearched.

He chanced a subtle glance up and saw, just beyond the rim of his cap, the Warden turn away from the watchtower railing and disappear inside. Rufus smirked to himself, enjoying his triumph in the face of the hogs. *They won't touch me; the Warden has told them to lay off. But why? Is he an ALPHA agent or just naturally sympathetic to me?*

"Move, it! Stir your stumps!" a hog snorted.

The barrier rose and the Scarab Gang continued on their way, stopping only to collect their reward from the hog nestled in the kiosk. He begrudgingly coughed up five white tokens, pressing them into Rufus's expectant palm with special enmity. Beaming sarcastically at the kiosk-bound hog because he knew he could get away with it, Rufus passed the tokens around, taking special joy in seeing Tomek's handsome eyes light up at the prospect of a square meal and an imperium fix.

Tokens in paw, and unbelieving of their luck, Helmut and Madou hurriedly pushed the mine cart past the kiosk and along the spaghetti-junction of twisting rails before someone back there changed their mind. Within a few yards the multiple rails joined to form just one snaking towards the mouth of the cave and the outside world. Hogs milled around, watching the teams filing past to make sure nothing was removed from the carts and occasionally earning their keep by shouting.

"Move it!" they bellowed, or, "Hurry up, you maggots!" and other such equally unimaginative insults; Rufus was all but deaf to them by now.

After hours in heat and darkness working by feeble imperium lamps, the dazzling daylight and sharp mountain air overwhelmed Rufus and his crew. Their world was smudged by stinging tears into a twisted canvas of dreamy 'new art'. Slowly, and with much blinking, the camp proper came into focus; the long brown huts, the blasted erde quilted with lingering patches of white snow, the miles of grim fences and watchtowers, the high mountain peaks. Such was Gelb.

To the left an endless train of hundreds of ore-bearing hopper carriages waited, at once sparkling and dulled with streaks of imperium ash. The colossal locomotive coupled far ahead was already belching pollution, impatient to be on its way to Lupa with its much-needed load. Spread throughout the thousands of tonnes of ore were a few precious pounds of priceless white-imperium, which needed to be extracted, purified, diluted and packaged as venom stings for all the needy Howlers.

Rufus wondered how many sick wolves the crystal stowed in his stripy breeches might tide over. How many lives could he save by giving it up to Gelb's overlords as he ought to? How many Ivans, Uthers and Linuses will die because of your selfishness?

No, the hard half of his brain chided the soft, *you* have to survive first. You have to break Amael's plot or thousands will die in his purge. Besides, the hogs would just flog such a crystal on the black market to line their own filthy pockets – it would never make it to the veins of a worthy beast like Ivan and the other boys.

Whilst Rufus pondered, Madou and Helmut pushed the mine cart alongside the train whereupon their duty was done. The cart was snagged by a motorised chain running along the centre of the track and jolted from their grasp with frightening force. Thanks to the immense power of a chugging, belching imperium engine turning said chain, the cart quivered up a steep incline like an amusement ride and, by some other clever mechanism, automatically tipped sideways at the apex of the hill. The glittering ore rumbled out into the waiting hopper carriage and the empty cart rattled rapidly down the other side into a siding, joining hundreds of its wheeled brethren all awaiting the next shift. Rufus and the others were part of Shift A; the Shift B prisoners would soon take over. In such ways Gelb ran twenty-four hours.

Passing one last lacklustre checkpoint, the Scarabs left the mines for the prison camp, a bleak wilderness of miserable long huts and wire fences, flecked with snow and ash. Stripy prisoners shuffled to and fro, some sicker and more wretched than others, nearly all of them more so than the highly successful, and therefore rather healthy, the Scarab Gang. Rufus could feel countless jealous eyes watching Scarab's five-strong group cross the camp, wishing they were members instead of those hyenas, or that wolf, or that pig.

"Is lucky we get through!" Tomek whistled at Rufus, glancing back at the distant mouth of the mines.

"Luck had nothing to do with it," Rufus dismissed.

"What?"

"The Warden and I have an understanding."

Tomek nearly went cross-eyed, "Understanding?"

Rufus explained what was apparently obvious to him, "Yes, I think so. You see he has his own quota to fulfil. He needs chaps like us to stay healthy and find imperium veins so he can stay in his cushy job. To punish us would be counterproductive. So… I think he's marked us out for special treatment. Even if he suspects me of hiding the odd nugget down my breeches, he lets me go. The hogs will never search me, only you lot, just to maintain a front to the other crews."

Tomek looked at the others and they at him. "What?" he squeaked incredulously for them all, walking briskly alongside the strident Rufus. "How you know that? Did hogs tell you?"

"Nooo," Rufus woofed, pushing his cap back. "It's just my intuition. The Warden and I have developed a... a mutual, tacit concord of self-interest."

Tomek was mystified, perhaps mostly by Rufus's lofty vocabulary.

"Trust me," Rufus winked at the youth, patting his shoulder. "Now then, let's have this crystal distilled by Tack and get you a sting, Tomek."

"Is all right. I'm fine."

"Really? No pain at all."

Tomek shrugged. "I'm young," he said, "rot come from time to time, but... not much. One day, yes. But not yet."

"Wise words. Well in that case, young buck, you can exchange your share in the spoils for some embers, or whatever you fancy. As for me, I'm aching all over after today." Given a brief chuckle, Rufus turned to the other afflicted beast in the group, "How about you, Madou?"

The burly hyena glanced at Tomek, then pulling his cap down said, "I'm all right, chief. You can have my sting if you need it."

"Oh, that's very gracious, but-"

"And mine!" Tomek piped up, eager to match Madou's patronage. "You can have mine too."

Rufus glared at his fellow wolf.

"If you need it," the youngster added guardedly.

"Well I don't!" Rufus scolded, looking witheringly between Tomek and Madou. "I may be past it, but I'm not so far gone that I have to scrounge off you two!"

Paws rammed in pockets he stormed huffily ahead.

Giving the others a glance, Tomek hurried after Rufus. "I didn't mean it like that," he excused, gesturing with his paws as he fought to find the words. "You not, how you say, 'past it', Rufus, but... I'm not idiot. You older. Stronger. Everyone in Lupa know you are very powerful Howler. Real alpha wolf! You need more imperium than me. Is natural."

Rufus stopped and looked at Tomek.

The handsome, aquamarine-eyed youth spread a grey paw and said with easy confidence, "I know this. You famous."

"Flatterer," Rufus snorted.

"Is not flattery. Is truth!"

Running a finger round the inside of his stifling collar, Rufus turned to Helmut and the rest, "You lot go and join the canteen queue, get yourselves something to eat. I need to be rid of this crystal before my infuriating collar chokes me."

"I come with you," Tomek offered at once, already making to walk ahead.

"No Tomek," Rufus said.

"Someone should watch your back."

"Madou will. You go eat."

"But why Madou and not me?"

"Because he's so mean and ugly that nobody will come near me, isn't that right Madou?"

Madou grunted fondly, "I'm not as ugly as Helmut."

"Yes, well, he won't fit down Tack's hole."

"It's true, I tried," Helmut admitted, slapping his belly.

"Just tell me what you want," Rufus said to Tomek, like a father to his cub, "I'll get it off Tack if I can."

The anger on Tomek's hefty brows was plain, anger that he was being passed over for a hyena terrorist.

"Some chocolate perhaps?" Rufus suggested, slapping Tomek's arm.

A shrug, a nod.

"Chocolate then," Rufus decided.

Once the others had put in their own requests (embers for the skinny hyena who wasn't a Chakaa but was addicted to the kick of imperium, and a bottle of brandy for Helmut who's only addiction was a tipple) Rufus and Madou paired off and headed across to Gelb's anonymous brown huts, paws crunching on the snowy soil.

"Tomek hates me," Madou observed.

"What do you expect, you tried to kill him not very long ago," Rufus snorted.

"Zozizou didn't, yet Tomek hates him too!"

Zozizou – that tongue-twisting hyena name always made Rufus's ears prick. The thusly named skinny hyena back there was Madou's cousin twice removed, or some such, Rufus couldn't quite remember, but after bumping into his distant relation Madou had promised him a place on the gang and Rufus couldn't say no, even though he wasn't much use.

"I see it in his eyes," Madou went on. "He hates us for what we are, not what we do."

Rufus had heard enough. "Tomek saved my life, *and* yours, so you're going to look after him whatever he thinks of you. Is that clear?"

Madou grinned toothily, "It's all right, chief. Our people are used to Wolfen hatred." He spread a big paw, "But, if you could have a word with him. Make him see as *you* see."

"That's too dangerous."

"Why? He could join us. Doesn't he hate the Howlers for sending him down? Doesn't he want revenge?"

"Of course not."

"But he must-"

"No 'must' about it," Rufus scoffed. "You give our people no credit, do you? Tomek's still a wolf, loyal to Lupa despite his punishment. I don't want to drag him down any further than I already have. There's no way back for me, but he's only received a short stint for a decision I foisted upon him. If what you say is true, if THORN really is poised to bring change, he'll be safer here when the storm breaks. And if THORN fails, well, he'll soon be back on duty. Either way, he'll be all right."

Madou pushed his cap back, "You care a great deal for him. Is he what you wolves call a… beta?"

"I owe him," Rufus explained, pointing, "*You* owe him. Hyena honour dictates you pay back your debt."

Madou could but nod.

The wolf and the hyena, a questionable pairing anywhere else but Gelb, tramped up the stairs into one of the camp's fifty or so long huts. The draughty wooden structure contained rows of deserted bunk beds, with little square windows cut into the walls between them and a few naked gas lamps flickering overhead. Rufus and Madou creaked down the middle, homing in on two burly wolves sitting on opposite bunks, embers smouldering, cards in paws; a barrel served as a table between them. One was a scar-flecked grey fellow with rippling arms, the other a relatively chunky blonde chap, not unlike Linus, but with a healthy gut.

"Why if it isn't the Scarabs!" the grey one woofed, without so much as looking up from his cards – no doubt he'd sensed the approach of a fellow, powerful Howler, and his afflicted hyena friend. "Darlings of Gelb!" he mocked.

He dealt a card, flicking it onto the barrel between him and his friend. The card depicted a lovingly-rendered, anatomically accurate 'Queen of Bees', her six legs spread symmetrically astride a rich, warm, golden honeycomb. The blonde wolf responded by placing down a more modest 'Seven of Bees', the bees being arranged neatly in formation – modest, perhaps, but it still made his grey wolfen counterpart grunt in annoyance and scrutinise his own cards more closely.

"Whatcha found down there this time, oh master of miners?" the grey wolf asked Rufus, aggressively slapping down a nine of bees and waving a paw about. "The tomb of Ulf? The secret of eternal youth? Pray tell!"

Meanwhile, with a mischievous smile, the blonde wolf gently laid a 'Drone of Wasps' on the deck, similar to the Queen of Bees, but with a papery backdrop. The grey wolf grumbled and growled and tugged at his collar, but there was no way out. He picked up five cards from a second deck and added them to his growing paw, as the obtuse rules dictated.

"Well?" he snapped tetchily at Rufus, giving him a quick, pugnacious glare. "Hurry up; your hyena lackey is stinking up my air!"

With a glance at his hyena lackey, Rufus reached into his breeches and produced his catch. The pure, white-imperium crystal lit up the faces of the players. The blonde wolf's smouldering ember tumbled from his lower lip as he gaped in wonder, whilst the grey remained outwardly composed, just about.

"Well, lah di dah," he mocked, making a special effort to concentrate on his game as oppose to the fabulous chunk of life-extending imperium, "That doesn't impress me."

Rufus pocketed the gem. "I'll take it elsewhere then," he said, making to leave, "Come on, Madou."

"Chief."

With an eye-roll, the grey wolf stood up. "Wait, wait, wait," he sighed.

Rufus did so.

Without further fuss or mockery, the grey wolf cleared the cards away.

"Oi!" the blonde wolf piped in dismay.

"Clients, mate, can't be helped," his companion said, pocketing the decks. "Stand guard, yeah?"

Whilst the blonde wolf did so and went to the door to keep watch, his grey companion twisted the hefty barrel aside. He crouched down and hurriedly lifted the floorboards to reveal a wooden trapdoor. Lifting it by a rusted ring and opening a hole in the ground, he ushered his 'clients' inside.

"Quick!"

Removing his cap and tucking it down his shirt, Madou squeezed his powerful hyena frame through the orifice feet-first. The more svelte Rufus followed with relative ease. The trapdoor was immediately slammed behind them, plunging them into a damp, erde-reeking blackness. The scraping of wooden planks and the rumble of a barrel followed, as well as some muffled complaining.

"You could've left the cards on top."

"I didn't want 'em falling in the mud. Do you know how much they cost me? Ten meal tokens. Ten!"

"Just 'cause you were losing."

"Oh shut up and deal, you big baby. They're gonna be down there a good twenny minutes."

Leaving their fellow inmates to their distraction, Rufus and Madou crawled down the steep, pitch-black passage, heading for a dim light ahead. After months of mining, they were becoming accustomed to such claustrophobic spaces.

The way was barred by a rough, round wooden door with no external knob. Streaks of green light streamed through cracks in the wood, dividing up Rufus's wolfen face. With a glance at Madou, he rapped on the door.

"Password?" someone grunted from beyond.

"Caste," Rufus replied.

Given a brief pause, the door creaked open revealing a small, low, natural cave complete with well-worn stalagmites, some of which were sheared off altogether. Lighting came not from any lamp, but the slick, undulating walls themselves. They were laced with glowing veins of green-imperium, providing illumination enough to read by, if not comfortably. Nature's radiant marvels jostled for space with an invasion of dull, beast-made objects; boxes, barrels and burlap bags, some piled high in the corners. Wonky shelves crammed with bottles and trinkets lined the damp, dew-laced wall at the far end, behind what resembled a shop counter.

Rufus clambered into the cave on all fours. The ceiling was too low for him to stand. Preferring not to stoop, he instead sat against the nearest wall whilst Madou squeezed his mighty shoulders through the entrance and shuffled awkwardly into the cave.

The moment Madou was in, the door was gently shut behind him by the enormous paw of a bear. The big, black beast hunched menacingly over the hyena, crouching with his rounded ears touching the ceiling. He filled a good portion of the space down here and for the life of him Madou couldn't fathom how a bear had ever squeezed down a passage he himself had trouble managing. Smiling nervously, the hyena scooted backwards on his rump until he was sitting beside his wolfen friend. Rufus remained unconcerned as always, his muzzle slightly raised and graced with a confident smirk, one forearm resting on a knee.

"How are you, old chap?" he asked the bear, tipping his cap at him like a gentlebeast.

No reply, save a grunt.

"We'd like to see the professor, if he's not too busy."

As if on cue, a ragged green curtain behind the counter was whipped aside by a white cat without a collar. He peered in, his creamy face streaked with glittery imperium.

"You again?" he scoffed, disappearing at once. "Vhat do you vant now, Rufus? I am eeeextremely busy."

Rufus stood up and fearlessly ducked across the ghostly green cave to the white cat's wonky counter, whereupon he sat in a wicker chair nestled amongst the junk.

Giving the bear a glance, as if worried the giant might strike him down, Madou followed suit. He knelt upright beside Rufus, paws resting nobly on knees, as if posing for a traditional hyena portrait where the male knelt beside his seated and superior wife. The worldly Rufus noticed the chance similarity, but thought better than to point it out and offend Madou.

"Just a couple of things, Professor Tack," Rufus said cordially, "if you can stretch to it."

"Depends on vhat you've brought for me," the cat said pompously, his voice echoing from the adjoining cave. "You'd better not be vasting my time!"

Rufus had no idea how large Tack's secret abode was, but he supposed there was more to this place than two atriums. The white cat had been down here some years apparently, hidden from the hogs, the Warden and most inmates. Presumed lost in the endless mines by the official records, he had in fact faked his death and gone underground in a different manner to become the go-to beast for extra imperium stings. A once prestigious member of the Ark, Tack had been sent down for some illegal experiment or other, Rufus hadn't managed to get it out of him during his brief visits, but the cat's imperious knowledge meant he was one of the few beasts in Gelb able to distil imperium and bring added relief to those with the means to pay. Beasts brought him raw imperium, he took his share for his experiments, distributing useable stings and other commodities back.

"I found this little nugget," Rufus said airily, holding the imperium crystal between a finger and thumb.

Tack peeped through the tatty curtain. "Ach!" he hissed, scrabbling to lean over the counter. "Wunderbar!"

Before the fumbling feline Professor could take the monocular magnifier from around his neck and get a better look at Rufus's treasure, the wolf tucked it away.

"I want six stings," he demanded.

"Six!" Tack squeaked.

"Yes, standard fifty minims each, no skimping. And a few packs of embers – good ones mind."

"Impossible!"

"And a bottle of Hummel brandy. Oh, and chocolate."

"Nein, nein, nein."

"And I want them right now, up front, or I'm off to the hogs with this one."

"They'd hang you, Rufus, vor sneaking it through the checkpoint in the first place!"

"No, I don't think so," Rufus chuckled. "Lots of beasts go to them instead of you. But… I would *prefer* to continue to use your services, Professor, rather than line the pockets of those interminable bullies."

Tack's ash-stained whiskers hiked as he smirked with sympathy, "Naturalig."

"We've a deal then?"

"Ja, ja, all right. But you stretch me too var, Rufus. It's only because you are a fellow enlightened beast of science and reason vat I tolerate your cheek." Tack looked through Madou as if he wasn't even there to the big black bear looming silently and menacingly behind. "Remember," the Professor mewed with malice, "I could have Berg there snap your collared necks as easily as I snap mein fingers."

"I don't doubt it," Rufus grunted back, rubbing said collared neck, which was tighter than usual, "providing the ambient imperium in here doesn't throttle us first."

Tack smirked, "You know, I could remove your collars and replace them with counterfeits…

vor a price."

Madou's hefty face lit up, "You could?"

"Ja, ja."

"No," Rufus dismissed at once, "we're fine, thank you."

"But, chief-"

"What're we going to do, Madou, pretend to choke when the guards turn their little dials? We'd soon be found out."

Tack disagreed, "You vould be surprised how many have had the procedure and yet go undetected. It makes one's stay in this pit a little more… tolerable," the cat finished, ending on a high note, as if asking a question.

Rufus nodded, but said, "I'm afraid without it I would be sorely tempted to turn my imperious fire on the hogs and go down fighting. As it is, the notion of choking to death stays my paw and keeps me alive. Ironic, I know."

"Moronic, I fear; a most volfen trait I did not expect from a scientist like you."

"I'm a Howler first, sir."

"Ah. Then you *are* a fool."

⁂

With a knock on the roof and muffled protestations over yet another card game being interrupted, the trapdoor was flung open and muted sunlight poured in. Unable to see, Rufus was pulled blinking from the darkness into the light and Madou shortly after. The planks and barrel were hurriedly replaced by the grey and blonde wolves and the game continued between them as if nothing had occurred.

"Don't linger, you idiots," the grey wolf growled at them, his snout studiously buried in his cards already.

Nodding and blinking, Rufus and Madou took their leave, walking swiftly round the far end of the huts where they stood in the shade whilst their eyes adjusted. With a glance around for guards, Rufus dolled out the goods.

"Here," he said, passing Madou a sting, distilled and packaged by Tack; it almost looked official.

Madou gratefully received them. "Thank you, chief."

Despite Madou's earlier claims to the contrary, Rufus could see the relief in the hyena's violet eyes; relief that he could at last quench the pain and stave off the rot another month. It was against his hyena philosophy to take white-imperium, an affront to the Sky, but there was just no fighting the rot's agony. Madou was young and strong, but he and his fellow Chakaa brothers had been taking purple-imperium for years, drinking it in sacred chunta. They were as far gone as a Howler twice their age.

Well, at least now Madou was getting the good stuff, the best stuff. The poor boy will be all right.

By Ulf what's wrong with me? He's part of THORN. They're planning mass murder! Get a grip Rufus, you fool.

"Chief?"

"Mm?" Rufus hummed, "Sorry, I was miles away. Thinking of… elsewhere."

"I know the feeling," Madou grimaced, looking around the bleak, yet beautiful Sunrise Mountains beyond the Gelb fences and watchtowers. "I was just saying; you go ahead and eat with the others. I'm going to go take this now," he explained, flashing his sting a moment before hiding it again in his shaking paw. "I… I'm sorry, I-I-I have to."

Rufus nodded, "There's no shame in it."

With a slight scoff, the stocky Madou dipped his dark muzzle to his tan chest, then raised it, "I am ashamed to admit my weakness in front of the others, even Zozizou, and he's a mere addict! But not you, Red-mist; I can talk to you."

"I'm honoured, Madou."

"I trust you. I think of you as I do Nurka and Themba. You're one of us."

Rufus's smile faded a little. "Best take it now," he said, glancing around for guards, or anyone else for that matter, "I'll watch over you."

"No. I don't want you to see."

"See? But you just said you trust me-"

"Chief! Please, give me my dignity. You wouldn't want to be watched either, not after starving so long."

To that Rufus nodded.

The trembling Madou moved on, "I'll... I'll walk you to the canteen. I'm supposed to be watching your back-"

"Madou, I think I can make it to the canteen without being assaulted," Rufus assured. "I'll tell the others I ordered you to take your sting."

With a grateful woof and much nodding, Madou took his leave and disappeared round the side of a hut. Fondling the precious sting in one paw and tugging at his collar with the other, he walked swiftly through the desolation of Gelb, past wretched, sunken-eyed beasts who would gladly kill him for what he had hidden about his person, but who were too weak to tackle a hyena of his strength, or too afraid of the repercussions to try – Gelb's guards, despite to their own wanton use of their truncheons, looked unkindly on beasts who started fights.

Searching for a quiet corner free of prisoners and especially guards, Madou found a deserted spot behind a hut where not a soul was lingering. He ducked into the shadows, out of sight, and hurriedly tore open the cardboard sting. Asking for the Sky's forgiveness and parting the fur at his wrist, he slid the needle into his veins and the life-extending imperium into his blood.

Here it comes, Madou.

Dropping the syringe in the mud, Madou grasped at his collar, sliding his fingers down inside the metal band in a vain attempt to keep it at bay as the imperium rush took hold. He fell, scrabbling about the slick mud, unable to breathe, unable to think, his body wracked by imperious fire, his mind starved of oxygen. The world melted into a daub of coloured blurs and darkness encroached from the extremities, as if Madou were peering down a kaleidoscope.

It'll be over soon. It'll be over soon.

Someone appeared amidst the turmoil, a big beast looming large. In his feverish state Madou lashed out to be rid of the intruder, but the beast grabbed his wrists and held him firmer than anyone ever had in Madou's young life. He kicked and snarled, but the beast simply endured the blows.

"Stop it Madou!" they growled.

Starved of air and sanity, the choking Madou fell back in the freezing mud, tongue lolling.

The world went dark and quiet.

Light returned and the world reformed; forlorn fields and wind-whipped tents, bare trees stripped of leaves by poisonous ashen rain.

I'm back home, Madou realised, looking all around the hyena camp. I'm on the reservation! He looked down at his little dark-fingered paws, his puny body, a mighty hyena male no longer, but a feeble cub again, twelve or so, he couldn't quite tell. To his right stood Themba, tall and strong even for his age, and beyond him Nurka, his eyes tinged with more than imperium, with wisdom and foresight too.

"Madou!" someone growled ahead.

The youth looked up at the towering, powerful hyena in a fluttering vermillion red cloak, with his wondrous armour of black and white, shining spear jammed in the erde.

"Madou, stay with me!" he rumbled. "Be strong!"

"I am, my Prince!" Madou insisted, in his half-broken voice. "I am strong!"

"Madou! Madou!"

"I'll save our people! I will-"

The cloaked hyena reached down and cuffed Madou across the muzzle. The fields and tents were dashed aside, replaced by the wall of the wooden hut. Madou stared unblinking at the planks and slowly raised his muddied paws. They were big again, his arms muscled and strong, his body that of a powerful warrior, a Chakaa, not some helpless pup.

"Madou," someone said, in a hair-tingling baritone.

Madou turned to see, to confirm what he dared not yet believe his ears were telling him.

There he was, such a handsome hyena, so strong, so healthy, holding his head on his long, powerful neck with such grace and assurance even whilst kneeling in mud.

"Prince Noss?" Madou mouthed.

The hyena nodded, "It's... good to see you again, Chakaa Madou."

Given a moment's eye-darting hesitation, Madou scrabbled to his feet only to dive forward in the filth to prostrate himself utterly. "Prince Noss!" he cried, his snout scraping the erde. "Wife of Arjana! Son of the Four Winds!" he spluttered, shaking his head side to side, "F-ffff-forgive me. I didn't know it was you! How could I know? I thought you... I thought... Oh, by the Sky, I'm still dreaming!"

Noss laid a big paw on the back of Madou's thick neck and stroked his coarse fur. "No dream."

"Forgive me, my Prince. I didn't mean to strike you-"

"There's nothing to forgive, you were confused," Noss hushed. "Now, calm yourself before your collar chokes you again."

Gulping hard against his stifling collar, but remaining prostrated, Madou said happily, "Nurka said they'd murdered you. The wolves all said it."

"Do I look murdered?" Noss grunted. "Well, perhaps I'm a ghost? Hahahahaaaa!"

Madou didn't know what to say, so he refrained.

"It's I who must beg *your* forgiveness," Noss went on, suddenly sober. "You and... all my tribe-"

"My Prince, you can't say such things!" Madou yelped.

"I can. I must."

"But you're a prince! You're infallible."

"Infallible? Yet you, a mere warrior, are telling an infallible prince of hyenas what to do, it seems."

"No, my Prince-"

"Be quiet, you disrespectful whelp! I'll have this out before the unbearable shame kills me."

Madou bit his tongue.

"I did what I did for my wife and cubs," Noss said. "I never wanted to kill Red-mist, but... they offered me a fortune. I didn't think of the consequences. It never even occurred to me that the wolves would use my 'treachery' as a stick to beat the tribes with. I thought it was about bumping off Rufus, not blackening my own people's reputation."

"My Prince-"

"I'm truly sorry for my stupidity," Noss went on. "I'm sorry that I abandoned you all. I don't deserve to be your prince, but-"

"Prince Noss, please stop-"

"But!" Noss over-talked the mortified Madou, "I know you won't accept anything less, because I know unlike me you honour our traditions, as a hyena should. So here I am, contrite but willing to serve. Though fat lot of good I am to you all now, eh? Hahaaaahahahahaa!"

Madou gulped back his many questions.

His laughter subsiding, Noss posed his own, "So, how did you wind up in Gelb, Madou?"

"Captured, my Prince. I was bitten by a sewer centipede and... well... taken by the Bloodfangs. Nurka and Themba only just escaped themselves, from what I hear."

"Why weren't you executed?"

Madou shook his head, "I wish I had been, but a wolf called Vladimir went out of his way to send me here. I tried to get myself killed but he spared me... twice. It's like he wanted me to suffer."

The taller Noss grasped Madou's muscled shoulders and raised the stocky fellow up, so that both were standing. The lower-ranking Madou kept his teary eyes averted down, as hyena etiquette dictated.

"Vladimir's got a use for you," Noss growled. "Perhaps he even falsified your death, like mine."

"My Prince?"

Looking around, Noss explained, "I'm only alive because of what I know. Vladimir thinks he can use me to bring Amael Balbus down someday, so he hid me away here. Since I haven't been sent for yet I assume Amael and the wolfen conspirators are merrily chugging along?"

Madou confirmed. "They grow stronger every day, my Prince, as does THORN. In fact, I... I may have been spared because Amael arranged it."

"Amael? Why would he save a hyena?"

"Because, we're allies now!" Madou woofed, his claim punctuated by a deep yet quick and giddy hyena laugh. "Haha! Can you believe it? Wolves and hyenas working together."

Noss snorted, "What do you mean?"

The Prince sounded displeased, but Madou confidently enlightened him, "Amael came to us alone, soon after your arrest and... well, execution. He apologised for what was done to you and bowed before Nurka, on his knees! I'd never seen a wolf do that before." Madou shrugged and chuckled, "Themba wanted to cave his head in of course, as did I, but Nurka was wiser and struck a deal with the wolfen conspirators."

"What kind of 'deal'?"

"To take over Lupa, together," Madou all but whispered, as if someone might overhear and scupper THORN's plans. "Amael's provided us with everything; we have kristahl weapons now, and even ancestral Jua-mata armour. He stole it from a museum. It was wonderful to wear, whilst I had it."

Noss grunted, "I dread to think where mine went."

Madou continued, "Amael's supplied information too. Train schedules and details of sting shipments, even routes in and out of the city. It's taken us this last year and many hyena lives, but now everything is in place. Lupa's white-imperium stocks are low, but Amael has hoarded his own private cache. All that remains is the final blow to initiate the takeover."

The Prince hiked a thick, dark, hyena eyebrow. "Final blow?"

"At the Pack Summit. It's being held in Everdor this year, in Hummelton Town, far away from Lupa. Nurka's going to kill the Den Fathers whilst they're there, all of them in once. Then, whilst the packs are confused and panicking back in Lupa, Amael will return to seize the city and use his sting cache to outlast any resistance. We'll make a new government with him, wolf and hyena alike."

"You trust Amael after what he did to me?"

"No... but I trust Nurka. He'll see through any wolfen trick, I know it."

Noss grumbled, "And how does one kill *all* the Den Fathers when they're guarded by countless Howlers? The Pack Summit will be impossible to penetrate, even in pokey little Hummelton."

Madou grimaced, "I'm... not sure. I only know Nurka's plan involves the black-imperium we stole."

"*Black-imperium!*"

"Yes, my Prince. We've built up a huge stockpile from all the raids. That's what we've been doing since you were taken. It's been dangerous work, but so far we've had no accidents."

A long pause ensued.

At last, and with a rub of the jaw, Noss grunted, "So what's Nurka going to do, bomb the Summit with it?"

"Only he knows how it's to be done, my Prince."

"You don't?"

Madou seethed in shame "No. If Nurka *had* trusted me with his plans I'd have given everything away to Vladimir by now and all would be lost. They... they racked me, then had hung me by my paws for days, I-I-I couldn't bear it. I had to tell them as much as I knew. I *had* to. The pain was...."

Madou's mighty chest heaved as he wept.

"It's all right," Noss said, grasping Madou's shoulders and gently shaking him. "You've nothing to be ashamed of. They broke me too."

"You?" Madou snuffled.

"I told Vladimir of Amael's ambitions when he had me; he promised to protect Arjana if I did.

Of course I didn't know much back then, only that he planned to take over Lupa somehow, not that Nurka was going to help him. Besides, what good is the word of a mad hyena prince to the Den Fathers, eh?"

Madou let out a scoff. "You bear the affliction with great dignity, my Prince."

Noss shrugged. "The strong imperium ambiance around here is something of a comfort, I find. My mind's never been clearer." He tapped Madou's chest, "It's also allowed me to pass undetected even by Red-mist's senses. Besides, he thinks me dead and would never think it was me who passed him in the mines. But I've watched you and him. Yes. You two seem very friendly."

Madou defended, "He's a great wolf. His blood burns with imperium and yet he has time for me, for everyone."

"I told you."

"I think he'd join us, given a chance."

"Rufus," Noss almost chirped, "betray wolfkind?"

"Well they've betrayed him; sent him down on false charges! They're afraid he'll find a cure for the rot, he says."

"Hah! Maybe he will."

"He's a noble wolf," Madou insisted, "I… I would be dead months ago but for him."

"Then I'm in his debt, again."

"And I."

Suddenly Noss grasped his head in both paws, "By the Wind, how can I face him after what I did? I never expected us to meet again. I expected to die that day. I expected us both to die and Arjana to go free and yet none of it came to be."

Madou could but wait in silence.

The prince pondered matters. "Go back to Rufus, say nothing of me," Noss instructed. "I'll face him when the time is right."

Madou bowed again. "As you say, Prince Noss," he said, adding giddily, "And thank the Wind you're alive. Nurka will be so happy, and Themba too!"

"I'll see them again in this life," Noss predicted cheerily.

Once Madou had bowed and scraped his way round the corner and disappeared, Noss collapsed against the hut wall and slipped down into the mud.

"Nurka you fool," he growled, punching the ground, "you'll destroy my whole people!"

Chapter 27

The citizens of the buzzing Common Ground looked up from their café tables and newspapers this fine Lupan morning as a monobike screeched by. To those in the know, the intermittent revving of the engine attested to an inexperienced rider, but he was still a Howler, and a Bloodfang at that. Even here in the Common Ground, safe from Bloodfang or any other jurisdiction save ALPHA's, this fellow was to be avoided and by no means mocked, and the well-practised citizens of every race averted their eyes to their breakfasts and papers as ever.

The monobike and its stocky, red-cloaked wolfen rider rumbled and popped along the main road, past the cinema, pubs, restaurants and such, before coming to a juddering halt outside a nondescript town house. Kicking out the stand and swinging his armoured legs off the bike, the Bloodfang crunched across the pavement to the building, muscled, blonde-furred arms swinging gently, baby-blue eyes taking in the ash-stained bricks and tall windows from beneath his imposing helmet, round shield bobbing at his back.

The only indication that this address was one where a lonely Howler like him might find paid comfort was the red-imperium lantern eternally standing sentinel over the door – a code for those with eyes to see.

This was a Lupanar – a Howler brothel.

Climbing the steps, this next probable customer rapped on the hefty door and waited, paws cupped behind him. Time, citizens and cars, passed.

A flap slid to one side and a pair of large, eyeliner encircled pink eyes obviously belonging to the face of an older white wolfess scrutinised the soliciting wolf.

"It's six in the morning, Howler," she crackled, in an ember-checked voice. "We're closed until sundown."

"I-I-I know," the Howler excused, "but may I see Rosa quickly?"

"Rosalina? Do you have an appointment?"

"No, marm, but tell her it's Linus, Uther's partner."

"Uther Bloodfang Wild-heart?" the wolfess snorted. "Haven't seen that rogue for months. Has he dropped dead?"

"Uh, no marm; he's just… away."

After a while the wolfess demanded, "Brooch, please."

Linus grasped his brooch and induced the red-imperium fang to glow, proving as much as was possible from afar that the brooch was real and he was a Howler.

Satisfied, the wolfess unlocked the door and beckoned him in, confirming herself to be, as Linus had suspected even through the door flap, comfortably old enough to be his mother. Her smart purple petticoat and dress were of top quality and gilded with golden thread woven into images of various bugs – there was clearly lots of money to be made in an establishment where rich, drunken Howlers emptied their capacious cloak pockets for a night's pleasure.

"I'm Lady Audrey," the wolfess said, breaking an ember off in her mouth and speaking through clouds of vapour. "I look after the girls here."

"Pleasure, marm," Linus said nobly.

"Is it indeed?" Audrey woofed, one arm folded, the other holding her ember. She cast her pink eyes over the client before her, "You fill out your cloak don't you, Howler? You're like a little bear."

Linus could but emit a worried scoff.

Winking mischievously, Audrey observed further, "I've never seen you in here before. I'd have remembered you."

"N-nnn-no, marm. I've never, uh… well…."

Audrey brushed Linus with a bony paw, "Say no more, love. Rosa's very good with your sort. Gentle lass, she is."

'My sort?' Linus thought, but made only agreeable noises.

Laughing hoarsely, Audrey beckoned her plainly inexperienced client through the lobby to a perfectly respectable bar, with little round tables and a crackling fire. It looked a cosy place for a cup of tea and a newspaper, not at all what Linus had expected. In an hour or two, he supposed, Howlers would emerge from their rooms to partake of breakfast and catch up on the news, just like beasts staying at any other hotel.

"Wait here, Howler," Audrey said, creaking upstairs.

Removing his helmet and nodding, Linus wandered aimlessly around the deserted bar, brushing the smooth tabletops with a paw. He pictured Uther in the far corner with Lorna draped over one shoulder, Rosalina the other, both hanging on his every word as he drank and smouldered, lightening his troubles and his wallet.

Turning over a crumpled edition of yesterday's paper, Linus flicked through the usual propaganda to an article on the looming Pack Summit. Grainy photos of Everdor, with its rolling farmland and biscuit-box villages, caught his roving eyes; the City of Hummelton too, capital district of the Pack Hummel, complete with a castle and tall town houses.

You'll be there a week from now, his brain told him. You'll see it for yourself. Fields of green plants, clean water, bugs at every turn. Everdor must be a marvellous place.

"Linus!"

That recognisable squeak brought Linus back to Erde, back to Lupa. "Rosa," he beamed without knowing it.

The little brown wolfess scuttled downstairs in a modest green petticoat, modest compared to the frilly attire Linus was used to seeing her in at any rate, and waddled over to the Howler. Grasping Linus's big arms in her delicate paws she kissed the bashful Howler on the cheek in the manner of a friend then drew back to look him over.

"How ya bin, handsome?" Rosa asked, looking all around and asking further, "Is Uther back, then?"

"Not yet, no," the 'handsome' Linus replied, a little flustered by that unexpected kiss.

Squeezing Linus's free paw in both of hers Rosa leant forward and chided playfully, "Well where's the rogue gone? I thought you said he'd only be two months!"

Linus muddled through, "I-I-I know, but… well, one never knows with these secret missions. If it's something to do with THORN then it must be a very tricky situation, and they'll have to think on their feet, him and Ivan," he said, as if he had the slightest inkling of what he was talking about.

Rosalina was convinced at any rate. "Oh, it sounds very daring, dun' it?" she marvelled. "He'll have some tall stories to tell when he gets back won't he?"

"Some very tall ones, knowing Uther."

Linus and Rosa shared a hearty laugh as Lorna moseyed down the stairs in a red petticoat.

"Howdy, Linus," she greeted, when only halfway down.

"Lorna," he replied, adding, "Uther's not back yet."

"Yeah, I heard ya'll talking from upstairs. You two are like a walking barn party. You're gonna wake our sleepy clients."

"Sorry," Linus excused.

As Lorna passed Rosalina she pinched her friend in the side. "Well it's mostly Miss Foghorn here," she tutted good-humouredly, before kissing Linus on the other cheek and saying, "not Lupa's truest gentlebeast."

Further flustered, Linus tugged at the neck of his red cloak and attempted to construct words with his lips, "Uhm, well uhm… I…."

Giving up, Linus reached into his cloak pocket and produced a rainbow wad of lupas.

"Here," he said, pushing them at the wolfesses.

Feasting their eyes on the spectrum of money, the girls exchanged baffled glances, before Lorna spread a paw over the nape of her elegant blonde neck and conquered her shock to mount the power of speech. "Linus, honey," she purred, brushing a paw on his mantle-clad chest, "you don't have to pay us all up front, sweetheart. We know *you're* good for it, if that's what you want. Though, truth be told it is a little early in the day, we'll need five minutes to spruce up."

"What?" Linus gasped, eyes darting about. "Oh! No, no, no, it's not that! I don't want that!"

"Whatcha mean?" Rosa squeaked indignantly at Linus.

"Nothing. I just want you two to be all right, what without Uther around to, well… uh…. You see, he told me to look after you, but I won't be here. I-I-I'm going away for a while and so… well, there it is."

Lorna put Linus out of his misery, "You're going on a secret mission as well?"

"No, just the Pack Summit," Linus exhaled. "I'm going as Vladimir's adjutant."

"You mean, all the way out to Everdor?" Rosalina asked.

Linus nodded at her. "To my honour," he said, with sudden resolve. "I never expected to do something this important so early in my Howlership. I just hope I don't embarrass Grand Howler Vladimir."

"Of course you won't, silly!" Rosalina scolded, pushing Linus's money away as if it were offensive to her eyes, "And put that away!"

"Please, I insist."

"We won't take it fer nothing, will we Lorna?"

Lorna eyed up the cash a while, before snapping from an apparent stupor. "Of course not!" she woofed, arms folded.

"See?" Rosalina piped, wagging a finger at Linus before placing her paws on her hips. "Payment is one thing, but we'll not take no charity. We have our dignity, Linus."

"Please, Rosa, it's what Uther would want if he knew I was going away."

"Well we'd turn him down too!"

Linus, eventually, let his paw of lupas flop down. "I've insulted you," he guessed.

"Of course you ain't, silly," Rosalina sighed. "We appreciate your kindness, really, but me 'n' Lorna can look after ourselves. Us Beehive girls, we all stick together here, just like you 'Owlers do over at your Dens."

Linus wished that last statement were true.

Shuffling over to the stocky Howler, Rosalina hugged him tight, her little arms barely encompassing his robust form. Linus stood stiffly at first, unable to move, even breathe in the embrace of a wolfess. Slowly he relaxed in Rosalina's hold and even returned her sweet hug.

This isn't so bad.

"You're too good a wolf to have the rot, Linus Bloodfang," Rosalina cooed warmly, nuzzling into his thick neck. "Too good by half. Have fun in Everdor, handsome. We'll be here when you get back, you 'n' that rogue Wild-heart and we'll hear all about your adventures. All right?"

"Be careful out there on the streets," Linus said. "Lupa's a dangerous place."

"We'll manage, you daft beast."

As they parted company, Rosa felt Linus tug on the back of her petticoat.

She thought nothing of it.

Once goodbyes were exchanged and Linus had donned his helmet and left the building, Lorna and Rosalina climbed the steps to return to their rooms.

Alighting upon the wooden landing, Rosalina noticed a lump in the back of her green petticoat, right between her shoulder blades. Squirming and tugging did nothing to shift the irritation.

"Lorna could you have a look round there?" Rosa said, turning around and jabbing at thumb at her shoulders. "I think me underclothes are snagged in me strings, love."

With a gasp, Lorna plucked at Rosa's petticoat, instantly relieving the tightness. "Well, you got *something* snagged," she laughed, waving a crumpled wad of notes in front of Rosalina's wide-eyes. "I think Linus dropped something."

"Ooooh, that naughty wolf!" Rosalina growled, snatching the money and dashing downstairs. "Linus! Linuuus! Come back here!"

"Rosa, be quiet," Lorna seethed, chasing her colleague.

The loud popping of a monobike engine coughing into life and thrumming away beat the wolfesses to the front door. By the time they made the dew-licked streets, Linus was whizzing down the golden, sunlit road, deaf to Rosa's shouts by choice if not by circumstance.

Once the Howler had vanished over the hill, Rosa deftly counted the money. "It's five hundred,

Lorna!" she groaned, at once ashamed and delighted. "Why'd he do that?"

"Maybe he loves yer?" Lorna suggested with a wry smile.

"Don't be daft."

"Well, he ain't no Uther Wild-heart, honey, he's a different kind of wolf."

Rosalina looked at the money, then pressed the lupas to her chest like a bunch of sweet flowers and sighed. "You dunno the half it, Lorna."

✦

Parking his Giacomo *Springtail* across the road, Linus walked to the florist opposite and ran his eye over the spring flowers festooning the stall. He supposed this was the done thing when meeting with a respectable wolfess.

A grey old doe rabbit in a floral-pattered headscarf and shawl emerged from behind the stall. "Fresh from Everdor, the finest blooms," she said, in a warm, crackly voice. "Guaranteed to last a week, Howler."

"They look wonderful," Linus replied, lifting his helmet just enough to press his nose to a daffodil's trumpet and take a sniff. It had a sweet, yet musky scent that spoke of a wild world Linus had almost forgotten. "And smell even better," he added, pushing his helmet back down.

"Buying a posy for your mother?" the doe asked him.

"No, no."

"Ah, the girlfriend?"

Linus emitted a slight scoff of amusement and cupping his paws behind him said, "It's not like that."

The smiling doe made noises and gestures that indicated she didn't quite believe Linus. "Where's the lucky wolfess from?"

"Everdor, actually," Linus replied.

"Ah, where my flowers are grown!" said the doe.

"Yes, I heard."

"Then for you, Howler, a special price."

"No need for that, citizen, I'm not of Eisbrand territory. I've no privileges here."

"I noticed," the doe cackled, fearlessly tapping Linus's brooch with a bony finger.

The Howler noticed the imperium fang within brighten for a moment and felt a crackle in his bones.

Odd.

"But, I have a good feeling about you, Bloodfang," the doe continued, "I can tell about someone straight away. It's a gift. You've a good heart."

Linus blurted, "Are you… afflicted, citizen?"

The citizen fussed with her shawl and flowers, fluffing the latter up like pillows. The rubbery stems squeaked as they jostled against one another. "Little beasts like us are not gifted like you," the doe hummed. "We do not share in the blessings of the Howlers."

"Not to the same degree perhaps, but I felt something."

"Ah, well. Who knows?"

Leaving things at that, the doe took a bunch of little white droopy flowers from a bucket. They were rather sad-looking, their teardrop-shaped heads hanging low.

"I suggest these for your wolfess."

"Snowdrops?" Linus chirped.

The doe was surprised, "You know your flowers?"

"Well, I-"

"A bright wolf like you would choose a discerning, intelligent wolfess, I think," the doe interrupted wryly, "and the snowdrops carpet the woods in Everdor this time of year like, well… snow! She will appreciate your thoughtfulness if you choose them and let it be known why."

Her advice given, the old doe deftly wrapped the snowdrops in paper and passed them to her customer, whilst at the same time proffering a withered paw for payment. Despite much humble protestation and shawl-fussing on the florist's part, Linus endowed her with a hefty tip of twenty lupas. She had been very helpful and deserved every penny, he insisted, as she bowed and thanked him multiple times.

"Briar go with you, Howler," she said, invoking the old god of rabbits.

Crossing the street, Linus could almost hear Uther's gruff voice now. 'Puh! Whatcha do that fer? You get suckered in every time, mate, every time!'

Mounting his mono and tucking the flowers between his legs, Linus rode slowly along the road so as to not damage the doe's beautiful blooms. The modest flats and shops either side gave way to finer establishments as the Howler neared the rich district surrounding the Ark and his destination.

Heath's flat swung into view. Parking outside, Linus's heart began to pound and flutter with trepidation. Don't be stupid, Howler, he told himself, it's not like that.

Before he knew it, Linus was up the dingy stairwell.

Knock! Knock! Knock!

"Coming!" Heath cooed, as brightly as his big bear voice allowed. Whilst tying his bow tie he crossed his flat and opened the front door. The professor was surprised to discover a Howler on the landing rather than the postbeast. "Linus," he said, recognising that stocky frame despite the helmet, "what a pleasant surprise."

"Good morning, Professor Heath," Linus replied, paws and snowdrops behind back. "How are you?"

"Fine, Howler. And you?"

"As well as can be expected, sir, all things considered."

"Indeed. I know the feeling."

Clearing his throat, Linus asked, "Is Sara around?"

"Sara?" Heath woofed. "Yes yes, but you've only just caught her, we're off to the Petra Square Science Exhibition in a minute."

"Yes, I know. I'm accompanying her."

Heath nearly went cross-eyed, "You are?"

Linus emitted an awkward guffaw, "I hope so. Unless she's changed her mind?"

"No no, I'm sure she hasn't, but she never told me," the baffled Professor chuckled, scratching a hefty eyebrow. "Uh, come in, come in."

Linus wiped his armoured feet and stepped inside.

"Make yourself at home," Heath insisted, gesturing to the sofa in passing, the one Linus had slept on before. "I'll go let Sara know you're here."

"Thank you."

Heath disappeared into the depths of his flat.

Sitting on the sofa, Linus rolled the snowdrops over in his blonde paws. He could taste the adrenaline on his breath. Is this the right thing to do, or am I about to make an utter fool of myself? Why do I get so nervous over such silly things? I'm a Howler, I fight terrorists, criminals and mad bugs every week and yet a little wolfess frightens me to death.

I bet Uther doesn't feel like this.

He stood up again. Arms swinging aimlessly, he wandered around Heath's living room taking in all the marvellous photos and trinkets once again. As he passed by the dark hall leading to the bedrooms and bathroom, Linus caught wind of a hushed conversation.

"Have you seen him since the symposium, then?" Heath grumbled.

"Aye," Sara said, none too quiet. *"Ah bumped into him down the Common Ground. We had a coffee."*

"Saraaa."

"What?"

"It could be dangerous, associating with a Bloodfang."

"How is he any different tae Rufus?" Sara huffed.

"We don't know him," Heath argued, *"That's how."*

"Aye, and that's why Ah've invited him along. He's a good 'un Professor, Ah can tell."

"Well, so's Tristan. Why didn't you invite him?"

Sara tutted, *"He's nae into science."*

"He's at least an Eisbrand of high rank. He can protect you, more than some... some Bloodfang Trooper."

"Professor, Ah love you, but you're nae mah dad. Ah get enough stick from mah mother without you trying tae tell me what Ah can and can't do."

"It's precisely because of who you are you need to take care. Beasts could use you against Hummel."

"And you think Linus would hurt me?"

"No, but...."

"Well then!"

Linus shuffled away from the corridor and across the room, not because he didn't want to hear, but because he didn't want Heath and Sara to know he had. It didn't surprise him to learn that even the great Professor Heath, scholarly and open-minded though he was, harboured certain negative preconceptions regards Howlers and their packs.

So did Sara, Linus realised, collapsing on the sofa for the second time, *it's just that I'm different, I'm a 'good 'un'.*

"Hello, again."

Linus looked up to see the elegant Olivia breezing into the room in a pink blazer and white breeches.

"Hello, miss," Linus said, hopping to his feet.

"For me?" Olivia gasped, looking at the snowdrops in Linus's paws. "You shouldn't have."

"Oh, uh... well...."

"I'm only joking," the tall wolfess laughed, "I know they're for Sara."

Linus forced a chuckle.

"Don't mind Heath," Olivia whispered, though hardly. "He doesn't mean anything by it."

Linus realised Olivia was referring to Heath's furtive conversation with Sara. "It's fine," he said. "I suppose a criminal *could* use Sara's background against Hummel, if they knew she was their Den Mother's daughter."

"That's why she keeps it to herself. Mind you if anyone did try anything funny Hummel would kick up billy-oh."

Linus chuckled, then asked, "Are you Hummel too?"

"Nooo," Olivia woofed, "I'm a Freiwolf; at least I was adopted by a couple of Freiwolves. They live on Greystone turf. My parents run Blake Eisenglanz Works."

"That's a big concern."

"Yes."

"You live on Greystone territory as well?" Linus assumed.

Olivia shook her head. "No, not for years. I... can't. I'm allergic to ash, you see. I always suspected I was, but it's been confirmed. The Greystone air would likely finish me off for good!"

"I'm sorry to hear that."

"It's all right. You've got things far worse, Linus."

"Maybe, but at least I enjoy the benefits of imperium as well as the inconveniences."

After some time Olivia said cryptically, "So I see."

She sat on the arm of Heath's lovely sofa and crossed her long legs. Her violet eyes looked a little puffy and watery to Linus even though the air was clear today. Perhaps Heath's flat was so impregnated with ash from his constant smouldering it affected her.

"Must be very convenient, being able to blow a beast twice your size across the room," Olivia marvelled.

Linus snorted, "It has its uses."

Casting her eyes over Linus, Olivia smiled and said, "I am thinking of moving to Everdor, actually, with Sara."

"That'll be good for your lungs."

"Yes, but I've decided to stay a while longer, at least until this until mess with Howler Rufus blows over," Olivia went on. "It was very upsetting for the Professor, more than he shows. He has no family and we thought he could use the company."

Linus nodded, "That's very kind," before tacking on, "You think Rufus will be released then?"

"Oh yes," Olivia said, waving a paw. "They'll have to let him out sooner or later. ALPHA's overstepped the mark this time and the Den Fathers won't stand for it. Thorvald's already building a consensus to vote for his freedom. They'll show ALPHA who's boss."

Linus fought to disguise his joy, "I see."

Olivia raised an eyebrow at him, "You're close to Rufus, aren't you?"

Memories of Vladimir's advice reverberated thought Linus's head – deny Rufus, forsake him.

Linus gave in to cowardice, "He was just my superior."

Olivia winced. "It's all right, you're amongst fellow dissidents here," she half-joked. Looking down the hall and then back to Linus, she said in a dulcet tone, "Piece of advice, don't toe the official line in front of Sara or she'll be through with you by midday. That is, if you *want* a proper wolfess instead of the Common Ground floosies you low-ranking Howlers usually have to settle for."

Linus stood speechless.

"Here she comes," Olivia whispered mischievously, standing up as if nothing had been said.

Sara entered the living room in a green blazer and white breeches – she and Olivia made quite the matching pair as they stood together, Linus thought.

"Hello, Linus," Sara beamed, head cocked to one side.

The Howler bashfully hid his snowdrops, "Hello, Sara."

"He's brought you flowers, dear," Olivia betrayed.

"What? Don't be daft, Olivia."

"He has, haven't you Linus? What a gentlebeast."

Thus revealed, Linus brought the snowdrops round front and passed them paw to paw, "I just… well… I was passing a stall and… uh… Well, there it is."

"Oooh, snowdrops!" Sara sighed, melting at a sight unseen in Lupa. Taking the delicate white blooms she gave them a hearty sniff. "Och! They're mah favourite, Linus. How did ye know?"

"I hear they carpet Everdor this time of year," he said, with a modicum of confidence.

"Aye, that they do."

Heath stood in the hall. "My my, snowdrops indeed. Have you been to Everdor then, Linus?" he asked.

"Not yet, sir, but soon. I'm going to the Summit next week. It's being held in Hummelton this year."

"Going as part of your Den Father's escort?"

"I suppose. I… I don't really know what I'll be doing, sir, just that I'm going."

Heath chuckled at the comment, "That's life in general. We are but a penny set spinning on its edge."

There was a brief silence. Proudly nursing her flowers, Sara looked between all concerned, then said to Linus, "Are ye going to hide under that helmet all day, Howler?"

"Sorry," Linus replied, hurriedly undoing the strap and peeling back his helm to reveal his flaxen face. "I forget I'm wearing it sometimes."

To the surprise of all, Sara politely pecked Linus on the cheek, "Thank ye for the flowers," and marched into the kitchen, shouting back, "Ah'll just put them in water and we'll go, all right gang?"

Heath grabbed his keys and jacket. "Have you shut Toggle in, Olivia?"

"Yes, Professor," the wolfess replied.

Giving Linus a knowing Charlie Cricket wink, Heath said humorously, "Good. We could do without a repeat of the great kitchen honey disaster, eh Linus?"

"Oh yes, sir, absolutely."

✦

Knock! Knock! Knock!

Nothing

Knock! Knock! Knock!

Tristan peered through the brass letter box into Professor's Heath's apparently deserted lounge.

"Sara? Professor Heath? Anyone there?"

Not a soul, just the ticking of a grandfather clock.

Unsure how to proceed Tristan stepped back and looked around the hall, as if he might find the answers written on the light-faded walls.

Am I too late? Have they all been arrested?

Hurrying down the stairwell, Tristan got no further than the third floor before he bumped into a trio of black clothed beasts heading up – a grey cat in a black coat flanked by two grim-looking ALPHA Prefects.

"Watch it, Howler!" one snarled.

"Watch it yourself, Prefect!" the heavily armoured Tristan shot fearlessly back; he was bigger than either wolf, as usual, and this was Eisbrand land after all.

The slim grey cat held up a paw to calm his muscular wolfen escorts. "Our apologies, Captain Tristan," he said, adjusting his tinted specs.

"Doctor Josef," Tristan acknowledged. "What're you doing here?" he demanded.

The cat glanced upstairs. "Nobody in, I take it?"

"What?"

Josef Grau mewed knowingly, "Checking on Sara, as usual? I shouldn't bother pursuing her if I were you. She's a clever girl; she's not going to be interested in a lumbering oaf of a wolf like you."

"And what would *you* know about her?"

"I used to teach Sara. Didn't she tell you? I thought you two were the best of friends."

Tristan growled, "I was charged with her protection by her mother, Cora Hummel. Perhaps you've heard of her? She's the Hummel Den Mother, so if I were you I'd leave Sara alone."

"I'm not interested in Sara," Josef airily dismissed, turning the conversation on its head, "Though, I wonder what the Hummel Den Mother would make of your... advances towards her daughter."

"There have been no advances!" Tristan barked, looming over Josef. "Watch your lying tongue, cat, or I'll have you and your Prefect jokers thrown off our land in disgrace!"

Tristan and the Prefects and exchanged growls.

Josef maintained order, raising a paw at his Prefects. "I am merely concerned for you, my friend."

"I'm sure," Tristan scoffed.

"I wouldn't want to see you come to harm over some silly infatuation."

"Is that a threat?"

"So you will of course not obstruct me in my duties!" Josef continued loudly, over-talking Tristan. "I could have you arrested with a click of my fingers; I need only speak to Janoah. Were it not for your cousin being a valued member of her circle she'd have dealt with *you* years ago."

"I'm trembling," Tristan mocked effortlessly.

Josef's white whiskers twisted in frustration; he could not frighten this wolf.

At length, Tristan asked, "State your business. I will be satisfied before you pass me, ALPHA or not."

Josef turned his back. "I've no need to pass, Howler. No doubt they've gone to the Science Exhibition."

"Science Exhibition?"

Beckoning his Prefects to follow him, Doctor Josef took his leave without further ado.

Kicking himself, Tristan also exited the flats, fighting to maintain outward calm and nonchalance. The Science Exhibition, of course they're there!

Thundering across the street, Tristan noticed a little *Springtail* in Bloodfang livery parked nearby, but thought no more of it as he leapt on his own meatier Giacomo *Dragonfly* and sped away.

Josef observed all from the nearest alley. He turned to his Prefects, "Call Janoah; tell her if she wants to get some proper dirt on Tristan, now's the time. He's hiding dodgers and Heath's flat must hold evidence. We'll arrest them all; I'll get my pure-blood, she'll have her spy."

Meryl Stroud gently excavated a hole in the soil with a small spade and placed the plant within. The little bush was a mass of silvery, blade-like leaves and smelt gorgeous – at least Rafe thought so, catching a whiff.

"Smells like perfume," the big wolf observed, crouching beside the tiny nurse, he in his breeches and black Prefect cloak, she her usual, almost clinical uniform. "Lavender, yeah?"

"You remembered," Meryl praised, glancing up at Rafe. "Do you know anything about gardening?"

"Nah," he guffawed freely.

Meryl scooped soil over the lavender's roots and pressed it firmly home. "You should learn," she suggested, giving Rafe a coy sideways look. "It'd be good for you."

"Why?"

"It's therapeutic."

After a while, Meryl cocked her head to one side and added, "Good morning, by the way."

"Yeah, morning."

"How're your eyes today?"

Rafe blinked, "Much better. Things are pretty sharp."

Dusting off her paws, Meryl cast her own healthy eyes around the modest courtyard of ALPHA HQ, with its brutal, simple architecture of brown concrete and metal, quite ugly in her opinion. Still, plants might do well in this sheltered position, though only hardy plants tolerant of imperium ash, as was explained to Rafe.

"Lavender's tough as old boots," Meryl said, "and has medicinal properties. It's a herb, really."

"Can you cook it, then?" Rafe asked.

"My aunt says you can lace cakes with it, but to be honest that sounds revolting."

"Must taste like old wolfesses."

"Rafe!" Meryl chided, hiding a smirk. "Come on, have a go," she instructed, grabbing another potted lavender, one of many lined up, and pushing in into Rafe's mighty brown paws.

"I don't wanna break it," he complained.

"You won't break it," his nurse huffed, immediately taking it back. "Look, you just tap the bottom of the pot and pull," she instructed, doing just that. The lavender popped from its pot amidst a shower of dirt. Meryl dug another hole in the flowerbed and placed the plant beside the first. "We need to make a row," she explained. "Lavender looks best when planted in a row. The bees love it; you might get some little ones visiting."

That pleased Rafe. Meryl watched him take one of the lavenders and ease it from its terracotta pot. For all his strength, he was very careful, a little too careful, to the point of being painfully slow. He would learn.

"Now dig a hole," Meryl directed primly. "Make it the same depth as the original pot. You mustn't cover the stem, you see, or it'll rot the plant and kill it."

Rafe's erect ears pricked still further, "Rot?"

"Not *the* rot," Meryl clarified, regretting her vocabulary choice. "The stem mustn't stay damp, that's all."

"Right."

Rafe didn't take offence; he never did.

Meryl watched him plant the lavender, scooping the soil around its root ball with great care and pressing it down with those big, scarred paws that could channel imperium enough to kill Meryl in a flash.

"Like that?" he chirped like a proud son.

"Very good," Meryl said at length, mother-like. "Do you want to do another?"

"Sure."

Meryl and Rafe took a plant each and set about their work, him doing his best to emulate her, glancing often at her deft paws; she doing her best not to outpace him too much and make him feel inferior. Slowly the row of lavenders grew and took shape.

"Looking good," Rafe commented.

"Yes," Meryl agreed.

"The plants ain't bad either."

After a moment's pause, Meryl reproached, "Behave yourself."

Rafe laughed; Meryl too, quite unable to resist.

At times like this it was easy to forget this wolf was the same beast that donned the frightening Eisenwolf mantle. A few weeks ago Rafe couldn't walk, couldn't even see, his bones and muscles choked by poisonous ash. Now look at him, bright as a button and joking as usual.

The rogue.

Whether Doctor Josef's treatment had helped or not, Rafe's was a miraculous recovery. But how many times could he claw his way back, Meryl wondered, as she watched him work Lupa's polluted soil. How long before he waded so deep into an imperium-fuelled stupor as to sink forever, and all in the name of 'justice'.

Years yet, Meryl convinced herself. He's still so young.

"Rafe!"

Meryl and her charge both looked up from their lavenders to see Janoah striding into the bleak ALPHA courtyard in full Prefect paraphernalia.

Rafe stood up and saluted, ALPHA-style. Meryl refrained, not that Janoah noticed, or cared.

"We've got a job, Stenton," she said. "You can plant daisies another day."

"Lavenders," Rafe tutted.

"What?"

"They're lavenders, Jan. 'En they Meryl?"

"Yes," Meryl replied absently. Kneading her grey paws she hurried over to Janoah, "Must you make him wear that horrid suit of armour again? He's been doing so well."

"Rafe knows his duty, Nurse Meryl," Janoah said patronisingly. "Do you know yours?"

"I do, Prefect, but-"

"Good, then you understand I wouldn't be asking for Rafe's help without reason."

"Of course not, but-"

"I'll return him to you in good health this time," Janoah over-talked. "I promise."

Meryl nodded a little – Janoah was surprised she could nod at all in that suffocating collar and cravat. The wolfess dressed more cat than wolf.

Rafe cupped a big paw on Meryl's shoulder. "See you later," he said with a wink and a click of the cheek.

"Don't you wink at me like Charlie Cricket," she chided, grasping his paw in both hers. "Just come back safe."

Rafe said nothing, but roguishly kissed the back of one of Meryl's soiled paws and rubbed it before accompanying Janoah across the courtyard.

"Gardening, Rafe?" Meryl heard Janoah sigh.

"Yeah," Rafe replied, "it's therapeutic."

※

Pushing the hefty metallic door open just enough to slip inside, Janoah turned the knob on the wall, fuelling the imperium gas lamps overhead. With a cough and sparkle they settled down, bathing the room in their steady off-white glow, unmasking the secrets of this deepest, darkest dungeon within the ALPHA HQ. Barrels and boxes were piled high, pipes wriggled across the ceiling like worms, and the air reeked of oil and imperium. Racks of tools hung on the walls, wrenches, screwdrivers and tortured shapes Janoah couldn't fathom. This was the mad Josef's lair; she and Rafe were but guests.

"Josef isn't here," Janoah informed Rafe, turning over the bundle of keys in her ruddy paws, looking for the right one to unlock the next door set in the wall ahead. "We might need Meryl's help to get you into it."

"Nah, we'll manage," Rafe dismissed at once, stepping inside ahead of Janoah, fingers already unpinning his cloak, as if he couldn't wait to be out of it.

It's been a few months, Janoah thought. Does he miss the power, the thrill?

Do I?

She watched the towering Rafe unpin his brooch and slip his limp, poncho-like mantle from about his mountainous shoulders. He wasn't wearing a tunic beneath; he often didn't bother. His rich brown fur was in good condition, slick and shiny and showing off his rippling back muscles as they rolled beneath his skin. Meryl had done her work and brought Janoah's champion back to health – the nagging little nurse had her uses.

Rafe thoughtlessly tossed his cloak over a barrel like a soiled rag, the brooch dangling down and hitting the side like a conker on a string.

Tutting, Janoah marched over and began to fold the cloak.

"What?" Rafe chirped, sensing her disapproval. "I'm gonna put it back on in a minute-"

"This cloak represents ALPHA; don't cast it aside like a snotty kerchief!" Janoah scolded. "In my old pack you'd be flogged if you got caught disrespecting the colours. You're lucky ALPHA is so forward-thinking. Beasts get away with murder, here."

Pouting, Rafe awkwardly rubbed a huge, muscled arm.

Laying the cloak tidily on a workbench, Janoah went to the second rusted door set in the far wall and, after finding the appropriate key, unlocked it and pulled it wide.

A huge metal wolf stood in the dark recess within, at once tall and strong, yet hanging limp and lifeless. Its grille-clad muzzle rested slightly askew upon its bulbous, metallic chest, which was pitted and scarred like the skin of an old apple. Its long legs were somewhat bent and crooked, knees pressing against the naked bricks of the recess, whilst its Rafe-sized arms hung heavily by its narrow wolfen waist. The tinted round eyes stared down at Janoah, past the cobwebs of a few months indolence, melancholic whether Rafe was inside or not.

"Are you sure you're all right to go again?" Janoah said, as if addressing the empty armour.

Rafe waited until Janoah looked back at him, then nodded and woofed confidently, yet softly, "Yeah."

Janoah nodded back and depressed a button on the inner recess wall.

With an electronic, mechanical whirring the hefty suit slowly eased forward on its armour rack, metal-capped toes dragging slightly on the floor, until it stood proud of the alcove. Janoah removed the helmet, disturbing a long-legged spider, which hurried out of the suit's empty neck and descended on a fine thread of web. Rafe ducked in and caught the tiny creature in both massive paws, ferrying it away to a dark corner.

Janoah rolled her eyes as Rafe returned bearing an innocent smile. "You're as bad as Rufus," she huffed at him. "Always putting bugs out the window instead of swotting them."

Rafe detected a fondness in her tone. "You still care about him, don't yer?"

Janoah flicked her head, but said nothing.

"What's he really like?" Rafe pushed

"It's not safe to talk about a condemned wolf, Rafe."

"Oh come on, who cares?"

"You'd be surprised."

"You can tell me about him. I won't let Silvermane or anyone know-"

"Rafe!" Janoah snapped, adding gently. "Leave it, all right?"

The youth tucked his paws behind him. "Fine."

With a snort, Janoah threw Rafe his hefty helmet like a rugby ball. It hit him square in his muscled belly, making him wheeze as he rushed to catch it.

"I see Meryl's nursing has made you soft, Eisenwolf," Janoah tutted playfully. "I'll soon fix that."

Rafe nodded, "Glad to be back at work, Prefect."

They shared a chuckle.

"Come on," Janoah said, "Josef's waiting."

In an ideal world, with money and trust flowing freely down from ALPHA's upper echelons, Janoah would have at her fingertips a loyal crew of engineers sworn to secrecy. As it was this experimental, backwater project had but Josef, Meryl and herself to dress Rafe and maintain his gear, with Grand Prefect Silvermane occasionally deigning to peer in from time to time. Even with their help, squeezing Rafe into his unyielding, half-inch-thick armour was a tricky business.

The lower half was simple enough. Rafe simply stepped into his Eisenwolf legs like a pair of metal breeches, the smooth, silk-lined rubber coating aiding his feet on their passage down to the snug boots at the bottom.

The middle was trickier. The cuirass was too heavy and unwieldy to lift over Rafe by paw, so Josef had rigged wire pulleys in the ceiling. Attaching the wires, Janoah turned the crank and lifted cuirass aloft, holding it in place. Rafe stood beneath the empty shell, arms up, whilst Janoah turned the crank again. Inch by inch the cuirass was lowered over Rafe's powerful body, like an iron jumper. The big wolf slipped his rippling arms through the padded sleeves and squeezed his broad head through the heavily padded neck – just about.

"You've grown," Janoah observed, removing the pulley wires. "We'll have to adjust it again."

"I'm a growing boy, Jan," Rafe beamed.

It wasn't a joke; this enormous wolf was still a cub.

Janoah hefted the suit's impervious metal arms from the rack and slipped them over Rafe's limbs of mere flesh and blood. With a twist, they clipped in place; left arm, then right. Rafe wiggled his fingers inside the gauntlets whilst Janoah lined up the waist of the breeches with that of the cuirass and twisted them together with a satisfying metallic 'clunk'.

Her Eisenwolf was really taking shape.

Next came the backpack; a grey, metallic tangle of tubes, canisters, grills and dials, the workings of which only Josef really understood, or at least partially understood. Janoah hefted it from the rack, one long, black, wobbly pipe trailing across the floor behind her, and mated it with the matching, opposite depression cut into Rafe's armoured back with another, even more gratifying 'clunk' than before.

"Is it full?" Rafe asked, jiggling up and down. "Feels heavy back there."

Janoah tapped the dial that read 'Liquid Imperium'. The needle stayed put. "Seventy-five percent," she said. "Will that do?"

"Depends," Rafe replied. "Who is this Tristan anyway? He sounds familiar somehow."

Janoah retrieved Rafe's helmet. With him leaning forward she slipped it over his brow, causing that warm, brown face to disappear beneath that cold, grey mask.

"A Howler of some talent," Janoah's said vaguely, pulling up the suit's concertina-like rubber collar that housed Rafe's thick, muscled neck. She clicked it into the underside of the helmet; the Eisenwolf mantle was now air-tight and water-tight. "I know he'll fight sooner than be arrested," Janoah finished, "but we need him alive-"

"Jan... I can't breath!" Rafe wheezed metallically, thumbing round his back. "Me air supply! Quick!"

"Oh!"

Janoah hurried round and grabbed a black pipe trailing from Rafe's backpack. She plugged it into the left side of his helmet, near his nose, then reached round and twisted the main valve on the backpack, the big red one. Within seconds the backpack thrummed into life. Dials whirred and the exhaust projecting near Rafe's left shoulder coughed forth a stale pall of glittering ash, clouding the room.

The chest segment of Rafe's mighty cuirass heaved over the narrow waist below as the huge wolf gulped down air filtered through his backpack. Whilst Janoah choked on the ash Rafe's suit excreted, he himself remained impervious. No gas bomb could affect him, no ash or poisonous vapour reached his lungs, not with his very own air supply filtered through a catalyst of white-imperium crystal mesh. Not even a black-imperium bomb could affect an Eisenwolf, Josef insisted.

"You all right?" Rafe asked the spluttering Janoah.

Waving a paw Janoah donned her helmet to filter out the ash; the mesh inside wasn't as good as Rafe's gear, but better than nothing.

"Fine," she rasped, through the bitter taste of ash.

Rafe fumbled with his loose, wobbling air tube, but his armoured fingers and hefty limbs lacked the deftness needed to sort it out.

"Here, let me," Janoah said.

With motherly care, she clipped the tube into place along the underside of Rafe's armoured jaw and ran it neatly down the left side of his mighty neck so that it wasn't exposed and liable to get snagged on anything.

Janoah fetched Rafe's folded cloak from the workbench and draped it over his hard, unyielding iron shoulders, obscuring the ugly backpack, the ungainly pipe and all the twisted workings round there at a stroke. Only Rafe's exhaust pipe remained, the funnel poking up through a specially-made hole in his mantle. The seams of the hole were reinforced with a ring of beautiful, pattered stitches – Meryl's work.

Securing Rafe's cloak with his ALPHA brooch, Janoah proudly took him all in, her towering champion of iron, muscle and imperium.

"Let's go to work, Stenton," she said, patting his chest.

"FOR THE REPUBLIC!" he declared.

"Yes… for the Republic."

~Blick V~

"G, H, E, G, S... D."

"Good. Next line, please."

"Z, D, F... no, B? Uhm, N, H."

"Uh huh. Next."

"Uhm... J-J... 2? No Z! Z, that is. No numbers, are there?"

"You tell me, Rafe."

A squint, a shrug, an exhale.

"You can't see past line three?" Meryl gasped, sitting beside Rafe.

"Nah. Sorry."

Doctor Josef wrapped up the eye-test, literally snapping the chart upwards like a window blind. "Hmm, perhaps you are developing myopia."

"My...opia?" Rafe repeated,

The cat sighed and tapped his own glasses. "Short-sightedness. You've never worn spectacles before, I take it?"

"No. I don't think so."

"You have or haven't?" Josef snapped. "It's a simple question."

"Well I don't remember, do I?" Rafe woofed back. "Not since you all...." he trailed off.

Meryl held Rafe's paw, cooling tensions.

Unmoved, Josef purred, "Well, you are reaching maturity and myopia can develop naturally in late teenagers. Your body has changed rapidly these past few months, which will happen quite apart from imperium uptake."

Meryl spoke up, "It's clearly the rot, Doctor. It must be. Bright light hurts his eyes, doesn't it Rafe?"

"Well... uh."

"He needs rest and recuperation. I mean look at his fur, it's lost its sheen! Janoah's pushing him too hard."

Josef sniffed, "I'm the Doctor here, nurse, not you."

"That's as may be, but I'm not a fool. Rafe's undergone too many tests and assignments. It's only a matter of time before he gives out altogether and then that'll be an end to your project! He needs a break like any other Howler, especially after what happened in that warehouse last week."

"How do you know about that?"

Rafe twiddled his thumbs and looked to the ceiling.

"I know," Meryl insisted. "It's a miracle Rafe's heart didn't give out. I don't know what Janoah's trying to prove running around a Dead Zone tracking down sting dealers when Rafe isn't ready-"

"The Alpha is watching us, girl!"

Meryl whirled round to see Janoah standing in Josef's door, wearing the stormiest frown.

"And we need to make an impression, for we have little time," she finished, saluting, ALPHA-style.

Meryl saluted also; Rafe too, eventually.

Janoah stepped inside and cast her eyes over her Eisenwolf as he stood up, cloak draping from the enormous muscles of his chest and shoulders like curtains; how he'd grown, even in six short months

"But you're quite right, Nurse Meryl," Janoah admitted, "Rafe deserves a break. He's worked very hard and we're all very impressed, even the Alpha."

Rafe beamed proudly.

Janoah continued, "The Alpha is not a beast to show his emotions, but Silvermane tells me Mad Bront's... 'elimination' has gone down very well. He'd been eluding justice in the Bloc for years.

Of course, ALPHA has not divulged the exact nature of his demise to the Den Fathers, but the point is it was successful and the Alpha knows who was responsible."

A short silence followed.

Janoah waved her paw, "Well off you go. Your holiday starts now, Stenton. You've got a week; go do... something."

Meryl looked up at Rafe, then to Janoah. "Where can he go, exactly?" she asked, uncertain. "Go?"

"Well, I mean away. He needs to go somewhere restful."

"Wherever you like. Just look after him, Meryl, that's your job it seems to me."

Meryl dipped her chin, "I... I have an aunt in New Tharona. They have a house by the sea."

"Don't all Eisbrands?" Janoah half-joked.

"My old allegiance is neither here or there, Prefect, the fresh air will do Rafe good. It'll be much better than lingering in Lupa."

At length Janoah huffed, "I'll get it past Silvermane, just go before anyone notices. And be discreet, for Ulf's sake, Rafe stands out in a crowd rather."

"He'll be as quiet as a mouse monk, won't you Rafe?" Meryl said.

"Aye."

Janoah saluted, "All right, Stenton, dismissed."

"Yeah. Later, Jan," Rafe replied cheerily, slapping her on the back in passing – Meryl tugged him into the corridor.

Janoah sighed at Stenton's dangerous informality; he was not himself. Then again, perhaps he was more himself when high on imperium than not, like an uninhibited drunk. He'd probably slap the Alpha himself on the back in this condition!

Amnesia and quirky behaviour was one thing, but the eyes? Could he be so far gone?

"Well?" Janoah hissed at Josef, once Rafe and Meryl had left earshot.

"His eyesight's damaged," the cat confirmed breathlessly.

"Irreparably?"

"Not yet. But if he deteriorates after every little exertion he won't be much use to us."

Janoah grimaced, "Little exertion? You weren't there, Josef, you didn't see it. The power he wields. He destroyed a Koda. Bront's body was wrapped around a pole like a rag. I've never seen the like, not even from Rufus."

Josef could but shrug. "Perhaps you're right. Still, Rafe may not last long enough to shape Lupa's destiny, as you hope."

"Is there anything else you can try?"

"Other than being frugal with his abilities? Well, there is my shock imperium therapy."

"That torture? No!"

"It might be your only option in a pinch. Even Rafe can metabolise only so many stings in any day. It's not torture if he accedes to it. You can only ask."

Nodding and taking her leave, Janoah lingered at Josef's door long enough to pat the frame and chuckle, "Well, let's see what the seaside air does for an Eisenwolf."

CHAPTER 28

The Scarab Gang had no trouble fulfilling their quota today thanks to Rufus's imperious senses and the combined muscle power of Madou, Helmut and Tomek. Zozizou pitched in, but it was a struggle for the little hyena.

A paw clapped on his bare shoulder. "You all right, Zozizou?" Rufus asked amiably.

"Yes, yes," he rasped – his Lupan was even poorer than Tomek's.

"Take a break if you're tired-"

"No. Fine, fine."

"All right," Rufus hummed, breaking out an ember and smouldering away. He offered a stick to Zozizou and the hyena gratefully accepted, as did everyone else.

Only Tomek refused. "Is not good for you," he puffed, shovelling ore Helmut and Madou were cutting from the wall with picks into the cart.

"I know," Rufus chuckled, removing his ember and looking at it. "I can't go five minutes without one usually, but lately I've cut down. You know, I think my stint down here has been beneficial for my health!"

Tomek laughed, but knew that couldn't be true. Rufus was looking more ragged with each passing week. His red and grey coat, once so shiny and groomed, was scruffy and dirty. He'd lost a lot of weight too. Tomek supposed he himself looked terrible. The dearth of mirrors around here was a blessing.

Bzzzzzzzzt!

The announcement from the speakers strung throughout the subterranean complex was so distorted by the meandering caves and poor speaker quality that nobody directly understood a word, but the mangled syllables made up the familiar pattern of, 'Time up, return to base, or else.'

The Scarabs downed tools and started back, their mine cart safely within quota, though Rufus hadn't found any imperium crystals today. Tomek felt ambivalent about that as donned his tatty stripy shirt. On the one paw no crystals meant no extra food or venom, but on the other paw there was no danger that Rufus was going to get in trouble at the checkpoint for smuggling.

"The crystals haven't had time to grow back," Rufus was saying to Helmut, himself an ex-miner of some skill. "This shaft needs a few months to recover."

"Recover?" Tomek chirped.

Rufus looked at him, "Yes. Gelb's an imperium plume, dear boy."

Tomek frowned, "Plume? What is plume?"

"By Ulf, what're they teaching you youngsters in school these days?" Helmut snorted, pushing the cart. "What's a plume indeed."

"I leave school when I was ten to work fields," Tomek defended. "Then I get rot and that's it, off to Howler Academy."

Rufus tutted gently and shook his head.

Helmet educated the young wolf. "Imperium wells up from the Erde, lad," he said. "It's dissolved in molten rock and boiling water. Places where that happens are called plumes, and Gelb is smack bang in the middle of a whopping one."

"The hot springs are laden with imperium," Rufus elaborated. "As the water cools and percolates through the rock, the imperium precipitates out, forming ore and crystals."

"Prez... Prezipitate?" Tomek struggled.

"It's left behind, like salt in a saucepan of water if you boil the water away."

"Oh! Yes, yes."

Rufus rambled on, enjoying the pleasure of educating young Usenko. "Beasts have come to these parts looking for imperium for centuries. In fact, sick old Howlers pop down to nearby Everdor to bathe in their famous hot springs. It supposedly heals their aching bodies. Does a beast no good, in my opinion. Too much imperium kills most things stone dead, hence the lack of any greenery around here. Gelb was a desolate place long before the Republic of Lupa mined it, and likely will remain so long after."

"After Lupa?" Tomek scoffed with amusement. "What you mean after?"

"The world will outlast beast and his squabbles, Tomek."

Ending on that prophecy, Rufus flicked his half-spent ember away into the gloom before any lingering guards caught him smouldering. Embers and other contraband were overlooked in the camp, within reason, but not down here. Rufus wasn't sure why, but pigs were notoriously petty. It amused the bullies amongst them to keep the prisoners guessing as to how to best avoid pain. In the morning they could be nice, turning the other cheek, even giving advice on what shaft to mine; come the afternoon they might hit you over the neck for no reason, or turn the dreaded dial on their correction boxes and watch you writhe.

Rufus had a mind to correct them, but knew that would end his mission, and his life.

Passing the guards without incident this time, Rufus and his gang entered the massive gaping cave that served as the base camp for every shaft, with all its checkpoints and rails converging ahead. The other teams filed out and lined up with today's offerings, until the cave was packed with hot bodies and stifled by the dank smell of wet fur – the mines literally ran with the imperium-rich water Rufus had been talking to Tomek about, and nobody emerged dry.

The mining teams shuffled resignedly forth with their carts and tokens were distributed accordingly. As Scarab neared their turn for inspection, Rufus felt a powerful imperious presence mingling with his own and sensed long before the Warden emerged onto the watchtower that he would do so. Out of the corner of his eyes, Rufus spied the cloaked wolf grasping the watchtower railing, looking down upon the stripy masses like some emperor, most especially Rufus's gang.

What does he want? Is he protecting us?

Rufus privately entertained the notion that the Warden was in on ALPHA's plan to thwart Amael's conspiracy. Yes, it was just possible Janoah or Silvermane had gotten to him, despite the risks. After all, there was no telling who was part of Amael's plot. One wrong move, one wrong word, to one wrong beast, could spell disaster for ALPHA's carefully-laid trap. If Amael's conspirators went to ground, ALPHA's chance to catch them would pass, and with it the safety and security of Lupa for years to come.

Rufus and company stepped up to the checkpoint, eyes down, caps straight – except Tomek's. The hogs rifled through the ore in the cart and then everyone's pockets, Madou, Zozizou, Helmut and Tomek, turning up nothing.

As usual, Rufus went conspicuously unmolested.

Theories as to why jostling for position in his mind, Rufus led the way through the checkpoint to collect the tokens owed him. Lost in thought he failed to notice the Warden raise a paw at the hogs below and make a cutting motion to his throat. One of the hogs nodded and tipped his cap in tacit understanding. He disappeared inside the checkpoint booth. Moments later, as Helmut and Madou were pushing the cart through the barrier, a buzzing alarm sounded within the booth.

Bzzzzzzzt!

"Halt!" the hog inside bellowed.

Rufus was so surprised by the clamour that he fumbled the tokens, spilling some on the floor.

Half a dozen hogs gathered at the buzzing booth. One of them immediately kicked Rufus on his back as he tried to gather the tokens he had dropped, making him drop the rest. He sat in the mud looking up at the offending hog, his face aghast and indignant.

The hogs pulled the dumbstruck Rufus to his feet by the back of his shirt and pushed him against the mine cart. They gathered Tomek and the others and made them look into the ore as well, like naughty children.

"So," one hog snorted with glee, patting his truncheon into a palm, "filled your cart with rocks instead of ore, did we Scarab?"

"What?" Tomek growled. "Who says so?"

"We didn't, sir," Rufus countered calmly, glaring at Tomek in an effort to keep him quiet and out of trouble. "There must be some mistake."

"Our imperium sensors don't make mistakes!" the lead hog snarled, grabbing Rufus by the scruff of the neck and shaking him. "Working for the terrorists, is that it, hyena-lover?" he accused, glaring next at Madou, "Filling our carts with useless krap to slow down production, is that your game? Don't you hyenas ever give up? You should all be rounded up and shot!"

Madou said nothing. He knew it was useless to protest. The hogs were going to have their fun. The best anyone could do was shut up and let things run their course and hopefully nobody would get beaten senseless.

"Do you know what the maximum punishment is for trying to deceive us?" the lead hog said, relishing every word. "Dismemberment by ant."

"Is not fair," Tomek growled under his breath.

The hog whirled on him, "Whatcha say, Usenko?"

"Is no such thing as 'imperium sensors'," Tomek replied, raising his chin and glaring at the lead hog. "I'm Watcher and if we had machine that could douse for imperium we would use it at Lupan Wall."

"Shut up, Tomek!" Rufus seethed through his teeth.

But Tomek wouldn't be silenced. "We use sniffer-ants and our own senses, because that all there is!" he proclaimed. "Unless you have ant in that booth, I say you lie to us. You just like beating Howlers up because outside Gelb you hogs are weaklings and pathetic-"

Whop!

Truncheon to the back of the head; down went Tomek. Three of the hogs were on him at once, kicking and stomping him as he rolled into a protective ball.

Somehow, he did not cry out.

"Stop it!" Rufus yelped. Dashed around the cart he tried to get between the guards and Tomek. "Please!" he begged, holding up his paws to them all. "He's just a stupid cub! He's a foreigner; he doesn't know what he's saying-"

One of the hogs smacked Rufus across the snout with a truncheon and pushed him away. He fell back into Madou, who picked him up and then had to hold him back as he tried to charge back into the fray.

"Don't!" he rasped in the wolf's ear.

Madou felt Rufus's mighty corona grow, felt it pushing up against his own like a billowing curtain. His cruel imperium collar reacted accordingly, tightening until Madou had to let Rufus go in favour of his own collar.

Freed, Rufus stepped forth with both paws raised, purple, imperious plasma licking between his red fingers, singeing his fur and flesh. The collar pulled tight around his neck until surely he could scarce draw breath, yet the Howler felt nothing of it. The red mist had descended, clouding his mind.

"Get off him, I said!"

Rufus approached the hogs that were beating Tomek senseless and simply touched the nearest on the shoulder with his right paw. With a loud snap and a bright flash the guard was blown across the mine, tumbling into a stripy throng of on-looking prisoners. A second hog received Rufus's left paw, clapped right to his flabby peach face as he turned to look.

"Woooagh!" he screamed.

The hog's bloated body jolted involuntarily as the plasma coursed through him, kicking him off the ground and up into the mine cart. He fell into the ore and flailed about like a landed fish, spilling rocks over the sides before going still.

The other guards fled in panic, save the lead hog who grabbed the dial hanging around his neck and cranked it up full-blast. There was a loud hum as the imperious energy stored inside the contraption was released, creating an invisible artificial field of immense power. Invisible, but Helmut, Madou and Zozizou felt it well-enough. They each fell about choking as their collars tightened, subduing them and many other prisoners standing too close to the action.

Rufus too fell to his knees, grasping at his collar with one paw, then the other. The lead hog walked closer to him, concentrating the artificial field on the snarling Rufus.

"You'll die for this, wolf!" he spat. "They'll stake you out for the ants!"

The words had no sooner left the hog's pink snout than Rufus cried out.

"Grrrraaagh!"

And with a bright flash and crack of plasma, split his collar cleanly down the middle with his bare paws!

"W-w-w-what?" the hog yelped, backing away.

Rufus threw the smouldering band at him with contempt and dived on him with equal fervour, knocking the hog to the floor and setting about him with his fists; left, right, left.

High above in the watchtower, Gelb's Warden looked upon the chaos with outward indifference, his Howler mask betraying nothing as the famous Howler Rufus laid into the hog he had at his mercy. Without looking away, the Warden gestured at the two wolfen Watchers behind who were dressed in yellow and white.

"Alive," he stipulated.

The wolves nodded and simply vaulted over the watchtower railing, softening their landing below with a blast of imperious energy, scattering dust in a perfect bubble around them. They hurried to the checkpoint and dived on the unruly Rufus, subduing him with their own choice blasts of energy and swiftly binding his paws and feet with bundles of Howler-proof wire.

It was all over as quickly as it had begun.

✦

Though the sun's strength was dulled by a distinctly yellow Lupan haze, it still provided warmth enough to draw record crowds to this year's Science Exhibition. Beasts of every sort came from all across Lupa to converge on Petra Square, heart of the Eisbrand's capital district.

The Square was not very far from the prestigious Arkady University, or Heath's modest flat, so he and the girls had taken the tram. They had seen it all before, the colourful awnings and fluttering marquees set up in the midst of Petra Square were nothing new, if still a transient novelty. It was Howler Mills who was all a wonder, head craning this way and that like an overwhelmed cub as he dodged citizens of every caste and took in the spectacle. The square was boxed in on all sides by towering luxury residences with beautiful marbled facades and blue tiled roofs, whilst the capital Howler Den of the Eisbrands overlooked it all, a glittering wedding cake of stone, metal and glass that put Riddle Den to shame. Indeed, poor old Riddle Market was a run-down slum compared to this clean, majestic space!

And just when Linus thought things couldn't get any grander, he spied a huge fountain jutting up from amongst the hubbub like a marble mountain. He instantly recalled from various sources that the centre of Petra Square was home to a spectacular fountain.

As Linus walked closer, the six white wolfen statues standing equidistantly around the rim of the fountain's pool took shape. They were posed as if in the midst of battle, swords, spears, shield or bow in paw, depending on the wolf. Their faces were masked by helmets that resembled that of a Howler, but these long-dead beasts harkened to a time before imperium technology, before Lupa, before the rot. Back then their helmets, greaves and bracers would've been made of mere bronze, not imperium-weave alloy, and their marvellously-muscled bodies would've been built without a monthly fix of the good stuff.

Linus comforted himself by remembering that these were idealised representations of the Six Founders, and likely bared little resemblance to reality. Still, the romantic in him liked to think otherwise.

A whiff of acrid ash brought Linus back down to Erde and reminded him that he and the citizens of Lupa had come to admire the future, not relics of the past. Many an imperium engine turned and hissed around them, belching ash up into the sky and sometimes, if the wind would have it so, into their many varied faces. One such quivering iron contraption was a generator, Linus learnt, as he joined a crowd listening to the inventor; a generator that created imperium plasma just like a Howler could, only on a much grander scale. It was used to power glass lanterns that shone without a flame, as was demonstrated.

Very impressive, Heath and the girls agreed, clapping along with the rest. Though he clapped too, Linus found it quietly disconcerting that a machine could emulate a Howler's unique and dangerous plasma powers. Perhaps Rufus was onto something when he said the age of the Howlers was in its autumnal years.

More modest appliances followed; imperium-powered ovens, an automatic clothes-washing machine, music machines, and even a pump that sucked up dust and dirt through a pipe and stored it in a disposable bag.

"A vacuum cleaner?" Linus read.

"Och!" Sara marvelled, having a whirl of noisy suction machine herself. "Penny would love one of these!"

Further in, near the fountain, Linus found cars to drool over; handsome, sleek beasts of the sort Grand Howlers and above were luxuriously ferried about in, though they might opt for the heftier armoured variants. The Howler absent-mindedly left Sara and the others behind to pick his way amongst the reflective maze of cars, occasionally peering in at their plush interiors and daring to dream that one day he might get to ride in one.

Disappointingly there were no 'Valerios' to be had, so far as the learner Linus could see. New releases from the finest monobike manufacturer in the world were few and far between, there being little serious competition. Would they ever replace the cheap and reliable, *Springtail*, or improve the legendary M-8 *Spider*?

More to the point, Linus wondered, will I ever be able to ride such a beast as Ivan's mono, let alone afford one?

Looking across the polished roofs of the cars, Linus searched for his lost party and noticed fellow Howlers lurking amongst the crowded marquees. Heavily armoured, surcoat-clad Eisbrands one and all, here to guard their citizens and make sure everything ran smoothly, no doubt.

One locked eyes with Linus, as if recognising him.

Tristan? Linus wondered. No, too small. The eyes were wrong too. He had marvellous duotone eyes that Tristan. Handsome chap.

The anonymous Eisbrand looked away. Linus supposed the unwelcome presence of a Bloodfang had been noted, nothing more concerning.

"Linus!"

Hearing Sara's voice, the Howler found her amongst the hubbub and waved back.

"Come on, this way!" the little wolfess beckoned impatiently.

Linus walked leisurely over, but upon arrival was immediately seized by Sara and yanked through the crowds by the arm.

"What's wrong?"

"Quickly or ye'll miss it!" Sara tutted.

"Miss what?"

"Monty and Penny's balloon. Och! There they go!"

As quickly as she'd dragged Linus along, Sara pulled him to a halt and pointed. There was little need; Linus could hardly miss the great silver balloon rising from amongst the crowds and marquees on the far side of the fair, taking to the sky with all the grace of lazy fish waking from its seabed slumber. It was shaped like a pointed bauble and had tail fins, the top one strung with steel supporting wires. It was smaller than a typical dirigible, by Linus's estimation, and judging by those wires probably lacked a skeleton, maintaining its shape by the sheer pressure of the gases within. The tiny gondola snuggled against the bulging canvas bore two familiar cats in long white coats. One of them leant out an open window to wave daintily at the masses below with a scarf, the other stoically commanded the wheel, twisting the red fins and revving the ash-belching, imperium-powered propellers whirring each side of the gondola.

There was no mistaking Penny and Monty.

"Awoooooo!" Linus howled, waving both paws at the Buttle couple, as if they might spot him amongst the thousands gathered below, even less hear him over the engines.

Surprised at the guarded Linus's enthusiasm, Sara joined in the waving and shouting. "Penny, Monty! Down here!"

Thrumming deafeningly overhead, the Buttle's airship cast a great shadow across Linus and Sara before passing over the sparkling fountain behind them and across the fair. With surprising speed it cleared the fancy town houses and circled around Petra Square, watched by every beast within.

Except for one.

A recognisably large Eisbrand Howler emerged from the masses and was on Sara and Linus in a heartbeat. Throwing Linus a stern duotone glare he took Sara to one side by the arm.

"Tristan!" she yelped.

"Oi!" Linus barked, "What're you doing-"

"Shut up, Bloodfang!" Tristan snarled at him. "I want to talk to Sara in private. You're in the heart of our capital territory; remember that before you say another word!"

With a snort, Linus looked at Sara.

"It's all right," the wolfess reassured him.

Watched by Linus, Tristan led Sara over to the side of marquee as if to hide from prying eyes. The Eisbrand glanced all about before saying, "Sara they're coming for Olivia. We have to get her to a safe house."

"What?" Sara gasped.

"That crook Maher betrayed her to ALPHA. I can't protect her from them; she'll have to go into hiding. Heath as well, they've got him down for providing a dodger with stings."

"But… but Olivia paid him-"

"Do you think Maher cares? He's an ex-pupil of Josef and an ALPHA informant. I knew I'd heard of him before."

"How do you know?"

"I know," Tristan said firmly. "What's more I bumped into Josef outside Heath's flat which confirms it. Ulf knows what that psychopath'll do to Olivia. The same thing he did to Bruno, I wager."

"Bruno?" Sara said, eyes darting about. "Do you know something?"

"Not now, Sara."

"Tristan, *please* tell me."

"I don't know yet Sara! But I *do* know I can't stop ALPHA if they want Olivia. She has to leave Lupa. And so should you, at least until this blows over. Your mother will protect you."

Sara looked back at Linus. He met her gaze, but could not hear a word over the crowds.

"You can ditch him for starters," Tristan grunted.

"Tristan, don't!" Sara woofed. "Linus is a good 'un, as good as Rufus."

"Maybe, but get rid of him," Tristan huffed, adding before Sara could protest, "for his safety. You wouldn't want him arrested and beaten up by ALPHA, would you? Because that's what we're up against here. We, all of us, even you, could be sent to Gelb if we're caught hiding a dodger."

Sara made to speak, then changed her mind and cupped her little paws over her dark muzzle.

"Shall I do it?" Tristan offered, referring to Linus.

"No, you'll only make it worse," Sara said. "Ah'll tell him… something."

"Tell him he's not your type. Too short, I'd have thought."

"Oh, be serious!"

Tristan allowed a rare chuckle. "Where's Olivia and the Professor?" he asked looking around.

Sara was too busy wondering what to tell Linus to think straight. "They, uh… they went down tae where the balloon took off. Ah was bringing Linus over tae see. They said they'd wait there for us."

"Right. I'll go get them. Stay near the fountain. If you see any ALPHA prefects, hide."

"Aye."

Giving Linus a last glance, Tristan weaved through the spectators, leaving Sara rubbing her arms with her paws. She made her way slowly back to Linus, who met her halfway.

"Everything all right?" he asked.

"Aye."

"Doesn't look it."

"Ah'm fine," Sara insisted, forcing a smile. "Really."

Linus threw his paws up a little, "Well what did he want?"

"Nothing. Listen Linus, you… we have tae go home."

"Pardon."

"Ah'm sorry, it's nae your fault. Something's come up. We're leaving early. All of us."

"Oh," Linus said, "Would it be presumptuous to ask why?"

Sara seethed, "It's a private matter."

"I see," Linus claimed, when of course he didn't. "Well, I-I-I'll walk you home-"

"No!" Sara said, a little too firmly and quickly, "Don't trouble yerself. Really."

Linus thumbed behind him, "It's no trouble. My mono's back at Heath's flat anyway."

"Aye. Well, you go ahead. We're staying here a little while."

"But… I thought you were leaving."

"We are; in a minute."

"Then I'll wait."

"There's no need."

"I don't mind-"

"Linus, just… just go, would ye?" Sara groaned, pushing him a little with her paws. "Please. Just go home."

Linus looked down at himself, as if Sara's shove had left a stain on his mantle. The Howler rolled his powerful shoulders and plucked at the chest of his cloak; he felt suddenly hot and bothered, "All right, what's going on? What did Tristan say to you? Did he threaten you?"

"No!"

"Did he say something about me?"

"No, Linus! Tristan's nae like that. He's a good 'un. He's always…." Sara paused a moment to take a breath, then finished, "He's always looked out for me."

Mollified, Linus backed off a little, "Then what is it? Are you in some kind of trouble?" he guessed.

"No."

"Is it Heath? Is he in trouble? Look, I know his outspokenness is frowned upon, but I'm not about to denounce him. You know how I feel about him. He's a hero of mine."

Sara waved her paws, "Would you please just leave?"

After some thought, Linus spoke with a clarity he never knew he possessed, "Sara, I'm not leaving you without an explanation. It's my duty as a Howler to protect the citizens of Lupa. Now either tell me what's going on, or I'm going to stay here and find out for myself."

"Just go away!" Sara growled, shoving Linus hard enough to make him stumble. "Go on, now!"

"Sara-"

"Go home!" she barked at him. "And don't come sniffing around the flat! Ah don't want tae see you. Is that clear, Howler? Stay away from me!"

Linus stood, dumbfounded. Beasts stared at him.

"W-w-what did I do?" he stammered at last, all clarity crumbling in the face of Sara's rebuff.

"If ye don't leave me alone right now, Ah'll call the nearest Eisbrands for help!" Sara threatened, fists by her sides. She looked down, "Just go, Linus Mills. Ah nae want tae see you again."

The wonder that was Monty's flying machine roared overhead once more, casting Linus and Sara into deafening shadows as the crowds cheered and clapped. Linus saw and heard none of it, his world had condescend down to Sara and her sudden, inexplicable, unnatural rejection.

"Go away!" she all but screamed at him.

Linus looked down and away, then right at Sara. "It was stupid of me to think a s-sss-stammering, s-sss-stupid, s-sss-sack of rot could be friends with such a n-nnn-noble wolfess," he struggled, donning his helmet in shame. "I'll go back to where I belong, then. If that's what you want so badly."

Sara said nothing, though she bit her bottom lip to keep from utterance. Linus waited few seconds in the hope she would change her mind and say something, anything.

Nothing.

"Take care, citizen," Linus said distantly, pushing through the crowds and out of sight.

Alone, Sara staggered over to the fountain and collapsed on its lip, exhausted from the confrontation. Tristan returned shortly with Professor Heath and Olivia in tow, both looking decidedly fidgety and anxious. As he spoke to Sara, Tristan glanced this way and that, ears swivelling, clearly searching the masses for someone.

He failed to spot Linus lurking behind a stripy marquee, and as the group moved off through the fair the Bloodfang followed them at a distance.

As did a bespectacled grey cat and two Prefects.

Codex: Greystone

Lupa's master builders, craftsbeasts and artisans, the Greystones strike beasts as gruff and common, the accent of their quarter being, some say, the definitive Lupan parlance. If you were born within the knell of the steam hammers that constantly bend and shape eisenglanz, then you are a true Lupan.

Whatever their vocal inflections, the Greystones are an infuriatingly enigmatic pack, with the obvious outward action of any Elder or Den Father often nothing but a front for some underlying motivation. Their greatest slight of paw, however, is in keeping the method of stabilising yellow-imperium secret for centuries now. Other packs have tried to unpick this greatest of Greystone mysteries, but meeting always with failure they are instead necessitated to sell yellow-imperium ore to the Greystones, only to buy back the processed forms later – a lucrative venture for the Greystones. More wealth is generated from rich territorial holdings to the south. The Greystones own the entire Pinnacles and half of Rostsonne, up to the yawning canyons that divide that land. With the sea wind keeping the Ashfall at bay, Rostsonne remains good country for little beasts to grow cereal crops, albeit with heavy irrigation, whilst the Pinnacle mines provide endless metal ores for the insatiable Greystones to smelt into cars, trains, rails and gas pipes to keep Lupa's ancient infrastructure functioning.

However, some say the Greystones are more responsible for Lupa's self-destruction of late than its construction, for they were the first pack make possible again the deadly phenomenon that is the Eisenwolf.

It's said the first suits of Eisenwolf armour were recovered by Greystone artisans who dared to explore a Dead City. The expedition cost the lives of all involved, the members dying of rot upon their return. The suits they brought back, later dubbed eisenpelz, were initially thought useless. Normal Howlers hadn't a corona strong enough to control them, nor even the physical strength to move within them.

Ultimately it was found that only the pure-bloods, those wolves born of two Howlers, could don the Eisenwolf mantle. They alone had the sheer strength and imperium tolerance demanded by the cruel eisenpelz.

Few pure-bloods survive to birth, and even those that do often die young, especially today when they are rarely adopted by a pack. But back in the glory days, whilst they lived and donned the eisenpelz, they were the supreme power in Lupa, the ultimate Howler, able to destroy all before them with nought but a raised paw. For a time they were revered as gods amongst wolves.

During successive Howler Wars and the intervening years, every pack raced to match the Greystones, gathering their own eisenpelz and breeding pure-bloods to work them. Most even encouraged their scarce female Howlers to marry male Howlers instead of a healthy Freiwolf partner, despite the terrible risk of miscarriages and birth defects the cubs of two Howlers run - the need for Eisenwolves to maintain one's borders was simply too great.

Eventually matters reached a head. Successive generations of Eisenwolves, the bloodline ageing and mad, turned in upon their packs, their friends, even their loved ones, destroying hundreds of Howlers in orgies of violence that levelled whole districts, before collapsing and self-destructing in a torrent of imperious energy.

When the dust had settled, the status of Eisenwolves was forever tarnished.

Since this last and most destructive episode in Lupa's history over a decade ago, eisenpelz have been banned by several cross-pack Lupan Laws. Relationships between male and female Howlers are frowned upon and marriage forbidden to discourage any union that might produce a pure-blood. Eisenpelz cannot function without pure-bloods to use them, thus they are now obsolete.

However, it is an open secret that every pack still maintains a small collection of eisenpelz, just in case attitudes shift, or some outside force should threaten Lupa. Moreover, pure-bloods still walk Lupa's streets, the unwanted results of illegal Howler liaisons with their fellow afflicted, often abandoned on doorsteps, their parents and pasts lost to them.

Chapter 29

Sometimes walking, often dragged, Rufus was bundled across Gelb by the Warden's two personal Howlers; if that's what they called themselves, he wasn't sure and didn't much care for all his cuts and bruises. They said not a word as they escorted him into a grim-looking concrete building, down stark corridors and up cracked stairs, no sign of any beautification until the trio burst into a plush, well-furnished, if rather dark office.

The Warden was already there, facing the window with a drink in paw, looking out over the prisoners milling around the camp below.

Rufus was pushed onto a chair, his paws still bound by Howler-wire. His escort backed off.

"Dismissed," the Warden ordered.

"But, sir-"

"I can manage him. Go on."

With a chest-salute, the Howlers took their leave, closing the door gently behind them.

Rufus leant back in his chair. What now?

The Warden swirled his drink, brandy by the looks, and took a surprisingly delicate sip for such a powerful-looking wolf. He was a typical Hummel wolf; black, well-built, with honey-gold eyes. Though the blood and culture of the packs was fading from centuries of intermingling, some still harboured a classic appearance which spoke of their origins as loudly as any uniform.

"I've never seen that before," the Warden said, breaking Rufus from his musings.

The prisoner licked his bloody nose.

"They said you were strong," the Warden went on, with no hint of a Hummel accent, "but to break a collar like a paper chain. You really are quite... remarkable."

Barely hearing for his pains, Rufus wondered where this was headed; wondered where he was headed; solitary confinement, a flogging, firing squad. What was it that pig had said; dismemberment by ant? So much for Janoah's plan.

Nicely done, husband, she'd scold, real smooth.

"I have rode the wind," the Warden said wistfully, pricking Rufus's ruddy ears, "seen forests far below, met great beasts and small. I have kissed the sun, felt its warmth on my wings... etcetera, etcetera." He ended with a chuckle and turned to Rufus, "Your favourite fable, isn't it?"

The inmate sat in bemused silence.

"Don't worry," the Warden said, "I'm a friend."

Rufus sat up a little and twisted his bound paws. "Friend?" he exhaled, "Sorry, do forgive me; I'm... not quite with it after having my head kicked in by your thugs."

"My apologies, but that's how things are done around here," said the Warden. "Simply bringing you to my office without cause would've been suspicious."

"Suspicious?"

"Yes. There are agents on all sides amongst the hogs, don't doubt it. I needed an excuse for a private meeting, so I told the hogs to take your gang to task because they're getting too big for their boots. We do that from time to time, lest talented miners forget their place."

Rufus emitted a scoff.

"You disapprove? An impartialist like you would. But I am dealing with barbarians, sir. Murderers and imperium-traffickers and terrorists; you are well-acquainted with the latter... hyena-lover."

Is the Warden my contact? Rufus thought. He's recited the poem but he's not mentioned Janoah or Silvermane.

The Warden turned to the window and huffed, "You should appreciate the predicament you've landed me in, Howler. I can't just release you from Gelb; I've had to arrange for you to be executed... or make it appear so."

"Terribly sorry," Rufus excused.

"You should mind what you say," the Warden growled. "Perhaps I've not made up my mind which side I'm on." He turned to Rufus, walking round his desk to stand behind him. "I could still dispose of you," he said, placing a hefty paw on Rufus's ruddy shoulder, "I could have you murdered and tell Amael Balbus that it was some mining accident. Then I could go to ALPHA and expose him. I'm sure the Alpha would be interested to hear all about his plans. I would omit the fact I've been diverting white-imperium to Amael's private cache and blame it on THORN infiltration. There's no paperwork to prove otherwise."

Rufus's hair tingled, his mind whirred. What is going on here? Just keep listening, Red-mist.

"You're not half as clever as you think you are," the Warden told him. "You know, I allowed you to pass the checkpoint unharmed when your breeches were stuffed with imperium, just as I allowed you to sell what you stole from me to that strange cat, Tack. What? Do you think I don't know about him? I let him exist, Howler, I let the prisoners think they're getting one over one me. It keeps them happy and our trains full of imperium ore."

Rufus proffered a false smile, "That's very clever."

The Warden walked around the room, admiring his many trinkets, "Ulf knows I'm wasted here." He turned and pointed at Rufus with his drink, "Do you know, I increased Gelb's annual production by over two-hundred-percent! *I* devised the gang system, the tokens; *I* gave the prisoners initiative to work! All this and I am rewarded by being left out here to rot year after year! I should be an Elder; I'm a beast of culture and civilisation, not a prison guard. No more icy winters out here in this smouldering fistula watching over scum, not when Amael Balbus gives me what I want... and he had better."

He looked to Rufus.

"If I do this," he said, "I want your assurance that I'll be brought into Amael's regime, as he promised me."

Rufus found his tongue, "My assurance?"

"Well yes," the Warden laughed. "Surely you'll have a say in the new order? Amael's told me how much he values you. You're like a brother to him, that's why he's getting you out of here early."

Goodness, this fellow has been out of the loop a long time, Rufus realised.

"Amael's my dearest friend," Rufus agreed breathlessly.

Smiling, the Warden went on, "So then, once Amael's in charge and the hyenas are disposed of also, you will be in his government and will bring me aboard. Amael's promised he'll make me the administrator of a territory, but I want a good one, mind, the Eisbrands, or the Common Ground perhaps, or all of Hummel, if that's not too much. I don't want that Greystone ash pile or his Bloodfang slums. If that's to be my reward I'm going straight to ALPHA!"

"I don't blame you," Rufus chuckled, adding, "I will of course put in a good word with Amael."

The Warden growled dangerously, "I want assurances, not 'good words'."

"You'll get what you deserve," Rufus promised. "On my honour as a Howler. After all, we cultured wolves must stick together."

A grunt, a smile, a sip of brandy.

"Any chance I could be untied?" Rufus asked hopefully.

"I'm afraid not," was the reply. "You're going to be executed in a minute."

"Twice in as many months! I *am* doing well."

"Hmm?"

Rufus chuckled, "I'll tell you about it when we're back in Lupa and all that."

The Warden nodded, then said, "Amael assures me you'll be rescued by his associates before the sentence is fully carried out. I hope, for your sake, your trust in him is well-placed Howler Rufus."

"Oh, we're like brothers, remember."

"We'll see."

On that note the Warden snatched his phone. "I'm done with him," he told somebody, putting the phone down just as quickly.

"What about my gang?" Rufus blurted.

"What about them?"

"Well, what's to become of them? Only, I've grown rather attached to one or two of them."

"To that handsome young Watcher no doubt," the Warden snorted meaningfully – he wasn't completely out of the loop after all. "I'll tell the hogs to go lightly on the lad, if that's what you want."

"Tomek doesn't belong here," Rufus excused. "It's my fault he was sent down, you see. I'd be dead if not for him."

"Then he'll come to no serious harm as long as I run Gelb. You've my assurance."

Rufus beamed amiably, "Much obliged, sir."

The door opened and the Howlers strode in, saluting their superior.

"Get this scum out of my sight!" the Warden told them, a consummate actor if ever Rufus had met one, "And bring me a warrant; let's get this over with."

✤

Tristan led Sara, Olivia and Professor Heath through the tight, lesser-known backstreets of the Eisbrand Territory, the hubbub of Petra Square receding rapidly behind them until even the whirring of Monty's balloon was no more than a distant thrum punctuated by occasional faint cheers.

At least the Buttles were having fun.

What Sara wouldn't give to be up in their machine. They could simply fly over Lupa's walls and away to safety like some giant bumblebee, who could stop them?

Oh no!

"Toggle!" Sara yelped, running over to Heath and grabbing one of his enormous bear paws. "Professor, what about Toggle? She's shut in our room!"

"I know, Sara. I know. It'll be all right."

"All right? We cannae leave her in there; she'll starve tae death!"

"Now don't be silly," Heath reassured Sara, patting her paw. "Look, once we're in Everdor I'll send someone from the university round. Someone's bound to come knocking the moment I don't turn up for work tomorrow anyway. They'll hear her buzzing about."

"That could be days. She'll be frantic. Ah have tae go back fer her."

Tristan whirled round. "Sara!"

"You go on ahead," Sara told Heath and Olivia, "Ah'll get the next train. Ah'll meet you at the other end."

"I'll come too," Olivia offered at once.

"No, it's you ALPHA want. You have tae go with Tristan."

"Sara-"

"Ah can't leave her, Olivia. I just can't."

"For Ulf's sake, you two!" Tristan howled, gnarling his armoured fingers at them both, "It's just a stupid bug!"

"She's nae a stupid bug!" Sara protested vehemently, fists by her sides. "She's mah friend. Not that Ah expect you tae understand, Tristan. Bruno would've."

"And what *you* don't understand is that the flat is being watched by ALPHA agents. They'll arrest you!"

"Ah'm nae afraid o' them bullies, nae more than you Howlers!"

With that, Sara stormed off to see about her rescue. She took not more than ten steps before Tristan caught up with her and grabbed her arm.

"Let me go!" she barked, twisting like a mealworm.

"Sara!"

"Let me go! Ah mean it!"

After suffering a shower of harmless, if annoying, slaps about his armoured face and shoulders, Tristan grasped Sara's little arms and said firmly, "Look, I'll go!"

He glanced up and down the street, hoping the few citizens not at the exhibition weren't ALPHA informants. The rat green grocer sweeping his doorstep looked down and away upon meeting Tristan's gaze, whilst a pig at a cafe buried his snout in a beer.

"I'll go back for her," Tristan promised

"You?"

"If you'll just get on that train like a good wolfess, I'll bring your bee along tomorrow."

"But… but you don't know how tae manage her."

"It can't be that hard."

Heath walked over and raised the obvious, "Won't ALPHA see you going into my flat, Tristan?"

"They won't bother me," the Howler claimed. He looked at Olivia, "I can just say I was after offering Olivia a Howlership after I found out she was a dodger. I'm within my rights to approach potential Howlers with an offer, even dodgers."

"Would it…." Olivia began. Everyone looked to her, which silenced her a moment. "Would it be so bad," she continued, "I mean… if I became a Howler? I could be an Eisbrand. Like you. I might look quite good in a surcoat-"

"Olivia!" Sara gasped.

"I don't want to get you all in trouble. Perhaps I should just give up now?"

Tristan stared at the girls for quite a stretch, then confronted Olivia, "You want to be a slave?"

"What?"

"That's all I am, Olivia, a slave. I must do as I'm told, or else."

"Like any soldier-"

"I'm no soldier, just a bully," Tristan scoffed, looking down the street. "I oppress the citizens of Lupa and uphold the law even when it sticks in my throat to do so. I put up with little beasts crossing the road ahead of me and cursing my existence because their wife, or son, or husband disappeared. I suffer it not out of love for Lupa, but out of fear. I'll do *anything* to get my rotting paws on a sting so I can stave off the pain, just for another week or two, because I'm too scared to face the end. I'm nothing but a miserable addict."

"But the power you wield-"

"An extension of my pack's will, not mine at all. I'm not free. I'm as petty as a train hog. We all are."

Olivia looked down at her feet.

"It's too late for me," Tristan said, "but you can still get away and put that mind of yours to use."

Onwards, down the narrow streets, mingling and blending with the citizens going about their business as best as two wolves, a bear and a sizeable Howler were able. It would be even worse if Sara was towing a huge bee behind her, Tristan thought, not relishing the inevitable clash with whatever agents Josef had posted at the flat. Another run-in would do little to improve his already questionable profile.

The group made the nearest station, a pokey backwater stop compared to the grand affair near the university, its walls and pillars running with streaks of ash. Passing train-hogs and barriers with impunity thanks to Tristan flashing his brooch, the Howler escorted Sara and company to the door of a run-down train.

"My associate in Riddle District will meet you," he said, closing the door.

Sara lingered at the windows, her breath steaming up the glass. Tristan swore he lip-read a 'thank you' through the clouds of ash.

"All aboard!" a train hog warned.

Not lingering to wave and draw unwanted attention, Tristan took his leave, passing through the station again. He failed to notice Linus slip from behind a pillar just as he left. Flashing his brooch at the hogs, the blonde wolf hurried to the nearest carriage, the one coupled ahead of Sara's, and boarded the train just as it began to chug away.

Two black-cloaked ALPHA wolves also boarded a few coaches further back, and a grey cat too.

✦

Watched by many a mumbling prisoner and guard, the remaining members of the Scarab Gang were led across the camp to a fenced-off corner of Gelb. Inside the square fence, set in the bare erde, was a rusted trapdoor. The trapdoor was flung open by the yellow-uniformed hogs, revealing nothing at all within, unless black nothingness was a thing.

As he was forced towards the ominous hole by two hogs, Watcher Tomek was able to discern a slick, oily surface below, like a pool of liquid black-imperium.

"In yer go, scum!" one of the Gelb hogs snorted. "Maybe a stint down the Pit'll learn you some respect. If not… well, you'll go the same way as Rufus, picked apart by ants. Think about that whilst you're down there. Maybe you'll be able to hear him scream. Hah!"

Tomek emitted a whine of terror as the hogs shoved him towards this 'Pit'. He glanced back at Madou, as if he could do something to stop it. Even were he inclined, the hyena's paws were bound tight and his neck collared still. Helmut and Zozizou were behind him and in the same predicament.

"Don't worry, boys," laughed another hog, "you're all going in together!"

With that, he whacked Tomek on the back of the legs with his truncheon so the youngster lost the power to stand. As he stumbled in pain, the hogs pushed him down the hole head-first. Tomek tumbled tail over torso for the briefest moment before his back slapped into a wall of icy water. The cold embraced him with its frosty fingers, invading his fur, his eyes, his ears, his mouth; blind, deaf and dumb he flailed in the confusing tumult, twisting his bound paws in the struggle to swim.

Suddenly Tomek's feet touched solid ground. He pushed and scrabbled about, righting himself, or so he hoped. His head broke the surface and he greedily gulped down air.

Expecting to see something, anything, as he blinked the water from his stinging eyes, Tomek's world proved nothing but an infinity of darkness and rippling water.

No, a square of light hovered ahead and above – the trapdoor. The opening was so bright compared to the blackness all around that it more resembled a light fixture in the ceiling rather than the sky.

"You no do this!" Tomek yelled, wading forward. "You no treat wolves like this!"

Much hoggish laughter and snorting ensued.

Moments later, Madou's unmistakably muscled silhouette momentarily blocked the light before tumbling down into the water with an immense and foamy splash. The hyena righted himself in a snarling instant and shook the water from his robust head and neck. He stood waist deep in the pool, some inches shorter than Tomek, if almost twice as hefty. Big Helmut followed, stirring up a tidal wave as his immense body displaced an equal quantity of water, whilst the skinny little hyena Zozizou caused barely a splash at first, but flailed about post-impact with enough noise and panic for all.

Madou sloshed over to his cousin and, biting the back of his neck for his paws were bound behind him, pulled Zozizou upright.

"Calm yourself, cousin!" Madou barked, whispering afterward. "Don't show them you're afraid."

The shivering Zozizou nodded quickly, water dripping off his dark snout.

Madou looked up, catching a final glimpse of the sacred Sky before it was shut away amidst a chorus of cruel laughter, and with it went every ray of light.

✧

Sara cast her eyes up and down the trembling train carriage for the umpteenth time. Little beasts hid behind their newspapers, afraid of even a tiny, ordinary wolf like her. They had perhaps seen Tristan escorting her, and anyone too friendly with the Howlers was shunned.

"I'm sorry," Olivia said, drawing Sara's gaze back. "All this fuss over me."

"Don't be daft," Sara chided, grasping her friend's paws.

Olivia looked out the window at the passing Greystone Territory, with all its smokestacks and industry, heaps of ash and scrap metal – it was her birthplace.

"I always knew it," she sighed.

Sara leant forward a little. "What?"

Olivia cocked her head sideways at Sara. "That I was afflicted," she claimed, turning to the window again. "Ever since I was little I've known. I could feel them, you see. I've *always* been able to feel them all."

"Who?" Sara asked.

"My kind!" Olivia tutted, looking to Sara again. "Tristan's quite the wolf. If only you could feel what I feel, Sara, maybe you'd appreciate what you have in him. Still, it's not your fault, I suppose."

Sara emitted a tiny gasp of surprise at Olivia's patronising tone, but said nothing.

"Linus isn't half bad either," she went on. "He's not as mature though. His corona lacks... refinement. It's very wobbly. It's as if he can't control his strength. Oh, it's so hard to explain it to a normal beast like you."

"Uh, aye," Sara croaked – she had to say something, if only to acknowledge Olivia's expectant gaze.

She's just confused, Sara convinced herself; she's overwhelmed by what's happening to her. She's ill. Don't pay her rudeness any mind.

"Everything'll be fine," Sara reassured Olivia, and by extension herself.

She looked across at Heath, sitting opposite. The studious bear was strangely silent, staring out the window as if in deep contemplation, yet fidgeting, tugging at his waistcoat and rubbing his thighs as the train rocked to and fro.

"Ye all right, Professor?" Sara asked him.

"Hmm? What?"

"Don't worry," Sara told him. "Once Olivia's safe, Tristan will sort everything out with Den Father Thorvald and ye'll be back in your flat in no time."

Heath humoured his student with a nod and smile, but said nothing. He stared out the window again, thumbs twiddling.

This isn't like him, Sara thought, dipping her chin to her chest. It dawned upon her then, at that moment, that this was deadly serious.

"Ah wonder who Tristan's contact in Riddle is," Sara whispered, desperate to make conversation – anything was preferable to the unbearable silence. "It must be someone we can trust, a real upstanding Howler. Tristan's very clever at this kind of thing; he's got all kinds of contacts all over Lupa. It'll be fine."

The words had no sooner left Sara's lips than Olivia stood up and looked behind her.

"Someone's coming," she said, ears erect.

"What?"

"I can feel them. It's a Howler... Maybe two."

Sara peered round her seat and down the carriage. She could see nobody, no cloaked wolf of justice, only little beasts hiding behind crumpled papers.

"Where?"

Olivia sat back down again. "I'm telling you, Sara, someone's coming," she whispered, pulling her blazer tightly around her, as if it could dampen her field. "And if I can feel them, they'll be able to feel me. What if it's ALPHA, the ones Tristan said were coming?"

Heath looked the other way to Sara – the door to the next carriage wasn't far. "We should move move," he declared, standing up and tugging the creases from his waistcoat.

Little beasts of every sort peeked over their newspapers as the odd group of two wolves and a bear vacated their seats and hurried past them, followed minutes later by a grey cat flanked by two black-cloaked wolves; ALPHA agents to be sure. They had entered the carriage at the opposite end to the exiting group, missing them by seconds.

The cat in spectacles moved slowly down the carriage, looking at every seat, every face. Little beasts buried their noses in their papers if they had them, or the passing scenery if they didn't.

"She's not here, Doctor Josef," one of the Prefects said to the cat. "I can't feel anything. She must've gone to the next carriage."

"She's onto us," the second Prefect growled. "Come on, she'll get away!"

The cat, Josef, stopped them with a raised paw, but didn't face them. "She's not going anywhere, you fools, this is a non-stop train to Riddle District. Careful you don't pass her; she's a pure-blood, yet she's been hiding in plain sight for years, undetected. I suspect she can suppress her corona and she could be able to wield it."

"Without Howler training?" a Prefect said doubtfully.

"It's possible Tristan trained her; he has likely been aware of her for some time," Josef theorised. "We'll find out once Janoah takes him in-"

"Wait," one Prefect said to the other, "I got a tingle, mate. Up ahead. You feel it?"

"Yeah, I do. Different though, 'en it?"

"Yeah. It's not her. Still powerful though."

Doctor Josef looked back at his wolfen accomplices in a withering sort of way, as if his reliance on their imperious talents was a burden. "What're you two drivelling about?" he sighed. "You saw Tristan; he didn't get on!"

"Nah, it's not him, sir. It's someone else. Strong."

Josef peered down the swaying carriage. "The sooner I perfect a reliable imperium detector, the better," he complained. "Very well, you two take the lead, but *don't* lose your heads. I don't want a scene; the Alpha will not be pleased if you start a fight on public transport. Let *me* do the talking."

"Aye, sir."

"Understood, sir."

The Prefects hurried along the carriage with Josef following at a leisurely pace. One of the Prefects stopped near the end to pull down a newspaper and ask the rabbit hiding behind it, "Citizen, did you see a bear and two wolfesses pass this way?"

"Y-y-yes, Howler," the rabbit said. "They w-w-went into the next carriage just now."

"Prefect, actually," the wolf corrected, tapping his white ALPHA brooch. "Please don't confuse us lads at ALPHA with those corrupt, decadent Howlers, citizen."

"Pardon me, Prefect. M-mmm-my mistake."

"Was anyone else with the group you saw?"

"N-nnn-no, Prefect."

"You sure?"

"Yes, Prefect. It was just them, sir. Two wolfesses and a bear, I'd swear to it."

"All right then. Good day citizen."

Nodding at one another, the Prefects opened the carriage door and crossed the noisy, wind-whipped void between the carriages. Josef pulled his coat tightly around him as he braved the elements – he despised the wind. Slamming the door behind him with contempt, the cat almost bumped into the backs of his Prefects, who had stopped immediately inside the next carriage.

"Sir," one said, pointing ahead.

"Looks like trouble, sir," the other confirmed.

Peering between their cloaked shoulders, Josef saw Heath, Sara and most importantly Olivia, all nestled at the end of the carriage. However, standing between Josef and the object of his fascination was a familiar blond wolf in a red cloak and Bloodfang helmet; a short, stocky, well-built fellow.

Josef squeezed between the Prefects.

"Careful, sir," one advised.

"It's all right, he's with us," Josef purred at his wolves. "Howler Linus," he said, walking over to the Bloodfang with a whisker-hiking smirk.

"Doctor Josef," Linus replied simply.

Josef patted the Howler's shoulder. "Well done, Mills. We can take things from here-"

As Josef tried to pass him, Linus clamped a paw on the head of the nearest seat, blocking the cat's passage. "What's going on here?" he asked.

A distinct, hairy pause. Josef looked down at Linus's muscled arm and followed the offending limb up to the wolf's helmet-clad face. "Didn't Janoah send you?" he whispered.

Silence.

"But, I saw you at the fair," Josef hissed. "I thought you were *her* wolf."

Linus scoffed at the notion. "Her wolf? I'm *nobody's* wolf, sir," he growled, thinking back to that night he'd been mocked for being Rufus's perceived beta. "I'm a Bloodfang, not one of your agents. I answer to Elder Amael Balbus."

"Well… precisely."

"Pardon me?"

"Nothing," Josef mewed, glancing behind. "Listen, Howler Linus, let us not make a scene. I know you're only doing your duty, but these citizens are criminals, and it's therefore your duty to apprehend them."

"Criminals? In what way?"

Josef looked beyond Linus, to Olivia. "She's a dodger," he pointed, "and they've been hiding her."

"So?" Linus urged.

"So by 'hiding' I mean of course misappropriating imperium on her behalf-"

"That's a lie!" Sara shouted, stepping forth, fists clenched. "He's lying Linus!"

"I have proof!" Josef spat back. "My dear old colleague Heath there has been skimming venom off the Arkady University stores; imperium destined for experiments diverted to his own selfish needs as well as Olivia's."

Heath raised his hefty brown chin.

Josef pressed his attack, "How are you coping? Still smouldering like a trooper, no doubt. Doesn't do the lungs any good, you know. But of course, you do rather more than smoulder these days-"

"That's enough, Josef!" Heath snorted. "There's no need to drag that up."

"Oh, but it's so relevant."

"It has no bearing on anything!"

Sara looked back at Heath, "Professor?"

"Sara, Olivia… I…."

"He's a gazer, my dear wolves," Josef revealed, tutting like a disappointed relative as he attempted to murder Heath's reputation. "Or will be, soon enough. Your omniscient Professor's been a sad imperium junkie for years."

Heath dipped his chin.

"Keeping Olivia for yourself, were we?" Josef went on. "Waiting for her to blossom so you could experiment on a pure-blood? Shame on you."

"That's outrageous!" Heath bellowed, wagging a finger. "You're the one who was cast out of the Ark for your deviant experimentations!"

"By an unimaginative faculty of dolts, like yourself? Of course!" Josef piped. "Oh it was hard going for a while, wandering from employer to employer, zipping up cadavers for a living, but I've found my feet now. We cats always do."

The red and white banners of the Bloodfang Territory fluttered by the windows – the train was neared its destination, spurring Josef on.

"Fascinating as this is, we'll conduct the rest of the interrogation at HQ," he said, adding harshly, "You're all under arrest!"

"Now wait just a minute," Linus protested. "Let's talk-"

"Help me apprehend the dissidents, Howler, or join them, I don't care which," Josef interrupted, retreating backwards behind his black-cloaked toughs. Safely out of reach he threatened in a purring, delighted tone, "Don't think I can't take *you* to task, little wolf. Howler Tristan is being dealt with as we speak for his role in this charade and he's leagues above you in rank *and* talent, not to mention powerful friends. Not even Den Father Thorvald can save him now, not for his crimes."

"Crimes?" Sara woofed in disbelief. "What crimes?"

"Sheltering dodgers, imperium smuggling, turning a blind eye to dissident citizens spreading hyena propaganda and, most heinous of all, aiding and abetting THORN terrorists."

Linus could scarce believe it, "What?"

Josef cackled, "Oh, Tristan's *quite* the rogue Howler. Helping these criminals is just his latest misdemeanour. I suggest you don't join him in his fate."

"Och! That's ridiculous!" Sara dismissed. "Don't listen tae him, Linus! Tristan's nae a traitor!"

"We shall see!" Josef said pompously. "ALPHA will tease the truth from him, from you all.

Perhaps if you cooperate now I'll arrange for a moderate sentence. I have influence with the Alpha himself, you know."

Sara couldn't find words to speak.

"Well, Howler, what's it to be?" Josef urged Linus.

Linus looked back at Sara and Olivia. They stared at him in silence. Their lips betrayed nothing, but their eyes revealed the fear, the despair, the outrage. Linus could hear Vladimir now, hear his sound advice. ALPHA's just another pack in all but name, out to gain power. Don't give them an excuse to take you to task because they will. Lay low, Linus, play ignorant, wait.

Impossible.

The train slowed, Riddle Station and crowds of passengers rolled into view.

"Get them!" Josef hissed.

The ALPHA Prefects closed the distance on Linus in a heartbeat, rapiers drawing on the way. Linus whipped his own sword out and slapped the first rapier aside, then slammed a fist into the Prefect.

Pffzaack!

With a hearty plasmatic blast, the first wolf was sent bowing into the second. The second quickly recovered, but the first was left wheezing and smouldering from Linus's mighty punch

The second Prefect drew his pistol. Thinking fast, Linus turned his back.

Crack! Poing!

The pellet deflected off his shield and pinged around the carriage!

Sara screamed.

Furious, Linus whirled round, pistol drawn. He pointed it firmly at Josef and the Prefect, advancing on them as they retreated, helpless in the face of a loaded weapon.

"Linus, no!" Heath warned. "Don't lower yourself, Howler."

Linus ceased his advance. "We're done here, I think," he sniffed officiously.

The train creaked to a painful halt and the train hogs on the platform opened the doors. Passengers piled aboard, avoiding the Howler and two Prefects like the rot whilst moving to their seats. Some citizens, sensing that something was about to go down in this carriage, performed an about face in the door and picked the next one along instead.

"Come on," Sara whispered, shepherding Sara and Heath to the exit. "Let's go everyone."

Linus stayed put, glaring at Josef.

"Come on, Howler," Sara said, grabbing his arm and pulling him down the aisle, "Escort us tae Riddle Den."

Eventually, Linus let himself be taken.

"You'll pay for this!" Josef hissed, squeezing between the Prefects and chasing Linus and Sara to the door. He leant out of the train and shouted after them, "This isn't over!"

✦

The Warden's office door opened and a big hyena was pushed in and forced to sit in the chair opposite the desk. His paws were wired before him, just in case.

"Leave us," the Warden said to his heavies.

The two Howlers vacated the room, leaving their boss with the hyena.

"You look well, Noss," the Warden said at length.

"What've you done with Red-mist?" Noss demanded. "Is he to be executed?"

The Warden huffed, "In a manner of speaking."

"What do you mean?"

"It's nothing you need concern yourself with; your only concern is surviving. You're only alive at all because I will it-"

"I'm only 'alive' so that you can use me against Amael or Nurka, depending on who comes out on top!" Noss growled toothily. "You're as bad as Vladimir. I should kill myself and stop everyone playing games with my worthless hide!"

"And doom your wife and cubs when I tell Vladimir you killed yourself?"

Noss looked down, then up again, "You'll kill me anyway when Amael takes charge."

The Warden moved on regardless. "There's a cub in Rufus's gang by the name of Tomek," he said. "I'm releasing him from the pit early. Take him into your gang."

"The Mosquitoes are full," Noss grunted.

"Then lose someone. I want the cub protected."

"Why?"

"Because Rufus asked me to… and shouldn't a dying wolf's wishes be honoured?" the Warden chuckled. "He's a handsome boy that Tomek, I must admit. I might take him for myself when everything's over."

Noss's nostrils flared in obvious disgust.

"You disapprove?" the Warden huffed. "How rich coming from a hyena; I can't even tell you from your wife! Besides, you admire Rufus and he's the worst offender."

"Rufus doesn't take," Noss explained, "he asks."

The Warden stared a while. Unable to mount a riposte to Noss's wit, he picked up his phone and called his toughs back in. "I'm done with him!" As the Howlers returned to drag Noss away, the Warden stipulated, "Give him a good beating before you turn him loose again."

"Big wolf aren't you?" Noss cackled, eyes alight. "Your time will come, coward! It will come!"

✢

Linus strode briskly along the pavement with Sara and company in tow. The Howler had no idea where he was leading them, just away from the station. He kept glancing nervously over his cloaked shoulder, searching the bobbing sea of passing pedestrians, expecting members of ALPHA to emerge from the masses and drag him into the back of a car.

"Stop!" Sara puffed, grabbing Linus's paw in a deserted side-alley, "Just… stop a minute, will ye."

Linus was grateful for her intervention. "Sorry," he said, "I-I-I don't know what I'm doing."

"Ye don't?" Sara laughed. "Looked pretty good from where Ah was standing."

Linus could but laugh too – my this is exhilarating.

Sara shook her head in wonder, "Ah had no idea you were working with Tristan all along."

Linus's elation faded to bafflement, "What?"

"When ye stepped out of nowhere on the train," Sara continued. "Och! Ah could nae believe it. Ah thought you and Tristan hated each other. You're such good actors, the both of ye. Is that tae throw ALPHA off the scent? 'Tis very clever."

With a tiny exhale of exasperation, Linus came clean. "I'm n-nnn-not working with anyone, Sara."

Silence.

"What?" she squeaked, eyes searching Linus's masked face for answers.

"I just followed you when you left the fair," Linus explained, blonde paws spread. "The way you were acting, I knew something was wrong. I had to follow you and make sure you'd be all right. I had no idea what was going on, but I've a fairly good inkling now."

Linus looked meaningfully at Olivia and Professor Heath.

"Then… then you're nae our contact in Riddle?" Sara said, drawing the Howler's blue-eyed gaze back to her.

"No."

"Then… are ye going turn us in tae the Bloodfangs?"

"Of course not!" Linus scoffed.

Sara dipped her chin and gasped gratefully. Kneading her paws she said, "Ah'm sorry Ah was so mean tae you back at the fair. Tristan didnae want ye involved that's all, he wanted tae protect you. He… he told me tae get rid of ye."

"Luckily I'm not so easy to put off."

"Aye!" Sara laughed. "You're a good 'un Linus."

"If by 'good 'un' you mean guilty of 'dereliction of duty', then I suppose I qualify-"

"You're nae guilty of anything! What's criminal in Lupa is that the Howlers control white-imperium leaving anyone outside the packs tae die."

"I agree," Linus said, "but… change comes slowly, with debate and reason, not violence. I tell you now, if Tristan's working with THORN I can't condone his actions and I w-www-will n-nnn-not protect him-"

Sara grabbed Linus's paw, "He's nae working with THORN! Josef's a filthy liar."

Linus nodded and dipped his chin – Josef hadn't been lying about Olivia, so why would he lie about Tristan? Still, he let Sara down gently.

"I believe you," he said, somehow without a stammer.

Sara nodded gratefully and patted Linus's paw.

In the following silence, Olivia looked between everyone, Sara, Heath, Linus, but settled on the Howler, for he was the only one wearing the cloak of authority. "What's going to happen to me?" she demanded of him.

Linus took a sharp breath, "What do you want to do?"

"Me?" Olivia replied. "Do I even have a choice?"

"Of course."

"But… I don't know. I don't know *what* to do."

"What Tristan said tae do," Sara insisted. "Ye don't want tae be a Howler, Olivia. You're too clever tae waste ye life plodding the streets and beating up little beasts!"

Linus averted his eyes a little.

"Not that they're all like that," Sara excused.

"Well I wouldn't be, would I?" Olivia maintained, hiking her chin, "I'd be a good Howler too."

"Olivia-"

"I don't want you to get arrested because of me!"

"It's too late now, Ah'm up tae me eyeballs!" Sara laughed, pinching Olivia's nose. "And Ah wouldn't want it any other way. You'd do the same for me."

Linus waited a moment, before pitching in, "I wasn't lying back there. If it's what you want, I'm sure we'd take you on at Bloodfang." He looked Olivia up and down, "It's so obvious now. I must be an idiot not to have felt you sooner."

"No, I can control it," Olivia claimed. "My corona, I mean."

Heath interjected in a curious tone, "Really?"

Olivia nodded eagerly, "Yes. I've been doing it for years. When Howlers look at me, I… I… shrink down and repress myself, somehow. It's so hard to explain-"

"I know exactly what you mean," Linus reassured her.

Olivia beamed happily at him, "You do?"

"Absolutely, coronal suppression is part of our training," he insisted. "Why does Josef want you specifically?"

"Puh!" Heath woofed, adjusting his spectacles.

Sara looked up at her teacher, questions dancing on the tip of her tongue. In the end all she needed to say was, "Professor?"

Heath volunteered what he knew. "I'm afraid Doctor Josef is obsessed with finding beasts of exceptional imperium tolerance, by which I mean able to accept high levels in their blood." Met with silence he continued, "Well, he was kicked out of the Ark when it came to light he had experimented on prisoners during the war. He'd been injecting beasts with imperium cocktails and blood taken from beasts with the rot, trying to turn healthy citizens into the afflicted or some such nonsense. It's an open secret he continues to experiment on beasts under the guise of ALPHA. I've no doubt he believes Olivia to be just another worthy subject. We can't let him take her, Linus; it'd be a death sentence."

Linus nodded. He looked Heath up and down, "Are you an addict, sir, like Josef claims?"

Heath nodded, "Yes. I am. Do you want to know why?"

Sara leant in and seethed, "Linus-"

"I just need to know where I stand," Linus explained. "Go on, Professor."

Clearing his throat, Heath did so, "It all stems from my own experiments on the rot, ones quite different to Josef's. As a young bear I was trying to effect a cure, you see, but to make sure the medicines I developed were safe for others I always tested them on myself first. Always." The bear averted his eyes in shame, "At some point, I don't know quite when, I developed an imperium addiction, most probably from my supposed antidotes. I… I don't have the rot, my body cannot metabolise it and pollute itself with black-imperium in the same way as yours, but I am compelled to sting myself from time to time simply... out of habit-"

"Habit?" Linus woofed, unbelieving of his ears. "Whilst Howlers die from the rot *you* w-www-waste imperium for leisure?"

Heath's hoary old face grimaced, "It's an addiction, young wolf. It's a different kind of pain, but just as real as yours."

"I have no choice, sir!"

"Nor do I, believe me, nor do thousands of sad Lupans you label gazers and addicts!"

Linus could but snort and huff with indignation as Sara tried to soften the blow. "It came from his experiments to find a cure, Linus," she explained. "Rufus knows. We all know. Josef wasn't telling us anything new. We're all guilty if Heath is. Rufus too."

The longest time passed.

"I... I can take you to my Den if you want," Linus finally sniffed, coming to terms with it all, "but I imagine you've some better arrangement."

Olivia exchanged looks with her fellow fugitives.

"Well?" Linus urged.

Sara spoke for all, "Tristan said someone would meet us and they'd sort things out."

"Where?" Linus asked, glancing about, "Who?"

"Well, *here*, or at the station, Ah suppose," Sara replied with a shrug. "He never said who."

"We should go back," Olivia suggested, a little panicked.

Linus disagreed. "No," he said flatly. "Josef could still be at the station."

"Then what do we do?" Heath crackled helplessly.

Linus pondered matters a moment. "I've a spot you can hide for now. Come on."

Between bites of his sandwich, Werner Schwartz watched from inside his Politzi car, watched Linus, Sara and the others crossing the road and heading down the nearest alley. Twirling his truncheon he locked his car and followed them.

~BLICK VI~

The bubbling hiss of waves percolating through pebbles soothed Meryl's ears as she strolled along New Tharona's seafront. Rafe walked sedately beside her – one of his strides made two of hers. Otters, rats and other seafaring types plied their trades from market stalls lining the cobbled street. Draped with colourful, stripy awnings they offered goods aplenty; fish, crabs, pearls, souvenirs carved from driftwood, it was all to be had for a haggled price. Were Rafe in uniform he might've been able to pass off his 'Howler' privileges to get a free meal, but Meryl had decided they shouldn't stand out. So black breeches and tunic it was for him, simple blue dress for her, the high collar discarded for once, though the cravat remained, as did Rafe's silk ribbon of a tail. Most assumed they were a holidaying couple, no doubt.

Many a wolf passed by; New Tharona was Eisbrand property after all. Some must have even been Eisbrand Howlers on leave. Afflicted or not they all threw the towering Rafe a second look; at least Meryl assumed they weren't looking at her. Passing a group of well-to-do wolfesses seated around a café table, all of whom stared at Rafe as a collective, the Eisenwolf said in his airy baritone, "All right, ladies?"

They nodded and made niceties, then once Rafe and Meryl had gone tittered at one another over their afternoon tea.

They probably think we make an silly-looking couple, Meryl thought. Awful bitches.

Rafe didn't seem to notice, even less care.

A rather big and obvious Eisbrand Howler was smouldering over a beer at the next, much cheaper-looking seafront eatery, along with a portly hog. The handsome Eisbrand stared at Rafe and Meryl with duotone blue and green eyes. The hog also looked up from his meal, all but dropping his cutlery as he ran his beady eyes slowly up Rafe's muscled frame.

"Meryl?" said the wolf, addressing Meryl but staring at Rafe.

"Tristan," Meryl replied, stopping with her ward. "How are you?" she asked, with forced amiability.

"Fine, fine. You?"

A nod. "Well enough." At length, Meryl remembered her manners. "This is Rafe, Rafe Stenton; Rafe, this is Tristan Donskoy, an... old friend."

"All right, mate?" Rafe chirped, big paw extending.

Tristan nodded and stood up to shake, ember smouldering on his lips. "Pleasure."

Rafe looked to the gob-smacked hog, "Have... we met before?"

"Don't think so, lad," the pig snorted at length, getting back to his dinner.

Rafe stared, vacant, struggling.

"Business," Tristan volunteered to Meryl, excusing the rude hog. He turned to Rafe, "Meryl and I used to fish for tiddlers in the rock pools together," he explained, if only to break the unbearable silence, "back when we were cubs."

Rafe snapped from his trance, "Oh yeah?"

Meryl waved a paw, "Seems a lifetime ago."

"For a Howler it is," Tristan claimed soberly, adding, "Well, I'll let you get back to your stroll."

"And you your leave," Meryl assumed. "Look after yourself, Tristan. Tell Ivan I said hello."

"I will."

The pairs parted company, Rafe giving the hog and Howler a last over-the-shoulder glance. "Nice fella."

"Yes."

Meryl sounded rather distracted.

"Graumeer, it's well-named," she said afresh.

"Yeah? What's it mean?" Rafe asked, looking out across the waters.

"Grey Sea. Look at it, even when the sun comes out it's still as grey as the Lupa."

"Polluted is it?"

"No, not really," Meryl shrugged. "Believe it or not the otters say good seawater is often grey or green; means there's lots of nutrients in the water being churned up by currents. It's good for the fish. Good for business."

"So… we can go in it then?"

"Go in it? You mean swim?"

"Yeah."

"Don't be daft, it's freezing this time of year!"

Rafe squinted at the sun, which hurt his eyes more than it ever did under Lupa's ashen haze. "Sun's out, 'en it?" he sniffed, wiping away some tears.

Meryl didn't notice, "Yes, but the water's never warm. It's fine for the otters, they don't feel a thing."

"Aww, come on, just a paddle. Get our feet wet. Yeah?"

With a cheeky grin, which made Meryl scoff with amusement, Rafe diverted them down some steps onto the pebbly beach. Some young otters were playing, jumping off an algae-coated jetty, but nobody else in their right mind braved the autumn Graumeer. It could be argued Rafe wasn't in his right mind, and had never been since his horrendous induction, but Meryl had no excuse as she slipped off her practical boots, hoisted her hem and joined Rafe in the surf.

"Oh!" she squeaked. "It's like ice!"

"Cor, 'en it?" Rafe seethed. "Oooh! Ah! Hahaha!" He looked to the otter cubs watching them from the jetty, "How'd you lot swim in this?"

After some uncertainty, a bold cub replied, "We otters be made of tougher stuff dan you 'Owlers!"

"You reckon?"

"Don't see no Lupans in da Graumeer, not even in summer! Yah all be soft landlubbers!"

The cubs laughed at wolfen expense; no little beast would dare but otters didn't see themselves thus, least of all their cubs.

"Oh yeah?" Rafe woofed, dashing ashore. "Right!"

"Rafe, what're you doing? Rafe!"

Before Meryl even made landfall, Rafe had discarded his tunic and picked his way along the jetty. For a second the otters looked worried they were about to be clouted, but the giant wolf leant on his knees and challenged them. "Bet yer a penny I don't even gasp."

The otters agreed – this was worth a penny.

"Rafe, don't!" Meryl shouted, hurrying along the jetty. "The currents are dangerous!"

The cubs went first, bounding to the end of the jetty and diving gracefully into the lazy swell with barely a splash. Pinching his nose Rafe fell in with all the grace of a potato sack falling off the back of a truck.

Ka-sploosh!

Chapter 30

In the blackness of 'the Pit' the insidious cold was starting to bite. First it nibbled away at Tomek's lower half, his toes, his legs, submerged in the icy water as they were, but then his fingers and paws followed. The young wolf twisted his bound wrists, trying to stimulate some semblance of feeling, to no avail.

"My p-ppp-paws are d-d-dropping off," he told Helmut, in a quasi-joking, worried kind of tone.

"Hold on, lad," the hog encouraged; he was completely invisible down in this pitch-black hole, but Tomek judged him to be looming slightly ahead and to the left, and above for his great height compared to Tomek. "Think warm thoughts," he added.

"Is hard," Tomek laughed, "but, I try."

"Good lad. It'll be over soon."

"It is… for Rufus."

"Don't be silly," Helmut scolded, "they're not going to execute him."

"You heard what they s-sss-said," Tomek sniffed. "Death by ant. They s-sss-stake him out in the wilderness. I'm a Watcher… I-I-I have seen it. Is nothing left after the ants come for you. Not even bone."

Helmut hushed the youth with reason, "They're just trying to scare us. You don't bump off a miner of Rufus's talent. Nooo! The Warden needs his like to meet his quota and keep his job. You wait and see; Rufe'll be chucked in a hole somewhere and roughed up, just like us, but he'll be back to work in a few days, humbled and compliant, or so they think. We know him better of course."

"You think so?"

"I know so. I also know Rufus won't be broken so easy, and nor will we. We'll serve our time and come through this with our heads held high."

Tomek nodded in the blackness, forgetting Helmut couldn't even see.

Unable to abide the grim silence and thoughts of Rufus's fate that followed, the young wolf made conversation. "W-www-what did you do, Helmut?"

"Eh?"

"To get s-sss-sent down."

"Imperium smuggling, of course. I thought everyone knew that by now."

"Not me."

"Ah, well," Helmut chuckled wistfully. "Used to run stings through the Lupan Wall, didn't I – probably snuck some past *your* nose once or twice, lad. Hahaha!"

Tomek allowed a tiny snort of mutual amusement.

"I only dabbled in the best stuff, mind," Helmut was quick to point out. "Proper white venom, nothing that'd hurt nobody. I have my principles. Them being everyone should have access to the good stuff, not just you Howlers. 'Tis a civil right, in my opinion. There'd be plenty to go around if it were rationed properly. I said as much at my trial. Didn't do me any favours, probably made things worse, but, well… a hog has to speak as he finds."

Tomek looked across the darkness. "At least you not trying to hurt nobody," he sniffed, fighting off his shivers long enough to speak with intent, "Is not like some."

If Madou and his cousin Zozizou understood Tomek's meaning they didn't deign to reply.

Silence returned to the Pit, save for Tomek's shivering breaths. The wolf was embarrassed that he alone seemed to be succumbing to the intoxicating cold. Helmut was a giant of a pig; doubtless it would take longer for the warmth to escape his thick hide. Madou was short, yes, but built like a rock, perhaps twice Tomek's weight, so being inferior to him was excusable too. But Zozizou, that skinny hyena? Tomek couldn't hear him shivering in the dark. No word of complaint left his lips. In fact he couldn't recall Zozizou ever complaining, not here in this icy tomb and not down the mines either. He never said a word to anyone. Silent as the grave. Uncomplaining.

By Ulf, is even Zozizou better than me, that sad, skinny addict? What is wrong with me? Pull yourself together, Tomek, you are a Watcher!

Tomek determined to stand up straight and be a wolf, but his body had other ideas.

"Gagh!"

A thunderous pain rumbled down Tomek's legs like a runaway train, boring deep into his bones, his marrow, sapping his strength in an instant and sending him down. Anywhere else it might not matter, save for the embarrassment, but here was not the time or place!

Splash!

"Tomek?" Helmet snorted, thrusting his snout where he judged the wolf ought to be standing and finding nothing but air. "Tomek, lad!"

Splashes and gasps filled the Pit; it sounded like Tomek was thrashing about in the water. Was he being attacked? Was something in the water?

"Helmut… help me!" he cried, his voice punctuated by watery gargles. "Gaahagh!"

Helmut followed the sounds across the Pit. "Where you at, lad!" he said, sloshing desperately around. "Keep talking!"

Nothing.

"Tomeeek!" Helmut squealed, searching the waters with his legs for his arms were tied. "Tomek, where are yah? Tomek!" The hog looked across the Pit even though there was no slither of light to see by. "Lads!" he piped at the hyenas. "Tomek's gone under. I-I-I can't find him!"

For a few disturbing seconds, though it felt an eternity to Helmut, the pig heard not a slosh of movement from the hyenas, even less a concerned word.

"Madou!" Helmut urged.

With a mumble aimed at Zozizou in the native hyena language Helmut didn't understand, Madou tramped nosily across the pit. Helmut could feel the hyena's body heat on his own naked skin.

"He's here somewhere!" the pig told him, sloshing to and fro, hoping against hope he might feel Tomek's body brush against his shins. "He just fell over. I think it's the rot."

Calmly, and without a word, Madou ducked under the water, as if bobbing for apples. Not a moment later he broke the surface. The sound of water running off a waterlogged body was interrupted only by the coughing and gasping of said body.

"You got him?" Helmut asked.

"Yesh!" Madou replied through a mouthful of Tomek – no doubt with his paws bound behind him the hyena had resorted to holding the wolf upright with his teeth, biting his shirt or the scruff of his neck, Helmut supposed.

Tomek didn't have to suppose, he could feel Madou's enormous hyena teeth against his skin. He was grateful for them, and for the air filling his lungs again.

"You all right, lad?" Helmut asked, his rubbery snout getting in Tomek's face. "Lad?"

"Yes…yes!" Tomek spluttered. "Let me go. I stand up."

"Let it pass. Don't be proud. Madou can hold you, can't you Madou?"

Madou grunted positively.

For some minutes he held Tomek aloft. The hyena was embarrassingly warm and solid, like a sun-bathed boulder pressing against Tomek's sodden back, revitalising the stricken wolf. Worse, his corona overwhelmed Tomek, swamping him in a fuzzy embrace that the young wolf realised was a further comfort in this horrid place.

"I'm all right," Tomek sniffed, suddenly wriggling and elbowing himself free of Madou's hold. "Is gone now."

Madou backed off.

For a while nothing was said. The only sounds were ripples slapping against the rock walls and drips from the saturated, bodies contained within them.

"Nice one, Madou," Helmut praised. "Well done, mate. How'd you do that? I couldn't find him for the life of me-"

"His corona," the hyena replied bluntly, saying further. "My debt's repaid, wolf."

Tomek said nothing.

"Debt?" Helmut queried. "What debt?"

Madou explained. "Tomek knows what I mean. He saved my life back at the Lupan Wall, Rufus's too. With him gone and my debt paid there's nothing to tie us. We'll go our separate ways once we're out of here."

Helmut could scarce believe his ears, "What're you on about, mate?"

"It's what he wants isn't it?" Madou growled at Helmut, whilst referring to Tomek. "Terrorist scum aren't we? Not that the indoctrinated idiot has ever stopped to think what it is that drives my people to fight!"

"Madou-"

"Zozizou and I will find another gang, one made up of our own kind. There's always places opening up with beasts dying left right and centre."

"But we need Rufus-"

"He's dead!" Madou scoffed. "He's ant food, Helmut, or didn't you hear your fellow hogs?"

"They wouldn't do that! It's barbaric."

"Don't kid yourself! You heard Tomek. He's seen it done. And if that's what you wolves and hogs are capable of doing to your own kind, we hyenas haven't a prayer. Rufus is... *was* different to other Lupans. He spoke truth and reason. And that's why they've got rid of him. Someone up high ordered his death. He obviously didn't wither away down the mines as quickly as they would like, so the Warden has been told to speed things up. And you wonder why I'm in THORN. Why I fight. Well... Lupa's going to change soon enough, my brothers in THORN will see to it, and believe me Rufus was all for it. He was on our side!"

"I doubt that, mate," Helmut said in the aftermath.

With nothing more to say, Madou sloshed back to his cousin. The hyenas whispered in their native tongue, excluding Helmut and Tomek.

So, is this how it was going to be without Rufus? That wolf was a leader all right; one in a million. What a waste, Helmut thought.

Suddenly a light!

Daylight poured in through the opening trapdoor, blinding Helmut and doubtless the others.

"Wakey, wakey!" the guards snorted, appearing to the prisoners as silhouettes blurred by a film of stinging tears. "How're we doing down there, boys? Comfortable? Hahahahaaa!"

Another of the guards pushed the first aside and said reasonably, "Where's the Watcher?"

The blinking prisoners exchanged looks.

"You, the wolf, Tomek 'en it?" the guard said, beckoning with a chubby finger. "Come here. Stand under the door, you're coming out."

Shaking his head Tomek backed fearfully out of the light.

"Come back, idiot!" the guard snorted, leaning in. "We're not gonna hurt yer. You're being let off. The Warden said to pull you up sharpish." The hog looked to his fellow guards and laughed under his breath, "The boss must fancy him or something."

Helmut nudged Tomek towards the light, "Go on, lad. Up you go now."

"B-b-but what about you?"

"I'll be fine. Tough as old boots I am."

"So am I."

"I know that. But you nearly bought it a minute ago on account o' the rot. That's not something anyone can help, however tough, not even Rufus." Helmut peered across at the hyenas and added with intent, "We can't rely on Madou no more, so you get out of here whilst you can, lad. Go on."

Slowly, reluctantly, Tomek trudged into the middle of the pool. The hogs lowered down a wooden pole with a noose on the end and commanded Tomek to bite it. He did so, and hanging on with his powerful jaws – a trait shared by most beasts, not least wolfkind – he was pulled up through the trapdoor and onto dry land.

No sooner had Tomek departed than the door was snapped shut behind him, casting Helmut, Madou and his cousin into darkness again.

✦

"Go on, gerroutofit!"

With a kick to the rump, Tomek was sent stumbling back into Gelb's compound. Even with paws unbound he was unable to save himself the indignity of a face full of mud. As he made to rise the hogs kicked him again and laughed cruelly, before the leader of the group told the others to lay off, lest the Warden was watching.

"He's marked him," the hog added quietly. "For what I don't know. Come on."

"Let that be a lesson to yer," one of the guards spat at Tomek. "Watch yer mouth in future."

The hogs took their leave, closing the gates behind them.

Shivering and aching, Tomek dragged himself from the caking mud and stumbled forth into the compound, along the rows of anonymous brown huts. Curious, collared faces watched him from the windows.

Tomek trudged up the creaky stairs to his usual hut, through the door and past the rows of occupied bunks, over to those beds in the far corner that the Scarab Gang had claimed as their own long ago. They were furthest from the draughty door and relatively cosy.

As he made to collapse onto his pathetic mattress, Tomek stayed himself.

There was a wolf in his bed!

"Hey!" Tomek piped, more surprised than indignant. "What you doing?"

The wolf sat up and sneered. "Get lost!"

"Is my bed. My bed!"

"Well 'is my bed' now!" the wolf mocked, producing a rusty knife from under the ragged sheets and twisting it under Tomek's flaring nose. "Wanna fight about it, eh boy?"

Paws raised, Tomek backed off.

The youth cast his eyes over the bunks that his gang used to occupy in the hope of finding an empty bed; he instead found them claimed by strangers. Clearly word of Scarab's fall had gotten round Gelb in a heartbeat and a new gang had moved in on their 'territory', that being the far end of a hut.

The invaders glared pugnaciously back at Tomek; wolf, hog and cat – the only one among them apparently unconcerned by his presence was a big, superbly-muscled hyena who was lying on his back with his paws tucked behind his head, his stripy shirt rolled up and serving as a meagre pillow to his thick, collared neck. Puffing away on an ember he stared not at Tomek but at the ceiling. His bright purple eyes were like Madou's.

Feeling robbed and wronged, Tomek wanted to threaten even him, wanted to say something like, 'Wait until my friends are back, we'll have you!' But, knowing Rufus was likely gone forever, Tomek thought better of it and slunk away to find a less desirable bunk.

The nearer the hut door he ventured the more ragged and pathetic the beasts cowering in the beds either side of Tomek became, until they were so thin, sick and lowly that he could easily turn any one of them out and claim their place for himself. But, he had not the stomach for such heartlessness.

Finding a ragged old bunk not far from the door, Tomek curled up on the thin, likely flea-ridden mattress. Wet, cold and starving, tears came easily to the young wolf. He was glad nobody could see him as darkness descended on Gelb. He thought of Helmut still down in that awful pit, and Rufus being swarmed by ants and eaten alive, the ancient punishment metered out to treacherous Howlers.

Madou's right, we Lupans are cruel.

Between feverish shivers and thoughts, Tomek suddenly felt a warm sheet settle over his frozen body – a quick visual check proved it to be a stripy prisoner's shirt.

How odd.

Tomek rolled over and seeing that gigantic purple-eyed hyena looming over him he scooted up the bed until his back was to the wooden wall.

"I sleep here!" he yelped. "Is no problem! Please."

"Shh!" the hyena hushed, looking down the rows of beds, then back at Tomek. "I'm not going to hurt you." He flicked a big finger at Tomek. "Put my shirt over you before you catch a fever, you've been in the pit haven't you?"

Unsure, Tomek pulled the warm top up to his collared neck until the hyena smiled toothily at him.

"Better?" he asked.

Nodding, Tomek's eyes flitted about. "W-w-what you want, hyena?" he sniffed. "I have n-nnn-nothing."

The hyena took a draught of his ember. "You're in Scarab, aren't you?" he asked Tomek, who replied with a nod. The hyena went on, "There's a rumour going round that Rufus is going to be fed to the ants tomorrow. Is it true?"

Tomek dipped his chin, "They say so."

"Beasts say many things; you mustn't always believe them," the hyena chuckled. He looked around the hut, as if checking for prying ears, then peered under the bed at Tomek again, "Is Madou still down the Pit?"

Tomek nodded.

The hyena grunted. "How's he doing?"

"Better than me," Tomek admitted with a false laugh. "Is friend of yours, then?"

"He is," the hyena replied, "as is Red-mist, and if you're his friend you're mine as well." He held out a huge paw, "I'm Noss, Prince of the Jua-mata."

"Prince?" Tomek snorted.

"I usually keep it quiet, but Madou will tell you when he gets out. What's your name?"

"Tomek Usenko."

"Howler?"

"Watcher."

"Watcher? I used to be a Watcher myself."

"You? But… you a hyena."

Noss flashed his bright eyes and teeth, "It's a long story, and we've more important things to talk about."

Prince Noss sat on the foot of the bunk; the tired, woodworm-eaten structure creaked alarmingly under his muscular weight. He took a puff of his ember and said, "You'll mine with my gang for now, the Mosquitoes. Don't worry about the others, they won't hurt you. I'm the leader and *I* say who works with us."

Tomek gasped, "Thank you… I'm hard worker."

"You'll have to be! I'm not quite as good at sniffing out imperium as Rufus, but until he returns I'm the best miner in Gelb, even if I say so myself… Hahahahaaaa!"

"Returns?"

Noss leant close and whispered, "Do you think a wolf who can break an imperium collar with his bare paws is so readily disposed of?" Blowing ember vapour towards the nearest dew-flecked window, he continued, "I happen to know why Rufus is here, and you can sure wherever he's going next it's not to his death. No, some arrangement has been made. I'll make inquiries tomorrow."

Tomek sat in bemused silence.

"We'll talk later," Noss assured him. "Come, meet my gang."

✤

After half an hour bumping along the dirt road leading from Gelb, the truck skidded to a sudden, gravely halt. With his paws tied by wire Rufus was unable to stop himself falling sideways from the inertia.

The condemned wolf levered his bruised body back to a sitting position just as the truck doors were flung open, revealing the red sky of dusk and the two Watchers that passed as the Warden's personal thugs.

"I assume we've reached the chosen execution grounds, gentlebeasts," Rufus said airily.

Wordlessly the Watchers climbed inside and pulled the prisoner to his feet by the shoulders, escorting him from the truck and onto the dusty road.

The truck had stopped in the midst of a rocky valley with the mountains surrounding Gelb rising all around, their snowy peaks licked by the last rays of pink sunlight. Up there it was doubtless freezing, but the valley was warm enough now for the nearby stream to flow and the odd speck of green to survive despite the imperium effluent from Gelb's mines polluting the water.

It was also warm enough for giant ants to forage, Rufus knew, at least during the day. The telltale mounds of disturbed erde upsetting the otherwise flat and uniform valley floor betrayed the nest entrances to those with eyes to see. No beast with sense would be caught out here during the day.

As the Watchers led Rufus away from the road and into the barren wilderness, one pulled out an imperium pistol and cocked the hammer.

The other noticed and piped, "What're you doing?"

"Let's just shoot him and be done with it," said the one with the pistol.

"The Boss wants it done properly. He was *very* explicit."

"He'll never know."

"You're gonna to take that chance are you? You'll be out here next."

"I'm not sticking around here!" came the one with the pistol. "The ants could come out any minute. Mate, I've seen 'em turn a truck over and drag beasts down their holes alive!"

"We're doing this properly."

"What difference does it make? We'll give him a soldier's death."

"It's our duty to-!"

"Gentlebeasts, if I may!" Rufus piped up, clearing his throat. "It's still too cold for the ants to emerge during the night. They won't appear until the sun strikes their mounds. You're quite safe, for now."

The Watchers exchanged incredulous glances. The one with the pistol waved it at Rufus and snorted, "How'd you know?"

Rufus flashed a smile, "I'm something of an expert in the matter of bugs, young wolf."

"Oh yeah?"

"Absolutely. And believe me, whilst I appreciate the offer of a soldier's death, I don't want to be responsible for anybody else joining me in my fate." Rufus looked down at his feet and said, "Please... carry out your duty. I'm ready and willing to face my punishment."

The wolf with the pistol shook his helmeted head and marvelled, "You're a strange one."

The other Watcher unsentimentally turned the prisoner around and roughly pushed him forward.

"Move it!"

For a moment Rufus cringed, his back tingling and burning with fear as he expected any moment to hear a crack and feel a pellet tear through his body, ending it all.

But no pellet, no end, was forthcoming, just another shove between the shoulder blades.

I'm going to live, at least until dawn.

The two Watchers led Rufus to a conspicuously barren concreted area with a metal post set in the middle. Some pioneering weeds were growing between the cracks in the concrete, indicating that this structure, if one was charitable enough to regard it a structure, had been here for some time. A chain and collar dangled from the metal post, ready to receive the latest condemned beast and hold him fast until the ants awoke and happened across him.

Ulf willing someone else will happen across me before them, Rufus thought, as the Watchers clipped the hefty collar about his neck. He could see no bones or evidence of previous victims – unlike beasts, bugs wasted nothing.

With unbecoming haste that betrayed their fear, the Watchers left Rufus to his fate and jogged swiftly back to the truck, glancing over their shoulders all the way lest the six legged horrors that stalked this desolate land broke the instinct of eons and emerged before dawn. The truck performed a swift U-turn, kicking up a cloud of ash and dust in its polluting wake. Within half a minute it had carried the Watchers safely around the side of the nearest mountain, leaving Rufus with nothing but his bruises and thoughts.

After a few fruitless tugs on the chain and collar which succeeded only in choking him, the weakened wolf collapsed against the unforgiving metal pole and settled in for a long, cold, sleepless night.

Perhaps his last.

✦

The street outside Heath's flat appeared deserted, but an ALPHA agent must be watching, Tristan knew, as he stood in the shadows across the way. Josef Grau would not leave the flat unguarded in the hope Olivia would foolishly return.

She wouldn't; only beast foolish enough to show their face here is you, Tristan thought whilst crossing the lamp-lit street. It's just a bee. What does it matter?

It matters to Sara.

Tristan saw the Bloodfang-stamped *Springtail* from earlier hadn't moved an inch, parked as it was under the nearest imperium gas lamp. One assumed it belonged to Linus, but if Sara had sent him packing at the fair why was it still here? No doubt any watching agent had noticed it too, no doubt they had written down the plate and no doubt Howler Linus was going on ALPHA's watch list, provided that was his *Springtail* – the only doubt Tristan had.

Passing the mono, the gate and the entrance to the flats, Tristan went unchallenged. He climbed the dark, creaking stairs as quietly as his hefty armoured form allowed, peering through the passing regimental balusters, checking always for an ALPHA Prefect, a suspicious beast, anyone.

There was no one.

Tristan made Heath's front door. The blue-imperium snowflake symbol adorning his helmet illuminated the door just a little. Its feeble light swept across the shiny wood like a distant lighthouse as the Howler glanced nervously left and right before trying the knob.

Locked.

Good; ALPHA hasn't turned the place over for evidence yet, so the bee must still be here. Bad; you don't have the key, Tristan.

No matter for a skilled Howler.

Grasping the knob in both paws and averting his helmet-clad face, Tristan channelled the imperium as he had a hundred-thousand times. With a blinding blast of white-hot plasma the lock mechanism exploded in his grasp.

With a shake of his throbbing paws, Tristan pushed the smouldering door aside and entered Heath's flat. It was as dark as black-imperium inside with the only the merest trickle of amber street light leaking through the drawn curtains. Tristan's paw groped for the light switch by the door, but at the last second he thought better of it and waved a paw over his snowflake brooch instead. It shone a pale blue, illuminating Heath's living room, with its sofa, photos and many cultural trinkets.

The silence of the flat was disturbed by loud, intermittent hums and rough, wooden scraping noises.

Bvvvt! Bvvvbvvvvt!

It was coming from dead ahead; the bedrooms if Tristan recalled rightly. He also recalled from conversations with Heath that Sara's pet bee was a bit of a madam, rather like the wolfess herself. What was it called, Toggle or something? Did it come when called, or are bees deaf? Crossing the living room, Tristan wished he'd paid attention during biology. Ulf knows the way to Sara's heart lay through knowledge. She likes brainy types, like that Linus, not thugs like you-

Click!

The imperium lamps set in the walls coughed into life, banishing both the darkness and Tristan's thoughts, and swamping the feeble glow of his brooch.

"Don't move," a strong, yet feminine voice warned.

Despite the instruction, Tristan instantly turned to face its source and found a black-cloaked, green-eyed, red-furred wolfess standing in the kitchen doorframe, one paw touching the nearby light switch, the other aiming a pistol at him.

"Janoah?" Tristan scoffed.

"Prefect Janoah," she corrected sharply, taking a step into the living room. "Paws up!"

Tristan raised his paws, just a little.

"That's better," Janoah said, giving the smouldering front door a tiny sideways glance. "It appears I can now add breaking and entering to your unbecoming catalogue of felons."

With a growl, Tristan demanded sarcastically, "And how did *you* get in here, did you climb in the window like the spider you are?"

"I picked the lock."

"How devious."

Janoah's green eyes narrowed. "It's called finesse, Howler, something lacking in you clunking great Eisbrands. You traipse around Lupa in your shiny armour still, as if you own the whole city! Always have."

"I'll take no lectures from a vile Bloodfang, thank you."

Janoah chuckled, "Even less would I a THORN spy! Or would you prefer 'activist'?"

"Pull the other one."

"I'd not be so glib if I were you, Donskoy. This is a most serious accusation."

"You've got nothing on me."

With a cock of her head, Janoah reached into her cloak and produced several unopened stings, still in their cardboard, wax-dipped packaging. "The Professor's secret stash," she explained, rolling them over in her paw. "He's a miserable addict and you've been supplying him his illegal fix."

"By Ulf, is that the best you can come up with?"

"That… and helping him hide that dodger wolfess from the authorities," Janoah said. "You came back here to dispose of the evidence before ALPHA agents rifled through Heath's dirty drawers."

"I didn't come back for that, I came back for…." Tristan trailed off.

"For what?"

Bvvv! Bvvvt!

It didn't matter now, so Tristan admitted it. "The bee," he said, clearing his throat. "It's in the spare room."

"Yes, I had a quick look. Can't say I'm surprised, Heath's a strange one."

"It's just a pet. He left it behind."

Janoah stifled a laugh, "What were you going to do, post it too him in Everdor?"

"I don't know where he's gone."

"We'll see what you know back at ALPHA HQ," Janoah said, flicking her pistol at the door. "After you, Howler."

"I don't think so," Tristan spat.

"Resisting arrest are we? That's guilty behaviour if I ever saw it."

"This is no 'arrest'. You've no warrant. Nothing! There should be an army of ALPHA Prefects here to take me, not just you. This is just your twisted vendetta against me for all the years I turned your husband's head, isn't it?"

Janoah growled, "Now that really *is* absurd."

Tristan's squinting eyes revealed the smile hiding beneath his helmet, "It kills you to know Rufus would have even me back before going near you, if I'd let him. You shouldn't take it personally, Janoah, it's not your fault Rufus can't bring himself to fancy a twisted bitch like you. How's his latest whim? Linus is it? Are you planning his downfall too?"

Janoah's eyes flitted a little. Her finger played with the pistol trigger. "You really are clueless," she said, even as her gulp betrayed the wound left by Tristan's insults. "I've better things to do than worry about Rufus's daft flings. I love him, yes… but I love Lupa more. My parents died for it, dozens of my friends died for it. I will not see it destroyed by selfish beasts like you! You're going down; you, THORN and anyone else who's in on this putrid plot. You're going down, legitimately, so that Lupans know justice is being done and they can sleep easy in their beds."

Tristan exploded, "Nobody can sleep easy as long as the current cartel continues to oppress the citizens and murder hyenas! If you truly want to preserve Lupa things must change."

"So you admit it?"

"Whatever I admit to you here, I'll deny it later," Tristan claimed smugly. "Besides, Adal Weiss won't let you embarrass ALPHA by throwing the book at me over such spurious claims. Thorvald will protect me and Adal knows it. There's not an Elder jury that'd convict me and so give him the nod to send down any Howler he pleases. The Den Fathers will not set such a precedent; they do not want to give Adal more power."

Janoah agreed, "Perhaps… but your THORN compatriots will soon incriminate you beyond all doubt and then not even Thorvald will want to save you, even if he could."

"Is that a fact?"

"Yes. When Nurka rescues Noss Jua-mata from Gelb, as he must, your small part in this plot will be confirmed to us. It will also spell the end of THORN."

Tristan's duotone eyes widened.

Janoah beamed, "Praying mantis got your tongue? You see my dear Donskoy, there's no way that terrorist Nurka could know about Noss's continued existence except through me, Vladimir or Josef. It was our little secret. However, I've long suspected a certain someone has been tapping into Riddle Den's phone lines. Yes, a certain pig, shall we say?" The wolfess rolled her eyes and sighed, "Vladimir and I can be *so* careless when we catch up, can't we? Nattering away on the phone together, we give so much away. Or perhaps, only what we want to."

Tristan hoped the surcoat folds gathered about his throat hid his gulp. "I don't know what you're talking about."

Janoah wagged a chiding finger, "Good old Werner told you about Noss, didn't he? Yes. And you've passed it on to THORN like a good little spy. Now Nurka will be compelled to bust Noss out of Gelb. Oh, but I'm counting on the mad prince being there. He might be off his head on chunta, but he's not so far gone; Rufus Valerio taught him better than that."

Tristan growled, "What do you mean?"

"Concerned for your terrorist allies, traitor?" Janoah cooed triumphantly. "You implicate yourself with every word." She readied her pistol, "Now I *really* can't let you go, lest you run back and tell. I'd kill you first, believe me. So… let's make a deal. Come quietly and put down all you know in a confession and I'll see to it you get off lightly. You're just a foolish boy, I'll say, you knew no better. It's what Blade-dancer would want and Ulf knows I owe him that much for all the stings he's given Rufus."

Tristan took a sharp, shaky breath, his eyes flitted down at Janoah's pistol. Something passed between them, a cue, a feeling, a quiver in their mingling coronas.

"Thump you!"

Tristan went for it, diving behind the sofa in the same instance Janoah fired!

Crack! Toing!

Janoah's pellet pinged harmlessly off Tristan's armoured shoulder, tearing his surcoat and embedding itself in one of Heath's many photos. The frame crashed to the floor with a cacophony of glass at the same instance Tristan hit the carpet. No sooner had he landed than Tristan rolled away from the sofa, saving himself from Janoah's blade as she leapt over the cushions and thrust her rapier at him in a follow-up assault.

Scrabbling to his feet amidst a flurry of cloth and cloak Tristan summoned a flare of plasma to his gauntlet-clad fingertips. The blinding arc of burning imperious energy crackled through the air and slammed into Janoah's chest, blasting her backwards over the head of the sofa and down onto the cushions.

"Ooaaaf!"

Whilst Janoah flailed about the sofa, Tristan seized the glaring opportunity and rushed to the door. Yanking it wide he was presented not by open space, but a metallic wall of heaving, riveted armour with a lupine head.

The Eisenwolf.

"You!" Tristan yelped, simultaneously backing up and drawing his sword as Janoah's clunking marriage of iron and wolf squeezed through the doorframe.

"Rafe!" Janoah gasped, holding her smouldering chest.

"YOU ALL RIGHT, JAN?" the Eisenwolf asked in his thick, tinny tenor.

She nodded, gulped, and snarled, "Get him!"

Rafe's blank round eyes turned on Tristan, his soulless mask peering down at him, somehow appearing much taller when there was but a few inches difference. The exhaust projecting from Rafe's mountainous, cloak-draped back popped open and vented a noxious cloud of ash, instantly fouling the air in Heath's flat and spraying a circle of black on the ceiling directly above him.

"PUT YOUR WEAPON DOWN, HOWLER," he commanded.

"Not on your life!" Tristan growled, paws nursing the hilt of his great sword.

"I DON'T WANT TO HURT YOU."

"Then step aside!"

Rafe shook his head a little. "I CAN'T DO THAT, MATE. PUT YOUR SWORD AWAY AND LET'S SORT THIS ALL OUT BACK AT HQ. NOBODY HAS TO GET HURT-"

"Wake up, Bruno!" Tristan woofed, adding, "That's your name, not 'Rafe'. You are Bruno Claybourne! Remember?"

Rafe said nothing, but his metal ears pricked, as did Janoah's.

"By Ulf, look at you," Tristan gulped, "look at what you've become; what you're doing! I could never tell her. It'd break her heart to know."

Rafe's interest was piqued, "WHO?"

"Sara, you fool!" the Howler before him shouted. "Sara and Olivia! I'm trying to help them. Don't you even care about them? Don't you remember them at all?"

Rafe remained motionless.

Tristan explained, "Sara was your girlfriend, for Ulf's sake. You loved her, didn't you? You came on the train to see her all the time. That's how we met, me and you." The Howler ripped his helmet off, revealing his grey and white face. "It's me, Howler Tristan. Remember? I tried to recruit you just before this… this manipulator got her claws into you and made you into a monster. I helped you get away from her agents that day, the day they took you away and… changed you."

Slowly, Rafe cocked his head to Janoah. "OI, WHAT'S HE ON ABOUT, JAN?"

"A desperate ploy by a cornered roach," Janoah huffed, rolling off the sofa and standing back with her rapier held towards Tristan. "Be careful though, he's strong."

Rafe stepped protectively forward, "STAY BACK, JAN, I'LL DEAL WITH HIM."

Janoah nodded.

"Sara wouldn't want this!" Tristan howled, scrabbling to don his helmet again as he backed across the room away from the giant. He bumped into a tiny table, knocking one of Heath's many exotic trinkets to the floor; a squat beetle-god statue carved of wood. "She wouldn't want us to fight!" Tristan asserted, sword ready in both paws.

"I DON'T EITHER, MATE," Rafe sniffed metallically, raising an iron-gloved paw. Purple plasma licked between his thick fingers, snapping and popping in a fearful display of imperious power. "STAND DOWN AND WE WON'T HAVE TO."

A tiny shake of the head and trembling intake of breath was all Tristan could manage in the face of Rafe's corona flooding across the room and smothering his own, penetrating him right down to the bone.

Rafe grunted, "FINE."

With a quick twist of the valve at his back, the massive Prefect squatted down and launched himself forward with unnatural speed and power. The very air behind him rippled and twisted, blasting pictures and paintings from the walls.

Tristan weaved to his right and swung his sword left at Rafe, plasma arcing down the blade, but the Eisenwolf parried the hefty blow aside with a twist of his armoured forearm and followed it up by jabbing his other plasma-licked fist into Tristan's breastplate.

"Gagh!"

The blinding blast of plasma punched the Howler off his feet and sent him tumbling across Heath's beautiful carpet to a cacophony of armour and rivets. His dented breastplate smouldering and blasted, Tristan scrambled to his feet as quickly as he'd fallen.

Prefect and Howler circled round one another, stepping sideways, Tristan with his sword held forth, Rafe with his mighty arms held stiffly and slightly away from his sides, like a circus bodybuilder walking into the ring.

It can't be easy to move in that suit, Tristan thought, but move Rafe did, bearing down on his quarry a second time and cleaving the air with a crackling pawful of plasma so potent as to set Tristan's fur standing on end beneath his armour!

Somehow the Eisbrand parried with his sword and hacked Rafe in the side, biting deep into his armour.

A hit!

In the next breath, if that, Rafe slammed his mighty arm down, trapping Tristan's sword under his armpit whilst reaching round with his other paw. He grabbed the naked blade and, looking dolefully at Tristan with that anonymous mask, sent a shocking torrent of plasma shooting along the sword and up Tristan's arms.

Yelping in agony the Howler released his weapon and staggered backwards, his arms at once numb and yet burning from the plasma. Falling to his knees he shook his paws and tucked them under his arms in a vain attempt to stem the pulsing waves of pain.

"Grrrrrfgh!"

Meanwhile, Rafe discarded Tristan's sword and checked his own wound – his armour was cut deeply. Down to the flesh beneath? The watching Janoah couldn't tell.

Either way, she knew it was all over.

The exhaust at Rafe's massive back vented another cloud of choking ash, blackening the ceiling and turning the air in Heath's flat an even unhealthier grey. Seeing this, Janoah retrieved her helmet from a table and slipped it on before she succumbed to the pollution. Then she stood guard by the door, rapier ready, lest the wakened Tristan thought to escape.

"HAD ENOUGH?" Rafe asked the wounded Howler.

With one paralysed arm held close to his body, Tristan reached under his cloak with a trembling paw, searching for the pistol tucked near his tail. "It'll take more than that you... you abomination," he growled.

"YOU CAN'T HURT ME WITH THAT POP-GUN," Rafe said, somehow without a hint of arrogance.

Tristan pulled his 'pop-gun' from the holster and aimed at the mechanical accumulation of metal before him in the hope it might keep him at bay regardless.

"Wrap it up, Rafe," Janoah said, glancing behind, "before we attract too much attention."

Tristan leapt on her words. "Did you hear that, Bruno?" he said, with a slight laugh. "Better cart me off before anyone sees. That's how she operates, picking off the strong, gaining influence and power-"

"That's rich coming from one of Amael's wolves," Janoah countered.

"I'm nobody's wolf... except Thorvald's."

"Yet you betray him?"

"Thorvald b-believes in fairness and equality!" Tristan stammered. "He'll understand when we help bring it to Lupa, wolf, hyena, little beast... we'll forge a new society based on democracy, as it was in ancient times."

Janoah woofed, triumphant, "That's a confession if I ever heard one. Did you hear that, Rafe?"

A metallic nod.

"That's two witnesses, Tristan. It's over."

"The time of the Howlers *will* come to end," Tristan went on, uncaring of his fate, "if not now then soon. Even Rufus says so; the rise of imperium technology will give power to the many and we'll be thrown on the scrap heap. The best we Howlers can do is let ourselves down gently and help create a fairer world by building a democratic state!"

"Democratic indeed," Janoah chuckled. "I fear Amael and THORN have been telling you fibs, Tristan. Amael's bent on dictatorship; I know, I lay with him! Moreover, do you think hyenas want to live in harmony with wolves? They'll tear us down and set themselves up in our stead the moment we let them, as would any rabbit or mouse were they able! Wolfkind created this city, the Founders fought and died so wolves could rule, that is our right! But... not one wolf alone. Never! Even if Amael proves benevolent his successor could be a mad dictator; that way madness lies. We packs may squabble, but in the end we rub along. Lupa remains stable. That's how it must be, and ALPHA will keep it that way, regardless of what so-called technology comes along."

"I think you're the one being fibbed to, Valerio," Tristan corrected darkly. "The Alpha is the one bent on dictatorship. I know... because I know the one who lays with him... and it's definitely not you, or any other wolfess."

Janoah's eyes narrowed.

Tristan chuckled and tapped his masked snout.

Enough was enough. "Not too rough, Stenton," Janoah commanded, "we need him in one piece."

Rafe nodded and stepped forward, as unruffled by Tristan and his pistol as he would be by a cub armed with a cork gun.

"EASY, MATE."

"You'll not take me!" Tristan vowed, pressing the pistol under his jaw, where his otherwise all-encompassing Howler helmet didn't protect him. "Grrrfgh!"

"Rafe!" Janoah barked.

In the instant he had, Rafe cast both paws at Tristan and released a blast of imperious energy so potent that the lamps all around the room flared up in a rainbow of colour. The air warped and twisted as Rafe's invisible field threw Tristan against the nearest wall like a rag doll, cracking the plaster and knocking down a dozen pictures which rained down upon the Howler's surcoat-clad back.

The pistol tumbled to the floor beside him and Rafe chipped it neatly aside with a metal boot.

Janoah leant sideways against the doorframe and sighed with relief, "By Ulf's fangs. I'm getting sick and tired of these THORN fanatics killing themselves. We'll have to check him for a capsule."

Rafe stood over the Howler and judged by his weakened corona alone that, "HE'S OUT COLD, JAN."

Janoah sheathed her rapier. "Good. Pick him up and throw him in the truck."

Rafe went to do so, but looked to his right, to the corridor adjoining the upturned living room. He looked back to Janoah and asked, "OI, WHAT'S THAT?"

"What?"

"THAT NOISE SOUNDS LIKE... BUZZING."

Bvvvt Bvvvvvvt!

"I dunno," Janoah lied, with a flick of her head, adding, "It's probably the gas pipes or central heating. Come on, I can't carry this Eisbrand oaf."

Undeterred, Rafe clomped down the corridor, exploring the dark recesses of Heath's flat.

"Stenton!"

"HANG ON."

After a quick aural search the Eisenwolf opened one of the doors and a great, furry, six-legged ball squeezed past his legs and trundled down the corridor, walking over Tristan without a care in the world and into the kitchen.

"OI, JAN, IT'S A MASSIVE BEE!" Rafe laughed, following it to the kitchen. Peering round the door he watched the creature prise open Heath's larder and turn out jar after jar of honey and jam, knocking them to the floor with its flailing, quivering legs until one of them smashed. The bee immediately pounced on the broken jar and stuck a long, black, tongue-like mouthpart inside, rapidly vacuuming up the contents.

"HAAHAHA! OI, LOOK AT THIS! AWW, 'EN IT CUTE?"

Rolling her eyes, Janoah moseyed over for a look with a paw on her hips. "Adorable, until it stings you and you die from an allergic reaction," she said, smacking her lips and tugging Rafe's arm. "Come along, Stenton."

"WE CAN'T LEAVE IT."

"Oh yes we can."

"IT'LL DIE THOUGH."

"Just... just leave a window open, it'll fly away. It's a bee for Ulf's sake!"

"ITS WING'S BROKE."

Janoah came back to the door and dismissed, "Where? Looks fine to me."

Rafe clapped a paw to his helmet then said, "SHE... SHE SAID IT WAS BROKE, AND IT DON'T GROW BACK."

"What? Who?"

"THAT WOLFESS," Rafe sniffed.

"What wolfess?"

No reply.

With a worried frown, Janoah reached round Rafe's vast back and twisted the red valve. "You're going silly again-"

"I'M FINE!"

With that sharp protest, Rafe clomped into the kitchen.

"Leave it!" Janoah shouted, snapping like a chiding mother, "Rafe Stenton will you do as you're told!"

The Eisenwolf unpinned his black mantle and threw it over the bee like a net. Tossing the buzzing, wriggling bundle over his right shoulder, he then returned to the living room and draped Tristan over his left.

"RIGHT. LET'S GO."

Janoah shook her head, "You're unbelievable sometimes, Stenton, you know that? Unbelievable! If Silvermane ever saw your insubordination in the field, you'd be finished."

"AWW, LEAVE IT OUT, JAN. COME ON, LET'S GET BACK TO HQ."

Whistling a ditty, Rafe moseyed out the door, Janoah following in his wake.

"Ulf almighty!" she cursed.

CHAPTER 31

Linus awoke with a start. It was still dark, but a hint of dawn stained the smoggy air outside the window with a pale green hue – four or five in the morning the Howler judged.

'I should go,' he thought, throwing his armoured legs off the bed and stretching. Linus had slept on top of the sheets, sword in paw, dressed but for his helmet, which he now grabbed from the bedside table and buckled about his wedge-shaped wolfen head. He checked his reliable shield; it had likely saved his life on the train yesterday and bore a fresh scar to prove it, the Bloodfang crest chipped by that overenthusiastic Prefect's pellet.

To the door and a timid glance up and down the narrow lamp-lit hall; there was nobody about. Howlers and their paid company were sleeping soundly in their beds. Linus felt the coronas of snoozing Howlers as he passed the numbered rooms, often feeble, rarely strong and never remarkable. Living and working in Riddle Den with some of the brightest Howlers had spoilt Linus, the young wolf sometimes thought. The fiery imperium furnaces of Uther, Ivan and Rufus reduced most other Howlers to spent embers smouldering in an ash tray by comparison, and to be away from them of late was to feel cold and lonely.

'ROOM 23'

Linus rapped gently on the door three times, then a pause, then once more – the agreed code. Within seconds the latch turned over and a brown wolfess in a green night dress opened the door enough to peep through – Rosalina

"They're still asleep," she whispered directly, glancing back into her room. "Shall I wake 'em?"

"No, it's all right," Linus replied, "I was just checking up on you all before I go."

Lorna appeared behind Rosalina. "You off, partner?" she asked, brushing her fur.

To which Linus nodded. "I've got to report back to the Den by six or I'll be done for skiving," he explained. "Tell Sara and the others that I'll try and get hold of Tristan once I'm off duty and send him this way, if he's inclined to come. One of us will drop by later, I promise."

Linus trailed off as a Howler tramped down the corridor in full regalia – a burly-looking Greystone, sandy yellow cloak hugging his thick, armoured body and pistols rattling about his thighs. He eyed Linus up in passing and descended the stairs to the lounge, doubtless heading out the door to return to his Den; just another satisfied customer.

"Don't let anyone know they're here," Linus finished. "Keep them in your room."

Lorna scoffed, "Well we can't lock 'em up, Linus, nor lock Audrey out."

"No but... you know what I mean."

"We do," Rosalina insisted, glancing back at Lorna. "Don't worry, Linus, you get back to Riddle. This ain't the first time we've hidden someone in trouble. We've done it for Uther."

"Thank you. I-I-I'll pay you back."

"Don't be daft. We'll see you later. Go on."

With much nodding and fussing with his cloak, Linus took his leave, following the path the Greystone had walked a minute ago, along the hall and down the creaking stairs into the lounge and bar.

"Enjoy yourself, Howler?"

Linus nearly leapt from his hide at the recognisably crackly ember-fuelled voice belonging to Lady Audrey, the head wolfess, or whatever one might call her – Linus wasn't sure. Whatever her usual role, she was wiping tabletops and setting them for breakfast at the minute.

"Yes," Linus replied at last, turning to her, "thank you."

"My girls pleased you then?" Audrey pressed further.

"The best night I've had in a while," Linus blustered, convincing nobody of his sincerity, least of all Audrey.

"Glad to hear it, Howler," she said, adding, "Only... I noticed you didn't stay in Rosa's room. Mind you it was likely a little bit crowded in there."

"Crowded?" Linus repeated.

"Yes," Audrey crackled slowly, "what with the two wolfesses you snuck in with yesterday."

"Oh, uhm. I-I-I can explain-"

"Look, love, this is your first time, so I won't make a fuss, but this is an establishment for Howlers only. So, if you wouldn't mind taking your 'friends' with you we'll say no more about it, all right? There's a good lad."

Kneading the back of a chair with both paws to calm his racing heart, Linus settled upon the only course of action left open to him and delved into his cloak for his wallet.

Audrey leant on the table she was polishing and watched the Howler count out a wad of colourful lupas, as if she fully expected it.

Linus approached the savvy old wolfess and pressed the money into those bony, ember-stained white paws. "I'd be grateful if my friends might stay awhile, Lady Audrey," he said with intent. "If they could be fed and watered as well, I'll remunerate you, but... I need you to be discreet about their presence here."

Audrey's slender muzzle cracked a smile. "Say no more, love," she said, slipping the crisp lupas down her purple petticoat. "I'll take good care of the young ladies."

"There's... also a bear round back," Linus hazarded clumsily.

"A what, love?"

"A bear; he's sleeping in the alley behind your establishment. If you could perhaps bring him inside and put him up in a room I'd be further in your debt-"

"I can't bring no ruddy great bear in here, Howler!" Audrey woofed. "This is a wolfen establishment!"

"Please. This is the last place anyone would look for him. I only came to you because Uther's often expressed to me what a-a-a kind and b-b-beautiful wolfess you are."

"Y'what? Uther said that?"

"Absolutely. He's told me a hundred times that Lorna and Rosa are lucky to have you to look out for them."

"Oh Howler, I do try to accommodate, but-"

"My friends will be gone in a few days. Please, marm."

At length, Audrey gave in. "Well... as you're partnered with that handsome rogue Wild-heart, I'll see what I can do this once. But don't make a habit of this, all right?"

Breathing a sigh of relief, Linus said, "I'm grateful. I should be back tonight, and if not me an Eisbrand by the name of Tristan – my friends know him."

"I'll keep an eye out, Howler," Audrey said. "You have a good day, now."

"And you, marm. Thanks again."

Linus took his leave via the front door and hurried down the steps, sneaking along the foggy street with his cloak hood pulled up over his helmet in a subconscious attempt to pass unseen. He felt awful, entrusting Sara and the others to the money-greased paws of a stranger like Audrey, but surely Rosalina and Lorna would keep things together. They were Audrey's best girls, Uther had once said over a pint, and had some clout with the 'wily old bag', as he had so indelicately put it.

Linus allowed a fond smile over his rough-tongued friend as he hurried along the path.

Beep! Beep!

A standard Politzi car in Bloodfang livery pulled up beside Linus, headlamps beaming, engine chugging.

By Ulf this is it, Linus thought, as the car matched his pace, *I'm being arrested for getting in ALPHA's way. No, stay calm; mere Politzi don't have the authority to mess with you.*

The car's dew-laden window was flipped open revealing a familiar rotund hog stuffed behind the wheel.

"Werner?" Linus piped in surprise.

"I thought I recognised that stocky outline," the hog snorted pleasantly, tipping his red cap. "Need a lift, sir?"

"I'm all right, thank you."

Werner checked his pocket watch. "You sure, sir? You're cutting it fine, if I may say. You need to be back at HQ and I'll be passing that way. Hop in."

Upon second thoughts, Linus accepted the offer. Werner stopped the car as the Howler ran round to the passenger side door and climbed in.

"Thanks."

"My pleasure, Howler."

Crunching gears, Werner pulled away down the street, the Bloodfang Territory in his sights. "I thought you had a mono now, sir," the hog hummed, nursing the steering wheel.

"I do. I just left it… somewhere."

"Can't remember?" Werner chortled, cocking his flabby jowls to one side. "Must've been a right knees-up, sir. You won't find it in this smog, I dare say. Can't see my snout in front of my face!"

"Indeed," Linus coughed, pushing back his hood. He knew perfectly well his *Springtail* was parked outside Heath's flat, but the less Werner or anyone else knew of his movements of late the better he could deny them. "What're you doing in the Common Ground?" he asked, attempting to deflect further inquiry.

"Same as yerself," Werner snorted wryly.

Linus looked at the hog and, after a brief exercise of his brain to comprehend what Werner meant, forced a polite chuckle – better to let him think anything but the truth.

✦

Dawn. The sun struck the mountain peaks first, transmuting their snowy caps to gold, before trickling down the valley slopes and warming the dozens of giant ant mounds erupting from the barren terrain like enormous barnacles.

Time was short.

Kneeling on the unforgiving concrete into which his stake was set, Rufus twisted his wire-bound wrists for the hundredth time. That they were raw and bleeding was of no consequence when facing dismemberment by ant. If he could just get his paws up to his throat he could at least risk blasting the collar off, or perhaps the chain. Rufus knew he would as likely remove his head along with it, or cripple his paws for life. He had been fortunate not to do so yesterday, but that had been no lucid decision. The hogs had pushed him over the edge and the red mist had descended.

A little swirl of that mist would be useful right now.

"Grrrrrffffgh!"

No use, the wire wouldn't give. Rufus fell back against his execution stake, panting and afraid. He was trapped in a giant ant field, unable to so much as raise his paws to protect himself.

"Schmutz!" he seethed, trying to recall his meeting with Silvermane and Janoah a couple of months ago. "How'd you talk me into this one, Jan?"

You know how, his brain replied. You soft fool.

The crunch of stones shifting somewhere over Rufus's shoulder set his frayed heart somersaulting.

Was it a scout ant? Am I a dead beast?

Rufus daren't turn around lest any sudden movement triggered an attack. Ants were deaf and almost blind, relying on vibration and scent to find their way. Taking heart that he was upwind in relation to the creature, Rufus breathed lightly and remained perfectly still, and prayed to the wolfen god he didn't even believe in for deliverance.

Whatever it was back there spoke.

"They say talking to oneself is the first sign of madness, Howler Rufus," it said, in a harsh, gravely tone.

Ants didn't talk.

Rufus turned around to find a robust hyena dressed in striking black and white attire. The powerful beast stood with one foot resting on a rock, paws tucked nobly behind him, purple eyes squinting with inquiry. His thick, armoured legs were pattered with a beautiful black and white zigzag decor, as was his handsome Howler-like cloak. His face was masked by a white helmet that resembled a skull, complete with a set of presumably fake teeth, leaving only his rounded-off ears and black lower jaw visible.

"Forgive our tardiness, Red-mist," he said, "but we had to be sure this wasn't a trap."

Rufus articulated a reply, "Trap?"

"Yes. If the plan was to use you as bait to capture us, I'm sure you'd have been extracted before dawn and the… ants. As it is you're still here. Amael Balbus's message must be genuine."

A second hyena crunched across the wastes, bigger than the first, tall and powerful, his cloak hugging his massive, rounded shoulders and chest. His armour and cloak were similar to the first hyena, but of a labyrinthine design, a dazzling maze of black and white right-angled passages. In his paws he held a hammer with a grip as long as Rufus was tall, its imperium-laced head the size of a brick.

"Is this him?" the fellow scoffed, in a deeper and yet softer tone. "He's so… small."

"Can't you feel his corona?" seethed the first.

"Humph."

"Forgive my comrade's rudeness," the leader excused. "My name is Nurka, this is Themba-"

"The two bullies who turned Uther over in the Riddle refinery, I know," Rufus replied brusquely, twisting his wrists. "Look, if we could skip the pleasantries and get on with it before the ants carry us off, I'd be grateful."

The hyenas exchanged purple-eyed glances. Themba stepped forward and growled, "Do you want me to crack your head in, wolf? You're addressing a chieftain!"

"Themba!" Nurka snapped.

"But he insults you!"

"Shut up and break the chain, I'll untie him."

With that, Nurka set about unravelling the bloody wire from Rufus's raw wrists. The Howler grunted in pain as Nurka observed sarcastically, "And yet *we're* cruel? Look to your own kind, wolf."

Rufus said nothing.

Meanwhile Themba lay the Howler's chain on the concrete and hefted his hammer, taking aim.

"What're you doing?" Rufus asked, barking, "Don't!"

Undeterred, Themba struck the chain, crushing it between hammerhead and concrete. With a flash and bang of imperious energy, the links exploded in a spray of molten sparks and Rufus was freed. The peal of the explosion tore across the valley floor, over the mounds and back again, like a distant imperium cannon.

Taking his paws from his ringing ears, Rufus seethed, "By Ulf's fangs; are you two stupid?"

Themba bellowed at him, "What did you say, wolf?"

"Shout and compound your idiocy, why not?" the Howler replied sarcastically, gathering up his loose chain and throwing it around his shoulders like an absurd iron scarf. "If the ants weren't stirring before they are now. Which way to your car?"

"Car?" Nurka repeated questioningly.

"Your monos then, truck, whatever you've got."

The hyenas exchanged looks. "We walked, Howler," Nurka said. "Any vehicle would kick up too much dust and we'd be discovered. We've been hiding in the mountains for days waiting for you to be staked out, as planned."

"It's a long walk back to camp," Themba added with malicious glee.

Silence.

"Marvellous," Rufus sniffed at length. "Well then, lead on, sir." He flicked his paws at the hyenas, "Quickly now. Come on, come on!"

Somewhat disconcerted by Rufus's audacity, Nurka fumbled a moment. "Yes… uh, follow me. Themba, you take the rear."

Themba grunted disapprovingly, but did as bidden.

The trio picked their way across the sun-glanced valley floor, their long shadows rippling over rocks and sparse vegetation, Nurka in the lead, Themba at the back, Rufus stumbling along in the middle, dishevelled and dirty compared to the magnificently-dressed hyenas.

"Looks like we've got away with it," the wolf whispered, passing a seemingly quiet ant hill. "And I thought hyenas were supposed to know a thing or two about the wilds. Is it customary amongst your tribe to ring the dinner bell in the middle of an ant field, or is it peculiar to THORN members?"

"What do you mean 'dinner bell'?" Nurka asked.

"Vibrations excite most bugs, my good hyena; and that chap back there just woke the dead with that almighty gong."

Nurka replied to Rufus's caustic tone in his considered, if naturally rough voice. "I understand you're a wolf trained in what you call science, but Themba and I grew up in the Reservations, Howler. No ants live there, just roaches and the occasional giant hundred-legs that come to carry cubs off in the night. I was warned these ants emerge at dawn, nothing more. I apologise for our ignorance."

Faced with Nurka's humility, Rufus guiltily cleared his throat, "Not at all. Live and learn, eh?"

The group filed silently past a mighty mound of erde and rocks the size of a house, larger than any so far, but still an ant hill. Rufus could tell by the regularity of the massive conical structure; no geological process piled rocks like that, no wolf or other beast either. The ants had dug a great tunnel system beneath Rufus's feet and simply piled the excavated rocks and dirt outside the nearest exit, thus slowly building up a mountain. The scale and scope of their endeavour was the equal of any civilised mine or erdeworks.

As Rufus admired nature's work, one of the mound's many constituent rocks tumbled down the loose, scree-like piles, rolling past him at speed.

Several more clacked down the slopes, drawing Rufus's eye up the mound to its summit. At the top he spied a pair of dark, club-like appendages tentatively stroking the rim of the sun-baked peak.

Another set appeared. They were the antennae of some giant insect and no mistake.

"Is that them?" Nurka whispered at Rufus.

"Yes," the Howler replied.

Unpinning his handsome zigzag cloak and letting it fall at his matching armoured feet, Nurka revealed not only his amazing physique but a beautiful metallic bow and quiver he had been concealing. The impressive hyena slipped the bow from about his body and an arrow from the quiver, and notching shaft to string drew back, taking aim at the ants. His arrow was tipped with a sharp yellow-imperium crystal, which glimmered in the sunshine like a wicked boiled sweet.

"Don't!" Rufus seethed, as loudly as he dared.

Keeping his string taught, Nurka looked sideways from under his skull-like mask at Rufus, but said nothing.

Themba growled for his chief, "What's wrong now, wolf?"

Looking between the young hyenas, Rufus explained quietly, "If you kill one it'll set the whole lot off. Dozens will pour out after us. We'll be swamped!"

"Then what do we do?" Nurka asked.

"Don't panic. Just keep going. They won't notice us."

Staring at the mound's rim and the ants lurking just beyond like soldiers cowering in a watchtower, Nurka growled, "I'm not afraid of these creatures, Howler."

"Well I am," Rufus snorted honestly. "Whilst the inside of an ant nest is likely a wonder to behold, I don't want to be dismembered at the end of the tour by the hungry homeowners. Do you?"

At length, Nurka lowered his mighty imperium bow and Rufus could breathe easy again.

Wrapping his cloak about his body and securing it again in a somehow huffy manner, Nurka led the way. The hyena conspicuously carried his bow and quiver in his paws from then on, even as the group left the giant ant mounds far behind. Over-the-shoulder glances confirmed the insects atop the largest mound remained unaware of the tasty morsels that had passed right under their noses.

The ants were merely standing guard at the entrance to their nest, Rufus explained confidently; it was still too cold for the scouts to emerge and begin foraging.

Perhaps with the intention of provoking Rufus a little (the Howler couldn't be sure) Nurka observed, "Your knowledge of nature's ways must be useless in Lupa."

"I'm wasted there," Rufus chuckled freely, parrying any intended insult at once.

"Is that why you want to change things?"

"Change things?"

Nurka climbed up a row of wind-cut boulders. "Amael's new order," he clarified, standing atop the rocks and offering a paw to Rufus.

Looking at Nurka's paw before taking it, Rufus said, "Amael can do what he wants, as long as I get my expedition."

"To the Dead Cities?"

"One of them."

"They're just a legend, Howler."

"Oh they're quite real, I assure you," Rufus said, as Nurka helped him onto the rocks. "Lost in the wilds they may be, but they're there, and perhaps great knowledge, even a cure."

Nurka waited a moment. "Then... you don't care for Amael's plans for Lupa?"

"I'll have a care for whoever funds my expedition," Rufus claimed. "Beasts may die in Amael's coup, but that's nothing compared to the scourge of the rot. We must try and find a cure. Besides, I don't see how Amael could do a worse job than the current regime."

"Amael told us you were like a brother to him."

"Pff! And you believed him? He thinks I'm a fool! It's my wife who's got him on my side."

"Wife?"

"Janoah; perhaps you've heard of her."

Nurka shook his head a little.

"Well, she's put in a good word, I know it. She and Amael are together now, you see. You know how it is. I don't mind a bit of course; good on her."

"Of course," Nurka replied, despite his utter bafflement.

Smiling, Rufus turned and offered Themba a paw, but the big hyena vaulted up onto the boulders without wolfen aid and towered imposingly beside Rufus – his size was no impediment to his athleticism, clearly.

"Well, whatever your aims," Nurka said to Rufus, perhaps only for the pugnacious Themba's benefit, "you've always spoken up for our people, Red-mist, that can't be denied. Our prince always spoke well of you, so I'm inclined to trust you, even over Amael."

"And I you after getting me out of that pickle," Rufus said amiably, slapping the hyena's massive, spotty arm. "I suppose I owe you chaps a drink."

Nurka forced a polite chuckle.

Themba was already walking across the boulder field, as if eager to be away from the wolf he doubtless thought obnoxious.

Nurka however lingered. "There's... something I need to ask you, Red-mist," he hazarded.

"Can't it wait?" Rufus replied, glancing around the wilderness. "We're not clear of Gelb yet; someone might come looking for us, and I don't mean ants."

Nurka grunted, "I'd rather Themba not hear what I have to ask you. Your answer might upset him."

Rufus watched Nurka's partner in crime pick his way across the field of smooth, yet regularly-cut, cobble-like boulders, stepping over the deep, dark cracks between them like a cub playing amongst rock pools at the beach, his hammer reminding Rufus of a net for catching tiddlers as oppose to a deadly imperium-laced weapon for cracking heads. Perhaps even my head, Rufus thought, knowing a wrong answer to Nurka's question might end this charade, and that he had no chance against these chaps in his weakened state.

"All right," he said. "What do you want to know?"

Nurka glanced across at Themba as he leapt over an especially wide crevice, then dipped his chin at Rufus. "I don't dare believe this true," he said, "but... I've heard that-"

"Gaaaagh!"

Themba's scream cut through the valley and whatever Nurka had in mind.

Some giant, hairy, many-legged spider-like creature had snatched one of Themba's feet with its twin sets of black pincers and was dragging him backwards into the last crevice he'd leapt over!

Before Nurka's mind could fathom the situation his legs were already carrying him across the rocks to his comrade hyena's aid.

Throwing his pesky collar chain over one shoulder again, Rufus followed suit. "It's a sun-spider!" he declared, not that Nurka cared to know.

As he was dragged along on his front, big Themba desperately swung his kristahl hammer backwards at the giant bug's shiny, armoured, hair-flecked face – a hit, but to no avail. The sandy-coloured sun-spider backed up, reversing leg over leg into the deep, dark fissure between two boulders and taking the flailing Themba foot-first with it.

"Yaaagh!"

Just when the helpless hyena should have disappeared into the crevice his sturdy hammer accidentally lodged against the opposing rock faces, forming a holdfast. Clutching the shaft with both paws like a gymnast about to perform on the high bar, Themba stayed his descent, hanging on for grim death as the sun-spider pulled on his snared leg.

"Grrrrrfgh!" he snarled in twisting pain. "Nurkaaa!"

Nurka arrived, and throwing himself on his belly reached down into the crevice, the terrifying serrated jaws and bead-like black eyes of the sun-spider lurking within no impediment to his courage.

Realising at once it was hopeless to try and pull Themba up, Nurka stood and notched an arrow to his bow. The gleaming missile had a flight made of iridescent blue insect wings. Pulling back, the chief sent a bolt of plasma down his spotty arm, charging the arrow and making its head shine white-hot.

Nurka aimed down, past Themba, and let loose just as Rufus arrived to witness the shimmering, plasmatic projectile ping uselessly off the armoured face of the sun-spider, before spiralling into the crevice, its point glowing in the darkness.

"Ragh!" Nurka cursed. "How? That was blue kristahl!"

He notched a second arrow, tipped with yellow-imperium this time, and pulled the bow string back to breaking point. The loosed arrow whipped by inches from the struggling Themba and bounced off the sun-spider's carapace yet again. This time, however, as the arrow tumbled into the crevice, the tip began to fizzle and burn, before exploding in a hail of glowing crystalline shards as yellow-imperium ever did.

"By the Wind, what's that thing made of?" Nurka asked rhetorically.

"Hit it in the abdomen," Rufus suggested, adding, "the backside, that is."

"Nurkaaa!" Themba cried, as the sun-spider's mandibles chewed on his leg. "Gaaagh!"

"Hang on!" Nurka replied shakily. He strafed along the edge of the crevice with his bow taught, looking for an angle to hit the creature in its rear, but the rock faces twisted and contrived in such ways as to make a clean shot impossible. Nurka tried anyway – the arrow clipped off the rocks and exploded uselessly.

With a hurried assessment of the crevice and seeing no other way down, Rufus said, "Lower me down, Nurka."

"What?"

"I'm lighter than you. You can hold me."

Winging the situation, Rufus unravelled the chain by which he had been fastened to the stake not half hour ago and gave the end to Nurka.

"Here, use this."

Somewhat baffled, Nurka did as bidden and held the chain firm as Rufus, against his better judgement, lowered himself over the edge of the crevice with the chain in his paws. He had about four feet of chain to play with – not much. It was still attached to his collar, of course, and Rufus supposed if he slipped and fell the force of the collar being jolted against his neck might break it.

With Themba's cries in his ears, Rufus lowered himself down, paw over bloodied, sore paw, with hazardous haste, until he had no more chain at his disposal.

Looking down into the pit, the Howler judged the floor to be some eight feet away.

"All right, let go!" he seethed, with great misgivings.

Nurka, thinking fast, and displaying great strength and poise, risked straddling the crevice, one armoured foot pressed to each lip. Like a living well's windlass, he allowed the chain to slide slowly and doubtless painfully through his powerful paws, right to the very last link, before letting it, and Rufus, fall into the blackness below.

Rufus's back slammed into the far wall and he slid to the floor, the chain raining down upon him. With the adrenaline pumping he felt nothing of his tumble and leapt to his feet like a wolf half his age. He found he was but a few feet from the sun-spider's nearest enormous hairy leg.

If it turns on me now, Rufus knew, I'll be minced between its jaws in seconds.

"The bow!" he called up to Nurka.

Down it came, the quiver too, clacking against the rock faces to the ground.

"Hurry!" Nurka begged.

Rufus needn't be solicited. Notching an arrow he took aim at the sun-spider's segmented, pulsing posterior and drew back, overcoming his bruises and hunger long enough to give the arrow the energy it needed to fly.

Thwip!

The shot was clear and true. The yellow-imperium arrowhead embedded itself in the sun-spider's relatively soft, leathery abdomen, fizzled and exploded, ejecting shards of burning imperium in all directions like a spectacular firework.

The sun spider released Themba with a terrible stridulating din that sounded like the clicking of a thousand tongues against the roofs of a thousand mouths. Scrabbling into an adjoining crevice to escape, the beast left behind its dinner and a trail of white blood.

It was over.

Nurka helped Themba to safety, pulling him over the side of the crevice and onto the rock, leaving his hammer lodged where it was for now. Expecting the worst, Nurka was overjoyed to find Themba's leg intact; the labyrinthine armour design scratched and pitted, yes, but in no way crushed or broken. There was no blood leaking through the rivets, nothing at all to indicate injury.

"Are you hurt?" Nurka asked.

Taking a moment to lie on his back with his paws to his masked face in abject relief, Themba suddenly sat up and experimentally rolled his aching ankle. "I'm fine," he panted, whilst opening and closing his quivering paws – every tendon in his forearms ached from the strain of hanging on. "I thought… I was going to come apart at the waist," he admitted, adding humorously, "I must be a little taller."

Nurka snorted, "You're tall enough already," and held Themba tight, patting and rubbing his vast back. "By the Wind, I thought you were taken from me."

Peeling his chief aside, Themba scolded gently, "Not in front of the wolf, chief."

Nodding and composing himself, Nurka went to the crevice and looked for 'the wolf'.

"Well done, Rufus!" he called, paws resting on zigzag knees. "He's all right!"

No reply.

Not hearing or seeing Rufus, Nurka looked along the crevice. "There must be a way up!" he said aloud.

Still nothing.

"Red-mist! Where are you?"

Time passed down in the crevice; Rufus knew not how much as lay on his side in the darkness, writhing like an abandoned infant, awash in the agony and confusion of rot pains.

"Stop… please make it stop!" the red wolf moaned, nuzzling into the cold, sandy erde, his flaring nostrils blowing aside sprays of sand as he snorted and panted. He grasped uselessly at his thighs, pressing at the layers of fur and flesh in a vain attempt to reach the dying bones deep within and somehow stem the creeping agony of the rot. "By Ulf's fangs, not now. Not now!"

Cast by sheer pain to the very edge of consciousness, the last Rufus comprehended before giving in were two dazzling black and white cloaked figures pushing their way along the narrow passage towards him.

✦

Vladimir busied himself with paperwork, signing this, amending that, or so he would have Josef believe. The bespectacled grey cat couldn't help but suspect, as he waited in the chair opposite with two ALPHA Prefects hovering behind him, that Vladimir was merely scribbling on scrap paper just to look important. He claimed to be very busy running Riddle District by himself since Rufus's downfall.

"But surely Amael has installed another Grand Howler by now?" Josef had purred in a needling kind of tone.

"Not officially," Vladimir had replied, not looking up from his work. "Boris is acting as my fellow Grand Howler, but of course he has better things to do as Amael's adjutant, so I'm left to pick up the slack."

"Slack? You mean Rufus actually did some work?"

"He was a consummate Grand Howler," Vladimir defended.

"But a criminal."

"So it would appear, doctor. Now, if you don't mind, I've a lot of work to do. I've sent for Howler Mills. Please be patient."

And thus silence reigned.

After clawing at the arms of his chair for some time – Vladimir noting the damage done – Josef stood up and looked out the window at the passing hubbub of Riddle. Seeing Vladimir's office plants on the windowsill before him, the cat felt their varied leaves with a, "Hmm." When the foliage bored him the cat took to pulling out random books from Vladimir's library and flicking through them, raising his eyebrows and sniffing on occasion, as if passing derisive judgement on the Howler's literary taste – Vladimir kept his head down and his mind on his work to prevent himself from saying something he'd regret.

Finally a knock at the door broke the unbearable rising tension.

"Come in," Vladimir woofed in relief.

The office door opened and Linus presented himself. The stocky blonde Howler passed Josef and the Prefects a worried sideways glance, before saluting Vladimir, fist to chest and out.

"You sent for me, Grand Howler?" he said.

"I did," Vladimir grunted.

"I'm sorry I'm late back, sir," Linus pre-emptively excused. "I got carried away last night."

"Indeed you did," Vladimir seconded, flicking his golden pen at Josef and the two Prefects. "These gentlebeasts are from ALPHA, as I'm sure you can see. They've a warrant for your arrest, Linus."

"Arrest, sir?" Linus scoffed with indignation. "On what charge?"

Josef hissed, "You know very well what charge."

"I'm afraid I don't."

"You lying little weasel. You're under arrest-"

"Doctor Josef!" Vladimir growled, before addressing his subordinate. "I'm told you obstructed ALPHA in their duty, Mills. Is this true?"

"In what way obstruct, sir?"

"By preventing the apprehension of three imperium-abusing citizens and aiding their escape."

"That's not the case at all, Grand Howler; I was merely carrying out my duty to the Bloodfangs."

"Duty?" Josef spluttered. "Is it a Bloodfang's duty to strike ALPHA Prefects?"

Vladimir mediated calmly. "Doctor, if you please, I've heard your version of events twice over. Now if you would allow Howler Mills to speak,"

"You've no authority to stand in our way, Vladimir," Josef told the Grand Howler. "We have a warrant signed by a Grand Prefect, we can take action."

"Nonetheless, we can at least agree to discuss this misunderstanding before taking it further," Vladimir replied with disarming charm, adding, "Unless ALPHA is more interested in its own pride than keeping the peace?"

Josef was silenced, for now.

"Now then, what exactly happened, Mills?" Vladimir asked Linus directly.

"Well, sir, as you've likely been told, I took it upon myself to intervene in the arrest of three citizens by Doctor Josef here. Two wolfesses and a bear, sir."

"So I gather. Did you know they were dodgers, these citizens?"

"I didn't, sir."

"Yes you did, I told you!" Josef accused.

Linus kept going regardless. "I only knew for certain that one of them was afflicted, sir; a Freiwolf by the name of Olivia."

Vladimir's dark ears pricked, "Afflicted wolfess, you say?"

"Yes, sir," Linus confirmed. "I offered to take her to our Den and present her to you, as my find, sir. I could feel her corona. I thought she had great potential."

Josef hissed, "This is nonsense!"

"It's the truth, sir. There's nothing illegal about headhunting talent."

"Then where's Olivia now, eh?" the cat pressed.

Vladimir looked to Linus, "Well, Mills?"

Linus dipped his chin a little, "She ran away, sir."

Josef snorted, "Hah!"

"She tricked me, sir. They all did."

"Tricked you?" Vladimir repeated.

Linus 'explained'. "When we got to Riddle, someone hit me over the head, sir, which as you can imagine knocked me for six. By the time I recovered my senses they were all gone. It's a little embarrassing to say the least. Doctor Josef was right to warn me that they were criminals, but I didn't listen on account of the opportunity to recruit a Howler. I... I wasn't going to report the incident. I know that's wrong in itself, but I know you've been horribly busy what with Rufus gone. I didn't want to bother you or Elder Amael leading up to the Summit with my stupidity."

"Indeed. Nonetheless you should've."

"Yes, sir. I humbly apologise to the Doctor, and his Prefects. I didn't realise I'd caused any real upset."

Josef adjusted his tinted spectacles. "You can fool Vladimir, Linus, but we both know what happened," he growled, "and you know exactly where Olivia is. Tell me, or else you're coming to ALPHA HQ!"

"I don't know where she is."

"We'll see," Josef purred maliciously.

Vladimir spread his paws, "Doctor, this is hardly necessary-"

"It is completely necessary! You haven't the least understanding what's at stake here!"

"Some lowly dodgers? I rather think we have bigger worries with THORN. Can you not shake paws with Linus and put this aside?"

"I have a warrant!" Josef snapped, flapping a rolled up sheet of paper under the Grand Howler's nose. "Do you want me to fetch one with your name on it as well, Vladimir?"

Silence.

Kneading the arms of his plush antique chair, Vladimir sighed, "I'm sorry, Linus, but you'll have to go with him."

"But, sir-"

"He has a warrant. We must comply. I'm sure it'll come to nothing."

"Yes, sir," Linus said, failing not to gulp.

Glaring at Josef, Vladimir said with a disapproving smack of his lips, "Of course... I'll inform Elder Amael of this wanton intrusion. I'm sure he'll be interested to hear it ahead of the Summit where the future of ALPHA is to be discussed and voted upon by the Den Fathers."

"You do that," Josef sniffed, stepping up to Linus, taller by a head but thinner by a body. "We've a car waiting in the courtyard, Howler. I suggest you do not try anything funny between here and there; my associates will not hesitate to bring you down."

Linus remained silent as Josef's 'associates' relieved him of his weapons and escorted him to the door.

"I expect ALPHA to observe due process, Grau," Vladimir warned, chin raised. "Don't get ahead of yourself."

"I wouldn't dream," Josef Grau replied, taking his leave.

Once his office door had closed, Vladimir twiddled his pen and nursed his furrowed brow, taking a moment to wrestle with the situation.

Against all reason and sense the Grand Howler plucked his telephone from the desk and dialled through to where he shouldn't. Listening to the stifled ring, he walked to the window with the phone cord trailing behind him and looked down into the Den's courtyard, at Josef's shiny black ALPHA car. The Doctor and his strong-arm Prefects appeared in short order, escorting the red-cloaked Linus to the car and ducking him inside. The youngster's paws had been bound with Howler-wire on the way, as if Josef knew what he was dealing with. *Is it really some dodger he's after, or is it Linus he wants?*

"Janoah here," the phone crackled tiresomely.

"It's Vladimir."

"What do you want? I'm very busy."

"I need you to do me a favour," Vladimir said hurriedly, as Josef's car drove away.

"If this is about Tristan you can forget it."

"What?"

"He's a traitor and he might have information. I'm not letting him go just because he's Ivan's cousin and Thorvald's favourite, so save your breath-"

"Humph!" Vladimir scoffed. "Keep him and let it be on your head when Thorvald kicks up a stink with Adal. It's Linus I'm worried about."

"Linus?"

"Josef just arrested him."

"Well," Janoah huffed, *"he must have good reason-"*

"A foolish mistake nothing more. You owe him, Janoah; get him out of this."

Silence.

"Besides," Vladimir grumbled, "you know what he is as well as I do. If he ever makes it, he'll thank us later."

~Blick VII~

Meryl Stroud set some hot fish soup down beside the window, the rising steam caught the afternoon sun. Shivering, Rafe sat warming himself by the imperium hearth, his hips and shoulders wrapped in fresh towels.

"'Get our feet wet'," *Meryl quoted, imitating Rafe's voice. She continued as normal,* "I told my aunt you fell in and the otters pulled you ashore."

"Yeah?"

"Only to save them getting in trouble, not you. Otters are mischievous folk, especially the youngsters. But I think you take the biscuit."

"They o-o-owe me a p-p-penny."

"They saved your life; I rather think that's a debt paid. Can't swim, indeed, what's a beast to do with you?"

Rafe laughed and sniffed snottily. "Sorry."

Meryl set about drying his ears and neck, like a mother would their cub after they had endured a bath. Once Rafe's fur was thoroughly ruffled, Meryl took the towel from his shoulders and laid it by the hearth, with his clothes and ribbon.

"Now eat your soup before you catch a cold. Janoah would kill me if she found out; I'm supposed to be making you better, not finishing you off!"

Rafe shuffled his chair over to the table and dutifully made a start on his soup. Blowing on the spoon, he watched the beasts of New Tharona go about their business, strolling along the sea front and down the pier. It was a far cry from Lupa, quiet, soothing, fresh, yet still Rafe itched, not from ash getting in his fur, but the need to get back and work.

Janoah had said it, the Alpha is watching.

"I feel much better," *Rafe blurted between great slurps of fish broth and hunks of bread.* "Compared to last week."

Meryl sounded hopeful, "You do?"

"Yeah."

"Well, that's good! How're your eyes?"

Rafe pointed out the window, "I can read the shop signs."

"Which one?"

"All of 'em," *the Eisenwolf claimed, chomping away and hoping Meryl believed him.*

A long silence.

"Did you really recognise that hog?" *Meryl asked out of left field.*

"Hog?"

"The one sitting at the café with Howler Tristan."

Rafe stirred his soup, shrugged, "Maybe."

"Well, I did," *Meryl revealed.* "He's a Politzi chief in Bloodfang territory now, but he used to be a rebel, back during the war."

"Rebel?"

"Yes. I mean, it's all passed now, of course, there was the amnesty, but… still, it's strange Tristan would be talking to someone like that, especially out here in New Tharona. It's as if he was being discreet about it."

"Maybe they're old friends?"

"Yes. Best not tell anyone about it, though. All right?"

Rafe turned to Meryl. "Why not?"

"Just promise you won't. Tristan's a dear friend, I wouldn't want him getting in trouble on our account."

A mock frown, "Who's Tristan?"

Meryl smiled and folded some clothes. "I'm sure it's nothing anyway-"

Knock! Knock! Knock!

Before Meryl could ask who was at the bedroom door, Janoah all but burst inside, flanked by two more grim-looking ALPHA Prefects.

"Jan!" Rafe woofed, wiping his mouth and standing to attention in nought but a towel.

Janoah cast her eye over him, "Am I interrupting something, Stenton?"

"No, Prefect."

Blinking disbelief from her eyes, Meryl half-lied, "Rafe... just had a bath."

A slow, careful, Janoah-brand nod, "He's not so infirm he can't wash himself?"

"No, Prefect, I was just delivering some soup."

"Ah."

Meryl tugged her dress, "May I ask what you're doing out here? Am I not to be trusted with Rafe alone, is that it?"

Janoah held up a paw, "I trust you implicitly, my dear. Grand Prefect Horst has it in for us, however. He's poured poison in someone's ear and made sure Rafe can't leave the city again, not without 'proper' authorisation. He's jealous that's all. Pathetic really."

"Then-"

"Yes, the holiday's over, I'm afraid."

"But Rafe's not been here a week!"

"I delayed as long as I could," *Janoah claimed.* "I even took a leisurely drive and a long walk along the seafront... but I'm here now." *She nodded at her Eisenwolf,* "Get dressed, Stenton, we're going home."

"Yes, marm."

"Marm and Prefect, is it? Sea air must've done you a world of good, you're beginning to sound like a soldier at last. Who'd have thought?"

Rafe smiled a little.

Saluting ALPHA-style, Janoah took her leave, "We'll be down on the seafront. Don't be too long packing."

Once the Prefects had quite gone, Meryl threw the clothes she had been folding down on the floor and sat on the bed. "It's not fair! They've no right to do this, you're owed leave like any other Howler or Prefect; more for what you've been through. I can't be held responsible if you fall ill."

Rafe woofed, "But I feel better. I really do."

"Even so!"

After a long silence and many a shrug and paw-spread, the tail-less wolfen giant that was Rafe sat beside Meryl, making the bed slump alarmingly. "Look, I had a lovely time."

She said nothing, but forced a smile.

"Thanks. For everything, I mean."

"Everything?"

"Yeah. Everything you've done for me since we met. I... I feel like I've known you forever."

Meryl laughed a little.

Rafe looked to the door, then back again. His eyes met Meryl's and he held her gaze. Slowly, imperceptibly, his broad muzzle moved nearer to hers, until their noses all but touched.

Meryl suddenly turned aside and stood up. "No."

"What?"

"No, Rafe. We mustn't."

Licking his lips, Rafe ran a paw over his ears then twiddled his thumbs on his lap, "Is it... is it because I've got the rot?"

Meryl tutted sincerely, "No."

"Is it because me tail's gone, then?"

"No! No, of course not, silly. It makes no difference to me if a wolf has two tails."

Rafe looked to the broth, "Do I have fishy breath?"

"No!"

"Well what then? Don't you fancy me at all?"

Meryl emitted a snort, "Rafe, I'm sure someone that looks like you do has kissed many a wolfess in his time."

He shrugged, "I couldn't tell yer if I had, Meryl."

The nurse leapt on his words, "That's why we mustn't. Don't you see? You're not yourself right now. You say you feel like you've known me forever, but in six months I... I don't even know if I've met the real Rafe Stenton yet. I would never forgive myself if something were to happen between us and you not even remember it a week later. It wouldn't be fair on you."

"Yeah, but... that'll never change, will it?"

Meryl dodged Rafe's simple logic. "Get dressed, all right? And finish your soup; it's a long drive back to Lupa."

Retrieving the clothes she'd discarded, the nurse closed the door with a gentle, caring smile. Once she had gone, Rafe flopped back on the bed, mortified by his misstep.

"Smooth, Rafe. Nice one. Idiot."

Chapter 32

"Twenny-five... twenny-six... twenny-seven... twenny-eight."

Whilst Uther used an overhanging rock ledge as an improvised gymnasium, methodically pulling himself up to its rugged lip then lowering himself down again, Ivan deftly sliced raw mushrooms into a fire-licked frying pan. The freshly-picked fungal fruits hissed and danced around on the broiling oil like little white boats weathering a rough, storm-tossed sea. In reality it was a beautiful morning. The warm sun played on the burbling stream and tender-leafed trees rustled, caressed by an unseasonably clement breeze.

The only intrusion was Uther's grunts. "Thirty-five... thirty-six... thirty-seven."

If the gym-fanatic was trying to impress Blade-dancer by counting out loud, Ivan paid no outward heed.

"Forty-nine," Uther growled, pulling himself up one last time, "fifty!" and let go. "Woo!" he sniffed, rolling his muscled shoulders and swinging his sore arms, "That's the way to start the day, mate."

"I'm impressed," Ivan replied, "I didn't know you could count to fifty."

Uther buttoned up his tunic and pinned his mantle about his athletic frame. Sauntering over to Ivan he sat in the grass nearby, paws knitted around his armoured knees. "What's cooking?" he puffed.

"I don't know. I'm making it up."

"Puh! Smells good, though."

"It'll do. At least Everdor provides forage, even if it is only roots and fungus this time of year."

Uther peered into the frying pan Ivan was rapidly filling with slices of various colourful vegetables; root, leaf and fungus. "Mate, I wouldn't know where to begin. Where'd you learn all this guff?"

Ivan waited a moment, "Noss."

Uther looked momentarily surprised, but said nothing. Breaking out an ember he took a few puffs, blowing minty green vapour to the wind.

"You smoulder too much," the ember-shy Ivan complained, as Uther's vapours stung his eyes and nose.

After a month breathing the clean air beyond Lupa, away from noxious smog and vapour-filled bars, a mere puff from an ember was akin to sticking one's face's in a monobike's exhaust plume.

"You shouldn't rely on them," Ivan added. "They only hasten the rot."

"Yes, Mum," Uther replied.

Whilst Ivan cooked, Uther lay on the grassy bank and cast his eyes over the lush glade he found himself in. Trees and bushes jostled for space, spring flowers bloomed by the waterside and small insects flitted between the waving reeds, their wings catching the sun like slivers of silver. *So this is Everdor, in colour, in reality. The stale, monochrome newsreels did it no justice.*

Despite the circumstances, Uther knew he was lucky to experience this slice of paradise. Howlers were not allowed to leave Lupa without permission from their Elder, and if one took it upon himself to go AWOL they'd better have a source of stings. It did happen of course. Despite the propaganda to the contrary, disgruntled Howlers escaped the grind all the time to live it up in some foreign clime.

Uther stared at his smouldering ember, rolling it between his dark, blue-grey fingers that were slightly stained with a rainbow of glittery imperious ash.

"You know, mate," he laughed, taking a deep draught of heady vapours, "we *could* do a runner."

Ivan paused stirring a moment, just a moment.

"We've got a pack full of stings," Uther went on, clouds of vapour punctuating his every word. "Nobody could stop us. Amael wouldn't know anything's happened until we didn't show up to do his dirty work, and even then he couldn't do anything. We'll never have a better chance."

Uther cast a paw at the lovely scene.

"I mean just look at that sky! Imagine waking up to that every day, instead of the usual Lupan schmutz. Puh!"

Ivan remained silent, pushing sizzling mushrooms around with a roughly-carved wooden spoon as if he hadn't been listening, or cared not to respond to Uther's clumsy floatation.

"I remember when we met you," he said suddenly, "or should I say, when that drooling Vito showed you to us like an object."

Silence.

Ivan chuckled, "Vito believed the rumours, that Rufus was the same depraved sort as him, a wolf who took whatever and whoever he wanted. You were strong and handsome, even then, but powerless, afraid, a cub really. I thought nothing of it, just another victim of Vito's lust, a pretty boy dragged in off the street by his corrupt adjutants to satisfy him for a few weeks before being sent on. I was just a cub myself, barely a Howler. I knew no better. The war had hardened my heart. The things I'd seen and done."

Ivan shook his head a little, eyes closing and opening.

"But that's no excuse," he sniffed. "Rufus had been through the same, maybe worse. Still he cared. He got you out of Vito's clutches and gave you a chance-"

"So now I have to be grateful forever?" Uther exploded, standing up and turning away, rubbing his arms. "No wolf will touch *me* again. Not even Rufus. Alpha is me, alpha! Never a beta. Never!"

A brief pause.

Ivan huffed, "Maybe you can abandon him, just as you've always spurned him, but I can't. Perhaps you're the stronger wolf for it, a 'real alpha'. I've never really bought into all that krap anyway."

Ivan breathed a sigh.

"Take half the stings," he grunted at last, "Don't worry; I can manage this alone. It's probably better that way. Rufus wouldn't want you to get hurt."

Uther threw his paws up in affected disgust. "By Ulf's fangs, will you shut up?" he moaned. "I was just joking. Can't you take a thumping joke? Puh!"

Nodding, Ivan dished up breakfast into some wooden bowls. Uther silently snatched his portion and aggressively tucked in by himself.

The Howlers ate in brooding silence.

Though full of vitamins and flavour, a pile of fried vegetables lacked calories and Ivan knew they would quickly hunger. Fortunately they were nearing the sleepy towns that dotted Everdor and it would be easy enough to find some proper food.

"Do you feel that?" Uther mumbled between chews.

"Yes," Ivan replied.

"Where's he at?"

"Somewhere over my right shoulder."

"I figured. Stay here."

Finishing his food, Uther unpinned his cloak and cast it aside. "I'm gonna go wash," he said aloud. "I'm humming after being on the road nearly two months."

"You're not wrong," Ivan agreed.

Uther scuttled down the bank and disappeared behind some rocks for privacy, or so it might seem. Ivan knew better; he could feel Wild-heart's potent corona growing fainter as he coasted to the right and round into the trees. The third presence remained stationary, and hopefully unaware. He might sense Uther's approach, but Ivan's perception was keener than most and Uther would dampen his own imperious corona by means unknown and unexplainable to those fortunate enough not to be afflicted.

Ivan tided up, coughed and sniffed and generally made distractions as Uther closed in.

"Gagh!"

"Gotcha!"

The bushes shook and rustled as a scuffle took place amidst their tangled leaves.

"*Gerroffofme!*" someone yelped.

"*Shut up before I stick yer!*" Uther snarled. "*Ivan! I got him! 'Gis a paw!*"

Calmly drawing his rapier, Ivan moseyed into the shadowy undergrowth and found Uther kneeling on a yellow-cloaked Howler, one knee pressed into the fellow's back the other pinning an arm.

"A Greystone," Ivan stated, as Uther relieved the stranger of his dual pistols, tossing them into the bushes.

"I'm on your side!" the downed wolf complained.

"Oh yeah?" Uther scoffed.

"Flaid sent me!"

"Who?"

"Elder Flaid! He's in with Amael! Right?"

"I dunno, is he?"

Ivan tapped his rapier's fine point on the Greystone's armoured nose. "We weren't meant to meet with you until we got nearer the time."

"I know. I'm early. I-I-I was just scoping you out."

"Clumsily," Ivan disparaged. "This doesn't bode well for your usefulness to us, Greystone."

"Yeah well, I-I-I underestimated you," the Greystone excused nervously. "The great Ivan Blade-dancer; I should've known better-"

"Flattery won't sway us!" Ivan warned. "What's the password?"

"Password?"

"To prove you're Flaid's agent."

"Uhm, yeah...uh... Wait, I-I-I know this."

"Best get your thinking cap on, cub. I'm not letting you up without the word."

"Not letting you live, more like," Uther growled.

"Hang on, hang on! What letter does it start with again?"

"You tell us!"

Eyes darting about, the pinned Greystone proffered a hopeful guess, "Tree?"

Ivan said nothing, but looked at Uther, who cocked his head to one side.

"No?" the Greystone chirped, yellow eyes darting between his captors.

"No," Ivan replied.

"No, no, it's, uhm.... Stream!"

"Nope."

"Forest?"

"This isn't eye-spy."

"No, no, I got it, I do! I just can't remember! Give me a chance! I can prove it!"

Silence.

"Sky?"

Ivan sheathed his imperium rapier and stepped clear of the bushes, "Oh let him up, Uther; he's embarrassing. Besides, nobody seriously trying to stop us would send such a buffoon."

"Ohw!" Wild-heart groaned in disappointment.

With the password in paw, or not, Uther helped the Greystone up and dusted down his cloak.

"No hard feelings, mate," he said, patting him on the back. "Had to be done; security n' all that."

"Yeah. Sure. No problem," the Greystone puffed. "What is the password, by the way?"

"There ain't one," Uther sniffed.

"What?"

"Ivan were just ribbing yer. Hahahaha!"

Uther joined Ivan back at the campfire and pinned his cloak about himself, whilst the Greystone fished his pistols from the tousled bushes.

Once everything was in order the newcomer stepped into the light with an impressive rifle in both paws and aimed loosely at the Bloodfangs.

"Pow!" he joked, lowering the gun and sniffing, "I could've, you know."

"You could've *one* of us," Ivan corrected airily, "provided you can shoot straight; the other would've got you before you could reload that… ridiculous contraption."

The Greystone slung his 'ridiculous contraption' over his shoulder and buckled it in place. "Yeah, well, I've a couple of pistols too for just such an occasion, and a sword. Still, we're all friends here, eh?"

Ivan huffed, "Let's not get carried away."

Still a little uncertain, the Greystone joined the Bloodfangs by the fire and removed his helmet, revealing his light brown features. He had a friendly, handsome look, a robust face free of scars save for a nick across an eyebrow – the result of a bar brawl perhaps, or hitting one's head on a cupboard door, there was no telling. His eyes were a translucent lemony yellow, like the yellow-imperium the Greystones coveted so jealously.

"I'm Gunnar anyway. Pleased to meetcha-"

"We don't care what you're called," Ivan cut in, shunning Gunnar's offered paw. "This is a marriage of convenience, Greystone, to be followed by a swift divorce once we're done."

After a moment, Uther took Gunnar's paw, "Uther, mate."

"Yeah," Gunnar gasped with awe, "I know."

"Oh yeah?"

"Of course, I heard you talking. Anyway you're the fastest wolf in Lupa. Everyone knows you."

"Oi, he's growing on me," Uther told Ivan, before saying to Gunnar. "Sit down, yeah? We've got a lot of walking ahead, so best rest whilst you can, mate."

Nodding, Gunnar scooted awkwardly round and sat in the grass beside Uther, giving Ivan a nervous glance or two.

Uther silently offered the guest an ember.

"Ta."

Nothing set company at ease so much as a shared smouldering and soon clouds of different coloured vapours mingled happily overhead, much to Ivan's displeasure.

"Come on," he huffed, suddenly standing up and snuffing out the fire with a pan of water, "let's go."

"Already?" Uther woofed.

"The summit's in a few days. We can't muck about."

Washing his cookware in the babbling brook and placing them in his satchel, Ivan struck off ahead following the flow of the water.

"He's eager," Gunnar joked quietly.

Donning his helmet as he walked after Ivan, Uther whispered, "It's… personal, mate."

"Vito?"

"Rufus," Uther clarified. Then he asked Gunnar, "Here, how'd you find us out here anyway?"

"Tracked yer," the youth beamed.

"Y'what? Like footprints 'n' stuff?"

"Yeah, something like that."

"Puh! I'm impressed."

"Thanks. I trained as a Watcher, but I switched to the Howlers to be where the action is. The Lupan Wall's all checkpoints, guard duty, and one-sided conversations with gazers."

"I hear yer. Welcome aboard anyway."

With that, Uther and Gunnar followed Ivan deeper into the lush tangle of Everdor.

✧

Madou flopped in the mud, a sodden heap of spotty fur and stripy prison rags. The feeble mountain sun overhead did little to alleviate his shivering, it only blinded him with its cold brilliance.

After a day in the freezing 'Pit', Madou hardly noticed the prison hogs kicking him in the side to get him moving, and it didn't work for all that. They resorted to lifting the hefty beast by the arms and dragging him from the Pit's mouth, across to the main compound, whereupon they dumped him on the unyielding erde, chin-down, his bound wrists bloodied from the Howler-wire which they at least had the courtesy to remove.

"Madou," someone said, shaking the hyena's shoulder. "Madou, come on, lad, you can't lay here."

Through his blinding tears, Madou saw a familiar outline.

"Helmut?"

"Aye," the hog confirmed. "Come on, to your feet."

Madou was about to ask after his cousin, but was at once relieved and upset to find Zozizou standing over him dripping wet and dishevelled, his magnificent mane flopping down, yet on his feet.

Not only has a lowly pig weathered the Pit better than you, Madou thought, as Helmut and Zozizou helped him stagger across the compound, but so has your skinny, imperium-addicted cousin who you were supposed to be protecting!

You must be further down the rot's road than you imagine, Chakaa Madou.

The group made landfall on their usual hut's stairs and clambered inside. Lusting after a dry bed, however flea-ridden, Madou felt strangely gratified to see Helmut and Zozizou collapse about undesirable, ever-vacant bunks just inside the doors, shivering and tired after all. How perverse, Madou thought, wishing others harm to make yourself feel better.

Time passed. Nobody spoke. Too tired. Too cold. The other prisoners stared at them in silence, offering not a blanket or crust of bread. Gelb was no place for charity.

Some minutes later the sounds of many approaching footsteps crunching over Gelb's gritty soil drew Helmut's attention. He got up and looked out the door windows; a group of prisoners were striding this way, a rival gang by the looks, with a mighty and rather handsome hyena at the lead.

For a moment Helmut sensed trouble, until he spied a wolf amongst the gang, an athletic grey wolf wearing his stripy cap at a recognisably jaunty angle.

Helmut waved, "Tomek!"

Looking for himself, Madou immediately scrabbled out the door and down the stairs to prostrate himself on all fours in front of that big hyena!

"My prince," he said.

Peeking outside, Zozizou hurried to join his cousin at the bottom of the stairs, nose in the dirt, and that's when Helmut realised this must be a hyena thing. For his part the hog stood in the doorway, arms folded, and nodded once at Tomek, who nodded back.

Tomek was carrying a blanket, which he immediately draped over the bowing Madou.

At first Madou was glad, but when he saw who it was giving him the blanket he cast it aside with a vicious snarl and continued to grovel as before.

The impressive hyena stranger growled, "Tomek is my friend, Madou. You'll accept his aid."

"But my Prince-"

"Accept his aid as if it were my own paw! I understand he saved your life, and that of Rufus. If you spurn him, you spurn me. Do you spurn me, Madou?"

Silence.

"No, my Prince," Madou conceded.

The 'Prince' nodded at Tomek, who placed the blanket over the shivering Madou a second time. The proud hyena left the blanket alone, even though it must've pained his ego no end to suffer its comfort.

Zozizou was given a blanket also. "Much obliged, Prince Noss… son of the Four Winds," he rasped, adding with a smile and a nod, "Tomek."

Smiling, Tomek tipped his cap in acknowledgement.

Helmut watched, baffled, but reassured by the way this was going. It all looked friendly.

Prince Noss turned his purple-eyed gaze on the hog. "Is this Helmut?" he asked Tomek directly.

"Yes."

"A friend of Rufus is a friend of mine," the prince declared, flashing a toothy smile and directing one of his followers to give Helmut a blanket too. "Even a furless hog!" he laughed, gesturing for Madou and Zozizou to rise, though they both kept their eyes respectfully down.

Despite the disparaging comment, Helmut accepted this hyena's kindness. "And who're you to

Rufus, exactly?" he sniffed snottily, cloaking himself from the cold.

"An old friend," Noss claimed.

"Old friend?"

"Rufus and I are very close."

Scratching his head, Helmut gruffed, "You new in Gelb, then?"

Noss laughed, "New? My good hog, I've been in this dive almost a year now."

"That long, eh?"

"Indeed. Seems... rather longer."

Helmut smelt a rat, "Well if you're Rufus's friend where've you been hiding? I've never even seen you before."

"We were on the night shift," Noss explained, gesturing to his rough-looking crew. "I've passed you by many times during switchover, but I didn't want Rufus to know I was here for... personal reasons."

"Like what?"

Noss flashed his teeth, "I tried to kill him once."

"Kill him?" Helmut huffed. "What kind of a friend is that?"

"Finding yourselves on different sides in a struggle is no barrier to friendship and respect amongst warriors. You desk-bound hogs don't understand the refined nuances of warrior races like wolves and hyenas-"

Helmut brandished a fist, "You wanna be lamped by this desk-bound hog, mate?"

Silence.

"Hahahaaaahahaha!" Noss laughed, slapping Tomek on the back and making him stumble. "I like your pig, Tomek. He has spunk, for a curly-tailed truffle-sniffer."

Tomek could but laugh awkwardly.

"In any case," Noss sniffed afresh, "now Red-mist's supposedly 'gone' I've been moved to day shift to plug the gap. I'm the best miner around now, so I suggest you all stick with me if you want to survive."

Helmut looked to Tomek. "Lad, is this nutter for real?"

The young wolf explained. "I'm already in his gang," he said. "You come too, please, all of you. We'll make two new teams together."

Helmut, Madou and Zozizou exchanged glances.

"All right, lad," Helmut said, with obvious misgivings, "I go where you go."

⁌

"Pfffcaaagh!"

Linus bent double from the punch to his gut, or as far forward as his bonds allowed. Any lesser wolf might've vomited there and then.

Elbows resting on the stark table in the middle of the bleak, off-white, windowless room, Doctor Josef rapped his grey fingers together in front of his dispassionate bespectacled gaze whilst Linus spluttered helplessly in the chair opposite.

One of the doctor's two black-cloaked Prefects pulled the wheezing Howler upright again by the scruff of his neck, somewhat bending him over the back of the contoured new-materials chair to which he was tied.

"Are you a traitor, Howler?" Josef sighed. "Is that what I'm going to have to put in this report?"

"No, sir," Linus vowed, nostrils flaring.

"And yet you deceive me."

"I do not."

"You're in league with Tristan and the THORN terrorists he's working for; you're helping them smuggle Olivia out of Lupa so they can use her. Yes... I see how it is now-"

"THORN? That's insane! I hardly even know Tristan. He hates me!"

"For the last time, where is Olivia Blake?"

"As I've said," Linus coughed, chest heaving, wrists twisting behind his back, "someone hit me over the head and they ran off. That's all there is to it, I'm afraid."

Josef nodded at his Prefects. One of them boxed Linus in the nose.

"Unfffgh!"

Whilst Linus seethed in pain the doctor sighed, "This is most tiresome." Kneading his paws and fussing with his coat he waited until Linus had recovered, before continuing in a reasonable tone, "Just cooperate and you can walk, Linus. I've no interest in testing the physical limits of an ordinary Howler like you. I've serious work to do."

Linus licked his bleeding nose, "I don't know where they went. I wish I did, believe me."

Josef sat back a moment, then leant forward again and shuffled his papers. "Well," he said, smacking his lips, "we'll see what you know on the rack."

"R-rrr-rack?"

"Yes. You'll last five minutes, if that."

"You can't!" Linus spluttered. "It's not legal! The Bloodfangs won't stand for it!"

"You're in ALPHA's paws now, idiot, and I can do whatever I want behind these doors!" Josef hissed, flapping his warrant about, as if it were the keys to Lupa. Calming himself he purred, "I could send you down for whatever crime came to mind, aiding dodgers, terrorists, even striking a Prefect. It's not difficult, it happens all the time. Do you remember Rufus, how high he was before someone around here decided to get rid of him? His fall sent ripples across Lupa, but you? You're nothing, a nobody Howler. You could be made to disappear and nobody would even look up from their breakfast!"

The bruised Linus gulped, hard.

Tucking his papers into a file, Josef made for the door. He waited a moment, one paw resting on its simple lever. "You've wasted enough of my time. Your colleague Tristan is keeping the rack warm just down the hall where my expertise is greatly needed," the cat said pompously. "He's a strong one; a most impressive specimen. If I don't get something out of him regarding Olivia Blake's whereabouts I'll come back for you. Consider that, Howler."

On that ominous note Josef stepped out.

The metal door closed, sealing Linus inside with the two Prefects, who set about their work without delay.

"Gagh!"

Suffering through another stomach-churning blow to the belly, which made Linus glad he'd skipped breakfast, one of the helmet-masked wolves grabbed his blonde ears and pulled him back over the chair.

"Grrrfffgh!"

With eyes watering and ears burning, the gasping Linus couldn't tell whether it was the torturer behind him or the one in front doing the talking.

"Come on, mate, where's the girl?" they asked. "We'll stop if you tell us, but not before."

"I... don't... know!" Linus seethed.

"Ah, but you do. You're just being stubborn. Silly young thing, ain't yer, eh? Do you fancy 'em or something? Is that it, Howler?"

"W-w-what?"

"Ahhh... they're not worth it, mate," the Prefect sniffed, it was the one in front; Linus could tell now. "Wolfesses, that is. Those two'll chew you up and spit you out; especially the little Hummel bitch. What? Think she's gonna touch a rotting scumbag like you, do yer? You're dreaming!"

Linus said nothing, but averted his eyes to the imperium light glowing overhead.

"Oh dear, he's got it bad," the Prefect tutted to his silent comrade. He looked at Linus again, "See, mate, the doctor ain't very good at this... interrogation lark. He only knows how to stick beasts on his rack and fry 'em. The rack doesn't leave a mark of course, so its use can be denied, but it doesn't get under a wolf's skin half as much as I can." The Prefect drew his sword and pushed its vicious point into Linus's chin, "If you get through a racking it'll be back to me. They'll let me cut you then. I'll take an ear, if I like, or a finger maybe. Do you like your tail?" The Prefect looked at Linus's tail dangling through the chair's tail-hole and lifted it with his sword. "'Tis a fine bushy one, I see. It'll look good pinned to my wall-"

Wham!

The door burst open and a black-cloaked Prefect strode in.

"Stand away!" they barked.

Immediately the other two Prefects stood back and saluted with the subtle ALPHA wave.

With his tormentors out of his face, Linus was able to sit forward and see the newcomer – a wolfess, slender and russet-furred, armed with a rapier and a disapproving frown.

"Janoah?" Linus mouthed, spitting blood-laced saliva.

"Out," Janoah commanded simply, flicking a finger at her ALPHA comrades.

The Prefects exchanged looks before the one standing nearest to Janoah elected to speak. "Doctor Josef said we were to interrogate this wolf-"

"I don't care what Josef said," Janoah interrupted. "That cat has no authority; he's not a proper ALPHA Agent, just a contracted researcher. You two shouldn't even be assisting him without my say-so."

"Yes, marm, but… he has a warrant, signed by Grand Prefect Nikita."

"Nikita? Where is it?"

"He has it on him, marm. Josef that is."

With nod, Janoah said, "Fine. I'll take full responsibility for what transpires. You're both reassigned. Go on. Go patrol the city or something until this blows over."

The nearest Prefect emitted a grateful, "Aye, marm."

With another salute, the Prefects took their leave without further protest. They obviously didn't particularly care about seeing their task through, only that they would be on the right side of any potential fallout for not doing so. Linus supposed from his own experience it was wise of them to remain on the formidable Janoah's side.

The elegant wolfess stood over the stocky wolf, paws cupped behind her as his were wired behind him.

"I thought you were smarter than this, Linus," Janoah growled. "Losing your head over some passing fancy? I never imagined you'd be so stupid."

Linus gulped, but said nothing.

"My husband's made a career out of that, as well you know, and look at him now. Digging up imperium until he rots, which I dare say shan't be long in his condition."

Linus dipped his chin, "You helped put him there."

"And you'll join him if you continue to break the law!"

"I've broken no laws-"

"Don't bother. I know you're protecting some dodger girl. I'd let Josef rack you to find out where she is if I cared to know myself, but I don't. I'm glad she's given that cat the slip; saves me having to eliminate her."

Linus sat bolt upright and snorted, "Eliminate her?"

"Ah, silly wolf, so you do care about her," Janoah chuckled. "It's a good thing I came when I did. You'd have tied yourself in knots."

Composing himself, Linus asked, "Why would you need to… to get rid of Olivia?"

"Two Eisenwolves is one Eisenwolf too many. I have the only one. Josef covets him, they all do, Nikita, Silvermane, even the Alpha I dare say… but Rafe's loyal only to me."

Linus had stopped listening at, "Two Eisenwolves?"

Janoah chuckled, then sighed, "I've said too much. Must be those pretty blue peepers of yours. If I weren't such a wily wolfess I could be taken in by them."

Linus's 'pretty blue peepers' nearly crossed in amazement.

Suddenly, Janoah whipped out her rapier! Linus imagined the Prefect was going to plunge her fine imperious blade into his heart and 'eliminate him' without a second thought, but she instead cut the ropes binding him to the chair in a trice and sheathed her sword as quickly.

Helping the shorter Linus up, Janoah gently unwound the wire from his sore wrists.

The bruised Howler winced a little.

"I know," Janoah said, screwing up the wire. Kicking away the bleak new-materials chair to which Linus had been secured, she added, "These things are so uncomfortable, aren't they?"

Rubbing his wrists, Linus thought he'd better say something, anything, to Janoah. "Thank you," was all that came to mind.

"Where's your gear?" was her evasive reply.

Linus visually searched the austere interrogation room for his helmet, shield and swords. "I don't know."

"Evidence room. Follow me."

Linus did so, knowing the only way out of ALPHA's Den (and Den it was in all but name) in one piece was at Janoah's back. His mind raced as he followed the enigmatic wolfess down the harsh, unadorned corridors, free of anything so much as a painting or potted plant, even the imperium gas lamps were devoid of beautification, their modesty preserved only by simple frosted glass shades. *Why's she helping me? Is it because I'm a Bloodfang? Because I'm posted at Riddle? Is she so sentimental?*

A large rectangular window broke the monotony of the wall on the right. Lost in thought and worry, Linus might've passed it by without a care, but a glaring flicker of purplish light drew his attention to the room beyond.

Inside the dark space stood a whole wall of machinery and consoles covered in dials and knobs. Pipes connected the mechanical mass to a metallic table in the middle. Shackled to said table, splayed out like a wolf condemned to some horrible lingering death of old, was Tristan Eisbrand Donskoy.

The big wolf arched his back in mute agony as bolts of imperious energy licked silently over his smouldering grey and white body. The lack of sound only added to the disturbing spectacle.

"A rack?" Linus said.

Recognising Josef Grau as the beast working the rack's controls, Linus hid himself behind the wall.

"It's all right," Janoah said, touching the window. "It's one-way glass. Sound-proofed as well. The Alpha was fed-up with screams embarrassing him in front of guests."

Linus growled, "Racking wolves is forbidden!"

"Spare me your wet Rufus rhetoric. I don't like it, but it's the only way to break this one. Just be glad he's on there, not you. You would've been next, but for me."

Linus slowly peeped into the room again.

"Why?" he said, as Tristan writhed in silence, before clarifying, "What's he done?"

"He's working for THORN."

Linus seethed, "What? That's preposterous! Tristan wouldn't do that."

"Know that for a fact do you, Woodlouse?"

"Well… n-nnn-no, but I know him-"

"You're a naive fool, cub!" Janoah snapped, adding gently, "You'll learn." She looked into the room, paws behind back, indifferent to the suffering within. "You see, Tristan hates being a Howler, hates everything about Lupa. He'd see thousands die to overturn centuries of wolfen rule and for what? So he can ditch his responsibility and get stung for free. That's what his dissident sort believe in, giving venom to all, no control, no borders, no work."

Despite his better judgement, Linus hazarded, "What's so wrong with that?"

Janoah explained, "Stupid boy. Do you think the proud hyenas will let us live in peace if we let them go free? Do you think the little beasts will let bygones be bygones after all these years under our boot? Do you think the noble cats of Felicia won't send their Valours to invade us immediately we drop our guard? The moment the Howlers falter is the moment the other races tear wolfkind down and set themselves up as masters of the continent. They'd all kill each other in the process. It'd be anarchy. Genocide. No. That can never be. Not on my watch."

Linus kept his opinions to himself this time, but asked, "Isn't there another way to do this?"

"To do what?"

Linus gestured inside at Tristan.

"You really are a soft fool, aren't you?" Janoah tutted. "Has Rufus rubbed off on you, or were you always so stupid?"

No reply.

"Tristan has no family, save Ivan," Janoah huffed, "and he knows we can't touch his famous cousin. Ivan's a darling to too many. Besides, the Blade-dancer's out of town." After a while, the

Prefect turned to Linus, "Do you know anyone Tristan cares about?"

"What?"

"He must care about someone other than himself."

Sara and Olivia flashed through Linus's inner eye. "I wouldn't know," he claimed insipidly.

Janoah pressed, "What about the two girls? Tell me where they are. It's all right, Mills, *I* don't want them, but if I know where they are I can at least threaten Tristan with their arrest and maybe convince him to talk-"

"I don't know, for Ulf's sake!" Linus snapped, before averting his face from both Janoah and the awful spectacle beyond the glass. "Rack me, or let me go. Don't question me all over again."

Silence.

"How bold you've grown," Janoah growled. "You used to stammer like a trembling cub at a school play. That day you came to me with that sting for Rufus I thought you were going to pass out from fright."

Linus said nothing.

"Fine," Janoah hissed.

On she walked, Linus eventually following. After a maze of corridors and stairs, passing the occasional cloaked Prefect at whom Janoah saluted regardless of rank, they arrived in an open office with a simple square window overlooking ALPHA HQ's grim central quadrangle. Linus observed that someone had taken the time to attempt to beautify the brutal concrete space with rows of lavenders.

Ahead was a huge door to a walk-in safe, tucked behind a long, partitioned desk and guarded by a pretty, prim-looking white wolfess in a Politzi-like ALPHA uniform.

Janoah walked over and exchanged salutes. The safe door was ajar, to her surprise.

"Who's in there?" she demanded of the white wolfess.

"Uh… Stenton, Prefect."

Surprised, Janoah queried, "Rafe? What for?"

"He just said it was for the Tristan case, marm"

Janoah slid the nearby ledger over and turned it around on the desk. Running her finger down the entries she said, "You obviously know Rafe's not authorised to go in there, since you've not logged his visit."

"No, Prefect."

"Explain yourself, agent."

"I… I just. Well, he said it couldn't hurt. I thought he must have your permission as usual, Prefect Janoah."

Prefect Janoah flicked the ledger shut. "I know Rafe can be charming, but fawning over our strapping Eisenwolf is ill-advised, my dear. You'll get in trouble."

"Yes, Prefect. Sorry, Prefect. I'll fetch him at once-"

"No, I'll go. Just this once let's both pretend this never happened."

The wolfess nodded gratefully and lifted the desk partition, allowing Janoah to pass. Linus stayed put until Janoah beckoned him through. The white wolfess asked no questions as she set the desk back and nervously waited.

Linus followed Janoah into the evidence locker, expecting nothing more than a dingy broom cupboard like at Riddle, but finding instead an immense, illuminated atrium lined with row upon row of metallic standing shelves stuffed with cardboard boxes and open trays of confiscated trinkets; swords, armour, pistols, even individual pellets bent and warped from impacting something, or someone, and everything sporting brown labels attached by string, annotated, catalogued, however tiny.

Every Howler Den had an evidence locker, but this put all else to shame. Linus supposed the wrongdoings of a whole city, of thousands of corrupt Howlers, amounted to a lot of evidence, however spurious that evidence might be.

As he followed Janoah through the labyrinth of confiscated equipment, Linus wondered if Rufus's gear was stashed here somewhere, a sad Bloodfang helmet, armour and cloak, tucked in a box under 'R', perhaps.

Towards the end of the rows was an open space with a table and chairs and a magnifying glass on an armature for inspecting tricky evidence. Sitting at the table was an immense chocolate-brown wolf. He was polishing a huge two-pawed imperium sword with the gathered front of his black ALPHA cloak.

Walking over to him Janoah hissed at once, "Rafe, what're you doing?"

"Just looking," he sniffed.

"That's Tristan's sword."

"Yeah. I saw 'em bring it in," Rafe said, beaming hopefully. "Can I have it?"

"What? No you can't; it's evidence."

Linus stayed back amongst the shelves, if only because the coils of imperious energy springing from the brown wolf pierced him down to the core, setting his bones and muscles tingling. Linus hung onto the nearest shelf to steady his nerve in the presence of such an awesome corona.

Rafe stood up, towering over Janoah, his cloak hanging off that barrel-like chest and rolling over those mountainous shoulders. He lifted Tristan's huge two-pawed sword with but one rippling arm and swung it effortlessly to and fro, before twirling it round like a baton.

Come the second or third twirl, Rafe fumbled the sword. It escaped his grasp, flying across the room and clattering deafeningly to the concrete floor. Cringing like a cub who'd put a football through a neighbour's window, Rafe hurried to retrieve the sword. "I need lessons," he freely admitted, feeling the shining blue-imperium snowflake emblem on the pommel.

"Lessons?" Janoah scoffed.

"Yeah. Sword lessons."

"Don't be ridiculous."

Rafe looked along the perfect blade, "Why ridiculous?"

Janoah marched over to her champion. "You don't need a sword. Your suit is weapon enough. It's more powerful than any sword."

"But I want a sword, like everyone else!" Rafe asserted, chin high and mighty. "Like a proper Prefect."

"You are a proper Prefect."

"I'm not, though! I'm nothing."

Janoah couldn't deny it. Rafe had no official rank. In fact, he didn't even officially exist, despite the growing rumours.

The Eisenwolf hefted the sword blade up to his broad nose and admired its terrible beauty. "I could do a better job and really impress the Alpha if I learnt to fight properly," he claimed, "I know I could."

Shaking her head a little, Janoah held both paws up, as if creating a wall. "I don't know where this idea has come from, but I don't have time for it right now."

She breezed past Rafe, delving further into the archives beyond and casting her eyes over the rows until she located 'Recent Additions', whereupon she searched carefully for Linus's belongings.

Still clinging onto his looted sword, Rafe wandered across the room until he noticed Linus. "Alright, mate?" he asked amiably, raising his chin in greeting.

Linus let go of the shelf and brushed down his cloak, trying to look presentable despite a bloody nose. "Yes, thank you."

"Bloodfang, yeah?"

"I am, yes."

Nodding, Rafe looked down the way at Janoah, then back to Linus again. "Jan getting you off the hook is she?"

Linus emitted a tiny scoff of surprise, but refrained to confirm Rafe's suspicions.

"Whatcha do?" the big wolf asked pleasantly.

"Nothing. I'm innocent."

"Ah, that's what they all say, mate," Rafe woofed, shouldering Tristan's sword and moseying towards Linus. He stopped beside the little, if burly blonde wolf. "Don't do it again, or they might send me after you," he warned, "and I wouldn't want to hurt a nice boy like you."

On he walked, his fiery corona fading at Linus's back like the sun ducking behind a cloud.

Another, less potent aura approached from the front. Lost in the rapture of the last, Linus barely noticed it until its owner spoke.

"Here," Janoah said, chucking a pile of Howler equipment on the table, short sword, pistol, a beautiful round Bloodfang shield, the straps and buckles of it all flopping about like a dead octopus' tentacles, "You're lucky nobody pinched anything. They usually nick the wallet at least."

No reply.

Noticing Linus's vacant stare, Janoah leant on the table and said, "You get used to him."

"What?"

"Rafe."

"Sorry, I...." the Howler trailed off. He looked to the exit, for Rafe, but he'd gone. "I-I-I thought he would look... uh...."

"What?" Janoah chuckled. "Like a monster?"

"No," Linus clarified, "just... more ill."

Surprised at this stocky little wolf's gentle insight, Janoah explained, "Rafe's in the rot's good graces at the moment. He has bad days and good days, like all of us. It's just his bad days would be the death of you or I."

"It must be hard."

Janoah averted her gaze a little. "He does it for Lupa, he suffers so others don't have to, like we all do," she asserted, slapping Linus's shield and heading out. "Come on, Mills, I'll walk you to the gate."

✢

Janoah pushed the black side gate open and Linus stepped through the gap, watched by the Prefects standing guard at the main gate nearby. Linus expected them to stop him, or for Josef to come running across the forecourt, waving his warrant and shouting 'halt'.

But no, Janoah shut the gate with a squeak, barring Linus from the assorted concrete blocks pocked with windows that was ALPHA HQ's facade; an ugly if modest building.

"I told you I would remember you," Janoah said through the bars, making to leave. "Now we're even. Don't expect my help again."

"Even?" Linus woofed after her.

The Prefect turned, one paw resting on rapier hilt, and snorted, "You've a short memory. Lucky for you I don't."

It came to Linus then, the reason for it all; the white-imperium he had given Rufus that day nearly a year ago still carried truck with his wife.

"You helped me because of the venom I gave Rufus?" Linus almost laughed.

Silence.

"But you arrested him! I-I-I thought you didn't even care about him!"

Janoah parted company with a shouted warning, "Just stay out of trouble, Woodlouse!"

Chapter 33

The first thing Rufus saw was the flapping brown canvas of a tent; the second was the narrow face of a white rabbit looking grimly down on him.

The fellow was crouched beside Rufus, little arms resting on those big rabbit legs. He was wearing a short brown jacket, black breeches and a bowler hat, and looked awfully familiar to the bed-bound wolf.

"Don't get up," he advised gruffly.

Rufus merely grunted; rot pains were taking hold as the analgesic respite of sleep let go.

Daring to lift his head and assess the situation, the Howler found he was lying on a thin mattress in an open tent, his head propped up by a rolled blanket. His collar had gone, along with the chain. His rank prison clothes had also been disposed of, replaced by a traditional hyena sarong of a dazzling black and white swirl pattern that represented the Four Winds, as far as Rufus recalled. The beautiful cloth was clipped neatly about his waist by a handsome beetle-shaped brooch made of gold; hyenas thought very well of noble beetles.

Rufus felt this was all good news. Hyenas didn't furnish any old guest with sarongs and brooches depicting their gods and totems, only those they respected.

'I'm in', he thought, almost wishing he wasn't, that this farce had ended in that sun-spider's crevice.

The game had just begun.

"Haven't got a drink, have you?" Rufus croaked.

The white rabbit offered up a hip-flask, which Rufus gratefully swigged from. It contained something alcoholic. Water might've been a wiser choice, but it hit the spot and wet one's whistle.

"Much obliged," Rufus said, lying gratefully back.

Glancing out the tent flaps at distant peaks, the white rabbit surreptitiously produced an imperium pistol from his jacket and pressed its cold barrel into Rufus's heaving ribs.

"I don't expect you remember me," he menaced.

It took a few seconds for Rufus to register this new state of affairs. "Of course I do, Citizen Casimir."

Citizen Casimir grunted, "Then maybe you know what I'm going to ask you."

"I've an inkling. Though a pistol in the ribs won't change my answer."

"We'll see-"

Suddenly a pair of zigzag-pattered armoured legs rattled over to the tent. Casimir stowed his pistol away the same moment Nurka whipped the tent flaps aside and ducked into the cosy space – at least Rufus assumed this was Nurka, the hyena wasn't wearing his usual skull helmet and Rufus had yet to glimpse his face.

He was handsome; Rufus wasn't the sort to pretend he couldn't tell a handsome hyena from an ugly one. Those bright eyes and beetling brows were possessed of intelligence, yet the broad nose perched on the end of that thick, dark muzzle conveyed nobility and strength, as did that long, spot-flecked neck. He had a short, roguishly untidy scramble of a mane sticking up between his pleasantly rounded-off ears. Perhaps removing his helmet had messed up his mane, or perhaps it was always thus. One thing was certain, Nurka was very young, his hide unblemished by scars or greys, or even the whiskers a beast in their twenties could expect whatever the race.

He's only a cub, Rufus realised, just like Madou.

Without a word, Nurka knelt before Rufus, paws on zigzag-armoured knees, and bowed – not too far, just halfway.

"Thank you, Red-mist," he said, adding graciously, "I bow because I know Themba never will. He's a proud warrior. It's not easy for him to admit that a wolf saved his life."

Rufus spread a paw, "Let's just call us even."

Nodding, Nurka moved on. "You had an attack, a bad one," he said. "We... do not have any white-imperium stings to give you. We of the Jua-mata believe-"

"That white-imperium is the tears of the Sky," Rufus beamed. "You're probably right."

Nurka's brow twisted, but he nodded a little.

Rufus grunted, "You gave me something though. I can feel it."

"Chunta," Nurka revealed.

"The sacred drink?"

"You came round and drank a little. You were feverish."

"I don't remember."

Glancing at Casimir, Nurka made to rise, saying, "There's more if you need it. I'll go fetch some-"

"No!" Rufus woofed, sitting up a little. "No, thank you, Nurka. I couldn't possibly."

Kneeling again, the hyena moved to allay the wolf's fears. "I know it does not sit well with your kind, so I made a mild batch," he claimed, spreading a hefty paw. "I apologise if I wronged you, but I was worried you would not awaken."

Rufus raised a paw, dismissing the notion. One drink of sacred chunta and the purple-imperium it contained would not drive him mad, but nor would it make much difference to a wolf as far down rot's road as him. White and only white sufficed.

"You honour me with your tribe's colours, chieftain," Rufus said, plucking at his stripy sarong.

"No more than you deserve," Nurka insisted. "You've always been a famous friend of my people. What you did this morning only proves you make no distinction between wolf and hyena."

"I merely find in this life that there's no distinction to be made by race, only character."

"A philosophy to which I too subscribe."

Rufus couldn't help himself. "In which case, Nurka, if you're the face of THORN, and I believe you are, your goal can't be the downfall of wolfkind as the pack propaganda spouts, but the current rotten regime. Correct?"

Nurka waited for clarification.

Rufus weathered a wave of pain as he continued, "You don't... agh... don't blame desperate Howlers and... and Watchers for the mistakes of the Den Fathers, do you?"

Nurka's violet eyes flitted just a little, "All we want is our freedom, Red-mist, and our land returned. If that happened tomorrow THORN would disband."

"Then... we can remain friends," Rufus decreed, twisting on his pillow and panting. "Amael was r-rrr-right to confide in you."

"And I him, I hope."

Rufus grunted and growled, "Sorry, couldn't s-s-sss-spare an ember could you?"

Nurka plucked a case from his cloak pocket.

"Strawberry, if you have it," Rufus stipulated.

He got what he wanted, Nurka passing an already smouldering red ember to Casimir, who gave it to the stricken wolf.

"Ta."

Whilst Rufus puffed away like a true trooper, Nurka and Casimir exchanged glances.

"I... hate to disturb you further," the hyena hesitated, "but I must ask you something, Red-mist."

"You as well?" Rufus guffawed.

Nurka looked questioningly at Casimir.

"It's nothing, Nurka," the rabbit dismissed. "You go first."

Curious, but eager to set his own mind at ease, Nurka went ahead. "Red-mist, I've heard from a reliable source that Prince Noss is still alive."

Rufus's ruddy ears pricked.

"He's been held in Gelb since...." Nurka trailed off and averted his purple eyes a little, perhaps embarrassed to mention Noss's bungled attempt on Rufus's life. "Did you see him there?"

Exhaling a cloud of toxic strawberry ember vapours, Rufus shook his head. "No."

A shuffle. "I understand there are many inmates and two shifts, night and day, perhaps you missed him-"

"I'd have felt him at some point, Nurka."

"But Gelb is an imperium mine," the chief reasoned. "The walls drip with the blood of the Erde. Even your legendary senses must be dulled by its fog."

"True," Rufus admitted. "But... Josef killed him. It was an accident, they claim."

"Did you see a body?"

Silence.

Rufus frowned. "No. By the time I was back on my feet it was all done and dusted."

"Then it is possible," Nurka said. He clenched his fists on his lap, "May the Wind and Sky forgive my transgression in contradicting a Prince of the blood, but... it was... a... a mistake for Noss to try and kill you. You've my abject apologies from our people."

Red-mist grimaced, "I don't hold it against him, he must've been desperate."

Nurka emitted a grunt at Rufus's magnanimous reply.

"Did Amael tell you Noss is alive?" Red-mist probed.

The hyena shook his head, "No. On the contrary Amael insists he's dead, despite what I've heard, which is what arouses my suspicions that our Prince is alive."

Casimir piped up, "How comes?"

Nurka explained. "It makes sense. If Amael were to hide Prince Noss from me he could produce him as a bargaining chip against my people at any time. Most hyenas would do anything to ensure his safety, even me."

"That does make sense," Rufus agreed, his mind racing. Feeling the rot creeping up his legs again, he growled through a wave of discomfort, "Then... who told you Noss is in Gelb?"

Nurka caged up, "I cannot betray my sources."

"I'm not about to tell Amael who's been going behind his back," Rufus chuckled. "I'm in no position to do anything. But this source could be lying. If it's someone I know I can at least tell you if they're trustworthy"

"I decide that, Red-mist."

After a pause, Rufus nodded – cub he may be, but Nurka spoke with the sureness of a Den Father. Red-mist offered something up to gain further trust, "Well, I don't know about Noss, but I can tell you Madou's alive back there."

Silence.

"What, our Madou?" Casimir said, looking to Nurka.

Rufus continued. "Rode with me down to Gelb; we were in the same carriage. We became well acquainted after a bit of a wonky start."

Nurka searched his memory. "But he was bitten. He was dead. I saw his lips go blue-"

"He was alive, just about," Rufus insisted, blowing a strawberry vapour ring and watching it dash off the sloped tent canvas above. "He was interrogated and told the Bloodfangs what he knew. Beasts always talk on the rack, Nurka."

"Maybe, but Madou knows only what he needed to know, no more," Nurka said, triumphant.

"Not the truth then?"

"The truth, but with omissions."

Rufus nodded. "I'm not sure how he avoided execution; perhaps Amael's hiding him away like you believe he has Noss."

After a moment's thought Nurka stood up, "Excuse my rudeness, Red-mist, but I must tell Themba the good news. I'll be back shortly. We'll talk more."

Rufus merely raised a paw, almost ALPHA-like.

Nurka took his leave, hurrying across the camp. The tent flaps had barely settled before Casimir said, "Well, you've got Nurka on-side already I see. You work fast, Rufus."

Rufus puffed on his ember, "What? No pistol this time?"

Out came the pistol, as if Casimir had forgotten. "What did you Bloodfang bastards do to my boy? Answer me!"

"The question's not what I did to Bruno," Rufus replied coolly, "but what I'm going to do, which is save his young life if I can."

Casimir's eyes darted all over Rufus, searching the arrogant Howler for an explanation, "What? Whaddaya mean?"

"He's alive. And he's in ALPHA."

"ALPHA? What're you saying?"

"They turned him into an Eisenwolf," Rufus said. He waited a moment, "I know from your eyes you know what that means."

Open-jawed, Casimir nodded a little. "That was him, wasn't it?" he realised, lowering his pistol. "The Eisenwolf back at Riddle Refinery!"

"You saw him?"

"Saw him? I thumping shot him!" Casimir howled, dropping his pistol altogether to grab at his long white ears. "I shot my own lad! I... I didn't know, I swear!"

Rufus guffawed, "I imagine you merely tickled him."

"But I-I used an imperium pearl! I blew him off a barge into the Lupa. He must've drowned! Oh, Briar forgive me!"

Rufus looked hard at Casimir. "I always thought I could feel someone in *The Warren* even when Bruno wasn't around. An afflicted rabbit, rare indeed."

Casimir wasn't listening, too busy weeping.

At length, and with some effort, Rufus sat up and placed a paw on Casimir's shoulder. "Whatever you did, Bruno was well enough to kill a sewer centipede after, so I wouldn't beat yourself up."

"But he went into the river!"

"Well, eisenpelz suits have their own air supply. Rafe was alive and talking when I saw him last."

"Rafe?"

A grimace, "That's what he's called now. Ivan spoke to him at length, more than I; he said Bruno didn't seem the same wolf. That's how it is when you live day to day with enough imperium in your blood to power a train. It... changes you."

Casimir wiped his eyes, "He's forgotten me, then?"

"He's forgotten everyone, I fear."

There was a mournful silence.

Rufus glanced beyond the tent flaps. "I won't ask why you joined THORN, I think I can guess, but if you want to see Bruno again you'd better stay out of my way. I have to come through this to save him – that's the deal I struck with ALPHA."

"What? But, aren't you with Amael?"

"Who I'm with or not makes no difference to you if you want to save your son. Just keep out of my affairs, or better yet go back to Lupa before you get killed! No offence, but Nurka won't miss you."

"I can't abandon Nurka. We're so close."

"Close?"

"To setting things right."

Rufus instantly grabbed Casimir's jacket and pulled him into his face. "Right?" he snarled. "What's 'right' about hoarding enough black-imperium to murder half of Lupa? What're you fools planning to do with it, eh?"

"I-I-I don't know."

"Come now! You *must* know! Someone must know. You can't all be in the dark about Nurka's plans!"

"Only he knows, that's his policy-"

Suddenly Rufus released Casimir and lay back down as if nothing had occurred.

The tent flaps whipped open and Nurka returned, fresh from spreading his good news. He noticed a flustered Casimir wiping his eyes and tugging his jacket.

"Casimir?" the hyena asked, crouching on one knee and cupping a paw to the rabbit's shoulder; Rufus was amazed by his concern for the little beast.

"I'm fine, Nurka," Casimir sniffed.

Nurka nodded a little, then asked, "I take it Red-mist's answer was a disappointment?"

After some time, Casimir dipped his chin.

Nurka nodded, "I'm sorry. Your son will be avenged when change comes to Lupa and justice is done. We'll find those responsible, I promise."

With a glance down at Rufus, who sternly met his eye, Casimir shakily stood up and excused himself from the suddenly stifling tent.

Well, that could've gone better, Rufus thought, but at least he didn't denounce me to Nurka. Perhaps he's on side.

"The authorities killed his son," Nurka explained, unaware of what had transpired between Casimir and Rufus. "Bruno was an afflicted wolf that Casimir kindly adopted. I assume he asked you about his fate?"

"Yes. I wish I could've given Casimir better news."

Nurka grunted, "I should go talk to him," and stood up again. "You'll join Themba and I for dinner this evening," he decided, on no uncertain terms. "We've much to discuss, Red-mist."

Nurka slipped through the tent flaps leaving Rufus as troubled by the respect this terrorist had shown him as the intelligence he had exhibited. There had been no hint of hyena hysterics or purple-imperium madness like Noss. This chap might swig chunta, but he still knows exactly what he's about.

Rufus stared at the tent canvas. Chakaa Noss, old friend, are you really out there?

✦

Navigating ALPHA HQ's bland corridors on her way to attend the pressing matter of Tristan, Janoah was blown off course by a strange exclamation.

"Toggle, din dins!"

Following what could only be Rafe's chipper yet mighty voice down the hall, Janoah soon picked up his corona, which guided her out onto the HQ's central quadrangle, with its lavender rows and gravel paths surrounded on all sides by stern concrete cladding and cheerless long windows. Standing on the stairs overlooking the modest garden, awash in muted afternoon sunlight, Janoah found her Eisenwolf on his knees before the giant bee he'd pinched from Heath's flat.

"Toggle, din dins!" he urged, tapping a platter of honey with a ladle. "Come on! Din dins!"

The prim Nurse Meryl watched from one side, arms folded in doubt. "Rafe, I think bees are deaf."

"No, they feel sound with their hairs."

"Feel sound with their hairs?"

"Yeah."

Surprised at Rafe's confidence in the matter, Meryl guffawed gently, "Where'd you get that from?"

"Dunno. Some wolfess."

"Some wolfess?"

"Yeah."

Filing this 'some wolfess' under one of Rafe's admirers from amongst ALPHA HQ's wolfen staff, Meryl sat on the crunchy gravel and adjusted her dress accordingly. "Well it's not moving," she said, pawing some of the cool stones.

The nurse felt quite safe sitting down near the bee, for it was just resting there, trembling like a mono ticking over by the kerb. Rafe had physically lifted it out here to see if the outdoors would stir its soul, but so far 'Toggle' remained stubbornly unresponsive.

"Toooggle!" Rafe groaned impatiently. "Din dins!"

"Try a different name," Meryl suggested.

"I like Toggle. It sounds… right."

"Well its owners must've named it something. Where did you get it from exactly?"

It was then that Janoah descended the stairs and made herself known. "Having trouble?" she said, her boots crunching on the gravel.

Meryl made to get up; Janoah waved a paw to indicate there was no need, but the nurse did so anyway, as if she felt more vulnerable sitting in Janoah's presence than before some giant, venomous insect.

Rafe stood up too, all of him, and complained, "He's not eating, Jan."

"That's because *she's* pining, Rafe," Janoah emphasised, walking over and tidying the big wolf's brooch and cloak. "She misses her owners. Give her time; she'll come round when she's hungry enough."

Rafe scratched an enormous brown ear and said with a crafty smirk, "How'd you know it's a she? She could be a he!"

"Trust me; I married an etymologist."

"Y'what?"

"Bug-doctor," Janoah clarified, adding, "Rufus isn't just a pretty face, he knows a thing or two. Just not how to stay out of trouble."

Rafe nodded silently.

Walking around her massive Eisenwolf, Janoah took his nurse to one side. "How is he?" she whispered.

Meryl cupped her paws over her apron as she and Janoah walked clear of Rafe's keen earshot. "Erratic," she said, giving her patient an over the shoulder glance, "but healthy enough, despite a spike in blood-ash levels."

"He's definitely not himself today."

"What did he do last night? He must've exerted himself."

Janoah hummed cagily, "Somewhat."

"He brought in Howler Tristan didn't he?" Meryl guessed. "Don't deny it. Nobody else could've done it."

"I'm not denying anything, my dear Miss Stroud."

"Den Father Thorvald won't stand for it-"

"ALPHA's duty is clear. Is yours?"

Meryl scoffed, "Never clearer, but Tristan's like a son to Thorvald; everyone knows it. Whatever he's done the Alpha will have to let him go to keep the packs happy, so you may as well do it now to save yourself the embarrassment-"

"Tristan is a traitor!" Janoah snapped, whirling on Meryl via one heel.

Rafe glanced over, ears pricked.

"I put my own husband down the mines for his transgressions!" Janoah hissed. "I do not pick and choose according to my feelings or anyone else's!"

Meryl huffed triumphantly, "And yet you let that Bloodfang go earlier."

"Bloodfang?"

"Josef's furious about it. He's gone to Nikita. Linus I think I heard him say."

Janoah tipped her head back and smiled. "That young buffoon? He pitied some dodger that's all, so I let him go to keep the Bloodfangs sweet." The Prefect's chin dipped and her smile melted, "But Tristan's no buffoon, Meryl. He's been feeding information to THORN activists for years. He believes in tearing down the Republic!" Glancing Rafe's way, Janoah said, "Your only duty is Rafe's well-being. He needs to be at his best for the week ahead."

"Why?"

"Because the Pack Summit's upon us. Ulf help us all."

Meryl's eyes searched Janoah's inscrutable ruddy face for clues whilst she waited for the Prefect to elaborate.

"THORN and the conspirators will make a move," Janoah admitted, walking on. "We can't be sure how, but Rafe must be ready to stop them."

Strolling beside Janoah, Meryl took in the news. "He'll be going to the Summit, then?" she supposed, at length.

"In secret, yes. The Alpha himself is attending. Rafe will travel as part of his entourage, disguised as a Prefect; keep that under your apron whatever you do."

"Of course," Meryl professed, probing hopefully, "What about me?"

"What about you?"

"Perhaps I should come. Rafe may need me."

"That… might raise suspicion amongst the plotters."

"Suspicion? But they can't know who I am, surely. I'm nobody special outside of ALPHA-"

"You'd be surprised how deep the corruption runs," Janoah sniffed vaguely, looking around.

"You mean… there are conspirators in ALPHA?"

"Let's just say if certain quarters realise Rafe is at the Summit they might try and eliminate him. Failing that they might even use you against him."

Meryl stopped in her tracks, "Me?"

Janoah swivelled round, paws behind back, and smiled wryly at her, "Let's not be coy. You've nursed Rafe through the worst excesses of the rot for nigh on a year. Read him stories, fed him, bathed him; that's got to leave an impression on a young wolf."

Meryl tugged at her high collar and cravat. "Prefect, I swear nothing improper has ever-"

"Save it," Janoah dismissed, one paw raised. Placing that same paw on the nurse's shoulder, she implored her to, "Take care of our Eisenwolf, *however* you do it. Not for my sake, but all the innocent beasts that may depend on him. If it comes down to a fight, Rafe may be our last hope."

A flustered Meryl promised, "I'll do my best for him, but-"

"Oi, Meryl!" Rafe suddenly woofed from afar, "Look, look, look! Quick!"

At last, Toggle trundled over the gravel towards her new master and stuck her snout into the honey dish!

"Hahahaaaa! That's it, girl!" Rafe laughed, stroking the bee's furry black brow. "Nom nom nom."

Meryl tutted, "Look at him, the great big fool."

Janoah just smiled.

Not bidding the preoccupied Rafe farewell, Janoah left Meryl to deal with the Eisenwolf and his bee whilst she dealt with secret matters of state – who had the harder task being anyone's guess.

⁕

As Linus picked his way through the Common Ground he was surprised to be joined by a Politzi car in red and black Bloodfang livery, which pulled up alongside him in the same manner as that morning.

Toot! Toot!

And in the exact same manner, Werner Schwartz put the window down and offered the Howler a ride.

"Hop in, Linus. Don't argue, mate, I know ALPHA's given you the once over."

Well, almost the same manner. The hog sounded strangely assertive compared to his usual ingratiating self.

Every step Linus took sent part of him throbbing; his nose, his stomach, his ears, his pride, each sorer than the last, so without quarrel the young Howler opened the car door and slipped gingerly onto the seat.

"Thanks," he growled, unbuckling his hefty shield and tossing it on the back seat.

Werner pulled the car gently away. "Let's get you home before they change their mind."

"Actually I need to swing by-"

"Oh I wouldn't go back to the girls; ALPHA will be watching your every move now."

Linus's hot wolfen heart somersaulted into his mouth.

Mistaking the Howler's silence for confusion as oppose to restrained panic, Werner explained himself. "I'm Tristan's contact," he revealed freely, crunching gears and turning the wheel, sending his Politzi car hurtling down an alleyway in an effort to lose any would-be tail. "I was meant to meet Heath and the girls at the station and take 'em to a safe house," he went on, "but when I saw you get off the train with 'em I thought better of it and followed yer to see what yer did." The Hog looked Linus over, "I was pleasantly surprised when ALPHA arrested you. Seems to me you're on our side. Tristan certainly kept that quiet."

Linus scoffed, "I'm not on any side. It just sort of… happened."

Werner grunted soberly, "It's called a conscience, sir. We're all born with one, but the system beats it out of us." The hog nursed the wheel and sighed, "I've only lately started listening to mine again."

Wondering where this was headed, Linus thought he should make himself clear. "Look," he said, the sight of Tristan writhing on the rack plaguing his mind, "I just want to help Sara and Olivia get out of Lupa and back to Everdor. I don't want to get involved in anything else."

"Fair enough, lad."

Linus frowned beneath his helmet, "Lad?"

Werner beamed apologetically, "Sorry, sir. I'm fond of you, is all. Anyone not half my age is just a lad, even if they could put me through a wall with their imperious powers."

"I see. Well, I'd never put you through a wall, Werner."

"Glad to hear it, Howler."

After negotiating some traffic, Werner hazarded, "I, uh… I take it Tristan's been taken in?"

Linus waited a moment, "That mad cat Josef's racking him as we speak."

"So much for Lupan Law," Werner said, shaking his head and making his flabby, collar-riding jowls wobble. "That puts me in a pickle. If he talks I'll have to disappear again."

"What do you mean?"

"I fought in the civil war – on the losing side. Had to lay low for years afterwards, me and my old friends. Even now they'd dig out papers and throw my past back at me. Torture me. I'd sooner top meself this time."

"But the amnesty," Linus said. "The records were all destroyed, that was part of the peace agreement-"

"Nooo, lad!" Werner laughed, recoiling at the Howler's naivety. "Don't be daft. The packs got it all squirrelled away, and if they do, ALPHA definitely does!"

Linus looked away, "I don't believe it."

"Believe it!"

After a brief silence, Werner asked, "Does Tristan know where you took Heath n' the girls?"

Nursing his bruises, Linus seethed, "No. That's what Josef wanted to know. Luckily Janoah stepped in before he chucked me on the rack."

"Janoah?" Werner snorted. "She got you off the hook?"

Linus simply nodded.

"Why?"

"She owed me a favour; an old one."

Werner blinked disbelief from his beady eyes. "That wolfess is a mystery to me. She always was. She arrests her husband, right, yet gets some nobody Howler off the hook – no offence. What's she about, lad? I don't get it."

Linus had no answers, only questions. "What'll become of Tristan?"

Werner's snout twisted, "I dunno. If he admits nothing maybe they'll have to let him go; ALPHA still needs evidence to convince a jury of Elders… for now."

Linus watched the streets of Lupa pass by, citizens, shops, ash-streaked terraced houses. "Is he guilty of treason?" he asked, turning slowly to Werner. "Are you?"

The pink pig glanced back at the blonde wolf, "Would it stop you helping Heath and the girls if I were?"

"No."

Werner tapped his snout and sniffed.

Linus pressed the matter, "Why do you want to help Olivia anyway?"

"Why do you?"

Linus shrugged, "Because… she doesn't want to be a Howler, I think. I certainly don't want Josef to force her."

"Aye, if she stays here he'll force her all right. He'll make a right Howler out of her and probably more besides."

"You mean an Eisenwolf? You can say it."

Werner half-confirmed, "Tristan reckons Olivia's right powerful. When them wolfen ladies get the rot boy do they get it! Aye and all that comes with it. I've seen that little sprite Janoah blow Howlers twice her size into next week. She holds back to keep healthy, but believe me when she has to she can floor an army."

Linus could believe it. "Of course, the rot is sex-linked, like colour-blindness," he said. "Boys are more likely to develop it, but girls that do get it often express greater capacity to wield and tolerate imperium." He spread a paw at Werner, "But there's dozens of phenotypes, you know."

"Phenotypes?" the hog guffawed.

"Combinations of genes," the wolf explained.

Snorting, gear-changing bafflement.

The bookish Linus distilled matters further. "Genes are what we inherit from our parents; they determine eye colour, fur colour, everything. Some genes probably protect us from the rot, others predispose us to it. It's all in Heath's work. It's pioneering stuff, you should read it-"

"Lad lad lad, I dunno much about science, but whatever Olivia's got going on inside her, every Howler, Watcher and dare I say it Eisenwolf that never comes to pass makes the packs weaker and gives us citizens space to breathe, which can only be a good thing."

Linus said nothing to that – but then he was no mere citizen.

Suddenly Werner pulled over by the side of the road. "Listen," he said, glancing about, "I need to tell you the plan before we get to Riddle Den."

"Plan?"

"I might not get another chance before you have to leave. Stop me now if you want out. I won't blame yer. There's no shame in it."

Linus offered his tacit acceptance.

"All right then," Werner sniffed, shifting his bulk and nervously nursing the wheel, "this is what we're gonna do."

Chapter 34

"We'd better make camp," Gunnar Greystone said.

Uther stopped hacking at vines and squinted at the setting sun glinting through the forest canopy like imperium crystals. "What?" he woofed, pressing on. "There's an hour of daylight left, at least!"

"Yeah but all the nasties come out at night, mate," the yellow-cloaked Gunnar explained, casting his eyes over the foliage whilst puffing on the last dregs of an ember. "Best we settle down before then."

Uther stopped hacking a second time, "Whatcha mean, nasties?"

"Scorpions, centipedes, rove beetles."

"Spiders," Ivan added with intent, throwing Uther a merrily malicious look despite his obscuring helmet – it was all in those icy eyes.

Uther's white snout twitched accordingly, "Spiders?"

"Widow spiders, trapdoor spiders, Gunnar listed confidently, "net-casting spiders." Blowing ember vapours to the still evening air he said, "Luckily most of 'em sit still and wait for dinner to come to them, so if we make camp and keep a fire going we'll be all right-"

The Greystone suddenly clapped a brown paw to his thick wolfen neck, swatting the bravest of many midges buzzing about the party.

"Pesky blood-suckers aside," Gunnar laughed, wiping his paw off.

"I brought mosquito nets," Ivan revealed.

Gunnar was pleasantly surprised. "Nice one. And there was I starting to think you two townies didn't have a clue! Most city-folk don't."

"He doesn't," Ivan said effortlessly, referring to Uther.

Gunnar hiked an eyebrow, but declined to pass further comment.

"Yeah, well," Uther asserted, wagging a sword at Ivan, "at least I can find my way round Lupa blindfolded, not to mention function in civilised society like a *normal* wolf unlike a certain weirdo… so there."

The trio made camp, Ivan taking care of a fire whilst Gunnar constructed a shelter. Starting with bare branches lashed together in a triangular frame, Gunnar laid leafy branches on top to keep out the worst of any rain, before covering the entrance to the simple structure with the gauzy mosquito nets Ivan had promised him. Uther helped gather and cut branches, but was otherwise out of his depth.

"I need water," Ivan said, holding out his saucepan in a lacklustre fashion, "make yourself useful, Wild-heart; I can't leave this fire."

Uther snatched the pan. "Will do, Blade-prancer," he teased, making his way down hill to the stream they had been following.

Checking Uther had quite gone, Gunnar asked Ivan, "Why's he called Wild-heart if he dunno the first thing about the wilds?"

Blowing on his struggling fire, Ivan dodged the question, "You'd have to ask the hyenas."

"Yeah. Only, I heard a rumour it's *not* a hyena name; that Uther just made it up to impress beasts."

"I ignore jealous tongues."

A nod, "And what about your name, 'Blade-dancer'?"

After some time poking the fire, Ivan said dead-pan, "Oh, I made it up."

Gunnar frowned, then laughed. "Hah! Yeah, right."

As twilight fell, Gunnar watched the frustrated Ivan fuss with his pathetic embers a little while longer before he moseyed over and knelt opposite, ears pricked and eyes wide, like a cub eager to provide assistance.

Sensing the Greystone's tacit judgement regarding his own wild skills, Ivan excused lamely, "Wood's damp."

The great Blade-dancer had hardly justified his failure before Gunnar produced a silvery canister from his cloak pocket. Removing the lid with a satisfying pop he poured a little heap of sparkling yellow sand into his paw and quickly threw it into the base of the fire.

Foof!

Blinding white flames and burning heat erupted from the conflagration, illuminating the trees as if by daylight, before settling down again as a perfect, cheery campfire.

Gunnar popped the lid back on the canister and blew any remaining dust from his paw. "'Tis magic!"

"Flash powder," Ivan corrected, blinking a rippling after-image from his bleary eyes. "It's just ground-up yellow-imperium, isn't it?"

"Yeah, kinda. Did you two run out, or something?"

"Run out? We never had any. Never do."

"What?" Gunnar woofed. "Flaid gave Amael a case of yellow-imperium, didn't he?"

"Yes."

"So what's he done with it?"

"I've no idea. Sold it to help balance Riddle's books, I suppose; Ulf forbid he furnish his Howlers with extra equipment."

At length, Gunnar tossed the sarcastic Ivan his canister of flash powder. "Keep it," he whistled.

Surprised, Ivan rolled it over in his paws. "I couldn't."

"I've loads," Gunnar dismissed. "Call it a little gift. Least I can do. You Bloodfangs saved me life when I were bitten by that centipede."

"You have Rufus to thank for that."

"I know. Why do you think I volunteered for this?"

Ivan stared at Gunnar through the flames, then dipped his chin and gaze a little and emitted a grunt – what passed as approval from Blade-dancer, Gunnar supposed.

He watched Ivan gingerly pour a little powder into his palm, enough to flavour some chips if it were salt, and flick it into the fire in the somewhat haphazard manner of someone unsure.

Foof!

"Here," Gunnar said, raising a finger and taking a second canister of flash-powder from his backpack. "I'll show you another trick, mate."

Sprinkling a little powder on his palm he stood up and cast it not into the burning fire but the cold dusk air. In the same instant a spark of imperious plasma shot down his armoured arm and contacted the glittering cloud, igniting it in a dazzling flash.

"Clever," Ivan admitted blinkingly, half-blinded and somewhat impressed. "You could blind an opponent with that."

"Aye, 'tis all in the timing," Gunnar sniffed. "Try it."

Ivan rose to the challenge, literally standing up and garnishing his paw with some powder.

"Takes a bit of practice," Gunnar warned, as Ivan flicked a sparkling pawful into the air – no sooner had the words left his lips than, with a snap of plasma from Ivan's fingers, the cloud ignited.

Foof!

Sniffing assertively, Ivan blew residual ash from his palm.

Gunnar laughed, "Beginner's luck. Can you do it without fail, though, in the middle of a fight?"

Undoing his canister again, Ivan had another go.

Foof!

The mysterious flashes from camp reached Uther down by the stream, silently illuminating the great boughs of ancient trees arcing overhead like distant lightning, penetrating even his eyelids as he splashed cold water on his face.

"What're they playing at?" he mumbled, trying to see what was going on.

Drying his muzzle with a length of his cloak, Uther hurriedly dunked Ivan's saucepan in the stream with a mind to fly back and see what he was missing. As he lifted the pan from the water, however, his freezing fingers fumbled the grip and it splashed into the torrent to be swiftly carried downstream.

Cursing – for Ivan would kill him if he lost the pan – Uther traipsed after it, following the stream a few tens of feet before chancing a lunge into the dark, icy waters.

"Gotcha!" the Howler hissed, as if he'd nicked a criminal on the streets of Lupa.

Oh for the twisting alleys and vapour-filled bars of old Riddle District, the sodden Uther thought, trudging miserably back to shore, cloak dripping pathetically. Polluted and grey skied it may be, but you're never far from a drink, a warm bed and good company, whatever the weather.

Whipping off and wringing out his near-indestructible imperium-weave mantle, Uther shook his head and grumbled to himself. "What are you, homesick or summat? Puh! Pull yourself together Wild-heart."

Adrift in his mental meanderings, the prey failed to notice the two enormous globular spheres amidst the foliage above. Six other smaller spheres dotted the hairy brown carapace that framed them, eyes one and all, staring, unblinking, lidless as they were. Uther and the forest roundabout were reflected in their smooth obsidian surface, distorted into a grotesque, multitude of warped parodies.

Four of the creature's eight long, deceptively delicate-looking brown legs were slowly, painstakingly extended, like a great mechanical claw. The silk strung between the legs, at first nothing but a saggy collection of tangled threads like bloomers on a washing like, was pulled taught as the four feet spread and took shape, forming a perfect net of concentric rectangles.

The trap was set.

The monster's four other legs clung to silken lines running hither and thither between the stiff boughs, the thick strands shimmering in the twilight like spun glass. It repositioned itself; moved lower, closer. Mandibles twitched with anticipation and fangs dripped with venom as the prey-item stirred below, every movement stimulating instincts in the mindless predator, triggering responses, firing synapses, until a crescendo of signals tipped its mere ganglion of a brain over the edge. The legs spread ever wider, the net broader still, lower and lower, closer and closer!

Another flash from the camp; Uther glanced over – at one and the same time he caught something out the corner of his wolfen eye, looming over him, large and white and growing larger and whiter.

"What the?"

Uther looked up just in time to see the beautiful geometric net and a collection of shining black eyes beyond. Before he could make sense of it all the net spread wide and descended upon him like the judgemental paw of Ulf, pinning him to the ground!

"Oofaaagh!"

No sooner had Uther hit the ground than the dazed wolf left it behind, hoisted into the air, tumbling head over foot, his limbs tangled in indistinct collections of fuzzy white ropes.

It came to him then – this is spider web!

"Ivaaaaaan!"

Swords, swords, swords! Kicking and squirming, Uther scrabbled for the swords nestled at his thighs as he was smothered in an ever-tightening ball of silk. The spider's long limbs whooshed by and with each pass laid on another untidy sheet of the soft, yielding and yet un-breaking bonds.

The silk clung to Uther's furry forelimbs as he tried to extract a sword from a sheath and angle it through the organic cloth. The constant, juddering, tumbling motion, one moment the right way up, the next upside down, disorientated him to the point of utter confusion, but the swords were at his hips and he focused on them.

Get them out, Uther, get them out!

"Ivaaan!" he screamed, expecting any second the bite of death to come tearing through the silk and into his flesh, injecting him with paralysing venom, as Linus had said. "Ivan! Help me you son of a maggot! Gaaagh!"

Sword! Free? Yes!

Uther jammed his trembling right paw armed with his quivering right sword into the silk and heaved it to and fro. The threads barely gave ground until the Howler resorted to releasing a surge of imperious energy, as much now in this desperate moment as he'd ever called upon in his short life. His sword sparked with arcs of plasma and the web flamed and retreated before the burning blade as Uther ran it up towards his grimacing white face.

Come on… come ooon! Ulf almighty, please!

Suddenly the flaming silken cocoon reached some critical structural failure and a yelping Uther tumbled out of the spider's silken trap. He stopped short of the ground, dangling upside-down by his legs amidst a cats-cradle of smouldering threads. What silk remained was clinging to his armoured legs, the thick strands snagged on rivets, belts and plates.

"Gaaaaghfffgh!"

The spider descended coolly after the kicking, twirling, snarling Uther, who began to slash up at the stubborn web. The most enduring strands were extraordinarily strong and every one took several hefty chops, but each that broke lowered the panting Howler still further to the ground, further from the spider's terrible face.

Not far enough. The spider was on Uther again, the legs teasing more silk forth from its bulbous rear-end and starting the parcelling process over with mechanical patience.

"Ivaaaaan!" Uther cried, his strength and will failing as the broad ropes of web closed in a second time, rolling him up as before, pinning his arms to his sides. "Grrrrrfffaaaagh!"

A flash, a bang!

Ka-crack!

Uther's stomach rose into his chest – he was falling! Within half a second the soft grassy bank rose to meet his body and with a loud exhale of air the winded wolf rolled down to the shore, the icy water shooting up his nose.

"Gagh! Pleh! Caagh!"

Someone grabbed him and tore at the silk, removing the springy strands from about his face.

It was Ivan.

"You all right?" the Blade-dancer asked. "Are you bitten?"

"Get it off, get it off!" Uther yowled, writhing in the organic bonds like a wolf tied up in a potato sack. "Get me out of this, for Ulf's sake!"

Taking Uther's liveliness as a definitive 'no' to the bitten question, Ivan ran his fine rapier up inside the silk and slowly cut his comrade free without resorting to wasting precious imperious energy. He could feel Uther shaking like a leaf

"It's all right," Ivan soothed, "Calm down. It's over."

"Th-th-thump m-mmm-me!" Uther stammered, for the first time Ivan had ever heard. Wild-heart craned his neck to look up the bank. "Is it d-d-dead?"

Ka-crack!

A second flash and bang from Gunnar Greystone's rifle led Ivan to conclude, "Yes."

Once Uther was freed of the main cocoon he sprung to his feet and set about ripping the remaining fine strands from his body, brushing down his arms and chest and neck and face, wildly clapping paws here and there and everywhere.

"My back, do my back!" he begged, dancing on the spot.

Ivan reluctantly brushed Uther's dark bluish back, but insisted that, "There's nothing there."

"I can feel it!"

"It's just web!" Ivan scoffed. "By Ulf half our clothes are made of silk."

"Yeah, from fuzzy caterpillars, not that thing!" Uther spat, as a shiver visibly crawled down his spine. "Yeeeuch!"

Leaving Uther to pull himself together and brush himself free of imagined fibres, Ivan climbed the bank to join Gunnar by his kill. The Greystone was standing by his impressive conquest; a brown spider the size of a car, lying on its back with its twitching legs still curling creepily inwards.

"Net-casting spider," Gunnar sniffed calmly, reloading his rifle and looking up at the trees. "They attack from above."

"Yes… I know," Ivan said.

Gunnar peered down at Uther, "He all right?"

"Fine."

"Looks shaken up to me."

"Yes, well… he's not fond of anything with more than two legs."

Gunnar flicked his dying ember away and said, "He should try an imperial centipede on for size. They just keep on coming. I speak from painful experience."

Grunting, Ivan trudged down the bank and caught Uther gingerly dousing his right paw in the stream.

"Are you hurt?" Ivan demanded.

"It's nothing," Uther seethed.

Ivan knelt down and grabbed his comrade's wrist with his usual lack of social tact. Expecting shrapnel from Gunnar's rifle bolt to have gone through Uther's paw, he was relieved to find his dark pads to be blistered and his fur singed, not in any way bleeding.

"Imperium burn," Ivan diagnosed flatly.

"I overdid it cutting my way out," Uther explained, forcing a tiny, uneasy guffaw, "I panicked."

"There's no such thing as overdoing it when you're fighting for your life," Ivan insisted kindly, patting Uther's sturdy back. "Come on, I'll patch you up."

✦

Noss took a draught of green vapours before passing the mint-flavoured ember across to Madou sitting on the bunk opposite. Madou stared longingly at the smouldering stick of relief, but shook his head and dipped his chin.

"Take it," Noss insisted.

"It's your last one, my Prince-"

"You need it more than me after a day down that hole. I'll get some more from Tack tomorrow."

With a trembling paw, Madou plucked the glowing ember from his Prince's fingers and turned it to his own lips. The heady vapours filled his lungs and rushed through his blood, dulling the rot pains nibbling at his bones in an instant. His paw ceased trembling even as Noss watched him, which made the prince smile.

"Better?"

"Much, thank you," Madou puffed, trying to pass it back but being waved away. There was no point arguing with the prince of the Four Winds, so Madou resigned himself to suffer his munificence.

Madou soon noticed the low-ranking Zozizou staring down at him from the bunk overhead – staring at his ember anyway. With a guilty sigh Madou passed it up to his puny cousin, who immediately and greedily vacuumed up the minty vapours like a beast twice his size, burning through what remained of the ember in seconds and lighting up half the cabin by its green glow. By the time it occurred to the coughing Zozizou to offer the ember back to Madou it had been reduced to a pathetic stump.

"Keep it," Madou sighed, his annoyance lost on Zozizou if not Noss, who chuckled heartily as he eased back on his bunk, paws tucked behind his mighty neck.

Madou checked out his new gang for tomorrow; Prince Noss, his cousin, Helmut and Tomek, the last two being asleep in their bunks or drifting that way. They would also be joined by a hog, a cat and wolf whose names Madou hadn't really caught yet. They were from Noss's original gang and the prince had no intention of abandoning them. However, a gang of eight was too big, five being the limit set by Gelb's officials, so it had been decided by Noss to split everyone into two groups of four with him leading his original crew, long-dubbed Mosquito, whilst Madou took charge of Rufus's old Scarab gang. The two teams would mine in the same spot and share their spoils, hopefully bringing home enough imperium to keep the hogs satisfied.

For now.

However, the Lupan Summit approached. Out there in the real world THORN was making ready to strike. Nurka, Themba, their ally Amael, and doubtless many a disgruntled wolf and hog stirred all across Lupa. Soon the clarion call would sound!

But, as the old regime collapsed, what would happen here in Gelb? Would the Warden free all the prisoners, execute them, or simply carry on as before? Surely Nurka would demand the release of all hyena inmates, just as he would the tribes, but might Amael keep them in bondage and use them as a bargaining chip? What side would the Warden take in any disagreement?

Madou felt so helpless.

"We'll get out of here before the storm breaks," Noss insisted, settling down to sleep. "Don't worry, Madou."

"But how?"

"I've a feeling. Now, go to sleep, warrior."

The word of a Prince was final. Madou lay on his woefully thin mattress and silently prayed to the Wind, Erde and Sky to see him through these final most dangerous days, so that he might meet Nurka and Themba again in this life.

⁂

Given a short spell in the waiting room smouldering away in every context, Janoah was sent through by the secretary. Discarding her ember, she marched down the stark corridor and after a preparatory breath knocked on the double doors to the Grand Prefect Chamber.

"Come in," someone beckoned sternly – not the Alpha's airy baritone but Nikita's hefty accent.

Surprised, Janoah entered with outward confidence.

Sure enough the Alpha's chair was occupied not by ALPHA's premier Prefect, but by his second. He was flanked by Grand Prefects Horst and Duncan. Silvermane sat on the end, officially their equal, but unofficially beneath them for his relative youth and inexperience.

The big mottle-furred Nikita bade Janoah to sit with a simple gesture. "Please," he said, pronouncing 'Plez'.

They're after me, Janoah thought, saluting and forcing them all to salute back whether they liked her or not. Her mind raced as she took her seat. The Alpha's indisposed arranging his trip to the Summit, so now's their chance to nail me without going through him. I see how it is.

She glanced at Horst. That flabby excuse for a Howler's had your number all along, he's a lost cause. What about Duncan? He's friendly, but what've they told him? The amiable black wolf looked unusually solemn today. What's Doctor Josef said about me? That blasted cat will pay for this! At least Silvermane's on your side – Ah, but he's got to watch his back. Look at him shuffling in his seat, squirming under pressure, checking his pocket watch. His career comes first and to protect it he'll let you go, you always knew that.

That left the unreadable Nikita, sitting in the middle, the epitome of calm. What's his agenda? Is he just covering for the Alpha or does he want rid of me?

"Prefect, you set prime suspect free this morning," Nikita said, fighting his thick Steppes inflection as ever. "You do this before Doctor Josef finish interrogation. Why?"

"Prime suspect, sir?" Janoah woofed. "I haven't let Tristan Eisbrand go. He's being racked as we speak."

"I mean Howler Linus, of Bloodfang–"

"She knows who you meant, Nikita," Horst interjected, looking Janoah over with disgust. "She's feigning ignorance, as usual. I'm well-versed in her tricks."

"You wrong me, Grand Prefect Horst," Janoah defended. "I was merely unaware that this Bloodfang cub had anything to do with the breaking of THORN, which is my one and only concern this side of the Pack Summit."

Glancing sideways at Horst, Nikita explained, "Doctor Josef believes Linus aided the escape of criminals; criminals I issue warrant for and you overturn."

Janoah guffawed gently, "Not at all, sir. We interrogated Linus and found his account of events credible."

"You didn't rack him," Horst pointed out.

"No. What would be the point of that, Grand Prefect?"

"To prise the truth from him! What else? This act of incompetence will fool nobody, Prefect; you've gone too far in your wanton defiance this time."

"I'm not in the habit of wantonly and *illegally* racking every wolf I arrest, Grand Prefect," Janoah explained. "If that's 'defiance', then I stand guilty as charged."

"Doctor Josef says–"

"Respectfully, Grand Prefect Horst, I wouldn't put too much faith in what Josef Grau says,"

Janoah interrupted, so politely as to be allowed to continue. "I've known that cat a *long* time and believe me he can't stand not getting his own way. He knows his imperious science, but like most cats is a proud, petty creature who will waste valuable time to get revenge over the smallest infraction." Janoah continued, "Fact is, Howler Mills acted on Bloodfang soil and was carrying out his duty, nothing more. I couldn't move against him even if I didn't believe him, which I do. He wasn't protecting the criminals, he was taking the afflicted wolfess in for his own pack, she merely eluded him."

Silvermane checked his pocket watch, as if he were waiting for something, only putting it away again when Nikita looked at him funny.

Sensing by Horst's silence that she was gaining the upper paw, Janoah pressed her defence. "Gentlebeasts, the Summit approaches and ALPHA's future is going to be decided by the Den Fathers. They could clip our wings, or even disband us altogether. Then where would Lupa be? Back to the bad old days of rampant corruption and greed, that's where. The last thing we should be doing is needlessly antagonising the-"

"It's not for you to dictate to us ALPHA's policy!" Horst growled. "Admit it, Prefect; you were helping an ex-comrade get off the hook."

"I've no love for the Bloodfangs, sir."

"Oh really? Yet you phone Riddle Den all the time!"

"Am I to understand I'm being spied upon?"

"Inquiries were made; the operators have testified you ring through to Riddle regularly. Explain that."

Janoah dipped her chin and did so, "I'm still married to Rufus, Grand Prefect. I've a duty to my husband as well as ALPHA."

"Indeed!" Horst blustered. "Yet Rufus has been in Gelb for two months; *still* you call Riddle Den!" The Grand Prefect looked down his snowy muzzle at Janoah, "How do you account for that?"

"I've merely been arranging to take charge of my husband's possessions since his arrest, and… initiating divorce proceedings, as the Alpha instructed me to. It's a lengthy process."

Picking up a sheet of paper Nikita said, "I believe you do not need to be proceeding further in your divorce, Prefect. You are already rid of Rufus by, as they say, default."

"What do you mean?" Janoah demanded, forgetting herself.

Nikita passed the paper across to the Prefect and clasping his paws together on the long table said, "Howler Rufus was executed yesterday morning."

Janoah felt the floor collapse under her, felt her stomach rise into her chest. The Grand Prefects vanished from her vision, replaced by a void of inconsequence. They didn't matter now. All she saw was the death warrant trembling in her grasp, signed and dated in red.

No, it couldn't be.

Slowly, painfully, Janoah's fingers crushed the paper, denying its existence. "There… there must be some mistake. That's not supposed to happen-"

"No mistake," Nikita assured her, adding, "My sympathies, Prefect, it was… beyond ALPHA's control."

Horst had no such compunctions. "It seems Rufus carried on in Gelb as he had in Lupa, thinking he's above the law! A thief and a vagabond to the end-"

Whop!

Silvermane thumped a paw on the tabletop. "A little respect, if you will, sir!" he chided.

"For a criminal, Silver?" Horst replied derisively.

"For *any* fallen wolf," the youngest grand Prefect clarified, "and those they leave behind. Rufus was a great Howler, once. Pray we don't stray as he did."

"I do not need prayers to a non-existent entity to guard *my* integrity!" Horst snorted, breaking out an ember. Puffing confidently away he looked to Duncan; the big black wolf was looking down and to one side. Nikita too seemed to be suffering a bout of awkwardness, chin dipped and thumbs twiddling.

It was only when Janoah's grief-tinged sniffs reached Horst's ears that he realised the cause of their discomfort.

"By Ulf," the flabby wolf marvelled, removing his ember from his wobbling jowls, "is she crying now?" He leant forward, "Do you think tears will distract us from your misconduct, Prefect Janoah?"

"F-fff-forgive me," Janoah snuffled. "It's come as a shock, that's all. I'm perfectly all right."

Horst remained unmoved regardless. "You will go to Riddle Den and you will re-arrest Howler Linus immediately, is that clear?" he growled.

Janoah stayed firm. "I believe that… w-www-would be a mistake. It would only antagonise relations-"

"These are your orders, you arrogant wolfess!" Horst bellowed, rapping the tabletop so vigorously his multiple medals danced on his chest. "You will carry them out or be dismissed from ALPHA in disgrace, if not fed to the ants like your husband before you!"

"No!" Janoah shrieked, clasping at her chest and bending double to stay her heart from being ripped away. "They didn't! They couldn't! Not like that! Not my Rufus!"

"What? Didn't you know? That's how they do it in Gelb. They're very old-fashioned."

"Ahohohooooow, nooooo!"

Silvermane rose. In silence and watched by all he marched around the table, physically pulled Janoah to her feet and shepherded the near-collapsed wolfess from the chamber.

Once the door had closed and Janoah's howling had faded, Horst rolled back in his creaking new-materials chair. "That fool, Silver," he derided. "She's got him wrapped around her little finger. A few tears and he falls at her knees. Well, that won't work on us!"

Duncan grumbled quietly, "That was a low-blow, Horst."

"One cannot stoop lower than her!" Horst countered, prodding the tabletop. "That wolfess has no love for ALPHA or our ideals. All she craves is power and she'll do anything to get it. Silver doesn't see it, he's dazzled by her wit, but I am not."

"Och! But tae break the news tae her like that."

"She needed to be told," Nikita grunted, adding, "Better than reading it in paper." He moved on, addressing Horst, "This wolfess Josef was trying to get hold of, is she true Eisenwolf candidate, or am I being made fool of here by Josef?"

Horst blew a vapour ring. "Who knows? But do you know what I think? I think Janoah was happy to let Linus get rid of the competition," he said matter-of-factly. "I think he might've even intercepted the girl and murdered her on Janoah's orders."

"Murdered her?" Nikita scoffed.

"Yes. Think about it. Janoah's got an Eisenwolf in her pocket, a completely loyal killing machine she could turn loose on anyone… even us."

"Och!" Duncan woofed. "Come on, now!"

"It's true!" Horst insisted. "She doesn't want anyone else to find another Eisenwolf and threaten her power, that's why she obstructed Josef. Arrest Howler Linus and rack him, Grand Prefect Nikita, he'll soon sing like a cricket in heat – if the girl is alive he'll know where she went-"

"Niet," Nikita disagreed in his native tongue.

"Pardon?"

"No. You must let this go, Horst."

"But-"

"The Alpha has much to do and cannot be disturbed by these internal squabbles! Janoah will go to him to get her way, believe me, and she's right, we cannot provoke the Bloodfangs so close to summit. Is bad for Adal's negotiations."

"Yes… yes of course."

Nikita shuffled some papers. "Go tell Janoah the good news," he said, clearing his throat. "We will leave her little Bloodfang friend alone... for now."

"Me?" Horst woofed, his ember falling into his lap.

"Yes. You pressed her, you will let her down."

"But *you* gave Josef his warrant, Nikita-"

"I am representing the Alpha here. I cannot personally give way to a Prefect Captain. You must take this fall."

"But I can't! Not after all that. I'll look ridiculous."

"Swallow your pride, Horst. Is not so difficult."

"Grand Prefect Nikita, please don't make me humiliate myself in front of that… that-"

"Oh for crying out loud, Ah'll do it!" Duncan groaned, throwing his paws up in the face of Horst's blubbering. Slamming his chair under the table and proffering a tiny salute he took his leave, "Excuse me, sir."

Nikita saluted gratefully back, "Duncan."

Striking through the double doors and down the hall, Duncan found Silvermane standing over Janoah in the waiting room. The wolfess sat knock-kneed in a chair weeping into a kerchief whilst Silvermane nursed one of her shoulders with a paw. It was a pitiable sight.

Entering the waiting room, Duncan whipped a finger at the on-looking secretary, indicating for her to leave. The baffled secretary saluted and vacated the room via the nearest door.

"Ah'm sorry for your loss, Prefect," Duncan said, walking over to Janoah, paws tucked behind him. "Ah should tell ye, ALPHA has nae power over what happens at Gelb. It's run by a wolf appointed by the Den Fathers. Nae even the Alpha himself has any say. All we do is bring forth the evidence, any punishment is still in the paws of the packs."

"Yes, I-I-I know," Janoah heaved, regaining some semblance of composure. "Thank you."

Duncan nodded a little. He glanced at Silvermane, then delivered his message. "It's been decided tae leave that Bloodfang lad alone. So don't worry about all that."

"Linus?" Silvermane clarified.

"Aye, that's the one."

"Why? Horst wanted him racked a minute ago."

"Nikita wants tae keep everyone sweet whilst he's in charge," Duncan said, proffering a disarming smile, "and nae bother the Alpha with 'internal squabbles'."

Silvermane checked his pocket watch. "It's a little late for that, I'm afraid."

"Oh aye?"

It was then that the door the secretary had exited through swung open, injecting a small, if robust brown and white wolf into the waiting room. He was cloaked in black and sported a red-imperium medal beneath his brooch – the Imperium Heart.

Silvermane and Duncan turned smartly to him and saluted ALPHA style.

"My Alpha," they said, in near-unison.

Janoah fought to stand and salute. "My Alpha," she said resolutely.

The Alpha saluted back and strode over to them all, assessing the situation on the way. "What's the problem, Silver?" he demanded.

"Nothing, my Alpha; the situation has been resolved."

"Resolved!" the Alpha woofed, trailing off as he noticed Janoah's teary face, "I'm glad to… hear it. Prefect, whatever's the matter?"

Janoah dipped her chin.

"Rufus Bloodfang is dead, my Alpha," Silvermane volunteered on her behalf. "Prefect Janoah is understandably distressed-"

"Dead?"

"Yes, my Alpha."

The Alpha glanced at Duncan; though Silvermane and Janoah knew Rufus had been sent to Gelb on a mission, Duncan did not, and could not, know.

"But it's only been two months," the Alpha said. "That's nothing to a wolf like him. I thought he'd make it."

Silvermane explained, "I regret to say he was executed, my Alpha… by ant."

"You're sure?"

A nod.

The Alpha blinked as he digested the news, but remained otherwise composed. "I see," he said, turning away and strolling about the room, paws tucked behind him. "I knew Gelb was harsh but… I thought such practices had passed into the history books," he sighed, looking to Janoah. "Prefect, you can be sure I'll raise this act of savagery during the Pack Summit. Such a wantonly cruel execution is hardly the mark of a civilised society anymore. If a beast must die for his crimes, let it be by the sword or the pistol, and his body returned to his family for proper rites. For what it's worth you have my sympathies."

Janoah dipped her chin, "Thank you, my Alpha. You're most kind."

"You should take some time away from your duties-"

"No!" Janoah barked, adding quieter, "No thank you, my Alpha. Not this side of the Pack Summit. Lives are depending on all of us."

"I see. Are you sure you can carry on?"

"Absolutely. I… I would rather work than dwell on it."

The Alpha nodded, "Very well, Prefect," and turned to the others. "Is that all, gentlebeasts?"

"Yes, my Alpha," Silvermane confirmed. "My apologies for disturbing you."

"Not at all, Silvermane. If you've no need of me I'll return to my negotiations. Good evening."

With a salute the Alpha was gone again, passing as swiftly as a spring shower.

The Alpha's sympathies couldn't wash away Janoah's hatred and sadness. She collapsed back into the chair, wishing the ground would swallow her up.

"I always knew it might end this way," she said blandly, adding with a false chuckle, "Rufus knew it too. We made that quite clear to him, didn't we Silvermane?"

Worried Janoah might reveal in front of Duncan that Rufus's arrest and downfall had been staged, Silvermane made a surreptitious cutting motion to his throat and growled with intent. "You should go to your quarters and rest, Prefect; you've had a trying day. I'll speak to the Alpha about what's happened later and see what else he has to say about it. All right?"

"Yes," Janoah said wearily, "Yes, of course."

Glancing at Duncan, Silvermane helped Janoah from the chair. They didn't take two steps towards the door before the secretary Duncan had dismissed entered with a small brown envelope. Saluting all present she cleared her throat and presented the envelope to Janoah.

"A telegram for you, Prefect."

Janoah waved it away, "Leave it on my desk, for Ulf's sake."

"It's marked urgent, marm," the secretary insisted, adding in a questioning manner, "Perhaps it's something to do with what's happened?"

Passing the secretary a sideways look, Janoah snatched the envelope and tore it open. Unfurling the paper within she read the simple message at a glance before Silvermane could peek.

'HE'S ALIVE. YOUR EMPEROR.'

Janoah immediately screwed it up.

"What is it?" Silvermane asked.

"Rubbish, sir," Janoah dismissed, walking briskly to the door, the old bounce in her gait returning. "An unreliable informant," she explained. "I'm… going to collect Rufus's things from Riddle Den. I may as well get it over with."

⁂

"I can't believe you! How could you be so stupid?"

"I thought you'd be pleased! By Ulf, do you want me to put him back?"

"Of course I don't!"

"Well then!"

Janoah had to break out an ember before she broke Amael's neck. Puffing clouds of spent imperium like Rafe in his iron suit, she marched around Riddle Den's Elder Chamber gathering her thoughts and composing herself at this dangerous time.

"What about Ivan and Uther?" she realised, whirling on the seated Amael.

Reclined in his chair behind the table, Elder Amael spread his grey paws, "What about them?"

"They're doing this for Rufus, not you! They think they're killing Vito to make you Den Father so you can get him out! That was the deal you struck with them."

"So I've got Rufus out early. Those two don't need to know this side of doing their job. I couldn't get word to them anyway; they could be anywhere in Everdor."

Janoah shook her head, "They won't forgive you for using them, Amael."

Amael huffed, "They'll have to. I'll be in charge of Lupa by the time they get back – *if* they get back."

"I see. Is this how you treat loyal wolves?"

"Loyal? Don't make me laugh, Jan. They're going to murder their Den Father. Some loyalty!"

"It's for the greater good-"

"You just said yourself it's for Rufus," Amael corrected bitterly. "For their love of *him*, their master, it has nothing to do with 'greater goodness', even less me." He poured himself a stiff drink and snorted, "Ivan looks at me the same way he would a tick in his fur." Then, knocking brandy back the, he gulped and exhaled, "He's a strange one."

"Don't you see? You've justified his attitude by going behind his back!" Janoah scoffed. "He'll never forgive you."

Amael said nothing to that.

Janoah sighed and sat opposite him. "Fine, so Rufus is with Nurka. Now what're we do?"

"Nothing. The hyenas will look after him until we're in control of the city and he can return to Lupa safely. He'll be right at home in the meantime, faffing around in the wilds with those barbarians. Right?"

"I imagine."

"And on his return he'll have his expedition to wherever he wants to go. Isn't that what you want for him? What you've pestered me for all this time?"

Janoah nodded a little, "Yes."

"Well then! Don't complain."

Amael watched Janoah for a while, smouldering away, rubbing her upper arm with her free paw.

"I'm… sorry if I scared you," Amael said, just about squeezing an apology past his pride. "His execution had to look genuine. Rufus was told what to expect, the Warden made things quite clear, but I couldn't tell anyone else."

Janoah took a deep breath and exhaled, "Well, you certainly fooled me."

Amael smiled, "And through your reaction everyone else. Now, when I present Rufus alive and well, his every admirer will fall at my feet in gratitude. He has the love of the little beasts and the hyenas, not to mention half the learned beasts in Lupa. His endorsement will go a long way towards maintaining peace in the new order."

"You're not the dullard you look," Janoah chuckled.

Amael frowned a moment, then laughed heartily.

Sharing a giggle, Janoah slowly let her mirth die away and cocked her head to one side. She seemed to have something on her mind still.

"What's wrong?" Amael enquired.

"Nothing."

"I can see it on your face. You can't fool old Balbus."

"I thought you weren't 'old', Elder."

Another chuckle and another drink.

Janoah waited a while before declaring afresh, "No more secrets."

Amael gulped his second brandy, "Secrets?"

"I can't help you if you surprise me at every turn and leave me out of your affairs," Janoah explained. "Not as much as I would like, anyway."

"You do enough."

"I could do more, so much more!"

"It's for your protection, Jan," Amael said, dipping his chin a little. "This isn't over yet. Not by a long shot. ALPHA could still march me out of here and rack me, and Ulf knows what I might say. They've arrested one of us already. He's low down on the ladder, but still… it's a worry for us all."

Janoah frowned, "Who?"

"Tristan Eisbrand."

"Ah… Yes, I saw him."

"Which one of those ALPHA bastards snatched him off the street? Was it that fat maggot Horst?"

"No idea," Janoah lied, shrugging. "I didn't realise he was one of yours. If I'd known I could've warned him."

Amael grunted.

Janoah stood up and climbed clean over the Elder Table to sit in Amael's lap. "See what I mean?" she cooed, stroking his furrowed brow. "It's time you let me in, Amael. By Ulf the hyenas know more about your plans than I do. Those barbarians coming before me; how is that fair?"

"Janoah-"

"If you fall they'll come for me anyway. I'll *want* them to come for me, because there'll be no point continuing to live in a Lupa without a future. You're its future. You and I and the reforms we'll bring. If Rufus is denied his expedition thousands will continue to die. If he and others like him can at least *try* for a cure there is hope. You're our only hope, Amael. That's why I follow you."

"Not love, then?" he grumbled humorously.

"Of course love. And if you love me you'll let me in, and prove to me I'm not some pawn in your games."

Another unreadable grunt. After an age spent searching Janoah's ruddy face, her green eyes, her wry smile, Amael poured a third brandy and sniffed, "It's not pretty."

"Pretty?"

"What must be done. To be honest, I didn't tell you because I thought… I thought…."

"What?" Janoah urged.

Amael looked up at her. "That I might lose you, Jan."

"Lose me? Oh Amael-"

"Promise me you won't turn your back on me for what I must do. I take no pleasure in the method, but it's the only way, the *only* way!"

"Stop it, you silly beast," Janoah tutted, kissing Amael's forehead like that of a naïve cub. "You forget that I was in the war as well. The things I saw, the friends I lost; I've the stomach of a wolf, not a wolfess."

Amael nodded, relieved somewhat.

Cupping his jaw in both paws Janoah implored, "Share your burden. Tell me… everything."

⁕

Clearing his throat, Rufus gulped his drink by lantern light, thumping his furry grey chest a few times to help both it and Nurka's news to go down.

It was official, THORN's plan was to kill the Den Fathers, and anyone else at the Summit, with black-imperium.

"That was my reaction too," Nurka said, sitting cross-legged, paws on knees, the tent canvas flapping overhead. "I wanted no part of Amael's proposal, until I realised the method of killing doesn't shift the guilt, it's still killing." The hyena glanced sideways across the tent to big Themba, who was staring always at Rufus, as if trying to penetrate his soul with those purple eyes. "They shot Themba's family," Nurka went on, "and tipped them into a pit. They sanction the murder of countless other hyenas every day, by sword and silent starvation. Little by little your Den Fathers are chipping away at the tribes whilst presenting a noble front to the Lupan populace with endless propaganda. When I remember what your people are doing to mine, Red-mist, my guilt subsides."

Rufus nodded and looked into his drink, before quaffing the lot. It was some kind of alcoholic fruit mix, a hyena delicacy apparently. The wolf didn't much care right now, it could've been mono engine oil and he still would've knocked it back to steady his nerve.

Wiping his ruddy muzzle he said, "As you say one death is much like another. But, must they all die? They're not all bad. Thorvald is a good wolf and my friend. I can't believe he knows the extent of hyena suffering-"

"Maybe not, but do you think he'll let bygones be bygones after we murder his fellow Den

Fathers?" Nurka interjected flatly. "No, they *all* have to go. Amael Balbus has to be the only wolf of rank left. Whilst the other packs are flailing around voting in their new leaders and squabbling, Amael will assume power with the natural authority granted a Den Father and release the tribes."

Rufus put his cup down by the fire. "But he's just an Elder, Nurka. He's not above the hundreds of other Elders running Lupa. They're all equal beneath the Den Fathers."

"Amael's arranged to become your pack's Den Father just before the Summit commences."

As well Rufus knew; Janoah had said as much, just not, "How?"

Nurka shrugged, "That is his business. I didn't probe. I assume it involves 'removing' your current leader, Den Father Vito, a notorious, how do you say it… 'drooler'?"

Rufus dipped his chin.

There was a brief quiet, broken only by the odd chirp of a distant desert cricket.

"How will you deliver the black-imperium, exactly?" Rufus risked asking.

Nurka huffed, "You'll see."

"It's tricky stuff. Do you even know what you're-"

"Wolves are not the only beasts who read imperiology," the hyena chief interjected, without a doubt insulted. He continued, more politely, "In fact I read many of your works growing up, Red-mist, you and your friend Professor Heath."

Rufus beamed, "I'm honoured."

A second prickly silence; this felt a dangerous game.

"Strange Amael didn't tell you any of this," Themba needled, supping his drink but staring always at Rufus even as he tipped his head back. "It's almost like you've got nothing to do with him."

Rufus batted him away, "As I said, Themba, I don't. All I want from Amael is my expedition, and all he wants from me is endorsement. I'll stand by him and wave to the little beasts for a week or two if it'll help settle things down, but then I want to be about my work."

"Finding a 'cure'?" the mighty hyena mocked. "You cannot cure that which the gods inflict on us, save through righting what they decide are wrongs."

"We'll never know if we never try."

"Beasts have long dreamt of it. All have failed."

"Beasts have long dreamt of flying too, Themba, and of late we've discovered a way. How many beasts jumped to their doom with wings tied to their arms before we started putting working dirigibles up? Don't confuse failure with lack of progress."

"Those ridiculous balloons?" Themba scoffed. "They are an affront to nature! Beasts mock the Sky, trying to match his grace."

Rufus spread a paw, "I find imitation to be the sincerest form of flattery-"

"We wish you luck in your endeavours, Red-mist," Nurka rasped, suddenly closing down the subject. Snatching the gourd of fermented fruit nearby, he topped up his cup and downed it in one. Turning to Themba he said, "It's decided then. If Prince Noss is in Gelb we must get him out before we strike."

"It's risky, chief," Themba grumbled. "Cannot Amael do the same trick as he did with Rufus and have the Gelb Warden leave him out for the ants?"

"Thembaaaa pay attention!" Nurka growled with mild exasperation.

"What?"

"Amael didn't tell us Prince Noss is alive, yet it was his Howlers who arrested him, who supposedly 'racked him to death'. He has lied to us. Why? Because he's hidden our Prince away to use as a bargaining chip later, that's why! I told you we cannot trust Amael. He doesn't trust us. We may be working together, but only whilst it remains convenient."

Themba scratched his hefty brow.

Rufus remained silent. Did Amael know Noss was alive, or was someone else playing a game? Jan, is it you? What're you and Vladimir up to? What didn't you tell me? Why not?

Nurka moved on. "We will say to Amael that some of our fanatical followers snatched Prince Noss in a raid of their own initiative from rumours they had heard. Then Amael can plead ignorance and save face, as can we."

Themba remained pessimistic. "But what if Prince Noss is *not* there? Red-mist has not seen him. If we try and break him out for nothing and get killed then what good is that?"

"I'll find out," Nurka rasped calmly.

"How?"

Nurka was likely making things up as he went along, yet his certain tone set Themba at ease like the wisdom of a considered Matriarch. "Gelb's guards can be bought as any others," he said. "I'll have our agents make contact and arrange everything. If Prince Noss is really in Gelb we'll know, and he'll know we're coming for him... and Madou too."

Themba growled, "Hahahaaa! Chakaa Madou. I can't believe he survived being bitten. He's a true warrior!"

"We'll be together again soon. All of us."

The hyenas bumped their heads together in accord and drank to the future.

Rufus sat in silence; Janoah and Silvermane were right, these stupid boys are planning to kill hundreds, even thousands, and in such an unspeakable manner. Amael and the wolfen conspirators can't afford to share the blame, they'll have to lay this atrocity at the door of THORN and then finish the hyena tribes off to quell the public's fury.

I have to get away, I have to get word out.

You can't, said the other half of Rufus's brain. You *can't* quit yet. Stay and play the game a while longer. Noss – he wouldn't approve of this madness, would he? I can't believe he would sanction Nurka's use of black-imperium.

By Ulf, maybe that's it!

If Noss is alive then perhaps, just perhaps, that's the way out of this mess – the sacred command of a hyena prince.

✦

Janoah entered Silvermane's office and upon seeing Josef sitting in one of the chairs immediately performed an about face to leave.

"Prefect Janoah!" Silvermane barked. "Walk out of here and you walk out of ALPHA."

"What's that cat doing here?" she spat back.

"I invited him, same as you. Now get in here and sit down, we're going to settle this mess."

After a few seconds, Janoah slammed the office door and stood before Silvermane's desk, arms folded. Josef remained seated and outwardly dispassionate as ever, fingers rapping together before his pink feline nose.

Satisfied Janoah was listening if not sitting, Silvermane begun. "We cannot afford in-fighting and squabbling at this time," he stated, adding gravely, "especially since, in light of Rufus's passing, Rafe could be our last hope to smash THORN before they strike, and Rafe depends on you two to function at his best."

"Well if I'd been *allowed* to pursue Olivia Blake we might have *two* Eisenwolves by now," Josef sniffed airily.

"In a week?" Janoah mocked. "Don't be ridiculous, it took Rafe a year to get to where he is."

"I've learnt a great deal since then."

"Oh? You've learned nothing of diplomacy. You can't traipse around Lupa arresting just anybody, especially since you're *not* a Prefect."

"You helped me!"

"Yes, because that dodger girl was a good smokescreen behind which to arrest Tristan Eisbrand *without* disturbing the conspirators. If you let her slip through your paws that's your problem, and it should've been the end of it. Arresting Howler Mills and going so far as to beat him up this side of the Pack Summit is beyond stupid."

"He's obviously a collaborator."

Janoah laughed, "Oh do give it up, cat." She looked to Silvermane and chirped disarmingly, "You know what they call him back at Riddle Den? Woodlouse. I mean, I ask you, does that sound like insurgent material?"

Silver's brows rose.

"Linus aided and abetted a dodger," Josef argued to Silvermane.

To which Janoah countered, "He had pity on a beautiful girl, nothing more. We're not all as immune to feelings as you, you sociopathic feline-"

"Now that is enough," Silvermane interposed, somehow as calm and understated as ever. "Whatever happened between you, it's of no consequence. That girl is gone, Josef, and I want to hear no more about it, and nor does Nikita, so don't go to him again. What I need from you both is harmony… and a plan." The Grand Prefect looked desperately to Janoah and, paws spread, implored despite knowing what her reply must be, "Amael's told you nothing more?"

Janoah emitted a sharp breath and looked down, then up again. "He has only told me that the Den Fathers will be eliminated at the Summit, by the hyenas."

"What day, what time, with what?"

"Black-imperium, but he refuses to tell me how exactly. He says he's protecting me in case he falls. The less I know, the more likely it is I could plausibly say I was just his lover and deny knowledge of the plot."

Josef mocked, "How 'noble' Amael is."

"Yes," Janoah agreed, "in his own way, he is."

"Perhaps he suspects you," Silvermane wondered aloud.

"No."

"How can you be so sure, Janoah?"

Janoah paused to think, as if skirting round some real reason to give a false one. "I just know."

Whatever he thought, Silvermane let it lie. "Well keep trying. If Tristan can't or won't talk then we're going into this trap blindfolded! The Alpha will be in mortal danger, and every Den Father too."

"Rafe will not let the Alpha come to harm," Janoah reassured. "He'll be near the whole time."

"He can't traipse around in his suit, Janoah!"

"No, sir, but it will be kept nearby."

"How?"

"We'll find a way to hide it. When the attack comes, however it comes, Rafe will be ready."

⁂

Sitting in the ALPHA HQ's boxed-in garden and blowing ember vapours at the midnight Lupan sky, Janoah felt both her imperious corona and the bench upon which she sat bend under a familiarly hefty presence.

"All right, Jan?" Rafe said, sitting casually beside her, muscled arms splayed over the back of the bench.

Janoah let slip a fond smirk, disguising it with a dip of the chin, "Hello trouble."

Following Janoah's previous upward gaze, Rafe took in the stars pricking the usually foggy heavens. "Cor, it's really clear tonight, 'en it?"

"Yes," Janoah replied absently, humouring her champion by looking up again. "I don't think I've ever seen Lupa so clear."

A few seconds passed, as many as ten.

"I… heard about Rufus," Rafe volunteered, "I'm sorry."

Janoah considered telling her Eisenwolf the truth, that Rufus was alive and in hyena custody.

"Well," she said instead, "we all knew it was coming."

"Not like that though."

Janoah chuckled wryly, "On the contrary, it's just like Rufus to go out in style. Withering away in Gelb didn't suit him. He's always wanted to see the inside of an ant nest anyway."

Rafe could but grimace.

"How's the bee?" Janoah said.

Perhaps she's eager to keep her mind off Rufus, Rafe thought, obliging her. "Fine," he beamed. "Meryl's set up a spare room for him next to mine."

"Her."

"Yeah. I meant her. She's got a little box to sleep in and everything, but she kinda just climbed up the wall and stayed there. She's so funny."

Janoah tutted, "I'm not sure the Grand Prefects will find it so funny." Sniffing, she looked sideways at a suddenly worried Rafe, "But... I'll have Josef say Toggle is part of your therapy, to keep you sane. That usually washes with the Alpha, and he's all that matters."

Rafe nodded gratefully.

"You've not let me down yet," Janoah said sternly. "Don't start now when Lupa needs you most."

"I won't," Rafe claimed breezily.

"Look after yourself. Do what Meryl tells you. You need to be strong. If we can't stop THORN before they strike we must stop them *as* they strike; whatever happens the Alpha must survive and the conspirators must be taken into custody."

"I'll protect him... and you."

A nod from Janoah, before she looked away and took a sharp breath.

Another break, longer perhaps; Janoah wasn't gauging the passing of time, only the mood of the wolf beside her and how best to approach him. He was just a boy, a foolish boy, and yet he had the power to sway history.

"Rafe," Janoah sniffed, looking at the ember she was twiddling between her ash-stained fingers.

"Yeah?"

"You'll stick with me, won't you? You won't abandon me for Josef or Silvermane, or anyone."

Rafe frowned, "Whatcha mean?"

"I mean you'd follow *my* orders, not theirs. Not even the Alpha's if it came down to it."

"Jan-"

"Promise me! And I mean *whatever* happens, however awful it seemed at the time, whatever side I picked in the end, you'd back me up."

"I promise. Of course I do. I don't owe them lot anything, only you... and Meryl."

"You'd listen to *me*, or Meryl?"

"Meryl's not a soldier," Rafe said, dodging the question; he was cleverer than he looked sometimes. "What's wrong; you in trouble?" he asked afresh.

Taking a last draught of her dying ember, Janoah said, "I'm on a tightrope, Stenton; I might make it all the way across, or I might fall one way or the other – don't you let me hit the ground."

~Blick VIII~

A stroll through HQ's concrete 'gardens' wasn't as pleasant as the seaside, but it would have to do.

"This place needs some greenery," Meryl declared, casting her eye over the stark, brutal facade of ALPHA's central quadrangle.

"Greenery?" Rafe scoffed, looking up at the equally brutal sky. It had been raining on and off, a really miserable Lupan day. "We're right under the Ashfall, 'en we?"

"Some things will still grow, especially if we water them with clean water; it washes the leaves off. Nothing we can eat mind, not unless you want a rotten tummy. Lavender's tough, I might ask if we can stretch to buying some."

"Lavender?"

"Yes. It was growing at my aunt's. The silvery bush in the rockery?"

"Oh!" Rafe said, his face grimacing. "Yeah."

Meryl supposed he didn't remember, or as likely didn't even notice in the first place.

Suddenly the Eisenwolf stopped walking.

"Rafe?" Meryl queried worriedly.

He waved a dismissive paw and continued, but took no more than a few steps before hopping to a halt and grasping at his left leg. Rafe was silent, but Meryl could see the excruciating pain on his face.

"I'll get a sting," she said, already turning to run.

"They're... all gone!" Rafe seethed, leaning on a low wall. "I used 'em all up."

"What?" Meryl piped. "You can't have! There were three on your ration book when we went to New Tharona."

"Ssssorry, Meryl. I needed 'em. Heh!"

The nurse looked on, eyes darting, searching. She put the facts together. "You've been training again, haven't you? You've not been back two weeks and you've been sneaking down the gym. Trying to impress Janoah, are we? Well I'm not impressed. Not one bit. You're killing yourself!"

A wolf popped up from behind the low wall; not very high, being a short, brown wolf with a white face. "Watch that bedside manner, Nurse Stroud," he advised, perchance slightly irreverent.

Meryl went momentarily white in the face herself! She raised her paw, ALPHA-style. "Yes, sir. I-I-I mean-"

"I thought our Eisenwolf had been recuperating on the Graumeer?" the wolf said, perplexed as to Rafe's condition.

"Well... he was, but... Grand Prefect Horst insisted we return before Rafe was fully rested."

"Oh?"

"He was doing so well there. He needs rest, that's all it is-"

"We at ALPHA have precious little time to rest, Miss Stroud, I myself haven't had a week off in... six years."

"Then perhaps you should set an example, sir?" Meryl scolded.

The white-faced wolf raised his pale brows at Meryl's cheek and chuckled. "Perhaps you're right." Glancing at the pain-wracked Rafe, who was by now on his knees, he reached into his cloak pocket and set a sting on the wall. "This is one example I shouldn't set, but... please, take this for our Eisenwolf. He clearly needs it and I've been feeling quite buoyant of late."

Meryl's eyes quivered with uncertainty, "But-"

"Please, I insist."

"That would be illegal-"

"This isn't a test. Take it. Just don't tell anyone."

Meryl caved in and snatched the sting from atop the wall, "Thank you, my Alpha. Thank you so much."

The Alpha batted Meryl's gratitude away and turned to leave.

"Oh," he chirped, clicking his fingers, "I was thinking about ordering some plants for the grounds come the spring. Too dreary around here, don't you agree? Lavender, perhaps. You'll plant them for us, won't you Miss Stroud?"

"Uh, yes, my Alpha. Gladly!"

"Excellent."

Once the Alpha had strolled across the grounds, Meryl tore open the sting and administered it to Rafe via the arm. She held him and stroked his brow as the relief surged through his body, until he came back to her, looked up at her sweet face.

"Was that him?" he panted, standing up and peering over the wall. "The Alpha?"

"Yes," Meryl whispered. "He gave you his sting, though he shouldn't have."

"Yeah, I know," Rafe said, thinking. "Why'd he do that?"

"I don't know, but we mustn't tell anyone."

"I won't."

The nurse took her patient's paw, "Come on, you need to have a lie down."

"No, I'm all right now."

"Rafe, for goodness sake-"

"Lying down makes me feel worse, Meryl! Best keep moving. Ask Janoah, she'll tell you it's the same for her."

"Well, all right, but no training. Not until your rations come in."

"Of course not."

Leading Rafe though the austere ALPHA grounds, Meryl held out a paw, "It's starting to rain again. Oh, it's been so horrid since we got back. It was lovely at the seaside."

"Yeah. Lupa's krap, 'en it?"

"Rafe!" Meryl scolded, then sniggered. "You're not wrong."

Before they made the double doors to enter the shelter of HQ, Silvermane exploded from said doors.

"Rafe!" he panted, saluting. "Time to suit up, Eisenwolf, ALPHA needs you."

"What for, sir?"

"THORN is raiding a refinery down in Riddle District. Janoah's there, she needs backup-"

"No!" Meryl snarled.

"Excuse me?" Silvermane woofed.

"I absolutely forbid it, Grand Prefect. Rafe's too ill!"

"Ill? He's just been on holiday, hasn't he?"

"That's neither here nor there. He had an attack a few minutes ago and he's out of stings. You can't put him back in that… that horrible eisenpelz suit, I won't allow it!"

"Miss Stroud-"

"I'll go to the Alpha if I have to!"

Silvermane's nostrils flared. "I wouldn't try going over my head, young lady," he warned silkily, "not unless you want a very short, sharp career here at ALPHA-"

"Oi, that's enough!" Rafe barked, adding, "Sir." He turned to Meryl, taking her aside, "I've gotta go; Jan needs me."

"Rafe-"

"It'll be all right; got the Alpha's sting in me step, 'en I? He must believe in me. You've got to believe in me too, Meryl. I'll never make a proper Prefect if you don't."

At length, Meryl nodded.

With a final wink and click of the cheek, Rafe took off with Silvermane, leaving his nurse standing alone, thankful that the Lupan drizzle masked her burgeoning tears.

Adam Browne

Part IV
LUPICIDE

Adam Browne

Diary Excerpt 3

This is the last I'll write before returning from the Summit, as I will be stowing this incriminating diary somewhere no Bloodfang Provost or ALPHA Prefect will find it. I am running the risk of arrest, even imprisonment, but I cannot stand by whilst Olivia is pressed into the Howlers, or perhaps a worse fate if Josef's record is anything to go by. Sara is convinced that Josef helped disappear her old friend Bruno Claybourne, a wolf who was himself very strongly afflicted – a pure-blood perhaps. What ultimately became of Bruno, Sara doesn't know. The Bloodfangs assert he was killed, run down by a car whilst fleeing the Politzi, but Sara and Olivia both agree the story spun by the newspapers was an obvious fabrication. Bruno was no criminal. In fact, he didn't even know he was a dodger! Remarkably his adoptive rabbit father, Casimir, administered him venom on the sly. Not by stings, Sara claims, but by mixing it in cough syrup, which Bruno always took for his ash allergy. The sweetness of the syrup must have masked the bitter taste of white-imperium. Sara also claims the body she identified was a fake, or at least not Bruno. It all sounds incredible, but less so in the light of Josef's efforts to snatch Olivia and then bring me down for daring to get in his way. I've asked Werner what he knows about this Bruno, but he refused to be drawn, which could mean nothing, or a lot. There is more going on between that hog's ears than most realise, just not too much, I hope.

If Bruno is alive, Sara has yet to receive a letter from him. Considering how he would always forward telephone numbers and addresses whenever he moved before, he is either dead, unable to communicate, or, at best, protecting Sara. If he was inducted, as Sara suspects, he could have forgotten her. I was fortunate that my own induction left my mind intact; I had a terrible time of it.

Regardless, Sara is determined Olivia not be snatched away too, whatever Bruno's fate.

There's nothing we can do about Tristan's arrest. Heath feels sure he will be released once Thorvald presses ALPHA, but if he has been working with THORN then should he be freed? I hope Janoah is mistaken; I have never known her to be.

Guilty or not, Sara is beside herself. She blames Tristan's arrest on letting him go back for Toggle, which he did only to appease Sara; he must care for her more than she thinks, and perhaps she him. I told Sara, and firmly believe it, that if ALPHA wanted to take Tristan in, they were going to arrest him sooner or later wherever he was. It's not her fault. They arrested Rufus right in front of Den Father Thorvald, after all. Red-mist's execution is hard to fathom. I don't want to believe it, it feels as unreal as his arrest, yet Janoah was in Riddle Den just yesterday for the reading of his will. She left tearfully despite carrying out his arrest herself. That wolfess is an enigma to me. Still, it seems Rufus really is gone.

As for Toggle, her whereabouts remain a mystery. I did not see her in ALPHA HQ, nor think to ask Janoah. I've had to convince Sara against sneaking back to the flat, lest that entangles her further with Tristan; he would not want Sara arrested, I'm sure. Besides, ALPHA will have turned the flat over and found anything so obvious as a giant bee. Most likely Janoah has guessed Toggle belongs to Heath, she's no fool. I just hope she had the heart to return her to Arkady University rather than have Josef dispose of her, or allow him run some perverse experiment. Heath says Josef was kicked out of Arkady on ethical grounds, though he would not be specific.

Still no word from Uther or Ivan. Whatever they're up to, I hope they're in less trouble than I am.

Well, everything is in place. Werner has supplied the papers and disguises the girls will need, and we've invented a convincing cover-story between us all. I just hope Vladimir doesn't see right through me. That wolf has a mind and a manner like no other. He is not malicious, and has in fact cut me some slack when he should have sent me to be flogged, or worse, but I do not know how far he can be pushed, even less fooled.

Next stop, Hummelton. Ulf willing I will return to write on these pages again.

Howler Linus Bloodfang Mills

Chapter 35

Vladimir Oromov loitered on the platform under the miserable morning drizzle, clad in his Grand Howler mantle of silver helmet and white cloak. Amael Balbus stood just ahead and to the right, flanked by his Den Guards, his red cloak edged with white, his helmet and armour beautified with gold and silver as befitted an Elder.

Underneath the glorious, incorruptible gold plating that harked back to olden times, Amael's armour was made of modern eisenglanz alloys, as was Vladimir's and any other Howler. The gold and silver was but an electroplated façade, for show, as with so many things wolfen. Even the act of standing out here in the rain when everyone could be snug inside the station foyer amounted to nothing more than theatre. A little rain? Puh! The Bloodfangs of Riddle District were unconcerned, or so Amael wanted those aboard the Elder Train to think as it eased into Riddle Station. Vladimir couldn't help but suspect everyone would instead think Amael an idiot as his dozen or so drowned Riddle District wolves dripped ashen water all over the Elder Train's glorious interior, ruining carpet and upholstery in their wake.

Vladimir felt a stirring in his corona. "There you are, Mills," he hummed without turning around. "I was starting to think you'd been arrested again on your way back from the toilet."

"No, Grand Howler."

"The Elder Train waits for no wolf. We'd have left you behind, which, considering your reputation of late, might've been wise."

"Yes, Grand Howler."

Linus Mills took position slightly behind and to the left of Vladimir, just within the Grand Howler's peripheral vision. The young wolf stood chest out, hood up, shield at his back, his sodden cloak sticking to his thickly muscled frame and every impressive contour. Was Linus becoming aware of his own imposing presence?

"Urrhem," Linus grunted, clearing his throat, "E-e-excuse me Grand Howler."

No, guess not.

"Yes?" Vladimir sighed, averting his gaze to the ash-streaked rails running from horizon to grim horizon. "What do you want now?"

"Uh, well... it's... uhm...."

Vladimir almost sang, "Spit it out, Linus."

Before Linus could, another voice interjected.

"Grand Howler Vladimir?" they said, in a strong and yet distinctly feminine tone.

Vladimir whirled round to discover a second Howler standing confidently beside Linus, tall and slender, not least compared to the stocky blonde wolf. She, for she had the shape of a she to accompany the voice, was wearing a broadly-striped red and white cloak – the mark of a Howler Cub, a Bloodfang Howler still attending the academy. Odd.

"I told you to wait inside," Linus said to the newcomer, before turning to Vladimir. "I'm sorry, sir, this recruit accosted me in the foyer. I couldn't get rid of her, that's why I was delayed."

"Accosted you?" Vladimir woofed, sighing, "By Ulf's fangs, Linus, you're supposed to be my adjutant and you can't even deal with a mere Cub."

"Sorry sir. She's very persistent."

"Is she, by Ulf?"

The 'persistent' recruit performed a salute, fist to chest then out, impeccably done, and removed her helmet, revealing a perfect brown-furred wolfen visage. "Howler Cub Livia reporting, Grand Howler Oromov," she said, fluttering her imperious violet eyes, "and may I express what an honour this is-"

"Stow it, Cub," Vladimir snorted. "Flattery will get you nowhere. Explain yourself this instant."

Howler Cub Livia bowed a little, "Forgive me, Grand Howler, I wouldn't presume to flatter so great a wolf as you. I was under the impression you would be expecting us, however."

"Us?"

"My classmate and I, Grand Howler," Livia said, gesturing to the station foyer behind where another rather dumpy-looking Howler Cub paced nervously to and fro. "We're journalists from the academy newspaper, *The Wesp*. We were hoping to write an article on the Pack Summit, you see, particularly from a Bloodfang standpoint."

Silence.

The wolfess raised her chin, "Howler Uther assured us that he would pass on our request to his Grand Howler and that it would be possible for us to accompany you if we turned up on the day."

"Uther!" Vladimir huffed, rolling his eyes. "Tell me, Cub, did you by chance bump into this 'Uther' in a Common Grounds bar?"

"Why yes, Grand Howler, during our term holiday. We met him several times."

"Of course you did."

"He was most kind."

"Of course he was."

Linus chipped in, "I've already explained that Uther hasn't the authority to grant any such thing, sir, and that he was most likely referring to Grand Howler Rufus, not you."

"No doubt he was," Vladimir agreed, saying to Livia, "I believe you've been had my unfortunate wolfess."

"Had, Grand Howler?" she squeaked.

"Yes. Now be on your way, please."

"But-"

"That's an order, recruit. Now get out of my sight before I lodge a complaint to your tutors over this brazen breach of protocol."

Looking to Linus a moment, as if imploring for aid, Livia saluted and about-faced back to the station foyer.

There followed an awkward, rain-flecked silence. Linus looked between Vladimir and the retreating wolfess several times before plucking up his courage. "If I m-mmm-may, sir," he stammered. "Perhaps it'd be a good idea to let them come along after all."

Turning his back to Elder Amael in an attempt to guard his voice, Vladimir grunted surreptitiously, "What? Are you mad? As if I've not got enough to worry about already without some stupid whelps tripping me over."

"But to send them away like that after Uther promised them so much."

"What of it? He's a rake and Rufus was worse. Their word means nothing."

"Even so, they might write something terrible about Riddle District, about *you* even."

"Humph! Let them. I'll put an end to their careers before they've even begun."

"Yes, sir, but... what they wrote would still be in circulation regardless," Linus reasoned. "It might look bad, especially for Elder Amael when he's trying to secure the pack's leadership." The young Howler shrugged, "Surely it'd be better if they went away satisfied?"

"Humph!"

Linus kept going, "I'll happily take charge of them. They can use my cabin."

Vladimir suddenly glared down upon the stocky blonde wolf beside him as if he'd that very moment pupated from a writhing plump golden grub into a different caste of creature, a lean and dangerous stinging insect.

"What're you playing at, boy?" the Grand Howler growled darkly.

"Pardon, sir?"

The Grand Howler cuffed Linus across the head. "How can you so be so stupid? Ungrateful wretch!"

"Sir?" Linus piped innocently.

Not fooled for a moment, Vladimir grabbed the scruff of Linus's cloak and yanked him away from Amael's earshot. "Who're they to you? Speak!"

"Sir, I protest!"

"Spies are they?"

"No, sir!"

"THORN activists? Are you throwing yourself behind that shower after everything I've done for you?"

Elder Amael cut in with his neck-tingling tenor, "What's going on, Oromov?"

Vladimir stood to attention, releasing Linus. "Nothing, Elder Balbus," the former insisted.

"Doesn't sound like nothing," Amael reckoned, barely turning away from the tracks, "Who was that girl?"

"Nobody. Just a Howler Cub, Elder."

"She's a student journalist, Elder, for *The Wesp*," Linus piped up, passing Vladimir a sideways glance, "She wanted to write an article on you."

"An article on me?" Amael gruffed humorously.

"Yes, Elder, reporting your time at the Summit-"

"I sent her away," Vladimir grunted.

"Then bring her back."

"Elder?"

"Are your ears rotting already, Oromov? Let the poor girl come and talk to me."

"Yes, Elder… of course."

Vladimir sent Linus after Livia by slapping him in the chest with the back of a paw.

Unconsciously rubbing his chest, Linus hesitated a moment before tramping across the puddle-strewn platform to the dripping marbled foyer. Vladimir watched him chat with the Cubs awhile, wishing he could hear.

Linus returned with the Cubs in tow, one tall, one short, shorter even than him. They stood to attention and smartly saluted Amael, the taller one doing a better job than the short and it was to her Amael seemed drawn, perhaps only because she had removed her helmet.

"I'm told you youngsters write for your student paper," Amael sniffed soberly, paws behind back.

"Yes, Elder Balbus," Livia replied.

"And you wish to write an article on me."

"It would be an honour, Elder."

"Indeed," Amael said, "and if I achieve what I set out to achieve it'll be a historic scoop."

Producing a notepad and pencil from her cloak, Livia stood ready, "And what is it you're setting out to achieve, Elder?"

Amael laughed at this wolfess' gall, "You'll see firstpaw, Cub. You'll be along for the ride."

Livia had hardly the chance to perform an overblown gasp of joy before the lofty Vladimir poked his silvery armoured nose into the conversation. "If I may take your student numbers, Cubs."

"Numbers, Vladimir?" Amael snapped.

"For security checks, Elder, to make sure these Cubs are who they *say* they are."

"There's no need for that."

Vladimir remained firm. "I cannot be responsible for your safety if I cannot do my job, Elder," he said, turning to the Cubs, "Numbers, please."

"43956, Livia," Livia said impeccably.

"Uh, ah…." her short comrade struggled.

"She's 43961, Tara," Livia said on her behalf.

"Oh, aye," the short one confirmed, "43… 96… 01."

Whilst Vladimir hurriedly rifled about his cloak pocket for his golden pen and something to write on, Livia jotted the numbers down on her reporter's notepad and tore off the sheet for him.

"Here you are, Grand Howler."

Still with a paw inside his white cloak, Vladimir eyed Livia up a moment, before taking the rain-flecked paper with the very tips of his fingers. "Humph."

With much throat-clearing, Linus clumsily barrelled in and held out a paw, "I'll do the check, sir, if you're too busy-"

"I'll manage, Howler," Vladimir assured him, tucking the paper safely away in his cloak pocket and patting his chest where both it and his pen were snugly sequestered. "Rest assured, I'll ring through when we get to the Lupan Wall."

Linus had no recourse and so stood back again.

"Two Howler wolfesses in the same place at the same time," Vladimir observed, looking the stripy pair over, "most unusual, wouldn't you say, Elder Amael?"

"Yes. We've only ever had one wolfess on Riddle's roster in my time and that was Janoah."

Livia explained the supposed anomaly away, "As with colour-blindness, sirs, the imperium gene is sex-linked and recessive. Males have the X and a Y chromosome whereas we females have two X's, giving us a greater chance of being born healthy-"

"We are well-aware of Lupine biology, Cub," Vladimir huffed.

"Of course, Grand Howler. What you may not appreciate, being of the masculine persuasion, is that we afflicted females tend to stick together for our own... protection." Livia raised a limp paw to her puckered brow, "The Howler Academy can be such a... a daunting place with so many virile young wolves and so few wolfesses to confide in." With a tiny gasp she looked affectionately to her comrade, "Tara and I have stuck together through thick and thin. We look out for each other, isn't that right Tara?"

"Oh, aye," the little one piped. "Thick and thin."

Whilst Vladimir remained unmoved, Amael predictably melted before Livia's performance. "It must be difficult," the Elder grunted warmly. "But I assure you, you'll be quite safe in the company of *my* Howlers. Wolves will be wolves, but I do not tolerate ungallant behaviour in Riddle's ranks. It's the rod for any wolf who dares disrespect a wolfess – you can put *that* in your paper."

Smiling appreciatively, Howler Cub Livia dutifully scribbled Amael's quote down in her increasingly damp and dishevelled notepad.

"The Elder Train approaches, sir!" one of the Den Guards announced, stomping a foot.

"Stand ready," Amael replied, raising a paw. He turned to Linus, "Trooper."

"Yes, Elder?"

"Take charge of our guests. Put them up in a spare cabin; we're a few Howlers short with Uther and Ivan away and Rufus out of the picture, so there should be room enough in our allotted carriage."

"Yes, Elder," Linus vowed, saluting extra-smartly.

His will expressed, Amael faced the tracks again and stood paws behind back as he often did, flanked by his Den Guards and the rest of his Howlers, five others in all. Vladimir stood ready also, but watched Linus and his charges out the corner of his eyes; watched them exchange knowing glances and nods when they thought nobody was looking.

"Foolish boy," Vladimir grunted to himself.

To the left of Linus and everyone else, a billowing black cloud chugged swiftly over the ragged roofs and twisted chimneys of Riddle District, mixing into the bland grey sky like too much iodine being injected into a solution by an overenthusiastic science pupil.

The source of the churning cloud slowly turned towards Linus, growing louder, chugging away, before a bright white light emerged from behind a signal station, reflecting off the rain-glazed tracks and dazzling the blue-eyed wolf into squinting somewhat.

The Elder Train!

The great crest of a wolf's skull and red fangs secured to the engine's growing face proclaimed to all that this train was the Bloodfang's premier locomotive. Every pack had their own Elder Train to ferry their leaders to and from special occasions such as the Pack Summit, or Winterfeast, or to meetings with dignitaries of other lands and kingdoms, if so invited. Linus had seen the Elder Trains of various packs pass his house as a boy, and from atop his late father's shoulders had perched high enough by the trackside to glimpse their marvellous wood-panelled interiors where Howlers smouldered in velvet luxury under crystal chandeliers.

Linus never imagined he might step aboard such a fabulous train back then, and now he cared not to. Consumed by burgeoning panic he hardly noticed the massive blood-red engine rumble by, an enormous tangle of pipes and armour with wheels the dimensions of dinner tables, every inch already streaked with glittering ash after doubtless being cleaned just this morning. The endless entourage of carriages, their windows glowing with an invitingly warm light and pocked with wolfen faces, filled him only with dread.

Vladimir's onto me. He's going to find out I'm helping a dodger and then I'm going to be arrested, tried and sent down the mines with Rufus.

No, stay calm; Werner said those numbers are good.

The train squealed to a stop amidst hisses and clouds of ash and smartly dressed Politzi hog conductors emerged from several carriages to facilitate the boarding of both Amael's wolves and their luggage.

The conductors saluted Amael and informed him that Riddle District had been assigned Sleeping Carriage 13 for this event, farthest from the Den Father at the very end of the train, bar the caboose, or brake car.

"Car Thirteen?" Amael woofed in disgust.

Despite his initial instinctive exclaim, Amael quickly calmed down and nodded in acceptance. There was no dishonour in it; carriages were assigned randomly to help preclude any favouritism, at least in theory. It wasn't impossible that someone had greased administrative paws to arrange the rising Amael be isolated at the end of the train, but if Amael himself hadn't bothered to fiddle the books he doubted anyone else had the guts or heart to. Most of those who had been outwardly against him before were in his pocket now. Armed with Janoah's damaging information about their private lives gleaned from ALPHA's secret archives, even Amael's enemies had no choice but to vote him into the mantle of Den Father when the time came, a time that would come sooner than they imagined.

The starting horn had sounded.

Grumbling surreptitiously under his helmet, Amael led the way along the station platform striding past carriages and windows, watched by one and all, friend and enemy. Vladimir kept pace whilst the suspicious Cubs stuck to the lagging Linus like glue, particularly the small one.

"Och! They're all staring at us," she fretted, keeping her head down.

"Don't worry, Sara," Linus said, despite worrying. "Put your helmet back on, Olivia."

"Nobody here knows my face," Olivia replied.

"You never know. ALPHA plants agents everywhere, just like any other pack. There could be an informant of Josef's aboard somewhere."

Olivia duly donned her austere, grey, student's helmet, becoming 'Livia' again.

After passing an eternity of carriages filled with wolfen faces and bearing countless imperious eyes burning into the top of their helmeted heads, Linus and the girls made the second to last carriage and joined Amael and his entourage as they filed aboard. The train hogs had rolled out a pristine red carpet, which quickly turned black under the pounding of two dozen ash-plastered Howler boots. Thirteen districts, thirteen Elders, thirteen red carpets ruined, Linus supposed, and that was just the Bloodfangs! The logistics of the Pack Summit, the sheer cost, was starting to crystallise in the young Howler's mind. The mathematics proved a welcome distraction, as did the glorious interior he found himself in.

Directly opposite Linus as he boarded the Elder Train was a coffee table flanked by two red armchairs and topped with decanter of complimentary brandy and crystal tumblers – knowing Elder Amael he'd be all over that any second. To Linus's right an invitingly plush red sofa beckoned with black pillows propped up on each arm – very nice. To the Howler's left, snug against the carriage's rear wall and overlooked by a Bloodfang crest, stood a writing desk proffering pens and paper – useful. All around imperium lamps shone dutifully, their warm glow shimmering on the polished wood panelling and quilted red walls. Red carpet lined with gold thread ran from here towards the engine end of the train, then off to the starboard side and down a corridor with doors to private cabins that likely made up the remainder of Carriage 13.

As far as Linus understood, this sleeper carriage was for Amael and his Riddle Den Howlers, whilst dining, grooming and other necessities took place in specialised cars towards the middle of the train. Though such amenities had to be shared by representatives from every district, Linus had read that this was seen as beneficial. The whole pack would be forced to mingle; over dinner in the dining car, over embers in the lounge car, and even over towels and glimmer bottles in the bathing car. Elders, however introvert and guarded, would naturally discuss their affairs, learn the Den

Father's will, influence him and each other, before arriving at the Summit to officially debate with other packs and cast votes for or against proposals that would affect all of Lupa. Thus, of all the annual Summits, it was Hummel's that beasts always remembered, simply because of the novelty and logistics involved in travelling so far. Bloodfang, Eisbrand, Greystone, their capital districts were a stone's throw away from one another; Hummel were on the other side of the Sunrise Mountains in Everdor, clean and verdant Everdor. It was an adventure even for the oldest, crustiest Elders.

Momentarily, Linus felt more excited than scared.

As predicted, Amael dived on the brandy before everyone was even aboard, deftly filling all the tumblers with his practised paw like a bar beast.

"Let's make a toast."

Whilst Amael's two Den Guards stiffly refused the offer of a tipple as their creed dictated, Amael all but forced Vladimir and Linus to partake in his impromptu toast by pressing tumblers into their paws regardless of the fact it wasn't even ten o'clock. The other Bloodfang Howlers lucky enough to be chosen for this trip were roped in the moment they stepped aboard, as were the Cubs – there were glasses enough for everyone.

"To Riddle," Amael said, removing his dripping helmet and slamming it on the coffee table.

Livia boldly stepped forward and raised her glass. "To the Bloodfangs!" she declared instead, with the fervour common to new recruits.

Whilst some of the Howlers lingering behind sniggered at the Cub, Amael looked appreciatively to her and raised his glass. "To Lupa," he bettered, adding, "as I'm sure Boris would say if he were here guarding my conscience and not looking after Riddle Den in my absence."

The Howlers removed, or in some cases merely lifted their helmets and sampled the brandy with differing enthusiasm, some knocking it back like the hardy Amael, others merely sipping the lip like the wary Vladimir, but all with the fervent cry.

"To Lupa!"

All bar one. Linus noticed Sara didn't join in, not even lifting her helmet for a second to sip the drink; for whatever reason she just stood there stiff as a statue. Was she terrified, or just a strict teetotaller? Either way, Linus swapped glasses and downed Sara's drink on her behalf – by Ulf he needed it.

Nobody noticed, or at least nobody cared, not even Sara.

The carpet was rolled up, the doors slammed shut, whistles blown. The Elder Train's exceptionally powerful engine jolted into motion, causing a few stumbles.

"What about our luggage?" Linus piped.

"Already in your cabin, Mills," Amael calmly assured him, breaking out an ember and a second drink. "You're on the Elder Train to Hummelton now," he said, raising his glass to his lips. "You'll want for nothing over the next few days… except perhaps your sanity."

✦

The Alpha saluted ALPHA-style, Nikita saluted back from the top of the HQ's bleak concrete stairs.

With one paw twiddling her cravat, Meryl Stroud imagined what passed between them as she watched from above through the rain-flecked window. Something along the lines of 'Good luck, my Alpha,' and 'I leave HQ in your capable paws, Nikita,' or some such. Then the short, brown-furred Alpha ducked into his motorcade with the big, black-furred Duncan and rotund, white-furred Horst, the latter looking even more overburdened with medals than per usual. The Alpha sported only the Imperium Heart, as always. Nikita and Silvermane waved them off, before turning to one another and chatting as they moseyed back into the foyer of ALPHA HQ and out of Meryl's sight.

Bvvvt!

She whirled round to see Toggle trundling along the corridor towards her, a jittering ball of shiny black carapace and fluff.

"Oh! And how did you get out?" the ALPHA nurse tutted at the bee.

Toggle replied with a brief flutter of her iridescent wings.

Bvvt!

Then nuzzling into Meryl's dress she trembled away like a parked car, as bees were in the habit of doing.

"Surely you can't be lonely," Meryl cooed, bending down and gingerly patting the bee's dimply armoured brow. She didn't quite trust the creature not to twist its plump abdomen round and sting her in the shin. However, since bees could sting only once before dying, Toggle would need to be in fear for the colony's survival to resort to self-sacrifice, and, since there was no colony, she wouldn't. Meryl hoped she had her facts straight regards this giant of a bee.

Suddenly a giant of a wolf approached, his familiarly hefty boot steps turning Meryl's pert ears long before the follow-up deep yet bright, "Oi, Meryl!"

"Oi indeed!" Meryl reproached fondly, standing up to receive Rafe Stenton as he clomped down the way in his smart Prefect's uniform; black cloak, greaves, helmet and all, his ribbon for a tail wafting behind. Cupping her paws together Meryl said, "I thought you'd already left."

Rafe woofed, "What? Not without saying bye."

"But I thought you were-" Meryl began, looking outside where the Alpha's long-gone car had been, then changing course, "Well, just be careful, won't you?"

"Aww, it's just a training exercise, Meryl."

Meryl knew the truth, that Rafe was to act as the Alpha's secret bodyguard, but she played her part and feigned ignorance. "Even so, watch your imperium levels," she advised, skirting as closely to the truth as she could without revealing her knowledge. "Don't push yourself too far."

"Doctor Josef's coming," the Eisenwolf replied, waving a big paw. "It'll be fine."

A prim, restrained sort of nod from Meryl; then, amidst a spread of her paws and a shrug, she half-joked, "After looking after you day and night for all these months I won't know what to do with myself whilst you're away. I'll be bored out of my mind-"

Bvvt! Bvv!

"Hah! Looks like Toggle'll keep you busy," Rafe laughed heartily. "She's taken a shine to you, en' she?"

Bvvvv-v-v-v!

Meryl swore that, "I shut her in with a bowl of honey. I've no idea how she got out."

"Wasn't me."

"Then she must've opened the door herself, somehow."

Bending down as Meryl had, Rafe patted Toggle's firm brow and cooed like a doting parent to a cub, "Who's a clever little bee? Yes you are! Yes you are!"

Bvvvvt! Bvv!

Toggle wobbled her rear-end about and turned in circles.

Bvvvvt! Bvv! Bvvvvvvt!

"What *is* she doing?" Meryl giggled. "Is she dancing?"

"I dunno. We're gonna need an expert."

"Yes. If we're to look after her properly I shall have to read up on beekeeping."

"Yeah, good idea," Rafe chirped, standing up and hiking a thumb behind him. "Look... I'd better go. Jan's waiting; she'll take me head off."

Meryl suddenly grasped Rafe's mighty arms with both paws. "Let me see your face before you go," she implored him, her own face as sober as he had ever seen it.

"What? Oh, yeah!"

Tutting at his perceived stupidity, Rafe unbuckled the strap of his plain black Prefect's helmet and slipped it off via his great daft ears.

"Sorry," he excused rubbing his untidy scalp, "I forgot I was wearing it. It's so light compared to me eisenpelz."

Meryl just stared, her eyes flitting hither and thither, exploring Rafe's prematurely weathered visage, with his imperfect fur and drawn, tired eyes that yet burnt with an imperious flame.

At length the big wolf cracked under the little nurse's scrutiny. "What?" he laughed, rubbing his neck.

"You look very smart."

Rafe smiled and winked roguishly, "Oi, now that *is* a compliment, coming from you, nurse prim 'n' proper."

Meryl laughed in kind, then suddenly dipped her chin, her smile cooling rapidly. "Rafe did you..." she began afresh, trailing off.

"What?"

"Did *you* tell Janoah about Tristan?"

"Who's Tristan?"

"Don't joke!" Meryl snapped. Checking her tone lest Rafe really had forgotten, she continued, "The wolf you arrested in Heath's flat was the same one we saw talking to that hog. Remember, back in New Tharona? I know you didn't have a choice in the matter, it's your job to carry out ALPHA's will, but if you told Janoah after-"

"I didn't," Rafe said, simple as that. "Look, I didn't even remember him until I walked into that flat." The big wolf kicked at the floor, "I was gentle with him. He... he tried to shoot himself-"

"Oh no!" Meryl gasped.

"It's all right, Meryl. I stopped him. I had to."

The nurse breathed out with relief, and yet sadness, "Then perhaps he *is* guilty."

Rafe shrugged a little. "This might sound funny coming from a boxer 'en all, but I don't like to hurt anyone, Meryl, not really. But when someone's out to cause Lupa harm I got to fight back. We all do. Even you, in your own way. You help me, so you're fighting too, you know. I couldn't do it without yer-"

"Oh Rafe stop it. You make me feel so guilty!"

"Guilty?"

"How can you stand me, snapping at you like that?" Meryl seethed, covering his eyes a moment. "You've been bedridden on and off for weeks; gone blind for days on end. You've suffered so much; more than any wolf your age should, even with the rot. Yet you've never once snarled, or said an angry word to me, not even at your lowest ebb. You've kept on smiling and joking, from the very first moment when Josef called me in that day, to now. You know, sometimes I wish... I wish I had the rot too."

"Don't be daft!" Rafe tutted, adding, "What for, eh?"

"Then I could sense your corona," Meryl explained, "like Janoah does. You two share something that I never will. She knows your pain; understands it." The nurse looked off into space, "I-I get so jealous. I try not to hate her, but when I see you two laughing and joking when it's *her* fault you get so ill, I just want to march over there and box her right on the-"

"Meryl!"

The nurse covered her muzzle with both paws lest she dug any deeper. The damage was done. *I've lost him. It's over. Why did I open my stupid mouth, by Ulf, why?*

Letting his helmet clatter the floor without a care, Rafe swept Meryl into his embrace. He held her tight, silent, unmoving. *Why? What did it mean?*

Slowly, the mighty Eisenwolf, ALPHA's champion, began to snuffle and shake.

"Oh Rafe!" Meryl realised. "Rafe, don't cry. I'm sorry!"

Meryl knotted her arms tight about her patient's vast ribcage as he heaved and trembled with the fitful snatched breaths of bottled-up grief and torment. For longest time nothing more was said, nothing need be; all was touch and knowing as nurse and patient rocked gently to and fro in the stark ALPHA corridor.

Suddenly Rafe snapped his head back and wiped his moist eyes, "Sorry."

"Don't be silly," Meryl sniffed back. "It's my fault, I shouldn't have said-"

"No, it's fine," Rafe beamed. "Really. I mean it."

Meryl smiled briefly.

"I-I-I dunno who I am half the time," her Eisenwolf admitted through a false, toothy smile. "Sometimes... it'd be so easy to give up. But I won't do it, Meryl, not with you to look after me. I've been given this power to protect others. It's a gift from Ulf. I believe that, I do! I'll fight as long as Lupa needs me."

Swallowing her tears, Meryl nodded appreciatively throughout Rafe's assertion. Rubbing the Eisenwolf's immense upper arms, as if trying to massage the rot from those big bones, she said through a slight laugh, "Well I'll always need you, even when Lupa's at peace, so you'd better go on fighting long after then. Do you hear me, Rafe Stenton?"

A smile, a nod, a laugh.

"Listen to me, I'm being so selfish," Meryl scolded herself.

"No you're not," Rafe snorted. "You give up so much time for me. Read to me. Everything."

"What else could any right-thinking nurse do?" Meryl dismissed modestly, "I'd do the same for anyone." She looked to the water-streaked window, seeing nothing but her own thoughts, "You know… I despise Doctor Josef now. I used to think he cared about you, but he's already searching for another Eisenwolf candidate. And him a doctor. It's disgusting."

Rafe grunted a little.

"I'd leave his employ, leave ALPHA," Meryl asserted, "but I worry what'll become of you. So I stay and help Josef despite my every natural inclination." She rubbed her arms and shivered, "To think I helped him induct you. He told me you were dying, you know, that to save you, you *had* to become a Howler. Often it's true, it is the only path left, but I realise now he lied. You were sick, yes, but you're so strong you could have survived, if you had moved to Everdor and lived a healthy life. You *could* have kept your memories, your old life, and Josef and Janoah knew it."

"I don't want that life-"

"You don't remember it!" Meryl shouted. She fought a wave of tears, "And we never asked you, Rafe. We never asked what you wanted, we just… foisted ALPHA's needs upon you as if we had right to. You must hate me for it."

Gently turning Meryl's steel-grey muzzle with a big brown paw, Rafe said, "Stop it," and pressed his lips to hers before another incriminating word passed them. Meryl's eyes opened wide in shock, but she didn't fight it.

This time it felt right.

Bvvvvvt! Bvv!

Upon Toggle's rude interruption, Rafe drew back as quickly as he'd dived in, "Sorry! That was stupid. I'm sorry, Meryl-"

"No," a dazed Meryl replied, swallowing, "not at all."

Rafe squirmed with mortification, wringing the front of his cloak he emitted a mirthful snort, "You look like you've seen a ghost. Did I do it wrong or something?"

"No no."

"I've never tried it before. Well, except that time last year."

"Last year?"

"Yeah, at your aunt's. Remember? I tried to land one on you and you bailed out."

Meryl could breathe at last, "Yes! Yes, of course I remember. I'm just glad you do to. So very glad."

"This is the real me, Meryl," Rafe insisted, leaning in. "I might forget a thing or two, even myself… but never you."

"Yes. I know that now."

Taking each other's paws they touched their noses together, Meryl rubbing Rafe's dark, plasma-scarred palms with her rough pink, washer-wolf's thumbs. Putting aside all inhibitions, every concern, every wolf but each other, they slowly joined, awash in the rain-warped light rippling through the window.

✦

"Took your sweet time, Stenton!" Janoah barked, as Rafe sprinted across the rain-lashed ALPHA courtyard and all but leapt into the back of Josef Grau's van, making the whole vehicle shake.

"Sorry," Rafe panted, sitting heavily on the bench beside Janoah.

Doctor Josef sat opposite in his black coat and tinted spectacles, umbrella at the ready; Rafe's empty Eisenwolf mantle hung limply beside him like a surreal sculpture.

"Did my assistant keep you?" the cat guessed expectantly.

"Nah," Rafe lied, raising his voice over the patting of rain on the roof, "I was just spending a penny."

Nodding at Rafe's plausible excuse, Janoah slammed the doors and rapped on the metal partition. "Let's go, and make it snappy!"

"Yes marm!" the driver replied.

Its engine being already started, the van pulled away without much ado, through ALPHA's gates and down the road. There were no windows in the back through which to see HQ shrinking into the distance, and the only light source was a lamp set in the ceiling.

Janoah rummaged around in a trunk. "Here," she said, passing Rafe a folded black cloth, "put it on."

Even with his face obscured by his helmet, Rafe was visibly confused as he unfurled what turned out to be a black Prefect's cloak, identical to the one he was wearing surely.

No… no it felt different, somehow – cold and heavy, almost like the finest chain mail.

"It's special," Janoah explained, since she knew Rafe would only ask. "It'll help dampen your corona. It'll still be strong, but hopefully nobody on the Elder Train will be suspicious of you."

Rafe held the cloak up, looking for some clue as to how it might go about dampening anything. "How's it work?" he asked inevitably.

Janoah broke out an ember, "Never you mind."

"It's one of my old inventions," Josef declared instantly, "black-imperium-weave. Quite illegal."

Rafe froze, save for his widening eyes.

"It's all right," his doctor purred, those short tidy whiskers rising as he smiled. "It won't kill you. Do you think I'd be sitting here in this enclosed space if I thought it could?"

"But how? I thought-"

"The black-imperium has been isolated, stabilised, within the body of the thread," Josef clarified, in distilled terms. "Even if minuscule amounts do escape, say when a thread breaks, it'll be no more damaging than breathing in a day's worth of Lupan air, say."

Even so, Rafe emitted a shaky breath. He'd seen the twisted corpses of suicidal THORN members and didn't relish such a death himself.

"Just keep it away from fire, whatever you do," Josef advised cryptically.

"Fire?" Rafe piped.

The doctor spread his grey paws, but didn't elaborate further than, "Trust me, it would be very bad."

Not wishing to probe further lest he didn't like what he heard, Rafe slipped his normal cloak from his shoulders, his damp fur steaming from the telltale body heat of vigorous exercise – he had dashed through HQ at quite a clip after leaving Meryl. With unusual care and Janoah's help, the Eisenwolf draped the new cloak about him. It weighed against his chest and shoulders with unnatural force.

"It's weird," Rafe breathed uneasily, adding in a jocular fashion, "Heavy, 'en it?"

"Dense," Josef corrected, "black-imperium is the densest material known to science. Given time it'll always find its way to the bottom of anything… rather like me."

Janoah pulled the loose lengths of Rafe's special cloak over his right shoulder and pinned it in place with his shining black and white ALPHA brooch; it behaved as any normal mantle.

"There," Janoah said, sitting back and running a paw down Rafe's body, "you look very smart; smart enough to stand with the Alpha."

"It's so… black," Rafe observed.

"Of course," Josef huffed, "it's black-imperium."

Rafe rubbed his cloaked chest, "Yeah. I guess so." He suddenly looked to Janoah and beamed even through his helmet, "Well?"

"Well what?"

"Is it working or what?"

Janoah didn't let on the sudden chill she felt now Rafe's burning corona had left her. It was still there all right, lingering on the peripheral of Janoah's field, pushing on her, but Rafe felt like a lesser wolf, diminished, like any number of Howlers she had passed in the street, their feeble shells of imperious energy unable to breach her own.

"Can't you tell?" she chuckled, side-stepping the question with her own. "I'm being blocked out as much you're being blocked in."

"Oh, right. Yeah."

"Don't worry," Janoah sighed, blowing orange ember vapours at the subtly flickering light. "You don't have to pretend you even notice my feeble corona these days."

Rafe could but snort sharply, "Don't be stupid, Jan; I can feel you across HQ."

Janoah could but smile, "Flatterer."

Josef quietly marvelled at Janoah; she didn't usually tolerate such familiarity from anyone but Rufus, certainly not being called 'Jan', let alone 'stupid'. Any wolf who'd dared would've been soundly slapped down, but not her Rafe. He had crossed a special threshold of late.

"I've another present for you," Janoah said, reaching under the bench and pulling out a long, clearly substantial object tied up in red velvety cloth and white ribbon.

Rafe felt its heft, "What is it?"

"Open it."

The Eisenwolf did so, yanking at the ribbon like a giant cub on his birthday. The fine red cloth fell away at the top end, revealing the marvellous black hilt and white grip of what had to be an enormous two-pawed sword!

Woofing in surprise Rafe glanced at Janoah, who chuckled in that knowing sort of way.

"The work of the finest Greystone smiths," she claimed proudly. "The sword of a traitor has been… repurposed for a worthy cause."

"Whatcha mean?"

Shrugging, Janoah went on, "You seemed rather taken with it the other day. And as you said, it only would've rusted away in the archives. So I spoke to the Alpha about it. Rafe needs a weapon worthy of him now he's a proper Prefect, I said. He agreed."

It hit Rafe then, whilst slipping the rest of the cloth from the gleaming, polished blade, that this was Tristan Eisbrand's marvellous sword! The silver hilt had been somehow turned black, and the blue-imperium snowflake etched into the crosspiece had vanished, presumably ground out, replaced with the A symbol of ALPHA, rendered in pure white-imperium crystal. It must've cost Janoah a small fortune, or had she put it on ALPHA's books?

Rafe held the sword up, its tapering tip nearly scraping the van's roof, "Aww, Jan, it's beautiful."

"You're welcome."

"I… I forgot all about it, you know."

"After making such a fuss?" Janoah hummed knowingly. "It's not your fault; the imperium's been doing the talking lately. Still, you're in good health now. We can't have any strange behaviour whilst you're guarding the Alpha. Try and keep it together."

Rafe angled the sword down. "I will," he said. Then something else hit him, "Proper Prefect, did you say?"

Puffing on her ember, Janoah explained, "The Alpha agreed to that as well."

"Wait. So… I'm a Prefect? Like you?"

"That you are. Welcome to ALPHA, 'proper' Prefect Bruno."

"Bruno?" Rafe woofed with yet more surprise.

"That's right. Get used to it. That's your cover name."

Rafe laughed at the novelty, but Janoah remained steadfastly serious.

"You'll stand out in a crowd whatever you're called," she said, "but we don't want the world and his wife to know Eisenwolf Rafe is defending the Alpha. At least under a different guise and with that cloak there'll be a modicum of doubt as to who you really are; especially with the Alpha telling anyone who'll listen that you're just one of his bodyguards, as he will be."

"Why Bruno though?"

"What?" Janoah huffed defensively, leading Rafe, or Bruno, to strongly suspect she had picked the name. "Don't you like it?"

"No, I do," Rafe professed, moving to mollify any hurt feelings. Looking along the length of his sword he raised the shining blade to his grille-clad snout, peering at his anonymous helmeted reflection. "Bruno... Bruno," he said, whilst Janoah and Josef exchanged a look across the width of the van, "It has a nice ring to it."

Whilst Rafe pondered his new identity, Janoah reached under the bench again. "One more thing," she said, presenting her champion with a furry, limp, brown caterpillar, or so it appeared for a moment.

"What's that?" Rafe woofed.

"A prosthetic tail," Janoah replied with a chuckle. "It won't wag, but it'll have to do."

"I'm not wearing that!"

"It's necessary for your disguise."

"But it's so stupid! I don't mind if beasts know I ain't got a tail, it's the hiding it that's embarrassing."

Janoah glanced at a smirking Josef, then hissed at Rafe, "If you walk about with a ribbon for a tail beasts will ask questions. Who is he, how did he lose his tail? Was it amputated so he could fit into an Eisenwolf suit?"

"Nobody's gonna say that," Rafe snorted.

"Some might. You're still just a rumour, Rafe; let's not become fact. Not yet. Legally ALPHA is not a pack and not bound by the laws that prohibit the Eisenwolves, but in theory you could still be arrested and executed merely for existing."

Rafe snatched the tail. "Fine," he sulked, wagging it at Janoah, "but I'm keeping me lucky ribbon on me."

Chapter 36

Linus slumped heavily on the bed, already exhausted by this pretence and the Elder Train hadn't even left the city yet!

Ash billowed by the tiny, rectangular window of his trembling cabin, partially obscuring the ramshackle roofs of a slum passing down below. Linus imagined the deprived residents jealously eying up the train, glimpsing through its glittering windows the finest interior décor Lupan taxes could buy, just as he had done as a cub. Now he was aboard, Howler Linus, couched in luxury with his very own bed, chest of drawers, bedside lamp, wardrobe, mirror, even a tiny grooming sink, all made of beautified wood, enamel and glass. It was cramped, yes, much like Linus's quarters back at Riddle Den, but leagues above the rotting corrugated piles down there.

The crosshatch struts of an iron bridge whistled by the rain-speckled window as the Elder Train chugged over the vast grey waters of the River Lupa, which looked grimmer than ever under the drizzling firmament.

Making landfall again, the train continued west, passing an industrial complex and some canals, before approaching an interior arm of the Lupan Wall, looming large and grey. In times of conflict these internal stretches of the Lupan Wall mattered, but during peacetime they were hardly more of an impediment than the invisible district lines. The great gates were already open and the Elder Train billowed through unchecked, thus departing Riddle District and the Bloodfang territory altogether.

They had now entered one of Lupa's most run-down areas – the so-called Bloc. The Bloc was home to packs with which Linus had had nothing to do with and knew little about. Bloodfang, Greystone, Eisbrand, Hummel, even ALPHA if Vladimir's measure of their ambition was right; these were the packs that held the most land and riches, the ones beasts remembered, sat up and took notice of. Yet, into a territory smaller than any other, save the Common Ground, were crammed a host of lesser packs all competing for the big five's table scraps. Holding puny lands denoted by ever-changing boundaries, often just a few districts, sometimes just one, each of the Bloc packs harboured funny ways and strange by-laws that were hopelessly outdated by the standards of the big five. It was a dangerous quarter for a Howler to serve in too; the war had never quite left it. The so-called 'Den Fathers' of the Bloc packs were being eternally murdered and setup anew by feuds and plots, to the effect that the stable big packs credited the weak, bickering Bloc lot with very little clout.

However, because there were so many Bloc packs, each ruled by their own relatively obscure Den Father, a compromise had been struck long ago whereby the Bloc would elect two Den Fathers from amongst their many to send to the Pack Summit. Those two would then vote on behalf of the whole Bloc. Otherwise, as previous generations had discovered the hard way, the dozens of Bloc Den Fathers, each with very little land, Howlers or citizens between them, would overwhelm the wishes of the four big packs by sheer force of voting numbers and thereby overturn the desires of most Lupans, seeding strife and wars aplenty.

Not everyone liked the current system, least of all the boxed-in Bloc itself, but under it Lupa had enjoyed a long period of peace – the last war aside, which had only erupted thanks to an imperium shortage.

An imperium shortage not unlike the current one, Linus couldn't help but think.

How're the girls getting on? Perhaps I'd better go check on them. No, I mustn't be seen to care too much. That'd be suspicious.

Click!

Regretfully Linus hadn't locked his cabin door, and nor did Vladimir knock; the Grand Howler just barrelled in and shut the door as quickly as he'd barged it aside.

"Looks like we're taking the scenic route," he chuckled loudly – Vladimir never chuckled, even less spoke loudly. He locked the door, "Going through the Bloc, Ulf help us. It must be to scare off any would-be assassins."

By the time Linus had gathered wits enough to stand up and salute, Vladimir was already on him, pushing him via the chest so he fell back on the bed.

"Well?" the Grand Howler growled under his breath.

"Sir?" Linus yelped.

"Are you going to tell me what's going on, or are you going to make me beat it out of you?"

Linus gulped, then said, "You can't do that."

"I can do whatever I want!" Vladimir claimed, wafting a sheet of paper, the one Livia had given him no doubt. "I could tell Amael these numbers are false, as I know they are, even without checking them. Amael might be soft around pretty girls, but I am not such a fool. I'll insist those 'Cubs' are removed from the train and investigated, and you'll soon follow, unless you tell me *exactly* what you're up to."

Linus remained tight-lipped.

Vladimir changed tack. "I can't believe you'd do anything to wilfully endanger our lives, or Lupa," he grumbled, letting the paper flop back down by his side. "It's not in you. You're an idealistic young fool, nothing more; that's why I got you out of ALPHA's clutches."

Now Linus spoke, "What?"

"Humph! Didn't Janoah tell you? I contacted her at great risk to myself and instructed her to get you off the hook. And this is how you repay me, with lies?"

"Not lies, sir-"

"Linus do not try my patience!" Vladimir barked, before calming himself. "If there's no danger I'll let this go, nobody need know, but I *must* be allowed in, otherwise I'll bash the door down. I can have no secrets at this time. Do you understand me?"

At length Linus sat forward on the bed and dipped his chin, thumbs twiddling in his lap.

"Is that them?" he heard Vladimir growl. "The ones Josef Grau was after?"

Linus looked up at Vladimir, which rather gave the game away.

"I see," the Grand Howler hummed. "Trying to protect them from ALPHA, is that it? How stupid. You finished top of your class; you're supposed to be intelligent."

Linus looked down at his armoured feet again, emitting a shaky, nervous breath as he did so.

"What are they, family?" Vladimir asked, waiting a moment before guessing further, "Lovers?"

"Sir!" Linus squeaked indignantly.

"Money then? They're paying you to get out-"

"No! They're just... friends."

Vladimir faced the little window. "Then you really are a fool," he said, watching the streets and buildings of the rough, downtrodden Bloc pass. "You've got your whole life and career ahead of you and you throw it away over nothing but some passing friendship. What am I to do with you?"

Linus averted his gaze. In twelve months Vladimir had administered nothing more than the occasional hot-tempered clout of correction and stern words, but then Linus had never gone so far wrong as now.

Except, it felt right. Does that make me a rebel? Am I a traitor to Lupa?

Oh dear.

"Still, sneaking them through on the Elder Train is somewhat ingenious," Vladimir hummed. "Brazen, but ingenious. Out of respect for Den Father Vito the train won't be inspected as it passes though the Lupan Wall, so they shan't be uncovered."

"That's the idea, sir. It wasn't mine, though."

"Whose was it then? Uther's?"

"This has nothing to do with Uther, sir," Linus insisted.

"But the girl said-"

"That's just her cover story. It's just the sort if thing Uther would do. I wasn't sure you'd swallow it."

A Vladimir-brand grunt ensued – he *had* swallowed it.

"The tall one is very strong," the Grand Howler moved on, glancing to the nearest wall, as if he could feel Linus' wards through the cabin partitions right now. "Livia is it?"

"Olivia," Linus said, emphasising, "Oh-livia."

"How singularly unimaginative," Vladimir marvelled, turning to Linus again and adding, "Even for you."

"She's hiding in plain sight, sir. The more audacious the better, we thought."

"Humph! I'm not getting anything from the little one."

Linus explained, "You won't, sir. Sara's not afflicted. She's perfectly healthy in fact."

"Sara?"

"Yes."

"Not Sara Hummel, surely."

A nod.

Vladimir snorted, incredulous, "Good Ulf, I know she's a little firebrand, but what's *she* done to incur ALPHA's wrath?"

"Nothing, sir."

"She must've. She's Cora Hummel's daughter, you don't arrest such a well-connected wolfess on a whim."

Linus spread his paws, "ALPHA wanted to arrest her for hiding Olivia. They wanted to arrest Professor Heath too; for imperium abuse-"

"Yes yes yes, I quite remember that part of Josef's ranting."

"It's utter nonsense!"

"Stretched truths, Linus, not utter nonsense," Vladimir corrected sternly. "Josef's many things, but he's no fool; at least not when it comes to science. Olivia must have potential for him to be interested. I can feel her. So can you."

Linus shared what he knew, "Well, Josef's convinced she's a pure-blood."

"Pure-blood? You mean… she's a full Rot phenotype, with all the genes expressed?"

"I-I-I don't know, sir."

"You don't know?"

Linus shrugged a little.

"I thought you were into imperiology?" Vladimir huffed in disappointment.

Linus explained, "I know what you're talking about, sir, I read all the latest imperiology and biology journals, but I have no idea if Olivia is anything unusual or not. It's not as if I've tested her. I don't even know what she knows."

A nod. "I see. Well, suffice to say if Olivia *is* a pure-blood, to use the old term, then it's no wonder Josef wants her. She'd be a solid Eisenwolf candidate."

"Like Rafe," Linus stated.

"Yes… just like 'Rafe', or whatever Janoah calls her toy soldier these days," Vladimir agreed cryptically. "I wouldn't be surprised if she was the one directing Josef's actions. With two Eisenwolves loyal to her she'd be invincible within ALPHA-"

"No, sir."

"No?"

"Janoah told me she doesn't want Olivia being taken in by ALPHA," Linus insisted. "She said two Eisenwolves is one too many. They all want Rafe for themselves over there, but he belongs to her. He's her strong arm, from what I can tell."

Vladimir gruffed, "She confides in you again, I see. Dear me, that one sting you donated to Rufus went a long way in securing Janoah's love didn't it?"

"I did it for him, not her."

At length, Vladimir strode to the cabin door in all of two long steps and opened it a little. After peeking up and down the swaying carriage corridor, he shut the flimsy door again. Then, to Linus's thought-derailing amazement, the Grand Howler sat on the bed beside him. Linus made to stand in respect, but Vladimir pulled him back down by the arm.

"Linus, fascinating as this is, we must put these concerns aside," he said. "I'll do your friends no harm, nobody need know, but in return for turning my cheek I need your silence and cooperation in the days to come. I need a wolf in which I can confide, utterly. Can you be that wolf?"

"Sir?"

"Answer me. Yes, or no."

"Yes, Grand Howler. Of course."

Taking a deep breath Vladimir nodded, fidgeted, pulled out his golden pen and twiddled it between his fingers as he did when thinking. Was he nervous? Why?

"Linus… our leader is a traitor," he dared. "Amael has allied himself with THORN and is planning a coup to take over Lupa in the next few days."

With a loud, almost hog-like snort of, "What?" Linus physically recoiled from Vladimir's accusation.

The Grand Howler calmly set out his stall, "So far as we can ascertain, it'll begin with an attack on the Pack Summit by THORN in which the Den Fathers will be eliminated. During the subsequent confusion the wolfen arm of the conspiracy will move swiftly to control the city. In preparation, Amael's been embezzling white-imperium shipments, stockpiling his own illegal supply, possibly with the Gelb Warden's help, though where it is nobody knows."

With his brain stumbling to catch up, Linus emitted an incredulous breath.

Vladimir grunted, "Do you know why?"

With much nodding, Linus replied, "He who controls the stings controls the Howlers, sir. It's obvious."

"Yes, I thought you'd understand," Vladimir praised. "All Amael has to do is turn off the tap until his enemies submit… or die."

"It's monstrous."

"It gets worse," Vladimir claimed. "We haven't pinned down exactly how THORN is going to go about their task-"

"They'll plant a black-imperium bomb, naturally," Linus interrupted, echoing Uther's and many other wolfen opinions of THORN's ultimate goal.

Vladimir wasn't so sure. "That's the obvious conclusion, except the security around the Summit will be exceptionally tight. Every inch will be searched and searched again for anything untoward by countless loyal eyes. It'll be difficult to hide such a device. Besides, a bomb may not be that effective."

"Then what?"

"All I know is those hyenas fear nothing; they'll happily kill themselves in some suicidal gamble."

"Yes," Linus seethed, recalling the refinery and hyena who'd taken his own life.

There was a quiet moment, but for the trembling carriage.

"You believe me then?" Vladimir said, adding hastily, "I have evidence."

Linus looked to him, "I believe you, sir."

It was Vladimir's turn to breathe out in relief. "You're part of a select group, now," he said. "Very few know the full extent of the danger."

"Who else does?"

"Amongst others, Janoah and I… and the Alpha," Vladimir begrudgingly confessed.

"The Alpha?"

"Regrettably his 'organisation' is the only group I could turn to. I couldn't go to the other packs because even if I could get the evidence high enough to start an investigation they would've immediately made a move and ruined everything, and I'd be a dead wolf when Amael found out. ALPHA has no vested interest in protecting names and reputations, if anything they thrive on tearing them down. With Janoah's help, and mine, they've amassed enough evidence to build a case against Amael."

Linus digested that and said boldly, "Then why doesn't ALPHA arrest him now?"

"It's not enough, Linus."

"Not enough? They arrest other wolves at the drop of a hat!"

"Impressionable, nobody Howlers like you, maybe; not seasoned well-liked Elders," Vladimir pointed out. "ALPHA can't break ranks, not yet. To move now would be to capture only Amael, leaving his allies to go to ground. No, the Alpha understands, as I do, that we must wait and hope the plotters show their guilt and yet give us time to stop them." He looked to the window, "We've agents placed within THORN and with luck they'll be able to get word to us regards the manner and timing of the attack. Until then we're flailing in the dark. All we can be is vigilant."

"I-I-I will be, sir."

Vladimir turned to Linus again, then dipped his eyes a little, "There's more."

"More?"

"I'm... sorry to say that Uther and Ivan may be involved in Amael's conspiracy."

Linus's blood turned to rot. "What?"

"As you know, Amael supposedly sent them on an errand to sabotage THORN activities. I believe they are in fact on a mission to murder our Den Father."

"No!" Linus yelped, leaping up to his feet, as if to distance himself from Vladimir's vile accusation lest the Grand Howler's lack of faith in his fellow wolf was contagious. "I don't believe it!"

"Humph! You believed the rest."

"But, sir-"

"Uther and Ivan are to clear the way to the Den Father's chair so Amael can sit in it before the coup. That'll give him the authority to control the Bloodfangs legitimately whilst he sets about suppressing the other packs illegitimately."

"This is impossible."

"Not at all," Vladimir woofed. "Amael's secured all the votes necessary. What Elders he hasn't cajoled he's bullied. By Ulf, our Den Father is a liability, overcome by rot and vice; his death can't come soon enough for our Elders. They'll *throw* the Den Father's mantle at Amael."

Linus gnarled his fingers, "No I mean... Uther would never... He's not a m-mmm-murderer, Grand Howler. He'd never agree to something like that!"

"You don't know him as I do, Trooper. He has a past."

"He's my partner. My best friend!"

"Which clouds your judgement!" Vladimir barked back, standing up also, towering over the stocky Linus. He checked the door and his tone, trusting in the rumbling train to muffle all speech. "Still... if what I'm told is correct, Uther's doing it for love, not hate – him and Ivan both. Take consolation in that, though the law won't make such nice distinctions."

"Love?" Linus said, latching onto that soft, hopeful word amongst Vladimir's bleak vocabulary as he searched his hard face. "What do you mean? Love for what?"

"For whom," Vladimir corrected, sighing contemptuously, "for *him*, of course, who else?"

Linus frowned, "Amael?"

"Noooo, you daft pup-"

The unlocked door burst open and, of all the wolves that could've, Elder Amael entered, cloaked and helmeted and magnificent as always.

"Linus have you seen-" he began, stopping upon sighting Vladimir and scoffing in surprise, "There you are, Grand Howler."

The Howlers, Grand and not, stood to attention.

"I was just advising Linus on how to conduct himself during the trip, Elder," Vladimir explained deftly. "This is his first time away from Lupa, let alone attending a Summit."

Amael barely listened anyway. "I need you to stand with me, both of you," he said. "I've just heard a disturbing rumour."

"Rumour, sir?"

"Word is ALPHA's going to inspect the train as we pass through the Bloc arm of the Lupan Wall."

"Inspect the train?" Linus barked. "They c-c-can't do that; this is the Elder Train! We're on Bloc Territory anyway, what right does ALPHA have to inspect us here?"

Amael appreciated Linus's gall. "That's *exactly* what I said, Trooper!" he growled, making a fist, unaware Linus's exclaim stemmed from a very different source than an affront to his honour – he was thinking of his stowaways. "The worst part is Den Father Vito agreed to it, apparently!" Amael woofed. "Well, they can search the other carriages, but they're not stepping foot in mine! If the so-called Alpha thinks he can get away with bullying me he's another thing coming! Gather everyone together, we'll show them!"

Once Amael had stormed down the corridor, Vladimir turned to Linus and grumbled, "If he wasn't trying to bring down Lupa and set it up anew in his image I could learn to admire that wolf. He's exactly the sort to keep ALPHA in check." He looked to the dreary heavens and sighed, "Ulf, you mock me."

"What do we do, now?" Linus whispered.

"Do?" Vladimir replied. "Stand with our Elder against ALPHA's harassment. What else?"

"But Den Father Vito's in danger-"

"We can give nothing away. Nothing! We cannot even warn Vito without exposing ourselves to Amael; any one of Vito's entourage may be a conspirator. We will just have to hope the attempt on Vito's life fails, even if it is Blade-dancer and Wild-heart who're going about it." Adjusting his mantle, Vladimir added rationally, "Besides, *you* need Amael to keep ALPHA from discovering your friends. That makes him your greatest ally for the next ten minutes."

Linus could but breathe, "By Ulf's fangs, what a mess."

"Ulf mocks you too?" Vladimir asked rhetorically. Walking to the door and placing a paw on its frame, he lingered long enough to huff, "If he gets us through this nightmare in one piece I might yet believe in him again."

✧

The massive Elder Train of the Bloodfangs slowly ground to a halt at an anonymous-looking Bloc station, billowing ash across the platform and ruffling the Alpha's black cloak. The stocky brown wolf stood with his paws cupped before him, flanked by Duncan and Horst and a pawful of meaner-looking Prefects sporting more scars on their muscled arms than the average veteran.

"This is so demeaning, my Alpha," Horst complained from under his helmet, shielding himself from the judgemental gaze of countless Bloodfang eyes with a paw to his brow. "We'll never live this down."

"Och! Who cares what they think?" Duncan said jovially.

"I do! We should have our own train."

The Alpha growled, "For the last time, Horst, I'll not squander money on such extravagance. We must remain above financial reproach – it's all that protects us."

"But it could be *any* train, my Alpha," Horst whined.

"Oh aye?" Duncan chortled, "Even a rusty old hulk?"

"Yes! Why not? Just so long as we didn't have to share it with anyone else. The engine doesn't matter; we only need a nice sleeping car. And maybe a nice lounge too-"

"A pathetic mockery of an Elder Train would be even worse than riding on the real thing!" the Alpha declared, whirling on Horst. "There's no shame in honest poverty, but much in the pretence of wealth. Now suck in your pride... and that gut, for Ulf's sake."

The leader of ALPHA finished by giving Horst the reproachful once-over with those ice-blue eyes, which, as always, signified an end to the debate, but not the lecture.

"The packs give us nothing to work with and yet what trouble we cause them, eh?" the Alpha rumbled on, even as the lead carriage's doors opened and the red carpet lolled forth like a gigantic tongue. "Our 'Den' is a leaky, mildew-ridden, concrete dump and we can't even pay our Prefects properly, yet ALPHA's are the loyalist of wolves," he continued, gesturing at the Prefects roundabout, who all stood extra smartly, chests out and ears pricked, whilst the Alpha himself sang their virtues. "They're here because they love justice and peace, Horst, not wealth and comfort. My bed is no better than theirs, my rations the same; even my cloak and armour no finer. That's how it should be. What joins ALPHA is the common wish to derail that trainload of decadence before you, not ride it! So don't talk to me of Elder Trains again you utter buffoon."

Horst raised his chin, "Yes, my Alpha."

"I knew I should've brought Silver along instead of you. If you hadn't been at my side so long, Horst, I would've."

"Yes, my Alpha."

"Just try and keep your mouth shut and let me do the talking."

"Yes, my Alpha."

The puny ALPHA contingent watched as a veritable army of Bloodfang Den Guards emerged from the splendid carriage and formed a line down each side of the red carpet. A Howler stepped into this living tunnel, a grey wolf in a red cloak and black armour, the armour being trimmed with white at the joints and seams – red, white and black, the Bloodfang tricolour.

It was Den Father Vito Bloodfang, no doubt about it!

As Vito walked along the carpet with surprising vigour for one rumoured to be a rot-ridden, senile old wreck, his guards peeled off behind him and formed a circle, raising a living barrier between their Den Father and any assassin. Short of mowing the entire retinue down or blowing them up it would be nigh on impossible to take Vito out.

The Alpha wondered how the treacherous Amael would manage to assassinate his leader even as he raised a paw in ALPHA-style greeting.

"Den Father Vito," he said. "You honour us."

Before any amongst Vito's swarming entourage could take offence, and despite his beliefs, the Alpha knelt as a wolf was expected to do before a Den Father. Duncan and Horst followed their leader's cue and swallowed their pride, the latter only after being surreptitiously slapped on the leg by the Alpha. The other Prefects did the same, however much it may have pained them to bow and scrape before the decadent old order it had to be seen to be done, for now.

The magnificent red, white and black Vito raised his helmeted head a little. He said nothing, but leant to one side, close to a member of his entourage.

"Den Prefect Adal," the lesser wolf whispered in Vito's pricked grey ear, "the leader of ALPHA."

"I know that!" Vito snapped back.

The Den Father waited, staring vacantly, trying to remember what all this was about – the Alpha could almost hear the rusty gears grinding between his rotten ears.

The second wolf, clearly Vito's adjutant, gently reminded his leader that, "ALPHA lacks an engine, sir, but have their own carriages. You decided they could attach their train onto ours and hitch a ride to the Pack Summit this year since it is being held so far out of a wolf's way in Hummelton."

"Did I, by Ulf?" Vito woofed, as if doubting his own decision.

The adjutant sniffed, "After lengthy negotiations, Den Father. No other pack would take them."

"Then why in Ulf's name are we?"

"Because we're the strongest and the most righteous of the packs; we've nothing to fear from them. Your own words, Den Father."

"Yes. Yes, it's becoming... clearer now."

"Such wise words couldn't have come from any other."

Vito waved away the sycophantic flattery and gestured for the meagre ALPHA contingent to rise. "The honour is mine, Grand Prefect... Adal," he said, the name almost escaping his memory again. He continued with more confidence, "You're welcome aboard our train, but I'll warn you now that I'll grant ALPHA no more powers. My mind is made up, so do not try to bend my ear during this trip."

"On the contrary, sir, my Prefects and I will keep to our own carriages," the Alpha promised, bowing a little. "You'll be left in peace."

"You'll not dine with us then?" Vito guffawed in a high-pitched tenor, perchance offended.

The Alpha spread a paw, "If so invited, Den Father, but I wouldn't presume to intrude further than I already have. Besides, I'm a wolf of... simple pleasures."

Vito slapped Adal on the arm like a rough old soldier and chuckled, "What could be simpler than dining? No, no, you shall be our guest. Anything less would be churlish, and the Bloodfangs are not churlish."

"You've proven that merely by allowing us to ride on your train, Den Father, which is magnificent, if I may say." the Alpha praised, casting his gaze along the Elder Train.

"Yes. She's not bad. We'll have to see about getting a train for you lot one day."

The Alpha laughed politely.

Things were proceeding swimmingly, until an upset arrived in the form of a Bloodfang Elder bullying his way to the front of the goings-on.

It was Amael.

"Den Father Vito!" he panted, kneeling perfunctorily before rising without being beckoned, and glaring at the three ALPHA wolves. "Den Father, I must protest!"

Vito replied airily, "Protest, Amael?"

"Allowing ALPHA to inspect this train is an affront to your high office. They've been allowed to traipse over everything else, but the Elder Train is sacred ground. I will not stand by and let such a precedent be set-"

"Calm yourself, Elder," Vito's adjutant grunted. "You misunderstand, there's to be no inspection."

Baffled, and not a little afraid he'd made a fool of himself in front of everyone, Amael huffed defensively, "Then what're they doing here, Den Father?"

"Hitchhiking," the Alpha freely admitted. He saluted Amael, ALPHA-style, then said, "You've nothing to fear from our presence, Elder Amael. Only guilty Howlers need fear the paw of ALPHA."

"Indeed," Amael replied. "Rooting out the corruption within Lupa's ranks is a necessary affair, but you lot go about it with too much zeal than is natural for a wolf."

The Alpha indignantly cupped a paw to his cloaked chest, like an affronted housewife, "We but meet the enemies of the republic with the same robustness as any Howler should, Elder. The only difference being our jurisdiction is limited to Howlers, who are still not used to being scrutinised and will grumble."

"But who scrutinises ALPHA?" Amael snorted haughtily, adding with street-side gruffness, "Eh?"

"The Den Fathers, sir," the Alpha responded deftly. "No wolf we bring charges against is convicted by us, but by a jury of Elders picked by the Den Fathers. If ALPHA's evidence is lacking then that wolf goes free. What more safeguards do you need on our power?"

"Gentlebeasts, the Bloc is no place for a debate," Den Father Vito declared, holding out his paws to the rain. "You'll have your say at the Summit, all of you. Save your breath for then." Turning to his adjutant and clapping a paw on his shoulder he said through a restrained, pained growl, "Take care of our guests, I'm… I'm going inside. This rain does not agree with my bones."

"Yes, Den Father."

The rot really was gnawing at Vito; one could hear it in his voice and see it in his checked walk as he hobbled back to the train amidst his swirling Den Guard. Still, he wasn't as far gone as Adal had been led to believe. Perhaps it was a good day? The rot had its good and bad days.

"Where are your carriages?" Vito's adjutant asked sharply, unwilling to say 'Alpha' or even Grand Prefect. "I would like to inspect them."

"You inspect *our* carriages?"

"Horst!" the Alpha grunted, before continuing to the adjutant, "By all means, sir."

"If you'd kindly point me to them."

"They're in a siding somewhere around here," the Alpha replied airily, looking about and shrugging. "Ask the local train hogs, I left all the arrangements to them."

"Ah know where they are," Duncan volunteered. "Follow me, lad."

"I'm not a 'lad', Grand Prefect!" the adjutant protested.

"Och! Pardon me, sir. Habit is all."

Amael lingered on the periphery. Once Duncan and Vito's adjutant had departed, he said, "You surprise me, Prefect Adal," intentionally omitting the 'Grand' prefix.

The Alpha icily met Amael's fiery gaze, "How so?"

"You must have many enemies after all the Howlers you've sent down. You should take more care and keep your transport well-guarded, especially in the Bloc."

"It is well-guarded," Adal insisted, adding, "as am I."

⚜

Rafe felt the van tip some twenty degrees or so and struggle up what had to be a ramp. With no windows he couldn't see what was happening, but the sound of the engine took on a distinctly tinny tenor, as if entering a metallic tunnel. As quickly as the van had tipped up it levelled out again and its engine shuddered to a stop.

The drivers got out, shutting their doors and walking around the van. Rafe expected them to open the back doors but instead a bigger-sounding door slammed shut and was bolted.

"What's going on?" Rafe whispered, a little unnerved.

"Shh," Janoah replied.

Time passed, minutes only, but an eternity in the claustrophobic space. There came voices outside, muffled beyond comprehension. Doors opened; the voices grew louder and clearer.

"What's this?" someone asked sharply tapping on the side of the van.

"For the Alpha's protection," someone replied – it sounded like Grand Prefect Duncan.

"Protection?" said the beast with him.

"Aye. His bodyguards travel in it; behind his car."

"Open it up."

"Ah'm afraid Ah don't have the keys."

"Then get them, Grand Prefect."

"Gladly, sir, but Ulf knows who has them. It could take me some time tae track them down. Maybe later?"

Duncan (surely) and the grumbling stranger moved on, clunking around the metallic space in their Howler boots. After more unintelligible words from both parties the big doors were shut and bolted again.

Silence.

Janoah passed Rafe a reassuring smile, whilst Josef sat twiddling his fine feline whiskers, perhaps contemplating some deep scientific truth, but more likely contemplating breakfast since everyone had skipped it in their rush to get ready. Rafe for one felt his stomach churning, but knew better than to complain right now.

The van rocked slightly, then a few seconds later Rafe detected a definite forward acceleration. He hadn't ridden a train for some time, but it felt to him like pulling away from a station. The sounds of rail joins clacking underneath confirmed his suspicions, though not all.

"Are we on the Elder Train?" he whispered.

"In a manner of speaking," Janoah confirmed circumspectly, standing up and throwing the van doors wide.

Expecting daylight to flood into the poorly lit van, Rafe was surprised to see utter blackness beyond. Glancing at Josef, he joined Janoah as she stepped out into the void. Both Prefects unconsciously brushed their white-imperium brooches with a paw, commanding them to shine and drive back the darkness. The metallic panelled interior of a freight carriage was revealed to Rafe, the rivets joining the plates running with streaks of rust and ash. It reeked of imperium fuel and oil, a heady mix.

The train was picking up speed, the carriage rocking to and fro. Janoah steadied herself against the ALPHA van as she walked round towards its front.

"This way," she said.

Rafe followed, as did Josef, the latter shutting the van doors. With Janoah in the lead all three edged their way around the van.

The remainder of the space was piled high with barrels and boxes strapped securely together, but there was enough space to walk through to the carriage's interconnecting front end door. Janoah opened it, letting in daylight, as well as a torrent of cold, rain-flecked air. With her mantle whipping about her shoulders, she stepped fearlessly across the small gap between this carriage and the next, sleepers blurring beneath her, and opened the next door.

Rafe was beckoned across the elemental breach. It should've been easy for someone as big and tall as he, let alone a wolf fearless enough to face hyena warriors and giant centipedes, yet Janoah's Eisenwolf hesitated all the same, head darting left and right as he gripped the railings.

"Come on!" Janoah encouraged.

Regaining his composure, Rafe stepped across to the next much nicer-looking carriage. "Where's all the buildings gone?" he woofed ungrammatically.

Janoah looked out at the passing scenery – flat, ashen wastes as far as the fog allowed her to see. There were no buildings, no nothing, save the odd dead tree and growing puddle. Even the Wall Slums had been left far behind.

Laughing gently at Rafe's delectable naivety, Janoah patted the giant wolf's arm and shouted over the wind, "We've left Lupa! This is the Ashfall, you daft lump!"

Rafe gasped, "I've never seen it."

"You must've, when you went to New Tharona. It'"

Janoah recognised that blank Rafe stare; he was trying to remember it, if not the whole holiday.

"The Ashfall's not as bad that side," Janoah excused.

She then encouraged Josef to step across the gap; the cat looked in need of it as the wind and noise buffeted him from all directions. That, combined with the rain and general danger, precipitated a rapid retreat back into the previous carriage.

"I'll stay here and… and make sure the suit is in good order!" he shouted nervously.

"For Ulf's sake, Doctor, it's just a little rain!"

"You go ahead! I'll wait until the next stop!"

Janoah turned to Rafe, "Help him across, would you?"

"Sure."

Stepping easily back across the gap, Rafe spread his big brown paws at the coated cat.

"Come on, Doctor Josef, I'll help you-"

"No!" Josef snapped, disappearing inside. "No, thank you, Rafe. I'll be fine here."

"I won't let you fall."

"Let me go! No! Get off me you wolfen oaf!"

Rafe emerged from the carriage with a squirming, hissing Josef slung over one shoulder and hopped across the gap to join Janoah in the next carriage.

"Cats," she sighed, shutting the door against the elements.

Expecting a carriage like any other, with rows of seats down each side, Rafe was surprised to find a well-lit open space, complete with carpet, sofas, tables and chairs, even a landscape painting or two. The furniture was not the usual preferred minimalist ALPHA style made from new moulded imperium compounds, but old-fashioned organics; decorative wood and green velvet. Though polished it was chipped and worn. The carpet, too, was faded, the curtains threadbare, and the paintings washed out.

This was some kind of posh carriage, Rafe supposed, albeit but one that had seen better days.

At the far end of said carriage, cosseted behind a desk set against an elaborate partition, beneath a banner bearing the A symbol of ALPHA, sat the Alpha himself – helmet off, tea steaming beside him, writing furiously. Grand Prefects Horst and Duncan, meanwhile, were sprawled over the comfortable-looking furniture, supping tea, smouldering embers and chatting, until they noticed Rafe and the others, whereupon Duncan extinguished his ember and stood up to greet them.

"Aye, 'tis the Eisenwolf himself!" he said, jovial as ever.

Horst scoffed sarcastically, "Yes, tell the whole world, why don't you?"

Ignoring Horst, Duncan crossed the swaying carriage to meet Janoah, Rafe and Doctor Josef, the last of whom Rafe only that second remembered to put down.

"Sorry," Rafe excused.

Whilst the indignant Josef brushed water from his black coat, simple, half-hearted ALPHA salutes were exchanged by all, except the Alpha himself, who didn't so much as look up from his pen and paper.

"He's working," Duncan whispered, looking mostly to Janoah, and referring to the Alpha. "His speech," he added with a wink, "best tae leave him to it-"

"I can manage two things at once, Duncan," the Alpha said, beckoning the newcomers. "I'm not so far gone as old Vito."

"You're but a wee slip of a lad, my Alpha," Duncan woofed.

"The rot'll come for us all one day," the Alpha said soberly. "Not before our work is done, Ulf willing."

"Aye."

Janoah and her comrades approached the Alpha's desk whilst Duncan lingered on the periphery. The big black wolf, usually the biggest in any room, was dwarfed by the bigger brown Rafe.

"Welcome aboard, comrades," the Alpha said, even whilst still writing. "We've been tacked onto the end of the train, as far from the Bloodfang Den Father as possible, though that suits me just fine." He looked up a moment, "What do you think of our accommodation?"

Janoah glanced about the opulent, if faded trappings of the carriage. "Tawdry," she hummed.

The Alpha chuckled appreciatively, "I'm afraid it's the best we could do. Silvermane sourced it from a Greystone scrap yard. Must be a hundred years old if it's a day. We didn't have the time or money to refit it with simpler furniture." He flicked his plain-looking silvery pen to one side, indicating the passage to his left, before continuing to write an unrelated yet coherent sentence even as he spoke, "Your cabins are down the hall. I'll leave you to decide who gets what room; they're all much the same." He looked up again, specifically at the towering Rafe and sat back in amazement, "By Ulf it really works. Well done, Josef."

Doctor Josef bowed a little, "Thank you, my Alpha."

After a tiny 'Mm' of approval, the Alpha continued. "Now, Rafe, as far as anyone outside this room is aware, you're just a Howler that's recently come over to us from the Greystones. I picked you out to be my bodyguard because, well, who wouldn't want a wolf the size of a house at their back?"

"Aye, sir," Rafe chirped – Janoah trod on his foot, spurring him to add, "my Alpha."

The Alpha let it slide. "You're Prefect Bruno Claybourne now, not Eisenwolf Rafe Stenton. Remember that."

"Yes, my Alpha."

"Best thing you can do is be quiet, look menacing, and stay close to me or Janoah."

"I will, my Alpha."

"Surely our own Prefects will suspect something," Horst snorted, swirling his drink. "They've all seen Rafe lingering about HQ with that prim little Nurse Stroud."

Rafe's ears pricked at Horst's tone.

"I'm sure the good doctor's cloak will give even them pause for thought," the Alpha replied, giving Josef and the black-imperium cloak he'd made for Rafe a decidedly guarded look. He returned his gaze and pen to his paper, "Be vigilant, Prefect Claybourne. Whatever is to happen will happen; all we can do now is meet it when it comes."

"Yes, my Alpha," Rafe replied – or was it Bruno?

✣

Given a quick glance up and down the swaying train corridor, Linus knocked on the door and entered the cabin at Olivia's behest. He hadn't even shut said door before 'Howler' Sara leapt to accost him.

"Well?" she pleaded, still disguised by her stripy Cub gear.

After too long a breath for Sara's frayed nerves, Linus declared that, "It's all right. We're through."

"Och!" Sara exhaled. "Thank goodness."

"Vladimir… he knows who you are," Linus admitted awkwardly, adding quickly, "but he's not interested. He's looking the other way. To be honest I… I think he likes me."

Olivia blurted, "Likes you?"

"Well, he trusts me at least. He's often confided in me. I don't know. Maybe I'm reading him wrong-"

"He could do worse than confide in you," Olivia said. Approaching Linus she grasped his shoulder and said, "I'm grateful for what you've done. Really, I am."

Linus stared at Olivia, wondering if she even knew what she was, if indeed she was anything. "It's nothing," he said.

"If I can repay you in any way-"

"Repay me by living a life free of imperium's grip from here on… if you can."

Olivia nodded a little.

"What about the Professor?" Sara asked. "Have ye heard anything?"

"I'm sure Werner's taking care of him," Linus reassured chirpily, paws raised. "Now, please, don't leave this cabin unless you have to. We'll be at Hummelton in a day and then you'd best disappear. Don't worry about goodbyes, just slip away."

"Ah'll be all right, mah mum will protect me," Sara said, taking Olivia's nearest paw, "but won't they look for Olivia, even out in Everdor?"

"I don't think so," Linus assured, looking out the window at the passing fog-bound wastes of the Ashfall. "I suspect they'll have other worries by then."

Olivia frowned, "What do you mean?"

"Nothing you need worry about. Just play your role. You're very good at it you know."

"I try."

After a shared chuckle and mutual stare, Linus took his leave. "I-I-I'd better go."

Once the real Howler had gone, the disguised Sara sat on the bed, paws resting on her armoured knees.

"He's rather sweet isn't he?" Olivia hummed.

Sara collapsed sideways on the bed and exhaled in disbelief, "Och, Olivia, not now!"

Codex: Hummel

Of the four great wolf packs of the Lupan continent, Hummel are the outliers in every respect, being both physically and psychologically removed from Lupa.

As Lupa and its ashen effluent expanded over the centuries, slowly transforming the once green plains to the grey desolation of the Far Ashfall today, so were most other packs and their citizens necessitated to migrate into Lupa to earn a living. Not so Hummel. Everdor, home of the Hummels, remains beyond the choking hold of the Ashfall, the pollution's spread being largely blocked by the Sunrise Mountains. Thus Hummel and their little beasts have stayed put, necessarily so, for someone has to sow seeds and provide food – an impossibility under the Ashfall.

Hummel territory is vast and Howlers thin on the ground, making Everdor hard to police despite the low crime-rate, especially at its fringes where the truly wild world begins to encroach. To maintain order, Hummel could have pursued one of two paths, indomitable cruelty or relative lenience; they chose the latter. The citizens of Everdor enjoy near-equality with their wolfen protectors, at least nominally. In truth, the little beasts would quickly be conquered without Hummel and its powerful Howlers to protect them, and thus a cult of quasi-monarchy has developed whereby the Hummel Den Father or Mother is regarded almost as a Wolf King or Queen. Even Hummelton, capital of Hummel, has a medieval vibe, with heavy industry strictly prohibited by law. Hummelton can never become a rival to Lupa, or else Everdor would wither under a second Ashfall and the race of wolfkind starve.

Hummel are notoriously insular regarding Howler uptake, recruiting almost exclusively from their own stock and not importing afflicted talent from the Steppes, Rostsonne, Lupa or anywhere else but Everdor. Curiously, and perhaps because of their pure breeding, Hummel Howlers are as likely to be female as male, whereas the rot mostly afflicts males amongst the city-based packs. For reasons Lupan science is only just beginning to grasp, females are able to remove imperium from their blood more readily than males, making them less likely to develop and maintain a corona. In Hummel this seems not to be the case and female Howlers are both common and deadly.

However, some wonder how Hummel matures enough Howlers to even maintain their borders. The low-pollution environment makes ambient imperium uptake slow and candidates hard to detect, as the rot can linger for decades before expressing itself. It is a question this secretive pack refuses to be drawn upon.

Chapter 37

Screaming across the endless Far Ashfall towards the Sunrise Mountains, twilight snapping at its wheels, the titanic Bloodfang Elder Train stopped for no beast. The occasional shanty town hugging the rails was briefly dazzled by the great, glowing, mechanical millipede, its inviting windows illuminating the faces of noble and little beast, filling them with awe and wonder alike, before choking them all with swirls of hot imperious ash.

There seemed to be quite the crowd gathered at the rail side, perhaps in anticipation of other Elder Trains to follow. Eisbrand, Greystone and the representatives of the Bloc, they each had their own. The Eisbrand's was the most magnificently decorated and luxurious of all, wolves said, but the Greystones had built a better engine, others countered. The Bloodfangs could lay claim to neither accolade, and the weak Bloc nothing much at all. Still, ALPHA didn't even have their own train. Pathetic!

That was the joke swilling around the vapour-clogged dining carriage this evening. It amused the Howlers no end, even reassured them, to know that those pesky Prefects spoiling everyone's fun of late couldn't even get to the Summit without a lift. It was only the munificence (or rot-induced senility some whispered) of Den Father Vito that had allowed them to attend with any sort of dignity at all. The other packs had refused to help, and to drive to Hummelton in their dour ALPHA trucks, or worse take some civilian train with all the riffraff coming and going from Lupa, would've made them appear even more ridiculous.

And yet, those with eyes saw the opposite. While the Howlers revelled in luxury, humble ALPHA lingered in the back of the train, in some modest carriage found in a scrap yard. Poor, noble, wronged ALPHA, doing what it could to uphold wolfen law, taking only what it had to, functioning on a shoestring, now as they'd always done since their inception.

It looked bad for the Howlers, but Vladimir knew he couldn't pick that fight yet.

ALPHA would have to wait their turn.

A rabbit waiter dressed in red and white pushed a trolley laden with cups and saucers and all things drink-related down the aisle. Stopping next at Vladimir's table he asked, "Coffee or tea, sir?" with impeccable poise, ears erect and all.

"Tea," Vladimir gruffed sharply.

"Rostsonne or Hummel?"

"Rostsonne."

A tiny teapot, a cup and saucer, honey pot and a soy milk jug, were all laid out before Vladimir, all so delicate and fine that Linus, sitting beside him, could see light from the table lamp diffusing through the translucent porcelain. Each piece was painted with an idyllic countryside scene, with rolling hills, trees and cottages.

The rabbit added tea leaves and boiling water to the teapot with near ritualistic care.

"And you, sir?" he asked Linus.

It took the Howler a moment to respond, "Uh… tea please."

"Rostsonne or Hummel?"

"Rostsonne, please."

The same rite was performed, the difference being that Linus added a "Thank you," afterwards, which surprised the rabbit enough for him to throw the golden wolf a questioning glance.

'Tara' was sitting opposite Linus. When asked, the black wolfess went for Hummel tea and said to the rabbit, "Thank you very much," with an acknowledging nod and smile, which sent the little beast's whiskers twisting in alarm.

'Livia' was last. "Coffee," she demanded, without so much as waiting to be asked, even less thanking anyone.

Now that's more like it.

His confidence in the system restored, the rabbit set about preparing Livia's beverage, comfortable in his place as a little beast and taxpayer, backbone of Lupa, not the brain. If only all citizens were so content, and if only the hyenas could accept wolfen leadership, all would be well. Someone had to be on top, if not wolves then someone else would take over. It was the natural order. Right?

Maybe not, Linus thought – only thought, mind you.

He observed the Elders sitting at the 'Elder Table' in the middle of the dining carriage, with Den Father Vito at the head. Whatever wolves said of his mind, Vito looked magnificent in his Den Father's mantle, his grey face scarred but strong, a seasoned wolf one felt safe following. Amael was there, drinking and mingling, laughing when applicable, fitting in convincingly with his fellow Elders, yet every movement, every word an act, surely. Was he really plotting the downfall of Vito Bloodfang, Thorvald Eisbrand, Cora Hummel, the newly elected Flaid Greystone and the other Den Fathers, the whole rotten system?

Lupa might change for the better, might it not?

No! Stop it, Linus! You're no rebel. You're helping Sara and Olivia get out and that's all it is, a favour for good friends. Uther would do no less.

But… Uther's conspiring, isn't he? Him and Ivan are with Amael, aren't they? No… no they *can't* be. Vladimir's got it wrong. They're about something all right, but it's for the best whatever it is. Perhaps they're double agents, working against Amael, waiting to spring into action against him. Yes. Or maybe they're just going along with Amael to placate him. Did he even give them a choice? Did he force them? Either way, what if I see them? What should I do?

Ulf, help me.

"No sign of Adal, yet."

Vladimir's words and over-the-shoulder glance brought Linus back into the carriage, to the hubbub, and the scenery rolling by the window.

"Adal, sir?" he said.

Vladimir looked Linus over. "The self-styled 'Alpha'," he said, derisively. "That's his *real* name; Den Prefect Adal Weiss. Make sure you call him that and not 'Alpha', should he design to turn up for dinner."

Livia sipped her steaming coffee. "Was he invited, sir?"

Vladimir looked at her, his eyes dancing over Olivia's fine brown features, before saying, "Apparently so."

"Puh!"

"You disapprove, Cub?"

"ALPHA are a bunch of common pigs, Grand Howler."

Vladimir cocked his head a little. Linus half expected his superior to explode in some kind of rage at Olivia for speaking so out of turn, but no.

"Maybe," Vladimir said, "but those pigs are dangerously close to snatching the strings of power."

Even though Vladimir knew who she was, and the girls knew that Vladimir knew who they were, neither party had formally acknowledged the fact, thus Olivia still played the part of a zealous young Howler perfectly, which was just as well for the benefit of any onlookers.

"ALPHA's rise will be halted at the Summit," she claimed haughtily. "The Den Fathers have had enough of their meddling, thank Ulf."

Vladimir stirred his tea. "I wouldn't be so sure. Adal is a clever wolf gifted with a silver tongue. He got on this train, one way or another, and now he's going to be fashionably late for dinner just to upstage everyone, perhaps by fabricating some crisis that needed his attention. They'll be angry at first, but within five minutes of sitting down he'll have Vito and most of the Elders eating from his paw like a herd of compliant, plump silkworms. He shan't fool Amael, of course, but that's neither here nor there."

"How do you know?"

"Intuition and experience. I could be wrong, but I doubt it."

Putting her coffee down and nursing the elegant cup, Olivia indicated beyond Vladimir with her violet eyes and said in a rather coy manner, "Looks like we're about to find out, Grand Howler."

The carriage-to-carriage door opened and the black-cloaked Adal entered the dining car, accompanied by his retinue, all in their full gear, minus weapons – Howler uniform was what Howlers wore to a posh dinner, and Prefects were no different there.

Vladimir recognised most of the Alpha's entourage; the bloated Horst with all his medals, the mighty Duncan, whose black fur melded with his black cloak, and of course little red Janoah, lingering at the back with some giant of a Prefect looming over her shoulder.

By Ulf, is it? No. She'd not be so foolish, would she?

The ALPHA contingent picked their way through the carriage, watched surreptitiously, or blatantly depending on who was doing the watching, by all. As they breezed by Vladimir's table the Grand Howler felt their coronas mingle with his, felt Janoah's familiar bubble of imperious energy push up against his own – one never forgot her flavour.

Yet, as that giant wolf bringing up the rear passed him Vladimir felt nothing particularly unusual, certainly not the overwhelming glacier of a corona that he had expected. He glanced up at that anonymous helmet-clad face, but gleaned no clues from its black, metallic surface.

Vladimir performed one last visual check by leaning down and sideways somewhat.

The fellow had a tail.

"What's wrong, sir?" Linus said, as Vladimir levered himself upright again.

"Nothing," the Grand Howler dismissed, tugging at his cloak. "Just drink your tea."

Sara, meanwhile, also turned to watch the representatives of ALPHA pass. Her wide eyes lingered exclusively on the huge wolf at the back, with his broad shoulders and confident rolling gait.

"Who's that?" she whispered.

"ALPHA," Linus said, surprised Sara didn't know. "Don't worry about them."

"No, Ah mean-"

Before Sara could continue, Olivia huffed none too quietly, "Bunch of pigs."

Vladimir glanced at the bold wolfess, but tendered neither rebuke nor praise for now. He instead strained to glean through the multicoloured, cacophonous fog of ember vapour and raucous chatter permeating the carriage what was said at the Elder table as the Alpha and his party presented themselves to Den Father Vito.

"Den Prefect Adal," Vito acknowledged, seated amongst his suddenly silent Elders, all of whom were cautiously eyeing Adal and his Prefects up like an approaching swarm of wasps. "Stand you stinking hyenas!" Vito snarled, glaring at his rude entourage. "This wolf wears the Imperium Heart. Exalt him!"

The Elders hurriedly stood, Amael Balbus noticeably last. Vito, as a Den Father, was not required to pay deference, not even to a bearer of the Imperium Heart.

"You're late for tea, Den Prefect," he said.

Removing his helmet to reveal his white, mask-like face, Adal Weiss bowed courteously. "My apologies, Den Father Vito; there were matters requiring my attention."

"All the way out here?"

"I've a stack of correspondence clogging up my in-tray. I needed to clear the most urgent matters before reaching the next stop, whereupon my orders will be wired to HQ."

"Working to root out traitors even now," Amael woofed mockingly. "Don't you ever rest?"

Adal replied to Amael, but spoke to Vito, "ALPHA never rests. We can't afford to."

"Oh! Such diligence."

"Is to be lauded, Balbus," old Vito added sternly, raising a paw slightly and throwing the sarcastic Amael a sideways glare. "If our own Provosts were as assiduous as ALPHA's Prefects in rooting out corruption, we would not *need* ALPHA to begin with. We may even have avoided the last war, such as it was."

"The very reason I get out of bed in the morning, Den Father," Adal insisted. "To suffer through one pack war is enough for a lifetime. The notion of Lupa crumbling again haunts me." His eyes flitted over Amael, "With this shortage our fair city teeters on the edge once again. There are those who might take advantage of her weakness. We must all be on our guard."

Whilst Amael calmly knocked back a brandy – no wet-eared tea-sipping for him – Vito nodded solemnly, "Well said, sir," and beckoned Adal to be seated at the Elder table as his guest for the evening.

The rest of the Alpha's entourage had to make do with an empty table near Vladimir and the other low-ranking Bloodfang flotsam, for the Elder table was strictly for the Den Father, his Elders, and, in this exceptional case, their guest Den Prefect Adal Weiss.

Horst, Duncan and Janoah took their places, but the anonymous giant of a Prefect accompanying them loomed over the Elder table, as if unwilling to leave the Alpha's side. Spotting her comrade's faux pas, Janoah leapt up and tugged him away to sit with her, rebuking him like some unruly toddler. Even then he kept glancing Adal's way, as if concerned the Elders might all leap up with knives and murder the Alpha any second.

"Who is that wolf," Vito asked Adal in a curious tone.

Adal feigned ignorance, "Which wolf, Den Father?"

Despite mumblings that his mind was going, Vito wasn't fooled and said flatly, "The one that's as big as a house, as well you know." He went on, "I don't recognise him as one of your Grand Prefects."

"Oh, don't mind Bruno," Adal guffawed lightly, as a rabbit waiter prepared his tea. The very act of someone else attending to his needs made an impartialist like Adal fidgety, but he persevered and blanked the waiter's very existence as was the Howler custom. "He's my bodyguard," he explained, kneading his brown paws.

"Bodyguard?" Vito crackled. "You've need of them, Adal?"

"As any wolf of rank."

"Just the one bodyguard?" Amael sideswiped.

"He's all I need. The just make enemies of the unjust; but the unjust make enemies of both," Adal possibly quoted. "You'll find the most corrupt wolves have to build the highest walls, Amael."

Whilst Amael simmered, Vito observed Bruno's continual glances across the way. "He seems keen."

"He's young," Adal replied disarmingly, "but strong."

"Bloodfang?"

"I believe he's of Greystone stock, actually."

"Then I'm glad it was Flaid that lost such a… magnificent wolf to ALPHA and not me."

Adal merely chuckled.

Looking across to Bruno as if trying to gauge his imperious mettle, and doubtless being foiled by Josef's black-imperium cloak, Vito changed subject, "And the wolfess?"

"Janoah, sir. One of our finest Prefects."

"Janoah… Janoah…."

Vito's adjutant was on paw to give the Den Father's rot-ravaged mind a subtle kick. "The widow of Grand Howler Rufus, Den Father."

"Ah… yes."

The mere name 'Rufus' was all it took to silence the table for a time. There was only one Rufus in Lupa that wolves either respected or loathed, but always recognised, even now he had been fed to the ants.

Or so you all think, Amael chuckled to himself.

Ah, but die Rufus must, he decided, even as he downed his brandy and pretended to care what Vito was rambling on about now. Rufus was killed in the midst of the coup, Jan, shot in the confusion. Yes, that's it. I'll get Nurka'll to take care of him for me, and then I'll take care of Nurka and THORN before they inevitably turn on me. Janoah will never know I ordered it. They failed to protect Rufus, I'll say. You can't blame me for hyena incompetence. She'll throw a tantrum, but she'll come round.

Look at her, supping her tea and making witty conversation at her table like the best Common Ground escort money could buy. She's wrapping that soppy Duncan around her finger, even Horst looks mollified for once. She's so clever, so strong, so beautiful… so wasted on that arse of a wolf, Rufus.

I'll free you from him, Janoah. You'll be mine, you and Lupa. We'll sweep the other packs aside and found a dynasty of Wolf Kings. The Bloodfangs will rule! No more votes, no more deals, no more packs, just a homogeneous wolfen society guided by the word of the Wolf King, the crown passed from one ruler to the next.

Stability. Certainty. Peace.

If I don't do it Adal will, and Ulf save us all from such a world as ALPHA would impose. Look at you, you short, pen-pushing, joyless grub! You may fool Vito and the others, but you don't fool me. Searching for the conspirators are we, Adal Weiss? There's two in the midst of your concrete hive and you don't even know it. Flailing around in the dark you are. No bodyguard can save you from what's coming, however strong he is; no twist of words either, however clever they are. Your white face will turn as black as that mantle you wear as you choke on imperium waste, I'll see to that.

You at least truly deserve it.

✣

Emerging from his fluttering tent and crossing THORN's windblown camp, Rufus stepped into the flickering glow of the nearest fire.

Nurka had furnished his wolfen guest with all he needed for the task ahead – Howler greaves, helmet and rapier. It was the most basic, unadorned gear of the lowliest anonymous Trooper, stolen during some raid, apparently, and marred by as many scratches and scuffs as Rufus's war-hardened hide. The dazzling stripy cloak of Nurka's tribe lent him a modicum of splendour, however.

Of the hyenas huddled roundabout, Nurka alone stood to greet Rufus.

"Red-mist," the powerful hyena said in his hoarse tone, his face obscured by his fierce Jua-mata skull helmet, though his violet imperium-polluted eyes shone through.

"Nurka," Rufus replied.

Wolf and hyena shared a mutual respectful nod.

Nestled upon Nurka's left shoulder, like a fluffy shoulder pad, was a beautiful white pepper moth, its furry body and broad feathery antennae quivering in defiance of the bitter mountain climate. A small box was strapped to the bug's broad back, rather like a rucksack.

Teasing the moth from its perch and allowing it to hang from his forearm, its elegant wings tapering down in an inverted V-shape, Nurka opened the box it carried and slipped a piece of paper inside. Locking the lid again, he launched the not insubstantial creature into the air with a gruff grunt. Amidst a puff of white scales, the bug hummed across the camp and disappeared into the night, like a winged ghost.

Nurka had obviously been in communication with his contacts, whoever they may be, via that homing moth and probably others.

"Beautiful creatures pepper moths," Rufus observed. "Did it bring any news?"

Nurka tipped his helmeted head back, declaring confidently and with a flash off teeth, "Our Prince is alive."

"You're certain?"

"As can be when relying on pigs as intermediaries. We paid them, but someone might yet pay them more."

Whatever he thought, Rufus nodded sympathetically. He looked past Nurka, glancing to Themba and especially Casimir, the latter of whom averted his gaze and nibbled some bread.

"We will enter Gelb by the back door," Nurka announced.

Turning to him again Rufus blinked once, "Back door?"

"Yes," Nurka said, habitually wandering back and forth, paws cupped behind him, tail flicking. "As you probably know, there are countless ancient tunnels and abandoned shafts running through the Sunrise Mountains. In places they still intersect with Gelb's active mines."

"Of course," Rufus confirmed.

"And as an inmate of Gelb yourself, you must also have seen that the old tunnels are sealed to prevent prisoners wandering off?"

A nod from Rufus, followed by information, "Only by rusted doors and rubble. The guards didn't worry too much about us escaping because the tunnels are a death-trap."

"Death trap?" Themba said worriedly.

Rufus explained, "Nobody can navigate the caves by pure chance; you'd die of thirst or hunger before finding the way out, provided you didn't fall down a pit first, or get eaten by a cave spider. That's where they thought Professor Tack went."

"Who's Tack?" Nurka said.

"Oh, just a cat of… questionable sanity; a merchant of Gelb's healthy black market. He used to be a great professor, before someone in Lupa sent him down. The Elders have a nasty habit of doing that."

Nurka nodded and grunted.

After a moment's pause, Rufus spread a paw, "Do you know a way through the old tunnels then, Nurka?"

The hyena cackled triumphantly, "I've a map, Red-mist."

"Can it be trusted, though?" Casimir piped up from across the campfire. "It's ancient."

"It's our only choice," Nurka replied. "We'll mark our passage through the tunnels so we won't get lost, regardless of the map's integrity."

"Aye," Casimir said, "that's all well and good, but those tunnels are crawling with dangerous bugs. There's no telling what we'll bump into."

"It's a chance we must take."

"For just one hyena? Nurka, you're putting the whole operation at risk."

"Not just a hyena, but Prince Noss of the Jua-mata!" Nurka snarled back. "I do not expect a lowly rabbit to understand why he matters, but you *will* respect him!"

"Gentlebeasts!" Rufus said, raising his paws for calm. "I can see you've been debating this for some time."

"Hours," big Themba said, somewhat sarcastically.

Given a pause and nod, Rufus continued, "It's not just a question of *how* we do this, Nurka, but *when*."

"When?"

Rufus shared his reasoning. "Once we make our move word will quickly get out. If the powers that be judge there's sufficient danger the Summit could be cancelled and the Den Fathers disperse before… before what must be done is done."

"Prince Noss will be extracted surgically," Nurka said matter-of-factly. "The disappearance of one inmate will not upset anybody."

"He's a very important inmate."

"Nobody knows who he is, except Amael."

"Don't bet on it. The Warden must know who he is as well, and I'm sure many a guard too – ones other than those in your pocket. The Warden may be sympathetic to our cause, but he's playing a double game, waiting to see which way the wind blows before declaring his allegiance. He might want to hang onto Prince Noss for himself."

Nurka raised his chin and said pugnaciously, "So what're you saying?"

"I'm merely saying once we have Noss, things may be set in motion."

Eventually, the chief nodded, "We are ready to strike, Red-mist, I merely wish Noss to be there when we do."

Big Themba growled, "Personally, I wouldn't bother with this cowardly 'back door' approach. I'd raze that vile prison to the ground in a frontal assault and bury all the guards in the mines, alive, especially this murderous Warden, who's doubtless dutifully staked out many a hyena, *and* wolf, for the ants." He looked up from the crackling fire and flashed Rufus a menacing smile of a calibre only his people could manage, what with their marvellous dentition. "That'd silence the whole lot of them for good," he cackled.

"Until the next train arrives from Lupa to collect imperium ore and discovers Gelb in ruins," Nurka gruffed simply, rising up on his armoured toes a moment, paws behind back, like a proper sergeant major. "You'd sacrifice our chance to change the world for a moment's revenge, as usual, Themba. It's that kind of myopic thinking that's kept our people in bondage for too long. Leave the tactics to me, if you please."

"And your pet wolf, chief?" Themba dared acidly.

Nurka didn't reply, save to quickly shake his head at Rufus, conveying 'ignore him'.

"Rest, all of you," the chief instructed. "We make final preparations in the morning. Those that wish to enter the tunnels with me, make your peace with Mother Erde." He looked witheringly between Themba and Rufus, "And especially each other."

✦

The evening had panned out as Vladimir forecast. The Alpha had arrived late, made his noble excuses, bore the butt of enquiry and ridicule from hostile wolves like Amael, before ingratiating himself with Den Father Vito and a good many of the other Bloodfang elite with witty banter and tales of wartime exploits. Den Prefect Adal was after all wearing the Imperium Heart. No wolf could take that away from him however much they despised him, no more than they could Rufus, another hero of Lupa.

"How did he win it?"

"Mm?"

Poking at his chocolate pudding dessert, Linus clarified his question. "The Imperium Heart, sir."

"The only way you can, Mills," Vladimir said, delicately dabbing his lips with a napkin, "an extreme act of bravery and self-sacrifice."

Chewing on his pudding, Linus stared at his superior with those baby-blue eyes, rather like an expectant cub waiting for his father to continue the narrative. Noticing the impostor Howler Cubs Olivia and Sara (for such were their real names, and Vladimir knew it) were also staring at him, the Grand Howler had no choice but to elaborate.

"I gather that during the war," he said quietly, folding his napkin and kneading his paws, "Adal, then a Bloodfang, killed a dozen dissident Howlers single-pawed, preventing several Den Fathers from being assassinated. This was during the early peace talks; had they been killed the war might've continued. Adal was horribly wounded and bed-bound for a month. He was blinded and paralysed from the ash in his blood; every breath was agony they say. Short of a cure he should've rotted, but… somehow he came back. Nobody knows quite how." With a smack of the lips and a cock of the head, Vladimir added, "So, that's what it takes to win an Imperium Heart."

Olivia whipped out her notepad and, Vladimir supposed, started to write down Adal's story. *Cease your tiresome charade, I know* exactly *who you are,* Vladimir thought, but did not say, for it was better for everyone at this table if the girls genuinely kept up their act, for now.

"Linus was wounded, weren't you Linus?" Olivia alleged playfully, glancing at Sara. "He fought a great mad hog and was stuck on its tusks."

"Uh… that was all Uther, really," Linus excused, looking down and prodding his pudding. "I mostly got gored by the fellow and lay in a ditch."

"I hear you killed several criminals before they took you down. It was very brave."

"Hardly Imperium Heart material, I'm sure."

"No hardly about it," Vladimir scoffed haughtily. "Illegally discharging an imperium pearl, and moreover carrying a pistol on the Common Ground, rather offset any good you did. If Uther had missed he could've taken down the bridge and then you'd both be in Gelb, if not executed." Looking down at the gob-smacked Linus, he woofed, "Oh don't gawk at me like I've just told you I'm a wolfess, Mills, I've *always* known what really happened that night. I overheard Uther telling Ivan the whole story. Just be grateful Amael didn't question me over the veracity of your account, I'd not have defended you, nor shall I if you're ever so foolish again."

"N-nnn-no, sir."

"Humph! As long as we're clear."

Olivia winked at Linus across the table, perchance indicating she disagreed with Vladimir's stuffy assessment, and teasing a smile from the bashful Howler.

Once Linus had gathered himself enough to look up he noticed Sara sitting and staring at her uneaten dessert of honey-drizzled waffles.

"You all right?" he asked.

"Aye," Sara heaved forcefully. "Ah'm fine. Thank you."

She was anything but, Linus knew. He wanted to reach across and hold Sara's paw, tell her everything was going to be all right despite the fact Heath was in hiding, Tristan was in ALPHA's clutches and Rufus was dead.

Linus peered across the carriage, spying Janoah sitting with her fellow ALPHA Prefects. She had taken her own husband to task in the name of the Republic and now Tristan too. If she was so spiteful and uncaring she could have let me go the same way, yet here I am, purportedly because I helped Rufus, a dead beast she arrested. It doesn't add up. None of it.

If Janoah's with us against Amael, then perhaps there's more Vladimir hasn't dared tell me.

Am I not fully trusted, then?

By Ulf, why is life so complicated? Why couldn't it be as simple as the propaganda reels made out? Hyenas are bad, Howlers are good, little beasts are happy in their place. Linus felt an idiot for not so long ago believing what the papers spewed. I was a happier beast back then, but a fool.

Ignorance really is bliss.

Suddenly Vladimir stood up, and everyone else too, Sara, Olivia, every Howler at every table, rising to their feet like in a wave of bodies. Linus felt Vladimir's rough paw grasp the scruff of his cloak and pull him from his daydreaming, urging him to cooperate in what was, Linus realised, a mark of respect for Den Father Vito, who was leaving the carriage to retire to his quarters.

By all means, Linus had no quarrel with the idea. But, try as he might, his legs would not lift him from his chair! Their strength was gone, overcome by sudden shooting pains.

Oh no, not again!

"Linus!" Vladimir growled through the side of his muzzle as loudly as he dared.

"Sir, I…."

"Stand for our Den Father!"

Somehow, between Vladimir's tug and his own push, Linus overcame what he knew to be an ill-timed attack and stood smartly to attention.

The magnificent-looking Den Father Vito and his entourage filed down the carpeted channel running between the tables, passing inches from Vladimir and Olivia, who respectfully kept their gaze forward. Even without training Olivia seemed to carry herself like a natural Howler.

Perhaps, yet Den Father Vito stopped at Vladimir's table and turned to face the four wolves standing there. He stared for an age, his imperious eyes burning into the side of Vladimir's skull, then Olivia's and Sara's.

Had he spotted something amiss?

Stepping backwards to the whispers and murmurings of on-looking wolves, Vito looked at Linus.

"Ah, so *that's* where the storm rages," he said cryptically, tipping his head back a little. "You bear the pain with great fortitude, young wolf. What's your name?"

Mentally twisting in the chains of torment, Linus had to be elbowed into a response by Vladimir.

"Trooper Linus Mills… Den Father," he seethed, standing firm. "F-fff-forgive my rudeness, sir."

Vito waved a paw in dismissal. "We've none of us control of the rot, Howler. It strikes us down when it pleases, even over dinner," he chuckled. "Sit down and let it pass; I'll take no offence."

Clapping a paw on the table to shore himself up, Linus grunted, "Thank you, sir. But I'll s-sss-stand if I may. It won't beat me."

Vito nodded. Wolves whispered roundabout.

Whilst Sara looked worriedly on, Linus slowly straightened up opposite her and stood firm again. She couldn't sense the imperious rages within him, for she wasn't afflicted, but she could read the pain etched on his furrowed brow well enough. Linus's features softened as the attack seemed to pass, which gladdened Sara more than she considered normal.

Vito whispered something to his ever-present adjutant, then flicking a friendly paw at Linus suggested, if not altogether ordered, "You'll take the waters with me in Everdor."

"Waters, sir?"

"The hot springs, Howler Mills," Vito explained. "It'll do those bones a world of good."

"Uh, ah, well…."

"I go for a dip every year. What do you say?"

"I-I-I would love to, but-"

"He'd be delighted, Den Father," Vladimir answered, bowing a little and not making eye-contact. "Please forgive Mills, he's a city boy; hardly seen a blade of grass in his life, let alone a hot spring! I'm sure the rot has momentarily confused him too."

"Yes of course," Vito acknowledged.

With a raise of the paw like some old king, Vito took his leave, ambling down the carriage and out of sight – whereupon Linus collapsed like a sack of potatoes, nearly pulling the tablecloth and everything with it as he fell about the carriage.

"Gagh!"

"Och, Linus!" Sara yelped, reaching for him.

Vladimir quickly supported the stricken youth and helped him to sit in his chair. "I thought it'd passed," he said, pouring Linus a stiff drink.

"So had I," Linus panted. Noticing Sara's concerned gaze he said, "I'll be all right… in a minute."

"Do you have any stings?" she asked.

"In my cabin."

"Ah'll go get them-"

"No… I'll go back myself in a minute."

"Linus-"

"I won't sting myself in front of everyone, Sara! It's… not the done thing."

Olivia said, "He's right. It's not."

Baffled and annoyed, Sara looked at Olivia, who urged her to sit back down.

"Don't worry, Linus," Vladimir huffed. "With any luck Vito will have forgotten all about you by tomorrow. I'm sure his adjutant is in no hurry to remind him. Just try and keep a low profile, for Ulf's sake."

"Yes, sir."

Chapter 38

Morning's light barely warmed the Sunrise Mountains, but the mouth of the cave to which Nurka had brought Rufus expelled a noticeably steamy breath. This bode well in the Howler's opinion – if this cave was connected to the same system as Gelb it ought to be of a similar temperature.

"I thought the caves would be cold," Nurka said, sniffing the air.

"Some are," Red-mist replied, watching the moist air from the cave condense into a rising cloud, "but Gelb's on top of a plume; the walls drip with water that's full of dissolved imperium. I've seen beasts reduced to licking the walls in there just to try and get a little more good stuff."

"Pathetic, is it not?" Nurka rasped. "All our troubles stem from such places. If we didn't steal Mother Erde's blood we would not get the rot. It's her curse upon us for our greed."

Rufus shrugged, "Imperium's been bubbling up on the surface since the dawn of time. White rises up, releases its energy and decays into black, which sinks back down into the core of the planet. Who can blame our ancestors for being attracted to a shining imperium crystal, or wanting to tap into its power? It was either that or live in a straw hut forever, and now we are where we are and our civilisation depends upon imperium… rot and all."

Expecting resistance, or some debate, Rufus provoked only a noncommittal grunt from Chief Nurka.

Chief of what, Rufus still wondered, chief of THORN or just this offshoot? Is Nurka the mastermind of it all? Could I kill him here and now and end Amael's ambitions?

Even if I could there's a better way, Ulf help me. The word of a Hyena Prince can stop this madness and save further bloodshed on all sides.

Noss, please be alive, and be your old self.

Even as he hoped and prayed Rufus unconsciously felt his left arm, his fingers tracing the scars torn in his muscled hide by Noss's cruel yellow-imperium bomb not so long ago. The word of a Hyena Prince *could* stop this, but the question was would it be given?

Out of nowhere and with barely a flutter, that beautiful pepper moth from last night dropped out of the sky and perched on Nurka's shoulder.

The hyena took the quivering moth down and opened the little casket it carried.

He read the message within, his violet eyes tracing back and forth as Rufus watched.

"Everything's in place," Nurka said, destroying the message with a flash of imperious plasma from his black fingers before Rufus was able to glimpse its contents. "There's nothing else to do but go."

Upon Nurka's word things moved quickly. Themba, the other hyenas and Casimir all gathered at the cave mouth, a dozen souls in all including Rufus. Imperium lanterns and rations were distributed, whilst Nurka unfurled his map on a rock and inspected, for the umpteenth time, the maze of passages and caverns crudely scrawled out in plan form. The map had been stolen from Lupa's vast records, apparently, and sent by moth to the hyenas by some hog, somewhere.

Even if the document was genuine it made no mention of the cave spiders and cave centipedes that Rufus as a naturalist knew frequented such warm, dark, dank places as Gelb. Bugs were not obliged to stay in one place for very long and couldn't be pinned down on a sheet of paper.

Anticipating trouble, Themba hefted his hammer whilst Nurka shouldered his marvellous imperium bow, keeping both a lantern and his map to paw. Casimir cocked a trusty pistol and the other hyenas sharpened their imperium-tipped spears.

Rufus felt the weight of his basic rapier – it was no masterpiece, but it'd channel plasma well enough.

Releasing his messenger moth to the sky with a final note for his allies, and with a last glance at the muted mountain sun, Nurka delved into the hot, reeking cave ahead of his brave followers, lantern held forth.

"Mother Erde, forgive us our trespass," he prayed.

✣

When Linus awoke he noticed a distinct change had come over the tiny yet luxurious cabin he'd occupied of late. There came no motion, no sound; the ornate crystal bedside lamp no longer quivered and tinkled to the rails clacking rhythmically beneath.

The Elder Train had stopped!

Casting aside his sheets like an overgrown cub on Wintertide morn, Linus knelt on the bed in his appropriately Bloodfang-red under-breeches, his golden tail slapping audibly side to side with excitement. Whipping the tiny velvet curtains aside he peered out at bright wide world beyond the narrow carriage window.

Fields, bushes, trees, a clear blue sky; Linus's hungry eyes lapped up the lot. The concrete paths and tarmac roads of Lupa's unforgiving streets had been replaced almost overnight by lush grass and soft erde, whilst the regimental brick walls of terrace houses had given way to the soft leafy borders of tangled copses and clumps of trees. Even the towering smokestacks of imperium refineries were no more, marked instead by the odd outlying redwood tree pumping out nothing more harmful than fresh air. It was as if Linus had shut the curtains on a theatre production yesterday and little beasts had changed the set whilst he slept.

This must be Everdor, and it's just like the pictures, except in glorious colour.

If only Uther were here.

Oh but he is, cooed the other side of Linus's brain, causing his stout heart to skip a beat. He's here with Ivan plotting the death of Den Father Vito at Amael's command. That is if Vladimir's correct, or even to be believed.

Linus couldn't be sure of anything anymore, except that he could be sure of nothing.

Knock, knock, knock!

Pulling himself from the beauty beyond the window, Linus sprung from his bed and rifled through his clothes for a tunic.

Knock, knock, knock!

"Just a minute."

"Howler Linus?" someone crackled – not Amael, not Vladimir, not anyone Linus easily recognised either.

"Yes. Who is it?"

"I shan't come in; you're clearly in bed still. I'm Den Father Vito's adjutant. Our leader requests your presence at the hot springs. Attend at once. Don't worry about bathing, that's what the springs are for."

"Uh, ah, r-rrr-right you are, sir. I'll be right there."

"Very well."

"Where are the springs, sir?"

"Don't worry, I'll escort you personally."

✧

Fwooosh!

Across the way from the resting Elder Train, which had stopped in a siding in the middle of an otherwise unremarkable bare field, lay an opaque-looking lake. Projecting from the lake's cloudy waters like an island volcano was a squat cone of smooth rock, from which spurted a great fountain of white water.

"A geyser," Linus marvelled to himself, stepping from carriage to ground.

The scalding jet blasted some fifty feet into the air for a good minute, its spray and foam glinting like crystals in a sunbeam, before gurgling back into the erde. On closer inspection Linus noticed the geyser's rocky cone shimmered with colour, reds, greens, blues and more. It was doubtless made of solid imperium minerals that had precipitated out of the water. Linus supposed the whole lake must be laden with imperium, which is why some afflicted beasts believed bathing here helped ease the rot. Now, whether immersing oneself in what amounted to poison did more harm than good was open to debate, but Linus had no choice in the matter. Den Father Vito had invited him along as his guest and that was not a thing to be refused lightly, if at all.

Searching amongst his fellow Howlers for Vito or his adjutant, Linus convinced himself that taking an imperium bath couldn't be any worse than taking an imperium sting.

As it happened, Vito's smartly-cloaked adjutant found Linus. "This way, Howler," he beckoned tiresomely, coming up behind a bewildered Linus and gesturing for him to follow with a flick of the paw.

Observed by the jealous eyes of other Howlers and especially Elders, the singled-out Linus stuck to Vito's adjutant like glue in a vain attempt to feel protected as he weaved his way along the train and then across the open field.

"Just a few ground rules... Linus, was it?" the fellow said, stopping suddenly, paws cupped before him.

Linus was taken aback, "Uhm rules, sir?"

"You are Den Father Vito's guest, but you will observe his personal space."

"Personal space?"

"Do *not* get too close and do *not* lay your paws upon him at any time. The Den Guard will not hesitate to act if you provoke them."

"I see."

"For your sake, you'd better," the adjutant sniffed. "And for Ulf's sake, boy, don't fill his head with ideas or ask impossible favours. Vito grows frailer each passing year and his mind is not what it was. I am the one who has to deal with his fanciful notions, not him. Give me a headache and I'll make your life difficult. Understand me?"

With a gulp and many nods, Linus replied, "I-I-I wouldn't dream of asking for anything, sir. The thought hadn't occurred to me."

"Good!" the adjutant woofed sharply. "See that it doesn't and we'll part ways amicably."

With a flick of the wrist he led on, skirting along the lapping shore of the lake towards a nearby wood. Following a well-beaten path and some rotting signposts through the gnarled trees, Linus and his guide happened across a collection of small, steaming rock pools, their smooth, toroidal rims resembling nothing so much as flaccid doughnuts coated with imperium frosting left melting in the sun. It appeared *this* was the place to bathe, not the open lake back there. Linus imagined it was at least somewhat private as he took in the concealed copse.

Beyond the sweltering pools stood an arc of ancient-looking log cabins, each no bigger than was necessary to change in. Moss clung to their roofs in desperate clumps, like swarms of green bees.

The door to the middle cabin was barred by two fierce-looking Den Guards. Vito must be in there, Linus surmised, just before the door creaked open and revealed the Bloodfang's Den Father in nought but a red towel. His magnificent Howler gear had been stripped away, revealing the battered, scarred body of a wolf long past his prime. Still, Vito was no withered husk, not yet, and his impressive corona reached clean across the pools to touch Linus, who bowed on one knee.

"Ah, Howler Linus," Vito greeted, striding around the pools with his two guards in tow – more guards lingered in the trees, Linus noticed out the corner of his eyes. "Up you get, young wolf, I don't want to be looking at your ears all morning."

Linus stood up nervously, wondering with every adrenaline-laden breath whether to tell Vito what he knew, that Amael was out to murder him and take over Lupa. But, as Vladimir had warned, even if Amael fell the rest of the conspirators wouldn't. They would survive and, whilst plotting afresh, make Amael's accusers disappear.

Thus Linus stayed silent. He felt like a coward, but he didn't want to be thrown into the Lupa with cement shoes by Amael or his conspiring allies.

Leave it to Vladimir and Janoah; they know what they're doing. Right?

"How goes the affliction with you today?"

Vito's question brought Linus back from his mental meanderings.

"Well, Den Father," he managed to chirp.

"Ah but you're still very young, very... strong," Vito mused, running his glowing eyes over the golden Linus. "It'll ravage even your fine young body one day, as it does every one of us, even me, long though I've lasted." After a few seconds the aged Vito snapped from some momentary stupor and cast a withered paw to the pools, "These imperium springs will stave rot off a little longer, for the both of us... or beasts say."

"So I've read, sir."

Vito raised a finger and boasted, "Not just anyone can come here, you realise, only those granted permission by the state, by me and the other Den Fathers. The waters and woods are guarded all year round by Hummel wolves, and have been for hundreds of years. This is a rare privilege."

Linus could but bow again, paw to chest, "Then I'm truly honoured, sir."

Vito chuckled and glanced at his adjutant. "He has a way with words this one."

The adjutant smiled meekly.

"Well then," Vito declared, walking by Linus and flicking a paw behind him, "to a cabin with you, Howler. You'll find all you need inside, hot towels and whatnot, but don't take too long; we mustn't hog the healing waters all day. Others will want their turn."

"Yes, sir," Linus replied, following Vito's adjutant to the nearest cabin and repressing with every step the bad feeling he felt in the pit of his stomach.

✦

Teams Scarab and Mosquito, led by Madou and Noss respectively, filed into the mines behind their trundling carts along with the rest of Gelb's reluctant inmates.

"What're you grinning at, hyena?" one of the guard hogs blustered at the passing prince.

"At the prospect of yet another day raping Mother Erde for the glorious Republic, of course!" Noss cackled, removing his big paws from the cart long enough to bow a little. "What could be better than such an honour?"

"Huh," the hog replied, scratching his brow before flicking a pink limb into the mines. "Well, get a move on!"

"With great celerity, sir!"

It was outrageous enough that a prince of hyenas should be reduced to this servitude, let alone bowing to some bloated hog, but Madou contained his rages by convincing himself Noss was mocking the fellow. Then again, he wasn't all there at the best of times; perhaps this morning the prince was on a delirious high?

Noss's light mood persisted as he led Madou, Zozizou, Tomek and Helmut, and the others in each team, through the main mine entrance to the spaghetti junction of rails that sinuously slithered into dozens of smaller caves. Which shaft would Noss choose to mine today? It was always him that chose, not just because his imperious instincts were the keenest in Gelb now that Rufus was gone, but because Prince Noss simply exuded natural confidence, and therefore leadership.

Scarab and Mosquito queued at the diverging rail junctions whilst the teams ahead of them picked a shaft for the day. When it was his turn, Noss gestured at the hogs stationed in the switch tower ahead. He signalled right, to switch to the right track, not just once but three times in a row. Despite obvious misgivings, the hogs pulled the appropriate levers, forcing Noss's cart down rightmost rail each time they split, sending him and his gang towards a shaft into which no others had ventured for months now.

Everyone knew that rightmost shaft was mined out and showed no signs of replenishing. It was dormant, if not dead; the imperium-laden waters had shifted elsewhere for some geological reason nobody could know.

Still, and despite a worried glance at Helmut, Madou followed his Prince's example and sent his cart down the same rail, right, right and right again.

If any other teams took note, they couldn't follow, for Madou's gang was the last to pass today.

As they approached, Madou spied a Gelb hog lingering near the otherwise deserted shaft entrance. When Noss passed him the apparent stranger tipped his yellow cap at Noss, who nodded back.

Strangely cordial that.

When Madou's gang passed, the same hog just stared and said nothing. Not even a rude word or mocking comment was aired over their apparently suicidal decision to dig in a dead mine shaft.

The pig may not have cared, but Madou burned with a desire to catch up to Noss and air his grievances over this madness. However, the prince of the Jua-mata Tribe had fared well in Gelb and was as strong as ever, charging ahead into the throat of Mother Erde, imperium lamps casting darkness aside. Even with Helmut's help pushing the cart, Madou was unable to catch up until Noss physically stopped and waited.

"Come on Madou," the prince cackled, breaking out an ember. "Don't you *want* to be free?"

"My Prince?" Madou panted, letting his hefty arms flop to his sides, mighty chest heaving. Putting Noss's comment down to the rot, Madou continued, "My Prince, this shaft is mined out. Can't you feel it? There's no imperium in the walls."

"The lad's right, Noss," Helmut seconded. "I'm not even afflicted, but even I can tell this shaft is stone cold n' bone dry. There'll be no imperium here."

Whilst a grinning Noss puffed away, Zozizou and the others in both teams made similar complaints to him, all except Tomek, who stood silently by, cap askew as always. Usually the first to voice his opinion on anything, Madou was struck by the wolf's silence now.

Tomek merely looked to Noss, expectantly, as if he knew things, secrets.

My imagination surely, Madou thought. Prince Noss wouldn't confide in some wolf before me.

Noss raised a black-fingered paw to silence everyone and declared, "We don't need to mine any imperium, because we're not going back."

"Eh?" Helmut snorted.

Grabbing a lantern from the side of the empty cart, Noss walked further into the dark mine. Following the tracks a fair way he veered off down a narrow passage and out of sight of the others.

He didn't return, nor beckon anyone to follow.

Shortly thereafter, distinctly hyena grunts and growls echoed around the corner, accompanied by the unmistakable xylophonic clatter of falling wood.

Madou and the others exchanged baffled glances before hurrying round to see what Noss was up to. They discovered him tearing planks of wood from a doorway set in the living rock, the long nails fastening them proving no impediment to one of his imperium-augmented strength. Any stubborn planks Noss happened across were blasted with a snap of imperious plasma, heating and softening the very nails and causing the wood to smoulder. Despite his imperious exertions the prince's collar didn't appear to bother him when it ought to have choked him into submission.

"Careful, my Prince!" Madou rasped, hurrying to aid his indomitable leader. "Mind your collar."

Noss merely grunted back.

Tomek arrived, only too eager to dive in and start peeling the wood from the door as well, as if he too were a Jua-mata hyena loyal to his prince.

Helmut, like the others, was less enthused. "What're you doing?" he asked, standing aloof.

"Leaving!" Noss cackled.

"Leaving? What… going off into the caves, you mean?"

"That's the idea."

"Huh! Are you out of your mind?"

Noss shrugged his massive shoulders, "So beasts say."

"But… but *nobody's* got out of Gelb via the caves; they're a death trap! They go on for miles and miles in all directions. You'll die before you see daylight."

Turning to throw some smouldering wood aside, Noss huffed, "Then stay here, pig."

"I will!" Helmut professed, muscled arms folding.

After some time, and some thought, the burly pig realised there must be more to Noss's strange turn than mere madness.

"So whatcha got, a map or something?"

Noss confessed, "Half a map."

"Half?"

"It's the best Tack had. It still cost me dear."

Helmut threw his arms wide, "Half a map's no good, you daft hyena!"

The daft hyena spoke soberly, with the clarity and surety of one who was anything but daft. "It'll get us as far as we need to go, which is out of Gelb. The Warden won't search for us or raise the alarm because nobody gets out via the caves, do they? We'll be presumed dead, lost in the caves, like so many other desperate fools."

Noss finished with a slightly manic laugh, which hardly set Helmut at ease.

"Aye, so we get out of Gelb," the hog scoffed. "But then what? Sit in the dark n' rot?"

Glancing at the other inmates behind Helmut, Noss pulled the last of the wood from the door. "If you stay here you'll rot for sure with your hefty sentences."

"Tomek won't," Helmut said. "He's got a light stint. He'll be out in a few months, won't yer Tomek?"

No reply.

"Lad?"

"That's no matter any more," Tomek said simply. "I get out of here now, Helmut."

And that was that. Indeed the young wolf obediently helped Noss and Madou yank the ancient doors open without protest, without question, as loyal to Noss as he had been to Rufus before him.

Whilst Helmut pondered matters, Tomek, Noss and Madou eked the long-abandoned doors open, inch by inch, tug by tug. Strange sounds accompanied every combined heave, like sheets of cotton being torn, a crackling, soft white noise that pricked the ears and alarmed the ancient senses.

Something other than rust had stiffened the doors – they were sealed with silk!

Madou released the door and almost fell on his tail in his haste to scoot backwards. "Ugh!" he woofed in disgust, wiping his paws on his stripy breeches.

Prince Noss reproached, "It's just web, Madou," holding his lantern up to the dark, web-lined void. Strands of silk clinging to the door frame wafted in the humid breath of the Erde, pointing back to the relative safety of Gelb like the withered fingers of forewarning ghosts. Ignoring their counsel, Noss stepped forth, his flickering lantern lighting the way, knowing that all it would take to spoil everything is for some Gelb hogs to wander down here and check on them now. The sooner they were away and too deep into the caves to find, the better.

He turned and appealed to his doubtful followers, "You have to trust me-"

"Look out!" Tomek yelped.

In a flash the Watcher leapt forward and pulled Noss from the door. Not knowing why Tomek should, but that he must have good reason, Noss instinctively span round and took on the defensive poise of a trained Howler, feet spaced, paws ready to box, lantern discarded.

The lantern clattered to the ground, the imperium within it mixing, flaring brightly, and reflecting eight-fold in the many-eyed glint of a giant spider the size of a bear!

"Waaaah!"

"Run!"

Despite the cries of the others behind, Noss and Tomek remained firm in the face of the spider. The creature dangled from the ceiling, its legs curled up on themselves to form a hairy cage.

"Is just skin!" Tomek announced, standing up straight and laughing, even whilst his heart secretly pounded. "Is only shed skin, look."

The young wolf tramped fearlessly over.

"Tomek!" Helmut piped in alarm, yanking the sides of his own cap down over his head.

"Is all right, Helmut," Tomek reassured, pushing on the giant crispy skin with a paw. It swayed to and fro like a horrifying paper lantern, crackling with the sound of autumnal leaves as it brushed against the cave walls. Even without Tomek's input the lifeless, dried husk continued to move, its legs agitated by the passing breeze.

How Tomek could stand there and poke that disgusting thing was beyond Helmut's comprehension.

"Don't touch it!" the pig seethed, his skin crawling.

Noss explained, "It's just an empty exoskeleton, Helmut, discarded by the spider as it grew," sounding like a teacher of nature, complete with lame pun, "An *ex*-exoskeleton, if you will," he cackled, retrieving his lantern. "Come on, there's no time to waste-"

"If that's just a skin where's the real thing?" one of Noss's gang piped up – the hyena prince didn't clock who amongst his followers it was, the wolf, the cat, the other pig, someone or other, he didn't care, his response would've been the same.

"Are you little beasts now?" he mocked, throwing them all one last purple-tinged glare. He saved his most withering look for the beast he expected the most from. "Madou?"

Raising his chin, and seeing Tomek wasn't afraid, the stocky Madou hurried over and knelt by Noss, "I go where you go, Prince of the Four Winds."

"And your cousin?"

After a quick snarl from Madou, the skinny Zozizou steeled himself and joined Madou at Prince Noss's feet, like a good hyena should.

Noss clenched a fist, "Better for a Jua-mata to die trying than cowering in fear!"

Madou nodded, whatever his misgivings. Death was one thing, but death by spider? Paralysed and bound in silk, waiting to be sucked dry, perhaps for days; was there anything in this world more horrific? Breaking a black-imperium capsule against one's teeth would be a blessed release in comparison.

Whilst Noss and the hyenas struck forth into the caves, Helmut stayed put with the remaining members of Mosquito and Scarab as they muttered their misgivings and debated whether to follow the questionably sane Noss.

"I ain't going in there if there's spiders."

"They're dead beasts."

Only Tomek dared join the escapees without a second thought.

"Tomek, don't go!" Helmut pleaded. Trotting to the door he seethed through his tusks. "Don't do this, lad. What's the point? You'll be getting out in no time!"

With every word the pig glanced worriedly at the spider husk wafting above, as if worried he might yet wake the empty skin from its hollow slumber.

Tomek turned around with a lantern held up and urged cheerily. "Come on, Helmut."

Helmet's lower jaw quivered. "I… I can't, lad."

"Is all right. Trust me."

The big pig shook his head and stepped back.

Tomek looked ahead to Noss – the hyena was waiting for nobody.

"I come back for you," Tomek promised hurriedly. "I come back when it all over. I say Helmut helped me. They get you out. You see."

"What? What're you on about?"

Tomek raised a finger to his lips, then tipped his wonky cap and took off after Noss. "Goodbye, my friend. Thank you for helping me through this place." With that he turned and chased after Noss.

"Aye," Helmut sighed, doffing his cap as if Tomek and the rest were dead already. "Good luck, lads."

Chapter 39

Ivan Donskoy slipped through the undergrowth, his rapier half pulled from its scabbard, his roaring imperious corona suppressed to a whimper.

Think of nothing, Rufus had instructed him all those years ago. Calm your mind, fold in on yourself and relax. Your corona will soon disappear.

Easy enough to achieve when reclined on a sofa, but somewhat taxing when stalking one's prey, heart racing, mouth dry. Still, Ivan supposed he must have managed it, for the Hummel Watcher yawning beside a tree remained unaware of their approaching doom.

Drawing his blade and touching it quickly yet gently to the surprised wolf's neck, Ivan released a blast of imperious energy, flashing down the sword and into his victim.

K-zapft!

With barely a yelp the Watcher hit the tree and collapsed in a heap of cloak and armour.

Ducking down lest he was seen, Ivan dragged his quarry away into a thicket just as Uther and Gunnar advanced through the trees to join him.

"Is he dead?" Gunnar whispered, with a gulp.

"Does it matter?" Ivan replied, sheathing his blade.

"He'll be fine, mate," Uther said with intent, even as he checked for a pulse. "Aye, just knocked out is all." He glared at Ivan, "We're not here to kill anyone but Vito, right?"

Ivan said nothing.

"Right?" Uther growled.

"I make no promises," Ivan huffed, "Nor should you."

"Well if I can help it-"

"You won't. Not in the heat of the moment. Not when your life depends on a clean kill."

Whilst his elders bickered, Gunnar looked the stunned wolf over. He was enrobed in a sage green cloak pinned by a golden brooch marked with a bee, its legs and wings spread. The bee was rendered in solid white-imperium. His armour too was white, albeit *not* made of white-imperium – no pack, no wolf even, was that wealthy.

"He's a Hummel 'en he?" Gunnar surmised.

"Yes, they guard the springs year-round," Ivan said, stealing ahead through the trees. "Come on."

Uther and Gunnar followed.

The trio were a long way from the springs and their target deep in the woods, but they had spied the Bloodfang Elder Train from afar and knew that Den Father Vito always partook of a dip in the supposedly healing waters here if ever he was passing this way.

That's what Amael had been counting on, what he had planned months ago, him and Janoah.

Now the moment had arrived.

✦

Whilst Den Father Vito soaked in the private woods out of sight, the rest of the Bloodfang delegation stretched their legs in the fields surrounding the Elder Train or paddled in the cool shores of geyser lake, depending on their disposition.

The ALPHA contingent kept their distance, setting up a flimsy array of new-materials tables and chairs by the waterside and enjoying tea and sandwiches served on plain white ALPHA tableware, not the decadent, highly decorated porcelain provided.

The Alpha supped his tea with Janoah, Horst and Duncan, guarded one and all by a colossal black-cloaked wolf looming nearby, a wolf Sara surely recognised.

She daren't believe it true, and yet here was another giant wolf of the same stature and colour as Bruno.

Coincidence?

She watched from a safe distance as Olivia attempted another pass, wandering within a few feet of the ALPHA group and her target.

The big wolf looked at her, but nothing more.

"I can't feel anything familiar," Olivia whispered, returning to Sara's side.

"Nothing?" Sara whined.

"Not from him, just… them. The Alpha, especially. He's some wolf, that one."

"But that makes nae sense. He's their bodyguard, he must be an imperium wielder. Right?"

"I know," Olivia sighed, theorising, "Well, maybe the Alpha's just overwhelmingly strong. Or… or maybe it's the imperium roundabout interfering with my senses."

Sara frowned, "Does that happen?"

"Oh yes, all the time. It's foggy round here. You can feel the energy in the air, crackling and… popping."

"Ah see."

Olivia waved a paw, "It can't be Bruno. I'd feel him."

Sara clasped her paws together, "Could ye not try once more?"

"I can't."

"Please. Just get as close as ye can."

Olivia indicated towards the Alpha and his cronies with her snout. "That red wolfess sitting with them is watching me. Her eyes are like daggers that one. I daren't push my luck. Linus told us to stay out of trouble."

Sara heaved an enormous sigh.

"Ah should've stood up for him," she all but whispered. "Ah should've swallowed mah pride and gone tae mah mother. She could've done something for Bruno. She's a Den Mother, beasts would've taken notice if she'd asked questions. Ah should've never signed those papers, it was nae even Bruno's body."

"Sara–"

"It was nae him, Olivia! It was nae. Tristan *made* me do it. He did it tae protect me, Ah know that, but… but ever since that day Ah've felt guilty. Guilty that Ah let them take Bruno away and never asked after him or told anyone."

Sara cupped her muzzle in her paws and fought back a surge of grief.

Olivia patted her back, "Oh, Sara."

The little black wolfess sucked it up. "Ah'm all right," she dismissed, looking at the giant of a wolf standing over the Alpha. "It's nae him. I mean, it can't be. What're the odds he'd turn up here? Ah'm just seeing what Ah want tae see. Every big, dark wolf Ah pass in the street is Bruno. Ah always look. 'Tis pathetic."

Sara's self-denying rant appeased nobody, least of all Olivia. "All right, one more try," she decided. "Just back me up if they get shirty."

"How?" Sara snuffled. "What do Ah say?"

"I dunno. We'll work it out. Stay here."

Meanwhile, at the Alpha's table, Janoah peered over the lip of her teacup, through the rising steam, past the Alpha dabbing his lips with a napkin and beyond the unmoving rock that was Rafe, to that nosy Bloodfang Cub.

"Here she comes again."

Horst's white ears swivelled on Janoah. "What?" he said between mouthfuls of cucumber sandwich fingers, looking all about. "Who?"

Janoah both sipped her tea and placed it down before deigning to reply. "That Howler Cub; she's buzzing around us like a wasp after a jam jar."

The laid-back Duncan had evidently already noticed, since he didn't even look. "Och, she's just curious of the great and noble Alpha," he said, spreading a big black paw. "Cubs will be Cubs, Janoah."

"I don't like it, sir. She could be a Bloodfang agent out to eavesdrop, or worse an assassin."

Chuckling at the notion, Duncan reached for a sandwich and chomped the dainty morsel down in a single bite. "The Bloodfangs would nae dare," he claimed.

Horst, to general amazement, including Janoah's, came down in her camp. "It's not loyal Bloodfangs but the conspirators we need to worry about," he said. "Who knows who Amael's gotten to by now. If a fanatic will swallow a black-imperium capsule they will as likely blow themselves up with a black-imperium bomb, taking us and more importantly the Alpha with them."

Pausing for thought, and a glance at the intruding Cub who was making yet another unsubtle pass, Duncan waved a cucumber finger at his fellow Prefects, "Then tell the lass tae buzz off."

"I'll do more than that, sir," Janoah claimed.

The Alpha offered no input – his protection was the duty of his Prefects – he merely sat and watched the geyser, timing its regular eruptions with his pocket watch like the amateur naturalist he claimed to be.

"Bruno," Janoah said, with a nod and a flick of the finger.

Nothing more substantial passed between Janoah and her well-trained henchbeast; Rafe left the table to intercept the nosy wolfess.

Olivia heard him coming, heard those boots crunching on the grass and gravel, but could hardly speed up or attempt to run away; there was nowhere to go, nowhere to hide, she was out in the wilderness hundreds of miles from Lupa. She acted natural, strolling along as before, pretending to take in the scenery but seeing nothing of it for her panicked thoughts.

The giant Prefect suddenly blocked her path.

"Come with me please, Cub," he said, his voice booming in defiance of his muffling ALPHA-black helmet.

Olivia recoiled with as much indignation and confusion as she could muster. "I beg your pardon?"

"Come with me, please," the Prefect stated, sterner.

He spread an enormous muscle-packed, brown-furred arm out from under his cloak. As said arm rose and the folds of the Prefect's cloak opened somewhat, so did Olivia feel the tendrils of an imperious presence reach out and pierce her corona down to the bone.

By Ulf, is that power coming from him?

Containing her surprise, if not working with it, Olivia cupped a paw to her chest and asked with eye-fluttering innocence, "Have I done something wrong, Prefect?"

"I dunno," he replied.

"I'm Elder Amael's guest, you see," Olivia excused. "I'm a student reporter, here to write an article about the Summit. I've never been to anything like this before."

The Prefect's initially stern front softened like chocolate under the sun. "Me neither," he admitted. "Oi look, I'm sure it'll be fine. Janoah's just being funny."

"Janoah?"

"My boss," the Prefect said, flicking his head towards the tables and half-joking, "Come on, or I'll get in trouble."

Disarmed by this wolf's familiar charm, Olivia allowed herself to be shepherded across to the little ALPHA enclave nestled by the lakeside. This could be the end. ALPHA could find out that I'm not a Howler in training and then we'll be for it. Linus won't be able to protect us now.

How could I be so stupid?

"What're you playing at, Cub?" the red wolfess at the table demanded. Olivia supposed she must be Janoah.

Before anything else, Olivia saluted like a good Howler Cub, fist to chest then out.

"Save your silly salutes, girl," Horst scoffed with reliable derision, even whilst devouring another sandwich. "We're ALPHA, not members of your decadent pack."

Janoah continued her interrogation. "Well? What're you doing lingering around? Yes, I saw you, walking by over and over. I see the other one too, hiding by the train. She looks very worried now. Spies are we?"

Olivia cast a glance at Sara, who was standing with her paws to her face, then chirped, "Spies? Of course not-"

"Oh? Assassins then?"

"Don't be absurd, marm."

"Excuse me?" Horst cut in again. "Do you know who you're talking to? You're in the presence of the Alpha and his Grand Prefects! The Alpha is the equivalent of your Den Father and we your Elders."

"Not quite, Grand Prefect."

"What?"

Olivia glanced at the wolves sitting about the table and decided to run with it; be bold, be brash, do not cower, know your rights as a Howler... if you were one.

"I mean no offence, sir," she said, "but Den Prefect Adal and yourselves are accountable to the Den Fathers, not the other way around."

Frowning hard, Horst sat forward. "Who are you?"

Olivia tipped her head back a little. "I'm Howler Cub Livia Bloodfang, student reporter."

"Reporter?" Horst blustered on.

"Yes, sir. I'm writing an article for the student paper-"

"About what?"

"The Summit, sir. Would you like me to include you in my article?"

"My dear, you'll be writing an article on the working conditions at Gelb from *inside* with your attitude-"

"That's enough, Horst," the Alpha sighed. "ALPHA does not exist to antagonise our fellow wolves, but to work with them to guard our fair city." Slipping his fine timepiece into his cloak pocket, the Alpha turned away from the dying geyser which he had been timing and beckoned Olivia round the table to stand before him, his handsome, white, mask-like face beaming warmly up at her. "Besides, we're guests aboard Den Father Vito's marvellous train and will be gracious to all his pack, including his Cubs."

Horst said nothing.

"Now then, Cub," the Alpha began, amiably but business-like, "if you're writing about the Summit you'll need a few interviews to go on, won't you?"

Olivia didn't know what else to do, save bow a little and say, "Yes, Alpha, sir, uh... Den Prefect Adal."

"Either will do," Adal chuckled. "Well, go get your friend and sit yourselves down."

"Sir?"

"You may interview me. How's that?"

"Oh, thank you so much, sir. I never dreamt I would so much as meet you as talk to you."

"Indeed. Off you go."

Another salute, then a bow, whatever came to mind, then Olivia scuttled away.

Duncan chuckled, "Och! That's very generous of ye, my Alpha."

"All the poor Cub wanted was to get near me," the Alpha replied, confident of his own importance. "I've nothing else to do whilst Vito toys with his new plaything."

Bruno turned and watched Livia traipse over to the train to fetch her friend – a short black wolfess in the same Howler Cub uniform. Words were spoken, gestures made, Bruno couldn't hear them nor lip-read, yet was unable shake off the creeping feeling of familiarity in the cut of the two Cubs.

"Something wrong, Bruno?" Janoah asked, bringing his attention back to the table.

"No," Rafe sniffed, standing to attention behind the Alpha.

"How're your eyes?" Janoah pressed. "It's very bright out here compared to Lupa."

"Fine."

"Josef's nearby if you need him-"

"I'm fine! Stop fussing me, Jan."

"You address her 'Prefect Janoah' or 'marm'," Horst tutted over his teacup, "not 'Jan', you ignoramus. You're a Prefect now, Bruno, start acting like it."

Rafe raised his chin, "Yes, Grand Prefect, sir!"

A nod, "Better."

Despite sensing Rafe was a bit off, Janoah settled again, at least outwardly to the wolves sitting around her. Inwardly she was a storm, her heart beating hot and cold.

She glanced across the fields, spied Amael standing by the lakeside with Vladimir and some others. She met Amael's hard eyes. He didn't nod or wink, but Janoah knew what he was going through too.

The vital moment steamed ever closer.

✦

Linus slipped nervously into the sweltering pool. Not willing to appear a limp-pawed weakling in front of Den Father Vito he suppressed the urge to yelp as the painfully hot water first infiltrated his breeches, then his guard fur and, finally, his water-repelling undercoat to scald his hide.

"Refreshing, no?" the scar-flecked Den Father Vito crackled, his wiry grey arms splayed over the pool's edge, ember smouldering between crooked lips.

Linus managed a convincing, "Yes, Den Father," fully expecting strips of flesh to peel off under the impenetrably green water and bob to the broiling surface like so much pasta. However, the pain soon passed and the water became at least bearable, if not at all 'refreshing'.

The young Howler wasn't quite sure what to expect from an imperium spring, despite having read about them. He couldn't see any imperium glowing in the murky green water, but it was of course daytime and the mixture must be extremely dilute in any case. Even so, Linus noticed his imperious senses fogging over. There was no direction to his inner eye anymore, no up or down, front or back, not even Den Father Vito's potent corona pushed through the imperious haze choking the air.

It was just like being inside the Riddle District imperium refinery, only worse.

"What're you expecting to see?" Vito laughed, watching his guest cup the spring water in his palms like a curious otter cub catching minnows. "The dissolved imperium?" Vito guessed before Linus could mount a response. "Oh, it's there. Can't you feel it?"

"I-I-I can. Yes."

Whilst Vito blew a cloud of vapour overhead and relaxed like a wolf at ease in his own bathroom, Linus stood stiffly in the water, wondering what next to do, what next to say. Two red- and white cloaked Den Guards loomed over the pool like lifeguards, imperium rapiers at the ready. So far as Linus could tell they were not directly watching him, their eyes scanning the surrounding woodland instead, but no doubt each stood poised to stick Vito's guest like a fish if he was so foolish as to make a wrong move.

"Sit down, relax," Vito encouraged, patting the smooth lip of the pool. "There's a bench under the water here by me, carved from the very rock. It's quite comfortable."

Linus glanced at the guards.

Vito sensed the youngster's unease. "Oh, don't mind them," he chuckled. "Despite what you may have heard from my overprotective adjutant we do not kill a beast for the merest infraction, uh... Linus."

Linus reciprocated Vito's humour with a slight laugh and waded through the chest-high water, the temperature of which felt more acceptable on his flaxen hide by the minute.

I could get used to this, Linus thought, seconds before scraping a kneecap against a rough and unyielding stone ledge somewhere down below – that'd be the bench then. Weathering the ensuing sting in silence, Linus settled on the submarine stone seating beside Vito whilst maintaining a respectable arm's length between himself and the Den Father.

Unfortunately, planting his posterior firmly on the bench-shaped rock resulted in the water level reaching Linus's chin. Feeling ridiculous, the short Howler brought his feet up and knelt on the bench instead, surreptitiously raising himself to chest-height, like Vito.

If the Den Father noticed Linus's sudden increase in stature, and he was watching throughout, he didn't pass comment, at least not regarding Linus's height or lack thereof.

"You've an impressive figure, Howler," he praised, casting his eyes over Linus's thick, rounded-off chest and shoulders. "You must train very hard."

"No harder than my partner, sir."

"Partner?"

"Howler Uther, sir. He's a far better wolf than me. P-p-perhaps you've heard of him?"

Raising his brow, Vito said, "Yes... rings a bell." He looked away for a time, then returned his attention to Linus. "Amael's fortunate to have such fine wolves as you serving him."

"I-I-I do my best, sir."

"How would you like to serve me instead?"

Vito's words went over Linus's head for a time, before his mind hurried to grab them back. "S-sss-serve you, Den Father?"

"Yes."

"I serve you through Amael, as I'm able-"

"Oh stop it, boy!" Vito tutted, flicking his spent ember into the water. He remained friendly, but stern, "Drop your tiresome act of false modesty and speak to me like a wolf, not a sycophant." Turning to face Linus properly, with one elbow resting on the pool's edge, the Den Father all but whispered over the bubbling pool, "You know what you are; what you're capable of. Rufus never just picked up any old Howler, he had exquisite taste that wolf."

Linus knelt in silence, heart thumping, mind racing, thinking, 'What've I got myself into now?'

Vito looked his prey over, those imperious eyes burning with hunger. "And now he's regrettably... gone," the Den Father crackled, with a minute shrug of his grey shoulders, "you need a new patron. It's only out of respect for Rufus that I never sent for you after the incident in the Common Ground. After all, Rufus found you first and we alphas don't tread on each other's toes."

"Incident, sir?"

"That Howler-killer in the Common Ground. You took care of him, you and Uther."

"That again?" Linus guffawed. "I did nothing, sir."

Vito growled, "What did I just say about false modesty?"

"I'm speaking truthfully, sir. I-I-I did nothing noteworthy. If Uther hadn't been there-"

"That's for others to decide, not you," Vito maintained. "And I, your Den Father, have decided you're most worthy.... Yes, most noteworthy indeed. You'll serve me, as my beta."

"Beta?" Linus gasped.

"Of course! What did you think I was talking about? Why do you think you're even here?"

"I-I-I... well...."

"It's a great honour to beta a Den Father. You'll get more out of the arrangement than that rogue Rufus could ever provide; respect, power, wealth, your own apartment and car, whatever you desire, within reason. Once we weary of each other, you can go your own way with all that was provided."

"B-b-but I-"

Vito over-talked the stuttering Linus. "Nobody will mock you as they did when you belonged to Rufus," he growled. "If anyone dares I'll slap them down so hard they'll find themselves in Gelb!"

On that crescendo, Vito glared hard at the Den Guards lingering about, as if warning them personally despite their oaths of discretion and loyalty.

"Does that satisfy you, Howler Linus?" he asked with a crooked smile, cupping a bony paw to Linus's thick neck. "Will you submit to me?"

Silence.

"Your friend Uther was mine too, you know," Vito claimed, cupping his paws on Linus's shoulders, "before I let Rufus take him. He was an ungrateful beta that one. I should've left him rotting in the gutter! But he was so... magnificent; more so now I hear. Still, you'll please your Den Father gladly, won't you?"

"N-nnn-no," Linus stammered.

Vito chuckled, yet conversely frowned, "What?"

Linus raised his chin. "No *thank you*, Den Father," he said levering Vito's searching paws aside of his stocky frame, "I can't be your beta, or indeed *anyone's* beta, that's not who I am." With a gulp he continued, "Whatever you've heard about me is untrue. Grand Howler Rufus was just my friend. There was nothing more to it I'm afraid."

Vito recoiled a little, "You expect me to believe that?"

"Whether you believe it or not, it doesn't change my answer, sir. I will submit to nothing-"

"Mind your tongue, boy. I'm your Den Father!"

"Be that as it may, sir, I must respectfully and humbly decline your most generous offer."

Vito laughed.

Linus remained stern.

"Who do you think you are?" Vito scoffed at Linus, looking him up and down. "Do you think you're an alpha, is that it, little wolf?"

"I've never given it much thought, sir-"

"Liar! Every wolf wishes to be an alpha. Few ever are and you certainly are not!"

Linus shrugged.

His silence only infuriated Vito further. "You've not the right to spurn me!" he snarled, wading into Linus, nose pressed to his. "You're a lowly Trooper hardly out of your Cub's mantle. Do you know what kind of power sleeps within my veins? I could destroy you with my bare paws-"

Thwip!

Vito's right ear inexplicably tore off of its own accord and spiralled through the air. Linus flinched as his face was flecked with blood.

What?

The thunderous blast of a rifle bolt followed shortly thereafter.

Ka-crack!

"Agh!" Vito yelped, clapping a paw to his bleeding skull and wading backwards from Linus, his face a mask of horror and shock. "Murderers! Assassins!" he accused, pointing at Linus in his pained confusion. "Seize him!"

✢

"ALPHA was set up for the packs, by the packs, to curb the excesses of the Howlers and protect the little beasts from abuse," the Alpha went on. "If we're disbanded the citizens will have no recourse for their grievances except revolt, and we all know what happens then." He sipped his tea, "I remember the war, Cub. I was there."

"Yet some argue ALPHA is too powerful," Olivia said confidently. "They claim you're just another pack now, serving your own interests. What do you say to such wolves?"

"My only ambition is Lupan stability. You see…."

Whilst Olivia made notes and asked the questions, acting the part she was apparently born to play, Sara stood behind in silence, that giant Prefect of her fascination looming anonymously over her. She could feel his presence without any aid of imperium, sense his eyes burrowing into her shoulders. Unable to bear it any longer Sara looked behind and followed the muscular bumps and folds of that unnaturally black cloak up to a thick brown chin nestled within a black helmet.

The towering Prefect cocked his head and hunched his mountainous shoulders a little in a friendly gesture.

Sara followed suit, even smiled. Words dallied on the tip of he tongue. What to say? Can I say? Should I just ask?

Ka-crrraaack!

The distant distorted echo of an imperium shot tore across the geyser lake, sending small crickets and grasshoppers leaping from the long grass in panic and causing every wolf at the ALPHA table to flinch.

Every wolf except Janoah.

Horst nearly fell off his chair, his bulk all but overturning the table as he and Duncan leapt to the Alpha's defence. "Into the train, my Alpha!" Horst urged, sword drawn, just barely. "Quickly, it could be a THORN attack!"

"Calm yourselves!" the Alpha scolded, tugging at his black cloak. "Probably nothing more than Hummels hunting game. This is their territory after all-"

Crack! Crack!

Two lesser shots ripped through the air, putting paid to the Alpha's theory.

"That's pistol fire," Duncan said.

"Nobody hunts with pistols, my Alpha," Horst seconded.

Without thinking, even less being command to do so, Rafe leapt into action, speeding across the fields towards the source of the disturbance with great, matchless strides.

Janoah sprang to her feet, "Rafe, no!" and gave chase.

✦

Vito's two Den Guards fired their pistols, but each missed the white ghost tearing across the clearing towards them. With a blast of imperious energy that punched his cloak billowing outwards the mysterious white wolf launched himself over the steaming pools and landed amidst the guards.

"Stop, assassin!" one cried, to no avail. The silent stranger set about him with his rapier, kristahl clashing, sparks of plasma flying. The air rippled with energy as the three wolves danced about the pools, trying to stick one another with their deadly blades.

Linus didn't linger to observe the insane melee, but instead blindly ushered Vito to safety, his mind and body seized by an instinctual desire to protect the Bloodfang's Den Father whatever had transpired.

"Go, sir!"

The baffled, bleeding Vito allowed himself to be pushed to the shore, where a third Den Guard waited with his paw outstretched, ready and desperate to pull his master from the water and flee.

"Take my paw, Den Father!" the Guard cried.

With Linus at his back, Vito scrabbled for the shore and reached for the aid being offered.

Bzzt! Crack!

"Gaaaaagh!"

With a flash and snap of plasma the Den Guard by the poolside was blasted tail over head into the water, landing on Linus and dragging him under the stiflingly hot waves.

Pushing the guard off him, Linus thrust himself to the surface and cleared his stinging eyes, whereupon he was met with a sight those eyes didn't believe despite everything Vladimir had said.

There at the pool's edge, left paw quivering with arcs of residual plasma, was a black and white-furred Bloodfang Howler. Linus saw right through his anonymous helmet and mantle, the cut of his athletic frame and the scent of his corona utterly unmistakable.

"Uther?" Linus yelped in horror.

"Linus?" Uther replied, equally aghast.

The trembling, bleeding Vito sloshed forward. "Uther, m-my finest beta," he said, spreading his paws on the pool's lip. He appeared strangely happy, his missing ear quite forgotten. "You've… come back to me, my child! You've come back now that Rufus has abandoned you, is that it? I-I told you he would." The Den Father reached up, "I'll take you back. Of course. Come… help me."

After a moment's ear-picked uncertainty, Wild-heart remembered what he was about. He drew a pistol from under his cloak and took aim at Vito. "Rot, you sick drooler!"

The Den Father's face sank.

Crack!

Amidst an explosion of ash, Vito clutched at his chest. Teetering in defiant disbelief, the Den Father glared murderously at Uther and raised a paw. Arcs of plasma trickled down his arm, the air and water rippled around him, but, before Vito could vent his fury one last time, he collapsed backwards into the pool. Linus watched helplessly as his leader rolled over, clouds of crimson pouring from a hole put right through him, front to back.

"By Ulf's fangs," Linus whined.

Uther's accomplice walked to the pool's edge, his rapier awash with the blood of the two other Den Guards lying dispatched on the ground behind him.

"Finish the job," he said.

"C-c-captain Ivan," Linus gulped shakily. Tall, elegant, white – it could be no other wolf but Blade-dancer.

Ivan didn't acknowledge the fact, nor even look at Linus, only at Uther. "Do you want to die a traitor's death, torn apart by ants? No witnesses, Wild-heart! They'll execute *him* as well for failing in his duties, don't you doubt it. Kill him, it'll be a kindness."

Uther stood stock still, unwilling, or unable.

"I should never have let you come," Ivan huffed, drawing his pistol and at last looking at Linus – aiming at Linus.

The witness closed his eyes, paws raised defensively if no doubt uselessly, but as Ivan pulled the trigger Uther lunged in and smacked his pistol aside.

Crack!

The pellet hit the surface beside a flinching Linus, sending up a shower of bloodied water.

Whirling on Uther, Ivan shoved him away. "Fool!"

Uther came right back, grabbing Ivan's cloak, "Touch him and I'll kill yer!"

"What are you now," Ivan spat acerbically, "his alpha?"

"Thump you, you arrogant ponce!"

The two assassins squared off against each other, chests touching, nostrils flaring.

Meanwhile, the Den Guard that Uther had stunned recovered his wherewithal and lunged ashore. Grabbing one of the dry pistols dropped by his comrades, he spluttered, "Die, assassin scum!"

Ka-crack!

The long-cloaked Den Guard span round in an explosion of blood and collapsed into the pool.

Shot, and dead for it, like Vito before him.

The trembling Linus turned this way and that, searching the woods until he saw a yellow-cloaked Greystone wolf standing just proud of the undergrowth, rifle smouldering in steady paws. Lowering the long barrel of his mighty weapon, he snapped from a momentary stupor and shouted, "Quit whining and move!" before fleeing into the trees.

Given one last mutual glare, Ivan and Uther made their escape with the Greystone, leaving Linus wallowing in the diluted blood of his slain leader, unable to speak, unable to think. This was a dream, an unreal nightmare!

I'm still alive, he realised, checking his body for holes, wounds, anything.

I survived!

Not for long, Linus thought, elation giving way to sobriety. You heard Ivan, you'll be executed for failing your Den Father so spectacularly, if not tortured first for information and you know things, Linus Mills, you knew this was to happen and you did nothing because of abject cowardice.

No! I won't let them get away with it! I won't let *Amael* get away with it!

Scrabbling for the shore and all but leaping from the bloody water where Vito's lifeless body floated limply, the sodden Linus snatched a rapier from one of the fallen Den Guards and sped into the dark woodlands after his comrades.

"Utheeeer!"

Chapter 40

The escapees pressed on through Gelb's dark caves, the light of their lanterns and Noss's map the only things keeping a lid on the growing unease. Rusting rails, abandoned mine carts and rotting wooden struts, all plentiful relics at first, began to thin out the further the group wandered from the active mines. Eventually all mining paraphernalia ceased to be and only bare, natural, un-worked rock passages remained – that and the odd wisp of ominous spider silk stretched between the slick walls.

The thought occurred to Madou, and he expressed it to his Prince, that they had nothing to protect themselves with. They had no weapons, not even their imperious paws – any exertion, any snap of plasma, and their collars would choke them into submission.

"I can get off one blast, maybe two," Madou said, tugging at his infuriating collar. "No more."

"Don't worry, Madou," Noss replied breezily, checking his map against the path ahead, "I had my collar replaced by Professor Tack ages ago."

Noss's revelation took a moment to sink through Madou's hefty skull. "It's fake?"

The Prince tapped the iridescent metal band hugging his thick neck, "No more dangerous than a bowtie; and I've worn one of those too! Rufus persuaded me into one for some Lupan function or other. Hahaha, yes. Those were the days."

Whilst his Prince reminisced, Madou claimed, "I was going to have Tack get rid of mine. I could have if I'd known we were going to escape, my Prince."

Noss dismissed at once, "You wouldn't have been able to afford Tack's prices."

"What did he want?" Madou replied, a little affronted.

"A white-imperium crystal, what else?" his Prince replied, flicking the map with the back of his dark fingers. "And this ragged thing cost me two! That cat is extortionate. Though without me and Rufus around to supply him with imperium he might have to drop his expectations in future."

Noss finished with a wide-eyed, hyena-brand cackle before leading on.

Madou looked across at Tomek and Zozizou, their faces lit by their glowing lanterns. "Well," he said in general, more to calm his own nerves than theirs, "as long as *one* of us can fight properly."

Nodding, Tomek cleared his throat and looked down.

Nothing was said, yet Madou sensed some awkwardness in the young Howler.

He's hiding something.

"Tomeeeek! Tomek! Wait fer me, lad!"

A gruff call echoed down the cave's throat, dashing Madou's immediate concerns over Tomek. The hyena instead turned to face the oncoming stranger, lantern held high and ready to strike.

No stranger, but a friend.

"Helmut!" Tomek chirped happily, recognising the hog long before anyone else. "What you doing?"

The big pig trotted over, somewhat breathless. "I changed my mind, lad," he panted, lantern swaying. "I couldn't convince the others, though. They went back."

At once amazed and concerned, Noss pushed his way to the fore. Looking beyond Helmut, down the winding passage that was one of countless forks in the caves, he demanded, "How'd you find us? We must be a mile in by now."

Helmut tapped his quivering porcine snout and sniffed, "No offence, but none of you smell too good right now. With my hog nose I could whiff you lot from the moon!"

Tomek scoffed, "You're one to talk."

"Huh! We pigs are very clean beasts, lad," Helmut insisted indignantly, fist to chest.

Laughing, Tomek slapped his friend on the back.

Noss, for once, wasn't tickled by the situation. "If you can find us, the Gelb hogs can too," he realised grimly, turning and picking up the pace. "Let's move!"

As quickly as he started, he suddenly stopped.

"And by the Wind snuff out some of those lanterns! We don't need them all. We're like a train of glow bugs down here. Everyone and their mother could find us."

The typically jovial hyena Prince shocked everyone with his outburst. Still, he was ever a little unstable.

Whatever their thoughts the party obeyed, putting out all but one of their lanterns. Only Zozizou – who with much head-shaking and paw-waving made it clear to cousin Madou that he wouldn't be denied his reassuring nightlight – and Noss himself lit the way.

They struck deeper into the caves, Madou's mind trapped between thoughts of Gelb hogs behind him and spiders ahead of him.

And perchance traitors beside him.

✢

Slashing aside leaves and saplings with the Den Guard's rapier, Linus tore through the undergrowth, twisted brambles clawing at his bare arms and legs like so much barbed wire. The further from the imperium spring he ventured the clearer his unknowable senses became, guiding him invisibly through the tangled labyrinth of anonymous tree trunks, like an ant following a scent trail.

Suddenly the auras faded. The panting Linus slowed down, stopped, spread his arms, tried to feel his way with his imperium-laced sword outstretched like an antenna. He felt presences in several directions, each fading fast as the assassins fled.

They've split up! I can't catch them all. Ulf knows I likely won't catch any of them. Uther, fastest wolf in Lupa, must already be halfway home.

Which way? Which one? Does it even matter?

With a growl of frustration Linus took off after the strongest and therefore presumably nearest corona. He immediately regretted his decision, for logically the strongest presence at any given distance ought to be Ivan.

And if I find him I'm a dead wolf.

✢

"Grrrffgh!"

Uther stumbled and rolled in the bushes. Not now! By Ulf's fangs, don't fail me now!

He tried to rise and carry on, but his rotting bones wouldn't have it. His right leg burning with sharp, shooting pains Wild-heart limped on.

It'll pass, he told himself. Just keep going. It'll pass.

He staggered into a sun-licked clearing dominated by a giant twisted cherry tree perched upon a hillock. The tree stood resplendent in blossom, its millions of delicate petals stained with the telltale rainbow iridescence of imperium. Its roots had perhaps tapped into a spring beneath the ground and taken up the rich imperious water hereabouts, leading to unnatural growth and colour.

At any other time and place even the cynical Uther might've marvelled at the strange tree's mesmerising beauty, but thoughts of capture and execution blinkered him, and he passed under its winding boughs with barely a glance.

Beyond the tree, like a ruined castle standing amidst the forest, rose an outcrop of gnarled rock with fingers and buttresses of pale, mossy limestone invading the woodland in radial spokes. The thought occurred to Uther to climb up and hide amongst the countless nooks and crannies until the rot passed and he could run again. No good hiding on the forest floor, the Bloodfangs would comb the area and sense any presence. Up there, perhaps, with his corona blocked by sheer rock and suppressed by calm meditation he might be able to conceal himself until nightfall.

It was as good a plan as any.

Grasping the rock with clammy paws the athletic Howler began his desperate ascent, his powerful arms compensating for his failing legs, pulling him up onto the first ledge. What he wouldn't give for a sting right now.

Uther hoped Ivan and Gunnar were faring better. Certainly they wouldn't have the bad luck to suffer an attack too. Gunnar was barely old enough to notice the rot and Uther had never seen Ivan succumb to any symptoms, never seen him succumb to anything, except Rufus.

Suddenly Wild-heart felt something at his back, an oh-so familiar corona.

"Uther!" it yapped from below.

Wild-heart froze, paws on the sun-warmed rock, ears twisting. He knew it was Linus; there was no need to look back and confirm the fact. With a gulp, he continued to climb.

"Utheeer!"

Still he ignored his friend and comrade.

After a pause, Linus panted nearer than before, "You're under arrest in the name of the Republic!"

Resting his back on the rock face Uther located Linus down there in the blossom-strewn clearing, standing proud with nothing to his name but his torn breeches and a stolen rapier. His glorious golden fur was sodden and filthy with mud and blood, his arms raked with scratches.

"Don't be daft, mate," Uther dismissed. "Just pretend you didn't see me."

He turned to climb again.

The trembling Linus raised his quivering rapier, pointing at Uther up there on the ledge. "Either come down here and give yourself up to me, quietly," he growled, barely containing his rage, "or I'll howl for all I'm worth. The rest of the pack'll come running and they'll tear you apart!"

Uther whirled around, "Puh! Is this the thanks I get for sparing your life? Ivan would've killed you-"

"Get down here you murderer!"

The longest time passed before Uther, heart thumping and bones throbbing beneath that façade of calm, raised his paws in defeat. Clambering down the way he'd climbed he jumped the last stretch to Erde, weathering a shooting pain in his thigh with barely a limp. He was glad his helmet masked his anguished expression in front of Linus, of all wolves.

Uther spread his paws at his soiled partner and said humorously, "You look a right state, dun yer?"

"I n-nnn-never believed it, Uther," Linus quavered, head shaking side to side, blue eyes wet with tears. "Not really. Not until now."

"Believed what?"

"That'd you'd murder a wolf for Amael's sake."

"Puh! Like I care about Amael."

"THORN then!"

"THORN?" Uther recoiled.

"You're working for them, you a-a-and Ivan. Vladimir told me everything. It's no good hiding it."

"You're clueless, Woodlouse. Aye, but you always was. Like I'd do anything for those hyena scumbags short of put a bullet through their skulls. Ulf almighty!"

Linus's eyes narrowed with realisation. It was true, Uther did hate hyenas, and was no fan of Amael's either, he had long said so ever since he and Linus had met.

"Why then?" Linus demanded. "Tell me the truth."

Uther waved a finger like a chiding parent. "You're not getting any more out of me, mate." He drew one of his twin swords in a flash, making Linus flinch. "Now," he said, eyes blazing from the shadows of his helm, "are you gonna howl your little heart out like a coward, or are you gonna face me like a *real* wolf?"

"Don't you dare!" Linus spat, tears wetting his flaxen cheeks. "There's no honour at stake here. You've not a shred left to your name!"

"That's rich coming from old Vito's latest fancy."

Linus exploded, "You just shot him dead, you murderous traitor! You've k-k-killed our Den Father!"

"Den Father my arse!" Uther gruffed back. "He was nothing but an empty shell, the rotten old bastard. Vito was scum, don't you doubt it! They all are, all them so-called Den 'Fathers'." He looked Linus up and down and goaded, "But you two were getting on sooo well. Did I interrupt something? Spoil your quick ticket to the top, eh? I never had you down as a beta for any price. Guess I was wrong!"

Disgusted, Linus said nothing. Instead he tipped his head back and howled for aid, "Awoooo!"

"Cowaaard!" Uther bellowed.

Drawing his second sword Wild-heart closed the distance between himself and Linus in a single, furious, imperium-powered bound, kicking up clouds of glimmering iridescent blossom in his wake. The Howlers clashed blades in an instant of mutual plasma-licked fury before parting, Linus scooting defensively backwards across the clearing with his rapier held forth in both paws, Uther remaining where he had landed.

"Look at you!" Wild-heart snorted, resting one sword on his shoulder and pointing with the other. "You dunno how to even hold that dainty thing. You're built for a sword n' shield, not that poncy needle. Puh!"

Shuffling from paw to paw, Linus twisted his neck a little and rolled his shoulders, saying nothing, but staring always at Uther.

"I don't wanna hurt you, mate," Uther claimed. "This is your last chance. Walk."

Still no word, only a tiny shake of the head.

Glancing at the trees roundabout, worried reinforcements might burst through the foliage any second, Uther nodded and growled, "Fine, I'll make this quick."

In a few strides he advanced on Linus a second time, thrusting and swinging his short blades with deadly intent. Linus remained on the back foot, parrying and weaving his way across the clearing, never once striking back with his long rapier. Imperium-steel clipped and clashed, sending up sparks of plasma, lighting the boughs of the blossom tree from beneath. Up and over the hillock they danced, skipping between the tree's twisted roots, one retreating as quickly as the other dared to advance.

A hit! Uther boxing Linus in the snout with the pommel of a sword.

"Gah!"

Knocked head over tail Linus tripped backwards and rolled down the mossy bank. Scrabbling to rise halfway down, he struck out blindly with his rapier lest Uther took the glaring advantage to hack him down – without armour or shield it would be an easy task.

Yet the Wild-heart refrained, he wasn't even in striking distance. He waited at the top of the hill until Linus recovered his stance, then circled down and round to the right, eyes gleaming, watching, smiling even.

Why hadn't he taken his chance to end it? Was it honour? Friendship? Did Uther believe he retained them even now after murdering a wolf in cold blood?

Wild-heart lunged to the attack, smashing Linus's thoughts in a shower of steel and colourful imperious sparks. Uther's plasma ran down the rapier hilt, shocking Linus's paw to numbness, but he held on.

As the Howlers exchanged blows their invisible fields mingled and wrestled, tearing at each other like rabid spirits. Linus's imperium-laden blood and bones boiled as he called upon the unnatural strength and speed of an afflicted wolf to keep Uther at bay. He couldn't know that Uther's blood burned hotter still, that his bones were already spent cinders, his muscles clogged with ash and pain from all his hardships of late, the travelling, the poor diet, the encounter with the net-casting spider.

It had all taken its toll.

The Wild-heart panted and laboured, every movement a chore as his body ceased up like a delicate timepiece dropped in seawater, gears grinding, scraping, ticking over with imperceptibly escalating tardiness as they fought the growing friction of the rot.

Then it happened.

"Grrrfgh!"

Linus struck home, felt the very tip of his needle-like rapier jamming momentarily into the firm flesh of Uther's ribcage, ripping muscle fibres and scraping bone. It was just a moment, a split second in time before Linus withdrew in horror, but the damage was done.

Dropping one sword to clutch his wound Uther staggered backwards, his remaining sword held defensively forward to ward Linus off.

"Puhaaahaha!" he cackled, checking his bloodied paw. "You got me, Woodlouse!"

Linus froze, staring, unbelieving, the furious red mist that had commanded his every thought and action of late dissipating under the hot, clean Everdor sun.

"Uther?" he whined through bloodied lips, as his friend, partner and traitor knelt in clearing, blossoms catching in the folds of his cloak.

"You win, mate," Uther panted from under his white-faced helm. "You've... come a long way. You're an alpha... always was... make no mistake."

Linus had no words left.

Neither did Uther. With a shaking, bloodied paw he reached round under his cloak and produced a pistol. For a moment Linus thought that he was the target, that Uther would shoot him and flee. Instead Wild-heart pressed the barrel to his own chin, and with deep breaths and tightly closed eyes prepared to pull the trigger. Better that than torture and being pulled apart by ants, as was the custom. No wolf who killed a Den Father could expect anything less.

Averting his eyes, Linus stood by and allowed his friend to take the honourable way out.

"Wha-?" Uther yelped in astonishment.

Linus looked back just in time to witness some invisible force yanked Uther's arm sideways, tearing the pistol from his quivering fingers! The weapon tumbled through the air and clapped satisfyingly into the spread pad of a light brown paw.

It was the Alpha!

"It's not that easy, I'm afraid," the black-cloaked wolf said, casually discarding the pistol over his shoulder and spreading his paw at Uther.

The Wild-heart's kristahl sword leapt from his desperate grip and skidded across the erde to Adal's armoured feet. Then, before he could so much as think to reach for it, Uther's second pistol wrenched itself free of the holster at his tail and punched through his cloak, spiralling off into the woods to land with a dull thud.

Linus stood dumbfounded as the very air about him crackled and warped with imperious energy. The Alpha's corona was incredible!

Gulping and panting, the wounded Uther scrabbled forwards, diving for his remaining sword that he'd dropped in battle, but it too deserted him, kicking up grass and blossom as it sped across the clearing and leapt clean into the Alpha's waiting paw.

Adal inspected the blade, feeling its keen edge with a curious thumb as three of his lesser ALPHA prefects burst through the undergrowth to join him, standing protectively about their leader, a cabal of black mantles.

"Stop, assassins!" one said.

"My Alpha?" another panted, eyeing up Uther and Linus, unsure how to proceed against them.

Adal pointed Uther out with the Howler's own sword, "Arrest that wolf; I've disarmed him."

"Yes, my Alpha."

The Prefects descended on Uther, who rose to meet them, fists raised in a boxing stance.

"Come on then, ALPHA scum!" he snarled.

Despite landing a good plasma-licked punch on the nearest Prefect's chest and diving bodily on the next to throttle him with his bare paws, the wounded Uther was quickly subdued by the third Prefect slapping him across the back of his helmeted head with a sword. It wasn't the physical blow of the steel but the snap of plasma that did it for him.

Bzz-tack!

Uther was sent down, his world spinning, paws quickly forced behind him and tied with wire.

Linus watched all this, aghast, and yet knowing it was the just thing. Uther had committed lupicide, and against a Den Father no less. He'd made his thorny bed and must lay in it.

With Uther restrained the Prefects turned on Linus. One grabbed his arm.

"Come here, you!"

Linus wrenched his muscled limb free with ease. "Get off me!" he spat.

"You're under arrest-"

"Leave him!" the Alpha barked, strolling over and explaining gently, "Howler Linus caught the traitor. He's to be commended for his bravery."

The Prefects backed off and instead pulled a dazed Uther to his feet, holding him fast between them.

"Well done, Howler," the Alpha said, standing before Linus and drawing his gaze. They proved to be the same stature, though the barrel-chested Linus certainly had the edge on sheer mass. "Do you know where the others went?" the Alpha asked.

Glancing at Uther, Linus said, "No, sir."

"Well, I'm sure Prefects Janoah and Bruno will track them down," the Alpha claimed airily. "Justice will be done; you've my assurance on that."

Linus wiped his bloody nose. "Mr. Alpha, sir, if… if I may," he sniffed, stammering through his sentence. "Our D-Den Father has been m-mmm-murdered. I-I-I believe this is a-a-a Bloodfang affair, not ALPHA's."

The Alpha cocked his helmeted head a little, the white A on his brow glowing, "Do you trust the wolves that wielded the knife to find the truth, Howler Linus?"

"Excuse me?"

"Vito is… was… a rotten, old, insatiable mad wolf, as you've likely just found out for yourself. He would've had his fill and discarded you within a month, leaving you without a shred of honour."

Wincing, Linus looked down.

The Alpha continued logically, paws behind his back, "My point being Vito has hindered and embarrassed the Bloodfangs for years. The other packs have benefited by his ineptitude, they would not want him dead. The Bloodfangs, however, will be relieved he's gone. This was an inside job, orchestrated by Vito's successor."

Linus looked up again.

Adal placed a paw on his bare shoulder and looking the dishevelled wolf in the eye said solemnly, "And we all know who that's expected to be, Howler."

✤

Amael Balbus watched Den Father Vito's sodden body being ferried from the scene of the crime under a bloody shroud, along with several Den Guards. None had survived. No witnesses could testify as to what had transpired. Vito's assassins would join him soon enough – unfortunate but necessary.

Amael noticed a Howler whispering in Vladimir's ear. The lofty Grand Howler nodded and approached his expectant Elder to report that, "Linus is alive, sir."

"Good," Amael lied at length, feigning relief.

Not fooled for a moment, but playing his own game, Vladimir stared awhile before adding, "Happily he seems to have caught one of the assassins."

A moment's silence.

"Who is it?" Amael said.

"It appears to be… Uther, sir."

"Uther? You mean *our* Uther? Wild-heart?"

"Yes, sir."

Amael feigned disbelief, "What in Ulf's name? He was supposed to be out hunting down THORN agents!"

"Yes, sir. It seems he had *other* ideas."

"That treacherous, murderous scum, what is he playing at! This could ruin me!"

Amael's acting was as transparent to Vladimir as the air between them, but having prior knowledge of the Elder's guilt was of course advantageous. Vladimir only wondered if Amael could fool an impartial observer, or if that even mattered when half the pack were in his pocket.

"Where is he?"

"Apparently ALPHA have him in custody."

"ALPHA? But you said Linus caught him."

"With Den Prefect Adal's help, I'm told. It seems like they intend to keep him as well."

With paws cupped before him, Vladimir watched Amael's devious mind tick over with great interest. What now for Lupa's would-be emperor? If ALPHA got to the truth of Vito's murder through Uther it might yet blot Amael's copybook and ruin his chances. Then again, perhaps the Elders were all so thoroughly blackmailed, or in Amael's pocket, that it wouldn't matter a fig.

"Well, we'll see about that!" Amael gruffed. "Come on!"

He marched off to rally his fellow Elders, most of whom flapped around the hot springs uselessly bellowing orders to comb the woods and protesting too much outrage over Vito's death to be believed. Only Vito's adjutant appeared truly bereft, if only for his own sake. The fellow stood by the bloody pool, helm in paws, doubtless contemplating his future now that his master had gone.

Following Amael in somehow lacklustre strides, Vladimir contemplated his own precarious future now that the game was nearing its end, one way or another.

✦

"Brunooo!"

Janoah searched the woods with eyes and soul, but saw and felt nothing.

"Rafe!" she snapped. She had not forgotten the cover name she had given her champion, but suspected *he* may have forgotten it himself. It was just possible he was having a funny turn – it was always possible. It was also possible he was dying in a ditch somewhere, shot or run through by Vito's assassins.

They were not just any assassins, but Blade-dancer and Wild-heart. *The stupid boy has no idea what he's up against.*

"Rafe! Answer me!"

A big all-black wolf stole through the trees with a huge sword – not Rafe, as Janoah hoped for a split second, but Duncan.

"Janoah," he panted, joining her.

"Grand Prefect Duncan," she replied, looking beyond him for the others. "Where's the Alpha?"

"He's searching south of here. Nae you worry about him, he can look after himself."

Janoah nodded. "I-I can't find Rafe," she explained, frantically running a paw over her ruddy ears. "It's that blasted cloak blocking his corona. I can't feel him! That idiot Josef and his ridiculous inventions."

"Aye," Duncan acknowledged. "Well, if Rafe's on someone's trail that someone's as good as done. Nobody can beat our Eisenwolf."

"Of course," Janoah replied, not convincing herself, nor containing her gulp.

"Did you see the mess back there?"

"Mess?"

"Vito," Duncan clarified. "He's belly-up in the water with a hole through him."

"I didn't linger longer than was necessary, sir," Janoah replied, detachedly. "I was trying to stay with Rafe. He went this direction, but he's too fast."

"Aye, well, let's just keep searching."

The pair struck out into the woods, weapons drawn.

With sudden realisation Janoah stopped. "Linus!" she seethed. "He was with Vito."

"The fair-furred lad? Ah didnae see him, did you?"

Janoah sighed loudly, perchance even worriedly – at least Duncan suspected.

"Perhaps he had a paw in it?" the Grand Prefect suggested.

"Don't be ridiculous!" Janoah snapped at him.

Duncan audibly huffed and puffed beneath his helmet.

Realising she'd overstepped the mark Janoah explained apologetically, "Sir, I've known Linus a long time. He's just not the sort to commit lupicide in cold blood."

A nod.

The Prefect and Grand Prefect continued to search the woods together, though only one of them actually cared to find the assassins, and it wasn't Janoah.

Rafe don't you spoil everything I've worked for. I'm not ready to choose yet.

✦

He's persistent, this one. Big chap. Not much of an corona though. Strange. Perhaps he's suppressing it. But why would he bother? I'm the one hiding.

Crouched on a bough of a giant, twisted tree, concealed amidst its rustling leaves, Ivan wondered such things as he watched the ALPHA Prefect of his fascination scour the woodland below.

The big Prefect stomped ungracefully about the undergrowth, sweeping aside bushes with swings of his mighty two-pawed sword, doubtless expecting to flush Ivan out like a roach from piles of Lupan garbage.

"I know you're here!" he panted in frustration, turning this way and that. "Come out!"

Ivan remained calm and still.

Skilled in the art though he was, even Blade-dancer couldn't dampen his corona down to nothing. Most wolves couldn't follow him if he didn't wish to be found, but this fellow had exceptional senses.

He's going to find me eventually. I may as well get it over with. He won't feel a thing.

As the Prefect passed underneath him again, Ivan slowly drew his rapier and stood up with graceful, gymnastic poise. Simply stepping off the branch into space he silently swooped upon his prey like a pouncing spider.

In the instant before Ivan's long rapier should've skewered him from shoulder to toe, the big Prefect whirled round and raised a glowing, plasma-licked paw. With an explosion of imperious energy that bent the very air and branches overhead, Ivan was blasted against the tree. His back slammed into the immovable trunk and he fell at its broad base, landing on his feet, crouched.

The Prefect leapt upon Ivan with a predictable follow-up assault, but Ivan was not called Blade-dancer by the hyenas for nothing. Weaving to one side he both nicked the Prefect's nearest arm with his sword and imperiously leapt some feet distant, all in one graceful movement.

Landing neatly, lightly, Ivan stood tall and proud, sword held loosely by his side.

There he waited.

The Prefect faced him, his huge and somehow familiar sword held up to his masked snout. He either didn't notice the small cut Ivan had dealt his upper arm, or just wished not to acknowledge the hit openly.

"Surrender, Howler," he said, in a light-toned yet profound voice, "I don't wanna hurt you."

Though his icy eyes narrowed curiously, Ivan didn't respond.

"Everyone's searching the woods, you can't get away," the Prefect claimed, creeping forth, foot over mud-flecked gaitered foot, as if hoping to close within striking distance without Ivan noticing. "Best you give up now."

Blade-dancer raised his sword a little. "Best for you," he suggested haughtily.

"For both of us, mate. I don't like hurting anyone."

A pause as Ivan contemplated the conflicting information converging in his mind. His instincts were telling him one thing, but logic another.

"You pack a decent punch for someone with such a feeble corona," he probed.

The Prefect huffed, "You dunno the half of it."

"Oh?"

"You don't stand a chance against me. I could end this right now. But I don't wanna kill you."

"You've a big head."

"It's just the truth, mate, I always speak as I find."

Ivan's eyes narrowed further, until they were reduced to mere slits of ice deep within his helm. "Prove it."

"What?"

"Show me your power, Prefect, if you even can."

Time passed. The Prefect's big brown ears twisted this way and that as he pondered the request.

"What for?" he scoffed, lowering his sword a little.

"I'll surrender, naturally," Ivan claimed ad-hoc, waving the tip of his rapier about as he constructed his terms. "If *I* believe I've no chance then I'll give up." He raised his chin, "Convince me. Or are you merely bragging after all, boy?"

That clinched it.

"All right, mate, you're on," the Prefect said, reaching for his brooch. He paused, ears pricked, "No tricks?"

Wondering what the brooch had to do with anything, Ivan confirmed nonetheless, "No 'tricks'."

Unpinning his ALPHA-marked brooch, the Prefect pulled his strangely hefty, leaden-looking cloak from his powerful, scar-flecked frame and tossed it aside, along with his sword belt. He stood, paws spread, the invisible tendrils of his imperious field striking through the woods and meshing with Ivan's own in an instant.

"So... it is you," Blade-dancer said, like a wolf unsurprised and unimpressed. "We meet again, Eisenwolf Rafe. Does Janoah go nowhere without her muscle these days?"

Rafe let his arms flop down, "Aye, and you are?"

"Ivan Donskoy. Don't remember me? No, I don't expect an imperium-fuelled mad-wolf to remember what he had for breakfast let alone who he's met lately. Nor will you remember the promise I made, to kill you if we ever met again."

"Just put your sword down, mate," Rafe commanded. "Come quietly."

"I think not," Ivan grunted.

"But you said–"

"You believe I'm scared of you? That you'll beat me? You're nothing without Josef Grau's contraption to protect you!" Blade-dancer growled. He pointed at Rafe's crumpled cloak, "Now put that illegal black-imperium rag back on and let me put you out of your misery. If I'm going to do *one* thing worthwhile this evening it'll be to rid Lupa of you before it's too late."

Rafe ignored his cloak – he had no need of it. "Fine, have it your way," he growled, sticking his great sword in the ground – he had no need of that either.

Spreading his big paws he summoned the dormant power within him. Arcs of purple-tinged plasma trickled down his mighty arms and played between his scarred fingers, highlighting every muscle and sinew of his incredible body.

"I'm sorry!" he shouted, over the crackles and pops of his imperious fury.

In an instant, Ivan plunged a paw into his cloak pocket and cast a fistful of sparkling yellow flash-powder into the air. With a snap of plasma he ignited the cloud in a blinding white flash!

Fwoof!

"Agh!"

No sooner did Rafe flinch away from the searing light than the most fantastic pain shot through his guts.

"Unffgh!" he grunted.

With blinded, rot-laden eyes pulsing and burning, the Eisenwolf bent double to grasp uselessly at whatever unseen object was causing him such agony. Something hard, cold and metallic had pierced him in the stomach.

Ivan's rapier!

The sword heated from ice-cold to poker-hot as Ivan channelled a torrent of energy down the hilt and into his impaled foe.

"Ooaaaagrrrfffgh!" Rafe cried, his back arching as rivulets of plasma danced all over his helpless body, as if he were being racked by Josef.

Ivan wasn't done yet. Clapping a bare paw to Rafe's helmeted brow he released a last thunderous snap of imperious power right between the Eisenwolf's burning eyes.

Crack!

Head whipping violently back from the blow, Rafe slid gently from Ivan's blade and collapsed. There he remained, a smoking heap of brown fur. Lifeless, Ivan judged, but for the odd twitch caused by residual plasma working its way through that great lupine body.

Ivan sheathed his beautiful, deadly rapier.

"No," Rafe heard him sigh, "I'm the sorry one, Bruno Claybourne."

CHAPTER 41

Casimir abruptly stopped in the midst of the passage with a paw pressed to his jacketed chest.

The dozen hyenas following Nurka's lead passed the little beast by with barely a glance, save for Themba, who was bringing up the rear with his kristahl hammer slung over a massive shoulder. "Casimir?"

"I-I'm fine, lad," the white rabbit insisted, forcing a feeble smile. "It's just a twinge in the old ticker. Was leaping about like a jumping bean there."

"Do not worry," Themba encouraged, his purple eyes alight in the darkness, "there are enough of us to fend off anything with more than two legs."

It sounded to Casimir like Themba savoured the idea of fighting a wild bug. The rabbit didn't, and hurried after Nurka and his lantern-carrying comrades for fear of left behind in the dark with who knows what lurking in the caves; spiders, centipedes, one's imagination ran wild with grim possibility.

Nurka seemed to know what he was about; striding forth at the head, taking definite decisions to go left or right when the caves presented him with a fork. If nothing else he had faith in that map, and his hyenas had faith in him. Not a word was said, not a doubt expressed.

They're devoted to their chief, Rufus realised, staring at the back of Nurka's helmeted head as he walked. But is this chief devoted to his prince?

Provided Noss really is alive... and not mad.

What do you say to a beast who tried to murder you? What does he say to you?

I wonder how Tomek's faring. Poor boy.

"Oop!"

Rufus's armoured right foot caught on something firm yet yielding, like a giant water balloon. Nurka span round and steadied the stumbling Howler with the reflexes of an afflicted beast.

"Red-mist," he said simply, with a nod of the head.

Assuming Rufus had merely tripped on uneven ground Nurka turned and made to walk on.

"Wait a second, Nurka," Rufus beseeched him.

The hyena chief waited, curious. His line of followers soon caught up and bunched at the spot Rufus had tripped, Themba included.

"What's the hold up?" the big hyena rumbled.

"Shh!" Rufus hushed, paw held up. He retraced his steps and crouched by a large white rock, barely discernable in the darkness. "Give us some light here."

With Nurka's silent nodding approval, one of the hyenas obliged the wolf, passing him a feeble imperium lantern.

Rufus held it up. With additional illumination the white rock took form in his light starved eyes, becoming an elongated, bean-shaped bag the dimensions of a pillow. It was somewhat translucent, like a glass of coconut milk, and its smooth surface glistened with a liquid glaze.

"It's an ant's egg," Rufus claimed.

"Ant's egg?" Casimir said.

"Shh. Quiet."

Rufus stood up and cast his lantern and eyes around the passage, revealing a pile of eggs lying against the wall; the one he'd tripped over was just an outlier.

"There must be a nest here," Rufus whispered, green eyes darting about as he theorised ad-hoc. "This warm and humid environment is ideal for raising young." He whirled on Nurka, "We should move, quickly."

With a nod and grunt the hyena chief beckoned his troops after him. Nothing more was said until the party had put some distance between them and the eggs.

"The map says nothing about ants," Nurka insisted, flicking the paper with his fingers.

"Bugs do as they please, they don't obey our maps and boundaries," Rufus replied, glancing over his shoulder.

Casimir looked to his taller compatriots. "What do we do now?" he asked nervously.

"We press on," Nurka replied without delay.

"But if they find us they'll swarm us!"

With Casimir's words ringing in the darkness the hyenas exchanged fearful glances.

Nurka instantly moved to rally them, "Dying by ant, by spider or hundred-legs, what difference does it make? We all knew *something* could be down here. I'm not about to abandon my Prince like a coward!" Casting his purple eyes over Themba and the others he rasped pugnaciously through his skull-helmet, "Are you?"

The hyenas stood firm. What other choice did they have? Peer pressure's a terrible and yet effective tool in the right paws, Rufus thought.

"Red-mist," Nurka said, somehow imploringly.

"Yes, Nurka?"

"What's the best thing to do if we happen across an ant down here?" the young chief asked, guessing, "Leave it alone like before, yes?"

"That… and pray, my good hyena."

※

After countless, winding, ever more claustrophobia-inducing passages that necessitated Noss and company proceed single file, even sideways on occasion, Madou for one was simultaneously relieved and surprised when the caves suddenly opened up into an enormous, high-vaulted atrium. The ceiling, some hundred feet above, was populated by so many stalactites that it resembled a petrified pine forest, albeit one turned upside-down.

The strange part wasn't the size of the space Madou found himself in, but rather that Noss's feeble lantern should reach so far as to light every facet of the translucent, white rocks this natural wonder consisted of.

"By the Wind," Madou mouthed, joining Prince Noss in the open. "It's so bright in here."

"Imperium veins," Noss explained simply. "The walls are glowing with ore."

"It's… beautiful."

"Why Madou, I never had you down as a romantic!" Noss cackled, slapping the stocky Madou's chest with the back of a hefty paw.

Tomek, Helmut and Zozizou took in the spectacle themselves.

"Would you look at that," Helmut whistled.

"Is amazing," Tomek seconded, removing his stripy cap, as if in respect of nature's wonder. "There must be enough imperium down here to feed the Howlers for months! No?"

"Aye, lad. Makes me wonder why they abandoned these caves in the first place."

"They can not know about it."

"Maybe… or maybe the Warden's been holding out on his superiors."

"What you mean?"

"He could be sitting on this for a reason, though I wouldn't like to guess what."

Madou was so preoccupied by what was above he failed to notice what lay ahead. To his horror he quickly realised the way was barred by precisely nothing – thin air – for a yawning black chasm cleaved the whole glittering atrium from one side to the other!

Walking tentatively to the edge of what he hoped was a mirage or trick of the light, Madou looked disappointedly down into a sheer black void. Gulping back primeval fears he searched left and right, up and down, but saw no bridge, no slither of rock breaching the gap, and no other passages to follow. There was no way to jump across; it was simply too far, even for an imperium-fuelled athlete, surely.

"Which way now, my Prince?" Madou asked, searching Noss's hefty features for answers.

"That way," Noss replied calmly, tipping his snout at the chasm.

"What?" Madou half-laughed.

Helmut joined in, "Oi! Whatcha mean?" He trotted as near to the frightening gulf as he dared, before drawing back with a gulp, lest the blackness sucked him down. "We can't get across there! Isn't there another way around?"

Noss flapped his map about, "Even if there is, I don't know the way out. This is as far as Tack ever got. So it's as far as I can take us."

"Then what do we do? I don't understand."

"We wait for help, hog."

"Aye, outside help?" Helmut guessed.

"That's right."

"From who?"

Noss beamed amiably, but vaguely, "Friends."

The prince's little party exchanged incredulous glances, all except Tomek, who remained strangely unconcerned in Madou's judgement.

Before Madou could question Tomek's behaviour of late, the sound of dozens of trotters clacking on stone echoed around the caves.

"Halt!"

"Stop!"

Several Gelb hogs hurried into the atrium armed with lanterns, truncheons and most dangerous of all their correction collar boxes.

"Hahaaa! Found yer!" the lead guard snorted, raising the box dangling from his corpulent neck. "My nose never fails me. Paws on your heads, scum! Hurry up!"

Declining to put his paws anywhere particular, the impressive Noss pushed his way to the front of his frightened comrades. "Amazing, some Gelb hogs with guts!" he cackled. "I thought the spider skins at the door would've scared you cowards away."

"Paws on your head or I'll drop you!" the lead hog threatened them.

"Go ahead," Noss goaded toothily.

"My Prince, you can't fight them alone!" Madou pleaded.

"I won't be alone, Madou."

Whilst Madou and the others placed their paws on their heads, Tomek stood silently with Noss. Together they advanced on the little hog army.

"Dead or alive, it doesn't matter to us!" the lead hog warned. "Nobody escapes Gelb!"

No reply. Just a knuckle-crack or two.

"Right! You asked for it!"

The hog cranked his correction box up to maximum. The device emitted a piercing hum and the caves lit up, the very walls glimmering with ripples of light as the imperium responded to the correction device's manufactured field. The imperium-collars responded too, throttling three out of five prisoners into submission – Helmut, Madou and his cousin Zozizou were downed in an instant.

Noss and Tomek remained strangely unaffected.

"What the-?" the lead hog snorted. He desperately twiddled the correction box's dial at them, but was deprived the sadistic pleasure of watching them writhe in agony.

"What's the matter? Is it broken?" Noss mocked. "Let me take a look at it."

With a flash of those mad eyes and mighty teeth, the hyena prince snatched the device from the fumbling hog, and with a blast of imperious energy sent the cruel machine out of the world.

Fzzzt! Bang!

"Oops, clumsy me," he said, dropping the smouldering box at his feet and dusting off his smoking paws. "Mother always told me I didn't know my own strength."

With that, Noss and Tomek set about the hogs, their bare paws weapons enough as they channelled blasts of imperious energy into flabby bellies and crooked snouts, sending the half dozen Gelb guards scattering and rolling in all directions. Truncheons or not they were no match for beasts marked by the rot.

With the correction box destroyed, Madou quickly recovered and joined the fray, snatching a discarded truncheon and braining every yellow-capped, pig-shaped head that crossed his maddened path.

"Aaahaaaagh!" he cried, chasing the fleeing hogs away into the caves.

"Madou!" Noss barked. "Let them go!"

Madou reluctantly obeyed. Panting and cursing and tugging at his stifling collar, he rejoined

Noss and the others. He was chiefly interested in Tomek – the wolf stood shaking his smouldering, doubtless throbbing paws, but remained unaffected by his collar.

"Why… weren't you choked too?" Madou snarled with suspicion. "Answer me!"

Tomek glanced at Noss, then shrugged, "I do not know. My collar must be broken-"

"Don't lie!" Madou accused, poking Tomek's chest with his truncheon. "You had it replaced by Tack. Who paid for it? Who're you working for? Tell me!"

"Madou!" Noss barked for the second time. "That's enough."

"My Prince, he couldn't afford to get his collar removed, not without help-"

"I paid for it."

Madou was silenced by surprise.

Noss explained, "I needed at least *one* beast who could fight besides me. Tomek is a Watcher, he can fight. So… I told him my plans and got his collar off."

Madou's rounded ears drooped, "But w-www-why not me? You picked a stranger – a wolf pup – over a brother warrior like me?"

"You were in the Pit at the time, Madou. Tomek wasn't. That's just how things fell. I didn't tell you because I knew you'd be hurt that I'd confided in him first."

"But-"

"That's the end of the matter!" Noss growled. "Accept it."

Tomek tried to paste over the cracks in Madou's hyena pride. "We get your collar off soon," he said, placing a paw on the warrior's huge, rounded shoulder. "Though you fight as good with it on as off, friend."

Madou pugnaciously shrugged him off and stomped away towards the chasm. Noss shook his head a little, conveying silently 'ignore him', but Tomek persisted, joining Madou in the open and looking up at the glorious imperium-laden rock formations sparkling overhead.

"I would be dead without you," Tomek said. "I would have drowned in Pit back in Gelb. Whatever happens I always remember you, Madou."

Madou grunted noncommittally and folded his mighty arms. It was his stubborn hyena pride, and he knew it. He'd suspected Tomek of hiding something, yet it was nothing malicious or spiteful.

Still nursing his throat, Helmut turned to Noss and demanded with his usual lack of reverence for a prince that wasn't his, "Who're these outside friends then, hyenas or what?"

"Does it matter?" Noss replied brusquely.

"Aye, it does. Are they THORN?"

"What's it to you? You're getting out aren't you?"

"I'm just thinking of Tomek. You're putting him in an awkward position. A Watcher hanging out with THORN terrorists, how's *that* gonna work? He was only a few months short of freedom anyway."

Noss's purple eyes flitted just a little. "Tomek knows what he's getting into," he whispered.

"Does he now?" Helmut whispered back. "And what exactly *are* you getting him into, eh?"

Rubbing his nose, Noss brushed past Helmut and changed subject before the pig could probe further. "We shouldn't stand around here," he said, loudly enough for all to hear. "They could be back with reinforcements, let's at least find a place to hide." He flicked a paw at Madou's cousin, "Zozizou, grab those truncheons. We may need them."

With a quick bow, the thickly-maned Zozizou scrabbled about on all fours, eagerly gathering the discarded weapons for his Prince. He stood up, truncheons clutched proudly to his chest – oh to be useful for one's sovereign!

Suddenly, Zozizou stopped in mid-stride.

"Ungh!"

He reached instinctively for his collared throat, the truncheons clattering at his feet.

"Gaaac-c-cgh!" he rasped.

Madou woofed in alarm, "What's wrong cousin?"

Even as the question left Madou's lips, Zozizou inexplicably rose into the air! He hovered on the spot, feet flailing a few inches from the ground, paws grasping at his constricted windpipe.

Then, with a strangled snarl he flew head-first across the cavern and slammed into its chalky walls with a sickening crack.

He flopped to the ground and rolled to a stop, tongue lolling.

"Zozizouuu!" Madou yowled, paws clapping to his head in horror. He ran to his cousin's aid, but his collar suddenly assumed the inertia of a mountain. "Gaaahaaagh!" he gargled, as he too was yanked to an inexplicable halt.

With a life all its own Madou's imperium collar winched him from the ground, just like Zozizou's had. The warrior squirmed and kicked as well, but to no avail. It was as though a spectral lynch mob had slung a rope around Madou's neck and hoisted him aloft for summary execution.

Through his blurred vision the hyena warrior spied three cloaked wolfen figures standing at the mouth of the atrium, one with their paw raised at him.

Madou braced himself for a sudden, violent end.

"Stop it!" Noss barked, stepping to the fore, his paws spread wide.

Whatever Noss did, if anything, Madou's collar loosened and the forces of nature returned to normal, pulling him to the ground, where he lay a moment, spluttering and gasping, half out of shock, half grief.

Clawing his way to the downed Zozizou, Madou cradled his cousin's bleeding head and looked murderously at the culprit as he stepped into the light.

The Warden of Gelb!

"That's as far as you go, Prince Noss," the black wolf declared in his tiresome tone. He was flanked by his two wolfen heavies, as ever. "Give yourself up before I lose my temper."

Satisfied Madou was all right, Noss let his mighty spotted arms flop down. "I'll come quietly," he said, glancing down at Madou and Zozizou. "If you let the others go. They're of no importance to anyone."

"Don't you dare try and bargain with me you wretch!" the Warden growled, casting a paw at Noss.

Nothing happened.

Noss smiled mischievously.

The Warden's bright eyes narrowed beneath his helmet. "A fake collar?" he surmised, allowing his paw to drop. "Tack's work no doubt. I'm surprised you could afford his prices. Did he sell you one of his useless maps too?"

"I'm surprised you know about him," Noss said, with a flash of those teeth. "Strange that you let him get away with running his little… tuck shop."

"It's a practical arrangement. Tack gets to experiment down in his hole, or whatever he does, whilst half the crystals he receives go to me. Without him every imperium nugget you dishonest miners squirrelled away for bargaining would disappear into the pockets of my corrupt guards. Have you ever met an honest pig? No, me neither. But pigs are all Lupa sends me! I make the best of a bad situation."

Noss nodded, "So, the prisoners think they're getting one over on you, when in fact they're merely giving you back what they stole for overpriced embers and confectionary. Very tidy, Warden."

"Indeed. Even the map you bought leads you here, a dead end. Nobody leaves Gelb unless *I* will it."

"Oh, evidently. No doubt you sell the venom Tack provides you on the black market and make a killing, even though each officially purified crystal could prolong a hundred good Howlers for a month. Very 'practical', Warden, if morally bankrupt."

"I'm not going to be dictated morals by treacherous hyena who tried to murder his own benefactor!" the Warden snarled. "You're only alive because I allow you to exist, you disgusting creature. 'Prince' indeed. You're nothing!"

"I see," Noss said, stepping slowly backwards. "Well, if I'm nothing, you won't mind should I spread myself over the floor of that chasm behind me."

Silence.

"What?" the Warden woofed.

"If you let my friends go," Noss bargained, "I'll return to Gelb with you. If not… I believe I might just end it all now."

"By Ulf's fangs!" the Warden laughed derisively, glancing at his two equally amused Howlers. "What're you threatening to do, throw yourself off that cliff?"

Noss shrugged, "And why not?"

"My prince, you can't!" Madou howled in dismay.

"Shut up, Madou."

The Warden stepped forward a little. "He's right. Hyenas can't commit suicide. It's against your custom."

Noss continued to walk backwards, closer and closer to the edge, "Ordinarily, but everyone knows I'm a bit… deranged. There's no telling what a seasoned Chakaa will do, is there?"

"But you'll have no honour," the Warden scoffed, a little worried now.

"Oh, I sold that *years* ago," Noss replied, with a nonchalant wave of the paw. "I've none left to lose!"

"Your tribe will be disgraced!"

"I've already disgraced them. They'll not bother to scrape my remains off the rocks, believe me."

"But… but you'll never meet your ancestors. You'll wander the eternal plains forever. Isn't that what you hyenas believe?"

"The empirical evidence for an afterlife is somewhat lacking," Noss said scientifically, turning around and jogging for the cliff. "So let's test the hypothesis shall we? Hahahahaaaahaha!"

The Warden reached out, "Alright alright! Stop! Stop! Please!"

Noss skidded to a halt inches from the black chasm, sending loose pebbles tumbling to their doom. He slowly turned around with a great big hyena grin slapped across his thick dark muzzle.

"Aww," he said, in mock disappointment – or at least the watching Madou hoped it was merely mock. "Hmm, it appears I'm more important than you claim, Warden," Noss boasted toothily. "Could it be that I'm valuable? It seems everyone wants a piece of me. THORN wants me alive; Amael wants me dead, or will do soon enough, whilst the wily Vladimir hasn't yet made up his mind! I'm your bargaining chip to use against everyone. However the dice fall you'll be safe, as long as you have an intact Prince to use against whoever wins and not a dismembered corpse blattered on the rocks below."

After the longest time huffing and puffing with fury the Warden conceded defeat. "What do you want?"

"Safe passage for the others," Noss sniffed, turning round to face the chasm again, arms folded. "I'll stay behind."

"Safe passage? To where? This is a dead end!"

Noss waved his map, before screwing it up and tossing it into the chasm. "We both know that's a lie; this place was explored by Lupan geologists centuries ago. I have friends coming in from the other side with the real map. When they arrive I want no trouble. You'll stand there looking pretty whilst they rescue everyone… except for me. You get to keep me. How delightful!"

"How do I know you won't kill yourself when they're gone?" the Warden growled, pointing at the gorge Noss remained inches from.

"Because I want to live, and I expect my side to win in the coming storm," Noss said wryly. "And when they do, you'll have to present me to them alive… or else."

"THORN won't win," the Warden maintained.

Noss said nothing.

Time passed. The standoff held. Eventually the frustrated Warden and his two wolves retreated to the atrium exit at Noss's behest, whilst a growing army of Gelb hogs gathered beyond, ready to rush in and overwhelm the fugitives if there was any sign of trickery.

Thus the five prisoners waited, trapped between a Gelb army and a bottomless pit – Noss most especially teetered on the edge, as if contemplating jumping still.

Madou tore strips of fabric from his shirt and bandaged his cousin's head, whilst Tomek rolled his up to fashion a pillow for the unconscious hyena.

"Thank you," Madou acknowledged.

Tomek merely tipped his stripy cap and looked across at the Warden standing in the cave.

"Give yourself up before you get hurt, cub," the Warden urged Tomek, beckoning with a paw. "Nobody's coming to rescue you. Noss there is a mad beast."

No reply.

"You'll be well treated. You won't have to mine ever again. I'll make you part of my household staff."

Still nothing.

"I mean it, boy, I was asked to look after you during your stay here."

That got Tomek's ear-twisting attention; Madou's too.

"You're a very handsome wolf, aren't you?" the Warden went on, loud enough for all to hear. "Yes. Just his sort. When this is all over he'll come calling for you, don't doubt it. I can protect you from him if you like."

"What you talking about?" Tomek spat at last.

"Howler Rufus, of course."

"What about him?"

"You're his wolf, aren't you? That's why he asked me to get you out of the Pit. He's taken a fancy to you."

Tomek barely reacted, but for an ear-twitch.

The Warden continued, "Of course if you *like* being his beta then that's fine too. Either way, I would rather salvage you from this situation in one piece than not; Rufus will thank me for it, and you will too, in time."

Tomek's young face twisted this way and that, before he waved a paw and walked off, his cap tugged shamefacedly down over his eyes.

Madou wasn't sure what that was all about, something distinctly wolfen, but he nonetheless took away one strange fact – according to the Warden, Rufus was still alive and Tomek didn't appear to be surprised by it.

What is going on here?

Suddenly a dejected-looking Helmut leapt to his trotters and pointed across the chasm. "I see 'em!"

Sure enough a contingent of hyenas entered the glowing atrium, a dozen or so, armed with spears and hammers and rifles. Two were especially robust-looking, wearing dazzling black and white cloaks, their faces masked by skull-shaped helmets.

The little army crossed the atrium and gathered by the opposite edge of the chasm that divided it. Whilst many cast their curious eyes to the shining ceiling, marvelling at its beauty, the hyena at their head cared only to stare at Noss.

"Prince Noss of the Four Winds," he said. "Is it really you?"

"Nurka?" Noss replied.

"Yes, my Prince," Nurka acknowledged, his raspy voice quavering with excitement.

Noss hiked his hefty brows, "You've grown."

Nurka allowed a brief giddy laugh, then fell to his knees and bowed. The rest of the group followed their chief, all but two of them – a red wolf and a white rabbit were left standing at the back.

Noss and the wolf stared at one another, their respectively purple and green eyes narrowing, their coronas reaching out and mingling as if no chasm parted them.

"Red-mist," Noss said – not asked, but stated.

The red wolf said nothing.

The rabbit looked between them, but neither he nor the wolf said a word before Nurka and his hyenas rose up again and obscured them from view.

"We've come for you, my Prince," Nurka declared.

"I should've guessed it was you behind the messages the guards kept passing me," Noss replied. "They never said your name, but I knew. Who else would bother to come for me but my old pupils?"

"Names are incriminating and dangerous to use, my Prince. It's not just us, but many allies across Lupa I must protect lest things should... unravel."

"Of course. You were always the clever one."

Leaving Zozizou a moment, Madou hurried to join his Prince. "Nurka, it's me!" he beamed, unable to contain himself.

"Madou!"

"Hahahaaaa!"

"Please forgive me for abandoning you in Riddle. I thought you were dead."

"So did I!" Madou professed. "It is good to see you."

Whilst his chief exchanged niceties across the divide, Themba spotted a problem lurking on Noss's side.

"Nurka," he said, pointing at the Warden and his small army of Gelb hogs gathered at the caves leading to the glowing atrium.

"I see them, Themba," Nurka replied, looking to Noss for an explanation.

"Don't mind the good Warden, we've come to an arrangement," the prince grunted vaguely. "He'll not disturb us."

Madou stepped in, "Nurka, he's not going to let Prince Noss go-"

"Shut up Madou!" Noss barked.

"But it's true, he's not!"

Nurka's wide purple eyes bared his alarm long before his mouth. "What do you mean? Madou, what's going on?"

Noss over-talked Madou and explained the precarious situation, that he was bargaining himself in place of Madou and the others, the Warden being unwilling to relinquish his guarantee against whatever force overtook Lupa, be it wolfen, hyena, or even the status quo.

"Then we'll kill him!" Themba growled.

"You'll do no such thing!" Noss chided. "I'm not going to be the cause of a bloodbath."

Nurka, for once, agreed with his second in command. "My Prince, we've risked everything coming down here. I'm not leaving without you."

"You'll do as your Prince commands, Nurka of the Jua-mata."

"Forgive me, but I must disobey you. Amael Balbus will use you against us once we've taken down the Den Fathers. He'll bargain with your life and bend THORN to his will. We must extract you *now*, whatever the cost."

"Don't concern yourself with me! You shouldn't have bothered to begin with. You should've left me to rot."

Nurka seethed, "My Prince!"

"It's the truth!" Noss looked down into the bottomless chasm, as if into his black soul. "I've caused nothing but heartache for my tribe since the day I sold my honour for a fistful of lupas. My betrayal of the Howlers brought new sanctions against my tribe. How many of you have suffered because of my selfishness?" Noss shook his head, "I'll have no more suffering and dying on my account. You'll leave me here, Nurka, and never look back. Take Madou and the others. Treat them as your friends, they've been mine."

Nurka dipped his chin to his cloaked chest. Usually so eloquent a beast, yet words wouldn't form on his lips for the anguish he felt.

His Prince and teacher was lost to him.

"Gentlebeasts," someone said in a gravely tone, "if I may."

It was Rufus, pushing his way to the fore with Casimir. The wolf cleared his throat.

"Let me talk to the Warden," he said.

"Talk?" Themba woofed. "You?"

"Yes, my good hyena, negotiate. You should try it sometime instead of hitting things with a hammer." With that scalding remark, Rufus turned to Nurka, "I might be able to talk him round."

"And if not?"

"We'll figure something out," Rufus chuckled, peering into the gulf. "Now, how does one traverse this little crack?"

Watched by an increasingly suspicious and fidgety Warden, Nurka set his hyenas to the task at paw. Setting aside his hammers, the powerful Themba threw a weighted rope to Madou on the opposite side of the chasm and instructed him to tie it off round one of the natural rock pillars that stretched all the way from dull floor to glowing ceiling. Themba did the same on the opposite side, thus creating the most rudimentary of crossings.

Nurka reached for the rope, but Themba stayed his paw.

"No chief," he said sternly. "If this goes south, you need to get away and carry on. Stay on this side."

With an eye-squinting pause for thought, Nurka accepted Themba's logic.

"Just be careful," the chief said.

Grunting in acknowledgement, Themba passed Nurka his splendid labyrinthine-patterned cloak and skull-helmet for safe-keeping. He grasped the rope overhead with both paws and took a few deep, nerve-calming breaths. Levering his armoured legs up, the powerful hyena hooked both feet over the taught, creaking twine and began to fearlessly shuttle himself across the chasm, paw over paw, like a living cable-car.

Themba made it look easy, but not everyone was convinced.

"Are you lot insane?" Helmut snorted. "I'm not going across there on a teensy rope!"

Tomek patted the hog on his mighty back, "You can do it, Helmut. Paw over paw. No problem."

"Well, w-w-what about Zoziwotsit? The lad's out cold! He can't do nowt."

Madou claimed nobly, "I'll carry him."

"How?"

"We'll tie him to my back."

Themba had by now crossed the perilous gorge, to general relief. He swung his legs down without a fuss and walked over to join Madou, embracing him then and there. After much back-thumping and shoulder-patting on both sides, the shortest and tallest of Nurka's followers parted.

Themba cast his wary eyes over Helmut and especially Tomek, then presented himself to Noss. "My Prince," he said, bowing again. It was as if prostrating himself from across the gorge wasn't good enough.

Noss averted his gaze to the pit. "Get my friends out of here, Themba. Look after them. Trust them."

"Even the wolf?"

"Especially him. Madou wouldn't be here if it wasn't for Tomek. He's one of us, now."

"Yes, my Prince."

One of the other hyenas made to cross over, but Rufus took the lead and told everyone to wait.

"Keep everyone on this side," Rufus said quietly to Nurka, swinging his legs up. "I've a plan."

"What're you gonna do?" Casimir butted-in.

"Fly."

With that cryptic reply, Rufus started his way across just as Themba had done, the folds of his tatty red cloak hanging down like an old tablecloth drying on a washing line.

Surprisingly, the athletic wolf proved somewhat less sure-footed than the preceding hefty hyena and for a moment one of his legs twanged away from the rope, causing him to twist alarmingly in space and sending something of a heart-stopping wobble rippling through the audience.

"I can't look," Helmut squealed, covering his beady eyes.

Rufus recovered his grip and continued as before, outwardly calm, inwardly frantic. He kept going, paw over paw, until he all but head-butted the pillar to which the rope was tied. With a quick over-the-shoulder glance to check the ground really was there, he peeled his numb legs and shaking paws from the line.

"Well," he woofed, dusting off his paws, "that's that."

Tomek hurried to greet him, tail wagging. After a quick embrace, which surprised Rufus no end, Tomek stood back and said bashfully, "Is good to see you, Rufus."

"Mutually, dear Tomek," Red-mist replied, setting Tomek's cap straight.

"I thought you were a goner, mate," Helmut whistled.

"Reports of my death have been greatly exaggerated."

"No I meant just now!"

Themba and Madou, meanwhile, saw to Zozizou. Themba scooped the wounded hyena up in his great, muscled spotty arms, scowling at the Warden the entire time.

"Did you do this?" he demanded pugnaciously.

"You're lucky I didn't tear his head off," the Warden replied. "No tricks, hyena, or I will."

Themba grunted, "I thought you were with Amael. We are too! We're all on the same side here, so why don't you let our Prince go?"

"Same side?" the Warden scoffed. "I'm on nobody's side hyena, not yet. I don't trust Amael any more than you do. He doesn't even know Noss is here; he was sent to me to be hidden. Noss is my security, *whatever* happens, and a good miner in the interim."

"You made him dig up imperium?" Themba snarled.

"Of course! What, do you think I'd let him sit on his rump being fanned by slaves? He's not *my* prince."

"Grrrfffg!"

Madou pulled the furious Themba away by the arm before the big hyena's temper snapped completely.

"Come on, Themba. Don't waste your breath on him. His time will come."

They returned to the gorge, whereupon Themba took it upon himself to ferry Zozizou to safety, citing Madou's weakened state and stifling collar. Tying Zozizou in front of him, Themba clambered onto the rope without further ado and whizzed across as before, the extra weight no impediment to him at all.

Passing Zozizou to his comrades, Themba went to cross yet again.

"No, Themba," Nurka rasped, grabbing him.

"What?"

"Stay here. Leave it to Red-mist."

"But-"

"Do as I say and be quiet! Please."

Themba, slowly, released the rope and reluctantly stood down. To leave his Prince's fate to a lowly wolf was a difficult thing indeed, but Themba bore the shame in silence.

"Get going, all of you," Rufus urged. "Come on, Helmut, nothing to it."

"I can't believe I'm doing this. I must be bonkers."

"It'll be fine. You're a big strong chap. Just do it like I did. Only... don't slip like me."

"Oh sure! Sound advice, Rufe. I feel so much better now."

Leaving Helmut with a pat on the back, Rufus slowly turned to Noss who was standing some distance away. The Prince of the Jua-mata kept his gaze averted, down into the blackness, ashamed, if not afraid. He could feel Red-mist's potent corona, sense those eyes burning unbearably into his thick spot-flecked neck, judging him for what he'd done in that backstreet café a year ago.

"How're your legs holding up, Noss?" Rufus crackled suddenly. "Do you remember what I taught you?"

Noss's rounded-off ears twisted. "What?" he sniffed.

"You'd better come with me," Red-mist went on, looking left and right. "We'll need a good run-up."

At once mystified and brimming with mortification, Noss mindlessly allowed Rufus to gently usher him away from the cliff and towards the waiting Warden, who was already emerging from the caves with his two Howlers in tow, eager to take charge of his princely hostage.

"What's he doing?" Themba growled, watching Rufus lead Noss away. "He's betrayed us!"

"Shh!" Nurka hushed. "Casimir," he whispered to the white rabbit, "tell everyone to ready their rifles. Don't make it obvious, just be ready."

"Aye."

Telling Noss to wait behind, Rufus walked the rest of the way alone and met the Warden, who stepped forward with his Howlers, leaving the Gelb hogs out of earshot.

"Rufus Bloodfang?" the Warden quizzed, unsure of his own senses in these imperium-laden caves.

"Hello again," Rufus acknowledged at length.

A moment's disbelief on the Warden's part, before he snarled, "What's going on? Amael's associates should've taken you to a safe house by now."

"These hyenas *are* Amael's associates. They're the very beasts he sent as part of our little… execution ruse."

"But then why-"

"I would like it very much," Rufus interrupted, playing the authority card, "if you'd accede to Chief Nurka's wishes and release Prince Noss into THORN's custody. Besides anything else Noss is a personal friend of mine."

The hyena prince looked on from behind, ears twisting.

"Friend?" came the incredulous Warden. "I know you're an associate of these… barbarians, Rufus, but didn't that one try and murder you?"

Rufus reasoned soberly, "It was Amael's signature on the bomb, amongst others. He bribed Noss to kill me to ruin the chances of the tribes being accepted into Lupan society, forcing them down a road of violent resistance and into his paws. It was nothing personal, just business. But you knew all that of course."

"Of course," the Warden said with a sniff, convincing nobody.

"It was a long time ago," Rufus said magnanimously. "We have to move on and let bygones be bygones for the good of Lupa. Isn't that so, Warden?"

No reply, save a noncommittal grunt.

"We'll be going then," Rufus declared, checking to make quite sure Helmut and the others had shimmied across the gorge to safety. "When the dust settles and I'm in the new government, I'll be sure to send for you-"

"I'm not done yet!" the Warden growled. "Do you think I'm stupid, Rufus?"

"Stupid?"

"I know how Amael's mind works. He's trying to exclude me from Nikita's table. Yes… he's found out about Noss hasn't he, and now he's sent you to trick me."

Nikita's table, did he say?

Rufus dwelt on that even as his lips uttered, "Trick you, my dear Warden?"

The 'dear' Warden explained. "If I have nothing left to bargain with, Amael can deny to Nikita that I so much as lifted a finger to help the cause and hang me out to dry. The fewer wolves in the new order the bigger the portions each will receive. Well, I want *my* portion. I want a rich territory of my own. By Ulf's fangs I've earned it! Ten years I've rotted in this dump, providing Lupa with imperium, turning the tap on and off at Nikita's command, risking my neck for his cause."

Casting a paw at the shining imperious atrium the Warden continued to rant.

"All this should've been mined out years ago, but it's still here, waiting for the signal to start production again once Nikita has control of the city. If anyone of consequence knew of this place I'd be executed. As it is nobody dares to check up on the rumours because they're afraid of being eaten by whatever Ulf-forsaken bugs crawl in the darkness! Bugs I will *personally* feed you too if you cross me again."

The Warden clicked his fingers, bringing his two grim Howlers to bear.

"No," he said sharply, "the prince stays with me. And tell Amael *and* Nikita I'll use Noss to turn THORN against them if they don't deal!"

Raising a calming paw, Rufus gently placed it on the Warden's heaving shoulder. "My dear Warden," he said, in his crackliest, most patronising tone, "I told you before… you'll get exactly what's coming to you-"

Pfffzzzzt! Crack!

With an incredible imperious blast Rufus sent the Warden tumbling and snarling across the atrium. His two Howler bodyguards followed suit, Rufus punching his right and left paws into each simultaneously.

Pfffzzzzt! Crack! Crack!

"Run!" Rufus snapped at Noss, tugging the hyena after him. "Come on, come on, come on!"

Noss picked his feet up and for the second time today did the most unnatural thing any beast, let alone a noble hyena, could do – ran headlong for a cliff!

"Stop them!" the smouldering Warden spluttered at his hogs.

Immediately the sound of pellets pinging off the rocks echoed around the atrium as several Gelb hogs drew pistols and opened fire. Nurka's troops spread out either side of their fleeing comrades and returned a volley, transforming the caves into a shooting gallery.

"You're insane, Red-mist!" Noss woofed with mad glee.

"You can do it!" Rufus encouraged, his armoured legs a blur of motion and imperious light as he sprinted with the speed of a true Howler. "Fly, Noss. Fly!"

At the last second, the final step before oblivion, Rufus bent his leading leg and with a blast of energy thrust himself into the air. His very corona reaching out like an extension of his being and pushing the erde away, rocketing him forward and across the yawning gap.

"By the Wind!" Nurka gasped, as Rufus bore down on the hyenas, cloak flapping like a flag in a gale.

"Mind out below!"

Landing heavily between Nurka and Themba, Rufus tripped and tumbled across the atrium like a Howler knocked from a speeding monobike, such was his velocity.

"Aaahaaaaahahaahhaaaa!" Noss yowled, kicking off the very tip of the cliff edge moments later, the ground disappearing beneath his flailing feet, replaced by the blackest of black pits.

He was airborne!

For a moment, as he sailed through space, Prince Noss was sure he glimpsed a glimmering white river meandering its way through the bottom of the gorge below, so many miles beneath it resembled a silver thread running through a cloak of black velvet.

White-imperium? Could it be the blood of Mother Erde herself, the very veins of the planet?

The wondrous sight vanished as quickly as it appeared, blocked by the rolling, uneven cliff faces of the chasm – cliffs off which Noss's body would doubtless bounce and break as he tumbled to his doom should his leap fall short of Red-mist's.

Alas, it did.

"Gaafffgh!"

The heftier Noss slammed belly-first into the cliff's rough, stony ledge, legs dangling, the wind punched from him. He clawed desperately at the weak rock with his dark fingers, pulling loose chalky masses of pebbles, which tumbled past him in miniature landslides.

"Gaaagh!" he yowled.

Finding no purchase, Noss slipped helplessly backwards towards the chasm and certain death. To fall into the planet and mingle with her blood, would it be so bad?

"Gotcha!"

Someone grasped the back of Noss's thick, furry, hyena neck, halting his slide.

It was Helmut.

"Oh no you don't," the big hog grunted, splayed on his front, teetering on oblivion. The cliff rapidly crumbled and shifted beneath his substantial bulk. "Woooagh!" he squealed, trotters kicking. "I'm slippin' I'm slippiiiin'!"

Tomek dived on Helmut.

Madou dived on them both.

Casimir dived on them all, for what it was worth.

Whilst Tomek, Madou and Casimir held Helmut fast, pellets ricocheting all around them, Themba reached over everyone with his long hammer and offered its brick-sized, imperium-laced head to Noss.

"Take the end, my Prince!" Nurka instructed calmly, even as a hyena beside him was hit by an imperium pellet and fell wounded. "Themba will pull you up!"

Coughing and spluttering, the winded Noss latched onto the lifeline with both paws. Themba dug in his heels and heaved with all his might, every muscle and sinew in his awesome body straining against his dusky, spot-flecked hide.

"Rrrraaagh!"

With Themba's help, Noss scrabbled up the cliff and made landfall, rolling to safety.

"Hahahaaaahaha!" he cackled. "Invigorating!"

Nurka barked, "Stay down, my Prince!" and drawing his bowstring back let an imperium-tipped arrow fly at the hogs on the opposite side. The volatile yellow-imperium missile exploded spectacularly on impact, sending the Warden's forces diving for cover.

"Let's go!" a panicked Casimir urged, tugging on his long ears. "Come on, come on, come oooon!"

"Cut the rope, someone!" Nurka rasped.

Howler Rufus obliged, slicing through said rope with a flick of his imperium rapier. Gathering their wounded, the hyenas and their allies fled into the caves, abandoning the Warden on the wrong side of the chasm, robbed of his bargaining chip and his dignity.

It was all over.

The Gelb hogs looked to the cheated Warden as he nursed his smouldering shoulder and ego.

"How'd they jump that?" one of his two Howlers whispered to the other. "I-I-I just can't believe it. That Rufus is some kinda super-"

"What now, sir?" the other asked, elbowing his comrade into silence.

Indeed, silence prevailed.

At last the Warden spoke. "I'm not finished yet," he growled at nobody in particular. "That hyena was Nurka; he's the one they're relying on to bring down the Den Fathers. If I can catch him I can bring down their whole conspiracy instead. Yes. I'll be a hero. The Den Fathers will reward me well enough, better than those treacherous worms Amael and Nikita."

He suddenly whirled round, cloak billowing.

"Cancel all mining operations and gather as many hogs as we can spare to keep order. We'll head them off at the exit."

Chapter 42

Saluting the ALPHA Prefects standing guard either side of the door, Janoah stepped across the precarious gap into what was fast becoming known as Josef's carriage – the cat hadn't left the windowless last car to so much as put in an appearance at dinner, so busy had he been working on Rafe's suit. He was nothing if not dedicated to his work, but nobody had expected Josef to have to repair the Eisenwolf himself.

"How is he?" Janoah demanded, looking down upon her wounded champion.

Rafe lay on a metal operating table in the midst of Josef's mobile garage, which reeked of imperium fuel and disinfectant. The big wolf's mighty chest heaved beneath a single, swaying imperium lamp. He had a respirator strapped over his thick, twitching muzzle and bandages binding his muscled midriff. The table and floor beneath him were smeared with his rich red blood, as were Josef's rubber gloves, though the latter wasn't a particularly unusual occurrence. The black ALPHA van which smuggled Rafe about Lupa loomed silently behind, like some giant, sad beetle mourning her partner's condition.

"Alive," Josef scoffed, peeling off his gory gloves and adding, "Just about. He's on enough stings and taubfene to euthanise an imperial centipede, though."

"He'll make it?" Janoah all but demanded.

"His wound was cauterised," the doctor explained curiously. "Whoever ran Rafe through inadvertently saved his life by burning many of the severed blood vessels closed. I assume they meant to kill him outright with an imperious shock, but they underestimated our Eisenwolf, as ever."

"It was Ivan," Janoah grunted.

"How do you know?"

"I *know*."

Josef hiked his whiskered brows.

"It's chaos out there," Janoah went on. "Amael's threatening to detach our carriages and strand us in a siding."

"He's behaving like a Den Father already!" Josef mewed with apparent delight. "But I suppose he's greased all the paws necessary to make it a done deal."

"He wants Uther, but the Alpha's not giving in."

Leaning on Rafe's table, Josef said guardedly, "The Alpha will have to interrogate Uther, if only for appearance's sake. He shan't do it himself, he never does."

"I know."

"Uther might break under torture. He might reveal to Horst or Duncan that you helped arrange Vito's murder-"

"Yes."

"Then what happens?"

"Then we are undone, my good doctor."

"We? You mean you!"

"Not at all," Janoah chuckled, leaning on the table as well, Rafe lying unconscious between her and his doctor. "Even though the Alpha knows how deeply I've had to involve myself with Amael, he can't be seen to condone my inaction when I could've warned Vito he was in danger. The Den Fathers would never understand the bigger picture; that to move now would be to send the conspirators to ground and endanger the whole Republic for some useless old drooler who was as good as dead anyway." Huffing, Janoah pushed off Rafe's table, making his mighty body wobble a bit. "The Alpha will throw me under the bus to maintain his position," she said resignedly, "And if I go, Rafe goes… then you, Doctor."

Josef cleared his throat. "What if we push to do the interrogation? I could kill Uther; a simple overdose."

Janoah entertained the notion. "Taubfene?" she assumed, raising her slender, ruddy chin.

"Two-hundred minims. He'd slip into a coma and die. Quite painless."

"No."

"Nobody would know. Uther swallowed a suicide capsule. Who's to contradict me? The Alpha will protect you from Horst and Amael will be glad to be rid of Uther; that'll calm him down too. Everybody wins-"

"I said, no!"

Josef's whiskers twisted, "Then what do you propose?"

Janoah thought for a moment, green eyes blinking once and slowly. "I'll ask the Alpha if I can interrogate Uther by myself. He should allow it. I can then guide his testimony and have him confess only what's expedient."

"That it was Amael who had Vito murdered and not you?"

"I didn't put my paw to this! I merely... turned the other cheek. I *had* to, for the Republic."

Josef said nothing – but was clearly enjoying himself.

Stroking Rafe's fevered brow Janoah moved on, "Do you have enough white-imperium for him?"

"I drained some from the suit."

Janoah nodded her approval and grunted.

"That does mean he'll have less in the tank when it's time to make the arrests," Josef pointed out.

"Rafe is more important. Ulf knows that lump of iron in there can't function by itself."

"No, but it'll be a marvel if Rafe recovers in time to use it before the Summit... if ever again."

Janoah spat, "He has to! You *have* to make him well!"

Josef adjusted his spectacles and pushing off Rafe's table grumbled something unintelligible.

"What did you say?" Janoah pressed him.

"Stroud," the cat hissed.

"Stroud? Nurse Meryl?"

With much whisker-twisting and paw wringing, Josef finally came out with it. "I need her. For all my medical skills and imperious knowledge it's *her*, blast her. It's her soft little voice that Rafe responds to. Her hot soup and... and brow-mopping and... and bedtime stories! He kept crying out for her until I hit him with enough taubfene to kill a bear. I've done all I can do; it's Meryl he needs now. I swear she has some power that I can't replicate, whether it's merely psychological or possibly even some imperious healing corona – such things have been recorded, you know."

Janoah planted her paws on her hips. "What, like the miracles of Ulf? You're not serious, Doctor."

"I never jest about my field, Janoah!" the cat said gravely, and not a little officiously.

Janoah looked down on Rafe, silent, pensive.

"I can call HQ at the next stop," Josef said.

"No," Janoah dismissed. "Meryl's too far away. It'd be pointless now, as well as suspicious; certain wolves back at HQ might ask questions, or worse."

"Then perhaps *you'd* better stay with Rafe."

"Me?"

"You're the next best thing to a friend he has, 'Jan'."

"I... I can't. I must remain with the Alpha. It's bad enough I've left his side at all during this crisis. Every second I'm gone Horst can poison his ear against me."

"Well I can't play nursemaid!" Josef spluttered.

Janoah suppressed a shudder at the thought. Looking up from feverish Rafe, she met Josef's smoky, bespectacled eyes. "No... but there might be someone aboard who can."

✧

"I'm going tae find Linus."

"We should stay here," Olivia seethed. "We've already drawn too much attention to ourselves."

Sliding the cabin door open, Sara said, "Ah don't care, Ah have tae know what's happened tae – agh!"

An ALPHA Prefect stepped into the doorframe – the red wolfess with the green eyes, the same one who'd been sitting with ALPHA's leaders earlier.

Pushing Sara inside the cabin she slid the door shut.

"Sara Hummel, I presume," she said loftily, casting her green eyes over the short black wolfess. "You look like your mother, albeit a dwarf," she chuckled, turning to the tall brown wolfess in a more convincing Howler Cub getup. "And Olivia Blake, is it?"

The girls exchanged looks, then Olivia said, "I'm sorry, Prefect, uh… whoever you are-"

"Janoah."

"Pleasure I'm sure, but you must have us confused with someone else."

Janoah beamed wryly, "Save it, girl, Vladimir's told me everything. Or should I say confirmed what I already suspected?" She locked the door behind her, "Don't worry, I'm a friend of his. And of Linus."

Another mutual glance passed between the girls. "How do we know?" Sara dared.

"Because were I not," Janoah explained, paws cupped before her like a school mistress, "I'd be compelled to inform my ALPHA colleagues, or the Bloodfangs, that we've two stowaways impersonating Howlers, which is a *very* grave offence punishable by a hefty jail sentence." Letting that sink in a moment she smacked her lips and continued, "As it is I require your help. In fact, Lupa's fate may turn on whether you are who I think you are, Sara."

Sara raised her chin nervously, "Which is?"

Janoah's searched for the appropriate term, settling for better or worse on, "Bruno's old flame."

✦

The dining carriage was divided into two camps, Amael and the Bloodfangs one end, the Alpha and his Prefects the other. The thought occurred to Vladimir that ALPHA was heavily outnumbered at least ten to one, but this was a diplomatic incident, not a war, and the peace held.

So far.

"This is a private Bloodfang affair," Amael growled again, slamming a paw on his end of the table.

"It is a Howler-on-Howler crime," Horst replied from the other end, "which therefore falls under ALPHA's jurisdiction. This is what we were set up to do!"

"By Ulf, our beloved Den Father has been murdered!"

"Rest assured we'll find the culprit."

"We already have. It was that mad dog, Uther!"

Horst huffed, "Uther is no friend of mine, but he is not mad like your Den Father was. Vito was a senile old drooler and an embarrassment to your pack, so it stands to reason-"

"How dare you!" Amael interrupted, rising to his feet with outrage.

"So it stands to reason," Horst barrelled on, looking Amael up and down, "that a Bloodfang Elder waiting for his chance to shine would benefit by Vito's death and nobody else! Giving Uther back to the Bloodfangs would guarantee only his convenient death and silence regarding who paid him to commit this most heinous deed."

Amael reached for his sword, "Are you accusing *me* of lupicide, you fat-"

"Gentlebeasts, if you please," the Alpha merely said, raising his paws and not his voice.

Still, he evoked silence.

Adal looked to Amael. "Elder Amael," he said calmly, his white mask-like face smiling somehow, even whilst solemn, "I assure you we are accusing nobody at this time. I hear and understand your concerns, but you must appreciate my position. The Lupan Laws state that this is indeed a Howler crime – it is Lupicide. Therefore, according to the legislation which Vito himself voted for at such a summit as we're shortly to attend, this regrettable incident falls to ALPHA to investigate. For me to do anything less would be a dereliction of my duties for which I could be impeached." He spread a paw, "Now, if you wish to *change* the law so that this quandary doesn't arise again, I suggest you elect Vito's successor in time for the Summit and lobby him to create a new motion to do so. Your pack is fractured and frightened; you need a leader. ALPHA will retire to our carriages and allow you to get on with the lengthy ballot process."

Amael absorbed Adal's speech, muzzle twitching with barely-contained rage. Oh to run you through, you arrogant son of a hyena, he thought.

"Fine," he sniffed, sitting back down, "but I warn you, Adal, when I'm elected Den Father your carriages will be promptly disconnected from my train and shunted into the nearest siding. Vito might've been soft, but I'm not ferrying you black-cloaked turds anywhere for free. You can get out and walk!"

"What?" Horst woofed, jowls wobbling. "How *dare* you speak to a winner of the Imperium Heart in this manner-"

"Horst!" the Alpha grunted at his Prefect, silencing him. He stared at Amael. "*When* you're elected, Elder Amael?" he said, one arm resting over the back of his chair, paw spread. "Don't you mean *if* you're elected? Or is your pack a dictatorship already?"

"Not at all, we're as democratic as the next pack," Amael replied, looking around at his Bloodfang comrades. "All those in favour of me succeeding Vito raise their paws."

The eleven remaining Bloodfang Elders raised their paws unanimously, even if some needed a glare from Amael or their comrades to do so.

Many others, Grand Howlers and Howlers alike, raised their paws and acclaimed Amael heartily.

"Aye!"

Vladimir managed to refrain; if anyone noticed they would put it down to his natural modesty and reticence.

He hoped.

"As you can see this lengthy ballot process won't take as long as you gambled," Amael gruffed confidently across the table. "If I were you, my 'Alpha', I'd start packing your bags and making new transport arrangements."

"You can't abandon us!" Horst blustered. "We're expected at the Summit!"

"Do you think any of the Den Fathers will miss you after your conduct of late?" Amael replied coolly. "Den Father Flaid despises you and you've even lost soft old Thorvald by arresting Tristan Eisbrand, clumsy oafs that you are. Mark my words, ALPHA; this summit will precipitate the end of your reign of terror." Amael pointed ahead, towards the tacked-on ALPHA carriages, "Now get to the back of my train where you belong!"

✢

Janoah had no sooner explained that she was responsible for Bruno's disappearance than the red mist of rage descended upon Sara, compelling her to cross the cabin in a heartbeat.

"Rot!" she spat, raising her arm to strike Janoah.

A noble effort, but the Prefect grabbed Sara's wrist well short of contact and pushed the little wolfess stumbling back into Olivia, dealing a small imperious shock for good measure.

"Agh!" Sara yelped, her arm tingling from paw to elbow.

"Next time," Janoah menaced, "I'll take it off."

Growling, Olivia stepped protectively in front of Sara, which amused Janoah greatly.

"Oh dear, I'm in trouble now," she mocked, cupping a paw to her cheek.

Knowing better than to try and fight a Howler of Janoah's famed power, Olivia instead demanded, "Why Bruno? What did he ever do to anyone?"

"The same reason Doctor Josef is after you; Rafe's got what it takes to bear the Eisenwolf mantle. Whether you do as well is… debatable."

Shaking her paw, Sara pushed to the fore again, "You stole him from us! From his father!"

"I did what I had to do, for Lupa."

"Lupa?"

"Yes, Lupa!" Janoah reiterated. "The only thing that holds this world together is wolfen domination." She looked Sara over with patronising disdain, "You may not believe it, limp-pawed Arkady-educated liberal that you are, but the hogs, hyenas and little beasts would all tear each other's throats out were it not for the Pax Lupi we've nurtured for centuries. For peace to continue, Lupa's dominion must continue. Doesn't matter what wolf rules or how it's done, provided Lupa flourishes. Rafe will help see to that; he's happy to, it gives him purpose."

Sara shook her head, "Why d'you keep calling him Rafe fer? It's Bruno! Bruno Claybourne!"

Janoah shrugged and huffed, "I didn't *pick* his name; it was mere happenstance."

Sara's dark little face scrunched up with bafflement.

"Bruno had to be seen to die," Janoah explained, with a tiresome air, "so that my... 'persistent' husband and various others interested in his talents wouldn't search for him, even less suspect I had him. The body you identified a year ago was that of some dying Howler called Rafe."

"What?"

"Josef applied a little makeup and swapped Rafe's and Bruno's papers, thus falsifying Bruno's death."

"That's disgusting!" Olivia gasped.

"I'm not proud of it, but needs must, my dear."

Sara stood dumbfounded for an epoch. "Ah knew it was nae him," she mouthed at last. "Ah knew it."

Janoah frowned curiously, "If you knew why'd you sign the papers, girl?"

Sara averted her eyes with shame, "Because Tristan told me to. He wanted tae protect me." She looked up at Janoah, "From you, Ah see that now."

Janoah chortled. "Tristan always was a bit of a flapper, unlike his unshakeable cousin. Rest assured, you've nothing to fear."

"Oh aye?"

"Cora Hummel's daughter you may be, but you're of no consequence to me," Janoah dismissed, adding, "To Bruno, on the other paw, you might mean a great deal... provided he even remembers you."

Olivia snorted, "Charming wolfess, aren't you?"

Janoah cocked her head a little. "What you think of me is neither here nor there, my dear, but if you care about Bruno as much as you claim you'll help him."

Sara shook her head, "How? What can we do?"

"Maybe nothing," Janoah admitted, "but you could at least try."

Sara looked to Olivia, who shrugged.

With great difficulty and much huffing and puffing, Janoah managed to squeeze a rather stale, "Please?" past her proud tongue.

"All right," Sara replied, daring to stipulate, "on one condition."

"What?"

"Let Tristan go. Ah know you arrested him. Get him out of ALPHA HQ like you did Linus."

"It's not the same," Janoah hissed, "Tristan's guilty-"

"Ah don't care!" Sara woofed. "You'll have tae let him go anyway; Thorvald will make ye. So do it sooner!"

Janoah frowned a moment, then smiled and said, "All right, girl, I'll see what I can do." Sliding the cabin door open and checking the way was clear, she beckoned, "This way."

✦

Josef Grau leapt to his feet from a snatched snooze amidst piles of boxes as Janoah opened the carriage door and allowed two Bloodfangs in.

"Who're you?" the cat demanded, tugging officiously at his lapels. "Get out of here! This is ALPHA territory!"

"Do calm down, Doctor," Janoah tutted, shutting the door and barring it. "They're here to help."

Josef stared suspiciously at the newcomers as Janoah beckoned them around the metal operating table upon which Rafe lay. As the Bloodfangs stepped into the light recognition hit Josef like a right hook.

"You!" he hissed, pointing at Olivia. "Stay right where you are, you're under arrest-"

"Not now, Doctor!" Janoah growled.

"But they're the ones-"

"I said not now!" the Howler reiterated firmly. "These citizens are under *my* protection. Leave them alone, is that clear?"

Silence and order prevailed.

With a nod from Janoah, Sara approached the table with some trepidation. She stood looking over Rafe for the longest time, studying his every powerful contour, his every scar, even going so far as to feel the rough, plasma-scarred pads of one of his big brown paws.

Suddenly Sara glared across at Janoah and Josef. "What've you done tae him?"

Before Janoah or Josef could respond, Rafe stirred.

"Meryl?" he grunted, lifting his head a moment before collapsing back. "Meryl... is that you?" he growled gently, eyes searching, fingers twitching.

Stroking Rafe's brow Janoah looked at Sara and said with intent, "Meryl's right here, Rafe. She'll sit with you."

"Jan... Jan, I-I-I can't see."

"I know, I know. Josef had to hit you with a lot of imperium, but it'll pass. Just rest easy Stenton and let your body heal. Meryl will sit with you, won't you Meryl?"

Overwhelmed, Sara could but nod regardless.

"Take his paw," Janoah urged under her breath.

Sara did so, both her tiny black paws vanishing amidst just one of Rafe's. Even as the giant wolf moaned in pain and tensed every mighty muscle hanging off his rotting bones, his grasp would no more bruise a peach than Sara's hide.

"Unngrrrfffgh!"

Sara looked helplessly to Janoah, "Och! What do Ah do?"

"Just stay with him," Janoah replied, looking to Olivia and back again, "Both of you. The rest is up to him."

"But Ah'm nae... 'Meryl'," Sara whispered.

"Whoever she is," Olivia added with a dismissive flick of the ear.

Janoah explained simply, "His nurse." Then spoke to Sara specifically, "My dear girl, Rafe... Bruno... hardly knows what's going on right now. Just mop his brow and hold his paw and let him believe whatever's convenient to his confused mind. He'll be all right."

Throwing a last warning glare at Doctor Josef, Janoah headed for the door and back to her ALPHA duties, saying unto herself, "He has to be all right."

✢

Panic had gripped ALPHA, or at least Horst. The rotund white wolf strode up and down the carriage gesturing with his paws and mopping his brow.

"We're finished," he woofed, medals tinkling, "washed up, kaput! Amael's going to leave us here in the middle of nowhere and turn everyone against us at the Summit in the meantime. The Den Fathers will vote to strip us of all power if not execute us!"

The Alpha reclined behind his desk, "Calm yourself, Horst, we're not done yet."

"My Alpha, without your rhetoric in the Den Fathers' ears to raise the spectre of the war and remind everyone why we exist, our purpose will be quickly forgotten for expediency. Nobody likes us rummaging through their dirty laundry, I understand the sentiment, but if someone doesn't hold the Howlers to account then Lupa is doomed to repeat the mistakes of the past!"

"If Amael succeeds, any vote made by the Den Fathers will be moot because they'll be dead," the Alpha pointed out. "So what difference would my 'rhetoric' make?"

"What if we were to assassinate Amael?" Horst suggested breathlessly.

Duncan laughed across the way, "What?"

Horst looked between him and Adal, blustering, "If he's gone, there'll be no uprising, even if THORN succeeds. Nurka needs Amael to run Lupa; nobody's going to listen to a bunch of hyena savages."

"Someone will just step sideways into Amael's boots," the Alpha said. "That's the point; we have to get them all in one fell swoop."

"But how can we? We've nothing left. No chances!"

"We have Rafe."

"Oh my Alpha, he's just *one* wolf-"

"He could upturn this entire train if I asked him."

"You mean if Janoah asked him," Horst grumbled. Reading the Alpha's angry face he continued, "Besides if we're left here so is Rafe, and he's in no fit state to do anything anyway-"

The carriage door opened and Janoah entered, saluting casually.

The Alpha saluted back, "How's Rafe?"

"Feverish, but recovering," she claimed guardedly.

"The fool, why did he run off like that?" Horst derided predictably. "Is he utterly mad now?"

"Hardly, Grand Prefect, Rafe wished only to protect weaker beasts and uphold the law, as we all should," Janoah defended with equal punctuality. "He wasn't to know Ivan Bloodfang isn't a wolf to trifle with."

"How do you know Ivan attacked him?" Horst said, walking over and raising his flabby chin.

"Because Uther didn't," Janoah replied, "which leaves Blade-dancer as the only suspect capable." She went on, "I know Amael sent him and Uther on a secret mission some months ago. He said it was to counter THORN activities, but I knew it must be something else. It appears he sent them to ambush Vito. Amael must've known the rotten old letch would bathe in the springs, as always, and in relative privacy because he likes to invite a 'guest' to join him, which just so happened to be Linus Mills."

"How do you know all this?"

"Deduction, Grand Prefect. It's what I'd have done if I were Amael and wanted to remove Vito."

"I see," Horst mused aloud. "Strange that Linus was with Vito, of all wolves. He seems to be in all the wrong places of late, and you always seem ready to bail him out. What should I deduce from that?"

"Vito chose Mills; we all saw it," Janoah dismissed, "no amount of planning by any wolf could make Vito pick his own assassin. No, Mills played no part in this except to run Uther down for which we should be grateful. He put aside personal friendship for justice. Linus Mills is a true Howler and nothing short of a hero."

"Hero!"

"Of the Republic," Janoah insisted coolly, studiously turning to the Alpha. "About transport, my Alpha-"

"I'm not finished yet," Horst growled.

"I am!" Janoah snarled sharply, continuing before Horst could erupt at her insolence, "My Alpha, if you're willing to compromise, I think we can still get to the Summit in time *and* honourably."

The Alpha's brown ears pricked. Raising a paw at a spluttering Horst to silence him he said to Janoah, "Go on."

Janoah glanced at Horst then said, "Release Tristan Eisbrand."

"What?" Horst woofed at once, then further, "Why?"

Janoah explained, "Den Father Thorvald loves him as a son. The Eisbrand train is due to pass; no doubt we can flag them down and strike a deal – Tristan's freedom for a ride to the Summit. Thorvald's an honourable wolf; he'll either refuse or comply, not cheat us."

Horst spread his paws, "But Tristan's a conspirator! You went out of your way to arrest him yourself!"

"A mere worker drone in their busy hive we can step over for the opportunity to squash Amael." On that brusque retort Janoah implored Adal, "My Alpha, we *must* attend the Summit at any cost. Whatever happens I assure you Rafe will do what he can to mitigate the loss of life and bring the conspirators to justice, but he can only do that if he's present."

Adal borrowed Horst's words, "He's but one wolf, Janoah."

"But an Eisenwolf, sir."

A pause.

Janoah huffed, "I signed up to ALPHA to make Lupa a safe, just place. Rafe goes through all his pains for the same. Let's not give up and let everything we've worked for slip away. We must fight, to the bitter end. We *must*, my Alpha!"

The Alpha's white face remained as placid and still as a porcelain mask throughout Janoah's impromptu speech.

"Agreed," he replied. "Though it pains me to lower myself to illegal backdoor dealing like some decrepit Den Father, I'll do as you ask… for Lupa."

"Thank you, my Alpha."

Janoah lingered; Adal could see something was on the tip of her tongue.

"Is there something else I can do for you, Prefect?" he enquired amiably.

Janoah came out with it. "Give Uther to me, my Alpha."

"Give him to you?"

"Let me interrogate him. In private. As an old comrade I know him better than anyone here. I can persuade him to testify against Amael."

The Alpha came across sterner than usual. "There'll be no deals with an assassin, Janoah. Howler Uther will pay the consequences for his crime whether he helps us or not."

"No deals, my Alpha, but Uther will say nothing if I don't intervene. I know him. He's too strong."

Horst scoffed, "No one is unbreakable."

"Yes," Janoah agreed, "but you won't beat a fighter like Uther into confessing. He has no family you can threaten to arrest and we've no rack back there either."

Horst leant close to Janoah's left ear, "Rack him? We'll pull out his claws, one by one, like in the good old days."

Flicking her ear, Janoah replied, "Grand Prefect, with respect, we know what Uther did and can guess at who told him to do it. What we need from him now is his future malleability so that when this all comes to trial he'll take the stand and indict Amael. How will it look if he hobbles into the box malnourished and crippled? How will ALPHA look? No, we must use reason and appeal to Uther's conscience."

"Conscience? That foul-mouthed, bed-leaping, murderous guttersnipe doesn't have one!"

"If that were so he'd have shot Linus as well, but he spared him over sentiment which Ivan didn't share because Ivan is not such a fool – Linus saw and heard everything."

"So it seems. Perhaps we should pull out Linus's claws too?"

With a roll of her eyes, Janoah implored the Alpha, "Let me work on Uther, my Alpha. I'll get him to sign a confession and more besides."

A nod and a salute, "Do as you will. It hardly matters this side of the Summit anyway."

"Thank you."

Once Janoah had taken her leave for the next carriage, Horst seethed through his fangs, "You give her too much, my Alpha!"

"I give her no more than her talent requires," Adal replied, standing up, paws on desk. "My dear friend, I suggest you channel your energies away from nursing your jealousies and redirect them towards our survival, because none of this will matter this time next week if we do not nail Amael and his followers to the wall! We'll be the ones having our claws pulled out if he succeeds. Do you understand me?"

Given much jaw-grinding and nostril-flaring, a chided Horst dipped his chin, "Yes, my Alpha."

Adal sat back down and loosened his black cloak from around his throat in a rare sign of stress, "Make yourself useful and draw me a hot bath before Amael disconnects us from the engine and leaves us to rot here in the wilderness without even the dignity of imperium power."

"Yes, my Alpha."

Once Horst had stepped forward into the same carriage as Janoah, the Alpha met eyes with Duncan sitting across the way; the big black wolf appeared as cool and collected as ever. Nothing ruffled him, not murders or politics or Horst's constant verbal backstabbing and manoeuvring.

"Mayhaps Ah'd best put the kettle on too, my Alpha?" he winked, standing up with a knee-slap. "Might be our last chance of a brew this side of getting our claws pulled out!"

⁂

It was simple enough to locate the cabin in which Uther was being held; the sounds of a muffled interrogation were as familiar to Janoah as traffic and honking horns beneath her office window. She listened at the door whilst the interrogator asked the prisoner a question; it was impossible to make out what was said over the sound of wheels on the track. Silence followed, then a coughing snarl as a fist was planted into Uther's stomach.

"Caaaghfffgh!"

One would always start small, with threats against family and friends, and work one's way up through violence and pain to the rack – everyone talked on the rack.

Just as well Josef didn't think to bring one, Janoah thought, entering the cabin.

The cramped space was stuffed with three wolfen bodies. Two were black-cloaked Prefects, one sitting on the bare bed filing his claws, the other standing with a knuckle-duster. The third was Uther, paws tied to the light fixture above his head with Howler-wire, stripped of his cloak, tunic and armour, his breeches and fur matted with blood.

"That's enough," Janoah said. "You're both dismissed. I'll take it from here."

The Prefects exchanged looks. One said, "He's a live one, marm, I think we ought to stay."

"I'm touched by your concern," Janoah replied, with a hint of sarcasm. She cast her eyes over the battered Uther, twisting in his cruel bonds as the train rocked to and fro, "But he appears thoroughly... subdued. I would rather you boys guard this carriage. It's possible whoever's behind Vito's murder will try and assassinate this cretin before he incriminates them. Allow no Bloodfangs to pass; can you do that for me?"

"Yes, marm."

Janoah's beseeching manner instilled the Prefects with a fresh sense of purpose and they eagerly went about their task, unknowingly leaving Uther with one of the few beasts who had reason to kill him.

This Wild-heart knew.

Watching Janoah shut the door and lock it, he grunted at her through bloodied teeth, "Just get it over with."

Saying nothing, Janoah wet a kerchief under the cabin's tiny sink and wrung it out. She approached Uther and gently mopped his white muzzle of blood. It was small comfort, and baffling to Uther.

"What're you doing?" he growled, twisting his wrists over his head.

"In trouble again, Wild-heart? What a surprise."

"Puh! Thanks to you."

"Oh? Then why didn't you just tell them about me?" Janoah asked.

"Should I have?"

"Is it because I'm Rufus's wife that you're protecting me, or are you actually loyal to me? Or are you just so pig-headed an alpha male you won't give up information to anyone without a fight?"

Uther swallowed, but said nothing.

"All of the above, perhaps?" Janoah cooed, returning to the sink to wash the cloth. "Unfortunately you've been betrayed, my dear Wild-heart. We both have."

"Betrayed?"

"Amael used you, and lied to me."

Uther looked on, his white muzzle slightly agape, dark grey ears erect, listening.

Janoah explained matter-of-factly. "He had Rufus extracted from Gelb weeks ago – the Warden there is in his pocket, you see. Oh it was very cleverly done; had me fooled. I won't bore you with the details, but sending you boys to kill Vito had nothing to do with Rufus and everything to do with power. Ivan wouldn't have murdered Vito for any other reason than to save Rufus's life, certainly not to make Amael Den Father, so Amael spun that yarn about getting Rufus out by some archaic legislation once he became Den Father."

Janoah checked her ruddy face in the tiny sink mirror. "Amael only saved Rufus because I asked him to," she said. "He loves me he says. Then again, perhaps he's just using me?"

Uther tipped his head back, blinking under the hot imperium light to which his paws were tied with unbreakable Howler-wire – his arms were numb, yet wracked with pain from the strain.

"Well, let's never mind me," Janoah chuckled, as if this were all a game. "I've no doubt Amael intended to eliminate you. There's probably someone waiting for Ivan at the agreed rendezvous point, though I'm confident Blade-dancer will outwit whatever goons Amael's hired."

"No!" Uther grunted. "That... double-crossing... bastard!"

"That irks you does it?" Janoah woofed. "You know, Josef suggested injecting you with a taubfene overdose to tidy up any loose ends. A tawdry solution I must say." Putting aside the cloth, the Prefect turned to the prisoner and said, "No, I can get you out of this… *if* you sign a confession."

"C-c-confession?"

"Lay Vito's death at Amael's door, but you must leave me out of the equation. That's all ALPHA needs."

"Puh! That's all *you* need."

"Would you prefer that injection?" Janoah threatened. "I'm trying to save your life!"

Silence.

"Besides, Rufus wouldn't forgive me if I let his handsome little Wild-heart die," Janoah sighed, sitting heavily on the bed. "He didn't save you from Vito's clutches all those years ago just to have you throw your life away."

"What're you on about now?" Uther growled.

Janoah hummed, "Oh it must've been very satisfying to finally get revenge on dirty old Vito for all the years of pain and humiliation. I told Amael you'd leap at his offer."

Uther gulped.

"What?" Janoah teased. "Think I didn't know?" She checked her claws, "Foolish boy, I've always known. I know everything there is to know about my old Riddle District crew, every tick and fancy, every skeleton in the cupboard. The mistake you made was conflating Rufus's two-way affection with the like of Vito's one-sided lust. You spurned my husband from the day you arrived in Riddle, fresh from the academy, such a strong, handsome wolf by then, not a frightened, wretched boy. I think you enjoyed hurting him, because you could. Rufus was a substitute for the untouchable Vito, a way to hit back at the establishment-"

"Shut up! You dunno nothing 'bout me!" Uther snarled, tugging at the wires that held him. "Nothin'!"

Janoah ignored his outburst. "I dare say Rufus won't be able to stand the sight of you when he finds out you're a cold-blooded murderer, even if it was the drooling Vito you done in. Now who'll be spurned, eh?"

Uther's chin dipped to his heaving chest as grief issued forth in fitful bursts.

"Grrfffggfffghh!"

"Oh there there, Wild-heart," Janoah tutted like a mother, standing up and drying the Howler's hot tears. Cupping her paws to his muzzle she said, "None of us are perfect. I have secrets too, you know. Terrible secrets."

Uther looked up from his grief and self-pity like that frightened, cub of yesteryear.

"Yes," Janoah insisted. "In fact I'm sitting on the fattest secret of all. Nobody knows as much as I do, not even wily old Vladimir. I have my ears to every wall, waiting, watching. It's very hard. Sometimes… I forget whose side I'm on, even who I am. It's enough to drive one mad! But I do it all for Lupa. I really do. All I want is for wolfkind to flourish. The thought of another war terrifies me."

The wolfess suddenly turned away, paw to mouth.

Uther watched, listened, eyes and cheeks wet, mouth agape in fascination. He'd never seen Janoah slip, never seen an emotion rule her mouth.

"Janoah… I… if it'll help then I'll do whatever you want. You know I will."

Whipping out her rapier, Janoah whirled round and cut the Howler-wire, sending Uther collapsing about the floor amidst a spray of sparks and pain. Pulling a pen from her cloak, she set it by Uther's trembling paws.

"Good," she sniffed, slapping some paper down, "now get to it, Wild-heart, or I'll string you back up by your ears!"

✦

"'Make yourself useful,'" Horst mocked in a whiney tone, swishing bathwater around in the carriage's communal washroom. "'Run me a hot bath.'" Drying his paws he grumbled, "He's developing such airs and graces, like a regular Den Father."

Leaving the washroom to fetch the Alpha, Horst bumped into Janoah as she emerged from the makeshift interrogation room with a piece of crumpled paper in her paws.

"Any progress?" Horst demanded.

Janoah wafted the paper about, "A signed confession, Grand Prefect."

"Already?"

"As you said, no one is unbreakable," Janoah nodded, bowing her head a little.

Unsure if Janoah was turning him a vague compliment, the rotund Horst grunted noncommittally. He leant forth and peered into the cabin, spying Uther lying on the bed in a foetal position, his broad, dark back shivering and heaving like a wolf waiting for death in a dying ward.

"Who cut him down?" Horst demanded, pulling back rapidly, as if fearing Uther had the strength to leap up and attack him like a mad wolf.

"I did," Janoah said.

"You? Explain yourself, this instant!"

"He couldn't very well write a confession with his paws tied over his head, Grand Prefect," Janoah patronised. "There's no need for claw-pulling or further barbarity, Uther's said all we need him to say, and without a sting he won't even be able to walk in his condition, let alone escape."

Horst cupped his paws behind him. "Sympathy for your old Riddle chums again Janoah?" he smirked. "Typical of a weak-willed wolfess."

"I've no love for this murderer, sir, but the kinder we are the better he'll cooperate come the trial. I'll have him well-guarded of course."

Horst huffed officiously, "See that you do!"

※

The vote was unanimous, every paw rising from the polished Elder Table in favour of Amael, the last elected Den Father of the Bloodfangs in twenty years.

"Aye!"

"Aye!"

"Aye!"

For so momentous an event the process felt strangely perfunctory, but a thin varnish of ceremony smoothing over the cracked and pitted edifice of Bloodfang democracy.

"My first act as Den Father will be to cut away the black rot of ALPHA from this train!" Amael announced, before Vito's cloak and brooch had even been draped around his shoulders. "Tell the driver to stop at the next station. We'll leave them there. Let them make their known way to the Summit, if they even can!"

Much cheering ensued – here was a wolf, at last, willing to stick it to those ALPHA bullies.

Ah, but how many of you know Amael's true ambition, to destroy our republic? Vladimir thought, watching proceedings from the corner of the carriage, helpless to change course, to speak out, for to say a word against Amael Balbus would be to mark himself for death in the inevitable purge.

No, not inevitable. We can still win.

Nervously twiddling his gold pen, Vladimir looked beyond the windows to the passing lush wilderness of Everdor, territory of Pack Hummel, seat of the Summit. Somewhere out there an underachieving Howler and a mad hyena prince were deciding Lupa's fate.

Ulf help us all.

CHAPTER 43

Thoughts of freedom spurred Noss on. The trial of Gelb was behind him. A year of torture, of surviving for his family's sake, was almost over.

Still, there was much to do.

The Prince stared at Rufus and Nurka walking ahead, side by side, wolf and hyena, friends.

Pity it was a terrible lie.

"Not far now," Casimir said, his voice quavering with relief. "Come on!" he gestured furiously, bounding ahead of Noss and the hyenas, lantern in paw.

"Mind the ants," Rufus reminded him.

"Ants?" Helmut snorted worriedly, looking to the Howler for an explanation.

Rufus spread a paw at the slick, dark walls and endless side-passages. "We stumbled across some eggs on the way in. These tunnels are part of an ant nursery, albeit on the periphery. We should be all right passing through, just don't agitate them."

"Whatcha mean agita-"

Rufus suddenly grabbed Helmut and pulled the big hog to one side with the augmented strength of an imperium-guzzling Howler.

"For starters don't step on their eggs, my good hog," he advised, pointing at a cluster of ghostly-white, bean-shaped objects which lay just shy of Helmut's hefty trotter, each one the approximate dimensions of a sleeping mouse. "Kick one of those and they'll not be best pleased."

"Cripes, big 'en they?"

Suddenly the oval head and nipping pincers of a giant ant reached out of the inky blackness!

"Wooagh!"

Helmut nearly fell backwards in fright, but Rufus held both himself and the hog firm.

"Don't panic!" he seethed, holding a paw up to Nurka and the others.

Everyone from Madou to Themba looked on as the bear-sized ant delicately stroked the eggs with her segmented, baton-like antennae, turning them, licking them, caring for them like a mother. Casimir's quivering lantern was reflected dozens of times in those two morose-looking compound eyes, yet the ant appeared unperturbed by the intruders.

"I'll kill it before it warns the rest," Themba growled, readying his hammer.

Tomek grabbed the hyena's arm, "No don't!"

"Get off me, wolf!"

"Is all right, friend," Tomek insisted. "She nearly blind and deaf, she probably not even see us."

The stocky Madou hiked his unconscious cousin Zozizou, whom he was carrying, further up his muscled shoulders and grumbled at the taller Tomek, "How'd you know?"

The young wolf tipped his stripy cap, "I worked with my ant every day. I raise her myself, from egg just like those. Ants not fight without reason. They attack only things they recognise as enemy, like centipedes."

"Stand down, Themba," Nurka rasped.

Meanwhile, Rufus ushered Helmut backwards, paw over paw, trotter over trotter. They and everyone else shuffled backwards, putting some distance between themselves and the ant, who continued her duties.

Then a second ant appeared from an adjoining passage and greeted the first. They tapped their antennae together, feeling each other's armoured faces, then the first ant scuttled down the nearest passage, leaving the second with the eggs. It was impossible to know whether they were simply unaware of the intruders or utterly untroubled by them.

"Like guards relieving each other," Rufus marvelled from a safe distance. "Heath will be green with envy."

Helmut snorted, "Can't they smell us?"

"Perhaps the ambient imperium levels interfere with their senses," Rufus theorised, removing his helmet to scratch his head. "Or maybe we're just downwind," he supposed instead, licking a finger and feeling for the airflow within the warm cave. "Either way", he said, replacing his helmet, "let's not overstay our welcome. Tomek's right, but these are wild ants and we're trespassing in their house. One false move could trigger an attack."

Themba held his hammer up. "I'll take a hundred down before they tear me apart!" he woofed, as if savouring the opportunity to die.

Prince Noss tiresomely pushed his hammer aside, "Boy, these creatures haven't the capacity to be impressed by your bluster. Besides there's a million of them in any given nest; they would not even notice a thousand losses."

Noss had been quiet since spectacularly leaping the ravine with Rufus, so everyone looked to him, surprised.

Unsure if his knowledge was being questioned, the hyena prince flashed a slightly manic, wide-eyed smile at the one beast everyone recognised as an expert in such matters, "Isn't that right, Red-mist?"

Returning Noss's purple-tinged gaze, Rufus confirmed flatly, "Yes," and turned to Themba, "I mean, what do you suppose the walls of Lupa were built for?"

Still mortified by his public, princely chiding, Themba said nothing.

Nurka, on the other paw, rasped confidently, "To pen in the citizens and control them, as slaves."

"Not at all, my good hyena," Rufus cheerily contradicted. "Lupa's walls were originally thrown up to keep bugs *out*, not citizens in."

The incredulous looks of the hyenas only impelled Rufus to continue.

"Before the Imperium Revolution reduced Lupa's surroundings to the polluted Ashfall of today, giant bugs of all sorts roamed about the city's hinterlands devouring crops and citizens alike. So the Founders built ever longer and higher walls around what was once a modest farming community. Wolves protected the little beasts in exchange for tribute, and the little beasts were our equals. It all began very nobly, I assure you." The Howler looked to Casimir, the only little beast present, "Of course, the foundations of mutual respect and cooperation have rotted under centuries of greed." He made a fist and growled, "Ulf willing we'll soon recapture the old ways with our own brand of 'revolution', a social revolution."

Rufus's little audience remained a calm sea of silence and stolen glances.

"Change *is* coming, Red-mist," Nurka promised vaguely, patting the Howler's shoulder in passing. "We should keep moving," he said, leading on. "Stay together and be mindful of the ants. Do not provoke them."

Tomek came alongside Rufus as they picked their way through the tunnels. "Is it true?" he asked, arms swinging. "Did Lupa really start that way, with everyone equal, even the little beasts?"

"Yes. The last two times, at least."

"Two times?"

Looking around, a somewhat distracted Rufus patted the youth's back, "Never mind. Let's just concentrate on getting out of here in one piece, all right?"

Tomek scoffed humorously, "You started it."

"Yes, well, one day you'll learn to ignore my waffling like everyone else."

"Never," Tomek said, tugging his cap down, perchance embarrassed to admit it, but admitting it all the same, "I missed your waffling."

Throwing Tomek a sideways look, Rufus tugged the young wolf's nearest ear. "Stop it," he chided fondly.

"What?"

"You know very well what, Usenko."

Leaving matters at that, Rufus rejoined Nurka at the head of the group, as if he were as much their leader as the hyena chief himself.

With every step the humid air grew fresher, the outside world beckoning, teasing, until that much-anticipated light at the end of the caves winked on, dispelling any creeping doubt in Nurka's map-reading skills. After hours navigating by cold imperium, be it beast-made lanterns or nature's rock formations, even the distant promise of the hot sun rendered Tomek's eyes momentarily useless as he hurried for the blinding slither of sky.

"Hahaaa!" the wolfen youth woofed, twirling with arms outstretched into the sun's golden embrace, before tossing his cap into the air and catching it again – an impressive feat when he could barely see for the glare. "We made it!"

Helmut trotted forth to join his mining buddy, not laughing, even less twirling. "I don't believe it," he snorted, squinting hot tears from his beady eyes, half from the sun, half from happiness. "Nobody gets out of Gelb. Nobody!"

"You're free, my friend."

The hog nodded soberly. "Aye… aye," he said, "but what now, mate?"

"What?"

"Where do I go? What do I do? What do *you* do? You can't go back home."

Tomek slapped the hog's mighty arm, "Don't worry about me. I've things to do."

"Aye, is that right?" Helmut snorted. Glancing back at Nurka and the others as they emerged squinting into the daylight, the hog pulled Tomek to one side whilst he had the brief opportunity. "Mate, we need to talk," he whispered.

"Talk?"

"This ain't no game. Now I *know* you're not thinking of joining these THORN creeps. That's not you. But whatever's going down beasts are gonna get hurt soon."

Tomek smiled as usual, "I'm Watcher, not you. Is my job to worry about this kind of thing, not you."

"Lad-"

"What's going on here?" Nurka suddenly rasped.

"What?" Helmut asked, innocently distancing himself from Tomek. "Whatcha mean?"

As a matter of fact, the hyena chieftain wasn't even addressing Helmut or Tomek, but Themba and Casimir who were walking beside him. "Where are they?" Nurka queried them further.

Big Themba kicked a smouldering campfire with his armoured toes whilst Casimir scanned the rough mountain terrain with his bleary eyes.

Nurka cupped his paws to his muzzle and called various hyena names.

"Mustaphaaaa? Tameeeer? Simooo?"

No reply. The Sunrise Mountains were silent but for a distant rockslide.

"What's up?" Helmut asked at last.

"I left half my warriors out here, at least twenty beasts," Nurka explained, purple eyes flitting about beneath his skull helmet. "They were supposed to wait until we returned."

"Maybe they came in after you?" Tomek supposed.

Nurka checked the sun and concluded that, "They can't have. We've not been gone that long. They had plenty of supplies too; they wouldn't need to forage."

Casimir bounded over to a strangely dark patch of otherwise grey pebbles. "Blood," he said, ears erect. "Nurka let's get-"

Crack!

Crack!

Crack!

The ground exploded all around Nurka and Themba in puffs of dust and dirt. The experienced hyenas knew from many a Lupan imperium raid when someone was shooting at them and immediately ducked.

"Back, back!" Nurka snarled, throwing a paw at Rufus and the others. "Ambush!"

Casimir zipped inside the caves and hopped behind the rocks, the hyenas hurrying after. Themba retreated backwards, unwilling to turn tail and run like a coward, until Nurka grabbed his arm and pulled him along.

"Run, Helmut!" Tomek yelped, dashing for safety, head down and zigzagging, just as he'd been taught in the Howler Academy. His bare back burned and tingled, not from the sun's hot rays, but the expectation that a pellet might tear through his body. Pebbles exploded left and right of Tomek as missiles impacted the ground.

Ting! Poing!

Into the cave and throwing himself behind a rock, the wolf landed heavily between Rufus and Madou.

Rufus checked the youngster for holes, "Are you all right?"

"Yes," Tomek panted, flinching from a final pellet exploding nearby. "I'm fine."

The shooting died down as quickly as it had begun.

Tomek looked around the cave mouth, at all his comrades new and old cowering in the shadows, pressed against the dank walls, rifles and pistols drawn if they had them, and that hyena, Nurka, readying his imperium bow.

Everyone seemed to be intact.

"Helmut?" Tomek gasped. He peered over the rocks, catching a glimpse of the huge hog lying snout-down in the open, motionless.

"No! Helmut! Helmut, I'm coming friend."

Rufus yanked Tomek back, "Get down you fool!"

A pellet pinged off the rock, showing them both with colourful imperious sparks.

"He was right behind me!" Tomek wailed. "Helmuuut! Helmut can you hear me? Helmut!"

"You can't help him now!"

"I have to!"

"Tomek! Rufus barked, grasping Tomek by both arms. "He's gone. I saw it."

"But-"

"I'm sorry. I'm so sorry, but keep your head down, please!"

Calm ensued. Tomek fell against the rocks and pulled his cap from his head.

"Schmutz!" he seethed to himself.

Rufus supposed Tomek had seen many beasts cut down before, being part of a firing squad, Rufus's firing squad at that, but perhaps he had never lost a friend.

Patting Tomek's shoulder, Rufus turned to Madou, "It must be the Warden. He knew where we were going to come out."

Madou set the unconscious Zozizou on the ground beside him, then grunted, "You should have killed him when you had the chance back there."

Rufus offered only a scornful scoff.

A few more pellets pinged off the cave walls, impelling everyone to duck and flinch.

"I know you could've!" Madou snarled afterwards. "Why do you always hold back, Red-mist? Why?"

"Well we're here now!" Rufus snapped, leaning against the rocks. "Ulf's fangs, he must have an army out there."

"We are army in here too!" a tearful Tomek replied, thumping his chest and tugging at his collar. "My collar is fake. I can fight! They have only two Howlers, three with Warden; the rest are just bullies with pistols."

Rufus shook his head, "And how many of us would be cut down by those pistols like Helmut?"

"I'm not coward!"

"Nor I, Tomek, but there must be a better way out of this."

Rufus peered across at Nurka, who was pressed against the far wall, bow in paws ready to shoot back.

"Stay here."

With that, Rufus scuttled across the cave mouth to join the hyena chief, throwing himself against the uneven wall, arms spread, like a giant starfish braving the tidal zone to eat a mussel.

Another few pellets pinged around the cave, after which Rufus turned around so his back was to the wall. "Helmut's down," he said.

"Dead," Nurka corrected, flicking his snout at the motionless body of the hog. "Your friend's been murdered, along with half my warriors," he added, referring to those he had left guarding the cave.

Rufus grimaced, then replied, "Your hyenas might've been taken hostage, Nurka-"

"No, Red-mist," the hyena chief replied darkly, his purple eyes squinting a little, "they knew what to do in the event of certain capture, we all do."

Rufus nearly spat, 'What's that, swallow their black-imperium capsules like mad-beasts?' but somehow refrained.

Casimir tugged his long white ears down around his cheeks like a bonnet, "Thump me, they're gonna throw a yellow-imperium bomb in here and then we'll be done for. Or worse, black-imperium. We'll be melted alive!"

To his right, Noss cackled, "How comes you little beasts are always so positive?"

"Well what's to stop them, eh?"

"The Warden needs me alive," Noss claimed. "Perhaps if I give myself up."

"I don't think we can fool him twice," Rufus said.

"I don't intend to fool him again. He can have me, if it will save lives-"

"No!" Nurka dismissed at once.

"No?" Noss growled pompously. "And who're you to tell me what to do, boy? I'm your prince!"

"I have lost many hyenas to get you this far; hyenas who believe you can unite the tribes," Nurka rasped, with the clarity of a beast, no boy. "I am not giving you back so that their lives are wasted, even less so that Amael can dictate terms with our prince in his paws!"

Silence prevailed, but for air whistling through thick, flaring hyena nostrils.

As if to change subject, Rufus snatched the map from Nurka's belt and searched its crinkled passages. "Nurka, is there another way out of here?"

The chief came-to, "Not on there, Red-mist."

"But there *must* be. Logically, if the ants aren't using this exit to get to the surface there must be other tunnels, perhaps some they have dug themselves. They need to forage above ground."

"I suppose they do, but would not the ants attack us if we tried to get by them?"

Themba hiked a thumb, "They didn't even notice us back there."

To which Prince Noss huffed, "They are more forgiving on the margins; they'd not take kindly to two dozen beasts traipsing right through their nest. If we provoke the ants too far we may trigger an attack. They could go into a frenzy and comb the mountain, killing anything not of their own scent. If you've ever trodden on a little ant hill by accident you'll know what I mean. Now imagine that, but with great ants. This whole place would become a death trap."

Nurka and Themba stared at their prince.

"If you do not believe your anointed prince, ask Red-mist!" he woofed, arms folding.

"Yes," Rufus replied, staring into space. Tapping the claw of his index finger on his helmeted nose to a metallic clink, he hummed rhetorically, "Yes… that might just work."

Grabbing a lantern from one of the hyenas, Red-mist precluded any questions with a command, "Keep them busy; if they negotiate draw it out as long as you can."

Questions came regardless.

"What're you going to do?" Nurka demanded to know.

"I need to find us a place to hide," Rufus replied cryptically. "Somewhere the ants won't go."

"What?"

"Trust me. I'll be as quick as I can."

Seeing Rufus peel off from the hyenas and head back into the cave, Tomek scrabbled to his feet and hurried after him, hugging the wall so as not to be seen or shot at.

"Rufus!"

"Tomek, stay there."

"Where you going?"

"To get us out of this," Rufus explained.

"I help," Tomek said, slapping his chest.

"No-"

"Please! Whatever it is, I *must* help. For Helmut. Please!"

With time of the essence, and Tomek's face irresistibly forlorn, Rufus caved in and beckoned the Watcher to follow him into the darkness once more, leaving Nurka and the others to hold the cave mouth.

"Water," Red-mist panted, as he hurried through the passages, waving his lantern at any dark rents and spaces in the rock as yet unexplored. "We need to find water."

"Water?" Tomek repeated.

"Yes. A pool of water, deep enough to swim in. The caves are running with it, there must be places it collects."

Baffled though he was, Tomek trusted Rufus knew what he was about. "Right. We split up, yes?" he suggested, taking in the many passages roundabout. "I search this way. You search that way."

The youngster made to dash off into one of many twisting side-passages.

"Wait! You need a light, you daft cub!"

"Oh! I go back for one."

"No, take mine," Rufus said, passing Tomek his lantern. "If you had a brain you'd be dangerous."

Tomek spread a paw, "What about you?"

Rufus answered him by running a paw over his mantle-fastening brooch. The tired imperium within the ancient metal rippled into life at the Howler's behest, shining with a barely useful red light suitable only for a dark room. Rufus had no idea to what pack this stolen armour might've once belonged, the circular symbol wasn't familiar, but it would serve.

"Don't go too far," he advised, grasping Tomek's shoulder. "Search a little way in and come back here to the start, all right? If you come to a fork in the caves mark the way back with a rock or something. If you find water, shout like mad."

Much nodding and a wave of the paw, then Tomek was away like a cub on a treasure hunt.

"Be careful!" Rufus called after him.

"I will!"

Waiting until the caves had swallowed Tomek and his lantern, Rufus picked his own passage to explore – they all looked the same. How easy it would be to get lost.

The red light of Rufus's brooch glimmered on the slick walls, making them appear almost visceral, as if he were exploring the innards of some giant creature. He tried not to dwell on what fate might befall Tomek. The eager cub could get lost forever, or fall down a pit never to be seen again, or be dismembered by a ferocious ant and carried off for tea.

Helmut, Zozizou and half Nurka's comrades, injured or dead. How many others will follow?

"If you must have blood, Ulf, take mine instead," Rufus bargained in the darkness, "All I ask is that you wait a little longer-"

"Praying, Red-mist?" someone huffed.

Whirling round, Rufus's red brooch illuminated the manic toothy grin of Noss Jua-mata, casting the hyena prince in shades of scarlet, save for his purple eyes which somehow resisted.

"That's not very scientific," he tutted, wagging a thick finger.

"What's going on back there?" Rufus demanded.

Noss shrugged, "I'm sure Nurka's capable of holding our Warden at bay," then glanced behind him, perhaps checking if someone had followed. "I excused myself from him to come tell you... I've kissed the sun."

Silence.

Noss went on theatrically, "I have kissed the sun, felt its warmth on *my* wings. I have known love with my mate and shared joy at their smile. Oh yes. And yet... there is so much more beyond the horizon, so much yet to see and do! This pond is but a puddle in a great ocean of green. Alas, I cannot go on. My time is done." He finished with a cackle, "Is that not the password?"

Rufus's emerald eyes squinted. "You?" he gasped, looking Noss up and down. "You're with Janoah? But how? If you've been in Gelb all this time, how could *you* be my contact?"

"Vladimir, that spider, plans well ahead. He faked my death and sent me to Gelb in secret, so that Amael wouldn't silence me."

"Because you'd testify against him," Rufus assumed.

Noss nodded, then dipped his chin, "I didn't... it was *not* hatred, that drove me to betray you Red-mist. Amael's camp came to me first. They offered me money, so *much* money! I just wanted to be free; free of my responsibilities as a prince, free of watching my people suffer and die and me being unable to do anything!"

Rufus let the tearful prince gather himself.

"I am a coward, I know," Noss self-flagellated. "I even betrayed Amael's camp by letting you live, but they had betrayed me anyway, arresting Arjana and the cubs. Vladimir saved them, but said if I wanted to see them again I had to survive Gelb, and wait on his word. Only, I never expected his 'word' would be this! I thought I would only have to testify against Amael when Vladimir brought him to trial, that was our deal. Now I'm supposed to help you bring THORN down from the inside, they say."

"They?"

"Vladimir's contacts in Gelb. He has spies everywhere."

"Spider indeed," Rufus agreed. "So then, will you help us?"

Noss growled, "Believe me, Nurka goes too far! I would stop him whether Vladimir said so or not. THORN's violent course will only destroy the tribes, not save them." He spread his paws, "I... I don't *want* to fight and kill anymore. I just want to live in a hut and raise my cubs with Arjana. That's all I have ever wanted."

Rufus gulped, his neck bobbing, "I knew you weren't so far gone that you'd murder innocent beasts. That's why you didn't throw a black-imperium grenade in *The Warren* that day. You couldn't do it, could you?"

Noss dipped his chin. "No, but... can you ever forgive me for what I *did* do?"

"What's done is done," Rufus replied, noncommittally. "Hundreds if not thousands of lives may depend on what we do next, that's what matters now. Understand?"

Noss nodded. Clearing his throat of residual grief he asked, "Is it just us, Red-mist?"

"Casimir's on our side," Rufus replied. "I had to convince him, but I think he can be relied upon."

"That cowardly rabbit?"

"Pessimistic, certainly."

Noss waited a moment, as if worried of the repercussions of his next sentence. "I... confided in Tomek before we broke out of Gelb. He's determined to help."

"Tomek? I wanted him left out of this!"

"He's a Watcher, Rufus, not some innocent cub you need to protect. He's shot beasts, executed them – *you* almost, he told me everything. He knows what's at stake."

"Does he?" Rufus scoffed. "Do *you* even know what's at stake?"

Noss said with some confidence, "Nurka's going to plant a black-imperium bomb at the Pack Summit, killing all the Den Fathers. Amael and his followers will leave before it explodes and head back to Lupa to take control in the power vacuum."

Rufus laughed a little, "Says who?"

"Madou," Noss said.

"Well, Madou may think so, and that's likely what he told Vladimir too, but a black-imperium bomb won't cut it, and Nurka knows that. He's read up on imperiology; he knows how black-imperium behaves. No, he's got something else in mind."

"Such as?"

"I'm... not sure yet, but it can't be a simple bomb-"

"Rufuuus! Rufus, I find it! Water!"

"Tomek?"

Returning to the main passage with Noss in tow, Rufus spied Tomek hurrying back from the very first cave he had disappeared down. Waving his lantern and a paw, the young wolf declared excitedly, "Is water this way!"

"Deep?" Rufus stipulated, meeting him at the mouth of the passage.

"Yes. There is waterfall with pool. Is quite big."

"Waterfall?"

"Yes, listen!"

Rufus listened, and sure enough detected a faint hiss on the air. "You're sure about this?" he asked.

"Come see," Tomek said, beckoning Rufus.

"No, I believe you," Red-mist assured Tomek, patting his shoulders. "Well done."

"What now?"

"Run back and bring Nurka and the others to the water you found," Rufus instructed. "Be ready to dive in, and I mean everyone, wounded or not."

"Right, I go!" Tomek said.

"Wait; Nurka might not listen to you alone!" Noss barked, chasing after the eager Watcher. He stopped long enough to say, "Good hunting, Red-mist."

Snorting, Rufus drew his sword and dashed the opposite way, vanishing into the dark.

As Tomek hurried through the caves as fast as was sensible by lantern light, he turned to Noss as the hyena caught up. "Do you know what we're doing, Noss?"

"Don't you?"

"Not really, no."

"Hahaaahahaa!" Noss cackled, "I like you, Tomek, you're an honest beast." Then he explained, for he knew the workings of Rufus's mind, as well as the habits of many a bug, "The ants won't go near water, so we can hide in there whilst the angry lot take care of the Warden and his pigs."

"Ants?"

"Yes, all Rufus need do is provoke them into defending their nest, then we wait out the storm in your pool."

"Sounds like it will work."

"I'm that convincing?" Noss laughed. "That's good to know."

Suddenly the hyena prince grabbed Tomek's arm, pulling him to a stop.

"Hey!" the Watcher yapped.

For a moment Noss was still and silent. "You know… we could end this now," he suddenly realised. "We could *not* tell Nurka. The ants would wipe him and the others out. It'd be an honourable death for a hyena, they wouldn't begrudge it. Then Amael's coup would collapse without Nurka completing his side of the bargain. It'd be over. We could all go home. It would be enough, wouldn't it?"

Tomek frowned and emitted a tiny scoff. "But… if Amael's coup is stopped too soon, then the traitors will not reveal themselves. That's what you told me."

Noss agreed with a nod. "I know. But, if we let this continue we risk Nurka and Amael succeeding. We may not get a better chance to end it."

Noss and Tomek stared at one another.

"What would Rufus do?" the latter asked.

"Rufus? He's just trying to get everyone through this unscathed. He's always been too soft. He just forgave me for trying to kill him! Anyone else would've run me through. I know his betas would've."

"His betas?"

Noss looked Tomek over, "Watch yourself. You're fast becoming one."

Silence and bafflement.

Noss fondly clipped Tomek's nearest ear with a paw, "Never mind, boy."

Whatever the hyena meant, Tomek moved on. "My mother always say… job worth doing is worth doing well," he said, in his typically chipper fashion. "We go on, to end, and do this properly. Like we planned."

Noss seconded, "To the end then. Hahahaaaahahaaa!"

✦

Rufus shone his feeble red brooch over the eggs Helmut had nearly trodden on. There was no sign of the nursery ants. They must be attending young elsewhere.

"Schmutz."

There was nothing else for it. Steeling himself for the task at paw, Rufus tentatively entered the passage near the clutch of eggs in search of the ants, kristahl rapier held forth, teeth clenched beneath his scratched and pitted helmet.

Rufus knew weapons and armour would do little to avail him against the fearsome jaws of countless furious sisters, for that's what ants were, daughters of the queen, sisters one and all, dedicated to the defence of her and the continuation of their underground realm. They would not take kindly to someone disturbing the peace.

After something of a steep climb necessitating Rufus crawl on all fours, the passage opened up into a larger atrium. The floor looked paler than the walls. As Rufus got his eye in he realised the whole cave was alive with movement! Fat, glistening, wriggling grubs, devoid of noticeable legs or eyes, lay amongst their un-hatched egg-bound sisters, like obese empresses lounging on piles of silk pillows, and all presided over by giant, six-legged slaves incessantly turning them, feeding them, cleaning them.

This was the nursery proper, most likely one of many. The eggs down the hall were but the beginnings of an extension for this growing colony.

Rufus watched, fascinated, wishing he had a camera and a flash, or even a sketchbook, with which to document the amazing sight. How many beasts can have seen the inside of a giant ant colony and lived to tell of it?

You still have to live, Rufus reminded himself.

Drawing his pistol, he aimed at one of the ants tending the grubs. Even though it was just a feeble-minded creature, an automaton controlled by pheromones and sensations with no higher thought than the very next thing to do, to wilfully shoot it went against every fibre of Rufus's being. He felt like a vandal throwing a brick through a hospital window into the baby ward, but it had to be done.

Lupa and countless lives may depend on it.

"Sorry, old girl," Rufus seethed, squeezing the trigger.

Crack!

The pistol exploded with a flash of light and sound, turning the whole atrium to day for a fraction of a second, every grub, egg and ant, illuminated. The one Rufus had selected for death fell over and curled into a tangle of legs. In its dying moments it chattered wildly, stridulating with its mouthparts like enormous maracas, while its grape-like abdomen pumped wildly, as if taking some final heaving breaths. The ant was in fact squirting an invisible pheromone into the air, a chemical message that carried a cry for help.

In seconds the nearest ant responded, rushing over to its dying sister and feeling her with its antennae. Then another came and another, each one chattering and releasing more chemical messages, drawing more and more ants to the fray like panicked mothers rushing from their houses to attend a youngster knocked down in the street. The sisters began to search for the cause of the disturbance; spider, centipede, another invading ant, whatever it was they massed to destroy it, running all over the nursery like creatures possessed.

Rufus promptly about-faced and slid into the tunnel as the caves thrummed to the chitinous feet of a hundred furious insect warriors.

The frenzy had begun.

✦

One of the Warden's two Howlers hurried up the mountainside to join his superior, who was overlooking the cave entrance from a safe distance. From this vantage point it was possible to see the dozens of Gelb hogs stationed around the rocks and escarpments that surrounded the cave, their pistols aimed at Nurka and the hyenas cowering within. It was also possible to see the bodies of the hyenas they had already dealt with, heaped to one side in a bloody pile.

The Warden was done with games and deals. Just kill them all was the order.

"Well?" he demanded of his Howler.

"They're... going back in, sir," the fellow puffed, a little short of breath after the climb.

"What?"

"They're retreating back into the caves, sir."

The Warden pondered the news. "They must be looking for another way out. Fools, they'll never see the light of day again. They'll expire in there, one way or another."

"Yes... sir."

For a time nothing more was said. The Howler fidgeted a little, shuffling from foot to gaiter-clad foot.

"What is it?" the frightening Warden grumbled at him.

"Nothing, sir."

"Out with it, Howler."

"Only that, well, Howler Rufus disappeared first sir, him and that cub he likes. Then after a few minutes the hyena prince ran after them both. I was just going to come tell you about it when those last two came back without Rufus and spoke to the hyenas, and then they all upped sticks and left together. They all looked pretty organised, sir, like they knew what they were about and where they were going to."

"I see."

"Maybe Howler Rufus knows a way out? He's pretty clever isn't he? One of the best there is, they say. He must be to leap that gorge sir; I ain't ever seen the like!"

The Warden glowered at his awed subordinate.

The Howler withered under his gaze, "Just a thought, sir."

"No… no you're right," the Warden admitted, paws on hips. "Maybe he does know a way out… or maybe he's just trying to draw us inside to ambush us."

The Howler waited for his orders.

"Take half the hogs and investigate," the Warden decided. "I'll stay here in case he's planning to hide somewhere and then double-back as you pass. Whatever he's thinking I won't underestimate him again, nor trust that worm Amael. Once this is over I'm going straight to the Den Fathers to inform them of the conspiracy. They'll have to reward my diligence then."

"Yes, sir."

Watching his two Howlers gather some hogs and enter the caves, the Warden growled to himself. "You're not going to best me, hyena-lover."

✦

Rufus scrabbled down the tunnel into the main passage as fast as his limbs could carry him. He avoided crushing the few ant eggs there, as if unwilling to compound murder with infanticide.

A mistake.

In the time it took Rufus to skirt politely around the pallid clutch, a furious ant burst from the tunnel in pursuit of him and in an instant lunged across, nipping his left arm neatly in her vice-like jaws and yanking him to a stop!

"Gaaaahaagh!" Rufus cried, falling about the place.

Round came the ant's abdomen, tucking under her legs, the sting unsheathed and ready to strike – ants had stings like wasps and bees and weren't shy about using them, but nor was Rufus shy about using his! Clapping his right paw to that rock-hard, armoured head, Rufus let the ant have it, blasting her with an plasmatic shock so potent that it blew her on her back and sent him tumbling across the caves until he slammed into its smooth, slick walls.

"Oof!"

Rolling momentarily into a ball of hurt, Rufus checked he had come away with his left arm and that it wasn't dangling from the jaws of the ant.

He still had both limbs, but neither was in a good state. With one bleeding and useless, and the other numbed by imperium shock, Rufus dragged himself to his feet and stumbled on with his arms folded to his chest. The adrenaline dulled the pain, but not the fear.

Dismembered by ants, what a way to go!

He glanced behind. Where one ant fell, ten others replaced her, filling the caves, antennae waving, searching. Find the intruder, protect the eggs! Whilst some set off to hunt down the enemy, others gathered the eggs in their jaws and ferried them up the tunnel, deeper into the nest, to safety.

So efficient, so organised, so deadly. Magnificent.

Rufus hurried on, the hiss of the waterfall and pool Tomek had promised tickling his ears. Tomek had come from the last passage on the right, as memory served, so that's where safety must lie. Rufus wished he had asked for directions. It's funny what one overlooks in the heat of the moment, he thought, hoping he had given Tomek and Noss enough time.

"Awoooo!"

Tomek? Howling to guide me? It must be!

Right, into the passage Tomek should have led Nurka, Themba and the others.

The dull chatter of countless armoured feet thumping on the floor and walls thundered past Rufus as the ants stampeded down the main passage he had only seconds ago left behind. Soon they'd search this tunnel too. They'd search everywhere, above and below, eliminating anything strange, anything not of the queen.

Keep running, Howler, don't look back.

"Awoooo!"

Definitely Tomek, louder, and with every step the hiss of falling water grew louder too. The tight tunnel opened up into a wide, black atrium, the feeble red light of Rufus's weary brooch unable to penetrate. He continued on, blind, hurting; he felt he was heading down a slight slope, for his feet were tilted forward. Light! Shapes! The glow of a lantern, the ripple of black water, the white foam of bubbles; slowly a waterfall and a lake crystallised in Rufus's eyes. Familiar beasts were wading into its depth, Noss, Nurka, Themba, Casimir!

"Rufus!" Tomek shouted, waving his lamp. "This way!"

Noss waved furiously too, beckoning Rufus into the water, as if the Howler needed encouragement like some timid bather concerned over temperature.

Suddenly, the prince snatched a spear from the nearest wading hyena and charged through the pool towards the subterranean shore, kicking up sprays of foam in his desperation, spear held overhead like a rifle.

"Behind you, Rufus!" he bellowed.

Something hit Rufus like a sandbag, he stumbled, fell, and tumbled down to the water's edge.

"Ofaagh!"

Then they were on him, several giant ants, a tangle of chitin and hairs, antennae beating him relentlessly like clubs. Their jaws nipped at his extremities, biting his flesh, seizing his limbs, an arm each, a leg each.

"Gaaahaaaaagh!"

Up Rufus rose, twisting in agony as the ants pulled in opposing directions, trying to tear him apart in a tug of war. He felt a shoulder crack, dislocate, his spine pop, tendons rip. With a last gasp of effort the Howler blasted them all with his imperious fury, sending waves of plasma rippling up each limb! Shocked right in the mouth by Rufus's energy the ants relented, dropping him and running in confused circles, their spiked legs kicking and tearing his broken body as they walked over and around him.

"Red-miiist!" Noss yelled, jamming his spear into one of the bewildered ants and releasing a blast of imperium that lit up the caves from stalagmite to stalactite. The stricken creature fell over sideways, its six legs curling up and antennae jittering as life took leave of its body.

Prince Noss whirled on the next giant bug fool enough to face him and struck it across the head with a thwack of his spear and a well-timed explosion of plasma. Legs curling in death it rolled down into the water and splashed in the shallows beside Tomek, who was hurrying to help.

Whilst Themba trudged for the shore, hammer in paws, Nurka calmly raised his imperium bow and shot past him, past Noss, past everyone, deep into the dark. A miss? No, the yellow-imperium arrow exploded in a spectacular flare, killing and confusing several more ants massing in the dark cave beyond.

"Hurry!" Nurka rasped, drawing another arrow. "Into the water!"

"Take him!" Noss bellowed at Tomek, jabbing his spear at another ant, and another.

Nodding and gesturing, Tomek pulled the disturbingly still and bloodied Rufus down to the water by his arms, whereupon the powerful Madou was on station to hoist the wounded wolf onto his shoulders and wade clear.

Big Themba joined Noss, smashing an ant 'skull' here, another there, and relishing it.

"Come at me!" he laughed wildly. "I am Thembaaaa of the Jua-mataaa! Remember it!"

Nurka shot another precious yellow-imperium arrow into the swarming ants whilst Casimir and the lesser hyenas fired a volley of pellets, lighting the underground lake with flashes of colour. Their efforts downed many an ant, but reinforcements were swift and ever more numerous. Some crawled on the walls, some even on the ceiling, their feet finding impossible purchases as they searched for the enemy.

"We're all gonna die!" someone shrieked – probably Casimir.

"Just stay in the water!" Nurka shouted over the falls, ushering everyone back. "Themba, stop showing off and get your arrogant tail into the water! Come on!"

Striking one last intrepid ant and snarling at another as if it had the mind to be intimidated, Themba waded backwards into the lake just ahead of Noss. The prince waved his spear left and right, the imperium tip glowing strongly with the energy he was imparting it. The light seemed to distract the ants, baffle them. Themba followed suit, channelling his energies up the hammer shaft to its brick-like kristahl head, so that it shone white-hot and reflected a million-fold in the compound eyes of a hundred ants.

To Nurka's surprise, and relief, the ants ceased their advance on Noss and Themba at the shoreline. They didn't dare to wade into the water a single inch, but checked its existence with their antennae and refused to go any further. No amount of pheromones could persuade them otherwise, and they instead broke off their advance to trundle around the dry areas of the cave in a vain search for something else to tear asunder.

"By the Wind, it's actually working!" Madou woofed, punching the foaming water from the falls that lapped at his waist. "Rufus was right. Hahahaaaa!"

"Of course I was," Rufus grunted indignantly atop his shoulders.

"Rufus!" Tomek yelped with delight, wading over. "How are you?"

"I've been... better."

Nurka's nervous band gathered into a tight circle in the midst of the subterranean lake, weapons presented outwards, lest the hydrophobic ants grew suddenly brave. The water here was cold and set many beasts shivering already. The wounded like Rufus and Zozizou were kept as clear of the icy water as their carriers were able, but there was nothing more anyone could do for them at present.

"N-n-now what?" the trembling Casimir complained, as the ants lingered on, searching, chattering.

Noss replied, "We wait for them to clean house."

⁂

The Warden descended from the escarpment to join his Gelb hogs by the cave mouth. "Remove this," he said, kicking the body of Helmut in passing. "Stick it with the others and burn it."

"But... but he's a hog, sir," a fellow hog pointed out.

"What?"

"Well, he's no hyena terrorist-"

"Sergeant, I'll stick Rufus himself on that pyre if he shows his face above ground. It makes no bones to me what these treacherous beasts are; they've all forfeited any right to a proper service as far as I'm concerned. Dispose of them at once!"

"Yes, sir."

A second hog enquired nervously, "What do we start a fire with, sir?"

The Warden growled despairingly, "Must I think of everything? Get the spare fuel tank from my car!"

"Yes, sir."

"Right away, sir."

The two hogs dragged the hefty Helmut away and round some rocks to where the dozen or so bodies of Nurka's hyena comrades were heaped, then set about dousing them with fuel fetched from the boot of the Warden's limo. Hyenas at least would not begrudge being returned to the wind and sky, but hogs like Helmut were the burying sort – much better to return to Mother Erde from whence life grew from, or so the old ways went.

The Warden had no time for the old ways, but hoped Rufus would be happy down there in his labyrinthine tomb. And if he dared come out, well, to the fire with his hyena-loving carcass. The only question remaining was whether to go to the Den Fathers or not. Without Nurka and the hyenas, Amael's coup was doomed, but was it best to stay silent and plead ignorance when the inevitable investigations began, or claim a conscience and rat on him first?

Whatever happens I'm the one sitting on Lupa's white-imperium. Nobody can touch me or I'll cut them off. I'll blow it all up, by Ulf!

It'll be fine. I'll be fine. Yes.

"Eyaaaagh!"

"Run! Run for your lives!"

Screams and then hogs burst from the cave, stumbling, arms-flailing into the light.

"Now what?" the Warden growled. Drawing his sword he seized the first hog that crossed his path. "What in Ulf's name are you doing?" he demanded.

The hog squirmed wildly, "Let me go! Let me go!"

Tickling the guard's bobbing pink throat with his rapier the Warden snarled, "Who gave you permission to retreat? Where's my Howlers? Answer me!"

"Th-th-they'll kill us all! We have to run!"

"Pull yourself together; they're just a bunch of-"

The blackness of the cave mouth came alive with shiny silhouettes, shifting, waving, like ripples on the water. The cloaked outline of a Howler emerged, hovering above the ground, upside down, arms trailing in the dust, like a deranged ghost.

No, it was but half a Howler, a dismembered and bloodied piece of flesh held aloft in the jaws of a giant ant. The beast chewed on its prey awhile, then dropped the carcass.

"Oh, by Ulf!" the Warden howled in horror, paw to mouth.

"Gaaaagh!" the hog squealed, wriggling free and running for the cliffs.

The cave erupted, spewing a chattering, living wave of giant ants into the open, clambering over flats and cliffs with equal ease. Gelb hogs fled in all directions, some escaped into the hills, most were run down and set upon by the ferocious ants, screaming, disappearing, dying quickly amidst a tangle of black bodies and legs.

Turning tail and sprinting for all he was worth, the Warden chanced a glance over the shoulder and immediately wished he hadn't. The killer ants were everywhere, combing the mountains high and low. So fast! So many! Gelb hogs fired their pistols and rifles in vain before being overcome by the hordes and carried away, some kicking and screaming as a whole, some in pieces and silent.

By Ulf, what can I do? Where do I go?

The car! The car!

Scrabbling madly up a scree-strewn hill towards the tidy black limo that had ferried him here from Gelb, the Warden slipped inside and locked the door behind him.

Seconds later the last of his two desperate Howlers arrived. Unable to open the door he bashed wildly on the window.

"Open the door, sir! Let me in! Please!"

The Warden thought about it, but then the first ants arrived and put paid to that!

In an instant one snatched the Howler away and carried him aloft kicking and screaming. The rest of the giant bugs clambered up and over limo's bonnet, their hard feet patting on the metalwork, their jagged jaws biting the windscreen wipers, tasting and feeling this foreign object that was not of their nest, nor even their world.

It didn't belong here.

"Away with you!" the Warden yelled, searching for the keys. "Get away you monsters!"

The limo rocked side to side as the ants set about attacking it like some great invading beetle that needed to be sent packing; chewing wheel-arches, biting bumpers and stinging tyres until they hissed back. Some of the insects came away with a prize of chrome or rubber and marched off proudly home, but most remained, shifting with every random tug and push this unknown, odd-smelling object away from the nest, away from the precious queen, towards the steep slope opposite the cave mouth.

"Stop it!" the creature cowering inside the hard shell commanded. "No! Please!"

The ants cared not, their commands came from a different plane, one of smells and instinct, not sound and reason. By accident or design they pushed the bizarre object and its screaming contents over the crest of the hill.

From the perspective of the ant sisters, the strange invader appeared to give up the fight and flee. It sped wildly down the loose rocky slope and crashed into a boulder, whereupon it overturned and tumbled wildly out of control, rolling and splashing into a shallow steam on its back, upturned.

All was still.

The ants investigated to the water's edge, then thought better of it and retreated to the caves.

The nest was safe again.

Chapter 44

As Den Father Amael Balbus had promised, the Elder Train stopped at the next station and ALPHA's carriages were duly shunted into a siding ready to be disconnected. The Alpha remained at his desk throughout, ignoring the view out the window of rusting train hulks and overgrown sheds in favour of writing furiously. Even as the carriage jerked against a buffer and sent his tea sloshing over the cup's rim he continued stoically penning without error.

"This is outrageous," Horst complained, striding up and down the carriage, paws behind back. "Amael will rue the day he took the law into his own paws."

From the comfort of a threadbare sofa, the big black Duncan watched his rotund white comrade pace. "There's nae law that says we have tae be at the Summit," he pointed out, somehow still smiling and jolly. "The Den Fathers nae want us there, we're never really welcome-"

"I know that!" Horst snapped. "But abandoning us in the middle of nowhere is utterly different to simply shunning us once we're there. It's not the done thing. Amael's not like the old Den Fathers. He has no scruples, no honour. He's a filthy guttersnipe!"

Duncan swigged from a tiny steel hip flask that was engraved with a bee. "Aye, but giving us a ride was nae Amael's deal," he sniffed, patting his chest to help the strong contents go down. "It was Vito's… and he's dead now."

Horst huffed, "Resigned to your fate are you? Giving up?"

"That's enough you two," the Alpha said, sealing his letter in an ALPHA envelope. "Whining won't solve anything. Horst, I want you to personally see about flagging down Thorvald."

"Me?"

The Alpha's white mask of a face scowled. "Yes you! Have someone change the signals. Ulf's teeth, lie on the tracks if you have to, just *stop* his train or we really will be resigned to our fate – that being summary execution at Amael's paws before the year is up."

"Yes, my Alpha."

"And take this," the Alpha said, sliding the A-marked envelope across the desk. "It's for Thorvald's eyes only, don't give it to anyone under him. It's my guarantee in writing that Howler Tristan will be released provided we are escorted safely to the Summit."

Taking the letter, Horst looked to Duncan, then back at the Alpha again. "Isn't that dangerous, my Alpha, to put it in writing?" he asked, flapping the envelope about. "Thorvald could use it against you."

"That'd be unwise," the Alpha dismissed. "It incriminates him as well. If he accepts my terms he's breaking the law too. I'm sure he will understand that."

"Yes, but if he *doesn't* accept it he could show everyone the letter!"

"And doom Tristan to Gelb? That wolf is like a son to Thorvald. No, he'll deal."

"With respect, my Alpha, this gamble is based on Janoah's assumptions-"

"On her *work*, Horst," Adal corrected, "which has thus far proven exemplary. I trust her judgement."

"But-"

"The matter is closed!"

As if on cue, the carriage door towards the front end of the train opened and allowed Prefect Janoah to enter. With the prerequisite salutes she breezed past the Alpha's desk and on towards the back of the train without a word being exchanged. Ignoring Horst's whispers behind her, she crossed into Josef's dingy carriage, where Rafe remained in a bad way.

"The Bloodfangs are leaving us here," she told Sara and Olivia, the latter springing to her feet from sitting upon one of many crates.

"Leaving us here?" Olivia scoffed.

"It's a long story. In any case you should get back to your train before you're stranded here with us. We could be stuck here until the end."

Sara was quick to declare, "Ah'm staying with Bruno."

"Me too," Olivia breathlessly agreed.

"Olivia!"

"I'm not going without you."

Sara seethed, "Monty and Penny are expecting you!"

"Well it won't hurt if I'm a few days late. We just said we'd arrive soon. They'll be dead busy preparing for the Summit anyway, Monty won't even notice."

Janoah hiked her brows at both wolves, but addressed Olivia specifically. "My dear, I thought you were trying to escape?"

"I am," Olivia asserted, adding, "I was."

Janoah waited for more.

Olivia continued, "But I'm here now. You know who I am, so I may as well stay with Sara and Bruno. I'm probably safer here with you than hiding amongst the Bloodfangs."

Janoah said nothing.

"Well what about Linus?" Sara asked. "He must be in a right state."

"I've sent word via Vladimir," Janoah replied, looking around the carriage. "Where's Josef got to? He's supposed to be looking after my Eisenwolf."

"He went into the van," Olivia said with a shrug.

"Ah. Fiddling with the suit, no doubt."

"Suit?"

Janoah said nothing. Joining the girls by the sick Eisenwolf's side, she stroked Rafe's fevered brow. "Monty and Penny?" she purred afresh, head cocked. "Who're they?"

"Nobody," Sara said simply, and all too quickly.

"Nobodies that want to hide a dodger."

"They're just old friends of ours. Farmers."

Janoah laughed at Sara's transparent lies. "My dear, farmers don't attend Summits," she said, glaring at Olivia, "Do they? No, I've heard those names somewhere before."

The girls exchanged looks.

Suddenly Josef Grau emerged from behind the van, wiping his greasy paws on an oily rag. "Are you talking about Montague Buttle?" he mewed. "That mad ginger cat?"

Janoah blinked rapidly at the Doctor, "Friend of yours as well, is he?"

"He's no friend of mine! He's that balloonist fool who's always on the newsreels. Thinks we're all going to sail about in his ridiculous, bloated contraptions."

"Balloonists?" Janoah pondered.

"They're nae ridiculous," Sara defended. "Monty and Penny Buttle are visionaries."

Josef spat, "Visionaries? No, no, no, if beasts are ever to fly it is by emulating nature, not fighting it. When was the last time you saw a bee inflate itself and float from flower to flower? Never! They have wings and flap with skill and purpose. Heavier than air flight is the *only* way to fly effectively, none of this balloon nonsense."

"They've been very successful Ah'll have ye know."

"Successful? All Monty's dirigibles do is catch fire and crash! I understand he's due to fly over the Summit as part of some self-promotional stunt."

Janoah repeated "Fly over the Summit?"

"Yes," Josef confirmed. "Don't be surprised if he comes down in flames, as per usual-"

"By Ulf!" Janoah woofed, slapping her brow. "That's it! That's how Amael's going to do it!" Suddenly she lurched across the table, over the unconscious Rafe, and grasped Sara's forearm. "Where are they?" she demanded of her.

Sara squeaked, "Let go of me-"

"Where do your friends keep this balloon? Answer me!"

"At their farm. Why?"

"*Where*, girl, the address! Spit it out!"

"What? Ah, Ah don't know exactly. It's just called Rumney Farm. It's… it's in the middle of nowhere, Monty and Penny usually pick me up." Sara thought for a moment, "It's in Grunrose District. Ah can probably show ye on a map-"

"Grunrose? That's on the other side of Everdor!" Janoah spat.

Releasing Sara, she ran for the door.

"Where are you going now?" Josef demanded.

Janoah stopped for nobody; there was no time. She strode through the ALPHA train as fast as dignity allowed, passing Prefects Grand and not, saluting the Alpha at his desk, blanking Horst, then on to the next carriage, past where Uther was being held, until she reached the door to the Bloodfang section of the train.

It was gone!

"Schmutz!" Janoah seethed.

Peering through the door's window, she watched the Bloodfang carriages ease away through the train yard, taking Vladimir and Linus with them. It can only just have decoupled.

What now? Think Janoah! There must be someone else; someone who can follow your hunch up without raising the alarm and ruining all your careful positioning. Who? Who!

Maybe. Could he? Yes, yes, maybe!

Janoah rushed back through the now decoupled and powerless Alpha cars, the lamps lining the corridor flickering either side of her as the gas pressure from the engine faded and the last dregs of imperium energy were burnt off. She came upon Uther's cell and the two prefects guarding him.

"Marm," they saluted.

"Hello boys," Janoah replied amiably, tapping the glass of a dying lamp. "Looks like the Alpha's defaulted on his gas bill."

"Puh! The cheek of them Bloodfangs!"

"Unbelievable that Balbus! He's a tyrant, marm."

"We'll show him yet," Janoah assured, heading inside the cabin under a smokescreen of friendly banter – no questions were even asked.

Once inside, Janoah closed the door and sat on Uther's bed, causing him to wake in alarm and roll against the wall for fear of being dragged out and beaten senseless again.

"Janoah," he gulped, eyes darting. "Whatcha want?"

No reply.

"I… I signed me confession. I did what you asked. Just leave me alone. Please."

Janoah produced a sting from her cloak pocket. The bloodied, bedraggled Uther eyed it hungrily as the wolfess waved it to and fro.

"You want to be a hero, Wild-heart?" she whispered. "Then shut up and listen, we've little time."

✦

Despite Amael's latest fit of pique, which Linus had heard through his thin cabin door, it had taken a good half hour for the Bloodfangs to gain clearance from the officious Hummel train hogs at the station and actually get underway. To simply manoeuvre onto the main line again as if driving a mere car about town invited disaster by risking a collision with another train.

Thus, despite dramatically decoupling, the Bloodfang train sat awhile within sight of the abandoned ALPHA carriages, both sides staring at one another through the windows in mutual disgust.

At last, the Elder Train pulled away from the station, leaving ALPHA behind as Amael so desired.

Linus fell back on his bed, exhausted. He almost wished Vladimir hadn't confided in him, that he had instead remained ignorant of the great affairs swirling around him.

He punched the bed and snarled with frustration, "Uther, you poor fool! How could you?"

The cabin door opened. Rising from his bed, Linus was met with none other than Vladimir.

"How are you?" the Grand Howler asked loftily, referring to Linus's recent interrogation at the paws of Bloodfangs. "Weren't too rough were they?"

"They didn't touch me," Linus replied.

"You said nothing?"

"Not about Amael's plot, if that's what you mean."

Vladimir nodded appreciatively. "I dare say bringing Uther down saved your life," he said.

"And the Alpha witnessing your actions proves your innocence… for now. Had you stayed whimpering over Vito's body, Amael could have blamed you for his murder and shot you here and now for expediency. Case closed. As it is, you're a hero."

Gulping, Linus excused himself, "I-I-I need to check on the girls."

"Don't bother," Vladimir sniffed, subtly locking the door. "They're gone."

"What?"

"They're back at the station."

"With ALPHA?" Linus woofed, looking out at the retreating station.

Vladimir raised a paw, urging Linus to keep his voice down, "With Janoah, specifically. They'll come to no harm, she's promised to protect them."

"And you believed her?"

"She's protected *you* enough times, hasn't she?"

That was true, Linus had to admit. "But why?" he asked, at last keeping his voice in check. "What's in it for her?"

Vladimir sighed with hefty scepticism, "Janoah has it in her head that Sara can help her."

"How?"

After a passing reluctance, Vladimir explained. "The Eisenwolf; Sara knows him… from before. Usually Janoah relies on Rafe's nurse to manage him, but she's back at HQ. Hopefully Sara can do something."

Scowling in bafflement, Linus shook his head a little, "W-what do you mean 'manage him'?"

It hadn't escaped Vladimir's notice that Linus had yet to address him as 'sir', but the Grand Howler put it down to the young wolf's frazzled nerves – he'd had a trying time.

"Rafe's a basket-case," Vladimir chirped. "Eisenwolves always are. The poisons in their blood push them to the edge of sanity, that's the reason they're illegal… or one reason. Not that ALPHA cares for *that* detail, even less does Janoah. In any case Rafe needs constant care. He's particularly bad after being stung to the eyeballs, which his injuries have necessitated. His body will recover… but his mind is another matter."

Linus nodded. "They told me one of ALPHA's wolves was attacked in the forest. Was that Rafe?"

"Yes."

"I didn't even know he was aboard."

"He was in disguise. We saw him at dinner. I'm not sure how he was able to suppress his corona so effectively, but there is a way, albeit an illegal one. Still, what's legality to ALPHA?"

Linus took a sharp breath and faced the cabin window, the trees rushing past like a horizontal green waterfall. "So, you told Janoah all about Sara and Olivia then?"

"Boy, we've been confiding whenever possible; words passed in carriage hallways and coded messages slipped in pockets," Vladimir sighed, no stranger to espionage. "We've built up our communication techniques over the years. Even a shoulder-barge from Janoah disguised as clumsy accident carries meaning to me these days."

"I-I-I had no idea, sir."

"Coming from a fool like you that's not surprising and hardly a compliment," Vladimir snorted. "Still, thanks to Amael's stunt we're on our own again for the time being. It's just me and you until we get to Hummelton, and even then we may not see Janoah again before the curtain falls."

Linus looked to Vladimir, "What can we do?"

"Watch, listen, wait," he grunted, "and pray beasts elsewhere are faring better than us."

✦

It was some hours before Nurka and his hyenas dared emerge from the subterranean pool and hurry through the caves with the wounded upon their shoulders. The ants had dispersed, taking with them any sign of the Warden and his hogs, the area around the cave's mouth being picked clean, save for discarded weapons and caps.

"Search the area," Nurka demanded of his troops.

Tomek hurried into the orange evening light. To his silent dismay Helmut's body had vanished. Perhaps the ants had carried him off with the rest of the spoils. Trying not to think about Helmut being carved up and fed to squirming ant grubs, Tomek stood where he had fallen and removed his stripy Gelb prisoner's cap in respect.

A recognisably hefty paw clapped on the young wolf's muscled shoulder. It was Madou. The hyena grunted stoically.

Tomek said nothing, but nodded.

With the cave secured, Rufus, Zozizou and the other wounded were laid out by some rocks and seen to despite Red-mist's insistence that they get clear of the ant nest before a scout discovered them.

"They'll keep… checking the area," he seethed. "Until they're sure it's safe."

"Shut up and sit still," Noss chided, removing Rufus's bloodied mantle and assessing his condition. The jaws of the ants had cut him to ribbons, but Noss sensed a deeper malaise – the rot. The blast Red-mist had administered to the ants to remove them from his wolfen self had left him in serious trouble.

"You need a sting," Noss advised.

"Nurka… only has… chunta."

"And what's wrong with chunta? Never did me any harm! Hahahahaaa!"

Rufus could but scoff humorously.

Noss chuckled too. "By the way, Red-mist," he said, "your left shoulder is dislocated."

"I know."

"I'll see to it—"

"Don't!" Rufus barked.

"Relax. I might be mad, but I haven't forgotten how to reset a put-out shoulder. I'll be as gentle as a summer breeze."

Somehow Noss's wild purple eyes didn't fill Rufus with confidence, but his shoulder had to be put back and the sooner the better. A quick nod set matters in motion and Noss to work. Casimir and some nearby hyenas watched curiously as the prince took Rufus's left arm and manipulated it out to one side and back again with extreme slowness and absolute care. There was nothing fast or brutal about it, no crack of bone or sinew, only a slight growl and flinch from the patient as his shoulder slotted back into its rightful place.

His work apparently done, Noss lay Rufus's ruddy arm across his grey chest. "See? It's no trouble putting right a delicate wolfen body like yours."

Rufus huffed back, "This delicate wolfen body could put you through a wall."

"Hahahahaaaa! I don't doubt it."

The banter between their prince and Red-mist both alarmed and fascinated the on-looking hyenas. That Noss could be so informal with a wolf, even going so far as to clean and dress his wounds, caused much confusion and whispering. Some turned to their chief for guidance and he gave it, dismissing their concerns.

"Prince Noss honours our guest," Nurka explained, "as we all should; he has saved our lives."

Rufus clocked everything, every look, every gesture, every word, assessing Noss's standing amongst the hyenas compared to Nurka – thus far not encouraging, Nurka seemed superior.

There was more bad news.

"I'm sorry," Casimir said, drawing Rufus's ears and eyes. "He's slipped away from us."

It was to Chakaa Madou whom Casimir spoke.

They were both crouched over Zozizou, who looked in no way changed, except that he lie utterly and unnaturally still. His wild mane stuck out from his bandaged head at crazy angles in death as in life. All through the caves Madou had bore him on his shoulders, all though Gelb in fact, propping up his weaker cousin with extra imperium rations, embers and food, and all for nought.

He was dead.

Reading events from afar, Nurka approached and comforted Madou with a simple paw on the shoulder.

"He'd become a miserable gazer," Madou sniffed, wiping his broad nose with a spotty forearm, "but he was still my cousin. We grew up together, you know, on the Reservation. He was my best friend. We did everything together."

"I remember, Madou."

"I should've protected him; I'm a Chakaa!"

"It's not your fault-"

"By the Wind!" Madou seethed, running a despairing paw through his short mane. "I thought he was going to make it. I thought it was just a bump to the head." He kicked at the pebbles, "Graaagh!"

Nurka grabbed Madou and took him to one side. Before the chief could administer a pep-talk, as the watching Rufus suspected he would, some hyenas hurried back from patrol with news. Whatever information they carried escaped Rufus's sharp wolfen ears, but not Tomek's. The young wolf sped off ahead of everyone, Madou and the other hyenas following behind.

"What's going on?" Rufus asked Noss.

"Nothing good, Red-mist," the prince replied grimly.

Directed by what he'd overheard, Tomek rounded some rocky outcrops and came across a scene of devastation. Twenty or so hyena bodies were piled up, their fur and clothes matted with blood. Even from a distance Tomek's nostrils flared at the acrid, heady fumes of imperium fuel. The bodies had been doused in it and the fuel can itself was lying nearby – as was a familiarly enormous hog.

"Helmut!" Tomek woofed, skidding to a halt in the dust beside his friend and cradling his bloody, fuel-drenched head. "Helmut! Helmut, is me, Tomek."

The big hog's beady eyes eased open. "Tomek… lad," he wheezed, blood frothing on his lips and tusks.

It looked bad.

"Yes, is me," Tomek said, smiling. "I'm here."

"I thought… you were all goners," Helmut gulped, looking about with just his eyes. "I heard 'em. They… they were gonna burn me. My fellow hogs. But yon giant ants came… killed 'em all." He frowned, "Didn't t-t-touch me, though."

"Is the fuel; ants not like it," Tomek beamed, checking Helmut over and wincing. "We get you fixed up now."

"Huh! D-d-don't b-be daft, lad."

"Is not daft-"

"Lad, I c-c-can't even breathe," Helmut rasped, grabbing Tomek's arm. "Just… s-sss-sit with me. Stay… 'til I go. Quiet like."

"Helmut-"

"Nah… nah… chin up, mate. Smile."

At length Tomek nodded, though his smiling lips quavered. The stocky Madou crunched over and loomed behind.

"You two… look out f-fff-fer each other," Helmut told them, looking mostly to Tomek. "Don't… do anything s-sss-silly, Tomek. You get th-through this, fer me."

A nod.

Helmut's eyes shut a little, then opened, "Rufe?"

Tomek croaked, "He's fine, Helmut."

"Good… that wolf's… right good 'un. S-sss-stick with…."

Breathing shallow, Helmut turned his eyes to clouds, their undersides lit by the setting sun in shades of red and yellow, their shadows blue and purple.

"Look, lad…. 'Tis like… imperium."

It was some minutes before Prince Noss slowly rounded the rocks and took in the grim scene of two dozen dead hyenas. Tomek and Madou stood over Helmut, the wolf with his cap in paw.

Nurka went to his Prince. "They were going to burn them heaped up like logs!" he rasped of the fallen hyenas. Nursing his head a moment, he composed himself, "The hog was able to make his peace, my Prince."

"That hog saved my life," Noss breathed. "I'd be down the bottom of Gelb's chasms but for him."

"I know."

"Set out our brothers properly and return them to the Sky," the prince decreed. "But Helmut goes into the ground, that is the hoggish custom. We will honour it."

Nurka nodded, "Of course, my Prince."

Some hyenas came up behind Noss. Bowing low in the dust to him, they addressed Nurka foremost, "Chief, it's the Warden."

"Warden?"

"Themba has found him, down in the stream."

They pointed away from the cave – in a trice, the furious Madou heard, saw and was away, tearing across the pebbly erde and scrabbling up and over the grey hills opposite the cave mouth!

"Madou!" Nurka barked.

Growling, the chief gave chase. Cresting with difficulty the loose hills he stopped and looked down upon a shallow river in a small valley. Themba and several hyenas were standing around an upturned limo in the midst of the shimmering water; a cloaked wolf lay at spear-point, half in, half out of the misshapen vehicle.

Battling to stay upright and not tumble head over tail, Nurka started downhill. Half running, half sliding, he descended the pebbly slope, causing something of a landslide – no doubt the loose piles were leftover from mining operations decades ago.

"Themba, stop!"

Down in the stream, Themba heard Nurka well enough, but ignored him. "What shall I do with this worm?" he asked Madou, poking the Warden with the butt of his hammer. The broken wolf lay half submerged in the shallows, spitting water and blood, his legs still within the mangled car from which he had crawled.

Stepping into the stream, the dishevelled Madou glanced behind at Nurka, then said to Themba, "My cousin's dead."

Themba snorted, "Little Zozizou?"

A tearful nod.

Silently, Themba offered Madou his hammer, but Madou shook his head. "I might… miss," he rasped, feeling his collared throat, which was constricting from sheer rage.

Themba nodded once and raised his hammer. "In the name of the Jua-mata, I sentence you to death!"

"No… p-p-p-please!" the Warden spluttered.

"Themba!" Nurka pealed across the waters.

No. Not this time. In a trice, Themba of the Jua-mata brought his weapon down with a mighty metallic thump and sickening crack; the Warden's eisenglanz helmet no protection against the blow of a kristahl hammer. Blood seeped into the fast-flowing water from the deformed helmet's every orifice, whilst imperious sparks played over its surface.

"Justice is done," Themba declared simply.

Then Nurka arrived, his paws latching onto Themba's labyrinthine cloak and pulling him all about to the metallic tinkle of belt buckles and body-piercings on both sides.

"By the Wind, must you smash everything?" he bellowed. "Have you no brains at all in that big empty head?"

He pushed Themba away, lest he punched him out.

"He killed Zozizou and all the others!" Themba defended, his chin raised proudly. "What else would you have me do? Spare him? This is no time for mercy!"

Nurka's purple eyes narrowed. "He knew where the white-imperium cache was. He's been siphoning it off Gelb shipments and sending it to Amael all this time, so he must have known *where* to send it, at least."

Themba and Madou stood in silence, perhaps unable to grasp Nurka's point.

"We could've had it!" the latter seethed, his dark fingers gnarling beneath his chin. "We could've stolen the white-imperium from under their noses."

"But it's no use to us, Nurka!" Themba dismissed. "It is sacred-"

"I'd have returned it to Mother Erde and denied Amael using it to fuel his Howlers against the tribes later, you fool! But you… you just had to go and….."

Unable to continue for his searing rage the chief turned to the setting sun peeping through the rolling mountains. Its calming disc proved no comfort.

"Chief, I'm sorry," Madou grunted guiltily. "I didn't know."

"Exactly!" Themba seconded. "Perhaps you should tell us all these plans you have, Nurka! We are not mind-readers. If I had but known the Warden was so important-"

"If I had," Nurka interrupted, "Madou here would have told the wolves everything under duress and all would be lost now! Must I carry the burden of your stupidity always? Can you not stop and think for a moment?"

Nursing his aching head, Nurka stormed through the water towards the bank.

Prince Noss was waiting there. Eyeing the Warden's crumpled remains, he said, "Can you blame them?"

Nurka exhaled in passing, "No, my Prince," and dejectedly climbed the pebbly bank, leaving Madou and Themba to wallow in the shame of their chief's contempt.

✦

"Marm!"

Lying on her bed in her full regalia, Janoah lowered the book she was reading by brooch-light to peer at the wide-eyed Prefect panting in the cabin doorway. "What?" she urged him.

"The assassin, marm. He's gone!"

Tossing her book aside, Janoah followed the panicked Prefect through the motionless and increasingly dingy ALPHA carriages, for they had no imperium power to light them without an engine and night was fast drawing in.

They arrived at the cabin where Uther Bloodfang was being held. Or not, as it turned out. Uther's cabin was instead home to a pair of writhing Prefects, their paws and feet bound by Howler-wire and muzzles tied shut. One of them had been stripped of his mantle, tunic and helmet, the other his greaves, boots and gaiters. Janoah wasn't sure which wolf looked more embarrassed.

"Search the surrounding countryside," she directed the other Prefects calmly. "Use lethal force if need be."

Orders given, Janoah moseyed inside and attended to one of the restrained Prefects, removing his gag. "What happened?" she growled, as if she didn't know.

"Uther just… c-c-came at us, marm, like lightning!" the young wolf spluttered. "He started groaning so… so I came inside and he'd gone. Then pow! He dropped down from nowhere and blasted me in the chest. The next thing I know we're both in here. I thought I was a goner!"

"All right, all right, calm down; nobody's blaming you," Janoah soothed. "When did this happen?"

"Ages ago, marm. It… it was when the Bloodfangs ditched us here, not long after you questioned him again. He'll be long gone by now."

"He can't get far; he's wounded."

"That's what I don't get!" the Prefect whined. "I thought he was messed up bad. How could he jump us like that? Where'd he get the energy? It's like someone slipped him a sting."

"It's my fault," Janoah said, as if about to confess, but of course doing no such thing. "I underestimated him," she sighed. "Horst was right. I should've left him bound up like a bug in a meat market. Instead I pitied an old comrade like the soft, foolish wolfess I am. Don't worry, boys, I'll take the heat for this."

✦

Luckily Grand Prefect Horst was attending to the small matter of flagging down the Eisbrand Elder Train and missed the bad news. Janoah felt she could stand the Alpha's fury without Horst there to fan the flames, provided Duncan was on paw to dampen them, which he was.

"By the stars, Janoah!" the Alpha shouted from behind his desk. "Uther was the reason Amael abandoned us here and now we don't even have him to show for it!"

"Yes, my Alpha," Janoah said. "Though… Amael would have seized upon any excuse to get rid of us-"

"That's not the point, is it?"

"No, my Alpha."

"He was our star witness against Amael. Now he's gone!"

Silence.

"This is ridiculous," the Alpha grumbled. "This entire excursion has been one disaster after another!" he went on, his voice rising with every word. "Why do I even bother? Why didn't I just stay a corrupt, money-grabbing, indolent Howler like everybody else instead of sticking my neck above the parapet and trying to change what Ulf *clearly* thinks is best for his people; a city of squalor and crime lorded over by droolers like Vito!"

Slamming his pen down the Alpha buried his white face in his brown paws.

By Ulf, it's like watching Amael throw one of his tantrums, Janoah thought; two wolves trying to achieve peace and harmony in Lupa yet somehow worlds apart. Ulf mocks me. If Duncan wasn't here I could explain my actions, that I set Uther free to chase down my hunch, but Duncan could be a traitor.

It could be anyone, except the Alpha.

Traitor or not, Janoah was hoping the amiable Duncan might step in and calm the Alpha down like he always did. However, the intense lights of a huge train beamed through the windows and slewed across the dark carriage, rousing everyone's attention.

"That's them," Duncan said, recognising the great snowflake crest of the Eisbrands adorning the train's circular face. And what a train! Painted pale blue and clean as a whistle, the great wheels plated with gold – it put the Bloodfang's grubby engine to shame.

For a horrifying moment Thorvald's fabulous engine appeared to pass by, as if somehow shunning the Alpha on principle – seeing that cretin Horst waving from the trackside would be impetus enough, Janoah supposed. But no, brakes screamed, carriages slowed and bright interiors came into sharp focus as the Eisbrand's home away from home eased into dock amidst swathes of vented ash.

"It's up to Horst to bluster his way through now," the Alpha said.

"Aye, he's the master," Duncan chuckled, moving to the window to watch. "There he goes. Look at him."

Curious, Janoah joined Duncan by the windows and watched Horst stride across the opposite side of the station with several Prefects in tow, helmet on, medals jingling at his chest, venting officiousness. He reached the leading carriage and rapped on the door.

"Open up! Open up in the name of the Republic! This is an emergency!"

The door opened up all right, and out tumbled several Eisbrand Den Guards, surrounding Horst and the drab black Prefects in a ring of long, blue surcoats and glittering gold and silver armour. Horst raised his paw to keep his wolves from drawing their swords or anything so foolish.

A final and most imposing Eisbrand Howler appeared in the door; Horst could sense his powerful corona. "What's the meaning of this Prefect?" the Howler growled, the word Prefect dripping through his silvery helmet grille with contempt.

"Grand Prefect, if you will," Horst corrected.

"Queen of Butterflies for all I care, now say your piece."

Containing his rage, the Prefect raised his chin, "I must speak to Den Father Thorvald."

"The Den Father is indisposed and cannot be disturbed. Speak to me or else."

Horst raised his ALPHA-marked envelope, as if it were a hall pass. "I carry a letter from the Alpha himself for Thorvald alone. This is a matter of national security. It would not be wise to obstruct me, Howler."

The affronted Eisbrand snorted, but said nothing. He secretly looked past Horst to the station, searching for clues as to the nature of this emergency. The ALPHA carriages, being without power and shunted into the siding opposite, were dark and obscure, resembling abandoned carriages amongst the rest of the run-down station's detritus. It looked for all the world as if Horst had appeared from thin air.

"I heard a rumour," the Eisbrand said loftily, "that the Alpha was too poor to run his own engine and had hitched a ride with mad old Vito and his backward Bloodfangs. Is that true, Grand

Prefect?"

Horst lowered the letter. "Den Father Vito is dead, I'll have you know! Furthermore if we at ALPHA are too poor it's because the packs, in their infinite wisdom, do not fund us adequately. Ulf knows we do not squander our budget on pretty uniforms and vast banquets like some!"

The Eisbrand raised a silencing paw. "Vito's dead?"

Horst explained, "Assassinated, mere hours ago. Now… are you going to let me through, or do I go back to the Alpha and explain I was unable to convey his correspondence to Thorvald Strom at this most perilous hour because of the petty officiousness of his bureaucrats?"

Back in the Alpha's dark carriage, Duncan clapped his paws once. "Och! He's in."

"Naturally," Adal said.

Why it was the Alpha couldn't just go across and solicit Thorvald himself was at once ridiculous and yet completely necessary. It was a matter of front. No Den Father would go begging for an audience; they sent lesser beasts. To be taken seriously the Alpha had to play the same game as the big boys, anything less would reduce him to a laughing stock. Only inside ALPHA's unassuming halls were such protocols considered outdated.

This Janoah knew, so it surprised her somewhat when, after a good five minutes, Horst emerged from the Eisbrand carriages with Thorvald Strom himself. The Den Father looked magnificent in his full glittering knight's panoply, flanked by a shield of ferocious Den Guards.

They crossed the dark, deserted station platform, Horst chatting and gesturing all the way; Thorvald nothing much.

"He's coming over!" Duncan woofed in horror, turning to the Alpha, who remained at his desk.

"Horst?" Adal asked.

"Aye, and Thorvald!"

"What? But Strom can't see us like this!"

"Well he's coming, Adal!"

"For the love of Ulf, Horst, what've you done?" the Alpha complained rhetorically, donning his helmet and tidying his cloak. "This is absurd. Get some lanterns in here. Quickly!"

Janoah was on it, rushing across into Josef's carriage and returning with some imperium lanterns from the cat's ample supplies, she hung them about the Alpha's mobile office so that Thorvald could at least see where he was going without resorting to his brooch.

Just in time. The door at the far end opened and Horst clambered inside, followed by Thorvald.

"Stay here," the Den Father was heard to tell his guards, refusing them entry. They protested, but Thorvald cut them down without delay. "This is a private matter! You will *not* insult Den Prefect Adal by questioning my safety in his presence. Stay here!"

Slamming the door on his contrite followers, Thorvald bade Horst to lead him down the corridor and into the Alpha's office. As they entered Adal stood up from his desk, whilst Duncan and Janoah looked on from a respectful distance, paws behind their backs. Everyone exchanged nods and salutes, Thorvald fist to chest and out, albeit casually, everyone else the even more casual ALPHA salute.

Casting those Eisbrand-blue eyes about the lantern-lit carriage in obvious curiosity, Thorvald said nothing disparaging about ALPHA's predicament whatever his private thoughts – wolves had long said of Strom that he was a class act.

"Den Father Thorvald," came the stocky Alpha, walking round his desk to greet the much taller Eisbrand.

"Den Prefect Adal," Thorvald replied, clearing his throat and looking back at the others.

Understanding at once, Adal nodded at Horst.

Horst leant forward as if hard of hearing, "Yes, my Alpha?"

"Leave us," Adal seethed, flicking a paw.

"Oh!"

Horst, Duncan and Janoah took their leave. This really was a private matter, distilled right down to the highest office in Lupa. Den Prefect and Den Father were going to hash out a deal without any prying ears – an illegal deal, and everyone knew it.

The lustre of ALPHA's self-professed purity was scuffed just a little that night.

Codex: ALPHA

Every pack has Provosts, Howlers that investigate and prosecute their own for crimes such as imperium skimming, murder and general abuse of their rights, but these pack-based internal investigators are open to bribes and bias, and even straight ones are often unable to bring charges against powerful Elders without putting their careers, even their lives, in danger.

The last Howler war, simply called 'The War' by this generation, came about because of the overreaching of the Howlers. Their cruelty towards little beasts in the form of heavy taxation, even downright theft and casual murder, led eventually to an explosion of violence – a rebellion. This rebellion, which began in the once contested Common Ground of Lupa and spread outwards, sparked an inter-pack war which lasted a decade. Lupa's heart was levelled in the conflict.

Once peace was restored, the Den Fathers met and agreed to form a multilateral regulatory body overseen and funded by all the packs. Thus ALPHA was born, the Agency for Lupan Peace and Howler Accountability.

ALPHA's independent 'Prefects' were granted the power to investigate errant Howlers, even Elders, across all packs equally and bring charges against them to a special court comprised of representatives from every pack. To this day ALPHA cannot punish, but they can bring a Howler's crimes to undoubted light.

By eliminating self-interested and corrupt courts, it was hoped, and still is by ALPHA's advocates, that no one Elder will again be allowed to overreach himself, that no Howler shall go unpunished, that no little beast feel wronged without recourse, thus dampening the same simmering resentment that led to the last war.

As for the devastated Common Ground, or Common, it was given to ALPHA to rebuild and maintain, since no other pack had any undoubted claim to it. Always a lawless place, the Common has since become a truly neutral territory where Howlers of every pack meet and mingle with impunity, leaving their troubles, but not their wallets, at the checkpoints. ALPHA makes little money from the Common, and the grants they rely upon dwindle with each passing Summit as the Den Fathers, under pressure from disgruntled Howlers tired of being investigated, pull ever tighter on the purse strings.

Unless ALPHA can prove itself, its current administrator, the popular impartialist and renowned recipient of the Imperium Heart, Adal Weiss, may well be the organisation's first and last Den Prefect to dare self-style himself as 'The Alpha'.

Chapter 45

Grand Prefect Silvermane wandered around the stark interrogation room, flipping through the pages of a file.

"Tristan Eisbrand Donskoy," he said, "Born at 422 Radoslav Avenue. Twenty-one years old. Parents deceased. No close family. Ah... but of course there's your good cousin Ivan, the so-called 'Blade-dancer'." Closing the file, Silvermane stood at the head of the rack and looked down on the restrained Tristan. "What epithet do you deserve, 'Imperium-peddler', 'Hyena-lover', 'Destroyer of Lupa?'"

"The Alpha is the one who'll destroy Lupa," Tristan seethed from the rack, twisting his bound paws. "Don't... think wolves can't see his transparent ambition."

"The Alpha's ambition, traitor, is to root out the likes of you before you plunge our fair city into the chaos of war as we suffered not so very long ago! Your parents died in that war, as did mine and countless other beasts of every race, sex and creed, afflicted or not! Yet you wish to repeat the mistakes of the past and tear things down with violence. I admit Lupa must change, we at ALPHA believe in equality for all, even the belligerent hyenas must eventually be accepted-"

"Pfff!" Tristan scoffed.

"But it will come at a well-defined pace, with debate and law guiding citizen and Howler alike, not anarchy!"

"The hyenas can't wait!" Tristan growled. "They are being massacred. Whole camps pitched into mass graves and at least some of the Den Fathers must know of it."

"Nonsense."

"I've *seen* evidence."

Reaching into his black cloak Silvermane unfolded a crumpled sheet of paper. "Like this pamphlet?" he snorted, waving it about. "Hyena propaganda, produced by THORN to gain sympathy. It does not convince."

Tristan turned his cheek, "I know beasts who have seen it with their own eyes. I believe them-"

"So you believe our race so vile we could do such things? Is that the state of your faith in wolfkind? What a disillusioned and sad individual you are. You disgust me."

Silvermane raised his paw at the 'doctor' in a lab coat standing over the same control panel where Josef usually worked the dials. He looked for all the world like Josef, except wolfen. He was even wearing the same tinted glasses – it helped to protect the eyes from the glare of the rack, apparently.

"Doctor Maher's new here," Silvermane claimed. "He's not as proficient with the rack as Josef. There's no telling what might go wrong. Isn't that right Doctor?"

Maher cleared his throat, "Well I'm actually-"

"Your eyes could explode out of your head!" Silvermane interrupted, leaning close to Tristan's ears. "Oh, I've seen it happen. I know I'm not much older than you, but I've seen many things you wouldn't believe, Donskoy."

Tristan closed his eyes and laughed darkly, "If it means I won't have to look up your nostrils for another two hours then by all means throw the switch and boil out my eyes!"

Silvermane huffed, then stood up straight. "For the last time, tell us what you know of Amael's plot. Name the conspirators. Testify against them. Save innocent lives, Tristan. You know it's the right thing to do!"

"I... know... *nothing*."

"You must. You admitted it to Janoah."

"That poisonous wolfess will say whatever she needs to garner her career."

"You tried to shoot yourself to avoid capture. Rafe stopped you. He corroborated Janoah's version of events-"

"You think Janoah can't school that slobbering monster into saying whatever she wants? He's her slave. Besides, getting rid of me has been on her to-do list for years. She hates me, always has, and Ivan too. Anyone who turns her husband's eye away from her for a second she can't stand."

Silvermane was surprised. "Rufus? You mean... you were one of his betas?"

Tristan's grey and white muzzle twisted and wrinkled in disgust. "Briefly."

"Goodness me. Quite the accolade."

"I was a foolish cub, but even I had the sense to know he was just using me. Rufus takes what he wants and moves on, he thinks only of himself! My cousin's a fool for putting up with him. Still he lingers on at Riddle District, begging for a wink of approval or a pat on the back from his 'alpha' when Rufus has no more interest in him these days than he would a dusty vase on his mantelpiece. Perhaps now Rufus is down in Gelb, Ivan will finally wake up and come home to Eisbrand, where he belongs."

Silvermane smacked his lips, "Rufus Valerio is no longer down in Gelb, but up in Ulf's Kingdom."

After a moment, Tristan frowned, "What?"

"He was executed. What's more your cousin has been implicated in the assassination of Vito Bloodfang and the murder of several Den Guards just this morning. Did you know that was to occur?"

Silvermane's news took some time to sink in. "No!" Tristan seethed. "Why in the world would Ivan...." He couldn't even finish his sentence, starting another instead, "That's impossible. This can't be right! You're lying! You have to be lying-"

"I do not appreciate being called a liar!" Silvermane interrupted, as loudly as his silky voice could. "Nor do I appreciate the slander of my fellow Prefects. Janoah is an exemplary Prefect and I will take her word over yours any day. She knows you have a spy in the Bloodfangs, she knows they work for THORN. Tell us who they are."

"Go cry at the moon, you ALPHA maggot! I've nothing to say to lying scum like you!"

Huffing, Silvermane nodded at Maher.

The switch was thrown, dials turned, the rack did its terrible work. Tristan twisted and screamed as the imperium in his blood burned.

"Grrrrrfgh!"

Silvermane waved a paw, the torture stopped as quickly as it'd begun.

So soon. Why?

As the panting Tristan came back down to Erde from his paroxysm of pain he saw someone standing in the doorway to the torture chamber.

It was Grand Prefect Nikita!

"Silvermane," he said, "there is phone call for you."

"I'm too busy-"

"For Adal even?" Nikita insisted in his broken dialect. "He has important news. Go; I take over here."

After some time, as if unduly reluctant to leave Tristan in the middle of the interrogation, Silvermane told Doctor Maher to, "Stay here and assist the Grand Prefect, I'll be back momentarily."

Maher nodded.

Walking briskly past Nikita into the stark ALPHA HQ corridors beyond, Silvermane happened across Nurse Meryl, who was going about her duties in the other direction.

The demure nurse proffered a lacklustre salute, "Grand Prefect Silver-!"

Silvermane took her to one side and whispered, "Watch them, Miss Stroud."

"I beg your pardon?"

"I'll be as fast as I can. Just keep an eye on Nikita, make sure he doesn't do anything... strange."

"Strange?"

"Please. I trust you."

Reading Silvermane's desperate eyes through his helmet, Meryl nodded, "I understand."

The Grand Prefect left her, striding down the hall and out of sight, rushing to his office as fast as dignity allowed.

The interrogation room door creaked shut. Mind and heart racing, Meryl crept along to the window and peered in on Nikita, Doctor Maher, and the helpless Tristan who was bound to the terrible rack. The glass was mirrored their side so nobody could see the little nurse as she spied on events, unable to hear much, but quite able to see everything.

What did Silvermane expect might happen?

Inside, Nikita walked over to Tristan and patted the young wolf's head – fondly if Meryl didn't know better. He then glided swiftly to the control panel.

"You are new here?" he asked Maher. "Doctor Josef send for you, no?"

"Yes, sir," Maher replied, tugging proudly at his coat lapels. "I was one of his star pupils at the Ark. We've been in close contact for years, ever since-"

"You know how to rack a beast?" Nikita interrupted.

"I've some experience yes. That's why Josef sent for me. He doesn't trust many beasts with his machinery. This new rack is marvellous. It's far more efficient than the old ones and much less dangerous for the, uhm… 'patient'."

Maher chuckled.

Nikita didn't. He shooed the doctor aside and immediately twiddled some dials. "It work the same way, yes?"

"More or less," Maher said, adding, "Careful now."

Nikita explained himself. "Silvermane has been too long interrogating this traitor. The Summit begins tomorrow. We do not have time to be gentle anymore. I will extract the information where he's failed."

Maher watched the Grand Prefect crank the dials all the way up into the red.

"Uh, you mustn't go that high, sir," Maher advised nervously.

"No?"

"That'll kill him. Immediately."

"Good. I do not want him to suffer long."

"What?"

The panting Tristan lifted his head from the rack and twisted to see and hear better what was happening. "Nikita?" he grunted, eyes darting to and fro. "Nikita? What're doing?"

"Goodbye, Tristan. I thank you."

"What? No… no wait, you can't! I… I haven't said anything. They've nothing on me. I swear!"

"I'm sorry."

"Nikita! Please! I-Ahhhaaaaghaaaaaagh!"

The switch was thrown, the rack burst into light, streaks of cruel purple plasma erupted from the rack and struck at Tristan's writhing body. So fierce were the bolts that they carved burning paths of shrivelled, smouldering fur wherever they struck.

"Are you insane?" Maher shouted over the cracks and pops of the rack. He barged Nikita aside and went for the dials. "Get away from there-agh!"

In a flash, Nikita cupped a big paw to the side of Maher's face and blasted the wolf across the room with a good old-fashioned discharge of natural imperious plasma.

The doctor slid to a stop by the door, which someone immediately opened, pushing Maher's quivering carcass aside with shuddering effort.

Nurse Meryl.

"Get out, wolfess!" Nikita commanded her.

Knowing she had no hope of reaching the controls, Meryl ran across to the pipes connecting the rack to the imperium gas mains and simply twisted a big, red lever-shaped valve.

Within seconds the machinery hissed and shut down, the lights winking out and dials returning to zero. Tristan collapsed about the rack, a quivering mass of smouldering fur.

Meryl stood protectively by the valve. Nikita held the controls – a standoff.

Footsteps thundered down the hallway outside.

"You care about your young Eisenwolf," the Grand Prefect said – it wasn't a question.

Meryl remained stock-still, grey ears pricked.

"If you want him surviving the coming change you will corroborate my story, Miss Stroud,"

Nikita threatened.

Meryl said nothing for a time. Words formed on her dry tongue but before they could come to anything of meaning several Prefects scrabbled into the interrogation room, boots squeaking on the floor, swords and pistols at the ready.

"Grand Prefect?" one gasped, glancing between all concerned – Nikita, Meryl and the downed Maher.

Nikita raised a paw. "Is all right," he said calmly. "Doctor Maher went mad."

"Mad, sir?"

"We were interrogating suspect when Maher try to kill him with rack. Perhaps he is in league with conspirators and was trying to silence him." Nikita looked to Meryl. "Nurse Stroud shut down rack just in time."

The Prefects believed Nikita regardless of Meryl, who in the end needn't nod or corroborate a thing. One of the wolves checked Maher's pulse.

"He's dead, sir!"

Nikita sighed, "Ulf's fangs. I did not mean to. I just had to stop him as fast as I could."

Sensing it was safe to do so, Meryl moved to the trembling Tristan and peeled open the Howler's eyelids, revealing first his green and then his blue eye; both were dilated.

"Tristan?" Meryl said. "Howler Tristan, stay with me!"

No reply. Foam began to form on his lips as his powerful body tensed fitted, tugging at the restraints.

Looking first at Nikita, then the Prefects, Meryl said, "We have to get him to the infirmary; he's having a seizure."

Silvermane returned to the corridor just as Meryl and the Prefects wheeled Tristan out on a stretcher. The nurse looked meaningfully at Silver in passing but revealed nothing verbally, for Nikita appeared in the doorway behind, watching, listening.

Silvermane kept walking, until he was beside his fellow Grand Prefect.

"What happened here?" he asked Nikita.

"Maher; he try to kill the prisoner," Nikita replied calmly, pointing at the doctor's curled-up body.

To which Silvermane scoffed, "What?"

"I am unfamiliar with this machinery, Silver. I did not realise Maher was turning up dials too high. Nurse Stroud, she come by just in time. She tried to stop Maher, but he kept on going. So *I* had to stop him... permanently."

"I see. He's dead, then?"

A simple nod and shrug – only a war-hardened wolf like Nikita could be so blasé about killing. "He must have been sent by Amael Balbus and the conspirators," he claimed.

Silvermane sighed, "We'll never know now."

"Unfortunate, but I had no choice."

"Of course, of course."

Nikita moved on with shocking speed, "What did Adal want?"

Silvermane's mind still reeled like a ship tossed by a hurricane. *I need to talk to Miss Stroud. What exactly happened; was it Nikita doing?* "He wants us to let Howler Tristan go," Silver said, with no hint of the turmoil within.

Another nod, as if Nikita were wholly unsurprised. "I thought he was your prime suspect?"

"That's neither here nor there; the Alpha's managed to strike a deal with Thorvald Strom."

"Deal?"

Silvermane explained, "Tristan's freedom for a lift to the Summit; they want it done tonight."

"That might be difficult, he's in bad way."

"Then Meryl had better be allowed to give him some white-imperium. I'll make the arrangements immediately."

Another nod, and a question, "What are our chances of stopping this conspiracy, Silver?"

Silvermane looked Nikita in the eye, "Oh, we're not finished yet. Not by a long shot."

✤

Under the cover of night, the hooded Ivan slipped out of the woods like an apparition and crossed the dirt road in a trice, pressing his back to the stone wall opposite. The red-imperium fangs adorning his helmet's white cheeks had been blotted out with a little sticky mud – one could dull them by suppressing one's corona, but Ivan hadn't trusted his concentration to hold all evening.

Headlights!

With an imperious bound Ivan silently scaled the wall and vaulted over into the farm complex beyond before the vehicle's light struck him.

It drove by, a truck by the sounds; probably nothing more than a civilian about their business. Hummel Howlers hunting assassins would descend on smart thrumming monobikes like any other pack, not dirty great trucks.

Relieved, Blade-dancer checked his rough map by red brooch light and took in the abandoned smallholding. This must be the place. There were several run-down wooden livestock buildings that must have once housed silkworms or the like and a stone farmhouse that had fallen into ruin, its thatched roof a collection of gaping wounds.

No lights, no activity, no life.

Good.

Ivan stole across the courtyard and cautiously entered the dilapidated farmhouse. The door was stiff with sheets of web, but a quick search by brooch light turned up no obvious spiders, just wispy cobwebs flapping at the windows like ethereal curtains. What little furniture remained was either upturned or broken, save for a kitchen table that was shrouded in dust and a cosy-looking chair by the collapsed fireplace.

Against his better judgement Ivan allowed himself a moment's respite. Removing his helmet and setting it on the kitchen table he slumped into the soft chair to rest his aching legs – that final jump back there hadn't helped. After months on the road, living and sleeping under the stars, come rain or shine, even this draughty ruin was a relief to behold. Yet the fresh air of the wilds had done him good too. Ivan felt somehow renewed between aches, his lungs felt bigger, his eyes and fur cleaner, free of grit and grime, as if he'd been holidaying on the Graumeer Coast. It was always supposed an afflicted beast could live a lot longer freed of the ash that clogged Lupa's streets. The rot was rarer out here and a single sting stretched a lot further without traces of industrially-produced black-imperium constantly assaulting one's body.

Was it worth it? Were the trains, hot baths and other modern conveniences worth the curse of rot? Was the thrill of a Giacomo Valerio G-8 *Spider* thrumming to one's corona reward enough for all the suffering? Just maybe. Ivan could hear Rufus now, debating such matters over a cup of tea – debating with himself that is. He always said a cure would change everything. Oh there would still be problems, still pollution and crime and greed, but no more dreaded rot, no more fighting over white-imperium to simply live.

Well, Ivan thought, you've got what you want, Amael. We did it. Now it's up to you with your newfound powers to get Rufus out of Gelb.

Ulf help you if you cross me.

The crunching of gravel in the courtyard sent Ivan ducking silently for cover.

If this was Lupa, Howlers would've locked down the district and combed every building for Vito's killers, Ivan had no doubt, but Everdor was a vast, empty wilderness overseen by no more Howlers than usual for a pack. The Bloodfangs had to move on and it was unlikely the thinly-spread Hummels were going to muster an army to help a rival pack find an assassin, especially at such a busy and dangerous time.

Still, Ivan remained hidden, just in case it wasn't Gunnar or Uther out there.

A cloaked wolf entered the farmhouse with a rifle in his paws and an ember smouldering at his lips, the orange glow lighting his chin. After a quick sweep of the room he moved to the table and picked up Ivan's helmet.

"Uther?" he guessed, looking around.

"It's bad luck to touch armour from another pack," Ivan growled, emerging from the darkness and snatching his helmet from Gunnar's paws.

"Bad luck for who?" the Greystone replied with a cheeky smile. "Me or you?"

Ivan didn't clarify.

Gunnar cast his eyes around the farmhouse. "Is the fastest wolf in Lupa here yet?"

"No."

"Huh. And I thought he'd be first."

"So did I," Ivan grunted worriedly, peering outside. "Did you have any trouble slipping away?"

"Nah. You?"

Ivan thought back to Rafe, "Not particularly."

Puffing on his ember, Gunnar posed the unfortunate question. "Think Uther made it out?"

"Well if you managed it what's to stop him?"

That was a thinly-veiled insult if ever there was one.

Pulling up a stool, Gunnar sat against the wall nearby and watched the door whilst Ivan took to a window.

Time passed.

"I missed," the Greystone sniffed at last, "I'm sorry."

Expecting the usual acerbic comment from Ivan, Gunnar was pleasantly surprised by the great wolf's magnanimous reply. "It wasn't your fault. Vito moved. Besides, I couldn't have done any better. In all probability I'd have taken Linus's head off instead, though that would've been just as well."

"Yeah, who was that cub anyway?"

Ivan waited a moment, then explained simply, "Uther's partner."

"What? You're kidding."

"Ulf knows what *he* was doing there, but Vito has a penchant for handsome young wolves... or had. You don't turn down the advances of a Den Father, not if you value your career, and your life. Vito was a rapacious old drooler quite capable abusing anyone, as Uther well-knows."

"Whatcha mean?"

Ivan looked back at Gunnar, then returned his icy gaze to the chilly night. "I did this for Rufus, fool that I am. Uther on the other paw had... better reasons."

"Like what?"

"You're singularly dense aren't you, Greystone? Let's just say it was personal, all right?"

Gunnar nodded, though he appeared baffled. Whether he grasped Ivan's nuanced meaning or not he couldn't press the matter without appearing both obtuse and nosy, so to save face on all fronts he let it go, just as Ivan hoped.

"You hungry?" the Greystone asked, eyeing up the fireplace and table. "I could whip up some grub."

Ivan sighed sarcastically, "Yes, light a fire. That'll attract attention to this supposedly derelict farm. Go wave a lantern out the window while you're at it."

Gunnar cocked his head to one side. "Mate, I've got a disposable yellow-imperium roaster in my satchel. No smoke and hardly any light, but it'll warm a tin of beans nicely. Whaddaya say?"

Ivan marvelled, "You carry a lot of toys don't you?"

"It's the Greystone way."

Gunnar dived through his backpack and turned out a metal canister about the diameter of a saucer, but much thicker. There was a ring-pull, which Gunnar used to tear off the foil lid and reveal a shallow bed of yellow-imperium nuggets.

Usually, when exposed to air, raw yellow-imperium would explode in seconds of course, but the secretive Greystone imperiologists had found ways and means of slowing the reaction down to nil and every degree above that. The nuggets in Gunnar's tin were of the gently smouldering variety, and warmed his and Ivan's faces like a charcoal grill, only without any smoke or noticeable fumes. Someone might smell the bubbling pan of baked beans Gunnar was soon stirring over the heat, but any search party would have to be so close as to be minded to scour the farm anyway, so that was a risk even Ivan was willing to take.

"Uther's gonna miss out," Gunnar cooed, spooning steaming beans into two new-materials bowls. "Maybe he got lost?" he said, passing one to Ivan.

"We went over everything a hundred times. Even Wild-heart can memorise a simple map."

"But this is the wilds, mate, not Lupa."

Ivan couldn't accept it. "It's probably a touch of rot slowing him up," he said, blowing on his beans. "His pins are bad sometimes, far worse than mine."

"Legs going already? I thought he was only twenny-odd."

Ivan huffed, "Uther's a fine wolf, but he pushes himself too hard. He's wearing his body out. He smoulders fifty a day and drinks heavily, amongst other pursuits. He invites the rot at every turn that one. I'd be surprised if he survives to thirty-five."

Gunnar stirred his beans thoughtfully, adopting that look Howlers had when confronted with the reality of their condition – Ivan saw it in their eyes all the time, and the mirror.

"Still," Ivan said, nibbling some beans, "there's life in Wild-heart yet. He'll make it."

✧

The night wind buffeted Uther's coarse fur and tore at his heavy cloak, as if trying to righteously rip the stolen ALPHA mantle from his sinewy shoulders. Clouds of ash billowed along the carriage roof and slammed into his face, but the black ALPHA helmet he'd also 'borrowed' for the sake of the Republic did its work and protected his eyes and nose from the imperium engine's poisonous fumes.

Janoah what've you talked me into now?

Suddenly the engine's lights dashed upon a hill and then vanished.

A tunnel!

Diving onto the carriage roof, Uther spread his arms and turned his head, embracing cold metal as the train plunged into the erde with a terrible scream. Bricks and mortar blurred past mere inches away, illuminated by the warm cabin lights below.

Uther tried not to think how any loose brick or projection in the tunnel's lining might smash his head open or scrape him off into oblivion in a heartbeat.

Beneath, Howlers and Elders dined unawares of the wind-blown stowaway, Amael Balbus among them, surrounded by a swarm of Den Guards and impossible to get to. He would not make the same mistake as the complacent old Vito and leave himself vulnerable. Oh no. Nor was he a mad, rot-ridden maggot of a wolf squirming uselessly, but a fit, powerful, centipede of a beast.

"He'd kill you himself if you crossed swords and where would that get anyone?" Janoah had said, cupping a paw to Uther's white face. *"Leave Amael to me; you've a greater task, Wild-heart. You might just save the whole Republic."*

✧

With a final metallic pop, the collar snapped open and slid down Madou's massive, spot-flecked, hyena neck.

"There, lad," Casimir said, pulling the thin iridescent band away and discarding it on the naked pebbly floor of the tent with a wobbly metallic clamour. "Who's next?" the rabbit gruffed, snipping the air with his cutters.

Noss gestured graciously at Tomek, "After you."

"No, after you," Tomek replied, adding chirpily. "Is fake anyway."

"And yet as fetching as the real deal."

With a wide-eyed chuckle, Noss sat on the tiny stool in the midst of the tent, elbows on thighs, and let Casimir do his work. The rabbit was a dab-paw at removing collars, one of many things he had learnt in the resistance.

"Just a little off the top," Noss joked, brushing his mane. "I don't want to look like Madou!" he laughed further, referring to Madou's pathetic little tuft of a mane which was woeful by hyena standards.

"You sound like Zozizou, my Prince," Madou replied, rubbing his freed neck. "He was always teasing me about my mane."

A moment's silence for the fallen Zozizou.

"Now *there* was a hyena with a magnificent do," Noss praised, grimacing as Casimir slipped his cutters up under the prince's collar and applied the first loud snip. "He's in a better place than we are, Madou, and no doubt impressing the ancestors with his mane as we speak."

Madou humoured Noss with a nod, then slipped through the tent flaps into the earliest feeble rays of clean dawn sunlight. Nobody had slept a wink, for they had been travelling all night to get to THORN's secret camp, which was a hive of activity. Hyenas were hurriedly packing up tents and piling goods onto trucks – they couldn't stay here with Gelb in such disarray not so very far away. With the Warden killed and many a hog missing, Howlers would be sent for, the mountains searched, security doubled. Madou felt bad for the prisoners who remained behind, but change was coming.

The day to strike was almost upon THORN, at last!

Even so, Madou had no idea what Nurka had in mind, where they were even headed. To the Summit, surely, Madou supposed, to do what had to be done; eliminate the Wolfen oligarchy with black-imperium bombs. *We may all die in the assault, Nurka, Themba, me, but the tribes will go on.*

I'm ready. I'll be with you soon, cousin. We can watch our people thrive together.

Crossing the camp with purposeful strides, Madou marched towards Nurka's flapping off-white tent with a mind to at last learn the details of Nurka's final plan. *We're at the last hurdle. He has to confide in me now. I'll demand it.*

"Chief?" Madou said, ducking into the tent.

To his surprise he found Nurka asleep with Themba awake beside him. Hyena beds were always untidy affairs consisting of a thick rug strewn with square pillows and sheets to nestle amongst, but even so it looked as though Nurka had collapsed atop it all from exhaustion, fully clothed – even his skull helmet remained strapped firmly about his chin!

"Shh," Themba hushed, standing up. "Give him five minutes, Madou."

The stocky Madou allowed himself to be ushered from the tent by the towering Themba.

"I'm exhausted myself," Madou admitted, "and starving."

"We can rest properly tonight," Themba replied, squinting in the sun. "We will need it." He plucked at Madou's revolting Gelb shirt. "Come on, you should get out of those rags and into something befitting a warrior, you and our Prince both."

"Gladly. What've you got?"

With a grunt and a flick of the head, Themba led Madou to another tent that was about to be taken down. Telling his hyena comrades to hold off, Themba ducked inside with Madou and rifled through a big trunk, turning out several neatly folded black and white cloaks. Some were zigzagged like Nurka's, some labyrinthine like Themba's own, some swirling, like the cloak Madou had lost when the Bloodfangs had seized him, others were different still. The specific meaning of any one pattern was lost on most wolves, but not a single hyena.

"May the Wind protect you," Themba said, reverently passing Madou the folded swirling-patterned cloak.

"And the Erde you," Madou replied.

Spare eisenglanz armour was trickier to come by than imperium-weave mantles. Madou had to settle for some generic plain grey gear instead of the fine matching leg armour and skull helmet of the Jua-mata warrior Nurka and Themba had. Still, it was better than meeting your ancestors in a smelly prison uniform.

"Any kristahl axes around here?" Madou hoped against hope, pinning his cloak about his powerful frame. "A spear will do. If it's good enough for Prince Noss, it's good enough for me-"

"We don't need weapons," Themba interrupted – somewhat bitterly, Madou felt.

"Come on, Themba. We have to get inside first. You'll have your chance of glory when we fight our way past the Den Guard."

"We won't have to. Nurka says he has another way."

Silence.

"What do you mean?"

Themba took out another cloak. "We will not be fighting anyone," he said, moving to the tent flaps. "Disappointed? I wanted to go down smashing wolfen skulls as well, but I believe in Nurka more than my own vain glory. I always have."

"He's told you then? What we're going to do exactly?"

"No," Themba replied, leaving Madou to finish dressing, "but I *still* believe in him."

Across camp Casimir cut Tomek's collar off. "You'd never know it was fake," he whistled, admiring the craft. "Is there no imperium in it at all?"

"No idea," Noss dismissed, sounding preoccupied. Peeping outside for a moment, he returned to grab Casimir's arm and pull him close. "Listen, rabbit, are you with us or are you against us?" he growled.

"What?"

"Rufus said you were one of us. Is that right?"

Casimir looked to Tomek for help. The young wolf appeared in no way willing, even less surprised by Noss's sudden aggressive turn.

"I'm on whatever side Rufus is on," the rabbit claimed, with a firm sniff. "He promised to see Bruno safe and that's all that matters to me now."

Noss's brow twisted, "Who's Bruno?"

"My son. The Howlers took him from me and made him into one their own. I want him back!"

"What would the Howlers want with a lowly rabbit?"

Casimir tutted, "Bruno's a wolf, genius; I adopted him!" Slowly his long ears wilted from shame. "I thought he was dead, see. That's what they had me believe. It were in the papers 'en all. I... I had nothing to live for. Nothing! So I paid a visit to the Politzi who arrested him. I was gonna kill him, I *swore* I was gonna shoot that treacherous, fat hog. But... but he said he was in THORN; said he could get me in too, so we could take Howlers to task together, like in the good old days." Casimir gnarled his fingers, "One thing led to another and before I knew it I was helping Nurka lift black-imperium. I thought I wanted to help, I thought I wanted this, but now... now I know Bruno's alive I just want him back and I don't care what else happens." Whipping his arm free of Noss, he said pugnaciously, "And if that's not good enough then you'd better just kill me hadn't yer?"

Noss cackled, "You have guts, for a rabbit." He looked to his partner, "Still, best you go with Tomek. You should be able to slip away at some point."

"Slip away?"

"To Hummelton; you have to find my contact and tell him what's been achieved... and what hasn't."

"Hummelton?" Casimir yelped. "You mean *walk* there?"

"Or better yet run!" Noss woofed, eyes wide for a mad second. "Hummelton isn't that far and Tomek knows the way. He's a Watcher like me, you know."

"Aye? And I've a bad leg you know!"

"So? I'm mad; never stopped me limping along," Noss growled through his teeth. "If you want to save your 'son', little beast, you'd better make an effort."

"Well... well what about you?" Casimir shot back. "What're you gonna do that's so important, eh?"

"Red-mist and I shall remain here and try to stop this madness from within. If we fail, you will at least have warned Vladimir what he can expect from us this end." Noss waited for a moment, then asked, "Has Nurka told you what he's planning to do precisely?"

"No."

"Didn't think so. Does *anyone* in THORN know?"

"He's kept it a secret from everyone, even Themba," Casimir despaired. "All I know is it involves black-imperium."

Noss pondered matters. "Vladimir already knows that," he grumbled. "Very well... I'll try to get something out of Nurka before you two leave. I mean, if a hyena can't confide in his Prince who can he confide in, eh? Hahahaaaaha!"

"Someone's coming!" Tomek hissed.

As Noss's laughter faded the tent flaps spat Themba inside, fully dressed in his labyrinthine cloak and armour.

"My Prince, is everything all right?" he asked.

"Yes, Themba."

Nodding and kneeling, Themba offering up a folded cloak. "This is for you."

Noss graciously received the heavy cloak and let it unfurl, revealing it to be exactly half black, half white. "Thank you, Themba. It's beautiful. Very fine work."

Themba was pleased to be of service. "There's armour as well if you want to have a look," he said standing up, tail flicking, "and some water to wash with."

"I will, I will," Noss insisted, turning the cloak over in his paws. "What about Tomek?"

"Tomek?"

"Yes, Tomek. Where's *his* cloak?"

Themba looked to the wolf, still wearing only his stripy yellow trousers and cap.

"He's a wolf, my Prince-"

"By the Wind, Themba!" Noss bellowed. "Tomek fought beside me and found the very waterfall that saved all our lives and *this* is how you treat him? Where is your honour?"

Themba instantly prostrated himself before his prince, all four paws on the ground. "Forgive me, my Prince, I wasn't thinking."

"Never was your strong point!" Noss snorted. "How's Red-mist faring? I hope he's being cared for better than poor Tomek here."

"Nurka saw to it personally."

Noss growled something unintelligible, but nodded. "Oh get up, get up," he gestured furiously. "Where *is* Nurka, I need to speak to him at once."

"He's asleep."

"Asleep? We've work to do!"

"He's exhausted, my Prince. We all are. We'll soon be on the road to Hummelton, though."

Noss grunted. "All right, but tell Nurka I want to go over his plans sooner rather than later. I might be the most handsome hyena in the tribes, but I didn't break out of Gelb just to stand around looking pretty. Hahahahaaa!"

※

Ivan snorted into wakefulness and quickly came to realise he had dozed off on the farmhouse windowsill. That could've been a deadly mistake.

"Gunnar?"

"Good morning," the Greystone acknowledged; he was still sitting on his stool, watching dawn's light advance across the decaying farmyard. "Sleep well?"

Embarrassed, Ivan cleared his throat and quickly diverted attention. "Where's Uther?"

Gunnar grimaced and shook his head almost imperceptibly.

Ivan exhaled a quick sigh of exasperation and searched out the window lest Uther should appear at that very moment.

"It can't be!" Blade-dancer growled. "Nobody catches him in a straight line, nobody!"

Gunnar waited a moment. "What now? We can't stick around here forever."

Ivan paced the alleys of his mind for answers, but found dead ends at every turn. To search was hopeless; if Uther was lying wounded or otherwise incapable he could be anywhere, and if he had been captured he was as good as dead; Amael would see to it, or Janoah, whoever got to him first, Ivan had no doubt.

"Let's go," he said, patting the windowsill a few times and donning his helmet.

Gunnar found his feet and his condolences, "I'm sorry. I know he's your friend-"

"Save it. He knew what he was getting into. We all did."

"Yeah. Still, he'll be fine, I'm sure of it."

The chipper Gunnar gathered his things, though not his rifle, for that had never once left his ready paws.

Ivan went to step out into the sunshine.

"Oi, we should leave a note," Gunnar said, clicking his fingers.

Ivan turned to him, "Note?"

"Well, in case Uther's just late. Best tell him we've gone on ahead and not to wait for us."

Nodding, Ivan grunted, "Got a pen and paper in that bottomless satchel of yours?"

"Nah."

Huffing, the Blade-dancer came back inside and searched around the kitchen. As luck would have it he turned up some old paper but no pens or pencils.

"Use the roaster," Gunnar suggested, watching Ivan fruitlessly open cupboards and drawers. "The imperium'll be cold by now; grab a spent nugget and write with it. I do it all the time. Bit of an artist I am, even if I say so myself."

"You draw with ash?"

"Yeah, it's better than charcoal."

'Humphing', Ivan silently took the roaster and upturned the ashes on the kitchen table. They were still hot, but some nuggets were cool enough. Ivan sorted one from the smouldering heaps and with it scrawled the beginnings of a message.

"Don't worry, mate," Gunnar said, stepping out with a fresh ember to his lips. "I'm sure Uther'll be along any-gagh-ugh!"

Ivan whirled round just as Gunnar fell back into the farmhouse clutching at his stomach.

"Gunnar!"

The Greystone was immediately stepped over by two hefty-looking Howlers in black.

"Don't move!" one of the strangers snarled, his pistol aimed at Ivan.

Ivan froze, assessing the situation. The Howlers were unmarked and anonymous, not members of Bloodfang or Hummel search parties, nor ALPHA by the looks. Whilst one dispassionately wiped his bloody rapier on Gunnar's yellow cloak and kicked the groaning wolf over to take his weapons, the other goon kept Ivan in his pistol sights.

"Where's the other one?" he demanded.

Ivan said nothing.

"Amael said there'd be a third one. We waited all night for him. I don't appreciate having to wait, Howler."

Still nothing, only Gunnar's grunts of pain

"We can make it quick and easy, or long and painful, it's up to you," the assassin said. "I'll shoot your knees out and work my way up – you'll talk before you die."

Ivan raised his chin a little and obviously looked past the strangers. "Now Uther!" he said to nobody.

The two assassins looked. It was a split second, a tiny mistake, but a lifetime for Blade-dancer. Snatching a paw of burning ash from the tabletop he cast it at the Howlers.

"Gaagh!"

Two imperious flashes from Ivan's kristahl sword later, he remained standing whilst the strangers fell about, their fur dashed with ash and blood. One of the two assassins stumbled out the door and into the farmyard in a bid to escape Blade-dancer's wrath.

Ivan went to the door and drew his pistol. There was nothing to say, not even halt.

Crack!

The assassin fell in the dust with a last spasm, his back punched through. The other crawled across the farmhouse a few feet before expiring from his wound – the Blade-dancer's lethality written in a trail of blood.

Satisfied nobody was going to run off and tell Amael he was still alive, Ivan attended to Gunnar, gently rolling the youngster over.

"Where'd they get you?"

"Gfffgh! They stuck me." Gunnar whined, lifting a bloody paw from his stomach. "I think it's bad. Agh!"

"You'll live."

Ivan searched the bodies of the lowly assassins; lowly assassins just like him. It was nothing personal; they had lost that's all, and there could be no quarter in this game.

Amael they'd said.

Amael!

Ivan's searching paws turned up some silver monobike keys, rolls of cash, and a sheet of crumpled paper. He unfurled the already familiar paper to reveal the exact same map of the imperium springs and surrounding countryside that Amael had supplied him. The ruined farmstead was circled.

Ivan stood up, his paws slowly, unconsciously, crushing the map into a ball.

To be captured and executed by the Bloodfangs was one thing; that was beyond Amael's control. To be marked for death from the outset was just plain rude.

A search along the road turned up two unmarked *Springtail* monobikes – the assassins'. Gunnar was in no fit state to ride by himself, so Ivan brought just one mono back to the farm, looking always over his shoulder. After injecting Gunnar with a field ration of painkilling taubfene, then disinfecting and sewing up his wound with the Greystone's own med kit, Ivan helped him limp from farmhouse to *Springtail*.

With revs and pops of engine, the chirpy mono and its two riders swerved out the farm and down the road.

"Lupa's… the other… way!" Gunnar shouted.

"We're not going to Lupa!" Ivan replied. "We're going to Hummelton!"

Adam Browne

PART V
BLACK RAIN

Adam Browne

Codex: The Jua-mata

The Jua-mata are the strongest of the many hyena tribes that once roamed free across the Lupan Continent. Though the tribes warred amongst themselves, they kept away from wolfen territory and concerns as they travelled place to place, following the seasons and migrating bugs, living in harmony with nature. Wolfkind was happy to tolerate the nomadic hyenas, even trade with them, provided they did not disturb wolfen territory or their little beasts. For centuries there was peace between tribe and pack.

Then came the second, or new 'black rain', as some hyenas call it, the Ashfall, spreading out from Lupa year by year, decade by decade, poisoning the land between the Sunrise and Sunset mountains little by little, until crops would not grow and most useful bugs died out. Wolves and little beasts not only headed to Lupa to earn a living, but also spread outwards, searching for clean land that was not already jealously guarded by Hummel. Soon strangers encroached on hyena migration routes; interests and swords clashed.

The guerrilla conflict with wolfkind, led by the Jua-mata, continued for decades, peaking at the end of the last Howler War when the hyenas sought to capitalise on the weakened and divided wolves. Ultimately, however, the lack of a structured, imperium-wielding force like the Howlers doomed the hyenas to failure. The Chakaa, those hyenas afflicted with the rot, are invariably powerful, but rare and largely untrained. They are frowned upon, even outcast by the tribes, who believe the plunder of Mother Erde for 'imperium', as wolves call it, a great sin.

Though afflicted hyenas are becoming ever more common as generations are exposed to the Ashfall, a Chakaa army is impossible to create and maintain whilst the tribes remain under close wolfen control on the Reservations. Wolfkind has attempted to co-opt the hyenas this way for over a decade, educating their cubs and even trying to assimilate some Chakaa into Howler Academies, a unique honour not afforded any other conquered race. These programmes have thus far failed and it seems some amongst wolfkind may have lost patience, for there are disturbing rumours that rather more than re-education goes on in the hyena Reservations.

Chapter 46

Cora Hummel slipped her sinewy black arms, those of a powerful afflicted wolfess, into the white and gold dressing gown held aloft by her Wolves of the Bedchamber. Rising from her bed she crossed to the sun-bathed half-hexagonal balcony, the railing being festooned with blooming wisteria.

The Den courtyard below was a bustle of activity as Hummel Howlers marched in neat formations, getting in some last-minute practice before the opening ceremony.

"Ateeeenchun!" a Grand Howler barked at his uniformed troopers. "Preseeent arms!"

The tidy block of wolfen warriors in green cloaks and white armour drew their swords and saluted to their mistress above.

"Long live Den Mother Cora!"

Den Mother Cora saluted calmly back. "You look very smart, mah handsome Howlers!" she called. "You make us proud tae lead Hummel!"

The Howlers saluted once more and continued their parade practice, whilst Cora cast her golden honey-like eyes across her domain, over the glistening tiled roofs and smoking chimneys, down the white marbled plaza and colourful awnings strewn with welcoming bunting, to Hummelton Station, columns standing tall, bee-adorned gold and green banners fluttering.

The first of the Elder Trains had arrived, judging by the ash clouds issuing from the station.

Cora turned slightly to her cloaked aids, female Howlers both; she needn't say a word before one of them volunteered the information she sought.

"The Bloodfangs, lady," the Howler said.

"Send them our felicitations."

"Eldress Brynn is at the station already, lady."

Cora nodded a little. "Any news of Vito's killers?" she asked at length.

"Not since the last telegram, lady."

Another nod, tinged with a disapproving huff, "Vito's nae even cold and they've already elected his successor."

"They cannae afford tae dally with the Summit approaching, lady."

"Aye," Cora agreed. "Ah'd best make ready tae receive this Amael. Fetch my things-"

Suddenly the bedchamber's double doors burst open and over half a dozen female cubs scurried inside. They filed up in a row from smallest tot, no older than three, to a fourteen-year-old lass, all in nightgowns.

"Good morning, mother," they sung in near-unison.

"Och! Mah babies!" Cora cooed, spreading her arms and beckoning them into an embrace. "Good morning, good morning tae ye all. Are ye excited for the goings-on?"

"Aye!" one of the smallest cubs squealed.

"Ahaahaha, well now, ye all must be on your best behaviour. Wear ye finest clothes and be *very* polite tae any of the Howlers from the other packs."

"Will Sara be coming, mummy?" a mid-sized cub asked.

Den Mother Cora's eyes flitted a little, "No dear, she's busy in Lupa."

"Ohhww."

"Nae pouting! She'll visit soon, Ah'm sure."

A big, middle-aged black wolf with silver hairs flecking his chin entered the chamber. He was wearing a smart green blazer with a white cravat and a pair of fine bone-white breeches.

"Good morning, wife," he beamed cordially, performing a noble bow.

"Good morning, husband," Cora replied, standing tall and formal again – as Den Mother of Hummel she needn't bow to anyone, but her Howler aids respectfully dipped their heads in the presence of her spouse.

"Ah tried tae stop this wee army here," he said, referring to his daughters, "but they evaded mah defences."

"We're ever glad tae receive our daughters," Cora replied, ruffling the perky ears of two of her many cubs.

Chuckling, Cora's husband wandered to the window. "Oh aye," he said, spying the heightened activity at the distant station, "looks like a more terrible invasion is well underway."

"And we're ever glad tae receive our brother and sister Howlers too," Cora replied, like the politician she was.

"Even mah no-good brother?"

The Den Mother huffed, "Duncan's a *fine* Prefect."

Scoffing, her husband leant on the window, "Who'd have thought jolly old Duncan would be snared by ALPHA's miserable web of dour killjoys, eh? He's got a tongue of silver that Adal. Ah'm telling ye, Cora, he'll nae stop undermining the power of the Den Fathers unless you all strip him of his office and disband his corrupt organisation altogether-"

"Angus!" Cora seethed. "Nae in front of the cubs!"

Angus Hummel stood silenced.

Her mate chastised, Cora looked down at her gathered daughters, "Pay your foolish father nae mind. You'll treat all our guests with honour, be they Bloodfang, Eisbrand, Greystone *or* ALPHA. Even the smallest pack from the Bloc that you've never before heard of is due our utmost regard, and you'll say nae a bad word against anyone, nae even in private. Is that clear?"

The girls all nodded and mumbled their agreement.

"Pardon? Ah cannae hear ye."

"Yes, mama!" they sang dutifully.

"And that goes double for you, Angus Hummel," Cora told her husband. "Leave the politics tae me."

Angus grunted.

In the following frosty silence Cora shooed her children and husband away. "Och! Now away with ye, all of you; Ah must dress tae receive our noble guests."

Retreating from the window, Angus walked over to Cora and took charge of their cubs, planting a quick assuaging kiss on his wife's cheek as he did so.

"You'll knock 'em dead."

✦

Ash swirled across the platform, the red carpet unfurled and Amael – Den Father Amael – stepped into the clean Hummelton sun resplendent in his 'new' red cloak and black armour. The ancient Bloodfang mantle had passed to him in the most literal sense, had been repurposed, the imperium-weave being too valuable to be interred with that old drooler Vito, or any Den Father before him stretching back centuries. The armour didn't fit Amael quite right; the helmet proved especially awkward and had been hastily re-padded to match his skull, but any formal adjustment would have to wait.

As Amael and his red-cloaked entourage disembarked the Elder Train, Hummel representatives approached through the last swirls of ash; a single Elder flanked by Howlers, all looking splendid in their green and gold cloaks and unusual white armour. Before Amael could so much as salute them, young wolfesses in white dresses emerged from behind the Hummel reception party, their ears draped with flower garlands and each carrying a wicker basket. Gently casting crocus petals in their wake they transformed a section of the white marbled station into a riot of spring colour, then formed up a line either side of the petal pathway and curtsied synchronously.

Amael nodded and chuckled at them. To his surprise the waiting Hummel Elder ahead bowed a little, whilst the Howlers got down on their knees.

Of course, Amael reminded himself, I'm a Den Father now; I bow to none and few equal me.

Soon no one will.

Chin high and entourage at his back, Amael stepped forth into his new role. As his pitted black boots kicked up the lush crocus petals, one of the adorable wolfesses lining the floral footpath caught his eye. She smiled bashfully and offered a whole crocus to Amael. He took it graciously.

In that moment an awful thought drilled its way into the Den Father's head, the thought that this modest flower maiden might choke along with her corrupt Elders, her youthful, innocent flesh rotting as the black-imperium cloud unpicked the very fabric of her being.

With a shiver, Amael turned his gaze and walked swiftly on, crocus twiddling in paw a moment before he let it slip discreetly to the ground.

The Hummel Elder stepped forward from the rest of her staff and saluted. "You and your Bloodfangs are welcome tae Hummelton, Den Father Amael," she greeted in a soft, feminine Hummel accent – judging by the curving contours of her body-hugging mantle she was indeed a wolfess and therefore an 'Eldress' in the strictest parlance. "Den Mother Cora extends both her solemn condolences over the loss of Den Father Vito," she went on, "and her joyous felicitations tae his successor."

"Thank you, Eldress," Amael replied, wondering what kind of wolfess was hiding beneath that pure white helmet – no Janoah, of that he was sure, probably more country bumpkin, but perhaps a pretty one. "I bear Vito's mantle with sadness and pride," Amael ad-libbed, "he was our pack's light in these dark times."

Nodding regardless of what she thought of Vito, which likely wasn't much for the decades of rumours, the Eldress spread a black paw. "Den Mother Cora will receive you at Hummel Den. Please allow me to escort your party through town. I have cars waiting."

Amael rolled a paw, "I would be honoured, Eldress…."

"Brynn, Eldress Brynn."

A nod, then Amael walked with Eldress Brynn. The Den Guard of each party formed up on their respective leader's side, exclusively male Bloodfangs for Amael and largely female Hummels for Brynn.

For reasons science couldn't yet explain, Hummel was the near-reverse of most packs; their ranks teemed with female Howlers whilst afflicted males were infrequent. Something in the pack's blood, or perhaps the comparatively pure environment, had turned the usual order of the wolfen world on its head. Yet not quite, for Hummel had somehow maintained the cult of respect for Howlers that had all but died in Lupa. Here they were not seen as diseased parasites preying off the labours of the little beasts, but kind benefactors and protectors, as it was in the old times, as it should be.

As it will be again, Amael promised himself.

He and Brynn passed through the grand station foyer and under reams of bunting stretched between the columns, coming to a waiting motorcade of open-topped Hummel cars flanked by Howlers riding green and white monobikes marked with a golden bee symbol. Green, gold and white banners depicting the same stylised bee fluttered from the tall town houses that lined the clean cobbled street. The condition of Hummelton was astonishing. There was hardly a streak of ash and not so much as a newspaper flapping in a gutter. Was Hummelton always so spotless, or had they tidied up because half of Lupa's finest were coming to stay?

Linus wondered such things as he tagged along with Vladimir, trying, failing, to remain inconspicuous. Amael's sudden rise had propelled his Howlers to the forefront of Bloodfang, whilst Vito's loyal staff had instantly faded to obscurity. Indeed, Riddle District would now be at the front of the queue for everything. Amael's rundown backwater, the slums of Bloodfang Territory, could even become the capital district if he decided not to move shop.

A moot thought, Linus knew, for Amael had bigger ambitions than that. What if he manages to pull off the unthinkable and rule as a Wolf King? What if he asks me to serve him? Can I refuse? Dare I?

"Linus," Vladimir said, beckoning his adjutant from his daydreams and into the chugging motorcar with Den Father Amael and Eldress Brynn.

Linus glanced round at the worthier Bloodfang Elders climbing into the second and third Hummel-branded cars. Linus, lowly Trooper Linus, was upstaging them all by riding with Amael. Unable to refuse, he climbed aboard the wonderful car and settled uneasily on the smooth green seat beside Vladimir. There was room enough for eight modest-sized beasts, Amael and Brynn sat opposite one another with some Den Guards each. They made polite conversation, Amael commenting on how beautiful Hummelton was and Brynn graciously asking what Riddle was like, for she had never been to Lupa.

"Dirty," Amael huffed, "like Lupa in general!"

Brynn chuckled courteously back.

Linus tried his own paw at breaking the ice by nodding and smiling at the anonymous Hummel Howler sitting opposite him.

"B-bbb-beautiful day!" he stammered over the hubbub of rumbling engines and slamming doors.

"Yes!" the Howler flatly confirmed. No more.

Awkward.

Linus blurted, "I'm a-a-a friend of Sara Hummel. Do you know her?"

A frown, a cock of the head. "Den Mother Cora's first daughter, ye mean?" the Howler queried, interested now.

Emboldened, Linus nodded vigorously, "We've been seeing each other for some time-"

Vladimir elbowed him firmly in the ribs.

Before Linus could fathom what he'd done wrong, the car pulled away under the care of the driver – a hog dressed in white. Beside the hog sat another Howler, male or female Linus couldn't tell, but they looked alert and ready to defend the motorcade against any would-be assassins.

The thought occurred to Linus, as he was whisked through sunny Hummelton, that a THORN sympathiser might leap out of the crowds of flag-waving little beasts lining the road and gas them all with a black-imperium bomb.

No, not with Amael in the car. Besides it was too early. If THORN was going to strike at all it would be during the actual Summit, when they could get everyone. Right?

Linus felt powerless, like a raft tossed in the current of fast-flowing events. The roar of an approaching waterfall foretold disaster and nobody seemed willing to pluck him from the water, even less dam the river.

I'm such a coward, sitting here whilst Amael gets away with murder, perhaps even mass murder. But what can I do?

'*You could shoot him, mate, as I shot Vito,*' Linus imagined Uther gruffing. '*He's sitting right there!*'

The Hummel motorcade trundled swiftly through the welcoming streets, Linus seeing none of the bunting and banners for his fevered thoughts. Within a few minutes the cars left the common folk behind and entered the exclusive courtyard of a great wedding-cake-like fortress. It resembled nothing so much as one of the countless castles the cats of Felicia were so fond of building for their extended royal dynasty – the royalist cats, unlike the republican wolves, hadn't lost their ancient buildings in civil wars past nor voluntarily knocked them down to make way for progress. Hummel's capital den, as Linus assumed it must be, looked a rare survivor of the old wolfen world, constructed not of brick and steel, but pale yellow stone. The many turrets and towers seemed to be hexagonal, their corners reinforced with handsome white masonry. Ivy and wisteria huddled in clusters around windows and balconies that were, again, hexagonal.

Pack Hummel certainly takes this whole bee thing seriously, Linus thought, as the car doors were opened and everyone spilled out. Amael and Brynn took the lead, climbing the steps to the Den's gaping main entrance even before the following cars had parked.

"Don't mention Sara again," Vladimir advised Linus, as they slowly climbed the steps, momentarily alone and out of earshot.

"Why not?"

"Because Den Mother Cora thinks Lupa is a sewer. She won't look kindly on a Bloodfang associating with her daughter. Howlers still behave like royalty here."

"Oh."

"By Ulf," Vladimir went on, "if they knew you'd helped Sara sneak a dodger out of Lupa into Hummel territory they'd lock you up themselves."

Linus's temper flared, "Oh what in Ulf's name does that matter now? The republic's in mortal danger!"

"Shh! Shut up."

"Sir we have to warn someone. Please. I… I *can't* sit idly by knowing Amael is-"

Grabbing Linus by the gathered neck of his cloak Vladimir snarled into his face, "You will *not* destroy everything I've worked for! Do you hear me? You'll shut up and sit on this, as I've done so for over a year!"

Vladimir released Linus just as rest of the Bloodfang guests, Elders, Howlers and all, climbed the broad stairs. Linus stood unmoving and undisturbed by their curious glances and muffled comments as they passed. They had seen enough to gather he was being told off by Vladimir, but had no idea why.

Linus wanted to scream.

Once they were alone again, Vladimir gently tidied Linus's cloak, father-like. "It's not long now, Mills," he said, suddenly so reasonable. "Amael and the conspirators will reveal themselves and the plot halted once they do, not before. Remember, I'm not acting alone. Trust me."

Linus breathed, "I'm trying, sir. I really am."

"Humph!"

On Vladimir's discordant huff they hurried inside to rejoin the main group.

Hummelton Den's doorway was a hexagon, naturally, and the glazed yellow tiles underfoot resembled, no doubt purposely, a sticky honeycomb. Remarkably, the vaulted ceiling of the hallway ahead was fashioned to mimic the twisting stems of plants, with sprouting leaves and flowers and the occasional petrified insect, all painted with pastel hues that penetrated the very stone, like a fresco.

Linus noticed beasts lurking in the dark recesses between the buttresses running down each side of the hall. Statues? No, two rows of huge, grim-looking Howlers. They were exceedingly large, heavily armoured wolves, somewhat like Eisbrands, but wearing green surcoats marked with an oak tree, and with black fur to a wolf, not the typical Eisbrand whites and greys. Each was armed with a kristahl halberd held rigid and upright, whilst their glowing bee brooches reflected manyfold in the contours of their magnificently polished armour.

"Halberdiers," Vladimir whispered to Linus, "Hummel's elite unit."

"I've heard something about them, sir."

"Good. Then you know to behave around them."

They walked forth, passing the silent 'Halberdiers' either side, wading through their frightfully strong coronas. It was like swimming in pins and treacle. That was the idea, to intimidate visitors and project Hummel power; country bumpkins we are not, silly little city wolves. The Bloodfangs that had preceded Linus and Vladimir certainly looked subdued.

After the oppressive Halberdier-lined corridor the Den opened up into a high, vaulted atrium where stained glass windows and priceless white-imperium crystal chandeliers conspired to set the continuing theme of honeycomb tiles and floral buttresses ablaze with light. Hummel banners hung from a second floor walkway, which ran completely around the hexagonal atrium. The ceiling was a mosaic of the Hummel bee, its wings and six legs spread over a great single hexagonal cell. Though it looked a plump, friendly creature its abdomen bore a bright red sting. The message was plain; the Hummels loved peace but were not defenceless.

Vladimir and Linus tardily joined the Bloodfang party gathered in the middle of the hall. The mood had come over very quiet and solemn after the Halberdier hall and their boots clacked noticeably in the quiet, turning a few heads. Instead of rudely manoeuvring their way to the front, Vladimir decided he and Linus should remain at the back. Amael and Brynn were at the front.

Two of those scary Halberdiers stood either side of magnificent hexagonal door ahead. After an unbearable half minute or so, they tapped their mighty halberds on the ground three times, turned towards one another and pulled the doors wide with ceremonial precision.

"The Den Mother comes!" they declared.

"The 'queen bee' herself," Vladimir huffed under his breath.

Linus stood on his toes and craned his neck this way and that, searching for a clear view through the rolling landscape of wolfen heads and ears, until Vladimir clapped a paw on his shoulder and pushed his heels flat again.

Oh to be taller.

The familiar clink and squeak of armour and belts disturbed the silence as several Hummel

Howlers entered the hall in a neat line. They parted and knelt in two rows. Eldress Brynn knelt too, then all the Bloodfangs, Elder and Howler alike, in a wave of reverence rolling back to Vladimir and Linus.

Only two wolves remained standing; Amael in striking red, white and black, and his only present equal, Cora, the Hummel Den Mother, resplendent in white, green and gold.

"Den Father Amael," she greeted.

"Den Mother Cora," he replied.

With his head dipped Linus dared to peep from under his helmet – he could see now with everyone kneeling. Cora looked splendid. Her white armour was inlaid with green-imperium swirls, depicting the tendrils of a climbing plant. It was neither a feminine nor masculine design, but rather gender-neutral, Linus thought. Cora's Howler mantle was white, bordered with a sage green trim, and a subtle golden honeycomb pattern was woven throughout the white portion of the cloth. Her brooch and helmet were gold and inlaid with a white-imperium bee.

Cora's mantle may have been a sermon to bees, but Amael's striking red and black outfit made *him* look more like the venomous insect; a parasitic wasp that had come amongst the Hummel to wreck havoc.

And so he had.

Linus wanted to leap up and denounce him, but knew he would succeed only in appearing a swivel-eyed loon. He would be dismissed as deranged, duly arrested, then done in by Amael on the quiet. *So, this is why Vladimir says nothing, because he can't. It would be suicide. I see now.*

"Please accept mah condolences regarding Den Father Vito," Cora said sombrely.

"Thank you, Den Mother," Amael nodded, simple, gruff.

"Ah'm utterly ashamed that this could happen on Hummel land. Rest assured our Watchers are combing Everdor as we speak; they'll find the assassins."

"I'm most grateful, but this seems to have been an internal job perpetrated by disaffected Bloodfang youths. Hummel bears no responsibility."

"Then you know who was behind it?"

"One of the assassins, Uther Wild-heart, has a sordid history with our late Den Father. It seems likely to have been nothing more than… petty revenge."

Linus's ears pricked from afar. *Was that just another Amael-brand lie or had Uther been in it for revenge? Please be true, I could forgive him if it was. I could. Oh but what does it matter now, Linus?*

Uther's as good as dead.

Cora looked around the hall. Not seeing any black-cloaked wolves kneeling, she hazarded, "I understood ALPHA were on your train?"

"Were being the operative the word," Amael huffed. "Adal and I came to a… constitutional impasse. I was forced to expel his party from Bloodfang territory, as is my right as Den Father. Our train is sovereign Bloodfang land and he was no longer welcome, you understand."

"Of course, but what kind of 'impasse'?"

Amael explained, "Prefect Adal stuck his nose in where it was not needed and seized Vito's assassin. He then refused to give the scum up for interrogation, despite our entreaties to do so." The Den Father shrugged his cloaked shoulders, "His implication, of course, is that we Bloodfangs are incapable of conducting a thorough and fair investigation. I could not tolerate such an insult. So, as my first act, I shunted ALPHA's carriages into the nearest siding somewhere along the tracks and left them there. Don't ask me where. They can hitch a lift on a passing ash train for all I care."

Cora digested the surprising news, "Ah see."

"You're shocked?" Amael asked, continuing before Cora could confirm or deny it. "However, I have to tell you, Den Mother, that unlike Vito I will not tolerate ALPHA's naked power grab, and nor will my Elders. We must work to put Adal's bullies in their place this year. I will be putting forth a motion to restrict their powers and I hope I can count on the votes of you and the Hummel Elders."

Cora made no clear commitment, but nodded politely.

"Och! Rise, please," she said afresh, gesturing at her still-kneeling guests. "You're welcome tae mah home. What's Hummel's is yours, mah Bloodfang brothers."

Everyone rose at their own pace, young Howlers springing up as if in defiance of authority, older, more respectful Elders taking their time, afraid standing too fast might be taken as an insult to the great Cora Hummel.

Whatever Cora thought of Amael's hasty dealings with ALPHA, the Den Mother remained gracious. "Would ye care tae walk with me awhile, Amael?" she asked, slipping her golden helmet from her black, bright-eyed face and passing it to one of her aides; a gesture of friendship and trust. "Ah would be glad tae show you and your fine wolves around whilst we wait for the rest of the packs tae arrive."

Amael also removed his helmet, revealing his tough, steel-grey features. "I take it we're the first?" he asked, walking with Cora through the main doors, Hummels and Bloodfangs mingling in tow.

"That ye are," Cora confirmed. "We didnae expect anyone until the afternoon."

Amael explained the blunder, "Our train departed Lupa early so that Den Father Vito could visit the springs. We planned to stay there some time before moving on. Naturally we didn't linger longer than necessary after…." Amael grimaced and sniffed, "That place will forever hold bad memories for me now."

Cora shook her head. "It's a tragedy," she sighed. "But life goes on; the fir makes way for the sapling. What we must do tae honour Vito is work tae keep such happenings rare, and nae let murder and intrigue become commonplace as it was when we were young."

Time and pawsteps passed.

"You know," Amael began afresh, "I'm eager to see where you keep your famous bees, Den Mother."

"Have ye nae seen the Den Apiary before?"

"No; too busy arguing and voting last time I came here."

Cora chuckled, "Aye, there'll be plenty of time for that come tomorrow. This way then, follow me."

✦

"Unnngh."

Sara heard a groan, but balanced somewhere between dreams and reality she put it down to imagination and unconsciously elected to remain where she was, her head resting on her folded arms.

The next she knew a great hefty paw clapped on the back of her neck!

"Meryl?" it said.

"Bruno!" Sara gasped, sitting bolt upright and grabbing that big paw in both of hers. "You're awake."

Bruno's muscled torso crumpled like an accordion as he levered himself into a half-sitting-up posture. He was wearing a blindfold, yet seemed to look right at Sara.

"You're… not Meryl," he croaked.

Sara shook her head, "Nae, it's me, Sara."

No reply.

"Do you nae remember me? Sara Hummel. We used tae be best friends."

Bruno dipped his chin a little.

"Look at me," Sara said. "Take off your blindfold-"

"No it'll burn!" Bruno yelped, pushing her paws away. He then explained, "My eyes are bad."

"Aye. Sorry."

Bruno groped blindly in front of him whilst trying to slip his legs from the table. "Where's Meryl?"

"She's nae here," Sara explained. "Bruno, you cannae get up! Bruno, no!"

"Meryl! Jan? Unnnghfffgh!"

"There now you've hurt yourself!" Sara scolded, pushing Bruno back onto the table. "Lay down, for Ulf's sake. Lay down before you split your stitches."

"It's all right," Bruno growled. "I'm not like you... I'm not normal."

"Oh aye? Nothing's changed there then, ye great useless lump!"

"What?"

"Look, Ah don't care if ye are a big shot Eisenwolf these days, you were run through by a sword, mister! You're in nae fit state tae stand. Now lay down and be still; Ah'll go fetch someone."

Clasping at his bandaged body, Bruno allowed Sara to lift his hefty legs back onto the table and generally reorientate him in the manner of a patient. Coughing and clearing his throat he lay under the glow of the feeble imperium lamp, his eyes protected by his blindfold.

"You're from before," he rasped – it wasn't a question.

Sara froze for a moment. She cocked her head to one side and stood over Bruno again. "Before?" she urged, wondering if she should.

"Before I changed," Bruno clarified. He frowned, then smiled with amusement, "Small... small and dark... and kinda bossy. Yeah, that's you, 'en it?"

"Oh aye, and you're perfect Ah suppose?"

Laughing a little, Bruno reached up and felt Sara's cheek with a big scarred thumb, as if trying to see with touch. "I can't feel you; you've got no corona."

"Ah'm nae afflicted," Sara explained.

"I can see Meryl, though. Don't tell anyone, but I can feel her and she's not ill. I daren't tell her, in case it scares her. I don't like to scare her. I wouldn't want her to get the rot, but she's not invisible like you are. Must be something going on."

Bruno's rambling died off and he let his paw flop down. With a tiny gasp, Sara blurted, "Bruno Ah'm so sorry. Ah'm sorry Ah never asked after you."

"Whatcha mean?"

"When they took you away. Ah should've done more, Ah should've said something tae someone! Instead Ah kept quiet and pretended you were dead, like they wanted. Ah went along with it and I shouldn't have. Och, Ah'm so ashamed-"

"Hey hey hey, shhh!" Bruno soothed. "Don't get upset, yeah? I hate it when Meryl cries. It's like I tell her, this all happened for a reason. Jan found me... she made me into something. I-I-I was nothing before she came along, just a nobody cook. I remember... s-sss-standing over a griddle... and... making waffles all day. And there was this white rabbit in an apron always telling me what to do. Cor he was bossy-"

"Och! That's ye dad, Bruno. That's Casimir!"

"Casimir?"

"Aye, he adopted ye," Sara explained. "Do you remember when he found you? He told me the story a hundred times. You were trapped in rubble, whimpering away and he dug ye out. It was back during the war, do ye nae remember?"

Bruno pondered matters, big dark brow twisting this way and that. "It doesn't matter," he seethed, writhing free of the memories. "None of that does. What matters is that I can make a difference now, me and Janoah. I got to get well again. Get Josef, I need another sting."

"More?"

"Jan needs me to be strong for her. I can't let her down, she's counting on me-"

"Jan, Jan, Jan, is she all you care about?" Sara huffed with frustration. "Don't you understand? She's the one who ruined your life! She took ye from me, from Casimir, from everyone who loved ye and had you pumped with imperium until you forgot us. She's killing you-"

"Such shocking ignorance!" Janoah barked, emerging from the shadows of the windowless carriage. "And you a university-educated wolf? What is the world coming to when the best and brightest in Lupa do not even understand basic biology? Fact is, girl, Rafe was dying, Josef and I saved him, and more besides."

Had Janoah been listening in the whole time, could she have heard everything? Indeed she could've, for Sara at last realised the carriage was as still and silent as a tomb.

The train's stopped! We must be in Hummelton. I'm home. Mum and Dad are near.

I'm safe now.

Emboldened Sara stood up straight. "Ah'm nae afraid of you," she told Janoah, walking round Bruno's makeshift bed and pointing back at him. "Ah'm going tae expose what you did tae Bruno."

"Aww, deedums. Going to tell your mummy and daddy about the nasty Prefect?" Janoah mocked. "Your parents can't touch me, girl, I have no case to answer. Eisenwolves are a legally grey area. Besides, they'd as likely kill Rafe as not. Is that what you want?"

"Kill him?"

"Your ignorance knows no bounds does it?" Janoah huffed at Sara, brushing past her to stand over Rafe and stroke his ears. "I'm here, Stenton."

"Jan," Rafe croaked, grabbing her arm, "I need more imperium."

"No, you can't have any more. No more taubfene either."

"But I have to-"

"Josef's stung you up to the eyeballs already! Your body's used the imperium to heal itself, but you're full of ash now. You won't be able to see for weeks... but you'll live."

"I can't f-fff-fight like this!"

"You may not have to," Janoah said. "When the time comes all you need do is stand behind me. You can do that, can't you?"

Rafe was baffled, "S-sss-stand behind you?"

"Amael and the others won't know the difference; they won't know you're ill. They just have to see you at my back, my Eisenwolf, invincible in his suit! They won't *dare* raise a paw against us... whatever we decide."

"Decide?"

"Shh! Rest. Don't worry yourself with the details, leave that to me. I'll get you some food from the catering carriage."

"I'm not hungry."

"You must eat. Besides, we're on the Eisbrand train now; you wouldn't believe the food. Even their leftovers are better than ALPHA rations."

Rafe laughed.

Janoah turned to Sara and looked the little wolfess up and down.

"You can stop playing dress-up now," she derided. "Take Olivia and go. Nobody will stop you."

"Ah'm staying here."

"I thought you were going to go tell on me?"

"Well there's nae point if it'll do nae good!" Sara admitted angrily. She looked down at her feet, "Look, Ah just... Ah just want Bruno tae be all right. Ah know what's happening is bigger than any one wolf, but promise me you'll do your best for him. Please... be a good 'un."

"Good 'un?" Janoah chirped with amusement. "Well you're a bold 'un all right, I'll give you that."

Glancing at Rafe, Janoah ushered Sara out through the carriage door, which she closed. Standing with Sara on the ledge between the sunbathed stationary carriages she continued, "If being a 'good 'un' means I won't let Lupa sink into hyena-ruled chaos then I am that, I promise you," she said, "but understand this: Rafe is what he is, not what he was. He has Meryl and his new life now. Whatever sentimental mush you fill his head with won't make a blind bit difference, except to confuse and upset him. If you love him, my dear, you'll let him go. I don't say you can't see him, but don't try and change him."

Sara closed her eyes and squeezed a tear out.

"It's your other friend you should cry for," Janoah said, wiping Sara's dark cheek with a finger. "You went through all this nonsense to protect her, didn't you?"

"Olivia?"

Casting her eyes over sunny Hummelton, Janoah nodded and explained. "I can't keep Josef away from her forever. The moment my back is turned he's going to go after her."

Sara growled afresh, "Ah won't let him take her!"

"Oh but he won't; she'll go willingly."

"Never!"

"Are you sure about that?" Janoah cooed. "Josef will offer her the Eisenwolf mantle, the chance to be like Rafe, a God amongst beasts! I think she'll take it. I see it in her eyes, the greed, the ambition. She's not like my Rafe."

"God amongst beasts? Bruno's as good as bed-bound!"

Janoah sighed. "Poor, healthy wolfess, you really don't get what it is to be a Howler do you? We afflicted all endure suffering; strong or weak we rot just the same. But Rafe? Oh, he may suffer, but he could turn this train over if the mood stuck! He can shape wolfen destiny with a flick of his paw. By Ulf, if he only had a brain he'd be dangerous! As it is this rare power has fallen to a… dim lamp, shall we say." Janoah paused for a fond chuckle, then said soberly, "What would young Olivia Blake choose, a slow decline like a dying fire, or a shooting star that is an Eisenwolf?"

Silence.

"See?" Janoah said. "Not so sure are you?"

"But she'll die young!" Sara argued, searching Janoah's face for a denial. "Won't she?"

Janoah opened the next carriage door, but lingered long enough to say, "You're fond of my husband aren't you? You should heed his favourite fable. It's Rafe's too, you know… and mine."

With that Janoah crossed into the Alpha's carriage and shut the door.

Sara squinted at the familiar sunny townscape of Hummelton, banners and bunting fluttering, little beasts milling to and fro, and the yellow, hexagonal towers of Hummel's capital den standing over the rolling rooftops like pencils in a colossal desk tidy. Sara remembered playing in the Den's endless corridors as a cub, a privileged princess in all but name. She had dreamt of bringing Bruno here for years, to walk the clean streets, breathe the fresh air and sup the sweet water. Now here he was. Too late.

Sara returned to Bruno's side. After the sunshine and fresh air it took some time to adjust to the gloom of Josef's awful carriage, to the gloom and the heady fumes of engine oil.

"You'd better find Olivia," Rafe grunted. "Jan's right, Josef's dying for a new patient. He's bored of me."

Sara's little jaw dropped open. "You heard us?"

"I might be blind, but my ears can hear a pin drop," Rafe boasted, with a smile. "Oi listen, Jan says a lot of stuff she don't mean, but you can believe her when she says she's a good 'un. She's… she's always tried to protect me from myself. She thinks I'm too thick to take the truth, but I just don't tell her what I remember about… old me. Bruno, en it? I try not to think about him too much. It's better this way. It's better for me, better for Meryl, better for Lupa to let him die. I'm Rafe now."

Sara waited a moment. "Can't you be both?"

"Eh?"

"We all forget things, you know, not just you. Only the odd memory stays with me from day tae day; Ah forget what Ah say tae beasts and what Ah had for breakfast! You're nae different, nae really; Bruno is still there. He's still you."

Rafe raised his brow, "You know… I never forgot you, nor Dad. The names faded, but not the faces. I mean that."

Heartened by Bruno's words, Sara took his paw and held it tight. "And Ah never gave up hope you were alive. Ah thought you were in a Howler Academy somewhere. Ah hoped one day you'd turn up at the university, like you used tae, only looking all handsome in a Howler mantle."

"Weren't far wrong," Bruno seethed.

Suddenly he arched his back and growled in pain.

"Bruno!" Sara yelped. "Bruno ye all right?"

"Agh… sssfff… it's fine. You go get Olivia, yeah? I can't f-fff-feel her; she must be up the train somewhere. Bring her back here so you can keep an eye on her."

"You'll be all right alone?"

"Yeah. Go on."

With some misgivings, Sara hurried out to search the train, leaving Bruno to pant and seethe through a resurgence of bone-burning rot.

⚜

The Den Apiary was a marvel to behold. For some reason Linus expected Cora's famous bees to live in great wooden huts out in the open, but they actually lived underground, within the Den's foundations.

The Den's cellars harboured ancient observation corridors, dim subterranean passages cut eons ago and pocked with small, glazed hexagonal windows that allowed Linus and the other Bloodfang guests to peep into the domain of Hummel's great bees. The light was poor, and the windows smeared with wax, but Linus could see the floor and walls beyond the windows were a rolling landscape of golden honeycombs watched over by countless hairy bees just like Toggle all jostling for space. Some of them trundled from cell to hexagonal cell, regurgitating nectar. Others fanned said cells with their wings, drying the nectar, thickening it into honey. Others capped the cells with beeswax, or built new cells, both by using their skilful mouthparts. Still others danced in circles like wild hyena warriors round a campfire, shaking their bodies and buzzing. They were communicating, as far as Linus understood from his private studies, telling other bees where to find flowers in a language of gesture and sound beyond the understanding of 'higher' beasts.

It was wonderful, but even this marvel of nature couldn't distract Linus from the torment coiling in his guts.

Amael seemed perfectly at ease.

"Where's the queen?" he asked the white-cloaked Cora.

"She's drowsy at present," she replied. "'Tis early in the season, the colony has only just awoken after winter."

"Slacking, eh?" Amael joked, tapping the window with a finger. "They'd best get on, Lupa needs sweet honey almost as much as it needs venom."

Cora frowned a moment, then explained, "We don't take honey from these bees anymore. Once, long ago now, the honey was used by our ancestors tae ease the rot. It was thought tae be a cure, but it was later discovered it merely contains white-imperium."

"There's imperium in that honey?"

"Aye, but a little. The plants the bees visit grow near imperium aquifers, so the nectar contains small amounts, which is then concentrated in the honey and wax – that's why our bees grow so big. Of course, we have superior methods of obtaining white-imperium these days... albeit less elegant."

"What's the point of keeping them then?" Amael snorted.

Den Mother Cora patiently bore Amael's metropolitan ignorance. "We don't keep them; we simply co-exist. Bees are the sacred symbol of our pack going back generations. It's said as long as they thrive, Hummel will stand."

Amael tipped his head back a little. "This... boorish city-beast has offended you, Den Mother," he sniffed. "Please accept my apologies, I didn't mean any disrespect."

Cora nodded a little, "None taken, Amael. Ah appreciate your curiosity, in fact."

A brief, awkward silence.

Thankfully some Hummel Howlers emerged from the gloomy tunnels and whispered in their mistress' dark ears. Nodding and dismissing them, Cora announced, "Ah'm afraid we'll have tae end the tour here, Howlers. The Eisbrands have arrived, as have ALPHA."

"ALPHA?" Amael snorted at once

"It seems so, yes."

Amael chuckled caustically, "Ridden Thorvald's cloak to Everdor have they? I can't believe he'd allow it!"

Cora frowned, "What do you mean?"

"ALPHA arrested one of Thorvald's best Howlers just the other day, compounding the insult they dealt by taking Rufus at the Arkady Symposium. Adal's impertinence knows no bounds, Den Mother. We *must* stop him, together."

Cora nodded, "Maybe so, but Ah must extend Den Prefect Adal the same courtesy as you for now-"

"You should bar your gates to him *and* his thugs!"

"That would nae be wise!" Cora said firmly. "If ye'll excuse me, Den Father Amael, Ah must greet our guests."

Amael backed off a step, "Not at all, Den Mother. I've kept you long enough. My Howlers and I need to head back to our train and unpack in any case."

"Our cars are at your disposal."

"Thank you. We'll walk back however. I wish to take in the sights before the Summit."

Cora nodded graciously and took her leave.

Flicking a paw, Amael led his Bloodfangs from the viewing tunnels too.

Vladimir lingered with Linus by a hexagonal window. "I underestimated him," the Grand Howler murmured.

"Sir?" Linus urged, baffled.

The lofty Vladimir looked down at Linus as if he had only just noticed his presence. "Amael," he grunted, "even though he plans for Cora and all the rest of the Den Fathers to be dead come the opening ceremony he still behaves as if the Summit will happen, as if this back-door dealing matters." The Grand Howler sighed and shook his head, "I knew he was a degenerate, but the wolf seems to have buried what remained of his conscience along with Vito. Not a fleck of guilt, not a nervous moment. You'd never know what he was up to. And I thought Janoah was a consummate actor."

Linus held out one last hope for Amael's soul. "Is he mad with rot, do you think?"

Vladimir walked on, "I wish that he were. I think, however, he knows exactly what he's doing, which makes him the worst kind of villain – a sane one."

Chapter 47

Taking her pocket watch in one paw and Tristan's wrist in the other, Meryl measured the wounded Howler's pulse.

Slow, but steady.

The door to the ward opened and Silvermane crept over in his black Alpha gear. "How is he?" he asked, as Meryl adjusted the air flow of Tristan's respirator.

"Stable," the nurse replied, casting her eyes over Tristan. His heaving body was dressed in long, rambling bandages, like white centipedes with tape legs. Each one covered a river-like plasma burn that had been carved into his hide by the rack, and there were many more tiny wounds and strips of burnt fur.

"He should be dead," Meryl went on. "I was a good ten seconds shutting the machine off."

Silvermane nodded and glanced over his cloaked shoulder, before continuing, "Was it on purpose?"

Meryl dipped her delicate chin over her collar until it touched her cravat, "Yes."

"Nikita?"

Another, smaller nod.

Silvermane took a sharp breath, "He tried to silence a fellow conspirator and make it look like Maher did it. So… Nikita is one of them. The Alpha will be devastated."

"He threatened me," Meryl revealed. "He said if I didn't corroborate his story he would see to it Rafe died, or words to that effect."

"He's in no position to threaten Rafe, nor will he ever be," Silvermane assured. "But… corroborate is what you'll do for now. I'll pretend I believe your account."

Meryl turned to Silvermane and seethed, "You have to tell the Alpha."

"No. Nikita must have spies everywhere; Horst and Duncan could be against us too. I shall carry on as before. Things will come to a head soon enough."

"But what about me? What about Tristan?"

"You'll be fine, just let Nikita believe he's got you over a barrel. It's Tristan we must protect. I believe he'll be in the mood to talk after Nikita tried to cook him."

Meryl pointed out to her superior that, "The Eisbrands want him released immediately; that was the deal the Alpha stuck with Thorvald, you *can't* keep him here any longer."

"Surely he's too sick to be moved?"

"Perhaps, but-"

"Then I'll explain to our Eisbrand brothers that Tristan must stay here for the sake of his own health," Silvermane sniffed. "Besides, if he's returned to the Eisbrands now the collaborators amidst their ranks will likely kill him before sundown. His best chance is to stay here."

"And how will you explain his wounds?"

"I'll tell them he resisted arrest."

"You can say what you like, Grand Prefect, but Thorvald will know he was racked in the end. ALPHA can't hide it this time; he'll be scarred for life you know."

"Let's not pretend the Eisbrands don't rack anyone."

"I don't deny it, Grand Prefect, but ALPHA shouldn't!"

"They *all* do it-"

"To maintain the moral high ground ALPHA should obey the Lupan Laws, not flout them!" Meryl dared, looking Silvermane up and down like a proper madam. "Every day we go on behaving as the other packs do we undermine the reason for our inception and invite more wolves like Amael Balbus to rise up. We're supposed to set an example, not sink to their level."

Silvermane stared at the bold little nurse a moment. "Stay with him," he instructed with a smack of the lips, neatly side-stepping Meryl's dangerous words. "Don't let anyone take Tristan, not even Nikita. I'll say my orders come down from the Alpha."

Meryl visibly recoiled at Silvermane's refusal to engage her grievances. Perhaps now was not the time, but there never seemed to be a time! Step by step, act by act, ALPHA was becoming that which it hated. Even Rafe, bless his heart, was a symptom of ALPHA's rot, his eisenpelz a forbidden weapon that the packs could and would match if need be. If ALPHA's allowed an Eisenwolf so are we, they might say, dusting off their suits and scouring their ranks for candidates once more. It'll be an arms-race.

"I'll be in touch," Silvermane assured. "If he wakes up send for me immediately and don't let Nikita know."

Meryl didn't nod.

Regardless, Silvermane took his leave, lingering at the ward door a moment, watching as Meryl mopped the brow of that traitorous Tristan with as much care and diligence as she would Rafe.

✦

The trucks rolled to a stop in the woods, dappled sunlight rolling across metal and canvas, wheels pushing aside great mounds of mud like chocolate biscuit dough. The hyenas disembarked, Nurka, Themba, the newly rescued Madou and their loyal followers.

THORN had arrived in Everdor.

Where in Everdor the feverish Rufus had no idea. His squinting eyes swivelled this way and that, absorbing everything as Nurka's hyenas ferried him through the woods on a stretcher. Hummelton must be within striking distance, what with the Summit being tomorrow and all, yet this looked to be the deepest darkest wilderness, far from the Hummel capital district. *We must be in the wilds; how else could the hyenas have a camp here and yet go unnoticed?*

Rufus's mental ramblings were derailed as the hyenas set his stretcher down on a table in a large circular tent.

The skull-mask and muscled shoulders of Nurka loomed over him, purple eyes gleaming as ever. "How are you, Red-mist?" he rasped.

"Never better," Rufus lied. "Where am I?"

"Everdor, but you knew that. This is our chief THORN encampment. I've never allowed outsiders here before. Not even Amael knows where we are."

"And… y-you didn't make me wear a blindfold?" Rufus chuckled drily, seething in pain.

"We're past that, I think," Nurka cackled, with a tiny scoff and nod. "You're no outsider. I owe you Themba's life, my Prince's freedom… many things." The hyena chief added soberly, "Besides, even were you a spy you're not going anywhere in your condition, and even if you could we're a long way from a telephone. You're no threat to us."

"Very reassuring."

"It's not *me* that needs reassuring; I'm just voicing my arguments aloud."

"Well if it helps, I'm convinced of my own impotence."

"Humph."

"Since I'm no threat, where are we exactly?"

Nurka unpinned his zigzagged cloak, "What Hummels call Grunrose District."

Rufus lifted his head. "Grunrose?" he said, piecing his Lupan geography together. "But… that's on the northern edge of Hummel territory. We're hundreds of miles away from Hummelton."

"Yes," Nurka confirmed, beating clouds of brown Gelb dust from his cloak. "It's very quiet up here on the borders of civilisation. For over a year now we've been travelling the Sunrise Mountains, past Gelb and down the river to Lupa, then back again to Everdor, each time adding to our cache."

"Cache?" Rufus repeated. "You mean… the black-imperium?"

Nurka nodded.

By Ulf, Rufus thought, *all THORN's labours are stowed in a tent or buried underground somewhere around here*. He laid back down with some unease, as if this very tent might be pitched above a secret hoard of lethal black-imperium. *If it could be found and destroyed, the canisters split open out here far from civilisation, that'd end Nurka's venture, and Amael's with him, yet cause minimal harm. However, breaking open the canisters like barrels of beer would be suicide for the beast wielding the axe.*

It'll have to be me. I can't ask Noss, even less Tomek.

"So, how are you planning to get to the Summit?" Rufus asked, somehow maintaining conversation even whilst his mind explored every path. Arriving always at his own demise his heart sank. I'll never go on my expedition now; never see the Dead Cities. "We're... h-half a day away by truck and you'll be stopped by Howlers," he struggled on. "The security around Hummelton will be tight. They won't let a fly pass, let alone truckload of hyenas and black-imperium."

Donning his cloak again Nurka huffed, "Do you think I spent years planning the downfall of Lupa's corrupt regime and yet overlooked such things?"

Rufus grimaced, "I'm merely concerned, my good hyena."

His good hyena grunted, "Prince Noss is equally concerned. Forgive me, but I must explain my plans to him before anyone, even Themba and Madou. It would be an affront to Prince Noss's rank to overlook him. He is our prince, after all and you're a... well a...."

"An outsider, yes."

Nurka bowed a little, "I'm glad you understand. I'll return as soon as I've put the prince's mind at ease." He made to leave, but lingered, "My hyenas will tend to your needs, but is there anything specific I can do for you?"

"No, no I'm quite alright just lying here."

"Very well-"

"Wait, uh... send Tomek in, would you?"

"Tomek?"

Rufus explained, "I just want to make sure he's all right after... everything. He's the sort to bottle things up, you see. Proud chap. He's only a cub, you know."

A nod, then Nurka slipped through the tent flaps.

Within no time at all the grey Tomek burst inside, anxiety pasted across those dark, caterpillar-like brows, as if Nurka had informed him Rufus was dying and about to cross the eternal plains and sit with his ancestors, as hyena beliefs maintained.

"Rufus!" he woofed, rushing to his friend's side and looking him over. "You all right?"

"As can be," Rufus replied, taking Tomek all in. He was wearing a stripy hyena cloak and greaves, no less! "Well, well look at you. Defected have we, Usenko?"

Tomek looked down at himself. "No no, is not like that. I-I-I had nothing to wear and-"

"Calm down, Tomek, I'm only pulling your leg. It's much better than those rank Gelb rags."

A nod, a shrug, a handsome wink – the rogue. "Black and white suits me, no?"

"Most becoming. You're a regular hyena warrior now."

"Hahaha!"

Checking the tent flaps for real hyena warriors, Rufus suddenly grabbed Tomek and pulled him close. "Listen, whatever happens next keep your head down," he seethed, his rough voice resembling car tyres rolling slowly down a gravel drive. Weathering resurgent rot pains he soldiered on, "I-I-I didn't want you involved in all this... but you're here now... I know that."

"Rufus, I have to tell you-"

"You've been a great help, Tomek. Really! Just don't do anything foolish. You can't fight Nurka, you can't do *anything*. They're too strong. Leave this to Noss and myself."

"You?" Tomek scoffed. "But your wounds-"

"I'll be fine," Rufus dismissed. "It'll pass."

"Pass? The ants cut you up, Rufus!"

"Look, just sit quietly and ride this out and you'll be back in Lupa in no time. All right? I'll get your record cleared in a heartbeat... and Helmut's too."

"Helmut?"

"He deserves to be pardoned. It's not much good now, but there it is. Perhaps his family will appreciate a posthumous medal. But I'm not losing you as well, so stay out of it-"

"I can't, I'm Janoah's agent!" Tomek growled.

Rufus's eyes darted all over the Watcher, "What?"

Glancing behind, Tomek leant close and seethed through his fangs, "Rufus I'm sorry, but I am... I am ALPHA agent."

Nurka shepherded Noss through the forested camp. Hyenas cooking over fires and sharpening imperium spears looked up and, upon recognising their prince, dropped everything to grovel in the erde.

Noss hoped it was for him they bowed, not Nurka.

"After you, my Prince," the chief said, stopping by a larger and finer tent than the rest.

Noss ducked inside. To his surprise the interior was magnificent, the floor-level bed being piled high with plush white pillows and velvety black blankets, whilst thick rugs bearing patterns of insects and plants knotted in red and gold covered every square inch with no bare erde to be seen. In the corner, by the bed, was a small, beautifully-carved wooden table housing a hookah pipe full of purple-imperium, and fine crystal decanters containing colourful translucent drinks, ready to pour into equally fine tumblers. There was a bigger albeit very low table in the middle of the room on which papers could be spread and plans made no doubt – hyenas didn't wander around gesticulating like wolves, nor even sit, they knelt respectfully and humbly. Even so, Nurka seemed to enjoy the good life.

"It's like a matriarch's hut in here!" Noss cackled at him, taking it all in. "Very nice, Nurka."

Nurka didn't react, save to silently spread a paw at the mattresses – sleeping and seating were one and the same to hyenas.

Sighing loudly, Noss gladly fell amidst the soft pillows, paws behind his head – after a year in Gelb it was paradise. With a start, he sat up again.

"Forgive me, Nurka," he chuckled. "My privations have been... long."

"Not at all my Prince," Nurka replied simply, kneeling beside him. "Drink?"

"Please."

Removing his helmet, as Noss did his, Nurka poured them both a stiff-smelling drink.

By the Wind he's still so young, Noss realised, taking in Nurka's handsome, unblemished face again for the first time in over a year. He had the mind of a beast twice his age and the extraordinarily muscular physique of a Chakaa to back his assertions up; it was so easy to forget just how young he was when disguised by that ferocious Jua-mata skull helmet.

"To THORN," Nurka said, raising his glass.

Noss raised his in kind, "To the Jua-mata."

Chinking their glasses they knocked back their drinks in a single gulp.

"Not bad," Noss said. "Hummel liquor, isn't it?"

"Yes. I believe so."

"A filthy wolfen beverage? You surprise me, Nurka."

The youngster allowed a rare chuckle, "My Prince, it's not wolves I hate, but the regime. An ally like Rufus wouldn't be alive if I was so simple."

"Simple like Themba?" Noss goaded, slapping Nurka on his nearest massive spotty arm and adding quickly, "I'm teasing! He's come on leaps and bounds."

Nurka forced a quick, polite laugh, and set his empty glass aside. "Wolfkind is enslaved by Lupa's corruption as much as anyone," he said, gravely. "There are good and bad in all, even hyenas. I haven't forgotten what you taught me, nor allowed Themba and Madou to forget. One must see beneath the hide, beneath the colours, spots, shapes and manners that separate us hardly at all... to the soul that does."

Noss nodded, "I am relieved to hear that." He took a sharp breath and asked, "How goes the affliction with you three?"

"Well, my Prince."

"Are you in pain?"

"It comes and goes."

Noss tapped his skull and flashed a manic smile, "And what of the mind, Nurka? Does that come and go too?"

With a twitch of a purple eye, the chief spread a paw at the low tabletop. "You wanted to know what we're to do; I'll show you," he said, changing subject.

"What about Madou and Themba-"

"I must confide in you first, my Prince, as is your right. They will understand," Nurka said, all but interrupting.

Noss dipped his chin and grunted.

Shuffling to the table, the prince watched the chieftain roll out some paper and quickly sketch the beginnings of a simple map using a traditional reed dipped in ink. One could add drafting to Nurka's list of abilities, as the young hyena swiftly laid ink lines hither and thither with quick and daring strokes that a master cat calligrapher of the east would envy. A bushy forest took shape, then a river in a single broad wavy stroke; farmland dotted with sprigs of grass appeared and what looked like a farm. Then, far across the other side, a quick collection of blocks, houses; a castle and a city wall – Hummelton?

"We are here," Nurka said, placing a tent in the forest.

"I gathered that," Noss cackled.

Nurka smiled and shuffled a little, he seemed nervous for the first time Noss had seen.

Strange.

The chief scratched an X elsewhere in the forest, north of the camp, by a rocky outcrop.

"This is the black-imperium cache," he revealed, adding a mouth to the rock. "It's in a cave north of here. Of the hyenas that went on raids only I know where the cache is, just in case anyone was captured. Not even Madou knows, yet."

Noss nodded, "I'm honoured by your trust, Nurka."

"You're our Prince," Nurka explained simply, moving the tip of his reed down to the farm he had sketched. "This is Rumney Farm. It's not far from here on the inside border of Grunrose, an hour or so by road."

"What's there, more imperium?" Noss guessed.

Nurka waited a moment, then looked up at the slightly taller Noss kneeling across the table from him and said, "A dirigible, my Prince."

Silence prevailed.

"What?"

"A dirigible; a balloon, a lighter-than-air flying machine, call it what you will-"

"I know what a dirigible is!" Noss said sharply, his dark hyena brow furrowing as he tried to fathom what was going through Nurka's mind. "We're to *fly* to Hummelton?"

"Yes."

"At night?"

"Daytime, my Prince."

Nurka's Prince could but laugh and scoff, "In broad daylight, in front of the whole world?"

"Doubtless."

His smile fading, Noss supposed he was missing something. "You know how to pilot a balloon?"

"No, but Montague Buttle does."

"Who?"

"The famous cat pilot, him and his wife. Forgive me, you've been indisposed of late."

Noss cast his mind back, "The names ring a bell."

Grunting, Nurka continued, "The farm is theirs. They have converted one of the silkworm barns into a secret hanger for their latest dirigible. They've been building it for over a year now. From the blueprints I've seen, it is enormous."

"All the better for a grand entrance!" Noss joked.

Unsmiling, Nurka calmly pointed to Hummelton with his ink-stained reed. "The Summit opening ceremony is tomorrow. It begins at midday and ends two hours later. It's a small window of opportunity, but it is the *only* time the Den Fathers of every pack and all their officers will be together… and yet out in the open."

Noss's bafflement only grew as Nurka slowly revealed his cards. "Out in the open?" the prince said. "What good is that? Black-imperium's best used in confined spaces, same as any bomb. When they asked me to kill Rufus I made sure he was in a café for a reason."

"We are not going to use bombs, my Prince. We never were. If the Lupans assume we are all the better; they'll be looking under benches and searching bags when they should be looking up."

Noss sat in silence.

Nurka patiently returned his reed to the forest and the cave therein. "The black-imperium rests in temporary holding flasks. Such flasks are not meant to leave the refinery; they're pressurised and highly dangerous. All one has to do, my Prince, is turn a valve and black-imperium will be released." The chief traced a path from the cave and out of the forest, terminating at Rumney Farm. "Tomorrow morning we will drive to the Buttle's farm and load the flasks onto their dirigible, as many as it can carry. Montague Buttle will then fly it to Hummelton."

"He's one of us, then?" Noss assumed.

"No, my Prince. The cat may be a Felician and Lupa's old enemy, but he relies on Lupa for sponsorship since the Queen of Felicia has forbidden his balloons. He has nothing to gain by helping us."

Noss spread a paw, "Then why should he fly you anywhere, Nurka?"

"Because to protect his wife he will do whatever we ask!" the chief rasped suddenly, looking to Noss with narrowed purple eyes burning. "Besides," he continued calmer, "the cats will not be told what we are to do. They will believe we are merely dropping propaganda leaflets from their balloon."

Noss frowned. "But you won't," he said, wiping his dry lips.

"We shall, my Prince, but not over the Summit; the dead have no use for propaganda. No, the leaflets are to be dropped over Lupa, for the citizens there to digest."

A pause, a nod, a question, "The dead, Nurka?"

With his Prince's undivided attention, Nurka slowly, painfully scratched his inky reed across to Hummelton. "The dirigible is due to fly over Hummelton during the opening ceremony bearing the flags of all the packs as an expression of Lupa's forward-thinking, enlightened people," he spat, the words sticking in his throat. "The Den Fathers are expecting a show. They will think nothing amiss as we pass over, until we loosen the imperium flasks in the balloon's hold and the sky turns black with ashen rain the like of which has never been seen! They'll all rot where they stand!"

Nurka's reed snapped on Hummelton's ink walls. He cast it aside with a trembling paw and looked at the silent, still Prince Noss across the table.

"Then... all that remains is Amael," Nurka sniffed, flexing and massaging his writing paw, dark fingers clenching and spreading. "He plans to leave the ceremony long before we arrive – there's nothing I can do about that. He knows what's coming. That's why when I heard you were alive I had to get you out, my Prince. In the struggle to come you'll be there to inspire the tribes and pull them together. They'll follow you. If Amael still had you he could've held you hostage. As it is our people will have a fair chance now. With Hummel destroyed and polluted beyond repair there'll be no food imports for Lupa, no Hummel Watchers to attack us from behind as we lay siege to the city's arteries of rail and road. Amael may have venom coming out his ears, but he'll starve. Our people know how to live off the land, and our Chakaa have plenty of purple-imperium. We will outlast him. Lupa will fall."

Noss stared, unflinching.

"It's... good to finally tell someone," Nurka heaved weightily, emitting a quick laugh and cupping a paw to his aching head. "To keep it from everyone, e-even Themba and Madou, and organising everything without revealing to anyone my entire thinking. It's been... trying."

Reaching across the low table, Noss cupped a paw to Nurka's thick neck. "It's a grand plan, Chakaa Nurka," he assured, shaking him fondly. "You really are the clever one. I'm proud of you."

"Proud?"

A nod, a smile... a gulp.

✣

"Tomeeeek," Rufus growled, cupping his paws to his face as he lay on the stretcher still. "Why did you let Janoah talk you into it?" he growled. "Why?"

Tomek could but stand with his paws behind his back, shrugging and shuffling as Rufus chided him. In the end the young Watcher whispered, "She worried for you. I am happy do it, for Lupa. I help you for Lupa."

"I felt so guilty. You wouldn't believe how awful I felt thinking I'd gotten you in trouble. All this time you made me suffer when you were a mere actor?"

"Not always!" Tomek defended indignantly, checking the tent flaps for stray hyenas before subduing his voice. "I not act when I stop Madou; that was real. Janoah not speak to me until after that day. I am no more actor than you. My story, it just fit. I had upset Elder Watcher by helping you and he had punished me; that's what we decided. Janoah arrange everything and I was sent down, just like you. It was all pretend, yes; I lied, yes; but I still mean what I say and do."

Rufus turned his cheek and sighed, "Well… you're here now. You're a grown up, I suppose. Like Noss said you've shot beasts; nearly shot *me* back at the wall that time."

Tomek shrugged and dipped his chin, "I not aim at you. I aimed over your head."

"Grateful, I'm sure."

"No. I always aim above prisoners. I have… never shot anyone before."

Rufus chuckled, "And I thought I was special for a moment there. What if you boys had all aimed over my head, what'd happen then, a pardon perhaps?"

"It not happened so far."

Rufus grunted, changed subject. "In any case you've done your bit. You're a Watcher so you know how to survive out here in Everdor, don't you?"

A nod, "I can survive in Ashfall. This place? Looks easy."

"Right. First opportunity you get you slip away and head back to civilisation. I mean it."

Expecting resistance, Rufus was surprised when Tomek replied, "That's our plan."

"Oh. Well, good," Red-mist sniffed officiously, settling down. "Who's plan?" he snorted, sitting up a little.

"Noss."

"You've been talking. What's he up to?"

The tent flaps parted and Casimir limped inside. The white rabbit nodded and saluted at Rufus, then looked to Tomek and hiked his thumb over his shoulder. "Can I borrow you, lad?" he asked simply.

Tomek hurried out at once, stopping only to look back at Rufus and salute him roguishly as ever.

"Tomek!" the wounded Rufus yelped, trying, failing to get up and give chase. "Tomek, wait a minute-agh!"

It was no good; Rufus was out of the loop.

Slipping across the THORN camp with Casimir, Tomek went unhindered by the hyenas. Those that had accompanied Nurka into the mines knew Tomek had been instrumental in getting Prince Noss and everyone else out, whilst those that didn't know of him yet at least recognised Casimir as Nurka's trusted ally – he wouldn't be up to no good with any treacherous, untrustworthy wolfen agent.

So, they went about their business. Even the pugnacious Themba paid no heed, save to look up from a quickly stolen meal by a campfire and sniff, "Welcome to Kambi Mata, little Casimir. You're one of us now."

"Aye, what a let down," the little beast gruffed in passing. "Just a lot of tents 'en it!"

Themba frowned, then laughed.

"Kambi Mata?" Tomek whispered, as he and Casimir walked swiftly on.

"Never mind, just keep moving," the rabbit hissed.

Into a tent, Noss was waiting inside, pacing on a rug. He whirled on Casimir and Tomek, looked beyond them. "Rufus?" he inquired.

"Still laid up bad," Casimir replied. "I couldn't risk him hobbling across camp for all to see."

Noss nodded, "It's probably for the best, he'll only disapprove. I'll speak to him if I get a chance." The hyena spread a paw about, gesturing to a pillow-strewn hyena bed and a low table complete with drinks. "My quarters," he cackled, "Nurka wanted to give me his luxurious pad; I refused."

"Should've accepted and asserted your authority," Casimir snorted, snatching a drink from the table and knocking it back – he needed it. "Shouldn't yer?" he added.

"By refusing him I *have* asserted my authority," Noss explained. He checked outside for any listening ears, then returned. "You've lived amongst my kind all this time and yet learnt nothing of our ways, rabbit."

Casimir defended, "I'm not as cosy with THORN as you think 'hyena'. I've never been here before."

"What do you mean?"

"This camp; Kambi Mata. This is THORN's main HQ, you realise that?"

"Camp of the dead?" Noss said, with a curious frown.

Tomek repeated, "Camp of the dead?"

"In our tongue, that's what Kambi Mata means."

"Reassuring, eh lad?" Casimir chucked at Tomek, pouring another drink. "Told yer not to ask."

"Then... Jua-mata means?"

"Dead Sun."

Tomek snorted at Noss, "That is your tribe's name?"

"And what of it, boy?"

"Nothing. Well, is not very...."

"Friendly?" the prince cackled. "And 'Bloodfang' is, I suppose? It's no good calling yourselves the Fluffy Wuffy Bees; well, unless you're Hummel!"

Tomek smiled and dipped his chin – Hummel's bee symbol always had been a bit of a giggle amongst the city packs.

Knocking his second drink back, Casimir said, "Nurka's never let me come this far in before. Usually I'm dumped in the outer camps with the other raiders whilst he and Themba carry on deeper into the forest with the black-imperium flasks. Aside from them, the only hyenas allowed into Kambi Mata were the ones who never went on raids and so would never be captured. I dunno why he's so lax now. I mean, you're his Prince 'en all so it makes sense fer you, but Rufus and Tomek? Nurka's usually paranoid about outsiders."

"He's getting careless," Noss theorised, peering outside again at distant hyenas milling about – he could feel no coronas, save Tomek's. "He was desperate to tell me his plan, you know; it was a relief for him. He feels safe now. He thinks nobody can stop him. He's right – we're in the middle of nowhere, miles from a phone, and nobody can get word out before the Summit tomorrow-"

"No, he's wrong!" Tomek growled, clenching a fist. "We will stop him. We have to."

Noss agreed with a hearty nod, "You two have to get away and warn the Howlers."

"I stay with you, no?" Tomek offered. "Back you up in case of a fight?"

"No, Tomek, you and Casimir will have to split up and search for help – you'll cover more ground that way. Slip away as soon as you can. Find a road, a house, a farm, even a Howler; there'll be something out here, there must be. Get word to Hummelton, specifically Vladimir – he alone will take you seriously."

Tomek reluctantly agreed.

Looking between the wolf and hyena, Casimir threw his pale paws wide, "What do we say to this 'Vladimir'?"

For once not smiling, Noss raised his dark chin a little, and his purple, imperium-laden eyes searched the stained canvas ceiling, "Tell him to look up."

✧

They were in the tent for some time, chatting, gesticulating, then the flaps parted, spitting Tomek and Casimir into the open. Madou kept a wary eye on the wolf and rabbit as they took a seat by the fire with Themba and partook of some food.

Madou remained discreet until Nurka fetched Noss from his tent and led the prince across the camp.

"Chief!" Madou puffed, running over, hefty arms swaying.

"Yes, Madou?" Nurka sighed with forced patience, whirling on his comrade, paws behind back.

"My Prince," Madou added, bowing.

"Madou," Noss acknowledged.

After an extended awkward silence, the stocky Madou clumsily articulated to his chief, "What's happening now?"

"Happening?" he replied.

"What's everyone doing?"

"Resting?" Nurka suggested, nodding at Themba by the fire. The big hyena was stirring a small pot emitting purple fumes. "Go and sit down, Madou, drink some chunta with Themba. You need to regain your strength after your time in Gelb."

Madou glanced between Noss and Nurka, "Haven't we got to discuss the plan?"

"When I'm ready."

"But the Summit's tomorrow-"

"*When I'm ready*," Nurka re-iterated sternly. He slapped Madou on the shoulder and gestured to the best tent in the camp. "I know this camp's new to you too, but the Qu-... *my* tent's just over there; you're welcome to it."

Madou accepted his lot, "Chief," and watched Nurka lead Noss through the forest. Noss was the centre of Nurka's world now it seemed.

He's our Prince, Madou told himself. It's only right.

Crossing the camp, leg armour rattling, Madou went to Nurka's rather grand-looking tent. It was even grander on the inside, rugs, pillows and other fineries jostling for Madou's attention. He didn't think too much of it as he sat amongst the pillows, only that this wasn't very Nurka. The chief had always been a hard, if learned hyena, surrounding himself with books rather than pillows. Perhaps power is going to his head? Perhaps he's starting to think he's some kind of prince himself after leading THORN so long? He had spoken to Noss out of turn at times, even contempt back in the caves. That sort of attitude would get a hyena in trouble, usually.

Madou lay back and allowed himself to relax, even sleep, despite his feverish thoughts.

✣

It proved a long, winding walk into the deepest darkest Everdor woodland before Nurka stopped at no place in particular and veered off to the left. Noss had tried to memorise the route, eyes searching secretly for landmarks; rocks, strange trees, anything. The only real standout feature for Noss, apart from a giant, black millipede trundling through the ferns nearby like an Elder Train, was the very cave he now found himself standing before. Nurka parted the thick thorn bushes obscuring its mouth and pushed through them into the gaping limestone maw.

"My Prince," he urged, parting the foliage from the other side like a beast peeping out from behind a green stage curtain to check the mood of the audience. "This way."

Looking over this low, moss-cloaked collection of stones that could barely be called a cave, Noss pushed through the thorn bushes. The usually sessile wall of spiked branches tore at his fur like things suddenly motile, almost pulling the prince's dazzling duotone mantle clean from his shoulders as he twisted his body to freedom on the other side; his legs and face were armoured, but his arms suffered many scratches.

"By the Wind, Nurka," Noss complained, rubbing at his stinging arms. "You must be red-raw coming in and out of here after an imperium raid."

"You grow accustomed to it, my Prince."

Lighting the way with their brooches, chieftain and prince dared the pale, glistening, limestone cave; Noss hoped this one didn't twist as deeply into Mother Erde as Gelb, he'd had quite enough of all that.

"It's not far," Nurka reassured, as if reading his Prince's mind.

"Lead on," Noss replied amiably.

I could kill you now, he thought, looking at the back of Nurka's helmet-clad head, but that won't stop you; Themba and Madou will carry on your mad mission. I must either challenge you openly, or else destroy your imperium cache in secret tonight. I won't get a chance to do both, but Tomek and Casimir will be on their way and one of them will succeed in warning the Howlers.

Someone must.

Nurka stopped by a small cavity in the side of the otherwise smooth cave passage. He stood to one side, rasping, "Here, my Prince."

Suppressing a primeval gulp of fear for what he was about to look upon, Noss peered into the side atrium.

There they were, dozens of spherical canisters marked with the deadly 'X' denoting black-imperium, all stacked neatly together. They resembled the tanks of anaesthetic gas Noss had seen used in Lupa's hospitals to soothe the moans of the wounded, but a whiff from one of these would do rather more than put a beast under.

There looked enough to douse Hummelton good and proper and then a fair portion of Lupa beyond – Nurka had casually mentioned, as he and Noss had traipsed through the woods as if engaged in an afternoon stroll, attempting a second gas attack against Lupa itself if all went well regards Hummelton tomorrow, perhaps eliminating Amael. Noss had but nodded and grunted, even as his guts twisted with horror.

Did Nurka truly understand what he was proposing? Elder, Howler and citizen; healthy, rotten, guilty or innocent; wolf, hyena and little beast; the poisonous rain would make no nice distinctions. Everything it touched would rot and any infrastructure so contaminated would remain unusable for millennia.

Nurka was out to make his very own Dead City, to create utter desolation and call it victory.

✢

Madou awoke with a snort and glanced about the tent. *How long have I been asleep? Not long, I think.*

Extracting himself from the pillows, Madou went to the tent flaps and looked blinkingly to the campfire where Themba sat tending his pot of sacred chunta.

With a quick glance up and down the camp, Madou hurried over. "Where'd they go?"

Themba looked up from the heady purple fumes, "Who?"

"Tomek and Casimir?"

The big hyena frowned slowly. "They went to rest. You should be resting too; we've a big day tomorrow. Come, sit and drink with me, Madou. It could be the last time we ever do in this life."

Madou glanced about, "Where'd they go exactly?"

"Who?"

"Ragh! Tomek and Casimir, you chunta-drunk fool!"

"I don't know!" Themba growled, looking the short Madou up and down. "What's wrong with you?" He ladled out some rich, purple chunta into a bowl. "Drink, Madou."

Rejecting the offer, Madou continued his search, half-walking, half-jogging about the camp, glancing in tents at sleeping hyenas and checking every fire, asking beasts if the grey wolf and the white rabbit had passed this way until he was directed to the edge of the camp and the dirt track that the trucks had trundled down to get here. No sign of Tomek or Casimir, just a winding dirt road cutting an arboreal tunnel through the ferny woodland.

Madou hurried down the muddy road, puddles splashing underfoot, until some fearsome, skull-painted THORN hyenas leapt out of the ferns and barred his path with their imperium spears.

Madou expected nothing less. In his native hyena tongue he asked them if a wolf and a rabbit passed though here, Casimir – you all know Casimir the white rabbit.

Yes, the hyenas replied in kind, Casimir had passed through with a Chakaa wolf honoured with our colours.

Where were they going? Madou pressed.

To the outer camp, where Casimir's old tent was; he was going to fetch his things here now that he was allowed into Kambi Mata.

Thanking his THORN brothers, Madou sped down the road towards the second camp.

✢

The outer camp was a mile down the track; running would look suspicious so Casimir checked his and Tomek's pace. The forest either side was crawling with watching THORN terrorists and booby traps had been laid all over; spike pits, tripwires attached to yellow-imperium bombs, ash grenades and falling logs, the list was comprehensive. The only safe way out of THORN territory was down the road and through the camp, preferably on wheels if they could get some.

"I'm one of the few experienced drivers and I've driven the black-imperium trucks before," Casimir explained to Tomek, as he limped nervously along. "They shouldn't think it unusual that Nurka's asked me to drive something somewhere."

"Uh huh," Tomek breathed.

"We'll have to go back if they stop us, and try again later."

"Yeah."

Casimir glanced up at the taller Tomek. "You remind me of my lad," he said fondly. "Wolf of few words, Bruno, and brave as could be. I like to think if he's one of you now he's a good 'un, even if he is an Eisenwolf."

Tomek smiled; Casimir could not see it beneath the wolf's helmet, but his eyes squinted at least.

"Airship," Casimir said, looking up at the sky through the branches, perhaps eager to change subject. "Nurka's a genius, but thumping mad."

"You really did not know of Nurka's plan?"

"No, lad. Nobody did."

"Would you have helped THORN if you did?"

Casimir stayed silent for a time, "At the time... maybe. Now I know Bruno's alive it's different. I got him to fight for again."

Tomek said nothing.

"You must despise me," Casimir grunted.

"You make mistake," Tomek reasoned, looking all around. "Is natural. I make many mistakes in life also. But we make good now, both of us."

The outer camp appeared through the trees; tents, wooden fences, some tree houses. Hyenas emerged from the forest to check what Casimir was up to; he got past them speaking in their native tongue which Tomek didn't understand. Satisfied with Casimir's story, the hyenas let him and his wolfen guest pass before melting into the trees again.

So far so good.

Into the camp, past hyenas milling about; Tomek always on the receiving end of funny looks, but he was with the white rabbit so all must be well. These were the raiders, Casimir told Tomek, those that had accompanied him and Nurka to Lupa time and again, stockpiling black-imperium without knowing exactly why. They didn't know its location or what Chakaa Nurka had in mind, only that their chief had a grand plan to smash wolfkind using the cursed blood of Mother Erde, her black, imperious fury. Tomorrow the plan would be revealed to them and the end of their trials was near. Excitement was running high. Hyenas danced and drank, laughed and whooped, more so tonight than any other night before a planned raid that Casimir could remember. There were no females though; a filthy camp in the middle of Everdor was no place for even the lowliest hyeness.

An unusually dark, drunk hyena painted like a skeleton stumbled into Tomek with a gourd sloshing in his paws. He looked the wide-eyed wolf up and down, said something Tomek didn't understand, then slapping his cloaked shoulders staggered away again.

"What did he say?" Tomek asked Casimir, craning his neck to follow the stumbling hyena visually.

"It was complimentary," the rabbit assured, tugging the wolf along. "Sort of."

As Casimir led him through the camp towards lines of trucks and bikes – some monos but mostly ordinary two-wheelers – Tomek passed many more hyenas drinking and laughing, drowning their sorrows and fears. Some sat quietly twiddling their thumbs or sharpening weapons, others cried whilst looking at photos or fondling trinkets. They weren't monsters or idiots, but beasts, each as complex and whole as Madou or Noss. Even Nurka was no mad beast, he was as erudite and measured as Rufus. What has Lupa done to drive Nurka to this desperate act? Were the Reservations and re-education camps so bad? Maybe, but poisoning thousands and starting another war is no way to solve anything.

Tomek remembered that day, not long after Rufus had passed through the Lupan Wall on his way to Gelb, being called into the Elder Watcher's office to meet ALPHA Prefect Janoah Valerio, leaving his loyal ant Scuttle outside.

"*What do you think of hyenas?*" Janoah had asked him, looking out the window at the passing trains.

"*I... think they... well... uh....*" Tomek had stumbled, standing to attention.

"*Pity they can't just fall into line, isn't it?*" Janoah had urged mischievously.

Relieved to be directed, Tomek had agreed, "*It better for them to do so, Prefect.*"

"*Better than being wiped out?*" Janoah had suggested further. "*Because that's what'll happen if THORN succeeds, you know. If hyenas are ever to be tolerated, as my husband desires, we must first save them from themselves, and from Amael.*" She had turned to Tomek, looked him up and down with her marvellous green eyes. "*You're quite a wolf... for a cub. You've been of great assistance to me and my husband, but you could do more. You could be a wolfen hero and save our great Republic. Does that interest you, Usenko?*"

"Lad!"

Tomek came back to the present, to the truck that Casimir was climbing inside.

"Stop daydreaming and crank the engine!" the gruff rabbit commanded, wiggling an S-shaped crank-shaft down at him from the cabin. "Hurry before we're seen."

"Right," Tomek nodded, dashing round front and inserting the dirty old truck's manual crank into the hole just beneath the grille – there weren't many vehicles like this anymore, it was an antique! Nonetheless, with a few vigorous rotations the engine rumbled into tremulous life, spluttering clouds of choking ash into the once-pristine undergrowth.

A tent nearby parted and an ash-stained hyena with goggles on his head dashed over to Tomek. He waved his oily paws and spluttered hyena syllables that were nonsensical to Tomek's pricked ears.

The young wolf shrugged and spread his paws as the hyena berated him. "Sorry, I not speak hyena."

Rapping on the truck window to gain the goggled hyena's attention, Casimir beckoned him round to the open door. The hyena stormed over and had it out with the rabbit, exchanging heated words for a good minute, wasting precious time.

This won't do.

Tomek came up behind the hyena and, with a glance about, tapped the crankshaft to his goggled head.

Pfzzzt!

Channelling a blast of plasma down the shaft, Tomek sent the fellow down, catching him before he hit the ground – the rumbling truck and rowdy party veiled the violent action.

"What've you done?" Casimir yelped, tugging on his ears.

"Is fine," Tomek excused, dragging the unconscious fellow away and dumping him in the damp ferns. He climbed inside the trembling truck and slammed its rusty door, "Let's go."

"I had everything under control."

"Go! Come on!"

Adrenaline pumping, Casimir revved the engine and directed the gurgling, ash-billowing, open-backed truck through the camp and onto the anonymous Everdor road. Nobody stopped them.

"We're on our way, lad."

Tomek watched the THORN camp's entrance retreat rapidly in the mirror.

As the road bent and obscured the camp from view, Tomek thought he caught a glimpse a familiarly hefty, stocky hyena standing at the gate.

Madou?

✦

The sunny platforms of Hummelton Station darkened under rolling clouds of ash as the magnificent Greystone Elder Train eased into dock, huffing and puffing to a controlled halt between the polished blue Eisbrand and black Bloodfang engines parked either side. The enormous Greystone contrivance dwarfed them, with its twelve gigantic sets of driving wheels as oppose to the eight and six of the Eisbrand and Bloodfang machines respectively, and sporting an imperium tender as large as a normal carriage to boot. Its sooty flanks were slashed by great gills that spurted ribbons of ash like an industrial shark choking on embers, and so tangled with pipes, valves and rivets was it that the engine appeared naked, as if the outer hull had been stripped away to reveal its secret inner workings. The Greystones were a practical pack, less concerned by the beauty of their trains and cars than being able to quickly access and fix problems. The Bloodfang train, no sleek beauty itself, looked fancy by comparison, whilst the contoured Eisbrand engine looked a positive dandy.

Linus made such comparisons as he stood at the Bloodfang dining car windows, watching the Greystones disembarking and being greeted by the same Hummel Eldress that had escorted Amael that very morning. Den Father Flaid, recently elected, stepped down from his carriage in a dour dark Grey cloak and light grey armour with yellow-imperium highlights. A tall, very powerful brown wolf whose muscular arms were flecked with scars, Flaid cut an imposing and vigorous figure indeed. He and Eldress Brynn shook paws and hugged – it was nothing personal, the Greystones were a tactile lot, a family pack, and Hummel simply accommodated. Thorvald had been welcomed by Cora with stiff Eisbrand protocol and ALPHA their simple salutes, before driving to the Den together. Linus had noted everything whilst helping cheerful Hummel little beasts sort the Bloodfang luggage and load it onto cars for the short drive to Hummelton's Den.

It wasn't so much the Elders Linus was interested in, but Sara. He looked up and down the station platforms, searching, always searching. If ALPHA were here then Sara should be too, somewhere.

Perhaps she's slipped back to Hummel, to her mother, and taken Olivia with her. Perhaps Den Mother Cora would sort everything out now, for Sara's sake.

Maybe they'd be safe.

"Gelb's been raided," huffed Vladimir, entering the dining car and shutting the door.

Linus peeled his eyes from the goings-on outside, "Sir?"

His superior walked over and ducked to peer through the windows at the Greystones himself. "THORN has attacked the prison for some reason, perhaps to rescue dissidents. The Warden was found in a river with his head caved in and half the hog guards are missing, and those they did find have been horrifically dismembered, torn into pieces they say."

Linus scoffed, "By hyenas?"

"Unlikely," Vladimir dismissed. "Most likely it was the ants that live around Gelb scavenging their bodies, but the papers won't let facts like that get in the way of blackening hyenas further. As I've said, every action THORN takes backfires against their own people. The worst is yet to come."

Vladimir heaved a sigh. He continued.

"Cora, Thorvald and Amael have agreed there's to be a curfew tonight – I'm sure Flaid will agree to it as well."

"Curfew, sir?"

"Yes, Mills. We're to pack our bags and head back to our assigned rooms at the Den; only Hummel Howlers and beasts with the correct papers will be allowed to roam about after dark, no outsiders." Vladimir pondered further, "I'm surprised Amael didn't protest the idea. Perhaps that means his fellow conspirators have already planted a bomb."

"Or they're crooked Hummel Howlers, sir, or just beasts with the correct papers."

A considered Vladimir nod.

Linus dipped his chin, "I… I feel so out of my depth."

"Oh?" Vladimir said, taking his leave. "That's how I've felt every day for months."

Linus worked his way through the dining saloon and many a specialised carriage; a lounge car with plush sofas, a library car with bureaus for writing, even a bathing car which, Linus was ashamed to say, he hadn't utilised; the water was rationed anyway, a minute of hot water, thirty seconds to soap, thirty to rinse, it was better to just use Glimmer and a comb.

Arriving in the sleeper car Linus ducked into his cabin. The door closed rapidly behind him.

The wind?

Linus turned in time to see an all-black Howler slap him in the side of the head with a rapier and a spark of imperious plasma.

Bzz-tack!

Chapter 48

"Noss?"

The kneeling hyena Prince looked up from his prayers to see a Howler peer into his tent. For a second Noss thought it was Tomek. Had he failed to get away? Had Casimir? *Am I rumbled?*

"Red-mist," Noss realised, chuckling, "You're walking!"

Glancing over his shoulder, Rufus slipped inside the prince's tent. His cloak and helm obscured any sign of wounds and bandages, but his limp and slight sideways stoop gave the pain away.

"What's going on?" he demanded. "Where's Tomek?"

Noss smiled a little and dipped his chin; he was rumbled, albeit in a different way. "Gone, I hope," he whispered.

"Gone?"

"I sent him and the rabbit to warn the Howlers of THORN's intentions whilst I try and talk Nurka down. I know what he's going to do; he's told me… everything."

Noss didn't get any further before Rufus dived on him, grabbing his cloak and pulling the massive hyena to his feet in defiance of his injuries.

"You had no right to put Tomek in danger!" Rufus seethed furiously. "You're not even a Howler; you're nothing but a criminal!"

Noss weathered the storm, then replied calmly, "Tomek wants to help protect your precious Republic. He's not a boy, he's an ALPHA agent. Janoah got to him, or didn't you know-"

"She had no right either; he's *sixteen* for Ulf's sake!"

"So? Will you sacrifice thousands of innocent lives just to keep one of your handsome betas safe? Are you that self-indulgent? Tomek for one would rather fight than cower. I admire his bravery as much as I do Nurka's."

Rufus frowned beneath his helm.

"Yes, Red-mist," Noss grunted, "Nurka, Themba and Madou are as dear to me as your betas, and every bit the warriors I hoped they would be. Yet I must save my people from them. If we are seen to kill thousands of innocents it's not just wolfkind that will never forgive us, but every other race too. The cats of Felicia will not be seen to deal with such a degenerate regime, save to cross the sea with half their Valours to destroy it! And no little beast will ever turn a wheel or sew a field for us, not if we stoop so low. Amael; he knows this. He'll blame my people for everything, pin it all on Nurka, and make himself out to be Lupa's saviour. When all other Den Fathers died, he alone survived and brought Lupa back together – that's his sick dream. There is no other way for him to commit genocide and yet remain in power."

Rufus slowly removed his paws from Noss, "Yes… I know," and nursing his wounds grunted, "What is Nurka's plan?"

Tidying his duotone cloak about his great chest, Noss glanced at the tent flaps and growled as soberly as Rufus had ever heard a hyena, "He's going to drop black-imperium on Hummelton, tomorrow, during the opening ceremony."

Silence reigned.

"Drop?"

"From the sky," Noss said, eyes looking up, "from an… airship."

Rufus scoffed in amazement, then clapped a paw to his helmeted head with a metallic ding. "By Ulf that's it! Why didn't I see it? Not a bomb, but a chemical rain!" He turned away, ashamed of his own dim-wittedness, "Heath and I once discussed using dirigibles to spray farmland with white-imperium to increase crop yield. Heath pointed out that all you'd need do is swap out white for black and you could kill thousands and desolate hundreds of square miles of land for centuries. How did it not occur to me that someone else would think of the very same thing?"

"Because you're a benign fool, Red-mist. What matters is what we do about it, you and I."

"You know what to do!" Red-mist asserted. "You have to face Nurka down. Use your position as the prince to pull rank on him. That's why I helped him get you out, because you can end this without a shot being fired. You and only you, Noss."

Noss turned away, "A sound theory, but... I'm nothing to them now."

"Don't be absurd!" Rufus woofed. "Nurka got you out of Gelb because you're the most important hyena alive. He thinks you'll help provide him with authority, but you'll do the exact opposite. Even if he doesn't obey you, the others will. They have to."

"Maybe."

"Are you blind? They all bow to you as you pass; Madou scrapes his nose in the mud for you and he's no pushover. You have to try, Noss."

Noss paced to and fro, "I fully intend to, but... I also know where the black-imperium is hidden."

"Nurka showed you," Rufus said; it wasn't so much a question as a statement.

"Yes."

"Where is it?"

Noss ceased pacing. "In a small cave north of here, hidden behind some thorn bushes; I broke fern fronds and scuffed my feet in the mud to leave tracks."

Rufus chirped, "Good thinking."

"Now I don't know what to do; destroy the imperium or face Nurka. I cannot do both, if I shoot my bolt it can only be one or the other."

"Why?"

A toothy, Noss-brand grin, "Because breaking one of the canisters will not only pollute the cave and the whole cache beyond retrieval, but kill whoever does it. I cannot face Nurka if I'm dead, Red-mist."

"That has occurred to me."

Noss spread his big paws, "What should I do?"

Rufus looked into nowhere, into the thinking space between worlds. "The hyenas will need you when this is all over. Forget the cache; face Nurka. The worst he can do is refuse to listen. He can't harm you – you're sacrosanct."

"I'm no coward," Noss growled.

"Talking Nurka down from this madness is a braver thing than betraying him, believe me."

After some foot-shuffles and nods, Noss said, "I'll have to make my move soon, before Tomek and Casimir are missed. My people won't appreciate a wolf interfering, not even one honoured by our colours. You had best stay out of it. Go whilst you can."

Rufus beamed, "I'll make myself scarce, but I'll not abandon you." He held out a paw, "Whatever happens, I'll be with you, Noss of the Jua-mata."

The massive hyena eventually grasped the svelte wolf's ruddy paw and pulled him into a firm embrace, "Thank you, Red-mist. I do not deserve such trust, not after... I betrayed you-"

"Oh don't get all soppy, you big spotty flannel!"

"Grrfghahahahaaaaa!"

Rufus winced for his wounds, and the private knowledge that he would never see Noss again whatever happened, nor Janoah, Ivan or anyone else.

✤

The late afternoon sun glittered sideways through regiments of rapidly-passing trees, painting Casimir's truck in flickering veins of gold and blue. The fact the setting sun was even visible meant the forest was thinning – the open plains of Everdor were near.

We're going to make it, Tomek thought.

The truck's engine began to pop and thrum, quietly at first, but with growing strength until Tomek could feel the vibrations in his cloaked chest.

It wasn't the truck at all.

"That's a mono engine," the young wolf realised, his wolfen heart leaping into his fangs.

"I hear it," Casimir said shakily, peering in the nearest wing mirror.

Doing the same, Tomek spied a fluttering cloaked figure coming up fast, the glint of a monobike's polished shell nestled between his armoured legs. The flicker of sunlight and shadow made the rider's colour and form hard to discern.

"Maybe is Hummel Watcher?" Tomek Bloodfang hoped against hope.

With one eye on the road and another on the mono, Casimir fondled for his pistol, "I don't think so, lad. That's one of the Chakaa. Rest of the hyenas won't be far behind, I bet."

Tomek didn't have a weapon, but was never without the corona of a Howler. He raised a paw and clenched his fingers several times, bracing himself for the necessary pain.

There came a sudden surge from monobike engine – the rider was attempting to overtake!

"Block him, Casimir!" Tomek advised.

"I'll thumping try, lad!"

The truck swerved this way and that as Casimir attempted to thwart the rider from getting ahead, but the mono was as the nimble ant to a ponderous beetle and whipped past on the inside of a turn.

"Sneaky maggot!" Casimir cursed, readying his pistol.

The now obviously hyena rider manoeuvred in front like a Howler pulling over a speeding vehicle. With a long straight in the road ahead he matched the truck's speed, twisted his body with a pistol in his paw, and took aim at the cabin.

"That's Madou!" Tomek woofed, recognising that stocky build. He wound down the window and shouted, "Madou stop! Please! Hear us out!"

Casimir pulled Tomek back, "Get down, lad!"

At the last second Madou changed his mind and lowered his aim to the wheels.

Crack!

Its left tyre deflating fast, the truck veered wildly, threatening to tumble into a muddy ditch running parallel to the road. Casimir dropped his pistol in his lap and with both paws on the wheel skilfully wrestled back control, even as the tyre beneath him collapsed hopelessly, churning up mud and pebbles. Teeth clenched, the rabbit changed down a gear or two and returned to the road. Tossing his pistol to Tomek he shouted with conviction and bloodlust no little beast was supposed to possess, "Take him out, lad, I got my paws full!"

Nodding, panting, his throat dry with adrenaline, Tomek leant out the window and aimed at Madou's cloaked back. He hesitated, his mind flitting back to the day Madou had saved him in Gelb's infamous Pit.

Madou's not an unfortunate prisoner tied to a stake anymore, he's a free terrorist out to help THORN murder thousands. This is no time to aim high, Tomek Usenko, nobody else will shoot him if you do not.

It's up to you.

Tomek fired, he was certain, yet heard nothing. The ash from his pistol was instantly whipped away by the rushing wind and Madou jolted forward, swerved wildly in front of the truck, nearly going under its deadly wheels altogether.

Recovering, he accelerated to safety and glared back at Tomek with wide, purple eyes.

With a gulp Tomek ducked inside again. Before he could inquire after a reload, Madou and his monobike slowed down and came alongside Casimir at the driver-side door. The rabbit dared not ram the hyena, for to do so would be to consign the barely driveable truck to a ditch, or a tree trunk. Rather than risk it Casimir tried to speed up, pressing his paw to the imperium gas, but Madou stayed with him easily.

Suddenly the burly hyena stood up on his bike, which stayed right and steady as only a gyroscopic mono could, and like a circus performer he leapt bravely, if not madly, from saddle to cabin door!

"Jua-mataaaa!"

Madou slammed into the truck door, latching on, and with all his imperium-fuelled might put a spotty elbow though the window, showering Casimir with glass and residual bolts of plasma. The little rabbit imagined he would be pulled from his seat and tossed into the woods like a rag doll; instead a determined Madou leant in and grabbed the top of the steering wheel in a big paw.

He pulled.

The truck lurched to the left, leaving the road and rolling to the right. The cabin instantly transformed into a tumbling cacophony of breaking glass and crumpling metal. Dirt, stones and fern leaves flew past the yelping Tomek, with no up or down, no rhyme or reason. Light, dark, light… dark.

Motionless.

The engine crackled and smoked, choked and died.

Silence.

Dazed and hurting, Tomek blinked hot stinging blood from his eyes and twisted in the cabin, trying to right himself even though he knew not which way was up. Piecing the world together he came to realise he was lying on the mangled passenger door, which was flush to the ferny ground – the way out was the driver-side door above.

Casimir was nowhere to be seen, nor was Madou. Had they been thrown clear?

Tomek had more sense than to call out for help. Grunting and panting, the strong young wolf pulled his way through the twisted cabin, much like the awful Gelb caves he had endured for months, only sharper. Up over the wheel he climbed to the broken driver door window and freedom.

He leapt down into the ferns, looked about – the trees ended sharply just feet away, the open fields of Everdor, and perhaps some scant hint of civilisation, began.

Run for it.

What about Casimir?

Leave him, the Republic comes first.

No.

Quelling the debate in his head, Tomek searched around the truck, the ditch, the road, staying always in the ferns.

Madou's monobike chugged by, the gyroscope within keeping it upright as it rolled to a halt like a giant penny; it sat there, trembling, inviting Tomek to leap on its back and go.

"Tomek!"

Casimir rolled out of the ferns into the ditch, his white fur muddied and bloodied.

"Go, lad! Hurry!"

As quickly as Tomek ran towards Casimir an imperious presence grew, butting up against Tomek's own like two ethereal barges on a canal. The Watcher stopped halfway to the citizen rabbit, expecting trouble, which sure enough emerged from the ferns in the cloaked form of Chakaa Madou.

The thickset hyena was dripping blood, his leg armour stained with rivulets of red.

"I… was starting to think I could trust you, like Rufus," he seethed. "After everything we've been through I thought maybe I was wrong to look sideways at you."

Tomek said nothing; he just stared, taking in Madou's obvious wounds.

Did I hit him?

"Our own Prince is a traitor," Madou growled, laughing for a moment. "Don't deny it! I saw you all whispering in the tent with him. You took advantage of his madness, didn't you? You twisted his mind whilst I was in the Pit, even after I saved your life down there. Filthy backstabbing wolf!"

"Madou… Nurka is going to kill many thousands," Tomek breathed, stepping backwards as Madou advanced on him, step by metallic, armoured step. "He is the mad one, *not* Noss. Nurka want to drop black-imperium from a balloon; spray it onto Hummelton and the fields. Everyone will die. Innocent beasts will die, not just Howlers. And all the bees that pollinate crops too! Without Hummel to run plantations everyone in Lupa will starve. Even the Hyenas will starve-"

"Lies!"

"Is truth!" Tomek barked. "Yes, Noss is here to stop Nurka, but that his decision, not mine. THORN goes to far, even for you. I know you'd not want to kill innocent citizens."

"What do you know about me?"

"I know you're good beast! I know wolfkind has wronged your people, I *know* this, I see it every day at Lupan Wall, but more killing will not fix it-"

A snarling Madou lunged to the attack. Tomek scrabbled away onto the road and skidded into a wrestling pose, hunched down, tail flicking, paws spread, ready to deal imperious blows.

"Hahahaaa! Let's see what you're made of, Chakaa Tomek!" Madou laughed, stepping onto the pebbly road in the same manner and circling his prey, like a crab. "We'll fight like true warriors, then. Only a fool trusts his life to a weapon, that's what Prince Noss taught us before you sneaky wolves turned him!"

Tomek replied, "What about Rufus? Did he turn him too?"

"Red-mist is one of us!"

"You really think so? I feel sorry for you if you think Rufus is murderer like Nurka!"

"Shut uuup!"

The fight was on, Madou closing the distance in a cloak-billowing bound and striking Tomek in the ribs as the young wolf tried to duck sideways and evade him.

Tomek yelped as Madou's imperious blast tore through even his tough Howler body, sending him rolling across the road. He righted himself neatly, staggered back in pain, and only just recovered his wherewithal in time to receive Madou's follow-up assault. The hyena barrelled into the wolf and together they tumbled off the road into the ditch near Casimir, exchanging kicks and punches all the way.

The rabbit looked on in horror as Madou laid into Tomek, punching him with flashing plasmatic fists, knocking his helmeted head left then right and paying no mind to his own bleeding, smouldering knuckles.

Casimir climbed up the ditch in a bid to escape whilst he could. At the lip of the ditch he hunched his back.

It was no use.

Bounding over in defiance of his gammy leg, Casimir Claybourne planted his white paws on a baffled Madou's shoulders.

"Get off him!" he cried, his arms channelling a bolt of plasma worthy of any Howler or Chakaa. *Bffzzzt!*

Now it was Madou's turn to fly, leaving the ground and Tomek behind he slid backwards through the slick stinking mud of the ditch.

"Come on, lad, get up!" Casimir begged, tugging on Tomek's cloak, dragging the dazed wolf along a little. "There's his mono. I can ride it, just hop on with me. Come on!"

"Go!" Tomek spluttered, levering himself up, blood dribbling out from under his helmet grille. "I stay."

"He'll kill yer, Tomek!"

"No. I stay... finish this; is what I must... do. You go, quickly."

As Madou rolled on all fours, Casimir looked between Tomek and the monobike. The pops and cracks of approaching bikes filled the forest – more hyenas? Sure enough Casimir could see them approaching on normal two-wheeled bikes, with Themba at their head on his own mono.

"Lad-"

"Go!" Tomek snarled, pushing the rabbit away. "Get away from here!"

Nodding, Casimir hurried across the road to Madou's plain-looking monobike and clambered aboard. To Tomek's relief and amazement, the little beast twisted the accelerator and sped down the road. He wobbled wildly for a stretch, but soon regained control and sped away.

Thank Ulf.

The moment Casimir crossed into the fields was the moment Tomek felt Madou's huge spotty-furred forearm lock around his neck and pull him back into the one-sided fight.

"It's over, Tomeeek!" Madou declared.

With a last plasmatic blast to his spine, the outmatched Tomek flew head over tail and collapsed in the ditch, smoke rising from his trembling, heaving body.

It was indeed over.

"M-Madou...." Tomek spluttered, as the stocky hyena stood over him shaking a smoking paw. "Let C-C-Casimir go. Please. He just... little beast; he can't do anything. But I am right. You will see. Ask Nurka... I am telling truth."

The panting Madou said nothing.

Themba and several hyenas arrived, pulling up by the overturned truck. "Madou!" Themba called, running over and jumping into the ditch with a tinkle of piercings. "What is this?"

"I took care of it," Madou sniffed, kicking Tomek in the ribs and levering the paralysed Howler onto his front. "He won't be getting up."

"Traitor?"

A nod, "I knew something was up. I've been watching him ever since Gelb." Looking left and right and nursing his wounds, Madou eventually added, "Casimir's dead, Themba."

"Dead? Where?"

"He... was dragged under the truck when it rolled over, along with my bike."

Themba made to check.

"Don't bother," Madou grimaced, "it'll be a mess."

Themba grunted, "Humph. I cannot believe it; Casimir was with us so long. Nurka will be very upset."

Madou nodded.

"I'd better finish this one," Themba said of Tomek, wielding his hammer.

Madou stayed his brother hyena's paw. "No, let's bring him back with us. We can execute him later; if he's lying I'll do it myself."

"Lying?"

"Prince Noss needs to explain a few things to me, or maybe Nurka does. Depends."

Themba frowned, "Madou, what is all this?"

"Did Nurka tell you his final plan whilst I was in Gelb?"

"Yes."

"All of it?" Madou pressed.

"Well... no," Themba admitted, squirming under his cloak and claims. "Not *all* of it," he rowed back, adding with cub-like eagerness, "but he will tonight. We will all know."

Madou nodded, dipped his chin, sniffed back blood. He looked up at the lesser hyenas lingering at the edge of the ditch, peering in on him and Tomek like curious beasts after a playground brawl.

"You're wounded," Themba observed.

Madou lifted his cloak enough to check the graze torn in his hip. "A scratch," he grunted, "the wolf missed more or less. He fought well though, for a treacherous Howler."

Themba silently shepherded the wounded Madou away. "Tie the wolf up," he growled at the others.

The hyenas dutifully jumped in the ditch and wired Tomek paw and foot.

✦

Linus lifted his heavy, helmet-clad head and shook the stars from his eyes. Slowly the dim cabin returned to focus, as did an a dark wolf with a ghost-white face.

"Uther?"

As Linus made to rise, Wild-heart used a rapier to push him back onto the bed. "Ah ah ah."

Linus twisted his arms, quickly discovering they were bound behind his back with a belt, one from his own wardrobe perhaps. Anything short of Howler-wire would hardly hold a Linus a minute, but that was long enough to leave him at another's mercy.

As he lay back, he contemplated shouting for help, but the cabin was in near-darkness and the station quiet. Evening had come, everyone else was probably settled at Hummelton Den since a curfew would soon be in effect; shouting for help with an unhinged murderer holding a rapier to one's throat was perhaps less than wise even in a crowd.

"What do you want?" Linus asked instead, looking Uther over and adding, "Come for revenge, is that it?"

"Puh!" the Wild-heart snorted, whipping his obviously stolen sword away – his whole kit was stolen, an ALPHA Prefect's mantle to be sure. "Listen to you! Think very well of yourself, doncha? High n' mighty Linus, hanging out on the Elder Train with all his important new friends. It's gone to your head already."

"How'd you even get here?"

"It weren't easy, I tell you that-"

"Kill someone else to acquire that kit did you?" Linus accused, sitting up a little.

Uther's nostrils flared, "Oi! I stopped Ivan killing you back at the springs. I'm not a murderer like him."

"Not a murderer? You shot Den Father Vito!"

"He deserved it!" Uther snarled, pushing Linus down with his sword tip again. "He had it comin'... he did," the Wild-heart sniffed quietly. "I never thought it'd be me, never thought I'd get that chance, but I'd do it again for what he did to me and who knows how many others! Rufus saved me from that life and I *had* to do something. I *had* to get him out of Gelb. You've no right to judge me, Linus. No thumping right! You've had it all good, you have, not like me. Not like me."

Linus frowned, "I've had it all good?" he repeated. "My parents died of rot when I was a cub and my whole hometown got sick and withered before my eyes! Oh, yes all good here Uther. Ideal childhood for me!"

Surprised at Linus's sarcastic wallop, Uther withdrew his sword and looked at his feet like a contrite cub, "I... I didn't mean it like that. You don't understand."

Sighing, Linus flicked his chin, "Then tell me. What did Vito do? Tell me why you and Ivan did what you did. If it wasn't for Amael then what was it all for?"

Uther looked away, then back again, "Rufus."

"Rufus?"

"He's alive, mate."

"What?"

"He's with the hyenas, with Nurka n' THORN, him and that Prince that tried to kill him. Noss was it?"

"But... but Rufus was executed, and Noss too-"

"No, no, no, it's all fake, mate. All of it."

"Fake?"

Wild-heart sat on the cabin bed. "Rufus was sent down as part of Janoah's plan. THORN had to think he was gonna turn, didn't they? So ALPHA faked his arrest and everything, made it look like he had nothing to lose so he'd be willing to join THORN. Vladimir sent that mad Noss down the same way; Josef didn't kill him, they packed him off to Gelb to keep him from Amael so he could testify against the conspirators later. It was all kept secret, see?"

Linus scoffed, "But Vladimir told me you and Ivan were in league with Amael!"

"Aye, we were! We helped him get into power so he could pardon Rufus; that was the deal. Only he got Rufus out of Gelb early and didn't even send word. Jan didn't plan that. She tried to have us recalled, but Amael didn't wanna know. He let us kill Vito anyway so he could become Den Father. The sneaky git used us, mate."

Linus waited; a captive audience in every sense.

Uther suddenly stood up and swished the air with his rapier. "I wanted Vito dead, aye, but I thought I was getting Rufus out too. That's what Jan thought, *and* Ivan – that's the only reason Blade-dancer said yes." Wild-heart shook his head and marvelled, "All I've really done is make Amael stronger. Still, ALPHA's just waiting to bring the whole lot down; Amael, THORN, all the conspirators. Jan's got everything covered." Pinching the air, Uther added, "'Cept one thing. Me and you Linus, we got to go help Rufus. That's what Jan told me. We could be Lupa's only chance, you know that? Me 'n you, heroes she said. Hahahahaaaa!"

Linus's brow twisted this way and that as he tried to make sense of Uther's rant. Whatever his score with Vito, Wild-heart wasn't telling – his pride wouldn't allow it.

Shoulders rolling with chuckles Uther turned, presenting his back and with it a chance to escape. Linus's own pride wouldn't allow him to lay here bound a moment longer.

"Grrrragh!"

Simultaneously kicking Uther in the rump with both feet, Linus blew apart the belt restraining his wrists with a snap of paw-scorching, bed-burning plasma.

Pfzzzat!

His blood up, he bodily dived on Uther, dragging him to the floor of the cabin. With ingrained wrestling skills honed in the Howler Academy and the strength gained from a year of all but living in Riddle Den's gym, Linus twisted Wild-heart into a hold, forearm locked to throat, rapier prised out of paw, snarling and grunting all the way down.

"I should snap your neck!" Linus seethed in Uther's twitching ear.

"Go on then… Woodlouse," he croaked. "But I could've killed you three times over lately. I didn't though, did I?"

After much nostril-flaring, Linus released Uther with a push and stood over him.

"Two times, at most," he corrected, chin raised.

"Hahaha! You keep telling yerself that if it makes you feel better."

Linus angrily snatched the rapier from the floor and pointed it at the criminal kneeling at his feet. "All right, Uther, I'm listening," he said. "Start from the top and tell me *exactly* what's going on. Take it slow."

"There's no time."

"Make time-"

"Linus! For Ulf's sake if I just wanted to escape I'd be halfway across the Teich by now. I got a mission to do. I came to you because nobody else is gonna believe me. Janoah can't come back me up; she can't take off across Everdor, she's gotta keep up appearances or Amael might get spooked. I'm her only chance. You've gotta trust me, mate."

Linus heaved his chest, "What is this mission?"

Uther stood up, determined. "Find Rumney Farm. Find the balloon. Take it out." He spread his paws, "That's all Janoah could give me; it's just a hunch, but it's what she'd do if she were Nurka, she said."

Linus had stopped listening at balloon. "Balloon?" he woofed. "What balloon?"

"Monty Buttle's balloon. Remember him?"

Linus was at once aghast and confused, his baby-blue eyes searching Uther's white face for clues.

"I don't understand, what's that to do with anything?"

Uther took his stolen ALPHA helmet from the bed, strapped it in place and grunted, "Look I'll explain on the way, but we need to *find* the way first. Like most wolfesses, Jan don't give proper directions; all we got to go on is a district and the name of this thumping farm-"

"I never said I was going to let you go!" Linus said, raising the rapier again. "Let alone help."

"No? Then stab me… again," Uther said, nursing the last wound Linus had dealt him; it had healed somewhat thanks to Janoah's sting. "But be it on your head when Amael steps over thousands of bodies to become king of Lupa. That what you want?"

Sniffing and turning slowly away, Uther exited the cabin and stole down the deserted carriage hall, passing through shafts of light from the station lanterns outside.

Ulf almighty, Linus whined in his head, rapier drooping like his tail. Grabbing his Bloodfang sword and shield, he started after his one-time partner.

"Uther wait!"

Uther stopped. Catching up to him, Linus said, "All right, but I'd better tell Vladimir all this."

"No time fer that."

"I can't just go-"

"Vlad can't do anything! He can't send Howlers to go investigate, Amael will know, and if Amael knows he's been rumbled he'll call the whole thing off and kill us. He's the Den Father now; ALPHA can't touch him. If we don't catch him red-pawed he'll have Janoah killed, Vladimir killed, you killed; *anyone* who got in his way is dead. Then when the air is clear he'll try again, they all will. Understand?"

Linus could but scoff.

"It's up to us," Uther said, raising a paw. "Now are you with me, Woodlouse?"

Linus, eventually, clasped Uther's paw, "Wild-heart."

✦

Puffing ember vapour from her lips like one of the many engines lined up in the station, Janoah crossed the platform and located the front of the sleek blue Eisbrand train – ALPHA's carriages were tacked on the end still, as was Rafe therefore.

Janoah started her way down.

"Who goes there?"

Sighing, the Prefect flashed her brooch at the white-cloaked Hummel Howlers speeding across the station to intercept her. "Prefect Captain Janoah Valerio," she said, saluting.

"There's a curfew in effect, Prefect," the Hummels replied. "Return to the Den, at once."

"I intend to, but the Alpha forgot his papers and sent me to collect them." Janoah slowly produced a letter from her black cloak, one sealed with the A of ALPHA. "You'll find this is signed by him."

The Howlers checked it out and exchanged looks.

"Arrest me if you must," Janoah said curtly, "but the Alpha wants those papers and if I don't get them he'll only have to disturb Den Mother Cora in the middle of the reception banquet-"

"Just hurry up," the Hummels said, returning the letter.

A nod.

Janoah continued, passing twenty or so magnificent Eisbrand carriages on her way to the drab and rusty ALPHA hulks clinging to the end like the crinkled, dry, shed skin on the posterior of a colourful caterpillar. She climbed not into the Alpha's office car to see about those phantom papers, but went straight into Josef's lair to see about her Eisenwolf.

They were all there, Sara, Olivia and Rafe – Josef could be heard tinkering inside his van.

"How is he?" Janoah enquired, stepping into the glow of the single overhead light.

"Sleeping," Sara whispered.

Janoah checked Rafe for herself, stroked his brow. The giant wolf frowned and licked his lips. He said something about Meryl, as usual, but Janoah couldn't decipher it.

"You should go home," she told Sara, without even looking at her. "You should be with Den Mother Cora and your little sisters. You hardly see them these days."

How it was Janoah knew such things Sara daren't guess, but the Prefect seemed to know all.

"Ah'm staying here with Bruno," the little Hummel wolfess replied with Meryl-like primness.

"And I," Olivia matched, hopping off a crate to stand with Sara.

"Don't care for your family much?" Janoah needled.

"Ah'm staying here *because* Ah care. Bruno needs tae be better tae help stop this, doesn't he?"

The Prefect conceded a nod.

"Well then. Anyway, mum n' dad can manage. They got all of Hummel tae worry about, they don't need little old me getting under their feet. They never have."

Janoah cocked her head a little, "Thank you… for sitting with him."

Sara looked up, blinking amazement from her eyes.

Regretting her words immediately, Janoah huffed, "Don't expect anything from me in return," and sauntered round the back of the black van.

A bright white light flashed from the seams in the van doors as Josef welded something to something else.

Janoah tried the doors, they were locked. "Doctor?"

"Go away!" came a tinny reply.

"It's me!"

"I'm busy!"

"Open up!"

With a feline growl one door opened, revealing Josef covered in grease and ash, with a welding mask strapped about his frowning face. Janoah worriedly peered past him to discover Rafe's suit in pieces on the floor; the torso here, the arms there, the backpack an unrecognisable heap of parts!

"What're you doing?" Janoah all but shrieked, stepping aboard.

"Making adjustments-"

"Adjustments? It's in pieces! Put it back together at once!"

"Do you want him to take on Amael and win, or die trying?" Josef mewed. "Rafe's not going up against some nothing hyenas with pop-guns, but a dozen of Lupa's most talented Howlers. In his state he won't be able to fight effectively as it is. He needs a boost."

"Boost?"

Josef's whiskers hiked with glee. Like a professor of anatomy he went to the arms and pointed out some metallic tendons running down the inside. "I am increasing the plasma output, which means the arms need more conductors, or they will melt under the extra load," he explained. "I've ran some extra ones down, as you can see."

"Right."

"I've also added an coronal field scabbard to the backpack."

"A what?" Janoah huffed.

Josef hefted Rafe's massive sword, just about, and held it gently over the backpack lying on the floor. Suddenly the sword was pulled down, mating with a slot in the backpack amidst sparks of plasma! Josef leapt back in shock, then adjusted his spectacles and laughed. Rubbing his paws and raising a finger at Janoah, he tried to pull the sword away - it would not budge.

"You try," he said, gesturing politely.

Janoah looked wary.

"It's quite safe."

Steeling herself, Janoah picked her way through the pieces of Rafe's deconstructed suit like a mother stepping through her child's toys, and grasped the hilt of the sword.

"A good tug," Josef stipulated.

Janoah pulled – the sword came away without complaint, save for an arc of plasma or two and a kind of stickiness, like invisible treacle.

"How?" the Prefect marvelled.

Josef spread a paw, "Your corona counteracts the backpack's attractive field. Only a Howler can remove the sword, if the backpack is turned on. I was considering for some time how to conveniently hitch such a long sword to Rafe's back without ungainly belts. I think it's an elegant solution."

Thrusting the sword at Josef, Janoah raised her paws as if washing her hands of it all. "Look, do whatever you have to do, Grau, but get it back together by morning! It'd better be working or Ulf help you."

As Janoah about-faced, she found Olivia peering inside the secretive van, like a cub at a sweet shop window. Stepping down, Janoah pushed Olivia aside and slammed the door firmly behind her.

Josef locked it.

Janoah walked wordlessly on, leaving Olivia transfixed by the pops and flashes of Josef's unabated welding. The white light beamed through the door cracks lighting up half her gaping face.

On her way out, Janoah stopped beside Sara and threw a green-eyed glance back at the van. "You should keep your friend away from there, if you know what's good for her."

Suddenly, Rafe spluttered into wakefulness.

"Jan!"

"Rafe?" Janoah said, coming over. "I'm here. It's all right."

"Someone's... outside," the blindfolded Rafe grunted, twisting on the table. "Powerful... familiar. Yeah, yeah, he was at the refinery."

"One of the Chakaa hyenas?"

"Dunno... can't remember. It's getting stronger."

Janoah drew her rapier and hurried to the carriage's coupling doors.

She scanned the station.

Yes, someone was out here; *two* someone's, their cloaked shapes stealing across the platform. Janoah hopped across and hid against the opposite carriage. She waited for the strangers to pass her, then jumped down with her pistol.

"Hold it right there," she said.

The figures froze.

"Paws up. Slowly, mind. Turn around-"

"Jan, it's me."

A frown, a scoff, "Uther?"

"Aye."

Both wolves turned around.

"Linus?" Janoah seethed in further incredulity.

"Marm," replied the blonde Howler; his red cloak appeared almost black in the feeble light, and his build resembled a hyena more than the average wolf.

Janoah looked about for Hummels, then beckoned her ex-comrades over into the shadows. "By Ulf you should be halfway across Everdor by now!" she hissed at Uther. "The farm's in Grunrose, you fool, not Hummelton. What're you still doing here?"

"I couldn't waltz about in plain sight; the station was crawling with beasts. I had to wait for nightfall."

"You're in disguise!"

"Puh! ALPHA uniform is like a beacon out here, not a disguise. This is Hummelton, not Lupa, even I know that."

Exasperated, Janoah turned to Linus, "And what do *you* want, Mills?"

"To help," he replied.

"Help? You?"

"If what Uther says is true, then I'd rather do something than sit here waiting to be gassed from the sky."

"Then you know," Janoah breathed. "It's just a theory. I could be wrong, but it's-"

"What you'd do," Linus finished. "Sounds logical."

The Prefect nodded, glanced around, moved on. "Grunrose is on the other side of Everdor; you'll need transport to make it before dawn. I don't care *who* you have to clonk over the head, just get on a mono and get going, now!"

"W-www-we need a map," Linus stammered for the first time in a while; it was Janoah, she was simply too intimidating for words!

"Map?" she spat, looking at Linus as if he were a perfect idiot.

"Well d-d-directions, m-mmm-marm. Anything."

"By Ulf's fangs *ask* someone when you get to Grunrose. Stop at a village. Use your brains, Howlers-"

"Ah can help."

Everyone looked up at Sara, peering down at them from the carriage door.

"Ah can get ye a bike," she claimed boldly, "and Ah know the way tae Rumney Farm, more or less."

Chapter 49

Noss paced Nurka's tent, steeling himself for the task at paw, planning his words. Suddenly he was disturbed by hyena snarls and whoops filling the cold night air of Kambi Mata. Peering through the tent flaps, the prince was horrified to see Madou and Themba at the head of a gang of hyenas dragging a muddied, bound Howler after them.

Tomek!

Noss emerged at once, striding towards Madou. "What's going on here?"

"You tell me, my Prince," Madou replied, his voice tinged with a caustic, sarcastic sting well above his rank.

Big Themba bowed and grumbled, "This... traitor stole a truck, my Prince, him and Casimir."

Tomek was duly dropped to the ground and kicked.

"Touch him again and I'll kill you!" Noss barked at the lesser hyenas, making them bow and scrape at once. He could see no sign of Casimir, which meant he was either dead, or on his way to Hummelton. "Stole a truck?" the prince mocked his fellow Chakaa. "For what purpose?"

"To escape and warn the Howlers of our intention to attack tomorrow," Themba explained, or just assumed.

"But the Howlers surely know we're to attack the Summit."

"They know when," Madou corrected, "but not how."

"None of us know Nurka's plan, certainly not Tomek."

"Not even you, my Prince?" Madou asked.

Noss dodged the question, "Madou, Themba, this must be a misunderstanding. Nurka obviously sent Casimir to fulfil some task and Tomek joined him."

"I don't think so, my Prince."

"Well I do, Madou!" Noss said, flashing his teeth. "This wolf saved all our lives, including mine, and this is how you repay him, with doubt and brutality?"

Madou said soberly, "It's because he did those things in the caves that he's not already dead."

Noss growled, "And where's the rabbit, Casimir?"

"He *is* dead."

"By your paw, Chakaa Madou?"

Chakaa Madou said nothing, but averted his purple eyes to the camp. "Where's Nurka? Find him someone; we must have this out with him here to listen-"

"We'll have this out now!" Noss snarled. "Untie this wolf at once."

"No."

"Madou... do you defy me, your anointed Prince?"

A sharp breath, a raised chin, "I do."

Noss nodded, grunted, then suddenly reached out with a big paw, slapping it to Madou's chest with a spectacular blast of plasma.

Pfffzaack!

"Gahaaagh-gah!" Madou somersaulted through the night air and thudded on his back. Sitting up at once he coughed and kicked his way back a few feet, grasping at his throbbing chest all the way, his cloak blackened and smouldering in the shape of Noss's paw.

"My Prince!" Themba snarled indignantly, turning on Noss with his hammer in paws.

"You too?" Noss enquired, focussing his furious eyes on Themba. "Usurper are we, Chakaa Themba?"

The big hyena withered before the prince's glare. "Tomek was... he was trying to escape-"

Grasping Themba's hammer in one paw, Noss channelled an imperious bolt down the shaft, shocking Themba into letting go with a painful yelp.

"Yowffgh!"

The Prince swung the hefty hammer away with contempt, flinging it across the camp like a champion athlete, which he was, an imperium-fuelled one. "Wave your hammer at me again, boy, and I'll kill you!" he bellowed. He looked at Themba, Madou and the lesser hyenas cowering roundabout, most of them with their noses touching mud by now. "Be glad a Prince rules you. When my ferocious grandmother ruled the Jua-mata, she had hyenas staked out in the sun for so much as a curt word against our royal blood! How soft we've grown. How fat. No wonder we're reduced to such cowardly acts as gassing beasts with black-imperium to get our own way! It disgusts me that you stoop even this low, but Nurka... he would have you crawl lower yet, on your bellies, like worms!"

At that moment Nurka himself strode into the camp at the head of a swarm of hyenas, a hundred or more by the looks. With black and white banners tied to glowing imperium spears like an army of old, they filed into Kambi Mata.

One of the banners depicted a black circle ringed by tight, eye-watering zigzags that bent one's vision. Looking out from the centre of this dazzling, sun-like halo was the painted white face of a hyena, eyeless like a skull, yet furred, as if half rotted, the dry hide still clinging to the bleached bones. It resembled the living hyenas standing beneath, only far more terrifying. The flag was effective not for its fangs, but for its haunting, dead-eyed gaze.

Upon meeting said gaze, Prince Noss felt he was looking upon an old friend. This was the flag of his once mighty tribe, the Jua-mata, banned from the Reservations and not seen flying for years. What a glorious sight!

And yet how wretched, Noss thought, flying under THORN.

Nurka stopped some yards distant from the transfixed Noss, and raising his right paw halted his hyena army behind him. The column ceased their advance and stood in silence.

"What's going on here?" Nurka rasped, paws tucked behind back as usual. He looked between Themba and Madou, then to Noss, drawing his eyes from the flag at last, "I step out for five minutes and you're all at each other's throats, even you my Prince."

Madou scrabbled to his feet and clasping his aching chest stumbled over to Nurka. "Chief," he said.

"Madou, you're wounded."

"Chief... Tomek and Casimir-"

"Yes, I know," Nurka cut him short, clapping a paw to Madou's burly shoulder and shaking him. "Well done running them down, not that it matters." He looked to Noss, "Amael's conspirators have infiltrated Hummel as completely as the rest of the packs; Howlers, Watchers, Politzi, there are sympathisers posted at all key positions. Any warning will be intercepted and not passed to their Den Mother Cora, or anyone else." Brushing past Madou, Nurka spread a reasonable paw at Noss, "My Prince, the rot must be bad with you today. I propose we go to your tent and speak privately-"

"My mind has never been clearer!" Noss replied, with a menacing tooth-flash. "The white-imperium I was necessitated to take in Gelb, may the Sky forgive me, has... reinvigorated my mind. I swear, I'm like a new hyena. Hahahahaaa!"

Nurka's nostrils flared beneath his skull helm. "As you must be, my Prince, to laugh at such a sacrilegious act!"

"Do you judge me, Nurka, your Prince?"

"As I would any traitor!"

With audible gasps reverberating about the camp, Noss gestured at the muttering hyenas all around, "Why don't you tell them, Nurka? Why don't you tell them what it is our noble race is to do tomorrow, what they have been working towards all this time?"

Nurka agreed with a nod, "That is precisely why I've gathered everybody here. I confided in you first, Prince Noss, as is your right, but you have betrayed us by sending Tomek and Casimir on an errand for your Lupan masters – I had you watched, so do not deny it." The chief nodded at Tomek, lying in the mud, "I can respect the wolf's decision, it's his kind at stake, and Casimir was but a flighty little beast, but you, a noble hyena prince, siding with those who keep us in bondage? I prayed to the Wind I was mistaken, or that you might even admit to me the circumstances you had been forced into. Regrettably you have failed my test of trust."

Noss raised his chin, "Nobody is *my* judge, boy."

"Oh? Not even Vladimir of the Bloodfangs? Doesn't he have you under his paw? Doesn't he claim to have Princess Arjana and her sacred cubs at his mercy? Does he not control you through them?"

Silence.

"Mantis got your tongue, I see," Nurka scoffed. "When I learnt from my sources you were alive I also learnt who stood to gain by sparing your life – Vladimir Bloodfang."

Noss's eyes twitched.

Emboldened, Nurka went on, "You struck a bargain with this Vladimir to spare your family and testify against Amael when he was brought down. He later asked you to betray THORN. He knew I would rescue you and is relying on you to provide him with intelligence, is that not so? That is why you live, because Vladimir needs you." Nurka spread a paw, "Still, I understand your predicament. Come, let's go to my tent and talk this over in private. There's something you must know-"

"Touch me and I'll shoot a bolt of plasma through your body so hearty your eyes will boil out your pretty face," Noss said – he just said it, no raised voice.

Nurka withdrew his paw, tucked it behind him. He cleared his throat. "I wish only to make peace here, my Prince."

"Peace? You and Amael would make a desolation," Noss replied steadily. He gestured at the banners, "You shame the Jua-mata, flying our flag under the name of THORN, as if you have the backing of the Matriarchs."

"My Prince, you do not understand-"

"Do not 'my Prince' me and then call me an idiot!" Noss barked. He took a sharp, calming breath, "I understand, Nurka, what you clearly do not, that I am your Prince, regardless of all other considerations. That is the law of our people punishable by the gods with damnation." He pointed above, at the Wind and Sky, then down at Mother Erde, "They command me, and I you, whether I be mad, or sane or somewhere in-between, as we Chakaa all are." He cackled a little, casting his unnatural purple eyes about the camp, at the sea of hyena faces, their combined gaze averted down in respect. "Jua-mata, members of THORN, you will lay down your arms, all of you. There is to be no final plan, no stealing of an airship, no abuse of black-imperium; none of the madness Nurka described to me in that tent! He speaks to me of sickness, yet *he's* the beast who plans to indiscriminately gas thousands of innocent citizens. It's true! He plans to drop black-imperium on Hummelton, from the sacred Sky, killing not only the oppressive Howlers but the whole city and no doubt the land itself for a hundred miles around. He plans on doing the same to Lupa, killing millions! This is the work of a sick mind consumed by hatred and fear. It is the work of a coward and mad beast that you will not follow a day longer. Yes… wolfkind oppresses us, I feel your pain, but Nurka's plan would destroy our whole people and bring ruin on us for generations! What race would deal with us after we had betrayed decency itself? None! We would be outcast from civilisation, hunted down and destroyed, like locusts. Amael knows this and will blame us and us alone for the war to come." Noss growled finally, "As your anointed Prince my word is law and I utterly reject and forbid this venture. We will find another way out; an *honourable* way."

Only the fluttering skull banner of the Jua-mata disturbed the peace.

As the dust of Noss's pitch settled, Madou limped over to Nurka. "Is it true?" he grunted. "Is *that* your plan?"

Nurka said nothing.

"Chief!" Madou snarled, grabbing his leader's arm. "Tell me he's lying. That Tomek's lying too. Please!"

The chief's burning eyes flitted to Madou, like a beast waking up from a trance. He turned away and gestured to his equally dazed followers to bring something forward.

Madou demanded again, "Chief!"

Nurka ignored him but for a glance and the words, "Shut up and bow, Madou."

Then, to Madou's bewilderment, Nurka faced his army and prostrated himself in the mud. Had he given in to Prince Noss's authority? If so, he was facing the wrong way. How strange.

"Chief?" Madou piped in confusion.

Noss, meanwhile, looked on as the gathered THORN hyenas parted ways, shuffling aside as someone or something nestled in the midst of Nurka's army came to the fore.

Slowly, the apex of a small, black and white tent emerged from the forest of imperium spears – a royal litter.

It couldn't be.

The striped litter was carried aloft on ornate wooden poles by a team of muscled hyenas in traditional garb, their necks and arms rattling with necklaces and bracelets made of insect wings, fangs and carapaces. They walked slowly and reverently into the open and, without the slightest wobble, set the litter down somewhat shy of Nurka and Madou. They then bowed on all fours.

Madou's legs inevitably gave way under the crushing weight of hyena custom as it dawned upon him what this must be. He fell to his knees beside Nurka, equals before a greater authority. Themba and the rest of the hyenas followed suit, bending like stalks of corn under a gust of wind.

Only Prince Noss remained standing.

The litter stirred, the flaps parted, and a marvellous beast stepped elegantly into the open – no hyena, but a hyeness. She was wreathed in magnificent, flowing garbs of pure black that devoured the sunlight falling upon her, like so much black-imperium. Her face, conversely, was painted gold, fur, nose and lips, all sparkling as the sun on wet sand. Perched upon her head stood a tall cylindrical crown marked with swirling patterns of black and white depicting, as all here well-knew, the sacred wind.

Her face was the sun, her robes the black erde, her crown the wind and sky; in this sacred hyeness were embodied all the Gods, not just one or two, for she was above Princes, Chiefs and Matriarchs, she was a Hyena Queen.

To Noss she was yet more. Even with a face of gold he recognised her features, her poise.

"Arjana?"

Queen Arjana said nothing as she approached Noss, foot over bejewelled sandalled foot, calm and self-possessed, her golden face unmoving even as she looked upon her mate for the first time in a year, even as Noss's hefty brow twisted and quivered in unbelieving comprehension.

"You're free?" he articulated at last.

"Yes, my husband," Arjana replied, detachedly. "And a Queen, as I was destined to become."

"Our cubs?"

Arjana's golden eyelids flitted. "Taken from me, by the guards."

"Taken?"

"They tore them from my arms in the re-education camp as punishment for refusing to raise them as… citizens," Arjana choked on the word citizen. "My servants too. Everyone. The hogs locked me away, beat me and starved me. They enjoyed it. I suffered great indignities unbefitting even the lowliest rank before our Nurka was were able to find and extract me. He lost many good hyenas doing so." She turned a little, looking down on her saviour with her golden face, "We are grateful to Chief Nurka for our deliverance, and yours. When I learned you were alive I sent for him to save you at any cost, which he did without question." Arjana raised her chin a little, looking Noss over, "I am grieved to hear the poisonous words of the wolf Vladimir and the cursed imperium in your veins have both turned your wits against us, but it is no fault of your own. How could you know he lied to you? That I was free? But I know you will do what is right now that you too are free to act upon your own wishes again."

Noss's mouth moved, but no words came forward.

Arjana continued, "I am Queen; the last hyeness of royal blood, and you the last true prince. When Lupa falls we will process into the wolfen capital together and found a new dynasty. The hyenas will become the prime race on this continent, and a great tribe again-"

"Process into a capital made desolate by black-imperium?" Noss spluttered at once. "Arjana, my love, Nurka's mad, don't you see?"

"Mad?"

"He's going to gas thousands with black-imperium! Not just the Summit, but everyone for miles around-"

"With a balloon, yes."

Noss's eyes narrowed, "You know?"

"Of course I know my husband; I planned it," Arjana revealed, adding, "I commanded Nurka to make it so."

"What?"

"Part of our cubs' re-education were classes on the benefits of imperium science and technology – the justification for the rape of Mother Erde as told by Howlers." Arjana looked across to Tomek like a spider might upon her prey, bound up in silk and waiting to be finished off. She turned back to Noss, "They let the children visit me, hoping it would turn my wits as they turned yours, but I was stronger than that – my mind is not clouded by the rot. I listened as my children described the 'dirigible' they had seen on the moving pictures. Zuma was especially excited." The Queen smiled a moment, he composure crumpling under sweet memories. "He was so like you. If you could've seen him, Noss; such a fool, but so handsome and strong already." Her golden countenance hardened, "It was the last time I saw them, but I remembered their lesson well. When Nurka brought me here to safety and told me his plan to kill the Den Fathers with a black-imperium bomb I knew it would not be enough. I knew we must go further, further even than the traitor Amael. He must die too. He thinks we will stop at Hummelton, but we will go on to Lupa with the balloon and finish him with the rest. Every Howler Den will be showered with our black rain. No wolf of rank must survive. They will all rot and their city stand empty forever more, like the Dead Cities of old." Arjana stepped closer to Noss, "You are right we will not process into Lupa, my husband, that was a figure of speech. We will return to the wilds and live as beasts were meant to, healthy and free. All beasts will live that way again."

Noss shook his head. He raised his paws as if to grasp his wife by the shoulders and shake sense into her, but refrained at the last inch. "Arjanaaaa," he seethed, his paws flopping to his sides, "don't you understand? We cannot turn back the clock. We cannot go back to the wilds. How would we defend ourselves? The next race that came across the waters wielding imperium spears would conquer us in a heartbeat! The wolves have kept peace for centuries, as the cats have on their continent, both using imperium. They conquered *us* with it. Without it we are nothing as well. What are we without Chakaa? Mere little beasts without power. What you and Nurka propose is madness. Killing the Den Fathers… I could see that through. But to murder every living thing between here and Lupa, and in such a manner, should be beneath our contempt! If we go through with this we are no better than the cowards who daily bully and murder our brothers and sisters in the Reservations, who killed Themba's family, and Madou's and Nurka's."

The three Chakaa looked up a little.

"If we do this act," Noss said to all, "we will become the barbarians they say we are, and justify *everything* they have done to us up to this day. And we will not survive a year longer, let alone found a dynasty, because no race who commits such a crime as mass black-imperium poisoning will be allowed to exist lest we did the same to another." The prince then implored his wife, "Arjana, think of our cubs. Their future."

"Their future?" she replied. "Did you not understand me? They're dead, my love."

One could almost hear the wind being sucked from Noss's lungs as Arjana's words punched him in the gut, his muscle-packed belly no defence against the crippling blow.

"Dead?" he rasped at Arjana. "Our little Zuma and Anjali?"

"Your Howler, Vladimir, he came to me. When I begged for help, on my knees, he told me he could do nothing. The re-education camp the wolves had made for the moving pictures had been dismantled, the houses and roads and schools knocked down and every hyena in it… 'disposed of'." Arjana's glittering, golden cheek was wetted by a single tear, "He apologised and left me, promising he would work for my release if you kept to your end of his bargain. I should have killed myself, freeing you sooner. But then he would have killed you. I lived for you, my Prince. Only you."

"Heheheheeee," Noss chuckled. "Hahahahahaahaheehee!" He collapsed on his knees, his laughter dissolving into vents of anguish, "Hahahaaahohohoow! By the Wind, no! Nohohooo!"

Forgoing all protocol and etiquette expected of a female hyena of such unassailable rank, Arjana knelt with Noss and embraced his heaving shoulders. "We are young and you are still healthy, my sweet, mad Chakaa," she whispered in his ear, leaving a streak of gold where her nose touched his fur. "We will have more cubs. I'll bring them into a world where the wolves are not even reduced to our slaves, but gone." She finished with a growl, "I swear it!"

The Queen let her Prince cry into her black robes, before grasping his tear-streaked cheeks and making him look into her golden visage.

"See now? Do you understand the searing pain? You sided with the wolves for years and look what it's got you!" She stood up, the comforting wife no longer, but the hard Queen again, "No more doubts, Prince Noss of the Four Winds. I declare the Howler in you dead, and your love for that vile race with it. You will help Chakaa Nurka complete his task. I command you, as Queen. Kneel and swear you will."

Already kneeling, Noss remained so, tears rolling down his thick black muzzle and over his broad nose that bubbled with the mucous of grief.

"I swear," he croaked. "I swear it."

Nurka and Themba exchanged looks of relief.

Arjana, however, glanced sideways, "Now... kill the wolfen spy you conspired with, my husband."

Noss emitted a snort. He looked slowly up that black robe, to that golden face crowned with white. Beneath the guise of power was a hyeness once so beautiful to him, now she was barely recognisable for her bloodlust.

"Prove yourself," she said.

"Tomek... he s-sss-saved my life," Noss excused. "He saved all our lives. It would be dishonourable to-"

"If you are such a coward that you cannot kill *one* wolf you cannot kill a thousand!" Arjana blasted, huffing like a disappointed teacher. "You could not even kill Rufus Red-mist, I hear. Are you a hyena or a mouse?"

Noss dipped his chin with shame.

The Queen grunted, "I see." She turned slightly, "You, Chakaa Madou, isn't it?"

The blood-stained Madou stumbled forward, then knelt again, head low, "Yes, my Queen?"

"Show our soft-minded Prince how a warrior is meant to behave. Execute the wolfen spy."

A pause, an uncertain, "As you command, my Queen-"

"Madou!" Noss snapped, rising up. "Don't. I beg you, as your teacher and friend. Help me."

Madou stared for an age, but for all his power and supposed infallibility, Noss was merely a Prince; as with the ants and bees and wasps there were no kings amongst hyenas, only male consorts. Slowly turning and taking an imperium spear from a hyena, Madou walked over to the wounded Tomek – a quick thrust to the heart and his suffering would be over. It would be an honourable end for a wolf. Madou felt he would be glad of such a death. Besides, it was Queen Arjana's will. She could not be denied.

Madou raised his spear, hesitated, steeled himself again and made to strike.

Suddenly a paw on the shoulder turned him around. A second paw, a fist to be exact, struck him in the stomach whilst the first relieved him of his spear. Prince Noss then blasted the young hyena away with an imperious shock to his helmeted face, knocking him out cold, or worse.

Nurka and Themba leapt up as one, *"Madou!"*

"There will be no murder here today as long as I stand!" Noss snarled. Spear held forth he stood over Tomek and pointed at the hyenas, "I do not envy your choice brothers, your insane Queen, or your mad Prince, but at least I have the excuse of being a Chakaa. Hahahaaaahaha!"

"Noss, you fool!" Arjana cried, her litter bearers moving to protect her. "Bow to me, or I will end you, I swear it! I will not let even you destroy THORN'S dream!"

"The dream is over already, Arjana! The black-imperium is gone! It has been destroyed!"

Nurka rasped for all, "What?"

Noss grinned broadly, "Forgotten Red-mist, Nurka? I was merely a distraction! He fooled you all along, at every step, and yet you are so clever?" Swinging his spear overhead the prince laughed, "Hahahahahaaaaahaha! Now come at me, boy! End my suffering once and for all!"

Themba grunted, "Go Nurka. Quickly!"

Nurka nodded and said with strange calm, "Protect the Queen."

The chief then hurried into the woods with some hyenas in tow, leaving Themba and the others to trap a hysterical Noss in a closing circle of spears.

"Hahahaaahahaaaa!"

✦

Rufus pushed through the thorn bushes, and staggered into the cave's mouth – his already wounded frame totting up a few more scratches.

It won't matter soon, Red-mist.

Running a paw over his faded old brooch to light the path, the Howler picked his way gingerly along the passage. Left, Noss had said, on the left. *Does he know what I'm going to do? Has he guessed? If he manages to turn things around back at Kambi Mata I'll be doing this for nought. But if he doesn't, then this is for all. Even if we both fail, Tomek will get word out and give them a chance back at Hummelton.*

Stay safe, dear Jan. And goodbye.

A slit in the cave wall; Rufus stopped thinking, stopped moving, rooted by fear. Steeling himself, he edged over, his brooch light revealing them; dozens of black canisters, all marked with red X's and warnings. Each one contained a million drops of black-imperium, a million deadly doses, in theory enough to kill the entire population of Lupa.

The great taboo had been broken by the hyenas, of all the races they have been pushed here first, and by my own arrogant kind. War waged by black-imperium, chemical warfare, the end of civilisation, was knocking at the world's gate. It will start here today if I don't stop it. I have to save us from ourselves.

Rufus marched into the cave and seized one of the canisters by its bright red valve. *Just do it, Howler. Do it now!*

"Forgive me, Jan," Rufus whined, attacking the stiff valve with both paws. Flecks of rust fell away from the canister and arcs of plasma sparked off Rufus's powerful arms as he summoned all his imperious might to overcome both years of corrosion and the phobia of eons.

Pffffsssssssss!

The black cloud issued forth, the air went opaque, poisoning everything in the cave forever. Rufus kept twisting the valve, eyes closed, lungs held, resisting the will to take flight a moment longer even as every muscle in his legs turned to jelly.

Enough!

He whirled away, his breath held still, and staggered through the cave. His arms were blackened, though he dare not look close and witness them decomposing before his eyes. *It would start there and work its way through, you know it's true. There's no escape. None. If I can just see the stars again.*

Into the moonlight, through the thorn bushes, Rufus fell, rolled, trembling into a ball, his paws tucked close as if to try and shore them up against disintegration.

It doesn't hurt. That's good. Perhaps it doesn't hurt? Must be the adrenaline. Thank Ulf.

Time passed. Rufus panted. Shook.

He came to realise he was still here, still feeling, and apart from his old wounds no worse for wear. He slowly unravelled his arms and inspected his quivering paws before the light of his brooch.

They were black, but intact, fur and flesh still clinging to bone. *How could it be?*

"Don't worry, Red-mist," Nurka rasped – his voice was unmistakable even at a distance. "You'll live. Perhaps long enough to see Lupa fall."

Rufus remained where he lay as panting hyenas surrounded him with glowing imperious spear tips. Nurka stepped to the fore, paws behind back with outward calm, purple eyes shimmering with inner fury.

"They're just canisters of ash," he stated simply.

"A decoy," Rufus realised, falling back on the soil, relieved and yet appalled at his own gullibility.

"Correct," Nurka confirmed, reaching down and rubbing his fingers on a length of Rufus's blackened cloak, then tasting the acrid ash on his tongue, as if to prove it harmless. "I showed our prince this place. I see he told you where to find it. Ironic that I long-expected him, a hyena, to betray us, but not you, a wolf. I thought you were our only true friend amongst your kind. Live and learn."

"I'm a friend of justice," Rufus replied, a spear tickling his chin, "but this isn't the way, Nurka. Please... think of what you're embarking upon-"

"I've thought ten years about it!" Nurka blasted, shaking a plasmatic fist. "Since I watched your people pitch my family into their graves I've thought about nothing else!"

"My family was murdered too!"

Nurka paused a moment. "In your Wolfen Wars, in great combat between packs, as hyena tribes warring! What's that honourable end compared to being swept up and squashed like lice?"

Rufus shot back, "No, Nurka! No. My family was *murdered*. It was before the war, back when I was just a cub. My mother was killed for being a Howler, my father for being married to a Howler, and my siblings for being the offspring of Howlers. It didn't matter how guilty my mother was, or my father, or how innocent my brothers and sisters, they were all lumped in together as the enemy. And do you know who rounded them up and shot them as I hid in the loft like a coward?"

Silence.

"A mob of little beasts, just like Casimir, driven to hate by misery and oppression, as he was. But I do not hold it against his whole people. That way madness lies."

Nurka's nostrils flared.

"Drop your black death on Lupa," Rufus said, "and you will open the door to the end of civilisation. The Dead Cities stand as testament to that! Do you want to set us back a thousand years, or do you want to help find the answer?"

"Answer?"

"A cure, Nurka, for the rot. If anyone knew it, or was even close, our ancestors were. The technology that lies out there may hold the key to ending all our suffering-"

"Enough of your wolfen lies!" Nurka spat, snatching a spear and ramming the blunt butt into Rufus's raw belly, causing the Howler to curl up in pain.

"Gaaagffrrgh!"

"The answer is an end to your vile technology and of the rape of Mother Erde!" the chief decreed, throwing the spear down. "Wire him!" he sniffed at his hyenas. "Let our Queen decide what's to be done with him."

⁂

It was a good fight, but even Noss was no match for an army. For a time none dared look at him, let alone strike him, their infallible, untouchable Prince, but Arjana was Queen and if she decreed her husband was no longer fit to rule then that was as certain as the sun rising tomorrow. He was sick in his mind, she said. For his own protection he had to be taken down. We are doing him a favour. They attacked tentatively at first, their timid spears knocked aside by Noss's ferocious swings. Urged on by their Queen they grew bolder, until the dam of sanity broke all out fighting ensued with hyenas coming at Noss from all around. He sent them on their way with swift spear-blows to the head and neck, twisting, turning, spinning, plasma arcing down the shaft and ejecting challengers from the living arena. With every hyena that was felled Noss grew weaker, his paws burning, his soul sapping, until Big Themba himself overcame his last dregs of lingering respect and entered the fray with a great hammer-blow out of left field, breaking Noss's spear in two and diving on him.

"Hahahaaaahaha!" Noss bellowed as they rolled in the mud. "Come on then, Thembaaahahahaaaa!"

They wrestled with Themba's hammer, itself sparking with plasma. The head glowed red-hot, then the whole shaft became unbearable to hold and the two Chakaa had to let it fall sizzling in a puddle.

After a brief exchange of plasmatic thumps and blows to the snout, ribs and belly each, Themba kicked Noss away. They separated, circled one another, panting, paws smouldering, noses bleeding. Tomek lay forgotten, lost to Noss amongst the tumult of bodies, smell of gore and singed fur.

"My Prince!" Themba begged. "Stop this!"

"Stop?" Noss laughed. "My wife is mad, my pupils murderers and my children dead, there is nothing left to do now but die!" he seethed at Themba, thumping his mighty chest with both fists. "Come on, cub, you can do iiiit!"

As Themba steeled himself for a second bout, someone pushed through the hyenas and grabbed the hammer, now cooled in the puddle.

It was Madou!

In the noise and violence, Noss failed to notice the stocky hyena coming up behind him until the hammer struck him square in the back with a mighty blast. Amidst a distinctly hyena yelp, Noss flew forward and tumbled across the impromptu arena, hyenas retreating from his sacred body as he rolled to a stop, his back smoking from the blow. He tried to rise, chuckled a moment, then fell flat on his chin, his tongue lolling.

It was over.

Madou dropped the hammer with a start and looked at his offending paws.

"I struck… a prince!" he wailed. "What've I done? Themba, I've killed our Prince!"

Themba hurried over and held Madou's wrists firm, lest he used them to injure himself in retribution. "Calm yourself, Madou!"

"But-"

"It is the Queen's will! It is *her* will. You are absolved of any crime."

Madou both nodded and shook his head all at once.

The silent sea of shocked hyenas parted in a wave and bowed as Queen Arjana herself approached. Themba and Madou fell on their knees, grovelling at her black-robed passing. She glided over to the downed Noss and, after a considerable pause, knelt and placed a tentative paw on his back.

"The Prince lives," she declared, standing up and raising her paws to the sacred Sky in thanks. "Tend to him," she commanded, stepping back and allowing her hyenas to carry him away whilst she followed. "Take him to our tent. His madness will pass and he will see. When all is done, he *will* understand."

✦

Hummelton was under curfew and security around castle-like Den was tight, but Sara Hummel not only knew all the back alleys and passages of her humble home town, but also how to spin a convincing yarn as an accoutrement to her evidently formidable status around here.

"Who goes there?" a Hummel Howler growled – a Halberdier in fact, dripping with armour and looking ferocious indeed. "Sara?" he gasped, raising his kristahl halberd as the distinctively dinky daughter of Den Mother Cora crossed the gloomy courtyard and approached the Den's garage. An athletic Alpha Prefect and a barrel-chested Bloodfang accompanied Sara.

A strange trio to be sure.

"You're back," the Hummel Halberdier scoffed, eying up the competition, "and with company Ah see."

Sara beamed, "Aye, Grant, Ah'm back again," and flapped a paw about. "Ah'm just showing some friends around, is that all right?"

"Does yer mum know?" asked this big Grant chap, scowling at the two obvious city-slickers.

"Aye, of course! Anything tae get me out of her fur. Ah have nae been here fer five minutes and she's already full tae the back teeth with mah 'daft opinions'."

Big Grant woofed, "Ah'm sure that's nae true. Ah missed ye. We all have."

"Och, away with ye, charmer!"

"'Tis the truth! Us Halberdiers nae tell fibs."

Whilst Sara took Grant's keys from his belt and opened a small door built into the larger garage door, Grant tapped his halberd on the cobbles and said, "You know there's a curfew."

"Aye, but on the streets only, nae in here."

"Aye, but-"

"We'll be five minutes," Sara claimed, returning the keys. "Mah friends like bikes, is all.

They've nae seen our quaint Hummel monos before."

"What, our tracked bikes you mean?"

"Aye, the funny tracked sort."

"They're duo's, Sara, nae monos. Got two wheels. And they're nae 'quaint' at all or 'funny'."

"Aye, alright, whatever," Sara shrugged. "Ah'm nae into them like you are."

"Puh!" Uther tutted at Grant, "Wolfesses, eh mate?"

Snorting, Halberdier Grant looked Uther over with obvious disdain, but Sara drew his ire away with easy charm and distracting words, until, before the Halberdier knew it, she and the two strangers had disappeared inside the garage.

"Smooth 'en yer," Uther gruffed, once inside the dark, heady-smelling space.

"Smoother than you, you nearly blew it," Sara hissed back.

"Me?"

"Keep yer chauvinism fer Lupa, Howler, this is Hummel."

Linus kept the peace, paws raised, voice lowered, "What now, Sara?"

Sara answered by reaching for the imperium gas lamp dial, turning the lights up until two rows of white-bodied bikes emerged from the gloom.

"There's yer ride," she said, gesturing at them. "Ah'll distract Grant; Ah can get him away from the door for ten minutes whilst you slip out. We're… old friends."

Linus *had* to ask, "Old friends?"

Sara didn't answer, not the question at least. "Go slow n' quiet out the Den," she said, tidying her fur. "Nobody will stop ye, they only really care about those coming in, nae out. At night ye Howlers all look the same anyway-"

"Where's the keys?" Uther asked, jingling an invisible set in front of Sara's button nose.

"Keys?"

"Aye! For the monos."

"Oh, no, you just turn them on here."

"Puh! Whatcha mean?"

"This is Hummelton, nae Lupa," Sara explained. She showed Uther to the nearest vehicle and the big red button on the right-paw side of the kristahl steering bars. "Just press start. Alright?"

"Hah!" the street-wise Uther marvelled. "You Hummel lot wouldn't last five minutes in Lupa."

"Says more about Lupa than us," Sara countered deftly.

Grunting his acknowledgement, Uther knelt down and felt the Hummel bike's main wheel. The rubber tyre was absent, replaced by a caterpillar track slung between the large, dominant wheel and a small subsidiary wheel trailing behind, altogether forming a rounded-off triangle in profile. Possessed of two wheels, this was strictly speaking a duo in wolfen parlance, not a mono.

"Well, it sure ain't a Valerio," Uther said, grabbing a sloshing can of imperium fuel, "but it'll have to do. We got a long ride ahead of us, Linus, best top up, mate."

"Shouldn't we take the normal ones?" Linus argued, standing by a 'normal one', by which he meant a familiar, Giacomo *Springtail* mono.

"Not over rough terrain, mate. This is Everdor. We might need to go off-road and tracks are best."

"Right. Good thinking."

Sara said, "Give me a few minutes tae take care of Grant," before tugging on Linus's red hood. "Ye got the map?"

Linus delved into his cloak pocket and unfurled the map Sara had scrawled on a piece of paper earlier. Janoah had provided said paper from the Alpha's office and it was watermarked with their infamous 'A', as well as some discarded thoughts by the Alpha himself written in near-illegible doctor's script – the mark of a genius Janoah had insisted. Something about hyenas, camps, new age and coming together, Linus hadn't time to decipher it through Sara's road lines and landmarks.

"It's only a rough guide," Sara sighed. "It's all Ah can remember from out Monty's car window."

"It's fine," Linus assured, tucking it away.

"Ah could guide you if Ah came with you–"

"No! No it's too dangerous."

"For a wolfess?" Sara huffed.

Taking one of those black paws in his golden digits, Linus grunted soberly, "For anyone but a Howler."

A nod, a smile, a "Good luck," then Sara was away.

"And you," Linus replied.

Sara Hummel nodded, then stepped out via the small door nestled within the main door – Linus decided that he and Uther should squeeze their monos, or duos, through that same door instead of noisily opening the large garage door and disturbing half the Den.

Sara's muffled words were at first impossible to interpret, but Linus tuned in well enough to get the jist of things.

"Come on, let's snuggle," Sara chirped.

"What, now?" Grant replied.

"Aye. Just fer a minute. Ah've missed ye."

"Ah'm on duty."

"And Ah'm going back tae Lupa straight after the Summit."

A long silence.

"It's now or never, Grant."

"All right, but just a minute. I can't get caught again."

Sara giggled in a way Linus had never heard before, *"Nae here, silly, come on, round the corner."*

Their chatter and giggling faded into the distance, along with the Halberdier's hefty armoured footsteps. The wolfess had successfully coaxed the wolf away from his duties.

Uther chuckled drily and shook his head. Linus was not remotely amused, but consoled himself with the thought that Sara didn't mean it.

By Ulf, why do I care so much? We're just friends.

"You know," Linus grunted, mounting his bike, "when this is over, I'll have to arrest you again."

"You can try," Uther replied, pulling his hood up.

"You should slip away and leave this to me."

"What? And let you get pummelled by hyenas? I'd never forgive myself."

Linus dipped his chin and snorted with mirth; Uther laughed and then started his bike with a kick. "These duos are a bit different to monos, Woodlouse, but I'll go slow for ya until you stop wobbling, you still being a learner 'en all."

Linus started his own 'duo', "You just try and keep up with me."

"Haha-haaa! Woodlouse! Seems like only yesterday you were a right timid little louse."

Linus's ears drooped, "I was never *that* timid, was I?"

Uther thought back to the day he and Linus had faced down that Howler-killer. "No. No I guess you weren't. Heh."

Outside, in the pretty Hummelton Den gardens, beside a fountain decorated with stone insects, Sara kept Halberdier Grant busy with stolen affection. The thrum of bike engines was subdued by the clinking of glass and bawdy laughter from within the nearby great hall as Cora Hummel threw a welcoming feast for her fellow Howlers.

Out the corner of her eyes, Sara spied Linus and Uther ride sedately through the courtyard, engines popping. Their passing drew Halberdier Grant's attention for a moment, before Sara pulled him back into her embrace.

"Never mind them, ye daft beast," she said, kissing him firmly.

"Och! Sara."

Through the main gates Linus rode, Uther following, the Hummel Halberdiers there paying little heed. Sara was right, leaving the den was obviously still allowed for now. Even with a curfew, Hummel Howlers were still about their business. The quaint Hummelton roads were otherwise devoid of activity, no cars, no citizens, just the streetlights and stars for company, and the occasional Howler pair doing the rounds. Few were perturbed by the passing of two wolves on bikes – at a glance, and by intermittent yellowish imperium streetlamps, nobody could rightly tell Hummel from Bloodfang, or even a supposed Prefect. Besides, no doubt everyone had been instructed to look out for hyenas.

More fool them.

Linus ground to a halt in the midst of a road. Uther came alongside him. "What's the matter, Woodlouse?"

"Checkpoint," Linus breathed, nodding ahead.

Sure enough the road was barred by a kiosk and a simple arm-gate. Three Howlers were milling about, bored and smouldering various embers. The road was closed in by walls, but beyond lay nothing, only blackness – the Everdor countryside.

"They'll stop us," Linus said, plucking at his Bloodfang cloak. "If we only had Hummel cloaks."

"Just run it, mate," Uther replied.

"Run it?"

"Aye! Thump 'em!"

"But the gate, Uther!" Linus seethed.

"Duck."

"Duck?"

"Lean and duck, mate. Get down right low, yeah?"

Linus stared wide-eyed at Uther, horrified at the words tumbling from his helmet grille.

"Your instructor never taught you that?" Wild-heart scoffed.

"No."

"Schmutz!"

The Howlers at the checkpoint had noticed the strangers parked in the middle of the road. One beckoned them over with a wave, suspicious already. There was no going back now.

"Look, just do what I do," Uther growled.

"Uther!"

"You can do it, Woodlouse! 'Tis easy!"

"I c-c-can't!"

"You thumping can!"

With that, Wild-heart took off down the street, his tracked bike popping and churning heartily, though it was no match for his Giacomo *Dragonfly*, even less Ivan's purring *Spider*.

Linus hurriedly stepped on the gas and followed as closely as he dared, his eyes locked on Uther's flapping cloaked shoulders. As he approached the checkpoint at ramming speed, Uther suddenly ducked down and leant steeply to the right, his body in line with the bike's, itself remaining upright whilst the rider almost dismounted altogether, his right knee and elbow an inch from scraping on the cobbles!

Under the gate! He was through!

One of the Howlers raised a pistol and shot into the night, but Uther kept on going.

Before Linus had time to think the gate was upon him, the Howlers too, paws raised, pistols too, shouting their warnings for him to stop. Heart pounding, Linus raised his left foot and slipped sideways off the deafening, quivering bike. The mono, duo, whatever it was, remained defiantly upright as Linus leant lower and lower, as far as he dared, the cobbles a blur – if he fell now he was a dead wolf. He caught sight of a pistol flash, of sparks pinging off the bike's white bodywork and flying at his helmet-clad face like shooting stars.

The gate thrummed by overhead, an inch from Linus's blonde ears if that.

I'm through! I did it!

Behind, two of the Howlers leapt on their bikes and the third picked up a telephone – the race was on.

Chapter 50

The Alpha swirled his drink – apple juice – and watched the city packs stuff themselves on the back of Hummel hospitality. The freshest food, the finest wine, a roaring fire and plenty of bunting strung between the hexagonal pillars and balconies; the reception was a magnificent do as always. The Den Fathers of each pack sat with the white-cloaked Cora at the head of the U-shaped table, with the ranks diminishing in prestige the further one ventured away, through Elders, Grand Howlers, Howlers, right down to the puny ALPHA contingent, stuck disrespectfully at the end of the U on a hastily-set extra table. The excuse went that they had not been expected to even attend back when the plans had been made and nobody had corrected the oversight since.

A blatant lie.

Den Mother Cora had offered a hasty change-around, but Adal, playing up the injury dealt him, and highlighting his own humility in the face of it, refused to displace anyone else of their rightful position, much to Horst's dismay.

"Look at them all," he complained. "Bunch of pigs. They did this on purpose."

"Mind your tongue, that's mah sister-in-law you're calling a pig!" Duncan growled.

"I didn't mean *her*," Horst insisted, tugging his cloak and setting his medals jingling.

Duncan made his excuses again, "Mah Alpha, Ah'm sure it's just an oversight. Ah know how Hummel works, 'tis run behind the scenes by wee beasts, they do all the clerical box-ticking. Cora's nae concerned with seating arrangements."

"Indeed," Adal seconded. "No matter, Duncan, this makes us look good."

"Good, my Alpha?"

"Humble; as indeed we are. Are we not, Horst?"

"Of course, but this is ridiculous," Horst blustered, peering across at some yellow-cloaked Greystones opposite, snickering and elbowing each other. "Look at them lot over there, laughing at us. It's a big joke."

The Alpha sipped his juice, "Let them laugh."

An elegant feminine Prefect crossed the hall and joined the ALPHA table, sitting in the empty space along from Duncan.

"Janoaaah!" the latter roared, raising his glass – the Hummel brandy was taking hold by the sounds. "You've joined us at last."

"Grand Prefect," Janoah saluted, and again, "My Alpha."

The white-faced Adal raised a brown paw accordingly. "Where've you been, Prefect?"

"Checking on Stenton."

A nod.

"That useless lump of yours?" Horst scoffed, tearing some bread for his second course; soup. "Josef ought to put him out of his misery. It would be a kindness."

Janoah caught a passing rabbit waiter and demanded some soup also, then, and only then, replied, "You will change your mind if Stenton is all that stands between a Republic and Amael's dictatorship, Grand Prefect."

Horst spluttered through his bread, "Fat chance! Where is he then? He should be here, protecting the Alpha, lest hyenas descend from the rafters. Instead he is bedridden, as per usual."

"Rafe has time, sir. THORN will not attack tonight."

"You know that for a fact, do you?"

Janoah explained patiently, "If Nurka plans to use black-imperium, as all evidence suggests, he will not move until Amael and the other conspirators are clear of danger. It must all have been planned most carefully. We must watch Amael's movements tomorrow. His leaving is the signal."

"For what?"

Janoah tore her own bread, "Hopefully nothing, provided the Alpha and I have outmanoeuvred him."

Horst looked to his leader. "My Alpha, have you confided in Prefect Janoah before me?"

"Not now, Horst."

"She knows your intentions more than I, clearly-"

"Whatever is being done is now beyond my control, let alone Prefect Janoah's machinations," Adal said. "It is up to agents put in place weeks ago to fulfil their duties and avert disaster. Nothing I say or do can change our fate, except to alert Amael and the conspirators to our knowledge of their plot and allow them to evade justice, and *that* I will not do. Loose tongues lose wars, remember the old propaganda?" The Alpha sipped his apple juice. "Now shut up and eat your soup. For all we know it could be our last meal."

"My Alpha, how can you joke at a time like this?"

Adal Weiss went further and allowed a rare laugh, which could not be pinned on alcohol-free apple juice.

Over at the head of the table, Cora Hummel entertained her fellow Den Fathers, Thorvald Eisbrand, Flaid Greystone, Amael Bloodfang and the two Bloc representatives sent this year whose names escaped many, their packs being so puny and obscure as to be drowned in the greater eddies of Lupan politics, not that the diplomatic Cora let on. Her husband, Angus, was relegated to sitting some seats over, supplanted by even the lowly posteriors of the Bloc Den Fathers who, even in their obscurity, were more important than some spouse. Angus Hummel was merely the 'Queen Bee's' drone, kept around to provide Cora with company and cubs, and to nurture them whilst she got on and ran the vast Hummel territory of Everdor, everyone knew that. He did have her ear though, everyone knew that too, and thus took great heed of him despite his total inability to wield imperium, a rare thing in Howler circles.

Angus himself took heed of one Den Father in-particular. "Good for you, Amael!" he said, shouting across more than a few faces and raising his glass. "Sticking it tae ALPHA. That's what Ah like tae see."

"I've no intention of being bullied," the stone-grey Amael replied cordially.

"They will be suitably chastised," said the big, grey-cloaked Flaid, nestled between Amael and Cora. "Some form of cross-pack regulation is necessary, of course, but ALPHA's wings must be… clipped."

"Pulled off more like," Angus said.

Thorvald stayed out of the debate, thrumming his fingers on the tabletop and picking at his food, whilst Cora's lips remained sealed by well-timed sips of Hummel brandy. Did they disagree or were they just being gracious? It won't matter come this time tomorrow, Amael thought, none of this will.

Some Hummel Howlers approached, both female; one whispered in Cora's pricked black ears.

The Den Mother looked up with a start and mopping her mouth excused herself.

"What's wrong, Cora?" Thorvald asked with a familiarity bred from decades.

"Mah daughter's here," she replied, adding, "Aye, *that* daughter."

"Your eldest?"

"Aye. Ah was nae expecting her." The Den Mother threw aside her napkin. "If you'll excuse me gentlebeasts, Ah'll return shortly."

Angus also made to rise.

"Stay, Angus," his wife commanded, marching off with her fellow Howlers.

Sipping his brandy, Amael watched her go and looked to Flaid. "Where's she going?"

"Sounds like her eldest daughter is in town," Flaid grunted. "They don't get on, I hear."

✥

Glancing back at the ward doors, Meryl slapped Tristan on the cheek, gently, if rapidly.

"Tristan. Tristan wake up. Tristan!"

"Ungh… grrfffgh!" he snorted. "Meryl? What… w-www-where am I?"

"Sit up. Come on. Up you get, Howler."

"I can't. I feel so… tired."

"I've given you a little taubfene, enough to stop the pain but not knock you out. You'll feel odd, but you should be able to walk. Now get up. Come on!"

At length, little Meryl levered the huge, languid Howler upright; on top of her medical training she'd had a lot of practise of late shifting Rafe's unmanageable bulk.

The numbed Tristan noticed himself. "W-w-what've they done to me?" he yelped, horrified eyes searching his bandaged arms and scorched fur. "What happened? I... I remember-"

"Tristan, listen to me!" Meryl snapped, grasping his face. "Nikita tried to kill you. He tried to rack you to death to cover his tracks, do you understand? Do *not* go back to him or anyone else involved in the conspiracy, and stay away from the Eisbrands too, at least until things blow over and Thorvald returns... if he ever does."

Tristan shook his head, "Thorvald's not to be harmed, Meryl. I'd never put his life in-"

"I don't want to hear about it!" Meryl hissed, paws raised. "I don't care what you've done, just get dressed. I'll slip you out of ALPHA HQ, for old times' sake."

Tears streaked from Tristan's duotone eyes, "Oh, Meryl... I...."

"Save it, you foolish wolf. Now hurry, before the nightshift takes over."

✧

"Sara."

"Mum."

Mother and daughter met in a quiet side atrium, with Halberdier Grant and a few other Howlers, including the ones who had summoned the Den Mother hither.

"What's this Ah'm told?" Cora demanded sharply, looking between Sara and a shame-faced Grant. "Helping perfect strangers steal bikes tae go joy-riding, is that what you get up tae these days?"

"No!"

"Then what? Explain yourself, daughter, before Ah banish ye from Everdor forever!"

Sara looked about at Grant and the Howlers. "Can we have some privacy here?"

Cora replied, "Whatever need be said, can be said in front of our loyal Howlers-"

"Mum!" Sara piped. "This is the present day, nae the Dark Age. Speak tae me normally, all right?"

At length, Cora dismissed her followers. "Go on, now."

With salutes and heel-clicks, the Howlers exited. Grant also attempted to slink away.

"Don't go far, Halberdier, Ah'll speak tae ye after!" Cora growled dangerously, making Grant's shoulders hunch.

"Aye, marm."

Once they were alone, Cora took a sharp breath and brushed past her daughter to an antique sofa nestled between silken yellow curtains. Sitting with a hefty armoured clink, she patted the plush Hummel-themed upholstery, complete with a honeycomb pattern.

"All right, mah first born. Say your piece."

"Call off your Howlers," Sara implored instantly, stepping closer but not sitting down, as if her mother were a poisonous bug. "Let mah friends pass the checkpoints."

"The thieves that stole the bikes?" the Den Mother enquired, in a rising, incredulous tone.

Sara huffed, "Borrowed, Mum."

"Borrowed? Tae borrow means tae ask."

"We could nae ask, there was nae time. This is an emergency!"

"Och! Ye had time tae deceive Grant," Cora observed. "A daughter of mine, wielding her feminine charms like a weapon. Is this what life in Lupa has taught ye? Tae behave like all those Common Ground, Lupanar harlots-"

"Mum! Grant's an old friend, nae a perfect stranger."

"And that makes it all right then?"

Sara folded her arms. "See? This is why Ah went around ye, everything's always a gigantic fuss."

"Sara, Ah *want* tae help ye, just *talk* tae me-"

"If ye want tae help, Mum, telephone the checkpoints from here tae Grunrose and tell them tae let mah friends pass. They'll fight if they have tae!"

Cora scowled, "Oh aye, will they now? Then is it treason you're about, daughter?"

"Do you think Ah'd betray mah own family?"

"No, but these 'friends' might've taken ye for a fool."

Sara whirled away, calmed herself, then turned back with her paws to her muzzle. "There's something else," she began furtively.

"By Ulf, there's more?"

Parting her paws, Sara whispered, "Ah need some royal jelly."

Silence, but for the distant bustle of banqueting.

Cora looked to the exit, then seethed as loudly as she dared, "Out of the question!"

"It's for a close friend. He's dying from rot."

"Who isn't these days?"

"This is different! He's gone blind and everything! Ah cannae stand tae see him this way, Ah just can't."

Cora shot to her feet, "Ah cannae give out jelly on a whim, it does nae grow on trees!" she hissed. "Wolves would kill tae know our secret. You only know of it at all because you were given it that day and remembered. Ah had nae choice, Ah could nae see mah first born die."

"Ah feel the same way about Bruno!"

"Bruno? Nae that cook you used tae write me about, the one who disappeared."

"Aye, the very wolf." Sara dipped her chin, then raised it, tears on her cheek. "Ah missed him so much, Mum. Ah didnae even realise until now."

"Och, Sara dear."

"He's nae the same wolf. He's... ill and... and changed in his mind." Choosing her words carefully, Sara wiped her eyes, "Maybe the jelly will bring him back. Even if it doesn't he'll be better. Ah cannae see him suffer. Please, ye have tae help."

Drawing an exasperated breath, the hard Den Mother of Hummel dissolved before her daughter's tears. "Ah'll nae give ye a drop of jelly," she said, pointing at the sofa, "nae pick up any phone, *until* you sit down and tell me what you've got mixed up in this time, Sara Hummel."

Cora slowly, regally, sat again.

"Nae word for months and now suddenly all this stuff and nonsense. First Tristan Eisbrand is arrested and then you disappear. Even Professor Heath has vanished! They say you had a paw in it. Is that true?"

Silence.

"Your father's been fretting over it all," Cora went on, trying to tease forth the truth. "You know what *he* thinks of ALPHA. Ah told him there must be evidence against Tristan for him tae be taken in; Adal's nae a fool. Ah said you'd be all right; they would nae dare touch you for fear of me. But still, Ah've been concerned. If you're in trouble, if you need me tae talk tae Adal and get ALPHA tae back down, Ah will. Whatever you did it cannae be all that."

Sara took a deep breath, "Ah'll tell ye everything, but call off your Howlers first."

"With THORN threatening tae sneak into the Summit, are ye mad? Ah cannae lax security-"

"It makes nae difference. THORN won't sneak through checkpoints, Mum. They'll nae even come by road."

"Och! Will hyenas just fall from the sky then?"

"Aye," Sara claimed, "that they will!"

Cora blinked, frowned.

"Phone the checkpoints yourself," Sara instructed. "Don't go through anyone else. There could be a spy anywhere and if they find out what we're doing they'll... well... Ah dunno what they'd do, but you can bet it'll nae help us win!"

Cora made huffing noises and plucked at her cloak.

Suddenly Angus rounded the corner. "Ah'll see tae it," he grunted; he had evidently been listening in long enough. "Ah'll telephone ahead and clear the checkpoints for your two friends, just give me their names."

"Angus!" Cora chided.

"Thanks, Dad, you're a lifesaver," Sara breathed, cocking her head. "It's Uther and Linus; they're Bloodfangs, though one is in disguise as a Prefect."

"Disguise?"

"Aye."

Sighing, Angus grunted, "All right, but Ah expect you'll have explained yourself tae yer mother in the meantime," he warned, lingering long enough to add, "We'll talk about your behaviour later. Is that clear young lady?"

Sara offered a contrite, "Aye."

Once her peace-making father had departed, Sara approached and sat on the sofa with her exasperated mother, who was tugging furiously at her white cloak.

"Mum...." Sara began, faltering.

"You and your father will be the death of me, Ah swear tae Ulf. He's like putty in your paws!"

A pause, as Sara found courage and words. "What Ah have tae say cannae leave here. You cannae make a fuss, or tell anyone. Promise me. There could be spies anywhere, even amongst your closest Howlers and if anything were tae happen tae you because of me."

"Saraaa-"

"Ah'm nae crazy or been taken in, this is real!" Sara insisted, taking Cora's nearest paw and glancing about, lest anyone were lingering nearby. "If ye do nothing else, if ye nae even believe me, fine, but at least send mah sisters somewhere safe. Don't let them die too, nae like that!"

Perceiving the terror in Sara's watery eyes, Cora overcame stately protocol long enough to hug her daughter to her cloaked body. "Hush, child, hush now. Ah'll nae let anyone die, you daft wee thing." Offering Sara a kerchief, Cora raised that little chin with a finger and beamed, "Now, speak as daughter tae mother. The truth now. All of it."

⚜

Brrrrrrrrrr-rrrrrrr-rrrrrup! Ppp-ppp-p-p-p!

Engines thrumming and tracked wheels whirring between their gaitered legs, Linus and Uther sped across the black Everdor countryside, the stony road surface glittering by the twin beams of their fierce headlamps. They were the only light sources around, but for the stars and the occasional roadside establishment passing at speed, the glow of Hummelton being now firmly in the rear-view mirror.

One, then two, headlamps winked independently into existence – bikes.

Deafened by engines, Uther drew alongside Linus and gestured with a thumb over his shoulder. Linus signalled back, acknowledging he had spotted the company; no doubt Hummels from the checkpoint they had run, or others parked unseen elsewhere.

There was no choice but to keep going, the Howlers mutually, tacitly consented, simultaneously twisting their accelerators. Try as he might, Linus squeezed no more speed from his duo. The lights behind advanced, growing ever brighter. Uther pulled away at first, either because he was somehow a better rider or had, by chance, picked a better-tuned bike. However, seeing Linus lag behind, Wild-heart fell back, unwilling to abandon his friend.

Linus waved him forward, shouting, "Go! Go!"

To which Uther shook his head, drew a sword, and prepared to make stand.

Stomach churning at the prospect of fighting fellow Howlers, Linus readied his pistol and clung to reason and necessity to salve his conscience. There was no choice. To be arrested now was to doom any chance of making Rumney Farm in time and stopping THORN. If the conspiracy ran as deeply as Janoah and Vladimir claimed then even the very Howlers coming up fast could be traitors, sent to silence any bearers of bad tidings.

Life had been much simpler in the Academy.

A flash! Linus's right wing mirror exploded with all the colours of the imperionic spectrum. Someone back there had fired and meant to hit him!

"Come on then!" Uther snarled – at least Linus could swear that's what he heard over the throbbing engines.

Uther braked, falling rapidly back towards the first upcoming mono; Linus glanced over his shoulder to see the black-cloaked Wild-heart and a predominantly white Hummel Howler meet swords, slashing, thrusting, veering away on their bikes and then returning for a second bout as fierce as the first.

It was madness! One false move and Uther would be dismounted at breakneck speed, his flesh torn away on the road, bones shattered, winding up a mangled heap, just like those fresh young Howlers who went too fast in pursuit of justice on their shiny new *Springtails* and slammed into an oncoming bus or tram – Linus had read many a sad obituary.

The young Bloodfang readied his pistol and took aim, yet the thought occurred that he might simply kill an innocent Hummel instead, a wolf or wolfess just doing their job.

Suddenly the second pursuing Hummel advanced on Uther's flank, sword raised to strike!

In an instant of sheer instinct Linus aimed and fired.

Crack!

The second Hummel careened away into the night and disappeared, lost to grassy fields and darkness.

Linus flinched in horror. Did I kill them? Ulf forgive me.

Uther dispatched the other fellow by slashing down at his bike's tracked wheel with a great plasmatic strike. His acquired ALPHA rapier was sacrificed to the whirring mechanism, pinched by the tracks and dragged under, before pinging off into the night a twisted, imperiously-glowing parody of its former self. The blow did its work and the Hummel's tracked wheel disassembled, flinging pieces of itself in all directions until the anonymous Howler thought it wiser to drop out of the race, then out of sight, coming to a juddering stop.

Triumphant, Uther stuck his finger up at his vanquished foe and rejoined Linus. Cloak fluttering about him he saluted his partner and laughed.

Linus, despite his misgivings, felt that wave of euphoria only battle provided.

It was strangely addictive.

✦

Angus swung aside a small painting located on the wall beside Cora's huge four-poster bed. The painting depicted the last Den Mother to serve before Cora, a severe-looking wolfess dressed in the same armour and cloak of the incumbent Den Mother, it being passed down for centuries now. Sara would never inherit the Hummel mantle, or any other, being too healthy to wield imperium and all. She never knew how to feel about that. At least Mum always knew what she had to be; a Howler, Sara had to make her own way, take her own decisions.

Not that there was any choice now.

Behind the painting was a safe which Sara's smartly-attired father deftly twiddled his way into. He retrieved a tiny jewel-encrusted golden phial from within. Holding the pretty heirloom back from Sara's eager grasp a moment longer, he asked one last time, "Do you really know what you're about, mah girl?"

"Ah'm nae a fool, Dad."

"No… but you've put your mother in a bind, tae be sure. Ah know you'd nae do it lightly, nae make stories up, but this is ALPHA's word against the integrity of a Den Father. Can ye nae see how that slimy worm Adal stands tae gain by Amael's fall. Showing the Den Fathers up as corrupt is a sure way tae make ALPHA stronger."

"Amael *is* corrupt," Sara replied curtly. "Would ye rather he gassed us all and ruled as king?"

Angus hadn't the words to speak.

Sara looked to the door, "Ah believe Prefect Janoah's story, Ah really do."

"But she's a well-known schemer, lass!"

"Maybe, but she's dealt fair with me and Olivia. Besides, if Bruno says she's a good 'un, then she's a good 'un. He was never a wolf tae mince his words."

Grumbling, Angus Hummel slowly, reluctantly, surrendered the tiny golden phial to his daughter. "'Tis the nearest thing tae a cure in this world," he said. "Your mother was saving it for herself; Ah told her to. There's nae telling when the Queen Bee will make more."

Sara beamed, "Ah know, but mum's strong. You'll have tae put up with her for years tae come."

"Aye," Angus chuckled back. "Ah hope this Bruno's worth it."

Taking the phial, tiny Sara kissed her towering father on the cheek, "You'd better believe it."

Given a silent moment, Angus went to the bedroom door and gestured for someone to approach. A Hummel Howler walked in, saluted.

"Eldress Brynn?" Sara gasped, as if betrayed.

"Hallo, Miss Sara," Brynn replied with a nod.

"Brynn will escort ye through town," Angus explained.

"Dad, Ah said tell nobody-"

"Yer mother insisted, as do I. She'll be discreet, won't you Brynn?"

"Of course, sir."

Sara huffed, but accepted the compromise. At least nobody would stop her on account of the curfew with an Eldress by her side. Pocketing her precious cargo, she said her farewells to father and took her leave with Brynn.

✦

Den Mother Cora returned to her place at the reception dinner and, forgoing her usual dignified composure, nabbed a gulp of brandy.

"How's Sara?" Thorvald asked cordially.

"Och! That daughter of mine," Cora bristled back. "Nought but trouble that one."

"Nonsense. She's a star pupil at the Ark, I understand."

"She's been too long in the city, Thorvald, surrounded by addicts and troublemakers! Ah'm only aggrieved she's caused *you* such harm of late."

"Me, Cora?"

"Aye. Your Howler Tristan."

Thorvald still didn't entirely follow.

"It's because of Sara's dodger friend that he was arrested, is it not?" Cora explained. "He was only trying tae serve Sara, as he was instructed by you through me, but she has abused her position as mah daughter and taken advantage of him. Tristan must've been put in an impossible position, for which Ah'm truly sorry."

Nodding, Thorvald grunted, "Tristan's erred, as I'm sure Sara has, but naïve, well-meaning wolves will be taken in by Lupa's desperate addicts. It's all gotten out of paw, somewhat. I have already advised Den Prefect Adal to release Tristan with a warning, which he will, and drop all charges regarding this matter, which he has." The oldest Den Father leant forth to meet eyes with the youngest a few seats along, "You see, I also refuse to be bullied."

Amael nodded and raised his glass, "I'm gratified to hear that, Den Father Thorvald."

Cora raised her glass also, then looking to all, but resting mostly on Amael, said somewhat out of the blue, "Do you gentlebeasts realise there's tae be a great balloon flying over us tomorrow?"

"Balloon?" said Flaid, appearing genuinely surprised.

Amael gulped his drink and looked elsewhere with feigned disinterest.

"The famous Buttle cats have built a new flying machine, their biggest yet," Cora explained. "Ah'd almost forgotten, but seeing mah daughter reminded me; she's befriended them of late. Their balloons are one of the few healthy interests she has outside of bugs."

"Perhaps she should take it up as a career?" Thorvald laughed, joking, "Up, up and up some more!"

Cora cocked her head, "You laugh, Den Father, but it could well be the way of the future."

"Elder Trains replaced by Elder dirigibles, perchance?"

"Indeed. That's why we at Hummel have backed the enterprise, *despite* intense Felician pressure to banish Montague Buttle from our territory; they nae mention banishing his wife but she is, of course, royalty."

"Decadent and backward race," Amael gruffed.

"Cats will be proud, Amael," Thorvald said, noncommittally.

Flaid sat forward, apparently interested in where the discussion was suddenly headed, "Our finest Greystone engineers envisage heavier than air flight being more likely than these... unwieldy balloons the cats and others have dreamt up. Winged vehicles emulating insects, fast and nimble, will win out, not some gasbag at the mercy of the wind. Nature is ever our guide."

"And have your finest engineers produced such a machine to date, Flaid?" Thorvald needled – the old Howler enjoyed a good wind up.

Flaid smiled, "Don't confuse lack of success with lack of progress, Thorvald."

"Lack of evidence is my point."

Cora joined in the ribbing. "Of course, clouds are mere gas at the mercy of the wind, but they do travel further than any insect, and for free," she said artfully, asking, "What do you think Den Father Amael, balloons or wings?"

Amael Balbus spread a steel-grey paw. "Unlike Flaid and yourself I don't pretend to know much about these new machines, but I'm sure this 'flyover' of yours will be an historic event regardless."

Cora's bright eyes narrowed in her dark face, "Then we must none of us miss the occasion, must we?"

Amael squinted in bafflement, but nodded. "Not for the world, Den Mother."

"Ah'm glad tae hear it."

Elsewhere, Vladimir was eating his meal and sharing tales of administrative woe with fellow long-suffering Grand Howlers, when a Bloodfang approached and reported surreptitiously, "We're missing a Howler, sir."

"Mm?" Vladimir urged.

"Howler Linus, sir. He seems to have… disappeared. The Hummels have had some bikes stolen and one of the thieves was described as a Bloodfang, sir. Not confirmed, but that's what I've got out of 'em."

Vladimir nodded throughout, pondering the news with seeming calm. "Have you searched his room?"

"Yes, sir."

"The pubs and Lupanars?"

"Would do sir, but for the curfew. The Hummels said they're taking care of it."

"Then that's all there is to it, Howler. No doubt Linus will turn up drunk in a bar sooner or later, or a bed. What happened at the hot springs has quite affected him."

"Aye, sir."

The Howler saluted and left Vladimir to knock back some brandy – he needed it.

✦

"Schmutz!"

It was a rare thing to hear Linus curse, and Uther missed the momentous event on account of his ears being assaulted by clamouring engines and whistling wind.

The approaching cause of Linus's consternation was an elegant stone bridge arcing over a river, specifically the checkpoint kiosks and stripy arm-barriers barring both the near and far side.

From the gentle hill he and Uther were speeding down towards the river, Linus enjoyed a good view of the surroundings. Eddies of black water swirled beneath the bridge like octopus tentacles, reflecting the lights of a sleepy Everdor town nestled on the far side. Linus spied a turning watermill and a busy pub. *The Diving Beetle*, said the latter's illuminated sign, complete with an appropriate picture of a beetle swimming amongst weeds. Linus recalled these landmarks from Sara's map and was glad to be on track, albeit dismayed there was no way of avoiding the checkpoint without going into the deadly-looking river.

Well, there was one way.

Coming alongside Linus, Uther pointed ahead at the checkpoint and calmly motioned his paw as if to dive, like a diving beetle. Go under, he was saying. Despite his misgivings, Linus thumbed-up.

You've ducked a barrier once, Linus told himself, you can do it once more.

Twice more, even.

Uther pulled ahead, engine thrumming, leading the way. Expecting the bikes to slow down, the Hummel Howlers at the checkpoint looked up from their hot chocolates just in time to be blinded by Uther's headlamp.

Vrrrum!

Pulling the same stunt as before, Uther ducked under the barrier; Linus followed mere seconds later, a little more sedately.

Vrrrrrrum!

Cresting the bridge and down the other side to the second barrier. The Howlers there waved and hollered, but did not raise their weapons like those back at Hummelton. Uther ducked, defying them and their barrier.

Vrrrum!

Righting himself he zoomed past the pub, leaving the little beast patrons standing outside smouldering and drinking on this fairly clement night scratching their heads at the commotion.

A young miller mouse in flour-dusted dungarees and a cap left his table and ran into the road to catch a glimpse of the speeding bike.

"Cor! Did you see-"

Vrrrrrr!

A second bike was on him in a flash, lighting-up his terror-stricken face.

Screee! Kfff-ffff-f-f-fgh!

Desperate to avoid a collision, the bike and its rider twisted away and fell to one side, sliding past an inch from the cringing mouse. The bike spiralled wildly away across the street whilst its rider rolled to a fleshy stop on the cobbles. He came to rest flat on his back, blonde arms spread wide.

It was over in a moment.

The pub patrons hurried to the mouse and pulled him back into anonymity, lest he was set upon by the Howlers for causing an accident.

The first bike returned and its wolfen rider hopped off to attend his stricken comrade.

"Linus!" he cried, lifting his bloodied head. "Mate!"

The Hummel Howlers from the checkpoint soon surrounded them, rifles aimed and ready.

✧

Driven to the station with Eldress Brynn, Sara crossed the deserted platforms unchallenged and climbed aboard the last carriage of the Eisbrand Train.

"Ye must keep this under your cloak, Eldress," she told the white-cloaked Brynn, barring the doorway. "Nobody knows what's in this carriage."

"Ah'm only here tae protect ye, Sara," replied she.

"Stay here then."

"Ah cannae do that. Mah orders were specific."

Nodding, for there could be no arguing, Sara entered, Brynn just behind, the latter casting her gaze all around the boxes and barrels.

Sara hurried straight to Bruno, who was still lying on the metal table under the lamp, his eyes blindfolded against the light that was so painful to his rotten eyes.

"Sara?" Olivia said, emerging tiredly from the gloom.

"How is he?"

"Not too good, I think," was the disappointing reply, with a chirpier, "How'd it go with your mum?"

Sara puffed uneasily, "As well as can be expected. Mum knows now; Ah dunno if she believes half of what Ah said, but Ah could nae keep a lid on things for trying." She gestured at Brynn, "Don't worry, she's only here tae baby-sit me."

Olivia nodded at Brynn, who approached the prostrate Bruno laden with suspicion.

"This is Bruno," Sara explained, reading Brynn's bafflement. "He's... well...."

"ALPHA's Eisenwolf," Brynn guessed. "So it's true, they found a pure-blood." She held out a black paw. "His corona... by Ulf's fangs, it burns."

"Yes," Olivia agreed, smiling fondly. "He's quite something."

Brynn suddenly backed away and drew her rapier, threatening the darkness by the van. "Who goes there?"

Slowly a grey cat in a black coat stepped into the stark light whilst rubbing his paws on an oily cloth. "Put your sword away, Hummel, I'm on your side."

Brynn lowered her blade, "Doctor Josef Grau, right?"

"My name precedes me, as usual."

Reaching into her pocket, Sara turned to the cat and showed him the bejewelled phial. "Ah've brought Bruno something. It should help tae sort him out."

Josef peered witheringly over his spectacles. "White-imperium can't help him now," he scoffed. "He's already overdosed. The best we can do, short of my patented imperium shock therapy, is to leave him alone. If he can stand by tomorrow morning it'll be a marvel."

"It's nae white-imperium, doctor," Sara claimed flatly.

Unscrewing the sapphire-topped phial, the little Hummel wolfess pulled the lid away, revealing a delicate glass dipstick attached to the underside, like a perfume dabber. A waxy, golden substance clung to the dabber, and a sweet smell pervaded the dingy carriage, like incense.

Josef flew over. "Royal jelly?" he hissed, looking between Sara and the phial.

Sara laughed falsely, "Aye! Somehow Ah thought someone like you would recognise it."

"Where did you get it?" the doctor demanded, answering immediately, "Den Mother Cora no doubt. Yes, I bet she's sitting on a pretty stockpile of the stuff all for herself whilst the rest of the Den Fathers rot."

"Ah wish," Sara said. "This is the last."

Like a pupil at class, Olivia raised a finger, "Excuse me, but what's royal jelly?"

Sara tried to explain, but Josef pompously took over. "It's a waxy substance produced by a great queen bee when she wants to make daughter queens. She secretes it from glands on her head and feeds it to selected grubs."

"Lovely," Olivia said, sarcastically.

"It's remarkable stuff," Josef insisted. "It induces grubs to form into new queens, instead of mere workers," he lectured, peering longingly at the phial. "Ancient hyena stories tell of its restorative properties, that it's a cure for the rot, an aphrodisiac and more. I've tried for years to get hold of some to test its veracity, but since only great bees like those under Hummelton Den produce this particular brand of royal jelly, and even then only when the old queen is good and ready, it's rarer than worm's teeth!" The doctor smiled one of his menacing smiles, "Still, the Hummel Den Fathers and Mothers are renown for their longevity and unusual good fortune. Cora's not so old, but she has produced quite the brood when a Howler's cubs ought to die at a rate of at least a quarter, *even* with a healthy partner." Josef looked at Sara meaningfully, as if inspecting her health, and demanded, "Does it work then? How is it taken, orally or topically? Perhaps you'd best give it to me to administer."

Sara tucked the phial close to her chest, lest the frantic cat tried to snatch it from her. "Ah know what Ah'm doing, all right?" she growled. She looked down at the glittering phial in her paws, "Ah remember how it's used. Mah mum gave me some when Ah was a wee lass. Ah was in a fever for weeks and weeks. Ah was dying, everyone was sure. Dad sat with me for days, whilst Mum disappeared. Then one day, she came running in all muddy and messy, like… like from a battle, and rubbed this stuff tae mah lips." Sara touched her mouth, recalling the childhood memory, "Ah can remember the cold glass of the bottle, the sticky jelly, and… and just licking mah lips. Mum begged me tae swallow. It tasted a little sweet, but oily, like beeswax. The next Ah knew Ah woke up feeling grand again." She looked to Eldress Brynn, "Ah reckon Mum raided a great bee's nest in the wilds tae find some jelly. Pillaging nature; it goes against everything Hummel stands fer. Howlers probably died for me. Mum always denied it, but Ah know what's what happened. Ah'm nae a fool."

Eldress Brynn remained silent on the matter.

"So, you take it orally then," Josef surmised, quite unmoved. "I would suggest a small dose."

Sara scoffed, "Aye, because you want tae keep some tae study!"

"No, not at all!" the cat spat, whiskers hiked. "Though that would be expedient. There could be a cure in that very bottle. Wouldn't have to raid nests in future if the active ingredient was isolated and reproduced, would you?"

"Maybe not, but Bruno needs it all," Sara said. "Ah told mum he's a big lad. She said tae either give him all of it, or not tae bother. So, there it is."

"You might kill him, meddling with things you do not understand."

"It'll work!"

"Yes, it will," Brynn said, drawing her pistol. "That's why I cannot allow this monster tae have it."

"What?"

"Give me the jelly, Sara."

"But Eldress-"

"This... abomination is the same breed of horror that wreaked havoc during the Wolfen Wars. When an Eisenwolf goes mad, and they often do, there's nae a force in the land that can stop them. Their kind is nae fit tae walk Erde again, do you understand?" Brynn held out a dark paw, "Now give me the jelly."

Sara stood dumbfounded. Clutching the phial close she instinctively backed away.

"Sara!" Brynn growled. "These are my orders."

"Orders?"

"Your mother is nae so foolish as you think. She knew ALPHA had something tae hide. Now, give me the phial and come with me."

"No! You're lying! She'd nae trick me!"

"Give it here!" the Eldress growled, pressing her pistol to Bruno's temple, pushing his head to one side. "Give it over or Ah'll kill him this instant!"

"No! Please!"

"Give me the phial!"

"Ah will, Ah will, just don't hurt him."

Slowly, shakily, watched in shocked silence by Josef and Olivia, Sara passed Brynn the phial. The moment the royal jelly was in her paw, Brynn pocketed it safely in her cloak.

"Ah'm sorry," she said.

"Sorry?"

Brynn cocked her pistol and aimed at Bruno's head.

Olivia raised a paw, "No!"

Bvvsssstt!

With a blinding flash, Eldress Brynn was punched across the carriage and slammed into the far wall with a fleshy metallic thud, streaks of white-hot plasma coils following her all the way to her final resting place.

All fell silent as the grave.

Plasma trickled over Olivia's trembling, steaming paw. She turned it about and looked at her palm.

"By Ulf," she gasped.

"Olivia?" Sara said.

"Hahahahaaaahaha!" Josef burst out laughing, clapping his paws at Olivia. "Magnificent! I knew it. You just decked an Elder and you've not even had a day's training in your life; *that*, my wolfen girl, is raw talent!"

"I had to!" Olivia excused. "You all saw it. She was going to kill him."

Josef shrugged, paws wide, "By all means, do it whenever the mood strikes. I shan't complain."

Gathering her wits, and checking Bruno for holes, Sara fell upon the still form of Eldress Brynn and turned her cloak out for the phial. It was still in once piece. She then kicked away Brynn's pistol and removed her sword, dropping it into some box like it was diseased.

"Is she dead?" Olivia asked, with more curiosity than horror.

"Probably," Josef mewed.

"She's fine," Sara claimed, whether she knew that to be the case or not.

Acting quickly, lest more Hummels should seize upon the commotion in the carriage and stop proceedings within, Sara scuttled back to Bruno with the jewelled phial and removed the lid. Turning Bruno's thick jaws towards her, she dabbed the royal jelly on his lips, rather like a naughty cub applying makeup to a dozing father.

At once Bruno licked it away in his sleep and swallowed it.

Sara emitted a sharp breath and, scraping out the last of the jelly, dabbed his lips a second time. Again he took it in.

Josef stood back a little, expecting a violent reaction. But nothing happened, no fit, no eruption of coronal energy, just steady breathing.

"It really isn't venom," he marvelled, snatching the phial before Sara could stop him.

"Oi!"

"What's in it? I must know!"

"Keep it then, 'tis all gone anyway," Sara woofed. She stroked Bruno's feverish brow and whispered in his ear. "It's up tae you now, Bruno. Fight, mah friend. Fight."

⁂

The sharp aroma of smelling salts attacking his flaring nostrils brought Linus back into the world. He sat up on a bed with a start, then a growl as bone-deep bruises wracked his arms and back.

"Agh! Fssss!"

"Easy, mate," Uther said, beaming, "By Ulf you scared me for a minute."

Looking past Uther's white face, Linus judged he was upstairs in some house or tavern or somewhere. Hummel Howlers were lingering about the periphery, whilst a rabbit doctor in a bowler hat kept up the revolting smelling-salts until Linus pushed his paw away.

"That's enough," he said, adding, "Thank you, sir."

The rabbit was gently dismissed by a Hummel Grand Howler, who stood over Linus.

"You're lucky you weren't killed, Bloodfang," he said, in a distinctly unimpressed manner.

Rubbing his sore (and bandaged) head, Linus wondered why he wasn't wired up like an uncommon criminal. He looked to Uther, who seemed chirpier than he ought to be for a wolf under arrest, and freer too.

"Our Den Mother has sent word you're tae be allowed tae pass unhindered," the Hummel explained. "They weren't specific on the matter at paw, but… we understand it is a matter of territorial security."

"We need to get to Rumney Farm, sir, and fast."

"Aye, so your friend here said," the Hummel replied, looking to his wolves. "Ah've nae heard of it."

"It's in Grunrose," Linus grunted, swinging his armoured legs off the bed.

The Hummel woofed, "Grunrose! 'Tis miles away.

"We know," Uther acknowledged. "Look, just give us some bikes and tell everyone to get out of our way, mate."

The Grand Howler shook his head. "Why don't Ah just ring through to this farm?"

"I told yer, there's no phone near it for fifty thumping miles! It's on the edge of the wilds."

"Ah could have some Howlers sent there tae investigate or whatever's needed."

Linus asked pertly, "Do you run the District?"

"Well… no, of course not, Ah'm nae an Elder-"

"Then don't lift a finger, sir. The Elder there could be a traitor. In fact I'm almost certain he or she must be for THORN to have come and gone unimpeded for the last year."

The Hummel scowled, "THORN?"

"Yes sir, and if they're warned, someone may lie in wait for us, or worse they might bring their attack forward a few hours, or change tactics altogether. Our best chance lies in surprising them in the act."

The Hummel nodded sagely, yet worriedly.

Linus stood up, shoulders back. "Now, if you could show us to a fresh bike I would be most grateful."

The Hummel was amazed that Linus could stand.

"Is the mouse all right, by the way?" the youth asked, his blue eyes wide. "I-I-I didn't hit him, did I?"

Uther cackled and slapped Linus on the hollow of his broad back, making him wince. "Don't worry, Woodlouse, you only nearly killed yourself instead, is all."

Linus exhaled gratefully.

After some thought, the Grand Howler declared, "Ah'll escort you tae Grunrose; it will be safer that way. Name's Lachlan, pleased tae meet yer."

"And I you," Linus said, shaking paws. "Thank you."

✧

As the midnight hour drew near, Meryl stole across the ALPHA grounds with big Tristan in tow. He was cloaked in a Prefect's mantle and helmet so nobody would stop him. In fact, at a glance, any observers might've easily mistaken him for the resident Eisenwolf, since Rafe was often seen shadowing the prim little Miss Stroud, and Tristan's stature was similar – in the dark none could easily discern his colouration, nor the bandages.

Keys rattling, Meryl opened the rusty side gate with an uncomfortably loud squeak and Tristan slipped through onto the streets of the Common Ground.

"Thank you," he whispered, lingering dangerously. "I know you're an impartialist too, like Rufus," he added, nursing a bandaged arm. "You must understand why I-"

"I'm a pacifist first!" Meryl seethed. "I do not condone your violent actions, or THORN's, though I pity the hyenas."

Tristan huffed, "Pacifist? What about that monster you tend? How many has *he* killed in your name, Meryl?"

The nurse suddenly shut the gate and about-faced, "Goodbye, Tristan Donskoy!"

✧

Queen Arjana Jua-mata sat nobly enthroned in Nurka's fine tent, a tent that had always stood ready to receive her with all its regal splendour; it never had been the austere Nurka's after all.

Arjana gently stroked a white pepper moth nestled beside her; the very same moth Nurka had used to communicate back at the mines. He, Themba and the freshly-bandaged Madou knelt before their Queen, the low table between them and her strewn with the rolled papers and inky reeds of their final council.

All was in paw.

"Take him," Arjana declared, picking up her trembling messenger moth and placing it on her black, velvety lap.

Nurka stood, chin dipped to avoid eye-contact with his golden-faced Queen, and coaxed the beautiful moth onto his forearm, where it hung neatly, like a fine white tribal shield of ancient hyena origin.

"Send word to me when it is done," Arjana said, passing Nurka two message canisters, adding, "or not done."

Nurka bowed, fist to cloaked chest, "My Queen," and retreated from her presence.

"You are the last hope of the Jua-mata," Arjana told the three Chakaa. "Make the Black Rain fall again; cleanse the land of the wicked, as the Sky did once before, and we shall return the world to its wild heritage."

The Chakaa listened well to the Queen's latest tirade. Their old teacher, Noss, remained unconscious throughout proceedings. Madou dared look upon his Prince, lying off to the left, his mighty body nestled amongst the plethora of dichotomously-coloured pillows that constituted Arjana's bed. Noss had been stripped of his cloak and his paws bound at the Queen's command – for his own safety.

The madness would pass, Arjana claimed, the curse of the gods visited upon her Prince for years of drinking chunta rose and fell as the tides. During the affliction's next low ebb, Noss would see above the waves and realise THORN's actions were just.

Rufus and Tomek's prospects were bleaker; Madou could glimpse them through the wafting tent flaps. Each sat tied to a separate stake out in the camp, awaiting execution at Arjana's pleasure. A lingering death at the nibbling jaws of the forest denizens, or perhaps a merciful beheading; the Queen had yet to decide.

They had saved many lives. Was death for them just?

More doubts, like buzzing, biting mosquitoes, assaulted Madou's fevered mind. Was it right to kill so many innocents? This *is* a war, war is about killing the enemy, is it not? Am I going mad too? Am I weak, like Prince Noss?

"Madou!" Nurka hissed, as he and Themba made the tent flaps – they were leaving.

Gathering his wits, Madou got up and backed out, bowing and supplicating his way into the night.

Once clear of Arjana's majesty Nurka took his brother Chakaa to one side, like a naughty cub. "You're wounded," he reasoned. "Perhaps you should stay here and-"

"No!" Madou woofed, standing up straight. "I'm ready."

Nurka inspected Madou's thick hyena face for the longest time, then nodded, slapped his arm, and led the way with Themba following loyally. Chakaa Madou lingered long enough to notice Rufus and Tomek staring silently, judgingly, before he fled to the safety of Nurka's charisma.

"What now?" the bloody-nosed Tomek grunted, twisting his painfully-wired wrists and looking across to Rufus, tied in a similar fashion to the stake next-door.

"It's out of our paws, dear boy," Rufus replied, watching the Chakaa go. "We've done all we can."

Glancing about, young Watcher Usenko leant as close as he could and whispered, "Casimir... he get away. I see it. Madou lied to Themba."

Rufus frowned. "Then…." he snorted, getting no further.

Tomek nodded. "As you say, is out of *our* paws."

CHAPTER 51

Morning's light poured down the valley, sloshed between the trees and outbuildings of Rumney Farm, and filtered through the dusty windows of the hanger.

Big old rusty barn was a more apt description, Penny felt, for unless one was blind it was painfully obvious the hanger had been a silk worm house in a previous life. However, Penelope Buttle knew the power of shameless self-promotion, and outright fibs. Rumney Farm was sequestered away in the sticks, miles from civilisation, and few strangers happened across it, even fewer had glimpsed its secretive contents. Well-staged newspaper photographs and articles were all the distant folks of Lupa and Felicia knew, thus the illusion of total professionalism was maintained.

Just about.

Pfffffshhhh!

"Oh my! Pleh! Gagh! Turn it off! Turn it off, Sweetpea! I'm drowning down here!"

"Oh!"

Penny twisted the big red valve; the connected hosepipe ceased whipping around the hanger, though not before drenching everything high and low. Water ran down the side of the vast, bulging flank of the dirigible in rippling sheets, clinging to the taut grey fabric until the under hang reached about forty-five degrees, whereupon it dripped off onto Monty's sodden, capped head.

Penny hurried down the ladder, her steel-toed boots clinking on the rusty metal rungs. "Sorry, Monty dear," she excused, stifling a spontaneous giggle.

"I know you said I needed a bath before the flyover, but this is the limit."

"It's about time we got changed anyway," Penny said, plucking at her oily coveralls. "We can't fly over Hummelton dressed like this."

"You go; I'll be right there."

"Don't leave it until the last minute. At least wash your face, we could be meeting all the Den Fathers later."

"Yes, dear."

Leaving her husband to wring out his cap, Penny headed for the hanger's huge double-doors – certainly a new addition to the silk worm barn. It was a fair trot, more than half a dirigible's distance, and this was a *big* dirigible, Monty's biggest yet. Penny reckoned if it was stood on end it would be about height of the Arkady University's mighty clock tower, and probably broader.

The name of the ship was stencilled near her bright red nose cone.

'RF-4 *Nimbus*'

Nimbus was the catchy name for the pubic; the rest meant something only to the Buttles. The R signified rigid, for unlike the modest balloon Penny had waved from at the Science Exhibition, the *Nimbus* contained an internal skeleton. The light yet sturdy durametal ribs pressing against its grey canvas gave the *Nimbus* the segmented appearance of a giant, anonymous grub.

F stood for felitium, Penny's secret lifting gas. The *Nimbus'* internal bladders had been inflated just last night and without mishap, save for Monty squeaking like a baby mouse when he was necessitated to fix a leak. Felitium was harmless, but it did raise one's voice comically if so inhaled.

Finally, the 4 in RF-4 *Nimbus* stood for the current generation of Buttle-made balloon, three other rigid balloon designs had gone before this one, and many a soft balloon too, some more successful than others.

Monty had a good feeling about the *Nimbus*, but then he always did. He was the optimist, the partner with his head in the clouds, literally. The practical side was left to Penny, managing finances, sponsorship, inventing new lifting gases, even making sure Monty turned up to an event on time instead of tinkering until the last desperate minute.

In that spirit, Penny decided to open the great double doors now and generally get a move on.

"Reg, get the doors will you?" she called, passing under the conical nose of the ship and plucking her pocket watch from one of her countless coverall pockets. "It's nearly six 'o' clock already."

At Penny's word, a brown rat abseiled down the canvas flank of the *Nimbus* on a wire harness and peered across at her. "What if there's press outside?" he asked, lowering himself slowly to the ground on a thin steel wire, like a furry spider.

"It hardly matters now," the grey catess replied. "If anyone's snooping about waiting to catch a sneaky photo they couldn't even get their plate developed before the flyover, let alone to an editor and a printing press."

"That's true," Reg agreed, unclipping himself. "I'll get to it, then."

"Thank you," Penny chirped, slipping through a small side door. She came back, "You *are* going to come up with us this time, aren't you? Only you've worked for nothing these past months. We want you to be in the photographs with us."

"What? A little beast like me?"

"Of course! Everyone else left, but you stayed on, Reg. Besides, with a ship this size we might need more paws on deck!"

After a pause, Reg beamed, "Wouldn't miss it for the world."

"Splendid," Penny replied. "I'm going to get ready."

"Aye."

Spitting on his pink paws, Reg sighed heavily, then began turning a crank on the wall. The hanger's metal doors slowly rattled open, throwing sunlight on the RF-4's nose, as if it were a giant metallic mole tentatively sniffing the air outside its subterranean home. Penny stopped for a moment to take in the grand sight. History was being made, she supposed, but then she and Monty had launched enough balloons now that it felt almost routine. Still, Penny would have liked to take Sara up over her home town. Where had that girl gotten to?

Thinking her thoughts, Penny crossed the farm, passing between the burgeoning mulberry field, which would be harvested for silkworms, and the sugar cane plantation where wild aphids would be encouraged to set up a colony. The cane plants were but seedlings; soon they would be twenty feet high and infested with aphids as big as one's fist. Penny had spent many a happy afternoon with Sara walking between the mighty stalks tickling aphids and collecting the sugary nectar they produced. Every bottle sold helped raise funds and keep the infant *Buttle Skyways* aloft. Perhaps after today's publicity stunt the money woes would finally be over. A licence to fly from Hummelton to Lupa would be a start; Queens Town to Felicia would come later, when Penny's dear cousin the Queen and her Privy Council came round. If the wolves could be persuaded the cats would cave in as well, they would have to or else be left behind by the march of technological progress.

Penny emerged from the fields and crossed to the farm itself, a large, L-shaped house in the frontier style, with blue-painted wooden slatted walls and a roof made of tin tiles. Pretty wisteria and ivy clambered all over it. The house had been modernised as far as possible, Monty installing central heating and plumbing, but it remained a quaint throwback to a simpler, romantic, if dangerous time, when Grunrose District had been a wild place, with outlaws and danger abound. The Frontier had been pushed back over the last century, so that now, though still fairly isolated, the house was safely within the laws and protections afforded by Lupan civilisation.

Penny went inside, through the reception, the kitchen, upstairs to the bedroom and dressing room, passing heirlooms and knickknacks, vases, antique pistols and swords, paintings of great cats, some of them Penny's noble ancestors; she had taken half of Felicia with her, or so Monty never tired of joking to guests.

Penny had soon groomed and changed into her best frilly white dress and wide-brimmed hat, complete with lilac ribbons and gloves. She took a matching silk scarf to help wave to the public, as usual. Despite her chemical knowledge she knew her role today; she was the gentle, reassuring face. If a mere catess in a dress can stomach a ride on airship so can you, so don't be afraid, you big hairy Howlers. Penny wasn't sure if Den Mother Cora qualified as a big hairy Howler, she had heard she was very regal, almost queen-like.

Thinking her thoughts and setting her hat just so in the dressing room mirror, Penny hummed a little tune and descended the stairs, twirling a parasol and nodding at her ancestors.

At the foot of the stairs she noticed the front door was open. Monty must have come in to get changed; a small miracle.

"Monty?" Penny chirped, searching about the kitchen, then returning and calling upstairs, "Monty? Monty, dear, are you in the bathroo-?"

It was the burly, wild-looking figure filling in the door to the front room that caused Penny's tongue to stick.

A hyena!

He was tall, as hyenas went, and wore a marvellous cloak with labyrinthine patterns of black and white. Penny stood staring at the stranger for a time, her mind fathoming what this was; a harmless passing traveller, a thief, or a murderer?

Remain calm Penelope; let's not jump to conclusions, the noble catess told herself.

"How do you do, sir?" she hazarded. "Can I help you?"

The big hyena's fierce purple eyes widened in surprise; perhaps he had expected Penny to run and scream, or at the very least scream. He looked past her to another, shorter hyena, who appeared at the opposite doorway, dressed in a similar, if zigzagged cloak. His face was covered by a skull-shaped helmet.

"Mrs Buttle," the second fellow presumed, cordially enough. He removed his ferocious helm like a gentlebeast, revealing a young and dashing hyena beneath. "I am Chief Nurka of the Juamata tribe," he continued in his rough, sandpaper voice. "Themba and I mean you no harm. Please, come with us."

"Come with you, sir?" Penny scoffed.

Nurka smiled briefly. "We want to ride in your flying machine," he explained, gesturing at the distant hanger with his helmet. "You will take us up, you and your husband."

"Is that right?" Penny said, cocking her head, "I... take it we don't have a choice in the matter?"

Nurka shrugged, "I'm afraid not. Please, do not make this more difficult than it need be, for your sake."

Penny nodded, smiled. Then she turned and dashed up the stairs. "Monnnnty!"

"Themba, grab her!" Nurka grunted, flicking a paw.

Themba rushed after the catess and snatched the hem of her dress, pulling her to a stop. Shrieking, Penny whipped her parasol backwards, hitting the hyena in the face, the metal spike catching his right eye.

"Gaaagh! You bitch!"

Snarling and cursing, Themba fell about the stairs nursing his eye.

Another hyena replaced him.

"Don't hurt her, Madou!" Nurka warned.

"Chief," the stocky Madou acknowledged, clambering over the seething Themba.

Reaching the top of the stairs, Penny grabbed a priceless vase from a whatnot and threw it down at the second attacker, then pulled the whatnot down for good measure.

"Oof!" Madou wheezed, as the vase broke over his back and rained porcelain down on Nurka and Themba. The whatnot tumbled after, blocking the stairs. By the time Madou looked up, Penny had gone. He heard a door slam and lock. No real matter for an afflicted beast.

Madou traversed the whatnot and located the door that Penny had locked.

Whereupon he waited.

And waited.

"Madou?" Nurka barked, climbing the stairs.

"Locked chief," Madou excused, suddenly and furiously twisting the doorknob.

"Blow it then!"

"I'm trying, chief," Madou assured. "I'm... I'm still a bit weak, that's all."

Nurka brushed the floundering Madou aside and grasped the doorknob.

Pfffzzt! Bang!

The lock exploded in molten sparks and Nurka, shaking his smouldering paw, kicked in the door to a cloud of smoke. He saw Penny glance back at him through the haze, then drop out the window.

There was a feline yelp, then much complaining below.

"Get off me you brute! Let me go this instant, I say! Monnnty!"

Nurka and Madou ran to the window and saw Themba in the garden below with Mrs Buttle over one shoulder, her punches and kicks availing her nothing.

"Well done," Nurka said, flicking his snout in approval.

Themba squinted back at his chief with one good eye, the other being bruised half-shut and weeping. "You're quite the little warrior," he complimented Penny.

"Monnnt-mmph!"

Gagging the fairer half of the Buttle couple, Themba ferried her round to Nurka, Madou and the others exiting the house, whereupon they set out towards the hanger to find her husband and persuade him.

✦

Checkpoints had been few and far between since Hummelton, occurring only at district borders, and with a Grand Howler escorting Linus and Uther, interfering busybodies, hogs in the main, had proved no impediment to progress. But after riding all night Linus was exhausted, and his body ached terribly from his fall. He felt so stupid, but then again it had perhaps been a blessing in disguise. There was nothing to do but put the pain to the back of his mind. Uther was likely as weary.

Linus just hoped Grand Howler Lachlan and his dozen Hummel escorts were still fresh, for there could be a fight at Rumney Farm, a fight for the future of all Lupa.

A fight we must win, Linus thought.

The last barrier between here and Rumney Farm appeared; the entrance to Grunrose District itself. The Hummel banners fluttered, along with the smaller district flag depicting a pale-green rose. The hogs operating the checkpoint were surprisingly numerous and alert, comprising a veritable army, as if someone in this far-flung district was expecting trouble. With THORN afoot that didn't seem too unreasonable.

Grand Howler Lachlan slowed his bike and hailed the two-dozen hogs, speaking to one over the barrier arm and flashing his Hummel brooch.

Linus and Uther stopped behind with the rest of the Hummels. They could not hear what was said over the thrum of their stationary bikes let alone everyone else's; a chorus of twelve or so rumbling mono engines was hard on the ears even at rest.

Whilst Lachlan had it out with the officious hog, one of the bike's exhausts backfired loudly, making Linus jump.

Crack!

No, it was not the bike; Lachlan bent double and fell on his side, shot by the hog at the gate!

Then all the hogs stationed nearby produced pistols and rifles, the Hummels too.

Crack! Crack! Crack!

"Ulf Almighty!" Uther roared, falling off his bike and twisting it sideways, using it for cover. "Linus!"

Wild-heart dragged his stunned partner off his bike and to the floor with him before the young wolf was torn to shreds by the insane, close-quarters fire fight. Some Hummels fell wounded, as did some hogs, but it was the latter that miscalculated. Once the first volley had been expended the hogs had no redress save to retreat into nearby offices and reload; the furious Howlers, on the other paw, had their kristahl weapons. Some drew swords, others unfolded spears that Watchers, used to dealing with centipedes, were fond of carrying for that extra stabbing range. Either way they leapt over the barrier in defence of Grand Howler Lachlan and set about the fumbling hogs.

Uther joined in the battle; Linus stayed out of the ensuing slaughter, hurrying instead to Lachlan and dragging him behind a bike amidst sparks of pistol fire.

"Grrrfgh!" the Grand Howler groaned, clutching his bloodied cloak. "Traitors!" he declared.

"Are you all right?" Linus asked, feeling an idiot, but he didn't know how else to express concern.

"I'll live," Lachlan growled, checking his ribs. "He... agh... he said nobody could pass. Nobody, on order of the Elder. Then he shot me! Since when are hogs permitted tae carry such weapons let alone use them against a Howler?"

Linus had a theory. "As I said, the Elder of Grunrose must be helping THORN. Amael's got many beasts on-side, from the lowest little beast to the highest Elder."

"Aye, Ah can believe it now!"

"You didn't before?"

"Ah was nae sure, but... but this clinches it. Something's a brewin', lad. Och!"

Uther returned with the others, their imperium weaponry bloodied, slain hogs lying on the road behind them. Linus supposed his comrades had had no choice and all, but he also imagined if he and Uther failed now they would be branded murderers by Amael's regime. He would skew events according to his needs, just as the packs had always done in the newspapers.

Now there really was no going back.

Despite protests from his wolves, Lachlan mounted his bike, insisting he push forward with his Bloodfang guests. The wounded were hastily patched up, Lachlan being the worst off as it happened, and the barrier was raised.

Checking Sara's map, Linus and Uther rode on with Lachlan, into the rolling hills of Grunrose. It wasn't far now.

✤

"An amazing machine, you've built," Nurka praised, peering inside the gondola's windows at all the controls that commanded the *Nimbus*; buttons, levers, steel cables, even an old-fashioned ship's wheel, albeit one made of light brushed-effect durametal instead of wood. "I've followed her progress closely," the hyena claimed.

"Not closely enough, sir," Monty sniffed, chin raised. Two hyenas were standing menacingly either side of him, their paws clapped on his shoulders. "She's not yet airworthy, I'll have you know-"

"Spare me your lies!" Nurka rasped back. "I know today's the day you fly over Hummelton. You've already filled her with gas, and your wife here was getting ready for the occasion when we unexpectedly... dropped in. Though not entirely unexpectedly, right Reg?"

Reg the rat appeared amongst the hyenas, his cap doffed in shame, yet his long brown face looked determined.

Nurka explained, "Your trusted employees have kept us up to speed with the *Nimbus*. So, do not lie."

"Reg!" Monty mewed, as did Penny, through her gag. "Mmph!"

Reg seethed at them both, "Sorry Monty, but we've all had enough."

"Enough old chap? Enough of what?"

"Of being trodden on by the Howlers! Us and the hyenas and everyone else. It's not you, you're good 'un's, it's them. Time for a change and the hyenas are the beasts to do it."

"Hyenas? Since when are *they* friends of the wee beasts?"

"Since the wolves started massacring 'em, like they massacred my family in the war."

"Reg, I know what happened, but innocent wolves were murdered too. It was a bally war and-"

"You dunno nothing, Monty! You dunno the half of it-"

"That's enough!" Nurka barked, before patting Reg on the shoulder. "Let's not have a debate, my little friend, time is short. Get her ready to fly," he instructed gently, to which the rat nodded and went about his work. "Help him," Nurka told some of his followers.

The chief turned to another hyena and grabbed a pile of papers from his paws; there were several of the spotted chaps about with stacks of paper, Monty observed.

Nurka approached Montague with the papers; leaflets the cat saw, with photographs and text.

"We will drop these over the Summit," Nurka said. "We have mountains of evidence; the wolves cannot cover it all up with their lies. We will drop them on Lupa too, every town and city that we can. The world will see what wolfkind means by 're-educate'. They do not educate, they torture, and murder, by the thousand."

"But that's impossible-"

"Look at them!" Nurka bellowed, thrusting some papers into Monty's paws. "Look at the faces of my dead brothers and sisters and deny it, I dare you! I *dare* you."

Monty took hold of the leaflets, some dropping to the floor at his feet. They were all the same, a grainy photo of hyena corpses being shunted into a pit, but Nurka quickly snatched leaflets from other stacks and slapped them furiously into Monty's paws; destroyed villages, firing squads, hyenas reduced to walking skeletons for want of something to eat, it was all there, and all convincing.

"We mean you no ill will," Nurka assured the Buttle couple, looking between Monty and Penny, then to Themba and Madou, who looked sideways at each other. "All you have to do is fly," the chief went on. "Nobody will blame you; we held you against your will. Once it is done we will let you go and... give ourselves up."

"Give up?" Monty said, blinking the awful imagery from his eyes.

Nurka spread a paw. "The wolves won't be able to quietly murder us once this gets out. Even if they do, we are ready to die for the cause. But, with help from sympathetic Elders, we hope to precipitate a change of government. THORN stands for The Hyena organisation for Recognition of Nationhood, nothing more. All we want is our land returned, our people freed, and we will live side by side with wolfkind. For all they say about us we haven't the strength to fight them openly. So, we must live in peace and let bygones be bygones. Our Queen will see to that; she will decree what hyenas must do and they will do it. It's our way."

Monty nodded absently. "I see, old chap. I see." He licked his lips, "What about Reg?"

"Reg?"

"Well, what's he getting for all this, him and all the wee beasts? He sounded rather frantic."

Nurka smiled and nodded. "As little beasts will be. The wolves will treat his people kinder once the world sees their true colours; they will have to. Besides, the Elders sympathetic to our cause love the little beasts as much as... as Rufus Bloodfang himself! Red-mist is with us, you realise."

"Really?" Monty marvelled. "Rufus Valerio?"

"Yes. He helped us get to this point. Without him we'd have been killed to a beast in the Gelb mines."

"He's here then?"

Nurka waved a paw, "He was wounded and had to remain behind, but he will be in the new government."

"I see, well that *is* something. So... so there's not going to be any ballyhoo then?"

"Ballyhoo?"

"Fighting and whatnot. Just these leaflets."

Nurka bowed a little, "No fighting," he said. "No blood will be spilt by us, on my honour as a chief. May the ancestors curse me if I lie to you."

Themba raised his chin; Madou breathed a deep breath; an oath to the ancestors was a very serious thing to a hyena.

Monty still faltered.

"If you do not wish to help us I can sympathise," Nurka said, looking to Penny, "but we may be forced to take more drastic measures. Beasts may die. I hope you understand that, compared to the murder of hundreds of my kin, a few strangers here and there are... as nothing."

Monty gulped and nodded, "Absolutely. I quite see your point. Can't really argue with the facts when the beasts with the facts also have pistols."

Nurka cocked his head to one side, "You'll fly us?"

Monty could but acquiesce with a nod.

"Then we are friends. Come."

The hyena chief ordered Themba to remove Penny's gag and set her down, then he led them outside into the morning sunshine, Penny holding Monty's paw. They passed the trucks that had ferried the hyenas from Kambi Mata to the farm. Nurka's followers set about the trucks, gingerly unloading a wooden crate from each.

"That's a lot of leaflets!" Monty observed, trying to remain chipper for Penny's sake.

"Yes," Nurka agreed, ushering them out of sight. "We've a lot of eyes to open."

"She can't carry more than fifty tonnes, you know, the old *Nimbus*."

"Monty!" Penny seethed.

"Sweetpea, we have no choice, we have to get them off the ground. It'll be all right. It's just a… a propaganda coup."

Nurka assured the frightened Penny that it was, and that Reg had supplied all the specifications needed regardless of any further cooperation. The hyenas had no more than ten tonnes of cargo to load, plus themselves; there would be no problem lifting off. Nurka did not need to consult the cats to calculate that ten tonnes of black-imperium weighed the same as ten tonnes of paper, and nor did they need to know.

"Nurka!" Themba panted, rounding the towering hanger.

"Yes, Themba?"

"Howlers, chief, coming down the road, fast."

"What?"

Themba lifted his Jua-mata helmet a moment to rub the eye Penny had poked. "There's a lot of them… at least ten… and I do not need to remind you there's only three Chakaa amongst us."

Nurka assessed the dire situation, running his purple eyes over the hanger and the windows. "Inside," he said. "We'll be able to hold them off long enough to launch. Come along my good cats, it seems we'll be leaving a little earlier than scheduled."

"They'll shoot us down!" Penny asserted, as Themba dragged her along; a cloud of ash on the horizon signified the approach of monobikes. "The Nimbus will explode, don't you see?"

"Explode, by the Wind!" Nurka rasped sarcastically, ushering Monty along. "How strange. I was under the impression your wondrous new felitium was inert, Mrs Buttle. Aren't you something of an imperiologist?"

It seemed Nurka had done his homework.

"It's not as inert as all that," Penny claimed, as she was pushed inside, passing under the *Nimbus'* red nose cone and into the silver gondola. "In any case, they'll shoot the airbags and we'll sink. You're already lost, sir!"

"The ship has hundreds of small gas bags, one or two being punctured will not hurt," Nurka replied, stepping aboard with Monty. "I commend your bravery in trying to fool me, but please cooperate."

Silence.

"I have *seen* the blueprints!" Nurka rasped, the whine of approaching monobikes pushing him into a rage. He squared up to Monty, dwarfing the slender cat in mass though not height. "Now get this machine started, Mr. Buttle, or I will have your rat walk me through the procedure regardless. Mark my words, if we start sinking, the first ballast overboard will be two uncooperative cats. Fly and you're of use to me. Refuse and you are not. Do I make myself clear?"

Monty nodded and tipped his cap. "Jolly clear, sir."

"Excellent."

Penny pressed her pink nose to the gondola window, trying to see what was being loaded into the *Nimbus'* cargo bay – not leaflets, she was sure. Themba pulled her back from the cold glass and growled menacingly.

"Penny, be a dear and help me," Monty quavered.

"But Monty-"

"Please!" Monty mewed desperately. "Please, Sweetpea, just do as they say. It'll be all right."

Whilst the Buttles began to pull levers and cables, watched always by Themba and some lesser hyenas, Madou climbed aboard with a speckled white moth hanging off on an arm. He passed it to Nurka.

"Chief."

"Thank you, Madou," Nurka replied, the moth taking up residence on his shoulder. He looked his stocky companion over, "How are you feeling?"

Madou's eyes flitted, "Fine, chief."

"Good, good."

"Shall I stay and see to the Howlers?"

"No, you and Themba must come with me. You've earned this. The others know what to do. They are ready to die, as are we all."

Nurka patted Madou on the neck, then went to Themba and pulled him into a three-way conference.

"This is it," the chief rasped. "All we have worked for. Today we set things right!"

Madou could but smile, nod, dip his chin.

Crack! Ka-crack!

The Howlers arrived, pistols and rifles blazing. The battle had begun!

⁕

"We're too late!" Linus shouted, ducking with Uther behind a silkworm trough.

"Not yet, mate," Uther gruffed. "Not yet."

The dusty hanger windows were quickly smashed by spotted elbows and the hyenas within began shooting out at Lachlan's Howlers. The farmhouse too harboured a couple of hyena snipers upstairs, one of whom took a well-aimed rifle-shot at the Bloodfangs.

Ka-crack!

The mighty pellet punched through the trough, sending splinters flying.

"Ulf damn it!" Uther snarled, shaking a paw.

"You hit?"

Wild-heart checked his trembling, bleeding paw. "Just a graze, mate," he laughed, giving it another shake. "Bit of wood or something. Bastard's got a Greystone rifle; must have to go through wood this thick and be that accurate."

"Where'd he get that?"

"Ulf knows, but he's dangerous. I gotta take him out. Stay here, Woodlouse, won't be a minute."

"Uther!"

Too late, Uther was already tearing through the obscuring fields of mulberry and towards the Buttle farmhouse. Linus was about to follow when Lachlan grasped his shoulder and pulled him back behind the trough.

"Where's this airship?" the white-cloaked Hummel asked, flicking his head at the hanger. "In there?"

"I can only presume so," the red-cloaked Linus responded.

Lachlan checked his wound, then chanced a peek at the hanger and all the hyenas stationed at the windows taking pot-shots at his wolves, and them back.

"Well we're nae getting in easy," the Grand Howler judged. "Perhaps we should keep them pinned down and send for help?"

"Most likely help won't come in this district, sir," Linus said. "Besides, the hyenas must be about to take off in order to make the opening ceremony. There's no time."

"Can we nae shoot the thing down?"

Linus shook his head, "No, I don't think so."

"But, did nae one explode over Felicia? Aye, Ah read about it in the papers-"

"Yes it did, sir!" Linus snapped, frustrated and trying to think. "But that's been fixed since. The lifting gas is inert, it won't catch fire now."

Lachlan looked Linus over and asked, "And how do you know so much about it, lad?"

"The inventors are friends of mine," was the youth's reply. He dipped his chin and gulped, "In fact I should have seen this coming. I should have thought of it myself. It's so obvious now it's painful. I could have warned Monty and Penny. I could have stopped this before it even begun!"

He punched the floor with a spark of plasma.

"It's nae your fault lad," Lachlan soothed. "You've nae got a wicked mind, is all."

Linus shook his head, and his paw. "An imperium cannon might do the trick," he sniffed afresh.

"Och! Ah left it in mah other breeches."

The two guffawed nervously at the joke, knowing that they had no options open to them save rushing the hanger and seizing control of the airship by force. Many, if not all the Howlers would die in such an attempt, but far better than all of Hummelton and beyond.

"Ah'll tell the lads what's about," Lachlan said, scurrying to his Howlers.

Time passed, shots were fired, orders given.

Before Lachlan could organise the final assault, Uther returned, skidding behind the trough with an enormous rifle in his paws.

"Got him," he said.

Linus checked the farmhouse – the hyena sniper was draped out the window, brained or worse. "That was quick."

"Fastest wolf in Lupa, Woodlouse, you know that."

Linus hated to ask, lest his friends were dead. "Did you see Penny or Monty in the house?"

"No, mate."

"They must be in the hanger. Hostages, do you think?"

"Maybe. I saw a sneaky way in back there."

"What? Where? How?"

Whilst tearing open a cartridge to reload his rifle, Uther explained, "There's a water tower round back. I reckon I can climb up that and get on the roof; there's probably a skylight for ventilation. I'll drop in and surprise 'em, know what I mean? Oi, has Lachlan got any imperium bombs?"

"I don't know; it's not standard gear, Uther."

"Ah well, neither's this," Uther cackled, slapping his massive rifle. "This'll put a big hole in Nurka's balloon."

"Not big enough, I fear," Linus woofed. "It won't just explode you know."

"I know, but it'll leak won't it?"

"There'll be cylinders of felitium on board to refill the bags at the pull of a lever. It won't pop and deflate like a football, Uther, it's like… like putting a… a pinprick in a bucket of water, it will take hours to empty."

Uther growled, "Worth a try though!"

"By all means, I'll try anything. Lachlan's going to assault the place any minute."

"Aye, well, so am I – from the *inside* tell him."

Uther made to sneak away, but Linus grabbed him, "Wait!"

"Oi!"

"I'm coming too."

"Woodlouse, you ain't built for sneaking-"

"I'm coming, Uther, and that's an end to it! I'm not a cub, I'm your partner." Linus paused a moment; Uther was very much a criminal now, not his partner, but what did any of that matter in the light of THORN'S planned mass-murder? "We'll attack from within," Linus finished, "Lachlan from the outside."

The Wild-heart gave in and slapped Linus on the arm, "All right, partner."

Hurrying for cover behind an outbuilding, Linus and Uther informed Lachlan of their plan.

"Good luck," Lachlan replied, saluting, "For the Republic!"

Linus saluted firmly back, Uther just barely.

The Bloodfangs set off on their mission, stealing around the farm under the cover of fences and bushes, even piles of rusting machinery. The rising sun helped blind the hyenas to their presence.

Uther ducked behind a flapping sheet of tarpaulin that was stretched over some kind of large machine, like a pitched tent. Linus joined him shortly after.

Poing!

An imperium pellet pinged off a nearby barrel.

"Someone's seen us," Uther said. "I'll get him, hang on."

Whilst he waited, Linus, overcome by curiosity, peered under the tight tarpaulin and discovered a tiny red dirigible that had seen better days. Four large wings protruded from its corroded shell in a squashed X-shape. There was a propeller on the back.

Wait, it's not a dirigible at all, Linus realised, but a heavier-than-air craft!

"Uther, look! It's a aeroplane! I had no idea Monty was making these-"

"Not now, Linus!" Uther snarled, taking aim at the hyena who aiming back at him from the hanger. "Ulf's teeth, like I give a schmutz."

Ka-crack!

"Got him!" Wild-heart woofed. "Move, Linus! Come on, come on, come on!"

Leaving the aeroplane, Linus scrabbled after Uther, following his guidance, however mad, however reckless. Jumping a fence, tearing across the farm and dashing headlong for the hanger. Uther then Linus ducked along its sunny, east-facing wall, slipped round the narrower north face into the vast, cold shade of its west side.

Somehow it felt safer here – indeed there were no hyenas at the windows; Lachlan and his Howlers were keeping them occupied on the sunny side, pistols blazing.

Panting beneath his white-cheeked helmet, red fangs glowing in the relative darkness, Linus looked up at the promised water tower. It was a good few feet from the hanger and was connected to it by a pipe.

As Linus snuck along the wall with Uther, the shield at his back scraped over the corrugated metal. Uther glared at his clumsy cohort and jerked a paw; Linus duly stood proud of the wall a little.

They soon made the water tower. Checking the windows were clear of rifle-toting hyenas, Uther wasted no time latching onto the tower's rust-flecked ladder and racing up, paw over paw, Greystone rifle dancing at his shoulder. Linus followed suit, shield at his back, boots clinking on the metal. It had not occurred to him how high the hanger was until he was halfway up the adjacent water tower's flimsy ladder. Rosalina would not approve, Linus thought.

Uther made the water tank and helped Linus aboard. They stood atop the tower, cloaks fluttering, a whole world of green rolling around them. The hanger roof was glaring in the strengthening dawn sunshine, like wet cobbles on a Riddle District street the morning after rain, when the ash had been freshly rinsed from the air.

"Climb across, right?" Linus panted, looking at the connecting pipe.

"Nah, jump mate."

"Jump!"

"I don't trust that flimsy plumbing, especially you, you're no lightweight."

"Uther I-I-I can't! It's too far!"

"You can do it," Uther encouraged. "Standing jump, mate"

"Standing! That's impossible."

Looking the hefty Linus over, Uther craned his gaze to the top of the tower's water tank. "Come on, up there; there's a bit of room for a run-up," he said, clambering up a pipe to the tank's roof and helping Linus up after him. "Cor, you weigh a ton, Woodlouse."

"That's not helpful, Uther."

"Hahaha!"

They were even higher now, the hanger roof being a good ten feet lower than the water tower's shallow apex.

"It's not far," Uther puffed. "Watch me. Easy peasy."

Wild-heart clapped his paws, rolled his shoulders, rocked back and forth.

Then he sped across the tank's roof in a few steps, like a mad beast, and kicked off its lip! Sailing through the air he landed on the hanger roof and rolled once, before springing to his feet, paws spread, as if expecting an audience to applaud him.

"Come on!" he beckoned.

Linus backed up to the far edge of the tower, as near as he dared – his legs and feet tingling with primeval fear, or was it the rot? Not now, by Ulf, not now. Young Mills prepared himself as Uther had, shoulder rolling and all that, even clapping for what it was worth. He tried to imagine there was not deadly chasm ahead, but a benign sand pit, like the one back in the Academy Linus had practised coronal-assisted long-jumps in. It didn't help.

Poing!

An imperium pellet twanged off the tower, then another and another, making Linus flinch.

Poing! Ting!

The hyenas had spotted him! Spurred on by necessity, Linus dashed those few steps to the lip, then kicked off with all his might. The yawning gap passed in an instant, replaced by glaring metal, and he landed, rubber-soled boots gripping the roof all too well and friction catapulting him over onto his back. Linus scraped along on his shield, spinning like an upturned dung beetle on a tabletop, before rolling over and grasping the roof with his paws.

He was alive.

"See?" Uther cackled, pulling him up and slapping his arm. "Cleared it by miles, mate."

Linus looked – he had too – and he emitted a giddy laugh for it. By Ulf, this was exhilarating!

Knowing they had been seen, Uther quickly found a ventilation hatch and lifted it open. Linus hurried to peer inside as well. Beneath them was a bulging sheet of grey, ribbed fabric, stretching as far as the eye could see. It was unmistakably the top of a dirigible, even though its scale was beyond anything Linus had expected.

"It's enormous!"

"Aye, and it's moving."

"Moving?"

Sure enough the ribbed canvas was sliding by, slowly but surely. Linus could hear the roar of propellers, smell the imperium ash.

"They're launching," he surmised. "What do we do?"

Uther looked all about for another hatch, a different solution, but concluded. "Jump!"

"Jump? Jump where?"

"Down!"

Uther tucked his armoured legs into the hatch and lowered himself down. He hung by his arms a moment, winked at Linus, then dropped some twenty feet onto the canvas below! Uther softened his landing with an imperious blast of will that billowed the canvas in circular ripple, like a pebble dropped into a pond. He didn't even stumble. As the balloon moved ever more rapidly, so was Uther swept away from the hatch like driftwood. He walked along, beckoning Linus, his boots stretching the silvery material over the ribs below.

"Come on!" he seethed.

With every passing second the dirigible grew slimmer, pointier, as the tail end approached, and the fall grew longer, more dangerous.

It was now or never.

With a prayer to Ulf, Linus levered himself into the hatch as Uther had done. Even when hanging by his arms the dirigible seemed awfully far below.

Somehow, Linus commanded his fingers to release. He dropped, bounced on his rump and rolled. There was no purchase, just a sea of sloping canvas.

I'm going to die!

A strong paw latched onto Linus's hood, staying his uncontrolled slide. It was Uther of course, with one black paw grasping a durametal rib through the stretchy canvas, the other Linus.

"Come on, mate!" he barked through his helmet.

With tremulous, adrenaline-boosted limbs, Linus flailed over and gained a purchase on the dirigible skeleton that he could see pressed against the fabric, his boots rested on a horizontal rib, his paws a vertical. Nodding at Uther that he was all right now and not daring to look back, he clambered up the gentle, if treacherously smooth slope. Despite the nod, Uther kept a hold of Linus's hood until he was safely on the back of the vast flying machine.

And flying it was, faster and faster, higher and higher. The relative gloom of the hanger passed over, replaced by an infinite blue sky and a blast of cross-wind that sent the Howlers' cloaks fluttering and the canvas wobbling, slapping the skeleton beneath. To the right was a hill of grey, to the left the four fins that made up the airships tail, each pinned upright with steel wires.

Uther stood up and confidently advanced along the ship's spine like the fearless maniac he was; Linus followed, albeit low, almost on all fours. Uther crouched, allowing Linus to catch up and assess the predicament he had gotten himself into. All around was blue sky and green horizon, behind was the silvery silk worm barn that had served as hanger, its roof shining bright in the sun.

The airship tipped back a little and rapidly gained height, sending Linus clawing at the canvas.

He looked back and saw the smoky battle continuing below between Lachlan's Howlers and the THORN hyenas.

"We're on our own now!" Uther shouted over the wind and propellers churning somewhere below.

Linus could but nod.

Were Nurka and the other Chakaa aboard? Were Monty and Penny? How do we even get to them? All Linus saw from nose to fin was a sea of shimmering, rippling silver canvas with not a hatch or hole of any kind.

"How long will it take to get to there?" Uther shouted in Linus's ear.

"What?"

"To Hummelton?"

"I… I don't know!" Linus replied, calculating, or trying to calculate in any case, roughly how fast a dirigible could fly and how far away Hummelton was, and not how fast a wolf would fall and how far away the ground was. "We need to get inside!"

"Hatch?"

"Can't see any!"

Uther looked about, nodded, then pushed on the stretchy lozenge-shaped world of fabric. "Cut through?"

"The inside is just bladders of felitium! The gondola is at the very bottom!"

"Aye! So?"

"So we… we might suffocate inside the balloon, you can't breathe felitium."

"Poisonous is it?"

"No, but it's not air, Uther!"

Uther slung his rifle round and plucked the bayonet from the muzzle. With this he cut a long slit in the fabric and peered inside, looked about a bit, then withdrew. He gestured for his comrade to have a go. Like a maggot squirming into an open wound, Linus pushed his masked face into the fluttering incision and looked around. It was dark, but he could see huge, white, rectangular bladders, dozens of them stretching as far as was visible, all squashed neatly together like plant cells under a microscope. They were secured to the durametal skeleton by wires running through eyelets.

"I'm going in!" Uther shouted, as Linus pulled his head back into daylight.

"Uther-"

"Got a better idea?"

No, Linus did not.

"If I get the angle right," Uther said, "one shot from this rifle could go through half them bags. What you reckon?"

A nod, "Worth a try!"

"Chop the rest open, aye?"

"If we lose too much lift we'll crash!"

"That's the idea!" Uther replied with a laugh.

Linus thought about it, and supposed crashing here in the countryside was better than at Hummelton, but he also supposed the black-imperium canisters might burst upon any violent impact and melt everyone inside. Worse, if the fuel tanks exploded and sent the wreck up in flames, the black-imperium would be carried aloft in the smoke to rain down over many tens if not hundreds of square miles. It would be a lesser disaster that what the hyenas had in mind, but a disaster nonetheless.

Linus put his argument to Uther, who shouted defensively back, "What do you wanna do then?"

"Take them out?" Linus said.

"The hyenas?"

"If there's not too many! We should at least look! It's a few hours to Hummelton, I'm sure!"

After some time, Uther nodded his agreement.

Without further ado Wild-heart split the fabric further and slipped inside, dropping onto the nearest bladder and grasping one of the steel wires for support. Linus lowered his legs in and with half as much grace joined Uther within the strange world of the dirigible, with bulging white bladders for a floor, an arcing grey ceiling above, and the thrum of propellers constantly assaulting the ears. The bladders were unexpectedly firm underfoot, but it was still difficult to walk with any kind of sure-footed grace, even Uther struggled to move about as he searched for an obvious way down through the tightly-packed bags of felitium. Cutting one open was an obvious solution and Wild-heart readied his bayonet knife again.

Linus came alongside him and hung on a steel wire.

"I think-"

Choing!

The wire snapped, slashing Linus in the right arm and tearing the bladder beneath him wide open.

With a cloak-billowing blast of felitium, and a wolfen yelp of surprise, Linus fell straight through the sagging canvas of the bladder and plunged into blackness.

"Linus!" he heard Uther bark, but Wild-heart could not save him this time.

Tumbling in free space for a split-second, Linus bounced off another bladder and slammed back-first into some horizontal supporting strut – his shield took the blow, but he then fell forward onto another structural support just below that, raking if not breaking some ribs. Winded and unable to cling on for pain he fell again, landing on some metallic platform to an awful, somewhat fleshy clamour.

"Gahaaaghfffgh!"

Linus rolled agonisingly over, grasping at his slashed and profusely bleeding arm. He had landed on a walkway that he judged ran from nose to tail of the airship. All around were bladders, struts, pipes and wires.

There was no sign of Uther.

Suddenly the walkway rattled beneath Linus's back, alerting him to several guttural-sounding hyenas bearing down on him from both ends with rifles and pistols ready.

Not good.

Linus scrabbled to his feet and lurched over the walkway's railings – more durametal framework and bladders lay beneath, but what lay below that, mere flimsy canvas stretched over skeletal struts?

The desperate Howler contemplated throwing himself over; contemplated too long.

Crack! Crack! Crack!

Poing! Ting! Pang!

Pellets ricocheted off the walkway, piercing bladders and then the cringing, flinching Linus.

The Howler collapsed silently about the metal walkway, his left leg hit, his shoulder torn. They went numb and useless, then stung like fire, as if Linus had been whipped by burning hot plasmatic cables. Unable to stand for the pain but with a plan of escape to paw, Linus rolled blindly off into space amidst a shower of colourful sparks. One pellet deflected off his impervious Bloodfang shield, stripping some paint off just as its owner fell bravely into oblivion.

The attacking Hyenas gathered excitedly at the railing and aimed down.

"No!" Madou barked, pushing them all away. "You'll burst all the air sacks!"

The stocky Chakaa looked down at the white 'air sacks' and saw two were smeared with rich, dark blood where the enemy had slid over one and then between them both.

"Get back to work!" Madou ordered, climbing over the railing. "Tell Nurka I'll find him."

The lesser hyenas waited, uncertain.

"Go on! I can manage!"

With his followers dismissed, Madou lowered himself carefully into the belly of the ship.

High above, Uther watched helplessly as everything unravelled. Wild-heart was unable to reveal himself, not even for Linus; there was too much at stake.

Shouldering his rifle, Uther picked his way down the dirigible's framework, hoping against hope his friend and comrade might still be alive down there somewhere, but accepting it might not matter.

One way or another, this crate is going down.

Chapter 52

Werner looked at the ticking clock above the dusty, long-since abandoned bar; it was approaching eight.

The clock was one of the few things still functioning, water and imperium gas being cut off a year ago when Casimir and Bruno had disappeared and stopped paying the bills. The windows had been daubed inside with white paint and the door boarded up, but the clock's precious white-imperium battery would last decades yet. For the imperium alone it would have been looted long ago had not Werner taken special charge of *The Warren* for his own needs, and the needs of the cause. Condemned and locked down by the Politzi Chief it served now as a secret rebel enclave.

Casimir could have the premises back when the great deed was done, clock included.

"Not long now," one of Werner's fellow conspirators said – to any passer-by just another rat Politzi, but underneath he was one of many such officials that had joined the cause.

"Aye," Werner replied, casting his beady eyes over everyone lounging around the tables. Some tried to play cards by imperium lantern, pitting paper bees, wasps, ants and termites against one another in an attempt to stay calm, but most sat nervously clock-watching, nursing fears and pistols alike.

There came a creak on the stairs as Professor Heath joined the conspirators nestled around the café tables. The old bear didn't really belong, he was no rebel, but Werner had agreed to take the befuddled fellow in until his problems blew over.

"Any news?" he whispered, as if he had a clue.

"No," the rotund Werner replied. "You should stay upstairs, Professor."

"I can't sit all day. I need to move about."

"If a Howler sees you that'll be the end of it! I can explain us lot away as a secret knees-up, but you're a wanted beast."

Heath hiked his brows. "A secret knees-up," he observed, casting an eye over Werner's armed Politzi, "with no beer and illegal pistols? That'll wash."

"Just stay upstairs," Werner snorted. "You can jump out the bedroom window if we're rumbled."

"I wouldn't fit," Heath dismissed, wandering round the back of the bar. He noticed the time. "The Pack Summit will be getting under way soon."

"Aye and THORN will be dropping our evidence."

"Humph! Lot of good some pamphleteering will do, even if it is from a balloon or whatnot."

Werner looked to his fellow conspirators then gruffed at the sceptical Professor, "You'll see what good it'll do, mate."

Heath checked the cupboards for a drink or some morsel, turning up nothing but a small and quite inedible spider. "Pictures are strong evidence, Werner, but hyena-sympathisers have been giving them out for years and it's changed nothing," the Professor sighed, ferrying the delicate long-legged spider to a safe place and watching it to crawl up into the rafters. "If the Den Fathers know of the Reservation abuses, they will deny it; if not they will dismiss it as propaganda."

Werner claimed, "Aye, well, we've got more than leaflets. That's just the beginning of our Impartialist movement."

Heath folded his arms, "So I gather."

"Oh yeah?"

"I know a rebellion when I see one. I've lived through a few. I want no part in any violence."

"Aye! You're neutral. 'Tis fine, I can respect that. But like I said, stay out the way."

Letting his arms fall loose, Heath rowed back a little, "It's not that I don't *agree* with Impartialism, Werner. Of course I want Lupa to be a city for all, but it's very often intellectuals like me who are targeted in the inevitable purges!"

"Not under Nikita, mate," Werner revealed.

"Nikita?" Heath said, recoiling. "Nikita of ALPHA?"

"Aye."

"So... he's your leader?"

"That's right. He's gonna throw Adal and all the rest over. Hah! Nikita's a real Impartialist. He's not like Adal; he won't tell beasts what to think and when to think it."

"You're convinced of that, are you Constable, when Nikita himself arrested Rufus for 'dissenting remarks'?"

"It were Adal's orders! But he's in Hummelton now. Nikita is in charge and soon he'll have the whole city, with *our* help."

All was set, Werner explained to Heath. When word came from Nikita, Werner would seize Riddle Den and instruct the Politzi to lock down the district. The same would happen at many Dens across the great city as rebel Politzi and Howlers emerged. Control would be wrestled from the grasp of Boris and other weak placeholders left to watch over Lupa by the absent Den Fathers. ALPHA would assume control and run Lupa as a united single pack headed by Grand Prefect Nikita. Now *there's* a wolf Werner could get behind! A rabid impartialist raised on the wild Steppes amongst beasts of all kinds, Nikita had released countless dissidents from ALPHA's cells and turned the other cheek to venom smugglers and hyena-sympathisers alike. Nikita would rule, aye, but as an impartialist he would do so with the help of the pigs and the rabbits! Train hogs and Politzi hogs, rabbit clerks and tax collectors, the hogs and long-ears were everywhere, running everything, trade and civil service relied on them; whoever ruled needed the humble pigs and rabbits.

Heath sighed, "And what of the Den Fathers, Werner, are they just going to roll over?"

"Oh, don't you worry about them, sir."

"I'm not, I'm more worried this is the start of another war!"

Suddenly the front door burst open, the bell ringing overhead, and a big grey and white wolf in a black Prefect's uniform tumbled inside *The Warren* and fell about the place, knocking over a chair.

"It's me!" he panted, removing his helmet. "It's me, don't shoot!"

His face was bloodied and covered in dressings, but Heath quickly recognised the wolf. "Tristan!" he woofed, hurrying to his aid.

"He tried... to kill me!" the Howler exhaled, as Heath picked him up and led him to a bench. Werner peered down the street and shut the door.

Tristan rambled, desperate and afraid, "I-I-I didn't know where else to go. Not home; the Eisbrands would question me too. She let me get away, Meryl Stroud that is, the ALPHA nurse. She gave me this uniform and led me out and-"

"Slow down, lad, slow down," Werner said. "Were you followed?"

"No."

"Sure?"

"Yes! Yes! I waited round corners and everything."

"All right. Fine. Now, who tried to kill yer?"

"Nikita!" the bloodied Tristan yelped, collapsing on a green wall-bench. "He sent Silvermane out, then threw the switch and tried to cook me alive. He killed Josef's assistant to do it! Meryl... she saved my life. She risked everything for me. I don't think she's really with us... but.... Oh, I don't know what to think anymore!"

Tristan rocked on the bench, arms folded close.

Heath turned to Werner with exemplary sarcasm, "What a reasonable fellow, this 'Nikita', murdering his own comrades. Not at all like nasty Adal or the Den Fathers, oh no-"

"Shut up!" Werner snorted, turning to Tristan. "It must've been a mistake, lad."

"No mistake!" the wolf seethed, shaking his head. "No mistake, Werner. Nikita threw the switch right beside me. I begged him not to do it, I begged him-"

"It *were* a mistake!" the hog reiterated, laughing and patting Tristan's shoulder, looking reassuringly at everyone else's worried faces. "Probably wasn't even Nikita you saw. You all look the same you wolves in your cloaks 'n' helmets, eh? You were probably confused from all the racking, lad."

"Not with *his* accent, Werner!" Tristan snarled, standing up to his full height, his raw, bandaged features suddenly filled with a terrible fury. "Do you take me for a fool?"

"No, lad of course not-"

"I tell you as I'm standing here, Grand Prefect Nikita tried to kill me! He did *this* to me!" Tristan spread his bandaged arms and paws. "I'll be scarred for life, Werner!"

"I believe yer! I do!"

Silence.

"I'm... I'm not sure of anything now," Tristan said, dipping his chin and collapsing onto the seat again, paws clasped and thumbs twiddling. "If Nikita will dispose of me like an insect after all I did for the cause, how will he treat the Den Fathers? I... *I know* beasts will die, as in any great change there will be violence, I accept that. But I was told we would work with the Den Fathers for change, holding the white-imperium as leverage so Thorvald and the others would have to come to Nikita's table."

Werner trotted across to the dusty bar and leant on it a moment. Checking the time again he whirled round. "Look, Tristan, you may as well know the truth. All of yer may as well know, now it's too late to stop it."

"Stop what?" Heath said, pushing up his specs.

"I didn't want to tell yer," Werner excused, looking to all, "I didn't want yer to know in case things went south, see? You lads can't be held responsible if you know nothing; you can deny everything with a conscience at any future trial. So, if you don't wanna know what I know, if you wanna be able to live a quiet life and not have troubled sleep, leave now." The Politzi Chief looked Heath over, "That goes double fer you, Professor Heath."

"I'll stay, thank you," the bear said.

"Aye, as you will."

Everyone else stayed put; rats, hogs and all.

"Well?" Tristan growled. "What is it?"

Werner heaved a sigh and rubbed his jaw, "I'm one of the few that knows, outside of the inner circle. See, Nurka *had* to tell me, he needed my help to get proper maps of the Gelb mines so he could spring Prince Noss out. I wanted to know the truth. I forced it outta him. The truth I said, or I'm-"

"Stop bragging and get to the point, hog!" Tristan growled, rising up, stepping forward. "I understood Nurka was to disrupt the Summit and keep the Den Fathers away long enough for Lupa to fall to Nikita, whereupon negotiations for an Impartialist government and a free hyena state would begin. Now what is it I've not been told?"

"The black-imperium, mate."

Tristan scoffed, "Is to contaminate the Elder Trains and cars. It's to keep the Den Fathers trapped at Hummelton-"

"No, they're gonna use the balloon!"

Tristan's eyes squinted, "Yes, to drop the propaganda-"

"No! Well, not just that."

"Then what, Werner? Spit it out, pig before I hit you!"

Heath's jaw dropped. "Ye gods," he gasped, removing his spectacles, "they're going to make black rain."

✤

"Euuugh," Sara stirred.

Despite everything, tiredness had overcome Sara last night and sent her off beside Bruno; she awoke now in the near-darkness of Josef Grau's oppressive carriage to find her old friend's metal operating bed empty.

"Bruno?" the little wolfess gasped, spreading her clammy black paws on the bloodied steel. "Bruno, where are ye!"

"They're in the van," said Eldress Brynn, down to the right.

Sara stood and looked at her. Someone had wired the noble Eldress to the van, her paws being now attached to the bumper in front of her. Ulf knows when she had awoken after the almighty blast Olivia had delivered.

To think Olivia had such power and without the slightest training to temper her. It was frightening.

"Let me go, Sara," Brynn whispered, squirming and looking over her shoulder. "Quickly!"

Sara shook her head a little. "Ah cannae do that yet."

"You must! Your Father will wonder where I am-"

"Ah don't believe he sent yer, nae Mum. You did this by yerself. You could even be a conspirator."

"Conspirator!"

"Maybe. Maybe ye think Bruno can stop them."

"He's a monster, Sara-"

"Ah'll let you go soon enough, but you'll nae hurt him, nae tell anyone where we are."

"They *know* where I am."

"Oh aye? If anyone did they'd have come straight here," Sara countered. "Now be quiet, Eldress, or Ah'll have Olivia zap ye again!"

"You wouldn't dare!"

"After ye tried tae kill Bruno Ah would nae care if she killed ye, and that's a fact. So shut up!"

Sara wasn't sure herself if she was blustering or not, but it sounded pretty good, so she left things at that and hurried round the van.

"Bruno?"

The doors were shut; she tugged them open.

"Brun-och!"

A huge metal wolf loomed large beneath a dim overhead light, taller and broader than any Sara had seen, with lensed eyes of gold and a black Prefect's mantle set with a brooch of shining white-imperium. Sticking up from his back was a dirty great ash-stained exhaust pipe and the shining hilt of a huge black sword that was somehow very familiar. His nose was a grille, as with any Howler, only larger, and he looked to be sealed inside his armour completely, chin, neck and all.

Olivia and Josef stood either side, like squires dressing a wolf knight of old, only they were twisting valves and checking pipes rather than tightening belts and buckles.

"Bruno?" Sara hazarded

The giant's metallic ears swivelled and his blank eyes focused on Sara, as if he had been daydreaming and just that second noticed the doors had been thrown open.

"HEY," he said, his voice tinny, augmented, coming through a speaker perhaps, and yet with all Sara recognised it at once, that carefree, light, yet deep back of the throat knell that was Bruno. "YOU ALL RIGHT, YEAH?"

"By Ulf it's you," Sara gasped, paw rising to her neck. She stepped backwards, eyes roving, face twisting and frowning, baffled and afraid, relieved and appalled. "This is the Eisenwolf mantle?"

"An eisenpelz; isn't it magnificent?" Olivia said excitedly. "I helped Josef put it back together."

"Indeed, Olivia was most helpful," Josef mewed at Sara, his face as smug as it was triumphant. "I believe we three have come to the conclusion I have been much maligned. I am not a heartless butcher; ask Rafe yourself! I help him cope with his affliction daily. He would be dead without my help!"

Olivia walked over to Josef, "It's all right, Sara. Everything will be all right for me now. You'll see."

Sara looked between them, and knew at that moment something terrible had come to pass whilst she had been asleep.

I've lost her, Sara realised.

Stepping forward, her paws resting on the van's chrome back bumper, Sara Hummel looked to the only cause left to her in this van. "Ye all right in there?" she asked. "Is it you in there Bruno, or is it Rafe Ah'm talking to?"

The Eisenwolf said nothing for a time. "I FEEL… ALL RIGHT, ACTUALLY," he sniffed, noncommittally. "WHAT WAS IT YOU GAVE ME LAST NIGHT?"

"A family secret," Sara said.

Bruno rolled his mighty shoulders, "WHATEVER IT WAS, THANKS FOR GETTING IT."

"Just use this second chance wisely. Don't get in trouble again. All right?"

The Eisenwolf said nothing.

"Promise me?"

"I... I CAN'T DO THAT. I HAVE TO PROTECT LUPA. THAT'S WHAT I'M HERE FOR, WHAT I WAS GIVEN THIS GIFT FOR! YOU DON'T HAVE TO UNDERSTAND... BUT DON'T GET IN MY WAY."

Sara backed away at the rebuff. "Ah didn't mean tae get in the way; Ah know what you have tae do, Ah do," she claimed, meekly at first, but coming back to the van with growing confidence. "Just remember, Bruno... Rafe... *whoever* ye are in there, that you're nae a monster for what beasts say ye are, but what ye actually do. There are beasts that care for you out here, even if ye cannae remember us so well. Even if ye nae even remember our names, we remember yours, and we're watching you. You fight for Lupa, aye, but do right by us; don't do anything we'd be ashamed of! That's all we powerless beasts ask."

Rafe's ears twitched and swivelled. "JUST CALL ME BRUNO, YEAH? SINCE YOU KNEW ME BEFORE."

Sara guffawed and dipped her chin, "Aye, that Ah will, ye great lump."

Rafe looked to Josef, "DOC, I CAN HEAR A TRAIN STARTING UP."

Josef checked his pocket watch, "That'll be the Bloodfang's imperium engine warming up. Amael is planning to leave before the hyenas choke everyone."

Rafe somehow looked alarmed, even through an unmoving helmet – it was all in the ears.

"Oh don't worry," Josef assured him, "Janoah's going with him. She'll have this carriage attached to the Bloodfang train before they leave. Amael trusts her, and will be too busy to check inside. He'll have no idea that his fate has been sealed until *you* walk through the door and arrest him and all the conspirators, or kill them if they resist." The cat sighed, "Either way it'll be quite... quite glorious."

Rafe looked to Sara, then back to Josef.

"I'LL ARREST THEM," he asserted, "SO THAT THEY GO TO TRIAL. NOT KILL."

"You'll do whatever's expedient-"

"I'LL DO WHATEVER'S RIGHT, MATE," Rafe asserted, "RIGHT BY ALL LUPANS."

Sara chuckled, "Aye, now *that's* mah Bruno."

"We'll see," Josef huffed. "Now stop fidgeting and let me finish preparations."

✢

"No!" Tristan howled. "This is insane!"

"It's the way it has to be, lad!" Werner replied. "War is about killing the enemy any way you can; the winner can sort the history books out and make a nice story later. Believe me, the Howlers have done it enough times now. When Nurka flies over Hummelton all the Den Fathers, and I mean all of 'em, will be dead and gone. Lupa can start afresh under a true Impartialist regime-"

"But all the innocent beasts! There'll be cubs and-"

"Casualties of war, mate! Casualties of war. Like my family; murdered by Howlers, and my pal Casimir's too *and* Bruno's no doubt. Aye, and they came back too, the Howlers, and took Bruno from Casimir, as if taking everything else from them two weren't enough already." Werner shook his jowls. "And I helped 'em do it, to my shame. I helped 'em. Janoah thinks she's made it, thinks she's all that. She's clueless! Aye, she's had it now, along with all the rest of 'em. They've all had it this time."

"This isn't going to happen. Not in my name!"

"Aye? Well too late now, Donskoy! You knew what you were getting into when-"

"I knew nothing of this!" Tristan bellowed, grabbing Werner and shaking him by his jacket lapels. "By Ulf, what do you take me for? Sara's there you fool, her whole family, all her little sisters. I love her!" The wolf shook his teary face, "This ends now, do you hear me? It's not too late to warn Thorvald. I suggest you get out of town, Werner, because I'm calling time on this conspiracy and when I return I will kill you myself if you're not gone-"

Crack!

In a flash of imperium and puff of ash, Werner fired from the hip, hitting Tristan in the stomach. The already wounded Howler fell silently, bending-double at the pig's trotters.

"Tristan?" Heath shouted, kneeling and cradling the groaning wolf. "Tristan!"

"Anyone else got any funny ideas?" the quivering Werner shouted, stepping backwards and grabbing a second pistol from a pitted table. "Eh? Eh?"

"No chief," one of his rat followers said, paws up. "We're with yer all the way."

Others voiced their approval.

"The hyenas can do as they like!"

"Aye, down with the Howlers!"

"Kill 'em all!"

"Good lads," Werner approved. "I knew you were with me. We'll take this city, and our revenge, you'll see!"

✢

"Janoah?"

The wolfess turned from the window overlooking Hummelton.

"Come in!"

Amael stepped in. "Time to go," he said, crossing the generous Hummelton quarters, complete with four-poster bed and an en-suite.

Baffled, Janoah glanced out the window at the quiet early-morning town. "The Summit's not even begun yet."

"We're not attending the Summit," Amael whispered.

"I thought we were going to put in an appearance and then leave on some pretence-"

"That's what Nurka's been led to believe, but I do not trust that he will not come early to get rid of me as well as the rest. So we're leaving *now*." Before Janoah could say anything, Amael raised a paw, "It makes no difference to the Summit, it will go on regardless. And even if it doesn't everyone will be here when THORN strikes and… well… that's that."

Janoah moved close to Amael and whispered, "What exactly *are* the hyenas going to do anyway? Are they hiding around here waiting to leap out with black-imperium gas bombs?"

"Humph! Always so clever, yet you haven't worked it… out?"

Amael trailed off somewhat and looked to his right, at the bedroom's en-suite.

"Do you feel that?"

Janoah wrenched Amael's attention back with both a paw to that chin and some accompanying flattery, "You're too devious even for me, Balbus."

"Indeed," the Den Father cackled, the en-suite forgotten in favour of Janoah's ruddy visage. "I'm glad I can still surprise you. Grab your things and meet me out front, my love. If anyone asks there's been an emergency in Riddle-"

"And we're going home to sort it, I know, I know."

A nod, a smile, Amael kissed Janoah and made to take his leave.

"Oh, the Alpha's carriage!" Janoah hissed, grabbing Amael's arm and leading him to one side.

"Carriage?"

The Prefect explained, "On the end of the Eisbrand train, the last ALPHA carriage. We should take it. I can have it moved; I have the authority, just as long as you say it can be shunted onto your train, of course."

Amael woofed, "Whatever for, wolfess?"

"It's full of millions of lupas and white-imperium, my dear," Janoah said, tidying Amael's cloak. "All of Adal's worldly possessions. He'll shortly be dead and shan't need them. It would be a shame not to take a lasting souvenir of my employment under him."

"Hahahaha, Janoaaah!" Amael cooed, stroking her lovely chin. "And yet you say I am more devious?"

After a kiss the Den Father took his leave, saying, "My car's out front. Hurry, and be discreet, the fewer eyebrows raised the better."

A nod.

Once she was 'alone' and quite sure Amael's corona had receded down the Hummel corridors, Janoah turned to the window. "You can come out now."

The en-suite door to her right creaked open and Vladimir emerged.

"You kept your corona about as dampened as a roaring Greystone furnace," Janoah scoffed. "He must've thought it was Duncan or Horst next door that he could feel, definitely not that 'weak pen-pusher' Oromov."

Vladimir grunted and bowed a little, "I've carefully cultivated that reputation for just such times as now. He doesn't see me, even under his nose."

"Nor me," Janoah replied, turning and adding, "I hope."

"I didn't hear him say what THORN is going to do."

"No."

"But... you suppose it *is* the dirigible?"

"That's where I sent our boys, so it had better be."

Vladimir spread his paws and growled. "How could you not get it out of Amael? He was right here and yet-"

"It would have been pushy and suspicious. I don't try him too hard, Vladimir."

"You did to save Rufus!"

"Because Amael *knows* I love him. That was genuine."

Vladimir paced around, armour clinking. "That's a fine thing, but what am I supposed to do if the balloon appears on the horizon? How will I know if Uther and Linus failed, or if it's even a threat at all? If I advise Cora to shoot it down and all that rolls out of the burning wreckage are two dead cats of royal blood I will be as good as ant-food and Lupa at risk of war with Felicia!"

"Do as you will," Janoah said, grabbing her rapier, her pistol and her helm from the bed. "Word may yet come from Rufus and the boys, if not... do as your conscience dictates. I'll do as mine does; a wolf can do no more."

"You, a conscience? With that Eisenwolf monster you and Josef keep under the stairs? Don't make me laugh." Vladimir came up behind Janoah. "You know... I wouldn't be surprised if you know *exactly* where the attack will come from and that you plan to go all the way with Amael, leaving me and everyone else to rot here-"

Janoah whipped round and slapped him.

Vladimir weathered the blow, wiped his nose, sniffed, whilst Janoah donned her helmet and trotted out the door, leaving the Grand Howler unsure whether he had merely insulted the Prefect, or sailed too close to the truth.

✦

Janoah exited Hummelton Den and, with a last glance back at the ancient castle, joined Amael in the back of his car. The Elder Trains always packed a car and some monos in an engineering carriage so the Den Father could venture abroad; Vito had brought his gorgeous Bloodfang-emblazoned, smooth-seated, luxurious private car – now it was Amael's.

Soon all of Lupa would be, for keeps.

Several other presumably conspiratorial Bloodfang Elders were in the car with Amael already.

"Janoah?" one spluttered, recognising her from her years as a Bloodfang.

"Elder Duval," Janoah replied.

"What is the meaning-"

"She's with us, Elder Duval," Amael replied, raising a paw but not his voice, not yet.

"But she's with ALPHA, Den Father."

Now the thunderous voice was raised, "As is Grand Prefect Nikita! But he is one of us also, as are hundreds of others across Lupa and beyond; ALPHA, Greystone, Bloodfang and Eisbrand, even Hummel. Today is the day the righteous Howlers put aside their petty differences and rise up as one pack of the just, putting an end to the stinking corruption!"

Much nodding and chest-thumping and hear-hearing.

"Where's Flaid's car?" another asked, a very young-looking 'Elder'.

"Flaid is not coming, Elder Cohen."

"But I thought he was with us, Den Father."

Amael explained patiently, "He is a Den Father, and *two* Den Fathers is one too many. I cannot share power."

"Well then what about Nikita?" Cohen pressed.

With a glance at Amael, Janoah stepped in, "Even as the new 'Alpha', Nikita will be legally beneath Amael and controllable. Flaid would be an equal partner and a legal complication we do not need."

"As Prefect Janoah says," Amael seconded.

"But I thought-"

"Calm yourself Elders, all is in paw."

As her door was closed by the Den Guards, Janoah wasn't so sure that everything was in paw. "Won't Flaid try and follow as soon as he finds out we're gone?" she asked.

Amael looked to his partner in crime and bed and said fondly, "He does not know what I know. Besides, he will find his Elder Train mysteriously… temperamental this morning."

"Sabotage?"

A wink.

"Devious Amael," Janoah cooed, much to the confusion and vexation of the other Elders. They looked on in silent disgust as this lowly Prefect removed her helm and then the Den Father's and kissed him with the obvious familiarity of a seasoned lover.

The rumours were true.

Amael's followers dared say nothing as the car pulled away, flanked by Den Guards and Howlers on monos.

Janoah judged that not even half the Bloodfang away-team was present, just a smattering of Elders, Grand Howlers and Howlers, some traitors, some simply obliviously following their Den Father.

The rest were to die with the all other flotsam, it seemed to Janoah, dear Vladimir included. Amael had no love for his pen-pusher and never had; he had been a rival once.

A rival for me.

Through the gates, passing two mighty Hummel Halberdiers, their saluting forms reflecting comically in the car's polished bodywork. If they were concerned by Amael's sudden departure they were ultimately powerless to stop it; a Den Father's business was not to be curtailed by anyone, not even during last night's curfew. If Amael wanted to leave that was his concern. Just another reason why old Vito had to die, Janoah realised; even something as easy to overlook as escaping Hummelton, which would have been difficult a few days ago, was simple now that Amael was a Den Father, answerable to nobody.

By Ulf, he's worked it all out; every detail, every facet, and I didn't even help him with half of it. He's handsome, strong, ambitious and young enough. He's so like Rufus; by rights I should love such a wolf the same.

Could I learn to be happy with him?

Parting lips with Amael and smiling, Janoah peered sadly out the window as the daylight rose higher over the happy little town of Hummelton.

Perhaps its last happy day.

Chapter 53

Propellers thrumming outside, Madou followed the blood trail through the dark bowels of the *Nimbus*, squeezing his muscled frame between churning imperium pipes and bulging sacks of air, or whatever special gas was in them. Sometimes he was necessitated to step across yawning gaps in the durametal skeleton with only flapping canvas beneath. One false step and Madou might rip right through the flimsy-looking material and plunge a thousand feet to his death.

At last the Chakaa reached some kind of terra firma, a metal corridor, with a door ahead, an alcove to the left, and a window to the right – the beginnings of the gondola slung beneath the main balloon perhaps, Madou hadn't gotten a good look of the layout.

The blood smeared its way along and to the left.

Madou went to the corridor's edge. He thought twice about stepping round, lest the Howler lay in wait. He instead tore a strip from his cloak and waved it.

"I'm a friend!" he shouted over the propellers. "I want no part of this!"

No reply.

"I'm stepping out! Don't shoot!"

Still nothing, but Madou was no coward. Dropping the strip of cloak and removing his helmet, he slowly edged out into the open, his paws clearly raised, a vast hyena silhouette against the wobbling, new-materials window behind.

Tucked in a corner ahead of him, pistol raised in a quivering, bloodied paw, was the Howler, his golden fur matted with crusty gore, one leg limp and useless, one arm tucked close.

"Stay there!" he woofed, as Madou took a step forward.

Madou stayed his advance. "I'm on your side," he said, as loudly as he dared. Even as the words left his lips he felt his guts twist for the betrayal of his Chakaa brothers, for all the work they had done and all they had been through to get here.

The blue-eyed Howler squinted through his helmet. "You're… one of the Chakaa hyenas. From the refinery; the one… the one that was bitten, aren't you?"

Madou chuckled. "A wolf that doesn't pretend he can't tell two hyenas apart!" he grunted. "I like you already."

"I thought Amael had you… agh… executed."

"No, I was sent to Gelb. I met Rufus there, perhaps you know him, Bloodfang?"

A cautious nod; the Bloodfang Howler flicked his pistol, beckoning Madou closer so they could discourse easier.

"Go on."

"We're friends," Madou explained, paws still up. "I don't know if Red-mist is still alive. When I left the camp he was in trouble."

"Trouble?"

"My chief, Nurka, he discovered Rufus's betrayal, and my Prince's too, a-and Tomek's. You won't know them, but they were all working against THORN. I didn't know who to believe, or what to do, but I… I had no choice but to follow my Queen. I *had* to obey Queen Arjana's word, it is hyena law. So, I struck Noss down because she said so, though I despise myself for it now!" Twisting in the galling chains of conflicting loyalties, Madou seethed and shook his head, "None of that matters to you, Howler, what matters is stopping this madness. I want my people to be free, but not like this. You have to help me. Please."

The blonde wolf listened well, then scoffed, "You want my help? By Ulf, you came *this* far, hyena. You *knew* about the black-imperium, you helped steal it!"

Madou nodded slowly, "I knew we were to use black-imperium, of course, but I thought we were to bomb the Den Fathers at the Summit and then attack the Howlers, dying in honourable battle, not… not this!" Madou gestured at the walls. "They say we will kill thousands, all of this Hummelton place and then on to Lupa, all the citizens wolf to mouse. It's not honourable! We will all be damned by our ancestors. Nurka… he's not well. It must be the purple-imperium; the chunta must've clouded his mind! He is a noble hyena, but you wolves killed his family, and Themba's. I... I never really knew mine, it's true. My cousin's family took me in, then Prince Noss himself trained me. Perhaps I am less touched by the pain of our people's suffering, or perhaps I'm just a coward."

The wolf shook his head. "No. If you stand up for right... that is not... cowardice."

He lowered his pistol.

"Well, if this is a trick, hyena, now's the time to... to finish me off. Not that I'm much of a threat to anyone."

Madou smiled and lowered his paws, "No trick, friend. If I wanted you dead I'd have done it by now."

"Indeed," said the wolf, holding out a bloody paw. "I'm Linus."

Madou's hefty brow rose in surprise, but he went over and bent down to shake paws. "Chakaa Madou."

"Honoured, friend."

A wave of shame washed over Madou's soul. How many more wolves were there in Lupa's ranks like this one, like Rufus, Tomek, wolves of substance? Yet THORN wished to kill all and sundry without discrimination, without honour!

"Are you alone, Howler Linus?" Madou asked, kneeling before him.

"Yes," Linus lied, his eyes flitting upwards. "I-I-I leapt onto the balloon and cut my way in. Madness really, but... I had to do something."

A nod.

"What do you propose we do, Madou?" Linus asked.

"I was hoping you could tell me, Howler," Madou replied, glancing around. "I do not know where to begin, but if there are two of us that's already better than one."

"One and a half," the crippled Linus seethed. "Grrfgh! All right, how... how many hyenas are there aboard?"

"Maybe two dozen, including Nurka and Themba and me."

"And who's flying the ship; Monty and Penny?"

"Who?"

"The cats, yes?"

"Oh! Yes, the cat and his wife. Nurka has forced them to, they didn't want to."

Linus nodded, "Does anyone else know how to fly?"

Madou shrugged his mighty shoulders, "Nurka seems to know a lot about this machine. I know nothing and Themba can't do. None of us even knew about it, save Queen Arjana I presume."

Another nod, a grunt, a plan.

"Then... what we need to do, Madou," Linus said, "is take Nurka and Themba down... them being the only other Chakaa." He dipped his chin and looked at Madou, "They *are* the only ones, right?"

"Yes," he replied with certainty.

"Right. Good. The rest of the hyenas you and I should be able to keep out of the gondola whilst Monty lands the ship... or at least crashes it gently enough not to cause a fire. Once she's down we can sabotage it."

Madou sat forward, "Could we not just sabotage it now, break some imperium pipes perhaps? Isn't that what you were doing up in the roof, cutting the air out of the bags?"

"No... no I-I fell, Madou, a cable snapped," Linus said, somewhat embarrassed; unsure if bad luck or stupidity had caused his tumble. "If we go down too hard... there could be an imperium fuel fire... and that would be *very* bad, believe me. Pure black-imperium will not travel far, but bound to smoke particles it might carry for hundreds of miles. I think the wind is blowing towards Lupa today. The poisonous cloud could reach there; it would certainly reach Hummelton... and the miles of farmland before. How many would die, if not immediately then at least prematurely from eating and drinking black-imperium? Even a teaspoon can kill thousands. The cases of rot would be incalculable."

Madou took a sharp breath.

"I doubt your Chief Nurka truly appreciates what he's got back there," Linus said. "Black-imperium is a thing hardly seen in nature. We… create it in quantities that do not belong on the surface of this planet."

"Nurka would agree with you there," Madou insisted. "We all would, us hyenas."

"You'd have us go back to the pre-imperium era, I suppose?"

"I would."

"I prefer to believe in a post-imperium era," Linus chuckled, wincing further, "Some kind of clean energy, from the wind or the water, even the sun. Fanciful perhaps, but, so was flying once." The Howler sobered up with a sniff, "Madou, we'd better think of something. With the wind behind us we can't be more than an hour or two from Hummelton, and I'm bound to become more useless to you by the minute."

Madou nodded, "I'll bind your wounds."

"No… no, leave them. I… I might have an idea."

A break, but for the propellers and wind, as Linus put it together in his mind.

"Wire," he said. "We need wire."

"Wire?" Madou replied, looking all about and passage and overhead. "Why?"

"To look like Howler-wire; it will seem like you've caught me, when you haven't. You see where I'm going?"

"I think so."

Linus felt his wounded arm, cut by wire. "The air bags?" he suggested. "They're held by wire."

Madou was on it, stepping round the corner and drawing his imperium short sword he cut a wire holding the corner of the nearest air bag. The wire sprung back viciously and slashed open the bag just as it had with Linus, releasing a rising cloud of felitium gas that betrayed its presence only by the way it set the air wobbling fitfully, as above a flame.

Whilst Madou wrestled with the wire, Linus made a heroic effort to stand. Limping on one leg and dragging the other, and with one arm rendered useless at the shoulder and the other cut deeply, he hobbled to the flimsy new-materials window and leant his cut arm on it, imprinting a bloody smear like the first daub of paint on a new canvas.

Wincing and grunting, he took a moment to observe the fields and forests of Everdor passing miles below, the trees resembling tufts of moss, the fields of worked arable land a patchwork quilt. Linus swore he could see little beasts standing outside farmhouses and by the roadside, waving. Such a glorious sight, and one Linus had dreamt of ever since that day in the cinema.

So long ago, it seemed.

With every passing house and station, every road and mark of civilisation, the dirigible drew nearer Hummelton, hub of Everdor, breadbasket of Lupa.

Linus rolled round to face Madou, "Well?"

The hyena ripped the wire down and felt it. "It's springy, but maybe it will look right."

The wolf offered up his paws, "Make it look convincing."

✢

Cora Hummel sat slowly behind her ornate office desk; she was dressed for the Summit and appeared as magnificent as any, more so for her stunning white armour and cloak. She looked up at the Grand Howler standing smartly, yet nervously before her, his striking Bloodfang colours resembling a poisonous caterpillar to Cora's pastel butterfly.

"You're the third beast tae come tae me with this, Howler Vladimir," she said, spreading her black paws over the desk.

"Third, Den Mother?"

"Mah daughter warned me yesterday; she's nae a fool but she moves in… dissident circles. Mah Howlers also arrested a lunatic rabbit on a mono during the curfew last night. They would have paid him nae mind, but because he was on a mono word got round tae me."

Vladimir stood equally astonished, "A little beast riding a monobike?"

"Aye, and well apparently! He claims tae have been spying on THORN for some time." Cora leant back in her chair. "Now you come before me with the same tall tale; that this dirigible is loaded with black-imperium."

"Perhaps, Den Mother," Vladimir stipulated. "It is merely supposition from evidence, but-"

"Nae to the rabbit, he's adamant."

"Who is he, if I may ask?"

"Funny you should; he's been asking for you!"

Leaving Vladimir baffled, Cora picked up a beautiful mahogany telephone, the base of which was inlaid with lighter wood depicting bees, flowers and honeycombs. "Send the rabbit up. The mad one. Aye, on the mono. Quickly now."

She hung up, twiddled her thumbs. Similarly, Vladimir fondled his golden pen behind his back; it was scant comfort. He had revealed his knowledge and allegiance at last, he was no longer invisible; now if Amael succeeded he was a dead wolf regardless of survival here.

Brrring! Brrring!

Cora gently put her phone to an ear and listened; Vladimir watched her fine, dark-furred face twist, her ears flick.

"What do you mean?" she said. "When?"

Vladimir looked on; he knew what this must be.

Cora stood up with her phone and strode went to the window, cable trailing after her. "Is his train still here?" she asked the caller, craning to see Hummelton Station. "Well go find out, Howler, and make sure he *doesn't* leave!"

A pause.

"Ah don't care if Ulf himself is on that train; hold it until Ah get down there!"

Slamming the phone on the desk, Cora declared, "It seems Amael's trying tae sneak away."

"Escaping," Vladimir stated, not even feigning surprise.

"Maybe," Cora replied, still guarded. "Ah'm going tae have this out with the wolf himself, Den Father tae Den Mother-"

"That wouldn't be wise, Den Mother."

"Would nae be wise? And who're you tae tell me-"

"Amael *will* be stopped, Den Mother, by my fellow agents," Vladimir revealed, chin up, trying to appear confident despite himself. "There are wolves planted amongst his inner circle who will... arrest him. If you confront him personally your life could be in danger. There are conspirators all around us; anybody could strike you down."

"Would the traitors nae be on Amael's train by now?"

"Some, certainly, but he has left far too early. I believe he may be attempting to divest himself of the competition by leaving many of his fellow conspirators here to choke; Den Father Flaid amongst others."

"Flaid... a traitor?" Cora scowled, looking Vladimir up and down with sudden suspicion. "By Ulf, you accuse your superiors too readily, Howler!"

"I speak as evidence finds, marm!" Vladimir maintained perilously. "If you do not believe me, or your own daughter, I suggest you speak to Adal Weiss as well!"

Cora waited, baffled, but listening.

Though he hated to give away credit for his work, Vladimir felt he had no choice but to cite the powerful Adal.

"The Alpha has been instrumental in allowing me and my agents to investigate this plot," he said. "He will corroborate all I've said. I did not turn to ALPHA lightly, I am not fond of their constant bullying of the Howlers, but I could turn nowhere else when my own Elder was a traitor. If I had come to our pack's Provosts with my knowledge, Amael would have found out and I would have been disposed of. For a year now I have kept silent to all but my closest confidants, waiting for this day."

"So you knew and said nothing?" Cora hissed.

"Den Mother, it was decided, by all involved, *including* the Alpha, that the only way to catch the conspirators red-pawed and make the charges stick was watch and see who attempted to leave the Summit on the day of THORN's planned attack. It stands to reason that any beasts who leave *must* have prior knowledge of an attack, whatever the manner of it, and *must* be with Amael. Whoever the wolf, Howler, Elder, even Den Father, they will all prove their guilt without question the moment they get up. However, those who remain in their seats, ignorant of any concrete knowledge of danger, must be presumed innocent. Therefore, our duty, marm, is to maintain the Summit as if nothing is amiss. We should continue as before, with or without Amael, yet be prepared to fend off any THORN attack. I pray to Ulf this poisonous dirigible will not materialise on the horizon, but we must make ready to shoot it down as discreetly as possible and as far from Hummelton as we can. I'm not entirely sure shooting it down won't simply spread a black-imperium cloud far and wide, but at least it shan't work as THORN and Amael intended."

Cora stood still for an age, assessing Vladimir's face, considering his words. "This is… incredible," she said.

Vladimir mopped his brow. "So it must seem," he replied, with a slight chuckle. "I fear I've grown accustomed to Amael's despicable plot, having had knowledge of it for so long. But my conscience is clear, Den Mother. Do as you will, I can do no more than I have."

There was a knock at the office door and Cora bade two Hummel Howlers to enter. They were escorting a white rabbit in a jacket. The rabbit's paws were wired – if he could ride a mono he should also be able to wield imperium.

Vladimir looked at the little beast and immediately frowned, "I've seen your face before."

The rabbit said nothing as he glanced nervously about.

"What's his name?" Vladimir asked in general.

"Casimir Claybourne, sir," a Hummel replied.

"Yes, that's it. Your nephew Borce works for us, under Constable Werner."

Casimir dipped his chin, "Dunno what you're on about-"

Vladimir slapped him quite casually, "Liar!" and continued, his remarkable memory on form. "You used to run *The Warren* down in Riddle District a while back. You're the rabbit who adopted…" he broke off and chuckled. "Oh I see! Humph! Of course you *would* join them after that. Ah, but too monstrous was it? Haven't the stomach for the terrorist agenda? No I don't blame you. So now you come crawling back to wolfkind, how pathetic-"

"I need to speak to Vladimir!" Casimir barked. "Please! I have a message for Vladimir Oromov-"

"You're speaking to him!" Oromov growled.

After a pause for breath, his eyes darting over Vladimir, Casimir blurted, "Noss sent me!"

"Noss?"

"Aye. He says that he's doing all he can from within THORN, him and Rufus. They told me to warn you about the… the balloon. It's gonna fly over Hummelton and Nurka's gonna spray everyone with black-imperium. It'll be genocide. I've said it a hundred times to your Howlers, but they aren't listening!" He looked back at his captors. "I rode all night to get here, dodged checkpoints, got shot at, everything. I've done all I can do, now it's down to you lot, so Briar help you if you don't believe me!"

Silence.

"Well, *don't* you believe me?" Casimir gruffed.

"Forgive us, citizen, if we don't look surprised," Vladimir said. "It's because we suspected this was THORN's plan. You have confirmed it."

Cora stepped forward, "You're sure this is how THORN's tae attack mah fair city, citizen?"

"Aye, Prince Noss is certain as can be, marm," Casimir replied, with a tiny bow, unsure just how to act in front of so noble-a-looking wolfess. "Nurka confided in him, all the plans, everything."

"But Prince Noss is dead, is he not?"

Vladimir raised a paw, "That's a *long* story, Den Mother, and we have little time. I suggest we procure an imperium cannon or two and set them up to the East of town, and some distance from it. It can be excused as a gun salute."

"Aye," Cora agreed weightily. "The Consort Angus will help ye arrange that, Howler. Ah'll stay here and keep the Summit in order, as you say." She turned to one of the Howlers escorting Casimir, "Someone find Eldress Brynn, Ah need tae speak tae her, and summon Adal Weiss as well."

"Brynn's missing, Den Mother," the Howler in Cora's sights blurted back.

"Missing?"

"Since last night, Den Mother. Under the Consort Angus' instruction she escorted Sara from the Den and nobody's seen them since."

"Well find her! And find Sara! And gather mah daughters, they must be taken somewhere safe, do y'hear? Do it discreetly, mind, Ah want nae panic."

"Yes, Den Mother."

"And fetch Angus here, Ulf help him!"

"Yes, marm."

One of the two Hummel Howlers left to attend her mistress's wishes; Vladimir hoped that particular wolfess was no traitor, just about anyone could be.

Even Janoah, Ulf help me.

Cora turned to the Grand Howler, "If we survive Amael's bid tae overturn the Republic, Vladimir Oromov, Ah'll be sure tae recommend you tae whatever new Bloodfang Den Father is elected in his place."

Vladimir bowed, "I merely serve this great Republic, Den Mother."

"Aye, as do we all."

✦

The Bloodfang Elder train whistled and bellowed, spurting clouds of acrid ash tumbling across the sunny platform. She had been turned around and was ready to go.

As was Amael.

"After you," he told Janoah, leading her to the nearest carriage door, his queen.

"Oh!" Janoah chirped airily, as if the matter had quite slipped her mind, "Amael, we need to get the Alpha's carriage."

"I'll take care of it, Jan."

"Be sure you do, it's important."

"I know."

Smiling, Janoah reluctantly boarded the train – she could urge Amael no more without seeming irregular.

Moving through the sumptuous lounge carriage at the head of Amael's band of conspiratorial comrades, Janoah sat in a plush red chair facing a window and peered anxiously across the station platforms and parked trains. She could see the end of the Eisbrand train poking out beyond the others thanks to the extra ALPHA carriages tacked on.

He's right there, inside Josef's carriage. Is he ready? Can he even stand up?

It's time to choose a side, Rafe. You promised to stand with me, whatever happens.

Suddenly Janoah felt a disturbance in her corona, so familiar, but then it vanished. She looked up and saw the back of a rather tall Bloodfang Howler as he glided past, with pure white arms and tail.

Before Janoah could think to call him over, the Elders drew her attention with some commotion.

"Hummels!" one shouted.

"Looks like trouble," came another, pressing his nose to the windows on the opposite side to Janoah.

"We should call this whole thing off."

"Don't be a fool! It's begun; we'll do better to fight!"

Janoah got up, "Calm yourselves, my Elders," and crossed the carriage to observe the goings-on herself.

Amael and two Den Guards were facing down some officious-looking Hummel Howlers that had obviously rushed to the station; their monos were still ticking over on the platform behind. Muffled, if clearly heated words followed as Amael explained his unexpected departure; some unspecified, but vital emergency demanded his presence in Bloodfang territory. He was leaving half his Elders here to vote whilst he returned to Lupa to see to the matter. *In any case, if I want to go for a picnic in the woods, I'm a Den Father now and it's none of Cora Hummel's business!*

Or words to that effect, Janoah couldn't quite make it out.

Regardless, the flummoxed Hummels were powerless and dared not press a Den Father further.

Turning his back on the Hummels, Amael flicked his paw ahead, signalling to someone. He then entered the lounge carriage and walked amongst his fellow conspirators.

"We're leaving," he grunted soberly.

Janoah pushed off the window, "What about the carriage?"

"Carriage?"

"The Alpha's. We need to couple it to us."

"Forget it, Jan."

"But Amael it's worth millions-"

"I said forget it! Cora's on her way over and if she knows I've gone already that means Flaid could be next. We can't have a scene with him, it'll be war."

Amael passed Janoah, heading deeper into the train, his followers in tow.

Left alone, Janoah went to the opposite window and looked upon Josef's carriage, her mind racing, heart pumping. She contemplated dashing across and fetching Rafe, or simply slipping off the train and letting Amael go.

Suddenly the floor jolted beneath Janoah's feet sending her stumbling her into a chair.

We're moving. Time's up.

Amael returned, smiling reassuringly; Janoah was rooted by his gaze, her paws kneading the arms of her chair.

"Nervous?" Amael asked, sitting opposite.

Janoah could but shrug and smile back. She felt sick to her stomach as Rafe's carriage slowly passed, as if she were abandoning her own cub on a doorstep.

She placed a paw on the window.

Ignorant of the truth, Amael joked, "There goes a few million lupas." Chuckling, he leant forward and grasped Janoah's paws in his. "Don't worry, my love, you'll not want for anything once I'm your Emperor."

He leant across and kissed her; it felt empty, oh so empty.

※

"It's going!"

"NO IT'LL COME BACK. IT HAS TO COME BACK."

"It's going, Rafe, I'm telling you."

Josef joined Olivia and Rafe at the carriage door. He removed his spectacles and watched the Bloodfang Elder Train chug away. "It is going," he gasped. "Janoah, you treacherous maggot. She's deserting us!"

"NO SHE AIN'T!"

"She's left us to choke, Rafe! I *knew* she was with Amael. I should never have trusted her!"

"SHUT UP!" Rafe bellowed at Josef, his voice echoing and distorting like a wolf in a giant steel pipe. His backpack exhaust ejected a tiny puff of ash. Breathing heavily the Eisenwolf thought a moment, ears swivelling. "SOMETHING MUST BE WRONG. SHE MUST BE IN TROUBLE. WE HAVE TO GO AFTER HER, JOSEF."

The cat spread his grey paws, "How? Can you drive a train? No!"

"The van?" Olivia suggested, paws spread. "Well can't we chase them in that?"

"AYE!" Rafe said. "AYE, THE VAN. COME ON!"

By the time Sara thought to join the commotion at the door everyone was dashing back inside the gloomy carriage, though it did not remain gloomy for long. Josef pulled a lever, chains and gears whirred, and the right wall of the carriage fell open like a drawbridge, gaping onto the platform and allowing light to flood in.

"What on Erde?" Sara gasped, squinting. "Bruno, what's going on?"

"I GOTTA GO, SARA; THE ELDER TRAIN'S LEAVING WITHOUT ME."

Eldress Brynn was still tied to the van, so Bruno burnt through her supposedly Howler-proof bonds with a continuous snap of plasma from a single finger, like a blow-torch.

"What're you doing?" Brynn yelped.

Picking the astonished Eldress up, Bruno set her aside.

"TAKE HER," he told Sara, "AND GO BACK TO YOUR MUM."

"Bruno-"

"PLEASE! STAY SAFE, YEAH?"

"Get away from her, you abomination!" Brynn growled, throwing aside what was left of the wire. "Sara, run! Ah'll hold him off."

"Och, shut up!"

"He could kill you with a touch!"

"Aye, and you any time, but he didn't!"

Bruno looked to Brynn, then cupped an enormous iron-clad paw to Sara's little cheek. "EVERYTHING'LL BE ALL RIGHT."

Despite her trepidation, Sara wrapped her arms around Bruno's unyielding metallic body. "Be careful, Eisenwolf."

"I WILL."

Tossing aside the last securing chains, Josef started the ALPHA van with a shudder and a honk. "Rafe, get in!" he hissed out the window.

With a casual salute at Sara and Brynn, Rafe clomped round to the back of the van and leapt inside with surprising grace. The moment the van doors slammed, Josef turned the steering wheel hard over and shunted straight through the boxes and barrels that had served mostly as a disguise.

As the van passed Sara, she saw Olivia rise up in the passenger seat and wave!

"Olivia!" Sara called, giving chase. "Oliviaaa!"

The van screeched down the carriage's ramp and pulled away amidst a pall of ash, leaving Sara coughing in its wake. It sped across the station and down a cobblestone ramp onto the road, pursuing the fleeing Elder Train via the nearest street through Hummelton.

"Don't forget me, Bruno Claybourne," Sara said, watching the van disappear over a bridge. "Nae yourself."

Chapter 54

Chakaa Nurka stroked the white moth hanging on his shoulder as he scrutinised Montague and Penny Buttle working the *Nimbus'* controls. Monty gently turned the wheel, increasing thrust to the left or right engine as appropriate to maintain course; Penny, meanwhile, played the controls like a strange musical instrument, pulling wire cords that in their turn inflated felitium bags or dropped ballast.

Nurka had studied the blueprints and felt he had a grasp of the workings, enough to spot signs of sabotage. "Why are you dropping so much ballast?" he rasped, grabbing Penny's paw.

She turned to him and replied primly, "Because, Mr. Nurka, we're losing lift. The Howlers probably put some holes in us as we took off."

"Is it serious?" Nurka interrogated further.

Monty took that one. "No," he said proudly, turning the shining durametal wheel; the rolling Everdor landscape beyond the tremulous windows shifted as the ship turned. "In previous ships maybe, they had just a dozen or so big lifting bags, but *Nimbus* here has over a hundred. Takes a lot longer to pop a hundred balloons than twelve, eh? Haha!" The hostage winked at his captor, "Don't worry, sir, we'll drop your bally leaflets, though not if you stop me wife from keeping us airborne! Paws off the merchandise, if you please."

Nurka looked sideways at the semi-jolly and always polite Monty. It was almost as if the cat was on side! His wife's face, however, was remained thunderous.

"Reg?" Nurka said, turning to the rat.

"Sounds right to me," he replied.

Satisfied he was not being tricked, Nurka released his iron grasp and Penny continued her work.

"Held hostage by a hyena twice in twelve months," she complained, tugging a cord and watching a dial spin. The airship noticeably rose, Nurka could feel it. "If this is how you hyenas conduct yourselves, Mister Nurka," Penny went on, "you'll receive no sympathy from me."

"I do not expect sympathy from a spoilt catess raised in luxury, nor do I seek it."

Monty huffed, "This 'spoilt catess' could help you; she has influence with her cousin the Queen of Felicia, after all."

"Does she?" Nurka said, incredulous. "Yet your Queen does not let you fly your 'infernal contraptions' over her city."

"Well no."

"So not very much influence!" Nurka surmised.

Penny asked, "You hyenas have leaders too, don't you?"

"Yes. The Matriarchs, and our Queen."

"And sometimes they are swayed by misguided council from jealous and ambitious sorts, are they not?"

Nurka sighed, "Perhaps."

"Well, the same has occurred to my cousin regarding Monty's balloons. But as Queen, and what's more Empress of many foreign lands and races who are *not* cats, she's well-used to local customs and complex territorial issues. She's always sympathetic to the plight of the natives."

"Natives, Madam?" Nurka growled in offence.

"Yes, local conquered folk."

"Oh I see! Spear-chucking barbarians like me, is that it?"

Penny wouldn't be drawn on semantics. "Sir, if the hyenas had sent a delegation to Felicia with such evidence as you have shown me, my cousin would have pressured Lupa to treat your people fairly. If such... such *appalling* things as is on those papers are truly occurring then I do sympathise, and wholly, but kidnapping and terrorism and all that THORN has done is no way to go about winning hearts and minds-"

"By the Wind, just fly your ship, madam!"

"We could end this now and sensibly. We'll turn right around and fly straight to Queens Town.

You'll be under Felician law there and quite safe. We can then sail to Felicia and present a case-"

"Madam cat, do I look like a fool?" Nurka rasped, his purple eyes alight. "Your cousin and her council would not interfere in Wolfen affairs even if I took them on a tour of the disgusting conditions in the Reservations myself! The trade links between Lupa and Felicia are too valuable to disturb over some 'natives'. Now I will *not* say it again; be silent and fly, or you will shortly be put out a window and I will pull those cords myself!"

"If you believe that then why are we dropping your pamphlets at all? What good will they do?"

"Just do as he says, Sweetpea," Monty advised calmly.

"But Monty-"

"Penelope Buttle, be quiet! Please!"

Penny tugged on a cable extra hard, venting both gas and her fury. "Humph!"

The mighty, labyrinthine-cloaked Themba trudged into the gondola with his kristahl hammer. "Chief."

"Themba, have you prepared the... the leaflets?" Nurka asked, sliding a paw under his hyena-skull-shaped helmet to nurse his head.

A nod, as Themba equated leaflets as code for black-imperium. "You all right, chief?" he whispered, glancing at the cats, then at his fellow hyenas standing guard. "I heard shouting."

"Fine. Fine. Just... tired."

After a moment's thought, Themba leant close. "You should rest. Let me take over."

Nurka grunted negatively and clapped a paw on Themba's huge spotty arm. "The Howler," he said, focusing. "Did they find him?"

"That's what I came for; Madou's got him."

"Dead?"

Themba shook his head and beckoned through the door.

The stocky Madou escorted a similarly-built, blonde-furred Howler down the main walkway. The wolf's arms were bound with wire, and so infirm was he from his many grievous injuries that Madou had to help him stumble painfully into the Gondola, whereupon he balanced on one leg, his other foot barely touching the floor. Despite his lack of stature and crippling wounds, the Howler stood chin up and chest out, as nobly and proudly as he could.

Before Nurka could say a word, Penny whirled round and gasped, "Linus!" She tugged on her husband's sleeve. "Monty, it's Howler Linus!"

"Linus? What do you mean? Oh!"

"Monty, Penny," Linus replied. "Don't be afraid."

"Oh Linus, what've they done to you?" Penny mewed, her gloved paws finding her cheeks.

"Acquainted are we?" Nurka rasped, looking between all concerned. "Small world."

"Brute!" Penny scolded him. "Brutes, all of you!"

"Be quiet and fly, madam!"

"I will not! Not if this is how you carry on!" Penny insisted, clutching at her dress, "I'll... I'll... why I'll not pull another cord, and nor will my husband! I absolutely will not stand for this."

"Sweetpea-"

"Shut up, Monty!" Penny hissed, then to the hyenas, "If you're going to hurt anyone you might as well make good your threat and throw me overboard!"

"Now Penny-"

"Stand up for yourself, Monty! Really, I mean it!"

Glancing at Nurka, Themba stomped over to the cats and grabbed Penny by the arm. "As you wish!"

"Let me go, you brute! Let me go!"

"I say, paws off!" Monty said. "Let her go-oof!"

Themba shoved him away and holding Penny fast dragged her towards the gondola's left side door. "We had best lighten the load, Madam. Out you go!"

"No!" Linus barked. "Please, leave her, be!"

"Themba!" Nurka snapped, the white moth fluttering at his shoulder. "That's enough."

Grinning broadly, as if this were all an exhilarating game, Themba indicated to Reg. "The rat can fly us, Chief, him and yourself. We do not need these insufferable cats, even less the Howler weighing us down."

Nurka reiterated, "Behave yourself."

At length, Themba released Penny back to Monty's care with a flick of the paws and a menacing growl.

The cats embraced each other.

"This Howler might matter to somebody," Nurka said, looking to Linus. "He certainly matters to our pilots. Another hostage cannot hurt."

Themba pushed the cats back towards the controls. "Get back to work! Go on!"

Monty led Penny back to the controls and they corrected course, engines revving and cords tugging. As the landscape shifted like a painted theatre backdrop being rolled onto set, a distinctly grey smudge panned into centre stage, like a distant, low-lying cloud.

No cloud, but surely a town– Hummelton Town.

"That's it!" Nurka woofed, walking to the window. "That's Hummelton." He looked to the cats. "How far away is it?"

Silence.

"How far, cat!"

"Not sure," Monty replied at length, tapping the altimeter. "At this height we can see maybe… fifty miles."

Nurka searched the sea of twirling dials himself. "What's our speed?"

Monty glared at him, but said, "Faster than it says. The wind is at our tail. I'd say we're about half hour out from Hummelton."

"Good. Good."

A brief quiet.

"We're rather early, wouldn't you say?" Monty hazarded, chin up. "We're not expected to fly over until noon. Might they not think something amiss-"

"Hah! Good! Let the wolves be surprised!" Nurka laughed, turning to Themba. "Check on the others, make sure the bl… that *everything* is in order."

"Chief."

Staring at Linus and shoulder-barging him on the way past, Themba tramped out the gondola and down the walkway, passing under the gas balloons arcing overhead, like a triumphal arch made of marshmallows.

Stroking his quivering moth to calm it, Nurka addressed the similarly quivering cats. "If you do not want to incur Themba's temper again, leave the politics to me and speak only when spoken to."

"He's a brute, sir, as are you!" Penny snuffled from the control panels.

"And these Howlers who kill hyena cubs, Madam," Nurka replied, gesturing at Linus, "are they brutes too?"

Linus frowned under his helmet, but kept his tongue.

"Yes, if true, then they are," Penny admitted.

"Then you see, Themba and I have merely risen to the occasion."

"Lowered yourselves, you mean. Two wrongs do not make right, Mister Nurka, and Linus here is a good wolf, he is no killer of anyone let alone cubs."

Linus's frown abated somewhat.

"He is a Bloodfang, madam, amongst the most fearful and brutal of the packs, do not doubt it," Nurka argued, walking over to Linus, paws behind his back. He stepped left and right, inspecting the intruder, "Your pack seems to have given us the most trouble of all, Howler Linus, from Redmist to our own Prince Noss, yours is a nest of traitors and deceivers-"

"The Bloodfangs are loyal to the Republic."

"Even Amael?" Nurka seethed triumphantly, purple eyes widening deep in the sockets of his helmet. "You must know of his treachery to have even come here, Howler, there is no other way you can have known where to come."

"Not at all. Many know by now and they are ready. Amael will fail, as will you-"

Madou grabbed the scruff of the wolf's neck and pulled his head back, "Silence, scum!"

"No, no, Madou, let's have none of that," Nurka said, glancing at Penny. "We hyenas are not 'brutes'."

"No, Chief," Madou replied, releasing Linus. The wolf glanced at him.

"You're strong," Nurka observed, leaning close. "I can feel your corona, Linus; it crackles like... Red-mist's."

"As does yours, Chakaa."

"A compliment?" Nurka woofed, surprised.

"No," Linus denied. "Truth."

"Truth? Then whilst we're about 'truth' are you alone?"

"Yes."

"Liar! Howlers *always* work in pairs."

"My partner didn't make it aboard."

"Then how did you?"

"I jumped on the roof."

"And your partner?"

"He was... too afraid," Linus maintained.

Nurka laughed hoarsely. "Too afraid. Hahahaaahaha!"

Somewhat bemused by Nurka's mirth, a thing he was not known for, Madou spoke up, "He's telling the truth, Chief."

"How do you know, Madou?" Nurka snapped.

"Because... because if there *was* anyone up there they'd be cutting air bags open to sink us, like this one was trying to before he fell. Our warriors did more damage by shooting at him; they put holes in everything. Luckily I stopped them or we would be crashing into the ground by now."

"Indeed."

Madou licked his lips and suggested, "You should let me take their rifles away, Chief. They don't need them."

Nurka glanced at the two indignant-looking hyenas standing guard, then turned to the windows and the growing smudge that was Hummelton. "I think we can trust them now there's nobody to shoot at, Madou."

Madou breathed deep, "Yes, Chief." He looked at Linus, and drew his sword a little.

Linus shook his head subtly.

Reluctantly, Madou slid the sword back.

"Nurka, this is beneath the noble hyenas," Linus said.

"Noble are we?"

"Yes! Rufus, Red-mist, taught me many things about you. He always said the hyenas were wronged and I agree. Think about what you're doing-"

"By the Wind, Howler, I've thought about nothing else these past moons," Nurka replied tiresomely. "Do you honestly think you're going to change my mind?"

"And how is your mind, Chakaa, flooded with purple-imperium?" Linus said. "Do you even know what you're about anymore?"

"I have never been more lucid."

"Then listen! The Den Fathers have been warned, nobody will even be down there. Hummelton will be evacuated. You'll look like a mad fool and nothing more."

"Oh? Yet here you are trying, *failing*, to stop me."

Linus had no answer to that, save, "I'm merely the insurance policy; others are working below. Amael Balbus will not get away. It's over."

Nurka strode back and forth, stroking his moth, snorting, tail flicking, then in a fit of temper turned and thrust his skull-face into Linus. "Amael is nothing to me!" he seethed furiously. "And even if Hummelton *is* deserted, the point is it will *remain* so, uninhabitable forever. The plantations too will be rendered toxic as we pass over, just as the land in the hyena reservations has been by centuries of ashen rain, only this will be a thousand times worse. Where will your Den Fathers go, hmm? Back to Lupa? Let them scurry away! They will starve soon enough. Forget white-imperium shortages, Howler, your kind will squabble over mere food come the winter. The desperate little beasts will no longer be cowed when their bellies are growling. They will rise up against you, and Amael and Nikita, or even your Den Fathers, *whoever* is victorious, will preside over a warring wasteland. Wolfkind will live as roaches on a pile of ash whilst we hyenas return to the wilds where we belong!"

Silence, but for the propellers.

"By Ulf, Nurka, just listen to yourself," Linus spat in disgust. "Like a cub throwing a tantrum."

Nurka stepped back, blinking at the rebuke.

Linus looked past him. "Did you hear that, Monty and Penny?" he called. "Rendered uninhabitable, he said! We'll all starve to death! I know you wouldn't help him do such a thing for all the honey in Hummelton. What's he told you, that they're dropping silly propaganda leaflets? All these years of planning for some door-to-door sales pitch, don't make me laugh-offaaagh!"

Furious, Nurka silenced Linus with a plasmatic punch to the gut, bending him double.

"They've... got... black... imperi-gagh-aaagh!" Linus wheezed, as Nurka kicked him in the side with a second plasmatic blast, sending him flying against the wall. "Gaagh! Cagh! Pleh!"

Madou stood by, one paw fondling his sword hilt, sweat dripping off his nose. He was a moment from acting when Penny stepped in.

"Mister Linus!" she shrieked, running over and falling upon the squirming, smouldering Howler. "Stop it, you brute!" she scolded Nurka. "Stop it this instant! We'll do whatever you want, just leave him be!"

The furious, panting Nurka whirled away. "See... see how they lie, madam?" he rasped, pointing and laughing. "Black-imperium, he says! This wolf is so confounded by Lupan propaganda he believes *us* to be the monsters, not they who slaughter us like silkworms! You saw the leaflets. You saw them, didn't you? Say you saw them!"

"Yes! Yes I did!"

"And do you think we'd print out a million leaflets of lies just to deceive two puny cats?"

"No!"

"Then you will fly this ship?"

"Yes, of course! I'll do whatever you want, just don't kill him! Please! No more violence."

Nurka looked to a gulping Madou then down on the weeping Penny. "Nobody need die, Madam, as long as you cooperate. Now back to your post."

Leaving the groaning Linus where he lay, Penny slunk reluctantly back to the controls, her dress stained with Linus's blood. She looked at Monty, unable to speak for tears and shock but conveying her wide-eyed horror.

"Don't try anything," Reg warned them. "I'm watching you."

"Is it true, Reg old boy?" Monty sniffed. "Are we carrying the black stuff?"

"Look, just stay on course, Monty. It'll be over soon."

"Answer me, sir!"

"It's just leaflets! That's all it is. The Howler's a filthy liar. They all are."

"Not Howler Linus," Monty maintained stiffly, reaching across and taking Penny's paw. "Right, Sweetpea?"

"Right you are, dear."

"Ready?"

"If you are Monty."

With a nod from each cat, Monty turned the wheel as fast he could and Penny tugged every cable in reach.

"What're you doing?" Reg piped. "Stop it! Get off the controls! Nurkaaaa!"

Monty shoved the rat away and continued to spin the wheel until it was hard over. *The Nimbus* trembled, lurched, its engines whining in pain as the outside world rolled and tipped at a crazy angle. Nurka, Madou and the two other hyenas stumbled across the gondola, clinging to poles and cables, whilst Linus slid to the far side and into the wall.

The ship groaned metallic groans, cables snapped and felitium bags split, but Monty clung to the wheel with Penny.

"I love you Monty!"
"Hold on, Sweetpea. Hold on!"

✢

A white, open-topped Hummel car pulled up in a green field. Inside were Grand Howler Vladimir Oromov and the Consort Angus, husband of Cora.

"There it is," Vladimir said, standing up in the open car and shielding his eyes.

Angus stood up as well.

Together he and Vladimir watched a distant silver lozenge twist and dip alarmingly.

"It's going down!" Angus woofed excitedly. "Hahaaa your boys did it!"

"Maybe, sir," Vladimir replied guardedly.

Several trucks rumbled across the grass, passing the white car and parking nearby. Each one drew an artillery piece behind it; handsome green and white-painted imperium cannons that resembled antiques compared to the modern vehicles that towed them.

Crews hopped from the back of the trucks, little beasts one and all. Rats, mice, rabbits and more, dressed in smart white military uniforms with tall hats. They were not Politzi, as far as Vladimir understood matters, but rather members of Hummel's little beast army; the Everdor Guard. Hummel always was a little different to the Lupan packs, but with such a large territory to police they needed lesser beasts to behave, even participate. What better way than to make them feel valued and included by allowing them to fight for their own country?

The idea had merit.

One day they might even give their little beasts a vote, Vladimir chuckled in his head.

Some of the wee beasts were armed with ram-rods, others carried imperium charges and cannon balls. They set about decoupling the artillery from the trucks and lining them up at Angus' instruction, each pointing at the distant dirigible. The charges of imperium and cannon balls were piled up and rammed down the barrels, in that order.

"Stand ready, lads!" Angus commanded, peering through some silver binoculars. "She's still well out of range."

Vladimir looked behind at the walls of Hummelton and the ancient Den towering at its heart. He could hear distant music and fanfare.

The opening ceremony had begun.

✢

"Yes it's all true," Adal said, his white face all but glowing in the dark alcove, like a disembodied theatre mask.

Even as Howlers passed behind, busily heading to and from the Opening Ceremony, Cora was unable to keep herself from spluttering, "Adal, this is outrageous even for you!"

"I had no choice but to stay silent, Cora."

"You could have come tae me! We're old friends-"

"And you'd have sat on it, would you?" Adal derided quickly, and with uncompromising gall. "Not investigated, arrested, nor breathed a word to any beast?"

Silence.

"No, thought not."

The tall, black Cora loomed over the short, brown and white Adal, "Ah could have cancelled the flyover, or set an ambush for THORN at the Buttle's farm. Anything!"

Adal smirked, "Cora, you forget I didn't know about THORN's method of delivering our deaths, only the date. All that was known is that they had black-imperium and would use it today; everything else was a mystery. The rabbit you arrested has confirmed what Prefect Janoah only presumed. She's very clever that Janoah. She and Vladimir between them cracked this case wide open; ALPHA will not forget or forsake them, nor should the Republic at large."

Cora was unable to find fault with Adal's smooth reasoning, except to say, "If the Republic even survives your reckless gamble, Adal."

"Everything's in paw, Cora," he assured her.

Their clandestine meeting concluded, Cora and Adal swept back into the sunlight, climbing the wooden steps and rejoining the Den Fathers; Thorvald, Flaid and the Bloc pair, along with their ever-present Den Guard.

Amael was conspicuously absent.

The remaining leaders were seated in the highest tier of a grandstand, one of many erected in a rectangle within Hummelton Den's extensive grounds. The many lesser Elders, Howlers and other relative riffraff sat in the tiers below. Then came Freiwolves, then little beasts, swarms of them, clustering like so many bees. After the ceremony, the Howlers would go about amusing themselves in town whilst the Den Fathers and Elders would take their place inside the Den's great hall and get down to serious business – debating motions and voting.

Unless we're all gassed, Cora thought.

As she sat amongst her equals, watching the uniformed Everdor Guard blissfully parading and trumpeting down below, Cora's mind and heart secretly raced. She scanned the sky for the balloon and kept looking to Den Father Flaid seated nearby – the big wolf was still here and outwardly perfectly at ease.

If Adal was to be believed, Flaid numbered among the conspirators. Yet he had not fled like Amael. Was he innocent, outwitted, or suicidal?

"Now we watch," Adal whispered to Cora.

"And pray," she growled out the side of her mouth.

"If you must," Adal sighed. "To the Wind god perhaps? He might blow THORN's dirigible off course, though you can bet the hyenas aboard are praying just the opposite and the Wind is their god, not ours."

Cora prayed to Ulf – as she did so a paw clapped on her shoulder. The Den Mother looked round and up, as if expecting Ulf himself to have appeared, a shining saviour.

Not Ulf, just a short black wolfess in a green blazer.

"Sara?"

"Mum."

"Where've you been all this time? Where's Brynn?"

"Around," Sara said vaguely, and not a little angrily. "Mum can we talk?"

Cora glanced about. "Nae now. Sara, you have tae leave town. Your sisters have already been sent away. Ah want you tae look after them."

"But-"

"Behave and obey me for once in your life!" Cora hissed, pulling Sara down onto her seat.

Adal leant over, "Why if it isn't the young reporter!"

"Reporter?" Cora said.

Sara excused, "Long story, Mum."

"Tall story," Adal corrected. Raising his snout at the horizon, he added surreptitiously, "Don't look now, but I spy a balloon."

✦

As the world beyond the gondola windows spiralled and dipped like a mad fairground ride, Nurka pushed off a metal pole and climbed the sloping floor, defying the twisting forces that would have sent any lesser beast tumbling. In a few imperium-charged steps he was on the wheel and peeling first Penny and then Monty from it.

"Get off you fools!" he snarled.

Penny reeled across the gondola, but Monty snatched a pole and immediately came to wrestle with Nurka.

"No!" he mewed. "I won't... let... you!"

Pfzzt!

Nurka simply ejected the cat across the gondola with a blast of plasma.

"Monty!" Penny cried, as her husband fell smouldering to the deck and rolled limply into a support pole.

Nurka watched the fallen cat a moment, before turning the wheel back, paw over paw, to its default position. The airship slowly stopped spiralling, but the dials were still dropping.

"Reg!" Nurka called, casting his eyes over the confusing controls and whirring dials. "Reg, help me!"

The nimble rat scurried to the helm, whereupon he tugged levers, pulled cables and generally restored order. Most of the dials stopped spinning rapidly anticlockwise and reversed to a sedate clockwise motion.

Once the ship had calmed down, the rat breathed, "Turn us west, Nurka."

Panting beneath his skull helm more from fear than effort, Nurka picked out the compass from the many indicators and gently turned the wheel until 'W' wobbled into view. Outside, Hummelton swung round, and it was closer than ever. Nurka could see smoke rising from chimneys and distant glistening windows catching the sun. Even when locked in a mad death-spiral the wind had still been blowing the *Nimbus* rapidly closer to the countryside conurbation, like a boat caught inexorably in a current.

"Hahahahaaahaha!" Nurka laughed. It was the freest laugh to ever escape the uncommonly reserved hyena's throat; it disturbed even his own sensibilities. Rubbing his face under his helmet and sobering up, he glanced behind and located Madou, who was pulling himself to his feet after the mad tumble.

"Madou!" Nurka called. "Go check on Themba and the others. Make sure they're all right. I'll stay here."

The chief tugged the cable he had seen Penny use to dump water and thus increase lift, the ship noticeably rose.

"Madou?" he urged.

Nurka looked round just as Madou pressed his kristahl sword against his chieftain's broad zigzag-cloaked back.

"Sorry, Chief," he said.

"Madou, what is this?"

Howler Linus, meanwhile, had slipped his no doubt ineffectual bonds. Sitting by the wall, he held Nurka's other two hyenas at bay with his pistol.

"Don't move," the Howler advised them. He threw them his wire bonds, "One of you tie the other with that, please."

The two hyenas stood defiantly still.

"Do it!" Madou barked at them. "Or I'll kill Nurka!"

"Nobody move!" Nurka commanded over all. "Madou... Madou, listen to me-"

"Shut up, Chief!" Madou replied.

He shoved Reg stumbling away – the puny rat could do nothing to help, as was ever a little beast's lot.

"It's over, Chief," Madou continued. "Come on. Step away from the wheel."

Nurka only gripped the wheel more firmly. "When did they turn you? Was it when they tortured you?"

"No Chief."

"You cannot believe their promises, Madou."

"Nobody made any promises, Chief."

"Was it money?"

"Not money, not promises... just my own conscience. I'm listening to it, at last. So should you-"

"Conscience? You're a *traitor*, turncloak!"

Madou pushed his sword closer. "You're the one betraying our people! Prince Noss is right; no civilised race would do what we're about to do! Noss raised us, made us what we are, and you have betrayed his teachings! We all have."

"Perhaps," Nurka admitted. "But you're the one who struck him down, Madou."

"I wish I hadn't! I wish I'd struck Arjana instead!"

"By the Wind! Do you even know what you're saying?"

Madou took a sharp breath. "I was with you, Nurka. Every raid, every battle, every... every burning second on the rack; I suffered for our cause. The wolfen Den Fathers can all rot, I'd be happy to kill them myself, with my own paws, because they know what goes on in the Reservations! They must know."

Linus's ears twisted, but he said nothing.

"But not *everyone* is guilty, Chief," Madou sniffed, "not Rufus, or Tomek, or Linus there, and the Wind knows the little beasts are innocent. They suffer as we do. If we kill every mother and cub and harmless old beast, along with a guilty few, our people will be exiles from civilisation itself. Even the ancestors will turn their backs on us!"

Purple eyes flitting, Nurka cooed, "Madoouuu, there is no other way. No other way! By the Wind, brother, do you think I have not considered all this a thousand times? I've not slept easy for months!"

"Well maybe you should've asked for a second opinion! Like mine! Maybe if you had trusted *me*, told *me* from the beginning what you and Arjana had in mind, we wouldn't be here now because I would have said what I am saying now!"

"And then where would we be now? Twiddling our thumbs on the Reservation?"

"We'd have found another way. We'll *find* another way. There's still time."

"Wake up Madou!"

"No, Nurka, I'm the one awake; it's you who you needs wake up, you and Themba. The chunta is clouding your minds, you know it's true! I've been off it for some months. I feel… better. I see and think clearer. I'm a changed beast-"

"Hahahahaaaahahah!" Nurka laughed.

"It's true!"

"So you defile your body with white-imperium and now you're better than us? What shall we do, blasphemer, land and give up? Say we're sorry? We will be executed on the spot if we're lucky or fed to the ants if we're not! Now put that sword down, Chakaa, or else run me though!"

"So be it, Nurka! So be it!"

"No!" Penny shouted. "No more! I won't stand for it!"

Both Nurka and Madou's rounded hyena ears pricked, as did Linus's triangular set.

"Drop your leaflets, Mister Nurka," Penny said. "Drop your leaflets and *only* the leaflets, as you said to Monty. Make this a peaceful protest, an honourable one. No killing, no fighting, rise above it all. You can do it, all of you, and you'll be remembered as heroes, not villains." She looked down on the unconscious Monty and stroked his whiskered face. "My dear Monty fought in many wars you know, subduing the native races of the Feline continent. He used to be a warrior, just like you all, a soldier of Felicia, of our Queen. But he gave it all up to fight for truth and reason and… and progress. That's why I fell in love with him, he wasn't like everyone else. You don't have to be like everyone else either. You can be better than them. Show them all up. You can!"

The longest time passed, Nurka studied Linus, Madou, and especially Penny as she cradled her husband.

Running his paws up inside his helmet Nurka clutched his aching head. "Grrraaaaagh!" he groaned. "Madooou… Madou, do you think that… perhaps I… that we…."

The chief's voice trailed curiously off as he focused on several puffs of ash erupting from the fields ahead. From the direction of the silent explosions came several blurred streaks of yellow, racing towards the gondola in all of a few seconds.

"Artillery?" said Reg.

Then the window in front of the hapless rat exploded inwards.

Ka-fssssfgh!

Reg instantly disappeared amidst a metallic cacophony of carnage, as did the two hyenas Linus was holding at bay. Ears and eyes momentarily overwhelmed from the ferocious blast and rush of whistling air, Linus didn't even see or hear what exactly happened to the three, all he saw now was a gaping hole in the gondola where once they had been.

In the chaos, Nurka ducked round and blasted Madou away, thumping both plasmatic fists to his gut. The stocky hyena flew across the deck and slammed into the wall.

"Oaaghagh!"

As Madou fell unconscious, the damaged right side of the gondola collapsed further, the metal bending away, as if being peeled open from below by a curious giant.

Linus scrabbled backwards as the floor beneath him gave way to deadly a slope of oblivion. It advanced faster than the Howler's wounded body allowed him to move! Thinking fast, the crippled wolf limped and lurched across to a pole and latched on with his half-useful arms, overcoming the agony to cling on as the flimsy floor deserted him.

"Gaagh!"

Beneath Linus's flailing boots the green fields of Everdor rolled by; roads, houses, a sparkling river; his pistol slipped through his fumbling bloodied fingers and spiralled away.

"Madou!" he yelped, slipping. "Help me! Madou!"

"Linus!" Penny shouted, pulling the unconscious Monty away. "Linus, hold on!"

Calming his loyal pepper moth fluttering worriedly at his shoulder, Nurka seized the wheel and turned the Nimbus firmly towards Hummelton.

More puffs of smoke; shells rumbled by, most missing, but a glancing blow was struck to the left underside of the balloon, tearing the fabric and smashing one of the durametal ribs. The whole skeleton of the ship quivered, the wheel vibrating in Nurka's hefty hyena paws. Sparks rained down over the fields and thick support cables flopped out through the flapping canvas, trailing like the tentacles of a black jellyfish.

Very quickly smoke began to billow from the burning hole torn in the *Nimbus*.

Fire!

Breathing hard and fast, Nurka pulled cables and pushed levers, upping the lift and thrust; despite the damage the *Nimbus* responded, gaining speed and height. Shells screamed by below, missing entirely this time. Hummelton grew ever larger and dominated the horizon; town houses, bridges, and the Den rising at its heart, all took shape.

It was time.

Glancing back at the groaning Madou and wondering what to do with him, Nurka saw Themba enter the Gondola, hammer in paw. The big hyena took in the devastation, the gaping hole in the floor being most disconcerting.

"Chief?" he shouted worriedly, the wind whistling through the floor and up his cloak.

"Everything ready back there?" Nurka replied.

"Yes!"

Nodding, Nurka gestured with his paws. "Give me your hammer!"

Themba silently obeyed; Nurka passed him his fluttering moth for safekeeping.

Then the chief turned and unceremoniously smashed the wheel up, bending and warping it with several blows. He tried to turn it – it was jammed fast.

Good, nobody could alter course now.

Satisfied, Nurka swapped the hammer for the moth. Then he disarmed Madou, flicking his sword into the gulf – it passed within inches of Linus flailing below.

"Stay here and… and watch Madou, he's not well," Nurka told Themba. "Don't let him or anyone else touch the controls." He went to said controls and tugged one of the cables, "Pull this cord to raise us if we get too low. All right?"

Themba nodded.

"It's time, Themba," Nurka said, walking over to him.

Another nod, a gulp. "You should let me do it," Themba said, looking slightly away. "The tribe will need you. What good am I to anyone without you?"

Nurka grasped both Themba's arms, "Don't worry, Themba. I'm not going anywhere."

"But… but the black-imperium. I thought you said-"

"You'll see. Stay here."

"Help him!" Penny screamed, gesturing at Linus scrabbling uselessly below. With all his wounds the Howler was unable to gain a purchase, his bloodied boots slipping on the metal, his strength failing fast.

Nurka stared, eyes narrowing in contemplation.

"Please!" the cat begged of Nurka. "He could have shot you where you stood, but he didn't! Please!"

"Themba… pull the Howler up," Nurka commanded.

"Chief?"

"Don't argue, just do it!"

"By the Wind, what-"

"If you love me you'll do as I command!" Nurka said, cupping a paw to Themba's helmet-clad cheek. "And... you will forgive me."

Exiting the gondola, Nurka dashed down the main walkway towards the tail of the now smoke-filled interior of *Nimbus*, his striking zigzagged cloak being the last thing to vanish in the thickening haze.

Baffled, worried, but obedient, Themba walked gingerly over to Penny and the hole torn in the gondola.

"Down there!" she told the massive hyena, as cannon fire rushed by once again.

Another strike sent the Nimbus trembling and rocking.

"Oh!" Penny mewed. "It may not matter soon! She won't hold together much longer!"

Silently grasping a support pole, Themba peered into the breach and spied the wolf Nurka had sent him to rescue; the Howler looked back with desperate baby-blue eyes.

"Quickly!" Penny urged, shouting. "Linus! Linus, he's going to help you!"

Themba leant down and extended his kristahl hammer towards this Linus. Unable to hear a thing for the whistling wind, the wolf fully expected to be poked or blasted off to his doom. All he could see was Penny's mouth moving and a giant hyena looming over him, those purple eyes alight with menace and hatred.

Yet the hammer stayed put. Was this a lifeline?

Taking his chances, Linus extricated his best arm from the pole first and latched onto the hammerhead, then his rather weaker arm followed.

"Gahffffgh!"

All the hours in the Riddle Den's gym, all the pain and sacrifices combined with the mixed blessings of imperium, granted Linus Mills the strength to cling on despite such fatigue and agony as he had never before known. Pushing with his good leg he scaled the wobbling metal slope with Themba's aid and collapsed about the deck.

"Thank... you!" he panted.

Themba backed off, cut the air with a paw, and turned away. "I do not understand what Nurka is doing, but-"

Ka-crack!

Themba whirled round, his blood spattering against the gondola windows. The big beast fell upon the crooked wheel, then to the floor, chest heaving, paw clutching his body.

Penny screamed.

The exhausted Linus looked up and saw Uther standing in the entrance to the gondola, the barrel of his Greystone rifle smouldering. With Themba downed he calmly turned to the stirring Madou and went to unceremoniously bayonet him where he sat!

"No!" Penny shrieked, throwing herself in the way. "No, Howler! Don't!"

"Out the way, marm!"

"Uther?" the cat squeaked. "Uther is that you?"

"Aye! Now step aside, marm!"

"I absolutely will not, sir. He's a friend of Linus!"

Uther looked to Linus, who nodded, then collapsed about the deck. Puzzled beyond words, the Wild-heart lowered his rifle and went to him.

"Mate?"

"Uther," Linus grunted, as his partner cradled him. He looked to Themba. "He... he saved my life. They... both did. Don't kill them, Uther."

"What're you on about?" Uther squawked. "They're the ones from the refinery!"

"I know. I know, but... grrrffgh! I think... agh...."

"Don't talk," Uther chided. "Shut up and lay still. You look like krap, mate, and that's no joke."

Linus grabbed Uther's sinewy black arm, "The other one, Nurka," he spluttered, "he w-www-went to the back of the s-sss-ship. The black-imperium is down that way."

"Aye, but it looks like we're going down, mate. Someone's shooting us up bad. THORN's already lost."

"No! No, we may s-sss-still pass over Hummelton."

"He's right, Uther," Penny agreed, crawling over. "The cannons seem to have stopped as well."

"They can't aim... straight up," Linus panted. "Cannon are not designed to shoot up at the sky. Nothing so dangerous ever flew... until today."

He laughed a little.

"Where's Nurka gone exactly?" Uther asked.

"There's a cargo hatch on the bottom deck, towards the back of the ship," Penny said. "If he's going to drop anything, it'll be from there."

"Right."

The catess stood up and brushed down her dirty dress, "I'll show you, Uther."

"No chance, marm, it's too dangerous in there. Stay here, look after Linus and Monty."

"But-"

"Please! I'll find it. I *always* find my way."

Penny nodded.

With that, Uther reloaded his rifle and made to leave, but Linus pulled him back.

"Uther wait! Wait a m-mmm-minute."

"Yeah, mate?"

"Just... think," Linus spluttered, his body trembling as shock set in, shock from being shot, blasted and nearly falling to his death. "Think b-bbb-before... you... you act. But act... if you must."

"What?"

"Just... I don't quite know... I... Hahaha!"

Frowning, Uther picked the delirious Linus up and set him down by the door. He removed his black Prefect's cloak and laid it over him. "Rest mate. Penny's here."

Grabbing his rifle, Wild-heart hurried into the smoky bowels of the *Nimbus*.

✦

Vladimir watched the burning airship approach; the Hummel artillery pieces were now useless, being unable to aim higher than forty degrees or so, but they had made their mark on the dirigible.

Was it enough?

The little beasts turned their cannon around, ready to fire once the ship had passed overhead and into range on the other side, but Angus put paid to that idea.

"Och, no! You'll hit the town you fools!"

Thus everyone stood helpless, heads craned skyward, as the airship passed overhead at surprising speed, like a great mechanical fish, belching smoke, propellers thrumming.

Vladimir unconsciously covered his already grille-clad nose with a kerchief, as if that might guard against any cloud of deadly black-imperium – it would not. But there was as yet no such cloud, just light, hot, rising smoke that, to an experienced imperiologist like Vladimir, in no way resembled cold, dense, black-imperium vapours.

Something strange did catch Vladimir's eye. Fluttering white squares, like confetti, were raining down overhead.

Paper?

"What do you reckon?" Angus asked.

"I think it's going to make it," Vladimir replied.

"Aye, me too."

"It's not dropping black-imperium, though."

"Aye, not yet anyway," Angus puffed worriedly.

After a few minutes, some of the mysterious papers made landfall and rolled across the fields, catching on the long grass.

Vladimir chased one down and grabbed it.

"Ah'm going back tae town," Angus declared, climbing in the driving seat of the Hummel car. "You all stay here!" he told his bemused little beasts, some of whom were inspecting the tumbling papers for themselves.

Against his better judgement, Vladimir hurried over and joined Angus in the car just as he was pulling away.

"What's that?" the Consort asked, glancing at the sheet in Vladimir's paws.

"Propaganda."

"Aye? Is that good news or bad news?"

As the car turned onto the road, Vladimir looked up at the dirigible, "I'm not sure."

✦

"Hahaaaa!" old Thorvald gruffed, patting Den Father Flaid's shoulder. "Look at that, young Flaid, a marvel of the modern age. Not even you Greystones have such a device."

"Indeed," Flaid grunted, shuffling in his seat.

A panicked Greystone Howler whispered something in his Den Father's twitching brown ear, but Flaid irritably waved them away.

The Howler backed slowly away, then ran down the steps.

"What's up with him, Flaid?" Thorvald asked.

"Toilet."

"Hah! Indeed." Old Thorvald checked his silver pocket watch. "Yes, I thought so; it's early by an hour. Did you change the flyover time, Den Mother Cora?"

"Nae," Cora replied sharply, her fingers clawing at her seat.

"Hmm, must be the wind behind her. Still, I would've thought Monty had taken that into account. Got chatting to him at the symposium, you know. Fascinating beast, ex-soldier, been to all sorts of places. Made me feel quite sheltered-"

As Thorvald blathered on, ignorant of any danger, so the similarly uninformed crowds enthusiastically turned to witness the approaching spectacle.

Not all were so ignorant.

Cora and Adal watched tens of Howlers and Elders in the seating below begin to stand up and leave, pushing through the crowds with unseemly haste.

By Ulf it's true, Cora knew then. It's all true. Thank Ulf I sent the girls away.

Thorvald was right too, the balloon had come unexpectedly early even for the conspirators themselves. Did they know what it was carrying, that it was going to choke everyone, or was its arrival merely understood as a general signal for a THORN attack of some kind?

Either way, Adal noted the faces and the names of all the Elders that dared to leave, consigning them to his mind – he knew every last one of them by heart. Den Father Flaid remained stoically seated and calm. Was he too proud to run, or simply not involved at all?

To Adal's frustration Flaid stoically remained unreadable.

The Alpha looked down over the railing, watching Horst and Duncan most carefully. Neither moved a muscle, save to knock back beer and chat cheerfully to his neighbour in Duncan's case, or, in the event of Horst, to bluster and tug pompously at his medals.

All was well with them.

Adal sat back, mind whirring. So, it's just you, Nikita? Or has Silver played us all for fools. Maybe he's in with Janoah and her pet Eisenwolf. Maybe Rafe will run the world once we've all rotted!

The Alpha burst out laughing.

"What's so funny, Adal?" Cora hissed, as the balloon bore down on Hummelton, propellers fighting to be heard over the cheers of the crowds.

"Nervous laughter, Cora," the Alpha dismissed drily, looking up as the enormous sleek balloon eclipsed the morning sun. "Just nervous laughter."

Cora chuckled as well, "You're nae gonna run then?"

Adal just huffed and pulled down his ALPHA helmet, hoping against hope its white-imperium filter might yet protect him.

✦

The smoke inside *Nimbus* was getting thicker as her canvas shell burnt away. Hurrying along, Uther spotted wind-fanned flames glowing to the right of the main walkway, just beyond the felitium bags.

Suddenly one of the bags caught fire ahead of him, burst and deflated, falling limply on the walkway and staying Uther's advance. However, the felitium within didn't explode or even burn particularly, it was just the canvas on fire.

Penny knew her stuff.

Uther wasn't sure if that was good or bad. Better these hyenas go down in flames! But, then again, Linus had said if the dirigible burned-up with black-imperium aboard it would be carried far and wide.

Leaping over the burning canvas, Uther kept going.

Wild-heart's helmet filter guarded his lungs from the swirling smoke. However, unlike the three Chakaa and their modified Howler helmets, the ordinary hyenas aboard had no such protection, not even gas masks. But, even as they spluttered and choked in the smoky atmosphere, the THORN zealots fought on, some firing up at Uther from stairways with pistols and rifles, others charging wildly at him with their spears.

Saving his last pellet for Nurka, Wild-heart engaged his lesser hyenas paw-to-paw, or rather rifle to spear. Parrying thrusts and then clubbing or plasmatically blasting them aside as they came at him, the THORN fanatics proved no match for a well-trained Howler.

Twisting a final terrorist over the railing and not even stopping to watch him bounce off the gas bags below, Uther descended a compact spiralling staircase into the deepest reaches of the *Nimbus*.

It was suddenly quieter, and, as with any fire, the air was clearer down low. It was easier to breathe, but easier to be seen as well. Uther kept his rifle ready as he crept speedily along the narrow walkways beneath the lowest gas bags, ready to stab, parry, club or even shoot, depending on who emerged to challenge him next.

He felt nobody, but of course the un-afflicted hyenas had no auras to give them away.

In the end Uther made a clear run. There was nobody back here. Why not? 'Black-imperium', Uther's mind cheerfully replied, 'Nurka's sent everyone else far away so they don't rot when he opens up the canisters... like you will.'

Puh! Thank you brain.

Parking his worries, Uther approached a silvery door. It was shut. Locked; there was no obvious locking mechanism, but the door felt wedged.

Casting his eyes about for another way round, Uther quickly concluded there wasn't. If the door was barred Nurka must be behind it.

Slinging his rifle, Uther took a run up and shoulder-barged the door with all his might. To his yelp of surprise the door proved extremely light and flimsy. Breaking clean off its hinges it fell in two and Uther tumbled over the wreckage, flailing ungracefully into the dark space beyond.

Rolling once, he immediately sprang to his feet with his rifle up and ready.

The room was large, dark and with taping U-shaped walls consisting of the dirigible's ribs and stretched canvas shell. There was a blinding, rectangular blue light in the middle of the floor.

Not a light, but an opening to the sky beneath!

Standing courageously by this heavenly abyss, bathed in blue and green light like some god, was Chakaa Nurka. He was armed only with stacks of paper in his paws. A speckled a white moth clung to his shoulder, like a suckling infant, its lovely wings ruffled by the wind.

"Halt!" Uther barked, emerging from the gloom and taking aim at Nurka's head.

Nurka looked at him.

"Don't thumping move!" Wild-heart reiterated.

Taking a deep breath, Nurka simply parted his paws and let the papers slip through his dark fingers. The majority fell through as a solid stack, but the top and bottom leaves instantly peeled away and fluttered about the room.

Nurka stood, waiting for the end, paws trembling.

Uther's finger tickled the trigger, the immensely powerful Greystone rifle in his steady paws coming to within a whisker of blowing Nurka's head clean off.

No, something stayed Uther, the paw of Ulf, or Linus's words, he was not quite sure what it was.

"Paws up!" he commanded.

Nurka remained quite still, watching the town of Hummelton pan below him, the crowds, the mighty towers of the Den, all passing within a few brief seconds, and with it went his last chance.

He closed his eyes, "Thembaaaa... forgive me."

"I said paws up!" Uther reiterated. "Don't think I'm gonna miss at this range, mate!"

Suddenly, Nurka's unnervingly bright purple irises focused on Uther. "If you will not kill me, Howler," he pleaded, tears dripping out from under his helmeted chin, "then for the love of Mother Erde *help* me!"

Uther's brow twisted. His rifle lowered just a little and he heard himself utter, "What?"

Nurka carefully gestured left and right, and the ominous canisters standing in the darkness, their spherical sides marked with single black X's

"Help me! Please!"

✦

The dirigible thrummed over, low, fast and, the crowd at large came to realise, on fire!

"By Ulf's fangs!" Thorvald thundered.

Gasping, pointing, screaming even fainting, Howlers and little beasts alike stood in their droves and watched flames and debris erupting from the airship's left flank. The canvas skin peeled away in cinders like a newspaper tossed in a fire, slowly revealing a metal skeleton and releasing a great billowing pall of black smoke.

Black smoke, or perhaps something worse.

Adal and Cora, almost alone amongst a thousand, remained seated, even visibly shrinking into their chairs as the black clouds streaming from the dying dirigible played across the face of the sun and loomed large over Hummelton.

The airship vanished over the Den's towers, out of sight; the smoke continued to tumble and swirl in its wake, hanging forever. It floated west with the wind and gradually thinned out, dispersing, and certainly not raining down as it should have were it something more than smoke.

Slowly, but surely, Adal Weiss stood up. "That's just smoke," he said.

Cora followed suit. "You're sure?" she dared hope.

"Yes."

Flaid heard them and loosened his cloak a little.

Breathing a secret sigh of relief himself, Adal's eyes came to rest on a sheet of paper tumbling down from the smoky sky. There were hundreds of papers, thousands, rolling and twisting in the breeze, landing gently all across the fields, the town, the Den and the crowds gathered within, like so much litter.

One leaf fluttered within Adal's reach. He leant over the grandstand banister and snatched it.

Cora came over. "What is it?"

Adal passed it to her. "Not black-imperium, just black propaganda." Whilst Cora inspected the leaflet, the Alpha nursed the banister. "Or perhaps it's not so black?"

✦

The *Nimbus* was losing height as the fire spread, the ground rising to meet her; Nurka just hoped his memory of Everdor geography served.

"There's a lake to the west of Hummelton!" he called over the wind. "We can drop the imperium into it!"

"Puh!" Uther scoffed, rifle up. "So you wanna secretly pollute the water, then? Kill Hummelton that way?"

"No! The flasks can be retrieved intact, Howler."

"Give over!"

"By the Wind, use your brain! If I wanted to rot everyone I would have twisted open every canister I could before my flesh fell off. That was the plan. The black-imperium should be pouring into this room and blowing out through the hatch by now. You should have rotted the second you broke through that door. You didn't!"

Uther squinted, unsure. Was this some hyena trick?

Nurka went on, "If we throw the imperium onto land, or if we crash and burn with it aboard, it will be much worse for you, for *all* of us. The canisters should survive falling into water. But the lake is small. I cannot move all the flasks by myself in time. You must help me, Howler. Please!"

Uther's eyes explored the dark, checking the canisters, looking for some hidden hyena, or trap.

"I... apologise for what I did to you at the refinery," Nurka rasped over the howling wind, recognising that distinctive black and white coat. "Uther, is it? The Wild-heart?"

A nod.

"You're a great warrior, even Themba says so, and he's the greatest warrior I know!" Nurka cackled fondly. "He's killed more hundred-legs than anyone."

Uther declined to reveal he had shot that great warrior Themba a few minutes ago.

Nurka dipped his chin, stared beyond the hatch, at passing fields and woodland. "I... I have come to realise, too late perhaps, that we great warriors must not stoop to murdering helpless beasts, lest we become those that oppress us. Madam cat back there is right. Prince Noss, Red-mist, Tomek... Madou, all of them fought so hard to stop me. I outwitted and outfought all them and yet... and yet they were right and I was wrong. I should have listened. I *should* have asked others what they thought, not wrapped myself up in my own bed of hatred, as Arjana and so many others have done! I should have been better." He returned his gaze to Uther, "I will not disgrace my people any further. I have delivered THORN's message. It is enough. Now help me dispose of my mistake, Wild-heart. I ask you, as warrior to warrior. Help me."

Uther's rifle quivered slowly to one side, his trust fighting his prejudice all the way, until the rifle clacked to the metal floor.

"All right, mate. You got it."

Nurka nodded and stroked his moth, calming its nerves and perchance his own.

Suddenly the ground beneath the hatch transitioned from rolling hills of green to a flat calm of blue water.

"The lake!" Nurka barked. "Hurry!"

The hyena led the way, grasping the nearest, hefty, X-emblazoned canister and hurling it into the gulf like a mad beast. The lethal, round container tumbled silently for a few seconds, before splashing into the water.

No sooner had Nurka rid *Nimbus* of one unit of black-imperium than he threw another overboard, and another and another! His strength was phenomenal and Uther could not match him, even less fully overcome the primal fear in his gut that, at any moment, a canister might leak or even burst altogether, rotting them both where they stood.

Grabbing a canister on the opposite side of the hatch to Nurka, Uther rolled it towards the opening like a barrel of beer into a cellar, sending it overboard. After a few seconds spiralling and shrinking before Uther's eyes it splashed into the lake. Had it survived, or split open, poisoning the lake? There was no way to tell, Uther just had to trust Nurka's judgement.

Just another twenty to go.

As wolf and hyena ran back and forth, dumping the deadly cargo flask by flask by their own chosen method, Nurka suddenly stumbled to the right, canister in paws, and fell against one of the durametal ribs.

The canister, a sphere but for its feet, rolled away from his grasp, past Uther, and into a dark corner.

Uther hadn't noticed until now, but the dirigible was listing heavily to the left and nose-down, thus making his job of rolling flasks uphill harder. Just like water weighing down a sea ship on one side and capsizing her, so this air ship was losing felitium on one side faster than the other.

And with the felitium went altitude.

And time.

Realising Uther was struggling, Nurka offered to swap sides. The usually proud wolf didn't protest for once and set to work rolling flasks effortlessly downhill; all they needed was guidance so they did not miss the hatch. Nurka hefted the others up hill and threw them in, tireless.

Smoke began to fill the room, rising from nose to tail as the Nimbus sank. Uther's mind strayed to Linus, Penny and Monty back in the gondola; it seemed to him that the nose was the worst place to be.

"If we're going down nose-first they'll be killed!" Uther told Nurka.

"It will not... matter where... they are!" Nurka panted back. "Not if a black-imperium flask splits open.... Keep going, Wild-heart!"

Uther did, and soon he and Nurka had cleared the room but for the lone stray canister that had rolled away into the far corner of the cargo hold. With the *Nimbus'* growing list making things difficult, Uther and Nurka tackled the last flask together and as one ferried it towards the hatch.

"Chief!" someone bellowed.

Nurka froze, Uther too. "Themba?" the former replied.

Themba stood in the cargo hold's mangled doorway, blood staining his cloak. He staggered inside and looked about.

"Nurka. What're you doing? Where's the imperium? What is this?"

"Themba. Themba, listen to me!"

"Traitor! You're with them! They've turned you!"

"No, Themba!"

Themba charged across the hold like a beast possessed, barging Nurka aside and sweeping Uther up into a bear-hug. The black-imperium rolled away, back to the corner where it hit the wall with a loud metallic clang.

Uther's ALPHA helmet emitted a barely lesser clang as Themba threw him to the floor and set about punishing his body with both fists, punching him left and right, breaking ribs with gusto. Wild-heart didn't stand a chance and was quickly beaten into submission.

"Gaaghfffgah!

Nurka dived on Themba's back. "Stop it! Themba!"

Themba flicked his head back, chinning Nurka and shoving him away. The disturbed pepper moth took flight in a flurry of scales as Nurka stumbled and rolled across the deck, only to settle on him again once he came to a rest.

"Don't worry, Nurka!" Themba claimed furiously. "You're next! We'll open that canister together! Haahahaaaaahaha!"

Grabbing the spluttering Uther under the nose of his helmet, Themba dragged him to the hatch. The chin-strap choked the already winded Wild-heart as he kicked and struggled to right himself, to fight back, get away, anything. He could see the bright blue of the sky through the hatch, the odd tall tree passing miles away. Soon he would have a fine view of the lake racing to meet him, and unlike a solid steel imperium flask he would break, even on water.

"Aaaagh!" he roared, the wind whipping at his ears. He looked up and saw the bloodied Themba looming over him, his wide eyes full of terrible, imperium-fuelled mania.

"Stop!" someone called over the windy tumult. "Stop, I say, or I'll shoot!"

Deaf to reason, Themba didn't even look up.

Ka-crack!

"Ungh!"

From down below, Uther witnessed Themba's marvellous black and white cloak explode in red blood. The hyena fell instantly and heavily to his knees, his armoured legs rendered suddenly powerless.

Uther was free!

Making good his escape, the Howler rolled aside and searched the hold with his eyes, eventually spotting, of all the beasts gracing Ulf's green Erde, Montague Buttle across the way with the Greystone rifle held firmly in his ginger paws.

Nurka stood up, stepped forward. "Themba?" he gasped.

Holding his mangled torso together, Themba looked across at Nurka and managed a toothy, red-tinged hyena cackle.

Slowly, he fell forwards.

"No!" Nurka rasped. "Themba!"

Closing the distance in a few short bounds, Nurka grabbed the back of Themba's cloak. It was too much. Themba's dead weight and Nurka's momentum pulled them both off balance and into the blue void.

They disappeared, together, and in silence.

Everything happened so fast that Uther could scarce contemplate it. He and Monty peered into the hatch, the cat falling on all fours. Neither saw evidence of Nurka or Themba, only their pepper moth fluttering over the water, shedding scales that caught the sunlight like a shower of snow.

One thing was plain – the *Nimbus* was perilously low.

"The black-imperium!" Uther shouted at Monty, pointing to the corner. "We got to throw it overboard!"

Monty remained still, numb, long whiskers whipped by the ferocious wind.

Uther grabbed him, "Oi, wake up, Monty! Help me!"

"What? Yes! Right, right!"

Uther staggered over to the imperium and with Monty's help rolled it to the hatch and into oblivion. Uther nearly fell out with it he was so bruised and exhausted, but Monty grabbed him firmly and pulled him back.

"Come on, Uther," the cat said, tugging him along.

"Eh?"

"There's a way off the old *Nimbus* yet. The others are waiting. Quickly now!"

Monty led Uther along the lowest level of the ship, down to the belly some way forward. The creaking and groaning was deafening, the smoke thick and choking. It was dark and baffling, but Monty knew the way by heart and led his Howler friend to another, smaller hatch.

Peering down, Uther saw a red, four-winged flying machine with a propeller in the tail, like the one Linus had found on the farm. It was attached to the underside of the *Nimbus* with a scaffold. There were two seats, one behind the other. Penny sat in the front, her paws on some control sticks; Madou was crammed in the back, holding Linus. Below them the waters and forests of Everdor passed, ever larger, ever closer.

"What in the name of Ulf is that?"

"A plane, me good 'Owler. Penny was gonna drop it over Hummelton and whiz about in it for a surprise. Haha!"

"Monty, Uther!" a goggled Penny cried, starting the engine and beckoning. "Quick!"

"Coming, Sweetpea!" Monty hollered. "I'll send him down!"

Uther looked at Monty, "We can't all fit in that tiny thing!"

"You go!"

"Me?"

Monty pulled on a big beige backpack with countless strings and buckles rattling about. "Don't worry, I've got this!"

Now Uther was utterly confused.

Monty winked. "Trust me! Down you go; squeeze in with the wife!"

Reluctant, but knowing there was no time, Uther descended the wind-whipped ladder and manoeuvred into the front seat with Penny. It was a very snug fit.

No sooner had Uther glanced suspiciously back at Madou and Linus than Penny shouted, "Get the lever Mister Uther!"

"Lever?"

"That one above you. Give it a good hard tug!"

Uther located the lever, reached up and pulled. His stomach trailed behind as the flying machine nose-dived and dropped like a stone.

"Wooooooagh!"

Chapter 55

The Elder Train was picking up speed, perhaps from a slight decline in the gradient, or perhaps Amael had ordered the firebox stoked with more imperium to put distance between himself, Hummelton and any repercussions; Josef did not know the lay of the land, even less the lay of Amael's mind.

Or was it the twisted geography of Janoah's unfathomable mind everyone needed to worry about? What game was she playing now?

"It's getting away!"

At Olivia's urging, Josef changed up a gear and accelerated. Suddenly, the track and road that had run parallel since leaving Hummelton veered away from one another, thus did train and van part company. Olivia watched the Bloodfang Elder Train skew away across the fields of Everdor and through a forest, trailing plumes of ash.

"Does this road go back to the track?"

"I don't know."

Olivia turned in her seat and shunted aside a square flap in the partition between the driver cabin and the rear. "Bruno!" she called, then, "Rafe?"

The Eisenwolf's grey metallic face appeared in at the face-sized aperture. "YEAH?"

"What do you need us to do?"

"WHATCHA MEAN? GET ME NEAR THE TRAIN."

"Do you mean alongside it or what?"

Rafe paused, metal ears swivelling a bit.

"STOP ON A BRIDGE?" he suggested at length. "I CAN JUMP ON THE ROOF."

"It's going awfully fast."

"I'LL BE FINE."

Josef hissed, "I don't think we can get far enough ahead, I'm having enough trouble staying with it as it is."

"WELL PUT YOUR FOOT DOWN, THEN!"

"If we're seen going too fast we'll be stopped by Howlers and then what? They'll see you!"

"SO WHAT? NOW COME ON, JAN NEEDS ME!"

"You assume, Rafe."

"SHUT UP! I KNOW SHE DOES! NOW GET MOVING OR I'LL DRIVE!"

Josef scoffed, "You can't drive, you fool!"

"I CAN! I USED TO... I THINK."

"You did," Olivia said, grasping the flap. "You used to drive your dad's little truck."

"MY DAD?"

Olivia chuckled, "Well... a sort of dad anyway." She leant closer, "We used to know each other, you and I. Do you remember? You used to come to the Arkady University all the time to see Sar... to see me."

"YOU?"

"Oh yes. It was getting serious-"

A violent swerve threw Rafe and Olivia about and put paid to their trip down memory lane.

"Pothole," Josef excused, clearing his throat. He popped open the glove box and threw Olivia a hefty book. "Make yourself useful and find us a bridge."

Olivia read the book cover; it was a detailed roadmap of Lupa. "This is for Lupa."

"It has a Hummelton pullout in the back."

"Right."

Whilst Josef swung the ALPHA van round ever more quaint country lanes, forcing Rafe back there to sit down on his bench before he fell down, Olivia flicked through to the pullout of Hummelton. It was a small scale, charting only the main thoroughfares. Even so, roads splayed in all directions from Hummelton, resembling the legs of a spider squashed between the pages.

Olivia quickly located the railway line and followed it east towards the edge of the paper. The railway shunted suddenly south and a road intersected it.

Olivia excitedly tapped the page, "Got one."

"Where?" Josef demanded.

After a quick survey, his passenger nodded ahead, "Keep going straight on. The railway turns back into us in a few miles."

"A turn? Good, the train will slow down a bit."

Rafe came back to the hatch. "YOU GOT ONE?"

"Yes," Olivia confirmed proudly.

As the van rounded a corner, Josef was presented with a long, if hilly, straight road, at the end of which was trouble.

"Checkpoint."

"RAM IT," Rafe said flatly.

"Are you mad? They'll send Howlers after us! No, we'll talk our way through."

"THAT'LL TAKE AGES. JUST KEEP GOING."

"I'm not getting arrested, thank you!"

Suddenly Rafe's right arm burst through the hatch and grabbed the Doctor's coat lapels. "IF JAN IS HURT BECAUSE WE LOSE THAT TRAIN I'LL THUMPING STRANGLE YOU! I KNOW YOU HATE HER! I'M NOT AS THICK YOU THINK, YOU KNOW!"

"Strangle me? Without my expertise you'd die! Killing your saviour, that's a pretty thick move."

Rafe shook his doctor, "DON'T YOU STOP!"

"All right, all right!" the cat huffed. "Just let go!"

No sooner had Rafe withdrawn back into his cell like some circus monster than Josef put his foot down. The enormous ALPHA van accelerated along the lane, bearing down on the checkpoint and gushing a thick plume of ash. The pig in the little booth didn't even look up from his novel and packed lunch until the barrier exploded!

Olivia flinched as bits of stripy wood flew over the windscreen; she looked in the mirror and saw the pig in the booth drop his sandwich in favour of a telephone.

"We've gone and done it now," she laughed, turning to Josef. "Is it always like this in ALPHA?"

"More or less," the cat said.

After another mile or so racing along the hilly straight road and feeling quite sick on the sudden dips, the ALPHA party spotted the promised bridge. It was a modest brick and mortar affair spanning a narrow chalk gully, the white rocks stained with telltale streaks of ash.

Suddenly a great plume of ash raced by, punching the trees and bushes that clung desperately to the rocks, their branches waving like rail side spectators.

"The train!" Olivia gasped.

Skidding to a halt atop the bridge, Josef almost fell out the van and scrambled round to open the back door; Rafe clomped down and round to the apex of the bridge. He stepped up on the low wall and crouched with surprising, sure-footed grace. The carriages of the Elder Train rumbled beneath him as he quickly reached for the red valve on his backpack.

"Bruno!" Olivia said, hurrying over and twisting it for him. "There."

"THANKS."

Backpack exhaust puffing merrily away, Rafe glanced back, gave a metallic thumbs-up, then pushed off the wall with an almighty, air-warping punch of imperious power that knocked Olivia back a step.

"Agh!"

Recovering her balance, the wolfess ran to the wall with Josef and saw Rafe land neatly on the very last carriage. He didn't stumble, or even crouch; he just stood tall, arms down, cloak fluttering, tail ribbon trailing. Shortly he was lost to sight, vanishing amidst a sun-dappled collage of ash clouds and leafy branches.

"Magnificent!" Olivia heard herself blurt. "He's like a… a jumping spider. How can someone that big and heavy move like that?"

Josef adjusted his tinted specs. "Because... he is a pureblood phenotype in an eisenpelz," he said logically, turning to the wolfess. "You could be every bit as magnificent, perhaps even more so."

Olivia looked to the cat, then beyond him, to some approaching bikes. Two Hummel Watchers sped to the bridge on tracked duos and hopped off with pistols drawn.

"Halt!"

Josef and Olivia turned around and raised their paws accordingly. The Doctor immediately set about explaining away the situation. "Don't get excited, Howlers. We're ALPHA agents on a mission of Republic security."

"Aye! Like smashing up Howler property?" one replied.

"It was an emergency," Olivia excused, turning a little and pointing below. "We had to get to the bridge and-"

"Shhshssh!" Josef hissed.

"ALPHA agents on a mission you say?" came the other, walking round to the back and pulling out some pipes and strange tools. "What's all this?"

Josef raised a finger and went to move, "Don't touch that!"

"Stay where you are!" said the first Watcher. "Turn around, paws on the wall!"

The Hummel pair set about frisking the criminals.

"Spread your legs!"

"No!" Olivia protested.

"Spread 'em!"

"I don't have anything to hide!"

"Och!" the Hummel cooed, leaning close and pinching Olivia on the rump. "Then you won't mind me looking, will you mah lovely wolfess? Hahaha-gagh!"

Pfzzzt!

Pffzaack!

Josef flinched and ducked, thinking the bangs and flashes were shots were being fired. He soon gathered the truth, that the Hummels were lying about the road with Olivia Blake standing over them, her paws smoking and quivering.

Standing up and looking about, Josef said, "Now you really have done it." He grabbed Olivia by the arm, "Come on-"

The frightened wolfess whipped her limb away.

Fearing the same fate as the Hummels, Josef raised his paws and backed off. "I get it; you don't like to be touched," he deduced, looking at the smouldering Watchers. "But I can help you. That's all I ever wanted to do, you must see that now. Sara and that do-gooder Linus and kept getting the way, but they have me all wrong."

Olivia dipped her chin and looked at her burning paws. "Can... can you stop the pain, Doctor?"

A nod, "Somewhat. In ALPHA, under my supervision, you will have all the venom you will ever need. And besides, you're female, you will cope with the rot much better than Rafe."

"I will?"

"You're a trained imperiologist aren't you? You know how it works. I taught you the latest theories myself."

Olivia laughed a little, "Yes, I-I suppose you did."

Beaming broadly, Josef Grau slowly, gently, placed a paw on Olivia's back and marshalled his prize towards the ALPHA van. "Come along, my dear. We're going to do great things you and I; great things."

✦

The embers and brandy were already out in the plush and distinctly Bloodfang-themed lounge car. Passing Janoah her drink, Amael sat opposite and knocked his back in a heartbeat.

It was not a celebratory drink, but a nerve-calming drink, and Janoah needed it just as much as Amael.

As everyone drank and smouldered in awkward, tense silence, the Everdor scenery rolling by,

Janoah wondered if the other Elders, Den Guard and Howlers on the train knew what was being done in their name. I'm not even supposed to know the extent of it; rotting the Den Fathers and then taking control of Lupa during the subsequent confusion and power vacuum was all Amael had voluntarily revealed. When is he going to admit he's having all of Hummelton gassed by a balloon? Indeed, has Nurka succeeded? Did he even take off? There's no way of knowing until we come to a station with telephone or a telegraph.

"It must be nearly time," Janoah said, fishing for info.

Amael broke from a trance and checking a clock on the carriage wall replied, "Soon, unless Nurka came early to eliminate me, in which case our hyena friend will be in for a shock come future negotiations."

Janoah laughed a little, "My clever Amael."

He smiled.

More fishing. "What's to be done with Hummelton anyway?" Janoah asked.

"Done?"

"Who gets it?"

Amael smiled, "Why? Do you want it?"

"Hah! I'm no bumpkin."

"Just as well," the Den Father said, pointing with his ember. "The hyenas will turn the place over; probably loot everything. It'll be a mess. They might even claim it for themselves, but they will be dislodged in due course."

Janoah sat astonished by Amael's consummate acting. Not a twitch, not a pause for thought, just a smooth, plausible response from this now seasoned liar who knew Hummelton would be a dead zone within the hour.

Or maybe I'm wrong. Maybe Linus and Uther are twiddling their thumbs in a farmyard, thinking what an idiot I am for sending them halfway across the country over some crazy hunch, whilst a mad hyena unimaginatively drives a truckload of black-imperium into Hummelton's capital den and explodes, killing just the Den Fathers and their immediate entourage.

Perhaps Amael's not what I thought he was.

Either way I'm helpless. I can't even arrest anyone, not without Rafe. I'm trapped.

Screeeeee-e-e-e-e-e!

The breaks squealed, sending brandy slopping over tumblers onto waxed tabletops. Conspiratorial Elders clutched at the arms of their chairs and looked to one another in panic.

"We're stopping!"

"Why?"

"Maybe it's a Hummel blockade?"

Amael shot to his feet. "Shut up you cowards!" he snarled at them all, throwing his empty glass to the floor. "Probably a red signal, that's all. There's another train ahead that we've had to stop for."

"There are no services to and from Hummelton today," said Elder Duval. "It's the Summit's opening day, there's no freight or passenger services allowed for security's sake."

Amael grunted, "Humph! Leaves on the line then."

The train stopped entirely, then began to slowly reverse.

"Do we need to reverse for leaves?" Duval scoffed, standing up. "Something's wrong, Amael!"

The door leading forward opened and a Howler entered the lounge carriage, his rapier drawn.

Janoah recognised him, tall, white, icy-eyed.

It can't be, can it?

Elder Duval approached the newcomer. "Howler, what's going on up there? Why are we revers-"

Kffssst!

Casually flicking his sword against Duval's head, the Howler administered an effortless blast of imperious energy, sending the Elder down at a stroke. The Den Guards stationed about the carriage drew their swords, but the Howler drew a pistol and aimed it squarely at Amael.

"I won't shoot our Den Father unless you give me an excuse!" he bellowed, specifically to the

Den Guards, staying their action. "Though by all means try me!"

Amael woofed incredulously, "Donskoy?"

"Surprised to see me, Elder?" Ivan Donskoy replied. "I'm sorry, 'Den Father'. You do move unseemly fast. Vito's not even cold yet."

A second Howler limped into the carriage. He was brown-furred and armed with a rifle. He leant heavily against the doorway and took aim at Amael.

"Keep the Den Father in your sight, Gunnar," Ivan said.

"He's going nowhere, mate."

Amael growled, "What is this?"

With Gunnar backing him up, Ivan relaxed his aim a little and responded, "You tell me, you seem to be in a terrible hurry to go somewhere."

"We're on our way to Lupa," Amael maintained, adding triumphantly, "to take the city."

"Are you, by Ulf? Your appetite for power only grows with the eating." Ivan gestured at the passing scenery, "As you can see, sir, there's been a change of schedule. We're going back to Hummelton, where you will be arrested for the murder of Den Father Vito."

"Humph!" Amael woofed. "You fool, Ivan, Uther was the one who killed him."

"At your command; Gunnar and I will testify to that."

"And convict yourselves?"

"We have no choice. You have no intention of allowing us to live so we'll at least take you with us. Tell me, Den Father, would you have sent assassins after *our* assassins, and then more after them? Where would it have ended?"

Janoah leant forward, "What's he talking about, Amael?"

"Nothing. He's deranged!"

Ivan continued, unfazed, "Since you tried to kill us you must have no wish to get Rufus out of Gelb. You never had. You want him gone so you can have his wife. Well take her by Ulf! He never wanted her anyway!"

Janoah scowled, but remained silent.

Amael laughed, "Rufus is already out of Gelb! I had him extracted myself."

"Liar."

"Jan, tell the wolf before he bursts a blood vessel."

Janoah dipped her chin, "It's true, Ivan. Amael had the hyenas rescue Rufus."

Silence. Ivan's icy eyes twitched.

"He did it for me," Janoah added, standing up. "He did it before you boys even killed Vito. I told him to recall you, but he didn't. Getting rid of Vito had nothing to do with Rufus, that was a ploy to get you and Uther-"

"I rescued Rufus all the same, didn't I?" Amael interrupted. "I could have left him to rot!"

Janoah could not deny it.

Amael continued, "He can have his expedition, everything! Once things settle down, that is."

With that, the Den Father addressed Ivan. "Blade-dancer, listen to me. If we go back to Hummelton we're all dead, including you! One whiff of the air back there and you'll rot. It's a dead city now, full of dead beasts! Nobody will be arresting anyone."

"What do you mean, 'dead city'?" Ivan seethed.

Confident he had Blade-dancer's full attention; Amael slowly turned around and sat calmly in a red chair, as if it were his throne. "I'm the last Den Father," he sniffed pompously, spreading his paws. "THORN has taken care of the others; gassed them all with black-imperium dropped from a, how do you say, 'dirigible'."

Even as her brain reeled from confirmation of her hunch, Janoah remembered to play the part, "Dirigible?"

The 'last Den Father' waved a paw, "Details, my love, details." He looked to Ivan, Gunnar, the others Elders, everyone, "What matters is that I am the most powerful, *legitimately* elected wolf left alive. Not only that, but the Warden of Gelb and I have been stockpiling venom in a secret location for years now. Unfortunately for the Warden he's dead. No fault of mine; the hyenas did that all by themselves! Happily that means I am now also the only beast who knows where to find the white-imperium necessary to feed the insatiable Howlers over the next few months. Gelb is in total disarray and you can bet THORN will try and cut off imperium and food supplies completely and lay siege to Lupa to get their way. I know Nurka's mind; he wants to overthrow wolfkind, rule Lupa. But I shan't let him, nor will I let ALPHA take over Lupa from within! Nikita thinks he'll be in charge now Adal's dead, but he must either bow to me, or bow out of existence. They all must. The packs will hold out for a moon or two under newly elected Den Fathers, but they'll all rot without venom. Howlers will defect to the Bloodfangs in droves; we will be the only pack in town giving out imperium. Then our pack will rule, a one-pack Lupa. Just think of the possibilities, Ivan! No more petty fighting over scraps of that stinking city. No more civil wars. We'll project Wolfen power outwards, into the wilds, across the sea, spread our influence across the whole world! This is a difficult birth and many will die, and… I regret that, but it'll be worth it. I promise you."

Amael offered a stone-grey paw.

"Now, Ivan, for Ulf's sake, wolf, let's not fall out over a little housekeeping! You can have any district you like, any territory even. Elder Ivan! Has a nice ring to it."

Silence.

"Rufus is with us," Amael claimed afresh. "He's safe with the hyenas, which I'm sure you'll agree is to his liking. He'll have his expedition, as I've said. You wouldn't go against Rufus would you? Of course not. Now, put that pistol down and have a drink."

Pistol quivering in paw, Blade-dancer looked desperately to Janoah. "Is it true?" he asked. "Are you and Rufus in with this… this mad wolf?"

"Ivan I…."

Janoah's brow twitched.

There came a new, coiling corona, reaching invisibly and yet ever more powerfully into the carriage. It stayed Janoah's heart, her lips, her very mind.

"Stenton?" she whispered.

Strange sounds erupting from the aft carriages put everyone on edge. There was a battle taking place back there; swords clashing, plasma snapping, wolves yelping.

The aft carriage door slid open and a smouldering Howler staggered inside. "Mon-ster!" he coughed, collapsing.

Then the huge, grey form of Janoah's Eisenwolf ducked inside, chest heaving, backpack puffing ash.

"JAN?"

"Rafe!"

Everyone, Elders, Den Guard, Amael and Janoah, all turned from lowly Ivan to face this new outrage. Most could scarce believe their eyes.

Gunnar lowered his rifle. "The Eisenwolf who killed the sewer centipede," he said. "They said I dreamt it. I knew I hadn't. I knew!"

Ivan slowly backed up.

"So it's true!" Amael growled. "ALPHA's resurrected the Eisenwolves. That meddling mad cat Josef!"

Janoah huffed, "He's mine, actually, Josef just… helped."

"Yours, Jan?"

Fearlessly, Janoah hurried around the chairs and over to Rafe, as if greeting her cub at the school gate.

"YOU ALL RIGHT?" he asked, shielding her at once.

"I am now," Janoah replied, standing with him. "How did you get aboard?"

"I JUMPED."

A nod, a chuckle, then Janoah slowly manoeuvred herself behind her towering Eisenwolf. "I'm… sorry, Amael."

"Sorry?"

"I can't go any further with you. You're right; nobody will be arresting anyone. It's better this way."

"What're you talking about, wolfess?" Amael demanded.

"Rafe they've killed everyone," Janoah said, turning to her champion. "Your little friend Sara; she's dead."

Rafe's blank lensed gaze stared down at Janoah, ears pricked. "WHATCHA MEAN? I-I JUST LEFT HER-"

"All of Hummelton's dead, Rafe! THORN has just this minute dumped black-imperium on the whole town using a balloon. All the Den Fathers, the Alpha, Sara, everyone. They're all gone."

Whilst Rafe fathomed the depths of this horrific news, Janoah nodded at Amael and the conspirators, "These wolves arranged it. They cannot be allowed to live, or they will take over Lupa. Do you understand what I'm saying? You must eliminate them."

"You bitch!" Amael seethed.

"OI!" Rafe snarled ferociously. "MIND YER MOUTH!"

"Don't you talk to me like that! I'm a Den Father! You lay a finger on me and you'll be executed!"

Ignoring Amael, Rafe asked Janoah, "IF YOU'RE RIGHT, SHOULDN'T WE TRY AND ARREST 'EM?"

"For who?" Janoah woofed. "There's nobody left to pass sentence against them! There's only you and me standing between the Republic and a dictatorship."

"BUT-"

"You said you'd trust me whatever happens, *whoever* stood against me. Remember? Don't forsake me now, Stenton!"

Shaking his head, then nodding his head, Rafe raised a gloved paw. Plasma began to snap and arc between his metallic fingers, seemingly without effort.

"IN THE NAME OF THE REPUBLIC," he said, "I SENTENCE YOU ALL TO… TO…."

"To death," Janoah finished. "Get 'em, Stenton!"

Amael raised his paws, "Wait! Wait a minute! I can give you anything you want. Anything!"

"GRRRAAAGH!"

Rafe cast his paw forward. The air rippled and warped as a wave of coronal energy twisted along the carriage in a heartbeat. Chairs overturned, tables tumbled, windows smashed and wood panels splintered. The wolves standing nearer than Amael were knocked on their backs, but the Den Father stood firm. As imperium gas lamps flared and exploded all around him, Amael pulled his pistol and fired; the pellet bounced off Rafe's chest.

"Kill him!" Amael commanded. "He's only one wolf!"

Everyone grabbed their pistols and opened fire in kind, peppering Rafe and the carriage behind.

"GET DOWN, JAN!"

Janoah, sword drawn, scrabbled into a corner, whilst Rafe advanced, foot over metal booted foot. Before he got near the Elders, the loyal Den Guard barred his path, a wall of cloaks and blades. Rafe reached behind and drew his sword, the blade disconnecting with a snap and spark of plasma that caused everyone to flinch. He brought the sword round in both paws and said, "YOU'RE JUST DEN GUARD, DOING YOUR JOB. YOUR LEADERS ARE CROOKS; YOU DON'T HAVE TO FIGHT FOR THEM."

Silence.

"PLEASE!"

With everyone's attention drawn aft, Ivan grabbed Gunnar and slipped away to the next carriage. "Come on."

"Shouldn't we do something?" Gunnar grunted, as he hobbled through the dining car with Ivan's help.

"Against that monster? I ran him through and he's still alive. And don't think we're not on Janoah's hit list too. We know too much."

"Oh."

"She's right, though," Blade-dancer said, looking for viable escape options. "It's better this way."

He noticed the trees and fields fall away outside, replaced by the placid, flat calm of Lake

Hummel. The train was crossing an arm of the lake on its way back to Hummelton, the track being raised above the water on thick wooden stilts.

"You have to get off," Ivan said, peering out the windows. "I trust you can swim."

"With a hole in my gut? Sure! No problem, mate."

"You'll be fine. It's shallow enough."

"Wait... what about you?"

Declining to answer, Ivan opened a door and looked down at the shimmering marshlands blurring by beneath him.

In that instant, he saw something utterly bizarre reflected in the waters – a fiery, smoke-billowing, silvery fish!

What?

Baffled, Ivan looked to the sky and witnessed the very moment a burning, skeletal airship silently nose-dived into a forest on the far side of the lake, perhaps a mile or two distant. It collapsed and disappeared behind the tree line amidst flames and smoke.

"Schmutz!" Gunnar whistled.

On that expletive, Ivan pushed the young Greystone out the door.

"Woaaaagh!"

Gunnar aquaplaned across the marshes and rolled to a stop in some muddy reeds.

Ivan shut the door and dashed through the dining car, then the catering car and on through an empty service car. He ducked through the dark, tunnel-like tender, passing bunkers of glittering green-imperium ore, then stepped into the noisy cabin of the clunking, hissing, ash-bellowing imperium engine.

The train this way was deserted but for a stripy badger driver in orange coveralls.

"You again, Howler?" said the stout, blinking creature, turning to Ivan and pushing up his ash-stained goggles. "Everything all right back there?"

Ivan ran his icy eyes along the complex mass of levers, valves and pipes over which the badger had dominion. "Can we go backwards faster, citizen?"

"Faster? Yes, Howler. The engine runs as quickly in reverse as forwards."

"How? Show me."

"Hooohoo, an enthusiast are we?" the friendly badger whistled.

"Absolutely," Ivan maintained.

Touching an anonymous-looking lever with one hefty paw and pointing at a red valve with the other, the badger explained. "This lever here, sir Howler, controls the direction of the imperium flow, that is backwards an' forward. An' that big valve there opens up the flow; more means faster."

A nod. "Open it up."

The badger hesitated, "Oh. Well, w-www-we mustn't go too fast, sir, we're coming up on Hummelton. Don't wanna crash into the station now do we. Hohooo!"

Ivan clapped a paw on the badger's shoulder, "If you'll forgive me, citizen."

"Forgive you? What for-woooooooh!"

The Howler grabbed the driver and forcibly ejected him from the cabin. Not even waiting to see him splash down in the marshland below like Gunnar before him, Ivan returned to the controls and opened the 'big red valve'.

The engine began to accelerate backwards, Hummelton looming larger with every more rapid chug.

Satisfied, Ivan touched his kristahl rapier to the valve.

Pffzack-k-k-k!

With long, stuttering snaps of plasma, he welded the valve in place. He did the same to the lever, melting the very steel with bolts of energy – live or die, nobody was going to undo his work.

Meanwhile, the lounge car had degenerated into chaos.

"Die monster!" a Den Guard hollered, throwing himself at Rafe Stenton, only to be swept aside by that great sword and sent slamming into the wall.

Immediately, a second Guard attacked, taking advantage of Rafe's clumsy over-swing and jabbing at the Eisenwolf with his rapier. The tip stuck fast in the metal cuirass, but did not penetrate.

Rafe grasped the rapier's tip in his metal paw and bending it away channelled plasma through it, into his attacker. The shocked Den Guard staggered away, arm numbed and burning, his rapier falling smouldering and warped onto the carpet and quickly setting it aflame.

Smoke mixed with Rafe's ash-belching exhaust and spiralled around the carriage ceiling, before being sucked out the broken windows. The whistling wind cleared the air but fuelled the flames, which licked up heavy red curtains and across the splintered wood panelling.

Still the fight continued. Janoah watched as Den Guards and Howlers presented themselves to her champion as space allowed, loyally offering up their lives to keep the monstrous Eisenwolf from the Elders and Den Father Amael. One by one brave wolves fell against the walls and furniture, slashed, burnt and broken, a terrible sight, a terrible waste. Rafe's heaving armour became streaked with blood and ash as he cut down all in his path like a whirling imperium-powered farm implement that had careened out of control.

One of the Den Guard threw himself at Rafe, barging him into the growing conflagration that was consuming the right wall. If anyone thought fire would stop an Eisenwolf they were sorely mistaken, the only part of Rafe that suffered any damage was his black Howler mantle. The cloak quickly went up in flames, melting like wax and emitting a dense vapour that rolled unnaturally down across the floor.

Strange, Janoah thought.

"Rafe!" she gasped. "Rafe, run! Get out of there!"

Not waiting, Janoah recoiled across the carriage and shut the door behind her. Tuned to Janoah's voice, Amael heard her warning and slipped quietly into the dining car.

Both parties watched through the door windows as Rafe leapt free of the fire in fear of his life even though it could not hurt him. The heavy black gas coming from his cloak swirled in his wake, the tattered material falling away in smouldering, molten shreds. The Eisenwolf looked around, expecting to be set upon by the Den Guard, but found instead the remaining Bloodfangs falling about the place, coughing and spluttering beneath their helmets.

What in the world?

One of the Elders removed his Helmet in a desperate attempt to breathe. He fell upon Rafe, clinging to him with blackened fingers, his mouth, nostrils, tongue and eyes black and bleeding, the flesh falling away in decaying strips.

"Haaaaagh! Help meeheeee!"

Rafe stood rooted with fear, metal chest heaving rapidly, adrenaline reeking on his breath, unable to move or think as the spluttering creature before him fell rotting and gurgling at his feet. The mighty Eisenwolf dropped his sword and fell backwards over a burning chair, tumbling, yelping, head over backpack into the thick of the dense black cloud pouring across the carriage like an evil fog.

I'm dead, he thought. I'm a dead wolf!

Meanwhile, Amael about-faced and hurried through the dining carriage, upsetting the beautifully-set tables and chairs as he rushed between them, fleeing the sight of his fellow conspirators melting alive.

Ivan stepped into the car from the other side, his magnificent bluish rapier at the ready. "Den Father? You look perturbed."

Amael stumbled to a halt. "Ivan! Ivan they melted!"

"Melted, sir?" Blade-dancer huffed.

"Black-imperium! I saw it. The Eisenwolf; he made it. It came from him. He killed them all in seconds. They just... fell apart at his feet, like rotting corpses!"

Ivan nodded slowly, "Ah. Like everyone at Hummelton, then?"

"What?"

"Don't worry, sir, at this speed we'll arrive shortly. If the crash doesn't kill us, the black-imperium will. You can go the same way as all the wolves you have murdered. There'll be no Den Fathers at all then. What will Lupa do?"

"No," Amael mouthed, then loudly, "No! Turn the train around. We'll decouple the carriages and leave him here."

"I'd rather not."

Amael strode forward, "Out of my way-"

With a forceful twist of his corona, Ivan both physically and intangibly shoved his Den Father stumbling backwards. Falling into a table, Amael stood dumbfounded for a moment, checking his body, as if shocked Ivan should violate him so.

"How *dare* you touch me!" he snarled. "I am your anointed-"

"Shut up and draw your sword 'Den Father'," Ivan interjected.

Back in the devastated lounge car, the black cloud slowly dispersed, sucked out the broken windows, leaving only the hot smoke of the fire rolling overhead.

Time passed. The train rattled along. Rafe checked his shaking paws, breathed longer, deeper.

He was alive. The suit worked. It really worked.

"Rafe! Rafe!"

The Eisenwolf turned, looked to the door behind. Janoah was there, peering inside. She beckoned him. He clomped over, still somewhat unsure of his own continued existence.

"JAN. WHAT DID I DO WRONG? WHAT HAPPENED?"

"It was the cloak!" Janoah shouted through the window, her voice muffled. "It was black-imperium weave. Josef said not to burn it!"

Rafe felt for his cloak, it was completely gone.

"I can't come in!" Janoah said. "And don't you come near me! You're contaminated!"

"I KNOW."

"Stay in your suit, it'll protect you! We'll hose you down you later! All right? Don't panic!"

A nod. "I'M ALL RIGHT."

Janoah pointed ahead. "Rafe, you have to check the engine! We're going far too fast; something must be wrong! Go! Quickly!"

Rafe nodded, then about-faced and hurried through the smoke. As he retrieved his sword he tried not to glimpse the semi-skeletal bodies littering the carriage, tried to tell himself that their horrible deaths from black-imperium were not his fault. It was a mistake.

Rafe slid open one door and entered the connecting passage between carriages. There he stood, peering through the decorated window at two wolves in the next car, one with a rapier drawn, a pure-white wolf, tall and lofty.

Something made Rafe pause, a memory of a green forest. Pain. Such pain!

Inside, Amael flicked his rapier from its sheath. "Fine, I'll put you out of your misery. To be honest I've wanted to do this for years, you lowly, back-combing, beta of a wolf! It's limp-wristed wolves like you and Rufus that have corrupted Lupa and made us all weak. When I'm in charge, I'll outlaw your like. Round them up, like hyenas, and re-educate you all with a pellet to the head!"

Ivan remained stock still, rapier held loose and slightly to one side, his feet spread just-so.

He said nothing; there was nothing he had say to one such as Amael.

The Den Father bounced on his feet, tested Ivan, feigned an attack, withdrew, then another. Ivan barely flinched.

"Come on, beta!" Amael goaded. "Scared, eh?"

Silence, patience.

"I'll gut you!"

Snarling, Amael struck forward in a flurry of rapier thrusts and slashes, plasma and sparks flew as Ivan parried them all in a blinding display of skill.

Blade-dancer retaliated, jabbing his blade forth once, and only once.

"Gugh!" Amael yelped, staggering back with a paw to his throat.

He fell upon a table, his rapier clattering aside, blood pouring liberally from his neck, staining the tablecloth onto which he grasped for life. Lingering there for a few seconds, perhaps as many as ten, he emitted a gurgling laugh and fell, dragging the bloody tablecloth, a vase of flowers and all the plates and cutlery on top of him.

The brief reign of Amael Balbus had ended.

Ivan flicked his rapier tip dry on another tabletop. As he made to sheath his weapon, he noticed Rafe had entered the carriage.

"YOU!" the giant woofed metallically, striding forth, Amael's body and growing pool of blood of no interest to him whatever.

Ivan said nothing.

"YOU TRIED TO KILL ME. I REMEMBER."

"I did, and I now I'll finish the job."

"WHY?" Rafe growled. "WHAT'VE I DONE?"

Ivan grunted, "You just killed half of my pack's leaders and you ask me why?"

"BUT THEY WERE TRAITORS! THUMP ME, YOU JUST KILLED YOUR DEN FATHER-"

"He was a monster and so are you, an abomination of nature, one that Rufus should *never* have drawn Janoah's attention to!"

"I'M NOT A MONSTER!"

"Humph!"

"I FIGHT FOR THE REPUBLIC, NOT AGAINST IT. I FIGHT FOR PEACE."

Ivan pointed with his rapier, "Cease your whining, pup, and come at me."

Rafe stood still, "I NEED TO STOP THE TRAIN."

"Kill me first, if you even can! Come on, Eisenwolf!"

"NO! I'VE KILLED ENOUGH TODAY. NO MORE."

"I tried to kill you. You *must* have your revenge. Come on, boy! You can do better than Amael!"

Rafe shook his head, "SORRY MATE, I'M NOT INTERESTED IN ALL THAT SCHMUTZ. NOW STEP ASIDE AND LET ME SAVE LIVES. PLEASE."

Slowly, indiscernibly, Ivan's rapier lowered.

Suddenly buildings panned past the window, lampposts, cars, streets, citizens, *living* citizens, standing and pointing, aghast at the runaway train.

How was Hummelton still alive? Had the hyenas failed?

"LET ME STOP THE TRAIN, YEAH?" Rafe urged.

Ivan nodded, then conversely shook his head. "I welded the engine's controls in place!" he despaired.

"WHAT?"

"So Amael couldn't reverse them! I thought... I thought...."

With a nod, Rafe hurried past. Ivan made to follow, until the Eisenwolf raised his metal paws, "I'M COVERED IN BLACK-IMPERIUM, MATE."

Ivan instinctively recoiled. "Josef's cloak?" he guessed, noticing its disappearance from Rafe's shoulders.

"YEAH, SO STAY BACK."

Given a moment's thought, Ivan scoffed, "It hardly matters if we're going to crash; at this speed we're finished. Come on, I'll show you the controls. Perhaps you can shift them."

"I'LL TRY ANYTHING."

Ivan led Rafe through dining car, catering car and service car, to the front of the train and the wind-swept cabin from whence he had ejected the badger driver minutes earlier. Rafe only just fit through the low and oppressive tender, stray nuggets of green-imperium crunching beneath his eisenglanz-soled boots.

Blade-dancer tried the forward-reverse lever first, then the flow valve; both were stuck fast and still hot from being welded by his own reckless actions.

"Throw that!" Ivan said of the lever, shaking his scorched paws.

Nodding, Rafe pushed on the lever with all his might; he succeeded only in bending the solid length of iron into a banana.

"OOPS."

"The valve!" Ivan instructed next, touching it. "Turn it clockwise to cut off the imperium flow."

Nodding, Rafe attacked the valve with both paws.

"GRRRR-FFFFFGH!"

As he struggled, Rafe's backpack began churning out great clouds of ash, which were instantly sucked forwards and out of the cabin to join the exhaust from the reversing imperium engine. In his desperate throes, accidental arcs of plasma shot down Rafe's gauntlet-clad arms and into the engine controls.

Ivan stood back as energy bolts danced over the face of the dials and played between pipes. For a second the engine stuttered and whined, he was sure.

Choink!

Away came the valve, breaking clean off in Rafe's impossible grasp. "AWW, SCHMUTZ!" he cursed, tossing it away. "IS THERE A BRAKE?"

"Yes, in the tender, but brakes won't stop a running engine," Ivan explained. "They'll just melt."

Rafe spread his paws, at a loss.

At length, Ivan gestured at the engine's controls, "It stuttered."

"WHAT?"

"When you shocked it with your plasma, the engine stuttered. I saw the dials drop, I swear. Perhaps you damaged it."

Rafe stood thinking. He looked to the engine, then back to Ivan, then back to the engine again, the cogs of his mind whirring. Slowly, he raised his armoured paws over the profusion of pipes, levers, switches and dials.

"GET OUT."

Ivan understood at once. He retreated from cabin to adjoining tender, but remained within sight, standing amidst the bunkers of glittering imperium. To his dismay he noticed the castle-like towers of Hummel's capital den panning into view; Hummelton station was not even a mile down the line. Blade-dancer entertained the vain hope that some diligent train hog would change the points and send the runaway Bloodfang Train on towards Queens Town, buying time, but in all likelihood she remained on course for the termination from whence she had departed.

Without delay, Rafe called upon his internal fires. The imperium in his bones, his blood and the eisenpelz worked as one great well of energy to give life to blinding bolts of plasma the like of which Ivan had never seen! The engine's dials went wild as Rafe's power surged through him and into the system, overwhelming it, disrupting the imperium flow. His invisible corona reached out too, coiling through the air, twisting the very fabric of reality; Ivan could feel it slicing through him even from a safe distance. The cabin walls and roof, solid sheets of metal, began to buckle and twist around Rafe. Pipes split and exploded, venting burning ash and gases which would have killed stone-dead anyone but the amazing iron-clad Eisenwolf.

Groaning and whining, the imperium engine's chugs mistimed, then backfired and eventually died altogether! The ash from the funnels ceased to billow and instead vented gently, like so many giant embers.

Quiet, but for the tearing wind and clack of wheels.

His backpack expelling a continuous, audible jet of ash like a boiling kettle, Rafe lowered his shaking, smouldering paws and fell back against the cabin wall.

Ivan dashed in, "You did it; she's rolling-stock!"

He returned to the tender and pulled on what he hoped was the brake lever.

Screeeeeeeee!

The train jolted and began slowing. Was it enough?

Ivan went to the twisted cabin window and looked out, then turned to Rafe. "We need to get away from the engine; it'll crush these carriages like paper. Come on."

"ARE... WE... WE STILL GONNA CRASH?"

"Maybe."

Nodding, panting, Rafe lumbered after the nimble Ivan, into the service car, through the catering car and on to dining car. Halfway along the latter he fell over a nicely-set table, exhausted and dizzy.

Ivan dashed back and wrapping his paw in his cloak tugged on the contaminated Rafe. "Come on, boy!"

"AYE!"

Rafe staggered as far as the dining carriage door before the Elder Train reached the end of the line. Hummelton station blurred by; pillars, tiles, the rear carriages of other trains.

"Honoured to have known you, Bruno Claybourne," Ivan said.

The Eisenwolf took a shaky, tinny breath, "AND YOU... WHOEVER YOU ARE."

Blade-dancer emitted an amused scoff.

With a thunderous explosion everything not bolted down jolted violently forwards, tables, chairs, glass, cutlery, Amael, Ivan and Eisenwolf. The carriage shook and crumpled, catapulted violently upwards and over, like a log in a caber toss. The roof became the wall and the broken windows scraped along the ground, sparks flying, fires setting.

The last thing Rafe saw in his mind's eye before all sensation was beaten from him was Meryl.

Sweet Meryl.

✦

Vladimir and Angus pulled up in the white Hummel car as the enormous durametal skeleton of the *Nimbus* collapsed in a heap of flames. They had trailed it past town and across the lake, watching it burn and shed debris all the way.

Getting as close as they dared, Vladimir stepped out the car and walked cautiously across the fields, circling the crash site and searching for any signs of life, or black-imperium. Thankfully there was none of the latter, but alas none of the former either.

"Nobody's getting out of that alive," Angus said, shielding his eyes from the heat.

Vladimir could but grunt and sigh.

"I say! Over here!"

A ginger cat in coveralls and a cap came traipsing through the long grass towards the wolves. He was rolling up a mass of silk sheeting in his arms; the sheet was connected to his backpack via two dozen strings or so. What in the world it was Vladimir had no idea, but he recognised the cat even before he opened his mouth.

"Montague Buttle!" he declared. "How'd you do?"

"Grand Howler Vladimir."

"What a waste, eh?" said the cat, looking upon the sad sight. "Me balloon doncha know. Years of work gone up in smoke... again."

"Indeed."

Monty licked his lips, "We uh... we had a bit of trouble, 'Owler. Hijacked we were. Held hostage-"

"Where are the hyenas?" Vladimir asked directly.

Monty blinked, "You know what happened?"

"I've an inkling."

"Oh, well... the THORN chaps all bought it I'm afraid, one way or another," Monty sniffed, matter-of-factly. "Except that Madou."

"Madou?"

"Yes," Monty clucked, "nothing we could do for the others. Things just... got out of paw up there. Thought my fighting days were over. Terrible business. Had to do it, left me no choice. None."

Vladimir looked to Angus, then back to Monty again. "What about my Howlers?"

"'Owlers?"

"Linus and Uther," Vladimir clarified, with a nod at the flaming wreck of *Nimbus*. "Are they in that?"

"No, no," Monty mewed, scanning the sunny sky. "They're still up in the big blue yonder somewhere. Penny's just looking for a nice spot to land."

Vladimir and Angus looked up as well, then exchanged bewildered shrugs.

✦

Brrrrrr-r-r-r-r-r-r-r-p-p-p-p-p-p-p!

It was not a monobike, nor a car, but a propeller, Sara reckoned, yet higher pitched than a dirigible's, like a hoverfly was to a bee.

She looked up and out the car window and saw a huge winged silhouette swoop overhead.

"Och!" Sara cooed, following the machine across the windscreen and down in a field.

Sara's many little sisters all clambered across the back of the Hummel limo and fought to press their faces to the window, with much gasping, pointing and giggling.

"Stop the car!" Sara told Eldress Brynn, who was driving.

"Mah orders were tae get you away from here."

"Stop the car!"

"Sara-"

"That's one of Monty Buttle's planes. It must be them!"

"Or a hyena!"

"Oh aye, Brynn, because hyenas can fly planes and all. Pull over for Ulf's sake!"

Reluctantly, Eldress Brynn drew to a stop and Sara flew out the car and across the fields. Her sisters tried to follow, but Brynn barked at them to stay where they were – unlike their disobedient big sister, they stayed put. Brynn hurried after Sara, eager to protect the daughter of Hummel's long-standing Den Mother.

The plane bounced to stop on its flimsy-looking wheels and turned slightly to one side. The engine and propeller choked to a halt. Beasts moved inside, Sara recognising some of them, others a mystery, Penny was up front with some Howler, and a hyena was squeezed into the back with another wolf wrapped in a bundle of black cloak.

Sara stopped, unsure. Was the hyena holding Penny hostage? Was Brynn right?

Penny and the Howler climbed out, the latter throwing off his helmet and falling on his knees to kiss the grass – it was Linus's friend Uther, and no mistake. Sara was further reassured when Penny waved enthusiastically. The cat's dress was covered in ash and Ulf knows what, but she did not look like a beast under duress.

Sara hurried over and embraced Penny, then eyes searching the plane asked her, "Where's Monty? We saw the balloon go down over by the lake."

"He took the parachute," Penny replied. "Always a gentlebeast, my Monty."

"And the black-imperium?"

"Gone, dear."

"Gone?"

Uther stood up and said to Sara, "We took care of it, sweetheart. Should be fine."

A nod, a smile.

Eldress Brynn arrived, rapier brandished as usual. Sara expected her to threaten the hefty hyena in the back seat, but she stood aloof, quiet, waiting, but ready to step in.

The silent hyena passed his wolfen bundle down to Uther.

"Linus!" Sara yelped.

"Sara?" he replied groggily, blinking in the sun. "Did... did we s-sss-stop Nurka?"

She nodded, "Aye, Ah think so."

"No," Uther replied, looking to Madou and saying, "Nurka stopped himself."

✣

Prince Noss awoke to a cool, damp cloth mopping his brow and the beautiful visage of Arjana looking down upon him, her face devoid of golden makeup and more beautiful for it.

"Arjana?"

"Noss."

Twisting his bound wrists, Noss made to rise from the piles of pillows, but Arjana pushed him down. "Rest."

Noss looked down at himself; he was dressed in traditional attire, just a black and white sarong.

"My paws are tied, wife," he observed.

"Yes, husband. For your own safety."

"Hahaaahah! Of course!" the prince chortled, then grunted in pain. "My back feels like... a bear stepped on me."

Arjana wetted the cloth and wrung it out. "Chakaa Madou had to hit you. I commanded him to. You were out of your wits."

Noss almost disagreed, but mentally trod on his tongue. "I was?" he said instead, playing along.

"You said terrible things against me. You tried to incite everyone to abandon me. They almost listened, you being a Prince."

Noss looked away a little.

Arjana smiled briefly, "It's all right. It was just the madness. I forgive you, Noss; as always I must forgive and forget your antics. It is a wife's duty, even a queen's."

A grunt.

Arjana slowly lay on the pillows beside Noss and placed an arm across him. "I missed you," she whispered.

Noss blinked his purple eyes slowly, "And I you."

"Truly?"

"It's what got me through Gelb, why I did not throw myself down a pit. All I thought of was you and the...."

There was a long painful silence as Noss avoided mentioning his cubs. The tent fluttered overhead. Campfires crackled. It was peaceful.

So peaceful.

"They took our cubs," Arjana reminded him.

"Vladimir promised me. He promised me!"

"His promises were lies, this wolf, as always they are. But now their rule is destroyed we will have more cubs. We will have many fine Princes and Princesses and marry them to the other tribes. We are still young."

"I'm rotting, wife."

"No. Not for many years."

"My mind burns. I... I...." Noss grimaced and breathed deep, trying not to weep. "Perhaps you should find someone with a clearer mind than I? Take Chakaa Nurka, since you two seem to agree on what's to be done. He's young and strong and... not nearly as useless as I."

"He is a great hyena, but no Prince of the blood," Arjana dismissed, sitting up and looking down on Noss, a finger playing on his chest. "Besides, he's gone."

"Gone?" Noss scoffed.

"He will have rotted with the black rain over Hummelton."

The Prince frowned, "What? But why?"

"It was the only way, Noss. Nurka always knew that was his fate. After him Themba will do the same over Lupa; Nurka will have instructed him what to do. As Chakaa they can survive the poison long enough to open the canisters, longer than those weakling Howlers who cannot even stomach the chunta. Just one of our afflicted is worth three of theirs. And you, my Prince, are worth a hundred more. We are the superior race. That is why they keep us in bondage still when all others they have conquered walk among them. They fear us."

Noss closed his eyes. "It's... it's all over then?"

"Yes. The sun is setting, my Prince, you slept all day. The sun sets not only out here, but on wolfkind's empire. I await Nurka's message to confirm the fact. Then we will make our next move."

"And go where? Do what?"

Arjana beamed, "To the Reservations, to free the tribes and leave for the wilds, as I have said. Once the Matriarchs know Lupa is finished they will sanction a revolt. It is assured. It is that or starve, the wolves will not be able to feed us."

It was all so plausible, so sensible, so clever, and yet Noss felt sick to his stomach. The cold-hearted murder of all wolfkind and countless innocents besides; was it a fair bargain for hyena freedom, would the ancestors look well on the achievements of THORN?

Noss licked his lips as he remembered a friend. "What happened to Red-mist?"

Arjana huffed and turned her face, "Your wolfen obsession? I knew you would not be long without mentioning the teacher who poisoned your mind against us."

"He made me, Arjana. He saved my life-"

"Spare me your moaning, he is alive!" the Queen roared, then spoke softer, "Nurka begged me to spare him. Red-mist assisted you in the mines, I understand. You would be dead but for him, though it was all a ruse and *not* for our benefit."

"Can you blame him?"

"No, he is cunning." Arjana tapped Noss's nose, "Perhaps, if you behave, my foolish Prince, I will find it possible to let him go. One wolf, however cunning, will be no threat to the Jua-mata in a post-Lupa world. Though without the blood of the Erde in his veins he will quickly rot."

"As will I," Noss pointed out.

Arjana shook her head, "Unlike the wolves we will take from Mother Erde only what we must, not more than we deserve. I will enforce our laws."

"I'm sure that's how the wolves started, Arjana. We will become like them and grow with the eating. We will have to build a great city too, then an army of Chakaa, and enslave the little beasts to sustain us just the same, or be defeated by greater powers. It is the way of this cruel world."

Sighing, Arjana sweetly kissed Noss's neck, "Do not talk of death and the past, but life and the future!"

"I was."

"Everything is in paw, husband. You will see."

Noss nuzzled into his wife, savouring her warmth, her familiar scent, so long denied him.

Can I go on? Can I love her, despite all?

"Untie me," he said, twisting his spotty arms. "Let me touch you, wife. Let us make love and cubs anew."

Arjana laughed, Queen no longer, but a girl again.

Bvvvvvvpt!

The white moth fluttered softly into the tent and settled gently on the Queen's back, interrupting affairs.

"Soon, my Prince," Arjana said, extracting herself from Noss and the pillows. "Rest your poor back whist you can. We will soon be on the move again."

She leant down and kissed him firmly, parted slowly. He smiled a toothy grin.

Falling back, the aching Noss watched his beautiful wife take the moth from her back and hang the trembling creature on the tent's central pole. She removed the message box it was carrying and knelt before the low table where Nurka had shown Noss his maps and plans not more than a day ago.

Arjana upturned the tiny message box in her paw and something small and shiny fell heavily into her palm; Noss didn't catch what it was.

The Queen stared at her palm for the longest time. Suddenly she emitted a snort of anguish and held whatever was close in both paws.

Noss levered himself painfully upright, "Arjana?"

"It is… over," she snuffled, fighting to maintain her composure. "You have won, my mad, mad Noss."

"Won? Arjana, what-"

"Guards!"

Arjana's four mighty litter bearers entered the tent and bowed low.

"Escort our Prince from my presence," she commanded them. "When I am gone, you will obey him. He is the best equipped to lead you in this wolfen world; he… knows them as I never did. Love him, as you have loved me. That is my wish."

"My Queen, please-" one rasped.

"Silence! Go. Do not return, you must not gaze upon what is left. Leave me here… for the wind and… the rain."

Arjana placed something in her mouth.

"No!" Noss snarled in realisation, tugging on his bonds as the guards descended upon him, pulling him away. "Spit it out! Spit it out, Arjana!"

"Goodbye my sweet, mad Prince."

As Noss was barely dragged from the tent by the strength of four hyenas, he heard the terrible crack of glass, the fizzle of flesh and glimpsed through the flaps Arjana collapsing over the table amidst a hint of black vapours.

"Arjanaaaaahahahaaaa!" Noss cried, falling to his knees in the mud. "Graaaaaghagh!"

The white pepper moth burst from the polluted tent and over the prince's head, thrumming into the twilight firmament.

"Her spirit flies!" one of the guards wailed, drawing the attention of all who remained at *Kambi Mata*. "The Queen goes to the Sky!"

Hyenas raised their spears and uttered their terrible war-cry, resembling mad laughter, at least to ignorant Wolfen ears like Tomek's.

"What they doing?" the youth whispered, twisting in his bonds to look at Rufus, bound to the next stake along.

"Seeing off their Queen," Rufus replied.

"She is dead?"

"That moth carried Nurka's news, dear boy. I think it was bad news."

Time passed, tears fell, until the Prince of the Four Winds felt his paws being untwined. Arjana's guards then prostrated themselves before him, fully expecting death for the insult they had dealt Noss, even though it had been a queen's command.

Noss remained kneeling, without the will to stand, nor pass judgment. Everything was lost, Arjana, Nurka, Themba, Madou, the cubs, every last beast he cared about.

Almost.

Rising slowly to his feet, Noss said numbly, "Release the Howlers."

Surprised but obedient, his hyenas hurried to do their master's bidding, untying the prisoners. Rufus and Tomek were starving, thirsty, filthy and battered, but they knew they were safe with Noss in charge. They shuffled slowly over to the prince, rubbing their wrists all the way.

Rufus prevented the ever-curious Tomek from going anywhere near Arjana's tent, both out of respect and because it was a death-trap.

"I'm truly sorry, Noss," he said.

His cheeks and muzzle wetted, Noss smiled. "You have won, Red-mist. THORN is finished."

Rufus disagreed, "Nobody's in any position to gloat, Noss. We're all of us losers today."

*

Brrrring! Brr-

Werner snatched the phone from the bar, the only device still working in *The Warren*. The others watched his face twist as he listened, every rat, rabbit, hog and other conspirator, hanging on his word, to strike, or not.

Werner shakily put the phone down. "Get out of here, lads," he said. "It's all over."

"What?"

"It's over! They're coming. Get out whilst you can."

After a moment's pause, the conspirators, with surprising calm and dignity, scraped chairs under the tables, grabbed their coats and filed for the door. Once on the dark Lupan streets they shook paws and split in all directions. The Politzi amongst them would not report for duty come tomorrow morning, or ever turn up in Riddle District again. They would disappear into Lupa's underbelly, gain new papers, new names, new lives, whatever it took to escape the net and fight on for another day, for another little beast plot.

Professor Heath remained, cradling the weak and wounded Howler Tristan.

"Go on!" Werner snorted at him. "Take the cub with yer."

"I'm staying. I have nowhere to go."

"Puh! Suit yerself."

"What about you? Shouldn't you go?"

"I'm tired of running," Werner sighed, leaning on the bar and inspecting his pistol. "Been running since the war, one way or another. I'm done with it."

Heath cleared his throat. "Does this mean the black-imperium wasn't dropped on Hummelton?"

Werner nodded, "Aye."

"It was no fit way to start a revolution. You would have regretted it, all of you."

"Maybe you're right. Maybe, but I doubt it."

Shortly, a Politzi car pulled up outside *The Warren*. A uniformed brown rabbit hopped out and timidly opened the door to the dark, boarded-up property.

"Chief?"

"Borce?"

"Yes, sir. It's me, sir."

Werner gruffed, "Too late, lad, they've all gone! Come in, I won't shoot yer."

"No, chief," Borce replied, stepping nervously inside.

"You found me fast."

"They're arresting everyone back at HQ, sir, one of 'em talked and said this was your hideout." Borce looked to Heath and Tristan, then back to Werner. "I'm afraid I've got to take you all in, Chief. There's some Howlers on the way."

"I know. It's all over. I shan't resist."

"I dunno what it is you got involved in and I-I-I don't wanna know. Only, I thought you might want five minutes to, you know, hop out a window, like. You've always been really good to me and my uncle."

"Aye. Thanks Borce, I appreciate that." Werner gestured at Heath and Tristan, "These two are innocent; they tried to stop me. They're heroes. Put that in your report."

"Oh. Yes, sir. I will."

"Now scram before someone sees you. Go on."

Nodding, Constable Borce made to leave, but Werner kept him a moment longer.

"Oh! Be sure to take *The Warren* back; you or Casimir are welcome to it. I've had it wrapped up in Politzi red tape since it got bombed out. I uh... I shan't be needing it anymore. Files are in my desk, you can sort it out on the quiet."

"Thanks, sir, will do," Borce said, with insipid cheer. "Good luck then."

"Aye, and you."

The Politzi rabbit shut the front door and climbed into his car, ostensibly to wait for backup. One puny rabbit couldn't make such an arrest by himself – that was the excuse Borce had dreamt up anyway.

The youngster looked to *The Warren*, took a deep, shaky breath and checked his pocket watch. Howlers would be here any minute. Grand Howler Boris had already been arrested by ALPHA agents swooping on Riddle, and the district itself put under temporary ALPHA control. Whatever was going down, it was massive.

Bang!

Blades of light cut through the gaps in the boarded up windows, partitioning the street for a moment.

Overcoming his natural rabbit timidity, Borce burst inside *The Warren* just in time to witness Werner Schwartz drop his pistol on the bar and collapse heavily behind it, trotters clutching at his chest.

It was indeed all over, for him.

Chapter 56

The stiff-collared Meryl Stroud clopped through the shafts of morning sunlight in her practical footwear, breakfast tray in paws, flight-challenged bee trundling after her. ALPHA HQ never looked particularly marvellous, even with the lavender and spring sunshine, but with Rafe back everything was a little brighter again in the eyes of Meryl.

"Miss Stroud!"

Silvermane's voice stopped the nurse, and Toggle, in their tracks.

"Yes, Grand Prefect?"

Silvermane stole across the hallway, "Miss Str-"

Bvvvt!

Almost stepping on the bee and being duly told off, Silvermane tugged his cloak and continued, "Miss Stroud, I'm just going to question Grand Prefect Nikita."

"Again?"

"Yes... and again and again, until the Alpha is satisfied I've wrung every last name from him! Now, I need you to write down your statement, about the racking incident with Tristan and Maher."

"What for?"

"To show Nikita we have him on something, even if it's just murder. Something to make him deal."

"To break him, you mean."

"Yes, if you will."

Meryl grimaced and looked away. "I want no part of it if you're going to rack him."

"Need I remind you," Silvermane said meaningfully, "that Tristan escaped ALPHA custody under your watch?"

"It was nothing to do with me! I went to the loo and when I came back he was gone. I'm not a guard, I'm a nurse! What difference does it make? He was being released anyway-"

"To the Eisbrands, wolfess, not out the back door! Sign a statement and I will forget your lapse of judgement-"

"Fine!" Meryl barked. "Fine, I'll do whatever you want. Just let me take this to Rafe before it gets cold."

Silvermane saluted, ALPHA-style.

Meryl had her paws full – a good excuse – and thus took her leave with only a nod, and Toggle.

Whilst Silvermane went to the stark holding cells, Meryl made her way to ALPHA's almost equally depressing infirmary wing and Rafe's permanent private ward, with its tiny window, single lamp, and meagre accoutrements. Meryl had set spring flowers in the window to brighten the dingy atmosphere; Rafe could appreciate them, for despite his exertions his eyes were healthy. In fact he was doing very well.

"Hey," said the giant, sitting up in bed with a small blue book in his big brown paws.

"Good morning," Meryl replied. "Reading?" she chirped, most impressed. She glanced around, "Do you need more light? I can get another lamp."

Rafe set aside his book, making room for breakfast. "Nah, I'm done," he said, rubbing his thighs.

Meryl slid the tray onto Rafe's blanketed lap and unfurled a napkin. "What is it?"

"What?"

"The book."

Rafe adopted a mock-scholarly air, "*Ashes of the Gods*, by Giacomo Valerio."

Meryl paused in mid-napkin-flick, then tied it around Rafe's thick neck. "Where'd you get that from?"

"You left it here on the table last night."

"I did?"

"Yeah. Don't you remember?"

"Oh, I'm all over the shop at present," Meryl sighed.

"It's really good, 'en it?" Rafe said. "Well-written. Not too difficult to read."

"Yes, well, that's because it's Giacomo Valerio. He was an engineer who wrote for the common beast. The vocabulary is simple, but his writing is still magical. I must've read it… oh, ten times."

"Common beast, am I?" Rafe joked.

"Most uncommon," Meryl cooed, "as well you know."

"You're rarer still, Miss Stroud."

Rafe pulled the giggling Meryl close. They kissed briefly.

"I wonder what they're like," Rafe said, looking into nowhere.

"What?"

"Those Dead Cities, where Giacomo found the first monobike parts. Must be all kinds of things buried there. I know my eisenpelz comes from there too."

Meryl primly extricated herself from Rafe and picked up the book, slipping in into her apron pocket.

"What're you doing?" he complained. "Can't I borrow it?"

"No."

"I thought you'd read it ten times-"

"You shouldn't be seen reading this sort of thing!"

Surprised, Rafe snorted, "Why not?"

Glancing at the door, Meryl whispered, "Because it's impartialist material. It'll give you ideas, ideas that, knowing your big mouth, you'll spout at the wrong wolf, like Horst. After what's just happened it's best to keep quiet awhile."

Rafe spread a paw, "It's your book, Meryl."

"Yes, well… everyone around here already knows what I think; no point hiding it now. But you're different. You frighten them, you know, Horst and all that."

"Eh?"

"Your power, Rafe; I-I mean a wolf like you could…." Meryl checked herself. "Well, never you mind. Peaceful change is the right way to go. Just take THORN! Their pamphlets have done more damage than any amount of black-imperium. Even Silvermane's convinced and Rufus says he didn't believe a word of the rumours coming out of the Reservations before. Now whether the Den Fathers were even aware of the atrocities or not, the whole world's seen those pictures. Things have to change. They've got to, by Ulf!"

Rafe sat listening throughout, mighty arms folded. "I love it when you get all political," he said cheekily.

Meryl blushed and cleared her throat. "Your porridge is getting cold, mister."

No sooner had Rafe popped open a jar of honey and spooned some onto said porridge than up reared a giant bee, its spiky front legs snagging the sheets like fishhooks.

Bvvvt!

"All right, Toggle?"

Bvvt! Bvvvvv!"

"Whatcha want, mate? Honey?"

"Of course she does; it's all she has eyes for," Meryl huffed. "She had her head in my lavenders whilst you were away, which is right and proper for a bee, only she's so clumsy she ended up trampling them all down!"

"She's a big girl," Rafe maintained, pushing the jar within reach of Toggle's searching proboscis. Upon locating the jar she rapidly lapped up its contents. Rafe, meanwhile, lapped up his porridge in great big spoonfuls.

Meryl pulled up Rafe's chair and sat, watching the outsized duo eating in harmony together. "You look so well. I can't believe it."

Rafe flexed an arm, "I feel well, like a new wolf."

"I don't understand it, but I'm not going to complain."

The Eisenwolf munched away, then said through a raised chin and mouthful of porridge, "Oi, how's Jan?"

Meryl looked down and away. "Same," she sighed, tugging her apron. "Broken bones and a bad temper. She can't stand missing out on the arrests. Rufus visited yesterday and I heard her tell him that Silvermane's going to 'steal her glory' by rounding up the conspirators. He told her that's nonsense; she was there on the train with you, stopping Amael. Silvermane was here, shuffling papers and likely waiting to see how the wind blew – the Alpha's no fool, he knows Janoah's worth."

At length, Meryl enquired delicately, "Rufus wanted me to ask you; are you *sure* it was Ivan you saw on the train?"

"Yeah! It must've been."

Meryl looked incredulous.

"Jan saw him too!" Rafe woofed at her.

"That's not what she's saying, Rafe, not even to Rufus."

"Look, he was right in front of me; a tall white wolf. He killed Amael in a single stroke! Gotta be Blade-dancer, right?"

"Well, according to Janoah, Amael saw his plan had failed, then went mad and crashed the train on purpose. She says he cut his own throat, though not before throwing a black-imperium bomb at his allies. She only just escaped death leaping from the train."

Rafe dropped his spoon in his breakfast with a splodge. "Who's gonna believe that schmutz?"

Meryl exhaled, "Who's to question it? Everyone's dead."

Rafe tugged his napkin off and threw it down. "Aww, she's making me look like an idiot, Meryl! I remember it clear as day. I remember everything this time. I dunno why, but I can picture the whole thing. There's no fuzzy wall. I was fighting 'em all, then my cloak set fire and… and…." Rafe trailed off at some awful memory Meryl was not privy to. "For once I wish I couldn't remember," he said, staring into the face of that wolf, rotting alive.

"Rafe," Meryl said gently, brining him back, "have you considered Janoah might be protecting you?"

"Protecting me?"

"Yes. It's no small matter to have killed those Elders, even if they were conspirators, and even if it was an accident. You could get in trouble."

"But… I had to fight. For the Republic, Meryl. Jan said so. We thought everyone back in Hummelton was dead and Amael was gonna take over."

A nod.

Clinging to the hope that Rafe really was just confused and Janoah's unlikely story was the correct one, Meryl took Rafe's nearest paw and said noncommittally. "Just talk to her first before you make any more statements to Silvermane and the others. Get your story straight between you. Janoah's many things, but she does care about you."

"Yeah, I know that Meryl."

"Yes," the nurse said, "I was perhaps just reminding myself."

Bvvvt!

Clink!

Down went Toggle, and down went the jar, falling off the bed and breaking.

"Toggle!" Meryl scolded, to no discernable effect.

Whilst Toggle trundled off to clean her shiny face, Meryl snatched Rafe's napkin and set about cleaning up the sticky mess, complaining mildly. "For Ulf's sake, what kind of stupid beast adopts a giant bee anyway?"

Rafe innocently poured some tea and tucked into his breakfast apple.

As Meryl collected sticky glass shards and placed them on the napkin, the sounds of shouting and pistol fire echoed across ALPHA HQ.

"Halt!"

Crack! Crack!

Glancing at Rafe, Meryl hurried to the door and peered outside just as boots squeaked loudly along the corridor towards her.

Right into her!

"Oh! Rafe!" Meryl screamed, as a big mottled in bundled her into the room.

It was Grand Prefect Nikita!

Rafe pushed the tray aside and threw the sheets from his legs.

"Don't move, or I kill her!" Nikita barked at him, then at the Prefects arriving at the door to Rafe's room. Swinging Meryl round and holding her close to him with both paws pressed to her face as if trying to crush a melon, the fallen Grand Prefect backed into a corner and snarled. "I will bake her brain if anyone move!"

Silvermane pushed to the front of the Prefects. "It's over Nikita."

"Stay back!"

"There's nowhere to go."

"Get rid of them!" Nikita said, looking to the other Prefects. "You know I will do it, Silver! You know it! I have nothing to lose!"

"Do as he says," Rafe said, shouting, "Do it!"

Raising his paws to calm everyone, Silvermane dismissed the other Prefects from the doorway, leaving just himself and Rafe inside. "Now what, Nikita?" he scoffed. "You're only making this harder than it needs to be. Confess and-"

"Shut up, maggot!" Nikita bellowed, plasma playing on his fingers.

Meryl squirmed, "Aaagh! Rafe!"

"Stop it!" Rafe begged. "I'll do whatever you want!"

Now he had everyone's attention, Nikita set out his desperate stall. "Then get your suit, Eisenwolf."

"What?"

"Someone fetch Josef!" Nikita snarled. "You will wear your mantle and escort me out of Lupa and kill anyone who gets in our way. If not… I roast your little wench's head like baked potato. Do you understand?"

"Yeah, mate. I understand. Just calm down. Don't hurt her. Please."

Silvermane snorted, "You're out of your mind, Nikita."

"Shut up and get the suit, Ulf damn you!"

Rafe glared at Silvermane, thus Silvermane told his Prefects, "Get Josef Grau. Tell him it's an emergency."

Shaking the helpless Meryl, Nikita snapped, "The suit!"

"Rafe can't pop it on like a hat, you fool," Silvermane explained. "You will have to let him go to where it's stored and wait for Josef to dress him. It takes time."

Nikita nodded. "Then I will go with him to where it is stored." He flicked his muzzle, "Now get out and go down the corridor. Leave your pistols on the floor, all of you. Leave me a loaded one."

Silvermane shook his head, "I will not arm you."

"Do it! Or you will be responsible for her death. Do you hear that Rafe? It is *his* fault if Miss Stroud dies. You know who to blame, who to kill when you go mad with grief. I know you will. You are already insane, Eisenwolf."

Whatever he thought, Rafe nodded at Silvermane. "Do as he says, sir. I got this."

"Stenton-"

"Please!"

Sighing, Silvermane drew his pistol and placed it on the floor, then backed out the room and down the way with his Prefects.

Once they were some distance away, Nikita flicked his head. "You first, Eisenwolf."

Rafe stood up from the bed, a tall brown tower of muscle and sinew. Intimidating now as always.

"Slowly!" Nikita warned, backing off. "Paws up!"

"Yeah. Yeah. No problem, mate."

Rafe went to the door, stepped over Silvermane's pistol and out into the hall, his paws up, feet patting on the floor.

"Stop!" Nikita instructed. "Stay there."

A nod.

Nikita shuffled Meryl towards the door and grabbed the pistol. He checked it was loaded and with one paw grasping the scruff of Meryl's neck aimed at Rafe. Now he had them both in his power.

"Lead the way, Eisenwolf. Try anything and I shoot you and kill her after."

Rafe started to walk towards Silvermane and the others.

"Back off!" Nikita threatened them, pistol wagging. "Get away, all of you!"

Silvermane and the Prefects did as bidden, retreating as quickly as Rafe advanced.

As he walked backwards, Silver read Rafe's furious features, watched his brow twist, his tongue lick his nose. One could almost see the gears of his mind whirring. Would Rafe chance turning and blasting Nikita? He might kill Meryl along with him. Even knocking them both down might give Nikita time to retaliate. One thing felt assured; this situation would not hold, someone or something was going to snap.

Oblivious to the drama, Toggle traipsed merrily after Meryl in pursuit of her endless quest for honey. She bumped into the back of Nikita.

Bvvt! Bvvvvt!

"Eugh!"

Nikita booted the bee savagely away, sending it spinning across the hall on its back.

"Don't!" Meryl said. "She won't hurt you-"

"Shut up, wolfess!"

Confused, Toggle flipped to her feet no worse for wear and came back. Her clawed front feet grasped both at Meryl's dress and Nikita's legs, like a needy child.

Bvvvvbvv!

Disturbed by the quivering creature's many needle-like claws tugging at him, the Grand Prefect turned and administered a more powerful, plasmatically-charged kick, ejecting Toggle down the hall.

"Get away!"

Bvvv-vvvvv-v-v-vvvvv!

Toggle flailed around, useless wings buzzing, legs kicking, sting protruding from her heaving abdomen.

Then something snapped.

Amidst the momentary distraction, Meryl elbowed Nikita and twisted herself away.

"Oof!"

Head down she ran for all she was worth. "Rafe!"

The Eisenwolf whirled round and sweeping Meryl into one arm raised his other paw.

Crack!

The desperate Nikita fired at them, the pistol pellet streaking down the hall, hot and glowing.

It slowed unnaturally, impossibly, as if the wobbling, transparent coils of imperious power leaving Rafe's corona affected even it. The missile hit neither him nor Meryl, but exploded in sparks against the wall to their right.

Rafe's furious will tore down the hall, crossing the distance to Nikita in all of a heartbeat, cracking plaster and windows and thumping into the Grand Prefect like the fist of Ulf.

"Gaaagh!"

By a twist of fate, Nikita landed square on top of the flailing Toggle.

Bzzzbzvvvbt!

"Ahaagh!" Nikita yelped, rolling aside, his back arched in apparent pain.

Free, Toggle righted herself and hurriedly climbed the wall to safety, whilst Silvermane and the Prefects thundered past Rafe and over to Nikita. They descended upon him, but soon they realised his gasps and wheezes were not of someone winded or protesting their arrest, but those of someone in greater trouble.

Meryl peered past Rafe's protective embrace and watched the Grand Prefect fit and twist and gasp for air.

"Something's wrong," she told Rafe.

"Meryl."

"Let me go. It's all right."

Telling the baffled Prefects to give Nikita air, Meryl asked them to roll him over onto his front.

"What's wrong with him?" Silvermane demanded.

"I don't know."

"Do something! If he dies we'll lose vital information. I'd have shot him myself otherwise."

"I can't do anything here," Meryl replied. "Carry him to the ward. Quickly now!"

The Prefects picked Nikita up and ferried him down the hall. Meryl glanced back at Rafe, who nodded and let her go about her work. Once she and Silvermane had gone, Rafe fell on his knees and nursed the arm he had used to project his imperious might. His bones and muscles ached and burned, as always; it was worse without the Eisenwolf mantle to help channel and enhance the energy.

Rafe looked at the pellet in the wall, then his shaking paw, incredulous.

"Your power grows, Stenton," someone said behind.

Rafe turned round and saw a stocky brown wolf with a pleasing white face standing over him.

"Alpha, sir," Rafe said, standing to salute with the modest ALPHA salute. "My Alpha, I mean."

Adal waved in kind then touched the pellet in the wall. "I saw everything," he said, quickly withdrawing his finger and licking it; the pellet was still hot. "Very impressive, even for a wolf of your... imperious stature."

"Thank you, sir."

"Yes. We'll be sad to see you go."

"Go, sir?" Rafe replied, worriedly.

Adal nodded, "Don't you know? Janoah and Rufus came to some arrangement months ago."

Rafe just looked blank.

"Typical of Janoah to keep it to herself," the Alpha sighed, waving a paw. "Some deal Rufus struck on your behalf; his price for going into Gelb and all that. You're to receive an imperium pension, in any case."

"Pension?" Rafe grunted, nursing and twisting his aching arm. "What's that, sir?"

"Sting rations, for life, without having to lift a finger ever again. You've earned it. Few do."

Rafe emitted a surprised snort.

"Doesn't that please you, Prefect?"

"I... I haven't thought about it, my Alpha."

"You can stay on of course; we at ALPHA will gladly have you. But we also keep our word, as Thorvald knows. I let Tristan off the hook, though he shall always be carefully watched that one. Once a stray, always a stray."

A nod – Rafe thought it best to nod despite his ignorance.

Adal walked over to Toggle and stood beneath her, "This is your bee?"

"Yes sir. Well, not mine exactly she just kind of... hangs around."

"I can see that."

Rafe said nothing, but smiled.

Adal leant close, inspecting Toggle's hairy, heaving abdomen. "Bees are supposed to die when they sting, aren't they?"

"I dunno, sir."

"Unless they're a queen, of course. They can sting all they like."

Another shrug and surreptitious nurse of the arm; Rafe was no biologist. "She's got a broken wing, sir," he said, trying to spark conversation so as to not appear such a dunce in front of the great Alpha.

"Yes. Just a small bit missing, isn't there?"

"She can't fly, though."

"How sad. Perhaps there's something Josef Grau can do about that. I'll have to mention it, when he's not too busy with that new wolfess."

Rafe frowned, but said nothing.

After a thoughtful pause, Adal turned to Rafe and said afresh, "Apologies, I really must go. I need to speak to Prefect Janoah, or rather Grand Prefect Janoah, should she accept." He looked at Toggle, "We've just had a position open up."

"Sir."

Saluting, the Alpha walked on, saying, "Have a good think about what you want to do. Whatever you decide, I'll see to it the matter is closed."

✣

The Bloodfang car bumped across the Ashfall, passing through another chain-link fence guarded by Watchers, then on through the endless grey shanty towns that made up the Reservations. Hyenas peered out of tents and corrugated shelters, old and young, curious and fearful.

What was a Howler limo doing here?

Some cubs followed the car, running alongside it, waving and begging with paws cupped. The wolf inside eventually rolled down his window and tossed a chocolate bar to the nearest cub.

"Share it!" he stipulated, rolling up the window.

Within a few twists and turns, the car pulled up outside a nicer tent than the rest. It was one half black and the other white, as dichotomous as the beast lurking within.

"This it?" the wolf asked, surprised.

"Should be, Elder Oromov," the hog driver replied.

A Den Guard climbed out the passenger seat and went round to open Vladimir's door – one couldn't be seen dead opening his one's door anymore.

"The cubs, sir?" said the driver.

Vladimir waved a dismissive paw and walked round the front of the car, heading for the tent. Two huge, grim-faced hyenas ducked out of the flaps and barred his path.

"I need to see Prince Noss," Vladimir declared. "I'm told this is his... abode."

No reply.

"I've come to close our bargain-"

"Close our bargain!" someone snarled inside. Noss burst from the tent flaps, as impressive in a mere sarong as he was when equipped in Howler attire, if not more so. "By the Wind, it *is* you! Get out of my sight, Vladimir. Get off my land before I have my hyenas tear you apart!"

"Noss, now listen to me-"

The Prince grabbed Vladimir and lifting him physically by his cloak, slammed him against the side of the car. "I said go! Go before I kill you! You who tortured me, who used me!"

The Den Guard jumped to Vladimir's defence, rapier drawn.

"No!" Vladimir snapped, raising his paw. "Stand down! Stand down. It's all right."

The Den Guard backed off.

Noss waited, chest heaving, lips curling; fighting tears, expletives and the urge to kill Oromov.

Vladimir gulped, "I've come to tell you, no to *thank* you, and to-"

"Keep your empty words. I have nothing left. Nothing!"

"And to return these to you," Vladimir finished, tapping on the window.

Noss looked down. Two hyena cubs were staring up at him through the tinted glass, a boy and a girl.

The Prince dropped Vladimir like a poker and staggered backwards. Paw to mouth he glanced at the wolf, then back at the cubs, unwilling to believe his eyes.

"I was able to locate them," Vladimir explained, tugging his mantle back into shape. "Taking them from Arjana was not my doing. I thought they were safe in the re-education camps. I thought they were the best accommodation available. By the time I found out the camps had been razed, the cubs had disappeared and Arjana had escaped."

Hardly listening, Noss went for the car door and almost pulled it off its hinges.

He knelt. "Children, it's me, your father," he said.

The male cub slid out and embraced Noss, rasping and crying in his rough little hyena voice, "Father!"

"Zuma! My boy!"

The hyeness slipped out with such grace and dignity, standing before Noss with her chin held high. "I am glad to see you again, my noble father."

"Anjali," Noss marvelled, shaking his head, tears pouring from his eyes, "my proud little queen. How like your mother you already are! You have her noble bearing."

The hyenas at the tent flaps and within sight of the goings-on all bowed low before Princess Anjali, and even Prince Noss dipped his head before this most regal cub. Then he embraced his daughter as a father and together all three rocked to and fro, weeping with grief and joy. They had lost much, but gained one another.

Vladimir silently walked around to the car's opposite side, the Den Guard following and opening the door.

Hearing the car start, Noss shot up and looked across the top of its shiny roof, catching Vladimir just before he slipped inside.

"Thank you, Vladimir."

"Our business is concluded," Elder Vladimir sniffed. Sliding across the smooth back seat he reached for the opposite door and winding down its window a little, said, "Keep the tribes quiet for five minutes and you might be surprised by what can be achieved back in Lupa. There's talk of dissolving the Reservations and all sorts. Have patience, Noss."

The prince nodded once.

"Oh, and Rufus sends his regards."

With that, Vladimir shut the window and his car U-turned, heading back towards the grey blotch on the already blasted landscape that was Lupa.

The mighty Noss beamed toothily down at his cubs, "Come children; let's go surprise your Uncle Madou!"

✦

The sun was ducking behind the smoke stacks of Lupa, casting long, sinister shadows across the lavender-filled courtyard. Janoah's shadow looked especially monstrous, with crutches making her silhouette resemble some many legged mechanical spider.

Minding the fractured leg she'd picked up in the train crash, she eased onto the bench beside Rafe. "You should be in bed resting, Stenton," she scolded, casting her eyes over him. "You look tired."

Rafe looked Janoah over, with her crutches, bandages and unflattering bed gown. "Yeah? Well you're a right state."

"Mind your trap! I'm a *Grand* Prefect now."

"Yeah, I heard."

"How? Nobody knows yet!"

Rafe spread a big paw over his huge cloaked chest, "The Alpha and I had a chat."

"I see! Looks like we're both moving up in the world."

After a moment's mirth, Rafe's face sank. "Whatcha you lie for, Jan?"

"Lie?"

"About what happened on the train."

Blinking once, Janoah explained gently, "I had to; you can't be seen to have killed all those Elders, let alone a Den Father, however corrupt."

"But you-"

"It's bad enough you're an Eisenwolf at all! Let's not frighten the Den Fathers into closing our operation down."

Rafe dipped his chin. "Aye, Meryl said as much."

"Then she's a wise wolfess."

Silence, but for distant traffic.

Breaking out an ember, Janoah looked across the grim ALPHA HQ and puffed, "Nikita's snuffed it, by the way."

Rafe sat up, big ears pricked in alarm.

"Meryl's not sure why," Janoah huffed. "Some kind of fit or heart attack. He might've taken poison. Josef was going to do an autopsy, but the Alpha doesn't seem bothered. So that's that."

"Well I didn't do anything, I just-"

Janoah waved a paw; "It's a kindness. He would've been executed anyway. He and Amael have both escaped the noose. Nurka too, it seems."

Rafe took a deep, shaky breath, "Jan I...."

"Mm?" Janoah sat forward, leant on a crutch and patted her champion's knee. "What?"

"Is it over?"

"Over?"

"Is Lupa safe now? I mean, THORN and all that. That's all gone, 'en it?"

"I don't know," Janoah shrugged. "Besides, there's always someone out to cause trouble-"

"Then I'll stay," Rafe blurted.

After working out what her Eisenwolf was referring to, Janoah licked her lips, "You don't have to on my account."

"I want to. I *want* to make Lupa safe... for Meryl."

"She won't thank you for it."

"She'll understand. I can't go sit on the Graumeer coast and stare at the sea like an old wolf yet. I'm not even twenny! Maybe when the rot really starts to bite, but not yet. I have to use what Ulf gave me whilst I still have it."

Nodding, Janoah asked, "But are you happy here, Rafe?"

"Happy?"

"Yes. I'm sure Meryl only wants you to be happy. It's what Rufus wants too."

Frowning, Rafe glanced across the HQ and caught Meryl's sweet face. She was standing at the door to the courtyard, watching, waiting.

"Yeah," Rafe said, waving at her until she waved back, "I'm happy, Jan."

Janoah shrugged, "Then it's settled."

Looking into the trembling sun, she took Rafe's paw in hers. She could feel his fire, the imperium burning in his blood, the blessed curse.

"We've proven ourselves to the Alpha," Janoah said. "He's seen us. Now we must help him forge Lupa anew, not just for wolfkind, but for everyone who depends on us to sleep soundly in their beds."

"Yeah? Sounds like a plan, Jan."

"Amael had the right idea; to reform. He just had the grace of a hyena with a sledgehammer. ALPHA can do better. We can all do better. We must."

Epilogue: Diary Excerpt 4

It has been two months since the strange events at Hummelton and I am back in Riddle at last. As you can see I have dug out my diary from its hiding place, though of course I have made small entries on paper in Hummelton Hospital in the interim – I must remember to paste those in here.

After much rest and recuperation my right arm feels as good as new, but my left leg remains weak at the knee. Riddle's staff surgeon says the Hummel doctors did an excellent job patching me up, though when it comes to pellets shattering bones and tendons Rufus says things are never quite the same again, however talented one's surgeon. He would know; that wolf is peppered with shrapnel. I hope he's wrong on this occasion and my leg improves. Regardless, I am able to perform my duties again, albeit the duties of a Howler Captain since my promotion. I am not sure what the rank entails, but Rufus says I'll get the hang of it. I will try my best to meet his and Elder Vladimir's expectations.

I am staring at the Imperium Heart the Den Fathers awarded me. I feel a fraud, for Uther was the wolf who carried me that day, urging me on, as always. He deserves this more than me. It's enough, I am reliably told by Elder Vladimir, that Vito's assassination was quietly put down to 'unknown agents hired by Amael' and Uther allowed to go shot-free. Well, almost. He has been dishonourably discharged from the Bloodfangs and joined ALPHA; Grand Prefect Janoah collected him herself just yesterday. He has nowhere else to go. I hate to say it, but I think Uther will fit in well; taking errant Howlers to task sounds right up his street. Though, Rufus reckons he will have great difficulty saying 'my Alpha'.

Uther did not act alone, Ivan and an unknown Greystone took part in Vito's murder. I was the only witness and I will not contest the findings of the inquiry. I owe Uther that, especially since Elder Vladimir further informs me, though cautions me to keep it quiet, that Uther was abused as a cub by the late Vito. He was just one of many street cubs swept up in the Bloodfang Den Father's mad indulgences. I realise now that Uther tried to tell me this, even to warn me against such wolves as Vito. I'm sure he wanted me to guess, saving him the agony of telling me, but I was too dense to grasp his pain. This goes some way, in my mind, towards excusing his actions. As for Ivan, nobody knows where he's gone. He was not in the wreckage of the Elder Train, though the driver of the train claims a white wolf of Ivan's stature threw him from the engine's cabin and set the train to crash into Hummelton Station. It could be Ivan was amongst the unidentifiable corpses in the contaminated lounge car, but Janoah insists otherwise and Rufus is inclined to believe her. Olivia Blake has also disappeared, albeit into the paws of ALPHA. If she has gone by choice, as Janoah claims, then there is nothing more to be said. Sara's efforts were not for nought; she may have lost one friend, but she saved another, and perhaps through him all of Lupa.

Is Lupa worth saving? Yes, but she must adapt. Den Father Vito was a symptom of our diseased and corrupt social structure, which allows abuses to go unchallenged and unpunished, since a Den Father is above scrutiny. Amael saw himself as the cure, but a cure that kills the patient is no cure at all.

Whilst most of the conspirators have been rounded up, Den Father Flaid of the Greystones has not been confronted. Janoah says he colluded in Amael's plan, but there is little evidence. The Den Fathers all say he did not even attempt to leave the Summit as the dirigible passed over, when surely a guilty wolf would have. Perhaps Amael did not reveal to Flaid his full intentions; certainly Tristan Eisbrand was unaware of the full extent of Amael's lupicidal ambitions. I understand from Sara he has been pardoned by Thorvald Strom, albeit severely chastised and sent to police some lesser district than Arkady as penance.

Perhaps we can afford to forgive; the white-imperium shortage is over and tensions are easing. Not only had Amael been siphoning off shipments for his cache (as yet still missing), but the Warden had closed the richest Gelb caves upon Grand Prefect Nikita's secret instructions, choking Lupa and seeding unrest for years. According to Silvermane, who interrogated Nikita shortly before his strange death, Gelb was to enter full commercial production again once Nikita was in control of Lupa, so that he would be seen as the hero who brought stability, whilst Amael was to be blamed for the atrocity at Hummelton and executed. Each conspirator was only out for themselves, it seems. It makes me sick.

However, there is a ray of hope. Since the revelations of maltreatment and outright murder in the hyena camps there is an appetite for change sweeping Lupa that cannot be sated, not least since our powerful feline neighbours across the Teich in Felicia have launched a formal complaint, delivered from their Lupan embassy in a speech that could not be silenced. The bold action was taken thanks in no small part to Penny Buttle having a word with her cousin the Queen, or so rumour has it.

The Den Fathers are making noises towards easing restrictions on the tribes. From what they hear, Vladimir and Rufus believe the current Reservations located cruelly on the Ashfall will be entirely dissolved and the hyenas allowed to move south to a new, healthier territory. A likely candidate for resettlement is South Rostsonne, beyond the canyons, where I myself was born. It's a hard country, dry and cruel, with few inhabitants, but paradise compared to the deadly Ashfall. The hyenas may even be allowed to create a nation of sorts, which is all The Hyena Organisation for the Recognition of Nationhood, and Nurka, wanted.

I still wonder what would have happened had Nurka followed through with the conspiracy and dropped black-imperium on Hummelton, instead of mere photographs. Some have tried to dismiss THORN's evidence, but few believe they would have gone to such length as to commandeer a dirigible to deliver false propaganda. Indeed they did not; Nurka had the opportunity to go down in infamy as a mass murderer. He stepped back from the abyss, and for that alone shares this Imperium Heart with me, for all beastkind. The same cannot be said of Queen Arjana, but if I had been treated as abominably as she, perhaps I would have sanctioned the slaughter of thousands too. I cannot condemn her; I have no right.

Nurka's body was never found and officially the stolen black-imperium was never aboard the Nimbus, nor was it thrown into Lake Hummel despite Uther's statement to ALPHA. All has been denied. Rufus has heard from Sara that Lake Hummel has been dredged on the quiet and the canisters recovered and buried deep in the belly of Gelb's lesser-known chasms, returned, as it were to, Mother Erde. Indeed, the disposal of black-imperium, and the security of refineries and other such places, is under review across the packs. Never again can any one beast come into possession of so much dangerous material, not now there is a means of delivering it across such broad areas as to prove catastrophic. This is a new age, a more complex age, innocence and naivety are passing.

If we want to drive our cars and read by night, be whisked across continents by trains and airships, even live at all in the case of the afflicted, white-imperium, black-imperium and every grade on the spectrum in-between, remain a necessary evil. There are no easy answers to this or any other problem beasts face, even a cure for the rot itself would not banish the need for imperium fuel and the resulting ashen rain that desolates not only Lupa's hinterlands, but that of Felicia and every great conurbation growing upon the face of the world, like so many bleeding sores. The Dead Cities that stand forgotten and overcome by sand, forest and sea in the great wild places of the world are testament to our past failures. Rufus, Heath and others, even Adal Weiss if Janoah is to be believed, theorise that great civilisations once flourished all across the world, civilisations where all beasts were equal, and none went hungry – the power of Rafe's Eisenwolf suit only confirms how advanced these civilisations must have been, we are only just beginning to grasp their ideas. Those cities and those ideas died many millennia ago, poisoned by black-imperium, either slowly over time, or by a great war. Perhaps the 'black rain', as the hyenas call it in their legends, came from an army of airships, or planes, or even a thousand artillery shells. Then again, perhaps it was delivered by some contrivance of destruction as yet unimagined, something that makes even Rafe Stenton's remarkable eisenpelz look like a plaything.

If Rufus gains the permission and funds to go on his expedition to these long-lost cities, then perhaps he will not only find the answers to our past, but to our future.

I must leave it there. Sara and Heath are due any minute and I'm not remotely groomed. Rufus is taking us down to Citizen Casimir's newly renovated 'Warren' to discuss his latest expedition *pitch. That young Steppes wolf, Tomek, is supposed to be there with his pet ant. Rufus is full of praises for him and Sara says he's rather dashing, especially in a hat.*

Captain Linus Bloodfang Mills

THIS MATTER IS CLOSED

Adam Browne

LEXICON

Adam Browne

ALPHA: The Agency for Lupan Peace and Howler Accountability. An organisation set up by the packs after the last Howler war to independently police the Howlers.

Alpha: In the context of a wolfen culture, a natural leader and/or dominant partner, male or female.

The Alpha: The current administrator of ALPHA. Few know the origins of the self-styled title.

Arkady University: Colloquially the 'Ark', the oldest and most prestigious centre of learning still standing in Lupa, located in the eponymous Arkady District of Eisbrand territory.

Ash: Waste imperium, a glittering grey powder, very soft and somewhat cohesive, it blankets Lupa and the surrounding land, smothering plant life. When Howlers use imperium to create plasma or bend their corona, ash is produced in the bloodstream, which can cause great discomfort before being excreted in sweat and urea.

Ashfall: The area immediately around Lupa rendered dead and lifeless by the pollution.

The Beehive: A famous saloon on the Common where Howlers go to relieve their woes, classier than most.

Beta: In the context of wolfen culture, a natural follower and/or subservient partner, male or female.

Black-imperium: The lowest state of imperium, yet the most fearsome. Black-imperium devours not only other states of imperium in an effort to regain energy, but also living matter. This is what causes the rot. Any creature that ingests or inhales black-imperium will either immediately die, or develop rot symptoms. Prognosis is dependent on dose; trace levels are survivable. Howlers develop the rot when the imperium in their blood decays into minute quantities of black, a phenomenon accelerated by using the imperium stored in one's bones and blood to bend one's corona or generate plasma. In nature, black-imperium sinks back into the Erde, where forces as yet unknown are thought to re-energise it back to white.

Black Rain: The hyena name for the catastrophe that befell all the races eons ago. Scholars believe it may have some truth, perhaps referring to a previous gradual pollution of the world from ashen rain, or worse, some manner of disaster involving black-imperium. Some hyenas call today's Ashfall the second black rain.

The Bloc: The jumbled territory north of the river over which many small packs contest dominion. It is a very dangerous and tough place to live or do business; wolves from the main packs rarely venture there.

Bloodfang: The oldest pack on record. They dominate the east of Lupa and have monopolised most imperium and food imports; a worrying situation for the other packs.

Blue-imperium: Highly prized and quite rare, blue-imperium contains almost as much energy as purple, but without the psychotic effects. However it is seldom ingested on purpose, since it is more useful stabilised and melded with steel to create extremely hard and durable kristahl. The Eisbrands make much use of blue-imperium in their mighty swords.

Centipede: A predatory invertebrate with thirty to over a hundred legs, dependant on species. The imperial, or colloquially sewer centipede, is a giant species that actively seeks imperium any way it can, often devouring imperium addicts living in the Wall Slums, but also tackling Watchers,

Howlers and anyone else with a corona, or anything that threatens it. In the wild it feasts on giant millipedes, woodlice and other harmless browsers.

Chakaa: The hyena answer to the Howlers, they are forbidden to use white-imperium by their beliefs, but unlike wolves they cope well with the psychotic side effects of purple-imperium. Even so, Chakaa are often unstable and are sidelined by the exacting standards set by noble-born hyena society, and only tolerated at all for their great strength and usefulness in battle.

Chunta: A bitter drink laced with purple-imperium, which Chakaa quaff to replenish their strength and stave off the rot.

Citizen: Any beast, little or great, that is not a Howler, but has the right to live and work in Lupa.

The Common Ground: Colloquially called the Common, this contested ground left over from the war was gifted to ALPHA to administrate.

Corona: The invisible field of energy that pervades and surrounds imperium, especially in the context of Howlers, who can often sense one another's presence.

Dayfly: A waterborne insect with a long, two or three-pronged tail. Hatching in the spring, they take a year to reach maturity, whereupon they grow wings and take flight in great nuptial swarms over the water. The adults die within a day or two, the females laying their eggs upstream of where they hatched before they expire.

Dead Cities: The evidence of previous great civilisations are said to still stand in long-forgotten parts of the world, though few beasts venture there for fear of their lives.

Dead Zone: An area of Lupa sealed off to the citizens as a result of an industrial accident, usually a black-imperium spill. It is thought by some archaeologists that the Dead Cities were made uninhabitable by a similar, if catastrophic accident.

Den: Typically one per district, a Den is where Howlers work, train and live. If married, a Howler's family will usually live nearby, since Dens do not generally have excess accommodation, though Hummelton Den is a famously notable exception, being able to house all the Den Fathers, Elders and their retinues when it is their turn to host the Pack Summit.

Den Father: The 'father' of an entire pack, very often an old and potent Howler. They are voted into power by the Elders of the pack they serve, but once seated they cannot be removed save through death, abdication, or impeachment. Den Mothers are much rarer owing to the scarcity of female Howlers, though Pack Hummel currently enjoys the leadership of Den Mother Cora.

Den Guard: Elite Howlers who are sworn to guard the Elders and Den Father of their pack. They wear longer mantles than the average Howler.

Dirigible: A rigid balloon filled with lighter-than-air gas. Many companies are exploring flight, but none have yet devised a lifting gas that is not explosive.

District: An area of Lupa, or Hummel territory, governed by an Elder; there are rarely physical barriers between districts, only lines drawn on maps.

Donskoy: One of the great Eisbrand lines. Most Eisbrands are related to one of just a pawful of sprawling, extended families.

Eisbrand: The richest pack. Their territory is kept fairly clean by the coastal wind. They make their money importing fine silks and other luxury goods from across the water.

Eisenglanz: An alloy created by infusing imperium ash with steel or other metals, making it more durable and more able to resist plasmatic attacks. It cannot be lifted by a Howler's corona, nor easily melted.

Eisenpelz: The suit worn by Eisenwolves. The recipe for eisenpelz metal is unknown, but it is almost indestructible. Melting down an eisenpelz and recasting it compromises its strength, thus its durability is at least in part due to the manner by which it was originally moulded.

Eisenwolf: The name given to wolves of exceptional imperious power who don the ancient eisenpelz suits found in the Dead Cities. They have been outlawed under the Lupan Laws, though loopholes exist and few packs, if any, have destroyed their collection.

Elder: The wolfen governor of a district and its Den; usually a powerful Howler. There are traditionally thirteen per pack.

Ember: Self-combusting tubes of lung-rotting poison that serve as a stopgap between stings. Embers self-ignite with a yellow-imperium tip, which is not to be inhaled, and contain a further cocktail of low-grade imperium, fruit or menthol flavourings, plus a few minims of taubfene. The last ingredient offers relief from rot pains but makes them highly addictive.

Erde: The green world beasts and bug inhabit. The word is capitalised when referring to the planet, and not when referring to the soil under a beast's paws.

Far Ashfall: The polluted land stretching eastwards to the Sunrise Mountains, very few plants can survive here. Held by the Bloodfangs, it remains the only practical rail and road route between Lupa and Hummelton.

Felicia: The capital of the cats across the Teich. It is a sprawling city not unlike Lupa, with similar mounting problems of imperium pollution. Felicia is governed by a constitutional monarchy.

Founders: The six wolves who founded Lupa some time after the great calamity that destroyed civilisation. Most packs claim some of their own were amongst them, if not all. Their statues stand, amongst other places, in Petra Square.

Freiwolf: Usually a healthy wolf who does not adhere to any one pack, having no pack name, nor loyalties, therefore. In the past, if a Howler wished to have healthy cubs, he or she would often seek a Freiwolf, since two Howlers rarely produce viable offspring, though some used to try regardless. However, since the Lupan laws outlawed Howlers marrying and breeding with each other, the only option for amorous Howlers now is to marry a Freiwolf. The ancient quandary facing Freiwolves and their families has not changed. To accept a Howler's advances brings not only the protection and prestige of a pack name, but also the restrictions of loyalty and the danger of becoming a target in any future dispute between packs.

Gelb: An ancient, semi-natural mine complex in the Sunrise Mountains that has been exploited for imperium time and again over the centuries. Its tunnels extend for hundreds of miles and most of the passages now lie abandoned and uncharted. The entire region around Gelb is situated on an imperium plume, which continuously heats and replenishes the water table with imperium. Mineral-saturated groundwater percolates through porous limestone rock, depositing raw imperium. Today, Gelb is a specialist prison camp where errant Howlers, Watchers and other dangerous criminals are sent to work off their debt to Lupan society.

Giacomo Valerio Monocycles: The famous monobike manufacturer founded by the long-dead Giacomo Valerio, a pioneer of imperium technology. Giacomo supply most packs direct with all their monocycle needs, though the proud Greystones stubbornly use their own brand. The GVM-12 'Springtail' is the mono of choice in Lupa, being cheap, reliable and easy to control. Other extant models include the more powerful GVM-20 'Dragonfly' and special-order GVM-8 'Spider', the latter a legend in Howler circles, as only the most skilful riders can tame it.

Grand Howler: One rank down from Elder, there are typically two to four Grand Howlers per district.

Grand Prefect: There are five Grand Prefects in ALPHA including the Alpha himself. They are nominally equal, beneath the Alpha.

Graumeer: The sea to the east, often grey and stormy.

Green-imperium: The most common variety of useful and naturally-occurring imperium, forms green ore and semi-stable crystals which can be combusted raw from the Erde. Used in industrial processes and in the fireboxes of imperium engines.

Greystone: The largest pack by number, they dominate the south and control the importing of many raw materials, such as iron, which they smelt and turn into all Lupa's wares.

Howler: Wolves who have contracted the rot and serve a pack in return for a ration of white-imperium. Howlers are usually found and trained in their teens.

Howler Codex: The voluminous manual that describes a Howler's duty, memorised in detail by few.

Howler Cub: Howler recruits, accepted but still in training at one of the many academies.

Hummel: The only serious pack that lives apart from Lupa, they grow the food that keeps the great city ticking over.

Hummelton: Everdor's capital, yet it is only the size of a large Lupan district. The burning of imperium is strictly limited to protect the environment.

Induction: The process by which a candidate Howler's bloodstream is saturated with white-imperium for the first time. Once undertaken induction cannot be reversed, and a Howler becomes reliant on stings to survive for the rest of their lives even should they stop using their abilities altogether.

Imperium: A powerful, often beautiful mineral with many diverse properties still doubtless undiscovered. Imperium is both a blessing and a curse. Without it beasts would still live in mud huts, yet with it they suffer ill health and barren landscapes. Left to its own devices, imperium naturally grows into many forms, decays over time and returns to the Erde without causing much ill effect, even enhancing local flora and fauna. It is the meddling of beasts that upsets nature's delicate balance.

The Imperium Heart: A heart-shaped medal of pure red-imperium crystal. Though not intrinsically valuable, this highest and rarest accolade is awarded by the Den Fathers only to those Howlers who have performed some exceptional deed in the name of the Republic Lupi. The word 'EXALT' is inscribed above the heart, and Howlers are expected to stand whenever a bearer of the

Imperium Heart enters a room.

Jua-mata: The most powerful hyena tribe, now reduced to prisoners on the Reservations, but for a few THORN rebels.

Kristahl: Steel melded with imperium, which renders it stronger and more conductive. There are many recipes for kristahl and new discoveries are made every year, but the two most popular alloys are blue and red kristahl, created with blue and red-imperium respectively. The colours of the metal are almost indistinguishable, though when compared the eye can tell the cold sheen of an expensive blue-kristahl blade from the warm tones of a cheaper red-kristahl one.

Little Beasts: The encompassing term used by wolves and cats for creatures who are meek; rats, rabbits, mice etc. Some races fall into grey areas, like the surly hogs and free otters, but a simple test is ask yourself whether you have been conquered and have any territory or country still ruled by your kind. If not, you are probably a little beast. This is not a foolproof assessment, since the hyenas have been conquered and nobody in their right mind regards them as little. As with most things in life, it is not as simple as all that.

Lupa[1]: The sprawling capital city of wolfkind and the whole Lupine Continent. It is home to millions of beasts descended from those races the wolves have conquered and co-opted over the centuries. The tonnes of imperium burnt here every day rains down as ash, clogging the streets and killing most plant life.

Lupa[2]: The recognised currency of Lupa, consisting of colourful imperium-weave notes and kristahl coins. One lupa is one-hundred pennies.

Lupan Laws: The basic laws of wolfkind that cross pack boundaries and districts, sometimes overriding pack by-laws, sometimes not - as always in matters of litigation things are complex. However, if no pack can point to a territory as theirs, then the law there will always revert to Lupan Law. Large swathes of the Lupine Continent fall under these rules, including South Rostsonne, the Sunrise and Sunset Mountains, and parts of Everdor.

Lupan Wall: Lupa's city wall, which has shifted and grown several times over the centuries to encompass the expanding city. Sections have also been laid tangentially across the city to separate pack territories, whilst other interior arms have been raised to contain the dangerously polluted Dead Zones.

Mantle: The poncho-like cloak that Howlers wear, complete with a hood to guard from the ash and rain.

Matriarchs: The female hyenas that rule the tribes through council and advise the Queen. They are rarely seen, protected as they are by the fighting males. Chieftains, even Princes, must defer to the decisions of the Matriarchs, but can appeal to the Queen directly, who can overrule all.

Monobike: The prime transport of Howlers, 'monos' are one-wheeled bikes stabilised by gyroscopes. They are able to navigate the narrowest alleys and turn on a penny. Only Howlers can ride them so they are rarely stolen, save for their precious imperium components. Grand Howlers and up often ride in cars, though some still prefer the thrill of a monobike.

New Materials: The blanket term for the ever-growing range of cheap, imperium-based substances coming to market. New materials are produced by melding various metals and other compounds with imperium, and even its ash. They are often used to make moulded modern furniture and fireproof interiors.

New Tharona: Properly 'New T'arona', in Lutran dialect, an otter colony on the Graumeer coast named for T'arona, the capital city of otterkind located far to the south. New Tharona is not sovereign otter territory, but managed under Eisbrand law. Many Eisbrand families live there, and Howlers often visit to take in the clean sea air and bawdy pubs.

Pack Summit: The annual meeting of the Den Fathers and their Elders, cyclically held in each pack's capital territory. When it is Hummel's turn to host the Summit, once every four years, Lupa is, for a few days, emptied of authority above that of Elder.

Plasma: The energy released by a Howler when tapping into his or her imperium reserves. The actual visual phenomena – the arcing coils, flashes and explosions – are merely a result of the air heating up and glowing at temperatures of many thousands of degrees.

The Politzi: Lupa's police force, consisting largely of hogs, rats, rabbits and other lesser beasts who are for the most part unable to wield imperium directly.

Prefect: Members of ALPHA, Howlers in all but name granted the authority to investigate other Howlers for illegal activity.

Purple-imperium: Considered the next down from white, purple or violet imperium is slightly more common and its energy is easily tapped. However, it is undesirable for Howler consumption since it tends to accumulate in the brain where it can cause headaches, blackouts, fitting and even psychosis.

Queens Town: Cat colony on the east coast, independent of Lupan Law. It was allowed to remain sovereign Felician territory as part of an ancient peace settlement between Felicia and Lupa. It is the first port of entry for any cats, or other beasts, coming to the Lupine Continent from across the Teich.

Red-imperium: Similar to blue-imperium in its properties, red makes good kristahl, but is much cheaper since it is much more easily found. It is less conductive than blue-imperium, however, and takes greater energy on the part of the wielder to use.

The Reservations: After their final defeat by wolfkind, the hyena tribes were forcibly relocated to fenced-in territories near Lupa, where some claim they are not only being purposely starved to death, but actively murdered. This is vehemently denied by the officials overseeing the Reservations.

Riddle District: A rough border district that polices the Bloodfang-Greystone arm of the interior Lupan Wall. Riddle suffers from a high crime rate and is famous for recruiting and maintaining a retinue of exceptionally tough Howlers.

River Lupa: The filthy river than serves Lupa; no one is sure whether the city is named for the river, or the river for the city.

The Rot: A degenerative disease caused chiefly by black-imperium. The constant ingestion and inhalation of ash, which contains traces of black-imperium, will eventually induce the rot in any beast. Howlers paradoxically enhance and damage their bodies by purposely stinging themselves with imperium. This extra energy source encourages muscle growth, promotes faster wound-healing and maintains a corona that, whilst a scientifically understood phenomenon in Lupa and Felicia, is to some cultures indistinguishable from magic. The use of any imperium creates more ash and black-imperium in the bloodstream than accidental inhalation and ingestion alone, leading to rot symptoms such as shooting pains in the bones and muscles, poor vision, amnesia, nausea and, eventually, renal failure and death. To live a long life as a Howler it is best to practise self-restraint.

Royal Jelly: Mysterious waxy substance rarely produced by great bee queens that is said to have medicinal properties.

Sun Spider: Not a true spider, the sun spider, or solifugae, is a predatory arachnid that lives in dry desert conditions. It has long hairy legs, an armoured head and two vicious sets of pincer-like mouthparts. The abdomen is softer and Watchers know to attack the beasts there, not front-on.

Sting: Usually white-imperium, purified, measured and packaged for Howler use alone, but on the street can mean any imperium sealed in a glass phial for injection.

Taubfene: A potent painkiller derived from Everdor poppies; it is addictive and best used sparingly. Overdosing is an effective means of euthanasia sometimes employed to save a dying Howler the pain and indignity of slowly rotting.

The Teich: The sea to the east, separating Felicia and the Feline Continent from Lupa and Lupine Continent.

Territory: In the context of a pack, the entirety of their land over which they have dominion to apply taxes and by-laws which do not contravene any overriding Lupan Laws agreed at the Pack Summit.

THORN: The Hyena Organisation for the Recognition of Nationhood are what wolves would call a terrorist cell; they would call themselves freedom fighters.

Ulf: The old god of wolfkind, mostly forgotten but for expletives, though some still adhere to the old religion. Those who study history believe he is a semi-mythical figure, a beast who existed and did great things. They attribute Ulf's supposed magical powers and impossible deeds to an early case of the rot. Other races tell similar stories, the rabbits believing in Briar, a trickster; the bears and hogs in the overarching Gaia, spirit of the whole world; whilst hyenas see the Erde, Sun, Wind and Sky as separate deities, and even revere bugs as lowly as dung beetles.

Valerio: One of the few wolfen families with ancient links to the Feline Continent. Traditionally red furred and graceful, it is thought they brought rapiers to the Lupine Continent, which the artful Bloodfangs adopted. Some say they are the original Bloodfangs, before the waters were muddied by interbreeding.

Valours: The cat equivalent of Howlers, almost unseen on the Lupan Continent, save in Queens Town.

Venom: In the context of imperium a slang term for the contents of a sting, usually meaning white-imperium, but can refer to the lesser blue and purple.

Wall Slums: The shanty towns clinging to the outside of Lupa like parasites. Beasts who are not true citizens gather here waiting for a chance to enter the city, either legitimately by interviews and work permits, or by paying smugglers to slip them through the gates and set them up with forged papers.

Watchers: Most packs have one Watcher District managed by a single Elder Watcher, though the Eisbrands have two, simply because they alone own two city gates. Watchers oversee all imports and exports of goods and beasts through the Lupan Wall. They are necessarily tough wolves, having to deal not only with ruthless smugglers and Wall Slum gangs, but the imperial centipedes that stalk the Ashfall. Den Fathers who started as Watchers are rare, though Thorvald Strom is one such wolf.

White-imperium: The rarest naturally occurring form of imperium known, it contains plentiful energy and has minor negative effects whilst residing in the bloodstream, provided one does not overdose. The initial rush of white-imperium entering the blood and combining with black-imperium and other contaminants can cause a release of energy, even going so far as to make a Howler's corona briefly coil out of control.

Wolfkind: The race of wolves as a whole. Also Lupans, though this often refers to non-wolfen citizens of Lupa.

Yellow-imperium: Poisonous and unstable, yellow-imperium reacts and explodes even as you dig it up from the ground. Pure crystals form only in airless environments, such as bogs and river clays, but ores are plentiful. The Greystones alone have devised means of manipulating and even stabilising this most fickle state of imperium and thus process and sell it to the other packs in many forms, including powder for guns, shrapnel grenades and, most important of all, supplying the self-lighting tips for millions upon millions of embers.

Contact Us

Website:
www.imperiumlupi.com

If you have any queries, please email:
toggle@imperiumlupi.net

For business propositions:
dayfly@imperiumlupi.net

Cover artist:
www.mike-nash.com

ABOUT THE AUTHOR

Adam Browne lives and works with his partner in Kent, England. Besides writing, his other pursuits include natural history, human history, futurism, and blocky old video games.

Printed in Great Britain
by Amazon